I0819836

Henry James

Notable Works

Cover Artwork: Painting by Pierre-Auguste Renoir. La Liseuse

ISBN: 978-1-78139-371-0

Contents

THE AMERICAN

THE TURN OF THE SCREW

THE PORTRAIT OF A LADY

VOLUME I (of II)

THE PORTRAIT OF A LADY

VOLUME II (of II)

THE WINGS OF THE DOVE

VOLUME I

BOOK FIRST

BOOK SECOND

BOOK THIRD

BOOK FOURTH

BOOK FIFTH

THE WINGS OF THE DOVE

VOLUME II

BOOK SIXTH

BOOK SEVENTH

BOOK EIGHTH

BOOK NINTH

BOOK TENTH

DAISY MILLER: A STUDY

IN TWO PARTS

THE AMBASSADORS

Volume I

Book First

Book Second

Book Third

Book Fourth

Book Fifth

Book Sixth

THE AMBASSADORS

Volume II

Book Seventh

Book Eighth

Book Ninth

Book Tenth

Book Eleventh

Book Twelfth

THE BEAST IN THE JUNGLE

THE AMERICAN

CHAPTER I

On a brilliant day in May, in the year 1868, a gentleman was reclining at his ease on the great circular divan which at that period occupied the centre of the Salon Carre, in the Museum of the Louvre. This commodious ottoman has since been removed, to the extreme regret of all weak-kneed lovers of the fine arts, but the gentleman in question had taken serene possession of its softest spot, and, with his head thrown back and his legs outstretched, was staring at Murillo's beautiful moon-borne Madonna in profound enjoyment of his posture. He had removed his hat, and flung down beside him a little red guide-book and an opera-glass. The day was warm; he was heated with walking, and he repeatedly passed his handkerchief over his forehead, with a somewhat wearied gesture. And yet he was evidently not a man to whom fatigue was familiar; long, lean, and muscular, he suggested the sort of vigor that is commonly known as "toughness." But his exertions on this particular day had been of an unwonted sort, and he had performed great physical feats which left him less jaded than his tranquil stroll through the Louvre. He had looked out all the pictures to which an asterisk was affixed in those formidable pages of fine print in his Badeker; his attention had been strained and his eyes dazzled, and he had sat down with an aesthetic headache. He had looked, moreover, not only at all the pictures, but at all the copies that were going forward around them, in the hands of those innumerable young women in irreproachable toilets who devote themselves, in France, to the propagation of masterpieces, and if the truth must be told, he had often admired the copy much more than the original. His physiognomy would have sufficiently indicated that he was a shrewd and capable fellow, and in truth he had often sat up all night over a bristling bundle of accounts, and heard the cock crow without a yawn. But Raphael and Titian and Rubens were a new kind of arithmetic, and they inspired our friend, for the first time in his life, with a vague self-mistrust.

An observer with anything of an eye for national types would have had no difficulty in determining the local origin of this undeveloped connoisseur, and indeed such an observer might have felt a certain humorous relish of the almost ideal completeness with which he filled out the national mould. The gentleman on the divan was a powerful specimen of an American. But he was not only a fine American; he was in the first place, physically, a fine man. He appeared to possess that kind of health and strength which, when found in perfection, are the most impressive—the physical capital which the owner does nothing to "keep up." If he was a muscular Christian, it was quite without knowing it. If it was necessary to walk to a remote spot, he walked, but he had never known himself to "exercise." He had no theory with regard to cold bathing or the use of Indian clubs; he was neither an oarsman, a rifleman, nor a fencer—he had never had time for these amusements—and he was quite unaware that the saddle is recommended for certain forms of indigestion. He was by inclination a temperate man; but he had supped the night before his visit to the Louvre at the Cafe Anglais—some one had told him it was an experience not to be omitted—and he had slept none the less the sleep of the just. His usual attitude and carriage were of a rather relaxed and lounging kind, but when under a special inspiration, he straightened himself, he looked like a grenadier on parade. He never smoked. He had been assured—such things are said—that cigars were excellent for the health, and he was quite capable of believing it; but he knew as little about tobacco as about homeopathy. He had a very well-formed head, with a shapely, symmetrical balance of the frontal and the occipital development, and a good deal of straight, rather dry brown hair. His complexion was brown, and his nose had a bold well-marked arch. His eye was of a clear, cold gray, and save for a rather abundant mustache he was clean-shaved. He had the flat jaw and sinewy neck which are frequent in the American type; but the traces of national origin are a matter of expression even more than of feature, and it was in this respect that our friend's countenance was supremely eloquent. The discriminating observer we have been supposing might, however, perfectly have measured its expressiveness, and yet have been at a loss to describe it. It had that typical vagueness which is not vacuity, that blankness which is not simplicity, that look of being committed to nothing in particular, of standing in an attitude of general hospitality to the chances of life, of being very much at one's own disposal so characteristic of many American faces. It was our friend's eye that chiefly told his story; an eye in which innocence and experience were singularly blended. It was full of contradictory suggestions, and though it was by no means the glowing orb of a hero of romance, you could find in it almost anything you looked for. Frigid and yet friendly, frank yet cautious, shrewd yet credulous, positive yet skeptical, confident yet shy, extremely intelligent and extremely good-humored, there was something vaguely defiant in its concessions, and something profoundly reassuring in its reserve. The cut of this gentleman's mustache, with the two premature wrinkles in the cheek above it, and the fashion of his garments, in which an exposed shirt-front and a cerulean cravat played perhaps an obtrusive part, completed the conditions of his identity. We have approached him, perhaps, at a not especially favorable moment; he is by no means sitting for his portrait. But listless as he lounges there, rather baffled on the aesthetic question, and guilty of the damning fault (as we have lately discovered it to be) of confounding the merit of the artist with that of his work (for he admires the squinting Madonna of the young lady with the boyish coiffure, because he thinks the young lady herself uncommonly taking), he is a sufficiently promising acquaintance. Decision, salubrity, jocosity, prosperity, seem to hover within his call; he is evidently a practical man, but the idea in his case, has undefined and mysterious boundaries, which invite the imagination to bestir itself on his behalf.

As the little copyist proceeded with her work, she sent every now and then a responsive glance toward her admirer. The cultivation of the fine arts appeared to necessitate, to her mind, a great deal of byplay, a great standing off with folded arms and head drooping from side to side, stroking of a dimpled chin with a dimpled hand, sighing and frowning and patting of the foot, fumbling in disordered tresses for wandering hair-pins. These performances were accompanied by a restless glance, which lingered longer than elsewhere upon the gentleman we have described. At last he rose abruptly, put on his hat, and approached the young lady. He placed himself before her picture and looked at it for some moments, during which she pretended to be quite unconscious of his inspection. Then, addressing her with the single word which constituted the strength of his French vocabulary, and holding up one finger in a manner which appeared to him to illuminate his meaning, "Combien?" he abruptly demanded.

The artist stared a moment, gave a little pout, shrugged her shoulders, put down her palette and brushes, and stood rubbing her hands.

"How much?" said our friend, in English. "Combien?"

"Monsieur wishes to buy it?" asked the young lady in French.

"Very pretty, splendide. Combien?" repeated the American.

"It pleases monsieur, my little picture? It's a very beautiful subject," said the young lady.

"The Madonna, yes; I am not a Catholic, but I want to buy it. Combien? Write it here." And he took a pencil from his pocket and showed her the fly-leaf of his guide-book. She stood looking at him and scratching her chin with the pencil. "Is it not for sale?" he asked. And as she still stood reflecting, and looking at him with an eye which, in spite of her desire to treat this avidity of patronage as a very old story, betrayed an almost touching incredulity, he was afraid he had offended her. She simply trying to look indifferent, and wondering how far she might go. "I haven't made a mistake—pas insulte, no?" her interlocutor continued. "Don't you understand a little English?"

The young lady's aptitude for playing a part at short notice was remarkable. She fixed him with her conscious, perceptive eye and asked him if he spoke no French. Then, "Donnez!" she said briefly, and took the open guide-book. In the upper corner of the fly-leaf she traced a number, in a minute and extremely neat hand. Then she handed back the book and took up her palette again.

Our friend read the number: "2,000 francs." He said nothing for a time, but stood looking at the picture, while the copyist began actively to dabble with her paint. "For a copy, isn't that a good deal?" he asked at last. "Pas beaucoup?"

The young lady raised her eyes from her palette, scanned him from head to foot, and alighted with admirable sagacity upon exactly the right answer. "Yes, it's a good deal. But my copy has remarkable qualities, it is worth nothing less."

The gentleman in whom we are interested understood no French, but I have said he was intelligent, and here is a good chance to prove it. He apprehended, by a natural instinct, the meaning of the young woman's phrase, and it gratified him to think that she was so honest. Beauty, talent, virtue; she combined everything! "But you must finish it," he said. "FINISH, you know;" and he pointed to the unpainted hand of the figure.

"Oh, it shall be finished in perfection; in the perfection of perfections!" cried mademoiselle; and to confirm her promise, she deposited a rosy blotch in the middle of the Madonna's cheek.

But the American frowned. "Ah, too red, too red!" he rejoined. "Her complexion," pointing to the Murillo, "is—more delicate."

"Delicate? Oh, it shall be delicate, monsieur; delicate as Sevres biscuit. I am going to tone that down; I know all the secrets of my art. And where will you allow us to send it to you? Your address?"

"My address? Oh yes!" And the gentleman drew a card from his pocket-book and wrote something upon it. Then hesitating a moment he said, "If I don't like it when it it's finished, you know, I shall not be obliged to take it."

The young lady seemed as good a guesser as himself. "Oh, I am very sure that monsieur is not capricious," she said with a roguish smile.

"Capricious?" And at this monsieur began to laugh. "Oh no, I'm not capricious. I am very faithful. I am very constant. Comprenez?"

"Monsieur is constant; I understand perfectly. It's a rare virtue. To recompense you, you shall have your picture on the first possible day; next week—as soon as it is dry. I will take the card of monsieur." And she took it and read his name: "Christopher Newman." Then she tried to repeat it aloud, and laughed at her bad accent. "Your English names are so droll!"

"Droll?" said Mr. Newman, laughing too. "Did you ever hear of Christopher Columbus?"

"Bien sur! He invented America; a very great man. And is he your patron?"

"My patron?"

"Your patron-saint, in the calendar."

"Oh, exactly; my parents named me for him."

"Monsieur is American?"

"Don't you see it?" monsieur inquired.

"And you mean to carry my little picture away over there?" and she explained her phrase with a gesture.

"Oh, I mean to buy a great many pictures—beaucoup, beaucoup," said Christopher Newman.

"The honor is not less for me," the young lady answered, "for I am sure monsieur has a great deal of taste."

"But you must give me your card," Newman said; "your card, you know."

The young lady looked severe for an instant, and then said, "My father will wait upon you."

But this time Mr. Newman's powers of divination were at fault. "Your card, your address," he simply repeated.

"My address?" said mademoiselle. Then with a little shrug, "Happily for you, you are an American! It is the first time I ever gave my card to a gentleman." And, taking from her pocket a rather greasy porte-monnaie, she extracted from it a small glazed visiting card, and presented the latter to her patron. It was neatly inscribed in pencil, with a great many flourishes, "Mlle. Noemie Nioche." But Mr. Newman, unlike his companion, read the name with perfect gravity; all French names to him were equally droll.

"And precisely, here is my father, who has come to escort me home," said Mademoiselle Noemie. "He speaks English. He will arrange with you." And she turned to welcome a little old gentleman who came shuffling up, peering over his spectacles at Newman.

M. Nioche wore a glossy wig, of an unnatural color which overhung his little meek, white, vacant face, and left it hardly more expressive than the unfeatured block upon which these articles are displayed in the barber's window. He was an exquisite image of shabby gentility. His scant ill-made coat, desperately brushed, his darned gloves, his highly polished boots, his rusty, shapely hat, told the story of a person who had "had losses" and who clung to the spirit of nice habits even though the letter had been hopelessly effaced. Among other things M. Nioche had lost courage. Adversity had not only ruined him, it had frightened him, and he was evidently going through his remnant of life on tiptoe, for fear of waking up the hostile fates. If this strange gentleman was saying anything improper to his daughter, M. Nioche would entreat him huskily, as a particular favor, to forbear; but he would admit at the same time that he was very presumptuous to ask for particular favors.

"Monsieur has bought my picture," said Mademoiselle Noemie. "When it's finished you'll carry it to him in a cab."

"In a cab!" cried M. Nioche; and he stared, in a bewildered way, as if he had seen the sun rising at midnight.

"Are you the young lady's father?" said Newman. "I think she said you speak English."

"Speak English—yes," said the old man slowly rubbing his hands. "I will bring it in a cab."

"Say something, then," cried his daughter. "Thank him a little—not too much."

"A little, my daughter, a little?" said M. Nioche perplexed. "How much?"

"Two thousand!" said Mademoiselle Noemie. "Don't make a fuss or he'll take back his word."

"Two thousand!" cried the old man, and he began to fumble for his snuff-box. He looked at Newman from head to foot; he looked at his daughter and then at the picture. "Take care you don't spoil it!" he cried almost sublimely.

"We must go home," said Mademoiselle Noemie. "This is a good day's work. Take care how you carry it!" And she began to put up her utensils.

"How can I thank you?" said M. Nioche. "My English does not suffice."

"I wish I spoke French as well," said Newman, good-naturedly. "Your daughter is very clever."

"Oh, sir!" and M. Nioche looked over his spectacles with tearful eyes and nodded several times with a world of sadness. "She has had an education—tres-superieure! Nothing was spared. Lessons in pastel at ten francs the lesson, lessons in oil at twelve francs. I didn't look at the francs then. She's an artiste, ah!"

"Do I understand you to say that you have had reverses?" asked Newman.

"Reverses? Oh, sir, misfortunes—terrible."

"Unsuccessful in business, eh?"

"Very unsuccessful, sir."

"Oh, never fear, you'll get on your legs again," said Newman cheerily.

The old man drooped his head on one side and looked at him with an expression of pain, as if this were an unfeeling jest.

"What does he say?" demanded Mademoiselle Noemie.

M. Nioche took a pinch of snuff. "He says I will make my fortune again."

"Perhaps he will help you. And what else?"

"He says thou art very clever."

"It is very possible. You believe it yourself, my father?"

"Believe it, my daughter? With this evidence!" And the old man turned afresh, with a staring, wondering homage, to the audacious daub on the easel.

"Ask him, then, if he would not like to learn French."

"To learn French?"

"To take lessons."

"To take lessons, my daughter? From thee?"

"From you!"

"From me, my child? How should I give lessons?"

"Pas de raisons! Ask him immediately!" said Mademoiselle Noemie, with soft brevity.

M. Nioche stood aghast, but under his daughter's eye he collected his wits, and, doing his best to assume an agreeable smile, he executed her commands. "Would it please you to receive instruction in our beautiful language?" he inquired, with an appealing quaver.

"To study French?" asked Newman, staring.

M. Nioche pressed his finger-tips together and slowly raised his shoulders. "A little conversation!"

"Conversation—that's it!" murmured Mademoiselle Noemie, who had caught the word. "The conversation of the best society."

"Our French conversation is famous, you know," M. Nioche ventured to continue. "It's a great talent."

"But isn't it awfully difficult?" asked Newman, very simply.

"Not to a man of esprit, like monsieur, an admirer of beauty in every form!" and M. Nioche cast a significant glance at his daughter's Madonna.

"I can't fancy myself chattering French!" said Newman with a laugh. "And yet, I suppose that the more a man knows the better."

"Monsieur expresses that very happily. Helas, oui!"

"I suppose it would help me a great deal, knocking about Paris, to know the language."

"Ah, there are so many things monsieur must want to say: difficult things!"

"Everything I want to say is difficult. But you give lessons?"

Poor M. Nioche was embarrassed; he smiled more appealingly. "I am not a regular professor," he admitted. "I can't nevertheless tell him that I'm a professor," he said to his daughter.

"Tell him it's a very exceptional chance," answered Mademoiselle Noemie; "an homme du monde—one gentleman conversing with another! Remember what you are—what you have been!"

"A teacher of languages in neither case! Much more formerly and much less to-day! And if he asks the price of the lessons?"

"He won't ask it," said Mademoiselle Noemie.

"What he pleases, I may say?"

"Never! That's bad style."

"If he asks, then?"

Mademoiselle Noemie had put on her bonnet and was tying the ribbons. She smoothed them out, with her soft little chin thrust forward. "Ten francs," she said quickly.

"Oh, my daughter! I shall never dare."

"Don't dare, then! He won't ask till the end of the lessons, and then I will make out the bill."

M. Nioche turned to the confiding foreigner again, and stood rubbing his hands, with an air of seeming to plead guilty which was not intenser only because it was habitually so striking. It never occurred to Newman to ask him for a guarantee of his skill in imparting instruction; he supposed of course M. Nioche knew his own language, and his appealing forlornness was quite the perfection of what the American, for vague reasons, had always associated with all elderly foreigners of the lesson-giving class. Newman had never reflected upon philological processes. His chief impression with regard to ascertaining those mysterious correlatives of his familiar English vocables which were current in this extraordinary city of Paris was, that it was simply a matter of a good deal of unwonted and rather ridiculous muscular effort on his own part. "How did you learn English?" he asked of the old man.

"When I was young, before my miseries. Oh, I was wide awake, then. My father was a great commercant; he placed me for a year in a counting-house in England. Some of it stuck to me; but I have forgotten!"

"How much French can I learn in a month?"

"What does he say?" asked Mademoiselle Noemie.

M. Nioche explained.

"He will speak like an angel!" said his daughter.

But the native integrity which had been vainly exerted to secure M. Nioche's commercial prosperity flickered up again. "Dame, monsieur!" he answered. "All I can teach you!" And then, recovering himself at a sign from his daughter, "I will wait upon you at your hotel."

"Oh yes, I should like to learn French," Newman went on, with democratic confidingness. "Hang me if I should ever have thought of it! I took for granted it was impossible. But if you learned my language, why shouldn't I learn yours?" and his frank, friendly laugh drew the sting from the jest. "Only, if we are going to converse, you know, you must think of something cheerful to converse about."

"You are very good, sir; I am overcome!" said M. Nioche, throwing out his hands. "But you have cheerfulness and happiness for two!"

"Oh no," said Newman more seriously. "You must be bright and lively; that's part of the bargain."

M. Nioche bowed, with his hand on his heart. "Very well, sir; you have already made me lively."

"Come and bring me my picture then; I will pay you for it, and we will talk about that. That will be a cheerful subject!"

Mademoiselle Noemie had collected her accessories, and she gave the precious Madonna in charge to her father, who retreated backwards out of sight, holding it at arm's-length and reiterating his obeisance. The young lady gathered her shawl about her like a perfect Parisienne, and it was with the smile of a Parisienne that she took leave of her patron.

CHAPTER II

He wandered back to the divan and seated himself on the other side, in view of the great canvas on which Paul Veronese had depicted the marriage-feast of Cana. Wearied as he was he found the picture entertaining; it had an illusion for him; it satisfied his conception, which was ambitious, of what a splendid banquet should be. In the left-hand corner of the picture is a young woman with yellow tresses confined in a golden head-dress; she is bending forward and listening, with the smile of a charming woman at a dinner-party, to her neighbor. Newman detected her in the crowd, admired her, and perceived that she too had her votive copyist—a young man with his hair standing on end. Suddenly he became conscious of the germ of the mania of the "collector;" he had taken the first step; why should he not go on? It was only twenty minutes before that he had bought the first picture of his life, and now he was already thinking of art-patronage as a fascinating pursuit. His reflections quickened his good-humor, and he was on the point of approaching the young man with another "Combien?" Two or three facts in this relation are noticeable, although the logical chain which connects them may seem imperfect. He knew Mademoiselle Nioche had asked too much; he bore her no grudge for doing so, and he was determined to pay the young man exactly the proper sum. At this moment, however, his attention was attracted by a gentleman who had come from another part of the room and whose manner was that of a stranger to the gallery, although he was equipped with neither guide-book nor opera-glass. He carried a white sun-umbrella, lined with blue silk, and he strolled in front of the Paul Veronese, vaguely looking at it, but much too near to see anything but the grain of the canvas. Opposite to Christopher Newman he paused and turned, and then our friend, who had been observing him, had a chance to verify a suspicion aroused by an imperfect view of his face. The result of this larger scrutiny was that he presently sprang to his feet, strode across the room, and, with an outstretched hand, arrested the gentleman with the blue-lined umbrella. The latter stared, but put out his hand at a venture. He was corpulent and rosy, and though his countenance, which was ornamented with a beautiful flaxen beard, carefully divided in the middle and brushed outward at the sides, was not remarkable for intensity of expression, he looked like a person who would willingly shake hands with any one. I know not what Newman thought of his face, but he found a want of response in his grasp.

"Oh, come, come," he said, laughing; "don't say, now, you don't know me—if I have NOT got a white parasol!"

The sound of his voice quickened the other's memory, his face expanded to its fullest capacity, and he also broke into a laugh. "Why, Newman—I'll be blowed! Where in the world—I declare—who would have thought? You know you have changed."

"You haven't!" said Newman.

"Not for the better, no doubt. When did you get here?"

"Three days ago."

"Why didn't you let me know?"

"I had no idea YOU were here."

"I have been here these six years."

"It must be eight or nine since we met."

"Something of that sort. We were very young."

"It was in St. Louis, during the war. You were in the army."

"Oh no, not I! But you were."

"I believe I was."

"You came out all right?"

CHAPTER II

"I came out with my legs and arms—and with satisfaction. All that seems very far away."

"And how long have you been in Europe?"

"Seventeen days."

"First time?"

"Yes, very much so."

"Made your everlasting fortune?"

Christopher Newman was silent a moment, and then with a tranquil smile he answered, "Yes."

"And come to Paris to spend it, eh?"

"Well, we shall see. So they carry those parasols here—the menfolk?"

"Of course they do. They're great things. They understand comfort out here."

"Where do you buy them?"

"Anywhere, everywhere."

"Well, Tristram, I'm glad to get hold of you. You can show me the ropes. I suppose you know Paris inside out."

Mr. Tristram gave a mellow smile of self-gratulation. "Well, I guess there are not many men that can show me much. I'll take care of you."

"It's a pity you were not here a few minutes ago. I have just bought a picture. You might have put the thing through for me."

"Bought a picture?" said Mr. Tristram, looking vaguely round at the walls. "Why, do they sell them?"

"I mean a copy."

"Oh, I see. These," said Mr. Tristram, nodding at the Titians and Vandykes, "these, I suppose, are originals."

"I hope so," cried Newman. "I don't want a copy of a copy."

"Ah," said Mr. Tristram, mysteriously, "you can never tell. They imitate, you know, so deucedly well. It's like the jewelers, with their false stones. Go into the Palais Royal, there; you see 'Imitation' on half the windows. The law obliges them to stick it on, you know; but you can't tell the things apart. To tell the truth," Mr. Tristram continued, with a wry face, "I don't do much in pictures. I leave that to my wife."

"Ah, you have got a wife?"

"Didn't I mention it? She's a very nice woman; you must know her. She's up there in the Avenue d'Iena."

"So you are regularly fixed—house and children and all."

"Yes, a tip-top house and a couple of youngsters."

"Well," said Christopher Newman, stretching his arms a little, with a sigh, "I envy you."

"Oh no! you don't!" answered Mr. Tristram, giving him a little poke with his parasol.

"I beg your pardon; I do!"

"Well, you won't, then, when—when—"

"You don't certainly mean when I have seen your establishment?"

"When you have seen Paris, my boy. You want to be your own master here."

"Oh, I have been my own master all my life, and I'm tired of it."

"Well, try Paris. How old are you?"

"Thirty-six."

"C'est le bel age, as they say here."

"What does that mean?"

"It means that a man shouldn't send away his plate till he has eaten his fill."

"All that? I have just made arrangements to take French lessons."

"Oh, you don't want any lessons. You'll pick it up. I never took any."

"I suppose you speak French as well as English?"

"Better!" said Mr. Tristram, roundly. "It's a splendid language. You can say all sorts of bright things in it."

"But I suppose," said Christopher Newman, with an earnest desire for information, "that you must be bright to begin with."

"Not a bit; that's just the beauty of it."

The two friends, as they exchanged these remarks, had remained standing where they met, and leaning against the rail which protected the pictures. Mr. Tristram at last declared that he was overcome with fatigue and should be happy to sit down. Newman recommended in the highest terms the great divan on which he had been lounging, and they prepared to seat themselves. "This is a great place; isn't it?" said Newman, with ardor.

"Great place, great place. Finest thing in the world." And then, suddenly, Mr. Tristram hesitated and looked about him. "I suppose they won't let you smoke here."

Newman stared. "Smoke? I'm sure I don't know. You know the regulations better than I."

"I? I never was here before!"

"Never! in six years?"

"I believe my wife dragged me here once when we first came to Paris, but I never found my way back."

"But you say you know Paris so well!"

"I don't call this Paris!" cried Mr. Tristram, with assurance. "Come; let's go over to the Palais Royal and have a smoke."

"I don't smoke," said Newman.

"A drink, then."

And Mr. Tristram led his companion away. They passed through the glorious halls of the Louvre, down the staircases, along the cool, dim galleries of sculpture, and out into the enormous court. Newman looked about him as he went, but he made no comments, and it was only when they at last emerged into the open air that he said to his friend, "It seems to me that in your place I should have come here once a week."

"Oh, no you wouldn't!" said Mr. Tristram. "You think so, but you wouldn't. You wouldn't have had time. You would always mean to go, but you never would go. There's better fun than that, here in Paris. Italy's the place to see pictures; wait till you get there. There you have to go; you can't do anything else. It's an awful country; you can't get a decent cigar. I don't know why I went in there, to-day; I was strolling along, rather hard up for amusement. I sort of noticed the Louvre as I passed, and I thought I would go in and see what was going on. But if I hadn't found you there I should have felt rather sold. Hang it, I don't care for pictures; I prefer the reality!" And Mr. Tristram tossed off this happy formula with an assurance which the numerous class of persons suffering from an overdose of "culture" might have envied him.

The two gentlemen proceeded along the Rue de Rivoli and into the Palais Royal, where they seated themselves at one of the little tables stationed at the door of the cafe which projects into the great open quadrangle. The place was filled with people, the fountains were spouting, a band was playing, clusters of chairs were gathered beneath all the lime-trees, and buxom, white-capped nurses, seated along the benches, were offering to their infant charges the amplest facilities for nutrition. There was an easy, homely gayety in the whole scene, and Christopher Newman felt that it was most characteristically Parisian.

"And now," began Mr. Tristram, when they had tested the decoction which he had caused to be served to them, "now just give an account of yourself. What are your ideas, what are your plans, where have you come from and where are you going? In the first place, where are you staying?"

"At the Grand Hotel," said Newman.

Mr. Tristram puckered his plump visage. "That won't do! You must change."

"Change?" demanded Newman. "Why, it's the finest hotel I ever was in."

"You don't want a 'fine' hotel; you want something small and quiet and elegant, where your bell is answered and you—your person is recognized."

"They keep running to see if I have rung before I have touched the bell," said Newman "and as for my person they are always bowing and scraping to it."

"I suppose you are always tipping them. That's very bad style."

"Always? By no means. A man brought me something yesterday, and then stood loafing in a beggarly manner. I offered him a chair and asked him if he wouldn't sit down. Was that bad style?"

"Very!"

"But he bolted, instantly. At any rate, the place amuses me. Hang your elegance, if it bores me. I sat in the court of the Grand Hotel last night until two o'clock in the morning, watching the coming and going, and the people knocking about."

"You're easily pleased. But you can do as you choose—a man in your shoes. You have made a pile of money, eh?"

"I have made enough"

"Happy the man who can say that? Enough for what?"

CHAPTER II

"Enough to rest awhile, to forget the confounded thing, to look about me, to see the world, to have a good time, to improve my mind, and, if the fancy takes me, to marry a wife." Newman spoke slowly, with a certain dryness of accent and with frequent pauses. This was his habitual mode of utterance, but it was especially marked in the words I have just quoted.

"Jupiter! There's a programme!" cried Mr. Tristram. "Certainly, all that takes money, especially the wife; unless indeed she gives it, as mine did. And what's the story? How have you done it?"

Newman had pushed his hat back from his forehead, folded his arms, and stretched his legs. He listened to the music, he looked about him at the bustling crowd, at the plashing fountains, at the nurses and the babies. "I have worked!" he answered at last.

Tristram looked at him for some moments, and allowed his placid eyes to measure his friend's generous longitude and rest upon his comfortably contemplative face. "What have you worked at?" he asked.

"Oh, at several things."

"I suppose you're a smart fellow, eh?"

Newman continued to look at the nurses and babies; they imparted to the scene a kind of primordial, pastoral simplicity. "Yes," he said at last, "I suppose I am." And then, in answer to his companion's inquiries, he related briefly his history since their last meeting. It was an intensely Western story, and it dealt with enterprises which it will be needless to introduce to the reader in detail. Newman had come out of the war with a brevet of brigadier-general, an honor which in this case—without invidious comparisons—had lighted upon shoulders amply competent to bear it. But though he could manage a fight, when need was, Newman heartily disliked the business; his four years in the army had left him with an angry, bitter sense of the waste of precious things—life and time and money and "smartness" and the early freshness of purpose; and he had addressed himself to the pursuits of peace with passionate zest and energy. He was of course as penniless when he plucked off his shoulder-straps as when he put them on, and the only capital at his disposal was his dogged resolution and his lively perception of ends and means. Exertion and action were as natural to him as respiration; a more completely healthy mortal had never trod the elastic soil of the West. His experience, moreover, was as wide as his capacity; when he was fourteen years old, necessity had taken him by his slim young shoulders and pushed him into the street, to earn that night's supper. He had not earned it but he had earned the next night's, and afterwards, whenever he had had none, it was because he had gone without it to use the money for something else, a keener pleasure or a finer profit. He had turned his hand, with his brain in it, to many things; he had been enterprising, in an eminent sense of the term; he had been adventurous and even reckless, and he had known bitter failure as well as brilliant success; but he was a born experimentalist, and he had always found something to enjoy in the pressure of necessity, even when it was as irritating as the haircloth shirt of the mediaeval monk. At one time failure seemed inexorably his portion; ill-luck became his bed-fellow, and whatever he touched he turned, not to gold, but to ashes. His most vivid conception of a supernatural element in the world's affairs had come to him once when this pertinacity of misfortune was at its climax; there seemed to him something stronger in life than his own will. But the mysterious something could only be the devil, and he was accordingly seized with an intense personal enmity to this impertinent force. He had known what it was to have utterly exhausted his credit, to be unable to raise a dollar, and to find himself at nightfall in a strange city, without a penny to mitigate its strangeness. It was under these circumstances that he made his entrance into San Francisco, the scene, subsequently, of his happiest strokes of fortune. If he did not, like Dr. Franklin in Philadelphia, march along the street munching a penny-loaf, it was only because he had not the penny-loaf necessary to the performance. In his darkest days he had had but one simple, practical impulse—the desire, as he would have phrased it, to see the thing through. He did so at last, buffeted his way into smooth waters, and made money largely. It must be admitted, rather nakedly, that Christopher Newman's sole aim in life had been to make money; what he had been placed in the world for was, to his own perception, simply to wrest a fortune, the bigger the better, from defiant opportunity. This idea completely filled his horizon and satisfied his imagination. Upon the uses of money, upon what one might do with a life into which one had succeeded in injecting the golden stream, he had up to his thirty-fifth year very scantily reflected. Life had been for him an open game, and he had played for high stakes. He had won at last and carried off his winnings; and now what was he to do with them? He was a man to whom, sooner or later, the question was sure to present itself, and the answer to it belongs to our story. A vague sense that more answers were possible than his philosophy had hitherto dreamt of had already taken possession of him, and it seemed softly and agreeably to deepen as he lounged in this brilliant corner of Paris with his friend.

"I must confess," he presently went on, "that here I don't feel at all smart. My remarkable talents seem of no use. I feel as simple as a little child, and a little child might take me by the hand and lead me about."

"Oh, I'll be your little child," said Tristram, jovially; "I'll take you by the hand. Trust yourself to me."

"I am a good worker," Newman continued, "but I rather think I am a poor loafer. I have come abroad to amuse myself, but I doubt whether I know how."

"Oh, that's easily learned."

"Well, I may perhaps learn it, but I am afraid I shall never do it by rote. I have the best will in the world about it, but my genius doesn't lie in that direction. As a loafer I shall never be original, as I take it that you are."

"Yes," said Tristram, "I suppose I am original; like all those immoral pictures in the Louvre."

"Besides," Newman continued, "I don't want to work at pleasure, any more than I played at work. I want to take it easily. I feel deliciously lazy, and I should like to spend six months as I am now, sitting under a tree and listening to a band. There's only one thing; I want to hear some good music."

"Music and pictures! Lord, what refined tastes! You are what my wife calls intellectual. I ain't, a bit. But we can find something better for you to do than to sit under a tree. To begin with, you must come to the club."

"What club?"

"The Occidental. You will see all the Americans there; all the best of them, at least. Of course you play poker?"

"Oh, I say," cried Newman, with energy, "you are not going to lock me up in a club and stick me down at a card-table! I haven't come all this way for that."

"What the deuce HAVE you come for! You were glad enough to play poker in St. Louis, I recollect, when you cleaned me out."

"I have come to see Europe, to get the best out of it I can. I want to see all the great things, and do what the clever people do."

"The clever people? Much obliged. You set me down as a blockhead, then?"

Newman was sitting sidewise in his chair, with his elbow on the back and his head leaning on his hand. Without moving he looked a while at his companion with his dry, guarded, half-inscrutable, and yet altogether good-natured smile. "Introduce me to your wife!" he said at last.

Tristram bounced about in his chair. "Upon my word, I won't. She doesn't want any help to turn up her nose at me, nor do you, either!"

"I don't turn up my nose at you, my dear fellow; nor at any one, or anything. I'm not proud, I assure you I'm not proud. That's why I am willing to take example by the clever people."

"Well, if I'm not the rose, as they say here, I have lived near it. I can show you some clever people, too. Do you know General Packard? Do you know C. P. Hatch? Do you know Miss Kitty Upjohn?"

"I shall be happy to make their acquaintance; I want to cultivate society."

Tristram seemed restless and suspicious; he eyed his friend askance, and then, "What are you up to, any way?" he demanded. "Are you going to write a book?"

Christopher Newman twisted one end of his mustache a while, in silence, and at last he made answer. "One day, a couple of months ago, something very curious happened to me. I had come on to New York on some important business; it was rather a long story—a question of getting ahead of another party, in a certain particular way, in the stock-market. This other party had once played me a very mean trick. I owed him a grudge, I felt awfully savage at the time, and I vowed that, when I got a chance, I would, figuratively speaking, put his nose out of joint. There was a matter of some sixty thousand dollars at stake. If I put it out of his way, it was a blow the fellow would feel, and he really deserved no quarter. I jumped into a hack and went about my business, and it was in this hack—this immortal, historical hack—that the curious thing I speak of occurred. It was a hack like any other, only a trifle dirtier, with a greasy line along the top of the drab cushions, as if it had been used for a great many Irish funerals. It is possible I took a nap; I had been traveling all night, and though I was excited with my errand, I felt the want of sleep. At all events I woke up suddenly, from a sleep or from a kind of a reverie, with the most extraordinary feeling in the world—a mortal disgust for the thing I was going to do. It came upon me like THAT!" and he snapped his fingers—"as abruptly as an old wound that begins to ache. I couldn't tell the meaning of it; I only felt that I loathed the whole business and wanted to wash my hands of it. The idea of losing that sixty thousand dollars, of letting it utterly slide and scuttle and never hearing of it again, seemed the sweetest thing in the world. And all this took place quite independently of my will, and I sat watching it as if it were a play at the theatre. I could feel it going on inside of me. You may depend upon it that there are things going on inside of us that we understand mighty little about."

"Jupiter! you make my flesh creep!" cried Tristram. "And while you sat in your hack, watching the play, as you call it, the other man marched in and bagged your sixty thousand dollars?"

"I have not the least idea. I hope so, poor devil! but I never found out. We pulled up in front of the place I was going to in Wall Street, but I sat still in the carriage, and at last the driver scrambled down off his seat to see whether his carriage had not turned into a hearse. I couldn't have got out, any more than if I had been a corpse. What was the matter with me? Momentary idiocy, you'll say. What I wanted to get out of was Wall Street. I told the man to drive down to the Brooklyn ferry and to cross over. When we were over, I told him to drive me out into the country. As I had told him originally to drive for dear life down town, I suppose he thought me insane. Perhaps I was, but in that case I am insane still. I spent the morning looking at the first green leaves on Long Island. I was sick of business; I wanted to throw it all up and break off short; I had money enough, or if I hadn't I ought to have. I seemed to feel a new man inside my old skin, and I longed for a new world. When you want a thing so very badly you had better treat yourself to it. I didn't understand the matter, not in the least; but I gave the old horse the bridle and let him find his way. As soon as I could get out of the game I sailed for Europe. That is how I come to be sitting here."

"You ought to have bought up that hack," said Tristram; "it isn't a safe vehicle to have about. And you have really sold out, then; you have retired from business?"

"I have made over my hand to a friend; when I feel disposed, I can take up the cards again. I dare say that a twelvemonth hence the operation will be reversed. The pendulum will swing back again. I shall be sitting in a gondola or on a dromedary, and all of a sudden I shall want to clear out. But for the present I am perfectly free. I have even bargained that I am to receive no business letters."

"Oh, it's a real caprice de prince," said Tristram. "I back out; a poor devil like me can't help you to spend such very magnificent leisure as that. You should get introduced to the crowned heads."

Newman looked at him a moment, and then, with his easy smile, "How does one do it?" he asked.

"Come, I like that!" cried Tristram. "It shows you are in earnest."

"Of course I am in earnest. Didn't I say I wanted the best? I know the best can't be had for mere money, but I rather think money will do a good deal. In addition, I am willing to take a good deal of trouble."

"You are not bashful, eh?"

"I haven't the least idea. I want the biggest kind of entertainment a man can get. People, places, art, nature, everything! I want to see the tallest mountains, and the bluest lakes, and the finest pictures and the handsomest churches, and the most celebrated men, and the most beautiful women."

"Settle down in Paris, then. There are no mountains that I know of, and the only lake is in the Bois du Boulogne, and not particularly blue. But there is everything else: plenty of pictures and churches, no end of celebrated men, and several beautiful women."

"But I can't settle down in Paris at this season, just as summer is coming on."

"Oh, for the summer go up to Trouville."

"What is Trouville?"

"The French Newport. Half the Americans go."

"Is it anywhere near the Alps?"

"About as near as Newport is to the Rocky Mountains."

"Oh, I want to see Mont Blanc," said Newman, "and Amsterdam, and the Rhine, and a lot of places. Venice in particular. I have great ideas about Venice."

"Ah," said Mr. Tristram, rising, "I see I shall have to introduce you to my wife!"

CHAPTER III

He performed this ceremony on the following day, when, by appointment, Christopher Newman went to dine with him. Mr. and Mrs. Tristram lived behind one of those chalk-colored facades which decorate with their pompous sameness the broad avenues manufactured by Baron Haussmann in the neighborhood of the Arc de Triomphe. Their apartment was rich in the modern conveniences, and Tristram lost no time in calling his visitor's attention to their principal household treasures, the gas-lamps and the furnace-holes. "Whenever you feel homesick," he said, "you must come up here. We'll stick you down before a register, under a good big burner, and—"

"And you will soon get over your homesickness," said Mrs. Tristram.

Her husband stared; his wife often had a tone which he found inscrutable he could not tell for his life whether she was in jest or in earnest. The truth is that circumstances had done much to cultivate in Mrs. Tristram a marked tendency to irony. Her taste on many points differed from that of her husband, and though she made frequent concessions it must be confessed that her concessions were not always graceful. They were founded upon a vague project she had of some day doing something very positive, something a trifle passionate. What she meant to do she could by no means have told you; but meanwhile, nevertheless, she was buying a good conscience, by installments.

It should be added, without delay, to anticipate misconception, that her little scheme of independence did not definitely involve the assistance of another person, of the opposite sex; she was not saving up virtue to cover the expenses of a flirtation. For this there were various reasons. To begin with, she had a very plain face and she was entirely without illusions as to her appearance. She had taken its measure to a hair's breadth, she knew the worst and the best, she had accepted herself. It had not been, indeed, without a struggle. As a young girl she had spent hours with her back to her mirror, crying her eyes out; and later she had from desperation and bravado adopted the habit of proclaiming herself the most ill-favored of women, in order that she might—as in common politeness was inevitable—be contradicted and reassured. It was since she had come to live in Europe that she had begun to take the matter philosophically. Her observation, acutely exercised here, had suggested to her that a woman's first duty is not to be beautiful, but to be pleasing, and she encountered so many women who pleased without beauty that she began to feel that she had discovered her mission. She had once heard an enthusiastic musician, out of patience with a gifted bungler, declare that a fine voice is really an obstacle to singing properly; and it occurred to her that it might perhaps be equally true that a beautiful face is an obstacle to the acquisition of charming manners. Mrs. Tristram, then, undertook to be exquisitely agreeable, and she brought to the task a really touching devotion. How well she would have succeeded I am unable to say; unfortunately she broke off in the middle. Her own excuse was the want of encouragement in her immediate circle. But I am inclined to think that she had not a real genius for the matter, or she would have pursued the charming art for itself. The poor lady was very incomplete. She fell back upon the harmonies of the toilet, which she thoroughly understood, and contented herself with dressing in perfection. She lived in Paris, which she pretended to detest, because it was only in Paris that one could find things to exactly suit one's complexion. Besides out of Paris it was always more or less of a trouble to get ten-button gloves. When she railed at this serviceable city and you asked her where she would prefer to reside, she returned some very unexpected answer. She would say in Copenhagen, or in Barcelona; having, while making the tour of Europe, spent a couple of days at each of these places. On the whole, with her poetic furbelows and her misshapen, intelligent little face, she was, when you knew her, a decidedly interesting woman. She was naturally shy, and if she had been born a beauty, she would (having no vanity) probably have remained shy. Now, she was both diffident and importunate; extremely reserved sometimes with her friends, and strangely expansive with strangers. She despised her husband; despised him too much, for she had been perfectly at liberty not to marry him. She had been in love with a clever man who had slighted her, and she had married a fool in the hope that this thankless wit, reflecting on it, would conclude that she had no appreciation of merit, and that he had flattered himself in supposing that she cared for his own. Restless, discontented, visionary, without personal ambitions, but with a certain avidity of imagination, she was, as I have said before, eminently incomplete. She was full—both for good and for ill—of beginnings that came to nothing; but she had nevertheless, morally, a spark of the sacred fire.

Newman was fond, under all circumstances, of the society of women, and now that he was out of his native element and deprived of his habitual interests, he turned to it for compensation. He took a great fancy to Mrs. Tristram; she frankly repaid it, and after their first meeting he passed a great many hours in her drawing-room. After two or three talks they were fast friends. Newman's manner with women was peculiar, and it required some ingenuity on a lady's part to discover that he admired her. He had no gallantry, in the usual sense of the term; no compliments, no graces, no speeches. Very fond of what is called chaffing, in his dealings with men, he never found himself on a sofa beside a member of the softer sex without feeling extremely serious. He was not shy, and so far as awkwardness proceeds from a struggle with shyness, he was not awkward; grave, attentive, submissive, often silent, he was simply swimming in a sort of rapture of respect. This emotion was not at all theoretic, it was not even in a high degree sentimental; he had thought very little about the "position" of women, and he was not familiar either sympathetically or otherwise, with the image of a President in petticoats. His attitude was simply the flower of his general good-nature, and a part of his instinctive and genuinely democratic assumption of every one's right to lead an easy life. If a shaggy pauper had a right to bed and board and wages and a vote, women, of course, who were weaker than paupers, and whose physical tissue was in itself an appeal, should be maintained, sentimentally, at the public expense. Newman was willing to be taxed for this purpose, largely, in proportion to his means. Moreover, many of the common traditions with regard to women were with him fresh personal impressions; he had never read a novel! He had been struck with their acuteness, their subtlety, their tact, their felicity of judgment. They seemed to him exquisitely organized. If it is true that one must always have in one's work here below a religion, or at least an ideal, of some sort, Newman found his metaphysical inspiration in a vague acceptance of final responsibility to some illumined feminine brow.

He spent a great deal of time in listening to advice from Mrs. Tristram; advice, it must be added, for which he had never asked. He would have been incapable of asking for it, for he had no perception of difficulties, and consequently no curiosity about remedies. The complex Parisian world about him seemed a very simple affair; it was an immense, amazing spectacle, but it neither inflamed his imagination nor irritated his curiosity. He kept his hands in his pockets, looked on good-humoredly, desired to miss nothing important, observed a great many things narrowly, and never reverted to himself. Mrs. Tristram's "advice" was a part of the show, and a more entertaining element, in her abundant gossip, than the others. He enjoyed her talking about himself; it seemed a part of her beautiful ingenuity; but he never made an application of anything she said, or remembered it when he was away from her. For herself, she appropriated him; he was the most interesting thing she had had to think about in many a month. She wished to do something with him—she hardly knew what. There was so much of him; he was so rich and robust, so easy, friendly, well-disposed, that he kept her fancy constantly on the alert. For the present, the only thing she could do was to like him. She told him that he was "horribly Western," but in this compliment the adverb was tinged with insincerity. She led him about with her, introduced him to fifty people, and took extreme satisfaction in her conquest. Newman accepted every proposal, shook hands universally and promiscuously, and seemed equally unfamiliar with trepidation or with elation. Tom Tristram complained of his wife's avidity, and declared that he could never have a clear five minutes with his friend. If he had known how things were going to turn out, he never would have brought him to the Avenue d'Iena. The two men, formerly, had not been intimate, but Newman remembered his earlier impression of his host, and did Mrs. Tristram, who had by no means taken him into her confidence, but whose secret he presently discovered, the justice to admit that her husband was a rather degenerate mortal. At twenty-five he had been a good fellow, and in this respect he was unchanged; but of a man of his age one expected something more. People said he was sociable, but this was as much a matter of course as for a dipped sponge to expand; and it was not a high order of sociability. He was a great gossip and tattler, and to produce a laugh would hardly have spared the reputation of his aged mother. Newman had a kindness for old memories, but he found it impossible not to perceive that Tristram was nowadays a very light weight. His only aspirations were to hold out at poker, at his club, to know the names of all the cocottes, to shake hands all round, to ply his rosy gullet with truffles and champagne, and to create uncomfortable eddies and obstructions among the constituent atoms of the American colony. He was shamefully idle, spiritless, sensual, snobbish. He irritated our friend by the tone of his allusions to their native country, and Newman was at a loss to understand why the United States were not good enough for Mr. Tristram. He had never been a very conscious patriot, but it vexed him to see them treated as little better than a vulgar smell in his friend's nostrils, and he finally broke out and swore that they were the greatest country in the world, that they could put all Europe into their breeches' pockets, and that an American who spoke ill of them ought to be carried home in irons and compelled to live in Boston. (This, for Newman was putting it very vindictively.) Tristram was a comfortable man to snub, he bore no malice, and he continued to insist on Newman's finishing his evening at the Occidental Club.

Christopher Newman dined several times in the Avenue d'Iena, and his host always proposed an early adjournment to this institution. Mrs. Tristram protested, and declared that her husband exhausted his ingenuity in trying to displease her.

"Oh no, I never try, my love," he answered. "I know you loathe me quite enough when I take my chance."

Newman hated to see a husband and wife on these terms, and he was sure one or other of them must be very unhappy. He knew it was not Tristram. Mrs. Tristram had a balcony before her windows, upon which, during the June evenings, she was fond of sitting, and Newman used frankly to say that he preferred the balcony to the club. It had a fringe of perfumed plants in tubs, and enabled you to look up the broad street and see the Arch of Triumph vaguely massing its heroic sculptures in the summer starlight. Sometimes Newman kept his promise of following Mr. Tristram, in half an hour, to the Occidental, and sometimes he forgot it. His hostess asked him a great many questions about himself, but on this subject he was an indifferent talker. He was not what is called subjective, though when he felt that her interest was sincere, he made an almost heroic attempt to be. He told her a great many things he had done, and regaled her with anecdotes of Western life; she was from Philadelphia, and with her eight years in Paris, talked of herself as a languid Oriental. But some other person was always the hero of the tale, by no means always to his advantage; and Newman's own emotions were but scantily chronicled. She had an especial wish to know whether he had ever been in love—seriously, passionately—and, failing to gather any satisfaction from his allusions, she at last directly inquired. He hesitated a while, and at last he said, "No!" She declared that she was delighted to hear it, as it confirmed her private conviction that he was a man of no feeling.

"Really?" he asked, very gravely. "Do you think so? How do you recognize a man of feeling?"

"I can't make out," said Mrs. Tristram, "whether you are very simple or very deep."

"I'm very deep. That's a fact."

"I believe that if I were to tell you with a certain air that you have no feeling, you would implicitly believe me."

"A certain air?" said Newman. "Try it and see."

"You would believe me, but you would not care," said Mrs. Tristram.

"You have got it all wrong. I should care immensely, but I shouldn't believe you. The fact is I have never had time to feel things. I have had to DO them, to make myself felt."

"I can imagine that you may have done that tremendously, sometimes."

"Yes, there's no mistake about that."

"When you are in a fury it can't be pleasant."

"I am never in a fury."

"Angry, then, or displeased."

"I am never angry, and it is so long since I have been displeased that I have quite forgotten it."

"I don't believe," said Mrs. Tristram, "that you are never angry. A man ought to be angry sometimes, and you are neither good enough nor bad enough always to keep your temper."

"I lose it perhaps once in five years."

"The time is coming round, then," said his hostess. "Before I have known you six months I shall see you in a fine fury."

"Do you mean to put me into one?"

CHAPTER III

"I should not be sorry. You take things too coolly. It exasperates me. And then you are too happy. You have what must be the most agreeable thing in the world, the consciousness of having bought your pleasure beforehand and paid for it. You have not a day of reckoning staring you in the face. Your reckonings are over."

"Well, I suppose I am happy," said Newman, meditatively.

"You have been odiously successful."

"Successful in copper," said Newman, "only so-so in railroads, and a hopeless fizzle in oil."

"It is very disagreeable to know how Americans have made their money. Now you have the world before you. You have only to enjoy."

"Oh, I suppose I am very well off," said Newman. "Only I am tired of having it thrown up at me. Besides, there are several drawbacks. I am not intellectual."

"One doesn't expect it of you," Mrs. Tristram answered. Then in a moment, "Besides, you are!"

"Well, I mean to have a good time, whether or no," said Newman. "I am not cultivated, I am not even educated; I know nothing about history, or art, or foreign tongues, or any other learned matters. But I am not a fool, either, and I shall undertake to know something about Europe by the time I have done with it. I feel something under my ribs here," he added in a moment, "that I can't explain—a sort of a mighty hankering, a desire to stretch out and haul in."

"Bravo!" said Mrs. Tristram, "that is very fine. You are the great Western Barbarian, stepping forth in his innocence and might, gazing a while at this poor effete Old World and then swooping down on it."

"Oh, come," said Newman. "I am not a barbarian, by a good deal. I am very much the reverse. I have seen barbarians; I know what they are."

"I don't mean that you are a Comanche chief, or that you wear a blanket and feathers. There are different shades."

"I am a highly civilized man," said Newman. "I stick to that. If you don't believe it, I should like to prove it to you."

Mrs. Tristram was silent a while. "I should like to make you prove it," she said, at last. "I should like to put you in a difficult place."

"Pray do," said Newman.

"That has a little conceited sound!" his companion rejoined.

"Oh," said Newman, "I have a very good opinion of myself."

"I wish I could put it to the test. Give me time and I will." And Mrs. Tristram remained silent for some time afterwards, as if she was trying to keep her pledge. It did not appear that evening that she succeeded; but as he was rising to take his leave she passed suddenly, as she was very apt to do, from the tone of unsparing persiflage to that of almost tremulous sympathy. "Speaking seriously," she said, "I believe in you, Mr. Newman. You flatter my patriotism."

"Your patriotism?" Christopher demanded.

"Even so. It would take too long to explain, and you probably would not understand. Besides, you might take it—really, you might take it for a declaration. But it has nothing to do with you personally; it's what you represent. Fortunately you don't know all that, or your conceit would increase insufferably."

Newman stood staring and wondering what under the sun he "represented."

"Forgive all my meddlesome chatter and forget my advice. It is very silly in me to undertake to tell you what to do. When you are embarrassed, do as you think best, and you will do very well. When you are in a difficulty, judge for yourself."

"I shall remember everything you have told me," said Newman. "There are so many forms and ceremonies over here—"

"Forms and ceremonies are what I mean, of course."

"Ah, but I want to observe them," said Newman. "Haven't I as good a right as another? They don't scare me, and you needn't give me leave to violate them. I won't take it."

"That is not what I mean. I mean, observe them in your own way. Settle nice questions for yourself. Cut the knot or untie it, as you choose."

"Oh, I am sure I shall never fumble over it!" said Newman.

The next time that he dined in the Avenue d'Iena was a Sunday, a day on which Mr. Tristram left the cards unshuffled, so that there was a trio in the evening on the balcony. The talk was of many things, and at last Mrs. Tristram suddenly observed to Christopher Newman that it was high time he should take a wife.

"Listen to her; she has the audacity!" said Tristram, who on Sunday evenings was always rather acrimonious.

"I don't suppose you have made up your mind not to marry?" Mrs. Tristram continued.

"Heaven forbid!" cried Newman. "I am sternly resolved on it."

"It's very easy," said Tristram; "fatally easy!"

"Well, then, I suppose you do not mean to wait till you are fifty."

"On the contrary, I am in a great hurry."

"One would never suppose it. Do you expect a lady to come and propose to you?"

"No; I am willing to propose. I think a great deal about it."

"Tell me some of your thoughts."

"Well," said Newman, slowly, "I want to marry very well."

"Marry a woman of sixty, then," said Tristram.

"'Well' in what sense?"

"In every sense. I shall be hard to please."

"You must remember that, as the French proverb says, the most beautiful girl in the world can give but what she has."

"Since you ask me," said Newman, "I will say frankly that I want extremely to marry. It is time, to begin with: before I know it I shall be forty. And then I'm lonely and helpless and dull. But if I marry now, so long as I didn't do it in hot haste when I was twenty, I must do it with my eyes open. I want to do the thing in handsome style. I do not only want to make no mistakes, but I want to make a great hit. I want to take my pick. My wife must be a magnificent woman."

"Voila ce qui s'appelle parler!" cried Mrs. Tristram.

"Oh, I have thought an immense deal about it."

"Perhaps you think too much. The best thing is simply to fall in love."

"When I find the woman who pleases me, I shall love her enough. My wife shall be very comfortable."

"You are superb! There's a chance for the magnificent women."

"You are not fair." Newman rejoined. "You draw a fellow out and put him off guard, and then you laugh at him."

"I assure you," said Mrs. Tristram, "that I am very serious. To prove it, I will make you a proposal. Should you like me, as they say here, to marry you?"

"To hunt up a wife for me?"

"She is already found. I will bring you together."

"Oh, come," said Tristram, "we don't keep a matrimonial bureau. He will think you want your commission."

"Present me to a woman who comes up to my notions," said Newman, "and I will marry her tomorrow."

"You have a strange tone about it, and I don't quite understand you. I didn't suppose you would be so cold-blooded and calculating."

Newman was silent a while. "Well," he said, at last, "I want a great woman. I stick to that. That's one thing I CAN treat myself to, and if it is to be had I mean to have it. What else have I toiled and struggled for, all these years? I have succeeded, and now what am I to do with my success? To make it perfect, as I see it, there must be a beautiful woman perched on the pile, like a statue on a monument. She must be as good as she is beautiful, and as clever as she is good. I can give my wife a good deal, so I am not afraid to ask a good deal myself. She shall have everything a woman can desire; I shall not even object to her being too good for me; she may be cleverer and wiser than I can understand, and I shall only be the better pleased. I want to possess, in a word, the best article in the market."

"Why didn't you tell a fellow all this at the outset?" Tristram demanded. "I have been trying so to make you fond of ME!"

"This is very interesting," said Mrs. Tristram. "I like to see a man know his own mind."

"I have known mine for a long time," Newman went on. "I made up my mind tolerably early in life that a beautiful wife was the thing best worth having, here below. It is the greatest victory over circumstances. When

I say beautiful, I mean beautiful in mind and in manners, as well as in person. It is a thing every man has an equal right to; he may get it if he can. He doesn't have to be born with certain faculties, on purpose; he needs only to be a man. Then he needs only to use his will, and such wits as he has, and to try."

"It strikes me that your marriage is to be rather a matter of vanity."

"Well, it is certain," said Newman, "that if people notice my wife and admire her, I shall be mightily tickled."

"After this," cried Mrs. Tristram, "call any man modest!"

"But none of them will admire her so much as I."

"I see you have a taste for splendor."

Newman hesitated a little; and then, "I honestly believe I have!" he said.

"And I suppose you have already looked about you a good deal."

"A good deal, according to opportunity."

"And you have seen nothing that satisfied you?"

"No," said Newman, half reluctantly, "I am bound to say in honesty that I have seen nothing that really satisfied me."

"You remind me of the heroes of the French romantic poets, Rolla and Fortunio and all those other insatiable gentlemen for whom nothing in this world was handsome enough. But I see you are in earnest, and I should like to help you."

"Who the deuce is it, darling, that you are going to put upon him?" Tristram cried. "We know a good many pretty girls, thank Heaven, but magnificent women are not so common."

"Have you any objections to a foreigner?" his wife continued, addressing Newman, who had tilted back his chair and, with his feet on a bar of the balcony railing and his hands in his pockets, was looking at the stars.

"No Irish need apply," said Tristram.

Newman meditated a while. "As a foreigner, no," he said at last; "I have no prejudices."

"My dear fellow, you have no suspicions!" cried Tristram. "You don't know what terrible customers these foreign women are; especially the 'magnificent' ones. How should you like a fair Circassian, with a dagger in her belt?"

Newman administered a vigorous slap to his knee. "I would marry a Japanese, if she pleased me," he affirmed.

"We had better confine ourselves to Europe," said Mrs. Tristram. "The only thing is, then, that the person be in herself to your taste?"

"She is going to offer you an unappreciated governess!" Tristram groaned.

"Assuredly. I won't deny that, other things being equal, I should prefer one of my own countrywomen. We should speak the same language, and that would be a comfort. But I am not afraid of a foreigner. Besides, I rather like the idea of taking in Europe, too. It enlarges the field of selection. When you choose from a greater number, you can bring your choice to a finer point!"

"You talk like Sardanapalus!" exclaimed Tristram.

"You say all this to the right person," said Newman's hostess. "I happen to number among my friends the loveliest woman in the world. Neither more nor less. I don't say a very charming person or a very estimable woman or a very great beauty; I say simply the loveliest woman in the world."

"The deuce!" cried Tristram, "you have kept very quiet about her. Were you afraid of me?"

"You have seen her," said his wife, "but you have no perception of such merit as Claire's."

"Ah, her name is Claire? I give it up."

"Does your friend wish to marry?" asked Newman.

"Not in the least. It is for you to make her change her mind. It will not be easy; she has had one husband, and he gave her a low opinion of the species."

"Oh, she is a widow, then?" said Newman.

"Are you already afraid? She was married at eighteen, by her parents, in the French fashion, to a disagreeable old man. But he had the good taste to die a couple of years afterward, and she is now twenty-five."

"So she is French?"

"French by her father, English by her mother. She is really more English than French, and she speaks English as well as you or I—or rather much better. She belongs to the very top of the basket, as they say here. Her family, on each side, is of fabulous antiquity; her mother is the daughter of an English Catholic earl. Her father is dead, and since her widowhood she has lived with her mother and a married brother. There is another brother, younger, who I believe is wild. They have an old hotel in the Rue de l'Universite, but their fortune is small, and they make a common household, for economy's sake. When I was a girl I was put into a convent here for my education, while my father made the tour of Europe. It was a silly thing to do with me, but it had the advantage that it made me acquainted with Claire de Bellegarde. She was younger than I but we became fast friends. I took a tremendous fancy to her, and she returned my passion as far as she could. They kept such a tight rein on her that she could do very little, and when I left the convent she had to give me up. I was not of her monde; I am not now, either, but we sometimes meet. They are terrible people—her monde; all mounted upon stilts a mile high, and with pedigrees long in proportion. It is the skim of the milk of the old noblesse. Do you know what a Legitimist is, or an Ultramontane? Go into Madame de Cintre's drawing-room some afternoon, at five o'clock, and you will see the best preserved specimens. I say go, but no one is admitted who can't show his fifty quarterings."

"And this is the lady you propose to me to marry?" asked Newman. "A lady I can't even approach?"

"But you said just now that you recognized no obstacles."

Newman looked at Mrs. Tristram a while, stroking his mustache. "Is she a beauty?" he demanded.

"No."

"Oh, then it's no use—"

"She is not a beauty, but she is beautiful, two very different things. A beauty has no faults in her face, the face of a beautiful woman may have faults that only deepen its charm."

"I remember Madame de Cintre, now," said Tristram. "She is as plain as a pike-staff. A man wouldn't look at her twice."

"In saying that HE would not look at her twice, my husband sufficiently describes her," Mrs. Tristram rejoined.

"Is she good; is she clever?" Newman asked.

"She is perfect! I won't say more than that. When you are praising a person to another who is to know her, it is bad policy to go into details. I won't exaggerate. I simply recommend her. Among all women I have known she stands alone; she is of a different clay."

"I should like to see her," said Newman, simply.

"I will try to manage it. The only way will be to invite her to dinner. I have never invited her before, and I don't know that she will come. Her old feudal countess of a mother rules the family with an iron hand, and allows her to have no friends but of her own choosing, and to visit only in a certain sacred circle. But I can at least ask her."

At this moment Mrs. Tristram was interrupted; a servant stepped out upon the balcony and announced that there were visitors in the drawing-room. When Newman's hostess had gone in to receive her friends, Tom Tristram approached his guest.

"Don't put your foot into THIS, my boy," he said, puffing the last whiffs of his cigar. "There's nothing in it!"

Newman looked askance at him, inquisitive. "You tell another story, eh?"

"I say simply that Madame de Cintre is a great white doll of a woman, who cultivates quiet haughtiness."

"Ah, she's haughty, eh?"

"She looks at you as if you were so much thin air, and cares for you about as much."

"She is very proud, eh?"

"Proud? As proud as I'm humble."

"And not good-looking?"

Tristram shrugged his shoulders: "It's a kind of beauty you must be INTELLECTUAL to understand. But I must go in and amuse the company."

Some time elapsed before Newman followed his friends into the drawing-room. When he at last made his appearance there he remained but a short time, and during this period sat perfectly silent, listening to a lady to whom Mrs. Tristram had straightway introduced him and who chattered, without a pause, with the full force of an extraordinarily high-pitched voice. Newman gazed and attended. Presently he came to bid good-night to Mrs. Tristram.

"Who is that lady?" he asked.

CHAPTER III

"Miss Dora Finch. How do you like her?"

"She's too noisy."

"She is thought so bright! Certainly, you are fastidious," said Mrs. Tristram.

Newman stood a moment, hesitating. Then at last "Don't forget about your friend," he said, "Madame What's-her-name? the proud beauty. Ask her to dinner, and give me a good notice." And with this he departed.

Some days later he came back; it was in the afternoon. He found Mrs. Tristram in her drawing-room; with her was a visitor, a woman young and pretty, dressed in white. The two ladies had risen and the visitor was apparently taking her leave. As Newman approached, he received from Mrs. Tristram a glance of the most vivid significance, which he was not immediately able to interpret.

"This is a good friend of ours," she said, turning to her companion, "Mr. Christopher Newman. I have spoken of you to him and he has an extreme desire to make your acquaintance. If you had consented to come and dine, I should have offered him an opportunity."

The stranger turned her face toward Newman, with a smile. He was not embarrassed, for his unconscious sang-froid was boundless; but as he became aware that this was the proud and beautiful Madame de Cintre, the loveliest woman in the world, the promised perfection, the proposed ideal, he made an instinctive movement to gather his wits together. Through the slight preoccupation that it produced he had a sense of a long, fair face, and of two eyes that were both brilliant and mild.

"I should have been most happy," said Madame de Cintre. "Unfortunately, as I have been telling Mrs. Tristram, I go on Monday to the country."

Newman had made a solemn bow. "I am very sorry," he said.

"Paris is getting too warm," Madame de Cintre added, taking her friend's hand again in farewell.

Mrs. Tristram seemed to have formed a sudden and somewhat venturesome resolution, and she smiled more intensely, as women do when they take such resolution. "I want Mr. Newman to know you," she said, dropping her head on one side and looking at Madame de Cintre's bonnet ribbons.

Christopher Newman stood gravely silent, while his native penetration admonished him. Mrs. Tristram was determined to force her friend to address him a word of encouragement which should be more than one of the common formulas of politeness; and if she was prompted by charity, it was by the charity that begins at home. Madame de Cintre was her dearest Claire, and her especial admiration but Madame de Cintre had found it impossible to dine with her and Madame de Cintre should for once be forced gently to render tribute to Mrs. Tristram.

"It would give me great pleasure," she said, looking at Mrs. Tristram.

"That's a great deal," cried the latter, "for Madame de Cintre to say!"

"I am very much obliged to you," said Newman. "Mrs. Tristram can speak better for me than I can speak for myself."

Madame de Cintre looked at him again, with the same soft brightness. "Are you to be long in Paris?" she asked.

"We shall keep him," said Mrs. Tristram.

"But you are keeping ME!" and Madame de Cintre shook her friend's hand.

"A moment longer," said Mrs. Tristram.

Madame de Cintre looked at Newman again; this time without her smile. Her eyes lingered a moment. "Will you come and see me?" she asked.

Mrs. Tristram kissed her. Newman expressed his thanks, and she took her leave. Her hostess went with her to the door, and left Newman alone a moment. Presently she returned, rubbing her hands. "It was a fortunate chance," she said. "She had come to decline my invitation. You triumphed on the spot, making her ask you, at the end of three minutes, to her house."

"It was you who triumphed," said Newman. "You must not be too hard upon her."

Mrs. Tristram stared. "What do you mean?"

"She did not strike me as so proud. I should say she was shy."

"You are very discriminating. And what do you think of her face?"

"It's handsome!" said Newman.

"I should think it was! Of course you will go and see her."

"To-morrow!" cried Newman.

"No, not to-morrow; the next day. That will be Sunday; she leaves Paris on Monday. If you don't see her; it will at least be a beginning." And she gave him Madame de Cintre's address.

He walked across the Seine, late in the summer afternoon, and made his way through those gray and silent streets of the Faubourg St. Germain whose houses present to the outer world a face as impassive and as suggestive of the concentration of privacy within as the blank walls of Eastern seraglios. Newman thought it a queer way for rich people to live; his ideal of grandeur was a splendid facade diffusing its brilliancy outward too, irradiating hospitality. The house to which he had been directed had a dark, dusty, painted portal, which swung open in answer to his ring. It admitted him into a wide, graveled court, surrounded on three sides with closed windows, and with a doorway facing the street, approached by three steps and surmounted by a tin canopy. The place was all in the shade; it answered to Newman's conception of a convent. The portress could not tell him whether Madame de Cintre was visible; he would please to apply at the farther door. He crossed the court; a gentleman was sitting, bareheaded, on the steps of the portico, playing with a beautiful pointer. He rose as Newman approached, and, as he laid his hand upon the bell, said with a smile, in English, that he was afraid Newman would be kept waiting; the servants were scattered, he himself had been ringing, he didn't know what the deuce was in them. He was a young man, his English was excellent, and his smile very frank. Newman pronounced the name of Madame de Cintre.

"I think," said the young man, "that my sister is visible. Come in, and if you will give me your card I will carry it to her myself."

Newman had been accompanied on his present errand by a slight sentiment, I will not say of defiance—a readiness for aggression or defense, as they might prove needful—but of reflection, good-humored suspicion. He took from his pocket, while he stood on the portico, a card upon which, under his name, he had written the words "San Francisco," and while he presented it he looked warily at his interlocutor. His glance was singularly reassuring; he liked the young man's face; it strongly resembled that of Madame de Cintre. He was evidently her brother. The young man, on his side, had made a rapid inspection of Newman's person. He had taken the card and was about to enter the house with it when another figure appeared on the threshold—an older man, of a fine presence, wearing evening dress. He looked hard at Newman, and Newman looked at him. "Madame de Cintre," the younger man repeated, as an introduction of the visitor. The other took the card from his hand, read it in a rapid glance, looked again at Newman from head to foot, hesitated a moment, and then said, gravely but urbanely, "Madame de Cintre is not at home."

The younger man made a gesture, and then, turning to Newman, "I am very sorry, sir," he said.

Newman gave him a friendly nod, to show that he bore him no malice, and retraced his steps. At the porter's lodge he stopped; the two men were still standing on the portico.

"Who is the gentleman with the dog?" he asked of the old woman who reappeared. He had begun to learn French.

"That is Monsieur le Comte."

"And the other?"

"That is Monsieur le Marquis."

"A marquis?" said Christopher in English, which the old woman fortunately did not understand. "Oh, then he's not the butler!"

CHAPTER IV

Early one morning, before Christopher Newman was dressed, a little old man was ushered into his apartment, followed by a youth in a blouse, bearing a picture in a brilliant frame. Newman, among the distractions of Paris, had forgotten M. Nioche and his accomplished daughter; but this was an effective reminder.

"I am afraid you had given me up, sir," said the old man, after many apologies and salutations. "We have made you wait so many days. You accused us, perhaps, of inconstancy of bad faith. But behold me at last! And behold also the pretty Madonna. Place it on a chair, my friend, in a good light, so that monsieur may admire it." And M. Nioche, addressing his companion, helped him to dispose the work of art.

It had been endued with a layer of varnish an inch thick and its frame, of an elaborate pattern, was at least a foot wide. It glittered and twinkled in the morning light, and looked, to Newman's eyes, wonderfully splendid and precious. It seemed to him a very happy purchase, and he felt rich in the possession of it. He stood looking at it complacently, while he proceeded with his toilet, and M. Nioche, who had dismissed his own attendant, hovered near, smiling and rubbing his hands.

"It has wonderful finesse," he murmured, caressingly. "And here and there are marvelous touches, you probably perceive them, sir. It attracted great attention on the Boulevard, as we came along. And then a gradation of tones! That's what it is to know how to paint. I don't say it because I am her father, sir; but as one man of taste addressing another I cannot help observing that you have there an exquisite work. It is hard to produce such things and to have to part with them. If our means only allowed us the luxury of keeping it! I really may say, sir—" and M. Nioche gave a little feebly insinuating laugh—"I really may say that I envy you! You see," he added in a moment, "we have taken the liberty of offering you a frame. It increases by a trifle the value of the work, and it will save you the annoyance—so great for a person of your delicacy—of going about to bargain at the shops."

The language spoken by M. Nioche was a singular compound, which I shrink from the attempt to reproduce in its integrity. He had apparently once possessed a certain knowledge of English, and his accent was oddly tinged with the cockneyism of the British metropolis. But his learning had grown rusty with disuse, and his vocabulary was defective and capricious. He had repaired it with large patches of French, with words anglicized by a process of his own, and with native idioms literally translated. The result, in the form in which he in all humility presented it, would be scarcely comprehensible to the reader, so that I have ventured to trim and sift it. Newman only half understood it, but it amused him, and the old man's decent forlornness appealed to his democratic instincts. The assumption of a fatality in misery always irritated his strong good nature—it was almost the only thing that did so; and he felt the impulse to wipe it out, as it were, with the sponge of his own prosperity. The papa of Mademoiselle Noemie, however, had apparently on this occasion been vigorously indoctrinated, and he showed a certain tremulous eagerness to cultivate unexpected opportunities.

"How much do I owe you, then, with the frame?" asked Newman.

"It will make in all three thousand francs," said the old man, smiling agreeably, but folding his hands in instinctive suppliance.

"Can you give me a receipt?"

"I have brought one," said M. Nioche. "I took the liberty of drawing it up, in case monsieur should happen to desire to discharge his debt." And he drew a paper from his pocket-book and presented it to his patron. The document was written in a minute, fantastic hand, and couched in the choicest language.

Newman laid down the money, and M. Nioche dropped the napoleons one by one, solemnly and lovingly, into an old leathern purse.

"And how is your young lady?" asked Newman. "She made a great impression on me."

"An impression? Monsieur is very good. Monsieur admires her appearance?"

"She is very pretty, certainly."

"Alas, yes, she is very pretty!"

"And what is the harm in her being pretty?"

M. Nioche fixed his eyes upon a spot on the carpet and shook his head. Then looking up at Newman with a gaze that seemed to brighten and expand, "Monsieur knows what Paris is. She is dangerous to beauty, when beauty hasn't the sou."

"Ah, but that is not the case with your daughter. She is rich, now."

"Very true; we are rich for six months. But if my daughter were a plain girl I should sleep better all the same."

"You are afraid of the young men?"

"The young and the old!"

"She ought to get a husband."

"Ah, monsieur, one doesn't get a husband for nothing. Her husband must take her as she is: I can't give her a sou. But the young men don't see with that eye."

"Oh," said Newman, "her talent is in itself a dowry."

"Ah, sir, it needs first to be converted into specie!" and M. Nioche slapped his purse tenderly before he stowed it away. "The operation doesn't take place every day."

"Well, your young men are very shabby," said Newman; "that's all I can say. They ought to pay for your daughter, and not ask money themselves."

"Those are very noble ideas, monsieur; but what will you have? They are not the ideas of this country. We want to know what we are about when we marry."

"How big a portion does your daughter want?"

M. Nioche stared, as if he wondered what was coming next; but he promptly recovered himself, at a venture, and replied that he knew a very nice young man, employed by an insurance company, who would content himself with fifteen thousand francs.

"Let your daughter paint half a dozen pictures for me, and she shall have her dowry."

"Half a dozen pictures—her dowry! Monsieur is not speaking inconsiderately?"

"If she will make me six or eight copies in the Louvre as pretty as that Madonna, I will pay her the same price," said Newman.

Poor M. Nioche was speechless a moment, with amazement and gratitude, and then he seized Newman's hand, pressed it between his own ten fingers, and gazed at him with watery eyes. "As pretty as that? They shall be a thousand times prettier—they shall be magnificent, sublime. Ah, if I only knew how to paint, myself, sir, so that I might lend a hand! What can I do to thank you? Voyons!" And he pressed his forehead while he tried to think of something.

"Oh, you have thanked me enough," said Newman.

"Ah, here it is, sir!" cried M. Nioche. "To express my gratitude, I will charge you nothing for the lessons in French conversation."

"The lessons? I had quite forgotten them. Listening to your English," added Newman, laughing, "is almost a lesson in French."

"Ah, I don't profess to teach English, certainly," said M. Nioche. "But for my own admirable tongue I am still at your service."

"Since you are here, then," said Newman, "we will begin. This is a very good hour. I am going to have my coffee; come every morning at half-past nine and have yours with me."

"Monsieur offers me my coffee, also?" cried M. Nioche. "Truly, my beaux jours are coming back."

"Come," said Newman, "let us begin. The coffee is almighty hot. How do you say that in French?"

Every day, then, for the following three weeks, the minutely respectable figure of M. Nioche made its appearance, with a series of little inquiring and apologetic obeisances, among the aromatic fumes of Newman's morning beverage. I don't know how much French our friend learned, but, as he himself said, if the attempt did him no good, it could at any rate do him no harm. And it amused him; it gratified that irregularly sociable side of his nature which had always expressed itself in a relish for ungrammatical conversation, and which often, even in his busy and preoccupied days, had made him sit on rail fences in young Western towns, in the twilight, in gossip hardly less than fraternal with humorous loafers and obscure fortune-seekers. He had notions, wherever he went, about talking with the natives; he had been assured, and his judgment approved the advice, that in traveling abroad it was an excellent thing to look into the life of the country. M. Nioche was very much of a native and, though his life might not be particularly worth looking into, he was a palpable and smoothly-rounded unit in that picturesque Parisian civilization which offered our hero so much easy entertainment and propounded so many curious problems to his inquiring and practical mind. Newman was fond of statistics; he liked to know how things were done; it gratified him to learn what taxes were paid, what profits were gathered, what commercial habits prevailed, how the battle of life was fought. M. Nioche, as a reduced capitalist, was familiar with these considerations, and he formulated his information, which he was proud to be able to impart, in the neatest possible terms and with a pinch of snuff between finger and thumb. As a Frenchman—quite apart from Newman's napoleons—M. Nioche loved conversation, and even in his decay his urbanity had not grown rusty. As a Frenchman, too, he could give a clear account of things, and—still as a Frenchman—when his knowledge was at fault he could supply its lapses with the most convenient and ingenious hypotheses. The little shrunken financier was intensely delighted to have questions asked him, and he scraped together information, by frugal processes, and took notes, in his little greasy pocket-book, of incidents which might interest his munificent friend. He read old almanacs at the book-stalls on the quays, and he began to frequent another cafe, where more newspapers were taken and his postprandial demitasse cost him a penny extra, and where he used to con the tattered sheets for curious anecdotes, freaks of nature, and strange coincidences. He would relate with solemnity the next morning that a child of five years of age had lately died at Bordeaux, whose brain had been found to weigh sixty ounces—the brain of a Napoleon or a Washington! or that Madame P—, charcutiere in the Rue de Clichy, had found in the wadding of an old petticoat the sum of three hundred and sixty francs, which she had lost five years before. He pronounced his words with great distinctness and sonority, and Newman assured him that his way of dealing with the French tongue was very superior to the bewildering chatter that he heard in other mouths. Upon this M. Nioche's accent became more finely trenchant than ever, he offered to read extracts from Lamartine, and he protested that, although he did endeavor according to his feeble lights to cultivate refinement of diction, monsieur, if he wanted the real thing, should go to the Theatre Francais.

Newman took an interest in French thriftiness and conceived a lively admiration for Parisian economies. His own economic genius was so entirely for operations on a larger scale, and, to move at his ease, he needed so imperatively the sense of great risks and great prizes, that he found an ungrudging entertainment in the spectacle of fortunes made by the aggregation of copper coins, and in the minute subdivision of labor and profit. He questioned M. Nioche about his own manner of life, and felt a friendly mixture of compassion and respect over the recital of his delicate frugalities. The worthy man told him how, at one period, he and his daughter had supported existence comfortably upon the sum of fifteen sous per diem; recently, having succeeded in hauling ashore the last floating fragments of the wreck of his fortune, his budget had been a trifle more ample. But they still had to count their sous very narrowly, and M. Nioche intimated with a sigh that Mademoiselle Noemie did not bring to this task that zealous cooperation which might have been desired.

"But what will you have?'" he asked, philosophically. "One is young, one is pretty, one needs new dresses and fresh gloves; one can't wear shabby gowns among the splendors of the Louvre."

"But your daughter earns enough to pay for her own clothes," said Newman.

M. Nioche looked at him with weak, uncertain eyes. He would have liked to be able to say that his daughter's talents were appreciated, and that her crooked little daubs commanded a market; but it seemed a scandal to abuse the credulity of this free-handed stranger, who, without a suspicion or a question, had admitted him to equal social rights. He compromised, and declared that while it was obvious that Mademoiselle Noemie's reproductions of the old masters had only to be seen to be coveted, the prices which, in consideration of their altogether peculiar degree of finish, she felt obliged to ask for them had kept purchasers at a respectful distance. "Poor little one!" said M. Nioche, with a sigh; "it is almost a pity that her work is so perfect! It would be in her interest to paint less well."

"But if Mademoiselle Noemie has this devotion to her art," Newman once observed, "why should you have those fears for her that you spoke of the other day?"

M. Nioche meditated: there was an inconsistency in his position; it made him chronically uncomfortable. Though he had no desire to destroy the goose with the golden eggs—Newman's benevolent confidence—he felt a tremulous impulse to speak out all his trouble. "Ah, she is an artist, my dear sir, most assuredly," he declared. "But, to tell you the truth, she is also a franche coquette. I am sorry to say," he added in a moment, shaking his head with a world of harmless bitterness, "that she comes honestly by it. Her mother was one before her!"

"You were not happy with your wife?" Newman asked.

M. Nioche gave half a dozen little backward jerks of his head. "She was my purgatory, monsieur!"

"She deceived you?"

"Under my nose, year after year. I was too stupid, and the temptation was too great. But I found her out at last. I have only been once in my life a man to be afraid of; I know it very well; it was in that hour! Nevertheless I don't like to think of it. I loved her—I can't tell you how much. She was a bad woman."

"She is not living?"

"She has gone to her account."

"Her influence on your daughter, then," said Newman encouragingly, "is not to be feared."

"She cared no more for her daughter than for the sole of her shoe! But Noemie has no need of influence. She is sufficient to herself. She is stronger than I."

"She doesn't obey you, eh?"

"She can't obey, monsieur, since I don't command. What would be the use? It would only irritate her and drive her to some coup de tete. She is very clever, like her mother; she would waste no time about it. As a child—when I was happy, or supposed I was—she studied drawing and painting with first-class professors, and they assured me she had a talent. I was delighted to believe it, and when I went into society I used to carry her pictures with me in a portfolio and hand them round to the company. I remember, once, a lady thought I was offering them for sale, and I took it very ill. We don't know what we may come to! Then came my dark days, and my explosion with Madame Nioche. Noemie had no more twenty-franc lessons; but in the course of time, when she grew older, and it became highly expedient that she should do something that would help to keep us alive, she bethought herself of her palette and brushes. Some of our friends in the quartier pronounced the idea fantastic: they recommended her to try bonnet making, to get a situation in a shop, or—if she was more ambitious—to advertise for a place of dame de compagnie. She did advertise, and an old lady wrote her a letter and bade her come and see her. The old lady liked her, and offered her her living and six hundred francs a year; but Noemie discovered that she passed her life in her arm-chair and had only two visitors, her confessor and her nephew: the confessor very strict, and the nephew a man of fifty, with a broken nose and a government clerkship of two thousand francs. She threw her old lady over, bought a paint-box, a canvas, and a new dress, and went and set up her easel in the Louvre. There in one place and another, she has passed the last two years; I can't say it has made us millionaires. But Noemie tells me that Rome was not built in a day, that she is making great progress, that I must leave her to her own devices. The fact is, without prejudice to her genius, that she has no idea of burying herself alive. She likes to see the world, and to be seen. She says, herself, that she can't work in the dark. With her appearance it is very natural. Only, I can't help worrying and trembling and wondering what may happen to her there all alone, day after day, amid all that coming and going of strangers. I can't be always at her side. I go with her in the morning, and I come to fetch her away, but she won't have me near her in the interval; she says I make her nervous. As if it didn't make me nervous to wander about all day without her! Ah, if anything were to happen to her!" cried M. Nioche, clenching his two fists and jerking back his head again, portentously.

"Oh, I guess nothing will happen," said Newman.

"I believe I should shoot her!" said the old man, solemnly.

"Oh, we'll marry her," said Newman, "since that's how you manage it; and I will go and see her tomorrow at the Louvre and pick out the pictures she is to copy for me."

M. Nioche had brought Newman a message from his daughter, in acceptance of his magnificent commission, the young lady declaring herself his most devoted servant, promising her most zealous endeavor, and regretting that the proprieties forbade her coming to thank him in person. The morning after the conversation just narrated, Newman reverted to his intention of meeting Mademoiselle Noemie at the Louvre. M. Nioche appeared preoccupied, and left his budget of anecdotes unopened; he took a great deal of snuff, and sent certain oblique, appealing glances toward his stalwart pupil. At last, when he was taking his leave, he stood a moment, after he had polished his hat with his calico pocket-handkerchief, with his small, pale eyes fixed strangely upon Newman.

"What's the matter?" our hero demanded.

"Excuse the solicitude of a father's heart!" said M. Nioche. "You inspire me with boundless confidence, but I can't help giving you a warning. After all, you are a man, you are young and at liberty. Let me beseech you, then, to respect the innocence of Mademoiselle Nioche!"

Newman had wondered what was coming, and at this he broke into a laugh. He was on the point of declaring that his own innocence struck him as the more exposed, but he contented himself with promising to treat the young girl with nothing less than veneration. He found her waiting for him, seated upon the great divan in the Salon Carre. She was not in her working-day costume, but wore her bonnet and gloves and carried her parasol, in honor of the occasion. These articles had been selected with unerring taste, and a fresher, prettier image of youthful alertness and blooming discretion was not to be conceived. She made Newman a most respectful curtsey and expressed her gratitude for his liberality in a wonderfully graceful little speech. It annoyed him to have a charming young girl stand there thanking him, and it made him feel uncomfortable to think that this perfect young lady, with her excellent manners and her finished intonation, was literally in his pay. He assured her, in such French as he could muster, that the thing was not worth mentioning, and that he considered her services a great favor.

"Whenever you please, then," said Mademoiselle Noemie, "we will pass the review."

They walked slowly round the room, then passed into the others and strolled about for half an hour. Mademoiselle Noemie evidently relished her situation, and had no desire to bring her public interview with her striking-looking patron to a close. Newman perceived that prosperity agreed with her. The little thin-lipped, peremptory air with which she had addressed her father on the occasion of their former meeting had given place to the most lingering and caressing tones.

"What sort of pictures do you desire?" she asked. "Sacred, or profane?"

"Oh, a few of each," said Newman. "But I want something bright and gay."

"Something gay? There is nothing very gay in this solemn old Louvre. But we will see what we can find. You speak French to-day like a charm. My father has done wonders."

"Oh, I am a bad subject," said Newman. "I am too old to learn a language."

"Too old? Quelle folie!" cried Mademoiselle Noemie, with a clear, shrill laugh. "You are a very young man. And how do you like my father?"

"He is a very nice old gentleman. He never laughs at my blunders."

"He is very comme il faut, my papa," said Mademoiselle Noemie, "and as honest as the day. Oh, an exceptional probity! You could trust him with millions."

"Do you always obey him?" asked Newman.

"Obey him?"

"Do you do what he bids you?"

The young girl stopped and looked at him; she had a spot of color in either cheek, and in her expressive French eye, which projected too much for perfect beauty, there was a slight gleam of audacity. "Why do you ask me that?" she demanded.

"Because I want to know."

"You think me a bad girl?" And she gave a strange smile.

Newman looked at her a moment; he saw that she was pretty, but he was not in the least dazzled. He remembered poor M. Nioche's solicitude for her "innocence," and he laughed as his eyes met hers. Her face was the oddest mixture of youth and maturity, and beneath her candid brow her searching little smile seemed to contain a world of ambiguous intentions. She was pretty enough, certainly to make her father nervous; but, as regards her innocence, Newman felt ready on the spot to affirm that she had never parted with it. She had simply never had any; she had been looking at the world since she was ten years old, and he would have been a wise man who could tell her any secrets. In her long mornings at the Louvre she had not only studied Madonnas and St. Johns; she had kept an eye upon all the variously embodied human nature around her, and she had formed her conclusions. In a certain sense, it seemed to Newman, M. Nioche might be at rest; his daughter might do something very audacious, but she would never do anything foolish. Newman, with his long-drawn, leisurely smile, and his even, unhurried utterance, was always, mentally, taking his time; and he asked himself, now, what she was looking at him in that way for. He had an idea that she would like him to confess that he did think her a bad girl.

"Oh, no," he said at last; "it would be very bad manners in me to judge you that way. I don't know you."

"But my father has complained to you," said Mademoiselle Noemie.

"He says you are a coquette."

"He shouldn't go about saying such things to gentlemen! But you don't believe it."

"No," said Newman gravely, "I don't believe it."

She looked at him again, gave a shrug and a smile, and then pointed to a small Italian picture, a Marriage of St. Catherine. "How should you like that?" she asked.

"It doesn't please me," said Newman. "The young lady in the yellow dress is not pretty."

"Ah, you are a great connoisseur," murmured Mademoiselle Noemie.

"In pictures? Oh, no; I know very little about them."

"In pretty women, then."

"In that I am hardly better."

"What do you say to that, then?" the young girl asked, indicating a superb Italian portrait of a lady. "I will do it for you on a smaller scale."

"On a smaller scale? Why not as large as the original?"

Mademoiselle Noemie glanced at the glowing splendor of the Venetian masterpiece and gave a little toss of her head. "I don't like that woman. She looks stupid."

"I do like her," said Newman. "Decidedly, I must have her, as large as life. And just as stupid as she is there."

The young girl fixed her eyes on him again, and with her mocking smile, "It certainly ought to be easy for me to make her look stupid!" she said.

"What do you mean?" asked Newman, puzzled.

She gave another little shrug. "Seriously, then, you want that portrait—the golden hair, the purple satin, the pearl necklace, the two magnificent arms?"

"Everything—just as it is."

"Would nothing else do, instead?"

"Oh, I want some other things, but I want that too."

Mademoiselle Noemie turned away a moment, walked to the other side of the hall, and stood there, looking vaguely about her. At last she came back. "It must be charming to be able to order pictures at such a rate. Venetian portraits, as large as life! You go at it en prince. And you are going to travel about Europe that way?"

"Yes, I intend to travel," said Newman.

"Ordering, buying, spending money?"

"Of course I shall spend some money."

"You are very happy to have it. And you are perfectly free?"

"How do you mean, free?"

"You have nothing to bother you—no family, no wife, no fiancee?"

"Yes, I am tolerably free."

"You are very happy," said Mademoiselle Noemie, gravely.

"Je le veux bien!" said Newman, proving that he had learned more French than he admitted.

"And how long shall you stay in Paris?" the young girl went on.

"Only a few days more."

"Why do you go away?"

"It is getting hot, and I must go to Switzerland."

"To Switzerland? That's a fine country. I would give my new parasol to see it! Lakes and mountains, romantic valleys and icy peaks! Oh, I congratulate you. Meanwhile, I shall sit here through all the hot summer, daubing at your pictures."

"Oh, take your time about it," said Newman. "Do them at your convenience."

They walked farther and looked at a dozen other things. Newman pointed out what pleased him, and Mademoiselle Noemie generally criticised it, and proposed something else. Then suddenly she diverged and began to talk about some personal matter.

"What made you speak to me the other day in the Salon Carre?" she abruptly asked.

"I admired your picture."

"But you hesitated a long time."

"Oh, I do nothing rashly," said Newman.

"Yes, I saw you watching me. But I never supposed you were going to speak to me. I never dreamed I should be walking about here with you to-day. It's very curious."

"It is very natural," observed Newman.

"Oh, I beg your pardon; not to me. Coquette as you think me, I have never walked about in public with a gentleman before. What was my father thinking of, when he consented to our interview?"

"He was repenting of his unjust accusations," replied Newman.

Mademoiselle Noemie remained silent; at last she dropped into a seat. "Well then, for those five it is fixed," she said. "Five copies as brilliant and beautiful as I can make them. We have one more to choose. Shouldn't you like one of those great Rubenses—the marriage of Marie de Medicis? Just look at it and see how handsome it is."

"Oh, yes; I should like that," said Newman. "Finish off with that."

"Finish off with that—good!" And she laughed. She sat a moment, looking at him, and then she suddenly rose and stood before him, with her hands hanging and clasped in front of her. "I don't understand you," she said with a smile. "I don't understand how a man can be so ignorant."

"Oh, I am ignorant, certainly," said Newman, putting his hands into his pockets.

"It's ridiculous! I don't know how to paint."

"You don't know how?"

"I paint like a cat; I can't draw a straight line. I never sold a picture until you bought that thing the other day." And as she offered this surprising information she continued to smile.

Newman burst into a laugh. "Why do you tell me this?" he asked.

"Because it irritates me to see a clever man blunder so. My pictures are grotesque."

"And the one I possess—"

"That one is rather worse than usual."

"Well," said Newman, "I like it all the same!"

She looked at him askance. "That is a very pretty thing to say," she answered; "but it is my duty to warn you before you go farther. This order of yours is impossible, you know. What do you take me for? It is work for ten men. You pick out the six most difficult pictures in the Louvre, and you expect me to go to work as if I were sitting down to hem a dozen pocket handkerchiefs. I wanted to see how far you would go."

Newman looked at the young girl in some perplexity. In spite of the ridiculous blunder of which he stood convicted, he was very far from being a simpleton, and he had a lively suspicion that Mademoiselle Noemie's sudden frankness was not essentially more honest than her leaving him in error would have been. She was playing a game; she was not simply taking pity on his aesthetic verdancy. What was it she expected to win? The stakes were high and the risk was great; the prize therefore must have been commensurate. But even granting that the prize might be great, Newman could not resist a movement of admiration for his companion's intrepidity. She was throwing away with one hand, whatever she might intend to do with the other, a very handsome sum of money.

"Are you joking," he said, "or are you serious?"

"Oh, serious!" cried Mademoiselle Noemie, but with her extraordinary smile.

"I know very little about pictures or how they are painted. If you can't do all that, of course you can't. Do what you can, then."

"It will be very bad," said Mademoiselle Noemie.

"Oh," said Newman, laughing, "if you are determined it shall be bad, of course it will. But why do you go on painting badly?"

"I can do nothing else; I have no real talent."

"You are deceiving your father, then."

The young girl hesitated a moment. "He knows very well!"

"No," Newman declared; "I am sure he believes in you."

"He is afraid of me. I go on painting badly, as you say, because I want to learn. I like it, at any rate. And I like being here; it is a place to come to, every day; it is better than sitting in a little dark, damp room, on a court, or selling buttons and whalebones over a counter."

"Of course it is much more amusing," said Newman. "But for a poor girl isn't it rather an expensive amusement?"

"Oh, I am very wrong, there is no doubt about that," said Mademoiselle Noemie. "But rather than earn my living as some girls do—toiling with a needle, in little black holes, out of the world—I would throw myself into the Seine."

"There is no need of that," Newman answered; "your father told you my offer?"

"Your offer?"

"He wants you to marry, and I told him I would give you a chance to earn your dot."

"He told me all about it, and you see the account I make of it! Why should you take such an interest in my marriage?"

"My interest was in your father. I hold to my offer; do what you can, and I will buy what you paint."

She stood for some time, meditating, with her eyes on the ground. At last, looking up, "What sort of a husband can you get for twelve thousand francs?" she asked.

"Your father tells me he knows some very good young men."

"Grocers and butchers and little maitres de cafes! I will not marry at all if I can't marry well."

"I would advise you not to be too fastidious," said Newman. "That's all the advice I can give you."

"I am very much vexed at what I have said!" cried the young girl. "It has done me no good. But I couldn't help it."

"What good did you expect it to do you?"

"I couldn't help it, simply."

Newman looked at her a moment. "Well, your pictures may be bad," he said, "but you are too clever for me, nevertheless. I don't understand you. Good-by!" And he put out his hand.

She made no response, and offered him no farewell. She turned away and seated herself sidewise on a bench, leaning her head on the back of her hand, which clasped the rail in front of the pictures. Newman stood a moment and then turned on his heel and retreated. He had understood her better than he confessed; this singular scene was a practical commentary upon her father's statement that she was a frank coquette.

CHAPTER V

When Newman related to Mrs. Tristram his fruitless visit to Madame de Cintre, she urged him not to be discouraged, but to carry out his plan of "seeing Europe" during the summer, and return to Paris in the autumn and settle down comfortably for the winter. "Madame de Cintre will keep," she said; "she is not a woman who will marry from one day to another." Newman made no distinct affirmation that he would come back to Paris; he even talked about Rome and the Nile, and abstained from professing any especial interest in Madame de Cintre's continued widowhood. This circumstance was at variance with his habitual frankness, and may perhaps be regarded as characteristic of the incipient stage of that passion which is more particularly known as the mysterious one. The truth is that the expression of a pair of eyes that were at once brilliant and mild had become very familiar to his memory, and he would not easily have resigned himself to the prospect of never looking into them again. He communicated to Mrs. Tristram a number of other facts, of greater or less importance, as you choose; but on this particular point he kept his own counsel. He took a kindly leave of M. Nioche, having assured him that, so far as he was concerned, the blue-cloaked Madonna herself might have been present at his interview with Mademoiselle Noemie; and left the old man nursing his breast-pocket, in an ecstasy which the acutest misfortune might have been defied to dissipate. Newman then started on his travels, with all his usual appearance of slow-strolling leisure, and all his essential directness and intensity of aim. No man seemed less in a hurry, and yet no man achieved more in brief periods. He had certain practical instincts which served him excellently in his trade of tourist. He found his way in foreign cities by divination, his memory was excellent when once his attention had been at all cordially given, and he emerged from dialogues in foreign tongues, of which he had, formally, not understood a word, in full possession of the particular fact he had desired to ascertain. His appetite for facts was capacious, and although many of those which he noted would have seemed woefully dry and colorless to the ordinary sentimental traveler, a careful inspection of the list would have shown that he had a soft spot in his imagination. In the charming city of Brussels—his first stopping-place after leaving Paris—he asked a great many questions about the street-cars, and took extreme satisfaction in the reappearance of this familiar symbol of American civilization; but he was also greatly struck with the beautiful Gothic tower of the Hotel de Ville, and wondered whether it would not be possible to "get up" something like it in San Francisco. He stood for half an hour in the crowded square before this edifice, in imminent danger from carriage-wheels, listening to a toothless old cicerone mumble in broken English the touching history of Counts Egmont and Horn; and he wrote the names of these gentlemen—for reasons best known to himself—on the back of an old letter.

At the outset, on his leaving Paris, his curiosity had not been intense; passive entertainment, in the Champs Elysees and at the theatres, seemed about as much as he need expect of himself, and although, as he had said to Tristram, he wanted to see the mysterious, satisfying BEST, he had not the Grand Tour in the least on his conscience, and was not given to cross-questioning the amusement of the hour. He believed that Europe was made for him, and not he for Europe. He had said that he wanted to improve his mind, but he would have felt a certain embarrassment, a certain shame, even—a false shame, possibly—if he had caught himself looking intellectually into the mirror. Neither in this nor in any other respect had Newman a high sense of responsibility; it was his prime conviction that a man's life should be easy, and that he should be able to resolve privilege into a matter of course. The world, to his sense, was a great bazaar, where one might stroll about and purchase handsome things; but he was no more conscious, individually, of social pressure than he admitted the existence of such a thing as an obligatory purchase. He had not only a dislike, but a sort of moral mistrust, of uncomfortable thoughts, and it was both uncomfortable and slightly contemptible to feel obliged to square one's self with a standard. One's standard was the ideal of one's own good-humored prosperity, the prosperity which enabled one to give as well as take. To expand, without bothering about it—without shiftless timidity on one side, or loquacious eagerness on the other—to the full compass of what he would have called a "pleasant" experience, was Newman's most definite programme of life. He had always hated to hurry to catch railroad trains, and yet he had always caught them; and just so an undue solicitude for "culture" seemed a sort of silly dawdling at the station, a proceeding properly confined to women, foreigners, and other unpractical persons. All this admitted, Newman enjoyed his journey, when once he had fairly entered the current, as profoundly as the most zealous dilettante. One's theories, after all, matter little; it is one's humor that is the great thing. Our friend was intelligent, and he could not help that. He lounged through Belgium and Holland and the Rhineland, through Switzer-Switzerland and Northern Italy, planning about nothing, but seeing everything. The guides and valets de place found him an excellent subject. He was always approachable, for he was much addicted to standing about in the vestibules and porticos of inns, and he availed himself little of the opportunities for impressive seclusion which are so liberally offered in Europe to gentlemen who travel with long purses. When an excursion, a church, a gallery, a ruin, was proposed to him, the first thing Newman usually did, after surveying his postulant in silence, from head to foot, was to sit down at a little table and order something to drink. The cicerone, during this process, usually retreated to a respectful distance; otherwise I am not sure that Newman would not have bidden him sit down and have a glass also, and tell him as an honest fellow whether his church or his gallery was really worth a man's trouble. At last he rose and stretched his long legs, beckoned to the man of monuments, looked at his watch, and fixed his eye on his adversary. "What is it?" he asked. "How far?" And whatever the answer was, although he sometimes seemed to hesitate, he never declined. He stepped into an open cab, made his conductor sit beside him to answer questions, bade the driver go fast (he had a particular aversion to slow driving) and rolled, in all probability through a dusty suburb, to the goal of his pilgrimage. If the goal was a disappointment, if the church was meagre, or the ruin a heap of rubbish, Newman never protested or berated his cicerone; he looked with an impartial eye upon great monuments and small, made the guide recite his lesson, listened to it religiously, asked if there was nothing else to be seen in the neighborhood, and drove back again at a rattling pace. It is to be feared that his perception of the difference between good architecture and bad was not acute, and that he might sometimes have been seen gazing with culpable serenity at inferior productions. Ugly churches were a part of his pastime in Europe, as well as beautiful ones, and his tour was altogether a pastime. But there is sometimes nothing like the imagination of these people who have none, and Newman, now and then, in an unguided stroll in a foreign city, before some lonely, sad-towered church, or some angular image of one who had rendered civic service in an unknown past, had felt a singular inward tremor. It was not an excitement or a perplexity; it was a placid, fathomless sense of diversion.

He encountered by chance in Holland a young American, with whom, for a time, he formed a sort of traveler's partnership. They were men of a very different cast, but each, in his way, was so good a fellow that, for a few weeks at least, it seemed something of a pleasure to share the chances of the road. Newman's comrade, whose name was Babcock, was a young Unitarian minister, a small, spare, neatly-attired man, with a strikingly candid physiognomy. He was a native of Dorchester, Massachusetts, and had spiritual charge of a small congregation in another suburb of the New England metropolis. His digestion was weak and he lived chiefly on Graham bread and hominy—a regimen to which he was so much attached that his tour seemed to him destined to be blighted when, on landing on the Continent, he found that these delicacies did not flourish under the table d'hote system. In Paris he had purchased a bag of hominy at an establishment which called itself an American Agency, and at which the New York illustrated papers were also to be procured, and he had carried it about with him, and shown extreme serenity and fortitude in the somewhat delicate position of having his hominy prepared for him and served at anomalous hours, at the hotels he successively visited. Newman had once spent a morning, in the course of business, at Mr. Babcock's birthplace, and, for reasons too recondite to unfold, his visit there always assumed in his mind a jocular cast. To carry out his joke, which certainly seems poor so long as it is not explained, he used often to address his companion as "Dorchester." Fellow-travelers very soon grow intimate but it is highly improbable that at home these extremely dissimilar characters would have found any very convenient points of contact. They were, indeed, as different as possible. Newman, who never reflected on such matters, accepted the situation with great equanimity, but Babcock used to meditate over it privately; used often, indeed, to retire to his room early in the evening for the express purpose of considering it conscientiously and impartially. He was not sure that it was a good thing for him to associate with our hero, whose way of taking life was so little his own. Newman was an excellent, generous fellow; Mr. Babcock sometimes said to himself that he was a NOBLE fellow, and, certainly, it was impossible not to like him. But would it not be dedesirable to try to exert an influence upon him, to try to quicken his moral life and sharpen his sense of duty? He liked everything, he accepted everything, he found amusement in everything; he was not discriminating, he had not a high tone. The young man from Dorchester accused Newman of a fault which he considered very grave, and which he did his best to avoid: what he would have called a want of "moral reaction." Poor Mr. Babcock was extremely fond of pictures and churches, and carried Mrs. Jameson's works about in his trunk; he delighted in aesthetic analysis, and received peculiar impressions from everything he saw. But nevertheless in his secret soul he detested Europe, and he felt an irritating need to protest against Newman's gross intellectual hospitality. Mr. Babcock's moral malaise, I am afraid, lay deeper than where any definition of mine can reach it. He mistrusted the European temperament, he suffered from the European climate, he hated the European dinner-hour; European life seemed to him unscrupulous and impure. And yet he had an exquisite sense of beauty; and as beauty was often inextricably associated with the above displeasing conditions, as he wished, above all, to be just and dispassionate, and as he was, furthermore, extremely devoted to "culture," he could not bring himself to decide that Europe was utterly bad. But he thought it was very bad indeed, and his quarrel with Newman was that this unregulated epicure had a sadly insufficient perception of the bad. Babcock himself really knew as little about the bad, in any quarter of the world, as a nursing infant, his most vivid realization of evil had been the discovery that one of his college classmates, who was studying architecture in Paris had a love affair with a young woman who did not expect him to marry her. Babcock had related this incident to Newman, and our hero had applied an epithet of an unflattering sort to the young girl. The next day his companion asked him whether he was very sure he had used exactly the right word to characterize the young architect's mistress. Newman stared and laughed. "There are a great many words to express that idea," he said; "you can take your choice!"

"Oh, I mean," said Babcock, "was she possibly not to be considered in a different light? Don't you think she really expected him to marry her?"

"I am sure I don't know," said Newman. "Very likely she did; I have no doubt she is a grand woman." And he began to laugh again.

"I didn't mean that either," said Babcock, "I was only afraid that I might have seemed yesterday not to remember—not to consider; well, I think I will write to Percival about it."

And he had written to Percival (who answered him in a really impudent fashion), and he had reflected that it was somehow, raw and reckless in Newman to assume in that off-hand manner that the young woman in Paris might be "grand." The brevity of Newman's judgments very often shocked and discomposed him. He had a way of damning people without farther appeal, or of pronouncing them capital company in the face of uncomfortable symptoms, which seemed unworthy of a man whose conscience had been properly cultivated. And yet poor Babcock liked him, and remembered that even if he was sometimes perplexing and painful, this was not a reason for giving him up. Goethe recommended seeing human nature in the most various forms, and Mr. Babcock thought Goethe perfectly splendid. He often tried, in odd half-hours of conversation to infuse into Newman a little of his own spiritual starch, but Newman's personal texture was too loose to admit of stiffening. His mind could no more hold principles than a sieve can hold water. He admired principles extremely, and thought Babcock a mighty fine little fellow for having so many. He accepted all that his high-strung companion offered him, and put them away in what he supposed to be a very safe place; but poor Babcock never afterwards recognized his gifts among the articles that Newman had in daily use.

They traveled together through Germany and into Switzerland, where for three or four weeks they trudged over passes and lounged upon blue lakes. At last they crossed the Simplon and made their way to Venice. Mr. Babcock had become gloomy and even a trifle irritable; he seemed moody, absent, preoccupied; he got his plans into a tangle, and talked one moment of doing one thing and the next of doing another. Newman led his usual life, made acquaintances, took his ease in the galleries and churches, spent an unconscionable amount of time in strolling in the Piazza San Marco, bought a great many bad pictures, and for a fortnight enjoyed Venice grossly. One evening, coming back to his inn, he found Babcock waiting for him in the little garden beside it. The young man walked up to him, looking very dismal, thrust out his hand, and said with solemnity that he was afraid they must part. Newman expressed his surprise and regret, and asked why a parting had became necessary. "Don't be afraid I'm tired of you," he said.

"You are not tired of me?" demanded Babcock, fixing him with his clear gray eye.

"Why the deuce should I be? You are a very plucky fellow. Besides, I don't grow tired of things."

"We don't understand each other," said the young minister.

"Don't I understand you?" cried Newman. "Why, I hoped I did. But what if I don't; where's the harm?"

"I don't understand YOU," said Babcock. And he sat down and rested his head on his hand, and looked up mournfully at his immeasurable friend.

"Oh Lord, I don't mind that!" cried Newman, with a laugh.

"But it's very distressing to me. It keeps me in a state of unrest. It irritates me; I can't settle anything. I don't think it's good for me."

"You worry too much; that's what's the matter with you," said Newman.

"Of course it must seem so to you. You think I take things too hard, and I think you take things too easily. We can never agree."

"But we have agreed very well all along."

"No, I haven't agreed," said Babcock, shaking his head. "I am very uncomfortable. I ought to have separated from you a month ago."

"Oh, horrors! I'll agree to anything!" cried Newman.

Mr. Babcock buried his head in both hands. At last looking up, "I don't think you appreciate my position," he said. "I try to arrive at the truth about everything. And then you go too fast. For me, you are too passionate, too extravagant. I feel as if I ought to go over all this ground we have traversed again, by myself, alone. I am afraid I have made a great many mistakes."

"Oh, you needn't give so many reasons," said Newman. "You are simply tired of my company. You have a good right to be."

"No, no, I am not tired!" cried the pestered young divine. "It is very wrong to be tired."

"I give it up!" laughed Newman. "But of course it will never do to go on making mistakes. Go your way, by all means. I shall miss you; but you have seen I make friends very easily. You will be lonely, yourself; but drop me a line, when you feel like it, and I will wait for you anywhere."

"I think I will go back to Milan. I am afraid I didn't do justice to Luini."

"Poor Luini!" said Newman.

"I mean that I am afraid I overestimated him. I don't think that he is a painter of the first rank."

"Luini?" Newman exclaimed; "why, he's enchanting—he's magnificent! There is something in his genius that is like a beautiful woman. It gives one the same feeling."

Mr. Babcock frowned and winced. And it must be added that this was, for Newman, an unusually metaphysical flight; but in passing through Milan he had taken a great fancy to the painter. "There you are again!" said Mr. Babcock. "Yes, we had better separate." And on the morrow he retraced his steps and proceeded to tone down his impressions of the great Lombard artist.

A few days afterwards Newman received a note from his late companion which ran as follows:—

My Dear Mr. Newman,—I am afraid that my conduct at Venice, a week ago, seemed to you strange and ungrateful, and I wish to explain my position, which, as I said at the time, I do not think you appreciate. I had long had it on my mind to propose that we should part company, and this step was not really so abrupt as it seemed. In the first place, you know, I am traveling in Europe on funds supplied by my congregation, who kindly offered me a vacation and an opportunity to enrich my mind with the treasures of nature and art in the Old World. I feel, therefore, as if I ought to use my time to the very best advantage. I have a high sense of responsibility. You appear to care only for the pleasure of the hour, and you give yourself up to it with a violence which I confess I am not able to emulate. I feel as if I must arrive at some conclusion and fix my belief on certain points. Art and life seem to me intensely serious things, and in our travels in Europe we should especially remember the immense seriousness of Art. You seem to hold that if a thing amuses you for the moment, that is all you need ask for it, and your relish for mere amusement is also much higher than mine. You put, however, a kind of reckless confidence into your pleasure which at times, I confess, has seemed to me—shall I say it?—almost cynical. Your way at any rate is not my way, and it is unwise that we should attempt any longer to pull together. And yet, let me add that I know there is a great deal to be said for your way; I have felt its attraction, in your society, very strongly. But for this I should have left you long ago. But I was so perplexed. I hope I have not done wrong. I feel as if I had a great deal of lost time to make up. I beg you take all this as I mean it, which,

Heaven knows, is not invidiously. I have a great personal esteem for you and hope that some day, when I have recovered my balance, we shall meet again. I hope you will continue to enjoy your travels, only DO remember that Life and Art ARE extremely serious. Believe me your sincere friend and well-wisher,

BENJAMIN BABCOCK

P. S. I am greatly perplexed by Luini.

This letter produced in Newman's mind a singular mixture of exhilaration and awe. At first, Mr. Babcock's tender conscience seemed to him a capital farce, and his traveling back to Milan only to get into a deeper muddle appeared, as the reward of his pedantry, exquisitely and ludicrously just. Then Newman reflected that these are mighty mysteries, that possibly he himself was indeed that baleful and barely mentionable thing, a cynic, and that his manner of considering the treasures of art and the privileges of life was probably very base and immoral. Newman had a great contempt for immorality, and that evening, for a good half hour, as he sat watching the star-sheen on the warm Adriatic, he felt rebuked and depressed. He was at a loss how to answer Babcock's letter. His good nature checked his resenting the young minister's lofty admonitions, and his tough, inelastic sense of humor forbade his taking them seriously. He wrote no answer at all but a day or two afterward he found in a curiosity shop a grotesque little statuette in ivory, of the sixteenth century, which he sent off to Babcock without a commentary. It represented a gaunt, ascetic-looking monk, in a tattered gown and cowl, kneeling with clasped hands and pulling a portentously long face. It was a wonderfully delicate piece of carving, and in a moment, through one of the rents of his gown, you espied a fat capon hung round the monk's waist. In Newman's intention what did the figure symbolize? Did it mean that he was going to try to be as "high-toned" as the monk looked at first, but that he feared he should succeed no better than the friar, on a closer inspection, proved to have done? It is not supposable that he intended a satire upon Babcock's own asceticism, for this would have been a truly cynical stroke. He made his late companion, at any rate, a very valuable little present.

Newman, on leaving Venice, went through the Tyrol to Vienna, and then returned westward, through Southern Germany. The autumn found him at Baden-Baden, where he spent several weeks. The place was charming, and he was in no hurry to depart; besides, he was looking about him and deciding what to do for the winter. His summer had been very full, and he sat under the great trees beside the miniature river that trickles past the Baden flower-beds, he slowly rummaged it over. He had seen and done a great deal, enjoyed and observed a great deal; he felt older, and yet he felt younger too. He remembered Mr. Babcock and his desire to form conclusions, and he remembered also that he had profited very little by his friend's exhortation to cultivate the same respectable habit. Could he not scrape together a few conclusions? Baden-Baden was the prettiest place he had seen yet, and orchestral music in the evening, under the stars, was decidedly a great institution. This was one of his conclusions! But he went on to reflect that he had done very wisely to pull up stakes and come abroad; this seeing of the world was a very interesting thing. He had learned a great deal; he couldn't say just what, but he had it there under his hat-band. He had done what he wanted; he had seen the great things, and he had given his mind a chance to "improve," if it would. He cheerfully believed that it had improved. Yes, this seeing of the world was very pleasant, and he would willingly do a little more of it. Thirty-six years old as he was, he had a handsome stretch of life before him yet, and he need not begin to count his weeks. Where should he take the world next? I have said he remembered the eyes of the lady whom he had found standing in Mrs. Tristram's drawing-room; four months had elapsed, and he had not forgotten them yet. He had looked—he had made a point of looking—into a great many other eyes in the interval, but the only ones he thought of now were Madame de Cintre's. If he wanted to see more of the world, should he find it in Madame de Cintre's eyes? He would certainly find something there, call it this world or the next. Throughout these rather formless meditations he sometimes thought of his past life and the long array of years (they had begun so early) during which he had had nothing in his head but "enterprise." They seemed far away now, for his present attitude was more than a holiday, it was almost a rupture. He had told Tristram that the pendulum was swinging back and it appeared that the backward swing had not yet ended. Still "enterprise," which was over in the other quarter wore to his mind a different aspect at different hours. In its train a thousand forgotten episodes came trooping back into his memory. Some of them he looked complacently enough in the face; from some he averted his head. They were old efforts, old exploits, antiquated examples of "smartness" and sharpness. Some of them, as he looked at them, he felt decidedly proud of; he admired himself as if he had been looking at another man. And, in fact, many of the qualities that make a great deed were there: the decision, the resolution, the courage, the celerity, the clear eye, and the strong hand. Of certain other achievements it would be going too far to say that he was ashamed of them for Newman had never had a stomach for dirty work. He was blessed with a natural impulse to disfigure with a direct, unreasoning blow the comely visage of temptation. And certainly, in no man could a want of integrity have been less excusable. Newman knew the crooked from the straight at a glance, and the former had cost him, first and last, a great many moments of lively disgust. But none the less some of his memories seemed to wear at present a rather graceless and sordid mien, and it struck him that if he had never done anything very ugly, he had never, on the other hand, done anything particularly beautiful. He had spent his years in the unremitting effort to add thousands to thousands, and, now that he stood well outside of it, the business of money-getting appeared tolerably dry and sterile. It is very well to sneer at money-getting after you have filled your pockets, and Newman, it may be said, should have begun somewhat earlier to moralize thus delicately. To this it may be answered that he might have made another fortune, if he chose; and we ought to add that he was not exactly moralizing. It had come back to him simply that what he had been looking at all summer was a very rich and beautiful world, and that it had not all been made by sharp railroad men and stock-brokers.

During his stay at Baden-Baden he received a letter from Mrs. Tristram, scolding him for the scanty tidings he had sent to his friends of the Avenue d'Iena, and begging to be definitely informed that he had not concocted any horrid scheme for wintering in outlying regions, but was coming back sanely and promptly to the most comfortable city in the world. Newman's answer ran as follows:—

"I supposed you knew I was a miserable letter-writer, and didn't expect anything of me. I don't think I have written twenty letters of pure friendship in my whole life; in America I conducted my correspondence altogether by telegrams. This is a letter of pure friendship; you have got hold of a curiosity, and I hope you will value it. You want to know everything that has happened to me these three months. The best way to tell you, I think, would be to send you my half dozen guide-books, with my pencil-marks in the margin. Wherever you find a scratch or a cross, or a 'Beautiful!' or a 'So true!' or a 'Too thin!' you may know that I have had a sensation of some sort or other. That has been about my history, ever since I left you. Belgium, Holland, Switzerland, Germany, Italy, I have been through the whole list, and I don't think I am any the worse for it. I know more about Madonnas and church-steeples than I supposed any man could. I have seen some very pretty things, and shall perhaps talk them over this winter, by your fireside. You see, my face is not altogether set against Paris. I have had all kinds of plans and visions, but your letter has blown most of them away. 'L'appetit vient en mangeant,' says the French proverb, and I find that the more I see of the world the more I want to see. Now that I am in the shafts, why shouldn't I trot to the end of the course? Sometimes I think of the far East, and keep rolling the names of Eastern cities under my tongue: Damascus and Bagdad, Medina and Mecca. I spent a week last month in the company of a returned missionary, who told me I ought to be ashamed to be loafing about Europe when there are such big things to be seen out there. I do want to explore, but I think I would rather explore over in the Rue de l'Universite. Do you ever hear from that pretty lady? If you can get her to promise she will be at home the next time I call, I will go back to Paris straight. I am more than ever in the state of mind I told you about that evening; I want a first-class wife. I have kept an eye on all the pretty girls I have come across this summer, but none of them came up to my notion, or anywhere near it. I should have enjoyed all this a thousand times more if I had had the lady just mentioned by my side. The nearest approach to her was a Unitarian minister from Boston, who very soon demanded a separation, for incompatibility of temper. He told me I was low-minded, immoral, a devotee of 'art for art'—whatever that is: all of which greatly afflicted me, for he was really a sweet little fellow. But shortly afterwards I met an Englishman, with whom I struck up an acquaintance which at first seemed to promise well—a very bright man, who writes in the London papers and knows Paris nearly as well as Tristram. We knocked about for a week together, but he very soon gave me up in disgust. I was too virtuous by half; I was too stern a moralist. He told me, in a friendly way, that I was cursed with a conscience; that I judged things like a Methodist and talked about them like an old lady. This was rather bewildering. Which of my two critics was I to believe? I didn't worry about it and very soon made up my mind they were both idiots. But there is one thing in which no one will ever have the impudence to pretend I am wrong, that is, in being your faithful friend,

"C. N."

CHAPTER VI

Newman gave up Damascus and Bagdad and returned to Paris before the autumn was over. He established himself in some rooms selected for him by Tom Tristram, in accordance with the latter's estimate of what he called his social position. When Newman learned that his social position was to be taken into account, he professed himself utterly incompetent, and begged Tristram to relieve him of the care. "I didn't know I had a social position," he said, "and if I have, I haven't the smallest idea what it is. Isn't a social position knowing some two or three thousand people and inviting them to dinner? I know you and your wife and little old Mr. Nioche, who gave me French lessons last spring. Can I invite you to dinner to meet each other? If I can, you must come to-morrow."

"That is not very grateful to me," said Mrs. Tristram, "who introduced you last year to every creature I know."

"So you did; I had quite forgotten. But I thought you wanted me to forget," said Newman, with that tone of simple deliberateness which frequently marked his utterance, and which an observer would not have known whether to pronounce a somewhat mysteriously humorous affection of ignorance or a modest aspiration to knowledge; "you told me you disliked them all."

"Ah, the way you remember what I say is at least very flattering. But in future," added Mrs. Tristram, "pray forget all the wicked things and remember only the good ones. It will be easily done, and it will not fatigue your memory. But I forewarn you that if you trust my husband to pick out your rooms, you are in for something hideous."

"Hideous, darling?" cried Tristram.

"To-day I must say nothing wicked; otherwise I should use stronger language."

"What do you think she would say, Newman?" asked Tristram. "If she really tried, now? She can express displeasure, volubly, in two or three languages; that's what it is to be intellectual. It gives her the start of me completely, for I can't swear, for the life of me, except in English. When I get mad I have to fall back on our dear old mother tongue. There's nothing like it, after all."

Newman declared that he knew nothing about tables and chairs, and that he would accept, in the way of a lodging, with his eyes shut, anything that Tristram should offer him. This was partly veracity on our hero's part, but it was also partly charity. He knew that to pry about and look at rooms, and make people open windows, and poke into sofas with his cane, and gossip with landladies, and ask who lived above and who below—he knew that this was of all pastimes the dearest to Tristram's heart, and he felt the more disposed to put it in his way as he was conscious that, as regards his obliging friend, he had suffered the warmth of ancient good-fellowship somewhat to abate. Besides, he had no taste for upholstery; he had even no very exquisite sense of comfort or convenience. He had a relish for luxury and splendor, but it was satisfied by rather gross contrivances. He scarcely knew a hard chair from a soft one, and he possessed a talent for stretching his legs which quite dispensed with adventitious facilities. His idea of comfort was to inhabit very large rooms, have a great many of them, and be conscious of their possessing a number of patented mechanical devices—half of which he should never have occasion to use. The apartments should be light and brilliant and lofty; he had once said that he liked rooms in which you wanted to keep your hat on. For the rest, he was satisfied with the assurance of any respectable person that everything was "handsome." Tristram accordingly secured for him an apartment to which this epithet might be lavishly applied. It was situated on the Boulevard Haussmann, on the first floor, and consisted of a series of rooms, gilded from floor to ceiling a foot thick, draped in various light shades of satin, and chiefly furnished with mirrors and clocks. Newman thought them magnificent, thanked Tristram heartily, immediately took possession, and had one of his trunks standing for three months in his drawing-room.

One day Mrs. Tristram told him that her beautiful friend, Madame de Cintre, had returned from the country; that she had met her three days before, coming out of the Church of St. Sulpice; she herself having journeyed to that distant quarter in quest of an obscure lace-mender, of whose skill she had heard high praise.

"And how were those eyes?" Newman asked.

"Those eyes were red with weeping, if you please!" said Mrs. Tristram. "She had been to confession."

"It doesn't tally with your account of her," said Newman, "that she should have sins to confess."

"They were not sins; they were sufferings."

"How do you know that?"

"She asked me to come and see her; I went this morning."

"And what does she suffer from?"

"I didn't ask her. With her, somehow, one is very discreet. But I guessed, easily enough. She suffers from her wicked old mother and her Grand Turk of a brother. They persecute her. But I can almost forgive them, because, as I told you, she is a saint, and a persecution is all that she needs to bring out her saintliness and make her perfect."

"That's a comfortable theory for her. I hope you will never impart it to the old folks. Why does she let them bully her? Is she not her own mistress?"

"Legally, yes, I suppose; but morally, no. In France you must never say nay to your mother, whatever she requires of you. She may be the most abominable old woman in the world, and make your life a purgatory; but, after all, she is ma mere, and you have no right to judge her. You have simply to obey. The thing has a fine side to it. Madame de Cintre bows her head and folds her wings."

"Can't she at least make her brother leave off?"

"Her brother is the chef de la famille, as they say; he is the head of the clan. With those people the family is everything; you must act, not for your own pleasure, but for the advantage of the family."

"I wonder what my family would like me to do!" exclaimed Tristram.

"I wish you had one!" said his wife.

"But what do they want to get out of that poor lady?" Newman asked.

"Another marriage. They are not rich, and they want to bring more money into the family."

"There's your chance, my boy!" said Tristram.

"And Madame de Cintre objects," Newman continued.

"She has been sold once; she naturally objects to being sold again. It appears that the first time they made rather a poor bargain; M. de Cintre left a scanty property."

"And to whom do they want to marry her now?"

"I thought it best not to ask; but you may be sure it is to some horrid old nabob, or to some dissipated little duke."

"There's Mrs. Tristram, as large as life!" cried her husband. "Observe the richness of her imagination. She has not a single question—it's vulgar to ask questions—and yet she knows everything. She has the history of Madame de Cintre's marriage at her fingers' ends. She has seen the lovely Claire on her knees, with loosened tresses and streaming eyes, and the rest of them standing over her with spikes and goads and red-hot irons, ready to come down on her if she refuses the tipsy duke. The simple truth is that they made a fuss about her milliner's bill or refused her an opera-box."

Newman looked from Tristram to his wife with a certain mistrust in each direction. "Do you really mean," he asked of Mrs. Tristram, "that your friend is being forced into an unhappy marriage?"

"I think it extremely probable. Those people are very capable of that sort of thing."

"It is like something in a play," said Newman; "that dark old house over there looks as if wicked things had been done in it, and might be done again."

"They have a still darker old house in the country Madame de Cintre tells me, and there, during the summer this scheme must have been hatched."

"MUST have been; mind that!" said Tristram.

"After all," suggested Newman, after a silence, "she may be in trouble about something else."

"If it is something else, then it is something worse," said Mrs. Tristram, with rich decision.

CHAPTER VI

Newman was silent a while, and seemed lost in meditation. "Is it possible," he asked at last, "that they do that sort of thing over here? that helpless women are bullied into marrying men they hate?"

"Helpless women, all over the world, have a hard time of it," said Mrs. Tristram. "There is plenty of bullying everywhere."

"A great deal of that kind of thing goes on in New York," said Tristram. "Girls are bullied or coaxed or bribed, or all three together, into marrying nasty fellows. There is no end of that always going on in the Fifth Avenue, and other bad things besides. The Mysteries of the Fifth Avenue! Some one ought to show them up."

"I don't believe it!" said Newman, very gravely. "I don't believe that, in America, girls are ever subjected to compulsion. I don't believe there have been a dozen cases of it since the country began."

"Listen to the voice of the spread eagle!" cried Tristram.

"The spread eagle ought to use his wings," said Mrs. Tristram. "Fly to the rescue of Madame de Cintre!"

"To her rescue?"

"Pounce down, seize her in your talons, and carry her off. Marry her yourself."

Newman, for some moments, answered nothing; but presently, "I should suppose she had heard enough of marrying," he said. "The kindest way to treat her would be to admire her, and yet never to speak of it. But that sort of thing is infamous," he added; "it makes me feel savage to hear of it."

He heard of it, however, more than once afterward. Mrs. Tristram again saw Madame de Cintre, and again found her looking very sad. But on these occasions there had been no tears; her beautiful eyes were clear and still. "She is cold, calm, and hopeless," Mrs. Tristram declared, and she added that on her mentioning that her friend Mr. Newman was again in Paris and was faithful in his desire to make Madame de Cintre's acquaintance, this lovely woman had found a smile in her despair, and declared that she was sorry to have missed his visit in the spring and that she hoped he had not lost courage. "I told her something about you," said Mrs. Tristram.

"That's a comfort," said Newman, placidly. "I like people to know about me."

A few days after this, one dusky autumn afternoon, he went again to the Rue de l'Universite. The early evening had closed in as he applied for admittance at the stoutly guarded Hotel de Bellegarde. He was told that Madame de Cintre was at home; he crossed the court, entered the farther door, and was conducted through a vestibule, vast, dim, and cold, up a broad stone staircase with an ancient iron balustrade, to an apartment on the second floor. Announced and ushered in, he found himself in a sort of paneled boudoir, at one end of which a lady and gentleman were seated before the fire. The gentleman was smoking a cigarette; there was no light in the room save that of a couple of candles and the glow from the hearth. Both persons rose to welcome Newman, who, in the firelight, recognized Madame de Cintre. She gave him her hand with a smile which seemed in itself an illumination, and, pointing to her companion, said softly, "My brother." The gentleman offered Newman a frank, friendly greeting, and our hero then perceived him to be the young man who had spoken to him in the court of the hotel on his former visit and who had struck him as a good fellow.

"Mrs. Tristram has spoken to me a great deal of you," said Madame de Cintre gently, as she resumed her former place.

Newman, after he had seated himself, began to consider what, in truth, was his errand. He had an unusual, unexpected sense of having wandered into a strange corner of the world. He was not given, as a general thing, to anticipating danger, or forecasting disaster, and he had had no social tremors on this particular occasion. He was not timid and he was not impudent. He felt too kindly toward himself to be the one, and too good-naturedly toward the rest of the world to be the other. But his native shrewdness sometimes placed his ease of temper at its mercy; with every disposition to take things simply, it was obliged to perceive that some things were not so simple as others. He felt as one does in missing a step, in an ascent, where one expected to find it. This strange, pretty woman, sitting in fire-side talk with her brother, in the gray depths of her inhospitable-looking house—what had he to say to her? She seemed enveloped in a sort of fantastic privacy; on what grounds had he pulled away the curtain? For a moment he felt as if he had plunged into some medium as deep as the ocean, and as if he must exert himself to keep from sinking. Meanwhile he was looking at Madame de Cintre, and she was settling herself in her chair and drawing in her long dress and turning her face towards him. Their eyes met; a moment afterwards she looked away and motioned to her brother to put a log on the fire. But the moment, and the glance which traversed it, had been sufficient to relieve Newman of the first and the last fit of personal embarrassment he was ever to know. He performed the movement which was so frequent with him, and which was always a sort of symbol of his taking mental possession of a scene—he extended his legs. The impression Madame de Cintre had made upon him on their first meeting came back in an instant; it had been deeper than he knew. She was pleasing, she was interesting; he had opened a book and the first lines held his attention.

She asked him several questions: how lately he had seen Mrs. Tristram, how long he had been in Paris, how long he expected to remain there, how he liked it. She spoke English without an accent, or rather with that distinctively British accent which, on his arrival in Europe, had struck Newman as an altogether foreign tongue, but which, in women, he had come to like extremely. Here and there Madame de Cintre's utterance had a faint shade of strangeness but at the end of ten minutes Newman found himself waiting for these soft roughnesses. He enjoyed them, and he marveled to see that gross thing, error, brought down to so fine a point.

"You have a beautiful country," said Madame de Cintre, presently.

"Oh, magnificent!" said Newman. "You ought to see it."

"I shall never see it," said Madame de Cintre with a smile.

"Why not?" asked Newman.

"I don't travel; especially so far."

"But you go away sometimes; you are not always here?"

"I go away in summer, a little way, to the country."

Newman wanted to ask her something more, something personal, he hardly knew what. "Don't you find it rather—rather quiet here?" he said; "so far from the street?" Rather "gloomy," he was going to say, but he reflected that that would be impolite.

"Yes, it is very quiet," said Madame de Cintre; "but we like that."

"Ah, you like that," repeated Newman, slowly.

"Besides, I have lived here all my life."

"Lived here all your life," said Newman, in the same way.

"I was born here, and my father was born here before me, and my grandfather, and my great-grandfathers. Were they not, Valentin?" and she appealed to her brother.

"Yes, it's a family habit to be born here!" the young man said with a laugh, and rose and threw the remnant of his cigarette into the fire, and then remained leaning against the chimney-piece. An observer would have perceived that he wished to take a better look at Newman, whom he covertly examined, while he stood stroking his mustache.

"Your house is tremendously old, then," said Newman.

"How old is it, brother?" asked Madame de Cintre.

The young man took the two candles from the mantel-shelf, lifted one high in each hand, and looked up toward the cornice of the room, above the chimney-piece. This latter feature of the apartment was of white marble, and in the familiar rococo style of the last century; but above it was a paneling of an earlier date, quaintly carved, painted white, and gilded here and there. The white had turned to yellow, and the gilding was tarnished. On the top, the figures ranged themselves into a sort of shield, on which an armorial device was cut. Above it, in relief, was a date—1627. "There you have it," said the young man. "That is old or new, according to your point of view."

"Well, over here," said Newman, "one's point of view gets shifted round considerably." And he threw back his head and looked about the room. "Your house is of a very curious style of architecture," he said.

"Are you interested in architecture?" asked the young man at the chimney-piece.

"Well, I took the trouble, this summer," said Newman, "to examine—as well as I can calculate—some four hundred and seventy churches. Do you call that interested?"

"Perhaps you are interested in theology," said the young man.

"Not particularly. Are you a Roman Catholic, madam?" And he turned to Madame de Cintre.

"Yes, sir," she answered, gravely.

Newman was struck with the gravity of her tone; he threw back his head and began to look round the room again. "Had you never noticed that number up there?" he presently asked.

She hesitated a moment, and then, "In former years," she said.

Her brother had been watching Newman's movement. "Perhaps you would like to examine the house," he said.

Newman slowly brought down his eyes and looked at him; he had a vague impression that the young man at the chimney-piece was inclined to irony. He was a handsome fellow, his face wore a smile, his mustaches were curled up at the ends, and there was a little dancing gleam in his eye. "Damn his French impudence!" Newman was on the point of saying to himself. "What the deuce is he grinning at?" He glanced at Madame de Cintre; she was sitting with her eyes fixed on the floor. She raised them, they met his, and she looked at her brother. Newman turned again to this young man and observed that he strikingly resembled his sister. This was in his favor, and our hero's first impression of the Count Valentin, moreover, had been agreeable. His mistrust expired, and he said he would be very glad to see the house.

The young man gave a frank laugh, and laid his hand on one of the candlesticks. "Good, good!" he exclaimed. "Come, then."

But Madame de Cintre rose quickly and grasped his arm, "Ah, Valentin!" she said. "What do you mean to do?"

"To show Mr. Newman the house. It will be very amusing."

She kept her hand on his arm, and turned to Newman with a smile. "Don't let him take you," she said; "you will not find it amusing. It is a musty old house, like any other."

"It is full of curious things," said the count, resisting. "Besides, I want to do it; it is a rare chance."

"You are very wicked, brother," Madame de Cintre answered.

"Nothing venture, nothing have!" cried the young man. "Will you come?"

Madame de Cintre stepped toward Newman, gently clasping her hands and smiling softly. "Would you not prefer my society, here, by my fire, to stumbling about dark passages after my brother?"

"A hundred times!" said Newman. "We will see the house some other day."

The young man put down his candlestick with mock solemnity, and, shaking his head, "Ah, you have defeated a great scheme, sir!" he said.

"A scheme? I don't understand," said Newman.

"You would have played your part in it all the better. Perhaps some day I shall have a chance to explain it."

"Be quiet, and ring for the tea," said Madame de Cintre.

The young man obeyed, and presently a servant brought in the tea, placed the tray on a small table, and departed. Madame de Cintre, from her place, busied herself with making it. She had but just begun when the door was thrown open and a lady rushed in, making a loud rustling sound. She stared at Newman, gave a little nod and a "Monsieur!" and then quickly approached Madame de Cintre and presented her forehead to be kissed. Madame de Cintre saluted her, and continued to make tea. The new-comer was young and pretty, it seemed to Newman; she wore her bonnet and cloak, and a train of royal proportions. She began to talk rapidly in French. "Oh, give me some tea, my beautiful one, for the love of God! I'm exhausted, mangled, massacred." Newman found himself quite unable to follow her; she spoke much less distinctly than M. Nioche.

"That is my sister-in-law," said the Count Valentin, leaning towards him.

"She is very pretty," said Newman.

"Exquisite," answered the young man, and this time, again, Newman suspected him of irony.

His sister-in-law came round to the other side of the fire with her cup of tea in her hand, holding it out at arm's-length, so that she might not spill it on her dress, and uttering little cries of alarm. She placed the cup on the mantel-shelf and begun to unpin her veil and pull off her gloves, looking meanwhile at Newman.

"Is there any thing I can do for you, my dear lady?" the Count Valentin asked, in a sort of mock-caressing tone.

"Present monsieur," said his sister-in-law.

The young man answered, "Mr. Newman!"

"I can't courtesy to you, monsieur, or I shall spill my tea," said the lady. "So Claire receives strangers, like that?" she added, in a low voice, in French, to her brother-in-law.

"Apparently!" he answered with a smile. Newman stood a moment, and then he approached Madame de Cintre. She looked up at him as if she were thinking of something to say. But she seemed to think of nothing; so she simply smiled. He sat down near her and she handed him a cup of tea. For a few moments they talked about that, and meanwhile he looked at her. He remembered what Mrs. Tristram had told him of her "perfection" and of her having, in combination, all the brilliant things that he dreamed of finding. This made him observe her not only without mistrust, but without uneasy conjectures; the presumption, from the first moment he looked at her, had been in her favor. And yet, if she was beautiful, it was not a dazzling beauty. She was tall and moulded in long lines; she had thick fair hair, a wide forehead, and features with a sort of harmonious irregularity. Her clear gray eyes were strikingly expressive; they were both gentle and intelligent, and Newman liked them immensely; but they had not those depths of splendor—those many-colored rays—which illumine the brows of famous beauties. Madame de Cintre was rather thin, and she looked younger than probably she was. In her whole person there was something both youthful and subdued, slender and yet ample, tranquil yet shy; a mixture of immaturity and repose, of innocence and dignity. What had Tristram meant, Newman wondered, by calling her proud? She was certainly not proud now, to him; or if she was, it was of no use, it was lost upon him; she must pile it up higher if she expected him to mind it. She was a beautiful woman, and it was very easy to get on with her. Was she a countess, a marquise, a kind of historical formation? Newman, who had rarely heard these words used, had never been at pains to attach any particular image to them; but they occurred to him now and seemed charged with a sort of melodious meaning. They signified something fair and softly bright, that had easy motions and spoke very agreeably.

"Have you many friends in Paris; do you go out?" asked Madame de Cintre, who had at last thought of something to say.

"Do you mean do I dance, and all that?"

"Do you go dans le monde, as we say?"

"I have seen a good many people. Mrs. Tristram has taken me about. I do whatever she tells me."

"By yourself, you are not fond of amusements?"

"Oh yes, of some sorts. I am not fond of dancing, and that sort of thing; I am too old and sober. But I want to be amused; I came to Europe for that."

"But you can be amused in America, too."

"I couldn't; I was always at work. But after all, that was my amusement."

At this moment Madame de Bellegarde came back for another cup of tea, accompanied by the Count Valentin. Madame de Cintre, when she had served her, began to talk again with Newman, and recalling what he had last said, "In your own country you were very much occupied?" she asked.

"I was in business. I have been in business since I was fifteen years old."

"And what was your business?" asked Madame de Bellegarde, who was decidedly not so pretty as Madame de Cintre.

"I have been in everything," said Newman. "At one time I sold leather; at one time I manufactured wash-tubs."

Madame de Bellegarde made a little grimace. "Leather? I don't like that. Wash-tubs are better. I prefer the smell of soap. I hope at least they made your fortune." She rattled this off with the air of a woman who had the reputation of saying everything that came into her head, and with a strong French accent.

Newman had spoken with cheerful seriousness, but Madame de Bellegarde's tone made him go on, after a meditative pause, with a certain light grimness of jocularity. "No, I lost money on wash-tubs, but I came out pretty square on leather."

"I have made up my mind, after all," said Madame de Bellegarde, "that the great point is—how do you call it?—to come out square. I am on my knees to money; I don't deny it. If you have it, I ask no questions. For that I am a real democrat—like you, monsieur. Madame de Cintre is very proud; but I find that one gets much more pleasure in this sad life if one doesn't look too close."

"Just Heaven, dear madam, how you go at it," said the Count Valentin, lowering his voice.

"He's a man one can speak to, I suppose, since my sister receives him," the lady answered. "Besides, it's very true; those are my ideas."

"Ah, you call them ideas," murmured the young man.

"But Mrs. Tristram told me you had been in the army—in your war," said Madame de Cintre.

"Yes, but that is not business!" said Newman.

"Very true!" said M. de Bellegarde. "Otherwise perhaps I should not be penniless."

"Is it true," asked Newman in a moment, "that you are so proud? I had already heard it."

Madame de Cintre smiled. "Do you find me so?"

"Oh," said Newman, "I am no judge. If you are proud with me, you will have to tell me. Otherwise I shall not know it."

Madame de Cintre began to laugh. "That would be pride in a sad position!" she said.

"It would be partly," Newman went on, "because I shouldn't want to know it. I want you to treat me well."

CHAPTER VI

Madame de Cintre, whose laugh had ceased, looked at him with her head half averted, as if she feared what he was going to say.

"Mrs. Tristram told you the literal truth," he went on; "I want very much to know you. I didn't come here simply to call to-day; I came in the hope that you might ask me to come again."

"Oh, pray come often," said Madame de Cintre.

"But will you be at home?" Newman insisted. Even to himself he seemed a trifle "pushing," but he was, in truth, a trifle excited.

"I hope so!" said Madame de Cintre.

Newman got up. "Well, we shall see," he said smoothing his hat with his coat-cuff.

"Brother," said Madame de Cintre, "invite Mr. Newman to come again."

The Count Valentin looked at our hero from head to foot with his peculiar smile, in which impudence and urbanity seemed perplexingly commingled. "Are you a brave man?" he asked, eying him askance.

"Well, I hope so," said Newman.

"I rather suspect so. In that case, come again."

"Ah, what an invitation!" murmured Madame de Cintre, with something painful in her smile.

"Oh, I want Mr. Newman to come—particularly," said the young man. "It will give me great pleasure. I shall be desolate if I miss one of his visits. But I maintain he must be brave. A stout heart, sir!" And he offered Newman his hand.

"I shall not come to see you; I shall come to see Madame de Cintre," said Newman.

"You will need all the more courage."

"Ah, Valentin!" said Madame de Cintre, appealingly.

"Decidedly," cried Madame de Bellegarde, "I am the only person here capable of saying something polite! Come to see me; you will need no courage," she said.

Newman gave a laugh which was not altogether an assent, and took his leave. Madame de Cintre did not take up her sister's challenge to be gracious, but she looked with a certain troubled air at the retreating guest.

CHAPTER VII

One evening very late, about a week after his visit to Madame de Cintre, Newman's servant brought him a card. It was that of young M. de Bellegarde. When, a few moments later, he went to receive his visitor, he found him standing in the middle of his great gilded parlor and eying it from cornice to carpet. M. de Bellegarde's face, it seemed to Newman, expressed a sense of lively entertainment. "What the devil is he laughing at now?" our hero asked himself. But he put the question without acrimony, for he felt that Madame de Cintre's brother was a good fellow, and he had a presentiment that on this basis of good fellowship they were destined to understand each other. Only, if there was anything to laugh at, he wished to have a glimpse of it too.

"To begin with," said the young man, as he extended his hand, "have I come too late?"

"Too late for what?" asked Newman.

"To smoke a cigar with you."

"You would have to come early to do that," said Newman. "I don't smoke."

"Ah, you are a strong man!"

"But I keep cigars," Newman added. "Sit down."

"Surely, I may not smoke here," said M. de Bellegarde.

"What is the matter? Is the room too small?"

"It is too large. It is like smoking in a ball-room, or a church."

"That is what you were laughing at just now?" Newman asked; "the size of my room?"

"It is not size only," replied M. de Bellegarde, "but splendor, and harmony, and beauty of detail. It was the smile of admiration."

Newman looked at him a moment, and then, "So it IS very ugly?" he inquired.

"Ugly, my dear sir? It is magnificent."

"That is the same thing, I suppose," said Newman. "Make yourself comfortable. Your coming to see me, I take it, is an act of friendship. You were not obliged to. Therefore, if anything around here amuses you, it will be all in a pleasant way. Laugh as loud as you please; I like to see my visitors cheerful. Only, I must make this request: that you explain the joke to me as soon as you can speak. I don't want to lose anything, myself."

M. de Bellegarde stared, with a look of unresentful perplexity. He laid his hand on Newman's sleeve and seemed on the point of saying something, but he suddenly checked himself, leaned back in his chair, and puffed at his cigar. At last, however, breaking silence,—"Certainly," he said, "my coming to see you is an act of friendship. Nevertheless I was in a measure obliged to do so. My sister asked me to come, and a request from my sister is, for me, a law. I was near you, and I observed lights in what I supposed were your rooms. It was not a ceremonious hour for making a call, but I was not sorry to do something that would show I was not performing a mere ceremony."

"Well, here I am as large as life," said Newman, extending his legs.

"I don't know what you mean," the young man went on "by giving me unlimited leave to laugh. Certainly I am a great laugher, and it is better to laugh too much than too little. But it is not in order that we may laugh together—or separately—that I have, I may say, sought your acquaintance. To speak with almost impudent frankness, you interest me!" All this was uttered by M. de Bellegarde with the modulated smoothness of the man of the world, and in spite of his excellent English, of the Frenchman; but Newman, at the same time that he sat noting its harmonious flow, perceived that it was not mere mechanical urbanity. Decidedly, there was something in his visitor that he liked. M. de Bellegarde was a foreigner to his finger-tips, and if Newman had met him on a Western prairie he would have felt it proper to address him with a "How-d'ye-do, Mosseer?" But there was something in his physiognomy which seemed to cast a sort of aerial bridge over the impassable gulf produced by difference of race. He was below the middle height, and robust and agile in figure. Valentin de Bellegarde, Newman afterwards learned, had a mortal dread of the robustness overtaking the agility; he was afraid of growing stout; he was too short, as he said, to afford a belly. He rode and fenced and practiced gymnastics with unremitting zeal, and if you greeted him with a "How well you are looking" he started and turned pale. In your WELL he read a grosser monosyllable. He had a round head, high above the ears, a crop of hair at once dense and silky, a broad, low forehead, a short nose, of the ironical and inquiring rather than of the dogmatic or sensitive cast, and a mustache as delicate as that of a page in a romance. He resembled his sister not in feature, but in the expression of his clear, bright eye, completely void of introspection, and in the way he smiled. The great point in his face was that it was intensely alive—frankly, ardently, gallantly alive. The look of it was like a bell, of which the handle might have been in the young man's soul: at a touch of the handle it rang with a loud, silver sound. There was something in his quick, light brown eye which assured you that he was not economizing his consciousness. He was not living in a corner of it to spare the furniture of the rest. He was squarely encamped in the centre and he was keeping open house. When he smiled, it was like the movement of a person who in emptying a cup turns it upside down: he gave you the last drop of his jollity. He inspired Newman with something of the same kindness that our hero used to feel in his earlier years for those of his companions who could perform strange and clever tricks—make their joints crack in queer places or whistle at the back of their mouths.

"My sister told me," M. de Bellegarde continued, "that I ought to come and remove the impression that I had taken such great pains to produce upon you; the impression that I am a lunatic. Did it strike you that I behaved very oddly the other day?"

"Rather so," said Newman.

"So my sister tells me." And M. de Bellegarde watched his host for a moment through his smoke-wreaths. "If that is the case, I think we had better let it stand. I didn't try to make you think I was a lunatic, at all; on the contrary, I wanted to produce a favorable impression. But if, after all, I made a fool of myself, it was the intention of Providence. I should injure myself by protesting too much, for I should seem to set up a claim for wisdom which, in the sequel of our acquaintance, I could by no means justify. Set me down as a lunatic with intervals of sanity."

"Oh, I guess you know what you are about," said Newman.

"When I am sane, I am very sane; that I admit," M. de Bellegarde answered. "But I didn't come here to talk about myself. I should like to ask you a few questions. You allow me?"

"Give me a specimen," said Newman.

"You live here all alone?"

"Absolutely. With whom should I live?"

"For the moment," said M. de Bellegarde with a smile "I am asking questions, not answering them. You have come to Paris for your pleasure?"

Newman was silent a while. Then, at last, "Every one asks me that!" he said with his mild slowness. "It sounds so awfully foolish."

"But at any rate you had a reason."

"Oh, I came for my pleasure!" said Newman. "Though it is foolish, it is true."

"And you are enjoying it?"

Like any other good American, Newman thought it as well not to truckle to the foreigner. "Oh, so-so," he answered.

M. de Bellegarde puffed his cigar again in silence. "For myself," he said at last, "I am entirely at your service. Anything I can do for you I shall be very happy to do. Call upon me at your convenience. Is there any one you desire to know—anything you wish to see? It is a pity you should not enjoy Paris."

"Oh, I do enjoy it!" said Newman, good-naturedly. "I'm much obligated to you."

"Honestly speaking," M. de Bellegarde went on, "there is something absurd to me in hearing myself make you these offers. They represent a great deal of goodwill, but they represent little else. You are a successful man and I am a failure, and it's a turning of the tables to talk as if I could lend you a hand."

"In what way are you a failure?" asked Newman.

"Oh, I'm not a tragical failure!" cried the young man with a laugh. "I have fallen from a height, and my fiasco has made no noise. You, evidently, are a success. You have made a fortune, you have built up an edifice, you are a financial, commercial power, you can travel about the world until you have found a soft spot, and lie down in it with the consciousness of having earned your rest. Is not that true? Well, imagine the exact reverse of all that, and you have me. I have done nothing—I can do nothing!"

"Why not?"

"It's a long story. Some day I will tell you. Meanwhile, I'm right, eh? You are a success? You have made a fortune? It's none of my business, but, in short, you are rich?"

"That's another thing that it sounds foolish to say," said Newman. "Hang it, no man is rich!"

"I have heard philosophers affirm," laughed M. de Bellegarde, "that no man was poor; but your formula strikes me as an improvement. As a general thing, I confess, I don't like successful people, and I find clever men who have made great fortunes very offensive. They tread on my toes; they make me uncomfortable. But as soon as I saw you, I said to myself. 'Ah, there is a man with whom I shall get on. He has the good-nature of success and none of the morgue; he has not our confoundedly irritable French vanity.' In short, I took a fancy to you. We are very different, I'm sure; I don't believe there is a subject on which we think or feel alike. But I rather think we shall get on, for there is such a thing, you know, as being too different to quarrel."

"Oh, I never quarrel," said Newman.

"Never! Sometimes it's a duty—or at least it's a pleasure. Oh, I have had two or three delicious quarrels in my day!" and M. de Bellegarde's handsome smile assumed, at the memory of these incidents, an almost voluptuous intensity.

With the preamble embodied in his share of the foregoing fragment of dialogue, he paid our hero a long visit; as the two men sat with their heels on Newman's glowing hearth, they heard the small hours of the morning striking larger from a far-off belfry. Valentin de Bellegarde was, by his own confession, at all times a great chatterer, and on this occasion he was evidently in a particularly loquacious mood. It was a tradition of his race that people of its blood always conferred a favor by their smiles, and as his enthusiasms were as rare as his civility was constant, he had a double reason for not suspecting that his friendship could ever be importunate. Moreover, the flower of an ancient stem as he was, tradition (since I have used the word) had in his temperament nothing of disagreeable rigidity. It was muffled in sociability and urbanity, as an old dowager in her laces and strings of pearls. Valentin was what is called in France a gentilhomme, of the purest source, and his rule of life, so far as it was definite, was to play the part of a gentilhomme. This, it seemed to him, was enough to occupy comfortably a young man of ordinary good parts. But all that he was he was by instinct and not by theory, and the amiability of his character was so great that certain of the aristocratic virtues, which in some aspects seem rather brittle and trenchant, acquired in his application of them an extreme geniality. In his younger years he had been suspected of low tastes, and his mother had greatly feared he would make a slip in the mud of the highway and bespatter the family shield. He had been treated, therefore, to more than his share of schooling and drilling, but his instructors had not succeeded in mounting him upon stilts. They could not spoil his safe spontaneity, and he remained the least cautious and the most lucky of young nobles. He had been tied with so short a rope in his youth that he had now a mortal grudge against family discipline. He had been known to say, within the limits of the family, that, light-headed as he was, the honor of the name was safer in his hands than in those of some of it's other members, and that if a day ever came to try it, they should see. His talk was an odd mixture of almost boyish garrulity and of the reserve and discretion of the man of the world, and he seemed to Newman, as afterwards young members of the Latin races often seemed to him, now amusingly juvenile and now appallingly mature. In America, Newman reflected, lads of twenty-five and thirty have old heads and young hearts, or at least young morals; here they have young heads and very aged hearts, morals the most grizzled and wrinkled.

"What I envy you is your liberty," observed M. de Bellegarde, "your wide range, your freedom to come and go, your not having a lot of people, who take themselves awfully seriously, expecting something of you. I live," he added with a sigh, "beneath the eyes of my admirable mother."

"It is your own fault; what is to hinder your ranging?" said Newman.

"There is a delightful simplicity in that remark! Everything is to hinder me. To begin with, I have not a penny."

"I had not a penny when I began to range."

CHAPTER VII

"Ah, but your poverty was your capital. Being an American, it was impossible you should remain what you were born, and being born poor—do I understand it?—it was therefore inevitable that you should become rich. You were in a position that makes one's mouth water; you looked round you and saw a world full of things you had only to step up to and take hold of. When I was twenty, I looked around me and saw a world with everything ticketed 'Hands off!' and the deuce of it was that the ticket seemed meant only for me. I couldn't go into business, I couldn't make money, because I was a Bellegarde. I couldn't go into politics, because I was a Bellegarde—the Bellegardes don't recognize the Bonapartes. I couldn't go into literature, because I was a dunce. I couldn't marry a rich girl, because no Bellegarde had ever married a roturiere, and it was not proper that I should begin. We shall have to come to it, yet. Marriageable heiresses, de notre bord, are not to be had for nothing; it must be name for name, and fortune for fortune. The only thing I could do was to go and fight for the Pope. That I did, punctiliously, and received an apostolic flesh-wound at Castlefidardo. It did neither the Holy Father nor me any good, that I could see. Rome was doubtless a very amusing place in the days of Caligula, but it has sadly fallen off since. I passed three years in the Castle of St. Angelo, and then came back to secular life."

"So you have no profession—you do nothing," said Newman.

"I do nothing! I am supposed to amuse myself, and, to tell the truth, I have amused myself. One can, if one knows how. But you can't keep it up forever. I am good for another five years, perhaps, but I foresee that after that I shall lose my appetite. Then what shall I do? I think I shall turn monk. Seriously, I think I shall tie a rope round my waist and go into a monastery. It was an old custom, and the old customs were very good. People understood life quite as well as we do. They kept the pot boiling till it cracked, and then they put it on the shelf altogether."

"Are you very religious?" asked Newman, in a tone which gave the inquiry a grotesque effect.

M. de Bellegarde evidently appreciated the comical element in the question, but he looked at Newman a moment with extreme soberness. "I am a very good Catholic. I respect the Church. I adore the blessed Virgin. I fear the Devil."

"Well, then," said Newman, "you are very well fixed. You have got pleasure in the present and religion in the future; what do you complain of?"

"It's a part of one's pleasure to complain. There is something in your own circumstances that irritates me. You are the first man I have ever envied. It's singular, but so it is. I have known many men who, besides any factitious advantages that I may possess, had money and brains into the bargain; but somehow they have never disturbed my good-humor. But you have got something that I should have liked to have. It is not money, it is not even brains—though no doubt yours are excellent. It is not your six feet of height, though I should have rather liked to be a couple of inches taller. It's a sort of air you have of being thoroughly at home in the world. When I was a boy, my father told me that it was by such an air as that that people recognized a Bellegarde. He called my attention to it. He didn't advise me to cultivate it; he said that as we grew up it always came of itself. I supposed it had come to me, because I think I have always had the feeling. My place in life was made for me, and it seemed easy to occupy it. But you who, as I understand it, have made your own place, you who, as you told us the other day, have manufactured wash-tubs—you strike me, somehow, as a man who stands at his ease, who looks at things from a height. I fancy you going about the world like a man traveling on a railroad in which he owns a large amount of stock. You make me feel as if I had missed something. What is it?"

"It is the proud consciousness of honest toil—of having manufactured a few wash-tubs," said Newman, at once jocose and serious.

"Oh no; I have seen men who had done even more, men who had made not only wash-tubs, but soap—strong-smelling yellow soap, in great bars; and they never made me the least uncomfortable."

"Then it's the privilege of being an American citizen," said Newman. "That sets a man up."

"Possibly," rejoined M. de Bellegarde. "But I am forced to say that I have seen a great many American citizens who didn't seem at all set up or in the least like large stock-holders. I never envied them. I rather think the thing is an accomplishment of your own."

"Oh, come," said Newman, "you will make me proud!"

"No, I shall not. You have nothing to do with pride, or with humility—that is a part of this easy manner of yours. People are proud only when they have something to lose, and humble when they have something to gain."

"I don't know what I have to lose," said Newman, "but I certainly have something to gain."

"What is it?" asked his visitor.

Newman hesitated a while. "I will tell you when I know you better."

"I hope that will be soon! Then, if I can help you to gain it, I shall be happy."

"Perhaps you may," said Newman.

"Don't forget, then, that I am your servant," M. de Bellegarde answered; and shortly afterwards he took his departure.

During the next three weeks Newman saw Bellegarde several times, and without formally swearing an eternal friendship the two men established a sort of comradeship. To Newman, Bellegarde was the ideal Frenchman, the Frenchman of tradition and romance, so far as our hero was concerned with these mystical influences. Gallant, expansive, amusing, more pleased himself with the effect he produced than those (even when they were well pleased) for whom he produced it; a master of all the distinctively social virtues and a votary of all agreeable sensations; a devotee of something mysterious and sacred to which he occasionally alluded in terms more ecstatic even than those in which he spoke of the last pretty woman, and which was simply the beautiful though somewhat superannuated image of HONOR; he was irresistibly entertaining and enlivening, and he formed a character to which Newman was as capable of doing justice when he had once been placed in contact with it, as he was unlikely, in musing upon the possible mixtures of our human ingredients, mentally to have foreshadowed it. Bellegarde did not in the least cause him to modify his needful premise that all Frenchmen are of a frothy and imponderable substance; he simply reminded him that light materials may be beaten up into a most agreeable compound. No two companions could be more different, but their differences made a capital basis for a friendship of which the distinctive characteristic was that it was extremely amusing to each.

Valentin de Bellegarde lived in the basement of an old house in the Rue d'Anjou St. Honore, and his small apartments lay between the court of the house and an old garden which spread itself behind it—one of those large, sunless humid gardens into which you look unexpectingly in Paris from back windows, wondering how among the grudging habitations they find their space. When Newman returned Bellegarde's visit, he hinted that HIS lodging was at least as much a laughing matter as his own. But its oddities were of a different cast from those of our hero's gilded saloons on the Boulevard Haussmann: the place was low, dusky, contracted, and crowded with curious bric-a-brac. Bellegarde, penniless patrician as he was, was an insatiable collector, and his walls were covered with rusty arms and ancient panels and platters, his doorways draped in faded tapestries, his floors muffled in the skins of beasts. Here and there was one of those uncomfortable tributes to elegance in which the upholsterer's art, in France, is so prolific; a curtain recess with a sheet of looking-glass in which, among the shadows, you could see nothing; a divan on which, for its festoons and furbelows, you could not sit; a fireplace draped, flounced, and frilled to the complete exclusion of fire. The young man's possessions were in picturesque disorder, and his apartment was pervaded by the odor of cigars, mingled with perfumes more inscrutable. Newman thought it a damp, gloomy place to live in, and was puzzled by the obstructive and fragmentary character of the furniture.

Bellegarde, according to the custom of his country talked very generously about himself, and unveiled the mysteries of his private history with an unsparing hand. Inevitably, he had a vast deal to say about women, and he used frequently to indulge in sentimental and ironical apostrophes to these authors of his joys and woes. "Oh, the women, the women, and the things they have made me do!" he would exclaim with a lustrous eye. "C'est egal, of all the follies and stupidities I have committed for them I would not have missed one!" On this subject Newman maintained an habitual reserve; to expatiate largely upon it had always seemed to him a proceeding vaguely analogous to the cooing of pigeons and the chattering of monkeys, and even inconsistent with a fully developed human character. But Bellegarde's confidences greatly amused him, and rarely displeased him, for the generous young Frenchman was not a cynic. "I really think," he had once said, "that I am not more depraved than most of my contemporaries. They are tolerably depraved, my contemporaries!" He said wonderfully pretty things about his female friends, and, numerous and various as they had been, declared that on the whole there was more good in them than harm. "But you are not to take that as advice," he added. "As an authority I am very untrustworthy. I'm prejudiced in their favor; I'm an IDEALIST!" Newman listened to him with his impartial smile, and was glad, for his own sake, that he had fine feelings; but he mentally repudiated the idea of a Frenchman having discovered any merit in the amiable sex which he himself did not suspect. M. de Bellegarde, however, did not confine his conversation to the autobiographical channel; he questioned our hero largely as to the events of his own life, and Newman told him some better stories than any that Bellegarde carried in his budget. He narrated his career, in fact, from the beginning, through all its variations, and whenever his companion's credulity, or his habits of gentility, appeared to protest, it amused him to heighten the color of the episode. Newman had sat with Western humorists in knots, round cast-iron stoves, and seen "tall" stories grow taller without toppling over, and his own imagination had learned the trick of piling up consistent wonders. Bellegarde's regular attitude at last became that of laughing self-defense; to maintain his reputation as an all-knowing Frenchman, he doubted of everything, wholesale. The result of this was that Newman found it impossible to convince him of certain time-honored verities.

"But the details don't matter," said M. de Bellegarde. "You have evidently had some surprising adventures; you have seen some strange sides of life, you have revolved to and fro over a whole continent as I walked up and down the Boulevard. You are a man of the world with a vengeance! You have spent some deadly dull hours, and you have done some extremely disagreeable things: you have shoveled sand, as a boy, for supper, and you have eaten roast dog in a gold-diggers' camp. You have stood casting up figures for ten hours at a time, and you have sat through Methodist sermons for the sake of looking at a pretty girl in another pew. All that is rather stiff, as we say. But at any rate you have done something and you are something; you have used your will and you have made your fortune. You have not stupified yourself with debauchery and you have not mortgaged your fortune to social conveniences. You take things easily, and you have fewer prejudices even than I, who pretend to have none, but who in reality have three or four. Happy man, you are strong and you are free. But what the deuce," demanded the young man in conclusion, "do you propose to do with such advantages? Really to use them you need a better world than this. There is nothing worth your while here."

"Oh, I think there is something," said Newman.

"What is it?"

"Well," murmured Newman, "I will tell you some other time!"

In this way our hero delayed from day to day broaching a subject which he had very much at heart. Meanwhile, however, he was growing practically familiar with it; in other words, he had called again, three times, on Madame de Cintre. On only two of these occasions had he found her at home, and on each of them she had other visitors. Her visitors were numerous and extremely loquacious, and they exacted much of their hostess's attention. She found time, however, to bestow a little of it on Newman, in an occasional vague smile, the very vagueness of which pleased him, allowing him as it did to fill it out mentally, both at the time and afterwards, with such meanings as most pleased him. He sat by without speaking, looking at the entrances and exits, the greetings and chatterings, of Madame de Cintre's visitors. He felt as if he were at the play, and as if his own speaking would be an interruption; sometimes he wished he had a book, to follow the dialogue; he half expected to see a woman in a white cap and pink ribbons come and offer him one for two francs. Some of the ladies looked at him very hard—or very soft, as you please; others seemed profoundly unconscious of his presence. The men looked only at Madame de Cintre. This was inevitable; for whether one called her beautiful or not she entirely occupied and filled one's vision, just as an agreeable sound fills one's ear. Newman had but twenty distinct words with her, but he carried away an impression to which solemn promises could not have given a higher value. She was part of the play that he was seeing acted, quite as much as her companions; but how she filled the stage and how much better she did it! Whether she rose or seated herself; whether she went with her departing friends to the door and lifted up the heavy curtain as they passed out, and stood an instant looking after them and giving them the last nod; or whether she leaned back in her chair with her arms crossed and her eyes resting, listening and smiling; she gave Newman the feeling that he should like to have her always before him, moving slowly to and fro along the whole scale of expressive hospitality. If it might be TO him, it would be well; if it might be FOR him, it would be still better! She was so tall and yet so light, so active and yet so still, so elegant and yet so simple, so frank and yet so mysterious! It was the mystery—it was what she was off the stage, as it were—that interested Newman most of all. He could not have told you what warrant he had for talking about mysteries; if it had been his habit to express himself in poetic figures he might have said that in observing Madame de Cintre he seemed to see the vague circle which sometimes accompanies the partly-filled disk of the moon. It was not that she was reserved; on the contrary, she was as frank as flowing water. But he was sure she had qualities which she herself did not suspect.

He had abstained for several reasons from saying some of these things to Bellegarde. One reason was that before proceeding to any act he was always circumspect, conjectural, contemplative; he had little eagerness, as became a man who felt that whenever he really began to move he walked with long steps. And then, it simply pleased him not to speak—it occupied him, it excited him. But one day Bellegarde had been dining with him, at a restaurant, and they had sat long over their dinner. On rising from it, Bellegarde proposed that, to help them through the rest of the evening, they should go and see Madame Dandelard. Madame Dandelard was a little Italian lady who had married a Frenchman who proved to be a rake and a brute and the torment of her life. Her husband had spent all her money, and then, lacking the means of obtaining more expensive pleasures, had taken, in his duller hours, to beating her. She had a blue spot somewhere, which she showed to several persons, including Bellegarde. She had obtained a separation from her husband, collected the scraps of her fortune (they were very meagre) and come to live in Paris, where she was staying at a hotel garni. She was always looking for an apartment, and visiting, inquiringly, those of other people. She was very pretty, very childlike, and she made very extraordinary remarks. Bellegarde had made her acquaintance, and the source of his interest in her was, according to his own declaration, a curiosity as to what would become of her. "She is poor, she is pretty, and she is silly," he said, "it seems to me she can go only one way. It's a pity, but it can't be helped. I will give her six months. She has nothing to fear from me, but I am watching the process. I am curious to see just how things will go. Yes, I know what you are going to say: this horrible Paris hardens one's heart. But it quickens one's wits, and it ends by teaching one a refinement of observation! To see this little woman's little drama play itself out, now, is, for me, an intellectual pleasure."

"If she is going to throw herself away," Newman had said, "you ought to stop her."

"Stop her? How stop her?"

"Talk to her; give her some good advice."

Bellegarde laughed. "Heaven deliver us both! Imagine the situation! Go and advise her yourself."

It was after this that Newman had gone with Bellegarde to see Madame Dandelard. When they came away, Bellegarde reproached his companion. "Where was your famous advice?" he asked. "I didn't hear a word of it."

"Oh, I give it up," said Newman, simply.

"Then you are as bad as I!" said Bellegarde.

"No, because I don't take an 'intellectual pleasure' in her prospective adventures. I don't in the least want to see her going down hill. I had rather look the other way. But why," he asked, in a moment, "don't you get your sister to go and see her?"

Bellegarde stared. "Go and see Madame Dandelard—my sister?"

"She might talk to her to very good purpose."

Bellegarde shook his head with sudden gravity. "My sister can't see that sort of person. Madame Dandelard is nothing at all; they would never meet."

"I should think," said Newman, "that your sister might see whom she pleased." And he privately resolved that after he knew her a little better he would ask Madame de Cintre to go and talk to the foolish little Italian lady.

After his dinner with Bellegarde, on the occasion I have mentioned, he demurred to his companion's proposal that they should go again and listen to Madame Dandelard describe her sorrows and her bruises.

"I have something better in mind," he said; "come home with me and finish the evening before my fire."

Bellegarde always welcomed the prospect of a long stretch of conversation, and before long the two men sat watching the great blaze which scattered its scintillations over the high adornments of Newman's ball-room.

CHAPTER VIII

"Tell me something about your sister," Newman began abruptly.

Bellegarde turned and gave him a quick look. "Now that I think of it, you have never yet asked me a question about her."

"I know that very well."

"If it is because you don't trust me, you are very right," said Bellegarde. "I can't talk of her rationally. I admire her too much."

"Talk of her as you can," rejoined Newman. "Let yourself go."

"Well, we are very good friends; we are such a brother and sister as have not been seen since Orestes and Electra. You have seen her; you know what she is: tall, thin, light, imposing, and gentle, half a grande dame and half an angel; a mixture of pride and humility, of the eagle and the dove. She looks like a statue which had failed as stone, resigned itself to its grave defects, and come to life as flesh and blood, to wear white capes and long trains. All I can say is that she really possesses every merit that her face, her glance, her smile, the tone of her voice, lead you to expect; it is saying a great deal. As a general thing, when a woman seems very charming, I should say 'Beware!' But in proportion as Claire seems charming you may fold your arms and let yourself float with the current; you are safe. She is so good! I have never seen a woman half so perfect or so complete. She has everything; that is all I can say about her. There!" Bellegarde concluded; "I told you I should rhapsodize."

Newman was silent a while, as if he were turning over his companion's words. "She is very good, eh?" he repeated at last.

"Divinely good!"

"Kind, charitable, gentle, generous?"

"Generosity itself; kindness double-distilled!"

"Is she clever?"

"She is the most intelligent woman I know. Try her, some day, with something difficult, and you will see."

"Is she fond of admiration?"

"Parbleu!" cried Bellegarde; "what woman is not?"

"Ah, when they are too fond of admiration they commit all kinds of follies to get it."

"I did not say she was too fond!" Bellegarde exclaimed. "Heaven forbid I should say anything so idiotic. She is not too anything! If I were to say she was ugly, I should not mean she was too ugly. She is fond of pleasing, and if you are pleased she is grateful. If you are not pleased, she lets it pass and thinks the worst neither of you nor of herself. I imagine, though, she hopes the saints in heaven are, for I am sure she is incapable of trying to please by any means of which they would disapprove."

"Is she grave or gay?" asked Newman.

"She is both; not alternately, for she is always the same. There is gravity in her gayety, and gayety in her gravity. But there is no reason why she should be particularly gay."

"Is she unhappy?"

"I won't say that, for unhappiness is according as one takes things, and Claire takes them according to some receipt communicated to her by the Blessed Virgin in a vision. To be unhappy is to be disagreeable, which, for her, is out of the question. So she has arranged her circumstances so as to be happy in them."

"She is a philosopher," said Newman.

"No, she is simply a very nice woman."

"Her circumstances, at any rate, have been disagreeable?"

Bellegarde hesitated a moment—a thing he very rarely did. "Oh, my dear fellow, if I go into the history of my family I shall give you more than you bargain for."

"No, on the contrary, I bargain for that," said Newman.

"We shall have to appoint a special seance, then, beginning early. Suffice it for the present that Claire has not slept on roses. She made at eighteen a marriage that was expected to be brilliant, but that turned out like a lamp that goes out; all smoke and bad smell. M. de Cintre was sixty years old, and an odious old gentleman. He lived, however, but a short time, and after his death his family pounced upon his money, brought a lawsuit against his widow, and pushed things very hard. Their case was a good one, for M. de Cintre, who had been trustee for some of his relatives, appeared to have been guilty of some very irregular practices. In the course of the suit some revelations were made as to his private history which my sister found so displeasing that she ceased to defend herself and washed her hands of the property. This required some pluck, for she was between two fires, her husband's family opposing her and her own family forcing her. My mother and my brother wished her to cleave to what they regarded as her rights. But she resisted firmly, and at last bought her freedom—obtained my mother's assent to dropping the suit at the price of a promise."

"What was the promise?"

"To do anything else, for the next ten years, that was asked of her—anything, that is, but marry."

"She had disliked her husband very much?"

"No one knows how much!"

"The marriage had been made in your horrible French way," Newman continued, "made by the two families, without her having any voice?"

"It was a chapter for a novel. She saw M. de Cintre for the first time a month before the wedding, after everything, to the minutest detail, had been arranged. She turned white when she looked at him, and white remained till her wedding-day. The evening before the ceremony she swooned away, and she spent the whole night in sobs. My mother sat holding her two hands, and my brother walked up and down the room. I declared it was revolting and told my sister publicly that if she would refuse, downright, I would stand by her. I was told to go about my business, and she became Comtesse de Cintre."

"Your brother," said Newman, reflectively, "must be a very nice young man."

"He is very nice, though he is not young. He is upward of fifty, fifteen years my senior. He has been a father to my sister and me. He is a very remarkable man; he has the best manners in France. He is extremely clever; indeed he is very learned. He is writing a history of The Princesses of France Who Never Married." This was said by Bellegarde with extreme gravity, looking straight at Newman, and with an eye that betokened no mental reservation; or that, at least, almost betokened none.

Newman perhaps discovered there what little there was, for he presently said, "You don't love your brother."

"I beg your pardon," said Bellegarde, ceremoniously; "well-bred people always love their brothers."

"Well, I don't love him, then!" Newman answered.

"Wait till you know him!" rejoined Bellegarde, and this time he smiled.

"Is your mother also very remarkable?" Newman asked, after a pause.

"For my mother," said Bellegarde, now with intense gravity, "I have the highest admiration. She is a very extraordinary woman. You cannot approach her without perceiving it."

"She is the daughter, I believe, of an English nobleman."

"Of the Earl of St. Dunstan's."

"Is the Earl of St. Dunstan's a very old family?"

"So-so; the sixteenth century. It is on my father's side that we go back—back, back, back. The family antiquaries themselves lose breath. At last they stop, panting and fanning themselves, somewhere in the ninth century, under Charlemagne. That is where we begin."

"There is no mistake about it?" said Newman.

"I'm sure I hope not. We have been mistaken at least for several centuries."

"And you have always married into old families?"

"As a rule; though in so long a stretch of time there have been some exceptions. Three or four Bellegardes, in the seventeenth and eighteenth centuries, took wives out of the bourgoisie—married lawyers' daughters."

"A lawyer's daughter; that's very bad, is it?" asked Newman.

"Horrible! one of us, in the middle ages, did better: he married a beggar-maid, like King Cophetua. That was really better; it was like marrying a bird or a monkey; one didn't have to think about her family at all. Our women have always done well; they have never even gone into the petite noblesse. There is, I believe, not a case on record of a misalliance among the women."

Newman turned this over for a while, and, then at last he said, "You offered, the first time you came to see me to render me any service you could. I told you that some time I would mention something you might do. Do you remember?"

"Remember? I have been counting the hours."

"Very well; here's your chance. Do what you can to make your sister think well of me."

Bellegarde stared, with a smile. "Why, I'm sure she thinks as well of you as possible, already."

"An opinion founded on seeing me three or four times? That is putting me off with very little. I want something more. I have been thinking of it a good deal, and at last I have decided to tell you. I should like very much to marry Madame de Cintre."

Bellegarde had been looking at him with quickened expectancy, and with the smile with which he had greeted Newman's allusion to his promised request. At this last announcement he continued to gaze; but his smile went through two or three curious phases. It felt, apparently, a momentary impulse to broaden; but this it immediately checked. Then it remained for some instants taking counsel with itself, at the end of which it decreed a retreat. It slowly effaced itself and left a look of seriousness modified by the desire not to be rude. Extreme surprise had come into the Count Valentin's face; but he had reflected that it would be uncivil to leave it there. And yet, what the deuce was he to do with it? He got up, in his agitation, and stood before the chimney-piece, still looking at Newman. He was a longer time thinking what to say than one would have expected.

"If you can't render me the service I ask," said Newman, "say it out!"

"Let me hear it again, distinctly," said Bellegarde. "It's very important, you know. I shall plead your cause with my sister, because you want—you want to marry her? That's it, eh?"

"Oh, I don't say plead my cause, exactly; I shall try and do that myself. But say a good word for me, now and then—let her know that you think well of me."

At this, Bellegarde gave a little light laugh.

"What I want chiefly, after all," Newman went on, "is just to let you know what I have in mind. I suppose that is what you expect, isn't it? I want to do what is customary over here. If there is any thing particular to be done, let me know and I will do it. I wouldn't for the world approach Madame de Cintre without all the proper forms. If I ought to go and tell your mother, why I will go and tell her. I will go and tell your brother, even. I will go and tell any one you please. As I don't know any one else, I begin by telling you. But that, if it is a social obligation, is a pleasure as well."

"Yes, I see—I see," said Bellegarde, lightly stroking his chin. "You have a very right feeling about it, but I'm glad you have begun with me." He paused, hesitated, and then turned away and walked slowly the length of the room. Newman got up and stood leaning against the mantel-shelf, with his hands in his pockets, watching Bellegarde's promenade. The young Frenchman came back and stopped in front of him. "I give it up," he said; "I will not pretend I am not surprised. I am—hugely! Ouf! It's a relief."

"That sort of news is always a surprise," said Newman. "No matter what you have done, people are never prepared. But if you are so surprised, I hope at least you are pleased."

"Come!" said Bellegarde. "I am going to be tremendously frank. I don't know whether I am pleased or horrified."

"If you are pleased, I shall be glad," said Newman, "and I shall be—encouraged. If you are horrified, I shall be sorry, but I shall not be discouraged. You must make the best of it."

"That is quite right—that is your only possible attitude. You are perfectly serious?"

"Am I a Frenchman, that I should not be?" asked Newman. "But why is it, by the bye, that you should be horrified?"

Bellegarde raised his hand to the back of his head and rubbed his hair quickly up and down, thrusting out the tip of his tongue as he did so. "Why, you are not noble, for instance," he said.

"The devil I am not!" exclaimed Newman.

"Oh," said Bellegarde a little more seriously, "I did not know you had a title."

"A title? What do you mean by a title?" asked Newman. "A count, a duke, a marquis? I don't know anything about that, I don't know who is and who is not. But I say I am noble. I don't exactly know what you mean by it, but it's a fine word and a fine idea; I put in a claim to it."

"But what have you to show, my dear fellow, what proofs?"

"Anything you please! But you don't suppose I am going to undertake to prove that I am noble. It is for you to prove the contrary."

"That's easily done. You have manufactured wash-tubs."

Newman stared a moment. "Therefore I am not noble? I don't see it. Tell me something I have NOT done—something I cannot do."

"You cannot marry a woman like Madame de Cintre for the asking."

"I believe you mean," said Newman slowly, "that I am not good enough."

"Brutally speaking—yes!"

Bellegarde had hesitated a moment, and while he hesitated Newman's attentive glance had grown somewhat eager. In answer to these last words he for a moment said nothing. He simply blushed a little. Then he raised his eyes to the ceiling and stood looking at one of the rosy cherubs that was painted upon it. "Of course I don't expect to marry any woman for the asking," he said at last; "I expect first to make myself acceptable to her. She must like me, to begin with. But that I am not good enough to make a trial is rather a surprise."

Bellegarde wore a look of mingled perplexity, sympathy, and amusement. "You should not hesitate, then, to go up to-morrow and ask a duchess to marry you?"

"Not if I thought she would suit me. But I am very fastidious; she might not at all."

Bellegarde's amusement began to prevail. "And you should be surprised if she refused you?"

Newman hesitated a moment. "It sounds conceited to say yes, but nevertheless I think I should. For I should make a very handsome offer."

"What would it be?"

"Everything she wishes. If I get hold of a woman that comes up to my standard, I shall think nothing too good for her. I have been a long time looking, and I find such women are rare. To combine the qualities I require seems to be difficult, but when the difficulty is vanquished it deserves a reward. My wife shall have a good position, and I'm not afraid to say that I shall be a good husband."

"And these qualities that you require—what are they?"

"Goodness, beauty, intelligence, a fine education, personal elegance—everything, in a word, that makes a splendid woman."

"And noble birth, evidently," said Bellegarde.

"Oh, throw that in, by all means, if it's there. The more the better!"

"And my sister seems to you to have all these things?"

"She is exactly what I have been looking for. She is my dream realized."

"And you would make her a very good husband?"

"That is what I wanted you to tell her."

Bellegarde laid his hand on his companion's arm a moment, looked at him with his head on one side, from head to foot, and then, with a loud laugh, and shaking the other hand in the air, turned away. He walked again the length of the room, and again he came back and stationed himself in front of Newman. "All this is very interesting—it is very curious. In what I said just now I was speaking, not for myself, but for my tradition, my superstitions. For myself, really, your proposal tickles me. It startled me at first, but the more I think of it the more I see in it. It's no use attempting to explain anything; you won't understand me. After all, I don't see why you need; it's no great loss."

"Oh, if there is anything more to explain, try it! I want to proceed with my eyes open. I will do my best to understand."

"No," said Bellegarde, "it's disagreeable to me; I give it up. I liked you the first time I saw you, and I will abide by that. It would be quite odious for me to come talking to you as if I could patronize you. I have told you before that I envy you; vous m'imposez, as we say. I didn't know you much until within five minutes. So we will let things go, and I will say nothing to you that, if our positions were reversed, you would not say to me."

I do not know whether in renouncing the mysterious opportunity to which he alluded, Bellegarde felt that he was doing something very generous. If so, he was not rewarded; his generosity was not appreciated. Newman quite failed to recognize the young Frenchman's power to wound his feelings, and he had now no sense of escaping or coming off easily. He did not thank his companion even with a glance. "My eyes are open, though," he said, "so far as that you have practically told me that your family and your friends will turn up their noses at me. I have never thought much about the reasons that make it proper for people to turn up their noses, and so I can only decide the question off-hand. Looking at it in that way I can't see anything in it. I simply think, if you want to know, that I'm as good as the best. Who the best are, I don't pretend to say. I have never thought much about that either. To tell the truth, I have always had rather a good opinion of myself; a man who is successful can't help it. But I will admit that I was conceited. What I don't say yes to is that I don't stand high—as high as any one else. This is a line of speculation I should not have chosen, but you must remember you began it yourself. I should never have dreamed that I was on the defensive, or that I had to justify myself; but if your people will have it so, I will do my best."

"But you offered, a while ago, to make your court as we say, to my mother and my brother."

"Damn it!" cried Newman, "I want to be polite."

"Good!" rejoined Bellegarde; "this will go far, it will be very entertaining. Excuse my speaking of it in that cold-blooded fashion, but the matter must, of necessity, be for me something of a spectacle. It's positively exciting. But apart from that I sympathize with you, and I shall be actor, so far as I can, as well as spectator. You are a capital fellow; I believe in you and I back you. The simple fact that you appreciate my sister will serve as the proof I was asking for. All men are equal—especially men of taste!"

"Do you think," asked Newman presently, "that Madame de Cintre is determined not to marry?"

"That is my impression. But that is not against you; it's for you to make her change her mind."

"I am afraid it will be hard," said Newman, gravely.

"I don't think it will be easy. In a general way I don't see why a widow should ever marry again. She has gained the benefits of matrimony—freedom and consideration—and she has got rid of the drawbacks. Why should she put her head into the noose again? Her usual motive is ambition: if a man can offer her a great position, make her a princess or an ambassadress she may think the compensation sufficient."

"And—in that way—is Madame de Cintre ambitious?"

"Who knows?" said Bellegarde, with a profound shrug. "I don't pretend to say all that she is or all that she is not. I think she might be touched by the prospect of becoming the wife of a great man. But in a certain way, I believe, whatever she does will be the IMPROBABLE. Don't be too confident, but don't absolutely doubt. Your best chance for success will be precisely in being, to her mind, unusual, unexpected, original. Don't try to be any one else; be simply yourself, out and out. Something or other can't fail to come of it; I am very curious to see what."

"I am much obliged to you for your advice," said Newman. "And," he added with a smile, "I am glad, for your sake, I am going to be so amusing."

"It will be more than amusing," said Bellegarde; "it will be inspiring. I look at it from my point of view, and you from yours. After all, anything for a change! And only yesterday I was yawning so as to dislocate my jaw, and declaring that there was nothing new under the sun! If it isn't new to see you come into the family as a suitor, I am very much mistaken. Let me say that, my dear fellow; I won't call it anything else, bad or good; I will simply call it NEW" And overcome with a sense of the novelty thus foreshadowed, Valentin de Bellegarde threw himself into a deep arm-chair before the fire, and, with a fixed, intense smile, seemed to read a vision of it in the flame of the logs. After a while he looked up. "Go ahead, my boy; you have my good wishes," he said. "But it is really a pity you don't understand me, that you don't know just what I am doing."

"Oh," said Newman, laughing, "don't do anything wrong. Leave me to myself, rather, or defy me, out and out. I wouldn't lay any load on your conscience."

Bellegarde sprang up again; he was evidently excited; there was a warmer spark even than usual in his eye. "You never will understand—you never will know," he said; "and if you succeed, and I turn out to have helped you, you will never be grateful, not as I shall deserve you should be. You will be an excellent fellow always, but you will not be grateful. But it doesn't matter, for I shall get my own fun out of it." And he broke into an extravagant laugh. "You look puzzled," he added; "you look almost frightened."

"It IS a pity," said Newman, "that I don't understand you. I shall lose some very good jokes."

"I told you, you remember, that we were very strange people," Bellegarde went on. "I give you warning again. We are! My mother is strange, my brother is strange, and I verily believe that I am stranger than either.

You will even find my sister a little strange. Old trees have crooked branches, old houses have queer cracks, old races have odd secrets. Remember that we are eight hundred years old!"

"Very good," said Newman; "that's the sort of thing I came to Europe for. You come into my programme."

"Touchez-la, then," said Bellegarde, putting out his hand. "It's a bargain: I accept you; I espouse your cause. It's because I like you, in a great measure; but that is not the only reason!" And he stood holding Newman's hand and looking at him askance.

"What is the other one?"

"I am in the Opposition. I dislike some one else."

"Your brother?" asked Newman, in his unmodulated voice.

Bellegarde laid his fingers upon his lips with a whispered HUSH! "Old races have strange secrets!" he said. "Put yourself into motion, come and see my sister, and be assured of my sympathy!" And on this he took his leave.

Newman dropped into a chair before his fire, and sat a long time staring into the blaze.

CHAPTER IX

He went to see Madame de Cintre the next day, and was informed by the servant that she was at home. He passed as usual up the large, cold staircase and through a spacious vestibule above, where the walls seemed all composed of small door panels, touched with long-faded gilding; whence he was ushered into the sitting-room in which he had already been received. It was empty, and the servant told him that Madame la Comtesse would presently appear. He had time, while he waited, to wonder whether Bellegarde had seen his sister since the evening before, and whether in this case he had spoken to her of their talk. In this case Madame de Cintre's receiving him was an encouragement. He felt a certain trepidation as he reflected that she might come in with the knowledge of his supreme admiration and of the project he had built upon it in her eyes; but the feeling was not disagreeable. Her face could wear no look that would make it less beautiful, and he was sure beforehand that however she might take the proposal he had in reserve, she would not take it in scorn or in irony. He had a feeling that if she could only read the bottom of his heart and measure the extent of his good will toward her, she would be entirely kind.

She came in at last, after so long an interval that he wondered whether she had been hesitating. She smiled with her usual frankness, and held out her hand; she looked at him straight with her soft and luminous eyes, and said, without a tremor in her voice, that she was glad to see him and that she hoped he was well. He found in her what he had found before—that faint perfume of a personal shyness worn away by contact with the world, but the more perceptible the more closely you approached her. This lingering diffidence seemed to give a peculiar value to what was definite and assured in her manner; it made it seem like an accomplishment, a beautiful talent, something that one might compare to an exquisite touch in a pianist. It was, in fact, Madame de Cintre's "authority," as they say of artists, that especially impressed and fascinated Newman; he always came back to the feeling that when he should complete himself by taking a wife, that was the way he should like his wife to interpret him to the world. The only trouble, indeed, was that when the instrument was so perfect it seemed to interpose too much between you and the genius that used it. Madame de Cintre gave Newman the sense of an elaborate education, of her having passed through mysterious ceremonies and processes of culture in her youth, of her having been fashioned and made flexible to certain exalted social needs. All this, as I have affirmed, made her seem rare and precious—a very expensive article, as he would have said, and one which a man with an ambition to have everything about him of the best would find it highly agreeable to possess. But looking at the matter with an eye to private felicity, Newman wondered where, in so exquisite a compound, nature and art showed their dividing line. Where did the special intention separate from the habit of good manners? Where did urbanity end and sincerity begin? Newman asked himself these questions even while he stood ready to accept the admired object in all its complexity; he felt that he could do so in profound security, and examine its mechanism afterwards, at leisure.

"I am very glad to find you alone," he said. "You know I have never had such good luck before."

"But you have seemed before very well contented with your luck," said Madame de Cintre. "You have sat and watched my visitors with an air of quiet amusement. What have you thought of them?"

"Oh, I have thought the ladies were very elegant and very graceful, and wonderfully quick at repartee. But what I have chiefly thought has been that they only helped me to admire you." This was not gallantry on Newman's part—an art in which he was quite unversed. It was simply the instinct of the practical man, who had made up his mind what he wanted, and was now beginning to take active steps to obtain it.

Madame de Cintre started slightly, and raised her eyebrows; she had evidently not expected so fervid a compliment. "Oh, in that case," she said with a laugh, "your finding me alone is not good luck for me. I hope some one will come in quickly."

"I hope not," said Newman. "I have something particular to say to you. Have you seen your brother?"

"Yes, I saw him an hour ago."

"Did he tell you that he had seen me last night?"

"He said so."

"And did he tell you what we had talked about?"

Madame de Cintre hesitated a moment. As Newman asked these questions she had grown a little pale, as if she regarded what was coming as necessary, but not as agreeable. "Did you give him a message to me?" she asked.

"It was not exactly a message—I asked him to render me a service."

"The service was to sing your praises, was it not?" And she accompanied this question with a little smile, as if to make it easier to herself.

"Yes, that is what it really amounts to," said Newman. "Did he sing my praises?"

"He spoke very well of you. But when I know that it was by your special request, of course I must take his eulogy with a grain of salt."

"Oh, that makes no difference," said Newman. "Your brother would not have spoken well of me unless he believed what he was saying. He is too honest for that."

"Are you very deep?" said Madame de Cintre. "Are you trying to please me by praising my brother? I confess it is a good way."

"For me, any way that succeeds will be good. I will praise your brother all day, if that will help me. He is a noble little fellow. He has made me feel, in promising to do what he can to help me, that I can depend upon him."

"Don't make too much of that," said Madame de Cintre. "He can help you very little."

"Of course I must work my way myself. I know that very well; I only want a chance to. In consenting to see me, after what he told you, you almost seem to be giving me a chance."

"I am seeing you," said Madame de Cintre, slowly and gravely, "because I promised my brother I would."

"Blessings on your brother's head!" cried Newman. "What I told him last evening was this: that I admired you more than any woman I had ever seen, and that I should like immensely to make you my wife." He uttered these words with great directness and firmness, and without any sense of confusion. He was full of his idea, he had completely mastered it, and he seemed to look down on Madame de Cintre, with all her gathered elegance, from the height of his bracing good conscience. It is probable that this particular tone and manner were the very best he could have hit upon. Yet the light, just visibly forced smile with which his companion had listened to him died away, and she sat looking at him with her lips parted and her face as solemn as a tragic mask. There was evidently something very painful to her in the scene to which he was subjecting her, and yet her impatience of it found no angry voice. Newman wondered whether he was hurting her; he could not imagine why the liberal devotion he meant to express should be disagreeable. He got up and stood before her, leaning one hand on the chimney-piece. "I know I have seen you very little to say this," he said, "so little that it may make what I say seem disrespectful. That is my misfortune! I could have said it the first time I saw you. Really, I had seen you before; I had seen you in imagination; you seemed almost an old friend. So what I say is not mere gallantry and compliments and nonsense—I can't talk that way, I don't know how, and I wouldn't, to you, if I could. It's as serious as such words can be. I feel as if I knew you and knew what a beautiful, admirable woman you are. I shall know better, perhaps, some day, but I have a general notion now. You are just the woman I have been looking for, except that you are far more perfect. I won't make any protestations and vows, but you can trust me. It is very soon, I know, to say all this; it is almost offensive. But why not gain time if one can? And if you want time to reflect—of course you do—the sooner you begin, the better for me. I don't know what you think of me; but there is no great mystery about me; you see what I am. Your brother told me that my antecedents and occupations were against me; that your family stands, somehow, on a higher level than I do. That is an idea which of course I don't understand and don't accept. But you don't care anything about that. I can assure you that I am a very solid fellow, and that if I give my mind to it I can arrange things so that in a very few years I shall not need to waste time in explaining who I am and what I am. You will decide for yourself whether you like me or not. What there is you see before you. I honestly believe I have no hidden vices or nasty tricks. I am kind, kind, kind! Everything that a man can give a woman I will give you. I have a large fortune, a very large fortune; some day, if you will allow me, I will go into details. If you want brilliancy, everything in the way of brilliancy that money can give you, you shall have. And as regards anything you may give up, don't take for granted too much that its place cannot be filled. Leave that to me; I'll take care of you; I shall know what you need. Energy and ingenuity can arrange everything. I'm a strong man! There, I have said what I had on my heart! It was better to get it off. I am very sorry if it's disagreeable to you; but think how much better it is that things should be clear. Don't answer me now, if you don't wish it. Think about it, think about it as slowly as you please. Of course I haven't said, I can't say, half I mean, especially about my admiration for you. But take a favorable view of me; it will only be just."

During this speech, the longest that Newman had ever made, Madame de Cintre kept her gaze fixed upon him, and it expanded at the last into a sort of fascinated stare. When he ceased speaking she lowered her eyes and sat for some moments looking down and straight before her. Then she slowly rose to her feet, and a pair of exceptionally keen eyes would have perceived that she was trembling a little in the movement. She still looked extremely serious. "I am very much obliged to you for your offer," she said. "It seems very strange, but I am glad you spoke without waiting any longer. It is better the subject should be dismissed. I appreciate all you say; you do me great honor. But I have decided not to marry."

"Oh, don't say that!" cried Newman, in a tone absolutely naif from its pleading and caressing cadence. She had turned away, and it made her stop a moment with her back to him. "Think better of that. You are too young, too beautiful, too much made to be happy and to make others happy. If you are afraid of losing your freedom, I can assure you that this freedom here, this life you now lead, is a dreary bondage to what I will offer you. You shall do things that I don't think you have ever thought of. I will take you anywhere in the wide world that you propose. Are you unhappy? You give me a feeling that you are unhappy. You have no right to be, or to be made so. Let me come in and put an end to it."

Madame de Cintre stood there a moment longer, looking away from him. If she was touched by the way he spoke, the thing was conceivable. His voice, always very mild and interrogative, gradually became as soft and as tenderly argumentative as if he had been talking to a much-loved child. He stood watching her, and she presently turned round again, but this time she did not look at him, and she spoke in a quietness in which there was a visible trace of effort.

"There are a great many reasons why I should not marry," she said, "more than I can explain to you. As for my happiness, I am very happy. Your offer seems strange to me, for more reasons also than I can say. Of course you have a perfect right to make it. But I cannot accept it—it is impossible. Please never speak of this matter again. If you cannot promise me this, I must ask you not to come back."

"Why is it impossible?" Newman demanded. "You may think it is, at first, without its really being so. I didn't expect you to be pleased at first, but I do believe that if you will think of it a good while, you may be satisfied."

"I don't know you," said Madame de Cintre. "Think how little I know you."

"Very little, of course, and therefore I don't ask for your ultimatum on the spot. I only ask you not to say no, and to let me hope. I will wait as long as you desire. Meanwhile you can see more of me and know me better, look at me as a possible husband—as a candidate—and make up your mind."

Something was going on, rapidly, in Madame de Cintre's thoughts; she was weighing a question there, beneath Newman's eyes, weighing it and deciding it. "From the moment I don't very respectfully beg you to leave the house and never return," she said, "I listen to you, I seem to give you hope. I HAVE listened to you—against my judgment. It is because you are eloquent. If I had been told this morning that I should consent to consider you as a possible husband, I should have thought my informant a little crazy. I AM listening to you, you see!" And she threw her hands out for a moment and let them drop with a gesture in which there was just the slightest expression of appealing weakness.

"Well, as far as saying goes, I have said everything," said Newman. "I believe in you, without restriction, and I think all the good of you that it is possible to think of a human creature. I firmly believe that in marrying me you will be SAFE. As I said just now," he went on with a smile, "I have no bad ways. I can DO so much for you. And if you are afraid that I am not what you have been accustomed to, not refined and delicate and punctilious, you may easily carry that too far. I AM delicate! You shall see!"

Madame de Cintre walked some distance away, and paused before a great plant, an azalea, which was flourishing in a porcelain tub before her window. She plucked off one of the flowers and, twisting it in her fingers, retraced her steps. Then she sat down in silence, and her attitude seemed to be a consent that Newman should say more.

"Why should you say it is impossible you should marry?" he continued. "The only thing that could make it really impossible would be your being already married. Is it because you have been unhappy in marriage? That is all the more reason! Is it because your family exert a pressure upon you, interfere with you, annoy you? That is still another reason; you ought to be perfectly free, and marriage will make you so. I don't say anything against your family—understand that!" added Newman, with an eagerness which might have made a perspicacious observer smile. "Whatever way you feel toward them is the right way, and anything that you should wish me to do to make myself agreeable to them I will do as well as I know how. Depend upon that!"

Madame de Cintre rose again and came toward the fireplace, near which Newman was standing. The expression of pain and embarrassment had passed out of her face, and it was illuminated with something which, this time at least, Newman need not have been perplexed whether to attribute to habit or to intention, to art or to nature. She had the air of a woman who has stepped across the frontier of friendship and, looking around her, finds the region vast. A certain checked and controlled exaltation seemed mingled with the usual level radiance of her glance. "I will not refuse to see you again," she said, "because much of what you have said has given me pleasure. But I will see you only on this condition: that you say nothing more in the same way for a long time."

"For how long?"

"For six months. It must be a solemn promise."

"Very well, I promise."

"Good-by, then," she said, and extended her hand.

He held it a moment, as if he were going to say something more. But he only looked at her; then he took his departure.

That evening, on the Boulevard, he met Valentin de Bellegarde. After they had exchanged greetings, Newman told him that he had seen Madame de Cintre a few hours before.

"I know it," said Bellegarde. "I dined in the Rue de l'Universite." And then, for some moments, both men were silent. Newman wished to ask Bellegarde what visible impression his visit had made and the Count Valentin had a question of his own. Bellegarde spoke first.

"It's none of my business, but what the deuce did you say to my sister?"

"I am willing to tell you," said Newman, "that I made her an offer of marriage."

"Already!" And the young man gave a whistle. "'Time is money!' Is that what you say in America? And Madame de Cintre?" he added, with an interrogative inflection.

"She did not accept my offer."

"She couldn't, you know, in that way."

"But I'm to see her again," said Newman.

"Oh, the strangeness of woman!" exclaimed Bellegarde. Then he stopped, and held Newman off at arms'-length. "I look at you with respect!" he exclaimed. "You have achieved what we call a personal success! Immediately, now, I must present you to my brother."

"Whenever you please!" said Newman.

CHAPTER X

Newman continued to see his friends the Tristrams with a good deal of frequency, though if you had listened to Mrs. Tristram's account of the matter you would have supposed that they had been cynically repudiated for the sake of grander acquaintance. "We were all very well so long as we had no rivals—we were better than nothing. But now that you have become the fashion, and have your pick every day of three invitations to dinner, we are tossed into the corner. I am sure it is very good of you to come and see us once a month; I wonder you don't send us your cards in an envelope. When you do, pray have them with black edges; it will be for the death of my last illusion." It was in this incisive strain that Mrs. Tristram moralized over Newman's so-called neglect, which was in reality a most exemplary constancy. Of course she was joking, but there was always something ironical in her jokes, as there was always something jocular in her gravity.

"I know no better proof that I have treated you very well," Newman had said, "than the fact that you make so free with my character. Familiarity breeds contempt; I have made myself too cheap. If I had a little proper pride I would stay away a while, and when you asked me to dinner say I was going to the Princess Borealska's. But I have not any pride where my pleasure is concerned, and to keep you in the humor to see me—if you must see me only to call me bad names—I will agree to anything you choose; I will admit that I am the biggest snob in Paris." Newman, in fact, had declined an invitation personally given by the Princess Borealska, an inquiring Polish lady to whom he had been presented, on the ground that on that particular day he always dined at Mrs. Tristram's; and it was only a tenderly perverse theory of his hostess of the Avenue d'Iena that he was faithless to his early friendships. She needed the theory to explain a certain moral irritation by which she was often visited; though, if this explanation was unsound, a deeper analyst than I must give the right one. Having launched our hero upon the current which was bearing him so rapidly along, she appeared but half-pleased at its swiftness. She had succeeded too well; she had played her game too cleverly and she wished to mix up the cards. Newman had told her, in due season, that her friend was "satisfactory." The epithet was not romantic, but Mrs. Tristram had no difficulty in perceiving that, in essentials, the feeling which lay beneath it was. Indeed, the mild, expansive brevity with which it was uttered, and a certain look, at once appealing and inscrutable, that issued from Newman's half-closed eyes as he leaned his head against the back of his chair, seemed to her the most eloquent attestation of a mature sentiment that she had ever encountered. Newman was, according to the French phrase, only abounding in her own sense, but his temperate raptures exerted a singular effect upon the ardor which she herself had so freely manifested a few months before. She now seemed inclined to take a purely critical view of Madame de Cintre, and wished to have it understood that she did not in the least answer for her being a compendium of all the virtues. "No woman was ever so good as that woman seems," she said. "Remember what Shakespeare calls Desdemona; 'a supersubtle Venetian.' Madame de Cintre is a supersubtle Parisian. She is a charming woman, and she has five hundred merits; but you had better keep that in mind." Was Mrs. Tristram simply finding out that she was jealous of her dear friend on the other side of the Seine, and that in undertaking to provide Newman with an ideal wife she had counted too much on her own disinterestedness? We may be permitted to doubt it. The inconsistent little lady of the Avenue d'Iena had an insuperable need of changing her place, intellectually. She had a lively imagination, and she was capable, at certain times, of imagining the direct reverse of her most cherished beliefs, with a vividness more intense than that of conviction. She got tired of thinking aright; but there was no serious harm in it, as she got equally tired of thinking wrong. In the midst of her mysterious perversities she had admirable flashes of justice. One of these occurred when Newman related to her that he had made a formal proposal to Madame de Cintre. He repeated in a few words what he had said, and in a great many what she had answered. Mrs. Tristram listened with extreme interest.

"But after all," said Newman, "there is nothing to congratulate me upon. It is not a triumph."

"I beg your pardon," said Mrs. Tristram; "it is a great triumph. It is a great triumph that she did not silence you at the first word, and request you never to speak to her again."

"I don't see that," observed Newman.

"Of course you don't; Heaven forbid you should! When I told you to go on your own way and do what came into your head, I had no idea you would go over the ground so fast. I never dreamed you would offer yourself after five or six morning-calls. As yet, what had you done to make her like you? You had simply sat—not very straight—and stared at her. But she does like you."

"That remains to be seen."

"No, that is proved. What will come of it remains to be seen. That you should propose to marry her, without more ado, could never have come into her head. You can form very little idea of what passed through her mind as you spoke; if she ever really marries you, the affair will be characterized by the usual justice of all human beings towards women. You will think you take generous views of her; but you will never begin to know through what a strange sea of feeling she passed before she accepted you. As she stood there in front of you the other day, she plunged into it. She said 'Why not?' to something which, a few hours earlier, had been inconceivable. She turned about on a thousand gathered prejudices and traditions as on a pivot, and looked where she had never looked hitherto. When I think of it—when I think of Claire de Cintre and all that she represents, there seems to me something very fine in it. When I recommended you to try your fortune with her I of course thought well of you, and in spite of your sins I think so still. But I confess I don't see quite what you are and what you have done, to make such a woman do this sort of thing for you."

"Oh, there is something very fine in it!" said Newman with a laugh, repeating her words. He took an extreme satisfaction in hearing that there was something fine in it. He had not the least doubt of it himself, but he had already begun to value the world's admiration of Madame de Cintre, as adding to the prospective glory of possession.

It was immediately after this conversation that Valentin de Bellegarde came to conduct his friend to the Rue de l'Universite to present him to the other members of his family. "You are already introduced," he said, "and you have begun to be talked about. My sister has mentioned your successive visits to my mother, and it was an accident that my mother was present at none of them. I have spoken of you as an American of immense wealth, and the best fellow in the world, who is looking for something very superior in the way of a wife."

"Do you suppose," asked Newman, "that Madame de Cintre has related to your mother the last conversation I had with her?"

"I am very certain that she has not; she will keep her own counsel. Meanwhile you must make your way with the rest of the family. Thus much is known about you: you have made a great fortune in trade, you are a little eccentric, and you frankly admire our dear Claire. My sister-in-law, whom you remember seeing in Madame de Cintre's sitting-room, took, it appears, a fancy to you; she has described you as having beaucoup de cachet. My mother, therefore, is curious to see you."

"She expects to laugh at me, eh?" said Newman.

"She never laughs. If she does not like you, don't hope to purchase favor by being amusing. Take warning by me!"

This conversation took place in the evening, and half an hour later Valentin ushered his companion into an apartment of the house of the Rue de l'Universite into which he had not yet penetrated, the salon of the dowager Marquise de Bellegarde. It was a vast, high room, with elaborate and ponderous mouldings, painted a whitish gray, along the upper portion of the walls and the ceiling; with a great deal of faded and carefully repaired tapestry in the doorways and chair-backs; a Turkey carpet in light colors, still soft and deep, in spite of great antiquity, on the floor, and portraits of each of Madame de Bellegarde's children, at the age of ten, suspended against an old screen of red silk. The room was illumined, exactly enough for conversation, by half a dozen candles, placed in odd corners, at a great distance apart. In a deep armchair, near the fire, sat an old lady in black; at the other end of the room another person was seated at the piano, playing a very expressive waltz. In this latter person Newman recognized the young Marquise de Bellegarde.

CHAPTER X

Valentin presented his friend, and Newman walked up to the old lady by the fire and shook hands with her. He received a rapid impression of a white, delicate, aged face, with a high forehead, a small mouth, and a pair of cold blue eyes which had kept much of the freshness of youth. Madame de Bellegarde looked hard at him, and returned his hand-shake with a sort of British positiveness which reminded him that she was the daughter of the Earl of St. Dunstan's. Her daughter-in-law stopped playing and gave him an agreeable smile. Newman sat down and looked about him, while Valentin went and kissed the hand of the young marquise.

"I ought to have seen you before," said Madame de Bellegarde. "You have paid several visits to my daughter."

"Oh, yes," said Newman, smiling; "Madame de Cintre and I are old friends by this time."

"You have gone fast," said Madame de Bellegarde.

"Not so fast as I should like," said Newman, bravely.

"Oh, you are very ambitious," answered the old lady.

"Yes, I confess I am," said Newman, smiling.

Madame de Bellegarde looked at him with her cold fine eyes, and he returned her gaze, reflecting that she was a possible adversary and trying to take her measure. Their eyes remained in contact for some moments. Then Madame de Bellegarde looked away, and without smiling, "I am very ambitious, too," she said.

Newman felt that taking her measure was not easy; she was a formidable, inscrutable little woman. She resembled her daughter, and yet she was utterly unlike her. The coloring in Madame de Cintre was the same, and the high delicacy of her brow and nose was hereditary. But her face was a larger and freer copy, and her mouth in especial a happy divergence from that conservative orifice, a little pair of lips at once plump and pinched, that looked, when closed, as if they could not open wider than to swallow a gooseberry or to emit an "Oh, dear, no!" which probably had been thought to give the finishing touch to the aristocratic prettiness of the Lady Emmeline Atheling as represented, forty years before, in several Books of Beauty. Madame de Cintre's face had, to Newman's eye, a range of expression as delightfully vast as the wind-streaked, cloud-flecked distance on a Western prairie. But her mother's white, intense, respectable countenance, with its formal gaze, and its circumscribed smile, suggested a document signed and sealed; a thing of parchment, ink, and ruled lines. "She is a woman of conventions and proprieties," he said to himself as he looked at her; "her world is the world of things immutably decreed. But how she is at home in it, and what a paradise she finds it. She walks about in it as if it were a blooming park, a Garden of Eden; and when she sees 'This is genteel,' or 'This is improper,' written on a mile-stone she stops ecstatically, as if she were listening to a nightingale or smelling a rose." Madame de Bellegarde wore a little black velvet hood tied under her chin, and she was wrapped in an old black cashmere shawl.

"You are an American?" she said presently. "I have seen several Americans."

"There are several in Paris," said Newman jocosely.

"Oh, really?" said Madame de Bellegarde. "It was in England I saw these, or somewhere else; not in Paris. I think it must have been in the Pyrenees, many years ago. I am told your ladies are very pretty. One of these ladies was very pretty! such a wonderful complexion! She presented me a note of introduction from some one—I forgot whom—and she sent with it a note of her own. I kept her letter a long time afterwards, it was so strangely expressed. I used to know some of the phrases by heart. But I have forgotten them now, it is so many years ago. Since then I have seen no more Americans. I think my daughter-in-law has; she is a great gad-about, she sees every one."

At this the younger lady came rustling forward, pinching in a very slender waist, and casting idly preoccupied glances over the front of her dress, which was apparently designed for a ball. She was, in a singular way, at once ugly and pretty; she had protuberant eyes, and lips strangely red. She reminded Newman of his friend, Mademoiselle Nioche; this was what that much-obstructed young lady would have liked to be. Valentin de Bellegarde walked behind her at a distance, hopping about to keep off the far-spreading train of her dress.

"You ought to show more of your shoulders behind," he said very gravely. "You might as well wear a standing ruff as such a dress as that."

The young woman turned her back to the mirror over the chimney-piece, and glanced behind her, to verify Valentin's assertion. The mirror descended low, and yet it reflected nothing but a large unclad flesh surface. The young marquise put her hands behind her and gave a downward pull to the waist of her dress. "Like that, you mean?" she asked.

"That is a little better," said Bellegarde in the same tone, "but it leaves a good deal to be desired."

"Oh, I never go to extremes," said his sister-in-law. And then, turning to Madame de Bellegarde, "What were you calling me just now, madame?"

"I called you a gad-about," said the old lady. "But I might call you something else, too."

"A gad-about? What an ugly word! What does it mean?"

"A very beautiful person," Newman ventured to say, seeing that it was in French.

"That is a pretty compliment but a bad translation," said the young marquise. And then, looking at him a moment, "Do you dance?"

"Not a step."

"You are very wrong," she said, simply. And with another look at her back in the mirror she turned away.

"Do you like Paris?" asked the old lady, who was apparently wondering what was the proper way to talk to an American.

"Yes, rather," said Newman. And then he added with a friendly intonation, "Don't you?"

"I can't say I know it. I know my house—I know my friends—I don't know Paris."

"Oh, you lose a great deal," said Newman, sympathetically.

Madame de Bellegarde stared; it was presumably the first time she had been condoled with on her losses.

"I am content with what I have," she said with dignity.

Newman's eyes, at this moment, were wandering round the room, which struck him as rather sad and shabby; passing from the high casements, with their small, thickly-framed panes, to the sallow tints of two or three portraits in pastel, of the last century, which hung between them. He ought, obviously, to have answered that the contentment of his hostess was quite natural—she had a great deal; but the idea did not occur to him during the pause of some moments which followed.

"Well, my dear mother," said Valentin, coming and leaning against the chimney-piece, "what do you think of my dear friend Newman? Is he not the excellent fellow I told you?"

"My acquaintance with Mr. Newman has not gone very far," said Madame de Bellegarde. "I can as yet only appreciate his great politeness."

"My mother is a great judge of these matters," said Valentin to Newman. "If you have satisfied her, it is a triumph."

"I hope I shall satisfy you, some day," said Newman, looking at the old lady. "I have done nothing yet."

"You must not listen to my son; he will bring you into trouble. He is a sad scatterbrain."

"Oh, I like him—I like him," said Newman, genially.

"He amuses you, eh?"

"Yes, perfectly."

"Do you hear that, Valentin?" said Madame de Bellegarde. "You amuse Mr. Newman."

"Perhaps we shall all come to that!" Valentin exclaimed.

"You must see my other son," said Madame de Bellegarde. "He is much better than this one. But he will not amuse you."

"I don't know—I don't know!" murmured Valentin, reflectively. "But we shall very soon see. Here comes Monsieur mon frere."

The door had just opened to give ingress to a gentleman who stepped forward and whose face Newman remembered. He had been the author of our hero's discomfiture the first time he tried to present himself to Madame de Cintre. Valentin de Bellegarde went to meet his brother, looked at him a moment, and then, taking him by the arm, led him up to Newman.

"This is my excellent friend Mr. Newman," he said very blandly. "You must know him."

"I am delighted to know Mr. Newman," said the marquis with a low bow, but without offering his hand.

"He is the old woman at second-hand," Newman said to himself, as he returned M. de Bellegarde's greeting. And this was the starting-point of a speculative theory, in his mind, that the late marquis had been a very amiable foreigner, with an inclination to take life easily and a sense that it was difficult for the husband of the stilted little lady by the fire to do so. But if he had taken little comfort in his wife he had taken much in his two younger children, who were after his own heart, while Madame de Bellegarde had paired with her eldest-born.

"My brother has spoken to me of you," said M. de Bellegarde; "and as you are also acquainted with my sister, it was time we should meet." He turned to his mother and gallantly bent over her hand, touching it with his lips, and then he assumed an attitude before the chimney-piece. With his long, lean face, his high-bridged nose and his small, opaque eye he looked much like an Englishman. His whiskers were fair and glossy, and he had a large dimple, of unmistakably British origin, in the middle of his handsome chin. He was "distinguished" to the tips of his polished nails, and there was not a movement of his fine, perpendicular person that was not noble and majestic. Newman had never yet been confronted with such an incarnation of the art of taking one's self seriously; he felt a sort of impulse to step backward, as you do to get a view of a great facade.

"Urbain," said young Madame de Bellegarde, who had apparently been waiting for her husband to take her to her ball, "I call your attention to the fact that I am dressed."

"That is a good idea," murmured Valentin.

"I am at your orders, my dear friend," said M. de Bellegarde. "Only, you must allow me first the pleasure of a little conversation with Mr. Newman."

"Oh, if you are going to a party, don't let me keep you," objected Newman. "I am very sure we shall meet again. Indeed, if you would like to converse with me I will gladly name an hour." He was eager to make it known that he would readily answer all questions and satisfy all exactions.

M. de Bellegarde stood in a well-balanced position before the fire, caressing one of his fair whiskers with one of his white hands, and looking at Newman, half askance, with eyes from which a particular ray of observation made its way through a general meaningless smile. "It is very kind of you to make such an offer," he said. "If I am not mistaken, your occupations are such as to make your time precious. You are in—a—as we say, dans les affaires."

"In business, you mean? Oh no, I have thrown business overboard for the present. I am 'loafing,' as WE say. My time is quite my own."

"Ah, you are taking a holiday," rejoined M. de Bellegarde. "'Loafing.' Yes, I have heard that expression."

"Mr. Newman is American," said Madame de Bellegarde.

"My brother is a great ethnologist," said Valentin.

"An ethnologist?" said Newman. "Ah, you collect negroes' skulls, and that sort of thing."

The marquis looked hard at his brother, and began to caress his other whisker. Then, turning to Newman, with sustained urbanity, "You are traveling for your pleasure?" he asked.'

"Oh, I am knocking about to pick up one thing and another. Of course I get a good deal of pleasure out of it."

"What especially interests you?" inquired the marquis.

"Well, everything interests me," said Newman. "I am not particular. Manufactures are what I care most about."

"That has been your specialty?"

"I can't say I have any specialty. My specialty has been to make the largest possible fortune in the shortest possible time." Newman made this last remark very deliberately; he wished to open the way, if it were necessary, to an authoritative statement of his means.

M. de Bellegarde laughed agreeably. "I hope you have succeeded," he said.

"Yes, I have made a fortune in a reasonable time. I am not so old, you see."

"Paris is a very good place to spend a fortune. I wish you great enjoyment of yours." And M. de Bellegarde drew forth his gloves and began to put them on.

Newman for a few moments watched him sliding his white hands into the white kid, and as he did so his feelings took a singular turn. M. de Bellegarde's good wishes seemed to descend out of the white expanse of his sublime serenity with the soft, scattered movement of a shower of snow-flakes. Yet Newman was not irritated; he did not feel that he was being patronized; he was conscious of no especial impulse to introduce a discord into so noble a harmony. Only he felt himself suddenly in personal contact with the forces with which his friend Valentin had told him that he would have to contend, and he became sensible of their intensity. He wished to make some answering manifestation, to stretch himself out at his own length, to sound a note at the uttermost end of HIS scale. It must be added that if this impulse was not vicious or malicious, it was by no means void of humorous expectancy. Newman was quite as ready to give play to that loosely-adjusted smile of his, if his hosts should happen to be shocked, as he was far from deliberately planning to shock them.

"Paris is a very good place for idle people," he said, "or it is a very good place if your family has been settled here for a long time, and you have made acquaintances and got your relations round you; or if you have got a good big house like this, and a wife and children and mother and sister, and everything comfortable. I don't like that way of living all in rooms next door to each other. But I am not an idler. I try to be, but I can't manage it; it goes against the grain. My business habits are too deep-seated. Then, I haven't any house to call my own, or anything in the way of a family. My sisters are five thousand miles away, my mother died when I was a youngster, and I haven't any wife; I wish I had! So, you see, I don't exactly know what to do with myself. I am not fond of books, as you are, sir, and I get tired of dining out and going to the opera. I miss my business activity. You see, I began to earn my living when I was almost a baby, and until a few months ago I have never had my hand off the plow. Elegant leisure comes hard."

This speech was followed by a profound silence of some moments, on the part of Newman's entertainers. Valentin stood looking at him fixedly, with his hands in his pockets, and then he slowly, with a half-sidling motion, went out of the door. The marquis continued to draw on his gloves and to smile benignantly.

"You began to earn your living when you were a mere baby?" said the marquise.

"Hardly more—a small boy."

"You say you are not fond of books," said M. de Bellegarde; "but you must do yourself the justice to remember that your studies were interrupted early."

"That is very true; on my tenth birthday I stopped going to school. I thought it was a grand way to keep it. But I picked up some information afterwards," said Newman, reassuringly.

"You have some sisters?" asked old Madame de Bellegarde.

"Yes, two sisters. Splendid women!"

"I hope that for them the hardships of life commenced less early."

"They married very early, if you call that a hardship, as girls do in our Western country. One of them is married to the owner of the largest india-rubber house in the West."

"Ah, you make houses also of india-rubber?" inquired the marquise.

"You can stretch them as your family increases," said young Madame de Bellegarde, who was muffling herself in a long white shawl.

Newman indulged in a burst of hilarity, and explained that the house in which his brother-in-law lived was a large wooden structure, but that he manufactured and sold india-rubber on a colossal scale.

"My children have some little india-rubber shoes which they put on when they go to play in the Tuileries in damp weather," said the young marquise. "I wonder whether your brother-in-law made them."

"Very likely," said Newman; "if he did, you may be very sure they are well made."

"Well, you must not be discouraged," said M. de Bellegarde, with vague urbanity.

"Oh, I don't mean to be. I have a project which gives me plenty to think about, and that is an occupation." And then Newman was silent a moment, hesitating, yet thinking rapidly; he wished to make his point, and yet to do so forced him to speak out in a way that was disagreeable to him. Nevertheless he continued, addressing himself to old Madame de Bellegarde, "I will tell you my project; perhaps you can help me. I want to take a wife."

"It is a very good project, but I am no matchmaker," said the old lady.

Newman looked at her an instant, and then, with perfect sincerity, "I should have thought you were," he declared.

Madame de Bellegarde appeared to think him too sincere. She murmured something sharply in French, and fixed her eyes on her son. At this moment the door of the room was thrown open, and with a rapid step Valentin reappeared.

"I have a message for you," he said to his sister-in-law. "Claire bids me to request you not to start for your ball. She will go with you."

"Claire will go with us!" cried the young marquise. "En voila, du nouveau!"

"She has changed her mind; she decided half an hour ago, and she is sticking the last diamond into her hair," said Valentin.

"What has taken possession of my daughter?" demanded Madame de Bellegarde, sternly. "She has not been into the world these three years. Does she take such a step at half an hour's notice, and without consulting me?"

"She consulted me, dear mother, five minutes since," said Valentin, "and I told her that such a beautiful woman—she is beautiful, you will see—had no right to bury herself alive."

CHAPTER X

"You should have referred Claire to her mother, my brother," said M. de Bellegarde, in French. "This is very strange."

"I refer her to the whole company!" said Valentin. "Here she comes!" And he went to the open door, met Madame de Cintre on the threshold, took her by the hand, and led her into the room. She was dressed in white; but a long blue cloak, which hung almost to her feet, was fastened across her shoulders by a silver clasp. She had tossed it back, however, and her long white arms were uncovered. In her dense, fair hair there glittered a dozen diamonds. She looked serious and, Newman thought, rather pale; but she glanced round her, and, when she saw him, smiled and put out her hand. He thought her tremendously handsome. He had a chance to look at her full in the face, for she stood a moment in the centre of the room, hesitating, apparently, what she should do, without meeting his eyes. Then she went up to her mother, who sat in her deep chair by the fire, looking at Madame de Cintre almost fiercely. With her back turned to the others, Madame de Cintre held her cloak apart to show her dress.

"What do you think of me?" she asked.

"I think you are audacious," said the marquise. "It was but three days ago, when I asked you, as a particular favor to myself, to go to the Duchess de Lusignan's, that you told me you were going nowhere and that one must be consistent. Is this your consistency? Why should you distinguish Madame Robineau? Who is it you wish to please to-night?"

"I wish to please myself, dear mother," said Madame de Cintre. And she bent over and kissed the old lady.

"I don't like surprises, my sister," said Urbain de Bellegarde; "especially when one is on the point of entering a drawing-room."

Newman at this juncture felt inspired to speak. "Oh, if you are going into a room with Madame de Cintre, you needn't be afraid of being noticed yourself!"

M. de Bellegarde turned to his sister with a smile too intense to be easy. "I hope you appreciate a compliment that is paid you at your brother's expense," he said. "Come, come, madame." And offering Madame de Cintre his arm he led her rapidly out of the room. Valentin rendered the same service to young Madame de Bellegarde, who had apparently been reflecting on the fact that the ball dress of her sister-in-law was much less brilliant than her own, and yet had failed to derive absolute comfort from the reflection. With a farewell smile she sought the complement of her consolation in the eyes of the American visitor, and perceiving in them a certain mysterious brilliancy, it is not improbable that she may have flattered herself she had found it.

Newman, left alone with old Madame de Bellegarde, stood before her a few moments in silence. "Your daughter is very beautiful," he said at last.

"She is very strange," said Madame de Bellegarde.

"I am glad to hear it," Newman rejoined, smiling. "It makes me hope."

"Hope what?"

"That she will consent, some day, to marry me."

The old lady slowly rose to her feet. "That really is your project, then?"

"Yes; will you favor it?"

"Favor it?" Madame de Bellegarde looked at him a moment and then shook her head. "No!" she said, softly.

"Will you suffer it, then? Will you let it pass?"

"You don't know what you ask. I am a very proud and meddlesome old woman."

"Well, I am very rich," said Newman.

Madame de Bellegarde fixed her eyes on the floor, and Newman thought it probable she was weighing the reasons in favor of resenting the brutality of this remark. But at last, looking up, she said simply, "How rich?"

Newman expressed his income in a round number which had the magnificent sound that large aggregations of dollars put on when they are translated into francs. He added a few remarks of a financial character, which completed a sufficiently striking presentment of his resources.

Madame de Bellegarde listened in silence. "You are very frank," she said finally. "I will be the same. I would rather favor you, on the whole, than suffer you. It will be easier."

"I am thankful for any terms," said Newman. "But, for the present, you have suffered me long enough. Good night!" And he took his leave.

CHAPTER XI

Newman, on his return to Paris, had not resumed the study of French conversation with M. Nioche; he found that he had too many other uses for his time. M. Nioche, however, came to see him very promptly, having learned his whereabouts by a mysterious process to which his patron never obtained the key. The shrunken little capitalist repeated his visit more than once. He seemed oppressed by a humiliating sense of having been overpaid, and wished apparently to redeem his debt by the offer of grammatical and statistical information in small installments. He wore the same decently melancholy aspect as a few months before; a few months more or less of brushing could make little difference in the antique lustre of his coat and hat. But the poor old man's spirit was a trifle more threadbare; it seemed to have received some hard rubs during the summer. Newman inquired with interest about Mademoiselle Noemie; and M. Nioche, at first, for answer, simply looked at him in lachrymose silence.

"Don't ask me, sir," he said at last. "I sit and watch her, but I can do nothing."

"Do you mean that she misconducts herself?"

"I don't know, I am sure. I can't follow her. I don't understand her. She has something in her head; I don't know what she is trying to do. She is too deep for me."

"Does she continue to go to the Louvre? Has she made any of those copies for me?"

"She goes to the Louvre, but I see nothing of the copies. She has something on her easel; I suppose it is one of the pictures you ordered. Such a magnificent order ought to give her fairy-fingers. But she is not in earnest. I can't say anything to her; I am afraid of her. One evening, last summer, when I took her to walk in the Champs Elysees, she said some things to me that frightened me."

"What were they?"

"Excuse an unhappy father from telling you," said M. Nioche, unfolding his calico pocket-handkerchief.

Newman promised himself to pay Mademoiselle Noemie another visit at the Louvre. He was curious about the progress of his copies, but it must be added that he was still more curious about the progress of the young lady herself. He went one afternoon to the great museum, and wandered through several of the rooms in fruitless quest of her. He was bending his steps to the long hall of the Italian masters, when suddenly he found himself face to face with Valentin de Bellegarde. The young Frenchman greeted him with ardor, and assured him that he was a godsend. He himself was in the worst of humors and he wanted some one to contradict.

"In a bad humor among all these beautiful things?" said Newman. "I thought you were so fond of pictures, especially the old black ones. There are two or three here that ought to keep you in spirits."

"Oh, to-day," answered Valentin, "I am not in a mood for pictures, and the more beautiful they are the less I like them. Their great staring eyes and fixed positions irritate me. I feel as if I were at some big, dull party, in a room full of people I shouldn't wish to speak to. What should I care for their beauty? It's a bore, and, worse still, it's a reproach. I have a great many ennuis; I feel vicious."

"If the Louvre has so little comfort for you, why in the world did you come here?" Newman asked.

"That is one of my ennuis. I came to meet my cousin—a dreadful English cousin, a member of my mother's family—who is in Paris for a week for her husband, and who wishes me to point out the 'principal beauties.' Imagine a woman who wears a green crape bonnet in December and has straps sticking out of the ankles of her interminable boots! My mother begged I would do something to oblige them. I have undertaken to play valet de place this afternoon. They were to have met me here at two o'clock, and I have been waiting for them twenty minutes. Why doesn't she arrive? She has at least a pair of feet to carry her. I don't know whether to be furious at their playing me false, or delighted to have escaped them."

"I think in your place I would be furious," said Newman, "because they may arrive yet, and then your fury will still be of use to you. Whereas if you were delighted and they were afterwards to turn up, you might not know what to do with your delight."

"You give me excellent advice, and I already feel better. I will be furious; I will let them go to the deuce and I myself will go with you—unless by chance you too have a rendezvous."

"It is not exactly a rendezvous," said Newman. "But I have in fact come to see a person, not a picture."

"A woman, presumably?"

"A young lady."

"Well," said Valentin, "I hope for you with all my heart that she is not clothed in green tulle and that her feet are not too much out of focus."

"I don't know much about her feet, but she has very pretty hands."

Valentin gave a sigh. "And on that assurance I must part with you?"

"I am not certain of finding my young lady," said Newman, "and I am not quite prepared to lose your company on the chance. It does not strike me as particularly desirable to introduce you to her, and yet I should rather like to have your opinion of her."

"Is she pretty?"

"I guess you will think so."

Bellegarde passed his arm into that of his companion. "Conduct me to her on the instant! I should be ashamed to make a pretty woman wait for my verdict."

Newman suffered himself to be gently propelled in the direction in which he had been walking, but his step was not rapid. He was turning something over in his mind. The two men passed into the long gallery of the Italian masters, and Newman, after having scanned for a moment its brilliant vista, turned aside into the smaller apartment devoted to the same school, on the left. It contained very few persons, but at the farther end of it sat Mademoiselle Nioche, before her easel. She was not at work; her palette and brushes had been laid down beside her, her hands were folded in her lap, and she was leaning back in her chair and looking intently at two ladies on the other side of the hall, who, with their backs turned to her, had stopped before one of the pictures. These ladies were apparently persons of high fashion; they were dressed with great splendor, and their long silken trains and furbelows were spread over the polished floor. It was at their dresses Mademoiselle Noemie was looking, though what she was thinking of I am unable to say. I hazard the supposition that she was saying to herself that to be able to drag such a train over a polished floor was a felicity worth any price. Her reflections, at any rate, were disturbed by the advent of Newman and his companion. She glanced at them quickly, and then, coloring a little, rose and stood before her easel.

"I came here on purpose to see you," said Newman in his bad French, offering to shake hands. And then, like a good American, he introduced Valentin formally: "Allow me to make you acquainted with the Comte Valentin de Bellegarde."

Valentin made a bow which must have seemed to Mademoiselle Noemie quite in harmony with the impressiveness of his title, but the graceful brevity of her own response made no concession to underbred surprise. She turned to Newman, putting up her hands to her hair and smoothing its delicately-felt roughness. Then, rapidly, she turned the canvas that was on her easel over upon its face. "You have not forgotten me?" she asked.

"I shall never forget you," said Newman. "You may be sure of that."

"Oh," said the young girl, "there are a great many different ways of remembering a person." And she looked straight at Valentin de Bellegarde, who was looking at her as a gentleman may when a "verdict" is expected of him.

"Have you painted anything for me?" said Newman. "Have you been industrious?"

"No, I have done nothing." And taking up her palette, she began to mix her colors at hazard.

"But your father tells me you have come here constantly."

"I have nowhere else to go! Here, all summer, it was cool, at least."

"Being here, then," said Newman, "you might have tried something."

"I told you before," she answered, softly, "that I don't know how to paint."

"But you have something charming on your easel, now," said Valentin, "if you would only let me see it."

She spread out her two hands, with the fingers expanded, over the back of the canvas—those hands which Newman had called pretty, and which, in spite of several paint-stains, Valentin could now admire. "My painting is not charming," she said.

"It is the only thing about you that is not, then, mademoiselle," quoth Valentin, gallantly.

She took up her little canvas and silently passed it to him. He looked at it, and in a moment she said, "I am sure you are a judge."

"Yes," he answered, "I am."

"You know, then, that that is very bad."

"Mon Dieu," said Valentin, shrugging his shoulders "let us distinguish."

"You know that I ought not to attempt to paint," the young girl continued.

"Frankly, then, mademoiselle, I think you ought not."

She began to look at the dresses of the two splendid ladies again—a point on which, having risked one conjecture, I think I may risk another. While she was looking at the ladies she was seeing Valentin de Bellegarde. He, at all events, was seeing her. He put down the roughly-besmeared canvas and addressed a little click with his tongue, accompanied by an elevation of the eyebrows, to Newman.

"Where have you been all these months?" asked Mademoiselle Noemie of our hero. "You took those great journeys, you amused yourself well?"

"Oh, yes," said Newman. "I amused myself well enough."

"I am very glad," said Mademoiselle Noemie with extreme gentleness, and she began to dabble in her colors again. She was singularly pretty, with the look of serious sympathy that she threw into her face.

Valentin took advantage of her downcast eyes to telegraph again to his companion. He renewed his mysterious physiognomical play, making at the same time a rapid tremulous movement in the air with his fingers. He was evidently finding Mademoiselle Noemie extremely interesting; the blue devils had departed, leaving the field clear.

"Tell me something about your travels," murmured the young girl.

"Oh, I went to Switzerland,—to Geneva and Zermatt and Zurich and all those places you know; and down to Venice, and all through Germany, and down the Rhine, and into Holland and Belgium—the regular round. How do you say that, in French—the regular round?" Newman asked of Valentin.

Mademoiselle Nioche fixed her eyes an instant on Bellegarde, and then with a little smile, "I don't understand monsieur," she said, "when he says so much at once. Would you be so good as to translate?"

"I would rather talk to you out of my own head," Valentin declared.

"No," said Newman, gravely, still in his bad French, "you must not talk to Mademoiselle Nioche, because you say discouraging things. You ought to tell her to work, to persevere."

"And we French, mademoiselle," said Valentin, "are accused of being false flatterers!"

"I don't want any flattery, I want only the truth. But I know the truth."

"All I say is that I suspect there are some things that you can do better than paint," said Valentin.

"I know the truth—I know the truth," Mademoiselle Noemie repeated. And, dipping a brush into a clot of red paint, she drew a great horizontal daub across her unfinished picture.

"What is that?" asked Newman.

Without answering, she drew another long crimson daub, in a vertical direction, down the middle of her canvas, and so, in a moment, completed the rough indication of a cross. "It is the sign of the truth," she said at last.

The two men looked at each other, and Valentin indulged in another flash of physiognomical eloquence. "You have spoiled your picture," said Newman.

"I know that very well. It was the only thing to do with it. I had sat looking at it all day without touching it. I had begun to hate it. It seemed to me something was going to happen."

"I like it better that way than as it was before," said Valentin. "Now it is more interesting. It tells a story. Is it for sale?"

"Everything I have is for sale," said Mademoiselle Noemie.

"How much is this thing?"

"Ten thousand francs," said the young girl, without a smile.

CHAPTER XI

"Everything that Mademoiselle Nioche may do at present is mine in advance," said Newman. "It makes part of an order I gave her some months ago. So you can't have this."

"Monsieur will lose nothing by it," said the young girl, looking at Valentin. And she began to put up her utensils.

"I shall have gained a charming memory," said Valentin. "You are going away? your day is over?"

"My father is coming to fetch me," said Mademoiselle Noemie.

She had hardly spoken when, through the door behind her, which opens on one of the great white stone staircases of the Louvre, M. Nioche made his appearance. He came in with his usual even, patient shuffle, and he made a low salute to the two gentlemen who were standing before his daughter's easel. Newman shook his hands with muscular friendliness, and Valentin returned his greeting with extreme deference. While the old man stood waiting for Noemie to make a parcel of her implements, he let his mild, oblique gaze hover toward Bellegarde, who was watching Mademoiselle Noemie put on her bonnet and mantle. Valentin was at no pains to disguise his scrutiny. He looked at a pretty girl as he would have listened to a piece of music. Attention, in each case, was simple good manners. M. Nioche at last took his daughter's paint-box in one hand and the bedaubed canvas, after giving it a solemn, puzzled stare, in the other, and led the way to the door. Mademoiselle Noemie made the young men the salute of a duchess, and followed her father.

"Well," said Newman, "what do you think of her?"

"She is very remarkable. Diable, diable, diable!" repeated M. de Bellegarde, reflectively; "she is very remarkable."

"I am afraid she is a sad little adventuress," said Newman.

"Not a little one—a great one. She has the material." And Valentin began to walk away slowly, looking vaguely at the pictures on the walls, with a thoughtful illumination in his eye. Nothing could have appealed to his imagination more than the possible adventures of a young lady endowed with the "material" of Mademoiselle Nioche. "She is very interesting," he went on. "She is a beautiful type."

"A beautiful type? What the deuce do you mean?" asked Newman.

"I mean from the artistic point of view. She is an artist,—outside of her painting, which obviously is execrable."

"But she is not beautiful. I don't even think her very pretty."

"She is quite pretty enough for her purposes, and it is a face and figure on which everything tells. If she were prettier she would be less intelligent, and her intelligence is half of her charm."

"In what way," asked Newman, who was much amused at his companion's immediate philosophization of Mademoiselle Nioche, "does her intelligence strike you as so remarkable?"

"She has taken the measure of life, and she has determined to BE something—to succeed at any cost. Her painting, of course, is a mere trick to gain time. She is waiting for her chance; she wishes to launch herself, and to do it well. She knows her Paris. She is one of fifty thousand, so far as the mere ambition goes; but I am very sure that in the way of resolution and capacity she is a rarity. And in one gift—perfect heartlessness—I will warrant she is unsurpassed. She has not as much heart as will go on the point of a needle. That is an immense virtue. Yes, she is one of the celebrities of the future."

"Heaven help us!" said Newman, "how far the artistic point of view may take a man! But in this case I must request that you don't let it take you too far. You have learned a wonderful deal about Mademoiselle Noemie in a quarter of an hour. Let that suffice; don't follow up your researches."

"My dear fellow," cried Bellegarde with warmth, "I hope I have too good manners to intrude."

"You are not intruding. The girl is nothing to me. In fact, I rather dislike her. But I like her poor old father, and for his sake I beg you to abstain from any attempt to verify your theories."

"For the sake of that seedy old gentleman who came to fetch her?" demanded Valentin, stopping short. And on Newman's assenting, "Ah no, ah no," he went on with a smile. "You are quite wrong, my dear fellow; you needn't mind him."

"I verily believe that you are accusing the poor gentleman of being capable of rejoicing in his daughter's dishonor."

"Voyons," said Valentin; "who is he? what is he?"

"He is what he looks like: as poor as a rat, but very high-toned."

"Exactly. I noticed him perfectly; be sure I do him justice. He has had losses, des malheurs, as we say. He is very low-spirited, and his daughter is too much for him. He is the pink of respectability, and he has sixty years of honesty on his back. All this I perfectly appreciate. But I know my fellow-men and my fellow-Parisians, and I will make a bargain with you." Newman gave ear to his bargain and he went on. "He would rather his daughter were a good girl than a bad one, but if the worst comes to the worst, the old man will not do what Virginius did. Success justifies everything. If Mademoiselle Noemie makes a figure, her papa will feel—well, we will call it relieved. And she will make a figure. The old gentleman's future is assured."

"I don't know what Virginius did, but M. Nioche will shoot Miss Noemie," said Newman. "After that, I suppose his future will be assured in some snug prison."

"I am not a cynic; I am simply an observer," Valentin rejoined. "Mademoiselle Noemie interests me; she is extremely remarkable. If there is a good reason, in honor or decency, for dismissing her from my thoughts forever, I am perfectly willing to do it. Your estimate of the papa's sensibilities is a good reason until it is invalidated. I promise you not to look at the young girl again until you tell me that you have changed your mind about the papa. When he has given distinct proof of being a philosopher, you will raise your interdict. Do you agree to that?"

"Do you mean to bribe him?"

"Oh, you admit, then, that he is bribable? No, he would ask too much, and it would not be exactly fair. I mean simply to wait. You will continue, I suppose, to see this interesting couple, and you will give me the news yourself."

"Well," said Newman, "if the old man turns out a humbug, you may do what you please. I wash my hands of the matter. For the girl herself, you may be at rest. I don't know what harm she may do to me, but I certainly can't hurt her. It seems to me," said Newman, "that you are very well matched. You are both hard cases, and M. Nioche and I, I believe, are the only virtuous men to be found in Paris."

Soon after this M. de Bellegarde, in punishment for his levity, received a stern poke in the back from a pointed instrument. Turning quickly round he found the weapon to be a parasol wielded by a lady in green gauze bonnet. Valentin's English cousins had been drifting about unpiloted, and evidently deemed that they had a grievance. Newman left him to their mercies, but with a boundless faith in his power to plead his cause.

CHAPTER XII

Three days after his introduction to the family of Madame de Cintre, Newman, coming in toward evening, found upon his table the card of the Marquis de Bellegarde. On the following day he received a note informing him that the Marquise de Bellegarde would be grateful for the honor of his company at dinner.

He went, of course, though he had to break another engagement to do it. He was ushered into the room in which Madame de Bellegarde had received him before, and here he found his venerable hostess, surrounded by her entire family. The room was lighted only by the crackling fire, which illuminated the very small pink slippers of a lady who, seated in a low chair, was stretching out her toes before it. This lady was the younger Madame de Bellegarde. Madame de Cintre was seated at the other end of the room, holding a little girl against her knee, the child of her brother Urbain, to whom she was apparently relating a wonderful story. Valentin was sitting on a puff, close to his sister-in-law, into whose ear he was certainly distilling the finest nonsense. The marquis was stationed before the fire, with his head erect and his hands behind him, in an attitude of formal expectancy.

Old Madame de Bellegarde stood up to give Newman her greeting, and there was that in the way she did so which seemed to measure narrowly the extent of her condescension. "We are all alone, you see, we have asked no one else," she said, austerely.

"I am very glad you didn't; this is much more sociable," said Newman. "Good evening, sir," and he offered his hand to the marquis.

M. de Bellegarde was affable, but in spite of his dignity he was restless. He began to pace up and down the room, he looked out of the long windows, he took up books and laid them down again. Young Madame de Bellegarde gave Newman her hand without moving and without looking at him.

"You may think that is coldness," exclaimed Valentin; "but it is not, it is warmth. It shows she is treating you as an intimate. Now she detests me, and yet she is always looking at me."

"No wonder I detest you if I am always looking at you!" cried the lady. "If Mr. Newman does not like my way of shaking hands, I will do it again."

But this charming privilege was lost upon our hero, who was already making his way across the room to Madame de Cintre. She looked at him as she shook hands, but she went on with the story she was telling her little niece. She had only two or three phrases to add, but they were apparently of great moment. She deepened her voice, smiling as she did so, and the little girl gazed at her with round eyes.

"But in the end the young prince married the beautiful Florabella," said Madame de Cintre, "and carried her off to live with him in the Land of the Pink Sky. There she was so happy that she forgot all her troubles, and went out to drive every day of her life in an ivory coach drawn by five hundred white mice. Poor Florabella," she exclaimed to Newman, "had suffered terribly."

"She had had nothing to eat for six months," said little Blanche.

"Yes, but when the six months were over, she had a plum-cake as big as that ottoman," said Madame de Cintre. "That quite set her up again."

"What a checkered career!" said Newman. "Are you very fond of children?" He was certain that she was, but he wished to make her say it.

"I like to talk with them," she answered; "we can talk with them so much more seriously than with grown persons. That is great nonsense that I have been telling Blanche, but it is a great deal more serious than most of what we say in society."

"I wish you would talk to me, then, as if I were Blanche's age," said Newman, laughing. "Were you happy at your ball, the other night?"

"Ecstatically!"

"Now you are talking the nonsense that we talk in society," said Newman. "I don't believe that."

"It was my own fault if I was not happy. The ball was very pretty, and every one very amiable."

"It was on your conscience," said Newman, "that you had annoyed your mother and your brother."

Madame de Cintre looked at him a moment without answering. "That is true," she replied at last. "I had undertaken more than I could carry out. I have very little courage; I am not a heroine." She said this with a certain soft emphasis; but then, changing her tone, "I could never have gone through the sufferings of the beautiful Florabella," she added, not even for her prospective rewards.

Dinner was announced, and Newman betook himself to the side of the old Madame de Bellegarde. The dining-room, at the end of a cold corridor, was vast and sombre; the dinner was simple and delicately excellent. Newman wondered whether Madame de Cintre had had something to do with ordering the repast and greatly hoped she had. Once seated at table, with the various members of the ancient house of Bellegarde around him, he asked himself the meaning of his position. Was the old lady responding to his advances? Did the fact that he was a solitary guest augment his credit or diminish it? Were they ashamed to show him to other people, or did they wish to give him a sign of sudden adoption into their last reserve of favor? Newman was on his guard; he was watchful and conjectural; and yet at the same time he was vaguely indifferent. Whether they gave him a long rope or a short one he was there now, and Madame de Cintre was opposite to him. She had a tall candlestick on each side of her; she would sit there for the next hour, and that was enough. The dinner was extremely solemn and measured; he wondered whether this was always the state of things in "old families." Madame de Bellegarde held her head very high, and fixed her eyes, which looked peculiarly sharp in her little, finely-wrinkled white face, very intently upon the table-service. The marquis appeared to have decided that the fine arts offered a safe subject of conversation, as not leading to startling personal revelations. Every now and then, having learned from Newman that he had been through the museums of Europe, he uttered some polished aphorism upon the flesh-tints of Rubens and the good taste of Sansovino. His manners seemed to indicate a fine, nervous dread that something disagreeable might happen if the atmosphere were not purified by allusions of a thoroughly superior cast. "What under the sun is the man afraid of?" Newman asked himself. "Does he think I am going to offer to swap jack-knives with him?" It was useless to shut his eyes to the fact that the marquis was profoundly disagreeable to him. He had never been a man of strong personal aversions; his nerves had not been at the mercy of the mystical qualities of his neighbors. But here was a man towards whom he was irresistibly in opposition; a man of forms and phrases and postures; a man full of possible impertinences and treacheries. M. de Bellegarde made him feel as if he were standing bare-footed on a marble floor; and yet, to gain his desire, Newman felt perfectly able to stand. He wondered what Madame de Cintre thought of his being accepted, if accepted it was. There was no judging from her face, which expressed simply the desire to be gracious in a manner which should require as little explicit recognition as possible. Young Madame de Bellegarde had always the same manners; she was always preoccupied, distracted, listening to everything and hearing nothing, looking at her dress, her rings, her finger-nails, seeming rather bored, and yet puzzling you to decide what was her ideal of social diversion. Newman was enlightened on this point later. Even Valentin did not quite seem master of his wits; his vivacity was fitful and forced, yet Newman observed that in the lapses of his talk he appeared excited. His eyes had an intenser spark than usual. The effect of all this was that Newman, for the first time in his life, was not himself; that he measured his movements, and counted his words, and resolved that if the occasion demanded that he should appear to have swallowed a ramrod, he would meet the emergency.

After dinner M. de Bellegarde proposed to his guest that they should go into the smoking-room, and he led the way toward a small, somewhat musty apartment, the walls of which were ornamented with old hangings of stamped leather and trophies of rusty arms. Newman refused a cigar, but he established himself upon one of the divans, while the marquis puffed his own weed before the fire-place, and Valentin sat looking through the light fumes of a cigarette from one to the other.

"I can't keep quiet any longer," said Valentin, at last. "I must tell you the news and congratulate you. My brother seems unable to come to the point; he revolves around his announcement like the priest around the altar. You are accepted as a candidate for the hand of our sister."

CHAPTER XII

"Valentin, be a little proper!" murmured the marquis, with a look of the most delicate irritation contracting the bridge of his high nose.

"There has been a family council," the young man continued; "my mother and Urbain have put their heads together, and even my testimony has not been altogether excluded. My mother and the marquis sat at a table covered with green cloth; my sister-in-law and I were on a bench against the wall. It was like a committee at the Corps Legislatif. We were called up, one after the other, to testify. We spoke of you very handsomely. Madame de Bellegarde said that if she had not been told who you were, she would have taken you for a duke—an American duke, the Duke of California. I said that I could warrant you grateful for the smallest favors—modest, humble, unassuming. I was sure that you would know your own place, always, and never give us occasion to remind you of certain differences. After all, you couldn't help it if you were not a duke. There were none in your country; but if there had been, it was certain that, smart and active as you are, you would have got the pick of the titles. At this point I was ordered to sit down, but I think I made an impression in your favor."

M. de Bellegarde looked at his brother with dangerous coldness, and gave a smile as thin as the edge of a knife. Then he removed a spark of cigar-ash from the sleeve of his coat; he fixed his eyes for a while on the cornice of the room, and at last he inserted one of his white hands into the breast of his waistcoat. "I must apologize to you for the deplorable levity of my brother," he said, "and I must notify you that this is probably not the last time that his want of tact will cause you serious embarrassment."

"No, I confess I have no tact," said Valentin. "Is your embarrassment really painful, Newman? The marquis will put you right again; his own touch is deliciously delicate."

"Valentin, I am sorry to say," the marquis continued, "has never possessed the tone, the manner, that belongs to a young man in his position. It has been a great affliction to his mother, who is very fond of the old traditions. But you must remember that he speaks for no one but himself."

"Oh, I don't mind him, sir," said Newman, good-humoredly. "I know what he amounts to."

"In the good old times," said Valentin, "marquises and counts used to have their appointed fools and jesters, to crack jokes for them. Nowadays we see a great strapping democrat keeping a count about him to play the fool. It's a good situation, but I certainly am very degenerate."

M. de Bellegarde fixed his eyes for some time on the floor. "My mother informed me," he said presently, "of the announcement that you made to her the other evening."

"That I desired to marry your sister?" said Newman.

"That you wished to arrange a marriage," said the marquis, slowly, "with my sister, the Comtesse de Cintre. The proposal was serious, and required, on my mother's part, a great deal of reflection. She naturally took me into her counsels, and I gave my most zealous attention to the subject. There was a great deal to be considered; more than you appear to imagine. We have viewed the question on all its faces, we have weighed one thing against another. Our conclusion has been that we favor your suit. My mother has desired me to inform you of our decision. She will have the honor of saying a few words to you on the subject, herself. Meanwhile, by us, the heads of the family, you are accepted."

Newman got up and came nearer to the marquis. "You will do nothing to hinder me, and all you can to help me, eh?"

"I will recommend my sister to accept you."

Newman passed his hand over his face, and pressed it for a moment upon his eyes. This promise had a great sound, and yet the pleasure he took in it was embittered by his having to stand there so and receive his passport from M. de Bellegarde. The idea of having this gentleman mixed up with his wooing and wedding was more and more disagreeable to him. But Newman had resolved to go through the mill, as he imagined it, and he would not cry out at the first turn of the wheel. He was silent a while, and then he said, with a certain dryness which Valentin told him afterwards had a very grand air, "I am much obliged to you."

"I take note of the promise," said Valentin, "I register the vow."

M. de Bellegarde began to gaze at the cornice again; he apparently had something more to say. "I must do my mother the justice," he resumed, "I must do myself the justice, to say that our decision was not easy. Such an arrangement was not what we had expected. The idea that my sister should marry a gentleman—ah—in business was something of a novelty."

"So I told you, you know," said Valentin raising his finger at Newman.

"The novelty has not quite worn away, I confess," the marquis went on; "perhaps it never will, entirely. But possibly that is not altogether to be regretted," and he gave his thin smile again. "It may be that the time has come when we should make some concession to novelty. There had been no novelties in our house for a great many years. I made the observation to my mother, and she did me the honor to admit that it was worthy of attention."

"My dear brother," interrupted Valentin, "is not your memory just here leading you the least bit astray? Our mother is, I may say, distinguished for her small respect of abstract reasoning. Are you very sure that she replied to your striking proposition in the gracious manner you describe? You know how terribly incisive she is sometimes. Didn't she, rather, do you the honor to say, 'A fiddlestick for your phrases! There are better reasons than that'?"

"Other reasons were discussed," said the marquis, without looking at Valentin, but with an audible tremor in his voice; "some of them possibly were better. We are conservative, Mr. Newman, but we are not also bigots. We judged the matter liberally. We have no doubt that everything will be comfortable."

Newman had stood listening to these remarks with his arms folded and his eyes fastened upon M. de Bellegarde, "Comfortable?" he said, with a sort of grim flatness of intonation. "Why shouldn't we be comfortable? If you are not, it will be your own fault; I have everything to make ME so."

"My brother means that with the lapse of time you may get used to the change"—and Valentin paused, to light another cigarette.

"What change?" asked Newman in the same tone.

"Urbain," said Valentin, very gravely, "I am afraid that Mr. Newman does not quite realize the change. We ought to insist upon that."

"My brother goes too far," said M. de Bellegarde. "It is his fatal want of tact again. It is my mother's wish, and mine, that no such allusions should be made. Pray never make them yourself. We prefer to assume that the person accepted as the possible husband of my sister is one of ourselves, and that he should have no explanations to make. With a little discretion on both sides, everything, I think, will be easy. That is exactly what I wished to say—that we quite understand what we have undertaken, and that you may depend upon our adhering to our resolution."

Valentin shook his hands in the air and then buried his face in them. "I have less tact than I might have, no doubt; but oh, my brother, if you knew what you yourself were saying!" And he went off into a long laugh.

M. de Bellegarde's face flushed a little, but he held his head higher, as if to repudiate this concession to vulgar perturbability. "I am sure you understand me," he said to Newman.

"Oh no, I don't understand you at all," said Newman. "But you needn't mind that. I don't care. In fact, I think I had better not understand you. I might not like it. That wouldn't suit me at all, you know. I want to marry your sister, that's all; to do it as quickly as possible, and to find fault with nothing. I don't care how I do it. I am not marrying you, you know, sir. I have got my leave, and that is all I want."

"You had better receive the last word from my mother," said the marquis.

"Very good; I will go and get it," said Newman; and he prepared to return to the drawing-room.

M. de Bellegarde made a motion for him to pass first, and when Newman had gone out he shut himself into the room with Valentin. Newman had been a trifle bewildered by the audacious irony of the younger brother, and he had not needed its aid to point the moral of M. de Bellegarde's transcendent patronage. He had wit enough to appreciate the force of that civility which consists in calling your attention to the impertinences it spares you. But he had felt warmly the delicate sympathy with himself that underlay Valentin's fraternal irreverence, and he was most unwilling that his friend should pay a tax upon it. He paused a moment in the corridor, after he had gone a few steps, expecting to hear the resonance of M. de Bellegarde's displeasure; but he detected only a perfect stillness. The stillness itself seemed a trifle portentous; he reflected however that he had no right to stand listening, and he made his way back to the salon. In his absence several persons had come in. They were scattered about the room in groups, two or three of them having passed into a small boudoir, next to the drawing-room, which had now been lighted and opened. Old Madame de Bellegarde was in her place by the fire, talking to a very old gentleman in a wig and a profuse white neck cloth of the fashion of 1820. Madame de Cintre was bending a listening head to the historic confidences of an old lady who was presumably the wife of the old gentleman in the neckcloth, an old lady in a red satin dress and an ermine cape, who wore across her forehead a band with a topaz set in it. Young Madame de Bellegarde, when Newman came in, left some people among whom she was sitting, and took the place that she had occupied before dinner. Then she gave a little push to the puff that stood near her, and by a glance at Newman seemed to indicate that she had placed it in position for him. He went and took possession of it; the marquis's wife amused and puzzled him.

"I know your secret," she said, in her bad but charming English; "you need make no mystery of it. You wish to marry my sister-in-law. C'est un beau choix. A man like you ought to marry a tall, thin woman. You must know that I have spoken in your favor; you owe me a famous taper!"

"You have spoken to Madame de Cintre?" said Newman.

"Oh no, not that. You may think it strange, but my sister-in-law and I are not so intimate as that. No; I spoke to my husband and my mother-in-law; I said I was sure we could do what we chose with you."

"I am much, obliged to you," said Newman, laughing; "but you can't."

"I know that very well; I didn't believe a word of it. But I wanted you to come into the house; I thought we should be friends."

"I am very sure of it," said Newman.

"Don't be too sure. If you like Madame de Cintre so much, perhaps you will not like me. We are as different as blue and pink. But you and I have something in common. I have come into this family by marriage; you want to come into it in the same way."

"Oh no, I don't!" interrupted Newman. "I only want to take Madame de Cintre out of it."

"Well, to cast your nets you have to go into the water. Our positions are alike; we shall be able to compare notes. What do you think of my husband? It's a strange question, isn't it? But I shall ask you some stranger ones yet."

"Perhaps a stranger one will be easier to answer," said Newman. "You might try me."

"Oh, you get off very well; the old Comte de la Rochefidele, yonder, couldn't do it better. I told them that if we only gave you a chance you would be a perfect talon rouge. I know something about men. Besides, you and I belong to the same camp. I am a ferocious democrat. By birth I am vieille roche; a good little bit of the history of France is the history of my family. Oh, you never heard of us, of course! Ce que c'est que la gloire! We are much better than the Bellegardes, at any rate. But I don't care a pin for my pedigree; I want to belong to my time. I'm a revolutionist, a radical, a child of the age! I am sure I go beyond you. I like clever people, wherever they come from, and I take my amusement wherever I find it. I don't pout at the Empire; here all the world pouts at the Empire. Of course I have to mind what I say; but I expect to take my revenge with you." Madame de Bellegarde discoursed for some time longer in this sympathetic strain, with an eager abundance which seemed to indicate that her opportunities for revealing her esoteric philosophy were indeed rare. She hoped that Newman would never be afraid of her, however he might be with the others, for, really, she went very far indeed. "Strong people"—le gens forts—were in her opinion equal, all the world over. Newman listened to her with an attention at once beguiled and irritated. He wondered what the deuce she, too, was driving at, with her hope that he would not be afraid of her and her protestations of equality. In so far as he could understand her, she was wrong; a silly, rattling woman was certainly not the equal of a sensible man, preoccupied with an ambitious passion. Madame de Bellegarde stopped suddenly, and looked at him sharply, shaking her fan. "I see you don't believe me," she said, "you are too much on your guard. You will not form an alliance, offensive or defensive? You are very wrong; I could help you."

Newman answered that he was very grateful and that he would certainly ask for help; she should see. "But first of all," he said, "I must help myself." And he went to join Madame de Cintre.

"I have been telling Madame de la Rochefidele that you are an American," she said, as he came up. "It interests her greatly. Her father went over with the French troops to help you in your battles in the last century, and she has always, in consequence, wanted greatly to see an American. But she has never succeeded till to-night. You are the first—to her knowledge—that she has ever looked at."

Madame de la Rochefidele had an aged, cadaverous face, with a falling of the lower jaw which prevented her from bringing her lips together, and reduced her conversations to a series of impressive but inarticulate gutturals. She raised an antique eyeglass, elaborately mounted in chased silver, and looked at Newman from head to foot. Then she said something to which he listened deferentially, but which he completely failed to understand.

"Madame de la Rochefidele says that she is convinced that she must have seen Americans without knowing it," Madame de Cintre explained. Newman thought it probable she had seen a great many things without knowing it; and the old lady, again addressing herself to utterance, declared—as interpreted by Madame de Cintre—that she wished she had known it.

At this moment the old gentleman who had been talking to the elder Madame de Bellegarde drew near, leading the marquise on his arm. His wife pointed out Newman to him, apparently explaining his remarkable origin. M. de la Rochefidele, whose old age was rosy and rotund, spoke very neatly and clearly, almost as prettily, Newman thought, as M. Nioche. When he had been enlightened, he turned to Newman with an inimitable elderly grace.

"Monsieur is by no means the first American that I have seen," he said. "Almost the first person I ever saw—to notice him—was an American."

"Ah?" said Newman, sympathetically.

"The great Dr. Franklin," said M. de la Rochefidele. "Of course I was very young. He was received very well in our monde."

"Not better than Mr. Newman," said Madame de Bellegarde. "I beg he will offer his arm into the other room. I could have offered no higher privilege to Dr. Franklin."

Newman, complying with Madame de Bellegarde's request, perceived that her two sons had returned to the drawing-room. He scanned their faces an instant for traces of the scene that had followed his separation from them, but the marquise seemed neither more nor less frigidly grand than usual, and Valentin was kissing ladies' hands with at least his habitual air of self-abandonment to the act. Madame de Bellegarde gave a glance at her eldest son, and by the time she had crossed the threshold of her boudoir he was at her side. The room was now empty and offered a sufficient degree of privacy. The old lady disengaged herself from Newman's arm and rested her hand on the arm of the marquis; and in this position she stood a moment, holding her head high and biting her small under-lip. I am afraid the picture was lost upon Newman, but Madame de Bellegarde was, in fact, at this moment a striking image of the dignity which—even in the case of a little time-shrunken old lady—may reside in the habit of unquestioned authority and the absoluteness of a social theory favorable to yourself.

"My son has spoken to you as I desired," she said, "and you understand that we shall not interfere. The rest will lie with yourself."

"M. de Bellegarde told me several things I didn't understand," said Newman, "but I made out that. You will leave me open field. I am much obliged."

"I wish to add a word that my son probably did not feel at liberty to say," the marquise rejoined. "I must say it for my own peace of mind. We are stretching a point; we are doing you a great favor."

"Oh, your son said it very well; didn't you?" said Newman.

"Not so well as my mother," declared the marquis.

"I can only repeat—I am much obliged."

"It is proper I should tell you," Madame de Bellegarde went on, "that I am very proud, and that I hold my head very high. I may be wrong, but I am too old to change. At least I know it, and I don't pretend to anything else. Don't flatter yourself that my daughter is not proud. She is proud in her own way—a somewhat different way from mine. You will have to make your terms with that. Even Valentin is proud, if you touch the right spot—or the wrong one. Urbain is proud; that you see for yourself. Sometimes I think he is a little too proud; but I wouldn't change him. He is the best of my children; he cleaves to his old mother. But I have said enough to show you that we are all proud together. It is well that you should know the sort of people you have come among."

"Well," said Newman, "I can only say, in return, that I am NOT proud; I shan't mind you! But you speak as if you intended to be very disagreeable."

"I shall not enjoy having my daughter marry you, and I shall not pretend to enjoy it. If you don't mind that, so much the better."

"If you stick to your own side of the contract we shall not quarrel; that is all I ask of you," said Newman. "Keep your hands off, and give me an open field. I am very much in earnest, and there is not the slightest danger of my getting discouraged or backing out. You will have me constantly before your eyes; if you don't like it, I am sorry for you. I will do for your daughter, if she will accept me everything that a man can do for a woman. I am happy to tell you that, as a promise—a pledge. I consider that on your side you make me an equal pledge. You will not back out, eh?"

CHAPTER XII

"I don't know what you mean by 'backing out,'" said the marquise. "It suggests a movement of which I think no Bellegarde has ever been guilty."

"Our word is our word," said Urbain. "We have given it."

"Well, now," said Newman, "I am very glad you are so proud. It makes me believe that you will keep it."

The marquise was silent a moment, and then, suddenly, "I shall always be polite to you, Mr. Newman," she declared, "but, decidedly, I shall never like you."

"Don't be too sure," said Newman, laughing.

"I am so sure that I will ask you to take me back to my arm-chair without the least fear of having my sentiments modified by the service you render me." And Madame de Bellegarde took his arm, and returned to the salon and to her customary place.

M. de la Rochefidele and his wife were preparing to take their leave, and Madame de Cintre's interview with the mumbling old lady was at an end. She stood looking about her, asking herself, apparently to whom she should next speak, when Newman came up to her.

"Your mother has given me leave—very solemnly—to come here often," he said. "I mean to come often."

"I shall be glad to see you," she answered, simply. And then, in a moment. "You probably think it very strange that there should be such a solemnity—as you say—about your coming."

"Well, yes; I do, rather."

"Do you remember what my brother Valentin said, the first time you came to see me—that we were a strange, strange family?"

"It was not the first time I came, but the second," said Newman.

"Very true. Valentin annoyed me at the time, but now I know you better, I may tell you he was right. If you come often, you will see!" and Madame de Cintre turned away.

Newman watched her a while, talking with other people, and then he took his leave. He shook hands last with Valentin de Bellegarde, who came out with him to the top of the staircase. "Well, you have got your permit," said Valentin. "I hope you liked the process."

"I like your sister, more than ever. But don't worry your brother any more for my sake," Newman added. "I don't mind him. I am afraid he came down on you in the smoking-room, after I went out."

"When my brother comes down on me," said Valentin, "he falls hard. I have a peculiar way of receiving him. I must say," he continued, "that they came up to the mark much sooner than I expected. I don't understand it, they must have had to turn the screw pretty tight. It's a tribute to your millions."

"Well, it's the most precious one they have ever received," said Newman.

He was turning away when Valentin stopped him, looking at him with a brilliant, softly-cynical glance. "I should like to know whether, within a few days, you have seen your venerable friend M. Nioche."

"He was yesterday at my rooms," Newman answered.

"What did he tell you?"

"Nothing particular."

"You didn't see the muzzle of a pistol sticking out of his pocket?"

"What are you driving at?" Newman demanded. "I thought he seemed rather cheerful for him."

Valentin broke into a laugh. "I am delighted to hear it! I win my bet. Mademoiselle Noemie has thrown her cap over the mill, as we say. She has left the paternal domicile. She is launched! And M. Nioche is rather cheerful—FOR HIM! Don't brandish your tomahawk at that rate; I have not seen her nor communicated with her since that day at the Louvre. Andromeda has found another Perseus than I. My information is exact; on such matters it always is. I suppose that now you will raise your protest."

"My protest be hanged!" murmured Newman, disgustedly.

But his tone found no echo in that in which Valentin, with his hand on the door, to return to his mother's apartment, exclaimed, "But I shall see her now! She is very remarkable—she is very remarkable!"

CHAPTER XIII

Newman kept his promise, or his menace, of going often to the Rue de l'Universite, and during the next six weeks he saw Madame de Cintre more times than he could have numbered. He flattered himself that he was not in love, but his biographer may be supposed to know better. He claimed, at least, none of the exemptions and emoluments of the romantic passion. Love, he believed, made a fool of a man, and his present emotion was not folly but wisdom; wisdom sound, serene, well-directed. What he felt was an intense, all-consuming tenderness, which had for its object an extraordinarily graceful and delicate, and at the same time impressive, woman who lived in a large gray house on the left bank of the Seine. This tenderness turned very often into a positive heart-ache; a sign in which, certainly, Newman ought to have read the appellation which science has conferred upon his sentiment. When the heart has a heavy weight upon it, it hardly matters whether the weight be of gold or of lead; when, at any rate, happiness passes into that place in which it becomes identical with pain, a man may admit that the reign of wisdom is temporarily suspended. Newman wished Madame de Cintre so well that nothing he could think of doing for her in the future rose to the high standard which his present mood had set itself. She seemed to him so felicitous a product of nature and circumstance that his invention, musing on future combinations, was constantly catching its breath with the fear of stumbling into some brutal compression or mutilation of her beautiful personal harmony. This is what I mean by Newman's tenderness: Madame de Cintre pleased him so, exactly as she was, that his desire to interpose between her and the troubles of life had the quality of a young mother's eagerness to protect the sleep of her first-born child. Newman was simply charmed, and he handled his charm as if it were a music-box which would stop if one shook it. There can be no better proof of the hankering epicure that is hidden in every man's temperament, waiting for a signal from some divine confederate that he may safely peep out. Newman at last was enjoying, purely, freely, deeply. Certain of Madame de Cintre's personal qualities—the luminous sweetness of her eyes, the delicate mobility of her face, the deep liquidity of her voice—filled all his consciousness. A rose-crowned Greek of old, gazing at a marble goddess with his whole bright intellect resting satisfied in the act, could not have been a more complete embodiment of the wisdom that loses itself in the enjoyment of quiet harmonies.

He made no violent love to her—no sentimental speeches. He never trespassed on what she had made him understand was for the present forbidden ground. But he had, nevertheless, a comfortable sense that she knew better from day to day how much he admired her. Though in general he was no great talker, he talked much, and he succeeded perfectly in making her say many things. He was not afraid of boring her, either by his discourse or by his silence; and whether or no he did occasionally bore her, it is probable that on the whole she liked him only the better for his absense of embarrassed scruples. Her visitors, coming in often while Newman sat there, found a tall, lean, silent man in a half-lounging attitude, who laughed out sometimes when no one had meant to be droll, and remained grave in the presence of calculated witticisms, for appreciation of which he had apparently not the proper culture.

It must be confessed that the number of subjects upon which Newman had no ideas was extremely large, and it must be added that as regards those subjects upon which he was without ideas he was also perfectly without words. He had little of the small change of conversation, and his stock of ready-made formulas and phrases was the scantiest. On the other hand he had plenty of attention to bestow, and his estimate of the importance of a topic did not depend upon the number of clever things he could say about it. He himself was almost never bored, and there was no man with whom it would have been a greater mistake to suppose that silence meant displeasure. What it was that entertained him during some of his speechless sessions I must, however, confess myself unable to determine. We know in a general way that a great many things which were old stories to a great many people had the charm of novelty to him, but a complete list of his new impressions would probably contain a number of surprises for us. He told Madame de Cintre a hundred long stories; he explained to her, in talking of the United States, the working of various local institutions and mercantile customs. Judging by the sequel she was interested, but one would not have been sure of it beforehand. As regards her own talk, Newman was very sure himself that she herself enjoyed it: this was as a sort of amendment to the portrait that Mrs. Tristram had drawn of her. He discovered that she had naturally an abundance of gayety. He had been right at first in saying she was shy; her shyness, in a woman whose circumstances and tranquil beauty afforded every facility for well-mannered hardihood, was only a charm the more. For Newman it had lasted some time, and even when it went it left something behind it which for a while performed the same office. Was this the tearful secret of which Mrs. Tristram had had a glimpse, and of which, as of her friend's reserve, her high-breeding, and her profundity, she had given a sketch of which the outlines were, perhaps, rather too heavy? Newman supposed so, but he found himself wondering less every day what Madame de Cintre's secrets might be, and more convinced that secrets were, in themselves, hateful things to her. She was a woman for the light, not for the shade; and her natural line was not picturesque reserve and mysterious melancholy, but frank, joyous, brilliant action, with just so much meditation as was necessary, and not a grain more. To this, apparently, he had succeeded in bringing her back. He felt, himself, that he was an antidote to oppressive secrets; what he offered her was, in fact, above all things a vast, sunny immunity from the need of having any.

He often passed his evenings, when Madame de Cintre had so appointed it, at the chilly fireside of Madame de Bellegarde, contenting himself with looking across the room, through narrowed eyelids, at his mistress, who always made a point, before her family, of talking to some one else. Madame de Bellegarde sat by the fire conversing neatly and coldly with whomsoever approached her, and glancing round the room with her slowly-restless eye, the effect of which, when it lighted upon him, was to Newman's sense identical with that of a sudden spurt of damp air. When he shook hands with her he always asked her with a laugh whether she could "stand him" another evening, and she replied, without a laugh, that thank God she had always been able to do her duty. Newman, talking once of the marquise to Mrs. Tristram, said that after all it was very easy to get on with her; it always was easy to get on with out-and-out rascals.

"And is it by that elegant term," said Mrs. Tristram, "that you designate the Marquise de Bellegarde?"

"Well," said Newman, "she is wicked, she is an old sinner."

"What is her crime?" asked Mrs. Tristram.

"I shouldn't wonder if she had murdered some one—all from a sense of duty, of course."

"How can you be so dreadful?" sighed Mrs. Tristram.

"I am not dreadful. I am speaking of her favorably."

"Pray what will you say when you want to be severe?"

"I shall keep my severity for some one else—for the marquis. There's a man I can't swallow, mix the drink as I will."

"And what has HE done?"

"I can't quite make out; it is something dreadfully bad, something mean and underhand, and not redeemed by audacity, as his mother's misdemeanors may have been. If he has never committed murder, he has at least turned his back and looked the other way while some one else was committing it."

In spite of this invidious hypothesis, which must be taken for nothing more than an example of the capricious play of "American humor," Newman did his best to maintain an easy and friendly style of communication with M. de Bellegarde. So long as he was in personal contact with people he disliked extremely to have anything to forgive them, and he was capable of a good deal of unsuspected imaginative effort (for the sake of his own personal comfort) to assume for the time that they were good fellows. He did his best to treat the marquis as one; he believed honestly, moreover, that he could not, in reason, be such a confounded fool as he seemed. Newman's familiarity was never importunate; his sense of human equality was not an aggressive taste or an aesthetic theory, but something as natural and organic as a physical appetite which had never been put on a scanty allowance and consequently was innocent of ungraceful eagerness. His tranquil unsuspectingness of the relativity of his own place in the social scale was probably irritating to M. de Bellegarde, who saw himself reflected in the mind of his potential brother-in-law in a crude and colorless form, unpleasantly dissimilar to the impressive image projected upon his own intellectual mirror. He never forgot himself for an instant, and replied to what he must have considered Newman's "advances" with mechanical politeness. Newman, who was constantly forgetting himself, and indulging in an unlimited amount of irresponsible inquiry and conjecture, now and then found himself confronted by the conscious, ironical smile of his host. What the deuce M. de Bellegarde was smiling at he was at a loss to divine. M. de Bellegarde's smile may be supposed to have been, for himself, a compromise between a great many emotions. So long as he smiled he was polite, and it was proper he should be polite. A smile, moreover, committed him to nothing more than politeness, and left the degree of politeness agreeably vague. A smile, too, was neither dissent—which was too serious—nor agreement, which might have brought on terrible complications. And then a smile covered his own personal dignity, which in this critical situation he was resolved to keep immaculate; it was quite enough that the glory of his house should pass into eclipse. Between him and Newman, his whole manner seemed to declare there could be no interchange of opinion; he was holding his breath so as not to inhale the odor of democracy. Newman was far from being versed in European politics, but he liked to have a general idea of what was going on about him, and he accordingly asked M. de Bellegarde several times what he thought of public affairs. M. de Bellegarde answered with suave concision that he thought as ill of them as possible, that they were going from bad to worse, and that the age was rotten to its core. This gave Newman, for the moment, an almost kindly feeling for the marquis; he pitied a man for whom the world was so cheerless a place, and the next time he saw M. de Bellegarde he attempted to call his attention to some of the brilliant features of the time. The marquis presently replied that he had but a single political conviction, which was enough for him: he believed in the divine right of Henry of Bourbon, Fifth of his name, to the throne of France. Newman stared, and after this he ceased to talk politics with M. de Bellegarde. He was not horrified nor scandalized, he was not even amused; he felt as he should have felt if he had discovered in M. de Bellegarde a taste for certain oddities of diet; an appetite, for instance, for fishbones or nutshells. Under these circumstances, of course, he would never have broached dietary questions with him.

One afternoon, on his calling on Madame de Cintre, Newman was requested by the servant to wait a few moments, as his hostess was not at liberty. He walked about the room a while, taking up her books, smelling her flowers, and looking at her prints and photographs (which he thought prodigiously pretty), and at last he heard the opening of a door to which his back was turned. On the threshold stood an old woman whom he remembered to have met several times in entering and leaving the house. She was tall and straight and dressed in black, and she wore a cap which, if Newman had been initiated into such mysteries, would have been a sufficient assurance that she was not a Frenchwoman; a cap of pure British composition. She had a pale, decent, depressed-looking face, and a clear, dull, English eye. She looked at Newman a moment, both intently and timidly, and then she dropped a short, straight English curtsey.

"Madame de Cintre begs you will kindly wait," she said. "She has just come in; she will soon have finished dressing."

"Oh, I will wait as long as she wants," said Newman. "Pray tell her not to hurry."

"Thank you, sir," said the woman, softly; and then, instead of retiring with her message, she advanced into the room. She looked about her for a moment, and presently went to a table and began to arrange certain books and knick-knacks. Newman was struck with the high respectability of her appearance; he was afraid to address her as a servant. She busied herself for some moments with putting the table in order and pulling the curtains straight, while Newman walked slowly to and fro. He perceived at last from her reflection in the mirror, as he was passing that her hands were idle and that she was looking at him intently. She evidently wished to say something, and Newman, perceiving it, helped her to begin.

"You are English?" he asked.

"Yes, sir, please," she answered, quickly and softly; "I was born in Wiltshire."

"And what do you think of Paris?"

"Oh, I don't think of Paris, sir," she said in the same tone. "It is so long since I have been here."

"Ah, you have been here very long?"

"It is more than forty years, sir. I came over with Lady Emmeline."

"You mean with old Madame de Bellegarde?"

"Yes, sir. I came with her when she was married. I was my lady's own woman."

"And you have been with her ever since?"

"I have been in the house ever since. My lady has taken a younger person. You see I am very old. I do nothing regular now. But I keep about."

"You look very strong and well," said Newman, observing the erectness of her figure, and a certain venerable rosiness in her cheek.

"Thank God I am not ill, sir; I hope I know my duty too well to go panting and coughing about the house. But I am an old woman, sir, and it is as an old woman that I venture to speak to you."

"Oh, speak out," said Newman, curiously. "You needn't be afraid of me."

"Yes, sir. I think you are kind. I have seen you before."

"On the stairs, you mean?"

"Yes, sir. When you have been coming to see the countess. I have taken the liberty of noticing that you come often."

"Oh yes; I come very often," said Newman, laughing. "You need not have been wide-awake to notice that."

"I have noticed it with pleasure, sir," said the ancient tire-woman, gravely. And she stood looking at Newman with a strange expression of face. The old instinct of deference and humility was there; the habit of decent self-effacement and knowledge of her "own place." But there mingled with it a certain mild audacity, born of the occasion and of a sense, probably, of Newman's unprecedented approachableness, and, beyond this, a vague indifference to the old proprieties; as if my lady's own woman had at last begun to reflect that, since my lady had taken another person, she had a slight reversionary property in herself.

"You take a great interest in the family?" said Newman.

"A deep interest, sir. Especially in the countess."

"I am glad of that," said Newman. And in a moment he added, smiling, "So do I!"

"So I suppose, sir. We can't help noticing these things and having our ideas; can we, sir?"

"You mean as a servant?" said Newman.

"Ah, there it is, sir. I am afraid that when I let my thoughts meddle with such matters I am no longer a servant. But I am so devoted to the countess; if she were my own child I couldn't love her more. That is how I come to be so bold, sir. They say you want to marry her."

Newman eyed his interlocutress and satisfied himself that she was not a gossip, but a zealot; she looked anxious, appealing, discreet. "It is quite true," he said. "I want to marry Madame de Cintre."

"And to take her away to America?"

"I will take her wherever she wants to go."

"The farther away the better, sir!" exclaimed the old woman, with sudden intensity. But she checked herself, and, taking up a paper-weight in mosaic, began to polish it with her black apron. "I don't mean anything against the house or the family, sir. But I think a great change would do the poor countess good. It is very sad here."

"Yes, it's not very lively," said Newman. "But Madame de Cintre is gay herself."

"She is everything that is good. You will not be vexed to hear that she has been gayer for a couple of months past than she had been in many a day before."

Newman was delighted to gather this testimony to the prosperity of his suit, but he repressed all violent marks of elation. "Has Madame de Cintre been in bad spirits before this?" he asked.

"Poor lady, she had good reason. M. de Cintre was no husband for a sweet young lady like that. And then, as I say, it has been a sad house. It is better, in my humble opinion, that she were out of it. So, if you will excuse me for saying so, I hope she will marry you."

"I hope she will!" said Newman.

"But you must not lose courage, sir, if she doesn't make up her mind at once. That is what I wanted to beg of you, sir. Don't give it up, sir. You will not take it ill if I say it's a great risk for any lady at any time; all the more when she has got rid of one bad bargain. But if she can marry a good, kind, respectable gentleman, I think she had better make up her mind to it. They speak very well of you, sir, in the house, and, if you will allow me to say so, I like your face. You have a very different appearance from the late count, he wasn't five feet high. And they say your fortune is beyond everything. There's no harm in that. So I beseech you to be patient, sir, and bide your time. If I don't say this to you, sir, perhaps no one will. Of course it is not for me to make any promises. I can answer for nothing. But I think your chance is not so bad, sir. I am nothing but a weary old woman in my quiet corner, but one woman understands another, and I think I make out the countess. I received her in my arms when she came into the world and her first wedding day was the saddest of my life. She owes it to me to show me another and a brighter one. If you will hold firm, sir—and you look as if you would—I think we may see it."

"I am much obliged to you for your encouragement," said Newman, heartily. "One can't have too much. I mean to hold firm. And if Madame de Cintre marries me you must come and live with her."

The old woman looked at him strangely, with her soft, lifeless eyes. "It may seem a heartless thing to say, sir, when one has been forty years in a house, but I may tell you that I should like to leave this place."

"Why, it's just the time to say it," said Newman, fervently. "After forty years one wants a change."

"You are very kind, sir;" and this faithful servant dropped another curtsey and seemed disposed to retire. But she lingered a moment and gave a timid, joyless smile. Newman was disappointed, and his fingers stole half shyly half irritably into his waistcoat-pocket. His informant noticed the movement. "Thank God I am not a Frenchwoman," she said. "If I were, I would tell you with a brazen simper, old as I am, that if you please, monsieur, my information is worth something. Let me tell you so in my own decent English way. It IS worth something."

"How much, please?" said Newman.

"Simply this: a promise not to hint to the countess that I have said these things."

"If that is all, you have it," said Newman.

"That is all, sir. Thank you, sir. Good day, sir." And having once more slid down telescope-wise into her scanty petticoats, the old woman departed. At the same moment Madame de Cintre came in by an opposite door. She noticed the movement of the other portiere and asked Newman who had been entertaining him.

"The British female!" said Newman. "An old lady in a black dress and a cap, who curtsies up and down, and expresses herself ever so well."

"An old lady who curtsies and expresses herself?... Ah, you mean poor Mrs. Bread. I happen to know that you have made a conquest of her."

"Mrs. Cake, she ought to be called," said Newman. "She is very sweet. She is a delicious old woman."

Madame de Cintre looked at him a moment. "What can she have said to you? She is an excellent creature, but we think her rather dismal."

"I suppose," Newman answered presently, "that I like her because she has lived near you so long. Since your birth, she told me."

"Yes," said Madame de Cintre, simply; "she is very faithful; I can trust her."

Newman had never made any reflections to this lady upon her mother and her brother Urbain; had given no hint of the impression they made upon him. But, as if she had guessed his thoughts, she seemed careful to avoid all occasion for making him speak of them. She never alluded to her mother's domestic decrees; she never quoted the opinions of the marquis. They had talked, however, of Valentin, and she had made no secret of her extreme affection for her younger brother. Newman listened sometimes with a certain harmless jealousy; he would have liked to divert some of her tender allusions to his own credit. Once Madame de Cintre told him with a little air of triumph about something that Valentin had done which she thought very much to his honor. It was a service he had rendered to an old friend of the family; something more "serious" than Valentin was usually supposed capable of being. Newman said he was glad to hear of it, and then began to talk about something which lay upon his own heart. Madame de Cintre listened, but after a while she said, "I don't like the way you speak of my brother Valentin." Hereupon Newman, surprised, said that he had never spoken of him but kindly.

"It is too kindly," said Madame de Cintre. "It is a kindness that costs nothing; it is the kindness you show to a child. It is as if you didn't respect him."

"Respect him? Why I think I do."

"You think? If you are not sure, it is no respect."

"Do you respect him?" said Newman. "If you do, I do."

"If one loves a person, that is a question one is not bound to answer," said Madame de Cintre.

"You should not have asked it of me, then. I am very fond of your brother."

"He amuses you. But you would not like to resemble him."

"I shouldn't like to resemble any one. It is hard enough work resembling one's self."

"What do you mean," asked Madame de Cintre, "by resembling one's self?"

"Why, doing what is expected of one. Doing one's duty."

"But that is only when one is very good."

"Well, a great many people are good," said Newman. "Valentin is quite good enough for me."

CHAPTER XIII

Madame de Cintre was silent for a short time. "He is not good enough for me," she said at last. "I wish he would do something."

"What can he do?" asked Newman.

"Nothing. Yet he is very clever."

"It is a proof of cleverness," said Newman, "to be happy without doing anything."

"I don't think Valentin is happy, in reality. He is clever, generous, brave; but what is there to show for it? To me there is something sad in his life, and sometimes I have a sort of foreboding about him. I don't know why, but I fancy he will have some great trouble—perhaps an unhappy end."

"Oh, leave him to me," said Newman, jovially. "I will watch over him and keep harm away."

One evening, in Madame de Bellegarde's salon, the conversation had flagged most sensibly. The marquis walked up and down in silence, like a sentinel at the door of some smooth-fronted citadel of the proprieties; his mother sat staring at the fire; young Madame de Bellegarde worked at an enormous band of tapestry. Usually there were three or four visitors, but on this occasion a violent storm sufficiently accounted for the absence of even the most devoted habitues. In the long silences the howling of the wind and the beating of the rain were distinctly audible. Newman sat perfectly still, watching the clock, determined to stay till the stroke of eleven, but not a moment longer. Madame de Cintre had turned her back to the circle, and had been standing for some time within the uplifted curtain of a window, with her forehead against the pane, gazing out into the deluged darkness. Suddenly she turned round toward her sister-in-law.

"For Heaven's sake," she said, with peculiar eagerness, "go to the piano and play something."

Madame de Bellegarde held up her tapestry and pointed to a little white flower. "Don't ask me to leave this. I am in the midst of a masterpiece. My flower is going to smell very sweet; I am putting in the smell with this gold-colored silk. I am holding my breath; I can't leave off. Play something yourself."

"It is absurd for me to play when you are present," said Madame de Cintre. But the next moment she went to the piano and began to strike the keys with vehemence. She played for some time, rapidly and brilliantly; when she stopped, Newman went to the piano and asked her to begin again. She shook her head, and, on his insisting, she said, "I have not been playing for you; I have been playing for myself." She went back to the window again and looked out, and shortly afterwards left the room. When Newman took leave, Urbain de Bellegarde accompanied him, as he always did, just three steps down the staircase. At the bottom stood a servant with his overcoat. He had just put it on when he saw Madame de Cintre coming towards him across the vestibule.

"Shall you be at home on Friday?" Newman asked.

She looked at him a moment before answering his question. "You don't like my mother and my brother," she said.

He hesitated a moment, and then he said softly, "No."

She laid her hand on the balustrade and prepared to ascend the stairs, fixing her eyes on the first step.

"Yes, I shall be at home on Friday," and she passed up the wide dusky staircase.

On the Friday, as soon as he came in, she asked him to please to tell her why he disliked her family.

"Dislike your family?" he exclaimed. "That has a horrid sound. I didn't say so, did I? I didn't mean it, if I did."

"I wish you would tell me what you think of them," said Madame de Cintre.

"I don't think of any of them but you."

"That is because you dislike them. Speak the truth; you can't offend me."

"Well, I don't exactly love your brother," said Newman. "I remember now. But what is the use of my saying so? I had forgotten it."

"You are too good-natured," said Madame de Cintre gravely. Then, as if to avoid the appearance of inviting him to speak ill of the marquis, she turned away, motioning him to sit down.

But he remained standing before her and said presently, "What is of much more importance is that they don't like me."

"No—they don't," she said.

"And don't you think they are wrong?" Newman asked. "I don't believe I am a man to dislike."

"I suppose that a man who may be liked may also be disliked. And my brother—my mother," she added, "have not made you angry?"

"Yes, sometimes."

"You have never shown it."

"So much the better."

"Yes, so much the better. They think they have treated you very well."

"I have no doubt they might have handled me much more roughly," said Newman. "I am much obliged to them. Honestly."

"You are generous," said Madame de Cintre. "It's a disagreeable position."

"For them, you mean. Not for me."

"For me," said Madame de Cintre.

"Not when their sins are forgiven!" said Newman. "They don't think I am as good as they are. I do. But we shan't quarrel about it."

"I can't even agree with you without saying something that has a disagreeable sound. The presumption was against you. That you probably don't understand."

Newman sat down and looked at her for some time. "I don't think I really understand it. But when you say it, I believe it."

"That's a poor reason," said Madame de Cintre, smiling.

"No, it's a very good one. You have a high spirit, a high standard; but with you it's all natural and unaffected; you don't seem to have stuck your head into a vise, as if you were sitting for the photograph of propriety. You think of me as a fellow who has had no idea in life but to make money and drive sharp bargains. That's a fair description of me, but it is not the whole story. A man ought to care for something else, though I don't know exactly what. I cared for money-making, but I never cared particularly for the money. There was nothing else to do, and it was impossible to be idle. I have been very easy to others, and to myself. I have done most of the things that people asked me—I don't mean rascals. As regards your mother and your brother," Newman added, "there is only one point upon which I feel that I might quarrel with them. I don't ask them to sing my praises to you, but I ask them to let you alone. If I thought they talked ill of me to you, I should come down upon them."

"They have let me alone, as you say. They have not talked ill of you."

"In that case," cried Newman, "I declare they are only too good for this world!"

Madame de Cintre appeared to find something startling in his exclamation. She would, perhaps, have replied, but at this moment the door was thrown open and Urbain de Bellegarde stepped across the threshold. He appeared surprised at finding Newman, but his surprise was but a momentary shadow across the surface of an unwonted joviality. Newman had never seen the marquis so exhilarated; his pale, unlighted countenance had a sort of thin transfiguration. He held open the door for some one else to enter, and presently appeared old Madame de Bellegarde, leaning on the arm of a gentleman whom Newman had not seen before. He had already risen, and Madame de Cintre rose, as she always did before her mother. The marquis, who had greeted Newman almost genially, stood apart, slowly rubbing his hands. His mother came forward with her companion. She gave a majestic little nod at Newman, and then she released the strange gentleman, that he might make his bow to her daughter.

"My daughter," she said, "I have brought you an unknown relative, Lord Deepmere. Lord Deepmere is our cousin, but he has done only to-day what he ought to have done long ago—come to make our acquaintance."

Madame de Cintre smiled, and offered Lord Deepmere her hand. "It is very extraordinary," said this noble laggard, "but this is the first time that I have ever been in Paris for more than three or four weeks."

"And how long have you been here now?" asked Madame de Cintre.

"Oh, for the last two months," said Lord Deepmere.

These two remarks might have constituted an impertinence; but a glance at Lord Deepmere's face would have satisfied you, as it apparently satisfied Madame de Cintre, that they constituted only a naivete. When his companions were seated, Newman, who was out of the conversation, occupied himself with observing the newcomer. Observation, however, as regards Lord Deepmere's person; had no great range. He was a small, meagre man, of some three and thirty years of age, with a bald head, a short nose and no front teeth in the upper jaw; he had round, candid blue eyes, and several pimples on his chin. He was evidently very shy, and he laughed a great deal, catching his breath with an odd, startling sound, as the most convenient imitation of repose. His physiognomy denoted great simplicity, a certain amount of brutality, and probable failure in the past to profit by rare educational advantages. He remarked that Paris was awfully jolly, but that for real, thorough-paced entertainment it was nothing to Dublin. He even preferred Dublin to London. Had Madame de Cintre ever been to Dublin? They must all come over there some day, and he would show them some Irish sport. He always went to Ireland for the fishing, and he came to Paris for the new Offenbach things. They always brought them out in Dublin, but he couldn't wait. He had been nine times to hear La Pomme de Paris. Madame de Cintre, leaning back, with her arms folded, looked at Lord Deepmere with a more visibly puzzled face than she usually showed to society. Madame de Bellegarde, on the other hand, wore a fixed smile. The marquis said that among light operas his favorite was the Gazza Ladra. The marquise then began a series of inquiries about the duke and the cardinal, the old countess and Lady Barbara, after listening to which, and to Lord Deepmere's somewhat irreverent responses, for a quarter of an hour, Newman rose to take his leave. The marquis went with him three steps into the hall.

"Is he Irish?" asked Newman, nodding in the direction of the visitor.

"His mother was the daughter of Lord Finucane," said the marquis; "he has great Irish estates. Lady Bridget, in the complete absence of male heirs, either direct or collateral—a most extraordinary circumstance—came in for everything. But Lord Deepmere's title is English and his English property is immense. He is a charming young man."

Newman answered nothing, but he detained the marquis as the latter was beginning gracefully to recede. "It is a good time for me to thank you," he said, "for sticking so punctiliously to our bargain, for doing so much to help me on with your sister."

The marquis stared. "Really, I have done nothing that I can boast of," he said.

"Oh don't be modest," Newman answered, laughing. "I can't flatter myself that I am doing so well simply by my own merit. And thank your mother for me, too!" And he turned away, leaving M. de Bellegarde looking after him.

CHAPTER XIV

The next time Newman came to the Rue de l'Universite he had the good fortune to find Madame de Cintre alone. He had come with a definite intention, and he lost no time in executing it. She wore, moreover, a look which he eagerly interpreted as expectancy.

"I have been coming to see you for six months, now," he said, "and I have never spoken to you a second time of marriage. That was what you asked me; I obeyed. Could any man have done better?"

"You have acted with great delicacy," said Madame de Cintre.

"Well, I'm going to change, now," said Newman. "I don't mean that I am going to be indelicate; but I'm going to go back to where I began. I AM back there. I have been all round the circle. Or rather, I have never been away from here. I have never ceased to want what I wanted then. Only now I am more sure of it, if possible; I am more sure of myself, and more sure of you. I know you better, though I don't know anything I didn't believe three months ago. You are everything—you are beyond everything—I can imagine or desire. You know me now; you MUST know me. I won't say that you have seen the best—but you have seen the worst. I hope you have been thinking all this while. You must have seen that I was only waiting; you can't suppose that I was changing. What will you say to me, now? Say that everything is clear and reasonable, and that I have been very patient and considerate, and deserve my reward. And then give me your hand. Madame de Cintre do that. Do it."

"I knew you were only waiting," she said; "and I was very sure this day would come. I have thought about it a great deal. At first I was half afraid of it. But I am not afraid of it now." She paused a moment, and then she added, "It's a relief."

She was sitting on a low chair, and Newman was on an ottoman, near her. He leaned a little and took her hand, which for an instant she let him keep. "That means that I have not waited for nothing," he said. She looked at him for a moment, and he saw her eyes fill with tears. "With me," he went on, "you will be as safe—as safe"—and even in his ardor he hesitated a moment for a comparison—"as safe," he said, with a kind of simple solemnity, "as in your father's arms."

Still she looked at him and her tears increased. Then, abruptly, she buried her face on the cushioned arm of the sofa beside her chair, and broke into noiseless sobs. "I am weak—I am weak," he heard her say.

"All the more reason why you should give yourself up to me," he answered. "Why are you troubled? There is nothing but happiness. Is that so hard to believe?"

"To you everything seems so simple," she said, raising her head. "But things are not so. I like you extremely. I liked you six months ago, and now I am sure of it, as you say you are sure. But it is not easy, simply for that, to decide to marry you. There are a great many things to think about."

"There ought to be only one thing to think about—that we love each other," said Newman. And as she remained silent he quickly added, "Very good, if you can't accept that, don't tell me so."

"I should be very glad to think of nothing," she said at last; "not to think at all; only to shut both my eyes and give myself up. But I can't. I'm cold, I'm old, I'm a coward; I never supposed I should marry again, and it seems to me very strange I should ever have listened to you. When I used to think, as a girl, of what I should do if I were to marry freely, by my own choice, I thought of a very different man from you."

"That's nothing against me," said Newman with an immense smile; "your taste was not formed."

His smile made Madame de Cintre smile. "Have you formed it?" she asked. And then she said, in a different tone, "Where do you wish to live?"

"Anywhere in the wide world you like. We can easily settle that."

CHAPTER XIV

"I don't know why I ask you," she presently continued. "I care very little. I think if I were to marry you I could live almost anywhere. You have some false ideas about me; you think that I need a great many things—that I must have a brilliant, worldly life. I am sure you are prepared to take a great deal of trouble to give me such things. But that is very arbitrary; I have done nothing to prove that." She paused again, looking at him, and her mingled sound and silence were so sweet to him that he had no wish to hurry her, any more than he would have had a wish to hurry a golden sunrise. "Your being so different, which at first seemed a difficulty, a trouble, began one day to seem to me a pleasure, a great pleasure. I was glad you were different. And yet if I had said so, no one would have understood me; I don't mean simply to my family."

"They would have said I was a queer monster, eh?" said Newman.

"They would have said I could never be happy with you—you were too different; and I would have said it was just BECAUSE you were so different that I might be happy. But they would have given better reasons than I. My only reason"—and she paused again.

But this time, in the midst of his golden sunrise, Newman felt the impulse to grasp at a rosy cloud. "Your only reason is that you love me!" he murmured with an eloquent gesture, and for want of a better reason Madame de Cintre reconciled herself to this one.

Newman came back the next day, and in the vestibule, as he entered the house, he encountered his friend Mrs. Bread. She was wandering about in honorable idleness, and when his eyes fell upon her she delivered him one of her curtsies. Then turning to the servant who had admitted him, she said, with the combined majesty of her native superiority and of a rugged English accent, "You may retire; I will have the honor of conducting monsieur." In spite of this combination, however, it appeared to Newman that her voice had a slight quaver, as if the tone of command were not habitual to it. The man gave her an impertinent stare, but he walked slowly away, and she led Newman up-stairs. At half its course the staircase gave a bend, forming a little platform. In the angle of the wall stood an indifferent statue of an eighteenth-century nymph, simpering, sallow, and cracked. Here Mrs. Bread stopped and looked with shy kindness at her companion.

"I know the good news, sir," she murmured.

"You have a good right to be first to know it," said Newman. "You have taken such a friendly interest."

Mrs. Bread turned away and began to blow the dust off the statue, as if this might be mockery.

"I suppose you want to congratulate me," said Newman. "I am greatly obliged." And then he added, "You gave me much pleasure the other day."

She turned around, apparently reassured. "You are not to think that I have been told anything," she said; "I have only guessed. But when I looked at you, as you came in, I was sure I had guessed aright."

"You are very sharp," said Newman. "I am sure that in your quiet way you see everything."

"I am not a fool, sir, thank God. I have guessed something else beside," said Mrs. Bread.

"What's that?"

"I needn't tell you that, sir; I don't think you would believe it. At any rate it wouldn't please you."

"Oh, tell me nothing but what will please me," laughed Newman. "That is the way you began."

"Well, sir, I suppose you won't be vexed to hear that the sooner everything is over the better."

"The sooner we are married, you mean? The better for me, certainly."

"The better for every one."

"The better for you, perhaps. You know you are coming to live with us," said Newman.

"I'm extremely obliged to you, sir, but it is not of myself I was thinking. I only wanted, if I might take the liberty, to recommend you to lose no time."

"Whom are you afraid of?"

Mrs. Bread looked up the staircase and then down and then she looked at the undusted nymph, as if she possibly had sentient ears. "I am afraid of every one," she said.

"What an uncomfortable state of mind!" said Newman. "Does 'every one' wish to prevent my marriage?"

"I am afraid of already having said too much," Mrs. Bread replied. "I won't take it back, but I won't say any more." And she took her way up the staircase again and led him into Madame de Cintre's salon.

Newman indulged in a brief and silent imprecation when he found that Madame de Cintre was not alone. With her sat her mother, and in the middle of the room stood young Madame de Bellegarde, in her bonnet and mantle. The old marquise, who was leaning back in her chair with a hand clasping the knob of each arm, looked at him fixedly without moving. She seemed barely conscious of his greeting; she appeared to be musing intently. Newman said to himself that her daughter had been announcing her engagement and that the old lady found the morsel hard to swallow. But Madame de Cintre, as she gave him her hand gave him also a look by which she appeared to mean that he should understand something. Was it a warning or a request? Did she wish to enjoin speech or silence? He was puzzled, and young Madame de Bellegarde's pretty grin gave him no information.

"I have not told my mother," said Madame de Cintre abruptly, looking at him.

"Told me what?" demanded the marquise. "You tell me too little; you should tell me everything."

"That is what I do," said Madame Urbain, with a little laugh.

"Let ME tell your mother," said Newman.

The old lady stared at him again, and then turned to her daughter. "You are going to marry him?" she cried, softly.

"Oui ma mere," said Madame de Cintre.

"Your daughter has consented, to my great happiness," said Newman.

"And when was this arrangement made?" asked Madame de Bellegarde. "I seem to be picking up the news by chance!"

"My suspense came to an end yesterday," said Newman.

"And how long was mine to have lasted?" said the marquise to her daughter. She spoke without irritation; with a sort of cold, noble displeasure.

Madame de Cintre stood silent, with her eyes on the ground. "It is over now," she said.

"Where is my son—where is Urbain?" asked the marquise. "Send for your brother and inform him."

Young Madame de Bellegarde laid her hand on the bell-rope. "He was to make some visits with me, and I was to go and knock—very softly, very softly—at the door of his study. But he can come to me!" She pulled the bell, and in a few moments Mrs. Bread appeared, with a face of calm inquiry.

"Send for your brother," said the old lady.

But Newman felt an irresistible impulse to speak, and to speak in a certain way. "Tell the marquis we want him," he said to Mrs. Bread, who quietly retired.

Young Madame de Bellegarde went to her sister-in-law and embraced her. Then she turned to Newman, with an intense smile. "She is charming. I congratulate you."

"I congratulate you, sir," said Madame de Bellegarde, with extreme solemnity. "My daughter is an extraordinarily good woman. She may have faults, but I don't know them."

"My mother does not often make jokes," said Madame de Cintre; "but when she does they are terrible."

"She is ravishing," the Marquise Urbain resumed, looking at her sister-in-law, with her head on one side. "Yes, I congratulate you."

Madame de Cintre turned away, and, taking up a piece of tapestry, began to ply the needle. Some minutes of silence elapsed, which were interrupted by the arrival of M. de Bellegarde. He came in with his hat in his hand, gloved, and was followed by his brother Valentin, who appeared to have just entered the house. M. de Bellegarde looked around the circle and greeted Newman with his usual finely-measured courtesy. Valentin saluted his mother and his sisters, and, as he shook hands with Newman, gave him a glance of acute interrogation.

"Arrivez donc, messieurs!" cried young Madame de Bellegarde. "We have great news for you."

"Speak to your brother, my daughter," said the old lady.

Madame de Cintre had been looking at her tapestry. She raised her eyes to her brother. "I have accepted Mr. Newman."

"Your sister has consented," said Newman. "You see after all, I knew what I was about."

"I am charmed!" said M. de Bellegarde, with superior benignity.

"So am I," said Valentin to Newman. "The marquis and I are charmed. I can't marry, myself, but I can understand it. I can't stand on my head, but I can applaud a clever acrobat. My dear sister, I bless your union."

The marquis stood looking for a while into the crown of his hat. "We have been prepared," he said at last "but it is inevitable that in face of the event one should experience a certain emotion." And he gave a most unhilarious smile.

"I feel no emotion that I was not perfectly prepared for," said his mother.

"I can't say that for myself," said Newman, smiling but differently from the marquis. "I am happier than I expected to be. I suppose it's the sight of your happiness!"

CHAPTER XIV

"Don't exaggerate that," said Madame de Bellegarde, getting up and laying her hand upon her daughter's arm. "You can't expect an honest old woman to thank you for taking away her beautiful, only daughter."

"You forgot me, dear madame," said the young marquise demurely.

"Yes, she is very beautiful," said Newman.

"And when is the wedding, pray?" asked young Madame de Bellegarde; "I must have a month to think over a dress."

"That must be discussed," said the marquise.

"Oh, we will discuss it, and let you know!" Newman exclaimed.

"I have no doubt we shall agree," said Urbain.

"If you don't agree with Madame de Cintre, you will be very unreasonable."

"Come, come, Urbain," said young Madame de Bellegarde, "I must go straight to my tailor's."

The old lady had been standing with her hand on her daughter's arm, looking at her fixedly. She gave a little sigh, and murmured, "No, I did NOT expect it! You are a fortunate man," she added, turning to Newman, with an expressive nod.

"Oh, I know that!" he answered. "I feel tremendously proud. I feel like crying it on the housetops,—like stopping people in the street to tell them."

Madame de Bellegarde narrowed her lips. "Pray don't," she said.

"The more people that know it, the better," Newman declared. "I haven't yet announced it here, but I telegraphed it this morning to America."

"Telegraphed it to America?" the old lady murmured.

"To New York, to St. Louis, and to San Francisco; those are the principal cities, you know. To-morrow I shall tell my friends here."

"Have you many?" asked Madame de Bellegarde, in a tone of which I am afraid that Newman but partly measured the impertinence.

"Enough to bring me a great many hand-shakes and congratulations. To say nothing," he added, in a moment, "of those I shall receive from your friends."

"They will not use the telegraph," said the marquise, taking her departure.

M. de Bellegarde, whose wife, her imagination having apparently taken flight to the tailor's, was fluttering her silken wings in emulation, shook hands with Newman, and said with a more persuasive accent than the latter had ever heard him use, "You may count upon me." Then his wife led him away.

Valentin stood looking from his sister to our hero. "I hope you both reflected seriously," he said.

Madame de Cintre smiled. "We have neither your powers of reflection nor your depth of seriousness; but we have done our best."

"Well, I have a great regard for each of you," Valentin continued. "You are charming young people. But I am not satisfied, on the whole, that you belong to that small and superior class—that exquisite group composed of persons who are worthy to remain unmarried. These are rare souls; they are the salt of the earth. But I don't mean to be invidious; the marrying people are often very nice."

"Valentin holds that women should marry, and that men should not," said Madame de Cintre. "I don't know how he arranges it."

"I arrange it by adoring you, my sister," said Valentin ardently. "Good-by."

"Adore some one whom you can marry," said Newman. "I will arrange that for you some day. I foresee that I am going to turn apostle."

Valentin was on the threshold; he looked back a moment with a face that had turned grave. "I adore some one I can't marry!" he said. And he dropped the portiere and departed.

"They don't like it," said Newman, standing alone before Madame de Cintre.

"No," she said, after a moment; "they don't like it."

"Well, now, do you mind that?" asked Newman.

"Yes!" she said, after another interval.

"That's a mistake."

"I can't help it. I should prefer that my mother were pleased."

"Why the deuce," demanded Newman, "is she not pleased? She gave you leave to marry me."

"Very true; I don't understand it. And yet I do 'mind it,' as you say. You will call it superstitious."

"That will depend upon how much you let it bother you. Then I shall call it an awful bore."

"I will keep it to myself," said Madame de Cintre, "It shall not bother you." And then they talked of their marriage-day, and Madame de Cintre assented unreservedly to Newman's desire to have it fixed for an early date.

Newman's telegrams were answered with interest. Having dispatched but three electric missives, he received no less than eight gratulatory bulletins in return. He put them into his pocket-book, and the next time he encountered old Madame de Bellegarde drew them forth and displayed them to her. This, it must be confessed, was a slightly malicious stroke; the reader must judge in what degree the offense was venial. Newman knew that the marquise disliked his telegrams, though he could see no sufficient reason for it. Madame de Cintre, on the other hand, liked them, and, most of them being of a humorous cast, laughed at them immoderately, and inquired into the character of their authors. Newman, now that his prize was gained, felt a peculiar desire that his triumph should be manifest. He more than suspected that the Bellegardes were keeping quiet about it, and allowing it, in their select circle, but a limited resonance; and it pleased him to think that if he were to take the trouble he might, as he phrased it, break all the windows. No man likes being repudiated, and yet Newman, if he was not flattered, was not exactly offended. He had not this good excuse for his somewhat aggressive impulse to promulgate his felicity; his sentiment was of another quality. He wanted for once to make the heads of the house of Bellegarde FEEL him; he knew not when he should have another chance. He had had for the past six months a sense of the old lady and her son looking straight over his head, and he was now resolved that they should toe a mark which he would give himself the satisfaction of drawing.

"It is like seeing a bottle emptied when the wine is poured too slowly," he said to Mrs. Tristram. "They make me want to joggle their elbows and force them to spill their wine."

To this Mrs. Tristram answered that he had better leave them alone and let them do things in their own way. "You must make allowances for them," she said. "It is natural enough that they should hang fire a little. They thought they accepted you when you made your application; but they are not people of imagination, they could not project themselves into the future, and now they will have to begin again. But they are people of honor, and they will do whatever is necessary."

Newman spent a few moments in narrow-eyed meditation. "I am not hard on them," he presently said, "and to prove it I will invite them all to a festival."

"To a festival?"

"You have been laughing at my great gilded rooms all winter; I will show you that they are good for something. I will give a party. What is the grandest thing one can do here? I will hire all the great singers from the opera, and all the first people from the Theatre Francais, and I will give an entertainment."

"And whom will you invite?"

"You, first of all. And then the old lady and her son. And then every one among her friends whom I have met at her house or elsewhere, every one who has shown me the minimum of politeness, every duke of them and his wife. And then all my friends, without exception: Miss Kitty Upjohn, Miss Dora Finch, General Packard, C. P Hatch, and all the rest. And every one shall know what it is about, that is, to celebrate my engagement to the Countess de Cintre. What do you think of the idea?"

"I think it is odious!" said Mrs. Tristram. And then in a moment: "I think it is delicious!"

The very next evening Newman repaired to Madame de Bellegarde's salon. where he found her surrounded by her children, and invited her to honor his poor dwelling by her presence on a certain evening a fortnight distant.

The marquise stared a moment. "My dear sir," she cried, "what do you want to do to me?"

"To make you acquainted with a few people, and then to place you in a very easy chair and ask you to listen to Madame Frezzolini's singing."

"You mean to give a concert?"

"Something of that sort."

"And to have a crowd of people?"

"All my friends, and I hope some of yours and your daughter's. I want to celebrate my engagement."

It seemed to Newman that Madame de Bellegarde turned pale. She opened her fan, a fine old painted fan of the last century, and looked at the picture, which represented a fete champetre—a lady with a guitar, singing, and a group of dancers round a garlanded Hermes.

"We go out so little," murmured the marquis, "since my poor father's death."

"But MY dear father is still alive, my friend," said his wife. "I am only waiting for my invitation to accept it," and she glanced with amiable confidence at Newman. "It will be magnificent; I am very sure of that."

I am sorry to say, to the discredit of Newman's gallantry, that this lady's invitation was not then and there bestowed; he was giving all his attention to the old marquise. She looked up at last, smiling. "I can't think of letting you offer me a fete," she said, "until I have offered you one. We want to present you to our friends; we will invite them all. We have it very much at heart. We must do things in order. Come to me about the 25th; I will let you know the exact day immediately. We shall not have any one so fine as Madame Frezzolini, but we shall have some very good people. After that you may talk of your own fete." The old lady spoke with a certain quick eagerness, smiling more agreeably as she went on.

It seemed to Newman a handsome proposal, and such proposals always touched the sources of his good-nature. He said to Madame de Bellegarde that he should be glad to come on the 25th or any other day, and that it mattered very little whether he met his friends at her house or at his own. I have said that Newman was observant, but it must be admitted that on this occasion he failed to notice a certain delicate glance which passed between Madame de Bellegarde and the marquis, and which we may presume to have been a commentary upon the innocence displayed in that latter clause of his speech.

Valentin de Bellegarde walked away with Newman that evening, and when they had left the Rue de l'Universite some distance behind them he said reflectively, "My mother is very strong—very strong." Then in answer to an interrogative movement of Newman's he continued, "She was driven to the wall, but you would never have thought it. Her fete of the 25th was an invention of the moment. She had no idea whatever of giving a fete, but finding it the only issue from your proposal, she looked straight at the dose—excuse the expression—and bolted it, as you saw, without winking. She is very strong."

"Dear me!" said Newman, divided between relish and compassion. "I don't care a straw for her fete, I am willing to take the will for the deed."

"No, no," said Valentin, with a little inconsequent touch of family pride. "The thing will be done now, and done handsomely."

CHAPTER XV

Valentin de Bellegarde's announcement of the secession of Mademoiselle Nioche from her father's domicile and his irreverent reflections upon the attitude of this anxious parent in so grave a catastrophe, received a practical commentary in the fact that M. Nioche was slow to seek another interview with his late pupil. It had cost Newman some disgust to be forced to assent to Valentin's somewhat cynical interpretation of the old man's philosophy, and, though circumstances seemed to indicate that he had not given himself up to a noble despair, Newman thought it very possible he might be suffering more keenly than was apparent. M. Nioche had been in the habit of paying him a respectful little visit every two or three weeks and his absence might be a proof quite as much of extreme depression as of a desire to conceal the success with which he had patched up his sorrow. Newman presently learned from Valentin several details touching this new phase of Mademoiselle Noemie's career.

"I told you she was remarkable," this unshrinking observer declared, "and the way she has managed this performance proves it. She has had other chances, but she was resolved to take none but the best. She did you the honor to think for a while that you might be such a chance. You were not; so she gathered up her patience and waited a while longer. At last her occasion came along, and she made her move with her eyes wide open. I am very sure she had no innocence to lose, but she had all her respectability. Dubious little damsel as you thought her, she had kept a firm hold of that; nothing could be proved against her, and she was determined not to let her reputation go till she had got her equivalent. About her equivalent she had high ideas. Apparently her ideal has been satisfied. It is fifty years old, bald-headed, and deaf, but it is very easy about money."

"And where in the world," asked Newman, "did you pick up this valuable information?"

"In conversation. Remember my frivolous habits. In conversation with a young woman engaged in the humble trade of glove-cleaner, who keeps a small shop in the Rue St. Roch. M. Nioche lives in the same house, up six pair of stairs, across the court, in and out of whose ill-swept doorway Miss Noemie has been flitting for the last five years. The little glove-cleaner was an old acquaintance; she used to be the friend of a friend of mine, who has married and dropped such friends. I often saw her in his society. As soon as I espied her behind her clear little window-pane, I recollected her. I had on a spotlessly fresh pair of gloves, but I went in and held up my hands, and said to her, 'Dear mademoiselle, what will you ask me for cleaning these?' 'Dear count,' she answered immediately, 'I will clean them for you for nothing.' She had instantly recognized me, and I had to hear her history for the last six years. But after that, I put her upon that of her neighbors. She knows and admires Noemie, and she told me what I have just repeated."

A month elapsed without M. Nioche reappearing, and Newman, who every morning read two or three suicides in the "Figaro," began to suspect that, mortification proving stubborn, he had sought a balm for his wounded pride in the waters of the Seine. He had a note of M. Nioche's address in his pocket-book, and finding himself one day in the quartier, he determined in so far as he might to clear up his doubts. He repaired to the house in the Rue St. Roch which bore the recorded number, and observed in a neighboring basement, behind a dangling row of neatly inflated gloves, the attentive physiognomy of Bellegarde's informant—a sallow person in a dressing-gown—peering into the street as if she were expecting that amiable nobleman to pass again. But it was not to her that Newman applied; he simply asked of the portress if M. Nioche were at home. The portress replied, as the portress invariably replies, that her lodger had gone out barely three minutes before; but then, through the little square hole of her lodge-window taking the measure of Newman's fortunes, and seeing them, by an unspecified process, refresh the dry places of servitude to occupants of fifth floors on courts, she added that M. Nioche would have had just time to reach the Cafe de la Patrie, round the second corner to the left, at which establishment he regularly spent his afternoons. Newman thanked her for the information, took the second turning to the left, and arrived at the Cafe de la Patrie. He felt a momentary hesitation to go in; was it not rather mean to "follow up" poor old Nioche at that rate? But there passed across his vision an image of a haggard little septuagenarian taking measured sips of a glass of sugar and water and finding them quite impotent to sweeten his desolation. He opened the door and entered, perceiving nothing at first but a dense cloud of tobacco smoke. Across this, however, in a corner, he presently descried the figure of M. Nioche, stirring the contents of a deep glass, with a lady seated in front of him. The lady's back was turned to Newman, but M. Nioche very soon perceived and recognized his visitor. Newman had gone toward him, and the old man rose slowly, gazing at him with a more blighted expression even than usual.

"If you are drinking hot punch," said Newman, "I suppose you are not dead. That's all right. Don't move."

M. Nioche stood staring, with a fallen jaw, not daring to put out his hand. The lady, who sat facing him, turned round in her place and glanced upward with a spirited toss of her head, displaying the agreeable features of his daughter. She looked at Newman sharply, to see how he was looking at her, then—I don't know what she discovered—she said graciously, "How d' ye do, monsieur? won't you come into our little corner?"

"Did you come—did you come after ME?" asked M. Nioche very softly.

"I went to your house to see what had become of you. I thought you might be sick," said Newman.

"It is very good of you, as always," said the old man. "No, I am not well. Yes, I am SEEK."

"Ask monsieur to sit down," said Mademoiselle Nioche. "Garcon, bring a chair."

"Will you do us the honor to SEAT?" said M. Nioche, timorously, and with a double foreignness of accent.

Newman said to himself that he had better see the thing out and he took a chair at the end of the table, with Mademoiselle Nioche on his left and her father on the other side. "You will take something, of course," said Miss Noemie, who was sipping a glass of madeira. Newman said that he believed not, and then she turned to her papa with a smile. "What an honor, eh? he has come only for us." M. Nioche drained his pungent glass at a long draught, and looked out from eyes more lachrymose in consequence. "But you didn't come for me, eh?" Mademoiselle Noemie went on. "You didn't expect to find me here?"

Newman observed the change in her appearance. She was very elegant and prettier than before; she looked a year or two older, and it was noticeable that, to the eye, she had only gained in respectability. She looked "ladylike." She was dressed in quiet colors, and wore her expensively unobtrusive toilet with a grace that might have come from years of practice. Her present self-possession and aplomb struck Newman as really infernal, and he inclined to agree with Valentin de Bellegarde that the young lady was very remarkable. "No, to tell the truth, I didn't come for you," he said, "and I didn't expect to find you. I was told," he added in a moment "that you had left your father."

"Quelle horreur!" cried Mademoiselle Nioche with a smile. "Does one leave one's father? You have the proof of the contrary."

"Yes, convincing proof," said Newman glancing at M. Nioche. The old man caught his glance obliquely, with his faded, deprecating eye, and then, lifting his empty glass, pretended to drink again.

"Who told you that?" Noemie demanded. "I know very well. It was M. de Bellegarde. Why don't you say yes? You are not polite."

"I am embarrassed," said Newman.

"I set you a better example. I know M. de Bellegarde told you. He knows a great deal about me—or he thinks he does. He has taken a great deal of trouble to find out, but half of it isn't true. In the first place, I haven't left my father; I am much too fond of him. Isn't it so, little father? M. de Bellegarde is a charming young man; it is impossible to be cleverer. I know a good deal about him too; you can tell him that when you next see him."

"No," said Newman, with a sturdy grin; "I won't carry any messages for you."

"Just as you please," said Mademoiselle Nioche, "I don't depend upon you, nor does M. de Bellegarde either. He is very much interested in me; he can be left to his own devices. He is a contrast to you."

"Oh, he is a great contrast to me, I have no doubt" said Newman. "But I don't exactly know how you mean it."

"I mean it in this way. First of all, he never offered to help me to a dot and a husband." And Mademoiselle Nioche paused, smiling. "I won't say that is in his favor, for I do you justice. What led you, by the way, to make me such a queer offer? You didn't care for me."

"Oh yes, I did," said Newman.

"How so?"

"It would have given me real pleasure to see you married to a respectable young fellow."

"With six thousand francs of income!" cried Mademoiselle Nioche. "Do you call that caring for me? I'm afraid you know little about women. You were not galant; you were not what you might have been."

Newman flushed a trifle fiercely. "Come!" he exclaimed "that's rather strong. I had no idea I had been so shabby."

Mademoiselle Nioche smiled as she took up her muff. "It is something, at any rate, to have made you angry."

Her father had leaned both his elbows on the table, and his head, bent forward, was supported in his hands, the thin white fingers of which were pressed over his ears. In his position he was staring fixedly at the bottom of his empty glass, and Newman supposed he was not hearing. Mademoiselle Noemie buttoned her furred jacket and pushed back her chair, casting a glance charged with the consciousness of an expensive appearance first down over her flounces and then up at Newman.

"You had better have remained an honest girl," Newman said, quietly.

M. Nioche continued to stare at the bottom of his glass, and his daughter got up, still bravely smiling. "You mean that I look so much like one? That's more than most women do nowadays. Don't judge me yet a while," she added. "I mean to succeed; that's what I mean to do. I leave you; I don't mean to be seen in cafes, for one thing. I can't think what you want of my poor father; he's very comfortable now. It isn't his fault, either. Au revoir, little father." And she tapped the old man on the head with her muff. Then she stopped a minute, looking at Newman. "Tell M. de Bellegarde, when he wants news of me, to come and get it from ME!" And she turned and departed, the white-aproned waiter, with a bow, holding the door wide open for her.

M. Nioche sat motionless, and Newman hardly knew what to say to him. The old man looked dismally foolish. "So you determined not to shoot her, after all," Newman said, presently.

M. Nioche, without moving, raised his eyes and gave him a long, peculiar look. It seemed to confess everything, and yet not to ask for pity, nor to pretend, on the other hand, to a rugged ability to do without it. It might have expressed the state of mind of an innocuous insect, flat in shape and conscious of the impending pressure of a boot-sole, and reflecting that he was perhaps too flat to be crushed. M. Nioche's gaze was a profession of moral flatness. "You despise me terribly," he said, in the weakest possible voice.

"Oh no," said Newman, "it is none of my business. It's a good plan to take things easily."

"I made you too many fine speeches," M. Nioche added. "I meant them at the time."

"I am sure I am very glad you didn't shoot her," said Newman. "I was afraid you might have shot yourself. That is why I came to look you up." And he began to button his coat.

"Neither," said M. Nioche. "You despise me, and I can't explain to you. I hoped I shouldn't see you again."

"Why, that's rather shabby," said Newman. "You shouldn't drop your friends that way. Besides, the last time you came to see me I thought you particularly jolly."

"Yes, I remember," said M. Nioche, musingly; "I was in a fever. I didn't know what I said, what I did. It was delirium."

"Ah, well, you are quieter now."

M. Nioche was silent a moment. "As quiet as the grave," he whispered softly.

"Are you very unhappy?"

M. Nioche rubbed his forehead slowly, and even pushed back his wig a little, looking askance at his empty glass. "Yes—yes. But that's an old story. I have always been unhappy. My daughter does what she will with me. I take what she gives me, good or bad. I have no spirit, and when you have no spirit you must keep quiet. I shan't trouble you any more."

"Well," said Newman, rather disgusted at the smooth operation of the old man's philosophy, "that's as you please."

M. Nioche seemed to have been prepared to be despised but nevertheless he made a feeble movement of appeal from Newman's faint praise. "After all," he said, "she is my daughter, and I can still look after her. If she will do wrong, why she will. But there are many different paths, there are degrees. I can give her the benefit—give her the benefit"—and M. Nioche paused, staring vaguely at Newman, who began to suspect that his brain had softened—"the benefit of my experience," M. Nioche added.

"Your experience?" inquired Newman, both amused and amazed.

"My experience of business," said M. Nioche, gravely.

"Ah, yes," said Newman, laughing, "that will be a great advantage to her!" And then he said good-by, and offered the poor, foolish old man his hand.

M. Nioche took it and leaned back against the wall, holding it a moment and looking up at him. "I suppose you think my wits are going," he said. "Very likely; I have always a pain in my head. That's why I can't explain, I can't tell you. And she's so strong, she makes me walk as she will, anywhere! But there's this—there's this." And he stopped, still staring up at Newman. His little white eyes expanded and glittered for a moment like those of a cat in the dark. "It's not as it seems. I haven't forgiven her. Oh, no!"

"That's right; don't," said Newman. "She's a bad case."

"It's horrible, it's horrible," said M. Nioche; "but do you want to know the truth? I hate her! I take what she gives me, and I hate her more. To-day she brought me three hundred francs; they are here in my waistcoat pocket. Now I hate her almost cruelly. No, I haven't forgiven her."

"Why did you accept the money?" Newman asked.

"If I hadn't," said M. Nioche, "I should have hated her still more. That's what misery is. No, I haven't forgiven her."

"Take care you don't hurt her!" said Newman, laughing again. And with this he took his leave. As he passed along the glazed side of the cafe, on reaching the street, he saw the old man motioning the waiter, with a melancholy gesture, to replenish his glass.

One day, a week after his visit to the Cafe de la Patrie, he called upon Valentin de Bellegarde, and by good fortune found him at home. Newman spoke of his interview with M. Nioche and his daughter, and said he was afraid Valentin had judged the old man correctly. He had found the couple hobnobbing together in all amity; the old gentleman's rigor was purely theoretic. Newman confessed that he was disappointed; he should have expected to see M. Nioche take high ground.

"High ground, my dear fellow," said Valentin, laughing; "there is no high ground for him to take. The only perceptible eminence in M. Nioche's horizon is Montmartre, which is not an edifying quarter. You can't go mountaineering in a flat country."

"He remarked, indeed," said Newman, "that he has not forgiven her. But she'll never find it out."

"We must do him the justice to suppose he doesn't like the thing," Valentin rejoined. "Mademoiselle Nioche is like the great artists whose biographies we read, who at the beginning of their career have suffered opposition in the domestic circle. Their vocation has not been recognized by their families, but the world has done it justice. Mademoiselle Nioche has a vocation."

"Oh, come," said Newman, impatiently, "you take the little baggage too seriously."

"I know I do; but when one has nothing to think about, one must think of little baggages. I suppose it is better to be serious about light things than not to be serious at all. This little baggage entertains me."

"Oh, she has discovered that. She knows you have been hunting her up and asking questions about her. She is very much tickled by it. That's rather annoying."

"Annoying, my dear fellow," laughed Valentin; "not the least!"

"Hanged if I should want to have a greedy little adventuress like that know I was giving myself such pains about her!" said Newman.

"A pretty woman is always worth one's pains," objected Valentin. "Mademoiselle Nioche is welcome to be tickled by my curiosity, and to know that I am tickled that she is tickled. She is not so much tickled, by the way."

"You had better go and tell her," Newman rejoined. "She gave me a message for you of some such drift."

"Bless your quiet imagination," said Valentin, "I have been to see her—three times in five days. She is a charming hostess; we talk of Shakespeare and the musical glasses. She is extremely clever and a very curious type; not at all coarse or wanting to be coarse; determined not to be. She means to take very good care of herself. She is extremely perfect; she is as hard and clear-cut as some little figure of a sea-nymph in an antique intaglio, and I will warrant that she has not a grain more of sentiment or heart than if she was scooped out of a big amethyst. You can't scratch her even with a diamond. Extremely pretty,—really, when you know her, she is wonderfully pretty,—intelligent, determined, ambitious, unscrupulous, capable of looking at a man strangled without changing color, she is upon my honor, extremely entertaining."

"It's a fine list of attractions," said Newman; "they would serve as a police-detective's description of a favorite criminal. I should sum them up by another word than 'entertaining.'"

"Why, that is just the word to use. I don't say she is laudable or lovable. I don't want her as my wife or my sister. But she is a very curious and ingenious piece of machinery; I like to see it in operation."

"Well, I have seen some very curious machines too," said Newman; "and once, in a needle factory, I saw a gentleman from the city, who had stopped too near one of them, picked up as neatly as if he had been prodded by a fork, swallowed down straight, and ground into small pieces."

Reentering his domicile, late in the evening, three days after Madame de Bellegarde had made her bargain with him—the expression is sufficiently correct—touching the entertainment at which she was to present him to the world, he found on his table a card of goodly dimensions bearing an announcement that this lady would be at home on the 27th of the month, at ten o'clock in the evening. He stuck it into the frame of his mirror and eyed it with some complacency; it seemed an agreeable emblem of triumph, documentary evidence that his prize was gained. Stretched out in a chair, he was looking at it lovingly, when Valentin de Bellegarde was shown into the room. Valentin's glance presently followed the direction of Newman's, and he perceived his mother's invitation.

"And what have they put into the corner?" he asked. "Not the customary 'music,' 'dancing,' or 'tableaux vivants'? They ought at least to put 'An American.'"

"Oh, there are to be several of us," said Newman. "Mrs. Tristram told me to-day that she had received a card and sent an acceptance."

"Ah, then, with Mrs. Tristram and her husband you will have support. My mother might have put on her card 'Three Americans.' But I suspect you will not lack amusement. You will see a great many of the best people in France. I mean the long pedigrees and the high noses, and all that. Some of them are awful idiots; I advise you to take them up cautiously."

"Oh, I guess I shall like them," said Newman. "I am prepared to like every one and everything in these days; I am in high good-humor."

Valentin looked at him a moment in silence and then dropped himself into a chair with an unwonted air of weariness.

"Happy man!" he said with a sigh. "Take care you don't become offensive."

"If any one chooses to take offense, he may. I have a good conscience," said Newman.

"So you are really in love with my sister."

"Yes, sir!" said Newman, after a pause.

"And she also?"

"I guess she likes me," said Newman.

"What is the witchcraft you have used?" Valentin asked. "How do YOU make love?"

"Oh, I haven't any general rules," said Newman. "In any way that seems acceptable."

"I suspect that, if one knew it," said Valentin, laughing, "you are a terrible customer. You walk in seven-league boots."

"There is something the matter with you to-night," Newman said in response to this. "You are vicious. Spare me all discordant sounds until after my marriage. Then, when I have settled down for life, I shall be better able to take things as they come."

"And when does your marriage take place?"

"About six weeks hence."

Valentin was silent a while, and then he said, "And you feel very confident about the future?"

"Confident. I knew what I wanted, exactly, and I know what I have got."

"You are sure you are going to be happy?"

"Sure?" said Newman. "So foolish a question deserves a foolish answer. Yes!"

"You are not afraid of anything?"

"What should I be afraid of? You can't hurt me unless you kill me by some violent means. That I should indeed consider a tremendous sell. I want to live and I mean to live. I can't die of illness, I am too ridiculously tough; and the time for dying of old age won't come round yet a while. I can't lose my wife, I shall take too good care of her. I may lose my money, or a large part of it; but that won't matter, for I shall make twice as much again. So what have I to be afraid of?"

CHAPTER XV

"You are not afraid it may be rather a mistake for an American man of business to marry a French countess?"

"For the countess, possibly; but not for the man of business, if you mean me! But my countess shall not be disappointed; I answer for her happiness!" And as if he felt the impulse to celebrate his happy certitude by a bonfire, he got up to throw a couple of logs upon the already blazing hearth. Valentin watched for a few moments the quickened flame, and then, with his head leaning on his hand, gave a melancholy sigh. "Got a headache?" Newman asked.

"Je suis triste," said Valentin, with Gallic simplicity.

"You are sad, eh? It is about the lady you said the other night that you adored and that you couldn't marry?"

"Did I really say that? It seemed to me afterwards that the words had escaped me. Before Claire it was bad taste. But I felt gloomy as I spoke, and I feel gloomy still. Why did you ever introduce me to that girl?"

"Oh, it's Noemie, is it? Lord deliver us! You don't mean to say you are lovesick about her?"

"Lovesick, no; it's not a grand passion. But the cold-blooded little demon sticks in my thoughts; she has bitten me with those even little teeth of hers; I feel as if I might turn rabid and do something crazy in consequence. It's very low, it's disgustingly low. She's the most mercenary little jade in Europe. Yet she really affects my peace of mind; she is always running in my head. It's a striking contrast to your noble and virtuous attachment—a vile contrast! It is rather pitiful that it should be the best I am able to do for myself at my present respectable age. I am a nice young man, eh, en somme? You can't warrant my future, as you do your own."

"Drop that girl, short," said Newman; "don't go near her again, and your future will do. Come over to America and I will get you a place in a bank."

"It is easy to say drop her," said Valentin, with a light laugh. "You can't drop a pretty woman like that. One must be polite, even with Noemie. Besides, I'll not have her suppose I am afraid of her."

"So, between politeness and vanity, you will get deeper into the mud? Keep them both for something better. Remember, too, that I didn't want to introduce you to her: you insisted. I had a sort of uneasy feeling about it."

"Oh, I don't reproach you," said Valentin. "Heaven forbid! I wouldn't for the world have missed knowing her. She is really extraordinary. The way she has already spread her wings is amazing. I don't know when a woman has amused me more. But excuse me," he added in an instant; "she doesn't amuse you, at second hand, and the subject is an impure one. Let us talk of something else." Valentin introduced another topic, but within five minutes Newman observed that, by a bold transition, he had reverted to Mademoiselle Nioche, and was giving pictures of her manners and quoting specimens of her mots. These were very witty, and, for a young woman who six months before had been painting the most artless madonnas, startlingly cynical. But at last, abruptly, he stopped, became thoughtful, and for some time afterwards said nothing. When he rose to go it was evident that his thoughts were still running upon Mademoiselle Nioche. "Yes, she's a frightful little monster!" he said.

CHAPTER XVI

The next ten days were the happiest that Newman had ever known. He saw Madame de Cintre every day, and never saw either old Madame de Bellegarde or the elder of his prospective brothers-in-law. Madame de Cintre at last seemed to think it becoming to apologize for their never being present. "They are much taken up," she said, "with doing the honors of Paris to Lord Deepmere." There was a smile in her gravity as she made this declaration, and it deepened as she added, "He is our seventh cousin, you know, and blood is thicker than water. And then, he is so interesting!" And with this she laughed.

Newman met young Madame de Bellegarde two or three times, always roaming about with graceful vagueness, as if in search of an unattainable ideal of amusement. She always reminded him of a painted perfume-bottle with a crack in it; but he had grown to have a kindly feeling for her, based on the fact of her owing conjugal allegiance to Urbain de Bellegarde. He pitied M. de Bellegarde's wife, especially since she was a silly, thirstily-smiling little brunette, with a suggestion of an unregulated heart. The small marquise sometimes looked at him with an intensity too marked not to be innocent, for coquetry is more finely shaded. She apparently wanted to ask him something or tell him something; he wondered what it was. But he was shy of giving her an opportunity, because, if her communication bore upon the aridity of her matrimonial lot, he was at a loss to see how he could help her. He had a fancy, however, of her coming up to him some day and saying (after looking around behind her) with a little passionate hiss, "I know you detest my husband; let me have the pleasure of assuring you for once that you are right. Pity a poor woman who is married to a clock-image in papier-mache!" Possessing, however, in default of a competent knowledge of the principles of etiquette, a very downright sense of the "meanness" of certain actions, it seemed to him to belong to his position to keep on his guard; he was not going to put it into the power of these people to say that in their house he had done anything unpleasant. As it was, Madame de Bellegarde used to give him news of the dress she meant to wear at his wedding, and which had not yet, in her creative imagination, in spite of many interviews with the tailor, resolved itself into its composite totality. "I told you pale blue bows on the sleeves, at the elbows," she said. "But to-day I don't see my blue bows at all. I don't know what has become of them. To-day I see pink—a tender pink. And then I pass through strange, dull phases in which neither blue nor pink says anything to me. And yet I must have the bows."

"Have them green or yellow," said Newman.

"Malheureux!" the little marquise would cry. "Green bows would break your marriage—your children would be illegitimate!"

Madame de Cintre was calmly happy before the world, and Newman had the felicity of fancying that before him, when the world was absent, she was almost agitatedly happy. She said very tender things. "I take no pleasure in you. You never give me a chance to scold you, to correct you. I bargained for that, I expected to enjoy it. But you won't do anything dreadful; you are dismally inoffensive. It is very stupid; there is no excitement for me; I might as well be marrying some one else."

"I am afraid it's the worst I can do," Newman would say in answer to this. "Kindly overlook the deficiency." He assured her that he, at least, would never scold her; she was perfectly satisfactory. "If you only knew," he said, "how exactly you are what I coveted! And I am beginning to understand why I coveted it; the having it makes all the difference that I expected. Never was a man so pleased with his good fortune. You have been holding your head for a week past just as I wanted my wife to hold hers. You say just the things I want her to say. You walk about the room just as I want her to walk. You have just the taste in dress that I want her to have. In short, you come up to the mark, and, I can tell you, my mark was high."

CHAPTER XVI

These observations seemed to make Madame de Cintre rather grave. At last she said, "Depend upon it, I don't come up to the mark; your mark is too high. I am not all that you suppose; I am a much smaller affair. She is a magnificent woman, your ideal. Pray, how did she come to such perfection?"

"She was never anything else," Newman said.

"I really believe," Madame de Cintre went on, "that she is better than my own ideal. Do you know that is a very handsome compliment? Well, sir, I will make her my own!"

Mrs. Tristram came to see her dear Claire after Newman had announced his engagement, and she told our hero the next day that his good fortune was simply absurd. "For the ridiculous part of it is," she said, "that you are evidently going to be as happy as if you were marrying Miss Smith or Miss Thompson. I call it a brilliant match for you, but you get brilliancy without paying any tax upon it. Those things are usually a compromise, but here you have everything, and nothing crowds anything else out. You will be brilliantly happy as well." Newman thanked her for her pleasant, encouraging way of saying things; no woman could encourage or discourage better. Tristram's way of saying things was different; he had been taken by his wife to call upon Madame de Cintre, and he gave an account of the expedition.

"You don't catch me giving an opinion on your countess this time," he said; "I put my foot in it once. That's a d—d underhand thing to do, by the way—coming round to sound a fellow upon the woman you are going to marry. You deserve anything you get. Then of course you rush and tell her, and she takes care to make it pleasant for the poor spiteful wretch the first time he calls. I will do you the justice to say, however, that you don't seem to have told Madame de Cintre; or if you have she's uncommonly magnanimous. She was very nice; she was tremendously polite. She and Lizzie sat on the sofa, pressing each other's hands and calling each other chere belle, and Madame de Cintre sent me with every third word a magnificent smile, as if to give me to understand that I too was a handsome dear. She quite made up for past neglect, I assure you; she was very pleasant and sociable. Only in an evil hour it came into her head to say that she must present us to her mother—her mother wished to know your friends. I didn't want to know her mother, and I was on the point of telling Lizzie to go in alone and let me wait for her outside. But Lizzie, with her usual infernal ingenuity, guessed my purpose and reduced me by a glance of her eye. So they marched off arm in arm, and I followed as I could. We found the old lady in her arm-chair, twiddling her aristocratic thumbs. She looked at Lizzie from head to foot; but at that game Lizzie, to do her justice, was a match for her. My wife told her we were great friends of Mr. Newman. The marquise started a moment, and then said, 'Oh, Mr. Newman! My daughter has made up her mind to marry a Mr. Newman.' Then Madame de Cintre began to fondle Lizzie again, and said it was this dear lady that had planned the match and brought them together. 'Oh, 'tis you I have to thank for my American son-in-law,' the old lady said to Mrs. Tristram. 'It was a very clever thought of yours. Be sure of my gratitude.' And then she began to look at me and presently said, 'Pray, are you engaged in some species of manufacture?' I wanted to say that I manufactured broom-sticks for old witches to ride on, but Lizzie got in ahead of me. 'My husband, Madame la Marquise,' she said, 'belongs to that unfortunate class of persons who have no profession and no business, and do very little good in the world.' To get her poke at the old woman she didn't care where she shoved me. 'Dear me,' said the marquise, 'we all have our duties.' 'I am sorry mine compel me to take leave of you,' said Lizzie. And we bundled out again. But you have a mother-in-law, in all the force of the term."

"Oh," said Newman, "my mother-in-law desires nothing better than to let me alone."

Betimes, on the evening of the 27th, he went to Madame de Bellegarde's ball. The old house in the Rue de l'Universite looked strangely brilliant. In the circle of light projected from the outer gate a detachment of the populace stood watching the carriages roll in; the court was illumined with flaring torches and the portico carpeted with crimson. When Newman arrived there were but a few people present. The marquise and her two daughters were at the top of the staircase, where the sallow old nymph in the angle peeped out from a bower of plants. Madame de Bellegarde, in purple and fine laces, looked like an old lady painted by Vandyke; Madame de Cintre was dressed in white. The old lady greeted Newman with majestic formality, and looking round her, called several of the persons who were standing near. They were elderly gentlemen, of what Valentin de Bellegarde had designated as the high-nosed category; two or three of them wore cordons and stars. They approached with measured alertness, and the marquise said that she wished to present them to Mr. Newman, who was going to marry her daughter. Then she introduced successively three dukes, three counts, and a baron. These gentlemen bowed and smiled most agreeably, and Newman indulged in a series of impartial handshakes, accompanied by a "Happy to make your acquaintance, sir." He looked at Madame de Cintre, but she was not looking at him. If his personal self-consciousness had been of a nature to make him constantly refer to her, as the critic before whom, in company, he played his part, he might have found it a flattering proof of her confidence that he never caught her eyes resting upon him. It is a reflection Newman did not make, but we nevertheless risk it, that in spite of this circumstance she probably saw every movement of his little finger. Young Madame de Bellegarde was dressed in an audacious toilet of crimson crape, bestrewn with huge silver moons—thin crescent and full disks.

"You don't say anything about my dress," she said to Newman.

"I feel," he answered, "as if I were looking at you through a telescope. It is very strange."

"If it is strange it matches the occasion. But I am not a heavenly body."

"I never saw the sky at midnight that particular shade of crimson," said Newman.

"That is my originality; any one could have chosen blue. My sister-in-law would have chosen a lovely shade of blue, with a dozen little delicate moons. But I think crimson is much more amusing. And I give my idea, which is moonshine."

"Moonshine and bloodshed," said Newman.

"A murder by moonlight," laughed Madame de Bellegarde. "What a delicious idea for a toilet! To make it complete, there is the silver dagger, you see, stuck into my hair. But here comes Lord Deepmere," she added in a moment. "I must find out what he thinks of it." Lord Deepmere came up, looking very red in the face, and laughing. "Lord Deepmere can't decide which he prefers, my sister-in-law or me," said Madame de Bellegarde. "He likes Claire because she is his cousin, and me because I am not. But he has no right to make love to Claire, whereas I am perfectly disponible. It is very wrong to make love to a woman who is engaged, but it is very wrong not to make love to a woman who is married."

"Oh, it's very jolly making love to married women," said Lord Deepmere, "because they can't ask you to marry them."

"Is that what the others do, the spinsters?" Newman inquired.

"Oh dear, yes," said Lord Deepmere; "in England all the girls ask a fellow to marry them."

"And a fellow brutally refuses," said Madame de Bellegarde.

"Why, really, you know, a fellow can't marry any girl that asks him," said his lordship.

"Your cousin won't ask you. She is going to marry Mr. Newman."

"Oh, that's a very different thing!" laughed Lord Deepmere.

"You would have accepted HER, I suppose. That makes me hope that after all you prefer me."

"Oh, when things are nice I never prefer one to the other," said the young Englishman. "I take them all."

"Ah, what a horror! I won't be taken in that way; I must be kept apart," cried Madame de Bellegarde. "Mr. Newman is much better; he knows how to choose. Oh, he chooses as if he were threading a needle. He prefers Madame de Cintre to any conceivable creature or thing."

"Well, you can't help my being her cousin," said Lord Deepmere to Newman, with candid hilarity.

"Oh, no, I can't help that," said Newman, laughing back; "neither can she!"

"And you can't help my dancing with her," said Lord Deepmere, with sturdy simplicity.

"I could prevent that only by dancing with her myself," said Newman. "But unfortunately I don't know how to dance."

"Oh, you may dance without knowing how; may you not, milord?" said Madame de Bellegarde. But to this Lord Deepmere replied that a fellow ought to know how to dance if he didn't want to make an ass of himself; and at this moment Urbain de Bellegarde joined the group, slow-stepping and with his hands behind him.

"This is a very splendid entertainment," said Newman, cheerfully. "The old house looks very bright."

"If YOU are pleased, we are content," said the marquis, lifting his shoulders and bending them forward.

"Oh, I suspect every one is pleased," said Newman. "How can they help being pleased when the first thing they see as they come in is your sister, standing there as beautiful as an angel?"

"Yes, she is very beautiful," rejoined the marquis, solemnly. "But that is not so great a source of satisfaction to other people, naturally, as to you."

"Yes, I am satisfied, marquis, I am satisfied," said Newman, with his protracted enunciation. "And now tell me," he added, looking round, "who some of your friends are."

M. de Bellegarde looked about him in silence, with his head bent and his hand raised to his lower lip, which he slowly rubbed. A stream of people had been pouring into the salon in which Newman stood with his host, the rooms were filling up and the spectacle had become brilliant. It borrowed its splendor chiefly from the shining shoulders and profuse jewels of the women, and from the voluminous elegance of their dresses. There were no uniforms, as Madame de Bellegarde's door was inexorably closed against the myrmidons of the upstart power which then ruled the fortunes of France, and the great company of smiling and chattering faces was not graced by any very frequent suggestions of harmonious beauty. It is a pity, nevertheless, that Newman had not been a physiognomist, for a great many of the faces were irregularly agreeable, expressive, and suggestive. If the occasion had been different they would hardly have pleased him; he would have thought the women not pretty enough and the men too smirking; but he was now in a humor to receive none but agreeable impressions, and he looked no more narrowly than to perceive that every one was brilliant, and to feel that the sun of their brilliancy was a part of his credit. "I will present you to some people," said M. de Bellegarde after a while. "I will make a point of it, in fact. You will allow me?"

"Oh, I will shake hands with any one you want," said Newman. "Your mother just introduced me to half a dozen old gentlemen. Take care you don't pick up the same parties again."

"Who are the gentlemen to whom my mother presented you?"

"Upon my word, I forgot them," said Newman, laughing. "The people here look very much alike."

"I suspect they have not forgotten you," said the marquis. And he began to walk through the rooms. Newman, to keep near him in the crowd, took his arm; after which for some time, the marquis walked straight along, in silence. At last, reaching the farther end of the suite of reception-rooms, Newman found himself in the presence of a lady of monstrous proportions, seated in a very capacious arm-chair, with several persons standing in a semicircle round her. This little group had divided as the marquis came up, and M. de Bellegarde stepped forward and stood for an instant silent and obsequious, with his hat raised to his lips, as Newman had seen some gentlemen stand in churches as soon as they entered their pews. The lady, indeed, bore a very fair likeness to a reverend effigy in some idolatrous shrine. She was monumentally stout and imperturbably serene. Her aspect was to Newman almost formidable; he had a troubled consciousness of a triple chin, a small piercing eye, a vast expanse of uncovered bosom, a nodding and twinkling tiara of plumes and gems, and an immense circumference of satin petticoat. With her little circle of beholders this remarkable woman reminded him of the Fat Lady at a fair. She fixed her small, unwinking eyes at the new-comers.

"Dear duchess," said the marquis, "let me present you our good friend Mr. Newman, of whom you have heard us speak. Wishing to make Mr. Newman known to those who are dear to us, I could not possibly fail to begin with you."

"Charmed, dear friend; charmed, monsieur," said the duchess in a voice which, though small and shrill, was not disagreeable, while Newman executed his obeisance. "I came on purpose to see monsieur. I hope he appreciates the compliment. You have only to look at me to do so, sir," she continued, sweeping her person with a much-encompassing glance. Newman hardly knew what to say, though it seemed that to a duchess who joked about her corpulence one might say almost anything. On hearing that the duchess had come on purpose to see Newman, the gentlemen who surrounded her turned a little and looked at him with sympathetic curiosity. The marquis with supernatural gravity mentioned to him the name of each, while the gentleman who bore it bowed; they were all what are called in France beaux noms. "I wanted extremely to see you," the duchess went on. "C'est positif. In the first place, I am very fond of the person you are going to marry; she is the most charming creature in France. Mind you treat her well, or you shall hear some news of me. But you look as if you were good. I am told you are very remarkable. I have heard all sorts of extraordinary things about you. Voyons, are they true?"

"I don't know what you can have heard," said Newman.

"Oh, you have your legende. We have heard that you have had a career the most checkered, the most bizarre. What is that about your having founded a city some ten years ago in the great West, a city which contains to-day half a million of inhabitants? Isn't it half a million, messieurs? You are exclusive proprietor of this flourishing settlement, and are consequently fabulously rich, and you would be richer still if you didn't grant lands and houses free of rent to all newcomers who will pledge themselves never to smoke cigars. At this game, in three years, we are told, you are going to be made president of America."

The duchess recited this amazing "legend" with a smooth self-possession which gave the speech to Newman's mind, the air of being a bit of amusing dialogue in a play, delivered by a veteran comic actress. Before she had ceased speaking he had burst into loud, irrepressible laughter. "Dear duchess, dear duchess," the marquis began to murmur, soothingly. Two or three persons came to the door of the room to see who was laughing at the duchess. But the lady continued with the soft, serene assurance of a person who, as a duchess, was certain of being listened to, and, as a garrulous woman, was independent of the pulse of her auditors. "But I know you are very remarkable. You must be, to have endeared yourself to this good marquis and to his admirable world. They are very exacting. I myself am not very sure at this hour of really possessing it. Eh, Bellegarde? To please you, I see, one must be an American millionaire. But your real triumph, my dear sir, is pleasing the countess; she is as difficult as a princess in a fairy tale. Your success is a miracle. What is your secret? I don't ask you to reveal it before all these gentlemen, but come and see me some day and give me a specimen of your talents."

"The secret is with Madame de Cintre," said Newman. "You must ask her for it. It consists in her having a great deal of charity."

"Very pretty!" said the duchess. "That's a very nice specimen, to begin with. What, Bellegarde, are you already taking monsieur away?"

"I have a duty to perform, dear friend," said the marquis, pointing to the other groups.

"Ah, for you I know what that means. Well, I have seen monsieur; that is what I wanted. He can't persuade me that he isn't very clever. Farewell."

As Newman passed on with his host, he asked who the duchess was. "The greatest lady in France," said the marquis. M. de Bellegarde then presented his prospective brother-in-law to some twenty other persons of both sexes, selected apparently for their typically august character. In some cases this character was written in good round hand upon the countenance of the wearer; in others Newman was thankful for such help as his companion's impressively brief intimation contributed to the discovery of it. There were large, majestic men, and small demonstrative men; there were ugly ladies in yellow lace and quaint jewels, and pretty ladies with white shoulders from which jewels and every thing else were absent. Every one gave Newman extreme attention, every one smiled, every one was charmed to make his acquaintance, every one looked at him with that soft hardness of good society which puts out its hand but keeps its fingers closed over the coin. If the marquis was going about as a bear-leader, if the fiction of Beauty and the Beast was supposed to have found its companion-piece, the general impression appeared to be that the bear was a very fair imitation of humanity. Newman found his reception among the marquis's friends very "pleasant;" he could not have said more for it. It was pleasant to be treated with so much explicit politeness; it was pleasant to hear neatly turned civilities, with a flavor of wit, uttered from beneath carefully-shaped mustaches; it was pleasant to see clever Frenchwomen—they all seemed clever—turn their backs to their partners to get a good look at the strange American whom Claire de Cintre was to marry, and reward the object of the exhibition with a charming smile. At last, as he turned away from a battery of smiles and other amenities, Newman caught the eye of the marquis looking at him heavily; and thereupon, for a single instant, he checked himself. "Am I behaving like a d—d fool?" he asked himself. "Am I stepping about like a terrier on his hind legs?" At this moment he perceived Mrs. Tristram at the other side of the room, and he waved his hand in farewell to M. de Bellegarde and made his way toward her.

"Am I holding my head too high?" he asked. "Do I look as if I had the lower end of a pulley fastened to my chin?"

"You look like all happy men, very ridiculous," said Mrs. Tristram. "It's the usual thing, neither better nor worse. I have been watching you for the last ten minutes, and I have been watching M. de Bellegarde. He doesn't like it."

"The more credit to him for putting it through," replied Newman. "But I shall be generous. I shan't trouble him any more. But I am very happy. I can't stand still here. Please to take my arm and we will go for a walk."

He led Mrs. Tristram through all the rooms. There were a great many of them, and, decorated for the occasion and filled with a stately crowd, their somewhat tarnished nobleness recovered its lustre. Mrs. Tristram, looking about her, dropped a series of softly-incisive comments upon her fellow-guests. But Newman made vague answers; he hardly heard her, his thoughts were elsewhere. They were lost in a cheerful sense of success, of attainment and victory. His momentary care as to whether he looked like a fool passed away, leaving him simply with a rich contentment. He had got what he wanted. The savor of success had always been highly agreeable to him, and it had been his fortune to know it often. But it had never before been so sweet, been associated with so much that was brilliant and suggestive and entertaining. The lights, the flowers, the music, the crowd, the splendid women, the jewels, the strangeness even of the universal murmur of a clever foreign tongue were all a vivid symbol and assurance of his having grasped his purpose and forced along his groove. If Newman's smile was larger than usual, it was not tickled vanity that pulled the strings; he had no wish to be shown with the finger or to achieve a personal success. If he could have looked down at the scene, invisible, from a hole in the roof, he would have enjoyed it quite as much. It would have spoken to him about his own prosperity and deepened that easy feeling about life to which, sooner or later, he made all experience contribute. Just now the cup seemed full.

"It is a very pretty party," said Mrs. Tristram, after they had walked a while. "I have seen nothing objectionable except my husband leaning against the wall and talking to an individual whom I suppose he takes for a duke, but whom I more than suspect to be the functionary who attends to the lamps. Do you think you could separate them? Knock over a lamp!"

I doubt whether Newman, who saw no harm in Tristram's conversing with an ingenious mechanic, would have complied with this request; but at this moment Valentin de Bellegarde drew near. Newman, some weeks previously, had presented Madame de Cintre's youngest brother to Mrs. Tristram, for whose merits Valentin professed a discriminating relish and to whom he had paid several visits.

"Did you ever read Keats's Belle Dame sans Merci?" asked Mrs. Tristram. "You remind me of the hero of the ballad:—

'Oh, what can ail thee, knight-at-arms,
Alone and palely loitering?'"

"If I am alone, it is because I have been deprived of your society," said Valentin. "Besides it is good manners for no man except Newman to look happy. This is all to his address. It is not for you and me to go before the curtain."

"You promised me last spring," said Newman to Mrs. Tristram, "that six months from that time I should get into a monstrous rage. It seems to me the time's up, and yet the nearest I can come to doing anything rough now is to offer you a cafe glace."

"I told you we should do things grandly," said Valentin. "I don't allude to the cafes glaces. But every one is here, and my sister told me just now that Urbain had been adorable."

"He's a good fellow, he's a good fellow," said Newman. "I love him as a brother. That reminds me that I ought to go and say something polite to your mother."

"Let it be something very polite indeed," said Valentin. "It may be the last time you will feel so much like it!"

Newman walked away, almost disposed to clasp old Madame de Bellegarde round the waist. He passed through several rooms and at last found the old marquise in the first saloon, seated on a sofa, with her young kinsman, Lord Deepmere, beside her. The young man looked somewhat bored; his hands were thrust into his pockets and his eyes were fixed upon the toes of his shoes, his feet being thrust out in front of him. Madame de Bellegarde appeared to have been talking to him with some intensity and to be waiting for an answer to what she had said, or for some sign of the effect of her words. Her hands were folded in her lap, and she was looking at his lordship's simple physiognomy with an air of politely suppressed irritation.

Lord Deepmere looked up as Newman approached, met his eyes, and changed color.

"I am afraid I disturb an interesting interview," said Newman.

Madame de Bellegarde rose, and her companion rising at the same time, she put her hand into his arm. She answered nothing for an instant, and then, as he remained silent, she said with a smile, "It would be polite for Lord Deepmere to say it was very interesting."

"Oh, I'm not polite!" cried his lordship. "But it was interesting."

"Madame de Bellegarde was giving you some good advice, eh?" said Newman; "toning you down a little?"

"I was giving him some excellent advice," said the marquise, fixing her fresh, cold eyes upon our hero. "It's for him to take it."

"Take it, sir—take it," Newman exclaimed. "Any advice the marquise gives you to-night must be good. For to-night, marquise, you must speak from a cheerful, comfortable spirit, and that makes good advice. You see everything going on so brightly and successfully round you. Your party is magnificent; it was a very happy thought. It is much better than that thing of mine would have been."

"If you are pleased I am satisfied," said Madame de Bellegarde. "My desire was to please you."

"Do you want to please me a little more?" said Newman. "Just drop our lordly friend; I am sure he wants to be off and shake his heels a little. Then take my arm and walk through the rooms."

"My desire was to please you," the old lady repeated. And she liberated Lord Deepmere, Newman rather wondering at her docility. "If this young man is wise," she added, "he will go and find my daughter and ask her to dance."

"I have been indorsing your advice," said Newman, bending over her and laughing, "I suppose I must swallow that!"

Lord Deepmere wiped his forehead and departed, and Madame de Bellegarde took Newman's arm. "Yes, it's a very pleasant, sociable entertainment," the latter declared, as they proceeded on their circuit. "Every one seems to know every one and to be glad to see every one. The marquis has made me acquainted with ever so many people, and I feel quite like one of the family. It's an occasion," Newman continued, wanting to say something thoroughly kind and comfortable, "that I shall always remember, and remember very pleasantly."

"I think it is an occasion that we shall none of us forget," said the marquise, with her pure, neat enunciation.

People made way for her as she passed, others turned round and looked at her, and she received a great many greetings and pressings of the hand, all of which she accepted with the most delicate dignity. But though she smiled upon every one, she said nothing until she reached the last of the rooms, where she found her elder son. Then, "This is enough, sir," she declared with measured softness to Newman, and turned to the marquis. He put out both his hands and took both hers, drawing her to a seat with an air of the tenderest veneration. It was a most harmonious family group, and Newman discreetly retired. He moved through the rooms for some time longer, circulating freely, overtopping most people by his great height, renewing acquaintance with some of the groups to which Urbain de Bellegarde had presented him, and expending generally the surplus of his equanimity. He continued to find it all extremely agreeable; but the most agreeable things have an end, and the revelry on this occasion began to deepen to a close. The music was sounding its ultimate strains and people were looking for the marquise, to make their farewells. There seemed to be some difficulty in finding her, and Newman heard a report that she had left the ball, feeling faint. "She has succumbed to the emotions of the evening," he heard a lady say. "Poor, dear marquise; I can imagine all that they may have been for her!" But he learned immediately afterwards that she had recovered herself and was seated in an armchair near the doorway, receiving parting compliments from great ladies who insisted upon her not rising. He himself set out in quest of Madame de Cintre. He had seen her move past him many times in the rapid circles of a waltz, but in accordance with her explicit instructions he had exchanged no words with her since the beginning of the evening. The whole house having been thrown open, the apartments of the rez-de-chaussee were also accessible, though a smaller number of persons had gathered there. Newman wandered through them, observing a few scattered couples to whom this comparative seclusion appeared grateful and reached a small conservatory which opened into the garden. The end of the conservatory was formed by a clear sheet of glass, unmasked by plants, and admitting the winter starlight so directly that a person standing there would seem to have passed into the open air. Two persons stood there now, a lady and a gentleman; the lady Newman, from within the room and although she had turned her back to it, immediately recognized as Madame de Cintre. He hesitated as to whether he would advance, but as he did so she looked round, feeling apparently that he was there. She rested her eyes on him a moment and then turned again to her companion.

"It is almost a pity not to tell Mr. Newman," she said softly, but in a tone that Newman could hear.

"Tell him if you like!" the gentleman answered, in the voice of Lord Deepmere.

"Oh, tell me by all means!" said Newman advancing.

Lord Deepmere, he observed, was very red in the face, and he had twisted his gloves into a tight cord as if he had been squeezing them dry. These, presumably, were tokens of violent emotion, and it seemed to Newman that the traces of corresponding agitation were visible in Madame de Cintre's face. The two had been talking with much vivacity. "What I should tell you is only to my lord's credit," said Madame de Cintre, smiling frankly enough.

"He wouldn't like it any better for that!" said my lord, with his awkward laugh.

"Come; what's the mystery?" Newman demanded. "Clear it up. I don't like mysteries."

"We must have some things we don't like, and go without some we do," said the ruddy young nobleman, laughing still.

"It's to Lord Deepmere's credit, but it is not to every one's," said Madam de Cintre. "So I shall say nothing about it. You may be sure," she added; and she put out her hand to the Englishman, who took it half shyly, half impetuously. "And now go and dance!" she said.

"Oh yes, I feel awfully like dancing!" he answered. "I shall go and get tipsy." And he walked away with a gloomy guffaw.

"What has happened between you?" Newman asked.

"I can't tell you—now," said Madame de Cintre. "Nothing that need make you unhappy."

"Has the little Englishman been trying to make love to you?"

She hesitated, and then she uttered a grave "No! he's a very honest little fellow."

"But you are agitated. Something is the matter."

"Nothing, I repeat, that need make you unhappy. My agitation is over. Some day I will tell you what it was; not now. I can't now!"

"Well, I confess," remarked Newman, "I don't want to hear anything unpleasant. I am satisfied with everything—most of all with you. I have seen all the ladies and talked with a great many of them; but I am satisfied with you." Madame de Cintre covered him for a moment with her large, soft glance, and then turned her eyes away into the starry night. So they stood silent a moment, side by side. "Say you are satisfied with me," said Newman.

He had to wait a moment for the answer; but it came at last, low yet distinct: "I am very happy."

It was presently followed by a few words from another source, which made them both turn round. "I am sadly afraid Madame de Cintre will take a chill. I have ventured to bring a shawl." Mrs. Bread stood there softly solicitous, holding a white drapery in her hand.

"Thank you," said Madame de Cintre, "the sight of those cold stars gives one a sense of frost. I won't take your shawl, but we will go back into the house."

She passed back and Newman followed her, Mrs. Bread standing respectfully aside to make way for them. Newman paused an instant before the old woman, and she glanced up at him with a silent greeting. "Oh, yes," he said, "you must come and live with us."

"Well then, sir, if you will," she answered, "you have not seen the last of me!"

CHAPTER XVII

Newman was fond of music and went often to the opera. A couple of evenings after Madame de Bellegarde's ball he sat listening to "Don Giovanni," having in honor of this work, which he had never yet seen represented, come to occupy his orchestra-chair before the rising of the curtain. Frequently he took a large box and invited a party of his compatriots; this was a mode of recreation to which he was much addicted. He liked making up parties of his friends and conducting them to the theatre, and taking them to drive on high drags or to dine at remote restaurants. He liked doing things which involved his paying for people; the vulgar truth is that he enjoyed "treating" them. This was not because he was what is called purse-proud; handling money in public was on the contrary positively disagreeable to him; he had a sort of personal modesty about it, akin to what he would have felt about making a toilet before spectators. But just as it was a gratification to him to be handsomely dressed, just so it was a private satisfaction to him (he enjoyed it very clandestinely) to have interposed, pecuniarily, in a scheme of pleasure. To set a large group of people in motion and transport them to a distance, to have special conveyances, to charter railway-carriages and steamboats, harmonized with his relish for bold processes, and made hospitality seem more active and more to the purpose. A few evenings before the occasion of which I speak he had invited several ladies and gentlemen to the opera to listen to Madame Alboni—a party which included Miss Dora Finch. It befell, however, that Miss Dora Finch, sitting near Newman in the box, discoursed brilliantly, not only during the entr'actes, but during many of the finest portions of the performance, so that Newman had really come away with an irritated sense that Madame Alboni had a thin, shrill voice, and that her musical phrase was much garnished with a laugh of the giggling order. After this he promised himself to go for a while to the opera alone.

When the curtain had fallen upon the first act of "Don Giovanni" he turned round in his place to observe the house. Presently, in one of the boxes, he perceived Urbain de Bellegarde and his wife. The little marquise was sweeping the house very busily with a glass, and Newman, supposing that she saw him, determined to go and bid her good evening. M. de Bellegarde was leaning against a column, motionless, looking straight in front of him, with one hand in the breast of his white waistcoat and the other resting his hat on his thigh. Newman was about to leave his place when he noticed in that obscure region devoted to the small boxes which in France are called, not inaptly, "bathing-tubs," a face which even the dim light and the distance could not make wholly indistinct. It was the face of a young and pretty woman, and it was surmounted with a coiffure of pink roses and diamonds. This person was looking round the house, and her fan was moving to and fro with the most practiced grace; when she lowered it, Newman perceived a pair of plump white shoulders and the edge of a rose-colored dress. Beside her, very close to the shoulders and talking, apparently with an earnestness which it pleased her scantily to heed, sat a young man with a red face and a very low shirt-collar. A moment's gazing left Newman with no doubts; the pretty young woman was Noemie Nioche. He looked hard into the depths of the box, thinking her father might perhaps be in attendance, but from what he could see the young man's eloquence had no other auditor. Newman at last made his way out, and in doing so he passed beneath the baignoire of Mademoiselle Noemie. She saw him as he approached and gave him a nod and smile which seemed meant as an assurance that she was still a good-natured girl, in spite of her enviable rise in the world. Newman passed into the foyer and walked through it. Suddenly he paused in front of a gentleman seated on one of the divans. The gentleman's elbows were on his knees; he was leaning forward and staring at the pavement, lost apparently in meditations of a somewhat gloomy cast. But in spite of his bent head Newman recognized him, and in a moment sat down beside him. Then the gentleman looked up and displayed the expressive countenance of Valentin de Bellegarde.

CHAPTER XVII

"What in the world are you thinking of so hard?" asked Newman.

"A subject that requires hard thinking to do it justice," said Valentin. "My immeasurable idiocy."

"What is the matter now?"

"The matter now is that I am a man again, and no more a fool than usual. But I came within an inch of taking that girl au serieux."

"You mean the young lady below stairs, in a baignoire in a pink dress?" said Newman.

"Did you notice what a brilliant kind of pink it was?" Valentin inquired, by way of answer. "It makes her look as white as new milk."

"White or black, as you please. But you have stopped going to see her?"

"Oh, bless you, no. Why should I stop? I have changed, but she hasn't," said Valentin. "I see she is a vulgar little wretch, after all. But she is as amusing as ever, and one MUST be amused."

"Well, I am glad she strikes you so unpleasantly," Newman rejoiced. "I suppose you have swallowed all those fine words you used about her the other night. You compared her to a sapphire, or a topaz, or an amethyst—some precious stone; what was it?"

"I don't remember," said Valentin, "it may have been to a carbuncle! But she won't make a fool of me now. She has no real charm. It's an awfully low thing to make a mistake about a person of that sort."

"I congratulate you," Newman declared, "upon the scales having fallen from your eyes. It's a great triumph; it ought to make you feel better."

"Yes, it makes me feel better!" said Valentin, gayly. Then, checking himself, he looked askance at Newman. "I rather think you are laughing at me. If you were not one of the family I would take it up."

"Oh, no, I'm not laughing, any more than I am one of the family. You make me feel badly. You are too clever a fellow, you are made of too good stuff, to spend your time in ups and downs over that class of goods. The idea of splitting hairs about Miss Nioche! It seems to me awfully foolish. You say you have given up taking her seriously; but you take her seriously so long as you take her at all."

Valentin turned round in his place and looked a while at Newman, wrinkling his forehead and rubbing his knees. "Vous parlez d'or. But she has wonderfully pretty arms. Would you believe I didn't know it till this evening?"

"But she is a vulgar little wretch, remember, all the same," said Newman.

"Yes; the other day she had the bad taste to begin to abuse her father, to his face, in my presence. I shouldn't have expected it of her; it was a disappointment; heigho!"

"Why, she cares no more for her father than for her door-mat," said Newman. "I discovered that the first time I saw her."

"Oh, that's another affair; she may think of the poor old beggar what she pleases. But it was low in her to call him bad names; it quite threw me off. It was about a frilled petticoat that he was to have fetched from the washer-woman's; he appeared to have neglected this graceful duty. She almost boxed his ears. He stood there staring at her with his little blank eyes and smoothing his old hat with his coat-tail. At last he turned round and went out without a word. Then I told her it was in very bad taste to speak so to one's papa. She said she should be so thankful to me if I would mention it to her whenever her taste was at fault; she had immense confidence in mine. I told her I couldn't have the bother of forming her manners; I had had an idea they were already formed, after the best models. She had disappointed me. But I shall get over it," said Valentin, gayly.

"Oh, time's a great consoler!" Newman answered with humorous sobriety. He was silent a moment, and then he added, in another tone, "I wish you would think of what I said to you the other day. Come over to America with us, and I will put you in the way of doing some business. You have a very good head, if you will only use it."

Valentin made a genial grimace. "My head is much obliged to you. Do you mean the place in a bank?"

"There are several places, but I suppose you would consider the bank the most aristocratic."

Valentin burst into a laugh. "My dear fellow, at night all cats are gray! When one derogates there are no degrees."

Newman answered nothing for a minute. Then, "I think you will find there are degrees in success," he said with a certain dryness.

Valentin had leaned forward again, with his elbows on his knees, and he was scratching the pavement with his stick. At last he said, looking up, "Do you really think I ought to do something?"

Newman laid his hand on his companion's arm and looked at him a moment through sagaciously-narrowed eyelids. "Try it and see. You are not good enough for it, but we will stretch a point."

"Do you really think I can make some money? I should like to see how it feels to have a little."

"Do what I tell you, and you shall be rich," said Newman. "Think of it." And he looked at his watch and prepared to resume his way to Madame de Bellegarde's box.

"Upon my word I will think of it," said Valentin. "I will go and listen to Mozart another half hour—I can always think better to music—and profoundly meditate upon it."

The marquis was with his wife when Newman entered their box; he was bland, remote, and correct as usual; or, as it seemed to Newman, even more than usual.

"What do you think of the opera?" asked our hero. "What do you think of the Don?"

"We all know what Mozart is," said the marquis; "our impressions don't date from this evening. Mozart is youth, freshness, brilliancy, facility—a little too great facility, perhaps. But the execution is here and there deplorably rough."

"I am very curious to see how it ends," said Newman.

"You speak as if it were a feuilleton in the 'Figaro,'" observed the marquis. "You have surely seen the opera before?"

"Never," said Newman. "I am sure I should have remembered it. Donna Elvira reminds me of Madame de Cintre; I don't mean in her circumstances, but in the music she sings."

"It is a very nice distinction," laughed the marquis lightly. "There is no great possibility, I imagine, of Madame de Cintre being forsaken."

"Not much!" said Newman. "But what becomes of the Don?"

"The devil comes down—or comes up," said Madame de Bellegarde, "and carries him off. I suppose Zerlina reminds you of me."

"I will go to the foyer for a few moments," said the marquis, "and give you a chance to say that the commander—the man of stone—resembles me." And he passed out of the box.

The little marquise stared an instant at the velvet ledge of the balcony, and then murmured, "Not a man of stone, a man of wood." Newman had taken her husband's empty chair. She made no protest, and then she turned suddenly and laid her closed fan upon his arm. "I am very glad you came in," she said. "I want to ask you a favor. I wanted to do so on Thursday, at my mother-in-law's ball, but you would give me no chance. You were in such very good spirits that I thought you might grant my little favor then; not that you look particularly doleful now. It is something you must promise me; now is the time to take you; after you are married you will be good for nothing. Come, promise!"

"I never sign a paper without reading it first," said Newman. "Show me your document."

"No, you must sign with your eyes shut; I will hold your hand. Come, before you put your head into the noose. You ought to be thankful to me for giving you a chance to do something amusing."

"If it is so amusing," said Newman, "it will be in even better season after I am married."

"In other words," cried Madame de Bellegarde, "you will not do it at all. You will be afraid of your wife."

"Oh, if the thing is intrinsically improper," said Newman, "I won't go into it. If it is not, I will do it after my marriage."

"You talk like a treatise on logic, and English logic into the bargain!" exclaimed Madame de Bellegarde. "Promise, then, after you are married. After all, I shall enjoy keeping you to it."

"Well, then, after I am married," said Newman serenely.

The little marquise hesitated a moment, looking at him, and he wondered what was coming. "I suppose you know what my life is," she presently said. "I have no pleasure, I see nothing, I do nothing. I live in Paris as I might live at Poitiers. My mother-in-law calls me—what is the pretty word?—a gad-about? accuses me of going to unheard-of places, and thinks it ought to be joy enough for me to sit at home and count over my ancestors on my fingers. But why should I bother about my ancestors? I am sure they never bothered about me. I don't propose to live with a green shade on my eyes; I hold that things were made to look at. My husband, you know, has principles, and the first on the list is that the Tuileries are dreadfully vulgar. If the Tuileries are vulgar, his principles are tiresome. If I chose I might have principles quite as well as he. If they grew on one's family tree I should only have to give mine a shake to bring down a shower of the finest. At any rate, I prefer clever Bonapartes to stupid Bourbons."

"Oh, I see; you want to go to court," said Newman, vaguely conjecturing that she might wish him to appeal to the United States legation to smooth her way to the imperial halls.

The marquise gave a little sharp laugh. "You are a thousand miles away. I will take care of the Tuileries myself; the day I decide to go they will be very glad to have me. Sooner or later I shall dance in an imperial quadrille. I know what you are going to say: 'How will you dare?' But I SHALL dare. I am afraid of my husband; he is soft, smooth, irreproachable; everything that you know; but I am afraid of him—horribly afraid of him. And yet I shall arrive at the Tuileries. But that will not be this winter, nor perhaps next, and meantime I must live. For the moment, I want to go somewhere else; it's my dream. I want to go to the Bal Bullier."

"To the Bal Bullier?" repeated Newman, for whom the words at first meant nothing.

"The ball in the Latin Quarter, where the students dance with their mistresses. Don't tell me you have not heard of it."

"Oh yes," said Newman; "I have heard of it; I remember now. I have even been there. And you want to go there?"

"It is silly, it is low, it is anything you please. But I want to go. Some of my friends have been, and they say it is awfully drole. My friends go everywhere; it is only I who sit moping at home."

"It seems to me you are not at home now," said Newman, "and I shouldn't exactly say you were moping."

"I am bored to death. I have been to the opera twice a week for the last eight years. Whenever I ask for anything my mouth is stopped with that: Pray, madam, haven't you an opera box? Could a woman of taste want more? In the first place, my opera box was down in my contrat; they have to give it to me. To-night, for instance, I should have preferred a thousand times to go to the Palais Royal. But my husband won't go to the Palais Royal because the ladies of the court go there so much. You may imagine, then, whether he would take me to Bullier's; he says it is a mere imitation—and a bad one—of what they do at the Princess Kleinfuss's. But as I don't go to the Princess Kleinfuss's, the next best thing is to go to Bullier's. It is my dream, at any rate, it's a fixed idea. All I ask of you is to give me your arm; you are less compromising than any one else. I don't know why, but you are. I can arrange it. I shall risk something, but that is my own affair. Besides, fortune favors the bold. Don't refuse me; it is my dream!"

Newman gave a loud laugh. It seemed to him hardly worth while to be the wife of the Marquis de Bellegarde, a daughter of the crusaders, heiress of six centuries of glories and traditions, to have centred one's aspirations upon the sight of a couple of hundred young ladies kicking off young men's hats. It struck him as a theme for the moralist; but he had no time to moralize upon it. The curtain rose again; M. de Bellegarde returned, and Newman went back to his seat.

He observed that Valentin de Bellegarde had taken his place in the baignoire of Mademoiselle Nioche, behind this young lady and her companion, where he was visible only if one carefully looked for him. In the next act Newman met him in the lobby and asked him if he had reflected upon possible emigration. "If you really meant to meditate," he said, "you might have chosen a better place for it."

"Oh, the place was not bad," said Valentin. "I was not thinking of that girl. I listened to the music, and, without thinking of the play or looking at the stage, I turned over your proposal. At first it seemed quite fantastic. And then a certain fiddle in the orchestra—I could distinguish it—began to say as it scraped away, 'Why not, why not?' And then, in that rapid movement, all the fiddles took it up and the conductor's stick seemed to beat it in the air: 'Why not, why not?' I'm sure I can't say! I don't see why not. I don't see why I shouldn't do something. It appears to me really a very bright idea. This sort of thing is certainly very stale. And then I could come back with a trunk full of dollars. Besides, I might possibly find it amusing. They call me a raffine; who knows but that I might discover an unsuspected charm in shop-keeping? It would really have a certain romantic, picturesque side; it would look well in my biography. It would look as if I were a strong man, a first-rate man, a man who dominated circumstances."

"Never mind how it would look," said Newman. "It always looks well to have half a million of dollars. There is no reason why you shouldn't have them if you will mind what I tell you—I alone—and not talk to other parties." He passed his arm into that of his companion, and the two walked for some time up and down one of the less frequented corridors. Newman's imagination began to glow with the idea of converting his bright, impracticable friend into a first-class man of business. He felt for the moment a sort of spiritual zeal, the zeal of the propagandist. Its ardor was in part the result of that general discomfort which the sight of all uninvested capital produced in him; so fine an intelligence as Bellegarde's ought to be dedicated to high uses. The highest uses known to Newman's experience were certain transcendent sagacities in the handling of railway stock. And then his zeal was quickened by his personal kindness for Valentin; he had a sort of pity for him which he was well aware he never could have made the Comte de Bellegarde understand. He never lost a sense of its being pitiable that Valentin should think it a large life to revolve in varnished boots between the Rue d'Anjou and the Rue de l'Universite, taking the Boulevard des Italiens on the way, when over there in America one's promenade was a continent, and one's Boulevard stretched from New York to San Francisco. It mortified him, moreover, to think that Valentin lacked money; there was a painful grotesqueness in it. It affected him as the ignorance of a companion, otherwise without reproach, touching some rudimentary branch of learning would have done. There were things that one knew about as a matter of course, he would have said in such a case. Just so, if one pretended to be easy in the world, one had money as a matter of course, one had made it! There was something almost ridiculously anomalous to Newman in the sight of lively pretensions unaccompanied by large investments in railroads; though I may add that he would not have maintained that such investments were in themselves a proper ground for pretensions. "I will make you do something," he said to Valentin; "I will put you through. I know half a dozen things in which we can make a place for you. You will see some lively work. It will take you a little while to get used to the life, but you will work in before long, and at the end of six months—after you have done a thing or two on your own account—you will like it. And then it will be very pleasant for you, having your sister over there. It will be pleasant for her to have you, too. Yes, Valentin," continued Newman, pressing his friend's arm genially, "I think I see just the opening for you. Keep quiet and I'll push you right in."

Newman pursued this favoring strain for some time longer. The two men strolled about for a quarter of an hour. Valentin listened and questioned, many of his questions making Newman laugh loud at the naivete of his ignorance of the vulgar processes of money-getting; smiling himself, too, half ironical and half curious. And yet he was serious; he was fascinated by Newman's plain prose version of the legend of El Dorado. It is true, however, that though to accept an "opening" in an American mercantile house might be a bold, original, and in its consequences extremely agreeable thing to do, he did not quite see himself objectively doing it. So that when the bell rang to indicate the close of the entr'acte, there was a certain mock-heroism in his saying, with his brilliant smile, "Well, then, put me through; push me in! I make myself over to you. Dip me into the pot and turn me into gold."

They had passed into the corridor which encircled the row of baignoires, and Valentin stopped in front of the dusky little box in which Mademoiselle Nioche had bestowed herself, laying his hand on the doorknob. "Oh, come, are you going back there?" asked Newman.

"Mon Dieu, oui," said Valentin.

"Haven't you another place?"

"Yes, I have my usual place, in the stalls."

"You had better go and occupy it, then."

"I see her very well from there, too," added Valentin, serenely, "and to-night she is worth seeing. But," he added in a moment, "I have a particular reason for going back just now."

"Oh, I give you up," said Newman. "You are infatuated!"

"No, it is only this. There is a young man in the box whom I shall annoy by going in, and I want to annoy him."

"I am sorry to hear it," said Newman. "Can't you leave the poor fellow alone?"

"No, he has given me cause. The box is not his. Noemie came in alone and installed herself. I went and spoke to her, and in a few moments she asked me to go and get her fan from the pocket of her cloak, which the ouvreuse had carried off. In my absence this gentleman came in and took the chair beside Noemie in which I had been sitting. My reappearance disgusted him, and he had the grossness to show it. He came within an ace of being impertinent. I don't know who he is; he is some vulgar wretch. I can't think where she picks up such acquaintances. He has been drinking, too, but he knows what he is about. Just now, in the second act, he was unmannerly again. I shall put in another appearance for ten minutes—time enough to give him an opportunity to commit himself, if he feels inclined. I really can't let the brute suppose that he is keeping me out of the box."

"My dear fellow," said Newman, remonstrantly, "what child's play! You are not going to pick a quarrel about that girl, I hope."

"That girl has nothing to do with it, and I have no intention of picking a quarrel. I am not a bully nor a fire-eater. I simply wish to make a point that a gentleman must."

"Oh, damn your point!" said Newman. "That is the trouble with you Frenchmen; you must be always making points. Well," he added, "be short. But if you are going in for this kind of thing, we must ship you off to America in advance."

"Very good," Valentin answered, "whenever you please. But if I go to America, I must not let this gentleman suppose that it is to run away from him."

And they separated. At the end of the act Newman observed that Valentin was still in the baignoire. He strolled into the corridor again, expecting to meet him, and when he was within a few yards of Mademoiselle Nioche's box saw his friend pass out, accompanied by the young man who had been seated beside its fair occupant. The two gentlemen walked with some quickness of step to a distant part of the lobby, where Newman perceived them stop and stand talking. The manner of each was perfectly quiet, but the stranger, who looked flushed, had begun to wipe his face very emphatically with his pocket-handkerchief. By this time Newman was abreast of the baignoire; the door had been left ajar, and he could see a pink dress inside. He immediately went in. Mademoiselle Nioche turned and greeted him with a brilliant smile.

"Ah, you have at last decided to come and see me?" she exclaimed. "You just save your politeness. You find me in a fine moment. Sit down." There was a very becoming little flush in her cheek, and her eye had a noticeable spark. You would have said that she had received some very good news.

"Something has happened here!" said Newman, without sitting down.

"You find me in a very fine moment," she repeated. "Two gentlemen—one of them is M. de Bellegarde, the pleasure of whose acquaintance I owe to you—have just had words about your humble servant. Very big words too. They can't come off without crossing swords. A duel—that will give me a push!" cried Mademoiselle Noemie clapping her little hands. "C'est ca qui pose une femme!"

"You don't mean to say that Bellegarde is going to fight about YOU!" exclaimed Newman, disgustedly.

"Nothing else!" and she looked at him with a hard little smile. "No, no, you are not galant! And if you prevent this affair I shall owe you a grudge—and pay my debt!"

Newman uttered an imprecation which, though brief—it consisted simply of the interjection "Oh!" followed by a geographical, or more correctly, perhaps a theological noun in four letters—had better not be transferred to these pages. He turned his back without more ceremony upon the pink dress and went out of the box. In the corridor he found Valentin and his companion walking towards him. The latter was thrusting a card into his waistcoat pocket. Mademoiselle Noemie's jealous votary was a tall, robust young man with a thick nose, a prominent blue eye, a Germanic physiognomy, and a massive watch-chain. When they reached the box, Valentin with an emphasized bow made way for him to pass in first. Newman touched Valentin's arm as a sign that he wished to speak with him, and Bellegarde answered that he would be with him in an instant. Valentin entered the box after the robust young man, but a couple of minutes afterwards he reappeared, largely smiling.

"She is immensely tickled," he said. "She says we will make her fortune. I don't want to be fatuous, but I think it is very possible."

"So you are going to fight?" said Newman.

"My dear fellow, don't look so mortally disgusted. It was not my choice. The thing is all arranged."

"I told you so!" groaned Newman.

"I told HIM so," said Valentin, smiling.

"What did he do to you?"

"My good friend, it doesn't matter what. He used an expression—I took it up."

"But I insist upon knowing; I can't, as your elder brother, have you rushing into this sort of nonsense."

"I am very much obliged to you," said Valentin. "I have nothing to conceal, but I can't go into particulars now and here."

"We will leave this place, then. You can tell me outside."

"Oh no, I can't leave this place, why should I hurry away? I will go to my orchestra-stall and sit out the opera."

"You will not enjoy it; you will be preoccupied."

Valentin looked at him a moment, colored a little, smiled, and patted him on the arm. "You are delightfully simple! Before an affair a man is quiet. The quietest thing I can do is to go straight to my place."

"Ah," said Newman, "you want her to see you there—you and your quietness. I am not so simple! It is a poor business."

Valentin remained, and the two men, in their respective places, sat out the rest of the performance, which was also enjoyed by Mademoiselle Nioche and her truculent admirer. At the end Newman joined Valentin again, and they went into the street together. Valentin shook his head at his friend's proposal that he should get into Newman's own vehicle, and stopped on the edge of the pavement. "I must go off alone," he said; "I must look up a couple of friends who will take charge of this matter."

"I will take charge of it," Newman declared. "Put it into my hands."

"You are very kind, but that is hardly possible. In the first place, you are, as you said just now, almost my brother; you are about to marry my sister. That alone disqualifies you; it casts doubts on your impartiality. And if it didn't, it would be enough for me that I strongly suspect you of disapproving of the affair. You would try to prevent a meeting."

"Of course I should," said Newman. "Whoever your friends are, I hope they will do that."

"Unquestionably they will. They will urge that excuses be made, proper excuses. But you would be too good-natured. You won't do."

Newman was silent a moment. He was keenly annoyed, but he saw it was useless to attempt interference. "When is this precious performance to come off?" he asked.

"The sooner the better," said Valentin. "The day after to-morrow, I hope."

"Well," said Newman, "I have certainly a claim to know the facts. I can't consent to shut my eyes to the matter."

"I shall be most happy to tell you the facts," said Valentin. "They are very simple, and it will be quickly done. But now everything depends on my putting my hands on my friends without delay. I will jump into a cab; you had better drive to my room and wait for me there. I will turn up at the end of an hour."

Newman assented protestingly, let his friend go, and then betook himself to the picturesque little apartment in the Rue d'Anjou. It was more than an hour before Valentin returned, but when he did so he was able to announce that he had found one of his desired friends, and that this gentleman had taken upon himself the care of securing an associate. Newman had been sitting without lights by Valentin's faded fire, upon which he had thrown a log; the blaze played over the richly-encumbered little sitting-room and produced fantastic gleams and shadows. He listened in silence to Valentin's account of what had passed between him and the gentleman whose card he had in his pocket—M. Stanislas Kapp, of Strasbourg—after his return to Mademoiselle Nioche's box. This hospitable young lady had espied an acquaintance on the other side of the house, and had expressed her displeasure at his not having the civility to come and pay her a visit. "Oh, let him alone!" M. Stanislas Kapp had hereupon exclaimed. "There are too many people in the box already." And he had fixed his eyes with a demonstrative stare upon M. de Bellegarde. Valentin had promptly retorted that if there were too many people in the box it was easy for M. Kapp to diminish the number. "I shall be most happy to open the door for YOU!" M. Kapp exclaimed. "I shall be delighted to fling you into the pit!" Valentin had answered. "Oh, do make a rumpus and get into the papers!" Miss Noemie had gleefully ejaculated. "M. Kapp, turn him out; or, M. de Bellegarde, pitch him into the pit, into the orchestra—anywhere! I don't care who does which, so long as you make a scene." Valentin answered that they would make no scene, but that the gentleman would be so good as to step into the corridor with him. In the corridor, after a brief further exchange of words, there had been an exchange of cards. M. Stanislas Kapp was very stiff. He evidently meant to force his offence home.

"The man, no doubt, was insolent," Newman said; "but if you hadn't gone back into the box the thing wouldn't have happened."

"Why, don't you see," Valentin replied, "that the event proves the extreme propriety of my going back into the box? M. Kapp wished to provoke me; he was awaiting his chance. In such a case—that is, when he has been, so to speak, notified—a man must be on hand to receive the provocation. My not returning would simply have been tantamount to my saying to M. Stanislas Kapp, 'Oh, if you are going to be disagreeable'"—

"'You must manage it by yourself; damned if I'll help you!' That would have been a thoroughly sensible thing to say. The only attraction for you seems to have been the prospect of M. Kapp's impertinence," Newman went on. "You told me you were not going back for that girl."

"Oh, don't mention that girl any more," murmured Valentin. "She's a bore."

"With all my heart. But if that is the way you feel about her, why couldn't you let her alone?"

CHAPTER XVII

Valentin shook his head with a fine smile. "I don't think you quite understand, and I don't believe I can make you. She understood the situation; she knew what was in the air; she was watching us."

"A cat may look at a king! What difference does that make?"

"Why, a man can't back down before a woman."

"I don't call her a woman. You said yourself she was a stone," cried Newman.

"Well," Valentin rejoined, "there is no disputing about tastes. It's a matter of feeling; it's measured by one's sense of honor."

"Oh, confound your sense of honor!" cried Newman.

"It is vain talking," said Valentin; "words have passed, and the thing is settled."

Newman turned away, taking his hat. Then pausing with his hand on the door, "What are you going to use?" he asked.

"That is for M. Stanislas Kapp, as the challenged party, to decide. My own choice would be a short, light sword. I handle it well. I'm an indifferent shot."

Newman had put on his hat; he pushed it back, gently scratching his forehead, high up. "I wish it were pistols," he said. "I could show you how to lodge a bullet!"

Valentin broke into a laugh. "What is it some English poet says about consistency? It's a flower or a star, or a jewel. Yours has the beauty of all three!" But he agreed to see Newman again on the morrow, after the details of his meeting with M. Stanislas Kapp should have been arranged.

In the course of the day Newman received three lines from him, saying that it had been decided that he should cross the frontier, with his adversary, and that he was to take the night express to Geneva. He should have time, however, to dine with Newman. In the afternoon Newman called upon Madame de Cintre, but his visit was brief. She was as gracious and sympathetic as he had ever found her, but she was sad, and she confessed, on Newman's charging her with her red eyes, that she had been crying. Valentin had been with her a couple of hours before, and his visit had left her with a painful impression. He had laughed and gossiped, he had brought her no bad news, he had only been, in his manner, rather more affectionate than usual. His fraternal tenderness had touched her, and on his departure she had burst into tears. She had felt as if something strange and sad were going to happen; she had tried to reason away the fancy, and the effort had only given her a headache. Newman, of course, was perforce tongue-tied about Valentin's projected duel, and his dramatic talent was not equal to satirizing Madame de Cintre's presentiment as pointedly as perfect security demanded. Before he went away he asked Madame de Cintre whether Valentin had seen his mother.

"Yes," she said, "but he didn't make her cry."

It was in Newman's own apartment that Valentin dined, having brought his portmanteau, so that he might adjourn directly to the railway. M. Stanislas Kapp had positively declined to make excuses, and he, on his side, obviously, had none to offer. Valentin had found out with whom he was dealing. M. Stanislas Kapp was the son of and heir of a rich brewer of Strasbourg, a youth of a sanguineous—and sanguinary—temperament. He was making ducks and drakes of the paternal brewery, and although he passed in a general way for a good fellow, he had already been observed to be quarrelsome after dinner. "Que voulez-vous?" said Valentin. "Brought up on beer, he can't stand champagne." He had chosen pistols. Valentin, at dinner, had an excellent appetite; he made a point, in view of his long journey, of eating more than usual. He took the liberty of suggesting to Newman a slight modification in the composition of a certain fish-sauce; he thought it would be worth mentioning to the cook. But Newman had no thoughts for fish-sauce; he felt thoroughly discontented. As he sat and watched his amiable and clever companion going through his excellent repast with the delicate deliberation of hereditary epicurism, the folly of so charming a fellow traveling off to expose his agreeable young life for the sake of M. Stanislas and Mademoiselle Noemie struck him with intolerable force. He had grown fond of Valentin, he felt now how fond; and his sense of helplessness only increased his irritation.

"Well, this sort of thing may be all very well," he cried at last, "but I declare I don't see it. I can't stop you, perhaps, but at least I can protest. I do protest, violently."

"My dear fellow, don't make a scene," said Valentin. "Scenes in these cases are in very bad taste."

"Your duel itself is a scene," said Newman; "that's all it is! It's a wretched theatrical affair. Why don't you take a band of music with you outright? It's d—d barbarous and it's d—d corrupt, both."

"Oh, I can't begin, at this time of day, to defend the theory of dueling," said Valentin. "It is our custom, and I think it is a good thing. Quite apart from the goodness of the cause in which a duel may be fought, it has a kind of picturesque charm which in this age of vile prose seems to me greatly to recommend it. It's a remnant of a higher-tempered time; one ought to cling to it. Depend upon it, a duel is never amiss."

"I don't know what you mean by a higher-tempered time," said Newman. "Because your great-grandfather was an ass, is that any reason why you should be? For my part I think we had better let our temper take care of itself; it generally seems to me quite high enough; I am not afraid of being too meek. If your great-grandfather were to make himself unpleasant to me, I think I could manage him yet."

"My dear friend," said Valentin, smiling, "you can't invent anything that will take the place of satisfaction for an insult. To demand it and to give it are equally excellent arrangements."

"Do you call this sort of thing satisfaction?" Newman asked. "Does it satisfy you to receive a present of the carcass of that coarse fop? does it gratify you to make him a present of yours? If a man hits you, hit him back; if a man libels you, haul him up."

"Haul him up, into court? Oh, that is very nasty!" said Valentin.

"The nastiness is his—not yours. And for that matter, what you are doing is not particularly nice. You are too good for it. I don't say you are the most useful man in the world, or the cleverest, or the most amiable. But you are too good to go and get your throat cut for a prostitute."

Valentin flushed a little, but he laughed. "I shan't get my throat cut if I can help it. Moreover, one's honor hasn't two different measures. It only knows that it is hurt; it doesn't ask when, or how, or where."

"The more fool it is!" said Newman.

Valentin ceased to laugh; he looked grave. "I beg you not to say any more," he said. "If you do I shall almost fancy you don't care about—about"—and he paused.

"About what?"

"About that matter—about one's honor."

"Fancy what you please," said Newman. "Fancy while you are at it that I care about YOU—though you are not worth it. But come back without damage," he added in a moment, "and I will forgive you. And then," he continued, as Valentin was going, "I will ship you straight off to America."

"Well," answered Valentin, "if I am to turn over a new page, this may figure as a tail-piece to the old." And then he lit another cigar and departed.

"Blast that girl!" said Newman as the door closed upon Valentin.

CHAPTER XVIII

Newman went the next morning to see Madame de Cintre, timing his visit so as to arrive after the noonday breakfast. In the court of the hotel, before the portico, stood Madame de Bellegarde's old square carriage. The servant who opened the door answered Newman's inquiry with a slightly embarrassed and hesitating murmur, and at the same moment Mrs. Bread appeared in the background, dim-visaged as usual, and wearing a large black bonnet and shawl.

"What is the matter?" asked Newman. "Is Madame la Comtesse at home, or not?"

Mrs. Bread advanced, fixing her eyes upon him: he observed that she held a sealed letter, very delicately, in her fingers. "The countess has left a message for you, sir; she has left this," said Mrs. Bread, holding out the letter, which Newman took.

"Left it? Is she out? Is she gone away?"

"She is going away, sir; she is leaving town," said Mrs. Bread.

"Leaving town!" exclaimed Newman. "What has happened?"

"It is not for me to say, sir," said Mrs. Bread, with her eyes on the ground. "But I thought it would come."

"What would come, pray?" Newman demanded. He had broken the seal of the letter, but he still questioned. "She is in the house? She is visible?"

"I don't think she expected you this morning," the old waiting-woman replied. "She was to leave immediately."

"Where is she going?"

"To Fleurieres."

"To Fleurieres? But surely I can see her?"

Mrs. Bread hesitated a moment, and then clasping together her two hands, "I will take you!" she said. And she led the way upstairs. At the top of the staircase she paused and fixed her dry, sad eyes upon Newman. "Be very easy with her," she said; "she is most unhappy!" Then she went on to Madame de Cintre's apartment; Newman, perplexed and alarmed, followed her rapidly. Mrs. Bread threw open the door, and Newman pushed back the curtain at the farther side of its deep embrasure. In the middle of the room stood Madame de Cintre; her face was pale and she was dressed for traveling. Behind her, before the fire-place, stood Urbain de Bellegarde, looking at his finger-nails; near the marquis sat his mother, buried in an arm-chair, and with her eyes immediately fixing themselves upon Newman. He felt, as soon as he entered the room, that he was in the presence of something evil; he was startled and pained, as he would have been by a threatening cry in the stillness of the night. He walked straight to Madame de Cintre and seized her by the hand.

"What is the matter?" he asked, commandingly; "what is happening?"

Urbain de Bellegarde stared, then left his place and came and leaned upon his mother's chair, behind. Newman's sudden irruption had evidently discomposed both mother and son. Madame de Cintre stood silent, with her eyes resting upon Newman's. She had often looked at him with all her soul, as it seemed to him; but in this present gaze there was a sort of bottomless depth. She was in distress; it was the most touching thing he had ever seen. His heart rose into his throat, and he was on the point of turning to her companions, with an angry challenge; but she checked him, pressing the hand that held her own.

"Something very grave has happened," she said. "I cannot marry you."

Newman dropped her hand and stood staring, first at her and then at the others. "Why not?" he asked, as quietly as possible.

Madame de Cintre almost smiled, but the attempt was strange. "You must ask my mother, you must ask my brother."

"Why can't she marry me?" said Newman, looking at them.

Madame de Bellegarde did not move in her place, but she was as pale as her daughter. The marquis looked down at her. She said nothing for some moments, but she kept her keen, clear eyes upon Newman, bravely. The marquis drew himself up and looked at the ceiling. "It's impossible!" he said softly.

"It's improper," said Madame de Bellegarde.

Newman began to laugh. "Oh, you are fooling!" he exclaimed.

"My sister, you have no time; you are losing your train," said the marquis.

"Come, is he mad?" asked Newman.

"No; don't think that," said Madame de Cintre. "But I am going away."

"Where are you going?"

"To the country, to Fleurieres; to be alone."

"To leave me?" said Newman, slowly.

"I can't see you, now," said Madame de Cintre.

"NOW—why not?"

"I am ashamed," said Madame de Cintre, simply.

Newman turned toward the marquis. "What have you done to her—what does it mean?" he asked with the same effort at calmness, the fruit of his constant practice in taking things easily. He was excited, but excitement with him was only an intenser deliberateness; it was the swimmer stripped.

"It means that I have given you up," said Madame de Cintre. "It means that."

Her face was too charged with tragic expression not fully to confirm her words. Newman was profoundly shocked, but he felt as yet no resentment against her. He was amazed, bewildered, and the presence of the old marquise and her son seemed to smite his eyes like the glare of a watchman's lantern. "Can't I see you alone?" he asked.

"It would be only more painful. I hoped I should not see you—I should escape. I wrote to you. Good-by." And she put out her hand again.

Newman put both his own into his pockets. "I will go with you," he said.

She laid her two hands on his arm. "Will you grant me a last request?" and as she looked at him, urging this, her eyes filled with tears. "Let me go alone—let me go in peace. I can't call it peace—it's death. But let me bury myself. So—good-by."

Newman passed his hand into his hair and stood slowly rubbing his head and looking through his keenly-narrowed eyes from one to the other of the three persons before him. His lips were compressed, and the two lines which had formed themselves beside his mouth might have made it appear at a first glance that he was smiling. I have said that his excitement was an intenser deliberateness, and now he looked grimly deliberate. "It seems very much as if you had interfered, marquis," he said slowly. "I thought you said you wouldn't interfere. I know you don't like me; but that doesn't make any difference. I thought you promised me you wouldn't interfere. I thought you swore on your honor that you wouldn't interfere. Don't you remember, marquis?"

The marquis lifted his eyebrows; but he was apparently determined to be even more urbane than usual. He rested his two hands upon the back of his mother's chair and bent forward, as if he were leaning over the edge of a pulpit or a lecture-desk. He did not smile, but he looked softly grave. "Excuse me, sir," he said, "I assured you that I would not influence my sister's decision. I adhered, to the letter, to my engagement. Did I not, sister?"

"Don't appeal, my son," said the marquise, "your word is sufficient."

"Yes—she accepted me," said Newman. "That is very true, I can't deny that. At least," he added, in a different tone, turning to Madame de Cintre, "you DID accept me?"

Something in the tone seemed to move her strongly. She turned away, burying her face in her hands.

"But you have interfered now, haven't you?" inquired Newman of the marquis.

"Neither then nor now have I attempted to influence my sister. I used no persuasion then, I have used no persuasion to-day."

"And what have you used?"

"We have used authority," said Madame de Bellegarde in a rich, bell-like voice.

"Ah, you have used authority," Newman exclaimed. "They have used authority," he went on, turning to Madame de Cintre. "What is it? how did they use it?"

"My mother commanded," said Madame de Cintre.

"Commanded you to give me up—I see. And you obey—I see. But why do you obey?" asked Newman.

Madame de Cintre looked across at the old marquise; her eyes slowly measured her from head to foot. "I am afraid of my mother," she said.

Madame de Bellegarde rose with a certain quickness, crying, "This is a most indecent scene!"

"I have no wish to prolong it," said Madame de Cintre; and turning to the door she put out her hand again. "If you can pity me a little, let me go alone."

Newman shook her hand quietly and firmly. "I'll come down there," he said. The portiere dropped behind her, and Newman sank with a long breath into the nearest chair. He leaned back in it, resting his hands on the knobs of the arms and looking at Madame de Bellegarde and Urbain. There was a long silence. They stood side by side, with their heads high and their handsome eyebrows arched.

"So you make a distinction?" Newman said at last. "You make a distinction between persuading and commanding? It's very neat. But the distinction is in favor of commanding. That rather spoils it."

"We have not the least objection to defining our position," said M. de Bellegarde. "We understand that it should not at first appear to you quite clear. We rather expected, indeed, that you should not do us justice."

"Oh, I'll do you justice," said Newman. "Don't be afraid. Please proceed."

The marquise laid her hand on her son's arm, as if to deprecate the attempt to define their position. "It is quite useless," she said, "to try and arrange this matter so as to make it agreeable to you. It can never be agreeable to you. It is a disappointment, and disappointments are unpleasant. I thought it over carefully and tried to arrange it better; but I only gave myself a headache and lost my sleep. Say what we will, you will think yourself ill-treated, and you will publish your wrongs among your friends. But we are not afraid of that. Besides, your friends are not our friends, and it will not matter. Think of us as you please. I only beg you not to be violent. I have never in my life been present at a violent scene of any kind, and at my age I can't be expected to begin."

"Is THAT all you have got to say?" asked Newman, slowly rising out of his chair. "That's a poor show for a clever lady like you, marquise. Come, try again."

"My mother goes to the point, with her usual honesty and intrepidity," said the marquis, toying with his watch-guard. "But it is perhaps well to say a little more. We of course quite repudiate the charge of having broken faith with you. We left you entirely at liberty to make yourself agreeable to my sister. We left her quite at liberty to entertain your proposal. When she accepted you we said nothing. We therefore quite observed our promise. It was only at a later stage of the affair, and on quite a different basis, as it were, that we determined to speak. It would have been better, perhaps, if we had spoken before. But really, you see, nothing has yet been done."

"Nothing has yet been done?" Newman repeated the words, unconscious of their comical effect. He had lost the sense of what the marquis was saying; M. de Bellegarde's superior style was a mere humming in his ears. All that he understood, in his deep and simple indignation, was that the matter was not a violent joke, and that the people before him were perfectly serious. "Do you suppose I can take this?" he asked. "Do you suppose it can matter to me what you say? Do you suppose I can seriously listen to you? You are simply crazy!"

Madame de Bellegarde gave a rap with her fan in the palm of her hand. "If you don't take it you can leave it, sir. It matters very little what you do. My daughter has given you up."

"She doesn't mean it," Newman declared after a moment.

"I think I can assure you that she does," said the marquis.

"Poor woman, what damnable thing have you done to her?" cried Newman.

"Gently, gently!" murmured M. de Bellegarde.

"She told you," said the old lady. "I commanded her."

Newman shook his head, heavily. "This sort of thing can't be, you know," he said. "A man can't be used in this fashion. You have got no right; you have got no power."

"My power," said Madame de Bellegarde, "is in my children's obedience."

"In their fear, your daughter said. There is something very strange in it. Why should your daughter be afraid of you?" added Newman, after looking a moment at the old lady. "There is some foul play."

The marquise met his gaze without flinching, and as if she did not hear or heed what he said. "I did my best," she said, quietly. "I could endure it no longer."

"It was a bold experiment!" said the marquis.

Newman felt disposed to walk to him, clutch his neck with his fingers and press his windpipe with his thumb. "I needn't tell you how you strike me," he said; "of course you know that. But I should think you would be afraid of your friends—all those people you introduced me to the other night. There were some very nice people among them; you may depend upon it there were some honest men and women."

"Our friends approve us," said M. de Bellegarde, "there is not a family among them that would have acted otherwise. And however that may be, we take the cue from no one. The Bellegardes have been used to set the example not to wait for it."

"You would have waited long before any one would have set you such an example as this," exclaimed Newman. "Have I done anything wrong?" he demanded. "Have I given you reason to change your opinion? Have you found out anything against me? I can't imagine."

"Our opinion," said Madame de Bellegarde, "is quite the same as at first—exactly. We have no ill-will towards yourself; we are very far from accusing you of misconduct. Since your relations with us began you have been, I frankly confess, less—less peculiar than I expected. It is not your disposition that we object to, it is your antecedents. We really cannot reconcile ourselves to a commercial person. We fancied in an evil hour that we could; it was a great misfortune. We determined to persevere to the end, and to give you every advantage. I was resolved that you should have no reason to accuse me of want of loyalty. We let the thing certainly go very far; we introduced you to our friends. To tell the truth, it was that, I think, that broke me down. I succumbed to the scene that took place on Thursday night in these rooms. You must excuse me if what I say is disagreeable to you, but we cannot release ourselves without an explanation."

"There can be no better proof of our good faith," said the marquis, "than our committing ourselves to you in the eyes of the world the other evening. We endeavored to bind ourselves—to tie our hands, as it were."

"But it was that," added his mother, "that opened our eyes and broke our bonds. We should have been most uncomfortable! You know," she added in a moment, "that you were forewarned. I told you we were very proud."

Newman took up his hat and began mechanically to smooth it; the very fierceness of his scorn kept him from speaking. "You are not proud enough," he observed at last.

"In all this matter," said the marquis, smiling, "I really see nothing but our humility."

"Let us have no more discussion than is necessary," resumed Madame de Bellegarde. "My daughter told you everything when she said she gave you up."

"I am not satisfied about your daughter," said Newman; "I want to know what you did to her. It is all very easy talking about authority and saying you commanded her. She didn't accept me blindly, and she wouldn't have given me up blindly. Not that I believe yet she has really given me up; she will talk it over with me. But you have frightened her, you have bullied her, you have HURT her. What was it you did to her?"

"I did very little!" said Madame de Bellegarde, in a tone which gave Newman a chill when he afterwards remembered it.

"Let me remind you that we offered you these explanations," the marquis observed, "with the express understanding that you should abstain from violence of language."

"I am not violent," Newman answered, "it is you who are violent! But I don't know that I have much more to say to you. What you expect of me, apparently, is to go my way, thanking you for favors received, and promising never to trouble you again."

"We expect of you to act like a clever man," said Madame de Bellegarde. "You have shown yourself that already, and what we have done is altogether based upon your being so. When one must submit, one must. Since my daughter absolutely withdraws, what will be the use of your making a noise?"

"It remains to be seen whether your daughter absolutely withdraws. Your daughter and I are still very good friends; nothing is changed in that. As I say, I will talk it over with her."

"That will be of no use," said the old lady. "I know my daughter well enough to know that words spoken as she just now spoke to you are final. Besides, she has promised me."

"I have no doubt her promise is worth a great deal more than your own," said Newman; "nevertheless I don't give her up."

"Just as you please! But if she won't even see you,—and she won't,—your constancy must remain purely Platonic."

Poor Newman was feigning a greater confidence than he felt. Madame de Cintre's strange intensity had in fact struck a chill to his heart; her face, still impressed upon his vision, had been a terribly vivid image of renunciation. He felt sick, and suddenly helpless. He turned away and stood for a moment with his hand on the door; then he faced about and after the briefest hesitation broke out with a different accent. "Come, think of what this must be to me, and let her alone! Why should you object to me so—what's the matter with me? I can't hurt you. I wouldn't if I could. I'm the most unobjectionable fellow in the world. What if I am a commercial person? What under the sun do you mean? A commercial person? I will be any sort of a person you want. I never talked to you about business. Let her go, and I will ask no questions. I will take her away, and you shall never see me or hear of me again. I will stay in America if you like. I'll sign a paper promising never to come back to Europe! All I want is not to lose her!"

Madame de Bellegarde and her son exchanged a glance of lucid irony, and Urbain said, "My dear sir, what you propose is hardly an improvement. We have not the slightest objection to seeing you, as an amiable foreigner, and we have every reason for not wishing to be eternally separated from my sister. We object to the marriage; and in that way," and M. de Bellegarde gave a small, thin laugh, "she would be more married than ever."

"Well, then," said Newman, "where is this place of yours—Fleurieres? I know it is near some old city on a hill."

"Precisely. Poitiers is on a hill," said Madame de Bellegarde. "I don't know how old it is. We are not afraid to tell you."

"It is Poitiers, is it? Very good," said Newman. "I shall immediately follow Madame de Cintre."

"The trains after this hour won't serve you," said Urbain.

"I shall hire a special train!"

"That will be a very silly waste of money," said Madame de Bellegarde.

"It will be time enough to talk about waste three days hence," Newman answered; and clapping his hat on his head, he departed.

He did not immediately start for Fleurieres; he was too stunned and wounded for consecutive action. He simply walked; he walked straight before him, following the river, till he got out of the enceinte of Paris. He had a burning, tingling sense of personal outrage. He had never in his life received so absolute a check; he had never been pulled up, or, as he would have said, "let down," so short; and he found the sensation intolerable; he strode along, tapping the trees and lamp-posts fiercely with his stick and inwardly raging. To lose Madame de Cintre after he had taken such jubilant and triumphant possession of her was as great an affront to his pride as it was an injury to his happiness. And to lose her by the interference and the dictation of others, by an impudent old woman and a pretentious fop stepping in with their "authority"! It was too preposterous, it was too pitiful. Upon what he deemed the unblushing treachery of the Bellegardes Newman wasted little thought; he consigned it, once for all, to eternal perdition. But the treachery of Madame de Cintre herself amazed and confounded him; there was a key to the mystery, of course, but he groped for it in vain. Only three days had elapsed since she stood beside him in the starlight, beautiful and tranquil as the trust with which he had inspired her, and told him that she was happy in the prospect of their marriage. What was the meaning of the change? of what infernal potion had she tasted? Poor Newman had a terrible apprehension that she had really changed. His very admiration for her attached the idea of force and weight to her rupture. But he did not rail at her as false, for he was sure she was unhappy. In his walk he had crossed one of the bridges of the Seine, and he still followed, unheedingly, the long, unbroken quay. He had left Paris behind him, and he was almost in the country; he was in the pleasant suburb of Auteuil. He stopped at last, looked around him without seeing or caring for its pleasantness, and then slowly turned and at a slower pace retraced his steps. When he came abreast of the fantastic embankment known as the Trocadero, he reflected, through his throbbing pain, that he was near Mrs. Tristram's dwelling, and that Mrs. Tristram, on particular occasions, had much of a woman's kindness in her utterance. He felt that he needed to pour out his ire and he took the road to her house. Mrs. Tristram was at home and alone, and as soon as she had looked at him, on his entering the room, she told him that she knew what he had come for. Newman sat down heavily, in silence, looking at her.

"They have backed out!" she said. "Well, you may think it strange, but I felt something the other night in the air." Presently he told her his story; she listened, with her eyes fixed on him. When he had finished she said quietly, "They want her to marry Lord Deepmere." Newman stared. He did not know that she knew anything about Lord Deepmere. "But I don't think she will," Mrs. Tristram added.

"SHE marry that poor little cub!" cried Newman. "Oh, Lord! And yet, why did she refuse me?"

"But that isn't the only thing," said Mrs. Tristram. "They really couldn't endure you any longer. They had overrated their courage. I must say, to give the devil his due, that there is something rather fine in that. It was your commercial quality in the abstract they couldn't swallow. That is really aristocratic. They wanted your money, but they have given you up for an idea."

Newman frowned most ruefully, and took up his hat again. "I thought you would encourage me!" he said, with almost childlike sadness.

"Excuse me," she answered very gently. "I feel none the less sorry for you, especially as I am at the bottom of your troubles. I have not forgotten that I suggested the marriage to you. I don't believe that Madame de Cintre has any intention of marrying Lord Deepmere. It is true he is not younger than she, as he looks. He is thirty-three years old; I looked in the Peerage. But no—I can't believe her so horribly, cruelly false."

"Please say nothing against her," said Newman.

"Poor woman, she IS cruel. But of course you will go after her and you will plead powerfully. Do you know that as you are now," Mrs. Tristram pursued, with characteristic audacity of comment, "you are extremely eloquent, even without speaking? To resist you a woman must have a very fixed idea in her head. I wish I had done you a wrong, that you might come to me in that fine fashion! But go to Madame de Cintre at any rate, and tell her that she is a puzzle even to me. I am very curious to see how far family discipline will go."

Newman sat a while longer, leaning his elbows on his knees and his head in his hands, and Mrs. Tristram continued to temper charity with philosophy and compassion with criticism. At last she inquired, "And what does the Count Valentin say to it?" Newman started; he had not thought of Valentin and his errand on the Swiss frontier since the morning. The reflection made him restless again, and he took his leave. He went straight to his apartment, where, upon the table of the vestibule, he found a telegram. It ran (with the date and place) as follows: "I am seriously ill; please to come to me as soon as possible. V. B." Newman groaned at this miserable news, and at the necessity of deferring his journey to the Chateau de Fleurieres. But he wrote to Madame de Cintre these few lines; they were all he had time for:—

"I don't give you up, and I don't really believe you give me up. I don't understand it, but we shall clear it up together. I can't follow you to-day, as I am called to see a friend at a distance who is very ill, perhaps dying. But I shall come to you as soon as I can leave my friend. Why shouldn't I say that he is your brother? C. N."

After this he had only time to catch the night express to Geneva.

CHAPTER XIX

Newman possessed a remarkable talent for sitting still when it was necessary, and he had an opportunity to use it on his journey to Switzerland. The successive hours of the night brought him no sleep, but he sat motionless in his corner of the railway-carriage, with his eyes closed, and the most observant of his fellow-travelers might have envied him his apparent slumber. Toward morning slumber really came, as an effect of mental rather than of physical fatigue. He slept for a couple of hours, and at last, waking, found his eyes resting upon one of the snow-powdered peaks of the Jura, behind which the sky was just reddening with the dawn. But he saw neither the cold mountain nor the warm sky; his consciousness began to throb again, on the very instant, with a sense of his wrong. He got out of the train half an hour before it reached Geneva, in the cold morning twilight, at the station indicated in Valentin's telegram. A drowsy station-master was on the platform with a lantern, and the hood of his overcoat over his head, and near him stood a gentleman who advanced to meet Newman. This personage was a man of forty, with a tall lean figure, a sallow face, a dark eye, a neat mustache, and a pair of fresh gloves. He took off his hat, looking very grave, and pronounced Newman's name. Our hero assented and said, "You are M. de Bellegarde's friend?"

"I unite with you in claiming that sad honor," said the gentleman. "I had placed myself at M. de Bellegarde's service in this melancholy affair, together with M. de Grosjoyaux, who is now at his bedside. M. de Grosjoyaux, I believe, has had the honor of meeting you in Paris, but as he is a better nurse than I he remained with our poor friend. Bellegarde has been eagerly expecting you."

"And how is Bellegarde?" said Newman. "He was badly hit?"

"The doctor has condemned him; we brought a surgeon with us. But he will die in the best sentiments. I sent last evening for the cure of the nearest French village, who spent an hour with him. The cure was quite satisfied."

"Heaven forgive us!" groaned Newman. "I would rather the doctor were satisfied! And can he see me—shall he know me?"

"When I left him, half an hour ago, he had fallen asleep after a feverish, wakeful night. But we shall see." And Newman's companion proceeded to lead the way out of the station to the village, explaining as he went that the little party was lodged in the humblest of Swiss inns, where, however, they had succeeded in making M. de Bellegarde much more comfortable than could at first have been expected. "We are old companions in arms," said Valentin's second; "it is not the first time that one of us has helped the other to lie easily. It is a very nasty wound, and the nastiest thing about it is that Bellegarde's adversary was not shot. He put his bullet where he could. It took it into its head to walk straight into Bellegarde's left side, just below the heart."

As they picked their way in the gray, deceptive dawn, between the manure-heaps of the village street, Newman's new acquaintance narrated the particulars of the duel. The conditions of the meeting had been that if the first exchange of shots should fail to satisfy one of the two gentlemen, a second should take place. Valentin's first bullet had done exactly what Newman's companion was convinced he had intended it to do; it had grazed the arm of M. Stanislas Kapp, just scratching the flesh. M. Kapp's own projectile, meanwhile, had passed at ten good inches from the person of Valentin. The representatives of M. Stanislas had demanded another shot, which was granted. Valentin had then fired aside and the young Alsatian had done effective execution. "I saw, when we met him on the ground," said Newman's informant, "that he was not going to be commode. It is a kind of bovine temperament." Valentin had immediately been installed at the inn, and M. Stanislas and his friends had withdrawn to regions unknown. The police authorities of the canton had waited upon the party at the inn, had been extremely majestic, and had drawn up a long proces-verbal; but it was probable that they would wink at so very gentlemanly a bit of bloodshed. Newman asked whether a message had not been sent to Valentin's family, and learned that up to a late hour on the preceding evening Valentin had opposed it. He had refused to believe his wound was dangerous. But after his interview with the cure he had consented, and a telegram had been dispatched to his mother. "But the marquise had better hurry!" said Newman's conductor.

"Well, it's an abominable affair!" said Newman. "That's all I have to say!" To say this, at least, in a tone of infinite disgust was an irresistible need.

"Ah, you don't approve?" questioned his conductor, with curious urbanity.

"Approve?" cried Newman. "I wish that when I had him there, night before last, I had locked him up in my cabinet de toilette!"

Valentin's late second opened his eyes, and shook his head up and down two or three times, gravely, with a little flute-like whistle. But they had reached the inn, and a stout maid-servant in a night-cap was at the door with a lantern, to take Newman's traveling-bag from the porter who trudged behind him. Valentin was lodged on the ground-floor at the back of the house, and Newman's companion went along a stone-faced passage and softly opened a door. Then he beckoned to Newman, who advanced and looked into the room, which was lighted by a single shaded candle. Beside the fire sat M. de Grosjoyaux asleep in his dressing-gown—a little plump, fair man whom Newman had seen several times in Valentin's company. On the bed lay Valentin, pale and still, with his eyes closed—a figure very shocking to Newman, who had seen it hitherto awake to its finger tips. M. de Grosjoyaux's colleague pointed to an open door beyond, and whispered that the doctor was within, keeping guard. So long as Valentin slept, or seemed to sleep, of course Newman could not approach him; so our hero withdrew for the present, committing himself to the care of the half-waked bonne. She took him to a room above-stairs, and introduced him to a bed on which a magnified bolster, in yellow calico, figured as a counterpane. Newman lay down, and, in spite of his counterpane, slept for three or four hours. When he awoke, the morning was advanced and the sun was filling his window, and he heard, outside of it, the clucking of hens. While he was dressing there came to his door a messenger from M. de Grosjoyaux and his companion proposing that he should breakfast with them. Presently he went down-stairs to the little stone-paved dining-room, where the maid-servant, who had taken off her night-cap, was serving the repast. M. de Grosjoyaux was there, surprisingly fresh for a gentleman who had been playing sick-nurse half the night, rubbing his hands and watching the breakfast table attentively. Newman renewed acquaintance with him, and learned that Valentin was still sleeping; the surgeon, who had had a fairly tranquil night, was at present sitting with him. Before M. de Grosjoyaux's associate reappeared, Newman learned that his name was M. Ledoux, and that Bellegarde's acquaintance with him dated from the days when they served together in the Pontifical Zouaves. M. Ledoux was the nephew of a distinguished Ultramontane bishop. At last the bishop's nephew came in with a toilet in which an ingenious attempt at harmony with the peculiar situation was visible, and with a gravity tempered by a decent deference to the best breakfast that the Croix Helvetique had ever set forth. Valentin's servant, who was allowed only in scanty measure the honor of watching with his master, had been lending a light Parisian hand in the kitchen. The two Frenchmen did their best to prove that if circumstances might overshadow, they could not really obscure, the national talent for conversation, and M. Ledoux delivered a neat little eulogy on poor Bellegarde, whom he pronounced the most charming Englishman he had ever known.

"Do you call him an Englishman?" Newman asked.

M. Ledoux smiled a moment and then made an epigram. "C'est plus qu'un Anglais—c'est un Anglomane!" Newman said soberly that he had never noticed it; and M. de Grosjoyaux remarked that it was really too soon to deliver a funeral oration upon poor Bellegarde. "Evidently," said M. Ledoux. "But I couldn't help observing this morning to Mr. Newman that when a man has taken such excellent measures for his salvation as our dear friend did last evening, it seems almost a pity he should put it in peril again by returning to the world." M. Ledoux was a great Catholic, and Newman thought him a queer mixture. His countenance, by daylight, had a sort of amiably saturnine cast; he had a very large thin nose, and looked like a Spanish picture. He appeared to think dueling a very perfect arrangement, provided, if one should get hit, one could promptly see the priest. He seemed to take a great satisfaction in Valentin's interview with the cure, and yet his conversation did not at all indicate a sanctimonious habit of mind. M. Ledoux had evidently a high sense of the becoming, and was prepared to be urbane and tasteful on all points. He was always furnished with a smile (which pushed his mustache up under his nose) and an explanation. Savoir-vivre—knowing how to live—was his specialty, in which he included knowing how to die; but, as Newman reflected, with a good deal of dumb irritation, he seemed disposed to delegate to others the application of his learning on this latter point. M. de Grosjoyaux was of quite another complexion, and appeared to regard his friend's theological unction as the sign of an inaccessibly superior mind. He was evidently doing his utmost, with a kind of jovial tenderness, to make life agreeable to Valentin to the last, and help him as little as possible to miss the Boulevard des Italiens; but what chiefly occupied his mind was the mystery of a bungling brewer's son making so neat a shot. He himself could snuff a candle, etc., and yet he confessed that he could not have done better than this. He hastened to add that on the present occasion he would have made a point of not doing so well. It was not an occasion for that sort of murderous work, que diable! He would have picked out some quiet fleshy spot and just tapped it with a harmless ball. M. Stanislas Kapp had been deplorably heavy-handed; but really, when the world had come to that pass that one granted a meeting to a brewer's son!... This was M. de Grosjoyaux's nearest approach to a generalization. He kept looking through the window, over the shoulder of M. Ledoux, at a slender tree which stood at the end of a lane, opposite to the inn, and seemed to be measuring its distance from his extended arm and secretly wishing that, since the subject had been introduced, propriety did not forbid a little speculative pistol-practice.

Newman was in no humor to enjoy good company. He could neither eat nor talk; his soul was sore with grief and anger, and the weight of his double sorrow was intolerable. He sat with his eyes fixed upon his plate, counting the minutes, wishing at one moment that Valentin would see him and leave him free to go in quest of Madame de Cintre and his lost happiness, and mentally calling himself a vile brute the next, for the impatient egotism of the wish. He was very poor company, himself, and even his acute preoccupation and his general lack of the habit of pondering the impression he produced did not prevent him from reflecting that his companions must be puzzled to see how poor Bellegarde came to take such a fancy to this taciturn Yankee that he must needs have him at his death-bed. After breakfast he strolled forth alone into the village and looked at the fountain, the geese, the open barn doors, the brown, bent old women, showing their hugely darned stocking-heels at the ends of their slowly-clicking sabots, and the beautiful view of snowy Alps and purple Jura at either end of the little street. The day was brilliant; early spring was in the air and in the sunshine, and the winter's damp was trickling out of the cottage eaves. It was birth and brightness for all nature, even for chirping chickens and waddling goslings, and it was to be death and burial for poor, foolish, generous, delightful Bellegarde. Newman walked as far as the village church, and went into the small grave-yard beside it, where he sat down and looked at the awkward tablets which were planted around. They were all sordid and hideous, and Newman could feel nothing but the hardness and coldness of death. He got up and came back to the inn, where he found M. Ledoux having coffee and a cigarette at a little green table which he had caused to be carried into the small garden. Newman, learning that the doctor was still sitting with Valentin, asked M. Ledoux if he might not be allowed to relieve him; he had a great desire to be useful to his poor friend. This was easily arranged; the doctor was very glad to go to bed. He was a youthful and rather jaunty practitioner, but he had a clever face, and the ribbon of the Legion of Honor in his buttonhole; Newman listened attentively to the instructions he gave him before retiring, and took mechanically from his hand a small volume which the surgeon recommended as a help to wakefulness, and which turned out to be an old copy of "Faublas." Valentin was still lying with his eyes closed, and there was no visible change in his condition. Newman sat down near him, and for a long time narrowly watched him. Then his eyes wandered away with his thoughts upon his own situation, and rested upon the chain of the Alps, disclosed by the drawing of the scant white cotton curtain of the window, through which the sunshine passed and lay in squares upon the red-tiled floor. He tried to interweave his reflections with hope, but he only half succeeded. What had happened to him seemed to have, in its violence and audacity, the force of a real calamity—the strength and insolence of Destiny herself. It was unnatural and monstrous, and he had no arms against it. At last a sound struck upon the stillness, and he heard Valentin's voice.

"It can't be about me you are pulling that long face!" He found, when he turned, that Valentin was lying in the same position; but his eyes were open, and he was even trying to smile. It was with a very slender strength that he returned the pressure of Newman's hand. "I have been watching you for a quarter of an hour," Valentin went on; "you have been looking as black as thunder. You are greatly disgusted with me, I see. Well, of course! So am I!"

"Oh, I shall not scold you," said Newman. "I feel too badly. And how are you getting on?"

"Oh, I'm getting off! They have quite settled that; haven't they?"

"That's for you to settle; you can get well if you try," said Newman, with resolute cheerfulness.

"My dear fellow, how can I try? Trying is violent exercise, and that sort of thing isn't in order for a man with a hole in his side as big as your hat, that begins to bleed if he moves a hair's-breadth. I knew you would come," he continued; "I knew I should wake up and find you here; so I'm not surprised. But last night I was very impatient. I didn't see how I could keep still until you came. It was a matter of keeping still, just like this; as still as a mummy in his case. You talk about trying; I tried that! Well, here I am yet—these twenty hours. It seems like twenty days." Bellegarde talked slowly and feebly, but distinctly enough. It was visible, however, that he was in extreme pain, and at last he closed his eyes. Newman begged him to remain silent and spare himself; the doctor had left urgent orders. "Oh," said Valentin, "let us eat and drink, for to-morrow—to-morrow"—and he paused again. "No, not to-morrow, perhaps, but today. I can't eat and drink, but I can talk. What's to be gained, at this pass, by renun—renunciation? I mustn't use such big words. I was always a chatterer; Lord, how I have talked in my day!"

"That's a reason for keeping quiet now," said Newman. "We know how well you talk, you know."

But Valentin, without heeding him, went on in the same weak, dying drawl. "I wanted to see you because you have seen my sister. Does she know—will she come?"

Newman was embarrassed. "Yes, by this time she must know."

"Didn't you tell her?" Valentin asked. And then, in a moment, "Didn't you bring me any message from her?" His eyes rested upon Newman's with a certain soft keenness.

"I didn't see her after I got your telegram," said Newman. "I wrote to her."

"And she sent you no answer?"

Newman was obliged to reply that Madame de Cintre had left Paris. "She went yesterday to Fleurieres."

"Yesterday—to Fleurieres? Why did she go to Fleurieres? What day is this? What day was yesterday? Ah, then I shan't see her," said Valentin, sadly. "Fleurieres is too far!" And then he closed his eyes again. Newman sat silent, summoning pious invention to his aid, but he was relieved at finding that Valentin was apparently too weak to reason or to be curious. Bellegarde, however, presently went on. "And my mother—and my brother—will they come? Are they at Fleurieres?"

"They were in Paris, but I didn't see them, either," Newman answered. "If they received your telegram in time, they will have started this morning. Otherwise they will be obliged to wait for the night-express, and they will arrive at the same hour as I did."

"They won't thank me—they won't thank me," Valentin murmured. "They will pass an atrocious night, and Urbain doesn't like the early morning air. I don't remember ever in my life to have seen him before noon—before breakfast. No one ever saw him. We don't know how he is then. Perhaps he's different. Who knows? Posterity, perhaps, will know. That's the time he works, in his cabinet, at the history of the Princesses. But I had to send for them—hadn't I? And then I want to see my mother sit there where you sit, and say good-by to her. Perhaps, after all, I don't know her, and she will have some surprise for me. Don't think you know her yet, yourself; perhaps she may surprise YOU. But if I can't see Claire, I don't care for anything. I have been thinking of it—and in my dreams, too. Why did she go to Fleurieres to-day? She never told me. What has happened? Ah, she ought to have guessed I was here—this way. It is the first time in her life she ever disappointed me. Poor Claire!"

"You know we are not man and wife quite yet,—your sister and I," said Newman. "She doesn't yet account to me for all her actions." And, after a fashion, he smiled.

Valentin looked at him a moment. "Have you quarreled?"

"Never, never, never!" Newman exclaimed.

"How happily you say that!" said Valentin. "You are going to be happy—VA!" In answer to this stroke of irony, none the less powerful for being so unconscious, all poor Newman could do was to give a helpless and transparent stare. Valentin continued to fix him with his own rather over-bright gaze, and presently he said, "But something is the matter with you. I watched you just now; you haven't a bridegroom's face."

"My dear fellow," said Newman, "how can I show YOU a bridegroom's face? If you think I enjoy seeing you lie there and not being able to help you"—

"Why, you are just the man to be cheerful; don't forfeit your rights! I'm a proof of your wisdom. When was a man ever gloomy when he could say, 'I told you so?' You told me so, you know. You did what you could about it. You said some very good things; I have thought them over. But, my dear friend, I was right, all the same. This is the regular way."

"I didn't do what I ought," said Newman. "I ought to have done something else."

"For instance?"

"Oh, something or other. I ought to have treated you as a small boy."

"Well, I'm a very small boy, now," said Valentin. "I'm rather less than an infant. An infant is helpless, but it's generally voted promising. I'm not promising, eh? Society can't lose a less valuable member."

Newman was strongly moved. He got up and turned his back upon his friend and walked away to the window, where he stood looking out, but only vaguely seeing. "No, I don't like the look of your back," Valentin continued. "I have always been an observer of backs; yours is quite out of sorts."

Newman returned to his bedside and begged him to be quiet. "Be quiet and get well," he said. "That's what you must do. Get well and help me."

"I told you you were in trouble! How can I help you?" Valentin asked.

"I'll let you know when you are better. You were always curious; there is something to get well for!" Newman answered, with resolute animation.

Valentin closed his eyes and lay a long time without speaking. He seemed even to have fallen asleep. But at the end of half an hour he began to talk again. "I am rather sorry about that place in the bank. Who knows but what I might have become another Rothschild? But I wasn't meant for a banker; bankers are not so easy to kill. Don't you think I have been very easy to kill? It's not like a serious man. It's really very mortifying. It's like telling your hostess you must go, when you count upon her begging you to stay, and then finding she does no such thing. 'Really—so soon? You've only just come!' Life doesn't make me any such polite little speech."

Newman for some time said nothing, but at last he broke out. "It's a bad case—it's a bad case—it's the worst case I ever met. I don't want to say anything unpleasant, but I can't help it. I've seen men dying before—and I've seen men shot. But it always seemed more natural; they were not so clever as you. Damnation—damnation! You might have done something better than this. It's about the meanest winding-up of a man's affairs that I can imagine!"

Valentin feebly waved his hand to and fro. "Don't insist—don't insist! It is mean—decidedly mean. For you see at the bottom—down at the bottom, in a little place as small as the end of a wine-funnel—I agree with you!"

A few moments after this the doctor put his head through the half-opened door and, perceiving that Valentin was awake, came in and felt his pulse. He shook his head and declared that he had talked too much—ten times too much. "Nonsense!" said Valentin; "a man sentenced to death can never talk too much. Have you never read an account of an execution in a newspaper? Don't they always set a lot of people at the prisoner—lawyers, reporters, priests—to make him talk? But it's not Mr. Newman's fault; he sits there as mum as a death's-head."

The doctor observed that it was time his patient's wound should be dressed again; MM. de Grosjoyaux and Ledoux, who had already witnessed this delicate operation, taking Newman's place as assistants. Newman withdrew and learned from his fellow-watchers that they had received a telegram from Urbain de Bellegarde to the effect that their message had been delivered in the Rue de l'Universite too late to allow him to take the morning train, but that he would start with his mother in the evening. Newman wandered away into the village again, and walked about restlessly for two or three hours. The day seemed terribly long. At dusk he came back and dined with the doctor and M. Ledoux. The dressing of Valentin's wound had been a very critical operation; the doctor didn't really see how he was to endure a repetition of it. He then declared that he must beg of Mr. Newman to deny himself for the present the satisfaction of sitting with M. de Bellegarde; more than any one else, apparently, he had the flattering but inconvenient privilege of exciting him. M. Ledoux, at this, swallowed a glass of wine in silence; he must have been wondering what the deuce Bellegarde found so exciting in the American.

Newman, after dinner, went up to his room, where he sat for a long time staring at his lighted candle, and thinking that Valentin was dying down-stairs. Late, when the candle had burnt low, there came a soft rap at his door. The doctor stood there with a candlestick and a shrug.

"He must amuse himself, still!" said Valentin's medical adviser. "He insists upon seeing you, and I am afraid you must come. I think at this rate, that he will hardly outlast the night."

Newman went back to Valentin's room, which he found lighted by a taper on the hearth. Valentin begged him to light a candle. "I want to see your face," he said. "They say you excite me," he went on, as Newman complied with this request, "and I confess I do feel excited. But it isn't you—it's my own thoughts. I have been thinking—thinking. Sit down there, and let me look at you again." Newman seated himself, folded his arms, and bent a heavy gaze upon his friend. He seemed to be playing a part, mechanically, in a lugubrious comedy. Valentin looked at him for some time. "Yes, this morning I was right; you have something on your mind heavier than Valentin de Bellegarde. Come, I'm a dying man and it's indecent to deceive me. Something happened after I left Paris. It was not for nothing that my sister started off at this season of the year for Fleurieres. Why was it? It sticks in my crop. I have been thinking it over, and if you don't tell me I shall guess."

"I had better not tell you," said Newman. "It won't do you any good."

"If you think it will do me any good not to tell me, you are very much mistaken. There is trouble about your marriage."

"Yes," said Newman. "There is trouble about my marriage."

"Good!" And Valentin was silent again. "They have stopped it."

"They have stopped it," said Newman. Now that he had spoken out, he found a satisfaction in it which deepened as he went on. "Your mother and brother have broken faith. They have decided that it can't take place. They have decided that I am not good enough, after all. They have taken back their word. Since you insist, there it is!"

Valentin gave a sort of groan, lifted his hands a moment, and then let them drop.

"I am sorry not to have anything better to tell you about them," Newman pursued. "But it's not my fault. I was, indeed, very unhappy when your telegram reached me; I was quite upside down. You may imagine whether I feel any better now."

Valentin moaned gaspingly, as if his wound were throbbing. "Broken faith, broken faith!" he murmured. "And my sister—my sister?"

"Your sister is very unhappy; she has consented to give me up. I don't know why. I don't know what they have done to her; it must be something pretty bad. In justice to her you ought to know it. They have made her suffer. I haven't seen her alone, but only before them! We had an interview yesterday morning. They came out, flat, in so many words. They told me to go about my business. It seems to me a very bad case. I'm angry, I'm sore, I'm sick."

Valentin lay there staring, with his eyes more brilliantly lighted, his lips soundlessly parted, and a flush of color in his pale face. Newman had never before uttered so many words in the plaintive key, but now, in speaking to Valentin in the poor fellow's extremity, he had a feeling that he was making his complaint somewhere within the presence of the power that men pray to in trouble; he felt his outgush of resentment as a sort of spiritual privilege.

"And Claire,"—said Bellegarde,—"Claire? She has given you up?"

"I don't really believe it," said Newman.

"No. Don't believe it, don't believe it. She is gaining time; excuse her."

"I pity her!" said Newman.

"Poor Claire!" murmured Valentin. "But they—but they"—and he paused again. "You saw them; they dismissed you, face to face?"

"Face to face. They were very explicit."

"What did they say?"

"They said they couldn't stand a commercial person."

Valentin put out his hand and laid it upon Newman's arm. "And about their promise—their engagement with you?"

"They made a distinction. They said it was to hold good only until Madame de Cintre accepted me."

Valentin lay staring a while, and his flush died away. "Don't tell me any more," he said at last. "I'm ashamed."

"You? You are the soul of honor," said Newman simply.

Valentin groaned and turned away his head. For some time nothing more was said. Then Valentin turned back again and found a certain force to press Newman's arm. "It's very bad—very bad. When my people—when my race—come to that, it is time for me to withdraw. I believe in my sister; she will explain. Excuse her. If she can't—if she can't, forgive her. She has suffered. But for the others it is very bad—very bad. You take it very hard? No, it's a shame to make you say so." He closed his eyes and again there was a silence. Newman felt almost awed; he had evoked a more solemn spirit than he expected. Presently Valentin looked at him again, removing his hand from his arm. "I apologize," he said. "Do you understand? Here on my death-bed. I apologize for my family. For my mother. For my brother. For the ancient house of Bellegarde. Voila!" he added, softly.

Newman for an answer took his hand and pressed it with a world of kindness. Valentin remained quiet, and at the end of half an hour the doctor softly came in. Behind him, through the half-open door, Newman saw the two questioning faces of MM. de Grosjoyaux and Ledoux. The doctor laid his hand on Valentin's wrist and sat looking at him. He gave no sign and the two gentlemen came in, M. Ledoux having first beckoned to some one outside. This was M. le cure, who carried in his hand an object unknown to Newman, and covered with a white napkin. M. le cure was short, round, and red: he advanced, pulling off his little black cap to Newman, and deposited his burden on the table; and then he sat down in the best arm-chair, with his hands folded across his person. The other gentlemen had exchanged glances which expressed unanimity as to the timeliness of their presence. But for a long time Valentin neither spoke nor moved. It was Newman's belief, afterwards, that M. le cure went to sleep. At last abruptly, Valentin pronounced Newman's name. His friend went to him, and he said in French, "You are not alone. I want to speak to you alone." Newman looked at the doctor, and the doctor looked at the cure, who looked back at him; and then the doctor and the cure, together, gave a shrug. "Alone—for five minutes," Valentin repeated. "Please leave us."

The cure took up his burden again and led the way out, followed by his companions. Newman closed the door behind them and came back to Valentin's bedside. Bellegarde had watched all this intently.

"It's very bad, it's very bad," he said, after Newman had seated himself close to him. "The more I think of it the worse it is."

"Oh, don't think of it," said Newman.

But Valentin went on, without heeding him. "Even if they should come round again, the shame—the baseness—is there."

"Oh, they won't come round!" said Newman.

"Well, you can make them."

"Make them?"

"I can tell you something—a great secret—an immense secret. You can use it against them—frighten them, force them."

"A secret!" Newman repeated. The idea of letting Valentin, on his death-bed, confide him an "immense secret" shocked him, for the moment, and made him draw back. It seemed an illicit way of arriving at information, and even had a vague analogy with listening at a key-hole. Then, suddenly, the thought of "forcing" Madame de Bellegarde and her son became attractive, and Newman bent his head closer to Valentin's lips. For some time, however, the dying man said nothing more. He only lay and looked at his friend with his kindled, expanded, troubled eye, and Newman began to believe that he had spoken in delirium. But at last he said,—

"There was something done—something done at Fleurieres. It was foul play. My father—something happened to him. I don't know; I have been ashamed—afraid to know. But I know there is something. My mother knows—Urbain knows."

"Something happened to your father?" said Newman, urgently.

Valentin looked at him, still more wide-eyed. "He didn't get well."

"Get well of what?"

But the immense effort which Valentin had made, first to decide to utter these words and then to bring them out, appeared to have taken his last strength. He lapsed again into silence, and Newman sat watching him. "Do you understand?" he began again, presently. "At Fleurieres. You can find out. Mrs. Bread knows. Tell her I begged you to ask her. Then tell them that, and see. It may help you. If not, tell, every one. It will—it will"—here Valentin's voice sank to the feeblest murmur—"it will avenge you!"

The words died away in a long, soft groan. Newman stood up, deeply impressed, not knowing what to say; his heart was beating violently. "Thank you," he said at last. "I am much obliged." But Valentin seemed not to hear him, he remained silent, and his silence continued. At last Newman went and opened the door. M. le cure reentered, bearing his sacred vessel and followed by the three gentlemen and by Valentin's servant. It was almost processional.

CHAPTER XX

Valentin de Bellegarde died, tranquilly, just as the cold, faint March dawn began to illumine the faces of the little knot of friends gathered about his bedside. An hour afterwards Newman left the inn and drove to Geneva; he was naturally unwilling to be present at the arrival of Madame de Bellegarde and her first-born. At Geneva, for the moment, he remained. He was like a man who has had a fall and wants to sit still and count his bruises. He instantly wrote to Madame de Cintre, relating to her the circumstances of her brother's death—with certain exceptions—and asking her what was the earliest moment at which he might hope that she would consent to see him. M. Ledoux had told him that he had reason to know that Valentin's will—Bellegarde had a great deal of elegant personal property to dispose of—contained a request that he should be buried near his father in the church-yard of Fleurieres, and Newman intended that the state of his own relations with the family should not deprive him of the satisfaction of helping to pay the last earthly honors to the best fellow in the world. He reflected that Valentin's friendship was older than Urbain's enmity, and that at a funeral it was easy to escape notice. Madame de Cintre's answer to his letter enabled him to time his arrival at Fleurieres. This answer was very brief; it ran as follows:—

"I thank you for your letter, and for your being with Valentin. It is a most inexpressible sorrow to me that I was not. To see you will be nothing but a distress to me; there is no need, therefore, to wait for what you call brighter days. It is all one now, and I shall have no brighter days. Come when you please; only notify me first. My brother is to be buried here on Friday, and my family is to remain here. C. de C."

As soon as he received this letter Newman went straight to Paris and to Poitiers. The journey took him far southward, through green Touraine and across the far-shining Loire, into a country where the early spring deepened about him as he went. But he had never made a journey during which he heeded less what he would have called the lay of the land. He obtained lodging at the inn at Poitiers, and the next morning drove in a couple of hours to the village of Fleurieres. But here, preoccupied though he was, he could not fail to notice the picturesqueness of the place. It was what the French call a petit bourg; it lay at the base of a sort of huge mound on the summit of which stood the crumbling ruins of a feudal castle, much of whose sturdy material, as well as that of the wall which dropped along the hill to inclose the clustered houses defensively, had been absorbed into the very substance of the village. The church was simply the former chapel of the castle, fronting upon its grass-grown court, which, however, was of generous enough width to have given up its quaintest corner to a little graveyard. Here the very headstones themselves seemed to sleep, as they slanted into the grass; the patient elbow of the rampart held them together on one side, and in front, far beneath their mossy lids, the green plains and blue distances stretched away. The way to church, up the hill, was impracticable to vehicles. It was lined with peasants, two or three rows deep, who stood watching old Madame de Bellegarde slowly ascend it, on the arm of her elder son, behind the pall-bearers of the other. Newman chose to lurk among the common mourners who murmured "Madame la Comtesse" as a tall figure veiled in black passed before them. He stood in the dusky little church while the service was going forward, but at the dismal tomb-side he turned away and walked down the hill. He went back to Poitiers, and spent two days in which patience and impatience were singularly commingled. On the third day he sent Madame de Cintre a note, saying that he would call upon her in the afternoon, and in accordance with this he again took his way to Fleurieres. He left his vehicle at the tavern in the village street, and obeyed the simple instructions which were given him for finding the chateau.

"It is just beyond there," said the landlord, and pointed to the tree-tops of the park, above the opposite houses. Newman followed the first cross-road to the right—it was bordered with mouldy cottages—and in a few moments saw before him the peaked roofs of the towers. Advancing farther, he found himself before a vast iron gate, rusty and closed; here he paused a moment, looking through the bars. The chateau was near the road; this was at once its merit and its defect; but its aspect was extremely impressive. Newman learned afterwards, from a guide-book of the province, that it dated from the time of Henry IV. It presented to the wide, paved area which preceded it and which was edged with shabby farm-buildings an immense facade of dark time-stained brick, flanked by two low wings, each of which terminated in a little Dutch-looking pavilion capped with a fantastic roof. Two towers rose behind, and behind the towers was a mass of elms and beeches, now just faintly green. But the great feature was a wide, green river which washed the foundations of the chateau. The building rose from an island in the circling stream, so that this formed a perfect moat spanned by a two-arched bridge without a parapet. The dull brick walls, which here and there made a grand, straight sweep; the ugly little cupolas of the wings, the deep-set windows, the long, steep pinnacles of mossy slate, all mirrored themselves in the tranquil river. Newman rang at the gate, and was almost frightened at the tone with which a big rusty bell above his head replied to him. An old woman came out from the gate-house and opened the creaking portal just wide enough for him to pass, and he went in, across the dry, bare court and the little cracked white slabs of the causeway on the moat. At the door of the chateau he waited for some moments, and this gave him a chance to observe that Fleurieres was not "kept up," and to reflect that it was a melancholy place of residence. "It looks," said Newman to himself—and I give the comparison for what it is worth—"like a Chinese penitentiary." At last the door was opened by a servant whom he remembered to have seen in the Rue de l'Universite. The man's dull face brightened as he perceived our hero, for Newman, for indefinable reasons, enjoyed the confidence of the liveried gentry. The footman led the way across a great central vestibule, with a pyramid of plants in tubs in the middle of glass doors all around, to what appeared to be the principal drawing-room of the chateau. Newman crossed the threshold of a room of superb proportions, which made him feel at first like a tourist with a guide-book and a cicerone awaiting a fee. But when his guide had left him alone, with the observation that he would call Madame la Comtesse, Newman perceived that the salon contained little that was remarkable save a dark ceiling with curiously carved rafters, some curtains of elaborate, antiquated tapestry, and a dark oaken floor, polished like a mirror. He waited some minutes, walking up and down; but at length, as he turned at the end of the room, he saw that Madame de Cintre had come in by a distant door. She wore a black dress, and she stood looking at him. As the length of the immense room lay between them he had time to look at her before they met in the middle of it.

He was dismayed at the change in her appearance. Pale, heavy-browed, almost haggard with a sort of monastic rigidity in her dress, she had little but her pure features in common with the woman whose radiant good grace he had hitherto admired. She let her eyes rest on his own, and she let him take her hand; but her eyes looked like two rainy autumn moons, and her touch was portentously lifeless.

"I was at your brother's funeral," Newman said. "Then I waited three days. But I could wait no longer."

"Nothing can be lost or gained by waiting," said Madame de Cintre. "But it was very considerate of you to wait, wronged as you have been."

"I'm glad you think I have been wronged," said Newman, with that oddly humorous accent with which he often uttered words of the gravest meaning.

"Do I need to say so?" she asked. "I don't think I have wronged, seriously, many persons; certainly not consciously. To you, to whom I have done this hard and cruel thing, the only reparation I can make is to say, 'I know it, I feel it!' The reparation is pitifully small!"

"Oh, it's a great step forward!" said Newman, with a gracious smile of encouragement. He pushed a chair towards her and held it, looking at her urgently. She sat down, mechanically, and he seated himself near her; but in a moment he got up, restlessly, and stood before her. She remained seated, like a troubled creature who had passed through the stage of restlessness.

"I say nothing is to be gained by my seeing you," she went on, "and yet I am very glad you came. Now I can tell you what I feel. It is a selfish pleasure, but it is one of the last I shall have." And she paused, with her great misty eyes fixed upon him. "I know how I have deceived and injured you; I know how cruel and cowardly I have been. I see it as vividly as you do—I feel it to the ends of my fingers." And she unclasped her hands, which were locked together in her lap, lifted them, and dropped them at her side. "Anything that you may have said of me in your angriest passion is nothing to what I have said to myself."

"In my angriest passion," said Newman, "I have said nothing hard of you. The very worst thing I have said of you yet is that you are the loveliest of women." And he seated himself before her again, abruptly.

She flushed a little, but even her flush was pale. "That is because you think I will come back. But I will not come back. It is in that hope you have come here, I know; I am very sorry for you. I would do almost anything for you. To say that, after what I have done, seems simply impudent; but what can I say that will not seem impudent? To wrong you and apologize—that is easy enough. I should not have wronged you." She stopped a moment, looking at him, and motioned him to let her go on. "I ought never to have listened to you at first; that was the wrong. No good could come of it. I felt it, and yet I listened; that was your fault. I liked you too much; I believed in you."

"And don't you believe in me now?"

"More than ever. But now it doesn't matter. I have given you up."

Newman gave a powerful thump with his clenched fist upon his knee. "Why, why, why?" he cried. "Give me a reason—a decent reason. You are not a child—you are not a minor, nor an idiot. You are not obliged to drop me because your mother told you to. Such a reason isn't worthy of you."

"I know that; it's not worthy of me. But it's the only one I have to give. After all," said Madame de Cintre, throwing out her hands, "think me an idiot and forget me! That will be the simplest way."

Newman got up and walked away with a crushing sense that his cause was lost, and yet with an equal inability to give up fighting. He went to one of the great windows, and looked out at the stiffly embanked river and the formal gardens which lay beyond it. When he turned round, Madame de Cintre had risen; she stood there silent and passive. "You are not frank," said Newman; "you are not honest. Instead of saying that you are imbecile, you should say that other people are wicked. Your mother and your brother have been false and cruel; they have been so to me, and I am sure they have been so to you. Why do you try to shield them? Why do you sacrifice me to them? I'm not false; I'm not cruel. You don't know what you give up; I can tell you that—you don't. They bully you and plot about you; and I—I"—And he paused, holding out his hands. She turned away and began to leave him. "You told me the other day that you were afraid of your mother," he said, following her. "What did you mean?"

Madame de Cintre shook her head. "I remember; I was sorry afterwards."

"You were sorry when she came down and put on the thumb-screws. In God's name what IS it she does to you?"

"Nothing. Nothing that you can understand. And now that I have given you up, I must not complain of her to you."

"That's no reasoning!" cried Newman. "Complain of her, on the contrary. Tell me all about it, frankly and trustfully, as you ought, and we will talk it over so satisfactorily that you won't give me up."

Madame de Cintre looked down some moments, fixedly; and then, raising her eyes, she said, "One good at least has come of this: I have made you judge me more fairly. You thought of me in a way that did me great honor; I don't know why you had taken it into your head. But it left me no loophole for escape—no chance to be the common, weak creature I am. It was not my fault; I warned you from the first. But I ought to have warned you more. I ought to have convinced you that I was doomed to disappoint you. But I WAS, in a way, too proud. You see what my superiority amounts to, I hope!" she went on, raising her voice with a tremor which even then and there Newman thought beautiful. "I am too proud to be honest, I am not too proud to be faithless. I am timid and cold and selfish. I am afraid of being uncomfortable."

"And you call marrying me uncomfortable!" said Newman staring.

Madame de Cintre blushed a little and seemed to say that if begging his pardon in words was impudent, she might at least thus mutely express her perfect comprehension of his finding her conduct odious. "It is not marrying you; it is doing all that would go with it. It's the rupture, the defiance, the insisting upon being happy in my own way. What right have I to be happy when—when"—And she paused.

"When what?" said Newman.

"When others have been most unhappy!"

"What others?" Newman asked. "What have you to do with any others but me? Besides you said just now that you wanted happiness, and that you should find it by obeying your mother. You contradict yourself."

"Yes, I contradict myself; that shows you that I am not even intelligent."

"You are laughing at me!" cried Newman. "You are mocking me!"

CHAPTER XX

She looked at him intently, and an observer might have said that she was asking herself whether she might not most quickly end their common pain by confessing that she was mocking him. "No; I am not," she presently said.

"Granting that you are not intelligent," he went on, "that you are weak, that you are common, that you are nothing that I have believed you were—what I ask of you is not heroic effort, it is a very common effort. There is a great deal on my side to make it easy. The simple truth is that you don't care enough about me to make it."

"I am cold," said Madame de Cintre, "I am as cold as that flowing river."

Newman gave a great rap on the floor with his stick, and a long, grim laugh. "Good, good!" he cried. "You go altogether too far—you overshoot the mark. There isn't a woman in the world as bad as you would make yourself out. I see your game; it's what I said. You are blackening yourself to whiten others. You don't want to give me up, at all; you like me—you like me. I know you do; you have shown it, and I have felt it. After that, you may be as cold as you please! They have bullied you, I say; they have tortured you. It's an outrage, and I insist upon saving you from the extravagance of your own generosity. Would you chop off your hand if your mother requested it?"

Madame de Cintre looked a little frightened. "I spoke of my mother too blindly, the other day. I am my own mistress, by law and by her approval. She can do nothing to me; she has done nothing. She has never alluded to those hard words I used about her."

"She has made you feel them, I'll promise you!" said Newman.

"It's my conscience that makes me feel them."

"Your conscience seems to me to be rather mixed!" exclaimed Newman, passionately.

"It has been in great trouble, but now it is very clear," said Madame de Cintre. "I don't give you up for any worldly advantage or for any worldly happiness."

"Oh, you don't give me up for Lord Deepmere, I know," said Newman. "I won't pretend, even to provoke you, that I think that. But that's what your mother and your brother wanted, and your mother, at that villainous ball of hers—I liked it at the time, but the very thought of it now makes me rabid—tried to push him on to make up to you."

"Who told you this?" said Madame de Cintre softly.

"Not Valentin. I observed it. I guessed it. I didn't know at the time that I was observing it, but it stuck in my memory. And afterwards, you recollect, I saw Lord Deepmere with you in the conservatory. You said then that you would tell me at another time what he had said to you."

"That was before—before THIS," said Madame de Cintre.

"It doesn't matter," said Newman; "and, besides, I think I know. He's an honest little Englishman. He came and told you what your mother was up to—that she wanted him to supplant me; not being a commercial person. If he would make you an offer she would undertake to bring you over and give me the slip. Lord Deepmere isn't very intellectual, so she had to spell it out to him. He said he admired you 'no end,' and that he wanted you to know it; but he didn't like being mixed up with that sort of underhand work, and he came to you and told tales. That was about the amount of it, wasn't it? And then you said you were perfectly happy."

"I don't see why we should talk of Lord Deepmere," said Madame de Cintre. "It was not for that you came here. And about my mother, it doesn't matter what you suspect and what you know. When once my mind has been made up, as it is now, I should not discuss these things. Discussing anything, now, is very idle. We must try and live each as we can. I believe you will be happy again; even, sometimes, when you think of me. When you do so, think this—that it was not easy, and that I did the best I could. I have things to reckon with that you don't know. I mean I have feelings. I must do as they force me—I must, I must. They would haunt me otherwise," she cried, with vehemence; "they would kill me!"

"I know what your feelings are: they are superstitions! They are the feeling that, after all, though I AM a good fellow, I have been in business; the feeling that your mother's looks are law and your brother's words are gospel; that you all hang together, and that it's a part of the everlasting proprieties that they should have a hand in everything you do. It makes my blood boil. That is cold; you are right. And what I feel here," and Newman struck his heart and became more poetical than he knew, "is a glowing fire!"

A spectator less preoccupied than Madame de Cintre's distracted wooer would have felt sure from the first that her appealing calm of manner was the result of violent effort, in spite of which the tide of agitation was rapidly rising. On these last words of Newman's it overflowed, though at first she spoke low, for fear of her voice betraying her. "No. I was not right—I am not cold! I believe that if I am doing what seems so bad, it is not mere weakness and falseness. Mr. Newman, it's like a religion. I can't tell you—I can't! It's cruel of you to insist. I don't see why I shouldn't ask you to believe me—and pity me. It's like a religion. There's a curse upon the house; I don't know what—I don't know why—don't ask me. We must all bear it. I have been too selfish; I wanted to escape from it. You offered me a great chance—besides my liking you. It seemed good to change completely, to break, to go away. And then I admired you. But I can't—it has overtaken and come back to me." Her self-control had now completely abandoned her, and her words were broken with long sobs. "Why do such dreadful things happen to us—why is my brother Valentin killed, like a beast in the midst of his youth and his gayety and his brightness and all that we loved him for? Why are there things I can't ask about—that I am afraid to know? Why are there places I can't look at, sounds I can't hear? Why is it given to me to choose, to decide, in a case so hard and so terrible as this? I am not meant for that—I am not made for boldness and defiance. I was made to be happy in a quiet, natural way." At this Newman gave a most expressive groan, but Madame de Cintre went on. "I was made to do gladly and gratefully what is expected of me. My mother has always been very good to me; that's all I can say. I must not judge her; I must not criticize her. If I did, it would come back to me. I can't change!"

"No," said Newman, bitterly; "I must change—if I break in two in the effort!"

"You are different. You are a man; you will get over it. You have all kinds of consolation. You were born—you were trained, to changes. Besides—besides, I shall always think of you."

"I don't care for that!" cried Newman. "You are cruel—you are terribly cruel. God forgive you! You may have the best reasons and the finest feelings in the world; that makes no difference. You are a mystery to me; I don't see how such hardness can go with such loveliness."

Madame de Cintre fixed him a moment with her swimming eyes. "You believe I am hard, then?"

Newman answered her look, and then broke out, "You are a perfect, faultless creature! Stay by me!"

"Of course I am hard," she went on. "Whenever we give pain we are hard. And we MUST give pain; that's the world,—the hateful, miserable world! Ah!" and she gave a long, deep sigh, "I can't even say I am glad to have known you—though I am. That too is to wrong you. I can say nothing that is not cruel. Therefore let us part, without more of this. Good-by!" And she put out her hand.

Newman stood and looked at it without taking it, and raised his eyes to her face. He felt, himself, like shedding tears of rage. "What are you going to do?" he asked. "Where are you going?"

"Where I shall give no more pain and suspect no more evil. I am going out of the world."

"Out of the world?"

"I am going into a convent."

"Into a convent!" Newman repeated the words with the deepest dismay; it was as if she had said she was going into an hospital. "Into a convent—YOU!"

"I told you that it was not for my worldly advantage or pleasure I was leaving you."

But still Newman hardly understood. "You are going to be a nun," he went on, "in a cell—for life—with a gown and white veil?"

"A nun—a Carmelite nun," said Madame de Cintre. "For life, with God's leave."

The idea struck Newman as too dark and horrible for belief, and made him feel as he would have done if she had told him that she was going to mutilate her beautiful face, or drink some potion that would make her mad. He clasped his hands and began to tremble, visibly.

"Madame de Cintre, don't, don't!" he said. "I beseech you! On my knees, if you like, I'll beseech you."

She laid her hand upon his arm, with a tender, pitying, almost reassuring gesture. "You don't understand," she said. "You have wrong ideas. It's nothing horrible. It is only peace and safety. It is to be out of the world, where such troubles as this come to the innocent, to the best. And for life—that's the blessing of it! They can't begin again."

Newman dropped into a chair and sat looking at her with a long, inarticulate murmur. That this superb woman, in whom he had seen all human grace and household force, should turn from him and all the brightness that he offered her—him and his future and his fortune and his fidelity—to muffle herself in ascetic rags and entomb herself in a cell was a confounding combination of the inexorable and the grotesque. As the image deepened before him the grotesque seemed to expand and overspread it; it was a reduction to the absurd of the trial to which he was subjected. "You—you a nun!" he exclaimed; "you with your beauty defaced—you behind locks and bars! Never, never, if I can prevent it!" And he sprang to his feet with a violent laugh.

"You can't prevent it," said Madame de Cintre, "and it ought—a little—to satisfy you. Do you suppose I will go on living in the world, still beside you, and yet not with you? It is all arranged. Good-by, good-by."

This time he took her hand, took it in both his own. "Forever?" he said. Her lips made an inaudible movement and his own uttered a deep imprecation. She closed her eyes, as if with the pain of hearing it; then he drew her towards him and clasped her to his breast. He kissed her white face; for an instant she resisted and for a moment she submitted; then, with force, she disengaged herself and hurried away over the long shining floor. The next moment the door closed behind her.

Newman made his way out as he could.

CHAPTER XXI

There is a pretty public walk at Poitiers, laid out upon the crest of the high hill around which the little city clusters, planted with thick trees and looking down upon the fertile fields in which the old English princes fought for their right and held it. Newman paced up and down this quiet promenade for the greater part of the next day and let his eyes wander over the historic prospect; but he would have been sadly at a loss to tell you afterwards whether the latter was made up of coal-fields or of vineyards. He was wholly given up to his grievance, or which reflection by no means diminished the weight. He feared that Madame de Cintre was irretrievably lost; and yet, as he would have said himself, he didn't see his way clear to giving her up. He found it impossible to turn his back upon Fleurieres and its inhabitants; it seemed to him that some germ of hope or reparation must lurk there somewhere, if he could only stretch his arm out far enough to pluck it. It was as if he had his hand on a door-knob and were closing his clenched fist upon it: he had thumped, he had called, he had pressed the door with his powerful knee and shaken it with all his strength, and dead, damning silence had answered him. And yet something held him there—something hardened the grasp of his fingers. Newman's satisfaction had been too intense, his whole plan too deliberate and mature, his prospect of happiness too rich and comprehensive for this fine moral fabric to crumble at a stroke. The very foundation seemed fatally injured, and yet he felt a stubborn desire still to try to save the edifice. He was filled with a sorer sense of wrong than he had ever known, or than he had supposed it possible he should know. To accept his injury and walk away without looking behind him was a stretch of good-nature of which he found himself incapable. He looked behind him intently and continually, and what he saw there did not assuage his resentment. He saw himself trustful, generous, liberal, patient, easy, pocketing frequent irritation and furnishing unlimited modesty. To have eaten humble pie, to have been snubbed and patronized and satirized and have consented to take it as one of the conditions of the bargain—to have done this, and done it all for nothing, surely gave one a right to protest. And to be turned off because one was a commercial person! As if he had ever talked or dreamt of the commercial since his connection with the Bellegardes began—as if he had made the least circumstance of the commercial—as if he would not have consented to confound the commercial fifty times a day, if it might have increased by a hair's breadth the chance of the Bellegardes' not playing him a trick! Granted that being commercial was fair ground for having a trick played upon one, how little they knew about the class so designed and its enterprising way of not standing upon trifles! It was in the light of his injury that the weight of Newman's past endurance seemed so heavy; his actual irritation had not been so great, merged as it was in his vision of the cloudless blue that overarched his immediate wooing. But now his sense of outrage was deep, rancorous, and ever present; he felt that he was a good fellow wronged. As for Madame de Cintre's conduct, it struck him with a kind of awe, and the fact that he was powerless to understand it or feel the reality of its motives only deepened the force with which he had attached himself to her. He had never let the fact of her Catholicism trouble him; Catholicism to him was nothing but a name, and to express a mistrust of the form in which her religious feelings had moulded themselves would have seemed to him on his own part a rather pretentious affectation of Protestant zeal. If such superb white flowers as that could bloom in Catholic soil, the soil was not insalubrious. But it was one thing to be a Catholic, and another to turn nun—on your hand! There was something lugubriously comical in the way Newman's thoroughly contemporaneous optimism was confronted with this dusky old-world expedient. To see a woman made for him and for motherhood to his children juggled away in this tragic travesty—it was a thing to rub one's eyes over, a nightmare, an illusion, a hoax. But the hours passed away without disproving the thing, and leaving him only the after-sense of the vehemence with which he had embraced Madame de Cintre. He remembered her words and her looks; he turned them over and tried to shake the mystery out of them and to infuse them with an endurable meaning. What had she meant by her feeling being a kind of religion? It was the religion simply of the family laws, the religion of which her implacable little mother was the high priestess. Twist the thing about as her generosity would, the one certain fact was that they had used force against her. Her generosity had tried to screen them, but Newman's heart rose into his throat at the thought that they should go scot-free.

The twenty-four hours wore themselves away, and the next morning Newman sprang to his feet with the resolution to return to Fleurieres and demand another interview with Madame de Bellegarde and her son. He lost no time in putting it into practice. As he rolled swiftly over the excellent road in the little caleche furnished him at the inn at Poitiers, he drew forth, as it were, from the very safe place in his mind to which he had consigned it, the last information given him by poor Valentin. Valentin had told him he could do something with it, and Newman thought it would be well to have it at hand. This was of course not the first time, lately, that Newman had given it his attention. It was information in the rough,—it was dark and puzzling; but Newman was neither helpless nor afraid. Valentin had evidently meant to put him in possession of a powerful instrument, though he could not be said to have placed the handle very securely within his grasp. But if he had not really told him the secret, he had at least given him the clew to it—a clew of which that queer old Mrs. Bread held the other end. Mrs. Bread had always looked to Newman as if she knew secrets; and as he apparently enjoyed her esteem, he suspected she might be induced to share her knowledge with him. So long as there was only Mrs. Bread to deal with, he felt easy. As to what there was to find out, he had only one fear—that it might not be bad enough. Then, when the image of the marquise and her son rose before him again, standing side by side, the old woman's hand in Urbain's arm, and the same cold, unsociable fixedness in the eyes of each, he cried out to himself that the fear was groundless. There was blood in the secret at the very last! He arrived at Fleurieres almost in a state of elation; he had satisfied himself, logically, that in the presence of his threat of exposure they would, as he mentally phrased it, rattle down like unwound buckets. He remembered indeed that he must first catch his hare—first ascertain what there was to expose; but after that, why shouldn't his happiness be as good as new again? Mother and son would drop their lovely victim in terror and take to hiding, and Madame de Cintre, left to herself, would surely come back to him. Give her a chance and she would rise to the surface, return to the light. How could she fail to perceive that his house would be much the most comfortable sort of convent?

Newman, as he had done before, left his conveyance at the inn and walked the short remaining distance to the chateau. When he reached the gate, however, a singular feeling took possession of him—a feeling which, strange as it may seem, had its source in its unfathomable good nature. He stood there a while, looking through the bars at the large, time-stained face of the edifice, and wondering to what crime it was that the dark old house, with its flowery name, had given convenient occasion. It had given occasion, first and last, to tyrannies and sufferings enough, Newman said to himself; it was an evil-looking place to live in. Then, suddenly, came the reflection—What a horrible rubbish-heap of iniquity to fumble in! The attitude of inquisitor turned its ignobler face, and with the same movement Newman declared that the Bellegardes should have another chance. He would appeal once more directly to their sense of fairness, and not to their fear, and if they should be accessible to reason, he need know nothing worse about them than what he already knew. That was bad enough.

The gate-keeper let him in through the same stiff crevice as before, and he passed through the court and over the little rustic bridge on the moat. The door was opened before he had reached it, and, as if to put his clemency to rout with the suggestion of a richer opportunity, Mrs. Bread stood there awaiting him. Her face, as usual, looked as hopelessly blank as the tide-smoothed sea-sand, and her black garments seemed of an intenser sable. Newman had already learned that her strange inexpressiveness could be a vehicle for emotion, and he was not surprised at the muffled vivacity with which she whispered, "I thought you would try again, sir. I was looking out for you."

"I am glad to see you," said Newman; "I think you are my friend."

Mrs. Bread looked at him opaquely. "I wish you well sir; but it's vain wishing now."

"You know, then, how they have treated me?"

"Oh, sir," said Mrs. Bread, dryly, "I know everything."

Newman hesitated a moment. "Everything?"

Mrs. Bread gave him a glance somewhat more lucent. "I know at least too much, sir."

"One can never know too much. I congratulate you. I have come to see Madame de Bellegarde and her son," Newman added. "Are they at home? If they are not, I will wait."

"My lady is always at home," Mrs. Bread replied, "and the marquis is mostly with her."

"Please then tell them—one or the other, or both—that I am here and that I desire to see them."

Mrs. Bread hesitated. "May I take a great liberty, sir?"

"You have never taken a liberty but you have justified it," said Newman, with diplomatic urbanity.

Mrs. Bread dropped her wrinkled eyelids as if she were curtseying; but the curtsey stopped there; the occasion was too grave. "You have come to plead with them again, sir? Perhaps you don't know this—that Madame de Cintre returned this morning to Paris."

"Ah, she's gone!" And Newman, groaning, smote the pavement with his stick.

"She has gone straight to the convent—the Carmelites they call it. I see you know, sir. My lady and the marquis take it very ill. It was only last night she told them."

"Ah, she had kept it back, then?" cried Newman. "Good, good! And they are very fierce?"

"They are not pleased," said Mrs. Bread. "But they may well dislike it. They tell me it's most dreadful, sir; of all the nuns in Christendom the Carmelites are the worst. You may say they are really not human, sir; they make you give up everything—forever. And to think of HER there! If I was one that cried, sir, I could cry."

Newman looked at her an instant. "We mustn't cry, Mrs. Bread; we must act. Go and call them!" And he made a movement to enter farther.

But Mrs. Bread gently checked him. "May I take another liberty? I am told you were with my dearest Mr. Valentin, in his last hours. If you would tell me a word about him! The poor count was my own boy, sir; for the first year of his life he was hardly out of my arms; I taught him to speak. And the count spoke so well, sir! He always spoke well to his poor old Bread. When he grew up and took his pleasure he always had a kind word for me. And to die in that wild way! They have a story that he fought with a wine-merchant. I can't believe that, sir! And was he in great pain?"

"You are a wise, kind old woman, Mrs. Bread," said Newman. "I hoped I might see you with my own children in your arms. Perhaps I shall, yet." And he put out his hand. Mrs. Bread looked for a moment at his open palm, and then, as if fascinated by the novelty of the gesture, extended her own ladylike fingers. Newman held her hand firmly and deliberately, fixing his eyes upon her. "You want to know all about Mr. Valentin?" he said.

"It would be a sad pleasure, sir."

"I can tell you everything. Can you sometimes leave this place?"

"The chateau, sir? I really don't know. I never tried."

"Try, then; try hard. Try this evening, at dusk. Come to me in the old ruin there on the hill, in the court before the church. I will wait for you there; I have something very important to tell you. An old woman like you can do as she pleases."

Mrs. Bread stared, wondering, with parted lips. "Is it from the count, sir?" she asked.

"From the count—from his death-bed," said Newman.

"I will come, then. I will be bold, for once, for HIM."

She led Newman into the great drawing-room with which he had already made acquaintance, and retired to execute his commands. Newman waited a long time; at last he was on the point of ringing and repeating his request. He was looking round him for a bell when the marquis came in with his mother on his arm. It will be seen that Newman had a logical mind when I say that he declared to himself, in perfect good faith, as a result of Valentin's dark hints, that his adversaries looked grossly wicked. "There is no mistake about it now," he said to himself as they advanced. "They're a bad lot; they have pulled off the mask." Madame de Bellegarde and her son certainly bore in their faces the signs of extreme perturbation; they looked like people who had passed a sleepless night. Confronted, moreover, with an annoyance which they hoped they had disposed of, it was not natural that they should have any very tender glances to bestow upon Newman. He stood before them, and such eye-beams as they found available they leveled at him; Newman feeling as if the door of a sepulchre had suddenly been opened, and the damp darkness were being exhaled.

"You see I have come back," he said. "I have come to try again."

"It would be ridiculous," said M. de Bellegarde, "to pretend that we are glad to see you or that we don't question the taste of your visit."

"Oh, don't talk about taste," said Newman, with a laugh, "or that will bring us round to yours! If I consulted my taste I certainly shouldn't come to see you. Besides, I will make as short work as you please. Promise me to raise the blockade—to set Madame de Cintre at liberty—and I will retire instantly."

"We hesitated as to whether we would see you," said Madame de Bellegarde; "and we were on the point of declining the honor. But it seemed to me that we should act with civility, as we have always done, and I wished to have the satisfaction of informing you that there are certain weaknesses that people of our way of feeling can be guilty of but once."

"You may be weak but once, but you will be audacious many times, madam," Newman answered. "I didn't come however, for conversational purposes. I came to say this, simply: that if you will write immediately to your daughter that you withdraw your opposition to her marriage, I will take care of the rest. You don't want her to turn nun—you know more about the horrors of it than I do. Marrying a commercial person is better than that. Give me a letter to her, signed and sealed, saying you retract and that she may marry me with your blessing, and I will take it to her at the convent and bring her out. There's your chance—I call those easy terms."

"We look at the matter otherwise, you know. We call them very hard terms," said Urbain de Bellegarde. They had all remained standing rigidly in the middle of the room. "I think my mother will tell you that she would rather her daughter should become Soeur Catherine than Mrs. Newman."

But the old lady, with the serenity of supreme power, let her son make her epigrams for her. She only smiled, almost sweetly, shaking her head and repeating, "But once, Mr. Newman; but once!"

Nothing that Newman had ever seen or heard gave him such a sense of marble hardness as this movement and the tone that accompanied it. "Could anything compel you?" he asked. "Do you know of anything that would force you?"

"This language, sir," said the marquis, "addressed to people in bereavement and grief is beyond all qualification."

"In most cases," Newman answered, "your objection would have some weight, even admitting that Madame de Cintre's present intentions make time precious. But I have thought of what you speak of, and I have come here to-day without scruple simply because I consider your brother and you two very different parties. I see no connection between you. Your brother was ashamed of you. Lying there wounded and dying, the poor fellow apologized to me for your conduct. He apologized to me for that of his mother."

For a moment the effect of these words was as if Newman had struck a physical blow. A quick flush leaped into the faces of Madame de Bellegarde and her son, and they exchanged a glance like a twinkle of steel. Urbain uttered two words which Newman but half heard, but of which the sense came to him as it were in the reverberation of the sound, "Le miserable!"

"You show little respect for the living," said Madame de Bellegarde, "but at least respect the dead. Don't profane—don't insult—the memory of my innocent son."

"I speak the simple truth," Newman declared, "and I speak it for a purpose. I repeat it—distinctly. Your son was utterly disgusted—your son apologized."

Urbain de Bellegarde was frowning portentously, and Newman supposed he was frowning at poor Valentin's invidious image. Taken by surprise, his scant affection for his brother had made a momentary concession to dishonor. But not for an appreciable instant did his mother lower her flag. "You are immensely mistaken, sir," she said. "My son was sometimes light, but he was never indecent. He died faithful to his name."

"You simply misunderstood him," said the marquis, beginning to rally. "You affirm the impossible!"

"Oh, I don't care for poor Valentin's apology," said Newman. "It was far more painful than pleasant to me. This atrocious thing was not his fault; he never hurt me, or any one else; he was the soul of honor. But it shows how he took it."

"If you wish to prove that my poor brother, in his last moments, was out of his head, we can only say that under the melancholy circumstances nothing was more possible. But confine yourself to that."

"He was quite in his right mind," said Newman, with gentle but dangerous doggedness; "I have never seen him so bright and clever. It was terrible to see that witty, capable fellow dying such a death. You know I was very fond of your brother. And I have further proof of his sanity," Newman concluded.

The marquise gathered herself together majestically. "This is too gross!" she cried. "We decline to accept your story, sir—we repudiate it. Urbain, open the door." She turned away, with an imperious motion to her son, and passed rapidly down the length of the room. The marquis went with her and held the door open. Newman was left standing.

He lifted his finger, as a sign to M. de Bellegarde, who closed the door behind his mother and stood waiting. Newman slowly advanced, more silent, for the moment, than life. The two men stood face to face. Then Newman had a singular sensation; he felt his sense of injury almost brimming over into jocularity. "Come," he said, "you don't treat me well; at least admit that."

M. de Bellegarde looked at him from head to foot, and then, in the most delicate, best-bred voice, "I detest you, personally," he said.

"That's the way I feel to you, but for politeness sake I don't say it," said Newman. "It's singular I should want so much to be your brother-in-law, but I can't give it up. Let me try once more." And he paused a moment. "You have a secret—you have a skeleton in the closet." M. de Bellegarde continued to look at him hard, but Newman could not see whether his eyes betrayed anything; the look of his eyes was always so strange. Newman paused again, and then went on. "You and your mother have committed a crime." At this M. de Bellegarde's eyes certainly did change; they seemed to flicker, like blown candles. Newman could see that he was profoundly startled; but there was something admirable in his self-control.

"Continue," said M. de Bellegarde.

Newman lifted a finger and made it waver a little in the air. "Need I continue? You are trembling."

"Pray where did you obtain this interesting information?" M. de Bellegarde asked, very softly.

"I shall be strictly accurate," said Newman. "I won't pretend to know more than I do. At present that is all I know. You have done something that you must hide, something that would damn you if it were known, something that would disgrace the name you are so proud of. I don't know what it is, but I can find out. Persist in your present course and I WILL find out. Change it, let your sister go in peace, and I will leave you alone. It's a bargain?"

The marquis almost succeeded in looking untroubled; the breaking up of the ice in his handsome countenance was an operation that was necessarily gradual. But Newman's mildly-syllabled argumentation seemed to press, and press, and presently he averted his eyes. He stood some moments, reflecting.

"My brother told you this," he said, looking up.

Newman hesitated a moment. "Yes, your brother told me."

The marquis smiled, handsomely. "Didn't I say that he was out of his mind?"

"He was out of his mind if I don't find out. He was very much in it if I do."

M. de Bellegarde gave a shrug. "Eh, sir, find out or not, as you please."

"I don't frighten you?" demanded Newman.

"That's for you to judge."

"No, it's for you to judge, at your leisure. Think it over, feel yourself all round. I will give you an hour or two. I can't give you more, for how do we know how fast they may be making Madame de Cintre a nun? Talk it over with your mother; let her judge whether she is frightened. I don't believe she is as easily frightened, in general, as you; but you will see. I will go and wait in the village, at the inn, and I beg you to let me know as soon as possible. Say by three o'clock. A simple YES or NO on paper will do. Only, you know, in case of a yes I shall expect you, this time, to stick to your bargain." And with this Newman opened the door and let himself out. The marquis did not move, and Newman, retiring, gave him another look. "At the inn, in the village," he repeated. Then he turned away altogether and passed out of the house.

He was extremely excited by what he had been doing, for it was inevitable that there should be a certain emotion in calling up the spectre of dishonor before a family a thousand years old. But he went back to the inn and contrived to wait there, deliberately, for the next two hours. He thought it more than probable that Urbain de Bellegarde would give no sign; for an answer to his challenge, in either sense, would be a confession of guilt. What he most expected was silence—in other words defiance. But he prayed that, as he imagined it, his shot might bring them down. It did bring, by three o'clock, a note, delivered by a footman; a note addressed in Urbain de Bellegarde's handsome English hand. It ran as follows:—

"I cannot deny myself the satisfaction of letting you know that I return to Paris, to-morrow, with my mother, in order that we may see my sister and confirm her in the resolution which is the most effectual reply to your audacious pertinacity.

"HENRI-URBAIN DE BELLEGARDE."

CHAPTER XXI

Newman put the letter into his pocket, and continued his walk up and down the inn-parlor. He had spent most of his time, for the past week, in walking up and down. He continued to measure the length of the little salle of the Armes de Prance until the day began to wane, when he went out to keep his rendezvous with Mrs. Bread. The path which led up the hill to the ruin was easy to find, and Newman in a short time had followed it to the top. He passed beneath the rugged arch of the castle wall, and looked about him in the early dusk for an old woman in black. The castle yard was empty, but the door of the church was open. Newman went into the little nave and of course found a deeper dusk than without. A couple of tapers, however, twinkled on the altar and just enabled him to perceive a figure seated by one of the pillars. Closer inspection helped him to recognize Mrs. Bread, in spite of the fact that she was dressed with unwonted splendor. She wore a large black silk bonnet, with imposing bows of crape, and an old black satin dress disposed itself in vaguely lustrous folds about her person. She had judged it proper to the occasion to appear in her stateliest apparel. She had been sitting with her eyes fixed upon the ground, but when Newman passed before her she looked up at him, and then she rose.

"Are you a Catholic, Mrs. Bread?" he asked.

"No, sir; I'm a good Church-of-England woman, very Low," she answered. "But I thought I should be safer in here than outside. I was never out in the evening before, sir."

"We shall be safer," said Newman, "where no one can hear us." And he led the way back into the castle court and then followed a path beside the church, which he was sure must lead into another part of the ruin. He was not deceived. It wandered along the crest of the hill and terminated before a fragment of wall pierced by a rough aperture which had once been a door. Through this aperture Newman passed and found himself in a nook peculiarly favorable to quiet conversation, as probably many an earnest couple, otherwise assorted than our friends, had assured themselves. The hill sloped abruptly away, and on the remnant of its crest were scattered two or three fragments of stone. Beneath, over the plain, lay the gathered twilight, through which, in the near distance, gleamed two or three lights from the chateau. Mrs. Bread rustled slowly after her guide, and Newman, satisfying himself that one of the fallen stones was steady, proposed to her to sit upon it. She cautiously complied, and he placed himself upon another, near her.

CHAPTER XXII

"I am very much obliged to you for coming," Newman said. "I hope it won't get you into trouble."

"I don't think I shall be missed. My lady, in these days, is not fond of having me about her." This was said with a certain fluttered eagerness which increased Newman's sense of having inspired the old woman with confidence.

"From the first, you know," he answered, "you took an interest in my prospects. You were on my side. That gratified me, I assure you. And now that you know what they have done to me, I am sure you are with me all the more."

"They have not done well—I must say it," said Mrs. Bread. "But you mustn't blame the poor countess; they pressed her hard."

"I would give a million of dollars to know what they did to her!" cried Newman.

Mrs. Bread sat with a dull, oblique gaze fixed upon the lights of the chateau. "They worked on her feelings; they knew that was the way. She is a delicate creature. They made her feel wicked. She is only too good."

"Ah, they made her feel wicked," said Newman, slowly; and then he repeated it. "They made her feel wicked,—they made her feel wicked." The words seemed to him for the moment a vivid description of infernal ingenuity.

"It was because she was so good that she gave up—poor sweet lady!" added Mrs. Bread.

"But she was better to them than to me," said Newman.

"She was afraid," said Mrs. Bread, very confidently; "she has always been afraid, or at least for a long time. That was the real trouble, sir. She was like a fair peach, I may say, with just one little speck. She had one little sad spot. You pushed her into the sunshine, sir, and it almost disappeared. Then they pulled her back into the shade and in a moment it began to spread. Before we knew it she was gone. She was a delicate creature."

This singular attestation of Madame de Cintre's delicacy, for all its singularity, set Newman's wound aching afresh. "I see," he presently said; "she knew something bad about her mother."

"No, sir, she knew nothing," said Mrs. Bread, holding her head very stiff and keeping her eyes fixed upon the glimmering windows of the chateau.

"She guessed something, then, or suspected it."

"She was afraid to know," said Mrs. Bread.

"But YOU know, at any rate," said Newman.

She slowly turned her vague eyes upon Newman, squeezing her hands together in her lap. "You are not quite faithful, sir. I thought it was to tell me about Mr. Valentin you asked me to come here."

"Oh, the more we talk of Mr. Valentin the better," said Newman. "That's exactly what I want. I was with him, as I told you, in his last hour. He was in a great deal of pain, but he was quite himself. You know what that means; he was bright and lively and clever."

"Oh, he would always be clever, sir," said Mrs. Bread. "And did he know of your trouble?"

"Yes, he guessed it of himself."

"And what did he say to it?"

"He said it was a disgrace to his name—but it was not the first."

"Lord, Lord!" murmured Mrs. Bread.

"He said that his mother and his brother had once put their heads together and invented something even worse."

"You shouldn't have listened to that, sir."

"Perhaps not. But I DID listen, and I don't forget it. Now I want to know what it is they did."

Mrs. Bread gave a soft moan. "And you have enticed me up into this strange place to tell you?"

"Don't be alarmed," said Newman. "I won't say a word that shall be disagreeable to you. Tell me as it suits you, and when it suits you. Only remember that it was Mr. Valentin's last wish that you should."

"Did he say that?"

"He said it with his last breath—'Tell Mrs. Bread I told you to ask her.'"

"Why didn't he tell you himself?"

"It was too long a story for a dying man; he had no breath left in his body. He could only say that he wanted me to know—that, wronged as I was, it was my right to know."

"But how will it help you, sir?" said Mrs. Bread.

"That's for me to decide. Mr. Valentin believed it would, and that's why he told me. Your name was almost the last word he spoke."

Mrs. Bread was evidently awe-struck by this statement; she shook her clasped hands slowly up and down. "Excuse me, sir," she said, "if I take a great liberty. Is it the solemn truth you are speaking? I MUST ask you that; must I not, sir?"

"There's no offense. It is the solemn truth; I solemnly swear it. Mr. Valentin himself would certainly have told me more if he had been able."

"Oh, sir, if he knew more!"

"Don't you suppose he did?"

"There's no saying what he knew about anything," said Mrs. Bread, with a mild head-shake. "He was so mightily clever. He could make you believe he knew things that he didn't, and that he didn't know others that he had better not have known."

"I suspect he knew something about his brother that kept the marquis civil to him," Newman propounded; "he made the marquis feel him. What he wanted now was to put me in his place; he wanted to give me a chance to make the marquis feel ME."

"Mercy on us!" cried the old waiting-woman, "how wicked we all are!"

"I don't know," said Newman; "some of us are wicked, certainly. I am very angry, I am very sore, and I am very bitter, but I don't know that I am wicked. I have been cruelly injured. They have hurt me, and I want to hurt them. I don't deny that; on the contrary, I tell you plainly that it is the use I want to make of your secret."

Mrs. Bread seemed to hold her breath. "You want to publish them—you want to shame them?"

"I want to bring them down,—down, down, down! I want to turn the tables upon them—I want to mortify them as they mortified me. They took me up into a high place and made me stand there for all the world to see me, and then they stole behind me and pushed me into this bottomless pit, where I lie howling and gnashing my teeth! I made a fool of myself before all their friends; but I shall make something worse of them."

This passionate sally, which Newman uttered with the greater fervor that it was the first time he had had a chance to say all this aloud, kindled two small sparks in Mrs. Bread's fixed eyes. "I suppose you have a right to your anger, sir; but think of the dishonor you will draw down on Madame de Cintre."

"Madame de Cintre is buried alive," cried Newman. "What are honor or dishonor to her? The door of the tomb is at this moment closing behind her."

"Yes, it's most awful," moaned Mrs. Bread.

"She has moved off, like her brother Valentin, to give me room to work. It's as if it were done on purpose."

"Surely," said Mrs. Bread, apparently impressed by the ingenuity of this reflection. She was silent for some moments; then she added, "And would you bring my lady before the courts?"

"The courts care nothing for my lady," Newman replied. "If she has committed a crime, she will be nothing for the courts but a wicked old woman."

"And will they hang her, Sir?"

"That depends upon what she has done." And Newman eyed Mrs. Bread intently.

"It would break up the family most terribly, sir!"

"It's time such a family should be broken up!" said Newman, with a laugh.

"And me at my age out of place, sir!" sighed Mrs. Bread.

"Oh, I will take care of you! You shall come and live with me. You shall be my housekeeper, or anything you like. I will pension you for life."

"Dear, dear, sir, you think of everything." And she seemed to fall a-brooding.

Newman watched her a while, and then he said suddenly. "Ah, Mrs. Bread, you are too fond of my lady!"

She looked at him as quickly. "I wouldn't have you say that, sir. I don't think it any part of my duty to be fond of my lady. I have served her faithfully this many a year; but if she were to die to-morrow, I believe, before Heaven I shouldn't shed a tear for her." Then, after a pause, "I have no reason to love her!" Mrs. Bread added. "The most she has done for me has been not to turn me out of the house." Newman felt that decidedly his companion was more and more confidential—that if luxury is corrupting, Mrs. Bread's conservative habits were already relaxed by the spiritual comfort of this preconcerted interview, in a remarkable locality, with a free-spoken millionaire. All his native shrewdness admonished him that his part was simply to let her take her time—let the charm of the occasion work. So he said nothing; he only looked at her kindly. Mrs. Bread sat nursing her lean elbows. "My lady once did me a great wrong," she went on at last. "She has a terrible tongue when she is vexed. It was many a year ago, but I have never forgotten it. I have never mentioned it to a human creature; I have kept my grudge to myself. I dare say I have been wicked, but my grudge has grown old with me. It has grown good for nothing, too, I dare say; but it has lived along, as I have lived. It will die when I die,—not before!"

"And what IS your grudge?" Newman asked.

Mrs. Bread dropped her eyes and hesitated. "If I were a foreigner, sir, I should make less of telling you; it comes harder to a decent Englishwoman. But I sometimes think I have picked up too many foreign ways. What I was telling you belongs to a time when I was much younger and very different looking to what I am now. I had a very high color, sir, if you can believe it, indeed I was a very smart lass. My lady was younger, too, and the late marquis was youngest of all—I mean in the way he went on, sir; he had a very high spirit; he was a magnificent man. He was fond of his pleasure, like most foreigners, and it must be owned that he sometimes went rather below him to take it. My lady was often jealous, and, if you'll believe it, sir, she did me the honor to be jealous of me. One day I had a red ribbon in my cap, and my lady flew out at me and ordered me to take it off. She accused me of putting it on to make the marquis look at me. I don't know that I was impertinent, but I spoke up like an honest girl and didn't count my words. A red ribbon indeed! As if it was my ribbons the marquis looked at! My lady knew afterwards that I was perfectly respectable, but she never said a word to show that she believed it. But the marquis did!" Mrs. Bread presently added, "I took off my red ribbon and put it away in a drawer, where I have kept it to this day. It's faded now, it's a very pale pink; but there it lies. My grudge has faded, too; the red has all gone out of it; but it lies here yet." And Mrs. Bread stroked her black satin bodice.

Newman listened with interest to this decent narrative, which seemed to have opened up the deeps of memory to his companion. Then, as she remained silent, and seemed to be losing herself in retrospective meditation upon her perfect respectability, he ventured upon a short cut to his goal. "So Madame de Bellegarde was jealous; I see. And M. de Bellegarde admired pretty women, without distinction of class. I suppose one mustn't be hard upon him, for they probably didn't all behave so properly as you. But years afterwards it could hardly have been jealousy that turned Madame de Bellegarde into a criminal."

Mrs. Bread gave a weary sigh. "We are using dreadful words, sir, but I don't care now. I see you have your idea, and I have no will of my own. My will was the will of my children, as I called them; but I have lost my children now. They are dead—I may say it of both of them; and what should I care for the living? What is any one in the house to me now—what am I to them? My lady objects to me—she has objected to me these thirty years. I should have been glad to be something to young Madame de Bellegarde, though I never was nurse to the present marquis. When he was a baby I was too young; they wouldn't trust me with him. But his wife told her own maid, Mamselle Clarisse, the opinion she had of me. Perhaps you would like to hear it, sir."

"Oh, immensely," said Newman.

"She said that if I would sit in her children's schoolroom I should do very well for a penwiper! When things have come to that I don't think I need stand upon ceremony."

"Decidedly not," said Newman. "Go on, Mrs. Bread."

Mrs. Bread, however, relapsed again into troubled dumbness, and all Newman could do was to fold his arms and wait. But at last she appeared to have set her memories in order. "It was when the late marquis was an old man and his eldest son had been two years married. It was when the time came on for marrying Mademoiselle Claire; that's the way they talk of it here, you know, sir. The marquis's health was bad; he was very much broken down. My lady had picked out M. de Cintre, for no good reason that I could see. But there are reasons, I very well know, that are beyond me, and you must be high in the world to understand them. Old M. de Cintre was very high, and my lady thought him almost as good as herself; that's saying a good deal. Mr. Urbain took sides with his mother, as he always did. The trouble, I believe, was that my lady would give very little money, and all the other gentlemen asked more. It was only M. de Cintre that was satisfied. The Lord willed it he should have that one soft spot; it was the only one he had. He may have been very grand in his birth, and he certainly was very grand in his bows and speeches; but that was all the grandeur he had. I think he was like what I have heard of comedians; not that I have ever seen one. But I know he painted his face. He might paint it all he would; he could never make me like it! The marquis couldn't abide him, and declared that sooner than take such a husband as that Mademoiselle Claire should take none at all. He and my lady had a great scene; it came even to our ears in the servants' hall. It was not their first quarrel, if the truth must be told. They were not a loving couple, but they didn't often come to words, because, I think, neither of them thought the other's doings worth the trouble. My lady had long ago got over her jealousy, and she had taken to indifference. In this, I must say, they were well matched. The marquis was very easy-going; he had a most gentlemanly temper. He got angry only once a year, but then it was very bad. He always took to bed directly afterwards. This time I speak of he took to bed as usual, but he never got up again. I'm afraid the poor gentleman was paying for his dissipation; isn't it true they mostly do, sir, when they get old? My lady and Mr. Urbain kept quiet, but I know my lady wrote letters to M. de Cintre. The marquis got worse and the doctors gave him up. My lady, she gave him up too, and if the truth must be told, she gave up gladly. When once he was out of the way she could do what she pleased with her daughter, and it was all arranged that my poor innocent child should be handed over to M. de Cintre. You don't know what Mademoiselle was in those days, sir; she was the sweetest young creature in France, and knew as little of what was going on around her as the lamb does of the butcher. I used to nurse the marquis, and I was always in his room. It was here at Fleurieres, in the autumn. We had a doctor from Paris, who came and stayed two or three weeks in the house. Then there came two others, and there was a consultation, and these two others, as I said, declared that the marquis couldn't be saved. After this they went off, pocketing their fees, but the other one stayed and did what he could. The marquis himself kept crying out that he wouldn't die, that he didn't want to die, that he would live and look after his daughter. Mademoiselle Claire and the viscount—that was Mr. Valentin, you know—were both in the house. The doctor was a clever man,—that I could see myself,—and I think he believed that the marquis might get well. We took good care of him, he and I, between us, and one day, when my lady had almost ordered her mourning, my patient suddenly began to mend. He got better and better, till the doctor said he was out of danger. What was killing him was the dreadful fits of pain in his stomach. But little by little they stopped, and the poor marquis began to make his jokes again. The doctor found something that gave him great comfort—some white stuff that we kept in a great bottle on the chimney-piece. I used to give it to the marquis through a glass tube; it always made him easier. Then the doctor went away, after telling me to keep on giving him the mixture whenever he was bad. After that there was a little doctor from Poitiers, who came every day. So we were alone in the house—my lady and her poor husband and their three children. Young Madame de Bellegarde had gone away, with her little girl, to her mothers. You know she is very lively, and her maid told me that she didn't like to be where people were dying." Mrs. Bread paused a moment, and then she went on with the same quiet consistency. "I think you have guessed, sir, that when the marquis began to turn my lady was disappointed." And she paused again, bending upon Newman a face which seemed to grow whiter as the darkness settled down upon them.

Newman had listened eagerly—with an eagerness greater even than that with which he had bent his ear to Valentin de Bellegarde's last words. Every now and then, as his companion looked up at him, she reminded him of an ancient tabby cat, protracting the enjoyment of a dish of milk. Even her triumph was measured and decorous; the faculty of exultation had been chilled by disuse. She presently continued. "Late one night I was sitting by the marquis in his room, the great red room in the west tower. He had been complaining a little, and I gave him a spoonful of the doctor's dose. My lady had been there in the early part of the evening; she sat far more than an hour by his bed. Then she went away and left me alone. After midnight she came back, and her eldest son was with her. They went to the bed and looked at the marquis, and my lady took hold of his hand. Then she turned to me and said he was not so well; I remember how the marquis, without saying anything, lay staring at her. I can see his white face, at this moment, in the great black square between the bed-curtains. I said I didn't think he was very bad; and she told me to go to bed—she would sit a while with him. When the marquis saw me going he gave a sort of groan, and called out to me not to leave him; but Mr. Urbain opened the door for me and pointed the way out. The present marquis—perhaps you have noticed, sir—has a very proud way of giving orders, and I was there to take orders. I went to my room, but I wasn't easy; I couldn't tell you why. I didn't undress; I sat there waiting and listening. For what, would you have said, sir? I couldn't have told you; for surely a poor gentleman might be comfortable with his wife and his son. It was as if I expected to hear the marquis moaning after me again. I listened, but I heard nothing. It was a very still night; I never knew a night so still. At last the very stillness itself seemed to frighten me, and I came out of my room and went very softly down-stairs. In the anteroom, outside of the marquis's chamber, I found Mr. Urbain walking up and down. He asked me what I wanted, and I said I came back to relieve my lady. He said HE would relieve my lady, and ordered me back to bed; but as I stood there, unwilling to turn away, the door of the room opened and my lady came out. I noticed she was very pale; she was very strange. She looked a moment at the count and at me, and then she held out her arms to the count. He went to her, and she fell upon him and hid her face. I went quickly past her into the room and to the marquis's bed. He was lying there, very white, with his eyes shut, like a corpse. I took hold of his hand and spoke to him, and he felt to me like a dead man. Then I turned round; my lady and Mr. Urbain were there. 'My poor Bread,' said my lady, 'M. le Marquis is gone.' Mr. Urbain knelt down by the bed and said softly, 'Mon pere, mon pere.' I thought it wonderful strange, and asked my lady what in the world had happened, and why she hadn't called me. She said nothing had happened; that she had only been sitting there with the marquis, very quiet. She had closed her eyes, thinking she might sleep, and she had slept, she didn't know how long. When she woke up he was dead. 'It's death, my son, It's death,' she said to the count. Mr. Urbain said they must have the doctor, immediately, from Poitiers, and that he would ride off and fetch him. He kissed his father's face, and then he kissed his mother and went away. My lady and I stood there at the bedside. As I looked at the poor marquis it came into my head that he was not dead, that he was in a kind of swoon. And then my lady repeated, 'My poor Bread, it's death, it's death;' and I said, 'Yes, my lady, it's certainly death.' I said just the opposite to what I believed; it was my notion. Then my lady said we must wait for the doctor, and we sat there and waited. It was a long time; the poor marquis neither stirred nor changed. 'I have seen death before,' said my lady, 'and it's terribly like this.' 'Yes please, my lady,' said I; and I kept thinking. The night wore away without the count's coming back, and my lady began to be frightened. She was afraid he had had an accident in the dark, or met with some wild people. At last she got so restless that she went below to watch in the court for her son's return. I sat there alone and the marquis never stirred."

Here Mrs. Bread paused again, and the most artistic of romancers could not have been more effective. Newman made a movement as if he were turning over the page of a novel. "So he WAS dead!" he exclaimed.

"Three days afterwards he was in his grave," said Mrs. Bread, sententiously. "In a little while I went away to the front of the house and looked out into the court, and there, before long, I saw Mr. Urbain ride in alone. I waited a bit, to hear him come upstairs with his mother, but they stayed below, and I went back to the marquis's room. I went to the bed and held up the light to him, but I don't know why I didn't let the candlestick fall. The marquis's eyes were open—open wide! they were staring at me. I knelt down beside him and took his hands, and begged him to tell me, in the name of wonder, whether he was alive or dead. Still he looked at me a long time, and then he made me a sign to put my ear close to him: 'I am dead,' he said, 'I am dead. The marquise has killed me.' I was all in a tremble; I didn't understand him. He seemed both a man and a corpse, if you can fancy, sir. 'But you'll get well now, sir,' I said. And then he whispered again, ever so weak; 'I wouldn't get well for a kingdom. I wouldn't be that woman's husband again.' And then he said more; he said she had murdered him. I asked him what she had done to him, but he only replied, 'Murder, murder. And she'll kill my daughter,' he said; 'my poor unhappy child.' And he begged me to prevent that, and then he said that he was dying, that he was dead. I was afraid to move or to leave him; I was almost dead myself. All of a sudden he asked me to get a pencil and write for him; and then I had to tell him that I couldn't manage a pencil. He asked me to hold him up in bed while he wrote himself, and I said he could never, never do such a thing. But he seemed to have a kind of terror that gave him strength. I found a pencil in the room and a piece of paper and a book, and I put the paper on the book and the pencil into his hand, and moved the candle near him. You will think all this very strange, sir; and very strange it was. The strangest part of it was that I believed he was dying, and that I was eager to help him to write. I sat on the bed and put my arm round him, and held him up. I felt very strong; I believe I could have lifted him and carried him. It was a wonder how he wrote, but he did write, in a big scratching hand; he almost covered one side of the paper. It seemed a long time; I suppose it was three or four minutes. He was groaning, terribly, all the while. Then he said it was ended, and I let him down upon his pillows and he gave me the paper and told me to fold it, and hide it, and give it to those who would act upon it. 'Whom do you mean?' I said. 'Who are those who will act upon it?' But he only groaned, for an answer; he couldn't speak, for weakness. In a few minutes he told me to go and look at the bottle on the chimney-piece. I knew the bottle he meant; the white stuff that was good for his stomach. I went and looked at it, but it was empty. When I came back his eyes were open and he was staring at me; but soon he closed them and he said no more. I hid the paper in my dress; I didn't look at what was written upon it, though I can read very well, sir, if I haven't any handwriting. I sat down near the bed, but it was nearly half an hour before my lady and the count came in. The marquis looked as he did when they left him, and I never said a word about his having been otherwise. Mr. Urbain said that the doctor had been called to a person in child-birth, but that he promised to set out for Fleurieres immediately. In another half hour he arrived, and as soon as he had examined the marquis he said that we had had a false alarm. The poor gentleman was very low, but he was still living. I watched my lady and her son when he said this, to see if they looked at each other, and I am obliged to admit that they didn't. The doctor said there was no reason he should die; he had been going on so well. And then he wanted to know how he had suddenly fallen off; he had left him so very hearty. My lady told her little story again—what she had told Mr. Urbain and me—and the doctor looked at her and said nothing. He stayed all the next day at the chateau, and hardly left the marquis. I was always there. Mademoiselle and Mr. Valentin came and looked at their father, but he never stirred. It was a strange, deathly stupor. My lady was always about; her face was as white as her husband's, and she looked very proud, as I had seen her look when her orders or her wishes had been disobeyed. It was as if the poor marquis had defied her; and the way she took it made me afraid of her. The apothecary from Poitiers kept the marquis along through the day, and we waited for the other doctor from Paris, who, as I told you, had been staying at Fleurieres. They had telegraphed for him early in the morning, and in the evening he arrived. He talked a bit outside with the doctor from Poitiers, and then they came in to see the marquis together. I was with him, and so was Mr. Urbain. My lady had been to receive the doctor from Paris, and she didn't come back with him into the room. He sat down by the marquis; I can see him there now, with his hand on the marquis's wrist, and Mr. Urbain watching him with a little looking-glass in his hand. 'I'm sure he's better,' said the little doctor from Poitiers; 'I'm sure he'll come back.' A few moments after he had said this the marquis opened his eyes, as if he were waking up, and looked at us, from one to the other. I saw him look at me, very softly, as you'd say. At the same moment my lady came in on tiptoe; she came up to the bed and put in her head between me and the count. The marquis saw her and gave a long, most wonderful moan. He said something we couldn't understand, and he seemed to have a kind of spasm. He shook all over and then closed his eyes, and the doctor jumped up and took hold of my lady. He held her for a moment a bit roughly. The marquis was stone dead! This time there were those there that knew."

Newman felt as if he had been reading by starlight the report of highly important evidence in a great murder case. "And the paper—the paper!" he said, excitedly. "What was written upon it?"

"I can't tell you, sir," answered Mrs. Bread. "I couldn't read it; it was in French."

"But could no one else read it?"

"I never asked a human creature."

"No one has ever seen it?"

"If you see it you'll be the first."

Newman seized the old woman's hand in both his own and pressed it vigorously. "I thank you ever so much for that," he cried. "I want to be the first, I want it to be my property and no one else's! You're the wisest old woman in Europe. And what did you do with the paper?" This information had made him feel extraordinarily strong. "Give it to me quick!"

Mrs. Bread got up with a certain majesty. "It is not so easy as that, sir. If you want the paper, you must wait."

"But waiting is horrible, you know," urged Newman.

"I am sure I have waited; I have waited these many years," said Mrs. Bread.

"That is very true. You have waited for me. I won't forget it. And yet, how comes it you didn't do as M. de Bellegarde said, show the paper to some one?"

"To whom should I show it?" answered Mrs. Bread, mournfully. "It was not easy to know, and many's the night I have lain awake thinking of it. Six months afterwards, when they married Mademoiselle to her vicious old husband, I was very near bringing it out. I thought it was my duty to do something with it, and yet I was mightily afraid. I didn't know what was written on the paper or how bad it might be, and there was no one I could trust enough to ask. And it seemed to me a cruel kindness to do that sweet young creature, letting her know that her father had written her mother down so shamefully; for that's what he did, I suppose. I thought she would rather be unhappy with her husband than be unhappy that way. It was for her and for my dear Mr. Valentin I kept quiet. Quiet I call it, but for me it was a weary quietness. It worried me terribly, and it changed me altogether. But for others I held my tongue, and no one, to this hour, knows what passed between the poor marquis and me."

"But evidently there were suspicions," said Newman. "Where did Mr. Valentin get his ideas?"

"It was the little doctor from Poitiers. He was very ill-satisfied, and he made a great talk. He was a sharp Frenchman, and coming to the house, as he did day after day, I suppose he saw more than he seemed to see. And indeed the way the poor marquis went off as soon as his eyes fell on my lady was a most shocking sight for anyone. The medical gentleman from Paris was much more accommodating, and he hushed up the other. But for all he could do Mr. Valentin and Mademoiselle heard something; they knew their father's death was somehow against nature. Of course they couldn't accuse their mother, and, as I tell you, I was as dumb as that stone. Mr. Valentin used to look at me sometimes, and his eyes seemed to shine, as if he were thinking of asking me something. I was dreadfully afraid he would speak, and I always looked away and went about my business. If I were to tell him, I was sure he would hate me afterwards, and that I could never have borne. Once I went up to him and took a great liberty; I kissed him, as I had kissed him when he was a child. 'You oughtn't to look so sad, sir,' I said; 'believe your poor old Bread. Such a gallant, handsome young man can have nothing to be sad about.' And I think he understood me; he understood that I was begging off, and he made up his mind in his own way. He went about with his unasked question in his mind, as I did with my untold tale; we were both afraid of bringing dishonor on a great house. And it was the same with Mademoiselle. She didn't know what happened; she wouldn't know. My lady and Mr. Urbain asked me no questions because they had no reason. I was as still as a mouse. When I was younger my lady thought me a hussy, and now she thought me a fool. How should I have any ideas?"

"But you say the little doctor from Poitiers made a talk," said Newman. "Did no one take it up?"

"I heard nothing of it, sir. They are always talking scandal in these foreign countries you may have noticed—and I suppose they shook their heads over Madame de Bellegarde. But after all, what could they say? The marquis had been ill, and the marquis had died; he had as good a right to die as any one. The doctor couldn't say he had not come honestly by his cramps. The next year the little doctor left the place and bought a practice in Bordeaux, and if there has been any gossip it died out. And I don't think there could have been much gossip about my lady that any one would listen to. My lady is so very respectable."

Newman, at this last affirmation, broke into an immense, resounding laugh. Mrs. Bread had begun to move away from the spot where they were sitting, and he helped her through the aperture in the wall and along the homeward path. "Yes," he said, "my lady's respectability is delicious; it will be a great crash!" They reached the empty space in front of the church, where they stopped a moment, looking at each other with something of an air of closer fellowship—like two sociable conspirators. "But what was it," said Newman, "what was it she did to her husband? She didn't stab him or poison him."

"I don't know, sir; no one saw it."

"Unless it was Mr. Urbain. You say he was walking up and down, outside the room. Perhaps he looked through the keyhole. But no; I think that with his mother he would take it on trust."

"You may be sure I have often thought of it," said Mrs. Bread. "I am sure she didn't touch him with her hands. I saw nothing on him, anywhere. I believe it was in this way. He had a fit of his great pain, and he asked her for his medicine. Instead of giving it to him she went and poured it away, before his eyes. Then he saw what she meant, and, weak and helpless as he was, he was frightened, he was terrified. 'You want to kill me,' he said. 'Yes, M. le Marquis, I want to kill you,' says my lady, and sits down and fixes her eyes upon him. You know my lady's eyes, I think, sir; it was with them she killed him; it was with the terrible strong will she put into them. It was like a frost on flowers."

"Well, you are a very intelligent woman; you have shown great discretion," said Newman. "I shall value your services as housekeeper extremely."

CHAPTER XXII

They had begun to descend the hill, and Mrs. Bread said nothing until they reached the foot. Newman strolled lightly beside her; his head was thrown back and he was gazing at all the stars; he seemed to himself to be riding his vengeance along the Milky Way. "So you are serious, sir, about that?" said Mrs. Bread, softly.

"About your living with me? Why of course I will take care of you to the end of your days. You can't live with those people any longer. And you oughtn't to, you know, after this. You give me the paper, and you move away."

"It seems very flighty in me to be taking a new place at this time of life," observed Mrs. Bread, lugubriously. "But if you are going to turn the house upside down, I would rather be out of it."

"Oh," said Newman, in the cheerful tone of a man who feels rich in alternatives. "I don't think I shall bring in the constables, if that's what you mean. Whatever Madame de Bellegarde did, I am afraid the law can't take hold of it. But I am glad of that; it leaves it altogether to me!"

"You are a mighty bold gentleman, sir," murmured Mrs. Bread, looking at him round the edge of her great bonnet.

He walked with her back to the chateau; the curfew had tolled for the laborious villagers of Fleurieres, and the street was unlighted and empty. She promised him that he should have the marquis's manuscript in half an hour. Mrs. Bread choosing not to go in by the great gate, they passed round by a winding lane to a door in the wall of the park, of which she had the key, and which would enable her to enter the chateau from behind. Newman arranged with her that he should await outside the wall her return with the coveted document.

She went in, and his half hour in the dusky lane seemed very long. But he had plenty to think about. At last the door in the wall opened and Mrs. Bread stood there, with one hand on the latch and the other holding out a scrap of white paper, folded small. In a moment he was master of it, and it had passed into his waistcoat pocket. "Come and see me in Paris," he said; "we are to settle your future, you know; and I will translate poor M. de Bellegarde's French to you." Never had he felt so grateful as at this moment for M. Nioche's instructions.

Mrs. Bread's dull eyes had followed the disappearance of the paper, and she gave a heavy sigh. "Well, you have done what you would with me, sir, and I suppose you will do it again. You MUST take care of me now. You are a terribly positive gentleman."

"Just now," said Newman, "I'm a terribly impatient gentleman!" And he bade her good-night and walked rapidly back to the inn. He ordered his vehicle to be prepared for his return to Poitiers, and then he shut the door of the common salle and strode toward the solitary lamp on the chimney-piece. He pulled out the paper and quickly unfolded it. It was covered with pencil-marks, which at first, in the feeble light, seemed indistinct. But Newman's fierce curiosity forced a meaning from the tremulous signs. The English of them was as follows:—

"My wife has tried to kill me, and she has done it; I am dying, dying horribly. It is to marry my dear daughter to M. de Cintre. With all my soul I protest,—I forbid it. I am not insane,—ask the doctors, ask Mrs. B——. It was alone with me here, to-night; she attacked me and put me to death. It is murder, if murder ever was. Ask the doctors.

"HENRI-URBAIN DE BELLEGARDE"

CHAPTER XXIII

Newman returned to Paris the second day after his interview with Mrs. Bread. The morrow he had spent at Poitiers, reading over and over again the little document which he had lodged in his pocket-book, and thinking what he would do in the circumstances and how he would do it. He would not have said that Poitiers was an amusing place; yet the day seemed very short. Domiciled once more in the Boulevard Haussmann, he walked over to the Rue de l'Universite and inquired of Madame de Bellegarde's portress whether the marquise had come back. The portress told him that she had arrived, with M. le Marquis, on the preceding day, and further informed him that if he desired to enter, Madame de Bellegarde and her son were both at home. As she said these words the little white-faced old woman who peered out of the dusky gate-house of the Hotel de Bellegarde gave a small wicked smile—a smile which seemed to Newman to mean, "Go in if you dare!" She was evidently versed in the current domestic history; she was placed where she could feel the pulse of the house. Newman stood a moment, twisting his mustache and looking at her; then he abruptly turned away. But this was not because he was afraid to go in—though he doubted whether, if he did so, he should be able to make his way, unchallenged, into the presence of Madame de Cintre's relatives. Confidence—excessive confidence, perhaps—quite as much as timidity prompted his retreat. He was nursing his thunder-bolt; he loved it; he was unwilling to part with it. He seemed to be holding it aloft in the rumbling, vaguely-flashing air, directly over the heads of his victims, and he fancied he could see their pale, upturned faces. Few specimens of the human countenance had ever given him such pleasure as these, lighted in the lurid fashion I have hinted at, and he was disposed to sip the cup of contemplative revenge in a leisurely fashion. It must be added, too, that he was at a loss to see exactly how he could arrange to witness the operation of his thunder. To send in his card to Madame de Bellegarde would be a waste of ceremony; she would certainly decline to receive him. On the other hand he could not force his way into her presence. It annoyed him keenly to think that he might be reduced to the blind satisfaction of writing her a letter; but he consoled himself in a measure with the reflection that a letter might lead to an interview. He went home, and feeling rather tired—nursing a vengeance was, it must be confessed, a rather fatiguing process; it took a good deal out of one—flung himself into one of his brocaded fauteuils, stretched his legs, thrust his hands into his pockets, and, while he watched the reflected sunset fading from the ornate house-tops on the opposite side of the Boulevard, began mentally to compose a cool epistle to Madame de Bellegarde. While he was so occupied his servant threw open the door and announced ceremoniously, "Madame Brett!"

Newman roused himself, expectantly, and in a few moments perceived upon his threshold the worthy woman with whom he had conversed to such good purpose on the starlit hill-top of Fleurieres. Mrs. Bread had made for this visit the same toilet as for her former expedition. Newman was struck with her distinguished appearance. His lamp was not lit, and as her large, grave face gazed at him through the light dusk from under the shadow of her ample bonnet, he felt the incongruity of such a person presenting herself as a servant. He greeted her with high geniality and bade her come in and sit down and make herself comfortable. There was something which might have touched the springs both of mirth and of melancholy in the ancient maidenliness with which Mrs. Bread endeavored to comply with these directions. She was not playing at being fluttered, which would have been simply ridiculous; she was doing her best to carry herself as a person so humble that, for her, even embarrassment would have been pretentious; but evidently she had never dreamed of its being in her horoscope to pay a visit, at night-fall, to a friendly single gentleman who lived in theatrical-looking rooms on one of the new Boulevards.

"I truly hope I am not forgetting my place, sir," she murmured.

"Forgetting your place?" cried Newman. "Why, you are remembering it. This is your place, you know. You are already in my service; your wages, as housekeeper, began a fortnight ago. I can tell you my house wants keeping! Why don't you take off your bonnet and stay?"

"Take off my bonnet?" said Mrs. Bread, with timid literalness. "Oh, sir, I haven't my cap. And with your leave, sir, I couldn't keep house in my best gown."

"Never mind your gown," said Newman, cheerfully. "You shall have a better gown than that."

Mrs. Bread stared solemnly and then stretched her hands over her lustreless satin skirt, as if the perilous side of her situation were defining itself. "Oh, sir, I am fond of my own clothes," she murmured.

"I hope you have left those wicked people, at any rate," said Newman.

"Well, sir, here I am!" said Mrs. Bread. "That's all I can tell you. Here I sit, poor Catherine Bread. It's a strange place for me to be. I don't know myself; I never supposed I was so bold. But indeed, sir, I have gone as far as my own strength will bear me."

"Oh, come, Mrs. Bread," said Newman, almost caressingly, "don't make yourself uncomfortable. Now's the time to feel lively, you know."

She began to speak again with a trembling voice. "I think it would be more respectable if I could—if I could"—and her voice trembled to a pause.

"If you could give up this sort of thing altogether?" said Newman kindly, trying to anticipate her meaning, which he supposed might be a wish to retire from service.

"If I could give up everything, sir! All I should ask is a decent Protestant burial."

"Burial!" cried Newman, with a burst of laughter. "Why, to bury you now would be a sad piece of extravagance. It's only rascals who have to be buried to get respectable. Honest folks like you and me can live our time out—and live together. Come! Did you bring your baggage?"

"My box is locked and corded; but I haven't yet spoken to my lady."

"Speak to her, then, and have done with it. I should like to have your chance!" cried Newman.

"I would gladly give it you, sir. I have passed some weary hours in my lady's dressing-room; but this will be one of the longest. She will tax me with ingratitude."

"Well," said Newman, "so long as you can tax her with murder—"

"Oh, sir, I can't; not I," sighed Mrs. Bread.

"You don't mean to say anything about it? So much the better. Leave that to me."

"If she calls me a thankless old woman," said Mrs. Bread, "I shall have nothing to say. But it is better so," she softly added. "She shall be my lady to the last. That will be more respectable."

"And then you will come to me and I shall be your gentleman," said Newman; "that will be more respectable still!"

Mrs. Bread rose, with lowered eyes, and stood a moment; then, looking up, she rested her eyes upon Newman's face. The disordered proprieties were somehow settling to rest. She looked at Newman so long and so fixedly, with such a dull, intense devotedness, that he himself might have had a pretext for embarrassment. At last she said gently, "You are not looking well, sir."

"That's natural enough," said Newman. "I have nothing to feel well about. To be very indifferent and very fierce, very dull and very jovial, very sick and very lively, all at once,—why, it rather mixes one up."

Mrs. Bread gave a noiseless sigh. "I can tell you something that will make you feel duller still, if you want to feel all one way. About Madame de Cintre."

"What can you tell me?" Newman demanded. "Not that you have seen her?"

She shook her head. "No, indeed, sir, nor ever shall. That's the dullness of it. Nor my lady. Nor M. de Bellegarde."

"You mean that she is kept so close."

"Close, close," said Mrs. Bread, very softly.

These words, for an instant, seemed to check the beating of Newman's heart. He leaned back in his chair, staring up at the old woman. "They have tried to see her, and she wouldn't—she couldn't?"

"She refused—forever! I had it from my lady's own maid," said Mrs. Bread, "who had it from my lady. To speak of it to such a person my lady must have felt the shock. Madame de Cintre won't see them now, and now is her only chance. A while hence she will have no chance."

"You mean the other women—the mothers, the daughters, the sisters; what is it they call them?—won't let her?"

"It is what they call the rule of the house,—or of the order, I believe," said Mrs. Bread. "There is no rule so strict as that of the Carmelites. The bad women in the reformatories are fine ladies to them. They wear old brown cloaks—so the femme de chambre told me—that you wouldn't use for a horse blanket. And the poor countess was so fond of soft-feeling dresses; she would never have anything stiff! They sleep on the ground," Mrs. Bread went on; "they are no better, no better,"—and she hesitated for a comparison,—"they are no better than tinkers' wives. They give up everything, down to the very name their poor old nurses called them by. They give up father and mother, brother and sister,—to say nothing of other persons," Mrs. Bread delicately added. "They wear a shroud under their brown cloaks and a rope round their waists, and they get up on winter nights and go off into cold places to pray to the Virgin Mary. The Virgin Mary is a hard mistress!"

Mrs. Bread, dwelling on these terrible facts, sat dry-eyed and pale, with her hands clasped in her satin lap. Newman gave a melancholy groan and fell forward, leaning his head on his hands. There was a long silence, broken only by the ticking of the great gilded clock on the chimney-piece.

"Where is this place—where is the convent?" Newman asked at last, looking up.

"There are two houses," said Mrs. Bread. "I found out; I thought you would like to know—though it's poor comfort, I think. One is in the Avenue de Messine; they have learned that Madame de Cintre is there. The other is in the Rue d'Enfer. That's a terrible name; I suppose you know what it means."

Newman got up and walked away to the end of his long room. When he came back Mrs. Bread had got up, and stood by the fire with folded hands. "Tell me this," he said. "Can I get near her—even if I don't see her? Can I look through a grating, or some such thing, at the place where she is?"

It is said that all women love a lover, and Mrs. Bread's sense of the pre-established harmony which kept servants in their "place," even as planets in their orbits (not that Mrs. Bread had ever consciously likened herself to a planet), barely availed to temper the maternal melancholy with which she leaned her head on one side and gazed at her new employer. She probably felt for the moment as if, forty years before, she had held him also in her arms. "That wouldn't help you, sir. It would only make her seem farther away."

"I want to go there, at all events," said Newman. "Avenue de Messine, you say? And what is it they call themselves?"

"Carmelites," said Mrs. Bread.

"I shall remember that."

Mrs. Bread hesitated a moment, and then, "It's my duty to tell you this, sir," she went on. "The convent has a chapel, and some people are admitted on Sunday to the Mass. You don't see the poor creatures that are shut up there, but I am told you can hear them sing. It's a wonder they have any heart for singing! Some Sunday I shall make bold to go. It seems to me I should know her voice in fifty."

Newman looked at his visitor very gratefully; then he held out his hand and shook hers. "Thank you," he said. "If any one can get in, I will." A moment later Mrs. Bread proposed, deferentially, to retire, but he checked her and put a lighted candle into her hand. "There are half a dozen rooms there I don't use," he said, pointing through an open door. "Go and look at them and take your choice. You can live in the one you like best." From this bewildering opportunity Mrs. Bread at first recoiled; but finally, yielding to Newman's gentle, reassuring push, she wandered off into the dusk with her tremulous taper. She remained absent a quarter of an hour, during which Newman paced up and down, stopped occasionally to look out of the window at the lights on the Boulevard, and then resumed his walk. Mrs. Bread's relish for her investigation apparently increased as she proceeded; but at last she reappeared and deposited her candlestick on the chimney-piece.

"Well, have you picked one out?" asked Newman.

"A room, sir? They are all too fine for a dingy old body like me. There isn't one that hasn't a bit of gilding."

"It's only tinsel, Mrs. Bread," said Newman. "If you stay there a while it will all peel off of itself." And he gave a dismal smile.

"Oh, sir, there are things enough peeling off already!" rejoined Mrs. Bread, with a head-shake. "Since I was there I thought I would look about me. I don't believe you know, sir. The corners are most dreadful. You do want a housekeeper, that you do; you want a tidy Englishwoman that isn't above taking hold of a broom."

Newman assured her that he suspected, if he had not measured, his domestic abuses, and that to reform them was a mission worthy of her powers. She held her candlestick aloft again and looked around the salon with compassionate glances; then she intimated that she accepted the mission, and that its sacred character would sustain her in her rupture with Madame de Bellegarde. With this she curtsied herself away.

She came back the next day with her worldly goods, and Newman, going into his drawing-room, found her upon her aged knees before a divan, sewing up some detached fringe. He questioned her as to her leave-taking with her late mistress, and she said it had proved easier than she feared. "I was perfectly civil, sir, but the Lord helped me to remember that a good woman has no call to tremble before a bad one."

"I should think so!" cried Newman. "And does she know you have come to me?"

"She asked me where I was going, and I mentioned your name," said Mrs. Bread.

"What did she say to that?"

"She looked at me very hard, and she turned very red. Then she bade me leave her. I was all ready to go, and I had got the coachman, who is an Englishman, to bring down my poor box and to fetch me a cab. But when I went down myself to the gate I found it closed. My lady had sent orders to the porter not to let me pass, and by the same orders the porter's wife—she is a dreadful sly old body—had gone out in a cab to fetch home M. de Bellegarde from his club."

Newman slapped his knee. "She IS scared! she IS scared!" he cried, exultantly.

"I was frightened too, sir," said Mrs. Bread, "but I was also mightily vexed. I took it very high with the porter and asked him by what right he used violence to an honorable Englishwoman who had lived in the house for thirty years before he was heard of. Oh, sir, I was very grand, and I brought the man down. He drew his bolts and let me out, and I promised the cabman something handsome if he would drive fast. But he was terribly slow; it seemed as if we should never reach your blessed door. I am all of a tremble still; it took me five minutes, just now, to thread my needle."

Newman told her, with a gleeful laugh, that if she chose she might have a little maid on purpose to thread her needles; and he went away murmuring to himself again that the old woman WAS scared—she WAS scared!

He had not shown Mrs. Tristram the little paper that he carried in his pocket-book, but since his return to Paris he had seen her several times, and she had told him that he seemed to her to be in a strange way—an even stranger way than his sad situation made natural. Had his disappointment gone to his head? He looked like a man who was going to be ill, and yet she had never seen him more restless and active. One day he would sit hanging his head and looking as if he were firmly resolved never to smile again; another he would indulge in laughter that was almost unseemly and make jokes that were bad even for him. If he was trying to carry off his sorrow, he at such times really went too far. She begged him of all things not to be "strange." Feeling in a measure responsible as she did for the affair which had turned out so ill for him, she could endure anything but his strangeness. He might be melancholy if he would, or he might be stoical; he might be cross and cantankerous with her and ask her why she had ever dared to meddle with his destiny: to this she would submit; for this she would make allowances. Only, for Heaven's sake, let him not be incoherent. That would be extremely unpleasant. It was like people talking in their sleep; they always frightened her. And Mrs. Tristram intimated that, taking very high ground as regards the moral obligation which events had laid upon her, she proposed not to rest quiet until she should have confronted him with the least inadequate substitute for Madame de Cintre that the two hemispheres contained.

"Oh," said Newman, "we are even now, and we had better not open a new account! You may bury me some day, but you shall never marry me. It's too rough. I hope, at any rate," he added, "that there is nothing incoherent in this—that I want to go next Sunday to the Carmelite chapel in the Avenue de Messine. You know one of the Catholic ministers—an abbe, is that it?—I have seen him here, you know; that motherly old gentleman with the big waist-band. Please ask him if I need a special leave to go in, and if I do, beg him to obtain it for me."

Mrs. Tristram gave expression to the liveliest joy. "I am so glad you have asked me to do something!" she cried. "You shall get into the chapel if the abbe is disfrocked for his share in it." And two days afterwards she told him that it was all arranged; the abbe was enchanted to serve him, and if he would present himself civilly at the convent gate there would be no difficulty.

CHAPTER XXIV

Sunday was as yet two days off; but meanwhile, to beguile his impatience, Newman took his way to the Avenue de Messine and got what comfort he could in staring at the blank outer wall of Madame de Cintre's present residence. The street in question, as some travelers will remember, adjoins the Parc Monceau, which is one of the prettiest corners of Paris. The quarter has an air of modern opulence and convenience which seems at variance with the ascetic institution, and the impression made upon Newman's gloomily-irritated gaze by the fresh-looking, windowless expanse behind which the woman he loved was perhaps even then pledging herself to pass the rest of her days was less exasperating than he had feared. The place suggested a convent with the modern improvements—an asylum in which privacy, though unbroken, might be not quite identical with privation, and meditation, though monotonous, might be of a cheerful cast. And yet he knew the case was otherwise; only at present it was not a reality to him. It was too strange and too mocking to be real; it was like a page torn out of a romance, with no context in his own experience.

On Sunday morning, at the hour which Mrs. Tristram had indicated, he rang at the gate in the blank wall. It instantly opened and admitted him into a clean, cold-looking court, from beyond which a dull, plain edifice looked down upon him. A robust lay sister with a cheerful complexion emerged from a porter's lodge, and, on his stating his errand, pointed to the open door of the chapel, an edifice which occupied the right side of the court and was preceded by the high flight of steps. Newman ascended the steps and immediately entered the open door. Service had not yet begun; the place was dimly lighted, and it was some moments before he could distinguish its features. Then he saw it was divided by a large close iron screen into two unequal portions. The altar was on the hither side of the screen, and between it and the entrance were disposed several benches and chairs. Three or four of these were occupied by vague, motionless figures—figures that he presently perceived to be women, deeply absorbed in their devotion. The place seemed to Newman very cold; the smell of the incense itself was cold. Besides this there was a twinkle of tapers and here and there a glow of colored glass. Newman seated himself; the praying women kept still, with their backs turned. He saw they were visitors like himself and he would have liked to see their faces; for he believed that they were the mourning mothers and sisters of other women who had had the same pitiless courage as Madame de Cintre. But they were better off than he, for they at least shared the faith to which the others had sacrificed themselves. Three or four persons came in; two of them were elderly gentlemen. Every one was very quiet. Newman fastened his eyes upon the screen behind the altar. That was the convent, the real convent, the place where she was. But he could see nothing; no light came through the crevices. He got up and approached the partition very gently, trying to look through. But behind it there was darkness, with nothing stirring. He went back to his place, and after that a priest and two altar boys came in and began to say mass. Newman watched their genuflections and gyrations with a grim, still enmity; they seemed aids and abettors of Madame de Cintre's desertion; they were mouthing and droning out their triumph. The priest's long, dismal intonings acted upon his nerves and deepened his wrath; there was something defiant in his unintelligible drawl; it seemed meant for Newman himself. Suddenly there arose from the depths of the chapel, from behind the inexorable grating, a sound which drew his attention from the altar—the sound of a strange, lugubrious chant, uttered by women's voices. It began softly, but it presently grew louder, and as it increased it became more of a wail and a dirge. It was the chant of the Carmelite nuns, their only human utterance. It was their dirge over their buried affections and over the vanity of earthly desires. At first Newman was bewildered—almost stunned—by the strangeness of the sound; then, as he comprehended its meaning, he listened intently and his heart began to throb. He listened for Madame de Cintre's voice, and in the very heart of the tuneless harmony he imagined he made it out. (We are obliged to believe that he was wrong, inasmuch as she had obviously not yet had time to become a member of the invisible sisterhood.) The chant kept on, mechanical and monotonous, with dismal repetitions and despairing cadences. It was hideous, it was horrible; as it continued, Newman felt that he needed all his self-control. He was growing more agitated; he felt tears in his eyes. At last, as in its full force the thought came over him that this confused, impersonal wail was all that either he or the world she had deserted should ever hear of the voice he had found so sweet, he felt that he could bear it no longer. He rose abruptly and made his way out. On the threshold he paused, listened again to the dreary strain, and then hastily descended into the court. As he did so he saw the good sister with the high-colored cheeks and the fanlike frill to her coiffure, who had admitted him, was in conference at the gate with two persons who had just come in. A second glance informed him that these persons were Madame de Bellegarde and her son, and that they were about to avail themselves of that method of approach to Madame de Cintre which Newman had found but a mockery of consolation. As he crossed the court M. de Bellegarde recognized him; the marquis was coming to the steps, leading his mother. The old lady also gave Newman a look, and it resembled that of her son. Both faces expressed a franker perturbation, something more akin to the humbleness of dismay, than Newman had yet seen in them. Evidently he startled the Bellegardes, and they had not their grand behavior immediately in hand. Newman hurried past them, guided only by the desire to get out of the convent walls and into the street. The gate opened itself at his approach; he strode over the threshold and it closed behind him. A carriage which appeared to have been standing there, was just turning away from the sidewalk. Newman looked at it for a moment, blankly; then he became conscious, through the dusky mist that swam before his eyes, that a lady seated in it was bowing to him. The vehicle had turned away before he recognized her; it was an ancient landau with one half the cover lowered. The lady's bow was very positive and accompanied with a smile; a little girl was seated beside her. He raised his hat, and then the lady bade the coachman stop. The carriage halted again beside the pavement, and she sat there and beckoned to Newman—beckoned with the demonstrative grace of Madame Urbain de Bellegarde. Newman hesitated a moment before he obeyed her summons, during this moment he had time to curse his stupidity for letting the others escape him. He had been wondering how he could get at them; fool that he was for not stopping them then and there! What better place than beneath the very prison walls to which they had consigned the promise of his joy? He had been too bewildered to stop them, but now he felt ready to wait for them at the gate. Madame Urbain, with a certain attractive petulance, beckoned to him again, and this time he went over to the carriage. She leaned out and gave him her hand, looking at him kindly, and smiling.

"Ah, monsieur," she said, "you don't include me in your wrath? I had nothing to do with it."

"Oh, I don't suppose YOU could have prevented it!" Newman answered in a tone which was not that of studied gallantry.

"What you say is too true for me to resent the small account it makes of my influence. I forgive you, at any rate, because you look as if you had seen a ghost."

"I have!" said Newman.

"I am glad, then, I didn't go in with Madame de Bellegarde and my husband. You must have seen them, eh? Was the meeting affectionate? Did you hear the chanting? They say it's like the lamentations of the damned. I wouldn't go in: one is certain to hear that soon enough. Poor Claire—in a white shroud and a big brown cloak! That's the toilette of the Carmelites, you know. Well, she was always fond of long, loose things. But I must not speak of her to you; only I must say that I am very sorry for you, that if I could have helped you I would, and that I think every one has been very shabby. I was afraid of it, you know; I felt it in the air for a fortnight before it came. When I saw you at my mother-in-law's ball, taking it all so easily, I felt as if you were dancing on your grave. But what could I do? I wish you all the good I can think of. You will say that isn't much! Yes; they have been very shabby; I am not a bit afraid to say it; I assure you every one thinks so. We are not all like that. I am sorry I am not going to see you again; you know I think you very good company. I would prove it by asking you to get into the carriage and drive with me for a quarter of an hour, while I wait for my mother-in-law. Only if we were seen—considering what has passed, and every one knows you have been turned away—it might be thought I was going a little too far, even for me. But I shall see you sometimes—somewhere, eh? You know"—this was said in English—"we have a plan for a little amusement."

Newman stood there with his hand on the carriage-door listening to this consolatory murmur with an unlighted eye. He hardly knew what Madame de Bellegarde was saying; he was only conscious that she was chattering ineffectively. But suddenly it occurred to him that, with her pretty professions, there was a way of making her effective; she might help him to get at the old woman and the marquis. "They are coming back soon—your companions?" he said. "You are waiting for them?"

"They will hear the mass out; there is nothing to keep them longer. Claire has refused to see them."

"I want to speak to them," said Newman; "and you can help me, you can do me a favor. Delay your return for five minutes and give me a chance at them. I will wait for them here."

Madame de Bellegarde clasped her hands with a tender grimace. "My poor friend, what do you want to do to them? To beg them to come back to you? It will be wasted words. They will never come back!"

"I want to speak to them, all the same. Pray do what I ask you. Stay away and leave them to me for five minutes; you needn't be afraid; I shall not be violent; I am very quiet."

"Yes, you look very quiet! If they had le coeur tendre you would move them. But they haven't! However, I will do better for you than what you propose. The understanding is not that I shall come back for them. I am going into the Parc Monceau with my little girl to give her a walk, and my mother-in-law, who comes so rarely into this quarter, is to profit by the same opportunity to take the air. We are to wait for her in the park, where my husband is to bring her to us. Follow me now; just within the gates I shall get out of my carriage. Sit down on a chair in some quiet corner and I will bring them near you. There's devotion for you! Le reste vous regarde."

This proposal seemed to Newman extremely felicitous; it revived his drooping spirit, and he reflected that Madame Urbain was not such a goose as she seemed. He promised immediately to overtake her, and the carriage drove away.

The Parc Monceau is a very pretty piece of landscape-gardening, but Newman, passing into it, bestowed little attention upon its elegant vegetation, which was full of the freshness of spring. He found Madame de Bellegarde promptly, seated in one of the quiet corners of which she had spoken, while before her, in the alley, her little girl, attended by the footman and the lap-dog, walked up and down as if she were taking a lesson in deportment. Newman sat down beside the mamma, and she talked a great deal, apparently with the design of convincing him that—if he would only see it—poor dear Claire did not belong to the most fascinating type of woman. She was too tall and thin, too stiff and cold; her mouth was too wide and her nose too narrow. She had no dimples anywhere. And then she was eccentric, eccentric in cold blood; she was an Anglaise, after all. Newman was very impatient; he was counting the minutes until his victims should reappear. He sat silent, leaning upon his cane, looking absently and insensibly at the little marquise. At length Madame de Bellegarde said she would walk toward the gate of the park and meet her companions; but before she went she dropped her eyes, and, after playing a moment with the lace of her sleeve, looked up again at Newman.

"Do you remember," she asked, "the promise you made me three weeks ago?" And then, as Newman, vainly consulting his memory, was obliged to confess that the promise had escaped it, she declared that he had made her, at the time, a very queer answer—an answer at which, viewing it in the light of the sequel, she had fair ground for taking offense. "You promised to take me to Bullier's after your marriage. After your marriage—you made a great point of that. Three days after that your marriage was broken off. Do you know, when I heard the news, the first thing I said to myself? 'Oh heaven, now he won't go with me to Bullier's!' And I really began to wonder if you had not been expecting the rupture."

"Oh, my dear lady," murmured Newman, looking down the path to see if the others were not coming.

"I shall be good-natured," said Madame de Bellegarde. "One must not ask too much of a gentleman who is in love with a cloistered nun. Besides, I can't go to Bullier's while we are in mourning. But I haven't given it up for that. The partie is arranged; I have my cavalier. Lord Deepmere, if you please! He has gone back to his dear Dublin; but a few months hence I am to name any evening and he will come over from Ireland, on purpose. That's what I call gallantry!"

Shortly after this Madame de Bellegarde walked away with her little girl. Newman sat in his place; the time seemed terribly long. He felt how fiercely his quarter of an hour in the convent chapel had raked over the glowing coals of his resentment. Madame de Bellegarde kept him waiting, but she proved as good as her word. At last she reappeared at the end of the path, with her little girl and her footman; beside her slowly walked her husband, with his mother on his arm. They were a long time advancing, during which Newman sat unmoved. Tingling as he was with passion, it was extremely characteristic of him that he was able to moderate his expression of it, as he would have turned down a flaring gas-burner. His native coolness, shrewdness, and deliberateness, his life-long submissiveness to the sentiment that words were acts and acts were steps in life, and that in this matter of taking steps curveting and prancing were exclusively reserved for quadrupeds and foreigners—all this admonished him that rightful wrath had no connection with being a fool and indulging in spectacular violence. So as he rose, when old Madame de Bellegarde and her son were close to him, he only felt very tall and light. He had been sitting beside some shrubbery, in such a way as not to be noticeable at a distance; but M. de Bellegarde had evidently already perceived him. His mother and he were holding their course, but Newman stepped in front of them, and they were obliged to pause. He lifted his hat slightly, and looked at them for a moment; they were pale with amazement and disgust.

"Excuse me for stopping you," he said in a low tone, "but I must profit by the occasion. I have ten words to say to you. Will you listen to them?"

The marquis glared at him and then turned to his mother. "Can Mr. Newman possibly have anything to say that is worth our listening to?"

"I assure you I have something," said Newman, "besides, it is my duty to say it. It's a notification—a warning."

"Your duty?" said old Madame de Bellegarde, her thin lips curving like scorched paper. "That is your affair, not ours."

Madame Urbain meanwhile had seized her little girl by the hand, with a gesture of surprise and impatience which struck Newman, intent as he was upon his own words, with its dramatic effectiveness. "If Mr. Newman is going to make a scene in public," she exclaimed, "I will take my poor child out of the melee. She is too young to see such naughtiness!" and she instantly resumed her walk.

"You had much better listen to me," Newman went on. "Whether you do or not, things will be disagreeable for you; but at any rate you will be prepared."

"We have already heard something of your threats," said the marquis, "and you know what we think of them."

"You think a good deal more than you admit. A moment," Newman added in reply to an exclamation of the old lady. "I remember perfectly that we are in a public place, and you see I am very quiet. I am not going to tell your secret to the passers-by; I shall keep it, to begin with, for certain picked listeners. Any one who observes us will think that we are having a friendly chat, and that I am complimenting you, madam, on your venerable virtues."

The marquis gave three short sharp raps on the ground with his stick. "I demand of you to step out of our path!" he hissed.

Newman instantly complied, and M. de Bellegarde stepped forward with his mother. Then Newman said, "Half an hour hence Madame de Bellegarde will regret that she didn't learn exactly what I mean."

The marquise had taken a few steps, but at these words she paused, looking at Newman with eyes like two scintillating globules of ice. "You are like a peddler with something to sell," she said, with a little cold laugh which only partially concealed the tremor in her voice.

"Oh, no, not to sell," Newman rejoined; "I give it to you for nothing." And he approached nearer to her, looking her straight in the eyes. "You killed your husband," he said, almost in a whisper. "That is, you tried once and failed, and then, without trying, you succeeded."

Madame de Bellegarde closed her eyes and gave a little cough, which, as a piece of dissimulation, struck Newman as really heroic. "Dear mother," said the marquis, "does this stuff amuse you so much?"

"The rest is more amusing," said Newman. "You had better not lose it."

Madame de Bellegarde opened her eyes; the scintillations had gone out of them; they were fixed and dead. But she smiled superbly with her narrow little lips, and repeated Newman's word. "Amusing? Have I killed some one else?"

"I don't count your daughter," said Newman, "though I might! Your husband knew what you were doing. I have a proof of it whose existence you have never suspected." And he turned to the marquis, who was terribly white—whiter than Newman had ever seen any one out of a picture. "A paper written by the hand, and signed with the name, of Henri-Urbain de Bellegarde. Written after you, madame, had left him for dead, and while you, sir, had gone—not very fast—for the doctor."

The marquis looked at his mother; she turned away, looking vaguely round her. "I must sit down," she said in a low tone, going toward the bench on which Newman had been sitting.

"Couldn't you have spoken to me alone?" said the marquis to Newman, with a strange look.

"Well, yes, if I could have been sure of speaking to your mother alone, too," Newman answered. "But I have had to take you as I could get you."

Madame de Bellegarde, with a movement very eloquent of what he would have called her "grit," her steel-cold pluck and her instinctive appeal to her own personal resources, drew her hand out of her son's arm and went and seated herself upon the bench. There she remained, with her hands folded in her lap, looking straight at Newman. The expression of her face was such that he fancied at first that she was smiling; but he went and stood in front of her and saw that her elegant features were distorted by agitation. He saw, however, equally, that she was resisting her agitation with all the rigor of her inflexible will, and there was nothing like either fear or submission in her stony stare. She had been startled, but she was not terrified. Newman had an exasperating feeling that she would get the better of him still; he would not have believed it possible that he could so utterly fail to be touched by the sight of a woman (criminal or other) in so tight a place. Madame de Bellegarde gave a glance at her son which seemed tantamount to an injunction to be silent and leave her to her own devices. The marquis stood beside her, with his hands behind him, looking at Newman.

"What paper is this you speak of?" asked the old lady, with an imitation of tranquillity which would have been applauded in a veteran actress.

"Exactly what I have told you," said Newman. "A paper written by your husband after you had left him for dead, and during the couple of hours before you returned. You see he had the time; you shouldn't have stayed away so long. It declares distinctly his wife's murderous intent."

"I should like to see it," Madame de Bellegarde observed.

"I thought you might," said Newman, "and I have taken a copy." And he drew from his waistcoat pocket a small, folded sheet.

"Give it to my son," said Madame de Bellegarde. Newman handed it to the marquis, whose mother, glancing at him, said simply, "Look at it." M. de Bellegarde's eyes had a pale eagerness which it was useless for him to try to dissimulate; he took the paper in his light-gloved fingers and opened it. There was a silence, during which he read it. He had more than time to read it, but still he said nothing; he stood staring at it. "Where is the original?" asked Madame de Bellegarde, in a voice which was really a consummate negation of impatience.

"In a very safe place. Of course I can't show you that," said Newman. "You might want to take hold of it," he added with conscious quaintness. "But that's a very correct copy—except, of course, the handwriting. I am keeping the original to show some one else."

M. de Bellegarde at last looked up, and his eyes were still very eager. "To whom do you mean to show it?"

"Well, I'm thinking of beginning with the duchess," said Newman; "that stout lady I saw at your ball. She asked me to come and see her, you know. I thought at the moment I shouldn't have much to say to her; but my little document will give us something to talk about."

"You had better keep it, my son," said Madame de Bellegarde.

"By all means," said Newman; "keep it and show it to your mother when you get home."

"And after showing it to the duchess?"—asked the marquis, folding the paper and putting it away.

"Well, I'll take up the dukes," said Newman. "Then the counts and the barons—all the people you had the cruelty to introduce me to in a character of which you meant immediately to deprive me. I have made out a list."

For a moment neither Madame de Bellegarde nor her son said a word; the old lady sat with her eyes upon the ground; M. de Bellegarde's blanched pupils were fixed upon her face. Then, looking at Newman, "Is that all you have to say?" she asked.

"No, I want to say a few words more. I want to say that I hope you quite understand what I'm about. This is my revenge, you know. You have treated me before the world—convened for the express purpose—as if I were not good enough for you. I mean to show the world that, however bad I may be, you are not quite the people to say it."

Madame de Bellegarde was silent again, and then she broke her silence. Her self-possession continued to be extraordinary. "I needn't ask you who has been your accomplice. Mrs. Bread told me that you had purchased her services."

"Don't accuse Mrs. Bread of venality," said Newman. "She has kept your secret all these years. She has given you a long respite. It was beneath her eyes your husband wrote that paper; he put it into her hands with a solemn injunction that she was to make it public. She was too good-hearted to make use of it."

CHAPTER XXIV

The old lady appeared for an instant to hesitate, and then, "She was my husband's mistress," she said, softly. This was the only concession to self-defense that she condescended to make.

"I doubt that," said Newman.

Madame de Bellegarde got up from her bench. "It was not to your opinions I undertook to listen, and if you have nothing left but them to tell me I think this remarkable interview may terminate." And turning to the marquis she took his arm again. "My son," she said, "say something!"

M. de Bellegarde looked down at his mother, passing his hand over his forehead, and then, tenderly, caressingly, "What shall I say?" he asked.

"There is only one thing to say," said the Marquise. "That it was really not worth while to have interrupted our walk."

But the marquis thought he could improve this. "Your paper's a forgery," he said to Newman.

Newman shook his head a little, with a tranquil smile. "M. de Bellegarde," he said, "your mother does better. She has done better all along, from the first of my knowing you. You're a mighty plucky woman, madam," he continued. "It's a great pity you have made me your enemy. I should have been one of your greatest admirers."

"Mon pauvre ami," said Madame de Bellegarde to her son in French, and as if she had not heard these words, "you must take me immediately to my carriage."

Newman stepped back and let them leave him; he watched them a moment and saw Madame Urbain, with her little girl, come out of a by-path to meet them. The old lady stooped and kissed her grandchild. "Damn it, she is plucky!" said Newman, and he walked home with a slight sense of being balked. She was so inexpressively defiant! But on reflection he decided that what he had witnessed was no real sense of security, still less a real innocence. It was only a very superior style of brazen assurance. "Wait till she reads the paper!" he said to himself; and he concluded that he should hear from her soon.

He heard sooner than he expected. The next morning, before midday, when he was about to give orders for his breakfast to be served, M. de Bellegarde's card was brought to him. "She has read the paper and she has passed a bad night," said Newman. He instantly admitted his visitor, who came in with the air of the ambassador of a great power meeting the delegate of a barbarous tribe whom an absurd accident had enabled for the moment to be abominably annoying. The ambassador, at all events, had passed a bad night, and his faultlessly careful toilet only threw into relief the frigid rancor in his eyes and the mottled tones of his refined complexion. He stood before Newman a moment, breathing quickly and softly, and shaking his forefinger curtly as his host pointed to a chair.

"What I have come to say is soon said," he declared "and can only be said without ceremony."

"I am good for as much or for as little as you desire," said Newman.

The marquis looked round the room a moment, and then, "On what terms will you part with your scrap of paper?"

"On none!" And while Newman, with his head on one side and his hands behind him sounded the marquis's turbid gaze with his own, he added, "Certainly, that is not worth sitting down about."

M. de Bellegarde meditated a moment, as if he had not heard Newman's refusal. "My mother and I, last evening," he said, "talked over your story. You will be surprised to learn that we think your little document is—a"—and he held back his word a moment—"is genuine."

"You forget that with you I am used to surprises!" exclaimed Newman, with a laugh.

"The very smallest amount of respect that we owe to my father's memory," the marquis continued, "makes us desire that he should not be held up to the world as the author of so—so infernal an attack upon the reputation of a wife whose only fault was that she had been submissive to accumulated injury."

"Oh, I see," said Newman. "It's for your father's sake." And he laughed the laugh in which he indulged when he was most amused—a noiseless laugh, with his lips closed.

But M. de Bellegarde's gravity held good. "There are a few of my father's particular friends for whom the knowledge of so—so unfortunate an—inspiration—would be a real grief. Even say we firmly established by medical evidence the presumption of a mind disordered by fever, il en resterait quelque chose. At the best it would look ill in him. Very ill!"

"Don't try medical evidence," said Newman. "Don't touch the doctors and they won't touch you. I don't mind your knowing that I have not written to them."

Newman fancied that he saw signs in M. de Bellegarde's discolored mask that this information was extremely pertinent. But it may have been merely fancy; for the marquis remained majestically argumentative. "For instance, Madame d'Outreville," he said, "of whom you spoke yesterday. I can imagine nothing that would shock her more."

"Oh, I am quite prepared to shock Madame d'Outreville, you know. That's on the cards. I expect to shock a great many people."

M. de Bellegarde examined for a moment the stitching on the back of one of his gloves. Then, without looking up, "We don't offer you money," he said. "That we supposed to be useless."

Newman, turning away, took a few turns about the room and then came back. "What DO you offer me? By what I can make out, the generosity is all to be on my side."

The marquis dropped his arms at his side and held his head a little higher. "What we offer you is a chance—a chance that a gentleman should appreciate. A chance to abstain from inflicting a terrible blot upon the memory of a man who certainly had his faults, but who, personally, had done you no wrong."

"There are two things to say to that," said Newman. "The first is, as regards appreciating your 'chance,' that you don't consider me a gentleman. That's your great point you know. It's a poor rule that won't work both ways. The second is that—well, in a word, you are talking great nonsense!"

Newman, who in the midst of his bitterness had, as I have said, kept well before his eyes a certain ideal of saying nothing rude, was immediately somewhat regretfully conscious of the sharpness of these words. But he speedily observed that the marquis took them more quietly than might have been expected. M. de Bellegarde, like the stately ambassador that he was, continued the policy of ignoring what was disagreeable in his adversary's replies. He gazed at the gilded arabesques on the opposite wall, and then presently transferred his glance to Newman, as if he too were a large grotesque in a rather vulgar system of chamber-decoration. "I suppose you know that as regards yourself it won't do at all."

"How do you mean it won't do?"

"Why, of course you damn yourself. But I suppose that's in your programme. You propose to throw mud at us; you believe, you hope, that some of it may stick. We know, of course, it can't," explained the marquis in a tone of conscious lucidity; "but you take the chance, and are willing at any rate to show that you yourself have dirty hands."

"That's a good comparison; at least half of it is," said Newman. "I take the chance of something sticking. But as regards my hands, they are clean. I have taken the matter up with my finger-tips."

M. de Bellegarde looked a moment into his hat. "All our friends are quite with us," he said. "They would have done exactly as we have done."

"I shall believe that when I hear them say it. Meanwhile I shall think better of human nature."

The marquis looked into his hat again. "Madame de Cintre was extremely fond of her father. If she knew of the existence of the few written words of which you propose to make this scandalous use, she would demand of you proudly for his sake to give it up to her, and she would destroy it without reading it."

"Very possibly," Newman rejoined. "But she will not know. I was in that convent yesterday and I know what SHE is doing. Lord deliver us! You can guess whether it made me feel forgiving!"

M. de Bellegarde appeared to have nothing more to suggest; but he continued to stand there, rigid and elegant, as a man who believed that his mere personal presence had an argumentative value. Newman watched him, and, without yielding an inch on the main issue, felt an incongruously good-natured impulse to help him to retreat in good order.

"Your visit's a failure, you see," he said. "You offer too little."

"Propose something yourself," said the marquis.

"Give me back Madame de Cintre in the same state in which you took her from me."

M. de Bellegarde threw back his head and his pale face flushed. "Never!" he said.

"You can't!"

"We wouldn't if we could! In the sentiment which led us to deprecate her marriage nothing is changed."

"'Deprecate' is good!" cried Newman. "It was hardly worth while to come here only to tell me that you are not ashamed of yourselves. I could have guessed that!"

The marquis slowly walked toward the door, and Newman, following, opened it for him. "What you propose to do will be very disagreeable," M. de Bellegarde said. "That is very evident. But it will be nothing more."

"As I understand it," Newman answered, "that will be quite enough!"

M. de Bellegarde stood for a moment looking on the ground, as if he were ransacking his ingenuity to see what else he could do to save his father's reputation. Then, with a little cold sigh, he seemed to signify that he regretfully surrendered the late marquis to the penalty of his turpitude. He gave a hardly perceptible shrug, took his neat umbrella from the servant in the vestibule, and, with his gentlemanly walk, passed out. Newman stood listening till he heard the door close; then he slowly exclaimed, "Well, I ought to begin to be satisfied now!"

CHAPTER XXV

Newman called upon the comical duchess and found her at home. An old gentleman with a high nose and a gold-headed cane was just taking leave of her; he made Newman a protracted obeisance as he retired, and our hero supposed that he was one of the mysterious grandees with whom he had shaken hands at Madame de Bellegarde's ball. The duchess, in her arm-chair, from which she did not move, with a great flower-pot on one side of her, a pile of pink-covered novels on the other, and a large piece of tapestry depending from her lap, presented an expansive and imposing front; but her aspect was in the highest degree gracious, and there was nothing in her manner to check the effusion of his confidence. She talked to him about flowers and books, getting launched with marvelous promptitude; about the theatres, about the peculiar institutions of his native country, about the humidity of Paris about the pretty complexions of the American ladies, about his impressions of France and his opinion of its female inhabitants. All this was a brilliant monologue on the part of the duchess, who, like many of her country-women, was a person of an affirmative rather than an interrogative cast of mind, who made mots and put them herself into circulation, and who was apt to offer you a present of a convenient little opinion, neatly enveloped in the gilt paper of a happy Gallicism. Newman had come to her with a grievance, but he found himself in an atmosphere in which apparently no cognizance was taken of grievance; an atmosphere into which the chill of discomfort had never penetrated, and which seemed exclusively made up of mild, sweet, stale intellectual perfumes. The feeling with which he had watched Madame d'Outreville at the treacherous festival of the Bellegardes came back to him; she struck him as a wonderful old lady in a comedy, particularly well up in her part. He observed before long that she asked him no questions about their common friends; she made no allusion to the circumstances under which he had been presented to her. She neither feigned ignorance of a change in these circumstances nor pretended to condole with him upon it; but she smiled and discoursed and compared the tender-tinted wools of her tapestry, as if the Bellegardes and their wickedness were not of this world. "She is fighting shy!" said Newman to himself; and, having made the observation, he was prompted to observe, farther, how the duchess would carry off her indifference. She did so in a masterly manner. There was not a gleam of disguised consciousness in those small, clear, demonstrative eyes which constituted her nearest claim to personal loveliness, there was not a symptom of apprehension that Newman would trench upon the ground she proposed to avoid. "Upon my word, she does it very well," he tacitly commented. "They all hold together bravely, and, whether any one else can trust them or not, they can certainly trust each other."

Newman, at this juncture, fell to admiring the duchess for her fine manners. He felt, most accurately, that she was not a grain less urbane than she would have been if his marriage were still in prospect; but he felt also that she was not a particle more urbane. He had come, so reasoned the duchess—Heaven knew why he had come, after what had happened; and for the half hour, therefore, she would be charmante. But she would never see him again. Finding no ready-made opportunity to tell his story, Newman pondered these things more dispassionately than might have been expected; he stretched his legs, as usual, and even chuckled a little, appreciatively and noiselessly. And then as the duchess went on relating a mot with which her mother had snubbed the great Napoleon, it occurred to Newman that her evasion of a chapter of French history more interesting to himself might possibly be the result of an extreme consideration for his feelings. Perhaps it was delicacy on the duchess's part—not policy. He was on the point of saying something himself, to make the chance which he had determined to give her still better, when the servant announced another visitor. The duchess, on hearing the name—it was that of an Italian prince—gave a little imperceptible pout, and said to

Newman, rapidly: "I beg you to remain; I desire this visit to be short." Newman said to himself, at this, that Madame d'Outreville intended, after all, that they should discuss the Bellegardes together.

The prince was a short, stout man, with a head disproportionately large. He had a dusky complexion and a bushy eyebrow, beneath which his eye wore a fixed and somewhat defiant expression; he seemed to be challenging you to insinuate that he was top-heavy. The duchess, judging from her charge to Newman, regarded him as a bore; but this was not apparent from the unchecked flow of her conversation. She made a fresh series of mots, characterized with great felicity the Italian intellect and the taste of the figs at Sorrento, predicted the ultimate future of the Italian kingdom (disgust with the brutal Sardinian rule and complete reversion, throughout the peninsula, to the sacred sway of the Holy Father), and, finally, gave a history of the love affairs of the Princess X——. This narrative provoked some rectifications on the part of the prince, who, as he said, pretended to know something about that matter; and having satisfied himself that Newman was in no laughing mood, either with regard to the size of his head or anything else, he entered into the controversy with an animation for which the duchess, when she set him down as a bore, could not have been prepared. The sentimental vicissitudes of the Princess X——led to a discussion of the heart history of Florentine nobility in general; the duchess had spent five weeks in Florence and had gathered much information on the subject. This was merged, in turn, in an examination of the Italian heart per se. The duchess took a brilliantly heterodox view—thought it the least susceptible organ of its kind that she had ever encountered, related examples of its want of susceptibility, and at last declared that for her the Italians were a people of ice. The prince became flame to refute her, and his visit really proved charming. Newman was naturally out of the conversation; he sat with his head a little on one side, watching the interlocutors. The duchess, as she talked, frequently looked at him with a smile, as if to intimate, in the charming manner of her nation, that it lay only with him to say something very much to the point. But he said nothing at all, and at last his thoughts began to wander. A singular feeling came over him—a sudden sense of the folly of his errand. What under the sun had he to say to the duchess, after all? Wherein would it profit him to tell her that the Bellegardes were traitors and that the old lady, into the bargain was a murderess? He seemed morally to have turned a sort of somersault, and to find things looking differently in consequence. He felt a sudden stiffening of his will and quickening of his reserve. What in the world had he been thinking of when he fancied the duchess could help him, and that it would conduce to his comfort to make her think ill of the Bellegardes? What did her opinion of the Bellegardes matter to him? It was only a shade more important than the opinion the Bellegardes entertained of her. The duchess help him—that cold, stout, soft, artificial woman help him?—she who in the last twenty minutes had built up between them a wall of polite conversation in which she evidently flattered herself that he would never find a gate. Had it come to that—that he was asking favors of conceited people, and appealing for sympathy where he had no sympathy to give? He rested his arms on his knees, and sat for some minutes staring into his hat. As he did so his ears tingled—he had come very near being an ass. Whether or no the duchess would hear his story, he wouldn't tell it. Was he to sit there another half hour for the sake of exposing the Bellegardes? The Bellegardes be hanged! He got up abruptly, and advanced to shake hands with his hostess.

"You can't stay longer?" she asked, very graciously.

"I am afraid not," he said.

She hesitated a moment, and then, "I had an idea you had something particular to say to me," she declared.

Newman looked at her; he felt a little dizzy; for the moment he seemed to be turning his somersault again. The little Italian prince came to his help: "Ah, madam, who has not that?" he softly sighed.

"Don't teach Mr. Newman to say fadaises," said the duchess. "It is his merit that he doesn't know how."

"Yes, I don't know how to say fadaises," said Newman, "and I don't want to say anything unpleasant."

"I am sure you are very considerate," said the duchess with a smile; and she gave him a little nod for good-by with which he took his departure.

Once in the street, he stood for some time on the pavement, wondering whether, after all, he was not an ass not to have discharged his pistol. And then again he decided that to talk to any one whomsoever about the Bellegardes would be extremely disagreeable to him. The least disagreeable thing, under the circumstances, was to banish them from his mind, and never think of them again. Indecision had not hitherto been one of Newman's weaknesses, and in this case it was not of long duration. For three days after this he did not, or at least he tried not to, think of the Bellegardes. He dined with Mrs. Tristram, and on her mentioning their name, he begged her almost severely to desist. This gave Tom Tristram a much-coveted opportunity to offer his condolences.

He leaned forward, laying his hand on Newman's arm compressing his lips and shaking his head. "The fact is my dear fellow, you see, that you ought never to have gone into it. It was not your doing, I know—it was all my wife. If you want to come down on her, I'll stand off; I give you leave to hit her as hard as you like. You know she has never had a word of reproach from me in her life, and I think she is in need of something of the kind. Why didn't you listen to ME? You know I didn't believe in the thing. I thought it at the best an amiable delusion. I don't profess to be a Don Juan or a gay Lothario,—that class of man, you know; but I do pretend to know something about the harder sex. I have never disliked a woman in my life that she has not turned out badly. I was not at all deceived in Lizzie, for instance; I always had my doubts about her. Whatever you may think of my present situation, I must at least admit that I got into it with my eyes open. Now suppose you had got into something like this box with Madame de Cintre. You may depend upon it she would have turned out a stiff one. And upon my word I don't see where you could have found your comfort. Not from the marquis, my dear Newman; he wasn't a man you could go and talk things over with in a sociable, common-sense way. Did he ever seem to want to have you on the premises—did he ever try to see you alone? Did he ever ask you to come and smoke a cigar with him of an evening, or step in, when you had been calling on the ladies, and take something? I don't think you would have got much encouragement out of HIM. And as for the old lady, she struck one as an uncommonly strong dose. They have a great expression here, you know; they call it 'sympathetic.' Everything is sympathetic—or ought to be. Now Madame de Bellegarde is about as sympathetic as that mustard-pot. They're a d—d cold-blooded lot, any way; I felt it awfully at that ball of theirs. I felt as if I were walking up and down in the Armory, in the Tower of London! My dear boy, don't think me a vulgar brute for hinting at it, but you may depend upon it, all they wanted was your money. I know something about that; I can tell when people want one's money! Why they stopped wanting yours I don't know; I suppose because they could get some one else's without working so hard for it. It isn't worth finding out. It may be that it was not Madame de Cintre that backed out first, very likely the old woman put her up to it. I suspect she and her mother are really as thick as thieves, eh? You are well out of it, my boy; make up your mind to that. If I express myself strongly it is all because I love you so much; and from that point of view I may say I should as soon have thought of making up to that piece of pale high-mightiness as I should have thought of making up to the Obelisk in the Place des la Concorde."

Newman sat gazing at Tristram during this harangue with a lack-lustre eye; never yet had he seemed to himself to have outgrown so completely the phase of equal comradeship with Tom Tristram. Mrs. Tristram's glance at her husband had more of a spark; she turned to Newman with a slightly lurid smile. "You must at least do justice," she said, "to the felicity with which Mr. Tristram repairs the indiscretions of a too zealous wife."

But even without the aid of Tom Tristram's conversational felicities, Newman would have begun to think of the Bellegardes again. He could cease to think of them only when he ceased to think of his loss and privation, and the days had as yet but scantily lightened the weight of this incommodity. In vain Mrs. Tristram begged him to cheer up; she assured him that the sight of his countenance made her miserable.

"How can I help it?" he demanded with a trembling voice. "I feel like a widower—and a widower who has not even the consolation of going to stand beside the grave of his wife—who has not the right to wear so much mourning as a weed on his hat. I feel," he added in a moment "as if my wife had been murdered and her assassins were still at large."

Mrs. Tristram made no immediate rejoinder, but at last she said, with a smile which, in so far as it was a forced one, was less successfully simulated than such smiles, on her lips, usually were; "Are you very sure that you would have been happy?"

Newman stared a moment, and then shook his head. "That's weak," he said; "that won't do."

"Well," said Mrs. Tristram with a more triumphant bravery, "I don't believe you would have been happy."

Newman gave a little laugh. "Say I should have been miserable, then; it's a misery I should have preferred to any happiness."

Mrs. Tristram began to muse. "I should have been curious to see; it would have been very strange."

"Was it from curiosity that you urged me to try and marry her?"

"A little," said Mrs. Tristram, growing still more audacious. Newman gave her the one angry look he had been destined ever to give her, turned away and took up his hat. She watched him a moment, and then she said, "That sounds very cruel, but it is less so than it sounds. Curiosity has a share in almost everything I do. I wanted very much to see, first, whether such a marriage could actually take place; second, what would happen if it should take place."

"So you didn't believe," said Newman, resentfully.

"Yes, I believed—I believed that it would take place, and that you would be happy. Otherwise I should have been, among my speculations, a very heartless creature. BUT," she continued, laying her hand upon Newman's arm and hazarding a grave smile, "it was the highest flight ever taken by a tolerably bold imagination!"

Shortly after this she recommended him to leave Paris and travel for three months. Change of scene would do him good, and he would forget his misfortune sooner in absence from the objects which had witnessed it. "I really feel," Newman rejoined, "as if to leave YOU, at least, would do me good—and cost me very little effort. You are growing cynical, you shock me and pain me."

"Very good," said Mrs. Tristram, good-naturedly or cynically, as may be thought most probable. "I shall certainly see you again."

Newman was very willing to get away from Paris; the brilliant streets he had walked through in his happier hours, and which then seemed to wear a higher brilliancy in honor of his happiness, appeared now to be in the secret of his defeat and to look down upon it in shining mockery. He would go somewhere; he cared little where; and he made his preparations. Then, one morning, at haphazard, he drove to the train that would transport him to Boulogne and dispatch him thence to the shores of Britain. As he rolled along in the train he asked himself what had become of his revenge, and he was able to say that it was provisionally pigeon-holed in a very safe place; it would keep till called for.

He arrived in London in the midst of what is called "the season," and it seemed to him at first that he might here put himself in the way of being diverted from his heavy-heartedness. He knew no one in all England, but the spectacle of the mighty metropolis roused him somewhat from his apathy. Anything that was enormous usually found favor with Newman, and the multitudinous energies and industries of England stirred within him a dull vivacity of contemplation. It is on record that the weather, at that moment, was of the finest English quality; he took long walks and explored London in every direction; he sat by the hour in Kensington Gardens and beside the adjoining Drive, watching the people and the horses and the carriages; the rosy English beauties, the wonderful English dandies, and the splendid flunkies. He went to the opera and found it better than in Paris; he went to the theatre and found a surprising charm in listening to dialogue the finest points of which came within the range of his comprehension. He made several excursions into the country, recommended by the waiter at his hotel, with whom, on this and similar points, he had established confidential relations. He watched the deer in Windsor Forest and admired the Thames from Richmond Hill; he ate white-bait and brown-bread and butter at Greenwich, and strolled in the grassy shadow of the cathedral of Canterbury. He also visited the Tower of London and Madame Tussaud's exhibition. One day he thought he would go to Sheffield, and then, thinking again, he gave it up. Why should he go to Sheffield? He had a feeling that the link which bound him to a possible interest in the manufacture of cutlery was broken. He had no desire for an "inside view" of any successful enterprise whatever, and he would not have given the smallest sum for the privilege of talking over the details of the most "splendid" business with the shrewdest of overseers.

One afternoon he had walked into Hyde Park, and was slowly threading his way through the human maze which edges the Drive. The stream of carriages was no less dense, and Newman, as usual, marveled at the strange, dingy figures which he saw taking the air in some of the stateliest vehicles. They reminded him of what he had read of eastern and southern countries, in which grotesque idols and fetiches were sometimes taken out of their temples and carried abroad in golden chariots to be displayed to the multitude. He saw a great many pretty cheeks beneath high-plumed hats as he squeezed his way through serried waves of crumpled muslin; and sitting on little chairs at the base of the great serious English trees, he observed a number of quiet-eyed maidens who seemed only to remind him afresh that the magic of beauty had gone out of the world with Madame de Cintre: to say nothing of other damsels, whose eyes were not quiet, and who struck him still more as a satire on possible consolation. He had been walking for some time, when, directly in front of him, borne back by the summer breeze, he heard a few words uttered in that bright Parisian idiom from which his ears had begun to alienate themselves. The voice in which the words were spoken made them seem even more like a thing with which he had once been familiar, and as he bent his eyes it lent an identity to the commonplace elegance of the back hair and shoulders of a young lady walking in the same direction as himself. Mademoiselle Nioche, apparently, had come to seek a more rapid advancement in London, and another glance led Newman to suppose that she had found it. A gentleman was strolling beside her, lending a most attentive ear to her conversation and too entranced to open his lips. Newman did not hear his voice, but perceived that he presented the dorsal expression of a well-dressed Englishman. Mademoiselle Nioche was attracting attention: the ladies who passed her turned round to survey the Parisian perfection of her toilet. A great cataract of flounces rolled down from the young lady's waist to Newman's feet; he had to step aside to avoid treading upon them. He stepped aside, indeed, with a decision of movement which the occasion scarcely demanded; for even this imperfect glimpse of Miss Noemie had excited his displeasure. She seemed an odious blot upon the face of nature; he wanted to put her out of his sight. He thought of Valentin de Bellegarde, still green in the earth of his burial—his young life clipped by this flourishing impudence. The perfume of the young lady's finery sickened him; he turned his head and tried to deflect his course; but the pressure of the crowd kept him near her a few minutes longer, so that he heard what she was saying.

"Ah, I am sure he will miss me," she murmured. "It was very cruel in me to leave him; I am afraid you will think me a very heartless creature. He might perfectly well have come with us. I don't think he is very well," she added; "it seemed to me to-day that he was not very gay."

Newman wondered whom she was talking about, but just then an opening among his neighbors enabled him to turn away, and he said to himself that she was probably paying a tribute to British propriety and playing at tender solicitude about her papa. Was that miserable old man still treading the path of vice in her train? Was he still giving her the benefit of his experience of affairs, and had he crossed the sea to serve as her interpreter? Newman walked some distance farther, and then began to retrace his steps taking care not to traverse again the orbit of Mademoiselle Nioche. At last he looked for a chair under the trees, but he had some difficulty in finding an empty one. He was about to give up the search when he saw a gentleman rise from the seat he had been occupying, leaving Newman to take it without looking at his neighbors. He sat there for some time without heeding them; his attention was lost in the irritation and bitterness produced by his recent glimpse of Miss Noemie's iniquitous vitality. But at the end of a quarter of an hour, dropping his eyes, he perceived a small pug-dog squatted upon the path near his feet—a diminutive but very perfect specimen of its interesting species. The pug was sniffing at the fashionable world, as it passed him, with his little black muzzle, and was kept from extending his investigation by a large blue ribbon attached to his collar with an enormous rosette and held in the hand of a person seated next to Newman. To this person Newman transferred his attention, and immediately perceived that he was the object of all that of his neighbor, who was staring up at him from a pair of little fixed white eyes. These eyes Newman instantly recognized; he had been sitting for the last quarter of an hour beside M. Nioche. He had vaguely felt that some one was staring at him. M. Nioche continued to stare; he appeared afraid to move, even to the extent of evading Newman's glance.

"Dear me," said Newman; "are you here, too?" And he looked at his neighbor's helplessness more grimly than he knew. M. Nioche had a new hat and a pair of kid gloves; his clothes, too, seemed to belong to a more recent antiquity than of yore. Over his arm was suspended a lady's mantilla—a light and brilliant tissue, fringed with white lace—which had apparently been committed to his keeping; and the little dog's blue ribbon was wound tightly round his hand. There was no expression of recognition in his face—or of anything indeed save a sort of feeble, fascinated dread; Newman looked at the pug and the lace mantilla, and then he met the old man's eyes again. "You know me, I see," he pursued. "You might have spoken to me before." M. Nioche still said nothing, but it seemed to Newman that his eyes began faintly to water. "I didn't expect," our hero went on, "to meet you so far from—from the Cafe de la Patrie." The old man remained silent, but decidedly Newman had touched the source of tears. His neighbor sat staring and Newman added, "What's the matter, M. Nioche? You used to talk—to talk very prettily. Don't you remember you even gave lessons in conversation?"

At this M. Nioche decided to change his attitude. He stooped and picked up the pug, lifted it to his face and wiped his eyes on its little soft back. "I'm afraid to speak to you," he presently said, looking over the puppy's shoulder. "I hoped you wouldn't notice me. I should have moved away, but I was afraid that if I moved you would notice me. So I sat very still."

"I suspect you have a bad conscience, sir," said Newman.

The old man put down the little dog and held it carefully in his lap. Then he shook his head, with his eyes still fixed upon his interlocutor. "No, Mr. Newman, I have a good conscience," he murmured.

"Then why should you want to slink away from me?"

"Because—because you don't understand my position."

"Oh, I think you once explained it to me," said Newman. "But it seems improved."

"Improved!" exclaimed M. Nioche, under his breath. "Do you call this improvement?" And he glanced at the treasures in his arms.

"Why, you are on your travels," Newman rejoined. "A visit to London in the season is certainly a sign of prosperity."

M. Nioche, in answer to this cruel piece of irony, lifted the puppy up to his face again, peering at Newman with his small blank eye-holes. There was something almost imbecile in the movement, and Newman hardly knew whether he was taking refuge in a convenient affectation of unreason, or whether he had in fact paid for his dishonor by the loss of his wits. In the latter case, just now, he felt little more tenderly to the foolish old man than in the former. Responsible or not, he was equally an accomplice of his detestably mischievous daughter. Newman was going to leave him abruptly, when a ray of entreaty appeared to disengage itself from the old man's misty gaze. "Are you going away?" he asked.

"Do you want me to stay?" said Newman.

"I should have left you—from consideration. But my dignity suffers at your leaving me—that way."

"Have you got anything particular to say to me?"

M. Nioche looked around him to see that no one was listening, and then he said, very softly but distinctly, "I have NOT forgiven her!"

Newman gave a short laugh, but the old man seemed for the moment not to perceive it; he was gazing away, absently, at some metaphysical image of his implacability. "It doesn't much matter whether you forgive her or not," said Newman. "There are other people who won't, I assure you."

"What has she done?" M. Nioche softly questioned, turning round again. "I don't know what she does, you know."

"She has done a devilish mischief; it doesn't matter what," said Newman. "She's a nuisance; she ought to be stopped."

M. Nioche stealthily put out his hand and laid it very gently upon Newman's arm. "Stopped, yes," he whispered. "That's it. Stopped short. She is running away—she must be stopped." Then he paused a moment and looked round him. "I mean to stop her," he went on. "I am only waiting for my chance."

"I see," said Newman, laughing briefly again. "She is running away and you are running after her. You have run a long distance!"

But M. Nioche stared insistently: "I shall stop her!" he softly repeated.

He had hardly spoken when the crowd in front of them separated, as if by the impulse to make way for an important personage. Presently, through the opening, advanced Mademoiselle Nioche, attended by the gentleman whom Newman had lately observed. His face being now presented to our hero, the latter recognized the irregular features, the hardly more regular complexion, and the amiable expression of Lord Deepmere. Noemie, on finding herself suddenly confronted with Newman, who, like M. Nioche, had risen from his seat, faltered for a barely perceptible instant. She gave him a little nod, as if she had seen him yesterday, and then, with a good-natured smile, "Tiens, how we keep meeting!" she said. She looked consummately pretty, and the front of her dress was a wonderful work of art. She went up to her father, stretching out her hands for the little dog, which he submissively placed in them, and she began to kiss it and murmur over it: "To think of leaving him all alone,—what a wicked, abominable creature he must believe me! He has been very unwell," she added, turning and affecting to explain to Newman, with a spark of infernal impudence, fine as a needlepoint, in her eye. "I don't think the English climate agrees with him."

"It seems to agree wonderfully well with his mistress," said Newman.

"Do you mean me? I have never been better, thank you," Miss Noemie declared. "But with MILORD"—and she gave a brilliant glance at her late companion—"how can one help being well?" She seated herself in the chair from which her father had risen, and began to arrange the little dog's rosette.

Lord Deepmere carried off such embarrassment as might be incidental to this unexpected encounter with the inferior grace of a male and a Briton. He blushed a good deal, and greeted the object of his late momentary aspiration to rivalry in the favor of a person other than the mistress of the invalid pug with an awkward nod and a rapid ejaculation—an ejaculation to which Newman, who often found it hard to understand the speech of English people, was able to attach no meaning. Then the young man stood there, with his hand on his hip, and with a conscious grin, staring askance at Miss Noemie. Suddenly an idea seemed to strike him, and he said, turning to Newman, "Oh, you know her?"

"Yes," said Newman, "I know her. I don't believe you do."

"Oh dear, yes, I do!" said Lord Deepmere, with another grin. "I knew her in Paris—by my poor cousin Bellegarde you know. He knew her, poor fellow, didn't he? It was she you know, who was at the bottom of his affair. Awfully sad, wasn't it?" continued the young man, talking off his embarrassment as his simple nature permitted. "They got up some story about its being for the Pope; about the other man having said something against the Pope's morals. They always do that, you know. They put it on the Pope because Bellegarde was once in the Zouaves. But it was about HER morals—SHE was the Pope!" Lord Deepmere pursued, directing an eye illumined by this pleasantry toward Mademoiselle Nioche, who was bending gracefully over her lap-dog, apparently absorbed in conversation with it. "I dare say you think it rather odd that I should—a—keep up the acquaintance," the young man resumed. "But she couldn't help it, you know, and Bellegarde was only my twentieth cousin. I dare say you think it's rather cheeky, my showing with her in Hyde Park. But you see she isn't known yet, and she's in such very good form"—And Lord Deepmere's conclusion was lost in the attesting glance which he again directed toward the young lady.

Newman turned away; he was having more of her than he relished. M. Nioche had stepped aside on his daughter's approach, and he stood there, within a very small compass, looking down hard at the ground. It had never yet, as between him and Newman, been so apposite to place on record the fact that he had not forgiven his daughter. As Newman was moving away he looked up and drew near to him, and Newman, seeing the old man had something particular to say, bent his head for an instant.

"You will see it some day in the papers,'" murmured M. Nioche.

Our hero departed to hide his smile, and to this day, though the newspapers form his principal reading, his eyes have not been arrested by any paragraph forming a sequel to this announcement.

CHAPTER XXVI

In that uninitiated observation of the great spectacle of English life upon which I have touched, it might be supposed that Newman passed a great many dull days. But the dullness of his days pleased him; his melancholy, which was settling into a secondary stage, like a healing wound, had in it a certain acrid, palatable sweetness. He had company in his thoughts, and for the present he wanted no other. He had no desire to make acquaintances, and he left untouched a couple of notes of introduction which had been sent him by Tom Tristram. He thought a great deal of Madame de Cintre—sometimes with a dogged tranquillity which might have seemed, for a quarter of an hour at a time, a near neighbor to forgetfulness. He lived over again the happiest hours he had known—that silver chain of numbered days in which his afternoon visits, tending sensibly to the ideal result, had subtilized his good humor to a sort of spiritual intoxication. He came back to reality, after such reveries, with a somewhat muffled shock; he had begun to feel the need of accepting the unchangeable. At other times the reality became an infamy again and the unchangeable an imposture, and he gave himself up to his angry restlessness till he was weary. But on the whole he fell into a rather reflective mood. Without in the least intending it or knowing it, he attempted to read the moral of his strange misadventure. He asked himself, in his quieter hours, whether perhaps, after all, he WAS more commercial than was pleasant. We know that it was in obedience to a strong reaction against questions exclusively commercial that he had come out to pick up aesthetic entertainment in Europe; it may therefore be understood that he was able to conceive that a man might be too commercial. He was very willing to grant it, but the concession, as to his own case, was not made with any very oppressive sense of shame. If he had been too commercial, he was ready to forget it, for in being so he had done no man any wrong that might not be as easily forgotten. He reflected with sober placidity that at least there were no monuments of his "meanness" scattered about the world. If there was any reason in the nature of things why his connection with business should have cast a shadow upon a connection—even a connection broken—with a woman justly proud, he was willing to sponge it out of his life forever. The thing seemed a possibility; he could not feel it, doubtless, as keenly as some people, and it hardly seemed worth while to flap his wings very hard to rise to the idea; but he could feel it enough to make any sacrifice that still remained to be made. As to what such sacrifice was now to be made to, here Newman stopped short before a blank wall over which there sometimes played a shadowy imagery. He had a fancy of carrying out his life as he would have directed it if Madame de Cintre had been left to him—of making it a religion to do nothing that she would have disliked. In this, certainly, there was no sacrifice; but there was a pale, oblique ray of inspiration. It would be lonely entertainment—a good deal like a man talking to himself in the mirror for want of better company. Yet the idea yielded Newman several half hours' dumb exaltation as he sat, with his hands in his pockets and his legs stretched, over the relics of an expensively poor dinner, in the undying English twilight. If, however, his commercial imagination was dead, he felt no contempt for the surviving actualities begotten by it. He was glad he had been prosperous and had been a great man of business rather than a small one; he was extremely glad he was rich. He felt no impulse to sell all he had and give to the poor, or to retire into meditative economy and asceticism. He was glad he was rich and tolerably young; it was possible to think too much about buying and selling, it was a gain to have a good slice of life left in which not to think about them. Come, what should he think about now? Again and again Newman could think only of one thing; his thoughts always came back to it, and as they did so, with an emotional rush which seemed physically to express itself in a sudden upward choking, he leaned forward—the waiter having left the room—and, resting his arms on the table, buried his troubled face.

He remained in England till midsummer, and spent a month in the country, wandering about cathedrals, castles, and ruins. Several times, taking a walk from his inn into meadows and parks, he stopped by a well-worn stile, looked across through the early evening at a gray church tower, with its dusky nimbus of thick-circling swallows, and remembered that this might have been part of the entertainment of his honeymoon. He had never been so much alone or indulged so little in accidental dialogue. The period of recreation appointed by Mrs. Tristram had at last expired, and he asked himself what he should do now. Mrs. Tristram had written to him, proposing to him that he should join her in the Pyrenees; but he was not in the humor to return to France. The simplest thing was to repair to Liverpool and embark on the first American steamer. Newman made his way to the great seaport and secured his berth; and the night before sailing he sat in his room at the hotel, staring down, vacantly and wearily, at an open portmanteau. A number of papers were lying upon it, which he had been meaning to look over; some of them might conveniently be destroyed. But at last he shuffled them roughly together, and pushed them into a corner of the valise; they were business papers, and he was in no humor for sifting them. Then he drew forth his pocket-book and took out a paper of smaller size than those he had dismissed. He did not unfold it; he simply sat looking at the back of it. If he had momentarily entertained the idea of destroying it, the idea quickly expired. What the paper suggested was the feeling that lay in his innermost heart and that no reviving cheerfulness could long quench—the feeling that after all and above all he was a good fellow wronged. With it came a hearty hope that the Bellegardes were enjoying their suspense as to what he would do yet. The more it was prolonged the more they would enjoy it! He had hung fire once, yes; perhaps, in his present queer state of mind, he might hang fire again. But he restored the little paper to his pocket-book very tenderly, and felt better for thinking of the suspense of the Bellegardes. He felt better every time he thought of it after that, as he sailed the summer seas. He landed in New York and journeyed across the continent to San Francisco, and nothing that he observed by the way contributed to mitigate his sense of being a good fellow wronged.

He saw a great many other good fellows—his old friends—but he told none of them of the trick that had been played him. He said simply that the lady he was to have married had changed her mind, and when he was asked if he had changed his own, he said, "Suppose we change the subject." He told his friends that he had brought home no "new ideas" from Europe, and his conduct probably struck them as an eloquent proof of failing invention. He took no interest in chatting about his affairs and manifested no desire to look over his accounts. He asked half a dozen questions which, like those of an eminent physician inquiring for particular symptoms, showed that he still knew what he was talking about; but he made no comments and gave no directions. He not only puzzled the gentlemen on the stock exchange, but he was himself surprised at the extent of his indifference. As it seemed only to increase, he made an effort to combat it; he tried to interest himself and to take up his old occupations. But they appeared unreal to him; do what he would he somehow could not believe in them. Sometimes he began to fear that there was something the matter with his head; that his brain, perhaps, had softened, and that the end of his strong activities had come. This idea came back to him with an exasperating force. A hopeless, helpless loafer, useful to no one and detestable to himself—this was what the treachery of the Bellegardes had made of him. In his restless idleness he came back from San Francisco to New York, and sat for three days in the lobby of his hotel, looking out through a huge wall of plate-glass at the unceasing stream of pretty girls in Parisian-looking dresses, undulating past with little parcels nursed against their neat figures. At the end of three days he returned to San Francisco, and having arrived there he wished he had stayed away. He had nothing to do, his occupation was gone, and it seemed to him that he should never find it again. He had nothing to do here, he sometimes said to himself; but there was something beyond the ocean that he was still to do; something that he had left undone experimentally and speculatively, to see if it could content itself to remain undone. But it was not content: it kept pulling at his heartstrings and thumping at his reason; it murmured in his ears and hovered perpetually before his eyes. It interposed between all new resolutions and their fulfillment; it seemed like a stubborn ghost, dumbly entreating to be laid. Till that was done he should never be able to do anything else.

One day, toward the end of the winter, after a long interval, he received a letter from Mrs. Tristram, who apparently was animated by a charitable desire to amuse and distract her correspondent. She gave him much Paris gossip, talked of General Packard and Miss Kitty Upjohn, enumerated the new plays at the theatre, and inclosed a note from her husband, who had gone down to spend a month at Nice. Then came her signature, and after this her postscript. The latter consisted of these few lines: "I heard three days since from my friend, the Abbe Aubert, that Madame de Cintre last week took the veil at the Carmelites. It was on her twenty-seventh birthday, and she took the name of her, patroness, St. Veronica. Sister Veronica has a life-time before her!"

This letter came to Newman in the morning; in the evening he started for Paris. His wound began to ache with its first fierceness, and during his long bleak journey the thought of Madame de Cintre's "life-time," passed within prison walls on whose outer side he might stand, kept him perpetual company. Now he would fix himself in Paris forever; he would extort a sort of happiness from the knowledge that if she was not there, at least the stony sepulchre that held her was. He descended, unannounced, upon Mrs. Bread, whom he found keeping lonely watch in his great empty saloons on the Boulevard Haussmann. They were as neat as a Dutch village, Mrs. Bread's only occupation had been removing individual dust-particles. She made no complaint, however, of her loneliness, for in her philosophy a servant was but a mysteriously projected machine, and it would be as fantastic for a housekeeper to comment upon a gentleman's absences as for a clock to remark upon not being wound up. No particular clock, Mrs. Bread supposed, went all the time, and no particular servant could enjoy all the sunshine diffused by the career of an exacting master. She ventured, nevertheless, to express a modest hope that Newman meant to remain a while in Paris. Newman laid his hand on hers and shook it gently. "I mean to remain forever," he said.

He went after this to see Mrs. Tristram, to whom he had telegraphed, and who expected him. She looked at him a moment and shook her head. "This won't do," she said; "you have come back too soon." He sat down and asked about her husband and her children, tried even to inquire about Miss Dora Finch. In the midst of this— "Do you know where she is?" he asked, abruptly.

Mrs. Tristram hesitated a moment; of course he couldn't mean Miss Dora Finch. Then she answered, properly: "She has gone to the other house—in the Rue d'Enfer." After Newman had sat a while longer looking very sombre, she went on: "You are not so good a man as I thought. You are more—you are more—"

"More what?" Newman asked.

"More unforgiving."

"Good God!" cried Newman; "do you expect me to forgive?"

"No, not that. I have forgiven, so of course you can't. But you might forget! You have a worse temper about it than I should have expected. You look wicked—you look dangerous."

"I may be dangerous," he said; "but I am not wicked. No, I am not wicked." And he got up to go. Mrs. Tristram asked him to come back to dinner; but he answered that he did not feel like pledging himself to be present at an entertainment, even as a solitary guest. Later in the evening, if he should be able, he would come.

He walked away through the city, beside the Seine and over it, and took the direction of the Rue d'Enfer. The day had the softness of early spring; but the weather was gray and humid. Newman found himself in a part of Paris which he little knew—a region of convents and prisons, of streets bordered by long dead walls and traversed by a few wayfarers. At the intersection of two of these streets stood the house of the Carmelites—a dull, plain edifice, with a high-shouldered blank wall all round it. From without Newman could see its upper windows, its steep roof and its chimneys. But these things revealed no symptoms of human life; the place looked dumb, deaf, inanimate. The pale, dead, discolored wall stretched beneath it, far down the empty side street—a vista without a human figure. Newman stood there a long time; there were no passers; he was free to gaze his fill. This seemed the goal of his journey; it was what he had come for. It was a strange satisfaction, and yet it was a satisfaction; the barren stillness of the place seemed to be his own release from ineffectual longing. It told him that the woman within was lost beyond recall, and that the days and years of the future would pile themselves above her like the huge immovable slab of a tomb. These days and years, in this place, would always be just so gray and silent. Suddenly, from the thought of their seeing him stand there, again the charm utterly departed. He would never stand there again; it was gratuitous dreariness. He turned away with a heavy heart, but with a heart lighter than the one he had brought. Everything was over, and he too at last could rest. He walked down through narrow, winding streets to the edge of the Seine again, and there he saw, close above him, the soft, vast towers of Notre Dame. He crossed one of the bridges and stood a moment in the empty place before the great cathedral; then he went in beneath the grossly-imaged portals. He wandered some distance up the nave and sat down in the splendid dimness. He sat a long time; he heard far-away bells chiming off, at long intervals, to the rest of the world. He was very tired; this was the best place he could be in. He said no prayers; he had no prayers to say. He had nothing to be thankful for, and he had nothing to ask; nothing to ask, because now he must take care of himself. But a great cathedral offers a very various hospitality, and Newman sat in his place, because while he was there he was out of the world. The most unpleasant thing that had ever happened to him had reached its formal conclusion, as it were; he could close the book and put it away. He leaned his head for a long time on the chair in front of him; when he took it up he felt that he was himself again. Somewhere in his mind, a tight knot seemed to have loosened. He thought of the Bellegardes; he had almost forgotten them. He remembered them as people he had meant to do something to. He gave a groan as he remembered what he had meant to do; he was annoyed at having meant to do it; the bottom, suddenly, had fallen out of his revenge. Whether it was Christian charity or unregenerate good nature—what it was, in the background of his soul—I don't pretend to say; but Newman's last thought was that of course he would let the Bellegardes go. If he had spoken it aloud he would have said that he didn't want to hurt them. He was ashamed of having wanted to hurt them. They had hurt him, but such things were really not his game. At last he got up and came out of the darkening church; not with the elastic step of a man who had won a victory or taken a resolve, but strolling soberly, like a good-natured man who is still a little ashamed.

Going home, he said to Mrs. Bread that he must trouble her to put back his things into the portmanteau she had unpacked the evening before. His gentle stewardess looked at him through eyes a trifle bedimmed. "Dear me, sir," she exclaimed, "I thought you said that you were going to stay forever."

"I meant that I was going to stay away forever," said Newman kindly. And since his departure from Paris on the following day he has certainly not returned. The gilded apartments I have so often spoken of stand ready to receive him; but they serve only as a spacious residence for Mrs. Bread, who wanders eternally from room to room, adjusting the tassels of the curtains, and keeps her wages, which are regularly brought her by a banker's clerk, in a great pink Sevres vase on the drawing-room mantel-shelf.

Late in the evening Newman went to Mrs. Tristram's and found Tom Tristram by the domestic fireside. "I'm glad to see you back in Paris," this gentleman declared. "You know it's really the only place for a white man to live." Mr. Tristram made his friend welcome, according to his own rosy light, and offered him a convenient resume of the Franco-American gossip of the last six months. Then at last he got up and said he would go for half an hour to the club. "I suppose a man who has been for six months in California wants a little intellectual conversation. I'll let my wife have a go at you."

Newman shook hands heartily with his host, but did not ask him to remain; and then he relapsed into his place on the sofa, opposite to Mrs. Tristram. She presently asked him what he had done after leaving her. "Nothing particular," said Newman.

"You struck me," she rejoined, "as a man with a plot in his head. You looked as if you were bent on some sinister errand, and after you had left me I wondered whether I ought to have let you go."

"I only went over to the other side of the river—to the Carmelites," said Newman.

Mrs. Tristram looked at him a moment and smiled. "What did you do there? Try to scale the wall?"

"I did nothing. I looked at the place for a few minutes and then came away."

Mrs. Tristram gave him a sympathetic glance. "You didn't happen to meet M. de Bellegarde," she asked, "staring hopelessly at the convent wall as well? I am told he takes his sister's conduct very hard."

"No, I didn't meet him, I am happy to say," Newman answered, after a pause.

"They are in the country," Mrs. Tristram went on; "at—what is the name of the place?—Fleurieres. They returned there at the time you left Paris and have been spending the year in extreme seclusion. The little marquise must enjoy it; I expect to hear that she has eloped with her daughter's music-master!"

Newman was looking at the light wood-fire; but he listened to this with extreme interest. At last he spoke: "I mean never to mention the name of those people again, and I don't want to hear anything more about them." And then he took out his pocket-book and drew forth a scrap of paper. He looked at it an instant, then got up and stood by the fire. "I am going to burn them up," he said. "I am glad to have you as a witness. There they go!" And he tossed the paper into the flame.

Mrs. Tristram sat with her embroidery needle suspended. "What is that paper?" she asked.

Newman leaning against the fire-place, stretched his arms and drew a longer breath than usual. Then after a moment, "I can tell you now," he said. "It was a paper containing a secret of the Bellegardes—something which would damn them if it were known."

Mrs. Tristram dropped her embroidery with a reproachful moan. "Ah, why didn't you show it to me?"

"I thought of showing it to you—I thought of showing it to every one. I thought of paying my debt to the Bellegardes that way. So I told them, and I frightened them. They have been staying in the country as you tell me, to keep out of the explosion. But I have given it up."

Mrs. Tristram began to take slow stitches again. "Have you quite given it up?"

"Oh yes."

"Is it very bad, this secret?"

"Yes, very bad."

"For myself," said Mrs. Tristram, "I am sorry you have given it up. I should have liked immensely to see your paper. They have wronged me too, you know, as your sponsor and guarantee, and it would have served for my revenge as well. How did you come into possession of your secret?"

"It's a long story. But honestly, at any rate."

"And they knew you were master of it?"

"Oh, I told them."

"Dear me, how interesting!" cried Mrs. Tristram. "And you humbled them at your feet?"

Newman was silent a moment. "No, not at all. They pretended not to care—not to be afraid. But I know they did care—they were afraid."

"Are you very sure?"

Newman stared a moment. "Yes, I'm sure."

Mrs. Tristram resumed her slow stitches. "They defied you, eh?"

"Yes," said Newman, "it was about that."

"You tried by the threat of exposure to make them retract?" Mrs. Tristram pursued.

"Yes, but they wouldn't. I gave them their choice, and they chose to take their chance of bluffing off the charge and convicting me of fraud. But they were frightened," Newman added, "and I have had all the vengeance I want."

"It is most provoking," said Mrs. Tristram, "to hear you talk of the 'charge' when the charge is burnt up. Is it quite consumed?" she asked, glancing at the fire.

Newman assured her that there was nothing left of it. "Well then," she said, "I suppose there is no harm in saying that you probably did not make them so very uncomfortable. My impression would be that since, as you say, they defied you, it was because they believed that, after all, you would never really come to the point. Their confidence, after counsel taken of each other, was not in their innocence, nor in their talent for bluffing things off; it was in your remarkable good nature! You see they were right."

Newman instinctively turned to see if the little paper was in fact consumed; but there was nothing left of it.

THE TURN OF THE SCREW

THE TURN OF THE SCREW

The story had held us, round the fire, sufficiently breathless, but except the obvious remark that it was gruesome, as, on Christmas Eve in an old house, a strange tale should essentially be, I remember no comment uttered till somebody happened to say that it was the only case he had met in which such a visitation had fallen on a child. The case, I may mention, was that of an apparition in just such an old house as had gathered us for the occasion—an appearance, of a dreadful kind, to a little boy sleeping in the room with his mother and waking her up in the terror of it; waking her not to dissipate his dread and soothe him to sleep again, but to encounter also, herself, before she had succeeded in doing so, the same sight that had shaken him. It was this observation that drew from Douglas—not immediately, but later in the evening—a reply that had the interesting consequence to which I call attention. Someone else told a story not particularly effective, which I saw he was not following. This I took for a sign that he had himself something to produce and that we should only have to wait. We waited in fact till two nights later; but that same evening, before we scattered, he brought out what was in his mind.

"I quite agree—in regard to Griffin's ghost, or whatever it was—that its appearing first to the little boy, at so tender an age, adds a particular touch. But it's not the first occurrence of its charming kind that I know to have involved a child. If the child gives the effect another turn of the screw, what do you say to TWO children—?"

"We say, of course," somebody exclaimed, "that they give two turns! Also that we want to hear about them."

I can see Douglas there before the fire, to which he had got up to present his back, looking down at his interlocutor with his hands in his pockets. "Nobody but me, till now, has ever heard. It's quite too horrible." This, naturally, was declared by several voices to give the thing the utmost price, and our friend, with quiet art, prepared his triumph by turning his eyes over the rest of us and going on: "It's beyond everything. Nothing at all that I know touches it."

"For sheer terror?" I remember asking.

He seemed to say it was not so simple as that; to be really at a loss how to qualify it. He passed his hand over his eyes, made a little wincing grimace. "For dreadful—dreadfulness!"

"Oh, how delicious!" cried one of the women.

He took no notice of her; he looked at me, but as if, instead of me, he saw what he spoke of. "For general uncanny ugliness and horror and pain."

"Well then," I said, "just sit right down and begin."

He turned round to the fire, gave a kick to a log, watched it an instant. Then as he faced us again: "I can't begin. I shall have to send to town." There was a unanimous groan at this, and much reproach; after which, in his preoccupied way, he explained. "The story's written. It's in a locked drawer—it has not been out for years. I could write to my man and enclose the key; he could send down the packet as he finds it." It was to me in particular that he appeared to propound this—appeared almost to appeal for aid not to hesitate. He had broken a thickness of ice, the formation of many a winter; had had his reasons for a long silence. The others resented postponement, but it was just his scruples that charmed me. I adjured him to write by the first post and to agree with us for an early hearing; then I asked him if the experience in question had been his own. To this his answer was prompt. "Oh, thank God, no!"

"And is the record yours? You took the thing down?"

"Nothing but the impression. I took that HERE"—he tapped his heart. "I've never lost it."

"Then your manuscript—?"

"Is in old, faded ink, and in the most beautiful hand." He hung fire again. "A woman's. She has been dead these twenty years. She sent me the pages in question before she died." They were all listening now, and of course there was somebody to be arch, or at any rate to draw the inference. But if he put the inference by without a smile it was also without irritation. "She was a most charming person, but she was ten years older than I. She was my sister's governess," he quietly said. "She was the most agreeable woman I've ever known in her position; she would have been worthy of any whatever. It was long ago, and this episode was long before. I was at Trinity, and I found her at home on my coming down the second summer. I was much there that year—it was a beautiful one; and we had, in her off-hours, some strolls and talks in the garden—talks in which she struck me as awfully clever and nice. Oh yes; don't grin: I liked her extremely and am glad to this day to think she liked me, too. If she hadn't she wouldn't have told me. She had never told anyone. It wasn't simply that she said so, but that I knew she hadn't. I was sure; I could see. You'll easily judge why when you hear."

"Because the thing had been such a scare?"

He continued to fix me. "You'll easily judge," he repeated: "YOU will."

I fixed him, too. "I see. She was in love."

He laughed for the first time. "You ARE acute. Yes, she was in love. That is, she had been. That came out—she couldn't tell her story without its coming out. I saw it, and she saw I saw it; but neither of us spoke of it. I remember the time and the place—the corner of the lawn, the shade of the great beeches and the long, hot summer afternoon. It wasn't a scene for a shudder; but oh—!" He quitted the fire and dropped back into his chair.

"You'll receive the packet Thursday morning?" I inquired.

"Probably not till the second post."

"Well then; after dinner—"

"You'll all meet me here?" He looked us round again. "Isn't anybody going?" It was almost the tone of hope.

"Everybody will stay!"

"*I* will"—and "*I* will!" cried the ladies whose departure had been fixed. Mrs. Griffin, however, expressed the need for a little more light. "Who was it she was in love with?"

"The story will tell," I took upon myself to reply.

"Oh, I can't wait for the story!"

"The story WON'T tell," said Douglas; "not in any literal, vulgar way."

"More's the pity, then. That's the only way I ever understand."

"Won't YOU tell, Douglas?" somebody else inquired.

He sprang to his feet again. "Yes—tomorrow. Now I must go to bed. Good night." And quickly catching up a candlestick, he left us slightly bewildered. From our end of the great brown hall we heard his step on the stair; whereupon Mrs. Griffin spoke. "Well, if I don't know who she was in love with, I know who HE was."

"She was ten years older," said her husband.

"Raison de plus—at that age! But it's rather nice, his long reticence."

"Forty years!" Griffin put in.

"With this outbreak at last."

"The outbreak," I returned, "will make a tremendous occasion of Thursday night;" and everyone so agreed with me that, in the light of it, we lost all attention for everything else. The last story, however incomplete and like the mere opening of a serial, had been told; we handshook and "candlestuck," as somebody said, and went to bed.

I knew the next day that a letter containing the key had, by the first post, gone off to his London apartments; but in spite of—or perhaps just on account of—the eventual diffusion of this knowledge we quite let him alone till after dinner, till such an hour of the evening, in fact, as might best accord with the kind of emotion on which our hopes were fixed. Then he became as communicative as we could desire and indeed gave us his best reason for being so. We had it from him again before the fire in the hall, as we had had our mild wonders of the previous night. It appeared that the narrative he had promised to read us really required for a proper intelligence a few words of prologue. Let me say here distinctly, to have done with it, that this narrative, from an exact transcript of my own made much later, is what I shall presently give. Poor Douglas, before his death—when it was in sight—committed to me the manuscript that reached him on the third of these days and that, on the same spot, with immense effect, he began to read to our hushed little circle on the night of the fourth. The departing ladies who had said they would stay didn't, of course, thank heaven, stay: they departed, in consequence of arrangements made, in a rage of curiosity, as they professed, produced by the touches with which he had already worked us up. But that only made his little final auditory more compact and select, kept it, round the hearth, subject to a common thrill.

The first of these touches conveyed that the written statement took up the tale at a point after it had, in a manner, begun. The fact to be in possession of was therefore that his old friend, the youngest of several daughters of a poor country parson, had, at the age of twenty, on taking service for the first time in the schoolroom, come up to London, in trepidation, to answer in person an advertisement that had already placed her in brief correspondence with the advertiser. This person proved, on her presenting herself, for judgment, at a house in Harley Street, that impressed her as vast and imposing—this prospective patron proved a gentleman, a bachelor in the prime of life, such a figure as had never risen, save in a dream or an old novel, before a fluttered, anxious girl out of a Hampshire vicarage. One could easily fix his type; it never, happily, dies out. He was handsome and bold and pleasant, offhand and gay and kind. He struck her, inevitably, as gallant and splendid, but what took her most of all and gave her the courage she afterward showed was that he put the whole thing to her as a kind of favor, an obligation he should gratefully incur. She conceived him as rich, but as fearfully extravagant—saw him all in a glow of high fashion, of good looks, of expensive habits, of charming ways with women. He had for his own town residence a big house filled with the spoils of travel and the trophies of the chase; but it was to his country home, an old family place in Essex, that he wished her immediately to proceed.

He had been left, by the death of their parents in India, guardian to a small nephew and a small niece, children of a younger, a military brother, whom he had lost two years before. These children were, by the strangest of chances for a man in his position—a lone man without the right sort of experience or a grain of patience—very heavily on his hands. It had all been a great worry and, on his own part doubtless, a series of blunders, but he immensely pitied the poor chicks and had done all he could; had in particular sent them down to his other house, the proper place for them being of course the country, and kept them there, from the first, with the best people he could find to look after them, parting even with his own servants to wait on them and going down himself, whenever he might, to see how they were doing. The awkward thing was that they had practically no other relations and that his own affairs took up all his time. He had put them in possession of Bly, which was healthy and secure, and had placed at the head of their little establishment—but below stairs only—an excellent woman, Mrs. Grose, whom he was sure his visitor would like and who had formerly been maid to his mother. She was now housekeeper and was also acting for the time as superintendent to the little girl, of whom, without children of her own, she was, by good luck, extremely fond. There were plenty of people to help, but of course the young lady who should go down as governess would be in supreme authority. She would also have, in holidays, to look after the small boy, who had been for a term at school—young as he was to be sent, but what else could be done?—and who, as the holidays were about to begin, would be back from one day to the other. There had been for the two children at first a young lady whom they had had the misfortune to lose. She had done for them quite beautifully—she was a most respectable person—till her death, the great awkwardness of which had, precisely, left no alternative but the school for little Miles. Mrs. Grose, since then, in the way of manners and things, had done as she could for Flora; and there were, further, a cook, a housemaid, a dairywoman, an old pony, an old groom, and an old gardener, all likewise thoroughly respectable.

So far had Douglas presented his picture when someone put a question. "And what did the former governess die of?—of so much respectability?"

Our friend's answer was prompt. "That will come out. I don't anticipate."

"Excuse me—I thought that was just what you ARE doing."

"In her successor's place," I suggested, "I should have wished to learn if the office brought with it—"

"Necessary danger to life?" Douglas completed my thought. "She did wish to learn, and she did learn. You shall hear tomorrow what she learned. Meanwhile, of course, the prospect struck her as slightly grim. She was young, untried, nervous: it was a vision of serious duties and little company, of really great loneliness. She hesitated—took a couple of days to consult and consider. But the salary offered much exceeded her modest measure, and on a second interview she faced the music, she engaged." And Douglas, with this, made a pause that, for the benefit of the company, moved me to throw in—

"The moral of which was of course the seduction exercised by the splendid young man. She succumbed to it."

He got up and, as he had done the night before, went to the fire, gave a stir to a log with his foot, then stood a moment with his back to us. "She saw him only twice."

"Yes, but that's just the beauty of her passion."

A little to my surprise, on this, Douglas turned round to me. "It WAS the beauty of it. There were others," he went on, "who hadn't succumbed. He told her frankly all his difficulty—that for several applicants the conditions had been prohibitive. They were, somehow, simply afraid. It sounded dull—it sounded strange; and all the more so because of his main condition."

"Which was—?"

"That she should never trouble him—but never, never: neither appeal nor complain nor write about anything; only meet all questions herself, receive all moneys from his solicitor, take the whole thing over and let him alone. She promised to do this, and she mentioned to me that when, for a moment, disburdened, delighted, he held her hand, thanking her for the sacrifice, she already felt rewarded."

"But was that all her reward?" one of the ladies asked.

"She never saw him again."

"Oh!" said the lady; which, as our friend immediately left us again, was the only other word of importance contributed to the subject till, the next night, by the corner of the hearth, in the best chair, he opened the faded red cover of a thin old-fashioned gilt-edged album. The whole thing took indeed more nights than one, but on the first occasion the same lady put another question. "What is your title?"

"I haven't one."

"Oh, *I* have!" I said. But Douglas, without heeding me, had begun to read with a fine clearness that was like a rendering to the ear of the beauty of his author's hand.

I

I remember the whole beginning as a succession of flights and drops, a little seesaw of the right throbs and the wrong. After rising, in town, to meet his appeal, I had at all events a couple of very bad days—found myself doubtful again, felt indeed sure I had made a mistake. In this state of mind I spent the long hours of bumping, swinging coach that carried me to the stopping place at which I was to be met by a vehicle from the house. This convenience, I was told, had been ordered, and I found, toward the close of the June afternoon, a commodious fly in waiting for me. Driving at that hour, on a lovely day, through a country to which the summer sweetness seemed to offer me a friendly welcome, my fortitude mounted afresh and, as we turned into the avenue, encountered a reprieve that was probably but a proof of the point to which it had sunk. I suppose I had expected, or had dreaded, something so melancholy that what greeted me was a good surprise. I remember as a most pleasant impression the broad, clear front, its open windows and fresh curtains and the pair of maids looking out; I remember the lawn and the bright flowers and the crunch of my wheels on the gravel and the clustered treetops over which the rooks circled and cawed in the golden sky. The scene had a greatness that made it a different affair from my own scant home, and there immediately appeared at the door, with a little girl in her hand, a civil person who dropped me as decent a curtsy as if I had been the mistress or a distinguished visitor. I had received in Harley Street a narrower notion of the place, and that, as I recalled it, made me think the proprietor still more of a gentleman, suggested that what I was to enjoy might be something beyond his promise.

I had no drop again till the next day, for I was carried triumphantly through the following hours by my introduction to the younger of my pupils. The little girl who accompanied Mrs. Grose appeared to me on the spot a creature so charming as to make it a great fortune to have to do with her. She was the most beautiful child I had ever seen, and I afterward wondered that my employer had not told me more of her. I slept little that night—I was too much excited; and this astonished me, too, I recollect, remained with me, adding to my sense of the liberality with which I was treated. The large, impressive room, one of the best in the house, the great state bed, as I almost felt it, the full, figured draperies, the long glasses in which, for the first time, I could see myself from head to foot, all struck me—like the extraordinary charm of my small charge—as so many things thrown in. It was thrown in as well, from the first moment, that I should get on with Mrs. Grose in a relation over which, on my way, in the coach, I fear I had rather brooded. The only thing indeed that in this early outlook might have made me shrink again was the clear circumstance of her being so glad to see me. I perceived within half an hour that she was so glad—stout, simple, plain, clean, wholesome woman—as to be positively on her guard against showing it too much. I wondered even then a little why she should wish not to show it, and that, with reflection, with suspicion, might of course have made me uneasy.

But it was a comfort that there could be no uneasiness in a connection with anything so beatific as the radiant image of my little girl, the vision of whose angelic beauty had probably more than anything else to do with the restlessness that, before morning, made me several times rise and wander about my room to take in the whole picture and prospect; to watch, from my open window, the faint summer dawn, to look at such portions of the rest of the house as I could catch, and to listen, while, in the fading dusk, the first birds began to twitter, for the possible recurrence of a sound or two, less natural and not without, but within, that I had fancied I heard. There had been a moment when I believed I recognized, faint and far, the cry of a child; there had been another when I found myself just consciously starting as at the passage, before my door, of a light footstep. But these fancies were not marked enough not to be thrown off, and it is only in the light, or the gloom, I should rather say, of other and subsequent matters that they now come back to me. To watch, teach, "form" little Flora would too evidently be the making of a happy and useful life. It had been agreed between us downstairs that after this first occasion I should have her as a matter of course at night, her small white bed being already arranged, to that end, in my room. What I had undertaken was the whole care of her, and she had remained, just this last time, with Mrs. Grose only as an effect of our consideration for my inevitable strangeness and her natural timidity. In spite of this timidity—which the child herself, in the oddest way in the world, had been perfectly frank and brave about, allowing it, without a sign of uncomfortable consciousness, with the deep, sweet serenity indeed of one of Raphael's holy infants, to be discussed, to be imputed to her, and to determine us—I feel quite sure she would presently like me. It was part of what I already liked Mrs. Grose herself for, the pleasure I could see her feel in my admiration and wonder as I sat at supper with four tall candles and with my pupil, in a high chair and a bib, brightly facing me, between them, over bread and milk. There were naturally things that in Flora's presence could pass between us only as prodigious and gratified looks, obscure and roundabout allusions.

"And the little boy—does he look like her? Is he too so very remarkable?"

One wouldn't flatter a child. "Oh, miss, MOST remarkable. If you think well of this one!"—and she stood there with a plate in her hand, beaming at our companion, who looked from one of us to the other with placid heavenly eyes that contained nothing to check us.

"Yes; if I do—?"

"You WILL be carried away by the little gentleman!"

"Well, that, I think, is what I came for—to be carried away. I'm afraid, however," I remember feeling the impulse to add, "I'm rather easily carried away. I was carried away in London!"

I can still see Mrs. Grose's broad face as she took this in. "In Harley Street?"

"In Harley Street."

"Well, miss, you're not the first—and you won't be the last."

"Oh, I've no pretension," I could laugh, "to being the only one. My other pupil, at any rate, as I understand, comes back tomorrow?"

"Not tomorrow—Friday, miss. He arrives, as you did, by the coach, under care of the guard, and is to be met by the same carriage."

I forthwith expressed that the proper as well as the pleasant and friendly thing would be therefore that on the arrival of the public conveyance I should be in waiting for him with his little sister; an idea in which Mrs. Grose concurred so heartily that I somehow took her manner as a kind of comforting pledge—never falsified, thank heaven!—that we should on every question be quite at one. Oh, she was glad I was there!

What I felt the next day was, I suppose, nothing that could be fairly called a reaction from the cheer of my arrival; it was probably at the most only a slight oppression produced by a fuller measure of the scale, as I walked round them, gazed up at them, took them in, of my new circumstances. They had, as it were, an extent and mass for which I had not been prepared and in the presence of which I found myself, freshly, a little scared as well as a little proud. Lessons, in this agitation, certainly suffered some delay; I reflected that my first duty was, by the gentlest arts I could contrive, to win the child into the sense of knowing me. I spent the day with her out-of-doors; I arranged with her, to her great satisfaction, that it should be she, she only, who might show me the place. She showed it step by step and room by room and secret by secret, with droll, delightful, childish talk about it and with the result, in half an hour, of our becoming immense friends. Young as she was, I was struck, throughout our little tour, with her confidence and courage with the way, in empty chambers and dull corridors, on crooked staircases that made me pause and even on the summit of an old machicolated square tower that made me dizzy, her morning music, her disposition to tell me so many more things than she asked, rang out and led me on. I have not seen Bly since the day I left it, and I daresay that to my older and more informed eyes it would now appear sufficiently contracted. But as my little conductress, with her hair of gold and her frock of blue, danced before me round corners and pattered down passages, I had the view of a castle of romance inhabited by a rosy sprite, such a place as would somehow, for diversion of the young idea, take all color out of storybooks and fairytales. Wasn't it just a storybook over which I had fallen adoze and adream? No; it was a big, ugly, antique, but convenient house, embodying a few features of a building still older, half-replaced and half-utilized, in which I had the fancy of our being almost as lost as a handful of passengers in a great drifting ship. Well, I was, strangely, at the helm!

II

This came home to me when, two days later, I drove over with Flora to meet, as Mrs. Grose said, the little gentleman; and all the more for an incident that, presenting itself the second evening, had deeply disconcerted me. The first day had been, on the whole, as I have expressed, reassuring; but I was to see it wind up in keen apprehension. The postbag, that evening—it came late—contained a letter for me, which, however, in the hand of my employer, I found to be composed but of a few words enclosing another, addressed to himself, with a seal still unbroken. "This, I recognize, is from the headmaster, and the headmaster's an awful bore. Read him, please; deal with him; but mind you don't report. Not a word. I'm off!" I broke the seal with a great effort—so great a one that I was a long time coming to it; took the unopened missive at last up to my room and only attacked it just before going to bed. I had better have let it wait till morning, for it gave me a second sleepless night. With no counsel to take, the next day, I was full of distress; and it finally got so the better of me that I determined to open myself at least to Mrs. Grose.

"What does it mean? The child's dismissed his school."

She gave me a look that I remarked at the moment; then, visibly, with a quick blankness, seemed to try to take it back. "But aren't they all—?"

"Sent home—yes. But only for the holidays. Miles may never go back at all."

Consciously, under my attention, she reddened. "They won't take him?"

"They absolutely decline."

At this she raised her eyes, which she had turned from me; I saw them fill with good tears. "What has he done?"

I hesitated; then I judged best simply to hand her my letter—which, however, had the effect of making her, without taking it, simply put her hands behind her. She shook her head sadly. "Such things are not for me, miss."

My counselor couldn't read! I winced at my mistake, which I attenuated as I could, and opened my letter again to repeat it to her; then, faltering in the act and folding it up once more, I put it back in my pocket. "Is he really BAD?"

The tears were still in her eyes. "Do the gentlemen say so?"

"They go into no particulars. They simply express their regret that it should be impossible to keep him. That can have only one meaning." Mrs. Grose listened with dumb emotion; she forbore to ask me what this meaning might be; so that, presently, to put the thing with some coherence and with the mere aid of her presence to my own mind, I went on: "That he's an injury to the others."

At this, with one of the quick turns of simple folk, she suddenly flamed up. "Master Miles! HIM an injury?"

There was such a flood of good faith in it that, though I had not yet seen the child, my very fears made me jump to the absurdity of the idea. I found myself, to meet my friend the better, offering it, on the spot, sarcastically. "To his poor little innocent mates!"

"It's too dreadful," cried Mrs. Grose, "to say such cruel things! Why, he's scarce ten years old."

"Yes, yes; it would be incredible."

She was evidently grateful for such a profession. "See him, miss, first. THEN believe it!" I felt forthwith a new impatience to see him; it was the beginning of a curiosity that, for all the next hours, was to deepen almost to pain. Mrs. Grose was aware, I could judge, of what she had produced in me, and she followed it up with assurance. "You might as well believe it of the little lady. Bless her," she added the next moment—"LOOK at her!"

I turned and saw that Flora, whom, ten minutes before, I had established in the schoolroom with a sheet of white paper, a pencil, and a copy of nice "round o's," now presented herself to view at the open door. She expressed in her little way an extraordinary detachment from disagreeable duties, looking to me, however, with a great childish light that seemed to offer it as a mere result of the affection she had conceived for my person, which had rendered necessary that she should follow me. I needed nothing more than this to feel the full force of Mrs. Grose's comparison, and, catching my pupil in my arms, covered her with kisses in which there was a sob of atonement.

Nonetheless, the rest of the day I watched for further occasion to approach my colleague, especially as, toward evening, I began to fancy she rather sought to avoid me. I overtook her, I remember, on the staircase; we went down together, and at the bottom I detained her, holding her there with a hand on her arm. "I take what you said to me at noon as a declaration that YOU'VE never known him to be bad."

She threw back her head; she had clearly, by this time, and very honestly, adopted an attitude. "Oh, never known him—I don't pretend THAT!"

I was upset again. "Then you HAVE known him—?"

"Yes indeed, miss, thank God!"

On reflection I accepted this. "You mean that a boy who never is—?"

"Is no boy for ME!"

I held her tighter. "You like them with the spirit to be naughty?" Then, keeping pace with her answer, "So do I!" I eagerly brought out. "But not to the degree to contaminate—"

"To contaminate?"—my big word left her at a loss. I explained it. "To corrupt."

She stared, taking my meaning in; but it produced in her an odd laugh. "Are you afraid he'll corrupt YOU?" She put the question with such a fine bold humor that, with a laugh, a little silly doubtless, to match her own, I gave way for the time to the apprehension of ridicule.

But the next day, as the hour for my drive approached, I cropped up in another place. "What was the lady who was here before?"

"The last governess? She was also young and pretty—almost as young and almost as pretty, miss, even as you."

"Ah, then, I hope her youth and her beauty helped her!" I recollect throwing off. "He seems to like us young and pretty!"

"Oh, he DID," Mrs. Grose assented: "it was the way he liked everyone!" She had no sooner spoken indeed than she caught herself up. "I mean that's HIS way—the master's."

I was struck. "But of whom did you speak first?"

She looked blank, but she colored. "Why, of HIM."

"Of the master?"

"Of who else?"

There was so obviously no one else that the next moment I had lost my impression of her having accidentally said more than she meant; and I merely asked what I wanted to know. "Did SHE see anything in the boy—?"

"That wasn't right? She never told me."

I had a scruple, but I overcame it. "Was she careful—particular?"

Mrs. Grose appeared to try to be conscientious. "About some things—yes."

"But not about all?"

Again she considered. "Well, miss—she's gone. I won't tell tales."

"I quite understand your feeling," I hastened to reply; but I thought it, after an instant, not opposed to this concession to pursue: "Did she die here?"

"No—she went off."

I don't know what there was in this brevity of Mrs. Grose's that struck me as ambiguous. "Went off to die?" Mrs. Grose looked straight out of the window, but I felt that, hypothetically, I had a right to know what young persons engaged for Bly were expected to do. "She was taken ill, you mean, and went home?"

"She was not taken ill, so far as appeared, in this house. She left it, at the end of the year, to go home, as she said, for a short holiday, to which the time she had put in had certainly given her a right. We had then a young woman—a nursemaid who had stayed on and who was a good girl and clever; and SHE took the children altogether for the interval. But our young lady never came back, and at the very moment I was expecting her I heard from the master that she was dead."

I turned this over. "But of what?"

"He never told me! But please, miss," said Mrs. Grose, "I must get to my work."

III

Her thus turning her back on me was fortunately not, for my just preoccupations, a snub that could check the growth of our mutual esteem. We met, after I had brought home little Miles, more intimately than ever on the ground of my stupefaction, my general emotion: so monstrous was I then ready to pronounce it that such a child as had now been revealed to me should be under an interdict. I was a little late on the scene, and I felt, as he stood wistfully looking out for me before the door of the inn at which the coach had put him down, that I had seen him, on the instant, without and within, in the great glow of freshness, the same positive fragrance of purity, in which I had, from the first moment, seen his little sister. He was incredibly beautiful, and Mrs. Grose had put her finger on it: everything but a sort of passion of tenderness for him was swept away by his presence. What I then and there took him to my heart for was something divine that I have never found to the same degree in any child—his indescribable little air of knowing nothing in the world but love. It would have been impossible to carry a bad name with a greater sweetness of innocence, and by the time I had got back to Bly with him I remained merely bewildered—so far, that is, as I was not outraged—by the sense of the horrible letter locked up in my room, in a drawer. As soon as I could compass a private word with Mrs. Grose I declared to her that it was grotesque.

She promptly understood me. "You mean the cruel charge—?"

"It doesn't live an instant. My dear woman, LOOK at him!"

She smiled at my pretention to have discovered his charm. "I assure you, miss, I do nothing else! What will you say, then?" she immediately added.

"In answer to the letter?" I had made up my mind. "Nothing."

"And to his uncle?"

I was incisive. "Nothing."

"And to the boy himself?"

I was wonderful. "Nothing."

She gave with her apron a great wipe to her mouth. "Then I'll stand by you. We'll see it out."

"We'll see it out!" I ardently echoed, giving her my hand to make it a vow.

She held me there a moment, then whisked up her apron again with her detached hand. "Would you mind, miss, if I used the freedom—"

"To kiss me? No!" I took the good creature in my arms and, after we had embraced like sisters, felt still more fortified and indignant.

This, at all events, was for the time: a time so full that, as I recall the way it went, it reminds me of all the art I now need to make it a little distinct. What I look back at with amazement is the situation I accepted. I had undertaken, with my companion, to see it out, and I was under a charm, apparently, that could smooth away the extent and the far and difficult connections of such an effort. I was lifted aloft on a great wave of infatuation and pity. I found it simple, in my ignorance, my confusion, and perhaps my conceit, to assume that I could deal with a boy whose education for the world was all on the point of beginning. I am unable even to remember at this day what proposal I framed for the end of his holidays and the resumption of his studies. Lessons with me, indeed, that charming summer, we all had a theory that he was to have; but I now feel that, for weeks, the lessons must have been rather my own. I learned something—at first, certainly—that had not been one of the teachings of my small, smothered life; learned to be amused, and even amusing, and not to think for the morrow. It was the first time, in a manner, that I had known space and air and freedom, all the music of summer and all the mystery of nature. And then there was consideration—and consideration was sweet. Oh, it was a trap—not designed, but deep—to my imagination, to my delicacy, perhaps to my vanity; to whatever, in me, was most excitable. The best way to picture it all is to say that I was off my guard. They gave me so little trouble—they were of a gentleness so extraordinary. I used to speculate—but even this with a dim disconnectedness—as to how the rough future (for all futures are rough!) would handle them and might bruise them. They had the bloom of health and happiness; and yet, as if I had been in charge of a pair of little grandees, of princes of the blood, for whom everything, to be right, would have to be enclosed and protected, the only form that, in my fancy, the afteryears could take for them was that of a romantic, a really royal extension of the garden and the park. It may be, of course, above all, that what suddenly broke into this gives the previous time a charm of stillness—that hush in which something gathers or crouches. The change was actually like the spring of a beast.

In the first weeks the days were long; they often, at their finest, gave me what I used to call my own hour, the hour when, for my pupils, teatime and bedtime having come and gone, I had, before my final retirement, a small interval alone. Much as I liked my companions, this hour was the thing in the day I liked most; and I liked it best of all when, as the light faded—or rather, I should say, the day lingered and the last calls of the last birds sounded, in a flushed sky, from the old trees—I could take a turn into the grounds and enjoy, almost with a sense of property that amused and flattered me, the beauty and dignity of the place. It was a pleasure at these moments to feel myself tranquil and justified; doubtless, perhaps, also to reflect that by my discretion, my quiet good sense and general high propriety, I was giving pleasure—if he ever thought of it!—to the person to whose pressure I had responded. What I was doing was what he had earnestly hoped and directly asked of me, and that I COULD, after all, do it proved even a greater joy than I had expected. I daresay I fancied myself, in short, a remarkable young woman and took comfort in the faith that this would more publicly appear. Well, I needed to be remarkable to offer a front to the remarkable things that presently gave their first sign.

It was plump, one afternoon, in the middle of my very hour: the children were tucked away, and I had come out for my stroll. One of the thoughts that, as I don't in the least shrink now from noting, used to be with me in these wanderings was that it would be as charming as a charming story suddenly to meet someone. Someone would appear there at the turn of a path and would stand before me and smile and approve. I didn't ask more than that—I only asked that he should KNOW; and the only way to be sure he knew would be to see it, and the kind light of it, in his handsome face. That was exactly present to me—by which I mean the face was—when, on the first of these occasions, at the end of a long June day, I stopped short on emerging from one of the plantations and coming into view of the house. What arrested me on the spot—and with a shock much greater than any vision had allowed for—was the sense that my imagination had, in a flash, turned real. He did stand there!—but high up, beyond the lawn and at the very top of the tower to which, on that first morning, little Flora had conducted me. This tower was one of a pair—square, incongruous, crenelated structures—that were distinguished, for some reason, though I could see little difference, as the new and the old. They flanked opposite ends of the house and were probably architectural absurdities, redeemed in a measure indeed by not being wholly disengaged nor of a height too pretentious, dating, in their gingerbread antiquity, from a romantic revival that was already a respectable past. I admired them, had fancies about them, for we could all profit in a degree, especially when they loomed through the dusk, by the grandeur of their actual battlements; yet it was not at such an elevation that the figure I had so often invoked seemed most in place.

It produced in me, this figure, in the clear twilight, I remember, two distinct gasps of emotion, which were, sharply, the shock of my first and that of my second surprise. My second was a violent perception of the mistake of my first: the man who met my eyes was not the person I had precipitately supposed. There came to me thus a bewilderment of vision of which, after these years, there is no living view that I can hope to give. An unknown man in a lonely place is a permitted object of fear to a young woman privately bred; and the figure that faced me was—a few more seconds assured me—as little anyone else I knew as it was the image that had been in my mind. I had not seen it in Harley Street—I had not seen it anywhere. The place, moreover, in the strangest way in the world, had, on the instant, and by the very fact of its appearance, become a solitude. To me at least, making my statement here with a deliberation with which I have never made it, the whole feeling of the moment returns. It was as if, while I took in—what I did take in—all the rest of the scene had been stricken with death. I can hear again, as I write, the intense hush in which the sounds of evening dropped. The rooks stopped cawing in the golden sky, and the friendly hour lost, for the minute, all its voice. But there was no other change in nature, unless indeed it were a change that I saw with a stranger sharpness. The gold was still in the sky, the clearness in the air, and the man who looked at me over the battlements was as definite as a picture in a frame. That's how I thought, with extraordinary quickness, of each person that he might have been and that he was not. We were confronted across our distance quite long enough for me to ask myself with intensity who then he was and to feel, as an effect of my inability to say, a wonder that in a few instants more became intense.

The great question, or one of these, is, afterward, I know, with regard to certain matters, the question of how long they have lasted. Well, this matter of mine, think what you will of it, lasted while I caught at a dozen possibilities, none of which made a difference for the better, that I could see, in there having been in the house—and for how long, above all?—a person of whom I was in ignorance. It lasted while I just bridled a little with the sense that my office demanded that there should be no such ignorance and no such person. It lasted while this visitant, at all events—and there was a touch of the strange freedom, as I remember, in the sign of familiarity of his wearing no hat—seemed to fix me, from his position, with just the question, just the scrutiny through the fading light, that his own presence provoked. We were too far apart to call to each other, but there was a moment at which, at shorter range, some challenge between us, breaking the hush, would have been the right result of our straight mutual stare. He was in one of the angles, the one away from the house, very erect, as it struck me, and with both hands on the ledge. So I saw him as I see the letters I form on this page; then, exactly, after a minute, as if to add to the spectacle, he slowly changed his place—passed, looking at me hard all the while, to the opposite corner of the platform. Yes, I had the sharpest sense that during this transit he never took his eyes from me, and I can see at this moment the way his hand, as he went, passed from one of the crenelations to the next. He stopped at the other corner, but less long, and even as he turned away still markedly fixed me. He turned away; that was all I knew.

IV

It was not that I didn't wait, on this occasion, for more, for I was rooted as deeply as I was shaken. Was there a "secret" at Bly—a mystery of Udolpho or an insane, an unmentionable relative kept in unsuspected confinement? I can't say how long I turned it over, or how long, in a confusion of curiosity and dread, I remained where I had had my collision; I only recall that when I re-entered the house darkness had quite closed in. Agitation, in the interval, certainly had held me and driven me, for I must, in circling about the place, have walked three miles; but I was to be, later on, so much more overwhelmed that this mere dawn of alarm was a comparatively human chill. The most singular part of it, in fact—singular as the rest had been—was the part I became, in the hall, aware of in meeting Mrs. Grose. This picture comes back to me in the general train—the impression, as I received it on my return, of the wide white panelled space, bright in the lamplight and with its portraits and red carpet, and of the good surprised look of my friend, which immediately told me she had missed me. It came to me straightway, under her contact, that, with plain heartiness, mere relieved anxiety at my appearance, she knew nothing whatever that could bear upon the incident I had there ready for her. I had not suspected in advance that her comfortable face would pull me up, and I somehow measured the importance of what I had seen by my thus finding myself hesitate to mention it. Scarce anything in the whole history seems to me so odd as this fact that my real beginning of fear was one, as I may say, with the instinct of sparing my companion. On the spot, accordingly, in the pleasant hall and with her eyes on me, I, for a reason that I couldn't then have phrased, achieved an inward resolution—offered a vague pretext for my lateness and, with the plea of the beauty of the night and of the heavy dew and wet feet, went as soon as possible to my room.

Here it was another affair; here, for many days after, it was a queer affair enough. There were hours, from day to day—or at least there were moments, snatched even from clear duties—when I had to shut myself up to think. It was not so much yet that I was more nervous than I could bear to be as that I was remarkably afraid of becoming so; for the truth I had now to turn over was, simply and clearly, the truth that I could arrive at no account whatever of the visitor with whom I had been so inexplicably and yet, as it seemed to me, so intimately concerned. It took little time to see that I could sound without forms of inquiry and without exciting remark any domestic complications. The shock I had suffered must have sharpened all my senses; I felt sure, at the end of three days and as the result of mere closer attention, that I had not been practiced upon by the servants nor made the object of any "game." Of whatever it was that I knew, nothing was known around me. There was but one sane inference: someone had taken a liberty rather gross. That was what, repeatedly, I dipped into my room and locked the door to say to myself. We had been, collectively, subject to an intrusion; some unscrupulous traveler, curious in old houses, had made his way in unobserved, enjoyed the prospect from the best point of view, and then stolen out as he came. If he had given me such a bold hard stare, that was but a part of his indiscretion. The good thing, after all, was that we should surely see no more of him.

This was not so good a thing, I admit, as not to leave me to judge that what, essentially, made nothing else much signify was simply my charming work. My charming work was just my life with Miles and Flora, and through nothing could I so like it as through feeling that I could throw myself into it in trouble. The attraction of my small charges was a constant joy, leading me to wonder afresh at the vanity of my original fears, the distaste I had begun by entertaining for the probable gray prose of my office. There was to be no gray prose, it appeared, and no long grind; so how could work not be charming that presented itself as daily beauty? It was all the romance of the nursery and the poetry of the schoolroom. I don't mean by this, of course, that we studied only fiction and verse; I mean I can express no otherwise the sort of interest my companions inspired. How can I describe that except by saying that instead of growing used to them—and it's a marvel for a governess: I call the sisterhood to witness!—I made constant fresh discoveries. There was one direction, assuredly, in which these discoveries stopped: deep obscurity continued to cover the region of the boy's conduct at school. It had been promptly given me, I have noted, to face that mystery without a pang. Perhaps even it would be nearer the truth to say that—without a word—he himself had cleared it up. He had made the whole charge absurd. My conclusion bloomed there with the real rose flush of his innocence: he was only too fine and fair for the little horrid, unclean school world, and he had paid a price for it. I reflected acutely that the sense of such differences, such superiorities of quality, always, on the part of the majority—which could include even stupid, sordid headmasters—turn infallibly to the vindictive.

Both the children had a gentleness (it was their only fault, and it never made Miles a muff) that kept them—how shall I express it?—almost impersonal and certainly quite unpunishable. They were like the cherubs of the anecdote, who had—morally, at any rate—nothing to whack! I remember feeling with Miles in especial as if he had had, as it were, no history. We expect of a small child a scant one, but there was in this beautiful little boy something extraordinarily sensitive, yet extraordinarily happy, that, more than in any creature of his age I have seen, struck me as beginning anew each day. He had never for a second suffered. I took this as a direct disproof of his having really been chastised. If he had been wicked he would have "caught" it, and I should have caught it by the rebound—I should have found the trace. I found nothing at all, and he was therefore an angel. He never spoke of his school, never mentioned a comrade or a master; and I, for my part, was quite too much disgusted to allude to them. Of course I was under the spell, and the wonderful part is that, even at the time, I perfectly knew I was. But I gave myself up to it; it was an antidote to any pain, and I had more pains than one. I was in receipt in these days of disturbing letters from home, where things were not going well. But with my children, what things in the world mattered? That was the question I used to put to my scrappy retirements. I was dazzled by their loveliness.

There was a Sunday—to get on—when it rained with such force and for so many hours that there could be no procession to church; in consequence of which, as the day declined, I had arranged with Mrs. Grose that, should the evening show improvement, we would attend together the late service. The rain happily stopped, and I prepared for our walk, which, through the park and by the good road to the village, would be a matter of twenty minutes. Coming downstairs to meet my colleague in the hall, I remembered a pair of gloves that had required three stitches and that had received them—with a publicity perhaps not edifying—while I sat with the children at their tea, served on Sundays, by exception, in that cold, clean temple of mahogany and brass, the "grown-up" dining room. The gloves had been dropped there, and I turned in to recover them. The day was gray enough, but the afternoon light still lingered, and it enabled me, on crossing the threshold, not only to recognize, on a chair near the wide window, then closed, the articles I wanted, but to become aware of a person on the other side of the window and looking straight in. One step into the room had sufficed; my vision was instantaneous; it was all there. The person looking straight in was the person who had already appeared to me. He appeared thus again with I won't say greater distinctness, for that was impossible, but with a nearness that represented a forward stride in our intercourse and made me, as I met him, catch my breath and turn cold. He was the same—he was the same, and seen, this time, as he had been seen before, from the waist up, the window, though the dining room was on the ground floor, not going down to the terrace on which he stood. His face was close to the glass, yet the effect of this better view was, strangely, only to show me how intense the former had been. He remained but a few seconds—long enough to convince me he also saw and recognized; but it was as if I had been looking at him for years and had known him always. Something, however, happened this time that had not happened before; his stare into my face, through the glass and across the room, was as deep and hard as then, but it quitted me for a moment during which I could still watch it, see it fix successively several other things. On the spot there came to me the added shock of a certitude that it was not for me he had come there. He had come for someone else.

The flash of this knowledge—for it was knowledge in the midst of dread—produced in me the most extraordinary effect, started as I stood there, a sudden vibration of duty and courage. I say courage because I was beyond all doubt already far gone. I bounded straight out of the door again, reached that of the house, got, in an instant, upon the drive, and, passing along the terrace as fast as I could rush, turned a corner and came full in sight. But it was in sight of nothing now—my visitor had vanished. I stopped, I almost dropped, with the real relief of this; but I took in the whole scene—I gave him time to reappear. I call it time, but how long was it? I can't speak to the purpose today of the duration of these things. That kind of measure must have left me: they couldn't have lasted as they actually appeared to me to last. The terrace and the whole place, the lawn and the garden beyond it, all I could see of the park, were empty with a great emptiness. There were shrubberies and big trees, but I remember the clear assurance I felt that none of them concealed him. He was there or was not there: not there if I didn't see him. I got hold of this; then, instinctively, instead of returning as I had come, went to the window. It was confusedly present to me that I ought to place myself where he had stood. I did so; I applied my face to the pane and looked, as he had looked, into the room. As if, at this moment, to show me exactly what his range had been, Mrs. Grose, as I had done for himself just before, came in from the hall. With this I had the full image of a repetition of what had already occurred. She saw me as I had seen my own visitant; she pulled up short as I had done; I gave her something of the shock that I had received. She turned white, and this made me ask myself if I had blanched as much. She stared, in short, and retreated on just MY lines, and I knew she had then passed out and come round to me and that I should presently meet her. I remained where I was, and while I waited I thought of more things than one. But there's only one I take space to mention. I wondered why SHE should be scared.

V

Oh, she let me know as soon as, round the corner of the house, she loomed again into view. "What in the name of goodness is the matter—?" She was now flushed and out of breath.

I said nothing till she came quite near. "With me?" I must have made a wonderful face. "Do I show it?"

"You're as white as a sheet. You look awful."

I considered; I could meet on this, without scruple, any innocence. My need to respect the bloom of Mrs. Grose's had dropped, without a rustle, from my shoulders, and if I wavered for the instant it was not with what I kept back. I put out my hand to her and she took it; I held her hard a little, liking to feel her close to me. There was a kind of support in the shy heave of her surprise. "You came for me for church, of course, but I can't go."

"Has anything happened?"

"Yes. You must know now. Did I look very queer?"

"Through this window? Dreadful!"

"Well," I said, "I've been frightened." Mrs. Grose's eyes expressed plainly that SHE had no wish to be, yet also that she knew too well her place not to be ready to share with me any marked inconvenience. Oh, it was quite settled that she MUST share! "Just what you saw from the dining room a minute ago was the effect of that. What *I* saw—just before—was much worse."

Her hand tightened. "What was it?"

"An extraordinary man. Looking in."

"What extraordinary man?"

"I haven't the least idea."

Mrs. Grose gazed round us in vain. "Then where is he gone?"

"I know still less."

"Have you seen him before?"

"Yes—once. On the old tower."

She could only look at me harder. "Do you mean he's a stranger?"

"Oh, very much!"

"Yet you didn't tell me?"

"No—for reasons. But now that you've guessed—"

Mrs. Grose's round eyes encountered this charge. "Ah, I haven't guessed!" she said very simply. "How can I if YOU don't imagine?"

"I don't in the very least."

"You've seen him nowhere but on the tower?"

"And on this spot just now."

Mrs. Grose looked round again. "What was he doing on the tower?"

"Only standing there and looking down at me."

She thought a minute. "Was he a gentleman?"

I found I had no need to think. "No." She gazed in deeper wonder. "No."

"Then nobody about the place? Nobody from the village?"

"Nobody—nobody. I didn't tell you, but I made sure."

She breathed a vague relief: this was, oddly, so much to the good. It only went indeed a little way. "But if he isn't a gentleman—"

"What IS he? He's a horror."

V

"A horror?"

"He's—God help me if I know WHAT he is!"

Mrs. Grose looked round once more; she fixed her eyes on the duskier distance, then, pulling herself together, turned to me with abrupt inconsequence. "It's time we should be at church."

"Oh, I'm not fit for church!"

"Won't it do you good?"

"It won't do THEM—! I nodded at the house.

"The children?"

"I can't leave them now."

"You're afraid—?"

I spoke boldly. "I'm afraid of HIM."

Mrs. Grose's large face showed me, at this, for the first time, the faraway faint glimmer of a consciousness more acute: I somehow made out in it the delayed dawn of an idea I myself had not given her and that was as yet quite obscure to me. It comes back to me that I thought instantly of this as something I could get from her; and I felt it to be connected with the desire she presently showed to know more. "When was it—on the tower?"

"About the middle of the month. At this same hour."

"Almost at dark," said Mrs. Grose.

"Oh, no, not nearly. I saw him as I see you."

"Then how did he get in?"

"And how did he get out?" I laughed. "I had no opportunity to ask him! This evening, you see," I pursued, "he has not been able to get in."

"He only peeps?"

"I hope it will be confined to that!" She had now let go my hand; she turned away a little. I waited an instant; then I brought out: "Go to church. Goodbye. I must watch."

Slowly she faced me again. "Do you fear for them?"

We met in another long look. "Don't YOU?" Instead of answering she came nearer to the window and, for a minute, applied her face to the glass. "You see how he could see," I meanwhile went on.

She didn't move. "How long was he here?"

"Till I came out. I came to meet him."

Mrs. Grose at last turned round, and there was still more in her face. "*I* couldn't have come out."

"Neither could I!" I laughed again. "But I did come. I have my duty."

"So have I mine," she replied; after which she added: "What is he like?"

"I've been dying to tell you. But he's like nobody."

"Nobody?" she echoed.

"He has no hat." Then seeing in her face that she already, in this, with a deeper dismay, found a touch of picture, I quickly added stroke to stroke. "He has red hair, very red, close-curling, and a pale face, long in shape, with straight, good features and little, rather queer whiskers that are as red as his hair. His eyebrows are, somehow, darker; they look particularly arched and as if they might move a good deal. His eyes are sharp, strange—awfully; but I only know clearly that they're rather small and very fixed. His mouth's wide, and his lips are thin, and except for his little whiskers he's quite clean-shaven. He gives me a sort of sense of looking like an actor."

"An actor!" It was impossible to resemble one less, at least, than Mrs. Grose at that moment.

"I've never seen one, but so I suppose them. He's tall, active, erect," I continued, "but never—no, never!—a gentleman."

My companion's face had blanched as I went on; her round eyes started and her mild mouth gaped. "A gentleman?" she gasped, confounded, stupefied: "a gentleman HE?"

"You know him then?"

She visibly tried to hold herself. "But he IS handsome?"

I saw the way to help her. "Remarkably!"

"And dressed—?"

"In somebody's clothes." "They're smart, but they're not his own."

She broke into a breathless affirmative groan: "They're the master's!"

I caught it up. "You DO know him?"

She faltered but a second. "Quint!" she cried.

"Quint?"

"Peter Quint—his own man, his valet, when he was here!"

"When the master was?"

Gaping still, but meeting me, she pieced it all together. "He never wore his hat, but he did wear—well, there were waistcoats missed. They were both here—last year. Then the master went, and Quint was alone."

I followed, but halting a little. "Alone?"

"Alone with US." Then, as from a deeper depth, "In charge," she added.

"And what became of him?"

She hung fire so long that I was still more mystified. "He went, too," she brought out at last.

"Went where?"

Her expression, at this, became extraordinary. "God knows where! He died."

"Died?" I almost shrieked.

She seemed fairly to square herself, plant herself more firmly to utter the wonder of it. "Yes. Mr. Quint is dead."

VI

It took of course more than that particular passage to place us together in presence of what we had now to live with as we could—my dreadful liability to impressions of the order so vividly exemplified, and my companion's knowledge, henceforth—a knowledge half consternation and half compassion—of that liability. There had been, this evening, after the revelation left me, for an hour, so prostrate—there had been, for either of us, no attendance on any service but a little service of tears and vows, of prayers and promises, a climax to the series of mutual challenges and pledges that had straightway ensued on our retreating together to the schoolroom and shutting ourselves up there to have everything out. The result of our having everything out was simply to reduce our situation to the last rigor of its elements. She herself had seen nothing, not the shadow of a shadow, and nobody in the house but the governess was in the governess's plight; yet she accepted without directly impugning my sanity the truth as I gave it to her, and ended by showing me, on this ground, an awestricken tenderness, an expression of the sense of my more than questionable privilege, of which the very breath has remained with me as that of the sweetest of human charities.

What was settled between us, accordingly, that night, was that we thought we might bear things together; and I was not even sure that, in spite of her exemption, it was she who had the best of the burden. I knew at this hour, I think, as well as I knew later, what I was capable of meeting to shelter my pupils; but it took me some time to be wholly sure of what my honest ally was prepared for to keep terms with so compromising a contract. I was queer company enough—quite as queer as the company I received; but as I trace over what we went through I see how much common ground we must have found in the one idea that, by good fortune, COULD steady us. It was the idea, the second movement, that led me straight out, as I may say, of the inner chamber of my dread. I could take the air in the court, at least, and there Mrs. Grose could join me. Perfectly can I recall now the particular way strength came to me before we separated for the night. We had gone over and over every feature of what I had seen.

"He was looking for someone else, you say—someone who was not you?"

"He was looking for little Miles." A portentous clearness now possessed me. "THAT'S whom he was looking for."

"But how do you know?"

"I know, I know, I know!" My exaltation grew. "And YOU know, my dear!"

She didn't deny this, but I required, I felt, not even so much telling as that. She resumed in a moment, at any rate: "What if HE should see him?"

"Little Miles? That's what he wants!"

She looked immensely scared again. "The child?"

"Heaven forbid! The man. He wants to appear to THEM." That he might was an awful conception, and yet, somehow, I could keep it at bay; which, moreover, as we lingered there, was what I succeeded in practically proving. I had an absolute certainty that I should see again what I had already seen, but something within me said that by offering myself bravely as the sole subject of such experience, by accepting, by inviting, by surmounting it all, I should serve as an expiatory victim and guard the tranquility of my companions. The children, in especial, I should thus fence about and absolutely save. I recall one of the last things I said that night to Mrs. Grose.

"It does strike me that my pupils have never mentioned—"

She looked at me hard as I musingly pulled up. "His having been here and the time they were with him?"

"The time they were with him, and his name, his presence, his history, in any way."

"Oh, the little lady doesn't remember. She never heard or knew."

"The circumstances of his death?" I thought with some intensity. "Perhaps not. But Miles would remember—Miles would know."

"Ah, don't try him!" broke from Mrs. Grose.

I returned her the look she had given me. "Don't be afraid." I continued to think. "It IS rather odd."

"That he has never spoken of him?"

"Never by the least allusion. And you tell me they were 'great friends'?"

"Oh, it wasn't HIM!" Mrs. Grose with emphasis declared. "It was Quint's own fancy. To play with him, I mean—to spoil him." She paused a moment; then she added: "Quint was much too free."

This gave me, straight from my vision of his face—SUCH a face!—a sudden sickness of disgust. "Too free with MY boy?"

"Too free with everyone!"

I forbore, for the moment, to analyze this description further than by the reflection that a part of it applied to several of the members of the household, of the half-dozen maids and men who were still of our small colony. But there was everything, for our apprehension, in the lucky fact that no discomfortable legend, no perturbation of scullions, had ever, within anyone's memory attached to the kind old place. It had neither bad name nor ill fame, and Mrs. Grose, most apparently, only desired to cling to me and to quake in silence. I even put her, the very last thing of all, to the test. It was when, at midnight, she had her hand on the schoolroom door to take leave. "I have it from you then—for it's of great importance—that he was definitely and admittedly bad?"

"Oh, not admittedly. *I* knew it—but the master didn't."

"And you never told him?"

"Well, he didn't like tale-bearing—he hated complaints. He was terribly short with anything of that kind, and if people were all right to HIM—"

"He wouldn't be bothered with more?" This squared well enough with my impressions of him: he was not a trouble-loving gentleman, nor so very particular perhaps about some of the company HE kept. All the same, I pressed my interlocutress. "I promise you *I* would have told!"

She felt my discrimination. "I daresay I was wrong. But, really, I was afraid."

"Afraid of what?"

"Of things that man could do. Quint was so clever—he was so deep."

I took this in still more than, probably, I showed. "You weren't afraid of anything else? Not of his effect—?"

"His effect?" she repeated with a face of anguish and waiting while I faltered.

"On innocent little precious lives. They were in your charge."

"No, they were not in mine!" she roundly and distressfully returned. "The master believed in him and placed him here because he was supposed not to be well and the country air so good for him. So he had everything to say. Yes"—she let me have it—"even about THEM."

"Them—that creature?" I had to smother a kind of howl. "And you could bear it!"

"No. I couldn't—and I can't now!" And the poor woman burst into tears.

A rigid control, from the next day, was, as I have said, to follow them; yet how often and how passionately, for a week, we came back together to the subject! Much as we had discussed it that Sunday night, I was, in the immediate later hours in especial—for it may be imagined whether I slept—still haunted with the shadow of something she had not told me. I myself had kept back nothing, but there was a word Mrs. Grose had kept back. I was sure, moreover, by morning, that this was not from a failure of frankness, but because on every side there were fears. It seems to me indeed, in retrospect, that by the time the morrow's sun was high I had restlessly read into the fact before us almost all the meaning they were to receive from subsequent and more cruel occurrences. What they gave me above all was just the sinister figure of the living man—the dead one would keep awhile!—and of the months he had continuously passed at Bly, which, added up, made a formidable stretch. The limit of this evil time had arrived only when, on the dawn of a winter's morning, Peter Quint was found, by a laborer going to early work, stone dead on the road from the village: a catastrophe explained—superficially at least—by a visible wound to his head; such a wound as might have been produced—and as, on the final evidence, HAD been—by a fatal slip, in the dark and after leaving the public house, on the steepish icy slope, a wrong path altogether, at the bottom of which he lay. The icy slope, the turn mistaken at night and in liquor, accounted for much—practically, in the end and after the inquest and boundless chatter, for everything; but there had been matters in his life—strange passages and perils, secret disorders, vices more than suspected—that would have accounted for a good deal more.

I scarce know how to put my story into words that shall be a credible picture of my state of mind; but I was in these days literally able to find a joy in the extraordinary flight of heroism the occasion demanded of me. I now saw that I had been asked for a service admirable and difficult; and there would be a greatness in letting it be seen—oh, in the right quarter!—that I could succeed where many another girl might have failed. It was an immense help to me—I confess I rather applaud myself as I look back!—that I saw my service so strongly and so simply. I was there to protect and defend the little creatures in the world the most bereaved and the most lovable, the appeal of whose helplessness had suddenly become only too explicit, a deep, constant ache of one's own committed heart. We were cut off, really, together; we were united in our danger. They had nothing but me, and I—well, I had THEM. It was in short a magnificent chance. This chance presented itself to me in an image richly material. I was a screen—I was to stand before them. The more I saw, the less they would. I began to watch them in a stifled suspense, a disguised excitement that might well, had it continued too long, have turned to something like madness. What saved me, as I now see, was that it turned to something else altogether. It didn't last as suspense—it was superseded by horrible proofs. Proofs, I say, yes—from the moment I really took hold.

This moment dated from an afternoon hour that I happened to spend in the grounds with the younger of my pupils alone. We had left Miles indoors, on the red cushion of a deep window seat; he had wished to finish a book, and I had been glad to encourage a purpose so laudable in a young man whose only defect was an occasional excess of the restless. His sister, on the contrary, had been alert to come out, and I strolled with her half an hour, seeking the shade, for the sun was still high and the day exceptionally warm. I was aware afresh, with her, as we went, of how, like her brother, she contrived—it was the charming thing in both children—to let me alone without appearing to drop me and to accompany me without appearing to surround. They were never importunate and yet never listless. My attention to them all really went to seeing them amuse themselves immensely without me: this was a spectacle they seemed actively to prepare and that engaged me as an active admirer. I walked in a world of their invention—they had no occasion whatever to draw upon mine; so that my time was taken only with being, for them, some remarkable person or thing that the game of the moment required and that was merely, thanks to my superior, my exalted stamp, a happy and highly distinguished sinecure. I forget what I was on the present occasion; I only remember that I was something very important and very quiet and that Flora was playing very hard. We were on the edge of the lake, and, as we had lately begun geography, the lake was the Sea of Azof.

Suddenly, in these circumstances, I became aware that, on the other side of the Sea of Azof, we had an interested spectator. The way this knowledge gathered in me was the strangest thing in the world—the strangest, that is, except the very much stranger in which it quickly merged itself. I had sat down with a piece of work—for I was something or other that could sit—on the old stone bench which overlooked the pond; and in this position I began to take in with certitude, and yet without direct vision, the presence, at a distance, of a third person. The old trees, the thick shrubbery, made a great and pleasant shade, but it was all suffused with the brightness of the hot, still hour. There was no ambiguity in anything; none whatever, at least, in the conviction I from one moment to another found myself forming as to what I should see straight before me and across the lake as a consequence of raising my eyes. They were attached at this juncture to the stitching in which I was engaged, and I can feel once more the spasm of my effort not to move them till I should so have steadied myself as to be able to make up my mind what to do. There was an alien object in view—a figure whose right of presence I instantly, passionately questioned. I recollect counting over perfectly the possibilities, reminding myself that nothing was more natural, for instance, then the appearance of one of the men about the place, or even of a messenger, a postman, or a tradesman's boy, from the village. That reminder had as little effect on my practical certitude as I was conscious—still even without looking—of its having upon the character and attitude of our visitor. Nothing was more natural than that these things should be the other things that they absolutely were not.

Of the positive identity of the apparition I would assure myself as soon as the small clock of my courage should have ticked out the right second; meanwhile, with an effort that was already sharp enough, I transferred my eyes straight to little Flora, who, at the moment, was about ten yards away. My heart had stood still for an instant with the wonder and terror of the question whether she too would see; and I held my breath while I waited for what a cry from her, what some sudden innocent sign either of interest or of alarm, would tell me. I waited, but nothing came; then, in the first place—and there is something more dire in this, I feel, than in anything I have to relate—I was determined by a sense that, within a minute, all sounds from her had previously dropped; and, in the second, by the circumstance that, also within the minute, she had, in her play, turned her back to the water. This was her attitude when I at last looked at her—looked with the confirmed conviction that we were still, together, under direct personal notice. She had picked up a small flat piece of wood, which happened to have in it a little hole that had evidently suggested to her the idea of sticking in another fragment that might figure as a mast and make the thing a boat. This second morsel, as I watched her, she was very markedly and intently attempting to tighten in its place. My apprehension of what she was doing sustained me so that after some seconds I felt I was ready for more. Then I again shifted my eyes—I faced what I had to face.

VII

I got hold of Mrs. Grose as soon after this as I could; and I can give no intelligible account of how I fought out the interval. Yet I still hear myself cry as I fairly threw myself into her arms: "They KNOW—it's too monstrous: they know, they know!"

"And what on earth—?" I felt her incredulity as she held me.

"Why, all that WE know—and heaven knows what else besides!" Then, as she released me, I made it out to her, made it out perhaps only now with full coherency even to myself. "Two hours ago, in the garden"—I could scarce articulate—"Flora SAW!"

Mrs. Grose took it as she might have taken a blow in the stomach. "She has told you?" she panted.

"Not a word—that's the horror. She kept it to herself! The child of eight, THAT child!" Unutterable still, for me, was the stupefaction of it.

Mrs. Grose, of course, could only gape the wider. "Then how do you know?"

"I was there—I saw with my eyes: saw that she was perfectly aware."

"Do you mean aware of HIM?"

"No—of HER." I was conscious as I spoke that I looked prodigious things, for I got the slow reflection of them in my companion's face. "Another person—this time; but a figure of quite as unmistakable horror and evil: a woman in black, pale and dreadful—with such an air also, and such a face!—on the other side of the lake. I was there with the child—quiet for the hour; and in the midst of it she came."

"Came how—from where?"

"From where they come from! She just appeared and stood there—but not so near."

"And without coming nearer?"

"Oh, for the effect and the feeling, she might have been as close as you!"

My friend, with an odd impulse, fell back a step. "Was she someone you've never seen?"

"Yes. But someone the child has. Someone YOU have." Then, to show how I had thought it all out: "My predecessor—the one who died."

"Miss Jessel?"

"Miss Jessel. You don't believe me?" I pressed.

She turned right and left in her distress. "How can you be sure?"

This drew from me, in the state of my nerves, a flash of impatience. "Then ask Flora—SHE'S sure!" But I had no sooner spoken than I caught myself up. "No, for God's sake, DON'T! She'll say she isn't—she'll lie!"

Mrs. Grose was not too bewildered instinctively to protest. "Ah, how CAN you?"

"Because I'm clear. Flora doesn't want me to know."

"It's only then to spare you."

"No, no—there are depths, depths! The more I go over it, the more I see in it, and the more I see in it, the more I fear. I don't know what I DON'T see—what I DON'T fear!"

Mrs. Grose tried to keep up with me. "You mean you're afraid of seeing her again?"

"Oh, no; that's nothing—now!" Then I explained. "It's of NOT seeing her."

But my companion only looked wan. "I don't understand you."

"Why, it's that the child may keep it up—and that the child assuredly WILL—without my knowing it."

At the image of this possibility Mrs. Grose for a moment collapsed, yet presently to pull herself together again, as if from the positive force of the sense of what, should we yield an inch, there would really be to give way to. "Dear, dear—we must keep our heads! And after all, if she doesn't mind it—!" She even tried a grim joke. "Perhaps she likes it!"

"Likes SUCH things—a scrap of an infant!"

"Isn't it just a proof of her blessed innocence?" my friend bravely inquired.

She brought me, for the instant, almost round. "Oh, we must clutch at THAT—we must cling to it! If it isn't a proof of what you say, it's a proof of—God knows what! For the woman's a horror of horrors."

Mrs. Grose, at this, fixed her eyes a minute on the ground; then at last raising them, "Tell me how you know," she said.

"Then you admit it's what she was?" I cried.

"Tell me how you know," my friend simply repeated.

"Know? By seeing her! By the way she looked."

"At you, do you mean—so wickedly?"

"Dear me, no—I could have borne that. She gave me never a glance. She only fixed the child."

Mrs. Grose tried to see it. "Fixed her?"

"Ah, with such awful eyes!"

She stared at mine as if they might really have resembled them. "Do you mean of dislike?"

"God help us, no. Of something much worse."

"Worse than dislike?—this left her indeed at a loss.

"With a determination—indescribable. With a kind of fury of intention."

I made her turn pale. "Intention?"

"To get hold of her." Mrs. Grose—her eyes just lingering on mine—gave a shudder and walked to the window; and while she stood there looking out I completed my statement. "THAT'S what Flora knows."

After a little she turned round. "The person was in black, you say?"

"In mourning—rather poor, almost shabby. But—yes—with extraordinary beauty." I now recognized to what I had at last, stroke by stroke, brought the victim of my confidence, for she quite visibly weighed this. "Oh, handsome—very, very," I insisted; "wonderfully handsome. But infamous."

She slowly came back to me. "Miss Jessel—WAS infamous." She once more took my hand in both her own, holding it as tight as if to fortify me against the increase of alarm I might draw from this disclosure. "They were both infamous," she finally said.

So, for a little, we faced it once more together; and I found absolutely a degree of help in seeing it now so straight. "I appreciate," I said, "the great decency of your not having hitherto spoken; but the time has certainly come to give me the whole thing." She appeared to assent to this, but still only in silence; seeing which I went on: "I must have it now. Of what did she die? Come, there was something between them."

"There was everything."

"In spite of the difference—?"

"Oh, of their rank, their condition"—she brought it woefully out. "SHE was a lady."

I turned it over; I again saw. "Yes—she was a lady."

"And he so dreadfully below," said Mrs. Grose.

I felt that I doubtless needn't press too hard, in such company, on the place of a servant in the scale; but there was nothing to prevent an acceptance of my companion's own measure of my predecessor's abasement. There was a way to deal with that, and I dealt; the more readily for my full vision—on the evidence—of our employer's late clever, good-looking "own" man; impudent, assured, spoiled, depraved. "The fellow was a hound."

Mrs. Grose considered as if it were perhaps a little a case for a sense of shades. "I've never seen one like him. He did what he wished."

"With HER?"

"With them all."

It was as if now in my friend's own eyes Miss Jessel had again appeared. I seemed at any rate, for an instant, to see their evocation of her as distinctly as I had seen her by the pond; and I brought out with decision: "It must have been also what SHE wished!"

Mrs. Grose's face signified that it had been indeed, but she said at the same time: "Poor woman—she paid for it!"

"Then you do know what she died of?" I asked.

"No—I know nothing. I wanted not to know; I was glad enough I didn't; and I thanked heaven she was well out of this!"

"Yet you had, then, your idea—"

"Of her real reason for leaving? Oh, yes—as to that. She couldn't have stayed. Fancy it here—for a governess! And afterward I imagined—and I still imagine. And what I imagine is dreadful."

"Not so dreadful as what *I* do," I replied; on which I must have shown her—as I was indeed but too conscious—a front of miserable defeat. It brought out again all her compassion for me, and at the renewed touch of her kindness my power to resist broke down. I burst, as I had, the other time, made her burst, into tears; she took me to her motherly breast, and my lamentation overflowed. "I don't do it!" I sobbed in despair; "I don't save or shield them! It's far worse than I dreamed—they're lost!"

VIII

What I had said to Mrs. Grose was true enough: there were in the matter I had put before her depths and possibilities that I lacked resolution to sound; so that when we met once more in the wonder of it we were of a common mind about the duty of resistance to extravagant fancies. We were to keep our heads if we should keep nothing else—difficult indeed as that might be in the face of what, in our prodigious experience, was least to be questioned. Late that night, while the house slept, we had another talk in my room, when she went all the way with me as to its being beyond doubt that I had seen exactly what I had seen. To hold her perfectly in the pinch of that, I found I had only to ask her how, if I had "made it up," I came to be able to give, of each of the persons appearing to me, a picture disclosing, to the last detail, their special marks—a portrait on the exhibition of which she had instantly recognized and named them. She wished of course—small blame to her!—to sink the whole subject; and I was quick to assure her that my own interest in it had now violently taken the form of a search for the way to escape from it. I encountered her on the ground of a probability that with recurrence—for recurrence we took for granted—I should get used to my danger, distinctly professing that my personal exposure had suddenly become the least of my discomforts. It was my new suspicion that was intolerable; and yet even to this complication the later hours of the day had brought a little ease.

On leaving her, after my first outbreak, I had of course returned to my pupils, associating the right remedy for my dismay with that sense of their charm which I had already found to be a thing I could positively cultivate and which had never failed me yet. I had simply, in other words, plunged afresh into Flora's special society and there become aware—it was almost a luxury!—that she could put her little conscious hand straight upon the spot that ached. She had looked at me in sweet speculation and then had accused me to my face of having "cried." I had supposed I had brushed away the ugly signs: but I could literally—for the time, at all events—rejoice, under this fathomless charity, that they had not entirely disappeared. To gaze into the depths of blue of the child's eyes and pronounce their loveliness a trick of premature cunning was to be guilty of a cynicism in preference to which I naturally preferred to abjure my judgment and, so far as might be, my agitation. I couldn't abjure for merely wanting to, but I could repeat to Mrs. Grose—as I did there, over and over, in the small hours—that with their voices in the air, their pressure on one's heart, and their fragrant faces against one's cheek, everything fell to the ground but their incapacity and their beauty. It was a pity that, somehow, to settle this once for all, I had equally to re-enumerate the signs of subtlety that, in the afternoon, by the lake had made a miracle of my show of self-possession. It was a pity to be obliged to reinvestigate the certitude of the moment itself and repeat how it had come to me as a revelation that the inconceivable communion I then surprised was a matter, for either party, of habit. It was a pity that I should have had to quaver out again the reasons for my not having, in my delusion, so much as questioned that the little girl saw our visitant even as I actually saw Mrs. Grose herself, and that she wanted, by just so much as she did thus see, to make me suppose she didn't, and at the same time, without showing anything, arrive at a guess as to whether I myself did! It was a pity that I needed once more to describe the portentous little activity by which she sought to divert my attention—the perceptible increase of movement, the greater intensity of play, the singing, the gabbling of nonsense, and the invitation to romp.

Yet if I had not indulged, to prove there was nothing in it, in this review, I should have missed the two or three dim elements of comfort that still remained to me. I should not for instance have been able to asseverate to my friend that I was certain—which was so much to the good—that *I* at least had not betrayed myself. I should not have been prompted, by stress of need, by desperation of mind—I scarce know what to call it—to invoke such further aid to intelligence as might spring from pushing my colleague fairly to the wall. She had told me, bit by bit, under pressure, a great deal; but a small shifty spot on the wrong side of it all still sometimes brushed my brow like the wing of a bat; and I remember how on this occasion—for the sleeping house and the concentration alike of our danger and our watch seemed to help—I felt the importance of giving the last jerk to the curtain. "I don't believe anything so horrible," I recollect saying; "no, let us put it definitely, my dear, that I don't. But if I did, you know, there's a thing I should require now, just without sparing you the least bit more—oh, not a scrap, come!—to get out of you. What was it you had in mind when, in our distress, before Miles came back, over the letter from his school, you said, under my insistence, that you didn't pretend for him that he had not literally EVER been 'bad'? He has NOT literally 'ever,' in these weeks that I myself have lived with him and so closely watched him; he has been an imperturbable little prodigy of delightful, lovable goodness. Therefore you might perfectly have made the claim for him if you had not, as it happened, seen an exception to take. What was your exception, and to what passage in your personal observation of him did you refer?"

It was a dreadfully austere inquiry, but levity was not our note, and, at any rate, before the gray dawn admonished us to separate I had got my answer. What my friend had had in mind proved to be immensely to the purpose. It was neither more nor less than the circumstance that for a period of several months Quint and the boy had been perpetually together. It was in fact the very appropriate truth that she had ventured to criticize the propriety, to hint at the incongruity, of so close an alliance, and even to go so far on the subject as a frank overture to Miss Jessel. Miss Jessel had, with a most strange manner, requested her to mind her business, and the good woman had, on this, directly approached little Miles. What she had said to him, since I pressed, was that SHE liked to see young gentlemen not forget their station.

I pressed again, of course, at this. "You reminded him that Quint was only a base menial?"

"As you might say! And it was his answer, for one thing, that was bad."

"And for another thing?" I waited. "He repeated your words to Quint?"

"No, not that. It's just what he WOULDN'T!" she could still impress upon me. "I was sure, at any rate," she added, "that he didn't. But he denied certain occasions."

"What occasions?"

"When they had been about together quite as if Quint were his tutor—and a very grand one—and Miss Jessel only for the little lady. When he had gone off with the fellow, I mean, and spent hours with him."

"He then prevaricated about it—he said he hadn't?" Her assent was clear enough to cause me to add in a moment: "I see. He lied."

"Oh!" Mrs. Grose mumbled. This was a suggestion that it didn't matter; which indeed she backed up by a further remark. "You see, after all, Miss Jessel didn't mind. She didn't forbid him."

I considered. "Did he put that to you as a justification?"

At this she dropped again. "No, he never spoke of it."

"Never mentioned her in connection with Quint?"

She saw, visibly flushing, where I was coming out. "Well, he didn't show anything. He denied," she repeated; "he denied."

Lord, how I pressed her now! "So that you could see he knew what was between the two wretches?"

"I don't know—I don't know!" the poor woman groaned.

"You do know, you dear thing," I replied; "only you haven't my dreadful boldness of mind, and you keep back, out of timidity and modesty and delicacy, even the impression that, in the past, when you had, without my aid, to flounder about in silence, most of all made you miserable. But I shall get it out of you yet! There was something in the boy that suggested to you," I continued, "that he covered and concealed their relation."

"Oh, he couldn't prevent—"

"Your learning the truth? I daresay! But, heavens," I fell, with vehemence, athinking, "what it shows that they must, to that extent, have succeeded in making of him!"

"Ah, nothing that's not nice NOW!" Mrs. Grose lugubriously pleaded.

"I don't wonder you looked queer," I persisted, "when I mentioned to you the letter from his school!"

"I doubt if I looked as queer as you!" she retorted with homely force. "And if he was so bad then as that comes to, how is he such an angel now?"

"Yes, indeed—and if he was a fiend at school! How, how, how? Well," I said in my torment, "you must put it to me again, but I shall not be able to tell you for some days. Only, put it to me again!" I cried in a way that made my friend stare. "There are directions in which I must not for the present let myself go." Meanwhile I returned to her first example—the one to which she had just previously referred—of the boy's happy capacity for an occasional slip. "If Quint—on your remonstrance at the time you speak of—was a base menial, one of the things Miles said to you, I find myself guessing, was that you were another." Again her admission was so adequate that I continued: "And you forgave him that?"

"Wouldn't YOU?"

"Oh, yes!" And we exchanged there, in the stillness, a sound of the oddest amusement. Then I went on: "At all events, while he was with the man—"

"Miss Flora was with the woman. It suited them all!"

It suited me, too, I felt, only too well; by which I mean that it suited exactly the particularly deadly view I was in the very act of forbidding myself to entertain. But I so far succeeded in checking the expression of this view that I will throw, just here, no further light on it than may be offered by the mention of my final observation to Mrs. Grose. "His having lied and been impudent are, I confess, less engaging specimens than I had hoped to have from you of the outbreak in him of the little natural man. Still," I mused, "They must do, for they make me feel more than ever that I must watch."

It made me blush, the next minute, to see in my friend's face how much more unreservedly she had forgiven him than her anecdote struck me as presenting to my own tenderness an occasion for doing. This came out when, at the schoolroom door, she quitted me. "Surely you don't accuse HIM—"

"Of carrying on an intercourse that he conceals from me? Ah, remember that, until further evidence, I now accuse nobody." Then, before shutting her out to go, by another passage, to her own place, "I must just wait," I wound up.

IX

I waited and waited, and the days, as they elapsed, took something from my consternation. A very few of them, in fact, passing, in constant sight of my pupils, without a fresh incident, sufficed to give to grievous fancies and even to odious memories a kind of brush of the sponge. I have spoken of the surrender to their extraordinary childish grace as a thing I could actively cultivate, and it may be imagined if I neglected now to address myself to this source for whatever it would yield. Stranger than I can express, certainly, was the effort to struggle against my new lights; it would doubtless have been, however, a greater tension still had it not been so frequently successful. I used to wonder how my little charges could help guessing that I thought strange things about them; and the circumstances that these things only made them more interesting was not by itself a direct aid to keeping them in the dark. I trembled lest they should see that they WERE so immensely more interesting. Putting things at the worst, at all events, as in meditation I so often did, any clouding of their innocence could only be—blameless and foredoomed as they were—a reason the more for taking risks. There were moments when, by an irresistible impulse, I found myself catching them up and pressing them to my heart. As soon as I had done so I used to say to myself: "What will they think of that? Doesn't it betray too much?" It would have been easy to get into a sad, wild tangle about how much I might betray; but the real account, I feel, of the hours of peace that I could still enjoy was that the immediate charm of my companions was a beguilement still effective even under the shadow of the possibility that it was studied. For if it occurred to me that I might occasionally excite suspicion by the little outbreaks of my sharper passion for them, so too I remember wondering if I mightn't see a queerness in the traceable increase of their own demonstrations.

They were at this period extravagantly and preternaturally fond of me; which, after all, I could reflect, was no more than a graceful response in children perpetually bowed over and hugged. The homage of which they were so lavish succeeded, in truth, for my nerves, quite as well as if I never appeared to myself, as I may say, literally to catch them at a purpose in it. They had never, I think, wanted to do so many things for their poor protectress; I mean—though they got their lessons better and better, which was naturally what would please her most—in the way of diverting, entertaining, surprising her; reading her passages, telling her stories, acting her charades, pouncing out at her, in disguises, as animals and historical characters, and above all astonishing her by the "pieces" they had secretly got by heart and could interminably recite. I should never get to the bottom—were I to let myself go even now—of the prodigious private commentary, all under still more private correction, with which, in these days, I overscored their full hours. They had shown me from the first a facility for everything, a general faculty which, taking a fresh start, achieved remarkable flights. They got their little tasks as if they loved them, and indulged, from the mere exuberance of the gift, in the most unimposed little miracles of memory. They not only popped out at me as tigers and as Romans, but as Shakespeareans, astronomers, and navigators. This was so singularly the case that it had presumably much to do with the fact as to which, at the present day, I am at a loss for a different explanation: I allude to my unnatural composure on the subject of another school for Miles. What I remember is that I was content not, for the time, to open the question, and that contentment must have sprung from the sense of his perpetually striking show of cleverness. He was too clever for a bad governess, for a parson's daughter, to spoil; and the strangest if not the brightest thread in the pensive embroidery I just spoke of was the impression I might have got, if I had dared to work it out, that he was under some influence operating in his small intellectual life as a tremendous incitement.

If it was easy to reflect, however, that such a boy could postpone school, it was at least as marked that for such a boy to have been "kicked out" by a schoolmaster was a mystification without end. Let me add that in their company now—and I was careful almost never to be out of it—I could follow no scent very far. We lived in a cloud of music and love and success and private theatricals. The musical sense in each of the children was of the quickest, but the elder in especial had a marvelous knack of catching and repeating. The schoolroom piano broke into all gruesome fancies; and when that failed there were confabulations in corners, with a sequel of one of them going out in the highest spirits in order to "come in" as something new. I had had brothers myself, and it was no revelation to me that little girls could be slavish idolaters of little boys. What surpassed everything was that there was a little boy in the world who could have for the inferior age, sex, and intelligence so fine a consideration. They were extraordinarily at one, and to say that they never either quarreled or complained is to make the note of praise coarse for their quality of sweetness. Sometimes, indeed, when I dropped into coarseness, I perhaps came across traces of little understandings between them by which one of them should keep me occupied while the other slipped away. There is a naive side, I suppose, in all diplomacy; but if my pupils practiced upon me, it was surely with the minimum of grossness. It was all in the other quarter that, after a lull, the grossness broke out.

I find that I really hang back; but I must take my plunge. In going on with the record of what was hideous at Bly, I not only challenge the most liberal faith—for which I little care; but—and this is another matter—I renew what I myself suffered, I again push my way through it to the end. There came suddenly an hour after which, as I look back, the affair seems to me to have been all pure suffering; but I have at least reached the heart of it, and the straightest road out is doubtless to advance. One evening—with nothing to lead up or to prepare it—I felt the cold touch of the impression that had breathed on me the night of my arrival and which, much lighter then, as I have mentioned, I should probably have made little of in memory had my subsequent sojourn been less agitated. I had not gone to bed; I sat reading by a couple of candles. There was a roomful of old books at Bly—last-century fiction, some of it, which, to the extent of a distinctly deprecated renown, but never to so much as that of a stray specimen, had reached the sequestered home and appealed to the unavowed curiosity of my youth. I remember that the book I had in my hand was Fielding's Amelia; also that I was wholly awake. I recall further both a general conviction that it was horribly late and a particular objection to looking at my watch. I figure, finally, that the white curtain draping, in the fashion of those days, the head of Flora's little bed, shrouded, as I had assured myself long before, the perfection of childish rest. I recollect in short that, though I was deeply interested in my author, I found myself, at the turn of a page and with his spell all scattered, looking straight up from him and hard at the door of my room. There was a moment during which I listened, reminded of the faint sense I had had, the first night, of there being something undefinably astir in the house, and noted the soft breath of the open casement just move the half-drawn blind. Then, with all the marks of a deliberation that must have seemed magnificent had there been anyone to admire it, I laid down my book, rose to my feet, and, taking a candle, went straight out of the room and, from the passage, on which my light made little impression, noiselessly closed and locked the door.

I can say now neither what determined nor what guided me, but I went straight along the lobby, holding my candle high, till I came within sight of the tall window that presided over the great turn of the staircase. At this point I precipitately found myself aware of three things. They were practically simultaneous, yet they had flashes of succession. My candle, under a bold flourish, went out, and I perceived, by the uncovered window, that the yielding dusk of earliest morning rendered it unnecessary. Without it, the next instant, I saw that there was someone on the stair. I speak of sequences, but I required no lapse of seconds to stiffen myself for a third encounter with Quint. The apparition had reached the landing halfway up and was therefore on the spot nearest the window, where at sight of me, it stopped short and fixed me exactly as it had fixed me from the tower and from the garden. He knew me as well as I knew him; and so, in the cold, faint twilight, with a glimmer in the high glass and another on the polish of the oak stair below, we faced each other in our common intensity. He was absolutely, on this occasion, a living, detestable, dangerous presence. But that was not the wonder of wonders; I reserve this distinction for quite another circumstance: the circumstance that dread had unmistakably quitted me and that there was nothing in me there that didn't meet and measure him.

I had plenty of anguish after that extraordinary moment, but I had, thank God, no terror. And he knew I had not—I found myself at the end of an instant magnificently aware of this. I felt, in a fierce rigor of confidence, that if I stood my ground a minute I should cease—for the time, at least—to have him to reckon with; and during the minute, accordingly, the thing was as human and hideous as a real interview: hideous just because it WAS human, as human as to have met alone, in the small hours, in a sleeping house, some enemy, some adventurer, some criminal. It was the dead silence of our long gaze at such close quarters that gave the whole horror, huge as it was, its only note of the unnatural. If I had met a murderer in such a place and at such an hour, we still at least would have spoken. Something would have passed, in life, between us; if nothing had passed, one of us would have moved. The moment was so prolonged that it would have taken but little more to make me doubt if even *I* were in life. I can't express what followed it save by saying that the silence itself—which was indeed in a manner an attestation of my strength—became the element into which I saw the figure disappear; in which I definitely saw it turn as I might have seen the low wretch to which it had once belonged turn on receipt of an order, and pass, with my eyes on the villainous back that no hunch could have more disfigured, straight down the staircase and into the darkness in which the next bend was lost.

X

I remained awhile at the top of the stair, but with the effect presently of understanding that when my visitor had gone, he had gone: then I returned to my room. The foremost thing I saw there by the light of the candle I had left burning was that Flora's little bed was empty; and on this I caught my breath with all the terror that, five minutes before, I had been able to resist. I dashed at the place in which I had left her lying and over which (for the small silk counterpane and the sheets were disarranged) the white curtains had been deceivingly pulled forward; then my step, to my unutterable relief, produced an answering sound: I perceived an agitation of the window blind, and the child, ducking down, emerged rosily from the other side of it. She stood there in so much of her candor and so little of her nightgown, with her pink bare feet and the golden glow of her curls. She looked intensely grave, and I had never had such a sense of losing an advantage acquired (the thrill of which had just been so prodigious) as on my consciousness that she addressed me with a reproach. "You naughty: where HAVE you been?"—instead of challenging her own irregularity I found myself arraigned and explaining. She herself explained, for that matter, with the loveliest, eagerest simplicity. She had known suddenly, as she lay there, that I was out of the room, and had jumped up to see what had become of me. I had dropped, with the joy of her reappearance, back into my chair—feeling then, and then only, a little faint; and she had pattered straight over to me, thrown herself upon my knee, given herself to be held with the flame of the candle full in the wonderful little face that was still flushed with sleep. I remember closing my eyes an instant, yieldingly, consciously, as before the excess of something beautiful that shone out of the blue of her own. "You were looking for me out of the window?" I said. "You thought I might be walking in the grounds?"

"Well, you know, I thought someone was"—she never blanched as she smiled out that at me.

Oh, how I looked at her now! "And did you see anyone?"

"Ah, NO!" she returned, almost with the full privilege of childish inconsequence, resentfully, though with a long sweetness in her little drawl of the negative.

At that moment, in the state of my nerves, I absolutely believed she lied; and if I once more closed my eyes it was before the dazzle of the three or four possible ways in which I might take this up. One of these, for a moment, tempted me with such singular intensity that, to withstand it, I must have gripped my little girl with a spasm that, wonderfully, she submitted to without a cry or a sign of fright. Why not break out at her on the spot and have it all over?—give it to her straight in her lovely little lighted face? "You see, you see, you KNOW that you do and that you already quite suspect I believe it; therefore, why not frankly confess it to me, so that we may at least live with it together and learn perhaps, in the strangeness of our fate, where we are and what it means?" This solicitation dropped, alas, as it came: if I could immediately have succumbed to it I might have spared myself—well, you'll see what. Instead of succumbing I sprang again to my feet, looked at her bed, and took a helpless middle way. "Why did you pull the curtain over the place to make me think you were still there?"

Flora luminously considered; after which, with her little divine smile: "Because I don't like to frighten you!"

"But if I had, by your idea, gone out—?"

She absolutely declined to be puzzled; she turned her eyes to the flame of the candle as if the question were as irrelevant, or at any rate as impersonal, as Mrs. Marcet or nine-times-nine. "Oh, but you know," she quite adequately answered, "that you might come back, you dear, and that you HAVE!" And after a little, when she had got into bed, I had, for a long time, by almost sitting on her to hold her hand, to prove that I recognized the pertinence of my return.

X

You may imagine the general complexion, from that moment, of my nights. I repeatedly sat up till I didn't know when; I selected moments when my roommate unmistakably slept, and, stealing out, took noiseless turns in the passage and even pushed as far as to where I had last met Quint. But I never met him there again; and I may as well say at once that I on no other occasion saw him in the house. I just missed, on the staircase, on the other hand, a different adventure. Looking down it from the top I once recognized the presence of a woman seated on one of the lower steps with her back presented to me, her body half-bowed and her head, in an attitude of woe, in her hands. I had been there but an instant, however, when she vanished without looking round at me. I knew, nonetheless, exactly what dreadful face she had to show; and I wondered whether, if instead of being above I had been below, I should have had, for going up, the same nerve I had lately shown Quint. Well, there continued to be plenty of chance for nerve. On the eleventh night after my latest encounter with that gentleman—they were all numbered now—I had an alarm that perilously skirted it and that indeed, from the particular quality of its unexpectedness, proved quite my sharpest shock. It was precisely the first night during this series that, weary with watching, I had felt that I might again without laxity lay myself down at my old hour. I slept immediately and, as I afterward knew, till about one o'clock; but when I woke it was to sit straight up, as completely roused as if a hand had shook me. I had left a light burning, but it was now out, and I felt an instant certainty that Flora had extinguished it. This brought me to my feet and straight, in the darkness, to her bed, which I found she had left. A glance at the window enlightened me further, and the striking of a match completed the picture.

The child had again got up—this time blowing out the taper, and had again, for some purpose of observation or response, squeezed in behind the blind and was peering out into the night. That she now saw—as she had not, I had satisfied myself, the previous time—was proved to me by the fact that she was disturbed neither by my reillumination nor by the haste I made to get into slippers and into a wrap. Hidden, protected, absorbed, she evidently rested on the sill—the casement opened forward—and gave herself up. There was a great still moon to help her, and this fact had counted in my quick decision. She was face to face with the apparition we had met at the lake, and could now communicate with it as she had not then been able to do. What I, on my side, had to care for was, without disturbing her, to reach, from the corridor, some other window in the same quarter. I got to the door without her hearing me; I got out of it, closed it, and listened, from the other side, for some sound from her. While I stood in the passage I had my eyes on her brother's door, which was but ten steps off and which, indescribably, produced in me a renewal of the strange impulse that I lately spoke of as my temptation. What if I should go straight in and march to HIS window?—what if, by risking to his boyish bewilderment a revelation of my motive, I should throw across the rest of the mystery the long halter of my boldness?

This thought held me sufficiently to make me cross to his threshold and pause again. I preternaturally listened; I figured to myself what might portentously be; I wondered if his bed were also empty and he too were secretly at watch. It was a deep, soundless minute, at the end of which my impulse failed. He was quiet; he might be innocent; the risk was hideous; I turned away. There was a figure in the grounds—a figure prowling for a sight, the visitor with whom Flora was engaged; but it was not the visitor most concerned with my boy. I hesitated afresh, but on other grounds and only for a few seconds; then I had made my choice. There were empty rooms at Bly, and it was only a question of choosing the right one. The right one suddenly presented itself to me as the lower one—though high above the gardens—in the solid corner of the house that I have spoken of as the old tower. This was a large, square chamber, arranged with some state as a bedroom, the extravagant size of which made it so inconvenient that it had not for years, though kept by Mrs. Grose in exemplary order, been occupied. I had often admired it and I knew my way about in it; I had only, after just faltering at the first chill gloom of its disuse, to pass across it and unbolt as quietly as I could one of the shutters. Achieving this transit, I uncovered the glass without a sound and, applying my face to the pane, was able, the darkness without being much less than within, to see that I commanded the right direction. Then I saw something more. The moon made the night extraordinarily penetrable and showed me on the lawn a person, diminished by distance, who stood there motionless and as if fascinated, looking up to where I had appeared—looking, that is, not so much straight at me as at something that was apparently above me. There was clearly another person above me—there was a person on the tower; but the presence on the lawn was not in the least what I had conceived and had confidently hurried to meet. The presence on the lawn—I felt sick as I made it out—was poor little Miles himself.

XI

It was not till late next day that I spoke to Mrs. Grose; the rigor with which I kept my pupils in sight making it often difficult to meet her privately, and the more as we each felt the importance of not provoking—on the part of the servants quite as much as on that of the children—any suspicion of a secret flurry or that of a discussion of mysteries. I drew a great security in this particular from her mere smooth aspect. There was nothing in her fresh face to pass on to others my horrible confidences. She believed me, I was sure, absolutely: if she hadn't I don't know what would have become of me, for I couldn't have borne the business alone. But she was a magnificent monument to the blessing of a want of imagination, and if she could see in our little charges nothing but their beauty and amiability, their happiness and cleverness, she had no direct communication with the sources of my trouble. If they had been at all visibly blighted or battered, she would doubtless have grown, on tracing it back, haggard enough to match them; as matters stood, however, I could feel her, when she surveyed them, with her large white arms folded and the habit of serenity in all her look, thank the Lord's mercy that if they were ruined the pieces would still serve. Flights of fancy gave place, in her mind, to a steady fireside glow, and I had already begun to perceive how, with the development of the conviction that—as time went on without a public accident—our young things could, after all, look out for themselves, she addressed her greatest solicitude to the sad case presented by their instructress. That, for myself, was a sound simplification: I could engage that, to the world, my face should tell no tales, but it would have been, in the conditions, an immense added strain to find myself anxious about hers.

At the hour I now speak of she had joined me, under pressure, on the terrace, where, with the lapse of the season, the afternoon sun was now agreeable; and we sat there together while, before us, at a distance, but within call if we wished, the children strolled to and fro in one of their most manageable moods. They moved slowly, in unison, below us, over the lawn, the boy, as they went, reading aloud from a storybook and passing his arm round his sister to keep her quite in touch. Mrs. Grose watched them with positive placidity; then I caught the suppressed intellectual creak with which she conscientiously turned to take from me a view of the back of the tapestry. I had made her a receptacle of lurid things, but there was an odd recognition of my superiority—my accomplishments and my function—in her patience under my pain. She offered her mind to my disclosures as, had I wished to mix a witch's broth and proposed it with assurance, she would have held out a large clean saucepan. This had become thoroughly her attitude by the time that, in my recital of the events of the night, I reached the point of what Miles had said to me when, after seeing him, at such a monstrous hour, almost on the very spot where he happened now to be, I had gone down to bring him in; choosing then, at the window, with a concentrated need of not alarming the house, rather that method than a signal more resonant. I had left her meanwhile in little doubt of my small hope of representing with success even to her actual sympathy my sense of the real splendor of the little inspiration with which, after I had got him into the house, the boy met my final articulate challenge. As soon as I appeared in the moonlight on the terrace, he had come to me as straight as possible; on which I had taken his hand without a word and led him, through the dark spaces, up the staircase where Quint had so hungrily hovered for him, along the lobby where I had listened and trembled, and so to his forsaken room.

Not a sound, on the way, had passed between us, and I had wondered—oh, HOW I had wondered!—if he were groping about in his little mind for something plausible and not too grotesque. It would tax his invention, certainly, and I felt, this time, over his real embarrassment, a curious thrill of triumph. It was a sharp trap for the inscrutable! He couldn't play any longer at innocence; so how the deuce would he get out of it? There beat in me indeed, with the passionate throb of this question an equal dumb appeal as to how the deuce *I* should. I was confronted at last, as never yet, with all the risk attached even now to sounding my own horrid note. I remember in fact that as we pushed into his little chamber, where the bed had not been slept in at all and the window, uncovered to the moonlight, made the place so clear that there was no need of striking a match—I remember how I suddenly dropped, sank upon the edge of the bed from the force of the idea that he must know how he really, as they say, "had" me. He could do what he liked, with all his cleverness to help him, so long as I should continue to defer to the old tradition of the criminality of those caretakers of the young who minister to superstitions and fears. He "had" me indeed, and in a cleft stick; for who would ever absolve me, who would consent that I should go unhung, if, by the faintest tremor of an overture, I were the first to introduce into our perfect intercourse an element so dire? No, no: it was useless to attempt to convey to Mrs. Grose, just as it is scarcely less so to attempt to suggest here, how, in our short, stiff brush in the dark, he fairly shook me with admiration. I was of course thoroughly kind and merciful; never, never yet had I placed on his little shoulders hands of such tenderness as those with which, while I rested against the bed, I held him there well under fire. I had no alternative but, in form at least, to put it to him.

"You must tell me now—and all the truth. What did you go out for? What were you doing there?"

I can still see his wonderful smile, the whites of his beautiful eyes, and the uncovering of his little teeth shine to me in the dusk. "If I tell you why, will you understand?" My heart, at this, leaped into my mouth. WOULD he tell me why? I found no sound on my lips to press it, and I was aware of replying only with a vague, repeated, grimacing nod. He was gentleness itself, and while I wagged my head at him he stood there more than ever a little fairy prince. It was his brightness indeed that gave me a respite. Would it be so great if he were really going to tell me? "Well," he said at last, "just exactly in order that you should do this."

"Do what?"

"Think me—for a change—BAD!" I shall never forget the sweetness and gaiety with which he brought out the word, nor how, on top of it, he bent forward and kissed me. It was practically the end of everything. I met his kiss and I had to make, while I folded him for a minute in my arms, the most stupendous effort not to cry. He had given exactly the account of himself that permitted least of my going behind it, and it was only with the effect of confirming my acceptance of it that, as I presently glanced about the room, I could say—

"Then you didn't undress at all?"

He fairly glittered in the gloom. "Not at all. I sat up and read."

"And when did you go down?"

"At midnight. When I'm bad I AM bad!"

"I see, I see—it's charming. But how could you be sure I would know it?"

"Oh, I arranged that with Flora." His answers rang out with a readiness! "She was to get up and look out."

"Which is what she did do." It was I who fell into the trap!

"So she disturbed you, and, to see what she was looking at, you also looked—you saw."

"While you," I concurred, "caught your death in the night air!"

He literally bloomed so from this exploit that he could afford radiantly to assent. "How otherwise should I have been bad enough?" he asked. Then, after another embrace, the incident and our interview closed on my recognition of all the reserves of goodness that, for his joke, he had been able to draw upon.

XII

The particular impression I had received proved in the morning light, I repeat, not quite successfully presentable to Mrs. Grose, though I reinforced it with the mention of still another remark that he had made before we separated. "It all lies in half a dozen words," I said to her, "words that really settle the matter. 'Think, you know, what I MIGHT do!' He threw that off to show me how good he is. He knows down to the ground what he 'might' do. That's what he gave them a taste of at school."

"Lord, you do change!" cried my friend.

"I don't change—I simply make it out. The four, depend upon it, perpetually meet. If on either of these last nights you had been with either child, you would clearly have understood. The more I've watched and waited the more I've felt that if there were nothing else to make it sure it would be made so by the systematic silence of each. NEVER, by a slip of the tongue, have they so much as alluded to either of their old friends, any more than Miles has alluded to his expulsion. Oh, yes, we may sit here and look at them, and they may show off to us there to their fill; but even while they pretend to be lost in their fairytale they're steeped in their vision of the dead restored. He's not reading to her," I declared; "they're talking of THEM—they're talking horrors! I go on, I know, as if I were crazy; and it's a wonder I'm not. What I've seen would have made YOU so; but it has only made me more lucid, made me get hold of still other things."

My lucidity must have seemed awful, but the charming creatures who were victims of it, passing and repassing in their interlocked sweetness, gave my colleague something to hold on by; and I felt how tight she held as, without stirring in the breath of my passion, she covered them still with her eyes. "Of what other things have you got hold?"

"Why, of the very things that have delighted, fascinated, and yet, at bottom, as I now so strangely see, mystified and troubled me. Their more than earthly beauty, their absolutely unnatural goodness. It's a game," I went on; "it's a policy and a fraud!"

"On the part of little darlings—?"

"As yet mere lovely babies? Yes, mad as that seems!" The very act of bringing it out really helped me to trace it—follow it all up and piece it all together. "They haven't been good—they've only been absent. It has been easy to live with them, because they're simply leading a life of their own. They're not mine—they're not ours. They're his and they're hers!"

"Quint's and that woman's?"

"Quint's and that woman's. They want to get to them."

Oh, how, at this, poor Mrs. Grose appeared to study them! "But for what?"

"For the love of all the evil that, in those dreadful days, the pair put into them. And to ply them with that evil still, to keep up the work of demons, is what brings the others back."

"Laws!" said my friend under her breath. The exclamation was homely, but it revealed a real acceptance of my further proof of what, in the bad time—for there had been a worse even than this!—must have occurred. There could have been no such justification for me as the plain assent of her experience to whatever depth of depravity I found credible in our brace of scoundrels. It was in obvious submission of memory that she brought out after a moment: "They WERE rascals! But what can they now do?" she pursued.

"Do?" I echoed so loud that Miles and Flora, as they passed at their distance, paused an instant in their walk and looked at us. "Don't they do enough?" I demanded in a lower tone, while the children, having smiled and nodded and kissed hands to us, resumed their exhibition. We were held by it a minute; then I answered: "They can destroy them!" At this my companion did turn, but the inquiry she launched was a silent one, the effect of which was to make me more explicit. "They don't know, as yet, quite how—but they're trying hard. They're seen only across, as it were, and beyond—in strange places and on high places, the top of towers, the roof of houses, the outside of windows, the further edge of pools; but there's a deep design, on either side, to shorten the distance and overcome the obstacle; and the success of the tempters is only a question of time. They've only to keep to their suggestions of danger."

"For the children to come?"

"And perish in the attempt!" Mrs. Grose slowly got up, and I scrupulously added: "Unless, of course, we can prevent!"

Standing there before me while I kept my seat, she visibly turned things over. "Their uncle must do the preventing. He must take them away."

"And who's to make him?"

She had been scanning the distance, but she now dropped on me a foolish face. "You, miss."

"By writing to him that his house is poisoned and his little nephew and niece mad?"

"But if they ARE, miss?"

"And if I am myself, you mean? That's charming news to be sent him by a governess whose prime undertaking was to give him no worry."

Mrs. Grose considered, following the children again. "Yes, he do hate worry. That was the great reason—"

"Why those fiends took him in so long? No doubt, though his indifference must have been awful. As I'm not a fiend, at any rate, I shouldn't take him in."

My companion, after an instant and for all answer, sat down again and grasped my arm. "Make him at any rate come to you."

I stared. "To ME?" I had a sudden fear of what she might do. "'Him'?"

"He ought to BE here—he ought to help."

I quickly rose, and I think I must have shown her a queerer face than ever yet. "You see me asking him for a visit?" No, with her eyes on my face she evidently couldn't. Instead of it even—as a woman reads another—she could see what I myself saw: his derision, his amusement, his contempt for the breakdown of my resignation at being left alone and for the fine machinery I had set in motion to attract his attention to my slighted charms. She didn't know—no one knew—how proud I had been to serve him and to stick to our terms; yet she nonetheless took the measure, I think, of the warning I now gave her. "If you should so lose your head as to appeal to him for me—"

She was really frightened. "Yes, miss?"

"I would leave, on the spot, both him and you."

XIII

It was all very well to join them, but speaking to them proved quite as much as ever an effort beyond my strength—offered, in close quarters, difficulties as insurmountable as before. This situation continued a month, and with new aggravations and particular notes, the note above all, sharper and sharper, of the small ironic consciousness on the part of my pupils. It was not, I am as sure today as I was sure then, my mere infernal imagination: it was absolutely traceable that they were aware of my predicament and that this strange relation made, in a manner, for a long time, the air in which we moved. I don't mean that they had their tongues in their cheeks or did anything vulgar, for that was not one of their dangers: I do mean, on the other hand, that the element of the unnamed and untouched became, between us, greater than any other, and that so much avoidance could not have been so successfully effected without a great deal of tacit arrangement. It was as if, at moments, we were perpetually coming into sight of subjects before which we must stop short, turning suddenly out of alleys that we perceived to be blind, closing with a little bang that made us look at each other—for, like all bangs, it was something louder than we had intended—the doors we had indiscreetly opened. All roads lead to Rome, and there were times when it might have struck us that almost every branch of study or subject of conversation skirted forbidden ground. Forbidden ground was the question of the return of the dead in general and of whatever, in especial, might survive, in memory, of the friends little children had lost. There were days when I could have sworn that one of them had, with a small invisible nudge, said to the other: "She thinks she'll do it this time—but she WON'T!" To "do it" would have been to indulge for instance—and for once in a way—in some direct reference to the lady who had prepared them for my discipline. They had a delightful endless appetite for passages in my own history, to which I had again and again treated them; they were in possession of everything that had ever happened to me, had had, with every circumstance the story of my smallest adventures and of those of my brothers and sisters and of the cat and the dog at home, as well as many particulars of the eccentric nature of my father, of the furniture and arrangement of our house, and of the conversation of the old women of our village. There were things enough, taking one with another, to chatter about, if one went very fast and knew by instinct when to go round. They pulled with an art of their own the strings of my invention and my memory; and nothing else perhaps, when I thought of such occasions afterward, gave me so the suspicion of being watched from under cover. It was in any case over MY life, MY past, and MY friends alone that we could take anything like our ease—a state of affairs that led them sometimes without the least pertinence to break out into sociable reminders. I was invited—with no visible connection—to repeat afresh Goody Gosling's celebrated mot or to confirm the details already supplied as to the cleverness of the vicarage pony.

It was partly at such junctures as these and partly at quite different ones that, with the turn my matters had now taken, my predicament, as I have called it, grew most sensible. The fact that the days passed for me without another encounter ought, it would have appeared, to have done something toward soothing my nerves. Since the light brush, that second night on the upper landing, of the presence of a woman at the foot of the stair, I had seen nothing, whether in or out of the house, that one had better not have seen. There was many a corner round which I expected to come upon Quint, and many a situation that, in a merely sinister way, would have favored the appearance of Miss Jessel. The summer had turned, the summer had gone; the autumn had dropped upon Bly and had blown out half our lights. The place, with its gray sky and withered garlands, its bared spaces and scattered dead leaves, was like a theater after the performance—all strewn with crumpled playbills. There were exactly states of the air, conditions of sound and of stillness, unspeakable impressions of the KIND of ministering moment, that brought back to me, long enough to catch it, the feeling of the medium in which, that June evening out of doors, I had had my first sight of Quint, and in which, too, at those other instants, I had, after seeing him through the window, looked for him in vain in the circle of shrubbery. I recognized the signs, the portents—I recognized the moment, the spot. But they remained unaccompanied and empty, and I continued unmolested; if unmolested one could call a young woman whose sensibility had, in the most extraordinary fashion, not declined but deepened. I had said in my talk with Mrs. Grose on that horrid scene of Flora's by the lake—and had perplexed her by so saying—that it would from that moment distress me much more to lose my power than to keep it. I had then expressed what was vividly in my mind: the truth that, whether the children really saw or not—since, that is, it was not yet definitely proved—I greatly preferred, as a safeguard, the fullness of my own exposure. I was ready to know the very worst that was to be known. What I had then had an ugly glimpse of was that my eyes might be sealed just while theirs were most opened. Well, my eyes WERE sealed, it appeared, at present—a consummation for which it seemed blasphemous not to thank God. There was, alas, a difficulty about that: I would have thanked him with all my soul had I not had in a proportionate measure this conviction of the secret of my pupils.

How can I retrace today the strange steps of my obsession? There were times of our being together when I would have been ready to swear that, literally, in my presence, but with my direct sense of it closed, they had visitors who were known and were welcome. Then it was that, had I not been deterred by the very chance that such an injury might prove greater than the injury to be averted, my exultation would have broken out. "They're here, they're here, you little wretches," I would have cried, "and you can't deny it now!" The little wretches denied it with all the added volume of their sociability and their tenderness, in just the crystal depths of which—like the flash of a fish in a stream—the mockery of their advantage peeped up. The shock, in truth, had sunk into me still deeper than I knew on the night when, looking out to see either Quint or Miss Jessel under the stars, I had beheld the boy over whose rest I watched and who had immediately brought in with him—had straightway, there, turned it on me—the lovely upward look with which, from the battlements above me, the hideous apparition of Quint had played. If it was a question of a scare, my discovery on this occasion had scared me more than any other, and it was in the condition of nerves produced by it that I made my actual inductions. They harassed me so that sometimes, at odd moments, I shut myself up audibly to rehearse—it was at once a fantastic relief and a renewed despair—the manner in which I might come to the point. I approached it from one side and the other while, in my room, I flung myself about, but I always broke down in the monstrous utterance of names. As they died away on my lips, I said to myself that I should indeed help them to represent something infamous, if, by pronouncing them, I should violate as rare a little case of instinctive delicacy as any schoolroom, probably, had ever known. When I said to myself: "THEY have the manners to be silent, and you, trusted as you are, the baseness to speak!" I felt myself crimson and I covered my face with my hands. After these secret scenes I chattered more than ever, going on volubly enough till one of our prodigious, palpable hushes occurred—I can call them nothing else—the strange, dizzy lift or swim (I try for terms!) into a stillness, a pause of all life, that had nothing to do with the more or less noise that at the moment we might be engaged in making and that I could hear through any deepened exhilaration or quickened recitation or louder strum of the piano. Then it was that the others, the outsiders, were there. Though they were not angels, they "passed," as the French say, causing me, while they stayed, to tremble with the fear of their addressing to their younger victims some yet more infernal message or more vivid image than they had thought good enough for myself.

What it was most impossible to get rid of was the cruel idea that, whatever I had seen, Miles and Flora saw MORE—things terrible and unguessable and that sprang from dreadful passages of intercourse in the past. Such things naturally left on the surface, for the time, a chill which we vociferously denied that we felt; and we had, all three, with repetition, got into such splendid training that we went, each time, almost automatically, to mark the close of the incident, through the very same movements. It was striking of the children, at all events, to kiss me inveterately with a kind of wild irrelevance and never to fail—one or the other—of the precious question that had helped us through many a peril. "When do you think he WILL come? Don't you think we OUGHT to write?"—there was nothing like that inquiry, we found by experience, for carrying off an awkwardness. "He" of course was their uncle in Harley Street; and we lived in much profusion of theory that he might at any moment arrive to mingle in our circle. It was impossible to have given less encouragement than he had done to such a doctrine, but if we had not had the doctrine to fall back upon we should have deprived each other of some of our finest exhibitions. He never wrote to them—that may have been selfish, but it was a part of the flattery of his trust of me; for the way in which a man pays his highest tribute to a woman is apt to be but by the more festal celebration of one of the sacred laws of his comfort; and I held that I carried out the spirit of the pledge given not to appeal to him when I let my charges understand that their own letters were but charming literary exercises. They were too beautiful to be posted; I kept them myself; I have them all to this hour. This was a rule indeed which only added to the satiric effect of my being plied with the supposition that he might at any moment be among us. It was exactly as if my charges knew how almost more awkward than anything else that might be for me. There appears to me, moreover, as I look back, no note in all this more extraordinary than the mere fact that, in spite of my tension and of their triumph, I never lost patience with them. Adorable they must in truth have been, I now reflect, that I didn't in these days hate them! Would exasperation, however, if relief had longer been postponed, finally have betrayed me? It little matters, for relief arrived. I call it relief, though it was only the relief that a snap brings to a strain or the burst of a thunderstorm to a day of suffocation. It was at least change, and it came with a rush.

XIV

Walking to church a certain Sunday morning, I had little Miles at my side and his sister, in advance of us and at Mrs. Grose's, well in sight. It was a crisp, clear day, the first of its order for some time; the night had brought a touch of frost, and the autumn air, bright and sharp, made the church bells almost gay. It was an odd accident of thought that I should have happened at such a moment to be particularly and very gratefully struck with the obedience of my little charges. Why did they never resent my inexorable, my perpetual society? Something or other had brought nearer home to me that I had all but pinned the boy to my shawl and that, in the way our companions were marshaled before me, I might have appeared to provide against some danger of rebellion. I was like a gaoler with an eye to possible surprises and escapes. But all this belonged—I mean their magnificent little surrender—just to the special array of the facts that were most abysmal. Turned out for Sunday by his uncle's tailor, who had had a free hand and a notion of pretty waistcoats and of his grand little air, Miles's whole title to independence, the rights of his sex and situation, were so stamped upon him that if he had suddenly struck for freedom I should have had nothing to say. I was by the strangest of chances wondering how I should meet him when the revolution unmistakably occurred. I call it a revolution because I now see how, with the word he spoke, the curtain rose on the last act of my dreadful drama, and the catastrophe was precipitated. "Look here, my dear, you know," he charmingly said, "when in the world, please, am I going back to school?"

Transcribed here the speech sounds harmless enough, particularly as uttered in the sweet, high, casual pipe with which, at all interlocutors, but above all at his eternal governess, he threw off intonations as if he were tossing roses. There was something in them that always made one "catch," and I caught, at any rate, now so effectually that I stopped as short as if one of the trees of the park had fallen across the road. There was something new, on the spot, between us, and he was perfectly aware that I recognized it, though, to enable me to do so, he had no need to look a whit less candid and charming than usual. I could feel in him how he already, from my at first finding nothing to reply, perceived the advantage he had gained. I was so slow to find anything that he had plenty of time, after a minute, to continue with his suggestive but inconclusive smile: "You know, my dear, that for a fellow to be with a lady ALWAYS—!" His "my dear" was constantly on his lips for me, and nothing could have expressed more the exact shade of the sentiment with which I desired to inspire my pupils than its fond familiarity. It was so respectfully easy.

But, oh, how I felt that at present I must pick my own phrases! I remember that, to gain time, I tried to laugh, and I seemed to see in the beautiful face with which he watched me how ugly and queer I looked. "And always with the same lady?" I returned.

He neither blanched nor winked. The whole thing was virtually out between us. "Ah, of course, she's a jolly, 'perfect' lady; but, after all, I'm a fellow, don't you see? that's—well, getting on."

I lingered there with him an instant ever so kindly. "Yes, you're getting on." Oh, but I felt helpless!

I have kept to this day the heartbreaking little idea of how he seemed to know that and to play with it. "And you can't say I've not been awfully good, can you?"

I laid my hand on his shoulder, for, though I felt how much better it would have been to walk on, I was not yet quite able. "No, I can't say that, Miles."

"Except just that one night, you know—!"

"That one night?" I couldn't look as straight as he.

"Why, when I went down—went out of the house."

"Oh, yes. But I forget what you did it for."

"You forget?"—he spoke with the sweet extravagance of childish reproach. "Why, it was to show you I could!"

"Oh, yes, you could."

"And I can again."

I felt that I might, perhaps, after all, succeed in keeping my wits about me. "Certainly. But you won't."

"No, not THAT again. It was nothing."

"It was nothing," I said. "But we must go on."

He resumed our walk with me, passing his hand into my arm. "Then when AM I going back?"

I wore, in turning it over, my most responsible air. "Were you very happy at school?"

He just considered. "Oh, I'm happy enough anywhere!"

"Well, then," I quavered, "if you're just as happy here—!"

"Ah, but that isn't everything! Of course YOU know a lot—"

"But you hint that you know almost as much?" I risked as he paused.

"Not half I want to!" Miles honestly professed. "But it isn't so much that."

"What is it, then?"

"Well—I want to see more life."

"I see; I see." We had arrived within sight of the church and of various persons, including several of the household of Bly, on their way to it and clustered about the door to see us go in. I quickened our step; I wanted to get there before the question between us opened up much further; I reflected hungrily that, for more than an hour, he would have to be silent; and I thought with envy of the comparative dusk of the pew and of the almost spiritual help of the hassock on which I might bend my knees. I seemed literally to be running a race with some confusion to which he was about to reduce me, but I felt that he had got in first when, before we had even entered the churchyard, he threw out—

"I want my own sort!"

It literally made me bound forward. "There are not many of your own sort, Miles!" I laughed. "Unless perhaps dear little Flora!"

"You really compare me to a baby girl?"

This found me singularly weak. "Don't you, then, LOVE our sweet Flora?"

"If I didn't—and you, too; if I didn't—!" he repeated as if retreating for a jump, yet leaving his thought so unfinished that, after we had come into the gate, another stop, which he imposed on me by the pressure of his arm, had become inevitable. Mrs. Grose and Flora had passed into the church, the other worshippers had followed, and we were, for the minute, alone among the old, thick graves. We had paused, on the path from the gate, by a low, oblong, tablelike tomb.

"Yes, if you didn't—?"

He looked, while I waited, at the graves. "Well, you know what!" But he didn't move, and he presently produced something that made me drop straight down on the stone slab, as if suddenly to rest. "Does my uncle think what YOU think?"

I markedly rested. "How do you know what I think?"

"Ah, well, of course I don't; for it strikes me you never tell me. But I mean does HE know?"

"Know what, Miles?"

"Why, the way I'm going on."

I perceived quickly enough that I could make, to this inquiry, no answer that would not involve something of a sacrifice of my employer. Yet it appeared to me that we were all, at Bly, sufficiently sacrificed to make that venial. "I don't think your uncle much cares."

Miles, on this, stood looking at me. "Then don't you think he can be made to?"

"In what way?"

"Why, by his coming down."

"But who'll get him to come down?"

"*I* will!" the boy said with extraordinary brightness and emphasis. He gave me another look charged with that expression and then marched off alone into church.

XV

The business was practically settled from the moment I never followed him. It was a pitiful surrender to agitation, but my being aware of this had somehow no power to restore me. I only sat there on my tomb and read into what my little friend had said to me the fullness of its meaning; by the time I had grasped the whole of which I had also embraced, for absence, the pretext that I was ashamed to offer my pupils and the rest of the congregation such an example of delay. What I said to myself above all was that Miles had got something out of me and that the proof of it, for him, would be just this awkward collapse. He had got out of me that there was something I was much afraid of and that he should probably be able to make use of my fear to gain, for his own purpose, more freedom. My fear was of having to deal with the intolerable question of the grounds of his dismissal from school, for that was really but the question of the horrors gathered behind. That his uncle should arrive to treat with me of these things was a solution that, strictly speaking, I ought now to have desired to bring on; but I could so little face the ugliness and the pain of it that I simply procrastinated and lived from hand to mouth. The boy, to my deep discomposure, was immensely in the right, was in a position to say to me: "Either you clear up with my guardian the mystery of this interruption of my studies, or you cease to expect me to lead with you a life that's so unnatural for a boy." What was so unnatural for the particular boy I was concerned with was this sudden revelation of a consciousness and a plan.

That was what really overcame me, what prevented my going in. I walked round the church, hesitating, hovering; I reflected that I had already, with him, hurt myself beyond repair. Therefore I could patch up nothing, and it was too extreme an effort to squeeze beside him into the pew: he would be so much more sure than ever to pass his arm into mine and make me sit there for an hour in close, silent contact with his commentary on our talk. For the first minute since his arrival I wanted to get away from him. As I paused beneath the high east window and listened to the sounds of worship, I was taken with an impulse that might master me, I felt, completely should I give it the least encouragement. I might easily put an end to my predicament by getting away altogether. Here was my chance; there was no one to stop me; I could give the whole thing up—turn my back and retreat. It was only a question of hurrying again, for a few preparations, to the house which the attendance at church of so many of the servants would practically have left unoccupied. No one, in short, could blame me if I should just drive desperately off. What was it to get away if I got away only till dinner? That would be in a couple of hours, at the end of which—I had the acute prevision—my little pupils would play at innocent wonder about my nonappearance in their train.

"What DID you do, you naughty, bad thing? Why in the world, to worry us so—and take our thoughts off, too, don't you know?—did you desert us at the very door?" I couldn't meet such questions nor, as they asked them, their false little lovely eyes; yet it was all so exactly what I should have to meet that, as the prospect grew sharp to me, I at last let myself go.

I got, so far as the immediate moment was concerned, away; I came straight out of the churchyard and, thinking hard, retraced my steps through the park. It seemed to me that by the time I reached the house I had made up my mind I would fly. The Sunday stillness both of the approaches and of the interior, in which I met no one, fairly excited me with a sense of opportunity. Were I to get off quickly, this way, I should get off without a scene, without a word. My quickness would have to be remarkable, however, and the question of a conveyance was the great one to settle. Tormented, in the hall, with difficulties and obstacles, I remember sinking down at the foot of the staircase—suddenly collapsing there on the lowest step and then, with a revulsion, recalling that it was exactly where more than a month before, in the darkness of night and just so bowed with evil things, I had seen the specter of the most horrible of women. At this I was able to straighten myself; I went the rest of the way up; I made, in my bewilderment, for the schoolroom, where there were objects belonging to me that I should have to take. But I opened the door to find again, in a flash, my eyes unsealed. In the presence of what I saw I reeled straight back upon my resistance.

Seated at my own table in clear noonday light I saw a person whom, without my previous experience, I should have taken at the first blush for some housemaid who might have stayed at home to look after the place and who, availing herself of rare relief from observation and of the schoolroom table and my pens, ink, and paper, had applied herself to the considerable effort of a letter to her sweetheart. There was an effort in the way that, while her arms rested on the table, her hands with evident weariness supported her head; but at the moment I took this in I had already become aware that, in spite of my entrance, her attitude strangely persisted. Then it was—with the very act of its announcing itself—that her identity flared up in a change of posture. She rose, not as if she had heard me, but with an indescribable grand melancholy of indifference and detachment, and, within a dozen feet of me, stood there as my vile predecessor. Dishonored and tragic, she was all before me; but even as I fixed and, for memory, secured it, the awful image passed away. Dark as midnight in her black dress, her haggard beauty and her unutterable woe, she had looked at me long enough to appear to say that her right to sit at my table was as good as mine to sit at hers. While these instants lasted, indeed, I had the extraordinary chill of feeling that it was I who was the intruder. It was as a wild protest against it that, actually addressing her—"You terrible, miserable woman!"—I heard myself break into a sound that, by the open door, rang through the long passage and the empty house. She looked at me as if she heard me, but I had recovered myself and cleared the air. There was nothing in the room the next minute but the sunshine and a sense that I must stay.

XVI

I had so perfectly expected that the return of my pupils would be marked by a demonstration that I was freshly upset at having to take into account that they were dumb about my absence. Instead of gaily denouncing and caressing me, they made no allusion to my having failed them, and I was left, for the time, on perceiving that she too said nothing, to study Mrs. Grose's odd face. I did this to such purpose that I made sure they had in some way bribed her to silence; a silence that, however, I would engage to break down on the first private opportunity. This opportunity came before tea: I secured five minutes with her in the housekeeper's room, where, in the twilight, amid a smell of lately baked bread, but with the place all swept and garnished, I found her sitting in pained placidity before the fire. So I see her still, so I see her best: facing the flame from her straight chair in the dusky, shining room, a large clean image of the "put away"—of drawers closed and locked and rest without a remedy.

"Oh, yes, they asked me to say nothing; and to please them—so long as they were there—of course I promised. But what had happened to you?"

"I only went with you for the walk," I said. "I had then to come back to meet a friend."

She showed her surprise. "A friend—YOU?"

"Oh, yes, I have a couple!" I laughed. "But did the children give you a reason?"

"For not alluding to your leaving us? Yes; they said you would like it better. Do you like it better?"

My face had made her rueful. "No, I like it worse!" But after an instant I added: "Did they say why I should like it better?"

"No; Master Miles only said, 'We must do nothing but what she likes!'"

"I wish indeed he would. And what did Flora say?"

"Miss Flora was too sweet. She said, 'Oh, of course, of course!'—and I said the same."

I thought a moment. "You were too sweet, too—I can hear you all. But nonetheless, between Miles and me, it's now all out."

"All out?" My companion stared. "But what, miss?"

"Everything. It doesn't matter. I've made up my mind. I came home, my dear," I went on, "for a talk with Miss Jessel."

I had by this time formed the habit of having Mrs. Grose literally well in hand in advance of my sounding that note; so that even now, as she bravely blinked under the signal of my word, I could keep her comparatively firm. "A talk! Do you mean she spoke?"

"It came to that. I found her, on my return, in the schoolroom."

"And what did she say?" I can hear the good woman still, and the candor of her stupefaction.

"That she suffers the torments—!"

It was this, of a truth, that made her, as she filled out my picture, gape. "Do you mean," she faltered, "—of the lost?"

"Of the lost. Of the damned. And that's why, to share them-" I faltered myself with the horror of it.

But my companion, with less imagination, kept me up. "To share them—?"

"She wants Flora." Mrs. Grose might, as I gave it to her, fairly have fallen away from me had I not been prepared. I still held her there, to show I was. "As I've told you, however, it doesn't matter."

"Because you've made up your mind? But to what?"

"To everything."

"And what do you call 'everything'?"

"Why, sending for their uncle."

"Oh, miss, in pity do," my friend broke out. "ah, but I will, I WILL! I see it's the only way. What's 'out,' as I told you, with Miles is that if he thinks I'm afraid to—and has ideas of what he gains by that—he shall see he's mistaken. Yes, yes; his uncle shall have it here from me on the spot (and before the boy himself, if necessary) that if I'm to be reproached with having done nothing again about more school—"

"Yes, miss—" my companion pressed me.

"Well, there's that awful reason."

There were now clearly so many of these for my poor colleague that she was excusable for being vague. "But—a—which?"

"Why, the letter from his old place."

"You'll show it to the master?"

"I ought to have done so on the instant."

"Oh, no!" said Mrs. Grose with decision.

"I'll put it before him," I went on inexorably, "that I can't undertake to work the question on behalf of a child who has been expelled—"

"For we've never in the least known what!" Mrs. Grose declared.

"For wickedness. For what else—when he's so clever and beautiful and perfect? Is he stupid? Is he untidy? Is he infirm? Is he ill-natured? He's exquisite—so it can be only THAT; and that would open up the whole thing. After all," I said, "it's their uncle's fault. If he left here such people—!"

"He didn't really in the least know them. The fault's mine." She had turned quite pale.

"Well, you shan't suffer," I answered.

"The children shan't!" she emphatically returned.

I was silent awhile; we looked at each other. "Then what am I to tell him?"

"You needn't tell him anything. *I*'ll tell him."

I measured this. "Do you mean you'll write—?" Remembering she couldn't, I caught myself up. "How do you communicate?"

"I tell the bailiff. HE writes."

"And should you like him to write our story?"

My question had a sarcastic force that I had not fully intended, and it made her, after a moment, inconsequently break down. The tears were again in her eyes. "Ah, miss, YOU write!"

"Well—tonight," I at last answered; and on this we separated.

XVII

I went so far, in the evening, as to make a beginning. The weather had changed back, a great wind was abroad, and beneath the lamp, in my room, with Flora at peace beside me, I sat for a long time before a blank sheet of paper and listened to the lash of the rain and the batter of the gusts. Finally I went out, taking a candle; I crossed the passage and listened a minute at Miles's door. What, under my endless obsession, I had been impelled to listen for was some betrayal of his not being at rest, and I presently caught one, but not in the form I had expected. His voice tinkled out. "I say, you there—come in." It was a gaiety in the gloom!

I went in with my light and found him, in bed, very wide awake, but very much at his ease. "Well, what are YOU up to?" he asked with a grace of sociability in which it occurred to me that Mrs. Grose, had she been present, might have looked in vain for proof that anything was "out."

I stood over him with my candle. "How did you know I was there?"

"Why, of course I heard you. Did you fancy you made no noise? You're like a troop of cavalry!" he beautifully laughed.

"Then you weren't asleep?"

"Not much! I lie awake and think."

I had put my candle, designedly, a short way off, and then, as he held out his friendly old hand to me, had sat down on the edge of his bed. "What is it," I asked, "that you think of?"

"What in the world, my dear, but YOU?"

"Ah, the pride I take in your appreciation doesn't insist on that! I had so far rather you slept."

"Well, I think also, you know, of this queer business of ours."

I marked the coolness of his firm little hand. "Of what queer business, Miles?"

"Why, the way you bring me up. And all the rest!"

I fairly held my breath a minute, and even from my glimmering taper there was light enough to show how he smiled up at me from his pillow. "What do you mean by all the rest?"

"Oh, you know, you know!"

I could say nothing for a minute, though I felt, as I held his hand and our eyes continued to meet, that my silence had all the air of admitting his charge and that nothing in the whole world of reality was perhaps at that moment so fabulous as our actual relation. "Certainly you shall go back to school," I said, "if it be that that troubles you. But not to the old place—we must find another, a better. How could I know it did trouble you, this question, when you never told me so, never spoke of it at all?" His clear, listening face, framed in its smooth whiteness, made him for the minute as appealing as some wistful patient in a children's hospital; and I would have given, as the resemblance came to me, all I possessed on earth really to be the nurse or the sister of charity who might have helped to cure him. Well, even as it was, I perhaps might help! "Do you know you've never said a word to me about your school—I mean the old one; never mentioned it in any way?"

He seemed to wonder; he smiled with the same loveliness. But he clearly gained time; he waited, he called for guidance. "Haven't I?" It wasn't for ME to help him—it was for the thing I had met!

Something in his tone and the expression of his face, as I got this from him, set my heart aching with such a pang as it had never yet known; so unutterably touching was it to see his little brain puzzled and his little resources taxed to play, under the spell laid on him, a part of innocence and consistency. "No, never—from the hour you came back. You've never mentioned to me one of your masters, one of your comrades, nor the least little thing that ever happened to you at school. Never, little Miles—no, never—have you given me an inkling of anything that MAY have happened there. Therefore you can fancy how much I'm in the dark. Until you came out, that way, this morning, you had, since the first hour I saw you, scarce even made a reference to anything in your previous life. You seemed so perfectly to accept the present." It was extraordinary how my absolute conviction of his secret precocity (or whatever I might call the poison of an influence that I dared but half to phrase) made him, in spite of the faint breath of his inward trouble, appear as accessible as an older person—imposed him almost as an intellectual equal. "I thought you wanted to go on as you are."

It struck me that at this he just faintly colored. He gave, at any rate, like a convalescent slightly fatigued, a languid shake of his head. "I don't—I don't. I want to get away."

"You're tired of Bly?"

"Oh, no, I like Bly."

"Well, then—?"

"Oh, YOU know what a boy wants!"

I felt that I didn't know so well as Miles, and I took temporary refuge. "You want to go to your uncle?"

Again, at this, with his sweet ironic face, he made a movement on the pillow. "Ah, you can't get off with that!"

I was silent a little, and it was I, now, I think, who changed color. "My dear, I don't want to get off!"

"You can't, even if you do. You can't, you can't!"—he lay beautifully staring. "My uncle must come down, and you must completely settle things."

"If we do," I returned with some spirit, "you may be sure it will be to take you quite away."

"Well, don't you understand that that's exactly what I'm working for? You'll have to tell him—about the way you've let it all drop: you'll have to tell him a tremendous lot!"

The exultation with which he uttered this helped me somehow, for the instant, to meet him rather more. "And how much will YOU, Miles, have to tell him? There are things he'll ask you!"

He turned it over. "Very likely. But what things?"

"The things you've never told me. To make up his mind what to do with you. He can't send you back—"

"Oh, I don't want to go back!" he broke in. "I want a new field."

He said it with admirable serenity, with positive unimpeachable gaiety; and doubtless it was that very note that most evoked for me the poignancy, the unnatural childish tragedy, of his probable reappearance at the end of three months with all this bravado and still more dishonor. It overwhelmed me now that I should never be able to bear that, and it made me let myself go. I threw myself upon him and in the tenderness of my pity I embraced him. "Dear little Miles, dear little Miles—!"

My face was close to his, and he let me kiss him, simply taking it with indulgent good humor. "Well, old lady?"

"Is there nothing—nothing at all that you want to tell me?"

He turned off a little, facing round toward the wall and holding up his hand to look at as one had seen sick children look. "I've told you—I told you this morning."

Oh, I was sorry for him! "That you just want me not to worry you?"

He looked round at me now, as if in recognition of my understanding him; then ever so gently, "To let me alone," he replied.

There was even a singular little dignity in it, something that made me release him, yet, when I had slowly risen, linger beside him. God knows I never wished to harass him, but I felt that merely, at this, to turn my back on him was to abandon or, to put it more truly, to lose him. "I've just begun a letter to your uncle," I said.

"Well, then, finish it!"

I waited a minute. "What happened before?"

He gazed up at me again. "Before what?"

"Before you came back. And before you went away."

For some time he was silent, but he continued to meet my eyes. "What happened?"

It made me, the sound of the words, in which it seemed to me that I caught for the very first time a small faint quaver of consenting consciousness—it made me drop on my knees beside the bed and seize once more the chance of possessing him. "Dear little Miles, dear little Miles, if you KNEW how I want to help you! It's only that, it's nothing but that, and I'd rather die than give you a pain or do you a wrong—I'd rather die than hurt a hair of you. Dear little Miles"—oh, I brought it out now even if I SHOULD go too far—"I just want you to help me to save you!" But I knew in a moment after this that I had gone too far. The answer to my appeal was instantaneous, but it came in the form of an extraordinary blast and chill, a gust of frozen air, and a shake of the room as great as if, in the wild wind, the casement had crashed in. The boy gave a loud, high shriek, which, lost in the rest of the shock of sound, might have seemed, indistinctly, though I was so close to him, a note either of jubilation or of terror. I jumped to my feet again and was conscious of darkness. So for a moment we remained, while I stared about me and saw that the drawn curtains were unstirred and the window tight. "Why, the candle's out!" I then cried.

"It was I who blew it, dear!" said Miles.

XVIII

The next day, after lessons, Mrs. Grose found a moment to say to me quietly: "Have you written, miss?"

"Yes—I've written." But I didn't add—for the hour—that my letter, sealed and directed, was still in my pocket. There would be time enough to send it before the messenger should go to the village. Meanwhile there had been, on the part of my pupils, no more brilliant, more exemplary morning. It was exactly as if they had both had at heart to gloss over any recent little friction. They performed the dizziest feats of arithmetic, soaring quite out of MY feeble range, and perpetrated, in higher spirits than ever, geographical and historical jokes. It was conspicuous of course in Miles in particular that he appeared to wish to show how easily he could let me down. This child, to my memory, really lives in a setting of beauty and misery that no words can translate; there was a distinction all his own in every impulse he revealed; never was a small natural creature, to the uninitiated eye all frankness and freedom, a more ingenious, a more extraordinary little gentleman. I had perpetually to guard against the wonder of contemplation into which my initiated view betrayed me; to check the irrelevant gaze and discouraged sigh in which I constantly both attacked and renounced the enigma of what such a little gentleman could have done that deserved a penalty. Say that, by the dark prodigy I knew, the imagination of all evil HAD been opened up to him: all the justice within me ached for the proof that it could ever have flowered into an act.

He had never, at any rate, been such a little gentleman as when, after our early dinner on this dreadful day, he came round to me and asked if I shouldn't like him, for half an hour, to play to me. David playing to Saul could never have shown a finer sense of the occasion. It was literally a charming exhibition of tact, of magnanimity, and quite tantamount to his saying outright: "The true knights we love to read about never push an advantage too far. I know what you mean now: you mean that—to be let alone yourself and not followed up—you'll cease to worry and spy upon me, won't keep me so close to you, will let me go and come. Well, I 'come,' you see—but I don't go! There'll be plenty of time for that. I do really delight in your society, and I only want to show you that I contended for a principle." It may be imagined whether I resisted this appeal or failed to accompany him again, hand in hand, to the schoolroom. He sat down at the old piano and played as he had never played; and if there are those who think he had better have been kicking a football I can only say that I wholly agree with them. For at the end of a time that under his influence I had quite ceased to measure, I started up with a strange sense of having literally slept at my post. It was after luncheon, and by the schoolroom fire, and yet I hadn't really, in the least, slept: I had only done something much worse—I had forgotten. Where, all this time, was Flora? When I put the question to Miles, he played on a minute before answering and then could only say: "Why, my dear, how do *I* know?"—breaking moreover into a happy laugh which, immediately after, as if it were a vocal accompaniment, he prolonged into incoherent, extravagant song.

I went straight to my room, but his sister was not there; then, before going downstairs, I looked into several others. As she was nowhere about she would surely be with Mrs. Grose, whom, in the comfort of that theory, I accordingly proceeded in quest of. I found her where I had found her the evening before, but she met my quick challenge with blank, scared ignorance. She had only supposed that, after the repast, I had carried off both the children; as to which she was quite in her right, for it was the very first time I had allowed the little girl out of my sight without some special provision. Of course now indeed she might be with the maids, so that the immediate thing was to look for her without an air of alarm. This we promptly arranged between us; but when, ten minutes later and in pursuance of our arrangement, we met in the hall, it was only to report on either side that after guarded inquiries we had altogether failed to trace her. For a minute there, apart from observation, we exchanged mute alarms, and I could feel with what high interest my friend returned me all those I had from the first given her.

"She'll be above," she presently said—"in one of the rooms you haven't searched."

"No; she's at a distance." I had made up my mind. "She has gone out."

Mrs. Grose stared. "Without a hat?"

I naturally also looked volumes. "Isn't that woman always without one?"

"She's with HER?"

"She's with HER!" I declared. "We must find them."

My hand was on my friend's arm, but she failed for the moment, confronted with such an account of the matter, to respond to my pressure. She communed, on the contrary, on the spot, with her uneasiness. "And where's Master Miles?"

"Oh, HE'S with Quint. They're in the schoolroom."

"Lord, miss!" My view, I was myself aware—and therefore I suppose my tone—had never yet reached so calm an assurance.

"The trick's played," I went on; "they've successfully worked their plan. He found the most divine little way to keep me quiet while she went off."

"'Divine'?" Mrs. Grose bewilderedly echoed.

"Infernal, then!" I almost cheerfully rejoined. "He has provided for himself as well. But come!"

She had helplessly gloomed at the upper regions. "You leave him—?"

"So long with Quint? Yes—I don't mind that now."

She always ended, at these moments, by getting possession of my hand, and in this manner she could at present still stay me. But after gasping an instant at my sudden resignation, "Because of your letter?" she eagerly brought out.

I quickly, by way of answer, felt for my letter, drew it forth, held it up, and then, freeing myself, went and laid it on the great hall table. "Luke will take it," I said as I came back. I reached the house door and opened it; I was already on the steps.

My companion still demurred: the storm of the night and the early morning had dropped, but the afternoon was damp and gray. I came down to the drive while she stood in the doorway. "You go with nothing on?"

"What do I care when the child has nothing? I can't wait to dress," I cried, "and if you must do so, I leave you. Try meanwhile, yourself, upstairs."

"With THEM?" Oh, on this, the poor woman promptly joined me!

XIX

We went straight to the lake, as it was called at Bly, and I daresay rightly called, though I reflect that it may in fact have been a sheet of water less remarkable than it appeared to my untraveled eyes. My acquaintance with sheets of water was small, and the pool of Bly, at all events on the few occasions of my consenting, under the protection of my pupils, to affront its surface in the old flat-bottomed boat moored there for our use, had impressed me both with its extent and its agitation. The usual place of embarkation was half a mile from the house, but I had an intimate conviction that, wherever Flora might be, she was not near home. She had not given me the slip for any small adventure, and, since the day of the very great one that I had shared with her by the pond, I had been aware, in our walks, of the quarter to which she most inclined. This was why I had now given to Mrs. Grose's steps so marked a direction—a direction that made her, when she perceived it, oppose a resistance that showed me she was freshly mystified. "You're going to the water, Miss?—you think she's IN—?"

"She may be, though the depth is, I believe, nowhere very great. But what I judge most likely is that she's on the spot from which, the other day, we saw together what I told you."

"When she pretended not to see—?"

"With that astounding self-possession? I've always been sure she wanted to go back alone. And now her brother has managed it for her."

Mrs. Grose still stood where she had stopped. "You suppose they really TALK of them?"

"I could meet this with a confidence! They say things that, if we heard them, would simply appall us."

"And if she IS there—"

"Yes?"

"Then Miss Jessel is?"

"Beyond a doubt. You shall see."

"Oh, thank you!" my friend cried, planted so firm that, taking it in, I went straight on without her. By the time I reached the pool, however, she was close behind me, and I knew that, whatever, to her apprehension, might befall me, the exposure of my society struck her as her least danger. She exhaled a moan of relief as we at last came in sight of the greater part of the water without a sight of the child. There was no trace of Flora on that nearer side of the bank where my observation of her had been most startling, and none on the opposite edge, where, save for a margin of some twenty yards, a thick copse came down to the water. The pond, oblong in shape, had a width so scant compared to its length that, with its ends out of view, it might have been taken for a scant river. We looked at the empty expanse, and then I felt the suggestion of my friend's eyes. I knew what she meant and I replied with a negative headshake.

"No, no; wait! She has taken the boat."

My companion stared at the vacant mooring place and then again across the lake. "Then where is it?"

"Our not seeing it is the strongest of proofs. She has used it to go over, and then has managed to hide it."

"All alone—that child?"

"She's not alone, and at such times she's not a child: she's an old, old woman." I scanned all the visible shore while Mrs. Grose took again, into the queer element I offered her, one of her plunges of submission; then I pointed out that the boat might perfectly be in a small refuge formed by one of the recesses of the pool, an indentation masked, for the hither side, by a projection of the bank and by a clump of trees growing close to the water.

"But if the boat's there, where on earth's SHE?" my colleague anxiously asked.

"That's exactly what we must learn." And I started to walk further.

"By going all the way round?"

"Certainly, far as it is. It will take us but ten minutes, but it's far enough to have made the child prefer not to walk. She went straight over."

"Laws!" cried my friend again; the chain of my logic was ever too much for her. It dragged her at my heels even now, and when we had got halfway round—a devious, tiresome process, on ground much broken and by a path choked with overgrowth—I paused to give her breath. I sustained her with a grateful arm, assuring her that she might hugely help me; and this started us afresh, so that in the course of but few minutes more we reached a point from which we found the boat to be where I had supposed it. It had been intentionally left as much as possible out of sight and was tied to one of the stakes of a fence that came, just there, down to the brink and that had been an assistance to disembarking. I recognized, as I looked at the pair of short, thick oars, quite safely drawn up, the prodigious character of the feat for a little girl; but I had lived, by this time, too long among wonders and had panted to too many livelier measures. There was a gate in the fence, through which we passed, and that brought us, after a trifling interval, more into the open. Then, "There she is!" we both exclaimed at once.

Flora, a short way off, stood before us on the grass and smiled as if her performance was now complete. The next thing she did, however, was to stoop straight down and pluck—quite as if it were all she was there for—a big, ugly spray of withered fern. I instantly became sure she had just come out of the copse. She waited for us, not herself taking a step, and I was conscious of the rare solemnity with which we presently approached her. She smiled and smiled, and we met; but it was all done in a silence by this time flagrantly ominous. Mrs. Grose was the first to break the spell: she threw herself on her knees and, drawing the child to her breast, clasped in a long embrace the little tender, yielding body. While this dumb convulsion lasted I could only watch it—which I did the more intently when I saw Flora's face peep at me over our companion's shoulder. It was serious now—the flicker had left it; but it strengthened the pang with which I at that moment envied Mrs. Grose the simplicity of HER relation. Still, all this while, nothing more passed between us save that Flora had let her foolish fern again drop to the ground. What she and I had virtually said to each other was that pretexts were useless now. When Mrs. Grose finally got up she kept the child's hand, so that the two were still before me; and the singular reticence of our communion was even more marked in the frank look she launched me. "I'll be hanged," it said, "if *I*'ll speak!"

It was Flora who, gazing all over me in candid wonder, was the first. She was struck with our bareheaded aspect. "Why, where are your things?"

"Where yours are, my dear!" I promptly returned.

She had already got back her gaiety, and appeared to take this as an answer quite sufficient. "And where's Miles?" she went on.

There was something in the small valor of it that quite finished me: these three words from her were, in a flash like the glitter of a drawn blade, the jostle of the cup that my hand, for weeks and weeks, had held high and full to the brim that now, even before speaking, I felt overflow in a deluge. "I'll tell you if you'll tell ME—" I heard myself say, then heard the tremor in which it broke.

"Well, what?"

Mrs. Grose's suspense blazed at me, but it was too late now, and I brought the thing out handsomely. "Where, my pet, is Miss Jessel?"

XX

Just as in the churchyard with Miles, the whole thing was upon us. Much as I had made of the fact that this name had never once, between us, been sounded, the quick, smitten glare with which the child's face now received it fairly likened my breach of the silence to the smash of a pane of glass. It added to the interposing cry, as if to stay the blow, that Mrs. Grose, at the same instant, uttered over my violence—the shriek of a creature scared, or rather wounded, which, in turn, within a few seconds, was completed by a gasp of my own. I seized my colleague's arm. "She's there, she's there!"

Miss Jessel stood before us on the opposite bank exactly as she had stood the other time, and I remember, strangely, as the first feeling now produced in me, my thrill of joy at having brought on a proof. She was there, and I was justified; she was there, and I was neither cruel nor mad. She was there for poor scared Mrs. Grose, but she was there most for Flora; and no moment of my monstrous time was perhaps so extraordinary as that in which I consciously threw out to her—with the sense that, pale and ravenous demon as she was, she would catch and understand it—an inarticulate message of gratitude. She rose erect on the spot my friend and I had lately quitted, and there was not, in all the long reach of her desire, an inch of her evil that fell short. This first vividness of vision and emotion were things of a few seconds, during which Mrs. Grose's dazed blink across to where I pointed struck me as a sovereign sign that she too at last saw, just as it carried my own eyes precipitately to the child. The revelation then of the manner in which Flora was affected startled me, in truth, far more than it would have done to find her also merely agitated, for direct dismay was of course not what I had expected. Prepared and on her guard as our pursuit had actually made her, she would repress every betrayal; and I was therefore shaken, on the spot, by my first glimpse of the particular one for which I had not allowed. To see her, without a convulsion of her small pink face, not even feign to glance in the direction of the prodigy I announced, but only, instead of that, turn at ME an expression of hard, still gravity, an expression absolutely new and unprecedented and that appeared to read and accuse and judge me—this was a stroke that somehow converted the little girl herself into the very presence that could make me quail. I quailed even though my certitude that she thoroughly saw was never greater than at that instant, and in the immediate need to defend myself I called it passionately to witness. "She's there, you little unhappy thing—there, there, THERE, and you see her as well as you see me!" I had said shortly before to Mrs. Grose that she was not at these times a child, but an old, old woman, and that description of her could not have been more strikingly confirmed than in the way in which, for all answer to this, she simply showed me, without a concession, an admission, of her eyes, a countenance of deeper and deeper, of indeed suddenly quite fixed, reprobation. I was by this time—if I can put the whole thing at all together—more appalled at what I may properly call her manner than at anything else, though it was simultaneously with this that I became aware of having Mrs. Grose also, and very formidably, to reckon with. My elder companion, the next moment, at any rate, blotted out everything but her own flushed face and her loud, shocked protest, a burst of high disapproval. "What a dreadful turn, to be sure, miss! Where on earth do you see anything?"

I could only grasp her more quickly yet, for even while she spoke the hideous plain presence stood undimmed and undaunted. It had already lasted a minute, and it lasted while I continued, seizing my colleague, quite thrusting her at it and presenting her to it, to insist with my pointing hand. "You don't see her exactly as WE see?—you mean to say you don't now—NOW? She's as big as a blazing fire! Only look, dearest woman, LOOK—!" She looked, even as I did, and gave me, with her deep groan of negation, repulsion, compassion—the mixture with her pity of her relief at her exemption—a sense, touching to me even then, that she would have backed me up if she could. I might well have needed that, for with this hard blow of the proof that her eyes were hopelessly sealed I felt my own situation horribly crumble, I felt—I saw—my livid predecessor press, from her position, on my defeat, and I was conscious, more than all, of what I should have from this instant to deal with in the astounding little attitude of Flora. Into this attitude Mrs. Grose immediately and violently entered, breaking, even while there pierced through my sense of ruin a prodigious private triumph, into breathless reassurance.

"She isn't there, little lady, and nobody's there—and you never see nothing, my sweet! How can poor Miss Jessel—when poor Miss Jessel's dead and buried? WE know, don't we, love?"—and she appealed, blundering in, to the child. "It's all a mere mistake and a worry and a joke—and we'll go home as fast as we can!"

Our companion, on this, had responded with a strange, quick primness of propriety, and they were again, with Mrs. Grose on her feet, united, as it were, in pained opposition to me. Flora continued to fix me with her small mask of reprobation, and even at that minute I prayed God to forgive me for seeming to see that, as she stood there holding tight to our friend's dress, her incomparable childish beauty had suddenly failed, had quite vanished. I've said it already—she was literally, she was hideously, hard; she had turned common and almost ugly. "I don't know what you mean. I see nobody. I see nothing. I never HAVE. I think you're cruel. I don't like you!" Then, after this deliverance, which might have been that of a vulgarly pert little girl in the street, she hugged Mrs. Grose more closely and buried in her skirts the dreadful little face. In this position she produced an almost furious wail. "Take me away, take me away—oh, take me away from HER!"

"From ME?" I panted.

"From you—from you!" she cried.

Even Mrs. Grose looked across at me dismayed, while I had nothing to do but communicate again with the figure that, on the opposite bank, without a movement, as rigidly still as if catching, beyond the interval, our voices, was as vividly there for my disaster as it was not there for my service. The wretched child had spoken exactly as if she had got from some outside source each of her stabbing little words, and I could therefore, in the full despair of all I had to accept, but sadly shake my head at her. "If I had ever doubted, all my doubt would at present have gone. I've been living with the miserable truth, and now it has only too much closed round me. Of course I've lost you: I've interfered, and you've seen—under HER dictation"—with which I faced, over the pool again, our infernal witness—"the easy and perfect way to meet it. I've done my best, but I've lost you. Goodbye." For Mrs. Grose I had an imperative, an almost frantic "Go, go!" before which, in infinite distress, but mutely possessed of the little girl and clearly convinced, in spite of her blindness, that something awful had occurred and some collapse engulfed us, she retreated, by the way we had come, as fast as she could move.

Of what first happened when I was left alone I had no subsequent memory. I only knew that at the end of, I suppose, a quarter of an hour, an odorous dampness and roughness, chilling and piercing my trouble, had made me understand that I must have thrown myself, on my face, on the ground and given way to a wildness of grief. I must have lain there long and cried and sobbed, for when I raised my head the day was almost done. I got up and looked a moment, through the twilight, at the gray pool and its blank, haunted edge, and then I took, back to the house, my dreary and difficult course. When I reached the gate in the fence the boat, to my surprise, was gone, so that I had a fresh reflection to make on Flora's extraordinary command of the situation. She passed that night, by the most tacit, and I should add, were not the word so grotesque a false note, the happiest of arrangements, with Mrs. Grose. I saw neither of them on my return, but, on the other hand, as by an ambiguous compensation, I saw a great deal of Miles. I saw—I can use no other phrase—so much of him that it was as if it were more than it had ever been. No evening I had passed at Bly had the portentous quality of this one; in spite of which—and in spite also of the deeper depths of consternation that had opened beneath my feet—there was literally, in the ebbing actual, an extraordinarily sweet sadness. On reaching the house I had never so much as looked for the boy; I had simply gone straight to my room to change what I was wearing and to take in, at a glance, much material testimony to Flora's rupture. Her little belongings had all been removed. When later, by the schoolroom fire, I was served with tea by the usual maid, I indulged, on the article of my other pupil, in no inquiry whatever. He had his freedom now—he might have it to the end! Well, he did have it; and it consisted—in part at least—of his coming in at about eight o'clock and sitting down with me in silence. On the removal of the tea things I had blown out the candles and drawn my chair closer: I was conscious of a mortal coldness and felt as if I should never again be warm. So, when he appeared, I was sitting in the glow with my thoughts. He paused a moment by the door as if to look at me; then—as if to share them—came to the other side of the hearth and sank into a chair. We sat there in absolute stillness; yet he wanted, I felt, to be with me.

XXI

Before a new day, in my room, had fully broken, my eyes opened to Mrs. Grose, who had come to my bedside with worse news. Flora was so markedly feverish that an illness was perhaps at hand; she had passed a night of extreme unrest, a night agitated above all by fears that had for their subject not in the least her former, but wholly her present, governess. It was not against the possible re-entrance of Miss Jessel on the scene that she protested—it was conspicuously and passionately against mine. I was promptly on my feet of course, and with an immense deal to ask; the more that my friend had discernibly now girded her loins to meet me once more. This I felt as soon as I had put to her the question of her sense of the child's sincerity as against my own. "She persists in denying to you that she saw, or has ever seen, anything?"

My visitor's trouble, truly, was great. "Ah, miss, it isn't a matter on which I can push her! Yet it isn't either, I must say, as if I much needed to. It has made her, every inch of her, quite old."

"Oh, I see her perfectly from here. She resents, for all the world like some high little personage, the imputation on her truthfulness and, as it were, her respectability. 'Miss Jessel indeed—SHE!' Ah, she's 'respectable,' the chit! The impression she gave me there yesterday was, I assure you, the very strangest of all; it was quite beyond any of the others. I DID put my foot in it! She'll never speak to me again."

Hideous and obscure as it all was, it held Mrs. Grose briefly silent; then she granted my point with a frankness which, I made sure, had more behind it. "I think indeed, miss, she never will. She do have a grand manner about it!"

"And that manner"—I summed it up—"is practically what's the matter with her now!"

Oh, that manner, I could see in my visitor's face, and not a little else besides! "She asks me every three minutes if I think you're coming in."

"I see—I see." I, too, on my side, had so much more than worked it out. "Has she said to you since yesterday—except to repudiate her familiarity with anything so dreadful—a single other word about Miss Jessel?"

"Not one, miss. And of course you know," my friend added, "I took it from her, by the lake, that, just then and there at least, there WAS nobody."

"Rather! and, naturally, you take it from her still."

"I don't contradict her. What else can I do?"

"Nothing in the world! You've the cleverest little person to deal with. They've made them—their two friends, I mean—still cleverer even than nature did; for it was wondrous material to play on! Flora has now her grievance, and she'll work it to the end."

"Yes, miss; but to WHAT end?"

"Why, that of dealing with me to her uncle. She'll make me out to him the lowest creature—!"

I winced at the fair show of the scene in Mrs. Grose's face; she looked for a minute as if she sharply saw them together. "And him who thinks so well of you!"

"He has an odd way—it comes over me now," I laughed,"—of proving it! But that doesn't matter. What Flora wants, of course, is to get rid of me."

My companion bravely concurred. "Never again to so much as look at you."

"So that what you've come to me now for," I asked, "is to speed me on my way?" Before she had time to reply, however, I had her in check. "I've a better idea—the result of my reflections. My going WOULD seem the right thing, and on Sunday I was terribly near it. Yet that won't do. It's YOU who must go. You must take Flora."

My visitor, at this, did speculate. "But where in the world—?"

"Away from here. Away from THEM. Away, even most of all, now, from me. Straight to her uncle."

"Only to tell on you—?"

"No, not 'only'! To leave me, in addition, with my remedy."

She was still vague. "And what IS your remedy?"

"Your loyalty, to begin with. And then Miles's."

She looked at me hard. "Do you think he—?"

"Won't, if he has the chance, turn on me? Yes, I venture still to think it. At all events, I want to try. Get off with his sister as soon as possible and leave me with him alone." I was amazed, myself, at the spirit I had still in reserve, and therefore perhaps a trifle the more disconcerted at the way in which, in spite of this fine example of it, she hesitated. "There's one thing, of course," I went on: "they mustn't, before she goes, see each other for three seconds." Then it came over me that, in spite of Flora's presumable sequestration from the instant of her return from the pool, it might already be too late. "Do you mean," I anxiously asked, "that they HAVE met?"

At this she quite flushed. "Ah, miss, I'm not such a fool as that! If I've been obliged to leave her three or four times, it has been each time with one of the maids, and at present, though she's alone, she's locked in safe. And yet—and yet!" There were too many things.

"And yet what?"

"Well, are you so sure of the little gentleman?"

"I'm not sure of anything but YOU. But I have, since last evening, a new hope. I think he wants to give me an opening. I do believe that—poor little exquisite wretch!—he wants to speak. Last evening, in the firelight and the silence, he sat with me for two hours as if it were just coming."

Mrs. Grose looked hard, through the window, at the gray, gathering day. "And did it come?"

"No, though I waited and waited, I confess it didn't, and it was without a breach of the silence or so much as a faint allusion to his sister's condition and absence that we at last kissed for good night. All the same," I continued, "I can't, if her uncle sees her, consent to his seeing her brother without my having given the boy—and most of all because things have got so bad—a little more time."

My friend appeared on this ground more reluctant than I could quite understand. "What do you mean by more time?"

"Well, a day or two—really to bring it out. He'll then be on MY side—of which you see the importance. If nothing comes, I shall only fail, and you will, at the worst, have helped me by doing, on your arrival in town, whatever you may have found possible." So I put it before her, but she continued for a little so inscrutably embarrassed that I came again to her aid. "Unless, indeed," I wound up, "you really want NOT to go."

I could see it, in her face, at last clear itself; she put out her hand to me as a pledge. "I'll go—I'll go. I'll go this morning."

I wanted to be very just. "If you SHOULD wish still to wait, I would engage she shouldn't see me."

"No, no: it's the place itself. She must leave it." She held me a moment with heavy eyes, then brought out the rest. "Your idea's the right one. I myself, miss—"

"Well?"

"I can't stay."

The look she gave me with it made me jump at possibilities. "You mean that, since yesterday, you HAVE seen—?"

She shook her head with dignity. "I've HEARD—!"

"Heard?"

"From that child—horrors! There!" she sighed with tragic relief. "On my honor, miss, she says things—!" But at this evocation she broke down; she dropped, with a sudden sob, upon my sofa and, as I had seen her do before, gave way to all the grief of it.

It was quite in another manner that I, for my part, let myself go. "Oh, thank God!"

She sprang up again at this, drying her eyes with a groan. "'Thank God'?"

"It so justifies me!"

"It does that, miss!"

I couldn't have desired more emphasis, but I just hesitated. "She's so horrible?"

I saw my colleague scarce knew how to put it. "Really shocking."

"And about me?"

"About you, miss—since you must have it. It's beyond everything, for a young lady; and I can't think wherever she must have picked up—"

"The appalling language she applied to me? I can, then!" I broke in with a laugh that was doubtless significant enough.

It only, in truth, left my friend still more grave. "Well, perhaps I ought to also—since I've heard some of it before! Yet I can't bear it," the poor woman went on while, with the same movement, she glanced, on my dressing table, at the face of my watch. "But I must go back."

I kept her, however. "Ah, if you can't bear it—!"

"How can I stop with her, you mean? Why, just FOR that: to get her away. Far from this," she pursued, "far from THEM-"

"She may be different? She may be free?" I seized her almost with joy. "Then, in spite of yesterday, you BELIEVE—"

"In such doings?" Her simple description of them required, in the light of her expression, to be carried no further, and she gave me the whole thing as she had never done. "I believe."

Yes, it was a joy, and we were still shoulder to shoulder: if I might continue sure of that I should care but little what else happened. My support in the presence of disaster would be the same as it had been in my early need of confidence, and if my friend would answer for my honesty, I would answer for all the rest. On the point of taking leave of her, nonetheless, I was to some extent embarrassed. "There's one thing, of course—it occurs to me—to remember. My letter, giving the alarm, will have reached town before you."

I now perceived still more how she had been beating about the bush and how weary at last it had made her. "Your letter won't have got there. Your letter never went."

"What then became of it?"

"Goodness knows! Master Miles—"

"Do you mean HE took it?" I gasped.

She hung fire, but she overcame her reluctance. "I mean that I saw yesterday, when I came back with Miss Flora, that it wasn't where you had put it. Later in the evening I had the chance to question Luke, and he declared that he had neither noticed nor touched it." We could only exchange, on this, one of our deeper mutual soundings, and it was Mrs. Grose who first brought up the plumb with an almost elated "You see!"

"Yes, I see that if Miles took it instead he probably will have read it and destroyed it."

"And don't you see anything else?"

I faced her a moment with a sad smile. "It strikes me that by this time your eyes are open even wider than mine."

They proved to be so indeed, but she could still blush, almost, to show it. "I make out now what he must have done at school." And she gave, in her simple sharpness, an almost droll disillusioned nod. "He stole!"

I turned it over—I tried to be more judicial. "Well—perhaps."

She looked as if she found me unexpectedly calm. "He stole LETTERS!"

She couldn't know my reasons for a calmness after all pretty shallow; so I showed them off as I might. "I hope then it was to more purpose than in this case! The note, at any rate, that I put on the table yesterday," I pursued, "will have given him so scant an advantage—for it contained only the bare demand for an interview—that he is already much ashamed of having gone so far for so little, and that what he had on his mind last evening was precisely the need of confession." I seemed to myself, for the instant, to have mastered it, to see it all. "Leave us, leave us"—I was already, at the door, hurrying her off. "I'll get it out of him. He'll meet me—he'll confess. If he confesses, he's saved. And if he's saved—"

"Then YOU are?" The dear woman kissed me on this, and I took her farewell. "I'll save you without him!" she cried as she went.

XXII

Yet it was when she had got off—and I missed her on the spot—that the great pinch really came. If I had counted on what it would give me to find myself alone with Miles, I speedily perceived, at least, that it would give me a measure. No hour of my stay in fact was so assailed with apprehensions as that of my coming down to learn that the carriage containing Mrs. Grose and my younger pupil had already rolled out of the gates. Now I WAS, I said to myself, face to face with the elements, and for much of the rest of the day, while I fought my weakness, I could consider that I had been supremely rash. It was a tighter place still than I had yet turned round in; all the more that, for the first time, I could see in the aspect of others a confused reflection of the crisis. What had happened naturally caused them all to stare; there was too little of the explained, throw out whatever we might, in the suddenness of my colleague's act. The maids and the men looked blank; the effect of which on my nerves was an aggravation until I saw the necessity of making it a positive aid. It was precisely, in short, by just clutching the helm that I avoided total wreck; and I dare say that, to bear up at all, I became, that morning, very grand and very dry. I welcomed the consciousness that I was charged with much to do, and I caused it to be known as well that, left thus to myself, I was quite remarkably firm. I wandered with that manner, for the next hour or two, all over the place and looked, I have no doubt, as if I were ready for any onset. So, for the benefit of whom it might concern, I paraded with a sick heart.

The person it appeared least to concern proved to be, till dinner, little Miles himself. My perambulations had given me, meanwhile, no glimpse of him, but they had tended to make more public the change taking place in our relation as a consequence of his having at the piano, the day before, kept me, in Flora's interest, so beguiled and befooled. The stamp of publicity had of course been fully given by her confinement and departure, and the change itself was now ushered in by our nonobservance of the regular custom of the schoolroom. He had already disappeared when, on my way down, I pushed open his door, and I learned below that he had breakfasted—in the presence of a couple of the maids—with Mrs. Grose and his sister. He had then gone out, as he said, for a stroll; than which nothing, I reflected, could better have expressed his frank view of the abrupt transformation of my office. What he would not permit this office to consist of was yet to be settled: there was a queer relief, at all events—I mean for myself in especial—in the renouncement of one pretension. If so much had sprung to the surface, I scarce put it too strongly in saying that what had perhaps sprung highest was the absurdity of our prolonging the fiction that I had anything more to teach him. It sufficiently stuck out that, by tacit little tricks in which even more than myself he carried out the care for my dignity, I had had to appeal to him to let me off straining to meet him on the ground of his true capacity. He had at any rate his freedom now; I was never to touch it again; as I had amply shown, moreover, when, on his joining me in the schoolroom the previous night, I had uttered, on the subject of the interval just concluded, neither challenge nor hint. I had too much, from this moment, my other ideas. Yet when he at last arrived, the difficulty of applying them, the accumulations of my problem, were brought straight home to me by the beautiful little presence on which what had occurred had as yet, for the eye, dropped neither stain nor shadow.

To mark, for the house, the high state I cultivated I decreed that my meals with the boy should be served, as we called it, downstairs; so that I had been awaiting him in the ponderous pomp of the room outside of the window of which I had had from Mrs. Grose, that first scared Sunday, my flash of something it would scarce have done to call light. Here at present I felt afresh—for I had felt it again and again—how my equilibrium depended on the success of my rigid will, the will to shut my eyes as tight as possible to the truth that what I had to deal with was, revoltingly, against nature. I could only get on at all by taking "nature" into my confidence and my account, by treating my monstrous ordeal as a push in a direction unusual, of course, and unpleasant, but demanding, after all, for a fair front, only another turn of the screw of ordinary human virtue. No attempt, nonetheless, could well require more tact than just this attempt to supply, one's self, ALL the nature. How could I put even a little of that article into a suppression of reference to what had occurred? How, on the other hand, could I make reference without a new plunge into the hideous obscure? Well, a sort of answer, after a time, had come to me, and it was so far confirmed as that I was met, incontestably, by the quickened vision of what was rare in my little companion. It was indeed as if he had found even now—as he had so often found at lessons—still some other delicate way to ease me off. Wasn't there light in the fact which, as we shared our solitude, broke out with a specious glitter it had never yet quite worn?—the fact that (opportunity aiding, precious opportunity which had now come) it would be preposterous, with a child so endowed, to forego the help one might wrest from absolute intelligence? What had his intelligence been given him for but to save him? Mightn't one, to reach his mind, risk the stretch of an angular arm over his character? It was as if, when we were face to face in the dining room, he had literally shown me the way. The roast mutton was on the table, and I had dispensed with attendance. Miles, before he sat down, stood a moment with his hands in his pockets and looked at the joint, on which he seemed on the point of passing some humorous judgment. But what he presently produced was: "I say, my dear, is she really very awfully ill?"

"Little Flora? Not so bad but that she'll presently be better. London will set her up. Bly had ceased to agree with her. Come here and take your mutton."

He alertly obeyed me, carried the plate carefully to his seat, and, when he was established, went on. "Did Bly disagree with her so terribly suddenly?"

"Not so suddenly as you might think. One had seen it coming on."

"Then why didn't you get her off before?"

"Before what?"

"Before she became too ill to travel."

I found myself prompt. "She's NOT too ill to travel: she only might have become so if she had stayed. This was just the moment to seize. The journey will dissipate the influence"—oh, I was grand!—"and carry it off."

"I see, I see"—Miles, for that matter, was grand, too. He settled to his repast with the charming little "table manner" that, from the day of his arrival, had relieved me of all grossness of admonition. Whatever he had been driven from school for, it was not for ugly feeding. He was irreproachable, as always, today; but he was unmistakably more conscious. He was discernibly trying to take for granted more things than he found, without assistance, quite easy; and he dropped into peaceful silence while he felt his situation. Our meal was of the briefest—mine a vain pretense, and I had the things immediately removed. While this was done Miles stood again with his hands in his little pockets and his back to me—stood and looked out of the wide window through which, that other day, I had seen what pulled me up. We continued silent while the maid was with us—as silent, it whimsically occurred to me, as some young couple who, on their wedding journey, at the inn, feel shy in the presence of the waiter. He turned round only when the waiter had left us. "Well—so we're alone!"

XXIII

"Oh, more or less." I fancy my smile was pale. "Not absolutely. We shouldn't like that!" I went on.

"No—I suppose we shouldn't. Of course we have the others."

"We have the others—we have indeed the others," I concurred.

"Yet even though we have them," he returned, still with his hands in his pockets and planted there in front of me, "they don't much count, do they?"

I made the best of it, but I felt wan. "It depends on what you call 'much'!"

"Yes"—with all accommodation—"everything depends!" On this, however, he faced to the window again and presently reached it with his vague, restless, cogitating step. He remained there awhile, with his forehead against the glass, in contemplation of the stupid shrubs I knew and the dull things of November. I had always my hypocrisy of "work," behind which, now, I gained the sofa. Steadying myself with it there as I had repeatedly done at those moments of torment that I have described as the moments of my knowing the children to be given to something from which I was barred, I sufficiently obeyed my habit of being prepared for the worst. But an extraordinary impression dropped on me as I extracted a meaning from the boy's embarrassed back—none other than the impression that I was not barred now. This inference grew in a few minutes to sharp intensity and seemed bound up with the direct perception that it was positively HE who was. The frames and squares of the great window were a kind of image, for him, of a kind of failure. I felt that I saw him, at any rate, shut in or shut out. He was admirable, but not comfortable: I took it in with a throb of hope. Wasn't he looking, through the haunted pane, for something he couldn't see?—and wasn't it the first time in the whole business that he had known such a lapse? The first, the very first: I found it a splendid portent. It made him anxious, though he watched himself; he had been anxious all day and, even while in his usual sweet little manner he sat at table, had needed all his small strange genius to give it a gloss. When he at last turned round to meet me, it was almost as if this genius had succumbed. "Well, I think I'm glad Bly agrees with ME!"

"You would certainly seem to have seen, these twenty-four hours, a good deal more of it than for some time before. I hope," I went on bravely, "that you've been enjoying yourself."

"Oh, yes, I've been ever so far; all round about—miles and miles away. I've never been so free."

He had really a manner of his own, and I could only try to keep up with him. "Well, do you like it?"

He stood there smiling; then at last he put into two words—"Do YOU?"—more discrimination than I had ever heard two words contain. Before I had time to deal with that, however, he continued as if with the sense that this was an impertinence to be softened. "Nothing could be more charming than the way you take it, for of course if we're alone together now it's you that are alone most. But I hope," he threw in, "you don't particularly mind!"

"Having to do with you?" I asked. "My dear child, how can I help minding? Though I've renounced all claim to your company—you're so beyond me—I at least greatly enjoy it. What else should I stay on for?"

He looked at me more directly, and the expression of his face, graver now, struck me as the most beautiful I had ever found in it. "You stay on just for THAT?"

"Certainly. I stay on as your friend and from the tremendous interest I take in you till something can be done for you that may be more worth your while. That needn't surprise you." My voice trembled so that I felt it impossible to suppress the shake. "Don't you remember how I told you, when I came and sat on your bed the night of the storm, that there was nothing in the world I wouldn't do for you?"

XXIII

"Yes, yes!" He, on his side, more and more visibly nervous, had a tone to master; but he was so much more successful than I that, laughing out through his gravity, he could pretend we were pleasantly jesting. "Only that, I think, was to get me to do something for YOU!"

"It was partly to get you to do something," I conceded. "But, you know, you didn't do it."

"Oh, yes," he said with the brightest superficial eagerness, "you wanted me to tell you something."

"That's it. Out, straight out. What you have on your mind, you know."

"Ah, then, is THAT what you've stayed over for?"

He spoke with a gaiety through which I could still catch the finest little quiver of resentful passion; but I can't begin to express the effect upon me of an implication of surrender even so faint. It was as if what I had yearned for had come at last only to astonish me. "Well, yes—I may as well make a clean breast of it, it was precisely for that."

He waited so long that I supposed it for the purpose of repudiating the assumption on which my action had been founded; but what he finally said was: "Do you mean now—here?"

"There couldn't be a better place or time." He looked round him uneasily, and I had the rare—oh, the queer!—impression of the very first symptom I had seen in him of the approach of immediate fear. It was as if he were suddenly afraid of me—which struck me indeed as perhaps the best thing to make him. Yet in the very pang of the effort I felt it vain to try sternness, and I heard myself the next instant so gentle as to be almost grotesque. "You want so to go out again?"

"Awfully!" He smiled at me heroically, and the touching little bravery of it was enhanced by his actually flushing with pain. He had picked up his hat, which he had brought in, and stood twirling it in a way that gave me, even as I was just nearly reaching port, a perverse horror of what I was doing. To do it in ANY way was an act of violence, for what did it consist of but the obtrusion of the idea of grossness and guilt on a small helpless creature who had been for me a revelation of the possibilities of beautiful intercourse? Wasn't it base to create for a being so exquisite a mere alien awkwardness? I suppose I now read into our situation a clearness it couldn't have had at the time, for I seem to see our poor eyes already lighted with some spark of a prevision of the anguish that was to come. So we circled about, with terrors and scruples, like fighters not daring to close. But it was for each other we feared! That kept us a little longer suspended and unbruised. "I'll tell you everything," Miles said—"I mean I'll tell you anything you like. You'll stay on with me, and we shall both be all right, and I WILL tell you—I WILL. But not now."

"Why not now?"

My insistence turned him from me and kept him once more at his window in a silence during which, between us, you might have heard a pin drop. Then he was before me again with the air of a person for whom, outside, someone who had frankly to be reckoned with was waiting. "I have to see Luke."

I had not yet reduced him to quite so vulgar a lie, and I felt proportionately ashamed. But, horrible as it was, his lies made up my truth. I achieved thoughtfully a few loops of my knitting. "Well, then, go to Luke, and I'll wait for what you promise. Only, in return for that, satisfy, before you leave me, one very much smaller request."

He looked as if he felt he had succeeded enough to be able still a little to bargain. "Very much smaller—?"

"Yes, a mere fraction of the whole. Tell me"—oh, my work preoccupied me, and I was offhand!—"if, yesterday afternoon, from the table in the hall, you took, you know, my letter."

XXIV

My sense of how he received this suffered for a minute from something that I can describe only as a fierce split of my attention—a stroke that at first, as I sprang straight up, reduced me to the mere blind movement of getting hold of him, drawing him close, and, while I just fell for support against the nearest piece of furniture, instinctively keeping him with his back to the window. The appearance was full upon us that I had already had to deal with here: Peter Quint had come into view like a sentinel before a prison. The next thing I saw was that, from outside, he had reached the window, and then I knew that, close to the glass and glaring in through it, he offered once more to the room his white face of damnation. It represents but grossly what took place within me at the sight to say that on the second my decision was made; yet I believe that no woman so overwhelmed ever in so short a time recovered her grasp of the ACT. It came to me in the very horror of the immediate presence that the act would be, seeing and facing what I saw and faced, to keep the boy himself unaware. The inspiration—I can call it by no other name—was that I felt how voluntarily, how transcendently, I MIGHT. It was like fighting with a demon for a human soul, and when I had fairly so appraised it I saw how the human soul—held out, in the tremor of my hands, at arm's length—had a perfect dew of sweat on a lovely childish forehead. The face that was close to mine was as white as the face against the glass, and out of it presently came a sound, not low nor weak, but as if from much further away, that I drank like a waft of fragrance.

"Yes—I took it."

At this, with a moan of joy, I enfolded, I drew him close; and while I held him to my breast, where I could feel in the sudden fever of his little body the tremendous pulse of his little heart, I kept my eyes on the thing at the window and saw it move and shift its posture. I have likened it to a sentinel, but its slow wheel, for a moment, was rather the prowl of a baffled beast. My present quickened courage, however, was such that, not too much to let it through, I had to shade, as it were, my flame. Meanwhile the glare of the face was again at the window, the scoundrel fixed as if to watch and wait. It was the very confidence that I might now defy him, as well as the positive certitude, by this time, of the child's unconsciousness, that made me go on. "What did you take it for?"

"To see what you said about me."

"You opened the letter?"

"I opened it."

My eyes were now, as I held him off a little again, on Miles's own face, in which the collapse of mockery showed me how complete was the ravage of uneasiness. What was prodigious was that at last, by my success, his sense was sealed and his communication stopped: he knew that he was in presence, but knew not of what, and knew still less that I also was and that I did know. And what did this strain of trouble matter when my eyes went back to the window only to see that the air was clear again and—by my personal triumph—the influence quenched? There was nothing there. I felt that the cause was mine and that I should surely get ALL. "And you found nothing!"—I let my elation out.

He gave the most mournful, thoughtful little headshake. "Nothing."

"Nothing, nothing!" I almost shouted in my joy.

"Nothing, nothing," he sadly repeated.

I kissed his forehead; it was drenched. "So what have you done with it?"

"I've burned it."

"Burned it?" It was now or never. "Is that what you did at school?"

Oh, what this brought up! "At school?"

"Did you take letters?—or other things?"

"Other things?" He appeared now to be thinking of something far off and that reached him only through the pressure of his anxiety. Yet it did reach him. "Did I STEAL?"

I felt myself redden to the roots of my hair as well as wonder if it were more strange to put to a gentleman such a question or to see him take it with allowances that gave the very distance of his fall in the world. "Was it for that you mightn't go back?"

The only thing he felt was rather a dreary little surprise. "Did you know I mightn't go back?"

"I know everything."

He gave me at this the longest and strangest look. "Everything?"

"Everything. Therefore DID you—?" But I couldn't say it again.

Miles could, very simply. "No. I didn't steal."

My face must have shown him I believed him utterly; yet my hands—but it was for pure tenderness—shook him as if to ask him why, if it was all for nothing, he had condemned me to months of torment. "What then did you do?"

He looked in vague pain all round the top of the room and drew his breath, two or three times over, as if with difficulty. He might have been standing at the bottom of the sea and raising his eyes to some faint green twilight. "Well—I said things."

"Only that?"

"They thought it was enough!"

"To turn you out for?"

Never, truly, had a person "turned out" shown so little to explain it as this little person! He appeared to weigh my question, but in a manner quite detached and almost helpless. "Well, I suppose I oughtn't."

"But to whom did you say them?"

He evidently tried to remember, but it dropped—he had lost it. "I don't know!"

He almost smiled at me in the desolation of his surrender, which was indeed practically, by this time, so complete that I ought to have left it there. But I was infatuated—I was blind with victory, though even then the very effect that was to have brought him so much nearer was already that of added separation. "Was it to everyone?" I asked.

"No; it was only to—" But he gave a sick little headshake. "I don't remember their names."

"Were they then so many?"

"No—only a few. Those I liked."

Those he liked? I seemed to float not into clearness, but into a darker obscure, and within a minute there had come to me out of my very pity the appalling alarm of his being perhaps innocent. It was for the instant confounding and bottomless, for if he WERE innocent, what then on earth was *I*? Paralyzed, while it lasted, by the mere brush of the question, I let him go a little, so that, with a deep-drawn sigh, he turned away from me again; which, as he faced toward the clear window, I suffered, feeling that I had nothing now there to keep him from. "And did they repeat what you said?" I went on after a moment.

He was soon at some distance from me, still breathing hard and again with the air, though now without anger for it, of being confined against his will. Once more, as he had done before, he looked up at the dim day as if, of what had hitherto sustained him, nothing was left but an unspeakable anxiety. "Oh, yes," he nevertheless replied—"they must have repeated them. To those THEY liked," he added.

There was, somehow, less of it than I had expected; but I turned it over. "And these things came round—?"

"To the masters? Oh, yes!" he answered very simply. "But I didn't know they'd tell."

"The masters? They didn't—they've never told. That's why I ask you."

He turned to me again his little beautiful fevered face. "Yes, it was too bad."

"Too bad?"

"What I suppose I sometimes said. To write home."

I can't name the exquisite pathos of the contradiction given to such a speech by such a speaker; I only know that the next instant I heard myself throw off with homely force: "Stuff and nonsense!" But the next after that I must have sounded stern enough. "What WERE these things?"

My sternness was all for his judge, his executioner; yet it made him avert himself again, and that movement made ME, with a single bound and an irrepressible cry, spring straight upon him. For there again, against the glass, as if to blight his confession and stay his answer, was the hideous author of our woe—the white face of damnation. I felt a sick swim at the drop of my victory and all the return of my battle, so that the wildness of my veritable leap only served as a great betrayal. I saw him, from the midst of my act, meet it with a divination, and on the perception that even now he only guessed, and that the window was still to his own eyes free, I let the impulse flame up to convert the climax of his dismay into the very proof of his liberation. "No more, no more, no more!" I shrieked, as I tried to press him against me, to my visitant.

"Is she HERE?" Miles panted as he caught with his sealed eyes the direction of my words. Then as his strange "she" staggered me and, with a gasp, I echoed it, "Miss Jessel, Miss Jessel!" he with a sudden fury gave me back.

I seized, stupefied, his supposition—some sequel to what we had done to Flora, but this made me only want to show him that it was better still than that. "It's not Miss Jessel! But it's at the window—straight before us. It's THERE—the coward horror, there for the last time!"

At this, after a second in which his head made the movement of a baffled dog's on a scent and then gave a frantic little shake for air and light, he was at me in a white rage, bewildered, glaring vainly over the place and missing wholly, though it now, to my sense, filled the room like the taste of poison, the wide, overwhelming presence. "It's HE?"

I was so determined to have all my proof that I flashed into ice to challenge him. "Whom do you mean by 'he'?"

"Peter Quint—you devil!" His face gave again, round the room, its convulsed supplication. "WHERE?"

They are in my ears still, his supreme surrender of the name and his tribute to my devotion. "What does he matter now, my own?—what will he EVER matter? *I* have you," I launched at the beast, "but he has lost you forever!" Then, for the demonstration of my work, "There, THERE!" I said to Miles.

But he had already jerked straight round, stared, glared again, and seen but the quiet day. With the stroke of the loss I was so proud of he uttered the cry of a creature hurled over an abyss, and the grasp with which I recovered him might have been that of catching him in his fall. I caught him, yes, I held him—it may be imagined with what a passion; but at the end of a minute I began to feel what it truly was that I held. We were alone with the quiet day, and his little heart, dispossessed, had stopped.

THE PORTRAIT OF A LADY

VOLUME I (of II)

PREFACE

"The Portrait of a Lady" was, like "Roderick Hudson," begun in Florence, during three months spent there in the spring of 1879. Like "Roderick" and like "The American," it had been designed for publication in "The Atlantic Monthly," where it began to appear in 1880. It differed from its two predecessors, however, in finding a course also open to it, from month to month, in "Macmillan's Magazine"; which was to be for me one of the last occasions of simultaneous "serialisation" in the two countries that the changing conditions of literary intercourse between England and the United States had up to then left unaltered. It is a long novel, and I was long in writing it; I remember being again much occupied with it, the following year, during a stay of several weeks made in Venice. I had rooms on Riva Schiavoni, at the top of a house near the passage leading off to San Zaccaria; the waterside life, the wondrous lagoon spread before me, and the ceaseless human chatter of Venice came in at my windows, to which I seem to myself to have been constantly driven, in the fruitless fidget of composition, as if to see whether, out in the blue channel, the ship of some right suggestion, of some better phrase, of the next happy twist of my subject, the next true touch for my canvas, mightn't come into sight. But I recall vividly enough that the response most elicited, in general, to these restless appeals was the rather grim admonition that romantic and historic sites, such as the land of Italy abounds in, offer the artist a questionable aid to concentration when they themselves are not to be the subject of it. They are too rich in their own life and too charged with their own meanings merely to help him out with a lame phrase; they draw him away from his small question to their own greater ones; so that, after a little, he feels, while thus yearning toward them in his difficulty, as if he were asking an army of glorious veterans to help him to arrest a peddler who has given him the wrong change.

There are pages of the book which, in the reading over, have seemed to make me see again the bristling curve of the wide Riva, the large colour-spots of the balconied houses and the repeated undulation of the little hunchbacked bridges, marked by the rise and drop again, with the wave, of foreshortened clicking pedestrians. The Venetian footfall and the Venetian cry—all talk there, wherever uttered, having the pitch of a call across the water—come in once more at the window, renewing one's old impression of the delighted senses and the divided, frustrated mind. How can places that speak IN GENERAL so to the imagination not give it, at the moment, the particular thing it wants? I recollect again and again, in beautiful places, dropping into that wonderment. The real truth is, I think, that they express, under this appeal, only too much—more than, in the given case, one has use for; so that one finds one's self working less congruously, after all, so far as the surrounding picture is concerned, than in presence of the moderate and the neutral, to which we may lend something of the light of our vision. Such a place as Venice is too proud for such charities; Venice doesn't borrow, she but all magnificently gives. We profit by that enormously, but to do so we must either be quite off duty or be on it in her service alone. Such, and so rueful, are these reminiscences; though on the whole, no doubt, one's book, and one's "literary effort" at large, were to be the better for them. Strangely fertilising, in the long run, does a wasted effort of attention often prove. It all depends on HOW the attention has been cheated, has been squandered. There are high-handed insolent frauds, and there are insidious sneaking ones. And there is, I fear, even on the most designing artist's part, always witless enough good faith, always anxious enough desire, to fail to guard him against their deceits.

Trying to recover here, for recognition, the germ of my idea, I see that it must have consisted not at all in any conceit of a "plot," nefarious name, in any flash, upon the fancy, of a set of relations, or in any one of those situations that, by a logic of their own, immediately fall, for the fabulist, into movement, into a march or a rush, a patter of quick steps; but altogether in the sense of a single character, the character and aspect of a particular engaging young woman, to which all the usual elements of a "subject," certainly of a setting, were to need to be super added. Quite as interesting as the young woman herself at her best, do I find, I must again repeat, this projection of memory upon the whole matter of the growth, in one's imagination, of some such apology for a motive. These are the fascinations of the fabulist's art, these lurking forces of expansion, these necessities of upspringing in the seed, these beautiful determinations, on the part of the idea entertained, to grow as tall as possible, to push into the light and the air and thickly flower there; and, quite as much, these fine possibilities of recovering, from some good standpoint on the ground gained, the intimate history of the business—of retracing and reconstructing its steps and stages. I have always fondly remembered a remark that I heard fall years ago from the lips of Ivan Turgenieff in regard to his own experience of the usual origin of the fictive picture. It began for him almost always with the vision of some person or persons, who hovered before him, soliciting him, as the active or passive figure, interesting him and appealing to him just as they were and by what they were. He saw them, in that fashion, as disponibles, saw them subject to the chances, the complications of existence, and saw them vividly, but then had to find for them the right relations, those that would most bring them out; to imagine, to invent and select and piece together the situations most useful and favourable to the sense of the creatures themselves, the complications they would be most likely to produce and to feel.

"To arrive at these things is to arrive at my story," he said, "and that's the way I look for it. The result is that I'm often accused of not having 'story' enough. I seem to myself to have as much as I need—to show my people, to exhibit their relations with each other; for that is all my measure. If I watch them long enough I see them come together, I see them PLACED, I see them engaged in this or that act and in this or that difficulty. How they look and move and speak and behave, always in the setting I have found for them, is my account of them—of which I dare say, alas, que cela manque souvent d'architecture. But I would rather, I think, have too little architecture than too much—when there's danger of its interfering with my measure of the truth. The French of course like more of it than I give—having by their own genius such a hand for it; and indeed one must give all one can. As for the origin of one's wind-blown germs themselves, who shall say, as you ask, where THEY come from? We have to go too far back, too far behind, to say. Isn't it all we can say that they come from every quarter of heaven, that they are THERE at almost any turn of the road? They accumulate, and we are always picking them over, selecting among them. They are the breath of life—by which I mean that life, in its own way, breathes them upon us. They are so, in a manner prescribed and imposed—floated into our minds by the current of life. That reduces to imbecility the vain critic's quarrel, so often, with one's subject, when he hasn't the wit to accept it. Will he point out then which other it should properly have been?—his office being, essentially to point out. Il en serait bien embarrasse. Ah, when he points out what I've done or failed to do with it, that's another matter: there he's on his ground. I give him up my 'sarchitecture,'" my distinguished friend concluded, "as much as he will."

So this beautiful genius, and I recall with comfort the gratitude I drew from his reference to the intensity of suggestion that may reside in the stray figure, the unattached character, the image en disponibilite. It gave me higher warrant than I seemed then to have met for just that blest habit of one's own imagination, the trick of investing some conceived or encountered individual, some brace or group of individuals, with the germinal property and authority. I was myself so much more antecedently conscious of my figures than of their setting—a too preliminary, a preferential interest in which struck me as in general such a putting of the cart before the horse. I might envy, though I couldn't emulate, the imaginative writer so constituted as to see his fable first and to make out its agents afterwards. I could think so little of any fable that didn't need its agents positively to launch it; I could think so little of any situation that didn't depend for its interest on the nature of the persons situated, and thereby on their way of taking it. There are methods of so-called presentation, I believe among novelists who have appeared to flourish—that offer the situation as indifferent to that support; but I have not lost the sense of the value for me, at the time, of the admirable Russian's testimony to my not needing, all superstitiously, to try and perform any such gymnastic. Other echoes from the same source linger with me, I confess, as unfadingly—if it be not all indeed one much-embracing echo. It was impossible after that not to read, for one's uses, high lucidity into the tormented and disfigured and bemuddled question of the objective value, and even quite into that of the critical appreciation, of "subject" in the novel.

One had had from an early time, for that matter, the instinct of the right estimate of such values and of its reducing to the inane the dull dispute over the "immoral" subject and the moral. Recognising so promptly the one measure of the worth of a given subject, the question about it that, rightly answered, disposes of all others—is it valid, in a word, is it genuine, is it sincere, the result of some direct impression or perception of life?—I had found small edification, mostly, in a critical pretension that had neglected from the first all delimitation of ground and all definition of terms. The air of my earlier time shows, to memory, as darkened, all round, with that vanity—unless the difference to-day be just in one's own final impatience, the lapse of one's attention. There is, I think, no more nutritive or suggestive truth in this connexion than that of the perfect dependence of the "moral" sense of a work of art on the amount of felt life concerned in producing it. The question comes back thus, obviously, to the kind and the degree of the artist's prime sensibility, which is the soil out of which his subject springs. The quality and capacity of that soil, its ability to "grow" with due freshness and straightness any vision of life, represents, strongly or weakly, the projected morality. That element is but another name for the more or less close connexion of the subject with some mark made on the intelligence, with some sincere experience. By which, at the same time, of course, one is far from contending that this enveloping air of the artist's humanity—which gives the last touch to the worth of the work—is not a widely and wondrously varying element; being on one occasion a rich and magnificent medium and on another a comparatively poor and ungenerous one. Here we get exactly the high price of the novel as a literary form—its power not only, while preserving that form with closeness, to range through all the differences of the individual relation to its general subject-matter, all the varieties of outlook on life, of disposition to reflect and project, created by conditions that are never the same from man to man (or, so far as that goes, from man to woman), but positively to appear more true to its character in proportion as it strains, or tends to burst, with a latent extravagance, its mould.

The house of fiction has in short not one window, but a million—a number of possible windows not to be reckoned, rather; every one of which has been pierced, or is still pierceable, in its vast front, by the need of the individual vision and by the pressure of the individual will. These apertures, of dissimilar shape and size, hang so, all together, over the human scene that we might have expected of them a greater sameness of report than we find. They are but windows at the best, mere holes in a dead wall, disconnected, perched aloft; they are not hinged doors opening straight upon life. But they have this mark of their own that at each of them stands a figure with a pair of eyes, or at least with a field-glass, which forms, again and again, for observation, a unique instrument, insuring to the person making use of it an impression distinct from every other. He and his neighbours are watching the same show, but one seeing more where the other sees less, one seeing black where the other sees white, one seeing big where the other sees small, one seeing coarse where the other sees fine. And so on, and so on; there is fortunately no saying on what, for the particular pair of eyes, the window may NOT open; "fortunately" by reason, precisely, of this incalculability of range. The spreading field, the human scene, is the "choice of subject"; the pierced aperture, either broad or balconied or slit-like and low-browed, is the "literary form"; but they are, singly or together, as nothing without the posted presence of the watcher—without, in other words, the consciousness of the artist. Tell me what the artist is, and I will tell you of what he has BEEN conscious. Thereby I shall express to you at once his boundless freedom and his "moral" reference.

All this is a long way round, however, for my word about my dim first move toward "The Portrait," which was exactly my grasp of a single character—an acquisition I had made, moreover, after a fashion not here to be retraced. Enough that I was, as seemed to me, in complete possession of it, that I had been so for a long time, that this had made it familiar and yet had not blurred its charm, and that, all urgently, all tormentingly, I saw it in motion and, so to speak, in transit. This amounts to saying that I saw it as bent upon its fate—some fate or other; which, among the possibilities, being precisely the question. Thus I had my vivid individual—vivid, so strangely, in spite of being still at large, not confined by the conditions, not engaged in the tangle, to which we look for much of the impress that constitutes an identity. If the apparition was still all to be placed how came it to be vivid?—since we puzzle such quantities out, mostly, just by the business of placing them. One could answer such a question beautifully, doubtless, if one could do so subtle, if not so monstrous, a thing as to write the history of the growth of one's imagination. One would describe then what, at a given time, had extraordinarily happened to it, and one would so, for instance, be in a position to tell, with an approach to clearness, how, under favour of occasion, it had been able to take over (take over straight from life) such and such a constituted, animated figure or form. The figure has to that extent, as you see, BEEN placed—placed in the imagination that detains it, preserves, protects, enjoys it, conscious of its presence in the dusky, crowded, heterogeneous back-shop of the mind very much as a wary dealer in precious odds and ends, competent to make an "advance" on rare objects confided to him, is conscious of the rare little "piece" left in deposit by the reduced, mysterious lady of title or the speculative amateur, and which is already there to disclose its merit afresh as soon as a key shall have clicked in a cupboard-door.

That may he, I recognise, a somewhat superfine analogy for the particular "value" I here speak of, the image of the young feminine nature that I had had for so considerable a time all curiously at my disposal; but it appears to fond memory quite to fit the fact—with the recall, in addition, of my pious desire but to place my treasure right. I quite remind myself thus of the dealer resigned not to "realise," resigned to keeping the precious object locked up indefinitely rather than commit it, at no matter what price, to vulgar hands. For there ARE dealers in these forms and figures and treasures capable of that refinement. The point is, however, that this single small corner-stone, the conception of a certain young woman affronting her destiny, had begun with being all my outfit for the large building of "The Portrait of a Lady." It came to be a square and spacious house—or has at least seemed so to me in this going over it again; but, such as it is, it had to be put up round my young woman while she stood there in perfect isolation. That is to me, artistically speaking, the circumstance of interest; for I have lost myself once more, I confess, in the curiosity of analysing the structure. By what process of logical accretion was this slight "personality," the mere slim shade of an intelligent but presumptuous girl, to find itself endowed with the high attributes of a Subject?—and indeed by what thinness, at the best, would such a subject not be vitiated? Millions of presumptuous girls, intelligent or not intelligent, daily affront their destiny, and what is it open to their destiny to be, at the most, that we should make an ado about it? The novel is of its very nature an "ado," an ado about something, and the larger the form it takes the greater of course the ado. Therefore, consciously, that was what one was in for—for positively organising an ado about Isabel Archer.

One looked it well in the face, I seem to remember, this extravagance; and with the effect precisely of recognising the charm of the problem. Challenge any such problem with any intelligence, and you immediately see how full it is of substance; the wonder being, all the while, as we look at the world, how absolutely, how inordinately, the Isabel Archers, and even much smaller female fry, insist on mattering. George Eliot has admirably noted it—"In these frail vessels is borne onward through the ages the treasure of human affection." In "Romeo and Juliet" Juliet has to be important, just as, in "Adam Bede" and "The Mill on the Floss" and "Middlemarch" and "Daniel Deronda," Hetty Sorrel and Maggie Tulliver and Rosamond Vincy and Gwendolen Harleth have to be; with that much of firm ground, that much of bracing air, at the disposal all the while of their feet and their lungs. They are typical, none the less, of a class difficult, in the individual case, to make a centre of interest; so difficult in fact that many an expert painter, as for instance Dickens and Walter Scott, as for instance even, in the main, so subtle a hand as that of R. L. Stevenson, has preferred to leave the task unattempted. There are in fact writers as to whom we make out that their refuge from this is to assume it to be not worth their attempting; by which pusillanimity in truth their honour is scantly saved. It is never an attestation of a value, or even of our imperfect sense of one, it is never a tribute to any truth at all, that we shall represent that value badly. It never makes up, artistically, for an artist's dim feeling about a thing that he shall "do" the thing as ill as possible. There are better ways than that, the best of all of which is to begin with less stupidity.

It may be answered meanwhile, in regard to Shakespeare's and to George Eliot's testimony, that their concession to the "importance" of their Juliets and Cleopatras and Portias (even with Portia as the very type and model of the young person intelligent and presumptuous) and to that of their Hettys and Maggies and Rosamonds and Gwendolens, suffers the abatement that these slimnesses are, when figuring as the main props of the theme, never suffered to be sole ministers of its appeal, but have their inadequacy eked out with comic relief and underplots, as the playwrights say, when not with murders and battles and the great mutations of the world. If they are shown as "mattering" as much as they could possibly pretend to, the proof of it is in a hundred other persons, made of much stouter stuff; and each involved moreover in a hundred relations which matter to THEM concomitantly with that one. Cleopatra matters, beyond bounds, to Antony, but his colleagues, his antagonists, the state of Rome and the impending battle also prodigiously matter; Portia matters to Antonio, and to Shylock, and to the Prince of Morocco, to the fifty aspiring princes, but for these gentry there are other lively concerns; for Antonio, notably, there are Shylock and Bassanio and his lost ventures and the extremity of his predicament. This extremity indeed, by the same token, matters to Portia—though its doing so becomes of interest all by the fact that Portia matters to US. That she does so, at any rate, and that almost everything comes round to it again, supports my contention as to this fine example of the value recognised in the mere young thing. (I say "mere" young thing because I guess that even Shakespeare, preoccupied mainly though he may have been with the passions of princes, would scarce have pretended to found the best of his appeal for her on her high social position.) It is an example exactly of the deep difficulty braved—the difficulty of making George Eliot's "frail vessel," if not the all-in-all for our attention, at least the clearest of the call.

Now to see deep difficulty braved is at any time, for the really addicted artist, to feel almost even as a pang the beautiful incentive, and to feel it verily in such sort as to wish the danger intensified. The difficulty most worth tackling can only be for him, in these conditions, the greatest the case permits of. So I remember feeling here (in presence, always, that is, of the particular uncertainty of my ground), that there would be one way better than another—oh, ever so much better than any other!—of making it fight out its battle. The frail vessel, that charged with George Eliot's "treasure," and thereby of such importance to those who curiously approach it, has likewise possibilities of importance to itself, possibilities which permit of treatment and in fact peculiarly require it from the moment they are considered at all. There is always the escape from any close account of the weak agent of such spells by using as a bridge for evasion, for retreat and flight, the view of her relation to those surrounding her. Make it predominantly a view of THEIR relation and the trick is played: you give the general sense of her effect, and you give it, so far as the raising on it of a superstructure goes, with the maximum of ease. Well, I recall perfectly how little, in my now quite established connexion, the maximum of ease appealed to me, and how I seemed to get rid of it by an honest transposition of the weights in the two scales. "Place the centre of the subject in the young woman's own consciousness," I said to myself, "and you get as interesting and as beautiful a difficulty as you could wish. Stick to THAT—for the centre; put the heaviest weight into THAT scale, which will be so largely the scale of her relation to herself. Make her only interested enough, at the same time, in the things that are not herself, and this relation needn't fear to be too limited. Place meanwhile in the other scale the lighter weight (which is usually the one that tips the balance of interest): press least hard, in short, on the consciousness of your heroine's satellites, especially the male; make it an interest contributive only to the greater one. See, at all events, what can be done in this way. What better field could there be for a due ingenuity? The girl hovers, inextinguishable, as a charming creature, and the job will be to translate her into the highest terms of that formula, and as nearly as possible moreover into ALL of them. To depend upon her and her little concerns wholly to see you through will necessitate, remember, your really 'doing' her."

So far I reasoned, and it took nothing less than that technical rigour, I now easily see, to inspire me with the right confidence for erecting on such a plot of ground the neat and careful and proportioned pile of bricks that arches over it and that was thus to form, constructionally speaking, a literary monument. Such is the aspect that to-day "The Portrait" wears for me: a structure reared with an "architectural" competence, as Turgenieff would have said, that makes it, to the author's own sense, the most proportioned of his productions after "The Ambassadors" which was to follow it so many years later and which has, no doubt, a superior roundness. On one thing I was determined; that, though I should clearly have to pile brick upon brick for the creation of an interest, I would leave no pretext for saying that anything is out of line, scale or perspective. I would build large—in fine embossed vaults and painted arches, as who should say, and yet never let it appear that the chequered pavement, the ground under the reader's feet, fails to stretch at every point to the base of the walls. That precautionary spirit, on re-perusal of the book, is the old note that most touches me: it testifies so, for my own ear, to the anxiety of my provision for the reader's amusement. I felt, in view of the possible limitations of my subject, that no such provision could be excessive, and the development of the latter was simply the general form of that earnest quest. And I find indeed that this is the only account I can give myself of the evolution of the fable it is all under the head thus named that I conceive the needful accretion as having taken place, the right complications as having started. It was naturally of the essence that the young woman should be herself complex; that was rudimentary—or was at any rate the light in which Isabel Archer had originally dawned. It went, however, but a certain way, and other lights, contending, conflicting lights, and of as many different colours, if possible, as the rockets, the Roman candles and Catherine-wheels of a "pyrotechnic display," would be employable to attest that she was. I had, no doubt, a groping instinct for the right complications, since I am quite unable to track the footsteps of those that constitute, as the case stands, the general situation exhibited. They are there, for what they are worth, and as numerous as might be; but my memory, I confess, is a blank as to how and whence they came.

I seem to myself to have waked up one morning in possession of them—of Ralph Touchett and his parents, of Madame Merle, of Gilbert Osmond and his daughter and his sister, of Lord Warburton, Caspar Goodwood and Miss Stackpole, the definite array of contributions to Isabel Archer's history. I recognised them, I knew them, they were the numbered pieces of my puzzle, the concrete terms of my "plot." It was as if they had simply, by an impulse of their own, floated into my ken, and all in response to my primary question: "Well, what will she DO?" Their answer seemed to be that if I would trust them they would show me; on which, with an urgent appeal to them to make it at least as interesting as they could, I trusted them. They were like the group of attendants and entertainers who come down by train when people in the country give a party; they represented the contract for carrying the party on. That was an excellent relation with them—a possible one even with so broken a reed (from her slightness of cohesion) as Henrietta Stackpole. It is a familiar truth to the novelist, at the strenuous hour, that, as certain elements in any work are of the essence, so others are only of the form; that as this or that character, this or that disposition of the material, belongs to the subject directly, so to speak, so this or that other belongs to it but indirectly—belongs intimately to the treatment. This is a truth, however, of which he rarely gets the benefit—since it could be assured to him, really, but by criticism based upon perception, criticism which is too little of this world. He must not think of benefits, moreover, I freely recognise, for that way dishonour lies: he has, that is, but one to think of—the benefit, whatever it may be, involved in his having cast a spell upon the simpler, the very simplest, forms of attention. This is all he is entitled to; he is entitled to nothing, he is bound to admit, that can come to him, from the reader, as a result on the latter's part of any act of reflexion or discrimination. He may ENJOY this finer tribute—that is another affair, but on condition only of taking it as a gratuity "thrown in," a mere miraculous windfall, the fruit of a tree he may not pretend to have shaken. Against reflexion, against discrimination, in his interest, all earth and air conspire; wherefore it is that, as I say, he must in many a case have schooled himself, from the first, to work but for a "living wage." The living wage is the reader's grant of the least possible quantity of attention required for consciousness of a "spell." The occasional charming "tip" is an act of his intelligence over and beyond this, a golden apple, for the writer's lap, straight from the wind-stirred tree. The artist may of course, in wanton moods, dream of some Paradise (for art) where the direct appeal to the intelligence might be legalised; for to such extravagances as these his yearning mind can scarce hope ever completely to close itself. The most he can do is to remember they ARE extravagances.

All of which is perhaps but a gracefully devious way of saying that Henrietta Stackpole was a good example, in "The Portrait," of the truth to which I just adverted—as good an example as I could name were it not that Maria Gostrey, in "The Ambassadors," then in the bosom of time, may be mentioned as a better. Each of these persons is but wheels to the coach; neither belongs to the body of that vehicle, or is for a moment accommodated with a seat inside. There the subject alone is ensconced, in the form of its "hero and heroine," and of the privileged high officials, say, who ride with the king and queen. There are reasons why one would have liked this to be felt, as in general one would like almost anything to be felt, in one's work, that one has one's self contributively felt. We have seen, however, how idle is that pretension, which I should be sorry to make too much of. Maria Gostrey and Miss Stackpole then are cases, each, of the light ficelle, not of the true agent; they may run beside the coach "for all they are worth," they may cling to it till they are out of breath (as poor Miss Stackpole all so visibly does), but neither, all the while, so much as gets her foot on the step, neither ceases for a moment to tread the dusty road. Put it even that they are like the fishwives who helped to bring back to Paris from Versailles, on that most ominous day of the first half of the French Revolution, the carriage of the royal family. The only thing is that I may well be asked, I acknowledge, why then, in the present fiction, I have suffered Henrietta (of whom we have indubitably too much) so officiously, so strangely, so almost inexplicably, to pervade. I will presently say what I can for that anomaly—and in the most conciliatory fashion.

A point I wish still more to make is that if my relation of confidence with the actors in my drama who WERE, unlike Miss Stackpole, true agents, was an excellent one to have arrived at, there still remained my relation with the reader, which was another affair altogether and as to which I felt no one to be trusted but myself. That solicitude was to be accordingly expressed in the artful patience with which, as I have said, I piled brick upon brick. The bricks, for the whole counting-over—putting for bricks little touches and inventions and enhancements by the way—affect me in truth as well-nigh innumerable and as ever so scrupulously fitted together and packed-in. It is an effect of detail, of the minutest; though, if one were in this connexion to say all, one would express the hope that the general, the ampler air of the modest monument still survives. I do at least seem to catch the key to a part of this abundance of small anxious, ingenious illustration as I recollect putting my finger, in my young woman's interest, on the most obvious of her predicates. "What will she 'do'? Why, the first thing she'll do will be to come to Europe; which in fact will form, and all inevitably, no small part of her principal adventure. Coming to Europe is even for the 'frail vessels,' in this wonderful age, a mild adventure; but what is truer than that on one side—the side of their independence of flood and field, of the moving accident, of battle and murder and sudden death—her adventures are to be mild? Without her sense of them, her sense FOR them, as one may say, they are next to nothing at all; but isn't the beauty and the difficulty just in showing their mystic conversion by that sense, conversion into the stuff of drama or, even more delightful word still, of 'story'?" It was all as clear, my contention, as a silver bell. Two very good instances, I think, of this effect of conversion, two cases of the rare chemistry, are the pages in which Isabel, coming into the drawing-room at Gardencourt, coming in from a wet walk or whatever, that rainy afternoon, finds Madame Merle in possession of the place, Madame Merle seated, all absorbed but all serene, at the piano, and deeply recognises, in the striking of such an hour, in the presence there, among the gathering shades, of this personage, of whom a moment before she had never so much as heard, a turning-point in her life. It is dreadful to have too much, for any artistic demonstration, to dot one's i's and insist on one's intentions, and I am not eager to do it now; but the question here was that of producing the maximum of intensity with the minimum of strain.

The interest was to be raised to its pitch and yet the elements to be kept in their key; so that, should the whole thing duly impress, I might show what an "exciting" inward life may do for the person leading it even while it remains perfectly normal. And I cannot think of a more consistent application of that ideal unless it be in the long statement, just beyond the middle of the book, of my young woman's extraordinary meditative vigil on the occasion that was to become for her such a landmark. Reduced to its essence, it is but the vigil of searching criticism; but it throws the action further forward that twenty "incidents" might have done. It was designed to have all the vivacity of incidents and all the economy of picture. She sits up, by her dying fire, far into the night, under the spell of recognitions on which she finds the last sharpness suddenly wait. It is a representation simply of her motionlessly SEEING, and an attempt withal to make the mere still lucidity of her act as "interesting" as the surprise of a caravan or the identification of a pirate. It represents, for that matter, one of the identifications dear to the novelist, and even indispensable to him; but it all goes on without her being approached by another person and without her leaving her chair. It is obviously the best thing in the book, but it is only a supreme illustration of the general plan. As to Henrietta, my apology for whom I just left incomplete, she exemplifies, I fear, in her superabundance, not an element of my plan, but only an excess of my zeal. So early was to begin my tendency to OVERTREAT, rather than undertreat (when there was choice or danger) my subject. (Many members of my craft, I gather, are far from agreeing with me, but I have always held overtreating the minor disservice.) "Treating" that of "The Portrait" amounted to never forgetting, by any lapse, that the thing was under a special obligation to be amusing. There was the danger of the noted "thinness"—which was to be averted, tooth and nail, by cultivation of the lively. That is at least how I see it to-day. Henrietta must have been at that time a part of my wonderful notion of the lively. And then there was another matter. I had, within the few preceding years, come to live in London, and the "international" light lay, in those days, to my sense, thick and rich upon the scene. It was the light in which so much of the picture hung. But that IS another matter. There is really too much to say.

HENRY JAMES

CHAPTER I

Under certain circumstances there are few hours in life more agreeable than the hour dedicated to the ceremony known as afternoon tea. There are circumstances in which, whether you partake of the tea or not—some people of course never do,—the situation is in itself delightful. Those that I have in mind in beginning to unfold this simple history offered an admirable setting to an innocent pastime. The implements of the little feast had been disposed upon the lawn of an old English country-house, in what I should call the perfect middle of a splendid summer afternoon. Part of the afternoon had waned, but much of it was left, and what was left was of the finest and rarest quality. Real dusk would not arrive for many hours; but the flood of summer light had begun to ebb, the air had grown mellow, the shadows were long upon the smooth, dense turf. They lengthened slowly, however, and the scene expressed that sense of leisure still to come which is perhaps the chief source of one's enjoyment of such a scene at such an hour. From five o'clock to eight is on certain occasions a little eternity; but on such an occasion as this the interval could be only an eternity of pleasure. The persons concerned in it were taking their pleasure quietly, and they were not of the sex which is supposed to furnish the regular votaries of the ceremony I have mentioned. The shadows on the perfect lawn were straight and angular; they were the shadows of an old man sitting in a deep wicker-chair near the low table on which the tea had been served, and of two younger men strolling to and fro, in desultory talk, in front of him. The old man had his cup in his hand; it was an unusually large cup, of a different pattern from the rest of the set and painted in brilliant colours. He disposed of its contents with much circumspection, holding it for a long time close to his chin, with his face turned to the house. His companions had either finished their tea or were indifferent to their privilege; they smoked cigarettes as they continued to stroll. One of them, from time to time, as he passed, looked with a certain attention at the elder man, who, unconscious of observation, rested his eyes upon the rich red front of his dwelling. The house that rose beyond the lawn was a structure to repay such consideration and was the most characteristic object in the peculiarly English picture I have attempted to sketch.

It stood upon a low hill, above the river—the river being the Thames at some forty miles from London. A long gabled front of red brick, with the complexion of which time and the weather had played all sorts of pictorial tricks, only, however, to improve and refine it, presented to the lawn its patches of ivy, its clustered chimneys, its windows smothered in creepers. The house had a name and a history; the old gentleman taking his tea would have been delighted to tell you these things: how it had been built under Edward the Sixth, had offered a night's hospitality to the great Elizabeth (whose august person had extended itself upon a huge, magnificent and terribly angular bed which still formed the principal honour of the sleeping apartments), had been a good deal bruised and defaced in Cromwell's wars, and then, under the Restoration, repaired and much enlarged; and how, finally, after having been remodelled and disfigured in the eighteenth century, it had passed into the careful keeping of a shrewd American banker, who had bought it originally because (owing to circumstances too complicated to set forth) it was offered at a great bargain: bought it with much grumbling at its ugliness, its antiquity, its incommodity, and who now, at the end of twenty years, had become conscious of a real aesthetic passion for it, so that he knew all its points and would tell you just where to stand to see them in combination and just the hour when the shadows of its various protuberances which fell so softly upon the warm, weary brickwork—were of the right measure. Besides this, as I have said, he could have counted off most of the successive owners and occupants, several of whom were known to general fame; doing so, however, with an undemonstrative conviction that the latest phase of its destiny was not the least honourable. The front of the house overlooking that portion of the lawn with which we are concerned was not the entrance-front; this was in quite another quarter. Privacy here reigned supreme, and the wide carpet of turf that covered the level hill-top seemed but the extension of a luxurious interior. The great still oaks and beeches flung down a shade as dense as that of velvet curtains; and the place was furnished, like a room, with cushioned seats, with rich-coloured rugs, with the books and papers that lay upon the grass. The river was at some distance; where the ground began to slope the lawn, properly speaking, ceased. But it was none the less a charming walk down to the water.

The old gentleman at the tea-table, who had come from America thirty years before, had brought with him, at the top of his baggage, his American physiognomy; and he had not only brought it with him, but he had kept it in the best order, so that, if necessary, he might have taken it back to his own country with perfect confidence. At present, obviously, nevertheless, he was not likely to displace himself; his journeys were over and he was taking the rest that precedes the great rest. He had a narrow, clean-shaven face, with features evenly distributed and an expression of placid acuteness. It was evidently a face in which the range of representation was not large, so that the air of contented shrewdness was all the more of a merit. It seemed to tell that he had been successful in life, yet it seemed to tell also that his success had not been exclusive and invidious, but had had much of the inoffensiveness of failure. He had certainly had a great experience of men, but there was an almost rustic simplicity in the faint smile that played upon his lean, spacious cheek and lighted up his humorous eye as he at last slowly and carefully deposited his big tea-cup upon the table. He was neatly dressed, in well-brushed black; but a shawl was folded upon his knees, and his feet were encased in thick, embroidered slippers. A beautiful collie dog lay upon the grass near his chair, watching the master's face almost as tenderly as the master took in the still more magisterial physiognomy of the house; and a little bristling, bustling terrier bestowed a desultory attendance upon the other gentlemen.

One of these was a remarkably well-made man of five-and-thirty, with a face as English as that of the old gentleman I have just sketched was something else; a noticeably handsome face, fresh-coloured, fair and frank, with firm, straight features, a lively grey eye and the rich adornment of a chestnut beard. This person had a certain fortunate, brilliant exceptional look—the air of a happy temperament fertilised by a high civilisation—which would have made almost any observer envy him at a venture. He was booted and spurred, as if he had dismounted from a long ride; he wore a white hat, which looked too large for him; he held his two hands behind him, and in one of them—a large, white, well-shaped fist—was crumpled a pair of soiled dog-skin gloves.

His companion, measuring the length of the lawn beside him, was a person of quite a different pattern, who, although he might have excited grave curiosity, would not, like the other, have provoked you to wish yourself, almost blindly, in his place. Tall, lean, loosely and feebly put together, he had an ugly, sickly, witty, charming face, furnished, but by no means decorated, with a straggling moustache and whisker. He looked clever and ill—a combination by no means felicitous; and he wore a brown velvet jacket. He carried his hands in his pockets, and there was something in the way he did it that showed the habit was inveterate. His gait had a shambling, wandering quality; he was not very firm on his legs. As I have said, whenever he passed the old man in the chair he rested his eyes upon him; and at this moment, with their faces brought into relation, you would easily have seen they were father and son. The father caught his son's eye at last and gave him a mild, responsive smile.

"I'm getting on very well," he said.

"Have you drunk your tea?" asked the son.

"Yes, and enjoyed it."

"Shall I give you some more?"

The old man considered, placidly. "Well, I guess I'll wait and see." He had, in speaking, the American tone.

"Are you cold?" the son enquired.

The father slowly rubbed his legs. "Well, I don't know. I can't tell till I feel."

"Perhaps some one might feel for you," said the younger man, laughing.

"Oh, I hope some one will always feel for me! Don't you feel for me, Lord Warburton?"

"Oh yes, immensely," said the gentleman addressed as Lord Warburton, promptly. "I'm bound to say you look wonderfully comfortable."

"Well, I suppose I am, in most respects." And the old man looked down at his green shawl and smoothed it over his knees. "The fact is I've been comfortable so many years that I suppose I've got so used to it I don't know it."

"Yes, that's the bore of comfort," said Lord Warburton. "We only know when we're uncomfortable."

"It strikes me we're rather particular," his companion remarked.

"Oh yes, there's no doubt we're particular," Lord Warburton murmured. And then the three men remained silent a while; the two younger ones standing looking down at the other, who presently asked for more tea. "I should think you would be very unhappy with that shawl," Lord Warburton resumed while his companion filled the old man's cup again.

"Oh no, he must have the shawl!" cried the gentleman in the velvet coat. "Don't put such ideas as that into his head."

"It belongs to my wife," said the old man simply.

"Oh, if it's for sentimental reasons—" And Lord Warburton made a gesture of apology.

"I suppose I must give it to her when she comes," the old man went on.

"You'll please to do nothing of the kind. You'll keep it to cover your poor old legs."

"Well, you mustn't abuse my legs," said the old man. "I guess they are as good as yours."

"Oh, you're perfectly free to abuse mine," his son replied, giving him his tea.

"Well, we're two lame ducks; I don't think there's much difference."

"I'm much obliged to you for calling me a duck. How's your tea?"

"Well, it's rather hot."

"That's intended to be a merit."

"Ah, there's a great deal of merit," murmured the old man, kindly. "He's a very good nurse, Lord Warburton."

"Isn't he a bit clumsy?" asked his lordship.

"Oh no, he's not clumsy—considering that he's an invalid himself. He's a very good nurse—for a sick-nurse. I call him my sick-nurse because he's sick himself."

"Oh, come, daddy!" the ugly young man exclaimed.

"Well, you are; I wish you weren't. But I suppose you can't help it."

"I might try: that's an idea," said the young man.

"Were you ever sick, Lord Warburton?" his father asked.

Lord Warburton considered a moment. "Yes, sir, once, in the Persian Gulf."

"He's making light of you, daddy," said the other young man. "That's a sort of joke."

"Well, there seem to be so many sorts now," daddy replied, serenely. "You don't look as if you had been sick, any way, Lord Warburton."

"He's sick of life; he was just telling me so; going on fearfully about it," said Lord Warburton's friend.

"Is that true, sir?" asked the old man gravely.

"If it is, your son gave me no consolation. He's a wretched fellow to talk to—a regular cynic. He doesn't seem to believe in anything."

"That's another sort of joke," said the person accused of cynicism.

"It's because his health is so poor," his father explained to Lord Warburton. "It affects his mind and colours his way of looking at things; he seems to feel as if he had never had a chance. But it's almost entirely theoretical, you know; it doesn't seem to affect his spirits. I've hardly ever seen him when he wasn't cheerful—about as he is at present. He often cheers me up."

The young man so described looked at Lord Warburton and laughed. "Is it a glowing eulogy or an accusation of levity? Should you like me to carry out my theories, daddy?"

"By Jove, we should see some queer things!" cried Lord Warburton.

"I hope you haven't taken up that sort of tone," said the old man.

"Warburton's tone is worse than mine; he pretends to be bored. I'm not in the least bored; I find life only too interesting."

"Ah, too interesting; you shouldn't allow it to be that, you know!"

"I'm never bored when I come here," said Lord Warburton. "One gets such uncommonly good talk."

"Is that another sort of joke?" asked the old man. "You've no excuse for being bored anywhere. When I was your age I had never heard of such a thing."

"You must have developed very late."

"No, I developed very quick; that was just the reason. When I was twenty years old I was very highly developed indeed. I was working tooth and nail. You wouldn't be bored if you had something to do; but all you young men are too idle. You think too much of your pleasure. You're too fastidious, and too indolent, and too rich."

"Oh, I say," cried Lord Warburton, "you're hardly the person to accuse a fellow-creature of being too rich!"

"Do you mean because I'm a banker?" asked the old man.

"Because of that, if you like; and because you have—haven't you?—such unlimited means."

"He isn't very rich," the other young man mercifully pleaded. "He has given away an immense deal of money."

"Well, I suppose it was his own," said Lord Warburton; "and in that case could there be a better proof of wealth? Let not a public benefactor talk of one's being too fond of pleasure."

"Daddy's very fond of pleasure—of other people's."

The old man shook his head. "I don't pretend to have contributed anything to the amusement of my contemporaries."

"My dear father, you're too modest!"

"That's a kind of joke, sir," said Lord Warburton.

"You young men have too many jokes. When there are no jokes you've nothing left."

"Fortunately there are always more jokes," the ugly young man remarked.

"I don't believe it—I believe things are getting more serious. You young men will find that out."

"The increasing seriousness of things, then that's the great opportunity of jokes."

"They'll have to be grim jokes," said the old man. "I'm convinced there will be great changes, and not all for the better."

"I quite agree with you, sir," Lord Warburton declared. "I'm very sure there will be great changes, and that all sorts of queer things will happen. That's why I find so much difficulty in applying your advice; you know you told me the other day that I ought to 'take hold' of something. One hesitates to take hold of a thing that may the next moment be knocked sky-high."

"You ought to take hold of a pretty woman," said his companion. "He's trying hard to fall in love," he added, by way of explanation, to his father.

"The pretty women themselves may be sent flying!" Lord Warburton exclaimed.

"No, no, they'll be firm," the old man rejoined; "they'll not be affected by the social and political changes I just referred to."

"You mean they won't be abolished? Very well, then, I'll lay hands on one as soon as possible and tie her round my neck as a life-preserver."

"The ladies will save us," said the old man; "that is the best of them will—for I make a difference between them. Make up to a good one and marry her, and your life will become much more interesting."

A momentary silence marked perhaps on the part of his auditors a sense of the magnanimity of this speech, for it was a secret neither for his son nor for his visitor that his own experiment in matrimony had not been a happy one. As he said, however, he made a difference; and these words may have been intended as a confession of personal error; though of course it was not in place for either of his companions to remark that apparently the lady of his choice had not been one of the best.

"If I marry an interesting woman I shall be interested: is that what you say?" Lord Warburton asked. "I'm not at all keen about marrying—your son misrepresented me; but there's no knowing what an interesting woman might do with me."

"I should like to see your idea of an interesting woman," said his friend.

"My dear fellow, you can't see ideas—especially such highly ethereal ones as mine. If I could only see it myself—that would be a great step in advance."

"Well, you may fall in love with whomsoever you please; but you mustn't fall in love with my niece," said the old man.

His son broke into a laugh. "He'll think you mean that as a provocation! My dear father, you've lived with the English for thirty years, and you've picked up a good many of the things they say. But you've never learned the things they don't say!"

"I say what I please," the old man returned with all his serenity.

"I haven't the honour of knowing your niece," Lord Warburton said. "I think it's the first time I've heard of her."

"She's a niece of my wife's; Mrs. Touchett brings her to England."

Then young Mr. Touchett explained. "My mother, you know, has been spending the winter in America, and we're expecting her back. She writes that she has discovered a niece and that she has invited her to come out with her."

"I see,—very kind of her," said Lord Warburton. Is the young lady interesting?"

"We hardly know more about her than you; my mother has not gone into details. She chiefly communicates with us by means of telegrams, and her telegrams are rather inscrutable. They say women don't know how to write them, but my mother has thoroughly mastered the art of condensation. 'Tired America, hot weather awful, return England with niece, first steamer decent cabin.' That's the sort of message we get from her—that was the last that came. But there had been another before, which I think contained the first mention of the niece. 'Changed hotel, very bad, impudent clerk, address here. Taken sister's girl, died last year, go to Europe, two sisters, quite independent.' Over that my father and I have scarcely stopped puzzling; it seems to admit of so many interpretations."

"There's one thing very clear in it," said the old man; "she has given the hotel-clerk a dressing."

"I'm not sure even of that, since he has driven her from the field. We thought at first that the sister mentioned might be the sister of the clerk; but the subsequent mention of a niece seems to prove that the allusion is to one of my aunts. Then there was a question as to whose the two other sisters were; they are probably two of my late aunt's daughters. But who's 'quite independent,' and in what sense is the term used?—that point's not yet settled. Does the expression apply more particularly to the young lady my mother has adopted, or does it characterise her sisters equally?—and is it used in a moral or in a financial sense? Does it mean that they've been left well off, or that they wish to be under no obligations? or does it simply mean that they're fond of their own way?"

"Whatever else it means, it's pretty sure to mean that," Mr. Touchett remarked.

"You'll see for yourself," said Lord Warburton. "When does Mrs. Touchett arrive?"

"We're quite in the dark; as soon as she can find a decent cabin. She may be waiting for it yet; on the other hand she may already have disembarked in England."

"In that case she would probably have telegraphed to you."

"She never telegraphs when you would expect it—only when you don't," said the old man. "She likes to drop on me suddenly; she thinks she'll find me doing something wrong. She has never done so yet, but she's not discouraged."

"It's her share in the family trait, the independence she speaks of." Her son's appreciation of the matter was more favourable. "Whatever the high spirit of those young ladies may be, her own is a match for it. She likes to do everything for herself and has no belief in any one's power to help her. She thinks me of no more use than a postage-stamp without gum, and she would never forgive me if I should presume to go to Liverpool to meet her."

"Will you at least let me know when your cousin arrives?" Lord Warburton asked.

"Only on the condition I've mentioned—that you don't fall in love with her!" Mr. Touchett replied.

"That strikes me as hard, don't you think me good enough?"

"I think you too good—because I shouldn't like her to marry you. She hasn't come here to look for a husband, I hope; so many young ladies are doing that, as if there were no good ones at home. Then she's probably engaged; American girls are usually engaged, I believe. Moreover I'm not sure, after all, that you'd be a remarkable husband."

"Very likely she's engaged; I've known a good many American girls, and they always were; but I could never see that it made any difference, upon my word! As for my being a good husband," Mr. Touchett's visitor pursued, "I'm not sure of that either. One can but try!"

"Try as much as you please, but don't try on my niece," smiled the old man, whose opposition to the idea was broadly humorous.

"Ah, well," said Lord Warburton with a humour broader still, "perhaps, after all, she's not worth trying on!"

CHAPTER II

While this exchange of pleasantries took place between the two Ralph Touchett wandered away a little, with his usual slouching gait, his hands in his pockets and his little rowdyish terrier at his heels. His face was turned toward the house, but his eyes were bent musingly on the lawn; so that he had been an object of observation to a person who had just made her appearance in the ample doorway for some moments before he perceived her. His attention was called to her by the conduct of his dog, who had suddenly darted forward with a little volley of shrill barks, in which the note of welcome, however, was more sensible than that of defiance. The person in question was a young lady, who seemed immediately to interpret the greeting of the small beast. He advanced with great rapidity and stood at her feet, looking up and barking hard; whereupon, without hesitation, she stooped and caught him in her hands, holding him face to face while he continued his quick chatter. His master now had had time to follow and to see that Bunchie's new friend was a tall girl in a black dress, who at first sight looked pretty. She was bareheaded, as if she were staying in the house—a fact which conveyed perplexity to the son of its master, conscious of that immunity from visitors which had for some time been rendered necessary by the latter's ill-health. Meantime the two other gentlemen had also taken note of the new-comer.

"Dear me, who's that strange woman?" Mr. Touchett had asked.

"Perhaps it's Mrs. Touchett's niece—the independent young lady," Lord Warburton suggested. "I think she must be, from the way she handles the dog."

The collie, too, had now allowed his attention to be diverted, and he trotted toward the young lady in the doorway, slowly setting his tail in motion as he went.

"But where's my wife then?" murmured the old man.

"I suppose the young lady has left her somewhere: that's a part of the independence."

The girl spoke to Ralph, smiling, while she still held up the terrier. "Is this your little dog, sir?"

"He was mine a moment ago; but you've suddenly acquired a remarkable air of property in him."

"Couldn't we share him?" asked the girl. "He's such a perfect little darling."

Ralph looked at her a moment; she was unexpectedly pretty. "You may have him altogether," he then replied.

The young lady seemed to have a great deal of confidence, both in herself and in others; but this abrupt generosity made her blush. "I ought to tell you that I'm probably your cousin," she brought out, putting down the dog. "And here's another!" she added quickly, as the collie came up.

"Probably?" the young man exclaimed, laughing. "I supposed it was quite settled! Have you arrived with my mother?"

"Yes, half an hour ago."

"And has she deposited you and departed again?"

"No, she went straight to her room, and she told me that, if I should see you, I was to say to you that you must come to her there at a quarter to seven."

The young man looked at his watch. "Thank you very much; I shall be punctual." And then he looked at his cousin. "You're very welcome here. I'm delighted to see you."

She was looking at everything, with an eye that denoted clear perception—at her companion, at the two dogs, at the two gentlemen under the trees, at the beautiful scene that surrounded her. "I've never seen anything so lovely as this place. I've been all over the house; it's too enchanting."

"I'm sorry you should have been here so long without our knowing it."

"Your mother told me that in England people arrived very quietly; so I thought it was all right. Is one of those gentlemen your father?"

"Yes, the elder one—the one sitting down," said Ralph.

The girl gave a laugh. "I don't suppose it's the other. Who's the other?"

"He's a friend of ours—Lord Warburton."

"Oh, I hoped there would be a lord; it's just like a novel!" And then, "Oh you adorable creature!" she suddenly cried, stooping down and picking up the small dog again.

She remained standing where they had met, making no offer to advance or to speak to Mr. Touchett, and while she lingered so near the threshold, slim and charming, her interlocutor wondered if she expected the old man to come and pay her his respects. American girls were used to a great deal of deference, and it had been intimated that this one had a high spirit. Indeed Ralph could see that in her face.

"Won't you come and make acquaintance with my father?" he nevertheless ventured to ask. "He's old and infirm—he doesn't leave his chair."

"Ah, poor man, I'm very sorry!" the girl exclaimed, immediately moving forward. "I got the impression from your mother that he was rather intensely active."

Ralph Touchett was silent a moment. "She hasn't seen him for a year."

"Well, he has a lovely place to sit. Come along, little hound."

"It's a dear old place," said the young man, looking sidewise at his neighbour.

"What's his name?" she asked, her attention having again reverted to the terrier.

"My father's name?"

"Yes," said the young lady with amusement; "but don't tell him I asked you."

They had come by this time to where old Mr. Touchett was sitting, and he slowly got up from his chair to introduce himself.

"My mother has arrived," said Ralph, "and this is Miss Archer."

The old man placed his two hands on her shoulders, looked at her a moment with extreme benevolence and then gallantly kissed her. "It's a great pleasure to me to see you here; but I wish you had given us a chance to receive you."

"Oh, we were received," said the girl. "There were about a dozen servants in the hall. And there was an old woman curtseying at the gate."

"We can do better than that—if we have notice!" And the old man stood there smiling, rubbing his hands and slowly shaking his head at her. "But Mrs. Touchett doesn't like receptions."

"She went straight to her room."

"Yes—and locked herself in. She always does that. Well, I suppose I shall see her next week." And Mrs. Touchett's husband slowly resumed his former posture.

"Before that," said Miss Archer. "She's coming down to dinner—at eight o'clock. Don't you forget a quarter to seven," she added, turning with a smile to Ralph.

"What's to happen at a quarter to seven?"

"I'm to see my mother," said Ralph.

"Ah, happy boy!" the old man commented. "You must sit down—you must have some tea," he observed to his wife's niece.

"They gave me some tea in my room the moment I got there," this young lady answered. "I'm sorry you're out of health," she added, resting her eyes upon her venerable host.

"Oh, I'm an old man, my dear; it's time for me to be old. But I shall be the better for having you here."

She had been looking all round her again—at the lawn, the great trees, the reedy, silvery Thames, the beautiful old house; and while engaged in this survey she had made room in it for her companions; a comprehensiveness of observation easily conceivable on the part of a young woman who was evidently both intelligent and excited. She had seated herself and had put away the little dog; her white hands, in her lap, were folded upon her black dress; her head was erect, her eye lighted, her flexible figure turned itself easily this way and that, in sympathy with the alertness with which she evidently caught impressions. Her impressions were numerous, and they were all reflected in a clear, still smile. "I've never seen anything so beautiful as this."

"It's looking very well," said Mr. Touchett. "I know the way it strikes you. I've been through all that. But you're very beautiful yourself," he added with a politeness by no means crudely jocular and with the happy consciousness that his advanced age gave him the privilege of saying such things—even to young persons who might possibly take alarm at them.

What degree of alarm this young person took need not be exactly measured; she instantly rose, however, with a blush which was not a refutation. "Oh yes, of course I'm lovely!" she returned with a quick laugh. "How old is your house? Is it Elizabethan?"

"It's early Tudor," said Ralph Touchett.

She turned toward him, watching his face. "Early Tudor? How very delightful! And I suppose there are a great many others."

"There are many much better ones."

"Don't say that, my son!" the old man protested. "There's nothing better than this."

"I've got a very good one; I think in some respects it's rather better," said Lord Warburton, who as yet had not spoken, but who had kept an attentive eye upon Miss Archer. He slightly inclined himself, smiling; he had an excellent manner with women. The girl appreciated it in an instant; she had not forgotten that this was Lord Warburton. "I should like very much to show it to you," he added.

"Don't believe him," cried the old man; "don't look at it! It's a wretched old barrack—not to be compared with this."

"I don't know—I can't judge," said the girl, smiling at Lord Warburton.

In this discussion Ralph Touchett took no interest whatever; he stood with his hands in his pockets, looking greatly as if he should like to renew his conversation with his new-found cousin.

"Are you very fond of dogs?" he enquired by way of beginning. He seemed to recognise that it was an awkward beginning for a clever man.

"Very fond of them indeed."

"You must keep the terrier, you know," he went on, still awkwardly.

"I'll keep him while I'm here, with pleasure."

"That will be for a long time, I hope."

"You're very kind. I hardly know. My aunt must settle that."

"I'll settle it with her—at a quarter to seven." And Ralph looked at his watch again.

"I'm glad to be here at all," said the girl.

"I don't believe you allow things to be settled for you."

"Oh yes; if they're settled as I like them."

"I shall settle this as I like it," said Ralph. "It's most unaccountable that we should never have known you."

"I was there—you had only to come and see me."

"There? Where do you mean?"

"In the United States: in New York and Albany and other American places."

"I've been there—all over, but I never saw you. I can't make it out."

Miss Archer just hesitated. "It was because there had been some disagreement between your mother and my father, after my mother's death, which took place when I was a child. In consequence of it we never expected to see you."

"Ah, but I don't embrace all my mother's quarrels—heaven forbid!" the young man cried. "You've lately lost your father?" he went on more gravely.

"Yes; more than a year ago. After that my aunt was very kind to me; she came to see me and proposed that I should come with her to Europe."

"I see," said Ralph. "She has adopted you."

"Adopted me?" The girl stared, and her blush came back to her, together with a momentary look of pain which gave her interlocutor some alarm. He had underestimated the effect of his words. Lord Warburton, who appeared constantly desirous of a nearer view of Miss Archer, strolled toward the two cousins at the moment, and as he did so she rested her wider eyes on him.

"Oh no; she has not adopted me. I'm not a candidate for adoption."

"I beg a thousand pardons," Ralph murmured. "I meant—I meant—" He hardly knew what he meant.

"You meant she has taken me up. Yes; she likes to take people up. She has been very kind to me; but," she added with a certain visible eagerness of desire to be explicit, "I'm very fond of my liberty."

"Are you talking about Mrs. Touchett?" the old man called out from his chair. "Come here, my dear, and tell me about her. I'm always thankful for information."

The girl hesitated again, smiling. "She's really very benevolent," she answered; after which she went over to her uncle, whose mirth was excited by her words.

Lord Warburton was left standing with Ralph Touchett, to whom in a moment he said: "You wished a while ago to see my idea of an interesting woman. There it is!"

CHAPTER III

Mrs. Touchett was certainly a person of many oddities, of which her behaviour on returning to her husband's house after many months was a noticeable specimen. She had her own way of doing all that she did, and this is the simplest description of a character which, although by no means without liberal motions, rarely succeeded in giving an impression of suavity. Mrs. Touchett might do a great deal of good, but she never pleased. This way of her own, of which she was so fond, was not intrinsically offensive—it was just unmistakeably distinguished from the ways of others. The edges of her conduct were so very clear-cut that for susceptible persons it sometimes had a knife-like effect. That hard fineness came out in her deportment during the first hours of her return from America, under circumstances in which it might have seemed that her first act would have been to exchange greetings with her husband and son. Mrs. Touchett, for reasons which she deemed excellent, always retired on such occasions into impenetrable seclusion, postponing the more sentimental ceremony until she had repaired the disorder of dress with a completeness which had the less reason to be of high importance as neither beauty nor vanity were concerned in it. She was a plain-faced old woman, without graces and without any great elegance, but with an extreme respect for her own motives. She was usually prepared to explain these—when the explanation was asked as a favour; and in such a case they proved totally different from those that had been attributed to her. She was virtually separated from her husband, but she appeared to perceive nothing irregular in the situation. It had become clear, at an early stage of their community, that they should never desire the same thing at the same moment, and this appearance had prompted her to rescue disagreement from the vulgar realm of accident. She did what she could to erect it into a law—a much more edifying aspect of it—by going to live in Florence, where she bought a house and established herself; and by leaving her husband to take care of the English branch of his bank. This arrangement greatly pleased her; it was so felicitously definite. It struck her husband in the same light, in a foggy square in London, where it was at times the most definite fact he discerned; but he would have preferred that such unnatural things should have a greater vagueness. To agree to disagree had cost him an effort; he was ready to agree to almost anything but that, and saw no reason why either assent or dissent should be so terribly consistent. Mrs. Touchett indulged in no regrets nor speculations, and usually came once a year to spend a month with her husband, a period during which she apparently took pains to convince him that she had adopted the right system. She was not fond of the English style of life, and had three or four reasons for it to which she currently alluded; they bore upon minor points of that ancient order, but for Mrs. Touchett they amply justified non-residence. She detested bread-sauce, which, as she said, looked like a poultice and tasted like soap; she objected to the consumption of beer by her maid-servants; and she affirmed that the British laundress (Mrs. Touchett was very particular about the appearance of her linen) was not a mistress of her art. At fixed intervals she paid a visit to her own country; but this last had been longer than any of its predecessors.

She had taken up her niece—there was little doubt of that. One wet afternoon, some four months earlier than the occurrence lately narrated, this young lady had been seated alone with a book. To say she was so occupied is to say that her solitude did not press upon her; for her love of knowledge had a fertilising quality and her imagination was strong. There was at this time, however, a want of fresh taste in her situation which the arrival of an unexpected visitor did much to correct. The visitor had not been announced; the girl heard her at last walking about the adjoining room. It was in an old house at Albany, a large, square, double house, with a notice of sale in the windows of one of the lower apartments. There were two entrances, one of which had long been out of use but had never been removed. They were exactly alike—large white doors, with an arched frame and wide side-lights, perched upon little "stoops" of red stone, which descended sidewise to the brick pavement of the street. The two houses together formed a single dwelling, the party-wall having been removed and the rooms placed in communication. These rooms, above-stairs, were extremely numerous, and were painted all over exactly alike, in a yellowish white which had grown sallow with time. On the third floor there was a sort of arched passage, connecting the two sides of the house, which Isabel and her sisters used in their childhood to call the tunnel and which, though it was short and well lighted, always seemed to the girl to be strange and lonely, especially on winter afternoons. She had been in the house, at different periods, as a child; in those days her grandmother lived there. Then there had been an absence of ten years, followed by a return to Albany before her father's death. Her grandmother, old Mrs. Archer, had exercised, chiefly within the limits of the family, a large hospitality in the early period, and the little girls often spent weeks under her roof—weeks of which Isabel had the happiest memory. The manner of life was different from that of her own home—larger, more plentiful, practically more festal; the discipline of the nursery was delightfully vague and the opportunity of listening to the conversation of one's elders (which with Isabel was a highly-valued pleasure) almost unbounded. There was a constant coming and going; her grandmother's sons and daughters and their children appeared to be in the enjoyment of standing invitations to arrive and remain, so that the house offered to a certain extent the appearance of a bustling provincial inn kept by a gentle old landlady who sighed a great deal and never presented a bill. Isabel of course knew nothing about bills; but even as a child she thought her grandmother's home romantic. There was a covered piazza behind it, furnished with a swing which was a source of tremulous interest; and beyond this was a long garden, sloping down to the stable and containing peach-trees of barely credible familiarity. Isabel had stayed with her grandmother at various seasons, but somehow all her visits had a flavour of peaches. On the other side, across the street, was an old house that was called the Dutch House—a peculiar structure dating from the earliest colonial time, composed of bricks that had been painted yellow, crowned with a gable that was pointed out to strangers, defended by a rickety wooden paling and standing sidewise to the street. It was occupied by a primary school for children of both sexes, kept or rather let go, by a demonstrative lady of whom Isabel's chief recollection was that her hair was fastened with strange bedroomy combs at the temples and that she was the widow of some one of consequence. The little girl had been offered the opportunity of laying a foundation of knowledge in this establishment; but having spent a single day in it, she had protested against its laws and had been allowed to stay at home, where, in the September days, when the windows of the Dutch House were open, she used to hear the hum of childish voices repeating the multiplication table—an incident in which the elation of liberty and the pain of exclusion were indistinguishably mingled. The foundation of her knowledge was really laid in the idleness of her grandmother's house, where, as most of the other inmates were not reading people, she had uncontrolled use of a library full of books with frontispieces, which she used to climb upon a chair to take down. When she had found one to her taste—she was guided in the selection chiefly by the frontispiece—she carried it into a mysterious apartment which lay beyond the library and which was called, traditionally, no one knew why, the office. Whose office it had been and at what period it had flourished, she never learned; it was enough for her that it contained an echo and a pleasant musty smell and that it was a chamber of disgrace for old pieces of furniture whose infirmities were not always apparent (so that the disgrace seemed unmerited and rendered them victims of injustice) and with which, in the manner of children, she had established relations almost human, certainly dramatic. There was an old haircloth sofa in especial, to which she had confided a hundred childish sorrows. The place owed much of its mysterious melancholy to the fact that it was properly entered from the second door of the house, the door that had been condemned, and that it was secured by bolts which a particularly slender little girl found it impossible to slide. She knew that this silent, motionless portal opened into the street; if the sidelights had not been filled with green paper she might have looked out upon the little brown stoop and the well-worn brick pavement. But she had no wish to look out, for this would have interfered with her theory that there was a strange, unseen place on the other side—a place which became to the child's imagination, according to its different moods, a region of delight or of terror.

It was in the "office" still that Isabel was sitting on that melancholy afternoon of early spring which I have just mentioned. At this time she might have had the whole house to choose from, and the room she had selected was the most depressed of its scenes. She had never opened the bolted door nor removed the green paper (renewed by other hands) from its sidelights; she had never assured herself that the vulgar street lay beyond. A crude, cold rain fell heavily; the spring-time was indeed an appeal—and it seemed a cynical, insincere appeal—to patience. Isabel, however, gave as little heed as possible to cosmic treacheries; she kept her eyes on her book and tried to fix her mind. It had lately occurred to her that her mind was a good deal of a vagabond, and she had spent much ingenuity in training it to a military step and teaching it to advance, to halt, to retreat, to perform even more complicated manoeuvres, at the word of command. Just now she had given it marching orders and it had been trudging over the sandy plains of a history of German Thought. Suddenly she became aware of a step very different from her own intellectual pace; she listened a little and perceived that some one was moving in the library, which communicated with the office. It struck her first as the step of a person from whom she was looking for a visit, then almost immediately announced itself as the tread of a woman and a stranger—her possible visitor being neither. It had an inquisitive, experimental quality which suggested that it would not stop short of the threshold of the office; and in fact the doorway of this apartment was presently occupied by a lady who paused there and looked very hard at our heroine. She was a plain, elderly woman, dressed in a comprehensive waterproof mantle; she had a face with a good deal of rather violent point.

"Oh," she began, "is that where you usually sit?" She looked about at the heterogeneous chairs and tables.

"Not when I have visitors," said Isabel, getting up to receive the intruder.

She directed their course back to the library while the visitor continued to look about her. "You seem to have plenty of other rooms; they're in rather better condition. But everything's immensely worn."

"Have you come to look at the house?" Isabel asked. "The servant will show it to you."

"Send her away; I don't want to buy it. She has probably gone to look for you and is wandering about upstairs; she didn't seem at all intelligent. You had better tell her it's no matter." And then, since the girl stood there hesitating and wondering, this unexpected critic said to her abruptly: "I suppose you're one of the daughters?"

Isabel thought she had very strange manners. "It depends upon whose daughters you mean."

"The late Mr. Archer's—and my poor sister's."

"Ah," said Isabel slowly, "you must be our crazy Aunt Lydia!"

"Is that what your father told you to call me? I'm your Aunt Lydia, but I'm not at all crazy: I haven't a delusion! And which of the daughters are you?"

"I'm the youngest of the three, and my name's Isabel."

"Yes; the others are Lilian and Edith. And are you the prettiest?"

"I haven't the least idea," said the girl.

"I think you must be." And in this way the aunt and the niece made friends. The aunt had quarrelled years before with her brother-in-law, after the death of her sister, taking him to task for the manner in which he brought up his three girls. Being a high-tempered man he had requested her to mind her own business, and she had taken him at his word. For many years she held no communication with him and after his death had addressed not a word to his daughters, who had been bred in that disrespectful view of her which we have just seen Isabel betray. Mrs. Touchett's behaviour was, as usual, perfectly deliberate. She intended to go to America to look after her investments (with which her husband, in spite of his great financial position, had nothing to do) and would take advantage of this opportunity to enquire into the condition of her nieces. There was no need of writing, for she should attach no importance to any account of them she should elicit by letter; she believed, always, in seeing for one's self. Isabel found, however, that she knew a good deal about them, and knew about the marriage of the two elder girls; knew that their poor father had left very little money, but that the house in Albany, which had passed into his hands, was to be sold for their benefit; knew, finally, that Edmund Ludlow, Lilian's husband, had taken upon himself to attend to this matter, in consideration of which the young couple, who had come to Albany during Mr. Archer's illness, were remaining there for the present and, as well as Isabel herself, occupying the old place.

"How much money do you expect for it?" Mrs. Touchett asked of her companion, who had brought her to sit in the front parlour, which she had inspected without enthusiasm.

"I haven't the least idea," said the girl.

"That's the second time you have said that to me," her aunt rejoined. "And yet you don't look at all stupid."

"I'm not stupid; but I don't know anything about money."

"Yes, that's the way you were brought up—as if you were to inherit a million. What have you in point of fact inherited?"

"I really can't tell you. You must ask Edmund and Lilian; they'll be back in half an hour."

"In Florence we should call it a very bad house," said Mrs. Touchett; "but here, I dare say, it will bring a high price. It ought to make a considerable sum for each of you. In addition to that you must have something else; it's most extraordinary your not knowing. The position's of value, and they'll probably pull it down and make a row of shops. I wonder you don't do that yourself; you might let the shops to great advantage."

Isabel stared; the idea of letting shops was new to her. "I hope they won't pull it down," she said; "I'm extremely fond of it."

"I don't see what makes you fond of it; your father died here."

"Yes; but I don't dislike it for that," the girl rather strangely returned. "I like places in which things have happened—even if they're sad things. A great many people have died here; the place has been full of life."

"Is that what you call being full of life?"

"I mean full of experience—of people's feelings and sorrows. And not of their sorrows only, for I've been very happy here as a child."

"You should go to Florence if you like houses in which things have happened—especially deaths. I live in an old palace in which three people have been murdered; three that were known and I don't know how many more besides."

"In an old palace?" Isabel repeated.

"Yes, my dear; a very different affair from this. This is very bourgeois."

Isabel felt some emotion, for she had always thought highly of her grandmother's house. But the emotion was of a kind which led her to say: "I should like very much to go to Florence."

"Well, if you'll be very good, and do everything I tell you I'll take you there," Mrs. Touchett declared.

Our young woman's emotion deepened; she flushed a little and smiled at her aunt in silence. "Do everything you tell me? I don't think I can promise that."

"No, you don't look like a person of that sort. You're fond of your own way; but it's not for me to blame you."

"And yet, to go to Florence," the girl exclaimed in a moment, "I'd promise almost anything!"

Edmund and Lilian were slow to return, and Mrs. Touchett had an hour's uninterrupted talk with her niece, who found her a strange and interesting figure: a figure essentially—almost the first she had ever met. She was as eccentric as Isabel had always supposed; and hitherto, whenever the girl had heard people described as eccentric, she had thought of them as offensive or alarming. The term had always suggested to her something grotesque and even sinister. But her aunt made it a matter of high but easy irony, or comedy, and led her to ask herself if the common tone, which was all she had known, had ever been as interesting. No one certainly had on any occasion so held her as this little thin-lipped, bright-eyed, foreign-looking woman, who retrieved an insignificant appearance by a distinguished manner and, sitting there in a well-worn waterproof, talked with striking familiarity of the courts of Europe. There was nothing flighty about Mrs. Touchett, but she recognised no social superiors, and, judging the great ones of the earth in a way that spoke of this, enjoyed the consciousness of making an impression on a candid and susceptible mind. Isabel at first had answered a good many questions, and it was from her answers apparently that Mrs. Touchett derived a high opinion of her intelligence. But after this she had asked a good many, and her aunt's answers, whatever turn they took, struck her as food for deep reflexion. Mrs. Touchett waited for the return of her other niece as long as she thought reasonable, but as at six o'clock Mrs. Ludlow had not come in she prepared to take her departure.

"Your sister must be a great gossip. Is she accustomed to staying out so many hours?"

"You've been out almost as long as she," Isabel replied; "she can have left the house but a short time before you came in."

Mrs. Touchett looked at the girl without resentment; she appeared to enjoy a bold retort and to be disposed to be gracious. "Perhaps she hasn't had so good an excuse as I. Tell her at any rate that she must come and see me this evening at that horrid hotel. She may bring her husband if she likes, but she needn't bring you. I shall see plenty of you later."

CHAPTER IV

Mrs. Ludlow was the eldest of the three sisters, and was usually thought the most sensible; the classification being in general that Lilian was the practical one, Edith the beauty and Isabel the "intellectual" superior. Mrs. Keyes, the second of the group, was the wife of an officer of the United States Engineers, and as our history is not further concerned with her it will suffice that she was indeed very pretty and that she formed the ornament of those various military stations, chiefly in the unfashionable West, to which, to her deep chagrin, her husband was successively relegated. Lilian had married a New York lawyer, a young man with a loud voice and an enthusiasm for his profession; the match was not brilliant, any more than Edith's, but Lilian had occasionally been spoken of as a young woman who might be thankful to marry at all—she was so much plainer than her sisters. She was, however, very happy, and now, as the mother of two peremptory little boys and the mistress of a wedge of brown stone violently driven into Fifty-third Street, seemed to exult in her condition as in a bold escape. She was short and solid, and her claim to figure was questioned, but she was conceded presence, though not majesty; she had moreover, as people said, improved since her marriage, and the two things in life of which she was most distinctly conscious were her husband's force in argument and her sister Isabel's originality. "I've never kept up with Isabel—it would have taken all my time," she had often remarked; in spite of which, however, she held her rather wistfully in sight; watching her as a motherly spaniel might watch a free greyhound. "I want to see her safely married—that's what I want to see," she frequently noted to her husband.

"Well, I must say I should have no particular desire to marry her," Edmund Ludlow was accustomed to answer in an extremely audible tone.

"I know you say that for argument; you always take the opposite ground. I don't see what you've against her except that she's so original."

"Well, I don't like originals; I like translations," Mr. Ludlow had more than once replied. "Isabel's written in a foreign tongue. I can't make her out. She ought to marry an Armenian or a Portuguese."

"That's just what I'm afraid she'll do!" cried Lilian, who thought Isabel capable of anything.

She listened with great interest to the girl's account of Mrs. Touchett's appearance and in the evening prepared to comply with their aunt's commands. Of what Isabel then said no report has remained, but her sister's words had doubtless prompted a word spoken to her husband as the two were making ready for their visit. "I do hope immensely she'll do something handsome for Isabel; she has evidently taken a great fancy to her."

"What is it you wish her to do?" Edmund Ludlow asked. "Make her a big present?"

"No indeed; nothing of the sort. But take an interest in her—sympathise with her. She's evidently just the sort of person to appreciate her. She has lived so much in foreign society; she told Isabel all about it. You know you've always thought Isabel rather foreign."

"You want her to give her a little foreign sympathy, eh? Don't you think she gets enough at home?"

"Well, she ought to go abroad," said Mrs. Ludlow. "She's just the person to go abroad."

"And you want the old lady to take her, is that it?"

"She has offered to take her—she's dying to have Isabel go. But what I want her to do when she gets her there is to give her all the advantages. I'm sure all we've got to do," said Mrs. Ludlow, "is to give her a chance."

"A chance for what?"

"A chance to develop."

"Oh Moses!" Edmund Ludlow exclaimed. "I hope she isn't going to develop any more!"

"If I were not sure you only said that for argument I should feel very badly," his wife replied. "But you know you love her."

"Do you know I love you?" the young man said, jocosely, to Isabel a little later, while he brushed his hat.

"I'm sure I don't care whether you do or not!" exclaimed the girl; whose voice and smile, however, were less haughty than her words.

"Oh, she feels so grand since Mrs. Touchett's visit," said her sister.

But Isabel challenged this assertion with a good deal of seriousness. "You must not say that, Lily. I don't feel grand at all."

"I'm sure there's no harm," said the conciliatory Lily.

"Ah, but there's nothing in Mrs. Touchett's visit to make one feel grand."

"Oh," exclaimed Ludlow, "she's grander than ever!"

"Whenever I feel grand," said the girl, "it will be for a better reason."

Whether she felt grand or no, she at any rate felt different, as if something had happened to her. Left to herself for the evening she sat a while under the lamp, her hands empty, her usual avocations unheeded. Then she rose and moved about the room, and from one room to another, preferring the places where the vague lamplight expired. She was restless and even agitated; at moments she trembled a little. The importance of what had happened was out of proportion to its appearance; there had really been a change in her life. What it would bring with it was as yet extremely indefinite; but Isabel was in a situation that gave a value to any change. She had a desire to leave the past behind her and, as she said to herself, to begin afresh. This desire indeed was not a birth of the present occasion; it was as familiar as the sound of the rain upon the window and it had led to her beginning afresh a great many times. She closed her eyes as she sat in one of the dusky corners of the quiet parlour; but it was not with a desire for dozing forgetfulness. It was on the contrary because she felt too wide-eyed and wished to check the sense of seeing too many things at once. Her imagination was by habit ridiculously active; when the door was not open it jumped out of the window. She was not accustomed indeed to keep it behind bolts; and at important moments, when she would have been thankful to make use of her judgement alone, she paid the penalty of having given undue encouragement to the faculty of seeing without judging. At present, with her sense that the note of change had been struck, came gradually a host of images of the things she was leaving behind her. The years and hours of her life came back to her, and for a long time, in a stillness broken only by the ticking of the big bronze clock, she passed them in review. It had been a very happy life and she had been a very fortunate person—this was the truth that seemed to emerge most vividly. She had had the best of everything, and in a world in which the circumstances of so many people made them unenviable it was an advantage never to have known anything particularly unpleasant. It appeared to Isabel that the unpleasant had been even too absent from her knowledge, for she had gathered from her acquaintance with literature that it was often a source of interest and even of instruction. Her father had kept it away from her—her handsome, much loved father, who always had such an aversion to it. It was a great felicity to have been his daughter; Isabel rose even to pride in her parentage. Since his death she had seemed to see him as turning his braver side to his children and as not having managed to ignore the ugly quite so much in practice as in aspiration. But this only made her tenderness for him greater; it was scarcely even painful to have to suppose him too generous, too good-natured, too indifferent to sordid considerations. Many persons had held that he carried this indifference too far, especially the large number of those to whom he owed money. Of their opinions Isabel was never very definitely informed; but it may interest the reader to know that, while they had recognised in the late Mr. Archer a remarkably handsome head and a very taking manner (indeed, as one of them had said, he was always taking something), they had declared that he was making a very poor use of his life. He had squandered a substantial fortune, he had been deplorably convivial, he was known to have gambled freely. A few very harsh critics went so far as to say that he had not even brought up his daughters. They had had no regular education and no permanent home; they had been at once spoiled and neglected; they had lived with nursemaids and governesses (usually very bad ones) or had been sent to superficial schools, kept by the French, from which, at the end of a month, they had been removed in tears. This view of the matter would have excited Isabel's indignation, for to her own sense her opportunities had been large. Even when her father had left his daughters for three months at Neufchatel with a French bonne who had eloped with a Russian nobleman staying at the same hotel—even in this irregular situation (an incident of the girl's eleventh year) she had been neither frightened nor ashamed, but had thought it a romantic episode in a liberal education. Her father had a large way of looking at life, of which his restlessness and even his occasional incoherency of conduct had been only a proof. He wished his daughters, even as children, to see as much of the world as possible; and it was for this purpose that, before Isabel was fourteen, he had transported them three times across the Atlantic, giving them on each occasion, however, but a few months' view of the subject proposed: a course which had whetted our heroine's curiosity without enabling her to satisfy it. She ought to have been a partisan of her father, for she was the member of his trio who most "made up" to him for the disagreeables he didn't mention. In his last days his general willingness to take leave of a world in which the difficulty of doing as one liked appeared to increase as one grew older had been sensibly modified by the pain of separation from his clever, his superior, his remarkable girl. Later, when the journeys to Europe ceased, he still had shown his children all sorts of indulgence, and if he had been troubled about money-matters nothing ever disturbed their irreflective consciousness of many possessions. Isabel, though she danced very well, had not the recollection of having been in New York a successful member of the choreographic circle; her sister Edith was, as every one said, so very much more fetching. Edith was so striking an example of success that Isabel could have no illusions as to what constituted this advantage, or as to the limits of her own power to frisk and jump and shriek—above all with rightness of effect. Nineteen persons out of twenty (including the younger sister herself) pronounced Edith infinitely the prettier of the two; but the twentieth, besides reversing this judgement, had the entertainment of thinking all the others aesthetic vulgarians. Isabel had in the depths of her nature an even more unquenchable desire to please than Edith; but the depths of this young lady's nature were a very out-of-the-way place, between which and the surface communication was interrupted by a dozen capricious forces. She saw the young men who came in large numbers to see her sister; but as a general thing they were afraid of her; they had a belief that some special preparation was required for talking with her. Her reputation of reading a great deal hung about her like the cloudy envelope of a goddess in an epic; it was supposed to engender difficult questions and to keep the conversation at a low temperature. The poor girl liked to be thought clever, but she hated to be thought bookish; she used to read in secret and, though her memory was excellent, to abstain from showy reference. She had a great desire for knowledge, but she really preferred almost any source of information to the printed page; she had an immense curiosity about life and was constantly staring and wondering. She carried within herself a great fund of life, and her deepest enjoyment was to feel the continuity between the movements of her own soul and the agitations of the world. For this reason she was fond of seeing great crowds and large stretches of country, of reading about revolutions and wars, of looking at historical pictures—a class of efforts as to which she had often committed the conscious solecism of forgiving them much bad painting for the sake of the subject. While the Civil War went on she was still a very young girl; but she passed months of this long period in a state of almost passionate excitement, in which she felt herself at times (to her extreme confusion) stirred almost indiscriminately by the valour of either army. Of course the circumspection of suspicious swains had never gone the length of making her a social proscript; for the number of those whose hearts, as they approached her, beat only just fast enough to remind them they had heads as well, had kept her unacquainted with the supreme disciplines of her sex and age. She had had everything a girl could have: kindness, admiration, bonbons, bouquets, the sense of exclusion from none of the privileges of the world she lived in, abundant opportunity for dancing, plenty of new dresses, the London Spectator, the latest publications, the music of Gounod, the poetry of Browning, the prose of George Eliot.

These things now, as memory played over them, resolved themselves into a multitude of scenes and figures. Forgotten things came back to her; many others, which she had lately thought of great moment, dropped out of sight. The result was kaleidoscopic, but the movement of the instrument was checked at last by the servant's coming in with the name of a gentleman. The name of the gentleman was Caspar Goodwood; he was a straight young man from Boston, who had known Miss Archer for the last twelvemonth and who, thinking her the most beautiful young woman of her time, had pronounced the time, according to the rule I have hinted at, a foolish period of history. He sometimes wrote to her and had within a week or two written from New York. She had thought it very possible he would come in—had indeed all the rainy day been vaguely expecting him. Now that she learned he was there, nevertheless, she felt no eagerness to receive him. He was the finest young man she had ever seen, was indeed quite a splendid young man; he inspired her with a sentiment of high, of rare respect. She had never felt equally moved to it by any other person. He was supposed by the world in general to wish to marry her, but this of course was between themselves. It at least may be affirmed that he had travelled from New York to Albany expressly to see her; having learned in the former city, where he was spending a few days and where he had hoped to find her, that she was still at the State capital. Isabel delayed for some minutes to go to him; she moved about the room with a new sense of complications. But at last she presented herself and found him standing near the lamp. He was tall, strong and somewhat stiff; he was also lean and brown. He was not romantically, he was much rather obscurely, handsome; but his physiognomy had an air of requesting your attention, which it rewarded according to the charm you found in blue eyes of remarkable fixedness, the eyes of a complexion other than his own, and a jaw of the somewhat angular mould which is supposed to bespeak resolution. Isabel said to herself that it bespoke resolution to-night; in spite of which, in half an hour, Caspar Goodwood, who had arrived hopeful as well as resolute, took his way back to his lodging with the feeling of a man defeated. He was not, it may be added, a man weakly to accept defeat.

CHAPTER V

Ralph Touchett was a philosopher, but nevertheless he knocked at his mother's door (at a quarter to seven) with a good deal of eagerness. Even philosophers have their preferences, and it must be admitted that of his progenitors his father ministered most to his sense of the sweetness of filial dependence. His father, as he had often said to himself, was the more motherly; his mother, on the other hand, was paternal, and even, according to the slang of the day, gubernatorial. She was nevertheless very fond of her only child and had always insisted on his spending three months of the year with her. Ralph rendered perfect justice to her affection and knew that in her thoughts and her thoroughly arranged and servanted life his turn always came after the other nearest subjects of her solicitude, the various punctualities of performance of the workers of her will. He found her completely dressed for dinner, but she embraced her boy with her gloved hands and made him sit on the sofa beside her. She enquired scrupulously about her husband's health and about the young man's own, and, receiving no very brilliant account of either, remarked that she was more than ever convinced of her wisdom in not exposing herself to the English climate. In this case she also might have given way. Ralph smiled at the idea of his mother's giving way, but made no point of reminding her that his own infirmity was not the result of the English climate, from which he absented himself for a considerable part of each year.

He had been a very small boy when his father, Daniel Tracy Touchett, a native of Rutland, in the State of Vermont, came to England as subordinate partner in a banking-house where some ten years later he gained preponderant control. Daniel Touchett saw before him a life-long residence in his adopted country, of which, from the first, he took a simple, sane and accommodating view. But, as he said to himself, he had no intention of disamericanising, nor had he a desire to teach his only son any such subtle art. It had been for himself so very soluble a problem to live in England assimilated yet unconverted that it seemed to him equally simple his lawful heir should after his death carry on the grey old bank in the white American light. He was at pains to intensify this light, however, by sending the boy home for his education. Ralph spent several terms at an American school and took a degree at an American university, after which, as he struck his father on his return as even redundantly native, he was placed for some three years in residence at Oxford. Oxford swallowed up Harvard, and Ralph became at last English enough. His outward conformity to the manners that surrounded him was none the less the mask of a mind that greatly enjoyed its independence, on which nothing long imposed itself, and which, naturally inclined to adventure and irony, indulged in a boundless liberty of appreciation. He began with being a young man of promise; at Oxford he distinguished himself, to his father's ineffable satisfaction, and the people about him said it was a thousand pities so clever a fellow should be shut out from a career. He might have had a career by returning to his own country (though this point is shrouded in uncertainty) and even if Mr. Touchett had been willing to part with him (which was not the case) it would have gone hard with him to put a watery waste permanently between himself and the old man whom he regarded as his best friend. Ralph was not only fond of his father, he admired him—he enjoyed the opportunity of observing him. Daniel Touchett, to his perception, was a man of genius, and though he himself had no aptitude for the banking mystery he made a point of learning enough of it to measure the great figure his father had played. It was not this, however, he mainly relished; it was the fine ivory surface, polished as by the English air, that the old man had opposed to possibilities of penetration. Daniel Touchett had been neither at Harvard nor at Oxford, and it was his own fault if he had placed in his son's hands the key to modern criticism. Ralph, whose head was full of ideas which his father had never guessed, had a high esteem for the latter's originality. Americans, rightly or wrongly, are commended for the ease with which they adapt themselves to foreign conditions; but Mr. Touchett had made of the very limits of his pliancy half the ground of his general success. He had retained in their freshness most of his marks of primary pressure; his tone, as his son always noted with pleasure, was that of the more luxuriant parts of New England. At the end of his life he had become, on his own ground, as mellow as he was rich; he combined consummate shrewdness with the disposition superficially to fraternise, and his "social position," on which he had never wasted a care, had the firm perfection of an unthumbed fruit. It was perhaps his want of imagination and of what is called the historic consciousness; but to many of the impressions usually made by English life upon the cultivated stranger his sense was completely closed. There were certain differences he had never perceived, certain habits he had never formed, certain obscurities he had never sounded. As regards these latter, on the day he had sounded them his son would have thought less well of him.

Ralph, on leaving Oxford, had spent a couple of years in travelling; after which he had found himself perched on a high stool in his father's bank. The responsibility and honour of such positions is not, I believe, measured by the height of the stool, which depends upon other considerations: Ralph, indeed, who had very long legs, was fond of standing, and even of walking about, at his work. To this exercise, however, he was obliged to devote but a limited period, for at the end of some eighteen months he had become aware of his being seriously out of health. He had caught a violent cold, which fixed itself on his lungs and threw them into dire confusion. He had to give up work and apply, to the letter, the sorry injunction to take care of himself. At first he slighted the task; it appeared to him it was not himself in the least he was taking care of, but an uninteresting and uninterested person with whom he had nothing in common. This person, however, improved on acquaintance, and Ralph grew at last to have a certain grudging tolerance, even an undemonstrative respect, for him. Misfortune makes strange bedfellows, and our young man, feeling that he had something at stake in the matter—it usually struck him as his reputation for ordinary wit—devoted to his graceless charge an amount of attention of which note was duly taken and which had at least the effect of keeping the poor fellow alive. One of his lungs began to heal, the other promised to follow its example, and he was assured he might outweather a dozen winters if he would betake himself to those climates in which consumptives chiefly congregate. As he had grown extremely fond of London, he cursed the flatness of exile: but at the same time that he cursed he conformed, and gradually, when he found his sensitive organ grateful even for grim favours, he conferred them with a lighter hand. He wintered abroad, as the phrase is; basked in the sun, stopped at home when the wind blew, went to bed when it rained, and once or twice, when it had snowed overnight, almost never got up again.

A secret hoard of indifference—like a thick cake a fond old nurse might have slipped into his first school outfit—came to his aid and helped to reconcile him to sacrifice; since at the best he was too ill for aught but that arduous game. As he said to himself, there was really nothing he had wanted very much to do, so that he had at least not renounced the field of valour. At present, however, the fragrance of forbidden fruit seemed occasionally to float past him and remind him that the finest of pleasures is the rush of action. Living as he now lived was like reading a good book in a poor translation—a meagre entertainment for a young man who felt that he might have been an excellent linguist. He had good winters and poor winters, and while the former lasted he was sometimes the sport of a vision of virtual recovery. But this vision was dispelled some three years before the occurrence of the incidents with which this history opens: he had on that occasion remained later than usual in England and had been overtaken by bad weather before reaching Algiers. He arrived more dead than alive and lay there for several weeks between life and death. His convalescence was a miracle, but the first use he made of it was to assure himself that such miracles happen but once. He said to himself that his hour was in sight and that it behoved him to keep his eyes upon it, yet that it was also open to him to spend the interval as agreeably as might be consistent with such a preoccupation. With the prospect of losing them the simple use of his faculties became an exquisite pleasure; it seemed to him the joys of contemplation had never been sounded. He was far from the time when he had found it hard that he should be obliged to give up the idea of distinguishing himself; an idea none the less importunate for being vague and none the less delightful for having had to struggle in the same breast with bursts of inspiring self-criticism. His friends at present judged him more cheerful, and attributed it to a theory, over which they shook their heads knowingly, that he would recover his health. His serenity was but the array of wild flowers niched in his ruin.

It was very probably this sweet-tasting property of the observed thing in itself that was mainly concerned in Ralph's quickly-stirred interest in the advent of a young lady who was evidently not insipid. If he was consideringly disposed, something told him, here was occupation enough for a succession of days. It may be added, in summary fashion, that the imagination of loving—as distinguished from that of being loved—had still a place in his reduced sketch. He had only forbidden himself the riot of expression. However, he shouldn't inspire his cousin with a passion, nor would she be able, even should she try, to help him to one. "And now tell me about the young lady," he said to his mother. "What do you mean to do with her?"

Mrs. Touchett was prompt. "I mean to ask your father to invite her to stay three or four weeks at Garden-court."

"You needn't stand on any such ceremony as that," said Ralph. "My father will ask her as a matter of course."

"I don't know about that. She's my niece; she's not his."

"Good Lord, dear mother; what a sense of property! That's all the more reason for his asking her. But after that—I mean after three months (for its absurd asking the poor girl to remain but for three or four paltry weeks)—what do you mean to do with her?"

"I mean to take her to Paris. I mean to get her clothing."

"Ah yes, that's of course. But independently of that?"

"I shall invite her to spend the autumn with me in Florence."

"You don't rise above detail, dear mother," said Ralph. "I should like to know what you mean to do with her in a general way."

"My duty!" Mrs. Touchett declared. "I suppose you pity her very much," she added.

"No, I don't think I pity her. She doesn't strike me as inviting compassion. I think I envy her. Before being sure, however, give me a hint of where you see your duty."

"In showing her four European countries—I shall leave her the choice of two of them—and in giving her the opportunity of perfecting herself in French, which she already knows very well."

Ralph frowned a little. "That sounds rather dry—even allowing her the choice of two of the countries."

"If it's dry," said his mother with a laugh, "you can leave Isabel alone to water it! She is as good as a summer rain, any day."

"Do you mean she's a gifted being?"

"I don't know whether she's a gifted being, but she's a clever girl—with a strong will and a high temper. She has no idea of being bored."

"I can imagine that," said Ralph; and then he added abruptly: "How do you two get on?"

"Do you mean by that that I'm a bore? I don't think she finds me one. Some girls might, I know; but Isabel's too clever for that. I think I greatly amuse her. We get on because I understand her, I know the sort of girl she is. She's very frank, and I'm very frank: we know just what to expect of each other."

"Ah, dear mother," Ralph exclaimed, "one always knows what to expect of you! You've never surprised me but once, and that's to-day—in presenting me with a pretty cousin whose existence I had never suspected."

"Do you think her so very pretty?"

"Very pretty indeed; but I don't insist upon that. It's her general air of being some one in particular that strikes me. Who is this rare creature, and what is she? Where did you find her, and how did you make her acquaintance?"

"I found her in an old house at Albany, sitting in a dreary room on a rainy day, reading a heavy book and boring herself to death. She didn't know she was bored, but when I left her no doubt of it she seemed very grateful for the service. You may say I shouldn't have enlightened he—I should have let her alone. There's a good deal in that, but I acted conscientiously; I thought she was meant for something better. It occurred to me that it would be a kindness to take her about and introduce her to the world. She thinks she knows a great deal of it—like most American girls; but like most American girls she's ridiculously mistaken. If you want to know, I thought she would do me credit. I like to be well thought of, and for a woman of my age there's no greater convenience, in some ways, than an attractive niece. You know I had seen nothing of my sister's children for years; I disapproved entirely of the father. But I always meant to do something for them when he should have gone to his reward. I ascertained where they were to be found and, without any preliminaries, went and introduced myself. There are two others of them, both of whom are married; but I saw only the elder, who has, by the way, a very uncivil husband. The wife, whose name is Lily, jumped at the idea of my taking an interest in Isabel; she said it was just what her sister needed—that some one should take an interest in her. She spoke of her as you might speak of some young person of genius—in want of encouragement and patronage. It may be that Isabel's a genius; but in that case I've not yet learned her special line. Mrs. Ludlow was especially keen about my taking her to Europe; they all regard Europe over there as a land of emigration, of rescue, a refuge for their superfluous population. Isabel herself seemed very glad to come, and the thing was easily arranged. There was a little difficulty about the money-question, as she seemed averse to being under pecuniary obligations. But she has a small income and she supposes herself to be travelling at her own expense."

Ralph had listened attentively to this judicious report, by which his interest in the subject of it was not impaired. "Ah, if she's a genius," he said, "we must find out her special line. Is it by chance for flirting?"

"I don't think so. You may suspect that at first, but you'll be wrong. You won't, I think, in anyway, be easily right about her."

"Warburton's wrong then!" Ralph rejoicingly exclaimed. "He flatters himself he has made that discovery."

His mother shook her head. "Lord Warburton won't understand her. He needn't try."

"He's very intelligent," said Ralph; "but it's right he should be puzzled once in a while."

"Isabel will enjoy puzzling a lord," Mrs. Touchett remarked.

Her son frowned a little. "What does she know about lords?"

"Nothing at all: that will puzzle him all the more."

Ralph greeted these words with a laugh and looked out of the window. Then, "Are you not going down to see my father?" he asked.

"At a quarter to eight," said Mrs. Touchett.

Her son looked at his watch. "You've another quarter of an hour then. Tell me some more about Isabel." After which, as Mrs. Touchett declined his invitation, declaring that he must find out for himself, "Well," he pursued, "she'll certainly do you credit. But won't she also give you trouble?"

"I hope not; but if she does I shall not shrink from it. I never do that."

"She strikes me as very natural," said Ralph.

"Natural people are not the most trouble."

"No," said Ralph; "you yourself are a proof of that. You're extremely natural, and I'm sure you have never troubled any one. It takes trouble to do that. But tell me this; it just occurs to me. Is Isabel capable of making herself disagreeable?"

"Ah," cried his mother, "you ask too many questions! Find that out for yourself."

His questions, however, were not exhausted. "All this time," he said, "you've not told me what you intend to do with her."

"Do with her? You talk as if she were a yard of calico. I shall do absolutely nothing with her, and she herself will do everything she chooses. She gave me notice of that."

"What you meant then, in your telegram, was that her character's independent."

"I never know what I mean in my telegrams—especially those I send from America. Clearness is too expensive. Come down to your father."

"It's not yet a quarter to eight," said Ralph.

"I must allow for his impatience," Mrs. Touchett answered. Ralph knew what to think of his father's impatience; but, making no rejoinder, he offered his mother his arm. This put it in his power, as they descended together, to stop her a moment on the middle landing of the staircase—the broad, low, wide-armed staircase of time-blackened oak which was one of the most striking features of Gardencourt. "You've no plan of marrying her?" he smiled.

"Marrying her? I should be sorry to play her such a trick! But apart from that, she's perfectly able to marry herself. She has every facility."

"Do you mean to say she has a husband picked out?"

"I don't know about a husband, but there's a young man in Boston—!"

Ralph went on; he had no desire to hear about the young man in Boston. "As my father says, they're always engaged!"

His mother had told him that he must satisfy his curiosity at the source, and it soon became evident he should not want for occasion. He had a good deal of talk with his young kinswoman when the two had been left together in the drawing-room. Lord Warburton, who had ridden over from his own house, some ten miles distant, remounted and took his departure before dinner; and an hour after this meal was ended Mr. and Mrs. Touchett, who appeared to have quite emptied the measure of their forms, withdrew, under the valid pretext of fatigue, to their respective apartments. The young man spent an hour with his cousin; though she had been travelling half the day she appeared in no degree spent. She was really tired; she knew it, and knew she should pay for it on the morrow; but it was her habit at this period to carry exhaustion to the furthest point and confess to it only when dissimulation broke down. A fine hypocrisy was for the present possible; she was interested; she was, as she said to herself, floated. She asked Ralph to show her the pictures; there were a great many in the house, most of them of his own choosing. The best were arranged in an oaken gallery, of charming proportions, which had a sitting-room at either end of it and which in the evening was usually lighted. The light was insufficient to show the pictures to advantage, and the visit might have stood over to the morrow. This suggestion Ralph had ventured to make; but Isabel looked disappointed—smiling still, however—and said: "If you please I should like to see them just a little." She was eager, she knew she was eager and now seemed so; she couldn't help it. "She doesn't take suggestions," Ralph said to himself; but he said it without irritation; her pressure amused and even pleased him. The lamps were on brackets, at intervals, and if the light was imperfect it was genial. It fell upon the vague squares of rich colour and on the faded gilding of heavy frames; it made a sheen on the polished floor of the gallery. Ralph took a candlestick and moved about, pointing out the things he liked; Isabel, inclining to one picture after another, indulged in little exclamations and murmurs. She was evidently a judge; she had a natural taste; he was struck with that. She took a candlestick herself and held it slowly here and there; she lifted it high, and as she did so he found himself pausing in the middle of the place and bending his eyes much less upon the pictures than on her presence. He lost nothing, in truth, by these wandering glances, for she was better worth looking at than most works of art. She was undeniably spare, and ponderably light, and proveably tall; when people had wished to distinguish her from the other two Miss Archers they had always called her the willowy one. Her hair, which was dark even to blackness, had been an object of envy to many women; her light grey eyes, a little too firm perhaps in her graver moments, had an enchanting range of concession. They walked slowly up one side of the gallery and down the other, and then she said: "Well, now I know more than I did when I began!"

"You apparently have a great passion for knowledge," her cousin returned.

"I think I have; most girls are horridly ignorant."

"You strike me as different from most girls."

"Ah, some of them would—but the way they're talked to!" murmured Isabel, who preferred not to dilate just yet on herself. Then in a moment, to change the subject, "Please tell me—isn't there a ghost?" she went on.

"A ghost?"

"A castle-spectre, a thing that appears. We call them ghosts in America."

"So we do here, when we see them."

"You do see them then? You ought to, in this romantic old house."

"It's not a romantic old house," said Ralph. "You'll be disappointed if you count on that. It's a dismally prosaic one; there's no romance here but what you may have brought with you."

"I've brought a great deal; but it seems to me I've brought it to the right place."

"To keep it out of harm, certainly; nothing will ever happen to it here, between my father and me."

Isabel looked at him a moment. "Is there never any one here but your father and you?"

"My mother, of course."

"Oh, I know your mother; she's not romantic. Haven't you other people?"

"Very few."

"I'm sorry for that; I like so much to see people."

"Oh, we'll invite all the county to amuse you," said Ralph.

"Now you're making fun of me," the girl answered rather gravely. "Who was the gentleman on the lawn when I arrived?"

"A county neighbour; he doesn't come very often."

"I'm sorry for that; I liked him," said Isabel.

"Why, it seemed to me that you barely spoke to him," Ralph objected.

"Never mind, I like him all the same. I like your father too, immensely."

"You can't do better than that. He's the dearest of the dear."

"I'm so sorry he is ill," said Isabel.

"You must help me to nurse him; you ought to be a good nurse."

"I don't think I am; I've been told I'm not; I'm said to have too many theories. But you haven't told me about the ghost," she added.

Ralph, however, gave no heed to this observation. "You like my father and you like Lord Warburton. I infer also that you like my mother."

"I like your mother very much, because—because—" And Isabel found herself attempting to assign a reason for her affection for Mrs. Touchett.

"Ah, we never know why!" said her companion, laughing.

"I always know why," the girl answered. "It's because she doesn't expect one to like her. She doesn't care whether one does or not."

"So you adore her—out of perversity? Well, I take greatly after my mother," said Ralph.

"I don't believe you do at all. You wish people to like you, and you try to make them do it."

"Good heavens, how you see through one!" he cried with a dismay that was not altogether jocular.

"But I like you all the same," his cousin went on. "The way to clinch the matter will be to show me the ghost."

Ralph shook his head sadly. "I might show it to you, but you'd never see it. The privilege isn't given to every one; it's not enviable. It has never been seen by a young, happy, innocent person like you. You must have suffered first, have suffered greatly, have gained some miserable knowledge. In that way your eyes are opened to it. I saw it long ago," said Ralph.

"I told you just now I'm very fond of knowledge," Isabel answered.

"Yes, of happy knowledge—of pleasant knowledge. But you haven't suffered, and you're not made to suffer. I hope you'll never see the ghost!"

She had listened to him attentively, with a smile on her lips, but with a certain gravity in her eyes. Charming as he found her, she had struck him as rather presumptuous—indeed it was a part of her charm; and he wondered what she would say. "I'm not afraid, you know," she said: which seemed quite presumptuous enough.

"You're not afraid of suffering?"

"Yes, I'm afraid of suffering. But I'm not afraid of ghosts. And I think people suffer too easily," she added.

"I don't believe you do," said Ralph, looking at her with his hands in his pockets.

"I don't think that's a fault," she answered. "It's not absolutely necessary to suffer; we were not made for that."

"You were not, certainly."

"I'm not speaking of myself." And she wandered off a little.

"No, it isn't a fault," said her cousin. "It's a merit to be strong."

"Only, if you don't suffer they call you hard," Isabel remarked.

They passed out of the smaller drawing-room, into which they had returned from the gallery, and paused in the hall, at the foot of the staircase. Here Ralph presented his companion with her bedroom candle, which he had taken from a niche. "Never mind what they call you. When you do suffer they call you an idiot. The great point's to be as happy as possible."

She looked at him a little; she had taken her candle and placed her foot on the oaken stair. "Well," she said, "that's what I came to Europe for, to be as happy as possible. Good-night."

"Good-night! I wish you all success, and shall be very glad to contribute to it!"

She turned away, and he watched her as she slowly ascended. Then, with his hands always in his pockets, he went back to the empty drawing-room.

CHAPTER VI

Isabel Archer was a young person of many theories; her imagination was remarkably active. It had been her fortune to possess a finer mind than most of the persons among whom her lot was cast; to have a larger perception of surrounding facts and to care for knowledge that was tinged with the unfamiliar. It is true that among her contemporaries she passed for a young woman of extraordinary profundity; for these excellent people never withheld their admiration from a reach of intellect of which they themselves were not conscious, and spoke of Isabel as a prodigy of learning, a creature reported to have read the classic authors—in translations. Her paternal aunt, Mrs. Varian, once spread the rumour that Isabel was writing a book—Mrs. Varian having a reverence for books, and averred that the girl would distinguish herself in print. Mrs. Varian thought highly of literature, for which she entertained that esteem that is connected with a sense of privation. Her own large house, remarkable for its assortment of mosaic tables and decorated ceilings, was unfurnished with a library, and in the way of printed volumes contained nothing but half a dozen novels in paper on a shelf in the apartment of one of the Miss Varians. Practically, Mrs. Varian's acquaintance with literature was confined to The New York Interviewer; as she very justly said, after you had read the Interviewer you had lost all faith in culture. Her tendency, with this, was rather to keep the Interviewer out of the way of her daughters; she was determined to bring them up properly, and they read nothing at all. Her impression with regard to Isabel's labours was quite illusory; the girl had never attempted to write a book and had no desire for the laurels of authorship. She had no talent for expression and too little of the consciousness of genius; she only had a general idea that people were right when they treated her as if she were rather superior. Whether or no she were superior, people were right in admiring her if they thought her so; for it seemed to her often that her mind moved more quickly than theirs, and this encouraged an impatience that might easily be confounded with superiority. It may be affirmed without delay that Isabel was probably very liable to the sin of self-esteem; she often surveyed with complacency the field of her own nature; she was in the habit of taking for granted, on scanty evidence, that she was right; she treated herself to occasions of homage. Meanwhile her errors and delusions were frequently such as a biographer interested in preserving the dignity of his subject must shrink from specifying. Her thoughts were a tangle of vague outlines which had never been corrected by the judgement of people speaking with authority. In matters of opinion she had had her own way, and it had led her into a thousand ridiculous zigzags. At moments she discovered she was grotesquely wrong, and then she treated herself to a week of passionate humility. After this she held her head higher than ever again; for it was of no use, she had an unquenchable desire to think well of herself. She had a theory that it was only under this provision life was worth living; that one should be one of the best, should be conscious of a fine organisation (she couldn't help knowing her organisation was fine), should move in a realm of light, of natural wisdom, of happy impulse, of inspiration gracefully chronic. It was almost as unnecessary to cultivate doubt of one's self as to cultivate doubt of one's best friend: one should try to be one's own best friend and to give one's self, in this manner, distinguished company. The girl had a certain nobleness of imagination which rendered her a good many services and played her a great many tricks. She spent half her time in thinking of beauty and bravery and magnanimity; she had a fixed determination to regard the world as a place of brightness, of free expansion, of irresistible action: she held it must be detestable to be afraid or ashamed. She had an infinite hope that she should never do anything wrong. She had resented so strongly, after discovering them, her mere errors of feeling (the discovery always made her tremble as if she had escaped from a trap which might have caught her and smothered her) that the chance of inflicting a sensible injury upon another person, presented only as a contingency, caused her at moments to hold her breath. That always struck her as the worst thing that could happen to her. On the whole, reflectively, she was in no uncertainty about the things that were wrong. She had no love of their look, but when she fixed them hard she recognised them. It was wrong to be mean, to be jealous, to be false, to be cruel; she had seen very little of the evil of the world, but she had seen women who lied and who tried to hurt each other. Seeing such things had quickened her high spirit; it seemed indecent not to scorn them. Of course the danger of a high spirit was the danger of inconsistency—the danger of keeping up the flag after the place has surrendered; a sort of behaviour so crooked as to be almost a dishonour to the flag. But Isabel, who knew little of the sorts of artillery to which young women are exposed, flattered herself that such contradictions would never be noted in her own conduct. Her life should always be in harmony with the most pleasing impression she should produce; she would be what she appeared, and she would appear what she was. Sometimes she went so far as to wish that she might find herself some day in a difficult position, so that she should have the pleasure of being as heroic as the occasion demanded. Altogether, with her meagre knowledge, her inflated ideals, her confidence at once innocent and dogmatic, her temper at once exacting and indulgent, her mixture of curiosity and fastidiousness, of vivacity and indifference, her desire to look very well and to be if possible even better, her determination to see, to try, to know, her combination of the delicate, desultory, flame-like spirit and the eager and personal creature of conditions: she would be an easy victim of scientific criticism if she were not intended to awaken on the reader's part an impulse more tender and more purely expectant.

It was one of her theories that Isabel Archer was very fortunate in being independent, and that she ought to make some very enlightened use of that state. She never called it the state of solitude, much less of singleness; she thought such descriptions weak, and, besides, her sister Lily constantly urged her to come and abide. She had a friend whose acquaintance she had made shortly before her father's death, who offered so high an example of useful activity that Isabel always thought of her as a model. Henrietta Stackpole had the advantage of an admired ability; she was thoroughly launched in journalism, and her letters to the Interviewer, from Washington, Newport, the White Mountains and other places, were universally quoted. Isabel pronounced them with confidence "ephemeral," but she esteemed the courage, energy and good-humour of the writer, who, without parents and without property, had adopted three of the children of an infirm and widowed sister and was paying their school-bills out of the proceeds of her literary labour. Henrietta was in the van of progress and had clear-cut views on most subjects; her cherished desire had long been to come to Europe and write a series of letters to the Interviewer from the radical point of view—an enterprise the less difficult as she knew perfectly in advance what her opinions would be and to how many objections most European institutions lay open. When she heard that Isabel was coming she wished to start at once; thinking, naturally, that it would be delightful the two should travel together. She had been obliged, however, to postpone this enterprise. She thought Isabel a glorious creature, and had spoken of her covertly in some of her letters, though she never mentioned the fact to her friend, who would not have taken pleasure in it and was not a regular student of the Interviewer. Henrietta, for Isabel, was chiefly a proof that a woman might suffice to herself and be happy. Her resources were of the obvious kind; but even if one had not the journalistic talent and a genius for guessing, as Henrietta said, what the public was going to want, one was not therefore to conclude that one had no vocation, no beneficent aptitude of any sort, and resign one's self to being frivolous and hollow. Isabel was stoutly determined not to be hollow. If one should wait with the right patience one would find some happy work to one's hand. Of course, among her theories, this young lady was not without a collection of views on the subject of marriage. The first on the list was a conviction of the vulgarity of thinking too much of it. From lapsing into eagerness on this point she earnestly prayed she might be delivered; she held that a woman ought to be able to live to herself, in the absence of exceptional flimsiness, and that it was perfectly possible to be happy without the society of a more or less coarse-minded person of another sex. The girl's prayer was very sufficiently answered; something pure and proud that there was in her—something cold and dry an unappreciated suitor with a taste for analysis might have called it—had hitherto kept her from any great vanity of conjecture on the article of possible husbands. Few of the men she saw seemed worth a ruinous expenditure, and it made her smile to think that one of them should present himself as an incentive to hope and a reward of patience. Deep in her soul—it was the deepest thing there—lay a belief that if a certain light should dawn she could give herself completely; but this image, on the whole, was too formidable to be attractive. Isabel's thoughts hovered about it, but they seldom rested on it long; after a little it ended in alarms. It often seemed to her that she thought too much about herself; you could have made her colour, any day in the year, by calling her a rank egoist. She was always planning out her development, desiring her perfection, observing her progress. Her nature had, in her conceit, a certain garden-like quality, a suggestion of perfume and murmuring boughs, of shady bowers and lengthening vistas, which made her feel that introspection was, after all, an exercise in the open air, and that a visit to the recesses of one's spirit was harmless when one returned from it with a lapful of roses. But she was often reminded that there were other gardens in the world than those of her remarkable soul, and that there were moreover a great many places which were not gardens at all—only dusky pestiferous tracts, planted thick with ugliness and misery. In the current of that repaid curiosity on which she had lately been floating, which had conveyed her to this beautiful old England and might carry her much further still, she often checked herself with the thought of the thousands of people who were less happy than herself—a thought which for the moment made her fine, full consciousness appear a kind of immodesty. What should one do with the misery of the world in a scheme of the agreeable for one's self? It must be confessed that this question never held her long. She was too young, too impatient to live, too unacquainted with pain. She always returned to her theory that a young woman whom after all every one thought clever should begin by getting a general impression of life. This impression was necessary to prevent mistakes, and after it should be secured she might make the unfortunate condition of others a subject of special attention.

England was a revelation to her, and she found herself as diverted as a child at a pantomime. In her infantine excursions to Europe she had seen only the Continent, and seen it from the nursery window; Paris, not London, was her father's Mecca, and into many of his interests there his children had naturally not entered. The images of that time moreover had grown faint and remote, and the old-world quality in everything that she now saw had all the charm of strangeness. Her uncle's house seemed a picture made real; no refinement of the agreeable was lost upon Isabel; the rich perfection of Gardencourt at once revealed a world and gratified a need. The large, low rooms, with brown ceilings and dusky corners, the deep embrasures and curious casements, the quiet light on dark, polished panels, the deep greenness outside, that seemed always peeping in, the sense of well-ordered privacy in the centre of a "property"—a place where sounds were felicitously accidental, where the tread was muffed by the earth itself and in the thick mild air all friction dropped out of contact and all shrillness out of talk—these things were much to the taste of our young lady, whose taste played a considerable part in her emotions. She formed a fast friendship with her uncle, and often sat by his chair when he had had it moved out to the lawn. He passed hours in the open air, sitting with folded hands like a placid, homely household god, a god of service, who had done his work and received his wages and was trying to grow used to weeks and months made up only of off-days. Isabel amused him more than she suspected—the effect she produced upon people was often different from what she supposed—and he frequently gave himself the pleasure of making her chatter. It was by this term that he qualified her conversation, which had much of the "point" observable in that of the young ladies of her country, to whom the ear of the world is more directly presented than to their sisters in other lands. Like the mass of American girls Isabel had been encouraged to express herself; her remarks had been attended to; she had been expected to have emotions and opinions. Many of her opinions had doubtless but a slender value, many of her emotions passed away in the utterance; but they had left a trace in giving her the habit of seeming at least to feel and think, and in imparting moreover to her words when she was really moved that prompt vividness which so many people had regarded as a sign of superiority. Mr. Touchett used to think that she reminded him of his wife when his wife was in her teens. It was because she was fresh and natural and quick to understand, to speak—so many characteristics of her niece—that he had fallen in love with Mrs. Touchett. He never expressed this analogy to the girl herself, however; for if Mrs. Touchett had once been like Isabel, Isabel was not at all like Mrs. Touchett. The old man was full of kindness for her; it was a long time, as he said, since they had had any young life in the house; and our rustling, quickly-moving, clear-voiced heroine was as agreeable to his sense as the sound of flowing water. He wanted to do something for her and wished she would ask it of him. She would ask nothing but questions; it is true that of these she asked a quantity. Her uncle had a great fund of answers, though her pressure sometimes came in forms that puzzled him. She questioned him immensely about England, about the British constitution, the English character, the state of politics, the manners and customs of the royal family, the peculiarities of the aristocracy, the way of living and thinking of his neighbours; and in begging to be enlightened on these points she usually enquired whether they corresponded with the descriptions in the books. The old man always looked at her a little with his fine dry smile while he smoothed down the shawl spread across his legs.

"The books?" he once said; "well, I don't know much about the books. You must ask Ralph about that. I've always ascertained for myself—got my information in the natural form. I never asked many questions even; I just kept quiet and took notice. Of course I've had very good opportunities—better than what a young lady would naturally have. I'm of an inquisitive disposition, though you mightn't think it if you were to watch me: however much you might watch me I should be watching you more. I've been watching these people for upwards of thirty-five years, and I don't hesitate to say that I've acquired considerable information. It's a very fine country on the whole—finer perhaps than what we give it credit for on the other side. Several improvements I should like to see introduced; but the necessity of them doesn't seem to be generally felt as yet. When the necessity of a thing is generally felt they usually manage to accomplish it; but they seem to feel pretty comfortable about waiting till then. I certainly feel more at home among them than I expected to when I first came over; I suppose it's because I've had a considerable degree of success. When you're successful you naturally feel more at home."

"Do you suppose that if I'm successful I shall feel at home?" Isabel asked.

"I should think it very probable, and you certainly will be successful. They like American young ladies very much over here; they show them a great deal of kindness. But you mustn't feel too much at home, you know."

"Oh, I'm by no means sure it will satisfy me," Isabel judicially emphasised. "I like the place very much, but I'm not sure I shall like the people."

"The people are very good people; especially if you like them."

"I've no doubt they're good," Isabel rejoined; "but are they pleasant in society? They won't rob me nor beat me; but will they make themselves agreeable to me? That's what I like people to do. I don't hesitate to say so, because I always appreciate it. I don't believe they're very nice to girls; they're not nice to them in the novels."

"I don't know about the novels," said Mr. Touchett. "I believe the novels have a great deal but I don't suppose they're very accurate. We once had a lady who wrote novels staying here; she was a friend of Ralph's and he asked her down. She was very positive, quite up to everything; but she was not the sort of person you could depend on for evidence. Too free a fancy—I suppose that was it. She afterwards published a work of fiction in which she was understood to have given a representation—something in the nature of a caricature, as you might say—of my unworthy self. I didn't read it, but Ralph just handed me the book with the principal passages marked. It was understood to be a description of my conversation; American peculiarities, nasal twang, Yankee notions, stars and stripes. Well, it was not at all accurate; she couldn't have listened very attentively. I had no objection to her giving a report of my conversation, if she liked but I didn't like the idea that she hadn't taken the trouble to listen to it. Of course I talk like an American—I can't talk like a Hottentot. However I talk, I've made them understand me pretty well over here. But I don't talk like the old gentleman in that lady's novel. He wasn't an American; we wouldn't have him over there at any price. I just mention that fact to show you that they're not always accurate. Of course, as I've no daughters, and as Mrs. Touchett resides in Florence, I haven't had much chance to notice about the young ladies. It sometimes appears as if the young women in the lower class were not very well treated; but I guess their position is better in the upper and even to some extent in the middle."

"Gracious," Isabel exclaimed; "how many classes have they? About fifty, I suppose."

"Well, I don't know that I ever counted them. I never took much notice of the classes. That's the advantage of being an American here; you don't belong to any class."

"I hope so," said Isabel. "Imagine one's belonging to an English class!"

"Well, I guess some of them are pretty comfortable—especially towards the top. But for me there are only two classes: the people I trust and the people I don't. Of those two, my dear Isabel, you belong to the first."

"I'm much obliged to you," said the girl quickly. Her way of taking compliments seemed sometimes rather dry; she got rid of them as rapidly as possible. But as regards this she was sometimes misjudged; she was thought insensible to them, whereas in fact she was simply unwilling to show how infinitely they pleased her. To show that was to show too much. "I'm sure the English are very conventional," she added.

"They've got everything pretty well fixed," Mr. Touchett admitted. "It's all settled beforehand—they don't leave it to the last moment."

"I don't like to have everything settled beforehand," said the girl. "I like more unexpectedness."

Her uncle seemed amused at her distinctness of preference. "Well, it's settled beforehand that you'll have great success," he rejoined. "I suppose you'll like that."

"I shall not have success if they're too stupidly conventional. I'm not in the least stupidly conventional. I'm just the contrary. That's what they won't like."

"No, no, you're all wrong," said the old man. "You can't tell what they'll like. They're very inconsistent; that's their principal interest."

"Ah well," said Isabel, standing before her uncle with her hands clasped about the belt of her black dress and looking up and down the lawn—"that will suit me perfectly!"

CHAPTER VII

The two amused themselves, time and again, with talking of the attitude of the British public as if the young lady had been in a position to appeal to it; but in fact the British public remained for the present profoundly indifferent to Miss Isabel Archer, whose fortune had dropped her, as her cousin said, into the dullest house in England. Her gouty uncle received very little company, and Mrs. Touchett, not having cultivated relations with her husband's neighbours, was not warranted in expecting visits from them. She had, however, a peculiar taste; she liked to receive cards. For what is usually called social intercourse she had very little relish; but nothing pleased her more than to find her hall-table whitened with oblong morsels of symbolic pasteboard. She flattered herself that she was a very just woman, and had mastered the sovereign truth that nothing in this world is got for nothing. She had played no social part as mistress of Gardencourt, and it was not to be supposed that, in the surrounding country, a minute account should be kept of her comings and goings. But it is by no means certain that she did not feel it to be wrong that so little notice was taken of them and that her failure (really very gratuitous) to make herself important in the neighbourhood had not much to do with the acrimony of her allusions to her husband's adopted country. Isabel presently found herself in the singular situation of defending the British constitution against her aunt; Mrs. Touchett having formed the habit of sticking pins into this venerable instrument. Isabel always felt an impulse to pull out the pins; not that she imagined they inflicted any damage on the tough old parchment, but because it seemed to her her aunt might make better use of her sharpness. She was very critical herself—it was incidental to her age, her sex and her nationality; but she was very sentimental as well, and there was something in Mrs. Touchett's dryness that set her own moral fountains flowing.

"Now what's your point of view?" she asked of her aunt. "When you criticise everything here you should have a point of view. Yours doesn't seem to be American—you thought everything over there so disagreeable. When I criticise I have mine; it's thoroughly American!"

"My dear young lady," said Mrs. Touchett, "there are as many points of view in the world as there are people of sense to take them. You may say that doesn't make them very numerous! American? Never in the world; that's shockingly narrow. My point of view, thank God, is personal!"

Isabel thought this a better answer than she admitted; it was a tolerable description of her own manner of judging, but it would not have sounded well for her to say so. On the lips of a person less advanced in life and less enlightened by experience than Mrs. Touchett such a declaration would savour of immodesty, even of arrogance. She risked it nevertheless in talking with Ralph, with whom she talked a great deal and with whom her conversation was of a sort that gave a large licence to extravagance. Her cousin used, as the phrase is, to chaff her; he very soon established with her a reputation for treating everything as a joke, and he was not a man to neglect the privileges such a reputation conferred. She accused him of an odious want of seriousness, of laughing at all things, beginning with himself. Such slender faculty of reverence as he possessed centred wholly upon his father; for the rest, he exercised his wit indifferently upon his father's son, this gentleman's weak lungs, his useless life, his fantastic mother, his friends (Lord Warburton in especial), his adopted, and his native country, his charming new-found cousin. "I keep a band of music in my ante-room," he said once to her. "It has orders to play without stopping; it renders me two excellent services. It keeps the sounds of the world from reaching the private apartments, and it makes the world think that dancing's going on within." It was dance-music indeed that you usually heard when you came within ear-shot of Ralph's band; the liveliest waltzes seemed to float upon the air. Isabel often found herself irritated by this perpetual fiddling; she would have liked to pass through the ante-room, as her cousin called it, and enter the private apartments. It mattered little that he had assured her they were a very dismal place; she would have been glad to undertake to sweep them and set them in order. It was but half-hospitality to let her remain outside; to punish him for which Isabel administered innumerable taps with the ferule of her straight young wit. It must be said that her wit was exercised to a large extent in self-defence, for her cousin amused himself with calling her "Columbia" and accusing her of a patriotism so heated that it scorched. He drew a caricature of her in which she was represented as a very pretty young woman dressed, on the lines of the prevailing fashion, in the folds of the national banner. Isabel's chief dread in life at this period of her development was that she should appear narrow-minded; what she feared next afterwards was that she should really be so. But she nevertheless made no scruple of abounding in her cousin's sense and pretending to sigh for the charms of her native land. She would be as American as it pleased him to regard her, and if he chose to laugh at her she would give him plenty of occupation. She defended England against his mother, but when Ralph sang its praises on purpose, as she said, to work her up, she found herself able to differ from him on a variety of points. In fact, the quality of this small ripe country seemed as sweet to her as the taste of an October pear; and her satisfaction was at the root of the good spirits which enabled her to take her cousin's chaff and return it in kind. If her good-humour flagged at moments it was not because she thought herself ill-used, but because she suddenly felt sorry for Ralph. It seemed to her he was talking as a blind and had little heart in what he said. "I don't know what's the matter with you," she observed to him once; "but I suspect you're a great humbug."

"That's your privilege," Ralph answered, who had not been used to being so crudely addressed.

"I don't know what you care for; I don't think you care for anything. You don't really care for England when you praise it; you don't care for America even when you pretend to abuse it."

"I care for nothing but you, dear cousin," said Ralph.

"If I could believe even that, I should be very glad."

"Ah well, I should hope so!" the young man exclaimed.

Isabel might have believed it and not have been far from the truth. He thought a great deal about her; she was constantly present to his mind. At a time when his thoughts had been a good deal of a burden to him her sudden arrival, which promised nothing and was an open-handed gift of fate, had refreshed and quickened them, given them wings and something to fly for. Poor Ralph had been for many weeks steeped in melancholy; his outlook, habitually sombre, lay under the shadow of a deeper cloud. He had grown anxious about his father, whose gout, hitherto confined to his legs, had begun to ascend into regions more vital. The old man had been gravely ill in the spring, and the doctors had whispered to Ralph that another attack would be less easy to deal with. Just now he appeared disburdened of pain, but Ralph could not rid himself of a suspicion that this was a subterfuge of the enemy, who was waiting to take him off his guard. If the manoeuvre should succeed there would be little hope of any great resistance. Ralph had always taken for granted that his father would survive him—that his own name would be the first grimly called. The father and son had been close companions, and the idea of being left alone with the remnant of a tasteless life on his hands was not gratifying to the young man, who had always and tacitly counted upon his elder's help in making the best of a poor business. At the prospect of losing his great motive Ralph lost indeed his one inspiration. If they might die at the same time it would be all very well; but without the encouragement of his father's society he should barely have patience to await his own turn. He had not the incentive of feeling that he was indispensable to his mother; it was a rule with his mother to have no regrets. He bethought himself of course that it had been a small kindness to his father to wish that, of the two, the active rather than the passive party should know the felt wound; he remembered that the old man had always treated his own forecast of an early end as a clever fallacy, which he should be delighted to discredit so far as he might by dying first. But of the two triumphs, that of refuting a sophistical son and that of holding on a while longer to a state of being which, with all abatements, he enjoyed, Ralph deemed it no sin to hope the latter might be vouchsafed to Mr. Touchett.

These were nice questions, but Isabel's arrival put a stop to his puzzling over them. It even suggested there might be a compensation for the intolerable ennui of surviving his genial sire. He wondered whether he were harbouring "love" for this spontaneous young woman from Albany; but he judged that on the whole he was not. After he had known her for a week he quite made up his mind to this, and every day he felt a little more sure. Lord Warburton had been right about her; she was a really interesting little figure. Ralph wondered how their neighbour had found it out so soon; and then he said it was only another proof of his friend's high abilities, which he had always greatly admired. If his cousin were to be nothing more than an entertainment to him, Ralph was conscious she was an entertainment of a high order. "A character like that," he said to himself—"a real little passionate force to see at play is the finest thing in nature. It's finer than the finest work of art—than a Greek bas-relief, than a great Titian, than a Gothic cathedral. It's very pleasant to be so well treated where one had least looked for it. I had never been more blue, more bored, than for a week before she came; I had never expected less that anything pleasant would happen. Suddenly I receive a Titian, by the post, to hang on my wall—a Greek bas-relief to stick over my chimney-piece. The key of a beautiful edifice is thrust into my hand, and I'm told to walk in and admire. My poor boy, you've been sadly ungrateful, and now you had better keep very quiet and never grumble again." The sentiment of these reflexions was very just; but it was not exactly true that Ralph Touchett had had a key put into his hand. His cousin was a very brilliant girl, who would take, as he said, a good deal of knowing; but she needed the knowing, and his attitude with regard to her, though it was contemplative and critical, was not judicial. He surveyed the edifice from the outside and admired it greatly; he looked in at the windows and received an impression of proportions equally fair. But he felt that he saw it only by glimpses and that he had not yet stood under the roof. The door was fastened, and though he had keys in his pocket he had a conviction that none of them would fit. She was intelligent and generous; it was a fine free nature; but what was she going to do with herself? This question was irregular, for with most women one had no occasion to ask it. Most women did with themselves nothing at all; they waited, in attitudes more or less gracefully passive, for a man to come that way and furnish them with a destiny. Isabel's originality was that she gave one an impression of having intentions of her own. "Whenever she executes them," said Ralph, "may I be there to see!"

It devolved upon him of course to do the honours of the place. Mr. Touchett was confined to his chair, and his wife's position was that of rather a grim visitor; so that in the line of conduct that opened itself to Ralph duty and inclination were harmoniously mixed. He was not a great walker, but he strolled about the grounds with his cousin—a pastime for which the weather remained favourable with a persistency not allowed for in Isabel's somewhat lugubrious prevision of the climate; and in the long afternoons, of which the length was but the measure of her gratified eagerness, they took a boat on the river, the dear little river, as Isabel called it, where the opposite shore seemed still a part of the foreground of the landscape; or drove over the country in a phaeton—a low, capacious, thick-wheeled phaeton formerly much used by Mr. Touchett, but which he had now ceased to enjoy. Isabel enjoyed it largely and, handling the reins in a manner which approved itself to the groom as "knowing," was never weary of driving her uncle's capital horses through winding lanes and byways full of the rural incidents she had confidently expected to find; past cottages thatched and timbered, past alehouses latticed and sanded, past patches of ancient common and glimpses of empty parks, between hedgerows made thick by midsummer. When they reached home they usually found tea had been served on the lawn and that Mrs. Touchett had not shrunk from the extremity of handing her husband his cup. But the two for the most part sat silent; the old man with his head back and his eyes closed, his wife occupied with her knitting and wearing that appearance of rare profundity with which some ladies consider the movement of their needles.

One day, however, a visitor had arrived. The two young persons, after spending an hour on the river, strolled back to the house and perceived Lord Warburton sitting under the trees and engaged in conversation, of which even at a distance the desultory character was appreciable, with Mrs. Touchett. He had driven over from his own place with a portmanteau and had asked, as the father and son often invited him to do, for a dinner and a lodging. Isabel, seeing him for half an hour on the day of her arrival, had discovered in this brief space that she liked him; he had indeed rather sharply registered himself on her fine sense and she had thought of him several times. She had hoped she should see him again—hoped too that she should see a few others. Gardencourt was not dull; the place itself was sovereign, her uncle was more and more a sort of golden grandfather, and Ralph was unlike any cousin she had ever encountered—her idea of cousins having tended to gloom. Then her impressions were still so fresh and so quickly renewed that there was as yet hardly a hint of vacancy in the view. But Isabel had need to remind herself that she was interested in human nature and that her foremost hope in coming abroad had been that she should see a great many people. When Ralph said to her, as he had done several times, "I wonder you find this endurable; you ought to see some of the neighbours and some of our friends, because we have really got a few, though you would never suppose it"—when he offered to invite what he called a "lot of people" and make her acquainted with English society, she encouraged the hospitable impulse and promised in advance to hurl herself into the fray. Little, however, for the present, had come of his offers, and it may be confided to the reader that if the young man delayed to carry them out it was because he found the labour of providing for his companion by no means so severe as to require extraneous help. Isabel had spoken to him very often about "specimens;" it was a word that played a considerable part in her vocabulary; she had given him to understand that she wished to see English society illustrated by eminent cases.

"Well now, there's a specimen," he said to her as they walked up from the riverside and he recognised Lord Warburton.

"A specimen of what?" asked the girl.

"A specimen of an English gentleman."

"Do you mean they're all like him?"

"Oh no; they're not all like him."

"He's a favourable specimen then," said Isabel; "because I'm sure he's nice."

"Yes, he's very nice. And he's very fortunate."

The fortunate Lord Warburton exchanged a handshake with our heroine and hoped she was very well. "But I needn't ask that," he said, "since you've been handling the oars."

"I've been rowing a little," Isabel answered; "but how should you know it?"

"Oh, I know he doesn't row; he's too lazy," said his lordship, indicating Ralph Touchett with a laugh.

"He has a good excuse for his laziness," Isabel rejoined, lowering her voice a little.

"Ah, he has a good excuse for everything!" cried Lord Warburton, still with his sonorous mirth.

"My excuse for not rowing is that my cousin rows so well," said Ralph. "She does everything well. She touches nothing that she doesn't adorn!"

"It makes one want to be touched, Miss Archer," Lord Warburton declared.

"Be touched in the right sense and you'll never look the worse for it," said Isabel, who, if it pleased her to hear it said that her accomplishments were numerous, was happily able to reflect that such complacency was not the indication of a feeble mind, inasmuch as there were several things in which she excelled. Her desire to think well of herself had at least the element of humility that it always needed to be supported by proof.

Lord Warburton not only spent the night at Gardencourt, but he was persuaded to remain over the second day; and when the second day was ended he determined to postpone his departure till the morrow. During this period he addressed many of his remarks to Isabel, who accepted this evidence of his esteem with a very good grace. She found herself liking him extremely; the first impression he had made on her had had weight, but at the end of an evening spent in his society she scarce fell short of seeing him—though quite without luridity—as a hero of romance. She retired to rest with a sense of good fortune, with a quickened consciousness of possible felicities. "It's very nice to know two such charming people as those," she said, meaning by "those" her cousin and her cousin's friend. It must be added moreover that an incident had occurred which might have seemed to put her good-humour to the test. Mr. Touchett went to bed at half-past nine o'clock, but his wife remained in the drawing-room with the other members of the party. She prolonged her vigil for something less than an hour, and then, rising, observed to Isabel that it was time they should bid the gentlemen good-night. Isabel had as yet no desire to go to bed; the occasion wore, to her sense, a festive character, and feasts were not in the habit of terminating so early. So, without further thought, she replied, very simply—

"Need I go, dear aunt? I'll come up in half an hour."

"It's impossible I should wait for you," Mrs. Touchett answered.

"Ah, you needn't wait! Ralph will light my candle," Isabel gaily engaged.

"I'll light your candle; do let me light your candle, Miss Archer!" Lord Warburton exclaimed. "Only I beg it shall not be before midnight."

Mrs. Touchett fixed her bright little eyes upon him a moment and transferred them coldly to her niece. "You can't stay alone with the gentlemen. You're not—you're not at your blest Albany, my dear."

Isabel rose, blushing. "I wish I were," she said.

"Oh, I say, mother!" Ralph broke out.

"My dear Mrs. Touchett!" Lord Warburton murmured.

"I didn't make your country, my lord," Mrs. Touchett said majestically. "I must take it as I find it."

"Can't I stay with my own cousin?" Isabel enquired.

"I'm not aware that Lord Warburton is your cousin."

"Perhaps I had better go to bed!" the visitor suggested. "That will arrange it."

Mrs. Touchett gave a little look of despair and sat down again. "Oh, if it's necessary I'll stay up till midnight."

Ralph meanwhile handed Isabel her candlestick. He had been watching her; it had seemed to him her temper was involved—an accident that might be interesting. But if he had expected anything of a flare he was disappointed, for the girl simply laughed a little, nodded good-night and withdrew accompanied by her aunt. For himself he was annoyed at his mother, though he thought she was right. Above-stairs the two ladies separated at Mrs. Touchett's door. Isabel had said nothing on her way up.

"Of course you're vexed at my interfering with you," said Mrs. Touchett.

Isabel considered. "I'm not vexed, but I'm surprised—and a good deal mystified. Wasn't it proper I should remain in the drawing-room?"

"Not in the least. Young girls here—in decent houses—don't sit alone with the gentlemen late at night."

"You were very right to tell me then," said Isabel. "I don't understand it, but I'm very glad to know it.

"I shall always tell you," her aunt answered, "whenever I see you taking what seems to me too much liberty."

"Pray do; but I don't say I shall always think your remonstrance just."

"Very likely not. You're too fond of your own ways."

"Yes, I think I'm very fond of them. But I always want to know the things one shouldn't do."

"So as to do them?" asked her aunt.

"So as to choose," said Isabel.

CHAPTER VIII

As she was devoted to romantic effects Lord Warburton ventured to express a hope that she would come some day and see his house, a very curious old place. He extracted from Mrs. Touchett a promise that she would bring her niece to Lockleigh, and Ralph signified his willingness to attend the ladies if his father should be able to spare him. Lord Warburton assured our heroine that in the mean time his sisters would come and see her. She knew something about his sisters, having sounded him, during the hours they spent together while he was at Gardencourt, on many points connected with his family. When Isabel was interested she asked a great many questions, and as her companion was a copious talker she urged him on this occasion by no means in vain. He told her he had four sisters and two brothers and had lost both his parents. The brothers and sisters were very good people—"not particularly clever, you know," he said, "but very decent and pleasant;" and he was so good as to hope Miss Archer might know them well. One of the brothers was in the Church, settled in the family living, that of Lockleigh, which was a heavy, sprawling parish, and was an excellent fellow in spite of his thinking differently from himself on every conceivable topic. And then Lord Warburton mentioned some of the opinions held by his brother, which were opinions Isabel had often heard expressed and that she supposed to be entertained by a considerable portion of the human family. Many of them indeed she supposed she had held herself, till he assured her she was quite mistaken, that it was really impossible, that she had doubtless imagined she entertained them, but that she might depend that, if she thought them over a little, she would find there was nothing in them. When she answered that she had already thought several of the questions involved over very attentively he declared that she was only another example of what he had often been struck with—the fact that, of all the people in the world, the Americans were the most grossly superstitious. They were rank Tories and bigots, every one of them; there were no conservatives like American conservatives. Her uncle and her cousin were there to prove it; nothing could be more medieval than many of their views; they had ideas that people in England nowadays were ashamed to confess to; and they had the impudence moreover, said his lordship, laughing, to pretend they knew more about the needs and dangers of this poor dear stupid old England than he who was born in it and owned a considerable slice of it—the more shame to him! From all of which Isabel gathered that Lord Warburton was a nobleman of the newest pattern, a reformer, a radical, a contemner of ancient ways. His other brother, who was in the army in India, was rather wild and pig-headed and had not been of much use as yet but to make debts for Warburton to pay—one of the most precious privileges of an elder brother. "I don't think I shall pay any more," said her friend; "he lives a monstrous deal better than I do, enjoys unheard-of luxuries and thinks himself a much finer gentleman than I. As I'm a consistent radical I go in only for equality; I don't go in for the superiority of the younger brothers." Two of his four sisters, the second and fourth, were married, one of them having done very well, as they said, the other only so-so. The husband of the elder, Lord Haycock, was a very good fellow, but unfortunately a horrid Tory; and his wife, like all good English wives, was worse than her husband. The other had espoused a smallish squire in Norfolk and, though married but the other day, had already five children. This information and much more Lord Warburton imparted to his young American listener, taking pains to make many things clear and to lay bare to her apprehension the peculiarities of English life. Isabel was often amused at his explicitness and at the small allowance he seemed to make either for her own experience or for her imagination. "He thinks I'm a barbarian," she said, "and that I've never seen forks and spoons;" and she used to ask him artless questions for the pleasure of hearing him answer seriously. Then when he had fallen into the trap, "It's a pity you can't see me in my war-paint and feathers," she remarked; "if I had known how kind you are to the poor savages I would have brought over my native costume!" Lord Warburton had travelled through the United States and knew much more about them than Isabel; he was so good as to say that America was the most charming country in the world, but his recollections of it appeared to encourage the idea that Americans in England would need to have a great many things explained to them. "If I had only had you to explain things to me in America!" he said. "I was rather puzzled in your country; in fact I was quite bewildered, and the trouble was that the explanations only puzzled me more. You know I think they often gave me the wrong ones on purpose; they're rather clever about that over there. But when I explain you can trust me; about what I tell you there's no mistake." There was no mistake at least about his being very intelligent and cultivated and knowing almost everything in the world. Although he gave the most interesting and thrilling glimpses Isabel felt he never did it to exhibit himself, and though he had had rare chances and had tumbled in, as she put it, for high prizes, he was as far as possible from making a merit of it. He had enjoyed the best things of life, but they had not spoiled his sense of proportion. His quality was a mixture of the effect of rich experience—oh, so easily come by!—with a modesty at times almost boyish; the sweet and wholesome savour of which—it was as agreeable as something tasted—lost nothing from the addition of a tone of responsible kindness.

"I like your specimen English gentleman very much," Isabel said to Ralph after Lord Warburton had gone.

"I like him too—I love him well," Ralph returned. "But I pity him more."

Isabel looked at him askance. "Why, that seems to me his only fault—that one can't pity him a little. He appears to have everything, to know everything, to be everything."

"Oh, he's in a bad way!" Ralph insisted.

"I suppose you don't mean in health?"

"No, as to that he's detestably sound. What I mean is that he's a man with a great position who's playing all sorts of tricks with it. He doesn't take himself seriously."

"Does he regard himself as a joke?"

"Much worse; he regards himself as an imposition—as an abuse."

"Well, perhaps he is," said Isabel.

"Perhaps he is—though on the whole I don't think so. But in that case what's more pitiable than a sentient, self-conscious abuse planted by other hands, deeply rooted but aching with a sense of its injustice? For me, in his place, I could be as solemn as a statue of Buddha. He occupies a position that appeals to my imagination. Great responsibilities, great opportunities, great consideration, great wealth, great power, a natural share in the public affairs of a great country. But he's all in a muddle about himself, his position, his power, and indeed about everything in the world. He's the victim of a critical age; he has ceased to believe in himself and he doesn't know what to believe in. When I attempt to tell him (because if I were he I know very well what I should believe in) he calls me a pampered bigot. I believe he seriously thinks me an awful Philistine; he says I don't understand my time. I understand it certainly better than he, who can neither abolish himself as a nuisance nor maintain himself as an institution."

"He doesn't look very wretched," Isabel observed.

"Possibly not; though, being a man of a good deal of charming taste, I think he often has uncomfortable hours. But what is it to say of a being of his opportunities that he's not miserable? Besides, I believe he is."

"I don't," said Isabel.

"Well," her cousin rejoined, "if he isn't he ought to be!"

In the afternoon she spent an hour with her uncle on the lawn, where the old man sat, as usual, with his shawl over his legs and his large cup of diluted tea in his hands. In the course of conversation he asked her what she thought of their late visitor.

Isabel was prompt. "I think he's charming."

"He's a nice person," said Mr. Touchett, "but I don't recommend you to fall in love with him."

"I shall not do it then; I shall never fall in love but on your recommendation. Moreover," Isabel added, "my cousin gives me rather a sad account of Lord Warburton."

"Oh, indeed? I don't know what there may be to say, but you must remember that Ralph must talk."

"He thinks your friend's too subversive—or not subversive enough! I don't quite understand which," said Isabel.

The old man shook his head slowly, smiled and put down his cup. "I don't know which either. He goes very far, but it's quite possible he doesn't go far enough. He seems to want to do away with a good many things, but he seems to want to remain himself. I suppose that's natural, but it's rather inconsistent."

"Oh, I hope he'll remain himself," said Isabel. "If he were to be done away with his friends would miss him sadly."

"Well," said the old man, "I guess he'll stay and amuse his friends. I should certainly miss him very much here at Gardencourt. He always amuses me when he comes over, and I think he amuses himself as well. There's a considerable number like him, round in society; they're very fashionable just now. I don't know what they're trying to do—whether they're trying to get up a revolution. I hope at any rate they'll put it off till after I'm gone. You see they want to disestablish everything; but I'm a pretty big landowner here, and I don't want to be disestablished. I wouldn't have come over if I had thought they were going to behave like that," Mr. Touchett went on with expanding hilarity. "I came over because I thought England was a safe country. I call it a regular fraud if they are going to introduce any considerable changes; there'll be a large number disappointed in that case."

"Oh, I do hope they'll make a revolution!" Isabel exclaimed. "I should delight in seeing a revolution."

"Let me see," said her uncle, with a humorous intention; "I forget whether you're on the side of the old or on the side of the new. I've heard you take such opposite views."

"I'm on the side of both. I guess I'm a little on the side of everything. In a revolution—after it was well begun—I think I should be a high, proud loyalist. One sympathises more with them, and they've a chance to behave so exquisitely. I mean so picturesquely."

"I don't know that I understand what you mean by behaving picturesquely, but it seems to me that you do that always, my dear."

"Oh, you lovely man, if I could believe that!" the girl interrupted.

"I'm afraid, after all, you won't have the pleasure of going gracefully to the guillotine here just now," Mr. Touchett went on. "If you want to see a big outbreak you must pay us a long visit. You see, when you come to the point it wouldn't suit them to be taken at their word."

"Of whom are you speaking?"

"Well, I mean Lord Warburton and his friends—the radicals of the upper class. Of course I only know the way it strikes me. They talk about the changes, but I don't think they quite realise. You and I, you know, we know what it is to have lived under democratic institutions: I always thought them very comfortable, but I was used to them from the first. And then I ain't a lord; you're a lady, my dear, but I ain't a lord. Now over here I don't think it quite comes home to them. It's a matter of every day and every hour, and I don't think many of them would find it as pleasant as what they've got. Of course if they want to try, it's their own business; but I expect they won't try very hard."

"Don't you think they're sincere?" Isabel asked.

"Well, they want to FEEL earnest," Mr. Touchett allowed; "but it seems as if they took it out in theories mostly. Their radical views are a kind of amusement; they've got to have some amusement, and they might have coarser tastes than that. You see they're very luxurious, and these progressive ideas are about their biggest luxury. They make them feel moral and yet don't damage their position. They think a great deal of their position; don't let one of them ever persuade you he doesn't, for if you were to proceed on that basis you'd be pulled up very short."

Isabel followed her uncle's argument, which he unfolded with his quaint distinctness, most attentively, and though she was unacquainted with the British aristocracy she found it in harmony with her general impressions of human nature. But she felt moved to put in a protest on Lord Warburton's behalf. "I don't believe Lord Warburton's a humbug; I don't care what the others are. I should like to see Lord Warburton put to the test."

"Heaven deliver me from my friends!" Mr. Touchett answered. "Lord Warburton's a very amiable young man—a very fine young man. He has a hundred thousand a year. He owns fifty thousand acres of the soil of this little island and ever so many other things besides. He has half a dozen houses to live in. He has a seat in Parliament as I have one at my own dinner-table. He has elegant tastes—cares for literature, for art, for science, for charming young ladies. The most elegant is his taste for the new views. It affords him a great deal of pleasure—more perhaps than anything else, except the young ladies. His old house over there—what does he call it, Lockleigh?—is very attractive; but I don't think it's as pleasant as this. That doesn't matter, however—he has so many others. His views don't hurt any one as far as I can see; they certainly don't hurt himself. And if there were to be a revolution he would come off very easily. They wouldn't touch him, they'd leave him as he is: he's too much liked."

"Ah, he couldn't be a martyr even if he wished!" Isabel sighed. "That's a very poor position."

"He'll never be a martyr unless you make him one," said the old man.

Isabel shook her head; there might have been something laughable in the fact that she did it with a touch of melancholy. "I shall never make any one a martyr."

"You'll never be one, I hope."

"I hope not. But you don't pity Lord Warburton then as Ralph does?"

Her uncle looked at her a while with genial acuteness. "Yes, I do, after all!"

CHAPTER IX

The two Misses Molyneux, this nobleman's sisters, came presently to call upon her, and Isabel took a fancy to the young ladies, who appeared to her to show a most original stamp. It is true that when she described them to her cousin by that term he declared that no epithet could be less applicable than this to the two Misses Molyneux, since there were fifty thousand young women in England who exactly resembled them. Deprived of this advantage, however, Isabel's visitors retained that of an extreme sweetness and shyness of demeanour, and of having, as she thought, eyes like the balanced basins, the circles of "ornamental water," set, in parterres, among the geraniums.

"They're not morbid, at any rate, whatever they are," our heroine said to herself; and she deemed this a great charm, for two or three of the friends of her girlhood had been regrettably open to the charge (they would have been so nice without it), to say nothing of Isabel's having occasionally suspected it as a tendency of her own. The Misses Molyneux were not in their first youth, but they had bright, fresh complexions and something of the smile of childhood. Yes, their eyes, which Isabel admired, were round, quiet and contented, and their figures, also of a generous roundness, were encased in sealskin jackets. Their friendliness was great, so great that they were almost embarrassed to show it; they seemed somewhat afraid of the young lady from the other side of the world and rather looked than spoke their good wishes. But they made it clear to her that they hoped she would come to luncheon at Lockleigh, where they lived with their brother, and then they might see her very, very often. They wondered if she wouldn't come over some day, and sleep: they were expecting some people on the twenty-ninth, so perhaps she would come while the people were there.

"I'm afraid it isn't any one very remarkable," said the elder sister; "but I dare say you'll take us as you find us."

"I shall find you delightful; I think you're enchanting just as you are," replied Isabel, who often praised profusely.

Her visitors flushed, and her cousin told her, after they were gone, that if she said such things to those poor girls they would think she was in some wild, free manner practising on them: he was sure it was the first time they had been called enchanting.

"I can't help it," Isabel answered. "I think it's lovely to be so quiet and reasonable and satisfied. I should like to be like that."

"Heaven forbid!" cried Ralph with ardour.

"I mean to try and imitate them," said Isabel. "I want very much to see them at home."

She had this pleasure a few days later, when, with Ralph and his mother, she drove over to Lockleigh. She found the Misses Molyneux sitting in a vast drawing-room (she perceived afterwards it was one of several) in a wilderness of faded chintz; they were dressed on this occasion in black velveteen. Isabel liked them even better at home than she had done at Gardencourt, and was more than ever struck with the fact that they were not morbid. It had seemed to her before that if they had a fault it was a want of play of mind; but she presently saw they were capable of deep emotion. Before luncheon she was alone with them for some time, on one side of the room, while Lord Warburton, at a distance, talked to Mrs. Touchett.

"Is it true your brother's such a great radical?" Isabel asked. She knew it was true, but we have seen that her interest in human nature was keen, and she had a desire to draw the Misses Molyneux out.

"Oh dear, yes; he's immensely advanced," said Mildred, the younger sister.

"At the same time Warburton's very reasonable," Miss Molyneux observed.

Isabel watched him a moment at the other side of the room; he was clearly trying hard to make himself agreeable to Mrs. Touchett. Ralph had met the frank advances of one of the dogs before the fire that the temperature of an English August, in the ancient expanses, had not made an impertinence. "Do you suppose your brother's sincere?" Isabel enquired with a smile.

"Oh, he must be, you know!" Mildred exclaimed quickly, while the elder sister gazed at our heroine in silence.

"Do you think he would stand the test?"

"The test?"

"I mean for instance having to give up all this."

"Having to give up Lockleigh?" said Miss Molyneux, finding her voice.

"Yes, and the other places; what are they called?"

The two sisters exchanged an almost frightened glance. "Do you mean—do you mean on account of the expense?" the younger one asked.

"I dare say he might let one or two of his houses," said the other.

"Let them for nothing?" Isabel demanded.

"I can't fancy his giving up his property," said Miss Molyneux.

"Ah, I'm afraid he is an impostor!" Isabel returned. "Don't you think it's a false position?"

Her companions, evidently, had lost themselves. "My brother's position?" Miss Molyneux enquired.

"It's thought a very good position," said the younger sister. "It's the first position in this part of the county."

"I dare say you think me very irreverent," Isabel took occasion to remark. "I suppose you revere your brother and are rather afraid of him."

"Of course one looks up to one's brother," said Miss Molyneux simply.

"If you do that he must be very good—because you, evidently, are beautifully good."

"He's most kind. It will never be known, the good he does."

"His ability is known," Mildred added; "every one thinks it's immense."

"Oh, I can see that," said Isabel. "But if I were he I should wish to fight to the death: I mean for the heritage of the past. I should hold it tight."

"I think one ought to be liberal," Mildred argued gently. "We've always been so, even from the earliest times."

"Ah well," said Isabel, "you've made a great success of it; I don't wonder you like it. I see you're very fond of crewels."

When Lord Warburton showed her the house, after luncheon, it seemed to her a matter of course that it should be a noble picture. Within, it had been a good deal modernised—some of its best points had lost their purity; but as they saw it from the gardens, a stout grey pile, of the softest, deepest, most weather-fretted hue, rising from a broad, still moat, it affected the young visitor as a castle in a legend. The day was cool and rather lustreless; the first note of autumn had been struck, and the watery sunshine rested on the walls in blurred and desultory gleams, washing them, as it were, in places tenderly chosen, where the ache of antiquity was keenest. Her host's brother, the Vicar, had come to luncheon, and Isabel had had five minutes' talk with him—time enough to institute a search for a rich ecclesiasticism and give it up as vain. The marks of the Vicar of Lockleigh were a big, athletic figure, a candid, natural countenance, a capacious appetite and a tendency to indiscriminate laughter. Isabel learned afterwards from her cousin that before taking orders he had been a mighty wrestler and that he was still, on occasion—in the privacy of the family circle as it were—quite capable of flooring his man. Isabel liked him—she was in the mood for liking everything; but her imagination was a good deal taxed to think of him as a source of spiritual aid. The whole party, on leaving lunch, went to walk in the grounds; but Lord Warburton exercised some ingenuity in engaging his least familiar guest in a stroll apart from the others.

"I wish you to see the place properly, seriously," he said. "You can't do so if your attention is distracted by irrelevant gossip." His own conversation (though he told Isabel a good deal about the house, which had a very curious history) was not purely archaeological; he reverted at intervals to matters more personal—matters personal to the young lady as well as to himself. But at last, after a pause of some duration, returning for a moment to their ostensible theme, "Ah, well," he said, "I'm very glad indeed you like the old barrack. I wish you could see more of it—that you could stay here a while. My sisters have taken an immense fancy to you—if that would be any inducement."

"There's no want of inducements," Isabel answered; "but I'm afraid I can't make engagements. I'm quite in my aunt's hands."

"Ah, pardon me if I say I don't exactly believe that. I'm pretty sure you can do whatever you want."

"I'm sorry if I make that impression on you; I don't think it's a nice impression to make."

"It has the merit of permitting me to hope." And Lord Warburton paused a moment.

"To hope what?"

"That in future I may see you often."

"Ah," said Isabel, "to enjoy that pleasure I needn't be so terribly emancipated."

"Doubtless not; and yet, at the same time, I don't think your uncle likes me."

"You're very much mistaken. I've heard him speak very highly of you."

"I'm glad you have talked about me," said Lord Warburton. "But, I nevertheless don't think he'd like me to keep coming to Gardencourt."

"I can't answer for my uncle's tastes," the girl rejoined, "though I ought as far as possible to take them into account. But for myself I shall be very glad to see you."

"Now that's what I like to hear you say. I'm charmed when you say that."

"You're easily charmed, my lord," said Isabel.

"No, I'm not easily charmed!" And then he stopped a moment. "But you've charmed me, Miss Archer."

These words were uttered with an indefinable sound which startled the girl; it struck her as the prelude to something grave: she had heard the sound before and she recognised it. She had no wish, however, that for the moment such a prelude should have a sequel, and she said as gaily as possible and as quickly as an appreciable degree of agitation would allow her: "I'm afraid there's no prospect of my being able to come here again."

"Never?" said Lord Warburton.

"I won't say 'never'; I should feel very melodramatic."

"May I come and see you then some day next week?"

"Most assuredly. What is there to prevent it?"

"Nothing tangible. But with you I never feel safe. I've a sort of sense that you're always summing people up."

"You don't of necessity lose by that."

"It's very kind of you to say so; but, even if I gain, stern justice is not what I most love. Is Mrs. Touchett going to take you abroad?"

"I hope so."

"Is England not good enough for you?"

"That's a very Machiavellian speech; it doesn't deserve an answer. I want to see as many countries as I can."

"Then you'll go on judging, I suppose."

"Enjoying, I hope, too."

"Yes, that's what you enjoy most; I can't make out what you're up to," said Lord Warburton. "You strike me as having mysterious purposes—vast designs."

"You're so good as to have a theory about me which I don't at all fill out. Is there anything mysterious in a purpose entertained and executed every year, in the most public manner, by fifty thousand of my fellow-countrymen—the purpose of improving one's mind by foreign travel?"

"You can't improve your mind, Miss Archer," her companion declared. "It's already a most formidable instrument. It looks down on us all; it despises us."

"Despises you? You're making fun of me," said Isabel seriously.

"Well, you think us 'quaint'—that's the same thing. I won't be thought 'quaint,' to begin with; I'm not so in the least. I protest."

"That protest is one of the quaintest things I've ever heard," Isabel answered with a smile.

Lord Warburton was briefly silent. "You judge only from the outside—you don't care," he said presently. "You only care to amuse yourself." The note she had heard in his voice a moment before reappeared, and mixed with it now was an audible strain of bitterness—a bitterness so abrupt and inconsequent that the girl was afraid she had hurt him. She had often heard that the English are a highly eccentric people, and she had even read in some ingenious author that they are at bottom the most romantic of races. Was Lord Warburton suddenly turning romantic—was he going to make her a scene, in his own house, only the third time they had met? She was reassured quickly enough by her sense of his great good manners, which was not impaired by the fact that he had already touched the furthest limit of good taste in expressing his admiration of a young lady who had confided in his hospitality. She was right in trusting to his good manners, for he presently went on, laughing a little and without a trace of the accent that had discomposed her: "I don't mean of course that you amuse yourself with trifles. You select great materials; the foibles, the afflictions of human nature, the peculiarities of nations!"

"As regards that," said Isabel, "I should find in my own nation entertainment for a lifetime. But we've a long drive, and my aunt will soon wish to start." She turned back toward the others and Lord Warburton walked beside her in silence. But before they reached the others, "I shall come and see you next week," he said.

She had received an appreciable shock, but as it died away she felt that she couldn't pretend to herself that it was altogether a painful one. Nevertheless she made answer to his declaration, coldly enough, "Just as you please." And her coldness was not the calculation of her effect—a game she played in a much smaller degree than would have seemed probable to many critics. It came from a certain fear.

CHAPTER X

The day after her visit to Lockleigh she received a note from her friend Miss Stackpole—a note of which the envelope, exhibiting in conjunction the postmark of Liverpool and the neat calligraphy of the quick-fingered Henrietta, caused her some liveliness of emotion. "Here I am, my lovely friend," Miss Stackpole wrote; "I managed to get off at last. I decided only the night before I left New York—the Interviewer having come round to my figure. I put a few things into a bag, like a veteran journalist, and came down to the steamer in a street-car. Where are you and where can we meet? I suppose you're visiting at some castle or other and have already acquired the correct accent. Perhaps even you have married a lord; I almost hope you have, for I want some introductions to the first people and shall count on you for a few. The Interviewer wants some light on the nobility. My first impressions (of the people at large) are not rose-coloured; but I wish to talk them over with you, and you know that, whatever I am, at least I'm not superficial. I've also something very particular to tell you. Do appoint a meeting as quickly as you can; come to London (I should like so much to visit the sights with you) or else let me come to you, wherever you are. I will do so with pleasure; for you know everything interests me and I wish to see as much as possible of the inner life."

Isabel judged best not to show this letter to her uncle; but she acquainted him with its purport, and, as she expected, he begged her instantly to assure Miss Stackpole, in his name, that he should be delighted to receive her at Gardencourt. "Though she's a literary lady," he said, "I suppose that, being an American, she won't show me up, as that other one did. She has seen others like me."

"She has seen no other so delightful!" Isabel answered; but she was not altogether at ease about Henrietta's reproductive instincts, which belonged to that side of her friend's character which she regarded with least complacency. She wrote to Miss Stackpole, however, that she would be very welcome under Mr. Touchett's roof; and this alert young woman lost no time in announcing her prompt approach. She had gone up to London, and it was from that centre that she took the train for the station nearest to Gardencourt, where Isabel and Ralph were in waiting to receive her.

"Shall I love her or shall I hate her?" Ralph asked while they moved along the platform.

"Whichever you do will matter very little to her," said Isabel. "She doesn't care a straw what men think of her."

"As a man I'm bound to dislike her then. She must be a kind of monster. Is she very ugly?"

"No, she's decidedly pretty."

"A female interviewer—a reporter in petticoats? I'm very curious to see her," Ralph conceded.

"It's very easy to laugh at her but it is not easy to be as brave as she."

"I should think not; crimes of violence and attacks on the person require more or less pluck. Do you suppose she'll interview me?"

"Never in the world. She'll not think you of enough importance."

"You'll see," said Ralph. "She'll send a description of us all, including Bunchie, to her newspaper."

"I shall ask her not to," Isabel answered.

"You think she's capable of it then?"

"Perfectly."

"And yet you've made her your bosom-friend?"

"I've not made her my bosom-friend; but I like her in spite of her faults."

"Ah well," said Ralph, "I'm afraid I shall dislike her in spite of her merits."

"You'll probably fall in love with her at the end of three days."

"And have my love-letters published in the Interviewer? Never!" cried the young man.

The train presently arrived, and Miss Stackpole, promptly descending, proved, as Isabel had promised, quite delicately, even though rather provincially, fair. She was a neat, plump person, of medium stature, with a round face, a small mouth, a delicate complexion, a bunch of light brown ringlets at the back of her head and a peculiarly open, surprised-looking eye. The most striking point in her appearance was the remarkable fixedness of this organ, which rested without impudence or defiance, but as if in conscientious exercise of a natural right, upon every object it happened to encounter. It rested in this manner upon Ralph himself, a little arrested by Miss Stackpole's gracious and comfortable aspect, which hinted that it wouldn't be so easy as he had assumed to disapprove of her. She rustled, she shimmered, in fresh, dove-coloured draperies, and Ralph saw at a glance that she was as crisp and new and comprehensive as a first issue before the folding. From top to toe she had probably no misprint. She spoke in a clear, high voice—a voice not rich but loud; yet after she had taken her place with her companions in Mr. Touchett's carriage she struck him as not all in the large type, the type of horrid "headings," that he had expected. She answered the enquiries made of her by Isabel, however, and in which the young man ventured to join, with copious lucidity; and later, in the library at Gardencourt, when she had made the acquaintance of Mr. Touchett (his wife not having thought it necessary to appear) did more to give the measure of her confidence in her powers.

"Well, I should like to know whether you consider yourselves American or English," she broke out. "If once I knew I could talk to you accordingly."

"Talk to us anyhow and we shall be thankful," Ralph liberally answered.

She fixed her eyes on him, and there was something in their character that reminded him of large polished buttons—buttons that might have fixed the elastic loops of some tense receptacle: he seemed to see the reflection of surrounding objects on the pupil. The expression of a button is not usually deemed human, but there was something in Miss Stackpole's gaze that made him, as a very modest man, feel vaguely embarrassed—less inviolate, more dishonoured, than he liked. This sensation, it must be added, after he had spent a day or two in her company, sensibly diminished, though it never wholly lapsed. "I don't suppose that you're going to undertake to persuade me that you're an American," she said.

"To please you I'll be an Englishman, I'll be a Turk!"

"Well, if you can change about that way you're very welcome," Miss Stackpole returned.

"I'm sure you understand everything and that differences of nationality are no barrier to you," Ralph went on.

Miss Stackpole gazed at him still. "Do you mean the foreign languages?"

"The languages are nothing. I mean the spirit—the genius."

"I'm not sure that I understand you," said the correspondent of the Interviewer; "but I expect I shall before I leave."

"He's what's called a cosmopolite," Isabel suggested.

"That means he's a little of everything and not much of any. I must say I think patriotism is like charity—it begins at home."

"Ah, but where does home begin, Miss Stackpole?" Ralph enquired.

"I don't know where it begins, but I know where it ends. It ended a long time before I got here."

"Don't you like it over here?" asked Mr. Touchett with his aged, innocent voice.

"Well, sir, I haven't quite made up my mind what ground I shall take. I feel a good deal cramped. I felt it on the journey from Liverpool to London."

"Perhaps you were in a crowded carriage," Ralph suggested.

"Yes, but it was crowded with friends—party of Americans whose acquaintance I had made upon the steamer; a lovely group from Little Rock, Arkansas. In spite of that I felt cramped—I felt something pressing upon me; I couldn't tell what it was. I felt at the very commencement as if I were not going to accord with the atmosphere. But I suppose I shall make my own atmosphere. That's the true way—then you can breathe. Your surroundings seem very attractive."

"Ah, we too are a lovely group!" said Ralph. "Wait a little and you'll see."

Miss Stackpole showed every disposition to wait and evidently was prepared to make a considerable stay at Gardencourt. She occupied herself in the mornings with literary labour; but in spite of this Isabel spent many hours with her friend, who, once her daily task performed, deprecated, in fact defied, isolation. Isabel speedily found occasion to desire her to desist from celebrating the charms of their common sojourn in print, having discovered, on the second morning of Miss Stackpole's visit, that she was engaged on a letter to the Interviewer, of which the title, in her exquisitely neat and legible hand (exactly that of the copybooks which our heroine remembered at school) was "Americans and Tudors—Glimpses of Gardencourt." Miss Stackpole, with the best conscience in the world, offered to read her letter to Isabel, who immediately put in her protest.

"I don't think you ought to do that. I don't think you ought to describe the place."

Henrietta gazed at her as usual. "Why, it's just what the people want, and it's a lovely place."

"It's too lovely to be put in the newspapers, and it's not what my uncle wants."

"Don't you believe that!" cried Henrietta. "They're always delighted afterwards."

"My uncle won't be delighted—nor my cousin either. They'll consider it a breach of hospitality."

Miss Stackpole showed no sense of confusion; she simply wiped her pen, very neatly, upon an elegant little implement which she kept for the purpose, and put away her manuscript. "Of course if you don't approve I won't do it; but I sacrifice a beautiful subject."

"There are plenty of other subjects, there are subjects all round you. We'll take some drives; I'll show you some charming scenery."

"Scenery's not my department; I always need a human interest. You know I'm deeply human, Isabel; I always was," Miss Stackpole rejoined. "I was going to bring in your cousin—the alienated American. There's a great demand just now for the alienated American, and your cousin's a beautiful specimen. I should have handled him severely."

"He would have died of it!" Isabel exclaimed. "Not of the severity, but of the publicity."

"Well, I should have liked to kill him a little. And I should have delighted to do your uncle, who seems to me a much nobler type—the American faithful still. He's a grand old man; I don't see how he can object to my paying him honour."

Isabel looked at her companion in much wonderment; it struck her as strange that a nature in which she found so much to esteem should break down so in spots. "My poor Henrietta," she said, "you've no sense of privacy."

Henrietta coloured deeply, and for a moment her brilliant eyes were suffused, while Isabel found her more than ever inconsequent. "You do me great injustice," said Miss Stackpole with dignity. "I've never written a word about myself!"

"I'm very sure of that; but it seems to me one should be modest for others also!"

"Ah, that's very good!" cried Henrietta, seizing her pen again. "Just let me make a note of it and I'll put it in somewhere." she was a thoroughly good-natured woman, and half an hour later she was in as cheerful a mood as should have been looked for in a newspaper-lady in want of matter. "I've promised to do the social side," she said to Isabel; "and how can I do it unless I get ideas? If I can't describe this place don't you know some place I can describe?" Isabel promised she would bethink herself, and the next day, in conversation with her friend, she happened to mention her visit to Lord Warburton's ancient house. "Ah, you must take me there—that's just the place for me!" Miss Stackpole cried. "I must get a glimpse of the nobility."

"I can't take you," said Isabel; "but Lord Warburton's coming here, and you'll have a chance to see him and observe him. Only if you intend to repeat his conversation I shall certainly give him warning."

"Don't do that," her companion pleaded; "I want him to be natural."

"An Englishman's never so natural as when he's holding his tongue," Isabel declared.

It was not apparent, at the end of three days, that her cousin had, according to her prophecy, lost his heart to their visitor, though he had spent a good deal of time in her society. They strolled about the park together and sat under the trees, and in the afternoon, when it was delightful to float along the Thames, Miss Stackpole occupied a place in the boat in which hitherto Ralph had had but a single companion. Her presence proved somehow less irreducible to soft particles than Ralph had expected in the natural perturbation of his sense of the perfect solubility of that of his cousin; for the correspondent of the Interviewer prompted mirth in him, and he had long since decided that the crescendo of mirth should be the flower of his declining days. Henrietta, on her side, failed a little to justify Isabel's declaration with regard to her indifference to masculine opinion; for poor Ralph appeared to have presented himself to her as an irritating problem, which it would be almost immoral not to work out.

"What does he do for a living?" she asked of Isabel the evening of her arrival. "Does he go round all day with his hands in his pockets?"

"He does nothing," smiled Isabel; "he's a gentleman of large leisure."

"Well, I call that a shame—when I have to work like a car-conductor," Miss Stackpole replied. "I should like to show him up."

"He's in wretched health; he's quite unfit for work," Isabel urged.

"Pshaw! don't you believe it. I work when I'm sick," cried her friend. Later, when she stepped into the boat on joining the water-party, she remarked to Ralph that she supposed he hated her and would like to drown her.

"Ah no," said Ralph, "I keep my victims for a slower torture. And you'd be such an interesting one!"

"Well, you do torture me; I may say that. But I shock all your prejudices; that's one comfort."

"My prejudices? I haven't a prejudice to bless myself with. There's intellectual poverty for you."

"The more shame to you; I've some delicious ones. Of course I spoil your flirtation, or whatever it is you call it, with your cousin; but I don't care for that, as I render her the service of drawing you out. She'll see how thin you are."

"Ah, do draw me out!" Ralph exclaimed. "So few people will take the trouble."

Miss Stackpole, in this undertaking, appeared to shrink from no effort; resorting largely, whenever the opportunity offered, to the natural expedient of interrogation. On the following day the weather was bad, and in the afternoon the young man, by way of providing indoor amusement, offered to show her the pictures. Henrietta strolled through the long gallery in his society, while he pointed out its principal ornaments and mentioned the painters and subjects. Miss Stackpole looked at the pictures in perfect silence, committing herself to no opinion, and Ralph was gratified by the fact that she delivered herself of none of the little ready-made ejaculations of delight of which the visitors to Gardencourt were so frequently lavish. This young lady indeed, to do her justice, was but little addicted to the use of conventional terms; there was something earnest and inventive in her tone, which at times, in its strained deliberation, suggested a person of high culture speaking a foreign language. Ralph Touchett subsequently learned that she had at one time officiated as art critic to a journal of the other world; but she appeared, in spite of this fact, to carry in her pocket none of the small change of admiration. Suddenly, just after he had called her attention to a charming Constable, she turned and looked at him as if he himself had been a picture.

"Do you always spend your time like this?" she demanded.

"I seldom spend it so agreeably."

"Well, you know what I mean—without any regular occupation."

"Ah," said Ralph, "I'm the idlest man living."

Miss Stackpole directed her gaze to the Constable again, and Ralph bespoke her attention for a small Lancret hanging near it, which represented a gentleman in a pink doublet and hose and a ruff, leaning against the pedestal of the statue of a nymph in a garden and playing the guitar to two ladies seated on the grass. "That's my ideal of a regular occupation," he said.

Miss Stackpole turned to him again, and, though her eyes had rested upon the picture, he saw she had missed the subject. She was thinking of something much more serious. "I don't see how you can reconcile it to your conscience."

"My dear lady, I have no conscience!"

"Well, I advise you to cultivate one. You'll need it the next time you go to America."

"I shall probably never go again."

"Are you ashamed to show yourself?"

Ralph meditated with a mild smile. "I suppose that if one has no conscience one has no shame."

"Well, you've got plenty of assurance," Henrietta declared. "Do you consider it right to give up your country?"

"Ah, one doesn't give up one's country any more than one gives UP one's grandmother. They're both antecedent to choice—elements of one's composition that are not to be eliminated."

"I suppose that means that you've tried and been worsted. What do they think of you over here?"

"They delight in me."

"That's because you truckle to them."

"Ah, set it down a little to my natural charm!" Ralph sighed.

"I don't know anything about your natural charm. If you've got any charm it's quite unnatural. It's wholly acquired—or at least you've tried hard to acquire it, living over here. I don't say you've succeeded. It's a charm that I don't appreciate, anyway. Make yourself useful in some way, and then we'll talk about it." "Well, now, tell me what I shall do," said Ralph.

"Go right home, to begin with."

"Yes, I see. And then?"

"Take right hold of something."

"Well, now, what sort of thing?"

"Anything you please, so long as you take hold. Some new idea, some big work."

"Is it very difficult to take hold?" Ralph enquired.

"Not if you put your heart into it."

"Ah, my heart," said Ralph. "If it depends upon my heart—!"

"Haven't you got a heart?"

"I had one a few days ago, but I've lost it since."

"You're not serious," Miss Stackpole remarked; "that's what's the matter with you." But for all this, in a day or two, she again permitted him to fix her attention and on the later occasion assigned a different cause to her mysterious perversity. "I know what's the matter with you, Mr. Touchett," she said. "You think you're too good to get married."

"I thought so till I knew you, Miss Stackpole," Ralph answered; "and then I suddenly changed my mind."

"Oh pshaw!" Henrietta groaned.

"Then it seemed to me," said Ralph, "that I was not good enough."

"It would improve you. Besides, it's your duty."

"Ah," cried the young man, "one has so many duties! Is that a duty too?"

"Of course it is—did you never know that before? It's every one's duty to get married."

Ralph meditated a moment; he was disappointed. There was something in Miss Stackpole he had begun to like; it seemed to him that if she was not a charming woman she was at least a very good "sort." She was wanting in distinction, but, as Isabel had said, she was brave: she went into cages, she flourished lashes, like a spangled lion-tamer. He had not supposed her to be capable of vulgar arts, but these last words struck him as a false note. When a marriageable young woman urges matrimony on an unencumbered young man the most obvious explanation of her conduct is not the altruistic impulse.

"Ah, well now, there's a good deal to be said about that," Ralph rejoined.

"There may be, but that's the principal thing. I must say I think it looks very exclusive, going round all alone, as if you thought no woman was good enough for you. Do you think you're better than any one else in the world? In America it's usual for people to marry."

"If it's my duty," Ralph asked, "is it not, by analogy, yours as well?"

Miss Stackpole's ocular surfaces unwinkingly caught the sun. "Have you the fond hope of finding a flaw in my reasoning? Of course I've as good a right to marry as any one else."

"Well then," said Ralph, "I won't say it vexes me to see you single. It delights me rather."

"You're not serious yet. You never will be."

"Shall you not believe me to be so on the day I tell you I desire to give up the practice of going round alone?"

Miss Stackpole looked at him for a moment in a manner which seemed to announce a reply that might technically be called encouraging. But to his great surprise this expression suddenly resolved itself into an appearance of alarm and even of resentment. "No, not even then," she answered dryly. After which she walked away.

"I've not conceived a passion for your friend," Ralph said that evening to Isabel, "though we talked some time this morning about it."

"And you said something she didn't like," the girl replied.

Ralph stared. "Has she complained of me?"

"She told me she thinks there's something very low in the tone of Europeans towards women."

"Does she call me a European?"

"One of the worst. She told me you had said to her something that an American never would have said. But she didn't repeat it."

Ralph treated himself to a luxury of laughter. "She's an extraordinary combination. Did she think I was making love to her?"

"No; I believe even Americans do that. But she apparently thought you mistook the intention of something she had said, and put an unkind construction on it."

"I thought she was proposing marriage to me and I accepted her. Was that unkind?"

Isabel smiled. "It was unkind to me. I don't want you to marry."

"My dear cousin, what's one to do among you all?" Ralph demanded. "Miss Stackpole tells me it's my bounden duty, and that it's hers, in general, to see I do mine!"

"She has a great sense of duty," said Isabel gravely. "She has indeed, and it's the motive of everything she says. That's what I like her for. She thinks it's unworthy of you to keep so many things to yourself. That's what she wanted to express. If you thought she was trying to—to attract you, you were very wrong."

"It's true it was an odd way, but I did think she was trying to attract me. Forgive my depravity."

"You're very conceited. She had no interested views, and never supposed you would think she had."

"One must be very modest then to talk with such women," Ralph said humbly. "But it's a very strange type. She's too personal—considering that she expects other people not to be. She walks in without knocking at the door."

"Yes," Isabel admitted, "she doesn't sufficiently recognise the existence of knockers; and indeed I'm not sure that she doesn't think them rather a pretentious ornament. She thinks one's door should stand ajar. But I persist in liking her."

"I persist in thinking her too familiar," Ralph rejoined, naturally somewhat uncomfortable under the sense of having been doubly deceived in Miss Stackpole.

"Well," said Isabel, smiling, "I'm afraid it's because she's rather vulgar that I like her."

"She would be flattered by your reason!"

"If I should tell her I wouldn't express it in that way. I should say it's because there's something of the 'people' in her."

"What do you know about the people? and what does she, for that matter?"

"She knows a great deal, and I know enough to feel that she's a kind of emanation of the great democracy—of the continent, the country, the nation. I don't say that she sums it all up, that would be too much to ask of her. But she suggests it; she vividly figures it."

"You like her then for patriotic reasons. I'm afraid it is on those very grounds I object to her."

"Ah," said Isabel with a kind of joyous sigh, "I like so many things! If a thing strikes me with a certain intensity I accept it. I don't want to swagger, but I suppose I'm rather versatile. I like people to be totally different from Henrietta—in the style of Lord Warburton's sisters for instance. So long as I look at the Misses Molyneux they seem to me to answer a kind of ideal. Then Henrietta presents herself, and I'm straightway convinced by her; not so much in respect to herself as in respect to what masses behind her."

"Ah, you mean the back view of her," Ralph suggested.

"What she says is true," his cousin answered; "you'll never be serious. I like the great country stretching away beyond the rivers and across the prairies, blooming and smiling and spreading till it stops at the green Pacific! A strong, sweet, fresh odour seems to rise from it, and Henrietta—pardon my simile—has something of that odour in her garments."

Isabel blushed a little as she concluded this speech, and the blush, together with the momentary ardour she had thrown into it, was so becoming to her that Ralph stood smiling at her for a moment after she had ceased speaking. "I'm not sure the Pacific's so green as that," he said; "but you're a young woman of imagination. Henrietta, however, does smell of the Future—it almost knocks one down!"

CHAPTER XI

He took a resolve after this not to misinterpret her words even when Miss Stackpole appeared to strike the personal note most strongly. He bethought himself that persons, in her view, were simple and homogeneous organisms, and that he, for his own part, was too perverted a representative of the nature of man to have a right to deal with her in strict reciprocity. He carried out his resolve with a great deal of tact, and the young lady found in renewed contact with him no obstacle to the exercise of her genius for unshrinking enquiry, the general application of her confidence. Her situation at Gardencourt therefore, appreciated as we have seen her to be by Isabel and full of appreciation herself of that free play of intelligence which, to her sense, rendered Isabel's character a sister-spirit, and of the easy venerableness of Mr. Touchett, whose noble tone, as she said, met with her full approval—her situation at Gardencourt would have been perfectly comfortable had she not conceived an irresistible mistrust of the little lady for whom she had at first supposed herself obliged to "allow" as mistress of the house. She presently discovered, in truth, that this obligation was of the lightest and that Mrs. Touchett cared very little how Miss Stackpole behaved. Mrs. Touchett had defined her to Isabel as both an adventuress and a bore—adventuresses usually giving one more of a thrill; she had expressed some surprise at her niece's having selected such a friend, yet had immediately added that she knew Isabel's friends were her own affair and that she had never undertaken to like them all or to restrict the girl to those she liked.

"If you could see none but the people I like, my dear, you'd have a very small society," Mrs. Touchett frankly admitted; "and I don't think I like any man or woman well enough to recommend them to you. When it comes to recommending it's a serious affair. I don't like Miss Stackpole—everything about her displeases me; she talks so much too loud and looks at one as if one wanted to look at her—which one doesn't. I'm sure she has lived all her life in a boarding-house, and I detest the manners and the liberties of such places. If you ask me if I prefer my own manners, which you doubtless think very bad, I'll tell you that I prefer them immensely. Miss Stackpole knows I detest boarding-house civilisation, and she detests me for detesting it, because she thinks it the highest in the world. She'd like Gardencourt a great deal better if it were a boarding-house. For me, I find it almost too much of one! We shall never get on together therefore, and there's no use trying."

Mrs. Touchett was right in guessing that Henrietta disapproved of her, but she had not quite put her finger on the reason. A day or two after Miss Stackpole's arrival she had made some invidious reflexions on American hotels, which excited a vein of counter-argument on the part of the correspondent of the Interviewer, who in the exercise of her profession had acquainted herself, in the western world, with every form of caravansary. Henrietta expressed the opinion that American hotels were the best in the world, and Mrs. Touchett, fresh from a renewed struggle with them, recorded a conviction that they were the worst. Ralph, with his experimental geniality, suggested, by way of healing the breach, that the truth lay between the two extremes and that the establishments in question ought to be described as fair middling. This contribution to the discussion, however, Miss Stackpole rejected with scorn. Middling indeed! If they were not the best in the world they were the worst, but there was nothing middling about an American hotel.

"We judge from different points of view, evidently," said Mrs. Touchett. "I like to be treated as an individual; you like to be treated as a 'party.'"

"I don't know what you mean," Henrietta replied. "I like to be treated as an American lady."

"Poor American ladies!" cried Mrs. Touchett with a laugh. "They're the slaves of slaves."

"They're the companions of freemen," Henrietta retorted.

"They're the companions of their servants—the Irish chambermaid and the negro waiter. They share their work."

"Do you call the domestics in an American household 'slaves'?" Miss Stackpole enquired. "If that's the way you desire to treat them, no wonder you don't like America."

"If you've not good servants you're miserable," Mrs. Touchett serenely said. "They're very bad in America, but I've five perfect ones in Florence."

"I don't see what you want with five," Henrietta couldn't help observing. "I don't think I should like to see five persons surrounding me in that menial position."

"I like them in that position better than in some others," proclaimed Mrs. Touchett with much meaning.

"Should you like me better if I were your butler, dear?" her husband asked.

"I don't think I should: you wouldn't at all have the tenue."

"The companions of freemen—I like that, Miss Stackpole," said Ralph. "It's a beautiful description."

"When I said freemen I didn't mean you, sir!"

And this was the only reward that Ralph got for his compliment. Miss Stackpole was baffled; she evidently thought there was something treasonable in Mrs. Touchett's appreciation of a class which she privately judged to be a mysterious survival of feudalism. It was perhaps because her mind was oppressed with this image that she suffered some days to elapse before she took occasion to say to Isabel: "My dear friend, I wonder if you're growing faithless."

"Faithless? Faithless to you, Henrietta?"

"No, that would be a great pain; but it's not that."

"Faithless to my country then?"

"Ah, that I hope will never be. When I wrote to you from Liverpool I said I had something particular to tell you. You've never asked me what it is. Is it because you've suspected?"

"Suspected what? As a rule I don't think I suspect," said Isabel.

"I remember now that phrase in your letter, but I confess I had forgotten it. What have you to tell me?"

Henrietta looked disappointed, and her steady gaze betrayed it. "You don't ask that right—as if you thought it important. You're changed—you're thinking of other things."

"Tell me what you mean, and I'll think of that."

"Will you really think of it? That's what I wish to be sure of."

"I've not much control of my thoughts, but I'll do my best," said Isabel. Henrietta gazed at her, in silence, for a period which tried Isabel's patience, so that our heroine added at last: "Do you mean that you're going to be married?"

"Not till I've seen Europe!" said Miss Stackpole. "What are you laughing at?" she went on. "What I mean is that Mr. Goodwood came out in the steamer with me."

"Ah!" Isabel responded.

"You say that right. I had a good deal of talk with him; he has come after you."

"Did he tell you so?"

"No, he told me nothing; that's how I knew it," said Henrietta cleverly. "He said very little about you, but I spoke of you a good deal."

Isabel waited. At the mention of Mr. Goodwood's name she had turned a little pale. "I'm very sorry you did that," she observed at last.

"It was a pleasure to me, and I liked the way he listened. I could have talked a long time to such a listener; he was so quiet, so intense; he drank it all in."

"What did you say about me?" Isabel asked.

"I said you were on the whole the finest creature I know."

"I'm very sorry for that. He thinks too well of me already; he oughtn't to be encouraged."

"He's dying for a little encouragement. I see his face now, and his earnest absorbed look while I talked. I never saw an ugly man look so handsome."

"He's very simple-minded," said Isabel. "And he's not so ugly."

"There's nothing so simplifying as a grand passion."

"It's not a grand passion; I'm very sure it's not that."

"You don't say that as if you were sure."

Isabel gave rather a cold smile. "I shall say it better to Mr. Goodwood himself."

"He'll soon give you a chance," said Henrietta. Isabel offered no answer to this assertion, which her companion made with an air of great confidence. "He'll find you changed," the latter pursued. "You've been affected by your new surroundings."

"Very likely. I'm affected by everything."

"By everything but Mr. Goodwood!" Miss Stackpole exclaimed with a slightly harsh hilarity.

Isabel failed even to smile back and in a moment she said: "Did he ask you to speak to me?"

"Not in so many words. But his eyes asked it—and his handshake, when he bade me good-bye."

"Thank you for doing so." And Isabel turned away.

"Yes, you're changed; you've got new ideas over here," her friend continued.

"I hope so," said Isabel; "one should get as many new ideas as possible."

"Yes; but they shouldn't interfere with the old ones when the old ones have been the right ones."

Isabel turned about again. "If you mean that I had any idea with regard to Mr. Goodwood—!" But she faltered before her friend's implacable glitter.

"My dear child, you certainly encouraged him."

Isabel made for the moment as if to deny this charge; instead of which, however, she presently answered: "It's very true. I did encourage him." And then she asked if her companion had learned from Mr. Goodwood what he intended to do. It was a concession to her curiosity, for she disliked discussing the subject and found Henrietta wanting in delicacy.

"I asked him, and he said he meant to do nothing," Miss Stackpole answered. "But I don't believe that; he's not a man to do nothing. He is a man of high, bold action. Whatever happens to him he'll always do something, and whatever he does will always be right."

"I quite believe that." Henrietta might be wanting in delicacy, but it touched the girl, all the same, to hear this declaration.

"Ah, you do care for him!" her visitor rang out.

"Whatever he does will always be right," Isabel repeated. "When a man's of that infallible mould what does it matter to him what one feels?"

"It may not matter to him, but it matters to one's self."

"Ah, what it matters to me—that's not what we're discussing," said Isabel with a cold smile.

This time her companion was grave. "Well, I don't care; you have changed. You're not the girl you were a few short weeks ago, and Mr. Goodwood will see it. I expect him here any day."

"I hope he'll hate me then," said Isabel.

"I believe you hope it about as much as I believe him capable of it."

To this observation our heroine made no return; she was absorbed in the alarm given her by Henrietta's intimation that Caspar Goodwood would present himself at Gardencourt. She pretended to herself, however, that she thought the event impossible, and, later, she communicated her disbelief to her friend. For the next forty-eight hours, nevertheless, she stood prepared to hear the young man's name announced. The feeling pressed upon her; it made the air sultry, as if there were to be a change of weather; and the weather, socially speaking, had been so agreeable during Isabel's stay at Gardencourt that any change would be for the worse. Her suspense indeed was dissipated the second day. She had walked into the park in company with the sociable Bunchie, and after strolling about for some time, in a manner at once listless and restless, had seated herself on a garden-bench, within sight of the house, beneath a spreading beech, where, in a white dress ornamented with black ribbons, she formed among the flickering shadows a graceful and harmonious image. She entertained herself for some moments with talking to the little terrier, as to whom the proposal of an ownership divided with her cousin had been applied as impartially as possible—as impartially as Bunchie's own somewhat fickle and inconstant sympathies would allow. But she was notified for the first time, on this occasion, of the finite character of Bunchie's intellect; hitherto she had been mainly struck with its extent. It seemed to her at last that she would do well to take a book; formerly, when heavy-hearted, she had been able, with the help of some well-chosen volume, to transfer the seat of consciousness to the organ of pure reason. Of late, it was not to be denied, literature had seemed a fading light, and even after she had reminded herself that her uncle's library was provided with a complete set of those authors which no gentleman's collection should be without, she sat motionless and empty-handed, her eyes bent on the cool green turf of the lawn. Her meditations were presently interrupted by the arrival of a servant who handed her a letter. The letter bore the London postmark and was addressed in a hand she knew—that came into her vision, already so held by him, with the vividness of the writer's voice or his face. This document proved short and may be given entire.

MY DEAR MISS ARCHER—I don't know whether you will have heard of my coming to England, but even if you have not it will scarcely be a surprise to you. You will remember that when you gave me my dismissal at Albany, three months ago, I did not accept it. I protested against it. You in fact appeared to accept my protest and to admit that I had the right on my side. I had come to see you with the hope that you would let me bring you over to my conviction; my reasons for entertaining this hope had been of the best. But you disappointed it; I found you changed, and you were able to give me no reason for the change. You admitted that you were unreasonable, and it was the only concession you would make; but it was a very cheap one, because that's not your character. No, you are not, and you never will be, arbitrary or capricious. Therefore it is that I believe you will let me see you again. You told me that I'm not disagreeable to you, and I believe it; for I don't see why that should be. I shall always think of you; I shall never think of any one else. I came to England simply because you are here; I couldn't stay at home after you had gone: I hated the country because you were not in it. If I like this country at present it is only because it holds you. I have been to England before, but have never enjoyed it much. May I not come and see you for half an hour? This at present is the dearest wish of yours faithfully,

CASPAR GOODWOOD.

Isabel read this missive with such deep attention that she had not perceived an approaching tread on the soft grass. Looking up, however, as she mechanically folded it she saw Lord Warburton standing before her.

CHAPTER XII

She put the letter into her pocket and offered her visitor a smile of welcome, exhibiting no trace of discomposure and half surprised at her coolness.

"They told me you were out here," said Lord Warburton; "and as there was no one in the drawing-room and it's really you that I wish to see, I came out with no more ado."

Isabel had got up; she felt a wish, for the moment, that he should not sit down beside her. "I was just going indoors."

"Please don't do that; it's much jollier here; I've ridden over from Lockleigh; it's a lovely day." His smile was peculiarly friendly and pleasing, and his whole person seemed to emit that radiance of good-feeling and good fare which had formed the charm of the girl's first impression of him. It surrounded him like a zone of fine June weather.

"We'll walk about a little then," said Isabel, who could not divest herself of the sense of an intention on the part of her visitor and who wished both to elude the intention and to satisfy her curiosity about it. It had flashed upon her vision once before, and it had given her on that occasion, as we know, a certain alarm. This alarm was composed of several elements, not all of which were disagreeable; she had indeed spent some days in analysing them and had succeeded in separating the pleasant part of the idea of Lord Warburton's "making up" to her from the painful. It may appear to some readers that the young lady was both precipitate and unduly fastidious; but the latter of these facts, if the charge be true, may serve to exonerate her from the discredit of the former. She was not eager to convince herself that a territorial magnate, as she had heard Lord Warburton called, was smitten with her charms; the fact of a declaration from such a source carrying with it really more questions than it would answer. She had received a strong impression of his being a "personage," and she had occupied herself in examining the image so conveyed. At the risk of adding to the evidence of her self-sufficiency it must be said that there had been moments when this possibility of admiration by a personage represented to her an aggression almost to the degree of an affront, quite to the degree of an inconvenience. She had never yet known a personage; there had been no personages, in this sense, in her life; there were probably none such at all in her native land. When she had thought of individual eminence she had thought of it on the basis of character and wit—of what one might like in a gentleman's mind and in his talk. She herself was a character—she couldn't help being aware of that; and hitherto her visions of a completed consciousness had concerned themselves largely with moral images—things as to which the question would be whether they pleased her sublime soul. Lord Warburton loomed up before her, largely and brightly, as a collection of attributes and powers which were not to be measured by this simple rule, but which demanded a different sort of appreciation—an appreciation that the girl, with her habit of judging quickly and freely, felt she lacked patience to bestow. He appeared to demand of her something that no one else, as it were, had presumed to do. What she felt was that a territorial, a political, a social magnate had conceived the design of drawing her into the system in which he rather invidiously lived and moved. A certain instinct, not imperious, but persuasive, told her to resist—murmured to her that virtually she had a system and an orbit of her own. It told her other things besides—things which both contradicted and confirmed each other; that a girl might do much worse than trust herself to such a man and that it would be very interesting to see something of his system from his own point of view; that on the other hand, however, there was evidently a great deal of it which she should regard only as a complication of every hour, and that even in the whole there was something stiff and stupid which would make it a burden. Furthermore there was a young man lately come from America who had no system at all, but who had a character of which it was useless for her to try to persuade herself that the impression on her mind had been light. The letter she carried in her pocket all sufficiently reminded her of the contrary. Smile not, however, I venture to repeat, at this simple young woman from Albany who debated whether she should accept an English peer before he had offered himself and who was disposed to believe that on the whole she could do better. She was a person of great good faith, and if there was a great deal of folly in her wisdom those who judge her severely may have the satisfaction of finding that, later, she became consistently wise only at the cost of an amount of folly which will constitute almost a direct appeal to charity.

Lord Warburton seemed quite ready to walk, to sit or to do anything that Isabel should propose, and he gave her this assurance with his usual air of being particularly pleased to exercise a social virtue. But he was, nevertheless, not in command of his emotions, and as he strolled beside her for a moment, in silence, looking at her without letting her know it, there was something embarrassed in his glance and his misdirected laughter. Yes, assuredly—as we have touched on the point, we may return to it for a moment again—the English are the most romantic people in the world and Lord Warburton was about to give an example of it. He was about to take a step which would astonish all his friends and displease a great many of them, and which had superficially nothing to recommend it. The young lady who trod the turf beside him had come from a queer country across the sea which he knew a good deal about; her antecedents, her associations were very vague to his mind except in so far as they were generic, and in this sense they showed as distinct and unimportant. Miss Archer had neither a fortune nor the sort of beauty that justifies a man to the multitude, and he calculated that he had spent about twenty-six hours in her company. He had summed up all this—the perversity of the impulse, which had declined to avail itself of the most liberal opportunities to subside, and the judgement of mankind, as exemplified particularly in the more quickly-judging half of it: he had looked these things well in the face and then had dismissed them from his thoughts. He cared no more for them than for the rosebud in his buttonhole. It is the good fortune of a man who for the greater part of a lifetime has abstained without effort from making himself disagreeable to his friends, that when the need comes for such a course it is not discredited by irritating associations.

"I hope you had a pleasant ride," said Isabel, who observed her companion's hesitancy.

"It would have been pleasant if for nothing else than that it brought me here."

"Are you so fond of Gardencourt?" the girl asked, more and more sure that he meant to make some appeal to her; wishing not to challenge him if he hesitated, and yet to keep all the quietness of her reason if he proceeded. It suddenly came upon her that her situation was one which a few weeks ago she would have deemed deeply romantic: the park of an old English country-house, with the foreground embellished by a "great" (as she supposed) nobleman in the act of making love to a young lady who, on careful inspection, should be found to present remarkable analogies with herself. But if she was now the heroine of the situation she succeeded scarcely the less in looking at it from the outside.

"I care nothing for Gardencourt," said her companion. "I care only for you."

"You've known me too short a time to have a right to say that, and I can't believe you're serious."

These words of Isabel's were not perfectly sincere, for she had no doubt whatever that he himself was. They were simply a tribute to the fact, of which she was perfectly aware, that those he had just uttered would have excited surprise on the part of a vulgar world. And, moreover, if anything beside the sense she had already acquired that Lord Warburton was not a loose thinker had been needed to convince her, the tone in which he replied would quite have served the purpose.

"One's right in such a matter is not measured by the time, Miss Archer; it's measured by the feeling itself. If I were to wait three months it would make no difference; I shall not be more sure of what I mean than I am today. Of course I've seen you very little, but my impression dates from the very first hour we met. I lost no time, I fell in love with you then. It was at first sight, as the novels say; I know now that's not a fancy-phrase, and I shall think better of novels for evermore. Those two days I spent here settled it; I don't know whether you suspected I was doing so, but I paid-mentally speaking I mean—the greatest possible attention to you. Nothing you said, nothing you did, was lost upon me. When you came to Lockleigh the other day—or rather when you went away—I was perfectly sure. Nevertheless I made up my mind to think it over and to question myself narrowly. I've done so; all these days I've done nothing else. I don't make mistakes about such things; I'm a very judicious animal. I don't go off easily, but when I'm touched, it's for life. It's for life, Miss Archer, it's for life," Lord Warburton repeated in the kindest, tenderest, pleasantest voice Isabel had ever heard, and looking at her with eyes charged with the light of a passion that had sifted itself clear of the baser parts of emotion—the heat, the violence, the unreason—and that burned as steadily as a lamp in a windless place.

By tacit consent, as he talked, they had walked more and more slowly, and at last they stopped and he took her hand. "Ah, Lord Warburton, how little you know me!" Isabel said very gently. Gently too she drew her hand away.

"Don't taunt me with that; that I don't know you better makes me unhappy enough already; it's all my loss. But that's what I want, and it seems to me I'm taking the best way. If you'll be my wife, then I shall know you, and when I tell you all the good I think of you you'll not be able to say it's from ignorance."

"If you know me little I know you even less," said Isabel.

"You mean that, unlike yourself, I may not improve on acquaintance? Ah, of course that's very possible. But think, to speak to you as I do, how determined I must be to try and give satisfaction! You do like me rather, don't you?"

"I like you very much, Lord Warburton," she answered; and at this moment she liked him immensely.

"I thank you for saying that; it shows you don't regard me as a stranger. I really believe I've filled all the other relations of life very creditably, and I don't see why I shouldn't fill this one—in which I offer myself to you—seeing that I care so much more about it. Ask the people who know me well; I've friends who'll speak for me."

"I don't need the recommendation of your friends," said Isabel.

"Ah now, that's delightful of you. You believe in me yourself."

"Completely," Isabel declared. She quite glowed there, inwardly, with the pleasure of feeling she did.

The light in her companion's eyes turned into a smile, and he gave a long exhalation of joy. "If you're mistaken, Miss Archer, let me lose all I possess!"

She wondered whether he meant this for a reminder that he was rich, and, on the instant, felt sure that he didn't. He was thinking that, as he would have said himself; and indeed he might safely leave it to the memory of any interlocutor, especially of one to whom he was offering his hand. Isabel had prayed that she might not be agitated, and her mind was tranquil enough, even while she listened and asked herself what it was best she should say, to indulge in this incidental criticism. What she should say, had she asked herself? Her foremost wish was to say something if possible not less kind than what he had said to her. His words had carried perfect conviction with them; she felt she did, all so mysteriously, matter to him. "I thank you more than I can say for your offer," she returned at last. "It does me great honour."

"Ah, don't say that!" he broke out. "I was afraid you'd say something like that. I don't see what you've to do with that sort of thing. I don't see why you should thank me—it's I who ought to thank you for listening to me: a man you know so little coming down on you with such a thumper! Of course it's a great question; I must tell you that I'd rather ask it than have it to answer myself. But the way you've listened—or at least your having listened at all—gives me some hope."

"Don't hope too much," Isabel said.

"Oh Miss Archer!" her companion murmured, smiling again, in his seriousness, as if such a warning might perhaps be taken but as the play of high spirits, the exuberance of elation.

"Should you be greatly surprised if I were to beg you not to hope at all?" Isabel asked.

"Surprised? I don't know what you mean by surprise. It wouldn't be that; it would be a feeling very much worse."

Isabel walked on again; she was silent for some minutes. "I'm very sure that, highly as I already think of you, my opinion of you, if I should know you well, would only rise. But I'm by no means sure that you wouldn't be disappointed. And I say that not in the least out of conventional modesty; it's perfectly sincere."

"I'm willing to risk it, Miss Archer," her companion replied.

"It's a great question, as you say. It's a very difficult question."

"I don't expect you of course to answer it outright. Think it over as long as may be necessary. If I can gain by waiting I'll gladly wait a long time. Only remember that in the end my dearest happiness depends on your answer."

"I should be very sorry to keep you in suspense," said Isabel.

"Oh, don't mind. I'd much rather have a good answer six months hence than a bad one to-day."

"But it's very probable that even six months hence I shouldn't be able to give you one that you'd think good."

"Why not, since you really like me?"

"Ah, you must never doubt that," said Isabel.

"Well then, I don't see what more you ask!"

"It's not what I ask; it's what I can give. I don't think I should suit you; I really don't think I should."

"You needn't worry about that. That's my affair. You needn't be a better royalist than the king."

"It's not only that," said Isabel; "but I'm not sure I wish to marry any one."

"Very likely you don't. I've no doubt a great many women begin that way," said his lordship, who, be it averred, did not in the least believe in the axiom he thus beguiled his anxiety by uttering. "But they're frequently persuaded."

"Ah, that's because they want to be!" And Isabel lightly laughed. Her suitor's countenance fell, and he looked at her for a while in silence. "I'm afraid it's my being an Englishman that makes you hesitate," he said presently. "I know your uncle thinks you ought to marry in your own country."

Isabel listened to this assertion with some interest; it had never occurred to her that Mr. Touchett was likely to discuss her matrimonial prospects with Lord Warburton. "Has he told you that?"

"I remember his making the remark. He spoke perhaps of Americans generally."

"He appears himself to have found it very pleasant to live in England." Isabel spoke in a manner that might have seemed a little perverse, but which expressed both her constant perception of her uncle's outward felicity and her general disposition to elude any obligation to take a restricted view.

It gave her companion hope, and he immediately cried with warmth: "Ah, my dear Miss Archer, old England's a very good sort of country, you know! And it will be still better when we've furbished it up a little."

"Oh, don't furbish it, Lord Warburton—, leave it alone. I like it this way."

"Well then, if you like it, I'm more and more unable to see your objection to what I propose."

"I'm afraid I can't make you understand."

"You ought at least to try. I've a fair intelligence. Are you afraid—afraid of the climate? We can easily live elsewhere, you know. You can pick out your climate, the whole world over."

These words were uttered with a breadth of candour that was like the embrace of strong arms—that was like the fragrance straight in her face, and by his clean, breathing lips, of she knew not what strange gardens, what charged airs. She would have given her little finger at that moment to feel strongly and simply the impulse to answer: "Lord Warburton, it's impossible for me to do better in this wonderful world, I think, than commit myself, very gratefully, to your loyalty." But though she was lost in admiration of her opportunity she managed to move back into the deepest shade of it, even as some wild, caught creature in a vast cage. The "splendid" security so offered her was not the greatest she could conceive. What she finally bethought herself of saying was something very different—something that deferred the need of really facing her crisis. "Don't think me unkind if I ask you to say no more about this to-day."

"Certainly, certainly!" her companion cried. "I wouldn't bore you for the world."

"You've given me a great deal to think about, and I promise you to do it justice."

"That's all I ask of you, of course—and that you'll remember how absolutely my happiness is in your hands."

Isabel listened with extreme respect to this admonition, but she said after a minute: "I must tell you that what I shall think about is some way of letting you know that what you ask is impossible—letting you know it without making you miserable."

"There's no way to do that, Miss Archer. I won't say that if you refuse me you'll kill me; I shall not die of it. But I shall do worse; I shall live to no purpose."

"You'll live to marry a better woman than I."

"Don't say that, please," said Lord Warburton very gravely. "That's fair to neither of us."

"To marry a worse one then."

"If there are better women than you I prefer the bad ones. That's all I can say," he went on with the same earnestness. "There's no accounting for tastes."

His gravity made her feel equally grave, and she showed it by again requesting him to drop the subject for the present. "I'll speak to you myself—very soon. Perhaps I shall write to you."

"At your convenience, yes," he replied. "Whatever time you take, it must seem to me long, and I suppose I must make the best of that."

"I shall not keep you in suspense; I only want to collect my mind a little."

He gave a melancholy sigh and stood looking at her a moment, with his hands behind him, giving short nervous shakes to his hunting-crop. "Do you know I'm very much afraid of it—of that remarkable mind of yours?"

Our heroine's biographer can scarcely tell why, but the question made her start and brought a conscious blush to her cheek. She returned his look a moment, and then with a note in her voice that might almost have appealed to his compassion, "So am I, my lord!" she oddly exclaimed.

His compassion was not stirred, however; all he possessed of the faculty of pity was needed at home. "Ah! be merciful, be merciful," he murmured.

"I think you had better go," said Isabel. "I'll write to you."

"Very good; but whatever you write I'll come and see you, you know." And then he stood reflecting, his eyes fixed on the observant countenance of Bunchie, who had the air of having understood all that had been said and of pretending to carry off the indiscretion by a simulated fit of curiosity as to the roots of an ancient oak. "There's one thing more," he went on. "You know, if you don't like Lockleigh—if you think it's damp or anything of that sort—you need never go within fifty miles of it. It's not damp, by the way; I've had the house thoroughly examined; it's perfectly safe and right. But if you shouldn't fancy it you needn't dream of living in it. There's no difficulty whatever about that; there are plenty of houses. I thought I'd just mention it; some people don't like a moat, you know. Good-bye."

"I adore a moat," said Isabel. "Good-bye."

He held out his hand, and she gave him hers a moment—a moment long enough for him to bend his handsome bared head and kiss it. Then, still agitating, in his mastered emotion, his implement of the chase, he walked rapidly away. He was evidently much upset.

Isabel herself was upset, but she had not been affected as she would have imagined. What she felt was not a great responsibility, a great difficulty of choice; it appeared to her there had been no choice in the question. She couldn't marry Lord Warburton; the idea failed to support any enlightened prejudice in favour of the free exploration of life that she had hitherto entertained or was now capable of entertaining. She must write this to him, she must convince him, and that duty was comparatively simple. But what disturbed her, in the sense that it struck her with wonderment, was this very fact that it cost her so little to refuse a magnificent "chance." With whatever qualifications one would, Lord Warburton had offered her a great opportunity; the situation might have discomforts, might contain oppressive, might contain narrowing elements, might prove really but a stupefying anodyne; but she did her sex no injustice in believing that nineteen women out of twenty would have accommodated themselves to it without a pang. Why then upon her also should it not irresistibly impose itself? Who was she, what was she, that she should hold herself superior? What view of life, what design upon fate, what conception of happiness, had she that pretended to be larger than these large these fabulous occasions? If she wouldn't do such a thing as that then she must do great things, she must do something greater. Poor Isabel found ground to remind herself from time to time that she must not be too proud, and nothing could be more sincere than her prayer to be delivered from such a danger: the isolation and loneliness of pride had for her mind the horror of a desert place. If it had been pride that interfered with her accepting Lord Warburton such a betise was singularly misplaced; and she was so conscious of liking him that she ventured to assure herself it was the very softness, and the fine intelligence, of sympathy. She liked him too much to marry him, that was the truth; something assured her there was a fallacy somewhere in the glowing logic of the proposition—as he saw it—even though she mightn't put her very finest finger-point on it; and to inflict upon a man who offered so much a wife with a tendency to criticise would be a peculiarly discreditable act. She had promised him she would consider his question, and when, after he had left her, she wandered back to the bench where he had found her and lost herself in meditation, it might have seemed that she was keeping her vow. But this was not the case; she was wondering if she were not a cold, hard, priggish person, and, on her at last getting up and going rather quickly back to the house, felt, as she had said to her friend, really frightened at herself.

CHAPTER XIII

It was this feeling and not the wish to ask advice—she had no desire whatever for that—that led her to speak to her uncle of what had taken place. She wished to speak to some one; she should feel more natural, more human, and her uncle, for this purpose, presented himself in a more attractive light than either her aunt or her friend Henrietta. Her cousin of course was a possible confidant; but she would have had to do herself violence to air this special secret to Ralph. So the next day, after breakfast, she sought her occasion. Her uncle never left his apartment till the afternoon, but he received his cronies, as he said, in his dressing-room. Isabel had quite taken her place in the class so designated, which, for the rest, included the old man's son, his physician, his personal servant, and even Miss Stackpole. Mrs. Touchett did not figure in the list, and this was an obstacle the less to Isabel's finding her host alone. He sat in a complicated mechanical chair, at the open window of his room, looking westward over the park and the river, with his newspapers and letters piled up beside him, his toilet freshly and minutely made, and his smooth, speculative face composed to benevolent expectation.

She approached her point directly. "I think I ought to let you know that Lord Warburton has asked me to marry him. I suppose I ought to tell my aunt; but it seems best to tell you first."

The old man expressed no surprise, but thanked her for the confidence she showed him. "Do you mind telling me whether you accepted him?" he then enquired.

"I've not answered him definitely yet; I've taken a little time to think of it, because that seems more respectful. But I shall not accept him."

Mr. Touchett made no comment upon this; he had the air of thinking that, whatever interest he might take in the matter from the point of view of sociability, he had no active voice in it. "Well, I told you you'd be a success over here. Americans are highly appreciated."

"Very highly indeed," said Isabel. "But at the cost of seeming both tasteless and ungrateful, I don't think I can marry Lord Warburton."

"Well," her uncle went on, "of course an old man can't judge for a young lady. I'm glad you didn't ask me before you made up your mind. I suppose I ought to tell you," he added slowly, but as if it were not of much consequence, "that I've known all about it these three days."

"About Lord Warburton's state of mind?"

"About his intentions, as they say here. He wrote me a very pleasant letter, telling me all about them. Should you like to see his letter?" the old man obligingly asked.

"Thank you; I don't think I care about that. But I'm glad he wrote to you; it was right that he should, and he would be certain to do what was right."

"Ah well, I guess you do like him!" Mr. Touchett declared. "You needn't pretend you don't."

"I like him extremely; I'm very free to admit that. But I don't wish to marry any one just now."

"You think some one may come along whom you may like better. Well, that's very likely," said Mr. Touchett, who appeared to wish to show his kindness to the girl by easing off her decision, as it were, and finding cheerful reasons for it.

"I don't care if I don't meet any one else. I like Lord Warburton quite well enough." she fell into that appearance of a sudden change of point of view with which she sometimes startled and even displeased her interlocutors.

Her uncle, however, seemed proof against either of these impressions. "He's a very fine man," he resumed in a tone which might have passed for that of encouragement. "His letter was one of the pleasantest I've received for some weeks. I suppose one of the reasons I liked it was that it was all about you; that is all except the part that was about himself. I suppose he told you all that."

"He would have told me everything I wished to ask him," Isabel said.

"But you didn't feel curious?"

"My curiosity would have been idle—once I had determined to decline his offer."

"You didn't find it sufficiently attractive?" Mr. Touchett enquired.

She was silent a little. "I suppose it was that," she presently admitted. "But I don't know why."

"Fortunately ladies are not obliged to give reasons," said her uncle. "There's a great deal that's attractive about such an idea; but I don't see why the English should want to entice us away from our native land. I know that we try to attract them over there, but that's because our population is insufficient. Here, you know, they're rather crowded. However, I presume there's room for charming young ladies everywhere."

"There seems to have been room here for you," said Isabel, whose eyes had been wandering over the large pleasure-spaces of the park.

Mr. Touchett gave a shrewd, conscious smile. "There's room everywhere, my dear, if you'll pay for it. I sometimes think I've paid too much for this. Perhaps you also might have to pay too much."

"Perhaps I might," the girl replied.

That suggestion gave her something more definite to rest on than she had found in her own thoughts, and the fact of this association of her uncle's mild acuteness with her dilemma seemed to prove that she was concerned with the natural and reasonable emotions of life and not altogether a victim to intellectual eagerness and vague ambitions—ambitions reaching beyond Lord Warburton's beautiful appeal, reaching to something indefinable and possibly not commendable. In so far as the indefinable had an influence upon Isabel's behaviour at this juncture, it was not the conception, even unformulated, of a union with Caspar Goodwood; for however she might have resisted conquest at her English suitor's large quiet hands she was at least as far removed from the disposition to let the young man from Boston take positive possession of her. The sentiment in which She sought refuge after reading his letter was a critical view of his having come abroad; for it was part of the influence he had upon her that he seemed to deprive her of the sense of freedom. There was a disagreeably strong push, a kind of hardness of presence, in his way of rising before her. She had been haunted at moments by the image, by the danger, of his disapproval and had wondered—a consideration she had never paid in equal degree to any one else—whether he would like what she did. The difficulty was that more than any man she had ever known, more than poor Lord Warburton (she had begun now to give his lordship the benefit of this epithet), Caspar Goodwood expressed for her an energy—and she had already felt it as a power that was of his very nature. It was in no degree a matter of his "advantages"—it was a matter of the spirit that sat in his clear-burning eyes like some tireless watcher at a window. She might like it or not, but he insisted, ever, with his whole weight and force: even in one's usual contact with him one had to reckon with that. The idea of a diminished liberty was particularly disagreeable to her at present, since she had just given a sort of personal accent to her independence by looking so straight at Lord Warburton's big bribe and yet turning away from it. Sometimes Caspar Goodwood had seemed to range himself on the side of her destiny, to be the stubbornest fact she knew; she said to herself at such moments that she might evade him for a time, but that she must make terms with him at last—terms which would be certain to be favourable to himself. Her impulse had been to avail herself of the things that helped her to resist such an obligation; and this impulse had been much concerned in her eager acceptance of her aunt's invitation, which had come to her at an hour when she expected from day to day to see Mr. Goodwood and when she was glad to have an answer ready for something she was sure he would say to her. When she had told him at Albany, on the evening of Mrs. Touchett's visit, that she couldn't then discuss difficult questions, dazzled as she was by the great immediate opening of her aunt's offer of "Europe," he declared that this was no answer at all; and it was now to obtain a better one that he was following her across the sea. To say to herself that he was a kind of grim fate was well enough for a fanciful young woman who was able to take much for granted in him; but the reader has a right to a nearer and a clearer view.

He was the son of a proprietor of well-known cotton-mills in Massachusetts—a gentleman who had accumulated a considerable fortune in the exercise of this industry. Caspar at present managed the works, and with a judgement and a temper which, in spite of keen competition and languid years, had kept their prosperity from dwindling. He had received the better part of his education at Harvard College, where, however, he had gained renown rather as a gymnast and an oarsman than as a gleaner of more dispersed knowledge. Later on he had learned that the finer intelligence too could vault and pull and strain—might even, breaking the record, treat itself to rare exploits. He had thus discovered in himself a sharp eye for the mystery of mechanics, and had invented an improvement in the cotton-spinning process which was now largely used and was known by his name. You might have seen it in the newspapers in connection with this fruitful contrivance; assurance of which he had given to Isabel by showing her in the columns of the New York Interviewer an exhaustive article on the Goodwood patent—an article not prepared by Miss Stackpole, friendly as she had proved herself to his more sentimental interests. There were intricate, bristling things he rejoiced in; he liked to organise, to contend, to administer; he could make people work his will, believe in him, march before him and justify him. This was the art, as they said, of managing men—which rested, in him, further, on a bold though brooding ambition. It struck those who knew him well that he might do greater things than carry on a cotton-factory; there was nothing cottony about Caspar Goodwood, and his friends took for granted that he would somehow and somewhere write himself in bigger letters. But it was as if something large and confused, something dark and ugly, would have to call upon him: he was not after all in harmony with mere smug peace and greed and gain, an order of things of which the vital breath was ubiquitous advertisement. It pleased Isabel to believe that he might have ridden, on a plunging steed, the whirlwind of a great war—a war like the Civil strife that had overdarkened her conscious childhood and his ripening youth.

She liked at any rate this idea of his being by character and in fact a mover of men—liked it much better than some other points in his nature and aspect. She cared nothing for his cotton-mill—the Goodwood patent left her imagination absolutely cold. She wished him no ounce less of his manhood, but she sometimes thought he would be rather nicer if he looked, for instance, a little differently. His jaw was too square and set and his figure too straight and stiff: these things suggested a want of easy consonance with the deeper rhythms of life. Then she viewed with reserve a habit he had of dressing always in the same manner; it was not apparently that he wore the same clothes continually, for, on the contrary, his garments had a way of looking rather too new. But they all seemed of the same piece; the figure, the stuff, was so drearily usual. She had reminded herself more than once that this was a frivolous objection to a person of his importance; and then she had amended the rebuke by saying that it would be a frivolous objection only if she were in love with him. She was not in love with him and therefore might criticise his small defects as well as his great—which latter consisted in the collective reproach of his being too serious, or, rather, not of his being so, since one could never be, but certainly of his seeming so. He showed his appetites and designs too simply and artlessly; when one was alone with him he talked too much about the same subject, and when other people were present he talked too little about anything. And yet he was of supremely strong, clean make—which was so much she saw the different fitted parts of him as she had seen, in museums and portraits, the different fitted parts of armoured warriors—in plates of steel handsomely inlaid with gold. It was very strange: where, ever, was any tangible link between her impression and her act? Caspar Goodwood had never corresponded to her idea of a delightful person, and she supposed that this was why he left her so harshly critical. When, however, Lord Warburton, who not only did correspond with it, but gave an extension to the term, appealed to her approval, she found herself still unsatisfied. It was certainly strange.

The sense of her incoherence was not a help to answering Mr. Goodwood's letter, and Isabel determined to leave it a while unhonoured. If he had determined to persecute her he must take the consequences; foremost among which was his being left to perceive how little it charmed her that he should come down to Gardencourt. She was already liable to the incursions of one suitor at this place, and though it might be pleasant to be appreciated in opposite quarters there was a kind of grossness in entertaining two such passionate pleaders at once, even in a case where the entertainment should consist of dismissing them. She made no reply to Mr. Goodwood; but at the end of three days she wrote to Lord Warburton, and the letter belongs to our history.

DEAR LORD WARBURTON—A great deal of earnest thought has not led me to change my mind about the suggestion you were so kind as to make me the other day. I am not, I am really and truly not, able to regard you in the light of a companion for life; or to think of your home—your various homes—as the settled seat of my existence. These things cannot be reasoned about, and I very earnestly entreat you not to return to the subject we discussed so exhaustively. We see our lives from our own point of view; that is the privilege of the weakest and humblest of us; and I shall never be able to see mine in the manner you proposed. Kindly let this suffice you, and do me the justice to believe that I have given your proposal the deeply respectful consideration it deserves. It is with this very great regard that I remain sincerely yours,

ISABEL ARCHER.

While the author of this missive was making up her mind to dispatch it Henrietta Stackpole formed a resolve which was accompanied by no demur. She invited Ralph Touchett to take a walk with her in the garden, and when he had assented with that alacrity which seemed constantly to testify to his high expectations, she informed him that she had a favour to ask of him. It may be admitted that at this information the young man flinched; for we know that Miss Stackpole had struck him as apt to push an advantage. The alarm was unreasoned, however; for he was clear about the area of her indiscretion as little as advised of its vertical depth, and he made a very civil profession of the desire to serve her. He was afraid of her and presently told her so. "When you look at me in a certain way my knees knock together, my faculties desert me; I'm filled with trepidation and I ask only for strength to execute your commands. You've an address that I've never encountered in any woman."

"Well," Henrietta replied good-humouredly, "if I had not known before that you were trying somehow to abash me I should know it now. Of course I'm easy game—I was brought up with such different customs and ideas. I'm not used to your arbitrary standards, and I've never been spoken to in America as you have spoken to me. If a gentleman conversing with me over there were to speak to me like that I shouldn't know what to make of it. We take everything more naturally over there, and, after all, we're a great deal more simple. I admit that; I'm very simple myself. Of course if you choose to laugh at me for it you're very welcome; but I think on the whole I would rather be myself than you. I'm quite content to be myself; I don't want to change. There are plenty of people that appreciate me just as I am. It's true they're nice fresh free-born Americans!" Henrietta had lately taken up the tone of helpless innocence and large concession. "I want you to assist me a little," she went on. "I don't care in the least whether I amuse you while you do so; or, rather, I'm perfectly willing your amusement should be your reward. I want you to help me about Isabel."

"Has she injured you?" Ralph asked.

"If she had I shouldn't mind, and I should never tell you. What I'm afraid of is that she'll injure herself."

"I think that's very possible," said Ralph.

His companion stopped in the garden-walk, fixing on him perhaps the very gaze that unnerved him. "That too would amuse you, I suppose. The way you do say things! I never heard any one so indifferent."

"To Isabel? Ah, not that!"

"Well, you're not in love with her, I hope."

"How can that be, when I'm in love with Another?"

"You're in love with yourself, that's the Other!" Miss Stackpole declared. "Much good may it do you! But if you wish to be serious once in your life here's a chance; and if you really care for your cousin here's an opportunity to prove it. I don't expect you to understand her; that's too much to ask. But you needn't do that to grant my favour. I'll supply the necessary intelligence."

"I shall enjoy that immensely!" Ralph exclaimed. "I'll be Caliban and you shall be Ariel."

"You're not at all like Caliban, because you're sophisticated, and Caliban was not. But I'm not talking about imaginary characters; I'm talking about Isabel. Isabel's intensely real. What I wish to tell you is that I find her fearfully changed."

"Since you came, do you mean?"

"Since I came and before I came. She's not the same as she once so beautifully was."

"As she was in America?"

"Yes, in America. I suppose you know she comes from there. She can't help it, but she does."

"Do you want to change her back again?"

"Of course I do, and I want you to help me."

"Ah," said Ralph, "I'm only Caliban; I'm not Prospero."

"You were Prospero enough to make her what she has become. You've acted on Isabel Archer since she came here, Mr. Touchett."

"I, my dear Miss Stackpole? Never in the world. Isabel Archer has acted on me—yes; she acts on every one. But I've been absolutely passive."

"You're too passive then. You had better stir yourself and be careful. Isabel's changing every day; she's drifting away—right out to sea. I've watched her and I can see it. She's not the bright American girl she was. She's taking different views, a different colour, and turning away from her old ideals. I want to save those ideals, Mr. Touchett, and that's where you come in."

"Not surely as an ideal?"

"Well, I hope not," Henrietta replied promptly. "I've got a fear in my heart that she's going to marry one of these fell Europeans, and I want to prevent it.

"Ah, I see," cried Ralph; "and to prevent it you want me to step in and marry her?"

"Not quite; that remedy would be as bad as the disease, for you're the typical, the fell European from whom I wish to rescue her. No; I wish you to take an interest in another person—a young man to whom she once gave great encouragement and whom she now doesn't seem to think good enough. He's a thoroughly grand man and a very dear friend of mine, and I wish very much you would invite him to pay a visit here."

Ralph was much puzzled by this appeal, and it is perhaps not to the credit of his purity of mind that he failed to look at it at first in the simplest light. It wore, to his eyes, a tortuous air, and his fault was that he was not quite sure that anything in the world could really be as candid as this request of Miss Stackpole's appeared. That a young woman should demand that a gentleman whom she described as her very dear friend should be furnished with an opportunity to make himself agreeable to another young woman, a young woman whose attention had wandered and whose charms were greater—this was an anomaly which for the moment challenged all his ingenuity of interpretation. To read between the lines was easier than to follow the text, and to suppose that Miss Stackpole wished the gentleman invited to Gardencourt on her own account was the sign not so much of a vulgar as of an embarrassed mind. Even from this venial act of vulgarity, however, Ralph was saved, and saved by a force that I can only speak of as inspiration. With no more outward light on the subject than he already possessed he suddenly acquired the conviction that it would be a sovereign injustice to the correspondent of the Interviewer to assign a dishonourable motive to any act of hers. This conviction passed into his mind with extreme rapidity; it was perhaps kindled by the pure radiance of the young lady's imperturbable gaze. He returned this challenge a moment, consciously, resisting an inclination to frown as one frowns in the presence of larger luminaries. "Who's the gentleman you speak of?"

"Mr. Caspar Goodwood—of Boston. He has been extremely attentive to Isabel—just as devoted to her as he can live. He has followed her out here and he's at present in London. I don't know his address, but I guess I can obtain it."

"I've never heard of him," said Ralph.

"Well, I suppose you haven't heard of every one. I don't believe he has ever heard of you; but that's no reason why Isabel shouldn't marry him."

Ralph gave a mild ambiguous laugh. "What a rage you have for marrying people! Do you remember how you wanted to marry me the other day?"

"I've got over that. You don't know how to take such ideas. Mr. Goodwood does, however; and that's what I like about him. He's a splendid man and a perfect gentleman, and Isabel knows it."

"Is she very fond of him?"

"If she isn't she ought to be. He's simply wrapped up in her."

"And you wish me to ask him here," said Ralph reflectively.

"It would be an act of true hospitality."

"Caspar Goodwood," Ralph continued—"it's rather a striking name."

"I don't care anything about his name. It might be Ezekiel Jenkins, and I should say the same. He's the only man I have ever seen whom I think worthy of Isabel."

"You're a very devoted friend," said Ralph.

"Of course I am. If you say that to pour scorn on me I don't care."

"I don't say it to pour scorn on you; I'm very much struck with it."

"You're more satiric than ever, but I advise you not to laugh at Mr. Goodwood."

"I assure you I'm very serious; you ought to understand that," said Ralph.

In a moment his companion understood it. "I believe you are; now you're too serious."

"You're difficult to please."

"Oh, you're very serious indeed. You won't invite Mr. Goodwood."

"I don't know," said Ralph. "I'm capable of strange things. Tell me a little about Mr. Goodwood. What's he like?"

"He's just the opposite of you. He's at the head of a cotton-factory; a very fine one."

"Has he pleasant manners?" asked Ralph.

"Splendid manners—in the American style."

"Would he be an agreeable member of our little circle?"

"I don't think he'd care much about our little circle. He'd concentrate on Isabel."

"And how would my cousin like that?"

"Very possibly not at all. But it will be good for her. It will call back her thoughts."

"Call them back—from where?"

"From foreign parts and other unnatural places. Three months ago she gave Mr. Goodwood every reason to suppose he was acceptable to her, and it's not worthy of Isabel to go back on a real friend simply because she has changed the scene. I've changed the scene too, and the effect of it has been to make me care more for my old associations than ever. It's my belief that the sooner Isabel changes it back again the better. I know her well enough to know that she would never be truly happy over here, and I wish her to form some strong American tie that will act as a preservative."

"Aren't you perhaps a little too much in a hurry?" Ralph enquired. "Don't you think you ought to give her more of a chance in poor old England?"

"A chance to ruin her bright young life? One's never too much in a hurry to save a precious human creature from drowning."

"As I understand it then," said Ralph, "you wish me to push Mr. Goodwood overboard after her. Do you know," he added, "that I've never heard her mention his name?"

Henrietta gave a brilliant smile. "I'm delighted to hear that; it proves how much she thinks of him."

Ralph appeared to allow that there was a good deal in this, and he surrendered to thought while his companion watched him askance. "If I should invite Mr. Goodwood," he finally said, "it would be to quarrel with him."

"Don't do that; he'd prove the better man."

"You certainly are doing your best to make me hate him! I really don't think I can ask him. I should be afraid of being rude to him."

"It's just as you please," Henrietta returned. "I had no idea you were in love with her yourself."

"Do you really believe that?" the young man asked with lifted eyebrows.

"That's the most natural speech I've ever heard you make! Of course I believe it," Miss Stackpole ingeniously said.

"Well," Ralph concluded, "to prove to you that you're wrong I'll invite him. It must be of course as a friend of yours."

"It will not be as a friend of mine that he'll come; and it will not be to prove to me that I'm wrong that you'll ask him—but to prove it to yourself!"

These last words of Miss Stackpole's (on which the two presently separated) contained an amount of truth which Ralph Touchett was obliged to recognise; but it so far took the edge from too sharp a recognition that, in spite of his suspecting it would be rather more indiscreet to keep than to break his promise, he wrote Mr. Goodwood a note of six lines, expressing the pleasure it would give Mr. Touchett the elder that he should join a little party at Gardencourt, of which Miss Stackpole was a valued member. Having sent his letter (to the care of a banker whom Henrietta suggested) he waited in some suspense. He had heard this fresh formidable figure named for the first time; for when his mother had mentioned on her arrival that there was a story about the girl's having an "admirer" at home, the idea had seemed deficient in reality and he had taken no pains to ask questions the answers to which would involve only the vague or the disagreeable. Now, however, the native admiration of which his cousin was the object had become more concrete; it took the form of a young man who had followed her to London, who was interested in a cotton-mill and had manners in the most splendid of the American styles. Ralph had two theories about this intervenes. Either his passion was a sentimental fiction of Miss Stackpole's (there was always a sort of tacit understanding among women, born of the solidarity of the sex, that they should discover or invent lovers for each other), in which case he was not to be feared and would probably not accept the invitation; or else he would accept the invitation and in this event prove himself a creature too irrational to demand further consideration. The latter clause of Ralph's argument might have seemed incoherent; but it embodied his conviction that if Mr. Goodwood were interested in Isabel in the serious manner described by Miss Stackpole he would not care to present himself at Gardencourt on a summons from the latter lady. "On this supposition," said Ralph, "he must regard her as a thorn on the stem of his rose; as an intercessor he must find her wanting in tact."

Two days after he had sent his invitation he received a very short note from Caspar Goodwood, thanking him for it, regretting that other engagements made a visit to Gardencourt impossible and presenting many compliments to Miss Stackpole. Ralph handed the note to Henrietta, who, when she had read it, exclaimed: "Well, I never have heard of anything so stiff!"

"I'm afraid he doesn't care so much about my cousin as you suppose," Ralph observed.

"No, it's not that; it's some subtler motive. His nature's very deep. But I'm determined to fathom it, and I shall write to him to know what he means."

His refusal of Ralph's overtures was vaguely disconcerting; from the moment he declined to come to Gardencourt our friend began to think him of importance. He asked himself what it signified to him whether Isabel's admirers should be desperadoes or laggards; they were not rivals of his and were perfectly welcome to act out their genius. Nevertheless he felt much curiosity as to the result of Miss Stackpole's promised enquiry into the causes of Mr. Goodwood's stiffness—a curiosity for the present ungratified, inasmuch as when he asked her three days later if she had written to London she was obliged to confess she had written in vain. Mr. Goodwood had not replied.

"I suppose he's thinking it over," she said; "he thinks everything over; he's not really at all impetuous. But I'm accustomed to having my letters answered the same day." She presently proposed to Isabel, at all events, that they should make an excursion to London together. "If I must tell the truth," she observed, "I'm not seeing much at this place, and I shouldn't think you were either. I've not even seen that aristocrat—what's his name?—Lord Washburton. He seems to let you severely alone."

"Lord Warburton's coming to-morrow, I happen to know," replied her friend, who had received a note from the master of Lockleigh in answer to her own letter. "You'll have every opportunity of turning him inside out."

"Well, he may do for one letter, but what's one letter when you want to write fifty? I've described all the scenery in this vicinity and raved about all the old women and donkeys. You may say what you please, scenery doesn't make a vital letter. I must go back to London and get some impressions of real life. I was there but three days before I came away, and that's hardly time to get in touch."

As Isabel, on her journey from New York to Gardencourt, had seen even less of the British capital than this, it appeared a happy suggestion of Henrietta's that the two should go thither on a visit of pleasure. The idea struck Isabel as charming; he was curious of the thick detail of London, which had always loomed large and rich to her. They turned over their schemes together and indulged in visions of romantic hours. They would stay at some picturesque old inn—one of the inns described by Dickens—and drive over the town in those delightful hansoms. Henrietta was a literary woman, and the great advantage of being a literary woman was that you could go everywhere and do everything. They would dine at a coffee-house and go afterwards to the play; they would frequent the Abbey and the British Museum and find out where Doctor Johnson had lived, and Goldsmith and Addison. Isabel grew eager and presently unveiled the bright vision to Ralph, who burst into a fit of laughter which scarce expressed the sympathy she had desired.

"It's a delightful plan," he said. "I advise you to go to the Duke's Head in Covent Garden, an easy, informal, old-fashioned place, and I'll have you put down at my club."

"Do you mean it's improper?" Isabel asked. "Dear me, isn't anything proper here? With Henrietta surely I may go anywhere; she isn't hampered in that way. She has travelled over the whole American continent and can at least find her way about this minute island."

"Ah then," said Ralph, "let me take advantage of her protection to go up to town as well. I may never have a chance to travel so safely!"

CHAPTER XIV

Miss Stackpole would have prepared to start immediately; but Isabel, as we have seen, had been notified that Lord Warburton would come again to Gardencourt, and she believed it her duty to remain there and see him. For four or five days he had made no response to her letter; then he had written, very briefly, to say he would come to luncheon two days later. There was something in these delays and postponements that touched the girl and renewed her sense of his desire to be considerate and patient, not to appear to urge her too grossly; a consideration the more studied that she was so sure he "really liked" her. Isabel told her uncle she had written to him, mentioning also his intention of coming; and the old man, in consequence, left his room earlier than usual and made his appearance at the two o'clock repast. This was by no means an act of vigilance on his part, but the fruit of a benevolent belief that his being of the company might help to cover any conjoined straying away in case Isabel should give their noble visitor another hearing. That personage drove over from Lockleigh and brought the elder of his sisters with him, a measure presumably dictated by reflexions of the same order as Mr. Touchett's. The two visitors were introduced to Miss Stackpole, who, at luncheon, occupied a seat adjoining Lord Warburton's. Isabel, who was nervous and had no relish for the prospect of again arguing the question he had so prematurely opened, could not help admiring his good-humoured self-possession, which quite disguised the symptoms of that preoccupation with her presence it was natural she should suppose him to feel. He neither looked at her nor spoke to her, and the only sign of his emotion was that he avoided meeting her eyes. He had plenty of talk for the others, however, and he appeared to eat his luncheon with discrimination and appetite. Miss Molyneux, who had a smooth, nun-like forehead and wore a large silver cross suspended from her neck, was evidently preoccupied with Henrietta Stackpole, upon whom her eyes constantly rested in a manner suggesting a conflict between deep alienation and yearning wonder. Of the two ladies from Lockleigh she was the one Isabel had liked best; there was such a world of hereditary quiet in her. Isabel was sure moreover that her mild forehead and silver cross referred to some weird Anglican mystery—some delightful reinstitution perhaps of the quaint office of the canoness. She wondered what Miss Molyneux would think of her if she knew Miss Archer had refused her brother; and then she felt sure that Miss Molyneux would never know—that Lord Warburton never told her such things. He was fond of her and kind to her, but on the whole he told her little. Such, at least, was Isabel's theory; when, at table, she was not occupied in conversation she was usually occupied in forming theories about her neighbours. According to Isabel, if Miss Molyneux should ever learn what had passed between Miss Archer and Lord Warburton she would probably be shocked at such a girl's failure to rise; or no, rather (this was our heroine's last position) she would impute to the young American but a due consciousness of inequality.

Whatever Isabel might have made of her opportunities, at all events, Henrietta Stackpole was by no means disposed to neglect those in which she now found herself immersed. "Do you know you're the first lord I've ever seen?" she said very promptly to her neighbour. "I suppose you think I'm awfully benighted."

"You've escaped seeing some very ugly men," Lord Warburton answered, looking a trifle absently about the table.

"Are they very ugly? They try to make us believe in America that they're all handsome and magnificent and that they wear wonderful robes and crowns."

"Ah, the robes and crowns are gone out of fashion," said Lord Warburton, "like your tomahawks and revolvers."

"I'm sorry for that; I think an aristocracy ought to be splendid," Henrietta declared. "If it's not that, what is it?"

"Oh, you know, it isn't much, at the best," her neighbour allowed. "Won't you have a potato?"

"I don't care much for these European potatoes. I shouldn't know you from an ordinary American gentleman."

"Do talk to me as if I were one," said Lord Warburton. "I don't see how you manage to get on without potatoes; you must find so few things to eat over here."

Henrietta was silent a little; there was a chance he was not sincere. "I've had hardly any appetite since I've been here," she went on at last; "so it doesn't much matter. I don't approve of you, you know; I feel as if I ought to tell you that."

"Don't approve of me?"

"Yes; I don't suppose any one ever said such a thing to you before, did they? I don't approve of lords as an institution. I think the world has got beyond them—far beyond."

"Oh, so do I. I don't approve of myself in the least. Sometimes it comes over me—how I should object to myself if I were not myself, don't you know? But that's rather good, by the way—not to be vainglorious."

"Why don't you give it up then?" Miss Stackpole enquired.

"Give up—a—?" asked Lord Warburton, meeting her harsh inflexion with a very mellow one.

"Give up being a lord."

"Oh, I'm so little of one! One would really forget all about it if you wretched Americans were not constantly reminding one. However, I do think of giving it up, the little there is left of it, one of these days."

"I should like to see you do it!" Henrietta exclaimed rather grimly.

"I'll invite you to the ceremony; we'll have a supper and a dance."

"Well," said Miss Stackpole, "I like to see all sides. I don't approve of a privileged class, but I like to hear what they have to say for themselves."

"Mighty little, as you see!"

"I should like to draw you out a little more," Henrietta continued. "But you're always looking away. You're afraid of meeting my eye. I see you want to escape me."

"No, I'm only looking for those despised potatoes."

"Please explain about that young lady—your sister—then. I don't understand about her. Is she a Lady?"

"She's a capital good girl."

"I don't like the way you say that—as if you wanted to change the subject. Is her position inferior to yours?"

"We neither of us have any position to speak of; but she's better off than I, because she has none of the bother."

"Yes, she doesn't look as if she had much bother. I wish I had as little bother as that. You do produce quiet people over here, whatever else you may do."

"Ah, you see one takes life easily, on the whole," said Lord Warburton. "And then you know we're very dull. Ah, we can be dull when we try!"

"I should advise you to try something else. I shouldn't know what to talk to your sister about; she looks so different. Is that silver cross a badge?"

"A badge?"

"A sign of rank."

Lord Warburton's glance had wandered a good deal, but at this it met the gaze of his neighbour. "Oh yes," he answered in a moment; "the women go in for those things. The silver cross is worn by the eldest daughters of Viscounts." Which was his harmless revenge for having occasionally had his credulity too easily engaged in America. After luncheon he proposed to Isabel to come into the gallery and look at the pictures; and though she knew he had seen the pictures twenty times she complied without criticising this pretext. Her conscience now was very easy; ever since she sent him her letter she had felt particularly light of spirit. He walked slowly to the end of the gallery, staring at its contents and saying nothing; and then he suddenly broke out: "I hoped you wouldn't write to me that way."

"It was the only way, Lord Warburton," said the girl. "Do try and believe that."

"If I could believe it of course I should let you alone. But we can't believe by willing it; and I confess I don't understand. I could understand your disliking me; that I could understand well. But that you should admit you do—"

"What have I admitted?" Isabel interrupted, turning slightly pale.

"That you think me a good fellow; isn't that it?" She said nothing, and he went on: "You don't seem to have any reason, and that gives me a sense of injustice."

"I have a reason, Lord Warburton." She said it in a tone that made his heart contract.

"I should like very much to know it."

"I'll tell you some day when there's more to show for it."

"Excuse my saying that in the mean time I must doubt of it."

"You make me very unhappy," said Isabel.

"I'm not sorry for that; it may help you to know how I feel. Will you kindly answer me a question?" Isabel made no audible assent, but he apparently saw in her eyes something that gave him courage to go on. "Do you prefer some one else?"

"That's a question I'd rather not answer."

"Ah, you do then!" her suitor murmured with bitterness.

The bitterness touched her, and she cried out: "You're mistaken! I don't."

He sat down on a bench, unceremoniously, doggedly, like a man in trouble; leaning his elbows on his knees and staring at the floor. "I can't even be glad of that," he said at last, throwing himself back against the wall; "for that would be an excuse."

She raised her eyebrows in surprise. "An excuse? Must I excuse myself?"

He paid, however, no answer to the question. Another idea had come into his head. "Is it my political opinions? Do you think I go too far?"

"I can't object to your political opinions, because I don't understand them."

"You don't care what I think!" he cried, getting up. "It's all the same to you."

Isabel walked to the other side of the gallery and stood there showing him her charming back, her light slim figure, the length of her white neck as she bent her head, and the density of her dark braids. She stopped in front of a small picture as if for the purpose of examining it; and there was something so young and free in her movement that her very pliancy seemed to mock at him. Her eyes, however, saw nothing; they had suddenly been suffused with tears. In a moment he followed her, and by this time she had brushed her tears away; but when she turned round her face was pale and the expression of her eyes strange. "That reason that I wouldn't tell you—I'll tell it you after all. It's that I can't escape my fate."

"Your fate?"

"I should try to escape it if I were to marry you."

"I don't understand. Why should not that be your fate as well as anything else?"

"Because it's not," said Isabel femininely. "I know it's not. It's not my fate to give up—I know it can't be."

Poor Lord Warburton stared, an interrogative point in either eye. "Do you call marrying me giving up?"

"Not in the usual sense. It's getting—getting—getting a great deal. But it's giving up other chances."

"Other chances for what?"

"I don't mean chances to marry," said Isabel, her colour quickly coming back to her. And then she stopped, looking down with a deep frown, as if it were hopeless to attempt to make her meaning clear.

"I don't think it presumptuous in me to suggest that you'll gain more than you'll lose," her companion observed.

"I can't escape unhappiness," said Isabel. "In marrying you I shall be trying to."

"I don't know whether you'd try to, but you certainly would: that I must in candour admit!" he exclaimed with an anxious laugh.

"I mustn't—I can't!" cried the girl.

"Well, if you're bent on being miserable I don't see why you should make me so. Whatever charms a life of misery may have for you, it has none for me."

"I'm not bent on a life of misery," said Isabel. "I've always been intensely determined to be happy, and I've often believed I should be. I've told people that; you can ask them. But it comes over me every now and then that I can never be happy in any extraordinary way; not by turning away, by separating myself."

"By separating yourself from what?"

"From life. From the usual chances and dangers, from what most people know and suffer."

Lord Warburton broke into a smile that almost denoted hope. "Why, my dear Miss Archer," he began to explain with the most considerate eagerness, "I don't offer you any exoneration from life or from any chances or dangers whatever. I wish I could; depend upon it I would! For what do you take me, pray? Heaven help me, I'm not the Emperor of China! All I offer you is the chance of taking the common lot in a comfortable sort of way. The common lot? Why, I'm devoted to the common lot! Strike an alliance with me, and I promise you that you shall have plenty of it. You shall separate from nothing whatever—not even from your friend Miss Stackpole."

"She'd never approve of it," said Isabel, trying to smile and take advantage of this side-issue; despising herself too, not a little, for doing so.

"Are we speaking of Miss Stackpole?" his lordship asked impatiently. "I never saw a person judge things on such theoretic grounds."

"Now I suppose you're speaking of me," said Isabel with humility; and she turned away again, for she saw Miss Molyneux enter the gallery, accompanied by Henrietta and by Ralph.

Lord Warburton's sister addressed him with a certain timidity and reminded him she ought to return home in time for tea, as she was expecting company to partake of it. He made no answer—apparently not having heard her; he was preoccupied, and with good reason. Miss Molyneux—as if he had been Royalty—stood like a lady-in-waiting.

"Well, I never, Miss Molyneux!" said Henrietta Stackpole. "If I wanted to go he'd have to go. If I wanted my brother to do a thing he'd have to do it."

"Oh, Warburton does everything one wants," Miss Molyneux answered with a quick, shy laugh. "How very many pictures you have!" she went on, turning to Ralph.

"They look a good many, because they're all put together," said Ralph. "But it's really a bad way."

"Oh, I think it's so nice. I wish we had a gallery at Lockleigh. I'm so very fond of pictures," Miss Molyneux went on, persistently, to Ralph, as if she were afraid Miss Stackpole would address her again. Henrietta appeared at once to fascinate and to frighten her.

"Ah yes, pictures are very convenient," said Ralph, who appeared to know better what style of reflexion was acceptable to her.

"They're so very pleasant when it rains," the young lady continued. "It has rained of late so very often."

"I'm sorry you're going away, Lord Warburton," said Henrietta. "I wanted to get a great deal more out of you."

"I'm not going away," Lord Warburton answered.

"Your sister says you must. In America the gentlemen obey the ladies."

"I'm afraid we have some people to tea," said Miss Molyneux, looking at her brother.

"Very good, my dear. We'll go."

"I hoped you would resist!" Henrietta exclaimed. "I wanted to see what Miss Molyneux would do."

"I never do anything," said this young lady.

"I suppose in your position it's sufficient for you to exist!" Miss Stackpole returned. "I should like very much to see you at home."

"You must come to Lockleigh again," said Miss Molyneux, very sweetly, to Isabel, ignoring this remark of Isabel's friend. Isabel looked into her quiet eyes a moment, and for that moment seemed to see in their grey depths the reflexion of everything she had rejected in rejecting Lord Warburton—the peace, the kindness, the honour, the possessions, a deep security and a great exclusion. She kissed Miss Molyneux and then she said: "I'm afraid I can never come again."

"Never again?"

"I'm afraid I'm going away."

"Oh, I'm so very sorry," said Miss Molyneux. "I think that's so very wrong of you."

Lord Warburton watched this little passage; then he turned away and stared at a picture. Ralph, leaning against the rail before the picture with his hands in his pockets, had for the moment been watching him.

"I should like to see you at home," said Henrietta, whom Lord Warburton found beside him. "I should like an hour's talk with you; there are a great many questions I wish to ask you."

"I shall be delighted to see you," the proprietor of Lockleigh answered; "but I'm certain not to be able to answer many of your questions. When will you come?"

"Whenever Miss Archer will take me. We're thinking of going to London, but we'll go and see you first. I'm determined to get some satisfaction out of you."

"If it depends upon Miss Archer I'm afraid you won't get much. She won't come to Lockleigh; she doesn't like the place."

"She told me it was lovely!" said Henrietta.

Lord Warburton hesitated. "She won't come, all the same. You had better come alone," he added.

Henrietta straightened herself, and her large eyes expanded. "Would you make that remark to an English lady?" she enquired with soft asperity.

Lord Warburton stared. "Yes, if I liked her enough."

"You'd be careful not to like her enough. If Miss Archer won't visit your place again it's because she doesn't want to take me. I know what she thinks of me, and I suppose you think the same—that I oughtn't to bring in individuals." Lord Warburton was at a loss; he had not been made acquainted with Miss Stackpole's professional character and failed to catch her allusion. "Miss Archer has been warning you!" she therefore went on.

"Warning me?"

"Isn't that why she came off alone with you here—to put you on your guard?"

"Oh dear, no," said Lord Warburton brazenly; "our talk had no such solemn character as that."

"Well, you've been on your guard—intensely. I suppose it's natural to you; that's just what I wanted to observe. And so, too, Miss Molyneux—she wouldn't commit herself. You have been warned, anyway," Henrietta continued, addressing this young lady; "but for you it wasn't necessary."

"I hope not," said Miss Molyneux vaguely.

"Miss Stackpole takes notes," Ralph soothingly explained. "She's a great satirist; she sees through us all and she works us up."

"Well, I must say I never have had such a collection of bad material!" Henrietta declared, looking from Isabel to Lord Warburton and from this nobleman to his sister and to Ralph. "There's something the matter with you all; you're as dismal as if you had got a bad cable."

"You do see through us, Miss Stackpole," said Ralph in a low tone, giving her a little intelligent nod as he led the party out of the gallery. "There's something the matter with us all."

Isabel came behind these two; Miss Molyneux, who decidedly liked her immensely, had taken her arm, to walk beside her over the polished floor. Lord Warburton strolled on the other side with his hands behind him and his eyes lowered. For some moments he said nothing; and then, "Is it true you're going to London?" he asked.

"I believe it has been arranged."

"And when shall you come back?"

"In a few days; but probably for a very short time. I'm going to Paris with my aunt."

"When, then, shall I see you again?"

"Not for a good while," said Isabel. "But some day or other, I hope."

"Do you really hope it?"

"Very much."

He went a few steps in silence; then he stopped and put out his hand. "Good-bye."

"Good-bye," said Isabel.

Miss Molyneux kissed her again, and she let the two depart. After it, without rejoining Henrietta and Ralph, she retreated to her own room; in which apartment, before dinner, she was found by Mrs. Touchett, who had stopped on her way to the salon. "I may as well tell you," said that lady, "that your uncle has informed me of your relations with Lord Warburton."

Isabel considered. "Relations? They're hardly relations. That's the strange part of it: he has seen me but three or four times."

"Why did you tell your uncle rather than me?" Mrs. Touchett dispassionately asked.

Again the girl hesitated. "Because he knows Lord Warburton better."

"Yes, but I know you better."

"I'm not sure of that," said Isabel, smiling.

"Neither am I, after all; especially when you give me that rather conceited look. One would think you were awfully pleased with yourself and had carried off a prize! I suppose that when you refuse an offer like Lord Warburton's it's because you expect to do something better."

"Ah, my uncle didn't say that!" cried Isabel, smiling still.

CHAPTER XV

It had been arranged that the two young ladies should proceed to London under Ralph's escort, though Mrs. Touchett looked with little favour on the plan. It was just the sort of plan, she said, that Miss Stackpole would be sure to suggest, and she enquired if the correspondent of the Interviewer was to take the party to stay at her favourite boarding-house.

"I don't care where she takes us to stay, so long as there's local colour," said Isabel. "That's what we're going to London for."

"I suppose that after a girl has refused an English lord she may do anything," her aunt rejoined. "After that one needn't stand on trifles."

"Should you have liked me to marry Lord Warburton?" Isabel enquired.

"Of course I should."

"I thought you disliked the English so much."

"So I do; but it's all the greater reason for making use of them."

"Is that your idea of marriage?" And Isabel ventured to add that her aunt appeared to her to have made very little use of Mr. Touchett.

"Your uncle's not an English nobleman," said Mrs. Touchett, "though even if he had been I should still probably have taken up my residence in Florence."

"Do you think Lord Warburton could make me any better than I am?" the girl asked with some animation. "I don't mean I'm too good to improve. I mean that I don't love Lord Warburton enough to marry him."

"You did right to refuse him then," said Mrs. Touchett in her smallest, sparest voice. "Only, the next great offer you get, I hope you'll manage to come up to your standard."

"We had better wait till the offer comes before we talk about it. I hope very much I may have no more offers for the present. They upset me completely."

"You probably won't be troubled with them if you adopt permanently the Bohemian manner of life. However, I've promised Ralph not to criticise."

"I'll do whatever Ralph says is right," Isabel returned. "I've unbounded confidence in Ralph."

"His mother's much obliged to you!" this lady dryly laughed.

"It seems to me indeed she ought to feel it!" Isabel irrepressibly answered.

Ralph had assured her that there would be no violation of decency in their paying a visit—the little party of three—to the sights of the metropolis; but Mrs. Touchett took a different view. Like many ladies of her country who had lived a long time in Europe, she had completely lost her native tact on such points, and in her reaction, not in itself deplorable, against the liberty allowed to young persons beyond the seas, had fallen into gratuitous and exaggerated scruples. Ralph accompanied their visitors to town and established them at a quiet inn in a street that ran at right angles to Piccadilly. His first idea had been to take them to his father's house in Winchester Square, a large, dull mansion which at this period of the year was shrouded in silence and brown holland; but he bethought himself that, the cook being at Gardencourt, there was no one in the house to get them their meals, and Pratt's Hotel accordingly became their resting-place. Ralph, on his side, found quarters in Winchester Square, having a "den" there of which he was very fond and being familiar with deeper fears than that of a cold kitchen. He availed himself largely indeed of the resources of Pratt's Hotel, beginning his day with an early visit to his fellow travellers, who had Mr. Pratt in person, in a large bulging white waistcoat, to remove their dish-covers. Ralph turned up, as he said, after breakfast, and the little party made out a scheme of entertainment for the day. As London wears in the month of September a face blank but for its smears of prior service, the young man, who occasionally took an apologetic tone, was obliged to remind his companion, to Miss Stackpole's high derision, that there wasn't a creature in town.

"I suppose you mean the aristocracy are absent," Henrietta answered; "but I don't think you could have a better proof that if they were absent altogether they wouldn't be missed. It seems to me the place is about as full as it can be. There's no one here, of course, but three or four millions of people. What is it you call them—the lower-middle class? They're only the population of London, and that's of no consequence."

Ralph declared that for him the aristocracy left no void that Miss Stackpole herself didn't fill, and that a more contented man was nowhere at that moment to be found. In this he spoke the truth, for the stale September days, in the huge half-empty town, had a charm wrapped in them as a coloured gem might be wrapped in a dusty cloth. When he went home at night to the empty house in Winchester Square, after a chain of hours with his comparatively ardent friends, he wandered into the big dusky dining-room, where the candle he took from the hall-table, after letting himself in, constituted the only illumination. The square was still, the house was still; when he raised one of the windows of the dining-room to let in the air he heard the slow creak of the boots of a lone constable. His own step, in the empty place, seemed loud and sonorous; some of the carpets had been raised, and whenever he moved he roused a melancholy echo. He sat down in one of the armchairs; the big dark dining table twinkled here and there in the small candle-light; the pictures on the wall, all of them very brown, looked vague and incoherent. There was a ghostly presence as of dinners long since digested, of table-talk that had lost its actuality. This hint of the supernatural perhaps had something to do with the fact that his imagination took a flight and that he remained in his chair a long time beyond the hour at which he should have been in bed; doing nothing, not even reading the evening paper. I say he did nothing, and I maintain the phrase in the face of the fact that he thought at these moments of Isabel. To think of Isabel could only be for him an idle pursuit, leading to nothing and profiting little to any one. His cousin had not yet seemed to him so charming as during these days spent in sounding, tourist-fashion, the deeps and shallows of the metropolitan element. Isabel was full of premises, conclusions, emotions; if she had come in search of local colour she found it everywhere. She asked more questions than he could answer, and launched brave theories, as to historic cause and social effect, that he was equally unable to accept or to refute. The party went more than once to the British Museum and to that brighter palace of art which reclaims for antique variety so large an area of a monotonous suburb; they spent a morning in the Abbey and went on a penny-steamer to the Tower; they looked at pictures both in public and private collections and sat on various occasions beneath the great trees in Kensington Gardens. Henrietta proved an indestructible sight-seer and a more lenient judge than Ralph had ventured to hope. She had indeed many disappointments, and London at large suffered from her vivid remembrance of the strong points of the American civic idea; but she made the best of its dingy dignities and only heaved an occasional sigh and uttered a desultory "Well!" which led no further and lost itself in retrospect. The truth was that, as she said herself, she was not in her element. "I've not a sympathy with inanimate objects," she remarked to Isabel at the National Gallery; and she continued to suffer from the meagreness of the glimpse that had as yet been vouchsafed to her of the inner life. Landscapes by Turner and Assyrian bulls were a poor substitute for the literary dinner-parties at which she had hoped to meet the genius and renown of Great Britain.

"Where are your public men, where are your men and women of intellect?" she enquired of Ralph, standing in the middle of Trafalgar Square as if she had supposed this to be a place where she would naturally meet a few. "That's one of them on the top of the column, you say—Lord Nelson. Was he a lord too? Wasn't he high enough, that they had to stick him a hundred feet in the air? That's the past—I don't care about the past; I want to see some of the leading minds of the present. I won't say of the future, because I don't believe much in your future." Poor Ralph had few leading minds among his acquaintance and rarely enjoyed the pleasure of buttonholing a celebrity; a state of things which appeared to Miss Stackpole to indicate a deplorable want of enterprise. "If I were on the other side I should call," she said, "and tell the gentleman, whoever he might be, that I had heard a great deal about him and had come to see for myself. But I gather from what you say that this is not the custom here. You seem to have plenty of meaningless customs, but none of those that would help along. We are in advance, certainly. I suppose I shall have to give up the social side altogether;" and Henrietta, though she went about with her guidebook and pencil and wrote a letter to the Interviewer about the Tower (in which she described the execution of Lady Jane Grey), had a sad sense of falling below her mission.

The incident that had preceded Isabel's departure from Gardencourt left a painful trace in our young woman's mind: when she felt again in her face, as from a recurrent wave, the cold breath of her last suitor's surprise, she could only muffle her head till the air cleared. She could not have done less than what she did; this was certainly true. But her necessity, all the same, had been as graceless as some physical act in a strained attitude, and she felt no desire to take credit for her conduct. Mixed with this imperfect pride, nevertheless, was a feeling of freedom which in itself was sweet and which, as she wandered through the great city with her ill-matched companions, occasionally throbbed into odd demonstrations. When she walked in Kensington Gardens she stopped the children (mainly of the poorer sort) whom she saw playing on the grass; she asked them their names and gave them sixpence and, when they were pretty, kissed them. Ralph noticed these quaint charities; he noticed everything she did. One afternoon, that his companions might pass the time, he invited them to tea in Winchester Square, and he had the house set in order as much as possible for their visit. There was another guest to meet them, an amiable bachelor, an old friend of Ralph's who happened to be in town and for whom prompt commerce with Miss Stackpole appeared to have neither difficulty nor dread. Mr. Bantling, a stout, sleek, smiling man of forty, wonderfully dressed, universally informed and incoherently amused, laughed immoderately at everything Henrietta said, gave her several cups of tea, examined in her society the bric-a-brac, of which Ralph had a considerable collection, and afterwards, when the host proposed they should go out into the square and pretend it was a fete-champetre, walked round the limited enclosure several times with her and, at a dozen turns of their talk, bounded responsive—as with a positive passion for argument—to her remarks upon the inner life.

"Oh, I see; I dare say you found it very quiet at Gardencourt. Naturally there's not much going on there when there's such a lot of illness about. Touchett's very bad, you know; the doctors have forbidden his being in England at all, and he has only come back to take care of his father. The old man, I believe, has half a dozen things the matter with him. They call it gout, but to my certain knowledge he has organic disease so developed that you may depend upon it he'll go, some day soon, quite quickly. Of course that sort of thing makes a dreadfully dull house; I wonder they have people when they can do so little for them. Then I believe Mr. Touchett's always squabbling with his wife; she lives away from her husband, you know, in that extraordinary American way of yours. If you want a house where there's always something going on, I recommend you to go down and stay with my sister, Lady Pensil, in Bedfordshire. I'll write to her to-morrow and I'm sure she'll be delighted to ask you. I know just what you want—you want a house where they go in for theatricals and picnics and that sort of thing. My sister's just that sort of woman; she's always getting up something or other and she's always glad to have the sort of people who help her. I'm sure she'll ask you down by return of post: she's tremendously fond of distinguished people and writers. She writes herself, you know; but I haven't read everything she has written. It's usually poetry, and I don't go in much for poetry—unless it's Byron. I suppose you think a great deal of Byron in America," Mr. Bantling continued, expanding in the stimulating air of Miss Stackpole's attention, bringing up his sequences promptly and changing his topic with an easy turn of hand. Yet he none the less gracefully kept in sight of the idea, dazzling to Henrietta, of her going to stay with Lady Pensil in Bedfordshire. "I understand what you want; you want to see some genuine English sport. The Touchetts aren't English at all, you know; they have their own habits, their own language, their own food—some odd religion even, I believe, of their own. The old man thinks it's wicked to hunt, I'm told. You must get down to my sister's in time for the theatricals, and I'm sure she'll be glad to give you a part. I'm sure you act well; I know you're very clever. My sister's forty years old and has seven children, but she's going to play the principal part. Plain as she is she makes up awfully well—I will say for her. Of course you needn't act if you don't want to."

In this manner Mr. Bantling delivered himself while they strolled over the grass in Winchester Square, which, although it had been peppered by the London soot, invited the tread to linger. Henrietta thought her blooming, easy-voiced bachelor, with his impressibility to feminine merit and his splendid range of suggestion, a very agreeable man, and she valued the opportunity he offered her. "I don't know but I would go, if your sister should ask me. I think it would be my duty. What do you call her name?"

"Pensil. It's an odd name, but it isn't a bad one."

"I think one name's as good as another. But what's her rank?".

"Oh, she's a baron's wife; a convenient sort of rank. You're fine enough and you're not too fine."

"I don't know but what she'd be too fine for me. What do you call the place she lives in—Bedfordshire?"

"She lives away in the northern corner of it. It's a tiresome country, but I dare say you won't mind it. I'll try and run down while you're there."

All this was very pleasant to Miss Stackpole, and she was sorry to be obliged to separate from Lady Pensil's obliging brother. But it happened that she had met the day before, in Piccadilly, some friends whom she had not seen for a year: the Miss Climbers, two ladies from Wilmington, Delaware, who had been travelling on the Continent and were now preparing to re-embark. Henrietta had had a long interview with them on the Piccadilly pavement, and though the three ladies all talked at once they had not exhausted their store. It had been agreed therefore that Henrietta should come and dine with them in their lodgings in Jermyn Street at six o'clock on the morrow, and she now bethought herself of this engagement. She prepared to start for Jermyn Street, taking leave first of Ralph Touchett and Isabel, who, seated on garden chairs in another part of the enclosure, were occupied—if the term may be used—with an exchange of amenities less pointed than the practical colloquy of Miss Stackpole and Mr. Bantling. When it had been settled between Isabel and her friend that they should be reunited at some reputable hour at Pratt's Hotel, Ralph remarked that the latter must have a cab. She couldn't walk all the way to Jermyn Street.

"I suppose you mean it's improper for me to walk alone!" Henrietta exclaimed. "Merciful powers, have I come to this?"

"There's not the slightest need of your walking alone," Mr. Bantling gaily interposed. "I should be greatly pleased to go with you."

"I simply meant that you'd be late for dinner," Ralph returned. "Those poor ladies may easily believe that we refuse, at the last, to spare you."

"You had better have a hansom, Henrietta," said Isabel.

"I'll get you a hansom if you'll trust me," Mr. Bantling went on.

"We might walk a little till we meet one."

"I don't see why I shouldn't trust him, do you?" Henrietta enquired of Isabel.

"I don't see what Mr. Bantling could do to you," Isabel obligingly answered; "but, if you like, we'll walk with you till you find your cab."

"Never mind; we'll go alone. Come on, Mr. Bantling, and take care you get me a good one."

Mr. Bantling promised to do his best, and the two took their departure, leaving the girl and her cousin together in the square, over which a clear September twilight had now begun to gather. It was perfectly still; the wide quadrangle of dusky houses showed lights in none of the windows, where the shutters and blinds were closed; the pavements were a vacant expanse, and, putting aside two small children from a neighbouring slum, who, attracted by symptoms of abnormal animation in the interior, poked their faces between the rusty rails of the enclosure, the most vivid object within sight was the big red pillar-post on the southeast corner.

"Henrietta will ask him to get into the cab and go with her to Jermyn Street," Ralph observed. He always spoke of Miss Stackpole as Henrietta.

"Very possibly," said his companion.

"Or rather, no, she won't," he went on. "But Bantling will ask leave to get in."

"Very likely again. I'm glad very they're such good friends."

"She has made a conquest. He thinks her a brilliant woman. It may go far," said Ralph.

Isabel was briefly silent. "I call Henrietta a very brilliant woman, but I don't think it will go far. They would never really know each other. He has not the least idea what she really is, and she has no just comprehension of Mr. Bantling."

"There's no more usual basis of union than a mutual misunderstanding. But it ought not to be so difficult to understand Bob Bantling," Ralph added. "He is a very simple organism."

"Yes, but Henrietta's a simpler one still. And, pray, what am I to do?" Isabel asked, looking about her through the fading light, in which the limited landscape-gardening of the square took on a large and effective appearance. "I don't imagine that you'll propose that you and I, for our amusement, shall drive about London in a hansom."

"There's no reason we shouldn't stay here—if you don't dislike it. It's very warm; there will be half an hour yet before dark; and if you permit it I'll light a cigarette."

"You may do what you please," said Isabel, "if you'll amuse me till seven o'clock. I propose at that hour to go back and partake of a simple and solitary repast—two poached eggs and a muffin—at Pratt's Hotel."

"Mayn't I dine with you?" Ralph asked.

"No, you'll dine at your club."

They had wandered back to their chairs in the centre of the square again, and Ralph had lighted his cigarette. It would have given him extreme pleasure to be present in person at the modest little feast she had sketched; but in default of this he liked even being forbidden. For the moment, however, he liked immensely being alone with her, in the thickening dusk, in the centre of the multitudinous town; it made her seem to depend upon him and to be in his power. This power he could exert but vaguely; the best exercise of it was to accept her decisions submissively which indeed there was already an emotion in doing. "Why won't you let me dine with you?" he demanded after a pause.

"Because I don't care for it."

"I suppose you're tired of me."

"I shall be an hour hence. You see I have the gift of foreknowledge."

"Oh, I shall be delightful meanwhile," said Ralph.

But he said nothing more, and as she made no rejoinder they sat some time in a stillness which seemed to contradict his promise of entertainment. It seemed to him she was preoccupied, and he wondered what she was thinking about; there were two or three very possible subjects. At last he spoke again. "Is your objection to my society this evening caused by your expectation of another visitor?"

She turned her head with a glance of her clear, fair eyes. "Another visitor? What visitor should I have?"

He had none to suggest; which made his question seem to himself silly as well as brutal. "You've a great many friends that I don't know. You've a whole past from which I was perversely excluded."

"You were reserved for my future. You must remember that my past is over there across the water. There's none of it here in London."

"Very good, then, since your future is seated beside you. Capital thing to have your future so handy." And Ralph lighted another cigarette and reflected that Isabel probably meant she had received news that Mr. Caspar Goodwood had crossed to Paris. After he had lighted his cigarette he puffed it a while, and then he resumed. "I promised just now to be very amusing; but you see I don't come up to the mark, and the fact is there's a good deal of temerity in one's undertaking to amuse a person like you. What do you care for my feeble attempts? You've grand ideas—you've a high standard in such matters. I ought at least to bring in a band of music or a company of mountebanks."

"One mountebank's enough, and you do very well. Pray go on, and in another ten minutes I shall begin to laugh."

"I assure you I'm very serious," said Ralph. "You do really ask a great deal."

"I don't know what you mean. I ask nothing."

"You accept nothing," said Ralph. She coloured, and now suddenly it seemed to her that she guessed his meaning. But why should he speak to her of such things? He hesitated a little and then he continued: "There's something I should like very much to say to you. It's a question I wish to ask. It seems to me I've a right to ask it, because I've a kind of interest in the answer."

"Ask what you will," Isabel replied gently, "and I'll try to satisfy you."

"Well then, I hope you won't mind my saying that Warburton has told me of something that has passed between you."

Isabel suppressed a start; she sat looking at her open fan. "Very good; I suppose it was natural he should tell you."

"I have his leave to let you know he has done so. He has some hope still," said Ralph.

"Still?"

"He had it a few days ago."

"I don't believe he has any now," said the girl.

"I'm very sorry for him then; he's such an honest man."

"Pray, did he ask you to talk to me?"

"No, not that. But he told me because he couldn't help it. We're old friends, and he was greatly disappointed. He sent me a line asking me to come and see him, and I drove over to Lockleigh the day before he and his sister lunched with us. He was very heavy-hearted; he had just got a letter from you."

"Did he show you the letter?" asked Isabel with momentary loftiness.

"By no means. But he told me it was a neat refusal. I was very sorry for him," Ralph repeated.

For some moments Isabel said nothing; then at last, "Do you know how often he had seen me?" she enquired. "Five or six times."

"That's to your glory."

"It's not for that I say it."

"What then do you say it for. Not to prove that poor Warburton's state of mind's superficial, because I'm pretty sure you don't think that."

Isabel certainly was unable to say she thought it; but presently she said something else. "If you've not been requested by Lord Warburton to argue with me, then you're doing it disinterestedly—or for the love of argument."

"I've no wish to argue with you at all. I only wish to leave you alone. I'm simply greatly interested in your own sentiments."

"I'm greatly obliged to you!" cried Isabel with a slightly nervous laugh.

"Of course you mean that I'm meddling in what doesn't concern me. But why shouldn't I speak to you of this matter without annoying you or embarrassing myself? What's the use of being your cousin if I can't have a few privileges? What's the use of adoring you without hope of a reward if I can't have a few compensations? What's the use of being ill and disabled and restricted to mere spectatorship at the game of life if I really can't see the show when I've paid so much for my ticket? Tell me this," Ralph went on while she listened to him with quickened attention. "What had you in mind when you refused Lord Warburton?"

"What had I in mind?"

"What was the logic—the view of your situation—that dictated so remarkable an act?"

"I didn't wish to marry him—if that's logic."

"No, that's not logic—and I knew that before. It's really nothing, you know. What was it you said to yourself? You certainly said more than that."

Isabel reflected a moment, then answered with a question of her own. "Why do you call it a remarkable act? That's what your mother thinks too."

"Warburton's such a thorough good sort; as a man, I consider he has hardly a fault. And then he's what they call here no end of a swell. He has immense possessions, and his wife would be thought a superior being. He unites the intrinsic and the extrinsic advantages."

Isabel watched her cousin as to see how far he would go. "I refused him because he was too perfect then. I'm not perfect myself, and he's too good for me. Besides, his perfection would irritate me."

"That's ingenious rather than candid," said Ralph. "As a fact you think nothing in the world too perfect for you."

"Do you think I'm so good?"

"No, but you're exacting, all the same, without the excuse of thinking yourself good. Nineteen women out of twenty, however, even of the most exacting sort, would have managed to do with Warburton. Perhaps you don't know how he has been stalked."

"I don't wish to know. But it seems to me," said Isabel, "that one day when we talked of him you mentioned odd things in him." Ralph smokingly considered. "I hope that what I said then had no weight with you; for they were not faults, the things I spoke of: they were simply peculiarities of his position. If I had known he wished to marry you I'd never have alluded to them. I think I said that as regards that position he was rather a sceptic. It would have been in your power to make him a believer."

"I think not. I don't understand the matter, and I'm not conscious of any mission of that sort. You're evidently disappointed," Isabel added, looking at her cousin with rueful gentleness. "You'd have liked me to make such a marriage."

"Not in the least. I'm absolutely without a wish on the subject. I don't pretend to advise you, and I content myself with watching you—with the deepest interest."

She gave rather a conscious sigh. "I wish I could be as interesting to myself as I am to you!"

"There you're not candid again; you're extremely interesting to yourself. Do you know, however," said Ralph, "that if you've really given Warburton his final answer I'm rather glad it has been what it was. I don't mean I'm glad for you, and still less of course for him. I'm glad for myself."

"Are you thinking of proposing to me?"

"By no means. From the point of view I speak of that would be fatal; I should kill the goose that supplies me with the material of my inimitable omelettes. I use that animal as the symbol of my insane illusions. What I mean is that I shall have the thrill of seeing what a young lady does who won't marry Lord Warburton."

"That's what your mother counts upon too," said Isabel.

"Ah, there will be plenty of spectators! We shall hang on the rest of your career. I shall not see all of it, but I shall probably see the most interesting years. Of course if you were to marry our friend you'd still have a career—a very decent, in fact a very brilliant one. But relatively speaking it would be a little prosaic. It would be definitely marked out in advance; it would be wanting in the unexpected. You know I'm extremely fond of the unexpected, and now that you've kept the game in your hands I depend on your giving us some grand example of it."

"I don't understand you very well," said Isabel, "but I do so well enough to be able to say that if you look for grand examples of anything from me I shall disappoint you."

"You'll do so only by disappointing yourself and that will go hard with you!"

To this she made no direct reply; there was an amount of truth in it that would bear consideration. At last she said abruptly: "I don't see what harm there is in my wishing not to tie myself. I don't want to begin life by marrying. There are other things a woman can do."

"There's nothing she can do so well. But you're of course so many-sided."

"If one's two-sided it's enough," said Isabel.

"You're the most charming of polygons!" her companion broke out. At a glance from his companion, however, he became grave, and to prove it went on: "You want to see life—you'll be hanged if you don't, as the young men say."

"I don't think I want to see it as the young men want to see it. But I do want to look about me."

"You want to drain the cup of experience."

"No, I don't wish to touch the cup of experience. It's a poisoned drink! I only want to see for myself."

"You want to see, but not to feel," Ralph remarked.

"I don't think that if one's a sentient being one can make the distinction. I'm a good deal like Henrietta. The other day when I asked her if she wished to marry she said: 'Not till I've seen Europe!' I too don't wish to marry till I've seen Europe."

"You evidently expect a crowned head will be struck with you."

"No, that would be worse than marrying Lord Warburton. But it's getting very dark," Isabel continued, "and I must go home." She rose from her place, but Ralph only sat still and looked at her. As he remained there she stopped, and they exchanged a gaze that was full on either side, but especially on Ralph's, of utterances too vague for words.

"You've answered my question," he said at last. "You've told me what I wanted. I'm greatly obliged to you."

"It seems to me I've told you very little."

"You've told me the great thing: that the world interests you and that you want to throw yourself into it."

Her silvery eyes shone a moment in the dusk. "I never said that." "I think you meant it. Don't repudiate it. It's so fine!"

"I don't know what you're trying to fasten upon me, for I'm not in the least an adventurous spirit. Women are not like men."

Ralph slowly rose from his seat and they walked together to the gate of the square. "No," he said; "women rarely boast of their courage. Men do so with a certain frequency."

"Men have it to boast of!"

"Women have it too. You've a great deal."

"Enough to go home in a cab to Pratt's Hotel, but not more."

Ralph unlocked the gate, and after they had passed out he fastened it. "We'll find your cab," he said; and as they turned toward a neighbouring street in which this quest might avail he asked her again if he mightn't see her safely to the inn.

"By no means," she answered; "you're very tired; you must go home and go to bed."

The cab was found, and he helped her into it, standing a moment at the door. "When people forget I'm a poor creature I'm often incommoded," he said. "But it's worse when they remember it!"

CHAPTER XVI

She had had no hidden motive in wishing him not to take her home; it simply struck her that for some days past she had consumed an inordinate quantity of his time, and the independent spirit of the American girl whom extravagance of aid places in an attitude that she ends by finding "affected" had made her decide that for these few hours she must suffice to herself. She had moreover a great fondness for intervals of solitude, which since her arrival in England had been but meagrely met. It was a luxury she could always command at home and she had wittingly missed it. That evening, however, an incident occurred which—had there been a critic to note it—would have taken all colour from the theory that the wish to be quite by herself had caused her to dispense with her cousin's attendance. Seated toward nine o'clock in the dim illumination of Pratt's Hotel and trying with the aid of two tall candles to lose herself in a volume she had brought from Gardencourt, she succeeded only to the extent of reading other words than those printed on the page—words that Ralph had spoken to her that afternoon. Suddenly the well-muffed knuckle of the waiter was applied to the door, which presently gave way to his exhibition, even as a glorious trophy, of the card of a visitor. When this memento had offered to her fixed sight the name of Mr. Caspar Goodwood she let the man stand before her without signifying her wishes.

"Shall I show the gentleman up, ma'am?" he asked with a slightly encouraging inflexion.

Isabel hesitated still and while she hesitated glanced at the mirror. "He may come in," she said at last; and waited for him not so much smoothing her hair as girding her spirit.

Caspar Goodwood was accordingly the next moment shaking hands with her, but saying nothing till the servant had left the room. "Why didn't you answer my letter?" he then asked in a quick, full, slightly peremptory tone—the tone of a man whose questions were habitually pointed and who was capable of much insistence.

She answered by a ready question, "How did you know I was here?"

"Miss Stackpole let me know," said Caspar Goodwood. "She told me you would probably be at home alone this evening and would be willing to see me."

"Where did she see you—to tell you that?"

"She didn't see me; she wrote to me."

Isabel was silent; neither had sat down; they stood there with an air of defiance, or at least of contention. "Henrietta never told me she was writing to you," she said at last. "This is not kind of her."

"Is it so disagreeable to you to see me?" asked the young man.

"I didn't expect it. I don't like such surprises."

"But you knew I was in town; it was natural we should meet."

"Do you call this meeting? I hoped I shouldn't see you. In so big a place as London it seemed very possible."

"It was apparently repugnant to you even to write to me," her visitor went on.

Isabel made no reply; the sense of Henrietta Stackpole's treachery, as she momentarily qualified it, was strong within her. "Henrietta's certainly not a model of all the delicacies!" she exclaimed with bitterness. "It was a great liberty to take."

"I suppose I'm not a model either—of those virtues or of any others. The fault's mine as much as hers."

As Isabel looked at him it seemed to her that his jaw had never been more square. This might have displeased her, but she took a different turn. "No, it's not your fault so much as hers. What you've done was inevitable, I suppose, for you."

"It was indeed!" cried Caspar Goodwood with a voluntary laugh.

"And now that I've come, at any rate, mayn't I stay?"

"You may sit down, certainly."

She went back to her chair again, while her visitor took the first place that offered, in the manner of a man accustomed to pay little thought to that sort of furtherance. "I've been hoping every day for an answer to my letter. You might have written me a few lines."

"It wasn't the trouble of writing that prevented me; I could as easily have written you four pages as one. But my silence was an intention," Isabel said. "I thought it the best thing."

He sat with his eyes fixed on hers while she spoke; then he lowered them and attached them to a spot in the carpet as if he were making a strong effort to say nothing but what he ought. He was a strong man in the wrong, and he was acute enough to see that an uncompromising exhibition of his strength would only throw the falsity of his position into relief. Isabel was not incapable of tasting any advantage of position over a person of this quality, and though little desirous to flaunt it in his face she could enjoy being able to say "You know you oughtn't to have written to me yourself!" and to say it with an air of triumph.

Caspar Goodwood raised his eyes to her own again; they seemed to shine through the vizard of a helmet. He had a strong sense of justice and was ready any day in the year—over and above this—to argue the question of his rights. "You said you hoped never to hear from me again; I know that. But I never accepted any such rule as my own. I warned you that you should hear very soon."

"I didn't say I hoped NEVER to hear from you," said Isabel.

"Not for five years then; for ten years; twenty years. It's the same thing."

"Do you find it so? It seems to me there's a great difference. I can imagine that at the end of ten years we might have a very pleasant correspondence. I shall have matured my epistolary style."

She looked away while she spoke these words, knowing them of so much less earnest a cast than the countenance of her listener. Her eyes, however, at last came back to him, just as he said very irrelevantly; "Are you enjoying your visit to your uncle?"

"Very much indeed." She dropped, but then she broke out. "What good do you expect to get by insisting?"

"The good of not losing you."

"You've no right to talk of losing what's not yours. And even from your own point of view," Isabel added, "you ought to know when to let one alone."

"I disgust you very much," said Caspar Goodwood gloomily; not as if to provoke her to compassion for a man conscious of this blighting fact, but as if to set it well before himself, so that he might endeavour to act with his eyes on it.

"Yes, you don't at all delight me, you don't fit in, not in any way, just now, and the worst is that your putting it to the proof in this manner is quite unnecessary." It wasn't certainly as if his nature had been soft, so that pinpricks would draw blood from it; and from the first of her acquaintance with him, and of her having to defend herself against a certain air that he had of knowing better what was good for her than she knew herself, she had recognised the fact that perfect frankness was her best weapon. To attempt to spare his sensibility or to escape from him edgewise, as one might do from a man who had barred the way less sturdily—this, in dealing with Caspar Goodwood, who would grasp at everything of every sort that one might give him, was wasted agility. It was not that he had not susceptibilities, but his passive surface, as well as his active, was large and hard, and he might always be trusted to dress his wounds, so far as they required it, himself. She came back, even for her measure of possible pangs and aches in him, to her old sense that he was naturally plated and steeled, armed essentially for aggression.

"I can't reconcile myself to that," he simply said. There was a dangerous liberality about it; for she felt how open it was to him to make the point that he had not always disgusted her.

"I can't reconcile myself to it either, and it's not the state of things that ought to exist between us. If you'd only try to banish me from your mind for a few months we should be on good terms again."

"I see. If I should cease to think of you at all for a prescribed time, I should find I could keep it up indefinitely."

"Indefinitely is more than I ask. It's more even than I should like."

"You know that what you ask is impossible," said the young man, taking his adjective for granted in a manner she found irritating.

"Aren't you capable of making a calculated effort?" she demanded. "You're strong for everything else; why shouldn't you be strong for that?"

"An effort calculated for what?" And then as she hung fire, "I'm capable of nothing with regard to you," he went on, "but just of being infernally in love with you. If one's strong one loves only the more strongly."

"There's a good deal in that;" and indeed our young lady felt the force of it—felt it thrown off, into the vast of truth and poetry, as practically a bait to her imagination. But she promptly came round. "Think of me or not, as you find most possible; only leave me alone."

"Until when?"

"Well, for a year or two."

"Which do you mean? Between one year and two there's all the difference in the world."

"Call it two then," said Isabel with a studied effect of eagerness.

"And what shall I gain by that?" her friend asked with no sign of wincing.

"You'll have obliged me greatly."

"And what will be my reward?"

"Do you need a reward for an act of generosity?"

"Yes, when it involves a great sacrifice."

"There's no generosity without some sacrifice. Men don't understand such things. If you make the sacrifice you'll have all my admiration."

"I don't care a cent for your admiration—not one straw, with nothing to show for it. When will you marry me? That's the only question."

"Never—if you go on making me feel only as I feel at present."

"What do I gain then by not trying to make you feel otherwise?"

"You'll gain quite as much as by worrying me to death!" Caspar Goodwood bent his eyes again and gazed a while into the crown of his hat. A deep flush overspread his face; she could see her sharpness had at last penetrated. This immediately had a value—classic, romantic, redeeming, what did she know? for her; "the strong man in pain" was one of the categories of the human appeal, little charm as he might exert in the given case. "Why do you make me say such things to you?" she cried in a trembling voice. "I only want to be gentle—to be thoroughly kind. It's not delightful to me to feel people care for me and yet to have to try and reason them out of it. I think others also ought to be considerate; we have each to judge for ourselves. I know you're considerate, as much as you can be; you've good reasons for what you do. But I really don't want to marry, or to talk about it at all now. I shall probably never do it—no, never. I've a perfect right to feel that way, and it's no kindness to a woman to press her so hard, to urge her against her will. If I give you pain I can only say I'm very sorry. It's not my fault; I can't marry you simply to please you. I won't say that I shall always remain your friend, because when women say that, in these situations, it passes, I believe, for a sort of mockery. But try me some day."

Caspar Goodwood, during this speech, had kept his eyes fixed upon the name of his hatter, and it was not until some time after she had ceased speaking that he raised them. When he did so the sight of a rosy, lovely eagerness in Isabel's face threw some confusion into his attempt to analyse her words. "I'll go home—I'll go to-morrow—I'll leave you alone," he brought out at last. "Only," he heavily said, "I hate to lose sight of you!"

"Never fear. I shall do no harm."

"You'll marry some one else, as sure as I sit here," Caspar Goodwood declared.

"Do you think that a generous charge?"

"Why not? Plenty of men will try to make you."

"I told you just now that I don't wish to marry and that I almost certainly never shall."

"I know you did, and I like your 'almost certainly'! I put no faith in what you say."

"Thank you very much. Do you accuse me of lying to shake you off? You say very delicate things."

"Why should I not say that? You've given me no pledge of anything at all."

"No, that's all that would be wanting!"

"You may perhaps even believe you're safe—from wishing to be. But you're not," the young man went on as if preparing himself for the worst.

"Very well then. We'll put it that I'm not safe. Have it as you please."

"I don't know, however," said Caspar Goodwood, "that my keeping you in sight would prevent it."

"Don't you indeed? I'm after all very much afraid of you. Do you think I'm so very easily pleased?" she asked suddenly, changing her tone.

"No—I don't; I shall try to console myself with that. But there are a certain number of very dazzling men in the world, no doubt; and if there were only one it would be enough. The most dazzling of all will make straight for you. You'll be sure to take no one who isn't dazzling."

"If you mean by dazzling brilliantly clever," Isabel said—"and I can't imagine what else you mean—I don't need the aid of a clever man to teach me how to live. I can find it out for myself."

"Find out how to live alone? I wish that, when you have, you'd teach me!"

She looked at him a moment; then with a quick smile, "Oh, you ought to marry!" she said.

He might be pardoned if for an instant this exclamation seemed to him to sound the infernal note, and it is not on record that her motive for discharging such a shaft had been of the clearest. He oughtn't to stride about lean and hungry, however—she certainly felt THAT for him. "God forgive you!" he murmured between his teeth as he turned away.

Her accent had put her slightly in the wrong, and after a moment she felt the need to right herself. The easiest way to do it was to place him where she had been. "You do me great injustice—you say what you don't know!" she broke out. "I shouldn't be an easy victim—I've proved it."

"Oh, to me, perfectly."

"I've proved it to others as well." And she paused a moment. "I refused a proposal of marriage last week; what they call—no doubt—a dazzling one."

"I'm very glad to hear it," said the young man gravely.

"It was a proposal many girls would have accepted; it had everything to recommend it." Isabel had not proposed to herself to tell this story, but, now she had begun, the satisfaction of speaking it out and doing herself justice took possession of her. "I was offered a great position and a great fortune—by a person whom I like extremely."

Caspar watched her with intense interest. "Is he an Englishman?"

"He's an English nobleman," said Isabel.

Her visitor received this announcement at first in silence, but at last said: "I'm glad he's disappointed."

"Well then, as you have companions in misfortune, make the best of it."

"I don't call him a companion," said Casper grimly.

"Why not—since I declined his offer absolutely?"

"That doesn't make him my companion. Besides, he's an Englishman."

"And pray isn't an Englishman a human being?" Isabel asked.

"Oh, those people They're not of my humanity, and I don't care what becomes of them."

"You're very angry," said the girl. "We've discussed this matter quite enough."

"Oh yes, I'm very angry. I plead guilty to that!"

She turned away from him, walked to the open window and stood a moment looking into the dusky void of the street, where a turbid gaslight alone represented social animation. For some time neither of these young persons spoke; Caspar lingered near the chimney-piece with eyes gloomily attached. She had virtually requested him to go—he knew that; but at the risk of making himself odious he kept his ground. She was far too dear to him to be easily renounced, and he had crossed the sea all to wring from her some scrap of a vow. Presently she left the window and stood again before him. "You do me very little justice—after my telling you what I told you just now. I'm sorry I told you—since it matters so little to you."

"Ah," cried the young man, "if you were thinking of ME when you did it!" And then he paused with the fear that she might contradict so happy a thought.

"I was thinking of you a little," said Isabel.

"A little? I don't understand. If the knowledge of what I feel for you had any weight with you at all, calling it a 'little' is a poor account of it."

Isabel shook her head as if to carry off a blunder. "I've refused a most kind, noble gentleman. Make the most of that."

"I thank you then," said Caspar Goodwood gravely. "I thank you immensely."

"And now you had better go home."

"May I not see you again?" he asked.

"I think it's better not. You'll be sure to talk of this, and you see it leads to nothing."

"I promise you not to say a word that will annoy you."

Isabel reflected and then answered: "I return in a day or two to my uncle's, and I can't propose to you to come there. It would be too inconsistent."

Caspar Goodwood, on his side, considered. "You must do me justice too. I received an invitation to your uncle's more than a week ago, and I declined it."

She betrayed surprise. "From whom was your invitation?"

"From Mr. Ralph Touchett, whom I suppose to be your cousin. I declined it because I had not your authorisation to accept it. The suggestion that Mr. Touchett should invite me appeared to have come from Miss Stackpole."

"It certainly never did from me. Henrietta really goes very far," Isabel added.

"Don't be too hard on her—that touches ME."

"No; if you declined you did quite right, and I thank you for it." And she gave a little shudder of dismay at the thought that Lord Warburton and Mr. Goodwood might have met at Gardencourt: it would have been so awkward for Lord Warburton.

"When you leave your uncle where do you go?" her companion asked.

"I go abroad with my aunt—to Florence and other places."

The serenity of this announcement struck a chill to the young man's heart; he seemed to see her whirled away into circles from which he was inexorably excluded. Nevertheless he went on quickly with his questions. "And when shall you come back to America?"

"Perhaps not for a long time. I'm very happy here."

"Do you mean to give up your country?"

"Don't be an infant!"

"Well, you'll be out of my sight indeed!" said Caspar Goodwood.

"I don't know," she answered rather grandly. "The world—with all these places so arranged and so touching each other—comes to strike one as rather small."

"It's a sight too big for ME!" Caspar exclaimed with a simplicity our young lady might have found touching if her face had not been set against concessions.

This attitude was part of a system, a theory, that she had lately embraced, and to be thorough she said after a moment: "Don't think me unkind if I say it's just THAT—being out of your sight—that I like. If you were in the same place I should feel you were watching me, and I don't like that—I like my liberty too much. If there's a thing in the world I'm fond of," she went on with a slight recurrence of grandeur, "it's my personal independence."

But whatever there might be of the too superior in this speech moved Caspar Goodwood's admiration; there was nothing he winced at in the large air of it. He had never supposed she hadn't wings and the need of beautiful free movements—he wasn't, with his own long arms and strides, afraid of any force in her. Isabel's words, if they had been meant to shock him, failed of the mark and only made him smile with the sense that here was common ground. "Who would wish less to curtail your liberty than I? What can give me greater pleasure than to see you perfectly independent—doing whatever you like? It's to make you independent that I want to marry you."

"That's a beautiful sophism," said the girl with a smile more beautiful still.

"An unmarried woman—a girl of your age—isn't independent. There are all sorts of things she can't do. She's hampered at every step."

"That's as she looks at the question," Isabel answered with much spirit. "I'm not in my first youth—I can do what I choose—I belong quite to the independent class. I've neither father nor mother; I'm poor and of a serious disposition; I'm not pretty. I therefore am not bound to be timid and conventional; indeed I can't afford such luxuries. Besides, I try to judge things for myself; to judge wrong, I think, is more honourable than not to judge at all. I don't wish to be a mere sheep in the flock; I wish to choose my fate and know something of human affairs beyond what other people think it compatible with propriety to tell me." She paused a moment, but not long enough for her companion to reply. He was apparently on the point of doing so when she went on: "Let me say this to you, Mr. Goodwood. You're so kind as to speak of being afraid of my marrying. If you should hear a rumour that I'm on the point of doing so—girls are liable to have such things said about them—remember what I have told you about my love of liberty and venture to doubt it."

There was something passionately positive in the tone in which she gave him this advice, and he saw a shining candour in her eyes that helped him to believe her. On the whole he felt reassured, and you might have perceived it by the manner in which he said, quite eagerly: "You want simply to travel for two years? I'm quite willing to wait two years, and you may do what you like in the interval. If that's all you want, pray say so. I don't want you to be conventional; do I strike you as conventional myself? Do you want to improve your mind? Your mind's quite good enough for me; but if it interests you to wander about a while and see different countries I shall be delighted to help you in any way in my power."

"You're very generous; that's nothing new to me. The best way to help me will be to put as many hundred miles of sea between us as possible."

"One would think you were going to commit some atrocity!" said Caspar Goodwood.

"Perhaps I am. I wish to be free even to do that if the fancy takes me."

"Well then," he said slowly, "I'll go home." And he put out his hand, trying to look contented and confident.

Isabel's confidence in him, however, was greater than any he could feel in her. Not that he thought her capable of committing an atrocity; but, turn it over as he would, there was something ominous in the way she reserved her option. As she took his hand she felt a great respect for him; she knew how much he cared for her and she thought him magnanimous. They stood so for a moment, looking at each other, united by a hand-clasp which was not merely passive on her side. "That's right," she said very kindly, almost tenderly. "You'll lose nothing by being a reasonable man."

"But I'll come back, wherever you are, two years hence," he returned with characteristic grimness.

We have seen that our young lady was inconsequent, and at this she suddenly changed her note. "Ah, remember, I promise nothing—absolutely nothing!" Then more softly, as if to help him to leave her: "And remember too that I shall not be an easy victim!"

"You'll get very sick of your independence."

"Perhaps I shall; it's even very probable. When that day comes I shall be very glad to see you."

She had laid her hand on the knob of the door that led into her room, and she waited a moment to see whether her visitor would not take his departure. But he appeared unable to move; there was still an immense unwillingness in his attitude and a sore remonstrance in his eyes. "I must leave you now," said Isabel; and she opened the door and passed into the other room.

This apartment was dark, but the darkness was tempered by a vague radiance sent up through the window from the court of the hotel, and Isabel could make out the masses of the furniture, the dim shining of the mirror and the looming of the big four-posted bed. She stood still a moment, listening, and at last she heard Caspar Goodwood walk out of the sitting-room and close the door behind him. She stood still a little longer, and then, by an irresistible impulse, dropped on her knees before her bed and hid her face in her arms.

CHAPTER XVII

She was not praying; she was trembling—trembling all over. Vibration was easy to her, was in fact too constant with her, and she found herself now humming like a smitten harp. She only asked, however, to put on the cover, to case herself again in brown holland, but she wished to resist her excitement, and the attitude of devotion, which she kept for some time, seemed to help her to be still. She intensely rejoiced that Caspar Goodwood was gone; there was something in having thus got rid of him that was like the payment, for a stamped receipt, of some debt too long on her mind. As she felt the glad relief she bowed her head a little lower; the sense was there, throbbing in her heart; it was part of her emotion, but it was a thing to be ashamed of—it was profane and out of place. It was not for some ten minutes that she rose from her knees, and even when she came back to the sitting-room her tremor had not quite subsided. It had had, verily, two causes: part of it was to be accounted for by her long discussion with Mr. Goodwood, but it might be feared that the rest was simply the enjoyment she found in the exercise of her power. She sat down in the same chair again and took up her book, but without going through the form of opening the volume. She leaned back, with that low, soft, aspiring murmur with which she often uttered her response to accidents of which the brighter side was not superficially obvious, and yielded to the satisfaction of having refused two ardent suitors in a fortnight. That love of liberty of which she had given Caspar Goodwood so bold a sketch was as yet almost exclusively theoretic; she had not been able to indulge it on a large scale. But it appeared to her she had done something; she had tasted of the delight, if not of battle, at least of victory; she had done what was truest to her plan. In the glow of this consciousness the image of Mr. Goodwood taking his sad walk homeward through the dingy town presented itself with a certain reproachful force; so that, as at the same moment the door of the room was opened, she rose with an apprehension that he had come back. But it was only Henrietta Stackpole returning from her dinner.

Miss Stackpole immediately saw that our young lady had been "through" something, and indeed the discovery demanded no great penetration. She went straight up to her friend, who received her without a greeting. Isabel's elation in having sent Caspar Goodwood back to America presupposed her being in a manner glad he had come to see her; but at the same time she perfectly remembered Henrietta had had no right to set a trap for her. "Has he been here, dear?" the latter yearningly asked.

Isabel turned away and for some moments answered nothing. "You acted very wrongly," she declared at last.

"I acted for the best. I only hope you acted as well."

"You're not the judge. I can't trust you," said Isabel.

This declaration was unflattering, but Henrietta was much too unselfish to heed the charge it conveyed; she cared only for what it intimated with regard to her friend. "Isabel Archer," she observed with equal abruptness and solemnity, "if you marry one of these people I'll never speak to you again!"

"Before making so terrible a threat you had better wait till I'm asked," Isabel replied. Never having said a word to Miss Stackpole about Lord Warburton's overtures, she had now no impulse whatever to justify herself to Henrietta by telling her that she had refused that nobleman.

"Oh, you'll be asked quick enough, once you get off on the Continent. Annie Climber was asked three times in Italy—poor plain little Annie."

"Well, if Annie Climber wasn't captured why should I be?"

"I don't believe Annie was pressed; but you'll be."

"That's a flattering conviction," said Isabel without alarm.

"I don't flatter you, Isabel, I tell you the truth!" cried her friend. "I hope you don't mean to tell me that you didn't give Mr. Goodwood some hope."

"I don't see why I should tell you anything; as I said to you just now, I can't trust you. But since you're so much interested in Mr. Goodwood I won't conceal from you that he returns immediately to America."

"You don't mean to say you've sent him off?" Henrietta almost shrieked.

"I asked him to leave me alone; and I ask you the same, Henrietta." Miss Stackpole glittered for an instant with dismay, and then passed to the mirror over the chimney-piece and took off her bonnet. "I hope you've enjoyed your dinner," Isabel went on.

But her companion was not to be diverted by frivolous propositions. "Do you know where you're going, Isabel Archer?"

"Just now I'm going to bed," said Isabel with persistent frivolity.

"Do you know where you're drifting?" Henrietta pursued, holding out her bonnet delicately.

"No, I haven't the least idea, and I find it very pleasant not to know. A swift carriage, of a dark night, rattling with four horses over roads that one can't see—that's my idea of happiness."

"Mr. Goodwood certainly didn't teach you to say such things as that—like the heroine of an immoral novel," said Miss Stackpole. "You're drifting to some great mistake."

Isabel was irritated by her friend's interference, yet she still tried to think what truth this declaration could represent. She could think of nothing that diverted her from saying: "You must be very fond of me, Henrietta, to be willing to be so aggressive."

"I love you intensely, Isabel," said Miss Stackpole with feeling.

"Well, if you love me intensely let me as intensely alone. I asked that of Mr. Goodwood, and I must also ask it of you."

"Take care you're not let alone too much."

"That's what Mr. Goodwood said to me. I told him I must take the risks."

"You're a creature of risks—you make me shudder!" cried Henrietta. "When does Mr. Goodwood return to America?"

"I don't know—he didn't tell me."

"Perhaps you didn't enquire," said Henrietta with the note of righteous irony.

"I gave him too little satisfaction to have the right to ask questions of him."

This assertion seemed to Miss Stackpole for a moment to bid defiance to comment; but at last she exclaimed: "Well, Isabel, if I didn't know you I might think you were heartless!"

"Take care," said Isabel; "you're spoiling me."

"I'm afraid I've done that already. I hope, at least," Miss Stackpole added, "that he may cross with Annie Climber!"

Isabel learned from her the next morning that she had determined not to return to Gardencourt (where old Mr. Touchett had promised her a renewed welcome), but to await in London the arrival of the invitation that Mr. Bantling had promised her from his sister Lady Pensil. Miss Stackpole related very freely her conversation with Ralph Touchett's sociable friend and declared to Isabel that she really believed she had now got hold of something that would lead to something. On the receipt of Lady Pensil's letter—Mr. Bantling had virtually guaranteed the arrival of this document—she would immediately depart for Bedfordshire, and if Isabel cared to look out for her impressions in the Interviewer she would certainly find them. Henrietta was evidently going to see something of the inner life this time.

"Do you know where you're drifting, Henrietta Stackpole?" Isabel asked, imitating the tone in which her friend had spoken the night before.

"I'm drifting to a big position—that of the Queen of American Journalism. If my next letter isn't copied all over the West I'll swallow my penwiper!"

She had arranged with her friend Miss Annie Climber, the young lady of the continental offers, that they should go together to make those purchases which were to constitute Miss Climber's farewell to a hemisphere in which she at least had been appreciated; and she presently repaired to Jermyn Street to pick up her companion. Shortly after her departure Ralph Touchett was announced, and as soon as he came in Isabel saw he had something on his mind. He very soon took his cousin into his confidence. He had received from his mother a telegram to the effect that his father had had a sharp attack of his old malady, that she was much alarmed and that she begged he would instantly return to Gardencourt. On this occasion at least Mrs. Touchett's devotion to the electric wire was not open to criticism.

"I've judged it best to see the great doctor, Sir Matthew Hope, first," Ralph said; "by great good luck he's in town. He's to see me at half-past twelve, and I shall make sure of his coming down to Gardencourt—which he will do the more readily as he has already seen my father several times, both there and in London. There's an express at two-forty-five, which I shall take; and you'll come back with me or remain here a few days longer, exactly as you prefer."

"I shall certainly go with you," Isabel returned. "I don't suppose I can be of any use to my uncle, but if he's ill I shall like to be near him."

"I think you're fond of him," said Ralph with a certain shy pleasure in his face. "You appreciate him, which all the world hasn't done. The quality's too fine."

"I quite adore him," Isabel after a moment said.

"That's very well. After his son he's your greatest admirer." She welcomed this assurance, but she gave secretly a small sigh of relief at the thought that Mr. Touchett was one of those admirers who couldn't propose to marry her. This, however, was not what she spoke; she went on to inform Ralph that there were other reasons for her not remaining in London. She was tired of it and wished to leave it; and then Henrietta was going away—going to stay in Bedfordshire.

"In Bedfordshire?"

"With Lady Pensil, the sister of Mr. Bantling, who has answered for an invitation."

Ralph was feeling anxious, but at this he broke into a laugh. Suddenly, none the less, his gravity returned. "Bantling's a man of courage. But if the invitation should get lost on the way?"

"I thought the British post-office was impeccable."

"The good Homer sometimes nods," said Ralph. "However," he went on more brightly, "the good Bantling never does, and, whatever happens, he'll take care of Henrietta."

Ralph went to keep his appointment with Sir Matthew Hope, and Isabel made her arrangements for quitting Pratt's Hotel. Her uncle's danger touched her nearly, and while she stood before her open trunk, looking about her vaguely for what she should put into it, the tears suddenly rose to her eyes. It was perhaps for this reason that when Ralph came back at two o'clock to take her to the station she was not yet ready. He found Miss Stackpole, however, in the sitting-room, where she had just risen from her luncheon, and this lady immediately expressed her regret at his father's illness.

"He's a grand old man," she said; "he's faithful to the last. If it's really to be the last—pardon my alluding to it, but you must often have thought of the possibility—I'm sorry that I shall not be at Gardencourt."

"You'll amuse yourself much more in Bedfordshire."

"I shall be sorry to amuse myself at such a time," said Henrietta with much propriety. But she immediately added: "I should like so to commemorate the closing scene."

"My father may live a long time," said Ralph simply. Then, adverting to topics more cheerful, he interrogated Miss Stackpole as to her own future.

Now that Ralph was in trouble she addressed him in a tone of larger allowance and told him that she was much indebted to him for having made her acquainted with Mr. Bantling. "He has told me just the things I want to know," she said; "all the society items and all about the royal family. I can't make out that what he tells me about the royal family is much to their credit; but he says that's only my peculiar way of looking at it. Well, all I want is that he should give me the facts; I can put them together quick enough, once I've got them." And she added that Mr. Bantling had been so good as to promise to come and take her out that afternoon.

"To take you where?" Ralph ventured to enquire.

"To Buckingham Palace. He's going to show me over it, so that I may get some idea how they live."

"Ah," said Ralph, "we leave you in good hands. The first thing we shall hear is that you're invited to Windsor Castle."

"If they ask me, I shall certainly go. Once I get started I'm not afraid. But for all that," Henrietta added in a moment, "I'm not satisfied; I'm not at peace about Isabel."

"What is her last misdemeanour?"

"Well, I've told you before, and I suppose there's no harm in my going on. I always finish a subject that I take up. Mr. Goodwood was here last night."

Ralph opened his eyes; he even blushed a little—his blush being the sign of an emotion somewhat acute. He remembered that Isabel, in separating from him in Winchester Square, had repudiated his suggestion that her motive in doing so was the expectation of a visitor at Pratt's Hotel, and it was a new pang to him to have to suspect her of duplicity. On the other hand, he quickly said to himself, what concern was it of his that she should have made an appointment with a lover? Had it not been thought graceful in every age that young ladies should make a mystery of such appointments? Ralph gave Miss Stackpole a diplomatic answer. "I should have thought that, with the views you expressed to me the other day, this would satisfy you perfectly."

"That he should come to see her? That was very well, as far as it went. It was a little plot of mine; I let him know that we were in London, and when it had been arranged that I should spend the evening out I sent him a word—the word we just utter to the 'wise.' I hoped he would find her alone; I won't pretend I didn't hope that you'd be out of the way. He came to see her, but he might as well have stayed away."

"Isabel was cruel?"—and Ralph's face lighted with the relief of his cousin's not having shown duplicity.

"I don't exactly know what passed between them. But she gave him no satisfaction—she sent him back to America."

"Poor Mr. Goodwood!" Ralph sighed.

"Her only idea seems to be to get rid of him," Henrietta went on.

"Poor Mr. Goodwood!" Ralph repeated. The exclamation, it must be confessed, was automatic; it failed exactly to express his thoughts, which were taking another line.

"You don't say that as if you felt it. I don't believe you care."

"Ah," said Ralph, "you must remember that I don't know this interesting young man—that I've never seen him."

"Well, I shall see him, and I shall tell him not to give up. If I didn't believe Isabel would come round," Miss Stackpole added—"well, I'd give up myself. I mean I'd give HER up!"

CHAPTER XVIII

It had occurred to Ralph that, in the conditions, Isabel's parting with her friend might be of a slightly embarrassed nature, and he went down to the door of the hotel in advance of his cousin, who, after a slight delay, followed with the traces of an unaccepted remonstrance, as he thought, in her eyes. The two made the journey to Gardencourt in almost unbroken silence, and the servant who met them at the station had no better news to give them of Mr. Touchett—a fact which caused Ralph to congratulate himself afresh on Sir Matthew Hope's having promised to come down in the five o'clock train and spend the night. Mrs. Touchett, he learned, on reaching home, had been constantly with the old man and was with him at that moment; and this fact made Ralph say to himself that, after all, what his mother wanted was just easy occasion. The finer natures were those that shone at the larger times. Isabel went to her own room, noting throughout the house that perceptible hush which precedes a crisis. At the end of an hour, however, she came downstairs in search of her aunt, whom she wished to ask about Mr. Touchett. She went into the library, but Mrs. Touchett was not there, and as the weather, which had been damp and chill, was now altogether spoiled, it was not probable she had gone for her usual walk in the grounds. Isabel was on the point of ringing to send a question to her room, when this purpose quickly yielded to an unexpected sound—the sound of low music proceeding apparently from the saloon. She knew her aunt never touched the piano, and the musician was therefore probably Ralph, who played for his own amusement. That he should have resorted to this recreation at the present time indicated apparently that his anxiety about his father had been relieved; so that the girl took her way, almost with restored cheer, toward the source of the harmony. The drawing-room at Gardencourt was an apartment of great distances, and, as the piano was placed at the end of it furthest removed from the door at which she entered, her arrival was not noticed by the person seated before the instrument. This person was neither Ralph nor his mother; it was a lady whom Isabel immediately saw to be a stranger to herself, though her back was presented to the door. This back—an ample and well-dressed one—Isabel viewed for some moments with surprise. The lady was of course a visitor who had arrived during her absence and who had not been mentioned by either of the servants—one of them her aunt's maid—of whom she had had speech since her return. Isabel had already learned, however, with what treasures of reserve the function of receiving orders may be accompanied, and she was particularly conscious of having been treated with dryness by her aunt's maid, through whose hands she had slipped perhaps a little too mistrustfully and with an effect of plumage but the more lustrous. The advent of a guest was in itself far from disconcerting; she had not yet divested herself of a young faith that each new acquaintance would exert some momentous influence on her life. By the time she had made these reflexions she became aware that the lady at the piano played remarkably well. She was playing something of Schubert's—Isabel knew not what, but recognised Schubert—and she touched the piano with a discretion of her own. It showed skill, it showed feeling; Isabel sat down noiselessly on the nearest chair and waited till the end of the piece. When it was finished she felt a strong desire to thank the player, and rose from her seat to do so, while at the same time the stranger turned quickly round, as if but just aware of her presence.

"That's very beautiful, and your playing makes it more beautiful still," said Isabel with all the young radiance with which she usually uttered a truthful rapture.

"You don't think I disturbed Mr. Touchett then?" the musician answered as sweetly as this compliment deserved. "The house is so large and his room so far away that I thought I might venture, especially as I played just—just du bout des doigts."

"She's a Frenchwoman," Isabel said to herself; "she says that as if she were French." And this supposition made the visitor more interesting to our speculative heroine. "I hope my uncle's doing well," Isabel added. "I should think that to hear such lovely music as that would really make him feel better."

The lady smiled and discriminated. "I'm afraid there are moments in life when even Schubert has nothing to say to us. We must admit, however, that they are our worst."

"I'm not in that state now then," said Isabel. "On the contrary I should be so glad if you would play something more."

"If it will give you pleasure—delighted." And this obliging person took her place again and struck a few chords, while Isabel sat down nearer the instrument. Suddenly the new-comer stopped with her hands on the keys, half-turning and looking over her shoulder. She was forty years old and not pretty, though her expression charmed. "Pardon me," she said; "but are you the niece—the young American?"

"I'm my aunt's niece," Isabel replied with simplicity.

The lady at the piano sat still a moment longer, casting her air of interest over her shoulder. "That's very well; we're compatriots." And then she began to play.

"Ah then she's not French," Isabel murmured; and as the opposite supposition had made her romantic it might have seemed that this revelation would have marked a drop. But such was not the fact; rarer even than to be French seemed it to be American on such interesting terms.

The lady played in the same manner as before, softly and solemnly, and while she played the shadows deepened in the room. The autumn twilight gathered in, and from her place Isabel could see the rain, which had now begun in earnest, washing the cold-looking lawn and the wind shaking the great trees. At last, when the music had ceased, her companion got up and, coming nearer with a smile, before Isabel had time to thank her again, said: "I'm very glad you've come back; I've heard a great deal about you."

Isabel thought her a very attractive person, but nevertheless spoke with a certain abruptness in reply to this speech. "From whom have you heard about me?"

The stranger hesitated a single moment and then, "From your uncle," she answered. "I've been here three days, and the first day he let me come and pay him a visit in his room. Then he talked constantly of you."

"As you didn't know me that must rather have bored you."

"It made me want to know you. All the more that since then—your aunt being so much with Mr. Touchett—I've been quite alone and have got rather tired of my own society. I've not chosen a good moment for my visit."

A servant had come in with lamps and was presently followed by another bearing the tea-tray. On the appearance of this repast Mrs. Touchett had apparently been notified, for she now arrived and addressed herself to the tea-pot. Her greeting to her niece did not differ materially from her manner of raising the lid of this receptacle in order to glance at the contents: in neither act was it becoming to make a show of avidity. Questioned about her husband she was unable to say he was better; but the local doctor was with him, and much light was expected from this gentleman's consultation with Sir Matthew Hope.

"I suppose you two ladies have made acquaintance," she pursued. "If you haven't I recommend you to do so; for so long as we continue—Ralph and I—to cluster about Mr. Touchett's bed you're not likely to have much society but each other."

"I know nothing about you but that you're a great musician," Isabel said to the visitor.

"There's a good deal more than that to know," Mrs. Touchett affirmed in her little dry tone.

"A very little of it, I am sure, will content Miss Archer!" the lady exclaimed with a light laugh. "I'm an old friend of your aunt's. I've lived much in Florence. I'm Madame Merle." She made this last announcement as if she were referring to a person of tolerably distinct identity. For Isabel, however, it represented little; she could only continue to feel that Madame Merle had as charming a manner as any she had ever encountered.

"She's not a foreigner in spite of her name," said Mrs. Touchett.

"She was born—I always forget where you were born."

"It's hardly worth while then I should tell you."

"On the contrary," said Mrs. Touchett, who rarely missed a logical point; "if I remembered your telling me would be quite superfluous."

Madame Merle glanced at Isabel with a sort of world-wide smile, a thing that over-reached frontiers. "I was born under the shadow of the national banner."

"She's too fond of mystery," said Mrs. Touchett; "that's her great fault."

"Ah," exclaimed Madame Merle, "I've great faults, but I don't think that's one of then; it certainly isn't the greatest. I came into the world in the Brooklyn navy-yard. My father was a high officer in the United States Navy, and had a post—a post of responsibility—in that establishment at the time. I suppose I ought to love the sea, but I hate it. That's why I don't return to America. I love the land; the great thing is to love something."

Isabel, as a dispassionate witness, had not been struck with the force of Mrs. Touchett's characterisation of her visitor, who had an expressive, communicative, responsive face, by no means of the sort which, to Isabel's mind, suggested a secretive disposition. It was a face that told of an amplitude of nature and of quick and free motions and, though it had no regular beauty, was in the highest degree engaging and attaching. Madame Merle was a tall, fair, smooth woman; everything in her person was round and replete, though without those accumulations which suggest heaviness. Her features were thick but in perfect proportion and harmony, and her complexion had a healthy clearness. Her grey eyes were small but full of light and incapable of stupidity—incapable, according to some people, even of tears; she had a liberal, full-rimmed mouth which when she smiled drew itself upward to the left side in a manner that most people thought very odd, some very affected and a few very graceful. Isabel inclined to range herself in the last category. Madame Merle had thick, fair hair, arranged somehow "classically" and as if she were a Bust, Isabel judged—a Juno or a Niobe; and large white hands, of a perfect shape, a shape so perfect that their possessor, preferring to leave them unadorned, wore no jewelled rings. Isabel had taken her at first, as we have seen, for a Frenchwoman; but extended observation might have ranked her as a German—a German of high degree, perhaps an Austrian, a baroness, a countess, a princess. It would never have been supposed she had come into the world in Brooklyn—though one could doubtless not have carried through any argument that the air of distinction marking her in so eminent a degree was inconsistent with such a birth. It was true that the national banner had floated immediately over her cradle, and the breezy freedom of the stars and stripes might have shed an influence upon the attitude she there took towards life. And yet she had evidently nothing of the fluttered, flapping quality of a morsel of bunting in the wind; her manner expressed the repose and confidence which come from a large experience. Experience, however, had not quenched her youth; it had simply made her sympathetic and supple. She was in a word a woman of strong impulses kept in admirable order. This commended itself to Isabel as an ideal combination.

The girl made these reflexions while the three ladies sat at their tea, but that ceremony was interrupted before long by the arrival of the great doctor from London, who had been immediately ushered into the drawing-room. Mrs. Touchett took him off to the library for a private talk; and then Madame Merle and Isabel parted, to meet again at dinner. The idea of seeing more of this interesting woman did much to mitigate Isabel's sense of the sadness now settling on Gardencourt.

When she came into the drawing-room before dinner she found the place empty; but in the course of a moment Ralph arrived. His anxiety about his father had been lightened; Sir Matthew Hope's view of his condition was less depressed than his own had been. The doctor recommended that the nurse alone should remain with the old man for the next three or four hours; so that Ralph, his mother and the great physician himself were free to dine at table. Mrs. Touchett and Sir Matthew appeared; Madame Merle was the last.

Before she came Isabel spoke of her to Ralph, who was standing before the fireplace. "Pray who is this Madame Merle?"

"The cleverest woman I know, not excepting yourself," said Ralph.

"I thought she seemed very pleasant."

"I was sure you'd think her very pleasant."

"Is that why you invited her?"

"I didn't invite her, and when we came back from London I didn't know she was here. No one invited her. She's a friend of my mother's, and just after you and I went to town my mother got a note from her. She had arrived in England (she usually lives abroad, though she has first and last spent a good deal of time here), and asked leave to come down for a few days. She's a woman who can make such proposals with perfect confidence; she's so welcome wherever she goes. And with my mother there could be no question of hesitating; she's the one person in the world whom my mother very much admires. If she were not herself (which she after all much prefers), she would like to be Madame Merle. It would indeed be a great change."

"Well, she's very charming," said Isabel. "And she plays beautifully."

"She does everything beautifully. She's complete."

Isabel looked at her cousin a moment. "You don't like her."

"On the contrary, I was once in love with her."

"And she didn't care for you, and that's why you don't like her."

"How can we have discussed such things? Monsieur Merle was then living."

"Is he dead now?"

"So she says."

"Don't you believe her?"

"Yes, because the statement agrees with the probabilities. The husband of Madame Merle would be likely to pass away."

Isabel gazed at her cousin again. "I don't know what you mean. You mean something—that you don't mean. What was Monsieur Merle?"

"The husband of Madame."

"You're very odious. Has she any children?"

"Not the least little child—fortunately."

"Fortunately?"

"I mean fortunately for the child. She'd be sure to spoil it."

Isabel was apparently on the point of assuring her cousin for the third time that he was odious; but the discussion was interrupted by the arrival of the lady who was the topic of it. She came rustling in quickly, apologising for being late, fastening a bracelet, dressed in dark blue satin, which exposed a white bosom that was ineffectually covered by a curious silver necklace. Ralph offered her his arm with the exaggerated alertness of a man who was no longer a lover.

Even if this had still been his condition, however, Ralph had other things to think about. The great doctor spent the night at Gardencourt and, returning to London on the morrow, after another consultation with Mr. Touchett's own medical adviser, concurred in Ralph's desire that he should see the patient again on the day following. On the day following Sir Matthew Hope reappeared at Gardencourt, and now took a less encouraging view of the old man, who had grown worse in the twenty-four hours. His feebleness was extreme, and to his son, who constantly sat by his bedside, it often seemed that his end must be at hand. The local doctor, a very sagacious man, in whom Ralph had secretly more confidence than in his distinguished colleague, was constantly in attendance, and Sir Matthew Hope came back several times. Mr. Touchett was much of the time unconscious; he slept a great deal; he rarely spoke. Isabel had a great desire to be useful to him and was allowed to watch with him at hours when his other attendants (of whom Mrs. Touchett was not the least regular) went to take rest. He never seemed to know her, and she always said to herself "Suppose he should die while I'm sitting here;" an idea which excited her and kept her awake. Once he opened his eyes for a while and fixed them upon her intelligently, but when she went to him, hoping he would recognise her, he closed them and relapsed into stupor. The day after this, however, he revived for a longer time; but on this occasion Ralph only was with him. The old man began to talk, much to his son's satisfaction, who assured him that they should presently have him sitting up.

"No, my boy," said Mr. Touchett, "not unless you bury me in a sitting posture, as some of the ancients—was it the ancients?—used to do."

"Ah, daddy, don't talk about that," Ralph murmured. "You mustn't deny that you're getting better."

"There will be no need of my denying it if you don't say it," the old man answered. "Why should we prevaricate just at the last? We never prevaricated before. I've got to die some time, and it's better to die when one's sick than when one's well. I'm very sick—as sick as I shall ever be. I hope you don't want to prove that I shall ever be worse than this? That would be too bad. You don't? Well then."

Having made this excellent point he became quiet; but the next time that Ralph was with him he again addressed himself to conversation. The nurse had gone to her supper and Ralph was alone in charge, having just relieved Mrs. Touchett, who had been on guard since dinner. The room was lighted only by the flickering fire, which of late had become necessary, and Ralph's tall shadow was projected over wall and ceiling with an outline constantly varying but always grotesque.

"Who's that with me—is it my son?" the old man asked.

"Yes, it's your son, daddy."

"And is there no one else?"

"No one else."

Mr. Touchett said nothing for a while; and then, "I want to talk a little," he went on.

"Won't it tire you?" Ralph demurred.

"It won't matter if it does. I shall have a long rest. I want to talk about YOU."

Ralph had drawn nearer to the bed; he sat leaning forward with his hand on his father's. "You had better select a brighter topic."

"You were always bright; I used to be proud of your brightness. I should like so much to think you'd do something."

"If you leave us," said Ralph, "I shall do nothing but miss you."

"That's just what I don't want; it's what I want to talk about. You must get a new interest."

"I don't want a new interest, daddy. I have more old ones than I know what to do with."

The old man lay there looking at his son; his face was the face of the dying, but his eyes were the eyes of Daniel Touchett. He seemed to be reckoning over Ralph's interests. "Of course you have your mother," he said at last. "You'll take care of her."

"My mother will always take care of herself," Ralph returned.

"Well," said his father, "perhaps as she grows older she'll need a little help."

"I shall not see that. She'll outlive me."

"Very likely she will; but that's no reason—!" Mr. Touchett let his phrase die away in a helpless but not quite querulous sigh and remained silent again.

"Don't trouble yourself about us," said his son, "My mother and I get on very well together, you know."

"You get on by always being apart; that's not natural."

"If you leave us we shall probably see more of each other."

"Well," the old man observed with wandering irrelevance, "it can't be said that my death will make much difference in your mother's life."

"It will probably make more than you think."

"Well, she'll have more money," said Mr. Touchett. "I've left her a good wife's portion, just as if she had been a good wife."

"She has been one, daddy, according to her own theory. She has never troubled you."

"Ah, some troubles are pleasant," Mr. Touchett murmured. "Those you've given me for instance. But your mother has been less—less—what shall I call it? less out of the way since I've been ill. I presume she knows I've noticed it."

"I shall certainly tell her so; I'm so glad you mention it."

"It won't make any difference to her; she doesn't do it to please me. She does it to please—to please—" And he lay a while trying to think why she did it. "She does it because it suits her. But that's not what I want to talk about," he added. "It's about you. You'll be very well off."

"Yes," said Ralph, "I know that. But I hope you've not forgotten the talk we had a year ago—when I told you exactly what money I should need and begged you to make some good use of the rest."

"Yes, yes, I remember. I made a new will—in a few days. I suppose it was the first time such a thing had happened—a young man trying to get a will made against him."

"It is not against me," said Ralph. "It would be against me to have a large property to take care of. It's impossible for a man in my state of health to spend much money, and enough is as good as a feast."

"Well, you'll have enough—and something over. There will be more than enough for one—there will be enough for two."

"That's too much," said Ralph.

"Ah, don't say that. The best thing you can do; when I'm gone, will be to marry."

Ralph had foreseen what his father was coming to, and this suggestion was by no means fresh. It had long been Mr. Touchett's most ingenious way of taking the cheerful view of his son's possible duration. Ralph had usually treated it facetiously; but present circumstances proscribed the facetious. He simply fell back in his chair and returned his father's appealing gaze.

"If I, with a wife who hasn't been very fond of me, have had a very happy life," said the old man, carrying his ingenuity further still, "what a life mightn't you have if you should marry a person different from Mrs. Touchett. There are more different from her than there are like her." Ralph still said nothing; and after a pause his father resumed softly: "What do you think of your cousin?"

At this Ralph started, meeting the question with a strained smile. "Do I understand you to propose that I should marry Isabel?"

"Well, that's what it comes to in the end. Don't you like Isabel?"

"Yes, very much." And Ralph got up from his chair and wandered over to the fire. He stood before it an instant and then he stooped and stirred it mechanically. "I like Isabel very much," he repeated.

"Well," said his father, "I know she likes you. She has told me how much she likes you."

"Did she remark that she would like to marry me?"

"No, but she can't have anything against you. And she's the most charming young lady I've ever seen. And she would be good to you. I have thought a great deal about it."

"So have I," said Ralph, coming back to the bedside again. "I don't mind telling you that."

"You ARE in love with her then? I should think you would be. It's as if she came over on purpose."

"No, I'm not in love with her; but I should be if—if certain things were different."

"Ah, things are always different from what they might be," said the old man. "If you wait for them to change you'll never do anything. I don't know whether you know," he went on; "but I suppose there's no harm in my alluding to it at such an hour as this: there was some one wanted to marry Isabel the other day, and she wouldn't have him."

"I know she refused Warburton: he told me himself."

"Well, that proves there's a chance for somebody else."

"Somebody else took his chance the other day in London—and got nothing by it."

"Was it you?" Mr. Touchett eagerly asked.

"No, it was an older friend; a poor gentleman who came over from America to see about it."

"Well, I'm sorry for him, whoever he was. But it only proves what I say—that the way's open to you."

"If it is, dear father, it's all the greater pity that I'm unable to tread it. I haven't many convictions; but I have three or four that I hold strongly. One is that people, on the whole, had better not marry their cousins. Another is that people in an advanced stage of pulmonary disorder had better not marry at all."

The old man raised his weak hand and moved it to and fro before his face. "What do you mean by that? You look at things in a way that would make everything wrong. What sort of a cousin is a cousin that you had never seen for more than twenty years of her life? We're all each other's cousins, and if we stopped at that the human race would die out. It's just the same with your bad lung. You're a great deal better than you used to be. All you want is to lead a natural life. It is a great deal more natural to marry a pretty young lady that you're in love with than it is to remain single on false principles."

"I'm not in love with Isabel," said Ralph.

"You said just now that you would be if you didn't think it wrong. I want to prove to you that it isn't wrong."

"It will only tire you, dear daddy," said Ralph, who marvelled at his father's tenacity and at his finding strength to insist. "Then where shall we all be?"

"Where shall you be if I don't provide for you? You won't have anything to do with the bank, and you won't have me to take care of. You say you've so many interests; but I can't make them out."

Ralph leaned back in his chair with folded arms; his eyes were fixed for some time in meditation. At last, with the air of a man fairly mustering courage, "I take a great interest in my cousin," he said, "but not the sort of interest you desire. I shall not live many years; but I hope I shall live long enough to see what she does with herself. She's entirely independent of me; I can exercise very little influence upon her life. But I should like to do something for her."

"What should you like to do?"

"I should like to put a little wind in her sails."

"What do you mean by that?"

"I should like to put it into her power to do some of the things she wants. She wants to see the world for instance. I should like to put money in her purse."

"Ah, I'm glad you've thought of that," said the old man. "But I've thought of it too. I've left her a legacy—five thousand pounds."

"That's capital; it's very kind of you. But I should like to do a little more."

Something of that veiled acuteness with which it had been on Daniel Touchett's part the habit of a lifetime to listen to a financial proposition still lingered in the face in which the invalid had not obliterated the man of business. "I shall be happy to consider it," he said softly.

"Isabel's poor then. My mother tells me that she has but a few hundred dollars a year. I should like to make her rich."

"What do you mean by rich?"

"I call people rich when they're able to meet the requirements of their imagination. Isabel has a great deal of imagination."

"So have you, my son," said Mr. Touchett, listening very attentively but a little confusedly.

"You tell me I shall have money enough for two. What I want is that you should kindly relieve me of my superfluity and make it over to Isabel. Divide my inheritance into two equal halves and give her the second."

"To do what she likes with?"

"Absolutely what she likes."

"And without an equivalent?"

"What equivalent could there be?"

"The one I've already mentioned."

"Her marrying—some one or other? It's just to do away with anything of that sort that I make my suggestion. If she has an easy income she'll never have to marry for a support. That's what I want cannily to prevent. She wishes to be free, and your bequest will make her free."

"Well, you seem to have thought it out," said Mr. Touchett. "But I don't see why you appeal to me. The money will be yours, and you can easily give it to her yourself."

Ralph openly stared. "Ah, dear father, I can't offer Isabel money!"

The old man gave a groan. "Don't tell me you're not in love with her! Do you want me to have the credit of it?"

"Entirely. I should like it simply to be a clause in your will, without the slightest reference to me."

"Do you want me to make a new will then?"

"A few words will do it; you can attend to it the next time you feel a little lively."

"You must telegraph to Mr. Hilary then. I'll do nothing without my solicitor."

"You shall see Mr. Hilary to-morrow."

"He'll think we've quarrelled, you and I," said the old man.

"Very probably; I shall like him to think it," said Ralph, smiling; "and, to carry out the idea, I give you notice that I shall be very sharp, quite horrid and strange, with you."

The humour of this appeared to touch his father, who lay a little while taking it in. "I'll do anything you like," Mr. Touchett said at last; "but I'm not sure it's right. You say you want to put wind in her sails; but aren't you afraid of putting too much?"

"I should like to see her going before the breeze!" Ralph answered.

"You speak as if it were for your mere amusement."

"So it is, a good deal."

"Well, I don't think I understand," said Mr. Touchett with a sigh. "Young men are very different from what I was. When I cared for a girl—when I was young—I wanted to do more than look at her."

"You've scruples that I shouldn't have had, and you've ideas that I shouldn't have had either. You say Isabel wants to be free, and that her being rich will keep her from marrying for money. Do you think that she's a girl to do that?"

"By no means. But she has less money than she has ever had before. Her father then gave her everything, because he used to spend his capital. She has nothing but the crumbs of that feast to live on, and she doesn't really know how meagre they are—she has yet to learn it. My mother has told me all about it. Isabel will learn it when she's really thrown upon the world, and it would be very painful to me to think of her coming to the consciousness of a lot of wants she should be unable to satisfy."

"I've left her five thousand pounds. She can satisfy a good many wants with that."

"She can indeed. But she would probably spend it in two or three years."

"You think she'd be extravagant then?"

"Most certainly," said Ralph, smiling serenely.

Poor Mr. Touchett's acuteness was rapidly giving place to pure confusion. "It would merely be a question of time then, her spending the larger sum?"

"No—though at first I think she'd plunge into that pretty freely: she'd probably make over a part of it to each of her sisters. But after that she'd come to her senses, remember she has still a lifetime before her, and live within her means."

"Well, you HAVE worked it out," said the old man helplessly. "You do take an interest in her, certainly."

"You can't consistently say I go too far. You wished me to go further."

"Well, I don't know," Mr. Touchett answered. "I don't think I enter into your spirit. It seems to me immoral."

"Immoral, dear daddy?"

"Well, I don't know that it's right to make everything so easy for a person."

"It surely depends upon the person. When the person's good, your making things easy is all to the credit of virtue. To facilitate the execution of good impulses, what can be a nobler act?"

This was a little difficult to follow, and Mr. Touchett considered it for a while. At last he said: "Isabel's a sweet young thing; but do you think she's so good as that?"

"She's as good as her best opportunities," Ralph returned.

"Well," Mr. Touchett declared, "she ought to get a great many opportunities for sixty thousand pounds."

"I've no doubt she will."

"Of course I'll do what you want," said the old man. "I only want to understand it a little."

"Well, dear daddy, don't you understand it now?" his son caressingly asked. "If you don't we won't take any more trouble about it. We'll leave it alone."

Mr. Touchett lay a long time still. Ralph supposed he had given up the attempt to follow. But at last, quite lucidly, he began again. "Tell me this first. Doesn't it occur to you that a young lady with sixty thousand pounds may fall a victim to the fortune-hunters?"

"She'll hardly fall a victim to more than one."

"Well, one's too many."

"Decidedly. That's a risk, and it has entered into my calculation. I think it's appreciable, but I think it's small, and I'm prepared to take it."

Poor Mr. Touchett's acuteness had passed into perplexity, and his perplexity now passed into admiration. "Well, you have gone into it!" he repeated. "But I don't see what good you're to get of it."

Ralph leaned over his father's pillows and gently smoothed them; he was aware their talk had been unduly prolonged. "I shall get just the good I said a few moments ago I wished to put into Isabel's reach—that of having met the requirements of my imagination. But it's scandalous, the way I've taken advantage of you!"

CHAPTER XIX

As Mrs. Touchett had foretold, Isabel and Madame Merle were thrown much together during the illness of their host, so that if they had not become intimate it would have been almost a breach of good manners. Their manners were of the best, but in addition to this they happened to please each other. It is perhaps too much to say that they swore an eternal friendship, but tacitly at least they called the future to witness. Isabel did so with a perfectly good conscience, though she would have hesitated to admit she was intimate with her new friend in the high sense she privately attached to this term. She often wondered indeed if she ever had been, or ever could be, intimate with any one. She had an ideal of friendship as well as of several other sentiments, which it failed to seem to her in this case—it had not seemed to her in other cases—that the actual completely expressed. But she often reminded herself that there were essential reasons why one's ideal could never become concrete. It was a thing to believe in, not to see—a matter of faith, not of experience. Experience, however, might supply us with very creditable imitations of it, and the part of wisdom was to make the best of these. Certainly, on the whole, Isabel had never encountered a more agreeable and interesting figure than Madame Merle; she had never met a person having less of that fault which is the principal obstacle to friendship—the air of reproducing the more tiresome, the stale, the too-familiar parts of one's own character. The gates of the girl's confidence were opened wider than they had ever been; she said things to this amiable auditress that she had not yet said to any one. Sometimes she took alarm at her candour: it was as if she had given to a comparative stranger the key to her cabinet of jewels. These spiritual gems were the only ones of any magnitude that Isabel possessed, but there was all the greater reason for their being carefully guarded. Afterwards, however, she always remembered that one should never regret a generous error and that if Madame Merle had not the merits she attributed to her, so much the worse for Madame Merle. There was no doubt she had great merits—she was charming, sympathetic, intelligent, cultivated. More than this (for it had not been Isabel's ill-fortune to go through life without meeting in her own sex several persons of whom no less could fairly be said), she was rare, superior and preeminent. There are many amiable people in the world, and Madame Merle was far from being vulgarly good-natured and restlessly witty. She knew how to think—an accomplishment rare in women; and she had thought to very good purpose. Of course, too, she knew how to feel; Isabel couldn't have spent a week with her without being sure of that. This was indeed Madame Merle's great talent, her most perfect gift. Life had told upon her; she had felt it strongly, and it was part of the satisfaction to be taken in her society that when the girl talked of what she was pleased to call serious matters this lady understood her so easily and quickly. Emotion, it is true, had become with her rather historic; she made no secret of the fact that the fount of passion, thanks to having been rather violently tapped at one period, didn't flow quite so freely as of yore. She proposed moreover, as well as expected, to cease feeling; she freely admitted that of old she had been a little mad, and now she pretended to be perfectly sane.

"I judge more than I used to," she said to Isabel, "but it seems to me one has earned the right. One can't judge till one's forty; before that we're too eager, too hard, too cruel, and in addition much too ignorant. I'm sorry for you; it will be a long time before you're forty. But every gain's a loss of some kind; I often think that after forty one can't really feel. The freshness, the quickness have certainly gone. You'll keep them longer than most people; it will be a great satisfaction to me to see you some years hence. I want to see what life makes of you. One thing's certain—it can't spoil you. It may pull you about horribly, but I defy it to break you up."

Isabel received this assurance as a young soldier, still panting from a slight skirmish in which he has come off with honour, might receive a pat on the shoulder from his colonel. Like such a recognition of merit it seemed to come with authority. How could the lightest word do less on the part of a person who was prepared to say, of almost everything Isabel told her, "Oh, I've been in that, my dear; it passes, like everything else." On many of her interlocutors Madame Merle might have produced an irritating effect; it was disconcertingly difficult to surprise her. But Isabel, though by no means incapable of desiring to be effective, had not at present this impulse. She was too sincere, too interested in her judicious companion. And then moreover Madame Merle never said such things in the tone of triumph or of boastfulness; they dropped from her like cold confessions.

A period of bad weather had settled upon Gardencourt; the days grew shorter and there was an end to the pretty tea-parties on the lawn. But our young woman had long indoor conversations with her fellow visitor, and in spite of the rain the two ladies often sallied forth for a walk, equipped with the defensive apparatus which the English climate and the English genius have between them brought to such perfection. Madame Merle liked almost everything, including the English rain. "There's always a little of it and never too much at once," she said; "and it never wets you and it always smells good." She declared that in England the pleasures of smell were great—that in this inimitable island there was a certain mixture of fog and beer and soot which, however odd it might sound, was the national aroma, and was most agreeable to the nostril; and she used to lift the sleeve of her British overcoat and bury her nose in it, inhaling the clear, fine scent of the wool. Poor Ralph Touchett, as soon as the autumn had begun to define itself, became almost a prisoner; in bad weather he was unable to step out of the house, and he used sometimes to stand at one of the windows with his hands in his pockets and, from a countenance half-rueful, half-critical, watch Isabel and Madame Merle as they walked down the avenue under a pair of umbrellas. The roads about Gardencourt were so firm, even in the worst weather, that the two ladies always came back with a healthy glow in their cheeks, looking at the soles of their neat, stout boots and declaring that their walk had done them inexpressible good. Before luncheon, always, Madame Merle was engaged; Isabel admired and envied her rigid possession of her morning. Our heroine had always passed for a person of resources and had taken a certain pride in being one; but she wandered, as by the wrong side of the wall of a private garden, round the enclosed talents, accomplishments, aptitudes of Madame Merle. She found herself desiring to emulate them, and in twenty such ways this lady presented herself as a model. "I should like awfully to be so!" Isabel secretly exclaimed, more than once, as one after another of her friend's fine aspects caught the light, and before long she knew that she had learned a lesson from a high authority. It took no great time indeed for her to feel herself, as the phrase is, under an influence. "What's the harm," she wondered, "so long as it's a good one? The more one's under a good influence the better. The only thing is to see our steps as we take them—to understand them as we go. That, no doubt, I shall always do. I needn't be afraid of becoming too pliable; isn't it my fault that I'm not pliable enough?" It is said that imitation is the sincerest flattery; and if Isabel was sometimes moved to gape at her friend aspiringly and despairingly it was not so much because she desired herself to shine as because she wished to hold up the lamp for Madame Merle. She liked her extremely, but was even more dazzled than attracted. She sometimes asked herself what Henrietta Stackpole would say to her thinking so much of this perverted product of their common soil, and had a conviction that it would be severely judged. Henrietta would not at all subscribe to Madame Merle; for reasons she could not have defined this truth came home to the girl. On the other hand she was equally sure that, should the occasion offer, her new friend would strike off some happy view of her old: Madame Merle was too humorous, too observant, not to do justice to Henrietta, and on becoming acquainted with her would probably give the measure of a tact which Miss Stackpole couldn't hope to emulate. She appeared to have in her experience a touchstone for everything, and somewhere in the capacious pocket of her genial memory she would find the key to Henrietta's value. "That's the great thing," Isabel solemnly pondered; "that's the supreme good fortune: to be in a better position for appreciating people than they are for appreciating you." And she added that such, when one considered it, was simply the essence of the aristocratic situation. In this light, if in none other, one should aim at the aristocratic situation.

I may not count over all the links in the chain which led Isabel to think of Madame Merle's situation as aristocratic—a view of it never expressed in any reference made to it by that lady herself. She had known great things and great people, but she had never played a great part. She was one of the small ones of the earth; she had not been born to honours; she knew the world too well to nourish fatuous illusions on the article of her own place in it. She had encountered many of the fortunate few and was perfectly aware of those points at which their fortune differed from hers. But if by her informed measure she was no figure for a high scene, she had yet to Isabel's imagination a sort of greatness. To be so cultivated and civilised, so wise and so easy, and still make so light of it—that was really to be a great lady, especially when one so carried and presented one's self. It was as if somehow she had all society under contribution, and all the arts and graces it practised—or was the effect rather that of charming uses found for her, even from a distance, subtle service rendered by her to a clamorous world wherever she might be? After breakfast she wrote a succession of letters, as those arriving for her appeared innumerable: her correspondence was a source of surprise to Isabel when they sometimes walked together to the village post-office to deposit Madame Merle's offering to the mail. She knew more people, as she told Isabel, than she knew what to do with, and something was always turning up to be written about. Of painting she was devotedly fond, and made no more of brushing in a sketch than of pulling off her gloves. At Gardencourt she was perpetually taking advantage of an hour's sunshine to go out with a camp-stool and a box of water-colours. That she was a brave musician we have already perceived, and it was evidence of the fact that when she seated herself at the piano, as she always did in the evening, her listeners resigned themselves without a murmur to losing the grace of her talk. Isabel, since she had known her, felt ashamed of her own facility, which she now looked upon as basely inferior; and indeed, though she had been thought rather a prodigy at home, the loss to society when, in taking her place upon the music-stool, she turned her back to the room, was usually deemed greater than the gain. When Madame Merle was neither writing, nor painting, nor touching the piano, she was usually employed upon wonderful tasks of rich embroidery, cushions, curtains, decorations for the chimneypiece; an art in which her bold, free invention was as noted as the agility of her needle. She was never idle, for when engaged in none of the ways I have mentioned she was either reading (she appeared to Isabel to read "everything important"), or walking out, or playing patience with the cards, or talking with her fellow inmates. And with all this she had always the social quality, was never rudely absent and yet never too seated. She laid down her pastimes as easily as she took them up; she worked and talked at the same time, and appeared to impute scant worth to anything she did. She gave away her sketches and tapestries; she rose from the piano or remained there, according to the convenience of her auditors, which she always unerringly divined. She was in short the most comfortable, profitable, amenable person to live with. If for Isabel she had a fault it was that she was not natural; by which the girl meant, not that she was either affected or pretentious, since from these vulgar vices no woman could have been more exempt, but that her nature had been too much overlaid by custom and her angles too much rubbed away. She had become too flexible, too useful, was too ripe and too final. She was in a word too perfectly the social animal that man and woman are supposed to have been intended to be; and she had rid herself of every remnant of that tonic wildness which we may assume to have belonged even to the most amiable persons in the ages before country-house life was the fashion. Isabel found it difficult to think of her in any detachment or privacy, she existed only in her relations, direct or indirect, with her fellow mortals. One might wonder what commerce she could possibly hold with her own spirit. One always ended, however, by feeling that a charming surface doesn't necessarily prove one superficial; this was an illusion in which, in one's youth, one had but just escaped being nourished. Madame Merle was not superficial—not she. She was deep, and her nature spoke none the less in her behaviour because it spoke a conventional tongue. "What's language at all but a convention?" said Isabel. "She has the good taste not to pretend, like some people I've met, to express herself by original signs."

"I'm afraid you've suffered much," she once found occasion to say to her friend in response to some allusion that had appeared to reach far.

"What makes you think that?" Madame Merle asked with the amused smile of a person seated at a game of guesses. "I hope I haven't too much the droop of the misunderstood."

"No; but you sometimes say things that I think people who have always been happy wouldn't have found out."

"I haven't always been happy," said Madame Merle, smiling still, but with a mock gravity, as if she were telling a child a secret. "Such a wonderful thing!"

But Isabel rose to the irony. "A great many people give me the impression of never having for a moment felt anything."

"It's very true; there are many more iron pots certainly than porcelain. But you may depend on it that every one bears some mark; even the hardest iron pots have a little bruise, a little hole somewhere. I flatter myself that I'm rather stout, but if I must tell you the truth I've been shockingly chipped and cracked. I do very well for service yet, because I've been cleverly mended; and I try to remain in the cupboard—the quiet, dusky cupboard where there's an odour of stale spices—as much as I can. But when I've to come out and into a strong light—then, my dear, I'm a horror!"

I know not whether it was on this occasion or on some other that the conversation had taken the turn I have just indicated she said to Isabel that she would some day a tale unfold. Isabel assured her she should delight to listen to one, and reminded her more than once of this engagement. Madame Merle, however, begged repeatedly for a respite, and at last frankly told her young companion that they must wait till they knew each other better. This would be sure to happen, a long friendship so visibly lay before them. Isabel assented, but at the same time enquired if she mightn't be trusted—if she appeared capable of a betrayal of confidence.

"It's not that I'm afraid of your repeating what I say," her fellow visitor answered; "I'm afraid, on the contrary, of your taking it too much to yourself. You'd judge me too harshly; you're of the cruel age." She preferred for the present to talk to Isabel of Isabel, and exhibited the greatest interest in our heroine's history, sentiments, opinions, prospects. She made her chatter and listened to her chatter with infinite good nature. This flattered and quickened the girl, who was struck with all the distinguished people her friend had known and with her having lived, as Mrs. Touchett said, in the best company in Europe. Isabel thought the better of herself for enjoying the favour of a person who had so large a field of comparison; and it was perhaps partly to gratify the sense of profiting by comparison that she often appealed to these stores of reminiscence. Madame Merle had been a dweller in many lands and had social ties in a dozen different countries. "I don't pretend to be educated," she would say, "but I think I know my Europe;" and she spoke one day of going to Sweden to stay with an old friend, and another of proceeding to Malta to follow up a new acquaintance. With England, where she had often dwelt, she was thoroughly familiar, and for Isabel's benefit threw a great deal of light upon the customs of the country and the character of the people, who "after all," as she was fond of saying, were the most convenient in the world to live with.

"You mustn't think it strange her remaining here at such a time as this, when Mr. Touchett's passing away," that gentleman's wife remarked to her niece. "She is incapable of a mistake; she's the most tactful woman I know. It's a favour to me that she stays; she's putting off a lot of visits at great houses," said Mrs. Touchett, who never forgot that when she herself was in England her social value sank two or three degrees in the scale. "She has her pick of places; she's not in want of a shelter. But I've asked her to put in this time because I wish you to know her. I think it will be a good thing for you. Serena Merle hasn't a fault."

"If I didn't already like her very much that description might alarm me," Isabel returned.

"She's never the least little bit 'off.' I've brought you out here and I wish to do the best for you. Your sister Lily told me she hoped I would give you plenty of opportunities. I give you one in putting you in relation with Madame Merle. She's one of the most brilliant women in Europe."

"I like her better than I like your description of her," Isabel persisted in saying.

"Do you flatter yourself that you'll ever feel her open to criticism? I hope you'll let me know when you do."

"That will be cruel—to you," said Isabel.

"You needn't mind me. You won't discover a fault in her."

"Perhaps not. But I dare say I shan't miss it."

"She knows absolutely everything on earth there is to know," said Mrs. Touchett.

Isabel after this observed to their companion that she hoped she knew Mrs. Touchett considered she hadn't a speck on her perfection. On which "I'm obliged to you," Madame Merle replied, "but I'm afraid your aunt imagines, or at least alludes to, no aberrations that the clock-face doesn't register."

"So that you mean you've a wild side that's unknown to her?"

"Ah no, I fear my darkest sides are my tamest. I mean that having no faults, for your aunt, means that one's never late for dinner—that is for her dinner. I was not late, by the way, the other day, when you came back from London; the clock was just at eight when I came into the drawing-room: it was the rest of you that were before the time. It means that one answers a letter the day one gets it and that when one comes to stay with her one doesn't bring too much luggage and is careful not to be taken ill. For Mrs. Touchett those things constitute virtue; it's a blessing to be able to reduce it to its elements."

Madame Merle's own conversation, it will be perceived, was enriched with bold, free touches of criticism, which, even when they had a restrictive effect, never struck Isabel as ill-natured. It couldn't occur to the girl for instance that Mrs. Touchett's accomplished guest was abusing her; and this for very good reasons. In the first place Isabel rose eagerly to the sense of her shades; in the second Madame Merle implied that there was a great deal more to say; and it was clear in the third that for a person to speak to one without ceremony of one's near relations was an agreeable sign of that person's intimacy with one's self. These signs of deep communion multiplied as the days elapsed, and there was none of which Isabel was more sensible than of her companion's preference for making Miss Archer herself a topic. Though she referred frequently to the incidents of her own career she never lingered upon them; she was as little of a gross egotist as she was of a flat gossip.

"I'm old and stale and faded," she said more than once; "I'm of no more interest than last week's newspaper. You're young and fresh and of to-day; you've the great thing—you've actuality. I once had it—we all have it for an hour. You, however, will have it for longer. Let us talk about you then; you can say nothing I shall not care to hear. It's a sign that I'm growing old—that I like to talk with younger people. I think it's a very pretty compensation. If we can't have youth within us we can have it outside, and I really think we see it and feel it better that way. Of course we must be in sympathy with it—that I shall always be. I don't know that I shall ever be ill-natured with old people—I hope not; there are certainly some old people I adore. But I shall never be anything but abject with the young; they touch me and appeal to me too much. I give you carte blanche then; you can even be impertinent if you like; I shall let it pass and horribly spoil you. I speak as if I were a hundred years old, you say? Well, I am, if you please; I was born before the French Revolution. Ah, my dear, je viens de loin; I belong to the old, old world. But it's not of that I want to talk; I want to talk about the new. You must tell me more about America; you never tell me enough. Here I've been since I was brought here as a helpless child, and it's ridiculous, or rather it's scandalous, how little I know about that splendid, dreadful, funny country—surely the greatest and drollest of them all. There are a great many of us like that in these parts, and I must say I think we're a wretched set of people. You should live in your own land; whatever it may be you have your natural place there. If we're not good Americans we're certainly poor Europeans; we've no natural place here. We're mere parasites, crawling over the surface; we haven't our feet in the soil. At least one can know it and not have illusions. A woman perhaps can get on; a woman, it seems to me, has no natural place anywhere; wherever she finds herself she has to remain on the surface and, more or less, to crawl. You protest, my dear? you're horrified? you declare you'll never crawl? It's very true that I don't see you crawling; you stand more upright than a good many poor creatures. Very good; on the whole, I don't think you'll crawl. But the men, the Americans; je vous demande un peu, what do they make of it over here? I don't envy them trying to arrange themselves. Look at poor Ralph Touchett: what sort of a figure do you call that? Fortunately he has a consumption; I say fortunately, because it gives him something to do. His consumption's his carriere it's a kind of position. You can say: 'Oh, Mr. Touchett, he takes care of his lungs, he knows a great deal about climates.' But without that who would he be, what would he represent? 'Mr. Ralph Touchett: an American who lives in Europe.' That signifies absolutely nothing—it's impossible anything should signify less. 'He's very cultivated,' they say: 'he has a very pretty collection of old snuff-boxes.' The collection is all that's wanted to make it pitiful. I'm tired of the sound of the word; I think it's grotesque. With the poor old father it's different; he has his identity, and it's rather a massive one. He represents a great financial house, and that, in our day, is as good as anything else. For an American, at any rate, that will do very well. But I persist in thinking your cousin very lucky to have a chronic malady so long as he doesn't die of it. It's much better than the snuffboxes. If he weren't ill, you say, he'd do something?—he'd take his father's place in the house. My poor child, I doubt it; I don't think he's at all fond of the house. However, you know him better than I, though I used to know him rather well, and he may have the benefit of the doubt. The worst case, I think, is a friend of mine, a countryman of ours, who lives in Italy (where he also was brought before he knew better), and who is one of the most delightful men I know. Some day you must know him. I'll bring you together and then you'll see what I mean. He's Gilbert Osmond—he lives in Italy; that's all one can say about him or make of him. He's exceedingly clever, a man made to be distinguished; but, as I tell you, you exhaust the description when you say he's Mr. Osmond who lives tout betement in Italy. No career, no name, no position, no fortune, no past, no future, no anything. Oh yes, he paints, if you please—paints in water-colours; like me, only better than I. His painting's pretty bad; on the whole I'm rather glad of that. Fortunately he's very indolent, so indolent that it amounts to a sort of position. He can say, 'Oh, I do nothing; I'm too deadly lazy. You can do nothing to-day unless you get up at five o'clock in the morning.' In that way he becomes a sort of exception; you feel he might do something if he'd only rise early. He never speaks of his painting to people at large; he's too clever for that. But he has a little girl—a dear little girl; he does speak of her. He's devoted to her, and if it were a career to be an excellent father he'd be very distinguished. But I'm afraid that's no better than the snuff-boxes; perhaps not even so good. Tell me what they do in America," pursued Madame Merle, who, it must be observed parenthetically, did not deliver herself all at once of these reflexions, which are presented in a cluster for the convenience of the reader. She talked of Florence, where Mr. Osmond lived and where Mrs. Touchett occupied a medieval palace; she talked of Rome, where she herself had a little pied-a-terre with some rather good old damask. She talked of places, of people and even, as the phrase is, of "subjects"; and from time to time she talked of their kind old host and of the prospect of his recovery. From the first she had thought this prospect small, and Isabel had been struck with the positive, discriminating, competent way in which she took the measure of his remainder of life. One evening she announced definitely that he wouldn't live.

"Sir Matthew Hope told me so as plainly as was proper," she said; "standing there, near the fire, before dinner. He makes himself very agreeable, the great doctor. I don't mean his saying that has anything to do with it. But he says such things with great tact. I had told him I felt ill at my ease, staying here at such a time; it seemed to me so indiscreet—it wasn't as if I could nurse. 'You must remain, you must remain,' he answered; 'your office will come later.' Wasn't that a very delicate way of saying both that poor Mr. Touchett would go and that I might be of some use as a consoler? In fact, however, I shall not be of the slightest use. Your aunt will console herself; she, and she alone, knows just how much consolation she'll require. It would be a very delicate matter for another person to undertake to administer the dose. With your cousin it will be different; he'll miss his father immensely. But I should never presume to condole with Mr. Ralph; we're not on those terms." Madame Merle had alluded more than once to some undefined incongruity in her relations with Ralph Touchett; so Isabel took this occasion of asking her if they were not good friends.

"Perfectly, but he doesn't like me."

"What have you done to him?"

"Nothing whatever. But one has no need of a reason for that."

"For not liking you? I think one has need of a very good reason."

"You're very kind. Be sure you have one ready for the day you begin."

"Begin to dislike you? I shall never begin."

"I hope not; because if you do you'll never end. That's the way with your cousin; he doesn't get over it. It's an antipathy of nature—if I can call it that when it's all on his side. I've nothing whatever against him and don't bear him the least little grudge for not doing me justice. Justice is all I want. However, one feels that he's a gentleman and would never say anything underhand about one. Cartes sur table," Madame Merle subjoined in a moment, "I'm not afraid of him."

"I hope not indeed," said Isabel, who added something about his being the kindest creature living. She remembered, however, that on her first asking him about Madame Merle he had answered her in a manner which this lady might have thought injurious without being explicit. There was something between them, Isabel said to herself, but she said nothing more than this. If it were something of importance it should inspire respect; if it were not it was not worth her curiosity. With all her love of knowledge she had a natural shrinking from raising curtains and looking into unlighted corners. The love of knowledge coexisted in her mind with the finest capacity for ignorance.

But Madame Merle sometimes said things that startled her, made her raise her clear eyebrows at the time and think of the words afterwards. "I'd give a great deal to be your age again," she broke out once with a bitterness which, though diluted in her customary amplitude of ease, was imperfectly disguised by it. "If I could only begin again—if I could have my life before me!"

"Your life's before you yet," Isabel answered gently, for she was vaguely awe-struck.

"No; the best part's gone, and gone for nothing."

"Surely not for nothing," said Isabel.

"Why not—what have I got? Neither husband, nor child, nor fortune, nor position, nor the traces of a beauty that I never had."

"You have many friends, dear lady."

"I'm not so sure!" cried Madame Merle.

"Ah, you're wrong. You have memories, graces, talents—"

But Madame Merle interrupted her. "What have my talents brought me? Nothing but the need of using them still, to get through the hours, the years, to cheat myself with some pretence of movement, of unconsciousness. As for my graces and memories the less said about them the better. You'll be my friend till you find a better use for your friendship."

"It will be for you to see that I don't then," said Isabel.

"Yes; I would make an effort to keep you." And her companion looked at her gravely. "When I say I should like to be your age I mean with your qualities—frank, generous, sincere like you. In that case I should have made something better of my life."

"What should you have liked to do that you've not done?"

Madame Merle took a sheet of music—she was seated at the piano and had abruptly wheeled about on the stool when she first spoke—and mechanically turned the leaves. "I'm very ambitious!" she at last replied.

"And your ambitions have not been satisfied? They must have been great."

"They WERE great. I should make myself ridiculous by talking of them."

Isabel wondered what they could have been—whether Madame Merle had aspired to wear a crown. "I don't know what your idea of success may be, but you seem to me to have been successful. To me indeed you're a vivid image of success."

Madame Merle tossed away the music with a smile. "What's YOUR idea of success?"

"You evidently think it must be a very tame one. It's to see some dream of one's youth come true."

"Ah," Madame Merle exclaimed, "that I've never seen! But my dreams were so great—so preposterous. Heaven forgive me, I'm dreaming now!" And she turned back to the piano and began grandly to play. On the morrow she said to Isabel that her definition of success had been very pretty, yet frightfully sad. Measured in that way, who had ever succeeded? The dreams of one's youth, why they were enchanting, they were divine! Who had ever seen such things come to pass?

"I myself—a few of them," Isabel ventured to answer.

"Already? They must have been dreams of yesterday."

"I began to dream very young," Isabel smiled.

"Ah, if you mean the aspirations of your childhood—that of having a pink sash and a doll that could close her eyes."

"No, I don't mean that."

"Or a young man with a fine moustache going down on his knees to you."

"No, nor that either," Isabel declared with still more emphasis.

Madame Merle appeared to note this eagerness. "I suspect that's what you do mean. We've all had the young man with the moustache. He's the inevitable young man; he doesn't count."

Isabel was silent a little but then spoke with extreme and characteristic inconsequence. "Why shouldn't he count? There are young men and young men."

"And yours was a paragon—is that what you mean?" asked her friend with a laugh. "If you've had the identical young man you dreamed of, then that was success, and I congratulate you with all my heart. Only in that case why didn't you fly with him to his castle in the Apennines?"

"He has no castle in the Apennines."

"What has he? An ugly brick house in Fortieth Street? Don't tell me that; I refuse to recognise that as an ideal."

"I don't care anything about his house," said Isabel.

"That's very crude of you. When you've lived as long as I you'll see that every human being has his shell and that you must take the shell into account. By the shell I mean the whole envelope of circumstances. There's no such thing as an isolated man or woman; we're each of us made up of some cluster of appurtenances. What shall we call our 'self'? Where does it begin? where does it end? It overflows into everything that belongs to us—and then it flows back again. I know a large part of myself is in the clothes I choose to wear. I've a great respect for THINGS! One's self—for other people—is one's expression of one's self; and one's house, one's furniture, one's garments, the books one reads, the company one keeps—these things are all expressive."

This was very metaphysical; not more so, however, than several observations Madame Merle had already made. Isabel was fond of metaphysics, but was unable to accompany her friend into this bold analysis of the human personality. "I don't agree with you. I think just the other way. I don't know whether I succeed in expressing myself, but I know that nothing else expresses me. Nothing that belongs to me is any measure of me; everything's on the contrary a limit, a barrier, and a perfectly arbitrary one. Certainly the clothes which, as you say, I choose to wear, don't express me; and heaven forbid they should!"

"You dress very well," Madame Merle lightly interposed.

"Possibly; but I don't care to be judged by that. My clothes may express the dressmaker, but they don't express me. To begin with it's not my own choice that I wear them; they're imposed upon me by society."

"Should you prefer to go without them?" Madame Merle enquired in a tone which virtually terminated the discussion.

I am bound to confess, though it may cast some discredit on the sketch I have given of the youthful loyalty practised by our heroine toward this accomplished woman, that Isabel had said nothing whatever to her about Lord Warburton and had been equally reticent on the subject of Caspar Goodwood. She had not, however, concealed the fact that she had had opportunities of marrying and had even let her friend know of how advantageous a kind they had been. Lord Warburton had left Lockleigh and was gone to Scotland, taking his sisters with him; and though he had written to Ralph more than once to ask about Mr. Touchett's health the girl was not liable to the embarrassment of such enquiries as, had he still been in the neighbourhood, he would probably have felt bound to make in person. He had excellent ways, but she felt sure that if he had come to Gardencourt he would have seen Madame Merle, and that if he had seen her he would have liked her and betrayed to her that he was in love with her young friend. It so happened that during this lady's previous visits to Gardencourt—each of them much shorter than the present—he had either not been at Lockleigh or had not called at Mr. Touchett's. Therefore, though she knew him by name as the great man of that county, she had no cause to suspect him as a suitor of Mrs. Touchett's freshly-imported niece.

"You've plenty of time," she had said to Isabel in return for the mutilated confidences which our young woman made her and which didn't pretend to be perfect, though we have seen that at moments the girl had compunctions at having said so much. "I'm glad you've done nothing yet—that you have it still to do. It's a very good thing for a girl to have refused a few good offers—so long of course as they are not the best she's likely to have. Pardon me if my tone seems horribly corrupt; one must take the worldly view sometimes. Only don't keep on refusing for the sake of refusing. It's a pleasant exercise of power; but accepting's after all an exercise of power as well. There's always the danger of refusing once too often. It was not the one I fell into—I didn't refuse often enough. You're an exquisite creature, and I should like to see you married to a prime minister. But speaking strictly, you know, you're not what is technically called a parti. You're extremely good-looking and extremely clever; in yourself you're quite exceptional. You appear to have the vaguest ideas about your earthly possessions; but from what I can make out you're not embarrassed with an income. I wish you had a little money."

"I wish I had!" said Isabel, simply, apparently forgetting for the moment that her poverty had been a venial fault for two gallant gentlemen.

In spite of Sir Matthew Hope's benevolent recommendation Madame Merle did not remain to the end, as the issue of poor Mr. Touchett's malady had now come frankly to be designated. She was under pledges to other people which had at last to be redeemed, and she left Gardencourt with the understanding that she should in any event see Mrs. Touchett there again, or else in town, before quitting England. Her parting with Isabel was even more like the beginning of a friendship than their meeting had been. "I'm going to six places in succession, but I shall see no one I like so well as you. They'll all be old friends, however; one doesn't make new friends at my age. I've made a great exception for you. You must remember that and must think as well of me as possible. You must reward me by believing in me."

By way of answer Isabel kissed her, and, though some women kiss with facility, there are kisses and kisses, and this embrace was satisfactory to Madame Merle. Our young lady, after this, was much alone; she saw her aunt and cousin only at meals, and discovered that of the hours during which Mrs. Touchett was invisible only a minor portion was now devoted to nursing her husband. She spent the rest in her own apartments, to which access was not allowed even to her niece, apparently occupied there with mysterious and inscrutable exercises. At table she was grave and silent; but her solemnity was not an attitude—Isabel could see it was a conviction. She wondered if her aunt repented of having taken her own way so much; but there was no visible evidence of this—no tears, no sighs, no exaggeration of a zeal always to its own sense adequate. Mrs. Touchett seemed simply to feel the need of thinking things over and summing them up; she had a little moral account-book—with columns unerringly ruled and a sharp steel clasp—which she kept with exemplary neatness. Uttered reflection had with her ever, at any rate, a practical ring. "If I had foreseen this I'd not have proposed your coming abroad now," she said to Isabel after Madame Merle had left the house. "I'd have waited and sent for you next year."

"So that perhaps I should never have known my uncle? It's a great happiness to me to have come now."

"That's very well. But it was not that you might know your uncle that I brought you to Europe." A perfectly veracious speech; but, as Isabel thought, not as perfectly timed. She had leisure to think of this and other matters. She took a solitary walk every day and spent vague hours in turning over books in the library. Among the subjects that engaged her attention were the adventures of her friend Miss Stackpole, with whom she was in regular correspondence. Isabel liked her friend's private epistolary style better than her public; that is she felt her public letters would have been excellent if they had not been printed. Henrietta's career, however, was not so successful as might have been wished even in the interest of her private felicity; that view of the inner life of Great Britain which she was so eager to take appeared to dance before her like an ignis fatuus. The invitation from Lady Pensil, for mysterious reasons, had never arrived; and poor Mr. Bantling himself, with all his friendly ingenuity, had been unable to explain so grave a dereliction on the part of a missive that had obviously been sent. He had evidently taken Henrietta's affairs much to heart, and believed that he owed her a set-off to this illusory visit to Bedfordshire. "He says he should think I would go to the Continent," Henrietta wrote; "and as he thinks of going there himself I suppose his advice is sincere. He wants to know why I don't take a view of French life; and it's a fact that I want very much to see the new Republic. Mr. Bantling doesn't care much about the Republic, but he thinks of going over to Paris anyway. I must say he's quite as attentive as I could wish, and at least I shall have seen one polite Englishman. I keep telling Mr. Bantling that he ought to have been an American, and you should see how that pleases him. Whenever I say so he always breaks out with the same exclamation—'Ah, but really, come now!" A few days later she wrote that she had decided to go to Paris at the end of the week and that Mr. Banding had promised to see her off—perhaps even would go as far as Dover with her. She would wait in Paris till Isabel should arrive, Henrietta added; speaking quite as if Isabel were to start on her continental journey alone and making no allusion to Mrs. Touchett. Bearing in mind his interest in their late companion, our heroine communicated several passages from this correspondence to Ralph, who followed with an emotion akin to suspense the career of the representative of the Interviewer.

"It seems to me she's doing very well," he said, "going over to Paris with an ex-Lancer! If she wants something to write about she has only to describe that episode."

"It's not conventional, certainly," Isabel answered; "but if you mean that—as far as Henrietta is concerned—it's not perfectly innocent, you're very much mistaken. You'll never understand Henrietta."

"Pardon me, I understand her perfectly. I didn't at all at first, but now I've the point of view. I'm afraid, however, that Bantling hasn't; he may have some surprises. Oh, I understand Henrietta as well as if I had made her!"

Isabel was by no means sure of this, but she abstained from expressing further doubt, for she was disposed in these days to extend a great charity to her cousin. One afternoon less than a week after Madame Merle's departure she was seated in the library with a volume to which her attention was not fastened. She had placed herself in a deep window-bench, from which she looked out into the dull, damp park; and as the library stood at right angles to the entrance-front of the house she could see the doctor's brougham, which had been waiting for the last two hours before the door. She was struck with his remaining so long, but at last she saw him appear in the portico, stand a moment slowly drawing on his gloves and looking at the knees of his horse, and then get into the vehicle and roll away. Isabel kept her place for half an hour; there was a great stillness in the house. It was so great that when she at last heard a soft, slow step on the deep carpet of the room she was almost startled by the sound. She turned quickly away from the window and saw Ralph Touchett standing there with his hands still in his pockets, but with a face absolutely void of its usual latent smile. She got up and her movement and glance were a question.

"It's all over," said Ralph.

"Do you mean that my uncle...?" And Isabel stopped.

"My dear father died an hour ago."

"Ah, my poor Ralph!" she gently wailed, putting out her two hands to him.

CHAPTER XX

Some fortnight after this Madame Merle drove up in a hansom cab to the house in Winchester Square. As she descended from her vehicle she observed, suspended between the dining-room windows, a large, neat, wooden tablet, on whose fresh black ground were inscribed in white paint the words—"This noble freehold mansion to be sold"; with the name of the agent to whom application should be made. "They certainly lose no time," said the visitor as, after sounding the big brass knocker, she waited to be admitted; "it's a practical country!" And within the house, as she ascended to the drawing-room, she perceived numerous signs of abdication; pictures removed from the walls and placed upon sofas, windows undraped and floors laid bare. Mrs. Touchett presently received her and intimated in a few words that condolences might be taken for granted.

"I know what you're going to say—he was a very good man. But I know it better than any one, because I gave him more chance to show it. In that I think I was a good wife." Mrs. Touchett added that at the end her husband apparently recognised this fact. "He has treated me most liberally," she said; "I won't say more liberally than I expected, because I didn't expect. You know that as a general thing I don't expect. But he chose, I presume, to recognise the fact that though I lived much abroad and mingled—you may say freely—in foreign life, I never exhibited the smallest preference for any one else."

"For any one but yourself," Madame Merle mentally observed; but the reflexion was perfectly inaudible.

"I never sacrificed my husband to another," Mrs. Touchett continued with her stout curtness.

"Oh no," thought Madame Merle; "you never did anything for another!"

There was a certain cynicism in these mute comments which demands an explanation; the more so as they are not in accord either with the view—somewhat superficial perhaps—that we have hitherto enjoyed of Madame Merle's character or with the literal facts of Mrs. Touchett's history; the more so, too, as Madame Merle had a well-founded conviction that her friend's last remark was not in the least to be construed as a side-thrust at herself. The truth is that the moment she had crossed the threshold she received an impression that Mr. Touchett's death had had subtle consequences and that these consequences had been profitable to a little circle of persons among whom she was not numbered. Of course it was an event which would naturally have consequences; her imagination had more than once rested upon this fact during her stay at Gardencourt. But it had been one thing to foresee such a matter mentally and another to stand among its massive records. The idea of a distribution of property—she would almost have said of spoils—just now pressed upon her senses and irritated her with a sense of exclusion. I am far from wishing to picture her as one of the hungry mouths or envious hearts of the general herd, but we have already learned of her having desires that had never been satisfied. If she had been questioned, she would of course have admitted—with a fine proud smile—that she had not the faintest claim to a share in Mr. Touchett's relics. "There was never anything in the world between us," she would have said. "There was never that, poor man!"—with a fillip of her thumb and her third finger. I hasten to add, moreover, that if she couldn't at the present moment keep from quite perversely yearning she was careful not to betray herself. She had after all as much sympathy for Mrs. Touchett's gains as for her losses.

"He has left me this house," the newly-made widow said; "but of course I shall not live in it; I've a much better one in Florence. The will was opened only three days since, but I've already offered the house for sale. I've also a share in the bank; but I don't yet understand if I'm obliged to leave it there. If not I shall certainly take it out. Ralph, of course, has Gardencourt; but I'm not sure that he'll have means to keep up the place. He's naturally left very well off, but his father has given away an immense deal of money; there are bequests to a string of third cousins in Vermont. Ralph, however, is very fond of Gardencourt and would be quite capable of living there—in summer—with a maid-of-all-work and a gardener's boy. There's one remarkable clause in my husband's will," Mrs. Touchett added. "He has left my niece a fortune."

"A fortune!" Madame Merle softly repeated.

"Isabel steps into something like seventy thousand pounds." Madame Merle's hands were clasped in her lap; at this she raised them, still clasped, and held them a moment against her bosom while her eyes, a little dilated, fixed themselves on those of her friend. "Ah," she cried, "the clever creature!"

Mrs. Touchett gave her a quick look. "What do you mean by that?"

For an instant Madame Merle's colour rose and she dropped her eyes. "It certainly is clever to achieve such results—without an effort!"

"There assuredly was no effort. Don't call it an achievement."

Madame Merle was seldom guilty of the awkwardness of retracting what she had said; her wisdom was shown rather in maintaining it and placing it in a favourable light. "My dear friend, Isabel would certainly not have had seventy thousand pounds left her if she had not been the most charming girl in the world. Her charm includes great cleverness."

"She never dreamed, I'm sure, of my husband's doing anything for her; and I never dreamed of it either, for he never spoke to me of his intention," Mrs. Touchett said. "She had no claim upon him whatever; it was no great recommendation to him that she was my niece. Whatever she achieved she achieved unconsciously."

"Ah," rejoined Madame Merle, "those are the greatest strokes!" Mrs. Touchett reserved her opinion. "The girl's fortunate; I don't deny that. But for the present she's simply stupefied."

"Do you mean that she doesn't know what to do with the money?"

"That, I think, she has hardly considered. She doesn't know what to think about the matter at all. It has been as if a big gun were suddenly fired off behind her; she's feeling herself to see if she be hurt. It's but three days since she received a visit from the principal executor, who came in person, very gallantly, to notify her. He told me afterwards that when he had made his little speech she suddenly burst into tears. The money's to remain in the affairs of the bank, and she's to draw the interest."

Madame Merle shook her head with a wise and now quite benignant smile. "How very delicious! After she has done that two or three times she'll get used to it." Then after a silence, "What does your son think of it?" she abruptly asked.

"He left England before the will was read—used up by his fatigue and anxiety and hurrying off to the south. He's on his way to the Riviera and I've not yet heard from him. But it's not likely he'll ever object to anything done by his father."

"Didn't you say his own share had been cut down?"

"Only at his wish. I know that he urged his father to do something for the people in America. He's not in the least addicted to looking after number one."

"It depends upon whom he regards as number one!" said Madame Merle. And she remained thoughtful a moment, her eyes bent on the floor.

"Am I not to see your happy niece?" she asked at last as she raised them.

"You may see her; but you'll not be struck with her being happy. She has looked as solemn, these three days, as a Cimabue Madonna!" And Mrs. Touchett rang for a servant.

Isabel came in shortly after the footman had been sent to call her; and Madame Merle thought, as she appeared, that Mrs. Touchett's comparison had its force. The girl was pale and grave—an effect not mitigated by her deeper mourning; but the smile of her brightest moments came into her face as she saw Madame Merle, who went forward, laid her hand on our heroine's shoulder and, after looking at her a moment, kissed her as if she were returning the kiss she had received from her at Gardencourt. This was the only allusion the visitor, in her great good taste, made for the present to her young friend's inheritance.

Mrs. Touchett had no purpose of awaiting in London the sale of her house. After selecting from among its furniture the objects she wished to transport to her other abode, she left the rest of its contents to be disposed of by the auctioneer and took her departure for the Continent. She was of course accompanied on this journey by her niece, who now had plenty of leisure to measure and weigh and otherwise handle the windfall on which Madame Merle had covertly congratulated her. Isabel thought very often of the fact of her accession of means, looking at it in a dozen different lights; but we shall not now attempt to follow her train of thought or to explain exactly why her new consciousness was at first oppressive. This failure to rise to immediate joy was indeed but brief; the girl presently made up her mind that to be rich was a virtue because it was to be able to do, and that to do could only be sweet. It was the graceful contrary of the stupid side of weakness—especially the feminine variety. To be weak was, for a delicate young person, rather graceful, but, after all, as Isabel said to herself, there was a larger grace than that. Just now, it is true, there was not much to do—once she had sent off a cheque to Lily and another to poor Edith; but she was thankful for the quiet months which her mourning robes and her aunt's fresh widowhood compelled them to spend together. The acquisition of power made her serious; she scrutinised her power with a kind of tender ferocity, but was not eager to exercise it. She began to do so during a stay of some weeks which she eventually made with her aunt in Paris, though in ways that will inevitably present themselves as trivial. They were the ways most naturally imposed in a city in which the shops are the admiration of the world, and that were prescribed unreservedly by the guidance of Mrs. Touchett, who took a rigidly practical view of the transformation of her niece from a poor girl to a rich one. "Now that you're a young woman of fortune you must know how to play the part—I mean to play it well," she said to Isabel once for all; and she added that the girl's first duty was to have everything handsome. "You don't know how to take care of your things, but you must learn," she went on; this was Isabel's second duty. Isabel submitted, but for the present her imagination was not kindled; she longed for opportunities, but these were not the opportunities she meant.

Mrs. Touchett rarely changed her plans, and, having intended before her husband's death to spend a part of the winter in Paris, saw no reason to deprive herself—still less to deprive her companion—of this advantage. Though they would live in great retirement she might still present her niece, informally, to the little circle of her fellow countrymen dwelling upon the skirts of the Champs Elysees. With many of these amiable colonists Mrs. Touchett was intimate; she shared their expatriation, their convictions, their pastimes, their ennui. Isabel saw them arrive with a good deal of assiduity at her aunt's hotel, and pronounced on them with a trenchancy doubtless to be accounted for by the temporary exaltation of her sense of human duty. She made up her mind that their lives were, though luxurious, inane, and incurred some disfavour by expressing this view on bright Sunday afternoons, when the American absentees were engaged in calling on each other. Though her listeners passed for people kept exemplarily genial by their cooks and dressmakers, two or three of them thought her cleverness, which was generally admitted, inferior to that of the new theatrical pieces. "You all live here this way, but what does it lead to?" she was pleased to ask. "It doesn't seem to lead to anything, and I should think you'd get very tired of it."

Mrs. Touchett thought the question worthy of Henrietta Stackpole. The two ladies had found Henrietta in Paris, and Isabel constantly saw her; so that Mrs. Touchett had some reason for saying to herself that if her niece were not clever enough to originate almost anything, she might be suspected of having borrowed that style of remark from her journalistic friend. The first occasion on which Isabel had spoken was that of a visit paid by the two ladies to Mrs. Luce, an old friend of Mrs. Touchett's and the only person in Paris she now went to see. Mrs. Luce had been living in Paris since the days of Louis Philippe; she used to say jocosely that she was one of the generation of 1830—a joke of which the point was not always taken. When it failed Mrs. Luce used to explain—"Oh yes, I'm one of the romantics;" her French had never become quite perfect. She was always at home on Sunday afternoons and surrounded by sympathetic compatriots, usually the same. In fact she was at home at all times, and reproduced with wondrous truth in her well-cushioned little corner of the brilliant city, the domestic tone of her native Baltimore. This reduced Mr. Luce, her worthy husband, a tall, lean, grizzled, well-brushed gentleman who wore a gold eye-glass and carried his hat a little too much on the back of his head, to mere platonic praise of the "distractions" of Paris—they were his great word—since you would never have guessed from what cares he escaped to them. One of them was that he went every day to the American banker's, where he found a post-office that was almost as sociable and colloquial an institution as in an American country town. He passed an hour (in fine weather) in a chair in the Champs Elysees, and he dined uncommonly well at his own table, seated above a waxed floor which it was Mrs. Luce's happiness to believe had a finer polish than any other in the French capital. Occasionally he dined with a friend or two at the Cafe Anglais, where his talent for ordering a dinner was a source of felicity to his companions and an object of admiration even to the headwaiter of the establishment. These were his only known pastimes, but they had beguiled his hours for upwards of half a century, and they doubtless justified his frequent declaration that there was no place like Paris. In no other place, on these terms, could Mr. Luce flatter himself that he was enjoying life. There was nothing like Paris, but it must be confessed that Mr. Luce thought less highly of this scene of his dissipations than in earlier days. In the list of his resources his political reflections should not be omitted, for they were doubtless the animating principle of many hours that superficially seemed vacant. Like many of his fellow colonists Mr. Luce was a high—or rather a deep—conservative, and gave no countenance to the government lately established in France. He had no faith in its duration and would assure you from year to year that its end was close at hand. "They want to be kept down, sir, to be kept down; nothing but the strong hand—the iron heel—will do for them," he would frequently say of the French people; and his ideal of a fine showy clever rule was that of the superseded Empire. "Paris is much less attractive than in the days of the Emperor; HE knew how to make a city pleasant," Mr. Luce had often remarked to Mrs. Touchett, who was quite of his own way of thinking and wished to know what one had crossed that odious Atlantic for but to get away from republics.

"Why, madam, sitting in the Champs Elysees, opposite to the Palace of Industry, I've seen the court-carriages from the Tuileries pass up and down as many as seven times a day. I remember one occasion when they went as high as nine. What do you see now? It's no use talking, the style's all gone. Napoleon knew what the French people want, and there'll be a dark cloud over Paris, our Paris, till they get the Empire back again."

Among Mrs. Luce's visitors on Sunday afternoons was a young man with whom Isabel had had a good deal of conversation and whom she found full of valuable knowledge. Mr. Edward Rosier—Ned Rosier as he was called—was native to New York and had been brought up in Paris, living there under the eye of his father who, as it happened, had been an early and intimate friend of the late Mr. Archer. Edward Rosier remembered Isabel as a little girl; it had been his father who came to the rescue of the small Archers at the inn at Neufchatel (he was travelling that way with the boy and had stopped at the hotel by chance), after their bonne had gone off with the Russian prince and when Mr. Archer's whereabouts remained for some days a mystery. Isabel remembered perfectly the neat little male child whose hair smelt of a delicious cosmetic and who had a bonne all his own, warranted to lose sight of him under no provocation. Isabel took a walk with the pair beside the lake and thought little Edward as pretty as an angel—a comparison by no means conventional in her mind, for she had a very definite conception of a type of features which she supposed to be angelic and which her new friend perfectly illustrated. A small pink face surmounted by a blue velvet bonnet and set off by a stiff embroidered collar had become the countenance of her childish dreams; and she had firmly believed for some time afterwards that the heavenly hosts conversed among themselves in a queer little dialect of French-English, expressing the properest sentiments, as when Edward told her that he was "defended" by his bonne to go near the edge of the lake, and that one must always obey to one's bonne. Ned Rosier's English had improved; at least it exhibited in a less degree the French variation. His father was dead and his bonne dismissed, but the young man still conformed to the spirit of their teaching—he never went to the edge of the lake. There was still something agreeable to the nostrils about him and something not offensive to nobler organs. He was a very gentle and gracious youth, with what are called cultivated tastes—an acquaintance with old china, with good wine, with the bindings of books, with the Almanach de Gotha, with the best shops, the best hotels, the hours of railway-trains. He could order a dinner almost as well as Mr. Luce, and it was probable that as his experience accumulated he would be a worthy successor to that gentleman, whose rather grim politics he also advocated in a soft and innocent voice. He had some charming rooms in Paris, decorated with old Spanish altar-lace, the envy of his female friends, who declared that his chimney-piece was better draped than the high shoulders of many a duchess. He usually, however, spent a part of every winter at Pau, and had once passed a couple of months in the United States.

He took a great interest in Isabel and remembered perfectly the walk at Neufchatel, when she would persist in going so near the edge. He seemed to recognise this same tendency in the subversive enquiry that I quoted a moment ago, and set himself to answer our heroine's question with greater urbanity than it perhaps deserved. "What does it lead to, Miss Archer? Why Paris leads everywhere. You can't go anywhere unless you come here first. Every one that comes to Europe has got to pass through. You don't mean it in that sense so much? You mean what good it does you? Well, how can you penetrate futurity? How can you tell what lies ahead? If it's a pleasant road I don't care where it leads. I like the road, Miss Archer; I like the dear old asphalte. You can't get tired of it—you can't if you try. You think you would, but you wouldn't; there's always something new and fresh. Take the Hotel Drouot, now; they sometimes have three and four sales a week. Where can you get such things as you can here? In spite of all they say I maintain they're cheaper too, if you know the right places. I know plenty of places, but I keep them to myself. I'll tell you, if you like, as a particular favour; only you mustn't tell any one else. Don't you go anywhere without asking me first; I want you to promise me that. As a general thing avoid the Boulevards; there's very little to be done on the Boulevards. Speaking conscientiously—sans blague—I don't believe any one knows Paris better than I. You and Mrs. Touchett must come and breakfast with me some day, and I'll show you my things; je ne vous dis que ca! There has been a great deal of talk about London of late; it's the fashion to cry up London. But there's nothing in it—you can't do anything in London. No Louis Quinze—nothing of the First Empire; nothing but their eternal Queen Anne. It's good for one's bed-room, Queen Anne—for one's washing-room; but it isn't proper for a salon. Do I spend my life at the auctioneer's?" Mr. Rosier pursued in answer to another question of Isabel's. "Oh no; I haven't the means. I wish I had. You think I'm a mere trifler; I can tell by the expression of your face—you've got a wonderfully expressive face. I hope you don't mind my saying that; I mean it as a kind of warning. You think I ought to do something, and so do I, so long as you leave it vague. But when you come to the point you see you have to stop. I can't go home and be a shopkeeper. You think I'm very well fitted? Ah, Miss Archer, you overrate me. I can buy very well, but I can't sell; you should see when I sometimes try to get rid of my things. It takes much more ability to make other people buy than to buy yourself. When I think how clever they must be, the people who make ME buy! Ah no; I couldn't be a shopkeeper. I can't be a doctor; it's a repulsive business. I can't be a clergyman; I haven't got convictions. And then I can't pronounce the names right in the Bible. They're very difficult, in the Old Testament particularly. I can't be a lawyer; I don't understand—how do you call it?—the American procedure. Is there anything else? There's nothing for a gentleman in America. I should like to be a diplomatist; but American diplomacy—that's not for gentlemen either. I'm sure if you had seen the last min—"

Henrietta Stackpole, who was often with her friend when Mr. Rosier, coming to pay his compliments late in the afternoon, expressed himself after the fashion I have sketched, usually interrupted the young man at this point and read him a lecture on the duties of the American citizen. She thought him most unnatural; he was worse than poor Ralph Touchett. Henrietta, however, was at this time more than ever addicted to fine criticism, for her conscience had been freshly alarmed as regards Isabel. She had not congratulated this young lady on her augmentations and begged to be excused from doing so.

"If Mr. Touchett had consulted me about leaving you the money," she frankly asserted, "I'd have said to him 'Never!"

"I see," Isabel had answered. "You think it will prove a curse in disguise. Perhaps it will."

"Leave it to some one you care less for—that's what I should have said."

"To yourself for instance?" Isabel suggested jocosely. And then, "Do you really believe it will ruin me?" she asked in quite another tone.

"I hope it won't ruin you; but it will certainly confirm your dangerous tendencies."

"Do you mean the love of luxury—of extravagance?"

"No, no," said Henrietta; "I mean your exposure on the moral side. I approve of luxury; I think we ought to be as elegant as possible. Look at the luxury of our western cities; I've seen nothing over here to compare with it. I hope you'll never become grossly sensual; but I'm not afraid of that. The peril for you is that you live too much in the world of your own dreams. You're not enough in contact with reality—with the toiling, striving, suffering, I may even say sinning, world that surrounds you. You're too fastidious; you've too many graceful illusions. Your newly-acquired thousands will shut you up more and more to the society of a few selfish and heartless people who will be interested in keeping them up."

Isabel's eyes expanded as she gazed at this lurid scene. "What are my illusions?" she asked. "I try so hard not to have any."

"Well," said Henrietta, "you think you can lead a romantic life, that you can live by pleasing yourself and pleasing others. You'll find you're mistaken. Whatever life you lead you must put your soul in it—to make any sort of success of it; and from the moment you do that it ceases to be romance, I assure you: it becomes grim reality! And you can't always please yourself; you must sometimes please other people. That, I admit, you're very ready to do; but there's another thing that's still more important—you must often displease others. You must always be ready for that—you must never shrink from it. That doesn't suit you at all—you're too fond of admiration, you like to be thought well of. You think we can escape disagreeable duties by taking romantic views—that's your great illusion, my dear. But we can't. You must be prepared on many occasions in life to please no one at all—not even yourself."

Isabel shook her head sadly; she looked troubled and frightened. "This, for you, Henrietta," she said, "must be one of those occasions!"

VOLUME I (of II) CHAPTER XX

It was certainly true that Miss Stackpole, during her visit to Paris, which had been professionally more remunerative than her English sojourn, had not been living in the world of dreams. Mr. Bantling, who had now returned to England, was her companion for the first four weeks of her stay; and about Mr. Bantling there was nothing dreamy. Isabel learned from her friend that the two had led a life of great personal intimacy and that this had been a peculiar advantage to Henrietta, owing to the gentleman's remarkable knowledge of Paris. He had explained everything, shown her everything, been her constant guide and interpreter. They had breakfasted together, dined together, gone to the theatre together, supped together, really in a manner quite lived together. He was a true friend, Henrietta more than once assured our heroine; and she had never supposed that she could like any Englishman so well. Isabel could not have told you why, but she found something that ministered to mirth in the alliance the correspondent of the Interviewer had struck with Lady Pensil's brother; her amusement moreover subsisted in face of the fact that she thought it a credit to each of them. Isabel couldn't rid herself of a suspicion that they were playing somehow at cross-purposes—that the simplicity of each had been entrapped. But this simplicity was on either side none the less honourable. It was as graceful on Henrietta's part to believe that Mr. Bantling took an interest in the diffusion of lively journalism and in consolidating the position of lady-correspondents as it was on the part of his companion to suppose that the cause of the Interviewer—a periodical of which he never formed a very definite conception—was, if subtly analysed (a task to which Mr. Bantling felt himself quite equal), but the cause of Miss Stackpole's need of demonstrative affection. Each of these groping celibates supplied at any rate a want of which the other was impatiently conscious. Mr. Bantling, who was of rather a slow and a discursive habit, relished a prompt, keen, positive woman, who charmed him by the influence of a shining, challenging eye and a kind of bandbox freshness, and who kindled a perception of raciness in a mind to which the usual fare of life seemed unsalted. Henrietta, on the other hand, enjoyed the society of a gentleman who appeared somehow, in his way, made, by expensive, roundabout, almost "quaint" processes, for her use, and whose leisured state, though generally indefensible, was a decided boon to a breathless mate, and who was furnished with an easy, traditional, though by no means exhaustive, answer to almost any social or practical question that could come up. She often found Mr. Bantling's answers very convenient, and in the press of catching the American post would largely and showily address them to publicity. It was to be feared that she was indeed drifting toward those abysses of sophistication as to which Isabel, wishing for a good-humoured retort, had warned her. There might be danger in store for Isabel; but it was scarcely to be hoped that Miss Stackpole, on her side, would find permanent rest in any adoption of the views of a class pledged to all the old abuses. Isabel continued to warn her good-humouredly; Lady Pensil's obliging brother was sometimes, on our heroine's lips, an object of irreverent and facetious allusion. Nothing, however, could exceed Henrietta's amiability on this point; she used to abound in the sense of Isabel's irony and to enumerate with elation the hours she had spent with this perfect man of the world—a term that had ceased to make with her, as previously, for opprobrium. Then, a few moments later, she would forget that they had been talking jocosely and would mention with impulsive earnestness some expedition she had enjoyed in his company. She would say: "Oh, I know all about Versailles; I went there with Mr. Bantling. I was bound to see it thoroughly—I warned him when we went out there that I was thorough: so we spent three days at the hotel and wandered all over the place. It was lovely weather—a kind of Indian summer, only not so good. We just lived in that park. Oh yes; you can't tell me anything about Versailles." Henrietta appeared to have made arrangements to meet her gallant friend during the spring in Italy.

CHAPTER XXI

Mrs. Touchett, before arriving in Paris, had fixed the day for her departure and by the middle of February had begun to travel southward. She interrupted her journey to pay a visit to her son, who at San Remo, on the Italian shore of the Mediterranean, had been spending a dull, bright winter beneath a slow-moving white umbrella. Isabel went with her aunt as a matter of course, though Mrs. Touchett, with homely, customary logic, had laid before her a pair of alternatives.

"Now, of course, you're completely your own mistress and are as free as the bird on the bough. I don't mean you were not so before, but you're at present on a different footing—property erects a kind of barrier. You can do a great many things if you're rich which would be severely criticised if you were poor. You can go and come, you can travel alone, you can have your own establishment: I mean of course if you'll take a companion—some decayed gentlewoman, with a darned cashmere and dyed hair, who paints on velvet. You don't think you'd like that? Of course you can do as you please; I only want you to understand how much you're at liberty. You might take Miss Stackpole as your dame de compagnie; she'd keep people off very well. I think, however, that it's a great deal better you should remain with me, in spite of there being no obligation. It's better for several reasons, quite apart from your liking it. I shouldn't think you'd like it, but I recommend you to make the sacrifice. Of course whatever novelty there may have been at first in my society has quite passed away, and you see me as I am—a dull, obstinate, narrow-minded old woman."

"I don't think you're at all dull," Isabel had replied to this.

"But you do think I'm obstinate and narrow-minded? I told you so!" said Mrs. Touchett with much elation at being justified.

Isabel remained for the present with her aunt, because, in spite of eccentric impulses, she had a great regard for what was usually deemed decent, and a young gentlewoman without visible relations had always struck her as a flower without foliage. It was true that Mrs. Touchett's conversation had never again appeared so brilliant as that first afternoon in Albany, when she sat in her damp waterproof and sketched the opportunities that Europe would offer to a young person of taste. This, however, was in a great measure the girl's own fault; she had got a glimpse of her aunt's experience, and her imagination constantly anticipated the judgements and emotions of a woman who had very little of the same faculty. Apart from this, Mrs. Touchett had a great merit; she was as honest as a pair of compasses. There was a comfort in her stiffness and firmness; you knew exactly where to find her and were never liable to chance encounters and concussions. On her own ground she was perfectly present, but was never over-inquisitive as regards the territory of her neighbour. Isabel came at last to have a kind of undemonstrable pity for her; there seemed something so dreary in the condition of a person whose nature had, as it were, so little surface—offered so limited a face to the accretions of human contact. Nothing tender, nothing sympathetic, had ever had a chance to fasten upon it—no wind-sown blossom, no familiar softening moss. Her offered, her passive extent, in other words, was about that of a knife-edge. Isabel had reason to believe none the less that as she advanced in life she made more of those concessions to the sense of something obscurely distinct from convenience—more of them than she independently exacted. She was learning to sacrifice consistency to considerations of that inferior order for which the excuse must be found in the particular case. It was not to the credit of her absolute rectitude that she should have gone the longest way round to Florence in order to spend a few weeks with her invalid son; since in former years it had been one of her most definite convictions that when Ralph wished to see her he was at liberty to remember that Palazzo Crescentini contained a large apartment known as the quarter of the signorino.

"I want to ask you something," Isabel said to this young man the day after her arrival at San Remo—"something I've thought more than once of asking you by letter, but that I've hesitated on the whole to write about. Face to face, nevertheless, my question seems easy enough. Did you know your father intended to leave me so much money?"

Ralph stretched his legs a little further than usual and gazed a little more fixedly at the Mediterranean.

"What does it matter, my dear Isabel, whether I knew? My father was very obstinate."

"So," said the girl, "you did know."

"Yes; he told me. We even talked it over a little." "What did he do it for?" asked Isabel abruptly. "Why, as a kind of compliment."

"A compliment on what?"

"On your so beautifully existing."

"He liked me too much," she presently declared.

"That's a way we all have."

"If I believed that I should be very unhappy. Fortunately I don't believe it. I want to be treated with justice; I want nothing but that."

"Very good. But you must remember that justice to a lovely being is after all a florid sort of sentiment."

"I'm not a lovely being. How can you say that, at the very moment when I'm asking such odious questions? I must seem to you delicate!"

"You seem to me troubled," said Ralph.

"I am troubled."

"About what?"

For a moment she answered nothing; then she broke out: "Do you think it good for me suddenly to be made so rich? Henrietta doesn't."

"Oh, hang Henrietta!" said Ralph coarsely, "If you ask me I'm delighted at it."

"Is that why your father did it—for your amusement?"

"I differ with Miss Stackpole," Ralph went on more gravely. "I think it very good for you to have means."

Isabel looked at him with serious eyes. "I wonder whether you know what's good for me—or whether you care."

"If I know depend upon it I care. Shall I tell you what it is? Not to torment yourself."

"Not to torment you, I suppose you mean."

"You can't do that; I'm proof. Take things more easily. Don't ask yourself so much whether this or that is good for you. Don't question your conscience so much—it will get out of tune like a strummed piano. Keep it for great occasions. Don't try so much to form your character—it's like trying to pull open a tight, tender young rose. Live as you like best, and your character will take care of itself. Most things are good for you; the exceptions are very rare, and a comfortable income's not one of them." Ralph paused, smiling; Isabel had listened quickly. "You've too much power of thought—above all too much conscience," Ralph added. "It's out of all reason, the number of things you think wrong. Put back your watch. Diet your fever. Spread your wings; rise above the ground. It's never wrong to do that."

She had listened eagerly, as I say; and it was her nature to understand quickly. "I wonder if you appreciate what you say. If you do, you take a great responsibility."

"You frighten me a little, but I think I'm right," said Ralph, persisting in cheer.

"All the same what you say is very true," Isabel pursued. "You could say nothing more true. I'm absorbed in myself—I look at life too much as a doctor's prescription. Why indeed should we perpetually be thinking whether things are good for us, as if we were patients lying in a hospital? Why should I be so afraid of not doing right? As if it mattered to the world whether I do right or wrong!"

"You're a capital person to advise," said Ralph; "you take the wind out of my sails!"

She looked at him as if she had not heard him—though she was following out the train of reflexion which he himself had kindled. "I try to care more about the world than about myself—but I always come back to myself. It's because I'm afraid." She stopped; her voice had trembled a little. "Yes, I'm afraid; I can't tell you. A large fortune means freedom, and I'm afraid of that. It's such a fine thing, and one should make such a good use of it. If one shouldn't one would be ashamed. And one must keep thinking; it's a constant effort. I'm not sure it's not a greater happiness to be powerless."

"For weak people I've no doubt it's a greater happiness. For weak people the effort not to be contemptible must be great."

"And how do you know I'm not weak?" Isabel asked.

"Ah," Ralph answered with a flush that the girl noticed, "if you are I'm awfully sold!"

The charm of the Mediterranean coast only deepened for our heroine on acquaintance, for it was the threshold of Italy, the gate of admirations. Italy, as yet imperfectly seen and felt, stretched before her as a land of promise, a land in which a love of the beautiful might be comforted by endless knowledge. Whenever she strolled upon the shore with her cousin—and she was the companion of his daily walk—she looked across the sea, with longing eyes, to where she knew that Genoa lay. She was glad to pause, however, on the edge of this larger adventure; there was such a thrill even in the preliminary hovering. It affected her moreover as a peaceful interlude, as a hush of the drum and fife in a career which she had little warrant as yet for regarding as agitated, but which nevertheless she was constantly picturing to herself by the light of her hopes, her fears, her fancies, her ambitions, her predilections, and which reflected these subjective accidents in a manner sufficiently dramatic. Madame Merle had predicted to Mrs. Touchett that after their young friend had put her hand into her pocket half a dozen times she would be reconciled to the idea that it had been filled by a munificent uncle; and the event justified, as it had so often justified before, that lady's perspicacity. Ralph Touchett had praised his cousin for being morally inflammable, that is for being quick to take a hint that was meant as good advice. His advice had perhaps helped the matter; she had at any rate before leaving San Remo grown used to feeling rich. The consciousness in question found a proper place in rather a dense little group of ideas that she had about herself, and often it was by no means the least agreeable. It took perpetually for granted a thousand good intentions. She lost herself in a maze of visions; the fine things to be done by a rich, independent, generous girl who took a large human view of occasions and obligations were sublime in the mass. Her fortune therefore became to her mind a part of her better self; it gave her importance, gave her even, to her own imagination, a certain ideal beauty. What it did for her in the imagination of others is another affair, and on this point we must also touch in time. The visions I have just spoken of were mixed with other debates. Isabel liked better to think of the future than of the past; but at times, as she listened to the murmur of the Mediterranean waves, her glance took a backward flight. It rested upon two figures which, in spite of increasing distance, were still sufficiently salient; they were recognisable without difficulty as those of Caspar Goodwood and Lord Warburton. It was strange how quickly these images of energy had fallen into the background of our young lady's life. It was in her disposition at all times to lose faith in the reality of absent things; she could summon back her faith, in case of need, with an effort, but the effort was often painful even when the reality had been pleasant. The past was apt to look dead and its revival rather to show the livid light of a judgement-day. The girl moreover was not prone to take for granted that she herself lived in the mind of others—she had not the fatuity to believe she left indelible traces. She was capable of being wounded by the discovery that she had been forgotten; but of all liberties the one she herself found sweetest was the liberty to forget. She had not given her last shilling, sentimentally speaking, either to Caspar Goodwood or to Lord Warburton, and yet couldn't but feel them appreciably in debt to her. She had of course reminded herself that she was to hear from Mr. Goodwood again; but this was not to be for another year and a half, and in that time a great many things might happen. She had indeed failed to say to herself that her American suitor might find some other girl more comfortable to woo; because, though it was certain many other girls would prove so, she had not the smallest belief that this merit would attract him. But she reflected that she herself might know the humiliation of change, might really, for that matter, come to the end of the things that were not Caspar (even though there appeared so many of them), and find rest in those very elements of his presence which struck her now as impediments to the finer respiration. It was conceivable that these impediments should some day prove a sort of blessing in disguise—a clear and quiet harbour enclosed by a brave granite breakwater. But that day could only come in its order, and she couldn't wait for it with folded hands. That Lord Warburton should continue to cherish her image seemed to her more than a noble humility or an enlightened pride ought to wish to reckon with. She had so definitely undertaken to preserve no record of what had passed between them that a corresponding effort on his own part would be eminently just. This was not, as it may seem, merely a theory tinged with sarcasm. Isabel candidly believed that his lordship would, in the usual phrase, get over his disappointment. He had been deeply affected—this she believed, and she was still capable of deriving pleasure from the belief; but it was absurd that a man both so intelligent and so honourably dealt with should cultivate a scar out of proportion to any wound. Englishmen liked moreover to be comfortable, said Isabel, and there could be little comfort for Lord Warburton, in the long run, in brooding over a self-sufficient American girl who had been but a casual acquaintance. She flattered herself that, should she hear from one day to another that he had married some young woman of his own country who had done more to deserve him, she should receive the news without a pang even of surprise. It would have proved that he believed she was firm—which was what she wished to seem to him. That alone was grateful to her pride.

CHAPTER XXII

On one of the first days of May, some six months after old Mr. Touchett's death, a small group that might have been described by a painter as composing well was gathered in one of the many rooms of an ancient villa crowning an olive-muffled hill outside of the Roman gate of Florence. The villa was a long, rather blank-looking structure, with the far-projecting roof which Tuscany loves and which, on the hills that encircle Florence, when considered from a distance, makes so harmonious a rectangle with the straight, dark, definite cypresses that usually rise in groups of three or four beside it. The house had a front upon a little grassy, empty, rural piazza which occupied a part of the hill-top; and this front, pierced with a few windows in irregular relations and furnished with a stone bench lengthily adjusted to the base of the structure and useful as a lounging-place to one or two persons wearing more or less of that air of undervalued merit which in Italy, for some reason or other, always gracefully invests any one who confidently assumes a perfectly passive attitude—this antique, solid, weather-worn, yet imposing front had a somewhat incommunicative character. It was the mask, not the face of the house. It had heavy lids, but no eyes; the house in reality looked another way—looked off behind, into splendid openness and the range of the afternoon light. In that quarter the villa overhung the slope of its hill and the long valley of the Arno, hazy with Italian colour. It had a narrow garden, in the manner of a terrace, productive chiefly of tangles of wild roses and other old stone benches, mossy and sun-warmed. The parapet of the terrace was just the height to lean upon, and beneath it the ground declined into the vagueness of olive-crops and vineyards. It is not, however, with the outside of the place that we are concerned; on this bright morning of ripened spring its tenants had reason to prefer the shady side of the wall. The windows of the ground-floor, as you saw them from the piazza, were, in their noble proportions, extremely architectural; but their function seemed less to offer communication with the world than to defy the world to look in. They were massively cross-barred, and placed at such a height that curiosity, even on tiptoe, expired before it reached them. In an apartment lighted by a row of three of these jealous apertures—one of the several distinct apartments into which the villa was divided and which were mainly occupied by foreigners of random race long resident in Florence—a gentleman was seated in company with a young girl and two good sisters from a religious house. The room was, however, less sombre than our indications may have represented, for it had a wide, high door, which now stood open into the tangled garden behind; and the tall iron lattices admitted on occasion more than enough of the Italian sunshine. It was moreover a seat of ease, indeed of luxury, telling of arrangements subtly studied and refinements frankly proclaimed, and containing a variety of those faded hangings of damask and tapestry, those chests and cabinets of carved and time-polished oak, those angular specimens of pictorial art in frames as pedantically primitive, those perverse-looking relics of medieval brass and pottery, of which Italy has long been the not quite exhausted storehouse. These things kept terms with articles of modern furniture in which large allowance had been made for a lounging generation; it was to be noticed that all the chairs were deep and well padded and that much space was occupied by a writing-table of which the ingenious perfection bore the stamp of London and the nineteenth century. There were books in profusion and magazines and newspapers, and a few small, odd, elaborate pictures, chiefly in water-colour. One of these productions stood on a drawing-room easel before which, at the moment we begin to be concerned with her, the young girl I have mentioned had placed herself. She was looking at the picture in silence.

Silence—absolute silence—had not fallen upon her companions; but their talk had an appearance of embarrassed continuity. The two good sisters had not settled themselves in their respective chairs; their attitude expressed a final reserve and their faces showed the glaze of prudence. They were plain, ample, mild-featured women, with a kind of business-like modesty to which the impersonal aspect of their stiffened linen and of the serge that draped them as if nailed on frames gave an advantage. One of them, a person of a certain age, in spectacles, with a fresh complexion and a full cheek, had a more discriminating manner than her colleague, as well as the responsibility of their errand, which apparently related to the young girl. This object of interest wore her hat—an ornament of extreme simplicity and not at variance with her plain muslin gown, too short for her years, though it must already have been "let out." The gentleman who might have been supposed to be entertaining the two nuns was perhaps conscious of the difficulties of his function, it being in its way as arduous to converse with the very meek as with the very mighty. At the same time he was clearly much occupied with their quiet charge, and while she turned her back to him his eyes rested gravely on her slim, small figure. He was a man of forty, with a high but well-shaped head, on which the hair, still dense, but prematurely grizzled, had been cropped close. He had a fine, narrow, extremely modelled and composed face, of which the only fault was just this effect of its running a trifle too much to points; an appearance to which the shape of the beard contributed not a little. This beard, cut in the manner of the portraits of the sixteenth century and surmounted by a fair moustache, of which the ends had a romantic upward flourish, gave its wearer a foreign, traditionary look and suggested that he was a gentleman who studied style. His conscious, curious eyes, however, eyes at once vague and penetrating, intelligent and hard, expressive of the observer as well as of the dreamer, would have assured you that he studied it only within well-chosen limits, and that in so far as he sought it he found it. You would have been much at a loss to determine his original clime and country; he had none of the superficial signs that usually render the answer to this question an insipidly easy one. If he had English blood in his veins it had probably received some French or Italian commixture; but he suggested, fine gold coin as he was, no stamp nor emblem of the common mintage that provides for general circulation; he was the elegant complicated medal struck off for a special occasion. He had a light, lean, rather languid-looking figure, and was apparently neither tall nor short. He was dressed as a man dresses who takes little other trouble about it than to have no vulgar things.

"Well, my dear, what do you think of it?" he asked of the young girl. He used the Italian tongue, and used it with perfect ease; but this would not have convinced you he was Italian.

The child turned her head earnestly to one side and the other. "It's very pretty, papa. Did you make it yourself?"

"Certainly I made it. Don't you think I'm clever?"

"Yes, papa, very clever; I also have learned to make pictures." And she turned round and showed a small, fair face painted with a fixed and intensely sweet smile.

"You should have brought me a specimen of your powers."

"I've brought a great many; they're in my trunk."

"She draws very—very carefully," the elder of the nuns remarked, speaking in French.

"I'm glad to hear it. Is it you who have instructed her?"

"Happily no," said the good sister, blushing a little. "Ce n'est pas ma partie. I teach nothing; I leave that to those who are wiser. We've an excellent drawing-master, Mr.—Mr.—what is his name?" she asked of her companion.

Her companion looked about at the carpet. "It's a German name," she said in Italian, as if it needed to be translated.

"Yes," the other went on, "he's a German, and we've had him many years."

The young girl, who was not heeding the conversation, had wandered away to the open door of the large room and stood looking into the garden. "And you, my sister, are French," said the gentleman.

"Yes, sir," the visitor gently replied. "I speak to the pupils in my own tongue. I know no other. But we have sisters of other countries—English, German, Irish. They all speak their proper language."

The gentleman gave a smile. "Has my daughter been under the care of one of the Irish ladies?" And then, as he saw that his visitors suspected a joke, though failing to understand it, "You're very complete," he instantly added.

"Oh, yes, we're complete. We've everything, and everything's of the best."

"We have gymnastics," the Italian sister ventured to remark. "But not dangerous."

"I hope not. Is that YOUR branch?" A question which provoked much candid hilarity on the part of the two ladies; on the subsidence of which their entertainer, glancing at his daughter, remarked that she had grown.

"Yes, but I think she has finished. She'll remain—not big," said the French sister.

"I'm not sorry. I prefer women like books—very good and not too long. But I know," the gentleman said, "no particular reason why my child should be short."

The nun gave a temperate shrug, as if to intimate that such things might be beyond our knowledge. "She's in very good health; that's the best thing."

"Yes, she looks sound." And the young girl's father watched her a moment. "What do you see in the garden?" he asked in French.

"I see many flowers," she replied in a sweet, small voice and with an accent as good as his own.

"Yes, but not many good ones. However, such as they are, go out and gather some for ces dames."

The child turned to him with her smile heightened by pleasure. "May I, truly?"

"Ah, when I tell you," said her father.

The girl glanced at the elder of the nuns. "May I, truly, ma mere?"

"Obey monsieur your father, my child," said the sister, blushing again.

The child, satisfied with this authorisation, descended from the threshold and was presently lost to sight. "You don't spoil them," said her father gaily.

"For everything they must ask leave. That's our system. Leave is freely granted, but they must ask it."

"Oh, I don't quarrel with your system; I've no doubt it's excellent. I sent you my daughter to see what you'd make of her. I had faith."

"One must have faith," the sister blandly rejoined, gazing through her spectacles.

"Well, has my faith been rewarded What have you made of her?"

The sister dropped her eyes a moment. "A good Christian, monsieur."

Her host dropped his eyes as well; but it was probable that the movement had in each case a different spring. "Yes, and what else?"

He watched the lady from the convent, probably thinking she would say that a good Christian was everything; but for all her simplicity she was not so crude as that. "A charming young lady—a real little woman—a daughter in whom you will have nothing but contentment."

"She seems to me very gentille," said the father. "She's really pretty."

"She's perfect. She has no faults."

"She never had any as a child, and I'm glad you have given her none."

"We love her too much," said the spectacled sister with dignity.

"And as for faults, how can we give what we have not? Le couvent n'est pas comme le monde, monsieur. She's our daughter, as you may say. We've had her since she was so small."

"Of all those we shall lose this year she's the one we shall miss most," the younger woman murmured deferentially.

"Ah, yes, we shall talk long of her," said the other. "We shall hold her up to the new ones." And at this the good sister appeared to find her spectacles dim; while her companion, after fumbling a moment, presently drew forth a pocket-handkerchief of durable texture.

"It's not certain you'll lose her; nothing's settled yet," their host rejoined quickly; not as if to anticipate their tears, but in the tone of a man saying what was most agreeable to himself. "We should be very happy to believe that. Fifteen is very young to leave us."

"Oh," exclaimed the gentleman with more vivacity than he had yet used, "it is not I who wish to take her away. I wish you could keep her always!"

"Ah, monsieur," said the elder sister, smiling and getting up, "good as she is, she's made for the world. Le monde y gagnera."

"If all the good people were hidden away in convents how would the world get on?" her companion softly enquired, rising also.

This was a question of a wider bearing than the good woman apparently supposed; and the lady in spectacles took a harmonising view by saying comfortably: "Fortunately there are good people everywhere."

"If you're going there will be two less here," her host remarked gallantly.

For this extravagant sally his simple visitors had no answer, and they simply looked at each other in decent deprecation; but their confusion was speedily covered by the return of the young girl with two large bunches of roses—one of them all white, the other red.

"I give you your choice, mamman Catherine," said the child. "It's only the colour that's different, mamman Justine; there are just as many roses in one bunch as in the other."

The two sisters turned to each other, smiling and hesitating, with "Which will you take?" and "No, it's for you to choose."

"I'll take the red, thank you," said Catherine in the spectacles. "I'm so red myself. They'll comfort us on our way back to Rome."

"Ah, they won't last," cried the young girl. "I wish I could give you something that would last!"

"You've given us a good memory of yourself, my daughter. That will last!"

"I wish nuns could wear pretty things. I would give you my blue beads," the child went on.

"And do you go back to Rome to-night?" her father enquired.

"Yes, we take the train again. We've so much to do la-bas."

"Are you not tired?"

"We are never tired."

"Ah, my sister, sometimes," murmured the junior votaress.

"Not to-day, at any rate. We have rested too well here. Que Dieu vows garde, ma fine."

Their host, while they exchanged kisses with his daughter, went forward to open the door through which they were to pass; but as he did so he gave a slight exclamation, and stood looking beyond. The door opened into a vaulted ante-chamber, as high as a chapel and paved with red tiles; and into this antechamber a lady had just been admitted by a servant, a lad in shabby livery, who was now ushering her toward the apartment in which our friends were grouped. The gentleman at the door, after dropping his exclamation, remained silent; in silence too the lady advanced. He gave her no further audible greeting and offered her no hand, but stood aside to let her pass into the saloon. At the threshold she hesitated. "Is there any one?" she asked.

"Some one you may see."

She went in and found herself confronted with the two nuns and their pupil, who was coming forward, between them, with a hand in the arm of each. At the sight of the new visitor they all paused, and the lady, who had also stopped, stood looking at them. The young girl gave a little soft cry: "Ah, Madame Merle!"

The visitor had been slightly startled, but her manner the next instant was none the less gracious. "Yes, it's Madame Merle, come to welcome you home." And she held out two hands to the girl, who immediately came up to her, presenting her forehead to be kissed. Madame Merle saluted this portion of her charming little person and then stood smiling at the two nuns. They acknowledged her smile with a decent obeisance, but permitted themselves no direct scrutiny of this imposing, brilliant woman, who seemed to bring in with her something of the radiance of the outer world. "These ladies have brought my daughter home, and now they return to the convent," the gentleman explained.

"Ah, you go back to Rome? I've lately come from there. It's very lovely now," said Madame Merle.

The good sisters, standing with their hands folded into their sleeves, accepted this statement uncritically; and the master of the house asked his new visitor how long it was since she had left Rome. "She came to see me at the convent," said the young girl before the lady addressed had time to reply.

"I've been more than once, Pansy," Madame Merle declared. "Am I not your great friend in Rome?"

"I remember the last time best," said Pansy, "because you told me I should come away."

"Did you tell her that?" the child's father asked.

"I hardly remember. I told her what I thought would please her. I've been in Florence a week. I hoped you would come to see me."

"I should have done so if I had known you were there. One doesn't know such things by inspiration—though I suppose one ought. You had better sit down."

These two speeches were made in a particular tone of voice—a tone half-lowered and carefully quiet, but as from habit rather than from any definite need. Madame Merle looked about her, choosing her seat. "You're going to the door with these women? Let me of course not interrupt the ceremony. Je vous salue, mesdames," she added, in French, to the nuns, as if to dismiss them.

"This lady's a great friend of ours; you will have seen her at the convent," said their entertainer. "We've much faith in her judgement, and she'll help me to decide whether my daughter shall return to you at the end of the holidays."

"I hope you'll decide in our favour, madame," the sister in spectacles ventured to remark.

"That's Mr. Osmond's pleasantry; I decide nothing," said Madame Merle, but also as in pleasantry. "I believe you've a very good school, but Miss Osmond's friends must remember that she's very naturally meant for the world."

"That's what I've told monsieur," sister Catherine answered. "It's precisely to fit her for the world," she murmured, glancing at Pansy, who stood, at a little distance, attentive to Madame Merle's elegant apparel.

"Do you hear that, Pansy? You're very naturally meant for the world," said Pansy's father.

The child fixed him an instant with her pure young eyes. "Am I not meant for you, papa?"

Papa gave a quick, light laugh. "That doesn't prevent it! I'm of the world, Pansy."

"Kindly permit us to retire," said sister Catherine. "Be good and wise and happy in any case, my daughter."

"I shall certainly come back and see you," Pansy returned, recommencing her embraces, which were presently interrupted by Madame Merle.

"Stay with me, dear child," she said, "while your father takes the good ladies to the door."

Pansy stared, disappointed, yet not protesting. She was evidently impregnated with the idea of submission, which was due to any one who took the tone of authority; and she was a passive spectator of the operation of her fate. "May I not see mamman Catherine get into the carriage?" she nevertheless asked very gently.

"It would please me better if you'd remain with me," said Madame Merle, while Mr. Osmond and his companions, who had bowed low again to the other visitor, passed into the ante-chamber.

"Oh yes, I'll stay," Pansy answered; and she stood near Madame Merle, surrendering her little hand, which this lady took. She stared out of the window; her eyes had filled with tears.

"I'm glad they've taught you to obey," said Madame Merle. "That's what good little girls should do."

"Oh yes, I obey very well," cried Pansy with soft eagerness, almost with boastfulness, as if she had been speaking of her piano-playing. And then she gave a faint, just audible sigh.

Madame Merle, holding her hand, drew it across her own fine palm and looked at it. The gaze was critical, but it found nothing to deprecate; the child's small hand was delicate and fair. "I hope they always see that you wear gloves," she said in a moment. "Little girls usually dislike them."

"I used to dislike them, but I like them now," the child made answer.

"Very good, I'll make you a present of a dozen."

"I thank you very much. What colours will they be?" Pansy demanded with interest.

Madame Merle meditated. "Useful colours."

"But very pretty?"

"Are you very fond of pretty things?"

"Yes; but—but not too fond," said Pansy with a trace of asceticism.

"Well, they won't be too pretty," Madame Merle returned with a laugh. She took the child's other hand and drew her nearer; after which, looking at her a moment, "Shall you miss mother Catherine?" she went on.

"Yes—when I think of her."

"Try then not to think of her. Perhaps some day," added Madame Merle, "you'll have another mother."

"I don't think that's necessary," Pansy said, repeating her little soft conciliatory sigh. "I had more than thirty mothers at the convent."

Her father's step sounded again in the antechamber, and Madame Merle got up, releasing the child. Mr. Osmond came in and closed the door; then, without looking at Madame Merle, he pushed one or two chairs back into their places. His visitor waited a moment for him to speak, watching him as he moved about. Then at last she said: "I hoped you'd have come to Rome. I thought it possible you'd have wished yourself to fetch Pansy away."

"That was a natural supposition; but I'm afraid it's not the first time I've acted in defiance of your calculations."

"Yes," said Madame Merle, "I think you very perverse."

Mr. Osmond busied himself for a moment in the room—there was plenty of space in it to move about—in the fashion of a man mechanically seeking pretexts for not giving an attention which may be embarrassing. Presently, however, he had exhausted his pretexts; there was nothing left for him—unless he took up a book—but to stand with his hands behind him looking at Pansy. "Why didn't you come and see the last of mamman Catherine?" he asked of her abruptly in French.

Pansy hesitated a moment, glancing at Madame Merle. "I asked her to stay with me," said this lady, who had seated herself again in another place.

"Ah, that was better," Osmond conceded. With which he dropped into a chair and sat looking at Madame Merle; bent forward a little, his elbows on the edge of the arms and his hands interlocked.

"She's going to give me some gloves," said Pansy.

"You needn't tell that to every one, my dear," Madame Merle observed.

"You're very kind to her," said Osmond. "She's supposed to have everything she needs."

"I should think she had had enough of the nuns."

"If we're going to discuss that matter she had better go out of the room."

"Let her stay," said Madame Merle. "We'll talk of something else."

"If you like I won't listen," Pansy suggested with an appearance of candour which imposed conviction.

"You may listen, charming child, because you won't understand," her father replied. The child sat down, deferentially, near the open door, within sight of the garden, into which she directed her innocent, wistful eyes; and Mr. Osmond went on irrelevantly, addressing himself to his other companion. "You're looking particularly well."

"I think I always look the same," said Madame Merle.

"You always ARE the same. You don't vary. You're a wonderful woman."

"Yes, I think I am."

"You sometimes change your mind, however. You told me on your return from England that you wouldn't leave Rome again for the present."

"I'm pleased that you remember so well what I say. That was my intention. But I've come to Florence to meet some friends who have lately arrived and as to whose movements I was at that time uncertain."

"That reason's characteristic. You're always doing something for your friends."

Madame Merle smiled straight at her host. "It's less characteristic than your comment upon it which is perfectly insincere. I don't, however, make a crime of that," she added, "because if you don't believe what you say there's no reason why you should. I don't ruin myself for my friends; I don't deserve your praise. I care greatly for myself."

"Exactly; but yourself includes so many other selves—so much of every one else and of everything. I never knew a person whose life touched so many other lives."

"What do you call one's life?" asked Madame Merle. "One's appearance, one's movements, one's engagements, one's society?"

"I call YOUR life your ambitions," said Osmond.

Madame Merle looked a moment at Pansy. "I wonder if she understands that," she murmured.

"You see she can't stay with us!" And Pansy's father gave rather a joyless smile. "Go into the garden, mignonne, and pluck a flower or two for Madame Merle," he went on in French.

"That's just what I wanted to do," Pansy exclaimed, rising with promptness and noiselessly departing. Her father followed her to the open door, stood a moment watching her, and then came back, but remained standing, or rather strolling to and fro, as if to cultivate a sense of freedom which in another attitude might be wanting.

"My ambitions are principally for you," said Madame Merle, looking up at him with a certain courage.

"That comes back to what I say. I'm part of your life—I and a thousand others. You're not selfish—I can't admit that. If you were selfish, what should I be? What epithet would properly describe me?"

"You're indolent. For me that's your worst fault."

"I'm afraid it's really my best."

"You don't care," said Madame Merle gravely.

"No; I don't think I care much. What sort of a fault do you call that? My indolence, at any rate, was one of the reasons I didn't go to Rome. But it was only one of them."

"It's not of importance—to me at least—that you didn't go; though I should have been glad to see you. I'm glad you're not in Rome now—which you might be, would probably be, if you had gone there a month ago. There's something I should like you to do at present in Florence."

"Please remember my indolence," said Osmond.

"I do remember it; but I beg you to forget it. In that way you'll have both the virtue and the reward. This is not a great labour, and it may prove a real interest. How long is it since you made a new acquaintance?"

"I don't think I've made any since I made yours."

"It's time then you should make another. There's a friend of mine I want you to know."

Mr. Osmond, in his walk, had gone back to the open door again and was looking at his daughter as she moved about in the intense sunshine. "What good will it do me?" he asked with a sort of genial crudity.

Madame Merle waited. "It will amuse you." There was nothing crude in this rejoinder; it had been thoroughly well considered.

"If you say that, you know, I believe it," said Osmond, coming toward her. "There are some points in which my confidence in you is complete. I'm perfectly aware, for instance, that you know good society from bad."

"Society is all bad."

"Pardon me. That isn't—the knowledge I impute to you—a common sort of wisdom. You've gained it in the right way—experimentally; you've compared an immense number of more or less impossible people with each other."

"Well, I invite you to profit by my knowledge."

"To profit? Are you very sure that I shall?"

"It's what I hope. It will depend on yourself. If I could only induce you to make an effort!"

"Ah, there you are! I knew something tiresome was coming. What in the world—that's likely to turn up here—is worth an effort?"

Madame Merle flushed as with a wounded intention. "Don't be foolish, Osmond. No one knows better than you what IS worth an effort. Haven't I seen you in old days?"

"I recognise some things. But they're none of them probable in this poor life."

"It's the effort that makes them probable," said Madame Merle.

"There's something in that. Who then is your friend?"

"The person I came to Florence to see. She's a niece of Mrs. Touchett, whom you'll not have forgotten."

"A niece? The word niece suggests youth and ignorance. I see what you're coming to."

"Yes, she's young—twenty-three years old. She's a great friend of mine. I met her for the first time in England, several months ago, and we struck up a grand alliance. I like her immensely, and I do what I don't do every day—I admire her. You'll do the same."

"Not if I can help it."

"Precisely. But you won't be able to help it."

"Is she beautiful, clever, rich, splendid, universally intelligent and unprecedentedly virtuous? It's only on those conditions that I care to make her acquaintance. You know I asked you some time ago never to speak to me of a creature who shouldn't correspond to that description. I know plenty of dingy people; I don't want to know any more."

"Miss Archer isn't dingy; she's as bright as the morning. She corresponds to your description; it's for that I wish you to know her. She fills all your requirements."

"More or less, of course."

"No; quite literally. She's beautiful, accomplished, generous and, for an American, well-born. She's also very clever and very amiable, and she has a handsome fortune."

Mr. Osmond listened to this in silence, appearing to turn it over in his mind with his eyes on his informant. "What do you want to do with her?" he asked at last.

"What you see. Put her in your way."

"Isn't she meant for something better than that?"

"I don't pretend to know what people are meant for," said Madame Merle. "I only know what I can do with them."

"I'm sorry for Miss Archer!" Osmond declared.

Madame Merle got up. "If that's a beginning of interest in her I take note of it."

The two stood there face to face; she settled her mantilla, looking down at it as she did so. "You're looking very well," Osmond repeated still less relevantly than before. "You have some idea. You're never so well as when you've got an idea; they're always becoming to you."

In the manner and tone of these two persons, on first meeting at any juncture, and especially when they met in the presence of others, was something indirect and circumspect, as if they had approached each other obliquely and addressed each other by implication. The effect of each appeared to be to intensify to an appreciable degree the self-consciousness of the other. Madame Merle of course carried off any embarrassment better than her friend; but even Madame Merle had not on this occasion the form she would have liked to have—the perfect self-possession she would have wished to wear for her host. The point to be made is, however, that at a certain moment the element between them, whatever it was, always levelled itself and left them more closely face to face than either ever was with any one else. This was what had happened now. They stood there knowing each other well and each on the whole willing to accept the satisfaction of knowing as a compensation for the inconvenience—whatever it might be—of being known. "I wish very much you were not so heartless," Madame Merle quietly said. "It has always been against you, and it will be against you now."

"I'm not so heartless as you think. Every now and then something touches me—as for instance your saying just now that your ambitions are for me. I don't understand it; I don't see how or why they should be. But it touches me, all the same."

"You'll probably understand it even less as time goes on. There are some things you'll never understand. There's no particular need you should."

"You, after all, are the most remarkable of women," said Osmond. "You have more in you than almost any one. I don't see why you think Mrs. Touchett's niece should matter very much to me, when—when—" But he paused a moment.

"When I myself have mattered so little?"

"That of course is not what I meant to say. When I've known and appreciated such a woman as you."

"Isabel Archer's better than I," said Madame Merle.

Her companion gave a laugh. "How little you must think of her to say that!"

"Do you suppose I'm capable of jealousy? Please answer me that."

"With regard to me? No; on the whole I don't."

"Come and see me then, two days hence. I'm staying at Mrs. Touchett's—Palazzo Crescentini—and the girl will be there."

"Why didn't you ask me that at first simply, without speaking of the girl?" said Osmond. "You could have had her there at any rate."

Madame Merle looked at him in the manner of a woman whom no question he could ever put would find unprepared. "Do you wish to know why? Because I've spoken of you to her."

Osmond frowned and turned away. "I'd rather not know that." Then in a moment he pointed out the easel supporting the little water-colour drawing. "Have you seen what's there—my last?"

Madame Merle drew near and considered. "Is it the Venetian Alps—one of your last year's sketches?"

"Yes—but how you guess everything!"

She looked a moment longer, then turned away. "You know I don't care for your drawings."

"I know it, yet I'm always surprised at it. They're really so much better than most people's."

"That may very well be. But as the only thing you do—well, it's so little. I should have liked you to do so many other things: those were my ambitions."

"Yes; you've told me many times—things that were impossible."

"Things that were impossible," said Madame Merle. And then in quite a different tone: "In itself your little picture's very good." She looked about the room—at the old cabinets, pictures, tapestries, surfaces of faded silk. "Your rooms at least are perfect. I'm struck with that afresh whenever I come back; I know none better anywhere. You understand this sort of thing as nobody anywhere does. You've such adorable taste."

"I'm sick of my adorable taste," said Gilbert Osmond.

"You must nevertheless let Miss Archer come and see it. I've told her about it."

"I don't object to showing my things—when people are not idiots."

"You do it delightfully. As cicerone of your museum you appear to particular advantage."

Mr. Osmond, in return for this compliment, simply looked at once colder and more attentive. "Did you say she was rich?"

"She has seventy thousand pounds."

"En ecus bien comptes?"

"There's no doubt whatever about her fortune. I've seen it, as I may say."

"Satisfactory woman!—I mean you. And if I go to see her shall I see the mother?"

"The mother? She has none—nor father either."

"The aunt then—whom did you say?—Mrs. Touchett. I can easily keep her out of the way."

"I don't object to her," said Osmond; "I rather like Mrs. Touchett. She has a sort of old-fashioned character that's passing away—a vivid identity. But that long jackanapes the son—is he about the place?"

"He's there, but he won't trouble you."

"He's a good deal of a donkey."

"I think you're mistaken. He's a very clever man. But he's not fond of being about when I'm there, because he doesn't like me."

"What could he be more asinine than that? Did you say she has looks?" Osmond went on.

"Yes; but I won't say it again, lest you should be disappointed in them. Come and make a beginning; that's all I ask of you."

"A beginning of what?"

Madame Merle was silent a little. "I want you of course to marry her."

"The beginning of the end? Well, I'll see for myself. Have you told her that?"

"For what do you take me? She's not so coarse a piece of machinery—nor am I."

"Really," said Osmond after some meditation, "I don't understand your ambitions."

"I think you'll understand this one after you've seen Miss Archer. Suspend your judgement." Madame Merle, as she spoke, had drawn near the open door of the garden, where she stood a moment looking out. "Pansy has really grown pretty," she presently added.

"So it seemed to me."

"But she has had enough of the convent."

"I don't know," said Osmond. "I like what they've made of her. It's very charming."

"That's not the convent. It's the child's nature."

"It's the combination, I think. She's as pure as a pearl."

"Why doesn't she come back with my flowers then?" Madame Merle asked. "She's not in a hurry."

"We'll go and get them."

"She doesn't like me," the visitor murmured as she raised her parasol and they passed into the garden.

CHAPTER XXIII

Madame Merle, who had come to Florence on Mrs. Touchett's arrival at the invitation of this lady—Mrs. Touchett offering her for a month the hospitality of Palazzo Crescentini—the judicious Madame Merle spoke to Isabel afresh about Gilbert Osmond and expressed the hope she might know him; making, however, no such point of the matter as we have seen her do in recommending the girl herself to Mr. Osmond's attention. The reason of this was perhaps that Isabel offered no resistance whatever to Madame Merle's proposal. In Italy, as in England, the lady had a multitude of friends, both among the natives of the country and its heterogeneous visitors. She had mentioned to Isabel most of the people the girl would find it well to "meet"—of course, she said, Isabel could know whomever in the wide world she would—and had placed Mr. Osmond near the top of the list. He was an old friend of her own; she had known him these dozen years; he was one of the cleverest and most agreeable men—well, in Europe simply. He was altogether above the respectable average; quite another affair. He wasn't a professional charmer—far from it, and the effect he produced depended a good deal on the state of his nerves and his spirits. When not in the right mood he could fall as low as any one, saved only by his looking at such hours rather like a demoralised prince in exile. But if he cared or was interested or rightly challenged—just exactly rightly it had to be—then one felt his cleverness and his distinction. Those qualities didn't depend, in him, as in so many people, on his not committing or exposing himself. He had his perversities—which indeed Isabel would find to be the case with all the men really worth knowing—and didn't cause his light to shine equally for all persons. Madame Merle, however, thought she could undertake that for Isabel he would be brilliant. He was easily bored, too easily, and dull people always put him out; but a quick and cultivated girl like Isabel would give him a stimulus which was too absent from his life. At any rate he was a person not to miss. One shouldn't attempt to live in Italy without making a friend of Gilbert Osmond, who knew more about the country than any one except two or three German professors. And if they had more knowledge than he it was he who had most perception and taste—being artistic through and through. Isabel remembered that her friend had spoken of him during their plunge, at Gardencourt, into the deeps of talk, and wondered a little what was the nature of the tie binding these superior spirits. She felt that Madame Merle's ties always somehow had histories, and such an impression was part of the interest created by this inordinate woman. As regards her relations with Mr. Osmond, however, she hinted at nothing but a long-established calm friendship. Isabel said she should be happy to know a person who had enjoyed so high a confidence for so many years. "You ought to see a great many men," Madame Merle remarked; "you ought to see as many as possible, so as to get used to them."

"Used to them?" Isabel repeated with that solemn stare which sometimes seemed to proclaim her deficient in the sense of comedy. "Why, I'm not afraid of them—I'm as used to them as the cook to the butcher-boys."

"Used to them, I mean, so as to despise them. That's what one comes to with most of them. You'll pick out, for your society, the few whom you don't despise."

This was a note of cynicism that Madame Merle didn't often allow herself to sound; but Isabel was not alarmed, for she had never supposed that as one saw more of the world the sentiment of respect became the most active of one's emotions. It was excited, none the less, by the beautiful city of Florence, which pleased her not less than Madame Merle had promised; and if her unassisted perception had not been able to gauge its charms she had clever companions as priests to the mystery. She was—in no want indeed of esthetic illumination, for Ralph found it a joy that renewed his own early passion to act as cicerone to his eager young kinswoman. Madame Merle remained at home; she had seen the treasures of Florence again and again and had always something else to do. But she talked of all things with remarkable vividness of memory—she recalled the right-hand corner of the large Perugino and the position of the hands of the Saint Elizabeth in the picture next to it. She had her opinions as to the character of many famous works of art, differing often from Ralph with great sharpness and defending her interpretations with as much ingenuity as good-humour. Isabel listened to the discussions taking place between the two with a sense that she might derive much benefit from them and that they were among the advantages she couldn't have enjoyed for instance in Albany. In the clear May mornings before the formal breakfast—this repast at Mrs. Touchett's was served at twelve o'clock—she wandered with her cousin through the narrow and sombre Florentine streets, resting a while in the thicker dusk of some historic church or the vaulted chambers of some dispeopled convent. She went to the galleries and palaces; she looked at the pictures and statues that had hitherto been great names to her, and exchanged for a knowledge which was sometimes a limitation a presentiment which proved usually to have been a blank. She performed all those acts of mental prostration in which, on a first visit to Italy, youth and enthusiasm so freely indulge; she felt her heart beat in the presence of immortal genius and knew the sweetness of rising tears in eyes to which faded fresco and darkened marble grew dim. But the return, every day, was even pleasanter than the going forth; the return into the wide, monumental court of the great house in which Mrs. Touchett, many years before, had established herself, and into the high, cool rooms where the carven rafters and pompous frescoes of the sixteenth century looked down on the familiar commodities of the age of advertisement. Mrs. Touchett inhabited an historic building in a narrow street whose very name recalled the strife of medieval factions; and found compensation for the darkness of her frontage in the modicity of her rent and the brightness of a garden where nature itself looked as archaic as the rugged architecture of the palace and which cleared and scented the rooms in regular use. To live in such a place was, for Isabel, to hold to her ear all day a shell of the sea of the past. This vague eternal rumour kept her imagination awake.

Gilbert Osmond came to see Madame Merle, who presented him to the young lady lurking at the other side of the room. Isabel took on this occasion little part in the talk; she scarcely even smiled when the others turned to her invitingly; she sat there as if she had been at the play and had paid even a large sum for her place. Mrs. Touchett was not present, and these two had it, for the effect of brilliancy, all their own way. They talked of the Florentine, the Roman, the cosmopolite world, and might have been distinguished performers figuring for a charity. It all had the rich readiness that would have come from rehearsal. Madame Merle appealed to her as if she had been on the stage, but she could ignore any learnt cue without spoiling the scene—though of course she thus put dreadfully in the wrong the friend who had told Mr. Osmond she could be depended on. This was no matter for once; even if more had been involved she could have made no attempt to shine. There was something in the visitor that checked her and held her in suspense—made it more important she should get an impression of him than that she should produce one herself. Besides, she had little skill in producing an impression which she knew to be expected: nothing could be happier, in general, than to seem dazzling, but she had a perverse unwillingness to glitter by arrangement. Mr. Osmond, to do him justice, had a well-bred air of expecting nothing, a quiet ease that covered everything, even the first show of his own wit. This was the more grateful as his face, his head, was sensitive; he was not handsome, but he was fine, as fine as one of the drawings in the long gallery above the bridge of the Uffizi. And his very voice was fine—the more strangely that, with its clearness, it yet somehow wasn't sweet. This had had really to do with making her abstain from interference. His utterance was the vibration of glass, and if she had put out her finger she might have changed the pitch and spoiled the concert. Yet before he went she had to speak.

"Madame Merle," he said, "consents to come up to my hill-top some day next week and drink tea in my garden. It would give me much pleasure if you would come with her. It's thought rather pretty—there's what they call a general view. My daughter too would be so glad—or rather, for she's too young to have strong emotions, I should be so glad—so very glad." And Mr. Osmond paused with a slight air of embarrassment, leaving his sentence unfinished. "I should be so happy if you could know my daughter," he went on a moment afterwards.

Isabel replied that she should be delighted to see Miss Osmond and that if Madame Merle would show her the way to the hill-top she should be very grateful. Upon this assurance the visitor took his leave; after which Isabel fully expected her friend would scold her for having been so stupid. But to her surprise that lady, who indeed never fell into the mere matter-of-course, said to her in a few moments,

"You were charming, my dear; you were just as one would have wished you. You're never disappointing."

A rebuke might possibly have been irritating, though it is much more probable that Isabel would have taken it in good part; but, strange to say, the words that Madame Merle actually used caused her the first feeling of displeasure she had known this ally to excite. "That's more than I intended," she answered coldly. "I'm under no obligation that I know of to charm Mr. Osmond."

Madame Merle perceptibly flushed, but we know it was not her habit to retract. "My dear child, I didn't speak for him, poor man; I spoke for yourself. It's not of course a question as to his liking you; it matters little whether he likes you or not! But I thought you liked HIM."

"I did," said Isabel honestly. "But I don't see what that matters either."

"Everything that concerns you matters to me," Madame Merle returned with her weary nobleness; "especially when at the same time another old friend's concerned."

Whatever Isabel's obligations may have been to Mr. Osmond, it must be admitted that she found them sufficient to lead her to put to Ralph sundry questions about him. She thought Ralph's judgements distorted by his trials, but she flattered herself she had learned to make allowance for that.

"Do I know him?" said her cousin. "Oh, yes, I 'know' him; not well, but on the whole enough. I've never cultivated his society, and he apparently has never found mine indispensable to his happiness. Who is he, what is he? He's a vague, unexplained American who has been living these thirty years, or less, in Italy. Why do I call him unexplained? Only as a cover for my ignorance; I don't know his antecedents, his family, his origin. For all I do know he may be a prince in disguise; he rather looks like one, by the way—like a prince who has abdicated in a fit of fastidiousness and has been in a state of disgust ever since. He used to live in Rome; but of late years he has taken up his abode here; I remember hearing him say that Rome has grown vulgar. He has a great dread of vulgarity; that's his special line; he hasn't any other that I know of. He lives on his income, which I suspect of not being vulgarly large. He's a poor but honest gentleman that's what he calls himself. He married young and lost his wife, and I believe he has a daughter. He also has a sister, who's married to some small Count or other, of these parts; I remember meeting her of old. She's nicer than he, I should think, but rather impossible. I remember there used to be some stories about her. I don't think I recommend you to know her. But why don't you ask Madame Merle about these people? She knows them all much better than I."

"I ask you because I want your opinion as well as hers," said Isabel.

"A fig for my opinion! If you fall in love with Mr. Osmond what will you care for that?"

"Not much, probably. But meanwhile it has a certain importance. The more information one has about one's dangers the better."

"I don't agree to that—it may make them dangers. We know too much about people in these days; we hear too much. Our ears, our minds, our mouths, are stuffed with personalities. Don't mind anything any one tells you about any one else. Judge everyone and everything for yourself."

"That's what I try to do," said Isabel "but when you do that people call you conceited."

"You're not to mind them—that's precisely my argument; not to mind what they say about yourself any more than what they say about your friend or your enemy."

Isabel considered. "I think you're right; but there are some things I can't help minding: for instance when my friend's attacked or when I myself am praised."

"Of course you're always at liberty to judge the critic. Judge people as critics, however," Ralph added, "and you'll condemn them all!"

"I shall see Mr. Osmond for myself," said Isabel. "I've promised to pay him a visit."

"To pay him a visit?"

"To go and see his view, his pictures, his daughter—I don't know exactly what. Madame Merle's to take me; she tells me a great many ladies call on him."

"Ah, with Madame Merle you may go anywhere, de confiance," said Ralph. "She knows none but the best people."

Isabel said no more about Mr. Osmond, but she presently remarked to her cousin that she was not satisfied with his tone about Madame Merle. "It seems to me you insinuate things about her. I don't know what you mean, but if you've any grounds for disliking her I think you should either mention them frankly or else say nothing at all."

Ralph, however, resented this charge with more apparent earnestness than he commonly used. "I speak of Madame Merle exactly as I speak to her: with an even exaggerated respect."

"Exaggerated, precisely. That's what I complain of."

"I do so because Madame Merle's merits are exaggerated."

"By whom, pray? By me? If so I do her a poor service."

"No, no; by herself."

"Ah, I protest!" Isabel earnestly cried. "If ever there was a woman who made small claims—!"

"You put your finger on it," Ralph interrupted. "Her modesty's exaggerated. She has no business with small claims—she has a perfect right to make large ones."

"Her merits are large then. You contradict yourself."

"Her merits are immense," said Ralph. "She's indescribably blameless; a pathless desert of virtue; the only woman I know who never gives one a chance."

"A chance for what?"

"Well, say to call her a fool! She's the only woman I know who has but that one little fault."

Isabel turned away with impatience. "I don't understand you; you're too paradoxical for my plain mind."

"Let me explain. When I say she exaggerates I don't mean it in the vulgar sense—that she boasts, overstates, gives too fine an account of herself. I mean literally that she pushes the search for perfection too far—that her merits are in themselves overstrained. She's too good, too kind, too clever, too learned, too accomplished, too everything. She's too complete, in a word. I confess to you that she acts on my nerves and that I feel about her a good deal as that intensely human Athenian felt about Aristides the Just."

Isabel looked hard at her cousin; but the mocking spirit, if it lurked in his words, failed on this occasion to peep from his face. "Do you wish Madame Merle to be banished?"

"By no means. She's much too good company. I delight in Madame Merle," said Ralph Touchett simply.

"You're very odious, sir!" Isabel exclaimed. And then she asked him if he knew anything that was not to the honour of her brilliant friend.

"Nothing whatever. Don't you see that's just what I mean? On the character of every one else you may find some little black speck; if I were to take half an hour to it, some day, I've no doubt I should be able to find one on yours. For my own, of course, I'm spotted like a leopard. But on Madame Merle's nothing, nothing, nothing!"

"That's just what I think!" said Isabel with a toss of her head. "That is why I like her so much."

"She's a capital person for you to know. Since you wish to see the world you couldn't have a better guide."

"I suppose you mean by that that she's worldly?"

"Worldly? No," said Ralph, "she's the great round world itself!"

It had certainly not, as Isabel for the moment took it into her head to believe, been a refinement of malice in him to say that he delighted in Madame Merle. Ralph Touchett took his refreshment wherever he could find it, and he would not have forgiven himself if he had been left wholly unbeguiled by such a mistress of the social art. There are deep-lying sympathies and antipathies, and it may have been that, in spite of the administered justice she enjoyed at his hands, her absence from his mother's house would not have made life barren to him. But Ralph Touchett had learned more or less inscrutably to attend, and there could have been nothing so "sustained" to attend to as the general performance of Madame Merle. He tasted her in sips, he let her stand, with an opportuneness she herself could not have surpassed. There were moments when he felt almost sorry for her; and these, oddly enough, were the moments when his kindness was least demonstrative. He was sure she had been yearningly ambitious and that what she had visibly accomplished was far below her secret measure. She had got herself into perfect training, but had won none of the prizes. She was always plain Madame Merle, the widow of a Swiss negociant, with a small income and a large acquaintance, who stayed with people a great deal and was almost as universally "liked" as some new volume of smooth twaddle. The contrast between this position and any one of some half-dozen others that he supposed to have at various moments engaged her hope had an element of the tragical. His mother thought he got on beautifully with their genial guest; to Mrs. Touchett's sense two persons who dealt so largely in too-ingenious theories of conduct—that is of their own—would have much in common. He had given due consideration to Isabel's intimacy with her eminent friend, having long since made up his mind that he could not, without opposition, keep his cousin to himself; and he made the best of it, as he had done of worse things. He believed it would take care of itself; it wouldn't last forever. Neither of these two superior persons knew the other as well as she supposed, and when each had made an important discovery or two there would be, if not a rupture, at least a relaxation. Meanwhile he was quite willing to admit that the conversation of the elder lady was an advantage to the younger, who had a great deal to learn and would doubtless learn it better from Madame Merle than from some other instructors of the young. It was not probable that Isabel would be injured.

CHAPTER XXIV

It would certainly have been hard to see what injury could arise to her from the visit she presently paid to Mr. Osmond's hill-top. Nothing could have been more charming than this occasion—a soft afternoon in the full maturity of the Tuscan spring. The companions drove out of the Roman Gate, beneath the enormous blank superstructure which crowns the fine clear arch of that portal and makes it nakedly impressive, and wound between high-walled lanes into which the wealth of blossoming orchards over-drooped and flung a fragrance, until they reached the small superurban piazza, of crooked shape, where the long brown wall of the villa occupied in part by Mr. Osmond formed a principal, or at least a very imposing, object. Isabel went with her friend through a wide, high court, where a clear shadow rested below and a pair of light-arched galleries, facing each other above, caught the upper sunshine upon their slim columns and the flowering plants in which they were dressed. There was something grave and strong in the place; it looked somehow as if, once you were in, you would need an act of energy to get out. For Isabel, however, there was of course as yet no thought of getting out, but only of advancing. Mr. Osmond met her in the cold ante-chamber—it was cold even in the month of May—and ushered her, with her conductress, into the apartment to which we have already been introduced. Madame Merle was in front, and while Isabel lingered a little, talking with him, she went forward familiarly and greeted two persons who were seated in the saloon. One of these was little Pansy, on whom she bestowed a kiss; the other was a lady whom Mr. Osmond indicated to Isabel as his sister, the Countess Gemini. "And that's my little girl," he said, "who has just come out of her convent."

Pansy had on a scant white dress, and her fair hair was neatly arranged in a net; she wore her small shoes tied sandal-fashion about her ankles. She made Isabel a little conventual curtsey and then came to be kissed. The Countess Gemini simply nodded without getting up: Isabel could see she was a woman of high fashion. She was thin and dark and not at all pretty, having features that suggested some tropical bird—a long beak-like nose, small, quickly-moving eyes and a mouth and chin that receded extremely. Her expression, however, thanks to various intensities of emphasis and wonder, of horror and joy, was not inhuman, and, as regards her appearance, it was plain she understood herself and made the most of her points. Her attire, voluminous and delicate, bristling with elegance, had the look of shimmering plumage, and her attitudes were as light and sudden as those of a creature who perched upon twigs. She had a great deal of manner; Isabel, who had never known any one with so much manner, immediately classed her as the most affected of women. She remembered that Ralph had not recommended her as an acquaintance; but she was ready to acknowledge that to a casual view the Countess Gemini revealed no depths. Her demonstrations suggested the violent waving of some flag of general truce—white silk with fluttering streamers.

"You'll believe I'm glad to see you when I tell you it's only because I knew you were to be here that I came myself. I don't come and see my brother—I make him come and see me. This hill of his is impossible—I don't see what possesses him. Really, Osmond, you'll be the ruin of my horses some day, and if it hurts them you'll have to give me another pair. I heard them wheezing to-day; I assure you I did. It's very disagreeable to hear one's horses wheezing when one's sitting in the carriage; it sounds too as if they weren't what they should be. But I've always had good horses; whatever else I may have lacked I've always managed that. My husband doesn't know much, but I think he knows a horse. In general Italians don't, but my husband goes in, according to his poor light, for everything English. My horses are English—so it's all the greater pity they should be ruined. I must tell you," she went on, directly addressing Isabel, "that Osmond doesn't often invite me; I don't think he likes to have me. It was quite my own idea, coming to-day. I like to see new people, and I'm sure you're very new. But don't sit there; that chair's not what it looks. There are some very good seats here, but there are also some horrors."

These remarks were delivered with a series of little jerks and pecks, of roulades of shrillness, and in an accent that was as some fond recall of good English, or rather of good American, in adversity.

"I don't like to have you, my dear?" said her brother. "I'm sure you're invaluable."

"I don't see any horrors anywhere," Isabel returned, looking about her. "Everything seems to me beautiful and precious."

"I've a few good things," Mr. Osmond allowed; "indeed I've nothing very bad. But I've not what I should have liked."

He stood there a little awkwardly, smiling and glancing about; his manner was an odd mixture of the detached and the involved. He seemed to hint that nothing but the right "values" was of any consequence. Isabel made a rapid induction: perfect simplicity was not the badge of his family. Even the little girl from the convent, who, in her prim white dress, with her small submissive face and her hands locked before her, stood there as if she were about to partake of her first communion, even Mr. Osmond's diminutive daughter had a kind of finish that was not entirely artless.

"You'd have liked a few things from the Uffzi and the Pitti—that's what you'd have liked," said Madame Merle.

"Poor Osmond, with his old curtains and crucifixes!" the Countess Gemini exclaimed: she appeared to call her brother only by his family-name. Her ejaculation had no particular object; she smiled at Isabel as she made it and looked at her from head to foot.

Her brother had not heard her; he seemed to be thinking what he could say to Isabel. "Won't you have some tea?—you must be very tired," he at last bethought himself of remarking.

"No indeed, I'm not tired; what have I done to tire me?" Isabel felt a certain need of being very direct, of pretending to nothing; there was something in the air, in her general impression of things—she could hardly have said what it was—that deprived her of all disposition to put herself forward. The place, the occasion, the combination of people, signified more than lay on the surface; she would try to understand—she would not simply utter graceful platitudes. Poor Isabel was doubtless not aware that many women would have uttered graceful platitudes to cover the working of their observation. It must be confessed that her pride was a trifle alarmed. A man she had heard spoken of in terms that excited interest and who was evidently capable of distinguishing himself, had invited her, a young lady not lavish of her favours, to come to his house. Now that she had done so the burden of the entertainment rested naturally on his wit. Isabel was not rendered less observant, and for the moment, we judge, she was not rendered more indulgent, by perceiving that Mr. Osmond carried his burden less complacently than might have been expected. "What a fool I was to have let myself so needlessly in—!" she could fancy his exclaiming to himself.

"You'll be tired when you go home, if he shows you all his bibelots and gives you a lecture on each," said the Countess Gemini.

"I'm not afraid of that; but if I'm tired I shall at least have learned something."

"Very little, I suspect. But my sister's dreadfully afraid of learning anything," said Mr. Osmond.

"Oh, I confess to that; I don't want to know anything more—I know too much already. The more you know the more unhappy you are."

"You should not undervalue knowledge before Pansy, who has not finished her education," Madame Merle interposed with a smile. "Pansy will never know any harm," said the child's father. "Pansy's a little convent-flower."

"Oh, the convents, the convents!" cried the Countess with a flutter of her ruffles. "Speak to me of the convents! You may learn anything there; I'm a convent-flower myself. I don't pretend to be good, but the nuns do. Don't you see what I mean?" she went on, appealing to Isabel.

Isabel was not sure she saw, and she answered that she was very bad at following arguments. The Countess then declared that she herself detested arguments, but that this was her brother's taste—he would always discuss. "For me," she said, "one should like a thing or one shouldn't; one can't like everything, of course. But one shouldn't attempt to reason it out—you never know where it may lead you. There are some very good feelings that may have bad reasons, don't you know? And then there are very bad feelings, sometimes, that have good reasons. Don't you see what I mean? I don't care anything about reasons, but I know what I like."

"Ah, that's the great thing," said Isabel, smiling and suspecting that her acquaintance with this lightly flitting personage would not lead to intellectual repose. If the Countess objected to argument Isabel at this moment had as little taste for it, and she put out her hand to Pansy with a pleasant sense that such a gesture committed her to nothing that would admit of a divergence of views. Gilbert Osmond apparently took a rather hopeless view of his sister's tone; he turned the conversation to another topic. He presently sat down on the other side of his daughter, who had shyly brushed Isabel's fingers with her own; but he ended by drawing her out of her chair and making her stand between his knees, leaning against him while he passed his arm round her slimness. The child fixed her eyes on Isabel with a still, disinterested gaze which seemed void of an intention, yet conscious of an attraction. Mr. Osmond talked of many things; Madame Merle had said he could be agreeable when he chose, and to-day, after a little, he appeared not only to have chosen but to have determined. Madame Merle and the Countess Gemini sat a little apart, conversing in the effortless manner of persons who knew each other well enough to take their ease; but every now and then Isabel heard the Countess, at something said by her companion, plunge into the latter's lucidity as a poodle splashes after a thrown stick. It was as if Madame Merle were seeing how far she would go. Mr. Osmond talked of Florence, of Italy, of the pleasure of living in that country and of the abatements to the pleasure. There were both satisfactions and drawbacks; the drawbacks were numerous; strangers were too apt to see such a world as all romantic. It met the case soothingly for the human, for the social failure—by which he meant the people who couldn't "realise," as they said, on their sensibility: they could keep it about them there, in their poverty, without ridicule, as you might keep an heirloom or an inconvenient entailed place that brought you in nothing. Thus there were advantages in living in the country which contained the greatest sum of beauty. Certain impressions you could get only there. Others, favourable to life, you never got, and you got some that were very bad. But from time to time you got one of a quality that made up for everything. Italy, all the same, had spoiled a great many people; he was even fatuous enough to believe at times that he himself might have been a better man if he had spent less of his life there. It made one idle and dilettantish and second-rate; it had no discipline for the character, didn't cultivate in you, otherwise expressed, the successful social and other "cheek" that flourished in Paris and London. "We're sweetly provincial," said Mr. Osmond, "and I'm perfectly aware that I myself am as rusty as a key that has no lock to fit it. It polishes me up a little to talk with you—not that I venture to pretend I can turn that very complicated lock I suspect your intellect of being! But you'll be going away before I've seen you three times, and I shall perhaps never see you after that. That's what it is to live in a country that people come to. When they're disagreeable here it's bad enough; when they're agreeable it's still worse. As soon as you like them they're off again! I've been deceived too often; I've ceased to form attachments, to permit myself to feel attractions. You mean to stay—to settle? That would be really comfortable. Ah yes, your aunt's a sort of guarantee; I believe she may be depended on. Oh, she's an old Florentine; I mean literally an old one; not a modern outsider. She's a contemporary of the Medici; she must have been present at the burning of Savonarola, and I'm not sure she didn't throw a handful of chips into the flame. Her face is very much like some faces in the early pictures; little, dry, definite faces that must have had a good deal of expression, but almost always the same one. Indeed I can show you her portrait in a fresco of Ghirlandaio's. I hope you don't object to my speaking that way of your aunt, eh? I've an idea you don't. Perhaps you think that's even worse. I assure you there's no want of respect in it, to either of you. You know I'm a particular admirer of Mrs. Touchett."

While Isabel's host exerted himself to entertain her in this somewhat confidential fashion she looked occasionally at Madame Merle, who met her eyes with an inattentive smile in which, on this occasion, there was no infelicitous intimation that our heroine appeared to advantage. Madame Merle eventually proposed to the Countess Gemini that they should go into the garden, and the Countess, rising and shaking out her feathers, began to rustle toward the door. "Poor Miss Archer!" she exclaimed, surveying the other group with expressive compassion. "She has been brought quite into the family."

"Miss Archer can certainly have nothing but sympathy for a family to which you belong," Mr. Osmond answered, with a laugh which, though it had something of a mocking ring, had also a finer patience.

"I don't know what you mean by that! I'm sure she'll see no harm in me but what you tell her. I'm better than he says, Miss Archer," the Countess went on. "I'm only rather an idiot and a bore. Is that all he has said? Ah then, you keep him in good-humour. Has he opened on one of his favourite subjects? I give you notice that there are two or three that he treats a fond. In that case you had better take off your bonnet."

"I don't think I know what Mr. Osmond's favourite subjects are," said Isabel, who had risen to her feet.

The Countess assumed for an instant an attitude of intense meditation, pressing one of her hands, with the finger-tips gathered together, to her forehead. "I'll tell you in a moment. One's Machiavelli; the other's Vittoria Colonna; the next is Metastasio."

"Ah, with me," said Madame Merle, passing her arm into the Countess Gemini's as if to guide her course to the garden, "Mr. Osmond's never so historical."

"Oh you," the Countess answered as they moved away, "you yourself are Machiavelli—you yourself are Vittoria Colonna!"

"We shall hear next that poor Madame Merle is Metastasio!" Gilbert Osmond resignedly sighed.

Isabel had got up on the assumption that they too were to go into the garden; but her host stood there with no apparent inclination to leave the room, his hands in the pockets of his jacket and his daughter, who had now locked her arm into one of his own, clinging to him and looking up while her eyes moved from his own face to Isabel's. Isabel waited, with a certain unuttered contentedness, to have her movements directed; she liked Mr. Osmond's talk, his company: she had what always gave her a very private thrill, the consciousness of a new relation. Through the open doors of the great room she saw Madame Merle and the Countess stroll across the fine grass of the garden; then she turned, and her eyes wandered over the things scattered about her. The understanding had been that Mr. Osmond should show her his treasures; his pictures and cabinets all looked like treasures. Isabel after a moment went toward one of the pictures to see it better; but just as she had done so he said to her abruptly: "Miss Archer, what do you think of my sister?"

She faced him with some surprise. "Ah, don't ask me that—I've seen your sister too little."

"Yes, you've seen her very little; but you must have observed that there is not a great deal of her to see. What do you think of our family tone?" he went on with his cool smile. "I should like to know how it strikes a fresh, unprejudiced mind. I know what you're going to say—you've had almost no observation of it. Of course this is only a glimpse. But just take notice, in future, if you have a chance. I sometimes think we've got into a rather bad way, living off here among things and people not our own, without responsibilities or attachments, with nothing to hold us together or keep us up; marrying foreigners, forming artificial tastes, playing tricks with our natural mission. Let me add, though, that I say that much more for myself than for my sister. She's a very honest lady—more so than she seems. She's rather unhappy, and as she's not of a serious turn she doesn't tend to show it tragically: she shows it comically instead. She has got a horrid husband, though I'm not sure she makes the best of him. Of course, however, a horrid husband's an awkward thing. Madame Merle gives her excellent advice, but it's a good deal like giving a child a dictionary to learn a language with. He can look out the words, but he can't put them together. My sister needs a grammar, but unfortunately she's not grammatical. Pardon my troubling you with these details; my sister was very right in saying you've been taken into the family. Let me take down that picture; you want more light."

He took down the picture, carried it toward the window, related some curious facts about it. She looked at the other works of art, and he gave her such further information as might appear most acceptable to a young lady making a call on a summer afternoon. His pictures, his medallions and tapestries were interesting; but after a while Isabel felt the owner much more so, and independently of them, thickly as they seemed to overhang him. He resembled no one she had ever seen; most of the people she knew might be divided into groups of half a dozen specimens. There were one or two exceptions to this; she could think for instance of no group that would contain her aunt Lydia. There were other people who were, relatively speaking, original—original, as one might say, by courtesy such as Mr. Goodwood, as her cousin Ralph, as Henrietta Stackpole, as Lord Warburton, as Madame Merle. But in essentials, when one came to look at them, these individuals belonged to types already present to her mind. Her mind contained no class offering a natural place to Mr. Osmond—he was a specimen apart. It was not that she recognised all these truths at the hour, but they were falling into order before her. For the moment she only said to herself that this "new relation" would perhaps prove her very most distinguished. Madame Merle had had that note of rarity, but what quite other power it immediately gained when sounded by a man! It was not so much what he said and did, but rather what he withheld, that marked him for her as by one of those signs of the highly curious that he was showing her on the underside of old plates and in the corner of sixteenth-century drawings: he indulged in no striking deflections from common usage, he was an original without being an eccentric. She had never met a person of so fine a grain. The peculiarity was physical, to begin with, and it extended to impalpabilities. His dense, delicate hair, his overdrawn, retouched features, his clear complexion, ripe without being coarse, the very evenness of the growth of his beard, and that light, smooth slenderness of structure which made the movement of a single one of his fingers produce the effect of an expressive gesture—these personal points struck our sensitive young woman as signs of quality, of intensity, somehow as promises of interest. He was certainly fastidious and critical; he was probably irritable. His sensibility had governed him—possibly governed him too much; it had made him impatient of vulgar troubles and had led him to live by himself, in a sorted, sifted, arranged world, thinking about art and beauty and history. He had consulted his taste in everything—his taste alone perhaps, as a sick man consciously incurable consults at last only his lawyer: that was what made him so different from every one else. Ralph had something of this same quality, this appearance of thinking that life was a matter of connoisseurship; but in Ralph it was an anomaly, a kind of humorous excrescence, whereas in Mr. Osmond it was the keynote, and everything was in harmony with it. She was certainly far from understanding him completely; his meaning was not at all times obvious. It was hard to see what he meant for instance by speaking of his provincial side—which was exactly the side she would have taken him most to lack. Was it a harmless paradox, intended to puzzle her? or was it the last refinement of high culture? She trusted she should learn in time; it would be very interesting to learn. If it was provincial to have that harmony, what then was the finish of the capital? And she could put this question in spite of so feeling her host a shy personage; since such shyness as his—the shyness of ticklish nerves and fine perceptions—was perfectly consistent with the best breeding. Indeed it was almost a proof of standards and touchstones other than the vulgar: he must be so sure the vulgar would be first on the ground. He wasn't a man of easy assurance, who chatted and gossiped with the fluency of a superficial nature; he was critical of himself as well as of others, and, exacting a good deal of others, to think them agreeable, probably took a rather ironical view of what he himself offered: a proof into the bargain that he was not grossly conceited. If he had not been shy he wouldn't have effected that gradual, subtle, successful conversion of it to which she owed both what pleased her in him and what mystified her. If he had suddenly asked her what she thought of the Countess Gemini, that was doubtless a proof that he was interested in her; it could scarcely be as a help to knowledge of his own sister. That he should be so interested showed an enquiring mind; but it was a little singular he should sacrifice his fraternal feeling to his curiosity. This was the most eccentric thing he had done.

There were two other rooms, beyond the one in which she had been received, equally full of romantic objects, and in these apartments Isabel spent a quarter of an hour. Everything was in the last degree curious and precious, and Mr. Osmond continued to be the kindest of ciceroni as he led her from one fine piece to another and still held his little girl by the hand. His kindness almost surprised our young friend, who wondered why he should take so much trouble for her; and she was oppressed at last with the accumulation of beauty and knowledge to which she found herself introduced. There was enough for the present; she had ceased to attend to what he said; she listened to him with attentive eyes, but was not thinking of what he told her. He probably thought her quicker, cleverer in every way, more prepared, than she was. Madame Merle would have pleasantly exaggerated; which was a pity, because in the end he would be sure to find out, and then perhaps even her real intelligence wouldn't reconcile him to his mistake. A part of Isabel's fatigue came from the effort to appear as intelligent as she believed Madame Merle had described her, and from the fear (very unusual with her) of exposing—not her ignorance; for that she cared comparatively little—but her possible grossness of perception. It would have annoyed her to express a liking for something he, in his superior enlightenment, would think she oughtn't to like; or to pass by something at which the truly initiated mind would arrest itself. She had no wish to fall into that grotesqueness—in which she had seen women (and it was a warning) serenely, yet ignobly, flounder. She was very careful therefore as to what she said, as to what she noticed or failed to notice; more careful than she had ever been before.

They came back into the first of the rooms, where the tea had been served; but as the two other ladies were still on the terrace, and as Isabel had not yet been made acquainted with the view, the paramount distinction of the place, Mr. Osmond directed her steps into the garden without more delay. Madame Merle and the Countess had had chairs brought out, and as the afternoon was lovely the Countess proposed they should take their tea in the open air. Pansy therefore was sent to bid the servant bring out the preparations. The sun had got low, the golden light took a deeper tone, and on the mountains and the plain that stretched beneath them the masses of purple shadow glowed as richly as the places that were still exposed. The scene had an extraordinary charm. The air was almost solemnly still, and the large expanse of the landscape, with its garden-like culture and nobleness of outline, its teeming valley and delicately-fretted hills, its peculiarly human-looking touches of habitation, lay there in splendid harmony and classic grace. "You seem so well pleased that I think you can be trusted to come back," Osmond said as he led his companion to one of the angles of the terrace.

"I shall certainly come back," she returned, "in spite of what you say about its being bad to live in Italy. What was that you said about one's natural mission? I wonder if I should forsake my natural mission if I were to settle in Florence."

"A woman's natural mission is to be where she's most appreciated."

"The point's to find out where that is."

"Very true—she often wastes a great deal of time in the enquiry. People ought to make it very plain to her."

"Such a matter would have to be made very plain to me," smiled Isabel.

"I'm glad, at any rate, to hear you talk of settling. Madame Merle had given me an idea that you were of a rather roving disposition. I thought she spoke of your having some plan of going round the world."

"I'm rather ashamed of my plans; I make a new one every day."

"I don't see why you should be ashamed; it's the greatest of pleasures."

"It seems frivolous, I think," said Isabel. "One ought to choose something very deliberately, and be faithful to that."

"By that rule then, I've not been frivolous."

"Have you never made plans?"

"Yes, I made one years ago, and I'm acting on it to-day."

"It must have been a very pleasant one," Isabel permitted herself to observe.

"It was very simple. It was to be as quiet as possible."

"As quiet?" the girl repeated.

"Not to worry—not to strive nor struggle. To resign myself. To be content with little." He spoke these sentences slowly, with short pauses between, and his intelligent regard was fixed on his visitor's with the conscious air of a man who has brought himself to confess something.

"Do you call that simple?" she asked with mild irony.

"Yes, because it's negative."

"Has your life been negative?"

"Call it affirmative if you like. Only it has affirmed my indifference. Mind you, not my natural indifference—I HAD none. But my studied, my wilful renunciation."

She scarcely understood him; it seemed a question whether he were joking or not. Why should a man who struck her as having a great fund of reserve suddenly bring himself to be so confidential? This was his affair, however, and his confidences were interesting. "I don't see why you should have renounced," she said in a moment.

"Because I could do nothing. I had no prospects, I was poor, and I was not a man of genius. I had no talents even; I took my measure early in life. I was simply the most fastidious young gentleman living. There were two or three people in the world I envied—the Emperor of Russia, for instance, and the Sultan of Turkey! There were even moments when I envied the Pope of Rome—for the consideration he enjoys. I should have been delighted to be considered to that extent; but since that couldn't be I didn't care for anything less, and I made up my mind not to go in for honours. The leanest gentleman can always consider himself, and fortunately I was, though lean, a gentleman. I could do nothing in Italy—I couldn't even be an Italian patriot. To do that I should have had to get out of the country; and I was too fond of it to leave it, to say nothing of my being too well satisfied with it, on the whole, as it then was, to wish it altered. So I've passed a great many years here on that quiet plan I spoke of. I've not been at all unhappy. I don't mean to say I've cared for nothing; but the things I've cared for have been definite—limited. The events of my life have been absolutely unperceived by any one save myself; getting an old silver crucifix at a bargain (I've never bought anything dear, of course), or discovering, as I once did, a sketch by Correggio on a panel daubed over by some inspired idiot."

This would have been rather a dry account of Mr. Osmond's career if Isabel had fully believed it; but her imagination supplied the human element which she was sure had not been wanting. His life had been mingled with other lives more than he admitted; naturally she couldn't expect him to enter into this. For the present she abstained from provoking further revelations; to intimate that he had not told her everything would be more familiar and less considerate than she now desired to be—would in fact be uproariously vulgar. He had certainly told her quite enough. It was her present inclination, however, to express a measured sympathy for the success with which he had preserved his independence. "That's a very pleasant life," she said, "to renounce everything but Correggio!"

"Oh, I've made in my way a good thing of it. Don't imagine I'm whining about it. It's one's own fault if one isn't happy."

This was large; she kept down to something smaller. "Have you lived here always?"

"No, not always. I lived a long time at Naples, and many years in Rome. But I've been here a good while. Perhaps I shall have to change, however; to do something else. I've no longer myself to think of. My daughter's growing up and may very possibly not care so much for the Correggios and crucifixes as I. I shall have to do what's best for Pansy."

"Yes, do that," said Isabel. "She's such a dear little girl."

"Ah," cried Gilbert Osmond beautifully, "she's a little saint of heaven! She is my great happiness!"

CHAPTER XXV

While this sufficiently intimate colloquy (prolonged for some time after we cease to follow it) went forward Madame Merle and her companion, breaking a silence of some duration, had begun to exchange remarks. They were sitting in an attitude of unexpressed expectancy; an attitude especially marked on the part of the Countess Gemini, who, being of a more nervous temperament than her friend, practised with less success the art of disguising impatience. What these ladies were waiting for would not have been apparent and was perhaps not very definite to their own minds. Madame Merle waited for Osmond to release their young friend from her tete-a-tete, and the Countess waited because Madame Merle did. The Countess, moreover, by waiting, found the time ripe for one of her pretty perversities. She might have desired for some minutes to place it. Her brother wandered with Isabel to the end of the garden, to which point her eyes followed them.

"My dear," she then observed to her companion, "you'll excuse me if I don't congratulate you!"

"Very willingly, for I don't in the least know why you should."

"Haven't you a little plan that you think rather well of?" And the Countess nodded at the sequestered couple.

Madame Merle's eyes took the same direction; then she looked serenely at her neighbour. "You know I never understand you very well," she smiled.

"No one can understand better than you when you wish. I see that just now you DON'T wish."

"You say things to me that no one else does," said Madame Merle gravely, yet without bitterness.

"You mean things you don't like? Doesn't Osmond sometimes say such things?"

"What your brother says has a point."

"Yes, a poisoned one sometimes. If you mean that I'm not so clever as he you mustn't think I shall suffer from your sense of our difference. But it will be much better that you should understand me."

"Why so?" asked Madame Merle. "To what will it conduce?"

"If I don't approve of your plan you ought to know it in order to appreciate the danger of my interfering with it."

Madame Merle looked as if she were ready to admit that there might be something in this; but in a moment she said quietly: "You think me more calculating than I am."

"It's not your calculating I think ill of; it's your calculating wrong. You've done so in this case."

"You must have made extensive calculations yourself to discover that."

"No, I've not had time. I've seen the girl but this once," said the Countess, "and the conviction has suddenly come to me. I like her very much."

"So do I," Madame Merle mentioned.

"You've a strange way of showing it."

"Surely I've given her the advantage of making your acquaintance."

"That indeed," piped the Countess, "is perhaps the best thing that could happen to her!"

Madame Merle said nothing for some time. The Countess's manner was odious, was really low; but it was an old story, and with her eyes upon the violet slope of Monte Morello she gave herself up to reflection. "My dear lady," she finally resumed, "I advise you not to agitate yourself. The matter you allude to concerns three persons much stronger of purpose than yourself."

"Three persons? You and Osmond of course. But is Miss Archer also very strong of purpose?"

"Quite as much so as we."

"Ah then," said the Countess radiantly, "if I convince her it's her interest to resist you she'll do so successfully!"

"Resist us? Why do you express yourself so coarsely? She's not exposed to compulsion or deception."

"I'm not sure of that. You're capable of anything, you and Osmond. I don't mean Osmond by himself, and I don't mean you by yourself. But together you're dangerous—like some chemical combination."

"You had better leave us alone then," smiled Madame Merle.

"I don't mean to touch you—but I shall talk to that girl."

"My poor Amy," Madame Merle murmured, "I don't see what has got into your head."

"I take an interest in her—that's what has got into my head. I like her."

Madame Merle hesitated a moment. "I don't think she likes you."

The Countess's bright little eyes expanded and her face was set in a grimace. "Ah, you ARE dangerous—even by yourself!"

"If you want her to like you don't abuse your brother to her," said Madame Merle.

"I don't suppose you pretend she has fallen in love with him in two interviews."

Madame Merle looked a moment at Isabel and at the master of the house. He was leaning against the parapet, facing her, his arms folded; and she at present was evidently not lost in the mere impersonal view, persistently as she gazed at it. As Madame Merle watched her she lowered her eyes; she was listening, possibly with a certain embarrassment, while she pressed the point of her parasol into the path. Madame Merle rose from her chair. "Yes, I think so!" she pronounced.

The shabby footboy, summoned by Pansy—he might, tarnished as to livery and quaint as to type, have issued from some stray sketch of old-time manners, been "put in" by the brush of a Longhi or a Goya—had come out with a small table and placed it on the grass, and then had gone back and fetched the tea-tray; after which he had again disappeared, to return with a couple of chairs. Pansy had watched these proceedings with the deepest interest, standing with her small hands folded together upon the front of her scanty frock; but she had not presumed to offer assistance. When the tea-table had been arranged, however, she gently approached her aunt.

"Do you think papa would object to my making the tea?"

The Countess looked at her with a deliberately critical gaze and without answering her question. "My poor niece," she said, "is that your best frock?"

"Ah no," Pansy answered, "it's just a little toilette for common occasions."

"Do you call it a common occasion when I come to see you?—to say nothing of Madame Merle and the pretty lady yonder."

Pansy reflected a moment, turning gravely from one of the persons mentioned to the other. Then her face broke into its perfect smile. "I have a pretty dress, but even that one's very simple. Why should I expose it beside your beautiful things?"

"Because it's the prettiest you have; for me you must always wear the prettiest. Please put it on the next time. It seems to me they don't dress you so well as they might."

The child sparingly stroked down her antiquated skirt. "It's a good little dress to make tea—don't you think? Don't you believe papa would allow me?"

"Impossible for me to say, my child," said the Countess. "For me, your father's ideas are unfathomable. Madame Merle understands them better. Ask HER."

Madame Merle smiled with her usual grace. "It's a weighty question—let me think. It seems to me it would please your father to see a careful little daughter making his tea. It's the proper duty of the daughter of the house—when she grows up."

"So it seems to me, Madame Merle!" Pansy cried. "You shall see how well I'll make it. A spoonful for each." And she began to busy herself at the table.

"Two spoonfuls for me," said the Countess, who, with Madame Merle, remained for some moments watching her. "Listen to me, Pansy," the Countess resumed at last. "I should like to know what you think of your visitor."

"Ah, she's not mine—she's papa's," Pansy objected.

"Miss Archer came to see you as well," said Madame Merle.

"I'm very happy to hear that. She has been very polite to me."

"Do you like her then?" the Countess asked.

"She's charming—charming," Pansy repeated in her little neat conversational tone. "She pleases me thoroughly."

"And how do you think she pleases your father?"

"Ah really, Countess!" murmured Madame Merle dissuasively. "Go and call them to tea," she went on to the child.

"You'll see if they don't like it!" Pansy declared; and departed to summon the others, who had still lingered at the end of the terrace.

"If Miss Archer's to become her mother it's surely interesting to know if the child likes her," said the Countess.

"If your brother marries again it won't be for Pansy's sake," Madame Merle replied. "She'll soon be sixteen, and after that she'll begin to need a husband rather than a stepmother."

"And will you provide the husband as well?"

"I shall certainly take an interest in her marrying fortunately. I imagine you'll do the same."

"Indeed I shan't!" cried the Countess. "Why should I, of all women, set such a price on a husband?"

"You didn't marry fortunately; that's what I'm speaking of. When I say a husband I mean a good one."

"There are no good ones. Osmond won't be a good one."

Madame Merle closed her eyes a moment. "You're irritated just now; I don't know why," she presently said. "I don't think you'll really object either to your brother's or to your niece's marrying, when the time comes for them to do so; and as regards Pansy I'm confident that we shall some day have the pleasure of looking for a husband for her together. Your large acquaintance will be a great help."

"Yes, I'm irritated," the Countess answered. "You often irritate me. Your own coolness is fabulous. You're a strange woman."

"It's much better that we should always act together," Madame Merle went on.

"Do you mean that as a threat?" asked the Countess rising. Madame Merle shook her head as for quiet amusement. "No indeed, you've not my coolness!"

Isabel and Mr. Osmond were now slowly coming toward them and Isabel had taken Pansy by the hand. "Do you pretend to believe he'd make her happy?" the Countess demanded.

"If he should marry Miss Archer I suppose he'd behave like a gentleman."

The Countess jerked herself into a succession of attitudes. "Do you mean as most gentlemen behave? That would be much to be thankful for! Of course Osmond's a gentleman; his own sister needn't be reminded of that. But does he think he can marry any girl he happens to pick out? Osmond's a gentleman, of course; but I must say I've NEVER, no, no, never, seen any one of Osmond's pretensions! What they're all founded on is more than I can say. I'm his own sister; I might be supposed to know. Who is he, if you please? What has he ever done? If there had been anything particularly grand in his origin—if he were made of some superior clay—I presume I should have got some inkling of it. If there had been any great honours or splendours in the family I should certainly have made the most of them: they would have been quite in my line. But there's nothing, nothing, nothing. One's parents were charming people of course; but so were yours, I've no doubt. Every one's a charming person nowadays. Even I'm a charming person; don't laugh, it has literally been said. As for Osmond, he has always appeared to believe that he's descended from the gods."

"You may say what you please," said Madame Merle, who had listened to this quick outbreak none the less attentively, we may believe, because her eye wandered away from the speaker and her hands busied themselves with adjusting the knots of ribbon on her dress. "You Osmonds are a fine race—your blood must flow from some very pure source. Your brother, like an intelligent man, has had the conviction of it if he has not had the proofs. You're modest about it, but you yourself are extremely distinguished. What do you say about your niece? The child's a little princess. Nevertheless," Madame Merle added, "it won't be an easy matter for Osmond to marry Miss Archer. Yet he can try."

"I hope she'll refuse him. It will take him down a little."

"We mustn't forget that he is one of the cleverest of men."

"I've heard you say that before, but I haven't yet discovered what he has done."

"What he has done? He has done nothing that has had to be undone. And he has known how to wait."

"To wait for Miss Archer's money? How much of it is there?"

"That's not what I mean," said Madame Merle. "Miss Archer has seventy thousand pounds."

"Well, it's a pity she's so charming," the Countess declared. "To be sacrificed, any girl would do. She needn't be superior."

"If she weren't superior your brother would never look at her. He must have the best."

"Yes," returned the Countess as they went forward a little to meet the others, "he's very hard to satisfy. That makes me tremble for her happiness!"

CHAPTER XXVI

Gilbert Osmond came to see Isabel again; that is he came to Palazzo Crescentini. He had other friends there as well, and to Mrs. Touchett and Madame Merle he was always impartially civil; but the former of these ladies noted the fact that in the course of a fortnight he called five times, and compared it with another fact that she found no difficulty in remembering. Two visits a year had hitherto constituted his regular tribute to Mrs. Touchett's worth, and she had never observed him select for such visits those moments, of almost periodical recurrence, when Madame Merle was under her roof. It was not for Madame Merle that he came; these two were old friends and he never put himself out for her. He was not fond of Ralph—Ralph had told her so—and it was not supposable that Mr. Osmond had suddenly taken a fancy to her son. Ralph was imperturbable—Ralph had a kind of loose-fitting urbanity that wrapped him about like an ill-made overcoat, but of which he never divested himself; he thought Mr. Osmond very good company and was willing at any time to look at him in the light of hospitality. But he didn't flatter himself that the desire to repair a past injustice was the motive of their visitor's calls; he read the situation more clearly. Isabel was the attraction, and in all conscience a sufficient one. Osmond was a critic, a student of the exquisite, and it was natural he should be curious of so rare an apparition. So when his mother observed to him that it was plain what Mr. Osmond was thinking of, Ralph replied that he was quite of her opinion. Mrs. Touchett had from far back found a place on her scant list for this gentleman, though wondering dimly by what art and what process—so negative and so wise as they were—he had everywhere effectively imposed himself. As he had never been an importunate visitor he had had no chance to be offensive, and he was recommended to her by his appearance of being as well able to do without her as she was to do without him—a quality that always, oddly enough, affected her as providing ground for a relation with her. It gave her no satisfaction, however, to think that he had taken it into his head to marry her niece. Such an alliance, on Isabel's part, would have an air of almost morbid perversity. Mrs. Touchett easily remembered that the girl had refused an English peer; and that a young lady with whom Lord Warburton had not successfully wrestled should content herself with an obscure American dilettante, a middle-aged widower with an uncanny child and an ambiguous income, this answered to nothing in Mrs. Touchett's conception of success. She took, it will be observed, not the sentimental, but the political, view of matrimony—a view which has always had much to recommend it. "I trust she won't have the folly to listen to him," she said to her son; to which Ralph replied that Isabel's listening was one thing and Isabel's answering quite another. He knew she had listened to several parties, as his father would have said, but had made them listen in return; and he found much entertainment in the idea that in these few months of his knowing her he should observe a fresh suitor at her gate. She had wanted to see life, and fortune was serving her to her taste; a succession of fine gentlemen going down on their knees to her would do as well as anything else. Ralph looked forward to a fourth, a fifth, a tenth besieger; he had no conviction she would stop at a third. She would keep the gate ajar and open a parley; she would certainly not allow number three to come in. He expressed this view, somewhat after this fashion, to his mother, who looked at him as if he had been dancing a jig. He had such a fanciful, pictorial way of saying things that he might as well address her in the deaf-mute's alphabet.

"I don't think I know what you mean," she said; "you use too many figures of speech; I could never understand allegories. The two words in the language I most respect are Yes and No. If Isabel wants to marry Mr. Osmond she'll do so in spite of all your comparisons. Let her alone to find a fine one herself for anything she undertakes. I know very little about the young man in America; I don't think she spends much of her time in thinking of him, and I suspect he has got tired of waiting for her. There's nothing in life to prevent her marrying Mr. Osmond if she only looks at him in a certain way. That's all very well; no one approves more than I of one's pleasing one's self. But she takes her pleasure in such odd things; she's capable of marrying Mr. Osmond for the beauty of his opinions or for his autograph of Michael Angelo. She wants to be disinterested: as if she were the only person who's in danger of not being so! Will HE be so disinterested when he has the spending of her money? That was her idea before your father's death, and it has acquired new charms for her since. She ought to marry some one of whose disinterestedness she shall herself be sure; and there would be no such proof of that as his having a fortune of his own."

"My dear mother, I'm not afraid," Ralph answered. "She's making fools of us all. She'll please herself, of course; but she'll do so by studying human nature at close quarters and yet retaining her liberty. She has started on an exploring expedition, and I don't think she'll change her course, at the outset, at a signal from Gilbert Osmond. She may have slackened speed for an hour, but before we know it she'll be steaming away again. Excuse another metaphor."

Mrs. Touchett excused it perhaps, but was not so much reassured as to withhold from Madame Merle the expression of her fears. "You who know everything," she said, "you must know this: whether that curious creature's really making love to my niece."

"Gilbert Osmond?" Madame Merle widened her clear eyes and, with a full intelligence, "Heaven help us," she exclaimed, "that's an idea!"

"Hadn't it occurred to you?"

"You make me feel an idiot, but I confess it hadn't. I wonder," she added, "if it has occurred to Isabel."

"Oh, I shall now ask her," said Mrs. Touchett.

Madame Merle reflected. "Don't put it into her head. The thing would be to ask Mr. Osmond."

"I can't do that," said Mrs. Touchett. "I won't have him enquire of me—as he perfectly may with that air of his, given Isabel's situation—what business it is of mine."

"I'll ask him myself," Madame Merle bravely declared.

"But what business—for HIM—is it of yours?"

"It's being none whatever is just why I can afford to speak. It's so much less my business than any one's else that he can put me off with anything he chooses. But it will be by the way he does this that I shall know."

"Pray let me hear then," said Mrs. Touchett, "of the fruits of your penetration. If I can't speak to him, however, at least I can speak to Isabel."

Her companion sounded at this the note of warning. "Don't be too quick with her. Don't inflame her imagination."

"I never did anything in life to any one's imagination. But I'm always sure of her doing something—well, not of MY kind."

"No, you wouldn't like this," Madame Merle observed without the point of interrogation.

"Why in the world should I, pray? Mr. Osmond has nothing the least solid to offer."

Again Madame Merle was silent while her thoughtful smile drew up her mouth even more charmingly than usual toward the left corner. "Let us distinguish. Gilbert Osmond's certainly not the first comer. He's a man who in favourable conditions might very well make a great impression. He has made a great impression, to my knowledge, more than once."

"Don't tell me about his probably quite cold-blooded love-affairs; they're nothing to me!" Mrs. Touchett cried. "What you say's precisely why I wish he would cease his visits. He has nothing in the world that I know of but a dozen or two of early masters and a more or less pert little daughter."

"The early masters are now worth a good deal of money," said Madame Merle, "and the daughter's a very young and very innocent and very harmless person."

"In other words she's an insipid little chit. Is that what you mean? Having no fortune she can't hope to marry as they marry here; so that Isabel will have to furnish her either with a maintenance or with a dowry."

"Isabel probably wouldn't object to being kind to her. I think she likes the poor child."

"Another reason then for Mr. Osmond's stopping at home! Otherwise, a week hence, we shall have my niece arriving at the conviction that her mission in life's to prove that a stepmother may sacrifice herself—and that, to prove it, she must first become one."

"She would make a charming stepmother," smiled Madame Merle; "but I quite agree with you that she had better not decide upon her mission too hastily. Changing the form of one's mission's almost as difficult as changing the shape of one's nose: there they are, each, in the middle of one's face and one's character—one has to begin too far back. But I'll investigate and report to you."

All this went on quite over Isabel's head; she had no suspicions that her relations with Mr. Osmond were being discussed. Madame Merle had said nothing to put her on her guard; she alluded no more pointedly to him than to the other gentlemen of Florence, native and foreign, who now arrived in considerable numbers to pay their respects to Miss Archer's aunt. Isabel thought him interesting—she came back to that; she liked so to think of him. She had carried away an image from her visit to his hill-top which her subsequent knowledge of him did nothing to efface and which put on for her a particular harmony with other supposed and divined things, histories within histories: the image of a quiet, clever, sensitive, distinguished man, strolling on a moss-grown terrace above the sweet Val d'Arno and holding by the hand a little girl whose bell-like clearness gave a new grace to childhood. The picture had no flourishes, but she liked its lowness of tone and the atmosphere of summer twilight that pervaded it. It spoke of the kind of personal issue that touched her most nearly; of the choice between objects, subjects, contacts—what might she call them?—of a thin and those of a rich association; of a lonely, studious life in a lovely land; of an old sorrow that sometimes ached to-day; of a feeling of pride that was perhaps exaggerated, but that had an element of nobleness; of a care for beauty and perfection so natural and so cultivated together that the career appeared to stretch beneath it in the disposed vistas and with the ranges of steps and terraces and fountains of a formal Italian garden—allowing only for arid places freshened by the natural dews of a quaint half-anxious, half-helpless fatherhood. At Palazzo Crescentini Mr. Osmond's manner remained the same; diffident at first—oh self-conscious beyond doubt! and full of the effort (visible only to a sympathetic eye) to overcome this disadvantage; an effort which usually resulted in a great deal of easy, lively, very positive, rather aggressive, always suggestive talk. Mr. Osmond's talk was not injured by the indication of an eagerness to shine; Isabel found no difficulty in believing that a person was sincere who had so many of the signs of strong conviction—as for instance an explicit and graceful appreciation of anything that might be said on his own side of the question, said perhaps by Miss Archer in especial. What continued to please this young woman was that while he talked so for amusement he didn't talk, as she had heard people, for "effect." He uttered his ideas as if, odd as they often appeared, he were used to them and had lived with them; old polished knobs and heads and handles, of precious substance, that could be fitted if necessary to new walking-sticks—not switches plucked in destitution from the common tree and then too elegantly waved about. One day he brought his small daughter with him, and she rejoiced to renew acquaintance with the child, who, as she presented her forehead to be kissed by every member of the circle, reminded her vividly of an ingenue in a French play. Isabel had never seen a little person of this pattern; American girls were very different—different too were the maidens of England. Pansy was so formed and finished for her tiny place in the world, and yet in imagination, as one could see, so innocent and infantine. She sat on the sofa by Isabel; she wore a small grenadine mantle and a pair of the useful gloves that Madame Merle had given her—little grey gloves with a single button. She was like a sheet of blank paper—the ideal jeune fille of foreign fiction. Isabel hoped that so fair and smooth a page would be covered with an edifying text.

The Countess Gemini also came to call upon her, but the Countess was quite another affair. She was by no means a blank sheet; she had been written over in a variety of hands, and Mrs. Touchett, who felt by no means honoured by her visit, pronounced that a number of unmistakeable blots were to be seen upon her surface. The Countess gave rise indeed to some discussion between the mistress of the house and the visitor from Rome, in which Madame Merle (who was not such a fool as to irritate people by always agreeing with them) availed herself felicitously enough of that large licence of dissent which her hostess permitted as freely as she practised it. Mrs. Touchett had declared it a piece of audacity that this highly compromised character should have presented herself at such a time of day at the door of a house in which she was esteemed so little as she must long have known herself to be at Palazzo Crescentini. Isabel had been made acquainted with the estimate prevailing under that roof: it represented Mr. Osmond's sister as a lady who had so mismanaged her improprieties that they had ceased to hang together at all—which was at the least what one asked of such matters—and had become the mere floating fragments of a wrecked renown, incommoding social circulation. She had been married by her mother—a more administrative person, with an appreciation of foreign titles which the daughter, to do her justice, had probably by this time thrown off—to an Italian nobleman who had perhaps given her some excuse for attempting to quench the consciousness of outrage. The Countess, however, had consoled herself outrageously, and the list of her excuses had now lost itself in the labyrinth of her adventures. Mrs. Touchett had never consented to receive her, though the Countess had made overtures of old. Florence was not an austere city; but, as Mrs. Touchett said, she had to draw the line somewhere.

Madame Merle defended the luckless lady with a great deal of zeal and wit. She couldn't see why Mrs. Touchett should make a scapegoat of a woman who had really done no harm, who had only done good in the wrong way. One must certainly draw the line, but while one was about it one should draw it straight: it was a very crooked chalk-mark that would exclude the Countess Gemini. In that case Mrs. Touchett had better shut up her house; this perhaps would be the best course so long as she remained in Florence. One must be fair and not make arbitrary differences: the Countess had doubtless been imprudent, she had not been so clever as other women. She was a good creature, not clever at all; but since when had that been a ground of exclusion from the best society? For ever so long now one had heard nothing about her, and there could be no better proof of her having renounced the error of her ways than her desire to become a member of Mrs. Touchett's circle. Isabel could contribute nothing to this interesting dispute, not even a patient attention; she contented herself with having given a friendly welcome to the unfortunate lady, who, whatever her defects, had at least the merit of being Mr. Osmond's sister. As she liked the brother Isabel thought it proper to try and like the sister: in spite of the growing complexity of things she was still capable of these primitive sequences. She had not received the happiest impression of the Countess on meeting her at the villa, but was thankful for an opportunity to repair the accident. Had not Mr. Osmond remarked that she was a respectable person? To have proceeded from Gilbert Osmond this was a crude proposition, but Madame Merle bestowed upon it a certain improving polish. She told Isabel more about the poor Countess than Mr. Osmond had done, and related the history of her marriage and its consequences. The Count was a member of an ancient Tuscan family, but of such small estate that he had been glad to accept Amy Osmond, in spite of the questionable beauty which had yet not hampered her career, with the modest dowry her mother was able to offer—a sum about equivalent to that which had already formed her brother's share of their patrimony. Count Gemini since then, however, had inherited money, and now they were well enough off, as Italians went, though Amy was horribly extravagant. The Count was a low-lived brute; he had given his wife every pretext. She had no children; she had lost three within a year of their birth. Her mother, who had bristled with pretensions to elegant learning and published descriptive poems and corresponded on Italian subjects with the English weekly journals, her mother had died three years after the Countess's marriage, the father, lost in the grey American dawn of the situation, but reputed originally rich and wild, having died much earlier. One could see this in Gilbert Osmond, Madame Merle held—see that he had been brought up by a woman; though, to do him justice, one would suppose it had been by a more sensible woman than the American Corinne, as Mrs. Osmond had liked to be called. She had brought her children to Italy after her husband's death, and Mrs. Touchett remembered her during the year that followed her arrival. She thought her a horrible snob; but this was an irregularity of judgement on Mrs. Touchett's part, for she, like Mrs. Osmond, approved of political marriages. The Countess was very good company and not really the featherhead she seemed; all one had to do with her was to observe the simple condition of not believing a word she said. Madame Merle had always made the best of her for her brother's sake; he appreciated any kindness shown to Amy, because (if it had to be confessed for him) he rather felt she let down their common name. Naturally he couldn't like her style, her shrillness, her egotism, her violations of taste and above all of truth: she acted badly on his nerves, she was not HIS sort of woman. What was his sort of woman? Oh, the very opposite of the Countess, a woman to whom the truth should be habitually sacred. Isabel was unable to estimate the number of times her visitor had, in half an hour, profaned it: the Countess indeed had given her an impression of rather silly sincerity. She had talked almost exclusively about herself; how much she should like to know Miss Archer; how thankful she should be for a real friend; how base the people in Florence were; how tired she was of the place; how much she should like to live somewhere else—in Paris, in London, in Washington; how impossible it was to get anything nice to wear in Italy except a little old lace; how dear the world was growing everywhere; what a life of suffering and privation she had led. Madame Merle listened with interest to Isabel's account of this passage, but she had not needed it to feel exempt from anxiety. On the whole she was not afraid of the Countess, and she could afford to do what was altogether best—not to appear so.

Isabel had meanwhile another visitor, whom it was not, even behind her back, so easy a matter to patronise. Henrietta Stackpole, who had left Paris after Mrs. Touchett's departure for San Remo and had worked her way down, as she said, through the cities of North Italy, reached the banks of the Arno about the middle of May. Madame Merle surveyed her with a single glance, took her in from head to foot, and after a pang of despair determined to endure her. She determined indeed to delight in her. She mightn't be inhaled as a rose, but she might be grasped as a nettle. Madame Merle genially squeezed her into insignificance, and Isabel felt that in foreseeing this liberality she had done justice to her friend's intelligence. Henrietta's arrival had been announced by Mr. Bantling, who, coming down from Nice while she was at Venice, and expecting to find her in Florence, which she had not yet reached, called at Palazzo Crescentini to express his disappointment. Henrietta's own advent occurred two days later and produced in Mr. Bantling an emotion amply accounted for by the fact that he had not seen her since the termination of the episode at Versailles. The humorous view of his situation was generally taken, but it was uttered only by Ralph Touchett, who, in the privacy of his own apartment, when Bantling smoked a cigar there, indulged in goodness knew what strong comedy on the subject of the all-judging one and her British backer. This gentleman took the joke in perfectly good part and candidly confessed that he regarded the affair as a positive intellectual adventure. He liked Miss Stackpole extremely; he thought she had a wonderful head on her shoulders, and found great comfort in the society of a woman who was not perpetually thinking about what would be said and how what she did, how what they did—and they had done things!—would look. Miss Stackpole never cared how anything looked, and, if she didn't care, pray why should he? But his curiosity had been roused; he wanted awfully to see if she ever WOULD care. He was prepared to go as far as she—he didn't see why he should break down first.

Henrietta showed no signs of breaking down. Her prospects had brightened on her leaving England, and she was now in the full enjoyment of her copious resources. She had indeed been obliged to sacrifice her hopes with regard to the inner life; the social question, on the Continent, bristled with difficulties even more numerous than those she had encountered in England. But on the Continent there was the outer life, which was palpable and visible at every turn, and more easily convertible to literary uses than the customs of those opaque islanders. Out of doors in foreign lands, as she ingeniously remarked, one seemed to see the right side of the tapestry; out of doors in England one seemed to see the wrong side, which gave one no notion of the figure. The admission costs her historian a pang, but Henrietta, despairing of more occult things, was now paying much attention to the outer life. She had been studying it for two months at Venice, from which city she sent to the Interviewer a conscientious account of the gondolas, the Piazza, the Bridge of Sighs, the pigeons and the young boatman who chanted Tasso. The Interviewer was perhaps disappointed, but Henrietta was at least seeing Europe. Her present purpose was to get down to Rome before the malaria should come on—she apparently supposed that it began on a fixed day; and with this design she was to spend at present but few days in Florence. Mr. Bantling was to go with her to Rome, and she pointed out to Isabel that as he had been there before, as he was a military man and as he had had a classical education—he had been bred at Eton, where they study nothing but Latin and Whyte-Melville, said Miss Stackpole—he would be a most useful companion in the city of the Caesars. At this juncture Ralph had the happy idea of proposing to Isabel that she also, under his own escort, should make a pilgrimage to Rome. She expected to pass a portion of the next winter there—that was very well; but meantime there was no harm in surveying the field. There were ten days left of the beautiful month of May—the most precious month of all to the true Rome-lover. Isabel would become a Rome-lover; that was a foregone conclusion. She was provided with a trusty companion of her own sex, whose society, thanks to the fact of other calls on this lady's attention, would probably not be oppressive. Madame Merle would remain with Mrs. Touchett; she had left Rome for the summer and wouldn't care to return. She professed herself delighted to be left at peace in Florence; she had locked up her apartment and sent her cook home to Palestrina. She urged Isabel, however, to assent to Ralph's proposal, and assured her that a good introduction to Rome was not a thing to be despised. Isabel in truth needed no urging, and the party of four arranged its little journey. Mrs. Touchett, on this occasion, had resigned herself to the absence of a duenna; we have seen that she now inclined to the belief that her niece should stand alone. One of Isabel's preparations consisted of her seeing Gilbert Osmond before she started and mentioning her intention to him.

"I should like to be in Rome with you," he commented. "I should like to see you on that wonderful ground."

She scarcely faltered. "You might come then."

"But you'll have a lot of people with you."

"Ah," Isabel admitted, "of course I shall not be alone."

For a moment he said nothing more. "You'll like it," he went on at last. "They've spoiled it, but you'll rave about it."

"Ought I to dislike it because, poor old dear—the Niobe of Nations, you know—it has been spoiled?" she asked.

"No, I think not. It has been spoiled so often," he smiled. "If I were to go, what should I do with my little girl?"

"Can't you leave her at the villa?"

"I don't know that I like that—though there's a very good old woman who looks after her. I can't afford a governess."

"Bring her with you then," said Isabel promptly.

Mr. Osmond looked grave. "She has been in Rome all winter, at her convent; and she's too young to make journeys of pleasure."

"You don't like bringing her forward?" Isabel enquired.

"No, I think young girls should be kept out of the world."

"I was brought up on a different system."

"You? Oh, with you it succeeded, because you—you were exceptional."

"I don't see why," said Isabel, who, however, was not sure there was not some truth in the speech.

Mr. Osmond didn't explain; he simply went on: "If I thought it would make her resemble you to join a social group in Rome I'd take her there to-morrow."

"Don't make her resemble me," said Isabel. "Keep her like herself."

"I might send her to my sister," Mr. Osmond observed. He had almost the air of asking advice; he seemed to like to talk over his domestic matters with Miss Archer.

"Yes," she concurred; "I think that wouldn't do much towards making her resemble me!"

After she had left Florence Gilbert Osmond met Madame Merle at the Countess Gemini's. There were other people present; the Countess's drawing-room was usually well filled, and the talk had been general, but after a while Osmond left his place and came and sat on an ottoman half-behind, half-beside Madame Merle's chair. "She wants me to go to Rome with her," he remarked in a low voice.

"To go with her?"

"To be there while she's there. She proposed it.

"I suppose you mean that you proposed it and she assented."

"Of course I gave her a chance. But she's encouraging—she's very encouraging."

"I rejoice to hear it—but don't cry victory too soon. Of course you'll go to Rome."

"Ah," said Osmond, "it makes one work, this idea of yours!"

"Don't pretend you don't enjoy it—you're very ungrateful. You've not been so well occupied these many years."

"The way you take it's beautiful," said Osmond. "I ought to be grateful for that."

"Not too much so, however," Madame Merle answered. She talked with her usual smile, leaning back in her chair and looking round the room. "You've made a very good impression, and I've seen for myself that you've received one. You've not come to Mrs. Touchett's seven times to oblige me."

"The girl's not disagreeable," Osmond quietly conceded.

Madame Merle dropped her eye on him a moment, during which her lips closed with a certain firmness. "Is that all you can find to say about that fine creature?"

"All? Isn't it enough? Of how many people have you heard me say more?"

She made no answer to this, but still presented her talkative grace to the room. "You're unfathomable," she murmured at last. "I'm frightened at the abyss into which I shall have cast her."

He took it almost gaily. "You can't draw back—you've gone too far."

"Very good; but you must do the rest yourself."

"I shall do it," said Gilbert Osmond.

Madame Merle remained silent and he changed his place again; but when she rose to go he also took leave. Mrs. Touchett's victoria was awaiting her guest in the court, and after he had helped his friend into it he stood there detaining her. "You're very indiscreet," she said rather wearily; "you shouldn't have moved when I did."

He had taken off his hat; he passed his hand over his forehead. "I always forget; I'm out of the habit."

"You're quite unfathomable," she repeated, glancing up at the windows of the house, a modern structure in the new part of the town.

He paid no heed to this remark, but spoke in his own sense. "She's really very charming. I've scarcely known any one more graceful."

"It does me good to hear you say that. The better you like her the better for me."

"I like her very much. She's all you described her, and into the bargain capable, I feel, of great devotion. She has only one fault."

"What's that?"

"Too many ideas."

"I warned you she was clever."

"Fortunately they're very bad ones," said Osmond.

"Why is that fortunate?"

"Dame, if they must be sacrificed!"

Madame Merle leaned back, looking straight before her; then she spoke to the coachman. But her friend again detained her. "If I go to Rome what shall I do with Pansy?"

"I'll go and see her," said Madame Merle.

CHAPTER XXVII

I may not attempt to report in its fulness our young woman's response to the deep appeal of Rome, to analyse her feelings as she trod the pavement of the Forum or to number her pulsations as she crossed the threshold of Saint Peter's. It is enough to say that her impression was such as might have been expected of a person of her freshness and her eagerness. She had always been fond of history, and here was history in the stones of the street and the atoms of the sunshine. She had an imagination that kindled at the mention of great deeds, and wherever she turned some great deed had been acted. These things strongly moved her, but moved her all inwardly. It seemed to her companions that she talked less than usual, and Ralph Touchett, when he appeared to be looking listlessly and awkwardly over her head, was really dropping on her an intensity of observation. By her own measure she was very happy; she would even have been willing to take these hours for the happiest she was ever to know. The sense of the terrible human past was heavy to her, but that of something altogether contemporary would suddenly give it wings that it could wave in the blue. Her consciousness was so mixed that she scarcely knew where the different parts of it would lead her, and she went about in a repressed ecstasy of contemplation, seeing often in the things she looked at a great deal more than was there, and yet not seeing many of the items enumerated in her Murray. Rome, as Ralph said, confessed to the psychological moment. The herd of reechoing tourists had departed and most of the solemn places had relapsed into solemnity. The sky was a blaze of blue, and the plash of the fountains in their mossy niches had lost its chill and doubled its music. On the corners of the warm, bright streets one stumbled on bundles of flowers. Our friends had gone one afternoon—it was the third of their stay—to look at the latest excavations in the Forum, these labours having been for some time previous largely extended. They had descended from the modern street to the level of the Sacred Way, along which they wandered with a reverence of step which was not the same on the part of each. Henrietta Stackpole was struck with the fact that ancient Rome had been paved a good deal like New York, and even found an analogy between the deep chariot-ruts traceable in the antique street and the overjangled iron grooves which express the intensity of American life. The sun had begun to sink, the air was a golden haze, and the long shadows of broken column and vague pedestal leaned across the field of ruin. Henrietta wandered away with Mr. Bantling, whom it was apparently delightful to her to hear speak of Julius Caesar as a "cheeky old boy," and Ralph addressed such elucidations as he was prepared to offer to the attentive ear of our heroine. One of the humble archeologists who hover about the place had put himself at the disposal of the two, and repeated his lesson with a fluency which the decline of the season had done nothing to impair. A process of digging was on view in a remote corner of the Forum, and he presently remarked that if it should please the signori to go and watch it a little they might see something of interest. The proposal commended itself more to Ralph than to Isabel, weary with much wandering; so that she admonished her companion to satisfy his curiosity while she patiently awaited his return. The hour and the place were much to her taste—she should enjoy being briefly alone. Ralph accordingly went off with the cicerone while Isabel sat down on a prostrate column near the foundations of the Capitol. She wanted a short solitude, but she was not long to enjoy it. Keen as was her interest in the rugged relics of the Roman past that lay scattered about her and in which the corrosion of centuries had still left so much of individual life, her thoughts, after resting a while on these things, had wandered, by a concatenation of stages it might require some subtlety to trace, to regions and objects charged with a more active appeal. From the Roman past to Isabel Archer's future was a long stride, but her imagination had taken it in a single flight and now hovered in slow circles over the nearer and richer field. She was so absorbed in her thoughts, as she bent her eyes upon a row of cracked but not dislocated slabs covering the ground at her feet, that she had not heard the sound of approaching footsteps before a shadow was thrown across the line of her vision. She looked up and saw a gentleman—a gentleman who was not Ralph come back to say that the excavations were a bore. This personage was startled as she was startled; he stood there baring his head to her perceptibly pale surprise.

"Lord Warburton!" Isabel exclaimed as she rose.

"I had no idea it was you. I turned that corner and came upon you."

She looked about her to explain. "I'm alone, but my companions have just left me. My cousin's gone to look at the work over there."

"Ah yes; I see." And Lord Warburton's eyes wandered vaguely in the direction she had indicated. He stood firmly before her now; he had recovered his balance and seemed to wish to show it, though very kindly. "Don't let me disturb you," he went on, looking at her dejected pillar. "I'm afraid you're tired."

"Yes, I'm rather tired." She hesitated a moment, but sat down again. "Don't let me interrupt you," she added.

"Oh dear, I'm quite alone, I've nothing on earth to do. I had no idea you were in Rome. I've just come from the East. I'm only passing through."

"You've been making a long journey," said Isabel, who had learned from Ralph that Lord Warburton was absent from England.

"Yes, I came abroad for six months—soon after I saw you last. I've been in Turkey and Asia Minor; I came the other day from Athens." He managed not to be awkward, but he wasn't easy, and after a longer look at the girl he came down to nature. "Do you wish me to leave you, or will you let me stay a little?"

She took it all humanely. "I don't wish you to leave me, Lord Warburton; I'm very glad to see you."

"Thank you for saying that. May I sit down?"

The fluted shaft on which she had taken her seat would have afforded a resting-place to several persons, and there was plenty of room even for a highly-developed Englishman. This fine specimen of that great class seated himself near our young lady, and in the course of five minutes he had asked her several questions, taken rather at random and to which, as he put some of them twice over, he apparently somewhat missed catching the answer; had given her too some information about himself which was not wasted upon her calmer feminine sense. He repeated more than once that he had not expected to meet her, and it was evident that the encounter touched him in a way that would have made preparation advisable. He began abruptly to pass from the impunity of things to their solemnity, and from their being delightful to their being impossible. He was splendidly sunburnt; even his multitudinous beard had been burnished by the fire of Asia. He was dressed in the loose-fitting, heterogeneous garments in which the English traveller in foreign lands is wont to consult his comfort and affirm his nationality; and with his pleasant steady eyes, his bronzed complexion, fresh beneath its seasoning, his manly figure, his minimising manner and his general air of being a gentleman and an explorer, he was such a representative of the British race as need not in any clime have been disavowed by those who have a kindness for it. Isabel noted these things and was glad she had always liked him. He had kept, evidently in spite of shocks, every one of his merits—properties these partaking of the essence of great decent houses, as one might put it; resembling their innermost fixtures and ornaments, not subject to vulgar shifting and removable only by some whole break-up. They talked of the matters naturally in order; her uncle's death, Ralph's state of health, the way she had passed her winter, her visit to Rome, her return to Florence, her plans for the summer, the hotel she was staying at; and then of Lord Warburton's own adventures, movements, intentions, impressions and present domicile. At last there was a silence, and it said so much more than either had said that it scarce needed his final words. "I've written to you several times."

"Written to me? I've never had your letters."

"I never sent them. I burned them up."

"Ah," laughed Isabel, "it was better that you should do that than I!"

"I thought you wouldn't care for them," he went on with a simplicity that touched her. "It seemed to me that after all I had no right to trouble you with letters."

"I should have been very glad to have news of you. You know how I hoped that—that—" But she stopped; there would be such a flatness in the utterance of her thought.

"I know what you're going to say. You hoped we should always remain good friends." This formula, as Lord Warburton uttered it, was certainly flat enough; but then he was interested in making it appear so.

She found herself reduced simply to "Please don't talk of all that"; a speech which hardly struck her as improvement on the other.

"It's a small consolation to allow me!" her companion exclaimed with force.

"I can't pretend to console you," said the girl, who, all still as she sat there, threw herself back with a sort of inward triumph on the answer that had satisfied him so little six months before. He was pleasant, he was powerful, he was gallant; there was no better man than he. But her answer remained.

"It's very well you don't try to console me; it wouldn't be in your power," she heard him say through the medium of her strange elation.

"I hoped we should meet again, because I had no fear you would attempt to make me feel I had wronged you. But when you do that—the pain's greater than the pleasure." And she got up with a small conscious majesty, looking for her companions.

"I don't want to make you feel that; of course I can't say that. I only just want you to know one or two things—in fairness to myself, as it were. I won't return to the subject again. I felt very strongly what I expressed to you last year; I couldn't think of anything else. I tried to forget—energetically, systematically. I tried to take an interest in somebody else. I tell you this because I want you to know I did my duty. I didn't succeed. It was for the same purpose I went abroad—as far away as possible. They say travelling distracts the mind, but it didn't distract mine. I've thought of you perpetually, ever since I last saw you. I'm exactly the same. I love you just as much, and everything I said to you then is just as true. This instant at which I speak to you shows me again exactly how, to my great misfortune, you just insuperably charm me. There—I can't say less. I don't mean, however, to insist; it's only for a moment. I may add that when I came upon you a few minutes since, without the smallest idea of seeing you, I was, upon my honour, in the very act of wishing I knew where you were." He had recovered his self-control, and while he spoke it became complete. He might have been addressing a small committee—making all quietly and clearly a statement of importance; aided by an occasional look at a paper of notes concealed in his hat, which he had not again put on. And the committee, assuredly, would have felt the point proved.

"I've often thought of you, Lord Warburton," Isabel answered. "You may be sure I shall always do that." And she added in a tone of which she tried to keep up the kindness and keep down the meaning: "There's no harm in that on either side."

They walked along together, and she was prompt to ask about his sisters and request him to let them know she had done so. He made for the moment no further reference to their great question, but dipped again into shallower and safer waters. But he wished to know when she was to leave Rome, and on her mentioning the limit of her stay declared he was glad it was still so distant.

"Why do you say that if you yourself are only passing through?" she enquired with some anxiety.

"Ah, when I said I was passing through I didn't mean that one would treat Rome as if it were Clapham Junction. To pass through Rome is to stop a week or two."

"Say frankly that you mean to stay as long as I do!"

His flushed smile, for a little, seemed to sound her. "You won't like that. You're afraid you'll see too much of me."

"It doesn't matter what I like. I certainly can't expect you to leave this delightful place on my account. But I confess I'm afraid of you."

"Afraid I'll begin again? I promise to be very careful."

They had gradually stopped and they stood a moment face to face. "Poor Lord Warburton!" she said with a compassion intended to be good for both of them.

"Poor Lord Warburton indeed! But I'll be careful."

"You may be unhappy, but you shall not make ME so. That I can't allow."

"If I believed I could make you unhappy I think I should try it." At this she walked in advance and he also proceeded. "I'll never say a word to displease you."

"Very good. If you do, our friendship's at an end."

"Perhaps some day—after a while—you'll give me leave."

"Give you leave to make me unhappy?"

He hesitated. "To tell you again—" But he checked himself. "I'll keep it down. I'll keep it down always."

Ralph Touchett had been joined in his visit to the excavation by Miss Stackpole and her attendant, and these three now emerged from among the mounds of earth and stone collected round the aperture and came into sight of Isabel and her companion. Poor Ralph hailed his friend with joy qualified by wonder, and Henrietta exclaimed in a high voice "Gracious, there's that lord!" Ralph and his English neighbour greeted with the austerity with which, after long separations, English neighbours greet, and Miss Stackpole rested her large intellectual gaze upon the sunburnt traveller. But she soon established her relation to the crisis. "I don't suppose you remember me, sir."

"Indeed I do remember you," said Lord Warburton. "I asked you to come and see me, and you never came."

"I don't go everywhere I'm asked," Miss Stackpole answered coldly.

"Ah well, I won't ask you again," laughed the master of Lockleigh.

"If you do I'll go; so be sure!"

Lord Warburton, for all his hilarity, seemed sure enough. Mr. Bantling had stood by without claiming a recognition, but he now took occasion to nod to his lordship, who answered him with a friendly "Oh, you here, Bantling?" and a hand-shake.

"Well," said Henrietta, "I didn't know you knew him!"

"I guess you don't know every one I know," Mr. Bantling rejoined facetiously.

"I thought that when an Englishman knew a lord he always told you."

"Ah, I'm afraid Bantling was ashamed of me," Lord Warburton laughed again. Isabel took pleasure in that note; she gave a small sigh of relief as they kept their course homeward.

The next day was Sunday; she spent her morning over two long letters—one to her sister Lily, the other to Madame Merle; but in neither of these epistles did she mention the fact that a rejected suitor had threatened her with another appeal. Of a Sunday afternoon all good Romans (and the best Romans are often the northern barbarians) follow the custom of going to vespers at Saint Peter's; and it had been agreed among our friends that they would drive together to the great church. After lunch, an hour before the carriage came, Lord Warburton presented himself at the Hotel de Paris and paid a visit to the two ladies, Ralph Touchett and Mr. Bantling having gone out together. The visitor seemed to have wished to give Isabel a proof of his intention to keep the promise made her the evening before; he was both discreet and frank—not even dumbly importunate or remotely intense. He thus left her to judge what a mere good friend he could be. He talked about his travels, about Persia, about Turkey, and when Miss Stackpole asked him whether it would "pay" for her to visit those countries assured her they offered a great field to female enterprise. Isabel did him justice, but she wondered what his purpose was and what he expected to gain even by proving the superior strain of his sincerity. If he expected to melt her by showing what a good fellow he was, he might spare himself the trouble. She knew the superior strain of everything about him, and nothing he could now do was required to light the view. Moreover his being in Rome at all affected her as a complication of the wrong sort—she liked so complications of the right. Nevertheless, when, on bringing his call to a close, he said he too should be at Saint Peter's and should look out for her and her friends, she was obliged to reply that he must follow his convenience.

In the church, as she strolled over its tesselated acres, he was the first person she encountered. She had not been one of the superior tourists who are "disappointed" in Saint Peter's and find it smaller than its fame; the first time she passed beneath the huge leathern curtain that strains and bangs at the entrance, the first time she found herself beneath the far-arching dome and saw the light drizzle down through the air thickened with incense and with the reflections of marble and gilt, of mosaic and bronze, her conception of greatness rose and dizzily rose. After this it never lacked space to soar. She gazed and wondered like a child or a peasant, she paid her silent tribute to the seated sublime. Lord Warburton walked beside her and talked of Saint Sophia of Constantinople; she feared for instance that he would end by calling attention to his exemplary conduct. The service had not yet begun, but at Saint Peter's there is much to observe, and as there is something almost profane in the vastness of the place, which seems meant as much for physical as for spiritual exercise, the different figures and groups, the mingled worshippers and spectators, may follow their various intentions without conflict or scandal. In that splendid immensity individual indiscretion carries but a short distance. Isabel and her companions, however, were guilty of none; for though Henrietta was obliged in candour to declare that Michael Angelo's dome suffered by comparison with that of the Capitol at Washington, she addressed her protest chiefly to Mr. Bantling's ear and reserved it in its more accentuated form for the columns of the Interviewer. Isabel made the circuit of the church with his lordship, and as they drew near the choir on the left of the entrance the voices of the Pope's singers were borne to them over the heads of the large number of persons clustered outside the doors. They paused a while on the skirts of this crowd, composed in equal measure of Roman cockneys and inquisitive strangers, and while they stood there the sacred concert went forward. Ralph, with Henrietta and Mr.

Bantling, was apparently within, where Isabel, looking beyond the dense group in front of her, saw the afternoon light, silvered by clouds of incense that seemed to mingle with the splendid chant, slope through the embossed recesses of high windows. After a while the singing stopped and then Lord Warburton seemed disposed to move off with her. Isabel could only accompany him; whereupon she found herself confronted with Gilbert Osmond, who appeared to have been standing at a short distance behind her. He now approached with all the forms—he appeared to have multiplied them on this occasion to suit the place.

"So you decided to come?" she said as she put out her hand.

"Yes, I came last night and called this afternoon at your hotel. They told me you had come here, and I looked about for you."

"The others are inside," she decided to say.

"I didn't come for the others," he promptly returned.

She looked away; Lord Warburton was watching them; perhaps he had heard this. Suddenly she remembered it to be just what he had said to her the morning he came to Gardencourt to ask her to marry him. Mr. Osmond's words had brought the colour to her cheek, and this reminiscence had not the effect of dispelling it. She repaired any betrayal by mentioning to each companion the name of the other, and fortunately at this moment Mr. Bantling emerged from the choir, cleaving the crowd with British valour and followed by Miss Stackpole and Ralph Touchett. I say fortunately, but this is perhaps a superficial view of the matter; since on perceiving the gentleman from Florence Ralph Touchett appeared to take the case as not committing him to joy. He didn't hang back, however, from civility, and presently observed to Isabel, with due benevolence, that she would soon have all her friends about her. Miss Stackpole had met Mr. Osmond in Florence, but she had already found occasion to say to Isabel that she liked him no better than her other admirers—than Mr. Touchett and Lord Warburton, and even than little Mr. Rosier in Paris. "I don't know what it's in you," she had been pleased to remark, "but for a nice girl you do attract the most unnatural people. Mr. Goodwood's the only one I've any respect for, and he's just the one you don't appreciate."

"What's your opinion of Saint Peter's?" Mr. Osmond was meanwhile enquiring of our young lady.

"It's very large and very bright," she contented herself with replying.

"It's too large; it makes one feel like an atom."

"Isn't that the right way to feel in the greatest of human temples?" she asked with rather a liking for her phrase.

"I suppose it's the right way to feel everywhere, when one IS nobody. But I like it in a church as little as anywhere else."

"You ought indeed to be a Pope!" Isabel exclaimed, remembering something he had referred to in Florence.

"Ah, I should have enjoyed that!" said Gilbert Osmond.

Lord Warburton meanwhile had joined Ralph Touchett, and the two strolled away together. "Who's the fellow speaking to Miss Archer?" his lordship demanded.

"His name's Gilbert Osmond—he lives in Florence," Ralph said.

"What is he besides?"

"Nothing at all. Oh yes, he's an American; but one forgets that—he's so little of one."

"Has he known Miss Archer long?"

"Three or four weeks."

"Does she like him?"

"She's trying to find out."

"And will she?"

"Find out—?" Ralph asked.

"Will she like him?"

"Do you mean will she accept him?"

"Yes," said Lord Warburton after an instant; "I suppose that's what I horribly mean."

"Perhaps not if one does nothing to prevent it," Ralph replied.

His lordship stared a moment, but apprehended. "Then we must be perfectly quiet?"

"As quiet as the grave. And only on the chance!" Ralph added.

"The chance she may?"

"The chance she may not?"

Lord Warburton took this at first in silence, but he spoke again. "Is he awfully clever?"

"Awfully," said Ralph.

His companion thought. "And what else?"

"What more do you want?" Ralph groaned.

"Do you mean what more does SHE?"

Ralph took him by the arm to turn him: they had to rejoin the others. "She wants nothing that WE can give her."

"Ah well, if she won't have You—!" said his lordship handsomely as they went.

THE PORTRAIT OF A LADY

VOLUME II (of II)

CHAPTER XXVIII

On the morrow, in the evening, Lord Warburton went again to see his friends at their hotel, and at this establishment he learned that they had gone to the opera. He drove to the opera with the idea of paying them a visit in their box after the easy Italian fashion; and when he had obtained his admittance—it was one of the secondary theatres—looked about the large, bare, ill-lighted house. An act had just terminated and he was at liberty to pursue his quest. After scanning two or three tiers of boxes he perceived in one of the largest of these receptacles a lady whom he easily recognised. Miss Archer was seated facing the stage and partly screened by the curtain of the box; and beside her, leaning back in his chair, was Mr. Gilbert Osmond. They appeared to have the place to themselves, and Warburton supposed their companions had taken advantage of the recess to enjoy the relative coolness of the lobby. He stood a while with his eyes on the interesting pair; he asked himself if he should go up and interrupt the harmony. At last he judged that Isabel had seen him, and this accident determined him. There should be no marked holding off. He took his way to the upper regions and on the staircase met Ralph Touchett slowly descending, his hat at the inclination of ennui and his hands where they usually were.

"I saw you below a moment since and was going down to you. I feel lonely and want company," was Ralph's greeting.

"You've some that's very good which you've yet deserted."

"Do you mean my cousin? Oh, she has a visitor and doesn't want me. Then Miss Stackpole and Bantling have gone out to a cafe to eat an ice—Miss Stackpole delights in an ice. I didn't think they wanted me either. The opera's very bad; the women look like laundresses and sing like peacocks. I feel very low."

"You had better go home," Lord Warburton said without affectation.

"And leave my young lady in this sad place? Ah no, I must watch over her."

"She seems to have plenty of friends."

"Yes, that's why I must watch," said Ralph with the same large mock-melancholy.

"If she doesn't want you it's probable she doesn't want me."

"No, you're different. Go to the box and stay there while I walk about."

Lord Warburton went to the box, where Isabel's welcome was as to a friend so honourably old that he vaguely asked himself what queer temporal province she was annexing. He exchanged greetings with Mr. Osmond, to whom he had been introduced the day before and who, after he came in, sat blandly apart and silent, as if repudiating competence in the subjects of allusion now probable. It struck her second visitor that Miss Archer had, in operatic conditions, a radiance, even a slight exaltation; as she was, however, at all times a keenly-glancing, quickly-moving, completely animated young woman, he may have been mistaken on this point. Her talk with him moreover pointed to presence of mind; it expressed a kindness so ingenious and deliberate as to indicate that she was in undisturbed possession of her faculties. Poor Lord Warburton had moments of bewilderment. She had discouraged him, formally, as much as a woman could; what business had she then with such arts and such felicities, above all with such tones of reparation—preparation? Her voice had tricks of sweetness, but why play them on HIM? The others came back; the bare, familiar, trivial opera began again. The box was large, and there was room for him to remain if he would sit a little behind and in the dark. He did so for half an hour, while Mr. Osmond remained in front, leaning forward, his elbows on his knees, just behind Isabel. Lord Warburton heard nothing, and from his gloomy corner saw nothing but the clear profile of this young lady defined against the dim illumination of the house. When there was another interval no one moved. Mr. Osmond talked to Isabel, and Lord Warburton kept his corner. He did so but for a short time, however; after which he got up and bade good-night to the ladies. Isabel said nothing to detain him, but it didn't prevent his being puzzled again. Why should she mark so one of his values—quite the wrong one—when she would have nothing to do with another, which was quite the right? He was angry with himself for being puzzled, and then angry for being angry. Verdi's music did little to comfort him, and he left the theatre and walked homeward, without knowing his way, through the tortuous, tragic streets of Rome, where heavier sorrows than his had been carried under the stars.

"What's the character of that gentleman?" Osmond asked of Isabel after he had retired.

"Irreproachable—don't you see it?"

"He owns about half England; that's his character," Henrietta remarked. "That's what they call a free country!"

"Ah, he's a great proprietor? Happy man!" said Gilbert Osmond.

"Do you call that happiness—the ownership of wretched human beings?" cried Miss Stackpole. "He owns his tenants and has thousands of them. It's pleasant to own something, but inanimate objects are enough for me. I don't insist on flesh and blood and minds and consciences."

"It seems to me you own a human being or two," Mr. Bantling suggested jocosely. "I wonder if Warburton orders his tenants about as you do me."

"Lord Warburton's a great radical," Isabel said. "He has very advanced opinions."

"He has very advanced stone walls. His park's enclosed by a gigantic iron fence, some thirty miles round," Henrietta announced for the information of Mr. Osmond. "I should like him to converse with a few of our Boston radicals."

"Don't they approve of iron fences?" asked Mr. Bantling.

"Only to shut up wicked conservatives. I always feel as if I were talking to YOU over something with a neat top-finish of broken glass."

"Do you know him well, this unreformed reformer?" Osmond went on, questioning Isabel.

"Well enough for all the use I have for him."

"And how much of a use is that?"

"Well, I like to like him."

"'Liking to like'—why, it makes a passion!" said Osmond.

"No"—she considered—"keep that for liking to DISlike."

"Do you wish to provoke me then," Osmond laughed, "to a passion for HIM?"

She said nothing for a moment, but then met the light question with a disproportionate gravity. "No, Mr. Osmond; I don't think I should ever dare to provoke you. Lord Warburton, at any rate," she more easily added, "is a very nice man."

"Of great ability?" her friend enquired.

"Of excellent ability, and as good as he looks."

"As good as he's good-looking do you mean? He's very good-looking. How detestably fortunate!—to be a great English magnate, to be clever and handsome into the bargain, and, by way of finishing off, to enjoy your high favour! That's a man I could envy."

Isabel considered him with interest. "You seem to me to be always envying some one. Yesterday it was the Pope; to-day it's poor Lord Warburton."

"My envy's not dangerous; it wouldn't hurt a mouse. I don't want to destroy the people—I only want to BE them. You see it would destroy only myself."

"You'd like to be the Pope?" said Isabel.

"I should love it—but I should have gone in for it earlier. But why"—Osmond reverted—"do you speak of your friend as poor?"

"Women—when they are very, very good sometimes pity men after they've hurt them; that's their great way of showing kindness," said Ralph, joining in the conversation for the first time and with a cynicism so transparently ingenious as to be virtually innocent.

"Pray, have I hurt Lord Warburton?" Isabel asked, raising her eyebrows as if the idea were perfectly fresh.

"It serves him right if you have," said Henrietta while the curtain rose for the ballet.

Isabel saw no more of her attributive victim for the next twenty-four hours, but on the second day after the visit to the opera she encountered him in the gallery of the Capitol, where he stood before the lion of the collection, the statue of the Dying Gladiator. She had come in with her companions, among whom, on this occasion again, Gilbert Osmond had his place, and the party, having ascended the staircase, entered the first and finest of the rooms. Lord Warburton addressed her alertly enough, but said in a moment that he was leaving the gallery. "And I'm leaving Rome," he added. "I must bid you goodbye." Isabel, inconsequently enough, was now sorry to hear it. This was perhaps because she had ceased to be afraid of his renewing his suit; she was thinking of something else. She was on the point of naming her regret, but she checked herself and simply wished him a happy journey; which made him look at her rather unlightedly. "I'm afraid you'll think me very 'volatile.' I told you the other day I wanted so much to stop."

"Oh no; you could easily change your mind."

"That's what I have done."

"Bon voyage then."

"You're in a great hurry to get rid of me," said his lordship quite dismally.

"Not in the least. But I hate partings."

"You don't care what I do," he went on pitifully.

Isabel looked at him a moment. "Ah," she said, "you're not keeping your promise!"

He coloured like a boy of fifteen. "If I'm not, then it's because I can't; and that's why I'm going."

"Good-bye then."

"Good-bye." He lingered still, however. "When shall I see you again?"

Isabel hesitated, but soon, as if she had had a happy inspiration: "Some day after you're married."

"That will never be. It will be after you are."

"That will do as well," she smiled.

"Yes, quite as well. Good-bye."

They shook hands, and he left her alone in the glorious room, among the shining antique marbles. She sat down in the centre of the circle of these presences, regarding them vaguely, resting her eyes on their beautiful blank faces; listening, as it were, to their eternal silence. It is impossible, in Rome at least, to look long at a great company of Greek sculptures without feeling the effect of their noble quietude; which, as with a high door closed for the ceremony, slowly drops on the spirit the large white mantle of peace. I say in Rome especially, because the Roman air is an exquisite medium for such impressions. The golden sunshine mingles with them, the deep stillness of the past, so vivid yet, though it is nothing but a void full of names, seems to throw a solemn spell upon them. The blinds were partly closed in the windows of the Capitol, and a clear, warm shadow rested on the figures and made them more mildly human. Isabel sat there a long time, under the charm of their motionless grace, wondering to what, of their experience, their absent eyes were open, and how, to our ears, their alien lips would sound. The dark red walls of the room threw them into relief; the polished marble floor reflected their beauty. She had seen them all before, but her enjoyment repeated itself, and it was all the greater because she was glad again, for the time, to be alone. At last, however, her attention lapsed, drawn off by a deeper tide of life. An occasional tourist came in, stopped and stared a moment at the Dying Gladiator, and then passed out of the other door, creaking over the smooth pavement. At the end of half an hour Gilbert Osmond reappeared, apparently in advance of his companions. He strolled toward her slowly, with his hands behind him and his usual enquiring, yet not quite appealing smile. "I'm surprised to find you alone, I thought you had company.

"So I have—the best." And she glanced at the Antinous and the Faun.

"Do you call them better company than an English peer?"

"Ah, my English peer left me some time ago." She got up, speaking with intention a little dryly.

Mr. Osmond noted her dryness, which contributed for him to the interest of his question. "I'm afraid that what I heard the other evening is true: you're rather cruel to that nobleman."

Isabel looked a moment at the vanquished Gladiator. "It's not true. I'm scrupulously kind."

"That's exactly what I mean!" Gilbert Osmond returned, and with such happy hilarity that his joke needs to be explained. We know that he was fond of originals, of rarities, of the superior and the exquisite; and now that he had seen Lord Warburton, whom he thought a very fine example of his race and order, he perceived a new attraction in the idea of taking to himself a young lady who had qualified herself to figure in his collection of choice objects by declining so noble a hand. Gilbert Osmond had a high appreciation of this particular patriciate; not so much for its distinction, which he thought easily surpassable, as for its solid actuality. He had never forgiven his star for not appointing him to an English dukedom, and he could measure the unexpectedness of such conduct as Isabel's. It would be proper that the woman he might marry should have done something of that sort.

CHAPTER XXIX

Ralph Touchett, in talk with his excellent friend, had rather markedly qualified, as we know, his recognition of Gilbert Osmond's personal merits; but he might really have felt himself illiberal in the light of that gentleman's conduct during the rest of the visit to Rome. Osmond spent a portion of each day with Isabel and her companions, and ended by affecting them as the easiest of men to live with. Who wouldn't have seen that he could command, as it were, both tact and gaiety?—which perhaps was exactly why Ralph had made his old-time look of superficial sociability a reproach to him. Even Isabel's invidious kinsman was obliged to admit that he was just now a delightful associate. His good humour was imperturbable, his knowledge of the right fact, his production of the right word, as convenient as the friendly flicker of a match for your cigarette. Clearly he was amused—as amused as a man could be who was so little ever surprised, and that made him almost applausive. It was not that his spirits were visibly high—he would never, in the concert of pleasure, touch the big drum by so much as a knuckle: he had a mortal dislike to the high, ragged note, to what he called random ravings. He thought Miss Archer sometimes of too precipitate a readiness. It was pity she had that fault, because if she had not had it she would really have had none; she would have been as smooth to his general need of her as handled ivory to the palm. If he was not personally loud, however, he was deep, and during these closing days of the Roman May he knew a complacency that matched with slow irregular walks under the pines of the Villa Borghese, among the small sweet meadow-flowers and the mossy marbles. He was pleased with everything; he had never before been pleased with so many things at once. Old impressions, old enjoyments, renewed themselves; one evening, going home to his room at the inn, he wrote down a little sonnet to which he prefixed the title of "Rome Revisited." A day or two later he showed this piece of correct and ingenious verse to Isabel, explaining to her that it was an Italian fashion to commemorate the occasions of life by a tribute to the muse.

He took his pleasures in general singly; he was too often—he would have admitted that—too sorely aware of something wrong, something ugly; the fertilising dew of a conceivable felicity too seldom descended on his spirit. But at present he was happy—happier than he had perhaps ever been in his life, and the feeling had a large foundation. This was simply the sense of success—the most agreeable emotion of the human heart. Osmond had never had too much of it; in this respect he had the irritation of satiety, as he knew perfectly well and often reminded himself. "Ah no, I've not been spoiled; certainly I've not been spoiled," he used inwardly to repeat. "If I do succeed before I die I shall thoroughly have earned it." He was too apt to reason as if "earning" this boon consisted above all of covertly aching for it and might be confined to that exercise. Absolutely void of it, also, his career had not been; he might indeed have suggested to a spectator here and there that he was resting on vague laurels. But his triumphs were, some of them, now too old; others had been too easy. The present one had been less arduous than might have been expected, but had been easy—that is had been rapid—only because he had made an altogether exceptional effort, a greater effort than he had believed it in him to make. The desire to have something or other to show for his "parts"—to show somehow or other—had been the dream of his youth; but as the years went on the conditions attached to any marked proof of rarity had affected him more and more as gross and detestable; like the swallowing of mugs of beer to advertise what one could "stand." If an anonymous drawing on a museum wall had been conscious and watchful it might have known this peculiar pleasure of being at last and all of a sudden identified—as from the hand of a great master—by the so high and so unnoticed fact of style. His "style" was what the girl had discovered with a little help; and now, beside herself enjoying it, she should publish it to the world without his having any of the trouble. She should do the thing FOR him, and he would not have waited in vain.

Shortly before the time fixed in advance for her departure this young lady received from Mrs. Touchett a telegram running as follows: "Leave Florence 4th June for Bellaggio, and take you if you have not other views. But can't wait if you dawdle in Rome." The dawdling in Rome was very pleasant, but Isabel had different views, and she let her aunt know she would immediately join her. She told Gilbert Osmond that she had done so, and he replied that, spending many of his summers as well as his winters in Italy, he himself would loiter a little longer in the cool shadow of Saint Peter's. He would not return to Florence for ten days more, and in that time she would have started for Bellaggio. It might be months in this case before he should see her again. This exchange took place in the large decorated sitting-room occupied by our friends at the hotel; it was late in the evening, and Ralph Touchett was to take his cousin back to Florence on the morrow. Osmond had found the girl alone; Miss Stackpole had contracted a friendship with a delightful American family on the fourth floor and had mounted the interminable staircase to pay them a visit. Henrietta contracted friendships, in travelling, with great freedom, and had formed in railway-carriages several that were among her most valued ties. Ralph was making arrangements for the morrow's journey, and Isabel sat alone in a wilderness of yellow upholstery. The chairs and sofas were orange; the walls and windows were draped in purple and gilt. The mirrors, the pictures had great flamboyant frames; the ceiling was deeply vaulted and painted over with naked muses and cherubs. For Osmond the place was ugly to distress; the false colours, the sham splendour were like vulgar, bragging, lying talk. Isabel had taken in hand a volume of Ampere, presented, on their arrival in Rome, by Ralph; but though she held it in her lap with her finger vaguely kept in the place she was not impatient to pursue her study. A lamp covered with a drooping veil of pink tissue-paper burned on the table beside her and diffused a strange pale rosiness over the scene.

"You say you'll come back; but who knows?" Gilbert Osmond said.

"I think you're much more likely to start on your voyage round the world. You're under no obligation to come back; you can do exactly what you choose; you can roam through space."

"Well, Italy's a part of space," Isabel answered. "I can take it on the way."

"On the way round the world? No, don't do that. Don't put us in a parenthesis—give us a chapter to ourselves. I don't want to see you on your travels. I'd rather see you when they're over. I should like to see you when you're tired and satiated," Osmond added in a moment. "I shall prefer you in that state."

Isabel, with her eyes bent, fingered the pages of M. Ampere. "You turn things into ridicule without seeming to do it, though not, I think, without intending it. You've no respect for my travels—you think them ridiculous."

"Where do you find that?"

She went on in the same tone, fretting the edge of her book with the paper-knife. "You see my ignorance, my blunders, the way I wander about as if the world belonged to me, simply because—because it has been put into my power to do so. You don't think a woman ought to do that. You think it bold and ungraceful."

"I think it beautiful," said Osmond. "You know my opinions—I've treated you to enough of them. Don't you remember my telling you that one ought to make one's life a work of art? You looked rather shocked at first; but then I told you that it was exactly what you seemed to me to be trying to do with your own."

She looked up from her book. "What you despise most in the world is bad, is stupid art."

"Possibly. But yours seem to me very clear and very good."

"If I were to go to Japan next winter you would laugh at me," she went on.

Osmond gave a smile—a keen one, but not a laugh, for the tone of their conversation was not jocose. Isabel had in fact her solemnity; he had seen it before. "You have one!"

"That's exactly what I say. You think such an idea absurd."

"I would give my little finger to go to Japan; it's one of the countries I want most to see. Can't you believe that, with my taste for old lacquer?"

"I haven't a taste for old lacquer to excuse me," said Isabel.

"You've a better excuse—the means of going. You're quite wrong in your theory that I laugh at you. I don't know what has put it into your head."

"It wouldn't be remarkable if you did think it ridiculous that I should have the means to travel when you've not; for you know everything and I know nothing."

"The more reason why you should travel and learn," smiled Osmond. "Besides," he added as if it were a point to be made, "I don't know everything."

Isabel was not struck with the oddity of his saying this gravely; she was thinking that the pleasantest incident of her life—so it pleased her to qualify these too few days in Rome, which she might musingly have likened to the figure of some small princess of one of the ages of dress overmuffled in a mantle of state and dragging a train that it took pages or historians to hold up—that this felicity was coming to an end. That most of the interest of the time had been owing to Mr. Osmond was a reflexion she was not just now at pains to make; she had already done the point abundant justice. But she said to herself that if there were a danger they should never meet again, perhaps after all it would be as well. Happy things don't repeat themselves, and her adventure wore already the changed, the seaward face of some romantic island from which, after feasting on purple grapes, she was putting off while the breeze rose. She might come back to Italy and find him different—this strange man who pleased her just as he was; and it would be better not to come than run the risk of that. But if she was not to come the greater the pity that the chapter was closed; she felt for a moment a pang that touched the source of tears. The sensation kept her silent, and Gilbert Osmond was silent too; he was looking at her. "Go everywhere," he said at last, in a low, kind voice; "do everything; get everything out of life. Be happy,—be triumphant."

"What do you mean by being triumphant?"

"Well, doing what you like."

"To triumph, then, it seems to me, is to fail! Doing all the vain things one likes is often very tiresome."

"Exactly," said Osmond with his quiet quickness. "As I intimated just now, you'll be tired some day." He paused a moment and then he went on: "I don't know whether I had better not wait till then for something I want to say to you."

"Ah, I can't advise you without knowing what it is. But I'm horrid when I'm tired," Isabel added with due inconsequence.

"I don't believe that. You're angry, sometimes—that I can believe, though I've never seen it. But I'm sure you're never 'cross.'"

"Not even when I lose my temper?"

"You don't lose it—you find it, and that must be beautiful." Osmond spoke with a noble earnestness. "They must be great moments to see."

"If I could only find it now!" Isabel nervously cried.

"I'm not afraid; I should fold my arms and admire you. I'm speaking very seriously." He leaned forward, a hand on each knee; for some moments he bent his eyes on the floor. "What I wish to say to you," he went on at last, looking up, "is that I find I'm in love with you."

She instantly rose. "Ah, keep that till I am tired!"

"Tired of hearing it from others?" He sat there raising his eyes to her. "No, you may heed it now or never, as you please. But after all I must say it now." She had turned away, but in the movement she had stopped herself and dropped her gaze upon him. The two remained a while in this situation, exchanging a long look—the large, conscious look of the critical hours of life. Then he got up and came near her, deeply respectful, as if he were afraid he had been too familiar. "I'm absolutely in love with you."

He had repeated the announcement in a tone of almost impersonal discretion, like a man who expected very little from it but who spoke for his own needed relief. The tears came into her eyes: this time they obeyed the sharpness of the pang that suggested to her somehow the slipping of a fine bolt—backward, forward, she couldn't have said which. The words he had uttered made him, as he stood there, beautiful and generous, invested him as with the golden air of early autumn; but, morally speaking, she retreated before them—facing him still—as she had retreated in the other cases before a like encounter. "Oh don't say that, please," she answered with an intensity that expressed the dread of having, in this case too, to choose and decide. What made her dread great was precisely the force which, as it would seem, ought to have banished all dread—the sense of something within herself, deep down, that she supposed to be inspired and trustful passion. It was there like a large sum stored in a bank—which there was a terror in having to begin to spend. If she touched it, it would all come out.

"I haven't the idea that it will matter much to you," said Osmond. "I've too little to offer you. What I have—it's enough for me; but it's not enough for you. I've neither fortune, nor fame, nor extrinsic advantages of any kind. So I offer nothing. I only tell you because I think it can't offend you, and some day or other it may give you pleasure. It gives me pleasure, I assure you," he went on, standing there before her, considerately inclined to her, turning his hat, which he had taken up, slowly round with a movement which had all the decent tremor of awkwardness and none of its oddity, and presenting to her his firm, refined, slightly ravaged face. "It gives me no pain, because it's perfectly simple. For me you'll always be the most important woman in the world."

Isabel looked at herself in this character—looked intently, thinking she filled it with a certain grace. But what she said was not an expression of any such complacency. "You don't offend me; but you ought to remember that, without being offended, one may be incommoded, troubled." "Incommoded," she heard herself saying that, and it struck her as a ridiculous word. But it was what stupidly came to her.

"I remember perfectly. Of course you're surprised and startled. But if it's nothing but that, it will pass away. And it will perhaps leave something that I may not be ashamed of."

"I don't know what it may leave. You see at all events that I'm not overwhelmed," said Isabel with rather a pale smile. "I'm not too troubled to think. And I think that I'm glad I leave Rome to-morrow."

"Of course I don't agree with you there."

"I don't at all KNOW you," she added abruptly; and then she coloured as she heard herself saying what she had said almost a year before to Lord Warburton.

"If you were not going away you'd know me better."

"I shall do that some other time."

"I hope so. I'm very easy to know."

"No, no," she emphatically answered—"there you're not sincere. You're not easy to know; no one could be less so."

"Well," he laughed, "I said that because I know myself. It may be a boast, but I do."

"Very likely; but you're very wise."

"So are you, Miss Archer!" Osmond exclaimed.

"I don't feel so just now. Still, I'm wise enough to think you had better go. Good-night."

"God bless you!" said Gilbert Osmond, taking the hand which she failed to surrender. After which he added: "If we meet again you'll find me as you leave me. If we don't I shall be so all the same."

"Thank you very much. Good-bye."

There was something quietly firm about Isabel's visitor; he might go of his own movement, but wouldn't be dismissed. "There's one thing more. I haven't asked anything of you—not even a thought in the future; you must do me that justice. But there's a little service I should like to ask. I shall not return home for several days; Rome's delightful, and it's a good place for a man in my state of mind. Oh, I know you're sorry to leave it; but you're right to do what your aunt wishes."

"She doesn't even wish it!" Isabel broke out strangely.

Osmond was apparently on the point of saying something that would match these words, but he changed his mind and rejoined simply: "Ah well, it's proper you should go with her, very proper. Do everything that's proper; I go in for that. Excuse my being so patronising. You say you don't know me, but when you do you'll discover what a worship I have for propriety."

"You're not conventional?" Isabel gravely asked.

"I like the way you utter that word! No, I'm not conventional: I'm convention itself. You don't understand that?" And he paused a moment, smiling. "I should like to explain it." Then with a sudden, quick, bright naturalness, "Do come back again," he pleaded. "There are so many things we might talk about."

She stood there with lowered eyes. "What service did you speak of just now?"

"Go and see my little daughter before you leave Florence. She's alone at the villa; I decided not to send her to my sister, who hasn't at all my ideas. Tell her she must love her poor father very much," said Gilbert Osmond gently.

"It will be a great pleasure to me to go," Isabel answered. "I'll tell her what you say. Once more good-bye."

On this he took a rapid, respectful leave. When he had gone she stood a moment looking about her and seated herself slowly and with an air of deliberation. She sat there till her companions came back, with folded hands, gazing at the ugly carpet. Her agitation—for it had not diminished—was very still, very deep. What had happened was something that for a week past her imagination had been going forward to meet; but here, when it came, she stopped—that sublime principle somehow broke down. The working of this young lady's spirit was strange, and I can only give it to you as I see it, not hoping to make it seem altogether natural. Her imagination, as I say, now hung back: there was a last vague space it couldn't cross—a dusky, uncertain tract which looked ambiguous and even slightly treacherous, like a moorland seen in the winter twilight. But she was to cross it yet.

CHAPTER XXX

She returned on the morrow to Florence, under her cousin's escort, and Ralph Touchett, though usually restive under railway discipline, thought very well of the successive hours passed in the train that hurried his companion away from the city now distinguished by Gilbert Osmond's preference—hours that were to form the first stage in a larger scheme of travel. Miss Stackpole had remained behind; she was planning a little trip to Naples, to be carried out with Mr. Bantling's aid. Isabel was to have three days in Florence before the 4th of June, the date of Mrs. Touchett's departure, and she determined to devote the last of these to her promise to call on Pansy Osmond. Her plan, however, seemed for a moment likely to modify itself in deference to an idea of Madame Merle's. This lady was still at Casa Touchett; but she too was on the point of leaving Florence, her next station being an ancient castle in the mountains of Tuscany, the residence of a noble family of that country, whose acquaintance (she had known them, as she said, "forever") seemed to Isabel, in the light of certain photographs of their immense crenellated dwelling which her friend was able to show her, a precious privilege. She mentioned to this fortunate woman that Mr. Osmond had asked her to take a look at his daughter, but didn't mention that he had also made her a declaration of love.

"Ah, comme cela se trouve!" Madame Merle exclaimed. "I myself have been thinking it would be a kindness to pay the child a little visit before I go off."

"We can go together then," Isabel reasonably said: "reasonably" because the proposal was not uttered in the spirit of enthusiasm. She had prefigured her small pilgrimage as made in solitude; she should like it better so. She was nevertheless prepared to sacrifice this mystic sentiment to her great consideration for her friend.

That personage finely meditated. "After all, why should we both go; having, each of us, so much to do during these last hours?"

"Very good; I can easily go alone."

"I don't know about your going alone—to the house of a handsome bachelor. He has been married—but so long ago!"

Isabel stared. "When Mr. Osmond's away what does it matter?"

"They don't know he's away, you see."

"They? Whom do you mean?"

"Every one. But perhaps it doesn't signify."

"If you were going why shouldn't I?" Isabel asked.

"Because I'm an old frump and you're a beautiful young woman."

"Granting all that, you've not promised."

"How much you think of your promises!" said the elder woman in mild mockery.

"I think a great deal of my promises. Does that surprise you?"

"You're right," Madame Merle audibly reflected. "I really think you wish to be kind to the child."

"I wish very much to be kind to her."

"Go and see her then; no one will be the wiser. And tell her I'd have come if you hadn't. Or rather," Madame Merle added, "DON'T tell her. She won't care."

As Isabel drove, in the publicity of an open vehicle, along the winding way which led to Mr. Osmond's hilltop, she wondered what her friend had meant by no one's being the wiser. Once in a while, at large intervals, this lady, whose voyaging discretion, as a general thing, was rather of the open sea than of the risky channel, dropped a remark of ambiguous quality, struck a note that sounded false. What cared Isabel Archer for the vulgar judgements of obscure people? and did Madame Merle suppose that she was capable of doing a thing at all if it had to be sneakingly done? Of course not: she must have meant something else—something which in the press of the hours that preceded her departure she had not had time to explain. Isabel would return to this some day; there were sorts of things as to which she liked to be clear. She heard Pansy strumming at the piano in another place as she herself was ushered into Mr. Osmond's drawing-room; the little girl was "practising," and Isabel was pleased to think she performed this duty with rigour. She immediately came in, smoothing down her frock, and did the honours of her father's house with a wide-eyed earnestness of courtesy. Isabel sat there half an hour, and Pansy rose to the occasion as the small, winged fairy in the pantomime soars by the aid of the dissimulated wire—not chattering, but conversing, and showing the same respectful interest in Isabel's affairs that Isabel was so good as to take in hers. Isabel wondered at her; she had never had so directly presented to her nose the white flower of cultivated sweetness. How well the child had been taught, said our admiring young woman; how prettily she had been directed and fashioned; and yet how simple, how natural, how innocent she had been kept! Isabel was fond, ever, of the question of character and quality, of sounding, as who should say, the deep personal mystery, and it had pleased her, up to this time, to be in doubt as to whether this tender slip were not really all-knowing. Was the extremity of her candour but the perfection of self-consciousness? Was it put on to please her father's visitor, or was it the direct expression of an unspotted nature? The hour that Isabel spent in Mr. Osmond's beautiful empty, dusky rooms—the windows had been half-darkened, to keep out the heat, and here and there, through an easy crevice, the splendid summer day peeped in, lighting a gleam of faded colour or tarnished gilt in the rich gloom—her interview with the daughter of the house, I say, effectually settled this question. Pansy was really a blank page, a pure white surface, successfully kept so; she had neither art, nor guile, nor temper, nor talent—only two or three small exquisite instincts: for knowing a friend, for avoiding a mistake, for taking care of an old toy or a new frock. Yet to be so tender was to be touching withal, and she could be felt as an easy victim of fate. She would have no will, no power to resist, no sense of her own importance; she would easily be mystified, easily crushed: her force would be all in knowing when and where to cling. She moved about the place with her visitor, who had asked leave to walk through the other rooms again, where Pansy gave her judgement on several works of art. She spoke of her prospects, her occupations, her father's intentions; she was not egotistical, but felt the propriety of supplying the information so distinguished a guest would naturally expect.

"Please tell me," she said, "did papa, in Rome, go to see Madame Catherine? He told me he would if he had time. Perhaps he had not time. Papa likes a great deal of time. He wished to speak about my education; it isn't finished yet, you know. I don't know what they can do with me more; but it appears it's far from finished. Papa told me one day he thought he would finish it himself; for the last year or two, at the convent, the masters that teach the tall girls are so very dear. Papa's not rich, and I should be very sorry if he were to pay much money for me, because I don't think I'm worth it. I don't learn quickly enough, and I have no memory. For what I'm told, yes—especially when it's pleasant; but not for what I learn in a book. There was a young girl who was my best friend, and they took her away from the convent, when she was fourteen, to make—how do you say it in English?—to make a dot. You don't say it in English? I hope it isn't wrong; I only mean they wished to keep the money to marry her. I don't know whether it is for that that papa wishes to keep the money—to marry me. It costs so much to marry!" Pansy went on with a sigh; "I think papa might make that economy. At any rate I'm too young to think about it yet, and I don't care for any gentleman; I mean for any but him. If he were not my papa I should like to marry him; I would rather be his daughter than the wife of—of some strange person. I miss him very much, but not so much as you might think, for I've been so much away from him. Papa has always been principally for holidays. I miss Madame Catherine almost more; but you must not tell him that. You shall not see him again? I'm very sorry, and he'll be sorry too. Of everyone who comes here I like you the best. That's not a great compliment, for there are not many people. It was very kind of you to come to-day—so far from your house; for I'm really as yet only a child. Oh, yes, I've only the occupations of a child. When did YOU give them up, the occupations of a child? I should like to know how old you are, but I don't know whether it's right to ask. At the convent they told us that we must never ask the age. I don't like to do anything that's not expected; it looks as if one had not been properly taught. I myself—I should never like to be taken by surprise. Papa left directions for everything. I go to bed very early. When the sun goes off that side I go into the garden. Papa left strict orders that I was not to get scorched. I always enjoy the view; the mountains are so graceful. In Rome, from the convent, we saw nothing but roofs and bell-towers. I practise three hours. I don't play very well. You play yourself? I wish very much you'd play something for me; papa has the idea that I should hear good music. Madame Merle has played for me several times; that's what I like best about Madame Merle; she has great facility. I shall never have facility. And I've no voice—just a small sound like the squeak of a slate-pencil making flourishes."

Isabel gratified this respectful wish, drew off her gloves and sat down to the piano, while Pansy, standing beside her, watched her white hands move quickly over the keys. When she stopped she kissed the child good-bye, held her close, looked at her long. "Be very good," she said; "give pleasure to your father."

"I think that's what I live for," Pansy answered. "He has not much pleasure; he's rather a sad man."

Isabel listened to this assertion with an interest which she felt it almost a torment to be obliged to conceal. It was her pride that obliged her, and a certain sense of decency; there were still other things in her head which she felt a strong impulse, instantly checked, to say to Pansy about her father; there were things it would have given her pleasure to hear the child, to make the child, say. But she no sooner became conscious of these things than her imagination was hushed with horror at the idea of taking advantage of the little girl—it was of this she would have accused herself—and of exhaling into that air where he might still have a subtle sense for it any breath of her charmed state. She had come—she had come; but she had stayed only an hour. She rose quickly from the music-stool; even then, however, she lingered a moment, still holding her small companion, drawing the child's sweet slimness closer and looking down at her almost in envy. She was obliged to confess it to herself—she would have taken a passionate pleasure in talking of Gilbert Osmond to this innocent, diminutive creature who was so near him. But she said no other word; she only kissed Pansy once again. They went together through the vestibule, to the door that opened on the court; and there her young hostess stopped, looking rather wistfully beyond. "I may go no further. I've promised papa not to pass this door."

"You're right to obey him; he'll never ask you anything unreasonable."

"I shall always obey him. But when will you come again?"

"Not for a long time, I'm afraid."

"As soon as you can, I hope. I'm only a little girl," said Pansy, "but I shall always expect you." And the small figure stood in the high, dark doorway, watching Isabel cross the clear, grey court and disappear into the brightness beyond the big portone, which gave a wider dazzle as it opened.

CHAPTER XXXI

Isabel came back to Florence, but only after several months; an interval sufficiently replete with incident. It is not, however, during this interval that we are closely concerned with her; our attention is engaged again on a certain day in the late spring-time, shortly after her return to Palazzo Crescentini and a year from the date of the incidents just narrated. She was alone on this occasion, in one of the smaller of the numerous rooms devoted by Mrs. Touchett to social uses, and there was that in her expression and attitude which would have suggested that she was expecting a visitor. The tall window was open, and though its green shutters were partly drawn the bright air of the garden had come in through a broad interstice and filled the room with warmth and perfume. Our young woman stood near it for some time, her hands clasped behind her; she gazed abroad with the vagueness of unrest. Too troubled for attention she moved in a vain circle. Yet it could not be in her thought to catch a glimpse of her visitor before he should pass into the house, since the entrance to the palace was not through the garden, in which stillness and privacy always reigned. She wished rather to forestall his arrival by a process of conjecture, and to judge by the expression of her face this attempt gave her plenty to do. Grave she found herself, and positively more weighted, as by the experience of the lapse of the year she had spent in seeing the world. She had ranged, she would have said, through space and surveyed much of mankind, and was therefore now, in her own eyes, a very different person from the frivolous young woman from Albany who had begun to take the measure of Europe on the lawn at Gardencourt a couple of years before. She flattered herself she had harvested wisdom and learned a great deal more of life than this light-minded creature had even suspected. If her thoughts just now had inclined themselves to retrospect, instead of fluttering their wings nervously about the present, they would have evoked a multitude of interesting pictures. These pictures would have been both landscapes and figure-pieces; the latter, however, would have been the more numerous. With several of the images that might have been projected on such a field we are already acquainted. There would be for instance the conciliatory Lily, our heroine's sister and Edmund Ludlow's wife, who had come out from New York to spend five months with her relative. She had left her husband behind her, but had brought her children, to whom Isabel now played with equal munificence and tenderness the part of maiden-aunt. Mr. Ludlow, toward the last, had been able to snatch a few weeks from his forensic triumphs and, crossing the ocean with extreme rapidity, had spent a month with the two ladies in Paris before taking his wife home. The little Ludlows had not yet, even from the American point of view, reached the proper tourist-age; so that while her sister was with her Isabel had confined her movements to a narrow circle. Lily and the babies had joined her in Switzerland in the month of July, and they had spent a summer of fine weather in an Alpine valley where the flowers were thick in the meadows and the shade of great chestnuts made a resting-place for such upward wanderings as might be undertaken by ladies and children on warm afternoons. They had afterwards reached the French capital, which was worshipped, and with costly ceremonies, by Lily, but thought of as noisily vacant by Isabel, who in these days made use of her memory of Rome as she might have done, in a hot and crowded room, of a phial of something pungent hidden in her handkerchief.

Mrs. Ludlow sacrificed, as I say, to Paris, yet had doubts and wonderments not allayed at that altar; and after her husband had joined her found further chagrin in his failure to throw himself into these speculations. They all had Isabel for subject; but Edmund Ludlow, as he had always done before, declined to be surprised, or distressed, or mystified, or elated, at anything his sister-in-law might have done or have failed to do. Mrs. Ludlow's mental motions were sufficiently various. At one moment she thought it would be so natural for that young woman to come home and take a house in New York—the Rossiters', for instance, which had an elegant conservatory and was just round the corner from her own; at another she couldn't conceal her surprise at the girl's not marrying some member of one of the great aristocracies. On the whole, as I have said, she had fallen from high communion with the probabilities. She had taken more satisfaction in Isabel's accession of fortune than if the money had been left to herself; it had seemed to her to offer just the proper setting for her sister's slightly meagre, but scarce the less eminent figure. Isabel had developed less, however, than Lily had thought likely—development, to Lily's understanding, being somehow mysteriously connected with morning-calls and evening-parties. Intellectually, doubtless, she had made immense strides; but she appeared to have achieved few of those social conquests of which Mrs. Ludlow had expected to admire the trophies. Lily's conception of such achievements was extremely vague; but this was exactly what she had expected of Isabel—to give it form and body. Isabel could have done as well as she had done in New York; and Mrs. Ludlow appealed to her husband to know whether there was any privilege she enjoyed in Europe which the society of that city might not offer her. We know ourselves that Isabel had made conquests—whether inferior or not to those she might have effected in her native land it would be a delicate matter to decide; and it is not altogether with a feeling of complacency that I again mention that she had not rendered these honourable victories public. She had not told her sister the history of Lord Warburton, nor had she given her a hint of Mr. Osmond's state of mind; and she had had no better reason for her silence than that she didn't wish to speak. It was more romantic to say nothing, and, drinking deep, in secret, of romance, she was as little disposed to ask poor Lily's advice as she would have been to close that rare volume forever. But Lily knew nothing of these discriminations, and could only pronounce her sister's career a strange anti-climax—an impression confirmed by the fact that Isabel's silence about Mr. Osmond, for instance, was in direct proportion to the frequency with which he occupied her thoughts. As this happened very often it sometimes appeared to Mrs. Ludlow that she had lost her courage. So uncanny a result of so exhilarating an incident as inheriting a fortune was of course perplexing to the cheerful Lily; it added to her general sense that Isabel was not at all like other people.

Our young lady's courage, however, might have been taken as reaching its height after her relations had gone home. She could imagine braver things than spending the winter in Paris—Paris had sides by which it so resembled New York, Paris was like smart, neat prose—and her close correspondence with Madame Merle did much to stimulate such flights. She had never had a keener sense of freedom, of the absolute boldness and wantonness of liberty, than when she turned away from the platform at the Euston Station on one of the last days of November, after the departure of the train that was to convey poor Lily, her husband and her children to their ship at Liverpool. It had been good for her to regale; she was very conscious of that; she was very observant, as we know, of what was good for her, and her effort was constantly to find something that was good enough. To profit by the present advantage till the latest moment she had made the journey from Paris with the unenvied travellers. She would have accompanied them to Liverpool as well, only Edmund Ludlow had asked her, as a favour, not to do so; it made Lily so fidgety and she asked such impossible questions. Isabel watched the train move away; she kissed her hand to the elder of her small nephews, a demonstrative child who leaned dangerously far out of the window of the carriage and made separation an occasion of violent hilarity, and then she walked back into the foggy London street. The world lay before her—she could do whatever she chose. There was a deep thrill in it all, but for the present her choice was tolerably discreet; she chose simply to walk back from Euston Square to her hotel. The early dusk of a November afternoon had already closed in; the street-lamps, in the thick, brown air, looked weak and red; our heroine was unattended and Euston Square was a long way from Piccadilly. But Isabel performed the journey with a positive enjoyment of its dangers and lost her way almost on purpose, in order to get more sensations, so that she was disappointed when an obliging policeman easily set her right again. She was so fond of the spectacle of human life that she enjoyed even the aspect of gathering dusk in the London streets—the moving crowds, the hurrying cabs, the lighted shops, the flaring stalls, the dark, shining dampness of everything. That evening, at her hotel, she wrote to Madame Merle that she should start in a day or two for Rome. She made her way down to Rome without touching at Florence—having gone first to Venice and then proceeded southward by Ancona. She accomplished this journey without other assistance than that of her servant, for her natural protectors were not now on the ground. Ralph Touchett was spending the winter at Corfu, and Miss Stackpole, in the September previous, had been recalled to America by a telegram from the Interviewer. This journal offered its brilliant correspondent a fresher field for her genius than the mouldering cities of Europe, and Henrietta was cheered on her way by a promise from Mr. Bantling that he would soon come over to see her. Isabel wrote to Mrs. Touchett to apologise for not presenting herself just yet in Florence, and her aunt replied characteristically enough. Apologies, Mrs. Touchett intimated, were of no more use to her than bubbles, and she herself never dealt in such articles. One either did the thing or one didn't, and what one "would" have done belonged to the sphere of the irrelevant, like the idea of a future life or of the origin of things. Her letter was frank, but (a rare case with Mrs. Touchett) not so frank as it pretended. She easily forgave her niece for not stopping at Florence, because she took it for a sign that Gilbert Osmond was less in question there than formerly. She watched of course to see if he would now find a pretext for going to Rome, and derived some comfort from learning that he had not been guilty of an absence. Isabel, on her side, had not been a fortnight in Rome before she proposed to Madame Merle that they should make a little pilgrimage to the East. Madame Merle remarked that her friend was restless, but she added that she herself had always been consumed with the desire to visit Athens and Constantinople. The two ladies accordingly embarked on this expedition, and spent three months in Greece, in Turkey, in Egypt. Isabel found much to interest her in these countries, though Madame Merle continued to remark that even among the most classic sites, the scenes most calculated to suggest repose and reflexion, a certain incoherence prevailed in her. Isabel travelled rapidly and recklessly; she was like a thirsty person draining cup after cup. Madame Merle meanwhile, as lady-in-waiting to a princess circulating incognita, panted a little in her rear. It was on Isabel's invitation she had come, and she imparted all due dignity to the girl's uncountenanced state. She played her part with the tact that might have been expected of her, effacing herself and accepting the position of a companion whose expenses were profusely paid. The situation, however, had no hardships, and people who met this reserved though striking pair on their travels would not have been able to tell you which was patroness and which client. To say that Madame Merle improved on acquaintance states meagrely the impression she made on her friend, who had found her from the first so ample and so easy. At the end of an intimacy of three months Isabel felt she knew her better; her character had revealed itself, and the admirable woman had also at last redeemed her promise of relating her history from her own point of view—a consummation the more desirable as Isabel had already heard it related from the point of view of others. This history was so sad a one (in so far as it concerned the late M. Merle, a positive adventurer, she might say, though originally so plausible, who had taken advantage, years before, of her youth and of an inexperience in which doubtless those who knew her only now would find it difficult to believe); it abounded so in startling and lamentable incidents that her companion wondered a person so eprouvee could have kept so much of her freshness, her interest in life. Into this freshness of Madame Merle's she obtained a considerable insight; she seemed to see it as professional, as slightly mechanical, carried about in its case like the fiddle of the virtuoso, or blanketed and bridled like the "favourite" of the jockey. She liked her as much as ever, but there was a corner of the curtain that never was lifted; it was as if she had remained after all something of a public performer, condemned to emerge only in character and in costume. She had once said that she came from a distance, that she belonged to the "old, old" world, and Isabel never lost the impression that she was the product of a different moral or social clime from her own, that she had grown up under other stars.

She believed then that at bottom she had a different morality. Of course the morality of civilised persons has always much in common; but our young woman had a sense in her of values gone wrong or, as they said at the shops, marked down. She considered, with the presumption of youth, that a morality differing from her own must be inferior to it; and this conviction was an aid to detecting an occasional flash of cruelty, an occasional lapse from candour, in the conversation of a person who had raised delicate kindness to an art and whose pride was too high for the narrow ways of deception. Her conception of human motives might, in certain lights, have been acquired at the court of some kingdom in decadence, and there were several in her list of which our heroine had not even heard. She had not heard of everything, that was very plain; and there were evidently things in the world of which it was not advantageous to hear. She had once or twice had a positive scare; since it so affected her to have to exclaim, of her friend, "Heaven forgive her, she doesn't understand me!" Absurd as it may seem this discovery operated as a shock, left her with a vague dismay in which there was even an element of foreboding. The dismay of course subsided, in the light of some sudden proof of Madame Merle's remarkable intelligence; but it stood for a high-water-mark in the ebb and flow of confidence. Madame Merle had once declared her belief that when a friendship ceases to grow it immediately begins to decline—there being no point of equilibrium between liking more and liking less. A stationary affection, in other words, was impossible—it must move one way or the other. However that might be, the girl had in these days a thousand uses for her sense of the romantic, which was more active than it had ever been. I do not allude to the impulse it received as she gazed at the Pyramids in the course of an excursion from Cairo, or as she stood among the broken columns of the Acropolis and fixed her eyes upon the point designated to her as the Strait of Salamis; deep and memorable as these emotions had remained. She came back by the last of March from Egypt and Greece and made another stay in Rome. A few days after her arrival Gilbert Osmond descended from Florence and remained three weeks, during which the fact of her being with his old friend Madame Merle, in whose house she had gone to lodge, made it virtually inevitable that he should see her every day. When the last of April came she wrote to Mrs. Touchett that she should now rejoice to accept an invitation given long before, and went to pay a visit at Palazzo Crescentini, Madame Merle on this occasion remaining in Rome. She found her aunt alone; her cousin was still at Corfu. Ralph, however, was expected in Florence from day to day, and Isabel, who had not seen him for upwards of a year, was prepared to give him the most affectionate welcome.

CHAPTER XXXII

It was not of him, nevertheless, that she was thinking while she stood at the window near which we found her a while ago, and it was not of any of the matters I have rapidly sketched. She was not turned to the past, but to the immediate, impending hour. She had reason to expect a scene, and she was not fond of scenes. She was not asking herself what she should say to her visitor; this question had already been answered. What he would say to her—that was the interesting issue. It could be nothing in the least soothing—she had warrant for this, and the conviction doubtless showed in the cloud on her brow. For the rest, however, all clearness reigned in her; she had put away her mourning and she walked in no small shimmering splendour. She only, felt older—ever so much, and as if she were "worth more" for it, like some curious piece in an antiquary's collection. She was not at any rate left indefinitely to her apprehensions, for a servant at last stood before her with a card on his tray. "Let the gentleman come in," she said, and continued to gaze out of the window after the footman had retired. It was only when she had heard the door close behind the person who presently entered that she looked round.

Caspar Goodwood stood there—stood and received a moment, from head to foot, the bright, dry gaze with which she rather withheld than offered a greeting. Whether his sense of maturity had kept pace with Isabel's we shall perhaps presently ascertain; let me say meanwhile that to her critical glance he showed nothing of the injury of time. Straight, strong and hard, there was nothing in his appearance that spoke positively either of youth or of age; if he had neither innocence nor weakness, so he had no practical philosophy. His jaw showed the same voluntary cast as in earlier days; but a crisis like the present had in it of course something grim. He had the air of a man who had travelled hard; he said nothing at first, as if he had been out of breath. This gave Isabel time to make a reflexion: "Poor fellow, what great things he's capable of, and what a pity he should waste so dreadfully his splendid force! What a pity too that one can't satisfy everybody!" It gave her time to do more to say at the end of a minute: "I can't tell you how I hoped you wouldn't come!"

"I've no doubt of that." And he looked about him for a seat. Not only had he come, but he meant to settle.

"You must be very tired," said Isabel, seating herself, and generously, as she thought, to give him his opportunity.

"No, I'm not at all tired. Did you ever know me to be tired?"

"Never; I wish I had! When did you arrive?"

"Last night, very late; in a kind of snail-train they call the express. These Italian trains go at about the rate of an American funeral."

"That's in keeping—you must have felt as if you were coming to bury me!" And she forced a smile of encouragement to an easy view of their situation. She had reasoned the matter well out, making it perfectly clear that she broke no faith and falsified no contract; but for all this she was afraid of her visitor. She was ashamed of her fear; but she was devoutly thankful there was nothing else to be ashamed of. He looked at her with his stiff insistence, an insistence in which there was such a want of tact; especially when the dull dark beam in his eye rested on her as a physical weight.

"No, I didn't feel that; I couldn't think of you as dead. I wish I could!" he candidly declared.

"I thank you immensely."

"I'd rather think of you as dead than as married to another man."

"That's very selfish of you!" she returned with the ardour of a real conviction. "If you're not happy yourself others have yet a right to be."

"Very likely it's selfish; but I don't in the least mind your saying so. I don't mind anything you can say now—I don't feel it. The cruellest things you could think of would be mere pin-pricks. After what you've done I shall never feel anything—I mean anything but that. That I shall feel all my life."

Mr. Goodwood made these detached assertions with dry deliberateness, in his hard, slow American tone, which flung no atmospheric colour over propositions intrinsically crude. The tone made Isabel angry rather than touched her; but her anger perhaps was fortunate, inasmuch as it gave her a further reason for controlling herself. It was under the pressure of this control that she became, after a little, irrelevant. "When did you leave New York?"

He threw up his head as if calculating. "Seventeen days ago."

"You must have travelled fast in spite of your slow trains."

"I came as fast as I could. I'd have come five days ago if I had been able."

"It wouldn't have made any difference, Mr. Goodwood," she coldly smiled.

"Not to you—no. But to me."

"You gain nothing that I see."

"That's for me to judge!"

"Of course. To me it seems that you only torment yourself." And then, to change the subject, she asked him if he had seen Henrietta Stackpole. He looked as if he had not come from Boston to Florence to talk of Henrietta Stackpole; but he answered, distinctly enough, that this young lady had been with him just before he left America. "She came to see you?" Isabel then demanded.

"Yes, she was in Boston, and she called at my office. It was the day I had got your letter."

"Did you tell her?" Isabel asked with a certain anxiety.

"Oh no," said Caspar Goodwood simply; "I didn't want to do that. She'll hear it quick enough; she hears everything."

"I shall write to her, and then she'll write to me and scold me," Isabel declared, trying to smile again.

Caspar, however, remained sternly grave. "I guess she'll come right out," he said.

"On purpose to scold me?"

"I don't know. She seemed to think she had not seen Europe thoroughly."

"I'm glad you tell me that," Isabel said. "I must prepare for her."

Mr. Goodwood fixed his eyes for a moment on the floor; then at last, raising them, "Does she know Mr. Osmond?" he enquired.

"A little. And she doesn't like him. But of course I don't marry to please Henrietta," she added. It would have been better for poor Caspar if she had tried a little more to gratify Miss Stackpole; but he didn't say so; he only asked, presently, when her marriage would take place. To which she made answer that she didn't know yet. "I can only say it will be soon. I've told no one but yourself and one other person—an old friend of Mr. Osmond's."

"Is it a marriage your friends won't like?" he demanded.

"I really haven't an idea. As I say, I don't marry for my friends."

He went on, making no exclamation, no comment, only asking questions, doing it quite without delicacy. "Who and what then is Mr. Gilbert Osmond?"

"Who and what? Nobody and nothing but a very good and very honourable man. He's not in business," said Isabel. "He's not rich; he's not known for anything in particular."

She disliked Mr. Goodwood's questions, but she said to herself that she owed it to him to satisfy him as far as possible. The satisfaction poor Caspar exhibited was, however, small; he sat very upright, gazing at her. "Where does he come from? Where does he belong?"

She had never been so little pleased with the way he said "belawng." "He comes from nowhere. He has spent most of his life in Italy."

"You said in your letter he was American. Hasn't he a native place?"

"Yes, but he has forgotten it. He left it as a small boy."

"Has he never gone back?"

"Why should he go back?" Isabel asked, flushing all defensively. "He has no profession."

"He might have gone back for his pleasure. Doesn't he like the United States?"

"He doesn't know them. Then he's very quiet and very simple—he contents himself with Italy."

"With Italy and with you," said Mr. Goodwood with gloomy plainness and no appearance of trying to make an epigram. "What has he ever done?" he added abruptly.

"That I should marry him? Nothing at all," Isabel replied while her patience helped itself by turning a little to hardness. "If he had done great things would you forgive me any better? Give me up, Mr. Goodwood; I'm marrying a perfect nonentity. Don't try to take an interest in him. You can't."

"I can't appreciate him; that's what you mean. And you don't mean in the least that he's a perfect nonentity. You think he's grand, you think he's great, though no one else thinks so."

Isabel's colour deepened; she felt this really acute of her companion, and it was certainly a proof of the aid that passion might render perceptions she had never taken for fine. "Why do you always comeback to what others think? I can't discuss Mr. Osmond with you."

"Of course not," said Caspar reasonably. And he sat there with his air of stiff helplessness, as if not only this were true, but there were nothing else that they might discuss.

"You see how little you gain," she accordingly broke out—"how little comfort or satisfaction I can give you."

"I didn't expect you to give me much."

"I don't understand then why you came."

"I came because I wanted to see you once more—even just as you are."

"I appreciate that; but if you had waited a while, sooner or later we should have been sure to meet, and our meeting would have been pleasanter for each of us than this."

"Waited till after you're married? That's just what I didn't want to do. You'll be different then."

"Not very. I shall still be a great friend of yours. You'll see."

"That will make it all the worse," said Mr. Goodwood grimly.

"Ah, you're unaccommodating! I can't promise to dislike you in order to help you to resign yourself."

"I shouldn't care if you did!"

Isabel got up with a movement of repressed impatience and walked to the window, where she remained a moment looking out. When she turned round her visitor was still motionless in his place. She came toward him again and stopped, resting her hand on the back of the chair she had just quitted. "Do you mean you came simply to look at me? That's better for you perhaps than for me."

"I wished to hear the sound of your voice," he said.

"You've heard it, and you see it says nothing very sweet."

"It gives me pleasure, all the same." And with this he got up. She had felt pain and displeasure on receiving early that day the news he was in Florence and by her leave would come within an hour to see her. She had been vexed and distressed, though she had sent back word by his messenger that he might come when he would. She had not been better pleased when she saw him; his being there at all was so full of heavy implications. It implied things she could never assent to—rights, reproaches, remonstrance, rebuke, the expectation of making her change her purpose. These things, however, if implied, had not been expressed; and now our young lady, strangely enough, began to resent her visitor's remarkable self-control. There was a dumb misery about him that irritated her; there was a manly staying of his hand that made her heart beat faster. She felt her agitation rising, and she said to herself that she was angry in the way a woman is angry when she has been in the wrong. She was not in the wrong; she had fortunately not that bitterness to swallow; but, all the same, she wished he would denounce her a little. She had wished his visit would be short; it had no purpose, no propriety; yet now that he seemed to be turning away she felt a sudden horror of his leaving her without uttering a word that would give her an opportunity to defend herself more than she had done in writing to him a month before, in a few carefully chosen words, to announce her engagement. If she were not in the wrong, however, why should she desire to defend herself? It was an excess of generosity on Isabel's part to desire that Mr. Goodwood should be angry. And if he had not meanwhile held himself hard it might have made him so to hear the tone in which she suddenly exclaimed, as if she were accusing him of having accused her: "I've not deceived you! I was perfectly free!"

"Yes, I know that," said Caspar.

"I gave you full warning that I'd do as I chose."

"You said you'd probably never marry, and you said it with such a manner that I pretty well believed it."

She considered this an instant. "No one can be more surprised than myself at my present intention."

"You told me that if I heard you were engaged I was not to believe it," Caspar went on. "I heard it twenty days ago from yourself, but I remembered what you had said. I thought there might be some mistake, and that's partly why I came."

"If you wish me to repeat it by word of mouth, that's soon done. There's no mistake whatever."

"I saw that as soon as I came into the room."

"What good would it do you that I shouldn't marry?" she asked with a certain fierceness.

"I should like it better than this."

"You're very selfish, as I said before."

"I know that. I'm selfish as iron."

"Even iron sometimes melts! If you'll be reasonable I'll see you again."

"Don't you call me reasonable now?"

"I don't know what to say to you," she answered with sudden humility.

"I shan't trouble you for a long time," the young man went on. He made a step towards the door, but he stopped. "Another reason why I came was that I wanted to hear what you would say in explanation of your having changed your mind."

Her humbleness as suddenly deserted her. "In explanation? Do you think I'm bound to explain?"

He gave her one of his long dumb looks. "You were very positive. I did believe it."

"So did I. Do you think I could explain if I would?"

"No, I suppose not. Well," he added, "I've done what I wished. I've seen you."

"How little you make of these terrible journeys," she felt the poverty of her presently replying.

"If you're afraid I'm knocked up—in any such way as that—you may he at your ease about it." He turned away, this time in earnest, and no hand-shake, no sign of parting, was exchanged between them.

At the door he stopped with his hand on the knob. "I shall leave Florence to-morrow," he said without a quaver.

"I'm delighted to hear it!" she answered passionately. Five minutes after he had gone out she burst into tears.

CHAPTER XXXIII

Her fit of weeping, however, was soon smothered, and the signs of it had vanished when, an hour later, she broke the news to her aunt. I use this expression because she had been sure Mrs. Touchett would not be pleased; Isabel had only waited to tell her till she had seen Mr. Goodwood. She had an odd impression that it would not be honourable to make the fact public before she should have heard what Mr. Goodwood would say about it. He had said rather less than she expected, and she now had a somewhat angry sense of having lost time. But she would lose no more; she waited till Mrs. Touchett came into the drawing-room before the mid-day breakfast, and then she began. "Aunt Lydia, I've something to tell you."

Mrs. Touchett gave a little jump and looked at her almost fiercely. "You needn't tell me; I know what it is."

"I don't know how you know."

"The same way that I know when the window's open—by feeling a draught. You're going to marry that man."

"What man do you mean?" Isabel enquired with great dignity.

"Madame Merle's friend—Mr. Osmond."

"I don't know why you call him Madame Merle's friend. Is that the principal thing he's known by?"

"If he's not her friend he ought to be—after what she has done for him!" cried Mrs. Touchett. "I shouldn't have expected it of her; I'm disappointed."

"If you mean that Madame Merle has had anything to do with my engagement you're greatly mistaken," Isabel declared with a sort of ardent coldness.

"You mean that your attractions were sufficient, without the gentleman's having had to be lashed up? You're quite right. They're immense, your attractions, and he would never have presumed to think of you if she hadn't put him up to it. He has a very good opinion of himself, but he was not a man to take trouble. Madame Merle took the trouble for him."

"He has taken a great deal for himself!" cried Isabel with a voluntary laugh.

Mrs. Touchett gave a sharp nod. "I think he must, after all, to have made you like him so much."

"I thought he even pleased YOU."

"He did, at one time; and that's why I'm angry with him."

"Be angry with me, not with him," said the girl.

"Oh, I'm always angry with you; that's no satisfaction! Was it for this that you refused Lord Warburton?"

"Please don't go back to that. Why shouldn't I like Mr. Osmond, since others have done so?"

"Others, at their wildest moments, never wanted to marry him. There's nothing OF him," Mrs. Touchett explained.

"Then he can't hurt me," said Isabel.

"Do you think you're going to be happy? No one's happy, in such doings, you should know."

"I shall set the fashion then. What does one marry for?"

"What YOU will marry for, heaven only knows. People usually marry as they go into partnership—to set up a house. But in your partnership you'll bring everything."

"Is it that Mr. Osmond isn't rich? Is that what you're talking about?" Isabel asked.

"He has no money; he has no name; he has no importance. I value such things and I have the courage to say it; I think they're very precious. Many other people think the same, and they show it. But they give some other reason."

Isabel hesitated a little. "I think I value everything that's valuable. I care very much for money, and that's why I wish Mr. Osmond to have a little."

"Give it to him then; but marry some one else."

"His name's good enough for me," the girl went on. "It's a very pretty name. Have I such a fine one myself?"

"All the more reason you should improve on it. There are only a dozen American names. Do you marry him out of charity?"

"It was my duty to tell you, Aunt Lydia, but I don't think it's my duty to explain to you. Even if it were I shouldn't be able. So please don't remonstrate; in talking about it you have me at a disadvantage. I can't talk about it."

"I don't remonstrate, I simply answer you: I must give some sign of intelligence. I saw it coming, and I said nothing. I never meddle."

"You never do, and I'm greatly obliged to you. You've been very considerate."

"It was not considerate—it was convenient," said Mrs. Touchett. "But I shall talk to Madame Merle."

"I don't see why you keep bringing her in. She has been a very good friend to me."

"Possibly; but she has been a poor one to me."

"What has she done to you?"

"She has deceived me. She had as good as promised me to prevent your engagement."

"She couldn't have prevented it."

"She can do anything; that's what I've always liked her for. I knew she could play any part; but I understood that she played them one by one. I didn't understand that she would play two at the same time."

"I don't know what part she may have played to you," Isabel said; "that's between yourselves. To me she has been honest and kind and devoted."

"Devoted, of course; she wished you to marry her candidate. She told me she was watching you only in order to interpose."

"She said that to please you," the girl answered; conscious, however, of the inadequacy of the explanation.

"To please me by deceiving me? She knows me better. Am I pleased to-day?"

"I don't think you're ever much pleased," Isabel was obliged to reply. "If Madame Merle knew you would learn the truth what had she to gain by insincerity?"

"She gained time, as you see. While I waited for her to interfere you were marching away, and she was really beating the drum."

"That's very well. But by your own admission you saw I was marching, and even if she had given the alarm you wouldn't have tried to stop me."

"No, but some one else would."

"Whom do you mean?" Isabel asked, looking very hard at her aunt. Mrs. Touchett's little bright eyes, active as they usually were, sustained her gaze rather than returned it. "Would you have listened to Ralph?"

"Not if he had abused Mr. Osmond."

"Ralph doesn't abuse people; you know that perfectly. He cares very much for you."

"I know he does," said Isabel; "and I shall feel the value of it now, for he knows that whatever I do I do with reason."

"He never believed you would do this. I told him you were capable of it, and he argued the other way."

"He did it for the sake of argument," the girl smiled. "You don't accuse him of having deceived you; why should you accuse Madame Merle?"

"He never pretended he'd prevent it."

"I'm glad of that!" cried Isabel gaily. "I wish very much," she presently added, "that when he comes you'd tell him first of my engagement."

"Of course I'll mention it," said Mrs. Touchett. "I shall say nothing more to you about it, but I give you notice I shall talk to others."

"That's as you please. I only meant that it's rather better the announcement should come from you than from me."

"I quite agree with you; it's much more proper!" And on this the aunt and the niece went to breakfast, where Mrs. Touchett, as good as her word, made no allusion to Gilbert Osmond. After an interval of silence, however, she asked her companion from whom she had received a visit an hour before.

"From an old friend—an American gentleman," Isabel said with a colour in her cheek.

"An American gentleman of course. It's only an American gentleman who calls at ten o'clock in the morning."

"It was half-past ten; he was in a great hurry; he goes away this evening."

"Couldn't he have come yesterday, at the usual time?"

"He only arrived last night."

"He spends but twenty-four hours in Florence?" Mrs. Touchett cried. "He's an American gentleman truly."

"He is indeed," said Isabel, thinking with perverse admiration of what Caspar Goodwood had done for her.

Two days afterward Ralph arrived; but though Isabel was sure that Mrs. Touchett had lost no time in imparting to him the great fact, he showed at first no open knowledge of it. Their prompted talk was naturally of his health; Isabel had many questions to ask about Corfu. She had been shocked by his appearance when he came into the room; she had forgotten how ill he looked. In spite of Corfu he looked very ill to-day, and she wondered if he were really worse or if she were simply disaccustomed to living with an invalid. Poor Ralph made no nearer approach to conventional beauty as he advanced in life, and the now apparently complete loss of his health had done little to mitigate the natural oddity of his person. Blighted and battered, but still responsive and still ironic, his face was like a lighted lantern patched with paper and unsteadily held; his thin whisker languished upon a lean cheek; the exorbitant curve of his nose defined itself more sharply. Lean he was altogether, lean and long and loose-jointed; an accidental cohesion of relaxed angles. His brown velvet jacket had become perennial; his hands had fixed themselves in his pockets; he shambled and stumbled and shuffled in a manner that denoted great physical helplessness. It was perhaps this whimsical gait that helped to mark his character more than ever as that of the humorous invalid—the invalid for whom even his own disabilities are part of the general joke. They might well indeed with Ralph have been the chief cause of the want of seriousness marking his view of a world in which the reason for his own continued presence was past finding out. Isabel had grown fond of his ugliness; his awkwardness had become dear to her. They had been sweetened by association; they struck her as the very terms on which it had been given him to be charming. He was so charming that her sense of his being ill had hitherto had a sort of comfort in it; the state of his health had seemed not a limitation, but a kind of intellectual advantage; it absolved him from all professional and official emotions and left him the luxury of being exclusively personal. The personality so resulting was delightful; he had remained proof against the staleness of disease; he had had to consent to be deplorably ill, yet had somehow escaped being formally sick. Such had been the girl's impression of her cousin; and when she had pitied him it was only on reflection. As she reflected a good deal she had allowed him a certain amount of compassion; but she always had a dread of wasting that essence—a precious article, worth more to the giver than to any one else. Now, however, it took no great sensibility to feel that poor Ralph's tenure of life was less elastic than it should be. He was a bright, free, generous spirit, he had all the illumination of wisdom and none of its pedantry, and yet he was distressfully dying.

Isabel noted afresh that life was certainly hard for some people, and she felt a delicate glow of shame as she thought how easy it now promised to become for herself. She was prepared to learn that Ralph was not pleased with her engagement; but she was not prepared, in spite of her affection for him, to let this fact spoil the situation. She was not even prepared, or so she thought, to resent his want of sympathy; for it would be his privilege—it would be indeed his natural line—to find fault with any step she might take toward marriage. One's cousin always pretended to hate one's husband; that was traditional, classical; it was a part of one's cousin's always pretending to adore one. Ralph was nothing if not critical; and though she would certainly, other things being equal, have been as glad to marry to please him as to please any one, it would be absurd to regard as important that her choice should square with his views. What were his views after all? He had pretended to believe she had better have married Lord Warburton; but this was only because she had refused that excellent man. If she had accepted him Ralph would certainly have taken another tone; he always took the opposite. You could criticise any marriage; it was the essence of a marriage to be open to criticism. How well she herself, should she only give her mind to it, might criticise this union of her own! She had other employment, however, and Ralph was welcome to relieve her of the care. Isabel was prepared to be most patient and most indulgent. He must have seen that, and this made it the more odd he should say nothing. After three days had elapsed without his speaking our young woman wearied of waiting; dislike it as he would, he might at least go through the form. We, who know more about poor Ralph than his cousin, may easily believe that during the hours that followed his arrival at Palazzo Crescentini he had privately gone through many forms. His mother had literally greeted him with the great news, which had been even more sensibly chilling than Mrs. Touchett's maternal kiss. Ralph was shocked and humiliated; his calculations had been false and the person in the world in whom he was most interested was lost. He drifted about the house like a rudderless vessel in a rocky stream, or sat in the garden of the palace on a great cane chair, his long legs extended, his head thrown back and his hat pulled over his eyes. He felt cold about the heart; he had never liked anything less. What could he do, what could he say? If the girl were irreclaimable could he pretend to like it? To attempt to reclaim her was permissible only if the attempt should succeed. To try to persuade her of anything sordid or sinister in the man to whose deep art she had succumbed would be decently discreet only in the event of her being persuaded. Otherwise he should simply have damned himself. It cost him an equal effort to speak his thought and to dissemble; he could neither assent with sincerity nor protest with hope. Meanwhile he knew—or rather he supposed—that the affianced pair were daily renewing their mutual vows. Osmond at this moment showed himself little at Palazzo Crescentini; but Isabel met him every day elsewhere, as she was free to do after their engagement had been made public. She had taken a carriage by the month, so as not to be indebted to her aunt for the means of pursuing a course of which Mrs. Touchett disapproved, and she drove in the morning to the Cascine. This suburban wilderness, during the early hours, was void of all intruders, and our young lady, joined by her lover in its quietest part, strolled with him a while through the grey Italian shade and listened to the nightingales.

CHAPTER XXXIV

One morning, on her return from her drive, some half-hour before luncheon, she quitted her vehicle in the court of the palace and, instead of ascending the great staircase, crossed the court, passed beneath another archway and entered the garden. A sweeter spot at this moment could not have been imagined. The stillness of noontide hung over it, and the warm shade, enclosed and still, made bowers like spacious caves. Ralph was sitting there in the clear gloom, at the base of a statue of Terpsichore—a dancing nymph with taper fingers and inflated draperies in the manner of Bernini; the extreme relaxation of his attitude suggested at first to Isabel that he was asleep. Her light footstep on the grass had not roused him, and before turning away she stood for a moment looking at him. During this instant he opened his eyes; upon which she sat down on a rustic chair that matched with his own. Though in her irritation she had accused him of indifference she was not blind to the fact that he had visibly had something to brood over. But she had explained his air of absence partly by the languor of his increased weakness, partly by worries connected with the property inherited from his father—the fruit of eccentric arrangements of which Mrs. Touchett disapproved and which, as she had told Isabel, now encountered opposition from the other partners in the bank. He ought to have gone to England, his mother said, instead of coming to Florence; he had not been there for months, and took no more interest in the bank than in the state of Patagonia.

"I'm sorry I waked you," Isabel said; "you look too tired."

"I feel too tired. But I was not asleep. I was thinking of you."

"Are you tired of that?"

"Very much so. It leads to nothing. The road's long and I never arrive."

"What do you wish to arrive at?" she put to him, closing her parasol.

"At the point of expressing to myself properly what I think of your engagement."

"Don't think too much of it," she lightly returned.

"Do you mean that it's none of my business?"

"Beyond a certain point, yes."

"That's the point I want to fix. I had an idea you may have found me wanting in good manners. I've never congratulated you."

"Of course I've noticed that. I wondered why you were silent."

"There have been a good many reasons. I'll tell you now," Ralph said. He pulled off his hat and laid it on the ground; then he sat looking at her. He leaned back under the protection of Bernini, his head against his marble pedestal, his arms dropped on either side of him, his hands laid upon the rests of his wide chair. He looked awkward, uncomfortable; he hesitated long. Isabel said nothing; when people were embarrassed she was usually sorry for them, but she was determined not to help Ralph to utter a word that should not be to the honour of her high decision. "I think I've hardly got over my surprise," he went on at last. "You were the last person I expected to see caught."

"I don't know why you call it caught."

"Because you're going to be put into a cage."

"If I like my cage, that needn't trouble you," she answered.

"That's what I wonder at; that's what I've been thinking of."

"If you've been thinking you may imagine how I've thought! I'm satisfied that I'm doing well."

"You must have changed immensely. A year ago you valued your liberty beyond everything. You wanted only to see life."

"I've seen it," said Isabel. "It doesn't look to me now, I admit, such an inviting expanse."

"I don't pretend it is; only I had an idea that you took a genial view of it and wanted to survey the whole field."

"I've seen that one can't do anything so general. One must choose a corner and cultivate that."

"That's what I think. And one must choose as good a corner as possible. I had no idea, all winter, while I read your delightful letters, that you were choosing. You said nothing about it, and your silence put me off my guard."

"It was not a matter I was likely to write to you about. Besides, I knew nothing of the future. It has all come lately. If you had been on your guard, however," Isabel asked, "what would you have done?"

"I should have said 'Wait a little longer.'"

"Wait for what?"

"Well, for a little more light," said Ralph with rather an absurd smile, while his hands found their way into his pockets.

"Where should my light have come from? From you?"

"I might have struck a spark or two."

Isabel had drawn off her gloves; she smoothed them out as they lay upon her knee. The mildness of this movement was accidental, for her expression was not conciliatory. "You're beating about the bush, Ralph. You wish to say you don't like Mr. Osmond, and yet you're afraid."

"Willing to wound and yet afraid to strike? I'm willing to wound HIM, yes—but not to wound you. I'm afraid of you, not of him. If you marry him it won't be a fortunate way for me to have spoken."

"IF I marry him! Have you had any expectation of dissuading me?"

"Of course that seems to you too fatuous."

"No," said Isabel after a little; "it seems to me too touching."

"That's the same thing. It makes me so ridiculous that you pity me."

She stroked out her long gloves again. "I know you've a great affection for me. I can't get rid of that."

"For heaven's sake don't try. Keep that well in sight. It will convince you how intensely I want you to do well."

"And how little you trust me!"

There was a moment's silence; the warm noontide seemed to listen. "I trust you, but I don't trust him," said Ralph.

She raised her eyes and gave him a wide, deep look. "You've said it now, and I'm glad you've made it so clear. But you'll suffer by it."

"Not if you're just."

"I'm very just," said Isabel. "What better proof of it can there be than that I'm not angry with you? I don't know what's the matter with me, but I'm not. I was when you began, but it has passed away. Perhaps I ought to be angry, but Mr. Osmond wouldn't think so. He wants me to know everything; that's what I like him for. You've nothing to gain, I know that. I've never been so nice to you, as a girl, that you should have much reason for wishing me to remain one. You give very good advice; you've often done so. No, I'm very quiet; I've always believed in your wisdom," she went on, boasting of her quietness, yet speaking with a kind of contained exaltation. It was her passionate desire to be just; it touched Ralph to the heart, affected him like a caress from a creature he had injured. He wished to interrupt, to reassure her; for a moment he was absurdly inconsistent; he would have retracted what he had said. But she gave him no chance; she went on, having caught a glimpse, as she thought, of the heroic line and desiring to advance in that direction. "I see you've some special idea; I should like very much to hear it. I'm sure it's disinterested; I feel that. It seems a strange thing to argue about, and of course I ought to tell you definitely that if you expect to dissuade me you may give it up. You'll not move me an inch; it's too late. As you say, I'm caught. Certainly it won't be pleasant for you to remember this, but your pain will be in your own thoughts. I shall never reproach you."

"I don't think you ever will," said Ralph. "It's not in the least the sort of marriage I thought you'd make."

"What sort of marriage was that, pray?"

"Well, I can hardly say. I hadn't exactly a positive view of it, but I had a negative. I didn't think you'd decide for—well, for that type."

"What's the matter with Mr. Osmond's type, if it be one? His being so independent, so individual, is what I most see in him," the girl declared. "What do you know against him? You know him scarcely at all."

"Yes," Ralph said, "I know him very little, and I confess I haven't facts and items to prove him a villain. But all the same I can't help feeling that you're running a grave risk."

"Marriage is always a grave risk, and his risk's as grave as mine."

"That's his affair! If he's afraid, let him back out. I wish to God he would."

Isabel reclined in her chair, folding her arms and gazing a while at her cousin. "I don't think I understand you," she said at last coldly. "I don't know what you're talking about."

"I believed you'd marry a man of more importance."

Cold, I say, her tone had been, but at this a colour like a flame leaped into her face. "Of more importance to whom? It seems to me enough that one's husband should be of importance to one's self!"

Ralph blushed as well; his attitude embarrassed him. Physically speaking he proceeded to change it; he straightened himself, then leaned forward, resting a hand on each knee. He fixed his eyes on the ground; he had an air of the most respectful deliberation.

"I'll tell you in a moment what I mean," he presently said. He felt agitated, intensely eager; now that he had opened the discussion he wished to discharge his mind. But he wished also to be superlatively gentle.

Isabel waited a little—then she went on with majesty. "In everything that makes one care for people Mr. Osmond is pre-eminent. There may be nobler natures, but I've never had the pleasure of meeting one. Mr. Osmond's is the finest I know; he's good enough for me, and interesting enough, and clever enough. I'm far more struck with what he has and what he represents than with what he may lack."

"I had treated myself to a charming vision of your future," Ralph observed without answering this; "I had amused myself with planning out a high destiny for you. There was to be nothing of this sort in it. You were not to come down so easily or so soon."

"Come down, you say?"

"Well, that renders my sense of what has happened to you. You seemed to me to be soaring far up in the blue—to be, sailing in the bright light, over the heads of men. Suddenly some one tosses up a faded rosebud—a missile that should never have reached you—and straight you drop to the ground. It hurts me," said Ralph audaciously, "hurts me as if I had fallen myself!"

The look of pain and bewilderment deepened in his companion's face. "I don't understand you in the least," she repeated. "You say you amused yourself with a project for my career—I don't understand that. Don't amuse yourself too much, or I shall think you're doing it at my expense."

Ralph shook his head. "I'm not afraid of your not believing that I've had great ideas for you."

"What do you mean by my soaring and sailing?" she pursued.

"I've never moved on a higher plane than I'm moving on now. There's nothing higher for a girl than to marry a—a person she likes," said poor Isabel, wandering into the didactic.

"It's your liking the person we speak of that I venture to criticise, my dear cousin. I should have said that the man for you would have been a more active, larger, freer sort of nature." Ralph hesitated, then added: "I can't get over the sense that Osmond is somehow—well, small." He had uttered the last word with no great assurance; he was afraid she would flash out again. But to his surprise she was quiet; she had the air of considering.

"Small?" She made it sound immense.

"I think he's narrow, selfish. He takes himself so seriously!"

"He has a great respect for himself; I don't blame him for that," said Isabel. "It makes one more sure to respect others."

Ralph for a moment felt almost reassured by her reasonable tone.

"Yes, but everything is relative; one ought to feel one's relation to things—to others. I don't think Mr. Osmond does that."

"I've chiefly to do with his relation to me. In that he's excellent."

"He's the incarnation of taste," Ralph went on, thinking hard how he could best express Gilbert Osmond's sinister attributes without putting himself in the wrong by seeming to describe him coarsely. He wished to describe him impersonally, scientifically. "He judges and measures, approves and condemns, altogether by that."

"It's a happy thing then that his taste should be exquisite."

"It's exquisite, indeed, since it has led him to select you as his bride. But have you ever seen such a taste—a really exquisite one—ruffled?"

"I hope it may never be my fortune to fail to gratify my husband's."

At these words a sudden passion leaped to Ralph's lips. "Ah, that's wilful, that's unworthy of you! You were not meant to be measured in that way—you were meant for something better than to keep guard over the sensibilities of a sterile dilettante!"

Isabel rose quickly and he did the same, so that they stood for a moment looking at each other as if he had flung down a defiance or an insult. But "You go too far," she simply breathed.

"I've said what I had on my mind—and I've said it because I love you!"

Isabel turned pale: was he too on that tiresome list? She had a sudden wish to strike him off. "Ah then, you're not disinterested!"

"I love you, but I love without hope," said Ralph quickly, forcing a smile and feeling that in that last declaration he had expressed more than he intended.

Isabel moved away and stood looking into the sunny stillness of the garden; but after a little she turned back to him. "I'm afraid your talk then is the wildness of despair! I don't understand it—but it doesn't matter. I'm not arguing with you; it's impossible I should; I've only tried to listen to you. I'm much obliged to you for attempting to explain," she said gently, as if the anger with which she had just sprung up had already subsided. "It's very good of you to try to warn me, if you're really alarmed; but I won't promise to think of what you've said: I shall forget it as soon as possible. Try and forget it yourself; you've done your duty, and no man can do more. I can't explain to you what I feel, what I believe, and I wouldn't if I could." She paused a moment and then went on with an inconsequence that Ralph observed even in the midst of his eagerness to discover some symptom of concession. "I can't enter into your idea of Mr. Osmond; I can't do it justice, because I see him in quite another way. He's not important—no, he's not important; he's a man to whom importance is supremely indifferent. If that's what you mean when you call him 'small,' then he's as small as you please. I call that large—it's the largest thing I know. I won't pretend to argue with you about a person I'm going to marry," Isabel repeated. "I'm not in the least concerned to defend Mr. Osmond; he's not so weak as to need my defence. I should think it would seem strange even to yourself that I should talk of him so quietly and coldly, as if he were any one else. I wouldn't talk of him at all to any one but you; and you, after what you've said—I may just answer you once for all. Pray, would you wish me to make a mercenary marriage—what they call a marriage of ambition? I've only one ambition—to be free to follow out a good feeling. I had others once, but they've passed away. Do you complain of Mr. Osmond because he's not rich? That's just what I like him for. I've fortunately money enough; I've never felt so thankful for it as to-day. There have been moments when I should like to go and kneel down by your father's grave: he did perhaps a better thing than he knew when he put it into my power to marry a poor man—a man who has borne his poverty with such dignity, with such indifference. Mr. Osmond has never scrambled nor struggled—he has cared for no worldly prize. If that's to be narrow, if that's to be selfish, then it's very well. I'm not frightened by such words, I'm not even displeased; I'm only sorry that you should make a mistake. Others might have done so, but I'm surprised that you should. You might know a gentleman when you see one—you might know a fine mind. Mr. Osmond makes no mistakes! He knows everything, he understands everything, he has the kindest, gentlest, highest spirit. You've got hold of some false idea. It's a pity, but I can't help it; it regards you more than me." Isabel paused a moment, looking at her cousin with an eye illumined by a sentiment which contradicted the careful calmness of her manner—a mingled sentiment, to which the angry pain excited by his words and the wounded pride of having needed to justify a choice of which she felt only the nobleness and purity, equally contributed. Though she paused Ralph said nothing; he saw she had more to say. She was grand, but she was highly solicitous; she was indifferent, but she was all in a passion. "What sort of a person should you have liked me to marry?" she asked suddenly. "You talk about one's soaring and sailing, but if one marries at all one touches the earth. One has human feelings and needs, one has a heart in one's bosom, and one must marry a particular individual. Your mother has never forgiven me for not having come to a better understanding with Lord Warburton, and she's horrified at my contenting myself with a person who has none of his great advantages—no property, no title, no honours, no houses, nor lands, nor position, nor reputation, nor brilliant belongings of any sort. It's the total absence of all these things that pleases me. Mr. Osmond's simply a very lonely, a very cultivated and a very honest man—he's not a prodigious proprietor."

Ralph had listened with great attention, as if everything she said merited deep consideration; but in truth he was only half thinking of the things she said, he was for the rest simply accommodating himself to the weight of his total impression—the impression of her ardent good faith. She was wrong, but she believed; she was deluded, but she was dismally consistent. It was wonderfully characteristic of her that, having invented a fine thetheory, about Gilbert Osmond, she loved him not for what he really possessed, but for his very poverties dressed out as honours. Ralph remembered what he had said to his father about wishing to put it into her power to meet the requirements of her imagination. He had done so, and the girl had taken full advantage of the luxury. Poor Ralph felt sick; he felt ashamed. Isabel had uttered her last words with a low solemnity of conviction which virtually terminated the discussion, and she closed it formally by turning away and walking back to the house. Ralph walked beside her, and they passed into the court together and reached the big staircase. Here he stopped and Isabel paused, turning on him a face of elation—absolutely and perversely of gratitude. His opposition had made her own conception of her conduct clearer to her. "Shall you not come up to breakfast?" she asked.

"No; I want no breakfast; I'm not hungry."

"You ought to eat," said the girl; "you live on air."

"I do, very much, and I shall go back into the garden and take another mouthful. I came thus far simply to say this. I told you last year that if you were to get into trouble I should feel terribly sold. That's how I feel today."

"Do you think I'm in trouble?"

"One's in trouble when one's in error."

"Very well," said Isabel; "I shall never complain of my trouble to you!" And she moved up the staircase.

Ralph, standing there with his hands in his pockets, followed her with his eyes; then the lurking chill of the high-walled court struck him and made him shiver, so that he returned to the garden to breakfast on the Florentine sunshine.

CHAPTER XXXV

Isabel, when she strolled in the Cascine with her lover, felt no impulse to tell him how little he was approved at Palazzo Crescentini. The discreet opposition offered to her marriage by her aunt and her cousin made on the whole no great impression upon her; the moral of it was simply that they disliked Gilbert Osmond. This dislike was not alarming to Isabel; she scarcely even regretted it; for it served mainly to throw into higher relief the fact, in every way so honourable, that she married to please herself. One did other things to please other people; one did this for a more personal satisfaction; and Isabel's satisfaction was confirmed by her lover's admirable good conduct. Gilbert Osmond was in love, and he had never deserved less than during these still, bright days, each of them numbered, which preceded the fulfilment of his hopes, the harsh criticism passed upon him by Ralph Touchett. The chief impression produced on Isabel's spirit by this criticism was that the passion of love separated its victim terribly from every one but the loved object. She felt herself disjoined from every one she had ever known before—from her two sisters, who wrote to express a dutiful hope that she would be happy, and a surprise, somewhat more vague, at her not having chosen a consort who was the hero of a richer accumulation of anecdote; from Henrietta, who, she was sure, would come out, too late, on purpose to remonstrate; from Lord Warburton, who would certainly console himself, and from Caspar Goodwood, who perhaps would not; from her aunt, who had cold, shallow ideas about marriage, for which she was not sorry to display her contempt; and from Ralph, whose talk about having great views for her was surely but a whimsical cover for a personal disappointment. Ralph apparently wished her not to marry at all—that was what it really meant—because he was amused with the spectacle of her adventures as a single woman. His disappointment made him say angry things about the man she had preferred even to him: Isabel flattered herself that she believed Ralph had been angry. It was the more easy for her to believe this because, as I say, she had now little free or unemployed emotion for minor needs, and accepted as an incident, in fact quite as an ornament, of her lot the idea that to prefer Gilbert Osmond as she preferred him was perforce to break all other ties. She tasted of the sweets of this preference, and they made her conscious, almost with awe, of the invidious and remorseless tide of the charmed and possessed condition, great as was the traditional honour and imputed virtue of being in love. It was the tragic part of happiness; one's right was always made of the wrong of some one else.

The elation of success, which surely now flamed high in Osmond, emitted meanwhile very little smoke for so brilliant a blaze. Contentment, on his part, took no vulgar form; excitement, in the most self-conscious of men, was a kind of ecstasy of self-control. This disposition, however, made him an admirable lover; it gave him a constant view of the smitten and dedicated state. He never forgot himself, as I say; and so he never forgot to be graceful and tender, to wear the appearance—which presented indeed no difficulty—of stirred senses and deep intentions. He was immensely pleased with his young lady; Madame Merle had made him a present of incalculable value. What could be a finer thing to live with than a high spirit attuned to softness? For would not the softness be all for one's self, and the strenuousness for society, which admired the air of superiority? What could be a happier gift in a companion than a quick, fanciful mind which saved one repetitions and reflected one's thought on a polished, elegant surface? Osmond hated to see his thought reproduced literally—that made it look stale and stupid; he preferred it to be freshened in the reproduction even as "words" by music. His egotism had never taken the crude form of desiring a dull wife; this lady's intelligence was to be a silver plate, not an earthen one—a plate that he might heap up with ripe fruits, to which it would give a decorative value, so that talk might become for him a sort of served dessert. He found the silver quality in this perfection in Isabel; he could tap her imagination with his knuckle and make it ring. He knew perfectly, though he had not been told, that their union enjoyed little favour with the girl's relations; but he had always treated her so completely as an independent person that it hardly seemed necessary to express regret for the attitude of her family. Nevertheless, one morning, he made an abrupt allusion to it. "It's the difference in our fortune they don't like," he said. "They think I'm in love with your money."

"Are you speaking of my aunt—of my cousin?" Isabel asked. "How do you know what they think?"

"You've not told me they're pleased, and when I wrote to Mrs. Touchett the other day she never answered my note. If they had been delighted I should have had some sign of it, and the fact of my being poor and you rich is the most obvious explanation of their reserve. But of course when a poor man marries a rich girl he must be prepared for imputations. I don't mind them; I only care for one thing—for your not having the shadow of a doubt. I don't care what people of whom I ask nothing think—I'm not even capable perhaps of wanting to know. I've never so concerned myself, God forgive me, and why should I begin to-day, when I have taken to myself a compensation for everything? I won't pretend I'm sorry you're rich; I'm delighted. I delight in everything that's yours—whether it be money or virtue. Money's a horrid thing to follow, but a charming thing to meet. It seems to me, however, that I've sufficiently proved the limits of my itch for it: I never in my life tried to earn a penny, and I ought to be less subject to suspicion than most of the people one sees grubbing and grabbing. I suppose it's their business to suspect—that of your family; it's proper on the whole they should. They'll like me better some day; so will you, for that matter. Meanwhile my business is not to make myself bad blood, but simply to be thankful for life and love." "It has made me better, loving you," he said on another occasion; "it has made me wiser and easier and—I won't pretend to deny—brighter and nicer and even stronger. I used to want a great many things before and to be angry I didn't have them. Theoretically I was satisfied, as I once told you. I flattered myself I had limited my wants. But I was subject to irritation; I used to have morbid, sterile, hateful fits of hunger, of desire. Now I'm really satisfied, because I can't think of anything better. It's just as when one has been trying to spell out a book in the twilight and suddenly the lamp comes in. I had been putting out my eyes over the book of life and finding nothing to reward me for my pains; but now that I can read it properly I see it's a delightful story. My dear girl, I can't tell you how life seems to stretch there before us—what a long summer afternoon awaits us. It's the latter half of an Italian day—with a golden haze, and the shadows just lengthening, and that divine delicacy in the light, the air, the landscape, which I have loved all my life and which you love to-day. Upon my honour, I don't see why we shouldn't get on. We've got what we like—to say nothing of having each other. We've the faculty of admiration and several capital convictions. We're not stupid, we're not mean, we're not under bonds to any kind of ignorance or dreariness. You're remarkably fresh, and I'm remarkably well-seasoned. We've my poor child to amuse us; we'll try and make up some little life for her. It's all soft and mellow—it has the Italian colouring."

They made a good many plans, but they left themselves also a good deal of latitude; it was a matter of course, however, that they should live for the present in Italy. It was in Italy that they had met, Italy had been a party to their first impressions of each other, and Italy should be a party to their happiness. Osmond had the attachment of old acquaintance and Isabel the stimulus of new, which seemed to assure her a future at a high level of consciousness of the beautiful. The desire for unlimited expansion had been succeeded in her soul by the sense that life was vacant without some private duty that might gather one's energies to a point. She had told Ralph she had "seen life" in a year or two and that she was already tired, not of the act of living, but of that of observing. What had become of all her ardours, her aspirations, her theories, her high estimate of her independence and her incipient conviction that she should never marry? These things had been absorbed in a more primitive need—a need the answer to which brushed away numberless questions, yet gratified infinite desires. It simplified the situation at a stroke, it came down from above like the light of the stars, and it needed no explanation. There was explanation enough in the fact that he was her lover, her own, and that she should be able to be of use to him. She could surrender to him with a kind of humility, she could marry him with a kind of pride; she was not only taking, she was giving.

He brought Pansy with him two or three times to the Cascine—Pansy who was very little taller than a year before, and not much older. That she would always be a child was the conviction expressed by her father, who held her by the hand when she was in her sixteenth year and told her to go and play while he sat down a little with the pretty lady. Pansy wore a short dress and a long coat; her hat always seemed too big for her. She found pleasure in walking off, with quick, short steps, to the end of the alley, and then in walking back with a smile that seemed an appeal for approbation. Isabel approved in abundance, and the abundance had the personal touch that the child's affectionate nature craved. She watched her indications as if for herself also much depended on them—Pansy already so represented part of the service she could render, part of the responsibility she could face. Her father took so the childish view of her that he had not yet explained to her the new relation in which he stood to the elegant Miss Archer. "She doesn't know," he said to Isabel; "she doesn't guess; she thinks it perfectly natural that you and I should come and walk here together simply as good friends. There seems to me something enchantingly innocent in that; it's the way I like her to be. No, I'm not a failure, as I used to think; I've succeeded in two things. I'm to marry the woman I adore, and I've brought up my child, as I wished, in the old way."

He was very fond, in all things, of the "old way"; that had struck Isabel as one of his fine, quiet, sincere notes. "It occurs to me that you'll not know whether you've succeeded until you've told her," she said. "You must see how she takes your news, She may be horrified—she may be jealous."

"I'm not afraid of that; she's too fond of you on her own account. I should like to leave her in the dark a little longer—to see if it will come into her head that if we're not engaged we ought to be."

Isabel was impressed by Osmond's artistic, the plastic view, as it somehow appeared, of Pansy's innocence—her own appreciation of it being more anxiously moral. She was perhaps not the less pleased when he told her a few days later that he had communicated the fact to his daughter, who had made such a pretty little speech—"Oh, then I shall have a beautiful sister!" She was neither surprised nor alarmed; she had not cried, as he expected.

"Perhaps she had guessed it," said Isabel.

"Don't say that; I should be disgusted if I believed that. I thought it would be just a little shock; but the way she took it proves that her good manners are paramount. That's also what I wished. You shall see for yourself; to-morrow she shall make you her congratulations in person."

The meeting, on the morrow, took place at the Countess Gemini's, whither Pansy had been conducted by her father, who knew that Isabel was to come in the afternoon to return a visit made her by the Countess on learning that they were to become sisters-in-law. Calling at Casa Touchett the visitor had not found Isabel at home; but after our young woman had been ushered into the Countess's drawing-room Pansy arrived to say that her aunt would presently appear. Pansy was spending the day with that lady, who thought her of an age to begin to learn how to carry herself in company. It was Isabel's view that the little girl might have given lessons in deportment to her relative, and nothing could have justified this conviction more than the manner in which Pansy acquitted herself while they waited together for the Countess. Her father's decision, the year before, had finally been to send her back to the convent to receive the last graces, and Madame Catherine had evidently carried out her theory that Pansy was to be fitted for the great world.

"Papa has told me that you've kindly consented to marry him," said this excellent woman's pupil. "It's very delightful; I think you'll suit very well."

"You think I shall suit YOU?"

"You'll suit me beautifully; but what I mean is that you and papa will suit each other. You're both so quiet and so serious. You're not so quiet as he—or even as Madame Merle; but you're more quiet than many others. He should not for instance have a wife like my aunt. She's always in motion, in agitation—to-day especially; you'll see when she comes in. They told us at the convent it was wrong to judge our elders, but I suppose there's no harm if we judge them favourably. You'll be a delightful companion for papa."

"For you too, I hope," Isabel said.

"I speak first of him on purpose. I've told you already what I myself think of you; I liked you from the first. I admire you so much that I think it will be a good fortune to have you always before me. You'll be my model; I shall try to imitate you though I'm afraid it will be very feeble. I'm very glad for papa—he needed something more than me. Without you I don't see how he could have got it. You'll be my stepmother, but we mustn't use that word. They're always said to be cruel; but I don't think you'll ever so much as pinch or even push me. I'm not afraid at all."

"My good little Pansy," said Isabel gently, "I shall be ever so kind to you." A vague, inconsequent vision of her coming in some odd way to need it had intervened with the effect of a chill.

"Very well then, I've nothing to fear," the child returned with her note of prepared promptitude. What teaching she had had, it seemed to suggest—or what penalties for non-performance she dreaded!

Her description of her aunt had not been incorrect; the Countess Gemini was further than ever from having folded her wings. She entered the room with a flutter through the air and kissed Isabel first on the forehead and then on each cheek as if according to some ancient prescribed rite. She drew the visitor to a sofa and, looking at her with a variety of turns of the head, began to talk very much as if, seated brush in hand before an easel, she were applying a series of considered touches to a composition of figures already sketched in. "If you expect me to congratulate you I must beg you to excuse me. I don't suppose you care if I do or not; I believe you're supposed not to care—through being so clever—for all sorts of ordinary things. But I care myself if I tell fibs; I never tell them unless there's something rather good to be gained. I don't see what's to be gained with you—especially as you wouldn't believe me. I don't make professions any more than I make paper flowers or flouncey lampshades—I don't know how. My lampshades would be sure to take fire, my roses and my fibs to be larger than life. I'm very glad for my own sake that you're to marry Osmond; but I won't pretend I'm glad for yours. You're very brilliant—you know that's the way you're always spoken of; you're an heiress and very good-looking and original, not banal; so it's a good thing to have you in the family. Our family's very good, you know; Osmond will have told you that; and my mother was rather distinguished—she was called the American Corinne. But we're dreadfully fallen, I think, and perhaps you'll pick us up. I've great confidence in you; there are ever so many things I want to talk to you about. I never congratulate any girl on marrying; I think they ought to make it somehow not quite so awful a steel trap. I suppose Pansy oughtn't to hear all this; but that's what she has come to me for—to acquire the tone of society. There's no harm in her knowing what horrors she may be in for. When first I got an idea that my brother had designs on you I thought of writing to you, to recommend you, in the strongest terms, not to listen to him. Then I thought it would be disloyal, and I hate anything of that kind. Besides, as I say, I was enchanted for myself; and after all I'm very selfish. By the way, you won't respect me, not one little mite, and we shall never be intimate. I should like it, but you won't. Some day, all the same, we shall be better friends than you will believe at first. My husband will come and see you, though, as you probably know, he's on no sort of terms with Osmond. He's very fond of going to see pretty women, but I'm not afraid of you. In the first place I don't care what he does. In the second, you won't care a straw for him; he won't be a bit, at any time, your affair, and, stupid as he is, he'll see you're not his. Some day, if you can stand it, I'll tell you all about him. Do you think my niece ought to go out of the room? Pansy, go and practise a little in my boudoir."

"Let her stay, please," said Isabel. "I would rather hear nothing that Pansy may not!"

CHAPTER XXXVI

One afternoon of the autumn of 1876, toward dusk, a young man of pleasing appearance rang at the door of a small apartment on the third floor of an old Roman house. On its being opened he enquired for Madame Merle; whereupon the servant, a neat, plain woman, with a French face and a lady's maid's manner, ushered him into a diminutive drawing-room and requested the favour of his name. "Mr. Edward Rosier," said the young man, who sat down to wait till his hostess should appear.

The reader will perhaps not have forgotten that Mr. Rosier was an ornament of the American circle in Paris, but it may also be remembered that he sometimes vanished from its horizon. He had spent a portion of several winters at Pau, and as he was a gentleman of constituted habits he might have continued for years to pay his annual visit to this charming resort. In the summer of 1876, however, an incident befell him which changed the current not only of his thoughts, but of his customary sequences. He passed a month in the Upper Engadine and encountered at Saint Moritz a charming young girl. To this little person he began to pay, on the spot, particular attention: she struck him as exactly the household angel he had long been looking for. He was never precipitate, he was nothing if not discreet, so he forbore for the present to declare his passion; but it seemed to him when they parted—the young lady to go down into Italy and her admirer to proceed to Geneva, where he was under bonds to join other friends—that he should be romantically wretched if he were not to see her again. The simplest way to do so was to go in the autumn to Rome, where Miss Osmond was domiciled with her family. Mr. Rosier started on his pilgrimage to the Italian capital and reached it on the first of November. It was a pleasant thing to do, but for the young man there was a strain of the heroic in the enterprise. He might expose himself, unseasoned, to the poison of the Roman air, which in November lay, notoriously, much in wait. Fortune, however, favours the brave; and this adventurer, who took three grains of quinine a day, had at the end of a month no cause to deplore his temerity. He had made to a certain extent good use of his time; he had devoted it in vain to finding a flaw in Pansy Osmond's composition. She was admirably finished; she had had the last touch; she was really a consummate piece. He thought of her in amorous meditation a good deal as he might have thought of a Dresden-china shepherdess. Miss Osmond, indeed, in the bloom of her juvenility, had a hint of the rococo which Rosier, whose taste was predominantly for that manner, could not fail to appreciate. That he esteemed the productions of comparatively frivolous periods would have been apparent from the attention he bestowed upon Madame Merle's drawing-room, which, although furnished with specimens of every style, was especially rich in articles of the last two centuries. He had immediately put a glass into one eye and looked round; and then "By Jove, she has some jolly good things!" he had yearningly murmured. The room was small and densely filled with furniture; it gave an impression of faded silk and little statuettes which might totter if one moved. Rosier got up and wandered about with his careful tread, bending over the tables charged with knick-knacks and the cushions embossed with princely arms. When Madame Merle came in she found him standing before the fireplace with his nose very close to the great lace flounce attached to the damask cover of the mantel. He had lifted it delicately, as if he were smelling it.

"It's old Venetian," she said; "it's rather good."

"It's too good for this; you ought to wear it."

"They tell me you have some better in Paris, in the same situation."

"Ah, but I can't wear mine," smiled the visitor.

"I don't see why you shouldn't! I've better lace than that to wear."

His eyes wandered, lingeringly, round the room again. "You've some very good things."

"Yes, but I hate them."

"Do you want to get rid of them?" the young man quickly asked.

"No, it's good to have something to hate: one works it off!"

"I love my things," said Mr. Rosier as he sat there flushed with all his recognitions. "But it's not about them, nor about yours, that I came to talk to you." He paused a moment and then, with greater softness: "I care more for Miss Osmond than for all the bibelots in Europe!"

Madame Merle opened wide eyes. "Did you come to tell me that?"

"I came to ask your advice."

She looked at him with a friendly frown, stroking her chin with her large white hand. "A man in love, you know, doesn't ask advice."

"Why not, if he's in a difficult position? That's often the case with a man in love. I've been in love before, and I know. But never so much as this time—really never so much. I should like particularly to know what you think of my prospects. I'm afraid that for Mr. Osmond I'm not—well, a real collector's piece."

"Do you wish me to intercede?" Madame Merle asked with her fine arms folded and her handsome mouth drawn up to the left.

"If you could say a good word for me I should be greatly obliged. There will be no use in my troubling Miss Osmond unless I have good reason to believe her father will consent."

"You're very considerate; that's in your favour. But you assume in rather an off-hand way that I think you a prize."

"You've been very kind to me," said the young man. "That's why I came."

"I'm always kind to people who have good Louis Quatorze. It's very rare now, and there's no telling what one may get by it." With which the left-hand corner of Madame Merle's mouth gave expression to the joke.

But he looked, in spite of it, literally apprehensive and consistently strenuous. "Ah, I thought you liked me for myself!"

"I like you very much; but, if you please, we won't analyse. Pardon me if I seem patronising, but I think you a perfect little gentleman. I must tell you, however, that I've not the marrying of Pansy Osmond."

"I didn't suppose that. But you've seemed to me intimate with her family, and I thought you might have influence."

Madame Merle considered. "Whom do you call her family?"

"Why, her father; and—how do you say it in English?—her belle-mere."

"Mr. Osmond's her father, certainly; but his wife can scarcely be termed a member of her family. Mrs. Osmond has nothing to do with marrying her."

"I'm sorry for that," said Rosier with an amiable sigh of good faith. "I think Mrs. Osmond would favour me."

"Very likely—if her husband doesn't."

He raised his eyebrows. "Does she take the opposite line from him?"

"In everything. They think quite differently."

"Well," said Rosier, "I'm sorry for that; but it's none of my business. She's very fond of Pansy."

"Yes, she's very fond of Pansy."

"And Pansy has a great affection for her. She has told me how she loves her as if she were her own mother."

"You must, after all, have had some very intimate talk with the poor child," said Madame Merle. "Have you declared your sentiments?"

"Never!" cried Rosier, lifting his neatly-gloved hand. "Never till I've assured myself of those of the parents."

"You always wait for that? You've excellent principles; you observe the proprieties."

"I think you're laughing at me," the young man murmured, dropping back in his chair and feeling his small moustache. "I didn't expect that of you, Madame Merle."

She shook her head calmly, like a person who saw things as she saw them. "You don't do me justice. I think your conduct in excellent taste and the best you could adopt. Yes, that's what I think."

"I wouldn't agitate her—only to agitate her; I love her too much for that," said Ned Rosier.

"I'm glad, after all, that you've told me," Madame Merle went on. "Leave it to me a little; I think I can help you."

"I said you were the person to come to!" her visitor cried with prompt elation.

"You were very clever," Madame Merle returned more dryly. "When I say I can help you I mean once assuming your cause to be good. Let us think a little if it is."

"I'm awfully decent, you know," said Rosier earnestly. "I won't say I've no faults, but I'll say I've no vices."

"All that's negative, and it always depends, also, on what people call vices. What's the positive side? What's the virtuous? What have you got besides your Spanish lace and your Dresden teacups?"

"I've a comfortable little fortune—about forty thousand francs a year. With the talent I have for arranging, we can live beautifully on such an income."

"Beautifully, no. Sufficiently, yes. Even that depends on where you live."

"Well, in Paris. I would undertake it in Paris."

Madame Merle's mouth rose to the left. "It wouldn't be famous; you'd have to make use of the teacups, and they'd get broken."

"We don't want to be famous. If Miss Osmond should have everything pretty it would be enough. When one's as pretty as she one can afford—well, quite cheap faience. She ought never to wear anything but muslin—without the sprig," said Rosier reflectively.

"Wouldn't you even allow her the sprig? She'd be much obliged to you at any rate for that theory."

"It's the correct one, I assure you; and I'm sure she'd enter into it. She understands all that; that's why I love her."

"She's a very good little girl, and most tidy—also extremely graceful. But her father, to the best of my belief, can give her nothing."

Rosier scarce demurred. "I don't in the least desire that he should. But I may remark, all the same, that he lives like a rich man."

"The money's his wife's; she brought him a large fortune."

"Mrs. Osmond then is very fond of her stepdaughter; she may do something."

"For a love-sick swain you have your eyes about you!" Madame Merle exclaimed with a laugh.

"I esteem a dot very much. I can do without it, but I esteem it."

"Mrs. Osmond," Madame Merle went on, "will probably prefer to keep her money for her own children."

"Her own children? Surely she has none."

"She may have yet. She had a poor little boy, who died two years ago, six months after his birth. Others therefore may come."

"I hope they will, if it will make her happy. She's a splendid woman."

Madame Merle failed to burst into speech. "Ah, about her there's much to be said. Splendid as you like! We've not exactly made out that you're a parti. The absence of vices is hardly a source of income.

"Pardon me, I think it may be," said Rosier quite lucidly.

"You'll be a touching couple, living on your innocence!"

"I think you underrate me."

"You're not so innocent as that? Seriously," said Madame Merle, "of course forty thousand francs a year and a nice character are a combination to be considered. I don't say it's to be jumped at, but there might be a worse offer. Mr. Osmond, however, will probably incline to believe he can do better."

"HE can do so perhaps; but what can his daughter do? She can't do better than marry the man she loves. For she does, you know," Rosier added eagerly.

"She does—I know it."

"Ah," cried the young man, "I said you were the person to come to."

"But I don't know how you know it, if you haven't asked her," Madame Merle went on.

"In such a case there's no need of asking and telling; as you say, we're an innocent couple. How did YOU know it?"

"I who am not innocent? By being very crafty. Leave it to me; I'll find out for you."

Rosier got up and stood smoothing his hat. "You say that rather coldly. Don't simply find out how it is, but try to make it as it should be."

"I'll do my best. I'll try to make the most of your advantages."

"Thank you so very much. Meanwhile then I'll say a word to Mrs. Osmond."

"Gardez-vous-en bien!" And Madame Merle was on her feet. "Don't set her going, or you'll spoil everything."

Rosier gazed into his hat; he wondered whether his hostess HAD been after all the right person to come to. "I don't think I understand you. I'm an old friend of Mrs. Osmond, and I think she would like me to succeed."

"Be an old friend as much as you like; the more old friends she has the better, for she doesn't get on very well with some of her new. But don't for the present try to make her take up the cudgels for you. Her husband may have other views, and, as a person who wishes her well, I advise you not to multiply points of difference between them."

Poor Rosier's face assumed an expression of alarm; a suit for the hand of Pansy Osmond was even a more complicated business than his taste for proper transitions had allowed. But the extreme good sense which he concealed under a surface suggesting that of a careful owner's "best set" came to his assistance. "I don't see that I'm bound to consider Mr. Osmond so very much!" he exclaimed. "No, but you should consider HER. You say you're an old friend. Would you make her suffer?"

"Not for the world."

"Then be very careful, and let the matter alone till I've taken a few soundings."

"Let the matter alone, dear Madame Merle? Remember that I'm in love."

"Oh, you won't burn up! Why did you come to me, if you're not to heed what I say?"

"You're very kind; I'll be very good," the young man promised. "But I'm afraid Mr. Osmond's pretty hard," he added in his mild voice as he went to the door.

Madame Merle gave a short laugh. "It has been said before. But his wife isn't easy either."

"Ah, she's a splendid woman!" Ned Rosier repeated, for departure. He resolved that his conduct should be worthy of an aspirant who was already a model of discretion; but he saw nothing in any pledge he had given Madame Merle that made it improper he should keep himself in spirits by an occasional visit to Miss Osmond's home. He reflected constantly on what his adviser had said to him, and turned over in his mind the impression of her rather circumspect tone. He had gone to her de confiance, as they put it in Paris; but it was possible he had been precipitate. He found difficulty in thinking of himself as rash—he had incurred this reproach so rarely; but it certainly was true that he had known Madame Merle only for the last month, and that his thinking her a delightful woman was not, when one came to look into it, a reason for assuming that she would be eager to push Pansy Osmond into his arms, gracefully arranged as these members might be to receive her. She had indeed shown him benevolence, and she was a person of consideration among the girl's people, where she had a rather striking appearance (Rosier had more than once wondered how she managed it) of being intimate without being familiar. But possibly he had exaggerated these advantages. There was no particular reason why she should take trouble for him; a charming woman was charming to every one, and Rosier felt rather a fool when he thought of his having appealed to her on the ground that she had distinguished him. Very likely—though she had appeared to say it in joke—she was really only thinking of his bibelots. Had it come into her head that he might offer her two or three of the gems of his collection? If she would only help him to marry Miss Osmond he would present her with his whole museum. He could hardly say so to her outright; it would seem too gross a bribe. But he should like her to believe it.

It was with these thoughts that he went again to Mrs. Osmond's, Mrs. Osmond having an "evening"—she had taken the Thursday of each week—when his presence could be accounted for on general principles of civility. The object of Mr. Rosier's well-regulated affection dwelt in a high house in the very heart of Rome; a dark and massive structure overlooking a sunny piazzetta in the neighbourhood of the Farnese Palace. In a palace, too, little Pansy lived—a palace by Roman measure, but a dungeon to poor Rosier's apprehensive mind. It seemed to him of evil omen that the young lady he wished to marry, and whose fastidious father he doubted of his ability to conciliate, should be immured in a kind of domestic fortress, a pile which bore a stern old Roman name, which smelt of historic deeds, of crime and craft and violence, which was mentioned in "Murray" and visited by tourists who looked, on a vague survey, disappointed and depressed, and which had frescoes by Caravaggio in the piano nobile and a row of mutilated statues and dusty urns in the wide, nobly-arched loggia overhanging the damp court where a fountain gushed out of a mossy niche. In a less preoccupied frame of mind he could have done justice to the Palazzo Roccanera; he could have entered into the sentiment of Mrs. Osmond, who had once told him that on settling themselves in Rome she and her husband had chosen this habitation for the love of local colour. It had local colour enough, and though he knew less about architecture than about Limoges enamels he could see that the proportions of the windows and even the details of the cornice had quite the grand air. But Rosier was haunted by the conviction that at picturesque periods young girls had been shut up there to keep them from their true loves, and hen, under the threat of being thrown into convents, had been forced into unholy marriages. There was one point, however, to which he always did justice when once he found himself in Mrs. Osmond's warm, rich-looking reception-rooms, which were on the second floor. He acknowledged that these people were very strong in "good things." It was a taste of Osmond's own—not at all of hers; this she had told him the first time he came to the house, when, after asking himself for a quarter of an hour whether they had even better "French" than he in Paris, he was obliged on the spot to admit that they had, very much, and vanquished his envy, as a gentleman should, to the point of expressing to his hostess his pure admiration of her treasures. He learned from Mrs. Osmond that her husband had made a large collection before their marriage and that, though he had annexed a number of fine pieces within the last three years, he had achieved his greatest finds at a time when he had not the advantage of her advice. Rosier interpreted this information according to principles of his own. For "advice" read "cash," he said to himself; and the fact that Gilbert Osmond had landed his highest prizes during his impecunious season confirmed his most cherished doctrine—the doctrine that a collector may freely be poor if he be only patient. In general, when Rosier presented himself on a Thursday evening, his first recognition was for the walls of the saloon; there were three or four objects his eyes really yearned for. But after his talk with Madame Merle he felt the extreme seriousness of his position; and now, when he came in, he looked about for the daughter of the house with such eagerness as might be permitted a gentleman whose smile, as he crossed a threshold, always took everything comfortable for granted.

CHAPTER XXXVII

Pansy was not in the first of the rooms, a large apartment with a concave ceiling and walls covered with old red damask; it was here Mrs. Osmond usually sat—though she was not in her most customary place to-night—and that a circle of more especial intimates gathered about the fire. The room was flushed with subdued, diffused brightness; it contained the larger things and—almost always—an odour of flowers. Pansy on this occasion was presumably in the next of the series, the resort of younger visitors, where tea was served. Osmond stood before the chimney, leaning back with his hands behind him; he had one foot up and was warming the sole. Half a dozen persons, scattered near him, were talking together; but he was not in the conversation; his eyes had an expression, frequent with them, that seemed to represent them as engaged with objects more worth their while than the appearances actually thrust upon them. Rosier, coming in unannounced, failed to attract his attention; but the young man, who was very punctilious, though he was even exceptionally conscious that it was the wife, not the husband, he had come to see, went up to shake hands with him. Osmond put out his left hand, without changing his attitude.

"How d'ye do? My wife's somewhere about."

"Never fear; I shall find her," said Rosier cheerfully.

Osmond, however, took him in; he had never in his life felt himself so efficiently looked at. "Madame Merle has told him, and he doesn't like it," he privately reasoned. He had hoped Madame Merle would be there, but she was not in sight; perhaps she was in one of the other rooms or would come later. He had never especially delighted in Gilbert Osmond, having a fancy he gave himself airs. But Rosier was not quickly resentful, and where politeness was concerned had ever a strong need of being quite in the right. He looked round him and smiled, all without help, and then in a moment, "I saw a jolly good piece of Capo di Monte to-day," he said.

Osmond answered nothing at first; but presently, while he warmed his boot-sole, "I don't care a fig for Capo di Monte!" he returned.

"I hope you're not losing your interest?"

"In old pots and plates? Yes, I'm losing my interest."

Rosier for an instant forgot the delicacy of his position. "You're not thinking of parting with a—a piece or two?"

"No, I'm not thinking of parting with anything at all, Mr. Rosier," said Osmond, with his eyes still on the eyes of his visitor.

"Ah, you want to keep, but not to add," Rosier remarked brightly.

"Exactly. I've nothing I wish to match."

Poor Rosier was aware he had blushed; he was distressed at his want of assurance. "Ah, well, I have!" was all he could murmur; and he knew his murmur was partly lost as he turned away. He took his course to the adjoining room and met Mrs. Osmond coming out of the deep doorway. She was dressed in black velvet; she looked high and splendid, as he had said, and yet oh so radiantly gentle! We know what Mr. Rosier thought of her and the terms in which, to Madame Merle, he had expressed his admiration. Like his appreciation of her dear little stepdaughter it was based partly on his eye for decorative character, his instinct for authenticity; but also on a sense for uncatalogued values, for that secret of a "lustre" beyond any recorded losing or rediscovering, which his devotion to brittle wares had still not disqualified him to recognise. Mrs. Osmond, at present, might well have gratified such tastes. The years had touched her only to enrich her; the flower of her youth had not faded, it only hung more quietly on its stem. She had lost something of that quick eagerness to which her husband had privately taken exception—she had more the air of being able to wait. Now, at all events, framed in the gilded doorway, she struck our young man as the picture of a gracious lady. "You see I'm very regular," he said. "But who should be if I'm not?"

"Yes, I've known you longer than any one here. But we mustn't indulge in tender reminiscences. I want to introduce you to a young lady."

"Ah, please, what young lady?" Rosier was immensely obliging; but this was not what he had come for.

"She sits there by the fire in pink and has no one to speak to." Rosier hesitated a moment. "Can't Mr. Osmond speak to her? He's within six feet of her."

Mrs. Osmond also hesitated. "She's not very lively, and he doesn't like dull people."

"But she's good enough for me? Ah now, that's hard!"

"I only mean that you've ideas for two. And then you're so obliging."

"No, he's not—to me." And Mrs. Osmond vaguely smiled.

"That's a sign he should be doubly so to other women.

"So I tell him," she said, still smiling.

"You see I want some tea," Rosier went on, looking wistfully beyond.

"That's perfect. Go and give some to my young lady."

"Very good; but after that I'll abandon her to her fate. The simple truth is I'm dying to have a little talk with Miss Osmond."

"Ah," said Isabel, turning away, "I can't help you there!"

Five minutes later, while he handed a tea-cup to the damsel in pink, whom he had conducted into the other room, he wondered whether, in making to Mrs. Osmond the profession I have just quoted, he had broken the spirit of his promise to Madame Merle. Such a question was capable of occupying this young man's mind for a considerable time. At last, however, he became—comparatively speaking—reckless; he cared little what promises he might break. The fate to which he had threatened to abandon the damsel in pink proved to be none so terrible; for Pansy Osmond, who had given him the tea for his companion—Pansy was as fond as ever of making tea—presently came and talked to her. Into this mild colloquy Edward Rosier entered little; he sat by moodily, watching his small sweetheart. If we look at her now through his eyes we shall at first not see much to remind us of the obedient little girl who, at Florence, three years before, was sent to walk short distances in the Cascine while her father and Miss Archer talked together of matters sacred to elder people. But after a moment we shall perceive that if at nineteen Pansy has become a young lady she doesn't really fill out the part; that if she has grown very pretty she lacks in a deplorable degree the quality known and esteemed in the appearance of females as style; and that if she is dressed with great freshness she wears her smart attire with an undisguised appearance of saving it—very much as if it were lent her for the occasion. Edward Rosier, it would seem, would have been just the man to note these defects; and in point of fact there was not a quality of this young lady, of any sort, that he had not noted. Only he called her qualities by names of his own—some of which indeed were happy enough. "No, she's unique—she's absolutely unique," he used to say to himself; and you may be sure that not for an instant would he have admitted to you that she was wanting in style. Style? Why, she had the style of a little princess; if you couldn't see it you had no eye. It was not modern, it was not conscious, it would produce no impression in Broadway; the small, serious damsel, in her stiff little dress, only looked like an Infanta of Velasquez. This was enough for Edward Rosier, who thought her delightfully old-fashioned. Her anxious eyes, her charming lips, her slip of a figure, were as touching as a childish prayer. He had now an acute desire to know just to what point she liked him—a desire which made him fidget as he sat in his chair. It made him feel hot, so that he had to pat his forehead with his handkerchief; he had never been so uncomfortable. She was such a perfect jeune fille, and one couldn't make of a jeune fille the enquiry requisite for throwing light on such a point. A jeune fille was what Rosier had always dreamed of—a jeune fille who should yet not be French, for he had felt that this nationality would complicate the question. He was sure Pansy had never looked at a newspaper and that, in the way of novels, if she had read Sir Walter Scott it was the very most. An American jeune fille—what could be better than that? She would be frank and gay, and yet would not have walked alone, nor have received letters from men, nor have been taken to the theatre to see the comedy of manners. Rosier could not deny that, as the matter stood, it would be a breach of hospitality to appeal directly to this unsophisticated creature; but he was now in imminent danger of asking himself if hospitality were the most sacred thing in the world. Was not the sentiment that he entertained for Miss Osmond of infinitely greater importance? Of greater importance to him—yes; but not probably to the master of the house. There was one comfort; even if this gentleman had been placed on his guard by Madame Merle he would not have extended the warning to Pansy; it would not have been part of his policy to let her know that a prepossessing young man was in love with her. But he WAS in love with her, the prepossessing young man; and all these restrictions of circumstance had ended by irritating him. What had Gilbert Osmond meant by giving him two fingers of his left hand? If Osmond was rude, surely he himself might be bold. He felt extremely bold after the dull girl in so vain a disguise of rose-colour had responded to the call of her mother, who came in to say, with a significant simper at Rosier, that she must carry her off to other triumphs. The mother and daughter departed together, and now it depended only upon him that he should be virtually alone with Pansy. He had never been alone with her before; he had never been alone with a jeune fille. It was a great moment; poor Rosier began to pat his forehead again. There was another room beyond the one in which they stood—a small room that had been thrown open and lighted, but that, the company not being numerous, had remained empty all the evening. It was empty yet; it was upholstered in pale yellow; there were several lamps; through the open door it looked the very temple of authorised love. Rosier gazed a moment through this aperture; he was afraid that Pansy would run away, and felt almost capable of stretching out a hand to detain her. But she lingered where the other maiden had left them, making no motion to join a knot of visitors on the far side of the room. For a little it occurred to him that she was frightened—too frightened perhaps to move; but a second glance assured him she was not, and he then reflected that she was too innocent indeed for that. After a supreme hesitation he asked her if he might go and look at the yellow room, which seemed so attractive yet so virginal. He had been there already with Osmond, to inspect the furniture, which was of the First French Empire, and especially to admire the clock (which he didn't really admire), an immense classic structure of that period. He therefore felt that he had now begun to manoeuvre.

"Certainly, you may go," said Pansy; "and if you like I'll show you." She was not in the least frightened.

"That's just what I hoped you'd say; you're so very kind," Rosier murmured.

They went in together; Rosier really thought the room very ugly, and it seemed cold. The same idea appeared to have struck Pansy. "It's not for winter evenings; it's more for summer," she said. "It's papa's taste; he has so much."

He had a good deal, Rosier thought; but some of it was very bad. He looked about him; he hardly knew what to say in such a situation. "Doesn't Mrs. Osmond care how her rooms are done? Has she no taste?" he asked.

"Oh yes, a great deal; but it's more for literature," said Pansy—"and for conversation. But papa cares also for those things. I think he knows everything."

Rosier was silent a little. "There's one thing I'm sure he knows!" he broke out presently. "He knows that when I come here it's, with all respect to him, with all respect to Mrs. Osmond, who's so charming—it's really," said the young man, "to see you!"

"To see me?" And Pansy raised her vaguely troubled eyes.

"To see you; that's what I come for," Rosier repeated, feeling the intoxication of a rupture with authority.

Pansy stood looking at him, simply, intently, openly; a blush was not needed to make her face more modest. "I thought it was for that."

"And it was not disagreeable to you?"

"I couldn't tell; I didn't know. You never told me," said Pansy.

"I was afraid of offending you."

"You don't offend me," the young girl murmured, smiling as if an angel had kissed her.

"You like me then, Pansy?" Rosier asked very gently, feeling very happy.

"Yes—I like you."

They had walked to the chimney-piece where the big cold Empire clock was perched; they were well within the room and beyond observation from without. The tone in which she had said these four words seemed to him the very breath of nature, and his only answer could be to take her hand and hold it a moment. Then he raised it to his lips. She submitted, still with her pure, trusting smile, in which there was something ineffably passive. She liked him—she had liked him all the while; now anything might happen! She was ready—she had been ready always, waiting for him to speak. If he had not spoken she would have waited for ever; but when the word came she dropped like the peach from the shaken tree. Rosier felt that if he should draw her toward him and hold her to his heart she would submit without a murmur, would rest there without a question. It was true that this would be a rash experiment in a yellow Empire salottino. She had known it was for her he came, and yet like what a perfect little lady she had carried it off!

"You're very dear to me," he murmured, trying to believe that there was after all such a thing as hospitality.

She looked a moment at her hand, where he had kissed it. "Did you say papa knows?"

"You told me just now he knows everything."

"I think you must make sure," said Pansy.

"Ah, my dear, when once I'm sure of YOU!" Rosier murmured in her ear; whereupon she turned back to the other rooms with a little air of consistency which seemed to imply that their appeal should be immediate.

The other rooms meanwhile had become conscious of the arrival of Madame Merle, who, wherever she went, produced an impression when she entered. How she did it the most attentive spectator could not have told you, for she neither spoke loud, nor laughed profusely, nor moved rapidly, nor dressed with splendour, nor appealed in any appreciable manner to the audience. Large, fair, smiling, serene, there was something in her very tranquillity that diffused itself, and when people looked round it was because of a sudden quiet. On this occasion she had done the quietest thing she could do; after embracing Mrs. Osmond, which was more striking, she had sat down on a small sofa to commune with the master of the house. There was a brief exchange of commonplaces between these two—they always paid, in public, a certain formal tribute to the commonplace—and then Madame Merle, whose eyes had been wandering, asked if little Mr. Rosier had come this evening.

"He came nearly an hour ago—but he has disappeared," Osmond said.

"And where's Pansy?"

"In the other room. There are several people there."

"He's probably among them," said Madame Merle.

"Do you wish to see him?" Osmond asked in a provokingly pointless tone.

Madame Merle looked at him a moment; she knew each of his tones to the eighth of a note. "Yes, I should like to say to him that I've told you what he wants, and that it interests you but feebly."

"Don't tell him that. He'll try to interest me more—which is exactly what I don't want. Tell him I hate his proposal."

"But you don't hate it."

"It doesn't signify; I don't love it. I let him see that, myself, this evening; I was rude to him on purpose. That sort of thing's a great bore. There's no hurry."

"I'll tell him that you'll take time and think it over."

"No, don't do that. He'll hang on."

"If I discourage him he'll do the same."

"Yes, but in the one case he'll try to talk and explain—which would be exceedingly tiresome. In the other he'll probably hold his tongue and go in for some deeper game. That will leave me quiet. I hate talking with a donkey."

"Is that what you call poor Mr. Rosier?"

"Oh, he's a nuisance—with his eternal majolica."

Madame Merle dropped her eyes; she had a faint smile. "He's a gentleman, he has a charming temper; and, after all, an income of forty thousand francs!"

"It's misery—'genteel' misery," Osmond broke in. "It's not what I've dreamed of for Pansy."

"Very good then. He has promised me not to speak to her."

"Do you believe him?" Osmond asked absentmindedly.

"Perfectly. Pansy has thought a great deal about him; but I don't suppose you consider that that matters."

"I don't consider it matters at all; but neither do I believe she has thought of him."

"That opinion's more convenient," said Madame Merle quietly.

"Has she told you she's in love with him?"

"For what do you take her? And for what do you take me?" Madame Merle added in a moment.

Osmond had raised his foot and was resting his slim ankle on the other knee; he clasped his ankle in his hand familiarly—his long, fine forefinger and thumb could make a ring for it—and gazed a while before him. "This kind of thing doesn't find me unprepared. It's what I educated her for. It was all for this—that when such a case should come up she should do what I prefer."

"I'm not afraid that she'll not do it."

"Well then, where's the hitch?"

"I don't see any. But, all the same, I recommend you not to get rid of Mr. Rosier. Keep him on hand; he may be useful."

"I can't keep him. Keep him yourself."

"Very good; I'll put him into a corner and allow him so much a day." Madame Merle had, for the most part, while they talked, been glancing about her; it was her habit in this situation, just as it was her habit to interpose a good many blank-looking pauses. A long drop followed the last words I have quoted; and before it had ended she saw Pansy come out of the adjoining room, followed by Edward Rosier. The girl advanced a few steps and then stopped and stood looking at Madame Merle and at her father.

"He has spoken to her," Madame Merle went on to Osmond.

Her companion never turned his head. "So much for your belief in his promises. He ought to be horse-whipped."

"He intends to confess, poor little man!"

Osmond got up; he had now taken a sharp look at his daughter. "It doesn't matter," he murmured, turning away.

Pansy after a moment came up to Madame Merle with her little manner of unfamiliar politeness. This lady's reception of her was not more intimate; she simply, as she rose from the sofa, gave her a friendly smile.

"You're very late," the young creature gently said.

"My dear child, I'm never later than I intend to be."

Madame Merle had not got up to be gracious to Pansy; she moved toward Edward Rosier. He came to meet her and, very quickly, as if to get it off his mind, "I've spoken to her!" he whispered.

"I know it, Mr. Rosier."

"Did she tell you?"

"Yes, she told me. Behave properly for the rest of the evening, and come and see me to-morrow at a quarter past five." She was severe, and in the manner in which she turned her back to him there was a degree of contempt which caused him to mutter a decent imprecation.

He had no intention of speaking to Osmond; it was neither the time nor the place. But he instinctively wandered toward Isabel, who sat talking with an old lady. He sat down on the other side of her; the old lady was Italian, and Rosier took for granted she understood no English. "You said just now you wouldn't help me," he began to Mrs. Osmond. "Perhaps you'll feel differently when you know—when you know—!"

Isabel met his hesitation. "When I know what?"

"That she's all right."

"What do you mean by that?"

"Well, that we've come to an understanding."

"She's all wrong," said Isabel. "It won't do."

Poor Rosier gazed at her half-pleadingly, half-angrily; a sudden flush testified to his sense of injury. "I've never been treated so," he said. "What is there against me, after all? That's not the way I'm usually considered. I could have married twenty times."

"It's a pity you didn't. I don't mean twenty times, but once, comfortably," Isabel added, smiling kindly. "You're not rich enough for Pansy."

"She doesn't care a straw for one's money."

"No, but her father does."

"Ah yes, he has proved that!" cried the young man.

Isabel got up, turning away from him, leaving her old lady without ceremony; and he occupied himself for the next ten minutes in pretending to look at Gilbert Osmond's collection of miniatures, which were neatly arranged on a series of small velvet screens. But he looked without seeing; his cheek burned; he was too full of his sense of injury. It was certain that he had never been treated that way before; he was not used to being thought not good enough. He knew how good he was, and if such a fallacy had not been so pernicious he could have laughed at it. He searched again for Pansy, but she had disappeared, and his main desire was now to get out of the house. Before doing so he spoke once more to Isabel; it was not agreeable to him to reflect that he had just said a rude thing to her—the only point that would now justify a low view of him.

"I referred to Mr. Osmond as I shouldn't have done, a while ago," he began. "But you must remember my situation."

"I don't remember what you said," she answered coldly.

"Ah, you're offended, and now you'll never help me."

She was silent an instant, and then with a change of tone: "It's not that I won't; I simply can't!" Her manner was almost passionate.

"If you COULD, just a little, I'd never again speak of your husband save as an angel."

"The inducement's great," said Isabel gravely—inscrutably, as he afterwards, to himself, called it; and she gave him, straight in the eyes, a look which was also inscrutable. It made him remember somehow that he had known her as a child; and yet it was keener than he liked, and he took himself off.

CHAPTER XXXVIII

He went to see Madame Merle on the morrow, and to his surprise she let him off rather easily. But she made him promise that he would stop there till something should have been decided. Mr. Osmond had had higher expectations; it was very true that as he had no intention of giving his daughter a portion such expectations were open to criticism or even, if one would, to ridicule. But she would advise Mr. Rosier not to take that tone; if he would possess his soul in patience he might arrive at his felicity. Mr. Osmond was not favourable to his suit, but it wouldn't be a miracle if he should gradually come round. Pansy would never defy her father, he might depend on that; so nothing was to be gained by precipitation. Mr. Osmond needed to accustom his mind to an offer of a sort that he had not hitherto entertained, and this result must come of itself—it was useless to try to force it. Rosier remarked that his own situation would be in the meanwhile the most uncomfortable in the world, and Madame Merle assured him that she felt for him. But, as she justly declared, one couldn't have everything one wanted; she had learned that lesson for herself. There would be no use in his writing to Gilbert Osmond, who had charged her to tell him as much. He wished the matter dropped for a few weeks and would himself write when he should have anything to communicate that it might please Mr. Rosier to hear.

"He doesn't like your having spoken to Pansy, Ah, he doesn't like it at all," said Madame Merle.

"I'm perfectly willing to give him a chance to tell me so!"

"If you do that he'll tell you more than you care to hear. Go to the house, for the next month, as little as possible, and leave the rest to me."

"As little as possible? Who's to measure the possibility?"

"Let me measure it. Go on Thursday evenings with the rest of the world, but don't go at all at odd times, and don't fret about Pansy. I'll see that she understands everything. She's a calm little nature; she'll take it quietly."

Edward Rosier fretted about Pansy a good deal, but he did as he was advised, and awaited another Thursday evening before returning to Palazzo Roccanera. There had been a party at dinner, so that though he went early the company was already tolerably numerous. Osmond, as usual, was in the first room, near the fire, staring straight at the door, so that, not to be distinctly uncivil, Rosier had to go and speak to him.

"I'm glad that you can take a hint," Pansy's father said, slightly closing his keen, conscious eyes.

"I take no hints. But I took a message, as I supposed it to be."

"You took it? Where did you take it?"

It seemed to poor Rosier he was being insulted, and he waited a moment, asking himself how much a true lover ought to submit to. "Madame Merle gave me, as I understood it, a message from you—to the effect that you declined to give me the opportunity I desire, the opportunity to explain my wishes to you." And he flattered himself he spoke rather sternly.

"I don't see what Madame Merle has to do with it. Why did you apply to Madame Merle?"

"I asked her for an opinion—for nothing more. I did so because she had seemed to me to know you very well."

"She doesn't know me so well as she thinks," said Osmond.

"I'm sorry for that, because she has given me some little ground for hope."

Osmond stared into the fire a moment. "I set a great price on my daughter."

"You can't set a higher one than I do. Don't I prove it by wishing to marry her?"

"I wish to marry her very well," Osmond went on with a dry impertinence which, in another mood, poor Rosier would have admired.

"Of course I pretend she'd marry well in marrying me. She couldn't marry a man who loves her more—or whom, I may venture to add, she loves more."

"I'm not bound to accept your theories as to whom my daughter loves"—and Osmond looked up with a quick, cold smile.

"I'm not theorising. Your daughter has spoken."

"Not to me," Osmond continued, now bending forward a little and dropping his eyes to his boot-toes.

"I have her promise, sir!" cried Rosier with the sharpness of exasperation.

As their voices had been pitched very low before, such a note attracted some attention from the company. Osmond waited till this little movement had subsided; then he said, all undisturbed: "I think she has no recollection of having given it."

They had been standing with their faces to the fire, and after he had uttered these last words the master of the house turned round again to the room. Before Rosier had time to reply he perceived that a gentleman—a stranger—had just come in, unannounced, according to the Roman custom, and was about to present himself to his host. The latter smiled blandly, but somewhat blankly; the visitor had a handsome face and a large, fair beard, and was evidently an Englishman.

"You apparently don't recognise me," he said with a smile that expressed more than Osmond's.

"Ah yes, now I do. I expected so little to see you."

Rosier departed and went in direct pursuit of Pansy. He sought her, as usual, in the neighbouring room, but he again encountered Mrs. Osmond in his path. He gave his hostess no greeting—he was too righteously indignant, but said to her crudely: "Your husband's awfully cold-blooded."

She gave the same mystical smile he had noticed before. "You can't expect every one to be as hot as yourself."

"I don't pretend to be cold, but I'm cool. What has he been doing to his daughter?"

"I've no idea."

"Don't you take any interest?" Rosier demanded with his sense that she too was irritating.

For a moment she answered nothing; then, "No!" she said abruptly and with a quickened light in her eyes which directly contradicted the word.

"Pardon me if I don't believe that. Where's Miss Osmond?"

"In the corner, making tea. Please leave her there."

Rosier instantly discovered his friend, who had been hidden by intervening groups. He watched her, but her own attention was entirely given to her occupation. "What on earth has he done to her?" he asked again imploringly. "He declares to me she has given me up."

"She has not given you up," Isabel said in a low tone and without looking at him.

"Ah, thank you for that! Now I'll leave her alone as long as you think proper!"

He had hardly spoken when he saw her change colour, and became aware that Osmond was coming toward her accompanied by the gentleman who had just entered. He judged the latter, in spite of the advantage of good looks and evident social experience, a little embarrassed. "Isabel," said her husband, "I bring you an old friend."

Mrs. Osmond's face, though it wore a smile, was, like her old friend's, not perfectly confident. "I'm very happy to see Lord Warburton," she said. Rosier turned away and, now that his talk with her had been interrupted, felt absolved from the little pledge he had just taken. He had a quick impression that Mrs. Osmond wouldn't notice what he did.

Isabel in fact, to do him justice, for some time quite ceased to observe him. She had been startled; she hardly knew if she felt a pleasure or a pain. Lord Warburton, however, now that he was face to face with her, was plainly quite sure of his own sense of the matter; though his grey eyes had still their fine original property of keeping recognition and attestation strictly sincere. He was "heavier" than of yore and looked older; he stood there very solidly and sensibly.

"I suppose you didn't expect to see me," he said; "I've but just arrived. Literally, I only got here this evening. You see I've lost no time in coming to pay you my respects. I knew you were at home on Thursdays."

"You see the fame of your Thursdays has spread to England," Osmond remarked to his wife.

"It's very kind of Lord Warburton to come so soon; we're greatly flattered," Isabel said.

"Ah well, it's better than stopping in one of those horrible inns," Osmond went on.

"The hotel seems very good; I think it's the same at which I saw you four years since. You know it was here in Rome that we first met; it's a long time ago. Do you remember where I bade you good-bye?" his lordship asked of his hostess. "It was in the Capitol, in the first room."

"I remember that myself," said Osmond. "I was there at the time."

"Yes, I remember you there. I was very sorry to leave Rome—so sorry that, somehow or other, it became almost a dismal memory, and I've never cared to come back till to-day. But I knew you were living here," her old friend went on to Isabel, "and I assure you I've often thought of you. It must be a charming place to live in," he added with a look, round him, at her established home, in which she might have caught the dim ghost of his old ruefulness.

"We should have been glad to see you at any time," Osmond observed with propriety.

"Thank you very much. I haven't been out of England since then. Till a month ago I really supposed my travels over."

"I've heard of you from time to time," said Isabel, who had already, with her rare capacity for such inward feats, taken the measure of what meeting him again meant for her.

"I hope you've heard no harm. My life has been a remarkably complete blank."

"Like the good reigns in history," Osmond suggested. He appeared to think his duties as a host now terminated—he had performed them so conscientiously. Nothing could have been more adequate, more nicely measured, than his courtesy to his wife's old friend. It was punctilious, it was explicit, it was everything but natural—a deficiency which Lord Warburton, who, himself, had on the whole a good deal of nature, may be supposed to have perceived. "I'll leave you and Mrs. Osmond together," he added. "You have reminiscences into which I don't enter."

"I'm afraid you lose a good deal!" Lord Warburton called after him, as he moved away, in a tone which perhaps betrayed overmuch an appreciation of his generosity. Then the visitor turned on Isabel the deeper, the deepest, consciousness of his look, which gradually became more serious. "I'm really very glad to see you."

"It's very pleasant. You're very kind."

"Do you know that you're changed—a little?"

She just hesitated. "Yes—a good deal."

"I don't mean for the worse, of course; and yet how can I say for the better?"

"I think I shall have no scruple in saying that to YOU," she bravely returned.

"Ah well, for me—it's a long time. It would be a pity there shouldn't be something to show for it." They sat down and she asked him about his sisters, with other enquiries of a somewhat perfunctory kind. He answered her questions as if they interested him, and in a few moments she saw—or believed she saw—that he would press with less of his whole weight than of yore. Time had breathed upon his heart and, without chilling it, given it a relieved sense of having taken the air. Isabel felt her usual esteem for Time rise at a bound. Her friend's manner was certainly that of a contented man, one who would rather like people, or like her at least, to know him for such. "There's something I must tell you without more delay," he resumed. "I've brought Ralph Touchett with me."

"Brought him with you?" Isabel's surprise was great.

"He's at the hotel; he was too tired to come out and has gone to bed."

"I'll go to see him," she immediately said.

"That's exactly what I hoped you'd do. I had an idea you hadn't seen much of him since your marriage, that in fact your relations were a—a little more formal. That's why I hesitated—like an awkward Briton."

"I'm as fond of Ralph as ever," Isabel answered. "But why has he come to Rome?" The declaration was very gentle, the question a little sharp.

"Because he's very far gone, Mrs. Osmond."

"Rome then is no place for him. I heard from him that he had determined to give up his custom of wintering abroad and to remain in England, indoors, in what he called an artificial climate."

"Poor fellow, he doesn't succeed with the artificial! I went to see him three weeks ago, at Gardencourt, and found him thoroughly ill. He has been getting worse every year, and now he has no strength left. He smokes no more cigarettes! He had got up an artificial climate indeed; the house was as hot as Calcutta. Nevertheless he had suddenly taken it into his head to start for Sicily. I didn't believe in it—neither did the doctors, nor any of his friends. His mother, as I suppose you know, is in America, so there was no one to prevent him. He stuck to his idea that it would be the saving of him to spend the winter at Catania. He said he could take servants and furniture, could make himself comfortable, but in point of fact he hasn't brought anything. I wanted him at least to go by sea, to save fatigue; but he said he hated the sea and wished to stop at Rome. After that, though I thought it all rubbish, I made up my mind to come with him. I'm acting as—what do you call it in America?—as a kind of moderator. Poor Ralph's very moderate now. We left England a fortnight ago, and he has been very bad on the way. He can't keep warm, and the further south we come the more he feels the cold. He has got rather a good man, but I'm afraid he's beyond human help. I wanted him to take with him some clever fellow—I mean some sharp young doctor; but he wouldn't hear of it. If you don't mind my saying so, I think it was a most extraordinary time for Mrs. Touchett to decide on going to America."

Isabel had listened eagerly; her face was full of pain and wonder. "My aunt does that at fixed periods and lets nothing turn her aside. When the date comes round she starts; I think she'd have started if Ralph had been dying."

"I sometimes think he IS dying," Lord Warburton said.

Isabel sprang up. "I'll go to him then now."

He checked her; he was a little disconcerted at the quick effect of his words. "I don't mean I thought so to-night. On the contrary, to-day, in the train, he seemed particularly well; the idea of our reaching Rome—he's very fond of Rome, you know—gave him strength. An hour ago, when I bade him goodnight, he told me he was very tired, but very happy. Go to him in the morning; that's all I mean. I didn't tell him I was coming here; I didn't decide to till after we had separated. Then I remembered he had told me you had an evening, and that it was this very Thursday. It occurred to me to come in and tell you he's here, and let you know you had perhaps better not wait for him to call. I think he said he hadn't written to you." There was no need of Isabel's declaring that she would act upon Lord Warburton's information; she looked, as she sat there, like a winged creature held back. "Let alone that I wanted to see you for myself," her visitor gallantly added.

"I don't understand Ralph's plan; it seems to me very wild," she said. "I was glad to think of him between those thick walls at Gardencourt."

"He was completely alone there; the thick walls were his only company."

"You went to see him; you've been extremely kind."

"Oh dear, I had nothing to do," said Lord Warburton.

"We hear, on the contrary, that you're doing great things. Every one speaks of you as a great statesman, and I'm perpetually seeing your name in the Times, which, by the way, doesn't appear to hold it in reverence. You're apparently as wild a radical as ever."

"I don't feel nearly so wild; you know the world has come round to me. Touchett and I have kept up a sort of parliamentary debate all the way from London. I tell him he's the last of the Tories, and he calls me the King of the Goths—says I have, down to the details of my personal appearance, every sign of the brute. So you see there's life in him yet."

Isabel had many questions to ask about Ralph, but she abstained from asking them all. She would see for herself on the morrow. She perceived that after a little Lord Warburton would tire of that subject—he had a conception of other possible topics. She was more and more able to say to herself that he had recovered, and, what is more to the point, she was able to say it without bitterness. He had been for her, of old, such an image of urgency, of insistence, of something to be resisted and reasoned with, that his reappearance at first menaced her with a new trouble. But she was now reassured; she could see he only wished to live with her on good terms, that she was to understand he had forgiven her and was incapable of the bad taste of making pointed allusions. This was not a form of revenge, of course; she had no suspicion of his wishing to punish her by an exhibition of disillusionment; she did him the justice to believe it had simply occurred to him that she would now take a good-natured interest in knowing he was resigned. It was the resignation of a healthy, manly nature, in which sentimental wounds could never fester. British politics had cured him; she had known they would. She gave an envious thought to the happier lot of men, who are always free to plunge into the healing waters of action. Lord Warburton of course spoke of the past, but he spoke of it without implications; he even went so far as to allude to their former meeting in Rome as a very jolly time. And he told her he had been immensely interested in hearing of her marriage and that it was a great pleasure for him to make Mr. Osmond's acquaintance—since he could hardly be said to have made it on the other occasion. He had not written to her at the time of that passage in her history, but he didn't apologise to her for this. The only thing he implied was that they were old friends, intimate friends. It was very much as an intimate friend that he said to her, suddenly, after a short pause which he had occupied in smiling, as he looked about him, like a person amused, at a provincial entertainment, by some innocent game of guesses—

"Well now, I suppose you're very happy and all that sort of thing?"

Isabel answered with a quick laugh; the tone of his remark struck her almost as the accent of comedy. "Do you suppose if I were not I'd tell you?"

"Well, I don't know. I don't see why not."

"I do then. Fortunately, however, I'm very happy."

"You've got an awfully good house."

"Yes, it's very pleasant. But that's not my merit—it's my husband's."

"You mean he has arranged it?"

"Yes, it was nothing when we came."

"He must be very clever."

"He has a genius for upholstery," said Isabel.

"There's a great rage for that sort of thing now. But you must have a taste of your own."

"I enjoy things when they're done, but I've no ideas. I can never propose anything."

"Do you mean you accept what others propose?"

"Very willingly, for the most part."

"That's a good thing to know. I shall propose to you something."

"It will be very kind. I must say, however, that I've in a few small ways a certain initiative. I should like for instance to introduce you to some of these people."

"Oh, please don't; I prefer sitting here. Unless it be to that young lady in the blue dress. She has a charming face."

"The one talking to the rosy young man? That's my husband's daughter."

"Lucky man, your husband. What a dear little maid!"

"You must make her acquaintance."

"In a moment—with pleasure. I like looking at her from here." He ceased to look at her, however, very soon; his eyes constantly reverted to Mrs. Osmond. "Do you know I was wrong just now in saying you had changed?" he presently went on. "You seem to me, after all, very much the same."

"And yet I find it a great change to be married," said Isabel with mild gaiety.

"It affects most people more than it has affected you. You see I haven't gone in for that."

"It rather surprises me."

"You ought to understand it, Mrs. Osmond. But I do want to marry," he added more simply.

"It ought to be very easy," Isabel said, rising—after which she reflected, with a pang perhaps too visible, that she was hardly the person to say this. It was perhaps because Lord Warburton divined the pang that he generously forbore to call her attention to her not having contributed then to the facility.

Edward Rosier had meanwhile seated himself on an ottoman beside Pansy's tea-table. He pretended at first to talk to her about trifles, and she asked him who was the new gentleman conversing with her stepmother.

"He's an English lord," said Rosier. "I don't know more."

"I wonder if he'll have some tea. The English are so fond of tea."

"Never mind that; I've something particular to say to you."

"Don't speak so loud every one will hear," said Pansy.

"They won't hear if you continue to look that way: as if your only thought in life was the wish the kettle would boil."

"It has just been filled; the servants never know!"—and she sighed with the weight of her responsibility.

"Do you know what your father said to me just now? That you didn't mean what you said a week ago."

"I don't mean everything I say. How can a young girl do that? But I mean what I say to you."

"He told me you had forgotten me."

"Ah no, I don't forget," said Pansy, showing her pretty teeth in a fixed smile.

"Then everything's just the very same?"

"Ah no, not the very same. Papa has been terribly severe."

"What has he done to you?"

"He asked me what you had done to me, and I told him everything. Then he forbade me to marry you."

"You needn't mind that."

"Oh yes, I must indeed. I can't disobey papa."

"Not for one who loves you as I do, and whom you pretend to love?"

She raised the lid of the tea-pot, gazing into this vessel for a moment; then she dropped six words into its aromatic depths. "I love you just as much."

"What good will that do me?"

"Ah," said Pansy, raising her sweet, vague eyes, "I don't know that."

"You disappoint me," groaned poor Rosier.

She was silent a little; she handed a tea-cup to a servant. "Please don't talk any more."

"Is this to be all my satisfaction?"

"Papa said I was not to talk with you."

"Do you sacrifice me like that? Ah, it's too much!"

"I wish you'd wait a little," said the girl in a voice just distinct enough to betray a quaver.

"Of course I'll wait if you'll give me hope. But you take my life away."

"I'll not give you up—oh no!" Pansy went on.

"He'll try and make you marry some one else."

"I'll never do that."

"What then are we to wait for?"

She hesitated again. "I'll speak to Mrs. Osmond and she'll help us." It was in this manner that she for the most part designated her stepmother.

"She won't help us much. She's afraid."

"Afraid of what?"

"Of your father, I suppose."

Pansy shook her little head. "She's not afraid of any one. We must have patience."

"Ah, that's an awful word," Rosier groaned; he was deeply disconcerted. Oblivious of the customs of good society, he dropped his head into his hands and, supporting it with a melancholy grace, sat staring at the carpet. Presently he became aware of a good deal of movement about him and, as he looked up, saw Pansy making a curtsey—it was still her little curtsey of the convent—to the English lord whom Mrs. Osmond had introduced.

CHAPTER XXXIX

It will probably not surprise the reflective reader that Ralph Touchett should have seen less of his cousin since her marriage than he had done before that event—an event of which he took such a view as could hardly prove a confirmation of intimacy. He had uttered his thought, as we know, and after this had held his peace, Isabel not having invited him to resume a discussion which marked an era in their relations. That discussion had made a difference—the difference he feared rather than the one he hoped. It had not chilled the girl's zeal in carrying out her engagement, but it had come dangerously near to spoiling a friendship. No reference was ever again made between them to Ralph's opinion of Gilbert Osmond, and by surrounding this topic with a sacred silence they managed to preserve a semblance of reciprocal frankness. But there was a difference, as Ralph often said to himself—there was a difference. She had not forgiven him, she never would forgive him: that was all he had gained. She thought she had forgiven him; she believed she didn't care; and as she was both very generous and very proud these convictions represented a certain reality. But whether or no the event should justify him he would virtually have done her a wrong, and the wrong was of the sort that women remember best. As Osmond's wife she could never again be his friend. If in this character she should enjoy the felicity she expected, she would have nothing but contempt for the man who had attempted, in advance, to undermine a blessing so dear; and if on the other hand his warning should be justified the vow she had taken that he should never know it would lay upon her spirit such a burden as to make her hate him. So dismal had been, during the year that followed his cousin's marriage, Ralph's prevision of the future; and if his meditations appear morbid we must remember he was not in the bloom of health. He consoled himself as he might by behaving (as he deemed) beautifully, and was present at the ceremony by which Isabel was united to Mr. Osmond, and which was performed in Florence in the month of June. He learned from his mother that Isabel at first had thought of celebrating her nuptials in her native land, but that as simplicity was what she chiefly desired to secure she had finally decided, in spite of Osmond's professed willingness to make a journey of any length, that this characteristic would be best embodied in their being married by the nearest clergyman in the shortest time. The thing was done therefore at the little American chapel, on a very hot day, in the presence only of Mrs. Touchett and her son, of Pansy Osmond and the Countess Gemini. That severity in the proceedings of which I just spoke was in part the result of the absence of two persons who might have been looked for on the occasion and who would have lent it a certain richness. Madame Merle had been invited, but Madame Merle, who was unable to leave Rome, had written a gracious letter of excuses. Henrietta Stackpole had not been invited, as her departure from America, announced to Isabel by Mr. Goodwood, was in fact frustrated by the duties of her profession; but she had sent a letter, less gracious than Madame Merle's, intimating that, had she been able to cross the Atlantic, she would have been present not only as a witness but as a critic. Her return to Europe had taken place somewhat later, and she had effected a meeting with Isabel in the autumn, in Paris, when she had indulged—perhaps a trifle too freely—her critical genius. Poor Osmond, who was chiefly the subject of it, had protested so sharply that Henrietta was obliged to declare to Isabel that she had taken a step which put a barrier between them. "It isn't in the least that you've married—it is that you have married HIM," she had deemed it her duty to remark; agreeing, it will be seen, much more with Ralph Touchett than she suspected, though she had few of his hesitations and compunctions. Henrietta's second visit to Europe, however, was not apparently to have been made in vain; for just at the moment when Osmond had declared to Isabel that he really must object to that newspaper-woman, and Isabel had answered that it seemed to her he took Henrietta too hard, the good Mr. Bantling had appeared upon the scene and proposed that they should take a run down to Spain. Henrietta's letters from Spain had proved the most acceptable she had yet published, and there had been one in especial, dated from the Alhambra and entitled 'Moors and Moonlight,' which generally passed for her masterpiece. Isabel had been secretly disappointed at her husband's not seeing his way simply to take the poor girl for funny. She even wondered if his sense of fun, or of the funny—which would be his sense of humour, wouldn't it?—were by chance defective. Of course she herself looked at the matter as a person whose present happiness had nothing to grudge to Henrietta's violated conscience. Osmond had thought their alliance a kind of monstrosity; he couldn't imagine what they had in common. For him, Mr. Bantling's fellow tourist was simply the most vulgar of women, and he had also pronounced her the most abandoned. Against this latter clause of the verdict Isabel had appealed with an ardour that had made him wonder afresh at the oddity of some of his wife's tastes. Isabel could explain it only by saying that she liked to know people who were as different as possible from herself. "Why then don't you make the acquaintance of your washerwoman?" Osmond had enquired; to which Isabel had answered that she was afraid her washerwoman wouldn't care for her. Now Henrietta cared so much.

Ralph had seen nothing of her for the greater part of the two years that had followed her marriage; the winter that formed the beginning of her residence in Rome he had spent again at San Remo, where he had been joined in the spring by his mother, who afterwards had gone with him to England, to see what they were doing at the bank—an operation she couldn't induce him to perform. Ralph had taken a lease of his house at San Remo, a small villa which he had occupied still another winter; but late in the month of April of this second year he had come down to Rome. It was the first time since her marriage that he had stood face to face with Isabel; his desire to see her again was then of the keenest. She had written to him from time to time, but her letters told him nothing he wanted to know. He had asked his mother what she was making of her life, and his mother had simply answered that she supposed she was making the best of it. Mrs. Touchett had not the imagination that communes with the unseen, and she now pretended to no intimacy with her niece, whom she rarely encountered. This young woman appeared to be living in a sufficiently honourable way, but Mrs. Touchett still remained of the opinion that her marriage had been a shabby affair. It had given her no pleasure to think of Isabel's establishment, which she was sure was a very lame business. From time to time, in Florence, she rubbed against the Countess Gemini, doing her best always to minimise the contact; and the Countess reminded her of Osmond, who made her think of Isabel. The Countess was less talked of in these days; but Mrs. Touchett augured no good of that: it only proved how she had been talked of before. There was a more direct suggestion of Isabel in the person of Madame Merle; but Madame Merle's relations with Mrs. Touchett had undergone a perceptible change. Isabel's aunt had told her, without circumlocution, that she had played too ingenious a part; and Madame Merle, who never quarrelled with any one, who appeared to think no one worth it, and who had performed the miracle of living, more or less, for several years with Mrs. Touchett and showing no symptom of irritation—Madame Merle now took a very high tone and declared that this was an accusation from which she couldn't stoop to defend herself. She added, however (without stooping), that her behaviour had been only too simple, that she had believed only what she saw, that she saw Isabel was not eager to marry and Osmond not eager to please (his repeated visits had been nothing; he was boring himself to death on his hill-top and he came merely for amusement). Isabel had kept her sentiments to herself, and her journey to Greece and Egypt had effectually thrown dust in her companion's eyes. Madame Merle accepted the event—she was unprepared to think of it as a scandal; but that she had played any part in it, double or single, was an imputation against which she proudly protested. It was doubtless in consequence of Mrs. Touchett's attitude, and of the injury it offered to habits consecrated by many charming seasons, that Madame Merle had, after this, chosen to pass many months in England, where her credit was quite unimpaired. Mrs. Touchett had done her a wrong; there are some things that can't be forgiven. But Madame Merle suffered in silence; there was always something exquisite in her dignity.

Ralph, as I say, had wished to see for himself; but while engaged in this pursuit he had yet felt afresh what a fool he had been to put the girl on her guard. He had played the wrong card, and now he had lost the game. He should see nothing, he should learn nothing; for him she would always wear a mask. His true line would have been to profess delight in her union, so that later, when, as Ralph phrased it, the bottom should fall out of it, she might have the pleasure of saying to him that he had been a goose. He would gladly have consented to pass for a goose in order to know Isabel's real situation. At present, however, she neither taunted him with his fallacies nor pretended that her own confidence was justified; if she wore a mask it completely covered her face. There was something fixed and mechanical in the serenity painted on it; this was not an expression, Ralph said—it was a representation, it was even an advertisement. She had lost her child; that was a sorrow, but it was a sorrow she scarcely spoke of; there was more to say about it than she could say to Ralph. It belonged to the past, moreover; it had occurred six months before and she had already laid aside the tokens of mourning. She appeared to be leading the life of the world; Ralph heard her spoken of as having a "charming position." He obobserved that she produced the impression of being peculiarly enviable, that it was supposed, among many people, to be a privilege even to know her. Her house was not open to every one, and she had an evening in the week to which people were not invited as a matter of course. She lived with a certain magnificence, but you needed to be a member of her circle to perceive it; for there was nothing to gape at, nothing to criticise, nothing even to admire, in the daily proceedings of Mr. and Mrs. Osmond. Ralph, in all this, recognised the hand of the master; for he knew that Isabel had no faculty for producing studied impressions. She struck him as having a great love of movement, of gaiety, of late hours, of long rides, of fatigue; an eagerness to be entertained, to be interested, even to be bored, to make acquaintances, to see people who were talked about, to explore the neighbourhood of Rome, to enter into relation with certain of the mustiest relics of its old society. In all this there was much less discrimination than in that desire for comprehensiveness of development on which he had been used to exercise his wit. There was a kind of violence in some of her impulses, of crudity in some of her experiments, which took him by surprise: it seemed to him that she even spoke faster, moved faster, breathed faster, than before her marriage. Certainly she had fallen into exaggerations—she who used to care so much for the pure truth; and whereas of old she had a great delight in good-humoured argument, in intellectual play (she never looked so charming as when in the genial heat of discussion she received a crushing blow full in the face and brushed it away as a feather), she appeared now to think there was nothing worth people's either differing about or agreeing upon. Of old she had been curious, and now she was indifferent, and yet in spite of her indifference her activity was greater than ever. Slender still, but lovelier than before, she had gained no great maturity of aspect; yet there was an amplitude and a brilliancy in her personal arrangements that gave a touch of insolence to her beauty. Poor human-hearted Isabel, what perversity had bitten her? Her light step drew a mass of drapery behind it; her intelligent head sustained a majesty of ornament. The free, keen girl had become quite another person; what he saw was the fine lady who was supposed to represent something. What did Isabel represent? Ralph asked himself; and he could only answer by saying that she represented Gilbert Osmond. "Good heavens, what a function!" he then woefully exclaimed. He was lost in wonder at the mystery of things.

He recognised Osmond, as I say; he recognised him at every turn. He saw how he kept all things within limits; how he adjusted, regulated, animated their manner of life. Osmond was in his element; at last he had material to work with. He always had an eye to effect, and his effects were deeply calculated. They were produced by no vulgar means, but the motive was as vulgar as the art was great. To surround his interior with a sort of invidious sanctity, to tantalise society with a sense of exclusion, to make people believe his house was different from every other, to impart to the face that he presented to the world a cold originality—this was the ingenious effort of the personage to whom Isabel had attributed a superior morality. "He works with superior material," Ralph said to himself; "it's rich abundance compared with his former resources." Ralph was a clever man; but Ralph had never—to his own sense—been so clever as when he observed, in petto, that under the guise of caring only for intrinsic values Osmond lived exclusively for the world. Far from being its master as he pretended to be, he was its very humble servant, and the degree of its attention was his only measure of success. He lived with his eye on it from morning till night, and the world was so stupid it never suspected the trick. Everything he did was pose—pose so subtly considered that if one were not on the lookout one mistook it for impulse. Ralph had never met a man who lived so much in the land of consideration. His tastes, his studies, his accomplishments, his collections, were all for a purpose. His life on his hill-top at Florence had been the conscious attitude of years. His solitude, his ennui, his love for his daughter, his good manners, his bad manners, were so many features of a mental image constantly present to him as a model of impertinence and mystification. His ambition was not to please the world, but to please himself by exciting the world's curiosity and then declining to satisfy it. It had made him feel great, ever, to play the world a trick. The thing he had done in his life most directly to please himself was his marrying Miss Archer; though in this case indeed the gullible world was in a manner embodied in poor Isabel, who had been mystified to the top of her bent. Ralph of course found a fitness in being consistent; he had embraced a creed, and as he had suffered for it he could not in honour forsake it. I give this little sketch of its articles for what they may at the time have been worth. It was certain that he was very skilful in fitting the facts to his theory—even the fact that during the month he spent in Rome at this period the husband of the woman he loved appeared to regard him not in the least as an enemy.

For Gilbert Osmond Ralph had not now that importance. It was not that he had the importance of a friend; it was rather that he had none at all. He was Isabel's cousin and he was rather unpleasantly ill—it was on this basis that Osmond treated with him. He made the proper enquiries, asked about his health, about Mrs. Touchett, about his opinion of winter climates, whether he were comfortable at his hotel. He addressed him, on the few occasions of their meeting, not a word that was not necessary; but his manner had always the urbanity proper to conscious success in the presence of conscious failure. For all this, Ralph had had, toward the end, a sharp inward vision of Osmond's making it of small ease to his wife that she should continue to receive Mr. Touchett. He was not jealous—he had not that excuse; no one could be jealous of Ralph. But he made Isabel pay for her old-time kindness, of which so much was still left; and as Ralph had no idea of her paying too much, so when his suspicion had become sharp, he had taken himself off. In doing so he had deprived Isabel of a very interesting occupation: she had been constantly wondering what fine principle was keeping him alive. She had decided that it was his love of conversation; his conversation had been better than ever. He had given up walking; he was no longer a humorous stroller. He sat all day in a chair—almost any chair would serve, and was so dependent on what you would do for him that, had not his talk been highly contemplative, you might have thought he was blind. The reader already knows more about him than Isabel was ever to know, and the reader may therefore be given the key to the mystery. What kept Ralph alive was simply the fact that he had not yet seen enough of the person in the world in whom he was most interested: he was not yet satisfied. There was more to come; he couldn't make up his mind to lose that. He wanted to see what she would make of her husband—or what her husband would make of her. This was only the first act of the drama, and he was determined to sit out the performance. His determination had held good; it had kept him going some eighteen months more, till the time of his return to Rome with Lord Warburton. It had given him indeed such an air of intending to live indefinitely that Mrs. Touchett, though more accessible to confusions of thought in the matter of this strange, unremunerative—and unremunerated—son of hers than she had ever been before, had, as we have learned, not scrupled to embark for a distant land. If Ralph had been kept alive by suspense it was with a good deal of the same emotion—the excitement of wondering in what state she should find him—that Isabel mounted to his apartment the day after Lord Warburton had notified her of his arrival in Rome.

She spent an hour with him; it was the first of several visits. Gilbert Osmond called on him punctually, and on their sending their carriage for him Ralph came more than once to Palazzo Roccanera. A fortnight elapsed, at the end of which Ralph announced to Lord Warburton that he thought after all he wouldn't go to Sicily. The two men had been dining together after a day spent by the latter in ranging about the Campagna. They had left the table, and Warburton, before the chimney, was lighting a cigar, which he instantly removed from his lips.

"Won't go to Sicily? Where then will you go?"

"Well, I guess I won't go anywhere," said Ralph, from the sofa, all shamelessly.

"Do you mean you'll return to England?"

"Oh dear no; I'll stay in Rome."

"Rome won't do for you. Rome's not warm enough."

"It will have to do. I'll make it do. See how well I've been."

Lord Warburton looked at him a while, puffing a cigar and as if trying to see it. "You've been better than you were on the journey, certainly. I wonder how you lived through that. But I don't understand your condition. I recommend you to try Sicily."

"I can't try," said poor Ralph. "I've done trying. I can't move further. I can't face that journey. Fancy me between Scylla and Charybdis! I don't want to die on the Sicilian plains—to be snatched away, like Proserpine in the same locality, to the Plutonian shades."

"What the deuce then did you come for?" his lordship enquired.

"Because the idea took me. I see it won't do. It really doesn't matter where I am now. I've exhausted all remedies, I've swallowed all climates. As I'm here I'll stay. I haven't a single cousin in Sicily—much less a married one."

"Your cousin's certainly an inducement. But what does the doctor say?"

"I haven't asked him, and I don't care a fig. If I die here Mrs. Osmond will bury me. But I shall not die here."

"I hope not." Lord Warburton continued to smoke reflectively. "Well, I must say," he resumed, "for myself I'm very glad you don't insist on Sicily. I had a horror of that journey."

"Ah, but for you it needn't have mattered. I had no idea of dragging you in my train."

"I certainly didn't mean to let you go alone."

"My dear Warburton, I never expected you to come further than this," Ralph cried.

"I should have gone with you and seen you settled," said Lord Warburton.

"You're a very good Christian. You're a very kind man."

"Then I should have come back here."

"And then you'd have gone to England."

"No, no; I should have stayed."

"Well," said Ralph, "if that's what we are both up to, I don't see where Sicily comes in!"

His companion was silent; he sat staring at the fire. At last, looking up, "I say, tell me this," he broke out; "did you really mean to go to Sicily when we started?"

"Ah, vous m'en demandez trop! Let me put a question first. Did you come with me quite—platonically?"

"I don't know what you mean by that. I wanted to come abroad."

"I suspect we've each been playing our little game."

"Speak for yourself. I made no secret whatever of my desiring to be here a while."

"Yes, I remember you said you wished to see the Minister of Foreign Affairs."

"I've seen him three times. He's very amusing."

"I think you've forgotten what you came for," said Ralph.

"Perhaps I have," his companion answered rather gravely.

These two were gentlemen of a race which is not distinguished by the absence of reserve, and they had travelled together from London to Rome without an allusion to matters that were uppermost in the mind of each. There was an old subject they had once discussed, but it had lost its recognised place in their attention, and even after their arrival in Rome, where many things led back to it, they had kept the same half-diffident, half-confident silence.

"I recommend you to get the doctor's consent, all the same," Lord Warburton went on, abruptly, after an interval.

"The doctor's consent will spoil it. I never have it when I can help it."

"What then does Mrs. Osmond think?" Ralph's friend demanded. "I've not told her. She'll probably say that Rome's too cold and even offer to go with me to Catania. She's capable of that."

"In your place I should like it."

"Her husband won't like it."

"Ah well, I can fancy that; though it seems to me you're not bound to mind his likings. They're his affair."

"I don't want to make any more trouble between them," said Ralph.

"Is there so much already?"

"There's complete preparation for it. Her going off with me would make the explosion. Osmond isn't fond of his wife's cousin."

"Then of course he'd make a row. But won't he make a row if you stop here?"

"That's what I want to see. He made one the last time I was in Rome, and then I thought it my duty to disappear. Now I think it's my duty to stop and defend her."

"My dear Touchett, your defensive powers—!" Lord Warburton began with a smile. But he saw something in his companion's face that checked him. "Your duty, in these premises, seems to me rather a nice question," he observed instead.

Ralph for a short time answered nothing. "It's true that my defensive powers are small," he returned at last; "but as my aggressive ones are still smaller Osmond may after all not think me worth his gunpowder. At any rate," he added, "there are things I'm curious to see."

"You're sacrificing your health to your curiosity then?"

"I'm not much interested in my health, and I'm deeply interested in Mrs. Osmond."

"So am I. But not as I once was," Lord Warburton added quickly. This was one of the allusions he had not hitherto found occasion to make.

"Does she strike you as very happy?" Ralph enquired, emboldened by this confidence.

"Well, I don't know; I've hardly thought. She told me the other night she was happy."

"Ah, she told YOU, of course," Ralph exclaimed, smiling.

"I don't know that. It seems to me I was rather the sort of person she might have complained to."

"Complained? She'll never complain. She has done it—what she HAS done—and she knows it. She'll complain to you least of all. She's very careful."

"She needn't be. I don't mean to make love to her again."

"I'm delighted to hear it. There can be no doubt at least of YOUR duty."

"Ah no," said Lord Warburton gravely; "none!"

"Permit me to ask," Ralph went on, "whether it's to bring out the fact that you don't mean to make love to her that you're so very civil to the little girl?"

Lord Warburton gave a slight start; he got up and stood before the fire, looking at it hard. "Does that strike you as very ridiculous?"

"Ridiculous? Not in the least, if you really like her."

"I think her a delightful little person. I don't know when a girl of that age has pleased me more."

"She's a charming creature. Ah, she at least is genuine."

"Of course there's the difference in our ages—more than twenty years."

"My dear Warburton," said Ralph, "are you serious?"

"Perfectly serious—as far as I've got."

"I'm very glad. And, heaven help us," cried Ralph, "how cheered-up old Osmond will be!"

His companion frowned. "I say, don't spoil it. I shouldn't propose for his daughter to please HIM."

"He'll have the perversity to be pleased all the same."

"He's not so fond of me as that," said his lordship.

"As that? My dear Warburton, the drawback of your position is that people needn't be fond of you at all to wish to be connected with you. Now, with me in such a case, I should have the happy confidence that they loved me."

Lord Warburton seemed scarcely in the mood for doing justice to general axioms—he was thinking of a special case. "Do you judge she'll be pleased?"

"The girl herself? Delighted, surely."

"No, no; I mean Mrs. Osmond."

Ralph looked at him a moment. "My dear fellow, what has she to do with it?"

"Whatever she chooses. She's very fond of Pansy."

"Very true—very true." And Ralph slowly got up. "It's an interesting question—how far her fondness for Pansy will carry her." He stood there a moment with his hands in his pockets and rather a clouded brow. "I hope, you know, that you're very—very sure. The deuce!" he broke off. "I don't know how to say it."

"Yes, you do; you know how to say everything."

"Well, it's awkward. I hope you're sure that among Miss Osmond's merits her being—a—so near her step-mother isn't a leading one?"

"Good heavens, Touchett!" cried Lord Warburton angrily, "for what do you take me?"

CHAPTER XL

Isabel had not seen much of Madame Merle since her marriage, this lady having indulged in frequent absences from Rome. At one time she had spent six months in England; at another she had passed a portion of a winter in Paris. She had made numerous visits to distant friends and gave countenance to the idea that for the future she should be a less inveterate Roman than in the past. As she had been inveterate in the past only in the sense of constantly having an apartment in one of the sunniest niches of the Pincian—an apartment which often stood empty—this suggested a prospect of almost constant absence; a danger which Isabel at one period had been much inclined to deplore. Familiarity had modified in some degree her first impression of Madame Merle, but it had not essentially altered it; there was still much wonder of admiration in it. That personage was armed at all points; it was a pleasure to see a character so completely equipped for the social battle. She carried her flag discreetly, but her weapons were polished steel, and she used them with a skill which struck Isabel as more and more that of a veteran. She was never weary, never overcome with disgust; she never appeared to need rest or consolation. She had her own ideas; she had of old exposed a great many of them to Isabel, who knew also that under an appearance of extreme self-control her highly-cultivated friend concealed a rich sensibility. But her will was mistress of her life; there was something gallant in the way she kept going. It was as if she had learned the secret of it—as if the art of life were some clever trick she had guessed. Isabel, as she herself grew older, became acquainted with revulsions, with disgusts; there were days when the world looked black and she asked herself with some sharpness what it was that she was pretending to live for. Her old habit had been to live by enthusiasm, to fall in love with suddenly-perceived possibilities, with the idea of some new adventure. As a younger person she had been used to proceed from one little exaltation to the other: there were scarcely any dull places between. But Madame Merle had suppressed enthusiasm; she fell in love now-a-days with nothing; she lived entirely by reason and by wisdom. There were hours when Isabel would have given anything for lessons in this art; if her brilliant friend had been near she would have made an appeal to her. She had become aware more than before of the advantage of being like that—of having made one's self a firm surface, a sort of corselet of silver.

But, as I say, it was not till the winter during which we lately renewed acquaintance with our heroine that the personage in question made again a continuous stay in Rome. Isabel now saw more of her than she had done since her marriage; but by this time Isabel's needs and inclinations had considerably changed. It was not at present to Madame Merle that she would have applied for instruction; she had lost the desire to know this lady's clever trick. If she had troubles she must keep them to herself, and if life was difficult it would not make it easier to confess herself beaten. Madame Merle was doubtless of great use to herself and an ornament to any circle; but was she—would she be—of use to others in periods of refined embarrassment? The best way to profit by her friend—this indeed Isabel had always thought—was to imitate her, to be as firm and bright as she. She recognised no embarrassments, and Isabel, considering this fact, determined for the fiftieth time to brush aside her own. It seemed to her too, on the renewal of an intercourse which had virtually been interrupted, that her old ally was different, was almost detached—pushing to the extreme a certain rather artificial fear of being indiscreet. Ralph Touchett, we know, had been of the opinion that she was prone to exaggeration, to forcing the note—was apt, in the vulgar phrase, to overdo it. Isabel had never admitted this charge—had never indeed quite understood it; Madame Merle's conduct, to her perception, always bore the stamp of good taste, was always "quiet." But in this matter of not wishing to intrude upon the inner life of the Osmond family it at last occurred to our young woman that she overdid a little. That of course was not the best taste; that was rather violent. She remembered too much that Isabel was married; that she had now other interests; that though she, Madame

Merle, had known Gilbert Osmond and his little Pansy very well, better almost than any one, she was not after all of the inner circle. She was on her guard; she never spoke of their affairs till she was asked, even pressed—as when her opinion was wanted; she had a dread of seeming to meddle. Madame Merle was as candid as we know, and one day she candidly expressed this dread to Isabel.

"I MUST be on my guard," she said; "I might so easily, without suspecting it, offend you. You would be right to be offended, even if my intention should have been of the purest. I must not forget that I knew your husband long before you did; I must not let that betray me. If you were a silly woman you might be jealous. You're not a silly woman; I know that perfectly. But neither am I; therefore I'm determined not to get into trouble. A little harm's very soon done; a mistake's made before one knows it. Of course if I had wished to make love to your husband I had ten years to do it in, and nothing to prevent; so it isn't likely I shall begin to-day, when I'm so much less attractive than I was. But if I were to annoy you by seeming to take a place that doesn't belong to me, you wouldn't make that reflection; you'd simply say I was forgetting certain differences. I'm determined not to forget them. Certainly a good friend isn't always thinking of that; one doesn't suspect one's friends of injustice. I don't suspect you, my dear, in the least; but I suspect human nature. Don't think I make myself uncomfortable; I'm not always watching myself. I think I sufficiently prove it in talking to you as I do now. All I wish to say is, however, that if you were to be jealous—that's the form it would take—I should be sure to think it was a little my fault. It certainly wouldn't be your husband's."

Isabel had had three years to think over Mrs. Touchett's theory that Madame Merle had made Gilbert Osmond's marriage. We know how she had at first received it. Madame Merle might have made Gilbert Osmond's marriage, but she certainly had not made Isabel Archer's. That was the work of—Isabel scarcely knew what: of nature, providence, fortune, of the eternal mystery of things. It was true her aunt's complaint had been not so much of Madame Merle's activity as of her duplicity: she had brought about the strange event and then she had denied her guilt. Such guilt would not have been great, to Isabel's mind; she couldn't make a crime of Madame Merle's having been the producing cause of the most important friendship she had ever formed. This had occurred to her just before her marriage, after her little discussion with her aunt and at a time when she was still capable of that large inward reference, the tone almost of the philosophic historian, to her scant young annals. If Madame Merle had desired her change of state she could only say it had been a very happy thought. With her, moreover, she had been perfectly straightforward; she had never concealed her high opinion of Gilbert Osmond. After their union Isabel discovered that her husband took a less convenient view of the matter; he seldom consented to finger, in talk, this roundest and smoothest bead of their social rosary. "Don't you like Madame Merle?" Isabel had once said to him. "She thinks a great deal of you."

"I'll tell you once for all," Osmond had answered. "I liked her once better than I do to-day. I'm tired of her, and I'm rather ashamed of it. She's so almost unnaturally good! I'm glad she's not in Italy; it makes for relaxation—for a sort of moral detente. Don't talk of her too much; it seems to bring her back. She'll come back in plenty of time."

Madame Merle, in fact, had come back before it was too late—too late, I mean, to recover whatever advantage she might have lost. But meantime, if, as I have said, she was sensibly different, Isabel's feelings were also not quite the same. Her consciousness of the situation was as acute as of old, but it was much less satisfying. A dissatisfied mind, whatever else it may miss, is rarely in want of reasons; they bloom as thick as buttercups in June. The fact of Madame Merle's having had a hand in Gilbert Osmond's marriage ceased to be one of her titles to consideration; it might have been written, after all, that there was not so much to thank her for. As time went on there was less and less, and Isabel once said to herself that perhaps without her these things would not have been. That reflection indeed was instantly stifled; she knew an immediate horror at having made it. "Whatever happens to me let me not be unjust," she said; "let me bear my burdens myself and not shift them upon others!" This disposition was tested, eventually, by that ingenious apology for her present conduct which Madame Merle saw fit to make and of which I have given a sketch; for there was something irritating—there was almost an air of mockery—in her neat discriminations and clear convictions. In Isabel's mind to-day there was nothing clear; there was a confusion of regrets, a complication of fears. She felt helpless as she turned away from her friend, who had just made the statements I have quoted: Madame Merle knew so little what she was thinking of! She was herself moreover so unable to explain. Jealous of her—jealous of her with Gilbert? The idea just then suggested no near reality. She almost wished jealousy had been possible; it would have made in a manner for refreshment. Wasn't it in a manner one of the symptoms of happiness? Madame Merle, however, was wise, so wise that she might have been pretending to know Isabel better than Isabel knew herself. This young woman had always been fertile in resolutions—any of them of an elevated character; but at no period had they flourished (in the privacy of her heart) more richly than to-day. It is true that they all had a family likeness; they might have been summed up in the determination that if she was to be unhappy it should not be by a fault of her own. Her poor winged spirit had always had a great desire to do its best, and it had not as yet been seriously discouraged. It wished, therefore, to hold fast to justice—not to pay itself by petty revenges. To associate Madame Merle with its disappointment would be a petty revenge—especially as the pleasure to be derived from that would be perfectly insincere. It might feed her sense of bitterness, but it would not loosen her bonds. It was impossible to pretend that she had not acted with her eyes open; if ever a girl was a free agent she had been. A girl in love was doubtless not a free agent; but the sole source of her mistake had been within herself. There had been no plot, no snare; she had looked and considered and chosen. When a woman had made such a mistake, there was only one way to repair it—just immensely (oh, with the highest grandeur!) to accept it. One folly was enough, especially when it was to last for ever; a second one would not much set it off. In this vow of reticence there was a certain nobleness which kept Isabel going; but Madame Merle had been right, for all that, in taking her precautions.

One day about a month after Ralph Touchett's arrival in Rome Isabel came back from a walk with Pansy. It was not only a part of her general determination to be just that she was at present very thankful for Pansy—it was also a part of her tenderness for things that were pure and weak. Pansy was dear to her, and there was nothing else in her life that had the rightness of the young creature's attachment or the sweetness of her own clearness about it. It was like a soft presence—like a small hand in her own; on Pansy's part it was more than an affection—it was a kind of ardent coercive faith. On her own side her sense of the girl's dependence was more than a pleasure; it operated as a definite reason when motives threatened to fail her. She had said to herself that we must take our duty where we find it, and that we must look for it as much as possible. Pansy's sympathy was a direct admonition; it seemed to say that here was an opportunity, not eminent perhaps, but unmistakeable. Yet an opportunity for what Isabel could hardly have said; in general, to be more for the child than the child was able to be for herself. Isabel could have smiled, in these days, to remember that her little companion had once been ambiguous, for she now perceived that Pansy's ambiguities were simply her own grossness of vision. She had been unable to believe any one could care so much—so extraordinarily much—to please. But since then she had seen this delicate faculty in operation, and now she knew what to think of it. It was the whole creature—it was a sort of genius. Pansy had no pride to interfere with it, and though she was constantly extending her conquests she took no credit for them. The two were constantly together; Mrs. Osmond was rarely seen without her stepdaughter. Isabel liked her company; it had the effect of one's carrying a nosegay composed all of the same flower. And then not to neglect Pansy, not under any provocation to neglect her—this she had made an article of religion. The young girl had every appearance of being happier in Isabel's society than in that of any one save her father,—whom she admired with an intensity justified by the fact that, as paternity was an exquisite pleasure to Gilbert Osmond, he had always been luxuriously mild. Isabel knew how Pansy liked to be with her and how she studied the means of pleasing her. She had decided that the best way of pleasing her was negative, and consisted in not giving her trouble—a conviction which certainly could have had no reference to trouble already existing. She was therefore ingeniously passive and almost imaginatively docile; she was careful even to moderate the eagerness with which she assented to Isabel's propositions and which might have implied that she could have thought otherwise. She never interrupted, never asked social questions, and though she delighted in approbation, to the point of turning pale when it came to her, never held out her hand for it. She only looked toward it wistfully—an attitude which, as she grew older, made her eyes the prettiest in the world. When during the second winter at Palazzo Roccanera she began to go to parties, to dances, she always, at a reasonable hour, lest Mrs. Osmond should be tired, was the first to propose departure. Isabel appreciated the sacrifice of the late dances, for she knew her little companion had a passionate pleasure in this exercise, taking her steps to the music like a conscientious fairy. Society, moreover, had no drawbacks for her; she liked even the tiresome parts—the heat of ball-rooms, the dulness of dinners, the crush at the door, the awkward waiting for the carriage. During the day, in this vehicle, beside her stepmother, she sat in a small fixed, appreciative posture, bending forward and faintly smiling, as if she had been taken to drive for the first time.

On the day I speak of they had been driven out of one of the gates of the city and at the end of half an hour had left the carriage to await them by the roadside while they walked away over the short grass of the Campagna, which even in the winter months is sprinkled with delicate flowers. This was almost a daily habit with Isabel, who was fond of a walk and had a swift length of step, though not so swift a one as on her first coming to Europe. It was not the form of exercise that Pansy loved best, but she liked it, because she liked everything; and she moved with a shorter undulation beside her father's wife, who afterwards, on their return to Rome, paid a tribute to her preferences by making the circuit of the Pincian or the Villa Borghese. She had gathered a handful of flowers in a sunny hollow, far from the walls of Rome, and on reaching Palazzo Roccanera she went straight to her room, to put them into water. Isabel passed into the drawing-room, the one she herself usually occupied, the second in order from the large ante-chamber which was entered from the staircase and in which even Gilbert Osmond's rich devices had not been able to correct a look of rather grand nudity. Just beyond the threshold of the drawing-room she stopped short, the reason for her doing so being that she had received an impression. The impression had, in strictness, nothing unprecedented; but she felt it as something new, and the soundlessness of her step gave her time to take in the scene before she interrupted it. Madame Merle was there in her bonnet, and Gilbert Osmond was talking to her; for a minute they were unaware she had come in. Isabel had often seen that before, certainly; but what she had not seen, or at least had not noticed, was that their colloquy had for the moment converted itself into a sort of familiar silence, from which she instantly perceived that her entrance would startle them. Madame Merle was standing on the rug, a little way from the fire; Osmond was in a deep chair, leaning back and looking at her. Her head was erect, as usual, but her eyes were bent on his. What struck Isabel first was that he was sitting while Madame Merle stood; there was an anomaly in this that arrested her. Then she perceived that they had arrived at a desultory pause in their exchange of ideas and were musing, face to face, with the freedom of old friends who sometimes exchange ideas without uttering them. There was nothing to shock in this; they were old friends in fact. But the thing made an image, lasting only a moment, like a sudden flicker of light. Their relative positions, their absorbed mutual gaze, struck her as something detected. But it was all over by the time she had fairly seen it. Madame Merle had seen her and had welcomed her without moving; her husband, on the other hand, had instantly jumped up. He presently murmured something about wanting a walk and, after having asked their visitor to excuse him, left the room.

"I came to see you, thinking you would have come in; and as you hadn't I waited for you," Madame Merle said.

"Didn't he ask you to sit down?" Isabel asked with a smile.

Madame Merle looked about her. "Ah, it's very true; I was going away."

"You must stay now."

"Certainly. I came for a reason; I've something on my mind."

"I've told you that before," Isabel said—"that it takes something extraordinary to bring you to this house."

"And you know what I've told YOU; that whether I come or whether I stay away, I've always the same motive—the affection I bear you."

"Yes, you've told me that."

"You look just now as if you didn't believe it," said Madame Merle.

"Ah," Isabel answered, "the profundity of your motives, that's the last thing I doubt!"

"You doubt sooner of the sincerity of my words."

Isabel shook her head gravely. "I know you've always been kind to me."

"As often as you would let me. You don't always take it; then one has to let you alone. It's not to do you a kindness, however, that I've come to-day; it's quite another affair. I've come to get rid of a trouble of my own—to make it over to you. I've been talking to your husband about it."

"I'm surprised at that; he doesn't like troubles."

"Especially other people's; I know very well. But neither do you, I suppose. At any rate, whether you do or not, you must help me. It's about poor Mr. Rosier."

"Ah," said Isabel reflectively, "it's his trouble then, not yours."

"He has succeeded in saddling me with it. He comes to see me ten times a week, to talk about Pansy."

"Yes, he wants to marry her. I know all about it."

Madame Merle hesitated. "I gathered from your husband that perhaps you didn't."

"How should he know what I know? He has never spoken to me of the matter."

"It's probably because he doesn't know how to speak of it."

"It's nevertheless the sort of question in which he's rarely at fault."

"Yes, because as a general thing he knows perfectly well what to think. To-day he doesn't."

"Haven't you been telling him?" Isabel asked.

Madame Merle gave a bright, voluntary smile. "Do you know you're a little dry?"

"Yes; I can't help it. Mr. Rosier has also talked to me."

"In that there's some reason. You're so near the child."

"Ah," said Isabel, "for all the comfort I've given him! If you think me dry, I wonder what HE thinks."

"I believe he thinks you can do more than you have done."

"I can do nothing."

"You can do more at least than I. I don't know what mysterious connection he may have discovered between me and Pansy; but he came to me from the first, as if I held his fortune in my hand. Now he keeps coming back, to spur me up, to know what hope there is, to pour out his feelings."

"He's very much in love," said Isabel.

"Very much—for him."

"Very much for Pansy, you might say as well."

Madame Merle dropped her eyes a moment. "Don't you think she's attractive?"

"The dearest little person possible—but very limited."

"She ought to be all the easier for Mr. Rosier to love. Mr. Rosier's not unlimited."

"No," said Isabel, "he has about the extent of one's pocket-handkerchief—the small ones with lace borders." Her humour had lately turned a good deal to sarcasm, but in a moment she was ashamed of exercising it on so innocent an object as Pansy's suitor. "He's very kind, very honest," she presently added; "and he's not such a fool as he seems."

"He assures me that she delights in him," said Madame Merle.

"I don't know; I've not asked her."

"You've never sounded her a little?"

"It's not my place; it's her father's."

"Ah, you're too literal!" said Madame Merle.

"I must judge for myself."

Madame Merle gave her smile again. "It isn't easy to help you."

"To help me?" said Isabel very seriously. "What do you mean?"

"It's easy to displease you. Don't you see how wise I am to be careful? I notify you, at any rate, as I notified Osmond, that I wash my hands of the love-affairs of Miss Pansy and Mr. Edward Rosier. Je n'y peux rien, moi! I can't talk to Pansy about him. Especially," added Madame Merle, "as I don't think him a paragon of husbands."

Isabel reflected a little; after which, with a smile, "You don't wash your hands then!" she said. After which again she added in another tone: "You can't—you're too much interested."

Madame Merle slowly rose; she had given Isabel a look as rapid as the intimation that had gleamed before our heroine a few moments before. Only this time the latter saw nothing. "Ask him the next time, and you'll see."

"I can't ask him; he has ceased to come to the house. Gilbert has let him know that he's not welcome."

"Ah yes," said Madame Merle, "I forgot that—though it's the burden of his lamentation. He says Osmond has insulted him. All the same," she went on, "Osmond doesn't dislike him so much as he thinks." She had got up as if to close the conversation, but she lingered, looking about her, and had evidently more to say. Isabel perceived this and even saw the point she had in view; but Isabel also had her own reasons for not opening the way.

"That must have pleased him, if you've told him," she answered, smiling.

"Certainly I've told him; as far as that goes I've encouraged him. I've preached patience, have said that his case isn't desperate if he'll only hold his tongue and be quiet. Unfortunately he has taken it into his head to be jealous."

"Jealous?"

"Jealous of Lord Warburton, who, he says, is always here."

Isabel, who was tired, had remained sitting; but at this she also rose. "Ah!" she exclaimed simply, moving slowly to the fireplace. Madame Merle observed her as she passed and while she stood a moment before the mantel-glass and pushed into its place a wandering tress of hair.

"Poor Mr. Rosier keeps saying there's nothing impossible in Lord Warburton's falling in love with Pansy," Madame Merle went on. Isabel was silent a little; she turned away from the glass. "It's true—there's nothing impossible," she returned at last, gravely and more gently.

"So I've had to admit to Mr. Rosier. So, too, your husband thinks."

"That I don't know."

"Ask him and you'll see."

"I shall not ask him," said Isabel.

"Pardon me; I forgot you had pointed that out. Of course," Madame Merle added, "you've had infinitely more observation of Lord Warburton's behaviour than I."

"I see no reason why I shouldn't tell you that he likes my stepdaughter very much."

Madame Merle gave one of her quick looks again. "Likes her, you mean—as Mr. Rosier means?"

"I don't know how Mr. Rosier means; but Lord Warburton has let me know that he's charmed with Pansy."

"And you've never told Osmond?" This observation was immediate, precipitate; it almost burst from Madame Merle's lips.

Isabel's eyes rested on her. "I suppose he'll know in time; Lord Warburton has a tongue and knows how to express himself."

Madame Merle instantly became conscious that she had spoken more quickly than usual, and the reflection brought the colour to her cheek. She gave the treacherous impulse time to subside and then said as if she had been thinking it over a little: "That would be better than marrying poor Mr. Rosier."

"Much better, I think."

"It would be very delightful; it would be a great marriage. It's really very kind of him."

"Very kind of him?"

"To drop his eyes on a simple little girl."

"I don't see that."

"It's very good of you. But after all, Pansy Osmond—"

"After all, Pansy Osmond's the most attractive person he has ever known!" Isabel exclaimed.

Madame Merle stared, and indeed she was justly bewildered. "Ah, a moment ago I thought you seemed rather to disparage her."

"I said she was limited. And so she is. And so's Lord Warburton."

"So are we all, if you come to that. If it's no more than Pansy deserves, all the better. But if she fixes her affections on Mr. Rosier I won't admit that she deserves it. That will be too perverse."

"Mr. Rosier's a nuisance!" Isabel cried abruptly.

"I quite agree with you, and I'm delighted to know that I'm not expected to feed his flame. For the future, when he calls on me, my door shall be closed to him." And gathering her mantle together Madame Merle prepared to depart. She was checked, however, on her progress to the door, by an inconsequent request from Isabel.

"All the same, you know, be kind to him."

She lifted her shoulders and eyebrows and stood looking at her friend. "I don't understand your contradictions! Decidedly I shan't be kind to him, for it will be a false kindness. I want to see her married to Lord Warburton."

"You had better wait till he asks her."

"If what you say's true, he'll ask her. Especially," said Madame Merle in a moment, "if you make him."

"If I make him?"

"It's quite in your power. You've great influence with him."

Isabel frowned a little. "Where did you learn that?"

"Mrs. Touchett told me. Not you—never!" said Madame Merle, smiling.

"I certainly never told you anything of the sort."

"You MIGHT have done so—so far as opportunity went—when we were by way of being confidential with each other. But you really told me very little; I've often thought so since."

Isabel had thought so too, and sometimes with a certain satisfaction. But she didn't admit it now—perhaps because she wished not to appear to exult in it. "You seem to have had an excellent informant in my aunt," she simply returned.

"She let me know you had declined an offer of marriage from Lord Warburton, because she was greatly vexed and was full of the subject. Of course I think you've done better in doing as you did. But if you wouldn't marry Lord Warburton yourself, make him the reparation of helping him to marry some one else."

Isabel listened to this with a face that persisted in not reflecting the bright expressiveness of Madame Merle's. But in a moment she said, reasonably and gently enough: "I should be very glad indeed if, as regards Pansy, it could be arranged." Upon which her companion, who seemed to regard this as a speech of good omen, embraced her more tenderly than might have been expected and triumphantly withdrew.

CHAPTER XLI

Osmond touched on this matter that evening for the first time; coming very late into the drawing-room, where she was sitting alone. They had spent the evening at home, and Pansy had gone to bed; he himself had been sitting since dinner in a small apartment in which he had arranged his books and which he called his study. At ten o'clock Lord Warburton had come in, as he always did when he knew from Isabel that she was to be at home; he was going somewhere else and he sat for half an hour. Isabel, after asking him for news of Ralph, said very little to him, on purpose; she wished him to talk with her stepdaughter. She pretended to read; she even went after a little to the piano; she asked herself if she mightn't leave the room. She had come little by little to think well of the idea of Pansy's becoming the wife of the master of beautiful Lockleigh, though at first it had not presented itself in a manner to excite her enthusiasm. Madame Merle, that afternoon, had applied the match to an accumulation of inflammable material. When Isabel was unhappy she always looked about her—partly from impulse and partly by theory—for some form of positive exertion. She could never rid herself of the sense that unhappiness was a state of disease—of suffering as opposed to doing. To "do"—it hardly mattered what—would therefore be an escape, perhaps in some degree a remedy. Besides, she wished to convince herself that she had done everything possible to content her husband; she was determined not to be haunted by visions of his wife's limpness under appeal. It would please him greatly to see Pansy married to an English nobleman, and justly please him, since this nobleman was so sound a character. It seemed to Isabel that if she could make it her duty to bring about such an event she should play the part of a good wife. She wanted to be that; she wanted to be able to believe sincerely, and with proof of it, that she had been that. Then such an undertaking had other recommendations. It would occupy her, and she desired occupation. It would even amuse her, and if she could really amuse herself she perhaps might be saved. Lastly, it would be a service to Lord Warburton, who evidently pleased himself greatly with the charming girl. It was a little "weird" he should—being what he was; but there was no accounting for such impressions. Pansy might captivate any one—any one at least but Lord Warburton. Isabel would have thought her too small, too slight, perhaps even too artificial for that. There was always a little of the doll about her, and that was not what he had been looking for. Still, who could say what men ever were looking for? They looked for what they found; they knew what pleased them only when they saw it. No theory was valid in such matters, and nothing was more unaccountable or more natural than anything else. If he had cared for HER it might seem odd he should care for Pansy, who was so different; but he had not cared for her so much as he had supposed. Or if he had, he had completely got over it, and it was natural that, as that affair had failed, he should think something of quite another sort might succeed. Enthusiasm, as I say, had not come at first to Isabel, but it came to-day and made her feel almost happy. It was astonishing what happiness she could still find in the idea of procuring a pleasure for her husband. It was a pity, however, that Edward Rosier had crossed their path!

At this reflection the light that had suddenly gleamed upon that path lost something of its brightness. Isabel was unfortunately as sure that Pansy thought Mr. Rosier the nicest of all the young men—as sure as if she had held an interview with her on the subject. It was very tiresome she should be so sure, when she had carefully abstained from informing herself; almost as tiresome as that poor Mr. Rosier should have taken it into his own head. He was certainly very inferior to Lord Warburton. It was not the difference in fortune so much as the difference in the men; the young American was really so light a weight. He was much more of the type of the useless fine gentleman than the English nobleman. It was true that there was no particular reason why Pansy should marry a statesman; still, if a statesman admired her, that was his affair, and she would make a perfect little pearl of a peeress.

It may seem to the reader that Mrs. Osmond had grown of a sudden strangely cynical, for she ended by saying to herself that this difficulty could probably be arranged. An impediment that was embodied in poor Rosier could not anyhow present itself as a dangerous one; there were always means of levelling secondary obstacles. Isabel was perfectly aware that she had not taken the measure of Pansy's tenacity, which might prove to be inconveniently great; but she inclined to see her as rather letting go, under suggestion, than as clutching under deprecation—since she had certainly the faculty of assent developed in a very much higher degree than that of protest. She would cling, yes, she would cling; but it really mattered to her very little what she clung to. Lord Warburton would do as well as Mr. Rosier—especially as she seemed quite to like him; she had expressed this sentiment to Isabel without a single reservation; she had said she thought his conversation most interesting—he had told her all about India. His manner to Pansy had been of the rightest and easiest—Isabel noticed that for herself, as she also observed that he talked to her not in the least in a patronising way, reminding himself of her youth and simplicity, but quite as if she understood his subjects with that sufficiency with which she followed those of the fashionable operas. This went far enough for attention to the music and the barytone. He was careful only to be kind—he was as kind as he had been to another fluttered young chit at Gardencourt. A girl might well be touched by that; she remembered how she herself had been touched, and said to herself that if she had been as simple as Pansy the impression would have been deeper still. She had not been simple when she refused him; that operation had been as complicated as, later, her acceptance of Osmond had been. Pansy, however, in spite of HER simplicity, really did understand, and was glad that Lord Warburton should talk to her, not about her partners and bouquets, but about the state of Italy, the condition of the peasantry, the famous grist-tax, the pellagra, his impressions of Roman society. She looked at him, as she drew her needle through her tapestry, with sweet submissive eyes, and when she lowered them she gave little quiet oblique glances at his person, his hands, his feet, his clothes, as if she were considering him. Even his person, Isabel might have reminded her, was better than Mr. Rosier's. But Isabel contented herself at such moments with wondering where this gentleman was; he came no more at all to Palazzo Roccanera. It was surprising, as I say, the hold it had taken of her—the idea of assisting her husband to be pleased.

It was surprising for a variety of reasons which I shall presently touch upon. On the evening I speak of, while Lord Warburton sat there, she had been on the point of taking the great step of going out of the room and leaving her companions alone. I say the great step, because it was in this light that Gilbert Osmond would have regarded it, and Isabel was trying as much as possible to take her husband's view. She succeeded after a fashion, but she fell short of the point I mention. After all she couldn't rise to it; something held her and made this impossible. It was not exactly that it would be base or insidious; for women as a general thing practise such manoeuvres with a perfectly good conscience, and Isabel was instinctively much more true than false to the common genius of her sex. There was a vague doubt that interposed—a sense that she was not quite sure. So she remained in the drawing-room, and after a while Lord Warburton went off to his party, of which he promised to give Pansy a full account on the morrow. After he had gone she wondered if she had prevented something which would have happened if she had absented herself for a quarter of an hour; and then she pronounced—always mentally—that when their distinguished visitor should wish her to go away he would easily find means to let her know it. Pansy said nothing whatever about him after he had gone, and Isabel studiously said nothing, as she had taken a vow of reserve until after he should have declared himself. He was a little longer in coming to this than might seem to accord with the description he had given Isabel of his feelings. Pansy went to bed, and Isabel had to admit that she could not now guess what her stepdaughter was thinking of. Her transparent little companion was for the moment not to be seen through.

She remained alone, looking at the fire, until, at the end of half an hour, her husband came in. He moved about a while in silence and then sat down; he looked at the fire like herself. But she now had transferred her eyes from the flickering flame in the chimney to Osmond's face, and she watched him while he kept his silence. Covert observation had become a habit with her; an instinct, of which it is not an exaggeration to say that it was allied to that of self-defence, had made it habitual. She wished as much as possible to know his thoughts, to know what he would say, beforehand, so that she might prepare her answer. Preparing answers had not been her strong point of old; she had rarely in this respect got further than thinking afterwards of clever things she might have said. But she had learned caution—learned it in a measure from her husband's very countenance. It was the same face she had looked into with eyes equally earnest perhaps, but less penetrating, on the terrace of a Florentine villa; except that Osmond had grown slightly stouter since his marriage. He still, however, might strike one as very distinguished.

"Has Lord Warburton been here?" he presently asked.

"Yes, he stayed half an hour."

"Did he see Pansy?"

"Yes; he sat on the sofa beside her."

"Did he talk with her much?"

"He talked almost only to her."

"It seems to me he's attentive. Isn't that what you call it?"

"I don't call it anything," said Isabel; "I've waited for you to give it a name."

"That's a consideration you don't always show," Osmond answered after a moment.

"I've determined, this time, to try and act as you'd like. I've so often failed of that."

Osmond turned his head slowly, looking at her. "Are you trying to quarrel with me?"

"No, I'm trying to live at peace."

"Nothing's more easy; you know I don't quarrel myself."

"What do you call it when you try to make me angry?" Isabel asked.

"I don't try; if I've done so it has been the most natural thing in the world. Moreover I'm not in the least trying now."

Isabel smiled. "It doesn't matter. I've determined never to be angry again."

"That's an excellent resolve. Your temper isn't good."

"No—it's not good." She pushed away the book she had been reading and took up the band of tapestry Pansy had left on the table.

"That's partly why I've not spoken to you about this business of my daughter's," Osmond said, designating Pansy in the manner that was most frequent with him. "I was afraid I should encounter opposition—that you too would have views on the subject. I've sent little Rosier about his business."

"You were afraid I'd plead for Mr. Rosier? Haven't you noticed that I've never spoken to you of him?"

"I've never given you a chance. We've so little conversation in these days. I know he was an old friend of yours."

"Yes; he's an old friend of mine." Isabel cared little more for him than for the tapestry that she held in her hand; but it was true that he was an old friend and that with her husband she felt a desire not to extenuate such ties. He had a way of expressing contempt for them which fortified her loyalty to them, even when, as in the present case, they were in themselves insignificant. She sometimes felt a sort of passion of tenderness for memories which had no other merit than that they belonged to her unmarried life. "But as regards Pansy," she added in a moment, "I've given him no encouragement."

"That's fortunate," Osmond observed.

"Fortunate for me, I suppose you mean. For him it matters little."

"There's no use talking of him," Osmond said. "As I tell you, I've turned him out."

"Yes; but a lover outside's always a lover. He's sometimes even more of one. Mr. Rosier still has hope."

"He's welcome to the comfort of it! My daughter has only to sit perfectly quiet to become Lady Warburton."

"Should you like that?" Isabel asked with a simplicity which was not so affected as it may appear. She was resolved to assume nothing, for Osmond had a way of unexpectedly turning her assumptions against her. The intensity with which he would like his daughter to become Lady Warburton had been the very basis of her own recent reflections. But that was for herself; she would recognise nothing until Osmond should have put it into words; she would not take for granted with him that he thought Lord Warburton a prize worth an amount of effort that was unusual among the Osmonds. It was Gilbert's constant intimation that for him nothing in life was a prize; that he treated as from equal to equal with the most distinguished people in the world, and that his daughter had only to look about her to pick out a prince. It cost him therefore a lapse from consistency to say explicitly that he yearned for Lord Warburton and that if this nobleman should escape his equivalent might not be found; with which moreover it was another of his customary implications that he was never inconsistent. He would have liked his wife to glide over the point. But strangely enough, now that she was face to face with him and although an hour before she had almost invented a scheme for pleasing him, Isabel was not accommodating, would not glide. And yet she knew exactly the effect on his mind of her question: it would operate as an humiliation. Never mind; he was terribly capable of humiliating her—all the more so that he was also capable of waiting for great opportunities and of showing sometimes an almost unaccountable indifference to small ones. Isabel perhaps took a small opportunity because she would not have availed herself of a great one.

Osmond at present acquitted himself very honourably. "I should like it extremely; it would be a great marriage. And then Lord Warburton has another advantage: he's an old friend of yours. It would be pleasant for him to come into the family. It's very odd Pansy's admirers should all be your old friends."

"It's natural that they should come to see me. In coming to see me they see Pansy. Seeing her it's natural they should fall in love with her."

"So I think. But you're not bound to do so."

"If she should marry Lord Warburton I should be very glad," Isabel went on frankly. "He's an excellent man. You say, however, that she has only to sit perfectly still. Perhaps she won't sit perfectly still. If she loses Mr. Rosier she may jump up!"

Osmond appeared to give no heed to this; he sat gazing at the fire. "Pansy would like to be a great lady," he remarked in a moment with a certain tenderness of tone. "She wishes above all to please," he added.

"To please Mr. Rosier, perhaps."

"No, to please me."

"Me too a little, I think," said Isabel.

"Yes, she has a great opinion of you. But she'll do what I like."

"If you're sure of that, it's very well," she went on.

"Meantime," said Osmond, "I should like our distinguished visitor to speak."

"He has spoken—to me. He has told me it would be a great pleasure to him to believe she could care for him."

Osmond turned his head quickly, but at first he said nothing. Then, "Why didn't you tell me that?" he asked sharply.

"There was no opportunity. You know how we live. I've taken the first chance that has offered."

"Did you speak to him of Rosier?"

"Oh yes, a little."

"That was hardly necessary."

"I thought it best he should know, so that, so that—" And Isabel paused.

"So that what?"

"So that he might act accordingly."

"So that he might back out, do you mean?"

"No, so that he might advance while there's yet time."

"That's not the effect it seems to have had."

"You should have patience," said Isabel. "You know Englishmen are shy."

"This one's not. He was not when he made love to YOU."

She had been afraid Osmond would speak of that; it was disagreeable to her. "I beg your pardon; he was extremely so," she returned.

He answered nothing for some time; he took up a book and fingered the pages while she sat silent and occupied herself with Pansy's tapestry. "You must have a great deal of influence with him," Osmond went on at last. "The moment you really wish it you can bring him to the point."

This was more offensive still; but she felt the great naturalness of his saying it, and it was after all extremely like what she had said to herself. "Why should I have influence?" she asked. "What have I ever done to put him under an obligation to me?"

"You refused to marry him," said Osmond with his eyes on his book.

"I must not presume too much on that," she replied.

He threw down the book presently and got up, standing before the fire with his hands behind him. "Well, I hold that it lies in your hands. I shall leave it there. With a little good-will you may manage it. Think that over and remember how much I count on you." He waited a little, to give her time to answer; but she answered nothing, and he presently strolled out of the room.

CHAPTER XLII

She had answered nothing because his words had put the situation before her and she was absorbed in looking at it. There was something in them that suddenly made vibrations deep, so that she had been afraid to trust herself to speak. After he had gone she leaned back in her chair and closed her eyes; and for a long time, far into the night and still further, she sat in the still drawing-room, given up to her meditation. A servant came in to attend to the fire, and she bade him bring fresh candles and then go to bed. Osmond had told her to think of what he had said; and she did so indeed, and of many other things. The suggestion from another that she had a definite influence on Lord Warburton—this had given her the start that accompanies unexpected recognition. Was it true that there was something still between them that might be a handle to make him declare himself to Pansy—a susceptibility, on his part, to approval, a desire to do what would please her? Isabel had hitherto not asked herself the question, because she had not been forced; but now that it was directly presented to her she saw the answer, and the answer frightened her. Yes, there was something—something on Lord Warburton's part. When he had first come to Rome she believed the link that united them to be completely snapped; but little by little she had been reminded that it had yet a palpable existence. It was as thin as a hair, but there were moments when she seemed to hear it vibrate. For herself nothing was changed; what she once thought of him she always thought; it was needless this feeling should change; it seemed to her in fact a better feeling than ever. But he? had he still the idea that she might be more to him than other women? Had he the wish to profit by the memory of the few moments of intimacy through which they had once passed? Isabel knew she had read some of the signs of such a disposition. But what were his hopes, his pretensions, and in what strange way were they mingled with his evidently very sincere appreciation of poor Pansy? Was he in love with Gilbert Osmond's wife, and if so what comfort did he expect to derive from it? If he was in love with Pansy he was not in love with her stepmother, and if he was in love with her stepmother he was not in love with Pansy. Was she to cultivate the advantage she possessed in order to make him commit himself to Pansy, knowing he would do so for her sake and not for the small creature's own—was this the service her husband had asked of her? This at any rate was the duty with which she found herself confronted—from the moment she admitted to herself that her old friend had still an uneradicated predilection for her society. It was not an agreeable task; it was in fact a repulsive one. She asked herself with dismay whether Lord Warburton were pretending to be in love with Pansy in order to cultivate another satisfaction and what might be called other chances. Of this refinement of duplicity she presently acquitted him; she preferred to believe him in perfect good faith. But if his admiration for Pansy were a delusion this was scarcely better than its being an affectation. Isabel wandered among these ugly possibilities until she had completely lost her way; some of them, as she suddenly encountered them, seemed ugly enough. Then she broke out of the labyrinth, rubbing her eyes, and declared that her imagination surely did her little honour and that her husband's did him even less. Lord Warburton was as disinterested as he need be, and she was no more to him than she need wish. She would rest upon this till the contrary should be proved; proved more effectually than by a cynical intimation of Osmond's.

Such a resolution, however, brought her this evening but little peace, for her soul was haunted with terrors which crowded to the foreground of thought as quickly as a place was made for them. What had suddenly set them into livelier motion she hardly knew, unless it were the strange impression she had received in the afternoon of her husband's being in more direct communication with Madame Merle than she suspected. That impression came back to her from time to time, and now she wondered it had never come before. Besides this, her short interview with Osmond half an hour ago was a striking example of his faculty for making everything wither that he touched, spoiling everything for her that he looked at. It was very well to undertake to give him a proof of loyalty; the real fact was that the knowledge of his expecting a thing raised a presumption against it. It was as if he had had the evil eye; as if his presence were a blight and his favour a misfortune. Was the fault in himself, or only in the deep mistrust she had conceived for him? This mistrust was now the clearest result of their short married life; a gulf had opened between them over which they looked at each other with eyes that were on either side a declaration of the deception suffered. It was a strange opposition, of the like of which she had never dreamed—an opposition in which the vital principle of the one was a thing of contempt to the other. It was not her fault—she had practised no deception; she had only admired and believed. She had taken all the first steps in the purest confidence, and then she had suddenly found the infinite vista of a multiplied life to be a dark, narrow alley with a dead wall at the end. Instead of leading to the high places of happiness, from which the world would seem to lie below one, so that one could look down with a sense of exaltation and advantage, and judge and choose and pity, it led rather downward and earthward, into realms of restriction and depression where the sound of other lives, easier and freer, was heard as from above, and where it served to deepen the feeling of failure. It was her deep distrust of her husband—this was what darkened the world. That is a sentiment easily indicated, but not so easily explained, and so composite in its character that much time and still more suffering had been needed to bring it to its actual perfection. Suffering, with Isabel, was an active condition; it was not a chill, a stupor, a despair; it was a passion of thought, of speculation, of response to every pressure. She flattered herself that she had kept her failing faith to herself, however,—that no one suspected it but Osmond. Oh, he knew it, and there were times when she thought he enjoyed it. It had come gradually—it was not till the first year of their life together, so admirably intimate at first, had closed that she had taken the alarm. Then the shadows had begun to gather; it was as if Osmond deliberately, almost malignantly, had put the lights out one by one. The dusk at first was vague and thin, and she could still see her way in it. But it steadily deepened, and if now and again it had occasionally lifted there were certain corners of her prospect that were impenetrably black. These shadows were not an emanation from her own mind: she was very sure of that; she had done her best to be just and temperate, to see only the truth. They were a part, they were a kind of creation and consequence, of her husband's very presence. They were not his misdeeds, his turpitudes; she accused him of nothing—that is but of one thing, which was NOT a crime. She knew of no wrong he had done; he was not violent, he was not cruel: she simply believed he hated her. That was all she accused him of, and the miserable part of it was precisely that it was not a crime, for against a crime she might have found redress. He had discovered that she was so different, that she was not what he had believed she would prove to be. He had thought at first he could change her, and she had done her best to be what he would like. But she was, after all, herself—she couldn't help that; and now there was no use pretending, wearing a mask or a dress, for he knew her and had made up his mind. She was not afraid of him; she had no apprehension he would hurt her; for the ill-will he bore her was not of that sort. He would if possible never give her a pretext, never put himself in the wrong. Isabel, scanning the future with dry, fixed eyes, saw that he would have the better of her there. She would give him many pretexts, she would often put herself in the wrong. There were times when she almost pitied him; for if she had not deceived him in intention she understood how completely she must have done so in fact. She had effaced herself when he first knew her; she had made herself small, pretending there was less of her than there really was. It was because she had been under the extraordinary charm that he, on his side, had taken pains to put forth. He was not changed; he had not disguised himself, during the year of his courtship, any more than she. But she had seen only half his nature then, as one saw the disk of the moon when it was partly masked by the shadow of the earth. She saw the full moon now—she saw the whole man. She had kept still, as it were, so that he should have a free field, and yet in spite of this she had mistaken a part for the whole.

Ah, she had been immensely under the charm! It had not passed away; it was there still: she still knew perfectly what it was that made Osmond delightful when he chose to be. He had wished to be when he made love to her, and as she had wished to be charmed it was not wonderful he had succeeded. He had succeeded because he had been sincere; it never occurred to her now to deny him that. He admired her—he had told her why: because she was the most imaginative woman he had known. It might very well have been true; for during those months she had imagined a world of things that had no substance. She had had a more wondrous vision of him, fed through charmed senses and oh such a stirred fancy!—she had not read him right. A certain combination of features had touched her, and in them she had seen the most striking of figures. That he was poor and lonely and yet that somehow he was noble—that was what had interested her and seemed to give her her opportunity. There had been an indefinable beauty about him—in his situation, in his mind, in his face. She had felt at the same time that he was helpless and ineffectual, but the feeling had taken the form of a tenderness which was the very flower of respect. He was like a sceptical voyager strolling on the beach while he waited for the tide, looking seaward yet not putting to sea. It was in all this she had found her occasion. She would launch his boat for him; she would be his providence; it would be a good thing to love him. And she had loved him, she had so anxiously and yet so ardently given herself—a good deal for what she found in him, but a good deal also for what she brought him and what might enrich the gift. As she looked back at the passion of those full weeks she perceived in it a kind of maternal strain—the happiness of a woman who felt that she was a contributor, that she came with charged hands. But for her money, as she saw to-day, she would never have done it. And then her mind wandered off to poor Mr. Touchett, sleeping under English turf, the beneficent author of infinite woe! For this was the fantastic fact. At bottom her money had been a burden, had been on her mind, which was filled with the desire to transfer the weight of it to some other conscience, to some more prepared receptacle. What would lighten her own conscience more effectually than to make it over to the man with the best taste in the world? Unless she should have given it to a hospital there would have been nothing better she could do with it; and there was no charitable institution in which she had been as much interested as in Gilbert Osmond. He would use her fortune in a way that would make her think better of it and rub off a certain grossness attaching to the good luck of an unexpected inheritance. There had been nothing very delicate in inheriting seventy thousand pounds; the delicacy had been all in Mr. Touchett's leaving them to her. But to marry Gilbert Osmond and bring him such a portion—in that there would be delicacy for her as well. There would be less for him—that was true; but that was his affair, and if he loved her he wouldn't object to her being rich. Had he not had the courage to say he was glad she was rich?

Isabel's cheek burned when she asked herself if she had really married on a factitious theory, in order to do something finely appreciable with her money. But she was able to answer quickly enough that this was only half the story. It was because a certain ardour took possession of her—a sense of the earnestness of his affection and a delight in his personal qualities. He was better than any one else. This supreme conviction had filled her life for months, and enough of it still remained to prove to her that she could not have done otherwise. The finest—in the sense of being the subtlest—manly organism she had ever known had become her property, and the recognition of her having but to put out her hands and take it had been originally a sort of act of devotion. She had not been mistaken about the beauty of his mind; she knew that organ perfectly now. She had lived with it, she had lived IN it almost—it appeared to have become her habitation. If she had been captured it had taken a firm hand to seize her; that reflection perhaps had some worth. A mind more ingenious, more pliant, more cultivated, more trained to admirable exercises, she had not encountered; and it was this exquisite instrument she had now to reckon with. She lost herself in infinite dismay when she thought of the magnitude of HIS deception. It was a wonder, perhaps, in view of this, that he didn't hate her more. She remembered perfectly the first sign he had given of it—it had been like the bell that was to ring up the curtain upon the real drama of their life. He said to her one day that she had too many ideas and that she must get rid of them. He had told her that already, before their marriage; but then she had not noticed it: it had come back to her only afterwards. This time she might well have noticed it, because he had really meant it. The words had been nothing superficially; but when in the light of deepening experience she had looked into them they had then appeared portentous. He had really meant it—he would have liked her to have nothing of her own but her pretty appearance. She had known she had too many ideas; she had more even than he had supposed, many more than she had expressed to him when he had asked her to marry him. Yes, she HAD been hypocritical; she had liked him so much. She had too many ideas for herself; but that was just what one married for, to share them with some one else. One couldn't pluck them up by the roots, though of course one might suppress them, be careful not to utter them. It had not been this, however, his objecting to her opinions; this had been nothing. She had no opinions—none that she would not have been eager to sacrifice in the satisfaction of feeling herself loved for it. What he had meant had been the whole thing—her character, the way she felt, the way she judged. This was what she had kept in reserve; this was what he had not known until he had found himself—with the door closed behind, as it were—set down face to face with it. She had a certain way of looking at life which he took as a personal offence. Heaven knew that now at least it was a very humble, accommodating way! The strange thing was that she should not have suspected from the first that his own had been so different. She had thought it so large, so enlightened, so perfectly that of an honest man and a gentleman. Hadn't he assured her that he had no superstitions, no dull limitations, no prejudices that had lost their freshness? Hadn't he all the appearance of a man living in the open air of the world, indifferent to small considerations, caring only for truth and knowledge and believing that two intelligent people ought to look for them together and, whether they found them or not, find at least some happiness in the search? He had told her he loved the conventional; but there was a sense in which this seemed a noble declaration. In that sense, that of the love of harmony and order and decency and of all the stately offices of life, she went with him freely, and his warning had contained nothing ominous. But when, as the months had elapsed, she had followed him further and he had led her into the mansion of his own habitation, then, THEN she had seen where she really was.

She could live it over again, the incredulous terror with which she had taken the measure of her dwelling. Between those four walls she had lived ever since; they were to surround her for the rest of her life. It was the house of darkness, the house of dumbness, the house of suffocation. Osmond's beautiful mind gave it neither light nor air; Osmond's beautiful mind indeed seemed to peep down from a small high window and mock at her. Of course it had not been physical suffering; for physical suffering there might have been a remedy. She could come and go; she had her liberty; her husband was perfectly polite. He took himself so seriously; it was something appalling. Under all his culture, his cleverness, his amenity, under his good-nature, his facility, his knowledge of life, his egotism lay hidden like a serpent in a bank of flowers. She had taken him seriously, but she had not taken him so seriously as that. How could she—especially when she had known him better? She was to think of him as he thought of himself—as the first gentleman in Europe. So it was that she had thought of him at first, and that indeed was the reason she had married him. But when she began to see what it implied she drew back; there was more in the bond than she had meant to put her name to. It implied a sovereign contempt for every one but some three or four very exalted people whom he envied, and for everything in the world but half a dozen ideas of his own. That was very well; she would have gone with him even there a long distance; for he pointed out to her so much of the baseness and shabbiness of life, opened her eyes so wide to the stupidity, the depravity, the ignorance of mankind, that she had been properly impressed with the infinite vulgarity of things and of the virtue of keeping one's self unspotted by it. But this base, if noble world, it appeared, was after all what one was to live for; one was to keep it forever in one's eye, in order not to enlighten or convert or redeem it, but to extract from it some recognition of one's own superiority. On the one hand it was despicable, but on the other it afforded a standard. Osmond had talked to Isabel about his renunciation, his indifference, the ease with which he dispensed with the usual aids to success; and all this had seemed to her admirable. She had thought it a grand indifference, an exquisite independence. But indifference was really the last of his qualities; she had never seen any one who thought so much of others. For herself, avowedly, the world had always interested her and the study of her fellow creatures been her constant passion. She would have been willing, however, to renounce all her curiosities and sympathies for the sake of a personal life, if the person concerned had only been able to make her believe it was a gain! This at least was her present conviction; and the thing certainly would have been easier than to care for society as Osmond cared for it.

He was unable to live without it, and she saw that he had never really done so; he had looked at it out of his window even when he appeared to be most detached from it. He had his ideal, just as she had tried to have hers; only it was strange that people should seek for justice in such different quarters. His ideal was a conception of high prosperity and propriety, of the aristocratic life, which she now saw that he deemed himself always, in essence at least, to have led. He had never lapsed from it for an hour; he would never have recovered from the shame of doing so. That again was very well; here too she would have agreed; but they attached such different ideas, such different associations and desires, to the same formulas. Her notion of the aristocratic life was simply the union of great knowledge with great liberty; the knowledge would give one a sense of duty and the liberty a sense of enjoyment. But for Osmond it was altogether a thing of forms, a conscious, calculated attitude. He was fond of the old, the consecrated, the transmitted; so was she, but she pretended to do what she chose with it. He had an immense esteem for tradition; he had told her once that the best thing in the world was to have it, but that if one was so unfortunate as not to have it one must immediately proceed to make it. She knew that he meant by this that she hadn't it, but that he was better off; though from what source he had derived his traditions she never learned. He had a very large collection of them, however; that was very certain, and after a little she began to see. The great thing was to act in accordance with them; the great thing not only for him but for her. Isabel had an undefined conviction that to serve for another person than their proprietor traditions must be of a thoroughly superior kind; but she nevertheless assented to this intimation that she too must march to the stately music that floated down from unknown periods in her husband's past; she who of old had been so free of step, so desultory, so devious, so much the reverse of processional. There were certain things they must do, a certain posture they must take, certain people they must know and not know. When she saw this rigid system close about her, draped though it was in pictured tapestries, that sense of darkness and suffocation of which I have spoken took possession of her; she seemed shut up with an odour of mould and decay. She had resisted of course; at first very humorously, ironically, tenderly; then, as the situation grew more serious, eagerly, passionately, pleadingly. She had pleaded the cause of freedom, of doing as they chose, of not caring for the aspect and denomination of their life—the cause of other instincts and longings, of quite another ideal.

Then it was that her husband's personality, touched as it never had been, stepped forth and stood erect. The things she had said were answered only by his scorn, and she could see he was ineffably ashamed of her. What did he think of her—that she was base, vulgar, ignoble? He at least knew now that she had no traditions! It had not been in his prevision of things that she should reveal such flatness; her sentiments were worthy of a radical newspaper or a Unitarian preacher. The real offence, as she ultimately perceived, was her having a mind of her own at all. Her mind was to be his—attached to his own like a small garden-plot to a deer-park. He would rake the soil gently and water the flowers; he would weed the beds and gather an occasional nosegay. It would be a pretty piece of property for a proprietor already far-reaching. He didn't wish her to be stupid. On the contrary, it was because she was clever that she had pleased him. But he expected her intelligence to operate altogether in his favour, and so far from desiring her mind to be a blank he had flattered himself that it would be richly receptive. He had expected his wife to feel with him and for him, to enter into his opinions, his ambitions, his preferences; and Isabel was obliged to confess that this was no great insolence on the part of a man so accomplished and a husband originally at least so tender. But there were certain things she could never take in. To begin with, they were hideously unclean. She was not a daughter of the Puritans, but for all that she believed in such a thing as chastity and even as decency. It would appear that Osmond was far from doing anything of the sort; some of his traditions made her push back her skirts. Did all women have lovers? Did they all lie and even the best have their price? Were there only three or four that didn't deceive their husbands? When Isabel heard such things she felt a greater scorn for them than for the gossip of a village parlour—a scorn that kept its freshness in a very tainted air. There was the taint of her sister-in-law: did her husband judge only by the Countess Gemini? This lady very often lied, and she had practised deceptions that were not simply verbal. It was enough to find these facts assumed among Osmond's traditions—it was enough without giving them such a general extension. It was her scorn of his assumptions, it was this that made him draw himself up. He had plenty of contempt, and it was proper his wife should be as well furnished; but that she should turn the hot light of her disdain upon his own conception of things—this was a danger he had not allowed for. He believed he should have regulated her emotions before she came to it; and Isabel could easily imagine how his ears had scorched on his discovering he had been too confident. When one had a wife who gave one that sensation there was nothing left but to hate her.

She was morally certain now that this feeling of hatred, which at first had been a refuge and a refreshment, had become the occupation and comfort of his life. The feeling was deep, because it was sincere; he had had the revelation that she could after all dispense with him. If to herself the idea was startling, if it presented itself at first as a kind of infidelity, a capacity for pollution, what infinite effect might it not be expected to have had upon HIM? It was very simple; he despised her; she had no traditions and the moral horizon of a Unitarian minister. Poor Isabel, who had never been able to understand Unitarianism! This was the certitude she had been living with now for a time that she had ceased to measure. What was coming—what was before them? That was her constant question. What would he do—what ought SHE to do? When a man hated his wife what did it lead to? She didn't hate him, that she was sure of, for every little while she felt a passionate wish to give him a pleasant surprise. Very often, however, she felt afraid, and it used to come over her, as I have intimated, that she had deceived him at the very first. They were strangely married, at all events, and it was a horrible life. Until that morning he had scarcely spoken to her for a week; his manner was as dry as a burned-out fire. She knew there was a special reason; he was displeased at Ralph Touchett's staying on in Rome. He thought she saw too much of her cousin—he had told her a week before it was indecent she should go to him at his hotel. He would have said more than this if Ralph's invalid state had not appeared to make it brutal to denounce him; but having had to contain himself had only deepened his disgust. Isabel read all this as she would have read the hour on the clock-face; she was as perfectly aware that the sight of her interest in her cousin stirred her husband's rage as if Osmond had locked her into her room—which she was sure was what he wanted to do. It was her honest belief that on the whole she was not defiant, but she certainly couldn't pretend to be indifferent to Ralph. She believed he was dying at last and that she should never see him again, and this gave her a tenderness for him that she had never known before. Nothing was a pleasure to her now; how could anything be a pleasure to a woman who knew that she had thrown away her life? There was an everlasting weight on her heart—there was a livid light on everything. But Ralph's little visit was a lamp in the darkness; for the hour that she sat with him her ache for herself became somehow her ache for HIM. She felt to-day as if he had been her brother. She had never had a brother, but if she had and she were in trouble and he were dying, he would be dear to her as Ralph was. Ah yes, if Gilbert was jealous of her there was perhaps some reason; it didn't make Gilbert look better to sit for half an hour with Ralph. It was not that they talked of him—it was not that she complained. His name was never uttered between them. It was simply that Ralph was generous and that her husband was not. There was something in Ralph's talk, in his smile, in the mere fact of his being in Rome, that made the blasted circle round which she walked more spacious. He made her feel the good of the world; he made her feel what might have been. He was after all as intelligent as Osmond—quite apart from his being better. And thus it seemed to her an act of devotion to conceal her misery from him. She concealed it elaborately; she was perpetually, in their talk, hanging out curtains and before her again—it lived before her again,—it had never had time to die—that morning in the garden at Florence when he had warned her against Osmond. She had only to close her eyes to see the place, to hear his voice, to feel the warm, sweet air. How could he have known? What a mystery, what a wonder of wisdom! As intelligent as Gilbert? He was much more intelligent—to arrive at such a judgement as that. Gilbert had never been so deep, so just. She had told him then that from her at least he should never know if he was right; and this was what she was taking care of now. It gave her plenty to do; there was passion, exaltation, religion in it. Women find their religion sometimes in strange exercises, and Isabel at present, in playing a part before her cousin, had an idea that she was doing him a kindness. It would have been a kindness perhaps if he had been for a single instant a dupe. As it was, the kindness consisted mainly in trying to make him believe that he had once wounded her greatly and that the event had put him to shame, but that, as she was very generous and he was so ill, she bore him no grudge and even considerately forbore to flaunt her happiness in his face. Ralph smiled to himself, as he lay on his sofa, at this extraordinary form of consideration; but he forgave her for having forgiven him. She didn't wish him to have the pain of knowing she was unhappy: that was the great thing, and it didn't matter that such knowledge would rather have righted him.

For herself, she lingered in the soundless saloon long after the fire had gone out. There was no danger of her feeling the cold; she was in a fever. She heard the small hours strike, and then the great ones, but her vigil took no heed of time. Her mind, assailed by visions, was in a state of extraordinary activity, and her visions might as well come to her there, where she sat up to meet them, as on her pillow, to make a mockery of rest. As I have said, she believed she was not defiant, and what could be a better proof of it than that she should linger there half the night, trying to persuade herself that there was no reason why Pansy shouldn't be married as you would put a letter in the post-office? When the clock struck four she got up; she was going to bed at last, for the lamp had long since gone out and the candles burned down to their sockets. But even then she stopped again in the middle of the room and stood there gazing at a remembered vision—that of her husband and Madame Merle unconsciously and familiarly associated.

CHAPTER XLIII

Three nights after this she took Pansy to a great party, to which Osmond, who never went to dances, did not accompany them. Pansy was as ready for a dance as ever; she was not of a generalising turn and had not extended to other pleasures the interdict she had seen placed on those of love. If she was biding her time or hoping to circumvent her father she must have had a prevision of success. Isabel thought this unlikely; it was much more likely that Pansy had simply determined to be a good girl. She had never had such a chance, and she had a proper esteem for chances. She carried herself no less attentively than usual and kept no less anxious an eye upon her vaporous skirts; she held her bouquet very tight and counted over the flowers for the twentieth time. She made Isabel feel old; it seemed so long since she had been in a flutter about a ball. Pansy, who was greatly admired, was never in want of partners, and very soon after their arrival she gave Isabel, who was not dancing, her bouquet to hold. Isabel had rendered her this service for some minutes when she became aware of the near presence of Edward Rosier. He stood before her; he had lost his affable smile and wore a look of almost military resolution. The change in his appearance would have made Isabel smile if she had not felt his case to be at bottom a hard one: he had always smelt so much more of heliotrope than of gunpowder. He looked at her a moment somewhat fiercely, as if to notify her he was dangerous, and then dropped his eyes on her bouquet. After he had inspected it his glance softened and he said quickly: "It's all pansies; it must be hers!"

Isabel smiled kindly. "Yes, it's hers; she gave it to me to hold."

"May I hold it a little, Mrs. Osmond?" the poor young man asked.

"No, I can't trust you; I'm afraid you wouldn't give it back."

"I'm not sure that I should; I should leave the house with it instantly. But may I not at least have a single flower?"

Isabel hesitated a moment, and then, smiling still, held out the bouquet. "Choose one yourself. It's frightful what I'm doing for you."

"Ah, if you do no more than this, Mrs. Osmond!" Rosier exclaimed with his glass in one eye, carefully choosing his flower.

"Don't put it into your button-hole," she said. "Don't for the world!"

"I should like her to see it. She has refused to dance with me, but I wish to show her that I believe in her still."

"It's very well to show it to her, but it's out of place to show it to others. Her father has told her not to dance with you."

"And is that all YOU can do for me? I expected more from you, Mrs. Osmond," said the young man in a tone of fine general reference. "You know our acquaintance goes back very far—quite into the days of our innocent childhood."

"Don't make me out too old," Isabel patiently answered. "You come back to that very often, and I've never denied it. But I must tell you that, old friends as we are, if you had done me the honour to ask me to marry you I should have refused you on the spot."

"Ah, you don't esteem me then. Say at once that you think me a mere Parisian trifler!"

"I esteem you very much, but I'm not in love with you. What I mean by that, of course, is that I'm not in love with you for Pansy."

"Very good; I see. You pity me—that's all." And Edward Rosier looked all round, inconsequently, with his single glass. It was a revelation to him that people shouldn't be more pleased; but he was at least too proud to show that the deficiency struck him as general.

Isabel for a moment said nothing. His manner and appearance had not the dignity of the deepest tragedy; his little glass, among other things, was against that. But she suddenly felt touched; her own unhappiness, after all, had something in common with his, and it came over her, more than before, that here, in recognisable, if not in romantic form, was the most affecting thing in the world—young love struggling with adversity. "Would you really be very kind to her?" she finally asked in a low tone.

He dropped his eyes devoutly and raised the little flower that he held in his fingers to his lips. Then he looked at her. "You pity me; but don't you pity HER a little?"

"I don't know; I'm not sure. She'll always enjoy life."

"It will depend on what you call life!" Mr. Rosier effectively said. "She won't enjoy being tortured."

"There'll be nothing of that."

"I'm glad to hear it. She knows what she's about. You'll see."

"I think she does, and she'll never disobey her father. But she's coming back to me," Isabel added, "and I must beg you to go away."

Rosier lingered a moment till Pansy came in sight on the arm of her cavalier; he stood just long enough to look her in the face. Then he walked away, holding up his head; and the manner in which he achieved this sacrifice to expediency convinced Isabel he was very much in love.

Pansy, who seldom got disarranged in dancing, looking perfectly fresh and cool after this exercise, waited a moment and then took back her bouquet. Isabel watched her and saw she was counting the flowers; whereupon she said to herself that decidedly there were deeper forces at play than she had recognised. Pansy had seen Rosier turn away, but she said nothing to Isabel about him; she talked only of her partner, after he had made his bow and retired; of the music, the floor, the rare misfortune of having already torn her dress. Isabel was sure, however, she had discovered her lover to have abstracted a flower; though this knowledge was not needed to account for the dutiful grace with which she responded to the appeal of her next partner. That perfect amenity under acute constraint was part of a larger system. She was again led forth by a flushed young man, this time carrying her bouquet; and she had not been absent many minutes when Isabel saw Lord Warburton advancing through the crowd. He presently drew near and bade her good-evening; she had not seen him since the day before. He looked about him, and then "Where's the little maid?" he asked. It was in this manner that he had formed the harmless habit of alluding to Miss Osmond.

"She's dancing," said Isabel. "You'll see her somewhere."

He looked among the dancers and at last caught Pansy's eye. "She sees me, but she won't notice me," he then remarked. "Are you not dancing?"

"As you see, I'm a wall-flower."

"Won't you dance with me?"

"Thank you; I'd rather you should dance with the little maid."

"One needn't prevent the other—especially as she's engaged."

"She's not engaged for everything, and you can reserve yourself. She dances very hard, and you'll be the fresher."

"She dances beautifully," said Lord Warburton, following her with his eyes. "Ah, at last," he added, "she has given me a smile." He stood there with his handsome, easy, important physiognomy; and as Isabel observed him it came over her, as it had done before, that it was strange a man of his mettle should take an interest in a little maid. It struck her as a great incongruity; neither Pansy's small fascinations, nor his own kindness, his good-nature, not even his need for amusement, which was extreme and constant, were sufficient to account for it. "I should like to dance with you," he went on in a moment, turning back to Isabel; "but I think I like even better to talk with you."

"Yes, it's better, and it's more worthy of your dignity. Great statesmen oughtn't to waltz."

"Don't be cruel. Why did you recommend me then to dance with Miss Osmond?"

"Ah, that's different. If you danced with her it would look simply like a piece of kindness—as if you were doing it for her amusement. If you dance with me you'll look as if you were doing it for your own."

"And pray haven't I a right to amuse myself?"

"No, not with the affairs of the British Empire on your hands."

"The British Empire be hanged! You're always laughing at it."

"Amuse yourself with talking to me," said Isabel.

"I'm not sure it's really a recreation. You're too pointed; I've always to be defending myself. And you strike me as more than usually dangerous to-night. Will you absolutely not dance?"

"I can't leave my place. Pansy must find me here."

He was silent a little. "You're wonderfully good to her," he said suddenly.

Isabel stared a little and smiled. "Can you imagine one's not being?"

"No indeed. I know how one is charmed with her. But you must have done a great deal for her."

"I've taken her out with me," said Isabel, smiling still. "And I've seen that she has proper clothes."

"Your society must have been a great benefit to her. You've talked to her, advised her, helped her to develop."

"Ah yes, if she isn't the rose she has lived near it."

She laughed, and her companion did as much; but there was a certain visible preoccupation in his face which interfered with complete hilarity. "We all try to live as near it as we can," he said after a moment's hesitation.

Isabel turned away; Pansy was about to be restored to her, and she welcomed the diversion. We know how much she liked Lord Warburton; she thought him pleasanter even than the sum of his merits warranted; there was something in his friendship that appeared a kind of resource in case of indefinite need; it was like having a large balance at the bank. She felt happier when he was in the room; there was something reassuring in his approach; the sound of his voice reminded her of the beneficence of nature. Yet for all that it didn't suit her that he should be too near her, that he should take too much of her good-will for granted. She was afraid of that; she averted herself from it; she wished he wouldn't. She felt that if he should come too near, as it were, it might be in her to flash out and bid him keep his distance. Pansy came back to Isabel with another rent in her skirt, which was the inevitable consequence of the first and which she displayed to Isabel with serious eyes. There were too many gentlemen in uniform; they wore those dreadful spurs, which were fatal to the dresses of little maids. It hereupon became apparent that the resources of women are innumerable. Isabel devoted herself to Pansy's desecrated drapery; she fumbled for a pin and repaired the injury; she smiled and listened to her account of her adventures. Her attention, her sympathy were immediate and active; and they were in direct proportion to a sentiment with which they were in no way connected—a lively conjecture as to whether Lord Warburton might be trying to make love to her. It was not simply his words just then; it was others as well; it was the reference and the continuity. This was what she thought about while she pinned up Pansy's dress. If it were so, as she feared, he was of course unwitting; he himself had not taken account of his intention. But this made it none the more auspicious, made the situation none less impossible. The sooner he should get back into right relations with things the better. He immediately began to talk to Pansy—on whom it was certainly mystifying to see that he dropped a smile of chastened devotion. Pansy replied, as usual, with a little air of conscientious aspiration; he had to bend toward her a good deal in conversation, and her eyes, as usual, wandered up and down his robust person as if he had offered it to her for exhibition. She always seemed a little frightened; yet her fright was not of the painful character that suggests dislike; on the contrary, she looked as if she knew that he knew she liked him. Isabel left them together a little and wandered toward a friend whom she saw near and with whom she talked till the music of the following dance began, for which she knew Pansy to be also engaged. The girl joined her presently, with a little fluttered flush, and Isabel, who scrupulously took Osmond's view of his daughter's complete dependence, consigned her, as a precious and momentary loan, to her appointed partner. About all this matter she had her own imaginations, her own reserves; there were moments when Pansy's extreme adhesiveness made each of them, to her sense, look foolish. But Osmond had given her a sort of tableau of her position as his daughter's duenna, which consisted of gracious alternations of concession and contraction; and there were directions of his which she liked to think she obeyed to the letter. Perhaps, as regards some of them, it was because her doing so appeared to reduce them to the absurd.

After Pansy had been led away, she found Lord Warburton drawing near her again. She rested her eyes on him steadily; she wished she could sound his thoughts. But he had no appearance of confusion. "She has promised to dance with me later," he said.

"I'm glad of that. I suppose you've engaged her for the cotillion."

At this he looked a little awkward. "No, I didn't ask her for that. It's a quadrille."

"Ah, you're not clever!" said Isabel almost angrily. "I told her to keep the cotillion in case you should ask for it."

"Poor little maid, fancy that!" And Lord Warburton laughed frankly. "Of course I will if you like."

"If I like? Oh, if you dance with her only because I like it—!"

"I'm afraid I bore her. She seems to have a lot of young fellows on her book."

Isabel dropped her eyes, reflecting rapidly; Lord Warburton stood there looking at her and she felt his eyes on her face. She felt much inclined to ask him to remove them. She didn't do so, however; she only said to him, after a minute, with her own raised: "Please let me understand."

"Understand what?"

"You told me ten days ago that you'd like to marry my stepdaughter. You've not forgotten it!"

"Forgotten it? I wrote to Mr. Osmond about it this morning."

"Ah," said Isabel, "he didn't mention to me that he had heard from you."

Lord Warburton stammered a little. "I—I didn't send my letter."

"Perhaps you forgot THAT."

"No, I wasn't satisfied with it. It's an awkward sort of letter to write, you know. But I shall send it to-night."

"At three o'clock in the morning?"

"I mean later, in the course of the day."

"Very good. You still wish then to marry her?"

"Very much indeed."

"Aren't you afraid that you'll bore her?" And as her companion stared at this enquiry Isabel added: "If she can't dance with you for half an hour how will she be able to dance with you for life?"

"Ah," said Lord Warburton readily, "I'll let her dance with other people! About the cotillion, the fact is I thought that you—that you—"

"That I would do it with you? I told you I'd do nothing."

"Exactly; so that while it's going on I might find some quiet corner where we may sit down and talk."

"Oh," said Isabel gravely, "you're much too considerate of me."

When the cotillion came Pansy was found to have engaged herself, thinking, in perfect humility, that Lord Warburton had no intentions. Isabel recommended him to seek another partner, but he assured her that he would dance with no one but herself. As, however, she had, in spite of the remonstrances of her hostess, declined other invitations on the ground that she was not dancing at all, it was not possible for her to make an exception in Lord Warburton's favour.

"After all I don't care to dance," he said; "it's a barbarous amusement: I'd much rather talk." And he intimated that he had discovered exactly the corner he had been looking for—a quiet nook in one of the smaller rooms, where the music would come to them faintly and not interfere with conversation. Isabel had decided to let him carry out his idea; she wished to be satisfied. She wandered away from the ball-room with him, though she knew her husband desired she should not lose sight of his daughter. It was with his daughter's pretendant, however; that would make it right for Osmond. On her way out of the ball-room she came upon Edward Rosier, who was standing in a doorway, with folded arms, looking at the dance in the attitude of a young man without illusions. She stopped a moment and asked him if he were not dancing.

"Certainly not, if I can't dance with HER!" he answered.

"You had better go away then," said Isabel with the manner of good counsel.

"I shall not go till she does!" And he let Lord Warburton pass without giving him a look.

This nobleman, however, had noticed the melancholy youth, and he asked Isabel who her dismal friend was, remarking that he had seen him somewhere before.

"It's the young man I've told you about, who's in love with Pansy."

"Ah yes, I remember. He looks rather bad."

"He has reason. My husband won't listen to him."

"What's the matter with him?" Lord Warburton enquired. "He seems very harmless."

"He hasn't money enough, and he isn't very clever."

Lord Warburton listened with interest; he seemed struck with this account of Edward Rosier. "Dear me; he looked a well-set-up young fellow."

"So he is, but my husband's very particular."

"Oh, I see." And Lord Warburton paused a moment. "How much money has he got?" he then ventured to ask.

"Some forty thousand francs a year."

"Sixteen hundred pounds? Ah, but that's very good, you know."

"So I think. My husband, however, has larger ideas."

"Yes; I've noticed that your husband has very large ideas. Is he really an idiot, the young man?"

"An idiot? Not in the least; he's charming. When he was twelve years old I myself was in love with him."

"He doesn't look much more than twelve to-day," Lord Warburton rejoined vaguely, looking about him. Then with more point, "Don't you think we might sit here?" he asked.

"Wherever you please." The room was a sort of boudoir, pervaded by a subdued, rose-coloured light; a lady and gentleman moved out of it as our friends came in. "It's very kind of you to take such an interest in Mr. Rosier," Isabel said.

"He seems to me rather ill-treated. He had a face a yard long. I wondered what ailed him."

"You're a just man," said Isabel. "You've a kind thought even for a rival."

Lord Warburton suddenly turned with a stare. "A rival! Do you call him my rival?"

"Surely—if you both wish to marry the same person."

"Yes—but since he has no chance!"

"I like you, however that may be, for putting your self in his place. It shows imagination."

"You like me for it?" And Lord Warburton looked at her with an uncertain eye. "I think you mean you're laughing at me for it."

"Yes, I'm laughing at you a little. But I like you as somebody to laugh at."

"Ah well, then, let me enter into his situation a little more. What do you suppose one could do for him?"

"Since I have been praising your imagination I'll leave you to imagine that yourself," Isabel said. "Pansy too would like you for that."

"Miss Osmond? Ah, she, I flatter myself, likes me already."

"Very much, I think."

He waited a little; he was still questioning her face. "Well then, I don't understand you. You don't mean that she cares for him?"

A quick blush sprang to his brow. "You told me she would have no wish apart from her father's, and as I've gathered that he would favour me—!" He paused a little and then suggested "Don't you see?" through his blush.

"Yes, I told you she has an immense wish to please her father, and that it would probably take her very far."

"That seems to me a very proper feeling," said Lord Warburton.

"Certainly; it's a very proper feeling." Isabel remained silent for some moments; the room continued empty; the sound of the music reached them with its richness softened by the interposing apartments. Then at last she said: "But it hardly strikes me as the sort of feeling to which a man would wish to be indebted for a wife."

"I don't know; if the wife's a good one and he thinks she does well!"

"Yes, of course you must think that."

"I do; I can't help it. You call that very British, of course."

"No, I don't. I think Pansy would do wonderfully well to marry you, and I don't know who should know it better than you. But you're not in love."

"Ah, yes I am, Mrs. Osmond!"

Isabel shook her head. "You like to think you are while you sit here with me. But that's not how you strike me."

"I'm not like the young man in the doorway. I admit that. But what makes it so unnatural? Could any one in the world be more loveable than Miss Osmond?"

"No one, possibly. But love has nothing to do with good reasons."

"I don't agree with you. I'm delighted to have good reasons."

"Of course you are. If you were really in love you wouldn't care a straw for them."

"Ah, really in love—really in love!" Lord Warburton exclaimed, folding his arms, leaning back his head and stretching himself a little. "You must remember that I'm forty-two years old. I won't pretend I'm as I once was."

"Well, if you're sure," said Isabel, "it's all right."

He answered nothing; he sat there, with his head back, looking before him. Abruptly, however, he changed his position; he turned quickly to his friend. "Why are you so unwilling, so sceptical?" She met his eyes, and for a moment they looked straight at each other. If she wished to be satisfied she saw something that satisfied her;

she saw in his expression the gleam of an idea that she was uneasy on her own account—that she was perhaps even in fear. It showed a suspicion, not a hope, but such as it was it told her what she wanted to know. Not for an instant should he suspect her of detecting in his proposal of marrying her step-daughter an implication of increased nearness to herself, or of thinking it, on such a betrayal, ominous. In that brief, extremely personal gaze, however, deeper meanings passed between them than they were conscious of at the moment.

"My dear Lord Warburton," she said, smiling, "you may do, so far as I'm concerned, whatever comes into your head."

And with this she got up and wandered into the adjoining room, where, within her companion's view, she was immediately addressed by a pair of gentlemen, high personages in the Roman world, who met her as if they had been looking for her. While she talked with them she found herself regretting she had moved; it looked a little like running away—all the more as Lord Warburton didn't follow her. She was glad of this, however, and at any rate she was satisfied. She was so well satisfied that when, in passing back into the ball-room, she found Edward Rosier still planted in the doorway, she stopped and spoke to him again. "You did right not to go away. I've some comfort for you."

"I need it," the young man softly wailed, "when I see you so awfully thick with him!"

"Don't speak of him; I'll do what I can for you. I'm afraid it won't be much, but what I can I'll do."

He looked at her with gloomy obliqueness. "What has suddenly brought you round?"

"The sense that you are an inconvenience in doorways!" she answered, smiling as she passed him. Half an hour later she took leave, with Pansy, and at the foot of the staircase the two ladies, with many other departing guests, waited a while for their carriage. Just as it approached Lord Warburton came out of the house and assisted them to reach their vehicle. He stood a moment at the door, asking Pansy if she had amused herself; and she, having answered him, fell back with a little air of fatigue. Then Isabel, at the window, detaining him by a movement of her finger, murmured gently: "Don't forget to send your letter to her father!"

CHAPTER XLIV

The Countess Gemini was often extremely bored—bored, in her own phrase, to extinction. She had not been extinguished, however, and she struggled bravely enough with her destiny, which had been to marry an unaccommodating Florentine who insisted upon living in his native town, where he enjoyed such consideration as might attach to a gentleman whose talent for losing at cards had not the merit of being incidental to an obliging disposition. The Count Gemini was not liked even by those who won from him; and he bore a name which, having a measurable value in Florence, was, like the local coin of the old Italian states, without currency in other parts of the peninsula. In Rome he was simply a very dull Florentine, and it is not remarkable that he should not have cared to pay frequent visits to a place where, to carry it off, his dulness needed more explanation than was convenient. The Countess lived with her eyes upon Rome, and it was the constant grievance of her life that she had not an habitation there. She was ashamed to say how seldom she had been allowed to visit that city; it scarcely made the matter better that there were other members of the Florentine nobility who never had been there at all. She went whenever she could; that was all she could say. Or rather not all, but all she said she could say. In fact she had much more to say about it, and had often set forth the reasons why she hated Florence and wished to end her days in the shadow of Saint Peter's. They are reasons, however, that do not closely concern us, and were usually summed up in the declaration that Rome, in short, was the Eternal City and that Florence was simply a pretty little place like any other. The Countess apparently needed to connect the idea of eternity with her amusements. She was convinced that society was infinitely more interesting in Rome, where you met celebrities all winter at evening parties. At Florence there were no celebrities; none at least that one had heard of. Since her brother's marriage her impatience had greatly increased; she was so sure his wife had a more brilliant life than herself. She was not so intellectual as Isabel, but she was intellectual enough to do justice to Rome—not to the ruins and the catacombs, not even perhaps to the monuments and museums, the church ceremonies and the scenery; but certainly to all the rest. She heard a great deal about her sister-in-law and knew perfectly that Isabel was having a beautiful time. She had indeed seen it for herself on the only occasion on which she had enjoyed the hospitality of Palazzo Roccanera. She had spent a week there during the first winter of her brother's marriage, but she had not been encouraged to renew this satisfaction. Osmond didn't want her—that she was perfectly aware of; but she would have gone all the same, for after all she didn't care two straws about Osmond. It was her husband who wouldn't let her, and the money question was always a trouble. Isabel had been very nice; the Countess, who had liked her sister-in-law from the first, had not been blinded by envy to Isabel's personal merits. She had always observed that she got on better with clever women than with silly ones like herself; the silly ones could never understand her wisdom, whereas the clever ones—the really clever ones—always understood her silliness. It appeared to her that, different as they were in appearance and general style, Isabel and she had somewhere a patch of common ground that they would set their feet upon at last. It was not very large, but it was firm, and they should both know it when once they had really touched it. And then she lived, with Mrs. Osmond, under the influence of a pleasant surprise; she was constantly expecting that Isabel would "look down" on her, and she as constantly saw this operation postponed. She asked herself when it would begin, like fire-works, or Lent, or the opera season; not that she cared much, but she wondered what kept it in abeyance. Her sister-in-law regarded her with none but level glances and expressed for the poor Countess as little contempt as admiration. In reality Isabel would as soon have thought of despising her as of passing a moral judgement on a grasshopper. She was not indifferent to her husband's sister, however; she was rather a little afraid of her. She wondered at her; she thought her very extraordinary. The Countess seemed to her to have no soul; she was like a bright rare shell, with a polished surface and a remarkably pink lip, in which something would rattle when you shook it. This rattle was apparently the Countess's spiritual principle, a little loose nut that tumbled about inside of her. She was too odd for disdain, too anomalous for comparisons. Isabel would have invited her again (there was no question of inviting the Count); but Osmond, after his marriage, had not scrupled to say frankly that Amy was a fool of the worst species—a fool whose folly had the irrepressibility of genius. He said at another time that she had no heart; and he added in a moment that she had given it all away—in small pieces, like a frosted wedding-cake. The fact of not having been asked was of course another obstacle to the Countess's going again to Rome; but at the period with which this history has now to deal she was in receipt of an invitation to spend several weeks at Palazzo Roccanera. The proposal had come from Osmond himself, who wrote to his sister that she must be prepared to be very quiet. Whether or no she found in this phrase all the meaning he had put into it I am unable to say; but she accepted the invitation on any terms. She was curious, moreover; for one of the impressions of her former visit had been that her brother had found his match. Before the marriage she had been sorry for Isabel, so sorry as to have had serious thoughts—if any of the Countess's thoughts were serious—of putting her on her guard. But she had let that pass, and after a little she was reassured. Osmond was as lofty as ever, but his wife would not be an easy victim. The Countess was not very exact at measurements, but it seemed to her that if Isabel should draw herself up she would be the taller spirit of the two. What she wanted to learn now was whether Isabel had drawn herself up; it would give her immense pleasure to see Osmond overtopped.

Several days before she was to start for Rome a servant brought her the card of a visitor—a card with the simple superscription "Henrietta C. Stackpole." The Countess pressed her finger-tips to her forehead; she didn't remember to have known any such Henrietta as that. The servant then remarked that the lady had requested him to say that if the Countess should not recognise her name she would know her well enough on seeing her. By the time she appeared before her visitor she had in fact reminded herself that there was once a literary lady at Mrs. Touchett's; the only woman of letters she had ever encountered—that is the only modern one, since she was the daughter of a defunct poetess. She recognised Miss Stackpole immediately, the more so that Miss Stackpole seemed perfectly unchanged; and the Countess, who was thoroughly good-natured, thought it rather fine to be called on by a person of that sort of distinction. She wondered if Miss Stackpole had come on account of her mother—whether she had heard of the American Corinne. Her mother was not at all like Isabel's friend; the Countess could see at a glance that this lady was much more contemporary; and she received an impression of the improvements that were taking place—chiefly in distant countries—in the character (the professional character) of literary ladies. Her mother had been used to wear a Roman scarf thrown over a pair of shoulders timorously bared of their tight black velvet (oh the old clothes!) and a gold laurel-wreath set upon a multitude of glossy ringlets. She had spoken softly and vaguely, with the accent of her "Creole" ancestors, as she always confessed; she sighed a great deal and was not at all enterprising. But Henrietta, the Countess could see, was always closely buttoned and compactly braided; there was something brisk and business-like in her appearance; her manner was almost conscientiously familiar. It was as impossible to imagine her ever vaguely sighing as to imagine a letter posted without its address. The Countess could not but feel that the correspondent of the Interviewer was much more in the movement than the American Corinne. She explained that she had called on the Countess because she was the only person she knew in Florence, and that when she visited a foreign city she liked to see something more than superficial travellers. She knew Mrs. Touchett, but Mrs. Touchett was in America, and even if she had been in Florence Henrietta would not have put herself out for her, since Mrs. Touchett was not one of her admirations.

"Do you mean by that that I am?" the Countess graciously asked.

"Well, I like you better than I do her," said Miss Stackpole. "I seem to remember that when I saw you before you were very interesting. I don't know whether it was an accident or whether it's your usual style. At any rate I was a good deal struck with what you said. I made use of it afterwards in print."

"Dear me!" cried the Countess, staring and half-alarmed; "I had no idea I ever said anything remarkable! I wish I had known it at the time."

"It was about the position of woman in this city," Miss Stackpole remarked. "You threw a good deal of light upon it."

"The position of woman's very uncomfortable. Is that what you mean? And you wrote it down and published it?" the Countess went on. "Ah, do let me see it!"

"I'll write to them to send you the paper if you like," Henrietta said. "I didn't mention your name; I only said a lady of high rank. And then I quoted your views."

The Countess threw herself hastily backward, tossing up her clasped hands. "Do you know I'm rather sorry you didn't mention my name? I should have rather liked to see my name in the papers. I forget what my views were; I have so many! But I'm not ashamed of them. I'm not at all like my brother—I suppose you know my brother? He thinks it a kind of scandal to be put in the papers; if you were to quote him he'd never forgive you."

"He needn't be afraid; I shall never refer to him," said Miss Stackpole with bland dryness. "That's another reason," she added, "why I wanted to come to see you. You know Mr. Osmond married my dearest friend."

"Ah, yes; you were a friend of Isabel's. I was trying to think what I knew about you."

"I'm quite willing to be known by that," Henrietta declared. "But that isn't what your brother likes to know me by. He has tried to break up my relations with Isabel."

"Don't permit it," said the Countess.

"That's what I want to talk about. I'm going to Rome."

"So am I!" the Countess cried. "We'll go together."

"With great pleasure. And when I write about my journey I'll mention you by name as my companion."

The Countess sprang from her chair and came and sat on the sofa beside her visitor. "Ah, you must send me the paper! My husband won't like it, but he need never see it. Besides, he doesn't know how to read."

Henrietta's large eyes became immense. "Doesn't know how to read? May I put that into my letter?"

"Into your letter?"

"In the Interviewer. That's my paper."

"Oh yes, if you like; with his name. Are you going to stay with Isabel?"

Henrietta held up her head, gazing a little in silence at her hostess. "She has not asked me. I wrote to her I was coming, and she answered that she would engage a room for me at a pension. She gave no reason."

The Countess listened with extreme interest. "The reason's Osmond," she pregnantly remarked.

"Isabel ought to make a stand," said Miss Stackpole. "I'm afraid she has changed a great deal. I told her she would."

"I'm sorry to hear it; I hoped she would have her own way. Why doesn't my brother like you?" the Countess ingenuously added.

"I don't know and I don't care. He's perfectly welcome not to like me; I don't want every one to like me; I should think less of myself if some people did. A journalist can't hope to do much good unless he gets a good deal hated; that's the way he knows how his work goes on. And it's just the same for a lady. But I didn't expect it of Isabel."

"Do you mean that she hates you?" the Countess enquired.

"I don't know; I want to see. That's what I'm going to Rome for."

"Dear me, what a tiresome errand!" the Countess exclaimed.

"She doesn't write to me in the same way; it's easy to see there's a difference. If you know anything," Miss Stackpole went on, "I should like to hear it beforehand, so as to decide on the line I shall take."

The Countess thrust out her under lip and gave a gradual shrug. "I know very little; I see and hear very little of Osmond. He doesn't like me any better than he appears to like you."

"Yet you're not a lady correspondent," said Henrietta pensively.

"Oh, he has plenty of reasons. Nevertheless they've invited me—I'm to stay in the house!" And the Countess smiled almost fiercely; her exultation, for the moment, took little account of Miss Stackpole's disappointment.

This lady, however, regarded it very placidly. "I shouldn't have gone if she HAD asked me. That is I think I shouldn't; and I'm glad I hadn't to make up my mind. It would have been a very difficult question. I shouldn't have liked to turn away from her, and yet I shouldn't have been happy under her roof. A pension will suit me very well. But that's not all."

"Rome's very good just now," said the Countess; "there are all sorts of brilliant people. Did you ever hear of Lord Warburton?"

"Hear of him? I know him very well. Do you consider him very brilliant?" Henrietta enquired.

"I don't know him, but I'm told he's extremely grand seigneur. He's making love to Isabel."

"Making love to her?"

"So I'm told; I don't know the details," said the Countess lightly. "But Isabel's pretty safe."

Henrietta gazed earnestly at her companion; for a moment she said nothing. "When do you go to Rome?" she enquired abruptly.

"Not for a week, I'm afraid."

"I shall go to-morrow," Henrietta said. "I think I had better not wait."

"Dear me, I'm sorry; I'm having some dresses made. I'm told Isabel receives immensely. But I shall see you there; I shall call on you at your pension." Henrietta sat still—she was lost in thought; and suddenly the Countess cried: "Ah, but if you don't go with me you can't describe our journey!"

Miss Stackpole seemed unmoved by this consideration; she was thinking of something else and presently expressed it. "I'm not sure that I understand you about Lord Warburton."

"Understand me? I mean he's very nice, that's all."

"Do you consider it nice to make love to married women?" Henrietta enquired with unprecedented distinctness.

The Countess stared, and then with a little violent laugh: "It's certain all the nice men do it. Get married and you'll see!" she added.

"That idea would be enough to prevent me," said Miss Stackpole. "I should want my own husband; I shouldn't want any one else's. Do you mean that Isabel's guilty—guilty—?" And she paused a little, choosing her expression.

"Do I mean she's guilty? Oh dear no, not yet, I hope. I only mean that Osmond's very tiresome and that Lord Warburton, as I hear, is a great deal at the house. I'm afraid you're scandalised."

"No, I'm just anxious," Henrietta said.

"Ah, you're not very complimentary to Isabel! You should have more confidence. I'll tell you," the Countess added quickly: "if it will be a comfort to you I engage to draw him off."

Miss Stackpole answered at first only with the deeper solemnity of her gaze. "You don't understand me," she said after a while. "I haven't the idea you seem to suppose. I'm not afraid for Isabel—in that way. I'm only afraid she's unhappy—that's what I want to get at."

The Countess gave a dozen turns of the head; she looked impatient and sarcastic. "That may very well be; for my part I should like to know whether Osmond is." Miss Stackpole had begun a little to bore her.

"If she's really changed that must be at the bottom of it," Henrietta went on.

"You'll see; she'll tell you," said the Countess.

"Ah, she may NOT tell me—that's what I'm afraid of!"

"Well, if Osmond isn't amusing himself—in his own old way—I flatter myself I shall discover it," the Countess rejoined.

"I don't care for that," said Henrietta.

"I do immensely! If Isabel's unhappy I'm very sorry for her, but I can't help it. I might tell her something that would make her worse, but I can't tell her anything that would console her. What did she go and marry him for? If she had listened to me she'd have got rid of him. I'll forgive her, however, if I find she has made things hot for him! If she has simply allowed him to trample upon her I don't know that I shall even pity her. But I don't think that's very likely. I count upon finding that if she's miserable she has at least made HIM so."

Henrietta got up; these seemed to her, naturally, very dreadful expectations. She honestly believed she had no desire to see Mr. Osmond unhappy; and indeed he could not be for her the subject of a flight of fancy. She was on the whole rather disappointed in the Countess, whose mind moved in a narrower circle than she had imagined, though with a capacity for coarseness even there. "It will be better if they love each other," she said for edification.

"They can't. He can't love any one."

"I presumed that was the case. But it only aggravates my fear for Isabel. I shall positively start to-morrow."

"Isabel certainly has devotees," said the Countess, smiling very vividly. "I declare I don't pity her."

"It may be I can't assist her," Miss Stackpole pursued, as if it were well not to have illusions.

"You can have wanted to, at any rate; that's something. I believe that's what you came from America for," the Countess suddenly added.

"Yes, I wanted to look after her," Henrietta said serenely.

Her hostess stood there smiling at her with small bright eyes and an eager-looking nose; with cheeks into each of which a flush had come. "Ah, that's very pretty c'est bien gentil! Isn't it what they call friendship?"

"I don't know what they call it. I thought I had better come."

"She's very happy—she's very fortunate," the Countess went on. "She has others besides." And then she broke out passionately. "She's more fortunate than I! I'm as unhappy as she—I've a very bad husband; he's a great deal worse than Osmond. And I've no friends. I thought I had, but they're gone. No one, man or woman, would do for me what you've done for her."

Henrietta was touched; there was nature in this bitter effusion. She gazed at her companion a moment, and then: "Look here, Countess, I'll do anything for you that you like. I'll wait over and travel with you."

"Never mind," the Countess answered with a quick change of tone: "only describe me in the newspaper!"

Henrietta, before leaving her, however, was obliged to make her understand that she could give no fictitious representation of her journey to Rome. Miss Stackpole was a strictly veracious reporter. On quitting her she took the way to the Lung' Arno, the sunny quay beside the yellow river where the bright-faced inns familiar to tourists stand all in a row. She had learned her way before this through the streets of Florence (she was very quick in such matters), and was therefore able to turn with great decision of step out of the little square which forms the approach to the bridge of the Holy Trinity. She proceeded to the left, toward the Ponte Vecchio, and stopped in front of one of the hotels which overlook that delightful structure. Here she drew forth a small pocket-book, took from it a card and a pencil and, after meditating a moment, wrote a few words. It is our privilege to look over her shoulder, and if we exercise it we may read the brief query: "Could I see you this evening for a few moments on a very important matter?" Henrietta added that she should start on the morrow for Rome. Armed with this little document she approached the porter, who now had taken up his station in the doorway, and asked if Mr. Goodwood were at home. The porter replied, as porters always reply, that he had gone out about twenty minutes before; whereupon Henrietta presented her card and begged it might be handed him on his return. She left the inn and pursued her course along the quay to the severe portico of the Uffizi, through which she presently reached the entrance of the famous gallery of paintings. Making her way in, she ascended the high staircase which leads to the upper chambers. The long corridor, glazed on one side and decorated with antique busts, which gives admission to these apartments, presented an empty vista in which the bright winter light twinkled upon the marble floor. The gallery is very cold and during the midwinter weeks but scantily visited. Miss Stackpole may appear more ardent in her quest of artistic beauty than she has hitherto struck us as being, but she had after all her preferences and admirations. One of the latter was the little Correggio of the Tribune—the Virgin kneeling down before the sacred infant, who lies in a litter of straw, and clapping her hands to him while he delightedly laughs and crows. Henrietta had a special devotion to this intimate scene—she thought it the most beautiful picture in the world. On her way, at present, from New York to Rome, she was spending but three days in Florence, and yet reminded herself that they must not elapse without her paying another visit to her favourite work of art. She had a great sense of beauty in all ways, and it involved a good many intellectual obligations. She was about to turn into the Tribune when a gentleman came out of it; whereupon she gave a little exclamation and stood before Caspar Goodwood.

"I've just been at your hotel," she said. "I left a card for you."

"I'm very much honoured," Caspar Goodwood answered as if he really meant it.

"It was not to honour you I did it; I've called on you before and I know you don't like it. It was to talk to you a little about something."

He looked for a moment at the buckle in her hat. "I shall be very glad to hear what you wish to say."

"You don't like to talk with me," said Henrietta. "But I don't care for that; I don't talk for your amusement. I wrote a word to ask you to come and see me; but since I've met you here this will do as well."

"I was just going away," Goodwood stated; "but of course I'll stop." He was civil, but not enthusiastic.

Henrietta, however, never looked for great professions, and she was so much in earnest that she was thankful he would listen to her on any terms. She asked him first, none the less, if he had seen all the pictures.

"All I want to. I've been here an hour."

"I wonder if you've seen my Correggio," said Henrietta. "I came up on purpose to have a look at it." She went into the Tribune and he slowly accompanied her.

"I suppose I've seen it, but I didn't know it was yours. I don't remember pictures—especially that sort." She had pointed out her favourite work, and he asked her if it was about Correggio she wished to talk with him.

"No," said Henrietta, "it's about something less harmonious!" They had the small, brilliant room, a splendid cabinet of treasures, to themselves; there was only a custode hovering about the Medicean Venus. "I want you to do me a favour," Miss Stackpole went on.

Caspar Goodwood frowned a little, but he expressed no embarrassment at the sense of not looking eager. His face was that of a much older man than our earlier friend. "I'm sure it's something I shan't like," he said rather loudly.

"No, I don't think you'll like it. If you did it would be no favour."

"Well, let's hear it," he went on in the tone of a man quite conscious of his patience.

"You may say there's no particular reason why you should do me a favour. Indeed I only know of one: the fact that if you'd let me I'd gladly do you one." Her soft, exact tone, in which there was no attempt at effect, had an extreme sincerity; and her companion, though he presented rather a hard surface, couldn't help being touched by it. When he was touched he rarely showed it, however, by the usual signs; he neither blushed, nor looked away, nor looked conscious. He only fixed his attention more directly; he seemed to consider with added firmness. Henrietta continued therefore disinterestedly, without the sense of an advantage. "I may say now, indeed—it seems a good time—that if I've ever annoyed you (and I think sometimes I have) it's because I knew I was willing to suffer annoyance for you. I've troubled you—doubtless. But I'd TAKE trouble for you."

Goodwood hesitated. "You're taking trouble now."

"Yes, I am—some. I want you to consider whether it's better on the whole that you should go to Rome."

"I thought you were going to say that!" he answered rather artlessly.

"You HAVE considered it then?"

"Of course I have, very carefully. I've looked all round it. Otherwise I shouldn't have come so far as this. That's what I stayed in Paris two months for. I was thinking it over."

"I'm afraid you decided as you liked. You decided it was best because you were so much attracted."

"Best for whom, do you mean?" Goodwood demanded.

"Well, for yourself first. For Mrs. Osmond next."

"Oh, it won't do HER any good! I don't flatter myself that."

"Won't it do her some harm?—that's the question."

"I don't see what it will matter to her. I'm nothing to Mrs. Osmond. But if you want to know, I do want to see her myself."

"Yes, and that's why you go."

"Of course it is. Could there be a better reason?"

"How will it help you?—that's what I want to know," said Miss Stackpole.

"That's just what I can't tell you. It's just what I was thinking about in Paris."

"It will make you more discontented."

"Why do you say 'more' so?" Goodwood asked rather sternly. "How do you know I'm discontented?"

"Well," said Henrietta, hesitating a little, "you seem never to have cared for another."

"How do you know what I care for?" he cried with a big blush. "Just now I care to go to Rome."

Henrietta looked at him in silence, with a sad yet luminous expression. "Well," she observed at last, "I only wanted to tell you what I think; I had it on my mind. Of course you think it's none of my business. But nothing is any one's business, on that principle."

"It's very kind of you; I'm greatly obliged to you for your interest," said Caspar Goodwood. "I shall go to Rome and I shan't hurt Mrs. Osmond."

"You won't hurt her, perhaps. But will you help her?—that's the real issue."

"Is she in need of help?" he asked slowly, with a penetrating look.

"Most women always are," said Henrietta, with conscientious evasiveness and generalising less hopefully than usual. "If you go to Rome," she added, "I hope you'll be a true friend—not a selfish one!" And she turned off and began to look at the pictures.

Caspar Goodwood let her go and stood watching her while she wandered round the room; but after a moment he rejoined her. "You've heard something about her here," he then resumed. "I should like to know what you've heard."

Henrietta had never prevaricated in her life, and, though on this occasion there might have been a fitness in doing so, she decided, after thinking some minutes, to make no superficial exception. "Yes, I've heard," she answered; "but as I don't want you to go to Rome I won't tell you."

"Just as you please. I shall see for myself," he said. Then inconsistently, for him, "You've heard she's unhappy!" he added.

"Oh, you won't see that!" Henrietta exclaimed.

"I hope not. When do you start?"

"To-morrow, by the evening train. And you?"

Goodwood hung back; he had no desire to make his journey to Rome in Miss Stackpole's company. His indifference to this advantage was not of the same character as Gilbert Osmond's, but it had at this moment an equal distinctness. It was rather a tribute to Miss Stackpole's virtues than a reference to her faults. He thought her very remarkable, very brilliant, and he had, in theory, no objection to the class to which she belonged. Lady correspondents appeared to him a part of the natural scheme of things in a progressive country, and though he never read their letters he supposed that they ministered somehow to social prosperity. But it was this very eminence of their position that made him wish Miss Stackpole didn't take so much for granted. She took for granted that he was always ready for some allusion to Mrs. Osmond; she had done so when they met in Paris, six weeks after his arrival in Europe, and she had repeated the assumption with every successive opportunity. He had no wish whatever to allude to Mrs. Osmond; he was NOT always thinking of her; he was perfectly sure of that. He was the most reserved, the least colloquial of men, and this enquiring authoress was constantly flashing her lantern into the quiet darkness of his soul. He wished she didn't care so much; he even wished, though it might seem rather brutal of him, that she would leave him alone. In spite of this, however, he just now made other reflections—which show how widely different, in effect, his ill-humour was from Gilbert Osmond's. He desired to go immediately to Rome; he would have liked to go alone, in the night-train. He hated the European railway-carriages, in which one sat for hours in a vise, knee to knee and nose to nose with a foreigner to whom one presently found one's self objecting with all the added vehemence of one's wish to have the window open; and if they were worse at night even than by day, at least at night one could sleep and dream of an American saloon-car. But he couldn't take a night-train when Miss Stackpole was starting in the morning; it struck him that this would be an insult to an unprotected woman. Nor could he wait until after she had gone unless he should wait longer than he had patience for. It wouldn't do to start the next day. She worried him; she oppressed him; the idea of spending the day in a European railway-carriage with her offered a complication of irritations. Still, she was a lady travelling alone; it was his duty to put himself out for her. There could be no two questions about that; it was a perfectly clear necessity. He looked extremely grave for some moments and then said, wholly without the flourish of gallantry but in a tone of extreme distinctness, "Of course if you're going to-morrow I'll go too, as I may be of assistance to you."

"Well, Mr. Goodwood, I should hope so!" Henrietta returned imperturbably.

CHAPTER XLV

I have already had reason to say that Isabel knew her husband to be displeased by the continuance of Ralph's visit to Rome. That knowledge was very present to her as she went to her cousin's hotel the day after she had invited Lord Warburton to give a tangible proof of his sincerity; and at this moment, as at others, she had a sufficient perception of the sources of Osmond's opposition. He wished her to have no freedom of mind, and he knew perfectly well that Ralph was an apostle of freedom. It was just because he was this, Isabel said to herself, that it was a refreshment to go and see him. It will be perceived that she partook of this refreshment in spite of her husband's aversion to it, that is partook of it, as she flattered herself, discreetly. She had not as yet undertaken to act in direct opposition to his wishes; he was her appointed and inscribed master; she gazed at moments with a sort of incredulous blankness at this fact. It weighed upon her imagination, however; constantly present to her mind were all the traditionary decencies and sanctities of marriage. The idea of violating them filled her with shame as well as with dread, for on giving herself away she had lost sight of this contingency in the perfect belief that her husband's intentions were as generous as her own. She seemed to see, none the less, the rapid approach of the day when she should have to take back something she had solemnly bestown. Such a ceremony would be odious and monstrous; she tried to shut her eyes to it meanwhile. Osmond would do nothing to help it by beginning first; he would put that burden upon her to the end. He had not yet formally forbidden her to call upon Ralph; but she felt sure that unless Ralph should very soon depart this prohibition would come. How could poor Ralph depart? The weather as yet made it impossible. She could perfectly understand her husband's wish for the event; she didn't, to be just, see how he COULD like her to be with her cousin. Ralph never said a word against him, but Osmond's sore, mute protest was none the less founded. If he should positively interpose, if he should put forth his authority, she would have to decide, and that wouldn't be easy. The prospect made her heart beat and her cheeks burn, as I say, in advance; there were moments when, in her wish to avoid an open rupture, she found herself wishing Ralph would start even at a risk. And it was of no use that, when catching herself in this state of mind, she called herself a feeble spirit, a coward. It was not that she loved Ralph less, but that almost anything seemed preferable to repudiating the most serious act—the single sacred act—of her life. That appeared to make the whole future hideous. To break with Osmond once would be to break for ever; any open acknowledgement of irreconcilable needs would be an admission that their whole attempt had proved a failure. For them there could be no condonement, no compromise, no easy forgetfulness, no formal readjustment. They had attempted only one thing, but that one thing was to have been exquisite. Once they missed it nothing else would do; there was no conceivable substitute for that success. For the moment, Isabel went to the Hotel de Paris as often as she thought well; the measure of propriety was in the canon of taste, and there couldn't have been a better proof that morality was, so to speak, a matter of earnest appreciation. Isabel's application of that measure had been particularly free to-day, for in addition to the general truth that she couldn't leave Ralph to die alone she had something important to ask of him. This indeed was Gilbert's business as well as her own.

She came very soon to what she wished to speak of. "I want you to answer me a question. It's about Lord Warburton."

"I think I guess your question," Ralph answered from his arm-chair, out of which his thin legs protruded at greater length than ever.

"Very possibly you guess it. Please then answer it."

"Oh, I don't say I can do that."

"You're intimate with him," she said; "you've a great deal of observation of him."

"Very true. But think how he must dissimulate!"

"Why should he dissimulate? That's not his nature."

"Ah, you must remember that the circumstances are peculiar," said Ralph with an air of private amusement.

"To a certain extent—yes. But is he really in love?"

"Very much, I think. I can make that out."

"Ah!" said Isabel with a certain dryness.

Ralph looked at her as if his mild hilarity had been touched with mystification. "You say that as if you were disappointed."

Isabel got up, slowly smoothing her gloves and eyeing them thoughtfully. "It's after all no business of mine."

"You're very philosophic," said her cousin. And then in a moment: "May I enquire what you're talking about?"

Isabel stared. "I thought you knew. Lord Warburton tells me he wants, of all things in the world, to marry Pansy. I've told you that before, without eliciting a comment from you. You might risk one this morning, I think. Is it your belief that he really cares for her?"

"Ah, for Pansy, no!" cried Ralph very positively.

"But you said just now he did."

Ralph waited a moment. "That he cared for you, Mrs. Osmond."

Isabel shook her head gravely. "That's nonsense, you know."

"Of course it is. But the nonsense is Warburton's, not mine."

"That would be very tiresome." She spoke, as she flattered herself, with much subtlety.

"I ought to tell you indeed," Ralph went on, "that to me he has denied it."

"It's very good of you to talk about it together! Has he also told you that he's in love with Pansy?"

"He has spoken very well of her—very properly. He has let me know, of course, that he thinks she would do very well at Lockleigh."

"Does he really think it?"

"Ah, what Warburton really thinks—!" said Ralph.

Isabel fell to smoothing her gloves again; they were long, loose gloves on which she could freely expend herself. Soon, however, she looked up, and then, "Ah, Ralph, you give me no help!" she cried abruptly and passionately.

It was the first time she had alluded to the need for help, and the words shook her cousin with their violence. He gave a long murmur of relief, of pity, of tenderness; it seemed to him that at last the gulf between them had been bridged. It was this that made him exclaim in a moment: "How unhappy you must be!"

He had no sooner spoken than she recovered her self-possession, and the first use she made of it was to pretend she had not heard him. "When I talk of your helping me I talk great nonsense," she said with a quick smile. "The idea of my troubling you with my domestic embarrassments! The matter's very simple; Lord Warburton must get on by himself. I can't undertake to see him through."

"He ought to succeed easily," said Ralph.

Isabel debated. "Yes—but he has not always succeeded."

"Very true. You know, however, how that always surprised me. Is Miss Osmond capable of giving us a surprise?"

"It will come from him, rather. I seem to see that after all he'll let the matter drop."

"He'll do nothing dishonourable," said Ralph.

"I'm very sure of that. Nothing can be more honourable than for him to leave the poor child alone. She cares for another person, and it's cruel to attempt to bribe her by magnificent offers to give him up."

"Cruel to the other person perhaps—the one she cares for. But Warburton isn't obliged to mind that."

"No, cruel to her," said Isabel. "She would be very unhappy if she were to allow herself to be persuaded to desert poor Mr. Rosier. That idea seems to amuse you; of course you're not in love with him. He has the merit—for Pansy—of being in love with Pansy. She can see at a glance that Lord Warburton isn't."

"He'd be very good to her," said Ralph.

"He has been good to her already. Fortunately, however, he has not said a word to disturb her. He could come and bid her good-bye to-morrow with perfect propriety."

"How would your husband like that?"

"Not at all; and he may be right in not liking it. Only he must obtain satisfaction himself."

"Has he commissioned you to obtain it?" Ralph ventured to ask.

"It was natural that as an old friend of Lord Warburton's—an older friend, that is, than Gilbert—I should take an interest in his intentions."

"Take an interest in his renouncing them, you mean?"

Isabel hesitated, frowning a little. "Let me understand. Are you pleading his cause?"

"Not in the least. I'm very glad he shouldn't become your stepdaughter's husband. It makes such a very queer relation to you!" said Ralph, smiling. "But I'm rather nervous lest your husband should think you haven't pushed him enough."

Isabel found herself able to smile as well as he. "He knows me well enough not to have expected me to push. He himself has no intention of pushing, I presume. I'm not afraid I shall not be able to justify myself!" she said lightly.

Her mask had dropped for an instant, but she had put it on again, to Ralph's infinite disappointment. He had caught a glimpse of her natural face and he wished immensely to look into it. He had an almost savage desire to hear her complain of her husband—hear her say that she should be held accountable for Lord Warburton's defection. Ralph was certain that this was her situation; he knew by instinct, in advance, the form that in such an event Osmond's displeasure would take. It could only take the meanest and cruellest. He would have liked to warn Isabel of it—to let her see at least how he judged for her and how he knew. It little mattered that Isabel would know much better; it was for his own satisfaction more than for hers that he longed to show her he was not deceived. He tried and tried again to make her betray Osmond; he felt cold-blooded, cruel, dishonourable almost, in doing so. But it scarcely mattered, for he only failed. What had she come for then, and why did she seem almost to offer him a chance to violate their tacit convention? Why did she ask him his advice if she gave him no liberty to answer her? How could they talk of her domestic embarrassments, as it pleased her humorously to designate them, if the principal factor was not to be mentioned? These contradictions were themselves but an indication of her trouble, and her cry for help, just before, was the only thing he was bound to consider. "You'll be decidedly at variance, all the same," he said in a moment. And as she answered nothing, looking as if she scarce understood, "You'll find yourselves thinking very differently," he continued.

"That may easily happen, among the most united couples!" She took up her parasol; he saw she was nervous, afraid of what he might say. "It's a matter we can hardly quarrel about, however," she added; "for almost all the interest is on his side. That's very natural. Pansy's after all his daughter—not mine." And she put out her hand to wish him goodbye.

Ralph took an inward resolution that she shouldn't leave him without his letting her know that he knew everything: it seemed too great an opportunity to lose. "Do you know what his interest will make him say?" he asked as he took her hand. She shook her head, rather dryly—not discouragingly—and he went on. "It will make him say that your want of zeal is owing to jealousy." He stopped a moment; her face made him afraid.

"To jealousy?"

"To jealousy of his daughter."

She blushed red and threw back her head. "You're not kind," she said in a voice that he had never heard on her lips.

"Be frank with me and you'll see," he answered.

But she made no reply; she only pulled her hand out of his own, which he tried still to hold, and rapidly withdrew from the room. She made up her mind to speak to Pansy, and she took an occasion on the same day, going to the girl's room before dinner. Pansy was already dressed; she was always in advance of the time: it seemed to illustrate her pretty patience and the graceful stillness with which she could sit and wait. At present she was seated, in her fresh array, before the bed-room fire; she had blown out her candles on the completion of her toilet, in accordance with the economical habits in which she had been brought up sand which she was now more careful than ever to observe; so that the room was lighted only by a couple of logs. The rooms in Palazzo Roccanera were as spacious as they were numerous, and Pansy's virginal bower was an immense chamber with a dark, heavily-timbered ceiling. Its diminutive mistress, in the midst of it, appeared but a speck of humanity, and as she got up, with quick deference, to welcome Isabel, the latter was more than ever struck with her shy sincerity. Isabel had a difficult task—the only thing was to perform it as simply as possible. She felt bitter and angry, but she warned herself against betraying this heat. She was afraid even of looking too grave, or at least too stern; she was afraid of causing alarm. Put Pansy seemed to have guessed she had come more or less as a confessor; for after she had moved the chair in which she had been sitting a little nearer to the fire and Isabel had taken her place in it, she kneeled down on a cushion in front of her, looking up and resting her clasped hands on her stepmother's knees. What Isabel wished to do was to hear from her own lips that her mind was not occupied with Lord Warburton; but if she desired the assurance she felt herself by no means at liberty to provoke it. The girl's father would have qualified this as rank treachery; and indeed Isabel knew that if Pansy should display the smallest germ of a disposition to encourage Lord Warburton her own duty was to hold her tongue. It was difficult to interrogate without appearing to suggest; Pansy's supreme simplicity, an innocence even more complete than Isabel had yet judged it, gave to the most tentative enquiry something of the effect of an admonition. As she knelt there in the vague firelight, with her pretty dress dimly shining, her hands folded half in appeal and half in submission, her soft eyes, raised and fixed, full of the seriousness of the situation, she looked to Isabel like a childish martyr decked out for sacrifice and scarcely presuming even to hope to avert it. When Isabel said to her that she had never yet spoken to her of what might have been going on in relation to her getting married, but that her silence had not been indifference or ignorance, had only been the desire to leave her at liberty, Pansy bent forward, raised her face nearer and nearer, and with a little murmur which evidently expressed a deep longing, answered that she had greatly wished her to speak and that she begged her to advise her now.

"It's difficult for me to advise you," Isabel returned. "I don't know how I can undertake that. That's for your father; you must get his advice and, above all, you must act on it."

At this Pansy dropped her eyes; for a moment she said nothing. "I think I should like your advice better than papa's," she presently remarked.

"That's not as it should be," said Isabel coldly. "I love you very much, but your father loves you better."

"It isn't because you love me—it's because you're a lady," Pansy answered with the air of saying something very reasonable. "A lady can advise a young girl better than a man."

"I advise you then to pay the greatest respect to your father's wishes."

"Ah yes," said the child eagerly, "I must do that."

"But if I speak to you now about your getting married it's not for your own sake, it's for mine," Isabel went on. "If I try to learn from you what you expect, what you desire, it's only that I may act accordingly."

Pansy stared, and then very quickly, "Will you do everything I want?" she asked.

"Before I say yes I must know what such things are."

Pansy presently told her that the only thing she wanted in life was to marry Mr. Rosier. He had asked her and she had told him she would do so if her papa would allow it. Now her papa wouldn't allow it.

"Very well then, it's impossible," Isabel pronounced.

"Yes, it's impossible," said Pansy without a sigh and with the same extreme attention in her clear little face.

"You must think of something else then," Isabel went on; but Pansy, sighing at this, told her that she had attempted that feat without the least success.

"You think of those who think of you," she said with a faint smile. "I know Mr. Rosier thinks of me."

"He ought not to," said Isabel loftily. "Your father has expressly requested he shouldn't."

"He can't help it, because he knows I think of HIM."

"You shouldn't think of him. There's some excuse for him, perhaps; but there's none for you."

"I wish you would try to find one," the girl exclaimed as if she were praying to the Madonna.

"I should be very sorry to attempt it," said the Madonna with unusual frigidity. "If you knew some one else was thinking of you, would you think of him?"

"No one can think of me as Mr. Rosier does; no one has the right."

"Ah, but I don't admit Mr. Rosier's right!" Isabel hypocritically cried.

Pansy only gazed at her, evidently much puzzled; and Isabel, taking advantage of it, began to represent to her the wretched consequences of disobeying her father. At this Pansy stopped her with the assurance that she would never disobey him, would never marry without his consent. And she announced, in the serenest, simplest tone, that, though she might never marry Mr. Rosier, she would never cease to think of him. She appeared to have accepted the idea of eternal singleness; but Isabel of course was free to reflect that she had no conception of its meaning. She was perfectly sincere; she was prepared to give up her lover. This might seem an important step toward taking another, but for Pansy, evidently, it failed to lead in that direction. She felt no bitterness toward her father; there was no bitterness in her heart; there was only the sweetness of fidelity to Edward Rosier, and a strange, exquisite intimation that she could prove it better by remaining single than even by marrying him.

"Your father would like you to make a better marriage," said Isabel. "Mr. Rosier's fortune is not at all large."

"How do you mean better—if that would be good enough? And I have myself so little money; why should I look for a fortune?"

"Your having so little is a reason for looking for more." With which Isabel was grateful for the dimness of the room; she felt as if her face were hideously insincere. It was what she was doing for Osmond; it was what one had to do for Osmond! Pansy's solemn eyes, fixed on her own, almost embarrassed her; she was ashamed to think she had made so light of the girl's preference.

"What should you like me to do?" her companion softly demanded.

The question was a terrible one, and Isabel took refuge in timorous vagueness. "To remember all the pleasure it's in your power to give your father."

"To marry some one else, you mean—if he should ask me?"

For a moment Isabel's answer caused itself to be waited for; then she heard herself utter it in the stillness that Pansy's attention seemed to make. "Yes—to marry some one else."

The child's eyes grew more penetrating; Isabel believed she was doubting her sincerity, and the impression took force from her slowly getting up from her cushion. She stood there a moment with her small hands unclasped and then quavered out: "Well, I hope no one will ask me!"

"There has been a question of that. Some one else would have been ready to ask you."

"I don't think he can have been ready," said Pansy.

"It would appear so if he had been sure he'd succeed."

"If he had been sure? Then he wasn't ready!"

Isabel thought this rather sharp; she also got up and stood a moment looking into the fire. "Lord Warburton has shown you great attention," she resumed; "of course you know it's of him I speak." She found herself, against her expectation, almost placed in the position of justifying herself; which led her to introduce this nobleman more crudely than she had intended.

"He has been very kind to me, and I like him very much. But if you mean that he'll propose for me I think you're mistaken."

"Perhaps I am. But your father would like it extremely."

Pansy shook her head with a little wise smile. "Lord Warburton won't propose simply to please papa."

"Your father would like you to encourage him," Isabel went on mechanically.

"How can I encourage him?"

"I don't know. Your father must tell you that."

Pansy said nothing for a moment; she only continued to smile as if she were in possession of a bright assurance. "There's no danger—no danger!" she declared at last.

There was a conviction in the way she said this, and a felicity in her believing it, which conduced to Isabel's awkwardness. She felt accused of dishonesty, and the idea was disgusting. To repair her self-respect she was on the point of saying that Lord Warburton had let her know that there was a danger. But she didn't; she only said—in her embarrassment rather wide of the mark—that he surely had been most kind, most friendly.

"Yes, he has been very kind," Pansy answered. "That's what I like him for."

"Why then is the difficulty so great?"

"I've always felt sure of his knowing that I don't want—what did you say I should do?—to encourage him. He knows I don't want to marry, and he wants me to know that he therefore won't trouble me. That's the meaning of his kindness. It's as if he said to me: 'I like you very much, but if it doesn't please you I'll never say it again.' I think that's very kind, very noble," Pansy went on with deepening positiveness. "That is all we've said to each other. And he doesn't care for me either. Ah no, there's no danger."

Isabel was touched with wonder at the depths of perception of which this submissive little person was capable; she felt afraid of Pansy's wisdom—began almost to retreat before it. "You must tell your father that," she remarked reservedly.

"I think I'd rather not," Pansy unreservedly answered.

"You oughtn't to let him have false hopes."

"Perhaps not; but it will be good for me that he should. So long as he believes that Lord Warburton intends anything of the kind you say, papa won't propose any one else. And that will be an advantage for me," said the child very lucidly.

There was something brilliant in her lucidity, and it made her companion draw a long breath. It relieved this friend of a heavy responsibility. Pansy had a sufficient illumination of her own, and Isabel felt that she herself just now had no light to spare from her small stock. Nevertheless it still clung to her that she must be loyal to Osmond, that she was on her honour in dealing with his daughter. Under the influence of this sentiment she threw out another suggestion before she retired—a suggestion with which it seemed to her that she should have done her utmost.

"Your father takes for granted at least that you would like to marry a nobleman."

Pansy stood in the open doorway; she had drawn back the curtain for Isabel to pass. "I think Mr. Rosier looks like one!" she remarked very gravely.

CHAPTER XLVI

Lord Warburton was not seen in Mrs. Osmond's drawing-room for several days, and Isabel couldn't fail to observe that her husband said nothing to her about having received a letter from him. She couldn't fail to observe, either, that Osmond was in a state of expectancy and that, though it was not agreeable to him to betray it, he thought their distinguished friend kept him waiting quite too long. At the end of four days he alluded to his absence.

"What has become of Warburton? What does he mean by treating one like a tradesman with a bill?"

"I know nothing about him," Isabel said. "I saw him last Friday at the German ball. He told me then that he meant to write to you."

"He has never written to me."

"So I supposed, from your not having told me."

"He's an odd fish," said Osmond comprehensively. And on Isabel's making no rejoinder he went on to enquire whether it took his lordship five days to indite a letter. "Does he form his words with such difficulty?"

"I don't know," Isabel was reduced to replying. "I've never had a letter from him."

"Never had a letter? I had an idea that you were at one time in intimate correspondence."

She answered that this had not been the case, and let the conversation drop. On the morrow, however, coming into the drawing-room late in the afternoon, her husband took it up again.

"When Lord Warburton told you of his intention of writing what did you say to him?" he asked.

She just faltered. "I think I told him not to forget it.

"Did you believe there was a danger of that?"

"As you say, he's an odd fish."

"Apparently he has forgotten it," said Osmond. "Be so good as to remind him."

"Should you like me to write to him?" she demanded.

"I've no objection whatever."

"You expect too much of me."

"Ah yes, I expect a great deal of you."

"I'm afraid I shall disappoint you," said Isabel.

"My expectations have survived a good deal of disappointment."

"Of course I know that. Think how I must have disappointed myself! If you really wish hands laid on Lord Warburton you must lay them yourself."

For a couple of minutes Osmond answered nothing; then he said: "That won't be easy, with you working against me."

Isabel started; she felt herself beginning to tremble. He had a way of looking at her through half-closed eyelids, as if he were thinking of her but scarcely saw her, which seemed to her to have a wonderfully cruel intention. It appeared to recognise her as a disagreeable necessity of thought, but to ignore her for the time as a presence. That effect had never been so marked as now. "I think you accuse me of something very base," she returned.

"I accuse you of not being trustworthy. If he doesn't after all come forward it will be because you've kept him off. I don't know that it's base: it is the kind of thing a woman always thinks she may do. I've no doubt you've the finest ideas about it."

"I told you I would do what I could," she went on.

"Yes, that gained you time."

It came over her, after he had said this, that she had once thought him beautiful. "How much you must want to make sure of him!" she exclaimed in a moment.

She had no sooner spoken than she perceived the full reach of her words, of which she had not been conscious in uttering them. They made a comparison between Osmond and herself, recalled the fact that she had once held this coveted treasure in her hand and felt herself rich enough to let it fall. A momentary exultation took possession of her—a horrible delight in having wounded him; for his face instantly told her that none of the force of her exclamation was lost. He expressed nothing otherwise, however; he only said quickly: "Yes, I want it immensely."

At this moment a servant came in to usher a visitor, and he was followed the next by Lord Warburton, who received a visible check on seeing Osmond. He looked rapidly from the master of the house to the mistress; a movement that seemed to denote a reluctance to interrupt or even a perception of ominous conditions. Then he advanced, with his English address, in which a vague shyness seemed to offer itself as an element of good-breeding; in which the only defect was a difficulty in achieving transitions. Osmond was embarrassed; he found nothing to say; but Isabel remarked, promptly enough, that they had been in the act of talking about their visitor. Upon this her husband added that they hadn't known what was become of him—they had been afraid he had gone away. "No," he explained, smiling and looking at Osmond; "I'm only on the point of going." And then he mentioned that he found himself suddenly recalled to England: he should start on the morrow or the day after. "I'm awfully sorry to leave poor Touchett!" he ended by exclaiming.

For a moment neither of his companions spoke; Osmond only leaned back in his chair, listening. Isabel didn't look at him; she could only fancy how he looked. Her eyes were on their visitor's face, where they were the more free to rest that those of his lordship carefully avoided them. Yet Isabel was sure that had she met his glance she would have found it expressive. "You had better take poor Touchett with you," she heard her husband say, lightly enough, in a moment.

"He had better wait for warmer weather," Lord Warburton answered. "I shouldn't advise him to travel just now."

He sat there a quarter of an hour, talking as if he might not soon see them again—unless indeed they should come to England, a course he strongly recommended. Why shouldn't they come to England in the autumn?—that struck him as a very happy thought. It would give him such pleasure to do what he could for them—to have them come and spend a month with him. Osmond, by his own admission, had been to England but once; which was an absurd state of things for a man of his leisure and intelligence. It was just the country for him—he would be sure to get on well there. Then Lord Warburton asked Isabel if she remembered what a good time she had had there and if she didn't want to try it again. Didn't she want to see Gardencourt once more? Gardencourt was really very good. Touchett didn't take proper care of it, but it was the sort of place you could hardly spoil by letting it alone. Why didn't they come and pay Touchett a visit? He surely must have asked them. Hadn't asked them? What an ill-mannered wretch!—and Lord Warburton promised to give the master of Gardencourt a piece of his mind. Of course it was a mere accident; he would be delighted to have them. Spending a month with Touchett and a month with himself, and seeing all the rest of the people they must know there, they really wouldn't find it half bad. Lord Warburton added that it would amuse Miss Osmond as well, who had told him that she had never been to England and whom he had assured it was a country she deserved to see. Of course she didn't need to go to England to be admired—that was her fate everywhere; but she would be an immense success there, she certainly would, if that was any inducement. He asked if she were not at home: couldn't he say good-bye? Not that he liked good-byes—he always funked them. When he left England the other day he hadn't said good-bye to a two-legged creature. He had had half a mind to leave Rome without troubling Mrs. Osmond for a final interview. What could be more dreary than final interviews? One never said the things one wanted—one remembered them all an hour afterwards. On the other hand one usually said a lot of things one shouldn't, simply from a sense that one had to say something. Such a sense was upsetting; it muddled one's wits. He had it at present, and that was the effect it produced on him. If Mrs. Osmond didn't think he spoke as he ought she must set it down to agitation; it was no light thing to part with Mrs. Osmond. He was really very sorry to be going. He had thought of writing to her instead of calling—but he would write to her at any rate, to tell her a lot of things that would be sure to occur to him as soon as he had left the house. They must think seriously about coming to Lockleigh.

If there was anything awkward in the conditions of his visit or in the announcement of his departure it failed to come to the surface. Lord Warburton talked about his agitation; but he showed it in no other manner, and Isabel saw that since he had determined on a retreat he was capable of executing it gallantly. She was very glad for him; she liked him quite well enough to wish him to appear to carry a thing off. He would do that on any occasion—not from impudence but simply from the habit of success; and Isabel felt it out of her husband's power to frustrate this faculty. A complex operation, as she sat there, went on in her mind. On one side she listened to their visitor; said what was proper to him; read, more or less, between the lines of what he said himself; and wondered how he would have spoken if he had found her alone. On the other she had a perfect consciousness of Osmond's emotion. She felt almost sorry for him; he was condemned to the sharp pain of loss without the relief of cursing. He had had a great hope, and now, as he saw it vanish into smoke, he was obliged to sit and smile and twirl his thumbs. Not that he troubled himself to smile very brightly; he treated their friend on the whole to as vacant a countenance as so clever a man could very well wear. It was indeed a part of Osmond's cleverness that he could look consummately uncompromised. His present appearance, however, was not a confession of disappointment; it was simply a part of Osmond's habitual system, which was to be inexpressive exactly in proportion as he was really intent. He had been intent on this prize from the first; but he had never allowed his eagerness to irradiate his refined face. He had treated his possible son-in-law as he treated every one—with an air of being interested in him only for his own advantage, not for any profit to a person already so generally, so perfectly provided as Gilbert Osmond. He would give no sign now of an inward rage which was the result of a vanished prospect of gain—not the faintest nor subtlest. Isabel could be sure of that, if it was any satisfaction to her. Strangely, very strangely, it was a satisfaction; she wished Lord Warburton to triumph before her husband, and at the same time she wished her husband to be very superior before Lord Warburton. Osmond, in his way, was admirable; he had, like their visitor, the advantage of an acquired habit. It was not that of succeeding, but it was something almost as good—that of not attempting. As he leaned back in his place, listening but vaguely to the other's friendly offers and suppressed explanations—as if it were only proper to assume that they were addressed essentially to his wife—he had at least (since so little else was left him) the comfort of thinking how well he personally had kept out of it, and how the air of indifference, which he was now able to wear, had the added beauty of consistency. It was something to be able to look as if the leave-taker's movements had no relation to his own mind. The latter did well, certainly; but Osmond's performance was in its very nature more finished. Lord Warburton's position was after all an easy one; there was no reason in the world why he shouldn't leave Rome. He had had beneficent inclinations, but they had stopped short of fruition; he had never committed himself, and his honour was safe. Osmond appeared to take but a moderate interest in the proposal that they should go and stay with him and in his allusion to the success Pansy might extract from their visit. He murmured a recognition, but left Isabel to say that it was a matter requiring grave consideration. Isabel, even while she made this remark, could see the great vista which had suddenly opened out in her husband's mind, with Pansy's little figure marching up the middle of it.

Lord Warburton had asked leave to bid good-bye to Pansy, but neither Isabel nor Osmond had made any motion to send for her. He had the air of giving out that his visit must be short; he sat on a small chair, as if it were only for a moment, keeping his hat in his hand. But he stayed and stayed; Isabel wondered what he was waiting for. She believed it was not to see Pansy; she had an impression that on the whole he would rather not see Pansy. It was of course to see herself alone—he had something to say to her. Isabel had no great wish to hear it, for she was afraid it would be an explanation, and she could perfectly dispense with explanations. Osmond, however, presently got up, like a man of good taste to whom it had occurred that so inveterate a visitor might wish to say just the last word of all to the ladies. "I've a letter to write before dinner," he said; "you must excuse me. I'll see if my daughter's disengaged, and if she is she shall know you're here. Of course when you come to Rome you'll always look us up. Mrs. Osmond will talk to you about the English expedition: she decides all those things."

The nod with which, instead of a hand-shake, he wound up this little speech was perhaps rather a meagre form of salutation; but on the whole it was all the occasion demanded. Isabel reflected that after he left the room Lord Warburton would have no pretext for saying, "Your husband's very angry"; which would have been extremely disagreeable to her. Nevertheless, if he had done so, she would have said: "Oh, don't be anxious. He doesn't hate you: it's me that he hates!"

It was only when they had been left alone together that her friend showed a certain vague awkwardness—sitting down in another chair, handling two or three of the objects that were near him. "I hope he'll make Miss Osmond come," he presently remarked. "I want very much to see her."

"I'm glad it's the last time," said Isabel.

"So am I. She doesn't care for me."

"No, she doesn't care for you."

"I don't wonder at it," he returned. Then he added with inconsequence: "You'll come to England, won't you?"

"I think we had better not."

"Ah, you owe me a visit. Don't you remember that you were to have come to Lockleigh once, and you never did?"

"Everything's changed since then," said Isabel.

"Not changed for the worse, surely—as far as we're concerned. To see you under my roof"—and he hung fire but an instant—"would be a great satisfaction."

She had feared an explanation; but that was the only one that occurred. They talked a little of Ralph, and in another moment Pansy came in, already dressed for dinner and with a little red spot in either cheek. She shook hands with Lord Warburton and stood looking up into his face with a fixed smile—a smile that Isabel knew, though his lordship probably never suspected it, to be near akin to a burst of tears.

"I'm going away," he said. "I want to bid you good-bye."

"Good-bye, Lord Warburton." Her voice perceptibly trembled.

"And I want to tell you how much I wish you may be very happy."

"Thank you, Lord Warburton," Pansy answered.

He lingered a moment and gave a glance at Isabel. "You ought to be very happy—you've got a guardian angel."

"I'm sure I shall be happy," said Pansy in the tone of a person whose certainties were always cheerful.

"Such a conviction as that will take you a great way. But if it should ever fail you, remember—remember—" And her interlocutor stammered a little. "Think of me sometimes, you know!" he said with a vague laugh. Then he shook hands with Isabel in silence, and presently he was gone.

When he had left the room she expected an effusion of tears from her stepdaughter; but Pansy in fact treated her to something very different.

"I think you ARE my guardian angel!" she exclaimed very sweetly.

Isabel shook her head. "I'm not an angel of any kind. I'm at the most your good friend."

"You're a very good friend then—to have asked papa to be gentle with me."

"I've asked your father nothing," said Isabel, wondering.

"He told me just now to come to the drawing-room, and then he gave me a very kind kiss."

"Ah," said Isabel, "that was quite his own idea!"

She recognised the idea perfectly; it was very characteristic, and she was to see a great deal more of it. Even with Pansy he couldn't put himself the least in the wrong. They were dining out that day, and after their dinner they went to another entertainment; so that it was not till late in the evening that Isabel saw him alone. When Pansy kissed him before going to bed he returned her embrace with even more than his usual munificence, and Isabel wondered if he meant it as a hint that his daughter had been injured by the machinations of her stepmother. It was a partial expression, at any rate, of what he continued to expect of his wife. She was about to follow Pansy, but he remarked that he wished she would remain; he had something to say to her. Then he walked about the drawing-room a little, while she stood waiting in her cloak.

"I don't understand what you wish to do," he said in a moment. "I should like to know—so that I may know how to act."

"Just now I wish to go to bed. I'm very tired."

"Sit down and rest; I shall not keep you long. Not there—take a comfortable place." And he arranged a multitude of cushions that were scattered in picturesque disorder upon a vast divan. This was not, however, where she seated herself; she dropped into the nearest chair. The fire had gone out; the lights in the great room were few. She drew her cloak about her; she felt mortally cold. "I think you're trying to humiliate me," Osmond went on. "It's a most absurd undertaking."

"I haven't the least idea what you mean," she returned.

"You've played a very deep game; you've managed it beautifully."

"What is it that I've managed?"

"You've not quite settled it, however; we shall see him again." And he stopped in front of her, with his hands in his pockets, looking down at her thoughtfully, in his usual way, which seemed meant to let her know that she was not an object, but only a rather disagreeable incident, of thought.

"If you mean that Lord Warburton's under an obligation to come back you're wrong," Isabel said. "He's under none whatever."

"That's just what I complain of. But when I say he'll come back I don't mean he'll come from a sense of duty."

"There's nothing else to make him. I think he has quite exhausted Rome."

"Ah no, that's a shallow judgement. Rome's inexhaustible." And Osmond began to walk about again. "However, about that perhaps there's no hurry," he added. "It's rather a good idea of his that we should go to England. If it were not for the fear of finding your cousin there I think I should try to persuade you."

"It may be that you'll not find my cousin," said Isabel.

"I should like to be sure of it. However, I shall be as sure as possible. At the same time I should like to see his house, that you told me so much about at one time: what do you call it?—Gardencourt. It must be a charming thing. And then, you know, I've a devotion to the memory of your uncle: you made me take a great fancy to him. I should like to see where he lived and died. That indeed is a detail. Your friend was right. Pansy ought to see England."

"I've no doubt she would enjoy it," said Isabel.

"But that's a long time hence; next autumn's far off," Osmond continued; "and meantime there are things that more nearly interest us. Do you think me so very proud?" he suddenly asked.

"I think you very strange."

"You don't understand me."

"No, not even when you insult me."

"I don't insult you; I'm incapable of it. I merely speak of certain facts, and if the allusion's an injury to you the fault's not mine. It's surely a fact that you have kept all this matter quite in your own hands."

"Are you going back to Lord Warburton?" Isabel asked. "I'm very tired of his name."

"You shall hear it again before we've done with it."

She had spoken of his insulting her, but it suddenly seemed to her that this ceased to be a pain. He was going down—down; the vision of such a fall made her almost giddy: that was the only pain. He was too strange, too different; he didn't touch her. Still, the working of his morbid passion was extraordinary, and she felt a rising curiosity to know in what light he saw himself justified. "I might say to you that I judge you've nothing to say to me that's worth hearing," she returned in a moment. "But I should perhaps be wrong. There's a thing that would be worth my hearing—to know in the plainest words of what it is you accuse me."

"Of having prevented Pansy's marriage to Warburton. Are those words plain enough?"

"On the contrary, I took a great interest in it. I told you so; and when you told me that you counted on me—that I think was what you said—I accepted the obligation. I was a fool to do so, but I did it."

"You pretended to do it, and you even pretended reluctance to make me more willing to trust you. Then you began to use your ingenuity to get him out of the way."

"I think I see what you mean," said Isabel.

"Where's the letter you told me he had written me?" her husband demanded.

"I haven't the least idea; I haven't asked him."

"You stopped it on the way," said Osmond.

Isabel slowly got up; standing there in her white cloak, which covered her to her feet, she might have represented the angel of disdain, first cousin to that of pity. "Oh, Gilbert, for a man who was so fine—!" she exclaimed in a long murmur.

"I was never so fine as you. You've done everything you wanted. You've got him out of the say without appearing to do so, and you've placed me in the position in which you wished to see me—that of a man who has tried to marry his daughter to a lord, but has grotesquely failed."

"Pansy doesn't care for him. She's very glad he's gone," Isabel said.

"That has nothing to do with the matter."

"And he doesn't care for Pansy."

"That won't do; you told me he did. I don't know why you wanted this particular satisfaction," Osmond continued; "you might have taken some other. It doesn't seem to me that I've been presumptuous—that I have taken too much for granted. I've been very modest about it, very quiet. The idea didn't originate with me. He began to show that he liked her before I ever thought of it. I left it all to you."

"Yes, you were very glad to leave it to me. After this you must attend to such things yourself."

He looked at her a moment; then he turned away. "I thought you were very fond of my daughter."

"I've never been more so than to-day."

"Your affection is attended with immense limitations. However, that perhaps is natural."

"Is this all you wished to say to me?" Isabel asked, taking a candle that stood on one of the tables.

"Are you satisfied? Am I sufficiently disappointed?"

"I don't think that on the whole you're disappointed. You've had another opportunity to try to stupefy me."

"It's not that. It's proved that Pansy can aim high."

"Poor little Pansy!" said Isabel as she turned away with her candle.

CHAPTER XLVII

It was from Henrietta Stackpole that she learned how Caspar Goodwood had come to Rome; an event that took place three days after Lord Warburton's departure. This latter fact had been preceded by an incident of some importance to Isabel—the temporary absence, once again, of Madame Merle, who had gone to Naples to stay with a friend, the happy possessor of a villa at Posilippo. Madame Merle had ceased to minister to Isabel's happiness, who found herself wondering whether the most discreet of women might not also by chance be the most dangerous. Sometimes, at night, she had strange visions; she seemed to see her husband and her friend—his friend—in dim, indistinguishable combination. It seemed to her that she had not done with her; this lady had something in reserve. Isabel's imagination applied itself actively to this elusive point, but every now and then it was checked by a nameless dread, so that when the charming woman was away from Rome she had almost a consciousness of respite. She had already learned from Miss Stackpole that Caspar Goodwood was in Europe, Henrietta having written to make it known to her immediately after meeting him in Paris. He himself never wrote to Isabel, and though he was in Europe she thought it very possible he might not desire to see her. Their last interview, before her marriage, had had quite the character of a complete rupture; if she remembered rightly he had said he wished to take his last look at her. Since then he had been the most discordant survival of her earlier time—the only one in fact with which a permanent pain was associated. He had left her that morning with a sense of the most superfluous of shocks: it was like a collision between vessels in broad daylight. There had been no mist, no hidden current to excuse it, and she herself had only wished to steer wide. He had bumped against her prow, however, while her hand was on the tiller, and—to complete the metaphor—had given the lighter vessel a strain which still occasionally betrayed itself in a faint creaking. It had been horrid to see him, because he represented the only serious harm that (to her belief) she had ever done in the world: he was the only person with an unsatisfied claim on her. She had made him unhappy, she couldn't help it; and his unhappiness was a grim reality. She had cried with rage, after he had left her, at—she hardly knew what: she tried to think it had been at his want of consideration. He had come to her with his unhappiness when her own bliss was so perfect; he had done his best to darken the brightness of those pure rays. He had not been violent, and yet there had been a violence in the impression. There had been a violence at any rate in something somewhere; perhaps it was only in her own fit of weeping and in that after-sense of the same which had lasted three or four days.

The effect of his final appeal had in short faded away, and all the first year of her marriage he had dropped out of her books. He was a thankless subject of reference; it was disagreeable to have to think of a person who was sore and sombre about you and whom you could yet do nothing to relieve. It would have been different if she had been able to doubt, even a little, of his unreconciled state, as she doubted of Lord Warburton's; unfortunately it was beyond question, and this aggressive, uncompromising look of it was just what made it unattractive. She could never say to herself that here was a sufferer who had compensations, as she was able to say in the case of her English suitor. She had no faith in Mr. Goodwood's compensations and no esteem for them. A cotton factory was not a compensation for anything—least of all for having failed to marry Isabel Archer. And yet, beyond that, she hardly knew what he had—save of course his intrinsic qualities. Oh, he was intrinsic enough; she never thought of his even looking for artificial aids. If he extended his business—that, to the best of her belief, was the only form exertion could take with him—it would be because it was an enterprising thing, or good for the business; not in the least because he might hope it would overlay the past. This gave his figure a kind of bareness and bleakness which made the accident of meeting it in memory or in apprehension a peculiar concussion; it was deficient in the social drapery commonly muffling, in an overcivilized age, the sharpness of human contacts. His perfect silence, moreover, the fact that she never heard from him and very seldom heard any mention of him, deepened this impression of his loneliness. She asked Lily for news of him, from time to time; but Lily knew nothing of Boston—her imagination was all bounded on the east by Madison Avenue. As time went on Isabel had thought of him oftener, and with fewer restrictions; she had had more than once the idea of writing to him. She had never told her husband about him—never let Osmond know of his visits to her in Florence; a reserve not dictated in the early period by a want of confidence in Osmond, but simply by the consideration that the young man's disappointment was not her secret but his own. It would be wrong of her, she had believed, to convey it to another, and Mr. Goodwood's affairs could have, after all, little interest for Gilbert. When it had come to the point she had never written to him; it seemed to her that, considering his grievance, the least she could do was to let him alone. Nevertheless she would have been glad to be in some way nearer to him. It was not that it ever occurred to her that she might have married him; even after the consequences of her actual union had grown vivid to her that particular reflection, though she indulged in so many, had not had the assurance to present itself. But on finding herself in trouble he had become a member of that circle of things with which she wished to set herself right. I have mentioned how passionately she needed to feel that her unhappiness should not have come to her through her own fault. She had no near prospect of dying, and yet she wished to make her peace with the world—to put her spiritual affairs in order. It came back to her from time to time that there was an account still to be settled with Caspar, and she saw herself disposed or able to settle it to-day on terms easier for him than ever before. Still, when she learned he was coming to Rome she felt all afraid; it would be more disagreeable for him than for any one else to make out—since he WOULD make it out, as over a falsified balance-sheet or something of that sort—the intimate disarray of her affairs. Deep in her breast she believed that he had invested his all in her happiness, while the others had invested only a part. He was one more person from whom she should have to conceal her stress. She was reassured, however, after he arrived in Rome, for he spent several days without coming to see her.

Henrietta Stackpole, it may well be imagined, was more punctual, and Isabel was largely favoured with the society of her friend. She threw herself into it, for now that she had made such a point of keeping her conscience clear, that was one way of proving she had not been superficial—the more so as the years, in their flight, had rather enriched than blighted those peculiarities which had been humorously criticised by persons less interested than Isabel, and which were still marked enough to give loyalty a spice of heroism. Henrietta was as keen and quick and fresh as ever, and as neat and bright and fair. Her remarkably open eyes, lighted like great glazed railway-stations, had put up no shutters; her attire had lost none of its crispness, her opinions none of their national reference. She was by no means quite unchanged, however it struck Isabel she had grown vague. Of old she had never been vague; though undertaking many enquiries at once, she had managed to be entire and pointed about each. She had a reason for everything she did; she fairly bristled with motives. Formerly, when she came to Europe it was because she wished to see it, but now, having already seen it, she had no such excuse. She didn't for a moment pretend that the desire to examine decaying civilisations had anything to do with her present enterprise; her journey was rather an expression of her independence of the old world than of a sense of further obligations to it. "It's nothing to come to Europe," she said to Isabel; "it doesn't seem to me one needs so many reasons for that. It is something to stay at home; this is much more important." It was not therefore with a sense of doing anything very important that she treated herself to another pilgrimage to Rome; she had seen the place before and carefully inspected it; her present act was simply a sign of familiarity, of her knowing all about it, of her having as good a right as any one else to be there. This was all very well, and Henrietta was restless; she had a perfect right to be restless too, if one came to that. But she had after all a better reason for coming to Rome than that she cared for it so little. Her friend easily recognised it, and with it the worth of the other's fidelity. She had crossed the stormy ocean in midwinter because she had guessed that Isabel was sad. Henrietta guessed a great deal, but she had never guessed so happily as that. Isabel's satisfactions just now were few, but even if they had been more numerous there would still have been something of individual joy in her sense of being justified in having always thought highly of Henrietta. She had made large concessions with regard to her, and had yet insisted that, with all abatements, she was very valuable. It was not her own triumph, however, that she found good; it was simply the relief of confessing to this confidant, the first person to whom she had owned it, that she was not in the least at her ease. Henrietta had herself approached this point with the smallest possible delay, and had accused her to her face of being wretched. She was a woman, she was a sister; she was not Ralph, nor Lord Warburton, nor Caspar Goodwood, and Isabel could speak.

"Yes, I'm wretched," she said very mildly. She hated to hear herself say it; she tried to say it as judicially as possible.

"What does he do to you?" Henrietta asked, frowning as if she were enquiring into the operations of a quack doctor.

"He does nothing. But he doesn't like me."

"He's very hard to please!" cried Miss Stackpole. "Why don't you leave him?"

"I can't change that way," Isabel said.

"Why not, I should like to know? You won't confess that you've made a mistake. You're too proud."

"I don't know whether I'm too proud. But I can't publish my mistake. I don't think that's decent. I'd much rather die."

"You won't think so always," said Henrietta.

"I don't know what great unhappiness might bring me to; but it seems to me I shall always be ashamed. One must accept one's deeds. I married him before all the world; I was perfectly free; it was impossible to do anything more deliberate. One can't change that way," Isabel repeated.

"You HAVE changed, in spite of the impossibility. I hope you don't mean to say you like him."

Isabel debated. "No, I don't like him. I can tell you, because I'm weary of my secret. But that's enough; I can't announce it on the housetops."

Henrietta gave a laugh. "Don't you think you're rather too considerate?"

"It's not of him that I'm considerate—it's of myself!" Isabel answered.

It was not surprising Gilbert Osmond should not have taken comfort in Miss Stackpole; his instinct had naturally set him in opposition to a young lady capable of advising his wife to withdraw from the conjugal roof. When she arrived in Rome he had said to Isabel that he hoped she would leave her friend the interviewer alone; and Isabel had answered that he at least had nothing to fear from her. She said to Henrietta that as Osmond didn't like her she couldn't invite her to dine, but they could easily see each other in other ways. Isabel received Miss Stackpole freely in her own sitting-room, and took her repeatedly to drive, face to face with Pansy, who, bending a little forward, on the opposite seat of the carriage, gazed at the celebrated authoress with a respectful attention which Henrietta occasionally found irritating. She complained to Isabel that Miss Osmond had a little look as if she should remember everything one said. "I don't want to be remembered that way," Miss Stackpole declared; "I consider that my conversation refers only to the moment, like the morning papers. Your stepdaughter, as she sits there, looks as if she kept all the back numbers and would bring them out some day against me." She could not teach herself to think favourably of Pansy, whose absence of initiative, of conversation, of personal claims, seemed to her, in a girl of twenty, unnatural and even uncanny. Isabel presently saw that Osmond would have liked her to urge a little the cause of her friend, insist a little upon his receiving her, so that he might appear to suffer for good manners' sake. Her immediate acceptance of his objections put him too much in the wrong—it being in effect one of the disadvantages of expressing contempt that you cannot enjoy at the same time the credit of expressing sympathy. Osmond held to his credit, and yet he held to his objections—all of which were elements difficult to reconcile. The right thing would have been that Miss Stackpole should come to dine at Palazzo Roccanera once or twice, so that (in spite of his superficial civility, always so great) she might judge for herself how little pleasure it gave him. From the moment, however, that both the ladies were so unaccommodating, there was nothing for Osmond but to wish the lady from New York would take herself off. It was surprising how little satisfaction he got from his wife's friends; he took occasion to call Isabel's attention to it.

"You're certainly not fortunate in your intimates; I wish you might make a new collection," he said to her one morning in reference to nothing visible at the moment, but in a tone of ripe reflection which deprived the remark of all brutal abruptness. "It's as if you had taken the trouble to pick out the people in the world that I have least in common with. Your cousin I have always thought a conceited ass—besides his being the most ill-favoured animal I know. Then it's insufferably tiresome that one can't tell him so; one must spare him on account of his health. His health seems to me the best part of him; it gives him privileges enjoyed by no one else. If he's so desperately ill there's only one way to prove it; but he seems to have no mind for that. I can't say much more for the great Warburton. When one really thinks of it, the cool insolence of that performance was something rare! He comes and looks at one's daughter as if she were a suite of apartments; he tries the door-handles and looks out of the windows, raps on the walls and almost thinks he'll take the place. Will you be so good as to draw up a lease? Then, on the whole, he decides that the rooms are too small; he doesn't think he could live on a third floor; he must look out for a piano nobile. And he goes away after having got a month's lodging in the poor little apartment for nothing. Miss Stackpole, however, is your most wonderful invention. She strikes me as a kind of monster. One hasn't a nerve in one's body that she doesn't set quivering. You know I never have admitted that she's a woman. Do you know what she reminds me of? Of a new steel pen—the most odious thing in nature. She talks as a steel pen writes; aren't her letters, by the way, on ruled paper? She thinks and moves and walks and looks exactly as she talks. You may say that she doesn't hurt me, inasmuch as I don't see her. I don't see her, but I hear her; I hear her all day long. Her voice is in my ears; I can't get rid of it. I know exactly what she says, and every inflexion of the tone in which she says it. She says charming things about me, and they give you great comfort. I don't like at all to think she talks about me—I feel as I should feel if I knew the footman were wearing my hat."

Henrietta talked about Gilbert Osmond, as his wife assured him, rather less than he suspected. She had plenty of other subjects, in two of which the reader may be supposed to be especially interested. She let her friend know that Caspar Goodwood had discovered for himself that she was unhappy, though indeed her ingenuity was unable to suggest what comfort he hoped to give her by coming to Rome and yet not calling on her. They met him twice in the street, but he had no appearance of seeing them; they were driving, and he had a habit of looking straight in front of him, as if he proposed to take in but one object at a time. Isabel could have fancied she had seen him the day before; it must have been with just that face and step that he had walked out of Mrs. Touchett's door at the close of their last interview. He was dressed just as he had been dressed on that day, Isabel remembered the colour of his cravat; and yet in spite of this familiar look there was a strangeness in his figure too, something that made her feel it afresh to be rather terrible he should have come to Rome. He looked bigger and more overtopping than of old, and in those days he certainly reached high enough. She noticed that the people whom he passed looked back after him; but he went straight forward, lifting above them a face like a February sky.

Miss Stackpole's other topic was very different; she gave Isabel the latest news about Mr. Bantling. He had been out in the United States the year before, and she was happy to say she had been able to show him considerable attention. She didn't know how much he had enjoyed it, but she would undertake to say it had done him good; he wasn't the same man when he left as he had been when he came. It had opened his eyes and shown him that England wasn't everything. He had been very much liked in most places, and thought extremely simple—more simple than the English were commonly supposed to be. There were people who had thought him affected; she didn't know whether they meant that his simplicity was an affectation. Some of his questions were too discouraging; he thought all the chambermaids were farmers' daughters—or all the farmers' daughters were chambermaids—she couldn't exactly remember which. He hadn't seemed able to grasp the great school system; it had been really too much for him. On the whole he had behaved as if there were too much of everything—as if he could only take in a small part. The part he had chosen was the hotel system and the river navigation. He had seemed really fascinated with the hotels; he had a photograph of every one he had visited. But the river steamers were his principal interest; he wanted to do nothing but sail on the big boats. They had travelled together from New York to Milwaukee, stopping at the most interesting cities on the route; and whenever they started afresh he had wanted to know if they could go by the steamer. He seemed to have no idea of geography—had an impression that Baltimore was a Western city and was perpetually expecting to arrive at the Mississippi. He appeared never to have heard of any river in America but the Mississippi and was unprepared to recognise the existence of the Hudson, though obliged to confess at last that it was fully equal to the Rhine. They had spent some pleasant hours in the palace-cars; he was always ordering ice-cream from the coloured man. He could never get used to that idea—that you could get ice-cream in the cars. Of course you couldn't, nor fans, nor candy, nor anything in the English cars! He found the heat quite overwhelming, and she had told him she indeed expected it was the biggest he had ever experienced. He was now in England, hunting—"hunting round" Henrietta called it. These amusements were those of the American red men; we had left that behind long ago, the pleasures of the chase. It seemed to be generally believed in England that we wore tomahawks and feathers; but such a costume was more in keeping with English habits. Mr. Bantling would not have time to join her in Italy, but when she should go to Paris again he expected to come over. He wanted very much to see Versailles again; he was very fond of the ancient regime. They didn't agree about that, but that was what she liked Versailles for, that you could see the ancient regime had been swept away. There were no dukes and marquises there now; she remembered on the contrary one day when there were five American families, walking all round. Mr. Bantling was very anxious that she should take up the subject of England again, and he thought she might get on better with it now; England had changed a good deal within two or three years. He was determined that if she went there he should go to see his sister, Lady Pensil, and that this time the invitation should come to her straight. The mystery about that other one had never been explained.

Caspar Goodwood came at last to Palazzo Roccanera; he had written Isabel a note beforehand, to ask leave. This was promptly granted; she would be at home at six o'clock that afternoon. She spent the day wondering what he was coming for—what good he expected to get of it. He had presented himself hitherto as a person destitute of the faculty of compromise, who would take what he had asked for or take nothing. Isabel's hospitality, however, raised no questions, and she found no great difficulty in appearing happy enough to deceive him. It was her conviction at least that she deceived him, made him say to himself that he had been misinformed. But she also saw, so she believed, that he was not disappointed, as some other men, she was sure, would have been; he had not come to Rome to look for an opportunity. She never found out what he had come for; he offered her no explanation; there could be none but the very simple one that he wanted to see her. In other words he had come for his amusement. Isabel followed up this induction with a good deal of eagerness, and was delighted to have found a formula that would lay the ghost of this gentleman's ancient grievance. If he had come to Rome for his amusement this was exactly what she wanted; for if he cared for amusement he had got over his heartache. If he had got over his heartache everything was as it should be and her responsibilities were at an end. It was true that he took his recreation a little stiffly, but he had never been loose and easy and she had every reason to believe he was satisfied with what he saw. Henrietta was not in his confidence, though he was in hers, and Isabel consequently received no side-light upon his state of mind. He was open to little conversation on general topics; it came back to her that she had said of him once, years before, "Mr. Goodwood speaks a good deal, but he doesn't talk." He spoke a good deal now, but he talked perhaps as little as ever; considering, that is, how much there was in Rome to talk about. His arrival was not calculated to simplify her relations with her husband, for if Mr. Osmond didn't like her friends Mr. Goodwood had no claim upon his attention save as having been one of the first of them. There was nothing for her to say of him but that he was the very oldest; this rather meagre synthesis exhausted the facts. She had been obliged to introduce him to Gilbert; it was impossible she should not ask him to dinner, to her Thursday evenings, of which she had grown very weary, but to which her husband still held for the sake not so much of inviting people as of not inviting them.

To the Thursdays Mr. Goodwood came regularly, solemnly, rather early; he appeared to regard them with a good deal of gravity. Isabel every now and then had a moment of anger; there was something so literal about him; she thought he might know that she didn't know what to do with him. But she couldn't call him stupid; he was not that in the least; he was only extraordinarily honest. To be as honest as that made a man very different from most people; one had to be almost equally honest with HIM. She made this latter reflection at the very time she was flattering herself she had persuaded him that she was the most light-hearted of women. He never threw any doubt on this point, never asked her any personal questions. He got on much better with Osmond than had seemed probable. Osmond had a great dislike to being counted on; in such a case he had an irresistible need of disappointing you. It was in virtue of this principle that he gave himself the entertainment of taking a fancy to a perpendicular Bostonian whom he had been depended upon to treat with coldness. He asked Isabel if Mr. Goodwood also had wanted to marry her, and expressed surprise at her not having accepted him. It would have been an excellent thing, like living under some tall belfry which would strike all the hours and make a queer vibration in the upper air. He declared he liked to talk with the great Goodwood; it wasn't easy at first, you had to climb up an interminable steep staircase up to the top of the tower; but when you got there you had a big view and felt a little fresh breeze. Osmond, as we know, had delightful qualities, and he gave Caspar Goodwood the benefit of them all. Isabel could see that Mr. Goodwood thought better of her husband than he had ever wished to; he had given her the impression that morning in Florence of being inaccessible to a good impression. Gilbert asked him repeatedly to dinner, and Mr. Goodwood smoked a cigar with him afterwards and even desired to be shown his collections. Gilbert said to Isabel that he was very original; he was as strong and of as good a style as an English portmanteau,—he had plenty of straps and buckles which would never wear out, and a capital patent lock. Caspar Goodwood took to riding on the Campagna and devoted much time to this exercise; it was therefore mainly in the evening that Isabel saw him. She bethought herself of saying to him one day that if he were willing he could render her a service. And then she added smiling:

"I don't know, however, what right I have to ask a service of you."

"You're the person in the world who has most right," he answered. "I've given you assurances that I've never given any one else."

The service was that he should go and see her cousin Ralph, who was ill at the Hotel de Paris, alone, and be as kind to him as possible. Mr. Goodwood had never seen him, but he would know who the poor fellow was; if she was not mistaken Ralph had once invited him to Gardencourt. Caspar remembered the invitation perfectly, and, though he was not supposed to be a man of imagination, had enough to put himself in the place of a poor gentleman who lay dying at a Roman inn. He called at the Hotel de Paris and, on being shown into the presence of the master of Gardencourt, found Miss Stackpole sitting beside his sofa. A singular change had in fact occurred in this lady's relations with Ralph Touchett. She had not been asked by Isabel to go and see him, but on hearing that he was too ill to come out had immediately gone of her own motion. After this she had paid him a daily visit—always under the conviction that they were great enemies. "Oh yes, we're intimate enemies," Ralph used to say; and he accused her freely—as freely as the humour of it would allow—of coming to worry him to death. In reality they became excellent friends, Henrietta much wondering that she should never have liked him before. Ralph liked her exactly as much as he had always done; he had never doubted for a moment that she was an excellent fellow. They talked about everything and always differed; about everything, that is, but Isabel—a topic as to which Ralph always had a thin forefinger on his lips. Mr. Bantling on the other hand proved a great resource; Ralph was capable of discussing Mr. Bantling with Henrietta for hours. Discussion was stimulated of course by their inevitable difference of view—Ralph having amused himself with taking the ground that the genial ex-guardsman was a regular Machiavelli. Caspar Goodwood could contribute nothing to such a debate; but after he had been left alone with his host he found there were various other matters they could take up. It must be admitted that the lady who had just gone out was not one of these; Caspar granted all Miss Stackpole's merits in advance, but had no further remark to make about her. Neither, after the first allusions, did the two men expatiate upon Mrs. Osmond—a theme in which Goodwood perceived as many dangers as Ralph. He felt very sorry for that unclassable personage; he couldn't bear to see a pleasant man, so pleasant for all his queerness, so beyond anything to be done. There was always something to be done, for Goodwood, and he did it in this case by repeating several times his visit to the Hotel de Paris. It seemed to Isabel that she had been very clever; she had artfully disposed of the superfluous Caspar. She had given him an occupation; she had converted him into a caretaker of Ralph. She had a plan of making him travel northward with her cousin as soon as the first mild weather should allow it. Lord Warburton had brought Ralph to Rome and Mr. Goodwood should take him away. There seemed a happy symmetry in this, and she was now intensely eager that Ralph should depart. She had a constant fear he would die there before her eyes and a horror of the occurrence of this event at an inn, by her door, which he had so rarely entered. Ralph must sink to his last rest in his own dear house, in one of those deep, dim chambers of Gardencourt where the dark ivy would cluster round the edges of the glimmering window. There seemed to Isabel in these days something sacred in Gardencourt; no chapter of the past was more perfectly irrecoverable. When she thought of the months she had spent there the tears rose to her eyes. She flattered herself, as I say, upon her ingenuity, but she had need of all she could muster; for several events occurred which seemed to confront and defy her. The Countess Gemini arrived from Florence—arrived with her trunks, her dresses, her chatter, her falsehoods, her frivolity, the strange, the unholy legend of the number of her lovers. Edward Rosier, who had been away somewhere,—no one, not even Pansy, knew where,—reappeared in Rome and began to write her long letters, which she never answered. Madame Merle returned from Naples and said to her with a strange smile: "What on earth did you do with Lord Warburton?" As if it were any business of hers!

CHAPTER XLVIII

One day, toward the end of February, Ralph Touchett made up his mind to return to England. He had his own reasons for this decision, which he was not bound to communicate; but Henrietta Stackpole, to whom he mentioned his intention, flattered herself that she guessed them. She forbore to express them, however; she only said, after a moment, as she sat by his sofa: "I suppose you know you can't go alone?"

"I've no idea of doing that," Ralph answered. "I shall have people with me."

"What do you mean by 'people'? Servants whom you pay?"

"Ah," said Ralph jocosely, "after all, they're human beings."

"Are there any women among them?" Miss Stackpole desired to know.

"You speak as if I had a dozen! No, I confess I haven't a soubrette in my employment."

"Well," said Henrietta calmly, "you can't go to England that way. You must have a woman's care."

"I've had so much of yours for the past fortnight that it will last me a good while."

"You've not had enough of it yet. I guess I'll go with you," said Henrietta.

"Go with me?" Ralph slowly raised himself from his sofa.

"Yes, I know you don't like me, but I'll go with you all the same. It would be better for your health to lie down again."

Ralph looked at her a little; then he slowly relapsed. "I like you very much," he said in a moment.

Miss Stackpole gave one of her infrequent laughs. "You needn't think that by saying that you can buy me off. I'll go with you, and what is more I'll take care of you."

"You're a very good woman," said Ralph.

"Wait till I get you safely home before you say that. It won't be easy. But you had better go, all the same."

Before she left him, Ralph said to her: "Do you really mean to take care of me?"

"Well, I mean to try."

"I notify you then that I submit. Oh, I submit!" And it was perhaps a sign of submission that a few minutes after she had left him alone he burst into a loud fit of laughter. It seemed to him so inconsequent, such a conclusive proof of his having abdicated all functions and renounced all exercise, that he should start on a journey across Europe under the supervision of Miss Stackpole. And the great oddity was that the prospect pleased him; he was gratefully, luxuriously passive. He felt even impatient to start; and indeed he had an immense longing to see his own house again. The end of everything was at hand; it seemed to him he could stretch out his arm and touch the goal. But he wanted to die at home; it was the only wish he had left—to extend himself in the large quiet room where he had last seen his father lie, and close his eyes upon the summer dawn.

That same day Caspar Goodwood came to see him, and he informed his visitor that Miss Stackpole had taken him up and was to conduct him back to England. "Ah then," said Caspar, "I'm afraid I shall be a fifth wheel to the coach. Mrs. Osmond has made me promise to go with you."

"Good heavens—it's the golden age! You're all too kind."

"The kindness on my part is to her; it's hardly to you."

"Granting that, SHE'S kind," smiled Ralph.

"To get people to go with you? Yes, that's a sort of kindness," Goodwood answered without lending himself to the joke. "For myself, however," he added, "I'll go so far as to say that I would much rather travel with you and Miss Stackpole than with Miss Stackpole alone."

"And you'd rather stay here than do either," said Ralph. "There's really no need of your coming. Henrietta's extraordinarily efficient."

"I'm sure of that. But I've promised Mrs. Osmond."

"You can easily get her to let you off."

"She wouldn't let me off for the world. She wants me to look after you, but that isn't the principal thing. The principal thing is that she wants me to leave Rome."

"Ah, you see too much in it," Ralph suggested.

"I bore her," Goodwood went on; "she has nothing to say to me, so she invented that."

"Oh then, if it's a convenience to her I certainly will take you with me. Though I don't see why it should be a convenience," Ralph added in a moment.

"Well," said Caspar Goodwood simply, "she thinks I'm watching her."

"Watching her?"

"Trying to make out if she's happy."

"That's easy to make out," said Ralph. "She's the most visibly happy woman I know."

"Exactly so; I'm satisfied," Goodwood answered dryly. For all his dryness, however, he had more to say. "I've been watching her; I was an old friend and it seemed to me I had the right. She pretends to be happy; that was what she undertook to be; and I thought I should like to see for myself what it amounts to. I've seen," he continued with a harsh ring in his voice, "and I don't want to see any more. I'm now quite ready to go."

"Do you know it strikes me as about time you should?" Ralph rejoined. And this was the only conversation these gentlemen had about Isabel Osmond.

Henrietta made her preparations for departure, and among them she found it proper to say a few words to the Countess Gemini, who returned at Miss Stackpole's pension the visit which this lady had paid her in Florence.

"You were very wrong about Lord Warburton," she remarked to the Countess. "I think it right you should know that."

"About his making love to Isabel? My poor lady, he was at her house three times a day. He has left traces of his passage!" the Countess cried.

"He wished to marry your niece; that's why he came to the house."

The Countess stared, and then with an inconsiderate laugh: "Is that the story that Isabel tells? It isn't bad, as such things go. If he wishes to marry my niece, pray why doesn't he do it? Perhaps he has gone to buy the wedding-ring and will come back with it next month, after I'm gone."

"No, he'll not come back. Miss Osmond doesn't wish to marry him."

"She's very accommodating! I knew she was fond of Isabel, but I didn't know she carried it so far."

"I don't understand you," said Henrietta coldly, and reflecting that the Countess was unpleasantly perverse. "I really must stick to my point—that Isabel never encouraged the attentions of Lord Warburton."

"My dear friend, what do you and I know about it? All we know is that my brother's capable of everything."

"I don't know what your brother's capable of," said Henrietta with dignity.

"It's not her encouraging Warburton that I complain of; it's her sending him away. I want particularly to see him. Do you suppose she thought I would make him faithless?" the Countess continued with audacious insistence. "However, she's only keeping him, one can feel that. The house is full of him there; he's quite in the air. Oh yes, he has left traces; I'm sure I shall see him yet."

"Well," said Henrietta after a little, with one of those inspirations which had made the fortune of her letters to the Interviewer, "perhaps he'll be more successful with you than with Isabel!"

When she told her friend of the offer she had made Ralph Isabel replied that she could have done nothing that would have pleased her more. It had always been her faith that at bottom Ralph and this young woman were made to understand each other. "I don't care whether he understands me or not," Henrietta declared. "The great thing is that he shouldn't die in the cars."

"He won't do that," Isabel said, shaking her head with an extension of faith.

"He won't if I can help it. I see you want us all to go. I don't know what you want to do."

"I want to be alone," said Isabel.

"You won't be that so long as you've so much company at home."

"Ah, they're part of the comedy. You others are spectators."

"Do you call it a comedy, Isabel Archer?" Henrietta rather grimly asked.

"The tragedy then if you like. You're all looking at me; it makes me uncomfortable."

Henrietta engaged in this act for a while. "You're like the stricken deer, seeking the innermost shade. Oh, you do give me such a sense of helplessness!" she broke out.

"I'm not at all helpless. There are many things I mean to do."

"It's not you I'm speaking of; it's myself. It's too much, having come on purpose, to leave you just as I find you."

"You don't do that; you leave me much refreshed," Isabel said.

"Very mild refreshment—sour lemonade! I want you to promise me something."

"I can't do that. I shall never make another promise. I made such a solemn one four years ago, and I've succeeded so ill in keeping it."

"You've had no encouragement. In this case I should give you the greatest. Leave your husband before the worst comes; that's what I want you to promise."

"The worst? What do you call the worst?"

"Before your character gets spoiled."

"Do you mean my disposition? It won't get spoiled," Isabel answered, smiling. "I'm taking very good care of it. I'm extremely struck," she added, turning away, "with the off-hand way in which you speak of a woman's leaving her husband. It's easy to see you've never had one!"

"Well," said Henrietta as if she were beginning an argument, "nothing is more common in our Western cities, and it's to them, after all, that we must look in the future." Her argument, however, does not concern this history, which has too many other threads to unwind. She announced to Ralph Touchett that she was ready to leave Rome by any train he might designate, and Ralph immediately pulled himself together for departure. Isabel went to see him at the last, and he made the same remark that Henrietta had made. It struck him that Isabel was uncommonly glad to get rid of them all.

For all answer to this she gently laid her hand on his, and said in a low tone, with a quick smile: "My dear Ralph—!"

It was answer enough, and he was quite contented. But he went on in the same way, jocosely, ingenuously: "I've seen less of you than I might, but it's better than nothing. And then I've heard a great deal about you."

"I don't know from whom, leading the life you've done."

"From the voices of the air! Oh, from no one else; I never let other people speak of you. They always say you're 'charming,' and that's so flat."

"I might have seen more of you certainly," Isabel said. "But when one's married one has so much occupation."

"Fortunately I'm not married. When you come to see me in England I shall be able to entertain you with all the freedom of a bachelor." He continued to talk as if they should certainly meet again, and succeeded in making the assumption appear almost just. He made no allusion to his term being near, to the probability that he should not outlast the summer. If he preferred it so, Isabel was willing enough; the reality was sufficiently distinct without their erecting finger-posts in conversation. That had been well enough for the earlier time, though about this, as about his other affairs, Ralph had never been egotistic. Isabel spoke of his journey, of the stages into which he should divide it, of the precautions he should take. "Henrietta's my greatest precaution," he went on. "The conscience of that woman's sublime."

"Certainly she'll be very conscientious."

"Will be? She has been! It's only because she thinks it's her duty that she goes with me. There's a conception of duty for you."

"Yes, it's a generous one," said Isabel, "and it makes me deeply ashamed. I ought to go with you, you know."

"Your husband wouldn't like that."

"No, he wouldn't like it. But I might go, all the same."

"I'm startled by the boldness of your imagination. Fancy my being a cause of disagreement between a lady and her husband!"

"That's why I don't go," said Isabel simply—yet not very lucidly.

Ralph understood well enough, however. "I should think so, with all those occupations you speak of."

"It isn't that. I'm afraid," said Isabel. After a pause she repeated, as if to make herself, rather than him, hear the words: "I'm afraid."

Ralph could hardly tell what her tone meant; it was so strangely deliberate—apparently so void of emotion. Did she wish to do public penance for a fault of which she had not been convicted? or were her words simply an attempt at enlightened self-analysis? However this might be, Ralph could not resist so easy an opportunity. "Afraid of your husband?"

"Afraid of myself!" she said, getting up. She stood there a moment and then added: "If I were afraid of my husband that would be simply my duty. That's what women are expected to be."

"Ah yes," laughed Ralph; "but to make up for it there's always some man awfully afraid of some woman!"

She gave no heed to this pleasantry, but suddenly took a different turn. "With Henrietta at the head of your little band," she exclaimed abruptly, "there will be nothing left for Mr. Goodwood!"

"Ah, my dear Isabel," Ralph answered, "he's used to that. There is nothing left for Mr. Goodwood."

She coloured and then observed, quickly, that she must leave him. They stood together a moment; both her hands were in both of his. "You've been my best friend," she said.

"It was for you that I wanted—that I wanted to live. But I'm of no use to you."

Then it came over her more poignantly that she should not see him again. She could not accept that; she could not part with him that way. "If you should send for me I'd come," she said at last.

"Your husband won't consent to that."

"Oh yes, I can arrange it."

"I shall keep that for my last pleasure!" said Ralph.

In answer to which she simply kissed him. It was a Thursday, and that evening Caspar Goodwood came to Palazzo Roccanera. He was among the first to arrive, and he spent some time in conversation with Gilbert Osmond, who almost always was present when his wife received. They sat down together, and Osmond, talkative, communicative, expansive, seemed possessed with a kind of intellectual gaiety. He leaned back with his legs crossed, lounging and chatting, while Goodwood, more restless, but not at all lively, shifted his position, played with his hat, made the little sofa creak beneath him. Osmond's face wore a sharp, aggressive smile; he was as a man whose perceptions have been quickened by good news. He remarked to Goodwood that he was sorry they were to lose him; he himself should particularly miss him. He saw so few intelligent men—they were surprisingly scarce in Rome. He must be sure to come back; there was something very refreshing, to an inveterate Italian like himself, in talking with a genuine outsider.

"I'm very fond of Rome, you know," Osmond said; "but there's nothing I like better than to meet people who haven't that superstition. The modern world's after all very fine. Now you're thoroughly modern and yet are not at all common. So many of the moderns we see are such very poor stuff. If they're the children of the future we're willing to die young. Of course the ancients too are often very tiresome. My wife and I like everything that's really new—not the mere pretence of it. There's nothing new, unfortunately, in ignorance and stupidity. We see plenty of that in forms that offer themselves as a revelation of progress, of light. A revelation of vulgarity! There's a certain kind of vulgarity which I believe is really new; I don't think there ever was anything like it before. Indeed I don't find vulgarity, at all, before the present century. You see a faint menace of it here and there in the last, but to-day the air has grown so dense that delicate things are literally not recognised. Now, we've liked you—!" With which he hesitated a moment, laying his hand gently on Goodwood's knee and smiling with a mixture of assurance and embarrassment. "I'm going to say something extremely offensive and patronising, but you must let me have the satisfaction of it. We've liked you because—because you've reconciled us a little to the future. If there are to be a certain number of people like you—a la bonne heure! I'm talking for my wife as well as for myself, you see. She speaks for me, my wife; why shouldn't I speak for her? We're as united, you know, as the candlestick and the snuffers. Am I assuming too much when I say that I think I've understood from you that your occupations have been—a—commercial? There's a danger in that, you know; but it's the way you have escaped that strikes us. Excuse me if my little compliment seems in execrable taste; fortunately my wife doesn't hear me. What I mean is that you might have been—a—what I was mentioning just now. The whole American world was in a conspiracy to make you so. But you resisted, you've something about you that saved you. And yet you're so modern, so modern; the most modern man we know! We shall always be delighted to see you again."

I have said that Osmond was in good humour, and these remarks will give ample evidence of the fact. They were infinitely more personal than he usually cared to be, and if Caspar Goodwood had attended to them more closely he might have thought that the defence of delicacy was in rather odd hands. We may believe, however, that Osmond knew very well what he was about, and that if he chose to use the tone of patronage with a grossness not in his habits he had an excellent reason for the escapade. Goodwood had only a vague sense that he was laying it on somehow; he scarcely knew where the mixture was applied. Indeed he scarcely knew what Osmond was talking about; he wanted to be alone with Isabel, and that idea spoke louder to him than her husband's perfectly-pitched voice. He watched her talking with other people and wondered when she would be at liberty and whether he might ask her to go into one of the other rooms. His humour was not, like Osmond's, of the best; there was an element of dull rage in his consciousness of things. Up to this time he had not disliked Osmond personally; he had only thought him very well-informed and obliging and more than he had supposed like the person whom Isabel Archer would naturally marry. His host had won in the open field a great advantage over him, and Goodwood had too strong a sense of fair play to have been moved to underrate him on that account. He had not tried positively to think well of him; this was a flight of sentimental benevolence of which, even in the days when he came nearest to reconciling himself to what had happened, Goodwood was quite incapable. He accepted him as rather a brilliant personage of the amateurish kind, afflicted with a redundancy of leisure which it amused him to work off in little refinements of conversation. But he only half trusted him; he could never make out why the deuce Osmond should lavish refinements of any sort upon HIM. It made him suspect that he found some private entertainment in it, and it ministered to a general impression that his triumphant rival had in his composition a streak of perversity. He knew indeed that Osmond could have no reason to wish him evil; he had nothing to fear from him. He had carried off a supreme advantage and could afford to be kind to a man who had lost everything. It was true that Goodwood had at times grimly wished he were dead and would have liked to kill him; but Osmond had no means of knowing this, for practice had made the younger man perfect in the art of appearing inaccessible to-day to any violent emotion. He cultivated this art in order to deceive himself, but it was others that he deceived first. He cultivated it, moreover, with very limited success; of which there could be no better proof than the deep, dumb irritation that reigned in his soul when he heard Osmond speak of his wife's feelings as if he were commissioned to answer for them.

That was all he had had an ear for in what his host said to him this evening; he had been conscious that Osmond made more of a point even than usual of referring to the conjugal harmony prevailing at Palazzo Roccanera. He had been more careful than ever to speak as if he and his wife had all things in sweet community and it were as natural to each of them to say "we" as to say "I". In all this there was an air of intention that had puzzled and angered our poor Bostonian, who could only reflect for his comfort that Mrs. Osmond's relations with her husband were none of his business. He had no proof whatever that her husband misrepresented her, and if he judged her by the surface of things was bound to believe that she liked her life. She had never given him the faintest sign of discontent. Miss Stackpole had told him that she had lost her illusions, but writing for the papers had made Miss Stackpole sensational. She was too fond of early news. Moreover, since her arrival in Rome she had been much on her guard; she had pretty well ceased to flash her lantern at him. This indeed, it may be said for her, would have been quite against her conscience. She had now seen the reality of Isabel's situation, and it had inspired her with a just reserve. Whatever could be done to improve it the most useful form of assistance would not be to inflame her former lovers with a sense of her wrongs. Miss Stackpole continued to take a deep interest in the state of Mr. Goodwood's feelings, but she showed it at present only by sending him choice extracts, humorous and other, from the American journals, of which she received several by every post and which she always perused with a pair of scissors in her hand. The articles she cut out she placed in an envelope addressed to Mr. Goodwood, which she left with her own hand at his hotel. He never asked her a question about Isabel: hadn't he come five thousand miles to see for himself? He was thus not in the least authorised to think Mrs. Osmond unhappy; but the very absence of authorisation operated as an irritant, ministered to the harsh-ness with which, in spite of his theory that he had ceased to care, he now recognised that, so far as she was concerned, the future had nothing more for him. He had not even the satisfaction of knowing the truth; apparently he could not even be trusted to respect her if she WERE unhappy. He was hopeless, helpless, useless. To this last character she had called his attention by her ingenious plan for making him leave Rome. He had no objection whatever to doing what he could for her cousin, but it made him grind his teeth to think that of all the services she might have asked of him this was the one she had been eager to select. There had been no danger of her choosing one that would have kept him in Rome.

To-night what he was chiefly thinking of was that he was to leave her to-morrow and that he had gained nothing by coming but the knowledge that he was as little wanted as ever. About herself he had gained no knowledge; she was imperturbable, inscrutable, impenetrable. He felt the old bitterness, which he had tried so hard to swallow, rise again in his throat, and he knew there are disappointments that last as long as life. Osmond went on talking; Goodwood was vaguely aware that he was touching again upon his perfect intimacy with his wife. It seemed to him for a moment that the man had a kind of demonic imagination; it was impossible that without malice he should have selected so unusual a topic. But what did it matter, after all, whether he were demonic or not, and whether she loved him or hated him? She might hate him to the death without one's gaining a straw one's self. "You travel, by the by, with Ralph Touchett," Osmond said. "I suppose that means you'll move slowly?"

"I don't know. I shall do just as he likes."

"You're very accommodating. We're immensely obliged to you; you must really let me say it. My wife has probably expressed to you what we feel. Touchett has been on our minds all winter; it has looked more than once as if he would never leave Rome. He ought never to have come; it's worse than an imprudence for people in that state to travel; it's a kind of indelicacy. I wouldn't for the world be under such an obligation to Touchett as he has been to—to my wife and me. Other people inevitably have to look after him, and every one isn't so generous as you."

"I've nothing else to do," Caspar said dryly.

Osmond looked at him a moment askance. "You ought to marry, and then you'd have plenty to do! It's true that in that case you wouldn't be quite so available for deeds of mercy."

"Do you find that as a married man you're so much occupied?" the young man mechanically asked.

"Ah, you see, being married's in itself an occupation. It isn't always active; it's often passive; but that takes even more attention. Then my wife and I do so many things together. We read, we study, we make music, we walk, we drive—we talk even, as when we first knew each other. I delight, to this hour, in my wife's conversation. If you're ever bored take my advice and get married. Your wife indeed may bore you, in that case; but you'll never bore yourself. You'll always have something to say to yourself—always have a subject of reflection."

"I'm not bored," said Goodwood. "I've plenty to think about and to say to myself."

"More than to say to others!" Osmond exclaimed with a light laugh. "Where shall you go next? I mean after you've consigned Touchett to his natural caretakers—I believe his mother's at last coming back to look after him. That little lady's superb; she neglects her duties with a finish—! Perhaps you'll spend the summer in England?"

"I don't know. I've no plans."

"Happy man! That's a little bleak, but it's very free."

"Oh yes, I'm very free."

"Free to come back to Rome I hope," said Osmond as he saw a group of new visitors enter the room. "Remember that when you do come we count on you!"

Goodwood had meant to go away early, but the evening elapsed without his having a chance to speak to Isabel otherwise than as one of several associated interlocutors. There was something perverse in the inveteracy with which she avoided him; his unquenchable rancour discovered an intention where there was certainly no appearance of one. There was absolutely no appearance of one. She met his eyes with her clear hospitable smile, which seemed almost to ask that he would come and help her to entertain some of her visitors. To such suggestions, however, he opposed but a stiff impatience. He wandered about and waited; he talked to the few people he knew, who found him for the first time rather self-contradictory. This was indeed rare with Caspar Goodwood, though he often contradicted others. There was often music at Palazzo Roccanera, and it was usually very good. Under cover of the music he managed to contain himself; but toward the end, when he saw the people beginning to go, he drew near to Isabel and asked her in a low tone if he might not speak to her in one of the other rooms, which he had just assured himself was empty. She smiled as if she wished to oblige him but found her self absolutely prevented. "I'm afraid it's impossible. People are saying good-night, and I must be where they can see me."

"I shall wait till they are all gone then."

She hesitated a moment. "Ah, that will be delightful!" she exclaimed.

And he waited, though it took a long time yet. There were several people, at the end, who seemed tethered to the carpet. The Countess Gemini, who was never herself till midnight, as she said, displayed no consciousness that the entertainment was over; she had still a little circle of gentlemen in front of the fire, who every now and then broke into a united laugh. Osmond had disappeared—he never bade good-bye to people; and as the Countess was extending her range, according to her custom at this period of the evening, Isabel had sent Pansy to bed. Isabel sat a little apart; she too appeared to wish her sister-in-law would sound a lower note and let the last loiterers depart in peace.

"May I not say a word to you now?" Goodwood presently asked her. She got up immediately, smiling. "Certainly, we'll go somewhere else if you like." They went together, leaving the Countess with her little circle, and for a moment after they had crossed the threshold neither of them spoke. Isabel would not sit down; she stood in the middle of the room slowly fanning herself; she had for him the same familiar grace. She seemed to wait for him to speak. Now that he was alone with her all the passion he had never stifled surged into his senses; it hummed in his eyes and made things swim round him. The bright, empty room grew dim and blurred, and through the heaving veil he felt her hover before him with gleaming eyes and parted lips. If he had seen more distinctly he would have perceived her smile was fixed and a trifle forced—that she was frightened at what she saw in his own face. "I suppose you wish to bid me goodbye?" she said.

"Yes—but I don't like it. I don't want to leave Rome," he answered with almost plaintive honesty.

"I can well imagine. It's wonderfully good of you. I can't tell you how kind I think you."

For a moment more he said nothing. "With a few words like that you make me go."

"You must come back some day," she brightly returned.

"Some day? You mean as long a time hence as possible."

"Oh no; I don't mean all that."

"What do you mean? I don't understand! But I said I'd go, and I'll go," Goodwood added.

"Come back whenever you like," said Isabel with attempted lightness.

"I don't care a straw for your cousin!" Caspar broke out.

"Is that what you wished to tell me?"

"No, no; I didn't want to tell you anything; I wanted to ask you—" he paused a moment, and then—"what have you really made of your life?" he said, in a low, quick tone. He paused again, as if for an answer; but she said nothing, and he went on: "I can't understand, I can't penetrate you! What am I to believe—what do you want me to think?" Still she said nothing; she only stood looking at him, now quite without pretending to ease. "I'm told you're unhappy, and if you are I should like to know it. That would be something for me. But you yourself say you're happy, and you're somehow so still, so smooth, so hard. You're completely changed. You conceal everything; I haven't really come near you."

"You come very near," Isabel said gently, but in a tone of warning.

"And yet I don't touch you! I want to know the truth. Have you done well?"

"You ask a great deal."

"Yes—I've always asked a great deal. Of course you won't tell me. I shall never know if you can help it. And then it's none of my business." He had spoken with a visible effort to control himself, to give a considerate form to an inconsiderate state of mind. But the sense that it was his last chance, that he loved her and had lost her, that she would think him a fool whatever he should say, suddenly gave him a lash and added a deep vibration to his low voice. "You're perfectly inscrutable, and that's what makes me think you've something to hide. I tell you I don't care a straw for your cousin, but I don't mean that I don't like him. I mean that it isn't because I like him that I go away with him. I'd go if he were an idiot and you should have asked me. If you should ask me I'd go to Siberia tomorrow. Why do you want me to leave the place? You must have some reason for that; if you were as contented as you pretend you are you wouldn't care. I'd rather know the truth about you, even if it's damnable, than have come here for nothing. That isn't what I came for. I thought I shouldn't care. I came because I wanted to assure myself that I needn't think of you any more. I haven't thought of anything else, and you're quite right to wish me to go away. But if I must go, there's no harm in my letting myself out for a single moment, is there? If you're really hurt—if HE hurts you—nothing I say will hurt you. When I tell you I love you it's simply what I came for. I thought it was for something else; but it was for that. I shouldn't say it if I didn't believe I should never see you again. It's the last time—let me pluck a single flower! I've no right to say that, I know; and you've no right to listen. But you don't listen; you never listen, you're always thinking of something else. After this I must go, of course; so I shall at least have a reason. Your asking me is no reason, not a real one. I can't judge by your husband," he went on irrelevantly, almost incoherently; "I don't understand him; he tells me you adore each other. Why does he tell me that? What business is it of mine? When I say that to you, you look strange. But you always look strange. Yes, you've something to hide. It's none of my business—very true. But I love you," said Caspar Goodwood.

As he said, she looked strange. She turned her eyes to the door by which they had entered and raised her fan as if in warning.

"You've behaved so well; don't spoil it," she uttered softly.

"No one hears me. It's wonderful what you tried to put me off with. I love you as I've never loved you."

"I know it. I knew it as soon as you consented to go."

"You can't help it—of course not. You would if you could, but you can't, unfortunately. Unfortunately for me, I mean. I ask nothing—nothing, that is, I shouldn't. But I do ask one sole satisfaction:—that you tell me—that you tell me—!"

"That I tell you what?"

"Whether I may pity you."

"Should you like that?" Isabel asked, trying to smile again.

"To pity you? Most assuredly! That at least would be doing something. I'd give my life to it."

She raised her fan to her face, which it covered all except her eyes. They rested a moment on his. "Don't give your life to it; but give a thought to it every now and then." And with that she went back to the Countess Gemini.

CHAPTER XLIX

Madame Merle had not made her appearance at Palazzo Roccanera on the evening of that Thursday of which I have narrated some of the incidents, and Isabel, though she observed her absence, was not surprised by it. Things had passed between them which added no stimulus to sociability, and to appreciate which we must glance a little backward. It has been mentioned that Madame Merle returned from Naples shortly after Lord Warburton had left Rome, and that on her first meeting with Isabel (whom, to do her justice, she came immediately to see) her first utterance had been an enquiry as to the whereabouts of this nobleman, for whom she appeared to hold her dear friend accountable.

"Please don't talk of him," said Isabel for answer; "we've heard so much of him of late."

Madame Merle bent her head on one side a little, protestingly, and smiled at the left corner of her mouth. "You've heard, yes. But you must remember that I've not, in Naples. I hoped to find him here and to be able to congratulate Pansy."

"You may congratulate Pansy still; but not on marrying Lord Warburton."

"How you say that! Don't you know I had set my heart on it?" Madame Merle asked with a great deal of spirit, but still with the intonation of good-humour.

Isabel was discomposed, but she was determined to be good-humoured too. "You shouldn't have gone to Naples then. You should have stayed here to watch the affair."

"I had too much confidence in you. But do you think it's too late?"

"You had better ask Pansy," said Isabel.

"I shall ask her what you've said to her."

These words seemed to justify the impulse of self-defence aroused on Isabel's part by her perceiving that her visitor's attitude was a critical one. Madame Merle, as we know, had been very discreet hitherto; she had never criticised; she had been markedly afraid of intermeddling. But apparently she had only reserved herself for this occasion, since she now had a dangerous quickness in her eye and an air of irritation which even her admirable ease was not able to transmute. She had suffered a disappointment which excited Isabel's surprise—our heroine having no knowledge of her zealous interest in Pansy's marriage; and she betrayed it in a manner which quickened Mrs. Osmond's alarm. More clearly than ever before Isabel heard a cold, mocking voice proceed from she knew not where, in the dim void that surrounded her, and declare that this bright, strong, definite, worldly woman, this incarnation of the practical, the personal, the immediate, was a powerful agent in her destiny. She was nearer to her than Isabel had yet discovered, and her nearness was not the charming accident she had so long supposed. The sense of accident indeed had died within her that day when she happened to be struck with the manner in which the wonderful lady and her own husband sat together in private. No definite suspicion had as yet taken its place; but it was enough to make her view this friend with a different eye, to have been led to reflect that there was more intention in her past behaviour than she had allowed for at the time. Ah yes, there had been intention, there had been intention, Isabel said to herself; and she seemed to wake from a long pernicious dream. What was it that brought home to her that Madame Merle's intention had not been good? Nothing but the mistrust which had lately taken body and which married itself now to the fruitful wonder produced by her visitor's challenge on behalf of poor Pansy. There was something in this challenge which had at the very outset excited an answering defiance; a nameless vitality which she could see to have been absent from her friend's professions of delicacy and caution. Madame Merle had been unwilling to interfere, certainly, but only so long as there was nothing to interfere with. It will perhaps seem to the reader that Isabel went fast in casting doubt, on mere suspicion, on a sincerity proved by several years of good offices. She moved quickly indeed, and with reason, for a strange truth was filtering into her soul. Madame Merle's interest was identical with Osmond's: that was enough. "I think Pansy will tell you nothing that will make you more angry," she said in answer to her companion's last remark.

"I'm not in the least angry. I've only a great desire to retrieve the situation. Do you consider that Warburton has left us for ever?"

"I can't tell you; I don't understand you. It's all over; please let it rest. Osmond has talked to me a great deal about it, and I've nothing more to say or to hear. I've no doubt," Isabel added, "that he'll be very happy to discuss the subject with you."

"I know what he thinks; he came to see me last evening."

"As soon as you had arrived? Then you know all about it and you needn't apply to me for information."

"It isn't information I want. At bottom it's sympathy. I had set my heart on that marriage; the idea did what so few things do—it satisfied the imagination."

"Your imagination, yes. But not that of the persons concerned."

"You mean by that of course that I'm not concerned. Of course not directly. But when one's such an old friend one can't help having something at stake. You forget how long I've known Pansy. You mean, of course," Madame Merle added, "that YOU are one of the persons concerned."

"No; that's the last thing I mean. I'm very weary of it all."

Madame Merle hesitated a little. "Ah yes, your work's done."

"Take care what you say," said Isabel very gravely.

"Oh, I take care; never perhaps more than when it appears least. Your husband judges you severely."

Isabel made for a moment no answer to this; she felt choked with bitterness. It was not the insolence of Madame Merle's informing her that Osmond had been taking her into his confidence as against his wife that struck her most; for she was not quick to believe that this was meant for insolence. Madame Merle was very rarely insolent, and only when it was exactly right. It was not right now, or at least it was not right yet. What touched Isabel like a drop of corrosive acid upon an open wound was the knowledge that Osmond dishonoured her in his words as well as in his thoughts. "Should you like to know how I judge HIM?" she asked at last.

"No, because you'd never tell me. And it would be painful for me to know."

There was a pause, and for the first time since she had known her Isabel thought Madame Merle disagreeable. She wished she would leave her. "Remember how attractive Pansy is, and don't despair," she said abruptly, with a desire that this should close their interview.

But Madame Merle's expansive presence underwent no contraction. She only gathered her mantle about her and, with the movement, scattered upon the air a faint, agreeable fragrance. "I don't despair; I feel encouraged. And I didn't come to scold you; I came if possible to learn the truth. I know you'll tell it if I ask you. It's an immense blessing with you that one can count upon that. No, you won't believe what a comfort I take in it."

"What truth do you speak of?" Isabel asked, wondering.

"Just this: whether Lord Warburton changed his mind quite of his own movement or because you recommended it. To please himself I mean, or to please you. Think of the confidence I must still have in you, in spite of having lost a little of it," Madame Merle continued with a smile, "to ask such a question as that!" She sat looking at her friend, to judge the effect of her words, and then went on: "Now don't be heroic, don't be unreasonable, don't take offence. It seems to me I do you an honour in speaking so. I don't know another woman to whom I would do it. I haven't the least idea that any other woman would tell me the truth. And don't you see how well it is that your husband should know it? It's true that he doesn't appear to have had any tact whatever in trying to extract it; he has indulged in gratuitous suppositions. But that doesn't alter the fact that it would make a difference in his view of his daughter's prospects to know distinctly what really occurred. If Lord Warburton simply got tired of the poor child, that's one thing, and it's a pity. If he gave her up to please you it's another. That's a pity too, but in a different way. Then, in the latter case, you'd perhaps resign yourself to not being pleased—to simply seeing your step-daughter married. Let him off—let us have him!"

Madame Merle had proceeded very deliberately, watching her companion and apparently thinking she could proceed safely. As she went on Isabel grew pale; she clasped her hands more tightly in her lap. It was not that her visitor had at last thought it the right time to be insolent; for this was not what was most apparent. It was a worse horror than that. "Who are you—what are you?" Isabel murmured. "What have you to do with my husband?" It was strange that for the moment she drew as near to him as if she had loved him.

"Ah then, you take it heroically! I'm very sorry. Don't think, however, that I shall do so."

"What have you to do with me?" Isabel went on.

Madame Merle slowly got up, stroking her muff, but not removing her eyes from Isabel's face. "Everything!" she answered.

Isabel sat there looking up at her, without rising; her face was almost a prayer to be enlightened. But the light of this woman's eyes seemed only a darkness. "Oh misery!" she murmured at last; and she fell back, covering her face with her hands. It had come over her like a high-surging wave that Mrs. Touchett was right. Madame Merle had married her. Before she uncovered her face again that lady had left the room.

Isabel took a drive alone that afternoon; she wished to be far away, under the sky, where she could descend from her carriage and tread upon the daisies. She had long before this taken old Rome into her confidence, for in a world of ruins the ruin of her happiness seemed a less unnatural catastrophe. She rested her weariness upon things that had crumbled for centuries and yet still were upright; she dropped her secret sadness into the silence of lonely places, where its very modern quality detached itself and grew objective, so that as she sat in a sun-warmed angle on a winter's day, or stood in a mouldy church to which no one came, she could almost smile at it and think of its smallness. Small it was, in the large Roman record, and her haunting sense of the continuity of the human lot easily carried her from the less to the greater. She had become deeply, tenderly acquainted with Rome; it interfused and moderated her passion. But she had grown to think of it chiefly as the place where people had suffered. This was what came to her in the starved churches, where the marble columns, transferred from pagan ruins, seemed to offer her a companionship in endurance and the musty incense to be a compound of long-unanswered prayers. There was no gentler nor less consistent heretic than Isabel; the firmest of worshippers, gazing at dark altar-pictures or clustered candles, could not have felt more intimately the suggestiveness of these objects nor have been more liable at such moments to a spiritual visitation. Pansy, as we know, was almost always her companion, and of late the Countess Gemini, balancing a pink parasol, had lent brilliancy to their equipage; but she still occasionally found herself alone when it suited her mood and where it suited the place. On such occasions she had several resorts; the most accessible of which perhaps was a seat on the low parapet which edges the wide grassy space before the high, cold front of Saint John Lateran, whence you look across the Campagna at the far-trailing outline of the Alban Mount and at that mighty plain, between, which is still so full of all that has passed from it. After the departure of her cousin and his companions she roamed more than usual; she carried her sombre spirit from one familiar shrine to the other. Even when Pansy and the Countess were with her she felt the touch of a vanished world. The carriage, leaving the walls of Rome behind, rolled through narrow lanes where the wild honeysuckle had begun to tangle itself in the hedges, or waited for her in quiet places where the fields lay near, while she strolled further and further over the flower-freckled turf, or sat on a stone that had once had a use and gazed through the veil of her personal sadness at the splendid sadness of the scene—at the dense, warm light, the far gradations and soft confusions of colour, the motionless shepherds in lonely attitudes, the hills where the cloud-shadows had the lightness of a blush.

On the afternoon I began with speaking of, she had taken a resolution not to think of Madame Merle; but the resolution proved vain, and this lady's image hovered constantly before her. She asked herself, with an almost childlike horror of the supposition, whether to this intimate friend of several years the great historical epithet of wicked were to be applied. She knew the idea only by the Bible and other literary works; to the best of her belief she had had no personal acquaintance with wickedness. She had desired a large acquaintance with human life, and in spite of her having flattered herself that she cultivated it with some success this elementary privilege had been denied her. Perhaps it was not wicked—in the historic sense—to be even deeply false; for that was what Madame Merle had been—deeply, deeply, deeply. Isabel's Aunt Lydia had made this discovery long before, and had mentioned it to her niece; but Isabel had flattered herself at this time that she had a much richer view of things, especially of the spontaneity of her own career and the nobleness of her own interpretations, than poor stiffly-reasoning Mrs. Touchett. Madame Merle had done what she wanted; she had brought about the union of her two friends; a reflection which could not fail to make it a matter of wonder that she should so much have desired such an event. There were people who had the match-making passion, like the votaries of art for art; but Madame Merle, great artist as she was, was scarcely one of these. She thought too ill of marriage, too ill even of life; she had desired that particular marriage but had not desired others. She had therefore had a conception of gain, and Isabel asked herself where she had found her profit. It took her naturally a long time to discover, and even then her discovery was imperfect. It came back to her that Madame Merle, though she had seemed to like her from their first meeting at Gardencourt, had been doubly affectionate after Mr. Touchett's death and after learning that her young friend had been subject to the good old man's charity. She had found her profit not in the gross device of borrowing money, but in the more refined idea of introducing one of her intimates to the young woman's fresh and ingenuous fortune. She had naturally chosen her closest intimate, and it was already vivid enough to Isabel that Gilbert occupied this position. She found herself confronted in this manner with the conviction that the man in the world whom she had supposed to be the least sordid had married her, like a vulgar adventurer, for her money. Strange to say, it had never before occurred to her; if she had thought a good deal of harm of Osmond she had not done him this particular injury. This was the worst she could think of, and she had been saying to herself that the worst was still to come. A man might marry a woman for her money perfectly well; the thing was often done. But at least he should let her know. She wondered whether, since he had wanted her money, her money would now satisfy him. Would he take her money and let her go Ah, if Mr. Touchett's great charity would but help her to-day it would be blessed indeed! It was not slow to occur to her that if Madame Merle had wished to do Gilbert a service his recognition to her of the boon must have lost its warmth. What must be his feelings to-day in regard to his too zealous benefactress, and what expression must they have found on the part of such a master of irony? It is a singular, but a characteristic, fact that before Isabel returned from her silent drive she had broken its silence by the soft exclamation: "Poor, poor Madame Merle!"

Her compassion would perhaps have been justified if on this same afternoon she had been concealed behind one of the valuable curtains of time-softened damask which dressed the interesting little salon of the lady to whom it referred; the carefully-arranged apartment to which we once paid a visit in company with the discreet Mr. Rosier. In that apartment, towards six o'clock, Gilbert Osmond was seated, and his hostess stood before him as Isabel had seen her stand on an occasion commemorated in this history with an emphasis appropriate not so much to its apparent as to its real importance.

"I don't believe you're unhappy; I believe you like it," said Madame Merle.

"Did I say I was unhappy?" Osmond asked with a face grave enough to suggest that he might have been.

"No, but you don't say the contrary, as you ought in common gratitude."

"Don't talk about gratitude," he returned dryly. "And don't aggravate me," he added in a moment.

Madame Merle slowly seated herself, with her arms folded and her white hands arranged as a support to one of them and an ornament, as it were, to the other. She looked exquisitely calm but impressively sad. "On your side, don't try to frighten me. I wonder if you guess some of my thoughts."

"I trouble about them no more than I can help. I've quite enough of my own."

"That's because they're so delightful."

Osmond rested his head against the back of his chair and looked at his companion with a cynical directness which seemed also partly an expression of fatigue. "You do aggravate me," he remarked in a moment. "I'm very tired."

"Eh moi donc!" cried Madame Merle.

"With you it's because you fatigue yourself. With me it's not my own fault."

"When I fatigue myself it's for you. I've given you an interest. That's a great gift."

"Do you call it an interest?" Osmond enquired with detachment.

"Certainly, since it helps you to pass your time."

"The time has never seemed longer to me than this winter."

"You've never looked better; you've never been so agreeable, so brilliant."

"Damn my brilliancy!" he thoughtfully murmured. "How little, after all, you know me!"

"If I don't know you I know nothing," smiled Madame Merle. "You've the feeling of complete success."

"No, I shall not have that till I've made you stop judging me."

"I did that long ago. I speak from old knowledge. But you express yourself more too."

Osmond just hung fire. "I wish you'd express yourself less!"

"You wish to condemn me to silence? Remember that I've never been a chatterbox. At any rate there are three or four things I should like to say to you first. Your wife doesn't know what to do with herself," she went on with a change of tone.

"Pardon me; she knows perfectly. She has a line sharply drawn. She means to carry out her ideas."

"Her ideas to-day must be remarkable."

"Certainly they are. She has more of them than ever."

"She was unable to show me any this morning," said Madame Merle. "She seemed in a very simple, almost in a stupid, state of mind. She was completely bewildered."

"You had better say at once that she was pathetic."

"Ah no, I don't want to encourage you too much."

He still had his head against the cushion behind him; the ankle of one foot rested on the other knee. So he sat for a while. "I should like to know what's the matter with you," he said at last.

"The matter—the matter—!" And here Madame Merle stopped. Then she went on with a sudden outbreak of passion, a burst of summer thunder in a clear sky: "The matter is that I would give my right hand to be able to weep, and that I can't!"

"What good would it do you to weep?"

"It would make me feel as I felt before I knew you."

"If I've dried your tears, that's something. But I've seen you shed them."

"Oh, I believe you'll make me cry still. I mean make me howl like a wolf. I've a great hope, I've a great need, of that. I was vile this morning; I was horrid," she said.

"If Isabel was in the stupid state of mind you mention she probably didn't perceive it," Osmond answered.

"It was precisely my deviltry that stupefied her. I couldn't help it; I was full of something bad. Perhaps it was something good; I don't know. You've not only dried up my tears; you've dried up my soul."

"It's not I then that am responsible for my wife's condition," Osmond said. "It's pleasant to think that I shall get the benefit of your influence upon her. Don't you know the soul is an immortal principle? How can it suffer alteration?"

"I don't believe at all that it's an immortal principle. I believe it can perfectly be destroyed. That's what has happened to mine, which was a very good one to start with; and it's you I have to thank for it. You're VERY bad," she added with gravity in her emphasis.

"Is this the way we're to end?" Osmond asked with the same studied coldness.

"I don't know how we're to end. I wish I did—How do bad people end?—especially as to their COMMON crimes. You have made me as bad as yourself."

"I don't understand you. You seem to me quite good enough," said Osmond, his conscious indifference giving an extreme effect to the words.

Madame Merle's self-possession tended on the contrary to diminish, and she was nearer losing it than on any occasion on which we have had the pleasure of meeting her. The glow of her eye turners sombre; her smile betrayed a painful effort. "Good enough for anything that I've done with myself? I suppose that's what you mean."

"Good enough to be always charming!" Osmond exclaimed, smiling too.

"Oh God!" his companion murmured; and, sitting there in her ripe freshness, she had recourse to the same gesture she had provoked on Isabel's part in the morning: she bent her face and covered it with her hands.

"Are you going to weep after all?" Osmond asked; and on her remaining motionless he went on: "Have I ever complained to you?"

She dropped her hands quickly. "No, you've taken your revenge otherwise—you have taken it on HER."

Osmond threw back his head further; he looked a while at the ceiling and might have been supposed to be appealing, in an informal way, to the heavenly powers. "Oh, the imagination of women! It's always vulgar, at bottom. You talk of revenge like a third-rate novelist."

"Of course you haven't complained. You've enjoyed your triumph too much."

"I'm rather curious to know what you call my triumph."

"You've made your wife afraid of you."

Osmond changed his position; he leaned forward, resting his elbows on his knees and looking a while at a beautiful old Persian rug, at his feet. He had an air of refusing to accept any one's valuation of anything, even of time, and of preferring to abide by his own; a peculiarity which made him at moments an irritating person to converse with. "Isabel's not afraid of me, and it's not what I wish," he said at last. "To what do you want to provoke me when you say such things as that?"

"I've thought over all the harm you can do me," Madame Merle answered. "Your wife was afraid of me this morning, but in me it was really you she feared."

"You may have said things that were in very bad taste; I'm not responsible for that. I didn't see the use of your going to see her at all: you're capable of acting without her. I've not made you afraid of me that I can see," he went on; "how then should I have made her? You're at least as brave. I can't think where you've picked up such rubbish; one might suppose you knew me by this time." He got up as he spoke and walked to the chimney, where he stood a moment bending his eye, as if he had seen them for the first time, on the delicate specimens of rare porcelain with which it was covered. He took up a small cup and held it in his hand; then, still holding it and leaning his arm on the mantel, he pursued: "You always see too much in everything; you overdo it; you lose sight of the real. I'm much simpler than you think."

"I think you're very simple." And Madame Merle kept her eye on her cup. "I've come to that with time. I judged you, as I say, of old; but it's only since your marriage that I've understood you. I've seen better what you have been to your wife than I ever saw what you were for me. Please be very careful of that precious object."

"It already has a wee bit of a tiny crack," said Osmond dryly as he put it down. "If you didn't understand me before I married it was cruelly rash of you to put me into such a box. However, I took a fancy to my box myself; I thought it would be a comfortable fit. I asked very little; I only asked that she should like me."

"That she should like you so much!"

"So much, of course; in such a case one asks the maximum. That she should adore me, if you will. Oh yes, I wanted that."

"I never adored you," said Madame Merle.

"Ah, but you pretended to!"

"It's true that you never accused me of being a comfortable fit," Madame Merle went on.

"My wife has declined—declined to do anything of the sort," said Osmond. "If you're determined to make a tragedy of that, the tragedy's hardly for her."

"The tragedy's for me!" Madame Merle exclaimed, rising with a long low sigh but having a glance at the same time for the contents of her mantel-shelf.

"It appears that I'm to be severely taught the disadvantages of a false position."

"You express yourself like a sentence in a copybook. We must look for our comfort where we can find it. If my wife doesn't like me, at least my child does. I shall look for compensations in Pansy. Fortunately I haven't a fault to find with her."

"Ah," she said softly, "if I had a child—!"

Osmond waited, and then, with a little formal air, "The children of others may be a great interest!" he announced.

"You're more like a copy-book than I. There's something after all that holds us together."

"Is it the idea of the harm I may do you?" Osmond asked.

"No; it's the idea of the good I may do for you. It's that," Madame Merle pursued, "that made me so jealous of Isabel. I want it to be MY work," she added, with her face, which had grown hard and bitter, relaxing to its habit of smoothness.

Her friend took up his hat and his umbrella, and after giving the former article two or three strokes with his coat-cuff, "On the whole, I think," he said, "you had better leave it to me."

After he had left her she went, the first thing, and lifted from the mantel-shelf the attenuated coffee-cup in which he had mentioned the existence of a crack; but she looked at it rather abstractedly. "Have I been so vile all for nothing?" she vaguely wailed.

CHAPTER L

As the Countess Gemini was not acquainted with the ancient monuments Isabel occasionally offered to introduce her to these interesting relics and to give their afternoon drive an antiquarian aim. The Countess, who professed to think her sister-in-law a prodigy of learning, never made an objection, and gazed at masses of Roman brickwork as patiently as if they had been mounds of modern drapery. She had not the historic sense, though she had in some directions the anecdotic, and as regards herself the apologetic, but she was so delighted to be in Rome that she only desired to float with the current. She would gladly have passed an hour every day in the damp darkness of the Baths of Titus if it had been a condition of her remaining at Palazzo Roccanera. Isabel, however, was not a severe cicerone; she used to visit the ruins chiefly because they offered an excuse for talking about other matters than the love affairs of the ladies of Florence, as to which her companion was never weary of offering information. It must be added that during these visits the Countess forbade herself every form of active research; her preference was to sit in the carriage and exclaim that everything was most interesting. It was in this manner that she had hitherto examined the Coliseum, to the infinite regret of her niece, who—with all the respect that she owed her—could not see why she should not descend from the vehicle and enter the building. Pansy had so little chance to ramble that her view of the case was not wholly disinterested; it may be divined that she had a secret hope that, once inside, her parents' guest might be induced to climb to the upper tiers. There came a day when the Countess announced her willingness to undertake this feat—a mild afternoon in March when the windy month expressed itself in occasional puffs of spring. The three ladies went into the Coliseum together, but Isabel left her companions to wander over the place. She had often ascended to those desolate ledges from which the Roman crowd used to bellow applause and where now the wild flowers (when they are allowed) bloom in the deep crevices; and to-day she felt weary and disposed to sit in the despoiled arena. It made an intermission too, for the Countess often asked more from one's attention than she gave in return; and Isabel believed that when she was alone with her niece she let the dust gather for a moment on the ancient scandals of the Arnide. She so remained below therefore, while Pansy guided her undiscriminating aunt to the steep brick staircase at the foot of which the custodian unlocks the tall wooden gate. The great enclosure was half in shadow; the western sun brought out the pale red tone of the great blocks of travertine—the latent colour that is the only living element in the immense ruin. Here and there wandered a peasant or a tourist, looking up at the far sky-line where, in the clear stillness, a multitude of swallows kept circling and plunging. Isabel presently became aware that one of the other visitors, planted in the middle of the arena, had turned his attention to her own person and was looking at her with a certain little poise of the head which she had some weeks before perceived to be characteristic of baffled but indestructible purpose. Such an attitude, today, could belong only to Mr. Edward Rosier; and this gentleman proved in fact to have been considering the question of speaking to her. When he had assured himself that she was unaccompanied he drew near, remarking that though she would not answer his letters she would perhaps not wholly close her ears to his spoken eloquence. She replied that her stepdaughter was close at hand and that she could only give him five minutes; whereupon he took out his watch and sat down upon a broken block.

"It's very soon told," said Edward Rosier. "I've sold all my bibelots!" Isabel gave instinctively an exclamation of horror; it was as if he had told her he had had all his teeth drawn. "I've sold them by auction at the Hotel Drouot," he went on. "The sale took place three days ago, and they've telegraphed me the result. It's magnificent."

"I'm glad to hear it; but I wish you had kept your pretty things."

"I have the money instead—fifty thousand dollars. Will Mr. Osmond think me rich enough now?"

"Is it for that you did it?" Isabel asked gently.

"For what else in the world could it be? That's the only thing I think of. I went to Paris and made my arrangements. I couldn't stop for the sale; I couldn't have seen them going off; I think it would have killed me. But I put them into good hands, and they brought high prices. I should tell you I have kept my enamels. Now I have the money in my pocket, and he can't say I'm poor!" the young man exclaimed defiantly.

"He'll say now that you're not wise," said Isabel, as if Gilbert Osmond had never said this before.

Rosier gave her a sharp look. "Do you mean that without my bibelots I'm nothing? Do you mean they were the best thing about me? That's what they told me in Paris; oh they were very frank about it. But they hadn't seen HER!"

"My dear friend, you deserve to succeed," said Isabel very kindly.

"You say that so sadly that it's the same as if you said I shouldn't." And he questioned her eyes with the clear trepidation of his own. He had the air of a man who knows he has been the talk of Paris for a week and is full half a head taller in consequence, but who also has a painful suspicion that in spite of this increase of stature one or two persons still have the perversity to think him diminutive. "I know what happened here while I was away," he went on; "What does Mr. Osmond expect after she has refused Lord Warburton?"

Isabel debated. "That she'll marry another nobleman."

"What other nobleman?"

"One that he'll pick out."

Rosier slowly got up, putting his watch into his waistcoat-pocket. "You're laughing at some one, but this time I don't think it's at me."

"I didn't mean to laugh," said Isabel. "I laugh very seldom. Now you had better go away."

"I feel very safe!" Rosier declared without moving. This might be; but it evidently made him feel more so to make the announcement in rather a loud voice, balancing himself a little complacently on his toes and looking all round the Coliseum as if it were filled with an audience. Suddenly Isabel saw him change colour; there was more of an audience than he had suspected. She turned and perceived that her two companions had returned from their excursion. "You must really go away," she said quickly. "Ah, my dear lady, pity me!" Edward Rosier murmured in a voice strangely at variance with the announcement I have just quoted. And then he added eagerly, like a man who in the midst of his misery is seized by a happy thought: "Is that lady the Countess Gemini? I've a great desire to be presented to her."

Isabel looked at him a moment. "She has no influence with her brother."

"Ah, what a monster you make him out!" And Rosier faced the Countess, who advanced, in front of Pansy, with an animation partly due perhaps to the fact that she perceived her sister-in-law to be engaged in conversation with a very pretty young man.

"I'm glad you've kept your enamels!" Isabel called as she left him. She went straight to Pansy, who, on seeing Edward Rosier, had stopped short, with lowered eyes. "We'll go back to the carriage," she said gently.

"Yes, it's getting late," Pansy returned more gently still. And she went on without a murmur, without faltering or glancing back. Isabel, however, allowing herself this last liberty, saw that a meeting had immediately taken place between the Countess and Mr. Rosier. He had removed his hat and was bowing and smiling; he had evidently introduced himself, while the Countess's expressive back displayed to Isabel's eye a gracious inclination. These facts, none the less, were presently lost to sight, for Isabel and Pansy took their places again in the carriage. Pansy, who faced her stepmother, at first kept her eyes fixed on her lap; then she raised them and rested them on Isabel's. There shone out of each of them a little melancholy ray—a spark of timid passion which touched Isabel to the heart. At the same time a wave of envy passed over her soul, as she compared the tremulous longing, the definite ideal of the child with her own dry despair. "Poor little Pansy!" she affectionately said.

"Oh never mind!" Pansy answered in the tone of eager apology. And then there was a silence; the Countess was a long time coming. "Did you show your aunt everything, and did she enjoy it?" Isabel asked at last.

"Yes, I showed her everything. I think she was very much pleased."

"And you're not tired, I hope."

"Oh no, thank you, I'm not tired."

The Countess still remained behind, so that Isabel requested the footman to go into the Coliseum and tell her they were waiting. He presently returned with the announcement that the Signora Contessa begged them not to wait—she would come home in a cab!

About a week after this lady's quick sympathies had enlisted themselves with Mr. Rosier, Isabel, going rather late to dress for dinner, found Pansy sitting in her room. The girl seemed to have been awaiting her; she got up from her low chair. "Pardon my taking the liberty," she said in a small voice. "It will be the last—for some time."

Her voice was strange, and her eyes, widely opened, had an excited, frightened look. "You're not going away!" Isabel exclaimed.

"I'm going to the convent."

"To the convent?"

Pansy drew nearer, till she was near enough to put her arms round Isabel and rest her head on her shoulder. She stood this way a moment, perfectly still; but her companion could feel her tremble. The quiver of her little body expressed everything she was unable to say. Isabel nevertheless pressed her. "Why are you going to the convent?"

"Because papa thinks it best. He says a young girl's better, every now and then, for making a little retreat. He says the world, always the world, is very bad for a young girl. This is just a chance for a little seclusion—a little reflexion." Pansy spoke in short detached sentences, as if she could scarce trust herself; and then she added with a triumph of self-control: "I think papa's right; I've been so much in the world this winter."

Her announcement had a strange effect on Isabel; it seemed to carry a larger meaning than the girl herself knew. "When was this decided?" she asked. "I've heard nothing of it."

"Papa told me half an hour ago; he thought it better it shouldn't be too much talked about in advance. Madame Catherine's to come for me at a quarter past seven, and I'm only to take two frocks. It's only for a few weeks; I'm sure it will be very good. I shall find all those ladies who used to be so kind to me, and I shall see the little girls who are being educated. I'm very fond of little girls," said Pansy with an effect of diminutive grandeur. "And I'm also very fond of Mother Catherine. I shall be very quiet and think a great deal."

Isabel listened to her, holding her breath; she was almost awe-struck. "Think of ME sometimes."

"Ah, come and see me soon!" cried Pansy; and the cry was very different from the heroic remarks of which she had just delivered herself.

Isabel could say nothing more; she understood nothing; she only felt how little she yet knew her husband. Her answer to his daughter was a long, tender kiss.

Half an hour later she learned from her maid that Madame Catherine had arrived in a cab and had departed again with the signorina. On going to the drawing-room before dinner she found the Countess Gemini alone, and this lady characterised the incident by exclaiming, with a wonderful toss of the head, "En voila, ma chere, une pose!" But if it was an affectation she was at a loss to see what her husband affected. She could only dimly perceive that he had more traditions than she supposed. It had become her habit to be so careful as to what she said to him that, strange as it may appear, she hesitated, for several minutes after he had come in, to allude to his daughter's sudden departure: she spoke of it only after they were seated at table. But she had forbidden herself ever to ask Osmond a question. All she could do was to make a declaration, and there was one that came very naturally. "I shall miss Pansy very much."

He looked a while, with his head inclined a little, at the basket of flowers in the middle of the table. "Ah yes," he said at last, "I had thought of that. You must go and see her, you know; but not too often. I dare say you wonder why I sent her to the good sisters; but I doubt if I can make you understand. It doesn't matter; don't trouble yourself about it. That's why I had not spoken of it. I didn't believe you would enter into it. But I've always had the idea; I've always thought it a part of the education of one's daughter. One's daughter should be fresh and fair; she should be innocent and gentle. With the manners of the present time she is liable to become so dusty and crumpled. Pansy's a little dusty, a little dishevelled; she has knocked about too much. This bustling, pushing rabble that calls itself society—one should take her out of it occasionally. Convents are very quiet, very convenient, very salutary. I like to think of her there, in the old garden, under the arcade, among those tranquil virtuous women. Many of them are gentlewomen born; several of them are noble. She will have her books and her drawing, she will have her piano. I've made the most liberal arrangements. There is to be nothing ascetic; there's just to be a certain little sense of sequestration. She'll have time to think, and there's something I want her to think about." Osmond spoke deliberately, reasonably, still with his head on one side, as if he were looking at the basket of flowers. His tone, however, was that of a man not so much offering an explanation as putting a thing into words—almost into pictures—to see, himself, how it would look. He consid-considered a while the picture he had evoked and seemed greatly pleased with it. And then he went on: "The Catholics are very wise after all. The convent is a great institution; we can't do without it; it corresponds to an essential need in families, in society. It's a school of good manners; it's a school of repose. Oh, I don't want to detach my daughter from the world," he added; "I don't want to make her fix her thoughts on any other. This one's very well, as SHE should take it, and she may think of it as much as she likes. Only she must think of it in the right way."

Isabel gave an extreme attention to this little sketch; she found it indeed intensely interesting. It seemed to show her how far her husband's desire to be effective was capable of going—to the point of playing theoretic tricks on the delicate organism of his daughter. She could not understand his purpose, no—not wholly; but she understood it better than he supposed or desired, inasmuch as she was convinced that the whole proceeding was an elaborate mystification, addressed to herself and destined to act upon her imagination. He had wanted to do something sudden and arbitrary, something unexpected and refined; to mark the difference between his sympathies and her own, and show that if he regarded his daughter as a precious work of art it was natural he should be more and more careful about the finishing touches. If he wished to be effective he had succeeded; the incident struck a chill into Isabel's heart. Pansy had known the convent in her childhood and had found a happy home there; she was fond of the good sisters, who were very fond of her, and there was therefore for the moment no definite hardship in her lot. But all the same the girl had taken fright; the impression her father desired to make would evidently be sharp enough. The old Protestant tradition had never faded from Isabel's imagination, and as her thoughts attached themselves to this striking example of her husband's genius—she sat looking, like him, at the basket of flowers—poor little Pansy became the heroine of a tragedy. Osmond wished it to be known that he shrank from nothing, and his wife found it hard to pretend to eat her dinner. There was a certain relief presently, in hearing the high, strained voice of her sister-in-law. The Countess too, apparently, had been thinking the thing out, but had arrived at a different conclusion from Isabel.

"It's very absurd, my dear Osmond," she said, "to invent so many pretty reasons for poor Pansy's banishment. Why, don't you say at once that you want to get her out of my way? Haven't you discovered that I think very well of Mr. Rosier? I do indeed; he seems to me simpaticissimo. He has made me believe in true love; I never did before! Of course you've made up your mind that with those convictions I'm dreadful company for Pansy."

Osmond took a sip of a glass of wine; he looked perfectly good-humoured. "My dear Amy," he answered, smiling as if he were uttering a piece of gallantry, "I don't know anything about your convictions, but if I suspected that they interfere with mine it would be much simpler to banish YOU."

CHAPTER LI

The Countess was not banished, but she felt the insecurity of her tenure of her brother's hospitality. A week after this incident Isabel received a telegram from England, dated from Gardencourt and bearing the stamp of Mrs. Touchett's authorship. "Ralph cannot last many days," it ran, "and if convenient would like to see you. Wishes me to say that you must come only if you've not other duties. Say, for myself, that you used to talk a good deal about your duty and to wonder what it was; shall be curious to see whether you've found it out. Ralph is really dying, and there's no other company." Isabel was prepared for this news, having received from Henrietta Stackpole a detailed account of her journey to England with her appreciative patient. Ralph had arrived more dead than alive, but she had managed to convey him to Gardencourt, where he had taken to his bed, which, as Miss Stackpole wrote, he evidently would never leave again. She added that she had really had two patients on her hands instead of one, inasmuch as Mr. Goodwood, who had been of no earthly use, was quite as ailing, in a different way, as Mr. Touchett. Afterwards she wrote that she had been obliged to surrender the field to Mrs. Touchett, who had just returned from America and had promptly given her to understand that she didn't wish any interviewing at Gardencourt. Isabel had written to her aunt shortly after Ralph came to Rome, letting her know of his critical condition and suggesting that she should lose no time in returning to Europe. Mrs. Touchett had telegraphed an acknowledgement of this admonition, and the only further news Isabel received from her was the second telegram I have just quoted.

Isabel stood a moment looking at the latter missive; then, thrusting it into her pocket, she went straight to the door of her husband's study. Here she again paused an instant, after which she opened the door and went in. Osmond was seated at the table near the window with a folio volume before him, propped against a pile of books. This volume was open at a page of small coloured plates, and Isabel presently saw that he had been copying from it the drawing of an antique coin. A box of water-colours and fine brushes lay before him, and he had already transferred to a sheet of immaculate paper the delicate, finely-tinted disk. His back was turned toward the door, but he recognised his wife without looking round.

"Excuse me for disturbing you," she said.

"When I come to your room I always knock," he answered, going on with his work.

"I forgot; I had something else to think of. My cousin's dying."

"Ah, I don't believe that," said Osmond, looking at his drawing through a magnifying glass. "He was dying when we married; he'll outlive us all."

Isabel gave herself no time, no thought, to appreciate the careful cynicism of this declaration; she simply went on quickly, full of her own intention "My aunt has telegraphed for me; I must go to Gardencourt."

"Why must you go to Gardencourt?" Osmond asked in the tone of impartial curiosity.

"To see Ralph before he dies."

To this, for some time, he made no rejoinder; he continued to give his chief attention to his work, which was of a sort that would brook no negligence. "I don't see the need of it," he said at last. "He came to see you here. I didn't like that; I thought his being in Rome a great mistake. But I tolerated it because it was to be the last time you should see him. Now you tell me it's not to have been the last. Ah, you're not grateful!"

"What am I to be grateful for?"

Gilbert Osmond laid down his little implements, blew a speck of dust from his drawing, slowly got up, and for the first time looked at his wife. "For my not having interfered while he was here."

"Oh yes, I am. I remember perfectly how distinctly you let me know you didn't like it. I was very glad when he went away."

"Leave him alone then. Don't run after him."

Isabel turned her eyes away from him; they rested upon his little drawing. "I must go to England," she said, with a full consciousness that her tone might strike an irritable man of taste as stupidly obstinate.

"I shall not like it if you do," Osmond remarked.

"Why should I mind that? You won't like it if I don't. You like nothing I do or don't do. You pretend to think I lie."

Osmond turned slightly pale; he gave a cold smile. "That's why you must go then? Not to see your cousin, but to take a revenge on me."

"I know nothing about revenge."

"I do," said Osmond. "Don't give me an occasion."

"You're only too eager to take one. You wish immensely that I would commit some folly."

"I should be gratified in that case if you disobeyed me."

"If I disobeyed you?" said Isabel in a low tone which had the effect of mildness.

"Let it be clear. If you leave Rome to-day it will be a piece of the most deliberate, the most calculated, opposition."

"How can you call it calculated? I received my aunt's telegram but three minutes ago."

"You calculate rapidly; it's a great accomplishment. I don't see why we should prolong our discussion; you know my wish." And he stood there as if he expected to see her withdraw.

But she never moved; she couldn't move, strange as it may seem; she still wished to justify herself; he had the power, in an extraordinary degree, of making her feel this need. There was something in her imagination he could always appeal to against her judgement. "You've no reason for such a wish," said Isabel, "and I've every reason for going. I can't tell you how unjust you seem to me. But I think you know. It's your own opposition that's calculated. It's malignant."

She had never uttered her worst thought to her husband before, and the sensation of hearing it was evidently new to Osmond. But he showed no surprise, and his coolness was apparently a proof that he had believed his wife would in fact be unable to resist for ever his ingenious endeavour to draw her out. "It's all the more intense then," he answered. And he added almost as if he were giving her a friendly counsel: "This is a very important matter." She recognised that; she was fully conscious of the weight of the occasion; she knew that between them they had arrived at a crisis. Its gravity made her careful; she said nothing, and he went on. "You say I've no reason? I have the very best. I dislike, from the bottom of my soul, what you intend to do. It's dishonourable; it's indelicate; it's indecent. Your cousin is nothing whatever to me, and I'm under no obligation to make concessions to him. I've already made the very handsomest. Your relations with him, while he was here, kept me on pins and needles; but I let that pass, because from week to week I expected him to go. I've never liked him and he has never liked me. That's why you like him—because he hates me," said Osmond with a quick, barely audible tremor in his voice. "I've an ideal of what my wife should do and should not do. She should not travel across Europe alone, in defiance of my deepest desire, to sit at the bedside of other men. Your cousin's nothing to you; he's nothing to us. You smile most expressively when I talk about US, but I assure you that WE, WE, Mrs. Osmond, is all I know. I take our marriage seriously; you appear to have found a way of not doing so. I'm not aware that we're divorced or separated; for me we're indissolubly united. You are nearer to me than any human creature, and I'm nearer to you. It may be a disagreeable proximity; it's one, at any rate, of our own deliberate making. You don't like to be reminded of that, I know; but I'm perfectly willing, because—because—" And he paused a moment, looking as if he had something to say which would be very much to the point. "Because I think we should accept the consequences of our actions, and what I value most in life is the honour of a thing!"

He spoke gravely and almost gently; the accent of sarcasm had dropped out of his tone. It had a gravity which checked his wife's quick emotion; the resolution with which she had entered the room found itself caught in a mesh of fine threads. His last words were not a command, they constituted a kind of appeal; and, though she felt that any expression of respect on his part could only be a refinement of egotism, they represented something transcendent and absolute, like the sign of the cross or the flag of one's country. He spoke in the name of something sacred and precious—the observance of a magnificent form. They were as perfectly apart in feeling as two disillusioned lovers had ever been; but they had never yet separated in act. Isabel had not changed; her old passion for justice still abode within her; and now, in the very thick of her sense of her husband's blasphemous sophistry, it began to throb to a tune which for a moment promised him the victory. It came over her that in his wish to preserve appearances he was after all sincere, and that this, as far as it went, was a merit. Ten minutes before she had felt all the joy of irreflective action—a joy to which she had so long been a stranger; but action had been suddenly changed to slow renunciation, transformed by the blight of Osmond's touch. If she must renounce, however, she would let him know she was a victim rather than a dupe. "I know you're a master of the art of mockery," she said. "How can you speak of an indissoluble union—how can you speak of your being contented? Where's our union when you accuse me of falsity? Where's your contentment when you have nothing but hideous suspicion in your heart?"

"It is in our living decently together, in spite of such drawbacks."

"We don't live decently together!" cried Isabel.

"Indeed we don't if you go to England."

"That's very little; that's nothing. I might do much more."

He raised his eyebrows and even his shoulders a little: he had lived long enough in Italy to catch this trick. "Ah, if you've come to threaten me I prefer my drawing." And he walked back to his table, where he took up the sheet of paper on which he had been working and stood studying it.

"I suppose that if I go you'll not expect me to come back," said Isabel.

He turned quickly round, and she could see this movement at least was not designed. He looked at her a little, and then, "Are you out of your mind?" he enquired.

"How can it be anything but a rupture?" she went on; "especially if all you say is true?" She was unable to see how it could be anything but a rupture; she sincerely wished to know what else it might be.

He sat down before his table. "I really can't argue with you on the hypothesis of your defying me," he said. And he took up one of his little brushes again.

She lingered but a moment longer; long enough to embrace with her eye his whole deliberately indifferent yet most expressive figure; after which she quickly left the room. Her faculties, her energy, her passion, were all dispersed again; she felt as if a cold, dark mist had suddenly encompassed her. Osmond possessed in a supreme degree the art of eliciting any weakness. On her way back to her room she found the Countess Gemini standing in the open doorway of a little parlour in which a small collection of heterogeneous books had been arranged. The Countess had an open volume in her hand; she appeared to have been glancing down a page which failed to strike her as interesting. At the sound of Isabel's step she raised her head.

"Ah my dear," she said, "you, who are so literary, do tell me some amusing book to read! Everything here's of a dreariness—! Do you think this would do me any good?"

Isabel glanced at the title of the volume she held out, but without reading or understanding it. "I'm afraid I can't advise you. I've had bad news. My cousin, Ralph Touchett, is dying."

The Countess threw down her book. "Ah, he was so simpatico. I'm awfully sorry for you."

"You would be sorrier still if you knew."

"What is there to know? You look very badly," the Countess added. "You must have been with Osmond."

Half an hour before Isabel would have listened very coldly to an intimation that she should ever feel a desire for the sympathy of her sister-in-law, and there can be no better proof of her present embarrassment than the fact that she almost clutched at this lady's fluttering attention. "I've been with Osmond," she said, while the Countess's bright eyes glittered at her.

"I'm sure then he has been odious!" the Countess cried. "Did he say he was glad poor Mr. Touchett's dying?"

"He said it's impossible I should go to England."

The Countess's mind, when her interests were concerned, was agile; she already foresaw the extinction of any further brightness in her visit to Rome. Ralph Touchett would die, Isabel would go into mourning, and then there would be no more dinner-parties. Such a prospect produced for a moment in her countenance an expressive grimace; but this rapid, picturesque play of feature was her only tribute to disappointment. After all, she reflected, the game was almost played out; she had already overstayed her invitation. And then she cared enough for Isabel's trouble to forget her own, and she saw that Isabel's trouble was deep.

It seemed deeper than the mere death of a cousin, and the Countess had no hesitation in connecting her exasperating brother with the expression of her sister-in-law's eyes. Her heart beat with an almost joyous expectation, for if she had wished to see Osmond overtopped the conditions looked favourable now. Of course if Isabel should go to England she herself would immediately leave Palazzo Roccanera; nothing would induce her to remain there with Osmond. Nevertheless she felt an immense desire to hear that Isabel would go to England. "Nothing's impossible for you, my dear," she said caressingly. "Why else are you rich and clever and good?"

"Why indeed? I feel stupidly weak."

"Why does Osmond say it's impossible?" the Countess asked in a tone which sufficiently declared that she couldn't imagine.

From the moment she thus began to question her, however, Isabel drew back; she disengaged her hand, which the Countess had affectionately taken. But she answered this enquiry with frank bitterness. "Because we're so happy together that we can't separate even for a fortnight."

"Ah," cried the Countess while Isabel turned away, "when I want to make a journey my husband simply tells me I can have no money!"

Isabel went to her room, where she walked up and down for an hour. It may appear to some readers that she gave herself much trouble, and it is certain that for a woman of a high spirit she had allowed herself easily to be arrested. It seemed to her that only now she fully measured the great undertaking of matrimony. Marriage meant that in such a case as this, when one had to choose, one chose as a matter of course for one's husband. "I'm afraid—yes, I'm afraid," she said to herself more than once, stopping short in her walk. But what she was afraid of was not her husband—his displeasure, his hatred, his revenge; it was not even her own later judgement of her conduct a consideration which had often held her in check; it was simply the violence there would be in going when Osmond wished her to remain. A gulf of difference had opened between them, but nevertheless it was his desire that she should stay, it was a horror to him that she should go. She knew the nervous fineness with which he could feel an objection. What he thought of her she knew, what he was capable of saying to her she had felt; yet they were married, for all that, and marriage meant that a woman should cleave to the man with whom, uttering tremendous vows, she had stood at the altar. She sank down on her sofa at last and buried her head in a pile of cushions.

When she raised her head again the Countess Gemini hovered before her. She had come in all unperceived; she had a strange smile on her thin lips and her whole face had grown in an hour a shining intimation. She lived assuredly, it might be said, at the window of her spirit, but now she was leaning far out. "I knocked," she began, "but you didn't answer me. So I ventured in. I've been looking at you for the past five minutes. You're very unhappy."

"Yes; but I don't think you can comfort me."

"Will you give me leave to try?" And the Countess sat down on the sofa beside her. She continued to smile, and there was something communicative and exultant in her expression. She appeared to have a deal to say, and it occurred to Isabel for the first time that her sister-in-law might say something really human. She made play with her glittering eyes, in which there was an unpleasant fascination. "After all," she soon resumed, "I must tell you, to begin with, that I don't understand your state of mind. You seem to have so many scruples, so many reasons, so many ties. When I discovered, ten years ago, that my husband's dearest wish was to make me miserable—of late he has simply let me alone—ah, it was a wonderful simplification! My poor Isabel, you're not simple enough."

"No, I'm not simple enough," said Isabel.

"There's something I want you to know," the Countess declared—"because I think you ought to know it. Perhaps you do; perhaps you've guessed it. But if you have, all I can say is that I understand still less why you shouldn't do as you like."

"What do you wish me to know?" Isabel felt a foreboding that made her heart beat faster. The Countess was about to justify herself, and this alone was portentous.

But she was nevertheless disposed to play a little with her subject. "In your place I should have guessed it ages ago. Have you never really suspected?"

"I've guessed nothing. What should I have suspected? I don't know what you mean."

"That's because you've such a beastly pure mind. I never saw a woman with such a pure mind!" cried the Countess.

Isabel slowly got up. "You're going to tell me something horrible."

"You can call it by whatever name you will!" And the Countess rose also, while her gathered perversity grew vivid and dreadful. She stood a moment in a sort of glare of intention and, as seemed to Isabel even then, of ugliness; after which she said: "My first sister-in-law had no children."

Isabel stared back at her; the announcement was an anticlimax. "Your first sister-in-law?"

"I suppose you know at least, if one may mention it, that Osmond has been married before! I've never spoken to you of his wife; I thought it mightn't be decent or respectful. But others, less particular, must have done so. The poor little woman lived hardly three years and died childless. It wasn't till after her death that Pansy arrived."

Isabel's brow had contracted to a frown; her lips were parted in pale, vague wonder. She was trying to follow; there seemed so much more to follow than she could see. "Pansy's not my husband's child then?"

"Your husband's—in perfection! But no one else's husband's. Some one else's wife's. Ah, my good Isabel," cried the Countess, "with you one must dot one's i's!"

"I don't understand. Whose wife's?" Isabel asked.

"The wife of a horrid little Swiss who died—how long?—a dozen, more than fifteen, years ago. He never recognised Miss Pansy, nor, knowing what he was about, would have anything to say to her; and there was no reason why he should. Osmond did, and that was better; though he had to fit on afterwards the whole rigmarole of his own wife's having died in childbirth, and of his having, in grief and horror, banished the little girl from his sight for as long as possible before taking her home from nurse. His wife had really died, you know, of quite another matter and in quite another place: in the Piedmontese mountains, where they had gone, one August, because her health appeared to require the air, but where she was suddenly taken worse—fatally ill. The story passed, sufficiently; it was covered by the appearances so long as nobody heeded, as nobody cared to look into it. But of course I knew—without researches," the Countess lucidly proceeded; "as also, you'll understand, without a word said between us—I mean between Osmond and me. Don't you see him looking at me, in silence, that way, to settle it?—that is to settle ME if I should say anything. I said nothing, right or left—never a word to a creature, if you can believe that of me: on my honour, my dear, I speak of the thing to you now, after all this time, as I've never, never spoken. It was to be enough for me, from the first, that the child was my niece—from the moment she was my brother's daughter. As for her veritable mother—!" But with this Pansy's wonderful aunt dropped—as, involuntarily, from the impression of her sister-in-law's face, out of which more eyes might have seemed to look at her than she had ever had to meet.

She had spoken no name, yet Isabel could but check, on her own lips, an echo of the unspoken. She sank to her seat again, hanging her head. "Why have you told me this?" she asked in a voice the Countess hardly recognised.

"Because I've been so bored with your not knowing. I've been bored, frankly, my dear, with not having told you; as if, stupidly, all this time I couldn't have managed! Ca me depasse, if you don't mind my saying so, the things, all round you, that you've appeared to succeed in not knowing. It's a sort of assistance—aid to innocent ignorance—that I've always been a bad hand at rendering; and in this connexion, that of keeping quiet for my brother, my virtue has at any rate finally found itself exhausted. It's not a black lie, moreover, you know," the Countess inimitably added. "The facts are exactly what I tell you."

"I had no idea," said Isabel presently; and looked up at her in a manner that doubtless matched the apparent witlessness of this confession.

"So I believed—though it was hard to believe. Had it never occurred to you that he was for six or seven years her lover?"

"I don't know. Things HAVE occurred to me, and perhaps that was what they all meant."

"She has been wonderfully clever, she has been magnificent, about Pansy!" the Countess, before all this view of it, cried.

"Oh, no idea, for me," Isabel went on, "ever DEFINITELY took that form." She appeared to be making out to herself what had been and what hadn't. "And as it is—I don't understand."

She spoke as one troubled and puzzled, yet the poor Countess seemed to have seen her revelation fall below its possibilities of effect. She had expected to kindle some responsive blaze, but had barely extracted a spark. Isabel showed as scarce more impressed than she might have been, as a young woman of approved imagination, with some fine sinister passage of public history. "Don't you recognise how the child could never pass for HER husband's?—that is with M. Merle himself," her companion resumed. "They had been separated too long for that, and he had gone to some far country—I think to South America. If she had ever had children—which I'm not sure of—she had lost them. The conditions happened to make it workable, under stress (I mean at so awkward a pinch), that Osmond should acknowledge the little girl. His wife was dead—very true; but she had not been dead too long to put a certain accommodation of dates out of the question—from the moment, I mean, that suspicion wasn't started; which was what they had to take care of. What was more natural than that poor Mrs. Osmond, at a distance and for a world not troubling about trifles, should have left behind her, poverina, the pledge of her brief happiness that had cost her her life? With the aid of a change of residence—Osmond had been living with her at Naples at the time of their stay in the Alps, and he in due course left it for ever—the whole history was successfully set going. My poor sister-in-law, in her grave, couldn't help herself, and the real mother, to save HER skin, renounced all visible property in the child."

"Ah, poor, poor woman!" cried Isabel, who herewith burst into tears. It was a long time since she had shed any; she had suffered a high reaction from weeping. But now they flowed with an abundance in which the Countess Gemini found only another discomfiture.

"It's very kind of you to pity her!" she discordantly laughed. "Yes indeed, you have a way of your own—!"

"He must have been false to his wife—and so very soon!" said Isabel with a sudden check.

"That's all that's wanting—that you should take up her cause!" the Countess went on. "I quite agree with you, however, that it was much too soon."

"But to me, to me—?" And Isabel hesitated as if she had not heard; as if her question—though it was sufficiently there in her eyes—were all for herself.

"To you he has been faithful? Well, it depends, my dear, on what you call faithful. When he married you he was no longer the lover of another woman—SUCH a lover as he had been, cara mia, between their risks and their precautions, while the thing lasted! That state of affairs had passed away; the lady had repented, or at all events, for reasons of her own, drawn back: she had always had, too, a worship of appearances so intense that even Osmond himself had got bored with it. You may therefore imagine what it was—when he couldn't patch it on conveniently to ANY of those he goes in for! But the whole past was between them."

"Yes," Isabel mechanically echoed, "the whole past is between them."

"Ah, this later past is nothing. But for six or seven years, as I say, they had kept it up."

She was silent a little. "Why then did she want him to marry me?"

"Ah my dear, that's her superiority! Because you had money; and because she believed you would be good to Pansy."

"Poor woman—and Pansy who doesn't like her!" cried Isabel.

"That's the reason she wanted some one whom Pansy would like. She knows it; she knows everything."

"Will she know that you've told me this?"

"That will depend upon whether you tell her. She's prepared for it, and do you know what she counts upon for her defence? On your believing that I lie. Perhaps you do; don't make yourself uncomfortable to hide it. Only, as it happens this time, I don't. I've told plenty of little idiotic fibs, but they've never hurt any one but myself."

Isabel sat staring at her companion's story as at a bale of fantastic wares some strolling gypsy might have unpacked on the carpet at her feet. "Why did Osmond never marry her?" she finally asked.

"Because she had no money." The Countess had an answer for everything, and if she lied she lied well. "No one knows, no one has ever known, what she lives on, or how she has got all those beautiful things. I don't believe Osmond himself knows. Besides, she wouldn't have married him."

"How can she have loved him then?"

"She doesn't love him in that way. She did at first, and then, I suppose, she would have married him; but at that time her husband was living. By the time M. Merle had rejoined—I won't say his ancestors, because he never had any—her relations with Osmond had changed, and she had grown more ambitious. Besides, she has never had, about him," the Countess went on, leaving Isabel to wince for it so tragically afterwards—"she HAD never had, what you might call any illusions of INTELLIGENCE. She hoped she might marry a great man; that has always been her idea. She has waited and watched and plotted and prayed; but she has never succeeded. I don't call Madame Merle a success, you know. I don't know what she may accomplish yet, but at present she has very little to show. The only tangible result she has ever achieved—except, of course, getting to know every one and staying with them free of expense—has been her bringing you and Osmond together. Oh, she did that, my dear; you needn't look as if you doubted it. I've watched them for years; I know everything—everything. I'm thought a great scatterbrain, but I've had enough application of mind to follow up those two. She hates me, and her way of showing it is to pretend to be for ever defending me. When people say I've had fifteen lovers she looks horrified and declares that quite half of them were never proved. She has been afraid of me for years, and she has taken great comfort in the vile, false things people have said about me. She has been afraid I'd expose her, and she threatened me one day when Osmond began to pay his court to you. It was at his house in Florence; do you remember that afternoon when she brought you there and we had tea in the garden? She let me know then that if I should tell tales two could play at that game. She pretends there's a good deal more to tell about me than about her. It would be an interesting comparison! I don't care a fig what she may say, simply because I know YOU don't care a fig. You can't trouble your head about me less than you do already. So she may take her revenge as she chooses; I don't think she'll frighten you very much. Her great idea has been to be tremendously irreproachable—a kind of full-blown lily—the incarnation of propriety. She has always worshipped that god. There should be no scandal about Caesar's wife, you know; and, as I say, she has always hoped to marry Caesar. That was one reason she wouldn't marry Osmond; the fear that on seeing her with Pansy people would put things together—would even see a resemblance. She has had a terror lest the mother should betray herself. She has been awfully careful; the mother has never done so."

"Yes, yes, the mother has done so," said Isabel, who had listened to all this with a face more and more wan. "She betrayed herself to me the other day, though I didn't recognise her. There appeared to have been a chance of Pansy's making a great marriage, and in her disappointment at its not coming off she almost dropped the mask."

"Ah, that's where she'd dish herself!" cried the Countess. "She has failed so dreadfully that she's determined her daughter shall make it up."

Isabel started at the words "her daughter," which her guest threw off so familiarly. "It seems very wonderful," she murmured; and in this bewildering impression she had almost lost her sense of being personally touched by the story.

"Now don't go and turn against the poor innocent child!" the Countess went on. "She's very nice, in spite of her deplorable origin. I myself have liked Pansy; not, naturally, because she was hers, but because she had become yours."

"Yes, she has become mine. And how the poor woman must have suffered at seeing me—!" Isabel exclaimed while she flushed at the thought.

"I don't believe she has suffered; on the contrary, she has enjoyed. Osmond's marriage has given his daughter a great little lift. Before that she lived in a hole. And do you know what the mother thought? That you might take such a fancy to the child that you'd do something for her. Osmond of course could never give her a portion. Osmond was really extremely poor; but of course you know all about that. Ah, my dear," cried the Countess, "why did you ever inherit money?" She stopped a moment as if she saw something singular in Isabel's face. "Don't tell me now that you'll give her a dot. You're capable of that, but I would refuse to believe it. Don't try to be too good. Be a little easy and natural and nasty; feel a little wicked, for the comfort of it, once in your life!"

"It's very strange. I suppose I ought to know, but I'm sorry," Isabel said. "I'm much obliged to you."

"Yes, you seem to be!" cried the Countess with a mocking laugh. "Perhaps you are—perhaps you're not. You don't take it as I should have thought."

"How should I take it?" Isabel asked.

"Well, I should say as a woman who has been made use of." Isabel made no answer to this; she only listened, and the Countess went on. "They've always been bound to each other; they remained so even after she broke off—or HE did. But he has always been more for her than she has been for him. When their little carnival was over they made a bargain that each should give the other complete liberty, but that each should also do everything possible to help the other on. You may ask me how I know such a thing as that. I know it by the way they've behaved. Now see how much better women are than men! She has found a wife for Osmond, but Osmond has never lifted a little finger for HER. She has worked for him, plotted for him, suffered for him; she has even more than once found money for him; and the end of it is that he's tired of her. She's an old habit; there are moments when he needs her, but on the whole he wouldn't miss her if she were removed. And, what's more, today she knows it. So you needn't be jealous!" the Countess added humorously.

Isabel rose from her sofa again; she felt bruised and scant of breath; her head was humming with new knowledge. "I'm much obliged to you," she repeated. And then she added abruptly, in quite a different tone: "How do you know all this?"

This enquiry appeared to ruffle the Countess more than Isabel's expression of gratitude pleased her. She gave her companion a bold stare, with which, "Let us assume that I've invented it!" she cried. She too, however, suddenly changed her tone and, laying her hand on Isabel's arm, said with the penetration of her sharp bright smile: "Now will you give up your journey?"

Isabel started a little; she turned away. But she felt weak and in a moment had to lay her arm upon the mantel-shelf for support. She stood a minute so, and then upon her arm she dropped her dizzy head, with closed eyes and pale lips.

"I've done wrong to speak—I've made you ill!" the Countess cried.

"Ah, I must see Ralph!" Isabel wailed; not in resentment, not in the quick passion her companion had looked for; but in a tone of far-reaching, infinite sadness.

CHAPTER LII

There was a train for Turin and Paris that evening; and after the Countess had left her Isabel had a rapid and decisive conference with her maid, who was discreet, devoted and active. After this she thought (except of her journey) only of one thing. She must go and see Pansy; from her she couldn't turn away. She had not seen her yet, as Osmond had given her to understand that it was too soon to begin. She drove at five o'clock to a high floor in a narrow street in the quarter of the Piazza Navona, and was admitted by the portress of the convent, a genial and obsequious person. Isabel had been at this institution before; she had come with Pansy to see the sisters. She knew they were good women, and she saw that the large rooms were clean and cheerful and that the well-used garden had sun for winter and shade for spring. But she disliked the place, which affronted and almost frightened her; not for the world would she have spent a night there. It produced to-day more than before the impression of a well-appointed prison; for it was not possible to pretend Pansy was free to leave it. This innocent creature had been presented to her in a new and violent light, but the secondary effect of the revelation was to make her reach out a hand.

The portress left her to wait in the parlour of the convent while she went to make it known that there was a visitor for the dear young lady. The parlour was a vast, cold apartment, with new-looking furniture; a large clean stove of white porcelain, unlighted, a collection of wax flowers under glass, and a series of engravings from religious pictures on the walls. On the other occasion Isabel had thought it less like Rome than like Philadelphia, but to-day she made no reflexions; the apartment only seemed to her very empty and very soundless. The portress returned at the end of some five minutes, ushering in another person. Isabel got up, expecting to see one of the ladies of the sisterhood, but to her extreme surprise found herself confronted with Madame Merle. The effect was strange, for Madame Merle was already so present to her vision that her appearance in the flesh was like suddenly, and rather awfully, seeing a painted picture move. Isabel had been thinking all day of her falsity, her audacity, her ability, her probable suffering; and these dark things seemed to flash with a sudden light as she entered the room. Her being there at all had the character of ugly evidence, of handwritings, of profaned relics, of grim things produced in court. It made Isabel feel faint; if it had been necessary to speak on the spot she would have been quite unable. But no such necessity was distinct to her; it seemed to her indeed that she had absolutely nothing to say to Madame Merle. In one's relations with this lady, however, there were never any absolute necessities; she had a manner which carried off not only her own deficiencies but those of other people. But she was different from usual; she came in slowly, behind the portress, and Isabel instantly perceived that she was not likely to depend upon her habitual resources. For her too the occasion was exceptional, and she had undertaken to treat it by the light of the moment. This gave her a peculiar gravity; she pretended not even to smile, and though Isabel saw that she was more than ever playing a part it seemed to her that on the whole the wonderful woman had never been so natural. She looked at her young friend from head to foot, but not harshly nor defiantly; with a cold gentleness rather, and an absence of any air of allusion to their last meeting. It was as if she had wished to mark a distinction. She had been irritated then, she was reconciled now.

"You can leave us alone," she said to the portress; "in five minutes this lady will ring for you." And then she turned to Isabel, who, after noting what has just been mentioned, had ceased to notice and had let her eyes wander as far as the limits of the room would allow. She wished never to look at Madame Merle again. "You're surprised to find me here, and I'm afraid you're not pleased," this lady went on. "You don't see why I should have come; it's as if I had anticipated you. I confess I've been rather indiscreet—I ought to have asked your permission." There was none of the oblique movement of irony in this; it was said simply and mildly; but Isabel, far afloat on a sea of wonder and pain, could not have told herself with what intention it was uttered. "But I've not been sitting long," Madame Merle continued; "that is I've not been long with Pansy. I came to see her because it occurred to me this afternoon that she must be rather lonely and perhaps even a little miserable. It may be good for a small girl; I know so little about small girls; I can't tell. At any rate it's a little dismal. Therefore I came—on the chance. I knew of course that you'd come, and her father as well; still, I had not been told other visitors were forbidden. The good woman—what's her name? Madame Catherine—made no objection whatever. I stayed twenty minutes with Pansy; she has a charming little room, not in the least conventual, with a piano and flowers. She has arranged it delightfully; she has so much taste. Of course it's all none of my business, but I feel happier since I've seen her. She may even have a maid if she likes; but of course she has no occasion to dress. She wears a little black frock; she looks so charming. I went afterwards to see Mother Catherine, who has a very good room too; I assure you I don't find the poor sisters at all monastic. Mother Catherine has a most coquettish little toilet-table, with something that looked uncommonly like a bottle of eau-de-Cologne. She speaks delightfully of Pansy; says it's a great happiness for them to have her. She's a little saint of heaven and a model to the oldest of them. Just as I was leaving Madame Catherine the portress came to say to her that there was a lady for the signorina. Of course I knew it must be you, and I asked her to let me go and receive you in her place. She demurred greatly—I must tell you that—and said it was her duty to notify the Mother Superior; it was of such high importance that you should be treated with respect. I requested her to let the Mother Superior alone and asked her how she supposed I would treat you!"

So Madame Merle went on, with much of the brilliancy of a woman who had long been a mistress of the art of conversation. But there were phases and gradations in her speech, not one of which was lost upon Isabel's ear, though her eyes were absent from her companion's face. She had not proceeded far before Isabel noted a sudden break in her voice, a lapse in her continuity, which was in itself a complete drama. This subtle modulation marked a momentous discovery—the perception of an entirely new attitude on the part of her listener. Madame Merle had guessed in the space of an instant that everything was at end between them, and in the space of another instant she had guessed the reason why. The person who stood there was not the same one she had seen hitherto, but was a very different person—a person who knew her secret. This discovery was tremendous, and from the moment she made it the most accomplished of women faltered and lost her courage. But only for that moment. Then the conscious stream of her perfect manner gathered itself again and flowed on as smoothly as might be to the end. But it was only because she had the end in view that she was able to proceed. She had been touched with a point that made her quiver, and she needed all the alertness of her will to repress her agitation. Her only safety was in her not betraying herself. She resisted this, but the startled quality of her voice refused to improve—she couldn't help it—while she heard herself say she hardly knew what. The tide of her confidence ebbed, and she was able only just to glide into port, faintly grazing the bottom.

Isabel saw it all as distinctly as if it had been reflected in a large clear glass. It might have been a great moment for her, for it might have been a moment of triumph. That Madame Merle had lost her pluck and saw before her the phantom of exposure—this in itself was a revenge, this in itself was almost the promise of a brighter day. And for a moment during which she stood apparently looking out of the window, with her back half-turned, Isabel enjoyed that knowledge. On the other side of the window lay the garden of the convent; but this is not what she saw; she saw nothing of the budding plants and the glowing afternoon. She saw, in the crude light of that revelation which had already become a part of experience and to which the very frailty of the vessel in which it had been offered her only gave an intrinsic price, the dry staring fact that she had been an applied handled hung-up tool, as senseless and convenient as mere shaped wood and iron. All the bitterness of this knowledge surged into her soul again; it was as if she felt on her lips the taste of dishonour. There was a moment during which, if she had turned and spoken, she would have said something that would hiss like a lash. But she closed her eyes, and then the hideous vision dropped. What remained was the cleverest woman in the world standing there within a few feet of her and knowing as little what to think as the meanest. Isabel's only revenge was to be silent still—to leave Madame Merle in this unprecedented situation. She left her there for a period that must have seemed long to this lady, who at last seated herself with a movement which was in itself a confession of helplessness. Then Isabel turned slow eyes, looking down at her. Madame Merle was very pale; her own eyes covered Isabel's face. She might see what she would, but her danger was over. Isabel would never accuse her, never reproach her; perhaps because she never would give her the opportunity to defend herself.

"I'm come to bid Pansy good-bye," our young woman said at last. "I go to England to-night."

"Go to England to-night!" Madame Merle repeated sitting there and looking up at her.

"I'm going to Gardencourt. Ralph Touchett's dying."

"Ah, you'll feel that." Madame Merle recovered herself; she had a chance to express sympathy. "Do you go alone?"

"Yes; without my husband."

Madame Merle gave a low vague murmur; a sort of recognition of the general sadness of things. "Mr. Touchett never liked me, but I'm sorry he's dying. Shall you see his mother?"

"Yes; she has returned from America."

"She used to be very kind to me; but she has changed. Others too have changed," said Madame Merle with a quiet noble pathos. She paused a moment, then added: "And you'll see dear old Gardencourt again!"

"I shall not enjoy it much," Isabel answered.

"Naturally—in your grief. But it's on the whole, of all the houses I know, and I know many, the one I should have liked best to live in. I don't venture to send a message to the people," Madame Merle added; "but I should like to give my love to the place."

Isabel turned away. "I had better go to Pansy. I've not much time."

While she looked about her for the proper egress, the door opened and admitted one of the ladies of the house, who advanced with a discreet smile, gently rubbing, under her long loose sleeves, a pair of plump white hands. Isabel recognised Madame Catherine, whose acquaintance she had already made, and begged that she would immediately let her see Miss Osmond. Madame Catherine looked doubly discreet, but smiled very blandly and said: "It will be good for her to see you. I'll take you to her myself." Then she directed her pleased guarded vision to Madame Merle.

"Will you let me remain a little?" this lady asked. "It's so good to be here."

"You may remain always if you like!" And the good sister gave a knowing laugh.

She led Isabel out of the room, through several corridors, and up a long staircase. All these departments were solid and bare, light and clean; so, thought Isabel, are the great penal establishments. Madame Catherine gently pushed open the door of Pansy's room and ushered in the visitor; then stood smiling with folded hands while the two others met and embraced.

"She's glad to see you," she repeated; "it will do her good." And she placed the best chair carefully for Isabel. But she made no movement to seat herself; she seemed ready to retire. "How does this dear child look?" she asked of Isabel, lingering a moment.

"She looks pale," Isabel answered.

"That's the pleasure of seeing you. She's very happy. Elle eclaire la maison," said the good sister.

Pansy wore, as Madame Merle had said, a little black dress; it was perhaps this that made her look pale. "They're very good to me—they think of everything!" she exclaimed with all her customary eagerness to accommodate.

"We think of you always—you're a precious charge," Madame Catherine remarked in the tone of a woman with whom benevolence was a habit and whose conception of duty was the acceptance of every care. It fell with a leaden weight on Isabel's ears; it seemed to represent the surrender of a personality, the authority of the Church.

When Madame Catherine had left them together Pansy kneeled down and hid her head in her stepmother's lap. So she remained some moments, while Isabel gently stroked her hair. Then she got up, averting her face and looking about the room. "Don't you think I've arranged it well? I've everything I have at home."

"It's very pretty; you're very comfortable." Isabel scarcely knew what she could say to her. On the one hand she couldn't let her think she had come to pity her, and on the other it would be a dull mockery to pretend to rejoice with her. So she simply added after a moment: "I've come to bid you good-bye. I'm going to England."

Pansy's white little face turned red. "To England! Not to come back?"

"I don't know when I shall come back."

"Ah, I'm sorry," Pansy breathed with faintness. She spoke as if she had no right to criticise; but her tone expressed a depth of disappointment.

"My cousin, Mr. Touchett, is very ill; he'll probably die. I wish to see him," Isabel said.

"Ah yes; you told me he would die. Of course you must go. And will papa go?"

"No; I shall go alone."

For a moment the girl said nothing. Isabel had often wondered what she thought of the apparent relations of her father with his wife; but never by a glance, by an intimation, had she let it be seen that she deemed them deficient in an air of intimacy. She made her reflexions, Isabel was sure; and she must have had a conviction that there were husbands and wives who were more intimate than that. But Pansy was not indiscreet even in thought; she would as little have ventured to judge her gentle stepmother as to criticise her magnificent father. Her heart may have stood almost as still as it would have done had she seen two of the saints in the great picture in the convent chapel turn their painted heads and shake them at each other. But as in this latter case she would (for very solemnity's sake) never have mentioned the awful phenomenon, so she put away all knowledge of the secrets of larger lives than her own. "You'll be very far away," she presently went on.

"Yes; I shall be far away. But it will scarcely matter," Isabel explained; "since so long as you're here I can't be called near you."

"Yes, but you can come and see me; though you've not come very often."

"I've not come because your father forbade it. To-day I bring nothing with me. I can't amuse you."

"I'm not to be amused. That's not what papa wishes."

"Then it hardly matters whether I'm in Rome or in England."

"You're not happy, Mrs. Osmond," said Pansy.

"Not very. But it doesn't matter."

"That's what I say to myself. What does it matter? But I should like to come out."

"I wish indeed you might."

"Don't leave me here," Pansy went on gently.

Isabel said nothing for a minute; her heart beat fast. "Will you come away with me now?" she asked.

Pansy looked at her pleadingly. "Did papa tell you to bring me?"

"No; it's my own proposal."

"I think I had better wait then. Did papa send me no message?"

"I don't think he knew I was coming."

"He thinks I've not had enough," said Pansy. "But I have. The ladies are very kind to me and the little girls come to see me. There are some very little ones—such charming children. Then my room—you can see for yourself. All that's very delightful. But I've had enough. Papa wished me to think a little—and I've thought a great deal."

"What have you thought?"

"Well, that I must never displease papa."

"You knew that before."

"Yes; but I know it better. I'll do anything—I'll do anything," said Pansy. Then, as she heard her own words, a deep, pure blush came into her face. Isabel read the meaning of it; she saw the poor girl had been vanquished. It was well that Mr. Edward Rosier had kept his enamels! Isabel looked into her eyes and saw there mainly a prayer to be treated easily. She laid her hand on Pansy's as if to let her know that her look conveyed no diminution of esteem; for the collapse of the girl's momentary resistance (mute and modest thought it had been) seemed only her tribute to the truth of things. She didn't presume to judge others, but she had judged herself; she had seen the reality. She had no vocation for struggling with combinations; in the solemnity of sequestration there was something that overwhelmed her. She bowed her pretty head to authority and only asked of authority to be merciful. Yes; it was very well that Edward Rosier had reserved a few articles!

Isabel got up; her time was rapidly shortening. "Good-bye then. I leave Rome to-night."

Pansy took hold of her dress; there was a sudden change in the child's face. "You look strange, you frighten me."

"Oh, I'm very harmless," said Isabel.

"Perhaps you won't come back?"

"Perhaps not. I can't tell."

"Ah, Mrs. Osmond, you won't leave me!"

Isabel now saw she had guessed everything. "My dear child, what can I do for you?" she asked.

"I don't know—but I'm happier when I think of you."

"You can always think of me."

"Not when you're so far. I'm a little afraid," said Pansy.

"What are you afraid of?"

"Of papa—a little. And of Madame Merle. She has just been to see me."

"You must not say that," Isabel observed.

"Oh, I'll do everything they want. Only if you're here I shall do it more easily."

Isabel considered. "I won't desert you," she said at last. "Good-bye, my child."

Then they held each other a moment in a silent embrace, like two sisters; and afterwards Pansy walked along the corridor with her visitor to the top of the staircase. "Madame Merle has been here," she remarked as they went; and as Isabel answered nothing she added abruptly: "I don't like Madame Merle!"

Isabel hesitated, then stopped. "You must never say that—that you don't like Madame Merle."

Pansy looked at her in wonder; but wonder with Pansy had never been a reason for non-compliance. "I never will again," she said with exquisite gentleness. At the top of the staircase they had to separate, as it appeared to be part of the mild but very definite discipline under which Pansy lived that she should not go down. Isabel descended, and when she reached the bottom the girl was standing above. "You'll come back?" she called out in a voice that Isabel remembered afterwards.

"Yes—I'll come back."

Madame Catherine met Mrs. Osmond below and conducted her to the door of the parlour, outside of which the two stood talking a minute. "I won't go in," said the good sister. "Madame Merle's waiting for you."

At this announcement Isabel stiffened; she was on the point of asking if there were no other egress from the convent. But a moment's reflexion assured her that she would do well not to betray to the worthy nun her desire to avoid Pansy's other friend. Her companion grasped her arm very gently and, fixing her a moment with wise, benevolent eyes, said in French and almost familiarly: "Eh bien, chere Madame, qu'en pensez-vous?"

"About my step-daughter? Oh, it would take long to tell you."

"We think it's enough," Madame Catherine distinctly observed. And she pushed open the door of the parlour.

Madame Merle was sitting just as Isabel had left her, like a woman so absorbed in thought that she had not moved a little finger. As Madame Catherine closed the door she got up, and Isabel saw that she had been thinking to some purpose. She had recovered her balance; she was in full possession of her resources. "I found I wished to wait for you," she said urbanely. "But it's not to talk about Pansy."

Isabel wondered what it could be to talk about, and in spite of Madame Merle's declaration she answered after a moment: "Madame Catherine says it's enough."

"Yes; it also seems to me enough. I wanted to ask you another word about poor Mr. Touchett," Madame Merle added. "Have you reason to believe that he's really at his last?"

"I've no information but a telegram. Unfortunately it only confirms a probability."

"I'm going to ask you a strange question," said Madame Merle. "Are you very fond of your cousin?" And she gave a smile as strange as her utterance.

"Yes, I'm very fond of him. But I don't understand you."

She just hung fire. "It's rather hard to explain. Something has occurred to me which may not have occurred to you, and I give you the benefit of my idea. Your cousin did you once a great service. Have you never guessed it?"

"He has done me many services."

"Yes; but one was much above the rest. He made you a rich woman."

"HE made me—?"

Madame Merle appearing to see herself successful, she went on more triumphantly: "He imparted to you that extra lustre which was required to make you a brilliant match. At bottom it's him you've to thank." She stopped; there was something in Isabel's eyes.

"I don't understand you. It was my uncle's money."

"Yes; it was your uncle's money, but it was your cousin's idea. He brought his father over to it. Ah, my dear, the sum was large!"

Isabel stood staring; she seemed to-day to live in a world illumined by lurid flashes. "I don't know why you say such things. I don't know what you know."

"I know nothing but what I've guessed. But I've guessed that."

Isabel went to the door and, when she had opened it, stood a moment with her hand on the latch. Then she said—it was her only revenge: "I believed it was you I had to thank!"

Madame Merle dropped her eyes; she stood there in a kind of proud penance. "You're very unhappy, I know. But I'm more so."

"Yes; I can believe that. I think I should like never to see you again."

Madame Merle raised her eyes. "I shall go to America," she quietly remarked while Isabel passed out.

CHAPTER LIII

It was not with surprise, it was with a feeling which in other circumstances would have had much of the effect of joy, that as Isabel descended from the Paris Mail at Charing Cross she stepped into the arms, as it were—or at any rate into the hands—of Henrietta Stackpole. She had telegraphed to her friend from Turin, and though she had not definitely said to herself that Henrietta would meet her, she had felt her telegram would produce some helpful result. On her long journey from Rome her mind had been given up to vagueness; she was unable to question the future. She performed this journey with sightless eyes and took little pleasure in the countries she traversed, decked out though they were in the richest freshness of spring. Her thoughts followed their course through other countries—strange-looking, dimly-lighted, pathless lands, in which there was no change of seasons, but only, as it seemed, a perpetual dreariness of winter. She had plenty to think about; but it was neither reflexion nor conscious purpose that filled her mind. Disconnected visions passed through it, and sudden dull gleams of memory, of expectation. The past and the future came and went at their will, but she saw them only in fitful images, which rose and fell by a logic of their own. It was extraordinary the things she remembered. Now that she was in the secret, now that she knew something that so much concerned her and the eclipse of which had made life resemble an attempt to play whist with an imperfect pack of cards, the truth of things, their mutual relations, their meaning, and for the most part their horror, rose before her with a kind of architectural vastness. She remembered a thousand trifles; they started to life with the spontaneity of a shiver. She had thought them trifles at the time; now she saw that they had been weighted with lead. Yet even now they were trifles after all, for of what use was it to her to understand them? Nothing seemed of use to her today. All purpose, all intention, was suspended; all desire too save the single desire to reach her much-embracing refuge. Gardencourt had been her starting-point, and to those muffled chambers it was at least a temporary solution to return. She had gone forth in her strength; she would come back in her weakness, and if the place had been a rest to her before, it would be a sanctuary now. She envied Ralph his dying, for if one were thinking of rest that was the most perfect of all. To cease utterly, to give it all up and not know anything more—this idea was as sweet as the vision of a cool bath in a marble tank, in a darkened chamber, in a hot land.

She had moments indeed in her journey from Rome which were almost as good as being dead. She sat in her corner, so motionless, so passive, simply with the sense of being carried, so detached from hope and regret, that she recalled to herself one of those Etruscan figures couched upon the receptacle of their ashes. There was nothing to regret now—that was all over. Not only the time of her folly, but the time of her repentance was far. The only thing to regret was that Madame Merle had been so—well, so unimaginable. Just here her intelligence dropped, from literal inability to say what it was that Madame Merle had been. Whatever it was it was for Madame Merle herself to regret it; and doubtless she would do so in America, where she had announced she was going. It concerned Isabel no more; she only had an impression that she should never again see Madame Merle. This impression carried her into the future, of which from time to time she had a mutilated glimpse. She saw herself, in the distant years, still in the attitude of a woman who had her life to live, and these intimations contradicted the spirit of the present hour. It might be desirable to get quite away, really away, further away than little grey-green England, but this privilege was evidently to be denied her. Deep in her soul—deeper than any appetite for renunciation—was the sense that life would be her business for a long time to come. And at moments there was something inspiring, almost enlivening, in the conviction. It was a proof of strength—it was a proof she should some day be happy again. It couldn't be she was to live only to suffer; she was still young, after all, and a great many things might happen to her yet. To live only to suffer—only to feel the injury of life repeated and enlarged—it seemed to her she was too valuable, too capable, for that. Then she wondered if it were vain and stupid to think so well of herself. When had it even been a guarantee to be valuable? Wasn't all history full of the destruction of precious things? Wasn't it much more probable that if one were fine one would suffer? It involved then perhaps an admission that one had a certain grossness; but Isabel recognised, as it passed before her eyes, the quick vague shadow of a long future. She should never escape; she should last to the end. Then the middle years wrapped her about again and the grey curtain of her indifference closed her in.

Henrietta kissed her, as Henrietta usually kissed, as if she were afraid she should be caught doing it; and then Isabel stood there in the crowd, looking about her, looking for her servant. She asked nothing; she wished to wait. She had a sudden perception that she should be helped. She rejoiced Henrietta had come; there was something terrible in an arrival in London. The dusky, smoky, far-arching vault of the station, the strange, livid light, the dense, dark, pushing crowd, filled her with a nervous fear and made her put her arm into her friend's. She remembered she had once liked these things; they seemed part of a mighty spectacle in which there was something that touched her. She remembered how she walked away from Euston, in the winter dusk, in the crowded streets, five years before. She could not have done that to-day, and the incident came before her as the deed of another person.

"It's too beautiful that you should have come," said Henrietta, looking at her as if she thought Isabel might be prepared to challenge the proposition. "If you hadn't—if you hadn't; well, I don't know," remarked Miss Stackpole, hinting ominously at her powers of disapproval.

Isabel looked about without seeing her maid. Her eyes rested on another figure, however, which she felt she had seen before; and in a moment she recognised the genial countenance of Mr. Bantling. He stood a little apart, and it was not in the power of the multitude that pressed about him to make him yield an inch of the ground he had taken—that of abstracting himself discreetly while the two ladies performed their embraces.

"There's Mr. Bantling," said Isabel, gently, irrelevantly, scarcely caring much now whether she should find her maid or not.

"Oh yes, he goes everywhere with me. Come here, Mr. Bantling!" Henrietta exclaimed. Whereupon the gallant bachelor advanced with a smile—a smile tempered, however, by the gravity of the occasion. "Isn't it lovely she has come?" Henrietta asked. "He knows all about it," she added; "we had quite a discussion. He said you wouldn't, I said you would."

"I thought you always agreed," Isabel smiled in return. She felt she could smile now; she had seen in an instant, in Mr. Bantling's brave eyes, that he had good news for her. They seemed to say he wished her to remember he was an old friend of her cousin—that he understood, that it was all right. Isabel gave him her hand; she thought of him, extravagantly, as a beautiful blameless knight.

"Oh, I always agree," said Mr. Bantling. "But she doesn't, you know."

"Didn't I tell you that a maid was a nuisance?" Henrietta enquired. "Your young lady has probably remained at Calais."

"I don't care," said Isabel, looking at Mr. Bantling, whom she had never found so interesting.

"Stay with her while I go and see," Henrietta commanded, leaving the two for a moment together.

They stood there at first in silence, and then Mr. Bantling asked Isabel how it had been on the Channel.

"Very fine. No, I believe it was very rough," she said, to her companion's obvious surprise. After which she added: "You've been to Gardencourt, I know."

"Now how do you know that?"

"I can't tell you—except that you look like a person who has been to Gardencourt."

"Do you think I look awfully sad? It's awfully sad there, you know."

"I don't believe you ever look awfully sad. You look awfully kind," said Isabel with a breadth that cost her no effort. It seemed to her she should never again feel a superficial embarrassment.

Poor Mr. Bantling, however, was still in this inferior stage. He blushed a good deal and laughed, he assured her that he was often very blue, and that when he was blue he was awfully fierce. "You can ask Miss Stackpole, you know. I was at Gardencourt two days ago."

"Did you see my cousin?"

"Only for a little. But he had been seeing people; Warburton had been there the day before. Ralph was just the same as usual, except that he was in bed and that he looks tremendously ill and that he can't speak," Mr. Bantling pursued. "He was awfully jolly and funny all the same. He was just as clever as ever. It's awfully wretched."

Even in the crowded, noisy station this simple picture was vivid. "Was that late in the day?"

"Yes; I went on purpose. We thought you'd like to know."

"I'm greatly obliged to you. Can I go down tonight?"

"Ah, I don't think SHE'LL let you go," said Mr. Bantling. "She wants you to stop with her. I made Touchett's man promise to telegraph me to-day, and I found the telegram an hour ago at my club. 'Quiet and easy,' that's what it says, and it's dated two o'clock. So you see you can wait till to-morrow. You must be awfully tired."

"Yes, I'm awfully tired. And I thank you again."

"Oh," said Mr. Bantling, "We were certain you would like the last news." On which Isabel vaguely noted that he and Henrietta seemed after all to agree. Miss Stackpole came back with Isabel's maid, whom she had caught in the act of proving her utility. This excellent person, instead of losing herself in the crowd, had simply attended to her mistress's luggage, so that the latter was now at liberty to leave the station. "You know you're not to think of going to the country to-night," Henrietta remarked to her. "It doesn't matter whether there's a train or not. You're to come straight to me in Wimpole Street. There isn't a corner to be had in London, but I've got you one all the same. It isn't a Roman palace, but it will do for a night."

"I'll do whatever you wish," Isabel said.

"You'll come and answer a few questions; that's what I wish."

"She doesn't say anything about dinner, does she, Mrs. Osmond?" Mr. Bantling enquired jocosely.

Henrietta fixed him a moment with her speculative gaze. "I see you're in a great hurry to get your own. You'll be at the Paddington Station to-morrow morning at ten."

"Don't come for my sake, Mr. Bantling," said Isabel.

"He'll come for mine," Henrietta declared as she ushered her friend into a cab. And later, in a large dusky parlour in Wimpole Street—to do her justice there had been dinner enough—she asked those questions to which she had alluded at the station. "Did your husband make you a scene about your coming?" That was Miss Stackpole's first enquiry.

"No; I can't say he made a scene."

"He didn't object then?"

"Yes, he objected very much. But it was not what you'd call a scene."

"What was it then?"

"It was a very quiet conversation."

Henrietta for a moment regarded her guest. "It must have been hellish," she then remarked. And Isabel didn't deny that it had been hellish. But she confined herself to answering Henrietta's questions, which was easy, as they were tolerably definite. For the present she offered her no new information. "Well," said Miss Stackpole at last, "I've only one criticism to make. I don't see why you promised little Miss Osmond to go back."

"I'm not sure I myself see now," Isabel replied. "But I did then."

"If you've forgotten your reason perhaps you won't return."

Isabel waited a moment. "Perhaps I shall find another."

"You'll certainly never find a good one."

"In default of a better my having promised will do," Isabel suggested.

"Yes; that's why I hate it."

"Don't speak of it now. I've a little time. Coming away was a complication, but what will going back be?"

"You must remember, after all, that he won't make you a scene!" said Henrietta with much intention.

"He will, though," Isabel answered gravely. "It won't be the scene of a moment; it will be a scene of the rest of my life."

For some minutes the two women sat and considered this remainder, and then Miss Stackpole, to change the subject, as Isabel had requested, announced abruptly: "I've been to stay with Lady Pensil!"

"Ah, the invitation came at last!"

"Yes; it took five years. But this time she wanted to see me."

"Naturally enough."

"It was more natural than I think you know," said Henrietta, who fixed her eyes on a distant point. And then she added, turning suddenly: "Isabel Archer, I beg your pardon. You don't know why? Because I criticised you, and yet I've gone further than you. Mr. Osmond, at least, was born on the other side!"

It was a moment before Isabel grasped her meaning; this sense was so modestly, or at least so ingeniously, veiled. Isabel's mind was not possessed at present with the comicality of things; but she greeted with a quick laugh the image that her companion had raised. She immediately recovered herself, however, and with the right excess of intensity, "Henrietta Stackpole," she asked, "are you going to give up your country?"

"Yes, my poor Isabel, I am. I won't pretend to deny it; I look the fact: in the face. I'm going to marry Mr. Bantling and locate right here in London."

"It seems very strange," said Isabel, smiling now.

"Well yes, I suppose it does. I've come to it little by little. I think I know what I'm doing; but I don't know as I can explain."

"One can't explain one's marriage," Isabel answered. "And yours doesn't need to be explained. Mr. Bantling isn't a riddle."

"No, he isn't a bad pun—or even a high flight of American humour. He has a beautiful nature," Henrietta went on. "I've studied him for many years and I see right through him. He's as clear as the style of a good prospectus. He's not intellectual, but he appreciates intellect. On the other hand he doesn't exaggerate its claims. I sometimes think we do in the United States."

"Ah," said Isabel, "you're changed indeed! It's the first time I've ever heard you say anything against your native land."

"I only say that we're too infatuated with mere brain-power; that, after all, isn't a vulgar fault. But I AM changed; a woman has to change a good deal to marry."

"I hope you'll be very happy. You will at last—over here—see something of the inner life."

Henrietta gave a little significant sigh. "That's the key to the mystery, I believe. I couldn't endure to be kept off. Now I've as good a right as any one!" she added with artless elation. Isabel was duly diverted, but there was a certain melancholy in her view. Henrietta, after all, had confessed herself human and feminine, Henrietta whom she had hitherto regarded as a light keen flame, a disembodied voice. It was a disappointment to find she had personal susceptibilities, that she was subject to common passions, and that her intimacy with Mr. Bantling had not been completely original. There was a want of originality in her marrying him—there was even a kind of stupidity; and for a moment, to Isabel's sense, the dreariness of the world took on a deeper tinge. A little later indeed she reflected that Mr. Bantling himself at least was original. But she didn't see how Henrietta could give up her country. She herself had relaxed her hold of it, but it had never been her country as it had been Henrietta's. She presently asked her if she had enjoyed her visit to Lady Pensil.

"Oh yes," said Henrietta, "she didn't know what to make of me."

"And was that very enjoyable?"

"Very much so, because she's supposed to be a master mind. She thinks she knows everything; but she doesn't understand a woman of my modern type. It would be so much easier for her if I were only a little better or a little worse. She's so puzzled; I believe she thinks it's my duty to go and do something immoral. She thinks it's immoral that I should marry her brother; but, after all, that isn't immoral enough. And she'll never understand my mixture—never!"

"She's not so intelligent as her brother then," said Isabel. "He appears to have understood."

"Oh no, he hasn't!" cried Miss Stackpole with decision. "I really believe that's what he wants to marry me for—just to find out the mystery and the proportions of it. That's a fixed idea—a kind of fascination."

"It's very good in you to humour it."

"Oh well," said Henrietta, "I've something to find out too!" And Isabel saw that she had not renounced an allegiance, but planned an attack. She was at last about to grapple in earnest with England.

Isabel also perceived, however, on the morrow, at the Paddington Station, where she found herself, at ten o'clock, in the company both of Miss Stackpole and Mr. Bantling, that the gentleman bore his perplexities lightly. If he had not found out everything he had found out at least the great point—that Miss Stackpole would not be wanting in initiative. It was evident that in the selection of a wife he had been on his guard against this deficiency.

"Henrietta has told me, and I'm very glad," Isabel said as she gave him her hand.

"I dare say you think it awfully odd," Mr. Bantling replied, resting on his neat umbrella.

"Yes, I think it awfully odd."

"You can't think it so awfully odd as I do. But I've always rather liked striking out a line," said Mr. Bantling serenely.

CHAPTER LIV

Isabel's arrival at Gardencourt on this second occasion was even quieter than it had been on the first. Ralph Touchett kept but a small household, and to the new servants Mrs. Osmond was a stranger; so that instead of being conducted to her own apartment she was coldly shown into the drawing-room and left to wait while her name was carried up to her aunt. She waited a long time; Mrs. Touchett appeared in no hurry to come to her. She grew impatient at last; she grew nervous and scared—as scared as if the objects about her had begun to show for conscious things, watching her trouble with grotesque grimaces. The day was dark and cold; the dusk was thick in the corners of the wide brown rooms. The house was perfectly still—with a stillness that Isabel remembered; it had filled all the place for days before the death of her uncle. She left the drawing-room and wandered about—strolled into the library and along the gallery of pictures, where, in the deep silence, her footstep made an echo. Nothing was changed; she recognised everything she had seen years before; it might have been only yesterday she had stood there. She envied the security of valuable "pieces" which change by no hair's breadth, only grow in value, while their owners lose inch by inch youth, happiness, beauty; and she became aware that she was walking about as her aunt had done on the day she had come to see her in Albany. She was changed enough since then—that had been the beginning. It suddenly struck her that if her Aunt Lydia had not come that day in just that way and found her alone, everything might have been different. She might have had another life and she might have been a woman more blest. She stopped in the gallery in front of a small picture—a charming and precious Bonington—upon which her eyes rested a long time. But she was not looking at the picture; she was wondering whether if her aunt had not come that day in Albany she would have married Caspar Goodwood.

Mrs. Touchett appeared at last, just after Isabel had returned to the big uninhabited drawing-room. She looked a good deal older, but her eye was as bright as ever and her head as erect; her thin lips seemed a repository of latent meanings. She wore a little grey dress of the most undecorated fashion, and Isabel wondered, as she had wondered the first time, if her remarkable kinswoman resembled more a queen-regent or the matron of a gaol. Her lips felt very thin indeed on Isabel's hot cheek.

"I've kept you waiting because I've been sitting with Ralph," Mrs. Touchett said. "The nurse had gone to luncheon and I had taken her place. He has a man who's supposed to look after him, but the man's good for nothing; he's always looking out of the window—as if there were anything to see! I didn't wish to move, because Ralph seemed to be sleeping and I was afraid the sound would disturb him. I waited till the nurse came back. I remembered you knew the house."

"I find I know it better even than I thought; I've been walking everywhere," Isabel answered. And then she asked if Ralph slept much.

"He lies with his eyes closed; he doesn't move. But I'm not sure that it's always sleep."

"Will he see me? Can he speak to me?"

Mrs. Touchett declined the office of saying. "You can try him," was the limit of her extravagance. And then she offered to conduct Isabel to her room. "I thought they had taken you there; but it's not my house, it's Ralph's; and I don't know what they do. They must at least have taken your luggage; I don't suppose you've brought much. Not that I care, however. I believe they've given you the same room you had before; when Ralph heard you were coming he said you must have that one."

"Did he say anything else?"

"Ah, my dear, he doesn't chatter as he used!" cried Mrs. Touchett as she preceded her niece up the staircase.

It was the same room, and something told Isabel it had not been slept in since she occupied it. Her luggage was there and was not voluminous; Mrs. Touchett sat down a moment with her eyes upon it. "Is there really no hope?" our young woman asked as she stood before her.

"None whatever. There never has been. It has not been a successful life."

"No—it has only been a beautiful one." Isabel found herself already contradicting her aunt; she was irritated by her dryness.

"I don't know what you mean by that; there's no beauty without health. That is a very odd dress to travel in."

Isabel glanced at her garment. "I left Rome at an hour's notice; I took the first that came."

"Your sisters, in America, wished to know how you dress. That seemed to be their principal interest. I wasn't able to tell them—but they seemed to have the right idea: that you never wear anything less than black brocade."

"They think I'm more brilliant than I am; I'm afraid to tell them the truth," said Isabel. "Lily wrote me you had dined with her."

"She invited me four times, and I went once. After the second time she should have let me alone. The dinner was very good; it must have been expensive. Her husband has a very bad manner. Did I enjoy my visit to America? Why should I have enjoyed it? I didn't go for my pleasure."

These were interesting items, but Mrs. Touchett soon left her niece, whom she was to meet in half an hour at the midday meal. For this repast the two ladies faced each other at an abbreviated table in the melancholy dining-room. Here, after a little, Isabel saw her aunt not to be so dry as she appeared, and her old pity for the poor woman's inexpressiveness, her want of regret, of disappointment, came back to her. Unmistakeably she would have found it a blessing to-day to be able to feel a defeat, a mistake, even a shame or two. She wondered if she were not even missing those enrichments of consciousness and privately trying—reaching out for some after-taste of life, dregs of the banquet; the testimony of pain or the cold recreation of remorse. On the other hand perhaps she was afraid; if she should begin to know remorse at all it might take her too far. Isabel could perceive, however, how it had come over her dimly that she had failed of something, that she saw herself in the future as an old woman without memories. Her little sharp face looked tragical. She told her niece that Ralph had as yet not moved, but that he probably would be able to see her before dinner. And then in a moment she added that he had seen Lord Warburton the day before; an announcement which startled Isabel a little, as it seemed an intimation that this personage was in the neighbourhood and that an accident might bring them together. Such an accident would not be happy; she had not come to England to struggle again with Lord Warburton. She none the less presently said to her aunt that he had been very kind to Ralph; she had seen something of that in Rome.

"He has something else to think of now," Mrs. Touchett returned. And she paused with a gaze like a gimlet.

Isabel saw she meant something, and instantly guessed what she meant. But her reply concealed her guess; her heart beat faster and she wished to gain a moment. "Ah yes—the House of Lords and all that."

"He's not thinking of the Lords; he's thinking of the ladies. At least he's thinking of one of them; he told Ralph he's engaged to be married."

"Ah, to be married!" Isabel mildly exclaimed.

"Unless he breaks it off. He seemed to think Ralph would like to know. Poor Ralph can't go to the wedding, though I believe it's to take place very soon.

"And who's the young lady?"

"A member of the aristocracy; Lady Flora, Lady Felicia—something of that sort."

"I'm very glad," Isabel said. "It must be a sudden decision."

"Sudden enough, I believe; a courtship of three weeks. It has only just been made public."

"I'm very glad," Isabel repeated with a larger emphasis. She knew her aunt was watching her—looking for the signs of some imputed soreness, and the desire to prevent her companion from seeing anything of this kind enabled her to speak in the tone of quick satisfaction, the tone almost of relief. Mrs. Touchett of course followed the tradition that ladies, even married ones, regard the marriage of their old lovers as an offence to themselves. Isabel's first care therefore was to show that however that might be in general she was not offended now. But meanwhile, as I say, her heart beat faster; and if she sat for some moments thoughtful—she presently forgot Mrs. Touchett's observation—it was not because she had lost an admirer. Her imagination had traversed half Europe; it halted, panting, and even trembling a little, in the city of Rome. She figured herself announcing to her husband that Lord Warburton was to lead a bride to the altar, and she was of course not aware how extremely wan she must have looked while she made this intellectual effort. But at last she collected herself and said to her aunt: "He was sure to do it some time or other."

Mrs. Touchett was silent; then she gave a sharp little shake of the head. "Ah, my dear, you're beyond me!" she cried suddenly. They went on with their luncheon in silence; Isabel felt as if she had heard of Lord Warburton's death. She had known him only as a suitor, and now that was all over. He was dead for poor Pansy; by Pansy he might have lived. A servant had been hovering about; at last Mrs. Touchett requested him to leave them alone. She had finished her meal; she sat with her hands folded on the edge of the table. "I should like to ask you three questions," she observed when the servant had gone.

"Three are a great many."

"I can't do with less; I've been thinking. They're all very good ones."

"That's what I'm afraid of. The best questions are the worst," Isabel answered. Mrs. Touchett had pushed back her chair, and as her niece left the table and walked, rather consciously, to one of the deep windows, she felt herself followed by her eyes.

"Have you ever been sorry you didn't marry Lord Warburton?" Mrs. Touchett enquired.

Isabel shook her head slowly, but not heavily. "No, dear aunt."

"Good. I ought to tell you that I propose to believe what you say."

"Your believing me's an immense temptation," she declared, smiling still.

"A temptation to lie? I don't recommend you to do that, for when I'm misinformed I'm as dangerous as a poisoned rat. I don't mean to crow over you."

"It's my husband who doesn't get on with me," said Isabel.

"I could have told him he wouldn't. I don't call that crowing over YOU," Mrs. Touchett added. "Do you still like Serena Merle?" she went on.

"Not as I once did. But it doesn't matter, for she's going to America."

"To America? She must have done something very bad."

"Yes—very bad."

"May I ask what it is?"

"She made a convenience of me."

"Ah," cried Mrs. Touchett, "so she did of me! She does of every one."

"She'll make a convenience of America," said Isabel, smiling again and glad that her aunt's questions were over.

It was not till the evening that she was able to see Ralph. He had been dozing all day; at least he had been lying unconscious. The doctor was there, but after a while went away—the local doctor, who had attended his father and whom Ralph liked. He came three or four times a day; he was deeply interested in his patient. Ralph had had Sir Matthew Hope, but he had got tired of this celebrated man, to whom he had asked his mother to send word he was now dead and was therefore without further need of medical advice. Mrs. Touchett had simply written to Sir Matthew that her son disliked him. On the day of Isabel's arrival Ralph gave no sign, as I have related, for many hours; but toward evening he raised himself and said he knew that she had come.

How he knew was not apparent, inasmuch as for fear of exciting him no one had offered the information. Isabel came in and sat by his bed in the dim light; there was only a shaded candle in a corner of the room. She told the nurse she might go—she herself would sit with him for the rest of the evening. He had opened his eyes and recognised her, and had moved his hand, which lay helpless beside him, so that she might take it. But he was unable to speak; he closed his eyes again and remained perfectly still, only keeping her hand in his own. She sat with him a long time—till the nurse came back; but he gave no further sign. He might have passed away while she looked at him; he was already the figure and pattern of death. She had thought him far gone in Rome, and this was worse; there was but one change possible now. There was a strange tranquillity in his face; it was as still as the lid of a box. With this he was a mere lattice of bones; when he opened his eyes to greet her it was as if she were looking into immeasurable space. It was not till midnight that the nurse came back; but the hours, to Isabel, had not seemed long; it was exactly what she had come for. If she had come simply to wait she found ample occasion, for he lay three days in a kind of grateful silence. He recognised her and at moments seemed to wish to speak; but he found no voice. Then he closed his eyes again, as if he too were waiting for something—for something that certainly would come. He was so absolutely quiet that it seemed to her what was coming had already arrived; and yet she never lost the sense that they were still together. But they were not always together; there were other hours that she passed in wandering through the empty house and listening for a voice that was not poor Ralph's. She had a constant fear; she thought it possible her husband would write to her. But he remained silent, and she only got a letter from Florence and from the Countess Gemini. Ralph, however, spoke at last—on the evening of the third day.

"I feel better to-night," he murmured, abruptly, in the soundless dimness of her vigil; "I think I can say something." She sank upon her knees beside his pillow; took his thin hand in her own; begged him not to make an effort—not to tire himself. His face was of necessity serious—it was incapable of the muscular play of a smile; but its owner apparently had not lost a perception of incongruities. "What does it matter if I'm tired when I've all eternity to rest? There's no harm in making an effort when it's the very last of all. Don't people always feel better just before the end? I've often heard of that; it's what I was waiting for. Ever since you've been here I thought it would come. I tried two or three times; I was afraid you'd get tired of sitting there." He spoke slowly, with painful breaks and long pauses; his voice seemed to come from a distance. When he ceased he lay with his face turned to Isabel and his large unwinking eyes open into her own. "It was very good of you to come," he went on. "I thought you would; but I wasn't sure."

"I was not sure either till I came," said Isabel.

"You've been like an angel beside my bed. You know they talk about the angel of death. It's the most beautiful of all. You've been like that; as if you were waiting for me."

"I was not waiting for your death; I was waiting for—for this. This is not death, dear Ralph."

"Not for you—no. There's nothing makes us feel so much alive as to see others die. That's the sensation of life—the sense that we remain. I've had it—even I. But now I'm of no use but to give it to others. With me it's all over." And then he paused. Isabel bowed her head further, till it rested on the two hands that were clasped upon his own. She couldn't see him now; but his far-away voice was close to her ear. "Isabel," he went on suddenly, "I wish it were over for you." She answered nothing; she had burst into sobs; she remained so, with her buried face. He lay silent, listening to her sobs; at last he gave a long groan. "Ah, what is it you have done for me?"

"What is it you did for me?" she cried, her now extreme agitation half smothered by her attitude. She had lost all her shame, all wish to hide things. Now he must know; she wished him to know, for it brought them supremely together, and he was beyond the reach of pain. "You did something once—you know it. O Ralph, you've been everything! What have I done for you—what can I do to-day? I would die if you could live. But I don't wish you to live; I would die myself, not to lose you." Her voice was as broken as his own and full of tears and anguish.

"You won't lose me—you'll keep me. Keep me in your heart; I shall be nearer to you than I've ever been. Dear Isabel, life is better; for in life there's love. Death is good—but there's no love."

"I never thanked you—I never spoke—I never was what I should be!" Isabel went on. She felt a passionate need to cry out and accuse herself, to let her sorrow possess her. All her troubles, for the moment, became single and melted together into this present pain. "What must you have thought of me? Yet how could I know? I never knew, and I only know to-day because there are people less stupid than I."

"Don't mind people," said Ralph. "I think I'm glad to leave people."

She raised her head and her clasped hands; she seemed for a moment to pray to him. "Is it true—is it true?" she asked.

"True that you've been stupid? Oh no," said Ralph with a sensible intention of wit.

"That you made me rich—that all I have is yours?"

He turned away his head, and for some time said nothing. Then at last: "Ah, don't speak of that—that was not happy." Slowly he moved his face toward her again, and they once more saw each other. "But for that—but for that—!" And he paused. "I believe I ruined you," he wailed.

She was full of the sense that he was beyond the reach of pain; he seemed already so little of this world. But even if she had not had it she would still have spoken, for nothing mattered now but the only knowledge that was not pure anguish—the knowledge that they were looking at the truth together.

"He married me for the money," she said. She wished to say everything; she was afraid he might die before she had done so. He gazed at her a little, and for the first time his fixed eyes lowered their lids. But he raised them in a moment, and then, "He was greatly in love with you," he answered.

"Yes, he was in love with me. But he wouldn't have married me if I had been poor. I don't hurt you in saying that. How can I? I only want you to understand. I always tried to keep you from understanding; but that's all over."

"I always understood," said Ralph.

"I thought you did, and I didn't like it. But now I like it."

"You don't hurt me—you make me very happy." And as Ralph said this there was an extraordinary gladness in his voice. She bent her head again, and pressed her lips to the back of his hand. "I always understood," he continued, "though it was so strange—so pitiful. You wanted to look at life for yourself—but you were not allowed; you were punished for your wish. You were ground in the very mill of the conventional!"

"Oh yes, I've been punished," Isabel sobbed.

He listened to her a little, and then continued: "Was he very bad about your coming?"

"He made it very hard for me. But I don't care."

"It is all over then between you?"

"Oh no; I don't think anything's over."

"Are you going back to him?" Ralph gasped.

"I don't know—I can't tell. I shall stay here as long as I may. I don't want to think—I needn't think. I don't care for anything but you, and that's enough for the present. It will last a little yet. Here on my knees, with you dying in my arms, I'm happier than I have been for a long time. And I want you to be happy—not to think of anything sad; only to feel that I'm near you and I love you. Why should there be pain—? In such hours as this what have we to do with pain? That's not the deepest thing; there's something deeper."

Ralph evidently found from moment to moment greater difficulty in speaking; he had to wait longer to collect himself. At first he appeared to make no response to these last words; he let a long time elapse. Then he murmured simply: "You must stay here."

"I should like to stay—as long as seems right."

"As seems right—as seems right?" He repeated her words. "Yes, you think a great deal about that."

"Of course one must. You're very tired," said Isabel.

"I'm very tired. You said just now that pain's not the deepest thing. No—no. But it's very deep. If I could stay—"

"For me you'll always be here," she softly interrupted. It was easy to interrupt him.

But he went on, after a moment: "It passes, after all; it's passing now. But love remains. I don't know why we should suffer so much. Perhaps I shall find out. There are many things in life. You're very young."

"I feel very old," said Isabel.

"You'll grow young again. That's how I see you. I don't believe—I don't believe—" But he stopped again; his strength failed him.

She begged him to be quiet now. "We needn't speak to understand each other," she said.

"I don't believe that such a generous mistake as yours can hurt you for more than a little."

"Oh Ralph, I'm very happy now," she cried through her tears.

"And remember this," he continued, "that if you've been hated you've also been loved. Ah but, Isabel—ADORED!" he just audibly and lingeringly breathed.

"Oh my brother!" she cried with a movement of still deeper prostration.

CHAPTER LV

He had told her, the first evening she ever spent at Gardencourt, that if she should live to suffer enough she might some day see the ghost with which the old house was duly provided. She apparently had fulfilled the necessary condition; for the next morning, in the cold, faint dawn, she knew that a spirit was standing by her bed. She had lain down without undressing, it being her belief that Ralph would not outlast the night. She had no inclination to sleep; she was waiting, and such waiting was wakeful. But she closed her eyes; she believed that as the night wore on she should hear a knock at her door. She heard no knock, but at the time the darkness began vaguely to grow grey she started up from her pillow as abruptly as if she had received a summons. It seemed to her for an instant that he was standing there—a vague, hovering figure in the vagueness of the room. She stared a moment; she saw his white face—his kind eyes; then she saw there was nothing. She was not afraid; she was only sure. She quitted the place and in her certainty passed through dark corridors and down a flight of oaken steps that shone in the vague light of a hall-window. Outside Ralph's door she stopped a moment, listening, but she seemed to hear only the hush that filled it. She opened the door with a hand as gentle as if she were lifting a veil from the face of the dead, and saw Mrs. Touchett sitting motionless and upright beside the couch of her son, with one of his hands in her own. The doctor was on the other side, with poor Ralph's further wrist resting in his professional fingers. The two nurses were at the foot between them. Mrs. Touchett took no notice of Isabel, but the doctor looked at her very hard; then he gently placed Ralph's hand in a proper position, close beside him. The nurse looked at her very hard too, and no one said a word; but Isabel only looked at what she had come to see. It was fairer than Ralph had ever been in life, and there was a strange resemblance to the face of his father, which, six years before, she had seen lying on the same pillow. She went to her aunt and put her arm around her; and Mrs. Touchett, who as a general thing neither invited nor enjoyed caresses, submitted for a moment to this one, rising, as might be, to take it. But she was stiff and dry-eyed; her acute white face was terrible.

"Dear Aunt Lydia," Isabel murmured.

"Go and thank God you've no child," said Mrs. Touchett, disengaging herself.

Three days after this a considerable number of people found time, at the height of the London "season," to take a morning train down to a quiet station in Berkshire and spend half an hour in a small grey church which stood within an easy walk. It was in the green burial-place of this edifice that Mrs. Touchett consigned her son to earth. She stood herself at the edge of the grave, and Isabel stood beside her; the sexton himself had not a more practical interest in the scene than Mrs. Touchett. It was a solemn occasion, but neither a harsh nor a heavy one; there was a certain geniality in the appearance of things. The weather had changed to fair; the day, one of the last of the treacherous May-time, was warm and windless, and the air had the brightness of the hawthorn and the blackbird. If it was sad to think of poor Touchett, it was not too sad, since death, for him, had had no violence. He had been dying so long; he was so ready; everything had been so expected and prepared. There were tears in Isabel's eyes, but they were not tears that blinded. She looked through them at the beauty of the day, the splendour of nature, the sweetness of the old English churchyard, the bowed heads of good friends. Lord Warburton was there, and a group of gentlemen all unknown to her, several of whom, as she afterwards learned, were connected with the bank; and there were others whom she knew. Miss Stackpole was among the first, with honest Mr. Bantling beside her; and Caspar Goodwood, lifting his head higher than the rest—bowing it rather less. During much of the time Isabel was conscious of Mr. Goodwood's gaze; he looked at her somewhat harder than he usually looked in public, while the others had fixed their eyes upon the churchyard turf. But she never let him see that she saw him; she thought of him only to wonder that he was still in England. She found she had taken for granted that after accompanying Ralph to Gardencourt he had gone away; she remembered how little it was a country that pleased him. He was there, however, very distinctly there; and something in his attitude seemed to say that he was there with a complex intention. She wouldn't meet his eyes, though there was doubtless sympathy in them; he made her rather uneasy. With the dispersal of the little group he disappeared, and the only person who came to speak to her—though several spoke to Mrs. Touchett—was Henrietta Stackpole. Henrietta had been crying.

Ralph had said to Isabel that he hoped she would remain at Gardencourt, and she made no immediate motion to leave the place. She said to herself that it was but common charity to stay a little with her aunt. It was fortunate she had so good a formula; otherwise she might have been greatly in want of one. Her errand was over; she had done what she had left her husband to do. She had a husband in a foreign city, counting the hours of her absence; in such a case one needed an excellent motive. He was not one of the best husbands, but that didn't alter the case. Certain obligations were involved in the very fact of marriage, and were quite independent of the quantity of enjoyment extracted from it. Isabel thought of her husband as little as might be; but now that she was at a distance, beyond its spell, she thought with a kind of spiritual shudder of Rome. There was a penetrating chill in the image, and she drew back into the deepest shade of Gardencourt. She lived from day to day, postponing, closing her eyes, trying not to think. She knew she must decide, but she decided nothing; her coming itself had not been a decision. On that occasion she had simply started. Osmond gave no sound and now evidently would give none; he would leave it all to her. From Pansy she heard nothing, but that was very simple: her father had told her not to write.

Mrs. Touchett accepted Isabel's company, but offered her no assistance; she appeared to be absorbed in considering, without enthusiasm but with perfect lucidity, the new conveniences of her own situation. Mrs. Touchett was not an optimist, but even from painful occurrences she managed to extract a certain utility. This consisted in the reflexion that, after all, such things happened to other people and not to herself. Death was disagreeable, but in this case it was her son's death, not her own; she had never flattered herself that her own would be disagreeable to any one but Mrs. Touchett. She was better off than poor Ralph, who had left all the commodities of life behind him, and indeed all the security; since the worst of dying was, to Mrs. Touchett's mind, that it exposed one to be taken advantage of. For herself she was on the spot; there was nothing so good as that. She made known to Isabel very punctually—it was the evening her son was buried—several of Ralph's testamentary arrangements. He had told her everything, had consulted her about everything. He left her no money; of course she had no need of money. He left her the furniture of Gardencourt, exclusive of the pictures and books and the use of the place for a year; after which it was to be sold. The money produced by the sale was to constitute an endowment for a hospital for poor persons suffering from the malady of which he died; and of this portion of the will Lord Warburton was appointed executor. The rest of his property, which was to be withdrawn from the bank, was disposed of in various bequests, several of them to those cousins in Vermont to whom his father had already been so bountiful. Then there were a number of small legacies.

"Some of them are extremely peculiar," said Mrs. Touchett; "he has left considerable sums to persons I never heard of. He gave me a list, and I asked then who some of them were, and he told me they were people who at various times had seemed to like him. Apparently he thought you didn't like him, for he hasn't left you a penny. It was his opinion that you had been handsomely treated by his father, which I'm bound to say I think you were—though I don't mean that I ever heard him complain of it. The pictures are to be dispersed; he has distributed them about, one by one, as little keepsakes. The most valuable of the collection goes to Lord Warburton. And what do you think he has done with his library? It sounds like a practical joke. He has left it to your friend Miss Stackpole—'in recognition of her services to literature.' Does he mean her following him up from Rome? Was that a service to literature? It contains a great many rare and valuable books, and as she can't carry it about the world in her trunk he recommends her to sell it at auction. She will sell it of course at Christie's, and with the proceeds she'll set up a newspaper. Will that be a service to literature?"

This question Isabel forbore to answer, as it exceeded the little interrogatory to which she had deemed it necessary to submit on her arrival. Besides, she had never been less interested in literature than to-day, as she found when she occasionally took down from the shelf one of the rare and valuable volumes of which Mrs. Touchett had spoken. She was quite unable to read; her attention had never been so little at her command. One afternoon, in the library, about a week after the ceremony in the churchyard, she was trying to fix it for an hour; but her eyes often wandered from the book in her hand to the open window, which looked down the long avenue. It was in this way that she saw a modest vehicle approach the door and perceived Lord Warburton sitting, in rather an uncomfortable attitude, in a corner of it. He had always had a high standard of courtesy, and it was therefore not remarkable, under the circumstances, that he should have taken the trouble to come down from London to call on Mrs. Touchett. It was of course Mrs. Touchett he had come to see, and not Mrs. Osmond; and to prove to herself the validity of this thesis Isabel presently stepped out of the house and wandered away into the park. Since her arrival at Gardencourt she had been but little out of doors, the weather being unfavourable for visiting the grounds. This evening, however, was fine, and at first it struck her as a happy thought to have come out. The theory I have just mentioned was plausible enough, but it brought her little rest, and if you had seen her pacing about you would have said she had a bad conscience. She was not pacified when at the end of a quarter of an hour, finding herself in view of the house, she saw Mrs. Touchett emerge from the portico accompanied by her visitor. Her aunt had evidently proposed to Lord Warburton that they should come in search of her. She was in no humour for visitors and, if she had had a chance, would have drawn back behind one of the great trees. But she saw she had been seen and that nothing was left her but to advance. As the lawn at Gardencourt was a vast expanse this took some time; during which she observed that, as he walked beside his hostess, Lord Warburton kept his hands rather stiffly behind him and his eyes upon the ground. Both persons apparently were silent; but Mrs. Touchett's thin little glance, as she directed it toward Isabel, had even at a distance an expression. It seemed to say with cutting sharpness: "Here's the eminently amenable nobleman you might have married!" When Lord Warburton lifted his own eyes, however, that was not what they said. They only said "This is rather awkward, you know, and I depend upon you to help me." He was very grave, very proper and, for the first time since Isabel had known him, greeted her without a smile. Even in his days of distress he had always begun with a smile. He looked extremely selfconscious.

"Lord Warburton has been so good as to come out to see me," said Mrs. Touchett. "He tells me he didn't know you were still here. I know he's an old friend of yours, and as I was told you were not in the house I brought him out to see for himself."

"Oh, I saw there was a good train at 6.40, that would get me back in time for dinner," Mrs. Touchett's companion rather irrelevantly explained. "I'm so glad to find you've not gone."

"I'm not here for long, you know," Isabel said with a certain eagerness.

"I suppose not; but I hope it's for some weeks. You came to England sooner than—a—than you thought?"

"Yes, I came very suddenly."

Mrs. Touchett turned away as if she were looking at the condition of the grounds, which indeed was not what it should be, while Lord Warburton hesitated a little. Isabel fancied he had been on the point of asking about her husband—rather confusedly—and then had checked himself. He continued immitigably grave, either because he thought it becoming in a place over which death had just passed, or for more personal reasons. If he was conscious of personal reasons it was very fortunate that he had the cover of the former motive; he could make the most of that. Isabel thought of all this. It was not that his face was sad, for that was another matter; but it was strangely inexpressive.

"My sisters would have been so glad to come if they had known you were still here—if they had thought you would see them," Lord Warburton went on. "Do kindly let them see you before you leave England."

"It would give me great pleasure; I have such a friendly recollection of them."

"I don't know whether you would come to Lockleigh for a day or two? You know there's always that old promise." And his lordship coloured a little as he made this suggestion, which gave his face a somewhat more familiar air. "Perhaps I'm not right in saying that just now; of course you're not thinking of visiting. But I meant what would hardly be a visit. My sisters are to be at Lockleigh at Whitsuntide for five days; and if you could come then—as you say you're not to be very long in England—I would see that there should be literally no one else."

Isabel wondered if not even the young lady he was to marry would be there with her mamma; but she did not express this idea.

"Thank you extremely," she contented herself with saying; "I'm afraid I hardly know about Whitsuntide."

"But I have your promise—haven't I?—for some other time."

There was an interrogation in this; but Isabel let it pass. She looked at her interlocutor a moment, and the result of her observation was that—as had happened before—she felt sorry for him. "Take care you don't miss your train," she said. And then she added: "I wish you every happiness."

He blushed again, more than before, and he looked at his watch. "Ah yes, 6.40; I haven't much time, but I've a fly at the door. Thank you very much." It was not apparent whether the thanks applied to her having reminded him of his train or to the more sentimental remark. "Good-bye, Mrs. Osmond; good-bye." He shook hands with her, without meeting her eyes, and then he turned to Mrs. Touchett, who had wandered back to them. With her his parting was equally brief; and in a moment the two ladies saw him move with long steps across the lawn.

"Are you very sure he's to be married?" Isabel asked of her aunt.

"I can't be surer than he; but he seems sure. I congratulated him, and he accepted it."

"Ah," said Isabel, "I give it up!"—while her aunt returned to the house and to those avocations which the visitor had interrupted.

She gave it up, but she still thought of it—thought of it while she strolled again under the great oaks whose shadows were long upon the acres of turf. At the end of a few minutes she found herself near a rustic bench, which, a moment after she had looked at it, struck her as an object recognised. It was not simply that she had seen it before, nor even that she had sat upon it; it was that on this spot something important had happened to her—that the place had an air of association. Then she remembered that she had been sitting there, six years before, when a servant brought her from the house the letter in which Caspar Goodwood informed her that he had followed her to Europe; and that when she had read the letter she looked up to hear Lord Warburton announcing that he should like to marry her. It was indeed an historical, an interesting, bench; she stood and looked at it as if it might have something to say to her. She wouldn't sit down on it now—she felt rather afraid of it. She only stood before it, and while she stood the past came back to her in one of those rushing waves of emotion by which persons of sensibility are visited at odd hours. The effect of this agitation was a sudden sense of being very tired, under the influence of which she overcame her scruples and sank into the rustic seat. I have said that she was restless and unable to occupy herself; and whether or no, if you had seen her there, you would have admired the justice of the former epithet, you would at least have allowed that at this moment she was the image of a victim of idleness. Her attitude had a singular absence of purpose; her hands, hanging at her sides, lost themselves in the folds of her black dress; her eyes gazed vaguely before her. There was nothing to recall her to the house; the two ladies, in their seclusion, dined early and had tea at an indefinite hour. How long she had sat in this position she could not have told you; but the twilight had grown thick when she became aware that she was not alone. She quickly straightened herself, glancing about, and then saw what had become of her solitude. She was sharing it with Caspar Goodwood, who stood looking at her, a few yards off, and whose footfall on the unresonant turf, as he came near, she had not heard. It occurred to her in the midst of this that it was just so Lord Warburton had surprised her of old.

She instantly rose, and as soon as Goodwood saw he was seen he started forward. She had had time only to rise when, with a motion that looked like violence, but felt like—she knew not what, he grasped her by the wrist and made her sink again into the seat. She closed her eyes; he had not hurt her; it was only a touch, which she had obeyed. But there was something in his face that she wished not to see. That was the way he had looked at her the other day in the churchyard; only at present it was worse. He said nothing at first; she only felt him close to her—beside her on the bench and pressingly turned to her. It almost seemed to her that no one had ever been so close to her as that. All this, however, took but an instant, at the end of which she had disengaged her wrist, turning her eyes upon her visitant. "You've frightened me," she said.

"I didn't mean to," he answered, "but if I did a little, no matter. I came from London a while ago by the train, but I couldn't come here directly. There was a man at the station who got ahead of me. He took a fly that was there, and I heard him give the order to drive here. I don't know who he was, but I didn't want to come with him; I wanted to see you alone. So I've been waiting and walking about. I've walked all over, and I was just coming to the house when I saw you here. There was a keeper, or someone, who met me; but that was all right, because I had made his acquaintance when I came here with your cousin. Is that gentleman gone? Are you really alone? I want to speak to you." Goodwood spoke very fast; he was as excited as when they had parted in Rome. Isabel had hoped that condition would subside; and she shrank into herself as she perceived that, on the contrary, he had only let out sail. She had a new sensation; he had never produced it before; it was a feeling of danger. There was indeed something really formidable in his resolution. She gazed straight before her; he, with a hand on each knee, leaned forward, looking deeply into her face. The twilight seemed to darken round them. "I want to speak to you," he repeated; "I've something particular to say. I don't want to trouble you—as I did the other day in Rome. That was of no use; it only distressed you. I couldn't help it; I knew I was wrong. But I'm not wrong now; please don't think I am," he went on with his hard, deep voice melting a moment into entreaty. "I came here to-day for a purpose. It's very different. It was vain for me to speak to you then; but now I can help you."

She couldn't have told you whether it was because she was afraid, or because such a voice in the darkness seemed of necessity a boon; but she listened to him as she had never listened before; his words dropped deep into her soul. They produced a sort of stillness in all her being; and it was with an effort, in a moment, that she answered him. "How can you help me?" she asked in a low tone, as if she were taking what he had said seriously enough to make the enquiry in confidence.

"By inducing you to trust me. Now I know—to-day I know. Do you remember what I asked you in Rome? Then I was quite in the dark. But to-day I know on good authority; everything's clear to me to-day. It was a good thing when you made me come away with your cousin. He was a good man, a fine man, one of the best; he told me how the case stands for you. He explained everything; he guessed my sentiments. He was a member of your family and he left you—so long as you should be in England—to my care," said Goodwood as if he were making a great point. "Do you know what he said to me the last time I saw him—as he lay there where he died? He said: 'Do everything you can for her; do everything she'll let you.'"

Isabel suddenly got up. "You had no business to talk about me!"

"Why not—why not, when we talked in that way?" he demanded, following her fast. "And he was dying—when a man's dying it's different." She checked the movement she had made to leave him; she was listening more than ever; it was true that he was not the same as that last time. That had been aimless, fruitless passion, but at present he had an idea, which she scented in all her being. "But it doesn't matter!" he exclaimed, pressing her still harder, though now without touching a hem of her garment. "If Touchett had never opened his mouth I should have known all the same. I had only to look at you at your cousin's funeral to see what's the matter with you. You can't deceive me any more; for God's sake be honest with a man who's so honest with you. You're the most unhappy of women, and your husband's the deadliest of fiends."

She turned on him as if he had struck her. "Are you mad?" she cried.

"I've never been so sane; I see the whole thing. Don't think it's necessary to defend him. But I won't say another word against him; I'll speak only of you," Goodwood added quickly. "How can you pretend you're not heart-broken? You don't know what to do—you don't know where to turn. It's too late to play a part; didn't you leave all that behind you in Rome? Touchett knew all about it, and I knew it too—what it would cost you to come here. It will have cost you your life? Say it will"—and he flared almost into anger: "give me one word of truth! When I know such a horror as that, how can I keep myself from wishing to save you? What would you think of me if I should stand still and see you go back to your reward? 'It's awful, what she'll have to pay for it!'—that's what Touchett said to me. I may tell you that, mayn't I? He was such a near relation!" cried Goodwood, making his queer grim point again. "I'd sooner have been shot than let another man say those things to me; but he was different; he seemed to me to have the right. It was after he got home—when he saw he was dying, and when I saw it too. I understand all about it: you're afraid to go back. You're perfectly alone; you don't know where to turn. You can't turn anywhere; you know that perfectly. Now it is therefore that I want you to think of ME."

"To think of 'you'?" Isabel said, standing before him in the dusk. The idea of which she had caught a glimpse a few moments before now loomed large. She threw back her head a little; she stared at it as if it had been a comet in the sky.

"You don't know where to turn. Turn straight to me. I want to persuade you to trust me," Goodwood repeated. And then he paused with his shining eyes. "Why should you go back—why should you go through that ghastly form?"

"To get away from you!" she answered. But this expressed only a little of what she felt. The rest was that she had never been loved before. She had believed it, but this was different; this was the hot wind of the desert, at the approach of which the others dropped dead, like mere sweet airs of the garden. It wrapped her about; it lifted her off her feet, while the very taste of it, as of something potent, acrid and strange, forced open her set teeth.

At first, in rejoinder to what she had said, it seemed to her that he would break out into greater violence. But after an instant he was perfectly quiet; he wished to prove he was sane, that he had reasoned it all out. "I want to prevent that, and I think I may, if you'll only for once listen to me. It's too monstrous of you to think of sinking back into that misery, of going to open your mouth to that poisoned air. It's you that are out of your mind. Trust me as if I had the care of you. Why shouldn't we be happy—when it's here before us, when it's so easy? I'm yours for ever—for ever and ever. Here I stand; I'm as firm as a rock. What have you to care about? You've no children; that perhaps would be an obstacle. As it is you've nothing to consider. You must save what you can of your life; you mustn't lose it all simply because you've lost a part. It would be an insult to you to assume that you care for the look of the thing, for what people will say, for the bottomless idiocy of the world. We've nothing to do with all that; we're quite out of it; we look at things as they are. You took the great step in coming away; the next is nothing; it's the natural one. I swear, as I stand here, that a woman deliberately made to suffer is justified in anything in life—in going down into the streets if that will help her! I know how you suffer, and that's why I'm here. We can do absolutely as we please; to whom under the sun do we owe anything? What is it that holds us, what is it that has the smallest right to interfere in such a question as this? Such a question is between ourselves—and to say that is to settle it! Were we born to rot in our misery—were we born to be afraid? I never knew YOU afraid! If you'll only trust me, how little you will be disappointed! The world's all before us—and the world's very big. I know something about that."

Isabel gave a long murmur, like a creature in pain; it was as if he were pressing something that hurt her.

"The world's very small," she said at random; she had an immense desire to appear to resist. She said it at random, to hear herself say something; but it was not what she meant. The world, in truth, had never seemed so large; it seemed to open out, all round her, to take the form of a mighty sea, where she floated in fathomless waters. She had wanted help, and here was help; it had come in a rushing torrent. I know not whether she believed everything he said; but she believed just then that to let him take her in his arms would be the next best thing to her dying. This belief, for a moment, was a kind of rapture, in which she felt herself sink and sink. In the movement she seemed to beat with her feet, in order to catch herself, to feel something to rest on.

"Ah, be mine as I'm yours!" she heard her companion cry. He had suddenly given up argument, and his voice seemed to come, harsh and terrible, through a confusion of vaguer sounds.

This however, of course, was but a subjective fact, as the metaphysicians say; the confusion, the noise of waters, all the rest of it, were in her own swimming head. In an instant she became aware of this. "Do me the greatest kindness of all," she panted. "I beseech you to go away!"

"Ah, don't say that. Don't kill me!" he cried.

She clasped her hands; her eyes were streaming with tears. "As you love me, as you pity me, leave me alone!"

He glared at her a moment through the dusk, and the next instant she felt his arms about her and his lips on her own lips. His kiss was like white lightning, a flash that spread, and spread again, and stayed; and it was extraordinarily as if, while she took it, she felt each thing in his hard manhood that had least pleased her, each aggressive fact of his face, his figure, his presence, justified of its intense identity and made one with this act of possession. So had she heard of those wrecked and under water following a train of images before they sink. But when darkness returned she was free. She never looked about her; she only darted from the spot. There were lights in the windows of the house; they shone far across the lawn. In an extraordinarily short time—for the distance was considerable—she had moved through the darkness (for she saw nothing) and reached the door. Here only she paused. She looked all about her; she listened a little; then she put her hand on the latch. She had not known where to turn; but she knew now. There was a very straight path.

Two days afterwards Caspar Goodwood knocked at the door of the house in Wimpole Street in which Henrietta Stackpole occupied furnished lodgings. He had hardly removed his hand from the knocker when the door was opened and Miss Stackpole herself stood before him. She had on her hat and jacket; she was on the point of going out. "Oh, good-morning," he said, "I was in hopes I should find Mrs. Osmond."

Henrietta kept him waiting a moment for her reply; but there was a good deal of expression about Miss Stackpole even when she was silent. "Pray what led you to suppose she was here?"

"I went down to Gardencourt this morning, and the servant told me she had come to London. He believed she was to come to you."

Again Miss Stackpole held him—with an intention of perfect kindness—in suspense. "She came here yesterday, and spent the night. But this morning she started for Rome."

Caspar Goodwood was not looking at her; his eyes were fastened on the doorstep. "Oh, she started—?" he stammered. And without finishing his phrase or looking up he stiffly averted himself. But he couldn't otherwise move.

Henrietta had come out, closing the door behind her, and now she put out her hand and grasped his arm. "Look here, Mr. Goodwood," she said; "just you wait!"

On which he looked up at her—but only to guess, from her face, with a revulsion, that she simply meant he was young. She stood shining at him with that cheap comfort, and it added, on the spot, thirty years to his life. She walked him away with her, however, as if she had given him now the key to patience.

THE WINGS OF THE DOVE

VOLUME I

BOOK FIRST

I

She waited, Kate Croy, for her father to come in, but he kept her unconscionably, and there were moments at which she showed herself, in the glass over the mantel, a face positively pale with the irritation that had brought her to the point of going away without sight of him. It was at this point, however, that she remained; changing her place, moving from the shabby sofa to the armchair upholstered in a glazed cloth that gave at once—she had tried it—the sense of the slippery and of the sticky. She had looked at the sallow prints on the walls and at the lonely magazine, a year old, that combined, with a small lamp in coloured glass and a knitted white centre-piece wanting in freshness, to enhance the effect of the purplish cloth on the principal table; she had above all, from time to time, taken a brief stand on the small balcony to which the pair of long windows gave access. The vulgar little street, in this view, offered scant relief from the vulgar little room; its main office was to suggest to her that the narrow black house-fronts, adjusted to a standard that would have been low even for backs, constituted quite the publicity implied by such privacies. One felt them in the room exactly as one felt the room—the hundred like it or worse—in the street. Each time she turned in again, each time, in her impatience, she gave him up, it was to sound to a deeper depth, while she tasted the faint, flat emanation of things, the failure of fortune and of honour. If she continued to wait it was really, in a manner, that she might not add the shame of fear, of individual, personal collapse, to all the other shames. To feel the street, to feel the room, to feel the table-cloth and the centre-piece and the lamp, gave her a small, salutary sense, at least, of neither shirking nor lying. This whole vision was the worst thing yet—as including, in particular, the interview for which she had prepared herself; and for what had she come but for the worst? She tried to be sad, so as not to be angry; but it made her angry that she couldn't be sad. And yet where was misery, misery too beaten for blame and chalk-marked by fate like a "lot" at a common auction, if not in these merciless signs of mere mean, stale feelings?

Her father's life, her sister's, her own, that of her two lost brothers—the whole history of their house had the effect of some fine florid, voluminous phrase, say even a musical, that dropped first into words, into notes, without sense, and then, hanging unfinished, into no words, no notes at all. Why should a set of people have been put in motion, on such a scale and with such an air of being equipped for a profitable journey, only to break down without an accident, to stretch themselves in the wayside dust without a reason? The answer to these questions was not in Chirk Street, but the questions themselves bristled there, and the girl's repeated pause before the mirror and the chimney-place might have represented her nearest approach to an escape from them. Was it not in fact the partial escape from this "worst" in which she was steeped to be able to make herself out again as agreeable to see? She stared into the tarnished glass too hard indeed to be staring at her beauty alone. She readjusted the poise of her black, closely-feathered hat; retouched, beneath it, the thick fall of her dusky hair; kept her eyes, aslant, no less on her beautiful averted than on her beautiful presented oval. She was dressed altogether in black, which gave an even tone, by contrast, to her clear face and made her hair more harmoniously dark. Outside, on the balcony, her eyes showed as blue; within, at the mirror, they showed almost as black. She was handsome, but the degree of it was not sustained by items and aids; a circumstance moreover playing its part at almost any time in the impression she produced. The impression was one that remained, but as regards the sources of it no sum in addition would have made up the total. She had stature without height, grace without motion, presence without mass. Slender and simple, frequently soundless, she was somehow always in the line of the eye—she counted singularly for its pleasure. More "dressed," often, with fewer accessories, than other women, or less dressed, should occasion require, with more, she probably could not have given the key to these felicities. They were mysteries of which her friends were conscious—those friends whose general explanation was to say that she was clever, whether or no it were taken by the world as the cause or as the effect of her charm. If she saw more things than her fine face in the dull glass of her father's lodgings, she might have seen that, after all, she was not herself a fact in the collapse. She didn't judge herself cheap, she didn't make for misery. Personally, at least, she was not chalk-marked for the auction. She hadn't given up yet, and the broken sentence, if she was the last word, would end with a sort of meaning. There was a minute during which, though her eyes were fixed, she quite visibly lost herself in the thought of the way she might still pull things round had she only been a man. It was the name, above all, she would take in hand—the precious name she so liked and that, in spite of the harm her wretched father had done it, was not yet past praying for. She loved it in fact the more tenderly for that bleeding wound. But what could a penniless girl do with it but let it go?

When her father at last appeared she became, as usual, instantly aware of the futility of any effort to hold him to anything. He had written her that he was ill, too ill to leave his room, and that he must see her without delay; and if this had been, as was probable, the sketch of a design, he was indifferent even to the moderate finish required for deception. He had clearly wanted, for perversities that he called reasons, to see her, just as she herself had sharpened for a talk; but she now again felt, in the inevitability of the freedom he used with her, all the old ache, her poor mother's very own, that he couldn't touch you ever so lightly without setting up. No relation with him could be so short or so superficial as not to be somehow to your hurt; and this, in the strangest way in the world, not because he desired it to be—feeling often, as he surely must, the profit for him of its not being—but because there was never a mistake for you that he could leave unmade or a conviction of his impossibility in you that he could approach you without strengthening. He might have awaited her on the sofa in his sitting-room, or might have stayed in bed and received her in that situation. She was glad to be spared the sight of such *penetralia,* but it would have reminded her a little less that there was no truth in him. This was the weariness of every fresh meeting; he dealt out lies as he might the cards from the greasy old pack for the game of diplomacy to which you were to sit down with him. The inconvenience—as always happens in such cases—was not that you minded what was false, but that you missed what was true. He might be ill, and it might suit you to know it, but no contact with him, for this, could ever be straight enough. Just so he even might die, but Kate fairly wondered on what evidence of his own she would some day have to believe it.

He had not at present come down from his room, which she knew to be above the one they were in: he had already been out of the house, though he would either, should she challenge him, deny it or present it as a proof of his extremity. She had, however, by this time, quite ceased to challenge him; not only, face to face with him, vain irritation dropped, but he breathed upon the tragic consciousness in such a way that after a moment nothing of it was left. The difficulty was not less that he breathed in the same way upon the comic: she almost believed that with this latter she might still have found a foothold for clinging to him. He had ceased to be amusing—he was really too inhuman. His perfect look, which had floated him so long, was practically perfect still; but one had long since for every occasion taken it for granted. Nothing could have better shown than the actual how right one had been. He looked exactly as much as usual—all pink and silver as to skin and hair, all straitness and starch as to figure and dress—the man in the world least connected with anything unpleasant. He was so particularly the English gentleman and the fortunate, settled, normal person. Seen at a foreign *table d'hôte,* he suggested but one thing: "In what perfection England produces them!" He had kind, safe eyes, and a voice which, for all its clean fulness, told, in a manner, the happy history of its having never had once to raise itself. Life had met him so, half-way, and had turned round so to walk with him, placing a hand in his arm and fondly leaving him to choose the pace. Those who knew him a little said, "How he does dress!"—those who knew him better said, "How *does* he?" The one stray gleam of comedy just now in his daughter's eyes was the funny feeling he momentarily made her have of being herself "looked up" by him in sordid lodgings. For a minute after he came in it was as if the place were her own and he the visitor with susceptibilities. He gave you funny feelings, he had indescribable arts, that quite turned the tables: that had been always how he came to see her mother so long as her mother would see him. He came from places they had often not known about, but he patronised Lexham Gardens. Kate's only actual expression of impatience, however, was "I'm glad you're so much better!"

"I'm not so much better, my dear—I'm exceedingly unwell; the proof of which is, precisely, that I've been out to the chemist's—that beastly fellow at the corner." So Mr. Croy showed he could qualify the humble hand that assuaged him. "I'm taking something he has made up for me. It's just why I've sent for you—that you may see me as I really am."

"Oh papa, it's long since I've ceased to see you otherwise than as you really are! I think we've all arrived by this time at the right word for that: 'You're beautiful—*n'en parlons plus.'* You're as beautiful as ever—you look lovely." He judged meanwhile her own appearance, as she knew she could always trust him to do; recognising, estimating, sometimes disapproving, what she wore, showing her the interest he continued to take in her. He might really take none at all, yet she virtually knew herself the creature in the world to whom he was least indifferent. She had often enough wondered what on earth, at the pass he had reached, could give him pleasure, and she had come back, on these occasions, to that. It gave him pleasure that she was handsome, that she was, in her way, a sensible value. It was at least as marked, nevertheless, that he derived none from similar conditions, so far as they *were* similar, in his other child. Poor Marian might be handsome, but he certainly didn't care. The hitch here, of course, was that, with whatever beauty, her sister, widowed and almost in want, with four bouncing children, was not a sensible value. She asked him, the next thing, how long he had been in his actual quarters, though aware of how little it mattered, how little any answer he might make would probably have in common with the truth. She failed in fact to notice his answer, truthful or not, already occupied as she was with what she had on her own side to say to him. This was really what had made her wait—what superseded the small remainder of her resentment at his constant practical impertinence; the result of all of which was that, within a minute, she had brought it out. "Yes—even now I'm willing to go with you. I don't know what you may have wished to say to me, and even if you hadn't written you would within a day or two have heard from me. Things have happened, and I've only waited, for seeing you, till I should be quite sure. I *am* quite sure. I'll go with you."

It produced an effect. "Go with me where?"

"Anywhere. I'll stay with you. Even here." She had taken off her gloves and, as if she had arrived with her plan, she sat down.

Lionel Croy hung about in his disengaged way—hovered there as if, in consequence of her words, looking for a pretext to back out easily: on which she immediately saw she had discounted, as it might be called, what he had himself been preparing. He wished her not to come to him, still less to settle with him, and had sent for her to give her up with some style and state; a part of the beauty of which, however, was to have been his sacrifice to her own detachment. There was no style, no state, unless she wished to forsake him. His idea had accordingly been to surrender her to her wish with all nobleness; it had by no means been to have positively to keep her off. She cared, however, not a straw for his embarrassment—feeling how little, on her own part, she was moved by charity. She had seen him, first and last, in so many attitudes that she could now deprive him quite without compunction of the luxury of a new one. Yet she felt the disconcerted gasp in his tone as he said: "Oh my child, I can never consent to that!"

"What then are you going to do?"

"I'm turning it over," said Lionel Croy. "You may imagine if I'm not thinking."

"Haven't you thought then," his daughter asked, "of what I speak of? I mean of my being ready."

Standing before her with his hands behind him and his legs a little apart, he swayed slightly to and fro, inclined toward her as if rising on his toes. It had an effect of conscientious deliberation. "No. I haven't. I couldn't. I wouldn't." It was so respectable, a show that she felt afresh, and with the memory of their old despair, the despair at home, how little his appearance ever by any chance told about him. His plausibility had been the heaviest of her mother's crosses; inevitably so much more present to the world than whatever it was that was horrid—thank God they didn't really know!—that he had done. He had positively been, in his way, by the force of his particular type, a terrible husband not to live with; his type reflecting so invidiously on the woman who had found him distasteful. Had this thereby not kept directly present to Kate herself that it might, on some sides, prove no light thing for her to leave uncompanioned a parent with such a face and such a manner? Yet if there was much she neither knew nor dreamed of, it passed between them at this very moment that he was quite familiar with himself as the subject of such quandaries. If he recognised his younger daughter's happy aspect as a sensible value, he had from the first still more exactly appraised his own. The great wonder was not that in spite of everything his own had helped him; the great wonder was that it hadn't helped him more. However, it was, to its old, eternal, recurrent tune, helping him all the while; her drop into patience with him showed how it was helping him at this moment. She saw the next instant precisely the line he would take. "Do you really ask me to believe you've been making up your mind to that?"

She had to consider her own line. "I don't think I care, papa, what you believe. I never, for that matter, think of you as believing anything; hardly more," she permitted herself to add, "than I ever think of you as yourself believed. I don't know you, father, you see."

"And it's your idea that you may make that up?"

"Oh dear, no; not at all. That's no part of the question. If I haven't understood you by this time, I never shall, and it doesn't matter. It has seemed to me that you may be lived with, but not that you may be understood. Of course I've not the least idea how you get on."

"I don't get on," Mr. Croy almost gaily replied.

His daughter took in the place again, and it might well have seemed odd that in so little to meet the eye there should be so much to show. What showed was the ugliness—so positive and palpable that it was somehow sustaining. It was a medium, a setting, and to that extent, after all, a dreadful sign of life; so that it fairly put a point into her answer. "Oh, I beg your pardon. You flourish."

"Do you throw it up at me again," he pleasantly inquired, "that I've not made away with myself?"

She treated the question as needing no reply; she sat there for real things. "You know how all our anxieties, under mamma's will, have come out. She had still less to leave than she feared. We don't know how we lived. It all makes up about two hundred a year for Marian, and two for me, but I give up a hundred to Marian."

"Oh, you weak thing!" her father kindly sighed.

"For you and me together," she went on, "the other hundred would do something."

"And what would do the rest?"

"Can you yourself do nothing?" He gave her a look; then, slipping his hands into his pockets and turning away, stood for a little at the window she had left open. She said nothing more—she had placed him there with that question, and the silence lasted a minute, broken by the call of an appealing costermonger, which came in with the mild March air, with the shabby sunshine, fearfully unbecoming to the room, and with the small homely hum of Chirk Street. Presently he moved nearer, but as if her question had quite dropped. "I don't see what has so suddenly wound you up."

"I should have thought you might perhaps guess. Let me at any rate tell you. Aunt Maud has made me a proposal. But she has also made me a condition. She wants to keep me."

"And what in the world else *could* she possibly want?"

"Oh, I don't know—many things. I'm not so precious a capture," the girl a little dryly explained. "No one has ever wanted to keep me before."

Looking always what was proper, her father looked now still more surprised than interested. "You've not had proposals?" He spoke as if that were incredible of Lionel Croy's daughter; as if indeed such an admission scarce consorted, even in filial intimacy, with her high spirit and general form.

"Not from rich relations. She's extremely kind to me, but it's time, she says, that we should understand each other."

Mr. Croy fully assented. "Of course it is—high time; and I can quite imagine what she means by it."

"Are you very sure?"

"Oh, perfectly. She means that she'll 'do' for you handsomely if you'll break off all relations with me. You speak of her condition. Her condition's of course that."

"Well then," said Kate, "it's what has wound me up. Here I am."

He showed with a gesture how thoroughly he had taken it in; after which, within a few seconds, he had, quite congruously, turned the situation about. "Do you really suppose me in a position to justify your throwing yourself upon me?"

She waited a little, but when she spoke it was clear. "Yes."

"Well then, you're a bigger fool than I should have ventured to suppose you."

"Why so? You live. You flourish. You bloom."

"Ah, how you've all always hated me!" he murmured with a pensive gaze again at the window.

"No one could be less of a mere cherished memory," she declared as if she had not heard him. "You're an actual person, if there ever was one. We agreed just now that you're beautiful. You strike me, you know, as—in your own way—much more firm on your feet than I am. Don't put it to me therefore as monstrous that the fact that we are, after all, parent and child should at present in some manner count for us. My idea has been that it should have some effect for each of us. I don't at all, as I told you just now," she pursued, "make out your life; but whatever it is I hereby offer you to accept it. And, on my side, I'll do everything I can for you."

"I see," said Lionel Croy. Then, with the sound of extreme relevance, "And what *can* you?" She only, at this, hesitated, and he took up her silence. "You can describe yourself—*to* yourself—as, in a fine flight, giving up your aunt for me; but what good, I should like to know, would your fine flight do me?" As she still said nothing he developed a little. "We're not possessed of so much, at this charming pass, please to remember, as that we can afford not to take hold of any perch held out to us. I like the way you talk, my dear, about 'giving up!' One doesn't give up the use of a spoon because one's reduced to living on broth. And your spoon, that is your aunt, please consider, is partly mine as well." She rose now, as if in sight of the term of her effort, in sight of the futility and the weariness of many things, and moved back to the poor little glass with which she had communed before. She retouched here again the poise of her hat, and this brought to her father's lips another remark in which impatience, however, had already been replaced by a funny flare of appreciation. "Oh, you're all right! Don't muddle yourself up with *me!"*

His daughter turned round to him. "The condition Aunt Maud makes is that I shall have absolutely nothing to do with you; never see you, nor speak, nor write to you, never go near you nor make you a sign, nor hold any sort of communication with you. What she requires is that you shall simply cease to exist for me."

He had always seemed—it was one of the marks of what they called the "unspeakable" in him—to walk a little more on his toes, as if for jauntiness, in the presence of offence. Nothing, however, was more wonderful than what he sometimes would take for offence, unless it might be what he sometimes wouldn't. He walked at any rate on his toes now. "A very proper requirement of your Aunt Maud, my dear—I don't hesitate to say it!" Yet as this, much as she had seen, left her silent at first from what might have been a sense of sickness, he had time to go on: "That's her condition then. But what are her promises? Just what does she engage to do? You must work it, you know."

"You mean make her feel," Kate asked after a moment, "how much I'm attached to you?"

"Well, what a cruel, invidious treaty it is for you to sign. I'm a poor old dad to make a stand about giving up—I quite agree. But I'm not, after all, quite the old dad not to get something *for* giving up."

"Oh, I think her idea," said Kate almost gaily now, "is that I shall get a great deal."

He met her with his inimitable amenity. "But does she give you the items?"

The girl went through the show. "More or less, I think. But many of them are things I dare say I may take for granted—things women can do for each other and that you wouldn't understand."

"There's nothing I understand so well, always, as the things I needn't! But what I want to do, you see," he went on, "is to put it to your conscience that you've an admirable opportunity; and that it's moreover one for which, after all, damn you, you've really to thank *me."*

"I confess I don't see," Kate observed, "what my 'conscience' has to do with it."

"Then, my dear girl, you ought simply to be ashamed of yourself. Do you know what you're a proof of, all you hard, hollow people together?" He put the question with a charming air of sudden spiritual heat. "Of the deplorably superficial morality of the age. The family sentiment, in our vulgarised, brutalised life, has gone utterly to pot. There was a day when a man like me—by which I mean a parent like me—would have been for a daughter like you a quite distinct value; what's called in the business world, I believe, an 'asset.'" He continued sociably to make it out. "I'm not talking only of what you might, with the right feeling do *for* me, but of what you might—it's what I call your opportunity—do *with* me. Unless indeed," he the next moment imperturbably threw off, "they come a good deal to the same thing. Your duty as well as your chance, if you're capable of seeing it, is to use me. Show family feeling by seeing what I'm good for. If you had it as *I* have it you'd see I'm still good—well, for a lot of things. There's in fact, my dear," Mr. Croy wound up, "a coach-and-four to be got out of me." His drop, or rather his climax, failed a little of effect, indeed, through an undue precipitation of memory. Something his daughter had said came back to him. "You've settled to give away half your little inheritance?"

Her hesitation broke into laughter. "No—I haven't 'settled' anything."

"But you mean, practically, to let Marian collar it?" They stood there face to face, but she so denied herself to his challenge that he could only go on. "You've a view of three hundred a year for her in addition to what her husband left her with? Is *that,"* the remote progenitor of such wantonness audibly wondered, "your morality?"

Kate found her answer without trouble. "Is it your idea that I should give you everything?"

The "everything" clearly struck him—to the point even of determining the tone of his reply. "Far from it. How can you ask that when I refuse what you tell me you came to offer? Make of my idea what you can; I think I've sufficiently expressed it, and it's at any rate to take or to leave. It's the only one, I may nevertheless add; it's the basket with all my eggs. It's my conception, in short, of your duty."

The girl's tired smile watched the word as if it had taken on a small grotesque visibility. "You're wonderful on such subjects! I think I should leave you in no doubt," she pursued, "that if I were to sign my aunt's agreement I should carry it out, in honour, to the letter."

"Rather, my own love! It's just your honour that I appeal to. The only way to play the game *is* to play it. There's no limit to what your aunt can do for you."

"Do you mean in the way of marrying me?"

"What else should I mean? Marry properly——"

"And then?" Kate asked as he hung fire.

"And then—well, I *will* talk with you. I'll resume relations."

She looked about her and picked up her parasol. "Because you're not so afraid of any one else in the world as you are of *her?* My husband, if I should marry, would be, at the worst, less of a terror? If that's what you mean, there may be something in it. But doesn't it depend a little also on what you mean by my getting a proper one? However," Kate added as she picked out the frill of her little umbrella, "I don't suppose your idea of him is *quite* that he should persuade you to live with us."

"Dear no—not a bit." He spoke as not resenting either the fear or the hope she imputed; met both imputations, in fact, with a sort of intellectual relief. "I place the case for you wholly in your aunt's hands. I take her view, with my eyes shut; I accept in all confidence any man she selects. If he's good enough for *her*—elephantine snob as she is—he's good enough for me; and quite in spite of the fact that she'll be sure to select one who can be trusted to be nasty to me. My only interest is in your doing what she wants. You shan't be so beastly poor, my darling," Mr. Croy declared, "if I can help it."

"Well then, good-bye, papa," the girl said after a reflection on this that had perceptibly ended for her in a renunciation of further debate. "Of course you understand that it may be for long."

Her companion, hereupon, had one of his finest inspirations. "Why not, frankly, for ever? You must do me the justice to see that I don't do things, that I've never done them, by halves—that if I offer you to efface myself, it's for the final, fatal sponge that I ask, well saturated and well applied."

She turned her handsome, quiet face upon him at such length that it might well have been for the last time. "I don't know what you're like."

"No more do I, my dear. I've spent my life in trying, in vain, to discover. Like nothing—more's the pity. If there had been many of us, and we could have found each other out, there's no knowing what we mightn't have done. But it doesn't matter now. Good-bye, love." He looked even not sure of what she would wish him to suppose on the subject of a kiss, yet also not embarrassed by his uncertainty.

She forbore in fact for a moment longer to clear it up. "I wish there were some one here who might serve—for any contingency—as a witness that I *have* put it to you that I'm ready to come."

"Would you like me," her father asked, "to call the landlady?"

"You may not believe me," she pursued, "but I came really hoping you might have found some way. I'm very sorry, at all events, to leave you unwell." He turned away from her, on this, and, as he had done before, took refuge, by the window, in a stare at the street. "Let me put it—unfortunately without a witness," she added after a moment, "that there's only one word you really need speak."

When he took this up it was still with his back to her. "If I don't strike you as having already spoken it, our time has been singularly wasted."

"I'll engage with you in respect to my aunt exactly to what she wants of me in respect to you. She wants me to choose. Very well, I *will* choose. I'll wash my hands of her for you to just that tune."

He at last brought himself round. "Do you know, dear, you make me sick? I've tried to be clear, and it isn't fair."

But she passed this over; she was too visibly sincere. "Father!"

"I don't quite see what's the matter with you," he said, "and if you can't pull yourself together I'll—upon my honour—take you in hand. Put you into a cab and deliver you again safe at Lancaster Gate."

She was really absent, distant. "Father."

It was too much, and he met it sharply. "Well?"

"Strange as it may be to you to hear me say it, there's a good you can do me and a help you can render."

"Isn't it then exactly what I've been trying to make you feel?"

"Yes," she answered patiently, "but so in the wrong way. I'm perfectly honest in what I say, and I know what I'm talking about. It isn't that I'll pretend I could have believed a month ago in anything to call aid or support from you. The case is changed—that's what has happened; my difficulty's a new one. But even now it's not a question of anything I should ask you in a way to 'do.' It's simply a question of your not turning me away—taking yourself out of my life. It's simply a question of your saying: 'Yes then, since you will, we'll stand together. We won't worry in advance about how or where; we'll have a faith and find a way.' That's all—*that* would be the good you'd do me. I should *have* you, and it would be for my benefit. Do you see?"

If he didn't it was not for want of looking at her hard. "The matter with you is that you're in love, and that your aunt knows and—for reasons, I'm sure, perfect—hates and opposes it. Well she may! It's a matter in which I trust her with my eyes shut. Go, please." Though he spoke not in anger—rather in infinite sadness—he fairly turned her out. Before she took it up he had, as the fullest expression of what he felt, opened the door of the room. He had fairly, in his deep disapproval, a generous compassion to spare. "I'm sorry for her, deluded woman, if she builds on you."

Kate stood a moment in the draught. "She's not the person *I* pity most, for, deluded in many ways though she may be, she's not the person who's most so. I mean," she explained, "if it's a question of what you call building on me."

He took it as if what she meant might be other than her description of it. "You're deceiving *two* persons then, Mrs. Lowder and somebody else?"

She shook her head with detachment. "I've no intention of that sort with respect to any one now—to Mrs. Lowder least of all. If you fail me"—she seemed to make it out for herself—"that has the merit at least that it simplifies. I shall go my way—as I see my way."

"Your way, you mean then, will be to marry some blackguard without a penny?"

"You ask a great deal of satisfaction," she observed, "for the little you give."

It brought him up again before her as with a sense that she was not to be hustled; and, though he glared at her a little, this had long been the practical limit to his general power of objection. "If you're base enough to incur your aunt's disgust, you're base enough for my argument. What, if you're not thinking of an utterly improper person, do your speeches to me signify? Who *is* the beggarly sneak?" he demanded as her response failed. Her response, when it came, was cold but distinct. "He has every disposition to make the best of you. He only wants in fact to be kind to you."

"Then he *must* be an ass! And how in the world can you consider it to improve him for me," her father pursued, "that he's also destitute and impossible? There are asses and asses, even—the right and the wrong—and you appear to have carefully picked out one of the wrong. Your aunt knows *them,* by good fortune; I perfectly trust, as I tell you, her judgment for them; and you may take it from me once for all that I won't hear of any one of whom *she* won't." Which led up to his last word. "If you should really defy us both——!"

"Well, papa?"

"Well, my sweet child, I think that—reduced to insignificance as you may fondly believe me—I should still not be quite without some way of making you regret it."

She had a pause, a grave one, but not, as appeared, that she might measure this danger. "If I shouldn't do it, you know, it wouldn't be because I'm afraid of you."

"Oh, if you don't do it," he retorted, "you may be as bold as you like!"

"Then you can do nothing at all for me?"

He showed her, this time unmistakably—it was before her there on the landing, at the top of the tortuous stairs and in the midst of the strange smell that seemed to cling to them—how vain her appeal remained. "I've never pretended to do more than my duty; I've given you the best and the clearest advice." And then came up the spring that moved him. "If it only displeases you, you can go to Marian to be consoled." What he couldn't forgive was her dividing with Marian her scant share of the provision their mother had been able to leave them. She should have divided it with *him.*

II

She had gone to Mrs. Lowder on her mother's death—gone with an effort the strain and pain of which made her at present, as she recalled them, reflect on the long way she had travelled since then. There had been nothing else to do—not a penny in the other house, nothing but unpaid bills that had gathered thick while its mistress lay mortally ill, and the admonition that there was nothing she must attempt to raise money on, since everything belonged to the "estate." How the estate would turn out at best presented itself as a mystery altogether gruesome; it had proved, in fact, since then a residuum a trifle less scant than, with Marian, she had for some weeks feared; but the girl had had at the beginning rather a wounded sense of its being watched on behalf of Marian and her children. What on earth was it supposed that *she* wanted to do to it? She wanted in truth only to give up—to abandon her own interest, which she, no doubt, would already have done had not the point been subject to Aunt Maud's sharp intervention. Aunt Maud's intervention was all sharp now, and the other point, the great one, was that it was to be, in this light, either all put up with or all declined. Yet at the winter's end, nevertheless, she could scarce have said what stand she conceived she had taken. It wouldn't be the first time she had seen herself obliged to accept with smothered irony other people's interpretation of her conduct. She often ended by giving up to them—it seemed really the way to live—the version that met their convenience.

The tall, rich, heavy house at Lancaster Gate, on the other side of the Park and the long South Kensington stretches, had figured to her, through childhood, through girlhood, as the remotest limit of her vague young world. It was further off and more occasional than anything else in the comparatively compact circle in which she revolved, and seemed, by a rigour early marked, to be reached through long, straight, discouraging vistas, which kept lengthening and straightening, whereas almost everything else in life was either, at the worst, round about Cromwell Road, or, at the furthest, in the nearer parts of Kensington Gardens. Mrs. Lowder was her only "real" aunt, not the wife of an uncle, and had been thereby, both in ancient days and when the greater trouble came, the person, of all persons, properly to make some sign; in accord with which our young woman's feeling was founded on the impression, quite cherished for years, that the signs made across the interval just mentioned had never been really in the note of the situation. The main office of this relative, for the young Croys—apart from giving them their fixed measure of social greatness—had struck them as being to form them to a conception of what they were not to expect. When Kate came to think matters over with the aid of knowledge, she failed quite to see how Aunt Maud could have been different—she had rather perceived by this time how many other things might have been; yet she also made out that if they had all consciously lived under a liability to the chill breath of *ultima Thule* they couldn't, either, on the facts, very well have done less. What in the event appeared established was that if Mrs. Lowder had disliked them she had yet not disliked them so much as they supposed. It had at any rate been for the purpose of showing how she struggled with her aversion that she sometimes came to see them, that she at regular periods invited them to her house, and in short, as it now looked, kept them along on the terms that would best give her sister the perennial luxury of a grievance. This sister, poor Mrs. Croy, the girl knew, had always judged her resentfully, and had brought them up, Marian, the boys and herself, to the idea of a particular attitude, for signs of the practice of which they watched each other with awe. The attitude was to make plain to Aunt Maud, with the same regularity as her invitations, that they sufficed—thanks awfully—to themselves. But the ground of it, Kate lived to discern, was that this was only because *she* didn't suffice to them. The little she offered was to be accepted under protest, yet not, really, because it was excessive. It wounded them—there was the rub!—because it fell short.

The number of new things our young lady looked out on from the high south window that hung over the Park—this number was so great (though some of the things were only old ones altered and, as the phrase was of other matters, done up), that life at present turned to her view from week to week more and more the face of a striking and distinguished stranger. She had reached a great age—for it quite seemed to her that at twenty-five it was late to reconsider; and her most general sense was a shade of regret that she had not known earlier. The world was different—whether for worse or for better—from her rudimentary readings, and it gave her the feeling of a wasted past. If she had only known sooner she might have arranged herself more to meet it. She made, at all events, discoveries every day, some of which were about herself and others about other persons. Two of these—one under each head—more particularly engaged, in alternation, her anxiety. She saw as she had never seen before how material things spoke to her. She saw, and she blushed to see, that if, in contrast with some of its old aspects, life now affected her as a dress successfully "done up," this was exactly by reason of the trimmings and lace, was a matter of ribbons and silk and velvet. She had a dire accessibility to pleasure from such sources. She liked the charming quarters her aunt had assigned her—liked them literally more than she had in all her other days liked anything; and nothing could have been more uneasy than her suspicion of her relative's view of this truth. Her relative was prodigious—she had never done her relative justice. These larger conditions all tasted of her, from morning till night; but she was a person in respect to whom the growth of acquaintance could only—strange as it might seem—keep your heart in your mouth.

The girl's second great discovery was that, so far from having been for Mrs. Lowder a subject of superficial consideration, the blighted home in Lexham Gardens had haunted her nights and her days. Kate had spent, all winter, hours of observation that were not less pointed for being spent alone; recent events, which her mourning explained, assured her a measure of isolation, and it was in the isolation above all that her neighbour's influence worked. Sitting far downstairs Aunt Maud was yet a presence from which a sensitive niece could feel herself extremely under pressure. She knew herself now, the sensitive niece, as having been marked from far back. She knew more than she could have told you, by the upstairs fire, in a whole dark December afternoon. She knew so much that her knowledge was what fairly kept her there, making her at times more endlessly between the small silk-covered sofa that stood for her in the firelight and the great grey map of Middlesex spread beneath her lookout. To go down, to forsake her refuge, was to meet some of her discoveries half-way, to have to face them or fly before them; whereas they were at such a height only like the rumble of a far-off siege heard in the provisioned citadel. She had almost liked, in these weeks, what had created her suspense and her stress: the loss of her mother, the submersion of her father, the discomfort of her sister, the confirmation of their shrunken prospects, the certainty, in especial, of her having to recognise that, should she behave, as she called it, decently—that is still do something for others—she would be herself wholly without supplies. She held that she had a right to sadness and stillness; she nursed them for their postponing power. What they mainly postponed was the question of a surrender—though she could not yet have said exactly of what: a general surrender of everything—that was at moments the way it presented itself—to Aunt Maud's looming "personality." It was by her personality that Aunt Maud was prodigious, and the great mass of it loomed because, in the thick, the foglike air of her arranged existence, there were parts doubtless magnified and parts certainly vague. They represented at all events alike, the dim and the distinct, a strong will and a high hand. It was perfectly present to Kate that she might be devoured, and she likened herself to a trembling kid, kept apart a day or two till her turn should come, but sure sooner or later to be introduced into the cage of the lioness.

The cage was Aunt Maud's own room, her office, her counting-house, her battlefield, her especial scene, in fine, of action, situated on the ground-floor, opening from the main hall and figuring rather to our young woman on exit and entrance as a guard house or a toll-gate. The lioness waited—the kid had at least that consciousness; was aware of the neighbourhood of a morsel she had reason to suppose tender. She would have been meanwhile a wonderful lioness for a show, an extraordinary figure in a cage or anywhere; majestic, magnificent, high-coloured, all brilliant gloss, perpetual satin, twinkling bugles and flashing gems, with a lustre of agate eyes, a sheen of raven hair, a polish of complexion that was like that of well-kept china and that—as if the skin were too tight—told especially at curves and corners. Her niece had a quiet name for her—she kept it quiet; thinking of her, with a free fancy, as somehow typically insular, she talked to herself of Britannia of the Market Place—Britannia unmistakable, but with a pen in her ear, and felt she should not be happy till she might on some occasion add to the rest of the panoply a helmet, a shield, a trident and a ledger. It was not in truth, however, that the forces with which, as Kate felt, she would have to deal were those most suggested by an image simple and broad; she was learning, after all, each day, to know her companion, and what she had already most perceived was the mistake of trusting to easy analogies. There was a whole side of Britannia, the side of her florid philistinism, her plumes and her train, her fantastic furniture and heaving bosom, the false gods of her taste and false notes of her talk, the sole contemplation of which would be dangerously misleading. She was a complex and subtle Britannia, as passionate as she was practical, with a reticule for her prejudices as deep as that other pocket, the pocket full of coins stamped in her image, that the world best knew her by. She carried on, in short, behind her aggressive and defensive front, operations determined by her wisdom. It was in fact, we have hinted, as a besieger that our young lady, in the provisioned citadel, had for the present most to think of her, and what made her formidable in this character was that she was unscrupulous and immoral. So, at all events, in silent sessions and a youthful off-hand way, Kate conveniently pictured her: what this sufficiently represented being that her weight was in the scale of certain dangers—those dangers that, by our showing, made the younger woman linger and lurk above, while the elder, below, both militant and diplomatic, covered as much of the ground as possible. Yet what were the dangers, after all, but just the dangers of life and of London? Mrs. Lowder *was* London, *was* life—the roar of the siege and the thick of the fray. There were some things, after all, of which Britannia was afraid; but Aunt Maud was afraid of nothing—not even, it would appear, of arduous thought. These impressions, none the less, Kate kept so much to herself that she scarce shared them with poor Marian, the ostensible purpose of her frequent visits to whom yet continued to be to talk over everything. One of her reasons for holding off from the last concession to Aunt Maud was that she might be the more free to commit herself to this so much nearer and so much less fortunate relative, with whom Aunt Maud would have, directly, almost nothing to do. The sharpest pinch of her state, meanwhile, was exactly that all intercourse with her sister had the effect of casting down her courage and tying her hands, adding daily to her sense of the part, not always either uplifting or sweetening, that the bond of blood might play in one's life. She was face to face with it now, with the bond of blood; the consciousness of it was what she seemed most clearly to have "come into" by the death of her mother, much of that consciousness as her mother had absorbed and carried away. Her haunting, harrassing father, her menacing, uncompromising aunt, her portionless little nephews and nieces, were figures that caused the chord of natural piety superabundantly to vibrate. Her manner of putting it to herself—but more especially in respect to Marian—was that she saw what you might be brought to by the cultivation of consanguinity. She had taken, in the old days, as she supposed, the measure of this liability; those being the days when, as the second-born, she had thought no one in the world so pretty as Marian, no one so charming, so clever, so assured, in advance, of happiness and success. The view was different now, but her attitude had been obliged, for many reasons, to show as the same. The subject of this estimate was no longer pretty, as the reason for thinking her clever was no longer plain; yet, bereaved, disappointed, demoralised, querulous, she was all the more sharply and insistently Kate's elder and Kate's own. Kate's most constant feeling about her was that she would make her, Kate, do things; and always, in comfortless Chelsea, at the door of the small house the small rent of which she couldn't help having on her mind, she fatalistically asked herself, before going in, which thing it would probably be this time. She noticed with profundity that disappointment made people selfish; she marvelled at the serenity—it was the poor woman's only one—of what Marian took for granted: her own state of abasement as the second-born, her life reduced to mere inexhaustible sisterhood. She existed, in that view, wholly for the small house in Chelsea; the moral of which moreover, of course, was that the more one gave oneself the less of one was left. There were always people to snatch at one, and it would never occur to *them* that they were eating one up. They did that without tasting.

There was no such misfortune, or at any rate no such discomfort, she further reasoned, as to be formed at once for being and for seeing. You always saw, in this case, something else than what you were, and you got, in consequence, none of the peace of your condition. However, as she never really let Marian see what she was, Marian might well not have been aware that she herself saw. Kate was accordingly, to her own vision, not a hypocrite of virtue, for she gave herself up; but she was a hypocrite of stupidity, for she kept to herself everything that was not herself. What she most kept was the particular sentiment with which she watched her sister instinctively neglect nothing that would make for her submission to their aunt; a state of the spirit that perhaps marked most sharply how poor you might become when you minded so much the absence of wealth. It was through Kate that Aunt Maud should be worked, and nothing mattered less than what might become of Kate in the process. Kate was to burn her ships, in short, so that Marian should profit; and Marian's desire to profit was quite oblivious of a dignity that had, after all, its reasons—if it had only cared for them—for keeping itself a little stiff. Kate, to be properly stiff for both of them, would therefore have had to be selfish, have had to prefer an ideal of behaviour—than which nothing, ever, was more selfish—to the possibility of stray crumbs for the four small creatures. The tale of Mrs. Lowder's disgust at her elder niece's marriage to Mr. Condrip had lost little of its point; the incredibly fatuous behaviour of Mr. Condrip, the parson of a dull suburban parish, with a saintly profile which was always in evidence, being so distinctly on record to keep criticism consistent. He had presented his profile on system, having, goodness knew, nothing else to present—nothing at all to full-face the world with, no imagination of the propriety of living and minding his business. Criticism had remained on Aunt Maud's part consistent enough; she was not a person to regard such proceedings as less of a mistake for having acquired more of the privilege of pathos. She had not been forgiving, and the only approach she made to over-looking them was by overlooking—with the surviving delinquent—the solid little phalanx that now represented them. Of the two sinister ceremonies that she lumped together, the marriage and the interment, she had been present at the former, just as she had sent Marian, before it, a liberal cheque; but this had not been for her more than the shadow of an admitted link with Mrs. Condrip's course. She disapproved of clamorous children for whom there was no prospect; she disapproved of weeping widows who couldn't make their errors good; and she had thus put within Marian's reach one of the few luxuries left when so much else had gone, an easy pretext for a constant grievance. Kate Croy remembered well what their mother, in a different quarter, had made of it; and it was Marian's marked failure to pluck the fruit of resentment that committed them, as sisters, to an almost equal fellowship in abjection. If the theory was that, yes, alas, one of the pair had ceased to be noticed, but that the other was noticed enough to make up for it, who would fail to see that Kate couldn't separate herself without a cruel pride? That lesson became sharp for our young lady the day after her interview with her father.

"I can't imagine," Marian on this occasion said to her, "how you can think of anything else in the world but the horrid way we're situated."

"And, pray, how do you know," Kate inquired in reply, "anything about my thoughts? It seems to me I give you sufficient proof of how much I think of *you.* I don't, really, my dear, know what else you've to do with!"

Marian's retort, on this, was a stroke as to which she had supplied herself with several kinds of preparation, but there was, none the less, something of an unexpected note in its promptitude. She had foreseen her sister's general fear; but here, ominously, was the special one. "Well, your own business is of course your own business, and you may say there's no one less in a position than I to preach to you. But, all the same, if you wash your hands of me for ever for it, I won't, for this once, keep back that I don't consider you've a right, as we all stand, to throw yourself away."

It was after the children's dinner, which was also their mother's, but which their aunt mostly contrived to keep from ever becoming her own luncheon; and the two young women were still in the presence of the crumpled table-cloth, the dispersed pinafores, the scraped dishes, the lingering odour of boiled food. Kate had asked, with ceremony, if she might put up a window a little, and Mrs. Condrip had replied without it that she might do as she liked. She often received such inquiries as if they reflected in a manner on the pure essence of her little ones. The four had retired, with much movement and noise, under imperfect control of the small Irish governess whom their aunt had hunted out for them and whose brooding resolve not to prolong so uncrowned a martyrdom she already more than suspected. Their mother had become for Kate—who took it just for the effect of being their mother—quite a different thing from the mild Marian of the past: Mr. Condrip's widow expansively obscured that image. She was little more than a ragged relic, a plain, prosaic result of him, as if she had somehow been pulled through him as through an obstinate funnel, only to be left crumpled and useless and with nothing in her but what he accounted for. She had grown red and almost fat, which were not happy signs of mourning; less and less like any Croy, particularly a Croy in trouble, and sensibly like her husband's two unmarried sisters, who came to see her, in Kate's view, much too often and stayed too long, with the consequence of inroads upon the tea and bread-and-butter—matters as to which Kate, not unconcerned with the tradesmen's books, had feelings. About them, moreover, Marian *was* touchy, and her nearer relative, who observed and weighed things, noted as an oddity that she would have taken any reflection on them as a reflection on herself. If that was what marriage necessarily did to you, Kate Croy would have questioned marriage. It was a grave example, at any rate, of what a man—and such a man!—might make of a woman. She could see how the Condrip pair pressed their brother's widow on the subject of Aunt Maud—who wasn't, after all, *their* aunt; made her, over their interminable cups, chatter and even swagger about Lancaster Gate, made her more vulgar than it had seemed written that any Croy could possibly become on such a subject. They laid it down, they rubbed it in, that Lancaster Gate was to be kept in sight, and that she, Kate, was to keep it; so that, curiously, or at all events sadly, our young woman was sure of being, in her own person, more permitted to them as an object of comment than they would in turn ever be permitted to herself. The beauty of which, too, was that Marian didn't love them. But they were Condrips—they had grown near the rose; they were almost like Bertie and Maudie, like Kitty and Guy. They talked of the dead to her, which Kate never did; it being a relation in which Kate could but mutely listen. She couldn't indeed too often say to herself that if that was what marriage did to you——! It may easily be guessed, therefore, that the ironic light of such reserves fell straight across the field of Marian's warning. "I don't quite see," she answered, "where, in particular, it strikes you that my danger lies. I'm not conscious, I assure you, of the least 'disposition' to throw myself anywhere. I feel as if, for the present, I have been quite sufficiently thrown."

"You don't feel"—Marian brought it all out—"as if you would like to marry Merton Densher?"

Kate took a moment to meet this inquiry. "Is it your idea that if I should feel so I would be bound to give you notice, so that you might step in and head me off? Is that your idea?" the girl asked. Then, as her sister also had a pause, "I don't know what makes you talk of Mr. Densher," she observed.

"I talk of him just because you don't. That you never do, in spite of what I know—that's what makes me think of him. Or rather perhaps it's what makes me think of *you.* If you don't know by this time what I hope for you, what I dream of—my attachment being what it is—it's no use my attempting to tell you." But Marian had in fact warmed to her work, and Kate was sure she had discussed Mr. Densher with the Miss Condrips. "If I name that person I suppose it's because I'm so afraid of him. If you want really to know, he fills me with terror. If you want really to know, in fact, I dislike him as much as I dread him."

"And yet don't think it dangerous to abuse him to me?"

"Yes," Mrs. Condrip confessed, "I do think it dangerous; but how can I speak of him otherwise? I dare say, I admit, that I shouldn't speak of him at all. Only I do want you for once, as I said just now, to know."

"To know what, my dear?"

"That I should regard it," Marian promptly returned, "as far and away the worst thing that has happened to us yet."

"Do you mean because he hasn't money?"

"Yes, for one thing. And because I don't believe in him."

Kate was civil, but perfunctory. "What do you mean by not believing in him?"

"Well, being sure he'll never get it. And you *must* have it. You *shall* have it."

"To give it to you?"

Marian met her with a readiness that was practically pert. "To *have* it, first. Not, at any rate, to go on not having it. Then we should see."

"We should indeed!" said Kate Croy. It was talk of a kind she loathed, but if Marian chose to be vulgar what was one to do? It made her think of the Miss Condrips with renewed aversion. "I like the way you arrange things—I like what you take for granted. If it's so easy for us to marry men who want us to scatter gold, I wonder we any of us do anything else. I don't see so many of them about, nor what interest I might ever have for them. You live, my dear," she presently added, "in a world of vain thoughts."

"Not so much as you, Kate; for I see what I see, and you can't turn it off that way." The elder sister paused long enough for the younger's face to show, in spite of superiority, an apprehension. "I'm not talking of any man but Aunt Maud's man, nor of any money, even, if you like, but Aunt Maud's money. I'm not talking of anything but your doing what *she* wants. You're wrong if you speak of anything that I want of you; I want nothing but what she does. That's good enough for me!"—and Marian's tone struck her companion as dreadful. "If I don't believe in Merton Densher, I do at least in Mrs. Lowder."

"Your ideas are the more striking," Kate returned, "that they're the same as papa's. I had them from him, you may be interested to know—and with all the brilliancy you may imagine—yesterday."

Marian clearly was interested to know. "He has been to see you?"

"No, I went to him."

"Really?" Marian wondered. "For what purpose?"

"To tell him I'm ready to go to him."

Marian stared. "To leave Aunt Maud——?"

"For my father, yes."

She had fairly flushed, poor Mrs. Condrip, with horror. "You're ready——?"

"So I told him. I couldn't tell him less."

"And, pray, could you tell him more?" Marian gasped in her distress. "What in the world is he *to* us? You bring out such a thing as that this way?"

They faced each other—the tears were in Marian's eyes. Kate watched them there a moment and then said: "I had thought it well over—over and over. But you needn't feel injured. I'm not going. He won't have me."

Her companion still panted—it took time to subside. "Well, *I* wouldn't have you—wouldn't receive you at all, I can assure you—if he had made you any other answer. I do feel injured—at your having been willing. If you were to go to papa, my dear, you would have to stop coming to me." Marian put it thus, indefinably, as a picture of privation from which her companion might shrink. Such were the threats she could complacently make, could think herself masterful for making. "But if he won't take you," she continued, "he shows at least his sharpness."

Marian had always her views of sharpness; she was, as her sister privately commented, great on it. But Kate had her refuge from irritation. "He won't take me," she simply repeated. "But he believes, like you, in Aunt Maud. He threatens me with his curse if I leave her."

"So you *won't?"* As the girl at first said nothing her companion caught at it. "You won't, of course? I see you won't. But I don't see why, nevertheless, I shouldn't insist to you once for all on the plain truth of the whole matter. The truth, my dear, of your duty. Do you ever think about *that?* It's the greatest duty of all."

"There you are again," Kate laughed. "Papa's also immense on my duty."

"Oh, I don't pretend to be immense, but I pretend to know more than you do of life; more even perhaps than papa." Marian seemed to see that personage at this moment, nevertheless, in the light of a kinder irony. "Poor old papa!"

She sighed it with as many condonations as her sister's ear had more than once caught in her "Dear old Aunt Maud!" These were things that made Kate, for the time, turn sharply away, and she gathered herself now to go. They were the note again of the abject; it was hard to say which of the persons in question had most shown how little they liked her. The younger woman proposed, at any rate, to let discussion rest, and she believed that, for herself, she had done so during the ten minutes that, thanks to her wish not to break off short, elapsed before she could gracefully withdraw. It then appeared, however, that Marian had been discussing still, and there was something that, at the last, Kate had to take up. "Whom do you mean by Aunt Maud's young man?"

"Whom should I mean but Lord Mark?"

"And where do you pick up such vulgar twaddle?" Kate demanded with her clear face. "How does such stuff, in this hole, get to you?"

She had no sooner spoken than she asked herself what had become of the grace to which she had sacrificed. Marian certainly did little to save it, and nothing indeed was so inconsequent as her ground of complaint. She desired her to "work" Lancaster Gate as she believed that scene of abundance could be worked; but she now didn't see why advantage should be taken of the bloated connection to put an affront on her own poor home. She appeared in fact for the moment to take the position that Kate kept her in her "hole" and then heartlessly reflected on her being in it. Yet she didn't explain how she had picked up the report on which her sister had challenged her—so that it was thus left to her sister to see in it, once more, a sign of the creeping curiosity of the Miss Condrips. They lived in a deeper hole than Marian, but they kept their ear to the ground, they spent their days in prowling, whereas Marian, in garments and shoes that seemed steadily to grow looser and larger, never prowled. There were times when Kate wondered if the Miss Condrips were offered her by fate as a warning for her own future—to be taken as showing her what she herself might become at forty if she let things too recklessly go. What was expected of her by others—and by so many of them—could, all the same, on occasion, present itself as beyond a joke; and this was just now the aspect it particularly wore. She was not only to quarrel with Merton Densher to oblige her five spectators—with the Miss Condrips there were five; she was to set forth in pursuit of Lord Mark on some preposterous theory of the premium attached to success. Mrs. Lowder's hand had attached it, and it figured at the end of the course as a bell that would ring, break out into public clamour, as soon as touched. Kate reflected sharply enough on the weak points of this fond fiction, with the result at last of a certain chill for her sister's confidence; though Mrs. Condrip still took refuge in the plea—which was after all the great point—that their aunt would be munificent when their aunt should be pleased. The exact identity of her candidate was a detail; what was of the essence was her conception of the kind of match it was open to her niece to make with her aid. Marian always spoke of marriages as "matches," but that was again a detail. Mrs. Lowder's "aid" meanwhile awaited them—if not to light the way to Lord Mark, then to somebody better. Marian would put up, in fine, with somebody better; she only wouldn't put up with somebody so much worse. Kate had, once more, to go through all this before a graceful issue was reached. It was reached by her paying with the sacrifice of Mr. Densher for her reduction of Lord Mark to the absurd. So they separated softly enough. She was to be let off hearing about Lord Mark so long as she made it good that she wasn't underhand about anybody else. She had denied everything and every one, she reflected as she went away—and that was a relief; but it also made rather a clean sweep of the future. The prospect put on a bareness that already gave her something in common with the Miss Condrips.

BOOK SECOND

III

Merton Densher, who passed the best hours of each night at the office of his newspaper, had at times, during the day, to make up for it, a sense, or at least an appearance, of leisure, in accordance with which he was not infrequently to be met, in different parts of the town, at moments when men of business are hidden from the public eye. More than once, during the present winter's end, he had deviated, toward three o'clock, or toward four, into Kensington Gardens, where he might for a while, on each occasion, have been observed to demean himself as a person with nothing to do. He made his way indeed, for the most part, with a certain directness, over to the north side; but once that ground was reached his behaviour was noticeably wanting in point. He moved seemingly at random from alley to alley; he stopped for no reason and remained idly agaze; he sat down in a chair and then changed to a bench; after which he walked about again, only again to repeat both the vagueness and the vivacity. Distinctly, he was a man either with nothing at all to do or with ever so much to think about; and it was not to be denied that the impression he might often thus easily make had the effect of causing the burden of proof, in certain directions, to rest on him. It was a little the fault of his aspect, his personal marks, which made it almost impossible to name his profession.

He was a longish, leanish, fairish young Englishman, not unamenable, on certain sides, to classification—as for instance by being a gentleman, by being rather specifically one of the educated, one of the generally sound and generally pleasant; yet, though to that degree neither extraordinary nor abnormal, he would have failed to play straight into an observer's hands. He was young for the House of Commons, he was loose for the army. He was refined, as might have been said, for the city, and, quite apart from the cut of his cloth, he was sceptical, it might have been felt, for the church. On the other hand he was credulous for diplomacy, or perhaps even for science, while he was perhaps at the same time too much in his mere senses for poetry, and yet too little in them for art. You would have got fairly near him by making out in his eyes the potential recognition of ideas; but you would have quite fallen away again on the question of the ideas themselves. The difficulty with Densher was that he looked vague without looking weak—idle without looking empty. It was the accident, possibly, of his long legs, which were apt to stretch themselves; of his straight hair and his well-shaped head, never, the latter, neatly smooth, and apt, into the bargain, at the time of quite other calls upon it, to throw itself suddenly back and, supported behind by his uplifted arms and interlocked hands, place him for unconscionable periods in communion with the ceiling, the tree-tops, the sky. He was in short visibly absent-minded, irregularly clever, liable to drop what was near and to take up what was far; he was more a respecter, in general, than a follower of custom. He suggested above all, however, that wondrous state of youth in which the elements, the metals more or less precious, are so in fusion and fermentation that the question of the final stamp, the pressure that fixes the value, must wait for comparative coolness. And it was a mark of his interesting mixture that if he was irritable it was by a law of considerable subtlety—a law that, in intercourse with him, it might be of profit, though not easy, to master. One of the effects of it was that he had for you surprises of tolerance as well as of temper.

He loitered, on the best of the relenting days, the several occasions we speak of, along the part of the Gardens nearest to Lancaster Gate, and when, always, in due time, Kate Croy came out of her aunt's house, crossed the road and arrived by the nearest entrance, there was a general publicity in the proceeding which made it slightly anomalous. If their meeting was to be bold and free it might have taken place within doors; if it was to be shy or secret it might have taken place almost anywhere better than under Mrs. Lowder's windows. They failed indeed to remain attached to that spot; they wandered and strolled, taking in the course of more than one of these interviews a considerable walk, or else picked out a couple of chairs under one of the great trees and sat as much apart—apart from every one else—as possible. But Kate had, each time, at first, the air of wishing to expose herself to pursuit and capture if those things were in question. She made the point that she was not underhand, any more than she was vulgar; that the Gardens were charming in themselves and this use of them a matter of taste; and that, if her aunt chose to glare at her from the drawing-room or to cause her to be tracked and overtaken, she could at least make it convenient that this should be easily done. The fact was that the relation between these young persons abounded in such oddities as were not inaptly symbolised by assignations that had a good deal more appearance than motive. Of the strength of the tie that held them we shall sufficiently take the measure; but it was meanwhile almost obvious that if the great possibility had come up for them it had done so, to an exceptional degree, under the protection of the famous law of contraries. Any deep harmony that might eventually govern them would not be the result of their having much in common—having anything, in fact, but their affection; and would really find its explanation in some sense, on the part of each, of being poor where the other was rich. It is nothing new indeed that generous young persons often admire most what nature hasn't given them—from which it would appear, after all, that our friends were both generous.

Merton Densher had repeatedly said to himself—and from far back—that he should be a fool not to marry a woman whose value would be in her differences; and Kate Croy, though without having quite so philosophised, had quickly recognised in the young man a precious unlikeness. He represented what her life had never given her and certainly, without some such aid as his, never would give her; all the high, dim things she lumped together as of the mind. It was on the side of the mind that Densher was rich for her, and mysterious and strong; and he had rendered her in especial the sovereign service of making that element real. She had had, all her days, to take it terribly on trust; no creature she had ever encountered having been able in any degree to testify for it directly. Vague rumours of its existence had made their precarious way to her; but nothing had, on the whole, struck her as more likely than that she should live and die without the chance to verify them. The chance had come—it was an extraordinary one—on the day she first met Densher; and it was to the girl's lasting honour that she knew on the spot what she was in the presence of. That occasion indeed, for everything that straightway flowered in it, would be worthy of high commemoration; Densher's perception went out to meet the young woman's and quite kept pace with her own recognition. Having so often concluded on the fact of his weakness, as he called it, for life—his strength merely for thought—life, he logically opined, was what he must somehow arrange to annex and possess. This was so much a necessity that thought by itself only went on in the void; it was from the immediate air of life that it must draw its breath. So the young man, ingenious but large, critical but ardent too, made out both his case and Kate Croy's. They had originally met before her mother's death—an occasion marked for her as the last pleasure permitted by the approach of that event; after which the dark months had interposed a screen and, for all Kate knew, made the end one with the beginning.

The beginning—to which she often went back—had been a scene, for our young woman, of supreme brilliancy; a party given at a "gallery" hired by a hostess who fished with big nets. A Spanish dancer, understood to be at that moment the delight of the town, an American reciter, the joy of a kindred people, an Hungarian fiddler, the wonder of the world at large—in the name of these and other attractions the company in which, by a rare privilege, Kate found herself had been freely convoked. She lived under her mother's roof, as she considered, obscurely, and was acquainted with few persons who entertained on that scale; but she had had dealings with two or three connected, as appeared, with such—two or three through whom the stream of hospitality, filtered or diffused, could thus now and then spread to outlying receptacles. A good-natured lady in fine, a friend of her mother and a relative of the lady of the gallery, had offered to take her to the party in question and had there fortified her, further, with two or three of those introductions that, at large parties, lead to other things—that had at any rate, on this occasion, culminated for her in conversation with a tall, fair, slightly unbrushed and rather awkward, but on the whole not dreary, young man. The young man had affected her as detached, as—it was indeed what he called himself—awfully at sea, as much more distinct from what surrounded them than any one else appeared to be, and even as probably quite disposed to be making his escape when pulled up to be placed in relation with her. He gave her his word for it indeed, that same evening, that only their meeting had prevented his flight, but that now he saw how sorry he should have been to miss it. This point they had reached by midnight, and though in respect to such remarks everything was in the tone, the tone was by midnight there too. She had had originally her full apprehension of his coerced, certainly of his vague, condition—full apprehensions often being with her immediate; then she had had her equal consciousness that, within five minutes, something between them had—well, she couldn't call it anything but *come.* It was nothing, but it was somehow everything—it was that something for each of them had happened.

They had found themselves looking at each other straight, and for a longer time on end than was usual even at parties in galleries; but that, after all, would have been a small affair, if there hadn't been something else with it. It wasn't, in a word, simply that their eyes had met; other conscious organs, faculties, feelers had met as well, and when Kate afterwards imaged to herself the sharp, deep fact she saw it, in the oddest way, as a particular performance. She had observed a ladder against a garden wall, and had trusted herself so to climb it as to be able to see over into the probable garden on the other side. On reaching the top she had found herself face to face with a gentleman engaged in a like calculation at the same moment, and the two inquirers had remained confronted on their ladders. The great point was that for the rest of that evening they had been perched—they had not climbed down; and indeed, during the time that followed, Kate at least had had the perched feeling—it was as if she were there aloft without a retreat. A simpler expression of all this is doubtless but that they had taken each other in with interest; and without a happy hazard six months later the incident would have closed in that account of it. The accident, meanwhile, had been as natural as anything in London ever is: Kate had one afternoon found herself opposite Mr. Densher on the Underground Railway. She had entered the train at Sloane Square to go to Queen's Road, and the carriage in which she had found a place was all but full. Densher was already in it—on the other bench and at the furthest angle; she was sure of him before they had again started. The day and the hour were darkness, there were six other persons, and she had been busy placing herself; but her consciousness had gone to him as straight as if they had come together in some bright level of the desert. They had on neither part a second's hesitation; they looked across the choked compartment exactly as if she had known he would be there and he had expected her to come in; so that, though in the conditions they could only exchange the greeting of movements, smiles, silence, it would have been quite in the key of these passages that they should have alighted for ease at the very next station. Kate was in fact sure that the very next station was the young man's true goal—which made it clear that he was going on only from the wish to speak to her. He had to go on, for this purpose, to High Street, Kensington, as it was not till then that the exit of a passenger gave him his chance.

His chance put him, however, in quick possession of the seat facing her, the alertness of his capture of which seemed to show her his impatience. It helped them, moreover, with strangers on either side, little to talk; though this very restriction perhaps made such a mark for them as nothing else could have done. If the fact that their opportunity had again come round for them could be so intensely expressed between them without a word, they might very well feel on the spot that it had not come round for nothing. The extraordinary part of the matter was that they were not in the least meeting where they had left off, but ever so much further on, and that these added links added still another between High Street and Notting Hill Gate, and then between the latter station and Queen's Road an extension really inordinate. At Notting Hill Gate, Kate's right-hand neighbour descended, whereupon Densher popped straight into that seat; only there was not much gained when a lady, the next instant, popped into Densher's. He could say almost nothing to her—she scarce knew, at least, what he said; she was so occupied with a certainty that one of the persons opposite, a youngish man with a single eyeglass, which he kept constantly in position, had made her out from the first as visibly, as strangely affected. If such a person made her out, what then did Densher do?—a question in truth sufficiently answered when, on their reaching her station, he instantly followed her out of the train. That had been the real beginning—the beginning of everything else; the other time, the time at the party, had been but the beginning of *that.* Never in life before had she so let herself go; for always before—so far as small adventures could have been in question for her—there had been, by the vulgar measure, more to go upon. He had walked with her to Lancaster Gate, and then she had walked with him away from it—for all the world, she said to herself, like the housemaid giggling to the baker.

This appearance, she was afterwards to feel, had been all in order for a relation that might precisely best be described in the terms of the baker and the housemaid. She could say to herself that from that hour they had kept company; that had come to represent, technically speaking, alike the range and the limit of their tie. He had on the spot, naturally, asked leave to call upon her—which, as a young person who wasn't really young, who didn't pretend to be a sheltered flower, she as rationally gave. That—she was promptly clear about it—was now her only possible basis; she was just the contemporary London female, highly modern, inevitably battered, honourably free. She had of course taken her aunt straight into her confidence—had gone through the form of asking her leave; and she subsequently remembered that though, on this occasion, she had left the history of her new alliance as scant as the facts themselves, Mrs. Lowder had struck her at the time surprisingly mild. It had been, in every way, the occasion, full of the reminder that her hostess was deep: it was definitely then that she had begun to ask herself what Aunt Maud was, in vulgar parlance, "up to." "You may receive, my dear, whom you like"—that was what Aunt Maud, who in general objected to people's doing as they liked, had replied; and it bore, this unexpectedness, a good deal of looking into. There were many explanations, and they were all amusing—amusing, that is, in the line of the sombre and brooding amusement, cultivated by Kate in her actual high retreat. Merton Densher came the very next Sunday; but Mrs. Lowder was so consistently magnanimous as to make it possible to her niece to see him alone. She saw him, however, on the Sunday following, in order to invite him to dinner; and when, after dining, he came again—which he did three times, she found means to treat his visit as preponderantly to herself. Kate's conviction that she didn't like him made that remarkable; it added to the evidence, by this time voluminous, that she was remarkable all round. If she had been, in the way of energy, merely usual, she would have kept her dislike direct; whereas it was now as if she were seeking to know him in order to see best where to "have" him. That was one of the reflections made in our young woman's high retreat; she smiled from her lookout, in the silence that was only the fact of hearing irrelevant sounds, as she caught the truth that you could easily accept people when you wanted them so to be delivered to you. When Aunt Maud wished them despatched, it was not to be done by deputy; it was clearly always a matter reserved for her own hand. But what made the girl wonder most was the implications of so much diplomacy in respect to her own value. What view might she take of her position in the light of this appearance that her companion feared so, as yet, to upset her? It was as if Densher were accepted partly under the dread that if he hadn't been she would act in resentment. Hadn't her aunt considered the danger that she would in that case have broken off, have seceded? The danger was exaggerated—she would have done nothing so gross; but that, it seemed, was the way Mrs. Lowder saw her and believed her to be reckoned with. What importance therefore did she really attach to her, what strange interest could she take on their keeping on terms? Her father and her sister had their answer to this—even without knowing how the question struck her; they saw the lady of Lancaster Gate as panting to make her fortune, and the explanation of that appetite was that, on the accident of a nearer view than she had before enjoyed, she had been charmed, been dazzled. They approved, they admired in her one of the belated fancies of rich, capricious, violent old women—the more marked, moreover, because the result of no plot; and they piled up the possible results for the person concerned. Kate knew what to think of her own power thus to carry by storm; she saw herself as handsome, no doubt, but as hard, and felt herself as clever but as cold; and as so much too imperfectly ambitious, furthermore, that it was a pity, for a quiet life, she couldn't settle to be either finely or stupidly indifferent. Her intelligence sometimes kept her still—too still—but her want of it was restless; so that she got the good, it seemed to her, of neither extreme. She saw herself at present, none the less, in a situation, and even her sad, disillusioned mother, dying, but with Aunt Maud interviewing the nurse on the stairs, had not failed to remind her that it was of the essence of situations to be, under Providence, worked. The dear woman had died in the belief that she was actually working the one then produced.

Kate took one of her walks with Densher just after her visit to Mr. Croy; but most of it went, as usual, to their sitting in talk. They had, under the trees, by the lake, the air of old friends—phases of apparent earnestness, in particular, in which they might have been settling every question in their vast young world; and periods of silence, side by side, perhaps even more, when "a long engagement!" would have been the final reading of the signs on the part of a passer struck with them, as it was so easy to be. They would have presented themselves thus as very old friends rather than as young persons who had met for the first time but a year before and had spent most of the interval without contact. It was indeed for each, already, as if they were older friends; and though the succession of their meetings might, between them, have been straightened out, they only had a confused sense of a good many, very much alike, and a confused intention of a good many more, as little different as possible. The desire to keep them just as they were had perhaps to do with the fact that in spite of the presumed diagnosis of the stranger there had been for them as yet no formal, no final understanding. Densher had at the very first pressed the question, but that, it had been easy to reply, was too soon; so that a singular thing had afterwards happened. They had accepted their acquaintance as too short for an engagement, but they had treated it as long enough for almost anything else, and marriage was somehow before them like a temple without an avenue. They belonged to the temple and they met in the grounds; they were in the stage at which grounds in general offered much scattered refreshment. But Kate had meanwhile had so few confidants that she wondered at the source of her father's suspicions. The diffusion of rumour was of course, in London, remarkable, and for Marian not less—as Aunt Maud touched neither directly—the mystery had worked. No doubt she had been seen. Of course she had been seen. She had taken no trouble not to be seen, and it was a thing, clearly, she was incapable of taking. But she had been seen how?—and *what* was there to see? She was in love—she knew that: but it was wholly her own business, and she had the sense of having conducted herself, of still so doing, with almost violent conformity.

"I've an idea—in fact I feel sure—that Aunt Maud means to write to you; and I think you had better know it." So much as this she said to him as soon as they met, but immediately adding to it: "So as to make up your mind how to take her. I know pretty well what she'll say to you."

"Then will you kindly tell me?"

She thought a little. "I can't do that. I should spoil it. She'll do the best for her own idea."

"Her idea, you mean, that I'm a sort of a scoundrel; or, at the best, not good enough for you?"

They were side by side again in their penny chairs, and Kate had another pause. "Not good enough for *her.*"

"Oh, I see. And that's necessary."

He put it as a truth rather more than as a question; but there had been plenty of truths between them that each had contradicted. Kate, however, let this one sufficiently pass, only saying the next moment: "She has behaved extraordinarily."

"And so have we," Densher declared. "I think, you know, we've been awfully decent."

"For ourselves, for each other, for people in general, yes. But not for *her.* For her," said Kate, "we've been monstrous. She has been giving us rope. So if she does send for you," the girl repeated, "you must know where you are."

"That I always know. It's where *you* are that concerns me."

"Well," said Kate after an instant, "her idea of that is what you'll have from her." He gave her a long look, and whatever else people who wouldn't let her alone might have wished, for her advancement, his long looks were the thing in the world she could never have enough of. What she felt was that, whatever might happen, she must keep them, must make them most completely her possession; and it was already strange enough that she reasoned, or at all events began to act, as if she might work them in with other and alien things, privately cherish them, and yet, as regards the rigour of it, pay no price. She looked it well in the face, she took it intensely home, that they were lovers; she rejoiced to herself and, frankly, to him, in their wearing of the name; but, distinguished creature that, in her way, she was, she took a view of this character that scarce squared with the conventional. The character itself she insisted on as their right, taking that so for granted that it didn't seem even bold; but Densher, though he agreed with her, found himself moved to wonder at her simplifications, her values. Life might prove difficult—was evidently going to; but meanwhile they had each other, and that was everything. This was her reasoning, but meanwhile, for *him,* each other was what they didn't have, and it was just the point. Repeatedly, however, it was a point that, in the face of strange and special things, he judged it rather awkwardly gross to urge. It was impossible to keep Mrs. Lowder out of their scheme. She stood there too close to it and too solidly; it had to open a gate, at a given point, do what they would to take her in. And she came in, always, while they sat together rather helplessly watching her, as in a coach-in-four; she drove round their prospect as the principal lady at the circus drives round the ring, and she stopped the coach in the middle to alight with majesty. It was our young man's sense that she was magnificently vulgar, but yet, quite, that this wasn't all. It wasn't with her vulgarity that she felt his want of means, though that might have helped her richly to embroider it; nor was it with the same infirmity that she was strong, original, dangerous.

His want of means—of means sufficient for anyone but himself—was really the great ugliness, and was, moreover, at no time more ugly for him than when it rose there, as it did seem to rise, shameless, face to face with the elements in Kate's life colloquially and conveniently classed by both of them as funny. He sometimes indeed, for that matter, asked himself if these elements were as funny as the innermost fact, so often vivid to him, of his own consciousness—his private inability to believe he should ever be rich. His conviction on this head was in truth quite positive and a thing by itself; he failed, after analysis, to understand it, though he had naturally more lights on it than any one else. He knew how it subsisted in spite of an equal consciousness of his being neither mentally nor physically quite helpless, neither a dunce nor a cripple; he knew it to be absolute, though secret, and also, strange to say, about common undertakings, not discouraging, not prohibitive. Only now was he having to think if it were prohibitive in respect to marriage; only now, for the first time, had he to weigh his case in scales. The scales, as he sat with Kate, often dangled in the line of his vision; he saw them, large and black, while he talked or listened, take, in the bright air, singular positions. Sometimes the right was down and sometimes the left; never a happy equipoise—one or the other always kicking the beam. Thus was kept before him the question of whether it were more ignoble to ask a woman to take her chance with you, or to accept it from one's conscience that her chance could be at the best but one of the degrees of privation; whether, too, otherwise, marrying for money mightn't after all be a smaller cause of shame than the mere dread of marrying without. Through these variations of mood and view, all the same, the mark on his forehead stood clear; he saw himself remain without whether he married or not. It was a line on which his fancy could be admirably active; the innumerable ways of making money were beautifully present to him; he could have handled them, for his newspaper, as easily as he handled everything. He was quite aware how he handled everything; it was another mark on his forehead; the pair of smudges from the thumb of fortune, the brand on the passive fleece, dated from the primal hour and kept each other company. He wrote, as for print, with deplorable ease; since there had been nothing to stop him even at the age of ten, so there was as little at twenty; it was part of his fate in the first place and part of the wretched public's in the second. The innumerable ways of making money were, no doubt, at all events, what his imagination often was busy with after he had tilted his chair and thrown back his head with his hands clasped behind it. What would most have prolonged that attitude, moreover, was the reflection that the ways were ways only for others. Within the minute, now—however this might be—he was aware of a nearer view than he had yet quite had of those circumstances on his companion's part that made least for simplicity of relation. He saw above all how she saw them herself, for she spoke of them at present with the last frankness, telling him of her visit to her father and giving him, in an account of her subsequent scene with her sister, an instance of how she was perpetually reduced to patching up, in one way or another, that unfortunate woman's hopes.

"The tune," she exclaimed, "to which we're a failure as a family!" With which he had it again all from her—and this time, as it seemed to him, more than all: the dishonour her father had brought them, his folly and cruelty and wickedness; the wounded state of her mother, abandoned, despoiled and helpless, yet, for the management of such a home as remained to them, dreadfully unreasonable too; the extinction of her two young brothers—one, at nineteen, the eldest of the house, by typhoid fever, contracted at a poisonous little place, as they had afterwards found out, that they had taken for a summer; the other, the flower of the flock, a middy on the *Britannia,* dreadfully drowned, and not even by an accident at sea, but by cramp, unrescued, while bathing, too late in the autumn, in a wretched little river during a holiday visit to the home of a shipmate. Then Marian's unnatural marriage, in itself a kind of spiritless turning of the other cheek to fortune: her actual wretchedness and plaintiveness, her greasy children, her impossible claims, her odious visitors—these things completed the proof of the heaviness, for them all, of the hand of fate. Kate confessedly described them with an excess of impatience; it was much of her charm for Densher that she gave in general that turn to her descriptions, partly as if to amuse him by free and humorous colour, partly—and that charm was the greatest—as if to work off, for her own relief, her constant perception of the incongruity of things. She had seen the general show too early and too sharply, and she was so intelligent that she knew it and allowed for that misfortune; therefore when, in talk with him, she was violent and almost unfeminine, it was almost as if they had settled, for intercourse, on the short cut of the fantastic and the happy language of exaggeration. It had come to be definite between them at a primary stage that, if they could have no other straight way, the realm of thought at least was open to them. They could think whatever they liked about whatever they would—or, in other words, they could say it. Saying it for each other, for each other alone, only of course added to the taste. The implication was thereby constant that what they said when not together had no taste for them at all, and nothing could have served more to launch them, at special hours, on their small floating island than such an assumption that they were only making believe everywhere else. Our young man, it must be added, was conscious enough that it was Kate who profited most by this particular play of the fact of intimacy. It always seemed to him that she had more life than he to react from, and when she recounted the dark disasters of her house and glanced at the hard, odd offset of her present exaltation—since as exaltation it was apparently to be considered—he felt his own grey domestic annals to make little show. It was naturally, in all such reference, the question of her father's character that engaged him most, but her picture of her adventure in Chirk Street gave him a sense of how little as yet that character was clear to him. What was it, to speak plainly, that Mr. Croy had originally done?

"I don't know—and I don't want to. I only know that years and years ago—when I was about fifteen—something or other happened that made him impossible. I mean impossible for the world at large first, and then, little by little, for mother. We of course didn't know it at the time," Kate explained, "but we knew it later; and it was, oddly enough, my sister who first made out that he had done something. I can hear her now—the way, one cold, black Sunday morning when, on account of an extraordinary fog, we had not gone to church, she broke it to me by the school-room fire. I was reading a history-book by the lamp—when we didn't go to church we had to read history-books—and I suddenly heard her say, out of the fog, which was in the room, and *apropos* of nothing: 'Papa has done something wicked.' And the curious thing was that I believed it on the spot and have believed it ever since, though she could tell me nothing more—neither what was the wickedness, nor how she knew, nor what would happen to him, nor anything else about it. We had our sense, always, that all sorts of things *had* happened, were all the while happening, to him; so that when Marian only said she was sure, tremendously sure, that she had made it out for herself, but that that was enough, I took her word for it—it seemed somehow so natural. We were not, however, to ask mother—which made it more natural still, and I said never a word. But mother, strangely enough, spoke of it to me, in time, of her own accord very much later on. He hadn't been with us for ever so long, but we were used to that. She must have had some fear, some conviction that I had an idea, some idea of her own that it was the best thing to do. She came out as abruptly as Marian had done: 'If you hear anything against your father—anything I mean, except that he's odious and vile—remember it's perfectly false.' That was the way I knew—it was true, though I recall that I said to her then that I of course knew it wasn't. She might have told me it was true, and yet have trusted me to contradict fiercely enough any accusation of him that I should meet—to contradict it much more fiercely and effectively, I think, than she would have done herself. As it happens, however," the girl went on, "I've never had occasion, and I've been conscious of it with a sort of surprise. It has made the world, at times, seem more decent. No one has so much as breathed to me. That has been a part of the silence, the silence that surrounds him, the silence that, for the world, has washed him out. He doesn't exist for people. And yet I'm as sure as ever. In fact, though I know no more than I did then, I'm more sure. And that," she wound up, "is what I sit here and tell you about my own father. If you don't call it a proof of confidence I don't know what will satisfy you."

"It satisfies me beautifully," Densher declared, "but it doesn't, my dear child, very greatly enlighten me. You don't, you know, really tell me anything. It's so vague that what am I to think but that you may very well be mistaken? What has he done, if no one can name it?"

"He has done everything."

"Oh—everything! Everything's nothing."

"Well then," said Kate, "he has done some particular thing. It's known—only, thank God, not to us. But it has been the end of him. You could doubtless find out with a little trouble. You can ask about."

Densher for a moment said nothing; but the next moment he made it up. "I wouldn't find out for the world, and I'd rather lose my tongue than put a question."

"And yet it's a part of me," said Kate.

"A part of you?"

"My father's dishonour." Then she sounded for him, but more deeply than ever yet, her note of proud, still pessimism. "How can such a thing as that not be the great thing in one's life?"

She had to take from him again, on this, one of his long looks, and she took it to its deepest, its headiest dregs. "I shall ask you, for the great thing in your life," he said, "to depend on *me* a little more." After which, just hesitating, "Doesn't he belong to some club?" he inquired.

She had a grave headshake. "He used to—to many."

"But he has dropped them?"

"They've dropped *him.* Of that I'm sure. It ought to do for you. I offered him," the girl immediately continued—"and it was for that I went to him—to come and be with him, make a home for him so far as is possible. But he won't hear of it."

Densher took this in with visible, but generous, wonder. "You offered him—'impossible' as you describe him to me—to live with him and share his disadvantages?" The young man saw for the moment but the high beauty of it. "You *are* gallant!"

"Because it strikes you as being brave for him?" She wouldn't in the least have this. "It wasn't courage—it was the opposite. I did it to save myself—to escape."

He had his air, so constant at this stage, as of her giving him finer things than any one to think about. "Escape from what?"

"From everything."

"Do you by any chance mean from me?"

"No; I spoke to him of you, told him—or what amounted to it—that I would bring you, if he would allow it, with me."

"But he won't allow it," said Densher.

"Won't hear of it on any terms. He won't help me, won't save me, won't hold out a finger to me," Kate went on; "he simply wriggles away, in his inimitable manner, and throws me back."

"Back then, after all, thank goodness," Densher concurred, "on me."

But she spoke again as with the sole vision of the whole scene she had evoked. "It's a pity, because you'd like him. He's wonderful—he's charming." Her companion gave one of the laughs that marked in him, again, his feeling in her tone, inveterately, something that banished the talk of other women, so far as he knew other women, to the dull desert of the conventional, and she had already continued. "He would make himself delightful to you."

"Even while objecting to me?"

"Well, he likes to please," the girl explained—"personally. He would appreciate you and be clever with you. It's to *me* he objects—that is as to my liking you."

"Heaven be praised then," Densher exclaimed, "that you like me enough for the objection!"

But she met it after an instant with some inconsequence. "I don't. I offered to give you up, if necessary, to go to him. But it made no difference, and that's what I mean," she pursued, "by his declining me on any terms. The point is, you see, that I don't escape."

Densher wondered. "But if you didn't wish to escape *me?"*

"I wished to escape Aunt Maud. But he insists that it's through her and through her only that I may help him; just as Marian insists that it's through her, and through her only, that I can help *her.* That's what I mean," she again explained, "by their turning me back."

The young man thought. "Your sister turns you back too?"

"Oh, with a push!"

"But have you offered to live with your sister?"

"I would in a moment if she'd have me. That's all my virtue—a narrow little family feeling. I've a small stupid piety—I don't know what to call it." Kate bravely sustained it; she made it out. "Sometimes, alone, I've to smother my shrieks when I think of my poor mother. She went through things—they pulled her down; I know what they were now—I didn't then, for I was a pig; and my position, compared with hers, is an insolence of success. That's what Marian keeps before me; that's what papa himself, as I say, so inimitably does. My position's a value, a great value, for them both"—she followed and followed. Lucid and ironic, she knew no merciful muddle. "It's *the* value—the only one they have."

Everything between our young couple moved today, in spite of their pauses, their margin, to a quicker measure—the quickness and anxiety playing lightning-like in the sultriness. Densher watched, decidedly, as he had never done before. "And the fact you speak of holds you!"

"Of course, it holds me. It's a perpetual sound in my ears. It makes me ask myself if I've any right to personal happiness, any right to anything but to be as rich and overflowing, as smart and shining, as I can be made."

Densher had a pause. "Oh, you might, with good luck, have the personal happiness too."

Her immediate answer to this was a silence like his own; after which she gave him straight in the face, but quite simply and quietly: "Darling!"

It took him another moment; then he was also quiet and simple. "Will you settle it by our being married tomorrow—as we can, with perfect ease, civilly?"

"Let us wait to arrange it," Kate presently replied, "till after you've seen her."

"Do you call that adoring me?" Densher demanded.

They were talking, for the time, with the strangest mixture of deliberation and directness, and nothing could have been more in the tone of it than the way she at last said: "You're afraid of her yourself."

He gave a smile a trifle glassy. "For young persons of a great distinction and a very high spirit, we're a caution!"

"Yes," she took it straight up; "we're hideously intelligent. But there's fun in it too. We must get our fun where we can. I think," she added, and for that matter, not without courage, "our relation's beautiful. It's not a bit vulgar. I cling to some saving romance in things."

It made him break into a laugh which had more freedom than his smile. "How you must be afraid you'll chuck me!"

"No, no, *that* would be vulgar. But, of course, I do see my danger," she admitted, "of doing something base."

"Then what can be so base as sacrificing me?"

"I *shan't* sacrifice you; don't cry out till you're hurt. I shall sacrifice nobody and nothing, and that's just my situation, that I want and that I shall try for everything. That," she wound up, "is how I see myself, and how I see you quite as much, acting for them."

"For 'them'?" and the young man strongly, extravagantly marked his coldness. "Thank you!"

"Don't you care for them?"

"Why should I? What are they to me but a serious nuisance?"

As soon as he had permitted himself this qualification of the unfortunate persons she so perversely cherished, he repented of his roughness—and partly because he expected a flash from her. But it was one of her finest sides that she sometimes flashed with a mere mild glow. "I don't see why you don't make out a little more that if we avoid stupidity we may do *all.* We may keep her."

He stared. "Make her pension us?"

"Well, wait at least till we have seen."

He thought. "Seen what can be got out of her?"

Kate for a moment said nothing. "After all I never asked her; never, when our troubles were at the worst, appealed to her nor went near her. She fixed upon me herself, settled on me with her wonderful gilded claws."

"You speak," Densher observed, "as if she were a vulture."

"Call it an eagle—with a gilded beak as well, and with wings for great flights. If she's a thing of the air, in short—say at once a balloon—I never myself got into her car. I was her choice."

It had really, her sketch of the affair, a high colour and a great style; at all of which he gazed a minute as at a picture by a master. "What she must see in you!"

"Wonders!" And, speaking it loud, she stood straight up. "Everything. There it is."

Yes, there it was, and as she remained before him he continued to face it. "So that what you mean is that I'm to do my part in somehow squaring her?"

"See her, see her," Kate said with impatience.

"And grovel to her?"

"Ah, do what you like!" And she walked in her impatience away.

IV

His eyes had followed her at this time quite long enough, before he overtook her, to make out more than ever, in the poise of her head, the pride of her step—he didn't know what best to call it—a part, at least, of Mrs. Lowder's reasons. He consciously winced while he figured his presenting himself as a reason opposed to these; though, at the same moment, with the source of Aunt Maud's inspiration thus before him, he was prepared to conform, by almost any abject attitude or profitable compromise, to his companion's easy injunction. He would do as *she* liked—his own liking might come off as it would. He would help her to the utmost of his power; for, all the rest of that day and the next, her easy injunction, tossed off that way as she turned her beautiful back, was like the crack of a great whip in the blue air, the high element in which Mrs. Lowder hung. He wouldn't grovel perhaps—he wasn't quite ready for that; but he would be patient, ridiculous, reasonable, unreasonable, and above all deeply diplomatic. He would be clever, with all his cleverness—which he now shook hard, as he sometimes shook his poor, dear, shabby, old watch, to start it up again. It wasn't, thank goodness, as if there weren't plenty of that, and with what they could muster between them it would be little to the credit of their star, however pale, that defeat and surrender—surrender so early, so immediate—should have to ensue. It was not indeed that he thought of that disaster as, at the worst, a direct sacrifice of their possibilities: he imaged—it which was enough as some proved vanity, some exposed fatuity, in the idea of bringing Mrs. Lowder round. When, shortly afterwards, in this lady's vast drawing-room—the apartments at Lancaster Gate had struck him from the first as of prodigious extent—he awaited her, at her request, conveyed in a "reply-paid" telegram, his theory was that of their still clinging to their idea, though with a sense of the difficulty of it really enlarged to the scale of the place.

He had the place for a long time—it seemed to him a quarter of an hour—to himself; and while Aunt Maud kept him and kept him, while observation and reflection crowded on him, he asked himself what was to be expected of a person who could treat one like that. The visit, the hour were of her own proposing, so that her delay, no doubt, was but part of a general plan of putting him to inconvenience. As he walked to and fro, however, taking in the message of her massive, florid furniture, the immense expression of her signs and symbols, he had as little doubt of the inconvenience he was prepared to suffer. He found himself even facing the thought that he had nothing to fall back on, and that that was as great a humiliation in a good cause as a proud man could desire. It had not yet been so distinct to him that he made no show—literally not the smallest; so complete a show seemed made there all about him; so almost abnormally affirmative, so aggressively erect, were the huge, heavy objects that syllabled his hostess story. "When all's said and done, you know, she's colossally vulgar"—he had once all but said that of Mrs. Lowder to her niece; only just keeping it back at the last, keeping it to himself with all its danger about it. It mattered because it bore so directly, and he at all events quite felt it a thing that Kate herself would some day bring out to him. It bore directly at present, and really all the more that somehow, strangely, it didn't in the least imply that Aunt Maud was dull or stale. She was vulgar with freshness, almost with beauty, since there was beauty, to a degree, in the play of so big and bold a temperament. She was in fine quite the largest possible quantity to deal with; and he was in the cage of the lioness without his whip—the whip, in a word, of a supply of proper retorts. He had no retort but that he loved the girl—which in such a house as that was painfully cheap. Kate had mentioned to him more than once that her aunt was Passionate, speaking of it as a kind of offset and uttering it as with a capital P, marking it as something that he might, that he in fact ought to, turn about in some way to their advantage. He wondered at this hour to what advantage he could turn it; but the case grew less simple the longer he waited. Decidedly there was something he hadn't enough of. He stood as one fast.

His slow march to and fro seemed to give him the very measure; as he paced and paced the distance it became the desert of his poverty; at the sight of which expanse moreover he could pretend to himself as little as before that the desert looked redeemable. Lancaster Gate looked rich—that was all the effect; which it was unthinkable that any state of his own should ever remotely resemble. He read more vividly, more critically, as has been hinted, the appearances about him; and they did nothing so much as make him wonder at his aesthetic reaction. He hadn't known—and in spite of Kate's repeated reference to her own rebellions of taste—that he should "mind" so much how an independent lady might decorate her house. It was the language of the house itself that spoke to him, writing out for him, with surpassing breadth and freedom, the associations and conceptions, the ideals and possibilities of the mistress. Never, he flattered himself, had he seen anything so gregari-gregariously ugly—operatively, ominously so cruel. He was glad to have found this last name for the whole character; "cruel" somehow played into the subject for an article—that his impression put straight into his mind. He would write about the heavy horrors that could still flourish, that lifted their undiminished heads, in an age so proud of its short way with false gods; and it would be funny if what he should have got from Mrs. Lowder were to prove, after all, but a small amount of copy. Yet the great thing, really the dark thing, was that, even while he thought of the quick column he might add up, he felt it less easy to laugh at the heavy horrors than to quail before them. He couldn't describe and dismiss them collectively, call them either Mid-Victorian or Early; not being at all sure they were rangeable under one rubric. It was only manifest they were splendid and were furthermore conclusively British. They constituted an order and they abounded in rare material—precious woods, metals, stuffs, stones. He had never dreamed of anything so fringed and scalloped, so buttoned and corded, drawn everywhere so tight, and curled everywhere so thick. He had never dreamed of so much gilt and glass, so much satin and plush, so much rosewood and marble and malachite. But it was, above all, the solid forms, the wasted finish, the misguided cost, the general attestation of morality and money, a good conscience and a big balance. These things finally represented for him a portentous negation of his own world of thought—of which, for that matter, in the presence of them, he became as for the first time hopelessly aware. They revealed it to him by their merciless difference. His interview with Aunt Maud, none the less, took by no means the turn he had expected. Passionate though her nature, no doubt Mrs. Lowder, on this occasion, neither threatened nor appealed. Her arms of aggression, her weapons of defence, were presumably close at hand, but she left them untouched and unmentioned, and was in fact so bland that he properly perceived only afterwards how adroit she had been. He properly perceived something else as well, which complicated his case; he shouldn't have known what to call it if he hadn't called it her really imprudent good-nature. Her blandness, in other words, was not mere policy—he wasn't dangerous enough for policy; it was the result, he could see, of her fairly liking him a little. From the moment she did that she herself became more interesting; and who knew what might happen should he take to liking *her?* Well, it was a risk he naturally must face. She fought him, at any rate, but with one hand, with a few loose grains of stray powder. He recognised at the end of ten minutes, and even without her explaining it, that if she had made him wait it had not been to wound him; they had by that time almost directly met on the fact of her intention. She had wanted him to think for himself of what she proposed to say to him—not having otherwise announced it; wanted to let it come home to him on the spot, as she had shrewdly believed it would. Her first question, on appearing, had practically been as to whether he hadn't taken her hint, and this inquiry assumed so many things that it made discussion, immediately, frank and large. He knew, with the question put, that the hint was just what he *had* taken; knew that she had made him quickly forgive her the display of her power; knew that if he didn't take care he should understand her, and the strength of her purpose, to say nothing of that of her imagination, nothing of the length of her purse, only too well. Yet he pulled himself up with the thought, too, that he was not going to be afraid of understanding her; he was just going to understand and understand without detriment to the feeblest, even, of his passions. The play of one's mind let one in, at the best, dreadfully, in action, in the need of action, where simplicity was all; but when one couldn't prevent it the thing was to make it complete. There would never be mistakes but for the original fun of mistakes. What he must use his fatal intelligence for was to resist. Mrs. Lowder, meanwhile, might use it for whatever she liked.

It was after she had begun her statement of her own idea about Kate that he began, on his side, to reflect that—with her manner of offering it as really sufficient if he would take the trouble to embrace—it she couldn't half hate him. That was all, positively, she seemed to show herself for the time as attempting; clearly, if she did her intention justice, she would have nothing more disagreeable to do. "If I hadn't been ready to go very much further, you understand, I wouldn't have gone so far. I don't care what you repeat to her—the more you repeat to her, perhaps the better; and, at any rate, there's nothing she doesn't already know. I don't say it for her; I say it for you—when I want to reach my niece I know how to do it straight." So Aunt Maud delivered herself—as with homely benevolence, in the simplest, but the clearest terms; virtually conveying that, though a word to the wise was, doubtless, in spite of the advantage, *not* always enough, a word to the good could never fail to be. The sense our young man read into her words was that she liked him because he was good—was really, by her measure, good enough: good enough, that is, to give up her niece for her and go his way in peace. But *was* he good enough—by his own measure? He fairly wondered, while she more fully expressed herself, if it might be his doom to prove so. "She's the finest possible creature—of course you flatter yourself that you know it. But I know it, quite as well as you possibly can—by which I mean a good deal better yet; and the tune to which I'm ready to prove my faith compares favourably enough, I think, with anything *you* can do. I don't say it because she's my niece—that's nothing to me: I might have had fifty nieces, and I wouldn't have brought one of them to this place if I hadn't found her to my taste. I don't say I wouldn't have done something else, but I wouldn't have put up with her presence. Kate's presence, by good fortune, I marked early; Kate's presence—unluckily for *you*—is everything I could possibly wish; Kate's presence is, in short, as fine as you know, and I've been keeping it for the comfort of my declining years. I've watched it long; I've been saving it up and letting it, as you say of investments, appreciate, and you may judge whether, now it has begun to pay so, I'm likely to consent to treat for it with any but a high bidder. I can do the best with her, and I've my idea of the best."

"Oh, I quite conceive," said Densher, "that your idea of the best isn't me."

It was an oddity of Mrs. Lowder's that her face in speech was like a lighted window at night, but that silence immediately drew the curtain. The occasion for reply allowed by her silence was never easy to take; yet she was still less easy to interrupt. The great glaze of her surface, at all events, gave her visitor no present help. "I didn't ask you to come to hear what it isn't—I asked you to come to hear what it is."

"Of course," Densher laughed, "it's very great indeed."

His hostess went on as if his contribution to the subject were barely relevant. "I want to see her high, high up—high up and in the light."

"Ah, you naturally want to marry her to a duke, and are eager to smooth away any hitch."

She gave him so, on this, the mere effect of the drawn blind that it quite forced him, at first, into the sense, possibly just, of having affected her as flip pant, perhaps even as low. He had been looked at so, in blighted moments of presumptuous youth, by big cold public men, but never, so far as he could recall, by any private lady. More than anything yet it gave him the measure of his companion's subtlety, and thereby of Kate's possible career. "Don't be *too* impossible!"—he feared from his friend, for a moment, some such answer as that; and then felt, as she spoke otherwise, as if she were letting him off easily. "I want her to marry a great man." That was all; but, more and more, it was enough; and if it hadn't been her next words would have made it so. "And I think of her what I think. There you are."

They sat for a little face to face upon it, and he was conscious of something deeper still, of something she wished him to understand if he only would. To that extent she did appeal—appealed to the intelligence she desired to show she believed him to possess. He was meanwhile, at all events, not the man wholly to fail of comprehension. "Of course I'm aware how little I can answer to any fond, proud dream. You've a view—a magnificent one; into which I perfectly enter. I thoroughly understand what I'm not, and I'm much obliged to you for not reminding me of it in any rougher way." She said nothing—she kept that up; it might even have been to let him go further, if he was capable of it, in the way of poorness of spirit. It was one of those cases in which a man couldn't show, if he showed at all, save for poor; unless indeed he preferred to show for asinine. It was the plain truth: he *was*—on Mrs. Lowder's basis, the only one in question—a very small quantity, and he did know, damnably, what made quantities large. He desired to be perfectly simple; yet in the midst of that effort a deeper apprehension throbbed. Aunt Maud clearly conveyed it, though he couldn't later on have said how. "You don't really matter, I believe, so much as you think, and I'm not going to make you a martyr by banishing you. Your performances with Kate in the Park are ridiculous so far as they're meant as consideration for me; and I had much rather see you myself—since you're, in your way, my dear young man, delightful—and arrange with you, count with you, as I easily, as I perfectly should. Do you suppose me so stupid as to quarrel with you if it's not really necessary? It won't—it would be too absurd!—*be* necessary. I can bite your head off any day, any day I really open my mouth; and I'm dealing with you now, see—and successfully judge—without opening it. I do things handsomely all round—I place you in the presence of the plan with which, from the moment it's a case of taking you seriously, you're incompatible. Come then as near it as you like, walk all round it—don't be afraid you'll hurt it!—and live on with it before you."

He afterwards felt that if she hadn't absolutely phrased all this it was because she so soon made him out as going with her far enough. He was so pleasantly affected by her asking no promise of him, her not proposing he should pay for her indulgence by his word of honour not to interfere, that he gave her a kind of general assurance of esteem. Immediately afterwards, then, he spoke of these things to Kate, and what then came back to him first of all was the way he had said to her—he mentioned it to the girl—very much as one of a pair of lovers says in a rupture by mutual consent: "I hope immensely, of course, that you'll always regard me as a friend." This had perhaps been going far—he submitted it all to Kate; but really there had been so much in it that it was to be looked at, as they might say, wholly in its own light. Other things than those we have presented had come up before the close of his scene with Aunt Maud, but this matter of her not treating him as a peril of the first order easily predominated. There was moreover plenty to talk about on the occasion of his subsequent passage with our young woman, it having been put to him abruptly, the night before, that he might give himself a lift and do his newspaper a service—so flatteringly was the case expressed—by going, for fifteen or twenty weeks, to America. The idea of a series of letters from the United States from the strictly social point of view had for some time been nursed in the inner sanctuary at whose door he sat, and the moment was now deemed happy for letting it loose. The imprisoned thought had, in a word, on the opening of the door, flown straight out into Densher's face, or perched at least on his shoulder, making him look up in surprise from his mere inky office-table. His account of the matter to Kate was that he couldn't refuse—not being in a position, as yet, to refuse anything; but that his being chosen for such an errand confounded his sense of proportion. He was definite as to his scarce knowing how to measure the honour, which struck him as equivocal; he had not quite supposed himself the man for the class of job. This confused consciousness, he intimated, he had promptly enough betrayed to his manager; with the effect, however, of seeing the question surprisingly clear up. What it came to was that the sort of twaddle that was not in his chords was, unexpectedly, just what they happened this time not to want. They wanted his letters, for queer reasons, about as good as he could let them come; he was to play his own little tune and not be afraid; that was the whole point.

It would have been the whole, that is, had there not been a sharper one still in the circumstance that he was to start at once. His mission, as they called it at the office, would probably be over by the end of June, which was desirable; but to bring that about he must now not lose a week; his inquiries, he understood, were to cover the whole ground, and there were reasons of State—reasons operating at the seat of empire in Fleet Street—why the nail should be struck on the head. Densher made no secret to Kate of his having asked for a day to decide; and his account of that matter was that he felt he owed it to her to speak to her first. She assured him on this that nothing so much as that scruple had yet shown her how they were bound together; she was clearly proud of his letting a thing of such importance depend on her; but she was clearer still as to his instant duty. She rejoiced in his prospect and urged him to his task; she should miss him intensely—of course she should miss him; but she made so little of it that she spoke with jubilation of what he would see and would do. She made so much of this last quantity that he laughed at her innocence, though also with scarce the heart to give her the real size of his drop in the daily bucket. He was struck at the same time with her happy grasp of what had really occurred in Fleet Street—all the more that it was his own final reading. He was to pull the subject up—that was just what they wanted; and it would take more than all the United States together, visit them each as he might, to let *him* down. It was just because he didn't nose about and wasn't the usual gossipmonger that they had picked him out; it was a branch of their correspondence with which they evidently wished a new tone associated, such a tone as, from now on, it would have always to take from his example.

"How you ought indeed, when you understand so well, to be a journalist's wife!" Densher exclaimed in admiration, even while she struck him as fairly hurrying him off.

But she was almost impatient of the praise. "What do you expect one *not* to understand when one cares for you?"

"Ah then, I'll put it otherwise and say 'How much you care for me!'"

"Yes," she assented; "it fairly redeems my stupidity. I *shall,* with a chance to show it," she added, "have some imagination for you."

She spoke of the future this time as so little contingent, that he felt a queerness of conscience in making her the report that he presently arrived at on what had passed for him with the real arbiter of their destiny. The way for that had been blocked a little by his news from Fleet Street; but in the crucible of their happy discussion this element soon melted into the other, and in the mixture that ensued the parts were not to be distinguished. The young man moreover, before taking his leave, was to see why Kate had just spoken of the future as if they now really possessed it, and was to come to the vision by a devious way that deepened the final cheer. Their faces were turned to the illumined quarter as soon as he had answered her question in respect to the appearance of their being able to play a waiting game with success. It was for the possibility of that appearance that she had, a few days before, so earnestly pressed him to see her aunt; and if after his hour with that lady it had not struck Densher that he had seen her to the happiest purpose the poor facts flushed with a better meaning as Kate, one by one, took them up.

"If she consents to your coming, why isn't that everything?"

"It *is* everything; everything *she* thinks it. It's the probability—I mean as Mrs. Lowder measures probability—that I may be prevented from becoming a complication for her by some arrangement, *any* arrangement, through which you shall see me often and easily. She's sure of my want of money, and that gives her time. She believes in my having a certain amount of delicacy, in my wishing to better my state before I put the pistol to your head in respect to sharing it. The time that will take figures for her as the time that will help her if she doesn't spoil her chance by treating me badly. She doesn't at all wish moreover," Densher went on, "to treat me badly, for I believe, upon my honour, funny as it may sound to you, that she personally rather likes me, and that if you weren't in question I might almost become her pet young man. She doesn't disparage intellect and culture—quite the contrary; she wants them to adorn her board and be named in her programme; and I'm sure it has sometimes cost her a real pang that I should be so desirable, at once, and so impossible." He paused a moment, and his companion then saw that a strange smile was in his face—a smile as strange even as the adjunct, in her own, of this informing vision. "I quite suspect her of believing that, if the truth were known, she likes me literally better than—deep down—you yourself do: wherefore she does me the honour to think that I may be safely left to kill my own cause. There, as I say, comes in her margin. I'm not the sort of stuff of romance that wears, that washes, that survives use, that resists familiarity. Once in any degree admit that, and your pride and prejudice will take care of the rest! the pride fed full, meanwhile, by the system she means to practise with you, and the prejudice excited by the comparison she'll enable you to make, from which I shall come off badly. She likes me, but she'll never like me so much as when she succeeded a little better in making me look wretched. For then *you'll* like me less."

Kate showed for this evocation a due interest, but no alarm; and it was a little as if to pay his tender cynicism back in kind that she after an instant replied: "I see, I see; what an immense affair she must think me! One was aware, but you deepen the impression."

"I think you'll make no mistake," said Densher, "in letting it go as deep as it will."

He had given her indeed, she made no scruple of showing, plenty to consider. "Her facing the music, her making you boldly as welcome as you say—that's an awfully big theory, you know, and worthy of all the other big things that, in one's acquaintance with people, give her a place so apart."

"Oh, she's grand," the young man conceded; "she's on the scale, altogether, of the car of Juggernaut which was a kind of image that came to me yesterday while I waited for her at Lancaster Gate. The things in your drawing-room there were like the forms of the strange idols, the mystic excrescences, with which one may suppose the front of the car to bristle."

"Yes, aren't they?" the girl returned; and they had, over all that aspect of their wonderful lady, one of those deep and free interchanges that made everything but confidence a false note for them. There were complications, there were questions; but they were so much more together than they were anything else. Kate uttered for a while no word of refutation of Aunt Maud's "big" diplomacy, and they left it there, as they would have left any other fine product, for a monument to her powers. But, Densher related further, he had had in other respects too the car of Juggernaut to face; he omitted nothing from his account of his visit, least of all the way Aunt Maud had frankly at last—though indeed only under artful pressure—fallen foul of his very type, his want of the right marks, his foreign accidents, his queer antecedents. She had told him he was but half a Briton, which, he granted Kate, would have been dreadful if he hadn't so let himself in for it.

"I was really curious, you see," he explained, "to find out from her what sort of queer creature, what sort of social anomaly, in the light of such conventions as hers, such an education as mine makes one pass for."

Kate said nothing for a little; but then, "Why should you care?" she asked.

"Oh," he laughed, "I like her so much; and then, for a man of my trade, her views, her spirit, are essentially a thing to get hold of; they belong to the great public mind that we meet at every turn and that we must keep setting up 'codes' with. Besides," he added, "I want to please her personally."

"Ah, yes, we must please her personally!" his companion echoed; and the words may represent all their definite recognition, at the time, of Densher's politic gain. They had in fact between this and his start for New York many matters to handle, and the question he now touched upon came up for Kate above all. She looked at him as if he had really told her aunt more of his immediate personal story than he had ever told herself. That, if it were so, was an accident, and it put him, for half an hour, on as much of the picture of his early years abroad, his migratory parents, his Swiss schools, his German university, as she had easy attention for. A man, he intimated, a man of their world, would have spotted him straight as to many of these points; a man of their world, so far as they had a world, would have been through the English mill. But it was none the less charming to make his confession to a woman; women had, in fact, for such differences, so much more imagination. Kate showed at present all his case could require; when she had had it from beginning to end she declared that she now made out more than ever yet of what she loved him for. She had herself, as a child, lived with some continuity in the world across the Channel, coming home again still a child; and had participated after that, in her teens, in her mother's brief but repeated retreats to Dresden, to Florence, to Biarritz, weak and expensive attempts at economy from which there stuck to her—though in general coldly expressed, through the instinctive avoidance of cheap raptures—the religion of foreign things. When it was revealed to her how many more foreign things were in Merton Densher than he had hitherto taken the trouble to catalogue, she almost faced him as if he were a map of the continent or a handsome present of a delightful new "Murray." He hadn't meant to swagger, he had rather meant to plead, though with Mrs. Lowder he had meant also a little to explain. His father had been, in strange countries, in twenty settlements of the English, British chaplain, resident or occasional, and had had for years the unusual luck of never wanting a billet. His career abroad had therefore been unbroken, and, as his stipend had never been great, he had educated his children at the smallest cost, in the schools nearest; which was also a saving of railway fares. Densher's mother, it further appeared, had practised on her side a distinguished industry, to the success of which—so far as success ever crowned it—this period of exile had much contributed: she copied, patient lady, famous pictures in great museums, having begun with a happy natural gift and taking in betimes the scale of her opportunity. Copyists abroad of course swarmed, but Mrs. Densher had had a sense and a hand of her own, had arrived at a perfection that persuaded, that even deceived, and that made the disposal of her work blissfully usual. Her son, who had lost her, held her image sacred, and the effect of his telling Kate all about her, as well as about other matters until then mixed and dim, was to render his history rich, his sources full, his outline anything but common. He had come round, he had come back, he insisted abundantly, to being a Briton: his Cambridge years, his happy connection, as it had proved, with his father's college, amply certified to that, to say nothing of his subsequent plunge into London, which filled up the measure. But brave enough though his descent to English earth, he had passed, by the way, through zones of air that had left their ruffle on his wings, had been exposed to initiations ineffaceable. Something had happened to him that could never be undone.

When Kate Croy said to him as much he besought her not to insist, declaring that this indeed was what was too much the matter with him, that he had been but too probably spoiled for native, for insular use. On which, not unnaturally, she insisted the more, assuring him, without mitigation, that if he was complicated and brilliant she wouldn't for the world have had him any thing less; so that he was reduced in the end to accusing her of putting the dreadful truth to him in the hollow guise of flattery. She was making out how abnormal he was in order that she might eventually find him impossible; and, as she could fully make it out but with his aid, she had to bribe him by feigned delight to help her. If her last word for him, in the connection, was that the way he saw himself was just a precious proof the more of his having tasted of the tree and being thereby prepared to assist her to eat, this gives the happy tone of their whole talk, the measure of the flight of time in the near presence of his settled departure. Kate showed, however, that she was to be more literally taken when she spoke of the relief Aunt Maud would draw from the prospect of his absence.

"Yet one can scarcely see why," he replied, "when she fears me so little."

His friend weighed his objection. "Your idea is that she likes you so much that she'll even go so far as to regret losing you?"

Well, he saw it in their constant comprehensive way. "Since what she builds on is the gradual process of your alienation, she may take the view that the process constantly requires me. Mustn't I be there to keep it going? It's in my exile that it may languish."

He went on with that fantasy, but at this point Kate ceased to attend. He saw after a little that she had been following some thought of her own, and he had been feeling the growth of something determinant even through the extravagance of much of the pleasantry, the warm, transparent irony, into which their livelier intimacy kept plunging like a confident swimmer. Suddenly she said to him with extraordinary beauty: "I engage myself to you for ever."

The beauty was in everything, and he could have separated nothing—couldn't have thought of her face as distinct from the whole joy. Yet her face had a new light. "And I pledge you—I call God to witness!—every spark of my faith; I give you every drop of my life." That was all, for the moment, but it was enough, and it was almost as quiet as if it were nothing. They were in the open air, in an alley of the Gardens; the great space, which seemed to arch just then higher and spread wider for them, threw them back into deep concentration. They moved by a common instinct to a spot, within sight, that struck them as fairly sequestered, and there, before their time together was spent, they had extorted from concentration every advance it could make them. They had exchanged vows and tokens, sealed their rich compact, solemnized, so far as breathed words and murmured sounds and lighted eyes and clasped hands could do it, their agreement to belong only, and to belong tremendously, to each other. They were to leave the place accordingly an affianced couple; but before they left it other things still had passed. Densher had declared his horror of bringing to a premature end her happy relation with her aunt; and they had worked round together to a high level of wisdom and patience. Kate's free profession was that she wished not to deprive *him* of Mrs. Lowder's countenance, which, in the long run, she was convinced he would continue to enjoy; and as, by a blessed turn, Aunt Maud had demanded of him no promise that would tie his hands, they should be able to cultivate their destiny in their own way and yet remain loyal. One difficulty alone stood out, which Densher named.

"Of course it will never do—we must remember that—from the moment you allow her to found hopes of you for any one else in particular. So long as her view is content to remain as general as at present appears, I don't see that we deceive her. At a given moment, you see, she must be undeceived: the only thing therefore is to be ready for the moment and to face it. Only, after all, in that case," the young man observed, "one doesn't quite make out what we shall have got from her."

"What she'll have got from *us?"* Kate inquired with a smile. "What she'll have got from us," the girl went on, "is her own affair—it's for *her* to measure. I asked her for nothing," she added; "I never put myself upon her. She must take her risks, and she surely understands them. What we shall have got from her is what we've already spoken of," Kate further explained; "it's that we shall have gained time. And so, for that matter, will she."

Densher gazed a little at all this clearness; his gaze was not at the present hour into romantic obscurity. "Yes; no doubt, in our particular situation, time's everything. And then there's the joy of it."

She hesitated. "Of our secret?"

"Not so much perhaps of our secret in itself, but of what's represented and, as we must somehow feel, protected and made deeper and closer by it." And his fine face, relaxed into happiness, covered her with all his meaning. "Our being as we are."

It was as if for a moment she let the meaning sink into her. "So gone?"

"So gone. So extremely gone. However," he smiled, "we shall go a good deal further." Her answer to which was only the softness of her silence—a silence that looked out for them both at the far reach of their prospect. This was immense, and they thus took final possession of it. They were practically united and they were splendidly strong; but there were other things—things they were precisely strong enough to be able successfully to count with and safely to allow for; in consequence of which they would, for the present, subject to some better reason, keep their understanding to themselves. It was not indeed, however, till after one more observation of Densher's that they felt the question completely straightened out. "The only thing of course is that she may any day absolutely put it to you."

Kate considered. "Ask me where, on my honour, we are? She may, naturally; but I doubt if in fact she will. While you're away she'll make the most of it. She'll leave me alone."

"But there'll be my letters."

The girl faced his letters. "Very, very many?"

"Very, very, very many—more than ever; and you know what that is! And then," Densher added, "there'll be yours."

"Oh, I shan't leave mine on the hall-table. I shall post them myself."

He looked at her a moment. "Do you think then I had best address you elsewhere?" After which, before she could quite answer, he added with some emphasis: "I'd rather not, you know. It's straighter."

She might again have just waited. "Of course it's straighter. Don't be afraid I shan't be straight. Address me," she continued, "where you like. I shall be proud enough of its being known you write to me."

He turned it over for the last clearness. "Even at the risk of its really bringing down the inquisition?"

Well, the last clearness now filled her. "I'm not afraid of the inquisition. If she asks if there's anything definite between us, I know perfectly what I shall say."

"That I *am,* of course, 'gone' for you?"

"That I love you as I shall never in my life love any one else, and that she can make what she likes of that." She said it out so splendidly that it was like a new profession of faith, the fulness of a tide breaking through; and the effect of that, in turn, was to make her companion meet her with such eyes that she had time again before he could otherwise speak. "Besides, she's just as likely to ask *you."*

"Not while I'm away."

"Then when you come back."

"Well then," said Densher, "we shall have had our particular joy. But what I feel is," he candidly added, "that, by an idea of her own, her superior policy, she *won't* ask me. She'll let me off. I shan't have to lie to her."

"It will be left all to me?" asked Kate.

"All to you!" he tenderly laughed.

But it was, oddly, the very next moment as if he had perhaps been a shade too candid. His discrimination seemed to mark a possible, a natural reality, a reality not wholly disallowed by the account the girl had just given of her own intention. There *was* a difference in the air—even if none other than the supposedly usual difference in truth between man and woman; and it was almost as if the sense of this provoked her. She seemed to cast about an instant, and then she went back a little resentfully to something she had suffered to pass a minute before. She appeared to take up rather more seriously than she need the joke about her freedom to deceive. Yet she did this too in a beautiful way. "Men are too stupid—even you. You didn't understand just now why, if I post my letters myself, it won't be for any thing so vulgar as to hide them."

"Oh, you said—for the pleasure."

"Yes; but you didn't, you don't understand what the pleasure may be. There are refinements——!" she more patiently dropped. "I mean of consciousness, of sensation, of appreciation," she went on. "No," she sadly insisted—*"men* don't know. They know, in such matters, almost nothing but what women show them."

This was one of the speeches, frequent in her, that, liberally, joyfully, intensely adopted and, in itself, as might be, embraced, drew him again as close to her, and held him as long, as their conditions permitted. "Then that's exactly why we've such an abysmal need of you!"

BOOK THIRD

V

The two ladies who, in advance of the Swiss season, had been warned that their design was unconsidered, that the passes would not be clear, nor the air mild, nor the inns open—the two ladies who, characteristically, had braved a good deal of possibly interested remonstrance were finding themselves, as their adventure turned out, wonderfully sustained. It was the judgment of the head-waiters and other functionaries on the Italian lakes that approved itself now as interested; they themselves had been conscious of impatiences, of bolder dreams—at least the younger had; so that one of the things they made out together—making out as they did an endless variety—was that in those operatic palaces of the Villa d'Este, of Cadenabbia, of Pallanza and Stresa, lone women, however reinforced by a travelling-library of instructive volumes, were apt to be beguiled and undone. Their flights of fancy moreover had been modest; they had for instance risked nothing vital in hoping to make their way by the Brünig. They were making it in fact happily enough as we meet them, and were only wishing that, for the wondrous beauty of the early high-climbing spring, it might have been longer and the places to pause and rest more numerous.

Such at least had been the intimated attitude of Mrs. Stringham, the elder of the companions, who had her own view of the impatiences of the younger, to which, however, she offered an opposition but of the most circuitous. She moved, the admirable Mrs. Stringham, in a fine cloud of observation and suspicion; she was in the position, as she believed, of knowing much more about Milly Theale than Milly herself knew, and yet of having to darken her knowledge as well as make it active. The woman in the world least formed by nature, as she was quite aware, for duplicities and labyrinths, she found herself dedicated to personal subtlety by a new set of circumstances, above all by a new personal relation; had now in fact to recognise that an education in the occult—she could scarce say what to call it—had begun for her the day she left New York with Mildred. She had come on from Boston for that purpose; had seen little of the girl—or rather had seen her but briefly, for Mrs. Stringham, when she saw anything at all, saw much, saw everything—before accepting her proposal; and had accordingly placed herself, by her act, in a boat that she more and more estimated as, humanly speaking, of the biggest, though likewise, no doubt, in many ways, by reason of its size, of the safest. In Boston, the winter before, the young lady in whom we are interested had, on the spot, deeply, yet almost tacitly, appealed to her, dropped into her mind the shy conceit of some assistance, some devotion to render. Mrs. Stringham's little life had often been visited by shy conceits—secret dreams that had fluttered their hour between its narrow walls without, for any great part, so much as mustering courage to look out of its rather dim windows. But this imagination—the fancy of a possible link with the remarkable young thing from New York—*had* mustered courage: had perched, on the instant, at the clearest look-out it could find, and might be said to have remained there till, only a few months later, it had caught, in surprise and joy, the unmistakable flash of a signal.

Milly Theale had Boston friends, such as they were, and of recent making; and it was understood that her visit to them—a visit that was not to be meagre—had been undertaken, after a series of bereavements, in the interest of the particular peace that New York could not give. It was recognised, liberally enough, that there were many things—perhaps even too many—New York *could* give; but this was felt to make no difference in the constant fact that what you had most to do, under the discipline of life, or of death, was really to feel your situation as grave. Boston could help you to that as nothing else could, and it had extended to Milly, by every presumption, some such measure of assistance. Mrs. Stringham was never to forget—for the moment had not faded, nor the infinitely fine vibration it set up in any degree ceased—her own first sight of the striking apparition, then unheralded and unexplained: the slim, constantly pale, delicately haggard, anomalously, agreeably angular young person, of not more than two-and-twenty in spite of her marks, whose hair was some how exceptionally red even for the real thing, which it innocently confessed to being, and whose clothes were remarkably black even for robes of mourning, which was the meaning they expressed. It was New York mourning, it was New York hair, it was a New York history, confused as yet, but multitudinous, of the loss of parents, brothers, sisters, almost every human appendage, all on a scale and with a sweep that had required the greater stage; it was a New York legend of affecting, of romantic isolation, and, beyond everything, it was by most accounts, in respect to the mass of money so piled on the girl's back, a set of New York possibilities. She was alone, she was stricken, she was rich, and, in particular, she was strange—a combination in itself of a nature to engage Mrs. Stringham's attention. But it was the strangeness that most determined our good lady's sympathy, convinced as she was that it was much greater than any one else—any one but the sole Susan Stringham—supposed. Susan privately settled it that Boston was not in the least seeing her, was only occupied with her seeing Boston, and that any assumed affinity between the two characters was delusive and vain. She was seeing her, and she had quite the deepest moment of her life in now obeying the instinct to conceal the vision. She couldn't explain it—no one would understand. They would say clever Boston things—Mrs. Stringham was from Burlington, Vermont, which she boldly upheld as the real heart of New England, Boston being "too far south"—but they would only darken counsel.

There could be no better proof, than this quick intellectual split, of the impression made on our friend, who shone, herself, she was well aware, with but the reflected light of the admirable city. She too had had her discipline, but it had not made her striking; it had been prosaically usual, though doubtless a decent dose; and had only made her usual to match it—usual, that is, as Boston went. She had lost first her husband, and then her mother, with whom, on her husband's death, she had lived again; so that now, childless, she was but more sharply single than before. But she sat rather coldly light, having, as she called it, enough to live on—so far, that is, as she lived by bread alone: how little indeed she was regularly content with that diet appeared from the name she had made—Susan Shepherd Stringham—as a contributor to the best magazines. She wrote short stories, and she fondly believed she had her "note," the art of showing New England without showing it wholly in the kitchen. She had not herself been brought up in the kitchen; she knew others who had not; and to speak for them had thus become with her a literary mission. To *be* in truth literary had ever been her dearest thought, the thought that kept her bright little nippers perpetually in position. There were masters, models, celebrities, mainly foreign, whom she finely accounted so and in whose light she ingeniously laboured; there were others whom, however chattered about, she ranked with the inane, for she was full of discrimination; but all categories failed her—they ceased at least to signify—as soon as she found herself in presence of the real thing, the romantic life itself. That was what she saw in Mildred—what positively made her hand a while tremble too much for the pen. She had had, it seemed to her, a revelation—such as even New England refined and grammatical couldn't give; and, all made up as she was of small neat memories and ingenuities, little industries and ambitions, mixed with something moral, personal, that was still more intensely responsive, she felt her new friend would have done her an ill turn if their friendship shouldn't develop, and yet that nothing would be left of anything else if it should. It was for the surrender of everything else that she was, however, quite prepared, and while she went about her usual Boston business with her usual Boston probity she was really all the while holding herself. She wore her "handsome" felt hat, so Tyrolese, yet some how, though feathered from the eagle's wing, so truly domestic, with the same straightness and security; she attached her fur boa with the same honest precautions; she preserved her balance on the ice-slopes with the same practised skill; she opened, each evening, her "Transcript" with the same interfusion of suspense and resignation; she attended her almost daily concert with the same expenditure of patience and the same economy of passion; she flitted in and out of the Public Library with the air of conscientiously returning or bravely carrying off in her pocket the key of knowledge itself; and finally—it was what she most did—she watched the thin trickle of a fictive "love-interest" through that somewhat serpentine channel, in the magazines, which she mainly managed to keep clear for it. But the real thing, all the while, was elsewhere; the real thing had gone back to New York, leaving behind it the two unsolved questions, quite distinct, of why it *was* real, and whether she should ever be so near it again.

For the figure to which these questions attached themselves she had found a convenient description—she thought of it for herself, always, as that of a girl with a background. The great reality was in the fact that, very soon, after but two or three meetings, the girl with the background, the girl with the crown of old gold and the mourning that was not as the mourning of Boston, but at once more rebellious in its gloom and more frivolous in its frills, had told her she had never seen any one like her. They had met thus as opposed curiosities, and that simple remark of Milly's—if simple it was—became the most important thing that had ever happened to her; it deprived the love-interest, for the time, of actuality and even of pertinence; it moved her first, in short, in a high degree, to gratitude, and then to no small compassion. Yet in respect to this relation at least it was what did prove the key of knowledge; it lighted up as nothing else could do the poor young woman's history. That the potential heiress of all the ages should never have seen any one like a mere typical subscriber, after all, to the "Transcript" was a truth that—in especial as announced with modesty, with humility, with regret—described a situation. It laid upon the elder woman, as to the void to be filled, a weight of responsibility; but in particular it led her to ask whom poor Mildred *had* then seen, and what range of contacts it had taken to produce such queer surprises. That was really the inquiry that had ended by clearing the air: the key of knowledge was felt to click in the lock from the moment it flashed upon Mrs. Stringham that her friend had been starved for culture. Culture was what she herself represented for her, and it was living up to that principle that would surely prove the great business. She knew, the clever lady, what the principle itself represented, and the limits of her own store; and a certain alarm would have grown upon her if something else hadn't grown faster.

This was, fortunately for her—and we give it in her own words—the sense of a harrowing pathos. That, primarily, was what appealed to her, what seemed to open the door of romance for her still wider than any, than a still more reckless, connection with the "picture-papers." For such was essentially the point: it was rich, romantic, abysmal, to have, as was evident, thousands and thousands a year, to have youth and intelligence and if not beauty, at least, in equal measure, a high, dim, charming, ambiguous oddity, which was even better, and then on top of all to enjoy boundless freedom, the freedom of the wind in the desert—it was unspeakably touching to be so equipped and yet to have been reduced by fortune to little humble-minded mistakes.

It brought our friend's imagination back again to New York, where aberrations were so possible in the intellectual sphere, and it in fact caused a visit she presently paid there to overflow with interest. As Milly had beautifully invited her, so she would hold out if she could against the strain of so much confidence in her mind; and the remarkable thing was that even at the end of three weeks she *had* held out. But by this time her mind had grown comparatively bold and free; it was dealing with new quantities, a different proportion altogether—and that had made for refreshment: she had accordingly gone home in convenient possession of her subject. New York was vast, New York was startling, with strange histories, with wild cosmopolite backward generations that accounted for anything; and to have got nearer the luxuriant tribe of which the rare creature was the final flower, the immense, extravagant, unregulated cluster, with free-living ancestors, handsome dead cousins, lurid uncles, beautiful vanished aunts, persons all busts and curls, preserved, though so exposed, in the marble of famous French chisels—all this, to say nothing of the effect of closer growths of the stem, was to have had one's small world-space both crowded and enlarged. Our couple had at all events effected an exchange; the elder friend had been as consciously intellectual as possible, and the younger, abounding in personal revelation, had been as unconsciously distinguished. This was poetry—it was also history—Mrs. Stringham thought, to a finer tune even than Maeterlink and Pater, than Marbot and Gregorovius. She appointed occasions for the reading of these authors with her hostess, rather perhaps than actually achieved great spans; but what they managed and what they missed speedily sank for her into the dim depths of the merely relative, so quickly, so strongly had she clutched her central clue. All her scruples and hesitations, all her anxious enthusiasms, had reduced themselves to a single alarm—the fear that she really might act on her companion clumsily and coarsely. She was positively afraid of what she might do to her, and to avoid that, to avoid it with piety and passion, to do, rather, nothing at all, to leave her untouched because no touch one could apply, however light, however just, however earnest and anxious, would be half good enough, would be anything but an ugly smutch upon perfection—this now imposed itself as a consistent, an inspiring thought.

Less than a month after the event that had so determined Mrs. Stringham's attitude—close upon the heels, that is, of her return from New York—she was reached by a proposal that brought up for her the kind of question her delicacy might have to contend with. Would she start for Europe with her young friend at the earliest possible date, and should she be willing to do so without making conditions? The inquiry was launched by wire; explanations, in sufficiency, were promised; extreme urgency was suggested, and a general surrender invited. It was to the honour of her sincerity that she made the surrender on the spot, though it was not perhaps altogether to that of her logic. She had wanted, very consciously, from the first, to give something up for her new acquaintance, but she had now no doubt that she was practically giving up all. What settled this was the fulness of a particular impression, the impression that had throughout more and more supported her and which she would have uttered so far as she might by saying that the charm of the creature was positively in the creature's greatness. She would have been content so to leave it; unless indeed she had said, more familiarly, that Mildred was the biggest impression of her life. That was at all events the biggest account of her, and none but a big, clearly, would do. Her situation, as such things were called, was on the grand scale; but it still was not that. It was her nature, once for all—a nature that reminded Mrs. Stringham of the term always used in the newspapers about the great new steamers, the inordinate number of "feet of water" they drew; so that if, in your little boat, you had chosen to hover and approach, you had but yourself to thank, when once motion was started, for the way the draught pulled you. Milly drew the feet of water, and odd though it might seem that a lonely girl, who was not robust and who hated sound and show, should stir the stream like a leviathan, her companion floated off with the sense of rocking violently at her side. More than prepared, however, for that excitement, Mrs. Stringham mainly failed of ease in respect to her own consistency. To attach herself for an indefinite time seemed a roundabout way of holding her hands off. If she wished to be sure of neither touching nor smutching, the straighter plan would doubtless have been not to keep her friend within reach. This in fact she fully recognised, and with it the degree to which she desired that the girl should lead her life, a life certain to be so much finer than that of anybody else. The difficulty, however, by good fortune, cleared away as soon as she had further recognised, as she was speedily able to do, that she, Susan Shepherd—the name with which Milly for the most part amused herself—was *not* anybody else. She had renounced that character; she had now no life to lead; and she honestly believed that she was thus supremely equipped for leading Milly's own. No other person whatever, she was sure, had to an equal degree this qualification, and it was really to assert it that she fondly embarked.

Many things, though not in many weeks, had come and gone since then, and one of the best of them, doubtless, had been the voyage itself, by the happy southern course, to the succession of Mediterranean ports, with the dazzled wind-up at Naples. Two or three others had preceded this; incidents, indeed rather lively marks, of their last fortnight at home, and one of which had determined on Mrs. Stringham's part a rush to New York, forty-eight breathless hours there, previous to her final rally. But the great sustained sea-light had drunk up the rest of the picture, so that for many days other questions and other possibilities sounded with as little effect as a trio of penny whistles might sound in a Wagner overture. It was the Wagner overture that practically prevailed, up through Italy, where Milly had already been, still further up and across the Alps, which were also partly known to Mrs. Stringham; only perhaps "taken" to a time not wholly congruous, hurried in fact on account of the girl's high restlessness. She had been expected, she had frankly promised, to be restless—that was partly why she was "great"—or was a consequence, at any rate, if not a cause; yet she had not perhaps altogether announced herself as straining so hard at the cord. It was familiar, it was beautiful to Mrs. Stringham that she had arrears to make up, the chances that had lapsed for her through the wanton ways of forefathers fond of Paris, but not of its higher sides, and fond almost of nothing else; but the vagueness, the openness, the eagerness without point and the interest without pause—all a part of the charm of her oddity as at first presented—had become more striking in proportion as they triumphed over movement and change. She had arts and idiosyncrasies of which no great account could have been given, but which were a daily grace if you lived with them; such as the art of being almost tragically impatient and yet making it as light as air; of being inexplicably sad and yet making it as clear as noon; of being unmistakably gay, and yet making it as soft as dusk. Mrs. Stringham by this time understood everything, was more than ever confirmed in wonder and admiration, in her view that it was life enough simply to feel her companion's feelings; but there were special keys she had not yet added to her bunch, impressions that, of a sudden, were apt to affect her as new.

This particular day on the great Swiss road had been, for some reason, full of them, and they referred themselves, provisionally, to some deeper depth than she had touched—though into two or three such depths, it must be added, she had peeped long enough to find herself suddenly draw back. It was not Milly's unpacified state, in short, that now troubled her—though certainly, as Europe was the great American sedative, the failure was to some extent to be noted: it was the suspected presence of something behind it—which, however, could scarcely have taken its place there since their departure. What any fresh motive of unrest could suddenly have sprung from was, in short, not to be divined. It was but half an explanation to say that excitement, for each of them, had naturally dropped, and that what they had left behind, or tried to—the great serious facts of life, as Mrs. Stringham liked to call them—was once more coming into sight as objects loom through smoke when smoke begins to clear; for these were general appearances from which the girl's own aspect, her really larger vagueness, seemed rather to disconnect itself. The nearest approach to a personal anxiety indulged in as yet by the elder lady was on her taking occasion to wonder if what she had more than anything else got hold of mightn't be one of the finer, one of the finest, one of the rarest—as she called it so that she might call it nothing worse—cases of American intensity. She had just had a moment of alarm—asked herself if her young friend were merely going to treat her to some complicated drama of nerves. At the end of a week, however, with their further progress, her young friend had effectively answered the question and given her the impression, indistinct indeed as yet, of something that had a reality compared with which the nervous explanation would have been coarse. Mrs. Stringham found herself from that hour, in other words, in presence of an explanation that remained a muffled and intangible form, but that, assuredly, should it take on sharpness, would explain everything and more than everything, would become instantly the light in which Milly was to be read.

Such a matter as this may at all events speak of the style in which our young woman could affect those who were near her, may testify to the sort of interest she could inspire. She worked—and seemingly quite without design—upon the sympathy, the curiosity, the fancy of her associates, and we shall really ourselves scarce otherwise come closer to her than by feeling their impression and sharing, if need be, their confusion. She reduced them, Mrs. Stringham would have said, reduced them to a consenting bewilderment; which was precisely, for that good lady, on a last analysis, what was most in harmony with her greatness. She exceeded, escaped measure, was surprising only because *they* were so far from great. Thus it was that on this wondrous day on the Brünig the spell of watching her had grown more than ever irresistible; a proof of what—or of a part of what—Mrs. Stringham had, with all the rest, been reduced to. She had almost the sense of tracking her young friend as if at a given moment to pounce. She knew she shouldn't pounce, she hadn't come out to pounce; yet she felt her attention secretive, all the same, and her observation scientific. She struck herself as hovering like a spy, applying tests, laying traps, concealing signs. This would last, however, only till she should fairly know what was the matter; and to watch was, after all, meanwhile, a way of clinging to the girl, not less than an occupation, a satisfaction in itself. The pleasure of watching, moreover, if a reason were needed, came from a sense of her beauty. Her beauty hadn't at all originally seemed a part of the situation, and Mrs. Stringham had, even in the first flush of friendship, not named it, grossly, to any one; having seen early that, for stupid people—and who, she sometimes secretly asked herself, wasn't stupid?—it would take a great deal of explaining. She had learned not to mention it till it was mentioned first—which occasionally happened, but not too often; and then she was there in force. Then she both warmed to the perception that met her own perception, and disputed it, suspiciously, as to special items; while, in general, she had learned to refine even to the point of herself employing the word that most people employed. She employed it to pretend that she was also stupid and so have done with the matter; spoke of her friend as plain, as ugly even, in a case of especially dense insistence; but as, in appearance, so "awfully full of things." This was her own way of describing a face that, thanks, doubtless, to rather too much forehead, too much nose and too much mouth, together with too little mere conventional colour and conventional line, was expressive, irregular, exquisite, both for speech and for silence. When Milly smiled it was a public event—when she didn't it was a chapter of history. They had stopped, on the Brünig, for luncheon, and there had come up for them under the charm of the place the question of a longer stay.

Mrs. Stringham was now on the ground of thrilled recognitions, small sharp echoes of a past which she kept in a well-thumbed case, but which, on pressure of a spring and exposure to the air, still showed itself ticking as hard as an honest old watch. The embalmed "Europe" of her younger time had partly stood for three years of Switzerland, a term of continuous school at Vevey, with rewards of merit in the form of silver medals tied by blue ribbons and mild mountain-passes attacked with alpenstocks. It was the good girls who, in the holidays, were taken highest, and our friend could now judge, from what she supposed her familiarity with the minor peaks, that she had been one of the best. These reminiscences, sacred to-day because prepared in the hushed chambers of the past, had been part of the general train laid for the pair of sisters, daughters early fatherless, by their brave Vermont mother, who struck her at present as having apparently, almost like Columbus, worked out, all unassisted, a conception of the other side of the globe. She had focussed Vevey, by the light of nature, and with extraordinary completeness, at Burlington; after which she had embarked, sailed, landed, explored and, above all, made good her presence. She had given her daughters the five years in Switzerland and Germany that were to leave them ever afterwards a standard of comparison for all cycles of Cathay, and to stamp the younger in especial—Susan was the younger—with a character that, as Mrs. Stringham had often had occasion, through life, to say to herself, made all the difference. It made all the difference for Mrs. Stringham, over and over again and in the most remote connections, that, thanks to her parent's lonely, thrifty, hardy faith, she was a woman of the world. There were plenty of women who were all sorts of things that she wasn't, but who, on the other hand, were not that, and who didn't know *she* was (which she liked—it relegated them still further) and didn't know, either, how it enabled her to judge them. She had never seen herself so much in this light as during the actual phase of her associated, if slightly undirected, pilgrimage; and the consciousness gave perhaps to her plea for a pause more intensity than she knew. The irrecoverable days had come back to her from far off; they were part of the sense of the cool upper air and of everything else that hung like an indestructible scent to the torn garment of youth—the taste of honey and the luxury of milk, the sound of cattle-bells and the rush of streams, the fragrance of trodden balms and the dizziness of deep gorges.

Milly clearly felt these things too, but they affected her companion at moments—that was quite the way Mrs. Stringham would have expressed it—as the princess in a conventional tragedy might have affected the confidant if a personal emotion had ever been permitted to the latter. That a princess could only be a princess was a truth with which, essentially, a confidant, however responsive, had to live. Mrs. Stringham was a woman of the world, but Milly Theale was a princess, the only one she had yet had to deal with, and this in its way, too, made all the difference. It was a perfectly definite doom for the wearer—it was for every one else a perfectly palpable quality. It might have been, possibly, with its involved loneliness and other mysteries, the weight under which she fancied her companion's admirable head occasionally, and ever so submissively, bowed. Milly had quite assented at luncheon to their staying over, and had left her to look at rooms, settle questions, arrange about their keeping on their carriage and horses; cares that had now moreover fallen to Mrs. Stringham as a matter of course and that yet for some reason, on this occasion particularly, brought home to her—all agreeably, richly, almost grandly—what it was to live with the great. Her young friend had, in a sublime degree, a sense closed to the general question of difficulty, which she got rid of, furthermore, not in the least as one had seen many charming persons do, by merely passing it on to others. She kept it completely at a distance: it never entered the circle; the most plaintive confidant couldn't have dragged it in; and to tread the path of a confidant was accordingly to live exempt. Service was in other words so easy to render that the whole thing was like court life without the hardships. It came back of course to the question of money, and our observant lady had by this time repeatedly reflected that if one were talking of the "difference," it was just this, this incomparably and nothing else, that when all was said and done most made it. A less vulgarly, a less obviously purchasing or parading person she couldn't have imagined; but it was, all the same, the truth of truths that the girl couldn't get away from her wealth. She might leave her conscientious companion as freely alone with it as possible and never ask a question, scarce even tolerate a reference; but it was in the fine folds of the helplessly expensive little black frock that she drew over the grass as she now strolled vaguely off; it was in the curious and splendid coils of hair, "done" with no eye whatever to the *mode du jour,* that peeped from under the corresponding indifference of her hat, the merely personal tradition that suggested a sort of noble inelegance; it lurked between the leaves of the uncut but antiquated Tauchnitz volume of which, before going out, she had mechanically possessed herself. She couldn't dress it away, nor walk it away, nor read it away, nor think it away; she could neither smile it away in any dreamy absence nor blow it away in any softened sigh. She couldn't have lost it if she had tried—that was what it was to be really rich. It had to be *the* thing you were. When at the end of an hour she had not returned to the house Mrs. Stringham, though the bright afternoon was yet young, took, with precautions, the same direction, went to join her in case of her caring for a walk. But the purpose of joining her was in truth less distinct than that of a due regard for a possibly preferred detachment: so that, once more, the good lady proceeded with a quietness that made her slightly "underhand" even in her own eyes. She couldn't help that, however, and she didn't care, sure as she was that what she really wanted was not to overstep, but to stop in time. It was to be able to stop in time that she went softly, but she had on this occasion further to go than ever yet, for she followed in vain, and at last with some anxiety, the footpath she believed Milly to have taken. It wound up a hillside and into the higher Alpine meadows in which, all these last days, they had so often wanted, as they passed above or below, to stray; and then it obscured itself in a wood, but always going up, up, and with a small cluster of brown old high-perched chalets evidently for its goal. Mrs. Stringham reached in due course the chalets, and there received from a bewildered old woman, a very fearful person to behold, an indication that sufficiently guided her. The young lady had been seen not long before passing further on, over a crest and to a place where the way would drop again, as our unappeased inquirer found it, in fact, a quarter of an hour later, markedly and almost alarmingly to do. It led somewhere, yet apparently quite into space, for the great side of the mountain appeared, from where she pulled up, to fall away altogether, though probably but to some issue below and out of sight. Her uncertainty moreover was brief, for she next became aware of the presence on a fragment of rock, twenty yards off, of the Tauchnitz volume that the girl had brought out, and that therefore pointed to her shortly previous passage. She had rid herself of the book, which was an encumbrance, and meant of course to pick it up on her return; but as she hadn't yet picked it up what on earth had become of her? Mrs. Stringham, I hasten to add, was within a few moments to see; but it was quite an accident that she had not, before they were over, betrayed by her deeper agitation the fact of her own nearness.

The whole place, with the descent of the path and as a sequel to a sharp turn that was masked by rocks and shrubs, appeared to fall precipitously and to become a "view" pure and simple, a view of great extent and beauty, but thrown forward and vertiginous. Milly, with the promise of it from just above, had gone straight down to it, not stopping till it was all before her; and here, on what struck her friend as the dizzy edge of it, she was seated at her ease. The path somehow took care of itself and its final business, but the girl's seat was a slab of rock at the end of a short promontory or excrescence that merely pointed off to the right into gulfs of air and that was so placed by good fortune, if not by the worst, as to be at last completely visible. For Mrs. Stringham stifled a cry on taking in what she believed to be the danger of such a perch for a mere maiden; her liability to slip, to slide, to leap, to be precipitated by a single false movement, by a turn of the head—how could one tell? into whatever was beneath. A thousand thoughts, for the minute, roared in the poor lady's ears, but without reaching, as happened, Milly's. It was a commotion that left our observer intensely still and holding her breath. What had first been offered her was the possibility of a latent intention—however wild the idea—in such a posture; of some betrayed accordance of Milly's caprice with a horrible hidden obsession. But since Mrs. Stringham stood as motionless as if a sound, a syllable, must have produced the start that would be fatal, so even the lapse of a few seconds had a partly reassuring effect. It gave her time to receive the impression which, when she some minutes later softly retraced her steps, was to be the sharpest she carried away. This was the impression that if the girl was deeply and recklessly meditating there, she was not meditating a jump; she was on the contrary, as she sat, much more in a state of uplifted and unlimited possession that had nothing to gain from violence. She was looking down on the kingdoms of the earth, and though indeed that of itself might well go to the brain, it wouldn't be with a view of renouncing them. Was she choosing among them, or did she want them all? This question, before Mrs. Stringham had decided what to do, made others vain; in accordance with which she saw, or believed she did, that if it might be dangerous to call out, to sound in any way a surprise, it would probably be safe enough to withdraw as she had come. She watched a while longer, she held her breath, and she never knew afterwards what time had elapsed.

Not many minutes probably, yet they had not seemed few, and they had given her so much to think of, not only while creeping home, but while waiting afterwards at the inn, that she was still busy with them when, late in the afternoon, Milly reappeared. She had stopped at the point of the path where the Tauchnitz lay, had taken it up and, with the pencil attached to her watch-guard, had scrawled a word—*à bientôt!*—across the cover; then, even under the girl's continued delay, had measured time without a return of alarm. For she now saw that the great thing she had brought away was precisely a conviction that the future was not to exist for her princess in the form of any sharp or simple release from the human predicament. It wouldn't be for her a question of a flying leap and thereby of a quick escape. It would be a question of taking full in the face the whole assault of life, to the general muster of which indeed her face might have been directly presented as she sat there on her rock. Mrs. Stringham was thus able to say to herself, even after another interval of some length, that if her young friend still continued absent it wouldn't be because—whatever the opportunity—she had cut short the thread. She wouldn't have committed suicide; she knew herself unmistakably reserved for some more complicated passage; this was the very vision in which she had, with no little awe, been discovered. The image that thus remained with the elder lady kept the character of revelation. During the breathless minutes of her watch she had seen her companion afresh; the latter's type, aspect, marks, her history, her state, her beauty, her mystery, all unconsciously betrayed themselves to the Alpine air, and all had been gathered in again to feed Mrs. Stringham's flame. They are things that will more distinctly appear for us, and they are meanwhile briefly represented by the enthusiasm that was stronger on our friend's part than any doubt. It was a consciousness she was scarce yet used to carrying, but she had as beneath her feet a mine of something precious. She seemed to herself to stand near the mouth, not yet quite cleared. The mine but needed working and would certainly yield a treasure. She was not thinking, either, of Milly's gold.

VI

The girl said nothing, when they met, about the words scrawled on the Tauchnitz, and Mrs. Stringham then noticed that she had not the book with her. She had left it lying and probably would never remember it at all. Her comrade's decision was therefore quickly made not to speak of having followed her; and within five minutes of her return, wonderfully enough, the preoccupation denoted by her forgetfulness further declared itself. "Should you think me quite abominable if I were to say that after all——?"

Mrs. Stringham had already thought, with the first sound of the question, everything she was capable of thinking, and had immediately made such a sign that Milly's words gave place to visible relief at her assent. "You don't care for our stop here—you'd rather go straight on? We'll start then with the peep of to-morrow's dawn—or as early as you like; it's only rather late now to take the road again." And she smiled to show how she meant it for a joke that an instant onward rush was what the girl would have wished. "I bullied you into stopping," she added; "so it serves me right."

Milly made in general the most of her good friend's jokes; but she humoured this one a little absently. "Oh yes, you do bully me." And it was thus arranged between them, with no discussion at all, that they would resume their journey in the morning. The younger tourist's interest in the detail of the matter—in spite of a declaration from the elder that she would consent to be dragged anywhere—appeared almost immediately afterwards quite to lose itself; she promised, however, to think till supper of where, with the world all before them, they might go—supper having been ordered for such time as permitted of lighted candles. It had been agreed between them that lighted candles at wayside inns, in strange countries, amid mountain scenery, gave the evening meal a peculiar poetry—such being the mild adventures, the refinements of impression, that they, as they would have said, went in for. It was now as if, before this repast, Milly had designed to "lie down"; but at the end of three minutes more she was not lying down, she was saying instead, abruptly, with a transition that was like a jump of four thousand miles: "What was it that, in New York, on the ninth, when you saw him alone, Dr. Finch said to you?"

It was not till later that Mrs. Stringham fully knew why the question had startled her still more than its suddenness explained; though the effect of it even at the moment was almost to frighten her into a false answer. She had to think, to remember the occasion, the "ninth," in New York, the time she had seen Dr. Finch alone, and to recall what he had then said to her; and when everything had come back it was quite, at first, for a moment, as if he had said something that immensely mattered. He hadn't, however, in fact; it was only as if he might perhaps after all have been going to. It was on the sixth—within ten days of their sailing—that she had hurried from Boston under the alarm, a small but a sufficient shock, of hearing that Mildred had suddenly been taken ill, had had, from some obscure cause, such an upset as threatened to stay their journey. The bearing of the accident had happily soon announced itself as slight, and there had been, in the event, but a few hours of anxiety; the journey had been pronounced again not only possible, but, as representing "change," highly advisable; and if the zealous guest had had five minutes by herself with the doctor, that was, clearly, no more at his instance than at her own. Almost nothing had passed between them but an easy exchange of enthusiasms in respect to the remedial properties of "Europe"; and this assurance, as the facts came back to her, she was now able to give. "Nothing whatever, on my word of honour, that you mayn't know or mightn't then have known. I've no secret with him about you. What makes you suspect it? I don't quite make out how you know I did see him alone."

"No—you never told me," said Milly. "And I don't mean," she went on, "during the twenty-four hours while I was bad, when your putting your heads together was natural enough. I mean after I was better—the last thing before you went home."

Mrs. Stringham continued to wonder. "Who told you I saw him then?"

"He didn't himself—nor did you write me it afterwards. We speak of it now for the first time. That's exactly why!" Milly declared—with something in her face and voice that, the next moment, betrayed for her companion that she had really known nothing, had only conjectured and, chancing her charge, made a hit. Yet why had her mind been busy with the question? "But if you're not, as you now assure me, in his confidence," she smiled, "it's no matter."

"I'm not in his confidence, and he had nothing to confide. But are you feeling unwell?"

The elder woman was earnest for the truth, though the possibility she named was not at all the one that seemed to fit—witness the long climb Milly had just indulged in. The girl showed her constant white face, but that her friends had all learned to discount, and it was often brightest when superficially not bravest. She continued for a little mysteriously to smile. "I don't know—haven't really the least idea. But it might be well to find out."

Mrs. Stringham, at this, flared into sympathy. "Are you in trouble—in pain?"

"Not the least little bit. But I sometimes wonder——!"

"Yes"—she pressed: "wonder what?"

"Well, if I shall have much of it."

Mrs. Stringham stared. "Much of what? Not of pain?"

"Of everything. Of everything I have."

Anxiously again, tenderly, our friend cast about. "You 'have' everything; so that when you say 'much' of it——"

"I only mean," the girl broke in, "shall I have it for long? That is if I *have* got it."

She had at present the effect, a little, of confounding, or at least of perplexing her comrade, who was touched, who was always touched, by something helpless in her grace and abrupt in her turns, and yet actually half made out in her a sort of mocking light. "If you've got an ailment?"

"If I've got everything," Milly laughed.

"Ah, *that*—like almost nobody else."

"Then for how long?"

Mrs. Stringham's eyes entreated her; she had gone close to her, half enclosed her with urgent arms. "Do you want to see some one?" And then as the girl only met it with a slow headshake, though looking perhaps a shade more conscious: "We'll go straight to the best near doctor." This too, however, produced but a gaze of qualified assent and a silence, sweet and vague, that left everything open. Our friend decidedly lost herself. "Tell me, for God's sake, if you're in distress."

"I don't think I've really *everything,"* Milly said as if to explain—and as if also to put it pleasantly.

"But what on earth can I do for you?" The girl hesitated, then seemed on the point of being able to say; but suddenly changed and expressed herself otherwise. "Dear, dear thing—I'm only too happy!"

It brought them closer, but it rather confirmed Mrs. Stringham's doubt. "Then what's the matter?"

"That's the matter—that I can scarcely bear it."

"But what is it you think you haven't got?"

Milly waited another moment; then she found it, and found for it a dim show of joy. "The power to resist the bliss of what I *have!"*

Mrs. Stringham took it in—her sense of being "put off" with it, the possible, probable irony of it—and her tenderness renewed itself in the positive grimness of a long murmur. "Whom will you see?"—for it was as if they looked down from their height at a continent of doctors. "Where will you first go?"

Milly had for the third time her air of consideration; but she came back with it to her plea of some minutes before. "I'll tell you at supper—good-bye till then." And she left the room with a lightness that testified for her companion to something that again particularly pleased her in the renewed promise of motion. The odd passage just concluded, Mrs. Stringham mused as she once more sat alone with a hooked needle and a ball of silk, the "fine" work with which she was always provided—this mystifying mood had simply been precipitated, no doubt, by their prolonged halt, with which the girl hadn't really been in sympathy. One had only to admit that her complaint was in fact but the excess of the joy of life, and everything *did* then fit. She couldn't stop for the joy, but she could go on for it, and with the sense of going on she floated again, was restored to her great spaces. There was no evasion of any truth—so at least Susan Shepherd hoped—in one's sitting there while the twilight deepened and feeling still more finely that the position of this young lady was magnificent. The evening at that height had naturally turned to cold, and the travellers had bespoken a fire with their meal; the great Alpine road asserted its brave presence through the small panes of the low, clean windows, with incidents at the inn-door, the yellow *diligence,* the great waggons, the hurrying, hooded, private conveyances, reminders, for our fanciful friend, of old stories, old pictures, historic flights, escapes, pursuits, things that had happened, things indeed that by a sort of strange congruity helped her to read the meanings of the greatest interest into the relation in which she was now so deeply involved. It was natural that this record of the magnificence of her companion's position should strike her as, after all, the best meaning she could extract; for she herself was seated in the magnificence as in a court-carriage—she came back to that, and such a method of progression, such a view from crimson cushions, would evidently have a great deal more to give. By the time the candles were lighted for supper and the short, white curtains were drawn, Milly had reappeared, and the little scenic room had then all its romance. That charm moreover was far from broken by the words in which she, without further loss of time, satisfied her patient mate. "I want to go straight to London."

It was unexpected, corresponding with no view positively taken at their departure; when England had appeared, on the contrary, rather relegated and postponed—seen for the moment, as who should say, at the end of an avenue of preparations and introductions. London, in short, might have been supposed to be the crown, and to be achieved like a siege by gradual approaches. Milly's actual fine stride was therefore the more exciting, as any simplification almost always was to Mrs. Stringham; who, besides, was afterwards to recall as the very beginning of a drama the terms in which, between their smoky candles, the girl had put her preference and in which still other things had come up, come while the clank of waggon-chains in the sharp air reached their ears, with the stamp of hoofs, the rattle of buckets and the foreign questions, foreign answers, that were all alike a part of the cheery converse of the road. The girl brought it out in truth as she might have brought a huge confession, something she admitted herself shy about and that would seem to show her as frivolous; it had rolled over her that what she wanted of Europe was "people," so far as they were to be had, and that if her friend really wished to know, the vision of this same equivocal quantity was what had haunted her during their previous days, in museums and churches, and what was again spoiling for her the pure taste of scenery. She was all for scenery—yes; but she wanted it human and personal, and all she could say was that there would be in London—wouldn't there? more of that kind than anywhere else. She came back to her idea that if it wasn't for long—if nothing should happen to be so for *her*—why, the particular thing she spoke of would probably have most to give her in the time, would probably be less than anything else a waste of her remainder. She produced this last consideration indeed with such gaiety that Mrs. Stringham was not again disconcerted by it, was in fact quite ready—if talk of early dying was in order—to match it from her own future. Good, then; they would, eat and drink because of what might happen to-morrow; and they would direct their course from that moment with a view to such eating and drinking. They ate and drank that night, in truth, as if in the spirit of this decision; whereby the air, before they separated, felt itself the clearer.

It had cleared perhaps to a view only too extensive—extensive, that is, in proportion to the signs of life presented. The idea of "people" was not so entertained on Milly's part as to connect itself with particular persons, and the fact remained for each of the ladies that they would, completely unknown, disembark at Dover amid the completely unknowing. They had no relation already formed; this plea Mrs. Stringham put forward to see what it would produce. It produced nothing at first but the observation on the girl's side that what she had in mind was no thought of society nor of scraping acquaintance; nothing was further from her than to desire the opportunities represented for the compatriot in general by a trunkful of "letters." It wasn't a question, in short, of the people the compatriot was after; it was the human, the English picture itself, as they might see it in their own way—the world imagined always in what one had read and dreamed. Mrs. Stringham did every justice to this world, but when later on an occasion chanced to present itself, she made a point of not omitting to remark that it might be a comfort to know in advance even an individual. This still, however, failed in vulgar parlance, to "fetch" Milly, so that she had presently to go all the way. "Haven't I understood from you, for that matter, that you gave Mr. Densher something of a promise?"

There was a moment, on this, when Milly's look had to be taken as representing one of two things—either that she was completely vague about the promise or that Mr. Densher's name itself started no train. But she really couldn't be so vague about the promise, her interlocutress quickly saw, without attaching it to something; it had to be a promise to somebody in particular to be so repudiated. In the event, accordingly, she acknowledged Mr. Merton Densher, the so unusually clever young Englishman who had made his appearance in New York on some special literary business—wasn't it?—shortly before their departure, and who had been three or four times in her house during the brief period between her visit to Boston and her companion's subsequent stay with her; but she required much reminding before it came back to her that she had mentioned to this companion just afterwards the confidence expressed by the personage in question in her never doing so dire a thing as to come to London without, as the phrase was, looking a fellow up. She had left him the enjoyment of his confidence, the form of which might have appeared a trifle free—that she now reasserted; she had done nothing either to impair or to enhance it; but she had also left Mrs. Stringham, in the connection and at the time, rather sorry to have missed Mr. Densher. She had thought of him again after that, the elder woman; she had likewise gone so far as to notice that Milly appeared not to have done so—which the girl might easily have betrayed; and, interested as she was in everything that concerned her, she had made out for herself, for herself only and rather idly, that, but for interruptions, the young Englishman might have become a better acquaintance. His being an acquaintance at all was one of the signs that in the first days had helped to place Milly, as a young person with the world before her, for sympathy and wonder. Isolated, unmothered, unguarded, but with her other strong marks, her big house, her big fortune, her big freedom, she had lately begun to "receive," for all her few years, as an older woman might have done—as was done, precisely, by princesses who had public considerations to observe and who came of age very early. If it was thus distinct to Mrs. Stringham then that Mr. Densher had gone off somewhere else in connection with his errand before her visit to New York, it had been also not undiscoverable that he had come back for a day or two later on, that is after her own second excursion—that he had in fine reappeared on a single occasion on his way to the West: his way from Washington as she believed, though he was out of sight at the time of her joining her friend for their departure. It had not occurred to her before to exaggerate—it had not occurred to her that she could; but she seemed to become aware to-night that there had been just enough in this relation to meet, to provoke, the free conception of a little more.

She presently put it that, at any rate, promise or no promise, Milly would, at a pinch, be able, in London, to act on his permission to make him a sign; to which Milly replied with readiness that her ability, though evident, would be none the less quite wasted, inasmuch as the gentleman would, to a certainty, be still in America. He had a great deal to do there—which he would scarce have begun; and in fact she might very well not have thought of London at all if she hadn't been sure he wasn't yet near coming back. It was perceptible to her companion that the moment our young woman had so far committed herself she had a sense of having overstepped; which was not quite patched up by her saying the next minute, possibly with a certain failure of presence of mind, that the last thing she desired was the air of running after him. Mrs. Stringham wondered privately what question there could be of any such appearance—the danger of which thus suddenly came up; but she said, for the time, nothing of it—she only said other things: one of which was, for instance, that if Mr. Densher was away he was away, and that this was the end of it; also that of course they must be discreet at any price. But what was the measure of discretion, and how was one to be sure? So it was that, as they sat there, she produced her own case: *she* had a possible tie with London, which she desired as little to disown as she might wish to risk presuming on it. She treated her companion, in short, for their evening's end, to the story of Maud Manningham, the odd but interesting English girl who had formed her special affinity in the old days at the Vevey school; whom she had written to, after their separation, with a regularity that had at first faltered and then altogether failed, yet that had been for the time quite a fine case of crude constancy; so that it had in fact flickered up again of itself on the occasion of the marriage of each. They had then once more fondly, scrupulously written—Mrs. Lowder first; and even another letter or two had afterwards passed. This, however, had been the end—though with no rupture, only a gentle drop: Maud Manningham had made, she believed, a great marriage, while she herself had made a small; on top of which, moreover, distance, difference, diminished community and impossible reunion had done the rest of the work. It was but after all these years that reunion had begun to show as possible—if the other party to it, that is, should be still in existence. That was exactly what it now struck our friend as interesting to ascertain, as, with one aid and another, she believed she might. It was an experiment she would at all events now make if Milly didn't object.

Milly in general objected to nothing, and, though she asked a question or two, she raised no present plea. Her questions—or at least her own answers to them—kindled, on Mrs. Stringham's part, a backward train: she hadn't known till tonight how much she remembered, or how fine it might be to see what had become of large, high-coloured Maud, florid, exotic and alien—which had been just the spell—even to the perceptions of youth. There was the danger—she frankly touched it—that such a temperament mightn't have matured, with the years, all in the sense of fineness; it was the sort of danger that, in renewing relations after long breaks, one had always to look in the face. To gather in strayed threads was to take a risk—for which, however, she was prepared if Milly was. The possible "fun," she confessed, was by itself rather tempting; and she fairly sounded, with this—wound up a little as she was—the note of fun as the harmless final right of fifty years of mere New England virtue. Among the things she was afterwards to recall was the indescribable look dropped on her, at this, by her companion; she was still seated there between the candles and before the finished supper, while Milly moved about, and the look was long to figure for her as an inscrutable comment on *her* notion of freedom. Challenged, at any rate, as for the last wise word, Milly showed perhaps, musingly, charmingly, that, though her attention had been mainly soundless, her friend's story—produced as a resource unsuspected, a card from up the sleeve—half surprised, half beguiled her. Since the matter, such as it was, depended on that, she brought out, before she went to bed, an easy, a light "Risk everything!"

This quality in it seemed possibly a little to deny weight to Maud Lowder's evoked presence—as Susan Stringham, still sitting up, became, in excited reflection, a trifle more conscious. Something determinant, when the girl had left her, took place in her—nameless but, as soon as she had given way, coercive. It was as if she knew again, in this fulness of time, that she had been, after Maud's marriage, just sensibly outlived or, as people nowadays said, shunted. Mrs. Lowder had left her behind, and on the occasion, subsequently, of the corresponding date in her own life—not the second, the sad one, with its dignity of sadness, but the first, with the meagreness of its supposed felicity—she had been, in the same spirit, almost patronisingly pitied. If that suspicion, even when it had ceased to matter, had never quite died out for her, there was doubtless some oddity in its now offering itself as a link, rather than as another break, in the chain; and indeed there might well have been for her a mood in which the notion of the development of patronage in her quondam schoolmate would have settled her question in another sense. It was actually settled—if the case be worth our analysis—by the happy consummation, the poetic justice, the generous revenge, of her having at last something to show. Maud, on their parting company, had appeared to have so much, and would now—for wasn't it also, in general, quite the rich law of English life?—have, with accretions, promotions, expansions, ever so much more. Very good; such things might be; she rose to the sense of being ready for them. Whatever Mrs. Lowder might have to show—and one hoped one did the presumptions all justice—she would have nothing like Milly Theale, who constituted the trophy producible by poor Susan. Poor Susan lingered late—till the candles were low, and as soon as the table was cleared she opened her neat portfolio. She had not lost the old clue; there were connections she remembered, addresses she could try; so the thing was to begin. She wrote on the spot.

BOOK FOURTH

VII

It had all gone so fast after this that Milly uttered but the truth nearest to hand in saying to the gentleman on her right—who was, by the same token, the gentleman on her hostess's left—that she scarce even then knew where she was: the words marking her first full sense of a situation really romantic. They were already dining, she and her friend, at Lancaster Gate, and surrounded, as it seemed to her, with every English accessory; though her consciousness of Mrs. Lowder's existence, and still more of her remarkable identity, had been of so recent and so sudden a birth. Susie, as she was apt to call her companion for a lighter change, had only had to wave a neat little wand for the fairy-tale to begin at once; in consequence of which Susie now glittered—for, with Mrs. Stringham's new sense of success, it came to that—in the character of a fairy godmother. Milly had almost insisted on dressing her, for the present occasion, as one; and it was no fault of the girl's if the good lady had not now appeared in a peaked hat, a short petticoat and diamond shoe-buckles, brandishing the magic crutch. The good lady, in truth, bore herself not less contentedly than if these insignia had marked her work; and Milly's observation to Lord Mark had just been, doubtless, the result of such a light exchange of looks with her as even the great length of the table had not baffled. There were twenty persons between them, but this sustained passage was the sharpest sequel yet to that other comparison of views during the pause on the Swiss pass. It almost appeared to Milly that their fortune had been unduly precipitated—as if, properly, they were in the position of having ventured on a small joke and found the answer out of proportion grave. She could not at this moment, for instance, have said whether, with her quickened perceptions, she were more enlivened or oppressed; and the case might in fact have been serious had she not, by good fortune, from the moment the picture loomed, quickly made up her mind that what finally most concerned her was neither to seek nor to shirk, was not even to wonder too much, but was to let things come as they would, since there was little enough doubt of how they would go.

Lord Mark had been brought to her before dinner—not by Mrs. Lowder, but by the handsome girl, that lady's niece, who was now at the other end and on the same side as Susie; he had taken her in, and she meant presently to ask him about Miss Croy, the handsome girl, actually offered to her sight—though now in a splendid way—but for the second time. The first time had been the occasion—only three days before—of her calling at their hotel with her aunt and then making, for our other two heroines, a great impression of beauty and eminence. This impression had remained so with Milly that, at present, and although her attention was aware at the same time of everything else, her eyes were mainly engaged with Kate Croy when not engaged with Susie. That wonderful creature's eyes moreover readily met them—she ranked now as a wonderful creature; and it seemed a part of the swift prosperity of the American visitors that, so little in the original reckoning, she should yet appear conscious, charmingly, frankly conscious, of possibilities of friendship for them. Milly had easily and, as a guest, gracefully generalised: English girls had a special, strong beauty, and it particularly showed in evening dress—above all when, as was strikingly the case with this one, the dress itself was what it should be. That observation she had all ready for Lord Mark when they should, after a little, get round to it. She seemed even now to see that there might be a good deal they would get round to; the indication being that, taken up once for all with her other neighbour, their hostess would leave them much to themselves. Mrs. Lowder's other neighbour was the Bishop of Murrum—a real bishop, such as Milly had never seen, with a complicated costume, a voice like an old-fashioned wind instrument, and a face all the portrait of a prelate; while the gentleman on our young lady's left, a gentleman thick-necked, large and literal, who looked straight before him and as if he were not to be diverted by vain words from that pursuit, clearly counted as an offset to the possession of Lord Mark. As Milly made out these things—with a shade of exhilaration at the way she already fell in—she saw how she was justified of her plea for people and her love of life. It wasn't then, as the prospect seemed to show, so difficult to get into the current, or to stand, at any rate, on the bank. It was easy to get near—if they *were* near; and yet the elements were different enough from any of her old elements, and positively rich and strange.

She asked herself if her right-hand neighbour would understand what she meant by such a description of them, should she throw it off; but another of the things to which, precisely, her sense was awakened was that no, decidedly, he wouldn't. It was nevertheless by this time open to her that his line would be to be clever; and indeed, evidently, no little of the interest was going to be in the fresh reference and fresh effect both of people's cleverness and of their simplicity. She thrilled, she consciously flushed, and turned pale with the certitude—it had never been so present—that she should find herself completely involved: the very air of the place, the pitch of the occasion, had for her so positive a taste and so deep an undertone. The smallest things, the faces, the hands, the jewels of the women, the sound of words, especially of names, across the table, the shape of the forks, the arrangement of the flowers, the attitude of the servants, the walls of the room, were all touches in a picture and denotements in a play; and they marked for her, moreover, her alertness of vision. She had never, she might well believe, been in such a state of vibration; her sensibility was almost too sharp for her comfort: there were, for example, more indications than she could reduce to order in the manner of the friendly niece, who struck her as distinguished and interesting, as in fact surprisingly genial. This young woman's type had, visibly, other possibilities; yet here, of its own free movement, it had already sketched a relation. Were they, Miss Croy and she, to take up the tale where their two elders had left it off so many years before?—were they to find they liked each other and to try for themselves if a scheme of constancy on more modern lines could be worked? She had doubted, as they came to England, of Maud Manningham, had believed her a broken reed and a vague resource, had seen their dependence on her as a state of mind that would have been shamefully silly—so far as it *was* dependence—had they wished to do any thing so inane as "get into society." To have made their pilgrimage all for the sake of such society as Mrs. Lowder might have in reserve for them—that didn't bear thinking of at all, and she herself had quite chosen her course for curiosity about other matters. She would have described this curiosity as a desire to see the places she had read about, and *that* description of her motive she was prepared to give her neighbour—even though, as a consequence of it, he should find how little she had read. It was almost at present as if her poor prevision had been rebuked by the majesty—she could scarcely call it less—of the event, or at all events by the commanding character of the two figures—she could scarcely call *that* less either—mainly presented. Mrs. Lowder and her niece, however dissimilar, had at least in common that each was a great reality. That was true, primarily, of the aunt—so true that Milly wondered how her own companion had arrived, in other days, at so odd an alliance; yet she none the less felt Mrs. Lowder as a person of whom the mind might in two or three days roughly make the circuit. She would sit there massive, at least, while one attempted it; whereas Miss Croy, the handsome girl, would indulge in incalculable movements that might interfere with one's tour. She was real, none the less, and everything and everybody were real; and it served them right, no doubt, the pair of them, for having rushed into their adventure.

Lord Mark's intelligence meanwhile, however, had met her own quite sufficiently to enable him to tell her how little he could clear up her situation. He explained, for that matter—or at least he hinted—that there was no such thing, to-day in London, as saying where any one was. Every one was everywhere—nobody was anywhere. He should be put to it—yes, frankly—to give a name of any sort or kind to their hostess's "set." *Was* it a set at all, or wasn't it, and were there not really no such things as sets, in the place, any more?—was there any thing but the senseless shifting tumble, like that of some great greasy sea in mid-Channel, of an overwhelming melted mixture? He threw out the question, which seemed large; Milly felt that at the end of five minutes he had thrown out a great many, though he followed none more than a step or two; perhaps he would prove suggestive, but he helped her as yet to no discriminations: he spoke as if he had given them up from too much knowledge. He was thus at the opposite extreme from herself, but, as a consequence of it, also wandering and lost; and he was furthermore, for all his temporary incoherence, to which she guessed there would be some key, as great a reality as either Mrs. Lowder or Kate. The only light in which he placed the former of these ladies was that of an extraordinary woman—a most extraordinary woman, and "the more extraordinary the more one knows her," while of the latter he said nothing, for the moment, but that she was tremendously, yes, quite tremendously, good-looking. It was some time, she thought, before his talk showed his cleverness, and yet each minute she believed in it more, quite apart from what her hostess had told her on first naming him. Perhaps he was one of the cases she had heard of at home—those characteristic cases of people in England who concealed their play of mind so much more than they showed it. Even Mr. Densher a little did that. And what made Lord Mark, at any rate, so real either, when this was a thing he so definitely insisted on? His type some how, as by a life, a need, an intention of its own, insisted *for* him; but that was all. It was difficult to guess his age—whether he were a young man who looked old or an old man who looked young; it seemed to prove nothing, as against other things, that he was bald and, as might have been said, slightly stale, or, more delicately perhaps, dry: there was such a fine little fidget of preoccupied life in him, and his eyes, at moments—though it was an appearance they could suddenly lose—were as candid and clear as those of a pleasant boy. Very neat, very light, and so fair that there was little other indication of his moustache than his constantly feeling it—which was again boyish—he would have affected her as the most intellectual person present if he had not affected her as the most frivolous. The latter quality was rather in his look than in anything else, though he constantly wore his double eyeglass, which was, much more, Bostonian and thoughtful.

The idea of his frivolity had, no doubt, to do with his personal designation, which represented—as yet, for our young woman, a little confusedly—a connection with an historic patriciate, a class that, in turn, also confusedly, represented an affinity with a social element that she had never heard otherwise described than as "fashion." The supreme social element in New York had never known itself but as reduced to that category, and though Milly was aware that, as applied to a territorial and political aristocracy, the label was probably too simple, she had for the time none other at hand. She presently, it is true, enriched her idea with the perception that her interlocutor was indifferent; yet this, indifferent as aristocracies notoriously were, saw her but little further, inasmuch as she felt that, in the first place, he would much rather get on with her than not, and in the second was only thinking of too many matters of his own. If he kept her in view on the one hand and kept so much else on the other—the way he crumbed up his bread was a proof—why did he hover before her as a potentially insolent noble? She couldn't have answered the question, and it was precisely one of those that swarmed. They were complicated, she might fairly have said, by his visibly knowing, having known from afar off, that she was a stranger and an American, and by his none the less making no more of it than if she and her like were the chief of his diet. He took her, kindly enough, but imperturbably, irreclaimably, for granted, and it wouldn't in the least help that she herself knew him, as quickly, for having been in her country and threshed it out. There would be nothing for her to explain or attenuate or brag about; she could neither escape nor prevail by her strangeness; he would have, for that matter, on such a subject, more to tell her than to learn from her. She might learn from *him* why she was so different from the handsome girl—which she didn't know, being merely able to feel it; or at any rate might learn from him why the handsome girl was so different from her.

On these lines, however, they would move later; the lines immediately laid down were, in spite of his vagueness for his own convenience, definite enough. She was already, he observed to her, thinking what she should say on her other side—which was what Americans were always doing. She needn't in conscience say anything at all; but Americans never knew that, nor ever, poor creatures, yes (*she* had interposed the "poor creatures!") what not to do. The burdens they took on—the things, positively, they made an affair of! This easy and, after all, friendly jibe at her race was really for her, on her new friend's part, the note of personal recognition so far as she required it; and she gave him a prompt and conscious example of morbid anxiety by insisting that her desire to be, herself, "lovely" all round was justly founded on the lovely way Mrs. Lowder had met her. He was directly interested in that, and it was not till afterwards that she fully knew how much more information about their friend he had taken than given. Here again, for instance, was a pertinent note for her: she had, on the spot, with her first plunge into the obscure depths of a society constituted from far back, encountered the interesting phenomenon of complicated, of possibly sinister motive. However, Maud Manningham (her name, even in her presence, somehow still fed the fancy) *had,* all the same, been lovely, and one was going to meet her now quite as far on as one had one's self been met. She had been with them at their hotel—they were a pair—before even they had supposed she could have got their letter. Of course indeed they had written in advance, but they had followed that up very fast. She had thus engaged them to dine but two days later, and on the morrow again, without waiting for a return visit, waiting for anything, she had called with her niece. It was as if she really cared for them, and it was magnificent fidelity—fidelity to Mrs. Stringham, her own companion and Mrs. Lowder's former schoolmate, the lady with the charming face and the rather high dress down there at the end.

Lord Mark took in through his nippers these balanced attributes of Susie. "But isn't Mrs. Stringham's fidelity then equally magnificent?"

"Well, it's a beautiful sentiment; but it isn't as if she had anything to *give."*

"Hasn't she got you?" Lord Mark presently asked.

"Me—to give Mrs. Lowder?" Milly had clearly not yet seen herself in the light of such an offering. "Oh, I'm rather a poor present; and I don't feel as if, even at that, I've as yet quite been given."

"You've been shown, and if our friend has jumped at you it comes to the same thing." He made his jokes, Lord Mark, without amusement for himself; yet it wasn't that he was grim. "To be seen you must recognise, *is,* for you, to be jumped at; and, if it's a question of being shown, here you are again. Only it has now been taken out of your friend's hands; it's Mrs. Lowder, already, who's getting the benefit. Look round the table and you'll make out, I think, that you're being, from top to bottom, jumped at."

"Well, then," said Milly, "I seem also to feel that I like it better than being made fun of."

It was one of the things she afterwards saw—Milly was for ever seeing things afterwards—that her companion had here had some way of his own, quite unlike any one's else, of assuring her of his consideration. She wondered how he had done it, for he had neither apologised nor protested. She said to herself, at any rate, that he had led her on; and what was most odd was the question by which he had done so. "Does she know much about you?"

"No, she just likes us."

Even for this his travelled lordship, seasoned and saturated, had no laugh. "I mean *you* particularly. Has that lady with the charming face, which *is* charming, told her?"

Milly hesitated. "Told her what?"

"Everything."

This, with the way he dropped it, again considerably moved her—made her feel for a moment that, as a matter of course, she was a subject for disclosures. But she quickly found her answer. "Oh, as for that, you must ask *her."*

"Your clever companion?"

"Mrs. Lowder."

He replied to this that their hostess was a person with whom there were certain liberties one never took, but that he was none the less fairly upheld, inasmuch as she was for the most part kind to him and as, should he be very good for a while, she would probably herself tell him. "And I shall have, at any rate, in the meantime, the interest of seeing what she does with you. That will teach me more or less, you see, how much she knows."

Milly followed this—it was lucid; but it suggested something apart. "How much does she know about *you?"*

"Nothing," said Lord Mark serenely. "But that doesn't matter—for what she does with me." And then, as to anticipate Milly's question about the nature of such doing: "This, for instance—turning me straight on for *you."*

The girl thought. "And you mean she wouldn't if she did know——?"

He met it as if it were really a point. "No. I believe, to do her justice, she still would. So you can be easy."

Milly had the next instant, then, acted on the permission. "Because you're even at the worst the best thing she has?"

With this he was at last amused. "I was till you came. You're the best now."

It was strange his words should have given her the sense of his knowing, but it was positive that they did so, and to the extent of making her believe them, though still with wonder. That, really, from this first of their meetings, was what was most to abide with her: she accepted almost helplessly, she surrendered to the inevitability of being the sort of thing, as he might have said, that he at least thoroughly believed he had, in going about, seen here enough of for all practical purposes. Her submission was naturally, moreover, not to be impaired by her learning later on that he had paid at short intervals, though at a time apparently just previous to her own emergence from the obscurity of extreme youth, three separate visits to New York, where his nameable friends and his contrasted contacts had been numerous. His impression, his recollection of the whole mixed quantity, was still visibly rich. It had helped him to place her, and she was more and more sharply conscious of having—as with the door sharply slammed upon her and the guard's hand raised in signal to the train—been popped into the compartment in which she was to travel for him. It was a use of her that many a girl would have been doubtless quick to resent; and the kind of mind that thus, in our young lady, made all for mere seeing and taking is precisely one of the charms of our subject. Milly had practically just learned from him, had made out, as it were, from her rumbling compartment, that he gave her the highest place among their friend's actual properties. She was a success, that was what it came to, he presently assured her, and that was what it was to be a success: it always happened before one could know it. One's ignorance was in fact often the greatest part of it.

"You haven't had time yet," he said; "this is nothing. But you'll see. You'll see everything. You can, you know—everything you dream of."

He made her more and more wonder; she almost felt as if he were showing her visions while he spoke; and strangely enough, though it was visions that had drawn her on, she hadn't seen them in connection—that is in such preliminary and necessary connection—with such a face as Lord Mark's, such eyes and such a voice, such a tone and such a manner. He had for an instant the effect of making her ask herself if she were after all going to be afraid; so distinct was it for fifty seconds that a fear passed over her. There they were again—yes, certainly: Susie's overture to Mrs. Lowder had been their joke, but they had pressed in that gaiety an electric bell that continued to sound. Positively, while she sat there, she had the loud rattle in her ears, and she wondered, during these moments, why the others didn't hear it. They didn't stare, they didn't smile, and the fear in her that I speak of was but her own desire to stop it. That dropped, however, as if the alarm itself had ceased; she seemed to have seen in a quick, though tempered glare that there were two courses for her, one to leave London again the first thing in the morning, the other to do nothing at all. Well, she would do nothing at all; she was already doing it; more than that, she had already done it, and her chance was gone. She gave herself up—she had the strangest sense, on the spot, of so deciding; for she had turned a corner before she went on again with Lord Mark. Inexpressive, but intensely significant, he met as no one else could have done the very question she had suddenly put to Mrs. Stringham on the Brünig. Should she have it, whatever she did have, that question had been, for long? "Ah, so possibly not," her neighbour appeared to reply; "therefore, don't you see? *I'm* the way." It was vivid that he might be, in spite of his absence of flourish; the way being doubtless just *in* that absence. The handsome girl, whom she didn't lose sight of and who, she felt, kept her also in view—Mrs. Lowder's striking niece would, perhaps, be the way as well, for in her too was the absence of flourish, though she had little else, so far as one could tell, in common with Lord Mark. Yet how indeed *could* one tell, what did one understand, and of what was one, for that matter, provisionally conscious but of their being somehow together in what they represented? Kate Croy, fine but friendly, looked over at her as really with a guess at Lord Mark's effect on her. If she could guess this effect what then did she know about it and in what degree had she felt it herself? Did that represent, as between them, anything particular, and should she have to count with them as duplicating, as intensifying by a mutual intelligence, the relation into which she was sinking? Nothing was so odd as that she should have to recognise so quickly in each of these glimpses of an instant the various signs of a relation; and this anomaly itself, had she had more time to give to it, might well, might almost terribly have suggested to her that her doom was to live fast. It was queerly a question of the short run and the consciousness proportionately crowded.

These were immense excursions for the spirit of a young person at Mrs. Lowder's mere dinner-party; but what was so significant and so admonitory as the fact of their being possible? What could they have been but just a part, already, of the crowded consciousness? And it was just a part, likewise, that while plates were changed and dishes presented and periods in the banquet marked; while appearances insisted and phenomena multiplied and words reached her from here and there like plashes of a slow, thick tide; while Mrs. Lowder grew somehow more stout and more instituted and Susie, at her distance and in comparison, more thinly improvised and more different—different, that is, from every one and everything: it was just a part that while this process went forward our young lady alighted, came back, taking up her destiny again as if she had been able by a wave or two of her wings to place herself briefly in sight of an alternative to it. Whatever it was it had showed in this brief interval as better than the alternative; and it now presented itself altogether in the image and in the place in which she had left it. The image was that of her being, as Lord Mark had declared, a success. This depended more or less of course on his idea of the thing—into which at present, however, she wouldn't go. But, renewing soon, she had asked him what he meant then that Mrs. Lowder would do with her, and he had replied that this might safely be left. "She'll get back," he pleasantly said, "her money." He could say it too—which was singular—without affecting her either as vulgar or as "nasty "; and he had soon explained himself by adding: "Nobody here, you know, does anything for nothing."

"Ah, if you mean that we shall reward her as hard as ever we can, nothing is more certain. But she's an idealist," Milly continued, "and idealists, in the long run, I think, *don't* feel that they lose."

Lord Mark seemed, within the limits of his enthusiasm, to find this charming. "Ah, she strikes you as an idealist?"

"She idealises *us,* my friend and me, absolutely. She sees us in a light," said Milly. "That's all I've got to hold on by. So don't deprive me of it."

"I wouldn't for the world. But do you think," he continued as if it were suddenly important for him—"do you think she sees *me* in a light?"

She neglected his question for a little, partly because her attention attached itself more and more to the handsome girl, partly because, placed so near their hostess, she wished not to show as discussing her too freely. Mrs. Lowder, it was true, steering in the other quarter a course in which she called at subjects as if they were islets in an archipelago, continued to allow them their ease, and Kate Croy, at the same time, steadily revealed herself as interesting. Milly in fact found, of a sudden, her ease—found it all—as she bethought herself that what Mrs. Lowder was really arranging for was a report on her quality and, as perhaps might be said, her value from Lord Mark. She wished him, the wonderful lady, to have no pretext for not knowing what he thought of Miss Theale. Why his judgment so mattered remained to be seen; but it was this divination, in any case, that now determined Milly's rejoinder. "No. She knows you. She has probably reason to. And you all, here, know each other—I see that—so far as you know anything. You know what you're used to, and it's your being used to it—that, and that only—that makes you. But there are things you don't know."

He took it in as if it might fairly, to do him justice, be a point. "Things that *I* don't—with all the pains I take and the way I've run about the world to leave nothing unlearned?"

Milly thought, and it was perhaps the very truth of his claim—its not being negligible—that sharpened her impatience and thereby her wit. "You're *blasé,* but you're not enlightened. You're familiar with everything, but conscious, really of nothing. What I mean is that you've no imagination."

Lord Mark, at this, threw back his head, ranging with his eyes the opposite side of the room and showing himself at last so much more completely as diverted that it fairly attracted their hostess's notice. Mrs. Lowder, however, only smiled on Milly for a sign that something racy was what she had expected, and resumed, with a splash of her screw, her cruise among the islands. "Oh, I've heard that," the young man replied, "before!"

"There it is then. You've heard everything before. You've heard *me* of course before, in my country, often enough."

"Oh, never too often," he protested; "I'm sure I hope I shall still hear you again and again."

"But what good then has it done you?" the girl went on as if now frankly to amuse him.

"Oh, you'll see when you know me."

"But, most assuredly, I shall never know you."

"Then that will be exactly," he laughed, "the good!"

If it established thus that they couldn't, or Wouldn't, mix, why, none the less, did Milly feel, through it, a perverse quickening of the relation to which she had been, in spite of herself, appointed?

What queerer consequence of their not mixing than their talking—for it was what they had arrived at—almost intimately? She wished to get away from him, or indeed, much rather, away from herself so far as she was present to him. She saw already—wonderful creature, after all, herself too—that there would be a good deal more of him to come for her, and that the special sign of their intercourse would be to keep herself out of the question. Everything else might come in—only never that; and with such an arrangement they might even go far. This in fact might quite have begun, on the spot, with her returning again to the topic of the handsome girl. If she was to keep herself out she could naturally best do so by putting in somebody else. She accordingly put in Kate Croy, being ready to that extent—as she was not at all afraid for her—to sacrifice her if necessary. Lord Mark himself, for that matter, had made it easy by saying a little while before that no one among them did anything for nothing. "What then"—she was aware of being abrupt—"does Miss Croy, if she's so interested, do it for? What has she to gain by *her* lovely welcome? Look at her *now!"* Milly broke out with characteristic freedom of praise, though pulling herself up also with a compunctious "Oh!" as the direction thus given to their eyes happened to coincide with a turn of Kate's face to them. All she had meant to do was to insist that this face was fine; but what she had in fact done was to renew again her effect of showing herself to its possessor as conjoined with Lord Mark for some interested view of it. He had, however, promptly met her question.

"To gain? Why, your acquaintance."

"Well, what's my acquaintance to her? She can care for me—she must feel that—only by being sorry for me; and that's why she's lovely: to be already willing to take the trouble to be. It's the height of the disinterested."

There were more things in this than one that Lord Mark might have taken up; but in a minute he had made his choice. "Ah then, I'm nowhere, for I'm afraid *I'm* not sorry for you in the least. What do you make then," he asked, "of your success?"

"Why, just the great reason of all. It's just because our friend there sees it that she pities me. She understands," Milly said; "she's better than any of you. She's beautiful."

He appeared struck with this at last—with the point the girl made of it; to which she came back even after a diversion created by a dish presented between them. "Beautiful in character, I see. *Is* she so? You must tell me about her."

Milly wondered. "But haven't you known her longer than I? Haven't you seen her for yourself?"

"No—I've failed with her. It's no use. I don't make her out. And I assure you I really should like to." His assurance had in fact for his companion a positive suggestion of sincerity; he affected her as now saying something that he felt; and she was the more struck with it as she was still conscious of the failure even of curiosity he had just shown in respect to herself. She had meant something—though indeed for herself almost only—in speaking of their friend's natural pity; it had been a note, doubtless, of questionable taste, but it had quavered out in spite of her; and he had not so much as cared to inquire "Why 'natural'?" Not that it wasn't really much better for her that he shouldn't: explanations would in truth have taken her much too far. Only she now perceived that, in comparison, her word about this other person really "drew" him; and there were things in that, probably, many things, as to which she would learn more and which glimmered there already as part and parcel of that larger "real" with which, in her new situation, she was to be beguiled. It was in fact at the very moment, this element, not absent from what Lord Mark was further saying. "So you're wrong, you see, as to our knowing all about each other. There are cases where we break down. I at any rate give *her* up—up, that is, to you. You must do her for me—tell me, I mean, when you know more. You'll notice," he pleasantly wound up, "that I've confidence in you."

"Why shouldn't you have?" Milly asked, observing in this, as she thought, a fine, though, for such a man, a surprisingly artless, fatuity. It was as if there might have been a question of her falsifying for the sake of her own show—that is of her honesty not being proof against her desire to keep well with him herself. She didn't, none the less, otherwise protest against his remark; there was something else she was occupied in seeing. It was the handsome girl alone, one of his own species and his own society, who had made him feel uncertain; of his certainties about a mere little American, a cheap exotic, imported almost wholesale, and whose habitat, with its conditions of climate, growth, and cultivation, its immense profusion, but its few varieties and thin development, he was perfectly satisfied. The marvel was, too, that Milly understood his satisfaction—feeling that she expressed the truth in presently saying: "Of course; I make out that she must be difficult; just as I see that I myself must be easy." And that was what, for all the rest of this occasion, remained with her—as the most interesting thing that could remain. She was more and more content herself to be easy; she would have been resigned, even had it been brought straighter home to her, to passing for a cheap exotic. Provisionally, at any rate, that protected her wish to keep herself, with Lord Mark, in abeyance. They *had* all affected her as inevitably knowing each other, and if the handsome girl's place among them was something even their initiation couldn't deal with—why, then, she would indeed be a quantity.

VIII

That sense of quantities, separate or mixed, was indeed doubtless what most prevailed at first for our slightly gasping American pair; it found utterance for them in their frequent remark to each other that they had no one but themselves to thank. It dropped from Milly more than once that if she had ever known it was so easy—! though her exclamation mostly ended without completing her idea. This, however, was a trifle to Mrs. Stringham, who cared little whether she meant that in this case she would have come sooner. She couldn't have come sooner, and she perhaps, on the contrary, meant—for it would have been like her—that she wouldn't have come at all; why it was so easy being at any rate a matter as to which her companion had begun quickly to pick up views. Susie kept some of these lights for the present to herself, since, freely communicated, they might have been a little disturbing; with which, moreover, the quantities that we speak of as surrounding the two ladies were, in many cases, quantities of things—and of other things—to talk about. Their immediate lesson, accordingly, was that they just had been caught up by the incalculable strength of a wave that was actually holding them aloft and that would naturally dash them wherever it liked. They meanwhile, we hasten to add, make the best of their precarious position, and if Milly had had no other help for it she would have found not a little in the sight of Susan Shepherd's state. The girl had had nothing to say to her, for three days, about the "success" announced by Lord Mark—which they saw, besides, otherwise established; she was too taken up, too touched, by Susie's own exaltation. Susie glowed in the light of her justified faith; everything had happened that she had been acute enough to think least probable; she had appealed to a possible delicacy in Maud Manningham—a delicacy, mind you, but *barely* possible—and her appeal had been met in a way that was an honour to human nature. This proved sensibility of the lady of Lancaster Gate performed verily, for both our friends, during these first days, the office of a fine floating gold-dust, something that threw over the prospect a harmonising blur. The forms, the colours behind it were strong and deep—we have seen how they already stood out for Milly; but nothing, comparatively, had had so much of the dignity of truth as the fact of Maud's fidelity to a sentiment. That was what Susie was proud of, much more than of her great place in the world, which she was moreover conscious of not as yet wholly measuring. That was what was more vivid even than her being—in senses more worldly and in fact almost in the degree of a revelation—English and distinct and positive, with almost no inward, but with the finest outward resonance.

Susan Shepherd's word for her, again and again, was that she was "large"; yet it was not exactly a case, as to the soul, of echoing chambers: she might have been likened rather to a capacious receptacle, originally perhaps loose, but now drawn as tightly as possible over its accumulated contents—a packed mass, for her American admirer, of curious detail. When the latter good lady, at home, had handsomely figured her friends as not small—which was the way she mostly figured them—there was a certain implication that they were spacious because they were empty. Mrs. Lowder, by a different law, was spacious because she was full, because she had something in common, even in repose, with a projectile, of great size, loaded and ready for use. That indeed, to Susie's romantic mind, announced itself as half the charm of their renewal—a charm as of sitting in springtime, during a long peace, on the daisied, grassy bank of some great slumbering fortress. True to her psychological instincts, certainly, Mrs. Stringham had noted that the "sentiment" she rejoiced in on her old schoolmate's part was all a matter of action and movement, was not, save for the interweaving of a more frequent plump "dearest" than she would herself perhaps have used, a matter of much other embroidery. She brooded, with interest, on this further remark of race, feeling in her own spirit a different economy. The joy, for her, was to know *why* she acted—the reason was half the business; whereas with Mrs. Lowder there might have been no reason: "why" was the trivial seasoning-substance, the vanilla or the nutmeg, omittable from the nutritive pudding without spoiling it. Mrs. Lowder's desire was clearly sharp that their young companions should also prosper together; and Mrs. Stringham's account of it all to Milly, during the first days, was that when, at Lancaster Gate, she was not occupied in telling, as it were, about her, she was occupied in hearing much of the history of her hostess's brilliant niece.

They had plenty, on these lines, the two elder women, to give and to take, and it was even not quite clear to the pilgrim from Boston that what she should mainly have arranged for in London was not a series of thrills for herself. She had a bad conscience, indeed almost a sense of immorality, in having to recognise that she was, as she said, carried away. She laughed to Milly when she also said that she didn't know where it would end; and the principal of her uneasiness was that Mrs. Lowder's life bristled for her with elements that she was really having to look at for the first time. They represented, she believed, the world, the world that, as a consequence of the cold shoulder turned to it by the Pilgrim Fathers, had never yet boldly crossed to Boston—it would surely have sunk the stoutest Cunarder—and she couldn't pretend that she faced the prospect simply because Milly had had a caprice. She was in the act herself of having one, directed precisely to their present spectacle. She could but seek strength in the thought that she had never had one—or had never yielded to one, which came to the same thing—before. The sustaining sense of it all, moreover, as literary material—that quite dropped from her. She must wait, at any rate, she should see: it struck her, so far as she had got, as vast, obscure, lurid. She reflected in the watches of the night that she was probably just going to love it for itself—that is for itself and Milly. The odd thing was that she could think of Milly's loving it without dread—or with dread, at least not on the score of conscience, only on the score of peace. It was a mercy, at all events, for the hour, that their fancies jumped together.

While, for this first week that followed their dinner, she drank deep at Lancaster Gate, her companion was no less happily, appeared to be indeed on the whole quite as romantically, provided for. The handsome English girl from the heavy English house had been as a figure in a picture stepping by magic out of its frame: it was a case, in truth, for which Mrs. Stringham presently found the perfect image. She had lost none of her grasp, but quite the contrary, of that other conceit in virtue of which Milly was the wandering princess: so what could be more in harmony now than to see the princess waited upon at the city gate by the worthiest maiden, the chosen daughter of the burgesses? It was the real again, evidently, the amusement of the meeting for the princess too; princesses living for the most part, in such an appeased way, on the plane of mere elegant representation. That was why they pounced, at city gates, on deputed flower-strewing damsels; that was why, after effigies, processions, and other stately games, frank human company was pleasant to them. Kate Croy really presented herself to Milly—the latter abounded for Mrs. Stringham in accounts of it—as the wondrous London girl in person, by what she had conceived, from far back, of the London girl; conceived from the tales of travellers and the anecdotes of New York, from old porings over *Punch* and a liberal acquaintance with the fiction of the day. The only thing was that she was nicer, for the creature in question had rather been, to our young woman, an image of dread. She had thought of her, at her best, as handsome just as Kate was, with turns of head and tones of voice, felicities of stature and attitude, things "put on" and, for that matter, put off, all the marks of the product of a packed society who should be at the same time the heroine of a strong story. She placed this striking young person from the first in a story, saw her, by a necessity of the imagination, for a heroine, felt it the only character in which she wouldn't be wasted; and this in spite of the heroine's pleasant abruptness, her forbearance from gush, her umbrellas and jackets and shoes—as these things sketched themselves to Milly—and something rather of a breezy boy in the carriage of her arms and the occasional freedom of her slang.

When Milly had settled that the extent of her goodwill itself made her shy, she had found for the moment quite a sufficient key, and they were by that time thoroughly afloat together. This might well have been the happiest hour they were to know, attacking in friendly independence their great London—the London of shops and streets and suburbs oddly interesting to Milly, as well as of museums, monuments, "sights" oddly unfamiliar to Kate, while their elders pursued a separate course, both rejoicing in their intimacy and each thinking the other's young woman a great acquisition for her own. Milly expressed to Susan Shepherd more than once that Kate had some secret, some smothered trouble, besides all the rest of her history; and that if she had so good-naturedly helped Mrs. Lowder to meet them this was exactly to create a diversion, to give herself something else to think about. But on the case thus postulated our young American had as yet had no light: she only felt that when the light should come it would greatly deepen the colour; and she liked to think she was prepared for anything. What she already knew, moreover, was full to her vision, of English, of eccentric, of Thackerayan character, Kate Croy having gradually become not a little explicit on the subject of her situation, her past, her present, her general predicament, her small success, up to the present hour, in contenting at the same time her father, her sister, her aunt and herself. It was Milly's subtle guess, imparted to her Susie, that the girl had somebody else as well, as yet unnamed, to content, it being manifest that such a creature couldn't help having; a creature not perhaps, if one would, exactly formed to inspire passions, since that always implied a certain silliness, but essentially seen, by the admiring eye of friendship, under the clear shadow of some probably eminent male interest. The clear shadow, from whatever source projected, hung, at any rate, over Milly's companion the whole week, and Kate Croy's handsome face smiled out of it, under bland skylights, in the presence alike of old masters passive in their glory and of thoroughly new ones, the newest, who bristled restlessly with pins and brandished snipping shears.

It was meanwhile a pretty part of the intercourse of these young ladies that each thought the other more remarkable than herself—that each thought herself, or assured the other she did, a comparatively dusty object and the other a favourite of nature and of fortune. Kate was amused, amazed at the way her friend insisted on "taking" her, and Milly wondered if Kate were sincere in finding her the most extraordinary—quite apart from her being the most charming—person she had come across. They had talked, in long drives, and quantities of history had not been wanting—in the light of which Mrs. Lowder's niece might superficially seem to have had the best of the argument. Her visitor's American references, with their bewildering immensities, their confounding moneyed New York, their excitements of high pressure, their opportunities of wild freedom, their record of used-up relatives, parents, clever, eager, fair, slim brothers—these the most loved—all engaged, as well as successive superseded guardians, in a high extravagance of speculation and dissipation that had left this exquisite being her black dress, her white face and her vivid hair as the mere last broken link: such a picture quite threw into the shade the brief biography, however sketchily amplified, of a mere middle-class nobody in Bayswater. And though that indeed might be but a Bayswater way of putting it, in addition to which Milly was in the stage of interest in Bayswater ways, this critic so far prevailed that, like Mrs. Stringham herself, she fairly got her companion to accept from her that she was quite the nearest approach to a practical princess Bayswater could hope ever to know. It was a fact—it became one at the end of three days—that Milly actually began to borrow from the handsome girl a sort of view of her state; the handsome girl's impression of it was clearly so sincere. This impression was a tribute, a tribute positively to power, power the source of which was the last thing Kate treated as a mystery. There were passages, under all their skylights, the succession of their shops being large, in which the latter's easy, yet the least bit dry manner sufficiently gave out that if she had had so deep a pocket——!

It was not moreover by any means with not having the imagination of expenditure that she appeared to charge her friend, but with not having the imagination of terror, of thrift, the imagination or in any degree the habit of a conscious dependence on others. Such moments, when all Wigmore Street, for instance, seemed to rustle about and the pale girl herself to be facing the different rustlers, usually so undiscriminated, as individual Britons too, Britons personal, parties to a relation and perhaps even intrinsically remarkable—such moments in especial determined in Kate a perception of the high happiness of her companion's liberty. Milly's range was thus immense; she had to ask nobody for anything, to refer nothing to any one; her freedom, her fortune and her fancy were her law; an obsequious world surrounded her, she could sniff up at every step its fumes. And Kate, in these days, was altogether in the phase of forgiving her so much bliss; in the phase moreover of believing that, should they continue to go on together, she would abide in that generosity. She had, at such a point as this, no suspicion of a rift within the lute—by which we mean not only none of anything's coming between them, but none of any definite flaw in so much clearness of quality. Yet, all the same, if Milly, at Mrs. Lowder's banquet, had described herself to Lord Mark as kindly used by the young woman on the other side because of some faintly-felt special propriety in it, so there really did match with this, privately, on the young woman's part, a feeling not analysed but divided, a latent impression that Mildred Theale was not, after all, a person to change places, to change even chances with. Kate, verily, would perhaps not quite have known what she meant by this reservation, and she came near naming it only when she said to herself that, rich as Milly was, one probably wouldn't—which was singular—ever hate her for it. The handsome girl had, with herself, these felicities and crudities: it wasn't obscure to her that, without some very particular reason to help, it might have proved a test of one's philosophy not to be irritated by a mistress of millions, or whatever they were, who, as a girl, so easily might have been, like herself, only vague and fatally female. She was by no means sure of liking Aunt Maud as much as she deserved, and Aunt Maud's command of funds was obviously inferior to Milly's. There was thus clearly, as pleading for the latter, some influence that would later on become distinct; and meanwhile, decidedly, it was enough that she was as charming as she was queer and as queer as she was charming—all of which was a rare amusement; as well, for that matter, as further sufficient that there were objects of value she had already pressed on Kate's acceptance. A week of her society in these conditions—conditions that Milly chose to sum up as ministering immensely, for a blind, vague pilgrim, to aid and comfort—announced itself from an early hour as likely to become a week of presents, acknowledgments, mementos, pledges of gratitude and admiration that were all on one side. Kate as promptly embraced the propriety of making it clear that she must forswear shops till she should receive some guarantee that the contents of each one she entered as a humble companion should not be placed at her feet; yet that was in truth not before she had found herself in possession, under whatever protests, of several precious ornaments and other minor conveniences.

Great was the absurdity, too, that there should have come a day, by the end of the week, when it appeared that all Milly would have asked in definite "return," as might be said, was to be told a little about Lord Mark and to be promised the privilege of a visit to Mrs. Condrip. Far other amusements had been offered her, but her eagerness was shamelessly human, and she seemed really to count more on the revelation of the anxious lady of Chelsea than on the best nights of the opera. Kate admired, and showed it, such an absence of fear: to the fear of being bored, in such a connection, she would have been so obviously entitled. Milly's answer to this was the plea of her curiosities—which left her friend wondering as to their odd direction. Some among them, no doubt, were rather more intelligible, and Kate had heard without wonder that she was blank about Lord Mark. This young lady's account of him, at the same time, professed itself as frankly imperfect; for what they best knew him by at Lancaster Gate was a thing difficult to explain. One knew people in general by something they had to show, something that, either for them or against, could be touched or named or proved; and she could think of no other case of a value taken as so great and yet flourishing untested. His value was his future, which had somehow got itself as accepted by Aunt Maud as if it had been his good cook or his steam-launch. She, Kate, didn't mean she thought him a humbug; he might do great things—but they were all, as yet, so to speak, he had done. On the other hand it was of course something of an achievement, and not open to every one, to have got one's self taken so seriously by Aunt Maud. The best thing about him, doubtless, on the whole, was that Aunt Maud believed in him. She was often fantastic, but she knew a humbug, and—no, Lord Mark wasn't that. He had been a short time in the House, on the Tory side, but had lost his seat on the first opportunity, and this was all he had to point to. However, he pointed to nothing; which was very possibly just a sign of his real cleverness, one of those that the really clever had in common with the really void. Even Aunt Maud frequently admitted that there was a good deal, for her view of him, to come up in the rear. And he wasn't meanwhile himself indifferent—indifferent to himself—for he was working Lancaster Gate for all it was worth: just as it was, no doubt, working *him,* and just as the working and the worked were in London, as one might explain, the parties to every relation.

Kate did explain, for her listening friend: every one who had anything to give—it was true they were the fewest—made the sharpest possible bargain for it, got at least its value in return. The strangest thing, furthermore, was that this might be, in cases, a happy understanding. The worker in one connection was the worked in another; it was as broad as it was long—with the wheels of the system, as might be seen, wonderfully oiled. People could quite like each other in the midst of it, as Aunt Maud, by every appearance, quite liked Lord Mark, and as Lord Mark, it was to be hoped, liked Mrs. Lowder, since if he didn't he was a greater brute than one could believe. She, Kate, had not yet, it was true, made out what he was doing for her—besides which the dear woman needed him, even at the most he could do, much less than she imagined; so far as all of which went, moreover, there were plenty of things on every side she had not yet made out. She believed, on the whole, in any one Aunt Maud took up; and she gave it to Milly as worth thinking of that, whatever wonderful people this young lady might meet in the land, she would meet no more extraordinary woman. There were greater celebrities by the million, and of course greater swells, but a bigger *person,* by Kate's view, and a larger natural handful every way, would really be far to seek. When Milly inquired with interest if Kate's belief in *her* was primarily on the lines of what Mrs. Lowder "took up," her interlocutress could handsomely say yes, since by the same principle she believed in herself. Whom but Aunt Maud's niece, pre-eminently, had Aunt Maud taken up, and who was thus more in the current, with her, of working and of being worked? "You may ask," Kate said, "what in the world I have to give; and that indeed is just what I'm trying to learn. There must be something, for her to think she can get it out of me. She *will* get it—trust her; and then I shall see what it is; which I beg you to believe I should never have found out for myself." She declined to treat any question of Milly's own "paying" power as discussable; that Milly would pay a hundred per cent.—and even to the end, doubtless, through the nose—was just the beautiful basis on which they found themselves.

These were fine facilities, pleasantries, ironies, all these luxuries of gossip and philosophies of London and of life, and they became quickly, between the pair, the common form of talk, Milly professing herself delighted to know that something was to be done with her. If the most remarkable woman in England was to do it, so much the better, and if the most remarkable woman in England had them both in hand together, why, what could be jollier for each? When she reflected indeed a little on the oddity of her wanting two at once, Kate had the natural reply that it was exactly what showed her sincerity. She invariably gave way to feeling, and feeling had distinctly popped up in her on the advent of her girlhood's friend. The way the cat would jump was always, in presence of anything that moved her, interesting to see; visibly enough, moreover, for a long time, it hadn't jumped anything like so far. This, in fact, as we already know, remained the marvel for Milly Theale, who, on sight of Mrs. Lowder, found fifty links in respect to Susie absent from the chain of association. She knew so herself what she thought of Susie that she would have expected the lady of Lancaster Gate to think something quite different; the failure of which endlessly mystified her. But her mystification was the cause for her of another fine impression, inasmuch as when she went so far as to observe to Kate that Susan Shepherd—and especially Susan Shepherd emerging so uninvited from an irrelevant past—ought, by all the proprieties, simply to have bored Aunt Maud, her confidant agreed with her without a protest and abounded in the sense of her wonder. Susan Shepherd at least bored the niece—that was plain; this young woman saw nothing in her—nothing to account for anything, not even for Milly's own indulgence: which little fact became in turn to the latter's mind a fact of significance. It was a light on the handsome girl—representing more than merely showed—that poor Susie was simply as nought to her. This was, in a manner too, a general admonition to poor Susie's companion, who seemed to see marked by it the direction in which she had best most look out.

It just faintly rankled in her that a person who was good enough and to spare for Milly Theale shouldn't be good enough for another girl; though, oddly enough, she could easily have forgiven Mrs. Lowder herself the impatience. Mrs. Lowder didn't feel it, and Kate Croy felt it with ease; yet in the end, be it added, she grasped the reason, and the reason enriched her mind. Wasn't it sufficiently the reason that the handsome girl was, with twenty other splendid qualities, the least bit brutal too, and didn't she suggest, as no one yet had ever done for her new friend, that there might be a wild beauty in that, and even a strange grace? Kate wasn't brutally brutal—which Milly had hitherto benightedly supposed the only way; she wasn't even aggressively so, but rather indifferently, defensively and, as might be said, by the habit of anticipation. She simplified in advance, was beforehand with her doubts, and knew with singular quickness what she wasn't, as they said in New York, going to like. In that way at least people were clearly quicker in England than at home; and Milly could quite see, after a little, how such instincts might become usual in a world in which dangers abounded. There were more dangers, clearly, round about Lancaster Gate than one suspected in New York or could dream of in Boston. At all events, with more sense of them, there were more precautions, and it was a remarkable world altogether in which there could be precautions, on whatever ground, against Susie.

IX

She certainly made up with Susie directly, however, for any allowance she might have had privately to extend to tepid appreciation; since the late and long talks of these two embraced not only everything offered and suggested by the hours they spent apart, but a good deal more besides. She might be as detached as the occasion required at four o'clock in the afternoon, but she used no such freedom to any one about anything as she habitually used about everything to Susan Shepherd at midnight. All the same, it should with much less delay than this have been mentioned, she had not yet—had not, that is, at the end of six days—produced any news for her comrade to compare with an announcement made her by the latter as a result of a drive with Mrs. Lowder, for a change, in the remarkable Battersea Park. The elder friends had sociably revolved there while the younger ones followed bolder fancies in the admirable equipage appointed to Milly at the hotel—a heavier, more emblazoned, more amusing chariot than she had ever, with "stables" notoriously mismanaged, known at home; whereby, in the course of the circuit, more than once repeated, it had "come out," as Mrs. Stringham said, that the couple at Lancaster Gate were, of all people, acquainted with Mildred's other English friend—the gentleman, the one connected with the English newspaper (Susie hung fire a little over his name) who had been with her in New York so shortly previous to present adventures. He had been named of course in Battersea Park—else he couldn't have been identified; and Susie had naturally, before she could produce her own share in the matter as a kind of confession, to make it plain that her allusion was to Mr. Merton Densher. This was because Milly had at first a little air of not knowing whom she meant; and the girl really kept, as well, a certain control of herself while she remarked that the case was surprising, the chance one in a thousand. They knew him, both Maud and Miss Croy knew him, she gathered too, rather well, though indeed it was not on any show of intimacy that he had happened to be mentioned. It had not been—Susie made the point—she herself who brought him in: he had in fact not been brought in at all, but only referred to as a young journalist known to Mrs. Lowder and who had lately gone to their wonderful country—Mrs. Lowder always said "your wonderful country"—on behalf of his journal. But Mrs. Stringham had taken it up—with the tips of her fingers indeed; and that was the confession: she had, without meaning any harm, recognised Mr. Densher as an acquaintance of Milly's, though she had also pulled herself up before getting in too far. Mrs. Lowder had been struck, clearly—it wasn't too much to say; then she also, it had rather seemed, had pulled herself up; and there had been a little moment during which each might have been keeping something from the other. "Only," said Milly's mate, "I luckily remembered in time that I had nothing whatever to keep—which was much simpler and nicer. I don't know what Maud has, but there it is. She was interested, distinctly, in your knowing him—in his having met you over there with so little loss of time. But I ventured to tell her it hadn't been so long as to make you as yet great friends. I don't know if I was right."

Whatever time this explanation might have taken, there had been moments enough in the matter now—before the elder woman's conscience had done itself justice—to enable Milly to reply that although the fact in question doubtless had its importance she imagined they wouldn't find the importance overwhelming. It *was* odd that their one Englishman should so instantly fit; it wasn't, however, miraculous—they surely all had often seen that, as every one said, the world was extraordinarily "small." Undoubtedly, too, Susie had done just the plain thing in not letting his name pass. Why in the world should there be a mystery?—and what an immense one they would appear to have made if he should come back and find they had concealed their knowledge of him! "I don't know, Susie dear," the girl observed, "what you think I have to conceal."

"It doesn't matter, at a given moment," Mrs. Stringham returned, "what you know or don't know as to what I think; for you always find out the very next moment, and when you do find out, dearest, you never *really* care. Only," she presently asked, "have you heard of him from Miss Croy?"

"Heard of Mr. Densher? Never a word. We haven't mentioned him. Why should we?"

"That *you* haven't, I understand; but that she hasn't," Susie opined, "may mean something."

"May mean what?"

"Well," Mrs. Stringham presently brought out, "I tell you all when I tell you that Maud asks me to suggest to you that it may perhaps be better for the present not to speak of him: not to speak of him to her niece, that is, unless she herself speaks to you first. But Maud thinks she won't."

Milly was ready to engage for anything; but in respect to the facts—as they so far possessed them—it all sounded a little complicated. "Is it because there's anything between them?"

"No—I gather not; but Maud's state of mind is precautionary. She's afraid of something. Or perhaps it would be more correct to say she's afraid of everything."

"She's afraid, you mean," Milly asked, "of their—a—liking each other?"

Susie had an intense thought and then an effusion. "My dear child, we move in a labyrinth."

"Of course we do. That's just the fun of it!" said Milly with a strange gaiety. Then she added: "Don't tell me that—in this for instance—there are not abysses. I want abysses."

Her friend looked at her—it was not unfrequently the case—a little harder than the surface of the occasion seemed to require; and another person present at such times might have wondered to what inner thought of her own the good lady was trying to fit the speech. It was too much her disposition, no doubt, to treat her young companion's words as symptoms of an imputed malady. It was none the less, however, her highest law to be light when the girl was light. She knew how to be quaint with the new quaintness—the great Boston gift; it had been, happily, her note in the magazines; and Maud Lowder, to whom it was new indeed and who had never heard anything remotely like it, quite cherished her, as a social resource, for it. It should not therefore fail her now; with it in fact one might face most things. "Ah, then let us hope we shall sound the depths—I'm prepared for the worst—of sorrow and sin! But she would like her niece—we're not ignorant of that, are we?—to marry Lord Mark. Hasn't she told you so?"

"Hasn't Mrs. Lowder told me?"

"No; hasn't Kate? It isn't, you know, that she doesn't know it."

Milly had, under her comrade's eyes, a minute of mute detachment. She had lived with Kate Croy for several days in a state of intimacy as deep as it had been sudden, and they had clearly, in talk, in many directions, proceeded to various extremities. Yet it now came over her as in a clear cold way that there was a possible account of their relations in which the quantity her new friend had told her might have figured as small, as smallest, beside the quantity she hadn't. She couldn't say, at any rate, whether or no she had made the point that her aunt designed her for Lord Mark: it had only sufficiently come out—which had been, moreover, eminently guessable—that she was involved in her aunt's designs. Somehow, for Milly, brush it over nervously as she might and with whatever simplifying hand, this abrupt extrusion of Mr. Densher altered all proportions, had an effect on all values. It was fantastic of her to let it make a difference that she couldn't in the least have defined—and she was at least, even during these instants, rather proud of being able to hide, on the spot, the difference it did make. Yet, all the same, the effect for her was, almost violently, of Mr. Densher's having been there—having been where she had stood till now in her simplicity—before her. It would have taken but another free moment to make her see abysses—since abysses were what she wanted—in the mere circumstance of his own silence, in New York, about his English friends. There had really been in New York little time for anything; but, had she liked, Milly could have made it out for herself that he had avoided the subject of Miss Croy, and that Miss Croy was yet a subject it could never be natural to avoid. It was to be added at the same time that even if his silence had been labyrinthe—which was absurd in view of all the other things too he couldn't possibly have spoken of—this was exactly what must suit her, since it fell under the head of the plea she had just uttered to Susie. These things, however, came and went, and it set itself up between the companions, for the occasion, in the oddest way, both that their happening all to know Mr. Densher—except indeed that Susie didn't, but probably would,—was a fact belonging, in a world of rushing about, to one of the common orders of chance; and yet further that it was amusing—oh, awfully amusing!—to be able fondly to hope that there was "something in" its having been left to crop up with such suddenness. There seemed somehow a possibility that the ground or, as it were, the air might, in a manner, have undergone some pleasing preparation; though the question of this possibility would probably, after all, have taken some threshing out. The truth, moreover—and there they were, already, our pair, talking about it, the "truth!"—had not in fact quite cropped out. This, obviously, in view of Mrs. Lowder's request to her old friend.

It was accordingly on Mrs. Lowder's recommendation that nothing should be said to Kate—it was on this rich attitude of Aunt Maud's that the idea of an interesting complication might best hope to perch; and when, in fact, after the colloquy we have reported Milly saw Kate again without mentioning any name, her silence succeeded in passing muster with her as the beginning of a new sort of fun. The sort was all the newer by reason of its containing a small element of anxiety: when she had gone in for fun before it had been with her hands a little more free. Yet it *was,* none the less, rather exciting to be conscious of a still sharper reason for interest in the handsome girl, as Kate continued, even now, pre-eminently to remain for her; and a reason—this was the great point—of which the young woman herself could have no suspicion. Twice over, thus, for two or three hours together, Milly found herself seeing Kate, quite fixing her in the light of the knowledge that it was a face on which Mr. Densher's eyes had more or less familiarly rested and which, by the same token, had looked, rather *more* beautifully than less, into his own. She pulled herself up indeed with the thought that it had inevitably looked, as beautifully as one would, into thousands of faces in which one might one's self never trace it; but just the odd result of the thought was to intensify for the girl that side of her friend which she had doubtless already been more prepared than she quite knew to think of as the "other," the not wholly calculable. It was fantastic, and Milly was aware of this; but the other side was what had, of a sudden, been turned straight towards her by the show of Mr. Densher's propinquity. She hadn't the excuse of knowing it for Kate's own, since nothing whatever as yet proved it particularly to be such. Never mind; it was with this other side now fully presented that Kate came and went, kissed her for greeting and for parting, talked, as usual, of everything but—as it had so abruptly become for Milly—*the* thing. Our young woman, it is true, would doubtless not have tasted so sharply a difference in this pair of occasions had she not been tasting so peculiarly her own possible betrayals. What happened was that afterwards, on separation, she wondered if the matter had not mainly been that she herself was so "other," so taken up with the unspoken; the strangest thing of all being, still subsequently, that when she asked herself how Kate could have failed to feel it she became conscious of being here on the edge of a great darkness. She should never know how Kate truly felt about anything such a one as Milly Theale should give her to feel. Kate would never—and not from ill-will, nor from duplicity, but from a sort of failure of common terms—reduce it to such a one's comprehension or put it within her convenience.

It was as such a one, therefore, that, for three or four days more, Milly watched Kate as just such another; and it was presently as such a one that she threw herself into their promised visit, at last achieved, to Chelsea, the quarter of the famous Carlyle, the field of exercise of his ghost, his votaries, and the residence of "poor Marian," so often referred to and actually a somewhat incongruous spirit there. With our young woman's first view of poor Marian everything gave way but the sense of how, in England, apparently, the social situation of sisters could be opposed, how common ground, for a place in the world, could quite fail them: a state of things sagely perceived to be involved in an hierarchical, an aristocratic order. Just whereabouts in the order Mrs. Lowder had established her niece was a question not wholly void, as yet, no doubt, of ambiguity—though Milly was withal sure Lord Mark could exactly have fixed the point if he would, fixing it at the same time for Aunt Maud herself; but it was clear that Mrs. Condrip was, as might have been said, in quite another geography. She would not, in short, have been to be found on the same social map, and it was as if her visitors had turned over page after page together before the final relief of their benevolent "Here!" The interval was bridged, of course, but the bridge, verily, was needed, and the impression left Milly to wonder whether, in the general connection, it were of bridges or of intervals that the spirit not locally disciplined would find itself most conscious. It was as if at home, by contrast, there were neither—neither the difference itself, from position to position, nor, on either side, and particularly on one, the awfully good manner, the conscious sinking of a consciousness, that made up for it. The conscious sinking, at all events, and the awfully good manner, the difference, the bridge, the interval, the skipped leaves of the social atlas—these, it was to be confessed, had a little, for our young lady, in default of stouter stuff, to work themselves into the light literary legend—a mixed, wandering echo of Trollope, of Thackeray, perhaps mostly of Dickens—under favour of which her pilgrimage had so much appealed. She could relate to Susie later on, late the same evening, that the legend, before she had done with it, had run clear, that the adored author of *The Newcomes*, in fine, had been on the whole the note: the picture lacking thus more than she had hoped, or rather perhaps showing less than she had feared, a certain possibility of Pickwickian outline. She explained how she meant by this that Mrs. Condrip had not altogether proved another Mrs. Nickleby, nor even—for she might have proved almost anything, from the way poor worried Kate had spoken—a widowed and aggravated Mrs. Micawber.

Mrs. Stringham, in the midnight conference, intimated rather yearningly that, however the event might have turned, the side of English life such experiences opened to Milly were just those she herself seemed "booked"—as they were all, roundabout her now, always saying—to miss: she had begun to have a little, for her fellow-observer, these moments of fanciful reaction—reaction in which she was once more all Susan Shepherd—against the high sphere of colder conventions into which her overwhelming connection with Maud Manningham had rapt her. Milly never lost sight, for long, of the Susan Shepherd side of her, and was always there to meet it when it came up and vaguely, tenderly, impatiently to pat it, abounding in the assurance that they would still provide for it. They had, however, to-night, another matter in hand; which proved to be presently, on the girl's part, in respect to her hour of Chelsea, the revelation that Mrs. Condrip, taking a few minutes when Kate was away with one of the children, in bed upstairs for some small complaint, had suddenly, without its being in the least "led up to," broken ground on the subject of Mr. Densher, mentioned him with impatience as a person in love with her sister. "She wished me, if I cared for Kate, to know," Milly said—"for it would be quite too dreadful, and one might do something."

Susie wondered. "Prevent anything coming of it? That's easily said. Do what?"

Milly had a dim smile. "I think that what she would like is that I should come a good deal to see her about it."

"And doesn't she suppose you've anything else to do?"

The girl had by this time clearly made it out. "Nothing but to admire and make much of her sister—whom she doesn't, however, herself in the least understand—and give up one's time, and everything else, to it." It struck the elder friend that she spoke with an almost unprecedented approach to sharpness; as if Mrs. Condrip had been rather specially disconcerting. Never yet so much as just of late had Mrs. Stringham seen her companion as exalted, and by the very play of something within, into a vague golden air that left irritation below. That was the great thing with Milly—it was her characteristic poetry; or at least it was Susan Shepherd's. "But she made a point," the former continued, "of my keeping what she says from Kate. I'm not to mention that she has spoken."

"And why," Mrs. Stringham presently asked, "is Mr. Densher so dreadful?"

Milly had, she thought, an hesitation—something that suggested a fuller talk with Mrs. Condrip than she inclined perhaps to report. "It isn't so much he himself." Then the girl spoke a little as for the romance of it; one could never tell, with her, where romance would come in. "It's the state of his fortunes."

"And is that very bad?"

"He has no 'private means,' and no prospect of any. He has no income, and no ability, according to Mrs. Condrip, to make one. He's as poor, she calls it, as 'poverty,' and she says she knows what that is."

Again Mrs. Stringham considered, and it presently produced something. "But isn't he brilliantly clever?"

Milly had also then an instant that was not quite fruitless. "I haven't the least idea."

To which, for the time, Susie only answered "Oh!"—though by the end of a minute she had followed it with a slightly musing "I see"; and that in turn with: "It's quite what Maud Lowder thinks."

"That he'll never do anything?"

"No—quite the contrary: that he's exceptionally able."

"Oh yes; I know"—Milly had again, in reference to what her friend had already told her of this, her little tone of a moment before. "But Mrs. Condrip's own great point is that Aunt Maud herself won't hear of any such person. Mr. Densher, she holds that's the way, at any rate, it was explained to me—won't ever be either a public man or a rich man. If he were public she'd be willing, as I understand, to help him; if he were rich—without being anything else—she'd do her best to swallow him. As it is, she taboos him."

"In short," said Mrs. Stringham as with a private purpose, "she told you, the sister, all about it. But Mrs. Lowder likes him," she added.

"Mrs. Condrip didn't tell me that."

"Well, she does, all the same, my dear, extremely."

"Then there it is!" On which, with a drop and one of those sudden, slightly sighing surrenders to a vague reflux and a general fatigue that had recently more than once marked themselves for her companion, Milly turned away. Yet the matter was not left so, that night, between them, albeit neither perhaps could afterwards have said which had first come back to it. Milly's own nearest approach, at least, for a little, to doing so, was to remark that they appeared all—every one they saw—to think tremendously of money. This prompted in Susie a laugh, not untender, the innocent meaning of which was that it came, as a subject for indifference, money did, easier to some people than to others: she made the point in fairness, however, that you couldn't have told, by any too crude transparency of air, what place it held for Maud Manningham. She did her worldliness with grand proper silences—if it mightn't better be put perhaps that she did her detachment with grand occasional pushes. However Susie put it, in truth, she was really, in justice to herself, thinking of the difference, as favourites of fortune, between her old friend and her new. Aunt Maud sat somehow in the midst of her money, founded on it and surrounded by it, even if with a clever high manner about it, her manner of looking, hard and bright, as if it weren't there. Milly, about hers, had no manner at all—which was possibly, from a point of view, a fault: she was at any rate far away on the edge of it, and you hadn't, as might be said, in order to get at her nature, to traverse, by whatever avenue, any piece of her property. It was clear, on the other hand, that Mrs. Lowder was keeping her wealth as for purposes, imaginations, ambitions, that would figure as large, as honourably unselfish, on the day they should take effect. She would impose her will, but her will would be only that a person or two shouldn't lose a benefit by not submitting if they could be made to submit. To Milly, as so much younger, such far views couldn't be imputed: there was nobody she was supposable as interested for. It was too soon, since she wasn't interested for herself. Even the richest woman, at her age, lacked motive, and Milly's motive doubtless had plenty of time to arrive. She was meanwhile beautiful, simple, sublime without it—whether missing it and vaguely reaching out for it or not; and with it, for that matter, in the event, would really be these things just as much. Only then she might very well have, like Aunt Maud, a manner. Such were the connections, at all events, in which the colloquy of our two ladies freshly flickered up—in which it came round that the elder asked the younger if she had herself, in the afternoon, named Mr. Densher as an acquaintance.

"Oh no—I said nothing of having seen him. I remembered," the girl explained, "Mrs. Lowder's wish."

"But that," her friend observed after a moment, "was for silence to Kate."

"Yes—but Mrs. Condrip would immediately have told Kate."

"Why so?—since she must dislike to talk about him."

"Mrs. Condrip must?" Milly thought. "What she would like most is that her sister should be brought to think ill of him; and if anything she can tell her will help that—" But Milly dropped suddenly here, as if her companion would see.

Her companion's interest, however, was all for what she herself saw. "You mean she'll immediately speak?" Mrs. Stringham gathered that this was what Milly meant, but it left still a question. "How will it be against him that you know him?"

"Oh, I don't know. It won't be so much one's knowing him as one's having kept it out of sight."

"Ah," said Mrs. Stringham, as if for comfort, *"you* haven't kept it out of sight. Isn't it much rather Miss Croy herself who has?"

"It isn't my acquaintance with him," Milly smiled, "that she has dissimulated."

"She has dissimulated only her own? Well then, the responsibility's hers."

"Ah but," said the girl, not perhaps with marked consequence, "she has a right to do as she likes."

"Then so, my dear, have you!" smiled Susan Shepherd.

Milly looked at her as if she were almost venerably simple, but also as if this were what one loved her for. "We're not quarrelling about it, Kate and I, *yet."*

"I only meant," Mrs. Stringham explained, "that I don't see what Mrs. Condrip would gain."

"By her being able to tell Kate?" Milly thought. "I only meant that I don't see what I myself should gain."

"But it will have to come out—that he knows you both—some time."

Milly scarce assented. "Do you mean when he comes back?"

"He'll find you both here, and he can hardly be looked to, I take it, to 'cut' either of you for the sake of the other."

This placed the question at last on a basis more distinctly cheerful. "I might get at him somehow beforehand," the girl suggested; "I might give him what they call here the tip—that he's not to know me when we meet. Or, better still, I mightn't be here at all."

"Do you want to run away from him?"

It was, oddly enough, an idea Milly seemed half to accept. "I don't know *what* I want to run away from!"

It dispelled, on the spot—something, to the elder woman's ear, in the sad, sweet sound of it—any ghost of any need of explaining. The sense was constant for her that their relation was as if afloat, like some island of the south, in a great warm sea that made, for every conceivable chance, a margin, an outer sphere of general emotion; and the effect of the occurrence of anything in particular was to make the sea submerge the island, the margin flood the text. The great wave now for a moment swept over. "I'll go anywhere else in the world you like."

But Milly came up through it. "Dear old Susie—how I do work you!"

"Oh, this is nothing yet."

"No indeed—to what it will be."

"You're not—and it's vain to pretend," said dear old Susie, who had been taking her in, "as sound and strong as I insist on having you."

"Insist, insist—the more the better. But the day I *look* as sound and strong as that, you know," Milly went on—"on that day I shall be just sound and strong enough to take leave of you sweetly for ever. That's where one is," she continued thus agreeably to embroider, "when even one's *most* 'beaux moments' aren't such as to qualify, so far as appearance goes, for anything gayer than a handsome cemetery. Since I've lived all these years as if I were dead, I shall die, no doubt, as if I were alive—which will happen to be as you want me. So, you see," she wound up, "you'll never really know where I am. Except indeed when I'm gone; and then you'll only know where I'm not."

"I'd die *for* you," said Susan Shepherd after a moment.

"'Thanks awfully'! Then stay here for me."

"But we can't be in London for August, nor for many of all these next weeks."

"Then we'll go back."

Susie blenched. "Back to America?"

"No, abroad—to Switzerland, Italy, anywhere. I mean by your staying here for me," Milly pursued, "your staying with me wherever I may be, even though we may neither of us know at the time where it is. No," she insisted, "I *don't* know where I am, and you never will, and it doesn't matter—and I dare say it's quite true," she broke off, "that everything will have to come out." Her friend would have felt of her that she joked about it now, had not her scale from grave to gay been a thing of such unnamable shades that her contrasts were never sharp. She made up for failures of gravity by failures of mirth; if she hadn't, that is, been at times as earnest as might have been liked, so she was certain not to be at other times as easy as she would like herself. "I must face the music. It isn't, at any rate, its 'coming out,'" she added; "it's that Mrs. Condrip would put the fact before her to his injury."

Her companion wondered. "But how to *his?"*

"Why, if he pretends to love her——!"

"And does he only 'pretend'?"

"I mean if, trusted by her in strange countries, he forgets her so far as to make up to other people."

The amendment, however, brought Susie in, as if with gaiety, for a comfortable end. "Did he make up, the false creature, to *you?"*

"No—but the question isn't of that. It's of what Kate might be made to believe."

"That, given the fact that he evidently more or less followed up his acquaintance with you, to say nothing of your obvious weird charm, he must have been all ready if you had at all led him on?"

Milly neither accepted nor qualified this; she only said, after a moment, as with a conscious excess of the pensive: "No, I don't think she'd quite wish to suggest that I made up to *him;* for that I should have had to do so would only bring out his constancy. All I mean is," she added—and now at last, as with a supreme impatience "that her being able to make him out a little a person who could give cause for jealousy would evidently help her, since she's afraid of him, to do him in her sister's mind a useful ill turn."

Susan Shepherd perceived in this explanation such signs of an appetite for motive as would have sat gracefully even on one of her own New England heroines. It was seeing round several corners; but that was what New England heroines did, and it was moreover interesting for the moment to make out how many really her young friend had undertaken to see round. Finally, too, weren't they braving the deeps? They got their amusement where they could. "Isn't it only," she asked, "rather probable she'd see that Kate's knowing him as (what's the pretty old word?) *volage*——?"

"Well?" She hadn't filled out her idea, but neither, it seemed, could Milly.

"Well, might but do what that often does—by all *our* blessed little laws and arrangements at least; excite Kate's own sentiment instead of depressing it."

The idea was bright, yet the girl but beautifully stared. "Kate's own sentiment? Oh, she didn't speak of that. I don't think," she added as if she had been unconsciously giving a wrong impression, "I don't think Mrs. Condrip imagines *she's* in love."

It made Mrs. Stringham stare in turn. "Then what's her fear?"

"Well, only the fact of Mr. Densher's possibly himself keeping it up—the fear of some final result from *that.*

"Oh," said Susie, intellectually a little disconcerted—"she looks far ahead!"

At this, however, Milly threw off another of her sudden vague "sports." "No—it's only we who do."

"Well, don't let us be more interested for them than they are for themselves!"

"Certainly not"—the girl promptly assented. A certain interest nevertheless remained; she appeared to wish to be clear. "It wasn't of anything on Kate's own part she spoke."

"You mean she thinks her sister does *not* care for him?"

It was still as if, for an instant, Milly had to be sure of what she meant; but there it presently was. "If she did care Mrs. Condrip would have told me."

What Susan Shepherd seemed hereupon for a little to wonder was why then they had been talking so. "But did you ask her?"

"Ah, no!"

"Oh!" said Susan Shepherd.

Milly, however, easily explained that she wouldn't have asked her for the world.

BOOK FIFTH

X

Lord Mark looked at her to-day in particular as if to wring from her a confession that she had originally done him injustice; and he was entitled to whatever there might be in it of advantage or merit that his intention really in a manner took effect: he cared about something, that is, after all, sufficiently to make her feel absurdly as if she *were* confessing—all the while it was quite the case that neither justice nor injustice was what had been in question between them. He had presented himself at the hotel, had found her and had found Susan Shepherd at home, had been "civil" to Susan—it was just that shade, and Susan's fancy had fondly caught it; and then had come again and missed them, and then had come and found them once more: besides letting them easily see that if it hadn't by this time been the end of everything—which they could feel in the exhausted air, that of the season at its last gasp—the places they might have liked to go to were such as they would have had only to mention. Their feeling was—or at any rate their modest general plea—that there was no place they would have liked to go to; there was only the sense of finding they liked, wherever they were, the place to which they had been brought. Such was highly the case as to their current consciousness—which could be indeed, in an equally eminent degree, but a matter of course; impressions this afternoon having by a happy turn of their wheel been gathered for them into a splendid cluster, an offering like an armful of the rarest flowers. They were in presence of the offering—they had been led up to it; and if it had been still their habit to look at each other across distances for increase of unanimity his hand would have been silently named between them as the hand applied to the wheel. He had administered the touch that, under light analysis, made the difference—the difference of their not having lost, as Susie on the spot and at the hour phrased it again and again, both for herself and for such others as the question might concern, so beautiful and interesting an experience; the difference also, in fact, of Mrs. Lowder's not having lost it either, though it was with Mrs. Lowder, superficially, they had come, and though it was further with that lady that our young woman was directly engaged during the half-hour or so of her most agreeably inward response to the scene.

The great historic house had, for Milly, beyond terrace and garden, as the centre of an almost extravagantly grand Watteau-composition, a tone as of old gold kept "down" by the quality of the air, summer full-flushed, but attuned to the general perfect taste. Much, by her measure, for the previous hour, appeared, in connection with this revelation of it, to have happened to her—a quantity expressed in introductions of charming new people, in walks through halls of armour, of pictures, of cabinets, of tapestry, of tea-tables, in an assault of reminders that this largeness of style was the sign of *appointed* felicity. The largeness of style was the great containing vessel, while everything else, the pleasant personal affluence, the easy, murmurous welcome, the honoured age of illustrious host and hostess, all at once so distinguished and so plain, so public and so shy, became but this or that element of the infusion. The elements melted together and seasoned the draught, the essence of which might have struck the girl as distilled into the small cup of iced coffee she had vaguely accepted from somebody, while a fuller flood, somehow, kept bearing her up—all the freshness of response of her young life the freshness of the first and only prime. What had perhaps brought on just now a kind of climax was the fact of her appearing to make out, through Aunt Maud, what was really the matter. It couldn't be less than a climax for a poor shaky maiden to find it put to her of a sudden that she herself was the matter—for that was positively what, on Mrs. Lowder's part, it came to. Everything was great, of course, in great pictures, and it was doubtless precisely a part of the brilliant life—since the brilliant life, as one had faintly figured it, clearly *was* humanly led—that all impressions within its area partook of its brilliancy; still, letting that pass, it fairly stamped an hour as with the official seal for one to be able to take in so comfortably one's companion's broad blandness. "You must stay among us—you must stay; anything else is impossible and ridiculous; you don't know yet, no doubt—you can't; but you will soon enough: you can stay in *any* position." It had been as the murmurous consecration to follow the murmurous welcome; and even if it were but part of Aunt Maud's own spiritual ebriety—for the dear woman, one could see, was spiritually "keeping" the day—it served to Milly, then and afterwards, as a high-water mark of the imagination.

It was to be the end of the short parenthesis which had begun but the other day at Lancaster Gate with Lord Mark's informing her that she was a "success"—the key thus again struck; and though no distinct, no numbered revelations had crowded in, there had, as we have seen, been plenty of incident for the space and the time. There had been thrice as much, and all gratuitous and genial—if, in portions, not exactly hitherto *the* revelation—as three unprepared weeks could have been expected to produce. Mrs. Lowder had improvised a "rush" for them, but out of elements, as Milly was now a little more freely aware, somewhat roughly combined. Therefore if at this very instant she had her reasons for thinking of the parenthesis as about to close—reasons completely personal—she had on behalf of her companion a divination almost as deep. The parenthesis would close with this admirable picture, but the admirable picture still would show Aunt Maud as not absolutely sure either if she herself were destined to remain in it. What she was doing, Milly might even not have escaped seeming to see, was to talk herself into a sublimer serenity while she ostensibly talked Milly. It was fine, the girl fully felt, the way she did talk *her,* little as, at bottom, our young woman needed it or found other persuasions at fault. It was in particular during the minutes of her grateful absorption of iced coffee—qualified by a sharp doubt of her wisdom—that she most had in view Lord Mark's relation to her being there, or at least to the question of her being amused at it. It wouldn't have taken much by the end of five minutes quite to make her feel that this relation was charming. It might, once more, simply have been that everything, anything, was charming when one was so justly and completely charmed; but, frankly, she had not supposed anything so serenely sociable could define itself between them as the friendly understanding that was at present somehow in the air. They were, many of them together, near the marquee that had been erected on a stretch of sward as a temple of refreshment and that happened to have the property—which was all to the good of making Milly think of a "durbar"; her iced coffee had been a consequence of this connection, in which, further, the bright company scattered about fell thoroughly into place. Certain of its members might have represented the contingent of "native princes"—familiar, but scarce the less grandly gregarious term!—and Lord Mark would have done for one of these even though for choice he but presented himself as a supervisory friend of the family. The Lancaster Gate family, he clearly intended, in which he included its American recruits, and included above all Kate Croy—a young person blessedly easy to take care of. She knew people, and people knew her, and she was the handsomest thing there—this last a declaration made by Milly, in a sort of soft mid-summer madness, a straight skylark-flight of charity, to Aunt Maud.

Kate had, for her new friend's eyes, the extraordinary and attaching property of appearing at a given moment to show as a beautiful stranger, to cut her connections and lose her identity, letting the imagination for the time make what it would of them—make her merely a person striking from afar, more and more pleasing as one watched, but who was above all a subject for curiosity. Nothing could have given her, as a party to a relation, a greater freshness than this sense—which sprang up at its own hours—of being as curious about her as if one hadn't known her. It had sprung up, we have gathered, as soon as Milly had seen her after hearing from Mrs. Stringham of her knowledge of Merton Densher; she had *looked* then other and, as Milly knew the real critical mind would call it, more objective; and our young woman had foreseen it of her, on the spot, that she would often look so again. It was exactly what she was doing this afternoon; and Milly, who had amusements of thought that were like the secrecies of a little girl playing with dolls when conventionally "too big," could almost settle to the game of what one would suppose her, how one would place her, if one didn't know her. She became thus, intermittently, a figure conditioned only by the great facts of aspect, a figure to be waited for, named and fitted. This was doubtless but a way of feeling that it was of her essence to be peculiarly what the occasion, whatever it might be, demanded when its demand was highest. There were probably ways enough, on these lines, for such a consciousness; another of them would be, for instance, to say that she was made for great social uses. Milly was not wholly sure that she herself knew what great social uses might be—unless, as a good example, exerting just that sort of glamour in just that sort of frame were one of them: she would have fallen back on knowing sufficiently that they existed at all events for her friend. It imputed a primness, all round, to be reduced but to saying, by way of a translation of one's amusement, that she was always so *right*—since that, too often, was what the *insupportables* themselves were; yet it was, in overflow to Aunt Maud, what she had to content herself withal—save for the lame enhancement of saying she was lovely. It served, all the same, the purpose, strengthened the bond that for the time held the two ladies together, distilled in short its drop of rose-colour for Mrs. Lowder's own view. That was really the view Milly had, for most of the rest of the occasion, to give herself to immediately taking in; but it didn't prevent the continued play of those swift cross-lights, odd beguilements of the mind, at which we have already glanced.

Mrs. Lowder herself found it enough simply to reply, in respect to Kate, that she was indeed a luxury to take about the world: she expressed no more surprise than that at her "rightness" to-day. Wasn't it by this time sufficiently manifest that it was precisely as the very luxury she was proving that she had, from far back, been appraised and waited for? Crude elation, however, might be kept at bay, and the circumstance none the less demonstrated that they were all swimming together in the blue. It came back to Lord Mark again, as he seemed slowly to pass and repass and conveniently to linger before them; he was personally the note of the blue—like a suspended skein of silk within reach of the broiderer's hand. Aunt Maud's free-moving shuttle took a length of him at rhythmic intervals; and one of the intermixed truths that flickered across to Milly was that he ever so consentingly knew he was being worked in. This was almost like an understanding with her at Mrs. Lowder's expense, which she would have none of; she wouldn't for the world have had him make any such point as that he wouldn't have launched them at Matcham—or whatever it was he *had* done—only for Aunt Maud's *beaux yeux.* What he had done, it would have been guessable, was something he had for some time been desired in vain to do; and what they were all now profiting by was a change comparatively sudden, the cessation of hope delayed. What had caused the cessation easily showed itself as none of Milly's business; and she was luckily, for that matter, in no real danger of hearing from him directly that her individual weight had been felt in the scale. Why then indeed was it an effect of his diffused but subdued participation that he might absolutely have been saying to her "Yes, let the dear woman take her own tone? Since she's here she may stay," he might have been adding—"for whatever she can make of it. But you and I are different." Milly knew *she* was different in truth—his own difference was his own affair; but also she knew that, after all, even at their distinctest, Lord Mark's "tips" in this line would be tacit. He practically placed her—it came round again to that—under no obligation whatever. It was a matter of equal ease, moreover, her letting Mrs. Lowder take a tone. She might have taken twenty—they would have spoiled nothing.

"You must stay on with us; you *can,* you know, in any position you like; any, any, *any,* my dear child"—and her emphasis went deep. "You must make your home with us; and it's really open to you to make the most beautiful one in the world. You mustn't be under a mistake—under any of any sort; and you must let us all think for you a little, take care of you and watch over you. Above all you must help me with Kate, and you must stay a little *for* her; nothing for a long time has happened to me so good as that you and she should have become friends. It's beautiful; it's great; it's everything. What makes it perfect is that it should have come about through our dear delightful Susie, restored to me, after so many years, by such a miracle. No—that's more charming to me than even your hitting it off with Kate. God has been good to one—positively; for I couldn't, at my age, have made a new friend—undertaken, I mean, out of whole cloth, the real thing. It's like changing one's bankers—after fifty: one doesn't do that. That's why Susie has been kept for me, as you seem to keep people in your wonderful country, in lavender and pink paper—coming back at last as straight as out of a fairy-tale and with you as an attendant fairy." Milly hereupon replied appreciatively that such a description of herself made her feel as if pink paper were her dress and lavender its trimming; but Aunt Maud was not to be deterred by a weak joke from keeping it up. Her interlocutress could feel besides that she kept it up in perfect sincerity. She was somehow at this hour a very happy woman, and a part of her happiness might precisely have been that her affections and her views were moving as never before in concert. Unquestionably she loved Susie; but she also loved Kate and loved Lord Mark, loved their funny old host and hostess, loved every one within range, down to the very servant who came to receive Milly's empty iceplate—down, for that matter, to Milly herself, who was, while she talked, really conscious of the enveloping flap of a protective mantle, a shelter with the weight of an eastern carpet. An eastern carpet, for wishing-purposes of one's own, was a thing to be on rather than under; still, however, if the girl should fail of breath it wouldn't be, she could feel, by Mrs. Lowder's fault. One of the last things she was afterwards to recall of this was Aunt Maud's going on to say that she and Kate must stand together because together they could do anything. It was for Kate of course she was essentially planning; but the plan, enlarged and uplifted now, somehow required Milly's prosperity too for its full operation, just as Milly's prosperity at the same time involved Kate's. It was nebulous yet, it was slightly confused, but it was unmistakably free and genial, and it made our young woman understand things Kate had said of her aunt's possibilities as well as characterisations that had fallen from Susan Shepherd. One of the most frequent on the lips of the latter had been that dear Maud was a natural force.

XI

A prime reason, we must add, why sundry impressions were not to be fully present to the girl till later on was that they yielded at this stage, with an effect of sharp supersession, to a detached quarter of an hour—her only one—with Lord Mark. "Have you seen the picture in the house, the beautiful one that's so like you?"—he was asking that as he stood before her; having come up at last with his smooth intimation that any wire he had pulled and yet wanted not to remind her of wasn't quite a reason for his having no joy at all.

"I've been through rooms and I've seen pictures. But if I'm 'like' anything so beautiful as most of them seemed to me——!" It needed in short for Milly some evidence, which he only wanted to supply. She was the image of the wonderful Bronzino, which she must have a look at on every ground. He had thus called her off and led her away; the more easily that the house within was above all what had already drawn round her its mystic circle. Their progress, meanwhile, was not of the straightest; it was an advance, without haste, through innumerable natural pauses and soft concussions, determined for the most part by the appearance before them of ladies and gentlemen, singly, in couples, in groups, who brought them to a stand with an inveterate "I say, Mark." What they said she never quite made out; it was their all so domestically knowing him, and his knowing them, that mainly struck her, while her impression, for the rest, was but of fellow-strollers more vaguely afloat than themselves, supernumeraries mostly a little battered, whether as jaunty males or as ostensibly elegant women. They might have been moving a good deal by a momentum that had begun far back, but they were still brave and personable, still warranted for continuance as long again, and they gave her, in especial collectively, a sense of pleasant voices, pleasanter than those of actors, of friendly, empty words and kind, lingering eyes. The lingering eyes looked her over, the lingering eyes were what went, in almost confessed simplicity, with the pointless "I say, Mark "; and what was really most sensible of all was that, as a pleasant matter of course, if she didn't mind, he seemed to suggest their letting people, poor dear things, have the benefit of her.

The odd part was that he made her herself believe, for amusement, in the benefit, measured by him in mere manner—for wonderful, of a truth, was, as a means of expression, his slightness of emphasis—that her present good-nature conferred. It was, as she could easily see, a mild common carnival of good-nature—a mass of London people together, of sorts and sorts, but who mainly knew each other and who, in their way, did, no doubt, confess to curiosity. It had gone round that she was there; questions about her would be passing; the easiest thing was to run the gauntlet with *him*—just as the easiest thing was in fact to trust him generally. Couldn't she know for herself, passively, how little harm they meant her?—to that extent that it made no difference whether or not he introduced them. The strangest thing of all for Milly was perhaps the uplifted assurance and indifference with which she could simply give back the particular bland stare that appeared in such cases to mark civilisation at its highest. It was so little her fault, this oddity of what had "gone round" about her, that to accept it without question might be as good a way as another of feeling life. It was inevitable to supply the probable description—that of the awfully rich young American who was so queer to behold, but nice, by all accounts, to know; and she had really but one instant of speculation as to fables or fantasies perchance originally launched. She asked herself once only if Susie could, inconceivably, have been blatant about her; for the question, on the spot, was really blown away for ever. She knew in fact on the spot and with sharpness just why she had "elected" Susan Shepherd: she had had from the first hour the conviction of her being precisely the person in the world least possibly a trumpeter. So it wasn't their fault, it wasn't their fault, and anything might happen that would, and everything now again melted together, and kind eyes were always kind eyes—if it were never to be worse than that! She got with her companion into the house; they brushed, beneficently, past all their accidents. The Bronzino was, it appeared, deep within, and the long afternoon light lingered for them on patches of old colour and waylaid them, as they went, in nooks and opening vistas.

It was all the while for Milly as if Lord Mark had really had something other than this spoken pretext in view; as if there were something he wanted to say to her and were only—consciously yet not awkwardly, just delicately—hanging fire. At the same time it was as if the thing had practically been said by the moment they came in sight of the picture; since what it appeared to amount to was "Do let a fellow who isn't a fool take care of you a little." The thing somehow, with the aid of the Bronzino, was done; it hadn't seemed to matter to her before if he were a fool or no; but now, just where they were, she liked his not being; and it was all moreover none the worse for coming back to something of the same sound as Mrs. Lowder's so recent reminder. She too wished to take care of her—and wasn't it, *à peu près,* what all the people with the kind eyes were wishing? Once more things melted together—the beauty and the history and the facility and the splendid midsummer glow: it was a sort of magnificent maximum, the pink dawn of an apotheosis, coming so curiously soon. What in fact befell was that, as she afterwards made out, it was Lord Mark who said nothing in particular—it was she herself who said all. She couldn't help that—it came; and the reason it came was that she found herself, for the first moment, looking at the mysterious portrait through tears. Perhaps it was her tears that made it just then so strange and fair—as wonderful as he had said: the face of a young woman, all magnificently drawn, down to the hands, and magnificently dressed; a face almost livid in hue, yet handsome in sadness and crowned with a mass of hair rolled back and high, that must, before fading with time, have had a family resemblance to her own. The lady in question, at all events, with her slightly Michaelangelesque squareness, her eyes of other days, her full lips, her long neck, her recorded jewels, her brocaded and wasted reds, was a very great personage—only unaccompanied by a joy. And she was dead, dead, dead. Milly recognised her exactly in words that had nothing to do with her. "I shall never be better than this."

He smiled for her at the portrait. "Than she? You'd scarce need to be better, for surely that's well enough. But you *are,* one feels, as it happens, better; because, splendid as she is, one doubts if she was good."

He hadn't understood. She was before the picture, but she had turned to him, and she didn't care if, for the minute, he noticed her tears. It was probably as good a moment as she should ever have with him. It was perhaps as good a moment as she should have with any one, or have in any connection whatever. "I mean that everything this afternoon has been too beautiful, and that perhaps everything together will never be so right again. I'm very glad therefore you've been a part of it."

Though he still didn't understand her he was as nice as if he had; he didn't ask for insistence, and that was just a part of his looking after her. He simply protected her now from herself, and there was a world of practice in it. "Oh, we must talk about these things!"

Ah, they had already done that, she knew, as much as she ever would; and she was shaking her head at her pale sister the next moment with a world, on her side, of slowness. "I wish I could see the resemblance. Of course her complexion's green," she laughed; "but mine's several shades greener."

"It's down to the very hands," said Lord Mark.

"Her hands are large," Milly went on, "but mine are larger. Mine are huge."

"Oh, you go her, all round, 'one better'—which is just what I said. But you're a pair. You must surely catch it," he added as if it were important to his character as a serious man not to appear to have invented his plea.

"I don't know one never knows one's self. It's a funny fancy, and I don't imagine it would have occurred——"

"I see it *has* occurred"—he has already taken her up. She had her back, as she faced the picture, to one of the doors of the room, which was open, and on her turning, as he spoke, she saw that they were in the presence of three other persons, also, as appeared, interested inquirers. Kate Croy was one of these; Lord Mark had just become aware of her, and she, all arrested, had immediately seen, and made the best of it, that she was far from being first in the field. She had brought a lady and a gentleman to whom she wished to show what Lord Mark was showing Milly, and he took her straightway as a reinforcement. Kate herself had spoken, however, before he had had time to tell her so.

"You had noticed too?"—she smiled at him without looking at Milly. "Then I'm not original—which one always hopes one has been. But the likeness is so great." And now she looked at Milly—for whom again it was, all round indeed, kind, kind eyes. "Yes, there you are, my dear, if you want to know. And you're superb." She

took now but a glance at the picture, though it was enough to make her question to her friends not too straight. "Isn't she superb?"

"I brought Miss Theale," Lord Mark explained to the latter, "quite off my own bat."

"I wanted Lady Aldershaw," Kate continued to Milly, "to see for herself."

"Les grands esprits se rencontrent!" laughed her attendant gentleman, a high, but slightly stooping, shambling and wavering person, who represented urbanity by the liberal aid of certain prominent front teeth and whom Milly vaguely took for some sort of great man.

Lady Aldershaw meanwhile looked at Milly quite as if Milly had been the Bronzino and the Bronzino only Milly. "Superb, superb. Of course I had noticed you. It is wonderful," she went on with her back to the picture, but with some other eagerness which Milly felt gathering, directing her motions now. It was enough—they were introduced, and she was saying "I wonder if you could give us the pleasure of coming——" She was not fresh, for she was not young, even though she denied at every pore that she was old; but she was vivid and much bejewelled for the midsummer daylight; and she was all in the palest pinks and blues. She didn't think, at this pass, that she could "come" anywhere—Milly didn't; and she already knew that somehow Lord Mark was saving her from the question. He had interposed, taking the words out of the lady's mouth and not caring at all if the lady minded. That was clearly the right way to treat her—at least for him; as she had only dropped, smiling, and then turned away with him. She had been dealt with—it would have done an enemy good. The gentleman still stood, a little helpless, addressing himself to the intention of urbanity as if it were a large loud whistle; he had been signing sympathy, in his way, while the lady made her overture; and Milly had, in this light, soon arrived at their identity. They were Lord and Lady Aldershaw, and the wife was the clever one. A minute or two later the situation had changed, and she knew it afterwards to have been by the subtle operation of Kate. She was herself saying that she was afraid she must go now if Susie could be found; but she was sitting down on the nearest seat to say it. The prospect, through opened doors, stretched before her into other rooms, down the vista of which Lord Mark was strolling with Lady Aldershaw, who, close to him and much intent, seemed to show from behind as peculiarly expert. Lord Aldershaw, for his part, had been left in the middle of the room, while Kate, with her back to him, was standing before her with much sweetness of manner. The sweetness was all for *her;* she had the sense of the poor gentleman's having somehow been handled as Lord Mark had handled his wife. He dangled there, he shambled a little; then he bethought himself of the Bronzino, before which, with his eyeglass, he hovered. It drew from him an odd, vague sound, not wholly distinct from a grunt, and a "Humph—most remarkable!" which lighted Kate's face with amusement. The next moment he had creaked away, over polished floors, after the others, and Milly was feeling as if *she* had been rude. But Lord Aldershaw was in every way a detail, and Kate was saying to her that she hoped she wasn't ill.

Thus it was that, aloft there in the great gilded historic chamber and the presence of the pale personage on the wall, whose eyes all the while seemed engaged with her own, she found herself suddenly sunk in something quite intimate and humble and to which these grandeurs were strange enough witnesses. It had come up, in the form in which she had had to accept it, all suddenly, and nothing about it, at the same time, was more marked than that she had in a manner plunged into it to escape from something else. Something else, from her first vision of her friend's appearance three minutes before, had been present to her even through the call made by the others on her attention; something that was perversely *there,* she was more and more uncomfortably finding, at least for the first moments and by some spring of its own, with every renewal of their meeting. "Is it the way she looks to *him?"* she asked herself—the perversity being that she kept in remembrance that Kate was known to him. It wasn't a fault in Kate—nor in him assuredly; and she had a horror, being generous and tender, of treating either of them as if it had been. To Densher himself she couldn't make it up—he was too far away; but her secondary impulse was to make it up to Kate. She did so now with a strange soft energy—the impulse immediately acting. "Will you render me to-morrow a great service?"

"Any service, dear child, in the world."

"But it's a secret one—nobody must know. I must be wicked and false about it."

"Then I'm your woman," Kate smiled, "for that's the kind of thing I love. *Do* let us do something bad. You're impossibly without sin, you know."

Milly's eyes, on this, remained a little with their companion's. "Ah, I shan't perhaps come up to your idea. It's only to deceive Susan Shepherd."

"Oh!" said Kate as if this were indeed mild.

"But thoroughly—as thoroughly as I can."

"And for cheating," Kate asked, "my powers will contribute? Well, I'll do my best for you." In accordance with which it was presently settled between them that Milly should have the aid and comfort of her presence for a visit to Sir Luke Strett. Kate had needed a minute for enlightenment, and it was quite grand for her comrade that this name should have said nothing to her. To Milly herself it had for some days been secretly saying much. The personage in question was, as she explained, the greatest of medical lights if she had got hold, as she believed (and she had used to this end the wisdom of the serpent) of the right, the special man. She had written to him three days before, and he had named her an hour, eleven-twenty; only it had come to her, on the eve, that she couldn't go alone. Her maid, on the other hand, wasn't good enough, and Susie was too good. Kate had listened, above all, with high indulgence. "And I'm betwixt and between, happy thought! Too good for what?"

Milly thought. "Why, to be worried if it's nothing. And to be still more worried—I mean before she need be—if it isn't."

Kate fixed her with deep eyes. "What in the world is the matter with you?" It had inevitably a sound of impatience, as if it had been a challenge really to produce something; so that Milly felt her for the moment only as a much older person, standing above her a little, doubting the imagined ailments, suspecting the easy complaints, of ignorant youth. It somewhat checked her, further, that the matter with her was what exactly as yet she wanted knowledge about; and she immediately declared, for conciliation, that if she were merely fanciful Kate would see her put to shame. Kate vividly uttered, in return, the hope that, since she could come out and be so charming, could so universally dazzle and interest, she wasn't all the while in distress or in anxiety—didn't believe herself, in short, to be in any degree seriously menaced. "Well, I want to make out—to make out!" was all that this consistently produced. To which Kate made clear answer: "Ah then, let us by all means!"

"I thought," Milly said, "you would like to help me. But I must ask you, please, for the promise of absolute silence."

"And how, if you *are* ill, can your friends remain in ignorance?"

"Well, if I am, it must of course finally come out. But I can go for a long time." Milly spoke with her eyes again on her painted sister's—almost as if under their suggestion. She still sat there before Kate, yet not without a light in her face. "That will be one of my advantages. I think I could die without its being noticed."

"You're an extraordinary young woman," her friend, visibly held by her, declared at last. "What a remarkable time to talk of such things!"

"Well, we won't talk, precisely"—Milly got herself together again. "I only wanted to make sure of you."

"Here in the midst of——!" But Kate could only sigh for wonder—almost visibly too for pity.

It made a moment during which her companion waited on her word; partly as if from a yearning, shy but deep, to have her case put to her just as Kate was struck by it; partly as if the hint of pity were already giving a sense to her whimsical "shot," with Lord Mark, at Mrs. Lowder's first dinner. Exactly this—the handsome girl's compassionate manner, her friendly descent from her own strength—was what she had then foretold. She took Kate up as if positively for the deeper taste of it. "Here in the midst of what?"

"Of everything. There's nothing you can't have. There's nothing you can't do."

"So Mrs. Lowder tells me."

It just kept Kate's eyes fixed as possibly for more of that; then, however, without waiting, she went on. "We all adore you."

"You're wonderful—you dear things!" Milly laughed.

"No, it's *you."* And Kate seemed struck with the real interest of it. "In three weeks!"

Milly kept it up. "Never were people on such terms! All the more reason," she added, "that I shouldn't needlessly torment you."

"But me? what becomes of *me?"* said Kate.

"Well, you—" Milly thought—"if there's anything to bear, you'll bear it."

"But I *won't* bear it!" said Kate Croy.

"Oh yes, you will: all the same! You'll pity me awfully, but you'll help me very much. And I absolutely trust you. So there we are." There they were, then, since Kate had so to take it; but there, Milly felt, she herself in particular was; for it was just the point at which she had wished to arrive. She had wanted to prove to herself that she didn't horribly blame her friend for any reserve; and what better proof could there be than this quite special confidence? If she desired to show Kate that she really believed the latter liked her, how could she show it more than by asking her for help?

XII

What it really came to, on the morrow, this first time—the time Kate went with her—was that the great man had, a little, to excuse himself; had, by a rare accident—for he kept his consulting-hours in general rigorously free—but ten minutes to give her; ten mere minutes which he yet placed at her service in a manner that she admired even more than she could meet it: so crystal-clean the great empty cup of attention that he set between them on the table. He was presently to jump into his carriage, but he promptly made the point that he must see her again, see her within a day or two; and he named for her at once another hour—easing her off beautifully too even then in respect to her possibly failing of justice to her errand. The minutes affected her in fact as ebbing more swiftly than her little army of items could muster, and they would probably have gone without her doing much more than secure another hearing, had it not been for her sense, at the last, that she had gained above all an impression. The impression—all the sharp growth of the final few moments—was neither more nor less than that she might make, of a sudden, in quite another world, another straight friend, and a friend who would moreover be, wonderfully, the most appointed, the most thoroughly adjusted of the whole collection, inasmuch as he would somehow wear the character scientifically, ponderably, proveably—not just loosely and sociably. Literally, furthermore, it wouldn't really depend on herself, Sir Luke Strett's friendship, in the least; perhaps what made her most stammer and pant was its thus queerly coming over her that she might find she had interested him even beyond her intention, find she was in fact launched in some current that would lose itself in the sea of science. At the same time that she struggled, however, she also surrendered; there was a moment at which she almost dropped the form of stating, of explaining, and threw herself, without violence, only with a supreme pointless quaver that had turned, the next instant, to an intensity of interrogative stillness, upon his general goodwill. His large, settled face, though firm, was not, as she had thought at first, hard; he looked, in the oddest manner, to her fancy, half like a general and half like a bishop, and she was soon sure that, within some such handsome range, what it would show her would be what was good, what was best for her. She had established, in other words, in this time-saving way, a relation with it; and the relation was the special trophy that, for the hour, she bore off. It was like an absolute possession, a new resource altogether, something done up in the softest silk and tucked away under the arm of memory. She hadn't had it when she went in, and she had it when she came out; she had it there under her cloak, but dissimulated, invisibly carried, when smiling, smiling, she again faced Kate Croy. That young lady had of course awaited her in another room, where, as the great man was to absent himself, no one else was in attendance; and she rose for her with such a face of sympathy as might have graced the vestibule of a dentist. "Is it out?" she seemed to ask as if it had been a question of a tooth; and Milly indeed kept her in no suspense at all.

"He's a dear. I'm to come again."

"But what does he say?"

Milly was almost gay. "That I'm not to worry about anything in the world, and that if I'll be a good girl and do exactly what he tells me, he'll take care of me for ever and ever."

Kate wondered as if things scarce fitted. "But does he allow then that you're ill?"

"I don't know what he allows, and I don't care. I shall know, and whatever it is it will be enough. He knows all about me, and I like it. I don't hate it a bit."

Still, however, Kate stared. "But could he, in so few minutes, ask you enough——?"

"He asked me scarcely anything—he doesn't need to do anything so stupid," Milly said. "He can tell. He knows," she repeated; "and when I go back—for he'll have thought me over a little—it will be all right."

Kate, after a moment, made the best of this. "Then when are we to come?"

It just pulled her friend up, for even while they talked—at least it was one of the reasons—she stood there suddenly, irrelevantly, in the light of her *other* identity, the identity she would have for Mr. Densher. This was always, from one instant to another, an incalculable light, which, though it might go off faster than it came on, necessarily disturbed. It sprang, with a perversity all its own, from the fact that, with the lapse of hours and days, the chances themselves that made for his being named continued so oddly to fail. There were twenty, there were fifty, but none of them turned up. This, in particular, was of course not a juncture at which the least of them would naturally be present; but it would make, none the less, Milly saw, another day practically all stamped with avoidance. She saw in a quick glimmer, and with it all Kate's unconsciousness; and then she shook off the obsession. But it had lasted long enough to qualify her response. No, she had shown Kate how she trusted her; and that, for loyalty, would somehow do. "Oh, dear thing, now that the ice is broken I shan't trouble *you* again."

"You'll come alone?"

"Without a scruple. Only I shall ask you, please, for your absolute discretion still."

Outside, before the door, on the wide pavement of the great square, they had to wait again while their carriage, which Milly had kept, completed a further turn of exercise, engaged in by the coachman for reasons of his own. The footman was there, and had indicated that he was making the circuit; so Kate went on while they stood. "But don't you ask a good deal, darling, in proportion to what you give?"

This pulled Milly up still shorter—so short in fact that she yielded as soon as she had taken it in. But she continued to smile. "I see. Then you *can* tell."

"I don't want to 'tell,'" said Kate. "I'll be as silent as the tomb if I can only have the truth from you. All I want is that you shouldn't keep from me how you find out that you really are."

"Well then, I won't, ever. But you see for yourself," Milly went on, "how I really am. I'm satisfied. I'm happy."

Kate looked at her long. "I believe you like it. The way things turn out for you——!"

Milly met her look now without a thought of anything but the spoken. She had ceased to be Mr. Densher's image; she was all her own memento and she was none the less fine. Still, still, what had passed was a fair bargain, and it would do. "Of course I like it. I feel—I can't otherwise describe it—as if I had been, on my knees, to the priest. I've confessed and I've been absolved. It has been lifted off."

Kate's eyes never quitted her. "He must have liked *you."*

"Oh—doctors!" Milly said. "But I hope," she added, "he didn't like me too much." Then as if to escape a little from her friend's deeper sounding, or as impatient for the carriage, not yet in sight, her eyes, turning away, took in the great stale square. As its staleness, however, was but that of London fairly fatigued, the late hot London with its dance all danced and its story all told, the air seemed a thing of blurred pictures and mixed echoes, and an impression met the sense—an impression that broke, the next moment, through the girl's tightened lips. "Oh, it's a beautiful big world, and everyone, yes, everyone——!" It presently brought her back to Kate, and she hoped she didn't actually look as much as if she were crying as she must have looked to Lord Mark among the portraits at Matcham.

Kate at all events understood. "Everyone wants to be so nice?"

"So nice," said the grateful Milly.

"Oh," Kate laughed, "we'll pull you through! And won't you now bring Mrs. Stringham?"

But Milly after an instant was again clear about that. "Not till I've seen him once more."

She was to have found this preference, two days later, abundantly justified; and yet when, in prompt accordance with what had passed between them, she reappeared before her distinguished friend—that character having, for him, in the interval, built itself up still higher—the first thing he asked her was whether she had been accompanied. She told him, on this, straightway, everything; completely free at present from her first embarrassment, disposed even—as she felt she might become—to undue volubility, and conscious moreover of no alarm from his thus perhaps wishing that she had not come alone. It was exactly as if, in the forty-eight hours that had passed, her acquaintance with him had somehow increased, and his own knowledge in particular received mysterious additions. They had been together, before, scarce ten minutes; but the relation, the one the ten minutes had so beautifully created, was there to take straight up: and this not, on his own part, from mere professional heartiness, mere bedside manner, which she would have disliked—much rather from a quiet, pleasant air in him of having positively asked about her, asked here and there and found out. Of course he couldn't in the least have asked, or have wanted to; there was no source of information to his hand, and he had really needed none: he had found out simply by his genius—and found out, she meant, literally everything. Now she knew not only that she didn't dislike this—the state of being found out about; but that, on the contrary, it was truly what she had come for, and that, for the time at least, it would give her something firm to stand on. She struck herself as aware, aware as she had never been, of really not having had from the beginning anything firm. It would be strange for the firmness to come, after all, from her learning in these agreeable conditions that she was in some way doomed; but above all it would prove how little she had hitherto had to hold her up. If she was now to be held up by the mere process—since that was perhaps on the cards—of being let down, this would only testify in turn to her queer little history. *That* sense of loosely rattling had been no process at all; and it was ridiculously true that her thus sitting there to see her life put into the scales represented her first approach to the taste of orderly living. Such was Milly's romantic version—that her life, especially by the fact of this second interview, *was* put into the scales; and just the best part of the relation established might have been, for that matter, that the great grave charming man knew, had known at once, that it was romantic, and in that measure allowed for it. Her only doubt, her only fear, was whether he perhaps wouldn't even take advantage of her being a little romantic to treat her as romantic altogether. This doubtless was her danger with him; but she should see, and dangers in general meanwhile dropped and dropped.

The very place, at the end of a few minutes, the commodious, "handsome" room, far back in the fine old house, soundless from position, somewhat sallow with years of celebrity, somewhat sombre even at midsummer—the very place put on for her a look of custom and use, squared itself solidly round her as with promises and certainties. She had come forth to see the world, and this then was to be the world's light, the rich dusk of a London "back," these the world's walls, those the world's curtains and carpet. She should be intimate with the great bronze clock and mantel-ornaments, conspicuously presented in gratitude and long ago; she should be as one of the circle of eminent contemporaries, photographed, engraved, signatured, and in particular framed and glazed, who made up the rest of the decoration, and made up as well so much of the human comfort; and while she thought of all the clean truths, unfringed, unfingered, that the listening stillness, strained into pauses and waits, would again and again, for years, have kept distinct, she also wondered what she would eventually decide upon to present in gratitude. She would give something better at least than the brawny Victorian bronzes. This was precisely an instance of what she felt he knew of her before he had done with her: that she was secretly romancing at that rate, in the midst of so much else that was more urgent, all over the place. So much for her secrets with him, none of which really required to be phrased. It would have been, for example, a secret for her from any one else that without a dear lady she had picked up just before coming over she wouldn't have a decently near connection, of any sort, for such an appeal as she was making, to put forward: no one in the least, as it were, to produce for respectability. But *his* seeing it she didn't mind a scrap, and not a scrap either his knowing how she had left the dear lady in the dark. She had come alone, putting her friend off with a fraud: giving a pretext of shops, of a whim, of she didn't know what—the amusement of being for once in the streets by herself. The streets by herself were new to her—she had always had in them a companion, or a maid; and he was never to believe, moreover, that she couldn't take full in the face anything he might have to say. He was softly amused at her account of her courage; though he yet showed it somehow without soothing her too grossly. Still, he did want to know whom she had. Hadn't there been a lady with her on Wednesday?

"Yes—a different one. Not the one who's travelling with me. I've told *her.*"

Distinctly he was amused, and it added to his air—the greatest charm of all—of giving her lots of time. "You've told her what?"

"Well," said Milly, "that I visit you in secret."

"And how many persons will she tell?"

"Oh, she's devoted. Not one."

"Well, if she's devoted doesn't that make another friend for you?"

It didn't take much computation, but she nevertheless had to think a moment, conscious as she was that he distinctly *would* want to fill out his notion of her—even a little, as it were, to warm the air for her. That, however—and better early than late—he must accept as of no use; and she herself felt for an instant quite a competent certainty on the subject of any such warming. The air, for Milly Theale, was, from the very nature of the case, destined never to rid itself of a considerable chill. This she could tell him with authority, if she could tell him nothing else; and she seemed to see now, in short, that it would importantly simplify. "Yes, it makes another; but they all together wouldn't make—well, I don't know what to call it but the difference. I mean when one is—really alone. I've never seen anything like the kindness." She pulled up a minute while he waited—waited again as if with his reasons for letting her, for almost making her, talk. What she herself wanted was not, for the third time, to cry, as it were, in public. She *had* never seen anything like the kindness, and she wished to do it justice; but she knew what she was about, and justice was not wronged by her being able presently to stick to her point. "Only one's situation is what it is. It's me it concerns. The rest is delightful and useless. Nobody can really help. That's why I'm by myself to-day. I *want* to be—in spite of Miss Croy, who came with me last. If you can help, so much the better and also of course if one can, a little, one's self. Except for that—you and me doing our best—I like you to see me just as I am. Yes, I like it—and I don't exaggerate. Shouldn't one, at the start, show the worst—so that anything after that may be better? It wouldn't make any real difference—it *won't* make any, anything that may happen won't—to any one. Therefore I feel myself, this way, with you, just as I am; and—if you do in the least care to know—it quite positively bears me up." She put it as to his caring to know, because his manner seemed to give her all her chance, and the impression was there for her to take. It was strange and deep for her, this impression, and she did, accordingly, take it straight home. It showed him—showed him in spite of himself—as allowing, somewhere far within, things comparatively remote, things in fact quite, as she would have said, outside, delicately to weigh with him; showed him as interested, on her behalf, in other questions beside the question of what was the matter with her. She accepted such an interest as regular in the highest type of scientific mind—his *being* the even highest, magnificently because otherwise, obviously, it wouldn't be there; but she could at the same time take it as a direct source of light upon herself, even though that might present her a little as pretending to equal him. Wanting to know more about a patient than how a patient was constructed or deranged couldn't be, even on the part of the greatest of doctors, anything but some form or other of the desire to let the patient down easily. When that was the case the reason, in turn, could only be, too manifestly, pity; and when pity held up its tell-tale face like a head on a pike, in a French revolution, bobbing before a window, what was the inference but that the patient was bad? He might say what he would now—she would always have seen the head at the window; and in fact from this moment she only wanted him to say what he would. He might say it too with the greater ease to himself as there wasn't one of her divinations that—as her own—he would in any way put himself out for. Finally, if he was making her talk she *was* talking; and what it could, at any rate, come to for him was that she wasn't afraid. If he wanted to do the dearest thing in the world for her he would show her he believed she wasn't; which undertaking of hers—not to have misled him—was what she counted at the moment as her presumptuous little hint to him that she was as good as himself. It put forward the bold idea that he could really *be* misled; and there actually passed between them for some seconds a sign, a sign of the eyes only, that they knew together where they were. This made, in their brown old temple of truth, its momentary flicker; then what followed it was that he had her, all the same, in his pocket; and the whole thing wound up, for that consummation, with its kind dim smile. Such kindness was wonderful with such dimness; but brightness—that even of sharp steel—was of course for the other side of the business, and it would all come in for her in one way or another. "Do you mean," he asked, "that you've no relations at all?—not a parent, not a sister, not even a cousin nor an aunt?"

She shook her head as with the easy habit of an interviewed heroine or a freak of nature at a show. "Nobody whatever." But the last thing she had come for was to be dreary about it. "I'm a survivor—a survivor of a general wreck. You see," she added, "how that's to be taken into account—that everyone else *has* gone. When I was ten years old there were, with my father and my mother, six of us. I'm all that's left. But they died," she went on, to be fair all round, "of different things. Still, there it is. And, as I told you before, I'm American. Not that I mean that makes me worse. However, you'll probably know what it makes me."

"Yes," he discreetly indulged her; "I know perfectly what it makes you. It makes you, to begin with, a capital case."

She sighed, though gratefully, as if again before the social scene. "Ah, there you are!"

"Oh, no; there 'we' aren't at all. There I am only—but as much as you like. I've no end of American friends: there *they* are, if you please, and it's a fact that you couldn't very well be in a better place than in their company. It puts you with plenty of others—and that isn't pure solitude." Then he pursued: "I'm sure you've an excellent spirit; but don't try to bear more things than you need." Which after an instant he further explained. "Hard things have come to you in youth, but you mustn't think life will be for you all hard things. You've the right to be happy. You must make up your mind to it. You must accept any form in which happiness may come."

"Oh, I'll accept any whatever!" she almost gaily returned. "And it seems to me, for that matter, that I'm accepting a new one every day. Now *this!"* she smiled.

"This is very well so far as it goes. You can depend on me," the great man said, "for unlimited interest. But I'm only, after all, one element in fifty. We must gather in plenty of others. Don't mind who knows. Knows, I mean, that you and I are friends."

"Ah, you do want to see some one!" she broke out. "You want to get at some one who cares for me." With which, however, as he simply met this spontaneity in a manner to show that he had often had it from young persons of her race, and that he was familiar even with the possibilities of their familiarity, she felt her freedom rendered vain by his silence, and she immediately tried to think of the most reasonable thing she could say. This would be, precisely, on the subject of that freedom, which she now quickly spoke of as complete. "That's of course by itself a great boon; so please don't think I don't know it. I can do exactly what I like—anything in all the wide world. I haven't a creature to ask—there's not a finger to stop me. I can shake about till I'm black and blue. That perhaps isn't *all* joy; but lots of people, I know, would like to try it." He had appeared about to put a question, but then had let her go on, which she promptly did, for she understood him the next moment as having thus taken it from her that her means were as great as might be. She had simply given it to him so, and this was all that would ever pass between them on the odious head. Yet she couldn't help also knowing that an important effect, for his judgment, or at least for his amusement—which was his feeling, since, marvellously, he did have feeling—was produced by it. All her little pieces had now then fallen together for him like the morsels of coloured glass that used to make combinations, under the hand, in the depths of one of the polygonal peepshows of childhood. "So that if it's a question of my doing anything under the sun that will help——!"

"You'll *do* anything under the sun? Good." He took that beautifully, ever so pleasantly, for what it was worth; but time was needed—ten minutes or so were needed on the spot—to deal even provisionally, with the substantive question. It was convenient, in its degree, that there was nothing she wouldn't do; but it seemed also highly and agreeably vague that she should have to do anything. They thus appeared to be taking her, together, for the moment, and almost for sociability, as prepared to proceed to gratuitous extremities; the upshot of which was in turn, that after much interrogation, auscultation, exploration, much noting of his own sequences and neglecting of hers, had duly kept up the vagueness, they might have struck themselves, or may at least strike us, as coming back from an undeterred but useless voyage to the north pole. Milly was ready, under orders, for the north pole; which fact was doubtless what made a blinding anticlimax of her friend's actual abstention from orders. "No," she heard him again distinctly repeat it, "I don't want you for the present to do anything at all; anything, that is, but obey a small prescription or two that will be made clear to you, and let me within a few days come to see you at home."

It was at first heavenly. "Then you'll see Mrs. Stringham." But she didn't mind a bit now.

"Well, I shan't be afraid of Mrs. Stringham." And he said it once more as she asked once more: "Absolutely not; I 'send' you nowhere. England's all right—anywhere that's pleasant, convenient, decent, will be all right. You say you can do exactly as you like. Oblige me therefore by being so good as to do it. There's only one thing: you ought of course, now, as soon as I've seen you again, to get out of London."

Milly thought. "May I then go back to the continent?"

"By all means back to the continent. Do go back to the continent."

"Then how will you keep seeing me? But perhaps," she quickly added, "you won't want to keep seeing me."

He had it all ready; he had really everything all ready. "I shall follow you up; though if you mean that I don't want you to keep seeing *me*——"

"Well?" she asked.

It was only just here that he struck her the least bit as stumbling. "Well, see all you can. That's what it comes to. Worry about nothing. You *have* at least no worries. It's a great, rare chance."

She had got up, for she had had from him both that he would send her something and would advise her promptly of the date of his coming to her, by which she was virtually dismissed. Yet, for herself, one or two things kept her. "May I come back to England too?"

"Rather! Whenever you like. But always, when you do come, immediately let me know."

"Ah," said Milly, "it won't be a great going to and fro."

"Then if you'll stay with us, so much the better."

It touched her, the way he controlled his impatience of her; and the fact itself affected her as so precious that she yielded to the wish to get more from it. "So you don't think I'm out of my mind?"

"Perhaps that *is,"* he smiled, "all that's the matter."

She looked at him longer. "No, that's too good. Shall I, at any rate, suffer?"

"Not a bit."

"And yet then live?"

"My dear young lady," said her distinguished friend, "isn't to 'live' exactly what I'm trying to persuade you to take the trouble to do?"

XIII

She had gone out with these last words so in her ears that when once she was well away—back this time in the great square alone—it was as if some instant application of them had opened out there before her. It was positively, this effect, an excitement that carried her on; she went forward into space under the sense of an impulse received—an impulse simple and direct, easy above all to act upon. She was borne up for the hour, and now she knew why she had wanted to come by herself. No one in the world could have sufficiently entered into her state; no tie would have been close enough to enable a companion to walk beside her without some disparity. She literally felt, in this first flush, that her only company must be the human race at large, present all round her, but inspiringly impersonal, and that her only field must be, then and there, the grey immensity of London. Grey immensity had somehow of a sudden become her element; grey immensity was what her distinguished friend had, for the moment, furnished her world with and what the question of "living," as he put it to her, living by option, by volition, inevitably took on for its immediate face. She went straight before her, without weakness, altogether with strength; and still as she went she was more glad to be alone, for nobody—not Kate Croy, not Susan Shepherd either—would have wished to rush with her as she rushed. She had asked him at the last whether, being on foot, she might go home so, or elsewhere, and he had replied as if almost amused again at her extravagance: "You're active, luckily, by nature—it's beautiful: therefore rejoice in it. *Be* active, without folly—for you're not foolish: be as active as you can and as you like." That had been in fact the final push, as well as the touch that most made a mixture of her consciousness—a strange mixture that tasted at one and the same time of what she had lost and what had been given her. It was wonderful to her, while she took her random course, that these quantities felt so equal: she had been treated—hadn't she?—as if it were in her power to live; and yet one wasn't treated so—was one?—unless it came up, quite as much, that one might die. The beauty of the bloom had gone from the small old sense of safety—that was distinct: she had left it behind her there forever. But the beauty of the idea of a great adventure, a big dim experiment or struggle in which she might, more responsibly than ever before, take a hand, had been offered her instead. It was as if she had had to pluck off her breast, to throw away, some friendly ornament, a familiar flower, a little old jewel, that was part of her daily dress; and to take up and shoulder as a substitute some queer defensive weapon, a musket, a spear, a battle-axe conducive possibly in a higher degree to a striking appearance, but demanding all the effort of the military posture. She felt this instrument, for that matter, already on her back, so that she proceeded now in very truth as a soldier on a march—proceeded as if, for her initiation, the first charge had been sounded. She passed along unknown streets, over dusty littery ways, between long rows of fronts not enhanced by the August light; she felt good for miles and only wanted to get lost; there were moments at corners, where she stopped and chose her direction, in which she quite lived up to his injunction to rejoice that she was active. It was like a new pleasure to have so new a reason; she would affirm, without delay, her option, her volition; taking this personal possession of what surrounded her was a fair affirmation to start with; and she really didn't care if she made it at the cost of alarms for Susie. Susie would wonder in due course "whatever," as they said at the hotel, had become of her; yet this would be nothing either, probably, to wonderments still in store. Wonderments in truth, Milly felt, even now attended her steps: it was quite as if she saw in people's eyes the reflection of her appearance and pace. She found herself moving at times in regions visibly not haunted by odd-looking girls from New York, duskily draped, sable-plumed, all but incongruously shod and gazing about them with extravagance; she might, from the curiosity she clearly excited in byways, in side-streets peopled with grimy children and costermongers carts, which she hoped were slums, literally have had her musket on her shoulder, have announced herself as freshly on the warpath. But for the fear of overdoing this character she would here and there have begun conversation, have asked her way; in spite of the fact that, as that would help the requirements of adventure, her way was exactly what she wanted not to know. The difficulty was that she at last accidentally found it; she had come out, she presently saw, at the Regent's Park, round which, on two or three occasions with Kate Croy, her public chariot had solemnly rolled. But she went into it further now; this was the real thing; the real thing was to be quite away from the pompous roads, well within the centre and on the stretches of shabby grass. Here were benches and smutty sheep; here were idle lads at games of ball, with their cries mild in the thick air; here were wanderers, anxious and tired like herself; here doubtless were hundreds of others just in the same box. Their box, their great common anxiety, what was it, in this grim breathing-space, but the practical question of life? They could live if they would; that is, like herself, they had been told so; she saw them all about her, on seats, digesting the information, feeling it altered, assimilated, recognising it again as something, in a slightly different shape, familiar enough, the blessed old truth that they would live if they could. All she thus shared with them made her wish to sit in their company; which she so far did that she looked for a bench that was empty, eschewing a still emptier chair that she saw hard by and for which she would have paid, with superiority, a fee.

The last scrap of superiority had soon enough left her, if only because she before long knew herself for more tired than she had proposed. This and the charm, after a fashion, of the situation in itself made her linger and rest; there was a sort of spell in the sense that nobody in the world knew where she was. It was the first time in her life that this had happened; somebody, everybody appeared to have known before, at every instant of it, where she was; so that she was now suddenly able to put it to herself that that hadn't been a life. This present kind of thing therefore might be—which was where precisely her distinguished friend seemed to be wishing her to come out. He wished her also, it was true, not to make, as she was perhaps doing now, too much of her isolation; at the same time however as he clearly desired to deny her no decent source of interest. He was interested—she arrived at that—in her appealing to as many sources as possible; and it fairly filtered into her, as she sat and sat, that he was essentially propping her up. Had she been doing it herself she would have called it bolstering—the bolstering that was simply for the weak; and she thought and thought as she put together the proofs that it was as one of the weak he was treating her. It was of course as one of the weak that she had gone to him—but, oh, with how sneaking a hope that he might pronounce her, as to all indispensables, a veritable young lioness! What indeed she was really confronted with was the consciousness that he had not, after all, pronounced her anything: she nursed herself into the sense that he had beautifully got out of it. Did he think, however, she wondered, that he could keep out of it to the end?—though, as she weighed the question, she yet felt it a little unjust. Milly weighed, in this extraordinary hour, questions numerous and strange; but she had, happily, before she moved, worked round to a simplification. Stranger than anything, for instance, was the effect of its rolling over her that, when one considered it, he might perhaps have "got out" by one door but to come in with a beautiful, beneficent dishonesty by another. It kept her more intensely motionless there that what he might fundamentally be "up to" was some disguised intention of standing by her as a friend. Wasn't that what women always said they wanted to do when they deprecated the addresses of gentlemen they couldn't more intimately go on with? It was what they, no doubt, sincerely fancied they could make of men of whom they couldn't make husbands. And she didn't even reason that it was, by a similar law, the expedient of doctors in general for the invalids of whom they couldn't make patients: she was somehow so sufficiently aware that *her* doctor was—however fatuous it might sound—exceptionally moved. This was the damning little fact—if she could talk of damnation: that she could believe herself to have caught him in the act of irrelevantly liking her. She hadn't gone to him to be liked, she had gone to him to be judged; and he was quite a great enough man to be in the habit, as a rule, of observing the difference. She could like *him,* as she distinctly did—that was another matter; all the more that her doing so was now, so obviously for herself, compatible with judgment. Yet it would have been all portentously mixed had not, as we say, a final, merciful wave, chilling rather, but washing clear, come to her assistance.

It came, of a sudden, when all other thought was spent. She had been asking herself why, if her case was grave—and she knew what she meant by that—he should have talked to her at all about what she might with futility "do"; or why on the other hand, if it were light, he should attach an importance to the office of friendship. She had him, with her little lonely acuteness—as acuteness went during the dog-days in the Regent's Park—in a cleft stick: she either mattered, and then she was ill; or she didn't matter, and then she was well enough. Now he was "acting," as they said at home, as if she did matter—until he should prove the contrary. It was too evident that a person at his high pressure must keep his inconsistencies, which were probably his highest amusements, only for the very greatest occasions. Her prevision, in fine, of just where she should catch him furnished the light of that judgment in which we describe her as daring to indulge. And the judgment it was that made her sensation simple. He *had* distinguished her—that was the chill. He hadn't known—how could he?—that she was devilishly subtle, subtle exactly in the manner of the suspected, the suspicious, the condemned. He in fact confessed to it, in his way, as to an interest in her combinations, her funny race, her funny losses, her funny gains, her funny freedom, and, no doubt, above all, her funny manners—funny, like those of Americans at their best, without being vulgar, legitimating amiability and helping to pass it off. In his appreciation of these redundancies he dressed out for her the compassion he so signally permitted himself to waste; but its operation for herself was as directly divesting, denuding, exposing. It reduced her to her ultimate state, which was that of a poor girl with her rent to pay for example—staring before her in a great city. Milly had her rent to pay, her rent for her future; everything else but how to meet it fell away from her in pieces, in tatters. This was the sensation the great man had doubtless not purposed. Well, she must go home, like the poor girl, and see. There might after all be ways; the poor girl too would be thinking. It came back for that matter perhaps to views already presented. She looked about her again, on her feet, at her scattered, melancholy comrades—some of them so melancholy as to be down on their stomachs in the grass, turned away, ignoring, burrowing; she saw once more, with them, those two faces of the question between which there was so little to choose for inspiration. It was perhaps superficially more striking that one could live if one would; but it was more appealing, insinuating, irresistible, in short, that one would live if one could.

She found after this, for the day or two, more amusement than she had ventured to count on in the fact, if it were not a mere fancy, of deceiving Susie; and she presently felt that what made the difference was the mere fancy—as this *was* one—of a countermove to her great man. His taking on himself—should he do so—to get at her companion made her suddenly, she held, irresponsible, made any notion of her own all right for her; though indeed at the very moment she invited herself to enjoy this impunity she became aware of new matter for surprise, or at least for speculation. Her idea would rather have been that Mrs. Stringham would have looked at her hard—her sketch of the grounds of her long, independent excursion showing, she could feel, as almost cynically superficial. Yet the dear woman so failed, in the event, to avail herself of any right of criticism that it was sensibly tempting, for an hour, to wonder if Kate Croy had been playing perfectly fair. Hadn't she possibly, from motives of the highest benevolence, promptings of the finest anxiety, just given poor Susie what she would have called the straight tip? It must immediately be mentioned, however, that, quite apart from a remembrance of the distinctness of Kate's promise, Milly, the next thing, found her explanation in a truth that had the merit of being general. If Susie, at this crisis, suspiciously spared her, it was really that Susie was always suspiciously sparing her—yet occasionally, too, with portentous and exceptional mercies. The girl was conscious of how she dropped at times into inscrutable, impenetrable deferences—attitudes that, though without at all intending it, made a difference for familiarity, for the ease of intimacy. It was as if she recalled herself to manners, to the law of court-etiquette—which last note above all helped our young woman to a just appreciation. It was definite for her, even if not quite solid, that to treat her as a princess was a positive need of her companion's mind; wherefore she couldn't help it if this lady had her transcendent view of the way the class in question were treated. Susan had read history, had read Gibbon and Froude and Saint-Simon; she had highlights as to the special allowances made for the class, and, since she saw them, when young, as effete and overtutored, inevitably ironic and infinitely refined, one must take it for amusing if she inclined to an indulgence verily Byzantine. If one *could* only be Byzantine!—wasn't *that* what she insidiously led one on to sigh? Milly tried to oblige her—for it really placed Susan herself so handsomely to be Byzantine now. The great ladies of that race—it would be somewhere in Gibbon—weren't, apparently, questioned about their mysteries. But oh, poor Milly and hers! Susan at all events proved scarce more inquisitive than if she had been a mosaic at Ravenna. Susan was a porcelain monument to the odd moral that consideration might, like cynicism, have abysses. Besides, the Puritan finally disencumbered——! What starved generations wasn't Mrs. Stringham, in fancy, going to make up for?

Kate Croy came straight to the hotel—came that evening shortly before dinner; specifically and publicly moreover, in a hansom that, driven apparently very fast, pulled up beneath their windows almost with the clatter of an accident, a "smash." Milly, alone, as happened, in the great garnished void of their sitting-room, where, a little, really, like a caged Byzantine, she had been pacing through the queer, long-drawn, almost sinister delay of night, an effect she yet liked—Milly, at the sound, one of the French windows standing open, passed out to the balcony that overhung, with pretensions, the general entrance, and so was in time for the look that Kate, alighting, paying her cabman, happened to send up to the front. The visitor moreover had a shilling back to wait for, during which Milly, from the balcony, looked down at her, and a mute exchange, but with smiles and nods, took place between them on what had occurred in the morning. It was what Kate had called for, and the tone was thus, almost by accident, determined for Milly before her friend came up. What was also, however, determined for her was, again, yet irrepressibly again, that the image presented to her, the splendid young woman who looked so particularly handsome in impatience, with the fine freedom of her signal, was the peculiar property of somebody else's vision, that this fine freedom in short was the fine freedom she showed Mr. Densher. Just so was how she looked to him, and just so was how Milly was held by her—held as by the strange sense of seeing through that distant person's eyes. It lasted, as usual, the strange sense, but fifty seconds; yet in so lasting it produced an effect. It produced in fact more than one, and we take them in their order. The first was that it struck our young woman as absurd to say that a girl's looking so to a man could possibly be without connections; and the second was that by the time Kate had got into the room Milly was in mental possession of the main connection it must have for herself.

She produced this commodity on the spot—produced it, that is, in straight response to Kate's frank "Well, what?" The inquiry bore of course, with Kate's eagerness, on the issue of the morning's scene, the great man's latest wisdom, and it doubtless affected Milly a little as the cheerful demand for news is apt to affect troubled spirits when news is not, in one of the neater forms, prepared for delivery. She couldn't have said what it was exactly that, on the instant, determined her; the nearest description of it would perhaps have been as the more vivid impression of all her friend took for granted. The contrast between this free quantity and the maze of possibilities through which, for hours, she had herself been picking her way, put on, in short, for the moment, a grossness that even friendly forms scarce lightened: it helped forward in fact the revelation to herself that she absolutely had nothing to tell. Besides which, certainly, there was something else—an influence, at the particular juncture, still more obscure. Kate had lost, on the way upstairs, the look—*the* look—that made her young hostess so subtly think and one of the signs of which was that she never kept it for many moments at once; yet she stood there, none the less, so in her bloom and in her strength, so completely again the "handsome girl" beyond all others, the "handsome girl" for whom Milly had at first gratefully taken her, that to meet her now with the note of the plaintive would amount somehow to a surrender, to a confession. *She* would never in her life be ill; the greatest doctor would keep her, at the worst, the fewest minutes; and it was as if she had asked just *with* all this practical impeccability for all that was most mortal in her friend. These things, for Milly, inwardly danced their dance; but the vibration produced and the dust kicked up had lasted less than our account of them. Almost before she knew it she was answering, and answering, beautifully, with no consciousness of fraud, only as with a sudden flare of the famous "will-power" she had heard about, read about, and which was what her medical adviser had mainly thrown her back on. "Oh, it's all right. He's lovely."

Kate was splendid, and it would have been clear for Milly now, had the further presumption been needed, that she had said no word to Mrs. Stringham. "You mean you've been absurd?"

"Absurd." It was a simple word to say, but the consequence of it, for our young woman, was that she felt it, as soon as spoken, to have done something for her safety.

And Kate really hung on her lips. "There's nothing at all the matter?"

"Nothing to worry about. I shall take a little watching, but I shan't have to do anything dreadful, or even, in the least, inconvenient. I can do in fact as I like." It was wonderful for Milly how just to put it so made all its pieces fall at present quite properly into places.

Yet even before the full effect came Kate had seized, kissed, blessed her. "My love, you're too sweet! It's too dear! But it's as I was sure." Then she grasped the full beauty. "You can do as you like?"

"Quite. Isn't it charming?"

"Ah, but catch you," Kate triumphed with gaiety, *"not* doing——! And what *shall* you do?"

"For the moment simply enjoy it. Enjoy"—Milly was completely luminous—"having got out of my scrape."

"Learning, you mean, so easily, that you *are* well."

It was as if Kate had but too conveniently put the words into her mouth. "Learning, I mean, so easily, that I *am* well."

"Only, no one's of course well enough to stay in London now. He can't," Kate went on, "want this of you."

"Mercy, no—I'm to knock about. I'm to go to places."

"But not beastly 'climates'—Engadines, Rivieras, boredoms?"

"No; just, as I say, where I prefer. I'm to go in for pleasure."

"Oh, the duck!"—Kate, with her own shades of familiarity, abounded. "But what kind of pleasure?"

"The highest," Milly smiled.

Her friend met it as nobly. "Which is the highest?"

"Well, it's just our chance to find out. You must help me."

"What have I wanted to do but help you," Kate asked, "from the moment I first laid eyes on you?" Yet with this too Kate had her wonder. "I like your talking, though, about that. What help, with your luck all round, do you want?"

XIV

Milly indeed at last couldn't say; so that she had really for the time brought it along to the point so oddly marked for her by her visitor's arrival, the truth that she was enviably strong. She carried this out, from that evening, for each hour still left her, and the more easily perhaps that the hours were now narrowly numbered. All she actually waited for was Sir Luke Strett's promised visit; as to her proceeding on which, however, her mind was quite made up. Since he wanted to get at Susie he should have the freest access, and then perhaps he would see how he liked it. What was between *them* they might settle as between them, and any pressure it should lift from her own spirit they were at liberty to convert to their use. If the dear man wished to fire Susan Shepherd with a still higher ideal, he would only after all, at the worst, have Susan on his hands. If devotion, in a word, was what it would come up for the interested pair to organise, she was herself ready to consume it as the dressed and served dish. He had talked to her of her "appetite" her account of which, she felt, must have been vague. But for devotion, she could now see, this appetite would be of the best. Gross, greedy, ravenous—these were doubtless the proper names for her: she was at all events resigned in advance to the machinations of sympathy. The day that followed her lonely excursion was to be the last but two or three of their stay in London; and the evening of that day practically ranked for them as, in the matter of outside relations, the last of all. People were by this time quite scattered, and many of those who had so liberally manifested in calls, in cards, in evident sincerity about visits, later on, over the land, had positively passed in music out of sight; whether as members, these latter, more especially, of Mrs. Lowder's immediate circle or as members of Lord Mark's—our friends being by this time able to make the distinction. The general pitch had thus, decidedly, dropped, and the occasions still to be dealt with were special and few. One of these, for Milly, announced itself as the doctor's call already mentioned, as to which she had now had a note from him: the single other, of importance, was their appointed leave-taking—for the shortest separation—in respect to Mrs. Lowder and Kate. The aunt and the niece were to dine with them alone, intimately and easily—as easily as should be consistent with the question of their afterwards going on together to some absurdly belated party, at which they had had it from Aunt Maud that they would do well to show. Sir Luke was to make his appearance on the morrow of this, and in respect to that complication Milly had already her plan.

The night was, at all events, hot and stale, and it was late enough by the time the four ladies had been gathered in, for their small session, at the hotel, where the windows were still open to the high balconies and the flames of the candles, behind the pink shades—disposed as for the vigil of watchers—were motionless in the air in which the season lay dead. What was presently settled among them was that Milly, who betrayed on this occasion a preference more marked than usual, should not hold herself obliged to climb that evening the social stair, however it might stretch to meet her, and that, Mrs. Lowder and Mrs. Stringham facing the ordeal together, Kate Croy should remain with her and await their return. It was a pleasure to Milly, ever, to send Susan Shepherd forth; she saw her go with complacency, liked, as it were, to put people off with her, and noted with satisfaction, when she so moved to the carriage, the further denudation—a markedly ebbing tide—of her little benevolent back. If it wasn't quite Aunt Maud's ideal, moreover, to take out the new American girl's funny friend instead of the new American girl herself, nothing could better indicate the range of that lady's merit than the spirit in which—as at the present hour for instance—she made the best of the minor advantage. And she did this with a broad, cheerful absence of illusion; she did it—confessing even as much to poor Susie—because, frankly, she *was* good-natured. When Mrs. Stringham observed that her own light was too abjectly borrowed and that it was as a link alone, fortunately not missing, that she was valued, Aunt Maud concurred to the extent of the remark: "Well, my dear, you're better than nothing." To-night, furthermore, it came up for Milly that

Aunt Maud had something particular in mind. Mrs. Stringham, before adjourning with her, had gone off for some shawl or other accessory, and Kate, as if a little impatient for their withdrawal, had wandered out to the balcony, where she hovered, for the time, unseen, though with scarce more to look at than the dim London stars and the cruder glow, up the street, on a corner, of a small public-house, in front of which a fagged cab-horse was thrown into relief. Mrs. Lowder made use of the moment: Milly felt as soon as she had spoken that what she was doing was somehow for use.

"Dear Susan tells me that you saw, in America, Mr. Densher—whom I've never till now, as you may have noticed, asked you about. But do you mind at last, in connection with him, doing something for me?" She had lowered her fine voice to a depth, though speaking with all her rich glibness; and Milly, after a small sharpness of surprise, was already guessing the sense of her appeal. "Will you name him, in any way you like, to *her"*—and Aunt Maud gave a nod at the window; "so that you may perhaps find out whether he's back?"

Ever so many things, for Milly, fell into line at this; it was a wonder, she afterwards thought, that she could be conscious of so many at once. She smiled hard, however, for them all. "But I don't know that it's important to me to 'find out.'" The array of things was further swollen, however, even as she said this, by its striking her as too much to say. She therefore tried as quickly to say less. "Except you mean, of course, that it's important to *you."* She fancied Aunt Maud was looking at her almost as hard as she was herself smiling, and that gave her another impulse. "You know I never *have* yet named him to her; so that if I should break out now——"

"Well?"—Mrs. Lowder waited.

"Why, she may wonder what I've been making a mystery of. She hasn't mentioned him, you know," Milly went on, "herself."

"No"—her friend a little heavily weighed it—"she wouldn't. So it's she, you see then, who has made the mystery."

Yes, Milly but wanted to see; only there was so much. "There has been of course no particular reason." Yet that indeed was neither here nor there. "Do you think," she asked, "he is back?"

"It will be about his time, I gather, and rather a comfort to me definitely to know."

"Then can't you ask her yourself?"

"Ah, we never speak of him!"

It helped Milly for the moment to the convenience of a puzzled pause. "Do you mean he's an acquaintance of whom you disapprove for her?"

Aunt Maud, as well, just hung fire. "I disapprove of *her* for the poor young man. She doesn't care for him."

"And *he* cares so much——?"

"Too much, too much. And my fear is," said Mrs. Lowder, "that he privately besets her. She keeps it to herself, but I don't want her worried. Neither, in truth," she both generously and confidentially concluded, "do I want *him."*

Milly showed all her own effort to meet the case. "But what can *I* do?"

"You can find out where they are. If I myself try," Mrs. Lowder explained, "I shall appear to treat them as if I supposed them deceiving me."

"And you don't. You don't," Milly mused for her, "suppose them deceiving you."

"Well," said Aunt Maud, whose fine onyx eyes failed to blink, even though Milly's questions might have been taken as drawing her rather further than she had originally meant to go—"well, Kate is thoroughly aware of my views for her, and that I take her being with me, at present, in the way she is with me, if you know what I mean, as a loyal assent to them. Therefore as my views don't happen to provide a place, at all, for Mr. Densher, much, in a manner, as I like him"—therefore, therefore in short she had been prompted to this step, though she completed her sense, but sketchily, with the rattle of her large fan.

It assisted them perhaps, however, for the moment, that Milly was able to pick out of her sense what might serve as the clearest part of it. "You do like him then?"

"Oh dear, yes. Don't you?"

Milly hesitated, for the question was somehow as the sudden point of something sharp on a nerve that winced. She just caught her breath, but she had ground for joy afterwards, she felt, in not really having failed to choose with quickness sufficient, out of fifteen possible answers, the one that would best serve her. She was then almost proud, as well, that she had cheerfully smiled. "I did—three times—in New York." So came and went for her, in these simple words, the speech that was to figure for her, later on, that night, as the one she had ever uttered that cost her most. She was to lie awake, at all events, half the night, for the gladness of not having taken any line so really inferior as the denial of a happy impression.

For Mrs. Lowder also, moreover, her simple words were the right ones; they were at any rate, that lady's laugh showed, in the natural note of the racy. "You dear American thing! But people may be very good, and yet not good for what one wants."

"Yes," the girl assented, "even I suppose when what one wants is something very good."

"Oh, my child, it would take too long just now to tell you all *I* want! I want everything at once and together—and ever so much for you too, you know. But you've seen us," Aunt Maud continued; "you'll have made out."

"Ah," said Milly, "I *don't* make out"; for again—it came that way in rushes—she felt an obscurity in things. "Why, if our friend here doesn't like him——"

"Should I conceive her interested in keeping things from me?" Mrs. Lowder did justice to the question. "My dear, how can you ask? Put yourself in her place. She meets me, but on *her* terms. Proud young women are proud young women. And proud old ones are—well, what *I* am. Fond of you as we both are, you can help us."

Milly tried to be inspired. "Does it come back then to my asking her straight?"

At this, however, finally, Aunt Maud threw her up. "Oh, if you've so many reasons not——!"

"I've not so many," Milly smiled "but I've one. If I break out so suddenly as knowing him, what will she make of my not having spoken before?"

Mrs. Lowder looked blank at it. "Why should you care what she makes? You may have only been decently discreet."

"Ah, I *have* been," the girl made haste to say.

"Besides," her friend went on, "I suggested to you, through Susan, your line."

"Yes, that reason's a reason for *me."*

"And for *me,"* Mrs. Lowder insisted. "She's not therefore so stupid as not to do justice to grounds so marked. You can tell her perfectly that I had asked you to say nothing."

"And may I tell her that you've asked me now to speak?"

Mrs. Lowder might well have thought, yet, oddly, this pulled her up. "You can't do it without——?"

Milly was almost ashamed to be raising so many difficulties. "I'll do what I can if you'll kindly tell me one thing more." She faltered a little—it was so prying; but she brought it out. "Will he have been writing to her?"

"It's exactly, my dear, what I should like to know." Mrs. Lowder was at last impatient. "Push in for yourself, and I dare say she'll tell you."

Even now, all the same, Milly had not quite fallen back. "It will be pushing in," she continued to smile, "for *you"* She allowed her companion, however, no time to take this up. "The point will be that if he *has* been writing she may have answered."

"But what point, you subtle thing, is that?"

"It isn't subtle, it seems to me, but quite simple," Milly said, "that if she has answered she has very possibly spoken of me."

"Very certainly indeed. But what difference will it make?"

The girl had a moment, at this, of thinking it natural that her interlocutress herself should so fail of subtlety. "It will make the difference that he will have written to her in answer that he knows me. And that, in turn," our young woman explained, "will give an oddity to my own silence."

"How so, if she's perfectly aware of having given you no opening? The only oddity," Aunt Maud lucidly professed, "is for yourself. It's in *her* not having spoken."

"Ah, there we are!" said Milly.

And she had uttered it, evidently, in a tone that struck her friend. "Then it *has* troubled you?"

But ah, the inquiry had only to be made to bring the rare colour with fine inconsequence, to her face. "Not, really, the least little bit!" And, quickly feeling the need to abound in this sense, she was on the point, to cut short, of declaring that she cared, after all, no scrap how much she obliged. Only she felt at this instant too the intervention of still other things. Mrs. Lowder was, in the first place, already beforehand, already affected as by the sudden vision of her having herself pushed too far. Milly could never judge from her face of her uppermost motive—it was so little, in its hard, smooth sheen, that kind of human countenance. She looked hard when she spoke fair; the only thing was that when she spoke hard she likewise didn't look soft. Something, none the less, had arisen in her now—a full appreciable tide, entering by the rupture of some bar. She announced that if what she had asked was to prove in the least a bore her young friend was not to dream of it; making her young friend at the same time, by the change in her tone, dream on the spot more profusely. She spoke with a belated light, Milly could apprehend—she could always apprehend—from pity; and the result of that perception, for the girl, was singular: it proved to her as quickly that Kate, keeping her secret, had been straight with her. From Kate distinctly then, as to why she was to be pitied, Aunt Maud knew nothing, and was thereby simply putting in evidence the fine side of her own character. This fine side was that she could almost at any hour, by a kindled preference or a diverted energy, glow for another interest than her own. She exclaimed as well, at this moment, that Milly must have been thinking, round the case, much more than she had supposed; and this remark could, at once, affect the girl as sharply as any other form of the charge of weakness. It was what everyone, if she didn't look out, would soon be saying—"There's something the matter with you!" What one was therefore one's self concerned immediately to establish was that there was nothing at all. "I shall like to help you; I shall like, so far as that goes, to help Kate herself," she made such haste as she could to declare; her eyes wandering meanwhile across the width of the room to that dusk of the balcony in which their companion perhaps a little unaccountably lingered. She suggested hereby her impatience to begin; she almost overtly wondered at the length of the opportunity this friend was giving them—referring it, however, so far as words went, to the other friend, breaking off with an amused: "How tremendously Susie must be beautifying!"

It only marked Aunt Maud, none the less, as too preoccupied for her allusion. The onyx eyes were fixed upon her with a polished pressure that must signify some enriched benevolence. "Let it go, my dear. We shall, after all, soon enough see."

"If he *has* come back we shall certainly see," Milly after a moment replied; "for he'll probably feel that he can't quite civilly not come to see me. Then *there,"* she remarked, "we shall be. It wouldn't then, you see, come through Kate at all—it would come through him. Except," she wound up with a smile, "that he won't find me."

She had the most extraordinary sense of interesting her interlocutress, in spite of herself, more than she wanted; it was as if her doom so floated her on that she couldn't stop—by very much the same trick it had played her with her doctor. "Shall you run away from him?"

She neglected the question, wanting only now to get off. "Then," she went on, "you'll deal with Kate directly."

"Shall you run away from *her?"* Mrs. Lowder profoundly inquired, while they became aware of Susie's return through the room, opening out behind them, in which they had dined.

This affected Milly as giving her but an instant; and suddenly, with it, everything she felt in the connection rose to her lips in a question that, even as she put it, she knew she was failing to keep colourless. "Is it your own belief that he *is* with her?"

Aunt Maud took it in—took in, that is, everything of the tone that she just wanted her not to; and the result for some seconds, was but to make their eyes meet in silence. Mrs. Stringham had rejoined them and was asking if Kate had gone—an inquiry at once answered by this young lady's reappearance. They saw her again in the open window, where, looking at them, she had paused—producing thus, on Aunt Maud's part, almost too impressive a "Hush!" Mrs. Lowder indeed, without loss of time, smothered any danger in a sweeping retreat with Susie; but Milly's words to her, just uttered, about dealing with her niece directly, struck our young woman as already recoiling on herself. Directness, however evaded, would be, fully, for *her;* nothing in fact would ever have been for her so direct as the evasion. Kate had remained in the window, very handsome and upright, the outer dark framing in a highly favourable way her summery simplicities and lightnesses of dress. Milly had, given the relation of space, no real fear she had heard their talk; only she hovered there as with conscious eyes and some added advantage. Then indeed, with small delay, her friend sufficiently saw. The conscious eyes, the added advantage were but those she had now always at command—those proper to the person Milly knew as known to Merton Densher. It was for several seconds again as if the *total* of her identity had been that of the person known to him—a determination having for result another sharpness of its own. Kate had positively but to be there just as she was to tell her he had come back. It seemed to pass between them, in fine, without a word, that he was in London, that he was perhaps only round the corner; and surely therefore no dealing of Milly's with her would yet have been so direct.

XV

It was doubtless because this queer form of directness had in itself, for the hour, seemed so sufficient that Milly was afterwards aware of having really, all the while—during the strange, indescribable session before the return of their companions—done nothing to intensify it. If she was most aware only afterwards, under the long, discurtained ordeal of the morrow's dawn, that was because she had really, till their evening's end came, ceased, after a little, to miss anything from their ostensible comfort. What was behind showed but in gleams and glimpses; what was in front never at all confessed to not holding the stage. Three minutes had not passed before Milly quite knew she should have done nothing Aunt Maud had just asked her. She knew it moreover by much the same light that had acted for her with that lady and with Sir Luke Strett. It pressed upon her then and there that she was still in a current determined, through her indifference, timidity, bravery, generosity—she scarce could say which—by others; that not she but the current acted, and that somebody else, always, was the keeper of the lock or the dam. Kate for example had but to open the flood-gate: the current moved in its mass—the current, as it had been, of her doing as Kate wanted. What, somehow, in the most extraordinary way in the world, *had* Kate wanted but to be, of a sudden, more interesting than she had ever been? Milly, for their evening then, quite held her breath with the appreciation of it. If she hadn't been sure her companion would have had nothing, from her moments with Mrs. Lowder, to go by, she would almost have seen the admirable creature "cutting in" to anticipate a danger. This fantasy indeed, while they sat together, dropped after a little; even if only because other fantasies multiplied and clustered, making fairly, for our young woman, the buoyant medium in which her friend talked and moved. They sat together, I say, but Kate moved as much as she talked; she figured there, restless and charming, just perhaps a shade perfunctory, repeatedly quitting her place, taking slowly, to and fro, in the trailing folds of her light dress, the length of the room, and almost avowedly performing for the pleasure of her hostess.

Mrs. Lowder had said to Milly at Matcham that she and her niece, as allies, could practically conquer the world; but though it was a speech about which there had even then been a vague, grand glamour, the girl read into it at present more of an approach to a meaning. Kate, for that matter, by herself, could conquer anything, and *she,* Milly Theale, was probably concerned with the "world" only as the small scrap of it that most impinged on her and that was therefore first to be dealt with. On this basis of being dealt with she would doubtless herself do her share of the conquering: she would have something to supply, Kate something to take—each of them thus, to that tune, something for squaring with Aunt Maud's ideal. This in short was what it came to now—that the occasion, in the quiet late lamplight, had the quality of a rough rehearsal of the possible big drama. Milly knew herself dealt with—handsomely, completely: she surrendered to the knowledge, for so it was, she felt, that she supplied her helpful force. And what Kate had to take Kate took as freely and, to all appearance, as gratefully; accepting afresh, with each of her long, slow walks, the relation between them so established and consecrating her companion's surrender simply by the interest she gave it. The interest to Milly herself we naturally mean; the interest to Kate Milly felt as probably inferior. It easily and largely came for their present talk, for the quick flight of the hour before the breach of the spell—it all came, when considered, from the circumstance, not in the least abnormal, that the handsome girl was in extraordinary "form." Milly remembered her having said that she was at her best late at night; remembered it by its having, with its fine assurance, made her wonder when *she* was at her best and how happy people must be who had such a fixed time. She had no time at all; she was never at her best—unless indeed it were exactly, as now, in listening, watching, admiring, collapsing. If Kate moreover, quite mercilessly, had never been so good, the beauty and the marvel of it was that she had never really been so frank; being a person of such a calibre, as Milly would have said, that, even while "dealing" with you and thereby, as it were, picking her steps, she could let herself go, could, in irony, in confidence, in extravagance, tell you things she had never told before. That was the impression—that she was telling things, and quite conceivably for her own relief as well; almost as if the errors of vision, the mistakes of proportion, the residuary innocence of spirit still to be remedied on the part of her auditor had their moments of proving too much for her nerves. She went at them just now, these sources of irritation, with an amused energy that it would have been open to Milly to regard as cynical and that was nevertheless called for—as to this the other was distinct—by the way that in certain connections the American mind broke down. It seemed at least—the American mind as sitting there thrilled and dazzled in Milly—not to understand English society without a separate confrontation with *all* the cases. It couldn't proceed by—there was some technical term she lacked until Milly suggested both analogy and induction, and then, differently, instinct, none of which were right: it had to be led up and introduced to each aspect of the monster, enabled to walk all round it, whether for the consequent exaggerated ecstasy or for the still more as appeared to this critic disproportionate shock. It might, the monster, Kate conceded, loom large for those born amid forms less developed and therefore no doubt less amusing; it might on some sides be a strange and dreadful monster, calculated to devour the unwary, to abase the proud, to scandalize the good; but if one had to live with it one must, not to be for ever sitting up, learn how: which was virtually in short to-night what the handsome girl showed herself as teaching.

She gave away publicly, in this process, Lancaster Gate and everything it contained; she gave away, hand over hand, Milly's thrill continued to note, Aunt Maud and Aunt Maud's glories and Aunt Maud's complacencies; she gave herself away most of all, and it was naturally what most contributed to her candour. She didn't speak to her friend once more, in Aunt Maud's strain, of how they could scale the skies; she spoke, by her bright, perverse preference on this occasion, of the need, in the first place, of being neither stupid nor vulgar. It might have been a lesson, for our young American, in the art of seeing things as they were—a lesson so various and so sustained that the pupil had, as we have shown, but receptively to gape. The odd thing furthermore was that it could serve its purpose while explicitly disavowing every personal bias. It wasn't that she disliked Aunt Maud, who was everything she had on other occasions declared; but the dear woman, ineffaceably stamped by inscrutable nature and a dreadful art, wasn't—how *could* she be?—what she wasn't. She wasn't any one. She wasn't anything. She wasn't anywhere. Milly mustn't think it—one couldn't, as a good friend, let her. Those hours at Matcham were *inespérées,* were pure manna from heaven; or if not wholly that perhaps, with humbugging old Lord Mark as a backer, were vain as a ground for hopes and calculations. Lord Mark was very well, but he wasn't *the* cleverest creature in England, and even if he had been he still wouldn't have been the most obliging. He weighed it out in ounces, and indeed each of the pair was really waiting for what the other would put down.

"She has put down *you."* said Milly, attached to the subject still; "and I think what you mean is that, on the counter, she still keeps hold of you."

"Lest"—Kate took it up—"he should suddenly grab me and run? Oh, as he isn't ready to run, he's much less ready, naturally, to grab. I *am*—you're so far right as that—on the counter, when I'm not in the shop-window; in and out of which I'm thus conveniently, commercially whisked: the essence, all of it, of my position, and the price, as properly, of my aunt's protection." Lord Mark was substantially what she had begun with as soon as they were alone; the impression was even yet with Milly of her having sounded his name, having imposed it, as a topic, in direct opposition to the other name that Mrs. Lowder had left in the air and that all her own look, as we have seen, kept there at first for her companion. The immediate strange effect had been that of her consciously needing, as it were, an alibi—which, successfully, she so found. She had worked it to the end, ridden it to and fro across the course marked for Milly by Aunt Maud, and now she had quite, so to speak, broken it in. "The bore is that if she wants him so much—wants him, heaven forgive her! for *me*—he has put us all out, since your arrival, by wanting somebody else. I don't mean somebody else than you."

Milly threw off the charm sufficiently to shake her head. "Then I haven't made out who it is. If I'm any part of his alternative he had better stop where he is."

"Truly, truly?—always, always?"

Milly tried to insist with an equal gaiety. "Would you like me to swear?"

Kate appeared for a moment—though that was doubtless but gaiety too—to think. "Haven't we been swearing enough?"

"You have perhaps, but I haven't, and I ought to give you the equivalent. At any rate there it is. Truly, truly as you say—'always, always.' So I'm not in the way."

"Thanks," said Kate—"but that doesn't help me."

"Oh, it's as simplifying for *him* that I speak of it."

"The difficulty really is that he's a person with so many ideas that it's particularly hard to simplify for him. That's exactly of course what Aunt Maud has been trying. He won't," Kate firmly continued, "make up his mind about me."

"Well," Milly smiled, "give him time."

Her friend met it in perfection. "One is *doing* that—one *is*. But one remains, all the same, but one of his ideas."

"There's no harm in that," Milly returned, "if you come out in the end as the best of them. What's a man," she pursued, "especially an ambitious one, without a variety of ideas?"

"No doubt. The more the merrier." And Kate looked at her grandly. "One can but hope to come out, and do nothing to prevent it."

All of which made for the impression, fantastic or not, of the *alibi*. The splendour, the grandeur were, for Milly, the bold ironic spirit behind it, so interesting too in itself. What, moreover, was not less interesting was the fact, as our young woman noted it, that Kate confined her point to the difficulties, so far as *she* was concerned, raised only by Lord Mark. She referred now to none that her own taste might present; which circumstance again played its little part. She was doing what she liked in respect to another person, but she was in no way committed to the other person, and her furthermore talking of Lord Mark as not young and not true were only the signs of her clear self-consciousness, were all in the line of her slightly hard, but scarce the less graceful extravagance. She didn't wish to show too much her consent to be arranged for, but that was a different thing from not wishing sufficiently to give it. There was something moreover, on it all, that Milly still found occasion to say, "If your aunt has been, as you tell me, put out by me, I feel that she has remained remarkably kind."

"Oh, but she has—whatever might have happened in that respect—plenty of use for you! You put her in, my dear, more than you put her out. You don't half see it, but she has clutched your petticoat. You can do anything—you can do, I mean, lots that *we* can't. You're an outsider, independent and standing by yourself; you're not hideously relative to tiers and tiers of others." And Kate, facing in that direction, went further and further; wound up, while Milly gaped, with extraordinary words. "We're of no use to you—it's decent to tell you. You'd be of use to us, but that's a different matter. My honest advice to you would be—" she went indeed all lengths—"to drop us while you can. It would be funny if you didn't soon see how awfully better you can do. We've not really done for you the least thing worth speaking of—nothing you mightn't easily have had in some other way. Therefore you're under no obligation. You won't want us next year; we shall only continue to want *you*. But that's no reason for you, and you mustn't pay too dreadfully for poor Mrs. Stringham's having let you in. She has the best conscience in the world; she's enchanted with what she has done; but you shouldn't take your people from *her*. It has been quite awful to see you do it."

Milly tried to be amused, so as not—it was too absurd—to be fairly frightened. Strange enough indeed—if not natural enough—that, late at night thus, in a mere mercenary house, with Susie away, a want of confidence should possess her. She recalled, with all the rest of it, the next day, piecing things together in the dawn, that she had felt herself alone with a creature who paced like a panther. That was a violent image, but it made her a little less ashamed of having been scared. For all her scare, none the less, she had now the sense to find words. "And yet without Susie I shouldn't have had you."

It had been at this point, however, that Kate flickered highest. "Oh, you may very well loathe me yet!"

Really at last, thus, it had been too much; as, with her own least feeble flare, after a wondering watch, Milly had shown. She hadn't cared; she had too much wanted to know; and, though a small solemnity of reproach, a sombre strain, had broken into her tone, it was to figure as her nearest approach to serving Mrs. Lowder. "Why do you say such things to me?"

This unexpectedly had acted, by a sudden turn of Kate's attitude, as a happy speech. She had risen as she spoke, and Kate had stopped before her, shining at her instantly with a softer brightness. Poor Milly hereby enjoyed one of her views of how people, wincing oddly, were often touched by her. "Because you're a dove." With which she felt herself ever so delicately, so considerately, embraced; not with familiarity or as a liberty taken, but almost ceremonially and in the manner of an accolade; partly as if, though a dove who could perch on a finger, one were also a princess with whom forms were to be observed. It even came to her, through the touch of her companion's lips, that this form, this cool pressure, fairly sealed the sense of what Kate had just said. It was moreover, for the girl, like an inspiration: she found herself accepting as the right one, while she caught her breath with relief, the name so given her. She met it on the instant as she would have met the revealed truth; it lighted up the strange dusk in which she lately had walked. *That* was what was the matter with her. She was a dove. Oh, *wasn't* she?—it echoed within her as she became aware of the sound, outside, of the return of their friends. There was, the next thing, little enough doubt about it after Aunt Maud had been two minutes in the room. She had come up, Mrs. Lowder, with Susan—which she needn't have done, at that hour, instead of letting Kate come down to her; so that Milly could be quite sure it was to catch hold, in some way, of the loose end they had left. Well, the way she did catch was simply to make the point that it didn't now in the least matter. She had mounted the stairs for this, and she had her moment again with her younger hostess while Kate, on the spot, as the latter at the time noted, gave Susan Shepherd unwonted opportunities. Kate was in other words, as Aunt Maud engaged her friend, listening with the handsomest response to Mrs. Stringham's impression of the scene they had just quitted. It was in the tone of the fondest indulgence—almost, really, that of dove cooing to dove—that Mrs. Lowder expressed to Milly the hope that it had all gone beautifully. Her "all" had an ample benevolence; it soothed and simplified; she spoke as if it were the two young women, not she and her comrade, who had been facing the town together. But Milly's answer had prepared itself while Aunt Maud was on the stair; she had felt in a rush all the reasons that would make it the most dovelike; and she gave it, while she was about it, as earnest, as candid. "I don't *think,* dear lady, he's here."

It gave her straightway the measure of the success she could have as a dove: that was recorded in the long look of deep criticism, a look without a word, that Mrs. Lowder poured forth. And the word, presently, bettered it still. "Oh, you exquisite thing!" The luscious innuendo of it, almost startling, lingered in the room, after the visitors had gone, like an oversweet fragrance. But left alone with Mrs. Stringham Milly continued to breathe it: she studied again the dovelike and so set her companion to mere rich reporting that she averted all inquiry into her own case.

That, with the new day, was once more her law—though she saw before her, of course, as something of a complication, her need, each time, to decide. She should have to be clear as to how a dove *would* act. She settled it, she thought, well enough this morning by quite readopting her plan in respect to Sir Luke Strett. That, she was pleased to reflect, had originally been pitched in the key of a merely iridescent drab; and although Mrs. Stringham, after breakfast, began by staring at it as if it had been a priceless Persian carpet suddenly unrolled at her feet, she had no scruple, at the end of five minutes, in leaving her to make the best of it. "Sir Luke Strett comes, by appointment, to see me at eleven, but I'm going out on purpose. He's to be told, please, deceptively, that I'm at home, and, you, as my representative, when he comes up, are to see him instead. He will like that, this time, better. So do be nice to him." It had taken, naturally, more explanation, and the mention, above all, of the fact that the visitor was the greatest of doctors; yet when once the key had been offered Susie slipped it on her bunch, and her young friend could again feel her lovely imagination operate. It operated in truth very much as Mrs. Lowder's, at the last, had done the night before: it made the air heavy once more with the extravagance of assent. It might, afresh, almost have frightened our young woman to see how people rushed to meet her: *had* she then so little time to live that the road must always be spared her? It was as if they were helping her to take it out on the spot. Susie—she couldn't deny, and didn't pretend to—might, of a truth, on *her* side, have treated such news as a flash merely lurid; as to which, to do Susie justice, the pain of it was all there. But, none the less, the margin always allowed her young friend was all there as well; and the proposal now made her what was it in short but Byzantine? The vision of Milly's perception of the propriety of the matter had, at any rate, quickly engulfed, so far as her attitude was concerned, any surprise and any shock; so that she only desired, the next thing, perfectly to possess the facts. Milly could easily speak, on this, as if there were only one: she made nothing of such another as that she had felt herself menaced. The great fact, in fine, was that she *knew* him to desire just now, more than anything else, to meet, quite apart, some one interested in her. Who therefore so interested as her faithful Susan? The only other circumstance that, by the time she had quitted her friend, she had treated as worth mentioning was the circumstance of her having at first intended to keep quiet. She had originally best seen herself as sweetly secretive. As to that she had changed, and her present request was the result. She didn't say why she had changed, but she trusted her faithful Susan. Their visitor would trust her not less, and she herself would adore their visitor. Moreover he wouldn't—the girl felt sure—tell her anything dreadful. The worst would be that he was in love and that he needed a confidant to work it. And now she was going to the National Gallery.

XVI

The idea of the National Gallery had been with her from the moment of her hearing from Sir Luke Strett about his hour of coming. It had been in her mind as a place so meagrely visited, as one of the places that had seemed at home one of the attractions of Europe and one of its highest aids to culture, but that—the old story—the typical frivolous always ended by sacrificing to vulgar pleasures. She had had perfectly, at those whimsical moments on the Brünig, the half-shamed sense of turning her back on such opportunities for real improvement as had figured to her, from of old, in connection with the continental tour, under the general head of "pictures and things"; and now she knew for what she had done so. The plea had been explicit—she had done so for life, as opposed to learning; the upshot of which had been that life was now beautifully provided for. In spite of those few dips and dashes into the many-coloured stream of history for which of late Kate Croy had helped her to find time, there were possible great chances she had neglected, possible great moments she should, save for to-day, have all but missed. She might still, she had felt, overtake one or two of them among the Titians and the Turners; she had been honestly nursing the hour, and, once she was in the benignant halls, her faith knew itself justified. It was the air she wanted and the world she would now exclusively choose; the quiet chambers, nobly overwhelming, rich but slightly veiled, opened out round her and made her presently say "If I could lose myself *here!"* There were people, people in plenty, but, admirably, no personal question. It was immense, outside, the personal question; but she had blissfully left it outside, and the nearest it came, for a quarter of an hour, to glimmering again into sight was when she watched for a little one of the more earnest of the lady-copyists. Two or three in particular, spectacled, aproned, absorbed, engaged her sympathy to an absurd extent, seemed to show her for the time the right way to live. She should have been a lady copyist—it met so the case. The case was the case of escape, of living under water, of being at once impersonal and firm. There it was before one—one had only to stick and stick.

Milly yielded to this charm till she was almost ashamed; she watched the lady-copyists till she found herself wondering what would be thought by others of a young woman, of adequate aspect, who should appear to regard them as the pride of the place. She would have liked to talk to them, to get, as it figured to her, into their lives, and was deterred but by the fact that she didn't quite see herself as purchasing imitations and yet feared she might excite the expectation of purchase. She really knew before long that what held her was the mere refuge, that something within her was after all too weak for the Turners and Titians. They joined hands about her in a circle too vast, though a circle that a year before she would only have desired to trace. They were truly for the larger, not for the smaller life, the life of which the actual pitch, for example, was an interest, the interest of compassion, in misguided efforts. She marked absurdly her little stations, blinking, in her shrinkage of curiosity, at the glorious walls, yet keeping an eye on vistas and approaches, so that she shouldn't be flagrantly caught. The vistas and approaches drew her in this way from room to room, and she had been through many parts of the show, as she supposed, when she sat down to rest. There were chairs in scant clusters, places from which one could gaze. Milly indeed at present fixed her eyes more than elsewhere on the appearance, first, that she couldn't quite, after all, have accounted to an examiner for the order of her "schools," and then on that of her being more tired than she had meant, in spite of her having been so much less intelligent. They found, her eyes, it should be added, other occupation as well, which she let them freely follow: they rested largely, in her vagueness, on the vagueness of other visitors; they attached themselves in especial, with mixed results, to the surprising stream of her compatriots. She was struck with the circumstance that the great museum, early in August, was haunted with these pilgrims, as also with that of her knowing them from afar, marking them easily, each and all, and recognising not less promptly that they had ever new lights for her—new lights on their own darkness. She gave herself up at last, and it was a consummation like another: what she should have come to the National Gallery for to-day would be to watch the copyists and reckon the Baedekers. That perhaps was the moral of a menaced state of health—that one would sit in public places and count the Americans. It passed the time in a manner; but it seemed already the second line of defence, and this notwithstanding the pattern, so unmistakable, of her country-folk. They were cut out as by scissors, coloured, labelled, mounted; but their relation to her failed to act—they somehow did nothing for her. Partly, no doubt, they didn't so much as notice or know her, didn't even recognise their community of collapse with her, the sign on her, as she sat there, that for her too Europe was "tough." It came to her idly thus—for her humour could still play—that she didn't seem then the same success with them as with the inhabitants of London, who had taken her up on scarce more of an acquaintance. She could wonder if they would be different should she go back with that glamour attached; and she could also wonder, if it came to that, whether she should ever go back. Her friends straggled past, at any rate, in all the vividness of their absent criticism, and she had even at last the sense of taking a mean advantage. There was a finer instant, however, at which three ladies, clearly a mother and daughters, had paused before her under compulsion of a comment apparently just uttered by one of them and referring to some object on the other side of the room. Milly had her back to the object, but her face very much to her young compatriot, the one who had spoken and in whose look she perceived a certain gloom of recognition. Recognition, for that matter, sat confessedly in her own eyes: she *knew* the three, generically, as easily as a schoolboy with a crib in his lap would know the answer in class; she felt, like the schoolboy, guilty enough—questioned, as honour went, as to her right so to possess, to dispossess, people who hadn't consciously provoked her. She would have been able to say where they lived, and how, had the place and the way been but amenable to the positive; she bent tenderly, in imagination, over marital, paternal Mr. Whatever-he-was, at home, eternally named, with all the honours and placidities, but eternally unseen and existing only as some one who could be financially heard from. The mother, the puffed and composed whiteness of whose hair had no relation to her apparent age, showed a countenance almost chemically clean and dry; her companions wore an air of vague resentment humanised by fatigue; and the three were equally adorned with short cloaks of coloured cloth surmounted by little tartan hoods. The tartans were doubtless conceivable as different, but the cloaks, curiously, only thinkable as one. "Handsome? Well, if you choose to say so." It was the mother who had spoken, who herself added, after a pause during which Milly took the reference as to a picture: "In the English style." The three pair of eyes had converged, and their possessors had for an instant rested, with the effect of a drop of the subject, on this last characterisation—with that, too, of a gloom not less mute in one of the daughters than murmured in the other. Milly's heart went out to them while they turned their backs; she said to herself that they ought to have known her, that there was something between them they might have beautifully put together. But she had lost *them* also—they were cold; they left her in her weak wonder as to what they had been looking at. The "handsome" disposed her to turn—all the more that the "English style" would be the English school, which she liked; only she saw, before moving, by the array on the side facing her, that she was in fact among small Dutch pictures. The action of this was again appreciable—the dim surmise that it wouldn't then be by a picture that the spring in the three ladies had been pressed. It was at all events time she should go, and she turned as she got on her feet. She had had behind her one of the entrances and various visitors who had come in while she sat, visitors single and in pairs—by one of the former of whom she felt her eyes suddenly held.

This was a gentleman in the middle of the place, a gentleman who had removed his hat and was for a moment, while he glanced, absently, as she could see, at the top tier of the collection, tapping his forehead with his pocket-handkerchief. The occupation held him long enough to give Milly time to take for granted—and a few seconds sufficed—that his face was the object just observed by her friends. This could only have been because she concurred in their tribute, even qualified, and indeed "the English style" of the gentleman—perhaps by instant contrast to the American—was what had had the arresting power. This arresting power, at the same time—and that was the marvel—had already sharpened almost to pain, for in the very act of judging the bared head with detachment she felt herself shaken by a knowledge of it. It was Merton Densher's own, and he was standing there, standing long enough unconscious for her to fix him and then hesitate. These successions were swift, so that she could still ask herself in freedom if she had best let him see her. She could still reply to that that she shouldn't like him to catch her in the effort to prevent this; and she might further have decided that he was too preoccupied to see anything had not a perception intervened that surpassed the first in violence. She was unable to think afterwards how long she had looked at him before knowing herself as otherwise looked at;

all she was coherently to put together was that she had had a second recognition without his having noticed her. The source of this latter shock was nobody less than Kate Croy—Kate Croy who was suddenly also in the line of vision and whose eyes met her eyes at their next movement. Kate was but two yards off—Mr. Densher wasn't alone. Kate's face specifically said so, for after a stare as blank at first as Milly's it broke into a far smile. That was what, wonderfully—in addition to the marvel of their meeting—passed from her for Milly; the instant reduction to easy terms of the fact of their being there, the two young women, together. It was perhaps only afterwards that the girl fully felt the connection between this touch and her already established conviction that Kate was a prodigious person; yet on the spot she none the less, in a degree, knew herself handled and again, as she had been the night before, dealt with—absolutely even dealt with for her greater pleasure. A minute in fine hadn't elapsed before Kate had somehow made her provisionally take everything as natural. The provisional was just the charm—acquiring that character from one moment to the other; it represented happily so much that Kate would explain on the very first chance. This left moreover—and that was the greatest wonder—all due margin for amusement at the way things happened, the monstrous oddity of their turning up in such a place on the very heels of their having separated without allusion to it. The handsome girl was thus literally in control of the scene by the time Merton Densher was ready to exclaim with a high flush, or a vivid blush—one didn't distinguish the embarrassment from the joy—"Why, Miss Theale: fancy!" and "Why, Miss Theale: what luck!"

Miss Theale had meanwhile the sense that for him too, on Kate's part, something wonderful and unspoken was determinant; and this although, distinctly, his companion had no more looked at him with a hint than he had looked at her with a question. He had looked and he was looking only at Milly herself, ever so pleasantly and considerately—she scarce knew what to call it; but without prejudice to her consciousness, all the same, that women got out of predicaments better than men. The predicament of course wasn't definite or phraseable—and the way they let all phrasing pass was presently to recur to our young woman as a characteristic triumph of the civilised state; but she took it for granted, insistently, with a small private flare of passion, because the one thing she could think of to do for him was to show him how she eased him off. She would really, tired and nervous, have been much disconcerted, were it not that the opportunity in question had saved her. It was what had saved her most, what had made her, after the first few seconds, almost as brave for Kate as Kate was for her, had made her only ask herself what their friend would like of her. That he was at the end of three minutes, without the least complicated reference, so smoothly "their" friend was just the effect of their all being sublimely civilised. The flash in which he saw this was, for Milly, fairly inspiring—to that degree in fact that she was even now, on such a plane, yearning to be supreme. It took, no doubt, a big dose of inspiration to treat as not funny—or at least as not unpleasant—the anomaly, for Kate, that *she* knew their gentleman, and for herself, that Kate was spending the morning with him; but everything continued to make for this after Milly had tasted of her draught. She was to wonder in subsequent reflection what in the world they had actually said, since they had made such a success of what they didn't say; the sweetness of the draught for the time, at any rate, was to feel success assured. What depended on this for Mr. Densher was all obscurity to her, and she perhaps but invented the image of his need as a short cut to service. Whatever were the facts, their perfect manners, all round, saw them through. The finest part of Milly's own inspiration, it may further be mentioned, was the quick perception that what would be of most service was, so to speak, her own native wood-note. She had long been conscious with shame for her thin blood, or at least for her poor economy, of her unused margin as an American girl—closely indeed as, in English air, the text might appear to cover the page. She still had reserves of spontaneity, if not of comicality; so that all this cash in hand could now find employment. She became as spontaneous as possible and as American as it might conveniently appeal to Mr. Densher, after his travels, to find her. She said things in the air, and yet flattered herself that she struck him as saying them not in the tone of agitation but in the tone of New York. In the tone of New York agitation was beautifully discounted, and she had now a sufficient view of how much it might accordingly help her.

The help was fairly rendered before they left the place; when her friends presently accepted her invitation to adjourn with her to luncheon at her hotel, it was in the Fifth Avenue that the meal might have waited. Kate had never been there so straight, but Milly was at present taking her; and if Mr. Densher had been he had at least never had to come so fast. She proposed it as the natural thing—proposed it as the American girl; and she saw herself quickly justified by the pace at which she was followed. The beauty of the case was that to do it all she had only to appear to take Kate's hint. This had said, in its fine first smile, "Oh yes, our look is queer—but give me time;" and the American girl could give time as nobody else could. What Milly thus gave she therefore made them take—even if, as they might surmise, it was rather more than they wanted. In the porch of the museum she expressed her preference for a four-wheeler; they would take their course in that guise precisely to multiply the minutes. She was more than ever justified by the positive charm that her spirit imparted even to their use of this conveyance; and she touched her highest point—that is, certainly, for herself—as she ushered her companions into the presence of Susie. Susie was there with luncheon, with her return, in prospect; and nothing could now have filled her own consciousness more to the brim than to see this good friend take in how little she was abjectly anxious. The cup itself actually offered to this good friend might in truth well be startling, for it was composed beyond question of ingredients oddly mixed. She caught Susie fairly looking at her as if to know whether she had brought in guests to hear Sir Luke Strett's report. Well, it was better her companion should have too much than too little to wonder about; she had come out "anyway," as they said at home, for the interest of the thing; and interest truly sat in her eyes. Milly was none the less, at the sharpest crisis, a little sorry for her; she could of necessity extract from the odd scene so comparatively little of a soothing secret. She saw Mr. Densher suddenly popping up, but she saw nothing else that had happened. She saw in the same way her young friend indifferent to her young friend's doom, and she lacked what would explain it. The only thing to keep her in patience was the way, after luncheon, Kate almost, as might be said, made up to her. This was actually perhaps as well what most kept Milly herself in patience. It had in fact for our young woman a positive beauty—was so marked as a deviation from the handsome girl's previous courses. Susie had been a bore to the handsome girl, and the change was now suggestive. The two sat together, after they had risen from table, in the apartment in which they had lunched, making it thus easy for the other guest and his entertainer to sit in the room adjacent. This, for the latter personage, was the beauty; it was almost, on Kate's part, like a prayer to be relieved. If she honestly liked better to be "thrown with" Susan Shepherd than with their other friend, why that said practically everything. It didn't perhaps altogether say why she had gone out with him for the morning, but it said, as one thought, about as much as she could say to his face.

Little by little indeed, under the vividness of Kate's behaviour, the probabilities fell back into their order. Merton Densher was in love, and Kate couldn't help it—could only be sorry and kind: wouldn't that, without wild flurries, cover everything? Milly at all events tried it as a cover, tried it hard, for the time; pulled it over her, in the front, the larger room, drew it up to her chin with energy. If it didn't, so treated, do everything for her, it did so much that she could herself supply the rest. She made that up by the interest of her great question, the question of whether, seeing him once more, with all that, as she called it to herself, had come and gone, her impression of him would be different from the impression received in New York. That had held her from the moment of their leaving the museum; it kept her company through their drive and during luncheon; and now that she was a quarter of an hour alone with him it became acute. She was to feel at this crisis that no clear, no common answer, no direct satisfaction on this point, was to reach her; she was to see her question itself simply go to pieces. She couldn't tell if he were different or not, and she didn't know nor care if *she* were: these things had ceased to matter in the light of the only thing she did know. This was that she liked him, as she put it to herself, as much as ever; and if that were to amount to liking a new person the amusement would be but the greater. She had thought him at first very quiet, in spite of recovery from his original confusion; though even the shade of bewilderment, she yet perceived, had not been due to such vagueness on the subject of her reintensified identity as the probable sight, over there, of many thousands of her kind would sufficiently have justified. No, he was quiet, inevitably, for the first half of the time, because Milly's own lively line—the line of spontaneity—made everything else relative; and because too, so far as Kate was spontaneous, it was ever so finely in the air among them that the normal pitch must be kept. Afterwards, when they had got a little more used, as it were, to each other's separate felicity, he had begun to talk more, clearly bethought himself, at a given moment, of what *his* natural lively line would be. It would be to take for granted she must wish to hear of the States, and to give her, in its order, everything he had seen and done there. He abounded, of a sudden he almost insisted; he returned, after breaks, to the charge; and the effect was perhaps the more odd as he gave no clue whatever to what he had admired, as he went, or to what he hadn't. He simply drenched her with his sociable story—especially during the time they were away from the others. She had stopped then being American—all to let him be English; a permission of which he took, she could feel, both immense and unconscious advantage. She had really never cared less for the "States" than at this moment; but that had nothing to do with the matter. It would have been the occasion of her life to learn about them, for nothing could put him off, and he ventured on no reference to what had happened for herself. It might have been almost as if he had known that the greatest of all these adventures was her doing just what she did then.

It was at this point that she saw the smash of her great question as complete, saw that all she had to do with was the sense of being there with him. And there was no chill for this in what she also presently saw—that, however he had begun, he was now acting from a particular desire, determined either by new facts or new fancies, to be like everyone else, simplifyingly "kind" to her. He had caught on already as to manner—fallen into line with everyone else; and if his spirits verily *had* gone up it might well be that he had thus felt himself lighting on the remedy for all awkwardness. Whatever he did or he didn't, Milly knew she should still like him—there was no alternative to that; but her heart could none the less sink a little on feeling how much his view of her was destined to have in common with—as she now sighed over it—*the* view. She could have dreamed of his not having *the* view, of his having something or other, if need be quite viewless, of his own; but he might have what he could with least trouble, and *the* view wouldn't be, after all, a positive bar to her seeing him. The defect of it in general—if she might so ungraciously criticise—was that, by its sweet universality, it made relations rather prosaically a matter of course. It anticipated and superseded the—likewise sweet—operation of real affinities. It was this that was doubtless marked in her power to keep him now—this and her glassy lustre of attention to his pleasantness about the scenery in the Rockies. She was in truth a little measuring her success in detaining him by Kate's success in "standing" Susan. It would not be, if she could help it, Mr. Densher who should first break down. Such at least was one of the forms of the girl's inward tension; but beneath even this deep reason was a motive still finer. What she had left at home on going out to give it a chance was meanwhile still, was more sharply and actively, there. What had been at the top of her mind about it and then been violently pushed down—this quantity was again working up. As soon as their friends should go Susie would break out, and what she would break out upon wouldn't be—interested in that gentleman as she had more than once shown herself—the personal fact of Mr. Densher. Milly had found in her face at luncheon a feverish glitter, and it told what she was full of. She didn't care now for Mr. Densher's personal fact. Mr. Densher had risen before her only to find his proper place in her imagination already, of a sudden, occupied. His personal fact failed, so far as she was concerned, to be personal, and her companion noted the failure. This could only mean that she was full to the brim, of Sir Luke Strett, and of what she had had from him. What *had* she had from him? It was indeed now working upward again that Milly would do well to know, though knowledge looked stiff in the light of Susie's glitter. It was therefore, on the whole, because Densher's young hostess was divided from it by so thin a partition that she continued to cling to the Rockies.

THE WINGS OF THE DOVE

VOLUME II

BOOK SIXTH

I

"I say, you know, Kate—you *did* stay!" had been Merton Densher's punctual remark on their adventure after they had, as it were, got out of it; an observation which she not less promptly, on her side, let him see that she forgave in him only because he was a man. She had to recognise, with whatever disappointment, that it was doubtless the most helpful he could make in this character. The fact of the adventure was flagrant between them; they had looked at each other, on gaining the street, as people look who have just rounded together a dangerous corner, and there was therefore already enough unanimity sketched out to have lighted, for her companion, anything equivocal in her action. But the amount of light men *did* need!—Kate could have been eloquent at this moment about that. What, however, on his seeing more, struck him as most distinct in her was her sense that, reunited after his absence and having been now half the morning together, it behooved them to face without delay the question of handling their immediate future. That it would require some handling, that they should still have to deal, deal in a crafty manner, with difficulties and delays, was the great matter he had come back to, greater than any but the refreshed consciousness of their personal need of each other. This need had had twenty minutes, the afternoon before, to find out where it stood, and the time was fully accounted for by the charm of the demonstration. He had arrived at Euston at five, having wired her from Liverpool the moment he landed, and she had quickly decided to meet him at the station, whatever publicity might attend such an act. When he had praised her for it on alighting from his train she had answered frankly enough that such things should be taken at a jump. She didn't care to-day who saw her, and she profited by it for her joy. To-morrow, inevitably, she should have time to think and then, as inevitably, would become a baser creature, a creature of alarms and precautions. It was none the less for to-morrow at an early hour that she had appointed their next meeting, keeping in mind for the present a particular obligation to show at Lancaster Gate by six o'clock. She had given, with imprecations, her reason—people to tea, eternally, and a promise to Aunt Maud; but she had been liberal enough on the spot and had suggested the National Gallery for the morning quite as with an idea that had ripened in expectancy. They might be seen there too, but nobody would know them; just as, for that matter, now, in the refreshment-room to which they had adjourned, they would incur the notice but, at the worst, of the unacquainted. They would "have something" there for the facility it would give. Thus had it already come up for them again that they had no place of convenience.

He found himself on English soil with all sorts of feelings, but he hadn't quite faced having to reckon with a certain ruefulness in regard to that subject as one of the strongest. He was aware later on that there were questions his impatience had shirked; whereby it actually rather smote him, for want of preparation and assurance, that he had nowhere to "take" his love. He had taken it thus, at Euston—and on Kate's own suggestion—into the place where people had beer and buns, and had ordered tea at a small table in the corner; which, no doubt, as they were lost in the crowd, did well enough for a stop-gap. It perhaps did as well as her simply driving with him to the door of his lodging, which had had to figure as the sole device of his own wit. That wit, the truth was, had broken down a little at the sharp prevision that once at his door they would have to hang back. She would have to stop there, wouldn't come in with him, couldn't possibly; and he shouldn't be able to ask her, would feel he couldn't without betraying a deficiency of what would be called, even at their advanced stage, respect for her: that again was all that was clear except the further fact that it was maddening. Compressed and concentrated, confined to a single sharp pang or two, but none the less in wait for him there on the Euston platform and lifting its head as that of a snake in the garden, was the disconcerting sense that "respect," in their game, seemed somehow—he scarce knew what to call it—a fifth wheel to the coach. It was properly an inside thing, not an outside, a thing to make love greater, not to make happiness less. They had met again for happiness, and he distinctly felt, during his most lucid moment or two, how he must keep watch on anything that really menaced that boon. If Kate had consented to drive away with him and alight at his house there would probably enough have occurred for them, at the foot of his steps, one of those strange instants between man and woman that blow upon the red spark, the spark of conflict, ever latent in the depths of passion. She would have shaken her head—oh sadly, divinely—on the question of coming in; and he, though doing all justice to her refusal, would have yet felt his eyes reach further into her own than a possible word at such a time could reach. This would have meant the suspicion, the dread of the shadow, of an adverse will. Lucky therefore in the actual case that the scant minutes took another turn and that by the half-hour she did in spite of everything contrive to spend with him Kate showed so well how she could deal with things that maddened. She seemed to ask him, to beseech him, and all for his better comfort, to leave her, now and henceforth, to treat them in her own way.

She had still met it in naming so promptly, for their early convenience, one of the great museums; and indeed with such happy art that his fully seeing where she had placed him hadn't been till after he left her. His absence from her for so many weeks had had such an effect upon him that his demands, his desires had grown; and only the night before, as his ship steamed, beneath summer stars, in sight of the Irish coast, he had felt all the force of his particular necessity. He hadn't in other words at any point doubted he was on his way to say to her that really their mistake must end. Their mistake was to have believed that they *could hold out*—hold out, that is, not against Aunt Maud, but against an impatience that, prolonged and exasperated, made a man ill. He had known more than ever, on their separating in the court of the station, how ill a man, and even a woman, could feel from such a cause; but he struck himself as also knowing that he had already suffered Kate to begin finely to apply antidotes and remedies and subtle sedatives. It had a vulgar sound—as throughout, in love, the names of things, the verbal terms of intercourse, were, compared with love itself, horribly vulgar; but it was as if, after all, he might have come back to find himself "put off," though it would take him of course a day or two to see. His letters from the States had pleased whom it concerned, though not so much as he had meant they should; and he should be paid according to agreement and would now take up his money. It wasn't in truth very much to take up, so that he hadn't in the least come back flourishing a cheque-book; that new motive for bringing his mistress to terms he couldn't therefore pretend to produce. The ideal certainty would have been to be able to present a change of prospect as a warrant for the change of philosophy, and without it he should have to make shift but with the pretext of the lapse of time. The lapse of time—not so many weeks after all, she might always of course say—couldn't at any rate have failed to do something for him; and that consideration it was that had just now tided him over, all the more that he had his vision of what it had done personally for Kate. This had come out for him with a splendour that almost scared him even in their small corner of the room at Euston—almost scared him because it just seemed to blaze at him that waiting was the game of dupes. Not yet had she been so the creature he had originally seen; not yet had he felt so soundly safely sure. It was all there for him, playing on his pride of possession as a hidden master in a great dim church might play on the grandest organ. His final sense was that a woman couldn't be like that and then ask of one the impossible.

She had been like that afresh on the morrow; and so for the hour they had been able to float in the mere joy of contact—such contact as their situation in pictured public halls permitted. This poor makeshift for closeness confessed itself in truth, by twenty small signs of unrest even on Kate's part, inadequate; so little could a decent interest in the interesting place presume to remind them of its claims. They had met there in order not to meet in the streets and not again, with an equal want of invention and of style, at a railway-station; not again, either, in Kensington Gardens, which, they could easily and tacitly agree, would have had too much of the taste of their old frustrations. The present taste, the taste that morning in the pictured halls, had been a variation; yet Densher had at the end of a quarter of an hour fully known what to conclude from it. This fairly consoled him for their awkwardness, as if he had been watching it affect her. She might be as nobly charming as she liked, and he had seen nothing to touch her in the States; she couldn't pretend that in such conditions as those she herself *believed* it enough to appease him. She couldn't pretend she believed he would believe it enough to render her a like service. It wasn't enough for that purpose—she as good as showed him it wasn't. That was what he could be glad, by demonstration, to have brought her to. He would have said to her had he put it crudely and on the spot: "*Now* am I to understand you that you consider this sort of thing can go on?" It would have been open to her, no doubt, to reply that to have him with her again, to have him all kept and treasured, so still, under her grasping hand, as she had held him in their yearning interval, was a sort of thing that he must allow her to have no quarrel about; but that would be a mere gesture of her grace, a mere sport of her subtlety. She knew as well as he what they wanted; in spite of which indeed he scarce could have said how beautifully he mightn't once more have named it and urged it if she hadn't, at a given moment, blurred, as it were, the accord. They had soon seated themselves for better talk, and so they had remained a while, intimate and superficial. The immediate things to say had been many, for they hadn't exhausted them at Euston. They drew upon them freely now, and Kate appeared quite to forget—which was prodigiously becoming to her—to look about for surprises. He was to try afterwards, and try in vain, to remember what speech or what silence of his own, what natural sign of the eyes or accidental touch of the hand, had precipitated for her, in the midst of this, a sudden different impulse. She had got up, with inconsequence, as if to break the charm, though he wasn't aware of what he had done at the moment to make the charm a danger. She had patched it up agreeably enough the next minute by some odd remark about some picture, to which he hadn't so much as replied; it being quite independently of this that he had himself exclaimed on the dreadful closeness of the rooms. He had observed that they must go out again to breathe; and it was as if their common consciousness, while they passed into another part, was that of persons who, infinitely engaged together, had been startled and were trying to look natural. It was probably while they were so occupied—as the young man subsequently reconceived—that they had stumbled upon his little New York friend. He thought of her for some reason as little, though she was of about Kate's height, to which, any more than to any other felicity in his mistress, he had never applied the diminutive.

What was to be in the retrospect more distinct to him was the process by which he had become aware that Kate's acquaintance with her was greater than he had gathered. She had written of it in due course as a new and amusing one, and he had written back that he had met over there, and that he much liked, the young person; whereupon she had answered that he must find out about her at home. Kate, in the event, however, had not returned to that, and he had of course, with so many things to find out about, been otherwise taken up. Little Miss Theale's individual history was not stuff for his newspaper; besides which, moreover, he was seeing but too many little Miss Theales. They even went so far as to impose themselves as one of the groups of social phenomena that fell into the scheme of his public letters. For this group in especial perhaps—the irrepressible, the supereminent young persons—his best pen was ready. Thus it was that there could come back to him in London, an hour or two after their luncheon with the American pair, the sense of a situation for which Kate hadn't wholly prepared him. Possibly indeed as marked as this was his recovered perception that preparations, of more than one kind, had been exactly what, both yesterday and to-day, he felt her as having in hand. That appearance in fact, if he dwelt on it, so ministered to apprehension as to require some brushing away. He shook off the suspicion to some extent, on their separating first from their hostesses and then from each other, by the aid of a long and rather aimless walk. He was to go to the office later, but he had the next two or three hours, and he gave himself as a pretext that he had eaten much too much. After Kate had asked him to put her into a cab—which, as an announced, a resumed policy on her part, he found himself deprecating—he stood a while by a corner and looked vaguely forth at his London. There was always doubtless a moment for the absentee recaptured—*the* moment, that of the reflux of the first emotion—at which it was beyond disproof that one was back. His full parenthesis was closed, and he was once more but a sentence, of a sort, in the general text, the text that, from his momentary street-corner, showed as a great grey page of print that somehow managed to be crowded without being "fine." The grey, however, was more or less the blur of a point of view not yet quite seized again; and there would be colour enough to come out. He was back, flatly enough, but back to possibilities and prospects, and the ground he now somewhat sightlessly covered was the act of renewed possession.

He walked northward without a plan, without suspicion, quite in the direction his little New York friend, in her restless ramble, had taken a day or two before. He reached, like Milly, the Regent's Park; and though he moved further and faster he finally sat down, like Milly, from the force of thought. For him too in this position, be it added—and he might positively have occupied the same bench—various troubled fancies folded their wings. He had no more yet said what he really wanted than Kate herself had found time. She should hear enough of that in a couple of days. He had practically not pressed her as to what most concerned them; it had seemed so to concern them during these first hours but to hold each other, spiritually speaking, close. This at any rate was palpable, that there were at present more things rather than fewer between them. The explanation about the two ladies would be part of the lot, yet could wait with all the rest. They were not meanwhile certainly what most made him roam—the missing explanations weren't. That was what she had so often said before, and always with the effect of suddenly breaking off: "Now please call me a good cab." Their previous encounters, the times when they had reached in their stroll the south side of the park, had had a way of winding up with this special irrelevance. It was effectively what most divided them, for he would generally, but for her reasons, have been able to jump in with her. What did she think he wished to do to her?—it was a question he had had occasion to put. A small matter, however, doubtless—since, when it came to that, they didn't depend on cabs good or bad for the sense of union: its importance was less from the particular loss than as a kind of irritating mark of her expertness. This expertness, under providence, had been great from the first, so far as joining him was concerned; and he was critical only because it had been still greater, even from the first too, in respect to leaving him. He had put the question to her again that afternoon, on the repetition of her appeal—had asked her once more what she supposed he wished to do. He recalled, on his bench in the Regent's Park, the freedom of fancy, funny and pretty, with which she had answered; recalled the moment itself, while the usual hansom charged them, during which he felt himself, disappointed as he was, grimacing back at the superiority of her very "humour," in its added grace of gaiety, to the celebrated solemn American. Their fresh appointment had been at all events by that time made, and he should see what her choice in respect to it—a surprise as well as a relief—would do toward really simplifying. It meant either new help or new hindrance, though it took them at least out of the streets. And her naming this privilege had naturally made him ask if Mrs. Lowder knew of his return.

"Not from me," Kate had replied. "But I shall speak to her now." And she had argued, as with rather a quick fresh view, that it would now be quite easy. "We've behaved for months so properly that I've margin surely for my mention of you. You'll come to see *her*, and she'll leave you with me; she'll show her good nature, and her lack of betrayed fear, in that. With her, you know, you've never broken, quite the contrary, and she likes you as much as ever. We're leaving town; it will be the end; just now therefore it's nothing to ask. I'll ask to-night," Kate had wound up, "and if you'll leave it to me—my cleverness, I assure you, has grown infernal—I'll make it all right."

He had of course thus left it to her and he was wondering more about it now than he had wondered there in Brook Street. He repeated to himself that if it wasn't in the line of triumph it was in the line of muddle. This indeed, no doubt, was as a part of his wonder for still other questions. Kate had really got off without meeting his little challenge about the terms of their intercourse with her dear Milly. Her dear Milly, it was sensible, *was* somehow in the picture. Her dear Milly, popping up in his absence, occupied—he couldn't have said quite why he felt it—more of the foreground than one would have expected her in advance to find clear. She took up room, and it was almost as if room had been made for her. Kate had appeared to take for granted he would know why it had been made; but that was just the point. It was a foreground in which he himself, in which his connexion with Kate, scarce enjoyed a space to turn round. But Miss Theale was perhaps at the present juncture a possibility of the same sort as the softened, if not the squared, Aunt Maud. It might be true of her also that if she weren't a bore she'd be a convenience. It rolled over him of a sudden, after he had resumed his walk, that this might easily be what Kate had meant. The charming girl adored her—Densher had for himself made out that—and would protect, would lend a hand, to their interviews. These might take place, in other words, on her premises, which would remove them still better from the streets. *That* was an explanation which did hang together. It was impaired a little, of a truth, by this fact that their next encounter was rather markedly not to depend upon her. Yet this fact in turn would be accounted for by the need of more preliminaries. One of the things he conceivably should gain on Thursday at Lancaster Gate would be a further view of that propriety.

II

It was extraordinary enough that he should actually be finding himself, when Thursday arrived, none so wide of the mark. Kate hadn't come all the way to this for him, but she had come to a good deal by the end of a quarter of an hour. What she had begun with was her surprise at her appearing to have left him on Tuesday anything more to understand. The parts, as he now saw, under her hand, did fall more or less together, and it wasn't even as if she had spent the interval in twisting and fitting them. She was bright and handsome, not fagged and worn, with the general clearness; for it certainly stuck out enough that if the American ladies themselves weren't to be squared, which was absurd, they fairly imposed the necessity of trying Aunt Maud again. One couldn't say to them, kind as she had been to them: "We'll meet, please, whenever you'll let us, at your house; but we count on you to help us to keep it secret." They must in other terms inevitably speak to Aunt Maud—it would be of the last awkwardness to ask them not to: Kate had embraced all this in her choice of speaking first. What Kate embraced altogether was indeed wonderful to-day for Densher, though he perhaps struck himself rather as getting it out of her piece by piece than as receiving it in a steady light. He had always felt, however, that the more he asked of her the more he found her prepared, as he imaged it, to hand out. He had said to her more than once even before his absence: "You keep the key of the cupboard, and I foresee that when we're married you'll dole me out my sugar by lumps." She had replied that she rejoiced in his assumption that sugar would be his diet, and the domestic arrangement so prefigured might have seemed already to prevail. The supply from the cupboard at this hour was doubtless, of a truth, not altogether cloyingly sweet; but it met in a manner his immediate requirements. If her explanations at any rate prompted questions the questions no more exhausted them than they exhausted her patience. And they were naturally, of the series, the simpler; as for instance in his taking it from her that Miss Theale then could do nothing for them. He frankly brought out what he had ventured to think possible. "If we can't meet here and we've really exhausted the charms of the open air and the crowd, some such little raft in the wreck, some occasional opportunity like that of Tuesday, has been present to me these two days as better than nothing. But if our friends are so accountable to this house of course there's no more to be said. And it's one more nail, thank God, in the coffin of our odious delay." He was but too glad without more ado to point the moral. "Now I hope you see we can't work it anyhow."

If she laughed for this—and her spirits seemed really high—it was because of the opportunity that, at the hotel, he had most shown himself as enjoying. "Your idea's beautiful when one remembers that you hadn't a word except for Milly." But she was as beautifully good-humoured. "You might of course get used to her—you *will.* You're quite right—so long as they're with us or near us." And she put it, lucidly, that the dear things couldn't *help*, simply as charming friends, giving them a lift. "They'll speak to Aunt Maud, but they won't shut their doors to us: that would be another matter. A friend always helps—and she's a friend." She had left Mrs. Stringham by this time out of the question; she had reduced it to Milly. "Besides, she particularly likes us. She particularly likes *you.* I say, old boy, make something of that." He felt her dodging the ultimatum he had just made sharp, his definite reminder of how little, at the best, they could work it; but there were certain of his remarks—those mostly of the sharper penetration—that it had been quite her practice from the first not formally, not reverently to notice. She showed the effect of them in ways less trite. This was what happened now: he didn't think in truth that she wasn't really minding. She took him up, none the less, on a minor question. "You say we can't meet here, but you see it's just what we do. What could be more lovely than this?"

It wasn't to torment him—that again he didn't believe; but he had to come to the house in some discomfort, so that he frowned a little at her calling it thus a luxury. Wasn't there an element in it of coming back into bondage? The bondage might be veiled and varnished, but he knew in his bones how little the very highest privileges of Lancaster Gate could ever be a sign of their freedom. They were upstairs, in one of the smaller apartments of state, a room arranged as a boudoir, but visibly unused—it defied familiarity—and furnished in the ugliest of blues. He had immediately looked with interest at the closed doors, and Kate had met his interest with the assurance that it was all right, that Aunt Maud did them justice—so far, that was, as this particular time was concerned; that they should be alone and have nothing to fear. But the fresh allusion to this that he had drawn from her acted on him now more directly, brought him closer still to the question. They *were* alone—it *was* all right: he took in anew the shut doors and the permitted privacy, the solid stillness of the great house. They connected themselves on the spot with something made doubly vivid in him by the whole present play of her charming strong will. What it amounted to was that he couldn't have her—hanged if he could!—evasive. He couldn't and he wouldn't—wouldn't have her inconvenient and elusive. He didn't want her deeper than himself, fine as it might be as wit or as character; he wanted to keep her where their communications would be straight and easy and their intercourse independent. The effect of this was to make him say in a moment: "Will you take me just as I am?"

She turned a little pale for the tone of truth in it—which qualified to his sense delightfully the strength of her will; and the pleasure he found in this was not the less for her breaking out after an instant into a strain that stirred him more than any she had ever used with him. "Ah do let me try myself! I assure you I see my way—so don't spoil it: wait for me and give me time. Dear man," Kate said, "only believe in me, and it will be beautiful."

He hadn't come back to hear her talk of his believing in her as if he didn't; but he had come back—and it all was upon him now—to seize her with a sudden intensity that her manner of pleading with him had made, as happily appeared, irresistible. He laid strong hands upon her to say, almost in anger, "Do you love me, love me, love me?" and she closed her eyes as with the sense that he might strike her but that she could gratefully take it. Her surrender was her response, her response her surrender; and, though scarce hearing what she said, he so profited by these things that it could for the time be ever so intimately appreciable to him that he was keeping her. The long embrace in which they held each other was the rout of evasion, and he took from it the certitude that what she had from him was real to her. It was stronger than an uttered vow, and the name he was to give it in afterthought was that she had been sublimely sincere. *That* was all he asked—sincerity making a basis that would bear almost anything. This settled so much, and settled it so thoroughly, that there was nothing left to ask her to swear to. Oaths and vows apart, now they could talk. It seemed in fact only now that their questions were put on the table. He had taken up more expressly at the end of five minutes her plea for her own plan, and it was marked that the difference made by the passage just enacted was a difference in favour of her choice of means. Means had somehow suddenly become a detail—her province and her care; it had grown more consistently vivid that her intelligence was one with her passion. "I certainly don't want," he said—and he could say it with a smile of indulgence—"to be all the while bringing it up that I don't trust you."

"I should hope not! What do you think I want to do?"

He had really at this to make out a little what he thought, and the first thing that put itself in evidence was of course the oddity, after all, of their game, to which he could but frankly allude. "We're doing, at the best, in trying to temporise in so special a way, a thing most people would call us fools for." But his visit passed, all the same, without his again attempting to make "just as he was" serve. He had no more money just as he was than he had had just as he had been, or than he should have, probably, when it came to that, just as he always would be; whereas she, on her side, in comparison with her state of some months before, had measureably more to relinquish. He easily saw how their meeting at Lancaster Gate gave more of an accent to that quantity than their meeting at stations or in parks; and yet on the other hand he couldn't urge this against it. If Mrs. Lowder was indifferent her indifference added in a manner to what Kate's taking him as he was would call on her to sacrifice. Such in fine was her art with him that she seemed to put the question of their still waiting into quite other terms than the terms of ugly blue, of florid Sèvres, of complicated brass, in which their boudoir expressed it. She said almost all in fact by saying, on this article of Aunt Maud, after he had once more pressed her, that when he should see her, as must inevitably soon happen, he would understand. "Do you mean," he asked at this, "that there's any *definite* sign of her coming round? I'm not talking," he explained, "of mere hypocrisies in her, or mere brave duplicities. Remember, after all, that supremely clever as we are, and as strong a team, I admit, as there is going—remember that she can play with us quite as much as we play with her."

"She doesn't want to play with *me*, my dear," Kate lucidly replied; "she doesn't want to make me suffer a bit more than she need. She cares for me too much, and everything she does or doesn't do has a value. *This* has a value—her being as she has been about us to-day. I believe she's in her room, where she's keeping strictly to herself while you're here with me. But that isn't 'playing'—not a bit."

"What is it then," the young man returned—"from the moment it isn't her blessing and a cheque?"

Kate was complete. "It's simply her absence of smallness. There is something in her above trifles. She *generally* trusts us; she doesn't propose to hunt us into corners; and if we frankly ask for a thing—why," said Kate, "she shrugs, but she lets it go. She has really but one fault—she's indifferent, on such ground as she has taken about us, to details. However," the girl cheerfully went on, "it isn't in detail we fight her."

"It seems to me," Densher brought out after a moment's thought of this, "that it's in detail we deceive her"—a speech that, as soon as he had uttered it, applied itself for him, as also visibly for his companion, to the after-glow of their recent embrace.

Any confusion attaching to this adventure, however, dropped from Kate, whom, as he could see with sacred joy, it must take more than that to make compunctious. "I don't say we can do it again. I mean," she explained, "meet here."

Densher indeed had been wondering where they could do it again. If Lancaster Gate was so limited that issue reappeared. "I mayn't come back at all?"

"Certainly—to see her. It's she, really," his companion smiled, "who's in love with you."

But it made him—a trifle more grave—look at her a moment. "Don't make out, you know, that every one's in love with me."

She hesitated. "I don't say every one."

"You said just now Miss Theale."

"I said she liked you—yes."

"Well, it comes to the same thing." With which, however, he pursued: "Of course I ought to thank Mrs. Lowder in person. I mean for *this*—as from myself."

"Ah but, you know, not too much!" She had an ironic gaiety for the implications of his "this," besides wishing to insist on a general prudence. "She'll wonder what you're thanking her for!"

Densher did justice to both considerations. "Yes, I can't very well tell her all."

It was perhaps because he said it so gravely that Kate was again in a manner amused. Yet she gave out light. "You can't very well 'tell' her anything, and that doesn't matter. Only be nice to her. Please her; make her see how clever you are—only without letting her see that you're trying. If you're charming to her you've nothing else to do."

But she oversimplified too. "I can be 'charming' to her, so far as I see, only by letting her suppose I give you up—which I'll be hanged if I do! It *is*," he said with feeling, "a game."

"Of course it's a game. But she'll never suppose you give me up—or I give *you*—if you keep reminding her how you enjoy our interviews."

"Then if she has to see us as obstinate and constant," Densher asked, "what good does it do?"

Kate was for a moment checked. "What good does what—?"

"Does my pleasing her—does anything. I *can't*," he impatiently declared, "please her."

Kate looked at him hard again, disappointed at his want of consistency; but it appeared to determine in her something better than a mere complaint. "Then *I* can! Leave it to me." With which she came to him under the compulsion, again, that had united them shortly before, and took hold of him in her urgency to the same tender purpose. It was her form of entreaty renewed and repeated, which made after all, as he met it, their great fact clear. And it somehow clarified *all* things so to possess each other. The effect of it was that, once more, on these terms, he could only be generous. He had so on the spot then left everything to her that she reverted in the course of a few moments to one of her previous—and as positively seemed—her most precious ideas. "You accused me just now of saying that Milly's in love with you. Well, if you come to that, I do say it. So there you are. That's the good she'll do us. It makes a basis for her seeing you—so that she'll help us to go on."

Densher stared—she was wondrous all round. "And what sort of a basis does it make for my seeing *her?*"

"Oh I don't mind!" Kate smiled.

"Don't mind my leading her on?"

She put it differently. "Don't mind her leading *you.*"

"Well, she won't—so it's nothing not to mind. But how can that 'help,'" he pursued, "with what she knows?"

"What she knows? That needn't prevent."

He wondered. "Prevent her loving us?"

"Prevent her helping you. She's *like* that," Kate Croy explained.

It took indeed some understanding. "Making nothing of the fact that I love another?"

"Making everything," said Kate. "To console you."

"But for what?"

"For not getting your other."

He continued to stare. "But how does she know—?"

"That you *won't* get her? She doesn't; but on the other hand she doesn't know you will. Meanwhile she sees you baffled, for she knows of Aunt Maud's stand. *That*"—Kate was lucid—"gives her the chance to be nice to you."

"And what does it give *me*," the young man none the less rationally asked, "the chance to be? A brute of a humbug to her?"

Kate so possessed her facts, as it were, that she smiled at his violence. "You'll extraordinarily like her. She's exquisite. And there are reasons. I mean others."

"What others?"

"Well, I'll tell you another time. Those I give you," the girl added, "are enough to go on with."

"To go on to what?"

"Why, to seeing her again—say as soon as you can: which, moreover, on all grounds, is no more than decent of you."

He of course took in her reference, and he had fully in mind what had passed between them in New York. It had been no great quantity, but it had made distinctly at the time for his pleasure; so that anything in the nature of an appeal in the name of it could have a slight kindling consequence. "Oh I shall naturally call again without delay. Yes," said Densher, "her being in love with me is nonsense; but I must, quite independently of that, make every acknowledgement of favours received."

It appeared practically all Kate asked. "Then you see. I shall meet you there."

"I don't quite see," he presently returned, "why she should wish to receive you for it."

"She receives me for myself—that is for *her* self. She thinks no end of me. That I should have to drum it into you!"

Yet still he didn't take it. "Then I confess she's beyond me."

Well, Kate could but leave it as she saw it. "She regards me as already—in these few weeks—her dearest friend. It's quite separate. We're in, she and I, ever so deep." And it was to confirm this that, as if it had flashed upon her that he was somewhere at sea, she threw out at last her own real light. "She doesn't of course know I care for *you*. She thinks I care so little that it's not worth speaking of." That he had been somewhere at sea these remarks made quickly clear, and Kate hailed the effect with surprise. "Have you been supposing that she does know—?"

"About our situation? Certainly, if you're such friends as you show me—and if you haven't otherwise represented it to her." She uttered at this such a sound of impatience that he stood artlessly vague. "You *have* denied it to her?"

She threw up her arms at his being so backward. "'Denied it'? My dear man, we've never spoken of you."

"Never, never?"

"Strange as it may appear to your glory—never."

He couldn't piece it together. "But won't Mrs. Lowder have spoken?"

"Very probably. But of *you*. Not of me."

This struck him as obscure. "How does she know me but as part and parcel of you?"

"How?" Kate triumphantly asked. "Why exactly to make nothing of it, to have nothing to do with it, to stick consistently to her line about it. Aunt Maud's line is to keep all reality out of our relation—that is out of my being in danger from you—by not having so much as suspected or heard of it. She'll get rid of it, as she believes, by ignoring it and sinking it—if she only does so hard enough. Therefore *she*, in her manner, 'denies' it if you will. That's how she knows you otherwise than as part and parcel of me. She won't for a moment have allowed either to Mrs. Stringham or to Milly that I've in any way, as they say, distinguished you."

"And you don't suppose," said Densher, "that they must have made it out for themselves?"

"No, my dear, I don't; not even," Kate declared, "after Milly's so funnily bumping against us on Tuesday."

"She doesn't see from *that*—?"

"That you're, so to speak, mad about me. Yes, she sees, no doubt, that you regard me with a complacent eye—for you show it, I think, always too much and too crudely. But nothing beyond that. I don't show it too much; I don't perhaps—to please you completely where others are concerned—show it enough."

"Can you show it or not as you like?" Densher demanded.

It pulled her up a little, but she came out resplendent. "Not where *you* are concerned. Beyond seeing that you're rather gone," she went on, "Milly only sees that I'm decently good to you."

"Very good indeed she must think it!"

"Very good indeed then. She easily sees me," Kate smiled, "as very good indeed."

The young man brooded. "But in a sense to take some explaining."

"Then I explain." She was really fine; it came back to her essential plea for her freedom of action and his beauty of trust. "I mean," she added, "I *will* explain."

"And what will I do?"

"Recognise the difference it must make if she thinks." But here in truth Kate faltered. It was his silence alone that, for the moment, took up her apparent meaning; and before he again spoke she had returned to remembrance and prudence. They were now not to forget that, Aunt Maud's liberality having put them on their honour, they mustn't spoil their case by abusing it. He must leave her in time; they should probably find it would help them. But she came back to Milly too. "Mind you go to see her."

Densher still, however, took up nothing of this. "Then I may come again?"

"For Aunt Maud—as much as you like. But we can't again," said Kate, "play her *this trick*. I can't see you here alone."

"Then where?"

"Go to see Milly," she for all satisfaction repeated.

"And what good will that do me?"

"Try it and you'll see."

"You mean you'll manage to be there?" Densher asked. "Say you are, how will that give us privacy?"

"Try it—you'll see," the girl once more returned. "We must manage as we can."

"That's precisely what *I* feel. It strikes me we might manage better." His idea of this was a thing that made him an instant hesitate; yet he brought it out with conviction. "Why won't you come to *me?*"

It was a question her troubled eyes seemed to tell him he was scarce generous in expecting her definitely to answer, and by looking to him to wait at least she appealed to something that she presently made him feel as his pity. It was on that special shade of tenderness that he thus found himself thrown back; and while he asked of his spirit and of his flesh just what concession they could arrange she pressed him yet again on the subject of her singular remedy for their embarrassment. It might have been irritating had she ever struck him as having in her mind a stupid corner. "You'll see," she said, "the difference it will make."

Well, since she wasn't stupid she was intelligent; it was he who was stupid—the proof of which was that he would do what she liked. But he made a last effort to understand, her allusion to the "difference" bringing him round to it. He indeed caught at something subtle but strong even as he spoke. "Is what you meant a moment ago that the difference will be in her being made to believe you hate me?"

Kate, however, had simply, for this gross way of putting it, one of her more marked shows of impatience; with which in fact she sharply closed their discussion. He opened the door on a sign from her, and she accompanied him to the top of the stairs with an air of having so put their possibilities before him that questions were idle and doubts perverse. "I verily believe I *shall* hate you if you spoil for me the beauty of what I see!"

III

He was really, notwithstanding, to hear more from her of what she saw; and the very next occasion had for him still other surprises than that. He received from Mrs. Lowder on the morning after his visit to Kate the telegraphic expression of a hope that he might be free to dine with them that evening; and his freedom affected him as fortunate even though in some degree qualified by her missive. "Expecting American friends whom I'm so glad to find you know!" His knowledge of American friends was clearly an accident of which he was to taste the fruit to the last bitterness. This apprehension, however, we hasten to add, enjoyed for him, in the immediate event, a certain merciful shrinkage; the immediate event being that, at Lancaster Gate, five minutes after his due arrival, prescribed him for eight-thirty, Mrs. Stringham came in alone. The long daylight, the postponed lamps, the habit of the hour, made dinners late and guests still later; so that, punctual as he was, he had found Mrs. Lowder alone, with Kate herself not yet in the field. He had thus had with her several bewildering moments—bewildering by reason, fairly, of their tacit invitation to him to be supernaturally simple. This was exactly, goodness knew, what he wanted to be; but he had never had it so largely and freely—*so* supernaturally simply, for that matter—imputed to him as of easy achievement. It was a particular in which Aunt Maud appeared to offer herself as an example, appeared to say quite agreeably: "What I want of you, don't you see? is to be just exactly as *I* am." The quantity of the article required was what might especially have caused him to stagger—he liked so, in general, the quantities in which Mrs. Lowder dealt. He would have liked as well to ask her how feasible she supposed it for a poor young man to resemble her at any point; but he had after all soon enough perceived that he was doing as she wished by letting his wonder show just a little as silly. He was conscious moreover of a small strange dread of the results of discussion with her—strange, truly, because it was her good nature, not her asperity, that he feared. Asperity might have made him angry—in which there was always a comfort; good nature, in his conditions, had a tendency to make him ashamed—which Aunt Maud indeed, wonderfully, liking him for himself, quite struck him as having guessed. To spare him therefore she also avoided discussion; she kept him down by refusing to quarrel with him. This was what she now proposed to him to enjoy, and his secret discomfort was his sense that on the whole it was what would best suit him. Being kept down was a bore, but his great dread, verily, was of being ashamed, which was a thing distinct; and it mattered but little that he was ashamed of that too. It was of the essence of his position that in such a house as this the tables could always be turned on him. "What do you offer, what do you offer?"—the place, however muffled in convenience and decorum, constantly hummed for him with that thick irony. The irony was a renewed reference to obvious bribes, and he had already seen how little aid came to him from denouncing the bribes as ugly in form. That was what the precious metals—they alone—could afford to be; it was vain enough for him accordingly to try to impart a gloss to his own comparative brummagem. The humiliation of this impotence was precisely what Aunt Maud sought to mitigate for him by keeping him down; and as her effort to that end had doubtless never yet been so visible he had probably never felt so definitely placed in the world as while he waited with her for her half-dozen other guests. She welcomed him genially back from the States, as to his view of which her few questions, though not coherent, were comprehensive, and he had the amusement of seeing in her, as through a clear glass, the outbreak of a plan and the sudden consciousness of a curiosity. She became aware of America, under his eyes, as a possible scene for social operations; the idea of a visit to the wonderful country had clearly but just occurred to her, yet she was talking of it, at the end of a minute, as her favourite dream. He didn't believe in it, but he pretended to; this helped her as well as anything else to treat him as harmless and blameless. She was so engaged, with the further aid of a complete absence of allusions, when the highest effect was given her method by the beautiful entrance of Kate. The method therefore received support all round, for no young man could have been less formidable than the person to the relief of whose shyness her niece ostensibly came. The ostensible, in Kate, struck him altogether, on this occasion, as prodigious; while scarcely less prodigious, for that matter, was his own reading, on the spot, of the relation between his companions—a relation lighted for him by the straight look, not exactly loving nor lingering, yet searching and soft, that, on the part of their hostess, the girl had to reckon with as she advanced. It took her in from head to foot, and in doing so it told a story that made poor Densher again the least bit sick: it marked so something with which Kate habitually and consummately reckoned.

That was the story—that she was always, for her beneficent dragon, under arms; living up, every hour, but especially at festal hours, to the "value" Mrs. Lowder had attached to her. High and fixed, this estimate ruled on each occasion at Lancaster Gate the social scene; so that he now recognised in it something like the artistic idea, the plastic substance, imposed by tradition, by genius, by criticism, in respect to a given character, on a distinguished actress. As such a person was to dress the part, to walk, to look, to speak, in every way to express, the part, so all this was what Kate was to do for the character she had undertaken, under her aunt's roof, to represent. It was made up, the character, of definite elements and touches—things all perfectly ponderable to criticism; and the way for her to meet criticism was evidently at the start to be sure her make-up had had the last touch and that she looked at least no worse than usual. Aunt Maud's appreciation of that to-night was indeed managerial, and the performer's own contribution fairly that of the faultless soldier on parade. Densher saw himself for the moment as in his purchased stall at the play; the watchful manager was in the depths of a box and the poor actress in the glare of the footlights. But she *passed*, the poor performer—he could see how she always passed; her wig, her paint, her jewels, every mark of her expression impeccable, and her entrance accordingly greeted with the proper round of applause. Such impressions as we thus note for Densher come and go, it must be granted, in very much less time than notation demands; but we may none the less make the point that there was, still further, time among them for him to feel almost too scared to take part in the ovation. He struck himself as having lost, for the minute, his presence of mind—so that in any case he only stared in silence at the older woman's technical challenge and at the younger one's disciplined face. It was as if the drama—it thus came to him, for the fact of a drama there was no blinking—was between *them*, them quite preponderantly; with Merton Densher relegated to mere spectatorship, a paying place in front, and one of the most expensive. This was why his appreciation had turned for the instant to fear—had just turned, as we have said, to sickness; and in spite of the fact that the disciplined face did offer him over the footlights, as he believed, the small gleam, fine faint but exquisite, of a special intelligence. So might a practised performer, even when raked by double-barrelled glasses, seem to be all in her part and yet convey a sign to the person in the house she loved best.

The drama, at all events, as Densher saw it, meanwhile went on—amplified soon enough by the advent of two other guests, stray gentlemen both, stragglers in the rout of the season, who visibly presented themselves to Kate during the next moments as subjects for a like impersonal treatment and sharers in a like usual mercy. At opposite ends of the social course, they displayed, in respect to the "figure" that each, in his way, made, one the expansive, the other the contractile effect of the perfect white waistcoat. A scratch company of two innocuous youths and a pacified veteran was therefore what now offered itself to Mrs. Stringham, who rustled in a little breathless and full of the compunction of having had to come alone. Her companion, at the last moment, had been indisposed—positively not well enough, and so had packed her off, insistently, with excuses, with wild regrets. This circumstance of their charming friend's illness was the first thing Kate took up with Densher on their being able after dinner, without bravado, to have ten minutes "naturally," as she called it—which wasn't what *he* did—together; but it was already as if the young man had, by an odd impression, throughout the meal, not been wholly deprived of Miss Theale's participation. Mrs. Lowder had made dear Milly the topic, and it proved, on the spot, a topic as familiar to the enthusiastic younger as to the sagacious older man. Any knowledge they might lack Mrs. Lowder's niece was moreover alert to supply, while Densher himself was freely appealed to as the most privileged, after all, of the group. Wasn't it he who had in a manner invented the wonderful creature—through having seen her first, caught her in her native jungle? Hadn't he more or less paved the way for her by his prompt recognition of her rarity, by preceding her, in a friendly spirit—as he had the "ear" of society—with a sharp flashlight or two?

He met, poor Densher, these enquiries as he could, listening with interest, yet with discomfort; wincing in particular, dry journalist as he was, to find it seemingly supposed of him that he had put his pen—oh his "pen!"—at the service of private distinction. The ear of society?—they were talking, or almost, as if he had publicly paragraphed a modest young lady. They dreamt dreams, in truth, he appeared to perceive, that fairly waked *him* up, and he settled himself in his place both to resist his embarrassment and to catch the full revelation. His embarrassment came naturally from the fact that if he could claim no credit for Miss Theale's success, so neither could he gracefully insist on his not having been concerned with her. What touched him most nearly was that the occasion took on somehow the air of a commemorative banquet, a feast to celebrate a brilliant if brief career. There was of course more said about the heroine than if she hadn't been absent, and he found himself rather stupefied at the range of Milly's triumph. Mrs. Lowder had wonders to tell of it; the two wearers of the waistcoat, either with sincerity or with hypocrisy, professed in the matter an equal expertness; and Densher at last seemed to know himself in presence of a social "case." It was Mrs. Stringham, obviously, whose testimony would have been most invoked hadn't she been, as her friend's representative, rather confined to the function of inhaling the incense; so that Kate, who treated her beautifully, smiling at her, cheering and consoling her across the table, appeared benevolently both to speak and to interpret for her. Kate spoke as if she wouldn't perhaps understand *their* way of appreciating Milly, but would let them none the less, in justice to their good will, express it in their coarser fashion. Densher himself wasn't unconscious in respect to this of a certain broad brotherhood with Mrs. Stringham; wondering indeed, while he followed the talk, how it might move American nerves. He had only heard of them before, but in his recent tour he had caught them in the remarkable fact, and there was now a moment or two when it came to him that he had perhaps—and not in the way of an escape—taken a lesson from them. They quivered, clearly, they hummed and drummed, they leaped and bounded in Mrs. Stringham's typical organism—this lady striking him as before all things excited, as, in the native phrase, keyed-up, to a perception of more elements in the occasion than he was himself able to count. She was accessible to sides of it, he imagined, that were as yet obscure to him; for, though she unmistakeably rejoiced and soared, he none the less saw her at moments as even more agitated than pleasure required. It was a state of emotion in her that could scarce represent simply an impatience to report at home. Her little dry New England brightness—he had "sampled" all the shades of the American complexity, if complexity it were—had its actual reasons for finding relief most in silence; so that before the subject was changed he perceived (with surprise at the others) that they had given her enough of it. He had quite had enough of it himself by the time he was asked if it were true that their friend had really not made in her own country the mark she had chalked so large in London. It was Mrs. Lowder herself who addressed him that enquiry; while he scarce knew if he were the more impressed with her launching it under Mrs. Stringham's nose or with her hope that he would allow to London the honour of discovery. The less expansive of the white waistcoats propounded the theory that they saw in London—for all that was said—much further than in the States: it wouldn't be the first time, he urged, that they had taught the Americans to appreciate (especially when it was funny) some native product. He didn't mean that Miss Theale was funny—though she was weird, and this was precisely her magic; but it might very well be that New York, in having her to show, hadn't been aware of its luck. There *were* plenty of people who were nothing over there and yet were awfully taken up in England; just as—to make the balance right, thank goodness—they sometimes sent out beauties and celebrities who left the Briton cold. The Briton's temperature in truth wasn't to be calculated—a formulation of the matter that was not reached, however, without producing in Mrs. Stringham a final feverish sally. She announced that if the point of view for a proper admiration of her young friend *had* seemed to fail a little in New York, there was no manner of doubt of her having carried Boston by storm. It pointed the moral that Boston, for the finer taste, left New York nowhere; and the good lady, as the exponent of this doctrine—which she set forth at a certain length—made, obviously, to Densher's mind, her nearest approach to supplying the weirdness in which Milly's absence had left them deficient. She made it indeed effective for him by suddenly addressing him. "You know nothing, sir—but not the least little bit—about my friend."

He hadn't pretended he did, but there was a purity of reproach in Mrs. Stringham's face and tone, a purity charged apparently with solemn meanings; so that for a little, small as had been his claim, he couldn't but feel that she exaggerated. He wondered what she did mean, but while doing so he defended himself. "I certainly don't know enormously much—beyond her having been most kind to me, in New York, as a poor bewildered and newly landed alien, and my having tremendously appreciated it." To which he added, he scarce knew why, what had an immediate success. "Remember, Mrs. Stringham, that you weren't then present."

"Ah there you are!" said Kate with much gay expression, though what it expressed he failed at the time to make out.

"You weren't present *then*, dearest," Mrs. Lowder richly concurred. "You don't know," she continued with mellow gaiety, "how far things may have gone."

It made the little woman, he could see, really lose her head. She had more things in that head than any of them in any other; unless perhaps it were Kate, whom he felt as indirectly watching him during this foolish passage, though it pleased him—and because of the foolishness—not to meet her eyes. He met Mrs. Stringham's, which affected him: with her he could on occasion clear it up—a sense produced by the mute communion between them and really the beginning, as the event was to show, of something extraordinary. It was even already a little the effect of this communion that Mrs. Stringham perceptibly faltered in her retort to Mrs. Lowder's joke. "Oh it's precisely my point that Mr. Densher *can't* have had vast opportunities." And then she smiled at him. "I wasn't away, you know, long."

It made everything, in the oddest way in the world, immediately right for him. "And I wasn't *there* long, either." He positively saw with it that nothing for him, so far as she was concerned, would again be wrong. "She's beautiful, but I don't say she's easy to know."

"Ah she's a thousand and one things!" replied the good lady, as if now to keep well with him.

He asked nothing better. "She was off with you to these parts before I knew it. I myself was off too—away off to wonderful parts, where I had endlessly more to see."

"But you didn't forget her!" Aunt Maud interposed with almost menacing archness.

"No, of course I didn't forget her. One doesn't forget such charming impressions. But I never," he lucidly maintained, "chattered to others about her."

"She'll thank you for that, sir," said Mrs. Stringham with a flushed firmness.

"Yet doesn't silence in such a case," Aunt Maud blandly enquired, "very often quite prove the depth of the impression?"

He would have been amused, hadn't he been slightly displeased, at all they seemed desirous to fasten on him. "Well, the impression was as deep as you like. But I really want Miss Theale to know," he pursued for Mrs. Stringham, "that I don't figure by any consent of my own as an authority about her."

Kate came to his assistance—if assistance it was—before their friend had had time to meet this charge. "You're right about her not being easy to know. One *sees* her with intensity—sees her more than one sees almost any one; but then one discovers that that isn't knowing her and that one may know better a person whom one doesn't 'see,' as I say, half so much."

The discrimination was interesting, but it brought them back to the fact of her success; and it was at that comparatively gross circumstance, now so fully placed before them, that Milly's anxious companion sat and looked—looked very much as some spectator in an old-time circus might have watched the oddity of a Christian maiden, in the arena, mildly, caressingly, martyred. It was the nosing and fumbling not of lions and tigers but of domestic animals let loose as for the joke. Even the joke made Mrs. Stringham uneasy, and her mute communion with Densher, to which we have alluded, was more and more determined by it. He wondered afterwards if Kate had made this out; though it was not indeed till much later on that he found himself, in thought, dividing the things she might have been conscious of from the things she must have missed. If she actually missed, at any rate, Mrs. Stringham's discomfort, that but showed how her own idea held her. Her own idea was, by insisting on the fact of the girl's prominence as a feature of the season's end, to keep Densher in relation, for the rest of them, both to present and to past. "It's everything that has happened *since* that makes you naturally a little shy about her. You don't know what has happened since, but we do; we've seen it and followed it; we've a little been *of* it." The great thing for him, at this, as Kate gave it, *was* in fact quite irresistibly that the case was a real one—the kind of thing that, when one's patience was shorter than one's curiosity, one had vaguely taken for possible in London, but in which one had never been even to this small extent concerned. The little American's sudden social adventure, her happy and, no doubt, harmless flourish, had probably been favoured by several accidents, but it had been favoured above all by the simple spring-board of the scene, by one of those common caprices of the numberless foolish flock, gregarious movements as inscrutable as ocean-currents. The huddled herd had drifted to her blindly—it might as blindly have drifted away. There had been of course a signal, but the great reason was probably the absence at the moment of a larger lion. The bigger beast would come and the smaller would then incontinently vanish. It was at all events characteristic, and what was of the essence of it was grist to his scribbling mill, matter for his journalising hand. That hand already, in intention, played over it, the "motive," as a sign of the season, a feature of the time, of the purely expeditious and rough-and-tumble nature of the social boom. The boom as in *itself* required—that would be the note; the subject of the process a comparatively minor question. Anything was boomable enough when nothing else was more so: the author of the "rotten" book, the beauty who was no beauty, the heiress who was only that, the stranger who was for the most part saved from being inconveniently strange but by being inconveniently familiar, the American whose Americanism had been long desperately discounted, the creature in fine as to whom spangles or spots of any sufficiently marked and exhibited sort could be loudly enough predicated.

So he judged at least, within his limits, and the idea that what he had thus caught in the fact was the trick of fashion and the tone of society went so far as to make him take up again his sense of independence. He had supposed himself civilised; but if this was civilisation—! One could smoke one's pipe outside when twaddle was within. He had rather avoided, as we have remarked, Kate's eyes, but there came a moment when he would fairly have liked to put it, across the table, to her: "I say, light of my life, is *this* the great world?" There came another, it must be added—and doubtless as a result of something that, over the cloth, did hang between them—when she struck him as having quite answered: "Dear no—for what do you take me? Not the least little bit: only a poor silly, though quite harmless, imitation." What she might have passed for saying, however, was practically merged in what she did say, for she came overtly to his aid, very much as if guessing some of his thoughts. She enunciated, to relieve his bewilderment, the obvious truth that you couldn't leave London for three months at that time of the year and come back to find your friends just where they were. As they had *of course* been jigging away they might well be so red in the face that you wouldn't know them. She reconciled in fine his disclaimer about Milly with that honour of having discovered her which it was vain for him modestly to shirk. He *had* unearthed her, but it was they, all of them together, who had developed her. She was always a charmer, one of the greatest ever seen, but she wasn't the person he had "backed."

Densher was to feel sure afterwards that Kate had had in these pleasantries no conscious, above all no insolent purpose of making light of poor Susan Shepherd's property in their young friend—which property, by such remarks, was very much pushed to the wall; but he was also to know that Mrs. Stringham had secretly resented them, Mrs. Stringham holding the opinion, of which he was ultimately to have a glimpse, that all the Kate Croys in Christendom were but dust for the feet of her Milly. That, it was true, would be what she must reveal only when driven to her last entrenchments and well cornered in her passion—the rare passion of friendship, the sole passion of her little life save the one other, more imperturbably cerebral, that she entertained for the art of Guy de Maupassant. She slipped in the observation that her Milly was incapable of change, was just exactly, on the contrary, the same Milly; but this made little difference in the drift of Kate's contention. She was perfectly kind to Susie: it was as if she positively knew her as handicapped for any disagreement by feeling that she, Kate, had "type," and by being committed to admiration of type. Kate had occasion subsequently—she found it somehow—to mention to our young man Milly's having spoken to her of this view on the good lady's part. She would like—Milly had had it from her—to put Kate Croy in a book and see what she could so do with her. "Chop me up fine or serve me whole"—it was a way of being got at that Kate professed she dreaded. It would be Mrs. Stringham's, however, she understood, because Mrs. Stringham, oddly, felt that with such stuff as the strange English girl was made of, stuff that (in spite of Maud Manningham, who was full of sentiment) she had never known, there was none other to be employed. These things were of later evidence, yet Densher might even then have felt them in the air. They were practically in it already when Kate, waiving the question of her friend's chemical change, wound up with the comparatively unobjectionable proposition that he must now, having missed so much, take them all up, on trust, further on. He met it peacefully, a little perhaps as an example to Mrs. Stringham—"Oh as far on as you like!" This even had its effect: Mrs. Stringham appropriated as much of it as might be meant for herself. The nice thing about her was that she could measure how much; so that by the time dinner was over they had really covered ground.

IV

The younger of the other men, it afterwards appeared, was most in his element at the piano; so that they had coffee and comic songs upstairs—the gentlemen, temporarily relinquished, submitting easily in this interest to Mrs. Lowder's parting injunction not to sit too tight. Our especial young man sat tighter when restored to the drawing-room; he made it out perfectly with Kate that they might, off and on, foregather without offence. He had perhaps stronger needs in this general respect than she; but she had better names for the scant risks to which she consented. It was the blessing of a big house that intervals were large and, of an August night, that windows were open; whereby, at a given moment, on the wide balcony, with the songs sufficiently sung, Aunt Maud could hold her little court more freshly. Densher and Kate, during these moments, occupied side by side a small sofa—a luxury formulated by the latter as the proof, under criticism, of their remarkably good conscience. "To seem not to know each other—once you're here—would be," the girl said, "to overdo it"; and she arranged it charmingly that they *must* have some passage to put Aunt Maud off the scent. She would be wondering otherwise what in the world they found their account in. For Densher, none the less, the profit of snatched moments, snatched contacts, was partial and poor; there were in particular at present more things in his mind than he could bring out while watching the windows. It was true, on the other hand, that she suddenly met most of them—and more than he could see on the spot—by coming out for him with a reference to Milly that was not in the key of those made at dinner. "She's not a bit right, you know. I mean in health. Just see her to-night. I mean it looks grave. For you she would have come, you know, if it had been at all possible."

He took this in such patience as he could muster. "What in the world's the matter with her?"

But Kate continued without saying. "Unless indeed your being here has been just a reason for her funking it."

"What in the world's the matter with her?" Densher asked again.

"Why just what I've told you—that she likes you so much."

"Then why should she deny herself the joy of meeting me?"

Kate cast about—it would take so long to explain. "And perhaps it's true that she *is* bad. She easily may be."

"Quite easily, I should say, judging by Mrs. Stringham, who's visibly preoccupied and worried."

"Visibly enough. Yet it mayn't," said Kate, "be only for that."

"For what then?"

But this question too, on thinking, she neglected. "Why, if it's anything real, doesn't that poor lady go home? She'd be anxious, and she has done all she need to be civil."

"I think," Densher remarked, "she has been quite beautifully civil."

It made Kate, he fancied, look at him the least bit harder; but she was already, in a manner, explaining. "Her preoccupation is probably on two different heads. One of them would make her hurry back, but the other makes her stay. She's commissioned to tell Milly all about you."

"Well then," said the young man between a laugh and a sigh, "I'm glad I felt, downstairs, a kind of 'drawing' to her. Wasn't I rather decent to her?"

"Awfully nice. You've instincts, you fiend. It's all," Kate declared, "as it should be."

"Except perhaps," he after a moment cynically suggested, "that she isn't getting much good of me now. Will she report to Milly on *this?*" And then as Kate seemed to wonder what "this" might be: "On our present disregard for appearances."

"Ah leave appearances to me!" She spoke in her high way. "I'll make them all right. Aunt Maud, moreover," she added, "has her so engaged that she won't notice." Densher felt, with this, that his companion had indeed perceptive flights he couldn't hope to match—had for instance another when she still subjoined: "And Mrs. Stringham's appearing to respond just in order to make that impression."

"Well," Densher dropped with some humour, "life's very interesting! I hope it's really as much so for you as you make it for others; I mean judging by what you make it for me. You seem to me to represent it as thrilling for *ces dames*, and in a different way for each: Aunt Maud, Susan Shepherd, Milly. But what *is*," he wound up, "the matter? Do you mean she's as ill as she looks?"

Kate's face struck him as replying at first that his derisive speech deserved no satisfaction; then she appeared to yield to a need of her own—the need to make the point that "as ill as she looked" was what Milly scarce could be. If she had been as ill as she looked she could scarce be a question with them, for her end would in that case be near. She believed herself nevertheless—and Kate couldn't help believing her too—seriously menaced. There was always the fact that they had been on the point of leaving town, the two ladies, and had suddenly been pulled up. "We bade them good-bye—or all but—Aunt Maud and I, the night before Milly, popping so very oddly into the National Gallery for a farewell look, found you and me together. They were then to get off a day or two later. But they've not got off—they're not getting off. When I see them—and I saw them this morning—they have showy reasons. They do mean to go, but they've postponed it." With which the girl brought out: "They've postponed it for *you*." He protested so far as a man might without fatuity, since a protest was itself credulous; but Kate, as ever, understood herself. "You've made Milly change her mind. She wants not to miss you—though she wants also not to show she wants you; which is why, as I hinted a moment ago, she may consciously have hung back to-night. She doesn't know when she may see you again—she doesn't know she ever may. She doesn't see the future. It has opened out before her in these last weeks as a dark confused thing."

Densher wondered. "After the tremendous time you've all been telling me she has had?"

"That's it. There's a shadow across it."

"The shadow, you consider, of some physical break-up?"

"Some physical break-down. Nothing less. She's scared. She has so much to lose. And she wants more."

"Ah well," said Densher with a sudden strange sense of discomfort, "couldn't one say to her that she can't have everything?"

"No—for one wouldn't want to. She really," Kate went on, "has been somebody here. Ask Aunt Maud—you may think me prejudiced," the girl oddly smiled. "Aunt Maud will tell you—the world's before her. It has all come since you saw her, and it's a pity you've missed it, for it certainly would have amused you. She has really been a perfect success—I mean of course so far as possible in the scrap of time—and she has taken it like a perfect angel. If you can imagine an angel with a thumping bank-account you'll have the simplest expression of the kind of thing. Her fortune's absolutely huge; Aunt Maud has had all the facts, or enough of them, in the last confidence, from 'Susie,' and Susie speaks by book. Take them then, in the last confidence, from *me*. There she is." Kate expressed above all what it most came to. "It's open to her to make, you see, the very greatest marriage. I assure you we're not vulgar about her. Her possibilities are quite plain."

Densher showed he neither disbelieved nor grudged them. "But what good then on earth can I do her?"

Well, she had it ready. "You can console her."

"And for what?"

"For all that, if she's stricken, she must see swept away. I shouldn't care for her if she hadn't so much," Kate very simply said. And then as it made him laugh not quite happily: "I shouldn't trouble about her if there were one thing she did have." The girl spoke indeed with a noble compassion. "She has nothing."

"Not all the young dukes?"

"Well we must see—see if anything can come of them. She at any rate does love life. To have met a person like you," Kate further explained, "is to have felt you become, with all the other fine things, a part of life. Oh she has you arranged!"

"*You* have, it strikes me, my dear"—and he looked both detached and rueful. "Pray what am I to do with the dukes?"

"Oh the dukes will be disappointed!"

"Then why shan't I be?"

"You'll have expected less," Kate wonderfully smiled. "Besides, you *will* be. You'll have expected enough for that."

"Yet it's what you want to let me in for?"

"I want," said the girl, "to make things pleasant for her. I use, for the purpose, what I have. You're what I have of most precious, and you're therefore what I use most."

He looked at her long. "I wish I could use *you* a little more." After which, as she continued to smile at him, "Is it a bad case of lungs?" he asked.

Kate showed for a little as if she wished it might be. "Not lungs, I think. Isn't consumption, taken in time, now curable?"

"People are, no doubt, patched up." But he wondered. "Do you mean she has something that's past patching?" And before she could answer: "It's really as if her appearance put her outside of such things—being, in spite of her youth, that of a person who has been through all it's conceivable she should be exposed to. She affects one, I should say, as a creature saved from a shipwreck. Such a creature may surely, in these days, on the doctrine of chances, go to sea again with confidence. She has *had* her wreck—she has met her adventure."

"Oh I grant you her wreck!"—Kate was all response so far. "But do let her have still her adventure. There are wrecks that are not adventures."

"Well—if there be also adventures that are not wrecks!" Densher in short was willing, but he came back to his point. "What I mean is that she has none of the effect—on one's nerves or whatever—of an invalid."

Kate on her side did this justice. "No—that's the beauty of her."

"The beauty—?"

"Yes, she's so wonderful. She won't show for that, any more than your watch, when it's about to stop for want of being wound up, gives you convenient notice or shows as different from usual. She won't die, she won't live, by inches. She won't smell, as it were, of drugs. She won't taste, as it were, of medicine. No one will know."

"Then what," he demanded, frankly mystified now, "are we talking about? In what extraordinary state *is* she?"

Kate went on as if, at this, making it out in a fashion for herself. "I believe that if she's ill at all she's very ill. I believe that if she's bad she's not a *little* bad. I can't tell you why, but that's how I see her. She'll really live or she'll really not. She'll have it all or she'll miss it all. Now I don't think she'll have it all."

Densher had followed this with his eyes upon her, her own having thoughtfully wandered, and as if it were more impressive than lucid. "You 'think' and you 'don't think,' and yet you remain all the while without an inkling of her complaint?"

"No, not without an inkling; but it's a matter in which I don't want knowledge. She moreover herself doesn't want one to want it: she has, as to what may be preying upon her, a kind of ferocity of modesty, a kind of—I don't know what to call it—intensity of pride. And then and then—" But with this she faltered.

"And then what?"

"I'm a brute about illness. I hate it. It's well for you, my dear," Kate continued, "that you're as sound as a bell."

"Thank you!" Densher laughed. "It's rather good then for yourself too that you're as strong as the sea."

She looked at him now a moment as for the selfish gladness of their young immunities. It was all they had together, but they had it at least without a flaw—each had the beauty, the physical felicity, the personal virtue, love and desire of the other. Yet it was as if that very consciousness threw them back the next moment into pity for the poor girl who had everything else in the world, the great genial good they, alas, didn't have, but failed on the other hand of this. "How we're talking about her!" Kate compunctiously sighed. But there were the facts. "From illness I keep away."

"But you don't—since here you are, in spite of all you say, in the midst of it."

"Ah I'm only watching—!"

"And putting me forward in your place? Thank you!"

"Oh," said Kate, "I'm breaking you in. Let it give you the measure of what I shall expect of you. One can't begin too soon."

She drew away, as from the impression of a stir on the balcony, the hand of which he had a minute before possessed himself; and the warning brought him back to attention. "You haven't even an idea if it's a case for surgery?"

"I dare say it may be; that is that if it comes to anything it may come to that. Of course she's in the highest hands."

"The doctors are after her then?"

"She's after *them*—it's the same thing. I think I'm free to say it now—she sees Sir Luke Strett."

It made him quickly wince. "Ah fifty thousand knives!" Then after an instant: "One seems to guess."

Yes, but she waved it away. "Don't guess. Only do as I tell you."

For a moment now, in silence, he took it all in, might have had it before him. "What you want of me then is to make up to a sick girl."

"Ah but you admit yourself that she doesn't affect you as sick. You understand moreover just how much—and just how little."

"It's amazing," he presently answered, "what you think I understand."

"Well, if you've brought me to it, my dear," she returned, "that has been your way of breaking *me* in. Besides which, so far as making up to her goes, plenty of others will."

Densher for a little, under this suggestion, might have been seeing their young friend on a pile of cushions and in a perpetual tea-gown, amid flowers and with drawn blinds, surrounded by the higher nobility. "Others can follow their tastes. Besides, others are free."

"But so are you, my dear!"

She had spoken with impatience, and her suddenly quitting him had sharpened it; in spite of which he kept his place, only looking up at her. "You're prodigious!"

"Of course I'm prodigious!"—and, as immediately happened, she gave a further sign of it that he fairly sat watching. The door from the lobby had, as she spoke, been thrown open for a gentleman who, immediately finding her within his view, advanced to greet her before the announcement of his name could reach her companion. Densher none the less felt himself brought quickly into relation; Kate's welcome to the visitor became almost precipitately an appeal to her friend, who slowly rose to meet it. "I don't know whether you know Lord Mark." And then for the other party: "Mr. Merton Densher—who has just come back from America."

"Oh!" said the other party while Densher said nothing—occupied as he mainly was on the spot with weighing the sound in question. He recognised it in a moment as less imponderable than it might have appeared, as having indeed positive claims. It wasn't, that is, he knew, the "Oh!" of the idiot, however great the superficial resemblance: it was that of the clever, the accomplished man; it was the very specialty of the speaker, and a deal of expensive training and experience had gone to producing it. Densher felt somehow that, as a thing of value accidentally picked up, it would retain an interest of curiosity. The three stood for a little together in an awkwardness to which he was conscious of contributing his share; Kate failing to ask Lord Mark to be seated, but letting him know that he would find Mrs. Lowder, with some others, on the balcony.

"Oh and Miss Theale I suppose?—as I seemed to hear outside, from below, Mrs. Stringham's unmistakeable voice."

"Yes, but Mrs. Stringham's alone. Milly's unwell," the girl explained, "and was compelled to disappoint us."

"Ah 'disappoint'—rather!" And, lingering a little, he kept his eyes on Densher. "She isn't really bad, I trust?"

Densher, after all he had heard, easily supposed him interested in Milly; but he could imagine him also interested in the young man with whom he had found Kate engaged and whom he yet considered without visible intelligence. That young man concluded in a moment that he was doing what he wanted, satisfying himself as to each. To this he was aided by Kate, who produced a prompt: "Oh dear no; I think not. I've just been reassuring Mr. Densher," she added—"who's as concerned as the rest of us. I've been calming his fears."

"Oh!" said Lord Mark again—and again it was just as good. That was for Densher, the latter could see, or think he saw. And then for the others: "*My* fears would want calming. We must take great care of her. This way?"

She went with him a few steps, and while Densher, hanging about, gave them frank attention, presently paused again for some further colloquy. What passed between them their observer lost, but she was presently with him again, Lord Mark joining the rest. Densher was by this time quite ready for her. "It's *he* who's your aunt's man?"

"Oh immensely."

"I mean for *you.*"

"That's what I mean too," Kate smiled. "There he is. Now you can judge."

"Judge of what?"

"Judge of him."

"Why should I judge of him?" Densher asked. "I've nothing to do with him."

"Then why do you ask about him?"

"To judge of you—which is different."

Kate seemed for a little to look at the difference. "To take the measure, do you mean, of my danger?"

He hesitated; then he said: "I'm thinking, I dare say, of Miss Theale's. How does your aunt reconcile his interest in her—?"

"With his interest in me?"

"With her own interest in you," Densher said while she reflected. "If that interest—Mrs. Lowder's—takes the form of Lord Mark, hasn't he rather to look out for the forms *he* takes?"

Kate seemed interested in the question, but "Oh he takes them easily," she answered. "The beauty is that she doesn't trust him."

"That Milly doesn't?"

"Yes—Milly either. But I mean Aunt Maud. Not really."

Densher gave it his wonder. "Takes him to her heart and yet thinks he cheats?"

"Yes," said Kate—"that's the way people are. What they think of their enemies, goodness knows, is bad enough; but I'm still more struck with what they think of their friends. Milly's own state of mind, however," she went on, "is lucky. That's Aunt Maud's security, though she doesn't yet fully recognise it—besides being Milly's own."

"You conceive it a real escape then not to care for him?"

She shook her head in beautiful grave deprecation. "You oughtn't to make me say too much. But I'm glad I don't."

"Don't say too much?"

"Don't care for Lord Mark."

"Oh!" Densher answered with a sound like his lordship's own. To which he added: "You absolutely hold that that poor girl doesn't?"

"Ah you know what I hold about that poor girl!" It had made her again impatient.

Yet he stuck a minute to the subject. "You scarcely call him, I suppose, one of the dukes."

"Mercy, no—far from it. He's not, compared with other possibilities, 'in' it. Milly, it's true," she said, to be exact, "has no natural sense of social values, doesn't in the least understand our differences or know who's who or what's what."

"I see. That," Densher laughed, "is her reason for liking *me*."

"Precisely. She doesn't resemble me," said Kate, "who at least know what I lose."

Well, it had all risen for Densher to a considerable interest. "And Aunt Maud—why shouldn't *she* know? I mean that your friend there isn't really anything. Does she suppose him of ducal value?"

"Scarcely; save in the sense of being uncle to a duke. That's undeniably something. He's the best moreover we can get."

"Oh, oh!" said Densher; and his doubt was not all derisive.

"It isn't Lord Mark's grandeur," she went on without heeding this; "because perhaps in the line of that alone—as he has no money—more could be done. But she's not a bit sordid; she only counts with the sordidness of others. Besides, he's grand enough, with a duke in his family and at the other end of the string. *The* thing's his genius."

"And do you believe in that?"

"In Lord Mark's genius?" Kate, as if for a more final opinion than had yet been asked of her, took a moment to think. She balanced indeed so that one would scarce have known what to expect; but she came out in time with a very sufficient "Yes!"

"Political?"

"Universal. I don't know at least," she said, "what else to call it when a man's able to make himself without effort, without violence, without machinery of any sort, so intensely felt. He has somehow an effect without his being in any traceable way a cause."

"Ah but if the effect," said Densher with conscious superficiality, "isn't agreeable—?"

"Oh but it is!"

"Not surely for every one."

"If you mean not for you," Kate returned, "you may have reasons—and men don't count. Women don't know if it's agreeable or not."

"Then there you are!"

"Yes, precisely—that takes, on his part, genius."

Densher stood before her as if he wondered what everything she thus promptly, easily and above all amusingly met him with, would have been found, should it have come to an analysis, to "take." Something suddenly, as if under a last determinant touch, welled up in him and overflowed—the sense of his good fortune and her variety, of the future she promised, the interest she supplied. "All women but you are stupid. How can I look at another? You're different and different—and then you're different again. No marvel Aunt Maud builds on you—except that you're so much too good for what she builds *for*. Even 'society' won't know how good for it you are; it's too stupid, and you're beyond it. You'd have to pull it uphill—it's you yourself who are at the top. The women one meets—what are they but books one has already read? You're a whole library of the unknown, the uncut." He almost moaned, he ached, from the depth of his content. "Upon my word I've a subscription!"

She took it from him with her face again giving out all it had in answer, and they remained once more confronted and united in their essential wealth of life. "It's you who draw me out. I exist in you. Not in others."

It had been, however, as if the thrill of their association itself pressed in him, as great felicities do, the sharp spring of fear. "See here, you know: don't, *don't*—!"

"Don't what?"

"Don't fail me. It would kill me."

She looked at him a minute with no response but her eyes. "So you think you'll kill *me* in time to prevent it?" She smiled, but he saw her the next instant as smiling through tears; and the instant after this she had got, in respect to the particular point, quite off. She had come back to another, which was one of her own; her own were so closely connected that Densher's were at best but parenthetic. Still she had a distance to go. "You do then see your way?" She put it to him before they joined—as was high time—the others. And she made him understand she meant his way with Milly.

He had dropped a little in presence of the explanation; then she had brought him up to a sort of recognition. He could make out by this light something of what he saw, but a dimness also there was, undispelled since his return. "There's something you must definitely tell me. If our friend knows that all the while—?"

She came straight to his aid, formulating for him his anxiety, though quite to smooth it down. "All the while she and I here were growing intimate, you and I were in unmentioned relation? If she knows that, yes, she knows our relation must have involved your writing to me."

"Then how could she suppose you weren't answering?"

"She doesn't suppose it."

"How then can she imagine you never named her?"

"She doesn't. She knows now I did name her. I've told her everything. She's in possession of reasons that will perfectly do."

Still he just brooded. "She takes things from you exactly as I take them?"

"Exactly as you take them."

"She's just such another victim?"

"Just such another. You're a pair."

"Then if anything happens," said Densher, "we can console each other?"

"Ah something *may* indeed happen," she returned, "if you'll only go straight!"

He watched the others an instant through the window. "What do you mean by going straight?"

"Not worrying. Doing as you like. Try, as I've told you before, and you'll see. You'll have me perfectly, always, to refer to."

"Oh rather, I hope! But if she's going away?"

It pulled Kate up but a moment. "I'll bring her back. There you are. You won't be able to say I haven't made it smooth for you."

He faced it all, and certainly it was queer. But it wasn't the queerness that after another minute was uppermost. He was in a wondrous silken web, and it was amusing. "You spoil me!"

He wasn't sure if Mrs. Lowder, who at this juncture reappeared, had caught his word as it dropped from him; probably not, he thought, her attention being given to Mrs. Stringham, with whom she came through and who was now, none too soon, taking leave of her. They were followed by Lord Mark and by the other men, but two or three things happened before any dispersal of the company began. One of these was that Kate found time to say to him with furtive emphasis: "You must go now!" Another was that she next addressed herself in all frankness to Lord Mark, drew near to him with an almost reproachful "Come and talk to *me!*"—a challenge resulting after a minute for Densher in a consciousness of their installation together in an out-of-the-way corner, though not the same he himself had just occupied with her. Still another was that Mrs. Stringham, in the random intensity of her farewells, affected him as looking at him with a small grave intimation, something into which he afterwards read the meaning that if he had happened to desire a few words with her after dinner he would have found her ready. This impression was naturally light, but it just left him with the sense of something by his own act overlooked, unappreciated. It gathered perhaps a slightly sharper shade from the mild formality of her "Good-night, sir!" as she passed him; a matter as to which there was now nothing more to be done, thanks to the alertness of the young man he by this time had appraised as even more harmless than himself. This personage had forestalled him in opening the door for her and was evidently—with a view, Densher might have judged, to ulterior designs on Milly—proposing to attend her to her carriage. What further occurred was that Aunt Maud, having released her, immediately had a word for himself. It was an imperative "Wait a minute," by which she both detained and dismissed him; she was particular about her minute, but he hadn't yet given her, as happened, a sign of withdrawal.

"Return to our little friend. You'll find her really interesting."

"If you mean Miss Theale," he said, "I shall certainly not forget her. But you must remember that, so far as her 'interest' is concerned, I myself discovered, I—as was said at dinner—invented her."

"Well, one seemed rather to gather that you hadn't taken out the patent. Don't, I only mean, in the press of other things, too much neglect her."

Affected, surprised by the coincidence of her appeal with Kate's, he asked himself quickly if it mightn't help him with her. He at any rate could but try. "You're all looking after my manners. That's exactly, you know, what Miss Croy has been saying to me. *She* keeps me up—she has had so much to say about them."

He found pleasure in being able to give his hostess an account of his passage with Kate that, while quite veracious, might be reassuring to herself. But Aunt Maud, wonderfully and facing him straight, took it as if her confidence were supplied with other props. If she saw his intention in it she yet blinked neither with doubt nor with acceptance; she only said imperturbably: "Yes, she'll herself do anything for her friend; so that she but preaches what she practises."

Densher really quite wondered if Aunt Maud knew how far Kate's devotion went. He was moreover a little puzzled by this special harmony; in face of which he quickly asked himself if Mrs. Lowder had bethought herself of the American girl as a distraction for him, and if Kate's mastery of the subject were therefore but an appearance addressed to her aunt. What might really *become* in all this of the American girl was therefore a question that, on the latter contingency, would lose none of its sharpness. However, questions could wait, and it was easy, so far as he understood, to meet Mrs. Lowder. "It isn't a bit, all the same, you know, that I resist. I find Miss Theale charming."

Well, it was all she wanted. "Then don't miss a chance."

"The only thing is," he went on, "that she's—naturally now—leaving town and, as I take it, going abroad."

Aunt Maud looked indeed an instant as if she herself had been dealing with this difficulty. "She won't go," she smiled in spite of it, "till she has seen you. Moreover, when she does go—" She paused, leaving him uncertain. But the next minute he was still more at sea. "We shall go too."

He gave a smile that he himself took for slightly strange. "And what good will that do *me?*"

"We shall be near them somewhere, and you'll come out to us."

"Oh!" he said a little awkwardly.

"I'll see that you do. I mean I'll write to you."

"Ah thank you, thank you!" Merton Densher laughed. She was indeed putting him on his honour, and his honour winced a little at the use he rather helplessly saw himself suffering her to believe she could make of it. "There are all sorts of things," he vaguely remarked, "to consider."

"No doubt. But there's above all the great thing."

"And pray what's that?"

"Why the importance of your not losing the occasion of your life. I'm treating you handsomely, I'm looking after it for you. I *can*—I can smooth your path. She's charming, she's clever and she's good. And her fortune's a real fortune."

Ah there she was, Aunt Maud! The pieces fell together for him as he felt her thus buying him off, and buying him—it would have been funny if it hadn't been so grave—with Miss Theale's money. He ventured, derisive, fairly to treat it as extravagant. "I'm much obliged to you for the handsome offer—"

"Of what doesn't belong to me?" She wasn't abashed. "I don't say it does—but there's no reason it shouldn't to *you*. Mind you, moreover"—she kept it up—"I'm not one who talks in the air. And you owe me something—if you want to know why."

Distinct he felt her pressure; he felt, given her basis, her consistency; he even felt, to a degree that was immediately to receive an odd confirmation, her truth. Her truth, for that matter, was that she believed him bribeable: a belief that for his own mind as well, while they stood there, lighted up the impossible. What then in this light did Kate believe him? But that wasn't what he asked aloud. "Of course I know I owe you thanks for a deal of kind treatment. Your inviting me for instance to-night—!"

"Yes, my inviting you to-night's a part of it. But you don't know," she added, "how far I've gone for you."

He felt himself red and as if his honour were colouring up; but he laughed again as he could. "I see how far you're going."

"I'm the most honest woman in the world, but I've nevertheless done for you what was necessary." And then as her now quite sombre gravity only made him stare: "To start you it *was* necessary. From *me* it has the weight." He but continued to stare, and she met his blankness with surprise. "Don't you understand me? I've told the proper lie for you." Still he only showed her his flushed strained smile; in spite of which, speaking with force and as if he must with a minute's reflexion see what she meant, she turned away from him. "I depend upon you now to make me right!"

The minute's reflexion he was of course more free to take after he had left the house. He walked up the Bayswater Road, but he stopped short, under the murky stars, before the modern church, in the middle of the square that, going eastward, opened out on his left. He had had his brief stupidity, but now he understood. She had guaranteed to Milly Theale through Mrs. Stringham that Kate didn't care for him. She had affirmed through the same source that the attachment was only his. He made it out, he made it out, and he could see what she meant by its starting him. She had described Kate as merely compassionate, so that Milly might be compassionate too. "Proper" indeed it was, her lie—the very properest possible and the most deeply, richly diplomatic. So Milly was successfully deceived.

V

To see her alone, the poor girl, he none the less promptly felt, was to see her after all very much on the old basis, the basis of his three visits in New York; the new element, when once he was again face to face with her, not really amounting to much more than a recognition, with a little surprise, of the positive extent of the old basis. Everything but that, everything embarrassing fell away after he had been present five minutes: it was in fact wonderful that their excellent, their pleasant, their permitted and proper and harmless American relation—the legitimacy of which he could thus scarce express in names enough—should seem so unperturbed by other matters. They had both since then had great adventures—such an adventure for him was his mental annexation of her country; and it was now, for the moment, as if the greatest of them all were this acquired consciousness of reasons other than those that had already served. Densher had asked for her, at her hotel, the day after Aunt Maud's dinner, with a rich, that is with a highly troubled, preconception of the part likely to be played for him at present, in any contact with her, by Kate's and Mrs. Lowder's so oddly conjoined and so really superfluous attempts to make her interesting. She had been interesting enough without them—that appeared to-day to come back to him; and, admirable and beautiful as was the charitable zeal of the two ladies, it might easily have nipped in the bud the germs of a friendship inevitably limited but still perfectly open to him. What had happily averted the need of his breaking off, what would as happily continue to avert it, was his own good sense and good humour, a certain spring of mind in him which ministered, imagination aiding, to understandings and allowances and which he had positively never felt such ground as just now to rejoice in the possession of. Many men—he practically made the reflexion—wouldn't have taken the matter that way, would have lost patience, finding the appeal in question irrational, exorbitant; and, thereby making short work with it, would have let it render any further acquaintance with Miss Theale impossible. He had talked with Kate of this young woman's being "sacrificed," and that would have been one way, so far as he was concerned, to sacrifice her. Such, however, had not been the tune to which his at first bewildered view had, since the night before, cleared itself up. It wasn't so much that he failed of being the kind of man who "chucked," for he knew himself as the kind of man wise enough to mark the case in which chucking might be the minor evil and the least cruelty. It was that he liked too much every one concerned willingly to show himself merely impracticable. He liked Kate, goodness knew, and he also clearly enough liked Mrs. Lowder. He liked in particular Milly herself; and hadn't it come up for him the evening before that he quite liked even Susan Shepherd? He had never known himself so generally merciful. It was a footing, at all events, whatever accounted for it, on which he should surely be rather a muff not to manage by one turn or another to escape disobliging. Should he find he couldn't work it there would still be time enough. The idea of working it crystallised before him in such guise as not only to promise much interest—fairly, in case of success, much enthusiasm; but positively to impart to failure an appearance of barbarity.

Arriving thus in Brook Street both with the best intentions and with a margin consciously left for some primary awkwardness, he found his burden, to his great relief, unexpectedly light. The awkwardness involved in the responsibility so newly and so ingeniously traced for him turned round on the spot to present him another face. This was simply the face of his old impression, which he now fully recovered—the impression that American girls, when, rare case, they had the attraction of Milly, were clearly the easiest people in the world. Had what had happened been that this specimen of the class was from the first so committed to ease that nothing subsequent *could* ever make her difficult? That affected him now as still more probable than on the occasion of the hour or two lately passed with her in Kate's society. Milly Theale had recognised no complication, to Densher's view, while bringing him, with his companion, from the National Gallery and entertaining them at luncheon; it was therefore scarce supposable that complications had become so soon too much for her. His pretext for presenting himself was fortunately of the best and simplest; the least he could decently do, given their happy acquaintance, was to call with an enquiry after learning that she had been prevented by illness from meeting him at dinner. And then there was the beautiful accident of her other demonstration; he must at any rate have given a sign as a sequel to the hospitality he had shared with Kate. Well, he was giving one now—such as it was; he was finding her, to begin with, accessible, and very naturally and prettily glad to see him. He had come, after luncheon, early, though not so early but that she might already be out if she were well enough; and she was well enough and yet was still at home. He had an inner glimpse, with this, of the comment Kate would have made on it; it wasn't absent from his thought that Milly would have been at home by *her* account because expecting, after a talk with Mrs. Stringham, that a certain person might turn up. He even—so pleasantly did things go—enjoyed freedom of mind to welcome, on that supposition, a fresh sign of the beautiful hypocrisy of women. He went so far as to enjoy believing the girl *might* have stayed in for him; it helped him to enjoy her behaving as if she hadn't. She expressed, that is, exactly the right degree of surprise; she didn't a bit overdo it: the lesson of which was, perceptibly, that, so far as his late lights had opened the door to any want of the natural in their meetings, he might trust her to take care of it for him as well as for herself. She had begun this, admirably, on his entrance, with her turning away from the table at which she had apparently been engaged in letter-writing; it was the very possibility of his betraying a concern for her as one of the afflicted that she had within the first minute conjured away. She was never, never—did he understand?—to be one of the afflicted for him; and the manner in which he understood it, something of the answering pleasure that he couldn't help knowing he showed, constituted, he was very soon after to acknowledge, something like a start for intimacy. When things like that could pass people had in truth to be equally conscious of a relation. It soon made one, at all events, when it didn't find one made. She had let him ask—there had been time for that, his allusion to her friend's explanatory arrival at Lancaster Gate without her being inevitable; but she had blown away, and quite as much with the look in her eyes as with the smile on her lips, every ground for anxiety and every chance for insistence. How was she?—why she was as he thus saw her and as she had reasons of her own, nobody else's business, for desiring to appear. Kate's account of her as too proud for pity, as fiercely shy about so personal a secret, came back to him; so that he rejoiced he could take a hint, especially when he wanted to. The question the girl had quickly disposed of—"Oh it was nothing: I'm all right, thank you!"—was one he was glad enough to be able to banish. It wasn't at all, in spite of the appeal Kate had made to him on it, his affair; for his interest had been invoked in the name of compassion, and the name of compassion was exactly what he felt himself at the end of two minutes forbidden so much as to whisper. He had been sent to see her in order to be sorry for her, and how sorry he might be, quite privately, he was yet to make out. Didn't that signify, however, almost not at all?—inasmuch as, whatever his upshot, he was never to give her a glimpse of it. Thus the ground was unexpectedly cleared; though it was not till a slightly longer time had passed that he read clear, at first with amusement and then with a strange shade of respect, what had most operated. Extraordinarily, quite amazingly, he began to see that if his pity hadn't had to yield to still other things it would have had to yield quite definitely to her own. That was the way the case had turned round: he had made his visit to be sorry for her, but he would repeat it—if he did repeat it—in order that she might be sorry for him. His situation made him, she judged—when once one liked him—a subject for that degree of tenderness: he felt this judgement in her, and felt it as something he should really, in decency, in dignity, in common honesty, have very soon to reckon with.

Odd enough was it certainly that the question originally before him, the question placed there by Kate, should so of a sudden find itself quite dislodged by another. This other, it was easy to see, came straight up with the fact of her beautiful delusion and her wasted charity; the whole thing preparing for him as pretty a case of conscience as he could have desired, and one at the prospect of which he was already wincing. If he was interesting it was because he was unhappy; and if he was unhappy it was because his passion for Kate had spent itself in vain; and if Kate was indifferent, inexorable, it was because she had left Milly in no doubt of it. That above all was what came up for him—how clear an impression of this attitude, how definite an account of his own failure, Kate must have given her friend. His immediate quarter of an hour there with the girl lighted up for him almost luridly such an inference; it was almost as if the other party to their remarkable understanding had been with them as they talked, had been hovering about, had dropped in to look after her work. The value of the work affected him as different from the moment he saw it so expressed in poor Milly. Since it was false that he wasn't loved, so his right was quite quenched to figure on that ground as important; and if he didn't look out he should find himself appreciating in a way quite at odds with straightness the good faith of Milly's benevolence. *There* was the place for scruples; there the need absolutely to mind what he was about. If it wasn't proper for him to enjoy consideration on a perfectly false footing, where was the guarantee that, if he kept on, he mightn't soon himself pretend to the grievance in order not to miss the sweet? Consideration—from a charming girl—was soothing on whatever theory; and it didn't take him far to remember that he had himself as yet done nothing deceptive. It was Kate's description of him, his defeated state, it was none of his own; his responsibility would begin, as he might say, only with acting it out. The sharp point was, however, in the difference between acting and not acting: this difference in fact it was that made the case of conscience. He saw it with a certain alarm rise before him that everything was acting that was not speaking the particular word. "If you like me because you think *she* doesn't, it isn't a bit true: she *does* like me awfully!"—that would have been the particular word; which there were at the same time but too palpably such difficulties about his uttering. Wouldn't it be virtually as indelicate to challenge her as to leave her deluded?—and this quite apart from the exposure, so to speak, of Kate, as to whom it would constitute a kind of betrayal. Kate's design was something so extraordinarily special to Kate that he felt himself shrink from the complications involved in judging it. Not to give away the woman one loved, but to back her up in her mistakes—once they had gone a certain length—that was perhaps chief among the inevitabilities of the abjection of love. Loyalty was of course supremely prescribed in presence of any design on her part, however roundabout, to do one nothing but good.

Densher had quite to steady himself not to be awestruck at the immensity of the good his own friend must on all this evidence have wanted to do him. Of one thing indeed meanwhile he was sure: Milly Theale wouldn't herself precipitate his necessity of intervention. She would absolutely never say to him: "*Is* it so impossible she shall ever care for you seriously?"—without which nothing could well be less delicate than for him aggressively to set her right. Kate would be free to do that if Kate, in some prudence, some contrition, for some better reason in fine, should revise her plan; but he asked himself what, failing this, *he* could do that wouldn't be after all more gross than doing nothing. This brought him round again to the acceptance of the fact that the poor girl liked him. She put it, for reasons of her own, on a simple, a beautiful ground, a ground that already supplied her with the pretext she required. The ground was there, that is, in the impression she had received, retained, cherished; the pretext, over and above it, was the pretext for acting on it. That she now believed as she did made her sure at last that she might act; so that what Densher therefore would have struck at would be the root, in her soul, of a pure pleasure. It positively lifted its head and flowered, this pure pleasure, while the young man now sat with her, and there were things she seemed to say that took the words out of his mouth. These were not all the things she did say; they were rather what such things meant in the light of what he knew. Her warning him for instance off the question of how she was, the quick brave little art with which she did that, represented to his fancy a truth she didn't utter. "I'm well for *you*—that's all you have to do with or need trouble about: I shall never be anything so horrid as ill for you. So there you are; worry about me, spare me, please, as little as you can. Don't be afraid, in short, to ignore my 'interesting' side. It isn't, you see, even now while you sit here, that there aren't lots of others. Only do *them* justice and we shall get on beautifully." This was what was folded finely up in her talk—all quite ostensibly about her impressions and her intentions. She tried to put Densher again on his American doings, but he wouldn't have that to-day. As he thought of the way in which, the other afternoon, before Kate, he had sat complacently "jawing," he accused himself of excess, of having overdone it, having made—at least apparently—more of a "set" at their entertainer than he was at all events then intending. He turned the tables, drawing her out about London, about her vision of life there, and only too glad to treat her as a person with whom he could easily have other topics than her aches and pains. He spoke to her above all of the evidence offered him at Lancaster Gate that she had come but to conquer; and when she had met this with full and gay assent—"How could I help being the feature of the season, the what-do-you-call-it, the theme of every tongue?"—they fraternised freely over all that had come and gone for each since their interrupted encounter in New York.

At the same time, while many things in quick succession came up for them, came up in particular for Densher, nothing perhaps was just so sharp as the odd influence of their present conditions on their view of their past ones. It was as if they hadn't known how "thick" they had originally become, as if, in a manner, they had really fallen to remembrance of more passages of intimacy than there had in fact at the time quite been room for. They were in a relation now so complicated, whether by what they said or by what they didn't say, that it might have been seeking to justify its speedy growth by reaching back to one of those fabulous periods in which prosperous states place their beginnings. He recalled what had been said at Mrs. Lowder's about the steps and stages, in people's careers, that absence caused one to miss, and about the resulting frequent sense of meeting them further on; which, with some other matters also recalled, he took occasion to communicate to Milly. The matters he couldn't mention mingled themselves with those he did; so that it would doubtless have been hard to say which of the two groups now played most of a part. He was kept face to face with this young lady by a force absolutely resident in their situation and operating, for his nerves, with the swiftness of the forces commonly regarded by sensitive persons as beyond their control. The current thus determined had positively become for him, by the time he had been ten minutes in the room, something that, but for the absurdity of comparing the very small with the very great, he would freely have likened to the rapids of Niagara. An uncriticised acquaintance between a clever young man and a responsive young woman could do nothing more, at the most, than go, and his actual experiment went and went and went. Nothing probably so conduced to make it go as the marked circumstance that they had spoken all the while not a word about Kate; and this in spite of the fact that, if it were a question for them of what had occurred in the past weeks, nothing had occurred comparable to Kate's predominance. Densher had but the night before appealed to her for instruction as to what he must do about her, but he fairly winced to find how little this came to. She had foretold him of course how little; but it was a truth that looked different when shown him by Milly. It proved to him that the latter had in fact been dealt with, but it produced in him the thought that Kate might perhaps again conveniently be questioned. He would have liked to speak to her before going further—to make sure she really meant him to succeed quite so much. With all the difference that, as we say, came up for him, it came up afresh, naturally, that he might make his visit brief and never renew it; yet the strangest thing of all was that the argument against that issue would have sprung precisely from the beautiful little eloquence involved in Milly's avoidances.

Precipitate these well might be, since they emphasised the fact that she was proceeding in the sense of the assurances she had taken. Over the latter she had visibly not hesitated, for hadn't they had the merit of giving her a chance? Densher quite saw her, felt her take it; the chance, neither more nor less, of help rendered him according to her freedom. It was what Kate had left her with: "Listen to him, *I?* Never! So do as you like." What Milly "liked" was to do, it thus appeared, as she was doing: our young man's glimpse of which was just what would have been for him not less a glimpse of the peculiar brutality of shaking her off. The choice exhaled its shy fragrance of heroism, for it was not aided by any question of parting with Kate. She would be charming to Kate as well as to Kate's adorer; she would incur whatever pain could dwell for her in the sight—should she continue to be exposed to the sight—of the adorer thrown with the adored. It wouldn't really have taken much more to make him wonder if he hadn't before him one of those rare cases of exaltation—food for fiction, food for poetry—in which a man's fortune with the woman who doesn't care for him is positively promoted by the woman who does. It was as if Milly had said to herself: "Well, he can at least meet her in my society, if that's anything to him; so that my line can only be to make my society attractive." She certainly couldn't have made a different impression if she *had* so reasoned. All of which, none the less, didn't prevent his soon enough saying to her, quite as if she were to be whirled into space: "And now, then, what becomes of you? Do you begin to rush about on visits to country-houses?"

She disowned the idea with a headshake that, put on what face she would, couldn't help betraying to him something of her suppressed view of the possibility—ever, ever perhaps—of any such proceedings. They weren't at any rate for her now. "Dear no. We go abroad for a few weeks somewhere of high air. That has been before us for many days; we've only been kept on by last necessities here. However, everything's done and the wind's in our sails."

"May you scud then happily before it! But when," he asked, "do you come back?"

She looked ever so vague; then as if to correct it: "Oh when the wind turns. And what do you do with your summer?"

"Ah I spend it in sordid toil. I drench it with mercenary ink. My work in your country counts for play as well. You see what's thought of the pleasure your country can give. My holiday's over."

"I'm sorry you had to take it," said Milly, "at such a different time from ours. If you could but have worked while we've been working—"

"I might be playing while you play? Oh the distinction isn't so great with me. There's a little of each for me, of work and of play, in either. But you and Mrs. Stringham, with Miss Croy and Mrs. Lowder—you all," he went on, "have been given up, like navvies or niggers, to real physical toil. Your rest is something you've earned and you need. My labour's comparatively light."

"Very true," she smiled; "but all the same I like mine."

"It doesn't leave you 'done'?"

"Not a bit. I don't get tired when I'm interested. Oh I could go far."

He bethought himself. "Then why don't you?—since you've got here, as I learn, the whole place in your pocket."

"Well, it's a kind of economy—I'm saving things up. I've enjoyed so what you speak of—though your account of it's fantastic—that I'm watching over its future, that I can't help being anxious and careful. I want—in the interest itself of what I've had and may still have—not to make stupid mistakes. The way not to make them is to get off again to a distance and see the situation from there. I shall keep it fresh," she wound up as if herself rather pleased with the ingenuity of her statement—"I shall keep it fresh, by that prudence, for my return."

"Ah then you *will* return? Can you promise one that?"

Her face fairly lighted at his asking for a promise; but she made as if bargaining a little. "Isn't London rather awful in winter?"

He had been going to ask her if she meant for the invalid; but he checked the infelicity of this and took the enquiry as referring to social life. "No—I like it, with one thing and another; it's less of a mob than later on; and it would have for *us* the merit—should you come here then—that we should probably see more of you. So do reappear for us—if it isn't a question of climate."

She looked at that a little graver. "If what isn't a question—?"

"Why the determination of your movements. You spoke just now of going somewhere for that."

"For better air?"—she remembered. "Oh yes, one certainly wants to get out of London in August."

"Rather, of course!"—he fully understood. "Though I'm glad you've hung on long enough for me to catch you. Try us at any rate," he continued, "once more."

"Whom do you mean by 'us'?" she presently asked.

It pulled him up an instant—representing, as he saw it might have seemed, an allusion to himself as conjoined with Kate, whom he was proposing not to mention any more than his hostess did. But the issue was easy. "I mean all of us together, every one you'll find ready to surround you with sympathy."

It made her, none the less, in her odd charming way, challenge him afresh. "Why do you say sympathy?"

"Well, it's doubtless a pale word. What we *shall* feel for you will be much nearer worship."

"As near then as you like!" With which at last Kate's name was sounded. "The people I'd most come back for are the people you know. I'd do it for Mrs. Lowder, who has been beautifully kind to me."

"So she has to *me*," said Densher. "I feel," he added as she at first answered nothing, "that, quite contrary to anything I originally expected, I've made a good friend of her."

"I didn't expect it either—its turning out as it has. But I did," said Milly, "with Kate. I shall come back for her too. I'd do anything"—she kept it up—"for Kate."

Looking at him as with conscious clearness while she spoke, she might for the moment have effectively laid a trap for whatever remains of the ideal straightness in him were still able to pull themselves together and operate. He was afterwards to say to himself that something had at that moment hung for him by a hair. "Oh I know what one would do for Kate!"—it had hung for him by a hair to break out with that, which he felt he had really been kept from by an element in his consciousness stronger still. The proof of the truth in question was precisely in his silence; resisting the impulse to break out was what he was doing for Kate. This at the time moreover came and went quickly enough; he was trying the next minute but to make Milly's allusion easy for herself. "Of course I know what friends you are—and of course I understand," he permitted himself to add, "any amount of devotion to a person so charming. That's the good turn then she'll do us all—I mean her working for your return."

"Oh you don't know," said Milly, "how much I'm really on her hands."

He could but accept the appearance of wondering how much he might show he knew. "Ah she's very masterful."

"She's great. Yet I don't say she bullies me."

"No—that's not the way. At any rate it isn't hers," he smiled. He remembered, however, then that an undue acquaintance with Kate's ways was just what he mustn't show; and he pursued the subject no further than to remark with a good intention that had the further merit of representing a truth: "I don't feel as if I knew her—really to call know."

"Well, if you come to that, I don't either!" she laughed. The words gave him, as soon as they were uttered, a sense of responsibility for his own; though during a silence that ensued for a minute he had time to recognise that his own contained after all no element of falsity. Strange enough therefore was it that he could go too far—if it *was* too far—without being false. His observation was one he would perfectly have made to Kate herself. And before he again spoke, and before Milly did, he took time for more still—for feeling how just here it was that he must break short off if his mind was really made up not to go further. It was as if he had been at a corner—and fairly put there by his last speech; so that it depended on him whether or no to turn it. The silence, if prolonged but an instant, might even have given him a sense of her waiting to see what he would do. It was filled for them the next thing by the sound, rather voluminous for the August afternoon, of the approach, in the street below them, of heavy carriage-wheels and of horses trained to "step." A rumble, a great shake, a considerable effective clatter, had been apparently succeeded by a pause at the door of the hotel, which was in turn accompanied by a due display of diminished prancing and stamping. "You've a visitor," Densher laughed, "and it must be at least an ambassador."

"It's only my own carriage; it does that—isn't it wonderful?—every day. But we find it, Mrs. Stringham and I, in the innocence of our hearts, very amusing." She had got up, as she spoke, to assure herself of what she said; and at the end of a few steps they were together on the balcony and looking down at her waiting chariot, which made indeed a brave show. "Is it very awful?"

It was to Densher's eyes—save for its absurd heaviness—only pleasantly pompous. "It seems to me delightfully rococo. But how do I know? You're mistress of these things, in contact with the highest wisdom. You occupy a position, moreover, thanks to which your carriage—well, by this time, in the eye of London, also occupies one." But she was going out, and he mustn't stand in her way. What had happened the next minute was first that she had denied she was going out, so that he might prolong his stay; and second that she had said she would go out with pleasure if he would like to drive—that in fact there were always things to do, that there had been a question for her to-day of several in particular, and that this in short was why the carriage had been ordered so early. They perceived, as she said these things, that an enquirer had presented himself, and, coming back, they found Milly's servant announcing the carriage and prepared to accompany her. This appeared to have for her the effect of settling the matter—on the basis, that is, of Densher's happy response. Densher's happy response, however, had as yet hung fire, the process we have described in him operating by this time with extreme intensity. The system of not pulling up, not breaking off, had already brought him headlong, he seemed to feel, to where they actually stood; and just now it was, with a vengeance, that he must do either one thing or the other. He had been waiting for some moments, which probably seemed to him longer than they were; this was because he was anxiously watching himself wait. He couldn't keep that up for ever; and since one thing or the other was what he must do, it was for the other that he presently became conscious of having decided. If he had been drifting it settled itself in the manner of a bump, of considerable violence, against a firm object in the stream. "Oh yes; I'll go with you with pleasure. It's a charming idea."

She gave no look to thank him—she rather looked away; she only said at once to her servant, "In ten minutes"; and then to her visitor, as the man went out, "We'll go somewhere—I shall like that. But I must ask of you time—as little as possible—to get ready." She looked over the room to provide for him, keep him there. "There are books and things—plenty; and I dress very quickly." He caught her eyes only as she went, on which he thought them pretty and touching.

Why especially touching at that instant he could certainly scarce have said; it was involved, it was lost in the sense of her wishing to oblige him. Clearly what had occurred was her having wished it so that she had made him simply wish, in civil acknowledgement, to oblige *her;* which he had now fully done by turning his corner. He was quite round it, his corner, by the time the door had closed upon her and he stood there alone. Alone he remained for three minutes more—remained with several very living little matters to think about. One of these was the phenomenon—typical, highly American, he would have said—of Milly's extreme spontaneity. It was perhaps rather as if he had sought refuge—refuge from another question—in the almost exclusive contemplation of this. Yet this, in its way, led him nowhere; not even to a sound generalisation about American girls. It was spontaneous for his young friend to have asked him to drive with her alone—since she hadn't mentioned her companion; but she struck him after all as no more advanced in doing it than Kate, for instance, who wasn't an American girl, might have struck him in not doing it. Besides, Kate *would* have done it, though Kate wasn't at all, in the same sense as Milly, spontaneous. And then in addition Kate *had* done it—or things very like it. Furthermore he was engaged to Kate—even if his ostensibly not being put her public freedom on other grounds. On all grounds, at any rate, the relation between Kate and freedom, between freedom and Kate, was a different one from any he could associate or cultivate, as to anything, with the girl who had just left him to prepare to give herself up to him. It had never struck him before, and he moved about the room while he thought of it, touching none of the books placed at his disposal. Milly was forward, as might be said, but not advanced; whereas Kate was backward—backward still, comparatively, as an English girl—and yet advanced in a high degree. However—though this didn't straighten it out—Kate was of course two or three years older; which at their time of life considerably counted.

Thus ingeniously discriminating, Densher continued slowly to wander; yet without keeping at bay for long the sense of having rounded his corner. He had so rounded it that he felt himself lose even the option of taking advantage of Milly's absence to retrace his steps. If he might have turned tail, vulgarly speaking, five minutes before, he couldn't turn tail now; he must simply wait there with his consciousness charged to the brim. Quickly enough moreover that issue was closed from without; in the course of three minutes more Miss Theale's servant had returned. He preceded a visitor whom he had met, obviously, at the foot of the stairs and whom, throwing open the door, he loudly announced as Miss Croy. Kate, on following him in, stopped short at sight of Densher—only, after an instant, as the young man saw with free amusement, not from surprise and still less from discomfiture. Densher immediately gave his explanation—Miss Theale had gone to prepare to drive—on receipt of which the servant effaced himself.

"And you're going with her?" Kate asked.

"Yes—with your approval; which I've taken, as you see, for granted."

"Oh," she laughed, "my approval's complete!" She was thoroughly consistent and handsome about it.

"What I mean is of course," he went on—for he was sensibly affected by her gaiety—"at your so lively instigation."

She had looked about the room—she might have been vaguely looking for signs of the duration, of the character of his visit, a momentary aid in taking a decision. "Well, instigation then, as much as you like." She treated it as pleasant, the success of her plea with him; she made a fresh joke of this direct impression of it. "So much so as that? Do you know I think I won't wait?"

"Not to see her—after coming?"

"Well, with you in the field—! I came for news of her, but she must be all right. If she *is*—"

But he took her straight up. "Ah how do I know?" He was moved to say more. "It's not I who am responsible for her, my dear. It seems to me it's you." She struck him as making light of a matter that had been costing him sundry qualms; so that they couldn't both be quite just. Either she was too easy or he had been too anxious. He didn't want at all events to feel a fool for that. "I'm doing nothing—and shall not, I assure you, do anything but what I'm told."

Their eyes met with some intensity over the emphasis he had given his words; and he had taken it from her the next moment that he really needn't get into a state. What in the world was the matter? She asked it, with interest, for all answer. "Isn't she better—if she's able to see you?"

"She assures me she's in perfect health."

Kate's interest grew. "I knew she would." On which she added: "It won't have been really for illness that she stayed away last night."

"For what then?"

"Well—for nervousness."

"Nervousness about what?"

"Oh you know!" She spoke with a hint of impatience, smiling however the next moment. "I've told you that."

He looked at her to recover in her face what she had told him; then it was as if what he saw there prompted him to say: "What have you told *her?*"

She gave him her controlled smile, and it was all as if they remembered where they were, liable to surprise, talking with softened voices, even stretching their opportunity, by such talk, beyond a quite right feeling. Milly's room would be close at hand, and yet they were saying things—! For a moment, none the less, they kept it up. "Ask *her*, if you like; you're free—she'll tell you. Act as you think best; don't trouble about what you think I may or mayn't have told. I'm all right with her," said Kate. "So there you are."

"If you mean *here* I am," he answered, "it's unmistakeable. If you also mean that her believing in you is all I have to do with you're so far right as that she certainly does believe in you."

"Well then take example by her."

"She's really doing it for you," Densher continued. "She's driving me out for you."

"In that case," said Kate with her soft tranquillity, "you can do it a little for *her*. I'm not afraid," she smiled.

He stood before her a moment, taking in again the face she put on it and affected again, as he had already so often been, by more things in this face and in her whole person and presence than he was, to his relief, obliged to find words for. It wasn't, under such impressions, a question of words. "I do nothing for any one in the world but you. But for you I'll do anything."

"Good, good," said Kate. "That's how I like you."

He waited again an instant. "Then you swear to it?"

"To 'it'? To what?"

"Why that you do 'like' me. Since it's all for that, you know, that I'm letting you do—well, God knows what with me."

She gave at this, with a stare, a disheartened gesture—the sense of which she immediately further expressed. "If you don't believe in me then, after all, hadn't you better break off before you've gone further?"

"Break off with you?"

"Break off with Milly. You might go now," she said, "and I'll stay and explain to her why it is."

He wondered—as if it struck him. "What would you say?"

"Why that you find you can't stand her, and that there's nothing for me but to bear with you as I best may."

He considered of this. "How much do you abuse me to her?"

"Exactly enough. As much as you see by her attitude."

Again he thought. "It doesn't seem to me I ought to mind her attitude."

"Well then, just as you like. I'll stay and do my best for you."

He saw she was sincere, was really giving him a chance; and that of itself made things clearer. The feeling of how far he had gone came back to him not in repentance, but in this very vision of an escape; and it Was not of what he had done, but of what Kate offered, that he now weighed the consequence. "Won't it make her—her not finding me here—be rather more sure there's something between us?"

Kate thought. "Oh I don't know. It will of course greatly upset her. But you needn't trouble about that. She won't die of it."

"Do you mean she *will?*" Densher presently asked.

"Don't put me questions when you don't believe what I say. You make too many conditions."

She spoke now with a shade of rational weariness that made the want of pliancy, the failure to oblige her, look poor and ugly; so that what it suddenly came back to for him was his deficiency in the things a man of any taste, so engaged, so enlisted, would have liked to make sure of being able to show—imagination, tact, positively even humour. The circumstance is doubtless odd, but the truth is none the less that the speculation uppermost with him at this juncture was: "What if I should begin to bore this creature?" And that, within a few seconds, had translated itself. "If you'll swear again you love me—!"

She looked about, at door and window, as if he were asking for more than he said. "Here? There's nothing between us here," Kate smiled.

"Oh *isn't* there?" Her smile itself, with this, had so settled something for him that he had come to her pleadingly and holding out his hands, which she immediately seized with her own as if both to check him and to keep him. It was by keeping him thus for a minute that she did check him; she held him long enough, while, with their eyes deeply meeting, they waited in silence for him to recover himself and renew his discretion. He coloured as with a return of the sense of where they were, and that gave her precisely one of her usual victories, which immediately took further form. By the time he had dropped her hands he had again taken hold, as it were, of Milly's. It was not at any rate with Milly he had broken. "I'll do all you wish," he declared as if to acknowledge the acceptance of his condition that he had practically, after all, drawn from her—a declaration on which she then, recurring to her first idea, promptly acted.

"If you *are* as good as that I go. You'll tell her that, finding you with her, I wouldn't wait. Say that, you know, from yourself. She'll understand."

She had reached the door with it—she was full of decision; but he had before she left him one more doubt. "I don't see how she can understand enough, you know, without understanding too much."

"You don't need to see."

He required then a last injunction. "I must simply go it blind?"

"You must simply be kind to her."

"And leave the rest to you?"

"Leave the rest to *her*," said Kate disappearing.

It came back then afresh to that, as it had come before. Milly, three minutes after Kate had gone, returned in her array—her big black hat, so little superstitiously in the fashion, her fine black garments throughout, the swathing of her throat, which Densher vaguely took for an infinite number of yards of priceless lace, and which, its folded fabric kept in place by heavy rows of pearls, hung down to her feet like the stole of a priestess. He spoke to her at once of their friend's visit and flight. "She hadn't known she'd find me," he said—and said at present without difficulty. He had so rounded his corner that it wasn't a question of a word more or less.

She took this account of the matter as quite sufficient; she glossed over whatever might be awkward. "I'm sorry—but I of course often see *her*." He felt the discrimination in his favour and how it justified Kate. This was Milly's tone when the matter was left to her. Well, it should now be wholly left.

BOOK SEVENTH

I

When Kate and Densher abandoned her to Mrs. Stringham on the day of her meeting them together and bringing them to luncheon, Milly, face to face with that companion, had had one of those moments in which the warned, the anxious fighter of the battle of life, as if once again feeling for the sword at his side, carries his hand straight to the quarter of his courage. She laid hers firmly on her heart, and the two women stood there showing each other a strange front. Susan Shepherd had received their great doctor's visit, which had been clearly no small affair for her; but Milly had since then, with insistence, kept in place, against communication and betrayal, as she now practically confessed, the barrier of their invited guests. "You've been too dear. With what I see you're full of you treated them beautifully. *Isn't* Kate charming when she wants to be?"

Poor Susie's expression, contending at first, as in a high fine spasm, with different dangers, had now quite let itself go. She had to make an effort to reach a point in space already so remote. "Miss Croy? Oh she was pleasant and clever. She knew," Mrs. Stringham added. "She knew."

Milly braced herself—but conscious above all, at the moment, of a high compassion for her mate. She made her out as struggling—struggling in all her nature against the betrayal of pity, which in itself, given her nature, could only be a torment. Milly gathered from the struggle how much there was of the pity, and how therefore it was both in her tenderness and in her conscience that Mrs. Stringham suffered. Wonderful and beautiful it was that this impression instantly steadied the girl. Ruefully asking herself on what basis of ease, with the drop of their barrier, they were to find themselves together, she felt the question met with a relief that was almost joy. The basis, the inevitable basis, was that she was going to be sorry for Susie, who, to all appearance, had been condemned in so much more uncomfortable a manner to be sorry for *her*. Mrs. Stringham's sorrow would hurt Mrs. Stringham, but how could her own ever hurt? She had, the poor girl, at all events, on the spot, five minutes of exaltation in which she turned the tables on her friend with a pass of the hand, a gesture of an energy that made a wind in the air. "Kate knew," she asked, "that you were full of Sir Luke Strett?"

"She spoke of nothing, but she was gentle and nice; she seemed to want to help me through." Which the good lady had no sooner said, however, than she almost tragically gasped at herself. She glared at Milly with a pretended pluck. "What I mean is that she saw one had been taken up with something. When I say she knows I should say she's a person who guesses." And her grimace was also, on its side, heroic. "But *she* doesn't matter, Milly."

The girl felt she by this time could face anything. "Nobody matters, Susie. Nobody." Which her next words, however, rather contradicted. "Did he take it ill that I wasn't here to see him? Wasn't it really just what he wanted—to have it out, so much more simply, with *you*?"

"We didn't have anything 'out,' Milly," Mrs. Stringham delicately quavered.

"Didn't he awfully like you," Milly went on, "and didn't he think you the most charming person I could possibly have referred him to for an account of me? Didn't you hit it off tremendously together and in fact fall quite in love, so that it will really be a great advantage for you to have me as a common ground? You're going to make, I can see, no end of a good thing of me."

"My own child, my own child!" Mrs. Stringham pleadingly murmured; yet showing as she did so that she feared the effect even of deprecation.

"Isn't he beautiful and good too himself?—altogether, whatever he may say, a lovely acquaintance to have made? You're just the right people for me—I see it now; and do you know what, between you, you must do?" Then as Susie still but stared, wonderstruck and holding herself: "You must simply see me through. Any way you choose. Make it out together. I, on my side, will be beautiful too, and we'll be—the three of us, with whatever others, oh as many as the case requires, any one you like!—a sight for the gods. I'll be as easy for you as carrying a feather." Susie took it for a moment in such silence that her young friend almost saw her—and scarcely withheld the observation—as taking it for "a part of the disease." This accordingly helped Milly to be, as she judged, definite and wise. "He's at any rate awfully interesting, isn't he?—which is so much to the good. We haven't at least—as we might have, with the way we tumbled into it—got hold of one of the dreary."

"Interesting, dearest?"—Mrs. Stringham felt her feet firmer. "I don't know if he's interesting or not; but I do know, my own," she continued to quaver, "that he's just as much interested as you could possibly desire."

"Certainly—that's it. Like all the world."

"No, my precious, not like all the world. Very much more deeply and intelligently."

"Ah there you are!" Milly laughed. "That's the way, Susie, I want you. So 'buck' up, my dear. We'll have beautiful times with him. Don't worry."

"I'm not worrying, Milly." And poor Susie's face registered the sublimity of her lie.

It was at this that, too sharply penetrated, her companion went to her, met by her with an embrace in which things were said that exceeded speech. Each held and clasped the other as if to console her for this unnamed woe, the woe for Mrs. Stringham of learning the torment of helplessness, the woe for Milly of having *her*, at such a time, to think of. Milly's assumption was immense, and the difficulty for her friend was that of not being able to gainsay it without bringing it more to the proof than tenderness and vagueness could permit. Nothing in fact came to the proof between them but that they could thus cling together—except indeed that, as we have indicated, the pledge of protection and support was all the younger woman's own. "I don't ask you," she presently said, "what he told you for yourself, nor what he told you to tell me, nor how he took it, really, that I had left him to you, nor what passed between you about me in any way. It wasn't to get that out of you that I took my means to make sure of your meeting freely—for there are things I don't want to know. I shall see him again and again and shall know more than enough. All I do want is that you shall see me through on *his* basis, whatever it is; which it's enough—for the purpose—that you yourself should know: that is with him to show you how. I'll make it charming for you—that's what I mean; I'll keep you up to it in such a way that half the time you won't know you're doing it. And for that you're to rest upon me. There. It's understood. We keep each other going, and you may absolutely feel of me that I shan't break down. So, with the way you haven't so much as a dig of the elbow to fear, how could you be safer?"

"He told me I *can* help you—of course he told me that," Susie, on her side, eagerly contended. "Why shouldn't he, and for what else have I come out with you? But he told me nothing dreadful—nothing, nothing, nothing," the poor lady passionately protested. "Only that you must do as you like and as he tells you—which *is* just simply to do as you like."

"I must keep in sight of him. I must from time to time go to him. But that's of course doing as I like. It's lucky," Milly smiled, "that I like going to him."

Mrs. Stringham was here in agreement; she gave a clutch at the account of their situation that most showed it as workable. "That's what *will* be charming for me, and what I'm sure he really wants of me—to help you to do as you like."

"And also a little, won't it be," Milly laughed, "to save me from the consequences? Of course," she added, "there must first *be* things I like."

"Oh I think you'll find some," Mrs. Stringham more bravely said. "I think there *are* some—as for instance just this one. I mean," she explained, "really having us so."

Milly thought. "Just as if I wanted you comfortable about *him*, and him the same about you? Yes—I shall get the good of it."

Susan Shepherd appeared to wander from this into a slight confusion. "Which of them are you talking of?"

Milly wondered an instant—then had a light. "I'm not talking of Mr. Densher." With which moreover she showed amusement. "Though if you can be comfortable about Mr. Densher too so much the better."

"Oh you meant Sir Luke Strett? Certainly he's a fine type. Do you know," Susie continued, "whom he reminds me of? Of *our* great man—Dr. Buttrick of Boston."

Milly recognised Dr. Buttrick of Boston, but she dropped him after a tributary pause. "What do you think, now that you've seen him, of Mr. Densher?"

It was not till after consideration, with her eyes fixed on her friend's, that Susie produced her answer. "I think he's very handsome."

Milly remained smiling at her, though putting on a little the manner of a teacher with a pupil. "Well, that will do for the first time. I *have* done," she went on, "what I wanted."

"Then that's all *we* want. You see there are plenty of things."

Milly shook her head for the "plenty." "The best is not to know—that includes them all. I don't—I don't know. Nothing about anything—except that you're *with* me. Remember that, please. There won't be anything that, on my side, for you, I shall forget. So it's all right."

The effect of it by this time was fairly, as intended, to sustain Susie, who dropped in spite of herself into the reassuring. "Most certainly it's all right. I think you ought to understand that he sees no reason—"

"Why I shouldn't have a grand long life?" Milly had taken it straight up, as to understand it and for a moment consider it. But she disposed of it otherwise. "Oh of course I know *that*." She spoke as if her friend's point were small.

Mrs. Stringham tried to enlarge it. "Well, what I mean is that he didn't say to me anything that he hasn't said to yourself."

"Really?—I would in his place!" She might have been disappointed, but she had her good humour. "He tells me to *live*"—and she oddly limited the word.

It left Susie a little at sea. "Then what do you want more?"

"My dear," the girl presently said, "I don't 'want,' as I assure you, anything. Still," she added, "I *am* living. Oh yes, I'm living."

It put them again face to face, but it had wound Mrs. Stringham up. "So am I then, you'll see!"—she spoke with the note of her recovery. Yet it was her wisdom now—meaning by it as much as she did—not to say more than that. She had risen by Milly's aid to a certain command of what was before them; the ten minutes of their talk had in fact made her more distinctly aware of the presence in her mind of a new idea. It was really perhaps an old idea with a new value; it had at all events begun during the last hour, though at first but feebly, to shine with a special light. That was because in the morning darkness had so suddenly descended—a sufficient shade of night to bring out the power of a star. The dusk might be thick yet, but the sky had comparatively cleared; and Susan Shepherd's star from this time on continued to twinkle for her. It was for the moment, after her passage with Milly, the one spark left in the heavens. She recognised, as she continued to watch it, that it had really been set there by Sir Luke Strett's visit and that the impressions immediately following had done no more than fix it. Milly's reappearance with Mr. Densher at her heels—or, so oddly perhaps, at Miss Croy's heels, Miss Croy being at Milly's—had contributed to this effect, though it was only with the lapse of the greater obscurity that Susie made that out. The obscurity had reigned during the hour of their friends' visit, faintly clearing indeed while, in one of the rooms, Kate Croy's remarkable advance to her intensified the fact that Milly and the young man were conjoined in the other. If it hadn't acquired on the spot all the intensity of which it was capable, this was because the poor lady still sat in her primary gloom, the gloom the great benignant doctor had practically left behind him.

The intensity the circumstance in question *might* wear to the informed imagination would have been sufficiently revealed for us, no doubt—and with other things to our purpose—in two or three of those confidential passages with Mrs. Lowder that she now permitted herself. She hadn't yet been so glad that she believed in her old friend; for if she hadn't had, at such a pass, somebody or other to believe in she should certainly have stumbled by the way. Discretion had ceased to consist of silence; silence was gross and thick, whereas wisdom should taper, however tremulously, to a point. She betook herself to Lancaster Gate the morning after the colloquy just noted; and there, in Maud Manningham's own sanctum, she gradually found relief in giving an account of herself. An account of herself was one of the things that she had long been in the habit of expecting herself regularly to give—the regularity depending of course much on such tests of merit as might, by laws beyond her control, rise in her path. She never spared herself in short a proper sharpness of conception of how she had behaved, and it was a statement that she for the most part found herself able to make. What had happened at present was that nothing, as she felt, was left of her to report to; she was all too sunk in the inevitable and the abysmal. To give an account of herself she must give it to somebody else, and her first instalment of it to her hostess was that she must please let her cry. She couldn't cry, with Milly in observation, at the hotel, which she had accordingly left for that purpose; and the power happily came to her with the good opportunity. She cried and cried at first—she confined herself to that; it was for the time the best statement of her business. Mrs. Lowder moreover intelligently took it as such, though knocking off a note or two more, as she said, while Susie sat near her table. She could resist the contagion of tears, but her patience did justice to her visitor's most vivid plea for it. "I shall never be able, you know, to cry again—at least not ever with *her;* so I must take it out when I can. Even if she does herself it won't be for me to give away; for what would that be but a confession of despair? I'm not with her for that—I'm with her to be regularly sublime. Besides, Milly won't cry herself."

"I'm sure I hope," said Mrs. Lowder, "that she won't have occasion to."

"She won't even if she does have occasion. She won't shed a tear. There's something that will prevent her."

"Oh!" said Mrs. Lowder.

"Yes, her pride," Mrs. Stringham explained in spite of her friend's doubt, and it was with this that her communication took consistent form. It had never been pride, Maud Manningham had hinted, that kept *her* from crying when other things made for it; it had only been that these same things, at such times, made still more for business, arrangements, correspondence, the ringing of bells, the marshalling of servants, the taking of decisions. "I might be crying now," she said, "if I weren't writing letters"—and this quite without harshness for her anxious companion, to whom she allowed just the administrative margin for difference. She had interrupted her no more than she would have interrupted the piano-tuner. It gave poor Susie time; and when Mrs. Lowder, to save appearances and catch the post, had, with her addressed and stamped notes, met at the door of the room the footman summoned by the pressure of a knob, the facts of the case were sufficiently ready for her. It took but two or three, however, given their importance, to lay the ground for the great one—Mrs. Stringham's interview of the day before with Sir Luke, who had wished to see her about Milly.

"He had wished it himself?"

"I think he was glad of it. Clearly indeed he was. He stayed a quarter of an hour. I could see that for *him* it was long. He's interested," said Mrs. Stringham.

"Do you mean in her case?"

"He says it *isn't* a case."

"What then is it?"

"It isn't, at least," Mrs. Stringham explained, "the case she believed it to be—thought it at any rate *might* be—when, without my knowledge, she went to see him. She went because there was something she was afraid of, and he examined her thoroughly—he has made sure. She's wrong—she hasn't what she thought."

"And what did she think?" Mrs. Lowder demanded.

"He didn't tell me."

"And you didn't ask?"

"I asked nothing," said poor Susie—"I only took what he gave me. He gave me no more than he had to—he was beautiful," she went on. "He *is*, thank God, interested."

"He must have been interested in *you*, dear," Maud Manningham observed with kindness.

Her visitor met it with candour. "Yes, love, I think he *is*. I mean that he sees what he can do with me."

Mrs. Lowder took it rightly. "For *her*."

"For her. Anything in the world he will or he must. He can use me to the last bone, and he likes at least that. He says the great thing for her is to be happy."

"It's surely the great thing for every one. Why, therefore," Mrs. Lowder handsomely asked, "should we cry so hard about it?"

"Only," poor Susie wailed, "that it's so strange, so beyond us. I mean if she can't be."

"She must be." Mrs. Lowder knew no impossibles. "She *shall* be."

"Well—if you'll help. He thinks, you know, we *can* help."

Mrs. Lowder faced a moment, in her massive way, what Sir Luke Strett thought. She sat back there, her knees apart, not unlike a picturesque ear-ringed matron at a market-stall; while her friend, before her, dropped their items, tossed the separate truths of the matter one by one, into her capacious apron. "But is that all he came to you for—to tell you she must be happy?"

"That she must be *made* so—that's the point. It seemed enough, as he told me," Mrs. Stringham went on; "he makes it somehow such a grand possible affair."

"Ah well, if he makes it possible!"

"I mean especially he makes it grand. He gave it to me, that is, as *my* part. The rest's his own."

"And what's the rest?" Mrs. Lowder asked.

"I don't know. *His* business. He means to keep hold of her."

"Then why do you say it isn't a 'case'? It must be very much of one."

Everything in Mrs. Stringham confessed to the extent of it. "It's only that it isn't *the* case she herself supposed."

"It's another?"

"It's another."

"Examining her for what she supposed he finds something else?"

"Something else."

"And what does he find?"

"Ah," Mrs. Stringham cried, "God keep me from knowing!"

"He didn't tell you that?"

But poor Susie had recovered herself. "What I mean is that if it's there I shall know in time. He's considering, but I can trust him for it—because he does, I feel, trust me. He's considering," she repeated.

"He's in other words not sure?"

"Well, he's watching. I think that's what he means. She's to get away now, but to come back to him in three months."

"Then I think," said Maud Lowder, "that he oughtn't meanwhile to scare us."

It roused Susie a little, Susie being already enrolled in the great doctor's cause. This came out at least in her glimmer of reproach. "Does it scare us to enlist us for her happiness?"

Mrs. Lowder was rather stiff for it. "Yes; it scares *me*. I'm always scared—I may call it so—till I understand. What happiness is he talking about?"

Mrs. Stringham at this came straight. "Oh you know!"

She had really said it so that her friend had to take it; which the latter in fact after a moment showed herself as having done. A strange light humour in the matter even perhaps suddenly aiding, she met it with a certain accommodation. "Well, say one seems to see. The point is—!" But, fairly too full now of her question, she dropped.

"The point is will it *cure?*"

"Precisely. Is it absolutely a remedy—the specific?"

"Well, I should think we might know!" Mrs. Stringham delicately declared.

"Ah but we haven't the complaint."

"Have you never, dearest, been in love?" Susan Shepherd enquired.

"Yes, my child; but not by the doctor's direction."

Maud Manningham had spoken perforce with a break into momentary mirth, which operated—and happily too—as a challenge to her visitor's spirit. "Oh of course we don't ask his leave to fall. But it's something to know he thinks it good for us."

"My dear woman," Mrs. Lowder cried, "it strikes me we know it without him. So that when *that's* all he has to tell us—!"

"Ah," Mrs. Stringham interposed, "it isn't 'all.' I feel Sir Luke will have more; he won't have put me off with anything inadequate. I'm to see him again; he as good as told me that he'll wish it. So it won't be for nothing."

"Then what will it be for? Do you mean he has somebody of his own to propose? Do you mean you told him nothing?"

Mrs. Stringham dealt with these questions. "I showed him I understood him. That was all I could do. I didn't feel at liberty to be explicit; but I felt, even though his visit so upset me, the comfort of what I had from you night before last."

"What I spoke to you of in the carriage when we had left her with Kate?"

"You had *seen*, apparently, in three minutes. And now that he's here, now that I've met him and had my impression of him, I feel," said Mrs. Stringham, "that you've been magnificent."

"Of course I've been magnificent. When," asked Maud Manningham, "was I anything else? But Milly won't be, you know, if she marries Merton Densher."

"Oh it's always magnificent to marry the man one loves. But we're going fast!" Mrs. Stringham woefully smiled.

"The thing *is* to go fast if I see the case right. What had I after all but my instinct of that on coming back with you, night before last, to pick up Kate? I felt what I felt—I knew in my bones the man had returned."

"That's just where, as I say, you're magnificent. But wait," said Mrs. Stringham, "till you've seen him."

"I shall see him immediately"—Mrs. Lowder took it up with decision. "What is then," she asked, "your impression?"

Mrs. Stringham's impression seemed lost in her doubts. "How can he ever care for her?"

Her companion, in her companion's heavy manner, sat on it. "By being put in the way of it."

"For God's sake then," Mrs. Stringham wailed, "*put* him in the way! You have him, one feels, in your hand."

Maud Lowder's eyes at this rested on her friend's. "Is that your impression of him?"

"It's my impression, dearest, of you. You handle every one."

Mrs. Lowder's eyes still rested, and Susan Shepherd now felt, for a wonder, not less sincere by seeing that she pleased her. But there was a great limitation. "I don't handle Kate."

It suggested something that her visitor hadn't yet had from her—something the sense of which made Mrs. Stringham gasp. "Do you mean Kate cares for *him?*"

That fact the lady of Lancaster Gate had up to this moment, as we know, enshrouded, and her friend's quick question had produced a change in her face. She blinked—then looked at the question hard; after which, whether she had inadvertently betrayed herself or had only reached a decision and then been affected by the quality of Mrs. Stringham's surprise, she accepted all results. What took place in her for Susan Shepherd was not simply that she made the best of them, but that she suddenly saw more in them to her purpose than she could have imagined. A certain impatience in fact marked in her this transition: she had been keeping back, very hard, an important truth, and wouldn't have liked to hear that she hadn't concealed it cleverly. Susie nevertheless felt herself pass as not a little of a fool with her for not having thought of it. What Susie indeed, however, most thought of at present, in the quick, new light of it, was the wonder of Kate's dissimulation. She had time for that view while she waited for an answer to her cry. "Kate thinks she cares. But she's mistaken. And no one knows it." These things, distinct and responsible, were Mrs. Lowder's retort. Yet they weren't all of it. "*You* don't know it—that must be your line. Or rather your line must be that you deny it utterly."

"Deny that she cares for him?"

"Deny that she so much as thinks that she does. Positively and absolutely. Deny that you've so much as heard of it."

Susie faced this new duty. "To Milly, you mean—if she asks?"

"To Milly, naturally. No one else *will* ask."

"Well," said Mrs. Stringham after a moment, "Milly won't."

Mrs. Lowder wondered. "Are you sure?"

"Yes, the more I think of it. And luckily for *me*. I lie badly."

"*I* lie well, thank God," Mrs. Lowder almost snorted, "when, as sometimes will happen, there's nothing else so good. One must always do the best. But without lies then," she went on, "perhaps we can work it out." Her interest had risen; her friend saw her, as within some minutes, more enrolled and inflamed—presently felt in her what had made the difference. Mrs. Stringham, it was true, descried this at the time but dimly; she only made out at first that Maud had found a reason for helping her. The reason was that, strangely, she might help Maud too, for which she now desired to profess herself ready even to lying. What really perhaps most came out for her was that her hostess was a little disappointed at her doubt of the social solidity of this appliance; and that in turn was to become a steadier light. The truth about Kate's delusion, as her aunt presented it, the delusion about the state of her affections, which might be removed—this was apparently the ground on which they now might more intimately meet. Mrs. Stringham saw herself recruited for the removal of Kate's delusion—by arts, however, in truth, that she as yet quite failed to compass. Or was it perhaps to be only for the removal of Mr. Densher's?—success in which indeed might entail other successes. Before that job, unfortunately, her heart had already failed. She felt that she believed in her bones what Milly believed, and what would now make working for Milly such a dreadful upward tug. All this within her was confusedly present—a cloud of questions out of which Maud Manningham's large seated self loomed, however, as a mass more and more definite, taking in fact for the consultative relation something of the form of an oracle. From the oracle the sound did come—or at any rate the sense did, a sense all accordant with the insufflation she had just seen working. "Yes," the sense was, "I'll help you for Milly, because if that comes off I shall be helped, by its doing so, for Kate"—a view into which Mrs. Stringham could now sufficiently enter. She found herself of a sudden, strange to say, quite willing to operate to Kate's harm, or at least to Kate's good as Mrs. Lowder with a noble anxiety measured it. She found herself in short not caring what became of Kate—only convinced at bottom of the predominance of Kate's star. Kate wasn't in danger, Kate wasn't pathetic; Kate Croy, whatever happened, would take care of Kate Croy. She saw moreover by this time that her friend was travelling even beyond her own speed. Mrs. Lowder had already, in mind, drafted a rough plan of action, a plan vividly enough thrown off as she said: "You must stay on a few days, and you must immediately, both of you, meet him at dinner." In addition to which Maud claimed the merit of having by an instinct of pity, of prescient wisdom, done much, two nights before, to prepare that ground. "The poor child, when I was with her there while you were getting your shawl, quite gave herself away to me."

"Oh I remember how you afterwards put it to me. Though it was nothing more," Susie did herself the justice to observe, "than what I too had quite felt."

But Mrs. Lowder fronted her so on this that she wondered what she had said. "I suppose I ought to be edified at what you can so beautifully give up."

"Give up?" Mrs. Stringham echoed. "Why, I give up nothing—I cling."

Her hostess showed impatience, turning again with some stiffness to her great brass-bound cylinder-desk and giving a push to an object or two disposed there. "I give up then. You know how little such a person as Mr. Densher was to be my idea for her. You know what I've been thinking perfectly possible."

"Oh you've been great"—Susie was perfectly fair. "A duke, a duchess, a princess, a palace: you've made me believe in them too. But where we break down is that *she* doesn't believe in them. Luckily for her—as it seems to be turning out—she doesn't want them. So what's one to do? I assure you I've had many dreams. But I've only one dream now."

Mrs. Stringham's tone in these last words gave so fully her meaning that Mrs. Lowder could but show herself as taking it in. They sat a moment longer confronted on it. "Her having what she does want?"

"If it *will* do anything for her."

Mrs. Lowder seemed to think what it might do; but she spoke for the instant of something else. "It does provoke me a bit, you know—for of course I'm a brute. And I had thought of all sorts of things. Yet it doesn't prevent the fact that we must be decent."

"We must take her"—Mrs. Stringham carried that out—"as she is."

"And we must take Mr. Densher as *he* is." With which Mrs. Lowder gave a sombre laugh. "It's a pity he isn't better!"

"Well, if he were better," her friend rejoined, "you'd have liked him for your niece; and in that case Milly would interfere. I mean," Susie added, "interfere with *you*."

"She interferes with me as it is—not that it matters now. But I saw Kate and her—really as soon as you came to me—set up side by side. I saw your girl—I don't mind telling—you helping my girl; and when I say that," Mrs. Lowder continued, "you'll probably put in for yourself that it was part of the reason of my welcome to you. So you see what I give up. I do give it up. But when I take that line," she further set forth, "I take it handsomely. So good-bye to it all. Good-day to Mrs. Densher! Heavens!" she growled.

Susie held herself a minute. "Even as Mrs. Densher my girl will be somebody."

"Yes, she won't be nobody. Besides," said Mrs. Lowder, "we're talking in the air."

Her companion sadly assented. "We're leaving everything out."

"It's nevertheless interesting." And Mrs. Lowder had another thought. "*He's* not quite nobody either." It brought her back to the question she had already put and which her friend hadn't at the time dealt with. "What in fact do you make of him?"

Susan Shepherd, at this, for reasons not clear even to herself, was moved a little to caution. So she remained general. "He's charming."

She had met Mrs. Lowder's eyes with that extreme pointedness in her own to which people resort when they are not quite candid—a circumstance that had its effect. "Yes; he's charming."

The effect of the words, however, was equally marked; they almost determined in Mrs. Stringham a return of amusement. "I thought you didn't like him!"

"I don't like him for Kate."

"But you don't like him for Milly either."

Mrs. Stringham rose as she spoke, and her friend also got up. "I like him, my dear, for myself."

"Then that's the best way of all."

"Well, it's one way. He's not good enough for my niece, and he's not good enough for you. One's an aunt, one's a wretch and one's a fool."

"Oh *I'm* not—not either," Susie declared.

But her companion kept on. "One lives for others. *You* do that. If I were living for myself I shouldn't at all mind him."

But Mrs. Stringham was sturdier. "Ah if I find him charming it's however I'm living."

Well, it broke Mrs. Lowder down. She hung fire but an instant, giving herself away with a laugh. "Of course he's all right in himself."

"That's all I contend," Susie said with more reserve; and the note in question—what Merton Densher was "in himself"—closed practically, with some inconsequence, this first of their councils.

II

It had at least made the difference for them, they could feel, of an informed state in respect to the great doctor, whom they were now to take as watching, waiting, studying, or at any rate as proposing to himself some such process before he should make up his mind. Mrs. Stringham understood him as considering the matter meanwhile in a spirit that, on this same occasion, at Lancaster Gate, she had come back to a rough notation of before retiring. She followed the course of his reckoning. If what they had talked of *could* happen—if Milly, that is, could have her thoughts taken off herself—it wouldn't do any harm and might conceivably do much good. If it couldn't happen—if, anxiously, though tactfully working, they themselves, conjoined, could do nothing to contribute to it—they would be in no worse a box than before. Only in this latter case the girl would have had her free range for the summer, for the autumn; she would have done her best in the sense enjoined on her, and, coming back at the end to her eminent man, would—besides having more to show him—find him more ready to go on with her. It was visible further to Susan Shepherd—as well as being ground for a second report to her old friend—that Milly did her part for a working view of the general case, inasmuch as she mentioned frankly and promptly that she meant to go and say good-bye to Sir Luke Strett and thank him. She even specified what she was to thank him for, his having been so easy about her behaviour.

"You see I didn't know that—for the liberty I took—I shouldn't afterwards get a stiff note from him."

So much Milly had said to her, and it had made her a trifle rash. "Oh you'll never get a stiff note from him in your life."

She felt her rashness, the next moment, at her young friend's question. "Why not, as well as any one else who has played him a trick?"

"Well, because he doesn't regard it as a trick. He could understand your action. It's all right, you see."

"Yes—I do see. It *is* all right. He's easier with me than with any one else, because that's the way to let me down. He's only making believe, and I'm not worth hauling up."

Rueful at having provoked again this ominous flare, poor Susie grasped at her only advantage. "Do you really accuse a man like Sir Luke Strett of trifling with you?"

She couldn't blind herself to the look her companion gave her—a strange half-amused perception of what she made of it. "Well, so far as it's trifling with me to pity me so much."

"He doesn't pity you," Susie earnestly reasoned. "He just—the same as any one else—likes you."

"He has no business then to like me. He's not the same as any one else."

"Why not, if he wants to work for you?"

Milly gave her another look, but this time a wonderful smile. "Ah there you are!" Mrs. Stringham coloured, for there indeed she was again. But Milly let her off. "Work for me, all the same—work for me! It's of course what I want." Then as usual she embraced her friend. "I'm not going to be as nasty as this to *him*."

"I'm sure I hope not!"—and Mrs. Stringham laughed for the kiss. "I've no doubt, however, he'd take it from you! It's *you*, my dear, who are not the same as any one else."

Milly's assent to which, after an instant, gave her the last word. "No, so that people can take anything from me." And what Mrs. Stringham did indeed resignedly take after this was the absence on her part of any account of the visit then paid. It was the beginning in fact between them of an odd independence—an independence positively of action and custom—on the subject of Milly's future. They went their separate ways with the girl's intense assent; this being really nothing but what she had so wonderfully put in her plea for after Mrs. Stringham's first encounter with Sir Luke. She fairly favoured the idea that Susie had or was to have other encounters—private pointed personal; she favoured every idea, but most of all the idea that she herself was to go on as if nothing were the matter. Since she was to be worked for that would be her way; and though her companions learned from herself nothing of it this was in the event her way with her medical adviser. She put her visit to him on the simplest ground; she had come just to tell him how touched she had been by his good nature. That required little explaining, for, as Mrs. Stringham had said, he quite understood he could but reply that it was all right.

"I had a charming quarter of an hour with that clever lady. You've got good friends."

"So each one of them thinks of all the others. But so I also think," Milly went on, "of all of them together. You're excellent for each other. And it's in that way, I dare say, that you're best for me."

There came to her on this occasion one of the strangest of her impressions, which was at the same time one of the finest of her alarms—the glimmer of a vision that if she should go, as it were, too far, she might perhaps deprive their relation of facility if not of value. Going too far was failing to try at least to remain simple. He would be quite ready to hate her if she did, by heading him off at every point, embarrass his exercise of a kindness that, no doubt, rather constituted for him a high method. Susie wouldn't hate her, since Susie positively wanted to suffer for her; Susie had a noble idea that she might somehow so do her good. Such, however, was not the way in which the greatest of London doctors was to be expected to wish to do it. He wouldn't have time even should he wish; whereby, in a word, Milly felt herself intimately warned. Face to face there with her smooth strong director, she enjoyed at a given moment quite such another lift of feeling as she had known in her crucial talk with Susie. It came round to the same thing; him too she would help to help her if that could possibly be; but if it couldn't possibly be she would assist also to make this right.

It wouldn't have taken many minutes more, on the basis in question, almost to reverse for her their characters of patient and physician. What *was* he in fact but patient, what was she but physician, from the moment she embraced once for all the necessity, adopted once for all the policy, of saving him alarms about her subtlety? She would leave the subtlety to him: he would enjoy his use of it, and she herself, no doubt, would in time enjoy his enjoyment. She went so far as to imagine that the inward success of these reflexions flushed her for the minute, to his eyes, with a certain bloom, a comparative appearance of health; and what verily next occurred was that he gave colour to the presumption. "Every little helps, no doubt!"—he noticed good-humouredly her harmless sally. "But, help or no help, you're looking, you know, remarkably well."

"Oh I thought I was," she answered; and it was as if already she saw his line. Only she wondered what he would have guessed. If he had guessed anything at all it would be rather remarkable of him. As for what there *was* to guess, he couldn't—if this was present to him—have arrived at it save by his own acuteness. That acuteness was therefore immense; and if it supplied the subtlety she thought of leaving him to, his portion would be none so bad. Neither, for that matter, would hers be—which she was even actually enjoying. She wondered if really then there mightn't be something for her. She hadn't been sure in coming to him that she was "better," and he hadn't used, he would be awfully careful not to use, that compromising term about her; in spite of all of which she would have been ready to say, for the amiable sympathy of it, "Yes, I *must* be," for he had this unaided sense of something that had happened to her. It was a sense unaided, because who could have told him of anything? Susie, she was certain, hadn't yet seen him again, and there were things it was impossible she could have told him the first time. Since such was his penetration, therefore, why shouldn't she gracefully, in recognition of it, accept the new circumstance, the one he was clearly wanting to congratulate her on, as a sufficient cause? If one nursed a cause tenderly enough it might produce an effect; and this, to begin with, would be a way of nursing. "You gave me the other day," she went on, "plenty to think over, and I've been doing that—thinking it over—quite as you'll have probably wished me. I think I must be pretty easy to treat," she smiled, "since you've already done me so much good."

The only obstacle to reciprocity with him was that he looked in advance so closely related to all one's possibilities that one missed the pleasure of really improving it. "Oh no, you're extremely difficult to treat. I've need with you, I assure you, of all my wit."

"Well, I mean I do come up." She hadn't meanwhile a bit believed in his answer, convinced as she was that if she *had* been difficult it would be the last thing he would have told her. "I'm doing," she said, "as I like."

"Then it's as *I* like. But you must really, though we're having such a decent month, get straight away." In pursuance of which, when she had replied with promptitude that her departure—for the Tyrol and then for Venice—was quite fixed for the fourteenth, he took her up with alacrity. "For Venice? That's perfect, for we shall meet there. I've a dream of it for October, when I'm hoping for three weeks off; three weeks during which, if I can get them clear, my niece, a young person who has quite the whip hand of me, is to take me where she prefers. I heard from her only yesterday that she expects to prefer Venice."

"That's lovely then. I shall expect you there. And anything that, in advance or in any way, I can do for you—!"

"Oh thank you. My niece, I seem to feel, does for me. But it will be capital to find you there."

"I think it ought to make you feel," she said after a moment, "that I *am* easy to treat."

But he shook his head again; he wouldn't have it. "You've not come to that *yet*."

"One has to be so bad for it?"

"Well, I don't think I've ever come to it—to 'ease' of treatment. I doubt if it's possible. I've not, if it is, found any one bad enough. The ease, you see, is for *you*."

"I see—I see."

They had an odd friendly, but perhaps the least bit awkward pause on it; after which Sir Luke asked: "And that clever lady—she goes with you?"

"Mrs. Stringham? Oh dear, yes. She'll stay with me, I hope, to the end."

He had a cheerful blankness. "To the end of what?"

"Well—of everything."

"Ah then," he laughed, "you're in luck. The end of everything is far off. This, you know, I'm hoping," said Sir Luke, "is only the beginning." And the next question he risked might have been a part of his hope. "Just you and she together?"

"No, two other friends; two ladies of whom we've seen more here than of any one and who are just the right people for us."

He thought a moment. "You'll be four women together then?"

"Ah," said Milly, "we're widows and orphans. But I think," she added as if to say what she saw would reassure him, "that we shall not be unattractive, as we move, to gentlemen. When you talk of 'life' I suppose you mean mainly gentlemen."

"When I talk of 'life,'" he made answer after a moment during which he might have been appreciating her raciness—"when I talk of life I think I mean more than anything else the beautiful show of it, in its freshness, made by young persons of your age. So go on as you are. I see more and more *how* you are. You can't," he went so far as to say for pleasantness, "better it."

She took it from him with a great show of peace. "One of our companions will be Miss Croy, who came with me here first. It's in *her* that life is splendid; and a part of that is even that she's devoted to me. But she's above all magnificent in herself. So that if you'd like," she freely threw out, "to see *her*—"

"Oh I shall like to see any one who's devoted to you, for clearly it will be jolly to be 'in' it. So that if she's to be at Venice I *shall* see her?"

"We must arrange it—I shan't fail. She moreover has a friend who may also be there"—Milly found herself going on to this. "He's likely to come, I believe, for he always follows her."

Sir Luke wondered. "You mean they're lovers?"

"*He* is," Milly smiled; "but not she. She doesn't care for him."

Sir Luke took an interest. "What's the matter with him?"

"Nothing but that she doesn't like him."

Sir Luke kept it up. "Is he all right?"

"Oh he's very nice. Indeed he's remarkably so."

"And he's to be in Venice?"

"So she tells me she fears. For if he is there he'll be constantly about with her."

"And she'll be constantly about with you?"

"As we're great friends—yes."

"Well then," said Sir Luke, "you won't be four women alone."

"Oh no; I quite recognise the chance of gentlemen. But he won't," Milly pursued in the same wondrous way, "have come, you see, for me."

"No—I see. But can't you help him?"

"Can't *you?*" Milly after a moment quaintly asked. Then for the joke of it she explained. "I'm putting you, you see, in relation with my entourage."

It might have been for the joke of it too, by this time, that her eminent friend fell in. "But if this gentleman *isn't* of your 'entourage '? I mean if he's of—what do you call her?—Miss Croy's. Unless indeed you also take an interest in him."

"Oh certainly I take an interest in him!"

"You think there may be then some chance for him?"

"I like him," said Milly, "enough to hope so."

"Then that's all right. But what, pray," Sir Luke next asked, "have I to do with him?"

"Nothing," said Milly, "except that if you're to be there, so may he be. And also that we shan't in that case be simply four dreary women."

He considered her as if at this point she a little tried his patience. "*You're* the least 'dreary' woman I've ever, ever seen. Ever, do you know? There's no reason why you shouldn't have a really splendid life."

"So every one tells me," she promptly returned.

"The conviction—strong already when I had seen you once—is strengthened in me by having seen your friend. There's no doubt about it. The world's before you."

"What did my friend tell you?" Milly asked.

"Nothing that wouldn't have given you pleasure. We talked about you—and freely. I don't deny that. But it shows me I don't require of you the impossible."

She was now on her feet. "I think I know what you require of me."

"Nothing, for you," he went on, "*is* impossible. So go on." He repeated it again—wanting her so to feel that to-day he saw it. "You're all right."

"Well," she smiled—"keep me so."

"Oh you'll get away from me."

"Keep me, keep me," she simply continued with her gentle eyes on him.

She had given him her hand for good-bye, and he thus for a moment did keep her. Something then, while he seemed to think if there were anything more, came back to him; though something of which there wasn't too much to be made. "Of course if there's anything I *can* do for your friend: I mean the gentleman you speak of—?" He gave out in short that he was ready.

"Oh Mr. Densher?" It was as if she had forgotten.

"Mr. Densher—is that his name?"

"Yes—but his case isn't so dreadful." She had within a minute got away from that.

"No doubt—if *you* take an interest." She had got away, but it was as if he made out in her eyes—though they also had rather got away—a reason for calling her back. "Still, if there's anything one can do—?"

She looked at him while she thought, while she smiled. "I'm afraid there's really nothing one can do."

III

Not yet so much as this morning had she felt herself sink into possession; gratefully glad that the warmth of the Southern summer was still in the high florid rooms, palatial chambers where hard cool pavements took reflexions in their lifelong polish, and where the sun on the stirred sea-water, flickering up through open windows, played over the painted "subjects" in the splendid ceilings—medallions of purple and brown, of brave old melancholy colour, medals as of old reddened gold, embossed and beribboned, all toned with time and all flourished and scolloped and gilded about, set in their great moulded and figured concavity (a nest of white cherubs, friendly creatures of the air) and appreciated by the aid of that second tier of smaller lights, straight openings to the front, which did everything, even with the Baedekers and photographs of Milly's party dreadfully meeting the eye, to make of the place an apartment of state. This at last only, though she had enjoyed the palace for three weeks, seemed to count as effective occupation; perhaps because it was the first time she had been alone—really to call alone—since she had left London, it ministered to her first full and unembarrassed sense of what the great Eugenio had done for her. The great Eugenio, recommended by grand-dukes and Americans, had entered her service during the last hours of all—had crossed from Paris, after multiplied *pourparlers* with Mrs. Stringham, to whom she had allowed more than ever a free hand, on purpose to escort her to the Continent and encompass her there, and had dedicated to her, from the moment of their meeting, all the treasures of his experience. She had judged him in advance—polyglot and universal, very dear and very deep—as probably but a swindler finished to the finger-tips; for he was forever carrying one well-kept Italian hand to his heart and plunging the other straight into her pocket, which, as she had instantly observed him to recognise, fitted it like a glove. The remarkable thing was that these elements of their common consciousness had rapidly gathered into an indestructible link, formed the ground of a happy relation; being by this time, strangely, grotesquely, delightfully, what most kept up confidence between them and what most expressed it.

She had seen quickly enough what was happening—the usual thing again, yet once again. Eugenio had, in an interview of five minutes, understood her, had got hold, like all the world, of the idea not so much of the care with which she must be taken up as of the care with which she must be let down. All the world understood her, all the world had got hold; but for nobody yet, she felt, would the idea have been so close a tie or won from herself so patient a surrender. Gracefully, respectfully, consummately enough—always with hands in position and the look, in his thick neat white hair, smooth fat face and black professional, almost theatrical eyes, as of some famous tenor grown too old to make love, but with an art still to make money—did he on occasion convey to her that she was, of all the clients of his glorious career, the one in whom his interest was most personal and paternal. The others had come in the way of business, but for her his sentiment was special. Confidence rested thus on her completely believing that: there was nothing of which she felt more sure. It passed between them every time they conversed; he was abysmal, but this intimacy lived on the surface. He had taken his place already for her among those who were to see her through, and meditation ranked him, in the constant perspective, for the final function, side by side with poor Susie—whom she was now pitying more than ever for having to be herself so sorry and to say so little about it. Eugenio had the general tact of a residuary legatee—which was a character that could be definitely worn; whereas she could see Susie, in the event of her death, in no character at all, Susie being insistently, exclusively concerned in her mere makeshift duration. This principle, for that matter, Milly at present, with a renewed flare of fancy, felt she should herself have liked to believe in. Eugenio had really done for her more than he probably knew—he didn't after all know everything—in having, for the wind-up of the autumn, on a weak word from her, so admirably, so perfectly established her. Her weak word, as a general hint, had been: "At Venice, please, if possible, no dreadful, no vulgar hotel; but, if it can be at all managed—you know what I mean—some fine old rooms, wholly independent, for a series of months. Plenty of them too, and the more interesting the better: part of a palace, historic and picturesque, but strictly inodorous, where we shall be to ourselves, with a cook, don't you know?—with servants, frescoes, tapestries, antiquities, the thorough make-believe of a settlement."

The proof of how he better and better understood her was in all the place; as to his masterly acquisition of which she had from the first asked no questions. She had shown him enough what she thought of it, and her forbearance pleased him; with the part of the transaction that mainly concerned her she would soon enough become acquainted, and his connexion with such values as she would then find noted could scarce help growing, as it were, still more residuary. Charming people, conscious Venice-lovers, evidently, had given up their house to her, and had fled to a distance, to other countries, to hide their blushes alike over what they had, however briefly, alienated, and over what they had, however durably, gained. They had preserved and consecrated, and she now—her part of it was shameless—appropriated and enjoyed. Palazzo Leporelli held its history still in its great lap, even like a painted idol, a solemn puppet hung about with decorations. Hung about with pictures and relics, the rich Venetian past, the ineffaceable character, was here the presence revered and served: which brings us back to our truth of a moment ago—the fact that, more than ever, this October morning, awkward novice though she might be, Milly moved slowly to and fro as the priestess of the worship. Certainly it came from the sweet taste of solitude, caught again and cherished for the hour; always a need of her nature, moreover, when things spoke to her with penetration. It was mostly in stillness they spoke to her best; amid voices she lost the sense. Voices had surrounded her for weeks, and she had tried to listen, had cultivated them and had answered back; these had been weeks in which there were other things they might well prevent her from hearing. More than the prospect had at first promised or threatened she had felt herself going on in a crowd and with a multiplied escort; the four ladies pictured by her to Sir Luke Strett as a phalanx comparatively closed and detached had in fact proved a rolling snowball, condemned from day to day to cover more ground. Susan Shepherd had compared this portion of the girl's excursion to the Empress Catherine's famous progress across the steppes of Russia; improvised settlements appeared at each turn of the road, villagers waiting with addresses drawn up in the language of London. Old friends in fine were in ambush, Mrs. Lowder's, Kate Croy's, her own; when the addresses weren't in the language of London they were in the more insistent idioms of American centres. The current was swollen even by Susie's social connexions; so that there were days, at hotels, at Dolomite picnics, on lake steamers, when she could almost repay to Aunt Maud and Kate with interest the debt contracted by the London "success" to which they had opened the door.

Mrs. Lowder's success and Kate's, amid the shock of Milly's and Mrs. Stringham's compatriots, failed but little, really, of the concert-pitch; it had gone almost as fast as the boom, over the sea, of the last great native novel. Those ladies were "so different"—different, observably enough, from the ladies so appraising them; it being throughout a case mainly of ladies, of a dozen at once sometimes, in Milly's apartment, pointing, also at once, that moral and many others. Milly's companions were acclaimed not only as perfectly fascinating in themselves, the nicest people yet known to the acclaimers, but as obvious helping hands, socially speaking, for the eccentric young woman, evident initiators and smoothers of her path, possible subduers of her eccentricity. Short intervals, to her own sense, stood now for great differences, and this renewed inhalation of her native air had somehow left her to feel that she already, that she mainly, struck the compatriot as queer and dissociated. She moved such a critic, it would appear, as to rather an odd suspicion, a benevolence induced by a want of complete trust: all of which showed her in the light of a person too plain and too ill-clothed for a thorough good time, and yet too rich and too befriended—an intuitive cunning within her managing this last—for a thorough bad one. The compatriots, in short, by what she made out, approved her friends for their expert wisdom with her; in spite of which judicial sagacity it was the compatriots who recorded themselves as the innocent parties. She saw things in these days that she had never seen before, and she couldn't have said why save on a principle too terrible to name; whereby she saw that neither Lancaster Gate was what New York took it for, nor New York what Lancaster Gate fondly fancied it in coquetting with the plan of a series of American visits. The plan might have been, humorously, on Mrs. Lowder's part, for the improvement of her social position—and it had verily in that direction lights that were perhaps but half a century too prompt; at all of which Kate Croy assisted with the cool controlled facility that went so well, as the others said, with her particular kind of good looks, the kind that led you to expect the person enjoying them *would* dispose of disputations, speculations, aspirations, in a few very neatly and brightly uttered words, so simplified in sense, however, that they sounded, even when guiltless, like rather aggravated slang. It wasn't that Kate hadn't pretended too that *she* should like to go to America; it was only that with this young woman Milly had constantly proceeded, and more than ever of late, on the theory of intimate confessions, private frank ironies that made up for their public grimaces and amid which, face to face, they wearily put off the mask.

These puttings-off of the mask had finally quite become the form taken by their moments together, moments indeed not increasingly frequent and not prolonged, thanks to the consciousness of fatigue on Milly's side whenever, as she herself expressed it, she got out of harness. They flourished their masks, the independent pair, as they might have flourished Spanish fans; they smiled and sighed on removing them; but the gesture, the smiles, the sighs, strangely enough, might have been suspected the greatest reality in the business. Strangely enough, we say, for the volume of effusion in general would have been found by either on measurement to be scarce proportional to the paraphernalia of relief. It was when they called each other's attention to their ceasing to pretend, it was then that what they were keeping back was most in the air. There was a difference, no doubt, and mainly to Kate's advantage: Milly didn't quite see what her friend could keep back, was possessed of, in fine, that would be so subject to retention; whereas it was comparatively plain sailing for Kate that poor Milly had a treasure to hide. This was not the treasure of a shy, an abject affection—concealment, on that head, belonging to quite another phase of such states; it was much rather a principle of pride relatively bold and hard, a principle that played up like a fine steel spring at the lightest pressure of too near a footfall. Thus insuperably guarded was the truth about the girl's own conception of her validity; thus was a wondering pitying sister condemned wistfully to look at her from the far side of the moat she had dug round her tower. Certain aspects of the connexion of these young women show for us, such is the twilight that gathers about them, in the likeness of some dim scene in a Maeterlinck play; we have positively the image, in the delicate dusk, of the figures so associated and yet so opposed, so mutually watchful: that of the angular pale princess, ostrich-plumed, black-robed, hung about with amulets, reminders, relics, mainly seated, mainly still, and that of the upright restless slow-circling lady of her court who exchanges with her, across the black water streaked with evening gleams, fitful questions and answers. The upright lady, with thick dark braids down her back, drawing over the grass a more embroidered train, makes the whole circuit, and makes it again, and the broken talk, brief and sparingly allusive, seems more to cover than to free their sense. This is because, when it fairly comes to not having others to consider, they meet in an air that appears rather anxiously to wait for their words. Such an impression as that was in fact grave, and might be tragic; so that, plainly enough, systematically at last, they settled to a care of what they said.

There could be no gross phrasing to Milly, in particular, of the probability that if she wasn't so proud she might be pitied with more comfort—more to the person pitying; there could be no spoken proof, no sharper demonstration than the consistently considerate attitude, that this marvellous mixture of her weakness and of her strength, her peril, if such it were, and her option, made her, kept her, irresistibly interesting. Kate's predicament in the matter was, after all, very much Mrs. Stringham's own, and Susan Shepherd herself indeed, in our Maeterlinck picture, might well have hovered in the gloaming by the moat. It may be declared for Kate, at all events, that her sincerity about her friend, through this time, was deep, her compassionate imagination strong; and that these things gave her a virtue, a good conscience, a credibility for herself, so to speak, that were later to be precious to her. She grasped with her keen intelligence the logic of their common duplicity, went unassisted through the same ordeal as Milly's other hushed follower, easily saw that for the girl to be explicit was to betray divinations, gratitudes, glimpses of the felt contrast between her fortune and her fear—all of which would have contradicted her systematic bravado. That was it, Kate wonderingly saw: to recognise was to bring down the avalanche—the avalanche Milly lived so in watch for and that might be started by the lightest of breaths; though less possibly the breath of her own stifled plaint than that of the vain sympathy, the mere helpless gaping inference of others. With so many suppressions as these, therefore, between them, their withdrawal together to unmask had to fall back, as we have hinted, on a nominal motive—which was decently represented by a joy at the drop of chatter. Chatter had in truth all along attended their steps, but they took the despairing view of it on purpose to have ready, when face to face, some view or other of something. The relief of getting out of harness—that was the moral of their meetings; but the moral of this, in turn, was that they couldn't so much as ask each other why harness need be worn. Milly wore it as a general armour.

She was out of it at present, for some reason, as she hadn't been for weeks; she was always out of it, that is, when alone, and her companions had never yet so much as just now affected her as dispersed and suppressed. It was as if still again, still more tacitly and wonderfully, Eugenio had understood her, taking it from her without a word and just bravely and brilliantly in the name, for instance, of the beautiful day: "Yes, get me an hour alone; take them off—I don't care where; absorb, amuse, detain them; drown them, kill them if you will: so that I may just a little, all by myself, see where I am." She was conscious of the dire impatience of it, for she gave up Susie as well as the others to him—Susie who would have drowned her very self for her; gave her up to a mercenary monster through whom she thus purchased respites. Strange were the turns of life and the moods of weakness; strange the flickers of fancy and the cheats of hope; yet lawful, all the same—weren't they?—those experiments tried with the truth that consisted, at the worst, but in practising on one's self. She was now playing with the thought that Eugenio might *inclusively* assist her: he had brought home to her, and always by remarks that were really quite soundless, the conception, hitherto ungrasped, of some complete use of her wealth itself, some use of it as a counter-move to fate. It had passed between them as preposterous that with so much money she should just stupidly and awkwardly *want*—any more want a life, a career, a consciousness, than want a house, a carriage or a cook. It was as if she had had from him a kind of expert professional measure of what he was in a position, at a stretch, to undertake for her; the thoroughness of which, for that matter, she could closely compare with a looseness on Sir Luke Strett's part that—at least in Palazzo Leporelli when mornings were fine—showed as almost amateurish. Sir Luke hadn't said to her "Pay enough money and leave the rest to *me*"—which was distinctly what Eugenio did say. Sir Luke had appeared indeed to speak of purchase and payment, but in reference to a different sort of cash. Those were amounts not to be named nor reckoned, and such moreover as she wasn't sure of having at her command. Eugenio—this was the difference—could name, could reckon, and prices of *his* kind were things she had never suffered to scare her. She had been willing, goodness knew, to pay enough for anything, for everything, and here was simply a new view of the sufficient quantity. She amused herself—for it came to that, since Eugenio was there to sign the receipt—with possibilities of meeting the bill. She was more prepared than ever to pay enough, and quite as much as ever to pay too much. What else—if such were points at which your most trusted servant failed—was the use of being, as the dear Susies of earth called you, a princess in a palace?

She made now, alone, the full circuit of the place, noble and peaceful while the summer sea, stirring here and there a curtain or an outer blind, breathed into its veiled spaces. She had a vision of clinging to it; that perhaps Eugenio could manage. She was *in* it, as in the ark of her deluge, and filled with such a tenderness for it that why shouldn't this, in common mercy, be warrant enough? She would never, never leave it—she would engage to that; would ask nothing more than to sit tight in it and float on and on. The beauty and intensity, the real momentary relief of this conceit, reached their climax in the positive purpose to put the question to Eugenio on his return as she had not yet put it; though the design, it must be added, dropped a little when, coming back to the great saloon from which she had started on her pensive progress, she found Lord Mark, of whose arrival in Venice she had been unaware, and who had now—while a servant was following her through empty rooms—been asked, in her absence, to wait. He had waited then, Lord Mark, he was waiting—oh unmistakeably; never before had he so much struck her as the man to do that on occasion with patience, to do it indeed almost as with gratitude for the chance, though at the same time with a sort of notifying firmness. The odd thing, as she was afterwards to recall, was that her wonder for what had brought him was not immediate, but had come at the end of five minutes; and also, quite incoherently, that she felt almost as glad to see him, and almost as forgiving of his interruption of her solitude, as if he had already been in her thought or acting at her suggestion. He was some-how, at the best, the end of a respite; one might like him very much and yet feel that his presence tempered precious solitude more than any other known to one: in spite of all of which, as he was neither dear Susie, nor dear Kate, nor dear Aunt Maud, nor even, for the least, dear Eugenio in person, the sight of him did no damage to her sense of the dispersal of her friends. She hadn't been so thoroughly alone with him since those moments of his showing her the great portrait at Matcham, the moments that had exactly made the high-water-mark of her security, the moments during which her tears themselves, those she had been ashamed of, were the sign of her consciously rounding her protective promontory, quitting the blue gulf of comparative ignorance and reaching her view of the troubled sea. His presence now referred itself to his presence then, reminding her how kind he had been, altogether, at Matcham, and telling her, unexpectedly, at a time when she could particularly feel it, that, for such kindness and for the beauty of what they remembered together, she hadn't lost him—quite the contrary. To receive him handsomely, to receive him there, to see him interested and charmed, as well, clearly, as delighted to have found her without some other person to spoil it—these things were so pleasant for the first minutes that they might have represented on her part some happy foreknowledge. She gave an account of her companions while he on his side failed to press her about them, even though describing his appearance, so unheralded, as the result of an impulse obeyed on the spot. He had been shivering at Carlsbad, belated there and blue, when taken by it; so that, knowing where they all were, he had simply caught the first train. He explained how he had known where they were; he had heard—what more natural?—from their friends, Milly's and his. He mentioned this betimes, but it was with his mention, singularly, that the girl became conscious of her inner question about his reason. She noticed his plural, which added to Mrs. Lowder or added to Kate; but she presently noticed also that it didn't affect her as explaining. Aunt Maud had written to him, Kate apparently—and this was interesting—had written to him; but their design presumably hadn't been that he should come and sit there as if rather relieved, so far as *they* were concerned, at postponements. He only said "Oh!" and again "Oh!" when she sketched their probable morning for him, under Eugenio's care and Mrs. Stringham's—sounding it quite as if any suggestion that he should overtake them at the Rialto or the Bridge of Sighs would leave him temporarily cold. This precisely it was that, after a little, operated for Milly as an obscure but still fairly direct check to confidence. He had known where they all were from the others, but it was not for the others that, in his actual dispositions, he had come. That, strange to say, was a pity; for, stranger still to say, she could have shown him more confidence if he himself had had less intention. His intention so chilled her, from the moment she found herself divining it, that, just for the pleasure of going on with him fairly, just for the pleasure of their remembrance together of Matcham and the Bronzino, the climax of her fortune, she could have fallen to pleading with him and to reasoning, to undeceiving him in time. There had been, for ten minutes, with the directness of her welcome to him and the way this clearly pleased him, something of the grace of amends made, even though he couldn't know it—amends for her not having been originally sure, for instance at that first dinner of Aunt Maud's, that he was adequately human. That first dinner of Aunt Maud's added itself to the hour at Matcham, added itself to other things, to consolidate, for her present benevolence, the ease of their relation, making it suddenly delightful that he had thus turned up. He exclaimed, as he looked about, on the charm of the place: "What a temple to taste and an expression of the pride of life, yet, with all that, what a jolly *home!*"—so that, for his entertainment, she could offer to walk him about though she mentioned that she had just been, for her own purposes, in a general prowl, taking everything in more susceptibly than before. He embraced her offer without a scruple and seemed to rejoice that he was to find her susceptible.

IV

She couldn't have said what it was, in the conditions, that renewed the whole solemnity, but by the end of twenty minutes a kind of wistful hush had fallen upon them, as before something poignant in which her visitor also participated. That was nothing verily but the perfection of the charm—or nothing rather but their excluded disinherited state in the presence of it. The charm turned on them a face that was cold in its beauty, that was full of a poetry never to be theirs, that spoke with an ironic smile of a possible but forbidden life. It all rolled afresh over Milly: "Oh the impossible romance—!" The romance for her, yet once more, would be to sit there for ever, through all her time, as in a fortress; and the idea became an image of never going down, of remaining aloft in the divine dustless air, where she would hear but the plash of the water against stone. The great floor on which they moved was at an altitude, and this prompted the rueful fancy. "Ah not to go down—never, never to go down!" she strangely sighed to her friend.

"But why shouldn't you," he asked, "with that tremendous old staircase in your court? There ought of course always to be people at top and bottom, in Veronese costumes, to watch you do it."

She shook her head both lightly and mournfully enough at his not understanding. "Not even for people in Veronese costumes. I mean that the positive beauty is that one needn't go down. I don't move in fact," she added—"now. I've not been out, you know. I stay up. That's how you happily found me."

Lord Mark wondered—he was, oh yes, adequately human. "You don't go about?"

She looked over the place, the storey above the apartments in which she had received him, the sala corresponding to the sala below and fronting the great canal with its gothic arches. The casements between the arches were open, the ledge of the balcony broad, the sweep of the canal, so overhung, admirable, and the flutter toward them of the loose white curtain an invitation to she scarce could have said what. But there was no mystery after a moment; she had never felt so invited to anything as to make that, and that only, just where she was, her adventure. It would be—to this it kept coming back—the adventure of not stirring. "I go about just here."

"Do you mean," Lord Mark presently asked, "that you're really not well?"

They were at the window, pausing, lingering, with the fine old faded palaces opposite and the slow Adriatic tide beneath; but after a minute, and before she answered, she had closed her eyes to what she saw and unresistingly dropped her face into her arms, which rested on the coping. She had fallen to her knees on the cushion of the window-place, and she leaned there, in a long silence, with her forehead down. She knew that her silence was itself too straight an answer, but it was beyond her now to say that she saw her way. She would have made the question itself impossible to others—impossible for example to such a man as Merton Densher; and she could wonder even on the spot what it was a sign of in her feeling for Lord Mark that from his lips it almost tempted her to break down. This was doubtless really because she cared for him so little; to let herself go with him thus, suffer his touch to make her cup overflow, would be the relief—since it was actually, for her nerves, a question of relief—that would cost her least. If he had come to her moreover with the intention she believed, or even if this intention had but been determined in him by the spell of their situation, he mustn't be mistaken about her value—for what value did she now have? It throbbed within her as she knelt there that she had none at all; though, holding herself, not yet speaking, she tried, even in the act, to recover what might be possible of it. With that there came to her a light: wouldn't her value, for the man who should marry her, be precisely in the ravage of her disease? *She* mightn't last, but her money would. For a man in whom the vision of her money should be intense, in whom it should be most of the ground for "making up" to her, any prospective failure on her part to be long for this world might easily count as a positive attraction. Such a man, proposing to please, persuade, secure her, appropriate her for such a time, shorter or longer, as nature and the doctors should allow, would make the best of her, ill, damaged, disagreeable though she might be, for the sake of eventual benefits: she being clearly a person of the sort esteemed likely to do the handsome thing by a stricken and sorrowing husband.

She had said to herself betimes, in a general way, that whatever habits her youth might form, that of seeing an interested suitor in every bush should certainly never grow to be one of them—an attitude she had early judged as ignoble, as poisonous. She had had accordingly in fact as little to do with it as possible and she scarce knew why at the present moment she should have had to catch herself in the act of imputing an ugly motive. It didn't sit, the ugly motive, in Lord Mark's cool English eyes; the darker side of it at any rate showed, to her imagination, but briefly. Suspicion moreover, with this, simplified itself: there was a beautiful reason—indeed there were two—why her companion's motive shouldn't matter. One was that even should he desire her without a penny she wouldn't marry him for the world; the other was that she felt him, after all, perceptively, kindly, very pleasantly and humanly, concerned for her. They were also two things, his wishing to be well, to be very well, with her, and his beginning to feel her as threatened, haunted, blighted; but they were melting together for him, making him, by their combination, only the more sure that, as he probably called it to himself, he liked her. That was presently what remained with her—his really doing it; and with the natural and proper incident of being conciliated by her weakness. Would she really have had him—she could ask herself that—disconcerted or disgusted by it? If he could only be touched enough to do what she preferred, not to raise, not to press any question, he might render her a much better service than by merely enabling her to refuse him. Again, again it was strange, but he figured to her for the moment as the one safe sympathiser. It would have made her worse to talk to others, but she wasn't afraid with him of how he might wince and look pale. She would keep him, that is, her one easy relation—in the sense of easy for himself. Their actual outlook had meanwhile such charm, what surrounded them within and without did so much toward making appreciative stillness as natural as at the opera, that she could consider she hadn't made him hang on her lips when at last, instead of saying if she were well or ill, she repeated: "I go about here. I don't get tired of it. I never should—it suits me so. I adore the place," she went on, "and I don't want in the least to give it up."

"Neither should I if I had your luck. Still, with that luck, for one's *all*—! Should you positively like to live here?"

"I think I should like," said poor Milly after an instant, "to die here."

Which made him, precisely, laugh. That was what she wanted—when a person did care: it was the pleasant human way, without depths of darkness. "Oh it's not good enough for *that!* That requires picking. But can't you keep it? It is, you know, the sort of place to see you in; you carry out the note, fill it, people it, quite by yourself, and you might do much worse—I mean for your friends—than show yourself here a while, three or four months, every year. But it's not my notion for the rest of the time. One has quite other uses for you."

"What sort of a use for me is it," she smilingly enquired, "to kill me?"

"Do you mean we should kill you in England?"

"Well, I've seen you and I'm afraid. You're too much for me—too many. England bristles with questions. This is more, as you say there, my form."

"Oho, oho!"—he laughed again as if to humour her. "Can't you then buy it—for a price? Depend upon it they'll treat for money. That is for money enough."

"I've exactly," she said, "been wondering if they won't. I think I shall try. But if I get it I shall cling to it." They were talking sincerely. "It will be my life—paid for as that. It will become my great gilded shell; so that those who wish to find me must come and hunt me up."

"Ah then you *will* be alive," said Lord Mark.

"Well, not quite extinct perhaps, but shrunken, wasted, wizened; rattling about here like the dried kernel of a nut."

"Oh," Lord Mark returned, "we, much as you mistrust us, can do better for you than that."

"In the sense that you'll feel it better for me really to have it over?"

He let her see now that she worried him, and after a look at her, of some duration, without his glasses—which always altered the expression of his eyes—he re-settled the nippers on his nose and went back to the view. But the view, in turn, soon enough released him. "Do you remember something I said to you that day at Matcham—or at least fully meant to?"

"Oh yes, I remember everything at Matcham. It's another life."

"Certainly it will be—I mean the kind of thing: what I then wanted it to represent for you. Matcham, you know," he continued, "is symbolic. I think I tried to rub that into you a little."

She met him with the full memory of what he had tried—not an inch, not an ounce of which was lost to her. "What I meant is that it seems a hundred years ago."

"Oh for me it comes in better. Perhaps a part of what makes me remember it," he pursued, "is that I was quite aware of what might have been said about what I was doing. I wanted you to take it from me that I should perhaps be able to look after you—well, rather better. Rather better, of course, than certain other persons in particular."

"Precisely—than Mrs. Lowder, than Miss Croy, even than Mrs. Stringham."

"Oh Mrs. Stringham's all right!" Lord Mark promptly amended.

It amused her even with what she had else to think of; and she could show him at all events how little, in spite of the hundred years, she had lost what he alluded to. The way he was with her at this moment made in fact the other moment so vivid as almost to start again the tears it had started at the time. "You could do so much for me, yes. I perfectly understood you."

"I wanted, you see," he despite this explained, "to *fix* your confidence. I mean, you know, in the right place."

"Well, Lord Mark, you did—it's just exactly now, my confidence, where you put it then. The only difference," said Milly, "is that I seem now to have no use for it. Besides," she then went on, "I do seem to feel you disposed to act in a way that would undermine it a little."

He took no more notice of these last words than if she hadn't said them, only watching her at present as with a gradual new light. "Are you *really* in any trouble?"

To this, on her side, she gave no heed. Making out his light was a little a light for herself. "Don't say, don't try to say, anything that's impossible. There are much better things you can do."

He looked straight at it and then straight over it. "It's too monstrous that one can't ask you as a friend what one wants so to know."

"What is it you want to know?" She spoke, as by a sudden turn, with a slight hardness. "Do you want to know if I'm badly ill?"

The sound of it in truth, though from no raising of her voice, invested the idea with a kind of terror, but a terror all for others. Lord Mark winced and flushed—clearly couldn't help it; but he kept his attitude together and spoke even with unwonted vivacity. "Do you imagine I can see you suffer and not say a word?"

"You won't see me suffer—don't be afraid. I shan't be a public nuisance. That's why I should have liked *this:* it's so beautiful in itself and yet it's out of the gangway. You won't know anything about anything," she added; and then as if to make with decision an end: "And you *don't!* No, not even you." He faced her through it with the remains of his expression, and she saw him as clearly—for *him*—bewildered; which made her wish to be sure not to have been unkind. She would be kind once for all; that would be the end. "I'm very badly ill."

"And you don't do anything?"

"I do everything. Everything's *this,*" she smiled. "I'm doing it now. One can't do more than live."

"Ah than live in the right way, no. But is that what you do? Why haven't you advice?"

He had looked about at the rococo elegance as if there were fifty things it didn't give her, so that he suggested with urgency the most absent. But she met his remedy with a smile. "I've the best advice in the world. I'm acting under it now. I act upon it in receiving you, in talking with you thus. One can't, as I tell you, do more than live."

"Oh live!" Lord Mark ejaculated.

"Well, it's immense for *me*." She finally spoke as if for amusement; now that she had uttered her truth, that he had learnt it from herself as no one had yet done, her emotion had, by the fact, dried up. There she was; but it was as if she would never speak again. "I shan't," she added, "have missed everything."

"Why should you have missed *anything?*" She felt, as he sounded this, to what, within the minute, he had made up his mind. "You're the person in the world for whom that's least necessary; for whom one would call it in fact most impossible; for whom 'missing' at all will surely require an extraordinary amount of misplaced good will. Since you believe in advice, for God's sake take *mine*. I know what you want."

Oh she knew he would know it. But she had brought it on herself—or almost. Yet she spoke with kindness. "I think I want not to be too much worried."

"You want to be adored." It came at last straight. "Nothing would worry you less. I mean as I shall do it. It *is* so"—he firmly kept it up. "You're not loved enough."

"Enough for what, Lord Mark?"

"Why to get the full good of it."

Well, she didn't after all mock at him. "I see what you mean. That full good of it which consists in finding one's self forced to love in return." She had grasped it, but she hesitated. "Your idea is that I might find myself forced to love *you?*"

"Oh 'forced'—!" He was so fine and so expert, so awake to anything the least ridiculous, and of a type with which the preaching of passion somehow so ill consorted—he was so much all these things that he had absolutely to take account of them himself. And he did so, in a single intonation, beautifully. Milly liked him again, liked him for such shades as that, liked him so that it was woeful to see him spoiling it, and still more woeful to have to rank him among those minor charms of existence that she gasped at moments to remember she must give up. "Is it inconceivable to you that you might try?"

"To be so favourably affected by you—?"

"To believe in me. To believe in me," Lord Mark repeated.

Again she hesitated. "To 'try' in return for your trying?"

"Oh I shouldn't have to!" he quickly declared. The prompt neat accent, however, his manner of disposing of her question, failed of real expression, as he himself the next moment intelligently, helplessly, almost comically saw—a failure pointed moreover by the laugh into which Milly was immediately startled. As a suggestion to her of a healing and uplifting passion it *was* in truth deficient; it wouldn't do as the communication of a force that should sweep them both away. And the beauty of him was that he too, even in the act of persuasion, of self-persuasion, could understand that, and could thereby show but the better as fitting into the pleasant commerce of prosperity. The way she let him see that she looked at him was a thing to shut him out, of itself, from services of danger, a thing that made a discrimination against him never yet made—made at least to any consciousness of his own. Born to float in a sustaining air, this would be his first encounter with a judgement formed in the sinister light of tragedy. The gathering dusk of *her* personal world presented itself to him, in her eyes, as an element in which it was vain for him to pretend he could find himself at home, since it was charged with depressions and with dooms, with the chill of the losing game. Almost without her needing to speak, and simply by the fact that there could be, in such a case, no decent substitute for a felt intensity, he had to take it from her that practically he was afraid—whether afraid to protest falsely enough, or only afraid of what might be eventually disagreeable in a compromised alliance, being a minor question. She believed she made out besides, wonderful girl, that he had never quite expected to have to protest about anything beyond his natural convenience—more, in fine, than his disposition and habits, his education as well, his personal *moyens*, in short, permitted. His predicament was therefore one he couldn't like, and also one she willingly would have spared him hadn't he brought it on himself. No man, she was quite aware, could enjoy thus having it from her that he wasn't good for what she would have called her reality. It wouldn't have taken much more to enable her positively to make out in him that he was virtually capable of hinting—had his innermost feeling spoken—at the propriety rather, in his interest, of some cutting down, some dressing up, of the offensive real. He would meet that halfway, but the real must also meet *him*. Milly's sense of it for herself, which was so conspicuously, so financially supported, couldn't, or wouldn't, so accommodate him, and the perception of that fairly showed in his face after a moment like the smart of a blow. It had marked the one minute during which he could again be touching to her. By the time he had tried once more, after all, to insist, he had quite ceased to be so.

By this time she had turned from their window to make a diversion, had walked him through other rooms, appealing again to the inner charm of the place, going even so far for that purpose as to point afresh her independent moral, to repeat that if one only had such a house for one's own and loved it and cherished it enough, it would pay one back in kind, would close one in from harm. He quite grasped for the quarter of an hour the perch she held out to him—grasped it with one hand, that is, while she felt him attached to his own clue with the other; he was by no means either so sore or so stupid, to do him all justice, as not to be able to behave more or less as if nothing had happened. It was one of his merits, to which she did justice too, that both his native and his acquired notion of behaviour rested on the general assumption that nothing—nothing to make a deadly difference for him—ever *could* happen. It was, socially, a working view like another, and it saw them easily enough through the greater part of the rest of their adventure. Downstairs again, however, with the limit of his stay in sight, the sign of his smarting, when all was said, reappeared for her—breaking out moreover, with an effect of strangeness, in another quite possibly sincere allusion to her state of health. He might for that matter have been seeing what he could do in the way of making it a grievance that she should snub him for a charity, on his own part, exquisitely roused. "It's true, you know, all the same, and I don't care a straw for your trying to freeze one up." He seemed to show her, poor man, bravely, how little he cared. "Everybody knows affection often makes things out when indifference doesn't notice. And that's why I know that *I* notice."

"Are you sure you've got it right?" the girl smiled. "I thought rather that affection was supposed to be blind."

"Blind to faults, not to beauties," Lord Mark promptly returned.

"And are my extremely private worries, my entirely domestic complications, which I'm ashamed to have given you a glimpse of—are they beauties?"

"Yes, for those who care for you—as every one does. Everything about you is a beauty. Besides which I don't believe," he declared, "in the seriousness of what you tell me. It's too absurd you should have *any* trouble about which something can't be done. If you can't get the right thing, who can, in all the world, I should like to know? You're the first young woman of your time. I mean what I say." He looked, to do him justice, quite as if he did; not ardent, but clear—simply so competent, in such a position, to compare, that his quiet assertion had the force not so much perhaps of a tribute as of a warrant. "We're all in love with you. I'll put it that way, dropping any claim of my own, if you can bear it better. I speak as one of the lot. You weren't born simply to torment us—you were born to make us happy. Therefore you must listen to us."

She shook her head with her slowness, but this time with all her mildness. "No, I mustn't listen to you—that's just what I mustn't do. The reason is, please, that it simply kills me. I must be as attached to you as you will, since you give that lovely account of yourselves. I give you in return the fullest possible belief of what it would be—" And she pulled up a little. "I give and give and give—there you are; stick to me as close as you like and see if I don't. Only I can't listen or receive or accept—I can't *agree.* I can't make a bargain. I can't really. You must believe that from me. It's all I've wanted to say to you, and why should it spoil anything?"

He let her question fall—though clearly, it might have seemed, because, for reasons or for none, there was so much that *was* spoiled. "You want somebody of your own." He came back, whether in good faith or in bad, to that; and it made her repeat her headshake. He kept it up as if his faith were of the best. "You want somebody, you want somebody."

She was to wonder afterwards if she hadn't been at this juncture on the point of saying something emphatic and vulgar—"Well, I don't at all events want *you!*" What somehow happened, nevertheless, the pity of it being greater than the irritation—the sadness, to her vivid sense, of his being so painfully astray, wandering in a desert in which there was nothing to nourish him—was that his error amounted to positive wrongdoing. She was moreover so acquainted with quite another sphere of usefulness for him that her having suffered him to insist almost convicted her of indelicacy. Why hadn't she stopped him off with her first impression of his purpose? She could do so now only by the allusion she had been wishing not to make. "Do you know I don't think you're doing very right?—and as a thing quite apart, I mean, from my listening to you. That's not right either—except that I'm *not* listening. You oughtn't to have come to Venice to see *me*—and in fact you've not come, and you mustn't behave as if you had. You've much older friends than I, and ever so much better. Really, if you've come at all, you can only have come—properly, and if I may say so honourably—for the best friend, as I believe her to be, that you have in the world."

When once she had said it he took it, oddly enough, as if he had been more or less expecting it. Still, he looked at her very hard, and they had a moment of this during which neither pronounced a name, each apparently determined that the other should. It was Milly's fine coercion, in the event, that was the stronger. "Miss Croy?" Lord Mark asked.

It might have been difficult to make out that she smiled. "Mrs. Lowder." He did make out something, and then fairly coloured for its attestation of his comparative simplicity. "I call *her* on the whole the best. I can't imagine a man's having a better."

Still with his eyes on her he turned it over. "Do you want me to marry Mrs. Lowder?"

At which it seemed to her that it was he who was almost vulgar! But she wouldn't in any way have that. "You know, Lord Mark, what I mean. One isn't in the least turning you out into the cold world. There's no cold world for you at all, I think," she went on; "nothing but a very warm and watchful and expectant world that's waiting for you at any moment you choose to take it up."

He never budged, but they were standing on the polished concrete and he had within a few minutes possessed himself again of his hat. "Do you want me to marry Kate Croy?"

"Mrs. Lowder wants it—I do no wrong, I think, in saying that; and she understands moreover that you know she does."

Well, he showed how beautifully he could take it; and it wasn't obscure to her, on her side, that it was a comfort to deal with a gentleman. "It's ever so kind of you to see such opportunities for me. But what's the use of my tackling Miss Croy?"

Milly rejoiced on the spot to be so able to point out. "Because she's the handsomest and cleverest and most charming creature I ever saw, and because if I were a man I should simply adore her. In fact I do as it is." It was a luxury of response.

"Oh, my dear lady, plenty of people adore her. But that can't further the case of *all.*"

"Ah," she went on, "I know about 'people.' If the case of one's bad, the case of another's good. I don't see what you have to fear from any one else," she said, "save through your being foolish, this way, about *me*."

So she said, but she was aware the next moment of what he was making of what she didn't see. "Is it your idea—since we're talking of these things in these ways—that the young lady you describe in such superlative terms is to be had for the asking?"

"Well, Lord Mark, try. She is a great person. But don't be humble." She was almost gay.

It was this apparently, at last, that was too much for him. "But don't you really *know?*"

As a challenge, practically, to the commonest intelligence she could pretend to, it made her of course wish to be fair. "I 'know' yes, that a particular person's very much in love with her."

"Then you must know by the same token that she's very much in love with a particular person."

"Ah I beg your pardon!"—and Milly quite flushed at having so crude a blunder imputed to her. "You're wholly mistaken."

"It's not true?"

"It's not true."

His stare became a smile. "Are you very, very sure?"

"As sure as one can be"—and Milly's manner could match it—"when one has every assurance. I speak on the best authority."

He hesitated. "Mrs. Lowder's?"

"No. I don't call Mrs. Lowder's the best."

"Oh I thought you were just now saying," he laughed, "that everything about her's so good."

"Good for you"—she was perfectly clear. "For you," she went on, "let her authority be the best. She doesn't believe what you mention, and you must know yourself how little she makes of it. So you can take it from her. *I* take it—" But Milly, with the positive tremor of her emphasis, pulled up.

"You take it from Kate?"

"From Kate herself."

"That she's thinking of no one at all?"

"Of no one at all." Then, with her intensity, she went on. "She has given me her word for it."

"Oh!" said Lord Mark. To which he next added: "And what do you call her word?"

It made Milly, on her side, stare—though perhaps partly but with the instinct of gaining time for the consciousness that she was already a little further "in" than she had designed. "Why, Lord Mark, what should *you* call her word?"

"Ah I'm not obliged to say. I've not asked her. You apparently have."

Well, it threw her on her defence—a defence that she felt, however, especially as of Kate. "We're very intimate," she said in a moment; "so that, without prying into each other's affairs, she naturally tells me things."

Lord Mark smiled as at a lame conclusion. "You mean then she made you of her own movement the declaration you quote?"

Milly thought again, though with hindrance rather than help in her sense of the way their eyes now met—met as for their each seeing in the other more than either said. What she most felt that she herself saw was the strange disposition on her companion's part to disparage Kate's veracity. She could be only concerned to "stand up" for that.

"I mean what I say: that when she spoke of her having no private interest—"

"She took her oath to you?" Lord Mark interrupted.

Milly didn't quite see why he should so catechise her; but she met it again for Kate. "She left me in no doubt whatever of her being free."

At this Lord Mark did look at her, though he continued to smile. "And thereby in no doubt of *your* being too?" It was as if as soon as he had said it, however, he felt it as something of a mistake, and she couldn't herself have told by what queer glare at him she had instantly signified that. He at any rate gave her glare no time to act further; he fell back on the spot, and with a light enough movement, within his rights. "That's all very well, but why in the world, dear lady, should she be swearing to you?"

She had to take this "dear lady" as applying to herself; which disconcerted her when he might now so gracefully have used it for the aspersed Kate. Once more it came to her that she must claim her own part of the aspersion. "Because, as I've told you, we're such tremendous friends."

"Oh," said Lord Mark, who for the moment looked as if that might have stood rather for an absence of such rigours. He was going, however, as if he had in a manner, at the last, got more or less what he wanted. Milly felt, while he addressed his next few words to leave-taking, that she had given rather more than she intended or than she should be able, when once more getting herself into hand, theoretically to defend. Strange enough in fact that he had had from her, about herself—and, under the searching spell of the place, infinitely straight—what no one else had had: neither Kate, nor Aunt Maud, nor Merton Densher, nor Susan Shepherd. He had made her within a minute, in particular, she was aware, lose her presence of mind, and she now wished he would take himself off, so that she might either recover it or bear the loss better in solitude. If he paused, however, she almost at the same time saw, it was because of his watching the approach, from the end of the sala, of one of the gondoliers, who, whatever excursions were appointed for the party with the attendance of the others, always, as the most decorative, most sashed and starched, remained at the palace on the theory that she might whimsically want him—which she never, in her caged freedom, had yet done. Brown Pasquale, slipping in white shoes over the marble and suggesting to her perpetually charmed vision she could scarce say what, either a mild Hindoo, too noiseless almost for her nerves, or simply a barefooted seaman on the deck of a ship—Pasquale offered to sight a small salver, which he obsequiously held out to her with its burden of a visiting-card. Lord Mark—and as if also for admiration of him—delayed his departure to let her receive it; on which she read it with the instant effect of another blow to her presence of mind. This precarious quantity was indeed now so gone that even for dealing with Pasquale she had to do her best to conceal its disappearance. The effort was made, none the less, by the time she had asked if the gentleman were below and had taken in the fact that he had come up. He had followed the gondolier and was waiting at the top of the staircase.

"I'll see him with pleasure." To which she added for her companion, while Pasquale went off: "Mr. Merton Densher."

"Oh!" said Lord Mark—in a manner that, making it resound through the great cool hall, might have carried it even to Densher's ear as a judgement of his identity heard and noted once before

BOOK EIGHTH

I

Densher became aware, afresh, that he disliked his hotel—and all the more promptly that he had had occasion of old to make the same discrimination. The establishment, choked at that season with the polyglot herd, cockneys of all climes, mainly German, mainly American, mainly English, it appeared as the corresponding sensitive nerve was touched, sounded loud and not sweet, sounded anything and everything but Italian, but Venetian. The Venetian was all a dialect, he knew; yet it was pure Attic beside some of the dialects at the bustling inn. It made, "abroad," both for his pleasure and his pain that he had to feel at almost any point how he had been through every thing before. He had been three or four times, in Venice, during other visits, through this pleasant irritation of paddling away—away from the concert of false notes in the vulgarised hall, away from the amiable American families and overfed German porters. He had in each case made terms for a lodging more private and not more costly, and he recalled with tenderness these shabby but friendly asylums, the windows of which he should easily know again in passing on canal or through campo. The shabbiest now failed of an appeal to him, but he found himself at the end of forty-eight hours forming views in respect to a small independent *quartiere*, far down the Grand Canal, which he had once occupied for a month with a sense of pomp and circumstance and yet also with a growth of initiation into the homelier Venetian mysteries. The humour of those days came back to him for an hour, and what further befell in this interval, to be brief, was that, emerging on a traghetto in sight of the recognised house, he made out on the green shutters of his old, of his young windows the strips of white pasted paper that figure in Venice as an invitation to tenants. This was in the course of his very first walk apart, a walk replete with impressions to which he responded with force. He had been almost without cessation, since his arrival, at Palazzo Leporelli, where, as happened, a turn of bad weather on the second day had kept the whole party continuously at home. The episode had passed for him like a series of hours in a museum, though without the fatigue of that; and it had also resembled something that he was still, with a stirred imagination, to find a name for. He might have been looking for the name while he gave himself up, subsequently, to the ramble—he saw that even after years he couldn't lose his way—crowned with his stare across the water at the little white papers.

He was to dine at the palace in an hour or two, and he had lunched there, at an early luncheon, that morning. He had then been out with the three ladies, the three being Mrs. Lowder, Mrs. Stringham and Kate, and had kept afloat with them, under a sufficient Venetian spell, until Aunt Maud had directed him to leave them and return to Miss Theale. Of two circumstances connected with this disposition of his person he was even now not unmindful; the first being that the lady of Lancaster Gate had addressed him with high publicity and as if expressing equally the sense of her companions, who had not spoken, but who might have been taken—yes, Susan Shepherd quite equally with Kate—for inscrutable parties to her plan. What he could as little contrive to forget was that he had, before the two others, as it struck him—that was to say especially before Kate—done exactly as he was bidden; gathered himself up without a protest and retraced his way to the palace. Present with him still was the question of whether he looked a fool for it, of whether the awkwardness he felt as the gondola rocked with the business of his leaving it—they could but make, in submission, for a landing-place that was none of the best—had furnished his friends with such entertainment as was to cause them, behind his back, to exchange intelligent smiles. He had found Milly Theale twenty minutes later alone, and he had sat with her till the others returned to tea. The strange part of this was that it had been very easy, extraordinarily easy. He knew it for strange only when he was away from her, because when he was away from her he was in contact with particular things that made it so. At the time, in her presence, it was as simple as sitting with his sister might have been, and not, if the point were urged, very much more thrilling. He continued to see her as he had first seen her—that remained ineffaceably behind. Mrs. Lowder, Susan Shepherd, his own Kate, might, each in proportion, see her as a princess, as an angel, as a star, but for himself, luckily, she hadn't as yet complications to any point of discomfort: the princess, the angel, the star, were muffled over, ever so lightly and brightly, with the little American girl who had been kind to him in New York and to whom certainly—though without making too much of it for either of them—he was perfectly willing to be kind in return. She appreciated his coming in on purpose, but there was nothing in that—from the moment she was always at home—that they couldn't easily keep up. The only note the least bit high that had even yet sounded between them was this admission on her part that she found it best to remain within. She wouldn't let him call it keeping quiet, for she insisted that her palace—with all its romance and art and history—had set up round her a whirlwind of suggestion that never dropped for an hour. It wasn't therefore, within such walls, confinement, it was the freedom of all the centuries: in respect to which Densher granted good-humouredly that they were then blown together, she and he, as much as she liked, through space.

Kate had found on the present occasion a moment to say to him that he suggested a clever cousin calling on a cousin afflicted, and bored for his pains; and though he denied on the spot the "bored" he could so far see it as an impression he might make that he wondered if the same image wouldn't have occurred to Milly. As soon as Kate appeared again the difference came up—the oddity, as he then instantly felt it, of his having sunk so deep. It was sinking because it was all doing what Kate had conceived for him; it wasn't in the least doing—and that had been his notion of his life—anything he himself had conceived. The difference, accordingly, renewed, sharp, sore, was the irritant under which he had quitted the palace and under which he was to make the best of the business of again dining there. He said to himself that he must make the best of everything; that was in his mind, at the traghetto, even while, with his preoccupation about changing quarters, he studied, across the canal, the look of his former abode. It had done for the past, would it do for the present? would it play in any manner into the general necessity of which he was conscious? That necessity of making the best was the instinct—as he indeed himself knew—of a man somehow aware that if he let go at one place he should let go everywhere. If he took off his hand, the hand that at least helped to hold it together, the whole queer fabric that built him in would fall away in a minute and admit the light. It was really a matter of nerves; it was exactly because he was nervous that he *could* go straight; yet if that condition should increase he must surely go wild. He was walking in short on a high ridge, steep down on either side, where the proprieties—once he could face at all remaining there—reduced themselves to his keeping his head. It was Kate who had so perched him, and there came up for him at moments, as he found himself planting one foot exactly before another, a sensible sharpness of irony as to her management of him. It wasn't that she had put him in danger—to be in real danger with her would have had another quality. There glowed for him in fact a kind of rage at what he wasn't having; an exasperation, a resentment, begotten truly by the very impatience of desire, in respect to his postponed and relegated, his so extremely manipulated state. It was beautifully done of her, but what was the real meaning of it unless that he was perpetually bent to her will? His idea from the first, from the very first of his knowing her, had been to be, as the French called it, *bon prince* with her, mindful of the good humour and generosity, the contempt, in the matter of confidence, for small outlays and small savings, that belonged to the man who wasn't generally afraid. There were things enough, goodness knew—for it was the moral of his plight—that he couldn't afford; but what had had a charm for him if not the notion of living handsomely, to make up for it, in another way? of not at all events reading the romance of his existence in a cheap edition. All he had originally felt in her came back to him, was indeed actually as present as ever—how he had admired and envied what he called to himself her pure talent for life, as distinguished from his own, a poor weak thing of the occasion, amateurishly patched up; only it irritated him the more that this was exactly what was now, ever so characteristically, standing out in her.

It was thanks to her pure talent for life, verily, that he was just where he was and that he was above all just *how* he was. The proof of a decent reaction in him against so much passivity was, with no great richness, that he at least knew—knew, that is, how he was, and how little he liked it as a thing accepted in mere helplessness. He was, for the moment, wistful—that above all described it; that was so large a part of the force that, as the autumn afternoon closed in, kept him, on his traghetto, positively throbbing with his question. His question connected itself, even while he stood, with his special smothered soreness, his sense almost of shame; and the soreness and the shame were less as he let himself, with the help of the conditions about him, regard it as serious. It was born, for that matter, partly of the conditions, those conditions that Kate had so almost insolently braved, had been willing, without a pang, to see him ridiculously—ridiculously so far as just complacently—

exposed to. How little it *could* be complacently he was to feel with the last thoroughness before he had moved from his point of vantage. His question, as we have called it, was the interesting question of whether he had really no will left. How could he know—that was the point—without putting the matter to the test? It had been right to be *bon prince,* and the joy, something of the pride, of having lived, in spirit, handsomely, was even now compatible with the impulse to look into their account; but he held his breath a little as it came home to him with supreme sharpness that, whereas he had done absolutely everything that Kate had wanted, she had done nothing whatever that he had. So it was in fine that his idea of the test by which he must try that possibility kept referring itself, in the warm early dusk, the approach of the Southern night—"conditions" these, such as we just spoke of—to the glimmer, more and more ghostly as the light failed, of the little white papers on his old green shutters. By the time he looked at his watch he had been for a quarter of an hour at this post of observation and reflexion; but by the time he walked away again he had found his answer to the idea that had grown so importunate. Since a proof of his will was wanted it was indeed very exactly in wait for him—it lurked there on the other side of the Canal. A ferryman at the little pier had from time to time accosted him; but it was a part of the play of his nervousness to turn his back on that facility. He would go over, but he walked, very quickly, round and round, crossing finally by the Rialto. The rooms, in the event, were unoccupied; the ancient padrona was there with her smile all a radiance but her recognition all a fable; the ancient rickety objects too, refined in their shabbiness, amiable in their decay, as to which, on his side, demonstrations were tenderly veracious; so that before he took his way again he had arranged to come in on the morrow.

He was amusing about it that evening at dinner—in spite of an odd first impulse, which at the palace quite melted away, to treat it merely as matter for his own satisfaction. This need, this propriety, he had taken for granted even up to the moment of suddenly perceiving, in the course of talk, that the incident would minister to innocent gaiety. Such was quite its effect, with the aid of his picture—an evocation of the quaint, of the humblest rococo, of a Venetian interior in the true old note. He made the point for his hostess that her own high chambers, though they were a thousand grand things, weren't really this; made it in fact with such success that she presently declared it his plain duty to invite her on some near day to tea. She had expressed as yet—he could feel it as felt among them all—no such clear wish to go anywhere, not even to make an effort for a parish feast, or an autumn sunset, nor to descend her staircase for Titian or Gianbellini. It was constantly Densher's view that, as between himself and Kate, things were understood without saying, so that he could catch in her, as she but too freely could in him, innumerable signs of it, the whole soft breath of consciousness meeting and promoting consciousness. This view was so far justified to-night as that Milly's offer to him of her company was to his sense taken up by Kate in spite of her doing nothing to show it. It fell in so perfectly with what she had desired and foretold that she was—and this was what most struck him—sufficiently gratified and blinded by it not to know, from the false quality of his response, from his tone and his very look, which for an instant instinctively sought her own, that he had answered inevitably, almost shamelessly, in a mere time-gaining sense. It gave him on the spot, her failure of perception, almost a beginning of the advantage he had been planning for—that is at least if she too were not darkly dishonest. She might, he was not unaware, have made out, from some deep part of her, the bearing, in respect to herself, of the little fact he had announced; for she was after all capable of that, capable of guessing and yet of simultaneously hiding her guess. It wound him up a turn or two further, none the less, to impute to her now a weakness of vision by which he could himself feel the stronger. Whatever apprehension of his motive in shifting his abode might have brushed her with its wings, she at all events certainly didn't guess that he was giving their friend a hollow promise. That was what she had herself imposed on him; there had been in the prospect from the first a definite particular point at which hollowness, to call it by its least compromising name, would have to begin. Therefore its hour had now charmingly sounded. Whatever in life he had recovered his old rooms for, he had not recovered them to receive Milly Theale: which made no more difference in his expression of happy readiness than if he had been—just what he was trying not to be—fully hardened and fully base. So rapid in fact was the rhythm of his inward drama that the quick vision of impossibility produced in him by his hostess's direct and unexpected appeal had the effect, slightly sinister, of positively scaring him. It gave him a measure of the intensity, the reality of his now mature motive. It prompted in him certainly no quarrel with these things, but it made them as vivid as if they already flushed with success. It was before the flush of success that his heart beat almost to dread. The dread was but the dread of the happiness to be compassed; only that was in itself a symptom. That a visit from Milly should, in this projection of necessities, strike him as of the last incongruity, quite as a hateful idea, and above all as spoiling, should one put it grossly, his game—the adoption of such a view might of course have an identity with one of those numerous ways of being a fool that seemed so to abound for him. It would remain none the less the way to which he should be in advance most reconciled. His mature motive, as to which he allowed himself no grain of illusion, had thus in an hour taken imaginative possession of the place: that precisely was how he saw it seated there, already unpacked and settled, for Milly's innocence, for Milly's beauty, no matter how short a time, to be housed with. There were things she would never recognise, never feel, never catch in the air; but this made no difference in the fact that her brushing against them would do nobody any good. The discrimination and the scruple were for *him*. So he felt all the parts of the case together, while Kate showed admirably as feeling none of them. Of course, however—when hadn't it to be his last word?—Kate was always sublime.

That came up in all connexions during the rest of these first days; came up in especial under pressure of the fact that each time our plighted pair snatched, in its passage, at the good fortune of half an hour together, they were doomed—though Densher felt it as all by *his* act—to spend a part of the rare occasion in wonder at their luck and in study of its queer character. This was the case after he might be supposed to have got, in a manner, used to it; it was the case after the girl—ready always, as we say, with the last word—had given him the benefit of her righting of every wrong appearance, a support familiar to him now in reference to other phases. It was still the case after he possibly might, with a little imagination, as she freely insisted, have made out, by the visible working of the crisis, what idea on Mrs. Lowder's part had determined it. Such as the idea was—and that it suited Kate's own book she openly professed—he had only to see how things were turning out to feel it strikingly justified. Densher's reply to all this vividness was that of course Aunt Maud's intervention hadn't been occult, even for *his* vividness, from the moment she had written him, with characteristic concentration, that if he should see his way to come to Venice for a fortnight she should engage he would find it no blunder. It took Aunt Maud really to do such things in such ways; just as it took him, he was ready to confess, to do such others as he must now strike them all—didn't he?—as committed to. Mrs. Lowder's admonition had been of course a direct reference to what she had said to him at Lancaster Gate before his departure the night Milly had failed them through illness; only it had at least matched that remarkable outbreak in respect to the quantity of good nature it attributed to him. The young man's discussions of his situation—which were confined to Kate; he had none with Aunt Maud herself—suffered a little, it may be divined, by the sense that he couldn't put everything off, as he privately expressed it, on other people. His ears, in solitude, were apt to burn with the reflexion that Mrs. Lowder had simply tested him, seen him as he was and made out what could be done with him. She had had but to whistle for him and he had come. If she had taken for granted his good nature she was as justified as Kate declared. This awkwardness of his conscience, both in respect to his general plasticity, the fruit of his feeling plasticity, within limits, to be a mode of life like another—certainly better than some, and particularly in respect to such confusion as might reign about what he had really come for—this inward ache was not wholly dispelled by the style, charming as that was, of Kate's poetic versions. Even the high wonder and delight of Kate couldn't set him right with himself when there was something quite distinct from these things that kept him wrong.

In default of being right with himself he had meanwhile, for one thing, the interest of seeing—and quite for the first time in his life—whether, on a given occasion, that might be quite so necessary to happiness as was commonly assumed and as he had up to this moment never doubted. He was engaged distinctly in an adventure—he who had never thought himself cut out for them, and it fairly helped him that he was able at moments to say to himself that he mustn't fall below it. At his hotel, alone, by night, or in the course of the few late strolls he was finding time to take through dusky labyrinthine alleys and empty *campi*, overhung with mouldering palaces, where he paused in disgust at his want of ease and where the sound of a rare footstep on the enclosed pavement was like that of a retarded dancer in a banquet-hall deserted—during these interludes he entertained cold views, even to the point, at moments, on the principle that the shortest follies are the best, of thinking of immediate departure as not only possible but as indicated. He had however only to cross again the threshold of Palazzo Leporelli to see all the elements of the business compose, as painters called it, differently. It began to strike him then that departure wouldn't curtail, but would signally coarsen his folly, and that above all, as he hadn't really "begun" anything, had only submitted, consented, but too generously indulged and condoned the beginnings of others, he had no call to treat himself with superstitious rigour. The single thing that was clear in complications was that, whatever happened, one was to behave as a gentleman—to which was added indeed the perhaps slightly less shining truth that complications might sometimes have their tedium beguiled by a study of the question of how a gentleman would behave. This question, I hasten to add, was not in the last resort Densher's greatest worry. Three women were looking to him at once, and, though such a predicament could never be, from the point of view of facility, quite the ideal, it yet had, thank goodness, its immediate workable law. The law was not to be a brute—in return for amiabilities. He hadn't come all the way out from England to be a brute. He hadn't thought of what it might give him to have a fortnight, however handicapped, with Kate in Venice, to be a brute. He hadn't treated Mrs. Lowder as if in responding to her suggestion he had understood her—he hadn't done that either to be a brute. And what he had prepared least of all for such an anti-climax was the prompt and inevitable, the achieved surrender—*as* a gentleman, oh that indubitably!—to the unexpected impression made by poor pale exquisite Milly as the mistress of a grand old palace and the dispenser of an hospitality more irresistible, thanks to all the conditions, than any ever known to him.

This spectacle had for him an eloquence, an authority, a felicity—he scarce knew by what strange name to call it—for which he said to himself that he had not consciously bargained. Her welcome, her frankness, sweetness, sadness, brightness, her disconcerting poetry, as he made shift at moments to call it, helped as it was by the beauty of her whole setting and by the perception at the same time, on the observer's part, that this element gained from her, in a manner, for effect and harmony, as much as it gave—her whole attitude had, to his imagination, meanings that hung about it, waiting upon her, hovering, dropping and quavering forth again, like vague faint snatches, mere ghosts of sound, of old-fashioned melancholy music. It was positively well for him, he had his times of reflecting, that he couldn't put it off on Kate and Mrs. Lowder, as a gentleman so conspicuously wouldn't, that—well, that he had been rather taken in by not having known in advance! There had been now five days of it all without his risking even to Kate alone any hint of what he ought to have known and of what in particular therefore had taken him in. The truth was doubtless that really, when it came to any free handling and naming of things, they were living together, the five of them, in an air in which an ugly effect of "blurting out" might easily be produced. He came back with his friend on each occasion to the blest miracle of renewed propinquity, which had a double virtue in that favouring air. He breathed on it as if he could scarcely believe it, yet the time had passed, in spite of this privilege, without his quite committing himself, for her ear, to any such comment on Milly's high style and state as would have corresponded with the amount of recognition it had produced in him. Behind everything for him was his renewed remembrance, which had fairly become a habit, that he had been the first to know her. This was what they had all insisted on, in her absence, that day at Mrs. Lowder's; and this was in especial what had made him feel its influence on his immediately paying her a second visit. Its influence had been all there, been in the high-hung, rumbling carriage with them, from the moment she took him to drive, covering them in together as if it had been a rug of softest silk. It had worked as a clear connexion with something lodged in the past, something already their own. He had more than once recalled how he had said to himself even at that moment, at some point in the drive, that he was not *there*, not just as he was in so doing it, through Kate and Kate's idea, but through Milly and Milly's own, and through himself and *his* own, unmistakeably—as well as through the little facts, whatever they had amounted to, of his time in New York.

II

There was at last, with everything that made for it, an occasion when he got from Kate, on what she now spoke of as his eternal refrain, an answer of which he was to measure afterwards the precipitating effect. His eternal refrain was the way he came back to the riddle of Mrs. Lowder's view of her profit—a view so hard to reconcile with the chances she gave them to meet. Impatiently, at this, the girl denied the chances, wanting to know from him, with a fine irony that smote him rather straight, whether he felt their opportunities as anything so grand. He looked at her deep in the eyes when she had sounded this note; it was the least he could let her off with for having made him visibly flush. For some reason then, with it, the sharpness dropped out of her tone, which became sweet and sincere. "'Meet,' my dear man," she expressively echoed; "does it strike you that we get, after all, so very much out of our meetings?"

"On the contrary—they're starvation diet. All I mean is—and it's all I've meant from the day I came—that we at least get more than Aunt Maud."

"Ah but you see," Kate replied, "you don't understand what Aunt Maud gets."

"Exactly so—and it's what I don't understand that keeps me so fascinated with the question. *She* gives me no light; she's prodigious. She takes everything as of a natural—!"

"She takes it as 'of a natural' that at this rate I shall be making my reflexions about you. There's every appearance for her," Kate went on, "that what she had made her mind up to as possible is possible; that what she had thought more likely than not to happen is happening. The very essence of her, as you surely by this time have made out for yourself, is that when she adopts a view she—well, to her own sense, really brings the thing about, fairly terrorizes with her view any other, any opposite view, and those, not less, who represent that. I've often thought success comes to her"—Kate continued to study the phenomenon—"by the spirit in her that dares and defies her idea not to prove the right one. One has seen it so again and again, in the face of everything, become the right one."

Densher had for this, as he listened, a smile of the largest response. "Ah my dear child, if you can explain I of course needn't not 'understand.' I'm condemned to that," he on his side presently explained, "only when understanding fails." He took a moment; then he pursued: "Does she think she terrorises *us?*" To which he added while, without immediate speech, Kate but looked over the place: "Does she believe anything so stiff as that you've really changed about me?" He knew now that he was probing the girl deep—something told him so; but that was a reason the more. "Has she got it into her head that you dislike me?"

To this, of a sudden, Kate's answer was strong. "You could yourself easily put it there!"

He wondered. "By telling her so?"

"No," said Kate as with amusement at his simplicity; "I don't ask that of you."

"Oh my dear," Densher laughed, "when you ask, you know, so little—!"

There was a full irony in this, on his own part, that he saw her resist the impulse to take up. "I'm perfectly justified in what I've asked," she quietly returned. "It's doing beautifully for you." Their eyes again intimately met, and the effect was to make her proceed. "You're not a bit unhappy."

"Oh ain't I?" he brought out very roundly.

"It doesn't practically show—which is enough for Aunt Maud. You're wonderful, you're beautiful," Kate said; "and if you really want to know whether I believe you're doing it you may take from me perfectly that I see it coming." With which, by a quick transition, as if she had settled the case, she asked him the hour.

"Oh only twelve-ten"—he had looked at his watch. "We've taken but thirteen minutes; we've time yet."

"Then we must walk. We must go toward them."

Densher, from where they had been standing, measured the long reach of the Square. "They're still in their shop. They're safe for half an hour."

"That shows then, that shows!" said Kate.

This colloquy had taken place in the middle of Piazza San Marco, always, as a great social saloon, a smooth-floored, blue-roofed chamber of amenity, favourable to talk; or rather, to be exact, not in the middle, but at the point where our pair had paused by a common impulse after leaving the great mosque-like church. It rose now, domed and pinnacled, but a little way behind them, and they had in front the vast empty space, enclosed by its arcades, to which at that hour movement and traffic were mostly confined. Venice was at breakfast, the Venice of the visitor and the possible acquaintance, and, except for the parties of importunate pigeons picking up the crumbs of perpetual feasts, their prospect was clear and they could see their companions hadn't yet been, and weren't for a while longer likely to be, disgorged by the lace-shop, in one of the *loggie*, where, shortly before, they had left them for a look-in—the expression was artfully Densher's—at Saint Mark's. Their morning had happened to take such a turn as brought this chance to the surface; yet his allusion, just made to Kate, hadn't been an overstatement of their general opportunity. The worst that could be said of their general opportunity was that it was essentially in presence—in presence of every one; every one consisting at this juncture, in a peopled world, of Susan Shepherd, Aunt Maud and Milly. But the proof how, even in presence, the opportunity could become special was furnished precisely by this view of the compatibility of their comfort with a certain amount of lingering. The others had assented to their not waiting in the shop; it was of course the least the others could do. What had really helped them this morning was the fact that, on his turning up, as he always called it, at the palace, Milly had not, as before, been able to present herself. Custom and use had hitherto seemed fairly established; on his coming round, day after day—eight days had been now so conveniently marked—their friends, Milly's and his, conveniently dispersed and left him to sit with her till luncheon. Such was the perfect operation of the scheme on which he had been, as he phrased it to himself, had out; so that certainly there was that amount of justification for Kate's vision of success. He *had*, for Mrs. Lowder—he couldn't help it while sitting there—the air, which was the thing to be desired, of no absorption in Kate sufficiently deep to be alarming. He had failed their young hostess each morning as little as she had failed him; it was only to-day that she hadn't been well enough to see him.

That had made a mark, all round; the mark was in the way in which, gathered in the room of state, with the place, from the right time, all bright and cool and beflowered, as always, to receive her descent, they—the rest of them—simply looked at each other. It was lurid—lurid, in all probability, for each of them privately—that they had uttered no common regrets. It was strange for our young man above all that, if the poor girl was indisposed to *that* degree, the hush of gravity, of apprehension, of significance of some sort, should be the most the case—that of the guests—could permit itself. The hush, for that matter, continued after the party of four had gone down to the gondola and taken their places in it. Milly had sent them word that she hoped they would go out and enjoy themselves, and this indeed had produced a second remarkable look, a look as of their knowing, one quite as well as the other, what such a message meant as provision for the alternative beguilement of Densher. She wished not to have spoiled his morning, and he had therefore, in civility, to take it as pleasantly patched up. Mrs. Stringham had helped the affair out, Mrs. Stringham who, when it came to that, knew their friend better than any of them. She knew her so well that she knew herself as acting in exquisite compliance with conditions comparatively obscure, approximately awful to them, by not thinking it necessary to stay at home. She had corrected that element of the perfunctory which was the slight fault, for all of them, of the occasion; she had invented a preference for Mrs. Lowder and herself; she had remembered the fond dreams of the visitation of lace that had hitherto always been brushed away by accidents, and it had come up as well for her that Kate had, the day before, spoken of the part played by fatality in her own failure of real acquaintance with the inside of Saint Mark's. Densher's sense of Susan Shepherd's conscious intervention had by this time a corner of his mind all to itself; something that had begun for them at Lancaster Gate was now a sentiment clothed in a shape; her action, ineffably discreet, had at all events a way of affecting him as for the most part subtly, even when not superficially, in his own interest. They were not, as a pair, as a "team," really united; there were too many persons, at least three, and too many things, between them; but meanwhile something was preparing that would draw them closer. He scarce knew what: probably nothing but his finding, at some hour when it would be a service to do so, that she had all the while understood him. He even had a presentiment of a juncture at which the understanding of every one else would fail and this deep little person's alone survive.

Such was to-day, in its freshness, the moral air, as we may say, that hung about our young friends; these had been the small accidents and quiet forces to which they owed the advantage we have seen them in some sort enjoying. It seemed in fact fairly to deepen for them as they stayed their course again; the splendid Square, which had so notoriously, in all the years, witnessed more of the joy of life than any equal area in Europe, furnished them, in their remoteness from earshot, with solitude and security. It was as if, being in possession, they could say what they liked; and it was also as if, in consequence of that, each had an apprehension of what the other wanted to say. It was most of all for them, moreover, as if this very quantity, seated on their lips in the bright historic air, where the only sign for their ears was the flutter of the doves, begot in the heart of each a fear. There might have been a betrayal of that in the way Densher broke the silence resting on her last words. "What did you mean just now that I can do to make Mrs. Lowder believe? For myself, stupidly, if you will, I don't see, from the moment I can't lie to her, what else there is but lying."

Well, she could tell him. "You can say something both handsome and sincere to her about Milly—whom you honestly like so much. That wouldn't be lying; and, coming from you, it would have an effect. You don't, you know, say much about her."

And Kate put before him the fruit of observation. "You don't, you know, speak of her at all."

"And has Aunt Maud," Densher asked, "told you so?" Then as the girl, for answer, only seemed to bethink herself, "You must have extraordinary conversations!" he exclaimed.

Yes, she had bethought herself. "We have extraordinary conversations."

His look, while their eyes met, marked him as disposed to hear more about them; but there was something in her own, apparently, that defeated the opportunity. He questioned her in a moment on a different matter, which had been in his mind a week, yet in respect to which he had had no chance so good as this. "Do you happen to know then, as such wonderful things pass between you, what she makes of the incident, the other day, of Lord Mark's so very superficial visit?—his having spent here, as I gather, but the two or three hours necessary for seeing our friend and yet taken no time at all, since he went off by the same night's train, for seeing any one else. What can she make of his not having waited to see *you*, or to see herself—with all he owes her?"

"Oh of course," said Kate, "she understands. He came to make Milly his offer of marriage—he came for nothing but that. As Milly wholly declined it his business was for the time at an end. He couldn't quite on the spot turn round to make up to *us*."

Kate had looked surprised that, as a matter of taste on such an adventurer's part, Densher shouldn't see it. But Densher was lost in another thought. "Do you mean that when, turning up myself, I found him leaving her, that was what had been taking place between them?"

"Didn't you make it out, my dear?" Kate enquired.

"What sort of a blundering weathercock then *is* he?" the young man went on in his wonder.

"Oh don't make too little of him!" Kate smiled. "Do you pretend that Milly didn't tell you?"

"How great an ass he had made of himself?"

Kate continued to smile. "You *are* in love with her, you know."

He gave her another long look. "Why, since she has refused him, should my opinion of Lord Mark show it? I'm not obliged, however, to think well of him for such treatment of the other persons I've mentioned, and I feel I don't understand from you why Mrs. Lowder should."

"She doesn't—but she doesn't care," Kate explained. "You know perfectly the terms on which lots of London people live together even when they're supposed to live very well. He's not committed to us—he was having his try. Mayn't an unsatisfied man," she asked, "always have his try?"

"And come back afterwards, with confidence in a welcome, to the victim of his inconstancy?"

Kate consented, as for argument, to be thought of as a victim. "Oh but he has *had* his try at *me*. So it's all right."

"Through your also having, you mean, refused him?"

She balanced an instant during which Densher might have just wondered if pure historic truth were to suffer a slight strain. But she dropped on the right side. "I haven't let it come to that. I've been too discouraging. Aunt Maud," she went on—now as lucid as ever—"considers, no doubt, that she has a pledge from him in respect to me; a pledge that would have been broken if Milly had accepted him. As the case stands that makes no difference."

Densher laughed out. "It isn't *his* merit that he has failed."

"It's still his merit, my dear, that he's Lord Mark. He's just what he was, and what he knew he was. It's not for me either to reflect on him after I've so treated him."

"Oh," said Densher impatiently, "you've treated him beautifully."

"I'm glad," she smiled, "that you can still be jealous." But before he could take it up she had more to say. "I don't see why it need puzzle you that Milly's so marked line gratifies Aunt Maud more than anything else can displease her. What does she see but that Milly herself recognises her situation with you as too precious to be spoiled? Such a recognition as that can't but seem to her to involve in some degree your own recognition. Out of which she therefore gets it that the more you have for Milly the less you have for me."

There were moments again—we know that from the first they had been numerous—when he felt with a strange mixed passion the mastery of her mere way of putting things. There was something in it that bent him at once to conviction and to reaction. And this effect, however it be named, now broke into his tone. "Oh if she began to know what I have for you—!"

It wasn't ambiguous, but Kate stood up to it. "Luckily for us we may really consider she doesn't. So successful have we been."

"Well," he presently said, "I take from you what you give me, and I suppose that, to be consistent—to stand on my feet where I do stand at all—I ought to thank you. Only, you know, what you give me seems to me, more than anything else, the larger and larger size of my job. It seems to me more than anything else what you expect of me. It never seems to me somehow what I may expect of *you*. There's so much you *don't* give me."

She appeared to wonder. "And pray what is it I don't—?"

"I give you proof," said Densher. "You give me none."

"What then do you call proof?" she after a moment ventured to ask.

"Your doing something for me."

She considered with surprise. "Am I not doing *this* for you? Do you call this nothing?"

"Nothing at all."

"Ah I risk, my dear, everything for it."

They had strolled slowly further, but he was brought up short. "I thought you exactly contend that, with your aunt so bamboozled, you risk nothing!"

It was the first time since the launching of her wonderful idea that he had seen her at a loss. He judged the next instant moreover that she didn't like it—either the being so or the being seen, for she soon spoke with an impatience that showed her as wounded; an appearance that produced in himself, he no less quickly felt, a sharp pang of indulgence. "What then do you wish me to risk?"

The appeal from danger touched him, but all to make him, as he would have said, worse. "What I wish is to be loved. How can I feel at this rate that I *am*?" Oh she understood him, for all she might so bravely disguise it, and that made him feel straighter than if she hadn't. Deep, always, was his sense of life with her—deep as it had been from the moment of those signs of life that in the dusky London of two winters ago they had originally exchanged. He had never taken her for unguarded, ignorant, weak; and if he put to her a claim for some intenser faith between them this was because he believed it could reach her and she could meet it. "I can go on perhaps," he said, "with help. But I can't go on without."

She looked away from him now, and it showed him how she understood. "We ought to be there—I mean when they come out."

"They *won't* come out—not yet. And I don't care if they do." To which he straightway added, as if to deal with the charge of selfishness that his words, sounding for himself, struck him as enabling her to make: "Why not have done with it all and face the music as we are?" It broke from him in perfect sincerity. "Good God, if you'd only *take* me!"

It brought her eyes round to him again, and he could see how, after all, somewhere deep within, she felt his rebellion more sweet than bitter. Its effect on her spirit and her sense was visibly to hold her an instant. "We've gone too far," she none the less pulled herself together to reply. "Do you want to kill her?"

He had an hesitation that wasn't all candid. "Kill, you mean, Aunt Maud?"

"You know whom I mean. We've told too many lies."

Oh at this his head went up. "I, my dear, have told none!"

He had brought it out with a sharpness that did him good, but he had naturally, none the less, to take the look it made her give him. "Thank you very much."

Her expression, however, failed to check the words that had already risen to his lips. "Rather than lay myself open to the least appearance of it I'll go this very night."

"Then go," said Kate Croy.

He knew after a little, while they walked on again together, that what was in the air for him, and disconcertingly, was not the violence, but much rather the cold quietness, of the way this had come from her. They walked on together, and it was for a minute as if their difference had become of a sudden, in all truth, a split—as if the basis of his departure had been settled. Then, incoherently and still more suddenly, recklessly moreover, since they now might easily, from under the arcades, be observed, he passed his hand into her arm with a force that produced for them another pause. "I'll tell any lie you want, any your idea requires, if you'll only come to me."

"Come to you?"

"Come to me."

"How? Where?"

She spoke low, but there was somehow, for his uncertainty, a wonder in her being so equal to him. "To my rooms, which are perfectly possible, and in taking which, the other day, I had you, as you must have felt, in view. We can arrange it—with two grains of courage. People in our case always arrange it." She listened as for the good information, and there was support for him—since it was a question of his going step by step—in the way she took no refuge in showing herself shocked. He had in truth not expected of her that particular vulgarity, but the absence of it only added the thrill of a deeper reason to his sense of possibilities. For the knowledge of what she was he had absolutely to *see* her now, incapable of refuge, stand there for him in all the light of the day and of his admirable merciless meaning. Her mere listening in fact made him even understand himself as he hadn't yet done. Idea for idea, his own was thus already, and in the germ, beautiful. "There's nothing for me possible but to feel that I'm not a fool. It's all I have to say, but you must know what it means. *With* you I can do it—I'll go as far as you demand or as you will yourself. Without you—I'll be hanged! And I must be sure."

She listened so well that she was really listening after he had ceased to speak. He had kept his grasp of her, drawing her close, and though they had again, for the time, stopped walking, his talk—for others at a distance—might have been, in the matchless place, that of any impressed tourist to any slightly more detached companion. On possessing himself of her arm he had made her turn, so that they faced afresh to Saint Mark's, over the great presence of which his eyes moved while she twiddled her parasol. She now, however, made a motion that confronted them finally with the opposite end. Then only she spoke—"Please take your hand out of my arm." He understood at once: she had made out in the shade of the gallery the issue of the others from their place of purchase. So they went to them side by side, and it was all right. The others had seen them as well and waited for them, complacent enough, under one of the arches. They themselves too—he argued that Kate would argue—looked perfectly ready, decently patient, properly accommodating. They themselves suggested nothing worse—always by Kate's system—than a pair of the children of a supercivilised age making the best of an awkwardness. They didn't nevertheless hurry—that would overdo it; so he had time to feel, as it were, what he felt. He felt, ever so distinctly—it was with this he faced Mrs. Lowder—that he was already in a sense possessed of what he wanted. There was more to come—everything; he had by no means, with his companion, had it all out. Yet what he was possessed of was real—the fact that she hadn't thrown over his lucidity the horrid shadow of cheap reprobation. Of this he had had so sore a fear that its being dispelled was in itself of the nature of bliss. The danger had dropped—it was behind him there in the great sunny space. So far she was good for what he wanted.

III

She was good enough, as it proved, for him to put to her that evening, and with further ground for it, the next sharpest question that had been on his lips in the morning—which his other preoccupation had then, to his consciousness, crowded out. His opportunity was again made, as befell, by his learning from Mrs. Stringham, on arriving, as usual, with the close of day, at the palace, that Milly must fail them again at dinner, but would to all appearance be able to come down later. He had found Susan Shepherd alone in the great saloon, where even more candles than their friend's large common allowance—she grew daily more splendid; they were all struck with it and chaffed her about it—lighted up the pervasive mystery of Style. He had thus five minutes with the good lady before Mrs. Lowder and Kate appeared—minutes illumined indeed to a longer reach than by the number of Milly's candles.

"*May* she come down—ought she if she isn't really up to it?"

He had asked that in the wonderment always stirred in him by glimpses—rare as were these—of the inner truth about the girl. There was of course a question of health—it was in the air, it was in the ground he trod, in the food he tasted, in the sounds he heard, it was everywhere. But it was everywhere with the effect of a request to him—to his very delicacy, to the common discretion of others as well as his own—that no allusion to it should be made. There had practically been none, that morning, on her explained non-appearance—the absence of it, as we know, quite monstrous and awkward; and this passage with Mrs. Stringham offered him his first licence to open his eyes. He had gladly enough held them closed; all the more that his doing so performed for his own spirit a useful function. If he positively wanted not to be brought up with his nose against Milly's facts, what better proof could he have that his conduct was marked by straightness? It was perhaps pathetic for her, and for himself was perhaps even ridiculous; but he hadn't even the amount of curiosity that he would have had about an ordinary friend. He might have shaken himself at moments to try, for a sort of dry decency, to have it; but that too, it appeared, wouldn't come. In what therefore was the duplicity? He was at least sure about his feelings—it being so established that he had none at all. They were all for Kate, without a feather's weight to spare. He was acting for Kate—not, by the deviation of an inch, for her friend. He was accordingly not interested, for had he been interested he would have cared, and had he cared he would have wanted to know. Had he wanted to know he wouldn't have been purely passive, and it was his pure passivity that had to represent his dignity and his honour. His dignity and his honour, at the same time, let us add, fortunately fell short to-night of spoiling his little talk with Susan Shepherd. One glimpse—it was as if she had wished to give him that; and it was as if, for himself, on current terms, he could oblige her by accepting it. She not only permitted, she fairly invited him to open his eyes. "I'm so glad you're here." It was no answer to his question, but it had for the moment to serve. And the rest was fully to come.

He smiled at her and presently found himself, as a kind of consequence of communion with her, talking her own language. "It's a very wonderful experience."

"Well"—and her raised face shone up at him—"that's all I want you to feel about it. If I weren't afraid," she added, "there are things I should like to say to you."

"And what are you afraid of, please?" he encouragingly asked.

"Of other things that I may possibly spoil. Besides, I don't, you know, seem to have the chance. You're always, you know, *with* her."

He was strangely supported, it struck him, in his fixed smile; which was the more fixed as he felt in these last words an exact description of his course. It was an odd thing to have come to, but he was always with her. "Ah," he none the less smiled, "I'm not with her now."

"No—and I'm so glad, since I get this from it. She's ever so much better."

"Better? Then she *has* been worse?"

Mrs. Stringham waited. "She has been marvellous—that's what she has been. She *is* marvellous. But she's really better."

"Oh then if she's really better—!" But he checked himself, wanting only to be easy about it and above all not to appear engaged to the point of mystification. "We shall miss her the more at dinner."

Susan Shepherd, however, was all there for him. "She's keeping herself. You'll see. You'll not really need to miss anything. There's to be a little party."

"Ah I do see—by this aggravated grandeur."

"Well, it *is* lovely, isn't it? I want the whole thing. She's lodged for the first time as she ought, from her type, to be; and doing it—I mean bringing out all the glory of the place—makes her really happy. It's a Veronese picture, as near as can be—with me as the inevitable dwarf, the small blackamoor, put into a corner of the foreground for effect. If I only had a hawk or a hound or something of that sort I should do the scene more honour. The old housekeeper, the woman in charge here, has a big red cockatoo that I might borrow and perch on my thumb for the evening." These explanations and sundry others Mrs. Stringham gave, though not all with the result of making him feel that the picture closed him in. What part was there for *him*, with his attitude that lacked the highest style, in a composition in which everything else would have it? "They won't, however, be at dinner, the few people she expects—they come round afterwards from their respective hotels; and Sir Luke Strett and his niece, the principal ones, will have arrived from London but an hour or two ago. It's for *him* she has wanted to do something—to let it begin at once. We shall see more of him, because she likes him; and I'm so glad—she'll be glad too—that *you're* to see him." The good lady, in connexion with it, was urgent, was almost unnaturally bright. "So I greatly hope—!" But her hope fairly lost itself in the wide light of her cheer.

He considered a little this appearance, while she let him, he thought, into still more knowledge than she uttered. "What is it you hope?"

"Well, that you'll stay on."

"Do you mean after dinner?" She meant, he seemed to feel, so much that he could scarce tell where it ended or began.

"Oh that, of course. Why we're to have music—beautiful instruments and songs; and not Tasso declaimed as in the guide-books either. She has arranged it—or at least I have. That is Eugenio has. Besides, you're in the picture."

"Oh—I!" said Densher almost with the gravity of a real protest.

"You'll be the grand young man who surpasses the others and holds up his head and the wine-cup. What we hope," Mrs. Stringham pursued, "is that you'll be faithful to us—that you've not come for a mere foolish few days."

Densher's more private and particular shabby realities turned, without comfort, he was conscious, at this touch, in the artificial repose he had in his anxiety about them but half-managed to induce. The way smooth ladies, travelling for their pleasure and housed in Veronese pictures, talked to plain embarrassed working-men, engaged in an unprecedented sacrifice of time and of the opportunity for modest acquisition! The things they took for granted and the general misery of explaining! He couldn't tell them how he had tried to work, how it was partly what he had moved into rooms for, only to find himself, almost for the first time in his life, stricken and sterile; because that would give them a false view of the source of his restlessness, if not of the degree of it. It would operate, indirectly perhaps, but infallibly, to add to that weight as of expected performance which these very moments with Mrs. Stringham caused more and more to settle on his heart. He had incurred it, the expectation of performance; the thing was done, and there was no use talking; again, again the cold breath of it was in the air. So there he was. And at best he floundered. "I'm afraid you won't understand when I say I've very tiresome things to consider. Botherations, necessities at home. The pinch, the pressure in London."

But she understood in perfection; she rose to the pinch and the pressure and showed how they had been her own very element. "Oh the daily task and the daily wage, the golden guerdon or reward? No one knows better than I how they haunt one in the flight of the precious deceiving days. Aren't they just what I myself have given up? I've given up all to follow *her*. I wish you could feel as I do. And can't you," she asked, "write about Venice?"

He very nearly wished, for the minute, that he could feel as she did; and he smiled for her kindly. "Do *you* write about Venice?"

"No; but I would—oh wouldn't I?—if I hadn't so completely given up. She's, you know, my princess, and to one's princess—"

"One makes the whole sacrifice?"

"Precisely. There you are!"

It pressed on him with this that never had a man been in so many places at once. "I quite understand that she's yours. Only you see she's not mine." He felt he could somehow, for honesty, risk that, as he had the moral certainty she wouldn't repeat it and least of all to Mrs. Lowder, who would find in it a disturbing implication. This was part of what he liked in the good lady, that she didn't repeat, and also that she gave him a delicate sense of her shyly wishing him to know it. That was in itself a hint of possibilities between them, of a relation, beneficent and elastic for him, which wouldn't engage him further than he could see. Yet even as he afresh made this out he felt how strange it all was. She wanted, Susan Shepherd then, as appeared, the same thing Kate wanted, only wanted it, as still further appeared, in so different a way and from a motive so different, even though scarce less deep. Then Mrs. Lowder wanted, by so odd an evolution of her exuberance, exactly what each of the others did; and he was between them all, he was in the midst. Such perceptions made occasions—well, occasions for fairly wondering if it mightn't be best just to consent, luxuriously, to *be* the ass the whole thing involved. Trying not to be and yet keeping in it was of the two things the more asinine. He was glad there was no male witness; it was a circle of petticoats; he shouldn't have liked a man to see him. He only had for a moment a sharp thought of Sir Luke Strett, the great master of the knife whom Kate in London had spoken of Milly as in commerce with, and whose renewed intervention at such a distance, just announced to him, required some accounting for. He had a vision of great London surgeons—if this one was a surgeon—as incisive all round; so that he should perhaps after all not wholly escape the ironic attention of his own sex. The most he might be able to do was not to care; while he was trying not to he could take that in. It was a train, however, that brought up the vision of Lord Mark as well. Lord Mark had caught him twice in the fact—the fact of his absurd posture; and that made a second male. But it was comparatively easy not to mind Lord Mark.

His companion had before this taken him up, and in a tone to confirm her discretion, on the matter of Milly's not being his princess. "Of course she's not. You must do something first."

Densher gave it his thought. "Wouldn't it be rather *she* who must?"

It had more than he intended the effect of bringing her to a stand. "I see. No doubt, if one takes it so." Her cheer was for the time in eclipse, and she looked over the place, avoiding his eyes, as in the wonder of what Milly could do. "And yet she has wanted to be kind."

It made him on the spot feel a brute. "Of course she has. No one could be more charming. She has treated me as if *I* were somebody. Call her my hostess as I've never had nor imagined a hostess, and I'm with you altogether. Of course," he added in the right spirit for her, "I do see that it's quite court life."

She promptly showed how this was almost all she wanted of him. "That's all I mean, if you understand it of such a court as never was: one of the courts of heaven, the court of a reigning seraph, a sort of a vice-queen of an angel. That will do perfectly."

"Oh well then I grant it. Only court life as a general thing, you know," he observed, "isn't supposed to pay."

"Yes, one has read; but this is beyond any book. That's just the beauty here; it's why she's the great and only princess. With her, at her court," said Mrs. Stringham, "it does pay." Then as if she had quite settled it for him: "You'll see for yourself."

He waited a moment, but said nothing to discourage her. "I think you were right just now. One must do something first."

"Well, you've done something."

"No—I don't see that. I can do more."

Oh well, she seemed to say, if he would have it so! "You can do everything, you know."

"Everything" was rather too much for him to take up gravely, and he modestly let it alone, speaking the next moment, to avert fatuity, of a different but a related matter. "Why has she sent for Sir Luke Strett if, as you tell me, she's so much better?"

"She hasn't sent. He has come of himself," Mrs. Stringham explained. "He has wanted to come."

"Isn't that rather worse then—if it means he mayn't be easy?"

"He was coming, from the first, for his holiday. She has known that these several weeks." After which Mrs. Stringham added: "You can *make* him easy."

"*I* can?" he candidly wondered. It was truly the circle of petticoats. "What have I to do with it for a man like that?"

"How do you know," said his friend, "what he's like? He's not like any one you've ever seen. He's a great beneficent being."

"Ah then he can do without me. I've no call, as an outsider, to meddle."

"Tell him, all the same," Mrs. Stringham urged, "what you think."

"What I think of Miss Theale?" Densher stared. It was, as they said, a large order. But he found the right note. "It's none of his business."

It did seem a moment for Mrs. Stringham too the right note. She fixed him at least with an expression still bright, but searching, that showed almost to excess what she saw in it; though what this might be he was not to make out till afterwards. "Say *that* to him then. Anything will do for him as a means of getting at you."

"And why should he get at me?"

"Give him a chance to. Let him talk to you. Then you'll see."

All of which, on Mrs. Stringham's part, sharpened his sense of immersion in an element rather more strangely than agreeably warm—a sense that was moreover, during the next two or three hours, to be fed to satiety by several other impressions. Milly came down after dinner, half a dozen friends—objects of interest mainly, it appeared, to the ladies of Lancaster Gate—having by that time arrived; and with this call on her attention, the further call of her musicians ushered by Eugenio, but personally and separately welcomed, and the supreme opportunity offered in the arrival of the great doctor, who came last of all, he felt her diffuse in wide warm waves the spell of a general, a beatific mildness. There was a deeper depth of it, doubtless, for some than for others; what he in particular knew of it was that he seemed to stand in it up to his neck. He moved about in it and it made no plash; he floated, he noiselessly swam in it, and they were all together, for that matter, like fishes in a crystal pool. The effect of the place, the beauty of the scene, had probably much to do with it; the golden grace of the high rooms, chambers of art in themselves, took care, as an influence, of the general manner, and made people bland without making them solemn. They were only people, as Mrs. Stringham had said, staying for the week or two at the inns, people who during the day had fingered their Baedekers, gaped at their frescoes and differed, over fractions of francs, with their gondoliers. But Milly, let loose among them in a wonderful white dress, brought them somehow into relation with something that made them more finely genial; so that if the Veronese picture of which he had talked with Mrs. Stringham was not quite constituted, the comparative prose of the previous hours, the traces of insensibility qualified by "beating down," were at last almost nobly disowned. There was perhaps something for him in the accident of his seeing her for the first time in white, but she hadn't yet had occasion—circulating with a clearness intensified—to strike him as so happily pervasive. She was different, younger, fairer, with the colour of her braided hair more than ever a not altogether lucky challenge to attention; yet he was loth wholly to explain it by her having quitted this once, for some obscure yet doubtless charming reason, her almost monastic, her hitherto inveterate black. Much as the change did for the value of her presence, she had never yet, when all was said, made it for *him*; and he was not to fail of the further amusement of judging her determined in the matter by Sir Luke Strett's visit. If he could in this connexion have felt jealous of Sir Luke Strett, whose strong face and type, less assimilated by the scene perhaps than any others, he was anon to study from the other side of the saloon, that would doubtless have been most amusing of all. But he couldn't be invidious, even to profit by so high a tide; he felt himself too much "in" it, as he might have said: a moment's reflexion put him more in than any one. The way Milly neglected him for other cares while Kate and Mrs. Lowder, without so much as the attenuation of a joke, introduced him to English ladies—that was itself a proof; for nothing really of so close a communion had up to this time passed between them as the single bright look and the three gay words (all ostensibly of the last lightness) with which her confessed consciousness brushed by him.

She was acquitting herself to-night as hostess, he could see, under some supreme idea, an inspiration which was half her nerves and half an inevitable harmony; but what he especially recognised was the character that had already several times broken out in her and that she so oddly appeared able, by choice or by instinctive affinity, to keep down or to display. She was the American girl as he had originally found her—found her at certain moments, it was true, in New York, more than at certain others; she was the American girl as, still more than then, he had seen her on the day of her meeting him in London and in Kate's company. It affected him as a large though queer social resource in her—such as a man, for instance, to his diminution, would never in the world be able to command; and he wouldn't have known whether to see it in an extension or a contraction of "personality," taking it as he did most directly for a confounding extension of surface. Clearly too it was the right thing this evening all round: that came out for him in a word from Kate as she approached him to wreak on him a second introduction. He had under cover of the music melted away from the lady toward whom she had first pushed him; and there was something in her to affect him as telling evasively a tale of their talk in the Piazza. To what did she want to coerce him as a form of penalty for what he had done to her there? It was thus in contact uppermost for him that he had done something; not only caused her perfect intelligence to act in his interest, but left her unable to get away, by any mere private effort, from his inattackable logic. With him thus in presence, and near him—and it had been as unmistakeable through dinner—there was no getting away for her at all, there was less of it than ever: so she could only either deal with the question straight, either frankly yield or ineffectually struggle or insincerely argue, or else merely express herself by following up the advantage she did possess. It was part of that advantage for the hour—a brief fallacious makeweight to his pressure—that there were plenty of things left in which he must feel her will. They only told him, these indications, how much she was, in such close quarters, feeling his; and it was enough for him again that her very aspect, as great a variation in its way as Milly's own, gave him back the sense of his action. It had never yet in life been granted him to know, almost materially to taste, as he could do in these minutes, the state of what was vulgarly called conquest. He had lived long enough to have been on occasion "liked," but it had never begun to be allowed him to be liked to any such tune in any such quarter. It was a liking greater than Milly's—or it would be: he felt it in him to answer for that. So at all events he read the case while he noted that Kate was somehow—for Kate—wanting in lustre. As a striking young presence she was practically superseded; of the mildness that Milly diffused she had assimilated all her share; she might fairly have been dressed to-night in the little black frock, superficially indistinguishable, that Milly had laid aside. This represented, he perceived, the opposite pole from such an effect as that of her wonderful entrance, under her aunt's eyes—he had never forgotten it—the day of their younger friend's failure at Lancaster Gate. She was, in her accepted effacement—it was actually her acceptance that made the beauty and repaired the damage—under her aunt's eyes now; but whose eyes were not effectually preoccupied? It struck him none the less certainly that almost the first thing she said to him showed an exquisite attempt to appear if not unconvinced at least self-possessed.

"Don't you think her good enough *now?*" Almost heedless of the danger of overt freedoms, she eyed Milly from where they stood, noted her in renewed talk, over her further wishes, with the members of her little orchestra, who had approached her with demonstrations of deference enlivened by native humours—things quite in the line of old Venetian comedy. The girl's idea of music had been happy—a real solvent of shyness, yet not drastic; thanks to the intermissions, discretions, a general habit of mercy to gathered barbarians, that reflected the good manners of its interpreters, representatives though these might be but of the order in which taste was natural and melody rank. It was easy at all events to answer Kate. "Ah my dear, you know how good I think her!"

"But she's *too* nice," Kate returned with appreciation. "Everything suits her so—especially her pearls. They go so with her old lace. I'll trouble you really to look at them." Densher, though aware he had seen them before, had perhaps not "really" looked at them, and had thus not done justice to the embodied poetry—his mind, for Milly's aspects, kept coming back to that—which owed them part of its style. Kate's face, as she considered them, struck him: the long, priceless chain, wound twice round the neck, hung, heavy and pure, down the front of the wearer's breast—so far down that Milly's trick, evidently unconscious, of holding and vaguely fingering and entwining a part of it, conduced presumably to convenience. "She's a dove," Kate went on, "and one somehow doesn't think of doves as bejewelled. Yet they suit her down to the ground."

"Yes—down to the ground is the word." Densher saw now how they suited her, but was perhaps still more aware of something intense in his companion's feeling about them. Milly was indeed a dove; this was the figure, though it most applied to her spirit. Yet he knew in a moment that Kate was just now, for reasons hidden from him, exceptionally under the impression of that element of wealth in her which was a power, which was a great power, and which was dove-like only so far as one remembered that doves have wings and wondrous flights, have them as well as tender tints and soft sounds. It even came to him dimly that such wings could in a given case—*had*, truly, in the case with which he was concerned—spread themselves for protection. Hadn't they, for that matter, lately taken an inordinate reach, and weren't Kate and Mrs. Lowder, weren't Susan Shepherd and he, wasn't he in particular, nestling under them to a great increase of immediate ease? All this was a brighter blur in the general light, out of which he heard Kate presently going on.

"Pearls have such a magic that they suit every one."

"They would uncommonly suit you," he frankly returned.

"Oh yes, I see myself!"

As she saw herself, suddenly, he saw her—she would have been splendid; and with it he felt more what she was thinking of. Milly's royal ornament had—under pressure now not wholly occult—taken on the character of a symbol of differences, differences of which the vision was actually in Kate's face. It might have been in her face too that, well as she certainly would look in pearls, pearls were exactly what Merton Densher would never be able to give her. Wasn't *that* the great difference that Milly to-night symbolised? She unconsciously represented to Kate, and Kate took it in at every pore, that there was nobody with whom she had less in common than a remarkably handsome girl married to a man unable to make her on any such lines as that the least little present. Of these absurdities, however, it was not till afterwards that Densher thought. He could think now, to any purpose, only of what Mrs. Stringham had said to him before dinner. He could but come back to his friend's question of a minute ago. "She's certainly good enough, as you call it, in the sense that I'm assured she's better. Mrs. Stringham, an hour or two since, was in great feather to me about it. She evidently believes her better."

"Well, if they choose to call it so—!"

"And what do *you* call it—as against them?"

"I don't call it anything to any one but you. I'm not 'against' them!" Kate added as with just a fresh breath of impatience for all he had to be taught.

"That's what I'm talking about," he said. "What do you call it to me?"

It made her wait a little. "She isn't better. She's worse. But that has nothing to do with it."

"Nothing to do?" He wondered.

But she was clear. "Nothing to do with us. Except of course that we're doing our best for her. We're making her want to live." And Kate again watched her. "To-night she does want to live." She spoke with a kindness that had the strange property of striking him as inconsequent—so much, and doubtless so unjustly, had all her clearness been an implication of the hard. "It's wonderful. It's beautiful."

"It's beautiful indeed."

He hated somehow the helplessness of his own note; but she had given it no heed. "She's doing it for *him*"—and she nodded in the direction of Milly's medical visitor. "She wants to be for him at her best. But she can't deceive him."

Densher had been looking too; which made him say in a moment: "And do you think *you* can? I mean, if he's to be with us here, about your sentiments. If Aunt Maud's so thick with him—!"

Aunt Maud now occupied in fact a place at his side and was visibly doing her best to entertain him, though this failed to prevent such a direction of his own eyes—determined, in the way such things happen, precisely by the attention of the others—as Densher became aware of and as Kate promptly marked. "He's looking at *you*. He wants to speak to you."

"So Mrs. Stringham," the young man laughed, "advised me he would."

"Then let him. Be right with him. I don't need," Kate went on in answer to the previous question, "to deceive him. Aunt Maud, if it's necessary, will do that. I mean that, knowing nothing about me, he can see me only as she sees me. She sees me now so well. He has nothing to do with me."

"Except to reprobate you," Densher suggested.

"For not caring for *you?* Perfectly. As a brilliant young man driven by it into your relation with Milly—as all *that* I leave you to him."

"Well," said Densher sincerely enough, "I think I can thank you for leaving me to some one easier perhaps with me than yourself."

She had been looking about again meanwhile, the lady having changed her place, for the friend of Mrs. Lowder's to whom she had spoken of introducing him. "All the more reason why I should commit you then to Lady Wells."

"Oh but wait." It was not only that he distinguished Lady Wells from afar, that she inspired him with no eagerness, and that, somewhere at the back of his head, he was fairly aware of the question, in germ, of whether this was the kind of person he should be involved with when they were married. It was furthermore that the consciousness of something he had not got from Kate in the morning, and that logically much concerned him, had been made more keen by these very moments—to say nothing of the consciousness that, with their general smallness of opportunity, he must squeeze each stray instant hard. If Aunt Maud, over there with Sir Luke, noted him as a little "attentive," that might pass for a futile demonstration on the part of a gentleman who had to confess to having, not very gracefully, changed his mind. Besides, just now, he didn't care for Aunt Maud except in so far as he was immediately to show. "How can Mrs. Lowder think me disposed of with any finality, if I'm disposed of only to a girl who's dying? If you're right about that, about the state of the case, you're wrong about Mrs. Lowder's being squared. If Milly, as you say," he lucidly pursued, "can't deceive a great surgeon, or whatever, the great surgeon won't deceive other people—not those, that is, who are closely concerned. He won't at any rate deceive Mrs. Stringham, who's Milly's greatest friend; and it will be very odd if Mrs. Stringham deceives Aunt Maud, who's her own."

Kate showed him at this the cold glow of an idea that really was worth his having kept her for. "Why will it be odd? I marvel at your seeing your way so little."

Mere curiosity even, about his companion, had now for him its quick, its slightly quaking intensities. He had compared her once, we know, to a "new book," an uncut volume of the highest, the rarest quality; and his emotion (to justify that) was again and again like the thrill of turning the page. "Well, you know how deeply I marvel at the way *you* see it!"

"It doesn't in the least follow," Kate went on, "that anything in the nature of what you call deception on Mrs. Stringham's part will be what you call odd. Why shouldn't she hide the truth?"

"From Mrs. Lowder?" Densher stared. "Why should she?"

"To please you."

"And how in the world can it please me?"

Kate turned her head away as if really at last almost tired of his density. But she looked at him again as she spoke. "Well then to please Milly." And before he could question: "Don't you feel by this time that there's nothing Susan Shepherd won't do for you?"

He had verily after an instant to take it in, so sharply it corresponded with the good lady's recent reception of him. It was queerer than anything again, the way they all came together round him. But that was an old story, and Kate's multiplied lights led him on and on. It was with a reserve, however, that he confessed this. "She's ever so kind. Only her view of the right thing may not be the same as yours."

"How can it be anything different if it's the view of serving you?"

Densher for an instant, but only for an instant, hung fire. "Oh the difficulty is that I don't, upon my honour, even yet quite make out how yours does serve me."

"It helps you—put it then," said Kate very simply—"to serve *me*. It gains you time."

"Time for what?"

"For everything!" She spoke at first, once more, with impatience; then as usual she qualified. "For anything that may happen."

Densher had a smile, but he felt it himself as strained. "You're cryptic, love!"

It made her keep her eyes on him, and he could thus see that, by one of those incalculable motions in her without which she wouldn't have been a quarter so interesting, they half-filled with tears from some source he had too roughly touched. "I'm taking a trouble for you I never dreamed I should take for any human creature."

Oh it went home, making him flush for it; yet he soon enough felt his reply on his lips. "Well, isn't my whole insistence to you now that I can conjure trouble away?" And he let it, his insistence, come out again; it had so constantly had, all the week, but its step or two to make. "There *need* be none whatever between us. There need be nothing but our sense of each other."

It had only the effect at first that her eyes grew dry while she took up again one of the so numerous links in her close chain. "You can tell her anything you like, anything whatever."

"Mrs. Stringham? I *have* nothing to tell her."

"You can tell her about *us*. I mean," she wonderfully pursued, "that you do still like me."

It was indeed so wonderful that it amused him. "Only not that you still like me."

She let his amusement pass. "I'm absolutely certain she wouldn't repeat it."

"I see. To Aunt Maud."

"You don't quite see. Neither to Aunt Maud nor to any one else." Kate then, he saw, was always seeing Milly much more, after all, than he was; and she showed it again as she went on. "*There*, accordingly, is your time."

She did at last make him think, and it was fairly as if light broke, though not quite all at once. "You must let me say I *do* see. Time for something in particular that I understand you regard as possible. Time too that, I further understand, is time for you as well."

"Time indeed for me as well." And encouraged visibly by his glow of concentration, she looked at him as through the air she had painfully made clear. Yet she was still on her guard. "Don't think, however, I'll do all the work for you. If you want things named you must name them."

He had quite, within the minute, been turning names over; and there was only one, which at last stared at him there dreadful, that properly fitted. "Since she's to die I'm to marry her?"

It struck him even at the moment as fine in her that she met it with no wincing nor mincing. She might for the grace of silence, for favour to their conditions, have only answered him with her eyes. But her lips bravely moved. "To marry her."

"So that when her death has taken place I shall in the natural course have money?"

It was before him enough now, and he had nothing more to ask; he had only to turn, on the spot, considerably cold with the thought that all along—to his stupidity, his timidity—it had been, it had been only, what she meant. Now that he was in possession moreover she couldn't forbear, strangely enough, to pronounce the words she hadn't pronounced: they broke through her controlled and colourless voice as if she should be ashamed, to the very end, to have flinched. "You'll in the natural course have money. We shall in the natural course be free."

"Oh, oh, oh!" Densher softly murmured.

"Yes, yes, yes." But she broke off. "Come to Lady Wells."

He never budged—there was too much else. "I'm to propose it then—marriage—on the spot?"

There was no ironic sound he needed to give it; the more simply he spoke the more he seemed ironic. But she remained consummately proof. "Oh I can't go into that with you, and from the moment you don't wash your hands of me I don't think you ought to ask me. You must act as you like and as you can."

He thought again. "I'm far—as I sufficiently showed you this morning—from washing my hands of you."

"Then," said Kate, "it's all right."

"All right?" His eagerness flamed. "You'll come?"

But he had had to see in a moment that it wasn't what she meant. "You'll have a free hand, a clear field, a chance—well, quite ideal."

"Your descriptions"—her "ideal" was such a touch!—"are prodigious. And what I don't make out is how, caring for me, you can like it."

"I don't like it, but I'm a person, thank goodness, who can do what I don't like."

It wasn't till afterwards that, going back to it, he was to read into this speech a kind of heroic ring, a note of character that belittled his own incapacity for action. Yet he saw indeed even at the time the greatness of knowing so well what one wanted. At the time too, moreover, he next reflected that he after all knew what *he* did. But something else on his lips was uppermost. "What I don't make out then is how you can even bear it."

"Well, when you know me better you'll find out how much I can bear." And she went on before he could take up, as it were, her too many implications. That it was left to him to know her, spiritually, "better" after his long sacrifice to knowledge—this for instance was a truth he hadn't been ready to receive so full in the face. She had mystified him enough, heaven knew, but that was rather by his own generosity than by hers. And what, with it, did she seem to suggest she might incur at his hands? In spite of these questions she was carrying him on. "All you'll have to do will be to stay."

"And proceed to my business under your eyes?"

"Oh dear no—we shall go."

"'Go?'" he wondered. "Go when, go where?"

"In a day or two—straight home. Aunt Maud wishes it now."

It gave him all he could take in to think of. "Then what becomes of Miss Theale?"

"What I tell you. She stays on, and you stay with her."

He stared. "All alone?"

She had a smile that was apparently for his tone. "You're old enough—with plenty of Mrs. Stringham."

Nothing might have been so odd for him now, could he have measured it, as his being able to feel, quite while he drew from her these successive cues, that he was essentially "seeing what she would say"—an instinct compatible for him therefore with that absence of a need to know her better to which she had a moment before done injustice. If it hadn't been appearing to him in gleams that she would somewhere break down, he probably couldn't have gone on. Still, as she wasn't breaking down there was nothing for him but to continue. "Is your going Mrs. Lowder's idea?"

"Very much indeed. Of course again you see what it does for us. And I don't," she added, "refer only to our going, but to Aunt Maud's view of the general propriety of it."

"I see again, as you say," Densher said after a moment. "It makes everything fit."

"Everything."

The word, for a little, held the air, and he might have seemed the while to be looking, by no means dimly now, at all it stood for. But he had in fact been looking at something else. "You leave her here then to die?"

"Ah she believes she won't die. Not if you stay. I mean," Kate explained, "Aunt Maud believes."

"And that's all that's necessary?"

Still indeed she didn't break down. "Didn't we long ago agree that what she believes is the principal thing for us?"

He recalled it, under her eyes, but it came as from long ago. "Oh yes. I can't deny it." Then he added: "So that if I stay—"

"It won't"—she was prompt—"be our fault."

"If Mrs. Lowder still, you mean, suspects us?"

"If she still suspects us. But she won't."

Kate gave it an emphasis that might have appeared to leave him nothing more; and he might in fact well have found nothing if he hadn't presently found: "But what if she doesn't accept me?"

It produced in her a look of weariness that made the patience of her tone the next moment touch him. "You can but try."

"Naturally I can but try. Only, you see, one has to try a little hard to propose to a dying girl."

"She isn't for you as if she's dying." It had determined in Kate the flash of *justesse* he could perhaps most, on consideration, have admired, since her retort touched the truth. There before him was the fact of how Milly to-night impressed him, and his companion, with her eyes in his own and pursuing his impression to the depths of them, literally now perched on the fact in triumph. She turned her head to where their friend was again in range, and it made him turn his, so that they watched a minute in concert. Milly, from the other side, happened at the moment to notice them, and she sent across toward them in response all the candour of her smile, the lustre of her pearls, the value of her life, the essence of her wealth. It brought them together again with faces made fairly grave by the reality she put into their plan. Kate herself grew a little pale for it, and they had for a time only a silence. The music, however, gay and vociferous, had broken out afresh and protected more than interrupted them. When Densher at last spoke it was under cover.

"I might stay, you know, without trying."

"Oh to stay *is* to try."

"To have for herself, you mean, the appearance of it?"

"I don't see how you can have the appearance more."

Densher waited. "You think it then possible she may *offer* marriage?"

"I can't think—if you really want to know—what she may *not* offer!"

"In the manner of princesses, who do such things?"

"In any manner you like. So be prepared."

Well, he looked as if he almost were. "It will be for me then to accept. But that's the way it must come."

Kate's silence, so far, let it pass; but she presently said: "You'll, on your honour, stay then?"

His answer made her wait, but when it came it was distinct. "Without you, you mean?"

"Without us."

"And you yourselves go at latest—?"

"Not later than Thursday."

It made three days. "Well," he said, "I'll stay, on my honour, if you'll come to me. On your honour."

Again, as before, this made her momentarily rigid, with a rigour out of which, at a loss, she vaguely cast about her. Her rigour was more to him, nevertheless, than all her readiness; for her readiness was the woman herself, and this other thing a mask, a stop-gap and a "dodge." She cast about, however, as happened, and not for the instant in vain. Her eyes, turned over the room, caught at a pretext. "Lady Wells is tired of waiting: she's coming—see—to *us*."

Densher saw in fact, but there was a distance for their visitor to cross, and he still had time. "If you decline to understand me I wholly decline to understand you. I'll do nothing."

"Nothing?" It was as if she tried for the minute to plead.

"I'll do nothing. I'll go off before you. I'll go to-morrow."

He was to have afterwards the sense of her having then, as the phrase was—and for vulgar triumphs too—seen he meant it. She looked again at Lady Wells, who was nearer, but she quickly came back. "And if I do understand?"

"I'll do everything."

She found anew a pretext in her approaching friend: he was fairly playing with her pride. He had never, he then knew, tasted, in all his relation with her, of anything so sharp—too sharp for mere sweetness—as the vividness with which he saw himself master in the conflict. "Well, I understand."

"On your honour?"

"On my honour."

"You'll come?"

"I'll come."

BOOK NINTH

I

It was after they had gone that he truly felt the difference, which was most to be felt moreover in his faded old rooms. He had recovered from the first a part of his attachment to this scene of contemplation, within sight, as it was, of the Rialto bridge, on the hither side of that arch of associations and the left going up the Canal; he had seen it in a particular light, to which, more and more, his mind and his hands adjusted it; but the interest the place now wore for him had risen at a bound, becoming a force that, on the spot, completely engaged and absorbed him, and relief from which—if relief was the name—he could find only by getting away and out of reach. What had come to pass within his walls lingered there as an obsession importunate to all his senses; it lived again, as a cluster of pleasant memories, at every hour and in every object; it made everything but itself irrelevant and tasteless. It remained, in a word, a conscious watchful presence, active on its own side, for ever to be reckoned with, in face of which the effort at detachment was scarcely less futile than frivolous. Kate had come to him; it was only once—and this not from any failure of their need, but from such impossibilities, for bravery alike and for subtlety, as there was at the last no blinking; yet she had come, that once, to stay, as people called it; and what survived of her, what reminded and insisted, was something he couldn't have banished if he had wished. Luckily he didn't wish, even though there might be for a man almost a shade of the awful in so unqualified a consequence of his act. It had simply *worked*, his idea, the idea he had made her accept; and all erect before him, really covering the ground as far as he could see, was the fact of the gained success that this represented. It was, otherwise, but the fact of the idea as directly applied, as converted from a luminous conception into an historic truth. He had known it before but as desired and urged, as convincingly insisted on for the help it would render; so that at present, *with* the help rendered, it seemed to acknowledge its office and to set up, for memory and faith, an insistence of its own. He had in fine judged his friend's pledge in advance as an inestimable value, and what he must now know his case for was that of a possession of the value to the full. Wasn't it perhaps even rather the value that possessed *him*, kept him thinking of it and waiting on it, turning round and round it and making sure of it again from this side and that?

It played for him—certainly in this prime afterglow—the part of a treasure kept at home in safety and sanctity, something he was sure of finding in its place when, with each return, he worked his heavy old key in the lock. The door had but to open for him to be with it again and for it to be all there; so intensely there that, as we say, no other act was possible to him than the renewed act, almost the hallucination, of intimacy. Wherever he looked or sat or stood, to whatever aspect he gave for the instant the advantage, it was in view as nothing of the moment, nothing begotten of time or of chance could be, or ever would; it was in view as, when the curtain has risen, the play on the stage is in view, night after night, for the fiddlers. He remained thus, in his own theatre, in his single person, perpetual orchestra to the ordered drama, the confirmed "run"; playing low and slow, moreover, in the regular way, for the situations of most importance. No other visitor was to come to him; he met, he bumped occasionally, in the Piazza or in his walks, against claimants to acquaintance, remembered or forgotten, at present mostly effusive, sometimes even inquisitive; but he gave no address and encouraged no approach; he couldn't for his life, he felt, have opened his door to a third person. Such a person would have interrupted him, would have profaned his secret or perhaps have guessed it; would at any rate have broken the spell of what he conceived himself—in the absence of anything "to show"—to be inwardly doing. He was giving himself up—that was quite enough—to the general feeling of his renewed engagement to fidelity. The force of the engagement, the quantity of the article to be supplied, the special solidity of the contract, the way, above all, as a service for which the price named by him had been magnificently paid, his equivalent office was to take effect—such items might well fill his consciousness when there was nothing from outside to interfere.

Never was a consciousness more rounded and fastened down over what filled it; which is precisely what we have spoken of as, in its degree, the oppression of success, the somewhat chilled state—tending to the solitary—of supreme recognition. If it was slightly awful to feel so justified, this was by the loss of the warmth of the element of mystery. The lucid reigned instead of it, and it was into the lucid that he sat and stared. He shook himself out of it a dozen times a day, tried to break by his own act his constant still communion. It wasn't still communion she had meant to bequeath him; it was the very different business of that kind of fidelity of which the other name was careful action.

Nothing, he perfectly knew, was less like careful action than the immersion he enjoyed at home. The actual grand queerness was that to be faithful to Kate he had positively to take his eyes, his arms, his lips straight off her—he had to let her alone. He had to remember it was time to go to the palace—which in truth was a mercy, since the check was not less effectual than imperative. What it came to, fortunately, as yet, was that when he closed the door behind him for an absence he always shut her in. Shut her out—it came to that rather, when once he had got a little away; and before he reached the palace, much more after hearing at his heels the bang of the greater *portone*, he felt free enough not to know his position as oppressively false. As Kate was *all* in his poor rooms, and not a ghost of her left for the grander, it was only on reflexion that the falseness came out; so long as he left it to the mercy of beneficent chance it offered him no face and made of him no claim that he couldn't meet without aggravation of his inward sense. This aggravation had been his original horror; yet what—in Milly's presence, each day—was horror doing with him but virtually letting him off? He shouldn't perhaps get off to the end; there was time enough still for the possibility of shame to pounce. Still, however, he did constantly a little more what he liked best, and that kept him for the time more safe. What he liked best was, in any case, to know why things were as he felt them; and he knew it pretty well, in this case, ten days after the retreat of his other friends. He then fairly perceived that—even putting their purity of motive at its highest—it was neither Kate nor he who made his strange relation to Milly, who made her own, so far as it might be, innocent; it was neither of them who practically purged it—if practically purged it was. Milly herself did everything—so far at least as he was concerned—Milly herself, and Milly's house, and Milly's hospitality, and Milly's manner, and Milly's character, and, perhaps still more than anything else, Milly's imagination, Mrs. Stringham and Sir Luke indeed a little aiding: whereby he knew the blessing of a fair pretext to ask himself what more he had to do. Something incalculable wrought for them—for him and Kate; something outside, beyond, above themselves, and doubtless ever so much better than they: which wasn't a reason, however—its being so much better—for them not to profit by it. Not to profit by it, so far as profit could be reckoned, would have been to go directly against it; and the spirit of generosity at present engendered in Densher could have felt no greater pang than by his having to go directly against Milly.

To go *with* her was the thing, so far as she could herself go; which, from the moment her tenure of her loved palace stretched on, was possible but by his remaining near her. This remaining was of course on the face of it the most "marked" of demonstrations—which was exactly why Kate had required it; it was so marked that on the very evening of the day it had taken effect Milly herself hadn't been able not to reach out to him, with an exquisite awkwardness, for some account of it. It was as if she had wanted from him some name that, now they were to be almost alone together, they could, for their further ease, know it and call it by—it being, after all, almost rudimentary that his presence, of which the absence of the others made quite a different thing, couldn't but have for himself some definite basis. She only wondered about the basis it would have for himself, and how he would describe it; that would quite do for her—it even would have done for her, he could see, had he produced some reason merely trivial, had he said he was waiting for money or clothes, for letters or for orders from Fleet Street, without which, as she might have heard, newspaper men never took a step. He hadn't in the event quite sunk to that; but he had none the less had there with her, that night, on Mrs. Stringham's leaving them alone—Mrs. Stringham proved really prodigious—his acquaintance with a shade of awkwardness darker than any Milly could know. He had supposed himself beforehand, on the question of what he was doing or pretending, in possession of some tone that would serve; but there were three minutes of his feeling incapable of promptness quite in the same degree in which a gentleman whose pocket has been picked feels incapable of purchase. It even didn't help him, oddly, that he was sure Kate would in some way have spoken for him—or rather not so much in some way as in one very particular way. He hadn't asked her, at the last, what she might, in the connexion, have said; nothing would have induced him to put such a question after she had been to see him: his lips were so sealed by that passage, his spirit in fact so hushed, in respect to any charge upon her freedom. There was something he could only therefore read back into the probabilities, and when he left the palace an hour afterwards it was with a sense of having breathed there, in the very air, the truth he had been guessing.

Just this perception it was, however, that had made him for the time ugly to himself in his awkwardness. It was horrible, with this creature, to *be* awkward; it was odious to be seeking excuses for the relation that involved it. Any relation that involved it was by the very fact as much discredited as a dish would be at dinner if one had to take medicine as a sauce. What Kate would have said in one of the young women's last talks was that—if Milly absolutely must have the truth about it—Mr. Densher was staying because she had really seen no way but to require it of him. If he stayed he didn't follow her—or didn't appear to her aunt to be doing so; and when she kept him from following her Mrs. Lowder couldn't pretend, in scenes, the renewal of which at this time of day was painful, that she after all didn't snub him as she might. She did nothing in fact *but* snub him—wouldn't that have been part of the story?—only Aunt Maud's suspicions were of the sort that had repeatedly to be dealt with. He had been, by the same token, reasonable enough—as he now, for that matter, well might; he had consented to oblige them, aunt and niece, by giving the plainest sign possible that he could exist away from London. To exist away from London was to exist away from Kate Croy—which was a gain, much appreciated, to the latter's comfort. There was a minute, at this hour, out of Densher's three, during which he knew the terror of Milly's uttering some such allusion to their friend's explanation as he must meet with words that wouldn't destroy it. To destroy it was to destroy everything, to destroy probably Kate herself, to destroy in particular by a breach of faith still uglier than anything else the beauty of their own last passage. He had given her his word of honour that if she would come to him he would act absolutely in her sense, and he had done so with a full enough vision of what her sense implied. What it implied for one thing was that to-night in the great saloon, noble in its half-lighted beauty, and straight in the white face of his young hostess, divine in her trust, or at any rate inscrutable in her mercy—what it implied was that he should lie with his lips. The single thing, of all things, that could save him from it would be Milly's letting him off after having thus scared him. What made her mercy inscrutable was that if she had already more than once saved him it was yet apparently without knowing how nearly he was lost.

These were transcendent motions, not the less blest for being obscure; whereby yet once more he was to feel the pressure lighten. He was kept on his feet in short by the felicity of her not presenting him with Kate's version as aversion to adopt. He couldn't stand up to lie—he felt as if he should have to go down on his knees. As it was he just sat there shaking a little for nervousness the leg he had crossed over the other. She was sorry for his suffered snub, but he had nothing more to subscribe to, to perjure himself about, than the three or four inanities he had, on his own side, feebly prepared for the crisis. He scrambled a little higher than the reference to money and clothes, letters and directions from his manager; but he brought out the beauty of the chance for him—there before him like a temptress painted by Titian—to do a little quiet writing. He was vivid for a moment on the difficulty of writing quietly in London; and he was precipitate, almost explosive, on his idea, long cherished, of a book.

The explosion lighted her face. "You'll do your book here?"

"I hope to begin it."

"It's something you haven't begun?"

"Well, only just."

"And since you came?"

She was so full of interest that he shouldn't perhaps after all be too easily let off. "I tried to think a few days ago that I had broken ground."

Scarcely anything, it was indeed clear, could have let him in deeper. "I'm afraid we've made an awful mess of your time."

"Of course you have. But what I'm hanging on for now is precisely to repair that ravage."

"Then you mustn't mind me, you know."

"You'll see," he tried to say with ease, "how little I shall mind anything."

"You'll want"—Milly had thrown herself into it—"the best part of your days."

He thought a moment: he did what he could to wreathe it in smiles. "Oh I shall make shift with the worst part. The best will be for *you*." And he wished Kate could hear him. It didn't help him moreover that he visibly, even pathetically, imaged to her by such touches his quest for comfort against discipline. He was to bury Kate's so signal snub, and also the hard law she had now laid on him, under a high intellectual effort. This at least was his crucifixion—that Milly was so interested. She was so interested that she presently asked him if he found his rooms propitious, while he felt that in just decently answering her he put on a brazen mask. He should need it quite particularly were she to express again her imagination of coming to tea with him—an extremity that he saw he was not to be spared. "We depend on you, Susie and I, you know, not to forget we're coming"—the extremity was but to face that remainder, yet it demanded all his tact. Facing their visit itself—to that, no matter what he might have to do, he would never consent, as we know, to be pushed; and this even though it might be exactly such a demonstration as would figure for him at the top of Kate's list of his proprieties. He could wonder freely enough, deep within, if Kate's view of that especial propriety had not been modified by a subsequent occurrence; but his deciding that it was quite likely not to have been had no effect on his own preference for tact. It pleased him to think of "tact" as his present prop in doubt; that glossed his predicament over, for it was of application among the sensitive and the kind. He wasn't inhuman, in fine, so long as it would serve. It had to serve now, accordingly, to help him not to sweeten Milly's hopes. He didn't want to be rude to them, but he still less wanted them to flower again in the particular connexion; so that, casting about him in his anxiety for a middle way to meet her, he put his foot, with unhappy effect, just in the wrong place. "Will it be safe for you to break into your custom of not leaving the house?"

"'Safe'—?" She had for twenty seconds an exquisite pale glare. Oh but he didn't need it, by that time, to wince; he had winced for himself as soon as he had made his mistake. He had done what, so unforgettably, she had asked him in London not to do; he had touched, all alone with her here, the supersensitive nerve of which she had warned him. He had not, since the occasion in London, touched it again till now; but he saw himself freshly warned that it was able to bear still less. So for the moment he knew as little what to do as he had ever known it in his life. He couldn't emphasise that he thought of her as dying, yet he couldn't pretend he thought of her as indifferent to precautions. Meanwhile too she had narrowed his choice. "You suppose me so awfully bad?"

He turned, in his pain, within himself; but by the time the colour had mounted to the roots of his hair he had found what he wanted. "I'll believe whatever you tell me."

"Well then, I'm splendid."

"Oh I don't need you to tell me that."

"I mean I'm capable of life."

"I've never doubted it."

"I mean," she went on, "that I want so to live—!"

"Well?" he asked while she paused with the intensity of it.

"Well, that I know I *can*."

"Whatever you do?" He shrank from solemnity about it.

"Whatever I do. If I want to."

"If you want to do it?"

"If I want to live. I *can*," Milly repeated.

He had clumsily brought it on himself, but he hesitated with all the pity of it. "Ah then that I believe."

"I will, I will," she declared; yet with the weight of it somehow turned for him to mere light and sound.

He felt himself smiling through a mist. "You simply must!"

It brought her straight again to the fact. "Well then, if you say it, why mayn't we pay you our visit?"

"Will it help you to live?"

"Every little helps," she laughed; "and it's very little for me, in general, to stay at home. Only I shan't want to miss it—!"

"Yes?"—she had dropped again.

"Well, on the day you give us a chance."

It was amazing what so brief an exchange had at this point done with him. His great scruple suddenly broke, giving way to something inordinately strange, something of a nature to become clear to him only when he had left her. "You can come," he said, "when you like."

What had taken place for him, however—the drop, almost with violence, of everything but a sense of her own reality—apparently showed in his face or his manner, and even so vividly that she could take it for something else. "I see how you feel—that I'm an awful bore about it and that, sooner than have any such upset, you'll go. So it's no matter."

"No matter? Oh!"—he quite protested now.

"If it drives you away to escape us. We want you not to go."

It was beautiful how she spoke for Mrs. Stringham. Whatever it was, at any rate, he shook his head. "I won't go."

"Then I won't go!" she brightly declared.

"You mean you won't come to me?"

"No—never now. It's over. But it's all right. I mean, apart from that," she went on, "that I won't do anything I oughtn't or that I'm not forced to."

"Oh who can ever force you?" he asked with his hand-to-mouth way, at all times, of speaking for her encouragement. "You're the least coercible of creatures."

"Because, you think, I'm so free?"

"The freest person probably now in the world. You've got everything."

"Well," she smiled, "call it so. I don't complain."

On which again, in spite of himself, it let him in. "No I know you don't complain."

As soon as he had said it he had himself heard the pity in it. His telling her she had "everything" was extravagant kind humour, whereas his knowing so tenderly that she didn't complain was terrible kind gravity. Milly felt, he could see, the difference; he might as well have praised her outright for looking death in the face. This was the way she just looked *him* again, and it was of no attenuation that she took him up more gently than ever. "It isn't a merit—when one sees one's way."

"To peace and plenty? Well, I dare say not."

"I mean to keeping what one has."

"Oh that's success. If what one has is good," Densher said at random, "it's enough to try for."

"Well, it's my limit. I'm not trying for more." To which then she added with a change: "And now about your book."

"My book—?" He had got in a moment so far from it.

"The one you're now to understand that nothing will induce either Susie or me to run the risk of spoiling."

He cast about, but he made up his mind. "I'm not doing a book."

"Not what you said?" she asked in a wonder. "You're not writing?"

He already felt relieved. "I don't know, upon my honour, what I'm doing."

It made her visibly grave; so that, disconcerted in another way, he was afraid of what she would see in it. She saw in fact exactly what he feared, but again his honour, as he called it, was saved even while she didn't know she had threatened it. Taking his words for a betrayal of the sense that he, on his side, *might* complain, what she clearly wanted was to urge on him some such patience as he should be perhaps able to arrive at with her indirect help. Still more clearly, however, she wanted to be sure of how far she might venture; and he could see her make out in a moment that she had a sort of test.

"Then if it's not for your book—?"

"What *am* I staying for?"

"I mean with your London work—with all you have to do. Isn't it rather empty for you?"

"Empty for me?" He remembered how Kate had held that she might propose marriage, and he wondered if this were the way she would naturally begin it. It would leave him, such an incident, he already felt, at a loss, and the note of his finest anxiety might have been in the vagueness of his reply. "Oh well—!"

"I ask too many questions?" She settled it for herself before he could protest. "You stay because you've got to."

He grasped at it. "I stay because I've got to." And he couldn't have said when he had uttered it if it were loyal to Kate or disloyal. It gave her, in a manner, away; it showed the tip of the ear of her plan. Yet Milly took it, he perceived, but as a plain statement of his truth. He was waiting for what Kate would have told her of—the permission from Lancaster Gate to come any nearer. To remain friends with either niece or aunt he mustn't stir without it. All this Densher read in the girl's sense of the spirit of his reply; so that it made him feel he was lying, and he had to think of something to correct that. What he thought of was, in an instant, "Isn't it enough, whatever may be one's other complications, to stay after all for *you?*"

"Oh you must judge."

He was by this time on his feet to take leave, and was also at last too restless. The speech in question at least wasn't disloyal to Kate; that was the very tone of their bargain. So was it, by being loyal, another kind of lie, the lie of the uncandid profession of a motive. He was staying so little "for" Milly that he was staying positively against her. He didn't, none the less, know, and at last, thank goodness, didn't care. The only thing he could say might make it either better or worse. "Well then, so long as I don't go, you must think of me all *as* judging!"

II

He didn't go home, on leaving her—he didn't want to; he walked instead, through his narrow ways and his *campi* with gothic arches, to a small and comparatively sequestered café where he had already more than once found refreshment and comparative repose, together with solutions that consisted mainly and pleasantly of further indecisions. It was a literal fact that those awaiting him there to-night, while he leaned back on his velvet bench with his head against a florid mirror and his eyes not looking further than the fumes of his tobacco, might have been regarded by him as a little less limp than usual. This wasn't because, before getting to his feet again, there was a step he had seen his way to; it was simply because the acceptance of his position took sharper effect from his sense of what he had just had to deal with. When half an hour before, at the palace, he had turned about to Milly on the question of the impossibility so inwardly felt, turned about on the spot and under her eyes, he had acted, by the sudden force of his seeing much further, seeing how little, how not at all, impossibilities mattered. It wasn't a case for pedantry; when people were at *her* pass everything was allowed. And her pass was now, as by the sharp click of a spring, just completely his own—to the extent, as he felt, of her deep dependence on him. Anything he should do or shouldn't would have close reference to her life, which was thus absolutely in his hands—and ought never to have reference to anything else. It was on the cards for him that he might kill her—that was the way he read the cards as he sat in his customary corner. The fear in this thought made him let everything go, kept him there actually, all motionless, for three hours on end. He renewed his consumption and smoked more cigarettes than he had ever done in the time. What had come out for him had come out, with this first intensity, as a terror; so that action itself, of any sort, the right as well as the wrong—if the difference even survived—had heard in it a vivid "Hush!" the injunction to keep from that moment intensely still. He thought in fact while his vigil lasted of several different ways for his doing so, and the hour might have served him as a lesson in going on tiptoe.

What he finally took home, when he ventured to leave the place, was the perceived truth that he might on any other system go straight to destruction. Destruction was represented for him by the idea of his really bringing to a point, on Milly's side, anything whatever. Nothing so "brought," he easily argued, but *must* be in one way or another a catastrophe. He was mixed up in her fate, or her fate, if that should be better, was mixed up in *him*, so that a single false motion might either way snap the coil. They helped him, it was true, these considerations, to a degree of eventual peace, for what they luminously amounted to was that he was to do nothing, and that fell in after all with the burden laid on him by Kate. He was only not to budge without the girl's leave—not, oddly enough at the last, to move without it, whether further or nearer, any more than without Kate's. It was to this his wisdom reduced itself—to the need again simply to be kind. That was the same as being still—as studying to create the minimum of vibration. He felt himself as he smoked shut up to a room on the wall of which something precious was too precariously hung. A false step would bring it down, and it must hang as long as possible. He was aware when he walked away again that even Fleet Street wouldn't at this juncture successfully touch him. His manager might wire that he was wanted, but he could easily be deaf to his manager. His money for the idle life might be none too much; happily, however, Venice was cheap, and it was moreover the queer fact that Milly in a manner supported him. The greatest of his expenses really was to walk to the palace to dinner. He didn't want, in short, to give that up, and he should probably be able, he felt, to stay his breath and his hand. He should be able to be still enough through everything.

He tried that for three weeks, with the sense after a little of not having failed. There had to be a delicate art in it, for he wasn't trying—quite the contrary—to be either distant or dull. That would not have been being "nice," which in its own form was the real law. That too might just have produced the vibration he desired to avert; so that he best kept everything in place by not hesitating or fearing, as it were, to let himself go—go in the direction, that is to say, of staying. It depended on where he went; which was what he meant by taking care. When one went on tiptoe one could turn off for retreat without betraying the manoeuvre. Perfect tact—the necessity for which he had from the first, as we know, happily recognised—was to keep all intercourse in the key of the absolutely settled. It was settled thus for instance that they were indissoluble good friends, and settled as well that her being the American girl was, just in time and for the relation they found themselves concerned in, a boon inappreciable. If, at least, as the days went on, she was to fall short of her prerogative of the great national, the great maidenly ease, if she didn't diviningly and responsively desire and labour to record herself as possessed of it, this wouldn't have been for want of Densher's keeping her, with his idea, well up to it—wouldn't have been in fine for want of his encouragement and reminder. He didn't perhaps in so many words speak to her of the quantity itself as of the thing she was least to intermit; but he talked of it, freely, in what he flattered himself was an impersonal way, and this held it there before her—since he was careful also to talk pleasantly. It was at once their idea, when all was said, and the most marked of their conveniences. The type was so elastic that it could be stretched to almost anything; and yet, not stretched, it kept down, remained normal, remained properly within bounds. And he *had* meanwhile, thank goodness, without being too much disconcerted, the sense, for the girl's part of the business, of the queerest conscious compliance, of her doing very much what he wanted, even though without her quite seeing why. She fairly touched this once in saying: "Oh yes, you like us to be as we are because it's a kind of facilitation to you that we don't quite measure: I think one would have to be English to measure it!"—and that too, strangely enough, without prejudice to her good nature. She might have been conceived as doing—that is of being—what he liked in order perhaps only to judge where it would take them. They really as it went on *saw* each other at the game; she knowing he tried to keep her in tune with his conception, and he knowing she thus knew it. Add that he again knew she knew, and yet that nothing was spoiled by it, and we get a fair impression of the line they found most completely workable. The strangest fact of all for us must be that the success he himself thus promoted was precisely what figured to his gratitude as the something above and beyond him, above and beyond Kate, that made for daily decency. There would scarce have been felicity—certainly too little of the right lubricant—had not the national character so invoked been, not less inscrutably than entirely, in Milly's chords. It made up her unity and was the one thing he could unlimitedly take for granted.

He did so then, daily, for twenty days, without deepened fear of the undue vibration that was keeping him watchful. He knew in his nervousness that he was living at best from day to day and from hand to mouth; yet he had succeeded, he believed, in avoiding a mistake. All women had alternatives, and Milly's would doubtless be shaky too; but the national character was firm in her, whether as all of her, practically, by this time, or but as a part; the national character that, in a woman still so young, made of the air breathed a virtual non-conductor. It wasn't till a certain occasion when the twenty days had passed that, going to the palace at tea-time, he was met by the information that the signorina padrona was not "receiving." The announcement met him, in the court, on the lips of one of the gondoliers, met him, he thought, with such a conscious eye as the knowledge of his freedoms of access, hitherto conspicuously shown, could scarce fail to beget. Densher had not been at Palazzo Leporelli among the mere receivable, but had taken his place once for all among the involved and included, so that on being so flagrantly braved he recognised after a moment the propriety of a further appeal. Neither of the two ladies, it appeared, received, and yet Pasquale was not prepared to say that either was *poco bene*. He was yet not prepared to say that either was anything, and he would have been blank, Densher mentally noted, if the term could ever apply to members of a race in whom vacancy was but a nest of darknesses—not a vain surface, but a place of withdrawal in which something obscure, something always ominous, indistinguishably lived. He felt afresh indeed at this hour the force of the veto laid within the palace on any mention, any cognition, of the liabilities of its mistress. The state of her health was never confessed to there as a reason. How much it might deeply be taken for one was another matter; of which he grew fully aware on carrying his question further. This appeal was to his friend Eugenio, whom he immediately sent for, with whom, for three rich minutes, protected from the weather, he was confronted in the gallery that led from the water-steps to the court, and whom he always called, in meditation, his friend; seeing it was so elegantly presumable he would have put an end to him if he could. That produced a relation which required a name of its own, an intimacy of consciousness in truth for each—an intimacy of eye, of ear, of general sensibility, of everything but tongue. It had been, in other words, for the five weeks, far from occult to our young man that Eugenio took a view of him not less finely formal than essentially vulgar, but which at the same time he couldn't himself raise an eyebrow to prevent. It was all in the air now again; it was as much between them as ever while Eugenio waited on him in the court.

The weather, from early morning, had turned to storm, the first sea-storm of the autumn, and Densher had almost invidiously brought him down the outer staircase—the massive ascent, the great feature of the court, to Milly's *piano nobile*. This was to pay him—it was the one chance—for all imputations; the imputation in particular that, clever, *tanto bello* and not rich, the young man from London was—by the obvious way—pressing Miss Theale's fortune hard. It was to pay him for the further ineffable intimation that a gentleman must take the young lady's most devoted servant (interested scarcely less in the high attraction) for a strangely casual appendage if he counted in such a connexion on impunity and prosperity. These interpretations were odious to Densher for the simple reason that they might have been so true of the attitude of an inferior man, and three things alone, accordingly, had kept him from righting himself. One of these was that his critic sought expression only in an impersonality, a positive inhumanity, of politeness; the second was that refinements of expression in a friend's servant were not a thing a visitor could take action on; and the third was the fact that the particular attribution of motive did him after all no wrong. It was his own fault if the vulgar view, the view that might have been taken of an inferior man, happened so incorrigibly to fit him. He apparently wasn't so different from inferior men as that came to. If therefore, in fine, Eugenio figured to him as "my friend" because he was conscious of his seeing so much of him, what he made him see on the same lines in the course of their present interview was ever so much more. Densher felt that he marked himself, no doubt, as insisting, by dissatisfaction with the gondolier's answer, on the pursuit taken for granted in him; and yet felt it only in the augmented, the exalted distance that was by this time established between them. Eugenio had of course reflected that a word to Miss Theale from such a pair of lips would cost him his place; but he could also bethink himself that, so long as the word never came—and it was, on the basis he had arranged, impossible—he enjoyed the imagination of mounting guard. He had never so mounted guard, Densher could see, as during these minutes in the damp *loggia* where the storm-gusts were strong; and there came in fact for our young man, as a result of his presence, a sudden sharp sense that everything had turned to the dismal. Something had happened—he didn't know what; and it wasn't Eugenio who would tell him. What Eugenio told him was that he thought the ladies—as if their liability had been equal—were a "leetle" fatigued, just a "leetle leetle," and without any cause named for it. It was one of the signs of what Densher felt in him that, by a profundity, a true deviltry of resource, he always met the latter's Italian with English and his English with Italian. He now, as usual, slightly smiled at him in the process—but ever so slightly this time, his manner also being attuned, our young man made out, to the thing, whatever it was, that constituted the rupture of peace.

This manner, while they stood a long minute facing each other over all they didn't say, played a part as well in the sudden jar to Densher's protected state. It was a Venice all of evil that had broken out for them alike, so that they were together in their anxiety, if they really could have met on it; a Venice of cold lashing rain from a low black sky, of wicked wind raging through narrow passes, of general arrest and interruption, with the people engaged in all the water-life huddled, stranded and wageless, bored and cynical, under archways and bridges. Our young man's mute exchange with his friend contained meanwhile such a depth of reference that, had the pressure been but slightly prolonged, they might have reached a point at which they were equally weak. Each had verily something in mind that would have made a hash of mutual suspicion and in presence of which, as a possibility, they were more united than disjoined. But it was to have been a moment for Densher that nothing could ease off—not even the formal propriety with which his interlocutor finally attended him to the *portone* and bowed upon his retreat. Nothing had passed about his coming back, and the air had made itself felt as a non-conductor of messages. Densher knew of course, as he took his way again, that Eugenio's invitation to return was not what he missed; yet he knew at the same time that what had happened to him was part of his punishment. Out in the square beyond the *fondamenta* that gave access to the land-gate of the palace, out where the wind was higher, he fairly, with the thought of it, pulled his umbrella closer down. It couldn't be, his consciousness, unseen enough by others—the base predicament of having, by a concatenation, just to *take* such things: such things as the fact that one very acute person in the world, whom he couldn't dispose of as an interested scoundrel, enjoyed an opinion of him that there was no attacking, no disproving, no (what was worst of all) even noticing. One had come to a queer pass when a servant's opinion so mattered. Eugenio's would have mattered even if, as founded on a low vision of appearances, it had been quite wrong. It was the more disagreeable accordingly that the vision of appearances was quite right, and yet was scarcely less low.

Such as it was, at any rate, Densher shook it off with the more impatience that he was independently restless. He had to walk in spite of weather, and he took his course, through crooked ways, to the Piazza, where he should have the shelter of the galleries. Here, in the high arcade, half Venice was crowded close, while, on the Molo, at the limit of the expanse, the old columns of the Saint Theodore and of the Lion were the frame of a door wide open to the storm. It was odd for him, as he moved, that it should have made such a difference—if the difference wasn't only that the palace had for the first time failed of a welcome. There was more, but it came from that; that gave the harsh note and broke the spell. The wet and the cold were now to reckon with, and it was to Densher precisely as if he had seen the obliteration, at a stroke, of the margin on a faith in which they were all living. The margin had been his name for it—for the thing that, though it had held out, could bear no shock. The shock, in some form, had come, and he wondered about it while, threading his way among loungers as vague as himself, he dropped his eyes sightlessly on the rubbish in shops. There were stretches of the gallery paved with squares of red marble, greasy now with the salt spray; and the whole place, in its huge elegance, the grace of its conception and the beauty of its detail, was more than ever like a great drawing-room, the drawing-room of Europe, profaned and bewildered by some reverse of fortune. He brushed shoulders with brown men whose hats askew, and the loose sleeves of whose pendent jackets, made them resemble melancholy maskers. The tables and chairs that overflowed from the cafés were gathered, still with a pretence of service, into the arcade, and here and there a spectacled German, with his coat-collar up, partook publicly of food and philosophy. These were impressions for Densher too, but he had made the whole circuit thrice before he stopped short, in front of Florian's, with the force of his sharpest. His eye had caught a face within the café—he had spotted an acquaintance behind the glass. The person he had thus paused long enough to look at twice was seated, well within range, at a small table on which a tumbler, half-emptied and evidently neglected, still remained; and though he had on his knee, as he leaned back, a copy of a French newspaper—the heading of the *Figaro* was visible—he stared straight before him at the little opposite rococo wall. Densher had him for a minute in profile, had him for a time during which his identity produced, however quickly, all the effect of establishing connexions—connexions startling and direct; and then, as if it were the one thing more needed, seized the look, determined by a turn of the head, that might have been a prompt result of the sense of being noticed. This wider view showed him *all* Lord Mark—Lord Mark as encountered, several weeks before, the day of the first visit of each to Palazzo Leporelli. For it had been all Lord Mark that was going out, on that occasion, as he came in—he had felt it, in the hall, at the time; and he was accordingly the less at a loss to recognise in a few seconds, as renewed meeting brought it to the surface, the same potential quantity.

It was a matter, the whole passage—it could only be—but of a few seconds; for as he might neither stand there to stare nor on the other hand make any advance from it, he had presently resumed his walk, this time to another pace. It had been for all the world, during his pause, as if he had caught his answer to the riddle of the day. Lord Mark had simply faced him—as he had faced *him*, not placed by him, not at first—as one of the damp shuffling crowd. Recognition, though hanging fire, had then clearly come; yet no light of salutation had been struck from these certainties. Acquaintance between them was scant enough for neither to take it up. That neither had done so was not, however, what now mattered, but that the gentleman at Florian's should be in the place at all. He couldn't have been in it long; Densher, as inevitably a haunter of the great meeting-ground, would in that case have seen him before. He paid short visits; he was on the wing; the question for him even as he sat there was of his train or of his boat. He had come back for something—as a sequel to his earlier visit; and whatever he had come back for it had had time to be done. He might have arrived but last night or that morning; he had already made the difference. It was a great thing for Densher to get this answer. He held it close, he hugged it, quite leaned on it as he continued to circulate. It kept him going and going—it made him no less restless. But it explained—and that was much, for with explanations he might somehow deal. The vice in the air, otherwise, was too much like the breath of fate. The weather had changed, the rain was ugly, the wind wicked, the sea impossible, *because* of Lord Mark. It was because of him, *a fortiori*, that the palace was closed. Densher went round again twice; he found the visitor each time as he had found him first. Once, that is, he was staring before him; the next time he was looking over his *Figaro*, which he had opened out. Densher didn't again stop, but left him apparently unconscious of his passage—on another repetition of which Lord Mark had disappeared. He had spent but the day; he would be off that night; he had now gone to his hotel for arrangements. These things were as plain to Densher as if he had had them in words. The obscure had cleared for him—if cleared it was; there was something he didn't see, the great thing; but he saw so round it and so close to it that this was almost as good. He had been looking at a man who had done what he had come for, and for whom, as done, it temporarily sufficed. The man had come again to see Milly, and Milly had received him. His visit would have taken place just before or just after luncheon, and it was the reason why he himself had found her door shut.

He said to himself that evening, he still said even on the morrow, that he only wanted a reason, and that with this perception of one he could now mind, as he called it, his business. His business, he had settled, as we know, was to keep thoroughly still; and he asked himself why it should prevent this that he could feel, in connexion with the crisis, so remarkably blameless. He gave the appearances before him all the benefit of being critical, so that if blame were to accrue he shouldn't feel he had dodged it. But it wasn't a bit he who, that day, had touched her, and if she was upset it wasn't a bit his act. The ability so to think about it amounted for Densher during several hours to a kind of exhilaration. The exhilaration was heightened fairly, besides, by the visible conditions—sharp, striking, ugly to him—of Lord Mark's return. His constant view of it, for all the next hours, of which there were many, was as a demonstration on the face of it sinister even to his own actual ignorance. He didn't need, for seeing it as evil, seeing it as, to a certainty, in a high degree "nasty," to know more about it than he had so easily and so wonderfully picked up. You couldn't drop on the poor girl that way without, by the fact, being brutal. Such a visit was a descent, an invasion, an aggression, constituting precisely one or other of the stupid shocks he himself had so decently sought to spare her. Densher had indeed drifted by the next morning to the reflexion—which he positively, with occasion, might have brought straight out—that the only delicate and honourable way of treating a person in such a state was to treat her as *he*, Merton Densher, did. With time, actually—for the impression but deepened—this sense of the contrast, to the advantage of Merton Densher, became a sense of relief, and that in turn a sense of escape. It was for all the world—and he drew a long breath on it—as if a special danger for him had passed. Lord Mark had, without in the least intending such a service, got it straight out of the way. It was *he*, the brute, who had stumbled into just the wrong inspiration and who had therefore produced, for the very person he had wished to hurt, an impunity that was comparative innocence, that was almost like purification. The person he had wished to hurt could only be the person so unaccountably hanging about. To keep still meanwhile was, for this person, more comprehensively, to keep it all up; and to keep it all up was, if that seemed on consideration best, not, for the day or two, to go back to the palace.

The day or two passed—stretched to three days; and with the effect, extraordinarily, that Densher felt himself in the course of them washed but the more clean. Some sign would come if his return should have the better effect; and he was at all events, in absence, without the particular scruple. It wouldn't have been meant for him by either of the women that he was to come back but to face Eugenio. That was impossible—the being again denied; for it made him practically answerable, and answerable was what he wasn't. There was no neglect either in absence, inasmuch as, from the moment he didn't get in, the one message he could send up would be some hope on the score of health. Since accordingly that sort of expression was definitely forbidden him he had only to wait—which he was actually helped to do by his feeling with the lapse of each day more and more wound up to it. The days in themselves were anything but sweet; the wind and the weather lasted, the fireless cold hinted at worse; the broken charm of the world about was broken into smaller pieces. He walked up and down his rooms and listened to the wind—listened also to tinkles of bells and watched for some servant of the palace. He might get a note, but the note never came; there were hours when he stayed at home not to miss it. When he wasn't at home he was in circulation again as he had been at the hour of his seeing Lord Mark. He strolled about the Square with the herd of refugees; he raked the approaches and the cafés on the chance the brute, as he now regularly imaged him, *might* be still there. He could only be there, he knew, to be received afresh; and that—one had but to think of it—would be indeed stiff. He had gone, however—it was proved; though Densher's care for the question either way only added to what was most acrid in the taste of his present ordeal. It all came round to what he was doing for Milly—spending days that neither relief nor escape could purge of a smack of the abject. What was it but abject for a man of his parts to be reduced to such pastimes? What was it but sordid for him, shuffling about in the rain, to have to peep into shops and to consider possible meetings? What was it but odious to find himself wondering what, as between him and another man, a possible meeting would produce? There recurred moments when in spite of everything he felt no straighter than another man. And yet even on the third day, when still nothing had come, he more than ever knew that he wouldn't have budged for the world.

He thought of the two women, in their silence, at last—he at all events thought of Milly—as probably, for her reasons, now intensely wishing him to go. The cold breath of her reasons was, with everything else, in the air; but he didn't care for them any more than for her wish itself, and he would stay in spite of her, stay in spite of odium, stay in spite perhaps of some final experience that would be, for the pain of it, all but unbearable. That would be his one way, purified though he was, to mark his virtue beyond any mistake. It would be accepting the disagreeable, and the disagreeable would be a proof; a proof of his not having stayed for the thing—the agreeable, as it were—that Kate had named. The thing Kate had named was not to have been the odium of staying in spite of hints. It was part of the odium as actual too that Kate was, for her comfort, just now well aloof. These were the first hours since her flight in which his sense of what she had done for him on the eve of that event was to incur a qualification. It was strange, it was perhaps base, to be thinking such things so soon; but one of the intimations of his solitude was that she had provided for herself. She was out of it all, by her act, as much as he was in it; and this difference grew, positively, as his own intensity increased. She had said in their last sharp snatch of talk—sharp though thickly muffled, and with every word in it final and deep, unlike even the deepest words they had ever yet spoken: "Letters? Never—*now*. Think of it. Impossible." So that as he had sufficiently caught her sense—into which he read, all the same, a strange inconsequence—they had practically wrapped their understanding in the breach of their correspondence. He had moreover, on losing her, done justice to her law of silence; for there was doubtless a finer delicacy in his not writing to her than in his writing as he must have written had he spoken of themselves. That would have been a turbid strain, and her idea had been to be noble; which, in a degree, was a manner. Only it left her, for the pinch, comparatively at ease. And it left *him*, in the conditions, peculiarly alone. He was alone, that is, till, on the afternoon of his third day, in gathering dusk and renewed rain, with his shabby rooms looking doubtless, in their confirmed dreariness, for the mere eyes of others, at their worst, the grinning padrona threw open the door and introduced Mrs. Stringham. That made at a bound a difference, especially when he saw that his visitor was weighted. It appeared part of her weight that she was in a wet waterproof, that she allowed her umbrella to be taken from her by the good woman without consciousness or care, and that her face, under her veil, richly rosy with the driving wind, was—and the veil too—as splashed as if the rain were her tears.

III

They came to it almost immediately; he was to wonder afterwards at the fewness of their steps. "She has turned her face to the wall."

"You mean she's worse?"

The poor lady stood there as she had stopped; Densher had, in the instant flare of his eagerness, his curiosity, all responsive at sight of her, waved away, on the spot, the padrona, who had offered to relieve her of her mackintosh. She looked vaguely about through her wet veil, intensely alive now to the step she had taken and wishing it not to have been in the dark, but clearly, as yet, seeing nothing. "I don't know *how* she is—and it's why I've come to you."

"I'm glad enough you've come," he said, "and it's quite—you make me feel—as if I had been wretchedly waiting for you."

She showed him again her blurred eyes—she had caught at his word. "Have you been wretched?"

Now, however, on his lips, the word expired. It would have sounded for him like a complaint, and before something he already made out in his visitor he knew his own trouble as small. Hers, under her damp draperies, which shamed his lack of a fire, was great, and he felt she had brought it all with her. He answered that he had been patient and above all that he had been still. "As still as a mouse—you'll have seen it for yourself. Stiller, for three days together, than I've ever been in my life. It has seemed to me the only thing."

This qualification of it as a policy or a remedy was straightway for his friend, he saw, a light that her own light could answer. "It has been best. I've wondered for you. But it has been best," she said again.

"Yet it has done no good?"

"I don't know. I've been afraid you were gone." Then as he gave a headshake which, though slow, was deeply mature: "You *won't* go?"

"Is to 'go,'" he asked, "to be still?"

"Oh I mean if you'll stay for me."

"I'll do anything for you. Isn't it for you alone now I can?"

She thought of it, and he could see even more of the relief she was taking from him. His presence, his face, his voice, the old rooms themselves, so meagre yet so charged, where Kate had admirably been to him—these things counted for her, now she had them, as the help she had been wanting: so that she still only stood there taking them all in. With it however popped up characteristically a throb of her conscience. What she thus tasted was almost a personal joy. It told Densher of the three days she on her side had spent. "Well, anything you do for me—*is* for her too. Only, only—!"

"Only nothing now matters?"

She looked at him a minute as if he were the fact itself that he expressed. "Then you know?"

"Is she dying?" he asked for all answer.

Mrs. Stringham waited—her face seemed to sound him. Then her own reply was strange. "She hasn't so much as named you. We haven't spoken."

"Not for three days?"

"No more," she simply went on, "than if it were all over. Not even by the faintest allusion."

"Oh," said Densher with more light, "you mean you haven't spoken about *me?*"

"About what else? No more than if you were dead."

"Well," he answered after a moment, "I *am* dead."

"Then I am," said Susan Shepherd with a drop of her arms on her waterproof.

It was a tone that, for the minute, imposed itself in its dry despair; it represented, in the bleak place, which had no life of its own, none but the life Kate had left—the sense of which, for that matter, by mystic channels, might fairly be reaching the visitor—the very impotence of their extinction. And Densher had nothing to oppose it withal, nothing but again: "Is she dying?"

It made her, however, as if these were crudities, almost material pangs, only say as before: "Then you know?"

"Yes," he at last returned, "I know. But the marvel to me is that *you* do. I've no right in fact to imagine or to assume that you do."

"You may," said Susan Shepherd, "all the same. I know."

"Everything?"

Her eyes, through her veil, kept pressing him. "No—not everything. That's why I've come."

"That I shall really tell you?" With which, as she hesitated and it affected him, he brought out in a groan a doubting "Oh, oh!" It turned him from her to the place itself, which was a part of what was in him, was the abode, the worn shrine more than ever, of the fact in possession, the fact, now a thick association, for which he had hired it. *That* was not for telling, but Susan Shepherd was, none the less, so decidedly wonderful that the sense of it might really have begun, by an effect already operating, to be a part of her knowledge. He saw, and it stirred him, that she hadn't come to judge him; had come rather, so far as she might dare, to pity. This showed him her own abasement—that, at any rate, of grief; and made him feel with a rush of friendliness that he liked to be with her. The rush had quickened when she met his groan with an attenuation.

"We shall at all events—if that's anything—be together."

It was his own good impulse in herself. "It's what I've ventured to feel. It's much." She replied in effect, silently, that it was whatever he liked; on which, so far as he had been afraid for anything, he knew his fear had dropped. The comfort was huge, for it gave back to him something precious, over which, in the effort of recovery, his own hand had too imperfectly closed. Kate, he remembered, had said to him, with her sole and single boldness—and also on grounds he hadn't then measured—that Mrs. Stringham was a person who *wouldn't*, at a pinch, in a stretch of confidence, wince. It was but another of the cases in which Kate was always showing. "You don't think then very horridly of me?"

And her answer was the more valuable that it came without nervous effusion—quite as if she understood what he might conceivably have believed. She turned over in fact what she thought, and that was what helped him. "Oh you've been extraordinary!"

It made him aware the next moment of how they had been planted there. She took off her cloak with his aid, though when she had also, accepting a seat, removed her veil, he recognised in her personal ravage that the words she had just uttered to him were the one flower she had to throw. They were all her consolation for him, and the consolation even still depended on the event. She sat with him at any rate in the grey clearance, as sad as a winter dawn, made by their meeting. The image she again evoked for him loomed in it but the larger. "She has turned her face to the wall."

He saw with the last vividness, and it was as if, in their silences, they were simply so leaving what he saw. "She doesn't speak at all? I don't mean not of me."

"Of nothing—of no one." And she went on, Susan Shepherd, giving it out as she had had to take it. "She doesn't *want* to die. Think of her age. Think of her goodness. Think of her beauty. Think of all she is. Think of all she *has*. She lies there stiffening herself and clinging to it all. So I thank God—!" the poor lady wound up with a wan inconsequence.

He wondered. "You thank God—?"

"That she's so quiet."

He continued to wonder. "*Is* she so quiet?"

"She's more than quiet. She's grim. It's what she has never been. So you see—all these days. I can't tell you—but it's better so. It would kill me if she *were* to tell me."

"To tell you?" He was still at a loss.

"How she feels. How she clings. How she doesn't want it."

"How she doesn't want to die? Of course she doesn't want it." He had a long pause, and they might have been thinking together of what they could even now do to prevent it. This, however, was not what he brought out. Milly's "grimness" and the great hushed palace were present to him; present with the little woman before him as she must have been waiting there and listening. "Only, what harm have *you* done her?"

Mrs. Stringham looked about in her darkness. "I don't know. I come and talk of her here with you."

It made him again hesitate. "Does she utterly hate me?"

"I don't know. How *can* I? No one ever will."

"She'll never tell?"

"She'll never tell."

Once more he thought. "She must be magnificent."

"She *is* magnificent."

His friend, after all, helped him, and he turned it, so far as he could, all over. "Would she see me again?"

It made his companion stare. "Should you like to see her?"

"You mean as you describe her?" He felt her surprise, and it took him some time. "No."

"Ah then!" Mrs. Stringham sighed.

"But if she could bear it I'd do anything."

She had for the moment her vision of this, but it collapsed. "I don't see what you can do."

"I don't either. But *she* might."

Mrs. Stringham continued to think. "It's too late."

"Too late for her to see—?"

"Too late."

The very decision of her despair—it was after all so lucid—kindled in him a heat. "But the doctor, all the while—?"

"Tacchini? Oh he's kind. He comes. He's proud of having been approved and coached by a great London man. He hardly in fact goes away; so that I scarce know what becomes of his other patients. He thinks her, justly enough, a great personage; he treats her like royalty; he's waiting on events. But she has barely consented to see him, and, though she has told him, generously—for she *thinks* of me, dear creature—that he may come, that he may stay, for my sake, he spends most of his time only hovering at her door, prowling through the rooms, trying to entertain me, in that ghastly saloon, with the gossip of Venice, and meeting me, in doorways, in the sala, on the staircase, with an agreeable intolerable smile. We don't," said Susan Shepherd, "talk of her."

"By her request?"

"Absolutely. I don't do what she doesn't wish. We talk of the price of provisions."

"By her request too?"

"Absolutely. She named it to me as a subject when she said, the first time, that if it would be any comfort to me he might stay as much as we liked."

Densher took it all in. "But he isn't any comfort to you!"

"None whatever. That, however," she added, "isn't his fault. Nothing's any comfort."

"Certainly," Densher observed, "as I but too horribly feel, *I'm* not."

"No. But I didn't come for that."

"You came for *me*."

"Well then call it that." But she looked at him a moment with eyes filled full, and something came up in her the next instant from deeper still. "I came at bottom of course—"

"You came at bottom of course for our friend herself. But if it's, as you say, too late for me to do anything?"

She continued to look at him, and with an irritation, which he saw grow in her, from the truth itself. "So I did say. But, with you here"—and she turned her vision again strangely about her—"with you here, and with everything, I feel we mustn't abandon her."

"God forbid we should abandon her."

"Then you *won't?*" His tone had made her flush again.

"How do you mean I 'won't,' if she abandons *me?* What can I do if she won't see me?"

"But you said just now you wouldn't like it."

"I said I shouldn't like it in the light of what you tell me. I shouldn't like it only to see her as you make me. I should like it if I could help her. But even then," Densher pursued without faith, "she would have to want it first herself. And there," he continued to make out, "is the devil of it. She *won't* want it herself. She *can't!*"

He had got up in his impatience of it, and she watched him while he helplessly moved. "There's one thing you can do. There's only that, and even for that there are difficulties. But there *is* that." He stood before her with his hands in his pockets, and he had soon enough, from her eyes, seen what was coming. She paused as if waiting for his leave to utter it, and as he only let her wait they heard in the silence, on the Canal, the renewed downpour of rain. She had at last to speak, but, as if still with her fear, she only half-spoke. "I think you really know yourself what it is."

He did know what it was, and with it even, as she said—rather!—there were difficulties. He turned away on them, on everything, for a moment; he moved to the other window and looked at the sheeted channel, wider, like a river, where the houses opposite, blurred and belittled, stood at twice their distance. Mrs. Stringham said nothing, was as mute in fact, for the minute, as if she had "had" him, and he was the first again to speak. When he did so, however, it was not in straight answer to her last remark—he only started from that. He said, as he came back to her, "Let me, you know, *see*—one must understand," almost as if he had for the time accepted it. And what he wished to understand was where, on the essence of the question, was the voice of Sir Luke Strett. If they talked of not giving her up shouldn't *he* be the one least of all to do it? "Aren't we, at the worst, in the dark without him?"

"Oh," said Mrs. Stringham, "it's he who has kept me going. I wired the first night, and he answered like an angel. He'll come like one. Only he can't arrive, at the nearest, till Thursday afternoon."

"Well then that's something."

She considered. "Something—yes. She likes him."

"Rather! I can see it still, the face with which, when he was here in October—that night when she was in white, when she had people there and those musicians—she committed him to my care. It was beautiful for both of us—she put us in relation. She asked me, for the time, to take him about; I did so, and we quite hit it off. That proved," Densher said with a quick sad smile, "that she liked him."

"He liked *you*," Susan Shepherd presently risked.

"Ah I know nothing about that."

"You ought to then. He went with you to galleries and churches; you saved his time for him, showed him the choicest things, and you perhaps will remember telling me myself that if he hadn't been a great surgeon he might really have been a great judge. I mean of the beautiful."

"Well," the young man admitted, "that's what he is—in having judged *her*. He hasn't," he went on, "judged her for nothing. His interest in her—which we must make the most of—can only be supremely beneficent."

He still roamed, while he spoke, with his hands in his pockets, and she saw him, on this, as her eyes sufficiently betrayed, trying to keep his distance from the recognition he had a few moments before partly confessed to. "I'm glad," she dropped, "you like him!"

There was something for him in the sound of it. "Well, I do no more, dear lady, than you do yourself. Surely *you* like him. Surely, when he was here, we all liked him."

"Yes, but I seem to feel I know what he thinks. And I should think, with all the time you spent with him, you'd know it," she said, "yourself."

Densher stopped short, though at first without a word. "We never spoke of her. Neither of us mentioned her, even to sound her name, and nothing whatever in connexion with her passed between us."

Mrs. Stringham stared up at him, surprised at this picture. But she had plainly an idea that after an instant resisted it. "That was his professional propriety."

"Precisely. But it was also my sense of that virtue in him, and it was something more besides." And he spoke with sudden intensity. "I couldn't *talk* to him about her!"

"Oh!" said Susan Shepherd.

"I can't talk to any one about her."

"Except to *me*," his friend continued.

"Except to you." The ghost of her smile, a gleam of significance, had waited on her words, and it kept him, for honesty, looking at her. For honesty too—that is for his own words—he had quickly coloured: he was sinking so, at a stroke, the burden of his discourse with Kate. His visitor, for the minute, while their eyes met, might have been watching him hold it down. And he *had* to hold it down—the effort of which, precisely, made him red. He couldn't let it come up; at least not yet. She might make what she would of it. He attempted to repeat his statement, but he really modified it. "Sir Luke, at all events, had nothing to tell me, and I had nothing to tell him. Make-believe talk was impossible for us, and—"

"And *real*"—she had taken him right up with a huge emphasis—"was more impossible still." No doubt—he didn't deny it; and she had straightway drawn her conclusion. "Then that proves what I say—that there were immensities between you. Otherwise you'd have chattered."

"I dare say," Densher granted, "we were both thinking of her."

"You were neither of you thinking of any one else. That's why you kept together."

Well, that too, if she desired, he took from her; but he came straight back to what he had originally said. "I haven't a notion, all the same, of what he thinks." She faced him, visibly, with the question into which he had already observed that her special shade of earnestness was perpetually flowering, right and left—"Are you *very* sure?"—and he could only note her apparent difference from himself. "You, I judge, believe that he thinks she's gone."

She took it, but she bore up. "It doesn't matter what I believe."

"Well, we shall see"—and he felt almost basely superficial. More and more, for the last five minutes, had he known she had brought something with her, and never in respect to anything had he had such a wish to postpone. He would have liked to put everything off till Thursday; he was sorry it was now Tuesday; he wondered if he were afraid. Yet it wasn't of Sir Luke, who was coming; nor of Milly, who was dying; nor of Mrs. Stringham, who was sitting there. It wasn't, strange to say, of Kate either, for Kate's presence affected him suddenly as having swooned or trembled away. Susan Shepherd's, thus prolonged, had cast on it some influence under which it had ceased to act. She was as absent to his sensibility as she had constantly been, since her departure, absent, as an echo or a reference, from the palace; and it was the first time, among the objects now surrounding him, that his sensibility so noted her. He knew soon enough that it was of himself he was afraid, and that even, if he didn't take care, he should infallibly be more so. "Meanwhile," he added for his companion, "it has been everything for me to see you." She slowly rose at the words, which might almost have conveyed to her the hint of his taking care. She stood there as if she had in fact seen him abruptly moved to dismiss her. But the abruptness would have been in this case so marked as fairly to offer ground for insistence to her imagination of his state. It would take her moreover, she clearly showed him she was thinking, but a minute or two to insist. Besides, she had already said it. "Will you do it if *he* asks you? I mean if Sir Luke himself puts it to you. And will you give him"—oh she was earnest now!—"the opportunity to put it to you?"

"The opportunity to put what?"

"That if you deny it to her, that may still do something."

Densher felt himself—as had already once befallen him in the quarter of an hour—turn red to the top of his forehead. Turning red had, however, for him, as a sign of shame, been, so to speak, discounted: his consciousness of it at the present moment was rather as a sign of his fear. It showed him sharply enough of what he was afraid. "If I deny what to her?"

Hesitation, on the demand, revived in her, for hadn't he all along been letting her see that he knew? "Why, what Lord Mark told her."

"And what did Lord Mark tell her?"

Mrs. Stringham had a look of bewilderment—of seeing him as suddenly perverse. "I've been judging that you yourself know." And it was she who now blushed deep.

It quickened his pity for her, but he was beset too by other things. "Then *you* know—"

"Of his dreadful visit?" She stared. "Why it's what has done it."

"Yes—I understand that. But you also know—"

He had faltered again, but all she knew she now wanted to say. "I'm speaking," she said soothingly, "of what he told her. It's *that* that I've taken you as knowing."

"Oh!" he sounded in spite of himself.

It appeared to have for her, he saw the next moment, the quality of relief, as if he had supposed her thinking of something else. Thereupon, straightway, that lightened it. "Oh you thought I've known it for *true!*"

Her light had heightened her flush, and he saw that he had betrayed himself. Not, however, that it mattered, as he immediately saw still better. There it was now, all of it at last, and this at least there was no postponing. They were left with her idea—the one she was wishing to make him recognise. He had expressed ten minutes before his need to understand, and she was acting after all but on that. Only what he was to understand was no small matter; it might be larger even than as yet appeared.

He took again one of his turns, not meeting what she had last said; he mooned a minute, as he would have called it, at a window; and of course she could see that she had driven him to the wall. She did clearly, without delay, see it; on which her sense of having "caught" him became as promptly a scruple, which she spoke as if not to press. "What I mean is that he told her you've been all the while engaged to Miss Croy."

He gave a jerk round; it was almost—to hear it—the touch of a lash; and he said—idiotically, as he afterwards knew—the first thing that came into his head. "All *what* while?"

"Oh it's not I who say it." She spoke in gentleness. "I only repeat to you what he told her."

Densher, from whom an impatience had escaped, had already caught himself up. "Pardon my brutality. Of course I know what you're talking about. I saw him, toward the evening," he further explained, "in the Piazza; only just saw him—through the glass at Florian's—without any words. In fact I scarcely know him—there wouldn't have been occasion. It was but once, moreover—he must have gone that night. But I knew he wouldn't have come for nothing, and I turned it over—what he would have come for."

Oh so had Mrs. Stringham. "He came for exasperation."

Densher approved. "He came to let her know that he knows better than she for whom it was she had a couple of months before, in her fool's paradise, refused him."

"How you *do* know!"—and Mrs. Stringham almost smiled.

"I know that—but I don't know the good it does him."

"The good, he thinks, if he has patience—not too much—may be to come. He doesn't know what he has done to her. Only *we*, you see, do that."

He saw, but he wondered. "She kept from him—what she felt?"

"She was able—I'm sure of it—not to show anything. He dealt her his blow, and she took it without a sign." Mrs. Stringham, it was plain, spoke by book, and it brought into play again her appreciation of what she related. "She's magnificent."

Densher again gravely assented. "Magnificent!"

"And *he*," she went on, "is an idiot of idiots."

"An idiot of idiots." For a moment, on it all, on the stupid doom in it, they looked at each other. "Yet he's thought so awfully clever."

"So awfully—it's Maud Lowder's own view. And he was nice, in London," said Mrs. Stringham, "to *me*. One could almost pity him—he has had such a good conscience."

"That's exactly the inevitable ass."

"Yes, but it wasn't—I could see from the only few things she first told me—that he meant *her* the least harm. He intended none whatever."

"That's always the ass at his worst," Densher returned. "He only of course meant harm to me."

"And good to himself—he thought that would come. He had been unable to swallow," Mrs. Stringham pursued, "what had happened on his other visit. He had been then too sharply humiliated."

"Oh I saw that."

"Yes, and he also saw you. He saw you received, as it were, while he was turned away."

"Perfectly," Densher said—"I've filled it out. And also that he has known meanwhile for *what* I was then received. For a stay of all these weeks. He had had it to think of."

"Precisely—it was more than he could bear. But he has it," said Mrs. Stringham, "to think of still."

"Only, after all," asked Densher, who himself somehow, at this point, was having more to think of even than he had yet had—"only, after all, how has he happened to know? That is, to know enough."

"What do you call enough?" Mrs. Stringham enquired.

"He can only have acted—it would have been his sole safety—from full knowledge."

He had gone on without heeding her question; but, face to face as they were, something had none the less passed between them. It was this that, after an instant, made her again interrogative. "What do you mean by full knowledge?"

Densher met it indirectly. "Where has he been since October?"

"I think he has been back to England. He came in fact, I've reason to believe, straight from there."

"Straight to do this job? All the way for his half-hour?"

"Well, to try again—with the help perhaps of a new fact. To make himself possibly right with her—a different attempt from the other. He had at any rate something to tell her, and he didn't know his opportunity would reduce itself to half an hour. Or perhaps indeed half an hour would be just what was most effective. It *has* been!" said Susan Shepherd.

Her companion took it in, understanding but too well; yet as she lighted the matter for him more, really, than his own courage had quite dared—putting the absent dots on several i's—he saw new questions swarm. They had been till now in a bunch, entangled and confused; and they fell apart, each showing for itself. The first he put to her was at any rate abrupt. "Have you heard of late from Mrs. Lowder."

"Oh yes, two or three times. She depends naturally upon news of Milly."

He hesitated. "And does she depend, naturally, upon news of *me?*"

His friend matched for an instant his deliberation.

"I've given her none that hasn't been decently good. This will have been the first."

"'This'?" Densher was thinking.

"Lord Mark's having been here, and her being as she is."

He thought a moment longer. "What has Mrs. Lowder written about him? Has she written that he has been with them?"

"She has mentioned him but once—it was in her letter before the last. Then she said something."

"And what did she say?"

Mrs. Stringham produced it with an effort. "Well it was in reference to Miss Croy. That she thought Kate was thinking of him. Or perhaps I should say rather that he was thinking of *her*—only it seemed this time to have struck Maud that he was seeing the way more open to him."

Densher listened with his eyes on the ground, but he presently raised them to speak, and there was that in his face which proved him aware of a queerness in his question. "Does she mean he has been encouraged to *propose* to her niece?"

"I don't know what she means."

"Of course not"—he recovered himself; "and I oughtn't to seem to trouble you to piece together what I can't piece myself. Only I 'guess,'" he added, "I *can* piece it."

She spoke a little timidly, but she risked it. "I dare say I can piece it too."

It was one of the things in her—and his conscious face took it from her as such—that from the moment of her coming in had seemed to mark for him, as to what concerned him, the long jump of her perception. They had parted four days earlier with many things, between them, deep down. But these things were now on their troubled surface, and it wasn't he who had brought them so quickly up. Women were wonderful—at least this one was. But so, not less, was Milly, was Aunt Maud; so, most of all, was his very Kate. Well, he already knew what he had been feeling about the circle of petticoats. They were all *such* petticoats! It was just the fineness of his tangle. The sense of that, in its turn, for us too, might have been not unconnected with his putting to his visitor a question that quite passed over her remark. "Has Miss Croy meanwhile written to our friend?"

"Oh," Mrs. Stringham amended, "*her* friend also. But not a single word that I know of."

He had taken it for certain she hadn't—the thing being after all but a shade more strange than his having himself, with Milly, never for six weeks mentioned the young lady in question. It was for that matter but a shade more strange than Milly's not having mentioned her. In spite of which, and however inconsequently, he blushed anew for Kate's silence. He got away from it in fact as quickly as possible, and the furthest he could get was by reverting for a minute to the man they had been judging. "How did he manage to get *at* her? She had only—with what had passed between them before—to say she couldn't see him."

"Oh she was disposed to kindness. She was easier," the good lady explained with a slight embarrassment, "than at the other time."

"Easier?"

"She was off her guard. There was a difference."

"Yes. But exactly not *the* difference."

"Exactly not the difference of her having to be harsh. Perfectly. She could afford to be the opposite." With which, as he said nothing, she just impatiently completed her sense. "She had had *you* here for six weeks."

"Oh!" Densher softly groaned.

"Besides, I think he must have written her first—written I mean in a tone to smooth his way. That it would be a kindness to himself. Then on the spot—"

"On the spot," Densher broke in, "he unmasked? The horrid little beast!"

It made Susan Shepherd turn slightly pale, though quickening, as for hope, the intensity of her look at him. "Oh he went off without an alarm."

"And he must have gone off also without a hope."

"Ah that, certainly."

"Then it *was* mere base revenge. Hasn't he known her, into the bargain," the young man asked—"didn't he, weeks before, see her, judge her, feel her, as having for such a suit as his not more perhaps than a few months to live?"

Mrs. Stringham at first, for reply, but looked at him in silence; and it gave more force to what she then remarkably added. "He has doubtless been aware of what you speak of, just as you have yourself been aware."

"He has wanted her, you mean, just *because*—?"

"Just because," said Susan Shepherd.

"The hound!" Merton Densher brought out. He moved off, however, with a hot face, as soon as he had spoken, conscious again of an intention in his visitor's reserve. Dusk was now deeper, and after he had once more taken counsel of the dreariness without he turned to his companion. "Shall we have lights—a lamp or the candles?"

"Not for me."

"Nothing?"

"Not for me."

He waited at the window another moment and then faced his friend with a thought. "He *will* have proposed to Miss Croy. That's what has happened."

Her reserve continued. "It's you who must judge."

"Well, I do judge. Mrs. Lowder will have done so too—only *she*, poor lady, wrong. Miss Croy's refusal of him will have struck him"—Densher continued to make it out—"as a phenomenon requiring a reason."

"And you've been clear to him *as* the reason?"

"Not too clear—since I'm sticking here and since that has been a fact to make his descent on Miss Theale relevant. But clear enough. He has believed," said Densher bravely, "that I may have been a reason at Lancaster Gate, and yet at the same time have been up to something in Venice."

Mrs. Stringham took her courage from his own. "'Up to' something? Up to what?"

"God knows. To some 'game,' as they say. To some deviltry. To some duplicity."

"Which of course," Mrs. Stringham observed, "is a monstrous supposition." Her companion, after a stiff minute—sensibly long for each—fell away from her again, and then added to it another minute, which he spent once more looking out with his hands in his pockets. This was no answer, he perfectly knew, to what she had dropped, and it even seemed to state for his own ears that no answer was possible. She left him to himself, and he was glad she had declined, for their further colloquy, the advantage of lights. These would have been an advantage mainly to herself. Yet she got her benefit too even from the absence of them. It came out in her very tone when at last she addressed him—so differently, for confidence—in words she had already used. "If Sir Luke himself asks it of you as something you can do for *him*, will you deny to Milly herself what she has been made so dreadfully to believe?"

Oh how he knew he hung back! But at last he said: "You're absolutely certain then that she does believe it?"

"Certain?" She appealed to their whole situation. "Judge!"

He took his time again to judge. "Do *you* believe it?"

He was conscious that his own appeal pressed her hard; it eased him a little that her answer must be a pain to her discretion. She answered none the less, and he was truly the harder pressed. "What I believe will inevitably depend more or less on your action. You can perfectly settle it—if you care. I promise to believe you down to the ground if, to save her life, you consent to a denial."

"But a denial, when it comes to that—confound the whole thing, don't you see!—of exactly what?"

It was as if he were hoping she would narrow; but in fact she enlarged. "Of everything."

Everything had never even yet seemed to him so incalculably much. "Oh!" he simply moaned into the gloom.

IV

The near Thursday, coming nearer and bringing Sir Luke Strett, brought also blessedly an abatement of other rigours. The weather changed, the stubborn storm yielded, and the autumn sunshine, baffled for many days, but now hot and almost vindictive, came into its own again and, with an almost audible paean, a suffusion of bright sound that was one with the bright colour, took large possession. Venice glowed and plashed and called and chimed again; the air was like a clap of hands, and the scattered pinks, yellows, blues, sea-greens, were like a hanging-out of vivid stuffs, a laying-down of fine carpets. Densher rejoiced in this on the occasion of his going to the station to meet the great doctor. He went after consideration, which, as he was constantly aware, was at present his imposed, his only, way of doing anything. That was where the event had landed him—where no event in his life had landed him before. He had thought, no doubt, from the day he was born, much more than he had acted; except indeed that he remembered thoughts—a few of them—which at the moment of their coming to him had thrilled him almost like adventures. But anything like his actual state he had not, as to the prohibition of impulse, accident, range—the prohibition in other words of freedom—hitherto known. The great oddity was that if he had felt his arrival, so few weeks back, especially as an adventure, nothing could now less resemble one than the fact of his staying. It would be an adventure to break away, to depart, to go back, above all, to London, and tell Kate Croy he had done so; but there was something of the merely, the almost meanly, obliged and involved sort in his going on as he was. That was the effect in particular of Mrs. Stringham's visit, which had left him as with such a taste in his mouth of what he couldn't do. It had made this quantity clear to him, and yet had deprived him of the sense, the other sense, of what, for a refuge, he possibly *could*.

It was but a small make-believe of freedom, he knew, to go to the station for Sir Luke. Nothing equally free, at all events, had he yet turned over so long. What then was his odious position but that again and again he was afraid? He stiffened himself under this consciousness as if it had been a tax levied by a tyrant. He hadn't at any time proposed to himself to live long enough for fear to preponderate in his life. Such was simply the advantage it had actually got of him. He was afraid for instance that an advance to his distinguished friend might prove for him somehow a pledge or a committal. He was afraid of it as a current that would draw him too far; yet he thought with an equal aversion of being shabby, being poor, through fear. What finally prevailed with him was the reflexion that, whatever might happen, the great man had, after that occasion at the palace, their young woman's brief sacrifice to society—and the hour of Mrs. Stringham's appeal had brought it well to the surface—shown him marked benevolence. Mrs. Stringham's comments on the relation in which Milly had placed them made him—it was unmistakeable—feel things he perhaps hadn't felt. It was in the spirit of seeking a chance to feel again adequately whatever it was he had missed—it was, no doubt, in that spirit, so far as it went a stroke for freedom, that Densher, arriving betimes, paced the platform before the train came in. Only, after it had come and he had presented himself at the door of Sir Luke's compartment with everything that followed—only, as the situation developed, the sense of an anti-climax to so many intensities deprived his apprehensions and hesitations even of the scant dignity they might claim. He could scarce have said if the visitor's manner less showed the remembrance that might have suggested expectation, or made shorter work of surprise in presence of the fact.

Sir Luke had clean forgotten—so Densher read—the rather remarkable young man he had formerly gone about with, though he picked him up again, on the spot, with one large quiet look. The young man felt himself so picked, and the thing immediately affected him as the proof of a splendid economy. Opposed to all the waste with which he was now connected the exhibition was of a nature quite nobly to admonish him. The eminent pilgrim, in the train, all the way, had used the hours as he needed, thinking not a moment in advance of what finally awaited him. An exquisite case awaited him—of which, in this queer way, the remarkable young man was an outlying part; but the single motion of his face, the motion into which Densher, from the platform, lightly stirred its stillness, was his first renewed cognition. If, however, he had suppressed the matter by leaving Victoria he would at once suppress now, in turn, whatever else suited. The perception of this became as a symbol of the whole pitch, so far as one might one's self be concerned, of his visit. One saw, our friend further meditated, everything that, in contact, he appeared to accept—if only, for much, not to trouble to sink it: what one missed was the inward use he made of it. Densher began wondering, at the great water-steps outside, what use he would make of the anomaly of their having there to separate. Eugenio had been on the platform, in the respectful rear, and the gondola from the palace, under his direction, bestirred itself, with its attaching mixture of alacrity and dignity, on their coming out of the station together. Densher didn't at all mind now that, he himself of necessity refusing a seat on the deep black cushions beside the guest of the palace, he had Milly's three emissaries for spectators; and this susceptibility, he also knew, it was something to have left behind. All he did was to smile down vaguely from the steps—they could see him, the donkeys, as shut out as they would. "I don't," he said with a sad headshake, "go there now."

"Oh!" Sir Luke Strett returned, and made no more of it; so that the thing was splendid, Densher fairly thought, as an inscrutability quite inevitable and unconscious. His friend appeared not even to make of it that he supposed it might be for respect to the crisis. He didn't moreover afterwards make much more of anything—after the classic craft, that is, obeying in the main Pasquale's inimitable stroke from the poop, had performed the manoeuvre by which it presented, receding, a back, so to speak, rendered positively graceful by the high black hump of its *felze*. Densher watched the gondola out of sight—he heard Pasquale's cry, borne to him across the water, for the sharp firm swerve into a side-canal, a short cut to the palace. He had no gondola of his own; it was his habit never to take one; and he humbly—as in Venice it *is* humble—walked away, though not without having for some time longer stood as if fixed where the guest of the palace had left him. It was strange enough, but he found himself as never yet, and as he couldn't have reckoned, in presence of the truth that was the truest about Milly. He couldn't have reckoned on the force of the difference instantly made—for it was all in the air as he heard Pasquale's cry and saw the boat disappear—by the mere visibility, on the spot, of the personage summoned to her aid. He hadn't only never been near the facts of her condition—which counted so as a blessing for him; he hadn't only, with all the world, hovered outside an impenetrable ring fence, within which there reigned a kind of expensive vagueness made up of smiles and silences and beautiful fictions and priceless arrangements, all strained to breaking; but he had also, with every one else, as he now felt, actively fostered suppressions which were in the direct interest of every one's good manner, every one's pity, every one's really quite generous ideal. It was a conspiracy of silence, as the *cliché* went, to which no one had made an exception, the great smudge of mortality across the picture, the shadow of pain and horror, finding in no quarter a surface of spirit or of speech that consented to reflect it. "The mere aesthetic instinct of mankind—!" our young man had more than once, in the connexion, said to himself; letting the rest of the proposition drop, but touching again thus sufficiently on the outrage even to taste involved in one's having to *see*. So then it had been—a general conscious fool's paradise, from which the specified had been chased like a dangerous animal. What therefore had at present befallen was that the specified, standing all the while at the gate, had now crossed the threshold as in Sir Luke Strett's person and quite on such a scale as to fill out the whole precinct. Densher's nerves, absolutely his heart-beats too, had measured the change before he on this occasion moved away.

The facts of physical suffering, of incurable pain, of the chance grimly narrowed, had been made, at a stroke, intense, and this was to be the way he was now to feel them. The clearance of the air, in short, making vision not only possible but inevitable, the one thing left to be thankful for was the breadth of Sir Luke's shoulders, which, should one be able to keep in line with them, might in some degree interpose. It was, however, far from plain to Densher for the first day or two that he was again to see his distinguished friend at all. That he couldn't, on any basis actually serving, return to the palace—this was as solid to him, every whit, as the other feature of his case, the fact of the publicity attaching to his proscription through his not having taken himself off. He had been seen often enough in the Leporelli gondola. As, accordingly, he was not on any presumption destined to meet Sir Luke about the town, where the latter would have neither time nor taste to lounge, nothing more would occur between them unless the great man should surprisingly wait upon him. His doing that, Densher further reflected, wouldn't even simply depend on Mrs. Stringham's having decided to—as they might say—turn him on. It would depend as well—for there would be practically some difference to her—on her actually attempting it; and it would depend above all on what Sir Luke would make of such an overture. Densher had for that matter his own view of the amount, to say nothing of the particular sort, of response it might expect from him. He had his own view of the ability of such a personage even to understand such an appeal. To what extent could he be prepared, and what importance in fine could he attach? Densher asked himself these questions, in truth, to put his own position at the worst. He should miss the great man completely unless the great man should come to see him, and the great man could only come to see him for a purpose unsupposable. Therefore he wouldn't come at all, and consequently there was nothing to hope.

It wasn't in the least that Densher invoked this violence to all probability; but it pressed on him that there were few possible diversions he could afford now to miss. Nothing in his predicament was so odd as that, incontestably afraid of himself, he was not afraid of Sir Luke. He had an impression, which he clung to, based on a previous taste of the visitor's company, that *he* would somehow let him off. The truth about Milly perched on his shoulders and sounded in his tread, became by the fact of his presence the name and the form, for the time, of everything in the place; but it didn't, for the difference, sit in his face, the face so squarely and easily turned to Densher at the earlier season. His presence on the first occasion, not as the result of a summons, but as a friendly whim of his own, had had quite another value; and though our young man could scarce regard that value as recoverable he yet reached out in imagination to a renewal of the old contact. He didn't propose, as he privately and forcibly phrased the matter, to be a hog; but there was something he after all did want for himself. It was something—this stuck to him—that Sir Luke would have had for him if it hadn't been impossible. These were his worst days, the two or three; those on which even the sense of the tension at the palace didn't much help him not to feel that his destiny made but light of him. He had never been, as he judged it, so down. In mean conditions, without books, without society, almost without money, he had nothing to do but to wait. His main support really was his original idea, which didn't leave him, of waiting for the deepest depth his predicament could sink him to. Fate would invent, if he but gave it time, some refinement of the horrible. It was just inventing meanwhile this suppression of Sir Luke. When the third day came without a sign he knew what to think. He had given Mrs. Stringham during her call on him no such answer as would have armed her faith, and the ultimatum she had described as ready for him when *he* should be ready was therefore—if on no other ground than her want of this power to answer for him—not to be presented. The presentation, heaven knew, was not what he desired.

That was not, either, we hasten to declare—as Densher then soon enough saw—the idea with which Sir Luke finally stood before him again. For stand before him again he finally did; just when our friend had gloomily embraced the belief that the limit of his power to absent himself from London obligations would have been reached. Four or five days, exclusive of journeys, represented the largest supposable sacrifice—to a head not crowned—on the part of one of the highest medical lights in the world; so that really when the personage in question, following up a tinkle of the bell, solidly rose in the doorway, it was to impose on Densher a vision that for the instant cut like a knife. It spoke, the fact, and in a single dreadful word, of the magnitude—he shrank from calling it anything else—of Milly's case. The great man had not gone then, and an immense surrender to her immense need was so expressed in it that some effect, some help, some hope, were flagrantly part of the expression. It was for Densher, with his reaction from disappointment, as if he were conscious of ten things at once—the foremost being that just conceivably, since Sir Luke *was* still there, she had been saved. Close upon its heels, however, and quite as sharply, came the sense that the crisis—plainly even now to be prolonged for him—was to have none of that sound simplicity. Not only had his visitor not dropped in to gossip about Milly, he hadn't dropped in to mention her at all; he had dropped in fairly to show that during the brief remainder of his stay, the end of which was now in sight, as little as possible of that was to be looked for. The demonstration, such as it was, was in the key of their previous acquaintance, and it was their previous acquaintance that had made him come. He was not to stop longer than the Saturday next at hand, but there were things of interest he should like to see again meanwhile. It was for these things of interest, for Venice and the opportunity of Venice, for a prowl or two, as he called it, and a turn about, that he had looked his young man up—producing on the latter's part, as soon as the case had, with the lapse of a further twenty-four hours, so defined itself, the most incongruous, yet most beneficent revulsion. Nothing could in fact have been more monstrous on the surface—and Densher was well aware of it—than the relief he found during this short period in the tacit drop of all reference to the palace, in neither hearing news nor asking for it. That was what had come out for him, on his visitor's entrance, even in the very seconds of suspense that were connecting the fact also directly and intensely with Milly's state. He had come to say he had saved her—he had come, as from Mrs. Stringham, to say how she might *be* saved—he had come, in spite of Mrs. Stringham, to say she was lost: the distinct throbs of hope, of fear, simultaneous for all their distinctness, merged their identity in a bound of the heart just as immediate and which remained after they had passed. It simply did wonders for him—this was the truth—that Sir Luke was, as he would have said, quiet.

The result of it was the oddest consciousness as of a blest calm after a storm. He had been trying for weeks, as we know, to keep superlatively still, and trying it largely in solitude and silence; but he looked back on it now as on the heat of fever. The real, the right stillness was this particular form of society. They walked together and they talked, looked up pictures again and recovered impressions—Sir Luke knew just what he wanted; haunted a little the dealers in old wares; sat down at Florian's for rest and mild drinks; blessed above all the grand weather, a bath of warm air, a pageant of autumn light. Once or twice while they rested the great man closed his eyes—keeping them so for some minutes while his companion, the more easily watching his face for it, made private reflexions on the subject of lost sleep. He had been up at night with her—he in person, for hours; but this was all he showed of it and was apparently to remain his nearest approach to an allusion. The extraordinary thing was that Densher could take it in perfectly as evidence, could turn cold at the image looking out of it; and yet that he could at the same time not intermit a throb of his response to accepted liberation. The liberation was an experience that held its own, and he continued to know why, in spite of his deserts, in spite of his folly, in spite of everything, he had so fondly hoped for it. He had hoped for it, had sat in his room there waiting for it, because he had thus divined in it, should it come, some power to let him off. He was *being* let off; dealt with in the only way that didn't aggravate his responsibility. The beauty was also that this wasn't on system or on any basis of intimate knowledge; it was just by being a man of the world and by knowing life, by feeling the real, that Sir Luke did him good. There had been in all the case too many women. A man's sense of it, another man's, changed the air; and he wondered what man, had he chosen, would have been more to his purpose than this one. He was large and easy—that was the benediction; he knew what mattered and what didn't; he distinguished between the essence and the shell, the just grounds and the unjust for fussing. One was thus—if one were concerned with him or exposed to him at all—in his hands for whatever he should do, and not much less affected by his mercy than one might have been by his rigour. The grand thing—it did come to that—was the way he carried off, as one might fairly call it, the business of making odd things natural. Nothing, if they hadn't taken it so, could have exceeded the unexplained oddity, between them, of Densher's now complete detachment from the poor ladies at the palace; nothing could have exceeded the no less marked anomaly of the great man's own abstentions of speech. He made, as he had done when they met at the station, nothing whatever of anything; and the effect of it, Densher would have said, was a relation with him quite resembling that of doctor and patient. One took the cue from him as one might have taken a dose—except that the cue was pleasant in the taking.

That was why one could leave it to his tacit discretion, why for the three or four days Densher again and again did so leave it; merely wondering a little, at the most, on the eve of Saturday, the announced term of the episode. Waiting once more on this latter occasion, the Saturday morning, for Sir Luke's reappearance at the station, our friend had to recognise the drop of his own borrowed ease, the result, naturally enough, of the prospect of losing a support. The difficulty was that, on such lines as had served them, the support was Sir Luke's personal presence. Would he go without leaving some substitute for that?—and without breaking, either, his silence in respect to his errand? Densher was in still deeper ignorance than at the hour of his call, and what was truly prodigious at so supreme a moment was that—as had immediately to appear—no gleam of light on what he had been living with for a week found its way out of him. What he had been doing was proof of a huge interest as well as of a huge fee; yet when the Leporelli gondola again, and somewhat tardily, approached, his companion, watching from the water-steps, studied his fine closed face as much as ever in vain. It was like a lesson, from the highest authority, on the subject of the relevant, so that its blankness affected Densher of a sudden almost as a cruelty, feeling it quite awfully compatible, as he did, with Milly's having ceased to exist. And the suspense continued after they had passed together, as time was short, directly into the station, where Eugenio, in the field early, was mounting guard over the compartment he had secured. The strain, though probably lasting, at the carriage-door, but a couple of minutes, prolonged itself so for our poor gentleman's nerves that he involuntarily directed a long look at Eugenio, who met it, however, as only Eugenio could. Sir Luke's attention was given for the time to the right bestowal of his numerous effects, about which he was particular, and Densher fairly found himself, so far as silence could go, questioning the representative of the palace. It didn't humiliate him now; it didn't humiliate him even to feel that that personage exactly knew how little he satisfied him. Eugenio resembled to that extent Sir Luke—to the extent of the extraordinary things with which his facial habit was compatible. By the time, however, that Densher had taken from it all its possessor intended Sir Luke was free and with a hand out for farewell. He offered the hand at first without speech; only on meeting his eyes could our young man see that they had never yet so completely looked at him. It was never, with Sir Luke, that they looked harder at one time than at another; but they looked longer, and this, even a shade of it, might mean on his part everything. It meant, Densher for ten seconds believed, that Milly Theale was dead; so that the word at last spoken made him start.

"I shall come back."

"Then she's better?"

"I shall come back within the month," Sir Luke repeated without heeding the question. He had dropped Densher's hand, but he held him otherwise still. "I bring you a message from Miss Theale," he said as if they hadn't spoken of her. "I'm commissioned to ask you from her to go and see her."

Densher's rebound from his supposition had a violence that his stare betrayed. "She asks me?"

Sir Luke had got into the carriage, the door of which the guard had closed; but he spoke again as he stood at the window, bending a little but not leaning out. "She told me she'd like it, and I promised that, as I expected to find you here, I'd let you know."

Densher, on the platform, took it from him, but what he took brought the blood into his face quite as what he had had to take from Mrs. Stringham. And he was also bewildered. "Then she can receive—?"

"She can receive you."

"And you're coming back—?"

"Oh because I must. She's not to move. She's to stay. I come to her."

"I see, I see," said Densher, who indeed did see—saw the sense of his friend's words and saw beyond it as well. What Mrs. Stringham had announced, and what he had yet expected not to have to face, *had* then come. Sir Luke had kept it for the last, but there it was, and the colourless compact form it was now taking—the tone of one man of the world to another, who, after what had happened, would understand—was but the characteristic manner of his appeal. Densher was to understand remarkably much; and the great thing certainly was to show that he did. "I'm particularly obliged, I'll go to-day." He brought that out, but in his pause, while they continued to look at each other, the train had slowly creaked into motion. There was time but for one more word, and the young man chose it, out of twenty, with intense concentration. "Then she's better?"

Sir Luke's face was wonderful. "Yes, she's better." And he kept it at the window while the train receded, holding him with it still. It was to be his nearest approach to the utter reference they had hitherto so successfully avoided. If it stood for everything; never had a face had to stand for more. So Densher, held after the train had gone, sharply reflected; so he reflected, asking himself into what abyss it pushed him, even while conscious of retreating under the maintained observation of Eugenio.

BOOK TENTH

I

"Then it has been—what do you say? a whole fortnight?—without your making a sign?"

Kate put that to him distinctly, in the December dusk of Lancaster Gate and on the matter of the time he had been back; but he saw with it straightway that she was as admirably true as ever to her instinct—which was a system as well—of not admitting the possibility between them of small resentments, of trifles to trip up their general trust. That by itself, the renewed beauty of it, would at this fresh sight of her have stirred him to his depths if something else, something no less vivid but quite separate, hadn't stirred him still more. It was in seeing her that he felt what their interruption had been, and that they met across it even as persons whose adventures, on either side, in time and space, of the nature of perils and exiles, had had a peculiar strangeness. He wondered if he were as different for her as she herself had immediately appeared: which was but his way indeed of taking in, with his thrill, that—even going by the mere first look—she had never been so handsome. That fact bloomed for him, in the firelight and lamplight that glowed their welcome through the London fog, as the flower of her difference; just as her difference itself—part of which was her striking him as older in a degree for which no mere couple of months could account—was the fruit of their intimate relation. If she was different it was because they had chosen together that she should be, and she might now, as a proof of their wisdom, their success, of the reality of what had happened—of what in fact, for the spirit of each, was still happening—been showing it to him for pride. His having returned and yet kept, for numbered days, so still, had been, he was quite aware, the first point he should have to tackle; with which consciousness indeed he had made a clean breast of it in finally addressing Mrs. Lowder a note that had led to his present visit. He had written to Aunt Maud as the finer way; and it would doubtless have been to be noted that he needed no effort not to write to Kate. Venice was three weeks behind him—he had come up slowly; but it was still as if even in London he must conform to her law. That was exactly how he was able, with his faith in her steadiness, to appeal to her feeling for the situation and explain his stretched delicacy. He had come to tell her everything, so far as occasion would serve them; and if nothing was more distinct than that his slow journey, his waits, his delay to reopen communication had kept pace with this resolve, so the inconsequence was doubtless at bottom but one of the elements of intensity. He was gathering everything up, everything he should tell her. That took time, and the proof was that, as he felt on the spot, he couldn't have brought it all with him before this afternoon. He *had* brought it, to the last syllable, and, out of the quantity it wouldn't be hard—as he in fact found—to produce, for Kate's understanding, his first reason.

"A fortnight, yes—it was a fortnight Friday; but I've only been keeping in, you see, with our wonderful system." He was so easily justified as that this of itself plainly enough prevented her saying she didn't see. Their wonderful system was accordingly still vivid for her; and such a gage of its equal vividness for himself was precisely what she must have asked. He hadn't even to dot his i's beyond the remark that on the very face of it, she would remember, their wonderful system attached no premium to rapidities of transition. "I couldn't quite—don't you know?—take my rebound with a rush; and I suppose I've been instinctively hanging off to minimise, for you as well as for myself, the appearances of rushing. There's a sort of fitness. But I knew you'd understand." It was presently as if she really understood so well that she almost appealed from his insistence—yet looking at him too, he was not unconscious, as if this mastery of fitnesses was a strong sign for her of what she had done to him. He might have struck her as expert for contingencies in the very degree of her having in Venice struck *him* as expert. He smiled over his plea for a renewal with stages and steps, a thing shaded, as they might say, and graduated; though—finely as she must respond—she met the smile but as she had met his entrance five minutes before. Her soft gravity at that moment—which was yet not solemnity, but the look of a consciousness charged with life to the brim and wishing not to overflow—had not qualified her welcome; what had done this being much more the presence in the room, for a couple of minutes, of the footman who had introduced him and who had been interrupted in preparing the tea-table.

Mrs. Lowder's reply to Densher's note had been to appoint the tea-hour, five o'clock on Sunday, for his seeing them. Kate had thereafter wired him, without a signature, "Come on Sunday *before* tea—about a quarter of an hour, which will help us"; and he had arrived therefore scrupulously at twenty minutes to five. Kate was alone in the room and hadn't delayed to tell him that Aunt Maud, as she had happily gathered, was to be, for the interval—not long but precious—engaged with an old servant, retired and pensioned, who had been paying her a visit and who was within the hour to depart again for the suburbs. They were to have the scrap of time, after the withdrawal of the footman, to themselves, and there was a moment when, in spite of their wonderful system, in spite of the proscription of rushes and the propriety of shades, it proclaimed itself indeed precious. And all without prejudice—that was what kept it noble—to Kate's high sobriety and her beautiful self-command. If he had his discretion she had her perfect manner, which was *her* decorum. Mrs. Stringham, he had, to finish with the question of his delay, furthermore observed, Mrs. Stringham would have written to Mrs. Lowder of his having quitted the place; so that it wasn't as if he were hoping to cheat them. They'd know he was no longer there.

"Yes, we've known it."

"And you continue to hear?"

"From Mrs. Stringham? Certainly. By which I mean Aunt Maud does."

"Then you've recent news?"

Her face showed a wonder. "Up to within a day or two I believe. But haven't *you?*"

"No—I've heard nothing." And it was now that he felt how much he had to tell her. "I don't get letters. But I've been sure Mrs. Lowder does." With which he added: "Then of course you know." He waited as if she would show what she knew; but she only showed in silence the dawn of a surprise that she couldn't control. There was nothing but for him to ask what he wanted. "Is Miss Theale alive?"

Kate's look at this was large. "Don't you *know?*"

"How should I, my dear—in the absence of everything?" And he himself stared as for light. "She's dead?" Then as with her eyes on him she slowly shook her head he uttered a strange "Not yet?"

It came out in Kate's face that there were several questions on her lips, but the one she presently put was: "Is it very terrible?"

"The manner of her so consciously and helplessly dying?" He had to think a moment. "Well, yes—since you ask me: very terrible to *me*—so far as, before I came away, I had any sight of it. But I don't think," he went on, "that—though I'll try—I *can* quite tell you what it was, what it is, for me. That's why I probably just sounded to you," he explained, "as if I hoped it might be over."

She gave him her quietest attention, but he by this time saw that, so far as telling her all was concerned, she would be divided between the wish and the reluctance to hear it; between the curiosity that, not unnaturally, would consume her and the opposing scruple of a respect for misfortune. The more she studied him too—and he had never so felt her closely attached to his face—the more the choice of an attitude would become impossible to her. There would simply be a feeling uppermost, and the feeling wouldn't be eagerness. This perception grew in him fast, and he even, with his imagination, had for a moment the quick forecast of her possibly breaking out at him, should he go too far, with a wonderful: "What horrors are you telling me?" It would have the sound—wouldn't it be open to him fairly to bring that out himself?—of a repudiation, for pity and almost for shame, of everything that in Venice had passed between them. Not that she would confess to any return upon herself; not that she would let compunction or horror give her away; but it was in the air for him—yes—that she wouldn't want details, that she positively wouldn't take them, and that, if he would generously understand it from her, she would prefer to keep him down. Nothing, however, was more definite for him than that at the same time he must remain down but so far as it suited him. Something rose strong within him against his not being free with her. She had been free enough about it all, three months before, with *him*. That was what she was at present only in the sense of treating him handsomely. "I can believe," she said with perfect consideration, "how dreadful for you much of it must have been."

He didn't however take this up; there were things about which he wished first to be clear. "There's no other possibility, by what you now know? I mean for her life." And he had just to insist—she would say as little as she could. "She *is* dying?"

"She's dying."

It was strange to him, in the matter of Milly, that Lancaster Gate could make him any surer; yet what in the world, in the matter of Milly, wasn't strange? Nothing was so much so as his own behaviour—his present as well as his past. He could but do as he must. "Has Sir Luke Strett," he asked, "gone back to her?"

"I believe he's there now."

"Then," said Densher, "it's the end."

She took it in silence for whatever he deemed it to be; but she spoke otherwise after a minute. "You won't know, unless you've perhaps seen him yourself, that Aunt Maud has been to him."

"Oh!" Densher exclaimed, with nothing to add to it.

"For real news," Kate herself after an instant added.

"She hasn't thought Mrs. Stringham's real?"

"It's perhaps only I who haven't. It was on Aunt Maud's trying again three days ago to see him that she heard at his house of his having gone. He had started I believe some days before."

"And won't then by this time be back?"

Kate shook her head. "She sent yesterday to know."

"He won't leave her then"—Densher had turned it over—"while she lives. He'll stay to the end. He's magnificent."

"I think *she* is," said Kate.

It had made them again look at each other long; and what it drew from him rather oddly was: "Oh you don't know!"

"Well, she's after all my friend."

It was somehow, with her handsome demur, the answer he had least expected of her; and it fanned with its breath, for a brief instant, his old sense of her variety. "I see. You would have been sure of it. You *were* sure of it."

"Of course I was sure of it."

And a pause again, with this, fell upon them; which Densher, however, presently broke. "If you don't think Mrs. Stringham's news 'real' what do you think of Lord Mark's?"

She didn't think anything. "Lord Mark's?"

"You haven't seen him?"

"Not since he saw her."

"You've known then of his seeing her?"

"Certainly. From Mrs. Stringham."

"And have you known," Densher went on, "the rest?"

Kate wondered. "What rest?"

"Why everything. It was his visit that she couldn't stand—it was what then took place that simply killed her."

"Oh!" Kate seriously breathed. But she had turned pale, and he saw that, whatever her degree of ignorance of these connexions, it wasn't put on. "Mrs. Stringham hasn't said *that*."

He observed none the less that she didn't ask what had then taken place; and he went on with his contribution to her knowledge. "The way it affected her was that it made her give up. She has given up beyond all power to care again, and that's why she's dying."

"Oh!" Kate once more slowly sighed, but with a vagueness that made him pursue.

"One can see now that she was living by will—which was very much what you originally told me of her."

"I remember. That was it."

"Well then her will, at a given moment, broke down, and the collapse was determined by that fellow's dastardly stroke. He told her, the scoundrel, that you and I are secretly engaged."

Kate gave a quick glare. "But he doesn't know it!"

"That doesn't matter. *She* did by the time he had left her. Besides," Densher added, "he does know it. When," he continued, "did you last see him?"

But she was lost now in the picture before her. "*That* was what made her worse?"

He watched her take it in—it so added to her sombre beauty. Then he spoke as Mrs. Stringham had spoken. "She turned her face to the wall."

"Poor Milly!" said Kate.

Slight as it was, her beauty somehow gave it style; so that he continued consistently: "She learned it, you see, too soon—since of course one's idea had been that she might never even learn it at all. And she *had* felt sure—through everything we had done—of there not being between us, so far at least as you were concerned, anything she need regard as a warning."

She took another moment for thought. "It wasn't through anything *you* did—whatever that may have been—that she gained her certainty. It was by the conviction she got from me."

"Oh it's very handsome," Densher said, "for you to take your share!"

"Do you suppose," Kate asked, "that I think of denying it?"

Her look and her tone made him for the instant regret his comment, which indeed had been the first that rose to his lips as an effect absolutely of what they would have called between them her straightness. Her straightness, visibly, was all his own loyalty could ask. Still, that was comparatively beside the mark. "Of course I don't suppose anything but that we're together in our recognitions, our responsibilities—whatever we choose to call them. It isn't a question for us of apportioning shares or distinguishing invidiously among such impressions as it was our idea to give."

"It wasn't *your* idea to give impressions," said Kate.

He met this with a smile that he himself felt, in its strained character, as queer. "Don't go into that!"

It was perhaps not as going into it that she had another idea—an idea born, she showed, of the vision he had just evoked. "Wouldn't it have been possible then to deny the truth of the information? I mean of Lord Mark's."

Densher wondered. "Possible for whom?"

"Why for you."

"To tell her he lied?"

"To tell her he's mistaken."

Densher stared—he was stupefied; the "possible" thus glanced at by Kate being exactly the alternative he had had to face in Venice and to put utterly away from him. Nothing was stranger than such a difference in their view of it. "And to lie myself, you mean, to do it? We *are*, my dear child," he said, "I suppose, still engaged."

"Of course we're still engaged. But to save her life—!"

He took in for a little the way she talked of it. Of course, it was to be remembered, she had always simplified, and it brought back his sense of the degree in which, to her energy as compared with his own, many things were easy; the very sense that so often before had moved him to admiration. "Well, if you must know—and I want you to be clear about it—I didn't even seriously think of a denial to her face. The question of it—*as* possibly saving her—was put to me definitely enough; but to turn it over was only to dismiss it. Besides," he added, "it wouldn't have done any good."

"You mean she would have had no faith in your correction?" She had spoken with a promptitude that affected him of a sudden as almost glib; but he himself paused with the overweight of all he meant, and she meanwhile went on. "Did you try?"

"I hadn't even a chance."

Kate maintained her wonderful manner, the manner of at once having it all before her and yet keeping it all at its distance. "She wouldn't see you?"

"Not after your friend had been with her."

She hesitated. "Couldn't you write?"

It made him also think, but with a difference. "She had turned her face to the wall."

This again for a moment hushed her, and they were both too grave now for parenthetic pity. But her interest came out for at least the minimum of light. "She refused even to let you speak to her?"

"My dear girl," Densher returned, "she was miserably, prohibitively ill."

"Well, that was what she had been before."

"And it didn't prevent? No," Densher admitted, "it didn't; and I don't pretend that she's not magnificent."

"She's prodigious," said Kate Croy.

He looked at her a moment. "So are you, my dear. But that's how it is," he wound up; "and there we are."

His idea had been in advance that she would perhaps sound him much more deeply, asking him above all two or three specific things. He had fairly fancied her even wanting to know and trying to find out how far, as the odious phrase was, he and Milly had gone, and how near, by the same token, they had come. He had asked himself if he were prepared to hear her do that, and had had to take for answer that he was prepared of course for everything. Wasn't he prepared for her ascertaining if her two or three prophecies had found time to be made true? He had fairly believed himself ready to say whether or no the overture on Milly's part promised according to the boldest of them had taken place. But what was in fact blessedly coming to him was that so far as such things were concerned his readiness wouldn't be taxed. Kate's pressure on the question of what had taken place remained so admirably general that even her present enquiry kept itself free of sharpness. "So then that after Lord Mark's interference you never again met?"

It was what he had been all the while coming to. "No; we met once—so far as it could be called a meeting. I had stayed—I didn't come away."

"That," said Kate, "was no more than decent."

"Precisely"—he felt himself wonderful; "and I wanted to be no less. She sent for me, I went to her, and that night I left Venice."

His companion waited. "Wouldn't *that* then have been your chance?"

"To refute Lord Mark's story? No, not even if before her there I had wanted to. What did it signify either? She was dying."

"Well," Kate in a manner persisted, "why not just *because* she was dying?" She had however all her discretion. "But of course I know that seeing her you could judge."

"Of course seeing her I could judge. And I did see her! If I had denied you moreover," Densher said with his eyes on her, "I'd have stuck to it."

She took for a moment the intention of his face. "You mean that to convince her you'd have insisted or somehow proved—?"

"I mean that to convince *you* I'd have insisted or somehow proved—!"

Kate looked for her moment at a loss. "To convince 'me'?"

"I wouldn't have made my denial, in such conditions, only to take it back afterwards."

With this quickly light came for her, and with it also her colour flamed. "Oh you'd have broken with me to make your denial a truth? You'd have 'chucked' me"—she embraced it perfectly—"to save your conscience?"

"I couldn't have done anything else," said Merton Densher. "So you see how right I was not to commit myself, and how little I could dream of it. If it ever again appears to you that I *might* have done so, remember what I say."

Kate again considered, but not with the effect at once to which he pointed. "You've fallen in love with her."

"Well then say so—with a dying woman. Why need you mind and what does it matter?"

It came from him, the question, straight out of the intensity of relation and the face-to-face necessity into which, from the first, from his entering the room, they had found themselves thrown; but it gave them their most extraordinary moment. "Wait till she is dead! Mrs. Stringham," Kate added, "is to telegraph." After which, in a tone still different, "For what then," she asked, "did Milly send for you?"

"It was what I tried to make out before I went. I must tell you moreover that I had no doubt of its really being to give me, as you say, a chance. She believed, I suppose, that I *might* deny; and what, to my own mind, was before me in going to her was the certainty that she'd put me to my test. She wanted from my own lips—so I saw it—the truth. But I was with her for twenty minutes, and she never asked me for it."

"She never wanted the truth"—Kate had a high headshake. "She wanted *you*. She would have taken from you what you could give her and been glad of it, even if she had known it false. You might have lied to her from pity, and she have seen you and felt you lie, and yet—since it was all for tenderness—she would have thanked you and blessed you and clung to you but the more. For that was your strength, my dear man—that she loves you with passion."

"Oh my 'strength'!" Densher coldly murmured.

"Otherwise, since she had sent for you, what was it to ask of you?" And then—quite without irony—as he waited a moment to say: "Was it just once more to look at you?"

"She had nothing to ask of me—nothing, that is, but not to stay any longer. She did to that extent want to see me. She had supposed at first—after he had been with her—that I had seen the propriety of taking myself off. Then since I hadn't—seeing my propriety as I did in another way—she found, days later, that I was still there. This," said Densher, "affected her."

"Of course it affected her."

Again she struck him, for all her dignity, as glib. "If it was somehow for *her* I was still staying, she wished that to end, she wished me to know how little there was need of it. And as a manner of farewell she wished herself to tell me so."

"And she did tell you so?"

"Face-to-face, yes. Personally, as she desired."

"And as *you* of course did."

"No, Kate," he returned with all their mutual consideration; "not as I did. I hadn't desired it in the least."

"You only went to oblige her?"

"To oblige her. And of course also to oblige you."

"Oh for myself certainly I'm glad."

"'Glad'?"—he echoed vaguely the way it rang out.

"I mean you did quite the right thing. You did it especially in having stayed. But that was all?" Kate went on. "That you mustn't wait?"

"That was really all—and in perfect kindness."

"Ah kindness naturally: from the moment she asked of you such a—well, such an effort. That you mustn't wait—that was the point," Kate added—"to see her die."

"That was the point, my dear," Densher said.

"And it took twenty minutes to make it?"

He thought a little. "I didn't time it to a second. I paid her the visit—just like another."

"Like another person?"

"Like another visit."

"Oh!" said Kate. Which had apparently the effect of slightly arresting his speech—an arrest she took advantage of to continue; making with it indeed her nearest approach to an enquiry of the kind against which he had braced himself. "Did she receive you—in her condition—in her room?"

"Not she," said Merton Densher. "She received me just as usual: in that glorious great *salone*, in the dress she always wears, from her inveterate corner of her sofa." And his face for the moment conveyed the scene, just as hers equally embraced it. "Do you remember what you originally said to me of her?"

"Ah I've said so many things."

"That she wouldn't smell of drugs, that she wouldn't taste of medicine. Well, she didn't."

"So that it was really almost happy?"

It took him a long time to answer, occupied as he partly was in feeling how nobody but Kate could have invested such a question with the tone that was perfectly right. She meanwhile, however, patiently waited. "I don't think I can attempt to say now what it was. Some day—perhaps. For it would be worth it for us."

"Some day—certainly." She seemed to record the promise. Yet she spoke again abruptly. "She'll recover."

"Well," said Densher, "you'll see."

She had the air an instant of trying to. "Did she show anything of her feeling? I mean," Kate explained, "of her feeling of having been misled."

She didn't press hard, surely; but he had just mentioned that he would have rather to glide. "She showed nothing but her beauty and her strength."

"Then," his companion asked, "what's the use of her strength?"

He seemed to look about for a use he could name; but he had soon given it up. "She must die, my dear, in her own extraordinary way."

"Naturally. But I don't see then what proof you have that she was ever alienated."

"I have the proof that she refused for days and days to see me."

"But she was ill."

"That hadn't prevented her—as you yourself a moment ago said—during the previous time. If it had been only illness it would have made no difference with her."

"She would still have received you?"

"She would still have received me."

"Oh well," said Kate, "if you know—!"

"Of course I know. I know moreover as well from Mrs. Stringham."

"And what does Mrs. Stringham know?"

"Everything."

She looked at him longer. "Everything?"

"Everything."

"Because you've told her?"

"Because she has seen for herself. I've told her nothing. She's a person who does see."

Kate thought. "That's by her liking you too. She as well is prodigious. You see what interest in a man does. It does it all round. So you needn't be afraid."

"I'm not afraid," said Densher.

Kate moved from her place then, looking at the clock, which marked five. She gave her attention to the tea-table, where Aunt Maud's huge silver kettle, which had been exposed to its lamp and which she had not soon enough noticed, was hissing too hard. "Well, it's all most wonderful!" she exclaimed as she rather too profusely—a sign her friend noticed—ladled tea into the pot. He watched her a moment at this occupation, coming nearer the table while she put in the steaming water. "You'll have some?"

He hesitated. "Hadn't we better wait—?"

"For Aunt Maud?" She saw what he meant—the deprecation, by their old law, of betrayals of the intimate note. "Oh you needn't mind now. We've done it!"

"Humbugged her?"

"Squared her. You've pleased her."

Densher mechanically accepted his tea. He was thinking of something else, and his thought in a moment came out. "What a brute then I must be!"

"A brute—?"

"To have pleased so many people."

"Ah," said Kate with a gleam of gaiety, "you've done it to please *me*." But she was already, with her gleam, reverting a little. "What I don't understand is—won't you have any sugar?"

"Yes, please."

"What I don't understand," she went on when she had helped him, "is what it was that had occurred to bring her round again. If she gave you up for days and days, what brought her back to you?"

She asked the question with her own cup in her hand, but it found him ready enough in spite of his sense of the ironic oddity of their going into it over the tea-table. "It was Sir Luke Strett who brought her back. His visit, his presence there did it."

"He brought her back then to life."

"Well, to what I saw."

"And by interceding for you?"

"I don't think he interceded. I don't indeed know what he did."

Kate wondered. "Didn't he tell you?"

"I didn't ask him. I met him again, but we practically didn't speak of her."

Kate stared. "Then how do you know?"

"I see. I feel. I was with him again as I had been before—"

"Oh and you pleased him too? That was it?"

"He understood," said Densher.

"But understood what?"

He waited a moment. "That I had meant awfully well."

"Ah, and made *her* understand? I see," she went on as he said nothing. "But how did he convince her?"

Densher put down his cup and turned away. "You must ask Sir Luke."

He stood looking at the fire and there was a time without sound. "The great thing," Kate then resumed, "is that she's satisfied. Which," she continued, looking across at him, "is what I've worked for."

"Satisfied to die in the flower of her youth?"

"Well, at peace with you."

"Oh 'peace'!" he murmured with his eyes on the fire.

"The peace of having loved."

He raised his eyes to her. "Is *that* peace?"

"Of having *been* loved," she went on. "That is. Of having," she wound up, "realised her passion. She wanted nothing more. She has had *all* she wanted."

Lucid and always grave, she gave this out with a beautiful authority that he could for the time meet with no words. He could only again look at her, though with the sense in so doing that he made her more than he intended take his silence for assent. Quite indeed as if she did so take it she quitted the table and came to the fire. "You may think it hideous that I should now, that I should *yet*"—she made a point of the word—"pretend to draw conclusions. But we've not failed."

"Oh!" he only again murmured.

She was once more close to him, close as she had been the day she came to him in Venice, the quickly returning memory of which intensified and enriched the fact. He could practically deny in such conditions nothing that she said, and what she said was, with it, visibly, a fruit of that knowledge. "We've succeeded." She spoke with her eyes deep in his own. "She won't have loved you for nothing." It made him wince, but she insisted. "And you won't have loved *me*."

II

He was to remain for several days under the deep impression of this inclusive passage, so luckily prolonged from moment to moment, but interrupted at its climax, as may be said, by the entrance of Aunt Maud, who found them standing together near the fire. The bearings of the colloquy, however, sharp as they were, were less sharp to his intelligence, strangely enough, than those of a talk with Mrs. Lowder alone for which she soon gave him—or for which perhaps rather Kate gave him—full occasion. What had happened on her at last joining them was to conduce, he could immediately see, to her desiring to have him to herself. Kate and he, no doubt, at the opening of the door, had fallen apart with a certain suddenness, so that she had turned her hard fine eyes from one to the other; but the effect of this lost itself, to his mind, the next minute, in the effect of his companion's rare alertness. She instantly spoke to her aunt of what had first been uppermost for herself, inviting her thereby intimately to join them, and doing it the more happily also, no doubt, because the fact she resentfully named gave her ample support. "Had you quite understood, my dear, that it's full three weeks—?" And she effaced herself as if to leave Mrs. Lowder to deal from her own point of view with this extravagance. Densher of course straightway noted that his cue for the protection of Kate was to make, no less, all of it he could; and their tracks, as he might have said, were fairly covered by the time their hostess had taken afresh, on his renewed admission, the measure of his scant eagerness. Kate had moved away as if no great showing were needed for her personal situation to be seen as delicate. She had been entertaining their visitor on her aunt's behalf—a visitor she had been at one time suspected of favouring too much and who had now come back to them as the stricken suitor of another person. It wasn't that the fate of the other person, her exquisite friend, didn't, in its tragic turn, also concern herself: it was only that her acceptance of Mr. Densher as a source of information could scarcely help having an awkwardness. She invented the awkwardness under Densher's eyes, and he marvelled on his side at the instant creation. It served her as the fine cloud that hangs about a goddess in an epic, and the young man was but vaguely to know at what point of the rest of his visit she had, for consideration, melted into it and out of sight.

He was taken up promptly with another matter—the truth of the remarkable difference, neither more nor less, that the events of Venice had introduced into his relation with Aunt Maud and that these weeks of their separation had caused quite richly to ripen for him. She had not sat down to her tea-table before he felt himself on terms with her that were absolutely new, nor could she press on him a second cup without her seeming herself, and quite wittingly, so to define and establish them. She regretted, but she quite understood, that what was taking place had obliged him to hang off; they had—after hearing of him from poor Susan as gone—been hoping for an early sight of him; they would have been interested, naturally, in his arriving straight from the scene. Yet she needed no reminder that the scene precisely—by which she meant the tragedy that had so detained and absorbed him, the memory, the shadow, the sorrow of it—was what marked him for unsociability. She thus presented him to himself, as it were, in the guise in which she had now adopted him, and it was the element of truth in the character that he found himself, for his own part, adopting. She treated him as blighted and ravaged, as frustrate and already bereft; and for him to feel that this opened for him a new chapter of frankness with her he scarce had also to perceive how it smoothed his approaches to Kate. It made the latter accessible as she hadn't yet begun to be; it set up for him at Lancaster Gate an association positively hostile to any other legend. It was quickly vivid to him that, were he minded, he could "work" this association: he had but to use the house freely for his prescribed attitude and he need hardly ever be out of it. Stranger than anything moreover was to be the way that by the end of a week he stood convicted to his own sense of a surrender to Mrs. Lowder's view. He had somehow met it at a point that had brought him on—brought him on a distance that he couldn't again retrace. He had private hours of wondering what had become of his sincerity; he had others of simply reflecting that he had it all in use. His only want of candour was Aunt Maud's wealth of sentiment. She was hugely sentimental, and the worst he did was to take it from her. He wasn't so himself—everything was too real; but it was none the less not false that he *had* been through a mill.

It was in particular not false for instance that when she had said to him, on the Sunday, almost cosily, from her sofa behind the tea, "I want you not to doubt, you poor dear, that I'm *with* you to the end!" his meeting her halfway had been the only course open to him. She was with him to the end—or she might be—in a way Kate wasn't; and even if it literally made her society meanwhile more soothing he must just brush away the question of why it shouldn't. Was he professing to her in any degree the possession of an aftersense that wasn't real? How in the world *could* he, when his aftersense, day by day, was his greatest reality? Such only was at bottom what there was between them, and two or three times over it made the hour pass. These were occasions—two and a scrap—on which he had come and gone without mention of Kate. Now that almost as never yet he had licence to ask for her, the queer turn of their affair made it a false note. It was another queer turn that when he talked with Aunt Maud about Milly nothing else seemed to come up. He called upon her almost avowedly for that purpose, and it was the queerest turn of all that the state of his nerves should require it. He liked her better; he was really behaving, he had occasion to say to himself, as if he liked her best. The thing was absolutely that she met *him* halfway. Nothing could have been broader than her vision, than her loquacity, than her sympathy. It appeared to gratify, to satisfy her to see him as he was; that too had its effect. It was all of course the last thing that could have seemed on the cards, a change by which he was completely *free* with this lady; and it wouldn't indeed have come about if—for another monstrosity—he hadn't ceased to be free with Kate. Thus it was that on the third time in especial of being alone with her he found himself uttering to the elder woman what had been impossible of utterance to the younger. Mrs. Lowder gave him in fact, on the ground of what he must keep from her, but one uneasy moment. That was when, on the first Sunday, after Kate had suppressed herself, she referred to her regret that he mightn't have stayed to the end. He found his reason difficult to give her, but she came after all to his help.

"You simply couldn't stand it?"

"I simply couldn't stand it. Besides you see—!" But he paused.

"Besides what?" He had been going to say more—then he saw dangers; luckily however she had again assisted him. "Besides—oh I know!—men haven't, in many relations, the courage of women."

"They haven't the courage of women."

"Kate or I would have stayed," she declared—"if we hadn't come away for the special reason that you so frankly appreciated."

Densher had said nothing about his appreciation: hadn't his behaviour since the hour itself sufficiently shown it? But he presently said—he couldn't help going so far: "I don't doubt, certainly, that Miss Croy would have stayed." And he saw again into the bargain what a marvel was Susan Shepherd. She did nothing but protect him—she had done nothing but keep it up. In copious communication with the friend of her youth she had yet, it was plain, favoured this lady with nothing that compromised him. Milly's act of renouncement she had described but as a change for the worse; she had mentioned Lord Mark's descent, as even without her it might be known, so that she mustn't appear to conceal it; but she had suppressed explanations and connexions, and indeed, for all he knew, blessed Puritan soul, had invented commendable fictions. Thus it was absolutely that he was at his ease. Thus it was that, shaking for ever, in the unrest that didn't drop, his crossed leg, he leaned back in deep yellow satin chairs and took such comfort as came. She asked, it was true, Aunt Maud, questions that Kate hadn't; but this was just the difference, that from her he positively liked them. He had taken with himself on leaving Venice the resolution to regard Milly as already dead to him—that being for his spirit the only thinkable way to pass the time of waiting. He had left her because it was what suited her, and it wasn't for him to go, as they said in America, behind this; which imposed on him but the sharper need to arrange himself with his interval. Suspense was the ugliest ache to him, and he would have nothing to do with it; the last thing he wished was to be unconscious of her—what he wished to ignore was her own consciousness, tortured, for all he knew, crucified by its pain. Knowingly to hang about in London while the pain went on—what would that do but make his days impossible? His scheme was accordingly to convince himself—and by some art about which he was vague—that the sense of waiting had passed. "What in fact," he restlessly reflected, "have I any further to do with it? Let me assume the thing actually over—as it at any moment may be—and I become good again for something at least to somebody. I'm good, as it is, for nothing to anybody, least of all to *her*." He consequently tried, so far as shutting his eyes and stalking grimly about was a trial; but his plan was carried out, it may well be guessed, neither with marked success nor with marked consistency. The days, whether lapsing or lingering, were a stiff reality; the suppression of anxiety was a thin idea; the taste of life itself was the taste of suspense. That he *was* waiting was in short at the bottom of everything; and it required no great sifting presently to feel that if he took so much more, as he called it, to Mrs. Lowder this was just for that reason.

She helped him to hold out, all the while that she was subtle enough—and he could see her divine it as what he wanted—not to insist on the actuality of their tension. His nearest approach to success was thus in being good for something to Aunt Maud, in default of any one better; her company eased his nerves even while they pretended together that they had seen their tragedy out. They spoke of the dying girl in the past tense; they said no worse of her than that she had *been* stupendous. On the other hand, however—and this was what wasn't for Densher pure peace—they insisted enough that stupendous was the word. It was the thing, this recognition, that kept him most quiet; he came to it with her repeatedly; talking about it against time and, in particular, we have noted, speaking of his supreme personal impression as he hadn't spoken to Kate. It was almost as if she herself enjoyed the perfection of the pathos; she sat there before the scene, as he couldn't help giving it out to her, very much as a stout citizen's wife might have sat, during a play that made people cry, in the pit or the family-circle. What most deeply stirred her was the way the poor girl must have wanted to live.

"Ah yes indeed—she did, she did: why in pity shouldn't she, with everything to fill her world? The mere *money* of her, the darling, if it isn't too disgusting at such a time to mention that—!"

Aunt Maud mentioned it—and Densher quite understood—but as fairly giving poetry to the life Milly clung to: a view of the "might have been" before which the good lady was hushed anew to tears. She had had her own vision of these possibilities, and her own social use for them, and since Milly's spirit had been after all so at one with her about them, what was the cruelty of the event but a cruelty, of a sort, to herself? That came out when he named, as *the* horrible thing to know, the fact of their young friend's unapproachable terror of the end, keep it down though she would; coming out therefore often, since in so naming it he found the strangest of reliefs. He allowed it all its vividness, as if on the principle of his not at least spiritually shirking. Milly had held with passion to her dream of a future, and she was separated from it, not shrieking indeed, but grimly, awfully silent, as one might imagine some noble young victim of the scaffold, in the French Revolution, separated at the prison-door from some object clutched for resistance. Densher, in a cold moment, so pictured the case for Mrs. Lowder, but no moment cold enough had yet come to make him so picture it to Kate. And it was the front so presented that had been, in Milly, heroic; presented with the highest heroism, Aunt Maud by this time knew, on the occasion of his taking leave of her. He had let her know, absolutely for the girl's glory, how he had been received on that occasion: with a positive effect—since she was indeed so perfectly the princess that Mrs. Stringham always called her—of princely state.

Before the fire in the great room that was all arabesques and cherubs, all gaiety and gilt, and that was warm at that hour too with a wealth of autumn sun, the state in question had been maintained and the situation—well, Densher said for the convenience of exquisite London gossip, sublime. The gossip—for it came to as much at Lancaster Gate—wasn't the less exquisite for his use of the silver veil, nor on the other hand was the veil, so touched, too much drawn aside. He himself for that matter took in the scene again at moments as from the page of a book. He saw a young man far off and in a relation inconceivable, saw him hushed, passive, staying his breath, but half understanding, yet dimly conscious of something immense and holding himself painfully together not to lose it. The young man at these moments so seen was too distant and too strange for the right identity; and yet, outside, afterwards, it was his own face Densher had known. He had known then at the same time what the young man had been conscious of, and he was to measure after that, day by day, how little he had lost. At present there with Mrs. Lowder he knew he had gathered all—that passed between them mutely as in the intervals of their associated gaze they exchanged looks of intelligence. This was as far as association could go, but it was far enough when she knew the essence. The essence was that something had happened to him too beautiful and too sacred to describe. He had been, to his recovered sense, forgiven, dedicated, blessed; but this he couldn't coherently express. It would have required an explanation—fatal to Mrs. Lowder's faith in him—of the nature of Milly's wrong. So, as to the wonderful scene, they just stood at the door. They had the sense of the presence within—they felt the charged stillness; after which, their association deepened by it, they turned together away.

That itself indeed, for our restless friend, became by the end of a week the very principle of reaction: so that he woke up one morning with such a sense of having played a part as he needed self-respect to gainsay. He hadn't in the least stated at Lancaster Gate that, as a haunted man—a man haunted with a memory—he was harmless; but the degree to which Mrs. Lowder accepted, admired and explained his new aspect laid upon him practically the weight of a declaration. What he hadn't in the least stated her own manner was perpetually stating; it was as haunted and harmless that she was constantly putting him down. There offered itself however to his purpose such an element as plain honesty, and he had embraced, by the time he dressed, his proper corrective. They were on the edge of Christmas, but Christmas this year was, as in the London of so many other years, disconcertingly mild; the still air was soft, the thick light was grey, the great town looked empty, and in the Park, where the grass was green, where the sheep browsed, where the birds multitudinously twittered, the straight walks lent themselves to slowness and the dim vistas to privacy. He held it fast this morning till he had got out, his sacrifice to honour, and then went with it to the nearest post-office and fixed it fast in a telegram; thinking of it moreover as a sacrifice only because he had, for reasons, felt it as an effort. Its character of effort it would owe to Kate's expected resistance, not less probable than on the occasion of past appeals; which was precisely why he—perhaps innocently—made his telegram persuasive. It had, as a recall of tender hours, to be, for the young woman at the counter, a trifle cryptic; but there was a good deal of it in one way and another, representing as it did a rich impulse and costing him a couple of shillings. There was also a moment later on, that day, when, in the Park, as he measured watchfully one of their old alleys, he might have been supposed by a cynical critic to be reckoning his chance of getting his money back. He was waiting—but he had waited of old; Lancaster Gate as a danger was practically at hand—but she had risked that danger before. Besides it was smaller now, with the queer turn of their affair; in spite of which indeed he was graver as he lingered and looked out.

Kate came at last by the way he had thought least likely, came as if she had started from the Marble Arch; but her advent was response—that was the great matter; response marked in her face and agreeable to him, even after Aunt Maud's responses, as nothing had been since his return to London. She had not, it was true, answered his wire, and he had begun to fear, as she was late, that with the instinct of what he might be again intending to press upon her she had decided—though not with ease—to deprive him of his chance. He would have of course, she knew, other chances, but she perhaps saw the present as offering her special danger. This, in fact, Densher could himself feel, was exactly why he had so prepared it, and he had rejoiced, even while he waited, in all that the conditions had to say to him of their simpler and better time. The shortest day of the year though it might be, it was, in the same place, by a whim of the weather, almost as much to their purpose as the days of sunny afternoons when they had taken their first trysts. This and that tree, within sight, on the grass, stretched bare boughs over the couple of chairs in which they had sat of old and in which—for they really could sit down again—they might recover the clearness of their prime. It was to all intents however this very reference that showed itself in Kate's face as, with her swift motion, she came toward him. It helped him, her swift motion, when it finally brought her nearer; helped him, for that matter, at first, if only by showing him afresh how terribly well she looked. It had been all along, he certainly remembered, a phenomenon of no rarity that he had felt her, at particular moments, handsomer than ever before; one of these for instance being still present to him as her entrance, under her aunt's eyes, at Lancaster Gate, the day of his dinner there after his return from America; and another her aspect on the same spot two Sundays ago—the light in which she struck the eyes he had brought back from Venice. In the course of a minute or two now he got, as he had got it the other times, his apprehension of the special stamp of the fortune of the moment.

Whatever it had been determined by as the different hours recurred to him, it took on at present a prompt connexion with an effect produced for him in truth more than once during the past week, only now much intensified. This effect he had already noted and named: it was that of the attitude assumed by his friend in the presence of the degree of response on his part to Mrs. Lowder's welcome which she couldn't possibly have failed to notice. She *had* noticed it, and she had beautifully shown him so; wearing in its honour the finest shade of studied serenity, a shade almost of gaiety over the workings of time. Everything of course was relative, with the shadow they were living under; but her condonation of the way in which he now, for confidence, distinguished Aunt Maud had almost the note of cheer. She had so by her own air consecrated the distinction, invidious in respect to herself though it might be; and nothing, really, more than this demonstration, could have given him had he still wanted it the measure of her superiority. It was doubtless for that matter this superiority alone that on the winter noon gave smooth decision to her step and charming courage to her eyes—a courage that deepened in them when he had presently got to what he did want. He had delayed after she had joined him not much more than long enough for him to say to her, drawing her hand into his arm and turning off where they had turned of old, that he wouldn't pretend he hadn't lately had moments of not quite believing he should ever again be so happy. She answered, passing over the reasons, whatever they had been, of his doubt, that her own belief was in high happiness for them if they would only have patience; though nothing at the same time could be dearer than his idea for their walk. It was only make-believe of course, with what had taken place for them, that they couldn't meet at home; she spoke of their opportunities as suffering at no point. He had at any rate soon let her know that he wished the present one to suffer at none, and in a quiet spot, beneath a great wintry tree, he let his entreaty come sharp.

"We've played our dreadful game and we've lost. We owe it to ourselves, we owe it to our feeling *for* ourselves and for each other, not to wait another day. Our marriage will—fundamentally, somehow, don't you see?—right everything that's wrong, and I can't express to you my impatience. We've only to announce it—and it takes off the weight."

"To 'announce' it?" Kate asked. She spoke as if not understanding, though she had listened to him without confusion.

"To accomplish it then—to-morrow if you will; *do* it and announce it as done. That's the least part of it—after it nothing will matter. We shall be so right," he said, "that we shall be strong; we shall only wonder at our past fear. It will seem an ugly madness. It will seem a bad dream."

She looked at him without flinching—with the look she had brought at his call; but he felt now the strange chill of her brightness. "My dear man, what has happened to you?"

"Well, that I can bear it no longer. *That's* simply what has happened. Something has snapped, has broken in me, and here I am. It's *as* I am that you must have me."

He saw her try for a time to appear to consider it; but he saw her also not consider it. Yet he saw her, felt her, further—he heard her, with her clear voice—try to be intensely kind with him. "I don't see, you know, what has changed." She had a large strange smile. "We've been going on together so well, and you suddenly desert me?"

It made him helplessly gaze. "You call it so 'well'? You've touches, upon my soul—!"

"I call it perfect—from my original point of view. I'm just where I was; and you must give me some better reason than you do, my dear, for *your* not being. It seems to me," she continued, "that we're only right as to what has been between us so long as we do wait. I don't think we wish to have behaved like fools." He took in while she talked her imperturbable consistency; which it was quietly, queerly hopeless to see her stand there and breathe into their mild remembering air. He had brought her there to be moved, and she was only immoveable—which was not moreover, either, because she didn't understand. She understood everything, and things he refused to; and she had reasons, deep down, the sense of which nearly sickened him. She had too again most of all her strange significant smile. "Of course if it's that you really *know* something—?" It was quite conceivable and possible to her, he could see, that he did. But he didn't even know what she meant, and he only looked at her in gloom. His gloom however didn't upset her. "You do, I believe, only you've a delicacy about saying it. Your delicacy to me, my dear, is a scruple too much. I should have no delicacy in hearing it, so that if you can *tell* me you know—"

"Well?" he asked as she still kept what depended on it.

"Why then I'll do what you want. We needn't, I grant you, in that case wait; and I can see what you mean by thinking it nicer of us not to. I don't even ask you," she continued, "for a proof. I'm content with your moral certainty."

By this time it had come over him—it had the force of a rush. The point she made was clear, as clear as that the blood, while he recognised it, mantled in his face. "I know nothing whatever."

"You've not an idea?"

"I've not an idea."

"I'd consent," she said—"I'd announce it to-morrow, to-day, I'd go home this moment and announce it to Aunt Maud, for an idea: I mean an idea straight *from* you, I mean as your own, given me in good faith. There, my dear!"—and she smiled again. "I call that really meeting you."

If it *was* then what she called it, it disposed of his appeal, and he could but stand there with his wasted passion—for it was in high passion that he had from the morning acted—in his face. She made it all out, bent upon her—the idea he didn't have, and the idea he had, and his failure of insistence when it brought up *that* challenge, and his sense of her personal presence, and his horror, almost, of her lucidity. They made in him a mix-mixture that might have been rage, but that was turning quickly to mere cold thought, thought which led to something else and was like a new dim dawn. It affected her then, and she had one of the impulses, in all sincerity, that had before this, between them, saved their position. When she had come nearer to him, when, putting her hand upon him, she made him sink with her, as she leaned to him, into their old pair of chairs, she prevented irresistibly, she forestalled, the waste of his passion. She had an advantage with his passion now.

III

He had said to her in the Park when challenged on it that nothing had "happened" to him as a cause for the demand he there made of her—happened he meant since the account he had given, after his return, of his recent experience. But in the course of a few days—they had brought him to Christmas morning—he was conscious enough, in preparing again to seek her out, of a difference on that score. Something had in this case happened to him, and, after his taking the night to think of it he felt that what it most, if not absolutely first, involved was his immediately again putting himself in relation with her. The fact itself had met him there—in his own small quarters—on Christmas Eve, and had not then indeed at once affected him as implying that consequence. So far as he on the spot and for the next hours took its measure—a process that made his night mercilessly wakeful—the consequences possibly implied were numerous to distraction. His spirit dealt with them, in the darkness, as the slow hours passed; his intelligence and his imagination, his soul and his sense, had never on the whole been so intensely engaged. It was his difficulty for the moment that he was face to face with alternatives, and that it was scarce even a question of turning from one to the other. They were not in a perspective in which they might be compared and considered; they were, by a strange effect, as close as a pair of monsters of whom he might have felt on either cheek the hot breath and the huge eyes. He saw them at once and but by looking straight before him; he wouldn't for that matter, in his cold apprehension, have turned his head by an inch. So it was that his agitation was still—was not, for the slow hours a matter of restless motion. He lay long, after the event, on the sofa where, extinguishing at a touch the white light of convenience that he hated, he had thrown himself without undressing. He stared at the buried day and wore out the time; with the arrival of the Christmas dawn moreover, late and grey, he felt himself somehow determined. The common wisdom had had its say to him—that safety in doubt was *not* action; and perhaps what most helped him was this very commonness. In his case there was nothing of *that*—in no case in his life had there ever been less: which association, from one thing to another, now worked for him as a choice. He acted, after his bath and his breakfast, in the sense of that marked element of the rare which he felt to be the sign of his crisis. And that is why, dressed with more state than usual and quite as if for church, he went out into the soft Christmas day.

Action, for him, on coming to the point, it appeared, carried with it a certain complexity. We should have known, walking by his side, that his final prime decision hadn't been to call at the door of Sir Luke Strett, and yet that this step, though subordinate, was none the less urgent. His prime decision was for another matter, to which impatience, once he was on the way, had now added itself; but he remained sufficiently aware that he must compromise with the perhaps excessive earliness. This, and the ferment set up within him, were together a reason for not driving; to say nothing of the absence of cabs in the dusky festal desert. Sir Luke's great square was not near, but he walked the Distance without seeing a hansom. He had his interval thus to turn over his view—the view to which what had happened the night before had not sharply reduced itself; but the complexity just mentioned was to be offered within the next few minutes another item to assimilate. Before Sir Luke's house, when he reached it, a brougham was drawn up—at the sight of which his heart had a lift that brought him for the instant to a stand. This pause wasn't long, but it was long enough to flash upon him a revelation in the light of which he caught his breath. The carriage, so possibly at such an hour and on such a day Sir Luke's own, had struck him as a sign that the great doctor was back. This would prove something else, in turn, still more intensely, and it was in the act of the double apprehension that Densher felt himself turn pale. His mind rebounded for the moment like a projectile that has suddenly been met by another: he stared at the strange truth that what he wanted *more* than to see Kate Croy was to see the witness who had just arrived from Venice. He wanted positively to be in his presence and to hear his voice—which was the spasm of his consciousness that produced the flash. Fortunately for him, on the spot, there supervened something in which the flash went out. He became aware within this minute that the coachman on the box of the brougham had a face known to him, whereas he had never seen before, to his knowledge, the great doctor's carriage. The carriage, as he came nearer, was simply Mrs. Lowder's; the face on the box was just the face that, in coming and going at Lancaster Gate, he would vaguely have noticed, outside, in attendance. With this the rest came: the lady of Lancaster Gate had, on a prompting not wholly remote from his own, presented herself for news; and news, in the house, she was clearly getting, since her brougham had stayed. Sir Luke *was* then back—only Mrs. Lowder was with him.

It was under the influence of this last reflexion that Densher again delayed; and it was while he delayed that something else occurred to him. It was all round, visibly—given his own new contribution—a case of pressure; and in a case of pressure Kate, for quicker knowledge, might have come out with her aunt. The possibility that in this event she might be sitting in the carriage—the thing most likely—had had the effect, before he could check it, of bringing him within range of the window. It wasn't there he had wished to see her; yet if she *was* there he couldn't pretend not to. What he had however the next moment made out was that if some one was there it wasn't Kate Croy. It was, with a sensible shock for him, the person who had last offered him a conscious face from behind the clear plate of a café in Venice. The great glass at Florian's was a medium less obscure, even with the window down, than the air of the London Christmas; yet at present also, none the less, between the two men, an exchange of recognitions could occur. Densher felt his own look a gaping arrest—which, he disgustedly remembered, his back as quickly turned, appeared to repeat itself as his special privilege. He mounted the steps of the house and touched the bell with a keen consciousness of being habitually looked at by Kate's friend from positions of almost insolent vantage. He forgot for the time the moment when, in Venice, at the palace, the encouraged young man had in a manner assisted at the departure of the disconcerted, since Lord Mark was not looking disconcerted now any more than he had looked from his bench at his café. Densher was thinking that *he* seemed to show as vagrant while another was ensconced. He was thinking of the other as—in spite of the difference of situation—more ensconced than ever; he was thinking of him above all as the friend of the person with whom his recognition had, the minute previous, associated him. The man was seated in the very place in which, beside Mrs. Lowder's, he had looked to find Kate, and that was a sufficient identity. Meanwhile at any rate the door of the house had opened and Mrs. Lowder stood before him. It was something at least that *she* wasn't Kate. She was herself, on the spot, in all her affluence; with presence of mind both to decide at once that Lord Mark, in the brougham, didn't matter and to prevent Sir Luke's butler, by a firm word thrown over her shoulder, from standing there to listen to her passage with the gentleman who had rung. "*I'll* tell Mr. Densher; you needn't wait!" And the passage, promptly and richly, took place on the steps.

"He arrives, travelling straight, to-morrow early. I couldn't not come to learn."

"No more," said Densher simply, "could I. On my way," he added, "to Lancaster Gate."

"Sweet of you." She beamed on him dimly, and he saw her face was attuned. It made him, with what she had just before said, know all, and he took the thing in while he met the air of portentous, of almost functional, sympathy that had settled itself as her medium with him and that yet had now a fresh glow. "So you *have* had your message?"

He knew so well what she meant, and so equally with it what he "*had* had" no less than what he hadn't, that, with but the smallest hesitation, he strained the point. "Yes—my message."

"Our dear dove then, as Kate calls her, has folded her wonderful wings."

"Yes—folded them."

It rather racked him, but he tried to receive it as she intended, and she evidently took his formal assent for self-control. "Unless it's more true," she accordingly added, "that she has spread them the wider."

He again but formally assented, though, strangely enough, the words fitted a figure deep in his own imagination. "Rather, yes—spread them the wider."

"For a flight, I trust, to some happiness greater—!"

"Exactly. Greater," Densher broke in; but now with a look, he feared, that did a little warn her off.

"You were certainly," she went on with more reserve, "entitled to direct news. Ours came late last night: I'm not sure otherwise I shouldn't have gone to you. But you're coming," she asked, "to *me?*"

He had had a minute by this time to think further, and the window of the brougham was still within range. Her rich "me," reaching him moreover through the mild damp, had the effect of a thump on his chest. "Squared," Aunt Maud? She was indeed squared, and the extent of it just now perversely enough took away his breath. His look from where they stood embraced the aperture at which the person sitting in the carriage might have shown, and he saw his interlocutress, on her side, understand the question in it, which he moreover then uttered. "Shall you be alone?" It was, as an immediate instinctive parley with the image of his condition that now flourished in her, almost hypocritical. It sounded as if he wished to come and overflow to her, yet this was exactly what he didn't. The need to overflow had suddenly—since the night before—dried up in him, and he had never been aware of a deeper reserve.

But she had meanwhile largely responded. "Completely alone. I should otherwise never have dreamed; feeling, dear friend, but too much!" Failing on her lips what she felt came out for him in the offered hand with which she had the next moment condolingly pressed his own. "Dear friend, dear friend!"—she was deeply "with" him, and she wished to be still more so: which was what made her immediately continue. "Or wouldn't you this evening, for the sad Christmas it makes us, dine with me *tête-à-tête?*"

It put the thing off, the question of a talk with her—making the difference, to his relief, of several hours; but it also rather mystified him. This however didn't diminish his need of caution. "Shall you mind if I don't tell you at once?"

"Not in the least—leave it open: it shall be as you may feel, and you needn't even send me word. I only *will* mention that to-day, of all days, I shall otherwise sit there alone."

Now at least he could ask. "Without Miss Croy?"

"Without Miss Croy. Miss Croy," said Mrs. Lowder, "is spending her Christmas in the bosom of her more immediate family."

He was afraid, even while he spoke, of what his face might show. "You mean she has left you?"

Aunt Maud's own face for that matter met the enquiry with a consciousness in which he saw a reflexion of events. He was made sure by it, even at the moment and as he had never been before, that since he had known these two women no confessed nor commented tension, no crisis of the cruder sort would really have taken form between them: which was precisely a high proof of how Kate had steered her boat. The situation exposed in Mrs. Lowder's present expression lighted up by contrast that superficial smoothness; which afterwards, with his time to think of it, was to put before him again the art, the particular gift, in the girl, now so placed and classed, so intimately familiar for him, as her talent for life. The peace, within a day or two—since his seeing her last—had clearly been broken; differences, deep down, kept there by a diplomacy on Kate's part as deep, had been shaken to the surface by some exceptional jar; with which, in addition, he felt Lord Mark's odd attendance at such an hour and season vaguely associated. The talent for life indeed, it at the same time struck him, would probably have shown equally in the breach, or whatever had occurred; Aunt Maud having suffered, he judged, a strain rather than a stroke. Of these quick thoughts, at all events, that lady was already abreast. "She went yesterday morning—and not with my approval, I don't mind telling you—to her sister: Mrs. Condrip, if you know who I mean, who lives somewhere in Chelsea. My other niece and her affairs—that I should have to say such things to-day!—are a constant worry; so that Kate, in consequence—well, of events!—has simply been called in. My own idea, I'm bound to say, was that with *such* events she need have, in her situation, next to nothing to do."

"But she differed with you?"

"She differed with me. And when Kate differs with you—!"

"Oh I can imagine." He had reached the point in the scale of hypocrisy at which he could ask himself why a little more or less should signify. Besides, with the intention he had had he *must* know. Kate's move, if he didn't know, might simply disconcert him; and of being disconcerted his horror was by this time fairly superstitious. "I hope you don't allude to events at all calamitous."

"No—only horrid and vulgar."

"Oh!" said Merton Densher.

Mrs. Lowder's soreness, it was still not obscure, had discovered in free speech to him a momentary balm. "They've the misfortune to have, I suppose you know, a dreadful horrible father."

"Oh!" said Densher again.

"He's too bad almost to name, but he has come upon Marian, and Marian has shrieked for help."

Densher wondered at this with intensity; and his curiosity compromised for an instant with his discretion. "Come upon her—for money?"

"Oh for that of course always. But, at *this* blessed season, for refuge, for safety: for God knows what. He's *there*, the brute. And Kate's with them. And that," Mrs. Lowder wound up, going down the steps, "is her Christmas."

She had stopped again at the bottom while he thought of an answer. "Yours then is after all rather better."

"It's at least more decent." And her hand once more came out. "But why do I talk of *our* troubles? Come if you can."

He showed a faint smile. "Thanks. If I can."

"And now—I dare say—you'll go to church?"

She had asked it, with her good intention, rather in the air and by way of sketching for him, in the line of support, something a little more to the purpose than what she had been giving him. He felt it as finishing off their intensities of expression that he found himself to all appearance receiving her hint as happy. "Why yes—I think I will": after which, as the door of the brougham, at her approach, had opened from within, he was free to turn his back. He heard the door, behind him, sharply close again and the vehicle move off in another direction than his own.

He had in fact for the time no direction; in spite of which indeed he was at the end of ten minutes aware of having walked straight to the south. That, he afterwards recognised, was, very sufficiently, because there had formed itself in his mind, even while Aunt Maud finally talked, an instant recognition of his necessary course. Nothing was open to him but to follow Kate, nor was anything more marked than the influence of the step she had taken on the emotion itself that possessed him. Her complications, which had fairly, with everything else, an awful sound—what were they, a thousand times over, but his own? His present business was to see that they didn't escape an hour longer taking their proper place in his life. He accordingly would have held his course hadn't it suddenly come over him that he had just lied to Mrs. Lowder—a term it perversely eased him to keep using—even more than was necessary. To what church was he going, to what church, in such a state of his nerves, *could* he go?—he pulled up short again, as he had pulled up in sight of Mrs. Lowder's carriage, to ask it. And yet the desire queerly stirred in him not to have wasted his word. He was just then however by a happy chance in the Brompton Road, and he bethought himself with a sudden light that the Oratory was at hand. He had but to turn the other way and he should find himself soon before it. At the door then, in a few minutes, his idea was really—as it struck him—consecrated: he was, pushing in, on the edge of a splendid service—the flocking crowd told of it—which glittered and resounded, from distant depths, in the blaze of altar-lights and the swell of organ and choir. It didn't match his own day, but it was much less of a discord than some other things actual and possible. The Oratory in short, to make him right, would do.

IV

The difference was thus that the dusk of afternoon—dusk thick from an early hour—had gathered when he knocked at Mrs. Condrip's door. He had gone from the church to his club, wishing not to present himself in Chelsea at luncheon-time and also remembering that he must attempt independently to make a meal. This, in the event, he but imperfectly achieved: he dropped into a chair in the great dim void of the club library, with nobody, up or down, to be seen, and there after a while, closing his eyes, recovered an hour of the sleep he had lost during the night. Before doing this indeed he had written—it was the first thing he did—a short note, which, in the Christmas desolation of the place, he had managed only with difficulty and doubt to commit to a messenger. He wished it carried by hand, and he was obliged, rather blindly, to trust the hand, as the messenger, for some reason, was unable to return with a gage of delivery. When at four o'clock he was face to face with Kate in Mrs. Condrip's small drawing-room he found to his relief that his notification had reached her. She was expectant and to that extent prepared; which simplified a little—if a little, at the present pass, counted. Her conditions were vaguely vivid to him from the moment of his coming in, and vivid partly by their difference, a difference sharp and suggestive, from those in which he had hitherto constantly seen her. He had seen her but in places comparatively great; in her aunt's pompous house, under the high trees of Kensington and the storied ceilings of Venice. He had seen her, in Venice, on a great occasion, as the centre itself of the splendid Piazza: he had seen her there, on a still greater one, in his own poor rooms, which yet had consorted with her, having state and ancientry even in their poorness; but Mrs. Condrip's interior, even by this best view of it and though not flagrantly mean, showed itself as a setting almost grotesquely inapt. Pale, grave and charming, she affected him at once as a distinguished stranger—a stranger to the little Chelsea street—who was making the best of a queer episode and a place of exile. The extraordinary thing was that at the end of three minutes he felt himself less appointedly a stranger in it than she.

A part of the queerness—this was to come to him in glimpses—sprang from the air as of a general large misfit imposed on the narrow room by the scale and mass of its furniture. The objects, the ornaments were, for the sisters, clearly relics and survivals of what would, in the case of Mrs. Condrip at least, have been called better days. The curtains that overdraped the windows, the sofas and tables that stayed circulation, the chimney-ornaments that reached to the ceiling and the florid chandelier that almost dropped to the floor, were so many mementoes of earlier homes and so many links with their unhappy mother. Whatever might have been in itself the quality of these elements Densher could feel the effect proceeding from them, as they lumpishly blocked out the decline of the dim day, to be ugly almost to the point of the sinister. They failed to accommodate or to compromise; they asserted their differences without tact and without taste. It was truly having a sense of Kate's own quality thus promptly to see them in reference to it. But that Densher had this sense was no new thing to him, nor did he in strictness need, for the hour, to be reminded of it. He only knew, by one of the tricks his imagination so constantly played him, that he was, so far as her present tension went, very specially sorry for her—which was not the view that had determined his start in the morning; yet also that he himself would have taken it all, as he might say, less hard. *He* could have lived in such a place; but it wasn't given to those of his complexion, so to speak, to be exiled anywhere. It was by their comparative grossness that they could somehow make shift. His natural, his inevitable, his ultimate home—left, that is, to itself—wasn't at all unlikely to be as queer and impossible as what was just round them, though doubtless in less ample masses. As he took in moreover how Kate wouldn't have been in the least the creature she was if what was just round them hadn't mismatched her, hadn't made for her a medium involving compunction in the spectator, so, by the same stroke, that became the very fact of her relation with her companions there, such a fact as filled him at once, oddly, both with assurance and with suspense. If he himself, on this brief vision, felt her as alien and as ever so unwittingly ironic, how must they not feel her and how above all must she not feel them?

Densher could ask himself that even after she had presently lighted the tall candles on the mantel-shelf. This was all their illumination but the fire, and she had proceeded to it with a quiet dryness that yet left play, visibly, to her implication between them, in their trouble and failing anything better, of the presumably genial Christmas hearth. So far as the genial went this had in strictness, given their conditions, to be all their geniality. He had told her in his note nothing but that he must promptly see her and that he hoped she might be able to make it possible; but he understood from the first look at her that his promptitude was already having for her its principal reference. "I was prevented this morning, in the few minutes," he explained, "asking Mrs. Lowder if she had let you know, though I rather gathered she had; and it's what I've been in fact since then assuming. It was because I was so struck at the moment with your having, as she did tell me, so suddenly come here."

"Yes, it was sudden enough." Very neat and fine in the contracted firelight, with her hands in her lap, Kate considered what he had said. He had spoken immediately of what had happened at Sir Luke Strett's door. "She has let me know nothing. But that doesn't matter—if it's what *you* mean."

"It's part of what I mean," Densher said; but what he went on with, after a pause during which she waited, was apparently not the rest of that. "She had had her telegram from Mrs. Stringham; late last night. But to me the poor lady hasn't wired. The event," he added, "will have taken place yesterday, and Sir Luke, starting immediately, one can see, and travelling straight, will get back to-morrow morning. So that Mrs. Stringham, I judge, is left to face in some solitude the situation bequeathed to her. But of course," he wound up, "Sir Luke couldn't stay."

Her look at him might have had in it a vague betrayal of the sense that he was gaining time. "Was your telegram from Sir Luke?"

"No—I've had no telegram."

She wondered. "But not a letter—?"

"Not from Mrs. Stringham—no." He failed again however to develop this—for which her forbearance from another question gave him occasion. From whom then had he heard? He might at last, confronted with her, really have been gaining time; and as if to show that she respected this impulse she made her enquiry different. "Should you like to go out to her—to Mrs. Stringham?"

About that at least he was clear. "Not at all. She's alone, but she's very capable and very courageous. Besides—!" He had been going on, but he dropped.

"Besides," she said, "there's Eugenio? Yes, of course one remembers Eugenio."

She had uttered the words as definitely to show them for not untender; and he showed equally every reason to assent. "One remembers him indeed, and with every ground for it. He'll be of the highest value to her—he's capable of anything. What I was going to say," he went on, "is that some of their people from America must quickly arrive."

On this, as happened, Kate was able at once to satisfy him. "Mr. Someone-or-other, the person principally in charge of Milly's affairs—her first trustee, I suppose—had just got there at Mrs. Stringham's last writing."

"Ah that then was after your aunt last spoke to me—I mean the last time before this morning. I'm relieved to hear it. So," he said, "they'll do."

"Oh they'll do." And it came from each still as if it wasn't what each was most thinking of. Kate presently got however a step nearer to that. "But if you had been wired to by nobody what then this morning had taken you to Sir Luke?"

"Oh something else—which I'll presently tell you. It's what made me instantly need to see you; it's what I've come to speak to you of. But in a minute. I feel too many things," he went on, "at seeing you in this place." He got up as he spoke; she herself remained perfectly still. His movement had been to the fire, and, leaning a little, with his back to it, to look down on her from where he stood, he confined himself to his point. "Is it anything very bad that has brought you?"

He had now in any case said enough to justify her wish for more; so that, passing this matter by, she pressed her own challenge. "Do you mean, if I may ask, that *she*, dying—?" Her face, wondering, pressed it more than her words.

"Certainly you may ask," he after a moment said. "What has come to me is what, as I say, I came expressly to tell you. I don't mind letting you know," he went on, "that my decision to do this took for me last night and this morning a great deal of thinking of. But here I am." And he indulged in a smile that couldn't, he was well aware, but strike her as mechanical.

She went straighter with him, she seemed to show, than he really went with her. "You didn't want to come?"

"It would have been simple, my dear"—and he continued to smile—"if it had been, one way or the other, only a question of 'wanting.' It took, I admit it, the idea of what I had best do, all sorts of difficult and portentous forms. It came up for me really—well, not at all for my happiness."

This word apparently puzzled her—she studied him in the light of it. "You look upset—you've certainly been tormented. You're not well."

"Oh—well enough!"

But she continued without heeding. "You hate what you're doing."

"My dear girl, you simplify"—and he was now serious enough. "It isn't so simple even as that."

She had the air of thinking what it then might be. "I of course can't, with no clue, know what it is." She remained none the less patient and still. "If at such a moment she could write you one's inevitably quite at sea. One doesn't, with the best will in the world, understand." And then as Densher had a pause which might have stood for all the involved explanation that, to his discouragement, loomed before him: "You *haven't* decided what to do."

She had said it very gently, almost sweetly, and he didn't instantly say otherwise. But he said so after a look at her. "Oh yes—I have. Only with this sight of you here and what I seem to see in it for you—!" And his eyes, as at suggestions that pressed, turned from one part of the room to another.

"Horrible place, isn't it?" said Kate.

It brought him straight back to his enquiry. "Is it for anything awful you've had to come?"

"Oh that will take as long to tell you as anything *you* may have. Don't mind," she continued, "the 'sight of me here,' nor whatever—which is more than I yet know myself—may be 'in it' for me. And kindly consider too that, after all, if you're in trouble I can a little wish to help you. Perhaps I can absolutely even do it."

"My dear child, it's just because of the sense of your wish—! I suppose I'm in trouble—I suppose that's it." He said this with so odd a suddenness of simplicity that she could only stare for it—which he as promptly saw. So he turned off as he could his vagueness. "And yet I oughtn't to be." Which sounded indeed vaguer still.

She waited a moment. "Is it, as you say for my own business, anything very awful?"

"Well," he slowly replied, "you'll tell me if you find it so. I mean if you find my idea—"

He was so slow that she took him up. "Awful?" A sound of impatience—the form of a laugh—at last escaped her. "I can't find it anything at all till I know what you're talking about."

It brought him then more to the point, though it did so at first but by making him, on the hearthrug before her, with his hands in his pockets, turn awhile to and fro. There rose in him even with this movement a recall of another time—the hour in Venice, the hour of gloom and storm, when Susan Shepherd had sat in his quarters there very much as Kate was sitting now, and he had wondered, in pain even as now, what he might say and mightn't. Yet the present occasion after all was somehow the easier. He tried at any rate to attach that feeling to it while he stopped before his companion. "The communication I speak of can't possibly belong—so far as its date is concerned—to these last days. The postmark, which is legible, does; but it isn't thinkable, for anything else, that she wrote—!" He dropped, looking at her as if she'd understand.

It was easy to understand. "On her deathbed?" But Kate took an instant's thought. "Aren't we agreed that there was never any one in the world like her?"

"Yes." And looking over her head he spoke clearly enough. "There was never any one in the world like her."

Kate, from her chair, always without a movement, raised her eyes to the unconscious reach of his own. Then when the latter again dropped to her she added a question. "And won't it further depend a little on what the communication is?"

"A little perhaps—but not much. It's a communication," said Densher.

"Do you mean a letter?"

"Yes, a letter. Addressed to me in her hand—in hers unmistakeably."

Kate thought. "Do you know her hand very well?"

"Oh perfectly."

It was as if his tone for this prompted—with a slight strangeness—her next demand. "Have you had many letters from her?"

"No. Only three notes." He spoke looking straight at her. "And very, very short ones."

"Ah," said Kate, "the number doesn't matter. Three lines would be enough if you're sure you remember."

"I'm sure I remember. Besides," Densher continued, "I've seen her hand in other ways. I seem to recall how you once, before she went to Venice, showed me one of her notes precisely *for* that. And then she once copied me something."

"Oh," said Kate almost with a smile, "I don't ask you for the detail of your reasons. One good one's enough." To which however she added as if precisely not to speak with impatience or with anything like irony: "And the writing has its usual look?"

Densher answered as if even to better that description of it. "It's beautiful."

"Yes—it *was* beautiful. Well," Kate, to defer to him still, further remarked, "it's not news to us now that she was stupendous. Anything's possible."

"Yes, anything's possible"—he appeared oddly to catch at it. "That's what I say to myself. It's what I've been believing you," he a trifle vaguely explained, "still more certain to feel."

She waited for him to say more, but he only, with his hands in his pockets, turned again away, going this time to the single window of the room, where in the absence of lamplight the blind hadn't been drawn. He looked out into the lamplit fog, lost himself in the small sordid London street—for sordid, with his other association, he felt it—as he had lost himself, with Mrs. Stringham's eyes on him, in the vista of the Grand Canal. It was present then to his recording consciousness that when he had last been driven to such an attitude the very depth of his resistance to the opportunity to give Kate away was what had so driven him. His waiting companion had on that occasion waited for him to say he *would*; and what he had meantime glowered forth at was the inanity of such a hope. Kate's attention, on her side, during these minutes, rested on the back and shoulders he thus familiarly presented—rested as with a view of their expression, a reference to things unimparted, links still missing and that she must ever miss, try to make them out as she would. The result of her tension was that she again took him up. "You received—what you spoke of—last night?"

It made him turn round. "Coming in from Fleet Street—earlier by an hour than usual—I found it with some other letters on my table. But my eyes went straight to it, in an extraordinary way, from the door. I recognised it, knew what it was, without touching it."

"One can understand." She listened with respect. His tone however was so singular that she presently added: "You speak as if all this while you *hadn't* touched it."

"Oh yes, I've touched it. I feel as if, ever since, I'd been touching nothing else. I quite firmly," he pursued as if to be plainer, "took hold of it."

"Then where is it?"

"Oh I have it here."

"And you've brought it to show me?"

"I've brought it to show you."

So he said with a distinctness that had, among his other oddities, almost a sound of cheer, yet making no movement that matched his words. She could accordingly but offer again her expectant face, while his own, to her impatience, seemed perversely to fill with another thought. "But now that you've done so you feel you don't want to."

"I want to immensely," he said. "Only you tell me nothing."

She smiled at him, with this, finally, as if he were an unreasonable child. "It seems to me I tell you quite as much as you tell me. You haven't yet even told me how it is that such explanations as you require don't come from your document itself." Then as he answered nothing she had a flash. "You mean you haven't read it?"

"I haven't read it."

She stared. "Then how am I to help you with it?"

Again leaving her while she never budged he paced five strides, and again he was before her. "By telling me *this*. It's something, you know, that you wouldn't tell me the other day."

She was vague. "The other day?"

"The first time after my return—the Sunday I came to you. What's he doing," Densher went on, "at that hour of the morning with her? What does his having been with her there mean?"

"Of whom are you talking?"

"Of that man—Lord Mark of course. What does it represent?"

"Oh with Aunt Maud?"

"Yes, my dear—and with you. It comes more or less to the same thing; and it's what you didn't tell me the other day when I put you the question."

Kate tried to remember the other day. "You asked me nothing about any hour."

"I asked you when it was you last saw him—previous, I mean, to his second descent at Venice. You wouldn't say, and as we were talking of a matter comparatively more important I let it pass. But the fact remains, you know, my dear, that you haven't told me."

Two things in this speech appeared to have reached Kate more distinctly than the others. "I 'wouldn't say'?—and you 'let it pass'?" She looked just coldly blank. "You really speak as if I were keeping something back."

"Well, you see," Densher persisted, "you're not even telling me now. All I want to know," he nevertheless explained, "is whether there was a connexion between that proceeding on his part, which was practically—oh beyond all doubt!—the shock precipitating for her what has now happened, and anything that had occurred with him previously for yourself. How in the world did he know we're engaged?"

V

Kate slowly rose; it was, since she had lighted the candles and sat down, the first movement she had made. "Are you trying to fix it on me that I must have told him?"

She spoke not so much in resentment as in pale dismay—which he showed he immediately took in. "My dear child, I'm not trying to 'fix' anything; but I'm extremely tormented and I seem not to understand. What has the brute to do with us anyway?"

"What has he indeed?" Kate asked.

She shook her head as if in recovery, within the minute, of some mild allowance for his unreason. There was in it—and for his reason really—one of those half-inconsequent sweetnesses by which she had often before made, over some point of difference, her own terms with him. Practically she was making them now, and essentially he was knowing it; yet inevitably, all the same, he was accepting it. She stood there close to him, with something in her patience that suggested her having supposed, when he spoke more appealingly, that he was going to kiss her. He hadn't been, it appeared; but his continued appeal was none the less the quieter. "What's he doing, from ten o'clock on Christmas morning, with Mrs. Lowder?"

Kate looked surprised. "Didn't she tell you he's staying there?"

"At Lancaster Gate?" Densher's surprise met it. "'Staying'?—since when?"

"Since day before yesterday. He was there before I came away." And then she explained—confessing it in fact anomalous. "It's an accident—like Aunt Maud's having herself remained in town for Christmas, but it isn't after all so monstrous. *We* stayed—and, with my having come here, she's sorry now—because we neither of us, waiting from day to day for the news you brought, seemed to want to be with a lot of people."

"You stayed for thinking of—Venice?"

"Of course we did. For what else? And even a little," Kate wonderfully added—"it's true at least of Aunt Maud—for thinking of you."

He appreciated. "I see. Nice of you every way. But whom," he enquired, "has Lord Mark stayed for thinking of?"

"His being in London, I believe, is a very commonplace matter. He has some rooms which he has had suddenly some rather advantageous chance to let—such as, with his confessed, his decidedly proclaimed want of money, he hasn't had it in him, in spite of everything, not to jump at."

Densher's attention was entire. "In spite of everything? In spite of what?"

"Well, I don't know. In spite, say, of his being scarcely supposed to do that sort of thing."

"To try to get money?"

"To try at any rate in little thrifty ways. Apparently however he has had for some reason to do what he can. He turned at a couple of days' notice out of his place, making it over to his tenant; and Aunt Maud, who's deeply in his confidence about all such matters, said: 'Come then to Lancaster Gate—to sleep at least—till, like all the world, you go to the country.' He was to have gone to the country—I think to Matcham—yesterday afternoon: Aunt Maud, that is, told me he was."

Kate had been somehow, for her companion, through this statement, beautifully, quite soothingly, suggestive. "Told you, you mean, so that you needn't leave the house?"

"Yes—so far as she had taken it into her head that his being there was part of my reason."

"And *was* it part of your reason?"

"A little if you like. Yet there's plenty here—as I knew there would be—without it. So that," she said candidly, "doesn't matter. I'm glad I am here: even if for all the good I do—!" She implied however that that didn't matter either. "He didn't, as you tell me, get off then to Matcham; though he may possibly, if it is possible, be going this afternoon. But what strikes me as most probable—and it's really, I'm bound to say, quite amiable of him—is that he has declined to leave Aunt Maud, as I've been so ready to do, to spend her Christmas alone. If moreover he has given up Matcham for her it's a *procédé* that won't please her less. It's small wonder therefore that she insists, on a dull day, in driving him about. I don't pretend to know," she wound up, "what may happen between them; but that's all I see in it."

"You see in everything, and you always did," Densher returned, "something that, while I'm with you at least, I always take from you as the truth itself."

She looked at him as if consciously and even carefully extracting the sting of his reservation; then she spoke with a quiet gravity that seemed to show how fine she found it. "Thank you." It had for him, like everything else, its effect. They were still closely face to face, and, yielding to the impulse to which he hadn't yielded just before, he laid his hands on her shoulders, held her hard a minute and shook her a little, far from untenderly, as if in expression of more mingled things, all difficult, than he could speak. Then bending his head he applied his lips to her cheek. He fell, after this, away for an instant, resuming his unrest, while she kept the position in which, all passive and as a statue, she had taken his demonstration. It didn't prevent her, however, from offering him, as if what she had had was enough for the moment, a further indulgence. She made a quiet lucid connexion and as she made it sat down again. "I've been trying to place exactly, as to its date, something that did happen to me while you were in Venice. I mean a talk with him. He spoke to me—spoke out."

"Ah there you are!" said Densher who had wheeled round.

"Well, if I'm 'there,' as you so gracefully call it, by having refused to meet him as he wanted—as he pressed—I plead guilty to being so. Would you have liked me," she went on, "to give him an answer that would have kept him from going?"

It made him a little awkwardly think. "Did you know he was going?"

"Never for a moment; but I'm afraid that—even if it doesn't fit your strange suppositions—I should have given him just the same answer if I had known. If it's a matter I haven't, since your return, thrust upon you, that's simply because it's not a matter in the memory of which I find a particular joy. I hope that if I've satisfied you about it," she continued, "it's not too much to ask of you to let it rest."

"Certainly," said Densher kindly, "I'll let it rest." But the next moment he pursued: "He saw something. He guessed."

"If you mean," she presently returned, "that he was unfortunately the one person we hadn't deceived, I can't contradict you."

"No—of course not. But *why*," Densher still risked, "was he unfortunately the one person—? He's not really a bit intelligent."

"Intelligent enough apparently to have seen a mystery, a riddle, in anything so unnatural as—all things considered and when it came to the point—my attitude. So he gouged out his conviction, and on his conviction he acted."

Densher seemed for a little to look at Lord Mark's conviction as if it were a blot on the face of nature. "Do you mean because you had appeared to him to have encouraged him?"

"Of course I had been decent to him. Otherwise where *were* we?"

"'Where'—?"

"You and I. What I appeared to him, however, hadn't mattered. What mattered was how I appeared to Aunt Maud. Besides, you must remember that he has had all along his impression of *you*. You can't help it," she said, "but you're after all—well, yourself."

"As much myself as you please. But when I took myself to Venice and kept myself there—what," Densher asked, "did he make of that?"

"Your being in Venice and liking to be—which is never on any one's part a monstrosity—was explicable for him in other ways. He was quite capable moreover of seeing it as dissimulation."

"In spite of Mrs. Lowder?"

"No," said Kate, "not in spite of Mrs. Lowder now. Aunt Maud, before what you call his second descent, hadn't convinced him—all the more that my refusal of him didn't help. But he came back convinced." And then as her companion still showed a face at a loss: "I mean after he had seen Milly, spoken to her and left her. Milly convinced him."

"Milly?" Densher again but vaguely echoed.

"That you were sincere. That it was *her* you loved." It came to him from her in such a way that he instantly, once more, turned, found himself yet again at his window. "Aunt Maud, on his return here," she meanwhile continued, "had it from him. And that's why you're now so well with Aunt Maud."

He only for a minute looked out in silence—after which he came away. "And why *you* are." It was almost, in its extremely affirmative effect between them, the note of recrimination; or it would have been perhaps rather if it hadn't been so much more the note of truth. It was sharp because it was true, but its truth appeared to impose it as an argument so conclusive as to permit on neither side a sequel. That made, while they faced each other over it without speech, the gravity of everything. It was as if there were almost danger, which the wrong word might start. Densher accordingly at last acted to better purpose: he drew, standing there before her, a pocket-book from the breast of his waistcoat and he drew from the pocket-book a folded letter to which her eyes attached themselves. He restored then the receptacle to its place and, with a movement not the less odd for being visibly instinctive and unconscious, carried the hand containing his letter behind him. What he thus finally spoke of was a different matter. "Did I understand from Mrs. Lowder that your father's in the house?"

If it never had taken her long in such excursions to meet him it was not to take her so now. "In the house, yes. But we needn't fear his interruption"—she spoke as if he had thought of that. "He's in bed."

"Do you mean with illness?"

She sadly shook her head. "Father's never ill. He's a marvel. He's only—endless."

Densher thought. "Can I in any way help you with him?"

"Yes." She perfectly, wearily, almost serenely, had it all. "By our making your visit as little of an affair as possible for him—and for Marian too."

"I see. They hate so your seeing me. Yet I couldn't—could I?—not have come."

"No, you couldn't not have come."

"But I can only, on the other hand, go as soon as possible?"

Quickly it almost upset her. "Ah don't, to-day, put ugly words into my mouth. I've enough of my trouble without it."

"I know—I know!" He spoke in instant pleading. "It's all only that I'm as troubled *for* you. When did he come?"

"Three days ago—after he hadn't been near her for more than a year, after he had apparently, and not regrettably, ceased to remember her existence; and in a state which made it impossible not to take him in."

Densher hesitated. "Do you mean in such want—?"

"No, not of food, of necessary things—not even, so far as his appearance went, of money. He looked as wonderful as ever. But he was—well, in terror."

"In terror of what?"

"I don't know. Of somebody—of something. He wants, he says, to be quiet. But his quietness is awful."

She suffered, but he couldn't not question. "What does he do?"

It made Kate herself hesitate. "He cries."

Again for a moment he hung fire, but he risked it. "What *has* he done?"

It made her slowly rise, and they were once more fully face to face. Her eyes held his own and she was paler than she had been. "If you love me—now—don't ask me about father."

He waited again a moment. "I love you. It's because I love you that I'm here. It's because I love you that I've brought you this." And he drew from behind him the letter that had remained in his hand.

But her eyes only—though he held it out—met the offer. "Why you've not broken the seal!"

"If I had broken the seal—exactly—I should know what's within. It's for *you* to break the seal that I bring it."

She looked—still not touching the thing—inordinately grave. "To break the seal of something to you from *her?*"

"Ah precisely because it's from her. I'll abide by whatever you think of it."

"I don't understand," said Kate. "What do you yourself think?" And then as he didn't answer: "It seems to me *I* think you know. You have your instinct. You don't need to read. It's the proof."

Densher faced her words as if they had been an accusation, an accusation for which he was prepared and which there was but one way to face. "I have indeed my instinct. It came to me, while I worried it out, last night. It came to me as an effect of the hour." He held up his letter and seemed now to insist more than to confess. "This thing had been timed."

"For Christmas Eve?"

"For Christmas Eve."

Kate had suddenly a strange smile. "The season of gifts!" After which, as he said nothing, she went on: "And had been written, you mean, while she could write, and kept to *be* so timed?"

Only meeting her eyes while he thought, he again didn't reply. "What do *you* mean by the proof?"

"Why of the beauty with which you've been loved. But I won't," she said, "break your seal."

"You positively decline?"

"Positively. Never." To which she added oddly: "I know without."

He had another pause. "And what is it you know?"

"That she announces to you she has made you rich."

His pause this time was longer. "Left me her fortune?"

"Not all of it, no doubt, for it's immense. But money to a large amount. I don't care," Kate went on, "to know how much." And her strange smile recurred. "I trust her."

"Did she tell you?" Densher asked.

"Never!" Kate visibly flushed at the thought. "That wouldn't, on my part, have been playing fair with her. And I did," she added, "play fair."

Densher, who had believed her—he couldn't help it—continued, holding his letter, to face her. He was much quieter now, as if his torment had somehow passed. "You played fair with me, Kate; and that's why—since we talk of proofs—I want to give *you* one. I've wanted to let you see—and in preference even to myself—something I feel as sacred."

She frowned a little. "I don't understand."

"I've asked myself for a tribute, for a sacrifice by which I can peculiarly recognise—"

"Peculiarly recognise what?" she demanded as he dropped.

"The admirable nature of your own sacrifice. You were capable in Venice of an act of splendid generosity."

"And the privilege you offer me with that document is my reward?"

He made a movement. "It's all I can do as a symbol of my attitude."

She looked at him long. "Your attitude, my dear, is that you're afraid of yourself. You've had to take yourself in hand. You've had to do yourself violence."

"So it is then you meet me?"

She bent her eyes hard a moment to the letter, from which her hand still stayed itself. "You absolutely *desire* me to take it?"

"I absolutely desire you to take it."

"To do what I like with it?"

"Short of course of making known its terms. It must remain—pardon my making the point—between you and me."

She had a last hesitation, but she presently broke it. "Trust me." Taking from him the sacred script she held it a little while her eyes again rested on those fine characters of Milly's that they had shortly before discussed. "To hold it," she brought out, "is to know."

"Oh I *know!*" said Merton Densher.

"Well then if we both do—!" She had already turned to the fire, nearer to which she had moved, and with a quick gesture had jerked the thing into the flame. He started—but only half—as to undo her action: his arrest was as prompt as the latter had been decisive. He only watched, with her, the paper burn; after which their eyes again met. "You'll have it all," Kate said, "from New York."

It was after he had in fact, two months later, heard from New York that she paid him a visit one morning at his own quarters—coming not as she had come in Venice, under his extreme solicitation, but as a need recognised in the first instance by herself, even though also as the prompt result of a missive delivered to her. This had consisted of a note from Densher accompanying a letter, "just to hand," addressed him by an eminent American legal firm, a firm of whose high character he had become conscious while in New York as of a thing in the air itself, and whose head and front, the principal executor of Milly Theale's copious will, had been duly identified at Lancaster Gate as the gentleman hurrying out, by the straight southern course, before the girl's death, to the support of Mrs. Stringham. Densher's act on receipt of the document in question—an act as to which and to the bearings of which his resolve had had time to mature—constituted in strictness, singularly enough, the first reference to Milly, or to what Milly might or might not have done, that had passed between our pair since they had stood together watching the destruction, in the little vulgar grate at Chelsea, of the undisclosed work of her hand. They had at the time, and in due deference now, on his part, to Kate's mention of her responsibility for his call, immediately separated, and when they met again the subject was made present to them—at all events till some flare of new light—only by the intensity with which it mutely expressed its absence. They were not moreover in these weeks to meet often, in spite of the fact that this had, during January and a part of February, actually become for them a comparatively easy matter. Kate's stay at Mrs. Condrip's prolonged itself under allowances from her aunt which would have been a mystery to Densher had he not been admitted, at Lancaster Gate, really in spite of himself, to the esoteric view of them. "It's her idea," Mrs. Lowder had there said to him as if she really despised ideas—which she didn't; "and I've taken up with my own, which is to give her her head till she has had enough of it. She *has* had enough of it, she had that soon enough; but as she's as proud as the deuce she'll come back when she has found some reason—having nothing in common with her disgust—of which she can make a show. She calls it her holiday, which she's spending in her own way—the holiday to which, once a year or so, as she says, the very maids in the scullery have a right. So we're taking it on that basis. But we shall not soon, I think, take another of the same sort. Besides, she's quite decent; she comes often—whenever I make her a sign; and she has been good, on the whole, this year or two, so that, to be decent myself, I don't complain. She has really been, poor dear, very much what one hoped; though I needn't, you know," Aunt Maud wound up, "tell *you*, after all, you clever creature, what that was."

It had been partly in truth to keep down the opportunity for this that Densher's appearances under the good lady's roof markedly, after Christmas, interspaced themselves. The phase of his situation that on his return from Venice had made them for a short time almost frequent was at present quite obscured, and with it the impulse that had then acted. Another phase had taken its place, which he would have been painfully at a loss as yet to name or otherwise set on its feet, but of which the steadily rising tide left Mrs. Lowder, for his desire, quite high and dry. There had been a moment when it seemed possible that Mrs. Stringham, returning to America under convoy, would pause in London on her way and be housed with her old friend; in which case he was prepared for some apparent zeal of attendance. But this danger passed—he had felt it a danger, and the person in the world whom he would just now have most valued seeing on his own terms sailed away westward from Genoa. He thereby only wrote to her, having broken, in this respect, after Milly's death, the silence as to the sense of which, before that event, their agreement had been so deep. She had answered him from Venice twice, and had had time to answer him twice again from New York. The last letter of her four had come by the same post as the document he sent on to Kate, but he hadn't gone into the question of also enclosing that. His correspondence with Milly's companion was somehow already presenting itself to him as a feature—as a factor, he would have said in his newspaper—of the time whatever it might be, long or short, in store for him; but one of his acutest current thoughts was apt to be devoted to his not having yet mentioned it to Kate. She had put him no question, no "Don't you ever hear?"—so that he hadn't been brought to the point. This he described to himself as a mercy, for he liked his secret. It was as a secret that, in the same personal privacy, he described his transatlantic commerce, scarce even wincing while he recognised it as the one connexion in which he wasn't straight. He had in fact for this connexion a vivid mental image—he saw it as a small emergent rock in the waste of waters, the bottomless grey expanse of straightness. The fact that he had on several recent occasions taken with Kate an out-of-the-way walk that was each time to define itself as more remarkable for what they didn't say than for what they did—this fact failed somehow to mitigate for him a strange consciousness of exposure. There was something deep within him that he had absolutely shown to no one—to the companion of these walks in particular not a bit more than he could help; but he was none the less haunted, under its shadow, with a dire apprehension of publicity. It was as if he had invoked that ugliness in some stupid good faith; and it was queer enough that on his emergent rock, clinging to it and to Susan Shepherd, he should figure himself as hidden from view. That represented no doubt his belief in her power, or in her delicate disposition to protect him. Only Kate at all events knew—what Kate did know, and she was also the last person interested to tell it; in spite of which it was as if his *act*, so deeply associated with her and never to be recalled nor recovered, was abroad on the winds of the world. His honesty, as he viewed it with Kate, was the very element of that menace:

to the degree that he saw at moments, as to their final impulse or their final remedy, the need to bury in the dark blindness of each other's arms the knowledge of each other that they couldn't undo.

Save indeed that the sense in which it was in these days a question of arms was limited, this might have been the intimate expedient to which they were actually resorting. It had its value, in conditions that made everything count, that thrice over, in Battersea Park—where Mrs. Lowder now never drove—he had adopted the usual means, in sequestered alleys, of holding her close to his side. She could make absences, on her present footing, without having too inordinately to account for them at home—which was exactly what gave them for the first time an appreciable margin. He supposed she could always say in Chelsea—though he didn't press it—that she had been across the town, in decency, for a look at her aunt; whereas there had always been reasons at Lancaster Gate for her not being able to plead the look at her other relatives. It was therefore between them a freedom of a purity as yet untasted; which for that matter also they made in various ways no little show of cherishing as such. They made the show indeed in every way but the way of a large use—an inconsequence that they almost equally gave time to helping each other to regard as natural. He put it to his companion that the kind of favour he now enjoyed at Lancaster Gate, the wonderful warmth of his reception there, cut in a manner the ground from under their feet. He was too horribly trusted—they had succeeded too well. He couldn't in short make appointments with her without abusing Aunt Maud, and he couldn't on the other hand haunt that lady without tying his hands. Kate saw what he meant just as he saw what she did when she admitted that she was herself, to a degree scarce less embarrassing, in the enjoyment of Aunt Maud's confidence. It was special at present—she was handsomely used; she confessed accordingly to a scruple about misapplying her licence. Mrs. Lowder then finally had found—and all unconsciously now—the way to baffle them. It wasn't however that they didn't meet a little, none the less, in the southern quarter, to point for their common benefit the moral of their defeat. They crossed the river; they wandered in neighbourhoods sordid and safe; the winter was mild, so that, mounting to the top of trams, they could rumble together to Clapham or to Greenwich. If at the same time their minutes had never been so counted it struck Densher that by a singular law their tone—he scarce knew what to call it—had never been so bland. Not to talk of what they *might* have talked of drove them to other ground; it was as if they used a perverse insistence to make up what they ignored. They concealed their pursuit of the irrelevant by the charm of their manner; they took precautions for the courtesy they had formerly left to come of itself; often, when he had quitted her, he stopped short, walking off, with the aftersense of their change. He would have described their change—had he so far faced it as to describe it—by their being so damned civil. That had even, with the intimate, the familiar at the point to which they had brought them, a touch almost of the droll. What danger had there ever been of their becoming rude—after each had long since made the other so tremendously tender? Such were the things he asked himself when he wondered what in particular he most feared.

Yet all the while too the tension had its charm—such being the interest of a creature who could bring one back to her by such different roads. It was her talent for life again; which found in her a difference for the differing time. She didn't give their tradition up; she but made of it something new. Frankly moreover she had never been more agreeable nor in a way—to put it prosaically—better company: he felt almost as if he were knowing her on that defined basis—which he even hesitated whether to measure as reduced or as extended; as if at all events he were admiring her as she was probably admired by people she met "out." He hadn't in fine reckoned that she would still have something fresh for him; yet this was what she had—that on the top of a tram in the Borough he felt as if he were next her at dinner. What a person she would be if they *had* been rich—with what a genius for the so-called great life, what a presence for the so-called great house, what a grace for the so-called great positions! He might regret at once, while he was about it, that they weren't princes or billionaires. She had treated him on their Christmas to a softness that had struck him at the time as of the quality of fine velvet, meant to fold thick, but stretched a little thin; at present, however, she gave him the impression of a contact multitudinous as only the superficial can be. She had throughout never a word for what went on at home. She came out of that and she returned to it, but her nearest reference was the look with which, each time, she bade him good-bye. The look was her repeated prohibition: "It's what I *have* to see and to know—so don't touch it. That but wakes up the old evil, which I keep still, in my way, by sitting by it. I go now—leave me alone!—to sit by it again. The way to pity me—if that's what you want—is to believe in me. If we could really *do* anything it would be another matter."

He watched her, when she went her way, with the vision of what she thus a little stiffly carried. It was confused and obscure, but how, with her head high, it made her hold herself! He really in his own person might at these moments have been swaying a little aloft as one of the objects in her poised basket. It was doubtless thanks to some such consciousness as this that he felt the lapse of the weeks, before the day of Kate's mounting of his stair, almost swingingly rapid. They contained for him the contradiction that, whereas periods of waiting are supposed in general to keep the time slow, it was the wait, actually, that made the pace trouble him. The secret of that anomaly, to be plain, was that he was aware of how, while the days melted, something rare went with them. This something was only a thought, but a thought precisely of such freshness and such delicacy as made the precious, of whatever sort, most subject to the hunger of time. The thought was all his own, and his intimate companion was the last person he might have shared it with. He kept it back like a favourite pang; left it behind him, so to say, when he went out, but came home again the sooner for the certainty of finding it there. Then he took it out of its sacred corner and its soft wrappings; he undid them one by one, handling them, handling *it*, as a father, baffled and tender, might handle a maimed child. But so it was before him—in his dread of who else might see it. Then he took to himself at such hours, in other words, that he should never, never know what had been in Milly's letter. The intention announced in it he should but too probably know; only that would have been, but for the depths of his spirit, the least part of it. The part of it missed for ever was the turn she would have given her act. This turn had possibilities that, somehow, by wondering about them, his imagination had extraordinarily filled out and refined. It had made of them a revelation the loss of which was like the sight of a priceless pearl cast before his eyes—his pledge given not to save it—into the fathomless sea, or rather even it was like the sacrifice of something sentient and throbbing, something that, for the spiritual ear, might have been audible as a faint far wail. This was the sound he cherished when alone in the stillness of his rooms. He sought and guarded the stillness, so that it might prevail there till the inevitable sounds of life, once more, comparatively coarse and harsh, should smother and deaden it—doubtless by the same process with which they would officiously heal the ache in his soul that was somehow one with it. It moreover deepened the sacred hush that he couldn't complain. He had given poor Kate her freedom.

The great and obvious thing, as soon as she stood there on the occasion we have already named, was that she was now in high possession of it. This would have marked immediately the difference—had there been nothing else to do it—between their actual terms and their other terms, the character of their last encounter in Venice. That had been *his* idea, whereas her present step was her own; the few marks they had in common were, from the first moment, to his conscious vision, almost pathetically plain. She was as grave now as before; she looked around her, to hide it, as before; she pretended, as before, in an air in which her words at the moment itself fell flat, to an interest in the place and a curiosity about his "things"; there was a recall in the way in which, after she had failed a little to push up her veil symmetrically and he had said she had better take it off altogether, she had acceded to his suggestion before the glass. It was just these things that were vain; and what was real was that his fancy figured her after the first few minutes as literally now providing the element of reassurance which had previously been his care. It was she, supremely, who had the presence of mind. She made indeed for that matter very prompt use of it. "You see I've not hesitated this time to break your seal."

She had laid on the table from the moment of her coming in the long envelope, substantially filled, which he had sent her enclosed in another of still ampler make. He had however not looked at it—his belief being that he wished never again to do so; besides which it had happened to rest with its addressed side up. So he "saw" nothing, and it was only into her eyes that her remark made him look, declining any approach to the object indicated. "It's not 'my' seal, my dear; and my intention—which my note tried to express—was all to treat it to you as not mine."

"Do you mean that it's to that extent mine then?"

"Well, let us call it, if we like, theirs—that of the good people in New York, the authors of our communication. If the seal is broken well and good; but we *might*, you know," he presently added, "have sent it back to them intact and inviolate. Only accompanied," he smiled with his heart in his mouth, "by an absolutely kind letter."

Kate took it with the mere brave blink with which a patient of courage signifies to the exploring medical hand that the tender place is touched. He saw on the spot that she was prepared, and with this signal sign that she was too intelligent not to be, came a flicker of possibilities. She was—merely to put it at that—intelligent enough for anything. "Is it what you're proposing we *should* do?"

"Ah it's too late to do it—well, ideally. Now, with that sign that we *know*—!"

"But you don't know," she said very gently.

"I refer," he went on without noticing it, "to what would have been the handsome way. Its being dispatched again, with no cognisance taken but one's assurance of the highest consideration, and the proof of this in the state of the envelope—*that* would have been really satisfying."

She thought an instant. "The state of the envelope proving refusal, you mean, not to be based on the insufficiency of the sum?"

Densher smiled again as for the play, however whimsical, of her humour. "Well yes—something of that sort."

"So that if cognisance *has* been taken—so far as I'm concerned—it spoils the beauty?"

"It makes the difference that I'm disappointed in the hope—which I confess I entertained—that you'd bring the thing back to me as you had received it."

"You didn't express that hope in your letter."

"I didn't want to. I wanted to leave it to yourself. I wanted—oh yes, if that's what you wish to ask me—to see what you'd do."

"You wanted to measure the possibilities of my departure from delicacy?"

He continued steady now; a kind of ease—from the presence, as in the air, of something he couldn't yet have named—had come to him. "Well, I wanted—in so good a case—to test you."

She was struck—it showed in her face—by his expression. "It *is* a good case. I doubt whether a better," she said with her eyes on him, "has ever been known."

"The better the case then the better the test!"

"How do you know," she asked in reply to this, "what I'm capable of?"

"I don't, my dear! Only with the seal unbroken I should have known sooner."

"I see"—she took it in. "But I myself shouldn't have known at all. And you wouldn't have known, either, what I do know."

"Let me tell you at once," he returned, "that if you've been moved to correct my ignorance I very particularly request you not to."

She just hesitated. "Are you afraid of the effect of the corrections? Can you only do it by doing it blindly?"

He waited a moment. "What is it that you speak of my doing?"

"Why the only thing in the world that I take you as thinking of. Not accepting—what she has done. Isn't there some regular name in such cases? Not taking up the bequest."

"There's something you forget in it," he said after a moment. "My asking you to join with me in doing so."

Her wonder but made her softer, yet at the same time didn't make her less firm. "How can I 'join' in a matter with which I've nothing to do?"

"How? By a single word."

"And what word?"

"Your consent to my giving up."

"My consent has no meaning when I can't prevent you."

"You can perfectly prevent me. Understand that well," he said.

She seemed to face a threat in it. "You mean you won't give up if I *don't* consent?"

"Yes. I do nothing."

"That, as I understand, is accepting."

Densher paused. "I do nothing formal."

"You won't, I suppose you mean, touch the money."

"I won't touch the money."

It had a sound—though he had been coming to it—that made for gravity. "Who then in such an event *will?*"

"Any one who wants or who can."

Again a little she said nothing: she might say too much. But by the time she spoke he had covered ground. "How can I touch it but *through* you?"

"You can't. Any more," he added, "than I can renounce it except through you."

"Oh ever so much less! There's nothing," she explained, "in my power."

"I'm in your power," Merton Densher said.

"In what way?"

"In the way I show—and the way I've always shown. When have I shown," he asked as with a sudden cold impatience, "anything else? You surely must feel—so that you needn't wish to appear to spare me in it—how you 'have' me."

"It's very good of you, my dear," she nervously laughed, "to put me so thoroughly up to it!"

"I put you up to nothing. I didn't even put you up to the chance that, as I said a few moments ago, I saw for you in forwarding that thing. Your liberty is therefore in every way complete."

It had come to the point really that they showed each other pale faces, and that all the unspoken between them looked out of their eyes in a dim terror of their further conflict. Something even rose between them in one of their short silences—something that was like an appeal from each to the other not to be too true. Their necessity was somehow before them, but which of them must meet it first? "Thank you!" Kate said for his word about her freedom, but taking for the minute no further action on it. It was blest at least that all ironies failed them, and during another slow moment their very sense of it cleared the air.

There was an effect of this in the way he soon went on. "You must intensely feel that it's the thing for which we worked together."

She took up the remark, however, no more than if it were commonplace; she was already again occupied with a point of her own. "Is it absolutely true—for if it is, you know, it's tremendously interesting—that you haven't so much as a curiosity about what she has done for you?"

"Would you like," he asked, "my formal oath on it?"

"No—but I don't understand. It seems to me in your place—!"

"Ah," he couldn't help breaking in, "what do you know of my place? Pardon me," he at once added; "my preference is the one I express."

She had in an instant nevertheless a curious thought. "But won't the facts be published?"

"'Published'?"—he winced.

"I mean won't you see them in the papers?"

"Ah never! I shall know how to escape that."

It seemed to settle the subject, but she had the next minute another insistence. "Your desire is to escape everything?"

"Everything."

"And do you need no more definite sense of what it is you ask me to help you to renounce?"

"My sense is sufficient without being definite. I'm willing to believe that the amount of money's not small."

"Ah there you are!" she exclaimed.

"If she was to leave me a remembrance," he quietly pursued, "it would inevitably not be meagre."

Kate waited as for how to say it. "It's worthy of her. It's what she was herself—if you remember what we once said *that* was."

He hesitated—as if there had been many things. But he remembered one of them. "Stupendous?"

"Stupendous." A faint smile for it—ever so small—had flickered in her face, but had vanished before the omen of tears, a little less uncertain, had shown themselves in his own. His eyes filled—but that made her continue. She continued gently. "I think that what it really is must be that you're afraid. I mean," she explained, "that you're afraid of *all* the truth. If you're in love with her without it, what indeed can you be more? And you're afraid—it's wonderful!—to be in love with her."

"I never was in love with her," said Densher.

She took it, but after a little she met it. "I believe that now—for the time she lived. I believe it at least for the time you were there. But your change came—as it might well—the day you last saw her; she died for you then that you might understand her. From that hour you *did*." With which Kate slowly rose. "And I do now. She did it *for* us." Densher rose to face her, and she went on with her thought. "I used to call her, in my stupidity—for want of anything better—a dove. Well she stretched out her wings, and it was to *that* they reached. They cover us."

"They cover us," Densher said.

"That's what I give you," Kate gravely wound up. "That's what I've done for you."

His look at her had a slow strangeness that had dried, on the moment, his tears. "Do I understand then—?"

"That I do consent?" She gravely shook her head. "No—for I see. You'll marry me without the money; you won't marry me with it. If I don't consent *you* don't."

"You lose me?" He showed, though naming it frankly, a sort of awe of her high grasp. "Well, you lose nothing else. I make over to you every penny."

Prompt was his own clearness, but she had no smile this time to spare. "Precisely—so that I must choose."

"You must choose."

Strange it was for him then that she stood in his own rooms doing it, while, with an intensity now beyond any that had ever made his breath come slow, he waited for her act. "There's but one thing that can save you from my choice."

"From your choice of my surrender to you?"

"Yes"—and she gave a nod at the long envelope on the table—"your surrender of that."

"What is it then?"

"Your word of honour that you're not in love with her memory."

"Oh—her memory!"

"Ah"—she made a high gesture—"don't speak of it as if you couldn't be. I could in your place; and you're one for whom it will do. Her memory's your love. You *want* no other."

He heard her out in stillness, watching her face but not moving. Then he only said: "I'll marry you, mind you, in an hour."

"As we were?"

"As we were."

But she turned to the door, and her headshake was now the end. "We shall never be again as we were!"

THE END

DAISY MILLER: A STUDY

IN TWO PARTS

PART I

At the little town of Vevey, in Switzerland, there is a particularly comfortable hotel. There are, indeed, many hotels, for the entertainment of tourists is the business of the place, which, as many travelers will remember, is seated upon the edge of a remarkably blue lake—a lake that it behooves every tourist to visit. The shore of the lake presents an unbroken array of establishments of this order, of every category, from the "grand hotel" of the newest fashion, with a chalk-white front, a hundred balconies, and a dozen flags flying from its roof, to the little Swiss pension of an elder day, with its name inscribed in German-looking lettering upon a pink or yellow wall and an awkward summerhouse in the angle of the garden. One of the hotels at Vevey, however, is famous, even classical, being distinguished from many of its upstart neighbors by an air both of luxury and of maturity. In this region, in the month of June, American travelers are extremely numerous; it may be said, indeed, that Vevey assumes at this period some of the characteristics of an American watering place. There are sights and sounds which evoke a vision, an echo, of Newport and Saratoga. There is a flitting hither and thither of "stylish" young girls, a rustling of muslin flounces, a rattle of dance music in the morning hours, a sound of high-pitched voices at all times. You receive an impression of these things at the excellent inn of the "Trois Couronnes" and are transported in fancy to the Ocean House or to Congress Hall. But at the "Trois Couronnes," it must be added, there are other features that are much at variance with these suggestions: neat German waiters, who look like secretaries of legation; Russian princesses sitting in the garden; little Polish boys walking about held by the hand, with their governors; a view of the sunny crest of the Dent du Midi and the picturesque towers of the Castle of Chillon.

I hardly know whether it was the analogies or the differences that were uppermost in the mind of a young American, who, two or three years ago, sat in the garden of the "Trois Couronnes," looking about him, rather idly, at some of the graceful objects I have mentioned. It was a beautiful summer morning, and in whatever fashion the young American looked at things, they must have seemed to him charming. He had come from Geneva the day before by the little steamer, to see his aunt, who was staying at the hotel—Geneva having been for a long time his place of residence. But his aunt had a headache—his aunt had almost always a headache—and now she was shut up in her room, smelling camphor, so that he was at liberty to wander about. He was some seven-and-twenty years of age; when his friends spoke of him, they usually said that he was at Geneva "studying." When his enemies spoke of him, they said—but, after all, he had no enemies; he was an extremely amiable fellow, and universally liked. What I should say is, simply, that when certain persons spoke of him they affirmed that the reason of his spending so much time at Geneva was that he was extremely devoted to a lady who lived there—a foreign lady—a person older than himself. Very few Americans—indeed, I think none—had ever seen this lady, about whom there were some singular stories. But Winterbourne had an old attachment for the little metropolis of Calvinism; he had been put to school there as a boy, and he had afterward gone to college there—circumstances which had led to his forming a great many youthful friendships. Many of these he had kept, and they were a source of great satisfaction to him.

After knocking at his aunt's door and learning that she was indisposed, he had taken a walk about the town, and then he had come in to his breakfast. He had now finished his breakfast; but he was drinking a small cup of coffee, which had been served to him on a little table in the garden by one of the waiters who looked like an attache. At last he finished his coffee and lit a cigarette. Presently a small boy came walking along the path—an urchin of nine or ten. The child, who was diminutive for his years, had an aged expression of countenance, a pale complexion, and sharp little features. He was dressed in knickerbockers, with red stockings, which displayed his poor little spindle-shanks; he also wore a brilliant red cravat. He carried in his hand a long alpenstock, the sharp point of which he thrust into everything that he approached—the flowerbeds, the garden benches, the trains of the ladies' dresses. In front of Winterbourne he paused, looking at him with a pair of bright, penetrating little eyes.

"Will you give me a lump of sugar?" he asked in a sharp, hard little voice—a voice immature and yet, somehow, not young.

Winterbourne glanced at the small table near him, on which his coffee service rested, and saw that several morsels of sugar remained. "Yes, you may take one," he answered; "but I don't think sugar is good for little boys."

This little boy stepped forward and carefully selected three of the coveted fragments, two of which he buried in the pocket of his knickerbockers, depositing the other as promptly in another place. He poked his alpenstock, lance-fashion, into Winterbourne's bench and tried to crack the lump of sugar with his teeth.

"Oh, blazes; it's har-r-d!" he exclaimed, pronouncing the adjective in a peculiar manner.

Winterbourne had immediately perceived that he might have the honor of claiming him as a fellow countryman. "Take care you don't hurt your teeth," he said, paternally.

"I haven't got any teeth to hurt. They have all come out. I have only got seven teeth. My mother counted them last night, and one came out right afterward. She said she'd slap me if any more came out. I can't help it. It's this old Europe. It's the climate that makes them come out. In America they didn't come out. It's these hotels."

Winterbourne was much amused. "If you eat three lumps of sugar, your mother will certainly slap you," he said.

"She's got to give me some candy, then," rejoined his young interlocutor. "I can't get any candy here—any American candy. American candy's the best candy."

"And are American little boys the best little boys?" asked Winterbourne.

"I don't know. I'm an American boy," said the child.

"I see you are one of the best!" laughed Winterbourne.

"Are you an American man?" pursued this vivacious infant. And then, on Winterbourne's affirmative reply—"American men are the best," he declared.

His companion thanked him for the compliment, and the child, who had now got astride of his alpenstock, stood looking about him, while he attacked a second lump of sugar. Winterbourne wondered if he himself had been like this in his infancy, for he had been brought to Europe at about this age.

"Here comes my sister!" cried the child in a moment. "She's an American girl."

Winterbourne looked along the path and saw a beautiful young lady advancing. "American girls are the best girls," he said cheerfully to his young companion.

"My sister ain't the best!" the child declared. "She's always blowing at me."

"I imagine that is your fault, not hers," said Winterbourne. The young lady meanwhile had drawn near. She was dressed in white muslin, with a hundred frills and flounces, and knots of pale-colored ribbon. She was bareheaded, but she balanced in her hand a large parasol, with a deep border of embroidery; and she was strikingly, admirably pretty. "How pretty they are!" thought Winterbourne, straightening himself in his seat, as if he were prepared to rise.

The young lady paused in front of his bench, near the parapet of the garden, which overlooked the lake. The little boy had now converted his alpenstock into a vaulting pole, by the aid of which he was springing about in the gravel and kicking it up not a little.

"Randolph," said the young lady, "what ARE you doing?"

"I'm going up the Alps," replied Randolph. "This is the way!" And he gave another little jump, scattering the pebbles about Winterbourne's ears.

"That's the way they come down," said Winterbourne.

"He's an American man!" cried Randolph, in his little hard voice.

The young lady gave no heed to this announcement, but looked straight at her brother. "Well, I guess you had better be quiet," she simply observed.

It seemed to Winterbourne that he had been in a manner presented. He got up and stepped slowly toward the young girl, throwing away his cigarette. "This little boy and I have made acquaintance," he said, with great civility. In Geneva, as he had been perfectly aware, a young man was not at liberty to speak to a young unmarried lady except under certain rarely occurring conditions; but here at Vevey, what conditions could be better than these?—a pretty American girl coming and standing in front of you in a garden. This pretty American girl, however, on hearing Winterbourne's observation, simply glanced at him; she then turned her head and looked over the parapet, at the lake and the opposite mountains. He wondered whether he had gone too far, but he decided that he must advance farther, rather than retreat. While he was thinking of something else to say, the young lady turned to the little boy again.

"I should like to know where you got that pole," she said.

"I bought it," responded Randolph.

"You don't mean to say you're going to take it to Italy?"

"Yes, I am going to take it to Italy," the child declared.

The young girl glanced over the front of her dress and smoothed out a knot or two of ribbon. Then she rested her eyes upon the prospect again. "Well, I guess you had better leave it somewhere," she said after a moment.

"Are you going to Italy?" Winterbourne inquired in a tone of great respect.

The young lady glanced at him again. "Yes, sir," she replied. And she said nothing more.

"Are you—a—going over the Simplon?" Winterbourne pursued, a little embarrassed.

"I don't know," she said. "I suppose it's some mountain. Randolph, what mountain are we going over?"

"Going where?" the child demanded.

"To Italy," Winterbourne explained.

"I don't know," said Randolph. "I don't want to go to Italy. I want to go to America."

"Oh, Italy is a beautiful place!" rejoined the young man.

"Can you get candy there?" Randolph loudly inquired.

"I hope not," said his sister. "I guess you have had enough candy, and mother thinks so too."

"I haven't had any for ever so long—for a hundred weeks!" cried the boy, still jumping about.

The young lady inspected her flounces and smoothed her ribbons again; and Winterbourne presently risked an observation upon the beauty of the view. He was ceasing to be embarrassed, for he had begun to perceive that she was not in the least embarrassed herself. There had not been the slightest alteration in her charming complexion; she was evidently neither offended nor flattered. If she looked another way when he spoke to her, and seemed not particularly to hear him, this was simply her habit, her manner. Yet, as he talked a little more and pointed out some of the objects of interest in the view, with which she appeared quite unacquainted, she gradually gave him more of the benefit of her glance; and then he saw that this glance was perfectly direct and unshrinking. It was not, however, what would have been called an immodest glance, for the young girl's eyes were singularly honest and fresh. They were wonderfully pretty eyes; and, indeed, Winterbourne had not seen for a long time anything prettier than his fair countrywoman's various features—her complexion, her nose, her ears, her teeth. He had a great relish for feminine beauty; he was addicted to observing and analyzing it; and as regards this young lady's face he made several observations. It was not at all insipid, but it was not exactly expressive; and though it was eminently delicate, Winterbourne mentally accused it—very forgivingly—of a want of finish. He thought it very possible that Master Randolph's sister was a coquette; he was sure she had a spirit of her own; but in her bright, sweet, superficial little visage there was no mockery, no irony. Before long it became obvious that she was much disposed toward conversation. She told him that they were going to Rome for the winter—she and her mother and Randolph. She asked him if he was a "real American"; she shouldn't have taken him for one; he seemed more like a German—this was said after a little hesitation—especially when he spoke. Winterbourne, laughing, answered that he had met Germans who spoke like Americans, but that he had not, so far as he remembered, met an American who spoke like a German. Then he asked her if she should not be more comfortable in sitting upon the bench which he had just quitted. She answered that she liked standing up and walking about; but she presently sat down. She told him she was from New York State—"if you know where that is." Winterbourne learned more about her by catching hold of her small, slippery brother and making him stand a few minutes by his side.

"Tell me your name, my boy," he said.

"Randolph C. Miller," said the boy sharply. "And I'll tell you her name;" and he leveled his alpenstock at his sister.

"You had better wait till you are asked!" said this young lady calmly.

"I should like very much to know your name," said Winterbourne.

"Her name is Daisy Miller!" cried the child. "But that isn't her real name; that isn't her name on her cards."

"It's a pity you haven't got one of my cards!" said Miss Miller.

"Her real name is Annie P. Miller," the boy went on.

"Ask him HIS name," said his sister, indicating Winterbourne.

But on this point Randolph seemed perfectly indifferent; he continued to supply information with regard to his own family. "My father's name is Ezra B. Miller," he announced. "My father ain't in Europe; my father's in a better place than Europe."

Winterbourne imagined for a moment that this was the manner in which the child had been taught to intimate that Mr. Miller had been removed to the sphere of celestial reward. But Randolph immediately added, "My father's in Schenectady. He's got a big business. My father's rich, you bet!"

"Well!" ejaculated Miss Miller, lowering her parasol and looking at the embroidered border. Winterbourne presently released the child, who departed, dragging his alpenstock along the path. "He doesn't like Europe," said the young girl. "He wants to go back."

"To Schenectady, you mean?"

"Yes; he wants to go right home. He hasn't got any boys here. There is one boy here, but he always goes round with a teacher; they won't let him play."

"And your brother hasn't any teacher?" Winterbourne inquired.

"Mother thought of getting him one, to travel round with us. There was a lady told her of a very good teacher; an American lady—perhaps you know her—Mrs. Sanders. I think she came from Boston. She told her of this teacher, and we thought of getting him to travel round with us. But Randolph said he didn't want a teacher traveling round with us. He said he wouldn't have lessons when he was in the cars. And we ARE in the cars about half the time. There was an English lady we met in the cars—I think her name was Miss Featherstone; perhaps you know her. She wanted to know why I didn't give Randolph lessons—give him 'instruction,' she called it. I guess he could give me more instruction than I could give him. He's very smart."

"Yes," said Winterbourne; "he seems very smart."

"Mother's going to get a teacher for him as soon as we get to Italy. Can you get good teachers in Italy?"

"Very good, I should think," said Winterbourne.

"Or else she's going to find some school. He ought to learn some more. He's only nine. He's going to college." And in this way Miss Miller continued to converse upon the affairs of her family and upon other topics. She sat there with her extremely pretty hands, ornamented with very brilliant rings, folded in her lap, and with her pretty eyes now resting upon those of Winterbourne, now wandering over the garden, the people who passed by, and the beautiful view. She talked to Winterbourne as if she had known him a long time. He found it very pleasant. It was many years since he had heard a young girl talk so much. It might have been said of this unknown young lady, who had come and sat down beside him upon a bench, that she chattered. She was very quiet; she sat in a charming, tranquil attitude; but her lips and her eyes were constantly moving. She had a soft, slender, agreeable voice, and her tone was decidedly sociable. She gave Winterbourne a history of her movements and intentions and those of her mother and brother, in Europe, and enumerated, in particular, the various hotels at which they had stopped. "That English lady in the cars," she said—"Miss Featherstone—asked me if we didn't all live in hotels in America. I told her I had never been in so many hotels in my life as since I came to Europe. I have never seen so many—it's nothing but hotels." But Miss Miller did not make this remark with a querulous accent; she appeared to be in the best humor with everything. She declared that the hotels were very good, when once you got used to their ways, and that Europe was perfectly sweet. She was not disappointed—not a bit. Perhaps it was because she had heard so much about it before. She had ever so many intimate friends that had been there ever so many times. And then she had had ever so many dresses and things from Paris. Whenever she put on a Paris dress she felt as if she were in Europe.

"It was a kind of a wishing cap," said Winterbourne.

"Yes," said Miss Miller without examining this analogy; "it always made me wish I was here. But I needn't have done that for dresses. I am sure they send all the pretty ones to America; you see the most frightful things here. The only thing I don't like," she proceeded, "is the society. There isn't any society; or, if there is, I don't know where it keeps itself. Do you? I suppose there is some society somewhere, but I haven't seen anything of it. I'm very fond of society, and I have always had a great deal of it. I don't mean only in Schenectady, but in New York. I used to go to New York every winter. In New York I had lots of society. Last winter I had seventeen dinners given me; and three of them were by gentlemen," added Daisy Miller. "I have more friends in New York than in Schenectady—more gentleman friends; and more young lady friends too," she resumed in a moment. She paused again for an instant; she was looking at Winterbourne with all her prettiness in her lively eyes and in her light, slightly monotonous smile. "I have always had," she said, "a great deal of gentlemen's society."

Poor Winterbourne was amused, perplexed, and decidedly charmed. He had never yet heard a young girl express herself in just this fashion; never, at least, save in cases where to say such things seemed a kind of demonstrative evidence of a certain laxity of deportment. And yet was he to accuse Miss Daisy Miller of actual or potential inconduite, as they said at Geneva? He felt that he had lived at Geneva so long that he had lost a good deal; he had become dishabituated to the American tone. Never, indeed, since he had grown old enough to appreciate things, had he encountered a young American girl of so pronounced a type as this. Certainly she was very charming, but how deucedly sociable! Was she simply a pretty girl from New York State? Were they all like that, the pretty girls who had a good deal of gentlemen's society? Or was she also a designing, an audacious, an unscrupulous young person? Winterbourne had lost his instinct in this matter, and his reason could not help him. Miss Daisy Miller looked extremely innocent. Some people had told him that, after all, American girls were exceedingly innocent; and others had told him that, after all, they were not. He was inclined to think Miss Daisy Miller was a flirt—a pretty American flirt. He had never, as yet, had any relations with young ladies of this category. He had known, here in Europe, two or three women—persons older than Miss Daisy Miller, and provided, for respectability's sake, with husbands—who were great coquettes—dangerous, terrible women, with whom one's relations were liable to take a serious turn. But this young girl was not a coquette in that sense; she was very unsophisticated; she was only a pretty American flirt. Winterbourne was almost grateful for having found the formula that applied to Miss Daisy Miller. He leaned back in his seat; he remarked to himself that she had the most charming nose he had ever seen; he wondered what were the regular conditions and limitations of one's intercourse with a pretty American flirt. It presently became apparent that he was on the way to learn.

"Have you been to that old castle?" asked the young girl, pointing with her parasol to the far-gleaming walls of the Chateau de Chillon.

"Yes, formerly, more than once," said Winterbourne. "You too, I suppose, have seen it?"

"No; we haven't been there. I want to go there dreadfully. Of course I mean to go there. I wouldn't go away from here without having seen that old castle."

"It's a very pretty excursion," said Winterbourne, "and very easy to make. You can drive, you know, or you can go by the little steamer."

"You can go in the cars," said Miss Miller.

"Yes; you can go in the cars," Winterbourne assented.

"Our courier says they take you right up to the castle," the young girl continued. "We were going last week, but my mother gave out. She suffers dreadfully from dyspepsia. She said she couldn't go. Randolph wouldn't go either; he says he doesn't think much of old castles. But I guess we'll go this week, if we can get Randolph."

"Your brother is not interested in ancient monuments?" Winterbourne inquired, smiling.

"He says he don't care much about old castles. He's only nine. He wants to stay at the hotel. Mother's afraid to leave him alone, and the courier won't stay with him; so we haven't been to many places. But it will be too bad if we don't go up there." And Miss Miller pointed again at the Chateau de Chillon.

"I should think it might be arranged," said Winterbourne. "Couldn't you get some one to stay for the afternoon with Randolph?"

Miss Miller looked at him a moment, and then, very placidly, "I wish YOU would stay with him!" she said.

Winterbourne hesitated a moment. "I should much rather go to Chillon with you."

"With me?" asked the young girl with the same placidity.

She didn't rise, blushing, as a young girl at Geneva would have done; and yet Winterbourne, conscious that he had been very bold, thought it possible she was offended. "With your mother," he answered very respectfully.

But it seemed that both his audacity and his respect were lost upon Miss Daisy Miller. "I guess my mother won't go, after all," she said. "She don't like to ride round in the afternoon. But did you really mean what you said just now—that you would like to go up there?"

"Most earnestly," Winterbourne declared.

"Then we may arrange it. If mother will stay with Randolph, I guess Eugenio will."

"Eugenio?" the young man inquired.

"Eugenio's our courier. He doesn't like to stay with Randolph; he's the most fastidious man I ever saw. But he's a splendid courier. I guess he'll stay at home with Randolph if mother does, and then we can go to the castle."

Winterbourne reflected for an instant as lucidly as possible—"we" could only mean Miss Daisy Miller and himself. This program seemed almost too agreeable for credence; he felt as if he ought to kiss the young lady's hand. Possibly he would have done so and quite spoiled the project, but at this moment another person, presumably Eugenio, appeared. A tall, handsome man, with superb whiskers, wearing a velvet morning coat and a brilliant watch chain, approached Miss Miller, looking sharply at her companion. "Oh, Eugenio!" said Miss Miller with the friendliest accent.

Eugenio had looked at Winterbourne from head to foot; he now bowed gravely to the young lady. "I have the honor to inform mademoiselle that luncheon is upon the table."

Miss Miller slowly rose. "See here, Eugenio!" she said; "I'm going to that old castle, anyway."

"To the Chateau de Chillon, mademoiselle?" the courier inquired. "Mademoiselle has made arrangements?" he added in a tone which struck Winterbourne as very impertinent.

Eugenio's tone apparently threw, even to Miss Miller's own apprehension, a slightly ironical light upon the young girl's situation. She turned to Winterbourne, blushing a little—a very little. "You won't back out?" she said.

"I shall not be happy till we go!" he protested.

"And you are staying in this hotel?" she went on. "And you are really an American?"

The courier stood looking at Winterbourne offensively. The young man, at least, thought his manner of looking an offense to Miss Miller; it conveyed an imputation that she "picked up" acquaintances. "I shall have the honor of presenting to you a person who will tell you all about me," he said, smiling and referring to his aunt.

"Oh, well, we'll go some day," said Miss Miller. And she gave him a smile and turned away. She put up her parasol and walked back to the inn beside Eugenio. Winterbourne stood looking after her; and as she moved away, drawing her muslin furbelows over the gravel, said to himself that she had the tournure of a princess.

He had, however, engaged to do more than proved feasible, in promising to present his aunt, Mrs. Costello, to Miss Daisy Miller. As soon as the former lady had got better of her headache, he waited upon her in her apartment; and, after the proper inquiries in regard to her health, he asked her if she had observed in the hotel an American family—a mamma, a daughter, and a little boy.

"And a courier?" said Mrs. Costello. "Oh yes, I have observed them. Seen them—heard them—and kept out of their way." Mrs. Costello was a widow with a fortune; a person of much distinction, who frequently intimated that, if she were not so dreadfully liable to sick headaches, she would probably have left a deeper impress upon her time. She had a long, pale face, a high nose, and a great deal of very striking white hair, which she wore in large puffs and rouleaux over the top of her head. She had two sons married in New York and another who was now in Europe. This young man was amusing himself at Hamburg, and, though he was on his travels, was rarely perceived to visit any particular city at the moment selected by his mother for her own appearance there. Her nephew, who had come up to Vevey expressly to see her, was therefore more attentive than those who, as she said, were nearer to her. He had imbibed at Geneva the idea that one must always be attentive to one's aunt. Mrs. Costello had not seen him for many years, and she was greatly pleased with him, manifesting her approbation by initiating him into many of the secrets of that social sway which, as she gave him to understand, she exerted in the American capital. She admitted that she was very exclusive; but, if he were acquainted with New York, he would see that one had to be. And her picture of the minutely hierarchical constitution of the society of that city, which she presented to him in many different lights, was, to Winterbourne's imagination, almost oppressively striking.

He immediately perceived, from her tone, that Miss Daisy Miller's place in the social scale was low. "I am afraid you don't approve of them," he said.

"They are very common," Mrs. Costello declared. "They are the sort of Americans that one does one's duty by not—not accepting."

"Ah, you don't accept them?" said the young man.

"I can't, my dear Frederick. I would if I could, but I can't."

"The young girl is very pretty," said Winterbourne in a moment.

"Of course she's pretty. But she is very common."

"I see what you mean, of course," said Winterbourne after another pause.

"She has that charming look that they all have," his aunt resumed. "I can't think where they pick it up; and she dresses in perfection—no, you don't know how well she dresses. I can't think where they get their taste."

"But, my dear aunt, she is not, after all, a Comanche savage."

"She is a young lady," said Mrs. Costello, "who has an intimacy with her mamma's courier."

"An intimacy with the courier?" the young man demanded.

"Oh, the mother is just as bad! They treat the courier like a familiar friend—like a gentleman. I shouldn't wonder if he dines with them. Very likely they have never seen a man with such good manners, such fine clothes, so like a gentleman. He probably corresponds to the young lady's idea of a count. He sits with them in the garden in the evening. I think he smokes."

Winterbourne listened with interest to these disclosures; they helped him to make up his mind about Miss Daisy. Evidently she was rather wild. "Well," he said, "I am not a courier, and yet she was very charming to me."

"You had better have said at first," said Mrs. Costello with dignity, "that you had made her acquaintance."

"We simply met in the garden, and we talked a bit."

"Tout bonnement! And pray what did you say?"

"I said I should take the liberty of introducing her to my admirable aunt."

"I am much obliged to you."

"It was to guarantee my respectability," said Winterbourne.

"And pray who is to guarantee hers?"

"Ah, you are cruel!" said the young man. "She's a very nice young girl."

"You don't say that as if you believed it," Mrs. Costello observed.

"She is completely uncultivated," Winterbourne went on. "But she is wonderfully pretty, and, in short, she is very nice. To prove that I believe it, I am going to take her to the Chateau de Chillon."

"You two are going off there together? I should say it proved just the contrary. How long had you known her, may I ask, when this interesting project was formed? You haven't been twenty-four hours in the house."

"I have known her half an hour!" said Winterbourne, smiling.

"Dear me!" cried Mrs. Costello. "What a dreadful girl!"

Her nephew was silent for some moments. "You really think, then," he began earnestly, and with a desire for trustworthy information—"you really think that—" But he paused again.

"Think what, sir?" said his aunt.

"That she is the sort of young lady who expects a man, sooner or later, to carry her off?"

"I haven't the least idea what such young ladies expect a man to do. But I really think that you had better not meddle with little American girls that are uncultivated, as you call them. You have lived too long out of the country. You will be sure to make some great mistake. You are too innocent."

"My dear aunt, I am not so innocent," said Winterbourne, smiling and curling his mustache.

"You are guilty too, then!"

Winterbourne continued to curl his mustache meditatively. "You won't let the poor girl know you then?" he asked at last.

"Is it literally true that she is going to the Chateau de Chillon with you?"

"I think that she fully intends it."

"Then, my dear Frederick," said Mrs. Costello, "I must decline the honor of her acquaintance. I am an old woman, but I am not too old, thank Heaven, to be shocked!"

"But don't they all do these things—the young girls in America?" Winterbourne inquired.

Mrs. Costello stared a moment. "I should like to see my granddaughters do them!" she declared grimly.

This seemed to throw some light upon the matter, for Winterbourne remembered to have heard that his pretty cousins in New York were "tremendous flirts." If, therefore, Miss Daisy Miller exceeded the liberal margin allowed to these young ladies, it was probable that anything might be expected of her. Winterbourne was impatient to see her again, and he was vexed with himself that, by instinct, he should not appreciate her justly.

Though he was impatient to see her, he hardly knew what he should say to her about his aunt's refusal to become acquainted with her; but he discovered, promptly enough, that with Miss Daisy Miller there was no great need of walking on tiptoe. He found her that evening in the garden, wandering about in the warm starlight like an indolent sylph, and swinging to and fro the largest fan he had ever beheld. It was ten o'clock. He had dined with his aunt, had been sitting with her since dinner, and had just taken leave of her till the morrow. Miss Daisy Miller seemed very glad to see him; she declared it was the longest evening she had ever passed.

"Have you been all alone?" he asked.

"I have been walking round with mother. But mother gets tired walking round," she answered.

"Has she gone to bed?"

"No; she doesn't like to go to bed," said the young girl. "She doesn't sleep—not three hours. She says she doesn't know how she lives. She's dreadfully nervous. I guess she sleeps more than she thinks. She's gone somewhere after Randolph; she wants to try to get him to go to bed. He doesn't like to go to bed."

"Let us hope she will persuade him," observed Winterbourne.

"She will talk to him all she can; but he doesn't like her to talk to him," said Miss Daisy, opening her fan. "She's going to try to get Eugenio to talk to him. But he isn't afraid of Eugenio. Eugenio's a splendid courier, but he can't make much impression on Randolph! I don't believe he'll go to bed before eleven." It appeared that Randolph's vigil was in fact triumphantly prolonged, for Winterbourne strolled about with the young girl for some time without meeting her mother. "I have been looking round for that lady you want to introduce me to," his companion resumed. "She's your aunt." Then, on Winterbourne's admitting the fact and expressing some curiosity as to how she had learned it, she said she had heard all about Mrs. Costello from the chambermaid. She was very quiet and very comme il faut; she wore white puffs; she spoke to no one, and she never dined at the table d'hote. Every two days she had a headache. "I think that's a lovely description, headache and all!" said Miss Daisy, chattering along in her thin, gay voice. "I want to know her ever so much. I know just what YOUR aunt would be; I know I should like her. She would be very exclusive. I like a lady to be exclusive; I'm dying to be exclusive myself. Well, we ARE exclusive, mother and I. We don't speak to everyone—or they don't speak to us. I suppose it's about the same thing. Anyway, I shall be ever so glad to know your aunt."

Winterbourne was embarrassed. "She would be most happy," he said; "but I am afraid those headaches will interfere."

The young girl looked at him through the dusk. "But I suppose she doesn't have a headache every day," she said sympathetically.

Winterbourne was silent a moment. "She tells me she does," he answered at last, not knowing what to say.

Miss Daisy Miller stopped and stood looking at him. Her prettiness was still visible in the darkness; she was opening and closing her enormous fan. "She doesn't want to know me!" she said suddenly. "Why don't you say so? You needn't be afraid. I'm not afraid!" And she gave a little laugh.

Winterbourne fancied there was a tremor in her voice; he was touched, shocked, mortified by it. "My dear young lady," he protested, "she knows no one. It's her wretched health."

The young girl walked on a few steps, laughing still. "You needn't be afraid," she repeated. "Why should she want to know me?" Then she paused again; she was close to the parapet of the garden, and in front of her was the starlit lake. There was a vague sheen upon its surface, and in the distance were dimly seen mountain forms. Daisy Miller looked out upon the mysterious prospect and then she gave another little laugh. "Gracious! she IS exclusive!" she said. Winterbourne wondered whether she was seriously wounded, and for a moment almost wished that her sense of injury might be such as to make it becoming in him to attempt to reassure and comfort her. He had a pleasant sense that she would be very approachable for consolatory purposes. He felt then, for the instant, quite ready to sacrifice his aunt, conversationally; to admit that she was a proud, rude woman, and to declare that they needn't mind her. But before he had time to commit himself to this perilous mixture of gallantry and impiety, the young lady, resuming her walk, gave an exclamation in quite another tone. "Well, here's Mother! I guess she hasn't got Randolph to go to bed." The figure of a lady appeared at a distance, very indistinct in the darkness, and advancing with a slow and wavering movement. Suddenly it seemed to pause.

"Are you sure it is your mother? Can you distinguish her in this thick dusk?" Winterbourne asked.

"Well!" cried Miss Daisy Miller with a laugh; "I guess I know my own mother. And when she has got on my shawl, too! She is always wearing my things."

The lady in question, ceasing to advance, hovered vaguely about the spot at which she had checked her steps.

"I am afraid your mother doesn't see you," said Winterbourne. "Or perhaps," he added, thinking, with Miss Miller, the joke permissible—"perhaps she feels guilty about your shawl."

"Oh, it's a fearful old thing!" the young girl replied serenely. "I told her she could wear it. She won't come here because she sees you."

"Ah, then," said Winterbourne, "I had better leave you."

"Oh, no; come on!" urged Miss Daisy Miller.

"I'm afraid your mother doesn't approve of my walking with you."

Miss Miller gave him a serious glance. "It isn't for me; it's for you—that is, it's for HER. Well, I don't know who it's for! But mother doesn't like any of my gentlemen friends. She's right down timid. She always makes a fuss if I introduce a gentleman. But I DO introduce them—almost always. If I didn't introduce my gentlemen friends to Mother," the young girl added in her little soft, flat monotone, "I shouldn't think I was natural."

"To introduce me," said Winterbourne, "you must know my name." And he proceeded to pronounce it.

"Oh, dear, I can't say all that!" said his companion with a laugh. But by this time they had come up to Mrs. Miller, who, as they drew near, walked to the parapet of the garden and leaned upon it, looking intently at the lake and turning her back to them. "Mother!" said the young girl in a tone of decision. Upon this the elder lady turned round. "Mr. Winterbourne," said Miss Daisy Miller, introducing the young man very frankly and prettily. "Common," she was, as Mrs. Costello had pronounced her; yet it was a wonder to Winterbourne that, with her commonness, she had a singularly delicate grace.

Her mother was a small, spare, light person, with a wandering eye, a very exiguous nose, and a large forehead, decorated with a certain amount of thin, much frizzled hair. Like her daughter, Mrs. Miller was dressed with extreme elegance; she had enormous diamonds in her ears. So far as Winterbourne could observe, she gave him no greeting—she certainly was not looking at him. Daisy was near her, pulling her shawl straight. "What are you doing, poking round here?" this young lady inquired, but by no means with that harshness of accent which her choice of words may imply.

"I don't know," said her mother, turning toward the lake again.

"I shouldn't think you'd want that shawl!" Daisy exclaimed.

"Well I do!" her mother answered with a little laugh.

"Did you get Randolph to go to bed?" asked the young girl.

"No; I couldn't induce him," said Mrs. Miller very gently. "He wants to talk to the waiter. He likes to talk to that waiter."

"I was telling Mr. Winterbourne," the young girl went on; and to the young man's ear her tone might have indicated that she had been uttering his name all her life.

"Oh, yes!" said Winterbourne; "I have the pleasure of knowing your son."

Randolph's mamma was silent; she turned her attention to the lake. But at last she spoke. "Well, I don't see how he lives!"

"Anyhow, it isn't so bad as it was at Dover," said Daisy Miller.

"And what occurred at Dover?" Winterbourne asked.

"He wouldn't go to bed at all. I guess he sat up all night in the public parlor. He wasn't in bed at twelve o'clock: I know that."

"It was half-past twelve," declared Mrs. Miller with mild emphasis.

"Does he sleep much during the day?" Winterbourne demanded.

"I guess he doesn't sleep much," Daisy rejoined.

"I wish he would!" said her mother. "It seems as if he couldn't."

"I think he's real tiresome," Daisy pursued.

Then, for some moments, there was silence. "Well, Daisy Miller," said the elder lady, presently, "I shouldn't think you'd want to talk against your own brother!"

"Well, he IS tiresome, Mother," said Daisy, quite without the asperity of a retort.

"He's only nine," urged Mrs. Miller.

"Well, he wouldn't go to that castle," said the young girl. "I'm going there with Mr. Winterbourne."

To this announcement, very placidly made, Daisy's mamma offered no response. Winterbourne took for granted that she deeply disapproved of the projected excursion; but he said to himself that she was a simple, easily managed person, and that a few deferential protestations would take the edge from her displeasure. "Yes," he began; "your daughter has kindly allowed me the honor of being her guide."

Mrs. Miller's wandering eyes attached themselves, with a sort of appealing air, to Daisy, who, however, strolled a few steps farther, gently humming to herself. "I presume you will go in the cars," said her mother.

"Yes, or in the boat," said Winterbourne.

"Well, of course, I don't know," Mrs. Miller rejoined. "I have never been to that castle."

"It is a pity you shouldn't go," said Winterbourne, beginning to feel reassured as to her opposition. And yet he was quite prepared to find that, as a matter of course, she meant to accompany her daughter.

"We've been thinking ever so much about going," she pursued; "but it seems as if we couldn't. Of course Daisy—she wants to go round. But there's a lady here—I don't know her name—she says she shouldn't think we'd want to go to see castles HERE; she should think we'd want to wait till we got to Italy. It seems as if there would be so many there," continued Mrs. Miller with an air of increasing confidence. "Of course we only want to see the principal ones. We visited several in England," she presently added.

"Ah yes! in England there are beautiful castles," said Winterbourne. "But Chillon here, is very well worth seeing."

"Well, if Daisy feels up to it—" said Mrs. Miller, in a tone impregnated with a sense of the magnitude of the enterprise. "It seems as if there was nothing she wouldn't undertake."

"Oh, I think she'll enjoy it!" Winterbourne declared. And he desired more and more to make it a certainty that he was to have the privilege of a tete-a-tete with the young lady, who was still strolling along in front of them, softly vocalizing. "You are not disposed, madam," he inquired, "to undertake it yourself?"

Daisy's mother looked at him an instant askance, and then walked forward in silence. Then—"I guess she had better go alone," she said simply. Winterbourne observed to himself that this was a very different type of maternity from that of the vigilant matrons who massed themselves in the forefront of social intercourse in the dark old city at the other end of the lake. But his meditations were interrupted by hearing his name very distinctly pronounced by Mrs. Miller's unprotected daughter.

"Mr. Winterbourne!" murmured Daisy.

"Mademoiselle!" said the young man.

"Don't you want to take me out in a boat?"

"At present?" he asked.

"Of course!" said Daisy.

"Well, Annie Miller!" exclaimed her mother.

"I beg you, madam, to let her go," said Winterbourne ardently; for he had never yet enjoyed the sensation of guiding through the summer starlight a skiff freighted with a fresh and beautiful young girl.

"I shouldn't think she'd want to," said her mother. "I should think she'd rather go indoors."

"I'm sure Mr. Winterbourne wants to take me," Daisy declared. "He's so awfully devoted!"

"I will row you over to Chillon in the starlight."

"I don't believe it!" said Daisy.

"Well!" ejaculated the elder lady again.

"You haven't spoken to me for half an hour," her daughter went on.

"I have been having some very pleasant conversation with your mother," said Winterbourne.

"Well, I want you to take me out in a boat!" Daisy repeated. They had all stopped, and she had turned round and was looking at Winterbourne. Her face wore a charming smile, her pretty eyes were gleaming, she was swinging her great fan about. No; it's impossible to be prettier than that, thought Winterbourne.

"There are half a dozen boats moored at that landing place," he said, pointing to certain steps which descended from the garden to the lake. "If you will do me the honor to accept my arm, we will go and select one of them."

Daisy stood there smiling; she threw back her head and gave a little, light laugh. "I like a gentleman to be formal!" she declared.

"I assure you it's a formal offer."

"I was bound I would make you say something," Daisy went on.

"You see, it's not very difficult," said Winterbourne. "But I am afraid you are chaffing me."

"I think not, sir," remarked Mrs. Miller very gently.

"Do, then, let me give you a row," he said to the young girl.

"It's quite lovely, the way you say that!" cried Daisy.

"It will be still more lovely to do it."

"Yes, it would be lovely!" said Daisy. But she made no movement to accompany him; she only stood there laughing.

"I should think you had better find out what time it is," interposed her mother.

"It is eleven o'clock, madam," said a voice, with a foreign accent, out of the neighboring darkness; and Winterbourne, turning, perceived the florid personage who was in attendance upon the two ladies. He had apparently just approached.

"Oh, Eugenio," said Daisy, "I am going out in a boat!"

Eugenio bowed. "At eleven o'clock, mademoiselle?"

"I am going with Mr. Winterbourne—this very minute."

"Do tell her she can't," said Mrs. Miller to the courier.

"I think you had better not go out in a boat, mademoiselle," Eugenio declared.

Winterbourne wished to Heaven this pretty girl were not so familiar with her courier; but he said nothing.

"I suppose you don't think it's proper!" Daisy exclaimed. "Eugenio doesn't think anything's proper."

"I am at your service," said Winterbourne.

"Does mademoiselle propose to go alone?" asked Eugenio of Mrs. Miller.

"Oh, no; with this gentleman!" answered Daisy's mamma.

The courier looked for a moment at Winterbourne—the latter thought he was smiling—and then, solemnly, with a bow, "As mademoiselle pleases!" he said.

"Oh, I hoped you would make a fuss!" said Daisy. "I don't care to go now."

"I myself shall make a fuss if you don't go," said Winterbourne.

"That's all I want—a little fuss!" And the young girl began to laugh again.

"Mr. Randolph has gone to bed!" the courier announced frigidly.

"Oh, Daisy; now we can go!" said Mrs. Miller.

Daisy turned away from Winterbourne, looking at him, smiling and fanning herself. "Good night," she said; "I hope you are disappointed, or disgusted, or something!"

He looked at her, taking the hand she offered him. "I am puzzled," he answered.

"Well, I hope it won't keep you awake!" she said very smartly; and, under the escort of the privileged Eugenio, the two ladies passed toward the house.

Winterbourne stood looking after them; he was indeed puzzled. He lingered beside the lake for a quarter of an hour, turning over the mystery of the young girl's sudden familiarities and caprices. But the only very definite conclusion he came to was that he should enjoy deucedly "going off" with her somewhere.

Two days afterward he went off with her to the Castle of Chillon. He waited for her in the large hall of the hotel, where the couriers, the servants, the foreign tourists, were lounging about and staring. It was not the place he should have chosen, but she had appointed it. She came tripping downstairs, buttoning her long gloves, squeezing her folded parasol against her pretty figure, dressed in the perfection of a soberly elegant traveling costume. Winterbourne was a man of imagination and, as our ancestors used to say, sensibility; as he looked at her dress and, on the great staircase, her little rapid, confiding step, he felt as if there were something romantic going forward. He could have believed he was going to elope with her. He passed out with her among all the idle people that were assembled there; they were all looking at her very hard; she had begun to chatter as soon as she joined him. Winterbourne's preference had been that they should be conveyed to Chillon in a carriage; but she expressed a lively wish to go in the little steamer; she declared that she had a passion for steamboats. There was always such a lovely breeze upon the water, and you saw such lots of people. The sail was not long, but Winterbourne's companion found time to say a great many things. To the young man himself their little excursion was so much of an escapade—an adventure—that, even allowing for her habitual sense of freedom, he had some expectation of seeing her regard it in the same way. But it must be confessed that, in this particular, he was disappointed. Daisy Miller was extremely animated, she was in charming spirits; but she was apparently not at all excited; she was not fluttered; she avoided neither his eyes nor those of anyone else; she blushed neither when she looked at him nor when she felt that people were looking at her. People continued to look at her a great deal, and Winterbourne took much satisfaction in his pretty companion's distinguished air. He had been a little afraid that she would talk loud, laugh overmuch, and even, perhaps, desire to move about the boat a good deal. But he quite forgot his fears; he sat smiling, with his eyes upon her face, while, without moving from her place, she delivered herself of a great number of original reflections. It was the most charming garrulity he had ever heard. He had assented to the idea that she was "common"; but was she so, after all, or was he simply getting used to her commonness? Her conversation was chiefly of what metaphysicians term the objective cast, but every now and then it took a subjective turn.

"What on EARTH are you so grave about?" she suddenly demanded, fixing her agreeable eyes upon Winterbourne's.

"Am I grave?" he asked. "I had an idea I was grinning from ear to ear."

"You look as if you were taking me to a funeral. If that's a grin, your ears are very near together."

"Should you like me to dance a hornpipe on the deck?"

"Pray do, and I'll carry round your hat. It will pay the expenses of our journey."

"I never was better pleased in my life," murmured Winterbourne.

She looked at him a moment and then burst into a little laugh. "I like to make you say those things! You're a queer mixture!"

In the castle, after they had landed, the subjective element decidedly prevailed. Daisy tripped about the vaulted chambers, rustled her skirts in the corkscrew staircases, flirted back with a pretty little cry and a shudder from the edge of the oubliettes, and turned a singularly well-shaped ear to everything that Winterbourne told her about the place. But he saw that she cared very little for feudal antiquities and that the dusky traditions of Chillon made but a slight impression upon her. They had the good fortune to have been able to walk about without other companionship than that of the custodian; and Winterbourne arranged with this functionary that they should not be hurried—that they should linger and pause wherever they chose. The custodian interpreted the bargain generously—Winterbourne, on his side, had been generous—and ended by leaving them quite to themselves. Miss Miller's observations were not remarkable for logical consistency; for anything she wanted to say she was sure to find a pretext. She found a great many pretexts in the rugged embrasures of Chillon for asking Winterbourne sudden questions about himself—his family, his previous history, his tastes, his habits, his intentions—and for supplying information upon corresponding points in her own personality. Of her own tastes, habits, and intentions Miss Miller was prepared to give the most definite, and indeed the most favorable account.

"Well, I hope you know enough!" she said to her companion, after he had told her the history of the unhappy Bonivard. "I never saw a man that knew so much!" The history of Bonivard had evidently, as they say, gone into one ear and out of the other. But Daisy went on to say that she wished Winterbourne would travel with them and "go round" with them; they might know something, in that case. "Don't you want to come and teach Randolph?" she asked. Winterbourne said that nothing could possibly please him so much, but that he had unfortunately other occupations. "Other occupations? I don't believe it!" said Miss Daisy. "What do you mean? You are not in business." The young man admitted that he was not in business; but he had engagements which, even within a day or two, would force him to go back to Geneva. "Oh, bother!" she said; "I don't believe it!" and she began to talk about something else. But a few moments later, when he was pointing out to her the pretty design of an antique fireplace, she broke out irrelevantly, "You don't mean to say you are going back to Geneva?"

"It is a melancholy fact that I shall have to return to Geneva tomorrow."

"Well, Mr. Winterbourne," said Daisy, "I think you're horrid!"

"Oh, don't say such dreadful things!" said Winterbourne—"just at the last!"

"The last!" cried the young girl; "I call it the first. I have half a mind to leave you here and go straight back to the hotel alone." And for the next ten minutes she did nothing but call him horrid. Poor Winterbourne was fairly bewildered; no young lady had as yet done him the honor to be so agitated by the announcement of his movements. His companion, after this, ceased to pay any attention to the curiosities of Chillon or the beauties of the lake; she opened fire upon the mysterious charmer in Geneva whom she appeared to have instantly taken it for granted that he was hurrying back to see. How did Miss Daisy Miller know that there was a charmer in Geneva? Winterbourne, who denied the existence of such a person, was quite unable to discover, and he was divided between amazement at the rapidity of her induction and amusement at the frankness of her persiflage. She seemed to him, in all this, an extraordinary mixture of innocence and crudity. "Does she never allow you more than three days at a time?" asked Daisy ironically. "Doesn't she give you a vacation in summer? There's no one so hard worked but they can get leave to go off somewhere at this season. I suppose, if you stay another day, she'll come after you in the boat. Do wait over till Friday, and I will go down to the landing to see her arrive!" Winterbourne began to think he had been wrong to feel disappointed in the temper in which the young lady had embarked. If he had missed the personal accent, the personal accent was now making its appearance. It sounded very distinctly, at last, in her telling him she would stop "teasing" him if he would promise her solemnly to come down to Rome in the winter.

"That's not a difficult promise to make," said Winterbourne. "My aunt has taken an apartment in Rome for the winter and has already asked me to come and see her."

"I don't want you to come for your aunt," said Daisy; "I want you to come for me." And this was the only allusion that the young man was ever to hear her make to his invidious kinswoman. He declared that, at any rate, he would certainly come. After this Daisy stopped teasing. Winterbourne took a carriage, and they drove back to Vevey in the dusk; the young girl was very quiet.

In the evening Winterbourne mentioned to Mrs. Costello that he had spent the afternoon at Chillon with Miss Daisy Miller.

"The Americans—of the courier?" asked this lady.

"Ah, happily," said Winterbourne, "the courier stayed at home."

"She went with you all alone?"

"All alone."

Mrs. Costello sniffed a little at her smelling bottle. "And that," she exclaimed, "is the young person whom you wanted me to know!"

PART II

Winterbourne, who had returned to Geneva the day after his excursion to Chillon, went to Rome toward the end of January. His aunt had been established there for several weeks, and he had received a couple of letters from her. "Those people you were so devoted to last summer at Vevey have turned up here, courier and all," she wrote. "They seem to have made several acquaintances, but the courier continues to be the most intime. The young lady, however, is also very intimate with some third-rate Italians, with whom she rackets about in a way that makes much talk. Bring me that pretty novel of Cherbuliez's—Paule Mere—and don't come later than the 23rd."

In the natural course of events, Winterbourne, on arriving in Rome, would presently have ascertained Mrs. Miller's address at the American banker's and have gone to pay his compliments to Miss Daisy. "After what happened at Vevey, I think I may certainly call upon them," he said to Mrs. Costello.

"If, after what happens—at Vevey and everywhere—you desire to keep up the acquaintance, you are very welcome. Of course a man may know everyone. Men are welcome to the privilege!"

"Pray what is it that happens—here, for instance?" Winterbourne demanded.

"The girl goes about alone with her foreigners. As to what happens further, you must apply elsewhere for information. She has picked up half a dozen of the regular Roman fortune hunters, and she takes them about to people's houses. When she comes to a party she brings with her a gentleman with a good deal of manner and a wonderful mustache."

"And where is the mother?"

"I haven't the least idea. They are very dreadful people."

Winterbourne meditated a moment. "They are very ignorant—very innocent only. Depend upon it they are not bad."

"They are hopelessly vulgar," said Mrs. Costello. "Whether or no being hopelessly vulgar is being 'bad' is a question for the metaphysicians. They are bad enough to dislike, at any rate; and for this short life that is quite enough."

The news that Daisy Miller was surrounded by half a dozen wonderful mustaches checked Winterbourne's impulse to go straightway to see her. He had, perhaps, not definitely flattered himself that he had made an ineffaceable impression upon her heart, but he was annoyed at hearing of a state of affairs so little in harmony with an image that had lately flitted in and out of his own meditations; the image of a very pretty girl looking out of an old Roman window and asking herself urgently when Mr. Winterbourne would arrive. If, however, he determined to wait a little before reminding Miss Miller of his claims to her consideration, he went very soon to call upon two or three other friends. One of these friends was an American lady who had spent several winters at Geneva, where she had placed her children at school. She was a very accomplished woman, and she lived in the Via Gregoriana. Winterbourne found her in a little crimson drawing room on a third floor; the room was filled with southern sunshine. He had not been there ten minutes when the servant came in, announcing "Madame Mila!" This announcement was presently followed by the entrance of little Randolph Miller, who stopped in the middle of the room and stood staring at Winterbourne. An instant later his pretty sister crossed the threshold; and then, after a considerable interval, Mrs. Miller slowly advanced.

"I know you!" said Randolph.

"I'm sure you know a great many things," exclaimed Winterbourne, taking him by the hand. "How is your education coming on?"

PART II

Daisy was exchanging greetings very prettily with her hostess, but when she heard Winterbourne's voice she quickly turned her head. "Well, I declare!" she said.

"I told you I should come, you know," Winterbourne rejoined, smiling.

"Well, I didn't believe it," said Miss Daisy.

"I am much obliged to you," laughed the young man.

"You might have come to see me!" said Daisy.

"I arrived only yesterday."

"I don't believe that!" the young girl declared.

Winterbourne turned with a protesting smile to her mother, but this lady evaded his glance, and, seating herself, fixed her eyes upon her son. "We've got a bigger place than this," said Randolph. "It's all gold on the walls."

Mrs. Miller turned uneasily in her chair. "I told you if I were to bring you, you would say something!" she murmured.

"I told YOU!" Randolph exclaimed. "I tell YOU, sir!" he added jocosely, giving Winterbourne a thump on the knee. "It IS bigger, too!"

Daisy had entered upon a lively conversation with her hostess; Winterbourne judged it becoming to address a few words to her mother. "I hope you have been well since we parted at Vevey," he said.

Mrs. Miller now certainly looked at him—at his chin. "Not very well, sir," she answered.

"She's got the dyspepsia," said Randolph. "I've got it too. Father's got it. I've got it most!"

This announcement, instead of embarrassing Mrs. Miller, seemed to relieve her. "I suffer from the liver," she said. "I think it's this climate; it's less bracing than Schenectady, especially in the winter season. I don't know whether you know we reside at Schenectady. I was saying to Daisy that I certainly hadn't found any one like Dr. Davis, and I didn't believe I should. Oh, at Schenectady he stands first; they think everything of him. He has so much to do, and yet there was nothing he wouldn't do for me. He said he never saw anything like my dyspepsia, but he was bound to cure it. I'm sure there was nothing he wouldn't try. He was just going to try something new when we came off. Mr. Miller wanted Daisy to see Europe for herself. But I wrote to Mr. Miller that it seems as if I couldn't get on without Dr. Davis. At Schenectady he stands at the very top; and there's a great deal of sickness there, too. It affects my sleep."

Winterbourne had a good deal of pathological gossip with Dr. Davis's patient, during which Daisy chattered unremittingly to her own companion. The young man asked Mrs. Miller how she was pleased with Rome. "Well, I must say I am disappointed," she answered. "We had heard so much about it; I suppose we had heard too much. But we couldn't help that. We had been led to expect something different."

"Ah, wait a little, and you will become very fond of it," said Winterbourne.

"I hate it worse and worse every day!" cried Randolph.

"You are like the infant Hannibal," said Winterbourne.

"No, I ain't!" Randolph declared at a venture.

"You are not much like an infant," said his mother. "But we have seen places," she resumed, "that I should put a long way before Rome." And in reply to Winterbourne's interrogation, "There's Zurich," she concluded, "I think Zurich is lovely; and we hadn't heard half so much about it."

"The best place we've seen is the City of Richmond!" said Randolph.

"He means the ship," his mother explained. "We crossed in that ship. Randolph had a good time on the City of Richmond."

"It's the best place I've seen," the child repeated. "Only it was turned the wrong way."

"Well, we've got to turn the right way some time," said Mrs. Miller with a little laugh. Winterbourne expressed the hope that her daughter at least found some gratification in Rome, and she declared that Daisy was quite carried away. "It's on account of the society—the society's splendid. She goes round everywhere; she has made a great number of acquaintances. Of course she goes round more than I do. I must say they have been very sociable; they have taken her right in. And then she knows a great many gentlemen. Oh, she thinks there's nothing like Rome. Of course, it's a great deal pleasanter for a young lady if she knows plenty of gentlemen."

By this time Daisy had turned her attention again to Winterbourne. "I've been telling Mrs. Walker how mean you were!" the young girl announced.

"And what is the evidence you have offered?" asked Winterbourne, rather annoyed at Miss Miller's want of appreciation of the zeal of an admirer who on his way down to Rome had stopped neither at Bologna nor at Florence, simply because of a certain sentimental impatience. He remembered that a cynical compatriot had once told him that American women—the pretty ones, and this gave a largeness to the axiom—were at once the most exacting in the world and the least endowed with a sense of indebtedness.

"Why, you were awfully mean at Vevey," said Daisy. "You wouldn't do anything. You wouldn't stay there when I asked you."

"My dearest young lady," cried Winterbourne, with eloquence, "have I come all the way to Rome to encounter your reproaches?"

"Just hear him say that!" said Daisy to her hostess, giving a twist to a bow on this lady's dress. "Did you ever hear anything so quaint?"

"So quaint, my dear?" murmured Mrs. Walker in the tone of a partisan of Winterbourne.

"Well, I don't know," said Daisy, fingering Mrs. Walker's ribbons. "Mrs. Walker, I want to tell you something."

"Mother-r," interposed Randolph, with his rough ends to his words, "I tell you you've got to go. Eugenio'll raise—something!"

"I'm not afraid of Eugenio," said Daisy with a toss of her head. "Look here, Mrs. Walker," she went on, "you know I'm coming to your party."

"I am delighted to hear it."

"I've got a lovely dress!"

"I am very sure of that."

"But I want to ask a favor—permission to bring a friend."

"I shall be happy to see any of your friends," said Mrs. Walker, turning with a smile to Mrs. Miller.

"Oh, they are not my friends," answered Daisy's mamma, smiling shyly in her own fashion. "I never spoke to them."

"It's an intimate friend of mine—Mr. Giovanelli," said Daisy without a tremor in her clear little voice or a shadow on her brilliant little face.

Mrs. Walker was silent a moment; she gave a rapid glance at Winterbourne. "I shall be glad to see Mr. Giovanelli," she then said.

"He's an Italian," Daisy pursued with the prettiest serenity. "He's a great friend of mine; he's the handsomest man in the world—except Mr. Winterbourne! He knows plenty of Italians, but he wants to know some Americans. He thinks ever so much of Americans. He's tremendously clever. He's perfectly lovely!"

It was settled that this brilliant personage should be brought to Mrs. Walker's party, and then Mrs. Miller prepared to take her leave. "I guess we'll go back to the hotel," she said.

"You may go back to the hotel, Mother, but I'm going to take a walk," said Daisy.

"She's going to walk with Mr. Giovanelli," Randolph proclaimed.

"I am going to the Pincio," said Daisy, smiling.

"Alone, my dear—at this hour?" Mrs. Walker asked. The afternoon was drawing to a close—it was the hour for the throng of carriages and of contemplative pedestrians. "I don't think it's safe, my dear," said Mrs. Walker.

"Neither do I," subjoined Mrs. Miller. "You'll get the fever, as sure as you live. Remember what Dr. Davis told you!"

"Give her some medicine before she goes," said Randolph.

The company had risen to its feet; Daisy, still showing her pretty teeth, bent over and kissed her hostess. "Mrs. Walker, you are too perfect," she said. "I'm not going alone; I am going to meet a friend."

"Your friend won't keep you from getting the fever," Mrs. Miller observed.

"Is it Mr. Giovanelli?" asked the hostess.

Winterbourne was watching the young girl; at this question his attention quickened. She stood there, smiling and smoothing her bonnet ribbons; she glanced at Winterbourne. Then, while she glanced and smiled, she answered, without a shade of hesitation, "Mr. Giovanelli—the beautiful Giovanelli."

"My dear young friend," said Mrs. Walker, taking her hand pleadingly, "don't walk off to the Pincio at this hour to meet a beautiful Italian."

"Well, he speaks English," said Mrs. Miller.

"Gracious me!" Daisy exclaimed, "I don't to do anything improper. There's an easy way to settle it." She continued to glance at Winterbourne. "The Pincio is only a hundred yards distant; and if Mr. Winterbourne were as polite as he pretends, he would offer to walk with me!"

Winterbourne's politeness hastened to affirm itself, and the young girl gave him gracious leave to accompany her. They passed downstairs before her mother, and at the door Winterbourne perceived Mrs. Miller's carriage drawn up, with the ornamental courier whose acquaintance he had made at Vevey seated within. "Goodbye, Eugenio!" cried Daisy; "I'm going to take a walk." The distance from the Via Gregoriana to the beautiful garden at the other end of the Pincian Hill is, in fact, rapidly traversed. As the day was splendid, however, and the concourse of vehicles, walkers, and loungers numerous, the young Americans found their progress much delayed. This fact was highly agreeable to Winterbourne, in spite of his consciousness of his singular situation. The slow-moving, idly gazing Roman crowd bestowed much attention upon the extremely pretty young foreign lady who was passing through it upon his arm; and he wondered what on earth had been in Daisy's mind when she proposed to expose herself, unattended, to its appreciation. His own mission, to her sense, apparently, was to consign her to the hands of Mr. Giovanelli; but Winterbourne, at once annoyed and gratified, resolved that he would do no such thing.

"Why haven't you been to see me?" asked Daisy. "You can't get out of that."

"I have had the honor of telling you that I have only just stepped out of the train."

"You must have stayed in the train a good while after it stopped!" cried the young girl with her little laugh. "I suppose you were asleep. You have had time to go to see Mrs. Walker."

"I knew Mrs. Walker—" Winterbourne began to explain.

"I know where you knew her. You knew her at Geneva. She told me so. Well, you knew me at Vevey. That's just as good. So you ought to have come." She asked him no other question than this; she began to prattle about her own affairs. "We've got splendid rooms at the hotel; Eugenio says they're the best rooms in Rome. We are going to stay all winter, if we don't die of the fever; and I guess we'll stay then. It's a great deal nicer than I thought; I thought it would be fearfully quiet; I was sure it would be awfully poky. I was sure we should be going round all the time with one of those dreadful old men that explain about the pictures and things. But we only had about a week of that, and now I'm enjoying myself. I know ever so many people, and they are all so charming. The society's extremely select. There are all kinds—English, and Germans, and Italians. I think I like the English best. I like their style of conversation. But there are some lovely Americans. I never saw anything so hospitable. There's something or other every day. There's not much dancing; but I must say I never thought dancing was everything. I was always fond of conversation. I guess I shall have plenty at Mrs. Walker's, her rooms are so small." When they had passed the gate of the Pincian Gardens, Miss Miller began to wonder where Mr. Giovanelli might be. "We had better go straight to that place in front," she said, "where you look at the view."

"I certainly shall not help you to find him," Winterbourne declared.

"Then I shall find him without you," cried Miss Daisy.

"You certainly won't leave me!" cried Winterbourne.

She burst into her little laugh. "Are you afraid you'll get lost—or run over? But there's Giovanelli, leaning against that tree. He's staring at the women in the carriages: did you ever see anything so cool?"

Winterbourne perceived at some distance a little man standing with folded arms nursing his cane. He had a handsome face, an artfully poised hat, a glass in one eye, and a nosegay in his buttonhole. Winterbourne looked at him a moment and then said, "Do you mean to speak to that man?"

"Do I mean to speak to him? Why, you don't suppose I mean to communicate by signs?"

"Pray understand, then," said Winterbourne, "that I intend to remain with you."

Daisy stopped and looked at him, without a sign of troubled consciousness in her face, with nothing but the presence of her charming eyes and her happy dimples. "Well, she's a cool one!" thought the young man.

"I don't like the way you say that," said Daisy. "It's too imperious."

"I beg your pardon if I say it wrong. The main point is to give you an idea of my meaning."

The young girl looked at him more gravely, but with eyes that were prettier than ever. "I have never allowed a gentleman to dictate to me, or to interfere with anything I do."

"I think you have made a mistake," said Winterbourne. "You should sometimes listen to a gentleman—the right one."

Daisy began to laugh again. "I do nothing but listen to gentlemen!" she exclaimed. "Tell me if Mr. Giovanelli is the right one?"

The gentleman with the nosegay in his bosom had now perceived our two friends, and was approaching the young girl with obsequious rapidity. He bowed to Winterbourne as well as to the latter's companion; he had a brilliant smile, an intelligent eye; Winterbourne thought him not a bad-looking fellow. But he nevertheless said to Daisy, "No, he's not the right one."

Daisy evidently had a natural talent for performing introductions; she mentioned the name of each of her companions to the other. She strolled alone with one of them on each side of her; Mr. Giovanelli, who spoke English very cleverly—Winterbourne afterward learned that he had practiced the idiom upon a great many American heiresses—addressed her a great deal of very polite nonsense; he was extremely urbane, and the young American, who said nothing, reflected upon that profundity of Italian cleverness which enables people to appear more gracious in proportion as they are more acutely disappointed. Giovanelli, of course, had counted upon something more intimate; he had not bargained for a party of three. But he kept his temper in a manner which suggested far-stretching intentions. Winterbourne flattered himself that he had taken his measure. "He is not a gentleman," said the young American; "he is only a clever imitation of one. He is a music master, or a penny-a-liner, or a third-rate artist. D__n his good looks!" Mr. Giovanelli had certainly a very pretty face; but Winterbourne felt a superior indignation at his own lovely fellow countrywoman's not knowing the difference between a spurious gentleman and a real one. Giovanelli chattered and jested and made himself wonderfully agreeable. It was true that, if he was an imitation, the imitation was brilliant. "Nevertheless," Winterbourne said to himself, "a nice girl ought to know!" And then he came back to the question whether this was, in fact, a nice girl. Would a nice girl, even allowing for her being a little American flirt, make a rendezvous with a presumably low-lived foreigner? The rendezvous in this case, indeed, had been in broad daylight and in the most crowded corner of Rome, but was it not impossible to regard the choice of these circumstances as a proof of extreme cynicism? Singular though it may seem, Winterbourne was vexed that the young girl, in joining her amoroso, should not appear more impatient of his own company, and he was vexed because of his inclination. It was impossible to regard her as a perfectly well-conducted young lady; she was wanting in a certain indispensable delicacy. It would therefore simplify matters greatly to be able to treat her as the object of one of those sentiments which are called by romancers "lawless passions." That she should seem to wish to get rid of him would help him to think more lightly of her, and to be able to think more lightly of her would make her much less perplexing. But Daisy, on this occasion, continued to present herself as an inscrutable combination of audacity and innocence.

She had been walking some quarter of an hour, attended by her two cavaliers, and responding in a tone of very childish gaiety, as it seemed to Winterbourne, to the pretty speeches of Mr. Giovanelli, when a carriage that had detached itself from the revolving train drew up beside the path. At the same moment Winterbourne perceived that his friend Mrs. Walker—the lady whose house he had lately left—was seated in the vehicle and was beckoning to him. Leaving Miss Miller's side, he hastened to obey her summons. Mrs. Walker was flushed; she wore an excited air. "It is really too dreadful," she said. "That girl must not do this sort of thing. She must not walk here with you two men. Fifty people have noticed her."

Winterbourne raised his eyebrows. "I think it's a pity to make too much fuss about it."

"It's a pity to let the girl ruin herself!"

"She is very innocent," said Winterbourne.

"She's very crazy!" cried Mrs. Walker. "Did you ever see anything so imbecile as her mother? After you had all left me just now, I could not sit still for thinking of it. It seemed too pitiful, not even to attempt to save her. I ordered the carriage and put on my bonnet, and came here as quickly as possible. Thank Heaven I have found you!"

"What do you propose to do with us?" asked Winterbourne, smiling.

"To ask her to get in, to drive her about here for half an hour, so that the world may see she is not running absolutely wild, and then to take her safely home."

"I don't think it's a very happy thought," said Winterbourne; "but you can try."

Mrs. Walker tried. The young man went in pursuit of Miss Miller, who had simply nodded and smiled at his interlocutor in the carriage and had gone her way with her companion. Daisy, on learning that Mrs. Walker wished to speak to her, retraced her steps with a perfect good grace and with Mr. Giovanelli at her side. She declared that she was delighted to have a chance to present this gentleman to Mrs. Walker. She immediately achieved the introduction, and declared that she had never in her life seen anything so lovely as Mrs. Walker's carriage rug.

"I am glad you admire it," said this lady, smiling sweetly. "Will you get in and let me put it over you?"

"Oh, no, thank you," said Daisy. "I shall admire it much more as I see you driving round with it."

"Do get in and drive with me!" said Mrs. Walker.

"That would be charming, but it's so enchanting just as I am!" and Daisy gave a brilliant glance at the gentlemen on either side of her.

"It may be enchanting, dear child, but it is not the custom here," urged Mrs. Walker, leaning forward in her victoria, with her hands devoutly clasped.

"Well, it ought to be, then!" said Daisy. "If I didn't walk I should expire."

"You should walk with your mother, dear," cried the lady from Geneva, losing patience.

"With my mother dear!" exclaimed the young girl. Winterbourne saw that she scented interference. "My mother never walked ten steps in her life. And then, you know," she added with a laugh, "I am more than five years old."

"You are old enough to be more reasonable. You are old enough, dear Miss Miller, to be talked about."

Daisy looked at Mrs. Walker, smiling intensely. "Talked about? What do you mean?"

"Come into my carriage, and I will tell you."

Daisy turned her quickened glance again from one of the gentlemen beside her to the other. Mr. Giovanelli was bowing to and fro, rubbing down his gloves and laughing very agreeably; Winterbourne thought it a most unpleasant scene. "I don't think I want to know what you mean," said Daisy presently. "I don't think I should like it."

Winterbourne wished that Mrs. Walker would tuck in her carriage rug and drive away, but this lady did not enjoy being defied, as she afterward told him. "Should you prefer being thought a very reckless girl?" she demanded.

"Gracious!" exclaimed Daisy. She looked again at Mr. Giovanelli, then she turned to Winterbourne. There was a little pink flush in her cheek; she was tremendously pretty. "Does Mr. Winterbourne think," she asked slowly, smiling, throwing back her head, and glancing at him from head to foot, "that, to save my reputation, I ought to get into the carriage?"

Winterbourne colored; for an instant he hesitated greatly. It seemed so strange to hear her speak that way of her "reputation." But he himself, in fact, must speak in accordance with gallantry. The finest gallantry, here, was simply to tell her the truth; and the truth, for Winterbourne, as the few indications I have been able to give have made him known to the reader, was that Daisy Miller should take Mrs. Walker's advice. He looked at her exquisite prettiness, and then he said, very gently, "I think you should get into the carriage."

Daisy gave a violent laugh. "I never heard anything so stiff! If this is improper, Mrs. Walker," she pursued, "then I am all improper, and you must give me up. Goodbye; I hope you'll have a lovely ride!" and, with Mr. Giovanelli, who made a triumphantly obsequious salute, she turned away.

Mrs. Walker sat looking after her, and there were tears in Mrs. Walker's eyes. "Get in here, sir," she said to Winterbourne, indicating the place beside her. The young man answered that he felt bound to accompany Miss Miller, whereupon Mrs. Walker declared that if he refused her this favor she would never speak to him again. She was evidently in earnest. Winterbourne overtook Daisy and her companion, and, offering the young girl his hand, told her that Mrs. Walker had made an imperious claim upon his society. He expected that in answer she would say something rather free, something to commit herself still further to that "recklessness" from which Mrs. Walker had so charitably endeavored to dissuade her. But she only shook his hand, hardly looking at him, while Mr. Giovanelli bade him farewell with a too emphatic flourish of the hat.

Winterbourne was not in the best possible humor as he took his seat in Mrs. Walker's victoria. "That was not clever of you," he said candidly, while the vehicle mingled again with the throng of carriages.

"In such a case," his companion answered, "I don't wish to be clever; I wish to be EARNEST!"

"Well, your earnestness has only offended her and put her off."

"It has happened very well," said Mrs. Walker. "If she is so perfectly determined to compromise herself, the sooner one knows it the better; one can act accordingly."

"I suspect she meant no harm," Winterbourne rejoined.

"So I thought a month ago. But she has been going too far."

"What has she been doing?"

"Everything that is not done here. Flirting with any man she could pick up; sitting in corners with mysterious Italians; dancing all the evening with the same partners; receiving visits at eleven o'clock at night. Her mother goes away when visitors come."

"But her brother," said Winterbourne, laughing, "sits up till midnight."

"He must be edified by what he sees. I'm told that at their hotel everyone is talking about her, and that a smile goes round among all the servants when a gentleman comes and asks for Miss Miller."

"The servants be hanged!" said Winterbourne angrily. "The poor girl's only fault," he presently added, "is that she is very uncultivated."

"She is naturally indelicate," Mrs. Walker declared.

"Take that example this morning. How long had you known her at Vevey?"

"A couple of days."

"Fancy, then, her making it a personal matter that you should have left the place!"

Winterbourne was silent for some moments; then he said, "I suspect, Mrs. Walker, that you and I have lived too long at Geneva!" And he added a request that she should inform him with what particular design she had made him enter her carriage.

"I wished to beg you to cease your relations with Miss Miller—not to flirt with her—to give her no further opportunity to expose herself—to let her alone, in short."

"I'm afraid I can't do that," said Winterbourne. "I like her extremely."

"All the more reason that you shouldn't help her to make a scandal."

"There shall be nothing scandalous in my attentions to her."

"There certainly will be in the way she takes them. But I have said what I had on my conscience," Mrs. Walker pursued. "If you wish to rejoin the young lady I will put you down. Here, by the way, you have a chance."

The carriage was traversing that part of the Pincian Garden that overhangs the wall of Rome and overlooks the beautiful Villa Borghese. It is bordered by a large parapet, near which there are several seats. One of the seats at a distance was occupied by a gentleman and a lady, toward whom Mrs. Walker gave a toss of her head. At the same moment these persons rose and walked toward the parapet. Winterbourne had asked the coachman to stop; he now descended from the carriage. His companion looked at him a moment in silence; then, while he raised his hat, she drove majestically away. Winterbourne stood there; he had turned his eyes toward Daisy and her cavalier. They evidently saw no one; they were too deeply occupied with each other. When they reached the low garden wall, they stood a moment looking off at the great flat-topped pine clusters of the Villa Borghese; then Giovanelli seated himself, familiarly, upon the broad ledge of the wall. The western sun in the opposite sky sent out a brilliant shaft through a couple of cloud bars, whereupon Daisy's companion took her parasol out of her hands and opened it. She came a little nearer, and he held the parasol over her; then, still holding it, he let it rest upon her shoulder, so that both of their heads were hidden from Winterbourne. This young man lingered a moment, then he began to walk. But he walked—not toward the couple with the parasol; toward the residence of his aunt, Mrs. Costello.

He flattered himself on the following day that there was no smiling among the servants when he, at least, asked for Mrs. Miller at her hotel. This lady and her daughter, however, were not at home; and on the next day after, repeating his visit, Winterbourne again had the misfortune not to find them. Mrs. Walker's party took place on the evening of the third day, and, in spite of the frigidity of his last interview with the hostess, Winterbourne was among the guests. Mrs. Walker was one of those American ladies who, while residing abroad, make a point, in their own phrase, of studying European society, and she had on this occasion collected several specimens of her diversely born fellow mortals to serve, as it were, as textbooks. When Winterbourne arrived, Daisy Miller was not there, but in a few moments he saw her mother come in alone, very shyly and ruefully. Mrs. Miller's hair above her exposed-looking temples was more frizzled than ever. As she approached Mrs. Walker, Winterbourne also drew near.

"You see, I've come all alone," said poor Mrs. Miller. "I'm so frightened; I don't know what to do. It's the first time I've ever been to a party alone, especially in this country. I wanted to bring Randolph or Eugenio, or someone, but Daisy just pushed me off by myself. I ain't used to going round alone."

"And does not your daughter intend to favor us with her society?" demanded Mrs. Walker impressively.

"Well, Daisy's all dressed," said Mrs. Miller with that accent of the dispassionate, if not of the philosophic, historian with which she always recorded the current incidents of her daughter's career. "She got dressed on purpose before dinner. But she's got a friend of hers there; that gentleman—the Italian—that she wanted to bring. They've got going at the piano; it seems as if they couldn't leave off. Mr. Giovanelli sings splendidly. But I guess they'll come before very long," concluded Mrs. Miller hopefully.

"I'm sorry she should come in that way," said Mrs. Walker.

"Well, I told her that there was no use in her getting dressed before dinner if she was going to wait three hours," responded Daisy's mamma. "I didn't see the use of her putting on such a dress as that to sit round with Mr. Giovanelli."

"This is most horrible!" said Mrs. Walker, turning away and addressing herself to Winterbourne. "Elle s'affiche. It's her revenge for my having ventured to remonstrate with her. When she comes, I shall not speak to her."

Daisy came after eleven o'clock; but she was not, on such an occasion, a young lady to wait to be spoken to. She rustled forward in radiant loveliness, smiling and chattering, carrying a large bouquet, and attended by Mr. Giovanelli. Everyone stopped talking and turned and looked at her. She came straight to Mrs. Walker. "I'm afraid you thought I never was coming, so I sent mother off to tell you. I wanted to make Mr. Giovanelli practice some things before he came; you know he sings beautifully, and I want you to ask him to sing. This is Mr. Giovanelli; you know I introduced him to you; he's got the most lovely voice, and he knows the most charming set of songs. I made him go over them this evening on purpose; we had the greatest time at the hotel." Of all this Daisy delivered herself with the sweetest, brightest audibleness, looking now at her hostess and now round the room, while she gave a series of little pats, round her shoulders, to the edges of her dress. "Is there anyone I know?" she asked.

"I think every one knows you!" said Mrs. Walker pregnantly, and she gave a very cursory greeting to Mr. Giovanelli. This gentleman bore himself gallantly. He smiled and bowed and showed his white teeth; he curled his mustaches and rolled his eyes and performed all the proper functions of a handsome Italian at an evening party. He sang very prettily half a dozen songs, though Mrs. Walker afterward declared that she had been quite unable to find out who asked him. It was apparently not Daisy who had given him his orders. Daisy sat at a distance from the piano, and though she had publicly, as it were, professed a high admiration for his singing, talked, not inaudibly, while it was going on.

"It's a pity these rooms are so small; we can't dance," she said to Winterbourne, as if she had seen him five minutes before.

"I am not sorry we can't dance," Winterbourne answered; "I don't dance."

"Of course you don't dance; you're too stiff," said Miss Daisy. "I hope you enjoyed your drive with Mrs. Walker!"

"No. I didn't enjoy it; I preferred walking with you."

"We paired off: that was much better," said Daisy. "But did you ever hear anything so cool as Mrs. Walker's wanting me to get into her carriage and drop poor Mr. Giovanelli, and under the pretext that it was proper? People have different ideas! It would have been most unkind; he had been talking about that walk for ten days."

"He should not have talked about it at all," said Winterbourne; "he would never have proposed to a young lady of this country to walk about the streets with him."

"About the streets?" cried Daisy with her pretty stare. "Where, then, would he have proposed to her to walk? The Pincio is not the streets, either; and I, thank goodness, am not a young lady of this country. The young ladies of this country have a dreadfully poky time of it, so far as I can learn; I don't see why I should change my habits for THEM."

"I am afraid your habits are those of a flirt," said Winterbourne gravely.

"Of course they are," she cried, giving him her little smiling stare again. "I'm a fearful, frightful flirt! Did you ever hear of a nice girl that was not? But I suppose you will tell me now that I am not a nice girl."

"You're a very nice girl; but I wish you would flirt with me, and me only," said Winterbourne.

"Ah! thank you—thank you very much; you are the last man I should think of flirting with. As I have had the pleasure of informing you, you are too stiff."

"You say that too often," said Winterbourne.

Daisy gave a delighted laugh. "If I could have the sweet hope of making you angry, I should say it again."

"Don't do that; when I am angry I'm stiffer than ever. But if you won't flirt with me, do cease, at least, to flirt with your friend at the piano; they don't understand that sort of thing here."

"I thought they understood nothing else!" exclaimed Daisy.

"Not in young unmarried women."

"It seems to me much more proper in young unmarried women than in old married ones," Daisy declared.

"Well," said Winterbourne, "when you deal with natives you must go by the custom of the place. Flirting is a purely American custom; it doesn't exist here. So when you show yourself in public with Mr. Giovanelli, and without your mother—"

"Gracious! poor Mother!" interposed Daisy.

"Though you may be flirting, Mr. Giovanelli is not; he means something else."

"He isn't preaching, at any rate," said Daisy with vivacity. "And if you want very much to know, we are neither of us flirting; we are too good friends for that: we are very intimate friends."

"Ah!" rejoined Winterbourne, "if you are in love with each other, it is another affair."

She had allowed him up to this point to talk so frankly that he had no expectation of shocking her by this ejaculation; but she immediately got up, blushing visibly, and leaving him to exclaim mentally that little American flirts were the queerest creatures in the world. "Mr. Giovanelli, at least," she said, giving her interlocutor a single glance, "never says such very disagreeable things to me."

Winterbourne was bewildered; he stood, staring. Mr. Giovanelli had finished singing. He left the piano and came over to Daisy. "Won't you come into the other room and have some tea?" he asked, bending before her with his ornamental smile.

Daisy turned to Winterbourne, beginning to smile again. He was still more perplexed, for this inconsequent smile made nothing clear, though it seemed to prove, indeed, that she had a sweetness and softness that reverted instinctively to the pardon of offenses. "It has never occurred to Mr. Winterbourne to offer me any tea," she said with her little tormenting manner.

"I have offered you advice," Winterbourne rejoined.

"I prefer weak tea!" cried Daisy, and she went off with the brilliant Giovanelli. She sat with him in the adjoining room, in the embrasure of the window, for the rest of the evening. There was an interesting performance at the piano, but neither of these young people gave heed to it. When Daisy came to take leave of Mrs. Walker, this lady conscientiously repaired the weakness of which she had been guilty at the moment of the young girl's arrival. She turned her back straight upon Miss Miller and left her to depart with what grace she might. Winterbourne was standing near the door; he saw it all. Daisy turned very pale and looked at her mother, but Mrs. Miller was humbly unconscious of any violation of the usual social forms. She appeared, indeed, to have felt an incongruous impulse to draw attention to her own striking observance of them. "Good night, Mrs. Walker," she said; "we've had a beautiful evening. You see, if I let Daisy come to parties without me, I don't want her to go away without me." Daisy turned away, looking with a pale, grave face at the circle near the door; Winterbourne saw that, for the first moment, she was too much shocked and puzzled even for indignation. He on his side was greatly touched.

"That was very cruel," he said to Mrs. Walker.

"She never enters my drawing room again!" replied his hostess.

Since Winterbourne was not to meet her in Mrs. Walker's drawing room, he went as often as possible to Mrs. Miller's hotel. The ladies were rarely at home, but when he found them, the devoted Giovanelli was always present. Very often the brilliant little Roman was in the drawing room with Daisy alone, Mrs. Miller being apparently constantly of the opinion that discretion is the better part of surveillance. Winterbourne noted, at first with surprise, that Daisy on these occasions was never embarrassed or annoyed by his own entrance; but he very presently began to feel that she had no more surprises for him; the unexpected in her behavior was the only thing to expect. She showed no displeasure at her tete-a-tete with Giovanelli being interrupted; she could chatter as freshly and freely with two gentlemen as with one; there was always, in her conversation, the same odd mixture of audacity and puerility. Winterbourne remarked to himself that if she was seriously interested in Giovanelli, it was very singular that she should not take more trouble to preserve the sanctity of their interviews; and he liked her the more for her innocent-looking indifference and her apparently inexhaustible good humor. He could hardly have said why, but she seemed to him a girl who would never be jealous. At the risk of exciting a somewhat derisive smile on the reader's part, I may affirm that with regard to the women who had hitherto interested him, it very often seemed to Winterbourne among the possibilities that, given certain contingencies, he should be afraid—literally afraid—of these ladies; he had a pleasant sense that he should never be afraid of Daisy Miller. It must be added that this sentiment was not altogether flattering to Daisy; it was part of his conviction, or rather of his apprehension, that she would prove a very light young person.

But she was evidently very much interested in Giovanelli. She looked at him whenever he spoke; she was perpetually telling him to do this and to do that; she was constantly "chaffing" and abusing him. She appeared completely to have forgotten that Winterbourne had said anything to displease her at Mrs. Walker's little party. One Sunday afternoon, having gone to St. Peter's with his aunt, Winterbourne perceived Daisy strolling about the great church in company with the inevitable Giovanelli. Presently he pointed out the young girl and her cavalier to Mrs. Costello. This lady looked at them a moment through her eyeglass, and then she said:

"That's what makes you so pensive in these days, eh?"

"I had not the least idea I was pensive," said the young man.

"You are very much preoccupied; you are thinking of something."

"And what is it," he asked, "that you accuse me of thinking of?"

"Of that young lady's—Miss Baker's, Miss Chandler's—what's her name?—Miss Miller's intrigue with that little barber's block."

"Do you call it an intrigue," Winterbourne asked—"an affair that goes on with such peculiar publicity?"

"That's their folly," said Mrs. Costello; "it's not their merit."

"No," rejoined Winterbourne, with something of that pensiveness to which his aunt had alluded. "I don't believe that there is anything to be called an intrigue."

"I have heard a dozen people speak of it; they say she is quite carried away by him."

"They are certainly very intimate," said Winterbourne.

Mrs. Costello inspected the young couple again with her optical instrument. "He is very handsome. One easily sees how it is. She thinks him the most elegant man in the world, the finest gentleman. She has never seen anything like him; he is better, even, than the courier. It was the courier probably who introduced him; and if he succeeds in marrying the young lady, the courier will come in for a magnificent commission."

"I don't believe she thinks of marrying him," said Winterbourne, "and I don't believe he hopes to marry her."

"You may be very sure she thinks of nothing. She goes on from day to day, from hour to hour, as they did in the Golden Age. I can imagine nothing more vulgar. And at the same time," added Mrs. Costello, "depend upon it that she may tell you any moment that she is 'engaged.'"

"I think that is more than Giovanelli expects," said Winterbourne.

"Who is Giovanelli?"

"The little Italian. I have asked questions about him and learned something. He is apparently a perfectly respectable little man. I believe he is, in a small way, a cavaliere avvocato. But he doesn't move in what are called the first circles. I think it is really not absolutely impossible that the courier introduced him. He is evidently immensely charmed with Miss Miller. If she thinks him the finest gentleman in the world, he, on his side, has never found himself in personal contact with such splendor, such opulence, such expensiveness as this young lady's. And then she must seem to him wonderfully pretty and interesting. I rather doubt that he dreams of marrying her. That must appear to him too impossible a piece of luck. He has nothing but his handsome face to offer, and there is a substantial Mr. Miller in that mysterious land of dollars. Giovanelli knows that he hasn't a title to offer. If he were only a count or a marchese! He must wonder at his luck, at the way they have taken him up."

"He accounts for it by his handsome face and thinks Miss Miller a young lady qui se passe ses fantaisies!" said Mrs. Costello.

"It is very true," Winterbourne pursued, "that Daisy and her mamma have not yet risen to that stage of—what shall I call it?—of culture at which the idea of catching a count or a marchese begins. I believe that they are intellectually incapable of that conception."

"Ah! but the avvocato can't believe it," said Mrs. Costello.

Of the observation excited by Daisy's "intrigue," Winterbourne gathered that day at St. Peter's sufficient evidence. A dozen of the American colonists in Rome came to talk with Mrs. Costello, who sat on a little portable stool at the base of one of the great pilasters. The vesper service was going forward in splendid chants and organ tones in the adjacent choir, and meanwhile, between Mrs. Costello and her friends, there was a great deal said about poor little Miss Miller's going really "too far." Winterbourne was not pleased with what he heard, but when, coming out upon the great steps of the church, he saw Daisy, who had emerged before him, get into an open cab with her accomplice and roll away through the cynical streets of Rome, he could not deny to himself that she was going very far indeed. He felt very sorry for her—not exactly that he believed that she had completely lost her head, but because it was painful to hear so much that was pretty, and undefended, and natural assigned to a vulgar place among the categories of disorder. He made an attempt after this to give a hint to Mrs. Miller. He met one day in the Corso a friend, a tourist like himself, who had just come out of the Doria Palace, where he had been walking through the beautiful gallery. His friend talked for a moment about the superb portrait of Innocent X by Velasquez which hangs in one of the cabinets of the palace, and then said, "And in the same cabinet, by the way, I had the pleasure of contemplating a picture of a different kind—that pretty American girl whom you pointed out to me last week." In answer to Winterbourne's inquiries, his friend narrated that the pretty American girl—prettier than ever—was seated with a companion in the secluded nook in which the great papal portrait was enshrined.

"Who was her companion?" asked Winterbourne.

"A little Italian with a bouquet in his buttonhole. The girl is delightfully pretty, but I thought I understood from you the other day that she was a young lady du meilleur monde."

"So she is!" answered Winterbourne; and having assured himself that his informant had seen Daisy and her companion but five minutes before, he jumped into a cab and went to call on Mrs. Miller. She was at home; but she apologized to him for receiving him in Daisy's absence.

"She's gone out somewhere with Mr. Giovanelli," said Mrs. Miller. "She's always going round with Mr. Giovanelli."

"I have noticed that they are very intimate," Winterbourne observed.

"Oh, it seems as if they couldn't live without each other!" said Mrs. Miller. "Well, he's a real gentleman, anyhow. I keep telling Daisy she's engaged!"

"And what does Daisy say?"

"Oh, she says she isn't engaged. But she might as well be!" this impartial parent resumed; "she goes on as if she was. But I've made Mr. Giovanelli promise to tell me, if SHE doesn't. I should want to write to Mr. Miller about it—shouldn't you?"

Winterbourne replied that he certainly should; and the state of mind of Daisy's mamma struck him as so unprecedented in the annals of parental vigilance that he gave up as utterly irrelevant the attempt to place her upon her guard.

After this Daisy was never at home, and Winterbourne ceased to meet her at the houses of their common acquaintances, because, as he perceived, these shrewd people had quite made up their minds that she was going too far. They ceased to invite her; and they intimated that they desired to express to observant Europeans the great truth that, though Miss Daisy Miller was a young American lady, her behavior was not representative—was regarded by her compatriots as abnormal. Winterbourne wondered how she felt about all the cold shoulders that were turned toward her, and sometimes it annoyed him to suspect that she did not feel at all. He said to himself that she was too light and childish, too uncultivated and unreasoning, too provincial, to have reflected upon her ostracism, or even to have perceived it. Then at other moments he believed that she carried about in her elegant and irresponsible little organism a defiant, passionate, perfectly observant consciousness of the impression she produced. He asked himself whether Daisy's defiance came from the consciousness of innocence, or from her being, essentially, a young person of the reckless class. It must be admitted that holding one's self to a belief in Daisy's "innocence" came to seem to Winterbourne more and more a matter of fine-spun gallantry. As I have already had occasion to relate, he was angry at finding himself reduced to chopping logic about this young lady; he was vexed at his want of instinctive certitude as to how far her eccentricities were generic, national, and how far they were personal. From either view of them he had somehow missed her, and now it was too late. She was "carried away" by Mr. Giovanelli.

A few days after his brief interview with her mother, he encountered her in that beautiful abode of flowering desolation known as the Palace of the Caesars. The early Roman spring had filled the air with bloom and perfume, and the rugged surface of the Palatine was muffled with tender verdure. Daisy was strolling along the top of one of those great mounds of ruin that are embanked with mossy marble and paved with monumental inscriptions. It seemed to him that Rome had never been so lovely as just then. He stood, looking off at the enchanting harmony of line and color that remotely encircles the city, inhaling the softly humid odors, and feeling the freshness of the year and the antiquity of the place reaffirm themselves in mysterious interfusion. It seemed to him also that Daisy had never looked so pretty, but this had been an observation of his whenever he met her. Giovanelli was at her side, and Giovanelli, too, wore an aspect of even unwonted brilliancy.

"Well," said Daisy, "I should think you would be lonesome!"

"Lonesome?" asked Winterbourne.

"You are always going round by yourself. Can't you get anyone to walk with you?"

"I am not so fortunate," said Winterbourne, "as your companion."

Giovanelli, from the first, had treated Winterbourne with distinguished politeness. He listened with a deferential air to his remarks; he laughed punctiliously at his pleasantries; he seemed disposed to testify to his belief that Winterbourne was a superior young man. He carried himself in no degree like a jealous wooer; he had obviously a great deal of tact; he had no objection to your expecting a little humility of him. It even seemed to Winterbourne at times that Giovanelli would find a certain mental relief in being able to have a private understanding with him—to say to him, as an intelligent man, that, bless you, HE knew how extraordinary was this young lady, and didn't flatter himself with delusive—or at least TOO delusive—hopes of matrimony and dollars. On this occasion he strolled away from his companion to pluck a sprig of almond blossom, which he carefully arranged in his buttonhole.

"I know why you say that," said Daisy, watching Giovanelli. "Because you think I go round too much with HIM." And she nodded at her attendant.

"Every one thinks so—if you care to know," said Winterbourne.

"Of course I care to know!" Daisy exclaimed seriously. "But I don't believe it. They are only pretending to be shocked. They don't really care a straw what I do. Besides, I don't go round so much."

"I think you will find they do care. They will show it disagreeably."

Daisy looked at him a moment. "How disagreeably?"

"Haven't you noticed anything?" Winterbourne asked.

"I have noticed you. But I noticed you were as stiff as an umbrella the first time I saw you."

"You will find I am not so stiff as several others," said Winterbourne, smiling.

"How shall I find it?"

"By going to see the others."

"What will they do to me?"

"They will give you the cold shoulder. Do you know what that means?"

Daisy was looking at him intently; she began to color. "Do you mean as Mrs. Walker did the other night?"

"Exactly!" said Winterbourne.

She looked away at Giovanelli, who was decorating himself with his almond blossom. Then looking back at Winterbourne, "I shouldn't think you would let people be so unkind!" she said.

"How can I help it?" he asked.

"I should think you would say something."

"I do say something;" and he paused a moment. "I say that your mother tells me that she believes you are engaged."

"Well, she does," said Daisy very simply.

Winterbourne began to laugh. "And does Randolph believe it?" he asked.

"I guess Randolph doesn't believe anything," said Daisy. Randolph's skepticism excited Winterbourne to further hilarity, and he observed that Giovanelli was coming back to them. Daisy, observing it too, addressed herself again to her countryman. "Since you have mentioned it," she said, "I AM engaged." Winterbourne looked at her; he had stopped laughing. "You don't believe!" she added.

He was silent a moment; and then, "Yes, I believe it," he said.

"Oh, no, you don't!" she answered. "Well, then—I am not!"

The young girl and her cicerone were on their way to the gate of the enclosure, so that Winterbourne, who had but lately entered, presently took leave of them. A week afterward he went to dine at a beautiful villa on the Caelian Hill, and, on arriving, dismissed his hired vehicle. The evening was charming, and he promised himself the satisfaction of walking home beneath the Arch of Constantine and past the vaguely lighted monuments of the Forum. There was a waning moon in the sky, and her radiance was not brilliant, but she was veiled in a thin cloud curtain which seemed to diffuse and equalize it. When, on his return from the villa (it was eleven o'clock), Winterbourne approached the dusky circle of the Colosseum, it recurred to him, as a lover of the picturesque, that the interior, in the pale moonshine, would be well worth a glance. He turned aside and walked to one of the empty arches, near which, as he observed, an open carriage—one of the little Roman streetcabs—was stationed. Then he passed in, among the cavernous shadows of the great structure, and emerged upon the clear and silent arena. The place had never seemed to him more impressive. One-half of the gigantic circus was in deep shade, the other was sleeping in the luminous dusk. As he stood there he began to murmur Byron's famous lines, out of "Manfred," but before he had finished his quotation he remembered that if nocturnal meditations in the Colosseum are recommended by the poets, they are deprecated by the doctors. The historic atmosphere was there, certainly; but the historic atmosphere, scientifically considered, was no better than a villainous miasma. Winterbourne walked to the middle of the arena, to take a more general glance, intending thereafter to make a hasty retreat. The great cross in the center was covered with shadow; it was only as he drew near it that he made it out distinctly. Then he saw that two persons were stationed upon the low steps which formed its base. One of these was a woman, seated; her companion was standing in front of her.

Presently the sound of the woman's voice came to him distinctly in the warm night air. "Well, he looks at us as one of the old lions or tigers may have looked at the Christian martyrs!" These were the words he heard, in the familiar accent of Miss Daisy Miller.

"Let us hope he is not very hungry," responded the ingenious Giovanelli. "He will have to take me first; you will serve for dessert!"

Winterbourne stopped, with a sort of horror, and, it must be added, with a sort of relief. It was as if a sudden illumination had been flashed upon the ambiguity of Daisy's behavior, and the riddle had become easy to read. She was a young lady whom a gentleman need no longer be at pains to respect. He stood there, looking at her—looking at her companion and not reflecting that though he saw them vaguely, he himself must have been more brightly visible. He felt angry with himself that he had bothered so much about the right way of regarding Miss Daisy Miller. Then, as he was going to advance again, he checked himself, not from the fear that he was doing her injustice, but from a sense of the danger of appearing unbecomingly exhilarated by this sudden revulsion from cautious criticism. He turned away toward the entrance of the place, but, as he did so, he heard Daisy speak again.

"Why, it was Mr. Winterbourne! He saw me, and he cuts me!"

What a clever little reprobate she was, and how smartly she played at injured innocence! But he wouldn't cut her. Winterbourne came forward again and went toward the great cross. Daisy had got up; Giovanelli lifted his hat. Winterbourne had now begun to think simply of the craziness, from a sanitary point of view, of a delicate young girl lounging away the evening in this nest of malaria. What if she WERE a clever little reprobate? that was no reason for her dying of the perniciosa. "How long have you been here?" he asked almost brutally.

Daisy, lovely in the flattering moonlight, looked at him a moment. Then—"All the evening," she answered, gently. "I never saw anything so pretty."

"I am afraid," said Winterbourne, "that you will not think Roman fever very pretty. This is the way people catch it. I wonder," he added, turning to Giovanelli, "that you, a native Roman, should countenance such a terrible indiscretion."

"Ah," said the handsome native, "for myself I am not afraid."

"Neither am I—for you! I am speaking for this young lady."

Giovanelli lifted his well-shaped eyebrows and showed his brilliant teeth. But he took Winterbourne's rebuke with docility. "I told the signorina it was a grave indiscretion, but when was the signorina ever prudent?"

"I never was sick, and I don't mean to be!" the signorina declared. "I don't look like much, but I'm healthy! I was bound to see the Colosseum by moonlight; I shouldn't have wanted to go home without that; and we have had the most beautiful time, haven't we, Mr. Giovanelli? If there has been any danger, Eugenio can give me some pills. He has got some splendid pills."

"I should advise you," said Winterbourne, "to drive home as fast as possible and take one!"

"What you say is very wise," Giovanelli rejoined. "I will go and make sure the carriage is at hand." And he went forward rapidly.

Daisy followed with Winterbourne. He kept looking at her; she seemed not in the least embarrassed. Winterbourne said nothing; Daisy chattered about the beauty of the place. "Well, I HAVE seen the Colosseum by moonlight!" she exclaimed. "That's one good thing." Then, noticing Winterbourne's silence, she asked him why he didn't speak. He made no answer; he only began to laugh. They passed under one of the dark archways; Giovanelli was in front with the carriage. Here Daisy stopped a moment, looking at the young American. "DID you believe I was engaged, the other day?" she asked.

"It doesn't matter what I believed the other day," said Winterbourne, still laughing.

"Well, what do you believe now?"

"I believe that it makes very little difference whether you are engaged or not!"

He felt the young girl's pretty eyes fixed upon him through the thick gloom of the archway; she was apparently going to answer. But Giovanelli hurried her forward. "Quick! quick!" he said; "if we get in by midnight we are quite safe."

Daisy took her seat in the carriage, and the fortunate Italian placed himself beside her. "Don't forget Eugenio's pills!" said Winterbourne as he lifted his hat.

"I don't care," said Daisy in a little strange tone, "whether I have Roman fever or not!" Upon this the cab driver cracked his whip, and they rolled away over the desultory patches of the antique pavement.

Winterbourne, to do him justice, as it were, mentioned to no one that he had encountered Miss Miller, at midnight, in the Colosseum with a gentleman; but nevertheless, a couple of days later, the fact of her having been there under these circumstances was known to every member of the little American circle, and commented accordingly. Winterbourne reflected that they had of course known it at the hotel, and that, after Daisy's return, there had been an exchange of remarks between the porter and the cab driver. But the young man was conscious, at the same moment, that it had ceased to be a matter of serious regret to him that the little American flirt should be "talked about" by low-minded menials. These people, a day or two later, had serious information to give: the little American flirt was alarmingly ill. Winterbourne, when the rumor came to him, immediately went to the hotel for more news. He found that two or three charitable friends had preceded him, and that they were being entertained in Mrs. Miller's salon by Randolph.

"It's going round at night," said Randolph—"that's what made her sick. She's always going round at night. I shouldn't think she'd want to, it's so plaguy dark. You can't see anything here at night, except when there's a moon. In America there's always a moon!" Mrs. Miller was invisible; she was now, at least, giving her daughter the advantage of her society. It was evident that Daisy was dangerously ill.

Winterbourne went often to ask for news of her, and once he saw Mrs. Miller, who, though deeply alarmed, was, rather to his surprise, perfectly composed, and, as it appeared, a most efficient and judicious nurse. She talked a good deal about Dr. Davis, but Winterbourne paid her the compliment of saying to himself that she was not, after all, such a monstrous goose. "Daisy spoke of you the other day," she said to him. "Half the time she doesn't know what she's saying, but that time I think she did. She gave me a message she told me to tell you. She told me to tell you that she never was engaged to that handsome Italian. I am sure I am very glad; Mr. Giovanelli hasn't been near us since she was taken ill. I thought he was so much of a gentleman; but I don't call that very polite! A lady told me that he was afraid I was angry with him for taking Daisy round at night. Well, so I am, but I suppose he knows I'm a lady. I would scorn to scold him. Anyway, she says she's not engaged. I don't know why she wanted you to know, but she said to me three times, 'Mind you tell Mr. Winterbourne.' And then she told me to ask if you remembered the time you went to that castle in Switzerland. But I said I wouldn't give any such messages as that. Only, if she is not engaged, I'm sure I'm glad to know it."

But, as Winterbourne had said, it mattered very little. A week after this, the poor girl died; it had been a terrible case of the fever. Daisy's grave was in the little Protestant cemetery, in an angle of the wall of imperial Rome, beneath the cypresses and the thick spring flowers. Winterbourne stood there beside it, with a number of other mourners, a number larger than the scandal excited by the young lady's career would have led you to expect. Near him stood Giovanelli, who came nearer still before Winterbourne turned away. Giovanelli was very pale: on this occasion he had no flower in his buttonhole; he seemed to wish to say something. At last he said, "She was the most beautiful young lady I ever saw, and the most amiable;" and then he added in a moment, "and she was the most innocent."

Winterbourne looked at him and presently repeated his words, "And the most innocent?"

"The most innocent!"

Winterbourne felt sore and angry. "Why the devil," he asked, "did you take her to that fatal place?"

Mr. Giovanelli's urbanity was apparently imperturbable. He looked on the ground a moment, and then he said, "For myself I had no fear; and she wanted to go."

"That was no reason!" Winterbourne declared.

The subtle Roman again dropped his eyes. "If she had lived, I should have got nothing. She would never have married me, I am sure."

"She would never have married you?"

"For a moment I hoped so. But no. I am sure."

Winterbourne listened to him: he stood staring at the raw protuberance among the April daisies. When he turned away again, Mr. Giovanelli, with his light, slow step, had retired.

Winterbourne almost immediately left Rome; but the following summer he again met his aunt, Mrs. Costello at Vevey. Mrs. Costello was fond of Vevey. In the interval Winterbourne had often thought of Daisy Miller and her mystifying manners. One day he spoke of her to his aunt—said it was on his conscience that he had done her injustice.

"I am sure I don't know," said Mrs. Costello. "How did your injustice affect her?"

"She sent me a message before her death which I didn't understand at the time; but I have understood it since. She would have appreciated one's esteem."

"Is that a modest way," asked Mrs. Costello, "of saying that she would have reciprocated one's affection?"

Winterbourne offered no answer to this question; but he presently said, "You were right in that remark that you made last summer. I was booked to make a mistake. I have lived too long in foreign parts."

Nevertheless, he went back to live at Geneva, whence there continue to come the most contradictory accounts of his motives of sojourn: a report that he is "studying" hard—an intimation that he is much interested in a very clever foreign lady.

THE AMBASSADORS

Volume I

Preface

Nothing is more easy than to state the subject of "The Ambassadors," which first appeared in twelve numbers of *The North American Review* (1903) and was published as a whole the same year. The situation involved is gathered up betimes, that is in the second chapter of Book Fifth, for the reader's benefit, into as few words as possible—planted or "sunk," stiffly and saliently, in the centre of the current, almost perhaps to the obstruction of traffic. Never can a composition of this sort have sprung straighter from a dropped grain of suggestion, and never can that grain, developed, overgrown and smothered, have yet lurked more in the mass as an independent particle. The whole case, in fine, is in Lambert Strether's irrepressible outbreak to little Bilham on the Sunday afternoon in Gloriani's garden, the candour with which he yields, for his young friend's enlightenment, to the charming admonition of that crisis. The idea of the tale resides indeed in the very fact that an hour of such unprecedented ease should have been felt by him AS a crisis, and he is at pains to express it for us as neatly as we could desire. The remarks to which he thus gives utterance contain the essence of "The Ambassadors," his fingers close, before he has done, round the stem of the full-blown flower; which, after that fashion, he continues officiously to present to us. "Live all you can; it's a mistake not to. It doesn't so much matter what you do in particular so long as you have your life. If you haven't had that what HAVE you had? I'm too old—too old at any rate for what I see. What one loses one loses; make no mistake about that. Still, we have the illusion of freedom; therefore don't, like me to-day, be without the memory of that illusion. I was either, at the right time, too stupid or too intelligent to have it, and now I'm a case of reaction against the mistake. Do what you like so long as you don't make it. For it WAS a mistake. Live, live!" Such is the gist of Strether's appeal to the impressed youth, whom he likes and whom he desires to befriend; the word "mistake" occurs several times, it will be seen, in the course of his remarks—which gives the measure of the signal warning he feels attached to his case. He has accordingly missed too much, though perhaps after all constitutionally qualified for a better part, and he wakes up to it in conditions that press the spring of a terrible question. WOULD there yet perhaps be time for reparation?—reparation, that is, for the injury done his character; for the affront, he is quite ready to say, so stupidly put upon it and in which he has even himself had so clumsy a hand? The answer to which is that he now at all events SEES; so that the business of my tale and the march of my action, not to say the precious moral of everything, is just my demonstration of this process of vision.

Nothing can exceed the closeness with which the whole fits again into its germ. That had been given me bodily, as usual, by the spoken word, for I was to take the image over exactly as I happened to have met it. A friend had repeated to me, with great appreciation, a thing or two said to him by a man of distinction, much his senior, and to which a sense akin to that of Strether's melancholy eloquence might be imputed—said as chance would have, and so easily might, in Paris, and in a charming old garden attached to a house of art, and on a Sunday afternoon of summer, many persons of great interest being present. The observation there listened to and gathered up had contained part of the "note" that I was to recognise on the spot as to my purpose—had contained in fact the greater part; the rest was in the place and the time and the scene they sketched: these constituents clustered and combined to give me further support, to give me what I may call the note absolute. There it stands, accordingly, full in the tideway; driven in, with hard taps, like some strong stake for the noose of a cable, the swirl of the current roundabout it. What amplified the hint to more than the bulk of hints in general was the gift with it of the old Paris garden, for in that token were sealed up values infinitely precious. There was of course the seal to break and each item of the packet to count over and handle and estimate; but somehow, in the light of the hint, all the elements of a situation of the sort most to my taste were there. I could even remember no occasion on which, so confronted, I had found it of a livelier interest to take stock, in this fashion, of suggested wealth. For I think, verily, that there are degrees of merit in subjects—in spite of the fact that to treat even one of the most ambiguous with due decency we must for the time, for the feverish and prejudiced hour, at least figure its merit and its dignity as POSSIBLY absolute. What it comes to, doubtless, is that even among the supremely good—since with such alone is it one's theory of one's honour to be concerned—there is an ideal BEAUTY of goodness the invoked action of which is to raise the artistic faith to its maximum. Then truly, I hold, one's theme may be said to shine, and that of "The Ambassadors," I confess, wore this glow for me from beginning to end. Fortunately thus I am able to estimate this as, frankly, quite the best, "all round," of all my productions; any failure of that justification would have made such an extreme of complacency publicly fatuous.

I recall then in this connexion no moment of subjective intermittence, never one of those alarms as for a suspected hollow beneath one's feet, a felt ingratitude in the scheme adopted, under which confidence fails and opportunity seems but to mock. If the motive of "The Wings of the Dove," as I have noted, was to worry me at moments by a sealing-up of its face—though without prejudice to its again, of a sudden, fairly grimacing with expression—so in this other business I had absolute conviction and constant clearness to deal with; it had been a frank proposition, the whole bunch of data, installed on my premises like a monotony of fine weather. (The order of composition, in these things, I may mention, was reversed by the order of publication; the earlier written of the two books having appeared as the later.) Even under the weight of my hero's years I could feel my postulate firm; even under the strain of the difference between those of Madame de Vionnet and those of Chad Newsome, a difference liable to be denounced as shocking, I could still feel it serene. Nothing resisted, nothing betrayed, I seem to make out, in this full and sound sense of the matter; it shed from any side I could turn it to the same golden glow. I rejoiced in the promise of a hero so mature, who would give me thereby the more to bite into—since it's only into thickened motive and accumulated character, I think, that the painter of life bites more than a little. My poor friend should have accumulated character, certainly; or rather would be quite naturally and handsomely possessed of it, in the sense that he would have, and would always have felt he had, imagination galore, and that this yet wouldn't have wrecked him. It was immeasurable, the opportunity to "do" a man of imagination, for if THERE mightn't be a chance to "bite," where in the world might it be? This personage of course, so enriched, wouldn't give me, for his type, imagination in PREDOMINANCE or as his prime faculty, nor should I, in view of other matters, have found that convenient. So particular a luxury—some occasion, that is, for study of the high gift in SUPREME command of a case or of a career—would still doubtless come on the day I should be ready to pay for it; and till then might, as from far back, remain hung up well in view and just out of reach. The comparative case meanwhile would serve—it was only on the minor scale that I had treated myself even to comparative cases.

I was to hasten to add however that, happy stopgaps as the minor scale had thus yielded, the instance in hand should enjoy the advantage of the full range of the major; since most immediately to the point was the question of that SUPPLEMENT of situation logically involved in our gentleman's impulse to deliver himself in the Paris garden on the Sunday afternoon—or if not involved by strict logic then all ideally and enchantingly implied in it. (I say "ideally," because I need scarce mention that for development, for expression of its maximum, my glimmering story was, at the earliest stage, to have nipped the thread of connexion with the possibilities of the actual reported speaker. HE remains but the happiest of accidents; his actualities, all too definite, precluded any range of possibilities; it had only been his charming office to project upon that wide field of the artist's vision—which hangs there ever in place like the white sheet suspended for the figures of a child's magic-lantern—a more fantastic and more moveable shadow.) No privilege of the teller of tales and the handler of puppets is more delightful, or has more of the suspense and the thrill of a game of difficulty breathlessly played, than just this business of looking for the unseen and the occult, in a scheme half-grasped, by the light or, so to speak, by the clinging scent, of the gage already in hand. No dreadful old pursuit of the hidden slave with bloodhounds and the rag of association can ever, for "excitement," I judge, have bettered it at its best. For the dramatist always, by the very law of his genius, believes not only in a possible right issue from the rightly-conceived tight place; he does much more than this—he believes, irresistibly, in the necessary, the precious "tightness" of the place (whatever the issue) on the strength of any respectable hint. It being thus the respectable hint that I had with such avidity picked up, what would be the story to which it would most inevitably form the centre? It is part of the charm attendant on such questions that the "story," with the omens true, as I say, puts on from this stage the authenticity of concrete existence. It then is, essentially—it begins to be, though it may more or less obscurely lurk, so that the point is not in the least what to make of it, but only, very delightfully and very damnably, where to put one's hand on it.

In which truth resides surely much of the interest of that admirable mixture for salutary application which we know as art. Art deals with what we see, it must first contribute full-handed that ingredient; it plucks its material, otherwise expressed, in the garden of life—which material elsewhere grown is stale and uneatable. But it has no sooner done this than it has to take account of a PROCESS—from which only when it's the basest of the servants of man, incurring ignominious dismissal with no "character," does it, and whether under some muddled pretext of morality or on any other, pusillanimously edge away. The process, that of the expression, the literal squeezing-out, of value is another affair—with which the happy luck of mere finding has little to do. The joys of finding, at this stage, are pretty well over; that quest of the subject as a whole by "matching," as the ladies say at the shops, the big piece with the snippet, having ended, we assume, with a capture. The subject is found, and if the problem is then transferred to the ground of what to do with it the field opens out for any amount of doing. This is precisely the infusion that, as I submit, completes the strong mixture. It is on the other hand the part of the business that can least be likened to the chase with horn and hound. It's all a sedentary part—involves as much ciphering, of sorts, as would merit the highest salary paid to a chief accountant. Not, however, that the chief accountant hasn't HIS gleams of bliss; for the felicity, or at least the equilibrium of the artist's state dwells less, surely, in the further delightful complications he can smuggle in than in those he succeeds in keeping out. He sows his seed at the risk of too thick a crop; wherefore yet again, like the gentlemen who audit ledgers, he must keep his head at any price. In consequence of all which, for the interest of the matter, I might seem here to have my choice of narrating my "hunt" for Lambert Strether, of describing the capture of the shadow projected by my friend's anecdote, or of reporting on the occurrences subsequent to that triumph. But I had probably best attempt a little to glance in each direction; since it comes to me again and again, over this licentious record, that one's bag of adventures, conceived or conceivable, has been only half-emptied by the mere telling of one's story. It depends so on what one means by that equivocal quantity. There is the story of one's hero, and then, thanks to the intimate connexion of things, the story of one's story itself. I blush to confess it, but if one's a dramatist one's a dramatist, and the latter imbroglio is liable on occasion to strike me as really the more objective of the two.

The philosophy imputed to him in that beautiful outbreak, the hour there, amid such happy provision, striking for him, would have been then, on behalf of my man of imagination, to be logically and, as the artless craft of comedy has it, "led up" to; the probable course to such a goal, the goal of so conscious a predicament, would have in short to be finely calculated. Where has he come from and why has he come, what is he doing (as we Anglo-Saxons, and we only, say, in our foredoomed clutch of exotic aids to expression) in that galere? To answer these questions plausibly, to answer them as under cross-examination in the witness-box by counsel for the prosecution, in other words satisfactorily to account for Strether and for his "peculiar tone," was to possess myself of the entire fabric. At the same time the clue to its whereabouts would lie in a certain principle of probability: he wouldn't have indulged in his peculiar tone without a reason; it would take a felt predicament or a false position to give him so ironic an accent. One hadn't been noting "tones" all one's life without recognising when one heard it the voice of the false position. The dear man in the Paris garden was then admirably and unmistakeably IN one—which was no small point gained; what next accordingly concerned us was the determination of THIS identity. One could only go by probabilities, but there was the advantage that the most general of the probabilities were virtual certainties. Possessed of our friend's nationality, to start with, there was a general probability in his narrower localism; which, for that matter, one had really but to keep under the lens for an hour to see it give up its secrets. He would have issued, our rueful worthy, from the very heart of New England—at the heels of which matter of course a perfect train of secrets tumbled for me into the light. They had to be sifted and sorted, and I shall not reproduce the detail of that process; but unmistakeably they were all there, and it was but a question, auspiciously, of picking among them. What the "position" would infallibly be, and why, on his hands, it had turned "false"—these inductive steps could only be as rapid as they were distinct. I accounted for everything—and "everything" had by this time become the most promising quantity—by the view that he had come to Paris in some state of mind which was literally undergoing, as a result of new and unexpected assaults and infusions, a change almost from hour to hour. He had come with a view that might have been figured by a clear green liquid, say, in a neat glass phial; and the liquid, once poured into the open cup of APPLICATION, once exposed to the action of another air, had begun to turn from green to red, or whatever, and might, for all he knew, be on its way to purple, to black, to yellow. At the still wilder extremes represented perhaps, for all he could say to the contrary, by a variability so violent, he would at first, naturally, but have gazed in surprise and alarm; whereby the SITUATION clearly would spring from the play of wildness and the development of extremes. I saw in a moment that, should this development proceed both with force and logic, my "story" would leave nothing to be desired. There is always, of course, for the story-teller, the irresistible determinant and the incalculable advantage of his interest in the story AS SUCH; it is ever, obviously, overwhelmingly, the prime and precious thing (as other than this I have never been able to see it); as to which what makes for it, with whatever headlong energy, may be said to pale before the energy with which it simply makes for itself. It rejoices, none the less, at its best, to seem to offer itself in a light, to seem to know, and with the very last knowledge, what it's about—liable as it yet is at moments to be caught by us with its tongue in its cheek and absolutely no warrant but its splendid impudence. Let us grant then that the impudence is always there—there, so to speak, for grace and effect and ALLURE; there, above all, because the Story is just the spoiled child of art, and because, as we are always disappointed when the pampered don't "play up," we like it, to that extent, to look all its character. It probably does so, in truth, even when we most flatter ourselves that we negotiate with it by treaty.

All of which, again, is but to say that the STEPS, for my fable, placed themselves with a prompt and, as it were, functional assurance—an air quite as of readiness to have dispensed with logic had I been in fact too stupid for my clue. Never, positively, none the less, as the links multiplied, had I felt less stupid than for the determination of poor Strether's errand and for the apprehension of his issue. These things continued to fall together, as by the neat action of their own weight and form, even while their commentator scratched his head about them; he easily sees now that they were always well in advance of him. As the case completed itself he had in fact, from a good way behind, to catch up with them, breathless and a little flurried, as he best could. THE false position, for our belated man of the world—belated because he had endeavoured so long to escape being one, and now at last had really to face his doom—the false position for him, I say, was obviously to have presented himself at the gate of that boundless menagerie primed with a moral scheme of the most approved pattern which was yet framed to break down on any approach to vivid facts; that is to any at all liberal appreciation of them. There would have been of course the case of the Strether prepared, wherever presenting himself, only to judge and to feel meanly; but HE would have moved for me, I confess, enveloped in no legend whatever. The actual man's note, from the first of our seeing it struck, is the note of discrimination, just as his drama is to become, under stress, the drama of discrimination. It would have been his blest imagination, we have seen, that had already helped him to discriminate; the element that was for so much of the pleasure of my cutting thick, as I have intimated, into his intellectual, into his moral substance. Yet here it was, at the same time, just here, that a shade for a moment fell across the scene.

There was the dreadful little old tradition, one of the platitudes of the human comedy, that people's moral scheme DOES break down in Paris; that nothing is more frequently observed; that hundreds of thousands of more or less hypocritical or more or less cynical persons annually visit the place for the sake of the probable catastrophe, and that I came late in the day to work myself up about it. There was in fine the TRIVIAL association, one of the vulgarest in the world; but which give me pause no longer, I think, simply because its vulgarity is so advertised. The revolution performed by Strether under the influence of the most interesting of great cities was to have nothing to do with any betise of the imputably "tempted" state; he was to be thrown forward, rather, thrown quite with violence, upon his lifelong trick of intense reflexion: which friendly test indeed was to bring him out, through winding passages, through alternations of darkness and light, very much IN Paris, but with the surrounding scene itself a minor matter, a mere symbol for more things than had been dreamt of in the philosophy of Woollett. Another surrounding scene would have done as well for our show could it have represented a place in which Strether's errand was likely to lie and his crisis to await him. The LIKELY place had the great merit of sparing me preparations; there would have been too many involved—not at all impossibilities, only rather worrying and delaying difficulties—in positing elsewhere Chad Newsome's interesting relation, his so interesting complexity of relations. Strether's appointed stage, in fine, could be but Chad's most luckily selected one. The young man had gone in, as they say, for circumjacent charm; and where he would have found it, by the turn of his mind, most "authentic," was where his earnest friend's analysis would most find HIM; as well as where, for that matter, the former's whole analytic faculty would be led such a wonderful dance.

"The Ambassadors" had been, all conveniently, "arranged for"; its first appearance was from month to month, in the *North American Review* during 1903, and I had been open from far back to any pleasant provocation for ingenuity that might reside in one's actively adopting—so as to make it, in its way, a small compositional law—recurrent breaks and resumptions. I had made up my mind here regularly to exploit and enjoy these often rather rude jolts—having found, as I believed an admirable way to it; yet every question of form and pressure, I easily remember, paled in the light of the major propriety, recognised as soon as really weighed; that of employing but one centre and keeping it all within my hero's compass. The thing was to be so much this worthy's intimate adventure that even the projection of his consciousness upon it from beginning to end without intermission or deviation would probably still leave a part of its value for him, and a fortiori for ourselves, unexpressed. I might, however, express every grain of it that there would be room for—on condition of contriving a splendid particular economy. Other persons in no small number were to people the scene, and each with his or her axe to grind, his or her situation to treat, his or her coherency not to fail of, his or her relation to my leading motive, in a word, to establish and carry on. But Strether's sense of these things, and Strether's only, should avail me for showing them; I should know them but through his more or less groping knowledge of them, since his very gropings would figure among his most interesting motions, and a full observance of the rich rigour I speak of would give me more of the effect I should be most "after" than all other possible observances together. It would give me a large unity, and that in turn would crown me with the grace to which the enlightened story-teller will at any time, for his interest, sacrifice if need be all other graces whatever. I refer of course to the grace of intensity, which there are ways of signally achieving and ways of signally missing—as we see it, all round us, helplessly and woefully missed. Not that it isn't, on the other hand, a virtue eminently subject to appreciation—there being no strict, no absolute measure of it; so that one may hear it acclaimed where it has quite escaped one's perception, and see it unnoticed where one has gratefully hailed it. After all of which I am not sure, either, that the immense amusement of the whole cluster of difficulties so arrayed may not operate, for the fond fabulist, when judicious not less than fond, as his best of determinants. That charming principle is always there, at all events, to keep interest fresh: it is a principle, we remember, essentially ravenous, without scruple and without mercy, appeased with no cheap nor easy nourishment. It enjoys the costly sacrifice and rejoices thereby in the very odour of difficulty—even as ogres, with their "Fee-faw-fum!" rejoice in the smell of the blood of Englishmen.

Thus it was, at all events, that the ultimate, though after all so speedy, definition of my gentleman's job—his coming out, all solemnly appointed and deputed, to "save" Chad, and his then finding the young man so disobligingly and, at first, so bewilderingly not lost that a new issue altogether, in the connexion, prodigiously faces them, which has to be dealt with in a new light—promised as many calls on ingenuity and on the higher branches of the compositional art as one could possibly desire. Again and yet again, as, from book to book, I proceed with my survey, I find no source of interest equal to this verification after the fact, as I may call it, and the more in detail the better, of the scheme of consistency "gone in" for. As always—since the charm never fails—the retracing of the process from point to point brings back the old illusion. The old intentions bloom again and flower—in spite of all the blossoms they were to have dropped by the way. This is the charm, as I say, of adventure TRANSPOSED—the thrilling ups and downs, the intricate ins and outs of the compositional problem, made after such a fashion admirably objective, becoming the question at issue and keeping the author's heart in his mouth. Such an element, for instance, as his intention that Mrs. Newsome, away off with her finger on the pulse of Massachusetts, should yet be no less intensely than circuitously present through the whole thing, should be no less felt as to be reckoned with than the most direct exhibition, the finest portrayal at first hand could make her, such a sign of artistic good faith, I say, once it's unmistakeably there, takes on again an actuality not too much impaired by the comparative dimness of the particular success. Cherished intention too inevitably acts and operates, in the book, about fifty times as little as I had fondly dreamt it might; but that scarce spoils for me the pleasure of recognising the fifty ways in which I had sought to provide for it. The mere charm of seeing such an idea constituent, in its degree; the fineness of the measures taken—a real extension, if successful, of the very terms and possibilities of representation and figuration—such things alone were, after this fashion, inspiring, such things alone were a gage of the probable success of that dissimulated calculation with which the whole effort was to square. But oh the cares begotten, none the less, of that same "judicious" sacrifice to a particular form of interest! One's work should have composition, because composition alone is positive beauty; but all the while—apart from one's inevitable consciousness too of the dire paucity of readers ever recognising or ever missing positive beauty—how, as to the cheap and easy, at every turn, how, as to immediacy and facility, and even as to the commoner vivacity, positive beauty might have to be sweated for and paid for! Once achieved and installed it may always be trusted to make the poor seeker feel he would have blushed to the roots of his hair for failing of it; yet, how, as its virtue can be essentially but the virtue of the whole, the wayside traps set in the interest of muddlement and pleading but the cause of the moment, of the particular bit in itself, have to be kicked out of the path! All the sophistications in life, for example, might have appeared to muster on behalf of the menace—the menace to a bright variety—involved in Strether's having all the subjective "say," as it were, to himself.

Had I, meanwhile, made him at once hero and historian, endowed him with the romantic privilege of the "first person"—the darkest abyss of romance this, inveterately, when enjoyed on the grand scale—variety, and many other queer matters as well, might have been smuggled in by a back door. Suffice it, to be brief, that the first person, in the long piece, is a form foredoomed to looseness and that looseness, never much my affair, had never been so little so as on this particular occasion. All of which reflexions flocked to the standard from the moment—a very early one—the question of how to keep my form amusing while sticking so close to my central figure and constantly taking its pattern from him had to be faced. He arrives (arrives at Chester) as for the dreadful purpose of giving his creator "no end" to tell about him—before which rigorous mission the serenest of creators might well have quailed. I was far from the serenest; I was more than agitated enough to reflect that, grimly deprived of one alternative or one substitute for "telling," I must address myself tooth and nail to another. I couldn't, save by implication, make other persons tell EACH OTHER about him—blest resource, blest necessity, of the drama, which reaches its effects of unity, all remarkably, by paths absolutely opposite to the paths of the novel: with other persons, save as they were primarily HIS persons (not he primarily but one of theirs), I had simply nothing to do. I had relations for him none the less, by the mercy of Providence, quite as much as if my exhibition was to be a muddle; if I could only by implication and a show of consequence make other persons tell each other about him, I could at least make him tell THEM whatever in the world he must; and could so, by the same token—which was a further luxury thrown in—see straight into the deep differences between what that could do for me, or at all events for HIM, and the large ease of "autobiography." It may be asked why, if one so keeps to one's hero, one shouldn't make a single mouthful of "method," shouldn't throw the reins on his neck and, letting them flap there as free as in "Gil Blas" or in "David Copperfield," equip him with the double privilege of subject and object—a course that has at least the merit of brushing away questions at a sweep. The answer to which is, I think, that one makes that surrender only if one is prepared NOT to make certain precious discriminations.

The "first person" then, so employed, is addressed by the author directly to ourselves, his possible readers, whom he has to reckon with, at the best, by our English tradition, so loosely and vaguely after all, so little respectfully, on so scant a presumption of exposure to criticism. Strether, on the other hand, encaged and provided for as "The Ambassadors" encages and provides, has to keep in view proprieties much stiffer and more salutary than any our straight and credulous gape are likely to bring home to him, has exhibitional conditions to meet, in a word, that forbid the terrible FLUIDITY of self-revelation. I may seem not to better the case for my discrimination if I say that, for my first care, I had thus inevitably to set him up a confidant or two, to wave away with energy the custom of the seated mass of explanation after the fact, the inserted block of merely referential narrative, which flourishes so, to the shame of the modern impatience, on the serried page of Balzac, but which seems simply to appal our actual, our general weaker, digestion. "Harking back to make up" took at any rate more doing, as the phrase is, not only than the reader of to-day demands, but than he will tolerate at any price any call upon him either to understand or remotely to measure; and for the beauty of the thing when done the current editorial mind in particular appears wholly without sense. It is not, however, primarily for either of these reasons, whatever their weight, that Strether's friend Waymarsh is so keenly clutched at, on the threshold of the book, or that no less a pounce is made on Maria Gostrey—without even the pretext, either, of HER being, in essence, Strether's friend. She is the reader's friend much rather—in consequence of dispositions that make him so eminently require one; and she acts in that capacity, and REALLY in that capacity alone, with exemplary devotion from beginning to and of the book. She is an enrolled, a direct, aid to lucidity; she is in fine, to tear off her mask, the most unmitigated and abandoned of ficelles. Half the dramatist's art, as we well know—since if we don't it's not the fault of the proofs that lie scattered about us—is in the use of ficelles; by which I mean in a deep dissimulation of his dependence on them. Waymarsh only to a slighter degree belongs, in the whole business, less to my subject than to my treatment of it; the interesting proof, in these connexions, being that one has but to take one's subject for the stuff of drama to interweave with enthusiasm as many Gostreys as need be.

The material of "The Ambassadors," conforming in this respect exactly to that of "The Wings of the Dove," published just before it, is taken absolutely for the stuff of drama; so that, availing myself of the opportunity given me by this edition for some prefatory remarks on the latter work, I had mainly to make on its behalf the point of its scenic consistency. It disguises that virtue, in the oddest way in the world, by just LOOKING, as we turn its pages, as little scenic as possible; but it sharply divides itself, just as the composition before us does, into the parts that prepare, that tend in fact to over-prepare, for scenes, and the parts, or otherwise into the scenes, that justify and crown the preparation. It may definitely be said, I think, that everything in it that is not scene (not, I of course mean, complete and functional scene, treating ALL the submitted matter, as by logical start, logical turn, and logical finish) is discriminated preparation, is the fusion and synthesis of picture. These alternations propose themselves all recogniseably, I think, from an early stage, as the very form and figure of "The Ambassadors"; so that, to repeat, such an agent as Miss Gostrey pre-engaged at a high salary, but waits in the draughty wing with her shawl and her smelling-salts. Her function speaks at once for itself, and by the time she has dined with Strether in London and gone to a play with him her intervention as a ficelle is, I hold, expertly justified. Thanks to it we have treated scenically, and scenically alone, the whole lumpish question of Strether's "past," which has seen us more happily on the way than anything else could have done; we have strained to a high lucidity and vivacity (or at least we hope we have) certain indispensable facts; we have seen our two or three immediate friends all conveniently and profitably in "action"; to say nothing of our beginning to descry others, of a remoter intensity, getting into motion, even if a bit vaguely as yet, for our further enrichment. Let my first point be here that the scene in question, that in which the whole situation at Woollett and the complex forces that have propelled my hero to where this lively extractor of his value and distiller of his essence awaits him, is normal and entire, is really an excellent STANDARD scene; copious, comprehensive, and accordingly never short, but with its office as definite as that of the hammer on the gong of the clock, the office of expressing ALL THAT IS IN the hour.

The "ficelle" character of the subordinate party is as artfully dissimulated, throughout, as may be, and to that extent that, with the seams or joints of Maria Gostrey's ostensible connectedness taken particular care of, duly smoothed over, that is, and anxiously kept from showing as "pieced on;" this figure doubtless achieves, after a fashion, something of the dignity of a prime idea: which circumstance but shows us afresh how many quite incalculable but none the less clear sources of enjoyment for the infatuated artist, how many copious springs of our never-to-be-slighted "fun" for the reader and critic susceptible of contagion, may sound their incidental plash as soon as an artistic process begins to enjoy free development. Exquisite—in illustration of this—the mere interest and amusement of such at once "creative" and critical questions as how and where and why to make Miss Gostrey's false connexion carry itself, under a due high polish, as a real one. Nowhere is it more of an artful expedient for mere consistency of form, to mention a case, than in the last "scene" of the book, where its function is to give or to add nothing whatever, but only to express as vividly as possible certain things quite other than itself and that are of the already fixed and appointed measure. Since, however, all art is EXPRESSION, and is thereby vividness, one was to find the door open here to any amount of delightful dissimulation. These verily are the refinements and ecstasies of method—amid which, or certainly under the influence of any exhilarated demonstration of which, one must keep one's head and not lose one's way. To cultivate an adequate intelligence for them and to make that sense operative is positively to find a charm in any produced ambiguity of appearance that is not by the same stroke, and all helplessly, an ambiguity of sense. To project imaginatively, for my hero, a relation that has nothing to do with the matter (the matter of my subject) but has everything to do with the manner (the manner of my presentation of the same) and yet to treat it, at close quarters and for fully economic expression's possible sake, as if it were important and essential—to do that sort of thing and yet muddle nothing may easily become, as one goes, a signally attaching proposition; even though it all remains but part and parcel, I hasten to recognise, of the merely general and related question of expressional curiosity and expressional decency.

I am moved to add after so much insistence on the scenic side of my labour that I have found the steps of re-perusal almost as much waylaid here by quite another style of effort in the same signal interest—or have in other words not failed to note how, even so associated and so discriminated, the finest proprieties and charms of the non-scenic may, under the right hand for them, still keep their intelligibility and assert their office. Infinitely suggestive such an observation as this last on the whole delightful head, where representation is concerned, of possible variety, of effective expressional change and contrast. One would like, at such an hour as this, for critical licence, to go into the matter of the noted inevitable deviation (from too fond an original vision) that the exquisite treachery even of the straightest execution may ever be trusted to inflict even on the most mature plan—the case being that, though one's last reconsidered production always seems to bristle with that particular evidence, "The Ambassadors" would place a flood of such light at my service. I must attach to my final remark here a different import; noting in the other connexion I just glanced at that such passages as that of my hero's first encounter with Chad Newsome, absolute attestations of the non-scenic form though they be, yet lay the firmest hand too—so far at least as intention goes—on representational effect. To report at all closely and completely of what "passes" on a given occasion is inevitably to become more or less scenic; and yet in the instance I allude to, WITH the conveyance, expressional curiosity and expressional decency are sought and arrived at under quite another law. The true inwardness of this may be at bottom but that one of the suffered treacheries has consisted precisely, for Chad's whole figure and presence, of a direct presentability diminished and compromised—despoiled, that is, of its PROPORTIONAL advantage; so that, in a word, the whole economy of his author's relation to him has at important points to be redetermined. The book, however, critically viewed, is touchingly full of these disguised and repaired losses, these insidious recoveries, these intensely redemptive consistencies. The pages in which Mamie Pocock gives her appointed and, I can't but think, duly felt lift to the whole action by the so inscrutably-applied side-stroke or short-cut of our just watching and as quite at an angle of vision as yet untried, her single hour of suspense in the hotel salon, in our partaking of her concentrated study of the sense of matters bearing on her own case, all the bright warm Paris afternoon, from the balcony that overlooks the Tuileries garden—these are as marked an example of the representational virtue that insists here and there on being, for the charm of opposition and renewal, other than the scenic. It wouldn't take much to make me further argue that from an equal play of such oppositions the book gathers an intensity that fairly adds to the dramatic—though the latter is supposed to be the sum of all intensities; or that has at any rate nothing to fear from juxtaposition with it. I consciously fail to shrink in fact from that extravagance—I risk it rather, for the sake of the moral involved; which is not that the particular production before us exhausts the interesting questions it raises, but that the Novel remains still, under the right persuasion, the most independent, most elastic, most prodigious of literary forms.

HENRY JAMES.

Book First

I

Strether's first question, when he reached the hotel, was about his friend; yet on his learning that Waymarsh was apparently not to arrive till evening he was not wholly disconcerted. A telegram from him bespeaking a room "only if not noisy," reply paid, was produced for the enquirer at the office, so that the understanding they should meet at Chester rather than at Liverpool remained to that extent sound. The same secret principle, however, that had prompted Strether not absolutely to desire Waymarsh's presence at the dock, that had led him thus to postpone for a few hours his enjoyment of it, now operated to make him feel he could still wait without disappointment. They would dine together at the worst, and, with all respect to dear old Waymarsh—if not even, for that matter, to himself—there was little fear that in the sequel they shouldn't see enough of each other. The principle I have just mentioned as operating had been, with the most newly disembarked of the two men, wholly instinctive—the fruit of a sharp sense that, delightful as it would be to find himself looking, after so much separation, into his comrade's face, his business would be a trifle bungled should he simply arrange for this countenance to present itself to the nearing steamer as the first "note," of Europe. Mixed with everything was the apprehension, already, on Strether's part, that it would, at best, throughout, prove the note of Europe in quite a sufficient degree.

That note had been meanwhile—since the previous afternoon, thanks to this happier device—such a consciousness of personal freedom as he hadn't known for years; such a deep taste of change and of having above all for the moment nobody and nothing to consider, as promised already, if headlong hope were not too foolish, to colour his adventure with cool success. There were people on the ship with whom he had easily consorted—so far as ease could up to now be imputed to him—and who for the most part plunged straight into the current that set from the landing-stage to London; there were others who had invited him to a tryst at the inn and had even invoked his aid for a "look round" at the beauties of Liverpool; but he had stolen away from every one alike, had kept no appointment and renewed no acquaintance, had been indifferently aware of the number of persons who esteemed themselves fortunate in being, unlike himself, "met," and had even independently, unsociably, alone, without encounter or relapse and by mere quiet evasion, given his afternoon and evening to the immediate and the sensible. They formed a qualified draught of Europe, an afternoon and an evening on the banks of the Mersey, but such as it was he took his potion at least undiluted. He winced a little, truly, at the thought that Waymarsh might be already at Chester; he reflected that, should he have to describe himself there as having "got in" so early, it would be difficult to make the interval look particularly eager; but he was like a man who, elatedly finding in his pocket more money than usual, handles it a while and idly and pleasantly chinks it before addressing himself to the business of spending. That he was prepared to be vague to Waymarsh about the hour of the ship's touching, and that he both wanted extremely to see him and enjoyed extremely the duration of delay—these things, it is to be conceived, were early signs in him that his relation to his actual errand might prove none of the simplest. He was burdened, poor Strether—it had better be confessed at the outset—with the oddity of a double consciousness. There was detachment in his zeal and curiosity in his indifference.

After the young woman in the glass cage had held up to him across her counter the pale-pink leaflet bearing his friend's name, which she neatly pronounced, he turned away to find himself, in the hall, facing a lady who met his eyes as with an intention suddenly determined, and whose features—not freshly young, not markedly fine, but on happy terms with each other—came back to him as from a recent vision. For a moment they stood confronted; then the moment placed her: he had noticed her the day before, noticed her at his previous inn, where—again in the hall—she had been briefly engaged with some people of his own ship's company. Nothing had actually passed between them, and he would as little have been able to say what had been the sign of her face for him on the first occasion as to name the ground of his present recognition. Recognition at any rate appeared to prevail on her own side as well—which would only have added to the mystery. All she now began by saying to him nevertheless was that, having chanced to catch his enquiry, she was moved to ask, by his leave, if it were possibly a question of Mr. Waymarsh of Milrose Connecticut—Mr. Waymarsh the American lawyer.

"Oh yes," he replied, "my very well-known friend. He's to meet me here, coming up from Malvern, and I supposed he'd already have arrived. But he doesn't come till later, and I'm relieved not to have kept him. Do you know him?" Strether wound up.

It wasn't till after he had spoken that he became aware of how much there had been in him of response; when the tone of her own rejoinder, as well as the play of something more in her face—something more, that is, than its apparently usual restless light—seemed to notify him. "I've met him at Milrose—where I used sometimes, a good while ago, to stay; I had friends there who were friends of his, and I've been at his house. I won't answer for it that he would know me," Strether's new acquaintance pursued; "but I should be delighted to see him. Perhaps," she added, "I shall—for I'm staying over." She paused while our friend took in these things, and it was as if a good deal of talk had already passed. They even vaguely smiled at it, and Strether presently observed that Mr. Waymarsh would, no doubt, be easily to be seen. This, however, appeared to affect the lady as if she might have advanced too far. She appeared to have no reserves about anything. "Oh," she said, "he won't care!"—and she immediately thereupon remarked that she believed Strether knew the Munsters; the Munsters being the people he had seen her with at Liverpool.

But he didn't, it happened, know the Munsters well enough to give the case much of a lift; so that they were left together as if over the mere laid table of conversation. Her qualification of the mentioned connexion had rather removed than placed a dish, and there seemed nothing else to serve. Their attitude remained, none the less, that of not forsaking the board; and the effect of this in turn was to give them the appearance of having accepted each other with an absence of preliminaries practically complete. They moved along the hall together, and Strether's companion threw off that the hotel had the advantage of a garden. He was aware by this time of his strange inconsequence: he had shirked the intimacies of the steamer and had muffled the shock of Waymarsh only to find himself forsaken, in this sudden case, both of avoidance and of caution. He passed, under this unsought protection and before he had so much as gone up to his room, into the garden of the hotel, and at the end of ten minutes had agreed to meet there again, as soon as he should have made himself tidy, the dispenser of such good assurances. He wanted to look at the town, and they would forthwith look together. It was almost as if she had been in possession and received him as a guest. Her acquaintance with the place presented her in a manner as a hostess, and Strether had a rueful glance for the lady in the glass cage. It was as if this personage had seen herself instantly superseded.

When in a quarter of an hour he came down, what his hostess saw, what she might have taken in with a vision kindly adjusted, was the lean, the slightly loose figure of a man of the middle height and something more perhaps than the middle age—a man of five-and-fifty, whose most immediate signs were a marked bloodless brownness of face, a thick dark moustache, of characteristically American cut, growing strong and falling low, a head of hair still abundant but irregularly streaked with grey, and a nose of bold free prominence, the even line, the high finish, as it might have been called, of which, had a certain effect of mitigation. A perpetual pair of glasses astride of this fine ridge, and a line, unusually deep and drawn, the prolonged pen-stroke of time, accompanying the curve of the moustache from nostril to chin, did something to complete the facial furniture that an attentive observer would have seen catalogued, on the spot, in the vision of the other party to Strether's appointment. She waited for him in the garden, the other party, drawing on a pair of singularly fresh soft and elastic light gloves and presenting herself with a superficial readiness which, as he approached her over the small smooth lawn and in the watery English sunshine, he might, with his rougher preparation, have marked as the model for such an occasion. She had, this lady, a perfect plain propriety, an expensive subdued suitability, that her companion was not free to analyse, but that struck him, so that his consciousness of it was instantly acute, as a quality quite new to him. Before reaching her he stopped on the grass and went through the form of feeling for something, possibly forgotten, in the light overcoat he carried on his arm; yet the essence of the act was no more than the impulse to gain time. Nothing could have been odder than Strether's sense of himself as at that moment launched in something of which the sense would be quite disconnected from the sense of his past and which was literally beginning there and then. It had begun in fact already upstairs and before the dressing glass that struck him as blocking further, so strangely, the dimness of the window of his dull bedroom; begun with a sharper survey of the elements of Appearance than he had for a long time been moved to make. He had during those moments felt these elements to be not so much to his hand as he should have liked, and then had fallen back on the thought that they were precisely a matter as to which help was supposed to come from what he was about to do. He was about to go up to London, so that hat and necktie might wait. What had come as straight to him as a ball in a well-played game—and caught moreover not less neatly—was just the air, in the person of his friend, of having seen and chosen, the air of achieved possession of those vague qualities and quantities that collectively figured to him as the advantage snatched from lucky chances. Without pomp or circumstance, certainly, as her original address to him, equally with his own response, had been, he would have sketched to himself his impression of her as: "Well, she's more thoroughly civilized—!" If "More thoroughly than WHOM?" would not have been for him a sequel to this remark, that was just by reason of his deep consciousness of the bearing of his comparison.

The amusement, at all events, of a civilisation intenser was what—familiar compatriot as she was, with the full tone of the compatriot and the rattling link not with mystery but only with dear dyspeptic Waymarsh—she appeared distinctly to promise. His pause while he felt in his overcoat was positively the pause of confidence, and it enabled his eyes to make out as much of a case for her, in proportion, as her own made out for himself. She affected him as almost insolently young; but an easily carried five-and-thirty could still do that. She was, however, like himself marked and wan; only it naturally couldn't have been known to him how much a spectator looking from one to the other might have discerned that they had in common. It wouldn't for such a spectator have been altogether insupposable that, each so finely brown and so sharply spare, each confessing so to dents of surface and aids to sight, to a disproportionate nose and a head delicately or grossly grizzled, they might have been brother and sister. On this ground indeed there would have been a residuum of difference; such a sister having surely known in respect to such a brother the extremity of separation, and such a brother now feeling in respect to such a sister the extremity of surprise. Surprise, it was true, was not on the other hand what the eyes of Strether's friend most showed him while she gave him, stroking her gloves smoother, the time he appreciated. They had taken hold of him straightway measuring him up and down as if they knew how; as if he were human material they had already in some sort handled. Their possessor was in truth, it may be communicated, the mistress of a hundred cases or categories, receptacles of the mind, subdivisions for convenience, in which, from a full experience, she pigeon-holed her fellow mortals with a hand as free as that of a compositor scattering type. She was as equipped in this particular as Strether was the reverse, and it made an opposition between them which he might well have shrunk from submitting to if he had fully suspected it. So far as he did suspect it he was on the contrary, after a short shake of his consciousness, as pleasantly passive as might be. He really had a sort of sense of what she knew. He had quite the sense that she knew things he didn't, and though this was a concession that in general he found not easy to make to women, he made it now as good-humouredly as if it lifted a burden. His eyes were so quiet behind his eternal nippers that they might almost have been absent without changing his face, which took its expression mainly, and not least its stamp of sensibility, from other sources, surface and grain and form. He joined his guide in an instant, and then felt she had profited still better than he by his having been for the moments just mentioned, so at the disposal of her intelligence. She knew even intimate things about him that he hadn't yet told her and perhaps never would. He wasn't unaware that he had told her rather remarkably many for the time, but these were not the real ones. Some of the real ones, however, precisely, were what she knew.

They were to pass again through the hall of the inn to get into the street, and it was here she presently checked him with a question. "Have you looked up my name?"

He could only stop with a laugh. "Have you looked up mine?"

"Oh dear, yes—as soon as you left me. I went to the office and asked. Hadn't YOU better do the same?"

He wondered. "Find out who you are?—after the uplifted young woman there has seen us thus scrape acquaintance!"

She laughed on her side now at the shade of alarm in his amusement. "Isn't it a reason the more? If what you're afraid of is the injury for me—my being seen to walk off with a gentleman who has to ask who I am—I assure you I don't in the least mind. Here, however," she continued, "is my card, and as I find there's something else again I have to say at the office, you can just study it during the moment I leave you."

She left him after he had taken from her the small pasteboard she had extracted from her pocket-book, and he had extracted another from his own, to exchange with it, before she came back. He read thus the simple designation "Maria Gostrey," to which was attached, in a corner of the card, with a number, the name of a street, presumably in Paris, without other appreciable identity than its foreignness. He put the card into his waistcoat pocket, keeping his own meanwhile in evidence; and as he leaned against the door-post he met with the smile of a straying thought what the expanse before the hotel offered to his view. It was positively droll to him that he should already have Maria Gostrey, whoever she was—of which he hadn't really the least idea—in a place of safe keeping. He had somehow an assurance that he should carefully preserve the little token he had just tucked in. He gazed with unseeing lingering eyes as he followed some of the implications of his act, asking himself if he really felt admonished to qualify it as disloyal. It was prompt, it was possibly even premature, and there was little doubt of the expression of face the sight of it would have produced in a certain person. But if it was "wrong"—why then he had better not have come out at all. At this, poor man, had he already—and even before meeting Waymarsh—arrived. He had believed he had a limit, but the limit had been transcended within thirty-six hours. By how long a space on the plane of manners or even of morals, moreover, he felt still more sharply after Maria Gostrey had come back to him and with a gay decisive "So now—!" led him forth into the world. This counted, it struck him as he walked beside her with his overcoat on an arm, his umbrella under another and his personal pasteboard a little stiffly retained between forefinger and thumb, this struck him as really, in comparison his introduction to things. It hadn't been "Europe" at Liverpool no—not even in the dreadful delightful impressive streets the night before—to the extent his present companion made it so. She hadn't yet done that so much as when, after their walk had lasted a few minutes and he had had time to wonder if a couple of sidelong glances from her meant that he had best have put on gloves she almost pulled him up with an amused challenge. "But why—fondly as it's so easy to imagine your clinging to it—don't you put it away? Or if it's an inconvenience to you to carry it, one's often glad to have one's card back. The fortune one spends in them!"

Then he saw both that his way of marching with his own prepared tribute had affected her as a deviation in one of those directions he couldn't yet measure, and that she supposed this emblem to be still the one he had received from her. He accordingly handed her the card as if in restitution, but as soon as she had it she felt the difference and, with her eyes on it, stopped short for apology. "I like," she observed, "your name."

"Oh," he answered, "you won't have heard of it!" Yet he had his reasons for not being sure but that she perhaps might.

Ah it was but too visible! She read it over again as one who had never seen it. "'Mr. Lewis Lambert Strether'"—she sounded it almost as freely as for any stranger. She repeated however that she liked it—"particularly the Lewis Lambert. It's the name of a novel of Balzac's."

"Oh I know that!" said Strether.

"But the novel's an awfully bad one."

"I know that too," Strether smiled. To which he added with an irrelevance that was only superficial: "I come from Woollett Massachusetts." It made her for some reason—the irrelevance or whatever—laugh. Balzac had described many cities, but hadn't described Woollett Massachusetts. "You say that," she returned, "as if you wanted one immediately to know the worst."

"Oh I think it's a thing," he said, "that you must already have made out. I feel it so that I certainly must look it, speak it, and, as people say there, 'act' it. It sticks out of me, and you knew surely for yourself as soon as you looked at me."

"The worst, you mean?"

"Well, the fact of where I come from. There at any rate it IS; so that you won't be able, if anything happens, to say I've not been straight with you."

"I see"—and Miss Gostrey looked really interested in the point he had made. "But what do you think of as happening?"

Though he wasn't shy—which was rather anomalous—Strether gazed about without meeting her eyes; a motion that was frequent with him in talk, yet of which his words often seemed not at all the effect. "Why that you should find me too hopeless." With which they walked on again together while she answered, as they went, that the most "hopeless" of her countryfolk were in general precisely those she liked best. All sorts of other pleasant small things-small things that were yet large for him—flowered in the air of the occasion, but the bearing of the occasion itself on matters still remote concerns us too closely to permit us to multiply our illustrations. Two or three, however, in truth, we should perhaps regret to lose. The tortuous wall—girdle, long since snapped, of the little swollen city, half held in place by careful civic hands—wanders in narrow file between parapets smoothed by peaceful generations, pausing here and there for a dismantled gate or a bridged gap, with rises and drops, steps up and steps down, queer twists, queer contacts, peeps into homely streets and under the brows of gables, views of cathedral tower and waterside fields, of huddled English town and ordered English country. Too deep almost for words was the delight of these things to Strether; yet as deeply mixed with it were certain images of his inward picture. He had trod this walks in the far-off time, at twenty-five; but that, instead of spoiling it, only enriched it for present feeling and marked his renewal as a thing substantial enough to share. It was with Waymarsh he should have shared it, and he was now accordingly taking from him something that was his due. He looked repeatedly at his watch, and when he had done so for the fifth time Miss Gostrey took him up.

"You're doing something that you think not right."

It so touched the place that he quite changed colour and his laugh grew almost awkward. "Am I enjoying it as much as THAT?"

"You're not enjoying it, I think, so much as you ought."

"I see"—he appeared thoughtfully to agree. "Great is my privilege."

"Oh it's not your privilege! It has nothing to do with me. It has to do with yourself. Your failure's general."

"Ah there you are!" he laughed. "It's the failure of Woollett. THAT'S general."

"The failure to enjoy," Miss Gostrey explained, "is what I mean."

"Precisely. Woollett isn't sure it ought to enjoy. If it were it would. But it hasn't, poor thing," Strether continued, "any one to show it how. It's not like me. I have somebody."

They had stopped, in the afternoon sunshine—constantly pausing, in their stroll, for the sharper sense of what they saw—and Strether rested on one of the high sides of the old stony groove of the little rampart. He leaned back on this support with his face to the tower of the cathedral, now admirably commanded by their station, the high red-brown mass, square and subordinately spired and crocketed, retouched and restored, but charming to his long-sealed eyes and with the first swallows of the year weaving their flight all round it. Miss Gostrey lingered near him, full of an air, to which she more and more justified her right, of understanding the effect of things. She quite concurred. "You've indeed somebody." And she added: "I wish you WOULD let me show you how!"

"Oh I'm afraid of you!" he cheerfully pleaded.

She kept on him a moment, through her glasses and through his own, a certain pleasant pointedness. "Ah no, you're not! You're not in the least, thank goodness! If you had been we shouldn't so soon have found ourselves here together. I think," she comfortably concluded, "you trust me."

"I think I do!—but that's exactly what I'm afraid of. I shouldn't mind if I didn't. It's falling thus in twenty minutes so utterly into your hands. I dare say," Strether continued, "it's a sort of thing you're thoroughly familiar with; but nothing more extraordinary has ever happened to me."

She watched him with all her kindness. "That means simply that you've recognised me—which IS rather beautiful and rare. You see what I am." As on this, however, he protested, with a good-humoured headshake, a resignation of any such claim, she had a moment of explanation. "If you'll only come on further as you HAVE come you'll at any rate make out. My own fate has been too many for me, and I've succumbed to it. I'm a general guide—to 'Europe,' don't you know? I wait for people—I put them through. I pick them up—I set them down. I'm a sort of superior 'courier-maid.' I'm a companion at large. I take people, as I've told you, about. I never sought it—it has come to me. It has been my fate, and one's fate one accepts. It's a dreadful thing to have to say, in so wicked a world, but I verily believe that, such as you see me, there's nothing I don't know. I know all the shops and the prices—but I know worse things still. I bear on my back the huge load of our national consciousness, or, in other words—for it comes to that—of our nation itself. Of what is our nation composed but of the men and women individually on my shoulders? I don't do it, you know, for any particular advantage. I don't do it, for instance—some people do, you know—for money."

Strether could only listen and wonder and weigh his chance. "And yet, affected as you are then to so many of your clients, you can scarcely be said to do it for love." He waited a moment. "How do we reward you?"

She had her own hesitation, but "You don't!" she finally returned, setting him again in motion. They went on, but in a few minutes, though while still thinking over what she had said, he once more took out his watch; mechanically, unconsciously and as if made nervous by the mere exhilaration of what struck him as her strange and cynical wit. He looked at the hour without seeing it, and then, on something again said by his companion, had another pause. "You're really in terror of him."

He smiled a smile that he almost felt to be sickly. "Now you can see why I'm afraid of you."

"Because I've such illuminations? Why they're all for your help! It's what I told you," she added, "just now. You feel as if this were wrong."

He fell back once more, settling himself against the parapet as if to hear more about it. "Then get me out!"

Her face fairly brightened for the joy of the appeal, but, as if it were a question of immediate action, she visibly considered. "Out of waiting for him?—of seeing him at all?"

"Oh no—not that," said poor Strether, looking grave. "I've got to wait for him—and I want very much to see him. But out of the terror. You did put your finger on it a few minutes ago. It's general, but it avails itself of particular occasions. That's what it's doing for me now. I'm always considering something else; something else, I mean, than the thing of the moment. The obsession of the other thing is the terror. I'm considering at present for instance something else than YOU."

She listened with charming earnestness. "Oh you oughtn't to do that!"

"It's what I admit. Make it then impossible."

She continued to think. "Is it really an 'order' from you?—that I shall take the job? WILL you give yourself up?"

Poor Strether heaved his sigh. "If I only could! But that's the deuce of it—that I never can. No—I can't."

She wasn't, however, discouraged. "But you want to at least?"

"Oh unspeakably!"

"Ah then, if you'll try!"—and she took over the job, as she had called it, on the spot. "Trust me!" she exclaimed, and the action of this, as they retraced their steps, was presently to make him pass his hand into her arm in the manner of a benign dependent paternal old person who wishes to be "nice" to a younger one. If he drew it out again indeed as they approached the inn this may have been because, after more talk had passed between them, the relation of age, or at least of experience—which, for that matter, had already played to and fro with some freedom—affected him as incurring a readjustment. It was at all events perhaps lucky that they arrived in sufficiently separate fashion within range of the hotel-door. The young lady they had left in the glass cage watched as if she had come to await them on the threshold. At her side stood a person equally interested, by his attitude, in their return, and the effect of the sight of whom was instantly to determine for Strether another of those responsive arrests that we have had so repeatedly to note. He left it to Miss Gostrey to name, with the fine full bravado as it almost struck him, of her "Mr. Waymarsh!" what was to have been, what—he more than ever felt as his short stare of suspended welcome took things in—would have been, but for herself, his doom. It was already upon him even at that distance—Mr. Waymarsh was for HIS part joyless.

II

He had none the less to confess to this friend that evening that he knew almost nothing about her, and it was a deficiency that Waymarsh, even with his memory refreshed by contact, by her own prompt and lucid allusions and enquiries, by their having publicly partaken of dinner in her company, and by another stroll, to which she was not a stranger, out into the town to look at the cathedral by moonlight—it was a blank that the resident of Milrose, though admitting acquaintance with the Munsters, professed himself unable to fill. He had no recollection of Miss Gostrey, and two or three questions that she put to him about those members of his circle had, to Strether's observation, the same effect he himself had already more directly felt—the effect of appearing to place all knowledge, for the time, on this original woman's side. It interested him indeed to mark the limits of any such relation for her with his friend as there could possibly be a question of, and it particularly struck him that they were to be marked altogether in Waymarsh's quarter. This added to his own sense of having gone far with her-gave him an early illustration of a much shorter course. There was a certitude he immediately grasped—a conviction that Waymarsh would quite fail, as it were, and on whatever degree of acquaintances to profit by her.

There had been after the first interchange among the three a talk of some five minutes in the hall, and then the two men had adjourned to the garden, Miss Gostrey for the time disappearing. Strether in due course accompanied his friend to the room he had bespoken and had, before going out, scrupulously visited; where at the end of another half-hour he had no less discreetly left him. On leaving him he repaired straight to his own room, but with the prompt effect of feeling the compass of that chamber resented by his condition. There he enjoyed at once the first consequence of their reunion. A place was too small for him after it that had seemed large enough before. He had awaited it with something he would have been sorry, have been almost ashamed not to recognise as emotion, yet with a tacit assumption at the same time that emotion would in the event find itself relieved. The actual oddity was that he was only more excited; and his excitement-to which indeed he would have found it difficult instantly to give a name—brought him once more downstairs and caused him for some minutes vaguely to wander. He went once more to the garden; he looked into the public room, found Miss Gostrey writing letters and backed out; he roamed, fidgeted and wasted time; but he was to have his more intimate session with his friend before the evening closed.

It was late—not till Strether had spent an hour upstairs with him—that this subject consented to betake himself to doubtful rest. Dinner and the subsequent stroll by moonlight—a dream, on Strether's part, of romantic effects rather prosaically merged in a mere missing of thicker coats—had measurably intervened, and this midnight conference was the result of Waymarsh's having (when they were free, as he put it, of their fashionable friend) found the smoking-room not quite what he wanted, and yet bed what he wanted less. His most frequent form of words was that he knew himself, and they were applied on this occasion to his certainty of not sleeping. He knew himself well enough to know that he should have a night of prowling unless he should succeed, as a preliminary, in getting prodigiously tired. If the effort directed to this end involved till a late hour the presence of Strether—consisted, that is, in the detention of the latter for full discourse—there was yet an impression of minor discipline involved for our friend in the picture Waymarsh made as he sat in trousers and shirt on the edge of his couch. With his long legs extended and his large back much bent, he nursed alternately, for an almost incredible time, his elbows and his beard. He struck his visitor as extremely, as almost wilfully uncomfortable; yet what had this been for Strether, from that first glimpse of him disconcerted in the porch of the hotel, but the predominant notes. The discomfort was in a manner contagious, as well as also in a manner inconsequent and unfounded; the visitor felt that unless he should get used to it—or unless Waymarsh himself should—it would constitute a menace for his own prepared, his own already confirmed, consciousness of the agreeable. On their first going up together to the room Strether had selected for him Waymarsh had looked it over in silence and with a sigh that represented for his companion, if not the habit of disapprobation, at least the despair of felicity; and this look had recurred to Strether as the key of much he had since observed. "Europe," he had begun to gather from these things, had up to now rather failed of its message to him; he hadn't got into tune with it and had at the end of three months almost renounced any such expectation.

He really appeared at present to insist on that by just perching there with the gas in his eyes. This of itself somehow conveyed the futility of single rectifications in a multiform failure. He had a large handsome head and a large sallow seamed face—a striking significant physiognomic total, the upper range of which, the great political brow, the thick loose hair, the dark fuliginous eyes, recalled even to a generation whose standard had dreadfully deviated the impressive image, familiar by engravings and busts, of some great national worthy of the earlier part of the mid-century. He was of the personal type—and it was an element in the power and promise that in their early time Strether had found in him—of the American statesman, the statesman trained in "Congressional halls," of an elder day. The legend had been in later years that as the lower part of his face, which was weak, and slightly crooked, spoiled the likeness, this was the real reason for the growth of his beard, which might have seemed to spoil it for those not in the secret. He shook his mane; he fixed, with his admirable eyes, his auditor or his observer; he wore no glasses and had a way, partly formidable, yet also partly encouraging, as from a representative to a constituent, of looking very hard at those who approached him. He met you as if you had knocked and he had bidden you enter. Strether, who hadn't seen him for so long an interval, apprehended him now with a freshness of taste, and had perhaps never done him such ideal justice. The head was bigger, the eyes finer, than they need have been for the career; but that only meant, after all, that the career was itself expressive. What it expressed at midnight in the gas-glaring bedroom at Chester was that the subject of it had, at the end of years, barely escaped, by flight in time, a general nervous collapse. But this very proof of the full life, as the full life was understood at Milrose, would have made to Strether's imagination an element in which Waymarsh could have floated easily had he only consented to float. Alas nothing so little resembled floating as the rigour with which, on the edge of his bed, he hugged his posture of prolonged impermanence. It suggested to his comrade something that always, when kept up, worried him—a person established in a railway-coach with a forward inclination. It represented the angle at which poor Waymarsh was to sit through the ordeal of Europe.

Thanks to the stress of occupation, the strain of professions, the absorption and embarrassment of each, they had not, at home, during years before this sudden brief and almost bewildering reign of comparative ease, found so much as a day for a meeting; a fact that was in some degree an explanation of the sharpness with which most of his friend's features stood out to Strether. Those he had lost sight of since the early time came back to him; others that it was never possible to forget struck him now as sitting, clustered and expectant, like a somewhat defiant family-group, on the doorstep of their residence. The room was narrow for its length, and the occupant of the bed thrust so far a pair of slippered feet that the visitor had almost to step over them in his recurrent rebounds from his chair to fidget back and forth. There were marks the friends made on things to talk about, and on things not to, and one of the latter in particular fell like the tap of chalk on the blackboard. Married at thirty, Waymarsh had not lived with his wife for fifteen years, and it came up vividly between them in the glare of the gas that Strether wasn't to ask about her. He knew they were still separate and that she lived at hotels, travelled in Europe, painted her face and wrote her husband abusive letters, of not one of which, to a certainty, that sufferer spared himself the perusal; but he respected without difficulty the cold twilight that had settled on this side of his companion's life. It was a province in which mystery reigned and as to which Waymarsh had never spoken the informing word. Strether, who wanted to do him the highest justice wherever he COULD do it, singularly admired him for the dignity of this reserve, and even counted it as one of the grounds—grounds all handled and numbered—for ranking him, in the range of their acquaintance, as a success. He WAS a success, Waymarsh, in spite of overwork, or prostration, of sensible shrinkage, of his wife's letters and of his not liking Europe. Strether would have reckoned his own career less futile had he been able to put into it anything so handsome as so much fine silence. One might one's self easily have left Mrs. Waymarsh; and one would assuredly have paid one's tribute to the ideal in covering with that attitude the derision of having been left by her. Her husband had held his tongue and had made a large income; and these were in especial the achievements as to which Strether envied him. Our friend had had indeed on his side too a subject for silence, which he fully appreciated; but it was a matter of a different sort, and the figure of the income he had arrived at had never been high enough to look any one in the face.

"I don't know as I quite see what you require it for. You don't appear sick to speak of." It was of Europe Waymarsh thus finally spoke.

"Well," said Strether, who fell as much as possible into step, "I guess I don't FEEL sick now that I've started. But I had pretty well run down before I did start."

Waymarsh raised his melancholy look. "Ain't you about up to your usual average?"

It was not quite pointedly sceptical, but it seemed somehow a plea for the purest veracity, and it thereby affected our friend as the very voice of Milrose. He had long since made a mental distinction—though never in truth daring to betray it—between the voice of Milrose and the voice even of Woollett. It was the former he felt, that was most in the real tradition. There had been occasions in his past when the sound of it had reduced him to temporary confusion, and the present, for some reason, suddenly became such another. It was nevertheless no light matter that the very effect of his confusion should be to make him again prevaricate. "That description hardly does justice to a man to whom it has done such a lot of good to see YOU."

Waymarsh fixed on his washing-stand the silent detached stare with which Milrose in person, as it were, might have marked the unexpectedness of a compliment from Woollett, and Strether for his part, felt once more like Woollett in person. "I mean," his friend presently continued, "that your appearance isn't as bad as I've seen it: it compares favourably with what it was when I last noticed it." On this appearance Waymarsh's eyes yet failed to rest; it was almost as if they obeyed an instinct of propriety, and the effect was still stronger when, always considering the basin and jug, he added: "You've filled out some since then."

"I'm afraid I have," Strether laughed: "one does fill out some with all one takes in, and I've taken in, I dare say, more than I've natural room for. I was dog-tired when I sailed." It had the oddest sound of cheerfulness.

"I was dog-tired," his companion returned, "when I arrived, and it's this wild hunt for rest that takes all the life out of me. The fact is, Strether—and it's a comfort to have you here at last to say it to; though I don't know, after all, that I've really waited; I've told it to people I've met in the cars—the fact is, such a country as this ain't my KIND of country anyway. There ain't a country I've seen over here that DOES seem my kind. Oh I don't say but what there are plenty of pretty places and remarkable old things; but the trouble is that I don't seem to feel anywhere in tune. That's one of the reasons why I suppose I've gained so little. I haven't had the first sign of that lift I was led to expect." With this he broke out more earnestly. "Look here—I want to go back."

His eyes were all attached to Strether's now, for he was one of the men who fully face you when they talk of themselves. This enabled his friend to look at him hard and immediately to appear to the highest advantage in his eyes by doing so. "That's a genial thing to say to a fellow who has come out on purpose to meet you!"

Nothing could have been finer, on this, than Waymarsh's sombre glow. "HAVE you come out on purpose?"

"Well—very largely."

"I thought from the way you wrote there was something back of it."

Strether hesitated. "Back of my desire to be with you?"

"Back of your prostration."

Strether, with a smile made more dim by a certain consciousness, shook his head. "There are all the causes of it!"

"And no particular cause that seemed most to drive you?"

Our friend could at last conscientiously answer. "Yes. One. There IS a matter that has had much to do with my coming out."

Waymarsh waited a little. "Too private to mention?"

"No, not too private—for YOU. Only rather complicated."

"Well," said Waymarsh, who had waited again, "I MAY lose my mind over here, but I don't know as I've done so yet."

"Oh you shall have the whole thing. But not tonight."

Waymarsh seemed to sit stiffer and to hold his elbows tighter. "Why not—if I can't sleep?"

"Because, my dear man, I CAN!"

"Then where's your prostration?"

"Just in that—that I can put in eight hours." And Strether brought it out that if Waymarsh didn't "gain" it was because he didn't go to bed: the result of which was, in its order, that, to do the latter justice, he permitted his friend to insist on his really getting settled. Strether, with a kind coercive hand for it, assisted him to this consummation, and again found his own part in their relation auspiciously enlarged by the smaller touches of lowering the lamp and seeing to a sufficiency of blanket. It somehow ministered for him to indulgence to feel Waymarsh, who looked unnaturally big and black in bed, as much tucked in as a patient in a hospital and, with his covering up to his chin, as much simplified by it He hovered in vague pity, to be brief, while his companion challenged him out of the bedclothes. "Is she really after you? Is that what's behind?"

Strether felt an uneasiness at the direction taken by his companion's insight, but he played a little at uncertainty. "Behind my coming out?"

"Behind your prostration or whatever. It's generally felt, you know, that she follows you up pretty close."

Strether's candour was never very far off. "Oh it has occurred to you that I'm literally running away from Mrs. Newsome?"

"Well, I haven't KNOWN but what you are. You're a very attractive man, Strether. You've seen for yourself," said Waymarsh "what that lady downstairs makes of it. Unless indeed," he rambled on with an effect between the ironic and the anxious, "it's you who are after HER. IS Mrs. Newsome OVER here?" He spoke as with a droll dread of her.

It made his friend—though rather dimly—smile. "Dear no she's safe, thank goodness—as I think I more and more feel—at home. She thought of coming, but she gave it up. I've come in a manner instead of her; and come to that extent—for you're right in your inference—on her business. So you see there IS plenty of connexion."

Waymarsh continued to see at least all there was. "Involving accordingly the particular one I've referred to?"

Strether took another turn about the room, giving a twitch to his companion's blanket and finally gaining the door. His feeling was that of a nurse who had earned personal rest by having made everything straight. "Involving more things than I can think of breaking ground on now. But don't be afraid—you shall have them from me: you'll probably find yourself having quite as much of them as you can do with. I shall—if we keep together—very much depend on your impression of some of them."

Waymarsh's acknowledgement of this tribute was characteristically indirect. "You mean to say you don't believe we WILL keep together?"

"I only glance at the danger," Strether paternally said, "because when I hear you wail to go back I seem to see you open up such possibilities of folly."

Waymarsh took it—silent a little—like a large snubbed child "What are you going to do with me?"

It was the very question Strether himself had put to Miss Gostrey, and he wondered if he had sounded like that. But HE at least could be more definite. "I'm going to take you right down to London."

"Oh I've been down to London!" Waymarsh more softly moaned. "I've no use, Strether, for anything down there."

"Well," said Strether, good-humouredly, "I guess you've some use for me."

"So I've got to go?"

"Oh you've got to go further yet."

"Well," Waymarsh sighed, "do your damnedest! Only you WILL tell me before you lead me on all the way—?"

Our friend had again so lost himself, both for amusement and for contrition, in the wonder of whether he had made, in his own challenge that afternoon, such another figure, that he for an instant missed the thread. "Tell you—?"

"Why what you've got on hand."

Strether hesitated. "Why it's such a matter as that even if I positively wanted I shouldn't be able to keep it from you."

Waymarsh gloomily gazed. "What does that mean then but that your trip is just FOR her?"

"For Mrs. Newsome? Oh it certainly is, as I say. Very much."

"Then why do you also say it's for me?"

Strether, in impatience, violently played with his latch. "It's simple enough. It's for both of you."

Waymarsh at last turned over with a groan. "Well, I won't marry you!"

"Neither, when it comes to that—!" But the visitor had already laughed and escaped.

III

He had told Miss Gostrey he should probably take, for departure with Waymarsh, some afternoon train, and it thereupon in the morning appeared that this lady had made her own plan for an earlier one. She had breakfasted when Strether came into the coffee-room; but, Waymarsh not having yet emerged, he was in time to recall her to the terms of their understanding and to pronounce her discretion overdone. She was surely not to break away at the very moment she had created a want. He had met her as she rose from her little table in a window, where, with the morning papers beside her, she reminded him, as he let her know, of Major Pendennis breakfasting at his club—a compliment of which she professed a deep appreciation; and he detained her as pleadingly as if he had already—and notably under pressure of the visions of the night—learned to be unable to do without her. She must teach him at all events, before she went, to order breakfast as breakfast was ordered in Europe, and she must especially sustain him in the problem of ordering for Waymarsh. The latter had laid upon his friend, by desperate sounds through the door of his room, dreadful divined responsibilities in respect to beefsteak and oranges—responsibilities which Miss Gostrey took over with an alertness of action that matched her quick intelligence. She had before this weaned the expatriated from traditions compared with which the matutinal beefsteak was but the creature of an hour, and it was not for her, with some of her memories, to falter in the path though she freely enough declared, on reflexion, that there was always in such cases a choice of opposed policies. "There are times when to give them their head, you know—!"

They had gone to wait together in the garden for the dressing of the meal, and Strether found her more suggestive than ever "Well, what?"

"Is to bring about for them such a complexity of relations-unless indeed we call it a simplicity!—that the situation HAS to wind itself up. They want to go back."

"And you want them to go!" Strether gaily concluded.

"I always want them to go, and I send them as fast as I can.'

"Oh I know—you take them to Liverpool."

"Any port will serve in a storm. I'm—with all my other functions—an agent for repatriation. I want to repeople our stricken country. What will become of it else? I want to discourage others."

The ordered English garden, in the freshness of the day, was delightful to Strether, who liked the sound, under his feet, of the tight fine gravel, packed with the chronic damp, and who had the idlest eye for the deep smoothness of turf and the clean curves of paths. "Other people?"

"Other countries. Other people—yes. I want to encourage our own."

Strether wondered. "Not to come? Why then do you 'meet' them—since it doesn't appear to be to stop them?"

"Oh that they shouldn't come is as yet too much to ask. What I attend to is that they come quickly and return still more so. I meet them to help it to be over as soon as possible, and though I don't stop them I've my way of putting them through. That's my little system; and, if you want to know," said Maria Gostrey, "it's my real secret, my innermost mission and use. I only seem, you see, to beguile and approve; but I've thought it all out and I'm working all the while underground. I can't perhaps quite give you my formula, but I think that practically I succeed. I send you back spent. So you stay back. Passed through my hands—"

"We don't turn up again?" The further she went the further he always saw himself able to follow. "I don't want your formula—I feel quite enough, as I hinted yesterday, your abysses. Spent!" he echoed. "If that's how you're arranging so subtly to send me I thank you for the warning."

For a minute, amid the pleasantness—poetry in tariffed items, but all the more, for guests already convicted, a challenge to consumption—they smiled at each other in confirmed fellowship. "Do you call it subtly? It's a plain poor tale. Besides, you're a special case."

"Oh special cases—that's weak!" She was weak enough, further still, to defer her journey and agree to accompany the gentlemen on their own, might a separate carriage mark her independence; though it was in spite of this to befall after luncheon that she went off alone and that, with a tryst taken for a day of her company in London, they lingered another night. She had, during the morning—spent in a way that he was to remember later on as the very climax of his foretaste, as warm with presentiments, with what he would have called collapses—had all sorts of things out with Strether; and among them the fact that though there was never a moment of her life when she wasn't "due" somewhere, there was yet scarce a perfidy to others of which she wasn't capable for his sake. She explained moreover that wherever she happened to be she found a dropped thread to pick up, a ragged edge to repair, some familiar appetite in ambush, jumping out as she approached, yet appeasable with a temporary biscuit. It became, on her taking the risk of the deviation imposed on him by her insidious arrangement of his morning meal, a point of honour for her not to fail with Waymarsh of the larger success too; and her subsequent boast to Strether was that she had made their friend fare—and quite without his knowing what was the matter—as Major Pendennis would have fared at the Megatherium. She had made him breakfast like a gentleman, and it was nothing, she forcibly asserted, to what she would yet make him do. She made him participate in the slow reiterated ramble with which, for Strether, the new day amply filled itself; and it was by her art that he somehow had the air, on the ramparts and in the Rows, of carrying a point of his own.

The three strolled and stared and gossiped, or at least the two did; the case really yielding for their comrade, if analysed, but the element of stricken silence. This element indeed affected Strether as charged with audible rumblings, but he was conscious of the care of taking it explicitly as a sign of pleasant peace. He wouldn't appeal too much, for that provoked stiffness; yet he wouldn't be too freely tacit, for that suggested giving up. Waymarsh himself adhered to an ambiguous dumbness that might have represented either the growth of a perception or the despair of one; and at times and in places—where the low-browed galleries were darkest, the opposite gables queerest, the solicitations of every kind densest—the others caught him fixing hard some object of minor interest, fixing even at moments nothing discernible, as if he were indulging it with a truce. When he met Strether's eye on such occasions he looked guilty and furtive, fell the next minute into some attitude of retractation. Our friend couldn't show him the right things for fear of provoking some total renouncement, and was tempted even to show him the wrong in order to make him differ with triumph. There were moments when he himself felt shy of professing the full sweetness of the taste of leisure, and there were others when he found himself feeling as if his passages of interchange with the lady at his side might fall upon the third member of their party very much as Mr. Burchell, at Dr. Primrose's fireside, was influenced by the high flights of the visitors from London. The smallest things so arrested and amused him that he repeatedly almost apologised—brought up afresh in explanation his plea of a previous grind. He was aware at the same time that his grind had been as nothing to Waymarsh's, and he repeatedly confessed that, to cover his frivolity, he was doing his best for his previous virtue. Do what he might, in any case, his previous virtue was still there, and it seemed fairly to stare at him out of the windows of shops that were not as the shops of Woollett, fairly to make him want things that he shouldn't know what to do with. It was by the oddest, the least admissible of laws demoralising him now; and the way it boldly took was to make him want more wants. These first walks in Europe were in fact a kind of finely lurid intimation of what one might find at the end of that process. Had he come back after long years, in something already so like the evening of life, only to be exposed to it? It was at all events over the shop-windows that he made, with Waymarsh, most free; though it would have been easier had not the latter most sensibly yielded to the appeal of the merely useful trades. He pierced with his sombre detachment the plate-glass of ironmongers and saddlers, while Strether flaunted an affinity with the dealers in stamped letter-paper and in smart neckties. Strether was in fact recurrently shameless in the presence of the tailors, though it was just over the heads of the tailors that his countryman most loftily looked. This gave Miss Gostrey a grasped opportunity to back up Waymarsh at his expense. The weary lawyer—it was unmistakeable—had a conception of dress; but that, in view of some of the features of the effect produced, was just what made the danger of insistence on it. Strether wondered if he by this time thought Miss Gostrey less fashionable or Lambert Strether more so; and it appeared probable that most of the remarks exchanged between this latter pair about passers, figures, faces, personal types, exemplified in their degree the disposition to talk as "society" talked.

Was what was happening to himself then, was what already HAD happened, really that a woman of fashion was floating him into society and that an old friend deserted on the brink was watching the force of the current? When the woman of fashion permitted Strether—as she permitted him at the most—the purchase of a pair of gloves, the terms she made about it, the prohibition of neckties and other items till she should be able to guide him through the Burlington Arcade, were such as to fall upon a sensitive ear as a challenge to just imputations. Miss Gostrey was such a woman of fashion as could make without a symptom of vulgar blinking an appointment for the Burlington Arcade. Mere discriminations about a pair of gloves could thus at any rate represent—always for such sensitive ears as were in question—possibilities of something that Strether could make a mark against only as the peril of apparent wantonness. He had quite the consciousness of his new friend, for their companion, that he might have had of a Jesuit in petticoats, a representative of the recruiting interests of the Catholic Church. The Catholic Church, for Waymarsh-that was to say the enemy, the monster of bulging eyes and far-reaching quivering groping tentacles—was exactly society, exactly the multiplication of shibboleths, exactly the discrimination of types and tones, exactly the wicked old Rows of Chester, rank with feudalism; exactly in short Europe.

There was light for observation, however, in an incident that occurred just before they turned back to luncheon. Waymarsh had been for a quarter of an hour exceptionally mute and distant, and something, or other—Strether was never to make out exactly what—proved, as it were, too much for him after his comrades had stood for three minutes taking in, while they leaned on an old balustrade that guarded the edge of the Row, a particularly crooked and huddled street-view. "He thinks us sophisticated, he thinks us worldly, he thinks us wicked, he thinks us all sorts of queer things," Strether reflected; for wondrous were the vague quantities our friend had within a couple of short days acquired the habit of conveniently and conclusively lumping together. There seemed moreover a direct connexion between some such inference and a sudden grim dash taken by Waymarsh to the opposite side. This movement was startlingly sudden, and his companions at first supposed him to have espied, to be pursuing, the glimpse of an acquaintance. They next made out, however, that an open door had instantly received him, and they then recognised him as engulfed in the establishment of a jeweller, behind whose glittering front he was lost to view. The fact had somehow the note of a demonstration, and it left each of the others to show a face almost of fear. But Miss Gostrey broke into a laugh. "What's the matter with him?"

"Well," said Strether, "he can't stand it."

"But can't stand what?"

"Anything. Europe."

"Then how will that jeweller help him?"

Strether seemed to make it out, from their position, between the interstices of arrayed watches, of close-hung dangling gewgaws. "You'll see."

"Ah that's just what—if he buys anything—I'm afraid of: that I shall see something rather dreadful."

Strether studied the finer appearances. "He may buy everything."

"Then don't you think we ought to follow him?"

"Not for worlds. Besides we can't. We're paralysed. We exchange a long scared look, we publicly tremble. The thing is, you see, we 'realise.' He has struck for freedom."

She wondered but she laughed. "Ah what a price to pay! And I was preparing some for him so cheap."

"No, no," Strether went on, frankly amused now; "don't call it that: the kind of freedom you deal in is dear." Then as to justify himself: "Am I not in MY way trying it? It's this."

"Being here, you mean, with me?"

"Yes, and talking to you as I do. I've known you a few hours, and I've known HIM all my life; so that if the ease I thus take with you about him isn't magnificent"—and the thought of it held him a moment—"why it's rather base."

"It's magnificent!" said Miss Gostrey to make an end of it. "And you should hear," she added, "the ease I take—and I above all intend to take—with Mr. Waymarsh."

Strether thought. "About ME? Ah that's no equivalent. The equivalent would be Waymarsh's himself serving me up—his remorseless analysis of me. And he'll never do that"—he was sadly clear. "He'll never remorselessly analyse me." He quite held her with the authority of this. "He'll never say a word to you about me."

She took it in; she did it justice; yet after an instant her reason, her restless irony, disposed of it. "Of course he won't. For what do you take people, that they're able to say words about anything, able remorselessly to analyse? There are not many like you and me. It will be only because he's too stupid."

It stirred in her friend a sceptical echo which was at the same time the protest of the faith of years. "Waymarsh stupid?"

"Compared with you."

Strether had still his eyes on the jeweller's front, and he waited a moment to answer. "He's a success of a kind that I haven't approached."

"Do you mean he has made money?"

"He makes it—to my belief. And I," said Strether, "though with a back quite as bent, have never made anything. I'm a perfectly equipped failure."

He feared an instant she'd ask him if he meant he was poor; and he was glad she didn't, for he really didn't know to what the truth on this unpleasant point mightn't have prompted her. She only, however, confirmed his assertion. "Thank goodness you're a failure—it's why I so distinguish you! Anything else to-day is too hideous. Look about you—look at the successes. Would you BE one, on your honour? Look, moreover," she continued, "at me."

For a little accordingly their eyes met. "I see," Strether returned. "You too are out of it."

"The superiority you discern in me," she concurred, "announces my futility. If you knew," she sighed, "the dreams of my youth! But our realities are what has brought us together. We're beaten brothers in arms."

He smiled at her kindly enough, but he shook his head. "It doesn't alter the fact that you're expensive. You've cost me already—!"

But he had hung fire. "Cost you what?"

"Well, my past—in one great lump. But no matter," he laughed: "I'll pay with my last penny."

Her attention had unfortunately now been engaged by their comrade's return, for Waymarsh met their view as he came out of his shop. "I hope he hasn't paid," she said, "with HIS last; though I'm convinced he has been splendid, and has been so for you."

"Ah no—not that!"

"Then for me?"

"Quite as little." Waymarsh was by this time near enough to show signs his friend could read, though he seemed to look almost carefully at nothing in particular.

"Then for himself?"

"For nobody. For nothing. For freedom."

"But what has freedom to do with it?"

Strether's answer was indirect. "To be as good as you and me. But different."

She had had time to take in their companion's face; and with it, as such things were easy for her, she took in all. "Different—yes. But better!"

If Waymarsh was sombre he was also indeed almost sublime. He told them nothing, left his absence unexplained, and though they were convinced he had made some extraordinary purchase they were never to learn its nature. He only glowered grandly at the tops of the old gables. "It's the sacred rage," Strether had had further time to say; and this sacred rage was to become between them, for convenient comprehension, the description of one of his periodical necessities. It was Strether who eventually contended that it did make him better than they. But by that time Miss Gostrey was convinced that she didn't want to be better than Strether.

Book Second

I

Those occasions on which Strether was, in association with the exile from Milrose, to see the sacred rage glimmer through would doubtless have their due periodicity; but our friend had meanwhile to find names for many other matters. On no evening of his life perhaps, as he reflected, had he had to supply so many as on the third of his short stay in London; an evening spent by Miss Gostrey's side at one of the theatres, to which he had found himself transported, without his own hand raised, on the mere expression of a conscientious wonder. She knew her theatre, she knew her play, as she had triumphantly known, three days running, everything else, and the moment filled to the brim, for her companion, that apprehension of the interesting which, whether or no the interesting happened to filter through his guide, strained now to its limits his brief opportunity. Waymarsh hadn't come with them; he had seen plays enough, he signified, before Strether had joined him—an affirmation that had its full force when his friend ascertained by questions that he had seen two and a circus. Questions as to what he had seen had on him indeed an effect only less favourable than questions as to what he hadn't. He liked the former to be discriminated; but how could it be done, Strether asked of their constant counsellor, without discriminating the latter?

Miss Gostrey had dined with him at his hotel, face to face over a small table on which the lighted candles had rose-coloured shades; and the rose-coloured shades and the small table and the soft fragrance of the lady—had anything to his mere sense ever been so soft?—were so many touches in he scarce knew what positive high picture. He had been to the theatre, even to the opera, in Boston, with Mrs. Newsome, more than once acting as her only escort; but there had been no little confronted dinner, no pink lights, no whiff of vague sweetness, as a preliminary: one of the results of which was that at present, mildly rueful, though with a sharpish accent, he actually asked himself WHY there hadn't. There was much the same difference in his impression of the noticed state of his companion, whose dress was "cut down," as he believed the term to be, in respect to shoulders and bosom, in a manner quite other than Mrs. Newsome's, and who wore round her throat a broad red velvet band with an antique jewel—he was rather complacently sure it was antique—attached to it in front. Mrs. Newsome's dress was never in any degree "cut down," and she never wore round her throat a broad red velvet band: if she had, moreover, would it ever have served so to carry on and complicate, as he now almost felt, his vision?

It would have been absurd of him to trace into ramifications the effect of the ribbon from which Miss Gostrey's trinket depended, had he not for the hour, at the best, been so given over to uncontrolled perceptions. What was it but an uncontrolled perception that his friend's velvet band somehow added, in her appearance, to the value of every other item—to that of her smile and of the way she carried her head, to that of her complexion, of her lips, her teeth, her eyes, her hair? What, certainly, had a man conscious of a man's work in the world to do with red velvet bands? He wouldn't for anything have so exposed himself as to tell Miss Gostrey how much he liked hers, yet he HAD none the less not only caught himself in the act—frivolous, no doubt, idiotic, and above all unexpected—of liking it: he had in addition taken it as a starting-point for fresh backward, fresh forward, fresh lateral flights. The manner in which Mrs. Newsome's throat WAS encircled suddenly represented for him, in an alien order, almost as many things as the manner in which Miss Gostrey's was. Mrs. Newsome wore, at operatic hours, a black silk dress—very handsome, he knew it was "handsome"—and an ornament that his memory was able further to identify as a ruche. He had his association indeed with the ruche, but it was rather imperfectly romantic. He had once said to the wearer—and it was as "free" a remark as he had ever made to her—that she looked, with her ruff and other matters, like Queen Elizabeth; and it had after this in truth been his fancy that, as a consequence of that tenderness and an acceptance of the idea, the form of this special tribute to the "frill" had grown slightly more marked. The connexion, as he sat there and let his imagination roam, was to strike him as vaguely pathetic; but there it all was, and pathetic was doubtless in the conditions the best thing it could possibly be. It had assuredly existed at any rate; for it seemed now to come over him that no gentleman of his age at Woollett could ever, to a lady of Mrs. Newsome's, which was not much less than his, have embarked on such a simile.

All sorts of things in fact now seemed to come over him, comparatively few of which his chronicler can hope for space to mention. It came over him for instance that Miss Gostrey looked perhaps like Mary Stuart: Lambert Strether had a candour of fancy which could rest for an instant gratified in such an antithesis. It came over him that never before—no, literally never—had a lady dined with him at a public place before going to the play. The publicity of the place was just, in the matter, for Strether, the rare strange thing; it affected him almost as the achievement of privacy might have affected a man of a different experience. He had married, in the far-away years, so young as to have missed the time natural in Boston for taking girls to the Museum; and it was absolutely true of hint that—even after the close of the period of conscious detachment occupying the centre of his life, the grey middle desert of the two deaths, that of his wife and that, ten years later, of his boy—he had never taken any one anywhere. It came over him in especial—though the monition had, as happened, already sounded, fitfully gleamed, in other forms—that the business he had come out on hadn't yet been so brought home to him as by the sight of the people about him. She gave him the impression, his friend, at first, more straight than he got it for himself—gave it simply by saying with off-hand illumination: "Oh yes, they're types!"—but after he had taken it he made to the full his own use of it; both while he kept silence for the four acts and while he talked in the intervals. It was an evening, it was a world of types, and this was a connexion above all in which the figures and faces in the stalls were interchangeable with those on the stage.

He felt as if the play itself penetrated him with the naked elbow of his neighbour, a great stripped handsome red-haired lady who conversed with a gentleman on her other side in stray dissyllables which had for his ear, in the oddest way in the world, so much sound that he wondered they hadn't more sense; and he recognised by the same law, beyond the footlights, what he was pleased to take for the very flush of English life. He had distracted drops in which he couldn't have said if it were actors or auditors who were most true, and the upshot of which, each time, was the consciousness of new contacts. However he viewed his job it was "types" he should have to tackle. Those before him and around him were not as the types of Woollett, where, for that matter, it had begun to seem to him that there must only have been the male and the female. These made two exactly, even with the individual varieties. Here, on the other hand, apart from the personal and the sexual range—which might be greater or less—a series of strong stamps had been applied, as it were, from without; stamps that his observation played with as, before a glass case on a table, it might have passed from medal to medal and from copper to gold. It befell that in the drama precisely there was a bad woman in a yellow frock who made a pleasant weak good-looking young man in perpetual evening dress do the most dreadful things. Strether felt himself on the whole not afraid of the yellow frock, but he was vaguely anxious over a certain kindness into which he found himself drifting for its victim. He hadn't come out, he reminded himself, to be too kind, or indeed to be kind at all, to Chadwick Newsome. Would Chad also be in perpetual evening dress? He somehow rather hoped it—it seemed so to add to THIS young man's general amenability; though he wondered too if, to fight him with his own weapons, he himself (a thought almost startling) would have likewise to be. This young man furthermore would have been much more easy to handle—at least for HIM—than appeared probable in respect to Chad.

It came up for him with Miss Gostrey that there were things of which she would really perhaps after all have heard, and she admitted when a little pressed that she was never quite sure of what she heard as distinguished from things such as, on occasions like the present, she only extravagantly guessed. "I seem with this freedom, you see, to have guessed Mr. Chad. He's a young man on whose head high hopes are placed at Woollett; a young man a wicked woman has got hold of and whom his family over there have sent you out to rescue. You've accepted the mission of separating him from the wicked woman. Are you quite sure she's very bad for him?"

Something in his manner showed it as quite pulling him up. "Of course we are. Wouldn't YOU be?"

"Oh I don't know. One never does—does one?—beforehand. One can only judge on the facts. Yours are quite new to me; I'm really not in the least, as you see, in possession of them: so it will be awfully interesting to have them from you. If you're satisfied, that's all that's required. I mean if you're sure you ARE sure: sure it won't do."

"That he should lead such a life? Rather!"

"Oh but I don't know, you see, about his life; you've not told me about his life. She may be charming—his life!"

"Charming?"—Strether stared before him. "She's base, venal-out of the streets."

"I see. And HE—?"

"Chad, wretched boy?"

"Of what type and temper is he?" she went on as Strether had lapsed.

"Well—the obstinate." It was as if for a moment he had been going to say more and had then controlled himself.

That was scarce what she wished. "Do you like him?"

This time he was prompt. "No. How CAN I?"

"Do you mean because of your being so saddled with him?"

"I'm thinking of his mother," said Strether after a moment. "He has darkened her admirable life." He spoke with austerity. "He has worried her half to death."

"Oh that's of course odious." She had a pause as if for renewed emphasis of this truth, but it ended on another note. "Is her life very admirable?"

"Extraordinarily."

There was so much in the tone that Miss Gostrey had to devote another pause to the appreciation of it. "And has he only HER? I don't mean the bad woman in Paris," she quickly added—"for I assure you I shouldn't even at the best be disposed to allow him more than one. But has he only his mother?"

"He has also a sister, older than himself and married; and they're both remarkably fine women."

"Very handsome, you mean?"

This promptitude—almost, as he might have thought, this precipitation, gave him a brief drop; but he came up again. "Mrs. Newsome, I think, is handsome, though she's not of course, with a son of twenty-eight and a daughter of thirty, in her very first youth. She married, however, extremely young."

"And is wonderful," Miss Gostrey asked, "for her age?"

Strether seemed to feel with a certain disquiet the pressure of it. "I don't say she's wonderful. Or rather," he went on the next moment, "I do say it. It's exactly what she IS—wonderful. But I wasn't thinking of her appearance," he explained—"striking as that doubtless is. I was thinking—well, of many other things." He seemed to look at these as if to mention some of them; then took, pulling himself up, another turn. "About Mrs. Pocock people may differ."

"Is that the daughter's name—'Pocock'?"

"That's the daughter's name," Strether sturdily confessed.

"And people may differ, you mean, about HER beauty?"

"About everything."

"But YOU admire her?"

He gave his friend a glance as to show how he could bear this "I'm perhaps a little afraid of her."

"Oh," said Miss Gostrey, "I see her from here! You may say then I see very fast and very far, but I've already shown you I do. The young man and the two ladies," she went on, "are at any rate all the family?"

"Quite all. His father has been dead ten years, and there's no brother, nor any other sister. They'd do," said Strether, "anything in the world for him."

"And you'd do anything in the world for THEM?"

He shifted again; she had made it perhaps just a shade too affirmative for his nerves. "Oh I don't know!"

"You'd do at any rate this, and the 'anything' they'd do is represented by their MAKING you do it."

"Ah they couldn't have come—either of them. They're very busy people and Mrs. Newsome in particular has a large full life. She's moreover highly nervous—and not at all strong."

"You mean she's an American invalid?"

He carefully distinguished. "There's nothing she likes less than to be called one, but she would consent to be one of those things, I think," he laughed, "if it were the only way to be the other."

"Consent to be an American in order to be an invalid?"

"No," said Strether, "the other way round. She's at any rate delicate sensitive high-strung. She puts so much of herself into everything—"

Ah Maria knew these things! "That she has nothing left for anything else? Of course she hasn't. To whom do you say it? High-strung? Don't I spend my life, for them, jamming down the pedal? I see moreover how it has told on you."

Strether took this more lightly. "Oh I jam down the pedal too!"

"Well," she lucidly returned, "we must from this moment bear on it together with all our might." And she forged ahead. "Have they money?"

But it was as if, while her energetic image still held him, her enquiry fell short. "Mrs. Newsome," he wished further to explain, "hasn't moreover your courage on the question of contact. If she had come it would have been to see the person herself."

"The woman? Ah but that's courage."

"No—it's exaltation, which is a very different thing. Courage," he, however, accommodatingly threw out, "is what YOU have."

She shook her head. "You say that only to patch me up—to cover the nudity of my want of exaltation. I've neither the one nor the other. I've mere battered indifference. I see that what you mean," Miss Gostrey pursued, "is that if your friend HAD come she would take great views, and the great views, to put it simply, would be too much for her."

Strether looked amused at her notion of the simple, but he adopted her formula. "Everything's too much for her."

"Ah then such a service as this of yours—"

"Is more for her than anything else? Yes—far more. But so long as it isn't too much for ME—!"

"Her condition doesn't matter? Surely not; we leave her condition out; we take it, that is, for granted. I see it, her condition, as behind and beneath you; yet at the same time I see it as bearing you up."

"Oh it does bear me up!" Strether laughed.

"Well then as yours bears ME nothing more's needed." With which she put again her question. "Has Mrs. Newsome money?"

This time he heeded. "Oh plenty. That's the root of the evil. There's money, to very large amounts, in the concern. Chad has had the free use of a great deal. But if he'll pull himself together and come home, all the same, he'll find his account in it."

She had listened with all her interest. "And I hope to goodness you'll find yours!"

"He'll take up his definite material reward," said Strether without acknowledgement of this. "He's at the parting of the ways. He can come into the business now—he can't come later."

"Is there a business?"

"Lord, yes—a big brave bouncing business. A roaring trade."

"A great shop?"

"Yes—a workshop; a great production, a great industry. The concern's a manufacture—and a manufacture that, if it's only properly looked after, may well be on the way to become a monopoly. It's a little thing they make—make better, it appears, than other people can, or than other people, at any rate, do. Mr. Newsome, being a man of ideas, at least in that particular line," Strether explained, "put them on it with great effect, and gave the place altogether, in his time, an immense lift."

"It's a place in itself?"

"Well, quite a number of buildings; almost a little industrial colony. But above all it's a thing. The article produced."

"And what IS the article produced?"

Strether looked about him as in slight reluctance to say; then the curtain, which he saw about to rise, came to his aid. "I'll tell you next time." But when the next time came he only said he'd tell her later on—after they should have left the theatre; for she had immediately reverted to their topic, and even for himself the picture of the stage was now overlaid with another image. His postponements, however, made her wonder—wonder if the article referred to were anything bad. And she explained that she meant improper or ridiculous or wrong. But Strether, so far as that went, could satisfy her. "Unmentionable? Oh no, we constantly talk of it; we are quite familiar and brazen about it. Only, as a small, trivial, rather ridiculous object of the commonest domestic use, it's just wanting in-what shall I say? Well, dignity, or the least approach to distinction. Right here therefore, with everything about us so grand—!" In short he shrank.

"It's a false note?"

"Sadly. It's vulgar."

"But surely not vulgarer than this." Then on his wondering as she herself had done: "Than everything about us." She seemed a trifle irritated. "What do you take this for?"

"Why for—comparatively—divine!"

"This dreadful London theatre? It's impossible, if you really want to know."

"Oh then," laughed Strether, "I DON'T really want to know!"

It made between them a pause, which she, however, still fascinated by the mystery of the production at Woollett, presently broke. "'Rather ridiculous'? Clothes-pins? Saleratus? Shoe-polish?"

It brought him round. "No—you don't even 'burn.' I don't think, you know, you'll guess it."

"How then can I judge how vulgar it is?"

"You'll judge when I do tell you"—and he persuaded her to patience. But it may even now frankly be mentioned that he in the sequel never WAS to tell her. He actually never did so, and it moreover oddly occurred that by the law, within her, of the incalculable, her desire for the information dropped and her attitude to the question converted itself into a positive cultivation of ignorance. In ignorance she could humour her fancy, and that proved a useful freedom. She could treat the little nameless object as indeed unnameable—she could make their abstention enormously definite. There might indeed have been for Strether the portent of this in what she next said.

"Is it perhaps then because it's so bad—because your industry as you call it, IS so vulgar—that Mr. Chad won't come back? Does he feel the taint? Is he staying away not to be mixed up in it?"

"Oh," Strether laughed, "it wouldn't appear—would it?—that he feels 'taints'! He's glad enough of the money from it, and the money's his whole basis. There's appreciation in that—I mean as to the allowance his mother has hitherto made him. She has of course the resource of cutting this allowance off; but even then he has unfortunately, and on no small scale, his independent supply—money left him by his grandfather, her own father."

"Wouldn't the fact you mention then," Miss Gostrey asked, "make it just more easy for him to be particular? Isn't he conceivable as fastidious about the source—the apparent and public source—of his income?"

Strether was able quite good-humouredly to entertain the proposition. "The source of his grandfather's wealth—and thereby of his own share in it—was not particularly noble."

"And what source was it?"

Strether cast about. "Well—practices."

"In business? Infamies? He was an old swindler?"

"Oh," he said with more emphasis than spirit, "I shan't describe HIM nor narrate his exploits."

"Lord, what abysses! And the late Mr. Newsome then?"

"Well, what about him?"

"Was he like the grandfather?"

"No—he was on the other side of the house. And he was different."

Miss Gostrey kept it up. "Better?"

Her friend for a moment hung fire. "No."

Her comment on his hesitation was scarce the less marked for being mute. "Thank you. NOW don't you see," she went on, "why the boy doesn't come home? He's drowning his shame."

"His shame? What shame?"

"What shame? Comment donc? THE shame."

"But where and when," Strether asked, "is 'THE shame'—where is any shame—to-day? The men I speak of—they did as every one does; and (besides being ancient history) it was all a matter of appreciation."

She showed how she understood. "Mrs. Newsome has appreciated?"

"Ah I can't speak for HER!"

"In the midst of such doings—and, as I understand you, profiting by them, she at least has remained exquisite?"

"Oh I can't talk of her!" Strether said.

"I thought she was just what you COULD talk of. You DON'T trust me," Miss Gostrey after a moment declared.

It had its effect. "Well, her money is spent, her life conceived and carried on with a large beneficence—"

"That's a kind of expiation of wrongs? Gracious," she added before he could speak, "how intensely you make me see her!"

"If you see her," Strether dropped, "it's all that's necessary."

She really seemed to have her. "I feel that. She IS, in spite of everything, handsome."

This at least enlivened him. "What do you mean by everything?"

"Well, I mean YOU." With which she had one of her swift changes of ground. "You say the concern needs looking after; but doesn't Mrs. Newsome look after it?"

"So far as possible. She's wonderfully able, but it's not her affair, and her life's a good deal overcharged. She has many, many things."

"And you also?"

"Oh yes—I've many too, if you will."

"I see. But what I mean is," Miss Gostrey amended, "do you also look after the business?"

"Oh no, I don't touch the business."

"Only everything else?"

"Well, yes—some things."

"As for instance—?"

Strether obligingly thought. "Well, the Review."

"The Review?—you have a Review?"

"Certainly. Woollett has a Review—which Mrs. Newsome, for the most part, magnificently pays for and which I, not at all magnificently, edit. My name's on the cover," Strether pursued, "and I'm really rather disappointed and hurt that you seem never to have heard of it."

She neglected for a moment this grievance. "And what kind of a Review is it?"

His serenity was now completely restored. "Well, it's green."

"Do you mean in political colour as they say here—in thought?"

"No; I mean the cover's green—of the most lovely shade."

"And with Mrs. Newsome's name on it too?"

He waited a little. "Oh as for that you must judge if she peeps out. She's behind the whole thing; but she's of a delicacy and a discretion—!"

Miss Gostrey took it all. "I'm sure. She WOULD be. I don't underrate her. She must be rather a swell."

"Oh yes, she's rather a swell!"

"A Woollett swell—bon! I like the idea of a Woollett swell. And you must be rather one too, to be so mixed up with her."

"Ah no," said Strether, "that's not the way it works."

But she had already taken him up. "The way it works—you needn't tell me!—is of course that you efface yourself."

"With my name on the cover?" he lucidly objected.

"Ah but you don't put it on for yourself."

"I beg your pardon—that's exactly what I do put it on for. It's exactly the thing that I'm reduced to doing for myself. It seems to rescue a little, you see, from the wreck of hopes and ambitions, the refuse-heap of disappointments and failures, my one presentable little scrap of an identity."

On this she looked at him as to say many things, but what she at last simply said was: "She likes to see it there. You're the bigger swell of the two," she immediately continued, "because you think you're not one. She thinks she IS one. However," Miss Gostrey added, "she thinks you're one too. You're at all events the biggest she can get hold of." She embroidered, she abounded. "I don't say it to interfere between you, but on the day she gets hold of a bigger one—!" Strether had thrown back his head as in silent mirth over something that struck him in her audacity or felicity, and her flight meanwhile was already higher. "Therefore close with her—!"

"Close with her?" he asked as she seemed to hang poised.

"Before you lose your chance."

Their eyes met over it. "What do you mean by closing?"

"And what do I mean by your chance? I'll tell you when you tell me all the things YOU don't. Is it her GREATEST fad?" she briskly pursued.

"The Review?" He seemed to wonder how he could best describe it. This resulted however but in a sketch. "It's her tribute to the ideal."

"I see. You go in for tremendous things."

"We go in for the unpopular side—that is so far as we dare."

"And how far DO you dare?"

"Well, she very far. I much less. I don't begin to have her faith. She provides," said Strether, "three fourths of that. And she provides, as I've confided to you, ALL the money."

It evoked somehow a vision of gold that held for a little Miss Gostrey's eyes, and she looked as if she heard the bright dollars shovelled in. "I hope then you make a good thing—"

"I NEVER made a good thing!" he at once returned.

She just waited. "Don't you call it a good thing to be loved?"

"Oh we're not loved. We're not even hated. We're only just sweetly ignored."

She had another pause. "You don't trust me!" she once more repeated.

"Don't I when I lift the last veil?—tell you the very secret of the prison-house?"

Again she met his eyes, but to the result that after an instant her own turned away with impatience. "You don't sell? Oh I'm glad of THAT!" After which however, and before he could protest, she was off again. "She's just a MORAL swell."

He accepted gaily enough the definition. "Yes—I really think that describes her."

But it had for his friend the oddest connexion. "How does she do her hair?"

He laughed out. "Beautifully!"

"Ah that doesn't tell me. However, it doesn't matter—I know. It's tremendously neat—a real reproach; quite remarkably thick and without, as yet, a single strand of white. There!"

He blushed for her realism, but gaped at her truth. "You're the very deuce."

"What else SHOULD I be? It was as the very deuce I pounced on you. But don't let it trouble you, for everything but the very deuce—at our age—is a bore and a delusion, and even he himself, after all, but half a joy." With which, on a single sweep of her wing, she resumed. "You assist her to expiate—which is rather hard when you've yourself not sinned."

"It's she who hasn't sinned," Strether replied. "I've sinned the most."

"Ah," Miss Gostrey cynically laughed, "what a picture of HER! Have you robbed the widow and the orphan?"

"I've sinned enough," said Strether.

"Enough for whom? Enough for what?"

"Well, to be where I am."

"Thank you!" They were disturbed at this moment by the passage between their knees and the back of the seats before them of a gentleman who had been absent during a part of the performance and who now returned for the close; but the interruption left Miss Gostrey time, before the subsequent hush, to express as a sharp finality her sense of the moral of all their talk. "I knew you had something up your sleeve!" This finality, however, left them in its turn, at the end of the play, as disposed to hang back as if they had still much to say; so that they easily agreed to let every one go before them—they found an interest in waiting. They made out from the lobby that the night had turned to rain; yet Miss Gostrey let her friend know that he wasn't to see her home. He was simply to put her, by herself, into a four-wheeler; she liked so in London, of wet nights after wild pleasures, thinking things over, on the return, in lonely four-wheelers. This was her great time, she intimated, for pulling herself together. The delays caused by the weather, the struggle for vehicles at the door, gave them occasion to subside on a divan at the back of the vestibule and just beyond the reach of the fresh damp gusts from the street. Here Strether's comrade resumed that free handling of the subject to which his own imagination of it already owed so much. "Does your young friend in Paris like you?"

It had almost, after the interval, startled him. "Oh I hope not! Why SHOULD he?"

"Why shouldn't he?" Miss Gostrey asked. "That you're coming down on him need have nothing to do with it."

"You see more in it," he presently returned, "than I."

"Of course I see you in it."

"Well then you see more in 'me'!"

"Than you see in yourself? Very likely. That's always one's right. What I was thinking of," she explained, "is the possible particular effect on him of his milieu."

"Oh his milieu—!" Strether really felt he could imagine it better now than three hours before.

"Do you mean it can only have been so lowering?"

"Why that's my very starting-point."

"Yes, but you start so far back. What do his letters say?"

"Nothing. He practically ignores us—or spares us. He doesn't write."

"I see. But there are all the same," she went on, "two quite distinct things that—given the wonderful place he's in—may have happened to him. One is that he may have got brutalised. The other is that he may have got refined."

Strether stared—this WAS a novelty. "Refined?"

"Oh," she said quietly, "there ARE refinements."

The way of it made him, after looking at her, break into a laugh. "YOU have them!"

"As one of the signs," she continued in the same tone, "they constitute perhaps the worst."

He thought it over and his gravity returned. "Is it a refinement not to answer his mother's letters?"

She appeared to have a scruple, but she brought it out. "Oh I should say the greatest of all."

"Well," said Strether, "I'M quite content to let it, as one of the signs, pass for the worst that I know he believes he can do what he likes with me."

This appeared to strike her. "How do you know it?"

"Oh I'm sure of it. I feel it in my bones."

"Feel he CAN do it?"

"Feel that he believes he can. It may come to the same thing!" Strether laughed.

She wouldn't, however, have this. "Nothing for you will ever come to the same thing as anything else." And she understood what she meant, it seemed, sufficiently to go straight on. "You say that if he does break he'll come in for things at home?"

"Quite positively. He'll come in for a particular chance—a chance that any properly constituted young man would jump at. The business has so developed that an opening scarcely apparent three years ago, but which his father's will took account of as in certain conditions possible and which, under that will, attaches to Chad's availing himself of it a large contingent advantage—this opening, the conditions having come about, now simply awaits him. His mother has kept it for him, holding out against strong pressure, till the last possible moment. It requires, naturally, as it carries with it a handsome 'part,' a large share in profits, his being on the spot and making a big effort for a big result. That's what I mean by his chance. If he misses it he comes in, as you say, for nothing. And to see that he doesn't miss it is, in a word, what I've come out for."

She let it all sink in. "What you've come out for then is simply to render him an immense service."

Well, poor Strether was willing to take it so. "Ah if you like."

"He stands, as they say, if you succeed with him, to gain—"

"Oh a lot of advantages." Strether had them clearly at his fingers' ends.

"By which you mean of course a lot of money."

"Well, not only. I'm acting with a sense for him of other things too. Consideration and comfort and security—the general safety of being anchored by a strong chain. He wants, as I see him, to be protected. Protected I mean from life."

"Ah voila!"—her thought fitted with a click. "From life. What you REALLY want to get him home for is to marry him."

"Well, that's about the size of it."

"Of course," she said, "it's rudimentary. But to any one in particular?"

He smiled at this, looking a little more conscious. "You get everything out."

For a moment again their eyes met. "You put everything in!"

He acknowledged the tribute by telling her. "To Mamie Pocock."

She wondered; then gravely, even exquisitely, as if to make the oddity also fit: "His own niece?"

"Oh you must yourself find a name for the relation. His brother-in-law's sister. Mrs. Jim's sister-in-law."

It seemed to have on Miss Gostrey a certain hardening effect. "And who in the world's Mrs. Jim?"

"Chad's sister—who was Sarah Newsome. She's married—didn't I mention it?—to Jim Pocock."

"Ah yes," she tacitly replied; but he had mentioned things—! Then, however, with all the sound it could have, "Who in the world's Jim Pocock?" she asked.

"Why Sally's husband. That's the only way we distinguish people at Woollett," he good-humoredly explained.

"And is it a great distinction—being Sally's husband?"

He considered. "I think there can be scarcely a greater—unless it may become one, in the future, to be Chad's wife."

"Then how do they distinguish YOU?"

"They DON'T—except, as I've told you, by the green cover."

Once more their eyes met on it, and she held him an instant. "The green cover won't—nor will ANY cover—avail you with ME. You're of a depth of duplicity!" Still, she could in her own large grasp of the real condone it. "Is Mamie a great parti?"

"Oh the greatest we have—our prettiest brightest girl."

Miss Gostrey seemed to fix the poor child. "I know what they CAN be. And with money?"

"Not perhaps with a great deal of that—but with so much of everything else that we don't miss it. We DON'T miss money much, you know," Strether added, "in general, in America, in pretty girls."

"No," she conceded; "but I know also what you do sometimes miss. And do you," she asked, "yourself admire her?"

It was a question, he indicated, that there might be several ways of taking; but he decided after an instant for the humorous. "Haven't I sufficiently showed you how I admire ANY pretty girl?"

Her interest in his problem was by this time such that it scarce left her freedom, and she kept close to the facts. "I supposed that at Woollett you wanted them—what shall I call it?—blameless. I mean your young men for your pretty girls."

"So did I!" Strether confessed. "But you strike there a curious fact—the fact that Woollett too accommodates itself to the spirit of the age and the increasing mildness of manners. Everything changes, and I hold that our situation precisely marks a date. We SHOULD prefer them blameless, but we have to make the best of them as we find them. Since the spirit of the age and the increasing mildness send them so much more to Paris—"

"You've to take them back as they come. When they DO come. Bon!" Once more she embraced it all, but she had a moment of thought. "Poor Chad!"

"Ah," said Strether cheerfully "Mamie will save him!"

She was looking away, still in her vision, and she spoke with impatience and almost as if he hadn't understood her. "YOU'LL save him. That's who'll save him."

"Oh but with Mamie's aid. Unless indeed you mean," he added, "that I shall effect so much more with yours!"

It made her at last again look at him. "You'll do more—as you're so much better—than all of us put together."

"I think I'm only better since I've known YOU!" Strether bravely returned.

The depletion of the place, the shrinkage of the crowd and now comparatively quiet withdrawal of its last elements had already brought them nearer the door and put them in relation with a messenger of whom he bespoke Miss Gostrey's cab. But this left them a few minutes more, which she was clearly in no mood not to use. "You've spoken to me of what—by your success—Mr. Chad stands to gain. But you've not spoken to me of what you do."

"Oh I've nothing more to gain," said Strether very simply.

She took it as even quite too simple. "You mean you've got it all 'down'? You've been paid in advance?"

"Ah don't talk about payment!" he groaned.

Something in the tone of it pulled her up, but as their messenger still delayed she had another chance and she put it in another way. "What—by failure—do you stand to lose?"

He still, however, wouldn't have it. "Nothing!" he exclaimed, and on the messenger's at this instant reappearing he was able to sink the subject in their responsive advance. When, a few steps up the street, under a lamp, he had put her into her four-wheeler and she had asked him if the man had called for him no second conveyance, he replied before the door was closed. "You won't take me with you?"

"Not for the world."

"Then I shall walk."

"In the rain?"

"I like the rain," said Strether. "Good-night!"

She kept him a moment, while his hand was on the door, by not answering; after which she answered by repeating her question. "What do you stand to lose?"

Why the question now affected him as other he couldn't have said; he could only this time meet it otherwise. "Everything."

"So I thought. Then you shall succeed. And to that end I'm yours—"

"Ah, dear lady!" he kindly breathed.

"Till death!" said Maria Gostrey. "Good-night."

II

Strether called, his second morning in Paris, on the bankers of the Rue Scribe to whom his letter of credit was addressed, and he made this visit attended by Waymarsh, in whose company he had crossed from London two days before. They had hastened to the Rue Scribe on the morrow of their arrival, but Strether had not then found the letters the hope of which prompted this errand. He had had as yet none at all; hadn't expected them in London, but had counted on several in Paris, and, disconcerted now, had presently strolled back to the Boulevard with a sense of injury that he felt himself taking for as good a start as any other. It would serve, this spur to his spirit, he reflected, as, pausing at the top of the street, he looked up and down the great foreign avenue, it would serve to begin business with. His idea was to begin business immediately, and it did much for him the rest of his day that the beginning of business awaited him. He did little else till night but ask himself what he should do if he hadn't fortunately had so much to do; but he put himself the question in many different situations and connexions. What carried him hither and yon was an admirable theory that nothing he could do wouldn't be in some manner related to what he fundamentally had on hand, or WOULD be—should he happen to have a scruple—wasted for it. He did happen to have a scruple—a scruple about taking no definite step till he should get letters; but this reasoning carried it off. A single day to feel his feet—he had felt them as yet only at Chester and in London—was he could consider, none too much; and having, as he had often privately expressed it, Paris to reckon with, he threw these hours of freshness consciously into the reckoning. They made it continually greater, but that was what it had best be if it was to be anything at all, and he gave himself up till far into the evening, at the theatre and on the return, after the theatre, along the bright congested Boulevard, to feeling it grow. Waymarsh had accompanied him this time to the play, and the two men had walked together, as a first stage, from the Gymnase to the Cafe Riche, into the crowded "terrace" of which establishment—the night, or rather the morning, for midnight had struck, being bland and populous—they had wedged themselves for refreshment. Waymarsh, as a result of some discussion with his friend, had made a marked virtue of his having now let himself go; and there had been elements of impression in their half-hour over their watered beer-glasses that gave him his occasion for conveying that he held this compromise with his stiffer self to have become extreme. He conveyed it—for it was still, after all, his stiffer self who gloomed out of the glare of the terrace—in solemn silence; and there was indeed a great deal of critical silence, every way, between the companions, even till they gained the Place de l'Opera, as to the character of their nocturnal progress.

This morning there WERE letters—letters which had reached London, apparently all together, the day of Strether's journey, and had taken their time to follow him; so that, after a controlled impulse to go into them in the reception-room of the bank, which, reminding him of the post-office at Woollett, affected him as the abutment of some transatlantic bridge, he slipped them into the pocket of his loose grey overcoat with a sense of the felicity of carrying them off. Waymarsh, who had had letters yesterday, had had them again to-day, and Waymarsh suggested in this particular no controlled impulses. The last one he was at all events likely to be observed to struggle with was clearly that of bringing to a premature close any visit to the Rue Scribe. Strether had left him there yesterday; he wanted to see the papers, and he had spent, by what his friend could make out, a succession of hours with the papers. He spoke of the establishment, with emphasis, as a post of superior observation; just as he spoke generally of his actual damnable doom as a device for hiding from him what was going on. Europe was best described, to his mind, as an elaborate engine for dissociating the confined American from that indispensable knowledge, and was accordingly only rendered bearable by these occasional stations of relief, traps for the arrest of wandering western airs. Strether, on his side, set himself to walk again—he had his relief in his pocket; and indeed, much as he had desired his budget, the growth of restlessness might have been marked in him from the moment he had assured himself of the superscription of most of the missives it contained. This restlessness became therefore his temporary law; he knew he should recognise as soon as see it the best place of all for settling down with his chief correspondent. He had for the next hour an accidental air of looking for it in the windows of shops; he came down the Rue de la Paix in the sun and, passing across the Tuileries and the river, indulged more than once—as if on finding himself determined—in a sudden pause before the book-stalls of the opposite quay. In the garden of the Tuileries he had lingered, on two or three spots, to look; it was as if the wonderful Paris spring had stayed him as he roamed. The prompt Paris morning struck its cheerful notes—in a soft breeze and a sprinkled smell, in the light flit, over the garden-floor, of bareheaded girls with the buckled strap of oblong boxes, in the type of ancient thrifty persons basking betimes where terrace-walls were warm, in the blue-frocked brass-labelled officialism of humble rakers and scrapers, in the deep references of a straight-pacing priest or the sharp ones of a white-gaitered red-legged soldier. He watched little brisk figures, figures whose movement was as the tick of the great Paris clock, take their smooth diagonal from point to point; the air had a taste as of something mixed with art, something that presented nature as a white-capped master-chef. The palace was gone, Strether remembered the palace; and when he gazed into the irremediable void of its site the historic sense in him might have been freely at play—the play under which in Paris indeed it so often winces like a touched nerve. He filled out spaces with dim symbols of scenes; he caught the gleam of white statues at the base of which, with his letters out, he could tilt back a straw-bottomed chair. But his drift was, for reasons, to the other side, and it floated him unspent up the Rue de Seine and as far as the Luxembourg. In the Luxembourg Gardens he pulled up; here at last he found his nook, and here, on a penny chair from which terraces, alleys, vistas, fountains, little trees in green tubs, little women in white caps and shrill little girls at play all sunnily "composed" together, he passed an hour in which the cup of his impressions seemed truly to overflow. But a week had elapsed since he quitted the ship, and there were more things in his mind than so few days could account for. More than once, during the time, he had regarded himself as admonished; but the admonition this morning was formidably sharp. It took as it hadn't done yet the form of a question—the question of what he was doing with such an extraordinary sense of escape. This sense was sharpest after he had read his letters, but that was also precisely why the question pressed. Four of the letters were from Mrs. Newsome and none of them short; she had lost no time, had followed on his heels while he moved, so expressing herself that he now could measure the probable frequency with which he should hear. They would arrive, it would seem, her communications, at the rate of several a week; he should be able to count, it might even prove, on more than one by each mail. If he had begun yesterday with a small grievance he had therefore an opportunity to begin to-day with its opposite. He read the letters successively and slowly, putting others back into his pocket but keeping these for a long time afterwards gathered in his lap. He held them there, lost in thought, as if to prolong the presence of what they gave him; or as if at the least to assure them their part in the constitution of some lucidity. His friend wrote admirably, and her tone was even more in her style than in her voice—he might almost, for the hour, have had to come this distance to get its full carrying quality; yet the plentitude of his consciousness of difference consorted perfectly with the deepened intensity of the connexion. It was the difference, the difference of being just where he was and AS he was, that formed the escape—this difference was so much greater than he had dreamed it would be; and what he finally sat there turning over was the strange logic of his finding himself so free. He felt it in a manner his duty to think out his state, to approve the process, and when he came in fact to trace the steps and add up the items they sufficiently accounted for the sum. He had never expected—that was the truth of it—again to find himself young, and all the years and other things it had taken to make him so were exactly his present arithmetic. He had to make sure of them to put his scruple to rest.

It all sprang at bottom from the beauty of Mrs. Newsome's desire that he should be worried with nothing that was not of the essence of his task; by insisting that he should thoroughly intermit and break she had so provided for his freedom that she would, as it were, have only herself to thank. Strether could not at this point indeed have completed his thought by the image of what she might have to thank herself FOR: the image, at best, of his own likeness-poor Lambert Strether washed up on the sunny strand by the waves of a single day, poor Lambert Strether thankful for breathing-time and stiffening himself while he gasped. There he was, and with nothing in his aspect or his posture to scandalise: it was only true that if he had seen Mrs. Newsome coming he would instinctively have jumped up to walk away a little. He would have come round and back to her bravely, but he would have had first to pull himself together. She abounded in news of the situation at home, proved to him how perfectly she was arranging for his absence, told him who would take up this and who take up that exactly where he had left it, gave him in fact chapter and verse for the moral that nothing would suffer. It filled for him, this tone of hers, all the air; yet it struck him at the same time as the hum of vain things. This latter effect was what he tried to justify—and with the success that, grave though the appearance, he at last lighted on a form that was happy. He arrived at it by the inevitable recognition of his having been a fortnight before one of the weariest of men. If ever a man had come off tired Lambert Strether was that man; and hadn't it been distinctly on the ground of his fatigue that his wonderful friend at home had so felt for him and so contrived? It seemed to him somehow at these instants that, could he only maintain with sufficient firmness his grasp of that truth, it might become in a manner his compass and his helm. What he wanted most was some idea that would simplify, and nothing would do this so much as the fact that he was done for and finished. If it had been in such a light that he had just detected in his cup the dregs of youth, that was a mere flaw of the surface of his scheme. He was so distinctly fagged-out that it must serve precisely as his convenience, and if he could but consistently be good for little enough he might do everything he wanted.

Everything he wanted was comprised moreover in a single boon—the common unattainable art of taking things as they came. He appeared to himself to have given his best years to an active appreciation of the way they didn't come; but perhaps—as they would seemingly here be things quite other—this long ache might at last drop to rest. He could easily see that from the moment he should accept the notion of his foredoomed collapse the last thing he would lack would be reasons and memories. Oh if he SHOULD do the sum no slate would hold the figures! The fact that he had failed, as he considered, in everything, in each relation and in half a dozen trades, as he liked luxuriously to put it, might have made, might still make, for an empty present; but it stood solidly for a crowded past. It had not been, so much achievement missed, a light yoke nor a short load. It was at present as if the backward picture had hung there, the long crooked course, grey in the shadow of his solitude. It had been a dreadful cheerful sociable solitude, a solitude of life or choice, of community; but though there had been people enough all round it there had been but three or four persons IN it. Waymarsh was one of these, and the fact struck him just now as marking the record. Mrs. Newsome was another, and Miss Gostrey had of a sudden shown signs of becoming a third. Beyond, behind them was the pale figure of his real youth, which held against its breast the two presences paler than itself—the young wife he had early lost and the young son he had stupidly sacrificed. He had again and again made out for himself that he might have kept his little boy, his little dull boy who had died at school of rapid diphtheria, if he had not in those years so insanely given himself to merely missing the mother. It was the soreness of his remorse that the child had in all likelihood not really been dull—had been dull, as he had been banished and neglected, mainly because the father had been unwittingly selfish. This was doubtless but the secret habit of sorrow, which had slowly given way to time; yet there remained an ache sharp enough to make the spirit, at the sight now and again of some fair young man just growing up, wince with the thought of an opportunity lost. Had ever a man, he had finally fallen into the way of asking himself, lost so much and even done so much for so little? There had been particular reasons why all yesterday, beyond other days, he should have had in one ear this cold enquiry. His name on the green cover, where he had put it for Mrs. Newsome, expressed him doubtless just enough to make the world—the world as distinguished, both for more and for less, from Woollett—ask who he was. He had incurred the ridicule of having to have his explanation explained. He was Lambert Strether because he was on the cover, whereas it should have been, for anything like glory, that he was on the cover because he was Lambert Strether. He would have done anything for Mrs. Newsome, have been still more ridiculous—as he might, for that matter, have occasion to be yet; which came to saying that this acceptance of fate was all he had to show at fifty-five.

He judged the quantity as small because it WAS small, and all the more egregiously since it couldn't, as he saw the case, so much as thinkably have been larger. He hadn't had the gift of making the most of what he tried, and if he had tried and tried again—no one but himself knew how often—it appeared to have been that he might demonstrate what else, in default of that, COULD be made. Old ghosts of experiments came back to him, old drudgeries and delusions, and disgusts, old recoveries with their relapses, old fevers with their chills, broken moments of good faith, others of still better doubt; adventures, for the most part, of the sort qualified as lessons. The special spring that had constantly played for him the day before was the recognition—frequent enough to surprise him—of the promises to himself that he had after his other visit never kept. The reminiscence to-day most quickened for him was that of the vow taken in the course of the pilgrimage that, newly-married, with the War just over, and helplessly young in spite of it, he had recklessly made with the creature who was so much younger still. It had been a bold dash, for which they had taken money set apart for necessities, but kept sacred at the moment in a hundred ways, and in none more so than by this private pledge of his own to treat the occasion as a relation formed with the higher culture and see that, as they said at Woollett, it should bear a good harvest. He had believed, sailing home again, that he had gained something great, and his theory—with an elaborate innocent plan of reading, digesting, coming back even, every few years—had then been to preserve, cherish and extend it. As such plans as these had come to nothing, however, in respect to acquisitions still more precious, it was doubtless little enough of a marvel that he should have lost account of that handful of seed. Buried for long years in dark corners at any rate these few germs had sprouted again under forty-eight hours of Paris. The process of yesterday had really been the process of feeling the general stirred life of connexions long since individually dropped. Strether had become acquainted even on this ground with short gusts of speculation—sudden flights of fancy in Louvre galleries, hungry gazes through clear plates behind which lemon-coloured volumes were as fresh as fruit on the tree.

There were instants at which he could ask whether, since there had been fundamentally so little question of his keeping anything, the fate after all decreed for him hadn't been only to BE kept. Kept for something, in that event, that he didn't pretend, didn't possibly dare as yet to divine; something that made him hover and wonder and laugh and sigh, made him advance and retreat, feeling half ashamed of his impulse to plunge and more than half afraid of his impulse to wait. He remembered for instance how he had gone back in the sixties with lemon-coloured volumes in general on the brain as well as with a dozen—selected for his wife too—in his trunk; and nothing had at the moment shown more confidence than this invocation of the finer taste. They were still somewhere at home, the dozen—stale and soiled and never sent to the binder; but what had become of the sharp initiation they represented? They represented now the mere sallow paint on the door of the temple of taste that he had dreamed of raising up—a structure he had practically never carried further. Strether's present highest flights were perhaps those in which this particular lapse figured to him as a symbol, a symbol of his long grind and his want of odd moments, his want moreover of money, of opportunity, of positive dignity. That the memory of the vow of his youth should, in order to throb again, have had to wait for this last, as he felt it, of all his accidents—that was surely proof enough of how his conscience had been encumbered. If any further proof were needed it would have been to be found in the fact that, as he perfectly now saw, he had ceased even to measure his meagreness, a meagreness that sprawled, in this retrospect, vague and comprehensive, stretching back like some unmapped Hinterland from a rough coast-settlement. His conscience had been amusing itself for the forty-eight hours by forbidding him the purchase of a book; he held off from that, held off from everything; from the moment he didn't yet call on Chad he wouldn't for the world have taken any other step. On this evidence, however, of the way they actually affected him he glared at the lemon-coloured covers in confession of the subconsciousness that, all the same, in the great desert of the years, he must have had of them. The green covers at home comprised, by the law of their purpose, no tribute to letters; it was of a mere rich kernel of economics, politics, ethics that, glazed and, as Mrs. Newsome maintained rather against HIS view, pre-eminently pleasant to touch, they formed the specious shell. Without therefore any needed instinctive knowledge of what was coming out, in Paris, on the bright highway, he struck himself at present as having more than once flushed with a suspicion: he couldn't otherwise at present be feeling so many fears confirmed. There were "movements" he was too late for: weren't they, with the fun of them, already spent? There were sequences he had missed and great gaps in the procession: he might have been watching it all recede in a golden cloud of dust. If the playhouse wasn't closed his seat had at least fallen to somebody else. He had had an uneasy feeling the night before that if he was at the theatre at all—though he indeed justified the theatre, in the specific sense, and with a grotesqueness to which his imagination did all honour, as something he owed poor Waymarsh—he should have been there with, and as might have been said, FOR Chad.

This suggested the question of whether he could properly have taken him to such a play, and what effect—it was a point that suddenly rose—his peculiar responsibility might be held in general to have on his choice of entertainment. It had literally been present to him at the Gymnase—where one was held moreover comparatively safe—that having his young friend at his side would have been an odd feature of the work of redemption; and this quite in spite of the fact that the picture presented might well, confronted with Chad's own private stage, have seemed the pattern of propriety. He clearly hadn't come out in the name of propriety but to visit unattended equivocal performances; yet still less had he done so to undermine his authority by sharing them with the graceless youth. Was he to renounce all amusement for the sweet sake of that authority? and WOULD such renouncement give him for Chad a moral glamour? The little problem bristled the more by reason of poor Strether's fairly open sense of the irony of things. Were there then sides on which his predicament threatened to look rather droll to him? Should he have to pretend to believe—either to himself or the wretched boy—that there was anything that could make the latter worse? Wasn't some such pretence on the other hand involved in the assumption of possible processes that would make him better? His greatest uneasiness seemed to peep at him out of the imminent impression that almost any acceptance of Paris might give one's authority away. It hung before him this morning, the vast bright Babylon, like some huge iridescent object, a jewel brilliant and hard, in which parts were not to be discriminated nor differences comfortably marked. It twinkled and trembled and melted together, and what seemed all surface one moment seemed all depth the next. It was a place of which, unmistakeably, Chad was fond; wherefore if he, Strether, should like it too much, what on earth, with such a bond, would become of either of them? It all depended of course—which was a gleam of light—on how the "too much" was measured; though indeed our friend fairly felt, while he prolonged the meditation I describe, that for himself even already a certain measure had been reached. It will have been sufficiently seen that he was not a man to neglect any good chance for reflexion. Was it at all possible for instance to like Paris enough without liking it too much? He luckily however hadn't promised Mrs. Newsome not to like it at all. He was ready to recognise at this stage that such an engagement WOULD have tied his hands. The Luxembourg Gardens were incontestably just so adorable at this hour by reason—in addition to their intrinsic charm—of his not having taken it. The only engagement he had taken, when he looked the thing in the face, was to do what he reasonably could.

It upset him a little none the less and after a while to find himself at last remembering on what current of association he had been floated so far. Old imaginations of the Latin Quarter had played their part for him, and he had duly recalled its having been with this scene of rather ominous legend that, like so many young men in fiction as well as in fact, Chad had begun. He was now quite out of it, with his "home," as Strether figured the place, in the Boulevard Malesherbes; which was perhaps why, repairing, not to fail of justice either, to the elder neighbourhood, our friend had felt he could allow for the element of the usual, the immemorial, without courting perturbation. He was not at least in danger of seeing the youth and the particular Person flaunt by together; and yet he was in the very air of which—just to feel what the early natural note must have been—he wished most to take counsel. It became at once vivid to him that he had originally had, for a few days, an almost envious vision of the boy's romantic privilege. Melancholy Murger, with Francine and Musette and Rodolphe, at home, in the company of the tattered, one—if he not in his single self two or three—of the unbound, the paper-covered dozen on the shelf; and when Chad had written, five years ago, after a sojourn then already prolonged to six months, that he had decided to go in for economy and the real thing, Strether's fancy had quite fondly accompanied him in this migration, which was to convey him, as they somewhat confusedly learned at Woollett, across the bridges and up the Montagne Sainte-Genevieve. This was the region—Chad had been quite distinct about it—in which the best French, and many other things, were to be learned at least cost, and in which all sorts of clever fellows, compatriots there for a purpose, formed an awfully pleasant set. The clever fellows, the friendly countrymen were mainly young painters, sculptors, architects, medical students; but they were, Chad sagely opined, a much more profitable lot to be with—even on the footing of not being quite one of them—than the "terrible toughs" (Strether remembered the edifying discrimination) of the American bars and banks roundabout the Opera. Chad had thrown out, in the communications following this one—for at that time he did once in a while communicate—that several members of a band of earnest workers under one of the great artists had taken him right in, making him dine every night, almost for nothing, at their place, and even pressing him not to neglect the hypothesis of there being as much "in him" as in any of them. There had been literally a moment at which it appeared there might be something in him; there had been at any rate a moment at which he had written that he didn't know but what a month or two more might see him enrolled in some atelier. The season had been one at which Mrs. Newsome was moved to gratitude for small mercies; it had broken on them all as a blessing that their absentee HAD perhaps a conscience—that he was sated in fine with idleness, was ambitious of variety. The exhibition was doubtless as yet not brilliant, but Strether himself, even by that time much enlisted and immersed, had determined, on the part of the two ladies, a temperate approval and in fact, as he now recollected, a certain austere enthusiasm.

But the very next thing that happened had been a dark drop of the curtain. The son and brother had not browsed long on the Montagne Sainte-Genevieve—his effective little use of the name of which, like his allusion to the best French, appeared to have been but one of the notes of his rough cunning. The light refreshment of these vain appearances had not accordingly carried any of them very far. On the other hand it had gained Chad time; it had given him a chance, unchecked, to strike his roots, had paved the way for initiations more direct and more deep. It was Strether's belief that he had been comparatively innocent before this first migration, and even that the first effects of the migration would not have been, without some particular bad accident, to have been deplored. There had been three months—he had sufficiently figured it out—in which Chad had wanted to try. He HAD tried, though not very hard—he had had his little hour of good faith. The weakness of this principle in him was that almost any accident attestedly bad enough was stronger. Such had at any rate markedly been the case for the precipitation of a special series of impressions. They had proved, successively, these impressions—all of Musette and Francine, but Musette and Francine vulgarised by the larger evolution of the type—irresistibly sharp: he had "taken up," by what was at the time to be shrinkingly gathered, as it was scantly mentioned, with one ferociously "interested" little person after another. Strether had read somewhere of a Latin motto, a description of the hours, observed on a clock by a traveller in Spain; and he had been led to apply it in thought to Chad's number one, number two, number three. Omnes vulnerant, ultima necat—they had all morally wounded, the last had morally killed. The last had been longest in possession—in possession, that is, of whatever was left of the poor boy's finer mortality. And it hadn't been she, it had been one of her early predecessors, who had determined the second migration, the expensive return and relapse, the exchange again, as was fairly to be presumed, of the vaunted best French for some special variety of the worst.

He pulled himself then at last together for his own progress back; not with the feeling that he had taken his walk in vain. He prolonged it a little, in the immediate neighbourhood, after he had quitted his chair; and the upshot of the whole morning for him was that his campaign had begun. He had wanted to put himself in relation, and he would be hanged if he were NOT in relation. He was that at no moment so much as while, under the old arches of the Odeon, he lingered before the charming open-air array of literature classic and casual. He found the effect of tone and tint, in the long charged tables and shelves, delicate and appetising; the impression—substituting one kind of low-priced consommation for another—might have been that of one of the pleasant cafes that overlapped, under an awning, to the pavement; but he edged along, grazing the tables, with his hands firmly behind him. He wasn't there to dip, to consume—he was there to reconstruct. He wasn't there for his own profit—not, that is, the direct; he was there on some chance of feeling the brush of the wing of the stray spirit of youth. He felt it in fact, he had it beside him; the old arcade indeed, as his inner sense listened, gave out the faint sound, as from far off, of the wild waving of wings. They were folded now over the breasts of buried generations; but a flutter or two lived again in the turned page of shock-headed slouch-hatted loiterers whose young intensity of type, in the direction of pale acuteness, deepened his vision, and even his appreciation, of racial differences, and whose manipulation of the uncut volume was too often, however, but a listening at closed doors. He reconstructed a possible groping Chad of three or four years before, a Chad who had, after all, simply—for that was the only way to see it—been too vulgar for his privilege. Surely it WAS a privilege to have been young and happy just there. Well, the best thing Strether knew of him was that he had had such a dream.

But his own actual business half an hour later was with a third floor on the Boulevard Malesherbes—so much as that was definite; and the fact of the enjoyment by the third-floor windows of a continuous balcony, to which he was helped by this knowledge, had perhaps something to do with his lingering for five minutes on the opposite side of the street. There were points as to which he had quite made up his mind, and one of these bore precisely on the wisdom of the abruptness to which events had finally committed him, a policy that he was pleased to find not at all shaken as he now looked at his watch and wondered. He HAD announced himself—six months before; had written out at least that Chad wasn't to be surprised should he see him some day turn up. Chad had thereupon, in a few words of rather carefully colourless answer, offered him a general welcome; and Strether, ruefully reflecting that he might have understood the warning as a hint to hospitality, a bid for an invitation, had fallen back upon silence as the corrective most to his own taste. He had asked Mrs. Newsome moreover not to announce him again; he had so distinct an opinion on his attacking his job, should he attack it at all, in his own way. Not the least of this lady's high merits for him was that he could absolutely rest on her word. She was the only woman he had known, even at Woollett, as to whom his conviction was positive that to lie was beyond her art. Sarah Pocock, for instance, her own daughter, though with social ideals, as they said, in some respects different—Sarah who WAS, in her way, aesthetic, had never refused to human commerce that mitigation of rigour; there were occasions when he had distinctly seen her apply it. Since, accordingly, at all events, he had had it from Mrs. Newsome that she had, at whatever cost to her more strenuous view, conformed, in the matter of preparing Chad, wholly to his restrictions, he now looked up at the fine continuous balcony with a safe sense that if the case had been bungled the mistake was at least his property. Was there perhaps just a suspicion of that in his present pause on the edge of the Boulevard and well in the pleasant light?

Many things came over him here, and one of them was that he should doubtless presently know whether he had been shallow or sharp. Another was that the balcony in question didn't somehow show as a convenience easy to surrender. Poor Strether had at this very moment to recognise the truth that wherever one paused in Paris the imagination reacted before one could stop it. This perpetual reaction put a price, if one would, on pauses; but it piled up consequences till there was scarce room to pick one's steps among them. What call had he, at such a juncture, for example, to like Chad's very house? High broad clear—he was expert enough to make out in a moment that it was admirably built—it fairly embarrassed our friend by the quality that, as he would have said, it "sprang" on him. He had struck off the fancy that it might, as a preliminary, be of service to him to be seen, by a happy accident, from the third-story windows, which took all the March sun, but of what service was it to find himself making out after a moment that the quality "sprung," the quality produced by measure and balance, the fine relation of part to part and space to space, was probably—aided by the presence of ornament as positive as it was discreet, and by the complexion of the stone, a cold fair grey, warmed and polished a little by life—neither more nor less than a case of distinction, such a case as he could only feel unexpectedly as a sort of delivered challenge? Meanwhile, however, the chance he had allowed for—the chance of being seen in time from the balcony—had become a fact. Two or three of the windows stood open to the violet air; and, before Strether had cut the knot by crossing, a young man had come out and looked about him, had lighted a cigarette and tossed the match over, and then, resting on the rail, had given himself up to watching the life below while he smoked. His arrival contributed, in its order, to keeping Strether in position; the result of which in turn was that Strether soon felt himself noticed. The young man began to look at him as in acknowledgement of his being himself in observation.

This was interesting so far as it went, but the interest was affected by the young man's not being Chad. Strether wondered at first if he were perhaps Chad altered, and then saw that this was asking too much of alteration. The young man was light bright and alert—with an air too pleasant to have been arrived at by patching. Strether had conceived Chad as patched, but not beyond recognition. He was in presence, he felt, of amendments enough as they stood; it was a sufficient amendment that the gentleman up there should be Chad's friend. He was young too then, the gentleman up there—he was very young; young enough apparently to be amused at an elderly watcher, to be curious even to see what the elderly watcher would do on finding himself watched. There was youth in that, there was youth in the surrender to the balcony, there was youth for Strether at this moment in everything but his own business; and Chad's thus pronounced association with youth had given the next instant an extraordinary quick lift to the issue. The balcony, the distinguished front, testified suddenly, for Strether's fancy, to something that was up and up; they placed the whole case materially, and as by an admirable image, on a level that he found himself at the end of another moment rejoicing to think he might reach. The young man looked at him still, he looked at the young man; and the issue, by a rapid process, was that this knowledge of a perched privacy appeared to him the last of luxuries. To him too the perched privacy was open, and he saw it now but in one light—that of the only domicile, the only fireside, in the great ironic city, on which he had the shadow of a claim. Miss Gostrey had a fireside; she had told him of it, and it was something that doubtless awaited him; but Miss Gostrey hadn't yet arrived—she mightn't arrive for days; and the sole attenuation of his excluded state was his vision of the small, the admittedly secondary hotel in the bye-street from the Rue de la Paix, in which her solicitude for his purse had placed him, which affected him somehow as all indoor chill, glass-roofed court and slippery staircase, and which, by the same token, expressed the presence of Waymarsh even at times when Waymarsh might have been certain to be round at the bank. It came to pass before he moved that Waymarsh, and Waymarsh alone, Waymarsh not only undiluted but positively strengthened, struck him as the present alternative to the young man in the balcony. When he did move it was fairly to escape that alternative. Taking his way over the street at last and passing through the porte-cochere of the house was like consciously leaving Waymarsh out. However, he would tell him all about it.

Book Third

I

Strether told Waymarsh all about it that very evening, on their dining together at the hotel; which needn't have happened, he was all the while aware, hadn't he chosen to sacrifice to this occasion a rarer opportunity. The mention to his companion of the sacrifice was moreover exactly what introduced his recital—or, as he would have called it with more confidence in his interlocutor, his confession. His confession was that he had been captured and that one of the features of the affair had just failed to be his engaging himself on the spot to dinner. As by such a freedom Waymarsh would have lost him he had obeyed his scruple; and he had likewise obeyed another scruple—which bore on the question of his himself bringing a guest.

Waymarsh looked gravely ardent, over the finished soup, at this array of scruples; Strether hadn't yet got quite used to being so unprepared for the consequences of the impression he produced. It was comparatively easy to explain, however, that he hadn't felt sure his guest would please. The person was a young man whose acquaintance he had made but that afternoon in the course of rather a hindered enquiry for another person—an enquiry his new friend had just prevented in fact from being vain. "Oh," said Strether, "I've all sorts of things to tell you!"—and he put it in a way that was a virtual hint to Waymarsh to help him to enjoy the telling. He waited for his fish, he drank of his wine, he wiped his long moustache, he leaned back in his chair, he took in the two English ladies who had just creaked past them and whom he would even have articulately greeted if they hadn't rather chilled the impulse; so that all he could do was—by way of doing something—to say "Merci, Francois!" out quite loud when his fish was brought. Everything was there that he wanted, everything that could make the moment an occasion, that would do beautifully—everything but what Waymarsh might give. The little waxed salle-a-manger was sallow and sociable; Francois, dancing over it, all smiles, was a man and a brother; the high-shouldered patronne, with her high-held, much-rubbed hands, seemed always assenting exuberantly to something unsaid; the Paris evening in short was, for Strether, in the very taste of the soup, in the goodness, as he was innocently pleased to think it, of the wine, in the pleasant coarse texture of the napkin and the crunch of the thick-crusted bread. These all were things congruous with his confession, and his confession was that he HAD—it would come out properly just there if Waymarsh would only take it properly—agreed to breakfast out, at twelve literally, the next day. He didn't quite know where; the delicacy of the case came straight up in the remembrance of his new friend's "We'll see; I'll take you somewhere!"—for it had required little more than that, after all, to let him right in. He was affected after a minute, face to face with his actual comrade, by the impulse to overcolour. There had already been things in respect to which he knew himself tempted by this perversity. If Waymarsh thought them bad he should at least have his reason for his discomfort; so Strether showed them as worse. Still, he was now, in his way, sincerely perplexed.

Chad had been absent from the Boulevard Malesherbes—was absent from Paris altogether; he had learned that from the concierge, but had nevertheless gone up, and gone up—there were no two ways about it—from an uncontrollable, a really, if one would, depraved curiosity. The concierge had mentioned to him that a friend of the tenant of the troisieme was for the time in possession; and this had been Strether's pretext for a further enquiry, an experiment carried on, under Chad's roof, without his knowledge. "I found his friend in fact there keeping the place warm, as he called it, for him; Chad himself being, as appears, in the south. He went a month ago to Cannes and though his return begins to be looked for it can't be for some days. I might, you see, perfectly have waited a week; might have beaten a retreat as soon as I got this essential knowledge. But I beat no retreat; I did the opposite; I stayed, I dawdled, I trifled; above all I looked round. I saw, in fine; and—I don't know what to call it—I sniffed. It's a detail, but it's as if there were something—something very good—TO sniff."

Waymarsh's face had shown his friend an attention apparently so remote that the latter was slightly surprised to find it at this point abreast with him. "Do you mean a smell? What of?"

"A charming scent. But I don't know."

Waymarsh gave an inferential grunt. "Does he live there with a woman?"

"I don't know."

Waymarsh waited an instant for more, then resumed. "Has he taken her off with him?"

"And will he bring her back?"—Strether fell into the enquiry. But he wound it up as before. "I don't know."

The way he wound it up, accompanied as this was with another drop back, another degustation of the Leoville, another wipe of his moustache and another good word for Francois, seemed to produce in his companion a slight irritation. "Then what the devil DO you know?"

"Well," said Strether almost gaily, "I guess I don't know anything!" His gaiety might have been a tribute to the fact that the state he had been reduced to did for him again what had been done by his talk of the matter with Miss Gostrey at the London theatre. It was somehow enlarging; and the air of that amplitude was now doubtless more or less—and all for Waymarsh to feel—in his further response. "That's what I found out from the young man."

"But I thought you said you found out nothing."

"Nothing but that—that I don't know anything."

"And what good does that do you?"

"It's just," said Strether, "what I've come to you to help me to discover. I mean anything about anything over here. I FELT that, up there. It regularly rose before me in its might. The young man moreover—Chad's friend—as good as told me so."

"As good as told you you know nothing about anything?" Waymarsh appeared to look at some one who might have as good as told HIM. "How old is he?"

"Well, I guess not thirty."

"Yet you had to take that from him?"

"Oh I took a good deal more—since, as I tell you, I took an invitation to dejeuner."

"And are you GOING to that unholy meal?"

"If you'll come with me. He wants you too, you know. I told him about you. He gave me his card," Strether pursued, "and his name's rather funny. It's John Little Bilham, and he says his two surnames are, on account of his being small, inevitably used together."

"Well," Waymarsh asked with due detachment from these details, "what's he doing up there?"

"His account of himself is that he's 'only a little artist-man.' That seemed to me perfectly to describe him. But he's yet in the phase of study; this, you know, is the great art-school—to pass a certain number of years in which he came over. And he's a great friend of Chad's, and occupying Chad's rooms just now because they're so pleasant. HE'S very pleasant and curious too," Strether added—"though he's not from Boston."

Waymarsh looked already rather sick of him. "Where is he from?"

Strether thought. "I don't know that, either. But he's 'notoriously,' as he put it himself, not from Boston."

"Well," Waymarsh moralised from dry depths, "every one can't notoriously be from Boston. Why," he continued, "is he curious?"

"Perhaps just for THAT—for one thing! But really," Strether added, "for everything. When you meet him you'll see."

"Oh I don't want to meet him," Waymarsh impatiently growled. "Why don't he go home?"

Strether hesitated. "Well, because he likes it over here."

This appeared in particular more than Waymarsh could bear. "He ought then to be ashamed of himself, and, as you admit that you think so too, why drag him in?"

Strether's reply again took time. "Perhaps I do think so myself—though I don't quite yet admit it. I'm not a bit sure—it's again one of the things I want to find out. I liked him, and CAN you like people—? But no matter." He pulled himself up. "There's no doubt I want you to come down on me and squash me."

Waymarsh helped himself to the next course, which, however proving not the dish he had just noted as supplied to the English ladies, had the effect of causing his imagination temporarily to wander. But it presently broke out at a softer spot. "Have they got a handsome place up there?"

"Oh a charming place; full of beautiful and valuable things. I never saw such a place"—and Strether's thought went back to it. "For a little artist-man—!" He could in fact scarce express it.

But his companion, who appeared now to have a view, insisted. "Well?"

"Well, life can hold nothing better. Besides, they're things of which he's in charge."

"So that he does doorkeeper for your precious pair? Can life," Waymarsh enquired, "hold nothing better than THAT?" Then as Strether, silent, seemed even yet to wonder, "Doesn't he know what SHE is?" he went on.

"I don't know. I didn't ask him. I couldn't. It was impossible. You wouldn't either. Besides I didn't want to. No more would you." Strether in short explained it at a stroke. "You can't make out over here what people do know."

"Then what did you come over for?"

"Well, I suppose exactly to see for myself—without their aid."

"Then what do you want mine for?"

"Oh," Strether laughed, "you're not one of THEM! I do know what you know."

As, however, this last assertion caused Waymarsh again to look at him hard—such being the latter's doubt of its implications—he felt his justification lame. Which was still more the case when Waymarsh presently said: "Look here, Strether. Quit this."

Our friend smiled with a doubt of his own. "Do you mean my tone?"

"No—damn your tone. I mean your nosing round. Quit the whole job. Let them stew in their juice. You're being used for a thing you ain't fit for. People don't take a fine-tooth comb to groom a horse."

"Am I a fine-tooth comb?" Strether laughed. "It's something I never called myself!"

"It's what you are, all the same. You ain't so young as you were, but you've kept your teeth."

He acknowledged his friend's humour. "Take care I don't get them into YOU! You'd like them, my friends at home, Waymarsh," he declared; "you'd really particularly like them. And I know"—it was slightly irrelevant, but he gave it sudden and singular force—"I know they'd like you!"

"Oh don't work them off on ME!" Waymarsh groaned.

Yet Strether still lingered with his hands in his pockets. "It's really quite as indispensable as I say that Chad should be got back."

"Indispensable to whom? To you?"

"Yes," Strether presently said.

"Because if you get him you also get Mrs. Newsome?"

Strether faced it. "Yes."

"And if you don't get him you don't get her?"

It might be merciless, but he continued not to flinch. "I think it might have some effect on our personal understanding. Chad's of real importance—or can easily become so if he will—to the business."

"And the business is of real importance to his mother's husband?"

"Well, I naturally want what my future wife wants. And the thing will be much better if we have our own man in it."

"If you have your own man in it, in other words," Waymarsh said, "you'll marry—you personally—more money. She's already rich, as I understand you, but she'll be richer still if the business can be made to boom on certain lines that you've laid down."

"I haven't laid them down," Strether promptly returned. "Mr. Newsome—who knew extraordinarily well what he was about—laid them down ten years ago."

Oh well, Waymarsh seemed to indicate with a shake of his mane, THAT didn't matter! "You're fierce for the boom anyway."

His friend weighed a moment in silence the justice of the charge. "I can scarcely be called fierce, I think, when I so freely take my chance of the possibility, the danger, of being influenced in a sense counter to Mrs. Newsome's own feelings."

Waymarsh gave this proposition a long hard look. "I see. You're afraid yourself of being squared. But you're a humbug," he added, "all the same."

"Oh!" Strether quickly protested.

"Yes, you ask me for protection—which makes you very interesting; and then you won't take it. You say you want to be squashed—"

"Ah but not so easily! Don't you see," Strether demanded "where my interest, as already shown you, lies? It lies in my not being squared. If I'm squared where's my marriage? If I miss my errand I miss that; and if I miss that I miss everything—I'm nowhere."

Waymarsh—but all relentlessly—took this in. "What do I care where you are if you're spoiled?"

Their eyes met on it an instant. "Thank you awfully," Strether at last said. "But don't you think HER judgement of that—?"

"Ought to content me? No."

It kept them again face to face, and the end of this was that Strether again laughed. "You do her injustice. You really MUST know her. Good-night."

He breakfasted with Mr. Bilham on the morrow, and, as inconsequently befell, with Waymarsh massively of the party. The latter announced, at the eleventh hour and much to his friend's surprise, that, damn it, he would as soon join him as do anything else; on which they proceeded together, strolling in a state of detachment practically luxurious for them to the Boulevard Malesherbes, a couple engaged that day with the sharp spell of Paris as confessedly, it might have been seen, as any couple among the daily thousands so compromised. They walked, wandered, wondered and, a little, lost themselves; Strether hadn't had for years so rich a consciousness of time—a bag of gold into which he constantly dipped for a handful. It was present to him that when the little business with Mr. Bilham should be over he would still have shining hours to use absolutely as he liked. There was no great pulse of haste yet in this process of saving Chad; nor was that effect a bit more marked as he sat, half an hour later, with his legs under Chad's mahogany, with Mr. Bilham on one side, with a friend of Mr. Bilham's on the other, with Waymarsh stupendously opposite, and with the great hum of Paris coming up in softness, vagueness-for Strether himself indeed already positive sweetness—through the sunny windows toward which, the day before, his curiosity had raised its wings from below. The feeling strongest with him at that moment had borne fruit almost faster than he could taste it, and Strether literally felt at the present hour that there was a precipitation in his fate. He had known nothing and nobody as he stood in the street; but hadn't his view now taken a bound in the direction of every one and of every thing?

"What's he up to, what's he up to?"—something like that was at the back of his head all the while in respect to little Bilham; but meanwhile, till he should make out, every one and every thing were as good as represented for him by the combination of his host and the lady on his left. The lady on his left, the lady thus promptly and ingeniously invited to "meet" Mr. Strether and Mr. Waymarsh—it was the way she herself expressed her case—was a very marked person, a person who had much to do with our friend's asking himself if the occasion weren't in its essence the most baited, the most gilded of traps. Baited it could properly be called when the repast was of so wise a savour, and gilded surrounding objects seemed inevitably to need to be when Miss Barrace—which was the lady's name—looked at them with convex Parisian eyes and through a glass with a remarkably long tortoise-shell handle. Why Miss Barrace, mature meagre erect and eminently gay, highly adorned, perfectly familiar, freely contradictions and reminding him of some last-century portrait of a clever head without powder—why Miss Barrace should have been in particular the note of a "trap" Strether couldn't on the spot have explained; he blinked in the light of a conviction that he should know later on, and know well—as it came over him, for that matter, with force, that he should need to. He wondered what he was to think exactly of either of his new friends; since the young man, Chad's intimate and deputy, had, in thus constituting the scene, practised so much more subtly than he had been prepared for, and since in especial Miss Barrace, surrounded clearly by every consideration, hadn't scrupled to figure as a familiar object. It was interesting to him to feel that he was in the presence of new measures, other standards, a different scale of relations, and that evidently here were a happy pair who didn't think of things at all as he and Waymarsh thought. Nothing was less to have been calculated in the business than that it should now be for him as if he and Waymarsh were comparatively quite at one.

The latter was magnificent—this at least was an assurance privately given him by Miss Barrace. "Oh your friend's a type, the grand old American—what shall one call it? The Hebrew prophet, Ezekiel, Jeremiah, who used when I was a little girl in the Rue Montaigne to come to see my father and who was usually the American Minister to the Tuileries or some other court. I haven't seen one these ever so many years; the sight of it warms my poor old chilled heart; this specimen is wonderful; in the right quarter, you know, he'll have a succes fou." Strether hadn't failed to ask what the right quarter might be, much as he required his presence of mind to meet such a change in their scheme. "Oh the artist-quarter and that kind of thing; HERE already, for instance, as you see." He had been on the point of echoing "'Here'?—is THIS the artist-quarter?" but she had already disposed of the question with a wave of all her tortoise-shell and an easy "Bring him to ME!" He knew on the spot how little he should be able to bring him, for the very air was by this time, to his sense, thick and hot with poor Way-Waymarsh's judgement of it. He was in the trap still more than his companion and, unlike his companion, not making the best of it; which was precisely what doubtless gave him his admirable sombre glow. Little did Miss Barrace know that what was behind it was his grave estimate of her own laxity. The general assumption with which our two friends had arrived had been that of finding Mr. Bilham ready to conduct them to one or other of those resorts of the earnest, the aesthetic fraternity which were shown among the sights of Paris. In this character it would have justified them in a proper insistence on discharging their score. Waymarsh's only proviso at the last had been that nobody should pay for him; but he found himself, as the occasion developed, paid for on a scale as to which Strether privately made out that he already nursed retribution. Strether was conscious across the table of what worked in him, conscious when they passed back to the small salon to which, the previous evening, he himself had made so rich a reference; conscious most of all as they stepped out to the balcony in which one would have had to be an ogre not to recognise the perfect place for easy aftertastes. These things were enhanced for Miss Barrace by a succession of excellent cigarettes—acknowledged, acclaimed, as a part of the wonderful supply left behind him by Chad—in an almost equal absorption of which Strether found himself blindly, almost wildly pushing forward. He might perish by the sword as well as by famine, and he knew that his having abetted the lady by an excess that was rare with him would count for little in the sum—as Waymarsh might so easily add it up—of her licence. Waymarsh had smoked of old, smoked hugely; but Waymarsh did nothing now, and that gave him his advantage over people who took things up lightly just when others had laid them heavily down. Strether had never smoked, and he felt as if he flaunted at his friend that this had been only because of a reason. The reason, it now began to appear even to himself, was that he had never had a lady to smoke with.

It was this lady's being there at all, however, that was the strange free thing; perhaps, since she WAS there, her smoking was the least of her freedoms. If Strether had been sure at each juncture of what—with Bilham in especial—she talked about, he might have traced others and winced at them and felt Waymarsh wince; but he was in fact so often at sea that his sense of the range of reference was merely general and that he on several different occasions guessed and interpreted only to doubt. He wondered what they meant, but there were things he scarce thought they could be supposed to mean, and "Oh no—not THAT!" was at the end of most of his ventures. This was the very beginning with him of a condition as to which, later on, it will be seen, he found cause to pull himself up; and he was to remember the moment duly as the first step in a process. The central fact of the place was neither more nor less, when analysed—and a pressure superficial sufficed—than the fundamental impropriety of Chad's situation, round about which they thus seemed cynically clustered. Accordingly, since they took it for granted, they took for granted all that was in connexion with it taken for granted at Woollett—matters as to which, verily, he had been reduced with Mrs. Newsome to the last intensity of silence. That was the consequence of their being too bad to be talked about, and was the accompaniment, by the same token, of a deep conception of their badness. It befell therefore that when poor Strether put it to himself that their badness was ultimately, or perhaps even insolently, what such a scene as the one before him was, so to speak, built upon, he could scarce shirk the dilemma of reading a roundabout echo of them into almost anything that came up. This, he was well aware, was a dreadful necessity; but such was the stern logic, he could only gather, of a relation to the irregular life.

It was the way the irregular life sat upon Bilham and Miss Barrace that was the insidious, the delicate marvel. He was eager to concede that their relation to it was all indirect, for anything else in him would have shown the grossness of bad manners; but the indirectness was none the less consonant—THAT was striking-with a grateful enjoyment of everything that was Chad's. They spoke of him repeatedly, invoking his good name and good nature, and the worst confusion of mind for Strether was that all their mention of him was of a kind to do him honour. They commended his munificence and approved his taste, and in doing so sat down, as it seemed to Strether, in the very soil out of which these things flowered. Our friend's final predicament was that he himself was sitting down, for the time, WITH them, and there was a supreme moment at which, compared with his collapse, Waymarsh's erectness affected him as really high. One thing was certain—he saw he must make up his mind. He must approach Chad, must wait for him, deal with him, master him, but he mustn't dispossess himself of the faculty of seeing things as they were. He must bring him to HIM—not go himself, as it were, so much of the way. He must at any rate be clearer as to what—should he continue to do that for convenience—he was still condoning. It was on the detail of this quantity—and what could the fact be but mystifying?-that Bilham and Miss Barrace threw so little light. So there they were.

II

When Miss Gostrey arrived, at the end of a week, she made him a sign; he went immediately to see her, and it wasn't till then that he could again close his grasp on the idea of a corrective. This idea however was luckily all before him again from the moment he crossed the threshold of the little entresol of the Quartier Marboeuf into which she had gathered, as she said, picking them up in a thousand flights and funny little passionate pounces, the makings of a final nest. He recognised in an instant that there really, there only, he should find the boon with the vision of which he had first mounted Chad's stairs. He might have been a little scared at the picture of how much more, in this place, he should know himself "in" hadn't his friend been on the spot to measure the amount to his appetite. Her compact and crowded little chambers, almost dusky, as they at first struck him, with accumulations, represented a supreme general adjustment to opportunities and conditions. Wherever he looked he saw an old ivory or an old brocade, and he scarce knew where to sit for fear of a misappliance. The life of the occupant struck him of a sudden as more charged with possession even than Chad's or than Miss Barrace's; wide as his glimpse had lately become of the empire of "things," what was before him still enlarged it; the lust of the eyes and the pride of life had indeed thus their temple. It was the innermost nook of the shrine—as brown as a pirate's cave. In the brownness were glints of gold; patches of purple were in the gloom; objects all that caught, through the muslin, with their high rarity, the light of the low windows. Nothing was clear about them but that they were precious, and they brushed his ignorance with their contempt as a flower, in a liberty taken with him, might have been whisked under his nose. But after a full look at his hostess he knew none the less what most concerned him. The circle in which they stood together was warm with life, and every question between them would live there as nowhere else. A question came up as soon as they had spoken, for his answer, with a laugh, was quickly: "Well, they've got hold of me!" Much of their talk on this first occasion was his development of that truth. He was extraordinarily glad to see her, expressing to her frankly what she most showed him, that one might live for years without a blessing unsuspected, but that to know it at last for no more than three days was to need it or miss it for ever. She was the blessing that had now become his need, and what could prove it better than that without her he had lost himself?

"What do you mean?" she asked with an absence of alarm that, correcting him as if he had mistaken the "period" of one of her pieces, gave him afresh a sense of her easy movement through the maze he had but begun to tread. "What in the name of all the Pococks have you managed to do?"

"Why exactly the wrong thing. I've made a frantic friend of little Bilham."

"Ah that sort of thing was of the essence of your case and to have been allowed for from the first." And it was only after this that, quite as a minor matter, she asked who in the world little Bilham might be. When she learned that he was a friend of Chad's and living for the time in Chad's rooms in Chad's absence, quite as if acting in Chad's spirit and serving Chad's cause, she showed, however, more interest. "Should you mind my seeing him? Only once, you know," she added.

"Oh the oftener the better: he's amusing—he's original."

"He doesn't shock you?" Miss Gostrey threw out.

"Never in the world! We escape that with a perfection—! I feel it to be largely, no doubt, because I don't half-understand him; but our modus vivendi isn't spoiled even by that. You must dine with me to meet him," Strether went on. "Then you'll see.'

"Are you giving dinners?"

"Yes—there I am. That's what I mean."

All her kindness wondered. "That you're spending too much money?"

"Dear no—they seem to cost so little. But that I do it to THEM. I ought to hold off."

She thought again—she laughed. "The money you must be spending to think it cheap! But I must be out of it—to the naked eye."

He looked for a moment as if she were really failing him. "Then you won't meet them?" It was almost as if she had developed an unexpected personal prudence.

She hesitated. "Who are they—first?"

"Why little Bilham to begin with." He kept back for the moment Miss Barrace. "And Chad—when he comes—you must absolutely see."

"When then does he come?"

"When Bilham has had time to write him, and hear from him about me. Bilham, however," he pursued, "will report favourably—favourably for Chad. That will make him not afraid to come. I want you the more therefore, you see, for my bluff."

"Oh you'll do yourself for your bluff." She was perfectly easy. "At the rate you've gone I'm quiet."

"Ah but I haven't," said Strether, "made one protest."

She turned it over. "Haven't you been seeing what there's to protest about?"

He let her, with this, however ruefully, have the whole truth. "I haven't yet found a single thing."

"Isn't there any one WITH him then?"

"Of the sort I came out about?" Strether took a moment. "How do I know? And what do I care?"

"Oh oh!"—and her laughter spread. He was struck in fact by the effect on her of his joke. He saw now how he meant it as a joke. SHE saw, however, still other things, though in an instant she had hidden them. "You've got at no facts at all?"

He tried to muster them. "Well, he has a lovely home."

"Ah that, in Paris," she quickly returned, "proves nothing. That is rather it DISproves nothing. They may very well, you see, the people your mission is concerned with, have done it FOR him."

"Exactly. And it was on the scene of their doings then that Waymarsh and I sat guzzling."

"Oh if you forbore to guzzle here on scenes of doings," she replied, "you might easily die of starvation." With which she smiled at him. "You've worse before you."

"Ah I've EVERYTHING before me. But on our hypothesis, you know, they must be wonderful."

"They ARE!" said Miss Gostrey. "You're not therefore, you see," she added, "wholly without facts. They've BEEN, in effect, wonderful."

To have got at something comparatively definite appeared at last a little to help—a wave by which moreover, the next moment, recollection was washed. "My young man does admit furthermore that they're our friend's great interest."

"Is that the expression he uses?"

Strether more exactly recalled. "No—not quite."

"Something more vivid? Less?"

He had bent, with neared glasses, over a group of articles on a small stand; and at this he came up. "It was a mere allusion, but, on the lookout as I was, it struck me. 'Awful, you know, as Chad is'—those were Bilham's words."

"'Awful, you know'—? Oh!"—and Miss Gostrey turned them over. She seemed, however, satisfied. "Well, what more do you want?"

He glanced once more at a bibelot or two, and everything sent him back. "But it is all the same as if they wished to let me have it between the eyes."

She wondered. "Quoi donc?"

"Why what I speak of. The amenity. They can stun you with that as well as with anything else."

"Oh," she answered, "you'll come round! I must see them each," she went on, "for myself. I mean Mr. Bilham and Mr. Newsome—Mr. Bilham naturally first. Once only—once for each; that will do. But face to face—for half an hour. What's Mr. Chad," she immediately pursued, "doing at Cannes? Decent men don't go to Cannes with the—well, with the kind of ladies you mean."

"Don't they?" Strether asked with an interest in decent men that amused her.

"No, elsewhere, but not to Cannes. Cannes is different. Cannes is better. Cannes is best. I mean it's all people you know—when you do know them. And if HE does, why that's different too. He must have gone alone. She can't be with him."

"I haven't," Strether confessed in his weakness, "the least idea." There seemed much in what she said, but he was able after a little to help her to a nearer impression. The meeting with little Bilham took place, by easy arrangement, in the great gallery of the Louvre; and when, standing with his fellow visitor before one of the splendid Titians—the overwhelming portrait of the young man with the strangely-shaped glove and the blue-grey eyes—he turned to see the third member of their party advance from the end of the waxed and gilded vista, he had a sense of having at last taken hold. He had agreed with Miss Gostrey—it dated even from Chester—for a morning at the Louvre, and he had embraced independently the same idea as thrown out by little Bilham, whom he had already accompanied to the museum of the Luxembourg. The fusion of these schemes presented no difficulty, and it was to strike him again that in little Bilham's company contrarieties in general dropped.

"Oh he's all right—he's one of US!" Miss Gostrey, after the first exchange, soon found a chance to murmur to her companion; and Strether, as they proceeded and paused and while a quick unanimity between the two appeared to have phrased itself in half a dozen remarks—Strether knew that he knew almost immediately what she meant, and took it as still another sign that he had got his job in hand. This was the more grateful to him that he could think of the intelligence now serving him as an acquisition positively new. He wouldn't have known even the day before what she meant—that is if she meant, what he assumed, that they were intense Americans together. He had just worked round—and with a sharper turn of the screw than any yet—to the conception of an American intense as little Bilham was intense. The young man was his first specimen; the specimen had profoundly perplexed him; at present however there was light. It was by little Bilham's amazing serenity that he had at first been affected, but he had inevitably, in his circumspection, felt it as the trail of the serpent, the corruption, as he might conveniently have said, of Europe; whereas the promptness with which it came up for Miss Gostrey but as a special little form of the oldest thing they knew justified it at once to his own vision as well. He wanted to be able to like his specimen with a clear good conscience, and this fully permitted it. What had muddled him was precisely the small artist-man's way—it was so complete—of being more American than anybody. But it now for the time put Strether vastly at his ease to have this view of a new way.

The amiable youth then looked out, as it had first struck Strether, at a world in respect to which he hadn't a prejudice. The one our friend most instantly missed was the usual one in favour of an occupation accepted. Little Bilham had an occupation, but it was only an occupation declined; and it was by his general exemption from alarm, anxiety or remorse on this score that the impression of his serenity was made. He had come out to Paris to paint—to fathom, that is, at large, that mystery; but study had been fatal to him so far as anything COULD be fatal, and his productive power faltered in proportion as his knowledge grew. Strether had gathered from him that at the moment of his finding him in Chad's rooms he hadn't saved from his shipwreck a scrap of anything but his beautiful intelligence and his confirmed habit of Paris. He referred to these things with an equal fond familiarity, and it was sufficiently clear that, as an outfit, they still served him. They were charming to Strether through the hour spent at the Louvre, where indeed they figured for him as an unseparated part of the charged iridescent air, the glamour of the name, the splendour of the space, the colour of the masters. Yet they were present too wherever the young man led, and the day after the visit to the Louvre they hung, in a different walk, about the steps of our party. He had invited his companions to cross the river with him, offering to show them his own poor place; and his own poor place, which was very poor, gave to his idiosyncrasies, for Strether—the small sublime indifference and independences that had struck the latter as fresh—an odd and engaging dignity. He lived at the end of an alley that went out of an old short cobbled street, a street that went in turn out of a new long smooth avenue—street and avenue and alley having, however, in common a sort of social shabbiness; and he introduced them to the rather cold and blank little studio which he had lent to a comrade for the term of his elegant absence. The comrade was another ingenuous compatriot, to whom he had wired that tea was to await them "regardless," and this reckless repast, and the second ingenuous compatriot, and the faraway makeshift life, with its jokes and its gaps, its delicate daubs and its three or four chairs, its overflow of taste and conviction and its lack of nearly all else—these things wove round the occasion a spell to which our hero unreservedly surrendered.

He liked the ingenuous compatriots—for two or three others soon gathered; he liked the delicate daubs and the free discriminations—involving references indeed, involving enthusiasms and execrations that made him, as they said, sit up; he liked above all the legend of good-humoured poverty, of mutual accommodation fairly raised to the romantic, that he soon read into the scene. The ingenuous compatriots showed a candour, he thought, surpassing even the candour of Woollett; they were red-haired and long-legged, they were quaint and queer and dear and droll; they made the place resound with the vernacular, which he had never known so marked as when figuring for the chosen language, he must suppose, of contemporary art. They twanged with a vengeance the aesthetic lyre—they drew from it wonderful airs. This aspect of their life had an admirable innocence; and he looked on occasion at Maria Gostrey to see to what extent that element reached her. She gave him however for the hour, as she had given him the previous day, no further sign than to show how she dealt with boys; meeting them with the air of old Parisian practice that she had for every one, for everything, in turn. Wonderful about the delicate daubs, masterful about the way to make tea, trustful about the legs of chairs and familiarly reminiscent of those, in the other time, the named, the numbered or the caricatured, who had flourished or failed, disappeared or arrived, she had accepted with the best grace her second course of little Bilham, and had said to Strether, the previous afternoon on his leaving them, that, since her impression was to be renewed, she would reserve judgement till after the new evidence.

The new evidence was to come, as it proved, in a day or two. He soon had from Maria a message to the effect that an excellent box at the Francais had been lent her for the following night; it seeming on such occasions not the least of her merits that she was subject to such approaches. The sense of how she was always paying for something in advance was equalled on Strether's part only by the sense of how she was always being paid; all of which made for his consciousness, in the larger air, of a lively bustling traffic, the exchange of such values as were not for him to handle. She hated, he knew, at the French play, anything but a box—just as she hated at the English anything but a stall; and a box was what he was already in this phase girding himself to press upon her. But she had for that matter her community with little Bilham: she too always, on the great issues, showed as having known in time. It made her constantly beforehand with him and gave him mainly the chance to ask himself how on the day of their settlement their account would stand. He endeavoured even now to keep it a little straight by arranging that if he accepted her invitation she should dine with him first; but the upshot of this scruple was that at eight o'clock on the morrow he awaited her with Waymarsh under the pillared portico. She hadn't dined with him, and it was characteristic of their relation that she had made him embrace her refusal without in the least understanding it. She ever caused her rearrangements to affect him as her tenderest touches. It was on that principle for instance that, giving him the opportunity to be amiable again to little Bilham, she had suggested his offering the young man a seat in their box. Strether had dispatched for this purpose a small blue missive to the Boulevard Malesherbes, but up to the moment of their passing into the theatre he had received no response to his message. He held, however, even after they had been for some time conveniently seated, that their friend, who knew his way about, would come in at his own right moment. His temporary absence moreover seemed, as never yet, to make the right moment for Miss Gostrey. Strether had been waiting till tonight to get back from her in some mirrored form her impressions and conclusions. She had elected, as they said, to see little Bilham once; but now she had seen him twice and had nevertheless not said more than a word.

Waymarsh meanwhile sat opposite him with their hostess between; and Miss Gostrey spoke of herself as an instructor of youth introducing her little charges to a work that was one of the glories of literature. The glory was happily unobjectionable, and the little charges were candid; for herself she had travelled that road and she merely waited on their innocence. But she referred in due time to their absent friend, whom it was clear they should have to give up. "He either won't have got your note," she said, "or you won't have got his: he has had some kind of hindrance, and, of course, for that matter, you know, a man never writes about coming to a box." She spoke as if, with her look, it might have been Waymarsh who had written to the youth, and the latter's face showed a mixture of austerity and anguish. She went on however as if to meet this. "He's far and away, you know, the best of them."

"The best of whom, ma'am?"

"Why of all the long procession—the boys, the girls, or the old men and old women as they sometimes really are; the hope, as one may say, of our country. They've all passed, year after year; but there has been no one in particular I've ever wanted to stop. I feel—don't YOU?—that I want to stop little Bilham; he's so exactly right as he is." She continued to talk to Waymarsh. "He's too delightful. If he'll only not spoil it! But they always WILL; they always do; they always have."

"I don't think Waymarsh knows," Strether said after a moment, "quite what it's open to Bilham to spoil."

"It can't be a good American," Waymarsh lucidly enough replied; "for it didn't strike me the young man had developed much in THAT shape."

"Ah," Miss Gostrey sighed, "the name of the good American is as easily given as taken away! What IS it, to begin with, to BE one, and what's the extraordinary hurry? Surely nothing that's so pressing was ever so little defined. It's such an order, really, that before we cook you the dish we must at least have your receipt. Besides the poor chicks have time! What I've seen so often spoiled," she pursued, "is the happy attitude itself, the state of faith and—what shall I call it?—the sense of beauty. You're right about him"—she now took in Strether; "little Bilham has them to a charm, we must keep little Bilham along." Then she was all again for Waymarsh. "The others have all wanted so dreadfully to do something, and they've gone and done it in too many cases indeed. It leaves them never the same afterwards; the charm's always somehow broken. Now HE, I think, you know, really won't. He won't do the least dreadful little thing. We shall continue to enjoy him just as he is. No—he's quite beautiful. He sees everything. He isn't a bit ashamed. He has every scrap of the courage of it that one could ask. Only think what he MIGHT do. One wants really—for fear of some accident—to keep him in view. At this very moment perhaps what mayn't he be up to? I've had my disappointments—the poor things are never really safe; or only at least when you have them under your eye. One can never completely trust them. One's uneasy, and I think that's why I most miss him now."

She had wound up with a laugh of enjoyment over her embroidery of her idea—an enjoyment that her face communicated to Strether, who almost wished none the less at this moment that she would let poor Waymarsh alone. HE knew more or less what she meant; but the fact wasn't a reason for her not pretending to Waymarsh that he didn't. It was craven of him perhaps, but he would, for the high amenity of the occasion, have liked Waymarsh not to be so sure of his wit. Her recognition of it gave him away and, before she had done with him or with that article, would give him worse. What was he, all the same, to do? He looked across the box at his friend; their eyes met; something queer and stiff, something that bore on the situation but that it was better not to touch, passed in silence between them. Well, the effect of it for Strether was an abrupt reaction, a final impatience of his own tendency to temporise. Where was that taking him anyway? It was one of the quiet instants that sometimes settle more matters than the outbreaks dear to the historic muse. The only qualification of the quietness was the synthetic "Oh hang it!" into which Strether's share of the silence soundlessly flowered. It represented, this mute ejaculation, a final impulse to burn his ships. These ships, to the historic muse, may seem of course mere cockles, but when he presently spoke to Miss Gostrey it was with the sense at least of applying the torch. "Is it then a conspiracy?"

"Between the two young men? Well, I don't pretend to be a seer or a prophetess," she presently replied; "but if I'm simply a woman of sense he's working for you to-night. I don't quite know how—but it's in my bones." And she looked at him at last as if, little material as she yet gave him, he'd really understand. "For an opinion THAT'S my opinion. He makes you out too well not to."

"Not to work for me to-night?" Strether wondered. "Then I hope he isn't doing anything very bad."

"They've got you," she portentously answered.

"Do you mean he IS—?"

"They've got you," she merely repeated. Though she disclaimed the prophetic vision she was at this instant the nearest approach he had ever met to the priestess of the oracle. The light was in her eyes. "You must face it now."

He faced it on the spot. "They HAD arranged—?"

"Every move in the game. And they've been arranging ever since. He has had every day his little telegram from Cannes."

It made Strether open his eyes. "Do you KNOW that?"

"I do better. I see it. This was, before I met him, what I wondered whether I WAS to see. But as soon as I met him I ceased to wonder, and our second meeting made me sure. I took him all in. He was acting—he is still—on his daily instructions."

"So that Chad has done the whole thing?"

"Oh no—not the whole. WE'VE done some of it. You and I and 'Europe.'"

"Europe—yes," Strether mused.

"Dear old Paris," she seemed to explain. But there was more, and, with one of her turns, she risked it. "And dear old Waymarsh. You," she declared, "have been a good bit of it."

He sat massive. "A good bit of what, ma'am?"

"Why of the wonderful consciousness of our friend here. You've helped too in your way to float him to where he is."

"And where the devil IS he?"

She passed it on with a laugh. "Where the devil, Strether, are you?"

He spoke as if he had just been thinking it out. "Well, quite already in Chad's hands, it would seem." And he had had with this another thought. "Will that be—just all through Bilham—the way he's going to work it? It would be, for him, you know, an idea. And Chad with an idea—!"

"Well?" she asked while the image held him.

"Well, is Chad—what shall I say?—monstrous?"

"Oh as much as you like! But the idea you speak of," she said, "won't have been his best. He'll have a better. It won't be all through little Bilham that he'll work it."

This already sounded almost like a hope destroyed. "Through whom else then?"

"That's what we shall see!" But quite as she spoke she turned, and Strether turned; for the door of the box had opened, with the click of the ouvreuse, from the lobby, and a gentleman, a stranger to them, had come in with a quick step. The door closed behind him, and, though their faces showed him his mistake, his air, which was striking, was all good confidence. The curtain had just again arisen, and, in the hush of the general attention, Strether's challenge was tacit, as was also the greeting, with a quickly deprecating hand and smile, of the unannounced visitor. He discreetly signed that he would wait, would stand, and these things and his face, one look from which she had caught, had suddenly worked for Miss Gostrey. She fitted to them all an answer for Strether's last question. The solid stranger was simply the answer—as she now, turning to her friend, indicated. She brought it straight out for him—it presented the intruder. "Why, through this gentleman!" The gentleman indeed, at the same time, though sounding for Strether a very short name, did practically as much to explain. Strether gasped the name back—then only had he seen Miss Gostrey had said more than she knew. They were in presence of Chad himself.

Our friend was to go over it afterwards again and again—he was going over it much of the time that they were together, and they were together constantly for three or four days: the note had been so strongly struck during that first half-hour that everything happening since was comparatively a minor development. The fact was that his perception of the young man's identity—so absolutely checked for a minute—had been quite one of the sensations that count in life; he certainly had never known one that had acted, as he might have said, with more of a crowded rush. And the rush though both vague and multitudinous, had lasted a long time, protected, as it were, yet at the same time aggravated, by the circumstance of its coinciding with a stretch of decorous silence. They couldn't talk without disturbing the spectators in the part of the balcony just below them; and it, for that matter, came to Strether—being a thing of the sort that did come to him—that these were the accidents of a high civilisation; the imposed tribute to propriety, the frequent exposure to conditions, usually brilliant, in which relief has to await its time. Relief was never quite near at hand for kings, queens, comedians and other such people, and though you might be yourself not exactly one of those, you could yet, in leading the life of high pressure, guess a little how they sometimes felt. It was truly the life of high pressure that Strether had seemed to feel himself lead while he sat there, close to Chad, during the long tension of the act. He was in presence of a fact that occupied his whole mind, that occupied for the half-hour his senses themselves all together; but he couldn't without inconvenience show anything—which moreover might count really as luck. What he might have shown, had he shown at all, was exactly the kind of emotion—the emotion of bewilderment—that he had proposed to himself from the first, whatever should occur, to show least. The phenomenon that had suddenly sat down there with him was a phenomenon of change so complete that his imagination, which had worked so beforehand, felt itself, in the connexion, without margin or allowance. It had faced every contingency but that Chad should not BE Chad, and this was what it now had to face with a mere strained smile and an uncomfortable flush.

He asked himself if, by any chance, before he should have in some way to commit himself, he might feel his mind settled to the new vision, might habituate it, so to speak, to the remarkable truth. But oh it was too remarkable, the truth; for what could be more remarkable than this sharp rupture of an identity? You could deal with a man as himself—you couldn't deal with him as somebody else. It was a small source of peace moreover to be reduced to wondering how little he might know in such an event what a sum he was setting you. He couldn't absolutely not know, for you couldn't absolutely not let him. It was a CASE then simply, a strong case, as people nowadays called such things,' a case of transformation unsurpassed, and the hope was but in the general law that strong cases were liable to control from without. Perhaps he, Strether himself, was the only person after all aware of it. Even Miss Gostrey, with all her science, wouldn't be, would she?—and he had never seen any one less aware of anything than Waymarsh as he glowered at Chad. The social sightlessness of his old friend's survey marked for him afresh, and almost in an humiliating way, the inevitable limits of direct aid from this source. He was not certain, however, of not drawing a shade of compensation from the privilege, as yet untasted, of knowing more about something in particular than Miss Gostrey did. His situation too was a case, for that matter, and he was now so interested, quite so privately agog, about it, that he had already an eye to the fun it would be to open up to her afterwards. He derived during his half-hour no assistance from her, and just this fact of her not meeting his eyes played a little, it must be confessed, into his predicament.

He had introduced Chad, in the first minutes, under his breath, and there was never the primness in her of the person unacquainted; but she had none the less betrayed at first no vision but of the stage, where she occasionally found a pretext for an appreciative moment that she invited Waymarsh to share. The latter's faculty of participation had never had, all round, such an assault to meet; the pressure on him being the sharper for this chosen attitude in her, as Strether judged it, of isolating, for their natural intercourse, Chad and himself. This intercourse was meanwhile restricted to a frank friendly look from the young man, something markedly like a smile, but falling far short of a grin, and to the vivacity of Strether's private speculation as to whether HE carried himself like a fool. He didn't quite see how he could so feel as one without somehow showing as one. The worst of that question moreover was that he knew it as a symptom the sense of which annoyed him. "If I'm going to be odiously conscious of how I may strike the fellow," he reflected, "it was so little what I came out for that I may as well stop before I begin." This sage consideration too, distinctly, seemed to leave untouched the fact that he WAS going to be conscious. He was conscious of everything but of what would have served him.

He was to know afterwards, in the watches of the night, that nothing would have been more open to him than after a minute or two to propose to Chad to seek with him the refuge of the lobby. He hadn't only not proposed it, but had lacked even the presence of mind to see it as possible. He had stuck there like a schoolboy wishing not to miss a minute of the show; though for that portion of the show then presented he hadn't had an instant's real attention. He couldn't when the curtain fell have given the slightest account of what had happened. He had therefore, further, not at that moment acknowledged the amenity added by this acceptance of his awkwardness to Chad's general patience. Hadn't he none the less known at the very time—known it stupidly and without reaction—that the boy was accepting something? He was modestly benevolent, the boy—that was at least what he had been capable of the superiority of making out his chance to be; and one had one's self literally not had the gumption to get in ahead of him. If we should go into all that occupied our friend in the watches of the night we should have to mend our pen; but an instance or two may mark for us the vividness with which he could remember. He remembered the two absurdities that, if his presence of mind HAD failed, were the things that had had most to do with it. He had never in his life seen a young man come into a box at ten o'clock at night, and would, if challenged on the question in advance, have scarce been ready to pronounce as to different ways of doing so. But it was in spite of this definite to him that Chad had had a way that was wonderful: a fact carrying with it an implication that, as one might imagine it, he knew, he had learned, how.

Here already then were abounding results; he had on the spot and without the least trouble of intention taught Strether that even in so small a thing as that there were different ways. He had done in the same line still more than this; had by a mere shake or two of the head made his old friend observe that the change in him was perhaps more than anything else, for the eye, a matter of the marked streaks of grey, extraordinary at his age, in his thick black hair; as well as that this new feature was curiously becoming to him, did something for him, as characterisation, also even—of all things in the world—as refinement, that had been a good deal wanted. Strether felt, however, he would have had to confess, that it wouldn't have been easy just now, on this and other counts, in the presence of what had been supplied, to be quite clear as to what had been missed. A reflexion a candid critic might have made of old, for instance, was that it would have been happier for the son to look more like the mother; but this was a reflexion that at present would never occur. The ground had quite fallen away from it, yet no resemblance whatever to the mother had supervened. It would have been hard for a young man's face and air to disconnect themselves more completely than Chad's at this juncture from any discerned, from any imaginable aspect of a New England female parent. That of course was no more than had been on the cards; but it produced in Strether none the less one of those frequent phenomena of mental reference with which all judgement in him was actually beset.

Again and again as the days passed he had had a sense of the pertinence of communicating quickly with Woollett—communicating with a quickness with which telegraphy alone would rhyme; the fruit really of a fine fancy in him for keeping things straight, for the happy forestalment of error. No one could explain better when needful, nor put more conscience into an account or a report; which burden of conscience is perhaps exactly the reason why his heart always sank when the clouds of explanation gathered. His highest ingenuity was in keeping the sky of life clear of them. Whether or no he had a grand idea of the lucid, he held that nothing ever was in fact—for any one else—explained. One went through the vain motions, but it was mostly a waste of life. A personal relation was a relation only so long as people either perfectly understood or, better still, didn't care if they didn't. From the moment they cared if they didn't it was living by the sweat of one's brow; and the sweat of one's brow was just what one might buy one's self off from by keeping the ground free of the wild weed of delusion. It easily grew too fast, and the Atlantic cable now alone could race with it. That agency would each day have testified for him to something that was not what Woollett had argued. He was not at this moment absolutely sure that the effect of the morrow's—or rather of the night's—appreciation of the crisis wouldn't be to determine some brief missive. "Have at last seen him, but oh dear!"—some temporary relief of that sort seemed to hover before him. It hovered somehow as preparing them all—yet preparing them for what? If he might do so more luminously and cheaply he would tick out in four words: "Awfully old—grey hair." To this particular item in Chad's appearance he constantly, during their mute half-hour, reverted; as if so very much more than he could have said had been involved in it. The most he could have said would have been: "If he's going to make me feel young—!" which indeed, however, carried with it quite enough. If Strether was to feel young, that is, it would be because Chad was to feel old; and an aged and hoary sinner had been no part of the scheme.

The question of Chadwick's true time of life was, doubtless, what came up quickest after the adjournment of the two, when the play was over, to a cafe in the Avenue de l'Opera. Miss Gostrey had in due course been perfect for such a step; she had known exactly what they wanted—to go straight somewhere and talk; and Strether had even felt she had known what he wished to say and that he was arranging immediately to begin. She hadn't pretended this, as she HAD pretended on the other hand, to have divined Waymarsh's wish to extend to her an independent protection homeward; but Strether nevertheless found how, after he had Chad opposite to him at a small table in the brilliant halls that his companion straightway selected, sharply and easily discriminated from others, it was quite, to his mind, as if she heard him speak; as if, sitting up, a mile away, in the little apartment he knew, she would listen hard enough to catch. He found too that he liked that idea, and he wished that, by the same token, Mrs. Newsome might have caught as well. For what had above all been determined in him as a necessity of the first order was not to lose another hour, nor a fraction of one; was to advance, to overwhelm, with a rush. This was how he would anticipate—by a night-attack, as might be—any forced maturity that a crammed consciousness of Paris was likely to take upon itself to assert on behalf of the boy. He knew to the full, on what he had just extracted from Miss Gostrey, Chad's marks of alertness; but they were a reason the more for not dawdling. If he was himself moreover to be treated as young he wouldn't at all events be so treated before he should have struck out at least once. His arms might be pinioned afterwards, but it would have been left on record that he was fifty. The importance of this he had indeed begun to feel before they left the theatre; it had become a wild unrest, urging him to seize his chance. He could scarcely wait for it as they went; he was on the verge of the indecency of bringing up the question in the street; he fairly caught himself going on—so he afterwards invidiously named it—as if there would be for him no second chance should the present be lost. Not till, on the purple divan before the perfunctory bock, he had brought out the words themselves, was he sure, for that matter, that the present would be saved.

Book Fourth

I

"I've come, you know, to make you break with everything, neither more nor less, and take you straight home; so you'll be so good as immediately and favourably to consider it!"—Strether, face to face with Chad after the play, had sounded these words almost breathlessly, and with an effect at first positively disconcerting to himself alone. For Chad's receptive attitude was that of a person who had been gracefully quiet while the messenger at last reaching him has run a mile through the dust. During some seconds after he had spoken Strether felt as if HE had made some such exertion; he was not even certain that the perspiration wasn't on his brow. It was the kind of consciousness for which he had to thank the look that, while the strain lasted, the young man's eyes gave him. They reflected—and the deuce of the thing was that they reflected really with a sort of shyness of kindness—his momentarily disordered state; which fact brought on in its turn for our friend the dawn of a fear that Chad might simply "take it out"—take everything out—in being sorry for him. Such a fear, any fear, was unpleasant. But everything was unpleasant; it was odd how everything had suddenly turned so. This however was no reason for letting the least thing go. Strether had the next minute proceeded as roundly as if with an advantage to follow up. "Of course I'm a busybody, if you want to fight the case to the death; but after all mainly in the sense of having known you and having given you such attention as you kindly permitted when you were in jackets and knickerbockers. Yes—it was knickerbockers, I'm busybody enough to remember that; and that you had, for your age—I speak of the first far-away time—tremendously stout legs. Well, we want you to break. Your mother's heart's passionately set upon it, but she has above and beyond that excellent arguments and reasons. I've not put them into her head—I needn't remind you how little she's a person who needs that. But they exist—you must take it from me as a friend both of hers and yours—for myself as well. I didn't invent them, I didn't originally work them out; but I understand them, I think I can explain them—by which I mean make you actively do them justice; and that's why you see me here. You had better know the worst at once. It's a question of an immediate rupture and an immediate return. I've been conceited enough to dream I can sugar that pill. I take at any rate the greatest interest in the question. I took it already before I left home, and I don't mind telling you that, altered as you are, I take it still more now that I've seen you. You're older and—I don't know what to call it!—more of a handful; but you're by so much the more, I seem to make out, to our purpose."

"Do I strike you as improved?" Strether was to recall that Chad had at this point enquired.

He was likewise to recall—and it had to count for some time as his greatest comfort—that it had been "given" him, as they said at Woollett, to reply with some presence of mind: "I haven't the least idea." He was really for a while to like thinking he had been positively hard. On the point of conceding that Chad had improved in appearance, but that to the question of appearance the remark must be confined, he checked even that compromise and left his reservation bare. Not only his moral, but also, as it were, his aesthetic sense had a little to pay for this, Chad being unmistakeably—and wasn't it a matter of the confounded grey hair again?—handsomer than he had ever promised. That however fell in perfectly with what Strether had said. They had no desire to keep down his proper expansion, and he wouldn't be less to their purpose for not looking, as he had too often done of old, only bold and wild. There was indeed a signal particular in which he would distinctly be more so. Strether didn't, as he talked, absolutely follow himself; he only knew he was clutching his thread and that he held it from moment to moment a little tighter; his mere uninterruptedness during the few minutes helped him to do that. He had frequently for a month, turned over what he should say on this very occasion, and he seemed at last to have said nothing he had thought of—everything was so totally different.

But in spite of all he had put the flag at the window. This was what he had done, and there was a minute during which he affected himself as having shaken it hard, flapped it with a mighty flutter, straight in front of his companion's nose. It gave him really almost the sense of having already acted his part. The momentary relief—as if from the knowledge that nothing of THAT at least could be undone—sprang from a particular cause, the cause that had flashed into operation, in Miss Gostrey's box, with direct apprehension, with amazed recognition, and that had been concerned since then in every throb of his consciousness. What it came to was that with an absolutely new quantity to deal with one simply couldn't know. The new quantity was represented by the fact that Chad had been made over. That was all; whatever it was it was everything. Strether had never seen the thing so done before—it was perhaps a speciality of Paris. If one had been present at the process one might little by little have mastered the result; but he was face to face, as matters stood, with the finished business. It had freely been noted for him that he might be received as a dog among skittles, but that was on the basis of the old quantity. He had originally thought of lines and tones as things to be taken, but these possibilities had now quite melted away. There was no computing at all what the young man before him would think or feel or say on any subject whatever. This intelligence Strether had afterwards, to account for his nervousness, reconstituted as he might, just as he had also reconstituted the promptness with which Chad had corrected his uncertainty. An extraordinarily short time had been required for the correction, and there had ceased to be anything negative in his companion's face and air as soon as it was made. "Your engagement to my mother has become then what they call here a fait accompli?"—it had consisted, the determinant touch, in nothing more than that.

Well, that was enough, Strether had felt while his answer hung fire. He had felt at the same time, however, that nothing could less become him than that it should hang fire too long. "Yes," he said brightly, "it was on the happy settlement of the question that I started. You see therefore to what tune I'm in your family. Moreover," he added, "I've been supposing you'd suppose it."

"Oh I've been supposing it for a long time, and what you tell me helps me to understand that you should want to do something. To do something, I mean," said Chad, "to commemorate an event so—what do they call it?—so auspicious. I see you make out, and not unnaturally," he continued, "that bringing me home in triumph as a sort of wedding-present to Mother would commemorate it better than anything else. You want to make a bonfire in fact," he laughed, "and you pitch me on. Thank you, thank you!" he laughed again.

He was altogether easy about it, and this made Strether now see how at bottom, and in spite of the shade of shyness that really cost him nothing, he had from the first moment been easy about everything. The shade of shyness was mere good taste. People with manners formed could apparently have, as one of their best cards, the shade of shyness too. He had leaned a little forward to speak; his elbows were on the table; and the inscrutable new face that he had got somewhere and somehow was brought by the movement nearer to his critics There was a fascination for that critic in its not being, this ripe physiognomy, the face that, under observation at least, he had originally carried away from Woollett. Strether found a certain freedom on his own side in defining it as that of a man of the world—a formula that indeed seemed to come now in some degree to his relief; that of a man to whom things had happened and were variously known. In gleams, in glances, the past did perhaps peep out of it; but such lights were faint and instantly merged. Chad was brown and thick and strong, and of old Chad had been rough. Was all the difference therefore that he was actually smooth? Possibly; for that he WAS smooth was as marked as in the taste of a sauce or in the rub of a hand. The effect of it was general—it had retouched his features, drawn them with a cleaner line. It had cleared his eyes and settled his colour and polished his fine square teeth—the main ornament of his face; and at the same time that it had given him a form and a surface, almost a design, it had toned his voice, established his accent, encouraged his smile to more play and his other motions to less. He had formerly, with a great deal of action, expressed very little; and he now expressed whatever was necessary with almost none at all. It was as if in short he had really, copious perhaps but shapeless, been put into a firm mould and turned successfully out. The phenomenon—Strether kept eyeing it as a phenomenon, an eminent case—was marked enough to be touched by the finger. He finally put his hand across the table and laid it on Chad's arm. "If you'll promise me—here on the spot and giving me your word of honour—to break straight off, you'll make the future the real right thing for all of us alike. You'll ease off the strain of this decent but none the less acute suspense in which I've for so many days been waiting for you, and let me turn in to rest. I shall leave you with my blessing and go to bed in peace."

Chad again fell back at this and, his hands pocketed, settled himself a little; in which posture he looked, though he rather anxiously smiled, only the more earnest. Then Strether seemed to see that he was really nervous, and he took that as what he would have called a wholesome sign. The only mark of it hitherto had been his more than once taking off and putting on his wide-brimmed crush hat. He had at this moment made the motion again to remove it, then had only pushed it back, so that it hung informally on his strong young grizzled crop. It was a touch that gave the note of the familiar—the intimate and the belated—to their quiet colloquy; and it was indeed by some such trivial aid that Strether became aware at the same moment of something else. The observation was at any rate determined in him by some light too fine to distinguish from so many others, but it was none the less sharply determined. Chad looked unmistakeably during these instants—well, as Strether put it to himself, all he was worth. Our friend had a sudden apprehension of what that would on certain sides be. He saw him in a flash as the young man marked out by women; and for a concentrated minute the dignity, the comparative austerity, as he funnily fancied it, of this character affected him almost with awe. There was an experience on his interlocutor's part that looked out at him from under the displaced hat, and that looked out moreover by a force of its own, the deep fact of its quantity and quality, and not through Chad's intending bravado or swagger. That was then the way men marked out by women WERE—and also the men by whom the women were doubtless in turn sufficiently distinguished. It affected Strether for thirty seconds as a relevant truth, a truth which, however, the next minute, had fallen into its relation. "Can't you imagine there being some questions," Chad asked, "that a fellow—however much impressed by your charming way of stating things—would like to put to you first?"

"Oh yes—easily. I'm here to answer everything. I think I can even tell you things, of the greatest interest to you, that you won't know enough to ask me. We'll take as many days to it as you like. But I want," Strether wound up, "to go to bed now."

"Really?"

Chad had spoken in such surprise that he was amused. "Can't you believe it?—with what you put me through?"

The young man seemed to consider. "Oh I haven't put you through much—yet."

"Do you mean there's so much more to come?" Strether laughed. "All the more reason then that I should gird myself." And as if to mark what he felt he could by this time count on he was already on his feet.

Chad, still seated, stayed him, with a hand against him, as he passed between their table and the next. "Oh we shall get on!"

The tone was, as who should say, everything Strether could have desired; and quite as good the expression of face with which the speaker had looked up at him and kindly held him. All these things lacked was their not showing quite so much as the fruit of experience. Yes, experience was what Chad did play on him, if he didn't play any grossness of defiance. Of course experience was in a manner defiance; but it wasn't, at any rate—rather indeed quite the contrary!—grossness; which was so much gained. He fairly grew older, Strether thought, while he himself so reasoned. Then with his mature pat of his visitor's arm he also got up; and there had been enough of it all by this time to make the visitor feel that something WAS settled. Wasn't it settled that he had at least the testimony of Chad's own belief in a settlement? Strether found himself treating Chad's profession that they would get on as a sufficient basis for going to bed. He hadn't nevertheless after this gone to bed directly; for when they had again passed out together into the mild bright night a check had virtually sprung from nothing more than a small circumstance which might have acted only as confirming quiescence. There were people, expressive sound, projected light, still abroad, and after they had taken in for a moment, through everything, the great clear architectural street, they turned off in tacit union to the quarter of Strether's hotel. "Of course," Chad here abruptly began, "of course Mother's making things out with you about me has been natural—and of course also you've had a good deal to go upon. Still, you must have filled out."

He had stopped, leaving his friend to wonder a little what point he wished to make; and this it was that enabled Strether meanwhile to make one. "Oh we've never pretended to go into detail. We weren't in the least bound to THAT. It was 'filling out' enough to miss you as we did."

But Chad rather oddly insisted, though under the high lamp at their corner, where they paused, he had at first looked as if touched by Strether's allusion to the long sense, at home, of his absence. "What I mean is you must have imagined."

"Imagined what?"

"Well—horrors."

It affected Strether: horrors were so little—superficially at least—in this robust and reasoning image. But he was none the less there to be veracious. "Yes, I dare say we HAVE imagined horrors. But where's the harm if we haven't been wrong?"

Chad raised his face to the lamp, and it was one of the moments at which he had, in his extraordinary way, most his air of designedly showing himself. It was as if at these instants he just presented himself, his identity so rounded off, his palpable presence and his massive young manhood, as such a link in the chain as might practically amount to a kind of demonstration. It was as if—and how but anomalously?—he couldn't after all help thinking sufficiently well of these things to let them go for what they were worth. What could there be in this for Strether but the hint of some self-respect, some sense of power, oddly perverted; something latent and beyond access, ominous and perhaps enviable? The intimation had the next thing, in a flash, taken on a name—a name on which our friend seized as he asked himself if he weren't perhaps really dealing with an irreducible young Pagan. This description—he quite jumped at it—had a sound that gratified his mental ear, so that of a sudden he had already adopted it. Pagan—yes, that was, wasn't it? what Chad WOULD logically be. It was what he must be. It was what he was. The idea was a clue and, instead of darkening the prospect, projected a certain clearness. Strether made out in this quick ray that a Pagan was perhaps, at the pass they had come to, the thing most wanted at Woollett. They'd be able to do with one—a good one; he'd find an opening—yes; and Strether's imagination even now prefigured and accompanied the first appearance there of the rousing personage. He had only the slight discomfort of feeling, as the young man turned away from the lamp, that his thought had in the momentary silence possibly been guessed. "Well, I've no doubt," said Chad, "you've come near enough. The details, as you say, don't matter. It HAS been generally the case that I've let myself go. But I'm coming round—I'm not so bad now." With which they walked on again to Strether's hotel.

"Do you mean," the latter asked as they approached the door, "that there isn't any woman with you now?"

"But pray what has that to do with it?"

"Why it's the whole question."

"Of my going home?" Chad was clearly surprised. "Oh not much! Do you think that when I want to go any one will have any power—"

"To keep you"—Strether took him straight up—"from carrying out your wish? Well, our idea has been that somebody has hitherto—or a good many persons perhaps—kept you pretty well from 'wanting.' That's what—if you're in anybody's hands—may again happen. You don't answer my question"—he kept it up; "but if you aren't in anybody's hands so much the better. There's nothing then but what makes for your going."

Chad turned this over. "I don't answer your question?" He spoke quite without resenting it. "Well, such questions have always a rather exaggerated side. One doesn't know quite what you mean by being in women's 'hands.' It's all so vague. One is when one isn't. One isn't when one is. And then one can't quite give people away." He seemed kindly to explain. "I've NEVER got stuck—so very hard; and, as against anything at any time really better, I don't think I've ever been afraid." There was something in it that held Strether to wonder, and this gave him time to go on. He broke out as with a more helpful thought. "Don't you know how I like Paris itself?"

The upshot was indeed to make our friend marvel. "Oh if THAT'S all that's the matter with you—!" It was HE who almost showed resentment.

Chad's smile of a truth more than met it. "But isn't that enough?"

Strether hesitated, but it came out. "Not enough for your mother!" Spoken, however, it sounded a trifle odd—the effect of which was that Chad broke into a laugh. Strether, at this, succumbed as well, though with extreme brevity. "Permit us to have still our theory. But if you ARE so free and so strong you're inexcusable. I'll write in the morning," he added with decision. "I'll say I've got you."

This appeared to open for Chad a new interest. "How often do you write?"

"Oh perpetually."

"And at great length?"

Strether had become a little impatient. "I hope it's not found too great."

"Oh I'm sure not. And you hear as often?"

Again Strether paused. "As often as I deserve."

"Mother writes," said Chad, "a lovely letter."

Strether, before the closed porte-cochere, fixed him a moment. "It's more, my boy, than YOU do! But our suppositions don't matter," he added, "if you're actually not entangled."

Chad's pride seemed none the less a little touched. "I never WAS that—let me insist. I always had my own way." With which he pursued: "And I have it at present."

"Then what are you here for? What has kept you," Strether asked, "if you HAVE been able to leave?"

It made Chad, after a stare, throw himself back. "Do you think one's kept only by women?" His surprise and his verbal emphasis rang out so clear in the still street that Strether winced till he remembered the safety of their English speech. "Is that," the young man demanded, "what they think at Woollett?" At the good faith in the question Strether had changed colour, feeling that, as he would have said, he had put his foot in it. He had appeared stupidly to misrepresent what they thought at Woollett; but before he had time to rectify Chad again was upon him. "I must say then you show a low mind!"

It so fell in, unhappily for Strether, with that reflexion of his own prompted in him by the pleasant air of the Boulevard Malesherbes, that its disconcerting force was rather unfairly great. It was a dig that, administered by himself—and administered even to poor Mrs. Newsome—was no more than salutary; but administered by Chad—and quite logically—it came nearer drawing blood. They HADn't a low mind—nor any approach to one; yet incontestably they had worked, and with a certain smugness, on a basis that might be turned against them. Chad had at any rate pulled his visitor up; he had even pulled up his admirable mother; he had absolutely, by a turn of the wrist and a jerk of the far-flung noose, pulled up, in a bunch, Woollett browsing in its pride. There was no doubt Woollett HAD insisted on his coarseness; and what he at present stood there for in the sleeping street was, by his manner of striking the other note, to make of such insistence a preoccupation compromising to the insisters. It was exactly as if they had imputed to him a vulgarity that he had by a mere gesture caused to fall from him. The devil of the case was that Strether felt it, by the same stroke, as falling straight upon himself. He had been wondering a minute ago if the boy weren't a Pagan, and he found himself wondering now if he weren't by chance a gentleman. It didn't in the least, on the spot, spring up helpfully for him that a person couldn't at the same time be both. There was nothing at this moment in the air to challenge the combination; there was everything to give it on the contrary something of a flourish. It struck Strether into the bargain as doing something to meet the most difficult of the questions; though perhaps indeed only by substituting another. Wouldn't it be precisely by having learned to be a gentleman that he had mastered the consequent trick of looking so well that one could scarce speak to him straight? But what in the world was the clue to such a prime producing cause? There were too many clues then that Strether still lacked, and these clues to clues were among them. What it accordingly amounted to for him was that he had to take full in the face a fresh attribution of ignorance. He had grown used by this time to reminders, especially from his own lips, of what he didn't know; but he had borne them because in the first place they were private and because in the second they practically conveyed a tribute. He didn't know what was bad, and—as others didn't know how little he knew it—he could put up with his state. But if he didn't know, in so important a particular, what was good, Chad at least was now aware he didn't; and that, for some reason, affected our friend as curiously public. It was in fact an exposed condition that the young man left him in long enough for him to feel its chill—till he saw fit, in a word, generously again to cover him. This last was in truth what Chad quite gracefully did. But he did it as with a simple thought that met the whole of the case. "Oh I'm all right!" It was what Strether had rather bewilderedly to go to bed on.

II

It really looked true moreover from the way Chad was to behave after this. He was full of attentions to his mother's ambassador; in spite of which, all the while, the latter's other relations rather remarkably contrived to assert themselves. Strether's sittings pen in hand with Mrs. Newsome up in his own room were broken, yet they were richer; and they were more than ever interspersed with the hours in which he reported himself, in a different fashion, but with scarce less earnestness and fulness, to Maria Gostrey. Now that, as he would have expressed it, he had really something to talk about he found himself, in respect to any oddity that might reside for him in the double connexion, at once more aware and more indifferent. He had been fine to Mrs. Newsome about his useful friend, but it had begun to haunt his imagination that Chad, taking up again for her benefit a pen too long disused, might possibly be finer. It wouldn't at all do, he saw, that anything should come up for him at Chad's hand but what specifically was to have come; the greatest divergence from which would be precisely the element of any lubrication of their intercourse by levity It was accordingly to forestall such an accident that he frankly put before the young man the several facts, just as they had occurred, of his funny alliance. He spoke of these facts, pleasantly and obligingly, as "the whole story," and felt that he might qualify the alliance as funny if he remained sufficiently grave about it. He flattered himself that he even exaggerated the wild freedom of his original encounter with the wonderful lady; he was scrupulously definite about the absurd conditions in which they had made acquaintance—their having picked each other up almost in the street; and he had (finest inspiration of all!) a conception of carrying the war into the enemy's country by showing surprise at the enemy's ignorance.

He had always had a notion that this last was the grand style of fighting; the greater therefore the reason for it, as he couldn't remember that he had ever before fought in the grand style. Every one, according to this, knew Miss Gostrey: how came it Chad didn't know her? The difficulty, the impossibility, was really to escape it; Strether put on him, by what he took for granted, the burden of proof of the contrary. This tone was so far successful as that Chad quite appeared to recognise her as a person whose fame had reached him, but against his acquaintance with whom much mischance had worked. He made the point at the same time that his social relations, such as they could be called, were perhaps not to the extent Strether supposed with the rising flood of their compatriots. He hinted at his having more and more given way to a different principle of selection; the moral of which seemed to be that he went about little in the "colony." For the moment certainly he had quite another interest. It was deep, what he understood, and Strether, for himself, could only so observe it. He couldn't see as yet how deep. Might he not all too soon! For there was really too much of their question that Chad had already committed himself to liking. He liked, to begin with, his prospective stepfather; which was distinctly what had not been on the cards. His hating him was the untowardness for which Strether had been best prepared; he hadn't expected the boy's actual form to give him more to do than his imputed. It gave him more through suggesting that he must somehow make up to himself for not being sure he was sufficiently disagreeable. That had really been present to him as his only way to be sure he was sufficiently thorough. The point was that if Chad's tolerance of his thoroughness were insincere, were but the best of devices for gaining time, it none the less did treat everything as tacitly concluded.

That seemed at the end of ten days the upshot of the abundant, the recurrent talk through which Strether poured into him all it concerned him to know, put him in full possession of facts and figures. Never cutting these colloquies short by a minute, Chad behaved, looked and spoke as if he were rather heavily, perhaps even a trifle gloomily, but none the less fundamentally and comfortably free. He made no crude profession of eagerness to yield, but he asked the most intelligent questions, probed, at moments, abruptly, even deeper than his friend's layer of information, justified by these touches the native estimate of his latent stuff, and had in every way the air of trying to live, reflectively, into the square bright picture. He walked up and down in front of this production, sociably took Strether's arm at the points at which he stopped, surveyed it repeatedly from the right and from the left, inclined a critical head to either quarter, and, while he puffed a still more critical cigarette, animadverted to his companion on this passage and that. Strether sought relief—there were hours when he required it—in repeating himself; it was in truth not to be blinked that Chad had a way. The main question as yet was of what it was a way TO. It made vulgar questions no more easy; but that was unimportant when all questions save those of his own asking had dropped. That he was free was answer enough, and it wasn't quite ridiculous that this freedom should end by presenting itself as what was difficult to move. His changed state, his lovely home, his beautiful things, his easy talk, his very appetite for Strether, insatiable and, when all was said, flattering—what were such marked matters all but the notes of his freedom? He had the effect of making a sacrifice of it just in these handsome forms to his visitor; which was mainly the reason the visitor was privately, for the time, a little out of countenance. Strether was at this period again and again thrown back on a felt need to remodel somehow his plan. He fairly caught himself shooting rueful glances, shy looks of pursuit, toward the embodied influence, the definite adversary, who had by a stroke of her own failed him and on a fond theory of whose palpable presence he had, under Mrs. Newsome's inspiration, altogether proceeded. He had once or twice, in secret, literally expressed the irritated wish that SHE would come out and find her.

He couldn't quite yet force it upon Woollett that such a career, such a perverted young life, showed after all a certain plausible side, DID in the case before them flaunt something like an impunity for the social man; but he could at least treat himself to the statement that would prepare him for the sharpest echo. This echo—as distinct over there in the dry thin air as some shrill "heading" above a column of print—seemed to reach him even as he wrote. "He says there's no woman," he could hear Mrs. Newsome report, in capitals almost of newspaper size, to Mrs. Pocock; and he could focus in Mrs. Pocock the response of the reader of the journal. He could see in the younger lady's face the earnestness of her attention and catch the full scepticism of her but slightly delayed "What is there then?" Just so he could again as little miss the mother's clear decision: "There's plenty of disposition, no doubt, to pretend there isn't." Strether had, after posting his letter, the whole scene out; and it was a scene during which, coming and going, as befell, he kept his eye not least upon the daughter. He had his fine sense of the conviction Mrs. Pocock would take occasion to reaffirm—a conviction bearing, as he had from the first deeply divined it to bear, on Mr. Strether's essential inaptitude. She had looked him in his conscious eyes even before he sailed, and that she didn't believe HE would find the woman had been written in her book. Hadn't she at the best but a scant faith in his ability to find women? It wasn't even as if he had found her mother—so much more, to her discrimination, had her mother performed the finding. Her mother had, in a case her private judgement of which remained educative of Mrs. Pocock's critical sense, found the man. The man owed his unchallenged state, in general, to the fact that Mrs. Newsome's discoveries were accepted at Woollett; but he knew in his bones, our friend did, how almost irresistibly Mrs. Pocock would now be moved to show what she thought of his own. Give HER a free hand, would be the moral, and the woman would soon be found.

His impression of Miss Gostrey after her introduction to Chad was meanwhile an impression of a person almost unnaturally on her guard. He struck himself as at first unable to extract from her what he wished; though indeed OF what he wished at this special juncture he would doubtless have contrived to make but a crude statement. It sifted and settled nothing to put to her, tout betement, as she often said, "Do you like him, eh?"—thanks to his feeling it actually the least of his needs to heap up the evidence in the young man's favour. He repeatedly knocked at her door to let her have it afresh that Chad's case—whatever else of minor interest it might yield—was first and foremost a miracle almost monstrous. It was the alteration of the entire man, and was so signal an instance that nothing else, for the intelligent observer, could—COULD it?—signify. "It's a plot," he declared—"there's more in it than meets the eye." He gave the rein to his fancy. "It's a plant!"

His fancy seemed to please her. "Whose then?"

"Well, the party responsible is, I suppose, the fate that waits for one, the dark doom that rides. What I mean is that with such elements one can't count. I've but my poor individual, my modest human means. It isn't playing the game to turn on the uncanny. All one's energy goes to facing it, to tracking it. One wants, confound it, don't you see?" he confessed with a queer face—"one wants to enjoy anything so rare. Call it then life"—he puzzled it out—"call it poor dear old life simply that springs the surprise. Nothing alters the fact that the surprise is paralysing, or at any rate engrossing—all, practically, hang it, that one sees, that one CAN see."

Her silences were never barren, nor even dull. "Is that what you've written home?"

He tossed it off. "Oh dear, yes!"

She had another pause while, across her carpets, he had another walk. "If you don't look out you'll have them straight over."

"Oh but I've said he'll go back."

"And WILL he?" Miss Gostrey asked.

The special tone of it made him, pulling up, look at her long. "What's that but just the question I've spent treasures of patience and ingenuity in giving you, by the sight of him—after everything had led up—every facility to answer? What is it but just the thing I came here to-day to get out of you? Will he?"

"No—he won't," she said at last. "He's not free."

The air of it held him. "Then you've all the while known—?"

"I've known nothing but what I've seen; and I wonder," she declared with some impatience, "that you didn't see as much. It was enough to be with him there—"

"In the box? Yes," he rather blankly urged.

"Well—to feel sure."

"Sure of what?"

She got up from her chair, at this, with a nearer approach than she had ever yet shown to dismay at his dimness. She even, fairly pausing for it, spoke with a shade of pity. "Guess!"

It was a shade, fairly, that brought a flush into his face; so that for a moment, as they waited together, their difference was between them. "You mean that just your hour with him told you so much of his story? Very good; I'm not such a fool, on my side, as that I don't understand you, or as that I didn't in some degree understand HIM. That he has done what he liked most isn't, among any of us, a matter the least in dispute. There's equally little question at this time of day of what it is he does like most. But I'm not talking," he reasonably explained, "of any mere wretch he may still pick up. I'm talking of some person who in his present situation may have held her own, may really have counted."

"That's exactly what I am!" said Miss Gostrey. But she as quickly made her point. "I thought you thought—or that they think at Woollett—that that's what mere wretches necessarily do. Mere wretches necessarily DON'T!" she declared with spirit. "There must, behind every appearance to the contrary, still be somebody—somebody who's not a mere wretch, since we accept the miracle. What else but such a somebody can such a miracle be?"

He took it in. "Because the fact itself IS the woman?"

"A woman. Some woman or other. It's one of the things that HAVE to be."

"But you mean then at least a good one."

"A good woman?" She threw up her arms with a laugh. "I should call her excellent!"

"Then why does he deny her?"

Miss Gostrey thought a moment. "Because she's too good to admit! Don't you see," she went on, "how she accounts for him?"

Strether clearly, more and more, did see; yet it made him also see other things. "But isn't what we want that he shall account for HER?"

"Well, he does. What you have before you is his way. You must forgive him if it isn't quite outspoken. In Paris such debts are tacit."

Strether could imagine; but still—! "Even when the woman's good?"

Again she laughed out. "Yes, and even when the man is! There's always a caution in such cases," she more seriously explained—"for what it may seem to show. There's nothing that's taken as showing so much here as sudden unnatural goodness."

"Ah then you're speaking now," Strether said, "of people who are NOT nice."

"I delight," she replied, "in your classifications. But do you want me," she asked, "to give you in the matter, on this ground, the wisest advice I'm capable of? Don't consider her, don't judge her at all in herself. Consider her and judge her only in Chad."

He had the courage at least of his companion's logic. "Because then I shall like her?" He almost looked, with his quick imagination as if he already did, though seeing at once also the full extent of how little it would suit his book. "But is that what I came out for?"

She had to confess indeed that it wasn't. But there was something else. "Don't make up your mind. There are all sorts of things. You haven't seen him all."

This on his side Strether recognised; but his acuteness none the less showed him the danger. "Yes, but if the more I see the better he seems?"

Well, she found something. "That may be—but his disavowal of her isn't, all the same, pure consideration. There's a hitch." She made it out. "It's the effort to sink her."

Strether winced at the image. "To 'sink'—?"

"Well, I mean there's a struggle, and a part of it is just what he hides. Take time—that's the only way not to make some mistake that you'll regret. Then you'll see. He does really want to shake her off."

Our friend had by this time so got into the vision that he almost gasped. "After all she has done for him?"

Miss Gostrey gave him a look which broke the next moment into a wonderful smile. "He's not so good as you think!"

They remained with him, these words, promising him, in their character of warning, considerable help; but the support he tried to draw from them found itself on each renewal of contact with Chad defeated by something else. What could it be, this disconcerting force, he asked himself, but the sense, constantly renewed, that Chad WAS—quite in fact insisted on being—as good as he thought? It seemed somehow as if he couldn't BUT be as good from the moment he wasn't as bad. There was a succession of days at all events when contact with him—and in its immediate effect, as if it could produce no other—elbowed out of Strether's consciousness everything but itself. Little Bilham once more pervaded the scene, but little Bilham became even in a higher degree than he had originally been one of the numerous forms of the inclusive relation; a consequence promoted, to our friend's sense, by two or three incidents with which we have yet to make acquaintance. Waymarsh himself, for the occasion, was drawn into the eddy; it absolutely, though but temporarily, swallowed him down, and there were days when Strether seemed to bump against him as a sinking swimmer might brush a submarine object. The fathomless medium held them—Chad's manner was the fathomless medium; and our friend felt as if they passed each other, in their deep immersion, with the round impersonal eye of silent fish. It was practically produced between them that Waymarsh was giving him then his chance; and the shade of discomfort that Strether drew from the allowance resembled not a little the embarrassment he had known at school, as a boy, when members of his family had been present at exhibitions. He could perform before strangers, but relatives were fatal, and it was now as if, comparatively, Waymarsh were a relative. He seemed to hear him say "Strike up then!" and to enjoy a foretaste of conscientious domestic criticism. He HAD struck up, so far as he actually could; Chad knew by this time in profusion what he wanted; and what vulgar violence did his fellow pilgrim expect of him when he had really emptied his mind? It went somehow to and fro that what poor Waymarsh meant was "I told you so—that you'd lose your immortal soul!" but it was also fairly explicit that Strether had his own challenge and that, since they must go to the bottom of things, he wasted no more virtue in watching Chad than Chad wasted in watching him. His dip for duty's sake—where was it worse than Waymarsh's own? For HE needn't have stopped resisting and refusing, needn't have parleyed, at that rate, with the foe.

The strolls over Paris to see something or call somewhere were accordingly inevitable and natural, and the late sessions in the wondrous troisieme, the lovely home, when men dropped in and the picture composed more suggestively through the haze of tobacco, of music more or less good and of talk more or less polyglot, were on a principle not to be distinguished from that of the mornings and the afternoons. Nothing, Strether had to recognise as he leaned back and smoked, could well less resemble a scene of violence than even the liveliest of these occasions. They were occasions of discussion, none the less, and Strether had never in his life heard so many opinions on so many subjects. There were opinions at Woollett, but only on three or four. The differences were there to match; if they were doubtless deep, though few, they were quiet—they were, as might be said, almost as shy as if people had been ashamed of them. People showed little diffidence about such things, on the other hand, in the Boulevard Malesherbes, and were so far from being ashamed of them—or indeed of anything else—that they often seemed to have invented them to avert those agreements that destroy the taste of talk. No one had ever done that at Woollett, though Strether could remember times when he himself had been tempted to it without quite knowing why. He saw why at present—he had but wanted to promote intercourse.

These, however, were but parenthetic memories, and the turn taken by his affair on the whole was positively that if his nerves were on the stretch it was because he missed violence. When he asked himself if none would then, in connexion with it, ever come at all, he might almost have passed as wondering how to provoke it. It would be too absurd if such a vision as THAT should have to be invoked for relief; it was already marked enough as absurd that he should actually have begun with flutters and dignities on the score of a single accepted meal. What sort of a brute had he expected Chad to be, anyway?—Strether had occasion to make the enquiry but was careful to make it in private. He could himself, comparatively recent as it was—it was truly but the fact of a few days since—focus his primal crudity; but he would on the approach of an observer, as if handling an illicit possession, have slipped the reminiscence out of sight. There were echoes of it still in Mrs. Newsome's letters, and there were moments when these echoes made him exclaim on her want of tact. He blushed of course, at once, still more for the explanation than for the ground of it: it came to him in time to save his manners that she couldn't at the best become tactful as quickly as he. Her tact had to reckon with the Atlantic Ocean, the General Post-Office and the extravagant curve of the globe. Chad had one day offered tea at the Boulevard Malesherbes to a chosen few, a group again including the unobscured Miss Barrace; and Strether had on coming out walked away with the acquaintance whom in his letters to Mrs. Newsome he always spoke of as the little artist-man. He had had full occasion to mention him as the other party, so oddly, to the only close personal alliance observation had as yet detected in Chad's existence. Little Bilham's way this afternoon was not Strether's, but he had none the less kindly come with him, and it was somehow a part of his kindness that as it had sadly begun to rain they suddenly found themselves seated for conversation at a cafe in which they had taken refuge. He had passed no more crowded hour in Chad's society than the one just ended; he had talked with Miss Barrace, who had reproached him with not having come to see her, and he had above all hit on a happy thought for causing Waymarsh's tension to relax. Something might possibly be extracted for the latter from the idea of his success with that lady, whose quick apprehension of what might amuse her had given Strether a free hand. What had she meant if not to ask whether she couldn't help him with his splendid encumbrance, and mightn't the sacred rage at any rate be kept a little in abeyance by thus creating for his comrade's mind even in a world of irrelevance the possibility of a relation? What was it but a relation to be regarded as so decorative and, in especial, on the strength of it, to be whirled away, amid flounces and feathers, in a coupe lined, by what Strether could make out, with dark blue brocade? He himself had never been whirled away—never at least in a coupe and behind a footman; he had driven with Miss Gostrey in cabs, with Mrs. Pocock, a few times, in an open buggy, with Mrs. Newsome in a four-seated cart and, occasionally up at the mountains, on a buckboard; but his friend's actual adventure transcended his personal experience. He now showed his companion soon enough indeed how inadequate, as a general monitor, this last queer quantity could once more feel itself.

"What game under the sun is he playing?" He signified the next moment that his allusion was not to the fat gentleman immersed in dominoes on whom his eyes had begun by resting, but to their host of the previous hour, as to whom, there on the velvet bench, with a final collapse of all consistency, he treated himself to the comfort of indiscretion. "Where do you see him come out?"

Little Bilham, in meditation, looked at him with a kindness almost paternal. "Don't you like it over here?"

Strether laughed out—for the tone was indeed droll; he let himself go. "What has that to do with it? The only thing I've any business to like is to feel that I'm moving him. That's why I ask you whether you believe I AM? Is the creature"—and he did his best to show that he simply wished to ascertain—"honest?"

His companion looked responsible, but looked it through a small dim smile. "What creature do you mean?"

It was on this that they did have for a little a mute interchange. "Is it untrue that he's free? How then," Strether asked wondering "does he arrange his life?"

"Is the creature you mean Chad himself?" little Bilham said.

Strether here, with a rising hope, just thought, "We must take one of them at a time." But his coherence lapsed. "IS there some woman? Of whom he's really afraid of course I mean—or who does with him what she likes."

"It's awfully charming of you," Bilham presently remarked, "not to have asked me that before."

"Oh I'm not fit for my job!"

The exclamation had escaped our friend, but it made little Bilham more deliberate. "Chad's a rare case!" he luminously observed. "He's awfully changed," he added.

"Then you see it too?"

"The way he has improved? Oh yes—I think every one must see it. But I'm not sure," said little Bilham, "that I didn't like him about as well in his other state."

"Then this IS really a new state altogether?"

"Well," the young man after a moment returned, "I'm not sure he was really meant by nature to be quite so good. It's like the new edition of an old book that one has been fond of—revised and amended, brought up to date, but not quite the thing one knew and loved. However that may be at all events," he pursued, "I don't think, you know, that he's really playing, as you call it, any game. I believe he really wants to go back and take up a career. He's capable of one, you know, that will improve and enlarge him still more. He won't then," little Bilham continued to remark, "be my pleasant well-rubbed old-fashioned volume at all. But of course I'm beastly immoral. I'm afraid it would be a funny world altogether—a world with things the way I like them. I ought, I dare say, to go home and go into business myself. Only I'd simply rather die—simply. And I've not the least difficulty in making up my mind not to, and in knowing exactly why, and in defending my ground against all comers. All the same," he wound up, "I assure you I don't say a word against it—for himself, I mean—to Chad. I seem to see it as much the best thing for him. You see he's not happy."

"DO I?"—Strether stared. "I've been supposing I see just the opposite—an extraordinary case of the equilibrium arrived at and assured."

"Oh there's a lot behind it."

"Ah there you are!" Strether exclaimed. "That's just what I want to get at. You speak of your familiar volume altered out of recognition. Well, who's the editor?"

Little Bilham looked before him a minute in silence. "He ought to get married. THAT would do it. And he wants to."

"Wants to marry her?"

Again little Bilham waited, and, with a sense that he had information, Strether scarce knew what was coming. "He wants to be free. He isn't used, you see," the young man explained in his lucid way, "to being so good."

Strether hesitated. "Then I may take it from you that he IS good?"

His companion matched his pause, but making it up with a quiet fulness. "DO take it from me."

"Well then why isn't he free? He swears to me he is, but meanwhile does nothing—except of course that he's so kind to me—to prove it; and couldn't really act much otherwise if he weren't. My question to you just now was exactly on this queer impression of his diplomacy: as if instead of really giving ground his line were to keep me on here and set me a bad example."

As the half-hour meanwhile had ebbed Strether paid his score, and the waiter was presently in the act of counting out change. Our friend pushed back to him a fraction of it, with which, after an emphatic recognition, the personage in question retreated. "You give too much," little Bilham permitted himself benevolently to observe.

"Oh I always give too much!" Strether helplessly sighed. "But you don't," he went on as if to get quickly away from the contemplation of that doom, "answer my question. Why isn't he free?"

Little Bilham had got up as if the transaction with the waiter had been a signal, and had already edged out between the table and the divan. The effect of this was that a minute later they had quitted the place, the gratified waiter alert again at the open door. Strether had found himself deferring to his companion's abruptness as to a hint that he should be answered as soon as they were more isolated. This happened when after a few steps in the outer air they had turned the next comer. There our friend had kept it up. "Why isn't he free if he's good?"

Little Bilham looked him full in the face. "Because it's a virtuous attachment."

This had settled the question so effectually for the time—that is for the next few days—that it had given Strether almost a new lease of life. It must be added however that, thanks to his constant habit of shaking the bottle in which life handed him the wine of experience, he presently found the taste of the lees rising as usual into his draught. His imagination had in other words already dealt with his young friend's assertion; of which it had made something that sufficiently came out on the very next occasion of his seeing Maria Gostrey. This occasion moreover had been determined promptly by a new circumstance—a circumstance he was the last man to leave her for a day in ignorance of. "When I said to him last night," he immediately began, "that without some definite word from him now that will enable me to speak to them over there of our sailing—or at least of mine, giving them some sort of date—my responsibility becomes uncomfortable and my situation awkward; when I said that to him what do you think was his reply?" And then as she this time gave it up: "Why that he has two particular friends, two ladies, mother and daughter, about to arrive in Paris—coming back from an absence; and that he wants me so furiously to meet them, know them and like them, that I shall oblige him by kindly not bringing our business to a crisis till he has had a chance to see them again himself. Is that," Strether enquired, "the way he's going to try to get off? These are the people," he explained, "that he must have gone down to see before I arrived. They're the best friends he has in the world, and they take more interest than any one else in what concerns him. As I'm his next best he sees a thousand reasons why we should comfortably meet. He hasn't broached the question sooner because their return was uncertain—seemed in fact for the present impossible. But he more than intimates that—if you can believe it—their desire to make my acquaintance has had to do with their surmounting difficulties."

"They're dying to see you?" Miss Gostrey asked.

"Dying. Of course," said Strether, "they're the virtuous attachment." He had already told her about that—had seen her the day after his talk with little Bilham; and they had then threshed out together the bearing of the revelation. She had helped him to put into it the logic in which little Bilham had left it slightly deficient Strether hadn't pressed him as to the object of the preference so unexpectedly described; feeling in the presence of it, with one of his irrepressible scruples, a delicacy from which he had in the quest of the quite other article worked himself sufficiently free. He had held off, as on a small principle of pride, from permitting his young friend to mention a name; wishing to make with this the great point that Chad's virtuous attachments were none of his business. He had wanted from the first not to think too much of his dignity, but that was no reason for not allowing it any little benefit that might turn up. He had often enough wondered to what degree his interference might pass for interested; so that there was no want of luxury in letting it be seen whenever he could that he didn't interfere. That had of course at the same time not deprived him of the further luxury of much private astonishment; which however he had reduced to some order before communicating his knowledge. When he had done this at last it was with the remark that, surprised as Miss Gostrey might, like himself, at first be, she would probably agree with him on reflexion that such an account of the matter did after all fit the confirmed appearances. Nothing certainly, on all the indications, could have been a greater change for him than a virtuous attachment, and since they had been in search of the "word" as the French called it, of that change, little Bilham's announcement—though so long and so oddly delayed—would serve as well as another. She had assured Strether in fact after a pause that the more she thought of it the more it did serve; and yet her assurance hadn't so weighed with him as that before they parted he hadn't ventured to challenge her sincerity. Didn't she believe the attachment was virtuous?—he had made sure of her again with the aid of that question. The tidings he brought her on this second occasion were moreover such as would help him to make surer still.

She showed at first none the less as only amused. "You say there are two? An attachment to them both then would, I suppose, almost necessarily be innocent."

Our friend took the point, but he had his clue. "Mayn't he be still in the stage of not quite knowing which of them, mother or daughter, he likes best?"

She gave it more thought. "Oh it must be the daughter—at his age."

"Possibly. Yet what do we know," Strether asked, "about hers? She may be old enough."

"Old enough for what?"

"Why to marry Chad. That may be, you know, what they want. And if Chad wants it too, and little Bilham wants it, and even we, at a pinch, could do with it—that is if she doesn't prevent repatriation—why it may be plain sailing yet."

It was always the case for him in these counsels that each of his remarks, as it came, seemed to drop into a deeper well. He had at all events to wait a moment to hear the slight splash of this one. "I don't see why if Mr. Newsome wants to marry the young lady he hasn't already done it or hasn't been prepared with some statement to you about it. And if he both wants to marry her and is on good terms with them why isn't he 'free'?"

Strether, responsively, wondered indeed. "Perhaps the girl herself doesn't like him."

"Then why does he speak of them to you as he does?"

Strether's mind echoed the question, but also again met it. "Perhaps it's with the mother he's on good terms."

"As against the daughter?"

"Well, if she's trying to persuade the daughter to consent to him, what could make him like the mother more? Only," Strether threw out, "why shouldn't the daughter consent to him?"

"Oh," said Miss Gostrey, "mayn't it be that every one else isn't quite so struck with him as you?"

"Doesn't regard him you mean as such an 'eligible' young man? Is that what I've come to?" he audibly and rather gravely sought to know. "However," he went on, "his marriage is what his mother most desires—that is if it will help. And oughtn't ANY marriage to help? They must want him"—he had already worked it out—"to be better off. Almost any girl he may marry will have a direct interest in his taking up his chances. It won't suit HER at least that he shall miss them."

Miss Gostrey cast about. "No—you reason well! But of course on the other hand there's always dear old Woollett itself."

"Oh yes," he mused—"there's always dear old Woollett itself."

She waited a moment. "The young lady mayn't find herself able to swallow THAT quantity. She may think it's paying too much; she may weigh one thing against another."

Strether, ever restless in such debates, took a vague turn "It will all depend on who she is. That of course—the proved ability to deal with dear old Woollett, since I'm sure she does deal with it—is what makes so strongly for Mamie."

"Mamie?"

He stopped short, at her tone, before her; then, though seeing that it represented not vagueness, but a momentary embarrassed fulness, let his exclamation come. "You surely haven't forgotten about Mamie!"

"No, I haven't forgotten about Mamie," she smiled. "There's no doubt whatever that there's ever so much to be said for her. Mamie's MY girl!" she roundly declared.

Strether resumed for a minute his walk. "She's really perfectly lovely, you know. Far prettier than any girl I've seen over here yet."

"That's precisely on what I perhaps most build." And she mused a moment in her friend's way. "I should positively like to take her in hand!"

He humoured the fancy, though indeed finally to deprecate it. "Oh but don't, in your zeal, go over to her! I need you most and can't, you know, be left."

But she kept it up. "I wish they'd send her out to me!"

"If they knew you," he returned, "they would."

"Ah but don't they?—after all that, as I've understood you you've told them about me?"

He had paused before her again, but he continued his course "They WILL—before, as you say, I've done." Then he came out with the point he had wished after all most to make. "It seems to give away now his game. This is what he has been doing—keeping me along for. He has been waiting for them."

Miss Gostrey drew in her lips. "You see a good deal in it!"

"I doubt if I see as much as you. Do you pretend," he went on, "that you don't see—?"

"Well, what?"—she pressed him as he paused.

"Why that there must be a lot between them—and that it has been going on from the first; even from before I came."

She took a minute to answer. "Who are they then—if it's so grave?"

"It mayn't be grave—it may be gay. But at any rate it's marked. Only I don't know," Strether had to confess, "anything about them. Their name for instance was a thing that, after little Bilham's information, I found it a kind of refreshment not to feel obliged to follow up."

"Oh," she returned, "if you think you've got off—!"

Her laugh produced in him a momentary gloom. "I don't think I've got off. I only think I'm breathing for about five minutes. I dare say I SHALL have, at the best, still to get on." A look, over it all, passed between them, and the next minute he had come back to good humour. "I don't meanwhile take the smallest interest in their name."

"Nor in their nationality?—American, French, English, Polish?"

"I don't care the least little 'hang,'" he smiled, "for their nationality. It would be nice if they're Polish!" he almost immediately added.

"Very nice indeed." The transition kept up her spirits. "So you see you do care."

He did this contention a modified justice. "I think I should if they WERE Polish. Yes," he thought—"there might be joy in THAT."

"Let us then hope for it." But she came after this nearer to the question. "If the girl's of the right age of course the mother can't be. I mean for the virtuous attachment. If the girl's twenty—and she can't be less—the mother must be at least forty. So it puts the mother out. SHE'S too old for him."

Strether, arrested again, considered and demurred. "Do you think so? Do you think any one would be too old for him? I'M eighty, and I'm too young. But perhaps the girl," he continued, "ISn't twenty. Perhaps she's only ten—but such a little dear that Chad finds himself counting her in as an attraction of the acquaintance. Perhaps she's only five. Perhaps the mother's but five-and-twenty—a charming young widow."

Miss Gostrey entertained the suggestion. "She IS a widow then?"

"I haven't the least idea!" They once more, in spite of this vagueness, exchanged a look—a look that was perhaps the longest yet. It seemed in fact, the next thing, to require to explain itself; which it did as it could. "I only feel what I've told you—that he has some reason."

Miss Gostrey's imagination had taken its own flight. "Perhaps she's NOT a widow."

Strether seemed to accept the possibility with reserve. Still he accepted it. "Then that's why the attachment—if it's to her—is virtuous."

But she looked as if she scarce followed. "Why is it virtuous if—since she's free—there's nothing to impose on it any condition?"

He laughed at her question. "Oh I perhaps don't mean as virtuous as THAT! Your idea is that it can be virtuous—in any sense worthy of the name—only if she's NOT free? But what does it become then," he asked, "for HER?"

"Ah that's another matter." He said nothing for a moment, and she soon went on. "I dare say you're right, at any rate, about Mr. Newsome's little plan. He HAS been trying you—has been reporting on you to these friends."

Strether meanwhile had had time to think more. "Then where's his straightness?"

"Well, as we say, it's struggling up, breaking out, asserting itself as it can. We can be on the side, you see, of his straightness. We can help him. But he has made out," said Miss Gostrey, "that you'll do."

"Do for what?"

"Why, for THEM—for ces dames. He has watched you, studied you, liked you—and recognised that THEY must. It's a great compliment to you, my dear man; for I'm sure they're particular. You came out for a success. Well," she gaily declared, "you're having it!"

He took it from her with momentary patience and then turned abruptly away. It was always convenient to him that there were so many fine things in her room to look at. But the examination of two or three of them appeared soon to have determined a speech that had little to do with them. "You don't believe in it!"

"In what?"

"In the character of the attachment. In its innocence."

But she defended herself. "I don't pretend to know anything about it. Everything's possible. We must see."

"See?" he echoed with a groan. "Haven't we seen enough?"

"I haven't," she smiled.

"But do you suppose then little Bilham has lied?"

"You must find out."

It made him almost turn pale. "Find out any MORE?"

He had dropped on a sofa for dismay; but she seemed, as she stood over him, to have the last word. "Wasn't what you came out for to find out ALL?"

Book Fifth

I

The Sunday of the next week was a wonderful day, and Chad Newsome had let his friend know in advance that he had provided for it. There had already been a question of his taking him to see the great Gloriani, who was at home on Sunday afternoons and at whose house, for the most part, fewer bores were to be met than elsewhere; but the project, through some accident, had not had instant effect, and now revived in happier conditions. Chad had made the point that the celebrated sculptor had a queer old garden, for which the weather—spring at last frank and fair—was propitious; and two or three of his other allusions had confirmed for Strether the expectation of something special. He had by this time, for all introductions and adventures, let himself recklessly go, cherishing the sense that whatever the young man showed him he was showing at least himself. He could have wished indeed, so far as this went, that Chad were less of a mere cicerone; for he was not without the impression—now that the vision of his game, his plan, his deep diplomacy, did recurrently assert itself—of his taking refuge from the realities of their intercourse in profusely dispensing, as our friend mentally phrased et panem et circenses. Our friend continued to feel rather smothered in flowers, though he made in his other moments the almost angry inference that this was only because of his odious ascetic suspicion of any form of beauty. He periodically assured himself—for his reactions were sharp—that he shouldn't reach the truth of anything till he had at least got rid of that.

He had known beforehand that Madame de Vionnet and her daughter would probably be on view, an intimation to that effect having constituted the only reference again made by Chad to his good friends from the south. The effect of Strether's talk about them with Miss Gostrey had been quite to consecrate his reluctance to pry; something in the very air of Chad's silence—judged in the light of that talk—offered it to him as a reserve he could markedly match. It shrouded them about with he scarce knew what, a consideration, a distinction; he was in presence at any rate—so far as it placed him there—of ladies; and the one thing that was definite for him was that they themselves should be, to the extent of his responsibility, in presence of a gentleman. Was it because they were very beautiful, very clever, or even very good—was it for one of these reasons that Chad was, so to speak, nursing his effect? Did he wish to spring them, in the Woollett phrase, with a fuller force—to confound his critic, slight though as yet the criticism, with some form of merit exquisitely incalculable? The most the critic had at all events asked was whether the persons in question were French; and that enquiry had been but a proper comment on the sound of their name. "Yes. That is no!" had been Chad's reply; but he had immediately added that their English was the most charming in the world, so that if Strether were wanting an excuse for not getting on with them he wouldn't in the least find one. Never in fact had Strether—in the mood into which the place had quickly launched him—felt, for himself, less the need of an excuse. Those he might have found would have been, at the worst, all for the others, the people before him, in whose liberty to be as they were he was aware that he positively rejoiced. His fellow guests were multiplying, and these things, their liberty, their intensity, their variety, their conditions at large, were in fusion in the admirable medium of the scene.

The place itself was a great impression—a small pavilion, clear-faced and sequestered, an effect of polished parquet, of fine white panel and spare sallow gilt, of decoration delicate and rare, in the heart of the Faubourg Saint-Germain and on the edge of a cluster of gardens attached to old noble houses. Far back from streets and unsuspected by crowds, reached by a long passage and a quiet court, it was as striking to the unprepared mind, he immediately saw, as a treasure dug up; giving him too, more than anything yet, the note of the range of the immeasurable town and sweeping away, as by a last brave brush, his usual landmarks and terms. It was in the garden, a spacious cherished remnant, out of which a dozen persons had already passed, that Chad's host presently met them while the tall bird-haunted trees, all of a twitter with the spring and the weather, and the high party-walls, on the other side of which grave hotels stood off for privacy, spoke of survival, transmission, association, a strong indifferent persistent order. The day was so soft that the little party had practically adjourned to the open air but the open air was in such conditions all a chamber of state. Strether had presently the sense of a great convent, a convent of missions, famous for he scarce knew what, a nursery of young priests, of scattered shade, of straight alleys and chapel-bells, that spread its mass in one quarter; he had the sense of names in the air, of ghosts at the windows, of signs and tokens, a whole range of expression, all about him, too thick for prompt discrimination.

This assault of images became for a moment, in the address of the distinguished sculptor, almost formidable: Gloriani showed him, in such perfect confidence, on Chad's introduction of him, a fine worn handsome face, a face that was like an open letter in a foreign tongue. With his genius in his eyes, his manners on his lips, his long career behind him and his honours and rewards all round, the great artist, in the course of a single sustained look and a few words of delight at receiving him, affected our friend as a dazzling prodigy of type. Strether had seen in museums—in the Luxembourg as well as, more reverently, later on, in the New York of the billionaires—the work of his hand; knowing too that after an earlier time in his native Rome he had migrated, in mid-career, to Paris, where, with a personal lustre almost violent, he shone in a constellation: all of which was more than enough to crown him, for his guest, with the light, with the romance, of glory. Strether, in contact with that element as he had never yet so intimately been, had the consciousness of opening to it, for the happy instant, all the windows of his mind, of letting this rather grey interior drink in for once the sun of a clime not marked in his old geography. He was to remember again repeatedly the medal-like Italian face, in which every line was an artist's own, in which time told only as tone and consecration; and he was to recall in especial, as the penetrating radiance, as the communication of the illustrious spirit itself, the manner in which, while they stood briefly, in welcome and response, face to face, he was held by the sculptor's eyes. He wasn't soon to forget them, was to think of them, all unconscious, unintending, preoccupied though they were, as the source of the deepest intellectual sounding to which he had ever been exposed. He was in fact quite to cherish his vision of it, to play with it in idle hours; only speaking of it to no one and quite aware he couldn't have spoken without appearing to talk nonsense. Was what it had told him or what it had asked him the greater of the mysteries? Was it the most special flare, unequalled, supreme, of the aesthetic torch, lighting that wondrous world for ever, or was it above all the long straight shaft sunk by a personal acuteness that life had seasoned to steel? Nothing on earth could have been stranger and no one doubtless more surprised than the artist himself, but it was for all the world to Strether just then as if in the matter of his accepted duty he had positively been on trial. The deep human expertness in Gloriani's charming smile—oh the terrible life behind it!—was flashed upon him as a test of his stuff.

Chad meanwhile, after having easily named his companion, had still more easily turned away and was already greeting other persons present. He was as easy, clever Chad, with the great artist as with his obscure compatriot, and as easy with every one else as with either: this fell into its place for Strether and made almost a new light, giving him, as a concatenation, something more he could enjoy. He liked Gloriani, but should never see him again; of that he was sufficiently sure. Chad accordingly, who was wonderful with both of them, was a kind of link for hopeless fancy, an implication of possibilities—oh if everything had been different! Strether noted at all events that he was thus on terms with illustrious spirits, and also that—yes, distinctly—he hadn't in the least swaggered about it. Our friend hadn't come there only for this figure of Abel Newsome's son, but that presence threatened to affect the observant mind as positively central. Gloriani indeed, remembering something and excusing himself, pursued Chad to speak to him, and Strether was left musing on many things. One of them was the question of whether, since he had been tested, he had passed. Did the artist drop him from having made out that he wouldn't do? He really felt just to-day that he might do better than usual. Hadn't he done well enough, so far as that went, in being exactly so dazzled? and in not having too, as he almost believed, wholly hidden from his host that he felt the latter's plummet? Suddenly, across the garden, he saw little Bilham approach, and it was a part of the fit that was on him that as their eyes met he guessed also HIS knowledge. If he had said to him on the instant what was uppermost he would have said: "HAVE I passed?—for of course I know one has to pass here." Little Bilham would have reassured him, have told him that he exaggerated, and have adduced happily enough the argument of little Bilham's own very presence; which, in truth, he could see, was as easy a one as Gloriani's own or as Chad's. He himself would perhaps then after a while cease to be frightened, would get the point of view for some of the faces—types tremendously alien, alien to Woollett—

that he had already begun to take in. Who were they all, the dispersed groups and couples, the ladies even more unlike those of Woollett than the gentlemen?—this was the enquiry that, when his young friend had greeted him, he did find himself making.

"Oh they're every one—all sorts and sizes; of course I mean within limits, though limits down perhaps rather more than limits up. There are always artists—he's beautiful and inimitable to the cher confrere; and then gros bonnets of many kinds—ambassadors, cabinet ministers, bankers, generals, what do I know? even Jews. Above all always some awfully nice women—and not too many; sometimes an actress, an artist, a great performer—but only when they're not monsters; and in particular the right femmes du monde. You can fancy his history on that side—I believe it's fabulous: they NEVER give him up. Yet he keeps them down: no one knows how he manages; it's too beautiful and bland. Never too many—and a mighty good thing too; just a perfect choice. But there are not in any way many bores; it has always been so; he has some secret. It's extraordinary. And you don't find it out. He's the same to every one. He doesn't ask questions.'

"Ah doesn't he?" Strether laughed.

Bilham met it with all his candour. "How then should I be here?

"Oh for what you tell me. You're part of the perfect choice."

Well, the young man took in the scene. "It seems rather good to-day."

Strether followed the direction of his eyes. "Are they all, this time, femmes du monde?"

Little Bilham showed his competence. "Pretty well."

This was a category our friend had a feeling for; a light, romantic and mysterious, on the feminine element, in which he enjoyed for a little watching it. "Are there any Poles?"

His companion considered. "I think I make out a 'Portuguee.' But I've seen Turks."

Strether wondered, desiring justice. "They seem—all the women—very harmonious."

"Oh in closer quarters they come out!" And then, while Strether was aware of fearing closer quarters, though giving himself again to the harmonies, "Well," little Bilham went on, "it IS at the worst rather good, you know. If you like it, you feel it, this way, that shows you're not in the least out But you always know things," he handsomely added, "immediately."

Strether liked it and felt it only too much; so "I say, don't lay traps for me!" he rather helplessly murmured.

"Well," his companion returned, "he's wonderfully kind to us."

"To us Americans you mean?"

"Oh no—he doesn't know anything about THAT. That's half the battle here—that you can never hear politics. We don't talk them. I mean to poor young wretches of all sorts. And yet it's always as charming as this; it's as if, by something in the air, our squalor didn't show. It puts us all back—into the last century."

"I'm afraid," Strether said, amused, "that it puts me rather forward: oh ever so far!"

"Into the next? But isn't that only," little Bilham asked, "because you're really of the century before?"

"The century before the last? Thank you!" Strether laughed. "If I ask you about some of the ladies it can't be then that I may hope, as such a specimen of the rococo, to please them."

"On the contrary they adore—we all adore here—the rococo, and where is there a better setting for it than the whole thing, the pavilion and the garden, together? There are lots of people with collections," little Bilham smiled as he glanced round. "You'll be secured!"

It made Strether for a moment give himself again to contemplation. There were faces he scarce knew what to make of. Were they charming or were they only strange? He mightn't talk politics, yet he suspected a Pole or two. The upshot was the question at the back of his head from the moment his friend had joined him. "Have Madame de Vionnet and her daughter arrived?"

"I haven't seen them yet, but Miss Gostrey has come. She's in the pavilion looking at objects. One can see SHE'S a collector," little Bilham added without offence.

"Oh yes, she's a collector, and I knew she was to come. Is Madame de Vionnet a collector?" Strether went on.

"Rather, I believe; almost celebrated." The young man met, on it, a little, his friend's eyes. "I happen to know—from Chad, whom I saw last night—that they've come back; but only yesterday. He wasn't sure—up to the last. This, accordingly," little Bilham went on, "will be—if they ARE here—their first appearance after their return."

Strether, very quickly, turned these things over. "Chad told you last night? To me, on our way here, he said nothing about it."

"But did you ask him?"

Strether did him the justice. "I dare say not."

"Well," said little Bilham, "you're not a person to whom it's easy to tell things you don't want to know. Though it is easy, I admit—it's quite beautiful," he benevolently added, "when you do want to."

Strether looked at him with an indulgence that matched his intelligence. "Is that the deep reasoning on which—about these ladies—you've been yourself so silent?"

Little Bilham considered the depth of his reasoning. "I haven't been silent. I spoke of them to you the other day, the day we sat together after Chad's tea-party."

Strether came round to it. "They then are the virtuous attachment?"

"I can only tell you that it's what they pass for. But isn't that enough? What more than a vain appearance does the wisest of us know? I commend you," the young man declared with a pleasant emphasis, "the vain appearance."

Strether looked more widely round, and what he saw, from face to face, deepened the effect of his young friend's words. "Is it so good?"

"Magnificent."

Strether had a pause. "The husband's dead?"

"Dear no. Alive."

"Oh!" said Strether. After which, as his companion laughed: "How then can it be so good?"

"You'll see for yourself. One does see."

"Chad's in love with the daughter?"

"That's what I mean."

Strether wondered. "Then where's the difficulty?"

"Why, aren't you and I—with our grander bolder ideas?"

"Oh mine—!" Strether said rather strangely. But then as if to attenuate: "You mean they won't hear of Woollett?"

Little Bilham smiled. "Isn't that just what you must see about?"

It had brought them, as she caught the last words, into relation with Miss Barrace, whom Strether had already observed—as he had never before seen a lady at a party—moving about alone. Coming within sound of them she had already spoken, and she took again, through her long-handled glass, all her amused and amusing possession. "How much, poor Mr. Strether, you seem to have to see about! But you can't say," she gaily declared, "that I don't do what I can to help you. Mr. Waymarsh is placed. I've left him in the house with Miss Gostrey."

"The way," little Bilham exclaimed, "Mr. Strether gets the ladies to work for him! He's just preparing to draw in another; to pounce—don't you see him?—on Madame de Vionnet."

"Madame de Vionnet? Oh, oh, oh!" Miss Barrace cried in a wonderful crescendo. There was more in it, our friend made out, than met the ear. Was it after all a joke that he should be serious about anything? He envied Miss Barrace at any rate her power of not being. She seemed, with little cries and protests and quick recognitions, movements like the darts of some fine high-feathered free-pecking bird, to stand before life as before some full shop-window. You could fairly hear, as she selected and pointed, the tap of her tortoise-shell against the glass. "It's certain that we do need seeing about; only I'm glad it's not I who have to do it. One does, no doubt, begin that way; then suddenly one finds that one has given it up. It's too much, it's too difficult. You're wonderful, you people," she continued to Strether, "for not feeling those things—by which I mean impossibilities. You never feel them. You face them with a fortitude that makes it a lesson to watch you."

"Ah but"—little Bilham put it with discouragement—"what do we achieve after all? We see about you and report—when we even go so far as reporting. But nothing's done."

"Oh you, Mr. Bilham," she replied as with an impatient rap on the glass, "you're not worth sixpence! You come over to convert the savages—for I know you verily did, I remember you—and the savages simply convert YOU."

"Not even!" the young man woefully confessed: "they haven't gone through that form. They've simply—the cannibals!—eaten me; converted me if you like, but converted me into food. I'm but the bleached bones of a Christian."

"Well then there we are! Only"—and Miss Barrace appealed again to Strether—"don't let it discourage you. You'll break down soon enough, but you'll meanwhile have had your moments. Il faut en avoir. I always like to see you while you last. And I'll tell you who WILL last."

"Waymarsh?"—he had already taken her up.

She laughed out as at the alarm of it. "He'll resist even Miss Gostrey: so grand is it not to understand. He's wonderful."

"He is indeed," Strether conceded. "He wouldn't tell me of this affair—only said he had an engagement; but with such a gloom, you must let me insist, as if it had been an engagement to be hanged. Then silently and secretly he turns up here with you. Do you call THAT 'lasting'?"

"Oh I hope it's lasting!" Miss Barrace said. "But he only, at the best, bears with me. He doesn't understand—not one little scrap. He's delightful. He's wonderful," she repeated.

"Michelangelesque!"—little Bilham completed her meaning. "He IS a success. Moses, on the ceiling, brought down to the floor; overwhelming, colossal, but somehow portable."

"Certainly, if you mean by portable," she returned, "looking so well in one's carriage. He's too funny beside me in his comer; he looks like somebody, somebody foreign and famous, en exil; so that people wonder—it's very amusing—whom I'm taking about. I show him Paris, show him everything, and he never turns a hair. He's like the Indian chief one reads about, who, when he comes up to Washington to see the Great Father, stands wrapt in his blanket and gives no sign. I might be the Great Father—from the way he takes everything." She was delighted at this hit of her identity with that personage—it fitted so her character; she declared it was the title she meant henceforth to adopt. "And the way he sits, too, in the corner of my room, only looking at my visitors very hard and as if he wanted to start something! They wonder what he does want to start. But he's wonderful," Miss Barrace once more insisted. "He has never started anything yet."

It presented him none the less, in truth, to her actual friends, who looked at each other in intelligence, with frank amusement on Bilham's part and a shade of sadness on Strether's. Strether's sadness sprang—for the image had its grandeur—from his thinking how little he himself was wrapt in his blanket, how little, in marble halls, all too oblivious of the Great Father, he resembled a really majestic aboriginal. But he had also another reflexion. "You've all of you here so much visual sense that you've somehow all 'run' to it. There are moments when it strikes one that you haven't any other."

"Any moral," little Bilham explained, watching serenely, across the garden, the several femmes du monde. "But Miss Barrace has a moral distinction," he kindly continued; speaking as if for Strether's benefit not less than for her own.

"HAVE you?" Strether, scarce knowing what he was about, asked of her almost eagerly.

"Oh not a distinction"—she was mightily amused at his tone—"Mr. Bilham's too good. But I think I may say a sufficiency. Yes, a sufficiency. Have you supposed strange things of me?"—and she fixed him again, through all her tortoise-shell, with the droll interest of it. "You ARE all indeed wonderful. I should awfully disappoint you. I do take my stand on my sufficiency. But I know, I confess," she went on, "strange people. I don't know how it happens; I don't do it on purpose; it seems to be my doom—as if I were always one of their habits: it's wonderful! I dare say moreover," she pursued with an interested gravity, "that I do, that we all do here, run too much to mere eye. But how can it be helped? We're all looking at each other—and in the light of Paris one sees what things resemble. That's what the light of Paris seems always to show. It's the fault of the light of Paris—dear old light!"

"Dear old Paris!" little Bilham echoed.

"Everything, every one shows," Miss Barrace went on.

"But for what they really are?" Strether asked.

"Oh I like your Boston 'reallys'! But sometimes—yes."

"Dear old Paris then!" Strether resignedly sighed while for a moment they looked at each other. Then he broke out: "Does Madame de Vionnet do that? I mean really show for what she is?"

Her answer was prompt. "She's charming. She's perfect."

"Then why did you a minute ago say 'Oh, oh, oh!' at her name?"

She easily remembered. "Why just because—! She's wonderful."

"Ah she too?"—Strether had almost a groan.

But Miss Barrace had meanwhile perceived relief. "Why not put your question straight to the person who can answer it best?"

"No," said little Bilham; "don't put any question; wait, rather—it will be much more fun—to judge for yourself. He has come to take you to her."

II

On which Strether saw that Chad was again at hand, and he afterwards scarce knew, absurd as it may seem, what had then quickly occurred. The moment concerned him, he felt, more deeply than he could have explained, and he had a subsequent passage of speculation as to whether, on walking off with Chad, he hadn't looked either pale or red. The only thing he was clear about was that, luckily, nothing indiscreet had in fact been said and that Chad himself was more than ever, in Miss Barrace's great sense, wonderful. It was one of the connexions—though really why it should be, after all, was none so apparent—in which the whole change in him came out as most striking. Strether recalled as they approached the house that he had impressed him that first night as knowing how to enter a box. Well, he impressed him scarce less now as knowing how to make a presentation. It did something for Strether's own quality—marked it as estimated; so that our poor friend, conscious and passive, really seemed to feel himself quite handed over and delivered; absolutely, as he would have said, made a present of, given away. As they reached the house a young woman, about to come forth, appeared, unaccompanied, on the steps; at the exchange with whom of a word on Chad's part Strether immediately perceived that, obligingly, kindly, she was there to meet them. Chad had left her in the house, but she had afterwards come halfway and then the next moment had joined them in the garden. Her air of youth, for Strether, was at first almost disconcerting, while his second impression was, not less sharply, a degree of relief at there not having just been, with the others, any freedom used about her. It was upon him at a touch that she was no subject for that, and meanwhile, on Chad's introducing him, she had spoken to him, very simply and gently, in an English clearly of the easiest to her, yet unlike any other he had ever heard. It wasn't as if she tried; nothing, he could see after they had been a few minutes together, was as if she tried; but her speech, charming correct and odd, was like a precaution against her passing for a Pole. There were precautions, he seemed indeed to see, only when there were really dangers.

Later on he was to feel many more of them, but by that time he was to feel other things besides. She was dressed in black, but in black that struck him as light and transparent; she was exceedingly fair, and, though she was as markedly slim, her face had a roundness, with eyes far apart and a little strange. Her smile was natural and dim; her hat not extravagant; he had only perhaps a sense of the clink, beneath her fine black sleeves, of more gold bracelets and bangles than he had ever seen a lady wear. Chad was excellently free and light about their encounter; it was one of the occasions on which Strether most wished he himself might have arrived at such ease and such humour: "Here you are then, face to face at last; you're made for each other—vous allez voir; and I bless your union." It was indeed, after he had gone off, as if he had been partly serious too. This latter motion had been determined by an enquiry from him about "Jeanne"; to which her mother had replied that she was probably still in the house with Miss Gostrey, to whom she had lately committed her. "Ah but you know," the young man had rejoined, "he must see her"; with which, while Strether pricked up his ears, he had started as if to bring her, leaving the other objects of his interest together. Strether wondered to find Miss Gostrey already involved, feeling that he missed a link; but feeling also, with small delay, how much he should like to talk with her of Madame de Vionnet on this basis of evidence.

The evidence as yet in truth was meagre; which, for that matter, was perhaps a little why his expectation had had a drop. There was somehow not quite a wealth in her; and a wealth was all that, in his simplicity, he had definitely prefigured. Still, it was too much to be sure already that there was but a poverty. They moved away from the house, and, with eyes on a bench at some distance, he proposed that they should sit down. "I've heard a great deal about you," she said as they went; but he had an answer to it that made her stop short. "Well, about YOU, Madame de Vionnet, I've heard, I'm bound to say, almost nothing"—those struck him as the only words he himself could utter with any lucidity; conscious as he was, and as with more reason, of the determination to be in respect to the rest of his business perfectly plain and go perfectly straight. It hadn't at any rate been in the least his idea to spy on Chad's proper freedom. It was possibly, however, at this very instant and under the impression of Madame de Vionnet's pause, that going straight began to announce itself as a matter for care. She had only after all to smile at him ever so gently in order to make him ask himself if he weren't already going crooked. It might be going crooked to find it of a sudden just only clear that she intended very definitely to be what he would have called nice to him. This was what passed between them while, for another instant, they stood still; he couldn't at least remember afterwards what else it might have been. The thing indeed really unmistakeable was its rolling over him as a wave that he had been, in conditions incalculable and unimaginable, a subject of discussion. He had been, on some ground that concerned her, answered for; which gave her an advantage he should never be able to match.

"Hasn't Miss Gostrey," she asked, "said a good word for me?"

What had struck him first was the way he was bracketed with that lady; and he wondered what account Chad would have given of their acquaintance. Something not as yet traceable, at all events, had obviously happened. "I didn't even know of her knowing you."

"Well, now she'll tell you all. I'm so glad you're in relation with her."

This was one of the things—the "all" Miss Gostrey would now tell him—that, with every deference to present preoccupation, was uppermost for Strether after they had taken their seat. One of the others was, at the end of five minutes, that she—oh incontestably, yes—DIFFERED less; differed, that is, scarcely at all—well, superficially speaking, from Mrs. Newsome or even from Mrs. Pocock. She was ever so much younger than the one and not so young as the other; but what WAS there in her, if anything, that would have made it impossible he should meet her at Woollett? And wherein was her talk during their moments on the bench together not the same as would have been found adequate for a Woollett garden-party?—unless perhaps truly in not being quite so bright. She observed to him that Mr. Newsome had, to her knowledge, taken extraordinary pleasure in his visit; but there was no good lady at Woollett who wouldn't have been at least up to that. Was there in Chad, by chance, after all, deep down, a principle of aboriginal loyalty that had made him, for sentimental ends, attach himself to elements, happily encountered, that would remind him most of the old air and the old soil? Why accordingly be in a flutter—Strether could even put it that way—about this unfamiliar phenomenon of the femme du monde? On these terms Mrs. Newsome herself was as much of one. Little Bilham verily had testified that they came out, the ladies of the type, in close quarters; but it was just in these quarters—now comparatively close—that he felt Madame de Vionnet's common humanity. She did come out, and certainly to his relief, but she came out as the usual thing. There might be motives behind, but so could there often be even at Woollett. The only thing was that if she showed him she wished to like him—as the motives behind might conceivably prompt—it would possibly have been more thrilling for him that she should have shown as more vividly alien. Ah she was neither Turk nor Pole!—which would be indeed flat once more for Mrs. Newsome and Mrs. Pocock. A lady and two gentlemen had meanwhile, however, approached their bench, and this accident stayed for the time further developments.

They presently addressed his companion, the brilliant strangers; she rose to speak to them, and Strether noted how the escorted lady, though mature and by no means beautiful, had more of the bold high look, the range of expensive reference, that he had, as might have been said, made his plans for. Madame de Vionnet greeted her as "Duchesse" and was greeted in turn, while talk started in French, as "Ma toute-belle"; little facts that had their due, their vivid interest for Strether. Madame de Vionnet didn't, none the less, introduce him—a note he was conscious of as false to the Woollett scale and the Woollett humanity; though it didn't prevent the Duchess, who struck him as confident and free, very much what he had obscurely supposed duchesses, from looking at him as straight and as hard—for it WAS hard—as if she would have liked, all the same, to know him. "Oh yes, my dear, it's all right, it's ME; and who are YOU, with your interesting wrinkles and your most effective (is it the handsomest, is it the ugliest?) of noses?"—some such loose handful of bright flowers she seemed, fragrantly enough, to fling at him. Strether almost wondered—at such a pace was he going—if some divination of the influence of either party were what determined Madame de Vionnet's abstention. One of the gentlemen, in any case, succeeded in placing himself in close relation with our friend's companion; a gentleman rather stout and importantly short, in a hat with a wonderful wide curl to its brim and a frock coat buttoned with an effect of superlative decision. His French had quickly turned to equal English, and it occurred to Strether that he might well be one of the ambassadors. His design was evidently to assert a claim to Madame de Vionnet's undivided countenance, and he made it good in the course of a minute—led her away with a trick of three words; a trick played with a social art of which Strether, looking after them as the four, whose backs were now all turned, moved off, felt himself no master.

He sank again upon his bench and, while his eyes followed the party, reflected, as he had done before, on Chad's strange communities. He sat there alone for five minutes, with plenty to think of; above all with his sense of having suddenly been dropped by a charming woman overlaid now by other impressions and in fact quite cleared and indifferent. He hadn't yet had so quiet a surrender; he didn't in the least care if nobody spoke to him more. He might have been, by his attitude, in for something of a march so broad that the want of ceremony with which he had just been used could fall into its place as but a minor incident of the procession. Besides, there would be incidents enough, as he felt when this term of contemplation was closed by the reappearance of little Bilham, who stood before him a moment with a suggestive "Well?" in which he saw himself reflected as disorganised, as possibly floored. He replied with a "Well!" intended to show that he wasn't floored in the least. No indeed; he gave it out, as the young man sat down beside him, that if, at the worst, he had been overturned at all, he had been overturned into the upper air, the sublimer element with which he had an affinity and in which he might be trusted a while to float. It wasn't a descent to earth to say after an instant and in sustained response to the reference: "You're quite sure her husband's living?"

"Oh dear, yes."

"Ah then—!"

"Ah then what?"

Strether had after all to think. "Well, I'm sorry for them." But it didn't for the moment matter more than that. He assured his young friend he was quite content. They wouldn't stir; were all right as they were. He didn't want to be introduced; had been introduced already about as far as he could go. He had seen moreover an immensity; liked Gloriani, who, as Miss Barrace kept saying, was wonderful; had made out, he was sure, the half-dozen other 'men who were distinguished, the artists, the critics and oh the great dramatist—HIM it was easy to spot; but wanted—no, thanks, really—to talk with none of them; having nothing at all to say and finding it would do beautifully as it was; do beautifully because what it was—well, was just simply too late. And when after this little Bilham, submissive and responsive, but with an eye to the consolation nearest, easily threw off some "Better late than never!" all he got in return for it was a sharp "Better early than late!" This note indeed the next thing overflowed for Strether into a quiet stream of demonstration that as soon as he had let himself go he felt as the real relief. It had consciously gathered to a head, but the reservoir had filled sooner than he knew, and his companion's touch was to make the waters spread. There were some things that had to come in time if they were to come at all. If they didn't come in time they were lost for ever. It was the general sense of them that had overwhelmed him with its long slow rush.

"It's not too late for YOU, on any side, and you don't strike me as in danger of missing the train; besides which people can be in general pretty well trusted, of course—with the clock of their freedom ticking as loud as it seems to do here—to keep an eye on the fleeting hour. All the same don't forget that you're young—blessedly young; be glad of it on the contrary and live up to it. Live all you can; it's a mistake not to. It doesn't so much matter what you do in particular, so long as you have your life. If you haven't had that what HAVE you had? This place and these impressions—mild as you may find them to wind a man up so; all my impressions of Chad and of people I've seen at HIS place—well, have had their abundant message for me, have just dropped THAT into my mind. I see it now. I haven't done so enough before—and now I'm old; too old at any rate for what I see. Oh I DO see, at least; and more than you'd believe or I can express. It's too late. And it's as if the train had fairly waited at the station for me without my having had the gumption to know it was there. Now I hear its faint receding whistle miles and miles down the line. What one loses one loses; make no mistake about that. The affair—I mean the affair of life—couldn't, no doubt, have been different for me; for it's at the best a tin mould, either fluted and embossed, with ornamental excrescences, or else smooth and dreadfully plain, into which, a helpless jelly, one's consciousness is poured—so that one 'takes' the form as the great cook says, and is more or less compactly held by it: one lives in fine as one can. Still, one has the illusion of freedom; therefore don't be, like me, without the memory of that illusion. I was either, at the right time, too stupid or too intelligent to have it; I don't quite know which. Of course at present I'm a case of reaction against the mistake; and the voice of reaction should, no doubt, always be taken with an allowance. But that doesn't affect the point that the right time is now yours. The right time is ANY time that one is still so lucky as to have. You've plenty; that's the great thing; you're, as I say, damn you, so happily and hatefully young. Don't at any rate miss things out of stupidity. Of course I don't take you for a fool, or I shouldn't be addressing you thus awfully. Do what you like so long as you don't make MY mistake. For it was a mistake. Live!" ... Slowly and sociably, with full pauses and straight dashes, Strether had so delivered himself; holding little Bilham from step to step deeply and gravely attentive. The end of all was that the young man had turned quite solemn, and that this was a contradiction of the innocent gaiety the speaker had wished to promote. He watched for a moment the consequence of his words, and then, laying a hand on his listener's knee and as if to end with the proper joke: "And now for the eye I shall keep on you!"

"Oh but I don't know that I want to be, at your age, too different from you!"

"Ah prepare while you're about it," said Strether, "to be more amusing."

Little Bilham continued to think, but at last had a smile. "Well, you ARE amusing—to ME."

"Impayable, as you say, no doubt. But what am I to myself?" Strether had risen with this, giving his attention now to an encounter that, in the middle of the garden, was in the act of taking place between their host and the lady at whose side Madame de Vionnet had quitted him. This lady, who appeared within a few minutes to have left her friends, awaited Gloriani's eager approach with words on her lips that Strether couldn't catch, but of which her interesting witty face seemed to give him the echo. He was sure she was prompt and fine, but also that she had met her match, and he liked—in the light of what he was quite sure was the Duchess's latent insolence—the good humour with which the great artist asserted equal resources. Were they, this pair, of the "great world"?—and was he himself, for the moment and thus related to them by his observation, IN it? Then there was something in the great world covertly tigerish, which came to him across the lawn and in the charming air as a waft from the jungle. Yet it made him admire most of the two, made him envy, the glossy male tiger, magnificently marked. These absurdities of the stirred sense, fruits of suggestion ripening on the instant, were all reflected in his next words to little Bilham. "I know—if we talk of that—whom I should enjoy being like!"

Little Bilham followed his eyes; but then as with a shade of knowing surprise: "Gloriani?"

Our friend had in fact already hesitated, though not on the hint of his companion's doubt, in which there were depths of critical reserve. He had just made out, in the now full picture, something and somebody else; another impression had been superimposed. A young girl in a white dress and a softly plumed white hat had suddenly come into view, and what was presently clear was that her course was toward them. What was clearer still was that the handsome young man at her side was Chad Newsome, and what was clearest of all was that she was therefore Mademoiselle de Vionnet, that she was unmistakeably pretty—bright gentle shy happy wonderful—and that Chad now, with a consummate calculation of effect, was about to present her to his old friend's vision. What was clearest of all indeed was something much more than this, something at the single stroke of which—and wasn't it simply juxtaposition?—all vagueness vanished. It was the click of a spring—he saw the truth. He had by this time also met Chad's look; there was more of it in that; and the truth, accordingly, so far as Bilham's enquiry was concerned, had thrust in the answer. "Oh Chad!"—it was that rare youth he should have enjoyed being "like." The virtuous attachment would be all there before him; the virtuous attachment would be in the very act of appeal for his blessing; Jeanne de Vionnet, this charming creature, would be exquisitely, intensely now—the object of it. Chad brought her straight up to him, and Chad was, oh yes, at this moment—for the glory of Woollett or whatever—better still even than Gloriani. He had plucked this blossom; he had kept it over-night in water; and at last as he held it up to wonder he did enjoy his effect. That was why Strether had felt at first the breath of calculation—and why moreover, as he now knew, his look at the girl would be, for the young man, a sign of the latter's success. What young man had ever paraded about that way, without a reason, a maiden in her flower? And there was nothing in his reason at present obscure. Her type sufficiently told of it—they wouldn't, they couldn't, want her to go to Woollett. Poor Woollett, and what it might miss!—though brave Chad indeed too, and what it might gain! Brave Chad however had just excellently spoken. "This is a good little friend of mine who knows all about you and has moreover a message for you. And this, my dear"—he had turned to the child herself—"is the best man in the world, who has it in his power to do a great deal for us and whom I want you to like and revere as nearly as possible as much as I do."

She stood there quite pink, a little frightened, prettier and prettier and not a bit like her mother. There was in this last particular no resemblance but that of youth to youth; and here was in fact suddenly Strether's sharpest impression. It went wondering, dazed, embarrassed, back to the woman he had just been talking with; it was a revelation in the light of which he already saw she would become more interesting. So slim and fresh and fair, she had yet put forth this perfection; so that for really believing it of her, for seeing her to any such developed degree as a mother, comparison would be urgent. Well, what was it now but fairly thrust upon him? "Mamma wishes me to tell you before we go," the girl said, "that she hopes very much you'll come to see us very soon. She has something important to say to you."

"She quite reproaches herself," Chad helpfully explained: "you were interesting her so much when she accidentally suffered you to be interrupted."

"Ah don't mention it!" Strether murmured, looking kindly from one to the other and wondering at many things.

"And I'm to ask you for myself," Jeanne continued with her hands clasped together as if in some small learnt prayer—"I'm to ask you for myself if you won't positively come."

"Leave it to me, dear—I'll take care of it!" Chad genially declared in answer to this, while Strether himself almost held his breath. What was in the girl was indeed too soft, too unknown for direct dealing; so that one could only gaze at it as at a picture, quite staying one's own hand. But with Chad he was now on ground—Chad he could meet; so pleasant a confidence in that and in everything did the young man freely exhale. There was the whole of a story in his tone to his companion, and he spoke indeed as if already of the family. It made Strether guess the more quickly what it might be about which Madame de Vionnet was so urgent. Having seen him then she had found him easy; she wished to have it out with him that some way for the young people must be discovered, some way that would not impose as a condition the transplantation of her daughter. He already saw himself discussing with this lady the attractions of Woollett as a residence for Chad's companion. Was that youth going now to trust her with the affair—so that it would be after all with one of his "lady-friends" that his mother's missionary should be condemned to deal? It was quite as if for an instant the two men looked at each other on this question. But there was no mistaking at last Chad's pride in the display of such a connexion. This was what had made him so carry himself while, three minutes before, he was bringing it into view; what had caused his friend, first catching sight of him, to be so struck with his air. It was, in a word, just when he thus finally felt Chad putting things straight off on him that he envied him, as he had mentioned to little Bilham, most. The whole exhibition however was but a matter of three or four minutes, and the author of it had soon explained that, as Madame de Vionnet was immediately going "on," this could be for Jeanne but a snatch. They would all meet again soon, and Strether was meanwhile to stay and amuse himself—"I'll pick you up again in plenty of time." He took the girl off as he had brought her, and Strether, with the faint sweet foreignness of her "Au revoir, monsieur!" in his ears as a note almost unprecedented, watched them recede side by side and felt how, once more, her companion's relation to her got an accent from it. They disappeared among the others and apparently into the house; whereupon our friend turned round to give out to little Bilham the conviction of which he was full. But there was no little Bilham any more; little Bilham had within the few moments, for reasons of his own, proceeded further: a circumstance by which, in its order, Strether was also sensibly affected.

III

Chad was not in fact on this occasion to keep his promise of coming back; but Miss Gostrey had soon presented herself with an explanation of his failure. There had been reasons at the last for his going off with ces dames; and he had asked her with much instance to come out and take charge of their friend. She did so, Strether felt as she took her place beside him, in a manner that left nothing to desire. He had dropped back on his bench, alone again for a time, and the more conscious for little Bilham's defection of his unexpressed thought; in respect to which however this next converser was a still more capacious vessel. "It's the child!" he had exclaimed to her almost as soon as she appeared; and though her direct response was for some time delayed he could feel in her meanwhile the working of this truth. It might have been simply, as she waited, that they were now in presence altogether of truth spreading like a flood and not for the moment to be offered her in the mere cupful; inasmuch as who should ces dames prove to be but persons about whom—once thus face to face with them—she found she might from the first have told him almost everything? This would have freely come had he taken the simple precaution of giving her their name. There could be no better example—and she appeared to note it with high amusement—than the way, making things out already so much for himself, he was at last throwing precautions to the winds. They were neither more nor less, she and the child's mother, than old school-friends—friends who had scarcely met for years but whom this unlooked-for chance had brought together with a rush. It was a relief, Miss Gostrey hinted, to feel herself no longer groping; she was unaccustomed to grope and as a general thing, he might well have seen, made straight enough for her clue. With the one she had now picked up in her hands there need be at least no waste of wonder. "She's coming to see me—that's for YOU," Strether's counsellor continued; "but I don't require it to know where I am."

The waste of wonder might be proscribed; but Strether, characteristically, was even by this time in the immensity of space. "By which you mean that you know where SHE is?"

She just hesitated. "I mean that if she comes to see me I shall—now that I've pulled myself round a bit after the shock—not be at home."

Strether hung poised. "You call it—your recognition—a shock?"

She gave one of her rare flickers of impatience. "It was a surprise, an emotion. Don't be so literal. I wash my hands of her."

Poor Strether's face lengthened. "She's impossible—?"

"She's even more charming than I remembered her."

"Then what's the matter?"

She had to think how to put it. "Well, I'M impossible. It's impossible. Everything's impossible."

He looked at her an instant. "I see where you're coming out. Everything's possible." Their eyes had on it in fact an exchange of some duration; after which he pursued: "Isn't it that beautiful child?" Then as she still said nothing: "Why don't you mean to receive her?"

Her answer in an instant rang clear. "Because I wish to keep out of the business."

It provoked in him a weak wail. "You're going to abandon me NOW?"

"No, I'm only going to abandon HER. She'll want me to help her with you. And I won't."

"You'll only help me with her? Well then—!" Most of the persons previously gathered had, in the interest of tea, passed into the house, and they had the gardens mainly to themselves. The shadows were long, the last call of the birds, who had made a home of their own in the noble interspaced quarter, sounded from the high trees in the other gardens as well, those of the old convent and of the old hotels; it was as if our friends had waited for the full charm to come out. Strether's impressions were still present; it was as if something had happened that "nailed" them, made them more intense; but he was to ask himself soon afterwards, that evening, what really HAD happened—conscious as he could after all remain that for a gentleman taken, and taken the first time, into the "great world," the world of ambassadors and duchesses, the items made a meagre total. It was nothing new to him, however, as we know, that a man might have—at all events such a man as he—an amount of experience out of any proportion to his adventures; so that, though it was doubtless no great adventure to sit on there with Miss Gostrey and hear about Madame de Vionnet, the hour, the picture, the immediate, the recent, the possible—as well as the communication itself, not a note of which failed to reverberate—only gave the moments more of the taste of history.

It was history, to begin with, that Jeanne's mother had been three-and-twenty years before, at Geneva, schoolmate and good girlfriend to Maria Gostrey, who had moreover enjoyed since then, though interruptedly and above all with a long recent drop, other glimpses of her. Twenty-three years put them both on, no doubt; and Madame de Vionnet—though she had married straight after school—couldn't be today an hour less than thirty-eight. This made her ten years older than Chad—though ten years, also, if Strether liked, older than she looked; the least, at any rate, that a prospective mother-in-law could be expected to do with. She would be of all mothers-in-law the most charming; unless indeed, through some perversity as yet insupposeable, she should utterly belie herself in that relation. There was none surely in which, as Maria remembered her, she mustn't be charming; and this frankly in spite of the stigma of failure in the tie where failure always most showed. It was no test there—when indeed WAS it a test there?—for Monsieur de Vionnet had been a brute. She had lived for years apart from him—which was of course always a horrid position; but Miss Gostrey's impression of the matter had been that she could scarce have made a better thing of it had she done it on purpose to show she was amiable. She was so amiable that nobody had had a word to say; which was luckily not the case for her husband. He was so impossible that she had the advantage of all her merits.

It was still history for Strether that the Comte de Vionnet—it being also history that the lady in question was a Countess—should now, under Miss Gostrey's sharp touch, rise before him as a high distinguished polished impertinent reprobate, the product of a mysterious order; it was history, further, that the charming girl so freely sketched by his companion should have been married out of hand by a mother, another figure of striking outline, full of dark personal motive; it was perhaps history most of all that this company was, as a matter of course, governed by such considerations as put divorce out of the question. "Ces gens-la don't divorce, you know, any more than they emigrate or abjure—they think it impious and vulgar"; a fact in the light of which they seemed but the more richly special. It was all special; it was all, for Strether's imagination, more or less rich. The girl at the Genevese school, an isolated interesting attaching creature, then both sensitive and violent, audacious but always forgiven, was the daughter of a French father and an English mother who, early left a widow, had married again—tried afresh with a foreigner; in her career with whom she had apparently given her child no example of comfort. All these people—the people of the English mother's side—had been of condition more or less eminent; yet with oddities and disparities that had often since made Maria, thinking them over, wonder what they really quite rhymed to. It was in any case her belief that the mother, interested and prone to adventure, had been without conscience, had only thought of ridding herself most quickly of a possible, an actual encumbrance. The father, by her impression, a Frenchman with a name one knew, had been a different matter, leaving his child, she clearly recalled, a memory all fondness, as well as an assured little fortune which was unluckily to make her more or less of a prey later on. She had been in particular, at school, dazzlingly, though quite booklessly, clever; as polyglot as a little Jewess (which she wasn't, oh no!) and chattering French, English, German, Italian, anything one would, in a way that made a clean sweep, if not of prizes and parchments, at least of every "part," whether memorised or improvised, in the curtained costumed school repertory, and in especial of all mysteries of race and vagueness of reference, all swagger about "home," among their variegated mates.

It would doubtless be difficult to-day, as between French and English, to name her and place her; she would certainly show, on knowledge, Miss Gostrey felt, as one of those convenient types who don't keep you explaining—minds with doors as numerous as the many-tongued cluster of confessionals at Saint Peter's. You might confess to her with confidence in Roumelian, and even Roumelian sins. Therefore—! But Strether's narrator covered her implication with a laugh; a laugh by which his betrayal of a sense of the lurid in the picture was also perhaps sufficiently protected. He had a moment of wondering, while his friend went on, what sins might be especially Roumelian. She went on at all events to the mention of her having met the young thing—again by some Swiss lake—in her first married state, which had appeared for the few intermediate years not at least violently disturbed. She had been lovely at that moment, delightful to HER, full of responsive emotion, of amused recognitions and amusing reminders, and then once more, much later, after a long interval, equally but differently charming—touching and rather mystifying for the five minutes of an encounter at a railway-station en province, during which it had come out that her life was all changed. Miss Gostrey had understood enough to see, essentially, what had happened, and yet had beautifully dreamed that she was herself faultless. There were doubtless depths in her, but she was all right; Strether would see if she wasn't. She was another person however—that had been promptly marked—from the small child of nature at the Geneva school, a little person quite made over (as foreign women WERE, compared with American) by marriage. Her situation too had evidently cleared itself up; there would have been—all that was possible—a judicial separation. She had settled in Paris, brought up her daughter, steered her boat. It was no very pleasant boat—especially there—to be in; but Marie de Vionnet would have headed straight. She would have friends, certainly—and very good ones. There she was at all events—and it was very interesting. Her knowing Mr. Chad didn't in the least prove she hadn't friends; what it proved was what good ones HE had. "I saw that," said Miss Gostrey, "that night at the Francais; it came out for me in three minutes. I saw HER—or somebody like her. And so," she immediately added, "did you."

"Oh no—not anybody like her!" Strether laughed. "But you mean," he as promptly went on, "that she has had such an influence on him?"

Miss Gostrey was on her feet; it was time for them to go. "She has brought him up for her daughter."

Their eyes, as so often, in candid conference, through their settled glasses, met over it long; after which Strether's again took in the whole place. They were quite alone there now. "Mustn't she rather—in the time then—have rushed it?"

"Ah she won't of course have lost an hour. But that's just the good mother—the good French one. You must remember that of her—that as a mother she's French, and that for them there's a special providence. It precisely however—that she mayn't have been able to begin as far back as she'd have liked—makes her grateful for aid."

Strether took this in as they slowly moved to the house on their way out. "She counts on me then to put the thing through?"

"Yes—she counts on you. Oh and first of all of course," Miss Gostrey added, "on her—well, convincing you."

"Ah," her friend returned, "she caught Chad young!"

"Yes, but there are women who are for all your 'times of life.' They're the most wonderful sort."

She had laughed the words out, but they brought her companion, the next thing, to a stand. "Is what you mean that she'll try to make a fool of me?"

"Well, I'm wondering what she WILL—with an opportunity—make."

"What do you call," Strether asked, "an opportunity? My going to see her?"

"Ah you must go to see her"—Miss Gostrey was a trifle evasive. "You can't not do that. You'd have gone to see the other woman. I mean if there had been one—a different sort. It's what you came out for."

It might be; but Strether distinguished. "I didn't come out to see THIS sort."

She had a wonderful look at him now. "Are you disappointed she isn't worse?"

He for a moment entertained the question, then found for it the frankest of answers. "Yes. If she were worse she'd be better for our purpose. It would be simpler."

"Perhaps," she admitted. "But won't this be pleasanter?"

"Ah you know," he promptly replied, "I didn't come out—wasn't that just what you originally reproached me with?—for the pleasant."

"Precisely. Therefore I say again what I said at first. You must take things as they come. Besides," Miss Gostrey added, "I'm not afraid for myself."

"For yourself—?"

"Of your seeing her. I trust her. There's nothing she'll say about me. In fact there's nothing she CAN."

Strether wondered—little as he had thought of this. Then he broke out. "Oh you women!"

There was something in it at which she flushed. "Yes—there we are. We're abysses." At last she smiled. "But I risk her!"

He gave himself a shake. "Well then so do I!" But he added as they passed into the house that he would see Chad the first thing in the morning.

This was the next day the more easily effected that the young man, as it happened, even before he was down, turned up at his hotel. Strether took his coffee, by habit, in the public room; but on his descending for this purpose Chad instantly proposed an adjournment to what he called greater privacy. He had himself as yet had nothing—they would sit down somewhere together; and when after a few steps and a turn into the Boulevard they had, for their greater privacy, sat down among twenty others, our friend saw in his companion's move a fear of the advent of Waymarsh. It was the first time Chad had to that extent given this personage "away"; and Strether found himself wondering of what it was symptomatic. He made out in a moment that the youth was in earnest as he hadn't yet seen him; which in its turn threw a ray perhaps a trifle startling on what they had each up to that time been treating as earnestness. It was sufficiently flattering however that the real thing—if this WAS at last the real thing—should have been determined, as appeared, precisely by an accretion of Strether's importance. For this was what it quickly enough came to—that Chad, rising with the lark, had rushed down to let him know while his morning consciousness was yet young that he had literally made the afternoon before a tremendous impression. Madame de Vionnet wouldn't, couldn't rest till she should have some assurance from him that he WOULD consent again to see her. The announcement was made, across their marble-topped table, while the foam of the hot milk was in their cups and its plash still in the air, with the smile of Chad's easiest urbanity; and this expression of his face caused our friend's doubts to gather on the spot into a challenge of the lips. "See here"—that was all; he only for the moment said again "See here." Chad met it with all his air of straight intelligence, while Strether remembered again that fancy of the first impression of him, the happy young Pagan, handsome and hard but oddly indulgent, whose mysterious measure he had under the street-lamp tried mentally to take. The young Pagan, while a long look passed between them, sufficiently understood. Strether scarce needed at last to say the rest—"I want to know where I am." But he said it, adding before any answer something more. "Are you engaged to be married—is that your secret?—to the young lady?"

Chad shook his head with the slow amenity that was one of his ways of conveying that there was time for everything. "I have no secret—though I may have secrets! I haven't at any rate that one. We're not engaged. No."

"Then where's the hitch?"

"Do you mean why I haven't already started with you?" Chad, beginning his coffee and buttering his roll, was quite ready to explain. "Nothing would have induced me—nothing will still induce me—not to try to keep you here as long as you can be made to stay. It's too visibly good for you." Strether had himself plenty to say about this, but it was amusing also to measure the march of Chad's tone. He had never been more a man of the world, and it was always in his company present to our friend that one was seeing how in successive connexions a man of the world acquitted himself. Chad kept it up beautifully. "My idea—voyons!—is simply that you should let Madame de Vionnet know you, simply that you should consent to know HER. I don't in the least mind telling you that, clever and charming as she is, she's ever so much in my confidence. All I ask of you is to let her talk to you. You've asked me about what you call my hitch, and so far as it goes she'll explain it to you. She's herself my hitch, hang it—if you must really have it all out. But in a sense," he hastened in the most wonderful manner to add, "that you'll quite make out for yourself. She's too good a friend, confound her. Too good, I mean, for me to leave without—without—" It was his first hesitation.

"Without what?"

"Well, without my arranging somehow or other the damnable terms of my sacrifice."

"It WILL be a sacrifice then?"

"It will be the greatest loss I ever suffered. I owe her so much."

It was beautiful, the way Chad said these things, and his plea was now confessedly—oh quite flagrantly and publicly—interesting. The moment really took on for Strether an intensity. Chad owed Madame de Vionnet so uch? What DID that do then but clear up the whole mystery? He was indebted for alterations, and she was in a position to have sent in her bill for expenses incurred in reconstruction. What was this at bottom been to be arrived at? Strether sat there arriving at it while he munched toast and stirred his sec- with the aid of Chad's pleasant earnest face was also to do more besides. No, never before ake him as he was. What was it that had suddenly so cleared up? It was just every- ody's but—in a measure—his own. Strether felt HIS character receive for the ings he had suspected or believed. The person to whom Chad owed it that to other persons—such a person was sufficiently raised above any "breath" by the nature of her work and the young man's steady light. All of which was vivid enough to come and go quickly; though indeed in the midst of it Strether could utter a question. "Have I your word of honour that if I surrender myself to Madame de Vionnet you'll surrender yourself to me?"

Chad laid his hand firmly on his friend's. "My dear man, you have it."

There was finally something in his felicity almost embarrassing and oppressive—Strether had begun to fidget under it for the open air and the erect posture. He had signed to the waiter that he wished to pay, and this transaction took some moments, during which he thoroughly felt, while he put down money and pretended—it was quite hollow—to estimate change, that Chad's higher spirit, his youth, his practice, his paganism, his felicity, his assurance, his impudence, whatever it might be, had consciously scored a success. Well, that was all right so far as it went; his sense of the thing in question covered our friend for a minute like a veil through which—as if he had been muffled—he heard his interlocutor ask him if he mightn't take him over about five. "Over" was over the river, and over the river was where Madame de Vionnet lived, and five was that very afternoon. They got at last out of the place—got out before he answered. He lighted, in the street, a cigarette, which again gave him more time. But it was already sharp for him that there was no use in time. "What does she propose to do to me?" he had presently demanded.

Chad had no delays. "Are you afraid of her?"

"Oh immensely. Don't you see it?"

"Well," said Chad, "she won't do anything worse to you than make you like her."

"It's just of that I'm afraid."

"Then it's not fair to me."

Strether cast about. "It's fair to your mother."

"Oh," said Chad, "are you afraid of HER?"

"Scarcely less. Or perhaps even more. But is this lady against your interests at home?" Strether went on.

"Not directly, no doubt; but she's greatly in favour of them here."

"And what—'here'—does she consider them to be?"

"Well, good relations!"

"With herself?"

"With herself."

"And what is it that makes them so good?"

"What? Well, that's exactly what you'll make out if you'll only go, as I'm supplicating you, to see her."

Strether stared at him with a little of the wanness, no doubt, that the vision of more to "make out" could scarce help producing. "I mean HOW good are they?"

"Oh awfully good."

Again Strether had faltered, but it was brief. It was all very well, but there was nothing now he wouldn't risk. "Excuse me, but I must really—as I began by telling you—know where I am. Is she bad?"

"'Bad'?"—Chad echoed it, but without a shock. "Is that what's implied—?"

"When relations are good?" Strether felt a little silly, and was even conscious of a foolish laugh, at having it imposed on him to have appeared to speak so. What indeed was he talking about? His stare had relaxed; he looked now all round him. But something in him brought him back, though he still didn't know quite how to turn it. The two or three ways he thought of, and one of them in particular, were, even with scruples dismissed, too ugly. He none the less at last found something. "Is her life without reproach?"

It struck him, directly he had found it, as pompous and priggish; so much so that he was thankful to Chad for taking it only in the right spirit. The young man spoke so immensely to the point that the effect was practically of positive blandness. "Absolutely without reproach. A beautiful life. Allez donc voir!"

These last words were, in the liberality of their confidence, so imperative that Strether went through no form of assent; but before they separated it had been confirmed that he should be picked up at a quarter to five.

Book Sixth

I

It was quite by half-past five—after the two men had been together in Madame de Vionnet's drawing-room not more than a dozen minutes—that Chad, with a look at his watch and then another at their hostess, said genially, gaily: "I've an engagement, and I know you won't complain if I leave him with you. He'll interest you immensely; and as for her," he declared to Strether, "I assure you, if you're at all nervous, she's perfectly safe."

He had left them to be embarrassed or not by this guarantee, as they could best manage, and embarrassment was a thing that Strether wasn't at first sure Madame de Vionnet escaped. He escaped it himself, to his surprise; but he had grown used by this time to thinking of himself as brazen. She occupied, his hostess, in the Rue de Bellechasse, the first floor of an old house to which our visitors had had access from an old clean court. The court was large and open, full of revelations, for our friend, of the habit of privacy, the peace of intervals, the dignity of distances and approaches; the house, to his restless sense, was in the high homely style of an elder day, and the ancient Paris that he was always looking for—sometimes intensely felt, sometimes more acutely missed—was in the immemorial polish of the wide waxed staircase and in the fine boiseries, the medallions, mouldings, mirrors, great clear spaces, of the greyish-white salon into which he had been shown. He seemed at the very outset to see her in the midst of possessions not vulgarly numerous, but hereditary cherished charming. While his eyes turned after a little from those of his hostess and Chad freely talked—not in the least about HIM, but about other people, people he didn't know, and quite as if he did know them—he found himself making out, as a background of the occupant, some glory, some prosperity of the First Empire, some Napoleonic glamour, some dim lustre of the great legend; elements clinging still to all the consular chairs and mythological brasses and sphinxes' heads and faded surfaces of satin striped with alternate silk.

The place itself went further back—that he guessed, and how old Paris continued in a manner to echo there; but the post-revolutionary period, the world he vaguely thought of as the world of Chateaubriand, of Madame de Stael, even of the young Lamartine, had left its stamp of harps and urns and torches, a stamp impressed on sundry small objects, ornaments and relics. He had never before, to his knowledge, had present to him relics, of any special dignity, of a private order—little old miniatures, medallions, pictures, books; books in leather bindings, pinkish and greenish, with gilt garlands on the back, ranged, together with other promiscuous properties, under the glass of brass-mounted cabinets. His attention took them all tenderly into account. They were among the matters that marked Madame de Vionnet's apartment as something quite different from Miss Gostrey's little museum of bargains and from Chad's lovely home; he recognised it as founded much more on old accumulations that had possibly from time to time shrunken than on any contemporary method of acquisition or form of curiosity. Chad and Miss Gostrey had rummaged and purchased and picked up and exchanged, sifting, selecting, comparing; whereas the mistress of the scene before him, beautifully passive under the spell of transmission—transmission from her father's line, he quite made up his mind—had only received, accepted and been quiet. When she hadn't been quiet she had been moved at the most to some occult charity for some fallen fortune. There had been objects she or her predecessors might even conceivably have parted with under need, but Strether couldn't suspect them of having sold old pieces to get "better" ones. They would have felt no difference as to better or worse. He could but imagine their having felt—perhaps in emigration, in proscription, for his sketch was slight and confused—the pressure of want or the obligation of sacrifice.

The pressure of want—whatever might be the case with the other force—was, however, presumably not active now, for the tokens of a chastened ease still abounded after all, many marks of a taste whose discriminations might perhaps have been called eccentric. He guessed at intense little preferences and sharp little exclusions, a deep suspicion of the vulgar and a personal view of the right. The general result of this was something for which he had no name on the spot quite ready, but something he would have come nearest to naming in speaking of it as the air of supreme respectability, the consciousness, small, still, reserved, but none the less distinct and diffused, of private honour. The air of supreme respectability—that was a strange blank wall for his adventure to have brought him to break his nose against. It had in fact, as he was now aware, filled all the approaches, hovered in the court as he passed, hung on the staircase as he mounted, sounded in the grave rumble of the old bell, as little electric as possible, of which Chad, at the door, had pulled the ancient but neatly-kept tassel; it formed in short the clearest medium of its particular kind that he had ever breathed. He would have answered for it at the end of a quarter of an hour that some of the glass cases contained swords and epaulettes of ancient colonels and generals; medals and orders once pinned over hearts that had long since ceased to beat; snuff-boxes bestowed on ministers and envoys; copies of works presented, with inscriptions, by authors now classic. At bottom of it all for him was the sense of her rare unlikeness to the women he had known. This sense had grown, since the day before, the more he recalled her, and had been above all singularly fed by his talk with Chad in the morning. Everything in fine made her immeasurably new, and nothing so new as the old house and the old objects. There were books, two or three, on a small table near his chair, but they hadn't the lemon-coloured covers with which his eye had begun to dally from the hour of his arrival and to the opportunity of a further acquaintance with which he had for a fortnight now altogether succumbed. On another table, across the room, he made out the great *Revue*; but even that familiar face, conspicuous in Mrs. Newsome's parlours, scarce counted here as a modern note. He was sure on the spot—and he afterwards knew he was right—that this was a touch of Chad's own hand. What would Mrs. Newsome say to the circumstance that Chad's interested "influence" kept her paper-knife in the *Revue*? The interested influence at any rate had, as we say, gone straight to the point—had in fact soon left it quite behind.

She was seated, near the fire, on a small stuffed and fringed chair one of the few modern articles in the room, and she leaned back in it with her hands clasped in her lap and no movement, in all her person, but the fine prompt play of her deep young face. The fire, under the low white marble, undraped and academic, had burnt down to the silver ashes of light wood, one of the windows, at a distance, stood open to the mildness and stillness, out of which, in the short pauses, came the faint sound, pleasant and homely, almost rustic, of a plash and a clatter of sabots from some coach-house on the other side of the court. Madame de Vionnet, while Strether sat there, wasn't to shift her posture by an inch. "I don't think you seriously believe in what you're doing," she said; "but all the same, you know, I'm going to treat you quite as if I did."

"By which you mean," Strether directly replied, "quite as if you didn't! I assure you it won't make the least difference with me how you treat me."

"Well," she said, taking that menace bravely and philosophically enough, "the only thing that really matters is that you shall get on with me."

"Ah but I don't!" he immediately returned.

It gave her another pause; which, however, she happily enough shook off. "Will you consent to go on with me a little—provisionally—as if you did?"

Then it was that he saw how she had decidedly come all the way; and there accompanied it an extraordinary sense of her raising from somewhere below him her beautiful suppliant eyes. He might have been perched at his door-step or at his window and she standing in the road. For a moment he let her stand and couldn't moreover have spoken. It had been sad, of a sudden, with a sadness that was like a cold breath in his face. "What can I do," he finally asked, "but listen to you as I promised Chadwick?"

"Ah but what I'm asking you," she quickly said, "isn't what Mr. Newsome had in mind." She spoke at present, he saw, as if to take courageously ALL her risk. "This is my own idea and a different thing."

It gave poor Strether in truth—uneasy as it made him too—something of the thrill of a bold perception justified. "Well," he answered kindly enough, "I was sure a moment since that some idea of your own had come to you."

She seemed still to look up at him, but now more serenely. "I made out you were sure—and that helped it to come. So you see," she continued, "we do get on."

"Oh but it appears to me I don't at all meet your request. How can I when I don't understand it?"

"It isn't at all necessary you should understand; it will do quite well enough if you simply remember it. Only feel I trust you—and for nothing so tremendous after all. Just," she said with a wonderful smile, "for common civility."

Strether had a long pause while they sat again face to face, as they had sat, scarce less conscious, before the poor lady had crossed the stream. She was the poor lady for Strether now because clearly she had some trouble, and her appeal to him could only mean that her trouble was deep. He couldn't help it; it wasn't his fault; he had done nothing; but by a turn of the hand she had somehow made their encounter a relation. And the relation profited by a mass of things that were not strictly in it or of it; by the very air in which they sat, by the high cold delicate room, by the world outside and the little plash in the court, by the First Empire and the relics in the stiff cabinets, by matters as far off as those and by others as near as the unbroken clasp of her hands in her lap and the look her expression had of being most natural when her eyes were most fixed. "You count upon me of course for something really much greater than it sounds."

"Oh it sounds great enough too!" she laughed at this.

He found himself in time on the point of telling her that she was, as Miss Barrace called it, wonderful; but, catching himself up, he said something else instead. "What was it Chad's idea then that you should say to me?"

"Ah his idea was simply what a man's idea always is—to put every effort off on the woman."

"The 'woman'—?" Strether slowly echoed.

"The woman he likes—and just in proportion as he likes her. In proportion too—for shifting the trouble—as she likes HIM."

Strether followed it; then with an abruptness of his own: "How much do you like Chad?"

"Just as much as THAT—to take all, with you, on myself." But she got at once again away from this. "I've been trembling as if we were to stand or fall by what you may think of me; and I'm even now," she went on wonderfully, "drawing a long breath—and, yes, truly taking a great courage—from the hope that I don't in fact strike you as impossible."

"That's at all events, clearly," he observed after an instant, "the way I don't strike YOU."

"Well," she so far assented, "as you haven't yet said you WON'T have the little patience with me I ask for—"

"You draw splendid conclusions? Perfectly. But I don't understand them," Strether pursued. "You seem to me to ask for much more than you need. What, at the worst for you, what at the best for myself, can I after all do? I can use no pressure that I haven't used. You come really late with your request. I've already done all that for myself the case admits of. I've said my say, and here I am."

"Yes, here you are, fortunately!" Madame de Vionnet laughed. "Mrs. Newsome," she added in another tone, "didn't think you can do so little."

He had an hesitation, but he brought the words out. "Well, she thinks so now."

"Do you mean by that—?" But she also hung fire.

"Do I mean what?"

She still rather faltered. "Pardon me if I touch on it, but if I'm saying extraordinary things, why, perhaps, mayn't I? Besides, doesn't it properly concern us to know?"

"To know what?" he insisted as after thus beating about the bush she had again dropped.

She made the effort. "Has she given you up?"

He was amazed afterwards to think how simply and quietly he had met it. "Not yet." It was almost as if he were a trifle disappointed—had expected still more of her freedom. But he went straight on. "Is that what Chad has told you will happen to me?"

She was evidently charmed with the way he took it. "If you mean if we've talked of it—most certainly. And the question's not what has had least to do with my wishing to see you."

"To judge if I'm the sort of man a woman CAN—?"

"Precisely," she exclaimed—"you wonderful gentleman! I do judge—I HAVE judged. A woman can't. You're safe—with every right to be. You'd be much happier if you'd only believe it."

Strether was silent a little; then he found himself speaking with a cynicism of confidence of which even at the moment the sources were strange to him. "I try to believe it. But it's a marvel," he exclaimed, "how YOU already get at it!"

Oh she was able to say. "Remember how much I was on the way to it through Mr. Newsome—before I saw you. He thinks everything of your strength."

"Well, I can bear almost anything!" our friend briskly interrupted. Deep and beautiful on this her smile came back, and with the effect of making him hear what he had said just as she had heard it. He easily enough felt that it gave him away, but what in truth had everything done but that? It had been all very well to think at moments that he was holding her nose down and that he had coerced her: what had he by this time done but let her practically see that he accepted their relation? What was their relation moreover—though light and brief enough in form as yet—but whatever she might choose to make it? Nothing could prevent her—certainly he couldn't—from making it pleasant. At the back of his head, behind everything, was the sense that she was—there, before him, close to him, in vivid imperative form—one of the rare women he had so often heard of, read of, thought of, but never met, whose very presence, look, voice, the mere contemporaneous FACT of whom, from the moment it was at all presented, made a relation of mere recognition. That was not the kind of woman he had ever found Mrs. Newsome, a contemporaneous fact who had been distinctly slow to establish herself; and at present, confronted with Madame de Vionnet, he felt the simplicity of his original impression of Miss Gostrey. She certainly had been a fact of rapid growth; but the world was wide, each day was more and more a new lesson. There were at any rate even among the stranger ones relations and relations. "Of course I suit Chad's grand way," he quickly added. "He hasn't had much difficulty in working me in."

She seemed to deny a little, on the young man's behalf, by the rise of her eyebrows, an intention of any process at all inconsiderate. "You must know how grieved he'd be if you were to lose anything. He believes you can keep his mother patient."

Strether wondered with his eyes on her. "I see. THAT'S then what you really want of me. And how am I to do it? Perhaps you'll tell me that."

"Simply tell her the truth."

"And what do you call the truth?"

"Well, any truth—about us all—that you see yourself. I leave it to you."

"Thank you very much. I like," Strether laughed with a slight harshness, "the way you leave things!"

But she insisted kindly, gently, as if it wasn't so bad. "Be perfectly honest. Tell her all."

"All?" he oddly echoed.

"Tell her the simple truth," Madame de Vionnet again pleaded.

"But what is the simple truth? The simple truth is exactly what I'm trying to discover."

She looked about a while, but presently she came back to him. "Tell her, fully and clearly, about US."

Strether meanwhile had been staring. "You and your daughter?"

"Yes—little Jeanne and me. Tell her," she just slightly quavered, "you like us."

"And what good will that do me? Or rather"—he caught himself up—"what good will it do YOU?"

She looked graver. "None, you believe, really?"

Strether debated. "She didn't send me out to 'like' you."

"Oh," she charmingly contended, "she sent you out to face the facts."

He admitted after an instant that there was something in that. "But how can I face them till I know what they are? Do you want him," he then braced himself to ask, "to marry your daughter?"

She gave a headshake as noble as it was prompt. "No—not that."

"And he really doesn't want to himself?"

She repeated the movement, but now with a strange light in her face. "He likes her too much."

Strether wondered. "To be willing to consider, you mean, the question of taking her to America?"

"To be willing to do anything with her but be immensely kind and nice—really tender of her. We watch over her, and you must help us. You must see her again."

Strether felt awkward. "Ah with pleasure—she's so remarkably attractive."

The mother's eagerness with which Madame de Vionnet jumped at this was to come back to him later as beautiful in its grace. "The dear thing DID please you?" Then as he met it with the largest "Oh!" of enthusiasm: "She's perfect. She's my joy."

"Well, I'm sure that—if one were near her and saw more of her—she'd be mine."

"Then," said Madame de Vionnet, "tell Mrs. Newsome that!"

He wondered the more. "What good will that do you?" As she appeared unable at once to say, however, he brought out something else. "Is your daughter in love with our friend?"

"Ah," she rather startlingly answered, "I wish you'd find out!"

He showed his surprise. "I? A stranger?"

"Oh you won't be a stranger—presently. You shall see her quite, I assure you, as if you weren't."

It remained for him none the less an extraordinary notion. "It seems to me surely that if her mother can't—"

"Ah little girls and their mothers to-day!" she rather inconsequently broke in. But she checked herself with something she seemed to give out as after all more to the point. "Tell her I've been good for him. Don't you think I have?"

It had its effect on him—more than at the moment he quite measured. Yet he was consciously enough touched. "Oh if it's all you—!"

"Well, it may not be 'all,'" she interrupted, "but it's to a great extent. Really and truly," she added in a tone that was to take its place with him among things remembered.

"Then it's very wonderful." He smiled at her from a face that he felt as strained, and her own face for a moment kept him so. At last she also got up. "Well, don't you think that for that—"

"I ought to save you?" So it was that the way to meet her—and the way, as well, in a manner, to get off—came over him. He heard himself use the exorbitant word, the very sound of which helped to determine his flight. "I'll save you if I can."

II

In Chad's lovely home, however, one evening ten days later, he felt himself present at the collapse of the question of Jeanne de Vionnet's shy secret. He had been dining there in the company of that young lady and her mother, as well as of other persons, and he had gone into the petit salon, at Chad's request, on purpose to talk with her. The young man had put this to him as a favour—"I should like so awfully to know what you think of her. It will really be a chance for you," he had said, "to see the jeune fille—I mean the type—as she actually is, and I don't think that, as an observer of manners, it's a thing you ought to miss. It will be an impression that—whatever else you take—you can carry home with you, where you'll find again so much to compare it with."

Strether knew well enough with what Chad wished him to compare it, and though he entirely assented he hadn't yet somehow been so deeply reminded that he was being, as he constantly though mutely expressed it, used. He was as far as ever from making out exactly to what end; but he was none the less constantly accompanied by a sense of the service he rendered. He conceived only that this service was highly agreeable to those who profited by it; and he was indeed still waiting for the moment at which he should catch it in the act of proving disagreeable, proving in some degree intolerable, to himself. He failed quite to see how his situation could clear up at all logically except by some turn of events that would give him the pretext of disgust. He was building from day to day on the possibility of disgust, but each day brought forth meanwhile a new and more engaging bend of the road. That possibility was now ever so much further from sight than on the eve of his arrival, and he perfectly felt that, should it come at all, it would have to be at best inconsequent and violent. He struck himself as a little nearer to it only when he asked himself what service, in such a life of utility, he was after all rendering Mrs. Newsome. When he wished to help himself to believe that he was still all right he reflected—and in fact with wonder—on the unimpaired frequency of their correspondence; in relation to which what was after all more natural than that it should become more frequent just in proportion as their problem became more complicated?

Certain it is at any rate that he now often brought himself balm by the question, with the rich consciousness of yesterday's letter, "Well, what can I do more than that—what can I do more than tell her everything?" To persuade himself that he did tell her, had told her, everything, he used to try to think of particular things he hadn't told her. When at rare moments and in the watches of the night he pounced on one it generally showed itself to be—to a deeper scrutiny—not quite truly of the essence. When anything new struck him as coming up, or anything already noted as reappearing, he always immediately wrote, as if for fear that if he didn't he would miss something; and also that he might be able to say to himself from time to time "She knows it NOW—even while I worry." It was a great comfort to him in general not to have left past things to be dragged to light and explained; not to have to produce at so late a stage anything not produced, or anything even veiled and attenuated, at the moment. She knew it now: that was what he said to himself to-night in relation to the fresh fact of Chad's acquaintance with the two ladies—not to speak of the fresher one of his own. Mrs. Newsome knew in other words that very night at Woollett that he himself knew Madame de Vionnet and that he had conscientiously been to see her; also that he had found her remarkably attractive and that there would probably be a good deal more to tell. But she further knew, or would know very soon, that, again conscientiously, he hadn't repeated his visit; and that when Chad had asked him on the Countess's behalf—Strether made her out vividly, with a thought at the back of his head, a Countess—if he wouldn't name a day for dining with her, he had replied lucidly: "Thank you very much—impossible." He had begged the young man would present his excuses and had trusted him to understand that it couldn't really strike one as quite the straight thing. He hadn't reported to Mrs. Newsome that he had promised to "save" Madame de Vionnet; but, so far as he was concerned with that reminiscence, he hadn't at any rate promised to haunt her house. What Chad had understood could only, in truth, be inferred from Chad's behaviour, which had been in this connexion as easy as in every other. He was easy, always, when he understood; he was easier still, if possible, when he didn't; he had replied that he would make it all right; and he had proceeded to do this by substituting the present occasion—as he was ready to substitute others—for any, for every occasion as to which his old friend should have a funny scruple.

"Oh but I'm not a little foreign girl; I'm just as English as I can be," Jeanne de Vionnet had said to him as soon as, in the petit salon, he sank, shyly enough on his own side, into the place near her vacated by Madame Gloriani at his approach. Madame Gloriani, who was in black velvet, with white lace and powdered hair, and whose somewhat massive majesty melted, at any contact, into the graciousness of some incomprehensible tongue, moved away to make room for the vague gentleman, after benevolent greetings to him which embodied, as he believed, in baffling accents, some recognition of his face from a couple of Sundays before. Then he had remarked—making the most of the advantage of his years—that it frightened him quite enough to find himself dedicated to the entertainment of a little foreign girl. There were girls he wasn't afraid of—he was quite bold with little Americans. Thus it was that she had defended herself to the end—"Oh but I'm almost American too. That's what mamma has wanted me to be—I mean LIKE that; for she has wanted me to have lots of freedom. She has known such good results from it."

She was fairly beautiful to him—a faint pastel in an oval frame: he thought of her already as of some lurking image in a long gallery, the portrait of a small old-time princess of whom nothing was known but that she had died young. Little Jeanne wasn't, doubtless, to die young, but one couldn't, all the same, bear on her lightly enough. It was bearing hard, it was bearing as HE, in any case, wouldn't bear, to concern himself, in relation to her, with the question of a young man. Odious really the question of a young man; one didn't treat such a person as a maid-servant suspected of a "follower." And then young men, young men—well, the thing was their business simply, or was at all events hers. She was fluttered, fairly fevered—to the point of a little glitter that came and went in her eyes and a pair of pink spots that stayed in her cheeks—with the great adventure of dining out and with the greater one still, possibly, of finding a gentleman whom she must think of as very, very old, a gentleman with eye-glasses, wrinkles, a long grizzled moustache. She spoke the prettiest English, our friend thought, that he had ever heard spoken, just as he had believed her a few minutes before to be speaking the prettiest French. He wondered almost wistfully if such a sweep of the lyre didn't react on the spirit itself; and his fancy had in fact, before he knew it, begun so to stray and embroider that he finally found himself, absent and extravagant, sitting with the child in a friendly silence. Only by this time he felt her flutter to have fortunately dropped and that she was more at her ease. She trusted him, liked him, and it was to come back to him afterwards that she had told him things. She had dipped into the waiting medium at last and found neither surge nor chill—nothing but the small splash she could herself make in the pleasant warmth, nothing but the safety of dipping and dipping again. At the end of the ten minutes he was to spend with her his impression—with all it had thrown off and all it had taken in—was complete. She had been free, as she knew freedom, partly to show him that, unlike other little persons she knew, she had imbibed that ideal. She was delightfully quaint about herself, but the vision of what she had imbibed was what most held him. It really consisted, he was soon enough to feel, in just one great little matter, the fact that, whatever her nature, she was thoroughly—he had to cast about for the word, but it came—bred. He couldn't of course on so short an acquaintance speak for her nature, but the idea of breeding was what she had meanwhile dropped into his mind. He had never yet known it so sharply presented. Her mother gave it, no doubt; but her mother, to make that less sensible, gave so much else besides, and on neither of the two previous occasions, extraordinary woman, Strether felt, anything like what she was giving tonight. Little Jeanne was a case, an exquisite case of education; whereas the Countess, whom it so amused him to think of by that denomination, was a case, also exquisite, of—well, he didn't know what.

"He has wonderful taste, notre jeune homme": this was what Gloriani said to him on turning away from the inspection of a small picture suspended near the door of the room. The high celebrity in question had just come in, apparently in search of Mademoiselle de Vionnet, but while Strether had got up from beside her their fellow guest, with his eye sharply caught, had paused for a long look. The thing was a landscape, of no size, but of the French school, as our friend was glad to feel he knew, and also of a quality—which he liked to think he should also have guessed; its frame was large out of proportion to the canvas, and he had never seen a person look at anything, he thought, just as Gloriani, with his nose very near and quick movements of the head from side to side and bottom to top, examined this feature of Chad's collection. The artist used that word the next moment smiling courteously, wiping his nippers and looking round him further—paying the place in short by the very manner of his presence and by something Strether fancied he could make out in this particular glance, such a tribute as, to the latter's sense, settled many things once for all. Strether was conscious at this instant, for that matter, as he hadn't yet been, of how, round about him, quite without him, they WERE consistently settled. Gloriani's smile, deeply Italian, he considered, and finely inscrutable, had had for him, during dinner, at which they were not neighbours, an indefinite greeting; but the quality in it was gone that had appeared on the other occasion to turn him inside out; it was as if even the momentary link supplied by the doubt between them had snapped. He was conscious now of the final reality, which was that there wasn't so much a doubt as a difference altogether; all the more that over the difference the famous sculptor seemed to signal almost condolingly, yet oh how vacantly! as across some great flat sheet of water. He threw out the bridge of a charming hollow civility on which Strether wouldn't have trusted his own full weight a moment. That idea, even though but transient and perhaps belated, had performed the office of putting Strether more at his ease, and the blurred picture had already dropped—dropped with the sound of something else said and with his becoming aware, by another quick turn, that Gloriani was now on the sofa talking with Jeanne, while he himself had in his ears again the familiar friendliness and the elusive meaning of the "Oh, oh, oh!" that had made him, a fortnight before, challenge Miss Barrace in vain. She had always the air, this picturesque and original lady, who struck him, so oddly, as both antique and modern—she had always the air of taking up some joke that one had already had out with her. The point itself, no doubt, was what was antique, and the use she made of it what was modern. He felt just now that her good-natured irony did bear on something, and it troubled him a little that she wouldn't be more explicit only assuring him, with the pleasure of observation so visible in her, that she wouldn't tell him more for the world. He could take refuge but in asking her what she had done with Waymarsh, though it must be added that he felt himself a little on the way to a clue after she had answered that this personage was, in the other room, engaged in conversation with Madame de Vionnet. He stared a moment at the image of such a conjunction; then, for Miss Barrace's benefit, he wondered. "Is she too then under the charm—?"

"No, not a bit"—Miss Barrace was prompt. "She makes nothing of him. She's bored. She won't help you with him."

"Oh," Strether laughed, "she can't do everything.

"Of course not—wonderful as she is. Besides, he makes nothing of HER. She won't take him from me—though she wouldn't, no doubt, having other affairs in hand, even if she could. I've never," said Miss Barrace, "seen her fail with any one before. And to-night, when she's so magnificent, it would seem to her strange—if she minded. So at any rate I have him all. Je suis tranquille!"

Strether understood, so far as that went; but he was feeling for his clue. "She strikes you to-night as particularly magnificent?"

"Surely. Almost as I've never seen her. Doesn't she you? Why it's FOR you."

He persisted in his candour. "'For' me—?"

"Oh, oh, oh!" cried Miss Barrace, who persisted in the opposite of that quality.

"Well," he acutely admitted, "she IS different. She's gay."

"She's gay!" Miss Barrace laughed. "And she has beautiful shoulders—though there's nothing different in that."

"No," said Strether, "one was sure of her shoulders. It isn't her shoulders."

His companion, with renewed mirth and the finest sense, between the puffs of her cigarette, of the drollery of things, appeared to find their conversation highly delightful. "Yes, it isn't her shoulders ."

"What then is it?" Strether earnestly enquired.

"Why, it's SHE—simply. It's her mood. It's her charm."

"Of course it's her charm, but we're speaking of the difference." "Well," Miss Barrace explained, "she's just brilliant, as we used to say. That's all. She's various. She's fifty women."

"Ah but only one"—Strether kept it clear—"at a time."

"Perhaps. But in fifty times—!"

"Oh we shan't come to that," our friend declared; and the next moment he had moved in another direction. "Will you answer me a plain question? Will she ever divorce?"

Miss Barrace looked at him through all her tortoise-shell. "Why should she?"

It wasn't what he had asked for, he signified; but he met it well enough. "To marry Chad."

"Why should she marry Chad?"

"Because I'm convinced she's very fond of him. She has done wonders for him."

"Well then, how could she do more? Marrying a man, or woman either," Miss Barrace sagely went on, "is never the wonder for any Jack and Jill can bring THAT off. The wonder is their doing such things without marrying."

Strether considered a moment this proposition. "You mean it's so beautiful for our friends simply to go on so?"

But whatever he said made her laugh. "Beautiful."

He nevertheless insisted. "And THAT because it's disinterested?"

She was now, however, suddenly tired of the question. "Yes then—call it that. Besides, she'll never divorce. Don't, moreover," she added, "believe everything you hear about her husband."

"He's not then," Strether asked, "a wretch?"

"Oh yes. But charming."

"Do you know him?"

"I've met him. He's bien aimable."

"To every one but his wife?"

"Oh for all I know, to her too—to any, to every woman. I hope you at any rate," she pursued with a quick change, "appreciate the care I take of Mr. Waymarsh."

"Oh immensely." But Strether was not yet in line. "At all events," he roundly brought out, "the attachment's an innocent one."

"Mine and his? Ah," she laughed, "don't rob it of ALL interest!"

"I mean our friend's here—to the lady we've been speaking of." That was what he had settled to as an indirect but none the less closely involved consequence of his impression of Jeanne. That was where he meant to stay. "It's innocent," he repeated—"I see the whole thing."

Mystified by his abrupt declaration, she had glanced over at Gloriani as at the unnamed subject of his allusion, but the next moment she had understood; though indeed not before Strether had noticed her momentary mistake and wondered what might possibly be behind that too. He already knew that the sculptor admired Madame de Vionnet; but did this admiration also represent an attachment of which the innocence was discussable? He was moving verily in a strange air and on ground not of the firmest. He looked hard for an instant at Miss Barrace, but she had already gone on. "All right with Mr. Newsome? Why of course she is!"—and she got gaily back to the question of her own good friend. "I dare say you're surprised that I'm not worn out with all I see—it being so much!—of Sitting Bull. But I'm not, you know—I don't mind him; I bear up, and we get on beautifully. I'm very strange; I'm like that; and often I can't explain. There are people who are supposed interesting or remarkable or whatever, and who bore me to death; and then there are others as to whom nobody can understand what anybody sees in them—in whom I see no end of things." Then after she had smoked a moment, "He's touching, you know," she said.

"'Know'?" Strether echoed—"don't I, indeed? We must move you almost to tears."

"Oh but I don't mean YOU!" she laughed.

"You ought to then, for the worst sign of all—as I must have it for you—is that you can't help me. That's when a woman pities."

"Ah but I do help you!" she cheerfully insisted.

Again he looked at her hard, and then after a pause: "No you don't!"

Her tortoise-shell, on its long chain, rattled down. "I help you with Sitting Bull. That's a good deal."

"Oh that, yes." But Strether hesitated. "Do you mean he talks of me?"

"So that I have to defend you? No, never.'

"I see," Strether mused. "It's too deep."

"That's his only fault," she returned—"that everything, with him, is too deep. He has depths of silence—which he breaks only at the longest intervals by a remark. And when the remark comes it's always something he has seen or felt for himself—never a bit banal THAT would be what one might have feared and what would kill me But never." She smoked again as she thus, with amused complacency, appreciated her acquisition. "And never about you. We keep clear of you. We're wonderful. But I'll tell you what he does do," she continued: "he tries to make me presents."

"Presents?" poor Strether echoed, conscious with a pang that HE hadn't yet tried that in any quarter.

"Why you see," she explained, "he's as fine as ever in the victoria; so that when I leave him, as I often do almost for hours—he likes it so—at the doors of shops, the sight of him there helps me, when I come out, to know my carriage away off in the rank. But sometimes, for a change, he goes with me into the shops, and then I've all I can do to prevent his buying me things."

"He wants to 'treat' you?" Strether almost gasped at all he himself hadn't thought of. He had a sense of admiration. "Oh he's much more in the real tradition than I. Yes," he mused, "it's the sacred rage."

"The sacred rage, exactly!"—and Miss Barrace, who hadn't before heard this term applied, recognised its bearing with a clap of her gemmed hands. "Now I do know why he's not banal. But I do prevent him all the same—and if you saw what he sometimes selects—from buying. I save him hundreds and hundreds. I only take flowers."

"Flowers?" Strether echoed again with a rueful reflexion. How many nosegays had her present converser sent?

"Innocent flowers," she pursued, "as much as he likes. And he sends me splendours; he knows all the best places—he has found them for himself; he's wonderful."

"He hasn't told them to me," her friend smiled, "he has a life of his own." But Strether had swung back to the consciousness that for himself after all it never would have done. Waymarsh hadn't Mrs. Waymarsh in the least to consider, whereas Lambert Strether had constantly, in the inmost honour of his thoughts, to consider Mrs. Newsome. He liked moreover to feel how much his friend was in the real tradition. Yet he had his conclusion. "WHAT a rage it is!" He had worked it out. "It's an opposition."

She followed, but at a distance. "That's what I feel. Yet to what?"

"Well, he thinks, you know, that I'VE a life of my own. And I haven't!"

"You haven't?" She showed doubt, and her laugh confirmed it. "Oh, oh, oh!"

"No—not for myself. I seem to have a life only for other people."

"Ah for them and WITH them! Just now for instance with—"

"Well, with whom?" he asked before she had had time to say.

His tone had the effect of making her hesitate and even, as he guessed, speak with a difference. "Say with Miss Gostrey. What do you do for HER?" It really made him wonder. "Nothing at all!"

III

Madame de Vionnet, having meanwhile come in, was at present close to them, and Miss Barrace hereupon, instead of risking a rejoinder, became again with a look that measured her from top to toe all mere long-handled appreciative tortoise-shell. She had struck our friend, from the first of her appearing, as dressed for a great occasion, and she met still more than on either of the others the conception reawakened in him at their garden-party, the idea of the femme du monde in her habit as she lived. Her bare shoulders and arms were white and beautiful; the materials of her dress, a mixture, as he supposed, of silk and crape, were of a silvery grey so artfully composed as to give an impression of warm splendour; and round her neck she wore a collar of large old emeralds, the green note of which was more dimly repeated, at other points of her apparel, in embroidery, in enamel, in satin, in substances and textures vaguely rich. Her head, extremely fair and exquisitely festal, was like a happy fancy, a notion of the antique, on an old precious medal, some silver coin of the Renaissance; while her slim lightness and brightness, her gaiety, her expression, her decision, contributed to an effect that might have been felt by a poet as half mythological and half conventional. He could have compared her to a goddess still partly engaged in a morning cloud, or to a sea-nymph waist-high in the summer surge. Above all she suggested to him the reflexion that the femme du monde—in these finest developments of the type—was, like Cleopatra in the play, indeed various and multifold. She had aspects, characters, days, nights—or had them at least, showed them by a mysterious law of her own, when in addition to everything she happened also to be a woman of genius. She was an obscure person, a muffled person one day, and a showy person, an uncovered person the next. He thought of Madame de Vionnet to-night as showy and uncovered, though he felt the formula rough, because, thanks to one of the short-cuts of genius she had taken all his categories by surprise. Twice during dinner he had met Chad's eyes in a longish look; but these communications had in truth only stirred up again old ambiguities—so little was it clear from them whether they were an appeal or an admonition. "You see how I'm fixed," was what they appeared to convey; yet how he was fixed was exactly what Strether didn't see. However, perhaps he should see now.

"Are you capable of the very great kindness of going to relieve Newsome, for a few minutes, of the rather crushing responsibility of Madame Gloriani, while I say a word, if he'll allow me, to Mr. Strether, of whom I've a question to ask? Our host ought to talk a bit to those other ladies, and I'll come back in a minute to your rescue." She made this proposal to Miss Barrace as if her consciousness of a special duty had just flickered-up, but that lady's recognition of Strether's little start at it—as at a betrayal on the speaker's part of a domesticated state—was as mute as his own comment; and after an instant, when their fellow guest had good-naturedly left them, he had been given something else to think of. "Why has Maria so suddenly gone? Do you know?" That was the question Madame de Vionnet had brought with her.

"I'm afraid I've no reason to give you but the simple reason I've had from her in a note—the sudden obligation to join in the south a sick friend who has got worse."

"Ah then she has been writing you?"

"Not since she went—I had only a brief explanatory word before she started. I went to see her," Strether explained—"it was the day after I called on you—but she was already on her way, and her concierge told me that in case of my coming I was to be informed she had written to me. I found her note when I got home."

Madame de Vionnet listened with interest and with her eyes on Strether's face; then her delicately decorated head had a small melancholy motion. "She didn't write to ME. I went to see her," she added, "almost immediately after I had seen you, and as I assured her I would do when I met her at Gloriani's. She hadn't then told me she was to be absent, and I felt at her door as if I understood. She's absent—with all respect to her sick friend, though I know indeed she has plenty—so that I may not see her. She doesn't want to meet me again. Well," she continued with a beautiful conscious mildness, "I liked and admired her beyond every one in the old time, and she knew it—perhaps that's precisely what has made her go—and I dare say I haven't lost her for ever." Strether still said nothing; he had a horror, as he now thought of himself, of being in question between women—was in fact already quite enough on his way to that, and there was moreover, as it came to him, perceptibly, something behind these allusions and professions that, should he take it in, would square but ill with his present resolve to simplify. It was as if, for him, all the same, her softness and sadness were sincere. He felt that not less when she soon went on: "I'm extremely glad of her happiness." But it also left him mute—sharp and fine though the imputation it conveyed. What it conveyed was that HE was Maria Gostrey's happiness, and for the least little in-instant he had the impulse to challenge the thought. He could have done so however only by saying "What then do you suppose to be between us?" and he was wonderfully glad a moment later not to have spoken. He would rather seem stupid any day than fatuous, and he drew back as well, with a smothered inward shudder, from the consideration of what women—of highly-developed type in particular—might think of each other. Whatever he had come out for he hadn't come to go into that; so that he absolutely took up nothing his interlocutress had now let drop. Yet, though he had kept away from her for days, had laid wholly on herself the burden of their meeting again, she hadn't a gleam of irritation to show him. "Well, about Jeanne now?" she smiled—it had the gaiety with which she had originally come in. He felt it on the instant to represent her motive and real errand. But he had been schooling her of a truth to say much in proportion to his little. "Do you make out that she has a sentiment? I mean for Mr. Newsome."

Almost resentful, Strether could at last be prompt. "How can I make out such things?"

She remained perfectly good-natured. "Ah but they're beautiful little things, and you make out—don't pretend—everything in the world. Haven't you," she asked, "been talking with her?"

"Yes, but not about Chad. At least not much."

"Oh you don't require 'much'!" she reassuringly declared. But she immediately changed her ground. "I hope you remember your promise of the other day."

"To 'save' you, as you called it?"

"I call it so still. You WILL?" she insisted. "You haven't repented?"

He wondered. "No—but I've been thinking what I meant."

She kept it up. "And not, a little, what I did?"

"No—that's not necessary. It will be enough if I know what I meant myself."

"And don't you know," she asked, "by this time?"

Again he had a pause. "I think you ought to leave it to me. But how long," he added, "do you give me?"

"It seems to me much more a question of how long you give ME. Doesn't our friend here himself, at any rate," she went on, "perpetually make me present to you?"

"Not," Strether replied, "by ever speaking of you to me."

"He never does that?"

"Never."

She considered, and, if the fact was disconcerting to her, effectually concealed it. The next minute indeed she had recovered. "No, he wouldn't. But do you NEED that?"

Her emphasis was wonderful, and though his eyes had been wandering he looked at her longer now. "I see what you mean."

"Of course you see what I mean."

Her triumph was gentle, and she really had tones to make justice weep. "I've before me what he owes you."

"Admit then that that's something," she said, yet still with the same discretion in her pride.

He took in this note but went straight on. "You've made of him what I see, but what I don't see is how in the world you've done it."

"Ah that's another question!" she smiled. "The point is of what use is your declining to know me when to know Mr. Newsome—as you do me the honour to find him—IS just to know me."

"I see," he mused, still with his eyes on her. "I shouldn't have met you to-night."

She raised and dropped her linked hands. "It doesn't matter. If I trust you why can't you a little trust me too? And why can't you also," she asked in another tone, "trust yourself?" But she gave him no time to reply. "Oh I shall be so easy for you! And I'm glad at any rate you've seen my child."

"I'm glad too," he said; "but she does you no good."

"No good?"—Madame de Vionnet had a clear stare. "Why she's an angel of light."

"That's precisely the reason. Leave her alone. Don't try to find out. I mean," he explained, "about what you spoke to me of—the way she feels."

His companion wondered. "Because one really won't?"

"Well, because I ask you, as a favour to myself, not to. She's the most charming creature I've ever seen. Therefore don't touch her. Don't know—don't want to know. And moreover—yes—you won't."

It was an appeal, of a sudden, and she took it in. "As a favour to you?"

"Well—since you ask me."

"Anything, everything you ask," she smiled. "I shan't know then—never. Thank you," she added with peculiar gentleness as she turned away.

The sound of it lingered with him, making him fairly feel as if he had been tripped up and had a fall. In the very act of arranging with her for his independence he had, under pressure from a particular perception, inconsistently, quite stupidly, committed himself, and, with her subtlety sensitive on the spot to an advantage, she had driven in by a single word a little golden nail, the sharp intention of which he signally felt. He hadn't detached, he had more closely connected himself, and his eyes, as he considered with some intensity this circumstance, met another pair which had just come within their range and which struck him as reflecting his sense of what he had done. He recognised them at the same moment as those of little Bilham, who had apparently drawn near on purpose to speak to him, and little Bilham wasn't, in the conditions, the person to whom his heart would be most closed. They were seated together a minute later at the angle of the room obliquely opposite the corner in which Gloriani was still engaged with Jeanne de Vionnet, to whom at first and in silence their attention had been benevolently given. "I can't see for my life," Strether had then observed, "how a young fellow of any spirit—such a one as you for instance—can be admitted to the sight of that young lady without being hard hit. Why don't you go in, little Bilham?" He remembered the tone into which he had been betrayed on the garden-bench at the sculptor's reception, and this might make up for that by being much more the right sort of thing to say to a young man worthy of any advice at all. "There WOULD be some reason."

"Some reason for what?"

"Why for hanging on here."

"To offer my hand and fortune to Mademoiselle de Vionnet?"

"Well," Strether asked, "to what lovelier apparition COULD you offer them? She's the sweetest little thing I've ever seen."

"She's certainly immense. I mean she's the real thing. I believe the pale pink petals are folded up there for some wondrous efflorescence in time; to open, that is, to some great golden sun. I'M unfortunately but a small farthing candle. What chance in such a field for a poor little painter-man?"

"Oh you're good enough," Strether threw out.

"Certainly I'm good enough. We're good enough, I consider, nous autres, for anything. But she's TOO good. There's the difference. They wouldn't look at me."

Strether, lounging on his divan and still charmed by the young girl, whose eyes had consciously strayed to him, he fancied, with a vague smile—Strether, enjoying the whole occasion as with dormant pulses at last awake and in spite of new material thrust upon him, thought over his companion's words. "Whom do you mean by 'they'? She and her mother?"

"She and her mother. And she has a father too, who, whatever else he may be, certainly can't be indifferent to the possibilities she represents. Besides, there's Chad."

Strether was silent a little. "Ah but he doesn't care for her—not, I mean, it appears, after all, in the sense I'm speaking of. He's NOT in love with her."

"No—but he's her best friend; after her mother. He's very fond of her. He has his ideas about what can be done for her."

"Well, it's very strange!" Strether presently remarked with a sighing sense of fulness.

"Very strange indeed. That's just the beauty of it. Isn't it very much the kind of beauty you had in mind," little Bilham went on, "when you were so wonderful and so inspiring to me the other day? Didn't you adjure me, in accents I shall never forget, to see, while I've a chance, everything I can?—and REALLY to see, for it must have been that only you meant. Well, you did me no end of good, and I'm doing my best. I DO make it out a situation."

"So do I!" Strether went on after a moment. But he had the next minute an inconsequent question. "How comes Chad so mixed up, anyway?"

"Ah, ah, ah!"—and little Bilham fell back on his cushions.

It reminded our friend of Miss Barrace, and he felt again the brush of his sense of moving in a maze of mystic closed allusions. Yet he kept hold of his thread. "Of course I understand really; only the general transformation makes me occasionally gasp. Chad with such a voice in the settlement of the future of a little countess—no," he declared, "it takes more time! You say moreover," he resumed, "that we're inevitably, people like you and me, out of the running. The curious fact remains that Chad himself isn't. The situation doesn't make for it, but in a different one he could have her if he would."

"Yes, but that's only because he's rich and because there's a possibility of his being richer. They won't think of anything but a great name or a great fortune."

"Well," said Strether, "he'll have no great fortune on THESE lines. He must stir his stumps."

"Is that," little Bilham enquired, "what you were saying to Madame de Vionnet?"

"No—I don't say much to her. Of course, however," Strether continued, "he can make sacrifices if he likes."

Little Bilham had a pause. "Oh he's not keen for sacrifices; or thinks, that is, possibly, that he has made enough."

"Well, it IS virtuous," his companion observed with some decision.

"That's exactly," the young man dropped after a moment, "what I mean."

It kept Strether himself silent a little. "I've made it out for myself," he then went on; "I've really, within the last half-hour, got hold of it. I understand it in short at last; which at first—when you originally spoke to me—I didn't. Nor when Chad originally spoke to me either."

"Oh," said little Bilham, "I don't think that at that time you believed me."

"Yes—I did; and I believed Chad too. It would have been odious and unmannerly—as well as quite perverse—if I hadn't. What interest have you in deceiving me?"

The young man cast about. "What interest have I?"

"Yes. Chad MIGHT have. But you?"

"Ah, ah, ah!" little Bilham exclaimed.

It might, on repetition, as a mystification, have irritated our friend a little, but he knew, once more, as we have seen, where he was, and his being proof against everything was only another attestation that he meant to stay there. "I couldn't, without my own impression, realise. She's a tremendously clever brilliant capable woman, and with an extraordinary charm on top of it all—the charm we surely all of us this evening know what to think of. It isn't every clever brilliant capable woman that has it. In fact it's rare with any woman. So there you are," Strether proceeded as if not for little Bilham's benefit alone. "I understand what a relation with such a woman—what such a high fine friendship—may be. It can't be vulgar or coarse, anyway—and that's the point."

"Yes, that's the point," said little Bilham. "It can't be vulgar or coarse. And, bless us and save us, it ISn't! It's, upon my word, the very finest thing I ever saw in my life, and the most distinguished."

Strether, from beside him and leaning back with him as he leaned, dropped on him a momentary look which filled a short interval and of which he took no notice. He only gazed before him with intent participation. "Of course what it has done for him," Strether at all events presently pursued, "of course what it has done for him—that is as to HOW it has so wonderfully worked—isn't a thing I pretend to understand. I've to take it as I find it. There he is."

"There he is!" little Bilham echoed. "And it's really and truly she. I don't understand either, even with my longer and closer opportunity. But I'm like you," he added; "I can admire and rejoice even when I'm a little in the dark. You see I've watched it for some three years, and especially for this last. He wasn't so bad before it as I seem to have made out that you think—"

"Oh I don't think anything now!" Strether impatiently broke in: "that is but what I DO think! I mean that originally, for her to have cared for him—"

"There must have been stuff in him? Oh yes, there was stuff indeed, and much more of it than ever showed, I dare say, at home. Still, you know," the young man in all fairness developed, "there was room for her, and that's where she came in. She saw her chance and took it. That's what strikes me as having been so fine. But of course," he wound up, "he liked her first."

"Naturally," said Strether.

"I mean that they first met somehow and somewhere—I believe in some American house—and she, without in the least then intending it, made her impression. Then with time and opportunity he made his; and after THAT she was as bad as he."

Strether vaguely took it up. "As 'bad'?"

"She began, that is, to care—to care very much. Alone, and in her horrid position, she found it, when once she had started, an interest. It was, it is, an interest, and it did—it continues to do—a lot for herself as well. So she still cares. She cares in fact," said little Bilham thoughtfully "more."

Strether's theory that it was none of his business was somehow not damaged by the way he took this. "More, you mean, than he?" On which his companion looked round at him, and now for an instant their eyes met. "More than he?" he repeated.

Little Bilham, for as long, hung fire. "Will you never tell any one?"

Strether thought. "Whom should I tell?"

"Why I supposed you reported regularly—"

"To people at home?"—Strether took him up. "Well, I won't tell them this."

The young man at last looked away. "Then she does now care more than he."

"Oh!" Strether oddly exclaimed.

But his companion immediately met it. "Haven't you after all had your impression of it? That's how you've got hold of him."

"Ah but I haven't got hold of him!"

"Oh I say!" But it was all little Bilham said.

"It's at any rate none of my business. I mean," Strether explained, "nothing else than getting hold of him is." It appeared, however, to strike him as his business to add: "The fact remains nevertheless that she has saved him."

Little Bilham just waited. "I thought that was what you were to do."

But Strether had his answer ready. "I'm speaking—in connexion with her—of his manners and morals, his character and life. I'm speaking of him as a person to deal with and talk with and live with—speaking of him as a social animal."

"And isn't it as a social animal that you also want him?"

"Certainly; so that it's as if she had saved him FOR us."

"It strikes you accordingly then," the young man threw out, "as for you all to save HER?"

"Oh for us 'all'—!" Strether could but laugh at that. It brought him back, however, to the point he had really wished to make. "They've accepted their situation—hard as it is. They're not free—at least she's not; but they take what's left to them. It's a friendship, of a beautiful sort; and that's what makes them so strong. They're straight, they feel; and they keep each other up. It's doubtless she, however, who, as you yourself have hinted, feels it most."

Little Bilham appeared to wonder what he had hinted. "Feels most that they're straight?"

"Well, feels that SHE is, and the strength that comes from it. She keeps HIM up—she keeps the whole thing up. When people are able to it's fine. She's wonderful, wonderful, as Miss Barrace says; and he is, in his way, too; however, as a mere man, he may sometimes rebel and not feel that he finds his account in it. She has simply given him an immense moral lift, and what that can explain is prodigious. That's why I speak of it as a situation. It IS one, if there ever was." And Strether, with his head back and his eyes on the ceiling, seemed to lose himself in the vision of it.

His companion attended deeply. "You state it much better than I could." "Oh you see it doesn't concern you."

Little Bilham considered. "I thought you said just now that it doesn't concern you either."

"Well, it doesn't a bit as Madame de Vionnet's affair. But as we were again saying just now, what did I come out for but to save him?"

"Yes—to remove him."

"To save him by removal; to win him over to HIMSELF thinking it best he shall take up business—thinking he must immediately do therefore what's necessary to that end."

"Well," said little Bilham after a moment, "you HAVE won him over. He does think it best. He has within a day or two again said to me as much."

"And that," Strether asked, "is why you consider that he cares less than she?"

"Cares less for her than she for him? Yes, that's one of the reasons. But other things too have given me the impression. A man, don't you think?" little Bilham presently pursued, "CAN'T, in such conditions, care so much as a woman. It takes different conditions to make him, and then perhaps he cares more. Chad," he wound up, "has his possible future before him."

"Are you speaking of his business future?"

"No—on the contrary; of the other, the future of what you so justly call their situation. M. de Vionnet may live for ever."

"So that they can't marry?"

The young man waited a moment. "Not being able to marry is all they've with any confidence to look forward to. A woman—a particular woman—may stand that strain. But can a man?" he propounded.

Strether's answer was as prompt as if he had already, for himself, worked it out. "Not without a very high ideal of conduct. But that's just what we're attributing to Chad. And how, for that matter," he mused, "does his going to America diminish the particular strain? Wouldn't it seem rather to add to it?"

"Out of sight out of mind!" his companion laughed. Then more bravely: "Wouldn't distance lessen the torment?" But before Strether could reply, "The thing is, you see, Chad ought to marry!" he wound up.

Strether, for a little, appeared to think of it. "If you talk of torments you don't diminish mine!" he then broke out. The next moment he was on his feet with a question. "He ought to marry whom?"

Little Bilham rose more slowly. "Well, some one he CAN—some thoroughly nice girl."

Strether's eyes, as they stood together, turned again to Jeanne. "Do you mean HER?"

His friend made a sudden strange face. "After being in love with her mother? No."

"But isn't it exactly your idea that he ISn't in love with her mother?"

His friend once more had a pause. "Well, he isn't at any rate in love with Jeanne."

"I dare say not."

"How CAN he be with any other woman?"

"Oh that I admit. But being in love isn't, you know, here"—little Bilham spoke in friendly reminder—"thought necessary, in strictness, for marriage."

"And what torment—to call a torment—can there ever possibly be with a woman like that?" As if from the interest of his own question Strether had gone on without hearing. "Is it for her to have turned a man out so wonderfully, too, only for somebody else?" He appeared to make a point of this, and little Bilham looked at him now. "When it's for each other that people give things up they don't miss them." Then he threw off as with an extravagance of which he was conscious: "Let them face the future together!"

Little Bilham looked at him indeed. "You mean that after all he shouldn't go back?"

"I mean that if he gives her up—!"

"Yes?"

"Well, he ought to be ashamed of himself." But Strether spoke with a sound that might have passed for a laugh.

THE AMBASSADORS

Volume II

Book Seventh

I

It wasn't the first time Strether had sat alone in the great dim church—still less was it the first of his giving himself up, so far as conditions permitted, to its beneficent action on his nerves. He had been to Notre Dame with Waymarsh, he had been there with Miss Gostrey, he had been there with Chad Newsome, and had found the place, even in company, such a refuge from the obsession of his problem that, with renewed pressure from that source, he had not unnaturally recurred to a remedy meeting the case, for the moment, so indirectly, no doubt, but so relievingly. He was conscious enough that it was only for the moment, but good moments—if he could call them good—still had their value for a man who by this time struck himself as living almost disgracefully from hand to mouth. Having so well learnt the way, he had lately made the pilgrimage more than once by himself—had quite stolen off, taking an unnoticed chance and making no point of speaking of the adventure when restored to his friends.

His great friend, for that matter, was still absent, as well as remarkably silent; even at the end of three weeks Miss Gostrey hadn't come back. She wrote to him from Mentone, admitting that he must judge her grossly inconsequent—perhaps in fact for the time odiously faithless; but asking for patience, for a deferred sentence, throwing herself in short on his generosity. For her too, she could assure him, life was complicated—more complicated than he could have guessed; she had moreover made certain of him—certain of not wholly missing him on her return—before her disappearance. If furthermore she didn't burden him with letters it was frankly because of her sense of the other great commerce he had to carry on. He himself, at the end of a fortnight, had written twice, to show how his generosity could be trusted; but he reminded himself in each case of Mrs. Newsome's epistolary manner at the times when Mrs. Newsome kept off delicate ground. He sank his problem, he talked of Waymarsh and Miss Barrace, of little Bilham and the set over the river, with whom he had again had tea, and he was easy, for convenience, about Chad and Madame de Vionnet and Jeanne. He admitted that he continued to see them, he was decidedly so confirmed a haunter of Chad's premises and that young man's practical intimacy with them was so undeniably great; but he had his reason for not attempting to render for Miss Gostrey's benefit the impression of these last days. That would be to tell her too much about himself—it being at present just from himself he was trying to escape.

This small struggle sprang not a little, in its way, from the same impulse that had now carried him across to Notre Dame; the impulse to let things be, to give them time to justify themselves or at least to pass. He was aware of having no errand in such a place but the desire not to be, for the hour, in certain other places; a sense of safety, of simplification, which each time he yielded to it he amused himself by thinking of as a private concession to cowardice. The great church had no altar for his worship, no direct voice for his soul; but it was none the less soothing even to sanctity; for he could feel while there what he couldn't elsewhere, that he was a plain tired man taking the holiday he had earned. He was tired, but he wasn't plain—that was the pity and the trouble of it; he was able, however, to drop his problem at the door very much as if it had been the copper piece that he deposited, on the threshold, in the receptacle of the inveterate blind beggar. He trod the long dim nave, sat in the splendid choir, paused before the cluttered chapels of the east end, and the mighty monument laid upon him its spell. He might have been a student under the charm of a museum—which was exactly what, in a foreign town, in the afternoon of life, he would have liked to be free to be. This form of sacrifice did at any rate for the occasion as well as another; it made him quite sufficiently understand how, within the precinct, for the real refugee, the things of the world could fall into abeyance. That was the cowardice, probably—to dodge them, to beg the question, not to deal with it in the hard outer light; but his own oblivions were too brief, too vain, to hurt any one but himself, and he had a vague and fanciful kindness for certain persons whom he met, figures of mystery and anxiety, and whom, with observation for his pastime, he ranked as those who were fleeing from justice. Justice was outside, in the hard light, and injustice too; but one was as absent as the other from the air of the long aisles and the brightness of the many altars.

Thus it was at all events that, one morning some dozen days after the dinner in the Boulevard Malesherbes at which Madame de Vionnet had been present with her daughter, he was called upon to play his part in an encounter that deeply stirred his imagination. He had the habit, in these contemplations, of watching a fellow visitant, here and there, from a respectable distance, remarking some note of behaviour, of penitence, of prostration, of the absolved, relieved state; this was the manner in which his vague tenderness took its course, the degree of demonstration to which it naturally had to confine itself. It hadn't indeed so felt its responsibility as when on this occasion he suddenly measured the suggestive effect of a lady whose supreme stillness, in the shade of one of the chapels, he had two or three times noticed as he made, and made once more, his slow circuit. She wasn't prostrate—not in any degree bowed, but she was strangely fixed, and her prolonged immobility showed her, while he passed and paused, as wholly given up to the need, whatever it was, that had brought her there. She only sat and gazed before her, as he himself often sat; but she had placed herself, as he never did, within the focus of the shrine, and she had lost herself, he could easily see, as he would only have liked to do. She was not a wandering alien, keeping back more than she gave, but one of the familiar, the intimate, the fortunate, for whom these dealings had a method and a meaning. She reminded our friend—since it was the way of nine tenths of his current impressions to act as recalls of things imagined—of some fine firm concentrated heroine of an old story, something he had heard, read, something that, had he had a hand for drama, he might himself have written, renewing her courage, renewing her clearness, in splendidly-protected meditation. Her back, as she sat, was turned to him, but his impression absolutely required that she should be young and interesting, and she carried her head moreover, even in the sacred shade, with a discernible faith in herself, a kind of implied conviction of consistency, security, impunity. But what had such a woman come for if she hadn't come to pray? Strether's reading of such matters was, it must be owned, confused; but he wondered if her attitude were some congruous fruit of absolution, of "indulgence." He knew but dimly what indulgence, in such a place, might mean; yet he had, as with a soft sweep, a vision of how it might indeed add to the zest of active rites. All this was a good deal to have been denoted by a mere lurking figure who was nothing to him; but, the last thing before leaving the church, he had the surprise of a still deeper quickening.

He had dropped upon a seat halfway down the nave and, again in the museum mood, was trying with head thrown back and eyes aloft, to reconstitute a past, to reduce it in fact to the convenient terms of Victor Hugo, whom, a few days before, giving the rein for once in a way to the joy of life, he had purchased in seventy bound volumes, a miracle of cheapness, parted with, he was assured by the shopman, at the price of the red-and-gold alone. He looked, doubtless, while he played his eternal nippers over Gothic glooms, sufficiently rapt in reverence; but what his thought had finally bumped against was the question of where, among packed accumulations, so multiform a wedge would be able to enter. Were seventy volumes in red-and-gold to be perhaps what he should most substantially have to show at Woollett as the fruit of his mission? It was a possibility that held him a minute—held him till he happened to feel that some one, unnoticed, had approached him and paused. Turning, he saw that a lady stood there as for a greeting, and he sprang up as he next took her, securely, for Madame de Vionnet, who appeared to have recognised him as she passed near him on her way to the door. She checked, quickly and gaily, a certain confusion in him, came to meet it, turned it back, by an art of her own; the confusion having threatened him as he knew her for the person he had lately been observing. She was the lurking figure of the dim chapel; she had occupied him more than she guessed; but it came to him in time, luckily, that he needn't tell her and that no harm, after all, had been done. She herself, for that matter, straightway showing she felt their encounter as the happiest of accidents, had for him a "You come here too?" that despoiled surprise of every awkwardness.

"I come often," she said. "I love this place, but I'm terrible, in general, for churches. The old women who live in them all know me; in fact I'm already myself one of the old women. It's like that, at all events, that I foresee I shall end." Looking about for a chair, so that he instantly pulled one nearer, she sat down with him again to the sound of an "Oh, I like so much your also being fond—!"

He confessed the extent of his feeling, though she left the object vague; and he was struck with the tact, the taste of her vagueness, which simply took for granted in him a sense of beautiful things. He was conscious of how much it was affected, this sense, by something subdued and discreet in the way she had arranged herself for her special object and her morning walk—he believed her to have come on foot; the way her slightly thicker veil was drawn—a mere touch, but everything; the composed gravity of her dress, in which, here and there, a dull wine-colour seemed to gleam faintly through black; the charming discretion of her small compact head; the quiet note, as she sat, of her folded, grey-gloved hands. It was, to Strether's mind, as if she sat on her own ground, the light honours of which, at an open gate, she thus easily did him, while all the vastness and mystery of the domain stretched off behind. When people were so completely in possession they could be extraordinarily civil; and our friend had indeed at this hour a kind of revelation of her heritage. She was romantic for him far beyond what she could have guessed, and again he found his small comfort in the conviction that, subtle though she was, his impression must remain a secret from her. The thing that, once more, made him uneasy for secrets in general was this particular patience she could have with his own want of colour; albeit that on the other hand his uneasiness pretty well dropped after he had been for ten minutes as colourless as possible and at the same time as responsive.

The moments had already, for that matter, drawn their deepest tinge from the special interest excited in him by his vision of his companion's identity with the person whose attitude before the glimmering altar had so impressed him. This attitude fitted admirably into the stand he had privately taken about her connexion with Chad on the last occasion of his seeing them together. It helped him to stick fast at the point he had then reached; it was there he had resolved that he WOULD stick, and at no moment since had it seemed as easy to do so. Unassailably innocent was a relation that could make one of the parties to it so carry herself. If it wasn't innocent why did she haunt the churches?—into which, given the woman he could believe he made out, she would never have come to flaunt an insolence of guilt. She haunted them for continued help, for strength, for peace—sublime support which, if one were able to look at it so, she found from day to day. They talked, in low easy tones and with lifted lingering looks, about the great monument and its history and its beauty—all of which, Madame de Vionnet professed, came to her most in the other, the outer view. "We'll presently, after we go," she said, "walk round it again if you like. I'm not in a particular hurry, and it will be pleasant to look at it well with you." He had spoken of the great romancer and the great romance, and of what, to his imagination, they had done for the whole, mentioning to her moreover the exorbitance of his purchase, the seventy blazing volumes that were so out of proportion.

"Out of proportion to what?"

"Well, to any other plunge." Yet he felt even as he spoke how at that instant he was plunging. He had made up his mind and was impatient to get into the air; for his purpose was a purpose to be uttered outside, and he had a fear that it might with delay still slip away from him. She however took her time; she drew out their quiet gossip as if she had wished to profit by their meeting, and this confirmed precisely an interpretation of her manner, of her mystery. While she rose, as he would have called it, to the question of Victor Hugo, her voice itself, the light low quaver of her deference to the solemnity about them, seemed to make her words mean something that they didn't mean openly. Help, strength, peace, a sublime support—she hadn't found so much of these things as that the amount wouldn't be sensibly greater for any scrap his appearance of faith in her might enable her to feel in her hand. Every little, in a long strain, helped, and if he happened to affect her as a firm object she could hold on by, he wouldn't jerk himself out of her reach. People in difficulties held on by what was nearest, and he was perhaps after all not further off than sources of comfort more abstract. It was as to this he had made up his mind; he had made it up, that is, to give her a sign. The sign would be that—though it was her own affair—he understood; the sign would be that—though it was her own affair—she was free to clutch. Since she took him for a firm object—much as he might to his own sense appear at times to rock—he would do his best to BE one.

The end of it was that half an hour later they were seated together for an early luncheon at a wonderful, a delightful house of entertainment on the left bank—a place of pilgrimage for the knowing, they were both aware, the knowing who came, for its great renown, the homage of restless days, from the other end of the town. Strether had already been there three times—first with Miss Gostrey, then with Chad, then with Chad again and with Waymarsh and little Bilham, all of whom he had himself sagaciously entertained; and his pleasure was deep now on learning that Madame de Vionnet hadn't yet been initiated. When he had said as they strolled round the church, by the river, acting at last on what, within, he had made up his mind to, "Will you, if you have time, come to dejeuner with me somewhere? For instance, if you know it, over there on the other side, which is so easy a walk"—and then had named the place; when he had done this she stopped short as for quick intensity, and yet deep difficulty, of response. She took in the proposal as if it were almost too charming to be true; and there had perhaps never yet been for her companion so unexpected a moment of pride—so fine, so odd a case, at any rate, as his finding himself thus able to offer to a person in such universal possession a new, a rare amusement. She had heard of the happy spot, but she asked him in reply to a further question how in the world he could suppose her to have been there. He supposed himself to have supposed that Chad might have taken her, and she guessed this the next moment to his no small discomfort.

"Ah, let me explain," she smiled, "that I don't go about with him in public; I never have such chances—not having them otherwise—and it's just the sort of thing that, as a quiet creature living in my hole, I adore." It was more than kind of him to have thought of it—though, frankly, if he asked whether she had time she hadn't a single minute. That however made no difference—she'd throw everything over. Every duty at home, domestic, maternal, social, awaited her; but it was a case for a high line. Her affairs would go to smash, but hadn't one a right to one's snatch of scandal when one was prepared to pay? It was on this pleasant basis of costly disorder, consequently, that they eventually seated themselves, on either side of a small table, at a window adjusted to the busy quay and the shining barge-burdened Seine; where, for an hour, in the matter of letting himself go, of diving deep, Strether was to feel he had touched bottom. He was to feel many things on this occasion, and one of the first of them was that he had travelled far since that evening in London, before the theatre, when his dinner with Maria Gostrey, between the pink-shaded candles, had struck him as requiring so many explanations. He had at that time gathered them in, the explanations—he had stored them up; but it was at present as if he had either soared above or sunk below them—he couldn't tell which; he could somehow think of none that didn't seem to leave the appearance of collapse and cynicism easier for him than lucidity. How could he wish it to be lucid for others, for any one, that he, for the hour, saw reasons enough in the mere way the bright clean ordered water-side life came in at the open window?—the mere way Madame de Vionnet, opposite him over their intensely white table-linen, their omelette aux tomates, their bottle of straw-coloured Chablis, thanked him for everything almost with the smile of a child, while her grey eyes moved in and out of their talk, back to the quarter of the warm spring air, in which early summer had already begun to throb, and then back again to his face and their human questions.

Their human questions became many before they had done—many more, as one after the other came up, than our friend's free fancy had at all foreseen. The sense he had had before, the sense he had had repeatedly, the sense that the situation was running away with him, had never been so sharp as now; and all the more that he could perfectly put his finger on the moment it had taken the bit in its teeth. That accident had definitely occurred, the other evening, after Chad's dinner; it had occurred, as he fully knew, at the moment when he interposed between this lady and her child, when he suffered himself so to discuss with her a matter closely concerning them that her own subtlety, marked by its significant "Thank you!" instantly sealed the occasion in her favour. Again he had held off for ten days, but the situation had continued out of hand in spite of that; the fact that it was running so fast being indeed just WHY he had held off. What had come over him as he recognised her in the nave of the church was that holding off could be but a losing game from the instant she was worked for not only by her subtlety, but by the hand of fate itself. If all the accidents were to fight on her side—and by the actual showing they loomed large—he could only give himself up. This was what he had done in privately deciding then and there to propose she should breakfast with him. What did the success of his proposal in fact resemble but the smash in which a regular runaway properly ends? The smash was their walk, their dejeuner, their omelette, the Chablis, the place, the view, their present talk and his present pleasure in it—to say nothing, wonder of wonders, of her own. To this tune and nothing less, accordingly, was his surrender made good. It sufficiently lighted up at least the folly of holding off. Ancient proverbs sounded, for his memory, in the tone of their words and the clink of their glasses, in the hum of the town and the plash of the river. It WAS clearly better to suffer as a sheep than as a lamb. One might as well perish by the sword as by famine.

"Maria's still away?"—that was the first thing she had asked him; and when he had found the frankness to be cheerful about it in spite of the meaning he knew her to attach to Miss Gostrey's absence, she had gone on to enquire if he didn't tremendously miss her. There were reasons that made him by no means sure, yet he nevertheless answered "Tremendously"; which she took in as if it were all she had wished to prove. Then, "A man in trouble MUST be possessed somehow of a woman," she said; "if she doesn't come in one way she comes in another."

"Why do you call me a man in trouble?"

"Ah because that's the way you strike me." She spoke ever so gently and as if with all fear of wounding him while she sat partaking of his bounty. "AREn't you in trouble?"

He felt himself colour at the question, and then hated that—hated to pass for anything so idiotic as woundable. Woundable by Chad's lady, in respect to whom he had come out with such a fund of indifference—was he already at that point? Perversely, none the less, his pause gave a strange air of truth to her supposition; and what was he in fact but disconcerted at having struck her just in the way he had most dreamed of not doing? "I'm not in trouble yet," he at last smiled. "I'm not in trouble now."

"Well, I'm always so. But that you sufficiently know." She was a woman who, between courses, could be graceful with her elbows on the table. It was a posture unknown to Mrs. Newsome, but it was easy for a femme du monde. "Yes—I am 'now'!"

"There was a question you put to me," he presently returned, "the night of Chad's dinner. I didn't answer it then, and it has been very handsome of you not to have sought an occasion for pressing me about it since."

She was instantly all there. "Of course I know what you allude to. I asked you what you had meant by saying, the day you came to see me, just before you left me, that you'd save me. And you then said—at our friend's—that you'd have really to wait to see, for yourself, what you did mean."

"Yes, I asked for time," said Strether. "And it sounds now, as you put it, like a very ridiculous speech."

"Oh!" she murmured—she was full of attenuation. But she had another thought. "If it does sound ridiculous why do you deny that you're in trouble?"

"Ah if I were," he replied, "it wouldn't be the trouble of fearing ridicule. I don't fear it."

"What then do you?"

"Nothing—now." And he leaned back in his chair.

"I like your 'now'!" she laughed across at him.

"Well, it's precisely that it fully comes to me at present that I've kept you long enough. I know by this time, at any rate, what I meant by my speech; and I really knew it the night of Chad's dinner."

"Then why didn't you tell me?"

"Because it was difficult at the moment. I had already at that moment done something for you, in the sense of what I had said the day I went to see you; but I wasn't then sure of the importance I might represent this as having."

She was all eagerness. "And you're sure now?"

"Yes; I see that, practically, I've done for you—had done for you when you put me your question—all that it's as yet possible to me to do. I feel now," he went on, "that it may go further than I thought. What I did after my visit to you," he explained, "was to write straight off to Mrs. Newsome about you, and I'm at last, from one day to the other, expecting her answer. It's this answer that will represent, as I believe, the consequences."

Patient and beautiful was her interest. "I see—the consequences of your speaking for me." And she waited as if not to hustle him.

He acknowledged it by immediately going on. "The question, you understand, was HOW I should save you. Well, I'm trying it by thus letting her know that I consider you worth saving."

"I see—I see." Her eagerness broke through.

"How can I thank you enough?" He couldn't tell her that, however, and she quickly pursued. "You do really, for yourself, consider it?"

His only answer at first was to help her to the dish that had been freshly put before them. "I've written to her again since then—I've left her in no doubt of what I think. I've told her all about you."

"Thanks—not so much. 'All about' me," she went on—"yes."

"All it seems to me you've done for him."

"Ah and you might have added all it seems to ME!" She laughed again, while she took up her knife and fork, as in the cheer of these assurances. "But you're not sure how she'll take it."

"No, I'll not pretend I'm sure."

"Voila." And she waited a moment. "I wish you'd tell me about her."

"Oh," said Strether with a slightly strained smile, "all that need concern you about her is that she's really a grand person."

Madame de Vionnet seemed to demur. "Is that all that need concern me about her?"

But Strether neglected the question. "Hasn't Chad talked to you?"

"Of his mother? Yes, a great deal—immensely. But not from your point of view."

"He can't," our friend returned, "have said any ill of her."

"Not the least bit. He has given me, like you, the assurance that she's really grand. But her being really grand is somehow just what hasn't seemed to simplify our case. Nothing," she continued, "is further from me than to wish to say a word against her; but of course I feel how little she can like being told of her owing me anything. No woman ever enjoys such an obligation to another woman."

This was a proposition Strether couldn't contradict. "And yet what other way could I have expressed to her what I felt? It's what there was most to say about you."

"Do you mean then that she WILL be good to me?"

"It's what I'm waiting to see. But I've little doubt she would," he added, "if she could comfortably see you."

It seemed to strike her as a happy, a beneficent thought. "Oh then couldn't that be managed? Wouldn't she come out? Wouldn't she if you so put it to her? DID you by any possibility?" she faintly quavered.

"Oh no"—he was prompt. "Not that. It would be, much more, to give an account of you that—since there's no question of YOUR paying the visit—I should go home first."

It instantly made her graver. "And are you thinking of that?"

"Oh all the while, naturally."

"Stay with us—stay with us!" she exclaimed on this. "That's your only way to make sure."

"To make sure of what?"

"Why that he doesn't break up. You didn't come out to do that to him."

"Doesn't it depend," Strether returned after a moment, "on what you mean by breaking up?"

"Oh you know well enough what I mean!"

His silence seemed again for a little to denote an understanding. "You take for granted remarkable things."

"Yes, I do—to the extent that I don't take for granted vulgar ones. You're perfectly capable of seeing that what you came out for wasn't really at all to do what you'd now have to do."

"Ah it's perfectly simple," Strether good-humouredly pleaded. "I've had but one thing to do—to put our case before him. To put it as it could only be put here on the spot—by personal pressure. My dear lady," he lucidly pursued, "my work, you see, is really done, and my reasons for staying on even another day are none of the best. Chad's in possession of our case and professes to do it full justice. What remains is with himself. I've had my rest, my amusement and refreshment; I've had, as we say at Woollett, a lovely time. Nothing in it has been more lovely than this happy meeting with you—in these fantastic conditions to which you've so delightfully consented. I've a sense of success. It's what I wanted. My getting all this good is what Chad has waited for, and I gather that if I'm ready to go he's the same."

She shook her head with a finer deeper wisdom. "You're not ready. If you're ready why did you write to Mrs. Newsome in the sense you've mentioned to me?"

Strether considered. "I shan't go before I hear from her. You're too much afraid of her," he added.

It produced between them a long look from which neither shrank. "I don't think you believe that—believe I've not really reason to fear her."

"She's capable of great generosity," Strether presently stated.

"Well then let her trust me a little. That's all I ask. Let her recognise in spite of everything what I've done."

"Ah remember," our friend replied, "that she can't effectually recognise it without seeing it for herself. Let Chad go over and show her what you've done, and let him plead with her there for it and, as it were, for YOU."

She measured the depth of this suggestion. "Do you give me your word of honour that if she once has him there she won't do her best to marry him?"

It made her companion, this enquiry, look again a while out at the view; after which he spoke without sharpness. "When she sees for herself what he is—"

But she had already broken in. "It's when she sees for herself what he is that she'll want to marry him most."

Strether's attitude, that of due deference to what she said, permitted him to attend for a minute to his luncheon. "I doubt if that will come off. It won't be easy to make it."

"It will be easy if he remains there—and he'll remain for the money. The money appears to be, as a probability, so hideously much."

"Well," Strether presently concluded, "nothing COULD really hurt you but his marrying."

She gave a strange light laugh. "Putting aside what may really hurt HIM."

But her friend looked at her as if he had thought of that too. "The question will come up, of course, of the future that you yourself offer him."

She was leaning back now, but she fully faced him. "Well, let it come up!"

"The point is that it's for Chad to make of it what he can. His being proof against marriage will show what he does make."

"If he IS proof, yes"—she accepted the proposition. "But for myself," she added, "the question is what YOU make."

"Ah I make nothing. It's not my affair."

"I beg your pardon. It's just there that, since you've taken it up and are committed to it, it most intensely becomes yours. You're not saving me, I take it, for your interest in myself, but for your interest in our friend. The one's at any rate wholly dependent on the other. You can't in honour not see me through," she wound up, "because you can't in honour not see HIM."

Strange and beautiful to him was her quiet soft acuteness. The thing that most moved him was really that she was so deeply serious. She had none of the portentous forms of it, but he had never come in contact, it struck him, with a force brought to so fine a head. Mrs. Newsome, goodness knew, was serious; but it was nothing to this. He took it all in, he saw it all together. "No," he mused, "I can't in honour not see him."

Her face affected him as with an exquisite light. "You WILL then?"

"I will."

At this she pushed back her chair and was the next moment on her feet. "Thank you!" she said with her hand held out to him across the table and with no less a meaning in the words than her lips had so particularly given them after Chad's dinner. The golden nail she had then driven in pierced a good inch deeper. Yet he reflected that he himself had only meanwhile done what he had made up his mind to on the same occasion. So far as the essence of the matter went he had simply stood fast on the spot on which he had then planted his feet.

II

He received three days after this a communication from America, in the form of a scrap of blue paper folded and gummed, not reaching him through his bankers, but delivered at his hotel by a small boy in uniform, who, under instructions from the concierge, approached him as he slowly paced the little court. It was the evening hour, but daylight was long now and Paris more than ever penetrating. The scent of flowers was in the streets, he had the whiff of violets perpetually in his nose; and he had attached himself to sounds and suggestions, vibrations of the air, human and dramatic, he imagined, as they were not in other places, that came out for him more and more as the mild afternoons deepened—a far-off hum, a sharp near click on the asphalt, a voice calling, replying, somewhere and as full of tone as an actor's in a play. He was to dine at home, as usual, with Waymarsh—they had settled to that for thrift and simplicity; and he now hung about before his friend came down.

He read his telegram in the court, standing still a long time where he had opened it and giving five minutes afterwards to the renewed study of it. At last, quickly, he crumpled it up as if to get it out of the way; in spite of which, however, he kept it there—still kept it when, at the end of another turn, he had dropped into a chair placed near a small table. Here, with his scrap of paper compressed in his fist and further concealed by his folding his arms tight, he sat for some time in thought, gazed before him so straight that Waymarsh appeared and approached him without catching his eye. The latter in fact, struck with his appearance, looked at him hard for a single instant and then, as if determined to that course by some special vividness in it, dropped back into the salon de lecture without addressing him. But the pilgrim from Milrose permitted himself still to observe the scene from behind the clear glass plate of that retreat. Strether ended, as he sat, by a fresh scrutiny of his compressed missive, which he smoothed out carefully again as he placed it on his table. There it remained for some minutes, until, at last looking up, he saw Waymarsh watching him from within. It was on this that their eyes met—met for a moment during which neither moved. But Strether then got up, folding his telegram more carefully and putting it into his waistcoat pocket.

A few minutes later the friends were seated together at dinner; but Strether had meanwhile said nothing about it, and they eventually parted, after coffee in the court, with nothing said on either side. Our friend had moreover the consciousness that even less than usual was on this occasion said between them, so that it was almost as if each had been waiting for something from the other. Waymarsh had always more or less the air of sitting at the door of his tent, and silence, after so many weeks, had come to play its part in their concert. This note indeed, to Strether's sense, had lately taken a fuller tone, and it was his fancy to-night that they had never quite so drawn it out. Yet it befell, none the less that he closed the door to confidence when his companion finally asked him if there were anything particular the matter with him. "Nothing," he replied, "more than usual."

On the morrow, however, at an early hour, he found occasion to give an answer more in consonance with the facts. What was the matter had continued to be so all the previous evening, the first hours of which, after dinner, in his room, he had devoted to the copious composition of a letter. He had quitted Waymarsh for this purpose, leaving him to his own resources with less ceremony than their wont, but finally coming down again with his letter unconcluded and going forth into the streets without enquiry for his comrade. He had taken a long vague walk, and one o'clock had struck before his return and his re-ascent to his room by the aid of the glimmering candle-end left for him on the shelf outside the porter's lodge. He had possessed himself, on closing his door, of the numerous loose sheets of his unfinished composition, and then, without reading them over, had torn them into small pieces. He had thereupon slept—as if it had been in some measure thanks to that sacrifice—the sleep of the just, and had prolonged his rest considerably beyond his custom. Thus it was that when, between nine and ten, the tap of the knob of a walking-stick sounded on his door, he had not yet made himself altogether presentable. Chad Newsome's bright deep voice determined quickly enough none the less the admission of the visitor. The little blue paper of the evening before, plainly an object the more precious for its escape from premature destruction, now lay on the sill of the open window, smoothed out afresh and kept from blowing away by the superincumbent weight of his watch. Chad, looking about with careless and competent criticism, as he looked wherever he went immediately espied it and permitted himself to fix it for a moment rather hard. After which he turned his eyes to his host. "It has come then at last?"

Strether paused in the act of pinning his necktie. "Then you know—? You've had one too?"

"No, I've had nothing, and I only know what I see. I see that thing and I guess. Well," he added, "it comes as pat as in a play, for I've precisely turned up this morning—as I would have done yesterday, but it was impossible—to take you."

"To take me?" Strether had turned again to his glass.

"Back, at last, as I promised. I'm ready—I've really been ready this month. I've only been waiting for you—as was perfectly right. But you're better now; you're safe—I see that for myself; you've got all your good. You're looking, this morning, as fit as a flea."

Strether, at his glass, finished dressing; consulting that witness moreover on this last opinion. WAS he looking preternaturally fit? There was something in it perhaps for Chad's wonderful eye, but he had felt himself for hours rather in pieces. Such a judgement, however, was after all but a contribution to his resolve; it testified unwittingly to his wisdom. He was still firmer, apparently—since it shone in him as a light—than he had flattered himself. His firmness indeed was slightly compromised, as he faced about to his friend, by the way this very personage looked—though the case would of course have been worse hadn't the secret of personal magnificence been at every hour Chad's unfailing possession. There he was in all the pleasant morning freshness of it—strong and sleek and gay, easy and fragrant and fathomless, with happy health in his colour, and pleasant silver in his thick young hair, and the right word for everything on the lips that his clear brownness caused to show as red. He had never struck Strether as personally such a success; it was as if now, for his definite surrender, he had gathered himself vividly together. This, sharply and rather strangely, was the form in which he was to be presented to Woollett. Our friend took him in again—he was always taking him in and yet finding that parts of him still remained out; though even thus his image showed through a mist of other things. "I've had a cable," Strether said, "from your mother."

"I dare say, my dear man. I hope she's well."

Strether hesitated. "No—she's not well, I'm sorry to have to tell you."

"Ah," said Chad, "I must have had the instinct of it. All the more reason then that we should start straight off."

Strether had now got together hat, gloves and stick, but Chad had dropped on the sofa as if to show where he wished to make his point. He kept observing his companion's things; he might have been judging how quickly they could be packed. He might even have wished to hint that he'd send his own servant to assist. "What do you mean," Strether enquired, "by 'straight off'?"

"Oh by one of next week's boats. Everything at this season goes out so light that berths will be easy anywhere."

Strether had in his hand his telegram, which he had kept there after attaching his watch, and he now offered it to Chad, who, however, with an odd movement, declined to take it. "Thanks, I'd rather not. Your correspondence with Mother's your own affair. I'm only WITH you both on it, whatever it is." Strether, at this, while their eyes met, slowly folded the missive and put it in his pocket; after which, before he had spoken again, Chad broke fresh ground. "Has Miss Gostrey come back?"

But when Strether presently spoke it wasn't in answer. "It's not, I gather, that your mother's physically ill; her health, on the whole, this spring, seems to have been better than usual. But she's worried, she's anxious, and it appears to have risen within the last few days to a climax. We've tired out, between us, her patience."

"Oh it isn't YOU!" Chad generously protested.

"I beg your pardon—it IS me." Strether was mild and melancholy, but firm. He saw it far away and over his companion's head. "It's very particularly me."

"Well then all the more reason. Marchons, marchons!" said the young man gaily. His host, however, at this, but continued to stand agaze; and he had the next thing repeated his question of a moment before. "Has Miss Gostrey come back?"

"Yes, two days ago."

"Then you've seen her?"

"No—I'm to see her to-day." But Strether wouldn't linger now on Miss Gostrey. "Your mother sends me an ultimatum. If I can't bring you I'm to leave you; I'm to come at any rate myself."

"Ah but you CAN bring me now," Chad, from his sofa, reassuringly replied.

Strether had a pause. "I don't think I understand you. Why was it that, more than a month ago, you put it to me so urgently to let Madame de Vionnet speak for you?"

"'Why'?" Chad considered, but he had it at his fingers' ends. "Why but because I knew how well she'd do it? It was the way to keep you quiet and, to that extent, do you good. Besides," he happily and comfortably explained, "I wanted you really to know her and to get the impression of her—and you see the good that HAS done you."

"Well," said Strether, "the way she has spoken for you, all the same—so far as I've given her a chance—has only made me feel how much she wishes to keep you. If you make nothing of that I don't see why you wanted me to listen to her."

"Why my dear man," Chad exclaimed, "I make everything of it! How can you doubt—?"

"I doubt only because you come to me this morning with your signal to start."

Chad stared, then gave a laugh. "And isn't my signal to start just what you've been waiting for?"

Strether debated; he took another turn. "This last month I've been awaiting, I think, more than anything else, the message I have here."

"You mean you've been afraid of it?"

"Well, I was doing my business in my own way. And I suppose your present announcement," Strether went on, "isn't merely the result of your sense of what I've expected. Otherwise you wouldn't have put me in relation—" But he paused, pulling up.

At this Chad rose. "Ah HER wanting me not to go has nothing to do with it! It's only because she's afraid—afraid of the way that, over there, I may get caught. But her fear's groundless."

He had met again his companion's sufficiently searching look. "Are you tired of her?"

Chad gave him in reply to this, with a movement of the head, the strangest slow smile he had ever had from him. "Never."

It had immediately, on Strether's imagination, so deep and soft an effect that our friend could only for the moment keep it before him. "Never?"

"Never," Chad obligingly and serenely repeated.

It made his companion take several more steps. "Then YOU'RE not afraid."

"Afraid to go?"

Strether pulled up again. "Afraid to stay."

The young man looked brightly amazed. "You want me now to 'stay'?"

"If I don't immediately sail the Pococks will immediately come out. That's what I mean," said Strether, "by your mother's ultimatum ."

Chad showed a still livelier, but not an alarmed interest. "She has turned on Sarah and Jim?"

Strether joined him for an instant in the vision. "Oh and you may be sure Mamie. THAT'S whom she's turning on."

This also Chad saw—he laughed out. "Mamie—to corrupt me?"

"Ah," said Strether, "she's very charming."

"So you've already more than once told me. I should like to see her."

Something happy and easy, something above all unconscious, in the way he said this, brought home again to his companion the facility of his attitude and the enviability of his state. "See her then by all means. And consider too," Strether went on, "that you really give your sister a lift in letting her come to you. You give her a couple of months of Paris, which she hasn't seen, if I'm not mistaken, since just after she was married, and which I'm sure she wants but the pretext to visit."

Chad listened, but with all his own knowledge of the world. "She has had it, the pretext, these several years, yet she has never taken it."

"Do you mean YOU?" Strether after an instant enquired.

"Certainly—the lone exile. And whom do you mean?" said Chad.

"Oh I mean ME. I'm her pretext. That is—for it comes to the same thing—I'm your mother's."

"Then why," Chad asked, "doesn't Mother come herself?"

His friend gave him a long look. "Should you like her to?" And as he for the moment said nothing: "It's perfectly open to you to cable for her."

Chad continued to think. "Will she come if I do?"

"Quite possibly. But try, and you'll see."

"Why don't YOU try?" Chad after a moment asked.

"Because I don't want to."

Chad thought. "Don't desire her presence here?"

Strether faced the question, and his answer was the more emphatic. "Don't put it off, my dear boy, on ME!"

"Well—I see what you mean. I'm sure you'd behave beautifully but you DON'T want to see her. So I won't play you that trick.'

"Ah," Strether declared, "I shouldn't call it a trick. You've a perfect right, and it would be perfectly straight of you." Then he added in a different tone: "You'd have moreover, in the person of Madame de Vionnet, a very interesting relation prepared for her."

Their eyes, on this proposition, continued to meet, but Chad's pleasant and bold, never flinched for a moment. He got up at last and he said something with which Strether was struck. "She wouldn't understand her, but that makes no difference. Madame de Vionnet would like to see her. She'd like to be charming to her. She believes she could work it."

Strether thought a moment, affected by this, but finally turning away. "She couldn't!"

"You're quite sure?" Chad asked.

"Well, risk it if you like!"

Strether, who uttered this with serenity, had urged a plea for their now getting into the air; but the young man still waited. "Have you sent your answer?"

"No, I've done nothing yet."

"Were you waiting to see me?"

"No, not that."

"Only waiting"—and Chad, with this, had a smile for him—"to see Miss Gostrey?"

"No—not even Miss Gostrey. I wasn't waiting to see any one. I had only waited, till now, to make up my mind—in complete solitude; and, since I of course absolutely owe you the information, was on the point of going out with it quite made up. Have therefore a little more patience with me. Remember," Strether went on, "that that's what you originally asked ME to have. I've had it, you see, and you see what has come of it. Stay on with me."

Chad looked grave. "How much longer?"

"Well, till I make you a sign. I can't myself, you know, at the best, or at the worst, stay for ever. Let the Pococks come," Strether repeated.

"Because it gains you time?"

"Yes—it gains me time."

Chad, as if it still puzzled him, waited a minute. "You don't want to get back to Mother?"

"Not just yet. I'm not ready."

"You feel," Chad asked in a tone of his own, "the charm of life over here?"

"Immensely." Strether faced it. "You've helped me so to feel it that that surely needn't surprise you."

"No, it doesn't surprise me, and I'm delighted. But what, my dear man," Chad went on with conscious queerness, "does it all lead to for you?"

The change of position and of relation, for each, was so oddly betrayed in the question that Chad laughed out as soon as he had uttered it—which made Strether also laugh. "Well, to my having a certitude that has been tested—that has passed through the fire. But oh," he couldn't help breaking out, "if within my first month here you had been willing to move with me—!"

"Well?" said Chad, while he broke down as for weight of thought.

"Well, we should have been over there by now."

"Ah but you wouldn't have had your fun!"

"I should have had a month of it; and I'm having now, if you want to know," Strether continued, "enough to last me for the rest of my days."

Chad looked amused and interested, yet still somewhat in the dark; partly perhaps because Strether's estimate of fun had required of him from the first a good deal of elucidation. "It wouldn't do if I left you—?"

"Left me?"—Strether remained blank.

"Only for a month or two—time to go and come. Madame de Vionnet," Chad smiled, "would look after you in the interval."

"To go back by yourself, I remaining here?" Again for an instant their eyes had the question out; after which Strether said: "Grotesque!"

"But I want to see Mother," Chad presently returned. "Remember how long it is since I've seen Mother."

"Long indeed; and that's exactly why I was originally so keen for moving you. Hadn't you shown us enough how beautifully you could do without it?"

"Oh but," said Chad wonderfully, "I'm better now."

There was an easy triumph in it that made his friend laugh out again. "Oh if you were worse I SHOULD know what to do with you. In that case I believe I'd have you gagged and strapped down, carried on board resisting, kicking. How MUCH," Strether asked, "do you want to see Mother?"

"How much?"—Chad seemed to find it in fact difficult to say.

"How much."

"Why as much as you've made me. I'd give anything to see her. And you've left me," Chad went on, "in little enough doubt as to how much SHE wants it."

Strether thought a minute. "Well then if those things are really your motive catch the French steamer and sail to-morrow. Of course, when it comes to that, you're absolutely free to do as you choose. From the moment you can't hold yourself I can only accept your flight."

"I'll fly in a minute then," said Chad, "if you'll stay here."

"I'll stay here till the next steamer—then I'll follow you."

"And do you call that," Chad asked, "accepting my flight?"

"Certainly—it's the only thing to call it. The only way to keep me here, accordingly," Strether explained, "is by staying yourself."

Chad took it in. "All the more that I've really dished you, eh?"

"Dished me?" Strether echoed as inexpressively as possible.

"Why if she sends out the Pococks it will be that she doesn't trust you, and if she doesn't trust you, that bears upon—well, you know what."

Strether decided after a moment that he did know what, and in consonance with this he spoke. "You see then all the more what you owe me."

"Well, if I do see, how can I pay?"

"By not deserting me. By standing by me."

"Oh I say—!" But Chad, as they went downstairs, clapped a firm hand, in the manner of a pledge, upon his shoulder. They descended slowly together and had, in the court of the hotel, some further talk, of which the upshot was that they presently separated. Chad Newsome departed, and Strether, left alone, looked about, superficially, for Waymarsh. But Waymarsh hadn't yet, it appeared, come down, and our friend finally went forth without sight of him.

III

At four o'clock that afternoon he had still not seen him, but he was then, as to make up for this, engaged in talk about him with Miss Gostrey. Strether had kept away from home all day, given himself up to the town and to his thoughts, wandered and mused, been at once restless and absorbed—and all with the present climax of a rich little welcome in the Quartier Marboeuf. "Waymarsh has been, 'unbeknown' to me, I'm convinced"—for Miss Gostrey had enquired—"in communication with Woollett: the consequence of which was, last night, the loudest possible call for me."

"Do you mean a letter to bring you home?"

"No—a cable, which I have at this moment in my pocket: a 'Come back by the first ship.'"

Strether's hostess, it might have been made out, just escaped changing colour. Reflexion arrived but in time and established a provisional serenity. It was perhaps exactly this that enabled her to say with duplicity: "And you're going—?"

"You almost deserve it when you abandon me so."

She shook her head as if this were not worth taking up. "My absence has helped you—as I've only to look at you to see. It was my calculation, and I'm justified. You're not where you were. And the thing," she smiled, "was for me not to be there either. You can go of yourself."

"Oh but I feel to-day," he comfortably declared, "that I shall want you yet."

She took him all in again. "Well, I promise you not again to leave you, but it will only be to follow you. You've got your momentum and can toddle alone."

He intelligently accepted it. "Yes—I suppose I can toddle. It's the sight of that in fact that has upset Waymarsh. He can bear it—the way I strike him as going—no longer. That's only the climax of his original feeling. He wants me to quit; and he must have written to Woollett that I'm in peril of perdition."

"Ah good!" she murmured. "But is it only your supposition?"

"I make it out—it explains."

"Then he denies?—or you haven't asked him?"

"I've not had time," Strether said; "I made it out but last night, putting various things together, and I've not been since then face to face with him."

She wondered. "Because you're too disgusted? You can't trust yourself?"

He settled his glasses on his nose. "Do I look in a great rage?"

"You look divine!"

"There's nothing," he went on, "to be angry about. He has done me on the contrary a service."

She made it out. "By bringing things to a head?"

"How well you understand!" he almost groaned. "Waymarsh won't in the least, at any rate, when I have it out with him, deny or extenuate. He has acted from the deepest conviction, with the best conscience and after wakeful nights. He'll recognise that he's fully responsible, and will consider that he has been highly successful; so that any discussion we may have will bring us quite together again—bridge the dark stream that has kept us so thoroughly apart. We shall have at last, in the consequences of his act, something we can definitely talk about."

She was silent a little. "How wonderfully you take it! But you're always wonderful."

He had a pause that matched her own; then he had, with an adequate spirit, a complete admission. "It's quite true. I'm extremely wonderful just now. I dare say in fact I'm quite fantastic, and I shouldn't be at all surprised if I were mad."

"Then tell me!" she earnestly pressed. As he, however, for the time answered nothing, only returning the look with which she watched him, she presented herself where it was easier to meet her. "What will Mr. Waymarsh exactly have done?"

"Simply have written a letter. One will have been quite enough. He has told them I want looking after."

"And DO you?"—she was all interest.

"Immensely. And I shall get it."

"By which you mean you don't budge?"

"I don't budge."

"You've cabled?"

"No—I've made Chad do it."

"That you decline to come?"

"That HE declines. We had it out this morning and I brought him round. He had come in, before I was down, to tell me he was ready—ready, I mean, to return. And he went off, after ten minutes with me, to say he wouldn't."

Miss Gostrey followed with intensity. "Then you've STOPPED him?"

Strether settled himself afresh in his chair. "I've stopped him. That is for the time. That"—he gave it to her more vividly—"is where I am."

"I see, I see. But where's Mr. Newsome? He was ready," she asked, "to go?"

"All ready."

"And sincerely—believing YOU'D be?"

"Perfectly, I think; so that he was amazed to find the hand I had laid on him to pull him over suddenly converted into an engine for keeping him still."

It was an account of the matter Miss Gostrey could weigh. "Does he think the conversion sudden?"

"Well," said Strether, "I'm not altogether sure what he thinks. I'm not sure of anything that concerns him, except that the more I've seen of him the less I've found him what I originally expected. He's obscure, and that's why I'm waiting."

She wondered. "But for what in particular?"

"For the answer to his cable."

"And what was his cable?"

"I don't know," Strether replied; "it was to be, when he left me, according to his own taste. I simply said to him: 'I want to stay, and the only way for me to do so is for you to.' That I wanted to stay seemed to interest him, and he acted on that."

Miss Gostrey turned it over. "He wants then himself to stay."

"He half wants it. That is he half wants to go. My original appeal has to that extent worked in him. Nevertheless," Strether pursued, "he won't go. Not, at least, so long as I'm here."

"But you can't," his companion suggested, "stay here always. I wish you could."

"By no means. Still, I want to see him a little further. He's not in the least the case I supposed, he's quite another case. And it's as such that he interests me." It was almost as if for his own intelligence that, deliberate and lucid, our friend thus expressed the matter. "I don't want to give him up."

Miss Gostrey but desired to help his lucidity. She had however to be light and tactful. "Up, you mean—a—to his mother?"

"Well, I'm not thinking of his mother now. I'm thinking of the plan of which I was the mouthpiece, which, as soon as we met, I put before him as persuasively as I knew how, and which was drawn up, as it were, in complete ignorance of all that, in this last long period, has been happening to him. It took no account whatever of the impression I was here on the spot immediately to begin to receive from him—impressions of which I feel sure I'm far from having had the last."

Miss Gostrey had a smile of the most genial criticism. "So your idea is—more or less—to stay out of curiosity?"

"Call it what you like! I don't care what it's called—"

"So long as you do stay? Certainly not then. I call it, all the same, immense fun," Maria Gostrey declared; "and to see you work it out will be one of the sensations of my life. It IS clear you can toddle alone!"

He received this tribute without elation. "I shan't be alone when the Pococks have come."

Her eyebrows went up. "The Pococks are coming?"

"That, I mean, is what will happen—and happen as quickly as possible—in consequence of Chad's cable. They'll simply embark. Sarah will come to speak for her mother—with an effect different from MY muddle."

Miss Gostrey more gravely wondered. "SHE then will take him back?"

"Very possibly—and we shall see. She must at any rate have the chance, and she may be trusted to do all she can."

"And do you WANT that?"

"Of course," said Strether, "I want it. I want to play fair."

But she had lost for a moment the thread. "If it devolves on the Pococks why do you stay?"

"Just to see that I DO play fair—and a little also, no doubt, that they do." Strether was luminous as he had never been. "I came out to find myself in presence of new facts—facts that have kept striking me as less and less met by our old reasons. The matter's perfectly simple. New reasons—reasons as new as the facts themselves—are wanted; and of this our friends at Woollett—Chad's and mine—were at the earliest moment definitely notified. If any are producible Mrs. Pocock will produce them; she'll bring over the whole collection. They'll be," he added with a pensive smile "a part of the 'fun' you speak of."

She was quite in the current now and floating by his side. "It's Mamie—so far as I've had it from you—who'll be their great card." And then as his contemplative silence wasn't a denial she significantly added: "I think I'm sorry for her."

"I think I am!"—and Strether sprang up, moving about a little as her eyes followed him. "But it can't be helped."

"You mean her coming out can't be?"

He explained after another turn what he meant. "The only way for her not to come is for me to go home—as I believe that on the spot I could prevent it. But the difficulty as to that is that if I do go home—"

"I see, I see"—she had easily understood. "Mr. Newsome will do the same, and that's not"—she laughed out now—"to be thought of."

Strether had no laugh; he had only a quiet comparatively placid look that might have shown him as proof against ridicule. "Strange, isn't it?"

They had, in the matter that so much interested them, come so far as this without sounding another name—to which however their present momentary silence was full of a conscious reference. Strether's question was a sufficient implication of the weight it had gained with him during the absence of his hostess; and just for that reason a single gesture from her could pass for him as a vivid answer. Yet he was answered still better when she said in a moment: "Will Mr. Newsome introduce his sister—?"

"To Madame de Vionnet?" Strether spoke the name at last. "I shall be greatly surprised if he doesn't."

She seemed to gaze at the possibility. "You mean you've thought of it and you're prepared."

"I've thought of it and I'm prepared."

It was to her visitor now that she applied her consideration. "Bon! You ARE magnificent!"

"Well," he answered after a pause and a little wearily, but still standing there before her—"well, that's what, just once in all my dull days, I think I shall like to have been!"

Two days later he had news from Chad of a communication from Woollett in response to their determinant telegram, this missive being addressed to Chad himself and announcing the immediate departure for France of Sarah and Jim and Mamie. Strether had meanwhile on his own side cabled; he had but delayed that act till after his visit to Miss Gostrey, an interview by which, as so often before, he felt his sense of things cleared up and settled. His message to Mrs. Newsome, in answer to her own, had consisted of the words: "Judge best to take another month, but with full appreciation of all re-enforcements." He had added that he was writing, but he was of course always writing; it was a practice that continued, oddly enough, to relieve him, to make him come nearer than anything else to the consciousness of doing something: so that he often wondered if he hadn't really, under his recent stress, acquired some hollow trick, one of the specious arts of make-believe. Wouldn't the pages he still so freely dispatched by the American post have been worthy of a showy journalist, some master of the great new science of beating the sense out of words? Wasn't he writing against time, and mainly to show he was kind?—since it had become quite his habit not to like to read himself over. On those lines he could still be liberal, yet it was at best a sort of whistling in the dark. It was unmistakeable moreover that the sense of being in the dark now pressed on him more sharply—creating thereby the need for a louder and livelier whistle. He whistled long and hard after sending his message; he whistled again and again in celebration of Chad's news; there was an interval of a fortnight in which this exercise helped him. He had no great notion of what, on the spot, Sarah Pocock would have to say, though he had indeed confused premonitions; but it shouldn't be in her power to say—it shouldn't be in any one's anywhere to say—that he was neglecting her mother. He might have written before more freely, but he had never written more copiously; and he frankly gave for a reason at Woollett that he wished to fill the void created there by Sarah's departure.

The increase of his darkness, however, and the quickening, as I have called it, of his tune, resided in the fact that he was hearing almost nothing. He had for some time been aware that he was hearing less than before, and he was now clearly following a process by which Mrs. Newsome's letters could but logically stop. He hadn't had a line for many days, and he needed no proof—though he was, in time, to have plenty—that she wouldn't have put pen to paper after receiving the hint that had determined her telegram. She wouldn't write till Sarah should have seen him and reported on him. It was strange, though it might well be less so than his own behaviour appeared at Woollett. It was at any rate significant, and what WAS remarkable was the way his friend's nature and manner put on for him, through this very drop of demonstration, a greater intensity. It struck him really that he had never so lived with her as during this period of her silence; the silence was a sacred hush, a finer clearer medium, in which her idiosyncrasies showed. He walked about with her, sat with her, drove with her and dined face-to-face with her—a rare treat "in his life," as he could perhaps have scarce escaped phrasing it; and if he had never seen her so soundless he had never, on the other hand, felt her so highly, so almost austerely, herself: pure and by the vulgar estimate "cold," but deep devoted delicate sensitive noble. Her vividness in these respects became for him, in the special conditions, almost an obsession; and though the obsession sharpened his pulses, adding really to the excitement of life, there were hours at which, to be less on the stretch, he directly sought forgetfulness. He knew it for the queerest of adventures—a circumstance capable of playing such a part only for Lambert Strether—that in Paris itself, of all places, he should find this ghost of the lady of Woollett more importunate than any other presence.

When he went back to Maria Gostrey it was for the change to something else. And yet after all the change scarcely operated for he talked to her of Mrs. Newsome in these days as he had never talked before. He had hitherto observed in that particular a discretion and a law; considerations that at present broke down quite as if relations had altered. They hadn't REALLY altered, he said to himself, so much as that came to; for if what had occurred was of course that Mrs. Newsome had ceased to trust him, there was nothing on the other hand to prove that he shouldn't win back her confidence. It was quite his present theory that he would leave no stone unturned to do so; and in fact if he now told Maria things about her that he had never told before this was largely because it kept before him the idea of the honour of such a woman's esteem. His relation with Maria as well was, strangely enough, no longer quite the same; this truth—though not too disconcertingly—had come up between them on the renewal of their meetings. It was all contained in what she had then almost immediately said to him; it was represented by the remark she had needed but ten minutes to make and that he hadn't been disposed to gainsay. He could toddle alone, and the difference that showed was extraordinary. The turn taken by their talk had promptly confirmed this difference; his larger confidence on the score of Mrs. Newsome did the rest; and the time seemed already far off when he had held out his small thirsty cup to the spout of her pail. Her pail was scarce touched now, and other fountains had flowed for him; she fell into her place as but one of his tributaries; and there was a strange sweetness—a melancholy mildness that touched him—in her acceptance of the altered order.

It marked for himself the flight of time, or at any rate what he was pleased to think of with irony and pity as the rush of experience; it having been but the day before yesterday that he sat at her feet and held on by her garment and was fed by her hand. It was the proportions that were changed, and the proportions were at all times, he philosophised, the very conditions of perception, the terms of thought. It was as if, with her effective little entresol and and her wide acquaintance, her activities, varieties, promiscuities, the duties and devotions that took up nine tenths of her time and of which he got, guardedly, but the side-wind—it was as if she had shrunk to a secondary element and had consented to the shrinkage with the perfection of tact. This perfection had never failed her; it had originally been greater than his prime measure for it; it had kept him quite apart, kept him out of the shop, as she called her huge general acquaintance, made their commerce as quiet, as much a thing of the home alone—the opposite of the shop—as if she had never another customer. She had been wonderful to him at first, with the memory of her little entresol, the image to which, on most mornings at that time, his eyes directly opened; but now she mainly figured for him as but part of the bristling total—though of course always as a person to whom he should never cease to be indebted. It would never be given to him certainly to inspire a greater kindness. She had decked him out for others, and he saw at this point at least nothing she would ever ask for. She only wondered and questioned and listened, rendering him the homage of a wistful speculation. She expressed it repeatedly; he was already far beyond her, and she must prepare herself to lose him. There was but one little chance for her.

Often as she had said it he met it—for it was a touch he liked—each time the same way. "My coming to grief?"

"Yes—then I might patch you up."

"Oh for my real smash, if it takes place, there will be no patching."

"But you surely don't mean it will kill you."

"No—worse. It will make me old."

"Ah nothing can do that! The wonderful and special thing about you is that you ARE, at this time of day, youth." Then she always made, further, one of those remarks that she had completely ceased to adorn with hesitations or apologies, and that had, by the same token, in spite of their extreme straightness, ceased to produce in Strether the least embarrassment. She made him believe them, and they became thereby as impersonal as truth itself. "It's just your particular charm."

His answer too was always the same. "Of course I'm youth—youth for the trip to Europe. I began to be young, or at least to get the benefit of it, the moment I met you at Chester, and that's what has been taking place ever since. I never had the benefit at the proper time—which comes to saying that I never had the thing itself. I'm having the benefit at this moment; I had it the other day when I said to Chad 'Wait'; I shall have it still again when Sarah Pocock arrives. It's a benefit that would make a poor show for many people; and I don't know who else but you and I, frankly, could begin to see in it what I feel. I don't get drunk; I don't pursue the ladies; I don't spend money; I don't even write sonnets. But nevertheless I'm making up late for what I didn't have early. I cultivate my little benefit in my own little way. It amuses me more than anything that has happened to me in all my life. They may say what they like—it's my surrender, it's my tribute, to youth. One puts that in where one can—it has to come in somewhere, if only out of the lives, the conditions, the feelings of other persons. Chad gives me the sense of it, for all his grey hairs, which merely make it solid in him and safe and serene; and SHE does the same, for all her being older than he, for all her marriageable daughter, her separated husband, her agitated history. Though they're young enough, my pair, I don't say they're, in the freshest way, their own absolutely prime adolescence; for that has nothing to do with it. The point is that they're mine. Yes, they're my youth; since somehow at the right time nothing else ever was. What I meant just now therefore is that it would all go—go before doing its work—if they were to fail me."

On which, just here, Miss Gostrey inveterately questioned. "What do you, in particular, call its work?"

"Well, to see me through."

"But through what?"—she liked to get it all out of him.

"Why through this experience." That was all that would come.

It regularly gave her none the less the last word. "Don't you remember how in those first days of our meeting it was I who was to see you through?"

"Remember? Tenderly, deeply"—he always rose to it. "You're just doing your part in letting me maunder to you thus."

"Ah don't speak as if my part were small; since whatever else fails you—"

"YOU won't, ever, ever, ever?"—he thus took her up. "Oh I beg your pardon; you necessarily, you inevitably WILL. Your conditions—that's what I mean—won't allow me anything to do for you."

"Let alone—I see what you mean—that I'm drearily dreadfully old. I AM, but there's a service—possible for you to render—that I know, all the same, I shall think of."

"And what will it be?"

This, in fine, however, she would never tell him. "You shall hear only if your smash takes place. As that's really out of the question, I won't expose myself"—a point at which, for reasons of his own, Strether ceased to press.

He came round, for publicity—it was the easiest thing—to the idea that his smash WAS out of the question, and this rendered idle the discussion of what might follow it. He attached an added importance, as the days elapsed, to the arrival of the Pococks; he had even a shameful sense of waiting for it insincerely and incorrectly. He accused himself of making believe to his own mind that Sarah's presence, her impression, her judgement would simplify and harmonise, he accused himself of being so afraid of what they MIGHT do that he sought refuge, to beg the whole question, in a vain fury. He had abundantly seen at home what they were in the habit of doing, and he had not at present the smallest ground. His clearest vision was when he made out that what he most desired was an account more full and free of Mrs. Newsome's state of mind than any he felt he could now expect from herself; that calculation at least went hand in hand with the sharp consciousness of wishing to prove to himself that he was not afraid to look his behaviour in the face. If he was by an inexorable logic to pay for it he was literally impatient to know the cost, and he held himself ready to pay in instalments. The first instalment would be precisely this entertainment of Sarah; as a consequence of which moreover, he should know vastly better how he stood.

Book Eighth

I

Strether rambled alone during these few days, the effect of the incident of the previous week having been to simplify in a marked fashion his mixed relations with Waymarsh. Nothing had passed between them in reference to Mrs. Newsome's summons but that our friend had mentioned to his own the departure of the deputation actually at sea—giving him thus an opportunity to confess to the occult intervention he imputed to him. Waymarsh however in the event confessed to nothing; and though this falsified in some degree Strether's forecast the latter amusedly saw in it the same depth of good conscience out of which the dear man's impertinence had originally sprung. He was patient with the dear man now and delighted to observe how unmistakeably he had put on flesh; he felt his own holiday so successfully large and free that he was full of allowances and charities in respect to those cabined and confined' his instinct toward a spirit so strapped down as Waymarsh's was to walk round it on tiptoe for fear of waking it up to a sense of losses by this time irretrievable. It was all very funny he knew, and but the difference, as he often said to himself, of tweedledum and tweedledee—an emancipation so purely comparative that it was like the advance of the door-mat on the scraper; yet the present crisis was happily to profit by it and the pilgrim from Milrose to know himself more than ever in the right.

Strether felt that when he heard of the approach of the Pococks the impulse of pity quite sprang up in him beside the impulse of triumph. That was exactly why Waymarsh had looked at him with eyes in which the heat of justice was measured and shaded. He had looked very hard, as if affectionately sorry for the friend—the friend of fifty-five—whose frivolity had had thus to be recorded; becoming, however, but obscurely sententious and leaving his companion to formulate a charge. It was in this general attitude that he had of late altogether taken refuge; with the drop of discussion they were solemnly sadly superficial; Strether recognised in him the mere portentous rumination to which Miss Barrace had so good-humouredly described herself as assigning a corner of her salon. It was quite as if he knew his surreptitious step had been divined, and it was also as if he missed the chance to explain the purity of his motive; but this privation of relief should be precisely his small penance: it was not amiss for Strether that he should find himself to that degree uneasy. If he had been challenged or accused, rebuked for meddling or otherwise pulled up, he would probably have shown, on his own system, all the height of his consistency, all the depth of his good faith. Explicit resentment of his course would have made him take the floor, and the thump of his fist on the table would have affirmed him as consciously incorruptible. Had what now really prevailed with Strether been but a dread of that thump—a dread of wincing a little painfully at what it might invidiously demonstrate? However this might be, at any rate, one of the marks of the crisis was a visible, a studied lapse, in Waymarsh, of betrayed concern. As if to make up to his comrade for the stroke by which he had played providence he now conspicuously ignored his movements, withdrew himself from the pretension to share them, stiffened up his sensibility to neglect, and, clasping his large empty hands and swinging his large restless foot, clearly looked to another quarter for justice.

This made for independence on Strether's part, and he had in truth at no moment of his stay been so free to go and come. The early summer brushed the picture over and blurred everything but the near; it made a vast warm fragrant medium in which the elements floated together on the best of terms, in which rewards were immediate and reckonings postponed. Chad was out of town again, for the first time since his visitor's first view of him; he had explained this necessity—without detail, yet also without embarrassment, the circumstance was one of those which, in the young man's life, testified to the variety of his ties. Strether wasn't otherwise concerned with it than for its so testifying—a pleasant multitudinous image in which he took comfort. He took comfort, by the same stroke, in the swing of Chad's pendulum back from that other swing, the sharp jerk towards Woollett, so stayed by his own hand. He had the entertainment of thinking that if he had for that moment stopped the clock it was to promote the next minute this still livelier motion. He himself did what he hadn't done before; he took two or three times whole days off—irrespective of others, of two or three taken with Miss Gostrey, two or three taken with little Bilham: he went to Chartres and cultivated, before the front of the cathedral, a general easy beatitude; he went to Fontainebleau and imagined himself on the way to Italy; he went to Rouen with a little handbag and inordinately spent the night.

One afternoon he did something quite different; finding himself in the neighbourhood of a fine old house across the river, he passed under the great arch of its doorway and asked at the porter's lodge for Madame de Vionnet. He had already hovered more than once about that possibility, been aware of it, in the course of ostensible strolls, as lurking but round the corner. Only it had perversely happened, after his morning at Notre Dame, that his consistency, as he considered and intended it, had come back to him; whereby he had reflected that the encounter in question had been none of his making; clinging again intensely to the strength of his position, which was precisely that there was nothing in it for himself. From the moment he actively pursued the charming associate of his adventure, from that moment his position weakened, for he was then acting in an interested way. It was only within a few days that he had fixed himself a limit: he promised himself his consistency should end with Sarah's arrival. It was arguing correctly to feel the title to a free hand conferred on him by this event. If he wasn't to be let alone he should be merely a dupe to act with delicacy. If he wasn't to be trusted he could at least take his ease. If he was to be placed under control he gained leave to try what his position MIGHT agreeably give him. An ideal rigour would perhaps postpone the trial till after the Pococks had shown their spirit; and it was to an ideal rigour that he had quite promised himself to conform.

Suddenly, however, on this particular day, he felt a particular fear under which everything collapsed. He knew abruptly that he was afraid of himself—and yet not in relation to the effect on his sensibilities of another hour of Madame de Vionnet. What he dreaded was the effect of a single hour of Sarah Pocock, as to whom he was visited, in troubled nights, with fantastic waking dreams. She loomed at him larger than life; she increased in volume as she drew nearer; she so met his eyes that, his imagination taking, after the first step, all, and more than all, the strides, he already felt her come down on him, already burned, under her reprobation, with the blush of guilt, already consented, by way of penance, to the instant forfeiture of everything. He saw himself, under her direction, recommitted to Woollett as juvenile offenders are committed to reformatories. It wasn't of course that Woollett was really a place of discipline; but he knew in advance that Sarah's salon at the hotel would be. His danger, at any rate, in such moods of alarm, was some concession, on this ground, that would involve a sharp rupture with the actual; therefore if he waited to take leave of that actual he might wholly miss his chance. It was represented with supreme vividness by Madame de Vionnet, and that is why, in a word, he waited no longer. He had seen in a flash that he must anticipate Mrs. Pocock. He was accordingly much disappointed on now learning from the portress that the lady of his quest was not in Paris. She had gone for some days to the country. There was nothing in this accident but what was natural; yet it produced for poor Strether a drop of all confidence. It was suddenly as if he should never see her again, and as if moreover he had brought it on himself by not having been quite kind to her.

It was the advantage of his having let his fancy lose itself for a little in the gloom that, as by reaction, the prospect began really to brighten from the moment the deputation from Woollett alighted on the platform of the station. They had come straight from Havre, having sailed from New York to that port, and having also, thanks to a happy voyage, made land with a promptitude that left Chad Newsome, who had meant to meet them at the dock, belated. He had received their telegram, with the announcement of their immediate further advance, just as he was taking the train for Havre, so that nothing had remained for him but to await them in Paris. He hastily picked up Strether, at the hotel, for this purpose, and he even, with easy pleasantry, suggested the attendance of Waymarsh as well—Waymarsh, at the moment his cab rattled up, being engaged, under Strether's contemplative range, in a grave perambulation of the familiar court. Waymarsh had learned from his companion, who had already had a note, delivered by hand, from Chad, that the Pococks were due, and had ambiguously, though, as always, impressively, glowered at him over the circumstance; carrying himself in a manner in which Strether was now expert enough to recognise his uncertainty, in the premises, as to the best tone. The only tone he aimed at with confidence was a full tone—which was necessarily difficult in the absence of a full knowledge. The Pococks were a quantity as yet unmeasured, and, as he had practically brought them over, so this witness had to that extent exposed himself. He wanted to feel right about it, but could only, at the best, for the time, feel vague. "I shall look to you, you know, immensely," our friend had said, "to help me with them," and he had been quite conscious of the effect of the remark, and of others of the same sort, on his comrade's sombre sensibility. He had insisted on the fact that Waymarsh would quite like Mrs. Pocock—one could be certain he would: he would be with her about everything, and she would also be with HIM, and Miss Barrace's nose, in short, would find itself out of joint.

Strether had woven this web of cheerfulness while they waited in the court for Chad; he had sat smoking cigarettes to keep himself quiet while, caged and leonine, his fellow traveller paced and turned before him. Chad Newsome was doubtless to be struck, when he arrived, with the sharpness of their opposition at this particular hour; he was to remember, as a part of it, how Waymarsh came with him and with Strether to the street and stood there with a face half-wistful and half-rueful. They talked of him, the two others, as they drove, and Strether put Chad in possession of much of his own strained sense of things. He had already, a few days before, named to him the wire he was convinced their friend had pulled—a confidence that had made on the young man's part quite hugely for curiosity and diversion. The action of the matter, moreover, Strether could see, was to penetrate; he saw that is, how Chad judged a system of influence in which Waymarsh had served as a determinant—an impression just now quickened again; with the whole bearing of such a fact on the youth's view of his relatives. As it came up between them that they might now take their friend for a feature of the control of these latter now sought to be exerted from Woollett, Strether felt indeed how it would be stamped all over him, half an hour later for Sarah Pocock's eyes, that he was as much on Chad's "side" as Waymarsh had probably described him. He was letting himself at present, go; there was no denying it; it might be desperation, it might be confidence; he should offer himself to the arriving travellers bristling with all the lucidity he had cultivated.

He repeated to Chad what he had been saying in the court to Waymarsh; how there was no doubt whatever that his sister would find the latter a kindred spirit, no doubt of the alliance, based on an exchange of views, that the pair would successfully strike up. They would become as thick as thieves—which moreover was but a development of what Strether remembered to have said in one of his first discussions with his mate, struck as he had then already been with the elements of affinity between that personage and Mrs. Newsome herself. "I told him, one day, when he had questioned me on your mother, that she was a person who, when he should know her, would rouse in him, I was sure, a special enthusiasm; and that hangs together with the conviction we now feel—this certitude that Mrs. Pocock will take him into her boat. For it's your mother's own boat that she's pulling."

"Ah," said Chad, "Mother's worth fifty of Sally!"

"A thousand; but when you presently meet her, all the same you'll be meeting your mother's representative—just as I shall. I feel like the outgoing ambassador," said Strether, "doing honour to his appointed successor." A moment after speaking as he had just done he felt he had inadvertently rather cheapened Mrs. Newsome to her son; an impression audibly reflected, as at first seen, in Chad's prompt protest. He had recently rather failed of apprehension of the young man's attitude and temper—remaining principally conscious of how little worry, at the worst, he wasted, and he studied him at this critical hour with renewed interest. Chad had done exactly what he had promised him a fortnight previous—had accepted without another question his plea for delay. He was waiting cheerfully and handsomely, but also inscrutably and with a slight increase perhaps of the hardness originally involved in his acquired high polish. He was neither excited nor depressed; was easy and acute and deliberate—unhurried unflurried unworried, only at most a little less amused than usual. Strether felt him more than ever a justification of the extraordinary process of which his own absurd spirit had been the arena; he knew as their cab rolled along, knew as he hadn't even yet known, that nothing else than what Chad had done and had been would have led to his present showing. They had made him, these things, what he was, and the business hadn't been easy; it had taken time and trouble, it had cost, above all, a price. The result at any rate was now to be offered to Sally; which Strether, so far as that was concerned, was glad to be there to witness. Would she in the least make it out or take it in, the result, or would she in the least care for it if she did? He scratched his chin as he asked himself by what name, when challenged—as he was sure he should be—he could call it for her. Oh those were determinations she must herself arrive at; since she wanted so much to see, let her see then and welcome. She had come out in the pride of her competence, yet it hummed in Strether's inner sense that she practically wouldn't see.

That this was moreover what Chad shrewdly suspected was clear from a word that next dropped from him. "They're children; they play at life!"—and the exclamation was significant and reassuring. It implied that he hadn't then, for his companion's sensibility, appeared to give Mrs. Newsome away; and it facilitated our friend's presently asking him if it were his idea that Mrs. Pocock and Madame de Vionnet should become acquainted. Strether was still more sharply struck, hereupon, with Chad's lucidity. "Why, isn't that exactly—to get a sight of the company I keep—what she has come out for?"

"Yes—I'm afraid it is," Strether unguardedly replied.

Chad's quick rejoinder lighted his precipitation. "Why do you say you're afraid?"

"Well, because I feel a certain responsibility. It's my testimony, I imagine, that will have been at the bottom of Mrs. Pocock's curiosity. My letters, as I've supposed you to understand from the beginning, have spoken freely. I've certainly said my little say about Madame de Vionnet."

All that, for Chad, was beautifully obvious. "Yes, but you've only spoken handsomely."

"Never more handsomely of any woman. But it's just that tone—!"

"That tone," said Chad, "that has fetched her? I dare say; but I've no quarrel with you about it. And no more has Madame de Vionnet. Don't you know by this time how she likes you?"

"Oh!"—and Strether had, with his groan, a real pang of melancholy. "For all I've done for her!"

"Ah you've done a great deal."

Chad's urbanity fairly shamed him, and he was at this moment absolutely impatient to see the face Sarah Pocock would present to a sort of thing, as he synthetically phrased it to himself, with no adequate forecast of which, despite his admonitions, she would certainly arrive. "I've done THIS!"

"Well, this is all right. She likes," Chad comfortably remarked, "to be liked."

It gave his companion a moment's thought. "And she's sure Mrs. Pocock WILL—?"

"No, I say that for you. She likes your liking her; it's so much, as it were," Chad laughed, "to the good. However, she doesn't despair of Sarah either, and is prepared, on her own side, to go all lengths."

"In the way of appreciation?"

"Yes, and of everything else. In the way of general amiability, hospitality and welcome. She's under arms," Chad laughed again; "she's prepared."

Strether took it in; then as if an echo of Miss Barrace were in the air: "She's wonderful."

"You don't begin to know HOW wonderful!"

There was a depth in it, to Strether's ear, of confirmed luxury—almost a kind of unconscious insolence of proprietorship; but the effect of the glimpse was not at this moment to foster speculation: there was something so conclusive in so much graceful and generous assurance. It was in fact a fresh evocation; and the evocation had before many minutes another consequence. "Well, I shall see her oftener now. I shall see her as much as I like—by your leave; which is what I hitherto haven't done."

"It has been," said Chad, but without reproach, "only your own fault. I tried to bring you together, and SHE, my dear fellow—I never saw her more charming to any man. But you've got your extraordinary ideas."

"Well, I DID have," Strether murmured, while he felt both how they had possessed him and how they had now lost their authority. He couldn't have traced the sequence to the end, but it was all because of Mrs. Pocock. Mrs. Pocock might be because of Mrs. Newsome, but that was still to be proved. What came over him was the sense of having stupidly failed to profit where profit would have been precious. It had been open to him to see so much more of her, and he had but let the good days pass. Fierce in him almost was the resolve to lose no more of them, and he whimsically reflected, while at Chad's side he drew nearer to his destination, that it was after all Sarah who would have quickened his chance. What her visit of inquisition might achieve in other directions was as yet all obscure—only not obscure that it would do supremely much to bring two earnest persons together. He had but to listen to Chad at this moment to feel it; for Chad was in the act of remarking to him that they of course both counted on him—he himself and the other earnest person—for cheer and support. It was brave to Strether to hear him talk as if the line of wisdom they had struck out was to make things ravishing to the Pococks. No, if Madame de Vionnet compassed THAT, compassed the ravishment of the Pococks, Madame de Vionnet would be prodigious. It would be a beautiful plan if it succeeded, and it all came to the question of Sarah's being really bribeable. The precedent of his own case helped Strether perhaps but little to consider she might prove so; it being distinct that her character would rather make for every possible difference. This idea of his own bribeability set him apart for himself; with the further mark in fact that his case was absolutely proved. He liked always, where Lambert Strether was concerned, to know the worst, and what he now seemed to know was not only that he was bribeable, but that he had been effectually bribed. The only difficulty was that he couldn't quite have said with what. It was as if he had sold himself, but hadn't somehow got the cash. That, however, was what, characteristically, WOULD happen to him. It would naturally be his kind of traffic. While he thought of these things he reminded Chad of the truth they mustn't lose sight of—the truth that, with all deference to her susceptibility to new interests, Sarah would have come out with a high firm definite purpose. "She hasn't come out, you know, to be bamboozled. We may all be ravishing—nothing perhaps can be more easy for us; but she hasn't come out to be ravished. She has come out just simply to take you home."

"Oh well, with HER I'll go," said Chad good-humouredly. "I suppose you'll allow THAT." And then as for a minute Strether said nothing: "Or is your idea that when I've seen her I shan't want to go?" As this question, however, again left his friend silent he presently went on: "My own idea at any rate is that they shall have while they're here the best sort of time."

It was at this that Strether spoke. "Ah there you are! I think if you really wanted to go—!"

"Well?" said Chad to bring it out.

"Well, you wouldn't trouble about our good time. You wouldn't care what sort of a time we have."

Chad could always take in the easiest way in the world any ingenious suggestion. "I see. But can I help it? I'm too decent."

"Yes, you're too decent!" Strether heavily sighed. And he felt for the moment as if it were the preposterous end of his mission.

It ministered for the time to this temporary effect that Chad made no rejoinder. But he spoke again as they came in sight of the station. "Do you mean to introduce her to Miss Gostrey?"

As to this Strether was ready. "No."

"But haven't you told me they know about her?"

"I think I've told you your mother knows."

"And won't she have told Sally?"

"That's one of the things I want to see."

"And if you find she HAS—?"

"Will I then, you mean, bring them together?"

"Yes," said Chad with his pleasant promptness: "to show her there's nothing in it."

Strether hesitated. "I don't know that I care very much what she may think there's in it."

"Not if it represents what Mother thinks?"

"Ah what DOES your mother think?" There was in this some sound of bewilderment.

But they were just driving up, and help, of a sort, might after all be quite at hand. "Isn't that, my dear man, what we're both just going to make out?"

II

Strether quitted the station half an hour later in different company. Chad had taken charge, for the journey to the hotel, of Sarah, Mamie, the maid and the luggage, all spaciously installed and conveyed; and it was only after the four had rolled away that his companion got into a cab with Jim. A strange new feeling had come over Strether, in consequence of which his spirits had risen; it was as if what had occurred on the alighting of his critics had been something other than his fear, though his fear had vet not been of an instant scene of violence. His impression had been nothing but what was inevitable—he said that to himself; yet relief and reassurance had softly dropped upon him. Nothing could be so odd as to be indebted for these things to the look of faces and the sound of voices that had been with him to satiety, as he might have said, for years; but he now knew, all the same, how uneasy he had felt; that was brought home to him by his present sense of a respite. It had come moreover in the flash of an eye, it had come in the smile with which Sarah, whom, at the window of her compartment, they had effusively greeted from the platform, rustled down to them a moment later, fresh and handsome from her cool June progress through the charming land. It was only a sign, but enough: she was going to be gracious and unallusive, she was going to play the larger game—which was still more apparent, after she had emerged from Chad's arms, in her direct greeting to the valued friend of her family.

Strether WAS then as much as ever the valued friend of her family, it was something he could at all events go on with; and the manner of his response to it expressed even for himself how little he had enjoyed the prospect of ceasing to figure in that likeness. He had always seen Sarah gracious—had in fact rarely seen her shy or dry, her marked thin-lipped smile, intense without brightness and as prompt to act as the scrape of a safety-match; the protrusion of her rather remarkably long chin, which in her case represented invitation and urbanity, and not, as in most others, pugnacity and defiance; the penetration of her voice to a distance, the general encouragement and approval of her manner, were all elements with which intercourse had made him familiar, but which he noted today almost as if she had been a new acquaintance. This first glimpse of her had given a brief but vivid accent to her resemblance to her mother; he could have taken her for Mrs. Newsome while she met his eyes as the train rolled into the station. It was an impression that quickly dropped; Mrs. Newsome was much handsomer, and while Sarah inclined to the massive her mother had, at an age, still the girdle of a maid; also the latter's chin was rather short, than long, and her smile, by good fortune, much more, oh ever so much more, mercifully vague. Strether had seen Mrs. Newsome reserved; he had literally heard her silent, though he had never known her unpleasant. It was the case with Mrs. Pocock that he had known HER unpleasant, even though he had never known her not affable. She had forms of affability that were in a high degree assertive; nothing for instance had ever been more striking than that she was affable to Jim.

What had told in any case at the window of the train was her high clear forehead, that forehead which her friends, for some reason, always thought of as a "brow"; the long reach of her eyes—it came out at this juncture in such a manner as to remind him, oddly enough, also of that of Waymarsh's; and the unusual gloss of her dark hair, dressed and hatted, after her mother's refined example, with such an avoidance of extremes that it was always spoken of at Woollett as "their own." Though this analogy dropped as soon as she was on the platform it had lasted long enough to make him feel all the advantage, as it were, of his relief. The woman at home, the woman to whom he was attached, was before him just long enough to give him again the measure of the wretchedness, in fact really of the shame, of their having to recognise the formation, between them, of a "split." He had taken this measure in solitude and meditation: but the catastrophe, as Sarah steamed up, looked for its seconds unprecedentedly dreadful—or proved, more exactly, altogether unthinkable; so that his finding something free and familiar to respond to brought with it an instant renewal of his loyalty. He had suddenly sounded the whole depth, had gasped at what he might have lost.

Well, he could now, for the quarter of an hour of their detention hover about the travellers as soothingly as if their direct message to him was that he had lost nothing. He wasn't going to have Sarah write to her mother that night that he was in any way altered or strange. There had been times enough for a month when it had seemed to him that he was strange, that he was altered, in every way; but that was a matter for himself; he knew at least whose business it was not; it was not at all events such a circumstance as Sarah's own unaided lights would help her to. Even if she had come out to flash those lights more than yet appeared she wouldn't make much headway against mere pleasantness. He counted on being able to be merely pleasant to the end, and if only from incapacity moreover to formulate anything different. He couldn't even formulate to himself his being changed and queer; it had taken place, the process, somewhere deep down; Maria Gostrey had caught glimpses of it; but how was he to fish it up, even if he desired, for Mrs. Pocock? This was then the spirit in which he hovered, and with the easier throb in it much indebted furthermore to the impression of high and established adequacy as a pretty girl promptly produced in him by Mamie. He had wondered vaguely—turning over many things in the fidget of his thoughts—if Mamie WERE as pretty as Woollett published her; as to which issue seeing her now again was to be so swept away by Woollett's opinion that this consequence really let loose for the imagination an avalanche of others. There were positively five minutes in which the last word seemed of necessity to abide with a Woollett represented by a Mamie. This was the sort of truth the place itself would feel; it would send her forth in confidence; it would point to her with triumph; it would take its stand on her with assurance; it would be conscious of no requirements she didn't meet, of no question she couldn't answer.

Well, it was right, Strether slipped smoothly enough into the cheerfulness of saying: granted that a community MIGHT be best represented by a young lady of twenty-two, Mamie perfectly played the part, played it as if she were used to it, and looked and spoke and dressed the character. He wondered if she mightn't, in the high light of Paris, a cool full studio-light, becoming yet treacherous, show as too conscious of these matters; but the next moment he felt satisfied that her consciousness was after all empty for its size, rather too simple than too mixed, and that the kind way with her would be not to take many things out of it, but to put as many as possible in. She was robust and conveniently tall; just a trifle too bloodlessly fair perhaps, but with a pleasant public familiar radiance that affirmed her vitality. She might have been "receiving" for Woollett, wherever she found herself, and there was something in her manner, her tone, her motion, her pretty blue eyes, her pretty perfect teeth and her very small, too small, nose, that immediately placed her, to the fancy, between the windows of a hot bright room in which voices were high—up at that end to which people were brought to be "presented." They were there to congratulate, these images, and Strether's renewed vision, on this hint, completed the idea. What Mamie was like was the happy bride, the bride after the church and just before going away. She wasn't the mere maiden, and yet was only as much married as that quantity came to. She was in the brilliant acclaimed festal stage. Well, might it last her long!

Strether rejoiced in these things for Chad, who was all genial attention to the needs of his friends, besides having arranged that his servant should reinforce him; the ladies were certainly pleasant to see, and Mamie would be at any time and anywhere pleasant to exhibit. She would look extraordinarily like his young wife—the wife of a honeymoon, should he go about with her; but that was his own affair—or perhaps it was hers; it was at any rate something she couldn't help. Strether remembered how he had seen him come up with Jeanne de Vionnet in Gloriani's garden, and the fancy he had had about that—the fancy obscured now, thickly overlaid with others; the recollection was during these minutes his only note of trouble. He had often, in spite of himself, wondered if Chad but too probably were not with Jeanne the object of a still and shaded flame. It was on the cards that the child MIGHT be tremulously in love, and this conviction now flickered up not a bit the less for his disliking to think of it, for its being, in a complicated situation, a complication the more, and for something indescribable in Mamie, something at all events straightway lent her by his own mind, something that gave her value, gave her intensity and purpose, as the symbol of an opposition. Little Jeanne wasn't really at all in question—how COULD she be?—yet from the moment Miss Pocock had shaken her skirts on the platform, touched up the immense bows of her hat and settled properly over her shoulder the strap of her morocco-and-gilt travelling-satchel, from that moment little Jeanne was opposed.

It was in the cab with Jim that impressions really crowded on Strether, giving him the strangest sense of length of absence from people among whom he had lived for years. Having them thus come out to him was as if he had returned to find them: and the droll promptitude of Jim's mental reaction threw his own initiation far back into the past. Whoever might or mightn't be suited by what was going on among them, Jim, for one, would certainly be: his instant recognition—frank and whimsical—of what the affair was for HIM gave Strether a glow of pleasure. "I say, you know, this IS about my shape, and if it hadn't been for YOU—!" so he broke out as the charming streets met his healthy appetite; and he wound up, after an expressive nudge, with a clap of his companion's knee and an "Oh you, you—you ARE doing it!" that was charged with rich meaning. Strether felt in it the intention of homage, but, with a curiosity otherwise occupied, postponed taking it up. What he was asking himself for the time was how Sarah Pocock, in the opportunity already given her, had judged her brother—from whom he himself, as they finally, at the station, separated for their different conveyances, had had a look into which he could read more than one message. However Sarah was judging her brother, Chad's conclusion about his sister, and about her husband and her husband's sister, was at the least on the way not to fail of confidence. Strether felt the confidence, and that, as the look between them was an exchange, what he himself gave back was relatively vague. This comparison of notes however could wait; everything struck him as depending on the effect produced by Chad. Neither Sarah nor Mamie had in any way, at the station—where they had had after all ample time—broken out about it; which, to make up for this, was what our friend had expected of Jim as soon as they should find themselves together.

It was queer to him that he had that noiseless brush with Chad; an ironic intelligence with this youth on the subject of his relatives, an intelligence carried on under their nose and, as might be said, at their expense—such a matter marked again for him strongly the number of stages he had come; albeit that if the number seemed great the time taken for the final one was but the turn of a hand. He had before this had many moments of wondering if he himself weren't perhaps changed even as Chad was changed. Only what in Chad was conspicuous improvement—well, he had no name ready for the working, in his own organism, of his own more timid dose. He should have to see first what this action would amount to. And for his occult passage with the young man, after all, the directness of it had no greater oddity than the fact that the young man's way with the three travellers should have been so happy a manifestation. Strether liked him for it, on the spot, as he hadn't yet liked him; it affected him while it lasted as he might have been affected by some light pleasant perfect work of art: to that degree that he wondered if they were really worthy of it, took it in and did it justice; to that degree that it would have been scarce a miracle if, there in the luggage-room, while they waited for their things, Sarah had pulled his sleeve and drawn him aside. "You're right; we haven't quite known what you mean, Mother and I, but now we see. Chad's magnificent; what can one want more? If THIS is the kind of thing—!" On which they might, as it were, have embraced and begun to work together.

Ah how much, as it was, for all her bridling brightness—which was merely general and noticed nothing—WOULD they work together? Strether knew he was unreasonable; he set it down to his being nervous: people couldn't notice everything and speak of everything in a quarter of an hour. Possibly, no doubt, also, he made too much of Chad's display. Yet, none the less, when, at the end of five minutes, in the cab, Jim Pocock had said nothing either—hadn't said, that is, what Strether wanted, though he had said much else—it all suddenly bounced back to their being either stupid or wilful. It was more probably on the whole the former; so that that would be the drawback of the bridling brightness. Yes, they would bridle and be bright; they would make the best of what was before them, but their observation would fail; it would be beyond them; they simply wouldn't understand. Of what use would it be then that they had come?—if they weren't to be intelligent up to THAT point: unless indeed he himself were utterly deluded and extravagant? Was he, on this question of Chad's improvement, fantastic and away from the truth? Did he live in a false world, a world that had grown simply to suit him, and was his present slight irritation—in the face now of Jim's silence in particular—but the alarm of the vain thing menaced by the touch of the real? Was this contribution of the real possibly the mission of the Pococks?—had they come to make the work of observation, as HE had practised observation, crack and crumble, and to reduce Chad to the plain terms in which honest minds could deal with him? Had they come in short to be sane where Strether was destined to feel that he himself had only been silly?

He glanced at such a contingency, but it failed to hold him long when once he had reflected that he would have been silly, in this case, with Maria Gostrey and little Bilham, with Madame de Vionnet and little Jeanne, with Lambert Strether, in fine, and above all with Chad Newsome himself. Wouldn't it be found to have made more for reality to be silly with these persons than sane with Sarah and Jim? Jim in fact, he presently made up his mind, was individually out of it; Jim didn't care; Jim hadn't come out either for Chad or for him; Jim in short left the moral side to Sally and indeed simply availed himself now, for the sense of recreation, of the fact that he left almost everything to Sally. He was nothing compared to Sally, and not so much by reason of Sally's temper and will as by that of her more developed type and greater acquaintance with the world. He quite frankly and serenely confessed, as he sat there with Strether, that he felt his type hang far in the rear of his wife's and still further, if possible, in the rear of his sister's. Their types, he well knew, were recognised and acclaimed; whereas the most a leading Woollett business-man could hope to achieve socially, and for that matter industrially, was a certain freedom to play into this general glamour.

The impression he made on our friend was another of the things that marked our friend's road. It was a strange impression, especially as so soon produced; Strether had received it, he judged, all in the twenty minutes; it struck him at least as but in a minor degree the work of the long Woollett years. Pocock was normally and consentingly though not quite wittingly out of the question. It was despite his being normal; it was despite his being cheerful; it was despite his being a leading Woollett business-man; and the determination of his fate left him thus perfectly usual—as everything else about it was clearly, to his sense, not less so. He seemed to say that there was a whole side of life on which the perfectly usual WAS for leading Woollett business-men to be out of the question. He made no more of it than that, and Strether, so far as Jim was concerned, desired to make no more. Only Strether's imagination, as always, worked, and he asked himself if this side of life were not somehow connected, for those who figured on it with the fact of marriage. Would HIS relation to it, had he married ten years before, have become now the same as Pocock's? Might it even become the same should he marry in a few months? Should he ever know himself as much out of the question for Mrs. Newsome as Jim knew himself—in a dim way—for Mrs. Jim?

To turn his eyes in that direction was to be personally reassured; he was different from Pocock; he had affirmed himself differently and was held after all in higher esteem. What none the less came home to him, however, at this hour, was that the society over there, that of which Sarah and Mamie—and, in a more eminent way, Mrs. Newsome herself—were specimens, was essentially a society of women, and that poor Jim wasn't in it. He himself Lambert Strether, WAS as yet in some degree—which was an odd situation for a man; but it kept coming back to him in a whimsical way that he should perhaps find his marriage had cost him his place. This occasion indeed, whatever that fancy represented, was not a time of sensible exclusion for Jim, who was in a state of manifest response to the charm of his adventure. Small and fat and constantly facetious, straw-coloured and destitute of marks, he would have been practically indistinguishable hadn't his constant preference for light-grey clothes, for white hats, for very big cigars and very little stories, done what it could for his identity. There were signs in him, though none of them plaintive, of always paying for others; and the principal one perhaps was just this failure of type. It was with this that he paid, rather than with fatigue or waste; and also doubtless a little with the effort of humour—never irrelevant to the conditions, to the relations, with which he was acquainted.

He gurgled his joy as they rolled through the happy streets; he declared that his trip was a regular windfall, and that he wasn't there, he was eager to remark, to hang back from anything: he didn't know quite what Sally had come for, but HE had come for a good time. Strether indulged him even while wondering if what Sally wanted her brother to go back for was to become like her husband. He trusted that a good time was to be, out and out, the programme for all of them; and he assented liberally to Jim's proposal that, disencumbered and irresponsible—his things were in the omnibus with those of the others—they should take a further turn round before going to the hotel. It wasn't for HIM to tackle Chad—it was Sally's job; and as it would be like her, he felt, to open fire on the spot, it wouldn't be amiss of them to hold off and give her time. Strether, on his side, only asked to give her time; so he jogged with his companion along boulevards and avenues, trying to extract from meagre material some forecast of his catastrophe. He was quick enough to see that Jim Pocock declined judgement, had hovered quite round the outer edge of discussion and anxiety, leaving all analysis of their question to the ladies alone and now only feeling his way toward some small droll cynicism. It broke out afresh, the cynicism—it had already shown a flicker—in a but slightly deferred: "Well, hanged if I would if I were he!"

"You mean you wouldn't in Chad's place—?"

"Give up this to go back and boss the advertising!" Poor Jim, with his arms folded and his little legs out in the open fiacre, drank in the sparkling Paris noon and carried his eyes from one side of their vista to the other. "Why I want to come right out and live here myself. And I want to live while I AM here too. I feel with YOU—oh you've been grand, old man, and I've twigged—that it ain't right to worry Chad. I don't mean to persecute him; I couldn't in conscience. It's thanks to you at any rate that I'm here, and I'm sure I'm much obliged. You're a lovely pair."

There were things in this speech that Strether let pass for the time. "Don't you then think it important the advertising should be thoroughly taken in hand? Chad WILL be, so far as capacity is concerned," he went on, "the man to do it."

"Where did he get his capacity," Jim asked, "over here?"

"He didn't get it over here, and the wonderful thing is that over here he hasn't inevitably lost it. He has a natural turn for business, an extraordinary head. He comes by that," Strether explained, "honestly enough. He's in that respect his father's son, and also—for she's wonderful in her way too—his mother's. He has other tastes and other tendencies; but Mrs. Newsome and your wife are quite right about his having that. He's very remarkable."

"Well, I guess he is!" Jim Pocock comfortably sighed. "But if you've believed so in his making us hum, why have you so prolonged the discussion? Don't you know we've been quite anxious about you?"

These questions were not informed with earnestness, but Strether saw he must none the less make a choice and take a line. "Because, you see, I've greatly liked it. I've liked my Paris, I dare say I've liked it too much."

"Oh you old wretch!" Jim gaily exclaimed.

"But nothing's concluded," Strether went on. "The case is more complex than it looks from Woollett."

"Oh well, it looks bad enough from Woollett!" Jim declared.

"Even after all I've written?"

Jim bethought himself. "Isn't it what you've written that has made Mrs. Newsome pack us off? That at least and Chad's not turning up?"

Strether made a reflexion of his own. "I see. That she should do something was, no doubt, inevitable, and your wife has therefore of course come out to act."

"Oh yes," Jim concurred—"to act. But Sally comes out to act, you know," he lucidly added, "every time she leaves the house. She never comes out but she DOES act. She's acting moreover now for her mother, and that fixes the scale." Then he wound up, opening all his senses to it, with a renewed embrace of pleasant Paris. "We haven't all the same at Woollett got anything like this."

Strether continued to consider. "I'm bound to say for you all that you strike me as having arrived in a very mild and reasonable frame of mind. You don't show your claws. I felt just now in Mrs. Pocock no symptom of that. She isn't fierce," he went on. "I'm such a nervous idiot that I thought she might be."

"Oh don't you know her well enough," Pocock asked, "to have noticed that she never gives herself away, any more than her mother ever does? They ain't fierce, either of 'em; they let you come quite close. They wear their fur the smooth side out—the warm side in. Do you know what they are?" Jim pursued as he looked about him, giving the question, as Strether felt, but half his care—"do you know what they are? They're about as intense as they can live."

"Yes"—and Strether's concurrence had a positive precipitation; "they're about as intense as they can live."

"They don't lash about and shake the cage," said Jim, who seemed pleased with his analogy; "and it's at feeding-time that they're quietest. But they always get there."

"They do indeed—they always get there!" Strether replied with a laugh that justified his confession of nervousness. He disliked to be talking sincerely of Mrs. Newsome with Pocock; he could have talked insincerely. But there was something he wanted to know, a need created in him by her recent intermission, by his having given from the first so much, as now more than ever appeared to him, and got so little. It was as if a queer truth in his companion's metaphor had rolled over him with a rush. She HAD been quiet at feeding-time; she had fed, and Sarah had fed with her, out of the big bowl of all his recent free communication, his vividness and pleasantness, his ingenuity and even his eloquence, while the current of her response had steadily run thin. Jim meanwhile however, it was true, slipped characteristically into shallowness from the moment he ceased to speak out of the experience of a husband.

"But of course Chad has now the advantage of being there before her. If he doesn't work that for all it's worth—!" He sighed with contingent pity at his brother-in-law's possible want of resource. "He has worked it on YOU, pretty well, eh?" and he asked the next moment if there were anything new at the Varieties, which he pronounced in the American manner. They talked about the Varieties—Strether confessing to a knowledge which produced again on Pocock's part a play of innuendo as vague as a nursery-rhyme, yet as aggressive as an elbow in his side; and they finished their drive under the protection of easy themes. Strether waited to the end, but still in vain, for any show that Jim had seen Chad as different; and he could scarce have explained the discouragement he drew from the absence of this testimony. It was what he had taken his own stand on, so far as he had taken a stand; and if they were all only going to see nothing he had only wasted his time. He gave his friend till the very last moment, till they had come into sight of the hotel; and when poor Pocock only continued cheerful and envious and funny he fairly grew to dislike him, to feel him extravagantly common. If they were ALL going to see nothing!—Strether knew, as this came back to him, that he was also letting Pocock represent for him what Mrs. Newsome wouldn't see. He went on disliking, in the light of Jim's commonness, to talk to him about that lady; yet just before the cab pulled up he knew the extent of his desire for the real word from Woollett.

"Has Mrs. Newsome at all given way—?"

"'Given way'?"—Jim echoed it with the practical derision of his sense of a long past.

"Under the strain, I mean, of hope deferred, of disappointment repeated and thereby intensified."

"Oh is she prostrate, you mean?"—he had his categories in hand. "Why yes, she's prostrate—just as Sally is. But they're never so lively, you know, as when they're prostrate."

"Ah Sarah's prostrate?" Strether vaguely murmured.

"It's when they're prostrate that they most sit up."

"And Mrs. Newsome's sitting up?"

"All night, my boy—for YOU!" And Jim fetched him, with a vulgar little guffaw, a thrust that gave relief to the picture. But he had got what he wanted. He felt on the spot that this WAS the real word from Woollett. "So don't you go home!" Jim added while he alighted and while his friend, letting him profusely pay the cabman, sat on in a momentary muse. Strether wondered if that were the real word too.

III

As the door of Mrs. Pocock's salon was pushed open for him, the next day, well before noon, he was reached by a voice with a charming sound that made him just falter before crossing the threshold. Madame de Vionnet was already on the field, and this gave the drama a quicker pace than he felt it as yet—though his suspense had increased—in the power of any act of his own to do. He had spent the previous evening with all his old friends together yet he would still have described himself as quite in the dark in respect to a forecast of their influence on his situation. It was strange now, none the less, that in the light of this unexpected note of her presence he felt Madame de Vionnet a part of that situation as she hadn't even yet been. She was alone, he found himself assuming, with Sarah, and there was a bearing in that—somehow beyond his control—on his personal fate. Yet she was only saying something quite easy and independent—the thing she had come, as a good friend of Chad's, on purpose to say. "There isn't anything at all—? I should be so delighted."

It was clear enough, when they were there before him, how she had been received. He saw this, as Sarah got up to greet him, from something fairly hectic in Sarah's face. He saw furthermore that they weren't, as had first come to him, alone together; he was at no loss as to the identity of the broad high back presented to him in the embrasure of the window furthest from the door. Waymarsh, whom he had to-day not yet seen, whom he only knew to have left the hotel before him, and who had taken part, the night previous, on Mrs. Pocock's kind invitation, conveyed by Chad, in the entertainment, informal but cordial, promptly offered by that lady—Waymarsh had anticipated him even as Madame de Vionnet had done, and, with his hands in his pockets and his attitude unaffected by Strether's entrance, was looking out, in marked detachment, at the Rue de Rivoli. The latter felt it in the air—it was immense how Waymarsh could mark things—that he had remained deeply dissociated from the overture to their hostess that we have recorded on Madame de Vionnet's side. He had, conspicuously, tact, besides a stiff general view; and this was why he had left Mrs. Pocock to struggle alone. He would outstay the visitor; he would unmistakeably wait; to what had he been doomed for months past but waiting? Therefore she was to feel that she had him in reserve. What support she drew from this was still to be seen, for, although Sarah was vividly bright, she had given herself up for the moment to an ambiguous flushed formalism. She had had to reckon more quickly than she expected; but it concerned her first of all to signify that she was not to be taken unawares. Strether arrived precisely in time for her showing it. "Oh you're too good; but I don't think I feel quite helpless. I have my brother—and these American friends. And then you know I've been to Paris. I KNOW Paris," said Sally Pocock in a tone that breathed a certain chill on Strether's heart.

"Ah but a woman, in this tiresome place where everything's always changing, a woman of good will," Madame de Vionnet threw off, "can always help a woman. I'm sure you 'know'—but we know perhaps different things." She too, visibly, wished to make no mistake; but it was a fear of a different order and more kept out of sight. She smiled in welcome at Strether; she greeted him more familiarly than Mrs. Pocock; she put out her hand to him without moving from her place; and it came to him in the course of a minute and in the oddest way that—yes, positively—she was giving him over to ruin. She was all kindness and ease, but she couldn't help so giving him; she was exquisite, and her being just as she was poured for Sarah a sudden rush of meaning into his own equivocations. How could she know how she was hurting him? She wanted to show as simple and humble—in the degree compatible with operative charm; but it was just this that seemed to put him on her side. She struck him as dressed, as arranged, as prepared infinitely to conciliate—with the very poetry of good taste in her view of the conditions of her early call. She was ready to advise about dressmakers and shops; she held herself wholly at the disposition of Chad's family. Strether noticed her card on the table—her coronet and her "Comtesse"—and the imagination was sharp in him of certain private adjustments in Sarah's mind. She had never, he was sure, sat with a "Comtesse" before, and such was the specimen of that class he had been keeping to play on her. She had crossed the sea very particularly for a look at her; but he read in Madame de Vionnet's own eyes that this curiosity hadn't been so successfully met as that she herself wouldn't now have more than ever need of him. She looked much as she had looked to him that morning at Notre Dame; he noted in fact the suggestive sameness of her discreet and delicate dress. It seemed to speak—perhaps a little prematurely or too finely—of the sense in which she would help Mrs. Pocock with the shops. The way that lady took her in, moreover, added depth to his impression of what Miss Gostrey, by their common wisdom, had escaped. He winced as he saw himself but for that timely prudence ushering in Maria as a guide and an example. There was however a touch of relief for him in his glimpse, so far as he had got it, of Sarah's line. She "knew Paris." Madame de Vionnet had, for that matter, lightly taken this up. "Ah then you've a turn for that, an affinity that belongs to your family. Your brother, though his long experience makes a difference, I admit, has become one of us in a marvellous way." And she appealed to Strether in the manner of a woman who could always glide off with smoothness into another subject. Wasn't HE struck with the way Mr. Newsome had made the place his own, and hadn't he been in a position to profit by his friend's wondrous expertness?

Strether felt the bravery, at the least, of her presenting herself so promptly to sound that note, and yet asked himself what other note, after all, she COULD strike from the moment she presented herself at all. She could meet Mrs. Pocock only on the ground of the obvious, and what feature of Chad's situation was more eminent than the fact that he had created for himself a new set of circumstances? Unless she hid herself altogether she could show but as one of these, an illustration of his domiciled and indeed of his confirmed condition. And the consciousness of all this in her charming eyes was so clear and fine that as she thus publicly drew him into her boat she produced in him such a silent agitation as he was not to fail afterwards to denounce as pusillanimous. "Ah don't be so charming to me!—for it makes us intimate, and after all what IS between us when I've been so tremendously on my guard and have seen you but half a dozen times?" He recognised once more the perverse law that so inveterately governed his poor personal aspects: it would be exactly LIKE the way things always turned out for him that he should affect Mrs. Pocock and Waymarsh as launched in a relation in which he had really never been launched at all. They were at this very moment—they could only be—attributing to him the full licence of it, and all by the operation of her own tone with him; whereas his sole licence had been to cling with intensity to the brink, not to dip so much as a toe into the flood. But the flicker of his fear on this occasion was not, as may be added, to repeat itself; it sprang up, for its moment, only to die down and then go out for ever. To meet his fellow visitor's invocation and, with Sarah's brilliant eyes on him, answer, WAS quite sufficiently to step into her boat. During the rest of the time her visit lasted he felt himself proceed to each of the proper offices, successively, for helping to keep the adventurous skiff afloat. It rocked beneath him, but he settled himself in his place. He took up an oar and, since he was to have the credit of pulling, pulled.

"That will make it all the pleasanter if it so happens that we DO meet," Madame de Vionnet had further observed in reference to Mrs. Pocock's mention of her initiated state; and she had immediately added that, after all, her hostess couldn't be in need with the good offices of Mr. Strether so close at hand. "It's he, I gather, who has learnt to know his Paris, and to love it, better than any one ever before in so short a time; so that between him and your brother, when it comes to the point, how can you possibly want for good guidance? The great thing, Mr. Strether will show you," she smiled, "is just to let one's self go."

"Oh I've not let myself go very far," Strether answered, feeling quite as if he had been called upon to hint to Mrs. Pocock how Parisians could talk. "I'm only afraid of showing I haven't let myself go far enough. I've taken a good deal of time, but I must quite have had the air of not budging from one spot." He looked at Sarah in a manner that he thought she might take as engaging, and he made, under Madame de Vionnet's protection, as it were, his first personal point. "What has really happened has been that, all the while, I've done what I came out for."

Yet it only at first gave Madame de Vionnet a chance immediately to take him up. "You've renewed acquaintance with your friend—you've learnt to know him again." She spoke with such cheerful helpfulness that they might, in a common cause, have been calling together and pledged to mutual aid.

Waymarsh, at this, as if he had been in question, straightway turned from the window. "Oh yes, Countess—he has renewed acquaintance with ME, and he HAS, I guess, learnt something about me, though I don't know how much he has liked it. It's for Strether himself to say whether he has felt it justifies his course."

"Oh but YOU," said the Countess gaily, "are not in the least what he came out for—is he really, Strether? and I hadn't you at all in my mind. I was thinking of Mr. Newsome, of whom we think so much and with whom, precisely, Mrs. Pocock has given herself the opportunity to take up threads. What a pleasure for you both!" Madame de Vionnet, with her eyes on Sarah, bravely continued.

Mrs. Pocock met her handsomely, but Strether quickly saw she meant to accept no version of her movements or plans from any other lips. She required no patronage and no support, which were but other names for a false position; she would show in her own way what she chose to show, and this she expressed with a dry glitter that recalled to him a fine Woollett winter morning. "I've never wanted for opportunities to see my brother. We've many things to think of at home, and great responsibilities and occupations, and our home's not an impossible place. We've plenty of reasons," Sarah continued a little piercingly, "for everything we do"—and in short she wouldn't give herself the least little scrap away. But she added as one who was always bland and who could afford a concession: "I've come because—well, because we do come."

"Ah then fortunately!"—Madame de Vionnet breathed it to the air. Five minutes later they were on their feet for her to take leave, standing together in an affability that had succeeded in surviving a further exchange of remarks; only with the emphasised appearance on Waymarsh's part of a tendency to revert, in a ruminating manner and as with an instinctive or a precautionary lightening of his tread, to an open window and his point of vantage. The glazed and gilded room, all red damask, ormolu, mirrors, clocks, looked south, and the shutters were bowed upon the summer morning; but the Tuileries garden and what was beyond it, over which the whole place hung, were things visible through gaps; so that the far-spreading presence of Paris came up in coolness, dimness and invitation, in the twinkle of gilt-tipped palings, the crunch of gravel, the click of hoofs, the crack of whips, things that suggested some parade of the circus. "I think it probable," said Mrs. Pocock, "that I shall have the opportunity of going to my brother's I've no doubt it's very pleasant indeed." She spoke as to Strether, but her face was turned with an intensity of brightness to Madame de Vionnet, and there was a moment during which, while she thus fronted her, our friend expected to hear her add: "I'm much obliged to you, I'm sure, for inviting me there." He guessed that for five seconds these words were on the point of coming; he heard them as clearly as if they had been spoken; but he presently knew they had just failed—knew it by a glance, quick and fine, from Madame de Vionnet, which told him that she too had felt them in the air, but that the point had luckily not been made in any manner requiring notice. This left her free to reply only to what had been said.

"That the Boulevard Malesherbes may be common ground for us offers me the best prospect I see for the pleasure of meeting you again."

"Oh I shall come to see you, since you've been so good": and Mrs. Pocock looked her invader well in the eyes. The flush in Sarah's cheeks had by this time settled to a small definite crimson spot that was not without its own bravery; she held her head a good deal up, and it came to Strether that of the two, at this moment, she was the one who most carried out the idea of a Countess. He quite took in, however, that she would really return her visitor's civility: she wouldn't report again at Woollett without at least so much producible history as that in her pocket.

"I want extremely to be able to show you my little daughter." Madame de Vionnet went on; "and I should have brought her with me if I hadn't wished first to ask your leave. I was in hopes I should perhaps find Miss Pocock, of whose being with you I've heard from Mr. Newsome and whose acquaintance I should so much like my child to make. If I have the pleasure of seeing her and you do permit it I shall venture to ask her to be kind to Jeanne. Mr. Strether will tell you"—she beautifully kept it up—"that my poor girl is gentle and good and rather lonely. They've made friends, he and she, ever so happily, and he doesn't, I believe, think ill of her. As for Jeanne herself he has had the same success with her that I know he has had here wherever he has turned." She seemed to ask him for permission to say these things, or seemed rather to take it, softly and happily, with the ease of intimacy, for granted, and he had quite the consciousness now that not to meet her at any point more than halfway would be odiously, basely to abandon her. Yes, he was WITH her, and, opposed even in this covert, this semi-safe fashion to those who were not, he felt, strangely and confusedly, but excitedly, inspiringly, how much and how far. It was as if he had positively waited in suspense for something from her that would let him in deeper, so that he might show her how he could take it. And what did in fact come as she drew out a little her farewell served sufficiently the purpose. "As his success is a matter that I'm sure he'll never mention for himself, I feel, you see, the less scruple; which it's very good of me to say, you know, by the way," she added as she addressed herself to him; "considering how little direct advantage I've gained from your triumphs with ME.

When does one ever see you? I wait at home and I languish. You'll have rendered me the service, Mrs. Pocock, at least," she wound up, "of giving me one of my much-too-rare glimpses of this gentleman."

"I certainly should be sorry to deprive you of anything that seems so much, as you describe it, your natural due. Mr. Strether and I are very old friends," Sarah allowed, "but the privilege of his society isn't a thing I shall quarrel about with any one."

"And yet, dear Sarah," he freely broke in, "I feel, when I hear you say that, that you don't quite do justice to the important truth of the extent to which—as you're also mine—I'm your natural due. I should like much better," he laughed, "to see you fight for me."

She met him, Mrs. Pocock, on this, with an arrest of speech—with a certain breathlessness, as he immediately fancied, on the score of a freedom for which she wasn't quite prepared. It had flared up—for all the harm he had intended by it—because, confoundedly, he didn't want any more to be afraid about her than he wanted to be afraid about Madame de Vionnet. He had never, naturally, called her anything but Sarah at home, and though he had perhaps never quite so markedly invoked her as his "dear," that was somehow partly because no occasion had hitherto laid so effective a trap for it. But something admonished him now that it was too late—unless indeed it were possibly too early; and that he at any rate shouldn't have pleased Mrs. Pocock the more by it. "Well, Mr. Strether—!" she murmured with vagueness, yet with sharpness, while her crimson spot burned a trifle brighter and he was aware that this must be for the present the limit of her response. Madame de Vionnet had already, however, come to his aid, and Waymarsh, as if for further participation, moved again back to them. It was true that the aid rendered by Madame de Vionnet was questionable; it was a sign that, for all one might confess to with her, and for all she might complain of not enjoying, she could still insidiously show how much of the material of conversation had accumulated between them.

"The real truth is, you know, that you sacrifice one without mercy to dear old Maria. She leaves no room in your life for anybody else. Do you know," she enquired of Mrs. Pocock, "about dear old Maria? The worst is that Miss Gostrey is really a wonderful woman."

"Oh yes indeed," Strether answered for her, "Mrs. Pocock knows about Miss Gostrey. Your mother, Sarah, must have told you about her; your mother knows everything," he sturdily pursued. "And I cordially admit," he added with his conscious gaiety of courage, "that she's as wonderful a woman as you like."

"Ah it isn't I who 'like,' dear Mr. Strether, anything to do with the matter!" Sarah Pocock promptly protested; "and I'm by no means sure I have—from my mother or from any one else—a notion of whom you're talking about."

"Well, he won't let you see her, you know," Madame de Vionnet sympathetically threw in. "He never lets me—old friends as we are: I mean as I am with Maria. He reserves her for his best hours; keeps her consummately to himself; only gives us others the crumbs of the feast."

"Well, Countess, I'VE had some of the crumbs," Waymarsh observed with weight and covering her with his large look; which led her to break in before he could go on.

"Comment donc, he shares her with YOU?" she exclaimed in droll stupefaction. "Take care you don't have, before you go much further, rather more of all ces dames than you may know what to do with!"

But he only continued in his massive way. "I can post you about the lady, Mrs. Pocock, so far as you may care to hear. I've seen her quite a number of times, and I was practically present when they made acquaintance. I've kept my eye on her right along, but I don't know as there's any real harm in her."

"'Harm'?" Madame de Vionnet quickly echoed. "Why she's the dearest and cleverest of all the clever and dear."

"Well, you run her pretty close, Countess," Waymarsh returned with spirit; "though there's no doubt she's pretty well up in things. She knows her way round Europe. Above all there's no doubt she does love Strether."

"Ah but we all do that—we all love Strether: it isn't a merit!" their fellow visitor laughed, keeping to her idea with a good conscience at which our friend was aware that he marvelled, though he trusted also for it, as he met her exquisitely expressive eyes, to some later light.

The prime effect of her tone, however—and it was a truth which his own eyes gave back to her in sad ironic play—could only be to make him feel that, to say such things to a man in public, a woman must practically think of him as ninety years old. He had turned awkwardly, responsively red, he knew, at her mention of Maria Gostrey; Sarah Pocock's presence—the particular quality of it—had made this inevitable; and then he had grown still redder in proportion as he hated to have shown anything at all. He felt indeed that he was showing much, as, uncomfortably and almost in pain, he offered up his redness to Waymarsh, who, strangely enough, seemed now to be looking at him with a certain explanatory yearning. Something deep—something built on their old old relation—passed, in this complexity, between them; he got the side-wind of a loyalty that stood behind all actual queer questions. Waymarsh's dry bare humour—as it gave itself to be taken—gloomed out to demand justice. "Well, if you talk of Miss Barrace I've MY chance too," it appeared stiffly to nod, and it granted that it was giving him away, but struggled to add that it did so only to save him. The sombre glow stared it at him till it fairly sounded out—"to save you, poor old man, to save you; to save you in spite of yourself." Yet it was somehow just this communication that showed him to himself as more than ever lost. Still another result of it was to put before him as never yet that between his comrade and the interest represented by Sarah there was already a basis. Beyond all question now, yes: Waymarsh had been in occult relation with Mrs. Newsome—out, out it all came in the very effort of his face. "Yes, you're feeling my hand"—he as good as proclaimed it; "but only because this at least I SHALL have got out of the damned Old World: that I shall have picked up the pieces into which it has caused you to crumble." It was as if in short, after an instant, Strether had not only had it from him, but had recognised that so far as this went the instant had cleared the air. Our friend understood and approved; he had the sense that they wouldn't otherwise speak of it. This would be all, and it would mark in himself a kind of intelligent generosity. It was with grim Sarah then—Sarah grim for all her grace—that Waymarsh had begun at ten o'clock in the morning to save him. Well—if he COULD, poor dear man, with his big bleak kindness! The upshot of which crowded perception was that Strether, on his own side, still showed no more than he absolutely had to. He showed the least possible by saying to Mrs. Pocock after an interval much briefer than our glance at the picture reflected in him: "Oh it's as true as they please!—There's no Miss Gostrey for any one but me—not the least little peep. I keep her to myself."

"Well, it's very good of you to notify me," Sarah replied without looking at him and thrown for a moment by this discrimination, as the direction of her eyes showed, upon a dimly desperate little community with Madame de Vionnet. "But I hope I shan't miss her too much."

Madame de Vionnet instantly rallied. "And you know—though it might occur to one—it isn't in the least that he's ashamed of her. She's really—in a way—extremely good-looking."

"Ah but extremely!" Strether laughed while he wondered at the odd part he found thus imposed on him.

It continued to be so by every touch from Madame de Vionnet. "Well, as I say, you know, I wish you would keep ME a little more to yourself. Couldn't you name some day for me, some hour—and better soon than late? I'll be at home whenever it best suits you. There—I can't say fairer."

Strether thought a moment while Waymarsh and Mrs. Pocock affected him as standing attentive. "I did lately call on you. Last week—while Chad was out of town."

"Yes—and I was away, as it happened, too. You choose your moments well. But don't wait for my next absence, for I shan't make another," Madame de Vionnet declared, "while Mrs. Pocock's here."

"That vow needn't keep you long, fortunately," Sarah observed with reasserted suavity. "I shall be at present but a short time in Paris. I have my plans for other countries. I meet a number of charming friends"—and her voice seemed to caress that description of these persons.

"Ah then," her visitor cheerfully replied, "all the more reason! To-morrow, for instance, or next day?" she continued to Strether. "Tuesday would do for me beautifully."

"Tuesday then with pleasure."

"And at half-past five?—or at six?"

It was ridiculous, but Mrs. Pocock and Waymarsh struck him as fairly waiting for his answer. It was indeed as if they were arranged, gathered for a performance, the performance of "Europe" by his confederate and himself. Well, the performance could only go on. "Say five forty-five."

"Five forty-five—good." And now at last Madame de Vionnet must leave them, though it carried, for herself, the performance a little further. "I DID hope so much also to see Miss Pocock. Mayn't I still?"

Sarah hesitated, but she rose equal. "She'll return your visit with me. She's at present out with Mr. Pocock and my brother."

"I see—of course Mr. Newsome has everything to show them. He has told me so much about her. My great desire's to give my daughter the opportunity of making her acquaintance. I'm always on the lookout for such chances for her. If I didn't bring her to-day it was only to make sure first that you'd let me." After which the charming woman risked a more intense appeal. "It wouldn't suit you also to mention some near time, so that we shall be sure not to lose you?" Strether on his side waited, for Sarah likewise had, after all, to perform; and it occupied him to have been thus reminded that she had stayed at home—and on her first morning of Paris—while Chad led the others forth. Oh she was up to her eyes; if she had stayed at home she had stayed by an understanding, arrived at the evening before, that Waymarsh would come and find her alone. This was beginning well—for a first day in Paris; and the thing might be amusing yet. But Madame de Vionnet's earnestness was meanwhile beautiful. "You may think me indiscreet, but I've SUCH a desire my Jeanne shall know an American girl of the really delightful kind. You see I throw myself for it on your charity."

The manner of this speech gave Strether such a sense of depths below it and behind it as he hadn't yet had—ministered in a way that almost frightened him to his dim divinations of reasons; but if Sarah still, in spite of it, faltered, this was why he had time for a sign of sympathy with her petitioner. "Let me say then, dear lady, to back your plea, that Miss Mamie is of the most delightful kind of all—is charming among the charming."

Even Waymarsh, though with more to produce on the subject, could get into motion in time. "Yes, Countess, the American girl's a thing that your country must at least allow ours the privilege to say we CAN show you. But her full beauty is only for those who know how to make use of her."

"Ah then," smiled Madame de Vionnet, "that's exactly what I want to do. I'm sure she has much to teach us."

It was wonderful, but what was scarce less so was that Strether found himself, by the quick effect of it, moved another way. "Oh that may be! But don't speak of your own exquisite daughter, you know, as if she weren't pure perfection. I at least won't take that from you. Mademoiselle de Vionnet," he explained, in considerable form, to Mrs. Pocock, "IS pure perfection. Mademoiselle de Vionnet IS exquisite."

It had been perhaps a little portentous, but "Ah?" Sarah simply glittered.

Waymarsh himself, for that matter, apparently recognised, in respect to the facts, the need of a larger justice, and he had with it an inclination to Sarah. "Miss Jane's strikingly handsome—in the regular French style."

It somehow made both Strether and Madame de Vionnet laugh out, though at the very moment he caught in Sarah's eyes, as glancing at the speaker, a vague but unmistakeable "You too?" It made Waymarsh in fact look consciously over her head. Madame de Vionnet meanwhile, however, made her point in her own way. "I wish indeed I could offer you my poor child as a dazzling attraction: it would make one's position simple enough! She's as good as she can be, but of course she's different, and the question is now—in the light of the way things seem to go—if she isn't after all TOO different: too different I mean from the splendid type every one is so agreed that your wonderful country produces. On the other hand of course Mr. Newsome, who knows it so well, has, as a good friend, dear kind man that he is, done everything he can—to keep us from fatal benightedness—for my small shy creature. Well," she wound up after Mrs. Pocock had signified, in a murmur still a little stiff, that she would speak to her own young charge on the question—"well, we shall sit, my child and I, and wait and wait and wait for you." But her last fine turn was for Strether. "Do speak of us in such a way—!"

"As that something can't but come of it? Oh something SHALL come of it! I take a great interest!" he further declared; and in proof of it, the next moment, he had gone with her down to her carriage.

Book Ninth

I

"The difficulty is," Strether said to Madame de Vionnet a couple of days later, "that I can't surprise them into the smallest sign of his not being the same old Chad they've been for the last three years glowering at across the sea. They simply won't give any, and as a policy, you know—what you call a parti pris, a deep game—that's positively remarkable."

It was so remarkable that our friend had pulled up before his hostess with the vision of it; he had risen from his chair at the end of ten minutes and begun, as a help not to worry, to move about before her quite as he moved before Maria. He had kept his appointment with her to the minute and had been intensely impatient, though divided in truth between the sense of having everything to tell her and the sense of having nothing at all. The short interval had, in the face of their complication, multiplied his impressions—it being meanwhile to be noted, moreover, that he already frankly, already almost publicly, viewed the complication as common to them. If Madame de Vionnet, under Sarah's eyes, had pulled him into her boat, there was by this time no doubt whatever that he had remained in it and that what he had really most been conscious of for many hours together was the movement of the vessel itself. They were in it together this moment as they hadn't yet been, and he hadn't at present uttered the least of the words of alarm or remonstrance that had died on his lips at the hotel. He had other things to say to her than that she had put him in a position; so quickly had his position grown to affect him as quite excitingly, altogether richly, inevitable. That the outlook, however—given the point of exposure—hadn't cleared up half so much as he had reckoned was the first warning she received from him on his arrival. She had replied with indulgence that he was in too great a hurry, and had remarked soothingly that if she knew how to be patient surely HE might be. He felt her presence, on the spot, he felt her tone and everything about her, as an aid to that effort; and it was perhaps one of the proofs of her success with him that he seemed so much to take his ease while they talked. By the time he had explained to her why his impressions, though multiplied, still baffled him, it was as if he had been familiarly talking for hours. They baffled him because Sarah—well, Sarah was deep, deeper than she had ever yet had a chance to show herself. He didn't say that this was partly the effect of her opening so straight down, as it were, into her mother, and that, given Mrs. Newsome's profundity, the shaft thus sunk might well have a reach; but he wasn't without a resigned apprehension that, at such a rate of confidence between the two women, he was likely soon to be moved to show how already, at moments, it had been for him as if he were dealing directly with Mrs. Newsome. Sarah, to a certainty, would have begun herself to feel it in him—and this naturally put it in her power to torment him the more. From the moment she knew he COULD be tormented—!

"But WHY can you be?"—his companion was surprised at his use of the word.

"Because I'm made so—I think of everything."

"Ah one must never do that," she smiled. "One must think of as few things as possible."

"Then," he answered, "one must pick them out right. But all I mean is—for I express myself with violence—that she's in a position to watch me. There's an element of suspense for me, and she can see me wriggle. But my wriggling doesn't matter," he pursued. "I can bear it. Besides, I shall wriggle out."

The picture at any rate stirred in her an appreciation that he felt to be sincere. "I don't see how a man can be kinder to a woman than you are to me."

Well, kind was what he wanted to be; yet even while her charming eyes rested on him with the truth of this he none the less had his humour of honesty. "When I say suspense I mean, you know," he laughed, "suspense about my own case too!"

"Oh yes—about your own case too!" It diminished his magnanimity, but she only looked at him the more tenderly.

"Not, however," he went on, "that I want to talk to you about that. It's my own little affair, and I mentioned it simply as part of Mrs. Pocock's advantage." No, no; though there was a queer present temptation in it, and his suspense was so real that to fidget was a relief, he wouldn't talk to her about Mrs. Newsome, wouldn't work off on her the anxiety produced in him by Sarah's calculated omissions of reference. The effect she produced of representing her mother had been produced—and that was just the immense, the uncanny part of it—without her having so much as mentioned that lady. She had brought no message, had alluded to no question, had only answered his enquiries with hopeless limited propriety. She had invented a way of meeting them—as if he had been a polite perfunctory poor relation, of distant degree—that made them almost ridiculous in him. He couldn't moreover on his own side ask much without appearing to publish how he had lately lacked news; a circumstance of which it was Sarah's profound policy not to betray a suspicion. These things, all the same, he wouldn't breathe to Madame de Vionnet—much as they might make him walk up and down. And what he didn't say—as well as what SHE didn't, for she had also her high decencies—enhanced the effect of his being there with her at the end of ten minutes more intimately on the basis of saving her than he had yet had occasion to be. It ended in fact by being quite beautiful between them, the number of things they had a manifest consciousness of not saying. He would have liked to turn her, critically, to the subject of Mrs. Pocock, but he so stuck to the line he felt to be the point of honour and of delicacy that he scarce even asked her what her personal impression had been. He knew it, for that matter, without putting her to trouble: that she wondered how, with such elements, Sarah could still have no charm, was one of the principal things she held her tongue about. Strether would have been interested in her estimate of the elements—indubitably there, some of them, and to be appraised according to taste—but he denied himself even the luxury of this diversion. The way Madame de Vionnet affected him to-day was in itself a kind of demonstration of the happy employment of gifts. How could a woman think Sarah had charm who struck one as having arrived at it herself by such different roads? On the other hand of course Sarah wasn't obliged to have it. He felt as if somehow Madame de Vionnet WAS. The great question meanwhile was what Chad thought of his sister; which was naturally ushered in by that of Sarah's apprehension of Chad. THAT they could talk of, and with a freedom purchased by their discretion in other senses. The difficulty however was that they were reduced as yet to conjecture. He had given them in the day or two as little of a lead as Sarah, and Madame de Vionnet mentioned that she hadn't seen him since his sister's arrival.

"And does that strike you as such an age?"

She met it in all honesty. "Oh I won't pretend I don't miss him. Sometimes I see him every day. Our friendship's like that. Make what you will of it!" she whimsically smiled; a little flicker of the kind, occasional in her, that had more than once moved him to wonder what he might best make of HER. "But he's perfectly right," she hastened to add, "and I wouldn't have him fail in any way at present for the world. I'd sooner not see him for three months. I begged him to be beautiful to them, and he fully feels it for himself."

Strether turned away under his quick perception; she was so odd a mixture of lucidity and mystery. She fell in at moments with the theory about her he most cherished, and she seemed at others to blow it into air. She spoke now as if her art were all an innocence, and then again as if her innocence were all an art. "Oh he's giving himself up, and he'll do so to the end. How can he but want, now that it's within reach, his full impression?—which is much more important, you know, than either yours or mine. But he's just soaking," Strether said as he came back; "he's going in conscientiously for a saturation. I'm bound to say he IS very good."

"Ah," she quietly replied, "to whom do you say it?" And then more quietly still: "He's capable of anything."

Strether more than reaffirmed—"Oh he's excellent. I more and more like," he insisted, "to see him with them;" though the oddity of this tone between them grew sharper for him even while they spoke. It placed the young man so before them as the result of her interest and the product of her genius, acknowledged so her part in the phenomenon and made the phenomenon so rare, that more than ever yet he might have been on the very point of asking her for some more detailed account of the whole business than he had yet received from her. The occasion almost forced upon him some question as to how she had managed and as to the appearance such miracles presented from her own singularly close place of survey. The moment in fact however passed, giving way to more present history, and he continued simply to mark his appreciation of the happy truth. "It's a tremendous comfort to feel how one can trust him." And then again while for a little she said nothing—as if after all to HER trust there might be a special limit: "I mean for making a good show to them."

"Yes," she thoughtfully returned—"but if they shut their eyes to it!"

Strether for an instant had his own thought. "Well perhaps that won't matter!"

"You mean because he probably—do what they will—won't like them?"

"Oh 'do what they will'—! They won't do much; especially if Sarah hasn't more—well, more than one has yet made out—to give."

Madame de Vionnet weighed it. "Ah she has all her grace!" It was a statement over which, for a little, they could look at each other sufficiently straight, and though it produced no protest from Strether the effect was somehow as if he had treated it as a joke. "She may be persuasive and caressing with him; she may be eloquent beyond words. She may get hold of him," she wound up—"well, as neither you nor I have."

"Yes, she MAY"—and now Strether smiled. "But he has spent all his time each day with Jim. He's still showing Jim round."

She visibly wondered. "Then how about Jim?"

Strether took a turn before he answered. "Hasn't he given you Jim? Hasn't he before this 'done' him for you?" He was a little at a loss. "Doesn't he tell you things?"

She hesitated. "No"—and their eyes once more gave and took. "Not as you do. You somehow make me see them—or at least feel them. And I haven't asked too much," she added; "I've of late wanted so not to worry him."

"Ah for that, so have I," he said with encouraging assent; so that—as if she had answered everything—they were briefly sociable on it. It threw him back on his other thought, with which he took another turn; stopping again, however, presently with something of a glow. "You see Jim's really immense. I think it will be Jim who'll do it."

She wondered. "Get hold of him?"

"No—just the other thing. Counteract Sarah's spell." And he showed now, our friend, how far he had worked it out. "Jim's intensely cynical."

"Oh dear Jim!" Madame de Vionnet vaguely smiled.

"Yes, literally—dear Jim! He's awful. What HE wants, heaven forgive him, is to help us."

"You mean"—she was eager—"help ME?"

"Well, Chad and me in the first place. But he throws you in too, though without as yet seeing you much. Only, so far as he does see you—if you don't mind—he sees you as awful."

"'Awful'?"—she wanted it all.

"A regular bad one—though of course of a tremendously superior kind. Dreadful, delightful, irresistible."

"Ah dear Jim! I should like to know him. I MUST."

"Yes, naturally. But will it do? You may, you know," Strether suggested, "disappoint him."

She was droll and humble about it. "I can but try. But my wickedness then," she went on, "is my recommendation for him?"

"Your wickedness and the charms with which, in such a degree as yours, he associates it. He understands, you see, that Chad and I have above all wanted to have a good time, and his view is simple and sharp. Nothing will persuade him—in the light, that is, of my behaviour—that I really didn't, quite as much as Chad, come over to have one before it was too late. He wouldn't have expected it of me; but men of my age, at Woollett—and especially the least likely ones—have been noted as liable to strange outbreaks, belated uncanny clutches at the unusual, the ideal. It's an effect that a lifetime of Woollett has quite been observed as having; and I thus give it to you, in Jim's view, for what it's worth. Now his wife and his mother-in-law," Strether continued to explain, "have, as in honour bound, no patience with such phenomena, late or early—which puts Jim, as against his relatives, on the other side. Besides," he added, "I don't think he really wants Chad back. If Chad doesn't come—"

"He'll have"—Madame de Vionnet quite apprehended—"more of the free hand?"

"Well, Chad's the bigger man."

"So he'll work now, en dessous, to keep him quiet?"

"No—he won't 'work' at all, and he won't do anything en dessous. He's very decent and won't be a traitor in the camp. But he'll be amused with his own little view of our duplicity, he'll sniff up what he supposes to be Paris from morning till night, and he'll be, as to the rest, for Chad—well, just what he is."

She thought it over. "A warning?"

He met it almost with glee. "You ARE as wonderful as everybody says!" And then to explain all he meant: "I drove him about for his first hour, and do you know what—all beautifully unconscious—he most put before me? Why that something like THAT is at bottom, as an improvement to his present state, as in fact the real redemption of it, what they think it may not be too late to make of our friend." With which, as, taking it in, she seemed, in her recurrent alarm, bravely to gaze at the possibility, he completed his statement. "But it IS too late. Thanks to you!"

It drew from her again one of her indefinite reflexions. "Oh 'me'—after all!"

He stood before her so exhilarated by his demonstration that he could fairly be jocular. "Everything's comparative. You're better than THAT."

"You"—she could but answer him—"are better than anything." But she had another thought. "WILL Mrs. Pocock come to me?"

"Oh yes—she'll do that. As soon, that is, as my friend Waymarsh—HER friend now—leaves her leisure."

She showed an interest. "Is he so much her friend as that?"

"Why, didn't you see it all at the hotel?"

"Oh"—she was amused—"'all' is a good deal to say. I don't know—I forget. I lost myself in HER."

"You were splendid," Strether returned—"but 'all' isn't a good deal to say: it's only a little. Yet it's charming so far as it goes. She wants a man to herself."

"And hasn't she got you?"

"Do you think she looked at me—or even at you—as if she had?" Strether easily dismissed that irony. "Every one, you see, must strike her as having somebody. You've got Chad—and Chad has got you."

"I see"—she made of it what she could. "And you've got Maria."

Well, he on his side accepted that. "I've got Maria. And Maria has got me. So it goes."

"But Mr. Jim—whom has he got?"

"Oh he has got—or it's as IF he had—the whole place."

"But for Mr. Waymarsh"—she recalled—"isn't Miss Barrace before any one else?"

He shook his head. "Miss Barrace is a raffinee, and her amusement won't lose by Mrs. Pocock. It will gain rather—especially if Sarah triumphs and she comes in for a view of it."

"How well you know us!" Madame de Vionnet, at this, frankly sighed.

"No—it seems to me it's we that I know. I know Sarah—it's perhaps on that ground only that my feet are firm. Waymarsh will take her round while Chad takes Jim—and I shall be, I assure you delighted for both of them. Sarah will have had what she requires—she will have paid her tribute to the ideal; and he will have done about the same. In Paris it's in the air—so what can one do less? If there's a point that, beyond any other, Sarah wants to make, it's that she didn't come out to be narrow. We shall feel at least that."

"Oh," she sighed, "the quantity we seem likely to 'feel'! But what becomes, in these conditions, of the girl?"

"Of Mamie—if we're all provided? Ah for that," said Strether, "you can trust Chad."

"To be, you mean, all right to her?"

"To pay her every attention as soon as he has polished off Jim. He wants what Jim can give him—and what Jim really won't—though he has had it all, and more than all, from me. He wants in short his own personal impression, and he'll get it—strong. But as soon as he has got it Mamie won't suffer."

"Oh Mamie mustn't SUFFER!" Madame de Vionnet soothingly emphasised.

But Strether could reassure her. "Don't fear. As soon as he has done with Jim, Jim will fall to me. And then you'll see."

It was as if in a moment she saw already; yet she still waited. Then "Is she really quite charming?" she asked.

He had got up with his last words and gathered in his hat and gloves. "I don't know; I'm watching. I'm studying the case, as it were—and I dare say I shall be able to tell you."

She wondered. "Is it a case?"

"Yes—I think so. At any rate I shall see.'

"But haven't you known her before?"

"Yes," he smiled—"but somehow at home she wasn't a case. She has become one since." It was as if he made it out for himself. "She has become one here."

"So very very soon?"

He measured it, laughing. "Not sooner than I did."

"And you became one—?"

"Very very soon. The day I arrived."

Her intelligent eyes showed her thought of it. "Ah but the day you arrived you met Maria. Whom has Miss Pocock met?"

He paused again, but he brought it out. "Hasn't she met Chad?"

"Certainly—but not for the first time. He's an old friend." At which Strether had a slow amused significant headshake that made her go on: "You mean that for HER at least he's a new person—that she sees him as different?"

"She sees him as different."

"And how does she see him?"

Strether gave it up. "How can one tell how a deep little girl sees a deep young man?"

"Is every one so deep? Is she too?"

"So it strikes me deeper than I thought. But wait a little—between us we'll make it out. You'll judge for that matter yourself."

Madame de Vionnet looked for the moment fairly bent on the chance. "Then she WILL come with her?—I mean Mamie with Mrs. Pocock?"

"Certainly. Her curiosity, if nothing else, will in any case work that. But leave it all to Chad."

"Ah," wailed Madame de Vionnet, turning away a little wearily, "the things I leave to Chad!"

The tone of it made him look at her with a kindness that showed his vision of her suspense. But he fell back on his confidence. "Oh well—trust him. Trust him all the way." He had indeed no sooner so spoken than the queer displacement of his point of view appeared again to come up for him in the very sound, which drew from him a short laugh, immediately checked. He became still more advisory. "When they do come give them plenty of Miss Jeanne. Let Mamie see her well."

She looked for a moment as if she placed them face to face. "For Mamie to hate her?"

He had another of his corrective headshakes. "Mamie won't. Trust THEM."

She looked at him hard, and then as if it were what she must always come back to: "It's you I trust. But I was sincere," she said, "at the hotel. I did, I do, want my child—"

"Well?"—Strether waited with deference while she appeared to hesitate as to how to put it.

"Well, to do what she can for me."

Strether for a little met her eyes on it; after which something that might have been unexpected to her came from him. "Poor little duck!"

Not more expected for himself indeed might well have been her echo of it. "Poor little duck! But she immensely wants herself," she said, "to see our friend's cousin."

"Is that what she thinks her?"

"It's what we call the young lady."

He thought again; then with a laugh: "Well, your daughter will help you."

And now at last he took leave of her, as he had been intending for five minutes. But she went part of the way with him, accompanying him out of the room and into the next and the next. Her noble old apartment offered a succession of three, the first two of which indeed, on entering, smaller than the last, but each with its faded and formal air, enlarged the office of the antechamber and enriched the sense of approach. Strether fancied them, liked them, and, passing through them with her more slowly now, met a sharp renewal of his original impression. He stopped, he looked back; the whole thing made a vista, which he found high melancholy and sweet—full, once more, of dim historic shades, of the faint faraway cannon-roar of the great Empire. It was doubtless half the projection of his mind, but his mind was a thing that, among old waxed parquets, pale shades of pink and green, pseudo-classic candelabra, he had always needfully to reckon with. They could easily make him irrelevant. The oddity, the originality, the poetry—he didn't know what to call it—of Chad's connexion reaffirmed for him its romantic side. "They ought to see this, you know. They MUST."

"The Pococks?"—she looked about in deprecation; she seemed to see gaps he didn't.

"Mamie and Sarah—Mamie in particular."

"My shabby old place? But THEIR things—!"

"Oh their things! You were talking of what will do something for you—"

"So that it strikes you," she broke in, "that my poor place may? Oh," she ruefully mused, "that WOULD be desperate!"

"Do you know what I wish?" he went on. "I wish Mrs. Newsome herself could have a look."

She stared, missing a little his logic. "It would make a difference?"

Her tone was so earnest that as he continued to look about he laughed. "It might!"

"But you've told her, you tell me—"

"All about you? Yes, a wonderful story. But there's all the indescribable—what one gets only on the spot."

"Thank you!" she charmingly and sadly smiled.

"It's all about me here," he freely continued. "Mrs. Newsome feels things."

But she seemed doomed always to come back to doubt. "No one feels so much as YOU. No—not any one."

"So much the worse then for every one. It's very easy."

They were by this time in the antechamber, still alone together, as she hadn't rung for a servant. The antechamber was high and square, grave and suggestive too, a little cold and slippery even in summer, and with a few old prints that were precious, Strether divined, on the walls. He stood in the middle, slightly lingering, vaguely directing his glasses, while, leaning against the door-post of the room, she gently pressed her cheek to the side of the recess. "YOU would have been a friend."

"I?"—it startled him a little.

"For the reason you say. You're not stupid." And then abruptly, as if bringing it out were somehow founded on that fact: "We're marrying Jeanne."

It affected him on the spot as a move in a game, and he was even then not without the sense that that wasn't the way Jeanne should be married. But he quickly showed his interest, though—as quickly afterwards struck him—with an absurd confusion of mind. "'You'? You and—a—not Chad?" Of course it was the child's father who made the 'we,' but to the child's father it would have cost him an effort to allude. Yet didn't it seem the next minute that Monsieur de Vionnet was after all not in question?—since she had gone on to say that it was indeed to Chad she referred and that he had been in the whole matter kindness itself.

"If I must tell you all, it is he himself who has put us in the way. I mean in the way of an opportunity that, so far as I can yet see, is all I could possibly have dreamed of. For all the trouble Monsieur de Vionnet will ever take!" It was the first time she had spoken to him of her husband, and he couldn't have expressed how much more intimate with her it suddenly made him feel. It wasn't much, in truth—there were other things in what she was saying that were far more; but it was as if, while they stood there together so easily in these cold chambers of the past, the single touch had shown the reach of her confidence. "But our friend," she asked, "hasn't then told you?"

"He has told me nothing."

"Well, it has come with rather a rush—all in a very few days; and hasn't moreover yet taken a form that permits an announcement. It's only for you—absolutely you alone—that I speak; I so want you to know." The sense he had so often had, since the first hour of his disembarkment, of being further and further "in," treated him again at this moment to another twinge; but in this wonderful way of her putting him in there continued to be something exquisitely remorseless. "Monsieur de Vionnet will accept what he MUST accept. He has proposed half a dozen things—each one more impossible than the other; and he wouldn't have found this if he lives to a hundred. Chad found it," she continued with her lighted, faintly flushed, her conscious confidential face, "in the quietest way in the world. Or rather it found HIM—for everything finds him; I mean finds him right. You'll think we do such things strangely—but at my age," she smiled, "one has to accept one's conditions. Our young man's people had seen her; one of his sisters, a charming woman—we know all about them—had observed her somewhere with me. She had spoken to her brother—turned him on; and we were again observed, poor Jeanne and I, without our in the least knowing it. It was at the beginning of the winter; it went on for some time; it outlasted our absence; it began again on our return; and it luckily seems all right. The young man had met Chad, and he got a friend to approach him—as having a decent interest in us. Mr. Newsome looked well before he leaped; he kept beautifully quiet and satisfied himself fully; then only he spoke. It's what has for some time past occupied us. It seems as if it were what would do; really, really all one could wish. There are only two or three points to be settled—they depend on her father. But this time I think we're safe."

Strether, consciously gaping a little, had fairly hung upon her lips. "I hope so with all my heart." And then he permitted himself: "Does nothing depend on HER?"

"Ah naturally; everything did. But she's pleased comme tout. She has been perfectly free; and he—our young friend—is really a combination. I quite adore him."

Strether just made sure. "You mean your future son-in-law?"

"Future if we all bring it off."

"Ah well," said Strether decorously, "I heartily hope you may." There seemed little else for him to say, though her communication had the oddest effect on him. Vaguely and confusedly he was troubled by it; feeling as if he had even himself been concerned in something deep and dim. He had allowed for depths, but these were greater: and it was as if, oppressively—indeed absurdly—he was responsible for what they had now thrown up to the surface. It was—through something ancient and cold in it—what he would have called the real thing. In short his hostess's news, though he couldn't have explained why, was a sensible shock, and his oppression a weight he felt he must somehow or other immediately get rid of. There were too many connexions missing to make it tolerable he should do anything else. He was prepared to suffer—before his own inner tribunal—for Chad; he was prepared to suffer even for Madame de Vionnet. But he wasn't prepared to suffer for the little girl So now having said the proper thing, he wanted to get away. She held him an instant, however, with another appeal.

"Do I seem to you very awful?"

"Awful? Why so?" But he called it to himself, even as he spoke, his biggest insincerity yet.

"Our arrangements are so different from yours."

"Mine?" Oh he could dismiss that too! "I haven't any arrangements."

"Then you must accept mine; all the more that they're excellent. They're founded on a vieille sagesse. There will be much more, if all goes well, for you to hear and to know, and everything, believe me, for you to like. Don't be afraid; you'll be satisfied." Thus she could talk to him of what, of her innermost life—for that was what it came to—he must "accept"; thus she could extraordinarily speak as if in such an affair his being satisfied had an importance. It was all a wonder and made the whole case larger. He had struck himself at the hotel, before Sarah and Waymarsh, as being in her boat; but where on earth was he now? This question was in the air till her own lips quenched it with another. "And do you suppose HE—who loves her so—would do anything reckless or cruel?"

He wondered what he supposed. "Do you mean your young man—?"

"I mean yours. I mean Mr. Newsome." It flashed for Strether the next moment a finer light, and the light deepened as she went on. "He takes, thank God, the truest tenderest interest in her."

It deepened indeed. "Oh I'm sure of that!"

"You were talking," she said, "about one's trusting him. You see then how I do."

He waited a moment—it all came. "I see—I see." He felt he really did see.

"He wouldn't hurt her for the world, nor—assuming she marries at all—risk anything that might make against her happiness. And—willingly, at least—he would never hurt ME."

Her face, with what he had by this time grasped, told him more than her words; whether something had come into it, or whether he only read clearer, her whole story—what at least he then took for such—reached out to him from it. With the initiative she now attributed to Chad it all made a sense, and this sense—a light, a lead, was what had abruptly risen before him. He wanted, once more, to get off with these things; which was at last made easy, a servant having, for his assistance, on hearing voices in the hall, just come forward. All that Strether had made out was, while the man opened the door and impersonally waited, summed up in his last word. "I don't think, you know, Chad will tell me anything."

"No—perhaps not yet."

"And I won't as yet speak to him."

"Ah that's as you'll think best. You must judge."

She had finally given him her hand, which he held a moment. "How MUCH I have to judge!"

"Everything," said Madame de Vionnet: a remark that was indeed—with the refined disguised suppressed passion of her face—what he most carried away.

II

So far as a direct approach was concerned Sarah had neglected him, for the week now about to end, with a civil consistency of chill that, giving him a higher idea of her social resource, threw him back on the general reflexion that a woman could always be amazing. It indeed helped a little to console him that he felt sure she had for the same period also left Chad's curiosity hanging; though on the other hand, for his personal relief, Chad could at least go through the various motions—and he made them extraordinarily numerous—of seeing she had a good time. There wasn't a motion on which, in her presence, poor Strether could so much as venture, and all he could do when he was out of it was to walk over for a talk with Maria. He walked over of course much less than usual, but he found a special compensation in a certain half-hour during which, toward the close of a crowded empty expensive day, his several companions seemed to him so disposed of as to give his forms and usages a rest. He had been with them in the morning and had nevertheless called on the Pococks in the afternoon; but their whole group, he then found, had dispersed after a fashion of which it would amuse Miss Gostrey to hear. He was sorry again, gratefully sorry she was so out of it—she who had really put him in; but she had fortunately always her appetite for news. The pure flame of the disinterested burned in her cave of treasures as a lamp in a Byzantine vault. It was just now, as happened, that for so fine a sense as hers a near view would have begun to pay. Within three days, precisely, the situation on which he was to report had shown signs of an equilibrium; the effect of his look in at the hotel was to confirm this appearance. If the equilibrium might only prevail! Sarah was out with Waymarsh, Mamie was out with Chad, and Jim was out alone. Later on indeed he himself was booked to Jim, was to take him that evening to the Varieties—which Strether was careful to pronounce as Jim pronounced them.

Miss Gostrey drank it in. "What then to-night do the others do?"

"Well, it has been arranged. Waymarsh takes Sarah to dine at Bignons."

She wondered. "And what do they do after? They can't come straight home."

"No, they can't come straight home—at least Sarah can't. It's their secret, but I think I've guessed it." Then as she waited: "The circus."

It made her stare a moment longer, then laugh almost to extravagance. "There's no one like you!"

"Like ME?"—he only wanted to understand.

"Like all of you together—like all of us: Woollett, Milrose and their products. We're abysmal—but may we never be less so! Mr. Newsome," she continued, "meanwhile takes Miss Pocock—?"

"Precisely—to the Francais: to see what you took Waymarsh and me to, a family-bill."

"Ah then may Mr. Chad enjoy it as I did!" But she saw so much in things. "Do they spend their evenings, your young people, like that, alone together?"

"Well, they're young people—but they're old friends."

"I see, I see. And do THEY dine—for a difference—at Brebant's?"

"Oh where they dine is their secret too. But I've my idea that it will be, very quietly, at Chad's own place."

"She'll come to him there alone?"

They looked at each other a moment. "He has known her from a child. Besides," said Strether with emphasis, "Mamie's remarkable. She's splendid."

She wondered. "Do you mean she expects to bring it off?"

"Getting hold of him? No—I think not."

"She doesn't want him enough?—or doesn't believe in her power?" On which as he said nothing she continued: "She finds she doesn't care for him?"

"No—I think she finds she does. But that's what I mean by so describing her. It's IF she does that she's splendid. But we'll see," he wound up, "where she comes out."

"You seem to show me sufficiently," Miss Gostrey laughed, "where she goes in! But is her childhood's friend," she asked, "permitting himself recklessly to flirt with her?"

"No—not that. Chad's also splendid. They're ALL splendid!" he declared with a sudden strange sound of wistfulness and envy. "They're at least HAPPY."

"Happy?"—it appeared, with their various difficulties, to surprise her.

"Well—I seem to myself among them the only one who isn't."

She demurred. "With your constant tribute to the ideal?"

He had a laugh at his tribute to the ideal, but he explained after a moment his impression. "I mean they're living. They're rushing about. I've already had my rushing. I'm waiting."

"But aren't you," she asked by way of cheer, "waiting with ME?"

He looked at her in all kindness. "Yes—if it weren't for that!"

"And you help me to wait," she said. "However," she went on, "I've really something for you that will help you to wait and which you shall have in a minute. Only there's something more I want from you first. I revel in Sarah."

"So do I. If it weren't," he again amusedly sighed, "for THAT—!"

"Well, you owe more to women than any man I ever saw. We do seem to keep you going. Yet Sarah, as I see her, must be great."

"She IS" Strether fully assented: "great! Whatever happens, she won't, with these unforgettable days, have lived in vain."

Miss Gostrey had a pause. "You mean she has fallen in love?"

"I mean she wonders if she hasn't—and it serves all her purpose."

"It has indeed," Maria laughed, "served women's purposes before!"

"Yes—for giving in. But I doubt if the idea—as an idea—has ever up to now answered so well for holding out. That's HER tribute to the ideal—we each have our own. It's her romance—and it seems to me better on the whole than mine. To have it in Paris too," he explained—"on this classic ground, in this charged infectious air, with so sudden an intensity: well, it's more than she expected. She has had in short to recognise the breaking out for her of a real affinity—and with everything to enhance the drama."

Miss Gostrey followed. "Jim for instance?"

"Jim. Jim hugely enhances. Jim was made to enhance. And then Mr. Waymarsh. It's the crowning touch—it supplies the colour. He's positively separated."

"And she herself unfortunately isn't—that supplies the colour too." Miss Gostrey was all there. But somehow—! "Is HE in love?"

Strether looked at her a long time; then looked all about the room; then came a little nearer. "Will you never tell any one in the world as long as ever you live?"

"Never." It was charming.

"He thinks Sarah really is. But he has no fear," Strether hastened to add.

"Of her being affected by it?"

"Of HIS being. He likes it, but he knows she can hold out. He's helping her, he's floating her over, by kindness."

Maria rather funnily considered it. "Floating her over in champagne? The kindness of dining her, nose to nose, at the hour when all Paris is crowding to profane delights, and in the—well, in the great temple, as one hears of it, of pleasure?"

"That's just IT, for both of them," Strether insisted—"and all of a supreme innocence. The Parisian place, the feverish hour, the putting before her of a hundred francs' worth of food and drink, which they'll scarcely touch—all that's the dear man's own romance; the expensive kind, expensive in francs and centimes, in which he abounds. And the circus afterwards—which is cheaper, but which he'll find some means of making as dear as possible—that's also HIS tribute to the ideal. It does for him. He'll see her through. They won't talk of anything worse than you and me."

"Well, we're bad enough perhaps, thank heaven," she laughed, "to upset them! Mr. Waymarsh at any rate is a hideous old coquette." And the next moment she had dropped everything for a different pursuit. "What you don't appear to know is that Jeanne de Vionnet has become engaged. She's to marry—it has been definitely arranged—young Monsieur de Montbron."

He fairly blushed. "Then—if you know it—it's 'out'?"

"Don't I often know things that are NOT out? However," she said, "this will be out to-morrow. But I see I've counted too much on your possible ignorance. You've been before me, and I don't make you jump as I hoped."

He gave a gasp at her insight. "You never fail! I've HAD my jump. I had it when I first heard."

"Then if you knew why didn't you tell me as soon as you came in?"

"Because I had it from her as a thing not yet to be spoken of."

Miss Gostrey wondered. "From Madame de Vionnet herself?"

"As a probability—not quite a certainty: a good cause in which Chad has been working. So I've waited."

"You need wait no longer," she returned. "It reached me yesterday—roundabout and accidental, but by a person who had had it from one of the young man's own people—as a thing quite settled. I was only keeping it for you."

"You thought Chad wouldn't have told me?"

She hesitated. "Well, if he hasn't—"

"He hasn't. And yet the thing appears to have been practically his doing. So there we are."

"There we are!" Maria candidly echoed.

"That's why I jumped. I jumped," he continued to explain, "because it means, this disposition of the daughter, that there's now nothing else: nothing else but him and the mother."

"Still—it simplifies."

"It simplifies"—he fully concurred. "But that's precisely where we are. It marks a stage in his relation. The act is his answer to Mrs. Newsome's demonstration."

"It tells," Maria asked, "the worst?"

"The worst."

"But is the worst what he wants Sarah to know?"

"He doesn't care for Sarah."

At which Miss Gostrey's eyebrows went up. "You mean she has already dished herself?"

Strether took a turn about; he had thought it out again and again before this, to the end; but the vista seemed each time longer. "He wants his good friend to know the best. I mean the measure of his attachment. She asked for a sign, and he thought of that one. There it is."

"A concession to her jealousy?"

Strether pulled up. "Yes—call it that. Make it lurid—for that makes my problem richer."

"Certainly, let us have it lurid—for I quite agree with you that we want none of our problems poor. But let us also have it clear. Can he, in the midst of such a preoccupation, or on the heels of it, have seriously cared for Jeanne?—cared, I mean, as a young man at liberty would have cared?"

Well, Strether had mastered it. "I think he can have thought it would be charming if he COULD care. It would be nicer."

"Nicer than being tied up to Marie?"

"Yes—than the discomfort of an attachment to a person he can never hope, short of a catastrophe, to marry. And he was quite right," said Strether. "It would certainly have been nicer. Even when a thing's already nice there mostly is some other thing that would have been nicer—or as to which we wonder if it wouldn't. But his question was all the same a dream. He COULDn't care in that way. He IS tied up to Marie. The relation is too special and has gone too far. It's the very basis, and his recent lively contribution toward establishing Jeanne in life has been his definite and final acknowledgement to Madame de Vionnet that he has ceased squirming. I doubt meanwhile," he went on, "if Sarah has at all directly attacked him."

His companion brooded. "But won't he wish for his own satisfaction to make his ground good to her?"

"No—he'll leave it to me, he'll leave everything to me. I 'sort of' feel"—he worked it out—"that the whole thing will come upon me. Yes, I shall have every inch and every ounce of it. I shall be USED for it—!" And Strether lost himself in the prospect. Then he fancifully expressed the issue. "To the last drop of my blood."

Maria, however, roundly protested. "Ah you'll please keep a drop for ME. I shall have a use for it!"—which she didn't however follow up. She had come back the next moment to another matter. "Mrs. Pocock, with her brother, is trusting only to her general charm?"

"So it would seem."

"And the charm's not working?"

Well, Strether put it otherwise, "She's sounding the note of home—which is the very best thing she can do."

"The best for Madame de Vionnet?"

"The best for home itself. The natural one; the right one."

"Right," Maria asked, "when it fails?"

Strether had a pause. "The difficulty's Jim. Jim's the note of home."

She debated. "Ah surely not the note of Mrs. Newsome."

But he had it all. "The note of the home for which Mrs. Newsome wants him—the home of the business. Jim stands, with his little legs apart, at the door of THAT tent; and Jim is, frankly speaking, extremely awful."

Maria stared. "And you in, you poor thing, for your evening with him?"

"Oh he's all right for ME!" Strether laughed. "Any one's good enough for ME. But Sarah shouldn't, all the same, have brought him. She doesn't appreciate him."

His friend was amused with this statement of it. "Doesn't know, you mean, how bad he is?"

Strether shook his head with decision. "Not really."

She wondered. "Then doesn't Mrs. Newsome?"

It made him frankly do the same. "Well, no—since you ask me."

Maria rubbed it in. "Not really either?"

"Not at all. She rates him rather high." With which indeed, immediately, he took himself up. "Well, he IS good too, in his way. It depends on what you want him for."

Miss Gostrey, however, wouldn't let it depend on anything—wouldn't have it, and wouldn't want him, at any price. "It suits my book," she said, "that he should be impossible; and it suits it still better," she more imaginatively added, "that Mrs. Newsome doesn't know he is."

Strether, in consequence, had to take it from her, but he fell back on something else. "I'll tell you who does really know."

"Mr. Waymarsh? Never!"

"Never indeed. I'm not ALWAYS thinking of Mr. Waymarsh; in fact I find now I never am." Then he mentioned the person as if there were a good deal in it. "Mamie."

"His own sister?" Oddly enough it but let her down. "What good will that do?"

"None perhaps. But there—as usual—we are!"

III

There they were yet again, accordingly, for two days more; when Strether, on being, at Mrs. Pocock's hotel, ushered into that lady's salon, found himself at first assuming a mistake on the part of the servant who had introduced him and retired. The occupants hadn't come in, for the room looked empty as only a room can look in Paris, of a fine afternoon when the faint murmur of the huge collective life, carried on out of doors, strays among scattered objects even as a summer air idles in a lonely garden. Our friend looked about and hesitated; observed, on the evidence of a table charged with purchases and other matters, that Sarah had become possessed—by no aid from HIM—of the last number of the salmon-coloured Revue; noted further that Mamie appeared to have received a present of Fromentin's "Maitres d'Autrefois" from Chad, who had written her name on the cover; and pulled up at the sight of a heavy letter addressed in a hand he knew. This letter, forwarded by a banker and arriving in Mrs. Pocock's absence, had been placed in evidence, and it drew from the fact of its being unopened a sudden queer power to intensify the reach of its author. It brought home to him the scale on which Mrs. Newsome—for she had been copious indeed this time—was writing to her daughter while she kept HIM in durance; and it had altogether such an effect upon him as made him for a few minutes stand still and breathe low. In his own room, at his own hotel, he had dozens of well-filled envelopes superscribed in that character; and there was actually something in the renewal of his interrupted vision of the character that played straight into the so frequent question of whether he weren't already disinherited beyond appeal. It was such an assurance as the sharp downstrokes of her pen hadn't yet had occasion to give him; but they somehow at the present crisis stood for a probable absoluteness in any decree of the writer. He looked at Sarah's name and address, in short, as if he had been looking hard into her mother's face, and then turned from it as if the face had declined to relax. But since it was in a manner as if Mrs. Newsome were thereby all the more, instead of the less, in the room, and were conscious, sharply and sorely conscious, of himself, so he felt both held and hushed, summoned to stay at least and take his punishment. By staying, accordingly, he took it—creeping softly and vaguely about and waiting for Sarah to come in. She WOULD come in if he stayed long enough, and he had now more than ever the sense of her success in leaving him a prey to anxiety. It wasn't to be denied that she had had a happy instinct, from the point of view of Woollett, in placing him thus at the mercy of her own initiative. It was very well to try to say he didn't care—that she might break ground when she would, might never break it at all if she wouldn't, and that he had no confession whatever to wait upon her with: he breathed from day to day an air that damnably required clearing, and there were moments when he quite ached to precipitate that process. He couldn't doubt that, should she only oblige him by surprising him just as he then was, a clarifying scene of some sort would result from the concussion.

He humbly circulated in this spirit till he suddenly had a fresh arrest. Both the windows of the room stood open to the balcony, but it was only now that, in the glass of the leaf of one of them, folded back, he caught a reflexion quickly recognised as the colour of a lady's dress. Somebody had been then all the while on the balcony, and the person, whoever it might be, was so placed between the windows as to be hidden from him; while on the other hand the many sounds of the street had covered his own entrance and movements. If the person were Sarah he might on the spot therefore be served to his taste. He might lead her by a move or two up to the remedy for his vain tension; as to which, should he get nothing else from it, he would at least have the relief of pulling down the roof on their heads. There was fortunately no one at hand to observe—in respect to his valour—that even on this completed reasoning he still hung fire. He had been waiting for Mrs. Pocock and the sound of the oracle; but he had to gird himself afresh—which he did in the embrasure of the window, neither advancing nor retreating—before provoking the revelation. It was apparently for Sarah to come more into view;

he was in that case there at her service. She did however, as meanwhile happened, come more into view; only she luckily came at the last minute as a contradiction of Sarah. The occupant of the balcony was after all quite another person, a person presented, on a second look, by a charming back and a slight shift of her position, as beautiful brilliant unconscious Mamie—Mamie alone at home, Mamie passing her time in her own innocent way, Mamie in short rather shabbily used, but Mamie absorbed interested and interesting. With her arms on the balustrade and her attention dropped to the street she allowed Strether to watch her, to consider several things, without her turning round.

But the oddity was that when he HAD so watched and considered he simply stepped back into the room without following up his advantage. He revolved there again for several minutes, quite as with something new to think of and as if the bearings of the possibility of Sarah had been superseded. For frankly, yes, it HAD bearings thus to find the girl in solitary possession. There was something in it that touched him to a point not to have been reckoned beforehand, something that softly but quite pressingly spoke to him, and that spoke the more each time he paused again at the edge of the balcony and saw her still unaware. Her companions were plainly scattered; Sarah would be off somewhere with Waymarsh and Chad off somewhere with Jim. Strether didn't at all mentally impute to Chad that he was with his "good friend"; he gave him the benefit of supposing him involved in appearances that, had he had to describe them—for instance to Maria—he would have conveniently qualified as more subtle. It came to him indeed the next thing that there was perhaps almost an excess of refinement in having left Mamie in such weather up there alone; however she might in fact have extemporised, under the charm of the Rue de Rivoli, a little makeshift Paris of wonder arid fancy. Our friend in any case now recognised—and it was as if at the recognition Mrs. Newsome's fixed intensity had suddenly, with a deep audible gasp, grown thin and vague—that day after day he had been conscious in respect to his young lady of something odd and ambiguous, yet something into which he could at last read a meaning. It had been at the most, this mystery, an obsession—oh an obsession agreeable; and it had just now fallen into its place as at the touch of a spring. It had represented the possibility between them of some communication baffled by accident and delay—the possibility even of some relation as yet unacknowledged.

There was always their old relation, the fruit of the Woollett years; but that—and it was what was strangest—had nothing whatever in common with what was now in the air. As a child, as a "bud," and then again as a flower of expansion, Mamie had bloomed for him, freely, in the almost incessantly open doorways of home; where he remembered her as first very forward, as then very backward—for he had carried on at one period, in Mrs. Newsome's parlours (oh Mrs. Newsome's phases and his own!) a course of English Literature re-enforced by exams and teas—and once more, finally, as very much in advance. But he had kept no great sense of points of contact; it not being in the nature of things at Woollett that the freshest of the buds should find herself in the same basket with the most withered of the winter apples. The child had given sharpness, above all, to his sense of the flight of time; it was but the day before yesterday that he had tripped up on her hoop, yet his experience of remarkable women—destined, it would seem, remarkably to grow—felt itself ready this afternoon, quite braced itself, to include her. She had in fine more to say to him than he had ever dreamed the pretty girl of the moment COULD have; and the proof of the circumstance was that, visibly, unmistakeably, she had been able to say it to no one else. It was something she could mention neither to her brother, to her sister-in-law nor to Chad; though he could just imagine that had she still been at home she might have brought it out, as a supreme tribute to age, authority and attitude, for Mrs. Newsome. It was moreover something in which they all took an interest; the strength of their interest was in truth just the reason of her prudence. All this then, for five minutes, was vivid to Strether, and it put before him that, poor child, she had now but her prudence to amuse her. That, for a pretty girl in Paris, struck him, with a rush, as a sorry state; so that under the impression he went out to her with a step as hypocritically alert, he was well aware, as if he had just come into the room. She turned with a start at his voice; preoccupied with him though she might be, she was just a scrap disappointed. "Oh I thought you were Mr. Bilham!"

The remark had been at first surprising and our friend's private thought, under the influence of it, temporarily blighted; yet we are able to add that he presently recovered his inward tone and that many a fresh flower of fancy was to bloom in the same air. Little Bilham—since little Bilham was, somewhat incongruously, expected—appeared behindhand; a circumstance by which Strether was to profit. They came back into the room together after a little, the couple on the balcony, and amid its crimson-and-gold elegance, with the others still absent, Strether passed forty minutes that he appraised even at the time as far, in the whole queer connexion, from his idlest. Yes indeed, since he had the other day so agreed with Maria about the inspiration of the lurid, here was something for his problem that surely didn't make it shrink and that was floated in upon him as part of a sudden flood. He was doubtless not to know till afterwards, on turning them over in thought, of how many elements his impression was composed; but he none the less felt, as he sat with the charming girl, the signal growth of a confidence. For she WAS charming, when all was said—and none the less so for the visible habit and practice of freedom and fluency. She was charming, he was aware, in spite of the fact that if he hadn't found her so he would have found her something he should have been in peril of expressing as "funny." Yes, she was funny, wonderful Mamie, and without dreaming it; she was bland, she was bridal—with never, that he could make out as yet, a bridegroom to support it; she was handsome and portly and easy and chatty, soft and sweet and almost disconcertingly reassuring. She was dressed, if we might so far discriminate, less as a young lady than as an old one—had an old one been supposable to Strether as so committed to vanity; the complexities of her hair missed moreover also the looseness of youth; and she had a mature manner of bending a little, as to encourage and reward, while she held neatly together in front of her a pair of strikingly polished hands: the combination of all of which kept up about her the glamour of her "receiving," placed her again perpetually between the windows and within sound of the ice-cream plates, suggested the enumeration of all the names, all the Mr. Brookses and Mr. Snookses, gregarious specimens of a single type, she was happy to "meet." But if all this was where she was funny, and if what was funnier than the rest was the contrast between her beautiful benevolent patronage—such a hint of the polysyllabic as might make her something of a bore toward middle age—and her rather flat little voice, the voice, naturally, unaffectedly yet, of a girl of fifteen; so Strether, none the less, at the end of ten minutes, felt in her a quiet dignity that pulled things bravely together. If quiet dignity, almost more than matronly, with voluminous, too voluminous clothes, was the effect she proposed to produce, that was an ideal one could like in her when once one had got into relation. The great thing now for her visitor was that this was exactly what he had done; it made so extraordinary a mixture of the brief and crowded hour. It was the mark of a relation that he had begun so quickly to find himself sure she was, of all people, as might have been said, on the side and of the party of Mrs. Newsome's original ambassador. She was in HIS interest and not in Sarah's, and some sign of that was precisely what he had been feeling in her, these last days, as imminent. Finally placed, in Paris, in immediate presence of the situation and of the hero of it—by whom Strether was incapable of meaning any one but Chad—she had accomplished, and really in a manner all unexpected to herself, a change of base; deep still things had come to pass within her, and by the time she had grown sure of them Strether had become aware of the little drama. When she knew where she was, in short, he had made it out; and he made it out at present still better; though with never a direct word passing between them all the while on the subject of his own predicament. There had been at first, as he sat there with her, a moment during which he wondered if she meant to break ground in respect to his prime undertaking. That door stood so strangely ajar that he was half-prepared to be conscious, at any juncture, of her having, of any one's having, quite bounced in. But, friendly, familiar, light of touch and happy of tact, she exquisitely stayed out; so that it was for all the world as if to show she could deal with him without being reduced to—well, scarcely anything.

It fully came up for them then, by means of their talking of everything BUT Chad, that Mamie, unlike Sarah, unlike Jim, knew perfectly what had become of him. It fully came up that she had taken to the last fraction of an inch the measure of the change in him, and that she wanted Strether to know what a secret she proposed to make of it. They talked most conveniently—as if they had had no chance yet—about Woollett; and that had virtually the effect of their keeping the secret more close. The hour took on for Strether, little by little, a queer sad sweetness of quality, he had such a revulsion in Mamie's favour and on behalf of her social value as might have come from remorse at some early injustice. She made him, as under the breath of some vague western whiff, homesick and freshly restless; he could really for the time have fancied himself stranded with her on a far shore, during an ominous calm, in a quaint community of shipwreck. Their little interview was like a picnic on a coral strand; they passed each other, with melancholy smiles and looks sufficiently allusive, such cupfuls of water as they had saved. Especially sharp in Strether meanwhile was the conviction that his companion really knew, as we have hinted, where she had come out. It was at a very particular place—only THAT she would never tell him; it would be above all what he should have to puzzle for himself. This was what he hoped for, because his interest in the girl wouldn't be complete without it. No more would the appreciation to which she was entitled—so assured was he that the more he saw of her process the more he should see of her pride. She saw, herself, everything; but she knew what she didn't want, and that it was that had helped her. What didn't she want?—there was a pleasure lost for her old friend in not yet knowing, as there would doubtless be a thrill in getting a glimpse. Gently and sociably she kept that dark to him, and it was as if she soothed and beguiled him in other ways to make up for it. She came out with her impression of Madame de Vionnet—of whom she had "heard so much"; she came out with her impression of Jeanne, whom she had been "dying to see": she brought it out with a blandness by which her auditor was really stirred that she had been with Sarah early that very afternoon, and after dreadful delays caused by all sorts of things, mainly, eternally, by the purchase of clothes—clothes that unfortunately wouldn't be themselves eternal—to call in the Rue de Bellechasse.

At the sound of these names Strether almost blushed to feel that he couldn't have sounded them first—and yet couldn't either have justified his squeamishness. Mamie made them easy as he couldn't have begun to do, and yet it could only have cost her more than he should ever have had to spend. It was as friends of Chad's, friends special, distinguished, desirable, enviable, that she spoke of them, and she beautifully carried it off that much as she had heard of them—though she didn't say how or where, which was a touch of her own—she had found them beyond her supposition. She abounded in praise of them, and after the manner of Woollett—which made the manner of Woollett a loveable thing again to Strether. He had never so felt the true inwardness of it as when his blooming companion pronounced the elder of the ladies of the Rue de Bellechasse too fascinating for words and declared of the younger that she was perfectly ideal, a real little monster of charm. "Nothing," she said of Jeanne, "ought ever to happen to her—she's so awfully right as she is. Another touch will spoil her—so she oughtn't to BE touched."

"Ah but things, here in Paris," Strether observed, "do happen to little girls." And then for the joke's and the occasion's sake: "Haven't you found that yourself?"

"That things happen—? Oh I'm not a little girl. I'm a big battered blowsy one. I don't care," Mamie laughed, "WHAT happens."

Strether had a pause while he wondered if it mightn't happen that he should give her the pleasure of learning that he found her nicer than he had really dreamed—a pause that ended when he had said to himself that, so far as it at all mattered for her, she had in fact perhaps already made this out. He risked accordingly a different question—though conscious, as soon as he had spoken, that he seemed to place it in relation to her last speech. "But that Mademoiselle de Vionnet is to be married—I suppose you've heard of THAT." For all, he then found, he need fear! "Dear, yes; the gentleman was there: Monsieur de Montbron, whom Madame de Vionnet presented to us."

"And was he nice?"

Mamie bloomed and bridled with her best reception manner. "Any man's nice when he's in love."

It made Strether laugh. "But is Monsieur de Montbron in love—already—with YOU?"

"Oh that's not necessary—it's so much better he should be so with HER: which, thank goodness, I lost no time in discovering for myself. He's perfectly gone—and I couldn't have borne it for her if he hadn't been. She's just too sweet."

Strether hesitated. "And through being in love too?"

On which with a smile that struck him as wonderful Mamie had a wonderful answer. "She doesn't know if she is or not."

It made him again laugh out. "Oh but YOU do!"

She was willing to take it that way. "Oh yes, I know everything." And as she sat there rubbing her polished hands and making the best of it—only holding her elbows perhaps a little too much out—the momentary effect for Strether was that every one else, in all their affair, seemed stupid.

"Know that poor little Jeanne doesn't know what's the matter with her?"

It was as near as they came to saying that she was probably in love with Chad; but it was quite near enough for what Strether wanted; which was to be confirmed in his certitude that, whether in love or not, she appealed to something large and easy in the girl before him. Mamie would be fat, too fat, at thirty; but she would always be the person who, at the present sharp hour, had been disinterestedly tender. "If I see a little more of her, as I hope I shall, I think she'll like me enough—for she seemed to like me to-day—to want me to tell her."

"And SHALL you?"

"Perfectly. I shall tell her the matter with her is that she wants only too much to do right. To do right for her, naturally," said Mamie, "is to please."

"Her mother, do you mean?"

"Her mother first."

Strether waited. "And then?"

"Well, 'then'—Mr. Newsome."

There was something really grand for him in the serenity of this reference. "And last only Monsieur de Montbron?"

"Last only"—she good-humouredly kept it up.

Strether considered. "So that every one after all then will be suited?"

She had one of her few hesitations, but it was a question only of a moment; and it was her nearest approach to being explicit with him about what was between them. "I think I can speak for myself. I shall be."

It said indeed so much, told such a story of her being ready to help him, so committed to him that truth, in short, for such use as he might make of it toward those ends of his own with which, patiently and trustfully, she had nothing to do—it so fully achieved all this that he appeared to himself simply to meet it in its own spirit by the last frankness of admiration. Admiration was of itself almost accusatory, but nothing less would serve to show her how nearly he understood. He put out his hand for good-bye with a "Splendid, splendid, splendid!" And he left her, in her splendour, still waiting for little Bilham.

Book Tenth

I

Strether occupied beside little Bilham, three evenings after his interview with Mamie Pocock, the same deep divan they had enjoyed together on the first occasion of our friend's meeting Madame de Vionnet and her daughter in the apartment of the Boulevard Malesherbes, where his position affirmed itself again as ministering to an easy exchange of impressions. The present evening had a different stamp; if the company was much more numerous, so, inevitably, were the ideas set in motion. It was on the other hand, however, now strongly marked that the talkers moved, in respect to such matters, round an inner, a protected circle. They knew at any rate what really concerned them to-night, and Strether had begun by keeping his companion close to it. Only a few of Chad's guests had dined—that is fifteen or twenty, a few compared with the large concourse offered to sight by eleven o'clock; but number and mass, quantity and quality, light, fragrance, sound, the overflow of hospitality meeting the high tide of response, had all from the first pressed upon Strether's consciousness, and he felt himself somehow part and parcel of the most festive scene, as the term was, in which he had ever in his life been engaged. He had perhaps seen, on Fourths of July and on dear old domestic Commencements, more people assembled, but he had never seen so many in proportion to the space, or had at all events never known so great a promiscuity to show so markedly as picked. Numerous as was the company, it had still been made so by selection, and what was above all rare for Strether was that, by no fault of his own, he was in the secret of the principle that had worked. He hadn't enquired, he had averted his head, but Chad had put him a pair of questions that themselves smoothed the ground. He hadn't answered the questions, he had replied that they were the young man's own affair; and he had then seen perfectly that the latter's direction was already settled.

Chad had applied for counsel only by way of intimating that he knew what to do; and he had clearly never known it better than in now presenting to his sister the whole circle of his society. This was all in the sense and the spirit of the note struck by him on that lady's arrival; he had taken at the station itself a line that led him without a break, and that enabled him to lead the Pococks—though dazed a little, no doubt, breathless, no doubt, and bewildered—to the uttermost end of the passage accepted by them perforce as pleasant. He had made it for them violently pleasant and mercilessly full; the upshot of which was, to Strether's vision, that they had come all the way without discovering it to be really no passage at all. It was a brave blind alley, where to pass was impossible and where, unless they stuck fast, they would have—which was always awkward—publicly to back out. They were touching bottom assuredly tonight; the whole scene represented the terminus of the cul-de-sac. So could things go when there was a hand to keep them consistent—a hand that pulled the wire with a skill at which the elder man more and more marvelled. The elder man felt responsible, but he also felt successful, since what had taken place was simply the issue of his own contention, six weeks before, that they properly should wait to see what their friends would have really to say. He had determined Chad to wait, he had determined him to see; he was therefore not to quarrel with the time given up to the business. As much as ever, accordingly, now that a fortnight had elapsed, the situation created for Sarah, and against which she had raised no protest, was that of her having accommodated herself to her adventure as to a pleasure-party surrendered perhaps even somewhat in excess to bustle and to "pace." If her brother had been at any point the least bit open to criticism it might have been on the ground of his spicing the draught too highly and pouring the cup too full. Frankly treating the whole occasion of the presence of his relatives as an opportunity for amusement, he left it, no doubt, but scant margin as an opportunity for anything else. He suggested, invented, abounded—yet all the while with the loosest easiest rein. Strether, during his own weeks, had gained a sense of knowing Paris; but he saw it afresh, and with fresh emotion, in the form of the knowledge offered to his colleague.

A thousand unuttered thoughts hummed for him in the air of these observations; not the least frequent of which was that Sarah might well of a truth not quite know whither she was drifting. She was in no position not to appear to expect that Chad should treat her handsomely; yet she struck our friend as privately stiffening a little each time she missed the chance of marking the great nuance. The great nuance was in brief that of course her brother must treat her handsomely—she should like to see him not; but that treating her handsomely, none the less, wasn't all in all—treating her handsomely buttered no parsnips; and that in fine there were moments when she felt the fixed eyes of their admirable absent mother fairly screw into the flat of her back. Strether, watching, after his habit, and overscoring with thought, positively had moments of his own in which he found himself sorry for her—occasions on which she affected him as a person seated in a runaway vehicle and turning over the question of a possible jump. WOULD she jump, could she, would THAT be a safe placed—this question, at such instants, sat for him in her lapse into pallor, her tight lips, her conscious eyes. It came back to the main point at issue: would she be, after all, to be squared? He believed on the whole she would jump; yet his alternations on this subject were the more especial stuff of his suspense. One thing remained well before him—a conviction that was in fact to gain sharpness from the impressions of this evening: that if she SHOULD gather in her skirts, close her eyes and quit the carriage while in motion, he would promptly enough become aware. She would alight from her headlong course more or less directly upon him; it would be appointed to him, unquestionably, to receive her entire weight. Signs and portents of the experience thus in reserve for him had as it happened, multiplied even through the dazzle of Chad's party. It was partly under the nervous consciousness of such a prospect that, leaving almost every one in the two other rooms, leaving those of the guests already known to him as well as a mass of brilliant strangers of both sexes and of several varieties of speech, he had desired five quiet minutes with little Bilham, whom he always found soothing and even a little inspiring, and to whom he had actually moreover something distinct and important to say.

He had felt of old—for it already seemed long ago—rather humiliated at discovering he could learn in talk with a personage so much his junior the lesson of a certain moral ease; but he had now got used to that—whether or no the mixture of the fact with other humiliations had made it indistinct, whether or no directly from little Bilham's example, the example of his being contentedly just the obscure and acute little Bilham he was. It worked so for him, Strether seemed to see; and our friend had at private hours a wan smile over the fact that he himself, after so many more years, was still in search of something that would work. However, as we have said, it worked just now for them equally to have found a corner a little apart. What particularly kept it apart was the circumstance that the music in the salon was admirable, with two or three such singers as it was a privilege to hear in private. Their presence gave a distinction to Chad's entertainment, and the interest of calculating their effect on Sarah was actually so sharp as to be almost painful. Unmistakeably, in her single person, the motive of the composition and dressed in a splendour of crimson which affected Strether as the sound of a fall through a skylight, she would now be in the forefront of the listening circle and committed by it up to her eyes. Those eyes during the wonderful dinner itself he hadn't once met; having confessedly—perhaps a little pusillanimously—arranged with Chad that he should be on the same side of the table. But there was no use in having arrived now with little Bilham at an unprecedented point of intimacy unless he could pitch everything into the pot. "You who sat where you could see her, what does she make of it all? By which I mean on what terms does she take it?"

"Oh she takes it, I judge, as proving that the claim of his family is more than ever justified."

"She isn't then pleased with what he has to show?"

"On the contrary; she's pleased with it as with his capacity to do this kind of thing—more than she has been pleased with anything for a long time. But she wants him to show it THERE. He has no right to waste it on the likes of us."

Strether wondered. "She wants him to move the whole thing over?"

"The whole thing—with an important exception. Everything he has 'picked up'—and the way he knows how. She sees no difficulty in that. She'd run the show herself, and she'll make the handsome concession that Woollett would be on the whole in some ways the better for it. Not that it wouldn't be also in some ways the better for Woollett. The people there are just as good."

"Just as good as you and these others? Ah that may be. But such an occasion as this, whether or no," Strether said, "isn't the people. It's what has made the people possible."

"Well then," his friend replied, "there you are; I give you my impression for what it's worth. Mrs. Pocock has SEEN, and that's to-night how she sits there. If you were to have a glimpse of her face you'd understand me. She has made up her mind—to the sound of expensive music."

Strether took it freely in. "Ah then I shall have news of her."

"I don't want to frighten you, but I think that likely. However," little Bilham continued, "if I'm of the least use to you to hold on by—!"

"You're not of the least!"—and Strether laid an appreciative hand on him to say it. "No one's of the least." With which, to mark how gaily he could take it, he patted his companion's knee. "I must meet my fate alone, and I SHALL—oh you'll see! And yet," he pursued the next moment, "you CAN help me too. You once said to me"—he followed this further—"that you held Chad should marry. I didn't see then so well as I know now that you meant he should marry Miss Pocock. Do you still consider that he should? Because if you do"—he kept it up—"I want you immediately to change your mind. You can help me that way."

"Help you by thinking he should NOT marry?"

"Not marry at all events Mamie."

"And who then?"

"Ah," Strether returned, "that I'm not obliged to say. But Madame de Vionnet—I suggest—when he can.'

"Oh!" said little Bilham with some sharpness.

"Oh precisely! But he needn't marry at all—I'm at any rate not obliged to provide for it. Whereas in your case I rather feel that I AM."

Little Bilham was amused. "Obliged to provide for my marrying?"

"Yes—after all I've done to you!"

The young man weighed it. "Have you done as much as that?"

"Well," said Strether, thus challenged, "of course I must remember what you've also done to ME. We may perhaps call it square. But all the same," he went on, "I wish awfully you'd marry Mamie Pocock yourself."

Little Bilham laughed out. "Why it was only the other night, in this very place, that you were proposing to me a different union altogether."

"Mademoiselle de Vionnet?" Well, Strether easily confessed it. "That, I admit, was a vain image. THIS is practical politics. I want to do something good for both of you—I wish you each so well; and you can see in a moment the trouble it will save me to polish you off by the same stroke. She likes you, you know. You console her. And she's splendid."

Little Bilham stared as a delicate appetite stares at an overheaped plate. "What do I console her for?"

It just made his friend impatient. "Oh come, you knows"

"And what proves for you that she likes me?"

"Why the fact that I found her three days ago stopping at home alone all the golden afternoon on the mere chance that you'd come to her, and hanging over her balcony on that of seeing your cab drive up. I don't know what you want more."

Little Bilham after a moment found it. "Only just to know what proves to you that I like HER."

"Oh if what I've just mentioned isn't enough to make you do it, you're a stony-hearted little fiend. Besides"—Strether encouraged his fancy's flight—"you showed your inclination in the way you kept her waiting, kept her on purpose to see if she cared enough for you."

His companion paid his ingenuity the deference of a pause. "I didn't keep her waiting. I came at the hour. I wouldn't have kept her waiting for the world," the young man honourably declared.

"Better still—then there you are!" And Strether, charmed, held him the faster. "Even if you didn't do her justice, moreover," he continued, "I should insist on your immediately coming round to it. I want awfully to have worked it. I want"—and our friend spoke now with a yearning that was really earnest—"at least to have done THAT."

"To have married me off—without a penny?"

"Well, I shan't live long; and I give you my word, now and here, that I'll leave you every penny of my own. I haven't many, unfortunately, but you shall have them all. And Miss Pocock, I think, has a few. I want," Strether went on, "to have been at least to that extent constructive even expiatory. I've been sacrificing so to strange gods that I feel I want to put on record, somehow, my fidelity—fundamentally unchanged after all—to our own. I feel as if my hands were embrued with the blood of monstrous alien altars—of another faith altogether.

There it is—it's done." And then he further explained. "It took hold of me because the idea of getting her quite out of the way for Chad helps to clear my ground."

The young man, at this, bounced about, and it brought them face to face in admitted amusement. "You want me to marry as a convenience to Chad?"

"No," Strether debated—"HE doesn't care whether you marry or not. It's as a convenience simply to my own plan FOR him."

"'Simply'!"—and little Bilham's concurrence was in itself a lively comment. "Thank you. But I thought," he continued, "you had exactly NO plan 'for' him."

"Well then call it my plan for myself—which may be well, as you say, to have none. His situation, don't you see? is reduced now to the bare facts one has to recognise. Mamie doesn't want him, and he doesn't want Mamie: so much as that these days have made clear. It's a thread we can wind up and tuck in."

But little Bilham still questioned. "YOU can—since you seem so much to want to. But why should I?"

Poor Strether thought it over, but was obliged of course to admit that his demonstration did superficially fail. "Seriously, there is no reason. It's my affair—I must do it alone. I've only my fantastic need of making my dose stiff."

Little Bilham wondered. "What do you call your dose?"

"Why what I have to swallow. I want my conditions unmitigated."

He had spoken in the tone of talk for talk's sake, and yet with an obscure truth lurking in the loose folds; a circumstance presently not without its effect on his young friend. Little Bilham's eyes rested on him a moment with some intensity; then suddenly, as if everything had cleared up, he gave a happy laugh. It seemed to say that if pretending, or even trying, or still even hoping, to be able to care for Mamie would be of use, he was all there for the job. "I'll do anything in the world for you!"

"Well," Strether smiled, "anything in the world is all I want. I don't know anything that pleased me in her more," he went on, "than the way that, on my finding her up there all alone, coming on her unawares and feeling greatly for her being so out of it, she knocked down my tall house of cards with her instant and cheerful allusion to the next young man. It was somehow so the note I needed—her staying at home to receive him."

"It was Chad of course," said little Bilham, "who asked the next young man—I like your name for me!—to call."

"So I supposed—all of which, thank God, is in our innocent and natural manners. But do you know," Strether asked, "if Chad knows—?" And then as this interlocutor seemed at a loss: "Why where she has come out."

Little Bilham, at this, met his face with a conscious look—it was as if, more than anything yet, the allusion had penetrated. "Do you know yourself?"

Strether lightly shook his head. "There I stop. Oh, odd as it may appear to you, there ARE things I don't know. I only got the sense from her of something very sharp, and yet very deep down, that she was keeping all to herself. That is I had begun with the belief that she HAD kept it to herself; but face to face with her there I soon made out that there was a person with whom she would have shared it. I had thought she possibly might with ME—but I saw then that I was only half in her confidence. When, turning to me to greet me—for she was on the balcony and I had come in without her knowing it—she showed me she had been expecting YOU and was proportionately disappointed, I got hold of the tail of my conviction. Half an hour later I was in possession of all the rest of it. You know what has happened." He looked at his young friend hard—then he felt sure. "For all you say, you're up to your eyes. So there you are."

Little Bilham after an instant pulled half round. "I assure you she hasn't told me anything."

"Of course she hasn't. For what do you suggest that I suppose her to take you? But you've been with her every day, you've seen her freely, you've liked her greatly—I stick to that—and you've made your profit of it. You know what she has been through as well as you know that she has dined here to-night—which must have put her, by the way, through a good deal more."

The young man faced this blast; after which he pulled round the rest of the way. "I haven't in the least said she hasn't been nice to me. But she's proud."

"And quite properly. But not too proud for that."

"It's just her pride that has made her. Chad," little Bilham loyally went on, "has really been as kind to her as possible. It's awkward for a man when a girl's in love with him."

"Ah but she isn't—now."

Little Bilham sat staring before him; then he sprang up as if his friend's penetration, recurrent and insistent, made him really after all too nervous. "No—she isn't now. It isn't in the least," he went on, "Chad's fault. He's really all right. I mean he would have been willing. But she came over with ideas. Those she had got at home. They had been her motive and support in joining her brother and his wife. She was to SAVE our friend."

"Ah like me, poor thing?" Strether also got to his feet.

"Exactly—she had a bad moment. It was very soon distinct to her, to pull her up, to let her down, that, alas, he was, he IS, saved. There's nothing left for her to do."

"Not even to love him?"

"She would have loved him better as she originally believed him."

Strether wondered "Of course one asks one's self what notion a little girl forms, where a young man's in question, of such a history and such a state."

"Well, this little girl saw them, no doubt, as obscure, but she saw them practically as wrong. The wrong for her WAS the obscure. Chad turns out at any rate right and good and disconcerting, while what she was all prepared for, primed and girded and wound up for, was to deal with him as the general opposite."

"Yet wasn't her whole point"—Strether weighed it—"that he was to be, that he COULD be, made better, redeemed?"

Little Bilham fixed it all a moment, and then with a small headshake that diffused a tenderness: "She's too late. Too late for the miracle."

"Yes"—his companion saw enough. "Still, if the worst fault of his condition is that it may be all there for her to profit by—?"

"Oh she doesn't want to 'profit,' in that flat way. She doesn't want to profit by another woman's work—she wants the miracle to have been her own miracle. THAT'S what she's too late for."

Strether quite felt how it all fitted, yet there seemed one loose piece. "I'm bound to say, you know, that she strikes one, on these lines, as fastidious—what you call here difficile."

Little Bilham tossed up his chin. "Of course she's difficile—on any lines! What else in the world ARE our Mamies—the real, the right ones?"

"I see, I see," our friend repeated, charmed by the responsive wisdom he had ended by so richly extracting. "Mamie is one of the real and the right."

"The very thing itself."

"And what it comes to then," Strether went on, "is that poor awful Chad is simply too good for her."

"Ah too good was what he was after all to be; but it was she herself, and she herself only, who was to have made him so."

It hung beautifully together, but with still a loose end. "Wouldn't he do for her even if he should after all break—"

"With his actual influence?" Oh little Bilham had for this enquiry the sharpest of all his controls. "How can he 'do'—on any terms whatever—when he's flagrantly spoiled?"

Strether could only meet the question with his passive, his receptive pleasure. "Well, thank goodness, YOU'RE not! You remain for her to save, and I come back, on so beautiful and full a demonstration, to my contention of just now—that of your showing distinct signs of her having already begun."

The most he could further say to himself—as his young friend turned away—was that the charge encountered for the moment no renewed denial. Little Bilham, taking his course back to the music, only shook his good-natured ears an instant, in the manner of a terrier who has got wet; while Strether relapsed into the sense—which had for him in these days most of comfort—that he was free to believe in anything that from hour to hour kept him going. He had positively motions and flutters of this conscious hour-to-hour kind, temporary surrenders to irony, to fancy, frequent instinctive snatches at the growing rose of observation, constantly stronger for him, as he felt, in scent and colour, and in which he could bury his nose even to wantonness. This last resource was offered him, for that matter, in the very form of his next clear perception—the vision of a prompt meeting, in the doorway of the room, between little Bilham and brilliant Miss Barrace, who was entering as Bilham withdrew. She had apparently put him a question, to which he had replied by turning to indicate his late interlocutor; toward whom, after an interrogation further aided by a resort to that optical machinery which seemed, like her other ornaments, curious and archaic, the genial lady, suggesting more than ever for her fellow guest the old French print, the historic portrait, directed herself with an intention that Strether instantly met. He knew in advance the first note she would sound, and took in as she approached all her need of sounding it. Nothing yet had been so "wonderful" between them as the present occasion; and it was her special sense of this quality in occasions that she was there, as she was in most places, to feed. That sense had already been so well fed by the situation about them that she had quitted the other room, forsaken the music, dropped out of the play, abandoned, in a word, the stage itself, that she might stand a minute behind the scenes with Strether and so perhaps figure as one of the famous augurs replying, behind the oracle, to the wink of the other. Seated near him presently where little Bilham had sat, she replied in truth to many things; beginning as soon as he had said to her—what he hoped he said without fatuity—"All you ladies are extraordinarily kind to me."

She played her long handle, which shifted her observation; she saw in an instant all the absences that left them free. "How can we be anything else? But isn't that exactly your plight? 'We ladies'—oh we're nice, and you must be having enough of us! As one of us, you know, I don't pretend I'm crazy about us. But Miss Gostrey at least to-night has left you alone, hasn't she?" With which she again looked about as if Maria might still lurk.

"Oh yes," said Strether; "she's only sitting up for me at home." And then as this elicited from his companion her gay "Oh, oh, oh!" he explained that he meant sitting up in suspense and prayer. "We thought it on the whole better she shouldn't be present; and either way of course it's a terrible worry for her." He abounded in the sense of his appeal to the ladies, and they might take their choice of his doing so from humility or from pride. "Yet she inclines to believe I shall come out."

"Oh I incline to believe too you'll come out!"—Miss Barrace, with her laugh, was not to be behind. "Only the question's about WHERE, isn't it? However," she happily continued, "if it's anywhere at all it must be very far on, mustn't it? To do us justice, I think, you know," she laughed, "we do, among us all, want you rather far on. Yes, yes," she repeated in her quick droll way; "we want you very, VERY far on!" After which she wished to know why he had thought it better Maria shouldn't be present.

"Oh," he replied, "it was really her own idea. I should have wished it. But she dreads responsibility."

"And isn't that a new thing for her?"

"To dread it? No doubt—no doubt. But her nerve has given way."

Miss Barrace looked at him a moment. "She has too much at stake." Then less gravely: "Mine, luckily for me, holds out."

"Luckily for me too"—Strether came back to that. "My own isn't so firm, MY appetite for responsibility isn't so sharp, as that I haven't felt the very principle of this occasion to be 'the more the merrier.' If we ARE so merry it's because Chad has understood so well."

"He has understood amazingly," said Miss Barrace.

"It's wonderful—Strether anticipated for her.

"It's wonderful!" she, to meet it, intensified; so that, face to face over it, they largely and recklessly laughed. But she presently added: "Oh I see the principle. If one didn't one would be lost. But when once one has got hold of it—"

"It's as simple as twice two! From the moment he had to do something—"

"A crowd"—she took him straight up—"was the only thing? Rather, rather: a rumpus of sound," she laughed, "or nothing. Mrs. Pocock's built in, or built out—whichever you call it; she's packed so tight she can't move. She's in splendid isolation"—Miss Barrace embroidered the theme.

Strether followed, but scrupulous of justice. "Yet with every one in the place successively introduced to her."

"Wonderfully—but just so that it does build her out. She's bricked up, she's buried alive!"

Strether seemed for a moment to look at it; but it brought him to a sigh. "Oh but she's not dead! It will take more than this to kill her."

His companion had a pause that might have been for pity. "No, I can't pretend I think she's finished—or that it's for more than to-night." She remained pensive as if with the same compunction. "It's only up to her chin." Then again for the fun of it: "She can breathe."

"She can breathe!"—he echoed it in the same spirit. "And do you know," he went on, "what's really all this time happening to me?—through the beauty of music, the gaiety of voices, the uproar in short of our revel and the felicity of your wit? The sound of Mrs. Pocock's respiration drowns for me, I assure you, every other. It's literally all I hear."

She focussed him with her clink of chains. "Well—!" she breathed ever so kindly.

"Well, what?"

"She IS free from her chin up," she mused; "and that WILL be enough for her."

"It will be enough for me!" Strether ruefully laughed. "Waymarsh has really," he then asked, "brought her to see you?"

"Yes—but that's the worst of it. I could do you no good. And yet I tried hard."

Strether wondered. "And how did you try?"

"Why I didn't speak of you."

"I see. That was better."

"Then what would have been worse? For speaking or silent," she lightly wailed, "I somehow 'compromise.' And it has never been any one but you."

"That shows"—he was magnanimous—"that it's something not in you, but in one's self. It's MY fault."

She was silent a little. "No, it's Mr. Waymarsh's. It's the fault of his having brought her."

"Ah then," said Strether good-naturedly, "why DID he bring her?"

"He couldn't afford not to."

"Oh you were a trophy—one of the spoils of conquest? But why in that case, since you do 'compromise'—"

"Don't I compromise HIM as well? I do compromise him as well," Miss Barrace smiled. "I compromise him as hard as I can. But for Mr. Waymarsh it isn't fatal. It's—so far as his wonderful relation with Mrs. Pocock is concerned—favourable." And then, as he still seemed slightly at sea: "The man who had succeeded with ME, don't you see? For her to get him from me was such an added incentive."

Strether saw, but as if his path was still strewn with surprises. "It's 'from' you then that she has got him?"

She was amused at his momentary muddle. "You can fancy my fight! She believes in her triumph. I think it has been part of her joy.

"Oh her joy!" Strether sceptically murmured.

"Well, she thinks she has had her own way. And what's to-night for her but a kind of apotheosis? Her frock's really good."

"Good enough to go to heaven in? For after a real apotheosis," Strether went on, "there's nothing BUT heaven. For Sarah there's only to-morrow."

"And you mean that she won't find to-morrow heavenly?"

"Well, I mean that I somehow feel to-night—on her behalf—too good to be true. She has had her cake; that is she's in the act now of having it, of swallowing the largest and sweetest piece. There won't be another left for her. Certainly I haven't one. It can only, at the best, be Chad." He continued to make it out as for their common entertainment. "He may have one, as it were, up his sleeve; yet it's borne in upon me that if he had—"

"He wouldn't"—she quite understood—"have taken all THIS trouble? I dare say not, and, if I may be quite free and dreadful, I very much hope he won't take any more. Of course I won't pretend now," she added, "not to know what it's a question of."

"Oh every one must know now," poor Strether thoughtfully admitted; "and it's strange enough and funny enough that one should feel everybody here at this very moment to be knowing and watching and waiting."

"Yes—isn't it indeed funny?" Miss Barrace quite rose to it. "That's the way we ARE in Paris." She was always pleased with a new contribution to that queerness. "It's wonderful! But, you know," she declared, "it all depends on you. I don't want to turn the knife in your vitals, but that's naturally what you just now meant by our all being on top of you. We know you as the hero of the drama, and we're gathered to see what you'll do."

Strether looked at her a moment with a light perhaps slightly obscured. "I think that must be why the hero has taken refuge in this corner. He's scared at his heroism—he shrinks from his part."

"Ah but we nevertheless believe he'll play it. That's why," Miss Barrace kindly went on, "we take such an interest in you. We feel you'll come up to the scratch." And then as he seemed perhaps not quite to take fire: "Don't let him do it."

"Don't let Chad go?"

"Yes, keep hold of him. With all this"—and she indicated the general tribute—"he has done enough. We love him here—he's charming."

"It's beautiful," said Strether, "the way you all can simplify when you will."

But she gave it to him back. "It's nothing to the way you will when you must."

He winced at it as at the very voice of prophecy, and it kept him a moment quiet. He detained her, however, on her appearing about to leave him alone in the rather cold clearance their talk had made. "There positively isn't a sign of a hero to-night; the hero's dodging and shirking, the hero's ashamed. Therefore, you know, I think, what you must all REALLY be occupied with is the heroine."

Miss Barrace took a minute. "The heroine?"

"The heroine. I've treated her," said Strether, "not a bit like a hero. Oh," he sighed, "I don't do it well!"

She eased him off. "You do it as you can." And then after another hesitation: "I think she's satisfied."

But he remained compunctious. "I haven't been near her. I haven't looked at her."

"Ah then you've lost a good deal!"

He showed he knew it. "She's more wonderful than ever?"

"Than ever. With Mr. Pocock."

Strether wondered. "Madame de Vionnet—with Jim?"

"Madame de Vionnet—with 'Jim.'" Miss Barrace was historic.

"And what's she doing with him?"

"Ah you must ask HIM!"

Strether's face lighted again at the prospect. "It WILL be amusing to do so." Yet he continued to wonder. "But she must have some idea."

"Of course she has—she has twenty ideas. She has in the first place," said Miss Barrace, swinging a little her tortoise-shell, "that of doing her part. Her part is to help YOU."

It came out as nothing had come yet; links were missing and connexions unnamed, but it was suddenly as if they were at the heart of their subject. "Yes; how much more she does it," Strether gravely reflected, "than I help HER!" It all came over him as with the near presence of the beauty, the grace, the intense, dissimulated spirit with which he had, as he said, been putting off contact. "SHE has courage."

"Ah she has courage!" Miss Barrace quite agreed; and it was as if for a moment they saw the quantity in each other's face.

But indeed the whole thing was present. "How much she must care!"

"Ah there it is. She does care. But it isn't, is it," Miss Barrace considerately added, "as if you had ever had any doubt of that?"

Strether seemed suddenly to like to feel that he really never had. "Why of course it's the whole point."

"Voila!" Miss Barrace smiled.

"It's why one came out," Strether went on. "And it's why one has stayed so long. And it's also"—he abounded—"why one's going home. It's why, it's why—"

"It's why everything!" she concurred. "It's why she might be to-night—for all she looks and shows, and for all your friend 'Jim' does—about twenty years old. That's another of her ideas; to be for him, and to be quite easily and charmingly, as young as a little girl."

Strether assisted at his distance. "'For him'? For Chad—?"

"For Chad, in a manner, naturally, always. But in particular to-night for Mr. Pocock." And then as her friend still stared: "Yes, it IS of a bravery But that's what she has: her high sense of duty." It was more than sufficiently before them. "When Mr. Newsome has his hands so embarrassed with his sister—"

"It's quite the least"—Strether filled it out—"that she should take his sister's husband? Certainly—quite the least. So she has taken him."

"She has taken him." It was all Miss Barrace had meant.

Still it remained enough. "It must be funny."

"Oh it IS funny." That of course essentially went with it.

But it brought them back. "How indeed then she must care!" In answer to which Strether's entertainer dropped a comprehensive "Ah!" expressive perhaps of some impatience for the time he took to get used to it. She herself had got used to it long before.

II

When one morning within the week he perceived the whole thing to be really at last upon him Strether's immediate feeling was all relief. He had known this morning that something was about to happen—known it, in a moment, by Waymarsh's manner when Waymarsh appeared before him during his brief consumption of coffee and a roll in the small slippery salle-a-manger so associated with rich rumination. Strether had taken there of late various lonely and absent-minded meals; he communed there, even at the end of June, with a suspected chill, the air of old shivers mixed with old savours, the air in which so many of his impressions had perversely matured; the place meanwhile renewing its message to him by the very circumstance of his single state. He now sat there, for the most part, to sigh softly, while he vaguely tilted his carafe, over the vision of how much better Waymarsh was occupied. That was really his success by the common measure—to have led this companion so on and on. He remembered how at first there had been scarce a squatting-place he could beguile him into passing; the actual outcome of which at last was that there was scarce one that could arrest him in his rush. His rush—as Strether vividly and amusedly figured it—continued to be all with Sarah, and contained perhaps moreover the word of the whole enigma, whipping up in its fine full-flavoured froth the very principle, for good or for ill, of his own, of Strether's destiny. It might after all, to the end, only be that they had united to save him, and indeed, so far as Waymarsh was concerned, that HAD to be the spring of action. Strether was glad at all events, in connexion with the case, that the saving he required was not more scant; so constituted a luxury was it in certain lights just to lurk there out of the full glare. He had moments of quite seriously wondering whether Waymarsh wouldn't in fact, thanks to old friendship and a conceivable indulgence, make about as good terms for him as he might make for himself. They wouldn't be the same terms of course; but they might have the advantage that he himself probably should be able to make none at all.

He was never in the morning very late, but Waymarsh had already been out, and, after a peep into the dim refectory, he presented himself with much less than usual of his large looseness. He had made sure, through the expanse of glass exposed to the court, that they would be alone; and there was now in fact that about him that pretty well took up the room. He was dressed in the garments of summer; and save that his white waistcoat was redundant and bulging these things favoured, they determined, his expression. He wore a straw hat such as his friend hadn't yet seen in Paris, and he showed a buttonhole freshly adorned with a magnificent rose. Strether read on the instant his story—how, astir for the previous hour, the sprinkled newness of the day, so pleasant at that season in Paris, he was fairly panting with the pulse of adventure and had been with Mrs. Pocock, unmistakeably, to the Marche aux Fleurs. Strether really knew in this vision of him a joy that was akin to envy; so reversed as he stood there did their old positions seem; so comparatively doleful now showed, by the sharp turn of the wheel, the posture of the pilgrim from Woollett. He wondered, this pilgrim, if he had originally looked to Waymarsh so brave and well, so remarkably launched, as it was at present the latter's privilege to appear. He recalled that his friend had remarked to him even at Chester that his aspect belied his plea of prostration; but there certainly couldn't have been, for an issue, an aspect less concerned than Waymarsh's with the menace of decay. Strether had at any rate never resembled a Southern planter of the great days—which was the image picturesquely suggested by the happy relation between the fuliginous face and the wide panama of his visitor. This type, it further amused him to guess, had been, on Waymarsh's part, the object of Sarah's care; he was convinced that her taste had not been a stranger to the conception and purchase of the hat, any more than her fine fingers had been guiltless of the bestowal of the rose. It came to him in the current of thought, as things so oddly did come, that HE had never risen with the lark to attend a brilliant woman to the Marche aux Fleurs; this could be fastened on him in connexion neither with Miss Gostrey nor with Madame de Vionnet; the practice of getting up early for adventures could indeed in no manner be fastened on him. It came to him in fact that just here was his usual case: he was for ever missing things through his general genius for missing them, while others were for ever picking them up through a contrary bent. And it was others who looked abstemious and he who looked greedy; it was he somehow who finally paid, and it was others who mainly partook. Yes, he should go to the scaffold yet for he wouldn't know quite whom. He almost, for that matter, felt on the scaffold now and really quite enjoying it. It worked out as BECAUSE he was anxious there—it worked out as for this reason that Waymarsh was so blooming. It was HIS trip for health, for a change, that proved the success—which was just what Strether, planning and exerting himself, had desired it should be. That truth already sat full-blown on his companion's lips; benevolence breathed from them as with the warmth of active exercise, and also a little as with the bustle of haste.

"Mrs. Pocock, whom I left a quarter of an hour ago at her hotel, has asked me to mention to you that she would like to find you at home here in about another hour. She wants to see you; she has something to say—or considers, I believe, that you may have: so that I asked her myself why she shouldn't come right round. She hasn't BEEN round yet—to see our place; and I took upon myself to say that I was sure you'd be glad to have her. The thing's therefore, you see, to keep right here till she comes."

The announcement was sociably, even though, after Waymarsh's wont, somewhat solemnly made; but Strether quickly felt other things in it than these light features. It was the first approach, from that quarter, to admitted consciousness; it quickened his pulse; it simply meant at last that he should have but himself to thank if he didn't know where he was. He had finished his breakfast; he pushed it away and was on his feet. There were plenty of elements of surprise, but only one of doubt. "The thing's for YOU to keep here too?" Waymarsh had been slightly ambiguous.

He wasn't ambiguous, however, after this enquiry; and Strether's understanding had probably never before opened so wide and effective a mouth as it was to open during the next five minutes. It was no part of his friend's wish, as appeared, to help to receive Mrs. Pocock; he quite understood the spirit in which she was to present herself, but his connexion with her visit was limited to his having—well, as he might say—perhaps a little promoted it. He had thought, and had let her know it, that Strether possibly would think she might have been round before. At any rate, as turned out, she had been wanting herself, quite a while, to come. "I told her," said Waymarsh, "that it would have been a bright idea if she had only carried it out before."

Strether pronounced it so bright as to be almost dazzling. "But why HASn't she carried it out before? She has seen me every day—she had only to name her hour. I've been waiting and waiting."

"Well, I told her you had. And she has been waiting too." It was, in the oddest way in the world, on the showing of this tone, a genial new pressing coaxing Waymarsh; a Waymarsh conscious with a different consciousness from any he had yet betrayed, and actually rendered by it almost insinuating. He lacked only time for full persuasion, and Strether was to see in a moment why. Meantime, however, our friend perceived, he was announcing a step of some magnanimity on Mrs. Pocock's part, so that he could deprecate a sharp question. It was his own high purpose in fact to have smoothed sharp questions to rest. He looked his old comrade very straight in the eyes, and he had never conveyed to him in so mute a manner so much kind confidence and so much good advice. Everything that was between them was again in his face, but matured and shelved and finally disposed of. "At any rate," he added, "she's coming now."

Considering how many pieces had to fit themselves, it all fell, in Strether's brain, into a close rapid order. He saw on the spot what had happened, and what probably would yet; and it was all funny enough. It was perhaps just this freedom of appreciation that wound him up to his flare of high spirits. "What is she coming FOR?—to kill me?"

"She's coming to be very VERY kind to you, and you must let me say that I greatly hope you'll not be less so to herself."

This was spoken by Waymarsh with much gravity of admonition, and as Strether stood there he knew he had but to make a movement to take the attitude of a man gracefully receiving a present. The present was that of the opportunity dear old Waymarsh had flattered himself he had divined in him the slight soreness of not having yet thoroughly enjoyed; so he had brought it to him thus, as on a little silver breakfast-tray, familiarly though delicately—without oppressive pomp; and he was to bend and smile and acknowledge, was to take and use and be grateful. He was not—that was the beauty of it—to be asked to deflect too much from his dignity. No wonder the old boy bloomed in this bland air of his own distillation. Strether felt for a moment as if Sarah were actually walking up and down outside. Wasn't she hanging about the porte-cochere while her friend thus summarily opened a way? Strether would meet her but to take it, and everything would be for the best in the best of possible worlds. He had never so much known what any one meant as, in the light of this demonstration, he knew what Mrs. Newsome did. It had reached Waymarsh from Sarah, but it had reached Sarah from her mother, and there was no break in the chain by which it reached HIM. "Has anything particular happened," he asked after a minute—"so suddenly to determine her? Has she heard anything unexpected from home?"

Waymarsh, on this, it seemed to him, looked at him harder than ever. "'Unexpected'?" He had a brief hesitation; then, however, he was firm. "We're leaving Paris."

"Leaving? That IS sudden."

Waymarsh showed a different opinion. "Less so than it may seem. The purpose of Mrs. Pocock's visit is to explain to you in fact that it's NOT."

Strether didn't at all know if he had really an advantage—anything that would practically count as one; but he enjoyed for the moment—as for the first time in his life—the sense of so carrying it off. He wondered—it was amusing—if he felt as the impudent feel. "I shall take great pleasure, I assure you, in any explanation. I shall be delighted to receive Sarah."

The sombre glow just darkened in his comrade's eyes; but he was struck with the way it died out again. It was too mixed with another consciousness—it was too smothered, as might be said, in flowers. He really for the time regretted it—poor dear old sombre glow! Something straight and simple, something heavy and empty, had been eclipsed in its company; something by which he had best known his friend. Waymarsh wouldn't BE his friend, somehow, without the occasional ornament of the sacred rage, and the right to the sacred rage—inestimably precious for Strether's charity—he also seemed in a manner, and at Mrs. Pocock's elbow, to have forfeited. Strether remembered the occasion early in their stay when on that very spot he had come out with his earnest, his ominous "Quit it!"—and, so remembering, felt it hang by a hair that he didn't himself now utter the same note. Waymarsh was having a good time—this was the truth that was embarrassing for him, and he was having it then and there, he was having it in Europe, he was having it under the very protection of circumstances of which he didn't in the least approve; all of which placed him in a false position, with no issue possible—none at least by the grand manner. It was practically in the manner of any one—it was all but in poor Strether's own—that instead of taking anything up he merely made the most of having to be himself explanatory. "I'm not leaving for the United States direct. Mr. and Mrs. Pocock and Miss Mamie are thinking of a little trip before their own return, and we've been talking for some days past of our joining forces. We've settled it that we do join and that we sail together the end of next month. But we start to-morrow for Switzerland. Mrs. Pocock wants some scenery. She hasn't had much yet."

He was brave in his way too, keeping nothing back, confessing all there was, and only leaving Strether to make certain connexions. "Is what Mrs. Newsome had cabled her daughter an injunction to break off short?"

The grand manner indeed at this just raised its head a little. "I know nothing about Mrs. Newsome's cables."

Their eyes met on it with some intensity—during the few seconds of which something happened quite out of proportion to the time. It happened that Strether, looking thus at his friend, didn't take his answer for truth—and that something more again occurred in consequence of THAT. Yes—Waymarsh just DID know about Mrs. Newsome's cables: to what other end than that had they dined together at Bignon's? Strether almost felt for the instant that it was to Mrs. Newsome herself the dinner had been given; and, for that matter, quite felt how she must have known about it and, as he might think, protected and consecrated it. He had a quick blurred view of daily cables, questions, answers, signals: clear enough was his vision of the expense that, when so wound up, the lady at home was prepared to incur. Vivid not less was his memory of what, during his long observation of her, some of her attainments of that high pitch had cost her. Distinctly she was at the highest now, and Waymarsh, who imagined himself an independent performer, was really, forcing his fine old natural voice, an overstrained accompanist. The whole reference of his errand seemed to mark her for Strether as by this time consentingly familiar to him, and nothing yet had so despoiled her of a special shade of consideration. "You don't know," he asked, "whether Sarah has been directed from home to try me on the matter of my also going to Switzerland?"

"I know," said Waymarsh as manfully as possible, "nothing whatever about her private affairs; though I believe her to be acting in conformity with things that have my highest respect." It was as manful as possible, but it was still the false note—as it had to be to convey so sorry a statement. He knew everything, Strether more and more felt, that he thus disclaimed, and his little punishment was just in this doom to a second fib. What falser position—given the man—could the most vindictive mind impose? He ended by squeezing through a passage in which three months before he would certainly have stuck fast. "Mrs Pocock will probably be ready herself to answer any enquiry you may put to her. But," he continued, "BUT—!" He faltered on it.

"But what? Don't put her too many?"

Waymarsh looked large, but the harm was done; he couldn't, do what he would, help looking rosy. "Don't do anything you'll be sorry for."

It was an attenuation, Strether guessed, of something else that had been on his lips; it was a sudden drop to directness, and was thereby the voice of sincerity. He had fallen to the supplicating note, and that immediately, for our friend, made a difference and reinstated him. They were in communication as they had been, that first morning, in Sarah's salon and in her presence and Madame de Vionnet's; and the same recognition of a great good will was again, after all, possible. Only the amount of response Waymarsh had then taken for granted was doubled, decupled now. This came out when he presently said: "Of course I needn't assure you I hope you'll come with us." Then it was that his implications and expectations loomed up for Strether as almost pathetically gross.

The latter patted his shoulder while he thanked him, giving the go-by to the question of joining the Pococks; he expressed the joy he felt at seeing him go forth again so brave and free, and he in fact almost took leave of him on the spot. "I shall see you again of course before you go; but I'm meanwhile much obliged to you for arranging so conveniently for what you've told me. I shall walk up and down in the court there—dear little old court which we've each bepaced so, this last couple of months, to the tune of our flights and our drops, our hesitations and our plunges: I shall hang about there, all impatience and excitement, please let Sarah know, till she graciously presents herself. Leave me with her without fear," he laughed; "I assure you I shan't hurt her. I don't think either she'll hurt ME: I'm in a situation in which damage was some time ago discounted. Besides, THAT isn't what worries you—but don't, don't explain! We're all right as we are: which was the degree of success our adventure was pledged to for each of us. We weren't, it seemed, all right as we were before; and we've got over the ground, all things considered, quickly. I hope you'll have a lovely time in the Alps."

Waymarsh fairly looked up at him as from the foot of them. "I don't know as I OUGHT really to go."

It was the conscience of Milrose in the very voice of Milrose, but, oh it was feeble and flat! Strether suddenly felt quite ashamed for him; he breathed a greater boldness. "LET yourself, on the contrary, go—in all agreeable directions. These are precious hours—at our age they mayn't recur. Don't have it to say to yourself at Milrose, next winter, that you hadn't courage for them." And then as his comrade queerly stared: "Live up to Mrs. Pocock."

"Live up to her?"

"You're a great help to her."

Waymarsh looked at it as at one of the uncomfortable things that were certainly true and that it was yet ironical to say. "It's more then than you are."

"That's exactly your own chance and advantage. Besides," said Strether, "I do in my way contribute. I know what I'm about."

Waymarsh had kept on his great panama, and, as he now stood nearer the door, his last look beneath the shade of it had turned again to darkness and warning. "So do I! See here, Strether."

"I know what you're going to say. 'Quit this'?"

"Quit this!" But it lacked its old intensity; nothing of it remained; it went out of the room with him.

III

Almost the first thing, strangely enough, that, about an hour later, Strether found himself doing in Sarah's presence was to remark articulately on this failure, in their friend, of what had been superficially his great distinction. It was as if—he alluded of course to the grand manner—the dear man had sacrificed it to some other advantage; which would be of course only for himself to measure. It might be simply that he was physically so much more sound than on his first coming out; this was all prosaic, comparatively cheerful and vulgar. And fortunately, if one came to that, his improvement in health was really itself grander than any manner it could be conceived as having cost him. "You yourself alone, dear Sarah"—Strether took the plunge—"have done him, it strikes me, in these three weeks, as much good as all the rest of his time together."

It was a plunge because somehow the range of reference was, in the conditions, "funny," and made funnier still by Sarah's attitude, by the turn the occasion had, with her appearance, so sensibly taken. Her appearance was really indeed funnier than anything else—the spirit in which he felt her to be there as soon as she was there, the shade of obscurity that cleared up for him as soon as he was seated with her in the small salon de lecture that had, for the most part, in all the weeks, witnessed the wane of his early vivacity of discussion with Waymarsh. It was an immense thing, quite a tremendous thing, for her to have come: this truth opened out to him in spite of his having already arrived for himself at a fairly vivid view of it. He had done exactly what he had given Waymarsh his word for—had walked and re-walked the court while he awaited her advent; acquiring in this exercise an amount of light that affected him at the time as flooding the scene. She had decided upon the step in order to give him the benefit of a doubt, in order to be able to say to her mother that she had, even to abjectness, smoothed the way for him. The doubt had been as to whether he mightn't take her as not having smoothed it—and the admonition had possibly come from Waymarsh's more detached spirit. Waymarsh had at any rate, certainly, thrown his weight into the scale—he had pointed to the importance of depriving their friend of a grievance. She had done justice to the plea, and it was to set herself right with a high ideal that she actually sat there in her state. Her calculation was sharp in the immobility with which she held her tall parasol-stick upright and at arm's length, quite as if she had struck the place to plant her flag; in the separate precautions she took not to show as nervous; in the aggressive repose in which she did quite nothing but wait for him. Doubt ceased to be possible from the moment he had taken in that she had arrived with no proposal whatever; that her concern was simply to show what she had come to receive. She had come to receive his submission, and Waymarsh was to have made it plain to him that she would expect nothing less. He saw fifty things, her host, at this convenient stage; but one of those he most saw was that their anxious friend hadn't quite had the hand required of him. Waymarsh HAD, however, uttered the request that she might find him mild, and while hanging about the court before her arrival he had turned over with zeal the different ways in which he could be so. The difficulty was that if he was mild he wasn't, for her purpose, conscious. If she wished him conscious—as everything about her cried aloud that she did—she must accordingly be at costs to make him so. Conscious he was, for himself—but only of too many things; so she must choose the one she required.

Practically, however, it at last got itself named, and when once that had happened they were quite at the centre of their situation. One thing had really done as well as another; when Strether had spoken of Waymarsh's leaving him, and that had necessarily brought on a reference to Mrs. Pocock's similar intention, the jump was but short to supreme lucidity. Light became indeed after that so intense that Strether would doubtless have but half made out, in the prodigious glare, by which of the two the issue had been in fact precipitated. It was, in their contracted quarters, as much there between them as if it had been something suddenly spilled with a crash and a splash on the floor. The form of his submission was to be an engagement to acquit himself within the twenty-four hours. "He'll go in a moment if you give him the word—he assures me on his honour he'll do that": this came in its order, out of its order, in respect to Chad, after the crash had occurred. It came repeatedly during the time taken by Strether to feel that he was even more fixed in his rigour than he had supposed—the time he was not above adding to a little by telling her that such a way of putting it on her brother's part left him sufficiently surprised. She wasn't at all funny at last—she was really fine; and he felt easily where she was strong—strong for herself. It hadn't yet so come home to him that she was nobly and appointedly officious. She was acting in interests grander and clearer than that of her poor little personal, poor little Parisian equilibrium, and all his consciousness of her mother's moral pressure profited by this proof of its sustaining force. She would be held up; she would be strengthened; he needn't in the least be anxious for her. What would once more have been distinct to him had he tried to make it so was that, as Mrs. Newsome was essentially all moral pressure, the presence of this element was almost identical with her own presence. It wasn't perhaps that he felt he was dealing with her straight, but it was certainly as if she had been dealing straight with HIM. She was reaching him somehow by the lengthened arm of the spirit, and he was having to that extent to take her into account; but he wasn't reaching her in turn, not making her take HIM; he was only reaching Sarah, who appeared to take so little of him. "Something has clearly passed between you and Chad," he presently said, "that I think I ought to know something more about. Does he put it all," he smiled, "on me?"

"Did you come out," she asked, "to put it all on HIM?"

But he replied to this no further than, after an instant, by saying: "Oh it's all right. Chad I mean's all right in having said to you—well anything he may have said. I'll TAKE it all—what he does put on me. Only I must see him before I see you again."

She hesitated, but she brought it out. "Is it absolutely necessary you should see me again?"

"Certainly, if I'm to give you any definite word about anything."

"Is it your idea then," she returned, "that I shall keep on meeting you only to be exposed to fresh humiliation?"

He fixed her a longer time. "Are your instructions from Mrs. Newsome that you shall, even at the worst, absolutely and irretrievably break with me?"

"My instructions from Mrs. Newsome are, if you please, my affair. You know perfectly what your own were, and you can judge for yourself of what it can do for you to have made what you have of them. You can perfectly see, at any rate, I'll go so far as to say, that if I wish not to expose myself I must wish still less to expose HER." She had already said more than she had quite expected; but, though she had also pulled up, the colour in her face showed him he should from one moment to the other have it all. He now indeed felt the high importance of his having it. "What is your conduct," she broke out as if to explain—"what is your conduct but an outrage to women like US? I mean your acting as if there can be a doubt—as between us and such another—of his duty?"

He thought a moment. It was rather much to deal with at once; not only the question itself, but the sore abysses it revealed. "Of course they're totally different kinds of duty."

"And do you pretend that he has any at all—to such another?"

"Do you mean to Madame de Vionnet?" He uttered the name not to affront her, but yet again to gain time—time that he needed for taking in something still other and larger than her demand of a moment before. It wasn't at once that he could see all that was in her actual challenge; but when he did he found himself just checking a low vague sound, a sound which was perhaps the nearest approach his vocal chords had ever known to a growl. Everything Mrs. Pocock had failed to give a sign of recognising in Chad as a particular part of a transformation—everything that had lent intention to this particular failure—affected him as gathered into a large loose bundle and thrown, in her words, into his face. The missile made him to that extent catch his breath; which however he presently recovered. "Why when a woman's at once so charming and so beneficent—"

"You can sacrifice mothers and sisters to her without a blush and can make them cross the ocean on purpose to feel the more and take from you the straighter, HOW you do it?"

Yes, she had taken him up as short and as sharply as that, but he tried not to flounder in her grasp. "I don't think there's anything I've done in any such calculated way as you describe. Everything has come as a sort of indistinguishable part of everything else. Your coming out belonged closely to my having come before you, and my having come was a result of our general state of mind. Our general state of mind had proceeded, on its side, from our queer ignorance, our queer misconceptions and confusions—from which, since then, an inexorable tide of light seems to have floated us into our perhaps still queerer knowledge. Don't you LIKE your brother as he is," he went on, "and haven't you given your mother an intelligible account of all that that comes to?"

It put to her also, doubtless, his own tone, too many things, this at least would have been the case hadn't his final challenge directly helped her. Everything, at the stage they had reached, directly helped her, because everything betrayed in him such a basis of intention. He saw—the odd way things came out!—that he would have been held less monstrous had he only been a little wilder. What exposed him was just his poor old trick of quiet inwardness, what exposed him was his THINKING such offence. He hadn't in the least however the desire to irritate that Sarah imputed to him, and he could only at last temporise, for the moment, with her indignant view. She was altogether more inflamed than he had expected, and he would probably understand this better when he should learn what had occurred for her with Chad. Till then her view of his particular blackness, her clear surprise at his not clutching the pole she held out, must pass as extravagant. "I leave you to flatter yourself," she returned, "that what you speak of is what YOU'VE beautifully done. When a thing has been already described in such a lovely way—!" But she caught herself up, and her comment on his description rang out sufficiently loud. "Do you consider her even an apology for a decent woman?"

Ah there it was at last! She put the matter more crudely than, for his own mixed purposes, he had yet had to do; but essentially it was all one matter. It was so much—so much; and she treated it, poor lady, as so little. He grew conscious, as he was now apt to do, of a strange smile, and the next moment he found himself talking like Miss Barrace. "She has struck me from the first as wonderful. I've been thinking too moreover that, after all, she would probably have represented even for yourself something rather new and rather good."

He was to have given Mrs. Pocock with this, however, but her best opportunity for a sound of derision. "Rather new? I hope so with all my heart!"

"I mean," he explained, "that she might have affected you by her exquisite amiability—a real revelation, it has seemed to myself; her high rarity, her distinction of every sort."

He had been, with these words, consciously a little "precious"; but he had had to be—he couldn't give her the truth of the case without them; and it seemed to him moreover now that he didn't care. He had at all events not served his cause, for she sprang at its exposed side. "A 'revelation'—to ME: I've come to such a woman for a revelation? You talk to me about 'distinction'—YOU, you who've had your privilege?—when the most distinguished woman we shall either of us have seen in this world sits there insulted, in her loneliness, by your incredible comparison!"

Strether forbore, with an effort, from straying; but he looked all about him. "Does your mother herself make the point that she sits insulted?"

Sarah's answer came so straight, so "pat," as might have been said, that he felt on the instant its origin. "She has confided to my judgement and my tenderness the expression of her personal sense of everything, and the assertion of her personal dignity."

They were the very words of the lady of Woollett—he would have known them in a thousand; her parting charge to her child. Mrs. Pocock accordingly spoke to this extent by book, and the fact immensely moved him. "If she does really feel as you say it's of course very very dreadful. I've given sufficient proof, one would have thought," he added, "of my deep admiration for Mrs. Newsome."

"And pray what proof would one have thought you'd CALL sufficient? That of thinking this person here so far superior to her?"

He wondered again; he waited. "Ah dear Sarah, you must LEAVE me this person here!"

In his desire to avoid all vulgar retorts, to show how, even perversely, he clung to his rag of reason, he had softly almost wailed this plea. Yet he knew it to be perhaps the most positive declaration he had ever made in his life, and his visitor's reception of it virtually gave it that importance. "That's exactly what I'm delighted to do. God knows WE don't want her! You take good care not to meet," she observed in a still higher key, "my question about their life. If you do consider it a thing one can even SPEAK of, I congratulate you on your taste!"

The life she alluded to was of course Chad's and Madame de Vionnet's, which she thus bracketed together in a way that made him wince a little; there being nothing for him but to take home her full intention. It was none the less his inconsequence that while he had himself been enjoying for weeks the view of the brilliant woman's specific action, he just suffered from any characterisation of it by other lips. "I think tremendously well of her, at the same time that I seem to feel her 'life' to be really none of my business. It's my business, that is, only so far as Chad's own life is affected by it; and what has happened, don't you see? is that Chad's has been affected so beautifully. The proof of the pudding's in the eating"—he tried, with no great success, to help it out with a touch of pleasantry, while she let him go on as if to sink and sink. He went on however well enough, as well as he could do without fresh counsel; he indeed shouldn't stand quite firm, he felt, till he should have re-established his communications with Chad. Still, he could always speak for the woman he had so definitely promised to "save." This wasn't quite for her the air of salvation; but as that chill fairly deepened what did it become but a reminder that one might at the worst perish WITH her? And it was simple enough—it was rudimentary: not, not to give her away. "I find in her more merits than you would probably have patience with my counting over. And do you know," he enquired, "the effect you produce on me by alluding to her in such terms? It's as if you had some motive in not recognising all she has done for your brother, and so shut your eyes to each side of the matter, in order, whichever side comes up, to get rid of the other. I don't, you must allow me to say, see how you can with any pretence to candour get rid of the side nearest you."

"Near me—THAT sort of thing?" And Sarah gave a jerk back of her head that well might have nullified any active proximity.

It kept her friend himself at his distance, and he respected for a moment the interval. Then with a last persuasive effort he bridged it. "You don't, on your honour, appreciate Chad's fortunate development?"

"Fortunate?" she echoed again. And indeed she was prepared. "I call it hideous."

Her departure had been for some minutes marked as imminent, and she was already at the door that stood open to the court, from the threshold of which she delivered herself of this judgement. It rang out so loud as to produce for the time the hush of everything else. Strether quite, as an effect of it, breathed less bravely; he could acknowledge it, but simply enough. "Oh if you think THAT—!"

"Then all's at an end? So much the better. I do think that!" She passed out as she spoke and took her way straight across the court, beyond which, separated from them by the deep arch of the porte-cochere the low victoria that had conveyed her from her own hotel was drawn up. She made for it with decision, and the manner of her break, the sharp shaft of her rejoinder, had an intensity by which Strether was at first kept in arrest. She had let fly at him as from a stretched cord, and it took him a minute to recover from the sense of being pierced. It was not the penetration of surprise; it was that, much more, of certainty; his case being put for him as he had as yet only put it to himself. She was away at any rate; she had distanced him—with rather a grand spring, an effect of pride and ease, after all; she had got into her carriage before he could overtake her, and the vehicle was already in motion. He stopped halfway; he stood there in the court only seeing her go and noting that she gave him no other look. The way he had put it to himself was that all quite MIGHT be at an end. Each of her movements, in this resolute rupture, reaffirmed, re-enforced that idea. Sarah passed out of sight in the sunny street while, planted there in the centre of the comparatively grey court, he continued merely to look before him. It probably WAS all at an end.

Book Eleventh

I

He went late that evening to the Boulevard Malesherbes, having his impression that it would be vain to go early, and having also, more than once in the course of the day, made enquiries of the concierge. Chad hadn't come in and had left no intimation; he had affairs, apparently, at this juncture—as it occurred to Strether he so well might have—that kept him long abroad. Our friend asked once for him at the hotel in the Rue de Rivoli, but the only contribution offered there was the fact that every one was out. It was with the idea that he would have to come home to sleep that Strether went up to his rooms, from which however he was still absent, though, from the balcony, a few moments later, his visitor heard eleven o'clock strike. Chad's servant had by this time answered for his reappearance; he HAD, the visitor learned, come quickly in to dress for dinner and vanish again. Strether spent an hour in waiting for him—an hour full of strange suggestions, persuasions, recognitions; one of those that he was to recall, at the end of his adventure, as the particular handful that most had counted. The mellowest lamplight and the easiest chair had been placed at his disposal by Baptiste, subtlest of servants; the novel half-uncut, the novel lemon-coloured and tender, with the ivory knife athwart it like the dagger in a contadina's hair, had been pushed within the soft circle—a circle which, for some reason, affected Strether as softer still after the same Baptiste had remarked that in the absence of a further need of anything by Monsieur he would betake himself to bed. The night was hot and heavy and the single lamp sufficient; the great flare of the lighted city, rising high, spending itself afar, played up from the Boulevard and, through the vague vista of the successive rooms, brought objects into view and added to their dignity. Strether found himself in possession as he never yet had been; he had been there alone, had turned over books and prints, had invoked, in Chad's absence, the spirit of the place, but never at the witching hour and never with a relish quite so like a pang.

He spent a long time on the balcony; he hung over it as he had seen little Bilham hang the day of his first approach, as he had seen Mamie hang over her own the day little Bilham himself might have seen her from below; he passed back into the rooms, the three that occupied the front and that communicated by wide doors; and, while he circulated and rested, tried to recover the impression that they had made on him three months before, to catch again the voice in which they had seemed then to speak to him. That voice, he had to note, failed audibly to sound; which he took as the proof of all the change in himself. He had heard, of old, only what he COULD then hear; what he could do now was to think of three months ago as a point in the far past. All voices had grown thicker and meant more things; they crowded on him as he moved about—it was the way they sounded together that wouldn't let him be still. He felt, strangely, as sad as if he had come for some wrong, and yet as excited as if he had come for some freedom. But the freedom was what was most in the place and the hour, it was the freedom that most brought him round again to the youth of his own that he had long ago missed. He could have explained little enough to-day either why he had missed it or why, after years and years, he should care that he had; the main truth of the actual appeal of everything was none the less that everything represented the substance of his loss put it within reach, within touch, made it, to a degree it had never been, an affair of the senses. That was what it became for him at this singular time, the youth he had long ago missed—a queer concrete presence, full of mystery, yet full of reality, which he could handle, taste, smell, the deep breathing of which he could positively hear. It was in the outside air as well as within; it was in the long watch, from the balcony, in the summer night, of the wide late life of Paris, the unceasing soft quick rumble, below, of the little lighted carriages that, in the press, always suggested the gamblers he had seen of old at Monte Carlo pushing up to the tables. This image was before him when he at last became aware that Chad was behind.

"She tells me you put it all on ME"—he had arrived after this promptly enough at that information; which expressed the case however quite as the young man appeared willing for the moment to leave it. Other things, with this advantage of their virtually having the night before them, came up for them, and had, as well, the odd effect of making the occasion, instead of hurried and feverish, one of the largest, loosest and easiest to which Strether's whole adventure was to have treated him. He had been pursuing Chad from an early hour and had overtaken him only now; but now the delay was repaired by their being so exceptionally confronted. They had foregathered enough of course in all the various times; they had again and again, since that first night at the theatre, been face to face over their question; but they had never been so alone together as they were actually alone—their talk hadn't yet been so supremely for themselves. And if many things moreover passed before them, none passed more distinctly for Strether than that striking truth about Chad of which he had been so often moved to take note: the truth that everything came happily back with him to his knowing how to live. It had been seated in his pleased smile—a smile that pleased exactly in the right degree—as his visitor turned round, on the balcony, to greet his advent; his visitor in fact felt on the spot that there was nothing their meeting would so much do as bear witness to that facility. He surrendered himself accordingly to so approved a gift; for what was the meaning of the facility but that others DID surrender themselves? He didn't want, luckily, to prevent Chad from living; but he was quite aware that even if he had he would himself have thoroughly gone to pieces. It was in truth essentially by bringing down his personal life to a function all subsidiary to the young man's own that he held together. And the great point, above all, the sign of how completely Chad possessed the knowledge in question, was that one thus became, not only with a proper cheerfulness, but with wild native impulses, the feeder of his stream. Their talk had accordingly not lasted three minutes without Strether's feeling basis enough for the excitement in which he had waited. This overflow fairly deepened, wastefully abounded, as he observed the smallness of anything corresponding to it on the part of his friend. That was exactly this friend's happy case; he "put out" his excitement, or whatever other emotion the matter involved, as he put out his washing; than which no arrangement could make more for domestic order. It was quite for Strether himself in short to feel a personal analogy with the laundress bringing home the triumphs of the mangle.

When he had reported on Sarah's visit, which he did very fully, Chad answered his question with perfect candour. "I positively referred her to you—told her she must absolutely see you. This was last night, and it all took place in ten minutes. It was our first free talk—really the first time she had tackled me. She knew I also knew what her line had been with yourself; knew moreover how little you had been doing to make anything difficult for her. So I spoke for you frankly—assured her you were all at her service. I assured her I was too," the young man continued; "and I pointed out how she could perfectly, at any time, have got at me. Her difficulty has been simply her not finding the moment she fancied."

"Her difficulty," Strether returned, "has been simply that she finds she's afraid of you. She's not afraid of ME, Sarah, one little scrap; and it was just because she has seen how I can fidget when I give my mind to it that she has felt her best chance, rightly enough to be in making me as uneasy as possible. I think she's at bottom as pleased to HAVE you put it on me as you yourself can possibly be to put it."

"But what in the world, my dear man," Chad enquired in objection to this luminosity, "have I done to make Sally afraid?"

"You've been 'wonderful, wonderful,' as we say—we poor people who watch the play from the pit; and that's what has, admirably, made her. Made her all the more effectually that she could see you didn't set about it on purpose—I mean set about affecting her as with fear."

Chad cast a pleasant backward glance over his possibilities of motive. "I've only wanted to be kind and friendly, to be decent and attentive—and I still only want to be."

Strether smiled at his comfortable clearness. "Well, there can certainly be no way for it better than by my taking the onus. It reduces your personal friction and your personal offence to almost nothing."

Ah but Chad, with his completer conception of the friendly, wouldn't quite have this! They had remained on the balcony, where, after their day of great and premature heat, the midnight air was delicious; and they leaned back in turn against the balustrade, all in harmony with the chairs and the flower-pots, the cigarettes and the starlight. "The onus isn't REALLY yours—after our agreeing so to wait together and judge together. That was all my answer to Sally," Chad pursued—"that we have been, that we are, just judging together."

"I'm not afraid of the burden," Strether explained; "I haven't come in the least that you should take it off me. I've come very much, it seems to me, to double up my fore legs in the manner of the camel when he gets down on his knees to make his back convenient. But I've supposed you all this while to have been doing a lot of special and private judging—about which I haven't troubled you; and I've only wished to have your conclusion first from you. I don't ask more than that; I'm quite ready to take it as it has come."

Chad turned up his face to the sky with a slow puff of his smoke. "Well, I've seen."

Strether waited a little. "I've left you wholly alone; haven't, I think I may say, since the first hour or two—when I merely preached patience—so much as breathed on you."

"Oh you've been awfully good!"

"We've both been good then—we've played the game. We've given them the most liberal conditions."

"Ah," said Chad, "splendid conditions! It was open to them, open to them"—he seemed to make it out, as he smoked, with his eyes still on the stars. He might in quiet sport have been reading their horoscope. Strether wondered meanwhile what had been open to them, and he finally let him have it. "It was open to them simply to let me alone; to have made up their minds, on really seeing me for themselves, that I could go on well enough as I was."

Strether assented to this proposition with full lucidity, his companion's plural pronoun, which stood all for Mrs. Newsome and her daughter, having no ambiguity for him. There was nothing, apparently, to stand for Mamie and Jim; and this added to our friend's sense of Chad's knowing what he thought. "But they've made up their minds to the opposite—that you CAN'T go on as you are."

"No," Chad continued in the same way; "they won't have it for a minute."

Strether on his side also reflectively smoked. It was as if their high place really represented some moral elevation from which they could look down on their recent past. "There never was the smallest chance, do you know, that they WOULD have it for a moment."

"Of course not—no real chance. But if they were willing to think there was—!"

"They weren't willing." Strether had worked it all out. "It wasn't for you they came out, but for me. It wasn't to see for themselves what you're doing, but what I'm doing. The first branch of their curiosity was inevitably destined, under my culpable delay, to give way to the second; and it's on the second that, if I may use the expression and you don't mind my marking the invidious fact, they've been of late exclusively perched. When Sarah sailed it was me, in other words, they were after."

Chad took it in both with intelligence and with indulgence. "It IS rather a business then—what I've let you in for!"

Strether had again a brief pause; which ended in a reply that seemed to dispose once for all of this element of compunction. Chad was to treat it, at any rate, so far as they were again together, as having done so. "I was 'in' when you found me."

"Ah but it was you," the young man laughed, "who found ME."

"I only found you out. It was you who found me in. It was all in the day's work for them, at all events, that they should come. And they've greatly enjoyed it," Strether declared.

"Well, I've tried to make them," said Chad.

His companion did himself presently the same justice. "So have I. I tried even this very morning—while Mrs. Pocock was with me. She enjoys for instance, almost as much as anything else, not being, as I've said, afraid of me; and I think I gave her help in that."

Chad took a deeper interest. "Was she very very nasty?"

Strether debated. "Well, she was the most important thing—she was definite. She was—at last—crystalline. And I felt no remorse. I saw that they must have come."

"Oh I wanted to see them for myself; so that if it were only for THAT—!" Chad's own remorse was as small.

This appeared almost all Strether wanted. "Isn't your having seen them for yourself then THE thing, beyond all others, that has come of their visit?"

Chad looked as if he thought it nice of his old friend to put it so. "Don't you count it as anything that you're dished—if you ARE dished? Are you, my dear man, dished?"

It sounded as if he were asking if he had caught cold or hurt his foot, and Strether for a minute but smoked and smoked. "I want to see her again. I must see her."

"Of course you must." Then Chad hesitated. "Do you mean—a—Mother herself?"

"Oh your mother—that will depend."

It was as if Mrs. Newsome had somehow been placed by the words very far off. Chad however endeavoured in spite of this to reach the place. "What do you mean it will depend on?"

Strether, for all answer, gave him a longish look. "I was speaking of Sarah. I must positively—though she quite cast me off—see HER again. I can't part with her that way."

"Then she was awfully unpleasant?"

Again Strether exhaled. "She was what she had to be. I mean that from the moment they're not delighted they can only be—well what I admit she was. We gave them," he went on, "their chance to be delighted, and they've walked up to it, and looked all round it, and not taken it."

"You can bring a horse to water—!" Chad suggested.

"Precisely. And the tune to which this morning Sarah wasn't delighted—the tune to which, to adopt your metaphor, she refused to drink—leaves us on that side nothing more to hope."

Chad had a pause, and then as if consolingly: "It was never of course really the least on the cards that they would be 'delighted.'"

"Well, I don't know, after all," Strether mused. "I've had to come as far round. However"—he shook it off—"it's doubtless MY performance that's absurd."

"There are certainly moments," said Chad, "when you seem to me too good to be true. Yet if you are true," he added, "that seems to be all that need concern me."

"I'm true, but I'm incredible. I'm fantastic and ridiculous—I don't explain myself even TO myself. How can they then," Strether asked, "understand me? So I don't quarrel with them."

"I see. They quarrel," said Chad rather comfortably, "with US." Strether noted once more the comfort, but his young friend had already gone on. "I should feel greatly ashamed, all the same, if I didn't put it before you again that you ought to think, after all, tremendously well. I mean before giving up beyond recall—" With which insistence, as from a certain delicacy, dropped.

Ah but Strether wanted it. "Say it all, say it all."

"Well, at your age, and with what—when all's said and done—Mother might do for you and be for you."

Chad had said it all, from his natural scruple, only to that extent; so that Strether after an instant himself took a hand. "My absence of an assured future. The little I have to show toward the power to take care of myself. The way, the wonderful way, she would certainly take care of me. Her fortune, her kindness, and the constant miracle of her having been disposed to go even so far. Of course, of course"—he summed it up. "There are those sharp facts."

Chad had meanwhile thought of another still. "And don't you really care—?"

His friend slowly turned round to him. "Will you go?"

"I'll go if you'll say you now consider I should. You know," he went on, "I was ready six weeks ago."

"Ah," said Strether, "that was when you didn't know I wasn't! You're ready at present because you do know it."

"That may be," Chad returned; "but all the same I'm sincere. You talk about taking the whole thing on your shoulders, but in what light do you regard me that you think me capable of letting you pay?" Strether patted his arm, as they stood together against the parapet, reassuringly—seeming to wish to contend that he HAD the wherewithal; but it was again round this question of purchase and price that the young man's sense of fairness continued to hover. "What it literally comes to for you, if you'll pardon my putting it so, is that you give up money. Possibly a good deal of money."

"Oh," Strether laughed, "if it were only just enough you'd still be justified in putting it so! But I've on my side to remind you too that YOU give up money; and more than 'possibly'—quite certainly, as I should suppose—a good deal."

"True enough; but I've got a certain quantity," Chad returned after a moment. "Whereas you, my dear man, you—"

"I can't be at all said"—Strether took him up—"to have a 'quantity' certain or uncertain? Very true. Still, I shan't starve."

"Oh you mustn't STARVE!" Chad pacifically emphasised; and so, in the pleasant conditions, they continued to talk; though there was, for that matter, a pause in which the younger companion might have been taken as weighing again the delicacy of his then and there promising the elder some provision against the possibility just mentioned. This, however, he presumably thought best not to do, for at the end of another minute they had moved in quite a different direction. Strether had broken in by returning to the subject of Chad's passage with Sarah and enquiring if they had arrived, in the event, at anything in the nature of a "scene." To this Chad replied that they had on the contrary kept tremendously polite; adding moreover that Sally was after all not the woman to have made the mistake of not being. "Her hands are a good deal tied, you see. I got so, from the first," he sagaciously observed, "the start of her."

"You mean she has taken so much from you?"

"Well, I couldn't of course in common decency give less: only she hadn't expected, I think, that I'd give her nearly so much. And she began to take it before she knew it."

"And she began to like it," said Strether, "as soon as she began to take it!"

"Yes, she has liked it—also more than she expected." After which Chad observed: "But she doesn't like ME. In fact she hates me."

Strether's interest grew. "Then why does she want you at home?"

"Because when you hate you want to triumph, and if she should get me neatly stuck there she WOULD triumph."

Strether followed afresh, but looking as he went. "Certainly—in a manner. But it would scarce be a triumph worth having if, once entangled, feeling her dislike and possibly conscious in time of a certain quantity of your own, you should on the spot make yourself unpleasant to her."

"Ah," said Chad, "she can bear ME—could bear me at least at home. It's my being there that would be her triumph. She hates me in Paris."

"She hates in other words—"

"Yes, THAT'S it!"—Chad had quickly understood this understanding; which formed on the part of each as near an approach as they had yet made to naming Madame de Vionnet. The limitations of their distinctness didn't, however, prevent its fairly lingering in the air that it was this lady Mrs. Pocock hated. It added one more touch moreover to their established recognition of the rare intimacy of Chad's association with her. He had never yet more twitched away the last light veil from this phenomenon than in presenting himself as confounded and submerged in the feeling she had created at Woollett. "And I'll tell you who hates me too," he immediately went on.

Strether knew as immediately whom he meant, but with as prompt a protest. "Ah no! Mamie doesn't hate—well," he caught himself in time—"anybody at all. Mamie's beautiful."

Chad shook his head. "That's just why I mind it. She certainly doesn't like me."

"How much do you mind it? What would you do for her?"

"Well, I'd like her if she'd like me. Really, really," Chad declared.

It gave his companion a moment's pause. "You asked me just now if I don't, as you said, 'care' about a certain person. You rather tempt me therefore to put the question in my turn. Don't YOU care about a certain other person?"

Chad looked at him hard in the lamplight of the window. "The difference is that I don't want to."

Strether wondered. "'Don't want' to?"

"I try not to—that is I HAVE tried. I've done my best. You can't be surprised," the young man easily went on, "when you yourself set me on it. I was indeed," he added, "already on it a little; but you set me harder. It was six weeks ago that I thought I had come out."

Strether took it well in. "But you haven't come out!"

"I don't know—it's what I WANT to know," said Chad. "And if I could have sufficiently wanted—by myself—to go back, I think I might have found out."

"Possibly"—Strether considered. "But all you were able to achieve was to want to want to! And even then," he pursued, "only till our friends there came. Do you want to want to still?" As with a sound half-dolorous, half-droll and all vague and equivocal, Chad buried his face for a little in his hands, rubbing it in a whimsical way that amounted to an evasion, he brought it out more sharply: "DO you?"

Chad kept for a time his attitude, but at last he looked up, and then abruptly, "Jim IS a damned dose!" he declared.

"Oh I don't ask you to abuse or describe or in any way pronounce on your relatives; I simply put it to you once more whether you're NOW ready. You say you've 'seen.' Is what you've seen that you can't resist?"

Chad gave him a strange smile—the nearest approach he had ever shown to a troubled one. "Can't you make me NOT resist?"

"What it comes to," Strether went on very gravely now and as if he hadn't heard him, "what it comes to is that more has been done for you, I think, than I've ever seen done—attempted perhaps, but never so successfully done—by one human being for another."

"Oh an immense deal certainly"—Chad did it full justice. "And you yourself are adding to it."

It was without heeding this either that his visitor continued. "And our friends there won't have it."

"No, they simply won't."

"They demand you on the basis, as it were, of repudiation and ingratitude; and what has been the matter with me," Strether went on, "is that I haven't seen my way to working with you for repudiation."

Chad appreciated this. "Then as you haven't seen yours you naturally haven't seen mine. There it is." After which he proceeded, with a certain abruptness, to a sharp interrogation. "NOW do you say she doesn't hate me?"

Strether hesitated. "'She'—?"

"Yes—Mother. We called it Sarah, but it comes to the same thing."

"Ah," Strether objected, "not to the same thing as her hating YOU."

On which—though as if for an instant it had hung fire—Chad remarkably replied: "Well, if they hate my good friend, THAT comes to the same thing." It had a note of inevitable truth that made Strether take it as enough, feel he wanted nothing more. The young man spoke in it for his "good friend" more than he had ever yet directly spoken, confessed to such deep identities between them as he might play with the idea of working free from, but which at a given moment could still draw him down like a whirlpool. And meanwhile he had gone on. "Their hating you too moreover—that also comes to a good deal."

"Ah," said Strether, "your mother doesn't."

Chad, however, loyally stuck to it—loyally, that is, to Strether. "She will if you don't look out."

"Well, I do look out. I am, after all, looking out. That's just why," our friend explained, "I want to see her again."

It drew from Chad again the same question. "To see Mother?"

"To see—for the present—Sarah."

"Ah then there you are! And what I don't for the life of me make out," Chad pursued with resigned perplexity, "is what you GAIN by it."

Oh it would have taken his companion too long to say! "That's because you have, I verily believe, no imagination. You've other qualities. But no imagination, don't you see? at all."

"I dare say. I do see." It was an idea in which Chad showed interest. "But haven't you yourself rather too much?"

"Oh RATHER—!" So that after an instant, under this reproach and as if it were at last a fact really to escape from, Strether made his move for departure.

II

One of the features of the restless afternoon passed by him after Mrs. Pocock's visit was an hour spent, shortly before dinner, with Maria Gostrey, whom of late, in spite of so sustained a call on his attention from other quarters, he had by no means neglected. And that he was still not neglecting her will appear from the fact that he was with her again at the same hour on the very morrow—with no less fine a consciousness moreover of being able to hold her ear. It continued inveterately to occur, for that matter, that whenever he had taken one of his greater turns he came back to where she so faithfully awaited him. None of these excursions had on the whole been livelier than the pair of incidents—the fruit of the short interval since his previous visit—on which he had now to report to her. He had seen Chad Newsome late the night before, and he had had that morning, as a sequel to this conversation, a second interview with Sarah. "But they're all off," he said, "at last."

It puzzled her a moment. "All?—Mr. Newsome with them?"

"Ah not yet! Sarah and Jim and Mamie. But Waymarsh with them—for Sarah. It's too beautiful," Strether continued; "I find I don't get over that—it's always a fresh joy. But it's a fresh joy too," he added, "that—well, what do you think? Little Bilham also goes. But he of course goes for Mamie."

Miss Gostrey wondered. "'For' her? Do you mean they're already engaged?"

"Well," said Strether, "say then for ME. He'll do anything for me; just as I will, for that matter—anything I can—for him. Or for Mamie either. SHE'LL do anything for me."

Miss Gostrey gave a comprehensive sigh. "The way you reduce people to subjection!"

"It's certainly, on one side, wonderful. But it's quite equalled, on another, by the way I don't. I haven't reduced Sarah, since yesterday; though I've succeeded in seeing her again, as I'll presently tell you. The others however are really all right. Mamie, by that blessed law of ours, absolutely must have a young man."

"But what must poor Mr. Bilham have? Do you mean they'll MARRY for you?"

"I mean that, by the same blessed law, it won't matter a grain if they don't—I shan't have in the least to worry."

She saw as usual what he meant. "And Mr. Jim?—who goes for him?"

"Oh," Strether had to admit, "I couldn't manage THAT. He's thrown, as usual, on the world; the world which, after all, by his account—for he has prodigious adventures—seems very good to him. He fortunately—'over here,' as he says—finds the world everywhere; and his most prodigious adventure of all," he went on, "has been of course of the last few days."

Miss Gostrey, already knowing, instantly made the connexion. "He has seen Marie de Vionnet again?"

"He went, all by himself, the day after Chad's party—didn't I tell you?—to tea with her. By her invitation—all alone."

"Quite like yourself!" Maria smiled.

"Oh but he's more wonderful about her than I am!" And then as his friend showed how she could believe it, filling it out, fitting it on to old memories of the wonderful woman: "What I should have liked to manage would have been HER going."

"To Switzerland with the party?"

"For Jim—and for symmetry. If it had been workable moreover for a fortnight she'd have gone. She's ready"—he followed up his renewed vision of her—"for anything."

Miss Gostrey went with him a minute. "She's too perfect!"

"She WILL, I think," he pursued, "go to-night to the station."

"To see him off?"

"With Chad—marvellously—as part of their general attention. And she does it"—it kept before him—"with a light, light grace, a free, free gaiety, that may well softly bewilder Mr. Pocock."

It kept her so before him that his companion had after an instant a friendly comment. "As in short it has softly bewildered a saner man. Are you really in love with her?" Maria threw off.

"It's of no importance I should know," he replied. "It matters so little—has nothing to do, practically, with either of us."

"All the same"—Maria continued to smile—"they go, the five, as I understand you, and you and Madame de Vionnet stay."

"Oh and Chad." To which Strether added: "And you."

"Ah 'me'!"—she gave a small impatient wail again, in which something of the unreconciled seemed suddenly to break out. "I don't stay, it somehow seems to me, much to my advantage. In the presence of all you cause to pass before me I've a tremendous sense of privation."

Strether hesitated. "But your privation, your keeping out of everything, has been—hasn't it?—by your own choice."

"Oh yes; it has been necessary—that is it has been better for you. What I mean is only that I seem to have ceased to serve you."

"How can you tell that?" he asked. "You don't know how you serve me. When you cease—"

"Well?" she said as he dropped.

"Well, I'll LET you know. Be quiet till then."

She thought a moment. "Then you positively like me to stay?"

"Don't I treat you as if I did?"

"You're certainly very kind to me. But that," said Maria, "is for myself. It's getting late, as you see, and Paris turning rather hot and dusty. People are scattering, and some of them, in other places want me. But if you want me here—!"

She had spoken as resigned to his word, but he had of a sudden a still sharper sense than he would have expected of desiring not to lose her. "I want you here."

She took it as if the words were all she had wished; as if they brought her, gave her something that was the compensation of her case. "Thank you," she simply answered. And then as he looked at her a little harder, "Thank you very much," she repeated.

It had broken as with a slight arrest into the current of their talk, and it held him a moment longer. "Why, two months, or whatever the time was, ago, did you so suddenly dash off? The reason you afterwards gave me for having kept away three weeks wasn't the real one."

She recalled. "I never supposed you believed it was. Yet," she continued, "if you didn't guess it that was just what helped you."

He looked away from her on this; he indulged, so far as space permitted, in one of his slow absences. "I've often thought of it, but never to feel that I could guess it. And you see the consideration with which I've treated you in never asking till now."

"Now then why DO you ask?"

"To show you how I miss you when you're not here, and what it does for me."

"It doesn't seem to have done," she laughed, "all it might! However," she added, "if you've really never guessed the truth I'll tell it you."

"I've never guessed it," Strether declared.

"Never?"

"Never."

"Well then I dashed off, as you say, so as not to have the confusion of being there if Marie de Vionnet should tell you anything to my detriment."

He looked as if he considerably doubted. "You even then would have had to face it on your return."

"Oh if I had found reason to believe it something very bad I'd have left you altogether."

"So then," he continued, "it was only on guessing she had been on the whole merciful that you ventured back?"

Maria kept it together. "I owe her thanks. Whatever her temptation she didn't separate us. That's one of my reasons," she went on "for admiring her so."

"Let it pass then," said Strether, "for one of mine as well. But what would have been her temptation?"

"What are ever the temptations of women?"

He thought—but hadn't, naturally, to think too long. "Men?"

"She would have had you, with it, more for herself. But she saw she could have you without it."

"Oh 'have' me!" Strether a trifle ambiguously sighed. "YOU," he handsomely declared, "would have had me at any rate WITH it."

"Oh 'have' you!"—she echoed it as he had done. "I do have you, however," she less ironically said, "from the moment you express a wish."

He stopped before her, full of the disposition. "I'll express fifty."

Which indeed begot in her, with a certain inconsequence, a return of her small wail. "Ah there you are!"

There, if it were so, he continued for the rest of the time to be, and it was as if to show her how she could still serve him that, coming back to the departure of the Pococks, he gave her the view, vivid with a hundred more touches than we can reproduce, of what had happened for him that morning. He had had ten minutes with Sarah at her hotel, ten minutes reconquered, by irresistible pressure, from the time over which he had already described her to Miss Gostrey as having, at the end of their interview on his own premises, passed the great sponge of the future. He had caught her by not announcing himself, had found her in her sitting-room with a dressmaker and a lingere whose accounts she appeared to have been more or less ingenuously settling and who soon withdrew. Then he had explained to her how he had succeeded, late the night before, in keeping his promise of seeing Chad. "I told her I'd take it all."

"You'd 'take' it?"

"Why if he doesn't go."

Maria waited. "And who takes it if he does?" she enquired with a certain grimness of gaiety.

"Well," said Strether, "I think I take, in any event, everything."

"By which I suppose you mean," his companion brought out after a moment, "that you definitely understand you now lose everything."

He stood before her again. "It does come perhaps to the same thing. But Chad, now that he has seen, doesn't really want it."

She could believe that, but she made, as always, for clearness. "Still, what, after all, HAS he seen?"

"What they want of him. And it's enough."

"It contrasts so unfavourably with what Madame de Vionnet wants?"

"It contrasts—just so; all round, and tremendously."

"Therefore, perhaps, most of all with what YOU want?"

"Oh," said Strether, "what I want is a thing I've ceased to measure or even to understand."

But his friend none the less went on. "Do you want Mrs. Newsome—after such a way of treating you?"

It was a straighter mode of dealing with this lady than they had as yet—such was their high form—permitted themselves; but it seemed not wholly for this that he delayed a moment. "I dare say it has been, after all, the only way she could have imagined."

"And does that make you want her any more?"

"I've tremendously disappointed her," Strether thought it worth while to mention.

"Of course you have. That's rudimentary; that was plain to us long ago. But isn't it almost as plain," Maria went on, "that you've even yet your straight remedy? Really drag him away, as I believe you still can, and you'd cease to have to count with her disappointment."

"Ah then," he laughed, "I should have to count with yours!"

But this barely struck her now. "What, in that case, should you call counting? You haven't come out where you are, I think, to please ME."

"Oh," he insisted, "that too, you know, has been part of it. I can't separate—it's all one; and that's perhaps why, as I say, I don't understand." But he was ready to declare again that this didn't in the least matter; all the more that, as he affirmed, he HADn't really as yet "come out." "She gives me after all, on its coming to the pinch, a last mercy, another chance. They don't sail, you see, for five or six weeks more, and they haven't—she admits that—expected Chad would take part in their tour. It's still open to him to join them, at the last, at Liverpool."

Miss Gostrey considered. "How in the world is it 'open' unless you open it? How can he join them at Liverpool if he but sinks deeper into his situation here?"

"He has given her—as I explained to you that she let me know yesterday—his word of honour to do as I say."

Maria stared. "But if you say nothing!"

Well, he as usual walked about on it. "I did say something this morning. I gave her my answer—the word I had promised her after hearing from himself what HE had promised. What she demanded of me yesterday, you'll remember, was the engagement then and there to make him take up this vow."

"Well then," Miss Gostrey enquired, "was the purpose of your visit to her only to decline?"

"No; it was to ask, odd as that may seem to you, for another delay."

"Ah that's weak!"

"Precisely!" She had spoken with impatience, but, so far as that at least, he knew where he was. "If I AM weak I want to find it out. If I don't find it out I shall have the comfort, the little glory, of thinking I'm strong."

"It's all the comfort, I judge," she returned, "that you WILL have!"

"At any rate," he said, "it will have been a month more. Paris may grow, from day to day, hot and dusty, as you say; but there are other things that are hotter and dustier. I'm not afraid to stay on; the summer here must be amusing in a wild—if it isn't a tame—way of its own; the place at no time more picturesque. I think I shall like it. And then," he benevolently smiled for her, "there will be always you."

"Oh," she objected, "it won't be as a part of the picturesqueness that I shall stay, for I shall be the plainest thing about you. You may, you see, at any rate," she pursued, "have nobody else. Madame de Vionnet may very well be going off, mayn't she?—and Mr. Newsome by the same stroke: unless indeed you've had an assurance from them to the contrary. So that if your idea's to stay for them"—it was her duty to suggest it—"you may be left in the lurch. Of course if they do stay"—she kept it up—"they would be part of the picturesqueness. Or else indeed you might join them somewhere."

Strether seemed to face it as if it were a happy thought; but the next moment he spoke more critically. "Do you mean that they'll probably go off together?"

She just considered. "I think it will be treating you quite without ceremony if they do; though after all," she added, "it would be difficult to see now quite what degree of ceremony properly meets your case."

"Of course," Strether conceded, "my attitude toward them is extraordinary."

"Just so; so that one may ask one's self what style of proceeding on their own part can altogether match it. The attitude of their own that won't pale in its light they've doubtless still to work out. The really handsome thing perhaps," she presently threw off, "WOULD be for them to withdraw into more secluded conditions, offering at the same time to share them with you." He looked at her, on this, as if some generous irritation—all in his interest—had suddenly again flickered in her; and what she next said indeed half-explained it. "Don't really be afraid to tell me if what now holds you IS the pleasant prospect of the empty town, with plenty of seats in the shade, cool drinks, deserted museums, drives to the Bois in the evening, and our wonderful woman all to yourself." And she kept it up still more. "The handsomest thing of ALL, when one makes it out, would, I dare say, be that Mr. Chad should for a while go off by himself. It's a pity, from that point of view," she wound up, "that he doesn't pay his mother a visit. It would at least occupy your interval." The thought in fact held her a moment. "Why doesn't he pay his mother a visit? Even a week, at this good moment, would do."

"My dear lady," Strether replied—and he had it even to himself surprisingly ready—"my dear lady, his mother has paid HIM a visit. Mrs. Newsome has been with him, this month, with an intensity that I'm sure he has thoroughly felt; he has lavishly entertained her, and she has let him have her thanks. Do you suggest he shall go back for more of them?"

Well, she succeeded after a little in shaking it off. "I see. It's what you don't suggest—what you haven't suggested. And you know."

"So would you, my dear," he kindly said, "if you had so much as seen her."

"As seen Mrs. Newsome?"

"No, Sarah—which, both for Chad and for myself, has served all the purpose."

"And served it in a manner," she responsively mused, "so extraordinary!"

"Well, you see," he partly explained, "what it comes to is that she's all cold thought—which Sarah could serve to us cold without its really losing anything. So it is that we know what she thinks of us."

Maria had followed, but she had an arrest. "What I've never made out, if you come to that, is what you think—I mean you personally—of HER. Don't you so much, when all's said, as care a little?"

"That," he answered with no loss of promptness, "is what even Chad himself asked me last night. He asked me if I don't mind the loss—well, the loss of an opulent future. Which moreover," he hastened to add, "was a perfectly natural question."

"I call your attention, all the same," said Miss Gostrey, "to the fact that I don't ask it. What I venture to ask is whether it's to Mrs. Newsome herself that you're indifferent."

"I haven't been so"—he spoke with all assurance. "I've been the very opposite. I've been, from the first moment, preoccupied with the impression everything might be making on her—quite oppressed, haunted, tormented by it. I've been interested ONLY in her seeing what I've seen. And I've been as disappointed in her refusal to see it as she has been in what has appeared to her the perversity of my insistence."

"Do you mean that she has shocked you as you've shocked her?"

Strether weighed it. "I'm probably not so shockable. But on the other hand I've gone much further to meet her. She, on her side, hasn't budged an inch."

"So that you're now at last"—Maria pointed the moral—"in the sad stage of recriminations."

"No—it's only to you I speak. I've been like a lamb to Sarah. I've only put my back to the wall. It's to THAT one naturally staggers when one has been violently pushed there."

She watched him a moment. "Thrown over?"

"Well, as I feel I've landed somewhere I think I must have been thrown."

She turned it over, but as hoping to clarify much rather than to harmonise. "The thing is that I suppose you've been disappointing—"

"Quite from the very first of my arrival? I dare say. I admit I was surprising even to myself."

"And then of course," Maria went on, "I had much to do with it."

"With my being surprising—?"

"That will do," she laughed, "if you're too delicate to call it MY being! Naturally," she added, "you came over more or less for surprises."

"Naturally!"—he valued the reminder.

"But they were to have been all for you"—she continued to piece it out—"and none of them for HER."

Once more he stopped before her as if she had touched the point. "That's just her difficulty—that she doesn't admit surprises. It's a fact that, I think, describes and represents her; and it falls in with what I tell you—that she's all, as I've called it, fine cold thought. She had, to her own mind, worked the whole thing out in advance, and worked it out for me as well as for herself. Whenever she has done that, you see, there's no room left; no margin, as it were, for any alteration. She's filled as full, packed as tight, as she'll hold and if you wish to get anything more or different either out or in—"

"You've got to make over altogether the woman herself?"

"What it comes to," said Strether, "is that you've got morally and intellectually to get rid of her."

"Which would appear," Maria returned, "to be practically what you've done."

But her friend threw back his head. "I haven't touched her. She won't BE touched. I see it now as I've never done; and she hangs together with a perfection of her own," he went on, "that does suggest a kind of wrong in ANY change of her composition. It was at any rate," he wound up, "the woman herself, as you call her the whole moral and intellectual being or block, that Sarah brought me over to take or to leave."

It turned Miss Gostrey to deeper thought. "Fancy having to take at the point of the bayonet a whole moral and intellectual being or block!"

"It was in fact," said Strether, "what, at home, I HAD done. But somehow over there I didn't quite know it."

"One never does, I suppose," Miss Gostrey concurred, "realise in advance, in such a case, the size, as you may say, of the block. Little by little it looms up. It has been looming for you more and more till at last you see it all."

"I see it all," he absently echoed, while his eyes might have been fixing some particularly large iceberg in a cool blue northern sea. "It's magnificent!" he then rather oddly exclaimed.

But his friend, who was used to this kind of inconsequence in him, kept the thread. "There's nothing so magnificent—for making others feel you—as to have no imagination."

It brought him straight round. "Ah there you are! It's what I said last night to Chad. That he himself, I mean, has none."

"Then it would appear," Maria suggested, "that he has, after all, something in common with his mother."

"He has in common that he makes one, as you say, 'feel' him. And yet," he added, as if the question were interesting, "one feels others too, even when they have plenty."

Miss Gostrey continued suggestive. "Madame de Vionnet?"

"SHE has plenty."

"Certainly—she had quantities of old. But there are different ways of making one's self felt."

"Yes, it comes, no doubt, to that. You now—"

He was benevolently going on, but she wouldn't have it. "Oh I DON'T make myself felt; so my quantity needn't be settled. Yours, you know," she said, "is monstrous. No one has ever had so much."

It struck him for a moment. "That's what Chad also thinks."

"There YOU are then—though it isn't for him to complain of it!"

"Oh he doesn't complain of it," said Strether.

"That's all that would be wanting! But apropos of what," Maria went on, "did the question come up?"

"Well, of his asking me what it is I gain."

She had a pause. "Then as I've asked you too it settles my case. Oh you HAVE," she repeated, "treasures of imagination."

But he had been for an instant thinking away from this, and he came up in another place. "And yet Mrs. Newsome—it's a thing to remember—HAS imagined, did, that is, imagine, and apparently still does, horrors about what I should have found. I was booked, by her vision—extraordinarily intense, after all—to find them; and that I didn't, that I couldn't, that, as she evidently felt, I wouldn't—this evidently didn't at all, as they say, 'suit' her book. It was more than she could bear. That was her disappointment."

"You mean you were to have found Chad himself horrible?"

"I was to have found the woman."

"Horrible?"

"Found her as she imagined her." And Strether paused as if for his own expression of it he could add no touch to that picture.

His companion had meanwhile thought. "She imagined stupidly—so it comes to the same thing."

"Stupidly? Oh!" said Strether.

But she insisted. "She imagined meanly."

He had it, however, better. "It couldn't but be ignorantly."

"Well, intensity with ignorance—what do you want worse?"

This question might have held him, but he let it pass. "Sarah isn't ignorant—now; she keeps up the theory of the horrible."

"Ah but she's intense—and that by itself will do sometimes as well. If it doesn't do, in this case, at any rate, to deny that Marie's charming, it will do at least to deny that she's good."

"What I claim is that she's good for Chad."

"You don't claim"—she seemed to like it clear—"that she's good for YOU."

But he continued without heeding. "That's what I wanted them to come out for—to see for themselves if she's bad for him."

"And now that they've done so they won't admit that she's good even for anything?"

"They do think," Strether presently admitted, "that she's on the whole about as bad for me. But they're consistent of course, inasmuch as they've their clear view of what's good for both of us."

"For you, to begin with"—Maria, all responsive, confined the question for the moment—"to eliminate from your existence and if possible even from your memory the dreadful creature that I must gruesomely shadow forth for them, even more than to eliminate the distincter evil—thereby a little less portentous—of the person whose confederate you've suffered yourself to become. However, that's comparatively simple. You can easily, at the worst, after all, give me up."

"I can easily at the worst, after all, give you up." The irony was so obvious that it needed no care. "I can easily at the worst, after all, even forget you."

"Call that then workable. But Mr. Newsome has much more to forget. How can HE do it?"

"Ah there again we are! That's just what I was to have made him do; just where I was to have worked with him and helped."

She took it in silence and without attenuation—as if perhaps from very familiarity with the facts; and her thought made a connexion without showing the links. "Do you remember how we used to talk at Chester and in London about my seeing you through?" She spoke as of far-off things and as if they had spent weeks at the places she named.

"It's just what you ARE doing."

"Ah but the worst—since you've left such a margin—may be still to come. You may yet break down."

"Yes, I may yet break down. But will you take me—?"

He had hesitated, and she waited. "Take you?"

"For as long as I can bear it."

She also debated "Mr. Newsome and Madame de Vionnet may, as we were saying, leave town. How long do you think you can bear it without them?"

Strether's reply to this was at first another question. "Do you mean in order to get away from me?"

Her answer had an abruptness. "Don't find me rude if I say I should think they'd want to!"

He looked at her hard again—seemed even for an instant to have an intensity of thought under which his colour changed. But he smiled. "You mean after what they've done to me?"

"After what SHE has."

At this, however, with a laugh, he was all right again. "Ah but she hasn't done it yet!"

III

He had taken the train a few days after this from a station—as well as to a station—selected almost at random; such days, whatever should happen, were numbered, and he had gone forth under the impulse—artless enough, no doubt—to give the whole of one of them to that French ruralism, with its cool special green, into which he had hitherto looked only through the little oblong window of the picture-frame. It had been as yet for the most part but a land of fancy for him—the background of fiction, the medium of art, the nursery of letters; practically as distant as Greece, but practically also well-nigh as consecrated. Romance could weave itself, for Strether's sense, out of elements mild enough; and even after what he had, as he felt, lately "been through," he could thrill a little at the chance of seeing something somewhere that would remind him of a certain small Lambinet that had charmed him, long years before, at a Boston dealer's and that he had quite absurdly never forgotten. It had been offered, he remembered, at a price he had been instructed to believe the lowest ever named for a Lambinet, a price he had never felt so poor as on having to recognise, all the same, as beyond a dream of possibility. He had dreamed—had turned and twisted possibilities for an hour: it had been the only adventure of his life in connexion with the purchase of a work of art. The adventure, it will be perceived, was modest; but the memory, beyond all reason and by some accident of association, was sweet. The little Lambinet abode with him as the picture he WOULD have bought—the particular production that had made him for the moment overstep the modesty of nature. He was quite aware that if he were to see it again he should perhaps have a drop or a shock, and he never found himself wishing that the wheel of time would turn it up again, just as he had seen it in the maroon-coloured, sky-lighted inner shrine of Tremont Street. It would be a different thing, however, to see the remembered mixture resolved back into its elements—to assist at the restoration to nature of the whole far-away hour: the dusty day in Boston, the background of the Fitchburg Depot, of the maroon-coloured sanctum, the special-green vision, the ridiculous price, the poplars, the willows, the rushes, the river, the sunny silvery sky, the shady woody horizon.

He observed in respect to his train almost no condition save that it should stop a few times after getting out of the banlieue; he threw himself on the general amiability of the day for the hint of where to alight. His theory of his excursion was that he could alight anywhere—not nearer Paris than an hour's run—on catching a suggestion of the particular note required. It made its sign, the suggestion—weather, air, light, colour and his mood all favouring—at the end of some eighty minutes; the train pulled up just at the right spot, and he found himself getting out as securely as if to keep an appointment. It will be felt of him that he could amuse himself, at his age, with very small things if it be again noted that his appointment was only with a superseded Boston fashion. He hadn't gone far without the quick confidence that it would be quite sufficiently kept. The oblong gilt frame disposed its enclosing lines; the poplars and willows, the reeds and river—a river of which he didn't know, and didn't want to know, the name—fell into a composition, full of felicity, within them; the sky was silver and turquoise and varnish; the village on the left was white and the church on the right was grey; it was all there, in short—it was what he wanted: it was Tremont Street, it was France, it was Lambinet. Moreover he was freely walking about in it. He did this last, for an hour, to his heart's content, making for the shady woody horizon and boring so deep into his impression and his idleness that he might fairly have got through them again and reached the maroon-coloured wall. It was a wonder, no doubt, that the taste of idleness for him shouldn't need more time to sweeten; but it had in fact taken the few previous days; it had been sweetening in truth ever since the retreat of the Pococks. He walked and walked as if to show himself how little he had now to do; he had nothing to do but turn off to some hillside where he might stretch himself and hear the poplars rustle, and whence—in the course of an afternoon so spent, an afternoon richly suffused too with the sense of a book in his pocket—he should sufficiently command the scene to be able to pick out just the right little rustic inn for an experiment in respect to dinner. There was a train back to Paris at 9.20, and he saw himself partaking, at the close of the day, with the enhancements of a coarse white cloth and a sanded door, of something fried and felicitous, washed down with authentic wine; after which he might, as he liked, either stroll back to his station in the gloaming or propose for the local carriole and converse with his driver, a driver who naturally wouldn't fail of a stiff clean blouse, of a knitted nightcap and of the genius of response—who, in fine, would sit on the shafts, tell him what the French people were thinking, and remind him, as indeed the whole episode would incidentally do, of Maupassant. Strether heard his lips, for the first time in French air, as this vision assumed consistency, emit sounds of expressive intention without fear of his company. He had been afraid of Chad and of Maria and of Madame de Vionnet; he had been most of all afraid of Waymarsh, in whose presence, so far as they had mixed together in the light of the town, he had never without somehow paying for it aired either his vocabulary or his accent. He usually paid for it by meeting immediately afterwards Waymarsh's eye.

Such were the liberties with which his fancy played after he had turned off to the hillside that did really and truly, as well as most amiably, await him beneath the poplars, the hillside that made him feel, for a murmurous couple of hours, how happy had been his thought. He had the sense of success, of a finer harmony in things; nothing but what had turned out as yet according to his plan. It most of all came home to him, as he lay on his back on the grass, that Sarah had really gone, that his tension was really relaxed; the peace diffused in these ideas might be delusive, but it hung about him none the less for the time. It fairly, for half an hour, sent him to sleep; he pulled his straw hat over his eyes—he had bought it the day before with a reminiscence of Waymarsh's—and lost himself anew in Lambinet. It was as if he had found out he was tired—tired not from his walk, but from that inward exercise which had known, on the whole, for three months, so little intermission. That was it—when once they were off he had dropped; this moreover was what he had dropped to, and now he was touching bottom. He was kept luxuriously quiet, soothed and amused by the consciousness of what he had found at the end of his descent. It was very much what he had told Maria Gostrey he should like to stay on for, the hugely-distributed Paris of summer, alternately dazzling and dusky, with a weight lifted for him off its columns and cornices and with shade and air in the flutter of awnings as wide as avenues. It was present to him without attenuation that, reaching out, the day after making the remark, for some proof of his freedom, he had gone that very afternoon to see Madame de Vionnet. He had gone again the next day but one, and the effect of the two visits, the after-sense of the couple of hours spent with her, was almost that of fulness and frequency. The brave intention of frequency, so great with him from the moment of his finding himself unjustly suspected at Woollett, had remained rather theoretic, and one of the things he could muse about under his poplars was the source of the special shyness that had still made him careful. He had surely got rid of it now, this special shyness; what had become of it if it hadn't precisely, within the week, rubbed off?

It struck him now in fact as sufficiently plain that if he had still been careful he had been so for a reason. He had really feared, in his behaviour, a lapse from good faith; if there was a danger of one's liking such a woman too much one's best safety was in waiting at least till one had the right to do so. In the light of the last few days the danger was fairly vivid; so that it was proportionately fortunate that the right was likewise established. It seemed to our friend that he had on each occasion profited to the utmost by the latter: how could he have done so more, he at all events asked himself, than in having immediately let her know that, if it was all the same to her, he preferred not to talk about anything tiresome? He had never in his life so sacrificed an armful of high interests as in that remark; he had never so prepared the way for the comparatively frivolous as in addressing it to Madame de Vionnet's intelligence. It hadn't been till later that he quite recalled how in conjuring away everything but the pleasant he had conjured away almost all they had hitherto talked about; it was not till later even that he remembered how, with their new tone, they hadn't so much as mentioned the name of Chad himself. One of the things that most lingered with him on his hillside was this delightful facility, with such a woman, of arriving at a new tone; he thought, as he lay on his back, of all the tones she might make possible if one were to try her, and at any rate of the probability that one could trust her to fit them to occasions. He had wanted her to feel that, as he was disinterested now, so she herself should be, and she had showed she felt it, and he had showed he was grateful, and it had been for all the world as if he were calling for the first time. They had had other, but irrelevant, meetings; it was quite as if, had they sooner known how much they REALLY had in common, there were quantities of comparatively dull matters they might have skipped. Well, they were skipping them now, even to graceful gratitude, even to handsome "Don't mention it!"—and it was amazing what could still come up without reference to what had been going on between them. It might have been, on analysis, nothing more than Shakespeare and the musical glasses; but it had served all the purpose of his appearing to have said to her: "Don't like me, if it's a question of liking me, for anything obvious and clumsy that I've, as they call it, 'done' for you: like me—well, like me, hang it, for anything else you choose. So, by the same propriety, don't be for me simply the person I've come to know through my awkward connexion with Chad—was ever anything, by the way, MORE awkward? Be for me, please, with all your admirable tact and trust, just whatever I may show you it's a present pleasure to me to think you." It had been a large indication to meet; but if she hadn't met it what HAD she done, and how had their time together slipped along so smoothly, mild but not slow, and melting, liquefying, into his happy illusion of idleness? He could recognise on the other hand that he had probably not been without reason, in his prior, his restricted state, for keeping an eye on his liability to lapse from good faith.

He really continued in the picture—that being for himself his situation—all the rest of this rambling day; so that the charm was still, was indeed more than ever upon him when, toward six o'clock he found himself amicably engaged with a stout white-capped deep-voiced woman at the door of the auberge of the biggest village, a village that affected him as a thing of whiteness, blueness and crookedness, set in coppery green, and that had the river flowing behind or before it—one couldn't say which; at the bottom, in particular, of the inn-garden. He had had other adventures before this; had kept along the height, after shaking off slumber; had admired, had almost coveted, another small old church, all steep roof and dim slate-colour without and all whitewash and paper flowers within; had lost his way and had found it again; had conversed with rustics who struck him perhaps a little more as men of the world than he had expected; had acquired at a bound a fearless facility in French; had had, as the afternoon waned, a watery bock, all pale and Parisian, in the cafe of the furthest village, which was not the biggest; and had meanwhile not once overstepped the oblong gilt frame. The frame had drawn itself out for him, as much as you please; but that was just his luck. He had finally come down again to the valley, to keep within touch of stations and trains, turning his face to the quarter from which he had started; and thus it was that he had at last pulled up before the hostess of the Cheval Blanc, who met him, with a rough readiness that was like the clatter of sabots over stones, on their common ground of a cotelette de veau a l'oseille and a subsequent lift. He had walked many miles and didn't know he was tired; but he still knew he was amused, and even that, though he had been alone all day, he had never yet so struck himself as engaged with others and in midstream of his drama. It might have passed for finished his drama, with its catastrophe all but reached: it had, however, none the less been vivid again for him as he thus gave it its fuller chance. He had only had to be at last well out of it to feel it, oddly enough, still going on.

For this had been all day at bottom the spell of the picture—that it was essentially more than anything else a scene and a stage, that the very air of the play was in the rustle of the willows and the tone of the sky. The play and the characters had, without his knowing it till now, peopled all his space for him, and it seemed somehow quite happy that they should offer themselves, in the conditions so supplied, with a kind of inevitability. It was as if the conditions made them not only inevitable, but so much more nearly natural and right as that they were at least easier, pleasanter, to put up with. The conditions had nowhere so asserted their difference from those of Woollett as they appeared to him to assert it in the little court of the Cheval Blanc while he arranged with his hostess for a comfortable climax. They were few and simple, scant and humble, but they were THE THING, as he would have called it, even to a greater degree than Madame de Vionnet's old high salon where the ghost of the Empire walked. "The" thing was the thing that implied the greatest number of other things of the sort he had had to tackle; and it was queer of course, but so it was—the implication here was complete. Not a single one of his observations but somehow fell into a place in it; not a breath of the cooler evening that wasn't somehow a syllable of the text. The text was simply, when condensed, that in THESE places such things were, and that if it was in them one elected to move about one had to make one's account with what one lighted on. Meanwhile at all events it was enough that they did affect one—so far as the village aspect was concerned—as whiteness, crookedness and blueness set in coppery green; there being positively, for that matter, an outer wall of the White Horse that was painted the most improbable shade. That was part of the amusement—as if to show that the fun was harmless; just as it was enough, further, that the picture and the play seemed supremely to melt together in the good woman's broad sketch of what she could do for her visitor's appetite. He felt in short a confidence, and it was general, and it was all he wanted to feel. It suffered no shock even on her mentioning that she had in fact just laid the cloth for two persons who, unlike Monsieur, had arrived by the river—in a boat of their own; who had asked her, half an hour before, what she could do for them, and had then paddled away to look at something a little further up—from which promenade they would presently return. Monsieur might meanwhile, if he liked, pass into the garden, such as it was, where she would serve him, should he wish it—for there were tables and benches in plenty—a "bitter" before his repast. Here she would also report to him on the possibility of a conveyance to his station, and here at any rate he would have the agrement of the river.

It may be mentioned without delay that Monsieur had the agrement of everything, and in particular, for the next twenty minutes, of a small and primitive pavilion that, at the garden's edge, almost overhung the water, testifying, in its somewhat battered state, to much fond frequentation. It consisted of little more than a platform, slightly raised, with a couple of benches and a table, a protecting rail and a projecting roof; but it raked the full grey-blue stream, which, taking a turn a short distance above, passed out of sight to reappear much higher up; and it was clearly in esteemed requisition for Sundays and other feasts. Strether sat there and, though hungry, felt at peace; the confidence that had so gathered for him deepened with the lap of the water, the ripple of the surface, the rustle of the reeds on the opposite bank, the faint diffused coolness and the slight rock of a couple of small boats attached to a rough landing-place hard by. The valley on the further side was all copper-green level and glazed pearly sky, a sky hatched across with screens of trimmed trees, which looked flat, like espaliers; and though the rest of the village straggled away in the near quarter the view had an emptiness that made one of the boats suggestive. Such a river set one afloat almost before one could take up the oars—the idle play of which would be moreover the aid to the full impression. This perception went so far as to bring him to his feet; but that movement, in turn, made him feel afresh that he was tired, and while he leaned against a post and continued to look out he saw something that gave him a sharper arrest.

IV

What he saw was exactly the right thing—a boat advancing round the bend and containing a man who held the paddles and a lady, at the stern, with a pink parasol. It was suddenly as if these figures, or something like them, had been wanted in the picture, had been wanted more or less all day, and had now drifted into sight, with the slow current, on purpose to fill up the measure. They came slowly, floating down, evidently directed to the landing-place near their spectator and presenting themselves to him not less clearly as the two persons for whom his hostess was already preparing a meal. For two very happy persons he found himself straightway taking them—a young man in shirt-sleeves, a young woman easy and fair, who had pulled pleasantly up from some other place and, being acquainted with the neighbourhood, had known what this particular retreat could offer them. The air quite thickened, at their approach, with further intimations; the intimation that they were expert, familiar, frequent—that this wouldn't at all events be the first time. They knew how to do it, he vaguely felt—and it made them but the more idyllic, though at the very moment of the impression, as happened, their boat seemed to have begun to drift wide, the oarsman letting it go. It had by this time none the less come much nearer—near enough for Strether to dream the lady in the stern had for some reason taken account of his being there to watch them. She had remarked on it sharply, yet her companion hadn't turned round; it was in fact almost as if our friend had felt her bid him keep still. She had taken in something as a result of which their course had wavered, and it continued to waver while they just stood off. This little effect was sudden and rapid, so rapid that Strether's sense of it was separate only for an instant from a sharp start of his own. He too had within the minute taken in something, taken in that he knew the lady whose parasol, shifting as if to hide her face, made so fine a pink point in the shining scene. It was too prodigious, a chance in a million, but, if he knew the lady, the gentleman, who still presented his back and kept off, the gentleman, the coatless hero of the idyll, who had responded to her start, was, to match the marvel, none other than Chad.

Chad and Madame de Vionnet were then like himself taking a day in the country—though it was as queer as fiction, as farce, that their country could happen to be exactly his; and she had been the first at recognition, the first to feel, across the water, the shock—for it appeared to come to that—of their wonderful accident. Strether became aware, with this, of what was taking place—that her recognition had been even stranger for the pair in the boat, that her immediate impulse had been to control it, and that she was quickly and intensely debating with Chad the risk of betrayal. He saw they would show nothing if they could feel sure he hadn't made them out; so that he had before him for a few seconds his own hesitation. It was a sharp fantastic crisis that had popped up as if in a dream, and it had had only to last the few seconds to make him feel it as quite horrible. They were thus, on either side, TRYING the other side, and all for some reason that broke the stillness like some unprovoked harsh note. It seemed to him again, within the limit, that he had but one thing to do—to settle their common question by some sign of surprise and joy. He hereupon gave large play to these things, agitating his hat and his stick and loudly calling out—a demonstration that brought him relief as soon as he had seen it answered. The boat, in mid-stream, still went a little wild—which seemed natural, however, while Chad turned round, half springing up; and his good friend, after blankness and wonder, began gaily to wave her parasol. Chad dropped afresh to his paddles and the boat headed round, amazement and pleasantry filling the air meanwhile, and relief, as Strether continued to fancy, superseding mere violence. Our friend went down to the water under this odd impression as of violence averted—the violence of their having "cut" him, out there in the eye of nature, on the assumption that he wouldn't know it. He awaited them with a face from which he was conscious of not being able quite to banish this idea that they would have gone on, not seeing and not knowing, missing their dinner and disappointing their hostess, had he himself taken a line to match. That at least was what darkened his vision for the moment. Afterwards, after they had bumped at the landing-place and he had assisted their getting ashore, everything found itself sponged over by the mere miracle of the encounter.

They could so much better at last, on either side, treat it as a wild extravagance of hazard, that the situation was made elastic by the amount of explanation called into play. Why indeed—apart from oddity—the situation should have been really stiff was a question naturally not practical at the moment, and in fact, so far as we are concerned, a question tackled, later on and in private, only by Strether himself. He was to reflect later on and in private that it was mainly HE who had explained—as he had had moreover comparatively little difficulty in doing. He was to have at all events meanwhile the worrying thought of their perhaps secretly suspecting him of having plotted this coincidence, taking such pains as might be to give it the semblance of an accident. That possibility—as their imputation—didn't of course bear looking into for an instant; yet the whole incident was so manifestly, arrange it as they would, an awkward one, that he could scarce keep disclaimers in respect to his own presence from rising to his lips. Disclaimers of intention would have been as tactless as his presence was practically gross; and the narrowest escape they either of them had was his lucky escape, in the event, from making any. Nothing of the sort, so far as surface and sound were involved, was even in question; surface and sound all made for their common ridiculous good fortune, for the general invraisemblance of the occasion, for the charming chance that they had, the others, in passing, ordered some food to be ready, the charming chance that he had himself not eaten, the charming chance, even more, that their little plans, their hours, their train, in short, from la-bas, would all match for their return together to Paris. The chance that was most charming of all, the chance that drew from Madame de Vionnet her clearest, gayest "Comme cela se trouve!" was the announcement made to Strether after they were seated at table, the word given him by their hostess in respect to his carriage for the station, on which he might now count. It settled the matter for his friends as well; the conveyance—it WAS all too lucky!—would serve for them; and nothing was more delightful than his being in a position to make the train so definite. It might have been, for themselves—to hear Madame de Vionnet—almost unnaturally vague, a detail left to be fixed; though Strether indeed was afterwards to remember that Chad had promptly enough intervened to forestall this appearance, laughing at his companion's flightiness and making the point that he had after all, in spite of the bedazzlement of a day out with her, known what he was about.

Strether was to remember afterwards further that this had had for him the effect of forming Chad's almost sole intervention; and indeed he was to remember further still, in subsequent meditation, many things that, as it were, fitted together. Another of them was for instance that the wonderful woman's overflow of surprise and amusement was wholly into French, which she struck him as speaking with an unprecedented command of idiomatic turns, but in which she got, as he might have said, somewhat away from him, taking all at once little brilliant jumps that he could but lamely match. The question of his own French had never come up for them; it was the one thing she wouldn't have permitted—it belonged, for a person who had been through much, to mere boredom; but the present result was odd, fairly veiling her identity, shifting her back into a mere voluble class or race to the intense audibility of which he was by this time inured. When she spoke the charming slightly strange English he best knew her by he seemed to feel her as a creature, among all the millions, with a language quite to herself, the real monopoly of a special shade of speech, beautifully easy for her, yet of a colour and a cadence that were both inimitable and matters of accident. She came back to these things after they had shaken down in the inn-parlour and knew, as it were, what was to become of them; it was inevitable that loud ejaculation over the prodigy of their convergence should at last wear itself out. Then it was that his impression took fuller form—the impression, destined only to deepen, to complete itself, that they had something to put a face upon, to carry off and make the best of, and that it was she who, admirably on the whole, was doing this. It was familiar to him of course that they had something to put a face upon; their friendship, their connexion, took any amount of explaining—that would have been made familiar by his twenty minutes with Mrs. Pocock if it hadn't already been so. Yet his theory, as we know, had bountifully been that the facts were specifically none of his business, and were, over and above, so far as one had to do with them, intrinsically beautiful; and this might have prepared him for anything, as well as rendered him proof against mystification. When he reached home that night, however, he knew he had been, at bottom, neither prepared nor proof; and since we have spoken of what he was, after his return, to recall and interpret, it may as well immediately be said that his real experience of these few hours put on, in that belated vision—for he scarce went to bed till morning—the aspect that is most to our purpose.

He then knew more or less how he had been affected—he but half knew at the time. There had been plenty to affect him even after, as has been said, they had shaken down; for his consciousness, though muffled, had its sharpest moments during this passage, a marked drop into innocent friendly Bohemia. They then had put their elbows on the table, deploring the premature end of their two or three dishes; which they had tried to make up with another bottle while Chad joked a little spasmodically, perhaps even a little irrelevantly, with the hostess. What it all came to had been that fiction and fable WERE, inevitably, in the air, and not as a simple term of comparison, but as a result of things said; also that they were blinking it, all round, and that they yet needn't, so much as that, have blinked it—though indeed if they hadn't Strether didn't quite see what else they could have done. Strether didn't quite see THAT even at an hour or two past midnight, even when he had, at his hotel, for a long time, without a light and without undressing, sat back on his bedroom sofa and stared straight before him. He was, at that point of vantage, in full possession, to make of it all what he could. He kept making of it that there had been simply a LIE in the charming affair—a lie on which one could now, detached and deliberate, perfectly put one's finger. It was with the lie that they had eaten and drunk and talked and laughed, that they had waited for their carriole rather impatiently, and had then got into the vehicle and, sensibly subsiding, driven their three or four miles through the darkening summer night. The eating and drinking, which had been a resource, had had the effect of having served its turn; the talk and laughter had done as much; and it was during their somewhat tedious progress to the station, during the waits there, the further delays, their submission to fatigue, their silences in the dim compartment of the much-stopping train, that he prepared himself for reflexions to come. It had been a performance, Madame de Vionnet's manner, and though it had to that degree faltered toward the end, as through her ceasing to believe in it, as if she had asked herself, or Chad had found a moment surreptitiously to ask her, what after all was the use, a performance it had none the less quite handsomely remained, with the final fact about it that it was on the whole easier to keep up than to abandon.

From the point of view of presence of mind it had been very wonderful indeed, wonderful for readiness, for beautiful assurance, for the way her decision was taken on the spot, without time to confer with Chad, without time for anything. Their only conference could have been the brief instants in the boat before they confessed to recognising the spectator on the bank, for they hadn't been alone together a moment since and must have communicated all in silence. It was a part of the deep impression for Strether, and not the least of the deep interest, that they COULD so communicate—that Chad in particular could let her know he left it to her. He habitually left things to others, as Strether was so well aware, and it in fact came over our friend in these meditations that there had been as yet no such vivid illustration of his famous knowing how to live. It was as if he had humoured her to the extent of letting her lie without correction—almost as if, really, he would be coming round in the morning to set the matter, as between Strether and himself, right. Of course he couldn't quite come; it was a case in which a man was obliged to accept the woman's version, even when fantastic; if she had, with more flurry than she cared to show, elected, as the phrase was, to represent that they had left Paris that morning, and with no design but of getting back within the day—if she had so sized-up, in the Woollett phrase, their necessity, she knew best her own measure. There were things, all the same, it was impossible to blink and which made this measure an odd one—the too evident fact for instance that she hadn't started out for the day dressed and hatted and shod, and even, for that matter, pink parasol'd, as she had been in the boat. From what did the drop in her assurance proceed as the tension increased—from what did this slightly baffled ingenuity spring but from her consciousness of not presenting, as night closed in, with not so much as a shawl to wrap her round, an appearance that matched her story? She admitted that she was cold, but only to blame her imprudence which Chad suffered her to give such account of as she might. Her shawl and Chad's overcoat and her other garments, and his, those they had each worn the day before, were at the place, best known to themselves—a quiet retreat enough, no doubt—at which they had been spending the twenty-four hours, to which they had fully meant to return that evening, from which they had so remarkably swum into Strether's ken, and the tacit repudiation of which had been thus the essence of her comedy. Strether saw how she had perceived in a flash that they couldn't quite look to going back there under his nose; though, honestly, as he gouged deeper into the matter, he was somewhat surprised, as Chad likewise had perhaps been, at the uprising of this scruple. He seemed even to divine that she had entertained it rather for Chad than for herself, and that, as the young man had lacked the chance to enlighten her, she had had to go on with it, he meanwhile mistaking her motive.

He was rather glad, none the less, that they had in point of fact not parted at the Cheval Blanc, that he hadn't been reduced to giving them his blessing for an idyllic retreat down the river. He had had in the actual case to make-believe more than he liked, but this was nothing, it struck him, to what the other event would have required. Could he, literally, quite have faced the other event? Would he have been capable of making the best of it with them? This was what he was trying to do now; but with the advantage of his being able to give more time to it a good deal counteracted by his sense of what, over and above the central fact itself, he had to swallow. It was the quantity of make-believe involved and so vividly exemplified that most disagreed with his spiritual stomach. He moved, however, from the consideration of that quantity—to say nothing of the consciousness of that organ—back to the other feature of the show, the deep, deep truth of the intimacy revealed. That was what, in his vain vigil, he oftenest reverted to: intimacy, at such a point, was LIKE that—and what in the world else would one have wished it to be like? It was all very well for him to feel the pity of its being so much like lying; he almost blushed, in the dark, for the way he had dressed the possibility in vagueness, as a little girl might have dressed her doll. He had made them—and by no fault of their own—momentarily pull it for him, the possibility, out of this vagueness; and must he not therefore take it now as they had had simply, with whatever thin attenuations, to give it to him? The very question, it may be added, made him feel lonely and cold. There was the element of the awkward all round, but Chad and Madame de Vionnet had at least the comfort that they could talk it over together. With whom could HE talk of such things?—unless indeed always, at almost any stage, with Maria? He foresaw that Miss Gostrey would come again into requisition on the morrow; though it wasn't to be denied that he was already a little afraid of her "What on earth—that's what I want to know now—had you then supposed?" He recognised at last that he had really been trying all along to suppose nothing. Verily, verily, his labour had been lost. He found himself supposing innumerable and wonderful things.

Book Twelfth

I

Strether couldn't have said he had during the previous hours definitely expected it; yet when, later on, that morning—though no later indeed than for his coming forth at ten o'clock—he saw the concierge produce, on his approach, a petit bleu delivered since his letters had been sent up, he recognised the appearance as the first symptom of a sequel. He then knew he had been thinking of some early sign from Chad as more likely, after all, than not; and this would be precisely the early sign. He took it so for granted that he opened the petit bleu just where he had stopped, in the pleasant cool draught of the porte-cochere—only curious to see where the young man would, at such a juncture, break out. His curiosity, however, was more than gratified; the small missive, whose gummed edge he had detached without attention to the address, not being from the young man at all, but from the person whom the case gave him on the spot as still more worth while. Worth while or not, he went round to the nearest telegraph-office, the big one on the Boulevard, with a directness that almost confessed to a fear of the danger of delay. He might have been thinking that if he didn't go before he could think he wouldn't perhaps go at all. He at any rate kept, in the lower side-pocket of his morning coat, a very deliberate hand on his blue missive, crumpling it up rather tenderly than harshly. He wrote a reply, on the Boulevard, also in the form of a petit bleu—which was quickly done, under pressure of the place, inasmuch as, like Madame de Vionnet's own communication, it consisted of the fewest words. She had asked him if he could do her the very great kindness of coming to see her that evening at half-past nine, and he answered, as if nothing were easier, that he would present himself at the hour she named. She had added a line of postscript, to the effect that she would come to him elsewhere and at his own hour if he preferred; but he took no notice of this, feeling that if he saw her at all half the value of it would be in seeing her where he had already seen her best. He mightn't see her at all; that was one of the reflexions he made after writing and before he dropped his closed card into the box; he mightn't see any one at all any more at all; he might make an end as well now as ever, leaving things as they were, since he was doubtless not to leave them better, and taking his way home so far as should appear that a home remained to him. This alternative was for a few minutes so sharp that if he at last did deposit his missive it was perhaps because the pressure of the place had an effect.

There was none other, however, than the common and constant pressure, familiar to our friend under the rubric of Postes et Telegraphes—the something in the air of these establishments; the vibration of the vast strange life of the town, the influence of the types, the performers concocting their messages; the little prompt Paris women, arranging, pretexting goodness knew what, driving the dreadful needle-pointed public pen at the dreadful sand-strewn public table: implements that symbolised for Strether's too interpretative innocence something more acute in manners, more sinister in morals, more fierce in the national life. After he had put in his paper he had ranged himself, he was really amused to think, on the side of the fierce, the sinister, the acute. He was carrying on a correspondence, across the great city, quite in the key of the Postes et Telegraphes in general; and it was fairly as if the acceptance of that fact had come from something in his state that sorted with the occupation of his neighbours. He was mixed up with the typical tale of Paris, and so were they, poor things—how could they all together help being? They were no worse than he, in short, and he no worse than they—if, queerly enough, no better; and at all events he had settled his hash, so that he went out to begin, from that moment, his day of waiting. The great settlement was, as he felt, in his preference for seeing his correspondent in her own best conditions. THAT was part of the typical tale, the part most significant in respect to himself. He liked the place she lived in, the picture that each time squared itself, large and high and clear, around her: every occasion of seeing it was a pleasure of a different shade. Yet what precisely was he doing with shades of pleasure now, and why hadn't he properly and logically compelled her to commit herself to whatever of disadvantage and penalty the situation might throw up? He might have proposed, as for Sarah Pocock, the cold hospitality of his own salon de lecture, in which the chill of Sarah's visit seemed still to abide and shades of pleasure were dim; he might have suggested a stone bench in the dusty Tuileries or a penny chair at the back part of the Champs Elysees. These things would have been a trifle stern, and sternness alone now wouldn't be sinister. An instinct in him cast about for some form of discipline in which they might meet—some awkwardness they would suffer from, some danger, or at least some grave inconvenience, they would incur. This would give a sense—which the spirit required, rather ached and sighed in the absence of—that somebody was paying something somewhere and somehow, that they were at least not all floating together on the silver stream of impunity. Just instead of that to go and see her late in the evening, as if, for all the world—well, as if he were as much in the swim as anybody else: this had as little as possible in common with the penal form.

Even when he had felt that objection melt away, however, the practical difference was small; the long stretch of his interval took the colour it would, and if he lived on thus with the sinister from hour to hour it proved an easier thing than one might have supposed in advance. He reverted in thought to his old tradition, the one he had been brought up on and which even so many years of life had but little worn away; the notion that the state of the wrongdoer, or at least this person's happiness, presented some special difficulty. What struck him now rather was the ease of it—for nothing in truth appeared easier. It was an ease he himself fairly tasted of for the rest of the day; giving himself quite up; not so much as trying to dress it out, in any particular whatever, as a difficulty; not after all going to see Maria—which would have been in a manner a result of such dressing; only idling, lounging, smoking, sitting in the shade, drinking lemonade and consuming ices. The day had turned to heat and eventual thunder, and he now and again went back to his hotel to find that Chad hadn't been there. He hadn't yet struck himself, since leaving Woollett, so much as a loafer, though there had been times when he believed himself touching bottom. This was a deeper depth than any, and with no foresight, scarcely with a care, as to what he should bring up. He almost wondered if he didn't LOOK demoralised and disreputable; he had the fanciful vision, as he sat and smoked, of some accidental, some motived, return of the Pococks, who would be passing along the Boulevard and would catch this view of him. They would have distinctly, on his appearance, every ground for scandal. But fate failed to administer even that sternness; the Pococks never passed and Chad made no sign. Strether meanwhile continued to hold off from Miss Gostrey, keeping her till to-morrow; so that by evening his irresponsibility, his impunity, his luxury, had become—there was no other word for them—immense.

Between nine and ten, at last, in the high clear picture—he was moving in these days, as in a gallery, from clever canvas to clever canvas—he drew a long breath: it was so presented to him from the first that the spell of his luxury wouldn't be broken. He wouldn't have, that is, to become responsible—this was admirably in the air: she had sent for him precisely to let him feel it, so that he might go on with the comfort (comfort already established, hadn't it been?) of regarding his ordeal, the ordeal of the weeks of Sarah's stay and of their climax, as safely traversed and left behind him. Didn't she just wish to assure him that SHE now took it all and so kept it; that he was absolutely not to worry any more, was only to rest on his laurels and continue generously to help her? The light in her beautiful formal room was dim, though it would do, as everything would always do; the hot night had kept out lamps, but there was a pair of clusters of candles that glimmered over the chimney-piece like the tall tapers of an altar. The windows were all open, their redundant hangings swaying a little, and he heard once more, from the empty court, the small plash of the fountain. From beyond this, and as from a great distance—beyond the court, beyond the corps de logis forming the front—came, as if excited and exciting, the vague voice of Paris. Strether had all along been subject to sudden gusts of fancy in connexion with such matters as these—odd starts of the historic sense, suppositions and divinations with no warrant but their intensity. Thus and so, on the eve of the great recorded dates, the days and nights of revolution, the sounds had come in, the omens, the beginnings broken out. They were the smell of revolution, the smell of the public temper—or perhaps simply the smell of blood.

It was at present queer beyond words, "subtle," he would have risked saying, that such suggestions should keep crossing the scene; but it was doubtless the effect of the thunder in the air, which had hung about all day without release. His hostess was dressed as for thunderous times, and it fell in with the kind of imagination we have just attributed to him that she should be in simplest coolest white, of a character so old-fashioned, if he were not mistaken, that Madame Roland must on the scaffold have worn something like it. This effect was enhanced by a small black fichu or scarf, of crape or gauze, disposed quaintly round her bosom and now completing as by a mystic touch the pathetic, the noble analogy. Poor Strether in fact scarce knew what analogy was evoked for him as the charming woman, receiving him and making him, as she could do such things, at once familiarly and gravely welcome, moved over her great room with her image almost repeated in its polished floor, which had been fully bared for summer. The associations of the place, all felt again; the gleam here and there, in the subdued light, of glass and gilt and parquet, with the quietness of her own note as the centre—these things were at first as delicate as if they had been ghostly, and he was sure in a moment that, whatever he should find he had come for, it wouldn't be for an impression that had previously failed him. That conviction held him from the outset, and, seeming singularly to simplify, certified to him that the objects about would help him, would really help them both. No, he might never see them again—this was only too probably the last time; and he should certainly see nothing in the least degree like them. He should soon be going to where such things were not, and it would be a small mercy for memory, for fancy, to have, in that stress, a loaf on the shelf. He knew in advance he should look back on the perception actually sharpest with him as on the view of something old, old, old, the oldest thing he had ever personally touched; and he also knew, even while he took his companion in as the feature among features, that memory and fancy couldn't help being enlisted for her. She might intend what she would, but this was beyond anything she could intend, with things from far back—tyrannies of history, facts of type, values, as the painters said, of expression—all working for her and giving her the supreme chance, the chance of the happy, the really luxurious few, the chance, on a great occasion, to be natural and simple. She had never, with him, been more so; or if it was the perfection of art it would never—and that came to the same thing—be proved against her.

What was truly wonderful was her way of differing so from time to time without detriment to her simplicity. Caprices, he was sure she felt, were before anything else bad manners, and that judgement in her was by itself a thing making more for safety of intercourse than anything that in his various own past intercourses he had had to reckon on. If therefore her presence was now quite other than the one she had shown him the night before, there was nothing of violence in the change—it was all harmony and reason. It gave him a mild deep person, whereas he had had on the occasion to which their interview was a direct reference a person committed to movement and surface and abounding in them; but she was in either character more remarkable for nothing than for her bridging of intervals, and this now fell in with what he understood he was to leave to her. The only thing was that, if he was to leave it ALL to her, why exactly had she sent for him? He had had, vaguely, in advance, his explanation, his view of the probability of her wishing to set something right, to deal in some way with the fraud so lately practised on his presumed credulity. Would she attempt to carry it further or would she blot it out? Would she throw over it some more or less happy colour; or would she do nothing about it at all? He perceived soon enough at least that, however reasonable she might be, she wasn't vulgarly confused, and it herewith pressed upon him that their eminent "lie," Chad's and hers, was simply after all such an inevitable tribute to good taste as he couldn't have wished them not to render. Away from them, during his vigil, he had seemed to wince at the amount of comedy involved; whereas in his present posture he could only ask himself how he should enjoy any attempt from her to take the comedy back. He shouldn't enjoy it at all; but, once more and yet once more, he could trust her. That is he could trust her to make deception right. As she presented things the ugliness—goodness knew why—went out of them; none the less too that she could present them, with an art of her own, by not so much as touching them. She let the matter, at all events, lie where it was—where the previous twenty-four hours had placed it; appearing merely to circle about it respectfully, tenderly, almost piously, while she took up another question.

She knew she hadn't really thrown dust in his eyes; this, the previous night, before they separated, had practically passed between them; and, as she had sent for him to see what the difference thus made for him might amount to, so he was conscious at the end of five minutes that he had been tried and tested. She had settled with Chad after he left them that she would, for her satisfaction, assure herself of this quantity, and Chad had, as usual, let her have her way. Chad was always letting people have their way when he felt that it would somehow turn his wheel for him; it somehow always did turn his wheel. Strether felt, oddly enough, before these facts, freshly and consentingly passive; they again so rubbed it into him that the couple thus fixing his attention were intimate, that his intervention had absolutely aided and intensified their intimacy, and that in fine he must accept the consequence of that. He had absolutely become, himself, with his perceptions and his mistakes, his concessions and his reserves, the droll mixture, as it must seem to them, of his braveries and his fears, the general spectacle of his art and his innocence, almost an added link and certainly a common priceless ground for them to meet upon. It was as if he had been hearing their very tone when she brought out a reference that was comparatively straight. "The last twice that you've been here, you know, I never asked you," she said with an abrupt transition—they had been pretending before this to talk simply of the charm of yesterday and of the interest of the country they had seen. The effort was confessedly vain; not for such talk had she invited him; and her impatient reminder was of their having done for it all the needful on his coming to her after Sarah's flight. What she hadn't asked him then was to state to her where and how he stood for her; she had been resting on Chad's report of their midnight hour together in the Boulevard Malesherbes. The thing therefore she at present desired was ushered in by this recall of the two occasions on which, disinterested and merciful, she hadn't worried him. To-night truly she WOULD worry him, and this was her appeal to him to let her risk it. He wasn't to mind if she bored him a little: she had behaved, after all—hadn't she?—so awfully, awfully well.

II

"Oh, you're all right, you're all right," he almost impatiently declared; his impatience being moreover not for her pressure, but for her scruple. More and more distinct to him was the tune to which she would have had the matter out with Chad: more and more vivid for him the idea that she had been nervous as to what he might be able to "stand." Yes, it had been a question if he had "stood" what the scene on the river had given him, and, though the young man had doubtless opined in favour of his recuperation, her own last word must have been that she should feel easier in seeing for herself. That was it, unmistakeably; she WAS seeing for herself. What he could stand was thus, in these moments, in the balance for Strether, who reflected, as he became fully aware of it, that he must properly brace himself. He wanted fully to appear to stand all he might; and there was a certain command of the situation for him in this very wish not to look too much at sea. She was ready with everything, but so, sufficiently, was he; that is he was at one point the more prepared of the two, inasmuch as, for all her cleverness, she couldn't produce on the spot—and it was surprising—an account of the motive of her note. He had the advantage that his pronouncing her "all right" gave him for an enquiry. "May I ask, delighted as I've been to come, if you've wished to say something special?" He spoke as if she might have seen he had been waiting for it—not indeed with discomfort, but with natural interest. Then he saw that she was a little taken aback, was even surprised herself at the detail she had neglected—the only one ever yet; having somehow assumed he would know, would recognise, would leave some things not to be said. She looked at him, however, an instant as if to convey that if he wanted them ALL—!

"Selfish and vulgar—that's what I must seem to you. You've done everything for me, and here I am as if I were asking for more. But it isn't," she went on, "because I'm afraid—though I AM of course afraid, as a woman in my position always is. I mean it isn't because one lives in terror—it isn't because of that one is selfish, for I'm ready to give you my word to-night that I don't care; don't care what still may happen and what I may lose. I don't ask you to raise your little finger for me again, nor do I wish so much as to mention to you what we've talked of before, either my danger or my safety, or his mother, or his sister, or the girl he may marry, or the fortune he may make or miss, or the right or the wrong, of any kind, he may do. If after the help one has had from you one can't either take care of one's self or simply hold one's tongue, one must renounce all claim to be an object of interest. It's in the name of what I DO care about that I've tried still to keep hold of you. How can I be indifferent," she asked, "to how I appear to you?" And as he found himself unable immediately to say: "Why, if you're going, NEED you, after all? Is it impossible you should stay on—so that one mayn't lose you?"

"Impossible I should live with you here instead of going home?"

"Not 'with' us, if you object to that, but near enough to us, somewhere, for us to see you—well," she beautifully brought out, "when we feel we MUST. How shall we not sometimes feel it? I've wanted to see you often when I couldn't," she pursued, "all these last weeks. How shan't I then miss you now, with the sense of your being gone forever?" Then as if the straightness of this appeal, taking him unprepared, had visibly left him wondering: "Where IS your 'home' moreover now—what has become of it? I've made a change in your life, I know I have; I've upset everything in your mind as well; in your sense of—what shall I call it?—all the decencies and possibilities. It gives me a kind of detestation—" She pulled up short.

Oh but he wanted to hear. "Detestation of what?"

"Of everything—of life."

"Ah that's too much," he laughed—"or too little!"

"Too little, precisely"—she was eager. "What I hate is myself—when I think that one has to take so much, to be happy, out of the lives of others, and that one isn't happy even then. One does it to cheat one's self and to stop one's mouth—but that's only at the best for a little. The wretched self is always there, always making one somehow a fresh anxiety. What it comes to is that it's not, that it's never, a happiness, any happiness at all, to TAKE. The only safe thing is to give. It's what plays you least false." Interesting, touching, strikingly sincere as she let these things come from her, she yet puzzled and troubled him—so fine was the quaver of her quietness. He felt what he had felt before with her, that there was always more behind what she showed, and more and more again behind that. "You know so, at least," she added, "where you are!"

"YOU ought to know it indeed then; for isn't what you've been giving exactly what has brought us together this way? You've been making, as I've so fully let you know I've felt," Strether said, "the most precious present I've ever seen made, and if you can't sit down peacefully on that performance you ARE, no doubt, born to torment yourself. But you ought," he wound up, "to be easy."

"And not trouble you any more, no doubt—not thrust on you even the wonder and the beauty of what I've done; only let you regard our business as over, and well over, and see you depart in a peace that matches my own? No doubt, no doubt, no doubt," she nervously repeated—"all the more that I don't really pretend I believe you couldn't, for yourself, NOT have done what you have. I don't pretend you feel yourself victimised, for this evidently is the way you live, and it's what—we're agreed—is the best way. Yes, as you say," she continued after a moment, "I ought to be easy and rest on my work. Well then here am I doing so. I AM easy. You'll have it for your last impression. When is it you say you go?" she asked with a quick change.

He took some time to reply—his last impression was more and more so mixed a one. It produced in him a vague disappointment, a drop that was deeper even than the fall of his elation the previous night. The good of what he had done, if he had done so much, wasn't there to enliven him quite to the point that would have been ideal for a grand gay finale. Women were thus endlessly absorbent, and to deal with them was to walk on water. What was at bottom the matter with her, embroider as she might and disclaim as she might—what was at bottom the matter with her was simply Chad himself. It was of Chad she was after all renewedly afraid; the strange strength of her passion was the very strength of her fear; she clung to HIM, Lambert Strether, as to a source of safety she had tested, and, generous graceful truthful as she might try to be, exquisite as she was, she dreaded the term of his being within reach. With this sharpest perception yet, it was like a chill in the air to him, it was almost appalling, that a creature so fine could be, by mysterious forces, a creature so exploited. For at the end of all things they WERE mysterious: she had but made Chad what he was—so why could she think she had made him infinite? She had made him better, she had made him best, she had made him anything one would; but it came to our friend with supreme queerness that he was none the less only Chad. Strether had the sense that HE, a little, had made him too; his high appreciation had as it were, consecrated her work The work, however admirable, was nevertheless of the strict human order, and in short it was marvellous that the companion of mere earthly joys, of comforts, aberrations (however one classed them) within the common experience should be so transcendently prized. It might have made Strether hot or shy, as such secrets of others brought home sometimes do make us; but he was held there by something so hard that it was fairly grim. This was not the discomposure of last night; that had quite passed—such discomposures were a detail; the real coercion was to see a man ineffably adored. There it was again—it took women, it took women; if to deal with them was to walk on water what wonder that the water rose? And it had never surely risen higher than round this woman. He presently found himself taking a long look from her, and the next thing he knew he had uttered all his thought. "You're afraid for your life!"

It drew out her long look, and he soon enough saw why. A spasm came into her face, the tears she had already been unable to hide overflowed at first in silence, and then, as the sound suddenly comes from a child, quickened to gasps, to sobs. She sat and covered her face with her hands, giving up all attempt at a manner. "It's how you see me, it's how you see me"—she caught her breath with it—"and it's as I AM, and as I must take myself, and of course it's no matter." Her emotion was at first so incoherent that he could only stand there at a loss, stand with his sense of having upset her, though of having done it by the truth. He had to listen to her in a silence that he made no immediate effort to attenuate, feeling her doubly woeful amid all her dim diffused elegance; consenting to it as he had consented to the rest, and even conscious of some vague inward irony in the presence of such a fine free range of bliss and bale. He couldn't say it was NOT no matter; for he was serving her to the end, he now knew, anyway—quite as if what he thought of her had nothing to do with it. It was actually moreover as if he didn't think of her at all, as if he could think of nothing but the passion, mature, abysmal, pitiful, she represented, and the possibilities she betrayed. She was older for him to-night, visibly less exempt from the touch of time; but she was as much as ever the finest and subtlest creature, the happiest apparition, it had been given him, in all his years, to meet; and yet he could see her there as vulgarly troubled, in very truth, as a maidservant crying for her young man. The only thing was that she judged herself as the maidservant wouldn't; the weakness of which wisdom too, the dishonour of which judgement, seemed but to sink her lower. Her collapse, however, no doubt, was briefer and she had in a manner recovered herself before he intervened. "Of course I'm afraid for my life. But that's nothing. It isn't that."

He was silent a little longer, as if thinking what it might be. "There's something I have in mind that I can still do."

But she threw off at last, with a sharp sad headshake, drying her eyes, what he could still do. "I don't care for that. Of course, as I've said, you're acting, in your wonderful way, for yourself; and what's for yourself is no more my business—though I may reach out unholy hands so clumsily to touch it—than if it were something in Timbuctoo. It's only that you don't snub me, as you've had fifty chances to do—it's only your beautiful patience that makes one forget one's manners. In spite of your patience, all the same," she went on, "you'd do anything rather than be with us here, even if that were possible. You'd do everything for us but be mixed up with us—which is a statement you can easily answer to the advantage of your own manners. You can say 'What's the use of talking of things that at the best are impossible?' What IS of course the use? It's only my little madness. You'd talk if you were tormented. And I don't mean now about HIM. Oh for him—!" Positively, strangely, bitterly, as it seemed to Strether, she gave "him," for the moment, away. "You don't care what I think of you; but I happen to care what you think of me. And what you MIGHT," she added. "What you perhaps even did."

He gained time. "What I did—?"

"Did think before. Before this. DIDn't you think—?"

But he had already stopped her. "I didn't think anything. I never think a step further than I'm obliged to."

"That's perfectly false, I believe," she returned—"except that you may, no doubt, often pull up when things become TOO ugly; or even, I'll say, to save you a protest, too beautiful. At any rate, even so far as it's true, we've thrust on you appearances that you've had to take in and that have therefore made your obligation. Ugly or beautiful—it doesn't matter what we call them—you were getting on without them, and that's where we're detestable. We bore you—that's where we are. And we may well—for what we've cost you. All you can do NOW is not to think at all. And I who should have liked to seem to you—well, sublime!"

He could only after a moment re-echo Miss Barrace. "You're wonderful!"

"I'm old and abject and hideous"—she went on as without hearing him. "Abject above all. Or old above all. It's when one's old that it's worst. I don't care what becomes of it—let what WILL; there it is. It's a doom—I know it; you can't see it more than I do myself. Things have to happen as they will." With which she came back again to what, face to face with him, had so quite broken down. "Of course you wouldn't, even if possible, and no matter what may happen to you, be near us. But think of me, think of me—!" She exhaled it into air.

He took refuge in repeating something he had already said and that she had made nothing of. "There's something I believe I can still do." And he put his hand out for good-bye.

She again made nothing of it; she went on with her insistence. "That won't help you. There's nothing to help you."

"Well, it may help YOU," he said.

She shook her head. "There's not a grain of certainty in my future—for the only certainty is that I shall be the loser in the end."

She hadn't taken his hand, but she moved with him to the door. "That's cheerful," he laughed, "for your benefactor!"

"What's cheerful for ME," she replied, "is that we might, you and I, have been friends. That's it—that's it. You see how, as I say, I want everything. I've wanted you too."

"Ah but you've HAD me!" he declared, at the door, with an emphasis that made an end.

III

His purpose had been to see Chad the next day, and he had prefigured seeing him by an early call; having in general never stood on ceremony in respect to visits at the Boulevard Malesherbes. It had been more often natural for him to go there than for Chad to come to the small hotel, the attractions of which were scant; yet it nevertheless, just now, at the eleventh hour, did suggest itself to Strether to begin by giving the young man a chance. It struck him that, in the inevitable course, Chad would be "round," as Waymarsh used to say—Waymarsh who already, somehow, seemed long ago. He hadn't come the day before, because it had been arranged between them that Madame de Vionnet should see their friend first; but now that this passage had taken place he would present himself, and their friend wouldn't have long to wait. Strether assumed, he became aware, on this reasoning, that the interesting parties to the arrangement would have met betimes, and that the more interesting of the two—as she was after all—would have communicated to the other the issue of her appeal. Chad would know without delay that his mother's messenger had been with her, and, though it was perhaps not quite easy to see how she could qualify what had occurred, he would at least have been sufficiently advised to feel he could go on. The day, however, brought, early or late, no word from him, and Strether felt, as a result of this, that a change had practically come over their intercourse. It was perhaps a premature judgement; or it only meant perhaps—how could he tell?—that the wonderful pair he protected had taken up again together the excursion he had accidentally checked. They might have gone back to the country, and gone back but with a long breath drawn; that indeed would best mark Chad's sense that reprobation hadn't rewarded Madame de Vionnet's request for an interview. At the end of the twenty-four hours, at the end of the forty-eight, there was still no overture; so that Strether filled up the time, as he had so often filled it before, by going to see Miss Gostrey.

He proposed amusements to her; he felt expert now in proposing amusements; and he had thus, for several days, an odd sense of leading her about Paris, of driving her in the Bois, of showing her the penny steamboats—those from which the breeze of the Seine was to be best enjoyed—that might have belonged to a kindly uncle doing the honours of the capital to an Intelligent niece from the country. He found means even to take her to shops she didn't know, or that she pretended she didn't; while she, on her side, was, like the country maiden, all passive modest and grateful—going in fact so far as to emulate rusticity in occasional fatigues and bewilderments. Strether described these vague proceedings to himself, described them even to her, as a happy interlude; the sign of which was that the companions said for the time no further word about the matter they had talked of to satiety. He proclaimed satiety at the outset, and she quickly took the hint; as docile both in this and in everything else as the intelligent obedient niece. He told her as yet nothing of his late adventure—for as an adventure it now ranked with him; he pushed the whole business temporarily aside and found his interest in the fact of her beautiful assent. She left questions unasked—she who for so long had been all questions; she gave herself up to him with an understanding of which mere mute gentleness might have seemed the sufficient expression. She knew his sense of his situation had taken still another step—of that he was quite aware; but she conveyed that, whatever had thus happened for him, it was thrown into the shade by what was happening for herself. This—though it mightn't to a detached spirit have seemed much—was the major interest, and she met it with a new directness of response, measuring it from hour to hour with her grave hush of acceptance. Touched as he had so often been by her before, he was, for his part too, touched afresh; all the more that though he could be duly aware of the principle of his own mood he couldn't be equally so of the principle of hers. He knew, that is, in a manner—knew roughly and resignedly—what he himself was hatching; whereas he had to take the chance of what he called to himself Maria's calculations. It was all he needed that she liked him enough for what they were doing, and even should they do a good deal more would still like him enough for that; the essential freshness of a relation so simple was a cool bath to the soreness produced by other relations. These others appeared to him now horribly complex; they bristled with fine points, points all unimaginable beforehand, points that pricked and drew blood; a fact that gave to an hour with his present friend on a bateau-mouche, or in the afternoon shade of the Champs Elysees, something of the innocent pleasure of handling rounded ivory. His relation with Chad personally—from the moment he had got his point of view—had been of the simplest; yet this also struck him as bristling, after a third and a fourth blank day had passed. It was as if at last however his care for such indications had dropped; there came a fifth blank day and he ceased to enquire or to heed.

They now took on to his fancy, Miss Gostrey and he, the image of the Babes in the Wood; they could trust the merciful elements to let them continue at peace. He had been great already, as he knew, at postponements; but he had only to get afresh into the rhythm of one to feel its fine attraction. It amused him to say to himself that he might for all the world have been going to die—die resignedly; the scene was filled for him with so deep a death-bed hush, so melancholy a charm. That meant the postponement of everything else—which made so for the quiet lapse of life; and the postponement in especial of the reckoning to come—unless indeed the reckoning to come were to be one and the same thing with extinction. It faced him, the reckoning, over the shoulder of much interposing experience—which also faced him; and one would float to it doubtless duly through these caverns of Kubla Khan. It was really behind everything; it hadn't merged in what he had done; his final appreciation of what he had done—his appreciation on the spot—would provide it with its main sharpness. The spot so focussed was of course Woollett, and he was to see, at the best, what Woollett would be with everything there changed for him. Wouldn't THAT revelation practically amount to the wind-up of his career? Well, the summer's end would show; his suspense had meanwhile exactly the sweetness of vain delay; and he had with it, we should mention, other pastimes than Maria's company—plenty of separate musings in which his luxury failed him but at one point. He was well in port, the outer sea behind him, and it was only a matter of getting ashore. There was a question that came and went for him, however, as he rested against the side of his ship, and it was a little to get rid of the obsession that he prolonged his hours with Miss Gostrey. It was a question about himself, but it could only be settled by seeing Chad again; it was indeed his principal reason for wanting to see Chad. After that it wouldn't signify—it was a ghost that certain words would easily lay to rest. Only the young man must be there to take the words. Once they were taken he wouldn't have a question left; none, that is, in connexion with this particular affair. It wouldn't then matter even to himself that he might now have been guilty of speaking BECAUSE of what he had forfeited. That was the refinement of his supreme scruple—he wished so to leave what he had forfeited out of account. He wished not to do anything because he had missed something else, because he was sore or sorry or impoverished, because he was maltreated or desperate; he wished to do everything because he was lucid and quiet, just the same for himself on all essential points as he had ever been. Thus it was that while he virtually hung about for Chad he kept mutely putting it: "You've been chucked, old boy; but what has that to do with it?" It would have sickened him to feel vindictive.

These tints of feeling indeed were doubtless but the iridescence of his idleness, and they were presently lost in a new light from Maria. She had a fresh fact for him before the week was out, and she practically met him with it on his appearing one night. He hadn't on this day seen her, but had planned presenting himself in due course to ask her to dine with him somewhere out of doors, on one of the terraces, in one of the gardens, of which the Paris of summer was profuse. It had then come on to rain, so that, disconcerted, he changed his mind; dining alone at home, a little stuffily and stupidly, and waiting on her afterwards to make up his loss. He was sure within a minute that something had happened; it was so in the air of the rich little room that he had scarcely to name his thought. Softly lighted, the whole colour of the place, with its vague values, was in cool fusion—an effect that made the visitor stand for a little agaze. It was as if in doing so now he had felt a recent presence—his recognition of the passage of which his hostess in turn divined. She had scarcely to say it—"Yes, she has been here, and this time I received her." It wasn't till a minute later that she added: "There being, as I understand you, no reason NOW—!"

"None for your refusing?"

"No—if you've done what you've had to do."

"I've certainly so far done it," Strether said, "as that you needn't fear the effect, or the appearance of coming between us. There's nothing between us now but what we ourselves have put there, and not an inch of room for anything else whatever. Therefore you're only beautifully WITH us as always—though doubtless now, if she has talked to you, rather more with us than less. Of course if she came," he added, "it was to talk to you."

"It was to talk to me," Maria returned; on which he was further sure that she was practically in possession of what he himself hadn't yet told her. He was even sure she was in possession of things he himself couldn't have told; for the consciousness of them was now all in her face and accompanied there with a shade of sadness that marked in her the close of all uncertainties. It came out for him more than ever yet that she had had from the first a knowledge she believed him not to have had, a knowledge the sharp acquisition of which might be destined to make a difference for him. The difference for him might not inconceivably be an arrest of his independence and a change in his attitude—in other words a revulsion in favour of the principles of Woollett. She had really prefigured the possibility of a shock that would send him swinging back to Mrs. Newsome. He hadn't, it was true, week after week, shown signs of receiving it, but the possibility had been none the less in the air. What Maria accordingly had had now to take in was that the shock had descended and that he hadn't, all the same, swung back. He had grown clear, in a flash, on a point long since settled for herself; but no reapproximation to Mrs. Newsome had occurred in consequence. Madame de Vionnet had by her visit held up the torch to these truths, and what now lingered in poor Maria's face was the somewhat smoky light of the scene between them. If the light however wasn't, as we have hinted, the glow of joy, the reasons for this also were perhaps discernible to Strether even through the blur cast over them by his natural modesty. She had held herself for months with a firm hand; she hadn't interfered on any chance—and chances were specious enough—that she might interfere to her profit. She had turned her back on the dream that Mrs. Newsome's rupture, their friend's forfeiture—the engagement the relation itself, broken beyond all mending—might furnish forth her advantage; and, to stay her hand from promoting these things, she had on private, difficult, but rigid, lines, played strictly fair. She couldn't therefore but feel that, though, as the end of all, the facts in question had been stoutly confirmed, her ground for personal, for what might have been called interested, elation remained rather vague. Strether might easily have made out that she had been asking herself, in the hours she had just sat through, if there were still for her, or were only not, a fair shade of uncertainty. Let us hasten to add, however, that what he at first made out on this occasion he also at first kept to himself. He only asked what in particular Madame de Vionnet had come for, and as to this his companion was ready.

"She wants tidings of Mr. Newsome, whom she appears not to have seen for some days."

"Then she hasn't been away with him again?"

"She seemed to think," Maria answered, "that he might have gone away with YOU."

"And did you tell her I know nothing of him?"

She had her indulgent headshake. "I've known nothing of what you know. I could only tell her I'd ask you."

"Then I've not seen him for a week—and of course I've wondered." His wonderment showed at this moment as sharper, but he presently went on. "Still, I dare say I can put my hand on him. Did she strike you," he asked, "as anxious?"

"She's always anxious."

"After all I've done for her?" And he had one of the last flickers of his occasional mild mirth. "To think that was just what I came out to prevent!"

She took it up but to reply. "You don't regard him then as safe?"

"I was just going to ask you how in that respect you regard Madame de Vionnet."

She looked at him a little. "What woman was EVER safe? She told me," she added—and it was as if at the touch of the connexion—"of your extraordinary meeting in the country. After that a quoi se fier?"

"It was, as an accident, in all the possible or impossible chapter," Strether conceded, "amazing enough. But still, but still—!"

"But still she didn't mind?"

"She doesn't mind anything."

"Well, then, as you don't either, we may all sink to rest!"

He appeared to agree with her, but he had his reservation. "I do mind Chad's disappearance."

"Oh you'll get him back. But now you know," she said, "why I went to Mentone." He had sufficiently let her see that he had by this time gathered things together, but there was nature in her wish to make them clearer still. "I didn't want you to put it to me."

"To put it to you—?"

"The question of what you were at last—a week ago—to see for yourself. I didn't want to have to lie for her. I felt that to be too much for me. A man of course is always expected to do it—to do it, I mean, for a woman; but not a woman for another woman; unless perhaps on the tit-for-tat principle, as an indirect way of protecting herself. I don't need protection, so that I was free to 'funk' you—simply to dodge your test. The responsibility was too much for me. I gained time, and when I came back the need of a test had blown over."

Strether thought of it serenely. "Yes; when you came back little Bilham had shown me what's expected of a gentleman. Little Bilham had lied like one."

"And like what you believed him?"

"Well," said Strether, "it was but a technical lie—he classed the attachment as virtuous. That was a view for which there was much to be said—and the virtue came out for me hugely There was of course a great deal of it. I got it full in the face, and I haven't, you see, done with it yet."

"What I see, what I saw," Maria returned, "is that you dressed up even the virtue. You were wonderful—you were beautiful, as I've had the honour of telling you before; but, if you wish really to know," she sadly confessed, "I never quite knew WHERE you were. There were moments," she explained, "when you struck me as grandly cynical; there were others when you struck me as grandly vague."

Her friend considered. "I had phases. I had flights."

"Yes, but things must have a basis."

"A basis seemed to me just what her beauty supplied."

"Her beauty of person?"

"Well, her beauty of everything. The impression she makes. She has such variety and yet such harmony."

She considered him with one of her deep returns of indulgence—returns out of all proportion to the irritations they flooded over. "You're complete."

"You're always too personal," he good-humouredly said; "but that's precisely how I wondered and wandered."

"If you mean," she went on, "that she was from the first for you the most charming woman in the world, nothing's more simple. Only that was an odd foundation."

"For what I reared on it?"

"For what you didn't!"

"Well, it was all not a fixed quantity. And it had for me—it has still—such elements of strangeness. Her greater age than his, her different world, traditions, association; her other opportunities, liabilities, standards."

His friend listened with respect to his enumeration of these disparities; then she disposed of them at a stroke. "Those things are nothing when a woman's hit. It's very awful. She was hit."

Strether, on his side, did justice to that plea. "Oh of course I saw she was hit. That she was hit was what we were busy with; that she was hit was our great affair. But somehow I couldn't think of her as down in the dust. And as put there by OUR little Chad!"

"Yet wasn't 'your' little Chad just your miracle?"

Strether admitted it. "Of course I moved among miracles. It was all phantasmagoric. But the great fact was that so much of it was none of my business—as I saw my business. It isn't even now."

His companion turned away on this, and it might well have been yet again with the sharpness of a fear of how little his philosophy could bring her personally. "I wish SHE could hear you!"

"Mrs. Newsome?"

"No—not Mrs. Newsome; since I understand you that it doesn't matter now what Mrs. Newsome hears. Hasn't she heard everything?"

"Practically—yes." He had thought a moment, but he went on. "You wish Madame de Vionnet could hear me?"

"Madame de Vionnet." She had come back to him. "She thinks just the contrary of what you say. That you distinctly judge her."

He turned over the scene as the two women thus placed together for him seemed to give it. "She might have known—!"

"Might have known you don't?" Miss Gostrey asked as he let it drop. "She was sure of it at first," she pursued as he said nothing; "she took it for granted, at least, as any woman in her position would. But after that she changed her mind; she believed you believed—"

"Well?"—he was curious.

"Why in her sublimity. And that belief had remained with her, I make out, till the accident of the other day opened your eyes. For that it did," said Maria, "open them—"

"She can't help"—he had taken it up—"being aware? No," he mused; "I suppose she thinks of that even yet."

"Then they WERE closed? There you are! However, if you see her as the most charming woman in the world it comes to the same thing. And if you'd like me to tell her that you do still so see her—!" Miss Gostrey, in short, offered herself for service to the end.

It was an offer he could temporarily entertain; but he decided. "She knows perfectly how I see her."

"Not favourably enough, she mentioned to me, to wish ever to see her again. She told me you had taken a final leave of her. She says you've done with her."

"So I have."

Maria had a pause; then she spoke as if for conscience. "She wouldn't have done with YOU. She feels she has lost you—yet that she might have been better for you."

"Oh she has been quite good enough!" Strether laughed.

"She thinks you and she might at any rate have been friends."

"We might certainly. That's just"—he continued to laugh—"why I'm going."

It was as if Maria could feel with this then at last that she had done her best for each. But she had still an idea. "Shall I tell her that?"

"No. Tell her nothing."

"Very well then." To which in the next breath Miss Gostrey added: "Poor dear thing!"

Her friend wondered; then with raised eyebrows: "Me?"

"Oh no. Marie de Vionnet."

He accepted the correction, but he wondered still. "Are you so sorry for her as that?"

It made her think a moment—made her even speak with a smile. But she didn't really retract. "I'm sorry for us all!"

IV

He was to delay no longer to re-establish communication with Chad, and we have just seen that he had spoken to Miss Gostrey of this intention on hearing from her of the young man's absence. It was not moreover only the assurance so given that prompted him; it was the need of causing his conduct to square with another profession still—the motive he had described to her as his sharpest for now getting away. If he was to get away because of some of the relations involved in staying, the cold attitude toward them might look pedantic in the light of lingering on. He must do both things; he must see Chad, but he must go. The more he thought of the former of these duties the more he felt himself make a subject of insistence of the latter. They were alike intensely present to him as he sat in front of a quiet little cafe into which he had dropped on quitting Maria's entresol. The rain that had spoiled his evening with her was over; for it was still to him as if his evening HAD been spoiled—though it mightn't have been wholly the rain. It was late when he left the cafe, yet not too late; he couldn't in any case go straight to bed, and he would walk round by the Boulevard Malesherbes—rather far round—on his way home. Present enough always was the small circumstance that had originally pressed for him the spring of so big a difference—the accident of little Bilham's appearance on the balcony of the mystic troisieme at the moment of his first visit, and the effect of it on his sense of what was then before him. He recalled his watch, his wait, and the recognition that had proceeded from the young stranger, that had played frankly into the air and had presently brought him up—things smoothing the way for his first straight step. He had since had occasion, a few times, to pass the house without going in; but he had never passed it without again feeling how it had then spoken to him. He stopped short to-night on coming to sight of it: it was as if his last day were oddly copying his first. The windows of Chad's apartment were open to the balcony—a pair of them lighted; and a figure that had come out and taken up little Bilham's attitude, a figure whose cigarette-spark he could see leaned on the rail and looked down at him. It denoted however no reappearance of his younger friend; it quickly defined itself in the tempered darkness as Chad's more solid shape; so that Chad's was the attention that after he had stepped forward into the street and signalled, he easily engaged; Chad's was the voice that, sounding into the night with promptness and seemingly with joy, greeted him and called him up.

That the young man had been visible there just in this position expressed somehow for Strether that, as Maria Gostrey had reported, he had been absent and silent; and our friend drew breath on each landing—the lift, at that hour, having ceased to work—before the implications of the fact. He had been for a week intensely away, away to a distance and alone; but he was more back than ever, and the attitude in which Strether had surprised him was something more than a return—it was clearly a conscious surrender. He had arrived but an hour before, from London, from Lucerne, from Homburg, from no matter where—though the visitor's fancy, on the staircase, liked to fill it out; and after a bath, a talk with Baptiste and a supper of light cold clever French things, which one could see the remains of there in the circle of the lamp, pretty and ultra-Parisian, he had come into the air again for a smoke, was occupied at the moment of Strether's approach in what might have been called taking up his life afresh. His life, his life!—Strether paused anew, on the last flight, at this final rather breathless sense of what Chad's life was doing with Chad's mother's emissary. It was dragging him, at strange hours, up the staircases of the rich; it was keeping him out of bed at the end of long hot days; it was transforming beyond recognition the simple, subtle, conveniently uniform thing that had anciently passed with him for a life of his own. Why should it concern him that Chad was to be fortified in the pleasant practice of smoking on balconies, of supping on salads, of feeling his special conditions agreeably reaffirm themselves, of finding reassurance in comparisons and contrasts? There was no answer to such a question but that he was still practically committed—he had perhaps never yet so much known it. It made him feel old, and he would buy his railway-ticket—feeling, no doubt, older—the next day; but he had meanwhile come up four flights, counting the entresol, at midnight and without a lift, for Chad's life. The young man, hearing him by this time, and with Baptiste sent to rest, was already at the door; so that Strether had before him in full visibility the cause in which he was labouring and even, with the troisieme fairly gained, panting a little.

Chad offered him, as always, a welcome in which the cordial and the formal—so far as the formal was the respectful—handsomely met; and after he had expressed a hope that he would let him put him up for the night Strether was in full possession of the key, as it might have been called, to what had lately happened. If he had just thought of himself as old Chad was at sight of him thinking of him as older: he wanted to put him up for the night just because he was ancient and weary. It could never be said the tenant of these quarters wasn't nice to him; a tenant who, if he might indeed now keep him, was probably prepared to work it all still more thoroughly. Our friend had in fact the impression that with the minimum of encouragement Chad would propose to keep him indefinitely; an impression in the lap of which one of his own possibilities seemed to sit. Madame de Vionnet had wished him to stay—so why didn't that happily fit? He could enshrine himself for the rest of his days in his young host's chambre d'ami and draw out these days at his young host's expense: there could scarce be greater logical expression of the countenance he had been moved to give. There was literally a minute—it was strange enough—during which he grasped the idea that as he WAS acting, as he could only act, he was inconsistent. The sign that the inward forces he had obeyed really hung together would be that—in default always of another career—he should promote the good cause by mounting guard on it. These things, during his first minutes, came and went; but they were after all practically disposed of as soon as he had mentioned his errand. He had come to say good-bye—yet that was only a part; so that from the moment Chad accepted his farewell the question of a more ideal affirmation gave way to something else. He proceeded with the rest of his business. "You'll be a brute, you know—you'll be guilty of the last infamy—if you ever forsake her."

That, uttered there at the solemn hour, uttered in the place that was full of her influence, was the rest of his business; and when once he had heard himself say it he felt that his message had never before been spoken. It placed his present call immediately on solid ground, and the effect of it was to enable him quite to play with what we have called the key. Chad showed no shade of embarrassment, but had none the less been troubled for him after their meeting in the country; had had fears and doubts on the subject of his comfort. He was disturbed, as it were, only FOR him, and had positively gone away to ease him off, to let him down—if it wasn't indeed rather to screw him up—the more gently. Seeing him now fairly jaded he had come, with characteristic good humour, all the way to meet him, and what Strether thereupon supremely made out was that he would abound for him to the end in conscientious assurances. This was what was between them while the visitor remained; so far from having to go over old ground he found his entertainer keen to agree to everything. It couldn't be put too strongly for him that he'd be a brute. "Oh rather!—if I should do anything of THAT sort. I hope you believe I really feel it."

"I want it," said Strether, "to be my last word of all to you. I can't say more, you know; and I don't see how I can do more, in every way, than I've done."

Chad took this, almost artlessly, as a direct allusion. "You've seen her?"

"Oh yes—to say good-bye. And if I had doubted the truth of what I tell you—"

"She'd have cleared up your doubt?" Chad understood—"rather"—again! It even kept him briefly silent. But he made that up. "She must have been wonderful."

"She WAS," Strether candidly admitted—all of which practically told as a reference to the conditions created by the accident of the previous week.

They appeared for a little to be looking back at it; and that came out still more in what Chad next said. "I don't know what you've really thought, all along; I never did know—for anything, with you, seemed to be possible. But of course—of course—" Without confusion, quite with nothing but indulgence, he broke down, he pulled up. "After all, you understand. I spoke to you originally only as I HAD to speak. There's only one way—isn't there?—about such things. However," he smiled with a final philosophy, "I see it's all right."

Strether met his eyes with a sense of multiplying thoughts. What was it that made him at present, late at night and after journeys, so renewedly, so substantially young? Strether saw in a moment what it was—it was that he was younger again than Madame de Vionnet. He himself said immediately none of the things that he was thinking; he said something quite different. "You HAVE really been to a distance?"

"I've been to England." Chad spoke cheerfully and promptly, but gave no further account of it than to say: "One must sometimes get off."

Strether wanted no more facts—he only wanted to justify, as it were, his question. "Of course you do as you're free to do. But I hope, this time, that you didn't go for ME."

"For very shame at bothering you really too much? My dear man," Chad laughed, "what WOULDn't I do for you?"

Strether's easy answer for this was that it was a disposition he had exactly come to profit by. "Even at the risk of being in your way I've waited on, you know, for a definite reason."

Chad took it in. "Oh yes—for us to make if possible a still better impression." And he stood there happily exhaling his full general consciousness. "I'm delighted to gather that you feel we've made it."

There was a pleasant irony in the words, which his guest, preoccupied and keeping to the point, didn't take up. "If I had my sense of wanting the rest of the time—the time of their being still on this side," he continued to explain—"I know now why I wanted it."

He was as grave, as distinct, as a demonstrator before a blackboard, and Chad continued to face him like an intelligent pupil. "You wanted to have been put through the whole thing."

Strether again, for a moment, said nothing; he turned his eyes away, and they lost themselves, through the open window, in the dusky outer air. "I shall learn from the Bank here where they're now having their letters, and my last word, which I shall write in the morning and which they're expecting as my ultimatum, will so immediately reach them." The light of his plural pronoun was sufficiently reflected in his companion's face as he again met it; and he completed his demonstration. He pursued indeed as if for himself. "Of course I've first to justify what I shall do."

"You're justifying it beautifully!" Chad declared.

"It's not a question of advising you not to go," Strether said, "but of absolutely preventing you, if possible, from so much as thinking of it. Let me accordingly appeal to you by all you hold sacred."

Chad showed a surprise. "What makes you think me capable—?"

"You'd not only be, as I say, a brute; you'd be," his companion went on in the same way, "a criminal of the deepest dye."

Chad gave a sharper look, as if to gauge a possible suspicion. "I don't know what should make you think I'm tired of her."

Strether didn't quite know either, and such impressions, for the imaginative mind, were always too fine, too floating, to produce on the spot their warrant. There was none the less for him, in the very manner of his host's allusion to satiety as a thinkable motive, a slight breath of the ominous. "I feel how much more she can do for you. She hasn't done it all yet. Stay with her at least till she has."

"And leave her THEN?"

Chad had kept smiling, but its effect in Strether was a shade of dryness. "Don't leave her BEFORE. When you've got all that can be got—I don't say," he added a trifle grimly. "That will be the proper time. But as, for you, from such a woman, there will always be something to be got, my remark's not a wrong to her." Chad let him go on, showing every decent deference, showing perhaps also a candid curiosity for this sharper accent. "I remember you, you know, as you were."

"An awful ass, wasn't I?"

The response was as prompt as if he had pressed a spring; it had a ready abundance at which he even winced; so that he took a moment to meet it. "You certainly then wouldn't have seemed worth all you've let me in for. You've defined yourself better. Your value has quintupled."

"Well then, wouldn't that be enough—?"

Chad had risked it jocosely, but Strether remained blank. "Enough?"

"If one SHOULD wish to live on one's accumulations?" After which, however, as his friend appeared cold to the joke, the young man as easily dropped it. "Of course I really never forget, night or day, what I owe her. I owe her everything. I give you my word of honour," he frankly rang out, "that I'm not a bit tired of her." Strether at this only gave him a stare: the way youth could express itself was again and again a wonder. He meant no harm, though he might after all be capable of much; yet he spoke of being "tired" of her almost as he might have spoken of being tired of roast mutton for dinner. "She has never for a moment yet bored me—never been wanting, as the cleverest women sometimes are, in tact. She has never talked about her tact—as even they too sometimes talk; but she has always had it. She has never had it more"—he handsomely made the point—"than just lately." And he scrupulously went further. "She has never been anything I could call a burden."

Strether for a moment said nothing; then he spoke gravely, with his shade of dryness deepened. "Oh if you didn't do her justice—!"

"I SHOULD be a beast, eh?"

Strether devoted no time to saying what he would be; THAT, visibly, would take them far. If there was nothing for it but to repeat, however, repetition was no mistake. "You owe her everything—very much more than she can ever owe you. You've in other words duties to her, of the most positive sort; and I don't see what other duties—as the others are presented to you—can be held to go before them."

Chad looked at him with a smile. "And you know of course about the others, eh?—since it's you yourself who have done the presenting."

"Much of it—yes—and to the best of my ability. But not all—from the moment your sister took my place."

"She didn't," Chad returned. "Sally took a place, certainly; but it was never, I saw from the first moment, to be yours. No one—with us—will ever take yours. It wouldn't be possible."

"Ah of course," sighed Strether, "I knew it. I believe you're right. No one in the world, I imagine, was ever so portentously solemn. There I am," he added with another sigh, as if weary enough, on occasion, of this truth. "I was made so."

Chad appeared for a little to consider the way he was made; he might for this purpose have measured him up and down. His conclusion favoured the fact. "YOU have never needed any one to make you better. There has never been any one good enough. They couldn't," the young man declared.

His friend hesitated. "I beg your pardon. They HAVE."

Chad showed, not without amusement, his doubt. "Who then?"

Strether—though a little dimly—smiled at him. "Women—too."

"'Two'?"—Chad stared and laughed. "Oh I don't believe, for such work, in any more than one! So you're proving too much. And what IS beastly, at all events," he added, "is losing you."

Strether had set himself in motion for departure, but at this he paused. "Are you afraid?"

"Afraid—?"

"Of doing wrong. I mean away from my eye." Before Chad could speak, however, he had taken himself up. "I AM, certainly," he laughed, "prodigious."

"Yes, you spoil us for all the stupid—!" This might have been, on Chad's part, in its extreme emphasis, almost too freely extravagant; but it was full, plainly enough, of the intention of comfort, it carried with it a protest against doubt and a promise, positively, of performance. Picking up a hat in the vestibule he came out with his friend, came downstairs, took his arm, affectionately, as to help and guide him, treating him if not exactly as aged and infirm, yet as a noble eccentric who appealed to tenderness, and keeping on with him, while they walked, to the next corner and the next. "You needn't tell me, you needn't tell me!"—this again as they proceeded, he wished to make Strether feel. What he needn't tell him was now at last, in the geniality of separation, anything at all it concerned him to know. He knew, up to the hilt—that really came over Chad; he understood, felt, recorded his vow; and they lingered on it as they had lingered in their walk to Strether's hotel the night of their first meeting. The latter took, at this hour, all he could get; he had given all he had had to give; he was as depleted as if he had spent his last sou. But there was just one thing for which, before they broke off, Chad seemed disposed slightly to bargain. His companion needn't, as he said, tell him, but he might himself mention that he had been getting some news of the art of advertisement. He came out quite suddenly with this announcement while Strether wondered if his revived interest were what had taken him, with strange inconsequence, over to London. He appeared at all events to have been looking into the question and had encountered a revelation. Advertising scientifically worked presented itself thus as the great new force. "It really does the thing, you know."

They were face to face under the street-lamp as they had been the first night, and Strether, no doubt, looked blank. "Affects, you mean, the sale of the object advertised?"

"Yes—but affects it extraordinarily; really beyond what one had supposed. I mean of course when it's done as one makes out that in our roaring age, it CAN be done. I've been finding out a little, though it doubtless doesn't amount to much more than what you originally, so awfully vividly—and all, very nearly, that first night—put before me. It's an art like another, and infinite like all the arts." He went on as if for the joke of it—

almost as if his friend's face amused him. "In the hands, naturally, of a master. The right man must take hold. With the right man to work it c'est un monde."

Strether had watched him quite as if, there on the pavement without a pretext, he had begun to dance a fancy step. "Is what you're thinking of that you yourself, in the case you have in mind, would be the right man?"

Chad had thrown back his light coat and thrust each of his thumbs into an armhole of his waistcoat; in which position his fingers played up and down. "Why, what is he but what you yourself, as I say, took me for when you first came out?"

Strether felt a little faint, but he coerced his attention. "Oh yes, and there's no doubt that, with your natural parts, you'd have much in common with him. Advertising is clearly at this time of day the secret of trade. It's quite possible it will be open to you—giving the whole of your mind to it—to make the whole place hum with you. Your mother's appeal is to the whole of your mind, and that's exactly the strength of her case."

Chad's fingers continued to twiddle, but he had something of a drop. "Ah we've been through my mother's case!"

"So I thought. Why then do you speak of the matter?"

"Only because it was part of our original discussion. To wind up where we began, my interest's purely platonic. There at any rate the fact is—the fact of the possible. I mean the money in it."

"Oh damn the money in it!" said Strether. And then as the young man's fixed smile seemed to shine out more strange: "Shall you give your friend up for the money in it?"

Chad preserved his handsome grimace as well as the rest of his attitude. "You're not altogether—in your so great 'solemnity'—kind. Haven't I been drinking you in—showing you all I feel you're worth to me? What have I done, what am I doing, but cleave to her to the death? The only thing is," he good-humouredly explained, "that one can't but have it before one, in the cleaving—the point where the death comes in. Don't be afraid for THAT. It's pleasant to a fellow's feelings," he developed, "to 'size-up' the bribe he applies his foot to."

"Oh then if all you want's a kickable surface the bribe's enormous."

"Good. Then there it goes!" Chad administered his kick with fantastic force and sent an imaginary object flying. It was accordingly as if they were once more rid of the question and could come back to what really concerned him. "Of course I shall see you tomorrow."

But Strether scarce heeded the plan proposed for this; he had still the impression—not the slighter for the simulated kick—of an irrelevant hornpipe or jig. "You're restless."

"Ah," returned Chad as they parted, "you're exciting."

V

He had, however, within two days, another separation to face. He had sent Maria Gostrey a word early, by hand, to ask if he might come to breakfast; in consequence of which, at noon, she awaited him in the cool shade of her little Dutch-looking dining-room. This retreat was at the back of the house, with a view of a scrap of old garden that had been saved from modern ravage; and though he had on more than one other occasion had his legs under its small and peculiarly polished table of hospitality, the place had never before struck him as so sacred to pleasant knowledge, to intimate charm, to antique order, to a neatness that was almost august. To sit there was, as he had told his hostess before, to see life reflected for the time in ideally kept pewter; which was somehow becoming, improving to life, so that one's eyes were held and comforted. Strether's were comforted at all events now—and the more that it was the last time—with the charming effect, on the board bare of a cloth and proud of its perfect surface, of the small old crockery and old silver, matched by the more substantial pieces happily disposed about the room. The specimens of vivid Delf, in particular had the dignity of family portraits; and it was in the midst of them that our friend resignedly expressed himself. He spoke even with a certain philosophic humour. "There's nothing more to wait for; I seem to have done a good day's work. I've let them have it all round. I've seen Chad, who has been to London and come back. He tells me I'm 'exciting,' and I seem indeed pretty well to have upset every one. I've at any rate excited HIM. He's distinctly restless."

"You've excited ME," Miss Gostrey smiled. "I'M distinctly restless."

"Oh you were that when I found you. It seems to me I've rather got you out of it. What's this," he asked as he looked about him, "but a haunt of ancient peace?"

"I wish with all my heart," she presently replied, "I could make you treat it as a haven of rest." On which they fronted each other, across the table, as if things unuttered were in the air.

Strether seemed, in his way, when he next spoke, to take some of them up. "It wouldn't give me—that would be the trouble—what it will, no doubt, still give you. I'm not," he explained, leaning back in his chair, but with his eyes on a small ripe round melon—"in real harmony with what surrounds me. You ARE. I take it too hard. You DON'T. It makes—that's what it comes to in the end—a fool of me." Then at a tangent, "What has he been doing in London?" he demanded.

"Ah one may go to London," Maria laughed. "You know I did."

Yes—he took the reminder. "And you brought ME back." He brooded there opposite to her, but without gloom. "Whom has Chad brought? He's full of ideas. And I wrote to Sarah," he added, "the first thing this morning. So I'm square. I'm ready for them."

She neglected certain parts of this speech in the interest of others. "Marie said to me the other day that she felt him to have the makings of an immense man of business."

"There it is. He's the son of his father!"

"But SUCH a father!"

"Ah just the right one from that point of view! But it isn't his father in him," Strether added, "that troubles me."

"What is it then?" He came back to his breakfast; he partook presently of the charming melon, which she liberally cut for him; and it was only after this that he met her question. Then moreover it was but to remark that he'd answer her presently. She waited, she watched, she served him and amused him, and it was perhaps with this last idea that she soon reminded him of his having never even yet named to her the article produced at Woollett. "Do you remember our talking of it in London—that night at the play?" Before he could say yes, however, she had put it to him for other matters. Did he remember, did he remember—this and that of their first days? He remembered everything, bringing up with humour even things of which she professed no recollection, things she vehemently denied; and falling back above all on the great interest of their early time, the curiosity felt by both of them as to where he would "come out." They had so assumed it was to be in some wonderful place—they had thought of it as so very MUCH out. Well, that was doubtless what it had been—since he had come out just there. He was out, in truth, as far as it was possible to be, and must now rather bethink himself of getting in again. He found on the spot the image of his recent history; he was like one of the figures of the old clock at Berne. THEY came out, on one side, at their hour, jigged along their little course in the public eye, and went in on the other side. He too had jigged his little course—him too a modest retreat awaited. He offered now, should she really like to know, to name the great product of Woollett. It would be a great commentary on everything. At this she stopped him off; she not only had no wish to know, but she wouldn't know for the world. She had done with the products of Woollett—for all the good she had got from them. She desired no further news of them, and she mentioned that Madame de Vionnet herself had, to her knowledge, lived exempt from the information he was ready to supply. She had never consented to receive it, though she would have taken it, under stress, from Mrs. Pocock. But it was a matter about which Mrs. Pocock appeared to have had little to say—never sounding the word—and it didn't signify now. There was nothing clearly for Maria Gostrey that signified now—save one sharp point, that is, to which she came in time. "I don't know whether it's before you as a possibility that, left to himself, Mr. Chad may after all go back. I judge that it IS more or less so before you, from what you just now said of him."

Her guest had his eyes on her, kindly but attentively, as if foreseeing what was to follow this. "I don't think it will be for the money." And then as she seemed uncertain: "I mean I don't believe it will be for that he'll give her up."

"Then he WILL give her up?"

Strether waited a moment, rather slow and deliberate now, drawing out a little this last soft stage, pleading with her in various suggestive and unspoken ways for patience and understanding. "What were you just about to ask me?"

"Is there anything he can do that would make you patch it up?"

"With Mrs. Newsome?"

Her assent, as if she had had a delicacy about sounding the name, was only in her face; but she added with it: "Or is there anything he can do that would make HER try it?"

"To patch it up with me?" His answer came at last in a conclusive headshake. "There's nothing any one can do. It's over. Over for both of us."

Maria wondered, seemed a little to doubt. "Are you so sure for her?"

"Oh yes—sure now. Too much has happened. I'm different for her."

She took it in then, drawing a deeper breath. "I see. So that as she's different for YOU—"

"Ah but," he interrupted, "she's not." And as Miss Gostrey wondered again: "She's the same. She's more than ever the same. But I do what I didn't before—I SEE her."

He spoke gravely and as if responsibly—since he had to pronounce; and the effect of it was slightly solemn, so that she simply exclaimed "Oh!" Satisfied and grateful, however, she showed in her own next words an acceptance of his statement. "What then do you go home to?"

He had pushed his plate a little away, occupied with another side of the matter; taking refuge verily in that side and feeling so moved that he soon found himself on his feet. He was affected in advance by what he believed might come from her, and he would have liked to forestall it and deal with it tenderly; yet in the presence of it he wished still more to be—though as smoothly as possible—deterrent and conclusive. He put her question by for the moment; he told her more about Chad. "It would have been impossible to meet me more than he did last night on the question of the infamy of not sticking to her."

"Is that what you called it for him—'infamy'?"

"Oh rather! I described to him in detail the base creature he'd be, and he quite agrees with me about it."

"So that it's really as if you had nailed him?"

"Quite really as if—! I told him I should curse him."

"Oh," she smiled, "you HAVE done it." And then having thought again: "You CAN'T after that propose—!" Yet she scanned his face.

"Propose again to Mrs. Newsome?"

She hesitated afresh, but she brought it out. "I've never believed, you know, that you did propose. I always believed it was really she—and, so far as that goes, I can understand it. What I mean is," she explained, "that with such a spirit—the spirit of curses!—your breach is past mending. She has only to know what you've done to him never again to raise a finger."

"I've done," said Strether, "what I could—one can't do more. He protests his devotion and his horror. But I'm not sure I've saved him. He protests too much. He asks how one can dream of his being tired. But he has all life before him."

Maria saw what he meant. "He's formed to please."

"And it's our friend who has formed him." Strether felt in it the strange irony.

"So it's scarcely his fault!"

"It's at any rate his danger. I mean," said Strether, "it's hers. But she knows it."

"Yes, she knows it. And is your idea," Miss Gostrey asked, "that there was some other woman in London?"

"Yes. No. That is I HAVE no ideas. I'm afraid of them. I've done with them." And he put out his hand to her. "Good-bye."

It brought her back to her unanswered question. "To what do you go home?"

"I don't know. There will always be something."

"To a great difference," she said as she kept his hand.

"A great difference—no doubt. Yet I shall see what I can make of it."

"Shall you make anything so good—?" But, as if remembering what Mrs. Newsome had done, it was as far as she went.

He had sufficiently understood. "So good as this place at this moment? So good as what YOU make of everything you touch?" He took a moment to say, for, really and truly, what stood about him there in her offer—which was as the offer of exquisite service, of lightened care, for the rest of his days—might well have tempted. It built him softly round, it roofed him warmly over, it rested, all so firm, on selection. And what ruled selection was beauty and knowledge. It was awkward, it was almost stupid, not to seem to prize such things; yet, none the less, so far as they made his opportunity they made it only for a moment. She'd moreover understand—she always understood.

That indeed might be, but meanwhile she was going on. "There's nothing, you know, I wouldn't do for you."

"Oh yes—I know."

"There's nothing," she repeated, "in all the world."

"I know. I know. But all the same I must go." He had got it at last. "To be right."

"To be right?"

She had echoed it in vague deprecation, but he felt it already clear for her. "That, you see, is my only logic. Not, out of the whole affair, to have got anything for myself."

She thought. "But with your wonderful impressions you'll have got a great deal."

"A great deal"—he agreed. "But nothing like YOU. It's you who would make me wrong!"

Honest and fine, she couldn't greatly pretend she didn't see it. Still she could pretend just a little. "But why should you be so dreadfully right?"

"That's the way that—if I must go—you yourself would be the first to want me. And I can't do anything else."

So then she had to take it, though still with her defeated protest. "It isn't so much your BEING 'right'—it's your horrible sharp eye for what makes you so."

"Oh but you're just as bad yourself. You can't resist me when I point that out."

She sighed it at last all comically, all tragically, away. "I can't indeed resist you."

"Then there we are!" said Strether.

THE BEAST IN THE JUNGLE

CHAPTER I

What determined the speech that startled him in the course of their encounter scarcely matters, being probably but some words spoken by himself quite without intention—spoken as they lingered and slowly moved together after their renewal of acquaintance. He had been conveyed by friends an hour or two before to the house at which she was staying; the party of visitors at the other house, of whom he was one, and thanks to whom it was his theory, as always, that he was lost in the crowd, had been invited over to luncheon. There had been after luncheon much dispersal, all in the interest of the original motive, a view of Weatherend itself and the fine things, intrinsic features, pictures, heirlooms, treasures of all the arts, that made the place almost famous; and the great rooms were so numerous that guests could wander at their will, hang back from the principal group and in cases where they took such matters with the last seriousness give themselves up to mysterious appreciations and measurements. There were persons to be observed, singly or in couples, bending toward objects in out-of-the-way corners with their hands on their knees and their heads nodding quite as with the emphasis of an excited sense of smell. When they were two they either mingled their sounds of ecstasy or melted into silences of even deeper import, so that there were aspects of the occasion that gave it for Marcher much the air of the "look round," previous to a sale highly advertised, that excites or quenches, as may be, the dream of acquisition. The dream of acquisition at Weatherend would have had to be wild indeed, and John Marcher found himself, among such suggestions, disconcerted almost equally by the presence of those who knew too much and by that of those who knew nothing. The great rooms caused so much poetry and history to press upon him that he needed some straying apart to feel in a proper relation with them, though this impulse was not, as happened, like the gloating of some of his companions, to be compared to the movements of a dog sniffing a cupboard. It had an issue promptly enough in a direction that was not to have been calculated.

It led, briefly, in the course of the October afternoon, to his closer meeting with May Bartram, whose face, a reminder, yet not quite a remembrance, as they sat much separated at a very long table, had begun merely by troubling him rather pleasantly. It affected him as the sequel of something of which he had lost the beginning. He knew it, and for the time quite welcomed it, as a continuation, but didn't know what it continued, which was an interest or an amusement the greater as he was also somehow aware—yet without a direct sign from her—that the young woman herself hadn't lost the thread. She hadn't lost it, but she wouldn't give it back to him, he saw, without some putting forth of his hand for it; and he not only saw that, but saw several things more, things odd enough in the light of the fact that at the moment some accident of grouping brought them face to face he was still merely fumbling with the idea that any contact between them in the past would have had no importance. If it had had no importance he scarcely knew why his actual impression of her should so seem to have so much; the answer to which, however, was that in such a life as they all appeared to be leading for the moment one could but take things as they came. He was satisfied, without in the least being able to say why, that this young lady might roughly have ranked in the house as a poor relation; satisfied also that she was not there on a brief visit, but was more or less a part of the establishment—almost a working, a remunerated part. Didn't she enjoy at periods a protection that she paid for by helping, among other services, to show the place and explain it, deal with the tiresome people, answer questions about the dates of the building, the styles of the furniture, the authorship of the pictures, the favourite haunts of the ghost? It wasn't that she looked as if you could have given her shillings—it was impossible to look less so. Yet when she finally drifted toward him, distinctly handsome, though ever so much older—older than when he had seen her before—it might have been as an effect of her guessing that he had, within the couple of hours, devoted more imagination to her than to all the others put together, and had thereby penetrated to a kind of truth that the others were too stupid for. She *was* there on harder terms than any one; she was there as a consequence of things suffered, one way and another, in the interval of years; and she remembered him very much as she was remembered—only a good deal better.

By the time they at last thus came to speech they were alone in one of the rooms—remarkable for a fine portrait over the chimney-place—out of which their friends had passed, and the charm of it was that even before they had spoken they had practically arranged with each other to stay behind for talk. The charm, happily, was in other things too—partly in there being scarce a spot at Weatherend without something to stay behind for. It was in the way the autumn day looked into the high windows as it waned; the way the red light, breaking at the close from under a low sombre sky, reached out in a long shaft and played over old wainscots, old tapestry, old gold, old colour. It was most of all perhaps in the way she came to him as if, since she had been turned on to deal with the simpler sort, he might, should he choose to keep the whole thing down, just take her mild attention for a part of her general business. As soon as he heard her voice, however, the gap was filled up and the missing link supplied; the slight irony he divined in her attitude lost its advantage. He almost jumped at it to get there before her. "I met you years and years ago in Rome. I remember all about it." She confessed to disappointment—she had been so sure he didn't; and to prove how well he did he began to pour forth the particular recollections that popped up as he called for them. Her face and her voice, all at his service now, worked the miracle—the impression operating like the torch of a lamplighter who touches into flame, one by one, a long row of gas-jets. Marcher flattered himself the illumination was brilliant, yet he was really still more pleased on her showing him, with amusement, that in his haste to make everything right he had got most things rather wrong. It hadn't been at Rome—it had been at Naples; and it hadn't been eight years before—it had been more nearly ten. She hadn't been, either, with her uncle and aunt, but with her mother and brother; in addition to which it was not with the Pembles *he* had been, but with the Boyers, coming down in their company from Rome—a point on which she insisted, a little to his confusion, and as to which she had her evidence in hand. The Boyers she had known, but didn't know the Pembles, though she had heard of them, and it was the people he was with who had made them acquainted. The incident of the thunderstorm that had raged round them with such violence as to drive them for refuge into an excavation—this incident had not occurred at the Palace of the Caesars, but at Pompeii, on an occasion when they had been present there at an important find.

He accepted her amendments, he enjoyed her corrections, though the moral of them was, she pointed out, that he *really* didn't remember the least thing about her; and he only felt it as a drawback that when all was made strictly historic there didn't appear much of anything left. They lingered together still, she neglecting her office—for from the moment he was so clever she had no proper right to him—and both neglecting the house, just waiting as to see if a memory or two more wouldn't again breathe on them. It hadn't taken them many minutes, after all, to put down on the table, like the cards of a pack, those that constituted their respective hands; only what came out was that the pack was unfortunately not perfect—that the past, invoked, invited, encouraged, could give them, naturally, no more than it had. It had made them anciently meet—her at twenty, him at twenty-five; but nothing was so strange, they seemed to say to each other, as that, while so occupied, it hadn't done a little more for them. They looked at each other as with the feeling of an occasion missed; the present would have been so much better if the other, in the far distance, in the foreign land, hadn't been so stupidly meagre. There weren't, apparently, all counted, more than a dozen little old things that had succeeded in coming to pass between them; trivialities of youth, simplicities of freshness, stupidities of ignorance, small possible germs, but too deeply buried—too deeply (didn't it seem?) to sprout after so many years. Marcher could only feel he ought to have rendered her some service—saved her from a capsized boat in the bay or at least recovered her dressing-bag, filched from her cab in the streets of Naples by a lazzarone with a stiletto. Or it would have been nice if he could have been taken with fever all alone at his hotel, and she could have come to look after him, to write to his people, to drive him out in convalescence. *Then* they would be in possession of the something or other that their actual show seemed to lack. It yet somehow presented itself, this show, as too good to be spoiled; so that they were reduced for a few minutes more to wondering a little helplessly why—since they seemed to know a certain number of the same people—their reunion had been so long averted. They didn't use that name for it, but their delay from minute to minute to join the others was a kind of confession that they didn't quite want it to be a failure. Their attempted supposition of reasons for their not having met but showed how little they knew of each other. There came in fact a moment when Marcher felt a positive pang. It was vain to pretend she was an old friend, for all the communities were wanting, in spite of which it was as an old friend that he saw she would have suited him. He had new ones enough—was surrounded with them for instance on the stage of the other house; as a new one he probably wouldn't have so much as noticed her. He would have liked to invent something, get her to make-believe with him that some passage of a romantic or critical kind *had* originally occurred. He was really almost reaching out in imagination—as against time—for something that would do, and saying to himself that if it didn't come this sketch of a fresh start would show for quite awkwardly bungled. They would separate, and now for no second or no third chance. They would have tried and not succeeded. Then it was, just at the turn, as he afterwards made it out to himself, that, everything else failing, she herself decided to take up the case and, as it were, save the situation. He felt as soon as she spoke that she had been consciously keeping back what she said and hoping to get on without it; a scruple in her that immensely touched him when, by the end of three or four minutes more, he was able to measure it. What she brought out, at any rate, quite cleared the air and supplied the link—the link it was so odd he should frivolously have managed to lose.

"You know you told me something I've never forgotten and that again and again has made me think of you since; it was that tremendously hot day when we went to Sorrento, across the bay, for the breeze. What I allude to was what you said to me, on the way back, as we sat under the awning of the boat enjoying the cool. Have you forgotten?"

He had forgotten, and was even more surprised than ashamed. But the great thing was that he saw in this no vulgar reminder of any "sweet" speech. The vanity of women had long memories, but she was making no claim on him of a compliment or a mistake. With another woman, a totally different one, he might have feared the recall possibly even some imbecile "offer." So, in having to say that he had indeed forgotten, he was conscious rather of a loss than of a gain; he already saw an interest in the matter of her mention. "I try to think—but I give it up. Yet I remember the Sorrento day."

"I'm not very sure you do," May Bartram after a moment said; "and I'm not very sure I ought to want you to. It's dreadful to bring a person back at any time to what he was ten years before. If you've lived away from it," she smiled, "so much the better."

"Ah if *you* haven't why should I?" he asked.

"Lived away, you mean, from what I myself was?"

"From what *I* was. I was of course an ass," Marcher went on; "but I would rather know from you just the sort of ass I was than—from the moment you have something in your mind—not know anything."

Still, however, she hesitated. "But if you've completely ceased to be that sort—?"

"Why I can then all the more bear to know. Besides, perhaps I haven't."

"Perhaps. Yet if you haven't," she added, "I should suppose you'd remember. Not indeed that *I* in the least connect with my impression the invidious name you use. If I had only thought you foolish," she explained, "the thing I speak of wouldn't so have remained with me. It was about yourself." She waited as if it might come to him; but as, only meeting her eyes in wonder, he gave no sign, she burnt her ships. "Has it ever happened?"

Then it was that, while he continued to stare, a light broke for him and the blood slowly came to his face, which began to burn with recognition.

"Do you mean I told you—?" But he faltered, lest what came to him shouldn't be right, lest he should only give himself away.

"It was something about yourself that it was natural one shouldn't forget—that is if one remembered you at all. That's why I ask you," she smiled, "if the thing you then spoke of has ever come to pass?"

Oh then he saw, but he was lost in wonder and found himself embarrassed. This, he also saw, made her sorry for him, as if her allusion had been a mistake. It took him but a moment, however, to feel it hadn't been, much as it had been a surprise. After the first little shock of it her knowledge on the contrary began, even if rather strangely, to taste sweet to him. She was the only other person in the world then who would have it, and she had had it all these years, while the fact of his having so breathed his secret had unaccountably faded from him. No wonder they couldn't have met as if nothing had happened. "I judge," he finally said, "that I know what you mean. Only I had strangely enough lost any sense of having taken you so far into my confidence."

"Is it because you've taken so many others as well?"

"I've taken nobody. Not a creature since then."

"So that I'm the only person who knows?"

"The only person in the world."

"Well," she quickly replied, "I myself have never spoken. I've never, never repeated of you what you told me." She looked at him so that he perfectly believed her. Their eyes met over it in such a way that he was without a doubt. "And I never will."

She spoke with an earnestness that, as if almost excessive, put him at ease about her possible derision. Somehow the whole question was a new luxury to him—that is from the moment she was in possession. If she didn't take the sarcastic view she clearly took the sympathetic, and that was what he had had, in all the long time, from no one whomsoever. What he felt was that he couldn't at present have begun to tell her, and yet could profit perhaps exquisitely by the accident of having done so of old. "Please don't then. We're just right as it is."

"Oh I am," she laughed, "if you are!" To which she added: "Then you do still feel in the same way?"

It was impossible he shouldn't take to himself that she was really interested, though it all kept coming as a perfect surprise. He had thought of himself so long as abominably alone, and lo he wasn't alone a bit. He hadn't been, it appeared, for an hour—since those moments on the Sorrento boat. It was she who had been, he seemed to see as he looked at her—she who had been made so by the graceless fact of his lapse of fidelity. To tell her what he had told her—what had it been but to ask something of her? something that she had given, in her charity, without his having, by a remembrance, by a return of the spirit, failing another encounter, so much as thanked her. What he had asked of her had been simply at first not to laugh at him. She had beautifully not done so for ten years, and she was not doing so now. So he had endless gratitude to make up. Only for that he must see just how he had figured to her. "What, exactly, was the account I gave—?"

"Of the way you did feel? Well, it was very simple. You said you had had from your earliest time, as the deepest thing within you, the sense of being kept for something rare and strange, possibly prodigious and terrible, that was sooner or later to happen to you, that you had in your bones the foreboding and the conviction of, and that would perhaps overwhelm you."

"Do you call that very simple?" John Marcher asked.

She thought a moment. "It was perhaps because I seemed, as you spoke, to understand it."

"You do understand it?" he eagerly asked.

Again she kept her kind eyes on him. "You still have the belief?"

"Oh!" he exclaimed helplessly. There was too much to say.

"Whatever it's to be," she clearly made out, "it hasn't yet come."

He shook his head in complete surrender now. "It hasn't yet come. Only, you know, it isn't anything I'm to do, to achieve in the world, to be distinguished or admired for. I'm not such an ass as *that*. It would be much better, no doubt, if I were."

"It's to be something you're merely to suffer?"

"Well, say to wait for—to have to meet, to face, to see suddenly break out in my life; possibly destroying all further consciousness, possibly annihilating me; possibly, on the other hand, only altering everything, striking at the root of all my world and leaving me to the consequences, however they shape themselves."

She took this in, but the light in her eyes continued for him not to be that of mockery. "Isn't what you describe perhaps but the expectation—or at any rate the sense of danger, familiar to so many people—of falling in love?"

John Marcher thought. "Did you ask me that before?"

"No—I wasn't so free-and-easy then. But it's what strikes me now."

"Of course," he said after a moment, "it strikes you. Of course it strikes *me*. Of course what's in store for me may be no more than that. The only thing is," he went on, "that I think if it had been that I should by this time know."

"Do you mean because you've *been* in love?" And then as he but looked at her in silence: "You've been in love, and it hasn't meant such a cataclysm, hasn't proved the great affair?"

"Here I am, you see. It hasn't been overwhelming."

"Then it hasn't been love," said May Bartram.

"Well, I at least thought it was. I took it for that—I've taken it till now. It was agreeable, it was delightful, it was miserable," he explained. "But it wasn't strange. It wasn't what my affair's to be."

"You want something all to yourself—something that nobody else knows or *has* known?"

CHAPTER I

"It isn't a question of what I 'want'—God knows I don't want anything. It's only a question of the apprehension that haunts me—that I live with day by day."

He said this so lucidly and consistently that he could see it further impose itself. If she hadn't been interested before she'd have been interested now.

"Is it a sense of coming violence?"

Evidently now too again he liked to talk of it. "I don't think of it as—when it does come—necessarily violent. I only think of it as natural and as of course above all unmistakeable. I think of it simply as *the* thing. *The* thing will of itself appear natural."

"Then how will it appear strange?"

Marcher bethought himself. "It won't—to *me*."

"To whom then?"

"Well," he replied, smiling at last, "say to you."

"Oh then I'm to be present?"

"Why you are present—since you know."

"I see." She turned it over. "But I mean at the catastrophe."

At this, for a minute, their lightness gave way to their gravity; it was as if the long look they exchanged held them together. "It will only depend on yourself—if you'll watch with me."

"Are you afraid?" she asked.

"Don't leave me now," he went on.

"Are you afraid?" she repeated.

"Do you think me simply out of my mind?" he pursued instead of answering. "Do I merely strike you as a harmless lunatic?"

"No," said May Bartram. "I understand you. I believe you."

"You mean you feel how my obsession—poor old thing—may correspond to some possible reality?"

"To some possible reality."

"Then you *will* watch with me?"

She hesitated, then for the third time put her question. "Are you afraid?"

"Did I tell you I was—at Naples?"

"No, you said nothing about it."

"Then I don't know. And I should like to know," said John Marcher. "You'll tell me yourself whether you think so. If you'll watch with me you'll see."

"Very good then." They had been moving by this time across the room, and at the door, before passing out, they paused as for the full wind-up of their understanding. "I'll watch with you," said May Bartram.

CHAPTER II

The fact that she "knew"—knew and yet neither chaffed him nor betrayed him—had in a short time begun to constitute between them a goodly bond, which became more marked when, within the year that followed their afternoon at Weatherend, the opportunities for meeting multiplied. The event that thus promoted these occasions was the death of the ancient lady her great-aunt, under whose wing, since losing her mother, she had to such an extent found shelter, and who, though but the widowed mother of the new successor to the property, had succeeded—thanks to a high tone and a high temper—in not forfeiting the supreme position at the great house. The deposition of this personage arrived but with her death, which, followed by many changes, made in particular a difference for the young woman in whom Marcher's expert attention had recognised from the first a dependent with a pride that might ache though it didn't bristle. Nothing for a long time had made him easier than the thought that the aching must have been much soothed by Miss Bartram's now finding herself able to set up a small home in London. She had acquired property, to an amount that made that luxury just possible, under her aunt's extremely complicated will, and when the whole matter began to be straightened out, which indeed took time, she let him know that the happy issue was at last in view. He had seen her again before that day, both because she had more than once accompanied the ancient lady to town and because he had paid another visit to the friends who so conveniently made of Weatherend one of the charms of their own hospitality. These friends had taken him back there; he had achieved there again with Miss Bartram some quiet detachment; and he had in London succeeded in persuading her to more than one brief absence from her aunt. They went together, on these latter occasions, to the National Gallery and the South Kensington Museum, where, among vivid reminders, they talked of Italy at large—not now attempting to recover, as at first, the taste of their youth and their ignorance. That recovery, the first day at Weatherend, had served its purpose well, had given them quite enough; so that they were, to Marcher's sense, no longer hovering about the head-waters of their stream, but had felt their boat pushed sharply off and down the current.

They were literally afloat together; for our gentleman this was marked, quite as marked as that the fortunate cause of it was just the buried treasure of her knowledge. He had with his own hands dug up this little hoard, brought to light—that is to within reach of the dim day constituted by their discretions and privacies—the object of value the hiding-place of which he had, after putting it into the ground himself, so strangely, so long forgotten. The rare luck of his having again just stumbled on the spot made him indifferent to any other question; he would doubtless have devoted more time to the odd accident of his lapse of memory if he hadn't been moved to devote so much to the sweetness, the comfort, as he felt, for the future, that this accident itself had helped to keep fresh. It had never entered into his plan that any one should "know", and mainly for the reason that it wasn't in him to tell any one. That would have been impossible, for nothing but the amusement of a cold world would have waited on it. Since, however, a mysterious fate had opened his mouth betimes, in spite of him, he would count that a compensation and profit by it to the utmost. That the right person *should* know tempered the asperity of his secret more even than his shyness had permitted him to imagine; and May Bartram was clearly right, because—well, because there she was. Her knowledge simply settled it; he would have been sure enough by this time had she been wrong. There was that in his situation, no doubt, that disposed him too much to see her as a mere confidant, taking all her light for him from the fact—the fact only—of her interest in his predicament; from her mercy, sympathy, seriousness, her consent not to regard him as the funniest of the funny. Aware, in fine, that her price for him was just in her giving him this constant sense of his being admirably spared, he was careful to remember that she had also a life of her own, with things that might happen to *her*, things that in friendship one should likewise take account of. Something fairly remarkable came to pass with him, for that matter, in this connexion—something represented by a certain passage of his consciousness, in the suddenest way, from one extreme to the other.

He had thought himself, so long as nobody knew, the most disinterested person in the world, carrying his concentrated burden, his perpetual suspense, ever so quietly, holding his tongue about it, giving others no glimpse of it nor of its effect upon his life, asking of them no allowance and only making on his side all those that were asked. He hadn't disturbed people with the queerness of their having to know a haunted man, though he had had moments of rather special temptation on hearing them say they were forsooth "unsettled." If they were as unsettled as he was—he who had never been settled for an hour in his life—they would know what it meant. Yet it wasn't, all the same, for him to make them, and he listened to them civilly enough. This was why he had such good—though possibly such rather colourless—manners; this was why, above all, he could regard himself, in a greedy world, as decently—as in fact perhaps even a little sublimely—unselfish. Our point is accordingly that he valued this character quite sufficiently to measure his present danger of letting it lapse, against which he promised himself to be much on his guard. He was quite ready, none the less, to be selfish just a little, since surely no more charming occasion for it had come to him. "Just a little," in a word, was just as much as Miss Bartram, taking one day with another, would let him. He never would be in the least coercive, and would keep well before him the lines on which consideration for her—the very highest—ought to proceed. He would thoroughly establish the heads under which her affairs, her requirements, her peculiarities—he went so far as to give them the latitude of that name—would come into their intercourse. All this naturally was a sign of how much he took the intercourse itself for granted. There was nothing more to be done about that. It simply existed; had sprung into being with her first penetrating question to him in the autumn light there at Weatherend. The real form it should have taken on the basis that stood out large was the form of their marrying. But the devil in this was that the very basis itself put marrying out of the question. His conviction, his apprehension, his obsession, in short, wasn't a privilege he could invite a woman to share; and that consequence of it was precisely what was the matter with him. Something or other lay in wait for him, amid the twists and the turns of the months and the years, like a crouching Beast in the Jungle. It signified little whether the crouching Beast were destined to slay him or to be slain. The definite point was the inevitable spring of the creature; and the definite lesson from that was that a man of feeling didn't cause himself to be accompanied by a lady on a tiger-hunt. Such was the image under which he had ended by figuring his life.

They had at first, none the less, in the scattered hours spent together, made no allusion to that view of it; which was a sign he was handsomely alert to give that he didn't expect, that he in fact didn't care, always to be talking about it. Such a feature in one's outlook was really like a hump on one's back. The difference it made every minute of the day existed quite independently of discussion. One discussed of course *like* a hunchback, for there was always, if nothing else, the hunchback face. That remained, and she was watching him; but people watched best, as a general thing, in silence, so that such would be predominantly the manner of their vigil. Yet he didn't want, at the same time, to be tense and solemn; tense and solemn was what he imagined he too much showed for with other people. The thing to be, with the one person who knew, was easy and natural—to make the reference rather than be seeming to avoid it, to avoid it rather than be seeming to make it, and to keep it, in any case, familiar, facetious even, rather than pedantic and portentous. Some such consideration as the latter was doubtless in his mind for instance when he wrote pleasantly to Miss Bartram that perhaps the great thing he had so long felt as in the lap of the gods was no more than this circumstance, which touched him so nearly, of her acquiring a house in London. It was the first allusion they had yet again made, needing any other hitherto so little; but when she replied, after having given him the news, that she was by no means satisfied with such a trifle as the climax to so special a suspense, she almost set him wondering if she hadn't even a larger conception of singularity for him than he had for himself. He was at all events destined to become aware little by little, as time went by, that she was all the while looking at his life, judging it, measuring it, in the light of the thing she knew, which grew to be at last, with the consecration of the years, never mentioned between them save as "the real truth" about him. That had always been his own form of reference to it, but she adopted the form so quietly that, looking back at the end of a period, he knew there was no moment at which it was traceable that she had, as he might say, got inside his idea, or exchanged the attitude of beautifully indulging for that of still more beautifully believing him.

It was always open to him to accuse her of seeing him but as the most harmless of maniacs, and this, in the long run—since it covered so much ground—was his easiest description of their friendship. He had a screw loose for her but she liked him in spite of it and was practically, against the rest of the world, his kind wise keeper, unremunerated but fairly amused and, in the absence of other near ties, not disreputably occupied. The rest of the world of course thought him queer, but she, she only, knew how, and above all why, queer; which was precisely what enabled her to dispose the concealing veil in the right folds. She took his gaiety from him—since it had to pass with them for gaiety—as she took everything else; but she certainly so far justified by her unerring touch his finer sense of the degree to which he had ended by convincing her. *She* at least never spoke of the secret of his life except as "the real truth about you," and she had in fact a wonderful way of making it seem, as such, the secret of her own life too. That was in fine how he so constantly felt her as allowing for him; he couldn't on the whole call it anything else. He allowed for himself, but she, exactly, allowed still more; partly because, better placed for a sight of the matter, she traced his unhappy perversion through reaches of its course into which he could scarce follow it. He knew how he felt, but, besides knowing that, she knew how he looked as well; he knew each of the things of importance he was insidiously kept from doing, but she could add up the amount they made, understand how much, with a lighter weight on his spirit, he might have done, and thereby establish how, clever as he was, he fell short. Above all she was in the secret of the difference between the forms he went through—those of his little office under Government, those of caring for his modest patrimony, for his library, for his garden in the country, for the people in London whose invitations he accepted and repaid—and the detachment that reigned beneath them and that made of all behaviour, all that could in the least be called behaviour, a long act of dissimulation. What it had come to was that he wore a mask painted with the social simper, out of the eye-holes of which there looked eyes of an expression not in the least matching the other features. This the stupid world, even after years, had never more than half discovered. It was only May Bartram who had, and she achieved, by an art indescribable, the feat of at once—or perhaps it was only alternately—meeting the eyes from in front and mingling her own vision, as from over his shoulder, with their peep through the apertures.

So while they grew older together she did watch with him, and so she let this association give shape and colour to her own existence. Beneath *her* forms as well detachment had learned to sit, and behaviour had become for her, in the social sense, a false account of herself. There was but one account of her that would have been true all the while and that she could give straight to nobody, least of all to John Marcher. Her whole attitude was a virtual statement, but the perception of that only seemed called to take its place for him as one of the many things necessarily crowded out of his consciousness. If she had moreover, like himself, to make sacrifices to their real truth, it was to be granted that her compensation might have affected her as more prompt and more natural. They had long periods, in this London time, during which, when they were together, a stranger might have listened to them without in the least pricking up his ears; on the other hand the real truth was equally liable at any moment to rise to the surface, and the auditor would then have wondered indeed what they were talking about. They had from an early hour made up their mind that society was, luckily, unintelligent, and the margin allowed them by this had fairly become one of their commonplaces. Yet there were still moments when the situation turned almost fresh—usually under the effect of some expression drawn from herself. Her expressions doubtless repeated themselves, but her intervals were generous. "What saves us, you know, is that we answer so completely to so usual an appearance: that of the man and woman whose friendship has become such a daily habit—or almost—as to be at last indispensable." That for instance was a remark she had frequently enough had occasion to make, though she had given it at different times different developments. What we are especially concerned with is the turn it happened to take from her one afternoon when he had come to see her in honour of her birthday. This anniversary had fallen on a Sunday, at a season of thick fog and general outward gloom; but he had brought her his customary offering, having known her now long enough to have established a hundred small traditions. It was one of his proofs to himself, the present he made her on her birthday, that he hadn't sunk into real selfishness. It was mostly nothing more than a small trinket, but it was always fine of its kind, and he was regularly careful to pay for it more than he thought he could afford. "Our habit saves you, at least, don't you see? because it makes you, after all, for the vulgar, indistinguishable from other men. What's the most inveterate mark of men in general? Why the capacity to spend endless time with dull women—to spend it I won't say without being bored, but without minding that they are, without being driven off at a tangent by it; which comes to the same thing. I'm your dull woman, a part of the daily bread for which you pray at church. That covers your tracks more than anything."

CHAPTER II

"And what covers yours?" asked Marcher, whom his dull woman could mostly to this extent amuse. "I see of course what you mean by your saving me, in this way and that, so far as other people are concerned—I've seen it all along. Only what is it that saves *you*? I often think, you know, of that."

She looked as if she sometimes thought of that too, but rather in a different way. "Where other people, you mean, are concerned?"

"Well, you're really so in with me, you know—as a sort of result of my being so in with yourself. I mean of my having such an immense regard for you, being so tremendously mindful of all you've done for me. I sometimes ask myself if it's quite fair. Fair I mean to have so involved and—since one may say it—interested you. I almost feel as if you hadn't really had time to do anything else."

"Anything else but be interested?" she asked. "Ah what else does one ever want to be? If I've been 'watching' with you, as we long ago agreed I was to do, watching's always in itself an absorption."

"Oh certainly," John Marcher said, "if you hadn't had your curiosity—! Only doesn't it sometimes come to you as time goes on that your curiosity isn't being particularly repaid?"

May Bartram had a pause. "Do you ask that, by any chance, because you feel at all that yours isn't? I mean because you have to wait so long."

Oh he understood what she meant! "For the thing to happen that never does happen? For the Beast to jump out? No, I'm just where I was about it. It isn't a matter as to which I can *choose*, I can decide for a change. It isn't one as to which there *can* be a change. It's in the lap of the gods. One's in the hands of one's law—there one is. As to the form the law will take, the way it will operate, that's its own affair."

"Yes," Miss Bartram replied; "of course one's fate's coming, of course it *has* come in its own form and its own way, all the while. Only, you know, the form and the way in your case were to have been—well, something so exceptional and, as one may say, so particularly *your* own."

Something in this made him look at her with suspicion. "You say 'were to *have* been,' as if in your heart you had begun to doubt."

"Oh!" she vaguely protested.

"As if you believed," he went on, "that nothing will now take place."

She shook her head slowly but rather inscrutably. "You're far from my thought."

He continued to look at her. "What then is the matter with you?"

"Well," she said after another wait, "the matter with me is simply that I'm more sure than ever my curiosity, as you call it, will be but too well repaid."

They were frankly grave now; he had got up from his seat, had turned once more about the little drawing-room to which, year after year, he brought his inevitable topic; in which he had, as he might have said, tasted their intimate community with every sauce, where every object was as familiar to him as the things of his own house and the very carpets were worn with his fitful walk very much as the desks in old counting-houses are worn by the elbows of generations of clerks. The generations of his nervous moods had been at work there, and the place was the written history of his whole middle life. Under the impression of what his friend had just said he knew himself, for some reason, more aware of these things; which made him, after a moment, stop again before her. "Is it possibly that you've grown afraid?"

"Afraid?" He thought, as she repeated the word, that his question had made her, a little, change colour; so that, lest he should have touched on a truth, he explained very kindly: "You remember that that was what you asked *me* long ago—that first day at Weatherend."

"Oh yes, and you told me you didn't know—that I was to see for myself. We've said little about it since, even in so long a time."

"Precisely," Marcher interposed—"quite as if it were too delicate a matter for us to make free with. Quite as if we might find, on pressure, that I *am* afraid. For then," he said, "we shouldn't, should we? quite know what to do."

She had for the time no answer to this question. "There have been days when I thought you were. Only, of course," she added, "there have been days when we have thought almost anything."

"Everything. Oh!" Marcher softly groaned, as with a gasp, half spent, at the face, more uncovered just then than it had been for a long while, of the imagination always with them. It had always had it's incalculable moments of glaring out, quite as with the very eyes of the very Beast, and, used as he was to them, they could still draw from him the tribute of a sigh that rose from the depths of his being. All they had thought, first and last, rolled over him; the past seemed to have been reduced to mere barren speculation. This in fact was what the place had just struck him as so full of—the simplification of everything but the state of suspense. That remained only by seeming to hang in the void surrounding it. Even his original fear, if fear it as had been, had lost itself in the desert. "I judge, however," he continued, "that you see I'm not afraid now."

"What I see, as I make it out, is that you've achieved something almost unprecedented in the way of getting used to danger. Living with it so long and so closely you've lost your sense of it; you know it's there, but you're indifferent, and you cease even, as of old, to have to whistle in the dark. Considering what the danger is," May Bartram wound up, "I'm bound to say I don't think your attitude could well be surpassed."

John Marcher faintly smiled. "It's heroic?"

"Certainly—call it that."

It was what he would have liked indeed to call it. "I *am* then a man of courage?"

"That's what you were to show me."

He still, however, wondered. "But doesn't the man of courage know what he's afraid of—or not afraid of? I don't know *that*, you see. I don't focus it. I can't name it. I only know I'm exposed."

"Yes, but exposed—how shall I say?—so directly. So intimately. That's surely enough."

"Enough to make you feel then—as what we may call the end and the upshot of our watch—that I'm not afraid?"

"You're not afraid. But it isn't," she said, "the end of our watch. That is it isn't the end of yours. You've everything still to see."

"Then why haven't you?" he asked. He had had, all along, to-day, the sense of her keeping something back, and he still had it. As this was his first impression of that it quite made a date. The case was the more marked as she didn't at first answer; which in turn made him go on. "You know something I don't." Then his voice, for that of a man of courage, trembled a little. "You know what's to happen." Her silence, with the face she showed, was almost a confession—it made him sure. "You know, and you're afraid to tell me. It's so bad that you're afraid I'll find out."

All this might be true, for she did look as if, unexpectedly to her, he had crossed some mystic line that she had secretly drawn round her. Yet she might, after all, not have worried; and the real climax was that he himself, at all events, needn't. "You'll never find out."

CHAPTER III

It was all to have made, none the less, as I have said, a date; which came out in the fact that again and again, even after long intervals, other things that passed between them were in relation to this hour but the character of recalls and results. Its immediate effect had been indeed rather to lighten insistence—almost to provoke a reaction; as if their topic had dropped by its own weight and as if moreover, for that matter, Marcher had been visited by one of his occasional warnings against egotism. He had kept up, he felt, and very decently on the whole, his consciousness of the importance of not being selfish, and it was true that he had never sinned in that direction without promptly enough trying to press the scales the other way. He often repaired his fault, the season permitting, by inviting his friend to accompany him to the opera; and it not infrequently thus happened that, to show he didn't wish her to have but one sort of food for her mind, he was the cause of her appearing there with him a dozen nights in the month. It even happened that, seeing her home at such times, he occasionally went in with her to finish, as he called it, the evening, and, the better to make his point, sat down to the frugal but always careful little supper that awaited his pleasure. His point was made, he thought, by his not eternally insisting with her on himself; made for instance, at such hours, when it befell that, her piano at hand and each of them familiar with it, they went over passages of the opera together. It chanced to be on one of these occasions, however, that he reminded her of her not having answered a certain question he had put to her during the talk that had taken place between them on her last birthday. "What is it that saves *you*?"—saved her, he meant, from that appearance of variation from the usual human type. If he had practically escaped remark, as she pretended, by doing, in the most important particular, what most men do—find the answer to life in patching up an alliance of a sort with a woman no better than himself—how had she escaped it, and how could the alliance, such as it was, since they must suppose it had been more or less noticed, have failed to make her rather positively talked about?

"I never said," May Bartram replied, "that it hadn't made me a good deal talked about."

"Ah well then you're not 'saved.'"

"It hasn't been a question for me. If you've had your woman I've had," she said, "my man."

"And you mean that makes you all right?"

Oh it was always as if there were so much to say!

"I don't know why it shouldn't make me—humanly, which is what we're speaking of—as right as it makes you."

"I see," Marcher returned. "'Humanly,' no doubt, as showing that you're living for something. Not, that is, just for me and my secret."

May Bartram smiled. "I don't pretend it exactly shows that I'm not living for you. It's my intimacy with you that's in question."

He laughed as he saw what she meant. "Yes, but since, as you say, I'm only, so far as people make out, ordinary, you're—aren't you? no more than ordinary either. You help me to pass for a man like another. So if I *am*, as I understand you, you're not compromised. Is that it?"

She had another of her waits, but she spoke clearly enough. "That's it. It's all that concerns me—to help you to pass for a man like another."

He was careful to acknowledge the remark handsomely. "How kind, how beautiful, you are to me! How shall I ever repay you?"

She had her last grave pause, as if there might be a choice of ways. But she chose. "By going on as you are."

It was into this going on as he was that they relapsed, and really for so long a time that the day inevitably came for a further sounding of their depths. These depths, constantly bridged over by a structure firm enough in spite of its lightness and of its occasional oscillation in the somewhat vertiginous air, invited on occasion, in the interest of their nerves, a dropping of the plummet and a measurement of the abyss. A difference had been made moreover, once for all, by the fact that she had all the while not appeared to feel the need of rebutting his charge of an idea within her that she didn't dare to express—a charge uttered just before one of the fullest of their later discussions ended. It had come up for him then that she "knew" something and that what she knew was bad—too bad to tell him. When he had spoken of it as visibly so bad that she was afraid he might find it out, her reply had left the matter too equivocal to be let alone and yet, for Marcher's special sensibility, almost too formidable again to touch. He circled about it at a distance that alternately narrowed and widened and that still wasn't much affected by the consciousness in him that there was nothing she could "know," after all, any better than he did. She had no source of knowledge he hadn't equally—except of course that she might have finer nerves. That was what women had where they were interested; they made out things, where people were concerned, that the people often couldn't have made out for themselves. Their nerves, their sensibility, their imagination, were conductors and revealers, and the beauty of May Bartram was in particular that she had given herself so to his case. He felt in these days what, oddly enough, he had never felt before, the growth of a dread of losing her by some catastrophe—some catastrophe that yet wouldn't at all be the catastrophe: partly because she had almost of a sudden begun to strike him as more useful to him than ever yet, and partly by reason of an appearance of uncertainty in her health, co-incident and equally new. It was characteristic of the inner detachment he had hitherto so successfully cultivated and to which our whole account of him is a reference, it was characteristic that his complications, such as they were, had never yet seemed so as at this crisis to thicken about him, even to the point of making him ask himself if he were, by any chance, of a truth, within sight or sound, within touch or reach, within the immediate jurisdiction, of the thing that waited.

When the day came, as come it had to, that his friend confessed to him her fear of a deep disorder in her blood, he felt somehow the shadow of a change and the chill of a shock. He immediately began to imagine aggravations and disasters, and above all to think of her peril as the direct menace for himself of personal privation. This indeed gave him one of those partial recoveries of equanimity that were agreeable to him—it showed him that what was still first in his mind was the loss she herself might suffer. "What if she should have to die before knowing, before seeing—?" It would have been brutal, in the early stages of her trouble, to put that question to her; but it had immediately sounded for him to his own concern, and the possibility was what most made him sorry for her. If she did "know," moreover, in the sense of her having had some—what should he think?—mystical irresistible light, this would make the matter not better, but worse, inasmuch as her original adoption of his own curiosity had quite become the basis of her life. She had been living to see what would *be* to be seen, and it would quite lacerate her to have to give up before the accomplishment of the vision. These reflexions, as I say, quickened his generosity; yet, make them as he might, he saw himself, with the lapse of the period, more and more disconcerted. It lapsed for him with a strange steady sweep, and the oddest oddity was that it gave him, independently of the threat of much inconvenience, almost the only positive surprise his career, if career it could be called, had yet offered him. She kept the house as she had never done; he had to go to her to see her—she could meet him nowhere now, though there was scarce a corner of their loved old London in which she hadn't in the past, at one time or another, done so; and he found her always seated by her fire in the deep old-fashioned chair she was less and less able to leave. He had been struck one day, after an absence exceeding his usual measure, with her suddenly looking much older to him than he had ever thought of her being; then he recognised that the suddenness was all on his side—he had just simply and suddenly noticed. She looked older because inevitably, after so many years, she *was* old, or almost; which was of course true in still greater measure of her companion. If she was old, or almost, John Marcher assuredly was, and yet it was her showing of the lesson, not his own, that brought the truth home to him. His surprises began here; when once they had begun they multiplied; they came rather with a rush: it was as if, in the oddest way in the world, they had all been kept back, sown in a thick cluster, for the late afternoon of life, the time at which for people in general the unexpected has died out.

One of them was that he should have caught himself—for he *had* so done—*really* wondering if the great accident would take form now as nothing more than his being condemned to see this charming woman, this admirable friend, pass away from him. He had never so unreservedly qualified her as while confronted in thought with such a possibility; in spite of which there was small doubt for him that as an answer to his long riddle the mere effacement of even so fine a feature of his situation would be an abject anticlimax. It would represent, as connected with his past attitude, a drop of dignity under the shadow of which his existence could only become the most grotesques of failures. He had been far from holding it a failure—long as he had waited for the appearance that was to make it a success. He had waited for quite another thing, not for such a thing as that. The breath of his good faith came short, however, as he recognised how long he had waited, or how long at least his companion had. That she, at all events, might be recorded as having waited in vain—this affected him sharply, and all the more because of his at first having done little more than amuse himself with the idea. It grew more grave as the gravity of her condition grew, and the state of mind it produced in him, which he himself ended by watching as if it had been some definite disfigurement of his outer person, may pass for another of his surprises. This conjoined itself still with another, the really stupefying consciousness of a question that he would have allowed to shape itself had he dared. What did everything mean—what, that is, did *she* mean, she and her vain waiting and her probable death and the soundless admonition of it all—unless that, at this time of day, it was simply, it was overwhelmingly too late? He had never at any stage of his queer consciousness admitted the whisper of such a correction; he had never till within these last few months been so false to his conviction as not to hold that what was to come to him had time, whether *he* struck himself as having it or not. That at last, at last, he certainly hadn't it, to speak of, or had it but in the scantiest measure—such, soon enough, as things went with him, became the inference with which his old obsession had to reckon: and this it was not helped to do by the more and more confirmed appearance that the great vagueness casting the long shadow in which he had lived had, to attest itself, almost no margin left. Since it was in Time that he was to have met his fate, so it was in Time that his fate was to have acted; and as he waked up to the sense of no longer being young, which was exactly the sense of being stale, just as that, in turn, was the sense of being weak, he waked up to another matter beside. It all hung together; they were subject, he and the great vagueness, to an equal and indivisible law. When the possibilities themselves had accordingly turned stale, when the secret of the gods had grown faint, had perhaps even quite evaporated, that, and that only, was failure. It wouldn't have been failure to be bankrupt, dishonoured, pilloried, hanged; it was failure not to be anything. And so, in the dark valley into which his path had taken its unlooked-for twist, he wondered not a little as he groped. He didn't care what awful crash might overtake him, with what ignominy or what monstrosity he might yet he associated—since he wasn't after all too utterly old to suffer—if it would only be decently proportionate to the posture he had kept, all his life, in the threatened presence of it. He had but one desire left—that he shouldn't have been "sold."

CHAPTER IV

Then it was that, one afternoon, while the spring of the year was young and new she met all in her own way his frankest betrayal of these alarms. He had gone in late to see her, but evening hadn't settled and she was presented to him in that long fresh light of waning April days which affects us often with a sadness sharper than the greyest hours of autumn. The week had been warm, the spring was supposed to have begun early, and May Bartram sat, for the first time in the year, without a fire; a fact that, to Marcher's sense, gave the scene of which she formed part a smooth and ultimate look, an air of knowing, in its immaculate order and cold meaningless cheer, that it would never see a fire again. Her own aspect—he could scarce have said why—intensified this note. Almost as white as wax, with the marks and signs in her face as numerous and as fine as if they had been etched by a needle, with soft white draperies relieved by a faded green scarf on the delicate tone of which the years had further refined, she was the picture of a serene and exquisite but impenetrable sphinx, whose head, or indeed all whose person, might have been powdered with silver. She was a sphinx, yet with her white petals and green fronds she might have been a lily too—only an artificial lily, wonderfully imitated and constantly kept, without dust or stain, though not exempt from a slight droop and a complexity of faint creases, under some clear glass bell. The perfection of household care, of high polish and finish, always reigned in her rooms, but they now looked most as if everything had been wound up, tucked in, put away, so that she might sit with folded hands and with nothing more to do. She was "out of it," to Marcher's vision; her work was over; she communicated with him as across some gulf or from some island of rest that she had already reached, and it made him feel strangely abandoned. Was it—or rather wasn't it—that if for so long she had been watching with him the answer to their question must have swum into her ken and taken on its name, so that her occupation was verily gone? He had as much as charged her with this in saying to her, many months before, that she even then knew something she was keeping from him. It was a point he had never since ventured to press, vaguely fearing as he did that it might become a difference, perhaps a disagreement, between them. He had in this later time turned nervous, which was what he in all the other years had never been; and the oddity was that his nervousness should have waited till he had begun to doubt, should have held off so long as he was sure. There was something, it seemed to him, that the wrong word would bring down on his head, something that would so at least ease off his tension. But he wanted not to speak the wrong word; that would make everything ugly. He wanted the knowledge he lacked to drop on him, if drop it could, by its own august weight. If she was to forsake him it was surely for her to take leave. This was why he didn't directly ask her again what she knew; but it was also why, approaching the matter from another side, he said to her in the course of his visit: "What do you regard as the very worst that at this time of day *can* happen to me?"

He had asked her that in the past often enough; they had, with the odd irregular rhythm of their intensities and avoidances, exchanged ideas about it and then had seen the ideas washed away by cool intervals, washed like figures traced in sea-sand. It had ever been the mark of their talk that the oldest allusions in it required but a little dismissal and reaction to come out again, sounding for the hour as new. She could thus at present meet his enquiry quite freshly and patiently. "Oh yes, I've repeatedly thought, only it always seemed to me of old that I couldn't quite make up my mind. I thought of dreadful things, between which it was difficult to choose; and so must you have done."

"Rather! I feel now as if I had scarce done anything else. I appear to myself to have spent my life in thinking of nothing but dreadful things. A great many of them I've at different times named to you, but there were others I couldn't name."

"They were too, too dreadful?"

"Too, too dreadful—some of them."

She looked at him a minute, and there came to him as he met it, an inconsequent sense that her eyes, when one got their full clearness, were still as beautiful as they had been in youth, only beautiful with a strange cold light—a light that somehow was a part of the effect, if it wasn't rather a part of the cause, of the pale hard sweetness of the season and the hour. "And yet," she said at last, "there are horrors we've mentioned."

It deepened the strangeness to see her, as such a figure in such a picture, talk of "horrors," but she was to do in a few minutes something stranger yet—though even of this he was to take the full measure but afterwards—and the note of it already trembled. It was, for the matter of that, one of the signs that her eyes were having again the high flicker of their prime. He had to admit, however, what she said. "Oh yes, there were times when we did go far." He caught himself in the act of speaking as if it all were over. Well, he wished it were; and the consummation depended for him clearly more and more on his friend.

But she had now a soft smile. "Oh far—!"

It was oddly ironic. "Do you mean you're prepared to go further?"

She was frail and ancient and charming as she continued to look at him, yet it was rather as if she had lost the thread. "Do you consider that we went far?"

"Why I thought it the point you were just making—that we *had* looked most things in the face."

"Including each other?" She still smiled. "But you're quite right. We've had together great imaginations, often great fears; but some of them have been unspoken."

"Then the worst—we haven't faced that. I *could* face it, I believe, if I knew what you think it. I feel," he explained, "as if I had lost my power to conceive such things." And he wondered if he looked as blank as he sounded. "It's spent."

"Then why do you assume," she asked, "that mine isn't?"

"Because you've given me signs to the contrary. It isn't a question for you of conceiving, imagining, comparing. It isn't a question now of choosing." At last he came out with it. "You know something I don't. You've shown me that before."

These last words had affected her, he made out in a moment, exceedingly, and she spoke with firmness. "I've shown you, my dear, nothing."

He shook his head. "You can't hide it."

"Oh, oh!" May Bartram sounded over what she couldn't hide. It was almost a smothered groan.

"You admitted it months ago, when I spoke of it to you as of something you were afraid I should find out. Your answer was that I couldn't, that I wouldn't, and I don't pretend I have. But you had something therefore in mind, and I see now how it must have been, how it still is, the possibility that, of all possibilities, has settled itself for you as the worst. This," he went on, "is why I appeal to you. I'm only afraid of ignorance to-day—I'm not afraid of knowledge." And then as for a while she said nothing: "What makes me sure is that I see in your face and feel here, in this air and amid these appearances, that you're out of it. You've done. You've had your experience. You leave me to my fate."

Well, she listened, motionless and white in her chair, as on a decision to be made, so that her manner was fairly an avowal, though still, with a small fine inner stiffness, an imperfect surrender. "It *would* be the worst," she finally let herself say. "I mean the thing I've never said."

It hushed him a moment. "More monstrous than all the monstrosities we've named?"

"More monstrous. Isn't that what you sufficiently express," she asked, "in calling it the worst?"

Marcher thought. "Assuredly—if you mean, as I do, something that includes all the loss and all the shame that are thinkable."

"It would if it *should* happen," said May Bartram. "What we're speaking of, remember, is only my idea."

"It's your belief," Marcher returned. "That's enough for me. I feel your beliefs are right. Therefore if, having this one, you give me no more light on it, you abandon me."

"No, no!" she repeated. "I'm with you—don't you see?—still." And as to make it more vivid to him she rose from her chair—a movement she seldom risked in these days—and showed herself, all draped and all soft, in her fairness and slimness. "I haven't forsaken you."

It was really, in its effort against weakness, a generous assurance, and had the success of the impulse not, happily, been great, it would have touched him to pain more than to pleasure. But the cold charm in her eyes had spread, as she hovered before him, to all the rest of her person, so that it was for the minute almost a recovery of youth. He couldn't pity her for that; he could only take her as she showed—as capable even yet of helping him. It was as if, at the same time, her light might at any instant go out; wherefore he must make the most of it. There passed before him with intensity the three or four things he wanted most to know; but the question that came of itself to his lips really covered the others. "Then tell me if I shall consciously suffer."

She promptly shook her head. "Never!"

It confirmed the authority he imputed to her, and it produced on him an extraordinary effect. "Well, what's better than that? Do you call that the worst?"

"You think nothing is better?" she asked.

She seemed to mean something so special that he again sharply wondered, though still with the dawn of a prospect of relief. "Why not, if one doesn't *know*?" After which, as their eyes, over his question, met in a silence, the dawn deepened, and something to his purpose came prodigiously out of her very face. His own, as he took it in, suddenly flushed to the forehead, and he gasped with the force of a perception to which, on the instant, everything fitted. The sound of his gasp filled the air; then he became articulate. "I see—if I don't suffer!"

In her own look, however, was doubt. "You see what?"

"Why what you mean—what you've always meant."

She again shook her head. "What I mean isn't what I've always meant. It's different."

"It's something new?"

She hung back from it a little. "Something new. It's not what you think. I see what you think."

His divination drew breath then; only her correction might be wrong. "It isn't that I *am* a blockhead?" he asked between faintness and grimness. "It isn't that it's all a mistake?"

"A mistake?" she pityingly echoed. *That* possibility, for her, he saw, would be monstrous; and if she guaranteed him the immunity from pain it would accordingly not be what she had in mind. "Oh no," she declared; "it's nothing of that sort. You've been right."

Yet he couldn't help asking himself if she weren't, thus pressed, speaking but to save him. It seemed to him he should be most in a hole if his history should prove all a platitude. "Are you telling me the truth, so that I shan't have been a bigger idiot than I can bear to know? I *haven't* lived with a vain imagination, in the most besotted illusion? I haven't waited but to see the door shut in my face?"

She shook her head again. "However the case stands *that* isn't the truth. Whatever the reality, it *is* a reality. The door isn't shut. The door's open," said May Bartram.

"Then something's to come?"

She waited once again, always with her cold sweet eyes on him. "It's never too late." She had, with her gliding step, diminished the distance between them, and she stood nearer to him, close to him, a minute, as if still charged with the unspoken. Her movement might have been for some finer emphasis of what she was at once hesitating and deciding to say. He had been standing by the chimney-piece, fireless and sparely adorned, a small perfect old French clock and two morsels of rosy Dresden constituting all its furniture; and her hand grasped the shelf while she kept him waiting, grasped it a little as for support and encouragement. She only kept him waiting, however; that is he only waited. It had become suddenly, from her movement and attitude, beautiful and vivid to him that she had something more to give him; her wasted face delicately shone with it—it glittered almost as with the white lustre of silver in her expression. She was right, incontestably, for what he saw in her face was the truth, and strangely, without consequence, while their talk of it as dreadful was still in the air, she appeared to present it as inordinately soft. This, prompting bewilderment, made him but gape the more gratefully for her revelation, so that they continued for some minutes silent, her face shining at him, her contact imponderably pressing, and his stare all kind but all expectant. The end, none the less, was that what he had expected failed to come to him. Something else took place instead, which seemed to consist at first in the mere closing of her eyes. She gave way at the same instant to a slow fine shudder, and though he remained staring—though he stared in fact but the harder—turned off and regained her chair. It was the end of what she had been intending, but it left him thinking only of that.

"Well, you don't say—?"

She had touched in her passage a bell near the chimney and had sunk back strangely pale. "I'm afraid I'm too ill."

CHAPTER IV

"Too ill to tell me?" it sprang up sharp to him, and almost to his lips, the fear she might die without giving him light. He checked himself in time from so expressing his question, but she answered as if she had heard the words.

"Don't you know—now?"

"'Now'—?" She had spoken as if some difference had been made within the moment. But her maid, quickly obedient to her bell, was already with them. "I know nothing." And he was afterwards to say to himself that he must have spoken with odious impatience, such an impatience as to show that, supremely disconcerted, he washed his hands of the whole question.

"Oh!" said May Bartram.

"Are you in pain?" he asked as the woman went to her.

"No," said May Bartram.

Her maid, who had put an arm round her as if to take her to her room, fixed on him eyes that appealingly contradicted her; in spite of which, however, he showed once more his mystification.

"What then has happened?"

She was once more, with her companion's help, on her feet, and, feeling withdrawal imposed on him, he had blankly found his hat and gloves and had reached the door. Yet he waited for her answer. "What *was* to," she said.

CHAPTER V

He came back the next day, but she was then unable to see him, and as it was literally the first time this had occurred in the long stretch of their acquaintance he turned away, defeated and sore, almost angry—or feeling at least that such a break in their custom was really the beginning of the end—and wandered alone with his thoughts, especially with the one he was least able to keep down. She was dying and he would lose her; she was dying and his life would end. He stopped in the Park, into which he had passed, and stared before him at his recurrent doubt. Away from her the doubt pressed again; in her presence he had believed her, but as he felt his forlornness he threw himself into the explanation that, nearest at hand, had most of a miserable warmth for him and least of a cold torment. She had deceived him to save him—to put him off with something in which he should be able to rest. What could the thing that was to happen to him be, after all, but just this thing that had began to happen? Her dying, her death, his consequent solitude—that was what he had figured as the Beast in the Jungle, that was what had been in the lap of the gods. He had had her word for it as he left her—what else on earth could she have meant? It wasn't a thing of a monstrous order; not a fate rare and distinguished; not a stroke of fortune that overwhelmed and immortalised; it had only the stamp of the common doom. But poor Marcher at this hour judged the common doom sufficient. It would serve his turn, and even as the consummation of infinite waiting he would bend his pride to accept it. He sat down on a bench in the twilight. He hadn't been a fool. Something had *been*, as she had said, to come. Before he rose indeed it had quite struck him that the final fact really matched with the long avenue through which he had had to reach it. As sharing his suspense and as giving herself all, giving her life, to bring it to an end, she had come with him every step of the way. He had lived by her aid, and to leave her behind would be cruelly, damnably to miss her. What could be more overwhelming than that?

Well, he was to know within the week, for though she kept him a while at bay, left him restless and wretched during a series of days on each of which he asked about her only again to have to turn away, she ended his trial by receiving him where she had always received him. Yet she had been brought out at some hazard into the presence of so many of the things that were, consciously, vainly, half their past, and there was scant service left in the gentleness of her mere desire, all too visible, to check his obsession and wind up his long trouble. That was clearly what she wanted; the one thing more for her own peace while she could still put out her hand. He was so affected by her state that, once seated by her chair, he was moved to let everything go; it was she herself therefore who brought him back, took up again, before she dismissed him, her last word of the other time. She showed how she wished to leave their business in order. "I'm not sure you understood. You've nothing to wait for more. It *has* come."

Oh how he looked at her! "Really?"

"Really."

"The thing that, as you said, *was* to?"

"The thing that we began in our youth to watch for."

Face to face with her once more he believed her; it was a claim to which he had so abjectly little to oppose. "You mean that it has come as a positive definite occurrence, with a name and a date?"

"Positive. Definite. I don't know about the 'name,' but, oh with a date!"

He found himself again too helplessly at sea. "But come in the night—come and passed me by?"

May Bartram had her strange faint smile. "Oh no, it hasn't passed you by!"

"But if I haven't been aware of it and it hasn't touched me—?"

CHAPTER V

"Ah your not being aware of it"—and she seemed to hesitate an instant to deal with this—"your not being aware of it is the strangeness in the strangeness. It's the wonder *of* the wonder." She spoke as with the softness almost of a sick child, yet now at last, at the end of all, with the perfect straightness of a sibyl. She visibly knew that she knew, and the effect on him was of something co-ordinate, in its high character, with the law that had ruled him. It was the true voice of the law; so on her lips would the law itself have sounded. "It *has* touched you," she went on. "It has done its office. It has made you all its own."

"So utterly without my knowing it?"

"So utterly without your knowing it." His hand, as he leaned to her, was on the arm of her chair, and, dimly smiling always now, she placed her own on it. "It's enough if *I* know it."

"Oh!" he confusedly breathed, as she herself of late so often had done.

"What I long ago said is true. You'll never know now, and I think you ought to be content. You've *had* it," said May Bartram.

"But had what?"

"Why what was to have marked you out. The proof of your law. It has acted. I'm too glad," she then bravely added, "to have been able to see what it's *not*."

He continued to attach his eyes to her, and with the sense that it was all beyond him, and that *she* was too, he would still have sharply challenged her hadn't he so felt it an abuse of her weakness to do more than take devoutly what she gave him, take it hushed as to a revelation. If he did speak, it was out of the foreknowledge of his loneliness to come. "If you're glad of what it's 'not' it might then have been worse?"

She turned her eyes away, she looked straight before her; with which after a moment: "Well, you know our fears."

He wondered. "It's something then we never feared?"

On this slowly she turned to him. "Did we ever dream, with all our dreams, that we should sit and talk of it thus?"

He tried for a little to make out that they had; but it was as if their dreams, numberless enough, were in solution in some thick cold mist through which thought lost itself. "It might have been that we couldn't talk."

"Well"—she did her best for him—"not from this side. This, you see," she said, "is the *other* side."

"I think," poor Marcher returned, "that all sides are the same to me." Then, however, as she gently shook her head in correction: "We mightn't, as it were, have got across—?"

"To where we are—no. We're *here*"—she made her weak emphasis.

"And much good does it do us!" was her friend's frank comment.

"It does us the good it can. It does us the good that *it* isn't here. It's past. It's behind," said May Bartram. "Before—" but her voice dropped.

He had got up, not to tire her, but it was hard to combat his yearning. She after all told him nothing but that his light had failed—which he knew well enough without her. "Before—?" he blankly echoed.

"Before you see, it was always to *come*. That kept it present."

"Oh I don't care what comes now! Besides," Marcher added, "it seems to me I liked it better present, as you say, than I can like it absent with *your* absence."

"Oh mine!"—and her pale hands made light of it.

"With the absence of everything." He had a dreadful sense of standing there before her for—so far as anything but this proved, this bottomless drop was concerned—the last time of their life. It rested on him with a weight he felt he could scarce bear, and this weight it apparently was that still pressed out what remained in him of speakable protest. "I believe you; but I can't begin to pretend I understand. *Nothing*, for me, is past; nothing *will* pass till I pass myself, which I pray my stars may be as soon as possible. Say, however," he added, "that I've eaten my cake, as you contend, to the last crumb—how can the thing I've never felt at all be the thing I was marked out to feel?"

She met him perhaps less directly, but she met him unperturbed. "You take your 'feelings' for granted. You were to suffer your fate. That was not necessarily to know it."

"How in the world—when what is such knowledge but suffering?"

She looked up at him a while in silence. "No—you don't understand."

"I suffer," said John Marcher.

"Don't, don't!"

"How can I help at least *that*?"

"*Don't*!" May Bartram repeated.

She spoke it in a tone so special, in spite of her weakness, that he stared an instant—stared as if some light, hitherto hidden, had shimmered across his vision. Darkness again closed over it, but the gleam had already become for him an idea. "Because I haven't the right—?"

"Don't *know*—when you needn't," she mercifully urged. "You needn't—for we shouldn't."

"Shouldn't?" If he could but know what she meant!

"No— it's too much."

"Too much?" he still asked but with a mystification that was the next moment of a sudden to give way. Her words, if they meant something, affected him in this light—the light also of her wasted face—as meaning *all*, and the sense of what knowledge had been for herself came over him with a rush which broke through into a question. "Is it of that then you're dying?"

She but watched him, gravely at first, as to see, with this, where he was, and she might have seen something or feared something that moved her sympathy. "I would live for you still—if I could." Her eyes closed for a little, as if, withdrawn into herself, she were for a last time trying. "But I can't!" she said as she raised them again to take leave of him.

She couldn't indeed, as but too promptly and sharply appeared, and he had no vision of her after this that was anything but darkness and doom. They had parted for ever in that strange talk; access to her chamber of pain, rigidly guarded, was almost wholly forbidden him; he was feeling now moreover, in the face of doctors, nurses, the two or three relatives attracted doubtless by the presumption of what she had to "leave," how few were the rights, as they were called in such cases, that he had to put forward, and how odd it might even seem that their intimacy shouldn't have given him more of them. The stupidest fourth cousin had more, even though she had been nothing in such a person's life. She had been a feature of features in *his*, for what else was it to have been so indispensable? Strange beyond saying were the ways of existence, baffling for him the anomaly of his lack, as he felt it to be, of producible claim. A woman might have been, as it were, everything to him, and it might yet present him, in no connexion that any one seemed held to recognise. If this was the case in these closing weeks it was the case more sharply on the occasion of the last offices rendered, in the great grey London cemetery, to what had been mortal, to what had been precious, in his friend. The concourse at her grave was not numerous, but he saw himself treated as scarce more nearly concerned with it than if there had been a thousand others. He was in short from this moment face to face with the fact that he was to profit extraordinarily little by the interest May Bartram had taken in him. He couldn't quite have said what he expected, but he hadn't surely expected this approach to a double privation. Not only had her interest failed him, but he seemed to feel himself unattended—and for a reason he couldn't seize—by the distinction, the dignity, the propriety, if nothing else, of the man markedly bereaved. It was as if, in the view of society he had not *been* markedly bereaved, as if there still failed some sign or proof of it, and as if none the less his character could never be affirmed nor the deficiency ever made up. There were moments as the weeks went by when he would have liked, by some almost aggressive act, to take his stand on the intimacy of his loss, in order that it *might* be questioned and his retort, to the relief of his spirit, so recorded; but the moments of an irritation more helpless followed fast on these, the moments during which, turning things over with a good conscience but with a bare horizon, he found himself wondering if he oughtn't to have begun, so to speak, further back.

He found himself wondering indeed at many things, and this last speculation had others to keep it company. What could he have done, after all, in her lifetime, without giving them both, as it were, away? He couldn't have made known she was watching him, for that would have published the superstition of the Beast. This was what closed his mouth now—now that the Jungle had been thrashed to vacancy and that the Beast had stolen away. It sounded too foolish and too flat; the difference for him in this particular, the extinction in his life of the element of suspense, was such as in fact to surprise him. He could scarce have said what the effect resembled; the abrupt cessation, the positive prohibition, of music perhaps, more than anything else, in some place all adjusted and all accustomed to sonority and to attention. If he could at any rate have conceived lifting the veil from his image at some moment of the past (what had he done, after all, if not lift it to *her*?) so to do this today, to talk to people at large of the Jungle cleared and confide to them that he now felt it as safe, would have been not only to see them listen as to a goodwife's tale, but really to hear himself tell one. What it presently came to in truth was that poor Marcher waded through his beaten grass, where no life stirred, where no breath sounded, where no evil eye seemed to gleam from a possible lair, very much as if vaguely looking for the Beast, and still more as if acutely missing it. He walked about in an existence that had grown strangely more spacious, and, stopping fitfully in places where the undergrowth of life struck him as closer, asked himself yearningly, wondered secretly and sorely, if it would have lurked here or there. It would have at all events sprung; what was at least complete was his belief in the truth itself of the assurance given him. The change from his old sense to his new was absolute and final: what was to happen had so absolutely and finally happened that he was as little able to know a fear for his future as to know a hope; so absent in short was any question of anything still to come. He was to live entirely with the other question, that of his unidentified past, that of his having to see his fortune impenetrably muffled and masked.

The torment of this vision became then his occupation; he couldn't perhaps have consented to live but for the possibility of guessing. She had told him, his friend, not to guess; she had forbidden him, so far as he might, to know, and she had even in a sort denied the power in him to learn: which were so many things, precisely, to deprive him of rest. It wasn't that he wanted, he argued for fairness, that anything past and done should repeat itself; it was only that he shouldn't, as an anticlimax, have been taken sleeping so sound as not to be able to win back by an effort of thought the lost stuff of consciousness. He declared to himself at moments that he would either win it back or have done with consciousness for ever; he made this idea his one motive in fine, made it so much his passion that none other, to compare with it, seemed ever to have touched him. The lost stuff of consciousness became thus for him as a strayed or stolen child to an unappeasable father; he hunted it up and down very much as if he were knocking at doors and enquiring of the police. This was the spirit in which, inevitably, he set himself to travel; he started on a journey that was to be as long as he could make it; it danced before him that, as the other side of the globe couldn't possibly have less to say to him, it might, by a possibility of suggestion, have more. Before he quitted London, however, he made a pilgrimage to May Bartram's grave, took his way to it through the endless avenues of the grim suburban necropolis, sought it out in the wilderness of tombs, and, though he had come but for the renewal of the act of farewell, found himself, when he had at last stood by it, beguiled into long intensities. He stood for an hour, powerless to turn away and yet powerless to penetrate the darkness of death; fixing with his eyes her inscribed name and date, beating his forehead against the fact of the secret they kept, drawing his breath, while he waited, as if some sense would in pity of him rise from the stones. He kneeled on the stones, however, in vain; they kept what they concealed; and if the face of the tomb did become a face for him it was because her two names became a pair of eyes that didn't know him. He gave them a last long look, but no palest light broke.

CHAPTER VI

He stayed away, after this, for a year; he visited the depths of Asia, spending himself on scenes of romantic interest, of superlative sanctity; but what was present to him everywhere was that for a man who had known what *he* had known the world was vulgar and vain. The state of mind in which he had lived for so many years shone out to him, in reflexion, as a light that coloured and refined, a light beside which the glow of the East was garish cheap and thin. The terrible truth was that he had lost—with everything else—a distinction as well; the things he saw couldn't help being common when he had become common to look at them. He was simply now one of them himself—he was in the dust, without a peg for the sense of difference; and there were hours when, before the temples of gods and the sepulchres of kings, his spirit turned for nobleness of association to the barely discriminated slab in the London suburb. That had become for him, and more intensely with time and distance, his one witness of a past glory. It was all that was left to him for proof or pride, yet the past glories of Pharaohs were nothing to him as he thought of it. Small wonder then that he came back to it on the morrow of his return. He was drawn there this time as irresistibly as the other, yet with a confidence, almost, that was doubtless the effect of the many months that had elapsed. He had lived, in spite of himself, into his change of feeling, and in wandering over the earth had wandered, as might be said, from the circumference to the centre of his desert. He had settled to his safety and accepted perforce his extinction; figuring to himself, with some colour, in the likeness of certain little old men he remembered to have seen, of whom, all meagre and wizened as they might look, it was related that they had in their time fought twenty duels or been loved by ten princesses. They indeed had been wondrous for others while he was but wondrous for himself; which, however, was exactly the cause of his haste to renew the wonder by getting back, as he might put it, into his own presence. That had quickened his steps and checked his delay. If his visit was prompt it was because he had been separated so long from the part of himself that alone he now valued.

It's accordingly not false to say that he reached his goal with a certain elation and stood there again with a certain assurance. The creature beneath the sod knew of his rare experience, so that, strangely now, the place had lost for him its mere blankness of expression. It met him in mildness—not, as before, in mockery; it wore for him the air of conscious greeting that we find, after absence, in things that have closely belonged to us and which seem to confess of themselves to the connexion. The plot of ground, the graven tablet, the tended flowers affected him so as belonging to him that he resembled for the hour a contented landlord reviewing a piece of property. Whatever had happened—well, had happened. He had not come back this time with the vanity of that question, his former worrying "What, *what*?" now practically so spent. Yet he would none the less never again so cut himself off from the spot; he would come back to it every month, for if he did nothing else by its aid he at least held up his head. It thus grew for him, in the oddest way, a positive resource; he carried out his idea of periodical returns, which took their place at last among the most inveterate of his habits. What it all amounted to, oddly enough, was that in his finally so simplified world this garden of death gave him the few square feet of earth on which he could still most live. It was as if, being nothing anywhere else for any one, nothing even for himself, he were just everything here, and if not for a crowd of witnesses or indeed for any witness but John Marcher, then by clear right of the register that he could scan like an open page. The open page was the tomb of his friend, and there were the facts of the past, there the truth of his life, there the backward reaches in which he could lose himself. He did this from time to time with such effect that he seemed to wander through the old years with his hand in the arm of a companion who was, in the most extraordinary manner, his other, his younger self; and to wander, which was more extraordinary yet, round and round a third presence—not wandering she, but stationary, still, whose eyes, turning with his revolution, never ceased to follow him, and whose seat was his point, so to speak, of orientation. Thus in short he settled to live—feeding all on the sense that he once *had* lived, and dependent on it not alone for a support but for an identity.

It sufficed him in its way for months and the year elapsed; it would doubtless even have carried him further but for an accident, superficially slight, which moved him, quite in another direction, with a force beyond any of his impressions of Egypt or of India. It was a thing of the merest chance—the turn, as he afterwards felt, of a hair, though he was indeed to live to believe that if light hadn't come to him in this particular fashion it would still have come in another. He was to live to believe this, I say, though he was not to live, I may not less definitely mention, to do much else. We allow him at any rate the benefit of the conviction, struggling up for him at the end, that, whatever might have happened or not happened, he would have come round of himself to the light. The incident of an autumn day had put the match to the train laid from of old by his misery. With the light before him he knew that even of late his ache had only been smothered. It was strangely drugged, but it throbbed; at the touch it began to bleed. And the touch, in the event, was the face of a fellow-mortal. This face, one grey afternoon when the leaves were thick in the alleys, looked into Marcher's own, at the cemetery, with an expression like the cut of a blade. He felt it, that is, so deep down that he winced at the steady thrust. The person who so mutely assaulted him was a figure he had noticed, on reaching his own goal, absorbed by a grave a short distance away, a grave apparently fresh, so that the emotion of the visitor would probably match it for frankness. This fact alone forbade further attention, though during the time he stayed he remained vaguely conscious of his neighbour, a middle-aged man apparently, in mourning, whose bowed back, among the clustered monuments and mortuary yews, was constantly presented. Marcher's theory that these were elements in contact with which he himself revived, had suffered, on this occasion, it may be granted, a marked, an excessive check. The autumn day was dire for him as none had recently been, and he rested with a heaviness he had not yet known on the low stone table that bore May Bartram's name. He rested without power to move, as if some spring in him, some spell vouchsafed, had suddenly been broken for ever. If he could have done that moment as he wanted he would simply have stretched himself on the slab that was ready to take him, treating it as a place prepared to receive his last sleep. What in all the wide world had he now to keep awake for? He stared before him with the question, and it was then that, as one of the cemetery walks passed near him, he caught the shock of the face.

His neighbour at the other grave had withdrawn, as he himself, with force enough in him, would have done by now, and was advancing along the path on his way to one of the gates. This brought him close, and his pace, was slow, so that—and all the more as there was a kind of hunger in his look—the two men were for a minute directly confronted. Marcher knew him at once for one of the deeply stricken—a perception so sharp that nothing else in the picture comparatively lived, neither his dress, his age, nor his presumable character and class; nothing lived but the deep ravage of the features that he showed. He *showed* them—that was the point; he was moved, as he passed, by some impulse that was either a signal for sympathy or, more possibly, a challenge to an opposed sorrow. He might already have been aware of our friend, might at some previous hour have noticed in him the smooth habit of the scene, with which the state of his own senses so scantly consorted, and might thereby have been stirred as by an overt discord. What Marcher was at all events conscious of was in the first place that the image of scarred passion presented to him was conscious too—of something that profaned the air; and in the second that, roused, startled, shocked, he was yet the next moment looking after it, as it went, with envy. The most extraordinary thing that had happened to him—though he had given that name to other matters as well—took place, after his immediate vague stare, as a consequence of this impression. The stranger passed, but the raw glare of his grief remained, making our friend wonder in pity what wrong, what wound it expressed, what injury not to be healed. What had the man *had*, to make him by the loss of it so bleed and yet live?

Something—and this reached him with a pang—that *he*, John Marcher, hadn't; the proof of which was precisely John Marcher's arid end. No passion had ever touched him, for this was what passion meant; he had survived and maundered and pined, but where had been *his* deep ravage? The extraordinary thing we speak of was the sudden rush of the result of this question. The sight that had just met his eyes named to him, as in letters of quick flame, something he had utterly, insanely missed, and what he had missed made these things a train of fire, made them mark themselves in an anguish of inward throbs. He had seen *outside* of his life, not learned it within, the way a woman was mourned when she had been loved for herself: such was the force of his conviction of the meaning of the stranger's face, which still flared for him as a smoky torch. It hadn't come to him, the knowledge, on the wings of experience; it had brushed him, jostled him, upset him, with the disrespect of chance, the insolence of accident. Now that the illumination had begun, however, it blazed to the zenith, and what he presently stood there gazing at was the sounded void of his life. He gazed, he drew breath, in pain; he turned in his dismay, and, turning, he had before him in sharper incision than ever the open page of his story. The name on the table smote him as the passage of his neighbour had done, and what it said to him, full in the face, was that she was what he had missed. This was the awful thought, the answer to all the past, the vision at the dread clearness of which he turned as cold as the stone beneath him. Everything fell together, confessed, explained, overwhelmed; leaving him most of all stupefied at the blindness he had cherished. The fate he had been marked for he had met with a vengeance—he had emptied the cup to the lees; he had been the man of his time, *the* man, to whom nothing on earth was to have happened. That was the rare stroke—that was his visitation. So he saw it, as we say, in pale horror, while the pieces fitted and fitted. So *she* had seen it while he didn't, and so she served at this hour to drive the truth home. It was the truth, vivid and monstrous, that all the while he had waited the wait was itself his portion. This the companion of his vigil had at a given moment made out, and she had then offered him the chance to baffle his doom. One's doom, however, was never baffled, and on the day she told him his own had come down she had seen him but stupidly stare at the escape she offered him.

The escape would have been to love her; then, *then* he would have lived. *She* had lived—who could say now with what passion?—since she had loved him for himself; whereas he had never thought of her (ah how it hugely glared at him!) but in the chill of his egotism and the light of her use. Her spoken words came back to him—the chain stretched and stretched. The Beast had lurked indeed, and the Beast, at its hour, had sprung; it had sprung in that twilight of the cold April when, pale, ill, wasted, but all beautiful, and perhaps even then recoverable, she had risen from her chair to stand before him and let him imaginably guess. It had sprung as he didn't guess; it had sprung as she hopelessly turned from him, and the mark, by the time he left her, had fallen where it *was* to fall. He had justified his fear and achieved his fate; he had failed, with the last exactitude, of all he was to fail of; and a moan now rose to his lips as he remembered she had prayed he mightn't know. This horror of waking—*this* was knowledge, knowledge under the breath of which the very tears in his eyes seemed to freeze. Through them, none the less, he tried to fix it and hold it; he kept it there before him so that he might feel the pain. That at least, belated and bitter, had something of the taste of life. But the bitterness suddenly sickened him, and it was as if, horribly, he saw, in the truth, in the cruelty of his image, what had been appointed and done. He saw the Jungle of his life and saw the lurking Beast; then, while he looked, perceived it, as by a stir of the air, rise, huge and hideous, for the leap that was to settle him. His eyes darkened—it was close; and, instinctively turning, in his hallucination, to avoid it, he flung himself, face down, on the tomb.

Joseph Conrad Collection including (unabridged): Heart of Darkness, Secret Agent, Lord Jim, Nostromo, Victory
Joseph Conrad
Benediction Classics, 2012
1092 pages
ISBN: 978-1-78139-329-1

Available from www.amazon.com, www.amazon.co.uk

Joseph Conrad (1857-1924) is considered to be one of the great novelists in English. His novels often have a nautical setting and his characters suffer trials in the midst of an indifferent universe. His masterful prose is second to none and his Polish background brings a romantic or tragic style that was previously unknown in English novels.

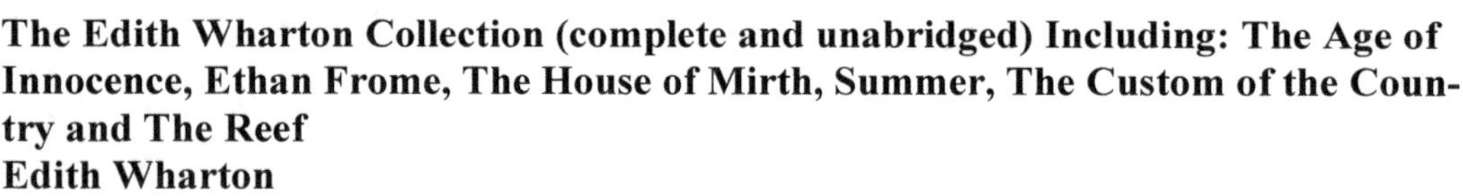

The Edith Wharton Collection (complete and unabridged) Including: The Age of Innocence, Ethan Frome, The House of Mirth, Summer, The Custom of the Country and The Reef
Edith Wharton
Benediction Classics, 2012
1188 pages
ISBN: 978-1-78139-340-6

Available from www.amazon.com, www.amazon.co.uk

Edith Wharton (1862 - 1937), was a Pulitzer Prize-winning American novelist and short story writer. She grew up in upper-class pre-WWI society and many of her stories critique this culture, using subtle irony. In this volume are brought together her six most acclaimed works: The Age of Innocence, Ethan Frome, The House of Mirth, Summer, The Custom of the Country and The Reef. Enjoy the beauty of Wharton's writing in this great collection, where the characters are beautifully captured, they struggle between duty and love in a society that dreads scandal more than disease and they wrestle courageously against their sometimes tragic fates. Wharton writes fine and intense narratives and is the greatest critic of her society.

Wilkie Collins Collection (complete and unabridged):The Woman in White, The Moonstone, No Name, Armadale
Wilkie Collins
Benediction Classics, 2012
1136 pages
ISBN: 978-1-78139-328-4

Available from www.amazon.com, www.amazon.co.uk

Wilkie Collins (1824-1889) is best known as the innovator of the detective novel.
He was a prolific writer, with 30 novels, more than 60 short stories, 14 plays, and more than 100 non-fiction pieces to his name. He was a close friend of Charles Dickens and one of the best known and loved Victorian Fiction writers. After his death, his popularity diminished as Dickens's grew. Now, Collins is once again becoming popular with most of his books in print and film, television and radio adaptations being made. There is much still to be discovered about this great author and this volume contains his four most popular novels.

Five Novels by Thomas Hardy - Far From The Madding Crowd, The Return of the Native, The Mayor of Casterbridge, Tess of the d'Urbervilles, Jude the Obscure (complete and unabridged)
Thomas Hardy
Benediction Classics, 2013
1114 pages
ISBN: 978-1-78139-356-7

Available from www.amazon.com, www.amazon.co.uk

Thomas Hardy, (1840 - 1928) was an English novelist and poet. He was highly critical of Victorian society and focussed mainly on the declining rural communities.

Famous Works - Mrs Dalloway, To the Lighthouse, Orlando, & A Room of One's Own
Virginia Woolf
Benediction Classics, 2012
454 pages
ISBN: 978-1-78139-207-2

Available from www.amazon.com, www.amazon.co.uk

Virginia Woolf is thought to be the foremost modernist writer of the twentieth century. Her most famous writings are reproduced in full in a single volume: Mrs Dalloway (1925), - A day in the life of a woman who is preparing a party. The novel stretches forwards and backwards in time as Clarissa wonders about the choices she has made. To the Lighthouse (1927) - a novel about loss and subjectivity. The Modern Library named it as No. 15 on its list of the 100 best English-language novels of the 20th century in 1998. It was also chosen by TIME magazine as one of the one hundred best English-language novels from 1923 to present in 2005. Orlando (1928) - a semi-biographical novel based in part on her bisexual lover Vita Sackville-West, it is considered to be Woolf's most accessible work. A Room of One's Own (1929) - a long essay based on talks that Woolf gave at Cambridge. It is seen as a feminist text, with women writers needing to find a place in a tradition dominated by men.

The Brontë Sisters: Famous Novels - unabridged - Wuthering Heights, Agnes Grey, The Tenant of Wildfell Hall, Jane Eyre
Charlotte Brontë
Benediction Classics, 2012
1130 pages
ISBN: 978-1-78139-250-8

Available from www.amazon.com, www.amazon.co.uk

The Brontës sisters, Charlotte (1816-55), Emily (1818-48), and Anne (1820-49), achieved literary renown for their novels which were passionate and original. Contained in this volume are the famous (or complete) novels - Wuthering Heights, Agnes Grey, The Tenant of Wildfell Hall, Jane Eyre.

Also from Benediction Books ...
Wandering Between Two Worlds: Essays on Faith and Art
Anita Mathias
Benediction Books, 2007
152 pages
ISBN: 0955373700

Available from www.amazon.com, www.amazon.co.uk

In these wide-ranging lyrical essays, Anita Mathias writes, in lush, lovely prose, of her naughty Catholic childhood in Jamshedpur, India; her large, eccentric family in Mangalore, a sea-coast town converted by the Portuguese in the sixteenth century; her rebellion and atheism as a teenager in her Himalayan boarding school, run by German missionary nuns, St. Mary's Convent, Nainital; and her abrupt religious conversion after which she entered Mother Teresa's convent in Calcutta as a novice. Later rich, elegant essays explore the dualities of her life as a writer, mother, and Christian in the United States-- Domesticity and Art, Writing and Prayer, and the experience of being "an alien and stranger" as an immigrant in America, sensing the need for roots.

About the Author

Anita Mathias is the author of *Wandering Between Two Worlds: Essays on Faith and Art.* She has a B.A. and M.A. in English from Somerville College, Oxford University, and an M.A. in Creative Writing from the Ohio State University, USA. Anita won a National Endowment of the Arts fellowship in Creative Nonfiction in 1997. She lives in Oxford, England with her husband, Roy, and her daughters, Zoe and Irene.

Anita's website:
http://www.anitamathias.com, and
Anita's blog Dreaming Beneath the Spires:
http://dreamingbeneaththespires.blogspot.com

The Church That Had Too Much
Anita Mathias
Benediction Books, 2010
52 pages
ISBN: 9781849026567

Available from www.amazon.com, www.amazon.co.uk

The Church That Had Too Much was very well-intentioned. She wanted to love God, she wanted to love people, but she was both hampered by her muchness and the abundance of her possessions, and beset by ambition, power struggles and snobbery. Read about the surprising way The Church That Had Too Much began to resolve her problems in this deceptively simple and enchanting fable.

About the Author

Anita Mathias is the author of *Wandering Between Two Worlds: Essays on Faith and Art*. She has a B.A. and M.A. in English from Somerville College, Oxford University, and an M.A. in Creative Writing from the Ohio State University, USA. Anita won a National Endowment of the Arts fellowship in Creative Nonfiction in 1997. She lives in Oxford, England with her husband, Roy, and her daughters, Zoe and Irene.

Anita's website:
 http://www.anitamathias.com, and
Anita's blog Dreaming Beneath the Spires:
 http://dreamingbeneaththespires.blogspot.com

www.ingramcontent.com/pod-product-compliance
Lightning Source LLC
Chambersburg PA
CBHW081132300726
48982CB00005B/944